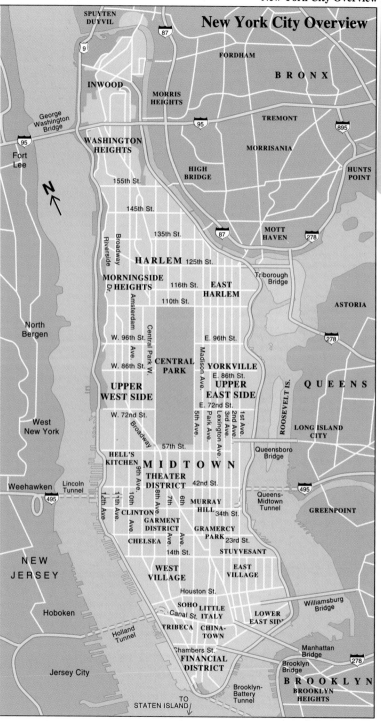

New York City Overview

KU-215-030

New York City Subways

Subways

Stops are not served by all trains at all times.
Refer to Transit Authority map for descriptions of express, local, and limited service.

Times Sq/42 St 7
Shuttle
Grand Central
57 St
50 St
42 St/8 Av
7 Av
5 Av
6 Av
Herald Sq
34 St
32 St
28 St
23 St
14 St/Union Sq
Astor Pl
3 Av
1 Av
2 Av
Lexington Av/53 St
L
14 St/8 Av
8 St/NYU
Broadway/Lafayette/Bleecker
Spring St
Bowery
Grand St
Essex St/Delancey St
E Broadway
Christopher St/Sheridan Sq
W 4 St/6 Av
Houston St
Prince St
Canal St
York St
High St/Bklyn Br
Jay St/Borough Hall
Lawrence Av
DeKalb Av
Bergen St
Atlantic Av
Pacific St
Schermerhorn St
Hoyt St
Franklin St
Chambers St
Park Pl
World Trade Center
Cortlandt St
Rector St
Wall St
Bowling Green
Canal St
Chambers St/City Hall 6
Fulton St
Broad St/J,Z
Wall St
Whitehall St/South Ferry
1,9 South Ferry
Court St/Borough Hall
Hoyt St/Fulton Mall
Borough Hall
4 Av/9 St

Dyre Av 5
Baychester
Gun Hill Rd
Pelham Pkwy
Morris Pk
Pelham Bay Park 6
Buhre Av
Middletown Rd
Westchester Sq
E Tremont Av
Zerega Av
Castle Hill Av
177 St/Parkchester
St Lawrence Av
Morrison Av/Sound View Av
Elder Av
Whitlock Av
241 St 2,5
Nereid Av
238 St
233 St
225 St
219 St
Gun Hill Rd
Woodlawn 4
Mosholu Pkwy
Bedford Pk D 205 St
Bedford Pk Blvd
C Pk
Kingsbridge Rd
Fordham Rd
182-183 St
Burke Av
Allerton Av
Pelham Pkwy
Bronx Pk E
E 180 St
E Tremont Av/Boston Rd
174 St
Freeman St
Simpson St
Intervale Av/163 St
Hunts Pt Av
Longwood Av
Prospect Av
E 149 St
Jackson Av
St Marys St/E 143 St
Cypress Av
Brook Av
3rd Av/138 St
242 St/Van Cortlandt Pk 1,9
238 St
231 St
225 St/Marble Hill
215 St
207 St A
Dyckman St
Kingsbridge Rd
Fordham Rd
183 St
182-183 St
176 St
Burnside Av
Mt Eden Av
170 St
167 St
161 St/Yankee Stadium
149 St/Concourse
138 St/Concourse
Bedford Pk Blvd
Kingsbridge Rd
Fordham Rd
Tremont Av
176 St
181 St
B 168 St
157 St
155 St
145 St
137 St/City College
125 St
116 St/Columbia
110 St/Cathedral Pkwy
103 St
96 St
86 St
79 St
72 St
66 St/Lincoln Ctr
59 St/Columbus Cir
190 St
181 St
175 St
168 St
145 St
137 St
125 St
116 St
110 St
103 St
96 St
86 St
81 St
72 St

Main St/Roosevelt Av/LIRR 7
Willets Pt/Shea Stadium
103 St/Corona Plaza
111 St
Junction Blvd
90 St/Elmhurst Av
82 St/Jackson Hts
74 St/Broadway
69 St
65 St
Northern Blvd
61 St
52 St
46 St
40 St
33 St
Ditmars Blvd N
Astoria Blvd/Hoyt Av
30 Av
Grand Av
36 Av
Washington
Steinway
Queensboro Plaza
Queens Plaza
Roosevelt Av
Grand Av
Court Hse Sq/45 Rd
Hunters Pt Av
Vernon Blvd/Jackson Av
Lexington Av
5 Av
57 St
7 Av
50 St
42 St/6 Av
Times Sq/42 St
34 St
Herald Sq
28 St
23 St
L
14 St/8 Av

Downtown Manhattan

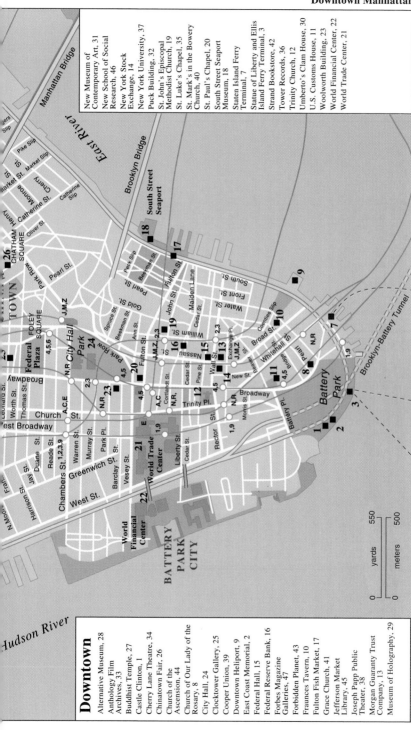

Midtown Manhattan

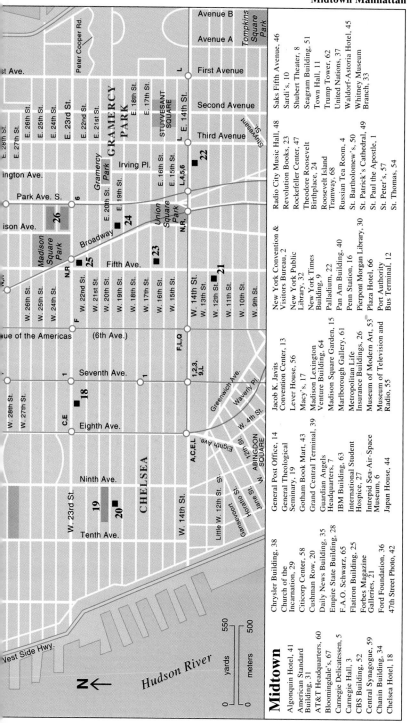

Midtown

- Algonquin Hotel, 41
- American Standard Building, 31
- AT&T Headquarters, 60
- Bloomingdale's, 67
- Carnegie Delicatessen, 5
- Carnegie Hall, 3
- CBS Building, 52
- Central Synagogue, 59
- Chanin Building, 34
- Chelsea Hotel, 18
- Chrysler Building, 38
- Church of the Incarnation, 29
- Citicorp Center, 58
- Cushman Row, 20
- Daily News Building, 35
- Empire State Building, 28
- F.A.O. Schwarz, 65
- Flatiron Building, 25
- Forbes Magazine Galleries, 21
- Ford Foundation, 36
- 47th Street Photo, 42
- General Post Office, 14
- General Theological Seminary, 19
- Gotham Book Mart, 43
- Grand Central Terminal, 39
- Guardian Angels Headquarters, 7
- IBM Building, 63
- International Student Hospice, 27
- Intrepid Sea-Air-Space Museum, 6
- Japan House, 44
- Jacob K. Javits Convention Center, 13
- Lever House, 56
- Macy's, 17
- Madison Lexington Venture Building, 64
- Madison Square Garden, 15
- Marlborough Gallery, 61
- Metropolitan Life Insurance Buildings, 26
- Museum of Modern Art, 53
- Museum of Television and Radio, 55
- New York Convention & Visitors Bureau, 2
- New York Public Library, 32
- New York Times Building, 9
- Palladium, 22
- Pan Am Building, 40
- Penn Station, 16
- Pierpont Morgan Library, 30
- Plaza Hotel, 66
- Port Authority Bus Terminal, 12
- Radio City Music Hall, 48
- Revolution Books, 23
- Rockefeller Center, 47
- Theodore Roosevelt Birthplace, 24
- Roosevelt Island Tramway, 68
- Russian Tea Room, 4
- St. Bartholomew's, 50
- St. Patrick's Cathedral, 49
- St. Paul the Apostle, 1
- St. Peter's, 57
- St. Thomas, 54
- Saks Fifth Avenue, 46
- Sardi's, 10
- Shubert Theater, 8
- Seagram Building, 51
- Town Hall, 11
- Trump Tower, 62
- United Nations, 37
- Waldorf-Astoria Hotel, 45
- Whitney Museum Branch, 33

Uptown

American Museum of Natural History, 53
The Ansonia, 55
The Arsenal, 25
Asia Society, 14
Belvedere Castle, 36
Bethesda Fountain, 33
Blockhouse No. 1, 42
Bloomingdale's, 22
Bridle Path, 30
Cathedral of St. John the Divine, 47
Central Park Zoo, 24
Chess and Checkers House, 28
Children's Museum of Manhattan, 51
Children's Zoo, 26
China House, 19

Cleopatra's Needle, 38
Columbia University, 46
Conservatory Garden, 2
Cooper-Hewitt Museum, 7
The Dairy, 27
Dakota Apartments, 56
Delacorte Theater, 37
El Museo del Barrio, 1
Fordham University, 60
Frick Museum, 13
Gracie Mansion, 10
Grant's Tomb, 45
Great Lawn, 39
Guggenheim Museum, 9
Hayden Planetarium (at the American Museum of Natural History), 53
Hector Memorial, 50
Hotel des Artistes, 57

Hunter College, 16
International Center of Photography, 5
Jewish Museum, 6
The Juilliard School (at Lincoln Center), 59
Lincoln Center, 59
Loeb Boathouse, 34
Masjid Malcolm Shabazz , 43
Metropolitan Museum of Art, 11
Mt. Sinai Hospital, 4
Museum of American Folk Art, 58
Museum of American Illustration, 21
Museum of the City of New York, 3
National Academy of Design, 8
New York Convention & Visitors Bureau, 61

New York Historical Society, 54
New York Hospital, 15
Plaza Hotel, 23
Police Station (Central Park), 40
Rockefeller University, 20
7th Regiment Armory, 17
Shakespeare Garden, 35
Soldiers and Sailors Monument, 49
Strawberry Fields, 32
Studio Museum in Harlem, 44
Symphony Space, 48
Tavern on the Green, 31
Temple Emanu-El, 18
Tennis Courts, 41
Whitney Museum of American Art, 12
Wollman Rink, 29
Zabar's, 52

Central Washington, D.C.

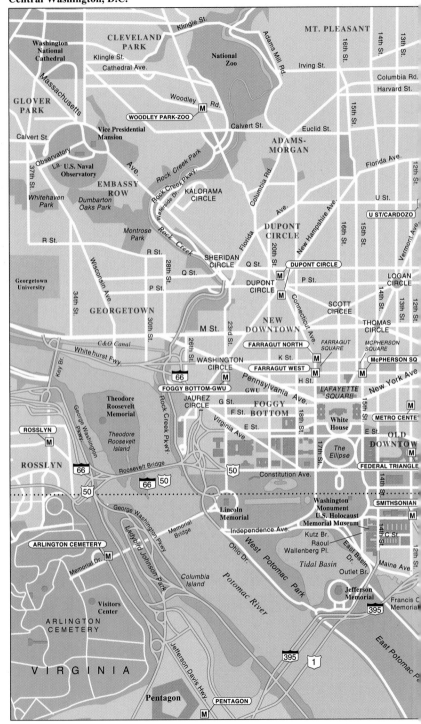

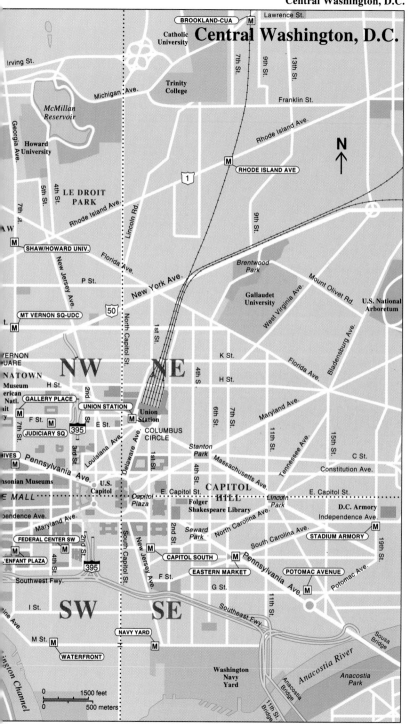

Central Washington, D.C.

The Mall Area, Washington, D.C.

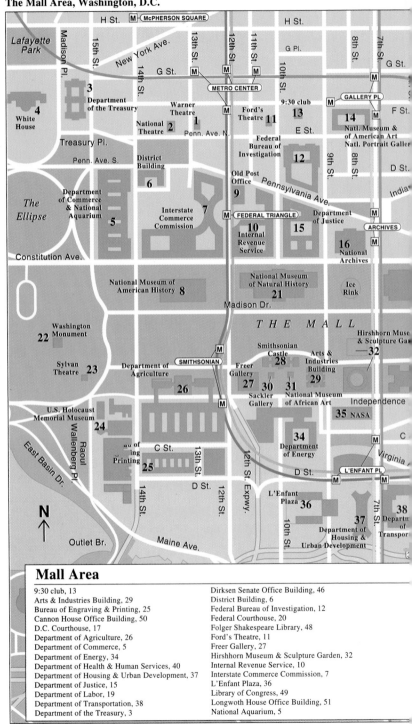

Mall Area

9:30 club, 13
Arts & Industries Building, 29
Bureau of Engraving & Printing, 25
Cannon House Office Building, 50
D.C. Courthouse, 17
Department of Agriculture, 26
Department of Commerce, 5
Department of Energy, 34
Department of Health & Human Services, 40
Department of Housing & Urban Development, 37
Department of Justice, 15
Department of Labor, 19
Department of Transportation, 38
Department of the Treasury, 3

Dirksen Senate Office Building, 46
District Building, 6
Federal Bureau of Investigation, 12
Federal Courthouse, 20
Folger Shakespeare Library, 48
Ford's Theatre, 11
Freer Gallery, 27
Hirshhorn Museum & Sculpture Garden, 32
Internal Revenue Service, 10
Interstate Commerce Commission, 7
L'Enfant Plaza, 36
Library of Congress, 49
Longwoth House Office Building, 51
National Aquarium, 5

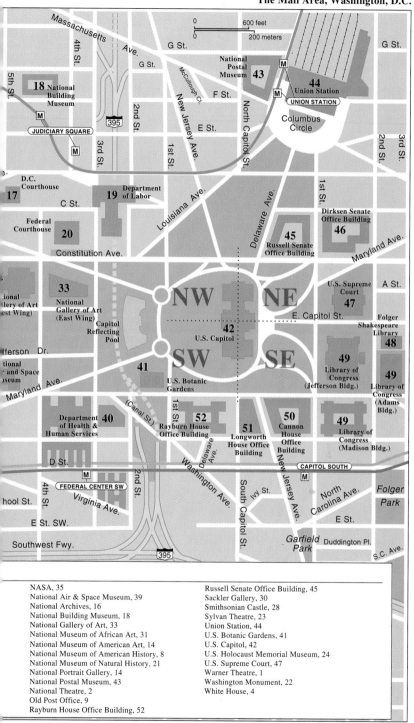

0   600 feet
0   200 meters

Massachusetts Ave.

4th St.
5th St.
G St.
G St.
G St.

National Postal Museum **43**

44 Union Station

M UNION STATION

McCullough Ct.
New Jersey Ave.
F St.
E St.
2nd St.
1st St.

North Capitol St.

Columbus Circle

18 National Building Museum

M
JUDICIARY SQUARE
M
3rd St.
395
2nd St.
3rd St.

2nd St.
3rd St.

D.C. Courthouse
17

C St.
19 Department of Labor

Federal Courthouse
20

Constitution Ave.

Louisiana Ave.
Delaware Ave.
1st St.

Dirksen Senate Office Building
46

45 Russell Senate Office Building

Maryland Ave.

33
National Gallery of Art (East Wing)

ional lery of Art est Wing)

Capitol Reflecting Pool

NW   **NE**

E. Capitol St.

U.S. Supreme Court
47

A St.

Folger Shakespeare Library
48

fferson Dr.
tional and Space useum
Maryland Ave.

41

42
U.S. Capitol

SW   **SE**

U.S. Botanic Gardens

49
Library of Congress (Jefferson Bldg.)

49
Library of Congress (Adams Bldg.)

Department of Health & Human Services
40

(Canal St.)

1st St.
52
Rayburn House Office Building

51
Longworth House Office Building

50
Cannon House Office Building

49
Library of Congress (Madison Bldg.)

D St.

M
FEDERAL CENTER SW

4th St.
hool St.
Virginia Ave.
2nd St.
Delaware Ave.

Washington Ave.

South Capitol St.

Ivy St.

CAPITOL SOUTH
M

New Jersey Ave.

North Carolina Ave.

Folger Park

E St. SW.

E St.

Southwest Fwy.

395

Garfield Park

Duddington Pl.

S.C. Ave.

NASA, 35
National Air & Space Museum, 39
National Archives, 16
National Building Museum, 18
National Gallery of Art, 33
National Museum of African Art, 31
National Museum of American Art, 14
National Museum of American History, 8
National Museum of Natural History, 21
National Portrait Gallery, 14
National Postal Museum, 43
National Theatre, 2
Old Post Office, 9
Rayburn House Office Building, 52

Russell Senate Office Building, 45
Sackler Gallery, 30
Smithsonian Castle, 28
Sylvan Theatre, 23
Union Station, 44
U.S. Botanic Gardens, 41
U.S. Capitol, 42
U.S. Holocaust Memorial Museum, 24
U.S. Supreme Court, 47
Warner Theatre, 1
Washington Monument, 22
White House, 4

White House Area, Foggy Bottom, and Nearby Arlington

N

GEORGETOWN

Prospect St.
33rd St.
N St.
31st St.
Olive St.
Old Stone House
M St.
Rock Creek

C&O Creek
South St.
L St.

Whitehurst Fwy.
K St. (under expressway)
26th St.
25th St.
24th St.

WASHINGTON CIRCLE
G.W. Hosp.

FOGGY BOTTOM-GWU
M
George Washing Univers

66

Potomac River

Thompson Boat Center
Watergate Hotel

JUAREZ CIRCLE

Watergate Hotel Complex

Rock Creek Pkwy.

FOGGY BOTTOM
Virgi

Theodore Roosevelt Memorial

Kennedy Center for the Performing Arts

Francis Scott Key Br.

Fort Myer Dr.
N. Lynn St.
N. Moore St.
19th St.
N. Kent St.

ROSSLYN
M

Wilson Blvd.

George Washington Pkwy.

Theodore Roosevelt Island

S Departme

ROSSLYN
Fairfax Dr.

Arlington Ridge Rd.

66

Theodore Roosevelt Br.

66 50

Natio Acade of Scie
50

N. Nash St.
Mead Dr.

50

NW
SW

Lincoln Memo

Marine Corps War Memorial (Iwo Jima Statue)

George Washington Memorial Pkwy.

Arlington Memorial Br.

12th St.

Netherlands Carillon

Ericsson Memorial

ARLINGTON

Ladybird Johnson Park

M
ARLINGTON CEMETERY

Memorial Dr.

Columbia Island

Grave of President John F. Kennedy

Jefferson Davis Hwy.

Arlington House

Robert E. Lee Memorial

■ Visitor Center

ARLINGTON NATIONAL CEMETERY

Tomb of the Unknown Soldier

Lyndon B. Johnson Memorial

V I R G I N I A

| 0 | 1500 feet |
| 0 | 500 meters |

Pentagon, National Airport

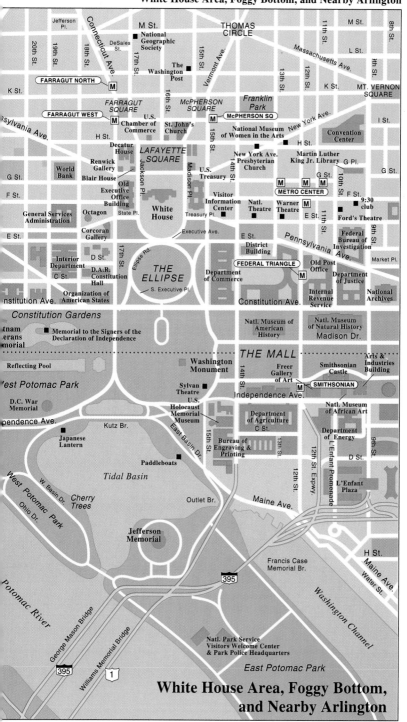

White House Area, Foggy Bottom, and Nearby Arlington

Metrorail System, Washington, D.C.

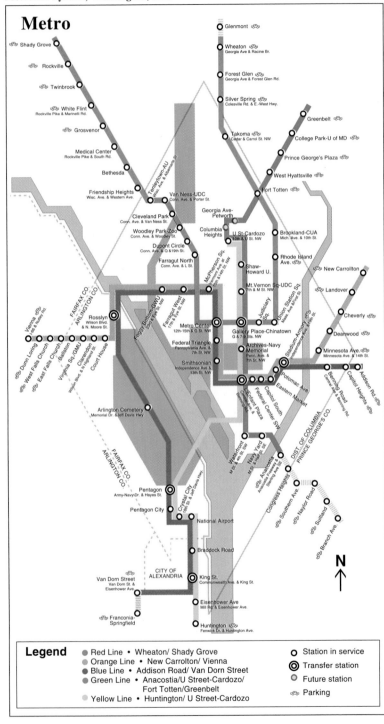

Metro

Legend

- Red Line • Wheaton/ Shady Grove
- Orange Line • New Carrolton/ Vienna
- Blue Line • Addison Road/ Van Dorn Street
- Green Line • Anacostia/U Street-Cardozo/ Fort Totten/Greenbelt
- Yellow Line • Huntington/ U Street-Cardozo

- ○ Station in service
- ◎ Transfer station
- ○ Future station
- Parking

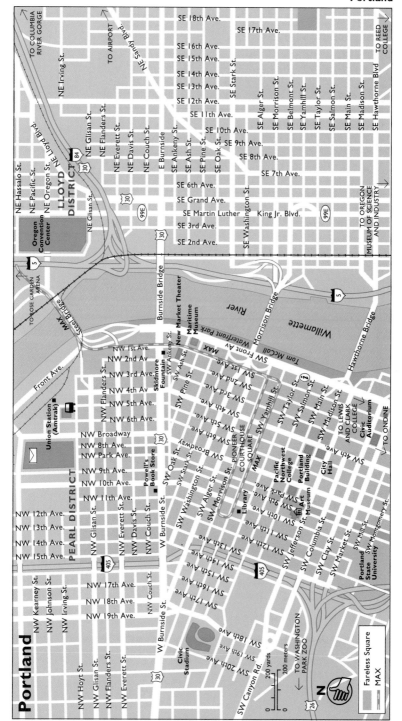

Portland

PEARL DISTRICT

LLOYD DISTRICT

NW Kearney St.
NW Johnson St.
NW Irving St.
NW Hoyt St.
NW Glisan St.
NW Flanders St.
NW Everett St.

NW 12th Ave.
NW 13th Ave.
NW 14th Ave.
NW 15th Ave.
NW 17th Ave.
NW 18th Ave.
NW 19th Ave.

NW Glisan St.
NW Everett St.
NW Davis St.
NW Couch St.

NW Broadway
NW 8th Ave.
NW Park Ave.
NW 9th Ave.
NW 10th Ave.
NW 11th Ave.

NW 1st Av
NW 2nd Av
NW 3rd Ave.
NW Flanders St.
NW 4th Ave.
NW 5th Ave.
NW 6th Ave.

NE Hassalo St.
NE Pacific St.
NE Oregon St.
NE Lloyd Blvd.
NE Glisan St.

NE Irving St.
NE Sandy Blvd.
NE Glisan St.
NE Flanders St.
NE Everett St.
NE Davis St.
NE Couch St.

SE 18th Ave.
SE 17th Ave.
SE 16th Ave.
SE 15th Ave.
SE 14th Ave.
SE 13th Ave.
SE 12th Ave.
SE 11th Ave.
SE 10th Ave.
SE 9th Ave.
SE 8th Ave.
SE 7th Ave.
SE 6th Ave.
SE Grand Ave.
SE Martin Luther King Jr. Blvd.
SE 3rd Ave.
SE 2nd Ave.

SE Stark St.
SE Alger St.
SE Morrison St.
SE Belmont St.
SE Yamhill St.
SE Taylor St.
SE Salmon St.
SE Main St.
SE Madison St.
SE Hawthorne Blvd

E Burnside
SE Ankeny St.
SE Ash St.
SE Pine St.
SE Oak St.

SE Washington St.

TO COLUMBIA RIVER GORGE
TO AIRPORT
TO REED COLLEGE
TO OREGON MUSEUM OF SCIENCE AND INDUSTRY

Oregon Convention Center
TO ROSE GARDEN ARENA
Union Station (Amtrak)
Steel Bridge
MAX
Front Ave.

Burnside Bridge
New Market Theater
Maritime Museum
Morrison Bridge
Hawthorne Bridge

Willamette River

Skidmore Fountain
SW Ankeny St.
SW Ash St.
SW Pine St.
SW Front Av
Tom McCall Waterfront Park
SW 1st Ave.
SW 2nd Ave.
SW 3rd Ave.

Powell's Book Store
SW Oak St.
SW Stark St.
SW Washington St.
SW Alger St.
SW Morrison St.
SW Broadway
SW 4th Ave.
SW 5th Ave.
SW 6th Ave.

PIONEER COURTHOUSE SQUARE
MAX
SW Yamhill St.
SW Taylor St.
SW Salmon St.
SW Main St.
SW Madison St.

Pacific Northwest College
Portland Building
City Hall
Civic Auditorium
TO LEWIS AND CLARK COLLEGE
TO ONDINE

Library
Art Museum
SW 9th Ave.
SW 10th Ave.
SW 11th Ave.
SW 12th Ave.
SW 13th Ave.
SW 14th Ave.
SW 15th Ave.
SW 16th Ave.
SW 17th Ave.
SW 18th Ave.
SW 19th Ave.
SW 20th Ave.

SW Park Ave.
SW Jefferson St.
SW Columbia St.
SW Clay St.
SW Market St.
SW Mill St.
SW Montgomery St.

Portland State University

W Burnside St.
NW Couch St.

Civic Stadium
SW Canyon Rd.
TO WASHINGTON PARK ZOO

N

Fareless Square
MAX

0   200 yards
0   200 meters

TO COLUMBIA RIVER GORGE

84
30
5
405
99E
26
i

Seattle

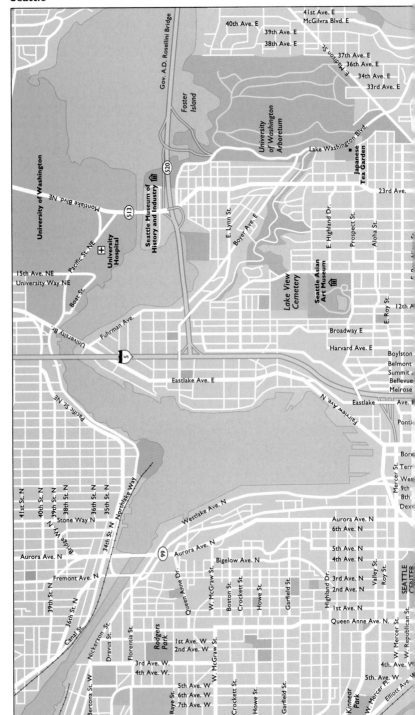

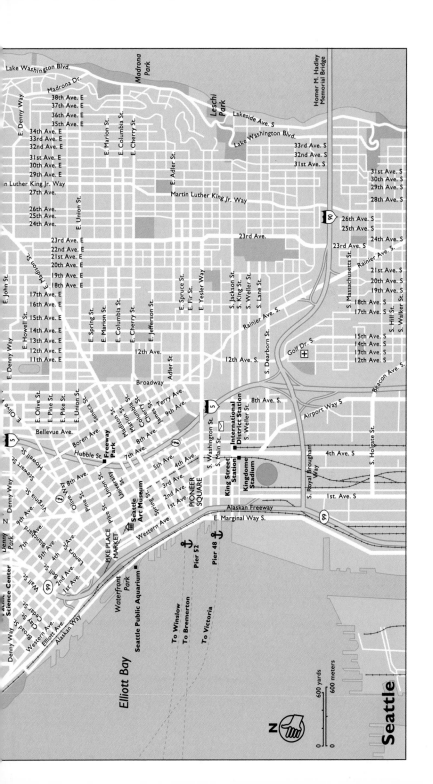

Seattle

Vancouver

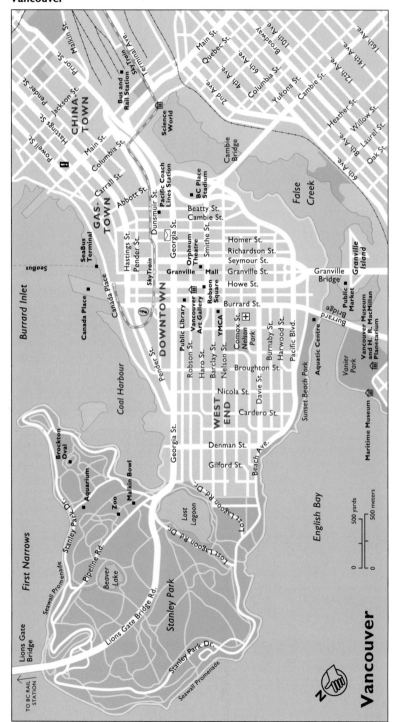

Vancouver

First Narrows

Lions Gate Bridge

TO BC RAIL STATION

Stanley Park

Stanley Park Dr.

Seawall Promenade

Lions Gate Bridge Rd.

Beaver Lake

Pipeline Rd.

Lost Lagoon Dr.

Stanley Park Dr.

Brockton Oval

Aquarium

Zoo

Malkin Bowl

Seawall Promenade

Burrard Inlet

Coal Harbour

Canada Place

SeaBus Terminal

Seabus

Canada Place

Pender St.

Georgia St.

Lost Lagoon

Lost Lagoon Rd. Dr.

English Bay

500 yards

500 meters

0

0

CHINA-TOWN

GAS-TOWN

DOWNTOWN

WEST END

Malkin St.

Prior St.

Jackson St.

Pender St.

Hastings St.

Powell St.

Main St.

Columbia St.

Carrall St.

Abbott St.

Dunsmuir St.

Hastings St.

Pender St.

SkyTrain

Bus and Rail Station

Terminal Ave.

SkyTrain Ave.

Science World

Pacific Coach Lines Station

BC Place Stadium

Beatty St.

Cambie St.

Georgia St.

Orpheum Theatre

Granville

Smithe St.

Mall

Public Library

Vancouver Art Gallery

Robson Square

YMCA

Comox St.

Nelson Park

Robson St.

Haro St.

Barclay St.

Nelson St.

Nicola St.

Cardero St.

Denman St.

Gilford St.

Broughton St.

Davie St.

Beach Ave.

Homer St.

Richardson St.

Seymour St.

Granville St.

Howe St.

Burrard St.

Burnaby St.

Harwood St.

Pacific Blvd.

Sunset Beach Park

Aquatic Centre

Granville Bridge

Burrard Bridge

Public Market

Granville Island

Vancouver Museum and H. R. MacMillan Planetarium

Vanier Park

Maritime Museum

False Creek

Cambie Bridge

Main St.

Quebec St.

Columbia St.

2nd Ave

4th Ave

6th Ave

Broadway

10th Ave

12th Ave

14th Ave

16th Ave

Yukon St.

Cambie St.

Heather St.

Willow St.

Laurel St.

Oak St.

8th Ave

6th Ave

Los Angeles

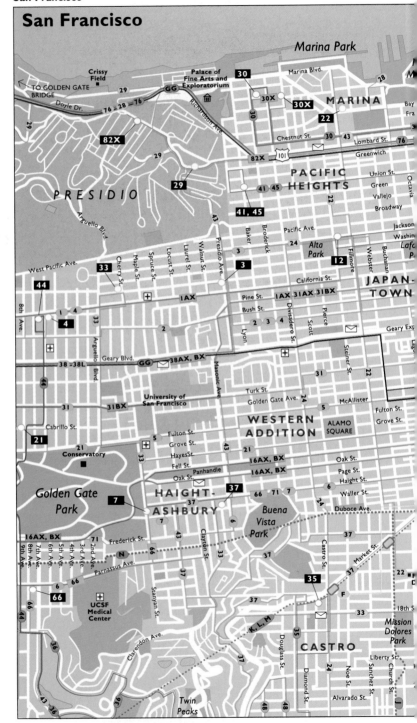

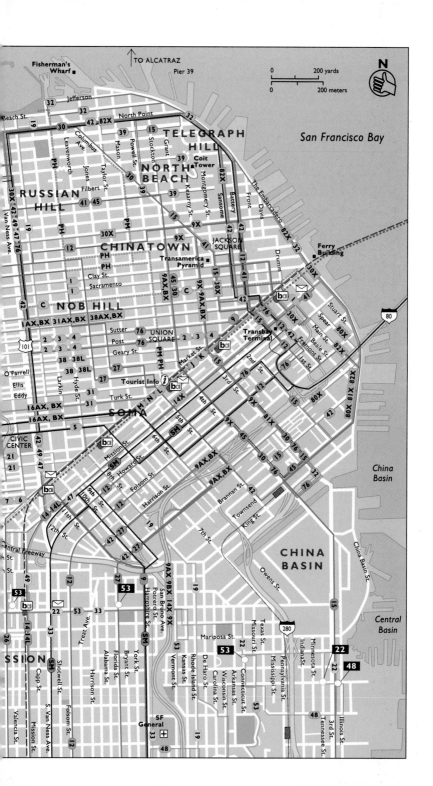

L.A. Westside

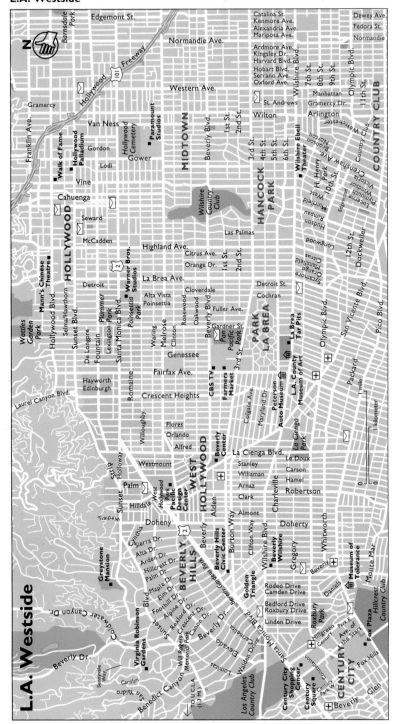

LET'S GO
USA

■ Let's Go writers travel on your budget.

"Guides that penetrate the veneer of the holiday brochures and mine the grit of real life."
—*The Economist*

"The writers seem to have experienced every rooster-packed bus and lunar-surfaced mattress about which they write."
—*The New York Times*

"All the dirt, dirt cheap."
—*People*

■ Great for independent travelers.

"The guides are aimed not only at young budget travelers but at the independent traveler, a sort of streetwise cookbook for traveling alone."
—*The New York Times*

"Flush with candor and irreverence, chock full of budget travel advice."
—*The Des Moines Register*

"An indispensable resource. *Let's Go*'s practical information can be used by every traveler."
—*The Chattanooga Free Press*

■ Let's Go is completely revised each year.

"Only *Let's Go* has the zeal to annually update every title on its list."
—*The Boston Globe*

"Unbeatable: good sight-seeing advice; up-to-date info on restaurants, hotels, and inns; a commitment to money-saving travel; and a wry style that brightens nearly every page."
—*The Washington Post*

■ All the important information you need.

"*Let's Go* authors provide a comedic element while still providing concise information and thorough coverage of the country. Anything you need to know about budget traveling is detailed in this book."
—*The Chicago Sun-Times*

"Value-packed, unbeatable, accurate, and comprehensive."
—*Los Angeles Times*

Let's Go Publications

Let's Go: Alaska & the Pacific Northwest 1999
Let's Go: Australia 1999
Let's Go: Austria & Switzerland 1999
Let's Go: Britain & Ireland 1999
Let's Go: California 1999
Let's Go: Central America 1999
Let's Go: Eastern Europe 1999
Let's Go: Ecuador & the Galápagos Islands 1999
Let's Go: Europe 1999
Let's Go: France 1999
Let's Go: Germany 1999
Let's Go: Greece 1999 **New title!**
Let's Go: India & Nepal 1999
Let's Go: Ireland 1999
Let's Go: Israel & Egypt 1999
Let's Go: Italy 1999
Let's Go: London 1999
Let's Go: Mexico 1999
Let's Go: New York City 1999
Let's Go: New Zealand 1999
Let's Go: Paris 1999
Let's Go: Rome 1999
Let's Go: South Africa 1999 **New title!**
Let's Go: Southeast Asia 1999
Let's Go: Spain & Portugal 1999
Let's Go: Turkey 1999 **New title!**
Let's Go: USA 1999
Let's Go: Washington, D.C. 1999

Let's Go Map Guides

Amsterdam	Madrid
Berlin	New Orleans
Boston	New York City
Chicago	Paris
Florence	Rome
London	San Francisco
Los Angeles	Washington, D.C.

Coming Soon: Prague, Seattle

Let's Go
Publications

Let's Go
USA
1999

Irene J. Hahn
Editor

T.J. Kelleher
Associate Editor

Kaya Stone
Associate Editor

Researcher-Writers:

Frank Beidler

Ann Schiff

Rebecca Glass

Matthew Ozug

Ruth Halikman

Jonathan B. Stein

Joe McCannon

Emily Ruth Von Kohorn

With:

Christian Reed Lorentzen

Alexander Z. Speier

Leeore Schnairson

Samantha Van Gerbig

Eliot Schrefer

Vivek Waglé

Macmillan

Published in Great Britain 1999 by Macmillan, an imprint of Macmillan General Books, 25 Eccleston Place, London, SW1W 9NF and Basingstoke.

Maps by David Lindroth copyright © 1999, 1998, 1997, 1996, 1995, 1994, 1993, 1992, 1991, 1990, 1989, 1988 by St. Martin's Press, Inc.

Published in the United States of America by St. Martin's Press, Inc.

ISBN: 0 333 74741 0

First edition
10 9 8 7 6 5 4 3 2 1

Let's Go: USA is written by Let's Go Publications, 67 Mount Auburn Street, Cambridge, MA 02138, USA.
Let's Go® and the thumb logo are trademarks of Let's Go, Inc. Printed in the USA on recycled paper with biodegradable soy ink.

About Let's Go

THIRTY-NINE YEARS OF WISDOM

Back in 1960, a few students at Harvard University banded together to produce a 20-page pamphlet offering a collection of tips on budget travel in Europe. This modest, mimeographed packet, offered as an extra to passengers on student charter flights to Europe, met with instant popularity. The following year, students traveling to Europe researched the first, full-fledged edition of *Let's Go: Europe,* a pocket-sized book featuring honest, irreverent writing and a decidedly youthful outlook on the world. Throughout the 60s, our guides reflected the times; the 1969 guide to America led off by inviting travelers to "dig the scene" at San Francisco's Haight-Ashbury. During the 70s and 80s, we gradually added regional guides and expanded coverage into the Middle East and Central America. With the addition of our in-depth city guides, handy map guides, and extensive coverage of Asia and Australia, the 90s are also proving to be a time of explosive growth for Let's Go, and there's certainly no end in sight. The maiden edition of *Let's Go: South Africa,* our pioneer guide to sub-Saharan Africa, hits the shelves this year, along with the first editions of *Let's Go: Greece* and *Let's Go: Turkey.*

We've seen a lot in 39 years. *Let's Go: Europe* is now the world's bestselling international guide, translated into seven languages. And our new guides bring Let's Go's total number of titles, with their spirit of adventure and their reputation for honesty, accuracy, and editorial integrity, to 44. But some things never change: our guides are still researched, written, and produced entirely by students who know first-hand how to see the world on the cheap.

HOW WE DO IT

Our series is completely revised and thoroughly updated every year by a well-traveled set of over 200 students. Every winter, we recruit over 160 researchers and 70 editors to write the books anew. After several months of training, researcher-writers hit the road for seven weeks of exploration, from Anchorage to Adelaide, Estonia to El Salvador, Iceland to Indonesia. Hired for their rare combination of budget travel sense, writing ability, stamina, and courage, these adventurous travelers know that train strikes, stolen luggage, food poisoning, and marriage proposals are all part of a day's work. Back at our offices, editors work from spring to fall, massaging copy written on Himalayan bus rides into witty yet informative prose. A student staff of typesetters, cartographers, publicists, and managers keeps our lively team together. In September, the collected efforts of the summer are delivered to our printer, who turns them into books in record time, so that you have the most up-to-date information available for your vacation. Even as you read this, work on next year's editions is well underway.

WHY WE DO IT

We don't think of budget travel as the last recourse of the destitute; we believe that it's the only way to travel. Living cheaply and simply brings you closer to the people and places you've been saving up to visit. Our books will ease your anxieties and answer your questions about the basics—so you can get off the beaten track and explore. Once you learn the ropes, we encourage you to put *Let's Go* down now and then to strike out on your own. You know as well as we that the best discoveries are often those you make yourself. When you find something worth sharing, please drop us a line. We're Let's Go Publications, 67 Mount Auburn St., Cambridge, MA 02138, USA (email: feedback@letsgo.com). For more info, visit our website, http://www.letsgo.com.

BANANA
BUNGALOW
Simply the Best!

Contents

ABOUT LET'S GO—V
HOW TO USE THIS BOOK—IX
LIST OF MAPS—XI
LET'S GO PICKS—XII

ESSENTIALS 1
PLANNING YOUR TRIP—1
When to Go, Useful Information, Documents and Formalities, Money Matters, Safety and Security, Health, Insurance, Alternatives to Tourism, Specific Concerns
GETTING THERE—21
Budget Travel Agencies, By Plane
ONCE THERE—28
Embassies and Consulates, Getting Around, Accommodations, Camping and the Outdoors, Lines of Communication

UNITED STATES 58
History, 1998's News, A Civics Primer, The Arts, The Media, Sports

NEW ENGLAND 67
MAINE—68
Maine Coast: Portland, South of Portland, Northern Maine Coast, Mt. Desert and Bar Harbor
NEW HAMPSHIRE—76
White Mountains
VERMONT—81
Burlington, Middlebury, Stowe, White River Junction, Brattleboro, Ski Resorts
MASSACHUSETTS—90
Eastern Massachusetts: Boston, Cambridge, Lexington and Concord, Salem, Plymouth. Cape Cod: Upper Cape, Lower Cape, Provincetown, Martha's Vineyard, Nantucket. Western Massachusetts: The Berkshires
RHODE ISLAND—118
Providence, Newport
CONNECTICUT—123
Hartford, New Haven, Mystic and the Connecticut Coast

MID-ATLANTIC 128
NEW YORK—128
New York City, Catskills, Albany, Cooperstown, Ithaca and the Finger Lakes, Buffalo, Niagara Falls, Northern New York, The Adirondacks, Lake Placid, Thousand Island Seaway
NEW JERSEY—188
Atlantic City, Cape May
PENNSYLVANIA—192
Philadelphia, Lancaster County, Gettysburg, Pittsburg, Ohiopyle
DELAWARE—211
Delaware Seashore
MARYLAND—213
Baltimore, Annapolis, Assateague Island, Ocean City
WASHINGTON, D.C.—222
VIRGINIA—236
Richmond, Williamsburg, Virginia Beach, Charlottesville, Shenandoah
WEST VIRGINIA—251
Harpers Ferry, New River Gorge, Monongahela National Forest

THE SOUTH 257
KENTUCKY—257
Louisville, Lexington, Daniel Boone National Forest, Cumberland Gap
TENNESSEE—269
Nashville, Knoxville, Great Smoky Mountains, Chattanooga, Memphis
NORTH CAROLINA—285
The Research Triangle, Charlotte, Carolina Mountains: Boone, Asheville, Outer Banks
SOUTH CAROLINA—298
Charleston, Columbia, Myrtle Beach and the Grand Strand
GEORGIA—305
Atlanta, Athens, Savannah, Brunswick and Environs
ALABAMA—318
Montgomery, Birmingham, Mobile
MISSISSIPPI—326
Jackson, Vicksburg, Natchez, Oxford
LOUISIANA—332
New Orleans, Baton Rouge. Acadiana: Lafayette, New Iberia and Environs
ARKANSAS—350
Little Rock, Hot Springs, Moutain View, Eureka Springs

FLORIDA 357
St. Augustine, Daytona Beach, Orlando, Cocoa Beach and Cape Canaveral, Fort Lauderdale, Miami and Miami Beach, Everglades, Florida Keys, Key Largo, Key West, Gulf Coast, Tampa, St. Petersburg and Clearwater, Gainesville, Panama City Beach

THE GREAT LAKES 394
OHIO—395
Cleveland, Columbus, Cincinnati
MICHIGAN—406
Detroit, Ann Arbor, Grand Rapids, Lake Michigan Shore, Isle Royale
INDIANA—423
Indianapolis, Bloomington
ILLINOIS—428
Chicago, Springfield
WISCONSIN—444
Milwaukee, Madison, Door County, Apostle Islands
MINNESOTA—455
Minneapolis and St. Paul, Duluth, Chippewa National Forest, Iron Range, Lake Superior North

THE GREAT PLAINS **467**
   NORTH DAKOTA—467
   Fargo, Theodore Roosevelt National Park
   SOUTH DAKOTA—472
   Sioux Falls, The Badlands, Wounded Knee, Black Hills Region: Mount Rushmore, Crazy Horse Memorial, Custer State Park, Wind Cave, Jewel Cave, Rapid City, Spearfish, Lead, Deadwood
   IOWA—481
   Des Moines, Spirit Lake and Okoboji, Iowa City, Amana Colonies
   NEBRASKA—488
   Omaha, Lincoln, Scotts Bluff
   KANSAS—494
   Wichita, Lawrence
   MISSOURI—498
   St. Louis, Hannibal, Kansas City, Branson
   OKLAHOMA—513
   Tulsa, Oklahoma City

TEXAS **519**
   Dallas, Austin, Houston, Galveston Island, San Antonio, Corpus Christi, Padre Island
   WESTERN TEXAS—543
   Amarillo, Guadalupe Mountains, El Paso, Ciudad Juárez, Big Bend

THE ROCKY MOUNTAINS **551**
   IDAHO—552
   Boise, McCall, Ketchum and Sun Valley, Sawtooth, Craters of the Moon
   MONTANA—560
   Billings, Little Big Horn, Bozeman, Missoula, Waterton-Glacier Peace Park
   WYOMING—570
   Yellowstone, Grand Teton, Jackson, Cody, Buffalo & Sheridan, Bighorn Mountains, Devils Tower, Thermopolis, Casper, Cheyenne
   COLORADO—590
   Denver, Boulder, Rocky Mountain National Park, Vail, Aspen, Glenwood Springs, Grand Junction, Colorado National Monument, Grand Mesa, Colorado Springs, Great Sand Dunes, San Juan Moutains, Black Canyon, Crested Butte, Telluride, Durango, Mesa Verde

THE SOUTHWEST **617**
   NEVADA—617
   Las Vegas, Reno
   UTAH—625
   Northern Utah: Salt Lake City, Timpanogos Cave, Park City, Dinosaur and Vernal, Flaming Gorge. Southern Utah: the Fab Five, Cedar City, Natural Bridges and Hovenweep
   ARIZONA—645
   Grand Canyon, Flagstaff, Navajo Reservation, Lake Powell and Page, Petrified Forest, Painted Desert, Sedona, Jerome, Phoenix, Organ Pipe Cactus National Monument, Tucson, Tombstone
   NEW MEXICO—671
   Santa Fe, Taos, Albuquerque, Gallup, Truth or Consequences, Gila Cliff Dwellings and Silver City, White Sands, Carlsbad Caverns

THE PACIFIC NORTHWEST **689**
   WASHINGTON—690
   Olympic Peninsula: Port Townsend, Olympic National Park. Cascade Range: Mount St. Helens, Mount Ranier National Park, North Cascades (Route 20). Eastern Washington: Spokae
   OREGON—715
   Portland, Mount Hood, Columbia River Gorge, Oregon Coast, Inland Oregon: Eugene, Crater Lake and Klamath Falls, Ashland, bend, Hells Canyon and Wallowa Mountains

CALIFORNIA **733**
   Southern California: Los Angeles, Orange County, Big Bear, San Diego, Tijuana, The California Desert: Palm Springs, Joshua Tree National Park, Death Valley, The Central Coast: Santa Barbara, San Luis Obispo, Big Sur, Monterey, Santa Cruz,San Francisco Bay Area: San Francisco, Berkeley, Oakland, San Jose, Palo Alto, San Mateo Coast, Marin County, Wine Country: Napa Valley, Sonoma Valley, Northern California: Mendocino, Avenue of the Giants, Redwood National Park, Gold Country, The Cascades, The Sierra Nevada: Lake Tahoe, Yosemite

ALASKA **829**
   Anchorage, Seward and Kanai Fjords, Wrangell-St. Elias, Denali, Fairbanks, Ketchikan, Juneau

HAWAII **842**
   Oahu, Honolulu, Beyond Honolulu, Maui, The Big Island, Kauai

CANADA **851**
   NOVA SCOTIA—854
   Atlantic Coast, Halifax
   NEW BRUNSWICK—860
   Saint John, Fundy
   PRINCE EDWARD ISLAND—864
   QUÉBEC—866
   Montréal, Québec City
   ONTARIO—884
   Toronto, Ottawa, Algonquin Provincial Park
   BRITISH COLUMBIA—903
   Vancouver, Vancouver Island, Victoria, Pacific Rim National Park, Southeastern British Columbia, Glacier National Park, Yoho National Park, Kootenay National Park, Prince Rupert, Alaska Approaches
   YUKON TERRITORY—915
   Whitehorse, Kluane NAtional Park, Dawson City
   ALBERTA—921
   Banff National Park, Jasper National Park, Edmonton, Calgary, Alberta Badlands

APPENDIX **930**
   Holidays, Festivals, Climate, Time Zones, Measurements3

INDEX **933**
   RESEARCHER-WRITERS—952
   ACKNOWLEDGMENTS—954
   THANKS TO OUR READERS—955

How to Use This Book

This book does not contain all there is to know about traveling in the USA. We came, we saw, we wrote down, but we did not cover it all. Stray from our directions; see the sights between the places we mention—the U.S. is full of undiscovered restaurants, inns, alien abduction sights, and particle accelerators waiting for exploration.

Let's Go: USA is divided into three parts. The first portion, **Essentials,** further splits in three. The chapter starts with information for planning a trip in the USA or Canada: necessary documents, entrance requirements, exchange rates, a description of certain laws and customs, health and safety advice, and travel advice for women, senior citizens, bisexuals, gays and lesbians, disabled travelers, and older travelers (p. 1). Information on getting to the USA and Canada, including listings for budget travel agencies, follows next (p. 21). The final section of **Essentials** offers advice on getting around, finding a bed, exploring the outdoors, and keeping in touch (p. 28).

Coverage of the **United States,** the book's hefty second part, begins with a primer on American culture and history. In all, 13 chapters, named after geographic regions, make up the coverage of the 50 states. The regions run north to south and progress east to west in the following order: **New England, Mid-Atlantic, The South, Florida, Great Lakes, Great Plains, Texas, Rocky Mountains, The Southwest, The Pacific Northwest, California, Alaska,** and **Hawaii.** The regions begin with **Highlights of the Region,** giving the lowdown on can't-miss towns, sights and experiences in each area. Each state's text opens with the largest, or most accessible, destination and fans outward. The index has an alphabetized list of the destinations covered.

The third section of the book contains locations in **Canada** which travelers often include in trips to the U.S. Following a description of Canadian culture and history, coverage runs east to west: **Nova Scotia, New Brunswick, Prince Edward Island, Québec, Ontario, Alberta, British Columbia,** and **The Yukon Territory.** Entries within the provinces generally move away form the American border.

We cap the book off with an **appendix,** filled with the scuttlebutt on climate, electricity, weights and measures, festivals, distances between cities, and holidays.

For all major destinations in the USA and in Canada, we include **Accommodations, Food, Sights,** and **Entertainment** headers. Within each of these categories, listings are ranked in order of value, according to our team's judgment. For extra-special establishments in large cities, we give the ol' thumbs up ℗. Our **Practical Information** will help you get around, find help, and keep in touch; tourist offices provide further help and, often, free maps. Sections entitled **"Near"** include suggestions for daytrips.

If you intend to travel extensively in one area, consider buying one of our regional guides, *Let's Go: Alaska & the Pacific Northwest* and *Let's Go: California;* one of our city guides, *Let's Go: New York City* and *Let's Go: Washington, D.C.;* or a *Let's Go Map Guide* to any of the following cities: Chicago, New Orleans, Boston, New York, Washington, D.C., San Francisco, or Los Angeles. Finally, as a supplement to our text, we recommend a good road map; it's an indispensable aid even for train/bus trippers. And now without further ado ("raise the curtain, kids!"), let's go USA.

A NOTE TO OUR READERS

The information for this book was gathered by *Let's Go's* researchers from May through August. Each listing is derived from the assigned researcher's opinion based upon his or her visit at a particular time. The opinions are expressed in a candid and forthright manner. Other travelers might disagree. Those traveling at a different time may have different experiences since prices, dates, hours, and conditions are always subject to change. You are urged to check beforehand to avoid inconvenience and surprises. Travel always involves a certain degree of risk, especially in low-cost areas. When traveling, especially on a budget, always take particular care to ensure your safety.

Maps

USA: Chapters xiii
The United States .... xiv-xv
USA National Park System .... xvi-xvii
New England 67
Boston 91
Mid-Atlantic 129
Lower Manhattan 131
Downtown Philadelphia 194
Central Baltimore 214
Central Washington, D.C. 221
The South 258-259
Nashville 270
Downtown Memphis 280
Downtown Atlanta 307
New Orleans 335
Downtown New Orleans 337
Florida Peninsula 358
Orlando Theme Parks 363
Miami 375
Great Lakes 394
Cleveland 396
Downtown Detroit 407
Downtown Chicago 429
Downtown Minneapolis & St. Paul 457
Great Plains 468
St. Louis Downtown 501
Kansas City 509
Texas 519
Downtown Dallas 521
Houston Museum District 530
Downtown San Antonio 536
Rocky Mountains 551
Denver 591
Southwest 618
Las Vegas: The $trip 620
Salt Lake City 627
National Parks of Utah 636

Downtown Phoenix 662
Santa Fe 673
Pacific Northwest 689
Seattle 691
Portland 717
California 735
Los Angeles Area 737
L.A. Westside 739
Downtown San Diego 761
Downtown San Francisco 781
Alaska 829
Hawaii 843
Eastern Canada 855
Vieux Montréal 874
Vieux-Québec 877
Ontario & Upstate New York 885
Toronto 886
Ottawa 896
British Columbia and the Yukon 902
Downtown Vancouver 904
Alberta, Saskatchewan, and Manitoba 919

Color Maps

Downtown Washington, D.C. .... color insert
Central Washington, D.C. .... color insert
Mall Area Washington, D.C. ...... color insert
White House Area,
    Foggy Bottom, Arlington ..... color insert
Metro Rail System, D.C. .... color insert
New York City Overview .... color insert
New York City Subways .... color insert
Downtown Manhattan .... color insert
Midtown Manhattan .... color insert
Uptown Manhattan .... color insert

Let's Go Picks

Here we tear off our veneer of objectivity and shamelessly declare our personal favorites—the sights, bites, and hostels we liked best.

Naturally Splendid: Denali National Park, AK (p. 835). Landscape, wildlife, and the largest vertical relief in the world; can you top 18,000 ft.? **Isle Royale,** MI (p. 422). Moose and wolf frolic in a natural setting unadulterated by humans. **Zion National Park,** UT (p. 641). Bow down to the Great White Throne amid countless vibrantly colored canyons.

Human-Made Wonders: Cross in the Woods, MI (p. 422). Truly God's country, the woods of Petoskey, MI, shelter the nation's tallest crucifix. **Carhenge,** NE (p. 494), where Druid meets Buick. **American Funeral Service Museum,** TX (p. 533). Entertainment for the faint of heart and pulse. The **Mall of America,** MN (p. 459). The country's largest mall with 2 mi. of shopping excitement.

Hospitable Hostels: Lake Louise Hostel, AB (p. 922), the best of Banff. **Shagawa Sam's,** Ely, MN (p. 464). So what if it's in the boondocks? There's a barbecue downstairs. **Shadowcliff Hostel,** CO (p. 600). A beautiful lodge with a view to write home about. **Hostel in the Forest,** GA (p. 317). Lodgers pine for these well-maintained tree houses.

Camp Here: Jenny Lake, Grand Teton National Park, WY (p. 576). This may be the most spectacular spot in the nation to pitch a tent. **Big Sur,** CA, (p. 775). Surrounded by Cali's redwoods and adjacent to the Pacific Ocean. **Padre Island,** TX (p. 542). Silky sands and crashing waves make this a southwestern paradise. **John Pennekamp State Park,** FL (p. 382). It has a beautiful campground lapped by the waters of the Florida Keys, and sits right next to a 25 mi. coral reef.

Towns We Hate to Leave: Austin, TX (p. 525). A pinch of politics, a peck of partying, a dose of hippies, and thousands of bats, brew together in this Texas town. **Stanley, ID** (p. 557). Surrounded by the Sawtooth Range, this untouristed gem, with terrific access to the outdoors, is well-nigh perfect. **Oxford, MS** (p. 332). With the Center for the Study of Southern Culture, Faulkner's home, and a place in the deep south, this burg earned a place in our hearts. **Ely, MN** (p. 464). This town, waiting in the Iron Range, home of Shagawa Sam and the International Wolf Center, cannot be missed.

Scenic Drives: Going-to-the-Sun Road, MT (p. 566). A mountainous jaunt through the peaks of Glacier National Park. **Telluride to Durango,** CO (p. 612). This bucolic journey is what road-tripping is all about. **Mt. Washington,** NH (p. 80). Has your car climbed Mt. Washington? **Route 20,** WA (p. 713). A verdant loop winding through the North Cascades. **Icefields Parkway,** AB (p. 923). Massive hunks of stone and ice line the road through Banff and Jasper National Parks. **Dempster Highway,** AK (p. 920). A spectacular pilgrimage into the Arctic.

Sustenance in Style: Arthur Bryant's, MO (p. 510). BBQ tasty enough for Jimmy Carter. **Blue Heaven,** FL (p. 384). Ernest Hemingway loved this place, and so did we. **No Name,** MA (p. 94). A seafood joint that exemplifies Beantown. **Bar Gernika,** ID (p. 554), hearty lip-smackin' Basque cuisine straight from the Pyrenees.

Fab Festivals: Testicle Festival, MT (p. 563). Bull testicles aren't just the stuff of legend; they're dinner. **Ashland Shakespeare Festival,** WA (p. 730). Year-round bard on the east bank of the Pacific, not the Thames. **Spoleto Festival USA,** SC (p. 301). 17 days of top-notch theater, music, opera and art.

The Foot's Fetish: Sourtoe Cocktail Club, YT (p. 920). They put a dismembered human toe in your drink; you drink your drink; the toe touches your lips; you gain membership to a club of 12,000 who have undergone aforementioned initiation.

Only in America: Bone-Marrow Patient 10% Discount, Bullock's, NC (p. 287). Barbecue does another service for America. **Funpigs,** Slickrock Campground, UT (p. 635). "A person who relaxes, has fun, and drives a four-wheel drive." **Red Carpet Washateria and Lanes,** MS (p. 330). Suds and bowling—a team that can't be beat.

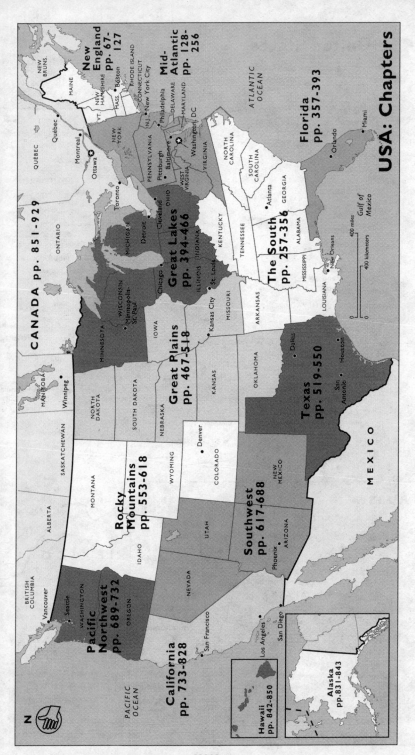

USA: Chapters

New England pp. 67-127

Mid-Atlantic pp. 128-256

Florida pp. 357-393

The South pp. 257-356

Great Lakes pp. 394-466

Great Plains pp. 467-518

Texas pp. 519-550

Rocky Mountains pp. 553-618

Southwest pp. 617-688

CANADA pp. 851-929

Pacific Northwest pp. 689-732

California pp. 733-828

Hawaii pp. 842-850

Alaska pp. 831-843

XIII

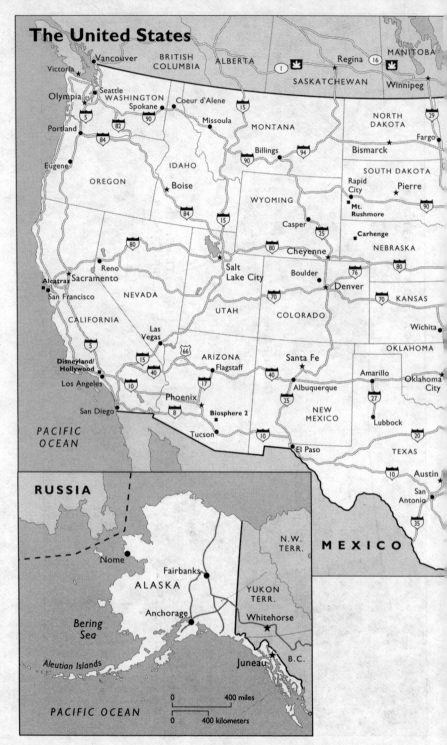

The United States

Vancouver
Victoria ★
BRITISH COLUMBIA
ALBERTA
SASKATCHEWAN
Regina (16)
MANITOBA
Winnipeg

Olympia
Seattle
WASHINGTON
Spokane
Coeur d'Alene
(15)
MONTANA
NORTH DAKOTA
Fargo

Portland
(84)
(82)
(90)
Missoula
Billings
(94)
Bismarck

Eugene
OREGON
IDAHO
★ Boise
(90)
WYOMING
SOUTH DAKOTA
Rapid City
■ Mt. Rushmore
★ Pierre
(90)

(84)
(15)
Casper
(25)
■ Carhenge
NEBRASKA

Reno
★ Sacramento
■ Alcatraz
San Francisco
NEVADA
(80)
Salt Lake City ★
UTAH
Boulder
Cheyenne ★
(80)
(76)
Denver
(80)
KANSAS
(70)

CALIFORNIA
(5)
Las Vegas
(15)
(66)
COLORADO
(70)
Wichita

Disneyland/ Hollywood
Los Angeles
(40)
ARIZONA
Flagstaff
(17)
Santa Fe ★
(40)
OKLAHOMA
Amarillo
Oklahoma City ★
(27)

(10)
San Diego
Phoenix
(8)
■ Biosphere 2
Albuquerque
(25)
NEW MEXICO
Lubbock

PACIFIC OCEAN
Tucson
(10)
El Paso
TEXAS
(20)

(10)
Austin ★
San Antonio
(35)

MEXICO

RUSSIA

Nome
Fairbanks
N.W. TERR.

ALASKA
Anchorage
YUKON TERR.
Whitehorse ★

Bering Sea
Juneau ★
B.C.

Aleutian Islands

PACIFIC OCEAN

0   400 miles
0   400 kilometers

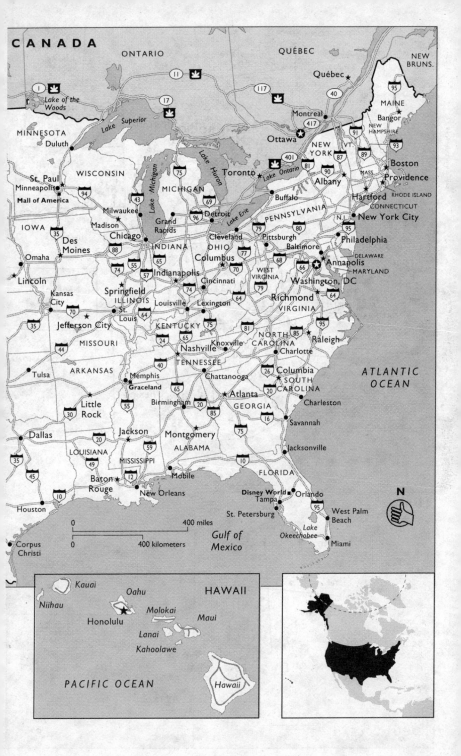

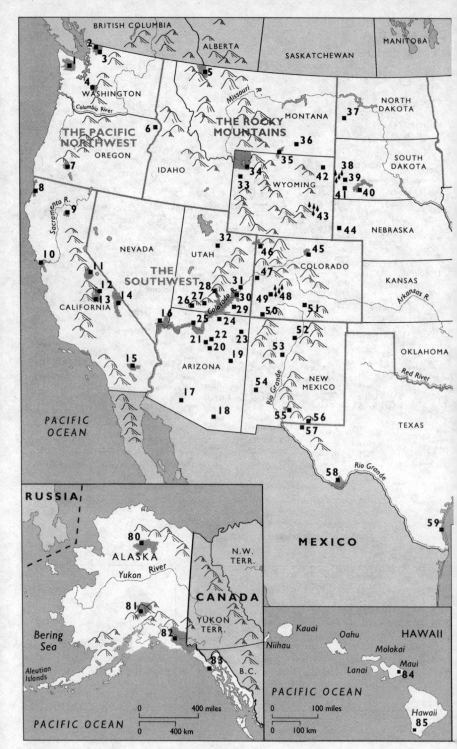

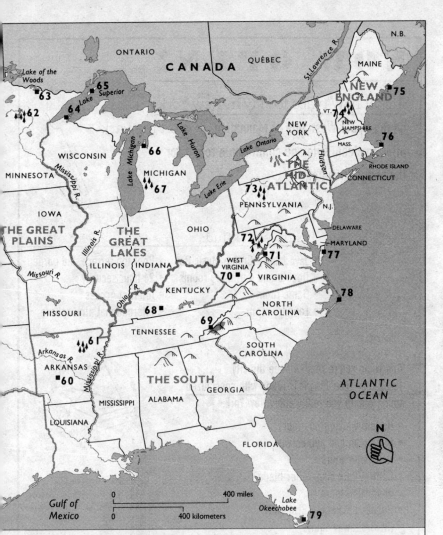

USA National Park System

National Monuments
Bandelier, NM, 52
Black Canyon, CO, 49
Canyon de Chelly, AZ, 23
Colorado, CO, 47
Devils Tower, WY, 42
Dinosaur, CO, 46
Gila Cliff Dwellings, NM, 54
Great Sand Dunes, CO, 51
Lassen Volcanic, CA, 9
Little Bighorn, MT, 36
Mt. Rushmore, SD, 39
Natural Bridges, UT, 29
Navajo, AZ, 24
Organ Pipe, AZ, 17
Petroglyph, NM, 22
Scotts Bluff, NE, 44
Sunset Crater, AZ, 21
Timpanogos Cave, UT, 32
Walnut Canyon, AZ, 20
White Sands, NM, 55
Wupatki, AZ, 53

National Parks
Acadia, ME, 75
Arches, UT, 31
Badlands, SD, 40
Big Bend, TX, 58
Bryce Canyon, UT, 27
Canyonlands, UT, 30
Capitol Reef, UT, 28
Carlsbad Caverns, NM, 56
Crater Lake, OR, 7
Death Valley, CA, 14
Denali, AK, 81
Everglades, FL, 79
Gates of the Arctic, AK, 80
Glacier, MT, 5
Glacier Bay, AK, 83
Grand Canyon, AZ, 25
Grand Teton, WY, 33
Great Smoky Mts., TN, 69
Guadalupe Mts., TX, 57
Haleakala, HI, 84
Hawaii Volcanoes, HI, 85
Hot Springs, AR, 60

Isle Royale, MI, 65
Joshua Tree, CA, 15
Kings Canyon, CA, 12
Mammoth Cave, KY, 68
Mesa Verde, CO, 50
Mt. Rainier, WA, 4
New River Gorge, WV, 70
North Cascades, WA, 2
Olympic, WA, 1
Petrified Forest, AZ, 19
Redwood, CA, 8
Rocky Mt., CO, 45
Saguaro, AZ, 18
Sequoia, CA, 13
Shenandoah, VA, 71
Theodore Roosevelt, ND, 37
Voyageurs, MN, 63
Wind Cave, SD, 41
Wrangell-St. Elias, AK, 82
Yellowstone, WY, 34
Yosemite, CA, 11
Zion, UT, 26

National Recreation Areas
Bighorn Canyon, MT, 35

Golden Gate, CA, 10
Hell's Canyon, OR, 6
Lake Mead, NV, 16
Ross Lake, WA, 3

National Forests
Allegheny, PA, 73
Black Hills, SD, 48
Chippewa, MN, 62
Grand Mesa, CO, 38
Manistee, MI, 67
Medicine Bow, WY, 43
Monongahela, WV, 72
Ozark, AR, 61
White Mts., NH, 74

National Lakeshores
Apostle Islands, WI, 64
Sleeping Bear Dunes, MI, 66

National Seashores
Assateague, MD, 77
Cape Cod, MA, 76
Cape Hatteras, NC, 78
Padre Island, TX, 59

ESSENTIALS

PLANNING YOUR TRIP

■ When to Go

Going to the right place at the right time makes all the difference when traveling. In most of the U.S., **tourist season** is from **Memorial Day** to **Labor Day** (May 31 to Sept. 6, 1999); expect things to be in full, camera-clicking swing. In the off season, hotels might be cheaper and sights less crowded, but those sights you traveled so far to see might also be closed. On national holidays, as well, many sights will be closed. In general, tourist offices are great resources for travelers. For a **climate chart, national holidays,** and a list of major **local festivals,** see the **Appendix,** p. 930.

■ Useful Information

GOVERNMENT INFORMATION OFFICES

Both Canada and the U.S. lack a central tourist info center. However, the states and the provinces all have their own well-stocked, professionally run offices. *Let's Go* includes info on these brochure oases in the **Practical Information** section for each state and province.

HITTING THE BOOKS

On the road, knowledge is power. The mail-order travel shops below offer books and supplies catering to special travel interests.

Adventurous Traveler Bookstore, P.O. Box 1468, Williston, VT 05495 (800-282-3963; http://www.AdventurousTraveler.com). Free 40-page catalogue upon request. Specializes in outdoor adventure travel books and maps for the U.S.

Bon Voyage!, 2069 W. Bullard Ave., Fresno, CA 93711-1200 (800-995-9716, from abroad 209-447-8441; fax 266-6460; email 70754.3511@compuserve.com). Annual mail-order catalogue offers a range of products. Books, travel accessories, luggage, electrical converters, maps, and videos. All merchandise may be returned for exchange or refund within 30 days of purchase, and prices are guaranteed.

Michelin Travel Publications, Michelin North America, P.O. Box 19008, Greenville, SC 29602-9008 (800-223-0987; fax 378-7471; http://www.michelin-travel.com). Publishes 4 major lines of travel-related material: *Green Guides,* for sight-seeing, maps, and driving itineraries; *Red Guides,* which rate hotels and restaurants; *In-Your-Pocket Guides;* and detailed, reliable road maps and atlases. All 4 are available at bookstores and distributors throughout the world.

Rand McNally, 150 S. Wacker Dr., Chicago, IL 60606 (800-333-0136; http://www.randmcnally.com). Publishes one of the most comprehensive road atlases of the U.S., Canada, and Mexico, available in their stores throughout the country and most bookstores for $10.

INTERNET RESOURCES

Along with everything else in the 90s, budget travel is moving rapidly into the Information Age, with the **Internet** as a leading travel resource. You can make your own airline, hotel, hostel, or car rental reservations on the Internet, and connect personally with others abroad (for airline-specific Web info, see p. 29). **NetTravel: How Travelers Use the Internet,** by Michael Shapiro, describes the Internet's different travel uses ($25).

ESSENTIALS

The **World Wide Web** has become the Internet forum of choice, although its lack of hierarchy makes it difficult to distinguish between the good, the bad, and the marketing. **Search engines** (services that search for webpages under specific subjects) can significantly aid the process. **Lycos** (http://a2z.lycos.com), **Infoseek** (http://guide.infoseek.com), and **HOTBOT** (http://www.hotbot.com) are a few of the most popular. **Yahoo!** is a slightly more organized search engine; check out its travel links at http://www.yahoo.com/Recreation/Travel. Another fruitful way to explore the Web's resources is to find a top site and use its links to other pages. **Let's Go's Web site** (http://www.letsgo.com) has info on our books and a list of links.

The **Student and Budget Travel Resource Guide** (http://asa.ugl.lib.umich.edu/chdocs/travel/travel-guide.html) is among the most helpful webpages; it has links to the CIA world factbook, consular info sheets, state travel advisories, Amtrak train schedules, the *Internet Guide to Hostelling*, a subway navigator, a jet lag diet, and more. **Shoestring Travel** (http://www.stratpub.com) is a budget travel e-zine (electronic magazine), with feature articles, links, user exchange, and accommodations advice. **City Net** (http://www.city.net) dispenses info on a wide array of cities and regions across the U.S. A similar set of services is provided by the **USA Citylink** page (http://www.USAcitylink.com). For Canada-specific travel info, consult the **Discover Canada** site (http://www.DiscoverCanada.com), or the **Canadian government's** surprisingly flashy info page (http://www.infocan.gc.ca).

Compare flight fares, look at maps, and make reservations through **Microsoft Expedia** (http://expedia.msn.com). FareTracker, a free service within Expedia, sends monthly mailings about the cheapest fares to any destination. **The CIA World Factbook** (http://www.odci.gov/cia/publications/factbook/index.html) has tons of vital statistics on the country you want to visit, from an overview of a country's economy to an explanation of their government system. **Cybercafe Guide** (http://www.cyberiacafe.net/cyberia/guide/ccafe.htm) can help you find cybercafes worldwide.

■ Documents and Formalities

EMBASSIES AND CONSULATES

Contact your nearest embassy or consulate to obtain info regarding visas and passports to the United States and Canada. The U.S. **State Dept.** publishes *Key Officers of Foreign Service Posts,* which lists detailed info on every overseas station ($3.75). To order a copy, write to the Superintendent of Documents, U.S. Government Printing Office, Washington, D.C. 20402 (202-512-1800; fax 512-2168), or consult the free Internet version at http://www.state.gov/www/about_state/contacts/index.html. A similar cyberlisting for the Canadian counterparts can be found at http://www.dfait-maeci.gc.ca/english/MISSIONS.

U.S. EMBASSIES: In **Australia,** Moonah Pl., Canberra, ACT 2600 (02 6214 5600; fax 6270 5970); in **Canada,** 100 Wellington St., Ottawa, ON K1P 5T1 (613-238-5335 or 238-4470; fax 238-5720); in **Ireland,** 42 Elgin Rd., Ballsbridge, Dublin (016 687 122); in **New Zealand,** 29 Fitzherbert Terr., Thorndon, Wellington (04 472 2068; fax 472 3537); in **South Africa,** 877 Pretorius St., Arcadio 0083; P.O. Box 9536, Pretoria 0001 (012 342 1048; fax 342 2244); in the **U.K.,** 24/31 Grosvenor Sq., London W1A 1AE (0171 499 9000; fax 409 1637).

U.S. CONSULATES: In **Australia,** MLC Centre, 19-29 Martin Pl., 59th fl., Sydney NSW 2000 (02 9373 9200; fax 9373 9125); 553 St. Kilda Rd., P.O. Box 6722, Melbourne, VIC 3004 (03 9526 5900; fax 9510 4646); 16 St. George Terr., 13th fl., Perth, WA 6000 (08 9231 9400; fax 9231 9444); in **Canada,** P.O. Box 65, Postal Station Desjardins, Montréal, QC H5B 1G1 (514-398-9695; fax 398-0973); 2 Pl. Terrasse Dufferin, CP939, Québec, QC G1R 4T9 (418-692-2095; fax 692-4640); 360 University Ave., Toronto, ON M5G 1S4 (416-595-1700; fax 595-0051); 1095 W. Pender St., Vancouver, BC V6E 2M6 (604-685-4311; fax 685-5285); in **New Zealand,** Yorkshire General Bldg.,

4th fl., corner of Shortland and O'Connell St., Auckland (09 303 2724; fax 366 0870); in **South Africa,** Broadway Industries Centre, Heerengracht, Foreshore, Capetown (021 214 280; fax 254 151); Kine Centre, 11th fl., P.O. Box 2155, Johannesburg (011 331 1327; fax 838 3920); in the **U.K.,** Queen's House, 14 Queen St., Belfast, N. Ireland BT1 6EQ (0123 232 8239; fax 224 8482); 3 Regent Terr., Edinburgh, Scotland EH7 5BW (0131 556 8315; fax 557 6023).

CANADIAN EMBASSIES: In **Australia,** Commonwealth Ave., Canberra, ACT 2600 (02 6273 3844; fax 6273 3285); in **Ireland,** Canada House, 65 St. Stephen's Green, Dublin 2 (014 781 988; fax 478 1285); in **New Zealand,** 61 Molesworth St., 3rd fl., Thorndon, Wellington (04 473 9577; fax 471 2082); in **South Africa,** 1103 Arcadia St., Hatfield, Pretoria 0083 (012 422 3000; fax 422 3052); in the **U.K.,** MacDonald House, 1 Grosvenor Sq., London W1X 0AA (0171 258 6600; fax 258 6333); in the **U.S.,** 501 Pennsylvania Ave., Washington, D.C. 20001 (202-682-1740; fax 682-7726).

CANADIAN CONSULATES: In **Australia,** Level 5, Quay West Bldg., 111 Harrington St., Sydney NSW, 2000 (02 9364 3000; fax 9364 3098); 123 Camberwell Rd., Hawthorn East, Melbourne, VIC 3123 (03 9811 9999; fax 9811 9969); 267 St. George Terr., 3rd fl., Perth, WA (08 9322 7930; fax 9261 7700); **New Zealand,** Level 9, Jetset Centre, 48 Emily Pl., Auckland (09 309 3690; fax 307 3111); in **South Africa,** Reserve Bank Bldg., 19th fl., 360 St. George's Mall St., Capetown 8001 (021 235 240; fax 234 893); in the **U.K.,** 3 George St., Edinburgh, Scotland EH2 2XZ (0131 220 4333; fax 245 6010); in the **U.S.,** 1251 Ave. of the Americas, New York, NY 10020 (212-596-1683; fax 596-1780); 550 S. Hope St., 18th fl., Los Angeles, CA 90071 (213-346-2700; fax 620-8827); 2 Prudential Plaza, 180 N. Stetson Ave., #2400, Chicago, IL 60601 (312-616-1860; fax 616-1877).

PASSPORTS

Be sure to file all applications several months in advance of your planned departure date. *Before you leave,* photocopy the page of your passport that contains your photograph, passport number, and other identifying info; this will help prove your citizenship and facilitate the issuing of a new passport if your old one is **lost** or **stolen.** Carry this photocopy in a safe place apart from your passport, and leave another copy at home. Consulates recommend that you also carry an expired passport or an official copy of your birth certificate. If you lose your passport, notify the local police and the nearest embassy or consulate of your home government *immediately.* To expedite its replacement, you will need to know all information previously recorded and show identification and proof of citizenship. A replacement may take weeks to process, and it may be valid only for a limited time. Some consulates can issue a new passport within 24 hours with proof of citizenship. Any visas stamped in your old passport will be irretrievably lost. In an emergency, ask for immediate temporary traveling papers that will permit you to return to your home country.

U.S. and Canadian citizens may cross the U.S.-Canada border with proof of citizenship, either birth certificate or passport. U.S. citizens under 18 need written consent of parent or guardian; Canadian citizens under 16 need notarized permission from both parents.

Australia: Apply for a passport in person at post office, passport office, or Australian diplomatic mission overseas. Appointment might be necessary. Passport offices located in Adelaide, Brisbane, Canberra City, Darwin, Hobart, Melbourne, Newcastle, Perth, and Sydney. Parents may file application for unmarried children under 18. Adult passports AUS$120 (for a 32-page passport) or AUS$180 (64-page). Child AUS$60 (32-page) or AUS$90 (64-page); prices change regularly. For more info, call toll-free (in Australia) 13 12 32, or visit http://www.austemb.org.

Ireland: Apply for passport by mail to either the Dept. of Foreign Affairs, Passport Office, Setanta Centre, Molesworth St., Dublin 2 (01 671 1633; fax 671 1092), or the Passport Office, Irish Life Bldg., 1A South Mall, Cork (02 127 2525; fax 127 5770). Obtain application at local Garda station or request one from passport office. The new Passport Express Service, available through post offices, allows citizens to get a passport in 2 weeks for an extra IR£3. Passports IR£45; valid for 5 years. Citizens under 18 or over 65 can request a 3-year passport IR£10.

New Zealand: Application forms available in New Zealand from travel agents and Dept. of Internal Affairs Link Centres in main cities and towns. Overseas, forms and passport services are provided by New Zealand embassies, high commissions, and consulates. Applications may be forwarded to Passport Office, P.O. Box 10526, Wellington. Standard processing time 10 working days. Adult NZ$80; child NZ$40. Urgent passport service available for extra NZ$80. Different fees apply at overseas post: 9 posts including London, Sydney, and Los Angeles offer both standard and urgent services (adult US$130, child US$65, plus US$130 if urgent). At other posts, adult urgent fee US$260, child US$195; issued within 3 working days. Children's names can no longer be endorsed on a parent's passport—they must apply for their own, which are valid for up to 5 years. Adult's passport valid for 10 years. More info is available on the Internet at http://www.govt.nz/agency_info/forms.

South Africa: Apply for a passport at any Home Affairs Office or South African Mission. Tourist passports, valid for 10 years, cost SAR80. Children under 16 must be issued their own passport, valid for 5 years, which costs SAR60. Emergency passport may be issued for SAR50. Time for the completion of an application is normally 3 months or more. Current passports less than 10 years old (counting from date of issuance) may be renewed until Dec. 31, 1999; every citizen whose passport's validity does not extend far beyond this date is urged to renew as soon as possible. Renewal is free, and turnaround time is usually 2 weeks. For further info, contact the nearest Dept. of Home Affairs Office.

United Kingdom: British citizens, British subjects, British Dependent Territories citizens, British Nationals (overseas), and British Overseas citizens may apply for a full passport, valid for 10 years (5 years if under 16). Forms available at passport offices, main post offices, many travel agents, and branches of Lloyds Bank and Artac World Choice. Apply by mail or in person (for an additional UK£10) to one of the passport offices, located in London, Liverpool, Newport, Peterborough, Glasgow, or Belfast. Fee is UK£31, UK£11 for children under 16. Children under 16 may no longer be included on parent's passport. London office offers same-day, walk-in rush service; arrive early. The British Visitor's Passport has been abolished; every traveler over 16 now needs a 10-year, standard passport. Contact U.K. Passport Agency at 0990 210 410.

U.S. AND CANADIAN ENTRANCE REQUIREMENTS

Foreign visitors to the United States and Canada are required to have a **passport** and **visa/proof of intent to leave.** To visit either country, you must be healthy and law-abiding, and demonstrate the ability to **support yourself financially** during your stay. A visa, stamped into a traveler's passport by the government of a host country, allows the bearer to stay in that country for a specified purpose and period of time. The **Center for International Business and Travel (CIBT),** 23201 New Mexico Ave. NW, Suite 210, Washington, D.C. 20016 (415-243-3900 or 800-925-2428), secures travel visas to and from all possible countries for a variable service charge. To obtain a U.S. or Canadian visa, contact the nearest embassy or consulate. According to U.S. law, **HIV-positive persons** are not permitted to enter the U.S. However, HIV testing is conducted only for those planning to immigrate permanently. Travelers from areas with particularly high concentrations of HIV-positive persons or persons with AIDS may be required to provide more info when applying. Travelers entering Canada who are suspected of being HIV-positive will be required to submit to HIV testing.

UNITED STATES Travelers from certain nations (including Australia, France, Germany, Ireland, Italy, Japan, New Zealand, and the U.K.) may enter the U.S. without a visa through the **Visa Waiver Pilot Program.** Visitors qualify as long as they are traveling for business or pleasure, are staying for 90 days or less, have proof of intent to leave (e.g., a returning plane ticket), a completed I-94W form (arrival/departure certificate attached to your visa upon arrival), and are traveling on particular air or sea carriers. Contact a U.S. consulate for more info; countries are added frequently.

Most visitors obtain a **B-2,** or "pleasure tourist," visa at the nearest U.S. consulate or embassy, which normally costs $45 and is usually valid for 6 months. For general visa inquiries, consult the Bureau of Consular Affair's Webpage (http://travel.state.gov/visa_services.html). If you lose your I-94 form, you can replace it at the nearest **Immigration and Naturalization Service (INS)** office, though it's very unlikely that the form will be replaced within the time of your stay. **Extensions** for visas are sometimes attainable with a completed I-539 form; call the forms request line 800-870-3676. For more info, contact the INS at 800-755-0777 or 202-307-1501 (http://www.ins.usdoj.gov).

CANADA Citizens of Australia, France, Germany, Ireland, Italy, Japan, Mexico, New Zealand, the U.K., and the U.S. may enter Canada without visas for stays of 90 days or less if they carry proof of intent to leave; South Africans need a visa to enter Canada. Citizens of other countries should contact their Canadian consulate for more info. Write to **Citizenship and Immigration Canada** for the useful booklet *Applying for a Visitor Visa* at Information Centre, Public Affairs Branch, Journal Tower South, 365 Laurier Ave. W., Ottawa, ON K1A 1L1 (888-242-2100 or 613-954-9019; fax 954-2221), or consult the electronic version at http://cicnet.ci.gc.ca. **Extensions** are sometimes granted; phone the nearest Canada Immigration Centre listed in the phone directory.

CUSTOMS: ENTERING

UNITED STATES It is illegal to transport many perishable foods, such as most fruits, vegetables, and meat products. Officials may seize articles made from certain protected species, so be ready to part with your illegally purchased cowboy boots or fur coat. Additional restrictions apply for goods that violate copyright or trademark laws. For a detailed description of the relevant codes, contact the **Animal and Plant Health Inspection Service (APHIS),** 4700 River Rd., Riverdale, MD 20737 (http://www.aphis.usda.gov/oa/travel.html).

You may bring the following into the U.S.: $100 in gifts and $200 in personal merchandise; 200 cigarettes (1 carton), 50 cigars, or 2kg of tobacco; and personal belongings such as clothes and jewelry. Travelers ages 21 and over may also bring up to 1L of alcohol, although state laws may further restrict the amount you may carry. Money (cash or traveler's checks) can be transported, but amounts over $10,000 must be reported. Customs officers may ask how much money you're carrying and your planned departure date in order to ensure that you'll be able to support yourself while in the U.S. The **U.S. Customs Service,** 1300 Pennsylvania Ave., Washington, D.C. 20229 (202-927-5580; http://www.customs.ustreas.gov), publishes the helpful brochure, *Customs Guidelines for Visitors to the United States*.

CANADA Besides items of a personal nature that you plan to use in Canada during your visit, the following items may be brought in free of duty: up to 1.14L of alcohol or a 24-pack of beer; 50 cigars or cigarillos, 200 cigarettes (1 carton), 200g of manufactured tobacco; and gifts valued less than CDN$60. If you exceed the limited amounts, you will be asked to pay a fine. For detailed info on Canadian customs and other travel booklets, write Canada Customs, 2265 St. Laurent Blvd., Ottawa, ON K1G 4K3. (800-461-9999 or 613-993-0534 outside Canada; fax 991-9062; http://www.rc.gc.ca.)

CUSTOMS: GOING HOME

Upon returning home, you must declare all articles you acquired abroad and must pay a duty on the value of those articles that exceed the allowance established by your country's customs service. Goods and gifts purchased at duty-free shops abroad are not exempt from duty or sales tax at your point of return, and should be declared. "Duty free" only means that you need not pay a tax in the country of purchase.

Australia: Citizens may import AUS$400 (under 18 AUS$200) of goods duty-free, in addition to 1.125L alcohol and 250 cigarettes or 250g tobacco. Any amount of Australian and/or foreign cash may be brought into or taken out of the country, but amounts of AUS$10,000 or more, or the equivalent in foreign currency, must be reported. All foodstuffs and animal products must be declared on arrival. For info, contact the

Regional Director, Australian Customs Service, G.P.O. Box 8, Sydney NSW 2001 (02 9213 2000; fax 9213 4000) or visit http://www.customs.gov.au.

Ireland: Citizens must declare everything in excess of IR£142 (IR£73 per traveler under 15 years of age) obtained outside the EU or duty- and tax-free in the EU above the following allowances: 200 cigarettes, 100 cigarillos, 50 cigars, or 250g tobacco; 1L liquor or 2L wine; 2L still wine; 50g perfume; and 250mL toilet water. Goods for which duty and tax were paid in another EU country up to a value of IR£460 (IR£115 per traveler under 15) will not be subject to additional customs duties. You must be over 17 to import tobacco or alcohol. For more info, contact The Revenue Commissioners, Dublin Castle (016 792 777; fax 712 021; email taxes@iol.ie; http://www.revenue.ie).

New Zealand: Citizens may import up to NZ$700 worth of goods duty-free if intended for personal use. The concession is 200 cigarettes (1 carton), 250g tobacco, 50 cigars, or a combination of all 3 not to exceed 250g. You may also bring in 4.5L of beer or wine and 1.125L of liquor. Only travelers over 17 may import tobacco or alcohol. For more info, contact New Zealand Customs, 50 Anzac Ave., Box 29, Auckland (09 377 3520; fax 309 2978).

South Africa: Citizens may import duty-free: 400 cigarettes, 50 cigars, 250g tobacco, 2L wine, 1L of spirits, 250mL toilet water, and 50mL perfume, and consumable items up to a value of SAR500. Goods up to a value of SAR10,000 over this duty-free allowance are dutiable at 20%; such goods are also exempted from payment of VAT. Items acquired abroad and sent to the Republic as unaccompanied baggage do not qualify for any allowances. You may not export or import South African bank notes in excess of SAR25,000. For more info, consult the free pamphlet *South African Customs Information,* available in airports or from the Commissioner for Customs and Excise, Private Bag X47, Pretoria 0001 (012 314 9911; fax 328 6478).

United Kingdom: Citizens or visitors arriving in the U.K. from outside the EU must declare goods in excess of the following allowances: 200 cigarettes, 100 cigarillos, 50 cigars, or 250g tobacco; still table wine (2L); strong liquors over 22% volume (1L), fortified or sparkling wine, other liquors (2L); perfume (60 cc/mL); toilet water (250 cc/mL); and UK£145 worth of all other goods including gifts and souvenirs. You must be over 17 to import liquor or tobacco. These allowances also apply to duty-free purchases within the EU, except for the last category, other goods, which then has an allowance of UK£75. Dutiable and taxable goods purchased for personal use (regulated according to set guide levels) within the EU do not require any further customs duty. For more info, contact Her Majesty's Customs and Excise, Custom House, Nettleton Road, Heathrow Airport, Hounslow, Middlesex TW6 2LA (0181 910 3602/3566; fax 910 3765) or at http://www.open.gov.uk.

YOUTH, STUDENT, & TEACHER IDENTIFICATION

Many U.S. establishments will honor an ordinary university student ID for student discounts. Still, two main forms of student and youth identification are extremely useful. Flashing the **International Student Identity Card (ISIC)** can procure discounts for sights, theaters, museums, accommodations, train, ferry, and airplane travel, and other services (1999 card valid Sept. 1998-Dec. 1999), and costs $20 (CDN$15). Ask about discounts even when none are advertised. Applicants must be at least 12 years old and degree-seeking students of a secondary or post-secondary school. Because of the proliferation of phony ISICs, many airlines and some other services require other proof of student identity, such as a signed letter from the registrar attesting to your student status and stamped with the school seal, and/or your school ID card. The card also provides a valuable insurance package (see **Insurance,** p. 14). In addition, cardholders have access to a toll-free **24hr. ISIC helpline** (800-626-2427 in the U.S. and Canada, elsewhere call collect 44 181 666 9025) whose multilingual staff can provide help in medical, legal, and financial emergencies overseas. When you apply for the card, ask for a copy of the *International Student Identity Card Handbook,* which lists some available discounts. Most of the **Budget Travel Agencies** (see p. 21) issue the ISIC. The **International Teacher Identity Card (ITIC)** is $20 and offers the similar but limited discounts, as well as medical insurance coverage. For more info on these handy cards, consult the organization's web site (http://www.istc.org) or email isicinfo@istc.org. Federation of International Youth Travel Organizations (FIYTO) issues a discount card to travelers who are under 26 but not students. Known as the **GO25 Card,** (http://www.go25.org), this one-year card offers many of the same benefits as the ISIC, and most organizations that sell the ISIC also sell the GO25 Card. A brochure that lists discounts is free when you purchase the card. To apply, you will need either a passport, valid driver's license, or copy of a birth certificate, and a passport-sized photo with your name printed on the back. The fee is $20. Information is available on the web at http://www.ciee.org, or by contacting Travel CUTS in Canada, STA Travel in the U.K., Council Travel in the U.S., or the **Federation of International Youth Travel Organizations (FIYTO),** Bredgade 25H, DK-1260 Copenhagen K, Denmark (453 333 9600; fax 393 9676; email mailbox@fiyto.org; http://www.fiyto.org or http://www.go25.org).

■ Money Matters

If you stay in hostels and prepare your own food, you can spend anywhere from $25-60 per person per day. Transportation will increase these figures. No matter how low your budget, if you plan to travel for more than a couple of days, you will need to keep handy a larger amount of cash than usual. Carrying it around with you, even in a money belt, is risky, and personal checks from another country, or even another state, will probably not be accepted no matter how many forms of identification you have (some banks even shy away from accepting checks).

Many Canadian shops, as well as vending machines and parking meters, accept U.S. coins at face value. Stores will often convert the price of your purchase for you, but they are not legally obligated to offer you a fair exchange. During the past several years, the Canadian dollar has been worth roughly 30% less than the U.S. dollar.

> All prices in the Canada section of this book are listed in Canadian dollars unless otherwise noted.

CURRENCY AND EXCHANGE

You'll get better rates exchanging for U.S. or Canadian dollars in the U.S. and Canada than at home, and wholesale rates offered at banks will be lower than those offered by other exchange agencies. However, converting some money before you go will allow you to zip through the airport while others languish in exchange lines. It's a good idea to bring enough foreign currency to last for the first 1 to 3 days of a trip. If you are planning to visit a little-touristed area, carry U.S. dollars from early on; bank tellers may not recognize or be willing to exchange foreign currencies. Shop around for the best commission and exchange rates possible. Banks generally have the best rates, but sometimes tourist offices or exchange kiosks offer better deals. Only go to banks or bureaux de change which have a 5% margin between their buy and sell prices; otherwise, they are making too much profit. Since you lose money with every transaction, convert in large sums, but don't convert more than you need, because it may be difficult to change it back to your home currency, or to a new one.

The Greenback (The U.S. Dollar)

CDN$1 = US$0.65	US$1 = CDN$1.54
UK£1 = US$1.68	US$1 = UK£0.60
IR£1 = US$1.45	US$1 = IR£0.69
AUS$1 = US$0.58	US$1 = AUS$1.72
NZ$1 = US$0.50	US$1 = NZ$2.00
SAR1 = US$0.16	US$1 = SAR6.21

The main unit of currency in the U.S. is the **dollar,** which is divided into 100 cents. Paper money is green in the U.S; bills come in denominations of $1, $5, $10, $20, $50, and $100. Coins are 1¢ (penny), 5¢ (nickel), 10¢ (dime), and 25¢ (quarter).

The Loonie (The Canadian Dollar)

US$1 = CDN$1.54	CDN$1 = US$0.65
UK£1 = CDN$2.58	CDN$1 = UK£0.39
IR£1 = CDN$2.23	CDN$1 = IR£0.45
AUS$1 = CDN$.90	CDN$1 = AUS$1.11
NZ$1 = CDN$0.77	CDN$1 = NZ$1.29
SAR1=CDN$0.25	CDN$1=SAR4.03

The main unit of currency in Canada is the **dollar**. Paper money comes in denominations of $5, $10, $20, $50, and $100, which are all the same size but color-coded by denomination. Coins come in denominations of 1¢, 5¢, 10¢, 25¢, $1, and $2. The $1 coin is known as the **Loonie.**

TRAVELER'S CHECKS

Traveler's checks are one of the safest and least troublesome means of carrying funds. Several agencies and many banks sell them, usually for face value plus a 1% commission. Members of the American Automobile Association (AAA) can get American Express checks commission-free (see **Automobile Clubs,** p. 35). Even in small towns, where traveler's checks might not be accepted, there will probably be at least one place in every town where you can exchange them for local currency.

Each agency provides refunds **if your checks are lost or stolen,** and many provide additional services. (Note that you may need a police report verifying the loss or theft.) Inquire about toll-free refund hotlines and refund centers, emergency message relay services, and stolen credit card assistance when you purchase your checks. Always keep your check receipts separate from your checks and store them in a safe place or with a traveling companion; record check numbers when you cash them and leave a list of check numbers with someone at home. Keep a separate supply of cash or traveler's checks for emergencies. Be sure never to countersign your checks until you're prepared to cash them.

American Express: Call 800-221-7282 in the U.S. and Canada, in Australia 800 25 19 02, in New Zealand 0800 441 068, in the U.K. 0800 521 313. Elsewhere, call U.S. collect 801-964-6665. The most widely recognized worldwide and the easiest to replace if lost or stolen. Checks can be purchased for a small fee at American Express Travel Service offices, banks, and AAA offices. They can also be obtained from American Express Dispensers at Travel Service Offices at airports by ordering over the phone (800-ORDER-TC/673-3782). American Express offices cash their checks commission-free, although they often offer slightly worse rates than banks. You can also buy *Cheques for Two,* which can be signed by either of two people traveling together. Visit their online travel offices (http://www.aexp.com).

Citicorp: Call 800-645-6556 in the U.S. and Canada; in Europe, the Middle East, or Africa, dial London office at 44 171 508 7007; from elsewhere call U.S. collect 813-623-1709. Commission 1-2% on check purchases. Checkholders become enrolled for 45 days in the Travel Assist Program (hotline 800-250-4377 or collect 202-296-8728), which provides travelers with an English-speaking doctor, lawyer, and interpreter referrals as well as check-refund assistance and general travel info. Citicorp's World Courier Service guarantees hand-delivery of traveler's checks when a refund location is not convenient. Call 24hr.

Thomas Cook MasterCard: Call 800-223-9920 in the U.S. and Canada; elsewhere call U.S. collect 609-987-7300; from the U.K. call 0800 622 101 free or 173 350 2995 collect or 173 331 8950 collect. Commission 1-2% for purchases. A Thomas Cook office will offer potentially lower commissions for purchases, and charge no commission for cashing checks.

CREDIT CARDS AND ATM CARDS

Credit cards are not accepted at many small, cheap locations where traveler's checks are welcomed. Still, credit cards can be extremely valuable in the U.S. and Canada, and are sometimes required (for example, at many car rental agencies). Credit cards are also useful when an emergency, such as necessary car repairs, leaves you temporarily without other resources. Major credit cards can be used to instantly extract cash advances from associated banks and ATM machines; this can be a great bargain for foreign travelers because credit card companies get the wholesale exchange rate, which is generally 5% better than the retail rate used by banks. However, a lost credit card can mean serious financial damage; cancel your card immediately if it is lost.

MasterCard (outside North America, "EuroCard" or "Access") and **Visa** ("Barclaycard" or "Carte Bleue") are the most widely accepted. For lost or stolen cards, call Visa at 800-336-8472 or Mastercard at 800-999-0454. **American Express** (800-843-2273) cards are less widely accepted, but card membership includes access to a 24hr. hotline offering medical and legal assistance in emergencies (800-554-2639 in U.S. and Canada). The card also offers extensive travel-related services, including assistance in changing airline, hotel, and car rental reservations, baggage loss and flight insurance, sending mailgrams and international cables, and holding mail at one of the more than 1700 AmEx offices around the world. Sign up for Express Cash for advances at many ATMs and all AmEx offices (see **Money From Home,** p. 11).

There are tens of thousands of **ATMs** (automatic teller machines) everywhere in the U.S., offering 24hr. service in banks, airports, grocery stores, gas stations, and elsewhere. ATMs allow you to withdraw cash from your bank account wherever you are, and happily get the same wholesale exchange rate as credit cards. There is often a limit on the amount of money you can withdraw per day (usually about $500, depending on the type of card and account). Two major ATM networks in the U.S. are **Cirrus** (800-4-CIRRUS/424-7787) and **PLUS** (800-843-7587). Inquire at your bank about fees charged for ATM transactions (usually $1-2, but can be as much as $5).

MONEY FROM HOME

If you run out of money on the road, you can have more mailed to you in the form of traveler's checks bought in your name, a certified check, or through postal money orders. **Certified checks** are redeemable at any bank, while postal **money orders** can be cashed at post offices upon display of two IDs (1 of which must be a photo ID). Keep receipts, since money orders are refundable if lost.

Wiring money can cost from around $10 (for domestic service) to $20 (international), depending on the bank, plus there will be a fee ($7-15) for receiving the money. Once you've found a bank that will accept a wire, write or telegram your home bank with your account number, the name and address of the bank to receive the wire, and a routing number. Also notify the bank of the form of ID that second bank should accept before paying the money. As a very last resort, most consulates will wire home for you and deduct the cost from the money you receive. **Western Union** (800-225-5227) is a well-known but expensive service that can be used to cable money with your Visa or MasterCard within the domestic United States. You or someone else can phone in a credit card number or bring cash to a Western Union office for pick-up at another Western Union location. The rates for sending cash are generally $10 cheaper than with a credit card. Rates to send money with a credit card are $40 to send $250, $53 to send $500, and $85 to send $1000. You will need ID to pick up the money. **American Express** is one of the easiest ways to get money from home. AmEx allows card holders to draw cash from their checking accounts at any of its major offices and many of its representatives' offices, up to $1000 every 21 days (no service charge; no interest). AmEx also offers **Express Cash,** with ATMs located in airports, hotels, banks, office complexes, and shopping areas. Express Cash withdrawals are automatically debited from the Cardmember's specified bank account or line of credit. Green card holders may withdraw up to $1000 in a 7-day period. There is a 2% transaction fee ($2.50 min./$20 max.) for each cash withdrawal. To enroll in Express Cash, Cardmembers may call 800-227-4669; outside the U.S. call collect 904-565-7875. Unless using the AmEx service, avoid cashing checks in foreign currencies; they usually take weeks and a $30 fee to clear.

TAXES

The U.S. **sales tax** is the equivalent of the European Value-Added Tax and ranges from 4-10% depending on the item and the place; in most states, groceries are not taxed. *Let's Go* lists sales tax rates in the introduction to each state.

In Canada, you'll quickly notice the 7% **goods and services tax (GST)** and an additional **sales tax** in some provinces. See the provinces' introductions for info on local taxes. Visitors can claim a rebate of the GST they pay on accommodations of less than 1 month and on most goods they buy and take home, so be sure to save your receipts and pick up a GST rebate form while in Canada. The total claim must be at least CDN\$7 of GST (equal to CDN\$100 in purchases) and must be made within 1 year of the date of the purchase; further goods must be exported from Canada within 60 days of purchase. A brochure detailing restrictions is available from local tourist offices or through **Revenue Canada, Visitor's Rebate Program,** 275 Pope Rd., Summerside, PEI C1N 6C6 (800-668-4748 or 902-432-5608 outside Canada).

Tipping and Bargaining

In the U.S., it is customary to **tip** waitstaff and cab drivers 15%, but at your discretion. At the airport, porters expect at least \$1 per bag tip to carry your bags. Tipping is less compulsory in Canada; a good tip signifies remarkable service. **Bargaining** is generally frowned upon and fruitless in both countries.

■ Safety and Security

STREET SMARTS

Tourists are particularly vulnerable to crime, because they often carry large amounts of cash and are not as street savvy as locals. To prevent easy theft, don't keep all of your valuables (money, important documents) in one place. To avoid unwanted attention, try to blend in as much as possible. Check a map indoors rather than on a street corner, and look over your map before setting out.

When walking at night, stick to busy, well-lit streets and avoid dark alleyways. Do not attempt to cross through parks, parking lots, or other large, deserted areas. A blissfully isolated beach can become a treacherous nightmare as night falls. Find out about unsafe areas from tourist information, from the manager of your hotel or hostel, or from a local whom you trust. You may want to carry a whistle to scare off attackers or attract attention. Whenever possible, *Let's Go* warns of unsafe neighborhoods and areas, but you should exercise your own judgment about the safety of your environs. Buildings in disrepair, vacant lots, and unpopulated areas are all bad signs. If you feel uncomfortable, leave as quickly and directly as you can, but don't allow fear of the unknown to turn you into a hermit. Careful, persistent exploration will build confidence and make your stay in an area more rewarding. *Let's Go* does not recommend **hitchhiking** under any circumstances, particularly for women—see **By Thumb** for more info, p. 39.

A good self-defense course will give you more concrete ways to react to different types of aggression, but it often carries a steep price tag. **Impact, Prepare, and Model Mugging** can refer you to local self-defense courses in the United States (800-345-KICK/5425), with prices from \$50-500.

In most of the U.S. and Canada, **call 911 for emergency medical help, police,** or **fire** toll-free (you don't have to put a coin in the pay phone). In some rural areas, the 911 system has not yet been introduced; if 911 doesn't work, dial the **operator (0),** who will contact the appropriate emergency service.

FINANCIAL SECURITY

Among the more colorful aspects of large cities are **con artists.** Con artists and hustlers often work in groups, and children are among the most effective. Be aware of certain classics: sob stories that require money, rolls of bills "found" on the street, mustard spilled (or saliva spit) onto your shoulder distracting you for enough time to snatch your bag. Be especially alert in these situations. Do not respond or make eye contact, walk quickly away, and keep a solid grip on your belongings. Contact the police if a hustler is particularly insistent or aggressive.

Don't put a wallet with money in your back pocket. If you carry a purse, buy a sturdy one with a secure clasp and carry it across the body, with the clasp against you. Secure your packs with combination padlocks which slip through the two zippers. (Even these precautions do not always suffice: moped riders who snatch purses and backpacks sometimes tote knives to cut the straps.) A **money belt** is the best way to carry cash; you can buy one at most camping supply stores. A **neck pouch** is equally safe, although far less accessible. Refrain from pulling out your neck pouch in public; if you must, be very discreet. Avoid keeping anything precious in a **fanny-pack** (even on your stomach): your valuables will be highly visible and easy to steal.

In city crowds and especially on public transportation, pick-pockets are amazingly deft at their craft. Rush hour is no excuse for strangers to press up against you on subways. If someone stands uncomfortably close, move to another car and hold your bags tightly. Also, be alert in public telephone booths. If you must say your calling-card number, do so very quietly; if you punch it in, make sure no one can look over your shoulder. **Photocopies** of important documents allow you to recover them in case they are lost or filched. Carry one copy separate from the documents and leave another copy at home. Keep some money separate from the rest to use in an emergency or in case of theft. Label every piece of luggage both inside and out.

Alcohol and Drugs

You must be 21 to drink in the U.S. *Even foreigners accustomed to observing no drinking age will be carded and will not be served without proper ID* (preferably some government document; a driver's license suffices, but a passport is best). **In Canada, you must be 19,** except in Alberta, Manitoba, and Québec, where you must be **18.** Some areas of the United States are "dry," meaning they do not permit the sale of alcohol at all, while other places do not allow it to be sold on Sundays. The possession or sale of marijuana, cocaine, LSD, and most opiates are serious crimes in the U.S. and Canada.

■ Health

Travelers complain most often about their feet and their gut, so take precautionary measures. Keep power chow handy, like trail mix, granola bars, bananas, or candy bars. Drinking lots of fluids can often prevent dehydration and constipation. Wearing sturdy shoes and clean socks and using talcum powder can help keep your feet dry and comfortable. To minimize the effects of jet lag, "reset" your body's clock by adopting the time of your destination immediately upon arrival. Many travelers experience fatigue, discomfort, or mild diarrhea upon arriving in a new area; unless symptoms are severe, allow time for your body to adjust before becoming worried. A compact **first-aid kit** should suffice for minor problems on the road. The following items are useful in many situations: multi-sized bandages, aspirin or other pain killers, antibiotic cream, a thermometer, a Swiss Army knife with tweezers, moleskin, a decongestant for colds, motion sickness remedy, medicine for diarrhea or stomach problems, sunscreen, insect repellent, and burn ointment.

Always have on hand the names of any people you wish to be contacted in case of a medical emergency and a list of any allergies or medical conditions of which doctors should be aware. Bring any **medication** you regularly take and may need while traveling, as well as a copy of the **prescription** and a statement of any pre-existing medical conditions, especially if you will be bringing insulin, syringes, or any narcotics into the U.S. or Canada. If you wear **glasses** or **contact lenses,** carry an extra prescription and arrange to have your doctor or a family member send a replacement pair in an emergency. If you wear contacts, be sure to carry a pair of glasses. The **American Red Cross,** 285 Columbus Ave., Boston, MA 02116-5114 (800-564-1234,

M-F 8:30am-4:30pm), sells invaluable first-aid and CPR books, which are also offered through their many well-taught and inexpensive first-aid and CPR courses. Obtain a subscription to the **Global Emergency Medical Services (GEMS),** 2001 Westside Dr., #120, Alpharetta, GA 30201 (800-860-1111 M-F 8:30am-5:30pm; fax 770-475-0058) for access to an emergency room registered nurse with on-line access to your personal medical history, your primary physician, and a worldwide network of English-speaking medical providers. For any dental problem, call 800-DENTIST/336-8478 for the dentist nearest you.

Acquired Immune Deficiency Syndrome/STDs

In the U.S. it is estimated that more than between 650,000 and 950,000 people are infected with HIV, and most do not realize that they are infected. The easiest mode of HIV transmission is through direct blood to blood contact with an HIV-positive person; never share intravenous drug, tattooing, or other needles. The most common mode of transmission is sexual intercourse. To lessen your chances of contracting HIV or any other sexually transmitted disease (STD), such as gonorrhea, chlamydia, genital warts, syphilis, and herpes, use a latex condom every time you have sex. Warning signs for STDs include: swelling, sores, bumps, or blisters on sex organs, rectum, or mouth; burning and pain during urination and bowel movements; itching around sex organs; swelling or redness in the throat; flu-like symptoms with fever, chills, and aches. Condoms are widely available in stores and at clinics in the U.S. and Canada, but it doesn't hurt to stock up before you set out. The **U.S. Center for Disease Control** (800-342-2437) can provide 24hr. info. By law, travelers with HIV cannot enter the U.S.

■ Insurance

Beware of buying unnecessary travel coverage—your regular insurance policies may extend to many travel-related accidents and property loss. **Medical insurance** (especially university policies) often cover costs incurred abroad; consult your provider.

ISIC and **ITIC** provide basic insurance benefits, including $100 per day of in-hospital sickness for a maximum of 60 days, and $3000 of accident-related medical reimbursement (see **Youth, Student, and Teacher Identification,** p. 8). **Council** and **STA** (see **Budget Travel Agencies,** p. 21) offer a range of plans that can supplement your basic insurance coverage, with options covering medical treatment and hospitalization, accidents, baggage loss, and even charter flights missed due to illness. Most **American Express** cardholders receive automatic car rental insurance (collision and theft, but not liability) and ground travel accident coverage ($100,000 in life insurance) on flight purchases made with the card (see **Renting,** p. 36).

Insurance companies usually require a copy of the police report for thefts, or evidence of having paid medical expenses (doctor's statements, receipts) before they will honor a claim and may have time limits on filing for reimbursement. Always carry policy numbers and proof of insurance. The **Traveler's Emergency Network,** 3100 Tower Blvd. Suite 1000B, Durham, NC 27707-9821, offers superlative, comprehensive, and flexible traveler's coverage starting at $30 for individuals, $50 for families. **Access America,** 6600 W. Broad St., P.O. Box 11188, Richmond, VA 23230 (800-284-8300; fax 804-673-1491), covers trip cancellation/interruption, on-the-spot hospital admittance costs, emergency medical evacuation, sickness, and baggage loss (24hr. hotline 804-673-1159 or 800-654-1908). The **Berkely Group/Carefree Travel Insurance,** 100 Garden City Plaza, P.O. Box 9366, Garden City, NY 11530-9366 (800-323-3149, 24hr.; fax 516-294-1095; email info@berkely.com; http://www.berkely.com), offers two comprehensive packages that include coverage for trip cancellation/interruption/delay, accident and sickness, medical, baggage loss, bag delay, accidental death, and dismemberment. Trip cancellation/interruption insurance may be purchased separately for $5.50 per $100 coverage.

■ Alternatives to Tourism

There's no better way to submerge yourself in a local culture than to become part of its economy. Job leads often come from local residents, hostel owners, employment offices, and chambers of commerce. Temporary agencies often hire for non-secretarial placement as well as for standard typing assignments. Marketable skills, i.e. touch-typing, dictation, computer knowledge, and experience with children, will prove very helpful (even necessary) in the search for a temporary job. Consult local newspapers and bulletin boards on college campuses for job listings.

WORKING IN THE U.S.

While volunteer (unpaid) jobs are readily available almost everywhere in the U.S., paid positions are more difficult to find, even with relatively low unemployment. Most job openings exist at the minimum wage level ($5.15/hr.). Some jobs provide room and board in exchange for labor. To work in the U.S., you **must** apply for a **work visa.** The place to start getting specific info on the jungle of paperwork surrounding **work visas** is your nearest U.S. embassy or consulate. Working or studying in the U.S. with only a B-2 (tourist) visa is grounds for deportation.

The **Council on International Education Exchange** (CIEE) offers a work and travel program and an internship USA program for non-U.S. citizens wishing to work in the U.S. CIEE, 205 E. 42nd St., New York, NY 10017-5706 (888-268-6245; fax 212-822-2699; email Info@ciee.org; http://www.ciee.org). Write to **Council Travel** (see **Budget Travel Agencies,** p. 21) for *Volunteer! The Comprehensive Guide to Voluntary Service in the U.S. and Abroad* ($14.45 including postage). Council also runs a summer travel/work program designed to provide students with the opportunity to spend their summers working in the U.S.; check your local Council agency.

WORKING IN CANADA

Most of the organizations and the literature discussed above are not aimed solely at those interested in working in the U.S.; many of the same programs that arrange volunteer and work programs in the U.S. are also active in Canada. Contact individual organizations and write for the publications which interest you most. Travel CUTS may also help you out (see **Budget Travel Agencies,** p. 21).

If you intend to work in Canada, you will need to obtain an **Employment Authorization** (CDN$125) before you enter the country. Visitors are ordinarily forbidden to change status once they have arrived. To obtain this authorization, your employer must submit a **letter of introduction** to Employment and Immigration and a **request for work permit.** Employment authorizations are only issued after it has been determined that qualified Canadian citizens and residents will not be adversely affected by the admission of a foreign worker. Your potential employer must contact the nearest **Canadian Employment Centre (CEC)** for approval of the employment offer. Main CEC office: 1 Front St. W, #100, Toronto, ON M57 2R7. For more info, contact the consulate or embassy in your home country. Residents of the U.S., Greenland, and St. Pierre/Miquelon may apply for an Employment Authorization at a port of entry.

STUDY OPPORTUNITIES

There are a number of paths for studying in the U.S. or in Canada. Almost all U.S. institutions accept applications from foreign students directly. If English is not your native language, you will likely be required to take the Test of English as a Foreign Language (TOEFL), which is administered in many countries. Requirements are set by each school. Contact **TOEFL/TSE Publications,** 225 Phillips Blvd., Ewing, NJ 08618 (609-771-7100; http://www.toefl.org).

World Learning, Inc., P.O. Box 676, Brattleboro, VT 05302-0676 (802-257-7751; fax 258-3248; email english@worldlearning.org; http://www.worldlearning.org), runs the International Students of English program, which offers intensive language courses at campuses in Massachusetts, Illinois, California, Idaho, Florida, Oregon, South Carolina, and Texas. The inclusive price of a 4-week program is $2145.

Institute of International Education (IIE), 809 United Nations Plaza, New York, NY 10017-3580 (212-984-5413 for recorded info; fax 984-5358). A non-profit, international, and cultural exchange agency, the IIE is an excellent source for info on studying in the U.S. and Canada. Publishes *Funding for U.S. Study: A Guide for Foreign Nationals,* available in most public and campus libraries, *Academic Year Abroad* ($43, plus $4 shipping), detailing over 2300 semester and year-long programs worldwide, and *Vacation Study Abroad* ($37, plus $4 shipping), which lists over 1800 short-term, summer, and language school programs. For book orders: IIE Books, Institute of International Education, P.O. Box 371, Annapolis Junction, MD 20701 (800-445-0443; fax 301-953-2838; email iie-books@iie.org).

Eurocentres, 101 N. Union St., #300, Alexandria, VA 22314 (800-648-4809; fax 684-1495; http://www.eurocentres.com), or Eurocentres, Head Office, Seestrasse 247, CH-8038 Zurich, Switzerland (411 485 5040; fax 481 6124). Coordinates language/ study programs and homestays for college students and adults throughout the U.S. Programs are between $500-5000 and last from 2 weeks to 3 months.

U.S. Student Visas

Foreign students who wish to study in the United States must apply for either a M-1 visa (vocational studies) or an F-1 visa (for full-time students enrolled in an academic or language program). An F-1 also allows you to work part-time in an on-campus position. To apply for an F-1, you must have a Form I-20 (an official endorsement by your prospective educational institution), verification of your proficiency in English (unless you are entering a language program), and proof of your financial capability to reside in the U.S. for a certain period of time. In addition, to apply for a visa, you will need the OF-156, available from U.S. consular offices, a valid passport, and one 37 x 37mm photo. Visas are processed with a $64 fee.

If you are studying in the U.S., you can take any on-campus job to help pay the bills once you have applied for a Social Security number and have completed an Employment Eligibility Form (I-9). If you are studying full-time in the U.S. on an F-1 visa, you can take any on-campus job provided you do not displace a U.S. resident. On-campus employment is limited to 20hr. per week while in session, but you may work full-time during vacation if you plan to return to school. For further info, contact the international students office at the institution you will be attending.

Canadian Student Visas

To study in Canada, you will need a **Student Authorization Certificate** plus any necessary entry visas. To obtain one, contact the nearest Canadian consulate or embassy. Apply at least four months ahead of time; it can take a long time for the paperwork to go through. There is a processing fee. You must also prove to the Canadian government that you are able to support yourself financially. Canadian immigration laws permit full-time students to seek on-campus employment. A student authorization is good for 1 year. If you plan to stay longer, it is very important that you do not let it expire before you apply for renewal. For specifics, contact the **Academic Relations Division at Foreign Affairs and International Trade Canada** (613-992-6142), the **Canadian Immigration Center (CIC),** or a consulate. **Residents of the U.S., Greenland,** and **St. Pierre/Miquelon** may apply for student authorization at a port of entry.

■ Specific Concerns

WOMEN TRAVELERS

Women exploring any area on their own often face heightened threats to personal safety. In all situations, it's best to trust your instincts; if you'd feel better somewhere else, move on. You may want to consider staying in hostels offering single rooms which lock from the inside, YWCAs, or other establishments that offer rooms for women only (most hostels are divided into single-sex sections). Stick to centrally located accommodations; avoid late-night treks or subway rides. Always carry change for the phone and money for a bus or taxi. Carry a whistle on your keychain. Look as if you know where you're going and consider approaching women or couples for directions if you're lost or feel uncomfortable. **Hitching** is never safe for lone women, or even for two women traveling together (see **By Thumb**, p. 39).

If you spend time in cities, you may be harassed no matter how you're dressed. Your best response to verbal harassment is no answer at all (a reaction is what the harasser wants). Don't hesitate to seek out a police officer or a passerby if you are being heckled. *Let's Go* lists emergency numbers (including rape crisis lines) in the **Practical Information** listings of most cities. These warnings should not discourage women from traveling alone—be adventurous—just avoid unnecessary risks.

For general info, contact the **National Organization for Women (NOW)**, (email now@now.org; http://now.org) which has branches across the country and can refer women travelers to rape crisis centers and counseling services and provide lists of feminist events in the area. Main offices include 105 E. 22nd St., #307, **New York**, NY 10010 (212-260-4422); 1000 16th St. NW, #700, **Washington, D.C.** 20036 (202-331-0066); and 3543 18th St., Box 27, **San Francisco**, CA 94110 (415-861-8960; fax 861-8969). **Journeywoman Online** (http://journeywoman.com) offers tips, tales and classifieds for women young and old who love to travel.

A Foxy Old Woman's Guide to Traveling Alone, by Jay Ben-Lesser, encompasses practically every specific concern, offering anecdotes and tips for anyone interested in solitary adventure. Available in bookstores and from Crossing Press (800-777-1048), in Freedom, CA, $11.

Handbook For Women Travelers, by Maggie and Gemma Moss ($18). Encyclopedic and well written. Available from Piatkus Books, 5 Windmill St., London W1P 1HF (0171 631 0710).

Women's Travel in Your Pocket, Ferrari Guides, P.O. Box 37887, Phoenix, AZ 85069 (602-863-2408; http://www.q-net.com), an annual guide for women (especially lesbians) traveling in the U.S., Canada, the Caribbean, and Mexico ($14).

OLDER TRAVELERS

Senior citizens are eligible for a wide range of discounts on transportation, museums, movies, theaters, concerts, restaurants, and accommodations. If you don't see a senior citizen price listed, ask and you may be delightfully surprised. Agencies for senior group travel include **Eldertreks**, 597 Markham St., Toronto, ON M6G 2L7, Canada (800-741-7956 or 416-588-5000; http://www.eldertreks.com), and **Walking the World**, P.O. Box 1186, Fort Collins, CO 80522 (970-498-0500). **Footloose** organizes outdoor excursions (see **Organized Adventure**, p. 51).

AARP (American Association of Retired Persons), 601 E St. NW, Washington, D.C. 20049 (202-434-2277). Members 50 and over receive benefits and services including the AARP Motoring Plan from AMOCO (800-334-3300), and discounts on lodging, car rental, and sight-seeing. Annual fee $8 per couple; $20 for 3 years; lifetime membership $75.

National Council of Senior Citizens, 8403 Colesville Rd., Silver Spring, MD 20910-31200 (301-578-8800; fax 578-8999). Membership $13 for 1 year, $33 for 3 years, lifetime membership $175. Individuals or couples receive hotel and auto rental discounts, a newsletter, and use of a discount travel agency.

No Problem! Worldwise Tips for Mature Adventurers, by Janice Kenyon. Advice and info on insurance, finances, security, health, and packing. Useful appendices. $16 from Orca Book Publishers, P.O. Box 468, Custer, WA 98240-0468.

Unbelievably Good Deals and Great Adventures That You Absolutely Can't Get Unless You're Over 50, by Joan Rattner Heilman. After you finish reading the title page, check inside for some great tips on senior discounts. $10 from Contemporary Publishing, 4255 Tuohey Ave., Lincolnwood, IL 60646 (847-679-5500)

BISEXUAL, GAY, AND LESBIAN TRAVELERS

Attitudes toward bisexual, gay, and lesbian travelers are, naturally, particular to each region and to the cities within it. Listed below are contact organizations and publishers which offer materials addressing those concerns. Homosexual sex is still illegal in many states, although such laws are rarely enforced.

Damron Travel Guides, P.O. Box 422458, San Francisco, CA 94142-2458 (415-255-0404 or 800-462-6654; http://www.damron.com). The *Damron Address Book* ($15) lists bars, restaurants, guest houses, and services in the U.S., Canada, and Mexico that cater to gay men. The *Damron Road Atlas* ($16) contains color maps of 56 major U.S. and Canadian cities with gay and lesbian resorts and listings of bars and accommodations. *The Women's Traveller* ($13) has over 7500 listings catering to lesbians. *Damron's Accomodations* ($19) lists gay and lesbian hotels around the world. Mail orders add $5 shipping charge.

Ferrari Guides, P.O. Box 37887, Phoenix, AZ 85069 (602-863-2408; fax 439-3952; e-mail ferrari@q-net.com; http://www.q-net.com). Gay and lesbian travel guides: *Ferrari Guides' Gay Travel A to Z* ($16), *Ferrari Guides' Men's Travel in Your Pocket* ($14), *Ferrari Guides' Women's Travel in Your Pocket* ($14), and *Ferrari Guides' Inn Places* ($16). Available in bookstores or by mail order. Postage/handling $4.50 for the first item, $1 for each additional item mailed within the U.S.

Gayellow Pages, P.O. Box 533, Village Station, New York, NY 10014 (212-674-0120; http://gayellowpages.com). An annually updated listing of accommodations, resorts, and other items of interest to the gay traveler. U.S./Canada edition $16.

Spartacus International Gay Guides ($33), published by Bruno Gmunder, Verlag GMBH, Leuschnerdamm 31, 10999 Berlin, Germany (030 615 0030). Lists bars, restaurants, hotels, and bookstores around the world catering to gays. Also lists hotlines for gays and relevant laws in various countries. Available by mail from Lambda Rising, 1625 Connecticut Ave. NW, Washington, D.C. 20009-1013 (202-462-6969).

DISABLED TRAVELERS

Hotels and hostels in the U.S. and Canada have become more and more accessible to disabled persons, and many sights are trying to make exploring less difficult. Call ahead to restaurants, hotels, parks, and other facilities to find out about the existence of ramps, the widths of doors, and the dimensions of elevators.

Amtrak (800-872-7245; see p. 31) and major airlines will accommodate disabled passengers if notified at least 72hr. in advance. Hearing-impaired travelers may contact Amtrak using teletype printers (800-872-7245). **Greyhound** (see p. 32) buses will provide free travel for a companion; if you are without a fellow traveler, call Greyhound (800-752-4841) at least 48hr., but no more than 1 week, before you plan to leave and they'll arrange assistance where needed. Hertz, National, and Avis **car rental agencies** have hand-controlled vehicles at some locations (see **Renting,** p. 36). For info on transportation availability in individual U.S. cities, contact the local chapter of the **Easter Seals Society** or look on the web at http://access-able.com. Local chapters' numbers are available from the national chapter at 800-221-6827. If you are planning to visit a national park or any other sight managed by the U.S. National Park Service, you can obtain a free **Golden Access Passport** (see **National Parks,** p. 47).

Directions Unlimited, 720 N. Bedford Rd., Bedford Hills, NY 10507 (914-241-1700 or 800-533-5343; fax 914-241-0243). Arranges individual and group vacations and tours for the physically disabled, as well as group tours for blind travelers.

Flying Wheels Travel Service, 143 W. Bridge St., Owatonne, MN 55060 (800-535-6790; fax 507-451-1685). Handles trips in the U.S. for groups or individuals in wheelchairs or those with other sorts of limited mobility.

Facts on File, 11 Penn Plaza, 15th fl., New York, NY 10001 (212-967-8800). Publishers of *Disability Resource,* a reference guide for travelers with disabilities ($45, plus shipping). Available at retail bookstores or by mail order.

Mobility International, USA (MIUSA), P.O. Box 10767, Eugene, OR 97440 (541-343-1284 voice and TDD; fax 343-6812; email info@miusa.org; http://www.miusa.org). Sells the 3rd edition of *A World of Options: A Guide to International Educational Exchange, Community Service, and Travel for Persons with Disabilities* (individuals $35; organizations $45).

Moss Rehab Hospital Travel Information Service (215-456-9600; TDD 456-9602). Telephone info resource center on travel accessibility and other travel-related concerns for those with disabilities.

Twin Peaks Press, P.O. Box 129, Vancouver, WA 98666-0129 (360-694-2462; fax 360-696-3210; email 73743.2634@compuserve.com; http://netm.com/mall/info-prod/twinpeak/helen.htm). *Travel for the Disabled* provides travel tips, lists of accessible tourist attractions, and advice on other resources for disabled travelers ($20). *Directory for Travel Agencies of the Disabled* ($20), *Wheelchair Vagabond* ($15), and *Directory of Accessible Van Rentals* ($10) also available. $4 shipping for first book, $2 for each additional book.

MINORITY TRAVELERS

Racial and ethnic minorities sometimes face blatant and, more often, subtle discrimination and/or harassment in new settings, though regions in the U.S. and Canada differ vastly in their general attitudes about race relations. Verbal harassment is now less common than unfair pricing, false info on accommodations, or inexcusably slow and unfriendly service at restaurants. The best way to deal with such encounters is to remain calm and report individuals to a supervisor and establishments to the Better Business Bureau for the region (411 will provide local listings); contact the police in extreme situations. *Let's Go* always welcomes reader input regarding discriminating establishments. Few travel publications list organizations geared toward the needs of minorities, though some might list cultural centers and restaurants of interest. **Go Girl! The Black Woman's Book of Travel and Adventure,** edited by Elaine Lee, includes 52 travelers' tales, advice on how to travel inexpensively and safely, and a discussion of issues of specific concern to black women. It's published by The Eighth Mountain Press, 624 SE 29th Ave., Portland, OR 97214 (503-233-3936; fax 233-0774).

In larger cities, African Americans can usually consult chapters of the **Urban League** and the **National Association for the Advancement of Colored People (NAACP)** (http://www.naacp.org) for info on events sponsored by or largely participated in by African Americans.

TRAVELERS WITH CHILDREN

Family vacations can be recipes for disaster, unless you slow your pace and plan ahead. If you pick a B&B for accommodation, call ahead and make sure it's child-friendly. If you rent a car, ask if the rental company provides a car seat for younger children. Consider using a papoose-style device to carry your baby on walking trips. Be sure that your child carries some sort of ID in case of an emergency or if he or she gets lost, and arrange a reunion spot in case of separation when sight-seeing. Restaurants, museums, tourist attractions, and airlines often have children's discounts. Breast-feeding is often a problem while traveling, so pack accordingly or search for mother-friendly spots.

Backpacking with Babies and Small Children ($10), published by Wilderness Press (for contact info, see **Useful Publications,** p. 43), is a useful guide for outdoor exploring with the younger set. The *Kidding Around* series ($8, postage under $5) of illustrated books about cities across the U.S. could prove invaluable for keeping little ones happy on long trips. (Published by John Muir Publications, P.O. Box 613, Santa Fe, NM 87504. Call 800-285-4078 or fax 505-988-1680.) Lonely Planet's *Travel with Children* ($12, plus $2.50 shipping) is also info-packed. Write to 150 Linden St., Oakland, CA 94607, or call 800-275-8555 or 510-893-8555 (fax 893-8563; email info@lonelyplanet.com; http://www.lonelyplanet.com).

DIETARY CONCERNS

Vegetarians should usually have no problem finding suitable cuisine on either coast and in most major cities, although small-town America might meet veggie requests with a long, blank stare. *Let's Go* notes restaurants with vegetarian-friendly selections in city listings. The **North American Vegetarian Society,** P.O. Box 72, Dolgeville, NY 13329 (518-568-7970), publishes *Transformative Adventures,* a guide to vacations and retreats ($15), the *Vegan Guide to New York City* ($4), and the *Vegetarian*

ESSENTIALS

Journal's Guide to Natural Food Restaurants in the U.S. and Canada ($12). Membership in the Society costs $20 (family membership $26); members receive a 10% discount on all publications.

Travelers who keep **kosher** should contact synagogues in larger cities for info on kosher restaurants; your own synagogue or college Hillel should have access to lists of Jewish institutions across the nation. If you are strict in your observance, consider preparing your own food on the road. **The Jewish Travel Guide** lists synagogues and kosher restaurants in over 80 countries. It is available from Sepher-Hermon Press, 1265 46th St., Brooklyn, NY 11219 (718-972-9010; $15, plus $3 shipping).

TRAVELING ALONE

There are many advantages to traveling alone, but you may also be a more visible target for robbery and harassment. Lone travelers need to be well organized and look confident at all times. If questioned, never admit that you are a solitary traveler. Maintain regular contact with someone at home who knows your itinerary. A number of organizations can find travel companions for solo travelers who so desire. **Connecting: News for Solo Travelers,** P.O. Box 29088, 1996 W. Broadway, Vancouver, BC V6J 5C2, Canada (604-737-7791 or 800-557-1757; http://www.travelwise.com/solo), publishes a bi-monthly newsletter with features and listings of singles looking for travel companions (subscription $25). The excellent **Traveling On Your Own,** by Eleanor Berman ($13), lists info resources for "singles" (old and young) and single parents. (Crown Publishers, Inc., 201 E 50th St., New York, NY 10022. Call 212-751-2600.)

GETTING THERE

■ Budget Travel Agencies

Council Travel (http://www.ciee.org/travel/index.htm), the travel division of Council, is a full-service travel agency specializing in youth and budget travel. They offer discount airfares on scheduled airlines, railpasses, hosteling cards, low-cost accommodations, guidebooks, budget tours, travel gear, and international student (ISIC), youth (GO25), and teacher (ITIC) identity cards. U.S. offices include: Emory Village, 1561 N. Decatur Rd., **Atlanta,** GA 30307 (404-377-9997); 2000 Guadalupe, **Austin,** TX 78705 (512-472-4931); 273 Newbury St., **Boston,** MA 02116 (617-266-1926); 1138 13th St., **Boulder,** CO 80302 (303-447-8101); 1153 N. Dearborn, **Chicago,** IL 60610 (312-951-0585); 10904 Lindbrook Dr., **Los Angeles,** CA 90024 (310-208-3551); 1501 University Ave. SE #300, **Minneapolis,** MN 55414 (612-379-2323); 205 E. 42nd St., **New York,** NY 10017 (212-822-2700); 953 Garnet Ave., **San Diego,** CA 92109 (619-270-6401); 530 Bush St., **San Francisco,** CA 94108 (415-421-3473); 1314 NE 43rd St. #210, **Seattle,** WA 98105 (206-632-2448); 3300 M St. NW, **Washington, D.C.** 20007 (202-337-6464). For U.S. cities not listed, call 800-2-COUNCIL/226-8624. Also 28A Poland St. (Oxford Circus), **London,** W1V 3DB (0171 287 3337); **Paris** (146 55 55 65); and **Munich** (089 39 50 22)

Travel CUTS (Canadian Universities Travel Services Limited), 187 College St., Toronto, ON M5T 1P7 (416-979-2406; fax 979-8167; email mail@travelcuts). Canada's national student travel bureau and equivalent of Council, with 40 offices across Canada. Also in the U.K., 295-A Regent St., **London** W1R 7YA (0171 637 31 61). Discounted domestic and international airfares open to all; special student fares to all destinations with valid ISIC. Issues ISIC, FIYTO, GO25, and HI hostel cards, as well as railpasses. Offers free *Student Traveler* magazine, as well as information on the Student Work Abroad Program (SWAP).

STA Travel, 6560 Scottsdale Rd. #F100, Scottsdale, AZ 85253 (800-777-0112 nationwide; fax 602-922-0793; http://sta-travel.com). A student and youth travel organization with over 150 offices worldwide offering discount airfares for young travelers, railpasses, accommodations, tours, insurance, and ISICs. U.S. offices include: 297

Newbury Street, **Boston,** MA 02115 (617-266-6014); 429 S. Dearborn St., **Chicago,** IL 60605 (312-786-9050); 7202 Melrose Ave., **Los Angeles,** CA 90046 (213-934-8722); 10 Downing St., Ste. G, **New York,** NY 10003 (212-627-3111); 4341 University Way NE, **Seattle,** WA 98105 (206-633-5000); 2401 Pennsylvania Ave., **Washington, D.C.** 20037 (202-887-0912); 51 Grant Ave., **San Francisco,** CA 94108 (415-391-8407). In the U.K., 6 Wrights Ln., **London** W8 6TA (0171 938 47 11 for North American travel). In New Zealand, 10 High St., **Auckland** (09 309 97 23). In Australia, 222 Faraday St., **Melbourne** VIC 3050 (03 349 69 11).

Let's Go Travel, Harvard Student Agencies, 17 Holyoke St., Cambridge, MA 02138 (617-495-9649; fax 495-7956; email travel@hsa.net; http://hsa.net/travel). Railpasses, HI-AYH memberships, ISICs, ITICs, FIYTO cards, guidebooks, maps, bargain flights, and a complete line of budget travel gear. All items available by mail; call or write for a catalogue (or see the catalogue in center of this publication).

Campus Travel, 52 Grosvenor Gardens, London SW1W 0AG (http://www.campus-travel.co.uk). 46 branches in the U.K. Student and youth fares on plane, train, boat, and bus travel. Maps, guides, discount and ID cards for students and youths, and travel insurance for students and under 35. Telephone booking service: in Europe, 0171 730 34 02; in North America, 0171 730 21 01; worldwide, 0171 730 81 11.

■ By Plane

Very generally, courier fares (if you can deal with restrictions) are the cheapest, followed by tickets bought from consolidators and stand-by seating. Last-minute specials, airfare wars, and charter flights can often beat these fares, however. Travelers will experience the least competition for inexpensive seats during the off-season. Peak-season rates go into effect between mid-May and early June and run until mid-September. Don't count on getting a seat right away during these months. The worst crunch leaving Europe takes place from mid-June to early July; August is uniformly tight for returning flights. (London is a major connecting point for budget flights to the U.S.; New York City is often the destination.) To make your way across the U.S., catch a coast-to-coast flight once you're in the country (see **By Plane,** p. 29).

Students and others under 26 should never need to pay full price for a ticket. Seniors can also get great deals; many airlines offer senior traveler clubs or airline passes with few restrictions and discounts for their companions as well. To research budget flights and outsmart airline reps, consult the phone-book-sized *Official Airline Guide* (at local libraries), a monthly guide for nearly every scheduled flight in the world and toll-free phone numbers for most airlines. More accessible and incredibly useful is Michael McColl's *The World-wide Guide to Cheap Airfare* ($15).

The *Official Airline Guide* also has a website (http://www.oag.com) that allows free access to flight schedules. The following sites have info on budget air travel: **TravelHUB,** http://www.travelhub.com; **Air Traveler's Handbook,** http://www.cs.cmu.edu/afs/cs.cmu.edu/user/mkant/Public/Travel/airfare.html; **Airlines of the Web,** http://www.itn.net/airlines; **Travelocity,** http://www.travelocity.com.

The commercial airlines' lowest regular offer is the **Advance Purchase Excursion Fare (APEX);** specials advertised in newspapers may be cheaper, but have more restrictions and fewer available seats. APEX fares provide you with confirmed reservations and allow "open-jaw" tickets (landing in and returning from different cities). Generally, reservations must be made 7-21 days in advance, with 7- to 14-day minimum and up to 90-day max. stay limits, and hefty cancellation and change penalties (fees rise in summer). Book APEX fares early during peak season; by May you will have a hard time getting the departure date you want for June through August.

TICKET CONSOLIDATORS

Ticket consolidators resell unsold tickets on commercial and charter airlines at unpublished fares; a 30-40% price reduction is not uncommon. Consolidators largely deal in international tickets; the deregulation of domestic U.S. airlines allowed them to discount their own fares. Consolidator tickets provide the greatest discounts over published fares when you are traveling: on short notice; on a high-priced trip; to an offbeat destination; or in the peak season, when published fares are jacked way up.

ESSENTIALS

There are rarely age constraints or stay limitations, but unlike tickets bought through an airline, you won't be able to use your tickets on another flight if you miss yours, and you will have to go back to the consolidator rather than the airline for a refund.

Not all consolidators deal with the general public; many only sell tickets through travel agents. **Bucket shops** are retail agencies that specialize in getting cheap tickets. Prices are marked up slightly, but bucket shops tend to have access to a larger market than would be available to the public and can also get tickets from wholesale consolidators. The **Association of Special Fares Agents (ASFA)** maintains a database of specialized dealers for particular regions (http://www.ntsltd.com/asfa). Look for bucket shops' tiny ads in the travel section of weekend papers; in the U.S., the Sunday *New York Times* is a good source. Kelly Monaghan's *Consolidators: Air Travel's Bargain Basement* is an invaluable source for more information and lists of consolidators by location and destination (US$8 plus $3.50 shipping) from the Intrepid Traveler, P.O. Box 438, New York, NY 10034 (email info@intrepidtraveler.com).

It is always best to contact specialists in your region, but the following agents provide general services. For destinations worldwide, try **Cheap Tickets,** with five offices in the U.S. (800-377-1000). **NOW Voyager,** 74 Varick St. #307, New York, NY 10013 (212-431-1616; fax 212-334-5243; email info@nowvoyagertravel.com; http://www.nowvoyagertravel.com) acts as a consolidator and books discounted international flights, mostly from New York, as well as courier flights (see **Courier Companies and Freighters** below), for an annual fee of US$50. For a processing fee, depending on the number of travelers and the itinerary, **Travel Avenue** (800-333-3335; fax 312-876-1254; http://www.travelavenue.com) will search for the lowest international airfare available, including consolidated prices, and will even give you a 5% rebate on fares over $350.

STAND-BY FLIGHTS

From Europe

Major airlines that tend to offer relatively inexpensive fares for a round-trip ticket from Europe include: **British Airways** (800-247-9297), **Continental** (800-525-0280), **Northwest** (800-225-2525), **TWA** (800-221-2000), and **United** (800-538-2929). Smaller, budget airlines often undercut major carriers by offering bargain fares on regularly scheduled flights. Competition for seats on these smaller carriers can be fierce. Other trans-Atlantic airlines include **Virgin Atlantic Airways** (800-862-8621) and **IcelandAir** (800-223-5500).

From Asia, Africa, and Australia

Whereas European travelers may choose from a variety of regular reduced fares, Asian, Australian, and African travelers must rely on APEX (see above). A good place to start searching for tickets is the local branch of an international budget travel agency (see **Budget Travel Agencies,** p. 21).

Qantas (800-227-4500), **United** (800-241-6522), and **Northwest** (800-225-2525) fly between Australia or New Zealand and the U.S. Advance purchase fares from Australia have extremely tough restrictions. If you are uncertain about your plans, pay extra for an advance purchase ticket that has only a 50% penalty for cancellation. Many travelers from Australia and New Zealand take **Singapore Air** (800-742-3333) or other East Asian-based carriers for the initial leg of the trip.

Delta Airlines (800-241-4141), **Japan Airlines** (800-525-3663), **Northwest** (800-225-2525), and **United** (800-538-2929) offer service from Japan. A round-trip ticket from Tokyo to L.A. usually ranges from $1250-2500. **South African Airways** (800-722-9675), **American** (800-433-7300), and **Northwest** connect South Africa with North America.

Stand-by brokers sell a promise that you will get to a destination near where you're intending to go, within a window of time (usually 5 days), from a location in a region you've specified. Call in before your date-range to hear all of your flight options for the next 7 days and the probability of boarding (you will not receive a ticket). Next,

ESSENTIALS

decide which flights you want to try to make and present a voucher at the airport which grants you the right to board a flight on a space-available basis. This procedure must be followed again for the return trip. Flexibility of schedule and destination is necessary, but all companies guarantee a flight or a refund if all available flights that fit your date and destination range are full when you arrive at the airport.

Airhitch, 2641 Broadway, 3rd fl., New York, NY 10025 (800-326-2009 or 212-864-2000; fax 864-5489), also has an office in L.A. (310-726-5000). There are several offices in **Europe,** so you can wait to register for your return; the main one is in **Paris** (147 00 16 30). **Air-Tech,** 588 Broadway, #204, New York, NY 10012 (212-219-7000; fax 219-0066; email fly@airtech.com; http://www.airtech.com), offers a similar service. Their travel window is one to four days. Upon registration and payment, Air-Tech sends out a FlightPass with a contact date that falls soon before your travel window, on which you are to call them for flight instructions. Air-Tech also arranges **courier flights** (see below) and regular confirmed-reserved flights at discount rates.

These stand-by agencies can also be used for travel within the U.S. Be sure to read all the fine print in your agreements with either company. It is difficult to receive refunds, and clients' vouchers will not be honored when an airline fails to receive payment in time. Keep in mind that there is not much certainty about your departure and arrival time and destination prior to your arrival at the airport.

CHARTER FLIGHTS

Charters are flights a tour operator contracts with an airline to fly extra loads of passengers to peak-season destinations. They are often cheaper than flights on scheduled airlines, especially during peak seasons. Some operate nonstop, and restrictions on minimum advance-purchase and minimum stay are more lenient. However, charter flights fly less frequently than major airlines, making refunds particularly difficult, and are almost always fully booked. Schedules and itineraries may also change or be cancelled at the last moment (as late as 48hr. before the trip, and without a full refund). In addition check-in, boarding, and baggage claim are often much slower. Pay with a credit card if you can and consider traveler's insurance against trip interruption.

Interworld (305-443-4929; fax 443-0351); **Travac** (800-872-8800; email mail@travac.com; http://www.travac.com); or **Rebel,** in Valencia, CA (800-227-3235; fax 294-0981; email travel@rebeltours.com; http://rebeltours.com), or in Orlando, FL (800-732-3588), are all options. **Council Charter,** 205 E. 42nd St., New York, NY 10017 (212-661-0311; fax 972-0194), offers a combination of inexpensive charter and scheduled airfares from a variety of U.S. gateways to and from most major destinations (see Council Travel in **Budget Travel Agencies,** p. 21).

Eleventh-hour **discount clubs** and **fare brokers** offer members savings on travel to and from Europe, including charter flights. **Last Minute Travel Service,** 100 Sylvan Rd., Woburn, MA 01801 (617-267-9800 or 800-527-8646), is one of the few travel clubs that don't charge a membership fee. Others include **Moment's Notice,** New York, NY (718-234-6295; fax 234-6450; http://www.moments-notice.com), for air tickets, tours, and hotels ($25 annual fee); and **Travelers Advantage,** Stamford, CT (800-548-1116; http://www.travelersadvantage.com; $49 annual fee). Study these organizations' contracts closely; you don't want to end up with an unwanted overnight layover.

COURIER COMPANIES AND FREIGHTERS

Those who travel light should consider flying as a **courier.** The company hiring you will use your checked luggage space for freight; you're usually only allowed to bring carry-ons, though some firms allow you to check luggage, depending on your trip. You are responsible for the safe delivery of the baggage claim slips (given to you by a courier company representative) to the representative waiting for you when you arrive. You will probably never see the cargo you are transporting—the company handles it all—and airport officials know that couriers are not responsible for the baggage checked for them. **Restrictions** to watch for: you must be over 18, have a valid passport, and procure your own visa (if necessary); most flights are round-trip with short fixed-length stays (usually 1 week); only single tickets are issued (although a

ESSENTIALS

companion may be able to get a next-day flight); and most flights are from New York. For a practical guide to air courier options, check out Kelly Monaghan's *Air Courier Bargains* ($15, plus $3.50 shipping), available from Intrepid Traveler (212-569-1081; email info@intrepidtraveler.com; http://intrepidtraveler.com), or consult the *Courier Air Travel Handbook* ($10, plus $3.50 shipping), published by Bookmasters, Inc., P.O. Box 2039, Mansfield, OH 44905 (800-507-2665; fax 419-281-6883). **NOW Voyager,** 74 Varick St., #307, New York, NY 10013 (212-431-1616; fax 334-5243; email info@nowvoyagertravel.com; http://www.nowvoyagertravel.com), acts as an agent for many courier flights worldwide (primarily from New York) and offers special last-minute deals to such cities as London, Paris, Rome, and Frankfurt for as little as $200 round-trip plus a $50 registration fee. They also act as a consolidator (see **Ticket Consolidators,** above).

ONCE THERE

■ Embassies and Consulates

For a more extensive list of embassies and consulates in the U.S., consult the website http://www.embassy.org. A similar compilation for the neighboring maple leaves can be found at http://www.impactconsulting.com/embassyott. Beauty, eh?

EMBASSIES IN U.S.: Australia, 1601 Massachusetts Ave. NW, Washington, D.C. 20036 (202-797-3000); **Canada,** 501 Pennsylvania Ave. NW, Washington, D.C. 20001 (202-682-1740); **Ireland,** 2234 Massachusetts Ave. NW, Washington, D.C. 20008 (202-462-3939); **New Zealand,** 37 Observatory Circle NW, Washington, D.C. 20008 (202-328-4800); **South Africa,** 3051 Massachusetts Ave. NW, Washington, D.C. 20008 (202-232-4400); **U.K.,** 3100 Massachusetts Ave. NW, Washington, D.C. 20008 (202-462-1340).

CONSULATES IN U.S.: Australia, 630 5th Ave., #420, New York, NY 10111 (212-408-8400) and Century Plaza Towers, 19th Fl., 2049 Century Park East, Los Angeles, CA 90067 (310-229-4800); **Canada,** 1251 Ave. of the Americas, Exxon Bldg., 16th fl., New York, NY 10020-1175 (212-596-1683), and 550 S. Hope St., 9th fl., Los Angeles, CA 90071 (213-346-2700); **Ireland,** 345 Park Ave., 17th fl., New York, NY 10154 (212-319-2552), and 44 Montgomery St., #3830, San Francisco, CA 94101 (415-392-4214); **New Zealand,** 12400 Wilshire Blvd., #1150, Los Angeles, CA 90025 (310-207-1605); **South Africa,** 333 E. 38th St., 9th fl., New York, NY 10016 (212-213-4880); **United Kingdom,** 845 3rd Ave., New York, NY 10022 (212-752-8400), and 11766 Wilshire Blvd., #400, Los Angeles, CA 90025 (213-385-7381).

EMBASSIES IN CANADA: Australia, 50 O'Connor St., #710, Ottawa, ON K1P 6L2 (613-236-0841); **Ireland,** 130 Albert St., #1105, Ottawa, ON K1P 5G4 (613-233-6281); **New Zealand,** 99 Bank St., #727, Ottawa, ON K1P 6G3 (613-238-5991); **South Africa,** 15 Sussex Dr., Ottawa, ON K1M 1M8 (613-744-0330); **United Kingdom,** 80 Elgin St., Ottawa, ON K1P 5K7 (613-237-1530); **United States,** 100 Wellington St., Ottawa, ON K1P 5T1 (613-238-4470).

CONSULATES IN CANADA: Australia, 175 Bloor St. E., # 314, Toronto, ON M4W 3R8 (416-323-1155); **New Zealand,** 888 Dunsmuir St., #1200, Vancouver, BC V6C 3K4 (604-684-7388); **South Africa,** 1 Pl. Ville Marie, #2615, Montreal, QC H3B 4S3 (514-878-9217; fax 878-4751), and 595 Burrard St., #3023, 3 Bentall Ctr., P.O. Box 49069, Vancouver, BC V7X 1G4 (604-6881301); **U.K.,** 1000 de la Gauchetiere W., #4200, Montreal, QC H3B 4W5 (514-866-5863), and 1111 Melville St., #800, Vancouver, BC V6E 3V6 (604-683-4421); **U.S.,** 2 Pl. Terrasse Dufferin, CP 939, Québec City, QC G1R 4T9 (418-692-2095), and 1095 West Pender St., Vancouver, BC V6E 2M6 (604-685-4311).

■ Getting Around

BY PLANE

When dealing with any commercial airline, buying in advance is best. Periodic **price wars** may lower prices in spring and early summer, but they're unpredictable; don't delay your purchase in hopes of catching one. For the cheapest fare, buy a round-trip ticket, stay over at least one Saturday, and travel at off-peak times (M-Th morning) and on off-peak hours (overnight **"red-eye"** flights can be cheaper and faster than prime-time). Chances of receiving discount fares increase on competitive routes. Fees for changing flight dates range from $25 for some domestic flights to $150 for many international flights. Most airlines allow those under 2 to fly free on an adult's lap.

Since travel peaks June to August and around holidays, reserve a seat several months in advance for these times. Try to secure the **Advance Purchase Excursion Fare (APEX),** the commercial carrier's cheapest fare (see **By Plane,** p. 23). Call the airline the day before your departure to confirm your flight reservation, and get to the airport at least 1hr. early to ensure you have a seat; airlines often overbook. (Of course, being "bumped" from a flight doesn't spell doom if your travel plans are flexible—you will probably leave on the next flight and get a free ticket or cash bonus. If you would like to be bumped to win a free ticket, check in early and let the airline officials know.) The following programs, services, and fares may be helpful for planning a reasonably priced airtrip, but be wary of deals that seem too good to be true:

Frequent flyer tickets: You cannot use frequent flyer tickets that are not in your name—all commercial airlines will check a photo ID, and you could find yourself paying for a new, full-fare ticket. If you have a frequent flyer account, make sure you're getting credit when you make the reservation and check in.

Air Passes: Many major U.S. airlines offer special **Visit USA** air passes and fares to international travelers. You must purchase these passes outside of North America, paying 1 price for a certain number of flight vouchers. Each voucher is good for 1 flight on an airline's domestic system; typically, all travel must be completed within 30-60 days.

The point of departure and destination for each coupon must be specified at the time of purchase, but dates of travel may be changed once travel has begun, usually at no extra charge. **USAirways** offers on-line packages (anywhere that USAirways travels). **United, Continental, Delta,** and **TWA** all sell vouchers as well. Call the airlines for specifics. TWA's **Youth Travel Pak** offers a similar deal to students 14-24, including North Americans. **Greyhound Air of Canada** (800-661-8747; http://www.grey-hound.ca) sells an international pass offering unlimited use of Greyhound flights over a certain period of time (7-day pass $209, 15-day $275, 30-day $375, 60-day $475).

Ticket Consolidators, Charter, Courier, and Stand-by-Flights: Although burdened by a number of restrictions, these low-cost ticket options are often bargains for travel within the U.S. and Canada. For info on **Ticket Consolidators,** see p. 23. For the lowdown on **Charter Flights,** see p. 27. **Courier Flight** info can be found on p. 27, while ultra-cheap **Stand-by Flights** are described on p. 25.

Student Fares: Secondary and post-secondary students have access to reduced fares on most major carriers. These bargain fares must be reserved at select travel agencies (see **Budget Travel Agencies,** p. 21).

Major Airlines

AirTran, Consumer Relations, Dept. INT, 9955 AirTran Blvd., Orlando, FL 32827 (800-247-8726; http://www.airtran.com). Special "X-Fares" for 18 to 22 year-olds.

Air Canada (800-776-3000; http://www.aircanada.ca). Discounts for youths ages 12-24 on stand-by tickets for flights within Canada; still, advance-purchase tickets may be cheaper.

Alaska Airlines, P.O. Box 68900, Seattle, WA 98168 (800-426-0333; http://www.alaska-air.com).

America West, 4000 E. Sky Harbor Blvd., Phoenix, AZ 85034 (800-235-9292; http://www.americawest.com). Serves primarily the western United States.

American, P.O. Box 619612, Dallas-Ft. Worth International Airport, TX 75261-9612 (800-433-7300; http://www.americanair.com).

Continental, 2929 Allen Pkwy., Houston, TX 77210 (800-525-0280; http://www.flycontinental.com). Great deals for senior citizens on coupon books and "Senior Passports" (800-248-8996).

Delta, Hartsfield International Airport, Atlanta, GA 30320 (800-241-4141; http://www.delta-air.com).

Northwest, 5101 Northwest Dr., St. Paul, MN 55111-3034 (800-225-2525; http://www.nwa.com).

Southwest, P.O. Box 36611, Dallas, TX 75235-1611 (800-435-9792; http://www.iflyswa.com). Lower fares, typically without assigned seating.

TWA, 1 City Center, 515 N. 6th St., St. Louis, MO 63101 (800-221-2000; http://www.twa.com).

United, P.O. Box 66100, Chicago, IL 60666 (800-241-6522; http://www.ual.com).

USAir, Office of Consumer Affairs, P.O. Box 1501, Winston-Salem, NC 27102-1501 (800-428-4322; http://www.usair.com).

BY TRAIN

Locomotion is still one of the cheapest ways to tour the U.S. and Canada, but keep in mind that discounted air travel, particularly on longer trips, may be cheaper than train travel. *As with airlines, you can save money by purchasing your tickets as far in advance as possible, so plan ahead and make reservations early.* It is essential to travel light on trains; not all stations will check your baggage.

Amtrak (800-872-7245; http://www.amtrak.com) is the only provider of intercity passenger train service in the U.S. Most cities have Amtrak offices which directly sell tickets, but tickets must be bought through an agent in some small towns. The informative webpage lists up-to-date schedules, fares, arrival and departure info, and makes reservations. **Discounts on full rail fares are given to:** senior citizens (15% off); students (15% off) with a Student Advantage Card (call 800-96-AMTRAK (26-8725) to purchase a card; $20); travelers with disabilities (15% off); children under 15 accompanied by a parent (50% off); children under age two (free); and current members of the U.S. armed forces, active-duty veterans, and their dependents (25% off). Amtrak also offers some **special packages:**

All-Aboard America: This fare divides the Continental U.S. into 3 regions—Eastern, Central, and Western.

Air-Rail Travel Plan: Amtrak and United Airlines allow you to travel in 1 direction by train and return by plane, or to fly to a distant point and return home by train. The train portion of the journey can last up to 30 days and include up to 3 stopovers. A multitude of variations are available; contact **Amtrak Vacations** (see below) for details.

North America Rail Pass: A 30-day discount option available only to those who aren't citizens of North America; the 15-day pass is available to all. It allows unlimited travel and unlimited stops over a period of either 15 or 30 days. A 30-day nationwide travel pass is $645 during peak season (June 1-Oct. 15) and $450 during the off-season; a 15-day nationwide pass is $400/$300. Call for regional variants.

Amtrak Vacations, 2211 Butterfield Rd., Downers Grove, IL 60515 (800-321-8684). An Amtrak-affiliated travel agency which offers packages in conjunction with airlines and hotel chains and, occasionally, discounts not to be found anywhere else. Programs vary throughout the year.

VIA Rail, P.O. Box 8116, Station A, Montreal, Québec H3C 3N3 (800-842-7733; http://www.viarail.ca), is Amtrak's Canadian analogue. **Discounts on full fares are given to:** students with ISIC card and youths under 24 (40% off full fare); seniors 60 and over (10% off); ages 2-15, accompanied by an adult (50% off); children under two (free on the lap of an adult). Reservations are required for first-class seats and sleeping car accommodations. Supersaver fares offer discounts of up to 50%. Call for details. The **Canrail Pass** allows unlimited travel on 12 to 15 days within a 30-day period. Between early June and mid-October, a 12-day pass costs CDN$569 (senior citizens, students and youths under 24 CDN$499). Off-season passes cost CDN$369 (seniors and youths CDN$339). Add CDN$44 for each additional day of travel. Call for information on seasonal promotions, such as discounts on Grayline Sightseeing Tours.

BY BUS

Buses generally offer the most frequent and complete service between the cities and towns of the U.S. and Canada. Often a bus is the only way to reach smaller locales without a car. In rural areas and across open spaces, however, bus lines tend to be sparse. *Russell's Official National Motor Coach Guide* ($15 including postage) is an invaluable tool for constructing an itinerary. Updated each month, *Russell's Guide* has schedules of every bus route (including Greyhound) between any two towns in the United States and Canada. Russell's also publishes two semiannual *Supplements,* one which includes a Directory of Bus Lines and Bus Stations ($6.25), and one which offers a series of Route Maps ($6.70). To order any of the above, write Russell's Guides, Inc., P.O. Box 278, Cedar Rapids, IA 52406 (319-364-6138; fax 364-4853).

Greyhound

Greyhound (800-231-2222; http://www.greyhound.com) operates the largest number of routes in the U.S., though local bus companies may provide more extensive services within specific regions. Schedule information is available at any Greyhound terminal, on the webpage, or by calling the 800 number. Reserve with a credit card over the phone at least 10 days in advance, and the ticket can be mailed anywhere in the U.S. Otherwise, reservations are available only up to 24hr. in advance. You can buy your ticket at the terminal, but arrive early.

If **boarding at a remote "flag stop,"** be sure you know exactly where the bus stops. You must call the nearest agency and let them know you'll be waiting and at what time. Catch the driver's attention by standing on the side of the road and flailing your arms wildly—better to be embarrassed than stranded. If a bus passes (usually because of over-crowding), a later, less-crowded bus should stop. Whatever you stow in compartments underneath the bus should be clearly marked; be sure to get a claim check for it and watch to make sure your luggage is on the same bus as you.

Advance purchase fares: Reserving space far ahead of time ensures a lower fare, although expect a smaller discount during the busy summer months (June 5-Sept. 15). For tickets purchased more than 21 days in advance, the one-way fare anywhere in the U.S. will not exceed $79, while the round-trip price is capped at $158 (from June-Sept., the one-way cap is $99 and the round-trip $198). Fares are also reduced for 14-day advance purchases on many popular routes; call the 800 number for up to the date pricing, or consult the user-friendly webpage.

Discounts on full fares: Senior citizens (10% off); children ages 2 to 11 (50% off); travelers with disabilities and special needs and their companions ride together for the price of 1. Active and retired U.S. military personnel and National Guard Reserves (10% off with valid ID) and their spouses and dependents may take a round-trip between any 2 points in the U.S. for $169. With a ticket purchased 3 or more days in advance, a friend can travel along for free; during the summer months, if purchased 7 days in advance, the free-loadin' friend gets half off.

Ameripass: Call 888-GLI-PASS (454-7277). Allows adults unlimited travel for 7 days ($199), 15 days ($299), 30 days ($409), or 60 days ($599). Prices for students with a valid college ID and for senior citizens are slightly less: 7 days ($179), 15 days ($269), 30 days ($369), or 60 days ($539). Children's passes are half the price of adults. The pass takes effect the first day used. Before purchasing an Ameripass, total up the separate bus fares between towns to make sure that the pass is really more economical, or at least worth the unlimited flexibility it provides. **TNMO Coaches, Vermont Transit, Carolina Trailways,** and **Valley Transit** are Greyhound subsidiaries, and as such will honor Ameripasses; actually, most bus companies in the U.S. will do so, but check for specifics.

International Ameripass: For travelers from outside North America. A 7-day pass is $179, 15-day pass $269, 30-day pass $369, 60-day pass $539. Call 888-GLI-PASS (454-7277) for schedule info. Primarily peddled in foreign countries by Greyhound-affiliated agencies; telephone numbers vary by country and are listed on the webpage. Order by email (to Dialcorp!jetpo01!Greyhound@jetsave.mail.att.net), or purchase in Greyhound's International Office, 625 Eighth Ave., New York, NY 10018 (800-246-8572 or 212-971-0492; fax 402-330-0919; email intlameripass@ greyhound.com). **Australia:** 049 342 088. **New Zealand:** 09 479 6555. **South Africa:** 011 331 2911. **United Kingdom:** 01342 317 317.

Greyhound Canada Transportation

Unrelated to Greyhound Lines, Greyhound Canada Transportation, 877 Greyhound Way, Calgary, AB T3C 3V8 (800-661-TRIP/8747; http://www.greyhound.ca) is Canada's main intercity bus company. The webpage has full schedule information.

Discounts: Seniors (10% off); students (10% off in Ontario, 25% off in West with purchase of CDN$15 discount card); a companion of a disabled person free; ages 3-7 50%; under 3 free. If reservations are made 7 days or more in advance, a friend travels ½-off. A child under 15 rides free with an adult if reserved 7 days in advance.

British Columbia student pass: Allows 4 one-way trips anywhere in the province (CDN$119); a similar pass exists for Alberta (CDN$99).

Canada Pass: Offers 7-, 15-, 30-, and 60-day unlimited travel on all routes for North American residents, including limited links to northern U.S. cities (7-day pass CDN$199; 15-day pass CDN$275; 30-day pass CDN$375; 60-day pass CDN$475).

International Canada Pass: For foreign visitors. Slightly lower prices (7-day pass CDN$199; 15-day pass CDN$270; 30-day pass CDN$365; 60-day pass CDN$465). The "Plus" pass adds travel to Québec and the Maritime provinces for a few dollars more; this can only be purchased overseas at select travel agencies, including those listed above for Greyhound Lines. Goods and services tax (GST) is added to fares.

Green Tortoise

Green Tortoise, 494 Broadway, San Francisco, CA 94133 (415-956-7500 or 800-867-8647; email tortoise@greentortoise.com), has "hostels on wheels" in remodeled diesel buses done up for living and eating on the road; meals are prepared communally. Prices include transportation, sleeping space on the bus, and tours of the regions through which you pass. Deposits ($100 most trips) are generally required, as space is tight. (Trips run May-Oct. From Hartford, Boston, or New York to San Francisco 10-14 days, $299-379 plus $101-111 for food.) Some round-trip vacation loops start and finish in San Francisco, winding through Yosemite National Park, Northern California, Baja California, the Grand Canyon, or Alaska along the way. Prepare for an earthy trip; buses have no toilets and little privacy. Reserve one to two months in advance; however, many trips have space available at departure. Reservations can be made over the phone or through the web at http://www.greentortoise.com.

East Coast Explorer

East Coast Explorer, 245 Eighth Ave., Suite 144, New York, NY 10011 (718-694-9667 or 800-610-2680 outside New York City; email llustig@delphi.com; http://hostels. com/transport/trans.ece.html), is an inexpensive way to tour the East Coast between New York City and Boston or Washington, D.C. (Reservations required. Two bags per person allowed.) For $3-7 more than Greyhound, you and 13 other passengers travel all day (10-11hr.) on back roads, stopping at natural and historic sites. Schedules vary by day of the week; call or check out the website for routes. Trips run in each direction between New York City and Washington, D.C. and between New York City and Boston ($29-32). The air-conditioned bus will pick up and drop off at most hostels and budget hotels.

Us Bus

Us Bus, 1050 Hancock St., Quincy, MA 02169 (617-773-8287 or in Europe 44 018 92 532 060; fax 773-7322; email TheUsbus@att.net), is a hop-on, hop-off travel pass system that takes passengers from door to door of youth hostels on major routes around the U.S. The 15-seat shuttle buses stop in over 50 American cities and national parks, with extensive service throughout the northeast, southeast, southwest and Pacific coast. Flexipasses are good for unlimited travel on a certain number of days over a period of time. (5 travel days over 15-day valid period $159; 10 days/25-day $279; 15 days/40-day $369; 45 days/90-day $699.) Book all trips in advance. Buses run May to October and stop in each location one to three times per day.

BY CAR

Let's Go lists U.S. highways thus: "I" (as in "I-90") refers to Interstate highways, "U.S." (as in "U.S. 1") to United States highways, and "Rte." (as in "Rte. 7") to state and local highways. For Canadian highways, "TCH" refers to the Trans-Canada Hwy., while "Hwy." or "autoroute" refers to standard automobile routes.

Automobile Clubs

American Automobile Association (AAA), 1050 Hingham St., Rocklin, MA 02370 (800-AAA-HELP/800-222-4357; http://www.aaa.com). Offers free trip-planning services, roadmaps and guidebooks, emergency road service anywhere in the U.S., free towing, and commission-free traveler's checks from American Express with over 1,000 offices scattered across the country. Discounts on Hertz car rental (5-20%), Amtrak tickets (10%), and various motel chains and theme parks. AAA has reciprocal agreements with the auto associations of many other countries, which often provide you with full benefits while in the U.S. AAA has 2 types of memberships, basic and plus, although the services do not differ greatly. Basic membership fees are $55 for the first year with $39 annual renewal; $30 yearly for associate (a family member in household); call 800-JOIN-AAA/800-564-6222 to sign up.

Canadian Automobile Association (CAA), 1145 Hunt Club Rd., #200, Ottowa, ON K1V0Y3 (800-CAA-HELP/800-222-4357; http://www.caa.ca). Affiliated with AAA (see above), the CAA provides nearly identical membership benefits, including 24hr. emergency roadside assistance, free maps and tourbooks, route planning, and various discounts. Basic membership is CDN$53 and CDN$34 for associates; call 800-JOIN-CAA (800-564-6222) to sign up.

Mobil Auto Club, 200 N. Martingale Rd., Schaumbourg, IL 60174 (800-621-5581). Benefits include locksmith reimbursement, towing (free up to 10 mi.), roadside service, and car-rental discounts. Annual fee ($79) covers you and another driver.

Montgomery Ward Auto Club, 200 N. Martingale Rd., Schaumbourg, IL 60173-2096 (800-621-5151). Provides 24hr. Emergency Roadside Assistance in any car, whether owned, rented, or borrowed, unlimited trip routing, and up to $1500 for travel emergencies. $79 yearly membership fee. Associate memberships available for driving-age children aged 16-23 for $24 annually.

On the Road

Tune up the car before you leave, make sure the tires are in good repair and have enough air, and get good maps. **Rand McNally's Road Atlas,** covering all of the U.S. and Canada, is one of the best (available at bookstores and gas stations, $10). A **compass** and a **car manual** can also be very useful. You should always carry a **spare tire** and **jack, jumper cables, extra oil, flares,** a **flashlight,** and **blankets** (in case you break down at night or in the winter). Those traveling long undeveloped stretches of road may want to consider renting a **car phone** in case of a breakdown. When traveling in the summer or in the desert bring five gallons of **water** for drinking and for the radiator. In extremely hot weather, use the air conditioner with restraint; if you see the car's temperature gauge climbing, turn it off. Turning the heater on full blast will help cool the engine. If radiator fluid is steaming, turn off the car for half an hour. *Never pour water over the engine to cool it.* Never lift a searing hot hood. In remote areas, remember to bring emergency food and water.

Sleeping in a car or van parked in the city is extremely dangerous—even the most dedicated budget traveler should not consider it an option. **Be sure to buckle up**—seat belts are required by law in many regions of the U.S. and Canada. The **speed limit in the U.S.** varies considerably from region to region. Most urban highways have a limit of 55 miles per hour (63km per hr.), while rural routes range from 65 mph (104kph) to 80 mph (128kph); Montana famously posts no speed limit, but basic speed laws, which require limiting speed according to road conditions, still apply. Heed the limit; not only does it save gas, but most local police forces and state troopers make frequent use of radar to catch speed demons. The **speed limit in Canada** is 100kph (63 mph). **Gas** in the U.S. costs about $1.25 per gallon ($0.33 per L), but prices vary widely according to state gasoline taxes. In Canada, gas costs CDN$0.60-65 per L (CDN$2-2.65 per gallon).

Drivers should take necessary precautions against **carjacking,** which has become one of the most frequent crimes committed in this country. Carjackers, who are usually armed, approach their victims in their vehicles, and force them to turn over the automobile. Carjackers prey on cars parked on the side of the road and cars stopped at red lights. If you are going to pull over on the side of the road, keep your doors locked and windows up at all times and do not pull over to help a car in the breakdown lane; call the police instead.

How to Navigate the Interstates

In the 1950s, President Eisenhower envisioned an **interstate system,** a federally funded network of highways designed primarily to subsidize American commerce. His dream has been realized, and there is actually an easily comprehensible, consistent system for numbering interstates. Even-numbered interstates run east-west and odd ones run north-south, decreasing in number toward the south and the west. North-south routes begin on the West Coast with I-5 and end with I-95 on the East Coast. The southernmost east-west route is I-4 in Florida. The northernmost east-west route is I-94, stretching from Montana to Wisconsin. Three-digit numbers signify branches of other interstates (e.g., I-285 is a branch of I-85), which are often a bypass skirting around a large city.

Renting

Although the cost of renting a car is often prohibitive for long distances, renting for local trips may be reasonable. **Auto rental agencies** fall into two categories: national companies with hundreds of branches, and local agencies that serve only one city or region.

National chains usually allow cars to be picked up in one city and dropped off in another (for a hefty charge, sometimes in excess of $1000); occasional promotions linked to coastal inventory imbalances may cut the fee dramatically. By calling a toll-free number, you can reserve a reliable car anywhere in the country. Generally, airport branches carry the cheapest rates. However, like airfares, car rental prices change constantly and often require scouting around for the best rate. Drawbacks include steep prices (a compact rents for about $45-80 per day) and high minimum ages for rentals (usually 25). Most branches rent to ages 21-24 with an additional fee, but policies and prices vary from agency to agency. If you're 21 or older and have a major credit card in your name, you may be able to rent where the minimum age would otherwise rule you out. **Alamo** (800-327-9633; http://www.goalamo.com) rents to ages 21-24 with a major credit card for an additional $20 per day. Some branches of **Avis** (800-230-4898; http://www.avis.com), in New York state and Québec province, and **Budget** (800-527-0700) rent to drivers under 25. **Hertz** (800-654-3131; http://www.hertz.com) policy varies with city. **Enterprise** (800-Rent-A-Car) rents to customers aged 21-24 with a variable surcharge. Most **Dollar** (800-8-00-4000; http://dollarcar.com) branches allow it, and various **Thrifty** (800-367-2277; http://www.thrifty.com) locations allow ages 21-24 to rent for an additional daily fee of about $20. **Rent-A-Wreck** (800-421-7253; email gene@raw.com; http://www.rent-a-wreck.com), specializes in supplying vehicles that are past their prime for lower-than-average prices; a bare-bones compact less than eight years old rents for around $20; cars, usually three to five years old, average under $25.

Most rental packages offer unlimited mileage, although some allow you a certain number of miles free before the usual charge of 25-40¢ per mile takes effect. Most quoted rates do not include gas or tax, so ask for the total cost before handing over the credit card; many large firms have added airport surcharges not covered by the designated fare. Return the car with a full tank unless you sign up for a fuel option plan that stipulates otherwise. And when dealing with any car rental company, be sure to ask whether the price includes insurance against theft and collision. There may be an additional charge, the collision and damage waiver (CDW), which usually comes to about $12-15 per day. If you use **American Express** to rent the car, they will automatically cover the CDW; call AmEx's car division (800-338-1670) for more information.

Buying

Adventures on Wheels, 42 Hwy. 36, Middletown, NJ 07748 (800-WHEELS-9/943-3579 or 732-583-8714; fax 583-8932; email info@wheels9.com; http://www. wheels9.com), will sell domestic and international travelers a motorhome, a camper or station wagon, organize its registration and provide insurance, and guarantee that they will buy it back from you after you have finished your travels. Buy a camper for $6-9000, use it for 5-6 months, and sell it back for $3000-5000. The main office is in New York/New Jersey; there are other offices in Los Angeles, San Francisco, and Miami. Vehicles can be picked up at one office and dropped off at another.

Auto Transport Companies

These services match drivers with car owners who need cars moved from one city to another. Would-be travelers give the company their desired destination and the company finds a car which needs to go there. The only expenses are gas, tolls, and your own living expenses. Some companies insure their cars; with others, your security deposit covers any breakdowns or damage. You must be at least 21, have a valid license, and agree to drive about 400 mi. per day on a fairly direct route. Companies regularly inspect current and past job references, take your fingerprints, and require a cash bond. Cars are available between most points, although it's easiest to find cars for traveling from coast to coast; New York and Los Angeles are popular transfer points. If offered a car, look it over first. Think twice about accepting a gas guzzler, since you'll be paying for the gas. With the company's approval, you may be able to share the cost with several companions.

> **Auto Driveaway Co.,** 310 S. Michigan Ave., Suite 1401, Chicago, IL 60604-4298 (800-346-2277; fax 312-341-9100; email autodrv@aol.com; http://www.autodrive-away.com).
>
> **Across America Driveaway,** 3626 Calumet Ave., Hammond, IN 46320 (800-619-7707 or 219-852-0134; fax 800-334-6931; http://www.schultz-international.com). Other offices in L.A. (800-964-7874 or 310-798-3377) and Dallas (214-745-8892).

BY BICYCLE

Before you pedal furiously onto the byways of America astride your banana-seat Huffy Desperado, remember that safe and secure cycling requires a quality helmet and lock. A good helmet costs about $40—much cheaper than critical head surgery. U-shaped **Kryptonite** or **Citadel** locks (about $30) carry insurance against theft for 1 or 2 years if your bike is registered with the police. **Bike Nashbar,** 4111 Simon Rd., Youngstown, OH 44512 (800-627-4227; fax 456-1223), will beat any nationally advertised in-stock price by 5¢, and ships anywhere in the U.S. and Canada. Their techline (330-788-6464; open M-F 8am-6pm) fields questions about repairs and maintenance.

Numerous publications will help you get the most out of your bicycle. *Bicycle Gearing: A Practical Guide* ($8.95), available from **The Mountaineers Books,** 300 3rd Ave. W., Seattle, WA 98134 (800-553-4453; fax 206-223-6306; email mbooks@ mountaineers.org; http://www.mountaineers.org/mbooks/mbooks.htm), discusses in lay terms how bicycle gears work, covering how to shift properly and get maximum propulsion from minimum exertion. *Anybody's Bike Book* ($11.95 plus $4.50 shipping), available from **Ten Speed Press,** Box 7123, Berkeley, CA 94707 (800-841-2665; fax 510-559-1629; email order@tenspeed.com; http://www.tenspeed.com), provides vital information on repair and maintenance during long-term bike sojourns. *The Packing Book* ($8.95) provides various checklists and suggested wardrobes, addresses safety concerns, and imparts packing techniques. **Rodale Press,** 33 E. Minor St., Emmaus, PA 18098-0099 (800-848-4735 or 610-967-5171), publishes a number of books for the intrepid would-be cyclist, including *Cycling for Women* ($8.95 plus shipping) and *Bicycle Repair* ($4.95 plus shipping).

Adventure Cycling Association, P.O. Box 8308-P, Missoula, MT 59807 (406-721-1776; fax 721-8754; email acabike@aol.com; http://www.adv-cycling.org). A national, non-profit organization that researches and maps long-distance routes and organizes bike tours for members. Membership $28 in the U.S., $35 in Canada and Mexico.

The Canadian Cycling Association, 1600 James Naismith Dr., #212A, Gloucester, ON K1B 5N4 (613-748-5629; fax 748-5692; email general@canadian-cycling.com; http://www.canadian-cycling.com). Distributes *The Canadian Cycling Association's Complete Guide to Bicycle Touring in Canada* (CDN$24), plus guides to specific regions of Canada, Alaska, and the Pacific Coast.

Backroads, 801 Cedar St., Berkeley, CA 94710-1800 (800-462-2848; fax 510-527-1444; email goactive@backroads.com; http://www.backroads.com), offers tours in 20 states, including Montana, Hawaii, California, Utah, and Maine. Travelers ride from accommodation to accommodation; prices include most meals, guide services, maps and directions, and van support.

BY MOTORCYCLE

It may be cheaper than car travel, but it takes a tenacious soul to endure a motorcycle tour. If you must carry a load, keep it low and forward where it won't distort the cycle's center of gravity. Fasten it either to the seat or over the rear axle in saddle or tank bags. Those considering a long journey should contact the **American Motorcyclist Association,** 33 Collegeview Rd., Westerville, OH 43801 (800-262-5646 or 614-891-2425 in Canada; fax 891-5012; email ama@ama-cycle.org; http://ama-cycle.org), the linchpin of U.S. biker culture. A full membership ($29 per year) includes a subscription to the extremely informative *American Motorcyclist* magazine, discounts on insurance, rentals, and hotels, and a kick-ass patch for your riding jacket. For an additional $25, members benefit from emergency roadside assistance, including pickup and delivery to a service shop.

Of course, **safety** should be your primary concern. Motorcycles are incredibly vulnerable to crosswinds, drunk drivers, and the blind spots of cars and trucks. *Always ride defensively.* Dangers skyrocket at night. **Helmets** are required by law in many states; wear the best one you can find. Americans should ask their State's Dept. of Motor Vehicles for a motorcycle operator's manual; the AMA webpage (see above) lists relevant laws and regulations for all 50 states.

Americade (email info@tourexpo.com; http://www.tourexpo.com) is an enormous week-long annual touring rally. In 1998 it was held June 1-6 in Lake George, NY. Call 518-656-3696 to register for 1999.

BY THUMB

Let's Go urges you to consider the great risks and disadvantages of **hitchhiking** before thumbing it. Hitching means entrusting your life to a randomly selected person who happens to stop beside you on the road. While this may be comparatively safe in some areas of Europe and Australia, it is generally *not* so in the U.S. We do not recommend it. We strongly urge you to find other means of transportation and to avoid situations where hitching is the only option.

■ Accommodations

Wherever you go, try to make reservations in advance, especially if you'll be traveling during peak tourist season. If you find yourself in truly dire financial straits, you can call the **Traveler's Aid Society** in some larger cities as a last resort; they will likely send you to a shelter. Local crisis hotlines may also be able to help.

HOTELS AND MOTELS

Many visitors centers, especially ones off major thoroughfares entering a state, have hotel coupons that can save you a bundle; if you don't see any, ask. Budget motels are usually clustered off the highway several miles outside of town, but the carless (and the light of wallet) may do better to try the hostels, YMCAs, YWCAs, and dorms downtown. The annually updated *National Directory of Budget Motels* ($13) covers over 2200 low-cost chain motels in the U.S. *The Hotel/Motel Special Program and Discount Guide* ($8) lists hotels and motels offering special discounts. Both are available in bookstores and on the web at http://www.amazon.com. Also look for the comprehensive *State by State Guide to Budget Motels* ($13) from Marlor Press, Inc., 4304 Brigadoon Dr., St. Paul, MN 55126 (651-484-4600 or 800-669-4908; fax 651-490-1182; email marlor@ix.net-com.com).

Chains usually adhere to a level of cleanliness and comfort more consistent than locally operated budget competitors. The cellar-level price of a single is about $30. Some budget chains are **Motel 6** (800-466-8356); **Super 8 Motels** (800-800-8000; http://www.super8motels.com/super8.html); **Choice Hotels International** (800-453-4511); and **Best Western International** (800-528-1234). **Great American Traveler,** P.O. Box 27965, Salt Lake City, UT 84127 (800-331-8867), offers a 50% discount at over 2000 hotels and motels worldwide with paid membership ($50 per year).

HOSTELS

For tight budgets and those lonesome traveling blues, hostels can't be beat. Hostels are generally dorm-style accommodations, often in single-sex large rooms with bunk beds; some hostels offer private rooms for families and couples. They often have kitchens and utensils for your use, bike or moped rentals, storage areas, and laundry facilities. There can be drawbacks; some hostels close during certain daytime "lock-out" hours, have a curfew, impose a maximum stay, or, less frequently, require that you do chores. Fees range from $5-25 per night, and hostels affiliated with one of the large hostel associations often have lower rates for members. *The Hostel Handbook for the U.S.A. & Canada,* by Jim Williams, available for $4 ($6 outside the U.S.) from Dept: IGH, 722 St. Nicholas Ave., New York, NY 10031 (email InfoHostel@aol.com; http://www.hos-

tels.com/handbook), lists over 500 hostels. If you have Internet access, check out the **Internet Guide to Hostelling** (http://hostels.com). Reservations for over 300 **Hostelling International (HI)** hostels (see listing below) may be made via the **International Booking Network (IBN),** a computerized reservation system, for a nominal fee (202-783-6161). If you plan to stay in hostels, consider joining one of these associations:

Hostelling International—American Youth Hostels (HI-AYH), 733 15th St. NW, #840, Washington, D.C. 20005 (202-783-6161; fax 783-6171; email hiayhserv@ hiayh.org; http://www.hiayh.org). 35 offices and over 150 hostels in the U.S. Memberships can be purchased at many travel agencies (see p. 21) or the national office in Washington, D.C. 1-year membership $25, under 18 $10, over 54 $15, family cards $35; includes *Hostelling North America: The Official Guide to Hostels in Canada and the United States.* Reserve by letter, phone, fax, or the International Booking Network (see above). Basic rules (with much local variation): check-in 5-8pm, check-out 9:30am (although most urban hostels have 24hr. access), 3-night max. stay, no pets or alcohol allowed on the premises. Fees $5-22 per night.

Hostelling International—Canada (HI-C), 400-205 Catherine St., Ottawa, ON K2P 1C3 (613-237-7884; fax 237-7868). Maintains 73 hostels throughout Canada. IBN booking centers in Edmonton, Montreal, Ottawa, and Vancouver; expect CDN$9-22.50 per night. Membership packages: CDN$25, under 18 CDN$12; 2-year CDN$35; lifetime CDN$175.

BED AND BREAKFASTS (B&B)

For a cozy alternative to impersonal hotel rooms, B&Bs (private homes with rooms available to travelers) range from the acceptable to the sublime. Hosts will sometimes go out of their way to be accommodating by accepting travelers with pets, giving personalized tours, or offering home-cooked meals. On the other hand, many B&Bs do not provide phones, TVs, or private bathrooms.

Several travel guides and reservation services specialize in B&Bs. Among the more extensive guides are *America's Best Bed and Breakfasts* ($18, CDN$25); *The Complete Guide to Bed and Breakfasts, Inns and Guesthouses in the U.S. and Canada* ($17), which lists over 11,000 B&Bs plus inns (available through Lanier Publications, P.O. Box D, Petaluma, CA 94953 (707-763-0271; fax 763-5762; email lanier@travelguides.com; http://www.travelguides.com); and *America's Favorite Inns, B&Bs, and Small Hotels* ($20, CDN$27). All three can be found in bookstores (see **Hitting the Books,** p. 1). **Bed and Breakfast: The National Network (TNN) of Reservation Services,** P.O. Box 4616, Springfield, MA 01101 (800-884-4288; fax 401-847-7309; email annas@wsii.com; http://www.tnn4bnb.com), can book reservations at over 7000 B&Bs throughout America and Canada.

YMCA AND YWCAS

Not all **Young Men's Christian Association (YMCA)** locations offer lodging; those that do are often located in urban downtowns, which can be convenient but a little gritty. YMCA rates are usually lower than a hotel's but higher than a hostel's, and may include use of pools, gyms, TVs, air conditioning (A/C), and other facilities. Many YMCAs accept women and families (group rates often available), and some (as in Los Angeles) will not lodge people under 18 without parental permission. All reservations must be made and paid for in advance, with a traveler's check (signed top and bottom), U.S. money order, certified check, Visa, or MasterCard. Call the local YMCA in question for fee info. For info or reservations (reservation fee $3, $6 overseas), contact **Y's Way International,** 224 E. 47th St., New York, NY 10017 (212-308-2899; fax 212-308-3161; http://www.ymca.int for links to branches worldwide). For Ys in **Canada,** contact the **Montréal YMCA** at 1450 Stanley St., Montréal, QC H3A 2W6 (514-849-8393; fax 849-8017) or the **YMCA of Stratford-Perth,** 204 Downie St., Stratford, ON M4Y 1T4 (519-271-0480).

Most **Young Women's Christian Associations (YWCAs)** accommodate only women or, sometimes, couples. Nonmembers are often required to join when lodging. For more

info or a world-wide directory ($10), write **YWCA-USA,** 726 Broadway, New York, NY 10003 (212-614-2700).

DORMS

Many **colleges and universities** open their residence halls to travelers during summer when school is not in session—some do so even in term-time. These dorms are often close to student areas—good sources for info on things to do, places to stay, and possible rides out of town—and are usually very clean. Getting a room may be difficult, but rates tend to be low, and many offer free local calls; call ahead. *Let's Go* lists colleges which rent dorm rooms among the accommodations for appropriate cities.

HOME EXCHANGE AND RENTALS

Home exchange offers the traveler with a home the opportunity to live like a native, and to dramatically cut down on accommodation fees—usually only an administration fee is paid to the matching service. Most companies have pictures of members and homes and info about the owners (some will even ask for your photo). A site listing many exchange companies can be found at http://www.aitec.edu.au/~bwechner/Documents/Travel/Lists/HomeExchangeClubs.html. **Renting a home** might be a good deal, depending on the length of stay and desired level of services.

Barclay International Group, 150 W 52nd St., New York, NY 10022 (212-832-3777 or 800-845-6636; fax 212-753-1139; email Barcintl@ix.netcom.com; http://www.barclay-web.com), arranges hotel alternative accommodations (apartment, condo, cottage, B&B, or villa rentals) in over 20 countries, including the U.S. and Canada. Most are equipped with kitchens, telephones, TV, and concierge and maid service. Rentals are pricey, starting around $700 per week in the off season.

The Invented City: International Home Exchange, 41 Sutter St., #1090, San Francisco, CA 94104 (800-788-CITY/2489 in the U.S. or 415-252-1141 elsewhere; fax 415-252-1171; email invented@aol.com). Listing of 1700 homes worldwide. For $50, you get your offer listed in 1 catalogue and receive 3 others.

■ Camping and the Outdoors

USEFUL PUBLICATIONS

Many publishing companies offer hiking guidebooks to meet the educational needs of novice or expert. The **Great Outdoors Recreation Pages** on the Web (http://www.gorp.com) overflows with camping-related info, including maps and fee data for national parks, forests, and some state park networks. The **Sierra Club Bookstore,** 85 2nd St. 2nd fl., San Francisco, CA 94105 (415-977-5600 or 800-935-1056; fax 977-5793; http://www.sierraclub.org/books), stocks guides to many national parks, several series on different regions of the U.S., and *Learning to Rock Climb* ($14), *The Sierra Club Family Outdoors Guide* ($12), and *Wildwater* ($12). **Wilderness Press,** 2440 Bancroft Way, Berkeley, CA 94704-1676 (510-843-8080 or 800-443-7227; fax 510-548-1355; email wpress@ix.netcom.com; http://www.wildernesspress.com), publishes over 100 hiking guides and maps to the western U.S., including *Backpacking Basics* ($11, including postage) and *Backpacking with Babies and Small Children* ($11). **Woodall Publications Corp.,** 13975 W. Polo Trail Dr., Lake Forest, IL 60045-5000 (800-323-9076; fax 847-362-8776; email emd@woodallpub.com; http://www.woodalls.com), puts out the ever-popular and annually updated *Woodall's Campground Directory* ($20) and *Woodall's Plan-it, Pack-it, Go!: Great Places to Tent, Fun Things To Do* ($13), which are generally available in American bookstores.

EQUIPMENT

At the core of your equipment is the **sleeping bag.** Your purchase should depend on the climate in which you plan to camp; sleeping bags are rated according to the lowest out-

ESSENTIALS

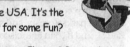

door temperature at which they will still keep you warm. If a bag's rating is not a temperature but a seasonal description, "summer" translates to a rating of 30-40°F, "three-season" means 0°F, and "winter" means below -50°F and are rarely necessary. Bags are made either of down (warmer and lighter) or of synthetic material (cheaper, heavier, more durable, and warmer when wet). Low prices for sleeping bags are $65-100 for a summer synthetic, $135-200 for a three-season synthetic; $150-225 for a three-season down bag; and upwards of $250-550 for a down winter-bag. **Sleeping bag pads** ($15-30) and **air mattresses** ($25-50) cushion your back and neck and insulate you from the ground. Another option is the part-foam, part air-mattress **Therm-A-Rest,** which inflates to full padding.

When you select a **tent,** your major considerations should be shape and size. The most user-friendly tents are free-standing, with their own frames and suspension systems. They set up quickly and require no staking (though staking adds security on windy days). Tents are also classified by season, which should be taken into account to avoid baking in a winter tent in the middle of the summer. Low-profile dome tents are especially efficient; when pitched, their internal space is almost entirely usable, which means little unnecessary bulk. Be sure your tent has a rain fly; seal the tent's seams with waterproofer. Two people *can* fit in a two-person tent, but will find life more pleasant in a four-person. If you're traveling by car, go for the bigger tent; if you're hiking, stick with a smaller tent that weighs no more than 3-4 lbs. Good two-person tents start at $150, four-person tents at $400, but you can sometimes find last year's model for half the price.

If you intend to do a lot of hiking, you should have a **frame backpack. Internal-frame packs** mold better to your back, keep a lower center of gravity, and can flex adequately to allow you to hike difficult trails that require a lot of bending and maneuvering. **External-frame packs** are more comfortable for long hikes over even terrain since they keep the weight higher and distribute it more evenly. Whichever you choose, make sure your pack has a strong, padded hip belt, which transfers the weight from the shoulders to the legs. Any serious backpacking requires a pack of at least 4000 cubic inches. Allow an additional 500 cubic inches for your sleeping bag in internal-frame packs. Sturdy backpacks cost anywhere from $125-500. This is one area where it doesn't pay to economize—cheaper packs may be less comfortable, and the straps are more likely to fray or rip. Before you buy any pack, try it on and imagine carrying it, full, a few miles up a rocky incline.

Buy **rain gear** in two pieces, a top and pants, rather than a poncho. **Synthetics,** like polypropylene tops, socks, and long underwear, along with a pile jacket, will keep you warm even when wet. When camping in autumn, winter, or spring, bring along a **"space blanket,"** which helps you to retain your body heat and doubles as a ground-cloth ($5-15). Plastic **canteens** or water bottles keep water cooler than metal ones do, and are virtually shatter- and leak-proof. Large, collapsible **water sacks** will significantly improve your lot in primitive campgrounds and weigh practically nothing when empty, though they can get bulky. Bring **water-purification tablets** for when you can't boil water. Though most campgrounds provide campfire sites, you may want to bring a small **metal grate** or **grill** of your own. For those places that forbid fires or the gathering of firewood, you'll need a **camp stove;** prices start at about $40. A **first aid kit, swiss army knife, insect repellent, calamine lotion,** and **waterproof matches** or a **lighter** are essential camping items. Other items include: a **battery-operated lantern,** a **plastic groundcloth,** a **nylon tarp,** a **waterproof backpack cover** (although you can also store your belongings in plastic bags inside your backpack), and a **"stuff sack"** or plastic bag to keep your sleeping bag dry.

Recreational Equipment, Inc. (REI) (800-426-4840; http://www.rei.com) stocks a comprehensive selection of REI brand and other leading brand equipment, clothing, and footwear for traveling, camping, cycling, paddling, climbing, and winter sports. In addition to mail order and an Internet commerce site, REI has 49 retail stores. The flagship store is at 222 Yale Ave. N., Seattle, WA 98109-5429.

ESSENTIALS

L.L. Bean, Casco St., Freeport, ME 04033-0001 (800-441-5713 in Canada or the U.S.; 0800 962 954 in the U.K.; 207-552-6878 elsewhere; fax 207-552-4080; http://www.llbean.com). Monolithic equipment and outdoor clothing supplier (see p. 72) offers high quality and loads of info. Customer-guaranteed satisfaction on all purchases, or they'll replace or refund it. Call for free catalogue. Open 24hr.

Campmor, P.O. Box 700, Saddle River, NJ 07458-0700 (888-CAMPMOR/226-7667 or 201-825-8300 outside the U.S.; email customer-service@campmor.com; http://www.campmor.com). Wide selection of name-brand equipment at low prices. 1-year guarantee on unused or defective merchandise.

Eastern Mountain Sports (EMS), 1 Vose Farm Rd., Peterborough, NH 03458 (603-924-7231; emsmail@emsonline.com; http://www.emsonline.com). Stores nationwide provide excellent service and guaranteed customer satisfaction on all items sold, though the prices are slightly higher. They don't have a catalogue, and they don't take mail or phone orders; call the above number for the branch nearest you.

A good source of info on **camping/recreational vehicles (RVs)** is the **National Association of RV Parks and Campgrounds,** 8605 Westwood Sector Dr., #201, Vienna, VA 22182 (703-734-3000; fax 734-3004). The association operates the **Go Camping America** listings, with info on over 3000 RV parks and campgrounds throughout North America (800-974-5151; http://www.gocampingamerica.com). Many of the larger U.S. rental firms (see **Renting,** p. 36) handle RV rentals, though rates vary widely by region, season (July and August are the most expensive months), and type.

NATIONAL PARKS

National Parks protect some of the most spectacular scenery in North America. Though their primary purpose is preservation, the parks also host recreational activities like ranger talks, guided hikes, skiing, and snowshoe expeditions. For info pertaining to the national park system, contact the **National Park Service,** Office of Public Inquiries, 1849 C St. NW, Room 1013, Washington, D.C. 20240 (202-208-4747). The slick and informative webpage (http://www.nps.gov) lists info on all the parks, detailed maps, and fee and reservation data. The **National Park Foundation,** 1101 L St., #1102, Washington, D.C. 20077 (202-785-4500), distributes *The Complete Guide to America's National Parks* by mail-order ($16, plus $3 shipping).

Entrance fees vary. The larger and more popular parks charge a $4-20 entry fee for cars and sometimes a $2-7 fee for pedestrians and cyclists. The **Golden Eagle Passport** ($50), available at park entrances, allows the passport-holder's party entry into all national parks for 1 year. U.S. citizens or residents 62 and over qualify for the lifetime **Golden Age Passport** ($10 one-time fee), which entitles the holder's party to free park entry, a 50% discount on camping, and 50% reductions on various recreational fees for the passport holder. Persons eligible for federal benefits on account of disabilities can enjoy the same privileges with the **Golden Access Passport** (free). Golden Age and Golden Access Passports must be purchased at a park entrance with proof of age or federal eligibility, respectively; Golden Eagle Passports can also be bought by writing to Golden Eagle Passport, 1100 Ohio Dr. SW, Room 138, Washington, D.C. 20242. All passports are also valid at National Monuments, Forests, Wildlife Preserves, and other national recreation sites.

Most national parks have both backcountry and developed tent **camping;** some welcome RVs, and a few offer grand lodges. At the more popular parks in the U.S. and Canada, reservations are essential, available through **DESTINET** (800-365-2267 or 619-452-8787 outside the U.S.) no sooner than 5 months in advance. Lodges and indoor accommodations should be reserved months in advance. Campgrounds often observe first come, first served policies. Many campgrounds fill up by late morning. Some limit your stay and/or the number of people in a group.

NATIONAL FORESTS
Often less accessible and less crowded, U.S. National Forests (http://www.fs.fed.us) are a purist's alternative to parks. While some have recreation facilities, most are equipped only for primitive camping—pit toilets and no water are the norm. Entrance fees, when charged, are $10-20, but camping is generally free, or $3-4.

Some specially designated wilderness areas have regulations barring all vehicles. Necessary wilderness permits for backpackers can be obtained at the U.S. Forest Service field office in the area. If you are interested in exploring a National Forest, call or write for a copy of *A Guide to Your National Forests* (publication *FS* #418): USDA, Forest Service, 1400 Independence Ave. SW, Washington, D.C. 20250 (ATTN: PAO, Public Publications; 202-205-0957; fax 205-0885). This booklet includes a list of all national forest addresses; request maps and other info directly from the forest(s) you plan to visit. **Reservations**, with a one-time $16.50 service fee, are available for most forests, but are usually unnecessary except during high season at the more popular sites. Write or call up to 1 year in advance to National Recreation Reservation Center, P.O. Box 900, Cumberland, MD 21501-0900 (800-280-2267; fax 301-722-9802).

CANADA'S NATIONAL PARKS Less trammeled than their southern counterparts, these parks boast at least as much natural splendor. Park entrance fees range from CDN$3-7 per person, with family and multi-day passes available. Reservations are being offered for a limited number of campgrounds on a trial basis for 1999 with a CDN$6.18 fee. For these reservations, or for info on the over 40 parks and countless historical sites in the network, call **Parks Canada,** 220 4th Ave. SE #552, Calgary, AB T2G 4X3 (800-748-7275), or consult the useful webpage (http://parkscanada.pch.gc.ca). A patchwork of regional passes are available at relevant parks; the best is the **Western Canada Pass,** which covers admission to all the parks in the Western provinces for a year (CDN$70 per vehicle, seniors CDN$53).

ROUGHING IT SAFELY

Stay warm, stay dry, stay hydrated. The vast majority of life-threatening wilderness problems stem from a failure to follow this advice. If you're going into an area that is not well traveled or well marked, let someone know where you're hiking and how long you intend to be out. *Never go camping or hiking by yourself for any significant time or distance.* On any hike, however brief, you should pack enough equipment to keep you alive should disaster befall. This includes **rain gear, hat** and **mittens, a first-aid kit,** a **reflector,** a **whistle, high energy food,** and **water.** Dress in warm layers of **synthetic materials** designed for the outdoors, or **wool.** Pile fleece jackets and Gore-Tex® raingear are excellent choices (see **Equipment** above). Never rely on **cotton** for warmth. This "death cloth" will be absolutely useless should it get wet. When camping, be sure to bring a proper tent with a rain-fly and warm sleeping bags. Check all equipment for any defects before embarking.

Check **weather forecasts** and pay attention to the skies when hiking; weather patterns can change instantly. If the weather turns nasty on a day hike, turn back. If on an overnight, start looking immediately for shelter. Whenever possible, let someone know when and where you are going hiking, whether a friend, your hostel, a park ranger, or a local hiking organization. Do not attempt a hike beyond your ability—you may be endangering your life.

ECO-TOURISM

While protecting yourself from the elements, take a moment to consider protecting the wilderness from you. At the very least, a responsible traveler practices **"minimum impact camping" or "leave no trace"** techniques. Because firewood is scarce in popular parks, campers should only make small fires using dead branches or brush. Using a campstove is a more efficient way to cook (if less fun). Use only existing fire pits and campsites to avoid creating new scars, and bury the ashes when leaving a site. Some parks prohibit campfires altogether. To avoid digging a rain trench for your tent, pitch it on high, dry ground. Don't cut vegetation or clear new campsites, and do not leave a trace of your presence when you leave a site. Make sure your campsite is at least 150 ft. from any water supply or body of water. If there are no toilet facilities, bury human waste at least 4 in. deep and 150 ft. or more from any water supply or campsite. Always pack your trash in a plastic bag and carry it with you until you reach the next trash can;

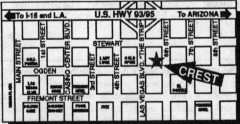

burning and burying pollute the environment. If nothing else, remember this mantra: "Leave only footprints, and take only pictures."

Responsible tourism means more than picking up your litter, however. Growing numbers of "ecotourists" are asking hard questions of resort owners and tour operators about how their policies affect local ecologies and local economies. Some try to give something back to the regions they enjoy by volunteering for environmental organizations at home or abroad. Above all, responsible tourism means being aware of your impact on the places you visit, and taking responsibility for your own actions. If you want to know more about "ecotourism" or responsible travel in a particular region, contact the **Partners in Responsible Tourism,** P.O. Box 419085-322, San Francisco, CA 94141 (http://www2.pirt.org/pirt/about.html).

BEAR IN MIND

Rangers and other local authorities will always be your best resource for learning how to behave safely around **bears** in a particular region. Ask local rangers for information on bear behavior before entering any park or wilderness area, and obey any posted warnings. No matter how tame a bear appears, don't be fooled—they're powerful and unpredictable animals who are not impressed or intimidated by humans. If you're close enough for a bear to be observing you, you're too close. To avoid a grizzly experience, keep your camp clean—no trash or food lying around—and don't cook near where you sleep. Try not to take the same path between your sleeping and eating areas—bears can follow those paths just as easily as you can. Park rangers can tell you how to identify bear trails—don't camp on them.

Never feed a bear or tempt it with such delicacies as open trash cans. **Bear-bagging,** which amounts to hanging edibles and other good-smelling objects from a tree, out of reach of hungry paws, is trickier than it sounds; park rangers or a salesperson at a wilderness store can show you how. Avoid greasy foods, especially bacon and ham; **grease** gets on everything, including your clothes and sleeping bag, and bears find it alluring. Bears are also attracted to any **perfume,** as are bugs—do without cologne, scented soap, deodorant, and hairspray while camping. If you see a bear at a distance, calmly walk (don't run) in the other direction. If you stumble upon a bear cub, leave immediately lest its over-protective mother stumble upon you.

Depending on the area you are in, bears are not the only animals that would-be campers should be wary of. In the west, **bison** may appear tame, but they are huge and fast, and, if provoked by tourists, can become dangerous. **Moose,** like bears, are also interested in your food. Do not feed them anything! Racoons, mice, and other smaller animals will happily raid food bags; even if there are no bears in the vicinity, food should be hung from a tree. On some trails, such as the Appalachian Trail, trail shelters are usually accompanied by a pole or rope for keeping food out reach.

ORGANIZED ADVENTURE

Organized adventure tours offer another way of exploring the wild. Activities include hiking, biking, skiing, canoeing, kayaking, rafting, climbing, photo safaris, and archaeological digs, and the trips go *everywhere*. Tourism bureaus can suggest parks, trails, and outfitters as well as answer more general questions; another good source for organized adventure options are the outdoors stores and organizations listed earlier. REI, EMS, or Sierra can inform you of a range of cheap, convenient trips. They often offer training programs for people who want an independent trip. Hundreds of operators worldwide are listed by the *Specialty Travel Index*, 305 San Anselmo Ave., Suite 313, San Anselmo, CA 94960 (800-442-4922 or 415-459-4900; fax 459-4974; email spectrav@ix.net-com.com; http://www.specialtytravel.com). **Backroads** handles organized **bicycle** treks; see p. 37 for more info. **Roadrunner International,** Quincy, MA, 02169 (800-TREK-USA/873-5782 in North America; (01892) 51 27 00 in Europe and the U.K.; fax 617-984-2045), offers hostel tour packages in the U.S. and Canada.

Sierra Club, 85 2nd St., 2nd fl., San Francisco, CA 94105-3441 (415-977-5630; http://www.sierraclub.org/outings), plans many adventure outings, both through its San Francisco headquarters and local branches in Canada and the U.S.

TrekAmerica, P.O. Box 189, Rockaway, NJ 07886 (800-221-0596; fax 973-983-8551; email info@trekamerica.com; http://www.trekamerica.com), organizes small group adventure camping tours throughout North America (trips from 7 days to 9 weeks). **Footloose** (http://www.footloose.com) is their open-age adult program.

■ Lines of Communication

U.S. AND CANADIAN MAIL

Offices of the **U.S. Postal Service** are usually open Monday to Friday from 9am to 5pm and sometimes on Saturday until about noon; branches in many larger cities open earlier and close later. If you don't want to make the trip to the post office, most hotels and hostel owners will send stamped postcards or letters home for you if you ask. **Postal rates within the U.S. are:** postcards 20¢, letters: 1 oz. 32¢, 23¢ per additional oz. Because of recent mail bomb scares, the Postal Service now requires that **overseas** letters be mailed directly from the post office and accompanied by a customs form. **Overseas rates are:** postcards 50¢, ½ oz. 60¢, 1 oz. $1, 40¢ per additional ½ oz. **Aerogrammes,** sheets that fold into envelopes and travel via air mail, are available at post offices for 50¢. Domestic mail generally takes 3-5 days; overseas mail, 7-14 days. **Postal rates (in CDN) within Canada are:** letters and postcards 30g 45¢, 50g 71¢; to U.S. 30g 52¢, 50g 77¢; to overseas destinations, 20g 90¢, 50g $1.37.

For both countries, write **"AIR MAIL"** on the front of the envelope for speediest delivery. If people want to get in touch with you, have them send mail **general delivery** to a city's main post office. You should bring a passport or other ID to pick up general delivery mail. *Always write "Hold for 30 Days" in a conspicuous spot on the envelope.* Family and friends can send letters to you labeled like this:

Elvis A. <u>PRESLEY</u> (underline and capitalize last name for accurate filing)
c/o general delivery
Post Office Street Address
Memphis, TN 38101 or VICTORIA, BC V8W 1L0
USA or Canada

In both the U.S. and Canada, **American Express** offices will act as a mail service for cardholders if you contact them in advance under the free **"Client Letter Service"** (see **American Express,** p. 10). If regular airmail is too slow, there are a few faster, more expensive, options. **Federal Express** (800-463-3339; http://www.fedex.com) is a reliable private courier service that guarantees overnight delivery anywhere in the continental U.S., at a price (a letter under ½ lb. sets you back $10.75-13.50). The cheaper but more sluggish U.S. Postal Service **Express Mail** will deliver a ½ lb. parcel in less than two days for $10.75 from any post office. For complete info on USPS rates, visit http://www.postcalc.usps.gov. The Canadian Postal Service offers **Priority Courier** (next day delivery), **XPress Post,** and **SkyPak** for destinations in the U.S. and other countries. Rates vary by destination and weight.

TELEPHONES

Telephone numbers in the U.S. and Canada consist of a 3-digit area code, a 3-digit exchange, and a 4-digit number, written as 123-456-7890. Numbers with **800** or **888** area codes are toll-free numbers. 900 numbers charge expensive per minute fees.

Local calls: Dial the last 7 digits. In some large cities, a 10-digit phone code is now required to make a local call.

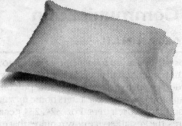

Long-distance calls within the U.S./Canada: 1 + area code + 7-digit number. Same area code calls are not always local; for long-distance calls within an area code: 1 + 7-digit number. For toll-free 800 or 888 numbers: 1 + 800 + 7-digit number.

International calls: Dial the universal international access code (011) followed by the country code, the city code, and the local number. Country codes and city codes may sometimes be listed with a zero in front (e.g. 033 for France), but when using 011, drop successive zeros (e.g., 011-33). In some areas you will need to give the number to the operator, who will then place the call for you. For country code listings, see the **Appendix,** p. 930.

Evening rates are considerably less than weekday rates (generally Su-F 5-11pm); **night and weekend rates** are cheaper than evening rates (generally M-F 11pm-8am, all day Sa, and all day Su except 5-11pm).

Dialing **"0"** will get you the **operator,** omnipotent in all matters connected with phones. To obtain specific local phone numbers or to find area codes for other cities, call **directory assistance** at **411** or look in the local **white pages** telephone directory; for **long-distance directory assistance,** dial **1-(area code)-555-1212.**

Pay phones are plentiful in most regions, most often stationed on street corners and in public areas. Put your coins (25-35¢ for a local call depending on the region) into the slot before dialing. If there is no answer or if you get a busy signal, you'll get your money back after hanging up, but not if you connect with an answering machine. If you are at a pay phone and don't have barrels of change, you can dial "0" for the operator and ask to place one of the following types of calls:

Collect call: If whoever picks up the phone call accepts the charges, he or she will be billed. The cheapest is MCI's 800-COLLECT/205-5328 service, which is 20-44% less expensive than other collect rates. AT&T's collect service, 800-CALL-ATT/225-5288, guarantees AT&T lines and rates for the call.

Person-to-person collect call: A little more expensive than a normal collect call, but a charge appears only if the person you wish to speak to is there (for example, if you want to speak to Michelle but not her parents).

Third-party billing: Bills the call to a 3rd party. Have the number of the place you want to call and the number of the place you want to bill the call to (e.g., home).

Most hotels charge exorbitant rates for phone calls. A calling **card** is probably your best and cheapest bet; your local long-distance service provider will have a number for you to dial while traveling (either toll-free or charged as a local call) to connect instantly to an operator in your home country. The calls (plus a small surcharge) are then billed either collect or to the calling card. For more info, call **AT&T** about its **USADirect** and **World Connect** services (888-288-4685; from abroad call 810-262-6644 collect); **Sprint** (800-877-4646; from abroad, call 913-624-5335 collect); or **MCI WorldPhone** and **World Reach** (800-444-4141; from abroad dial the country's MCI access number). Worldphone provides access to **Traveler's Assist,** which gives legal and medical advice, exchange rate info, and translation services. In Canada, contact Bell Canada's **Canada Direct** (800-565-4708); in the U.K., British Telecom's **BT Direct** (0800 345 144); in Ireland, Telecom Éireann's **Ireland Direct** (0800 250 250); in Australia, Telstra's **Australia Direct** (13 22 00); in New Zealand, **Telecom New Zealand** (123); and in South Africa, **Telkom South Africa** (09 03). Travelers with these accounts at home can use special **access numbers** to place calls from the U.S. through their home systems. All companies except Telkom South Africa have different access numbers depending on whether their cooperative partner in the U.S. is AT&T, MCI, or Sprint. Access numbers are: British Telecom (800-445-5667 AT&T, 800-444-2162 MCI, 800-800-0008 Sprint); Telecom Australia (800-682-2878 AT&T, 800-937-6822 MCI, 800-676-0061 Sprint); and Telkom South Africa (800-949-7027).

You can buy **pre-paid phone cards** from most gas stations and convenient stores, which carry a certain amount of phone time depending on the card's denomination. The card usually has a toll-free access telephone number and a personal identification number (PIN).

Some enterprising companies have created "callback" phone services. You call a specified number, ring once, and hang up; the company's computer calls back with a dial tone. You can then make as many calls as you want, at rates about 20-60% lower than you'd pay using credit cards or pay phones. This option is most economical for loquacious travelers, as services may include a $10-25 minimum billing per month. **America Tele-Fone** (800-321-5817) or **Telegroup** (800-338-0225) have services.

ELECTRONIC MAIL

With some computer knowledge and a little planning, you can beam messages anywhere for no per-message charges with **electronic mail (email). Traveltales.com** (http://traveltales.com) provides free, web-based email for travelers and maintains a list of cybercafes, travel links, and a travelers' chat room. Other free, web-based email providers include **Hotmail** (http://www.hotmail.com) and **USANET** (http://www.usa.net). Many free email providers are funded by advertising, and some may require subscribers to fill out a questionnaire. Search through http://www.cyberiacafe.net/cyberia/guide/ccafe.html to find a list of **cybercafes** around the world.

If you're hooked up to the infobahn, you should be able to find access numbers for your destination country; check with your Internet provider before leaving. If you're not connected, a comparatively cheap, easy-to-use provider is **America Online,** 8615 Westwood Center Dr., Vienna, VA 22070 (800-827-6364; http://www.aol.com).

Let's Go may be reached by email at feedback@letsgo.com.

UNITED STATES

Reaching from below the Tropic of Cancer to above the Arctic Circle and spanning the North American continent, the United States is big. It is a country defined by open spaces and an amazing breadth of terrain. Through decades of immigration, the U.S. has absorbed and integrated millions of immigrants to create the cultural amalgamation that now defines the population. Many ethnic and cultural narratives contribute to the proud spirit that pervades the country. As this child of many continents has risen from a colonial experiment to a position of supreme economic and political power, the **McCultural™ juggernaut** rolls on.

▋ History

IN THE BEGINNING

Archaeologists estimate that the first Americans crossed the Bering Sea from Siberia, either by land bridge or boat, during the last **Ice Age,** about 15,000 years ago. Recent archaeological digs have uncovered evidence of earlier habitation, but the data leaves room for doubt. By 9000 BC, populations of hunter-gatherers lived in every corner of North America. These settlers adapted remarkably to their new environment; on the plains, Native Americans hunted buffalo, and on the West Coast, Aleuts and Eskimos caught whales and other sea mammals. By the arrival of Europeans, around a hundred civilizations composed nine distinct cultural areas of North America.

EUROPEAN EXPLORATION AND COLONIZATION

The date of the first European exploration of North America is also disputed. The earliest Europeans to stumble upon the "New World" were likely sea voyagers blown off-course by storms. *The Saga of the Greenlanders* and *The Saga of Erik the Red* describe the travels of Icelanders who sailed to Greenland, the Labrador coast, and possibly northern New England, in 982. The traditional "discovery" of the Americas was in 1492, when **Christopher Columbus** found his voyage to the east blocked by Hispaniola in the Caribbean Sea. Believing he had reached the spice islands of the East Indies, he erroneously dubbed the inhabitants **"Indians."** In return for an efficient agricultural system, suitable for survival in the New World, the Europeans gave the Native Americans pestilence, persecution, and slavery.

Many Europeans came to the Americas (named after Italian explorer **Amerigo Vespucci**) in search of gold and silver; most were unsuccessful, but European colonization persisted. The Spanish originally boasted the most extensive American empire (today New Mexico, Arizona, California, and Florida). **St. Augustine** (p. 357), founded in Florida in 1565, was the first permanent European settlement in the present-day United States. Meanwhile, the French and Dutch created more modest empires to the north. It was the English, however, who most successfully settled the vast New World. After a few unsuccessful attempts, like the "lost colony" at **Roanoke** in North Carolina (p. 296), the English finally managed to establish a colony at **Jamestown** in 1607 (p. 242). Their success hinged on a strain of native American weed called tobacco, which achieved wild popularity in England. **English Puritans** landed first in **Provincetown** (p. 109) in 1620 (*not* **Plymouth Rock,** p. 105) in what is now Massachusetts, but quickly left for better land and sailed into the history books. Native Americans helped teach them to survive in a harsh land. The Pilgrims, grateful for their hard-won survival, celebrated with one of the most treasured holidays in modern American culture, **Thanks-**

giving. Though Britain's Empire grew to encompass 13 diverse colonies along the eastern seaboard, the New England Puritans exerted a strong political and cultural influence until well after the Revolution.

CONSOLIDATION AND REVOLUTION

Throughout the first half of the 18th century, the English colonies expanded as valleys were settled, fields plowed, and babies born. A quarter-million settlers had grown into 2.5 million by 1775. The expanding British colonies gradually imposed on the French, who also sought to expand their neighboring empire. Several military clashes resulted; the most explosive of these encounters was the **French and Indian War,** a side-show to the world-wide Seven Years' War. From 1756 to 1763, the English fought the French and their Native American allies, who joined the battle in exchange for French aid in inter-tribal conflicts. The British emerged victorious, and the 1763 **Peace of Paris** ceded French Canada to Britain's King George III.

Determined to make the colonists help pay the debts incurred in assuring their safety, the British government levied a number of taxes in the 1760s and early 1770s. The colonists reacted with indignation, protesting **"no taxation without representation."** Agitation over the taxes came to a head with the **Boston Massacre** in 1770 and then the **Boston Tea Party** in December of 1774, in which a group dressed as Native Americans dumped several shiploads of taxed English tea into Boston Harbor. The British response, dubbed the Intolerable Acts, was swift and harsh. Boston was effectively placed under siege, but the red-coated British soldiers who poured into town were met with armed rebellion, beginning in Lexington, MA, in April of 1775. On July 4, 1776, the Continental Congress formally issued the **Declaration of Independence,** announcing the 13 colonies' desire to be free of British rule. Initially a guerilla band composed of homespun militia known as **Minutemen,** the Continental forces eventually grew into an effective army under the leadership of **George Washington.** Despite many setbacks, the revolutionaries prevailed by vanquishing British General Lord Cornwallis at **Yorktown, Virginia** (p. 242), in 1781 with the help of the French fleet and a host of countries allied against the British.

LIFE, LIBERTY, AND THE CONSTITUTION

After experimenting with a loose confederate government until 1787, a distinguished group of 55 men convened to draft what is now the world's oldest written constitution. While the **Federalists** supported a strong central government uninfluenced by popular whim, their opposition, the **Jeffersonians** (Anti-Federalists), favored states' rights and feared the cutthroat individualism and domineering government that capitalism would bring.

The *Constitution*'s **Bill of Rights,** which included the rights to free speech, freedom of the press, and freedom of religion, remain a controversial cornerstone of the American political system. In spite of the supposed inalienability of these rights, the original words of the document's authors are still interpreted differently according to the political climate of each era. In 1896, **Justice Henry Billings Brown** used it to support the injustice in **Plessy v. Ferguson** whereas **Chief Justice Earl Warren** found the same document to destroy segregation in the 50s. The *Constitution,* with its malleability and responsiveness to changing mores, reflects the young country's contradictions, uniquely individualist ideals, and longing for just governance.

ONWARD AND OUTWARD: MANIFEST DESTINY

Looking toward the land beyond the Mississippi River, in 1803 **President Thomas Jefferson** purchased the **Louisiana Territory** (one-fourth of the present-day United States) from Napoleon for less than 3¢ an acre. After the War of 1812 with Britain, the westward movement gained momentum. **Manifest Destiny,** a belief that the United States was destined by God to rule the continent, captured the ideological imagination of the era. The annexation of Texas in 1846 and war with Mexico in 1848 added most of the Southwest and California to the territorial fold. Droves of people moved west in search of cheap, fertile land and a new life. **The Homestead Act** of 1862, which distributed tracts of government land to those who would develop and live on it, prompted the cultivation of the Great Plains. This large-scale settlement led to bloody battles with the Native Americans who had long inhabited these lands. Much of the legend of the Wild West revolves around tales of brave white settlers and stoic cowboys fending off attacks by the Indians. These stories are largely distortions, created to justify the actions of a government in displacing Native Americans through random surges of violence and breaches of treaties.

AMERICA'S BURDEN OF GUILT

The **first Africans** came to America in 1619, prisoners aboard a Dutch slave ship headed for Jamestown, VA. Their arrival marked the decline of indentured servitude, a system by which poor Europeans would pay for crossing the Atlantic with labor, typically for seven years. From the late 16th century and into the 17th century, as the demand for cheap labor increased, white settlers systematically invaded and terrorized Native American communities in search of "slaves." As white indentured servitude tapered off and Native Americans suffered fatally from European diseases, white America relied heavily on the African slave trade to fill the gap. The practice would last until the late 19th century, forming one of the most brutal chapters in the country's short history.

American victory in the Revolutionary War proved a mixed bag for African Americans. While northern blacks earned a large degree of freedom for themselves and their families as soldiers, nurses, and spies in the War, wealthy southern whites gained greater autonomy to exploit the enslaved population. Slavery was not an easy system for southerners to maintain. After contending with fierce uprisings, slaveowners struggled to outwit the more subtle, effective means of black rebellion that followed. Free African Americans and abolitionist whites formed the elusive **Underground Railroad,** an escape route into the free northern states. **Harriet Tubman,** a former slave, led at least a thousand African Americans on foot across the United States. Southerners who invaded the north to retrieve their "property" fueled existing tensions between North and South over slavery and states' rights. Two nations separated by economic and societal differences coexisted uneasily during the first half of the 19th century—it would take a fierce and bloody call to arms to decide which identity would prevail.

"A HOUSE DIVIDED"—THE CIVIL WAR

When an anti-slavery **Abraham Lincoln** was elected to the Presidency in 1860, South Carolina seceded from the Union. Twelve states (AL, AR, FL, GA, KY, LA, MS, MO, NC, TN, TX, and VA) followed in 1861, and 1862 witnessed the birth of a united Confederacy in the South. For four years, the country endured a savage and bloody war, fought by the North to restore the Union and by the South to break it. Lincoln issued the **Emancipation Proclamation** in 1863 to free slaves in Southern-held territory (but not in the few Union slave states, or occupied southern land). Despite the Proclamation's modest aims, blacks throughout the U.S. were encouraged by its promise; widespread plantation walk-outs ensued. The war claimed more American lives than any other in history, and many families suffered as brothers took up different uniforms and loyalties. After four bloody years of conflict, the North overcame the South. On April 9, 1865, **General Robert E. Lee,** the commander of the Army of Northern Virginia, the primary Confederate force, surrendered to **General Ulysses S. Grant** at Appomatox Court House, Virginia. Lincoln had led the North to victory, but the price was high. He was assassinated on April 14 by John Wilkes Booth, a Southern sympathizer. His legacy, the 13th Amendment, ended slavery in 1865.

INDUSTRIALIZATION AND WORLD WAR

The period after the war brought Reconstruction to the South, and Industrial Revolution to the North. The North's rapid transformation rendered it a formidable contender in the world economy, while the South's agricultural economy began a slow decline. During the North's **"Gilded Age,"** captains of industry such as George Vanderbilt, Andrew Carnegie, and John D. Rockefeller built commercial empires and enormous personal fortunes. The downside of the concentration of massive wealth in a few hands landed most heavily on workers—who faced low wages, violent strike break-ups, and unsafe working conditions—and hapless farmers.

Meanwhile, through victory in the Spanish-American War in 1898, the United States caught imperial fever, acquiring colonies in the Philippines, Puerto Rico, and Cuba. Progressives, who attacked the corruption and monopolistic practices of big business, found an ally in **President Theodore Roosevelt.**

After vowing to keep the U.S. out of "Europe's War," Wilson overcame a strong isolationist sentiment to convince Americans to join World War I. U.S. troops landed in Europe in 1917, and the war roared on for two more years until Germany's defeat.

ROARING 20S, GREAT DEPRESSION, AND WWII

As Americans found themselves tenuously seated in a political-economic world system, the winds of change began to ruffle their already unstable society. Women mobilized for the right to vote, which the **19th Amendment** to the *Constitution* granted in 1920. A pre-1970s sexual revolution produced higher hemlines and bare shoulders in women's fashion along with legalized birth control. European immigrants struggled to assimilate into an American identity, often by unifying to push black Americans and Asian immigrants out of Northern neighborhoods. Yet a common thread ran through each of these post-war communities; all grabbed for a slice of the seemingly abundant capitalist pie. The "Roaring 20s," however, was largely supported by overextended credit. The facade crumbled on Black Thursday, October 24, 1929, when the New York Stock Exchange crashed, launching the **Great Depression.**

Under the firm hand of President Franklin D. Roosevelt, the United States began a decade-long recovery. Roosevelt's **New Deal** implemented reform legislation and economic management through increased social spending. Farm prices were subsidized, financial institutions were put under federal jurisdiction, minimum wages were set, and the Social Security Act brought the U.S. into the era of the welfare state.

The German Nazi regime plowed through Europe; anxious Americans largely watched (though some volunteered to fight abroad). The Japanese attack on **Pearl Harbor,** Hawaii (p. 844), on December 7, 1941, brought America reluctantly into World War II. The war ended in Europe on May 8, 1945, about a week after Hitler committed suicide. The war in the Pacific continued until August, when the U.S., with the consent of Great Britain, detonated two newly developed nuclear bombs on Japan, killing 80,000 civilians. The war will always be remembered for **the Holocaust,** which killed millions of Jews, gypsies, homosexuals, and others, and for spawning the Nuclear Age.

THE COLD WAR AND CIVIL RIGHTS

Spared the wartime devastation of Europe and East Asia, the U.S. economy boomed in the post-war era, solidifying the status of the United States as the world's foremost economic and military power. But the ideological gulf between America and the other nuclear power, the Soviet Union, led to a half-century of worldwide skirmishes. Fears of Soviet expansion led to the **Red Scare** hysteria of the 1950s. Congressional committees saw communists everywhere: thousands of civil servants, writers, actors, and academics were blacklisted, and two American citizens, the Rosenbergs, were tried and sentenced to death for allegedly selling nuclear secrets to the Soviets. Fear of the left had grown in the U.S. since the Russian Revolution in 1917, but the feverish intensity it gained during the Cold War ultimately led to American military involvement in the Korean and Vietnam Wars and countless other interventions, including Reagan's "glorious" 1983 campaign in Grenada. Tensions between the U.S. and the USSR reached their peak during the **Cuban Missile Crisis** of 1962, when President **John Kennedy** and **Nikita Khrushchev** brought the world to the brink of nuclear war in a showdown over the deployment of Soviet nuclear missiles in Cuba.

Just a year later, an assassin's bullet claimed the charismatic President's young life. The 60s saw mounting social unrest linked to entrenched racism and the escalation of the Vietnam conflict. Sparked by Rosa Parks's refusal to give up a bus seat in Montgomery, Alabama (p. 319), in 1955, the **Civil Rights movement,** a time of intense protests by

African Americans, organized countless demonstrations, marches, and sit-ins in the heart of a defiant and often violent South. Activists were drenched with fire hoses, arrested, and even killed by local whites and policemen. The movement peaked with the **March on Washington** in 1963, where **Dr. Martin Luther King, Jr.** delivered his famous "I Have A Dream" speech, and the Mississippi Summer of 1964, a time of unyielding student activism and the birth of Black Power ideology. The movement's leader, Dr. King, was gunned down in Memphis (p. 278) in 1968 just as he became increasingly vocal about stifling poverty and the moral depravity of the Vietnam War. The mounting human costs of **Vietnam**—and growing suspicion of America's motives—catalyzed wrenching generational clashes reflected vividly in the stacks of burning draft cards. Despite a spate of civil rights legislation and anti-poverty measures passed under his watch, the specter of the war overshadowed—and eventually toppled—Lyndon B. Johnson's presidency. By the end of the next 11 years, the nation had suffered through the riots at the **1968 Democratic Convention**, 68,000 dead G.I.s, the killings at **Kent State**—and the collective weight of 7 million tons of bombs over Indochina, twice the amount used against America's World War II enemies. In 1972, 3 years before the war ended, five burglars were caught breaking into the Democratic National Convention Headquarters in the **Watergate** apartment complex, setting off a dramatic constitutional showdown that ultimately led to **President Richard "I Am Not A Crook" Nixon's resignation** in 1973.

The second wave of the **women's movement** accompanied the civil rights movement. Sparked by Betty Friedan's landmark book, *The Feminine Mystique,* American women sought to change the delineation between men's and women's roles in society, demanding access to male-dominated professions and equal pay. The sexual revolution, fueled by the development of the birth control pill, brought a woman's right to choose to the forefront of national debate; the 1973 Supreme Court decision **Roe v. Wade** legalized abortion, initiating a battle between abortion opponents and pro-choice advocates that divides the nation today.

BIG 80S

In 1980, actor and former California governor **Ronald Reagan** was elected to the White House. College campuses became quieter and more conservative as graduates flocked to Wall Street to become investment bankers. Though the decade's conservatives did embrace certain right-wing social goals like school prayer and the campaign against abortion, the Reagan revolution was essentially economic. Reaganomics handed tax breaks to big business, spurred short-term consumption, deregulated savings and loans, and laid the groundwork for economic disaster in the early 1990s. On the foreign policy front, Reagan aggressively swelled the military budget, sending weapons and aid to right-wing "freedom fighters" in Guatemala, Nicaragua, and Afghanistan, as well as selling arms to Iran.

LATELY...

Today, America faces a massive but shrinking deficit, an underfunded education system, a sustained assault on social spending, and battles over abortion, AIDS, gay rights, and persistent racism, though the economy continues to expand. At his election in 1992, a young, saxophone-toting **Bill Clinton** promised a new era of government interest and activism after years of laissez-faire rule. The promise of universal health care, the most ambitious of Clinton's policy goals, best captured the new attitude. By 1995, however, health care legislation was dead after vigorous lobbying from the health insurance industry, and the American Congress, a Democratic stronghold since mid-century, had been taken over by the Republican Party. An eager GOP attempted radical economic reforms and environmental rollbacks, which led to two government shut-downs between 1995 and 1996 and nationwide protests against the harsh proposals. A more conservative Clinton beat the Republicans at their own game in 1996, signing a welfare bill that ended the federal guarantee to the poor in exchange for bloc grants to the state—the administration's own estimate predicted that 1.2 million children would be thrown into poverty. The move enabled the savvy Clinton to capture the political center and an easy win in his 1996 reelection bid. He has cruised since, avoiding several attempts to assassinate his Presidency.

Right-wing extremist **Timothy McVeigh** went to prison for the April 1996 bombing of a federal building in Oklahoma City. The attack took the right-wing backlash of the 90s to a peak and increased fears of America's militia movements.

■ 1998's News

The most disturbing stories of the year were the multiple shootings occurring at schools nation-wide. Students have opened fire at schools in 10 states, spanning from Virginia to Alaska, leaving the nation searching for the cause of this latest plague.

1998 began with **Theodore Kaczynski,** a Harvard graduate and former math professor, pleading guilty to being the Unabomber, a famed anti-technology "activist." The Unabomber killed three and injured dozens with a series of package and letter bombs during a 17-year, one-man campaign against technological "progress," before being arrested in his Montana cabin in the spring of 1996.

The bombings of two U.S. Embassies in Africa have planted fears of terrorist attack in American hearts, and the retaliation by the U.S. military has prompted fears amongst Muslims of a cultural war against Islam.

President Bill Clinton continued to evade flack from his archnemesis, special prosecutor **Kenneth Starr,** who has launched a veritable crusade to bring down the Clinton presidency. After Starr's investigation into the Whitewater real estate "controversy" came to naught, a scandal that erupted early in 1998 gave Starr new ammunition and even spurred talk of impeachment. A story arose concerning 24-year-old former White House intern **Monica Lewinsky,** the President, and an affair that began in 1995. After months of rumor mongering in the press, Clinton admitted to an "improper relationship" on national TV, causing some to wonder if the President will survive this latest scandal.

Finally, on the lighter side, the nation's men rose up to say "I want a new drug," and **Viagra,** a pill to treat impotence, gained tremendous popularity across the country. It remains to be seen if they can replace the sport-utility vehicle as a source of male empowerment in the face of millenial fears.

And that, as Dennis Miller said, is the news.

■ A Civics Primer

The U.S. federal government has **three branches:** the executive, legislative, and judicial. The **executive branch** is headed by the **president** and **vice-president,** elected every 4 years. The executive branch administers most federal agencies, which fall under the jurisdiction of 13 departments of the government. The heads of these departments make up the Cabinet, and aid the president in policy decisions. The **House of Representatives** and the **Senate** comprise the **legislative branch,** where laws and budgets are debated. In the House, each state is allocated a number of seats proportional to its population, while every state sends two senators to Washington. Both senators and representatives are directly elected by the people of their state. The **judicial branch** consists of the **Supreme Court of the United States** and 90 district courts. The Supreme Court's nine justices, appointed for life by the President, hold the ultimate power to strike down laws that violate Constitutional principles.

Elected representatives in the U.S. are usually members of the **Republican** or **Democratic Parties,** which span a narrow (and right-leaning) political spectrum. The Republican Party is more conservative and divides into two warring camps: Christian traditionalists grudgingly share a tent with their libertarian, pro-business colleagues. The Democrats are also plagued by internal conflict, as the centrist, self-proclaimed New Democrats lock horns with the party's dwindling liberal contingent.

■ The Arts

LITERATURE

The **first best-seller** printed in America, the *Bay Psalm Book,* was published in Cambridge in 1640. Like much of the literature read and published in 17th- and 18th-century America, this chart buster was religious in nature. The early 1800s saw the rise of works that told the tale of the strong yet innocent American individual. **Herman Melville's** *Moby Dick,* **Walt Whitman's** *Leaves of Grass,* **James Fenimore Cooper's** *Last of the Mohicans,* and **Nathaniel Hawthorne's** *Scarlet Letter* all revolved around characters made unique by the American experience. While New England writers tried to portray a culture distinct from that of their European forebears, Midwestern humorists attempted to define the American character with larger-than-life tall tales set in the landscapes of the new continent. The most sophisticated practitioner of this genre was **Mark Twain,** whose works include the *Adventures of Huckleberry Finn.* As pioneers traveled farther west, authors like **Willa Cather** captured the stark beauty of the Plains, and the American desire to control, but care for, the land.

The early 20th century marked a reflective, self-centered movement in American literature. **F. Scott Fitzgerald's** works portray restless individuals, financially secure, but unfulfilled by their conspicuous consumption. Many writers moved abroad in search of refuge during this tumultuous time. The **"lost generation"** included **Ernest Hemingway, William Faulkner, Eudora Welty, T.S. Eliot, Ezra Pound, and Robert Frost.** During the 1920s, the **"Harlem Renaissance"** matched the excitement of the Jazz Age with the works of **Langston Hughes, Nella Larsen, and Zora Neale Hurston. Richard Wright's** *Black Boy* captured the harsher side of the times.

The **Beatniks** of the 50s, spearheaded by cult heroes **Jack Kerouac** and **Allen Ginsberg,** lived wildly through postwar America's dull conformity, while **Arthur Miller** looked into the American psyche with his poignant *Death of a Salesman* and *The Crucible,* an allegory of **McCarthyism.** Much recent literature explores the tensions between personal gender, ethnic, and cultural identities; **Toni Morrison,** a Nobel Prize winner, is a prime example.

American writing has forever been infused an obsession with the **outdoors,** from the fear of the early Puritans, to Cooper's *Leather Stocking Tales* and **Henry David Thoreau's** *Walden,* to **Aldo Leopold** and the late 20th century's **Edward Abbey.**

MUSIC

Although America is best known for its contribution to popular music, America has also nurtured classical composers of note. **Leonard Bernstein, George Gershwin, Aaron Copeland,** and **Charles Ives** have made their marks on the international score, blending classical forms and popular American genres.

However, it's **jazz** that's been called America's classical music. The blues, ragtime, and military brass bands combined in New Orleans and the Mississippi Delta to create this distinct American form, made famous by legendries like **Ella Fitzgerald, Miles Davis, Billie Holiday, Charlie Parker, John Coltrane,** and **Louis Armstrong,** to name a few. Rhythm & blues emerged from the African American gospel tradition to produce such greats as **Aretha Franklin, Otis Redding,** and a modern generation including **Boyz II Men.** A baby of the blues and country-western, **rock 'n' roll** produced many of America's music icons—first **Chuck Berry** and **Jerry Lee Lewis,** and eventually the King, **Elvis Presley.** Now, rock spans from **heavy metal** (Metallica) to **pop** (Madonna, Prince and Michael Jackson), but the likes of **Creedence Clearwater Revival, Bob Dylan,** and **Bruce Springsteen** still define the genre. Most recently, **hip-hop,** a distinctly young, African American genre, infiltrated styles around the world through the creative lyrics of **A Tribe Called Quest** and the late **Notorious B.I.G.** The West Coast spawned the revolutionary **"gangsta rap"** movement, sparking controversial debates throughout the country about the lyrics' espousal of violence and abusive treatment of women.

FILM

American film has come a long way since viewers were first amazed by Thomas Edison's 30-second film of a galloping horse. Film blossomed during the Golden Age of Hollywood, and became cloaked in glitz and glamour with the rise of **Marilyn Monroe, James Dean,** and **Elizabeth Taylor.** Today's movies are works of art and entertainment increasingly filled with computer-generated special effects. Animation, too, has found its way to the big screen with **Walt Disney/MGM Pictures** at the helm. Major production companies like **Columbia** and **Paramount** center their empires in California and New York City.

The influence of the multi-billion dollar American movie industry is undisputed as year after year records on openings, earnings, and fastest grossing movies are overturned. Celebrated movies of each genre include: **sci-fi** (*Star Wars, Alien*), **adventure** (*Raiders of the Lost Ark*), **thriller** (*Psycho, Silence of the Lambs*), **noir** (*The Maltese Falcon, Pulp Fiction, L.A. Confidential*) **drama** (*Casablanca, Titanic*), **horror** (*Friday the 13th*), **cult** (*The Rocky Horror Picture Show*), **historic** (*Glory, Schindler's List*), **comedy** (*National Lampoon's Vacation, Blazing Saddles*), **independent** (*Fargo*), **animated** (*Beauty and the Beast*), and the quintessential American **western** (*True Grit, Unforgiven*).

VISUAL ART

In the early 20th century, **Edward Hopper** and **Thomas Hart Benton** explored the innocence and mythic values of the United States during its emergence as a superpower. The abstract expressionism of **Arshile Gorky** and **Jackson Pollock** displays both the swaggering confidence and frenetic insecurity rampant in Cold War America. Pop Art, created by **Jasper Johns, Robert Rauschenberg, Roy Lichtenstein,** and **Andy Warhol,** satirizes the icons of American life and pop culture. Photography became medium of choice for artists concerned with improving desperate social conditions—**Dorothea Lange** and **Walker Evans's** photos captured the simple dignity of the Great Depression. American photographers have also used this tool to frame the remarkable natural environment. **Ansel Adams** revealed the grandiose beauty of the National Parks with his black and white photographs. **Robert Mapplethorpe's** use of nudes and flowers to create abstract images remains the center of controversy.

▓ The Media

U.S. radio, television, and print outlets are overwhelmingly dominated by huge commercial giants like General Electric, Disney, and Westinghouse—ten conglomerates, in fact, now control over half of all media output. The U.S. public media tradition is correspondingly weak, and recently a victim of the budget axe.

TELEVISION

There are television sets in 98% of U.S. homes. Competition between the six national networks (ABC, CBS, NBC, Fox, and two newcomers: UPN and WB), cable television, and satellite TV has triggered exponential growth in TV culture over the last few years. During prime time (8-11pm EST) you can find the most popular shows: the drama *ER,* the paranoid thriller *X-Files,* and *The Simpsons,* the wittiest animation ever to leave Springfield. **Day-time programming** is dominated by sensational talk shows—*Jerry Springer*'s sex and violence fest is in the vanguard—and steamy soap operas, including *Days of Our Lives* and *The Young and the Restless.* On cable you'll discover around-the-clock channels offering news, sports, movies, weather, and home shopping. **MTV,** offering dazzling displays of random visceral images, affords a glimpse into what parents countrywide fear represents the psyche of their wide-eyed children. **HBO** brings Hollywood into the living room, while **ESPN** satiates sports fans with round-the-clock sports coverage.

Television is the point of entry to world-wide news for most Americans. Twenty-four hour news coverage is available on **CNN**, a cable station. Each network presents local and national nightly news, while programs like *60 Minutes* and *Dateline* specialize in investigate reporting and undercover exposés.

The **Public Broadcasting Station** (PBS) is "commercial-free," funded by viewer contributions, the federal government, and grants from large corporations.

PRINT MEDIA

The most influential newspapers in the U.S. are the *New York Times, The Washington Post,* and the *Los Angeles Times.* They are all roughly centrist in slant, and have wide distributions throughout the U.S. *The Christian Science Monitor* and the *Wall Street Journal* are also well-respected dailies. *USA Today* is not as well respected, but is nationally the most readily available and easy to read. The three major weekly newsmagazines, *Time, Newsweek,* and *U.S. News & World Report,* cover national news and cultural trends in short, glossy articles. Other widely read magazines in the U.S. include *People,* which chronicles American gossip; *Spin* and *Rolling Stone,* which focus on the music industry; *Sports Illustrated;* and the *New Yorker,* which combines Big Apple happenings with short stories and essays on current events. Americans on the left read *The Nation* or *In These Times,* while conservatives subscribe to the *National Review* or Rupert Murdoch's new *Weekly Standard.* The business world reads *Fortune, Forbes,* and *Business Week.*

RADIO

Every major market's radio waves carry at least one rock, country, jazz, classic rock, easy listening, Top 40, classical, all-talk, and all-news station; however, most of the nation is dominated by country-western, rock, and Christian evangelism. Radio is generally divided into AM and FM; talk-radio compromises most of the low-frequency AM slots, and the high-powered FM stations feature most of the music. Each broadcaster owns a four-letter call-name, with "W" as the first letter for those east of the Mississippi River (as in WKRP), and "K" to the west (as in KPFA).

The U.S.'s public network, **National Public Radio (NPR)**, has a local station in every major market. Popular offerings include the hodge-podge feature *All Things Considered,* Ray Suarez's call-in *Talk of the Nation,* and the irreverent auto junkies Tom and Ray Magliozzi's *Car Talk.*

■ Sports

Year-round, millions of Americans live and die by their sports teams. Southern and midwestern states are known to shut down on autumn Saturdays to rally behind their state college's football team. Once considered America's pastime, baseball has been challenged in recent years by basketball and football for the hearts of Americans.

Most large cities sport professional teams in **Major League Baseball (MLB)**, the **National Basketball Association (NBA)**, the **National Football League (NFL)**, **National Hockey League (NHL)**, and, to a lesser extent, **Major League Soccer (MLS)** and **women's basketball (WNBA)**. However, **auto racing**, culminating with the **Indianapolis 500** (see p. 426) in late May, is America's most-watched spectator sport. Other major sporting events include the **Kentucky Derby** (see p. 262) in early May, tennis's **U.S. Open,** golf's **U.S. Open,** college football's **bowl games** and college basketball's **NCAA tournament,** better known as March Madness.

In 1998, superhuman **Michael Jordan** led his **Chicago Bulls** to its sixth NBA championship in the last eight years, while **John Elway** finally took home the Super Bowl crown for the **Denver Broncos.** In baseball, **Mark McGwire** and **Sammy Sosa** surpassed **Roger Maris's** record of 61 home runs in a single season, while the New York Yankees played the better than any team America has seen in decades.

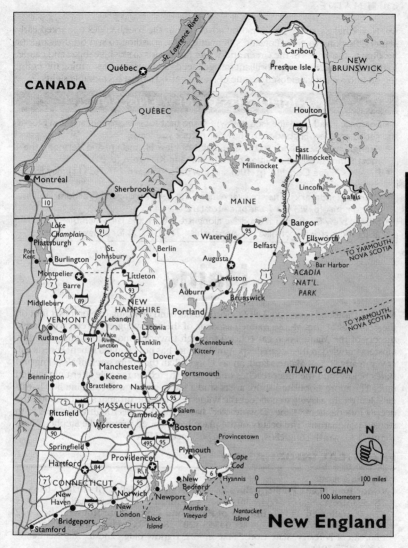

New England

NEW ENGLAND

New England has counted itself an intellectual and political center since before the States were United. Students and scholars nationwide funnel into New England's colleges each fall, and town meetings in rural villages still evoke the spirit of popular government which inspired American colonists to create a nation. Numerous scattered landmarks recount every step in the young country's break with the Old World.

Geographically, New England seems an unlikely cradle for any sort of civilization, with mountains wrinkling the land atop barren soil. The region's unpredictable climate can be particularly dismal during the harsh, wet winter from November to March, when rivers, campgrounds, and tourist attractions may slow down or freeze up. Nevertheless, today's visitors find adventure in the rough edges that irked early settlers, flocking to New England's dramatic, salty coastline to sun on the sand; or heading to the slopes of the Green and White Mountains to ski, hike, bike, and canoe. In the fall, the nation's most brilliant foliage bleeds and burns, transforming the entire region into a giant kaleidoscope, one of New England's most memorable sights.

🏞 HIGHLIGHTS OF NEW ENGLAND

- **Seafood.** Head to Maine (see below) for the best lobster around, and don't forget to try New England clam chowder before you leave.
- **Skiing.** Enthusiasts flock to the mountains of New Hampshire and Vermont; the most famous resorts include Stowe (p. 86) and Killington (p. 81).
- **Beaches.** Cape Cod, MA (p. 106) and Martha's Vineyard, MA (p. 111) may have the region's best.
- **Colonial landmarks.** They're everywhere, but a walk along the Freedom Trail in Boston, MA (p. 95) is a great place to start.
- **Scenic New England.** Take a drive along Rte. 100 in the fall, when the foliage is at its most striking, or hike the Appalachian Trail (p. 72) for a view on foot.

Maine

Nearly a thousand years ago, Leif Ericson and his band of Viking explorers set foot on the coasts of Maine. Moose roamed as kings of the sprawling evergreen wilderness, the cry of the Maine coon cat echoed through towering mountains, and countless lobsters crawled in the ocean deep. A millennium has not changed much. Forests still cover nearly 90% of Maine's land, an area larger than the entire stack of New England states below, and the inner reaches of the state stretch on for mile after uninhabited mile. The more populated shore areas stud a harsh and jagged coastline like barnacles. Rather than trying to conquer the wilderness like the urbanites to the south, the deeply independent Maine "Downeaster" has adapted to this rough wilderness with rugged pragmatism. The beauty of the place has inspired writers like Stephen King, Henry Wadsworth Longfellow, and Edna St. Vincent Millay.

PRACTICAL INFORMATION

Capital: Augusta.
Visitor Info: Maine Publicity Bureau, 325B Water St., Hallowell (207-623-0363 or 888-MAINE45/888-624-6345; http://www.visitmaine.com). Send mail to P.O. Box 2300, Hallowell 04347. **Bureau of Parks and Lands,** State House Station #22 (AMHI, Harlow Bldg.), Augusta 04333 (207-287-3821). **Maine Forest Service,** Bureau of Forestry, State House Station #22, Harlow Bldg., 2nd fl., Augusta 04333 (207-287-2791).
Emergency: 911.
Time Zone: Eastern. **Postal Abbreviation:** ME.
Sales Tax: 6%.

MAINE COAST

As the bird flies, the length of the Maine coast from Kittery to Lubec measures 228 miles, but if untangled, all of the convoluted inlets and rocky promontories would stretch out to a whopping 3478 miles. Fishing, the earliest business here, was later augmented by a vigorous shipbuilding industry; both traditions are still visible today. Unfortunately, rampant overfishing has catastrophically depleted the North Atlantic cod population and left fishermen wondering about the future of their livelihood. Lobster is still plentiful, however, and lobster by the pound is ubiquitous in coastal Maine. Stopping under one of the innumerable makeshift red wooden lobster signs that speckle the roadsides will reward visitors with a freshly boiled lobster to chow. Lobsters are tastiest before July, when most start to molt.

U.S. 1 hugs the coastline, stringing the port towns together. Lesser roads and small ferry lines connect the remote villages and offshore islands. Newly arrived visitors orient themselves at the **Maine Information Center** (207-439-1319), in Kittery, 3 mi. north of the Maine-New Hampshire bridge (open daily 8am-6pm; mid-Oct. to June 9am-5pm). **Greyhound** (800-231-2222) serves points between Portland and Bangor along I-95, the coastal town of Brunswick, and on to Boston. Reaching most coastal points of interest is virtually impossible by bus; a car or bike is necessary.

■ Portland

During the July 4th fireworks celebration of 1866, a young boy playing on Portland's wharf inadvertently started a fire which destroyed over three-fourths of the city before it was extinguished. Portland had to be rebuilt—for the fourth time (the old Portland fort had first been razed to the ground by Indians in 1632). Today, the Victorian reconstruction that survives in what is now called the Old Port Exchange stands in stark contrast to Portland's spirited youth culture. Ferries run to the nearby Casco Bay Islands; Sebago Lake provides sunning and water skiing opportunities.

ORIENTATION AND PRACTICAL INFORMATION

Downtown sits near the bay, along **Congress St.** between State and Pearl St. A few blocks south lies the **Old Port** on Commercial and Fore St. These two districts contain most of the city's sights and attractions. **I-295** (off I-95) forms the western boundary of downtown.

Buses: Concord Trailways, 100 Sewall St. (828-1151). To Boston (2hr., 10 per day, $16) and Bangor (2hr., 3 per day, $20). Offers discounts on round-trip fares for college students with ID. Metro buses #5 and #3 will transport you to and from the station (774-0351). Office open daily 5:30am-8:30pm. **Greyhound/Vermont Transit,** 950 Congress St. (772-6587 or 800-231-2222), on the western outskirts of town. *Be cautious here at night.* Take bus #1 "Congress St." downtown. Open daily 6:30am-7:15pm. To Boston (2¼hr., 8 per day, $13) and Bangor (2½-3½hr., 6 per day, $17).

Ferries: Prince of Fundy Cruises, P.O. Box 4216, 468 Commercial St. (800-341-7540, 800-482-0955 or 775-5616 in ME). Ferries to Yarmouth in southern Nova Scotia leave from the Portland International Ferry Terminal, on Commercial St. near the Million Dollar Bridge. Runs May to mid-June and mid-Sept. to late Oct. Fare $60, ages 5-14 $30, car $80, bike $7; late June to mid-Sept. $80/$40/$98/$10. Reservations strongly recommended. Boats depart Portland at 9pm; the 11hr. trip takes the whole night. Overnight cabins are available.

Public Transportation: Metro Bus (774-0351) offers service within and beyond the downtown area. Most routes run 6am-7pm. Fare $1, students 75¢, seniors 50¢, under 5 free, transfers free.

Visitor Info: Visitors Information Bureau, 305 Commercial St. (772-5800), at the corner of Center St. Open M-F 8am-6pm, Sa 10am-6pm, Su 10am-3pm; mid-Oct. to mid-May M-F 9am-5pm, Sa-Su 10am-5pm.

Hotlines: Rape Crisis, 774-3613. **Crisis Intervention Hotline,** 800-660-8500. Both 24hr.

Hospitals: Maine Medical Center, 22 Bramhall St. (871-0111). **Women's Community Health Services,** 773-7247 or 800-666-7247. Open daily 9am-5pm.

Internet Access: JavaNet Café, 37 Exchange St. (773-2469). Open M-Th 8am-11pm, F-Sa 8am-midnight, Su 8am-10pm. $6 per hr.

Post Office: 622 Congress St. (871-8449). Open M-F 8:30am-5pm, Sa 9am-noon. **ZIP code:** 04104. **Area code:** 207.

ACCOMMODATIONS AND CAMPGROUNDS

Portland has some inexpensive accommodations, but prices jump during the summer season. You can always try Exit 8 off I-95, where **Super 8** (854-1881) and budget rates (singles around $50-60) congregate.

◉**Portland Youth Hostel (HI-AYH),** 645 Congress St. (874-3281). Centrally located in a
university dorm. 39 beds in clean triples with bath and shower. Energetic and helpful
staff. Common room with TV, kitchen, bike storage. $16, nonmembers $19. $10 deposit
required. Check-out 11am. Free parking. Reservations recommended. Open June-Aug.

YMCA, 70 Forest Ave. (874-1111), on the north side of Congress St., 1 block from
post office. Men only. Access to kitchen, pool, and exercise facilities. 85 rooms.
Singles $26 per night, $87 per week. Key deposit $10. Check-in 11am-8:30pm.

The Inn at St. John, 939 Congress St. (773-6481), across from the bus station. An
upscale environment makes for a pricier alternative to the hostel. Free local calls
and parking. Continental breakfast included. Kitchen, laundry facilities, and bike
storage available. Tidy, tasteful singles and doubles start at $50, cheaper in winter.
Rooms with private bath slightly more expensive.

Wassamki Springs, 56 Saco St. (839-4276), in Scarborough. Closest campground
(10min. drive) to Portland. Drive 6 mi. west on Congress St. (becomes Rte. 22,
then County Rd.), then turn right on Saco St. Full facilities plus a sandy beach.
Flocks of migrant Winnebagos nest among cozy, fairly private sites that border the
lake. Sites $21 for 2 people, with hookup $23-25; $4 per additional person; add $2
for lakefront sites. Free showers. Reservations recommended 2 weeks in advance,
especially July-Aug. Open May to mid-Oct.

FOOD

Life is de bubbles for seafood lovers in Portland. One of the nation's leaders in restaurants per capita, Portland loves to chop *le poisson* and make it taste nice, as well as to
boil lobsters and sauté clams in ze spice. Do-it-yourselfers can buy seafood, dead or
alive, at the active port on **Commercial St.**

◉**Federal Spice,** 225 Federal St. (774-6404), just off Congress St. Whips up cheap, bold
home-cooking in a hurry using spicy hot elements from Caribbean, South American, and Asian cuisine. Healthsmart menu features less gluttonous versions of the
restaurant's burritos and tacos, all under $6. Open M-Sa 11am-9pm.

Gilbert's Chowder House, 92 Commercial St. (871-5636). The local choice for seafood. A large bowl of chowder in a bread bowl is a meal in itself ($5). On summer
nights Gilbert's patio on the water is one of the nicest spots in town. Open M-Th
11am-9pm, F-Sa 11am-10pm, Su noon-8pm; Oct.-May call for hrs.

Seamen's Club, 375 Fore St. (774-7777), at Exchange St. in the Old Port with a harbor
view. Top-notch seafood dining steeped in briny lore. Salads and sandwiches around $6,
dinner around $13. Fresh lobster year-round. Open M-F 10:30am-9:30pm, Sa-Su 10am-
10:30pm.

SIGHTS

Many of Portland's most spectacular sights lie outside the city proper, along the rugged coast or on the beautiful, secluded islands a short ferry ride offshore. **Two Lights
State Park** (799-5871), across the Million Dollar Bridge on State St. and south along
Rte. 77 to Cape Elizabeth, is a wonderful place to picnic and relax. **Casco Bay Lines**
(774-7871), on State Pier near the corner of Commercial and Franklin, America's oldest ferry service, runs year-round to the nearby islands. Daily **ferries** depart approximately every hour (M-Sa 5:45am-10:30pm) for nearby **Peaks Island** (round-trip
$5.25). On the island, you can rent a bike at **Brad's Recycled Bike Shop,** 115 Island
Ave. (766-5631; $4 per hr., $7.50 for up to 3hr., $10 per day). Waves crash on **Long
Island's** quiet, unpopulated beach. If you start at Long Island, you can island-hop by
catching later ferries to other islands (same price as Peaks ferry). Getting to more than
two islands will take all day.

You may feel the call of the sea the instant you arrive in Portland, but the city does
have activities for landlubbers. The **Portland Museum of Art,** 7 Congress Sq. (775-
6148); at the intersection of Congress, High, and Free St.; collects American art by
notables such as John Singer Sargent and Winslow Homer. *(Open May 31-Oct. 11 Tu-W
and Sa-Su 10am-5pm, Th-F 10am-9pm, M 10am-5pm. $6, students and seniors $5, ages 6-12
$1.)* The **Wadsworth-Longfellow House,** 489 Congress St. (879-0427), a museum of

social history and U.S. literature, zeroes in on late 18th- and 19th-century antiques as well as on the life of the poet. *(Purchase tickets at 489 Congress St. House open June-Oct. Tu-Su 10am-4pm. Gallery and museum store also open Nov.-May W-Sa noon-4pm. $5, seniors $4, under 12 $1. Price includes admission to a neighboring history museum with rotating exhibits. Tours every 30-40min.)* Henry lived in the house from infancy until age 19.

ENTERTAINMENT AND NIGHTLIFE

During the summer months, Portland brims with performing arts. Signs advertising concerts and theatrical productions are posted throughout the city, but the visitors center is the best place to find out about, well, just about everything (see **Practical Information,** above). The **Portland Symphony** (842-0800) presents concerts renowned throughout the northeast (50% student discount).

Traditionally held on the first Sunday in June, the **Old Port Festival** (772-6828) begins the summer with a bang, filling several blocks from Federal to Commercial St. with as many as 50,000 people. On summer afternoons, the **Noontime Performance Series** (772-6828) sees a variety of bands performs in Portland's Monument Sq. and Congress Sq. (mid-June to Aug.).

For a taste of the hometown spirit, the **Portland Sea Dogs,** an AA minor-league baseball team, take the field from April to mid-September at **Hadlock Field** on Park Ave. (tickets 874-9300; $4-6, under 17 $2-5).

After dark, the Old Port area, known as "the strip," especially **Fore St.** between Union and Exchange St., livens up with a high proportion of pleasant "shoppes" and a few good pubs. **Brian Boru,** 57 Center St. (780-1506), provides a mellow pub scene. The brew nachos ($5) are nice, as are $2 pints all day Sunday. (Open daily 11:30am-1am.) **Gritty MacDuff's,** 396 Fore St. (772-2739), brews its own sweet beer for adoring locals. These tasty pints are worth the $3. (Open daily 11:30am-1am.) There's an English pub around the corner at **Three Dollar Dewey's,** 241 Commercial St. (772-3310). Dewey's serves over 100 varieties of beer and ale (36 on tap at $3-3.50), along with great chili (cup $3.50) and free popcorn. (Open Su-Th 11:30am-midnight, F-Sa 11:30am-1am.) Info on Portland's jazz, blues, and club scene packs the *Casco Bay Weekly* and *FACE,* both of which are free in many restaurants and stores.

■ South of Portland

Ten miles south of Portland on U.S. 1, you'll find **Old Orchard Beach.** Most notable for its all-out tackiness, the plastic jewel in Old Orchard Beach's crown is the **Won-derland Arcade,** "the First Amusement Park in New England." Parking in Orchard Beach will cost you $3, and the cheapest hotels cost around $40 for a double. Much more tasteful is **Kennebunk,** and, 8 mi. east on Rte. 35, its coastal counterpart **Kennebunkport.** If you want to bypass busy U.S. 1, take the Maine Turnpike (I-95) south of Portland to Exit 3, then take Fletcher St. east into Kennebunk.

Spending the night in Kennebunk will make your trip significantly more expensive; avoid penury by camping. **Salty Acres Campground** (967-8623), 4½ mi. northeast of Kennebunkport on winding Rte. 9, offers swimming, a grocery store, laundry, phones, showers, and a convenient location about 1 mi. from beaches. This is a communal camping experience; sites are small and closely packed. (185 sites $16, with electricity $18, full hookup $22; $8 per additional adult after 2; $2 per additional child after 2. Open May to Oct. No reservations.) A little farther out is the **Mousam River Campground** (985-2507), on Alfred Rd. just west of Exit 3 off I-95 in west Kennebunk, with free showers, a small swimming pool, and tightly packed but very tidy campsites. (115 RV sites $22, $21 with AAA; $4 per additional adult after 2; $3 per additional person ages 13-17. Open mid-May to mid-Oct.)

The **Rachel Carson National Wildlife Refuge** (646-9226), ½ mi. off U.S. 1 on Rte. 9, provides a secluded escape from tourist throngs to the west. (Open M-F 8am-4:30pm, Sa-Su 10am-2pm; off-season M-F 8am-4:30pm.) A trail winds through the salt marsh home of over 200 species of shorebirds and waterfowl. The refuge is a tribute to the naturalist Rachel Carson, author of *Silent Spring,* the book which helped

The Appalachian Trail

Stretching 2160 unbroken miles from Mt. Katahdin, ME, to Springer Mountain, GA, the Appalachian Trail, or "AT," follows the path of the Appalachian Mountains along the eastern United States. Use of the AT is entirely free, although only foot travelers may access the trail. Along the way, the trail cuts through 14 states, eight national forests, and six national parks; 98% of the Trail is on public land. Three-sided first come, first served shelters dot the AT with about a day's journey in between, and hikers can take advantage of the many streams and nearby towns to stock up on water and supplies. White rectangular blazes mark rocks and trees along the entire length of the trail, while blue blazes mark side trails. Generally, the trail is very accessible, crossed by roads along its entire length except for the northernmost 100 mi. Although any part of the trail makes an excellent day hike, about 2500 people attempt a continuous hike of the Appalachian Trail annually. Numerous publications are available to facilitate your journey; contact the **Center for AT Studies**, P.O. Box 525, Hot Springs, NC 28743 (704-622-7601, staffed M-Sa 10am-10pm; fax 704-622-7601; email atcenter@trailplace.com; http://www.trailplace.com) for more information, including a list of publications.

launch the environmental movement. (Trail open daily sunrise-sunset. Free.) In nearby Wells the **National Estuarine Research Reserve,** at the junction of U.S. 1 and Rte. 9, sprawls over meadows and beaches and offers tours of the estuary, bird life, and wildflowers (open daily 8am-5pm).

Both of these towns are popular hideaways for wealthy authors and artists. A number of rare and used bookstores line U.S. 1 just south of Kennebunk, while art galleries fill the town itself. The blue-blooded (and gray-haired) meet at Kennebunkport, which reluctantly grew famous as the summer home of former President Bush, who owns an estate on Walker's Point. The **Kennebunk-Kennebunkport Chamber of Commerce,** 17 U.S. 100/Western Ave. (967-0857), in Kennebunkport, has a free guide to the area (open daily 9am-6pm; off-season 9am-5pm). South of Kennebunk on U.S. 1 lies **Ogunquit,** which means "beautiful place by the sea." The long, sandy shoreline is a definite must-see. A visit might begin at the **Ogunquit Information Bureau** (646-2939), on U.S. 1. (Open M-Th noon-5pm, F noon-6pm, Sa 10am-6pm, Su noon-6pm; early Sept. to late May daily 9am-5pm.) When weather permits, biking may be the best way to travel Maine's rocky shores and spare yourself the aggravation of thick summer traffic. **Wheels and Wares** (646-5774), U.S. 1 on the Wells/Ogunquit border, rents mountain bikes ($20 per day, $25 per 24hr.; open daily 10am-6pm). In the summer, a vibrant gay community inhabits Ogunquit. **Moody,** just south of Ogunquit, supplies some of the region's least expensive lodgings.

Nearby **Perkins Cove** charms the plaid socks off the polo shirt crowd with boutiques hawking seashell sculptures. The two **Barnacle Billy's** restaurants (646-5575), 20 yd. apart on Oar Weed Rd., practice an interesting division of labor. The original (a lobster pound) broils, bakes, and sautes lobsters, while their newer full-service location has a bigger menu. (Both open daily noon-9:30pm.) **Area code:** 207.

■ Northern Maine Coast

Much like the coastal region south of Portland, the north offers the traveler unforgettable beaches, windswept ocean vistas, and verdant forests—for a price. Lodging in L.L. Bean country isn't cheap, but camping or just passing through can give all the flavor, without the guilt of spending $70 at a hotel. Much of the region is unserviced by public transportation, but if you have a car, the drive along U.S. 1 offers a charming, unadulterated view of coastal Maine. However, congested traffic and winding roads make the drive up Maine's coast slow at times. The **area code** north of Portland: 207.

Freeport About 20 mi. north of Portland on I-95, Freeport once garnered glory as the "birthplace of Maine." The 1820 signing of documents declaring the state's independence from Massachusetts took place at the historic **Jameson Tavern,** 115 Main St.

(865-4196), right next to L. L. Bean. Dinner here will run you $15-23; the tap room has sandwiches for $6-11. Freeport is now known as the factory outlet capital of the world, with over 100 downtown stores. The grandaddy of them all, **L.L. Bean,** began manufacturing Maine Hunting Shoes in Freeport in 1912. Bean sells everything from clothes epitomizing preppy *haute couture* to sturdy tenting gear. The **factory outlet,** 11 Depot St. (865-4057), behind Bannister Shoes, is the place for bargains (open daily 9am-10pm; Jan. to late May 9am-9pm). The **retail store,** 95 Main St. (865-4761, 800-221-4221 for orders), stays open 24hr., 365 days a year. Only three events have ever caused the store to close (and only for a few hours each time): a nearby fire in the late 1980s, the death of President Kennedy, and the death of L.L. Bean founder Leon Leonwood (no wonder he went by L.L.) Bean.

In a town where even the fast food is fancy (McDonald's and Arby's are housed in stately Victorian mansions), unpretentious eateries are welcome sights. **DeRosier's,** 120 Main St. (865-6290), across from L.L. Bean, has good pizza and sandwiches, as well as ice cream, candy bars, and soda (open daily 9am-9pm, in winter closed Su). **Chowder Express and Sandwich Shop,** 2 Mechanic St. (865-3404), offers delicious sandwiches ($4-5) and steaming bowls of chowder ($3.75). If you want to spend a night in the area, the **Desert of Maine Campground,** 2 mi. west of Exit 19 off I-95, accommodates with 48 sites, nature trails, amazing dunes, a museum, and shuttles into downtown Freeport (sites $19, with hookup $25).

Camden In the summer, khaki-clad crowds flock to Camden, 100 mi. north of Portland, to dock their yachts alongside the tall-masted schooners in Penobscot Bay. Many of the cruises are out of the budgeteer's price range, but the **Rockport-Camden-Lincolnville Chamber of Commerce** (236-4404, outside ME 800-223-5459), on the public landing in Camden behind Cappy's Chowder House (see below), can tell you which are most affordable. They also have badly needed info on affordable accommodations. (Open M-F 9am-5pm, Sa 10am-5pm, Su noon-2pm; mid-Oct. to mid-May closed Su.) The **Camden Hills State Park** (236-3109; reservations 800-332-1501 for ME residents, 287-3824 out of state), 1¼ mi. north of town on U.S. 1, is almost always full in July and August, but you can be fairly certain to get a site if you arrive before 2pm. This beautiful coastal retreat offers more than 25 mi. of trails, including one trail which leads up to **Mt. Battie** and has a harbor view. Reservations can be made by phone with a credit card. (Sites $16, day use $2. Free showers. Open mid-May to mid-Oct.). The folks at **Maine Sports** (236-8797), on U.S. 1, in Rockport just south of Camden, teach/lead/rent/sell a wide array of sea-worthy vehicles. Kayak **rentals** only go to those with paddling experience (24hr. singles rental $40, doubles $55; ask about overnights to nearby islands). Kayaking **tours** are for everybody. (Open daily 8am-9pm; Sept.-May Su-Th 9am-6pm, F 9am-8pm. 2hr. harbor tour $30.)

Eating in Camden will never be cheap, but the oceanside experience may be worth it. In the heart of downtown Camden is **Cappy's Chowder House,** 1 Main St. (236-2254), a kindly, comfortable hangout where great seafood draws tourists and townspeople alike. The seasonal seafood pie ($9), made with scallops, shrimp, and clams, is exquisite. (Open daily 11am-midnight; in winter 11am-10pm.) **Fitzpatrick's** (236-2041), on Sharp's Wharf, has omelettes, sandwiches, and burgers, all for less than $7 (open May-Oct. Su-Th 7am-8pm, F-Sa 7am-8:30pm; call for winter hrs.).

The **Maine State Ferry Service** (624-7777 or 800-491-4883), 5 mi. north of Camden in Lincolnville, takes you across the Bay to Islesboro Island. (20min.; 7-9 per day; last return trip 4:30pm; round-trip $4.50, ages 5-11 $2, bike $4, car and driver $13. Parking $4.) The ferry also has an agency on U.S. 1 in **Rockland,** 517A Main St. (596-2202), that shuttles to North Haven, Vinalhaven, and Matinicus. Rates and schedules change with the weather.

Belfast Seventeen miles north of Camden on U.S. 1, Belfast is "real life" coastal Maine at its best. The **Belfast Area Chamber of Commerce** (338-5900), at the corner of Main St. and Front St., on the water, can help you with planning (open late May to Oct. daily 10am-6pm). There is no such thing as inexpensive accommodations within Belfast. However, U.S. 1 north of Belfast is littered with affordable motels (singles and doubles $35-50). A pricey but picturesque option is the beautiful and recently renovated **Hiram Alden Inn** (338-2151; singles from $70). U.S. 1 in Belfast and the surrounding towns allow you to stroll by the waterfront and watch the fishing boats come in, or enjoy the innumerable antique sales, flea markets, and plain old junk sales on summer weekends. **The Gothic,** 108 Main St. (338-4933), serves homemade baked goods and ice cream. If you're lucky, they'll have blueberry sorbet ($2) while you're in town. (Open Apr.-Dec. M-Sa 7:30am-8:30pm, Su 12:30-5:30pm.)

■ Mt. Desert Island and Bar Harbor

Mt. Desert Island is anything but deserted. During the summer, the island swarms with tourists lured by the thick forests and mountainous landscape. Roughly half of the island is covered by Acadia National Park, which harbors some of the last protected marine, mountain, and forest environments on the New England coast. The lively town of Bar Harbor, on the eastern side of the island, has the obligatory Maine lobster. Bar Harbor is by far the most crowded part of the island, sandwiched between the Blue Hill and Frenchmen Bays. Once a summer hamlet for the very wealthy, the town now welcomes a motley *mélange* of R&R-seekers; the monied have fled to the more secluded Northeast and Seal Harbor.

ORIENTATION AND PRACTICAL INFORMATION

Mt. Desert Island is shaped roughly like a lobster claw, 14 mi. long and 12 mi. wide. To the east on Rte. 3 lie Bar Harbor and Seal Harbor. South on Rte. 198 near the cleft is **Northeast Harbor.** Across Somes Sound on Rte. 102 is **Southwest Harbor,** where fishing and shipbuilding thrive without the taint of tacky tourism.

    Rte. 3 runs through Bar Harbor, becoming **Mt. Desert St.;** it and **Cottage St.** are the major east-west arteries. **Rte. 102** circuits the western half of the island.

Buses: Greyhound/Vermont Transit (800-451-3292) leaves for Bangor ($9) and Boston ($39) daily May-June and Sept.-Oct. 6:45am; July-Aug. 8am; in front of **Fox Run Travel,** 4 Kennebec St. (288-3366). Tickets are sold at Fox Run (open M-F 7:30am-5pm). 15% discount for students, 10% for seniors. Fox Run's owner comes to meet the bus for last-minute ticket purchases 30min. before departure.

Ferries: Beal & Bunker, from Northeast Harbor on the town dock (244-3575). To: Great Cranberry Island (20min.; 6 per day; $10, under 12 $5). Open late June to Sept. 6 M-F 7:30am-6pm, Sa-Su 10am-6pm; call for winter hrs. **Bay Ferries** (888-249-7245), Bar Harbor. To Yarmouth, NS (2½hr.; 2 per day June to mid-Oct., call for off-season schedule; $45, car $55, bike $10; $3 port tax per person). Reservations recommended, $5 fee.

Bike Rental: Bar Harbor Bicycle Shop, 141 Cottage St. (288-3886). Mountain bikes $10 for 4hr., $15 per day. Helmet, lock, and map. Driver's license, cash deposit, or credit card required. Open daily 8am-8pm; Sept.-June 9am-6pm.

National Park Canoe Rentals (244-5854), north end of Long Pond off Rte. 102. Cano rental $20-22 for 4hr., $30 per day; kayak rental $25 per ½-day, $50 per day. Open mid-May to mid-Oct. daily 8am-5pm.

Visitor Info: Acadia National Park Visitors Center (288-4932 or 288-5262; http://www.nps.gov/acad), 3 mi. north of Bar Harbor on Rte. 3. Open daily mid-June to mid-Sept. 8am-6pm; mid-Apr. to mid-June and mid-Sept. to Oct. 8am-4:30pm. **Park Headquarters** (288-3338), 3 mi. west of Bar Harbor on Rte. 233. Open M-F 8am-4:30pm. **Bar Harbor Chamber of Commerce** (288-5103), in the Marine Atlantic Ferry Terminal, Rte. 3. Open M-F 8am-5pm, Sa 10am-5pm, Su noon-5pm; in winter M-F 8am-4pm. **Mt. Desert Island Regional Chamber of Commerce** (288-3411), on Rte. 3 at the entrance to Thompson Island. In the same building, you'll find an **Acadia National Park Information Center** (288-9702). Both open daily July-Aug. 9am-8pm; mid-May to July and Sept. 6 to mid-Oct. 10am-6pm.

Hotlines: Downeast Sexual Assault Helpline, 800-228-2470. **Mental Health Crisis Line,** 800-245-8889. Both 24hr.

Emergency: Acadia National Park Law Enforcement, 288-3369.

Internet Access: Café Cyberway, 25 High St. (667-0718), 15 mi. outside of Mt. Desert Island in Ellsworth. $3 for 30min., $5 per hr.

Post Office: 55 Cottage St. (288-3122). Open M-F 8am-4:45pm, Sa 9am-noon. **ZIP code:** 04609. **Area code:** 207.

ACCOMMODATIONS AND CAMPGROUNDS

Grand hotels with grand prices linger from the island's exclusive resort days. Still, a few reasonable establishments do exist, particularly on **Rte. 3** north of Bar Harbor. Camping spots cover the island, especially **Rte. 198** and **102**, well west of town.

Bar Harbor Youth Hostel (HI-AYH), 27 Kennebec St. (288-5587), Bar Harbor; mailing address P.O. Box 32. In the parish house of St. Saviour's Episcopal Church, adjacent to the bus stop. 2 large dorm rooms which accommodate 20 in cheery red-and-white bunks. Common room, full kitchen, and a perfect location. Organized activities include movie nights. $12, nonmembers $15. Linen $2. Occasional pancake breakfast ($3). Lockout 9am-5pm. Curfew 11pm. Open mid-June to Sept.

Mt. Desert Island YWCA, 36 Mt. Desert St. (288-5008), Bar Harbor, near downtown. Women only. Extensive common space, full kitchen, laundry. Singles with hallway bath $30 per night; doubles $25 per person; solarium with 7 beds $20 per bed; weekly rates $90/$75/$65. $25 key/security deposit. Open daily 9am-9pm; off-season M-F 9am-4pm. Fills quickly; make reservations early.

White Birches Campground (244-3797), Southwest Harbor, on Seal Cove Rd. 1 mi. west of Rte. 102. 60 widely spaced, wooded sites offer an escape from the touristy areas. $16 for up to 4 people, with hookup $20; weekly $96/$120; $2 per additional person. Free hot showers, fireplace, bathrooms. Open mid-May to mid-Oct. daily 8am-9pm for check-in. Reservations recommended, especially in July-Aug.

Acadia National Park Campgrounds: Blackwoods (288-3274, reservations 800-365-2267), 5 mi. south of Bar Harbor on Rte. 3. Over 300 sites. Mid-June to mid-Sept. $16; mid-May to mid-June and mid-Sept. to mid-Oct. $14; mid-Dec. to mid-Mar. free. Group sites also available. Reservations highly recommended in summer. **Seawall** (244-3600), Rte. 102A on the western side of the island, 4 mi. south of Southwest Harbor. 10min. walk from the ocean. Toilets but no hookups. Showers available nearby; bring quarters ($1 per 6min.). First come, first served walk-in sites $10, drive-in $14, RV sites $14. Open late May to Sept. daily 7:15am-9pm.

FOOD, NIGHTLIFE, AND ENTERTAINMENT

Beal's (244-7178 or 800-245-7178), Southwest Harbor, at the end of Clark Point Rd. Superb prices for lobster. Pick your own live crustacean from a tank ($10-13); Beal's does the rest. Kitchen closed in off season, but fresh seafood is sold. Open daily mid-May to Sept. 6 9am-8pm; off-season 9am-5pm. Hrs. vary with weather.

Jordan's, 80 Cottage St. (288-3586), Bar Harbor. A favorite of locals and visitors, especially those who love muffins (6 for $4.25) and plate-sized blueberry pancakes ($3). Breakfast is served all day. Open daily 5am-2pm except for 3 weeks in Nov.

The Colonel's Deli Bakery and Restaurant (276-5147), on Main St. in Northeast Harbor. Sate thyself with sandwiches so big you'll have to squash the fresh baked bread to get one into your mouth (most around $4.50). The desserts are unusual and delicious ($1-2). Open mid-Apr. to Oct. daily 6:30am-9pm.

Most after dinner pleasures on the island are simple. **Ben and Bill's Chocolate Emporium,** 66 Main St. (288-3281), near Cottage St., boasts 50 flavors of homemade ice cream, including (no kidding) lobster (cone $2.50-3.75) and enough luscious chocolates to challenge Willy Wonka (open mid-Feb to Jan. daily 9am-11:30pm). **Geddy's Pub,** 19 Main St. (288-5077), is a three-tiered entertainment complex with a bar, dancing, and live music until 10:30pm; a DJ takes over until closing (no cover; open Apr.-Oct. daily 11:30-1am; winter hrs. vary). Locals prefer the less touristy **Lompoc Café & Brew Pub,** 36 Rodick St. (288-9392), off Cottage St., which features home-brewed Bar Harbor Real Ale and live jazz, blues, Celtic, rock, or folk (shows F-Sa nights; cover $1-2; open May-Oct. daily 11:30am-1am, winter hrs. vary). The Art Deco **Criterion Theatre** (288-3441), on Cottage St., shows movies in the summer. (Two evening shows daily. $6.50, under 12 $4, balcony seats $7.50, seniors $5.50. Box office open 30min. before show.)

NEW ENGLAND

SIGHTS

The staff at the **Mt. Desert Oceanarium** (244-7330), at the end of Clark Pt. Rd. near Beals in Southwest Harbor, knows its sea stuff. *(Open mid-May to late Oct. M-Sa 9am-5pm. Ticket for all 3 facilities $11.40, ages 4-12 $8.35; inquire about individual rates.)* The main museum, reminiscent of a grammar school science fair, fascinates children and some adults. Cruises head out to sea from a number of points. **Whale Watcher, Inc.,** 1 West St. (288-3322), Harbor Pl., offers sailing trips (2hr., $16); lobster fishing and seal watching trips (1½hr., $16.75); and whale-watching trips (3hr., $30; operates May-Oct.; reservations recommended; call for schedule). The **Acadian Whale Watcher** (288-9794), Golden Anchor Pier, West St., has occasional sunset cruises. *(Buy tickets at corner of Cottage and Main St. 4 trips per day, whale watch/puffin and whale tour combo $34. Operates May-Nov.)*

   Wildwood Stables (276-3622), along Park Loop Rd. in Seal Harbor, takes tourists to explore the island via horse and carriage. *(1hr. tour $13, seniors $12, ages 6-12 $7, ages 2-5 $4. 2hr. tour $16.50/$15.50/$8/$5. Reservations recommended.)*

■ Acadia National Park

The 33,000 acres that comprise Acadia National Park are a landlubber's dream, offering easy trails and challenging hikes. Millionaire and expert horseman John D. Rockefeller, fearing the island would someday be overrun by cars, funded all of the park's 120 mi. of trails. These **carriage roads** make for easy walking, fun mountain biking, and pleasant carriage rides.

   Precipice Trail, one of the most popular hikes, is closed June to late Aug. to accommodate nesting peregrine falcons. The 5 mi. **Eagle Lake Carriage Rd.** is graded for bicyclists. Touring the park by auto costs $10 for 7 days, $5 per pedestrian or cyclist. Seniors can purchase a lifetime pass for $10. The *Biking and Hiking Guide to the Carriage Roads* ($6), available at the visitors center and in bookstores, offers invaluable safety advice for the more labyrinthine trails.

   About 4 mi. south of Bar Harbor on Rte. 3, **Park Loop Rd.** runs along the shore of the island, where great waves crash against steep granite cliffs. The sea comes into **Thunder Hole** with a bang at half-tide. Swimming can be found in the relatively warm **Echo Lake** or at **Sand Beach,** both of which have lifeguards in the summer. To be the first person in the U.S. to see the sunrise, climb Cadillac Mountain just before dawn (4-4:30am in summer).

New Hampshire

New Hampshire bears only a slight likeness to the English county for which it was named. Pastoral fields give way to the White Mountains in the central and northern regions, while Mt. Washington, the highest point in the Appalachians (6288 ft.), surveys the Atlantic and five states. The first colony to declare independence from Great Britain, New Hampshire still embraces an individualistic ideal; the state motto, "Live Free or Die," is emblazoned on every license plate. Today, eager hordes descend upon the state year-round, drawn by a wealth of wilderness activities and an abundance of tax-free outlet shopping.

PRACTICAL INFORMATION

Capital: Concord.
Visitor Info: Office of Travel and Tourism, P.O. Box 856, Concord 03302 (603-271-2666 or 800-386-4664; http://www.visitnh.com). 24hr. recording provides fall foliage reports, daily ski conditions, snowmobile conditions, and special events. **Fish and Game Dept.,** 2 Hazen Dr., Concord 03301 (603-271-3421), furnishes info on hunting and fishing regulations and license fees. **U.S. Forest Service,** 719 Main St., Laconia 03246 (603-528-8721). Open M-F 8am-4:30pm.

Emergency: 911.
Time Zone: Eastern. **Postal Abbreviation:** NH.
Sales Tax: 0%; 8% on meals and rooms.

■ White Mountains

In the late 19th century, the White Mountains became an immensely popular summer retreat for wealthy New Englanders. Grand hotels peppered the rolling green landscape, and as many as 50 trains per day carried tourists through the region. The mountains are not quite as busy these days nor quite as fashionable. Unfortunately, the economics of vacationing here have not changed quite as drastically; affordable lodgings are as scarce as public transportation, and the notoriously unpredictable weather makes camping risky. Nevertheless, the area divided along the notches among the mountains still beckons the rugged and energetic adventurer.

PRACTICAL INFORMATION Finding the White Mountains by bus is considerably easier than getting around once there. **Concord Trailways** (228-3300 or 800-639-3317) runs from Boston to Concord (17 per day, $11); Conway (1-2 per day, $25); and Franconia (1 per day, $26). **Vermont Transit** (800-451-3292) stops its Boston-to-Vermont buses in Concord ($11) at the Trailways terminal, 30 Stickney Ave. The AMC runs a **shuttle service** (466-2727) among points within the mountains (service operates early June to early Oct. daily 8:45am-3:30pm; $7, nonmembers $8). Consult AMC's *The Guide* for a complete map of routes and times; reservations are recommended for all stops and required for some. Pertinent travel info can be obtained from the **White Mountain Attraction Center,** P.O. Box 10, N. Woodstock 03262 (745-8720), on Rte. 112 (open daily 8:30am-6pm). Another good resource is the regional office of the **U.S. Forest Service,** 719 Main St. (528-8721), Laconia, which lies south of the mountains. **Forest service ranger stations** dot the main highways throughout the forest: **Androscoggin** (466-2713), on Rte. 16, ½ mi. south of the U.S. 2 junction in Gorham; **Ammonoosuc** (869-2626), on Trudeau Rd. in Bethlehem, west of U.S. 3 on U.S. 302; and **Saco** (447-5448), on the Kancamangus Hwy. in Conway, 100 yd. off Rte. 16. Each station provides info on trail locations and conditions and a handy free guide to the local **backcountry facilities** (stations open daily 8am-4:30pm). **Pinkham Notch Visitors Center** (466-2725 or 466-2727 for reservations), 10 mi. north of Jackson on Rte. 16, is the area's best source of info on weather and trail conditions. The center also handles reservations at any of the AMC lodgings and sells the complete line of AMC books, trail maps ($3-9), and camping and hiking accessories. (Open daily 6:30am-10pm.) **Area code:** 603.

ACCOMMODATIONS AND CAMPGROUNDS The **Appalachian Mountains Club (AMC)** has its main base in the mountains at the Pinkham Notch Visitors Center, on Rte. 16 between Gorham and Jackson (see **Practical Information,** above). The area's primary source of info on camping, food, and lodging, the AMC also sells an assortment of camping and hiking accessories. The club runs two car-accessible lodgings in the White Mountains: **Joe Dodge Lodge** (see **Pinkham Notch,** p. 80) and the **Crawford Hostel** (846-7773, reservations 466-2721), adjoining the Crawford Notch Depot east of Bretton Woods on U.S. 302. ($14, nonmembers $18. 24 bunkbeds, toilets, metered showers, full kitchen. Bring a sleeping bag and food. Curfew 9:30pm. Reservations recommended.) The Depot has trail guides, maps, food, camping necessities, film, and restrooms (open May to early Oct. daily 9am-5pm). The AMC also operates a system of eight **huts,** spaced about a day's hike apart along the **Appalachian Trail.** Guests must provide their own sleeping bags or sheets. Meals at the huts, while not as good as those back at the Dodge lodge, are ample and appetizing. (Bunk with 2 meals $55, children $35; nonmembers $62/$39.) All huts stay open for full service June to mid-October; self-service rates with no meals provided are available at other times ($14, nonmembers $18; call for reservations).

Camping is free in a number of backcountry areas throughout the **White Mountains National Forest (WMNF).** Other campsites, mainly lean-tos and tent platforms with no showers or toilets, pepper the mountain trails. Most run $5 per night on a first come, first served basis, but many are free. The **U.S. Forest Service** (528-8721) or consult the AMC's free two-page handout, *Backpacker Shelters, Tent sites, Campsites, and Cabins in the White Mountains* are both good sources of info. Neither camping nor fires are allowed above the tree line (approximately 4000 ft.), within 200 ft. of a trail, or within ¼ mi. of roads, huts, shelters, tent platforms, lakes, or streams. Rules vary depending on forest conditions; backpackers should call the Forest Service before settling into a campsite. The Forest Service can also direct you to one of their 20 **designated campgrounds.** (Call 800-280-2267 for info. Sites $10-14. Bathrooms and firewood usually available. Reservation fee $8.65. Reserve 2 weeks in advance, especially July-Aug.)

HIKING AND BIKING If you intend to spend a lot of time in the area, and are planning to do significant hiking, the *AMC White Mountain Guide* is invaluable ($22; available in most bookstores and huts). The guide includes full maps and descriptions of all the mountain trails—you can pinpoint precisely where you are at any given time. Hikers should bring three layers of clothing in all seasons: one for wind, one for rain, and one for warmth, as weather conditions change at a moment's notice. Black flies and swarms of mosquitoes can ruin a trip, particularly in June.

Next to hiking, bicycling is the best way to see the mountains close up. According to some bikers, the approach to the WMNF from the north is slightly less steep than others. The *New Hampshire Bicycle* guide and map, available at info centers, the U.S. Forest Service's bike trail guides, or *30 Bicycle Tours in New Hampshire* ($13), available at local bookstores and outdoor equipment stores, can help with planning.

■ Franconia Notch Area

Formed by glacial movements that began during an ice age 400 million years ago, Franconia Notch encompasses imposing granite cliffs, waterfalls, endless woodlands, and the famous rocky profile of the "Old Man of the Mountain." The nearest town, Lincoln, lies just south of I-93 where Rte. 112 becomes the scenic Kancamagus Hwy. From Lincoln, the Kancamagus Hwy. branches east to Conway, twisting 35 mi. through the scenic **Pemigewasset Wilderness.** Attracting backpackers and skiers galore, 4000 ft. peaks rim the large basin. South of the highway, trails head into the **Sandwich Ranges,** including **Mt. Chocorua** (south along Rte. 16 near Ossippee), a dramatic peak and a favorite of 19th-century naturalist painters.

The **Flume Visitors Center** (745-8391), off I-93 north of Lincoln, screens an excellent 15min. film that acquaints visitors with the landscape (open daily July-Aug. 9am-5:30pm; Sept.-June 9am-5pm). While at the Center, you can purchase tickets to **The Flume,** a 2 mi. nature walk over hills, through a covered bridge, and to a boardwalk over a fantastic gorge walled by 90 ft. granite cliffs ($7, ages 6-12 $4). A 9 mi. recreational **bike path** begins at the Visitors Center and runs through the park.

The westernmost of the notches, Franconia is best known for the **Old Man of the Mountain,** a 40 ft. high human profile formed by five ledges of stone atop a 1200 ft. cliff north of The Flume. Nathaniel Hawthorne addressed this geological visage in his 1850 story "The Great Stone Face," and P.T. Barnum once offered to purchase the rock. Today, the Old Man is rather doddering; cables and turnbuckles support his forehead. **Profile Lake,** a 10min. walk from the base of the Cannon Mountain Aerial Tramway, has the best view of the geezer.

Unlike the Old Man, the **Great Cannon Cliff,** a 1000 ft. sheer drop into the cleft between **Mt. Lafayette** and **Cannon Mountain,** beckons more than just onlookers. Hands-on types test their technical skill and climb the cliff via the "Sticky Fingers" or "Meat Grinder" routes; less daring visitors opt to let the 80-passenger **Cannon Mountain Aerial Tramway** (823-5563) do the work. (Open daily late May to late Oct. 9am-5pm; early Dec. to mid-Apr. 8:30am-4:30pm. $7; round-trip $9, ages 6-12 $5.)

Myriad trails lead up into the mountains on both sides of the notch, providing excellent day hikes and spectacular views. Be prepared for severe weather, especially above 4000 ft. The **Lonesome Lake Trail,** a relatively easy hike, winds its way 1½ mi. from Lafayette Pl. to **Lonesome Lake** (a pleasant 1.8 mi. hike from The Basin), where the AMC operates its westernmost summer hut (see **Practical Information,** p. 77). The **Greenleaf Trail** (2½ mi.), which starts at the Aerial Tramway parking lot, and the **Old Bridle Path** (3 mi.), from Lafayette Place, are much more ambitious. Both lead up to the AMC's Greenleaf Hut near the summit of Mt. Lafayette overlooking Echo Lake, a favorite destination for sunset photographers. From Greenleaf, a 7½ mi. trek east along **Garfield Ridge** leads to the AMC's most remote hut, the **Galehead;** the area can keep you occupied for days. A campsite on Garfield ridge costs $5.

Just north of the southernmost end of Franconia Notch, **The Basin,** a waterfall in the Pemigewasset River and one of the park's most popular attractions, drops into a 15 ft. granite pool. The Basin's walls, smoothed by 25,000 years of sandy scouring, seem almost too perfect to be natural. The overlook is fully wheelchair-accessible.

The lifeguard-protected **beach** offers cool waters on the northern shore of **Echo Lake State Park** (356-2672), just north of Franconia Notch (open mid-June to Sept. daily 9am-7pm; park admission $2.50, under 12 and over 65 free).

Less renowned than the resorts of Mt. Washington Valley, the ski areas of Franconia Notch, collectively known as **Ski-93,** P.O. Box 517, Lincoln 13251 (745-8101 or 800-937-5493), offer multiple-area packages. Three miles east of I-93 on Rte. 112, **Loon Mountain** (745-8111) has summer activities including free beginner's rope tow, mountain bikes, an equestrian center, and live animal shows. By limiting lift ticket sales, Loon promises crowd-free skiing in winter. (Lift tickets M-F $38, Sa-Su $45; ages 13-21 $32/$40; ages 6-12 $25/$28). **Waterville Valley** (236-8311) offers cross-country skiing, plus some great downhill runs (lift tickets M-F $37, Sa-Su $44; ages 13-18 $34/$40; ages 6-12 $10). **Cannon Mountain** (823-5563), the northernmost point in the Notch on I-93, sports decent slopes and the New England Ski Museum. (Lift tickets M-F $28, Sa-Su $39; ages 13-18 and students $19/$32; ages 6-12 $19/$27.) Ski season at most resorts runs from mid-November through April.

Lafayette Campground (823-9513) is nestled smack in the middle of Franconia Notch. (Coin-operated showers. Sites for 2 $14, $7 per additional person. Call for reservations 1 week in advance. Open mid-May to mid-Oct., weather permitting.) If Lafayette is full, the more suburban **Fransted Campground** (823-5675), 1 mi. south of the village and 3 mi. north of the Notch, is nearby. (Showers and bathroom. Sites $18, with water and electricity $20. Open May to mid-Oct.) Hungry visitors to the area would be well-served to visit **Polly's Pancake Parlor** (823-5575), on Rt. 117 in Sugar Hill; the locals swear by the gigantic menu. The parlor offers a stack of six pancakes ($5), unlimited pancakes ($10) or waffles ($12), and a friendly staff. (Open M-F 7am-3pm, Sa-Su 7am-7pm; off-season Sa-Su 7am-7pm only.) **Area code:** 603.

■ North Conway

At first glance, North Conway, strung along the stretch of land shared by Rte. 16 and Rte. 302, seems like just another strip of motels and fast food joints on the way to somewhere else. Look again. This town, the largest city around, capitalizes on two of New Hampshire's most striking features: the terrain and the lack of sales tax. A number of very good cross-country and downhill ski centers await nearby. North Conway and Conway are two different towns, making addresses a bit confusing.

Though close to many ski areas, **Cranmore** (356-5543) is North Conway's resident mountain. (2-day lift tickets Su-F $58, Sa and holidays $72; children $28/$38. Open mid-Nov. to Apr. daily 10am-6pm.) **Attitash** (374-2368) offers the "smart credit ticket" and short-term options, 2½ mi. west on U.S. 302. (1-day pass M-F $39, Sa-Su $46, ages 6-12 $24/$28. Open Nov.-Apr. M-F 9am-4pm, Sa-Su 8am-4pm.) During the summer, speed demons enjoy the **Alpine Slide** at Attitash, a wild ¾ mi. sled ride down the mountain that tests the most adventurous souls. A one-day pass ($19) includes unlimited rides on the alpine slide and nearby waterslides. (Open daily 10am-6pm; in spring and fall Sa-Su only.) **Wildcat** (466-3326), known for having the area's largest lift capacity and a free novice skiing area, fronts Rte. 16 just south of Pinkham Notch State Park (lift tickets M-F $39, Sa-Su $46; ages 5-12 $25/$29). During the summer, Wildcat offers gondola rides ($9, ages 4-10 $4.50; operates mid-June to mid-Oct. 9:30am-4:30pm). All three areas offer special group and multi-day rates.

NEW ENGLAND

A number of stores in the North Conway area rent outdoor equipment. For downhill and cross-country skis, **Joe Jones** (356-9411), in North Conway on Main St. at Mechanic, is good. A second branch lies a few miles north of town on Rte. 302. (Alpine skis, boots, and poles $12 for 1 day, $22 for 2 days. Cross-country equipment $10/$16. Open July-Aug. daily 9am-9pm; Sept.-Nov. and Apr.-June Su-Th 10am-8pm, F-Sa 9am-8pm.) **Eastern Mountain Sports (EMS)** (356-5433), on Main St. in the Eastern Slope Inn, distributes free mountaineering pamphlets and books on the area. EMS also sells camping equipment and rents tents and sleeping bags. The knowledgeable staff can provide first-hand info on climbing and hiking in North Conway. (Open June-Sept. M-Sa 9am-9pm, Su 9am-6pm; Oct.-May Su-Th 9am-6pm, F-Sa 9am-9pm.)

White Mountains Hostel (HI-AYH), 36 Washington St. (447-1001 or 800-909-4776, ext. 51), sits 2 blocks from the bus station in Conway. Walk 2 blocks north on Main St./Rte. 16 to the first traffic light in Conway, then turn left on Washington St. A friendly staff, great proximity to the White Mountains, 43 well-kept bunks, and some genuine eco-love all converge at this haven for the hill-bound hosteler. (Kitchen and computer use. $16, nonmembers $19, includes light breakfast; private rooms $45/$48. Linen free. Reception 7-10am and 5-10pm. Check-out 10am. Reservations recommended during first 2 weeks in Oct. Open Dec.-Oct.) The **hostel** at the beautiful **Mt. Cranmore Lodge,** 859 Kearsarge Rd. (356-2044 or 800-356-3596), has 40 bunks. Associated with a lovely mountain inn, Mt. Cranmore offers a full breakfast, recreation room, pool, jacuzzi, tennis courts, duck pond, hiking and biking trails, cable, Sarah the cow, and three sheep, as well as easy access to nearby mountains. In winter, ski packages with nearby mountains are available. ($17. Linen and towel included. No curfew; no lockout; no smoking. Check-in 3pm. Check-out 11am.)

Breakfast and lunch spots line North Conway's Main St., but nearer to the hostel and bus stop is **Café Noche,** 147 Main St. (447-5050), notable for its upbeat border decor and sombrero-tilting spicy Mexican-American fare, like the Montezuma Pie (a sort of Mexican lasagna, $7) or the garden burger ($4.25; open M-F 11:30am-9pm, Sa-Su 11:30am-9:30pm). **Horsefeathers** (356-2687) serves hearty meals in the heart of North Conway. Burgers cost $7-7.50. (Kitchen open daily 11:30am-11:45pm; bar open until 1am.) After-dinner coffee is available across the street at the **Mourning Dew.** The crowd reconvenes at the pricey **Ledges Restaurant** (356-6260), in the Eastern Slope Inn. (Dinner specials $7-9. Dancing F-Sa. Food Su-Th noon-10pm, F-Sa noon-11pm; bar open 'til 1am. In summer open for breakfast Sa-Su.) **Area code:** 603.

■ Pinkham Notch

From just behind the Pinkham Notch Visitors Center all the way up to the summit of Mt. Washington, **Tuckerman's Ravine Trail** takes 4-5hr. of steep hiking each way. *Let's Go* urges caution when climbing—Mt. Washington claims at least one life every year. A gorgeous day here can suddenly turn into a chilling storm, with whipping winds and rumbling thunderclouds. It has never been warmer than 72°F atop Mt. Washington, and the average temperature on the peak is a bone-chilling 26.7°F. With an *average* wind speed of 35 mph and gusts that have been measured up to an astounding 231 mph, Mt. Washington ranks as the windiest place in the country. As long as you take proper measures, the climb is stellar and the view well worth it. Motorists can take the **Mt. Washington Auto Rd.** (466-3988), a paved and dirt road that winds 8 mi. to the summit. At the top, they sell a bumper sticker boasting "This Car Climbed Mt. Washington"—it's certain to impress folks when you cruise back through town, particularly if you're driving a jalopy. The road begins at Glen House, a short distance north of the visitors center on Rte. 16. (Road open daily mid-June to mid-Sept. 7:30am-6pm; mid-May to mid-June and mid-Sept. to mid-Oct. 8:30am-5pm. $15 per car and driver, $6 per passenger, ages 5-12 $4.) **Guided van tours** to the summit include a 30min. presentation on the mountain's natural history ($20, ages 5-12 $10). On the summit, you'll find strong wind, an info center, a **snack bar** (466-3347; open late May to mid-Oct. daily 8am-6pm), and a **museum** run by the **Mt. Washington Observatory** (466-3388; museum open late May to mid-Oct. daily 9am-7pm).

AMC's huts offer the best lodging on the mountain. At **Joe Dodge Lodge,** immediately behind the Pinkham Notch Visitors Center, a stay earns a comfy bunk with a delicious and sizeable breakfast and dinner. ($42, children $27; nonmembers $47/$31; off-season $37/$24/$42/$27; without meals $27/$18/$30/$20.) **Hermit's Lake Shelter,** situated about 2hr. up the Tuckerman Ravine Trail, has bathrooms but no shower, and sleeps 72 people in eight lean-tos and three tent platforms ($7 per night; buy nightly passes at the visitors center). **Carter Notch Hut** lies to the east of the visitors' center, a 4 mi. hike up the 19 mi. **Brook Trail.** Just 1½ mi. from Mt. Washington's summit sits **Lakes of the Clouds,** the largest, highest, and most popular of the AMC's huts (room for 90); additional sleeping space for six backpackers in its basement refuge room can be reserved from any other hut ($14, nonmembers $18).

New Hampshire's easternmost Notch lies in the shadow of Mt. Washington between Gorham and Jackson on Rte. 16. The home of AMC's main info center in the White Mountains and the starting point for most trips up Mt. Washington, Pinkham Notch's practicality gets more publicity than its beauty. To get to Pinkham Notch from I-93 S, take Exit 42 to U.S. 302 E, then follow Rte. 116 N to U.S. 2 E to Rte. 16 S. From I-93 N, take Exit 32 onto Rte. 112 E to Rte. 16 N. **Area code:** 603.

Vermont

Perhaps no other state is as aptly named as Vermont. The lineage of the name extends back to Samuel de Champlain, who in 1609 dubbed the area "green mountain" in his native French *(mont vert).* The Green Mountain range shapes and defines Vermont, spanning the length of the state from north to south and covering most of its width as well. Over the past few decades, ex-urbanite yuppies have invaded, creating some tension between the original, pristine Vermont and the packaged Vermont of organic food stores and mountaineering shops. Happily, the former still seems to prevail; visitors can frolic in any of the 30 state forests, 80 state parks, or the mammoth 186,000-acre Green Mountain National Forest.

PRACTICAL INFORMATION

Capital: Montpelier.
Visitor Info: Vermont Information Center, 134 State St., Montpelier 05602 (802-828-3237; http://www.travel-vermont.com). Open M-F 8am-8pm. **Dept. of Forests, Parks and Recreation,** 103 S. Main St., Waterbury 05676 (802-241-3670). Open M-F 7:45am-4:30pm. **Vermont Snowline** (802-229-0531). Nov.-May 24hr. recording on snow conditions.
Emergency: 911.
Time Zone: Eastern. **Postal Abbreviation:** VT.
Sales Tax: 5%; 9% on meals and lodgings.

■ Vermont Ski Resorts

Come winter, skiers pour into Vermont to hit some of the Northeast's finest resort areas, which become havens for bikers and hikers in the summer and fall. Numerous small towns feature accommodations options for travelers beyond the pricey inns and lodges at the resorts themselves; inquire about shared rooms with bunks, which cost significantly less than private rooms. For more information, contact **Ski Vermont,** P.O. Box 368, Montpelier 05601 (802-223-2439; fax 802-229-6917), or check out their comprehensive website at http://www.skivermont.com, which also provides links to the websites of major resorts. Other helpful organizations include the Vermont Information Center (see Vermont **Practical Information,** above), which can give you a free attractions packet; and the **Vermont Ski Areas Association,** 26 State St. (P.O. Box 368), Montpelier 05601 (802-223-2439; open M-F 7:45am-4:45pm).

Mt. Snow, on Rte. 100 in the town of West Dover (800-245-SNOW/7669), is located in southern Vermont west of **Brattleboro** (see p. 88). *(Open mid-Nov. to late Apr. M-F 9am-4pm, Sa-Su 8am-4pm. Adults $41 per ½-day, full-day $51.45 M-F, Sa-Su $54.60;*

ages 13-18 $41/$46.20/$24.50; seniors and under 13 $25.50/$32.55/$34.65. Prices include tax.) Benefiting from its proximity to the major metropolitan areas of the Northeast, this popular resort boasts 134 trails and 26 lifts, as well as the first snowboard park in the Northeast. In summer, bikers can take advantage of 45 mi. of trails across the "Mountain Biking Capital of the East." Moving north, the seven mountains of **Killington** (802-422-3333 or 800-621-MTNS/6867), at the junction of U.S. 4 and Rte. 100 N in Sherburne, host the East's longest ski season (mid-Oct. to early June), as well as the most terrain for novice and advanced skiers in New England. *(Adults $52 per day plus tax; call for other rates.)* Visitors bored with the slopes can ice-skate, snowshoe, or snowmobile, then choose from over 100 restaurants and clubs for *après* ski fun.

For some of the most reasonable lift ticket prices in Vermont, head to **Burke** (800-786-8338), off I-91 in northern Vermont. *(Season late Dec. to mid-Mar. M-F adults $15, students and seniors $15, children $15; Sa-Su $38/$33/$23; off-peak M-F $12/$12/$12, Sa-Su $33/$27/$17.)* In summer, visitors can partake in almost any recreational activity from rock climbing to fishing, as well as hike and bike across 200 mi. of trails. Far north, **Jay Peak** (800-451-4449 or 802-988-2611), in Jay on Rte. 242, sits just across the U.S. border with Canada in Vermont's Northeast Kingdom. *(Adults $44, under 15 $25, after 2:45pm $10; numerous special rates.)* Some of the East's most challenging Glades and ample opportunities for woods skiing make Jay Peak an appealing option for thrill-seekers; in summer, excellent fishing and mountain biking opportunities abound.

Other fine resorts include: **Stratton** (802-297-2200 or 800-787-2886; 90 trails, 12 lifts), on Rte. 30 N in Bondville; **Sugarbush** (802-583-2381 or 800-537-8427; 112 trails, 18 lifts, 4 mountains); **Stowe** (see p. 86); and **Middlebury College Snow Bowl** (p. 85). Cross-country resorts include the **Trapp Family Lodge,** Stowe (see p. 86); **Mountain Meadows,** Killington (802-745-7077; 90 mi. of trails); and **Woodstock** (802-457-6674 or 800-448-7900; 40 mi. of trails).

■ Burlington

Tucked between Lake Champlain and the Green Mountains, the largest city in Vermont successfully bridges the gap between the urban and the outdoors. Five colleges, including the University of Vermont (UVM), give the area a youthful, progressive flair; bead shops pop up next door to mainstream clothing stores without disrupting local harmony. Along Church St., numerous sidewalk cafes offer a taste of the middle-class hippie atmosphere, which transcends its paradoxical nature and colors this mellow villa.

PRACTICAL INFORMATION

Trains: Amtrak, 29 Railroad Ave., Essex Jct. (879-7298 or 800-872-7245), 5 mi. east of Burlington on Rte. 15. To New York (9¾hr., 1 per day, $56-62) and White River Junction (2hr., 1 per day, $13). Station open daily 7:30am-noon and 8-9pm. CCTA bus to downtown runs every 30min. M-F 5:55am-6:05pm, Sa 6:45am-7:40pm.

Buses: Vermont Transit, 345 Pine St. (864-6811 or 800-451-3292), at Main St. To: Boston (4¾hr., 5 per day, $45); Montreal (2½hr., 5 per day, $18-19); White River Junction (2hr., 5 per day, $14.50); Middlebury (1hr., 3 per day, $7.50); and Albany (4¾hr., 3 per day, $34). 15% discount with student ID. Connections made with Greyhound; Ameripasses accepted. Open daily 6am-8:15pm.

Public Transportation: Chittenden County Transit Authority (CCTA) (864-0211). Frequent, reliable service. Downtown hub at Cherry and Church St. Connections with Shelburne and other outlying areas. Buses operate every 30min. M-Sa roughly 6:15am-9:20pm, depending on routes. Fare $1; seniors, disabled, and under 18 50¢; under 5 free.

Bike Rental: Ski Rack, 85 Main St. (658-3313 or 800-882-4530). Mountain bikes $8 for 1hr., $14 for 4hr., and $22 for 24hr. Helmet and lock included. In-line skates $8 for 4hr., $12 per day. Credit card required for rental. Open M-Th 9am-8pm, F 9am-9pm, Sa 9am-6pm, Su 10am-5pm; mid-Aug. to mid-Apr. M-Th 10am-7pm, F 10am-8pm, Sa 9am-6pm, Su 11am-5pm.

Visitor Info: Lake Champlain Regional Chamber of Commerce, 60 Main St., Rte. 100 (863-3489), provides info on lodging, dining, and sights in and around Burlington. Open M-F 8:30am-5pm, Sa-Su 11am-3pm; Oct.-May M-F 8:30am-5pm.

Hotlines: Women's Rape Crisis Center, 863-1236. **Crises Services of Chittenden County,** 863-2400. Both 24hr.
Internet Access: Kinko's, 199 Main St. (658-2561). $12 per hr. Open 24hr.
Post Office: 11 Elmwood Ave. (863-6033), at Pearl St. Open M-F 8am-5pm, Sa 8am-1pm. **ZIP code:** 05401. **Area code:** 802.

A PLACE TO LAY YOUR HEAD

The chamber of commerce has the complete rundown on area accommodations. B&Bs are generally found in the outlying suburbs. Reasonably priced hotels and guest houses line **Shelburne Rd.** south of downtown. **Mrs. Farrell's Home Hostel (HI-AYH)** (865-3730), 3 mi. from downtown, is accessible by public transportation; she gives directions when you call for reservations. The six beds are split between a clean, comfortable basement and a lovely garden porch. The friendly, adventurous owner is sometimes hard to reach; call around 4-6pm. Even if she has no available beds, she can refer you to an overflow location. ($15, nonmembers $18. Handicapped-accessible room available for summer. Linen free. Showers, coffee, and bagels.) The **North Beach Campsites** (862-0942), on Institute Rd. 1½ mi. north of town by North Ave., have a spectacular view and access to a pristine beach on Lake Champlain. (136 sites. $16, with electricity $22, full hookup $25. Showers 25¢ per 5min. Beach is free but closes at 9pm, and parking costs $3. Open May to mid-Oct.) Take Rte. 127 to North Ave., or take the "North Ave." bus from the main terminal on Pine St. You can have your MTV at **Shelburne Campground** (985-2540), on Shelburne Rd., 1 mi. north of Shelburne and 5 mi. south of Burlington by Rte. 7; buses to Shelburne South stop right next to the campground. (Sites for 2 $16.80, with water and electricity $21-23, full hookup $27; $2 per additional person. Pool, laundry facilities. Open May-Oct.) See **Near Burlington,** p. 84, for more camping options.

FOOD AND ICE CREAM

At **Sweetwater's,** 120 Church St. (864-9800), incredibly high ceilings and vast wall paintings dwarf those who come for delicious $3-3.50 soups and $6-7 sandwiches. (Open M-Sa 11:30am-2am, Su 10:30am-midnight; food served M-Sa until 1am, Su until 11pm.) The **Oasis Diner,** 189 Bank St. (864-5308), has fried up the ultimate American diner experience since 1954. Hamburger, fries, and a small soda go for $5. The ghost of Elvis might enjoy the $3 grilled bacon and peanut butter sandwich. (Open M-F 5am-3pm, Sa 5am-2pm, Su 8am-2pm.) The **Vermont Pub and Brewery,** 144 College St. (865-0500), at St. Paul's St., offers affordable sandwiches and delicious homemade beers (pint $3). The free brewery tour offers more about Original Vermont Lager. (Pub open Su-F 11:30am-2am, Sa 11:30am-1am. Live entertainment Th-Sa 10pm. Tours W 8pm, Sa 4pm.) A bottle of wine sells for as little as $4 in the odorific warehouse of the **Cheese Outlet,** 400 Pine St. (863-3968), accompanying cheese and fresh bread, and cafe fare. (Veggie enchilada $6. Open M-Sa 8am-7pm, Su 10am-5pm.)

Although its original shop, a converted gas station at 169 Cherry St., has burned down and been abandoned, the Burlington **Ben & Jerry's,** 36 Church St. (862-9620), is still considered the company's birthplace (see p. 87). (Cones $2-3. Open Apr.-Nov. Su-Th 11am-11pm, F-Sa 11am-midnight; Dec.-Mar. Su-Th 11:30am-10pm, F-Sa 11:30am-11pm.)

SIGHTS, NIGHTLIFE, AND ENTERTAINMENT

Despite its suburban appearance, Burlington offers lively cultural and artistic entertainment. The popular pedestrian mall at historic **Church St. Marketplace** provides a haven for tie-dye and ice cream lovers and sells works by local artists. Amateur historians delight in Victorian **South Willard St.,** where you'll find **Champlain College** and the **University of Vermont** (656-3480), founded in 1797. **City Hall Park,** in the heart of downtown, and **Battery St. Park,** on Lake Champlain near the edge of downtown, are bucolic. For insomniac boaters, the **Burlington Community Boathouse** (865-3377), at the base of College St. at Lake Champlain, is open late to rent light craft for a cruise on the lake. *(Open June 2-Aug. 24hr.; mid-May to June 1 and Sept. to mid-Oct. daily 6am-10pm. Sailboats $20-35 per hr.)* The **Spirit of Ethan Allen** scenic cruise

(862-9685) departs from the boathouse at the bottom of College St. *(Cruises late May to mid-Oct. daily 10am, noon, 2, and 4pm. $8, ages 3-11 $4. Call about the more costly theme dinner and sunset cruises.)* The boat cruises along the Vermont coast, giving passengers a close-up view of the famous **Thrust Fault,** which is not visible from land.

The **Shelburne Museum** (985-3346), 7 mi. south of Burlington in Shelburne, houses one of the best collections of Americana in the country. *(Open daily 10am-5pm; late Oct. to late May, 1 tour daily at 1pm. Admission $17.50, students $10.50, ages 6-14 $7; AAA discount. Tours $7, ages 6-14 $3.)* Besides 37 buildings transported from all over New England, 45-acre Shelburne has a covered bridge from Cambridge, MA, a steamboat and lighthouse from Lake Champlain, and Degas, Cassatt, Manet, Monet, Rembrandt, and Whistler paintings. Tickets are valid for 2 consecutive days; you'll need the time to cover the 1 mi. exhibit. Five miles farther south on U.S. 7, the **Vermont Wildflower Farm** (425-3500) has a seed shop and 6½ acres of wildflower gardens. *(Open Apr.-Oct. daily 9:30am-5:30pm. $3, seniors $2.50, under 12 free; off-season admission only $1.50, but don't expect many blossoms.)*

The **Ethan Allen Homestead** (865-4556) rests northeast of Burlington on Rte. 127. *(Open mid-May to mid-June daily 1-5pm; June to mid-Oct. M-Sa 10am-5pm, Su 1-5pm. Last tour 4:15pm. Admission $4, seniors $3.50, ages 5-17 $2, families $12. Reserved tours available late Oct. to mid-May.)* In the 1780s, Allen, who forced the surrender of Fort Ticonderoga during the American Revolution and helped establish the state of Vermont, built his cabin in what is now the Winooski Valley Park.

Immortalized by ex-regulars Phish on their album *A Picture of Nectar,* **Nectar's,** 188 Main St. (658-4771), rocks with inexpensive food and nightly tunes (famous fries $2-4; no cover; open M-F 5:45am-2am, Sa-Su 7:30am-2am). Upstairs, **Club Metronome** (865-4563) ticks with live music (21+; cover varies).

Summer culture vultures won't want to miss the many festivities Burlington has to offer. The **Vermont Mozart Festival** (862-7352 or 800-639-9097) sends Bach, Beethoven, and Mozart to barns, farms, and meadows throughout the area July 11-August 1, 1999. From June 7-13, 1999, the **Discover Jazz Festival** (863-7992) features over 1000 international and Vermont musicians in both free and ticketed performances. The **Champlain Valley Folk Festival** (800-769-9176) entertains in early August. The **Flynn Theatre Box Office,** 153 Main St. (863-5966), handles sales for the Mozart and jazz performances (open M-F 10am-5pm, Sa 11am-4pm).

■ Near Burlington: Champlain Valley

Lake Champlain, a 100 mi. long lake between Vermont's Green Mountains and New York's Adirondacks, is often referred to as "Vermont's West Coast." **Lake Champlain Ferry** (864-9804), located on the dock at the bottom of King St., sails daily from Burlington to Port Kent, NY, and back. (1hr. Late June to Aug. 12-14 per day, 8am-7:30pm; mid-May to late June and Sept. to mid-Oct. 9 per day, 8am-6:35pm. $3.25, ages 6-12 $1.25, car $12.75.) The same company also sails from Grand Isle to Plattsburg, NY and 14 mi. south of Burlington from Charlotte, VT, to Essex, NY (either fare $2, ages 6-12 50¢, with car $6.75). Only the Grand Isle Ferry runs year-round.

Mt. Philo State Park (425-2390), 15 mi. south of Burlington on Rte. 7, offers pleasant camping and gorgeous views of the Champlain Valley; take the Vermont Transit bus from Burlington south along U.S. 7 toward Vergennes. (13 sites without hookups $11, 3 lean-tos $15. Entrance fee $2, ages 4-14 $1.50. Open mid-May to mid-Oct. daily 10am-sunset.) The marsh of the **Missisquoi National Wildlife Refuge** sits at the northern end of the lake near Swanton, VT. Also north of the lake, **Burton Island State Park** is accessible only by ferry from **Kill Kare State Park** (524-6353), 35 mi. north of Burlington and 3½ mi. southwest off U.S. 7 near St. Albans Bay (open late May to early Sept. daily 8:30am-6:30pm; $2; call for schedule). The campground has 17 tent sites ($13) and 26 lean-tos ($17; $4 per additional person). The state park on **Grand Isle** (372-4300), just off U.S. 2 north of Keeler Bay, also offers camping. (156 sites for 4 $13, $3 per additional person; 36 lean-tos $17/$4. Open mid-May to mid-Oct.)

∎ Middlebury

Unlike the many Vermont towns that seem to shy away from association with local colleges, Middlebury, "Vermont's Landmark College Town," welcomes the energy and culture stimulated by Middlebury College. The result is a traditional Vermont atmosphere tinged both with vitality and history.

PRACTICAL INFORMATION Middlebury stretches along U.S. 7, 42 mi. south of Burlington. **Vermont Transit** (388-4373) stops at the Exxon station, 16 Court St., west of Main St. (station open M-Sa 6am-9pm, Su 7am-9pm). Buses run to Burlington (1hr., 3 per day, $7.50); Rutland (1½hr., 3 per day, $7.50); Albany (3hr., 3 per day, $28); and Boston (6hr., 3 per day, $43). There is no public transportation in Middlebury, but the **Bike and Ski Touring Center,** 74 Main St. (388-6666), rents bikes and skis on the cheap (bikes as low as $15 per day and $50 per week; skis $10-15 per day). The staff at the **Addison County Chamber of Commerce,** 2 Court St. (388-7951; http://www.midvermont.com), in the historic Gamaliel Painter House, has area info (open M-F 9am-5pm; limited weekend hrs. in summer). **Post Office:** 10 Main St. (388-2681; open M-F 8am-5pm, Sa 8am-12:30pm). **ZIP code:** 05753. **Area code:** 802.

ACCOMMODATIONS AND CAMPGROUNDS Lodging with four walls and no mosquitoes does not come cheaply in Middlebury; prepare to trade an arm and a leg for an extended stay. The best budget accommodations are in the great outdoors. The new **Covered Bridge Home Hostel (HI-AYH),** 62 Seymour St. (388-0401) sits in a prime location for hiking, canoeing and kayaking next to the Green Mountain National Forest (6 beds $13-15). The **Sugar House Motor Inn** (388-2770), just north of Middlebury on Rte. 7, offers basic motel rooms with free local calls. (Singles $59-69; doubles $69-79; extra rollaway beds $15; prices jump to $90/$95 during fall foliage season and Middlebury graduation.) On the southern edge of Middlebury, the **Greystone Motel** (388-4935), 2 mi. south of the town center on Rte. 7, has 10 reasonably priced rooms (singles $57-60; doubles $67-70). Situated on a lake, **Branbury State Park** (247-5925), 7 mi. south on U.S. 7, then 4 mi. south on Rte. 53, is all abuzz with campers, picnickers, and water lovers. (40 sites $13. Lean-tos $17. Canoe rentals $5 per hr., $30 per day; paddleboats $5 per 30min. Open late May to mid-Oct.) **River's Bend Campground** (388-9092), 3 mi. north of Middlebury off Rte. 7 on the Pog Team Rd. in New Haven, is clean and appropriately named. (65 sites for 2 with water and electricity $20, river sites $24; $6 per additional adult. Showers 25¢ per 5min. Fishing, swimming, picnicking facilities $3. Canoe rental $6 per hr.)

FOOD AND NIGHTLIFE Middlebury's many fine restaurants cater chiefly to plump wallets, but the year-round presence of students ensures the survival of cheaper places. **Noonie's Deli** (388-0014), in the Marbleworks building just behind Main St., makes terrific sandwiches ($4-5) on homemade bread and follows up with fresh baked desserts (open daily 8am-8pm). A meal-to-go allows diners to eat overlooking the waterfall vista outside. Students flock to **Mister Up's** (388-6724), on Bakery Ln. just off Main St., for an impressively eclectic menu including sandwiches and hamburgers ($5-7) and an extensive salad bar ($7.50; open M-Sa 11:30am-midnight, Su 11am-midnight). **Amigos,** 4 Merchants Row (388-3624), befriends weary travelers with Mexican food ($5-12) and live local music 9:30pm-12:30am on summer Fridays and Saturdays. (Open M 11:30am-9pm, Tu-Sa 11:30am-10pm, Su 3-9pm; Sept.-May Tu-W 11:30am-9pm, Th-Sa 11:30am-9:30pm, Su 4-9pm. Bar open daily until 11pm.)

SIGHTS The **Vermont State Craft Center** (388-3177), at Frog Hollow, exhibits and sells the artistic productions of Vermonters (open M-Th 9:30am-5:30pm, F-Sa 9am-6pm, Su 11am-5pm). The nearby **Sheldon Museum,** 1 Park St. (388-2117), houses an extensive, sometimes macabre collection of Americana, including a set of teeth extracted in the 19th century. *(Open June-Oct. M-Sa 10am-5pm, occasionally Su 10am-4pm; Nov.-May M-F 10am-5pm. Guided tour $4, students and seniors $3.50, under 12 50¢. Self-guided tour of 1st fl. exhibition $2/$1.50/free.)* **Middlebury College** hosts cultural events; the architecturally striking concert hall in the college **Arts Center,** just outside of town, resonates with a terrific concert series. The campus **box office** (443-6433) has details on events sponsored by the college (open Sept.-May Tu-Sa 11am-4pm). Guided tours from the **Admissions Office** (443-3000), in Emma Willard Hall on S. Main St., showcase the campus. *(Tours Sept. to late May daily 10-11am and 2-3pm. Self-guided tour brochures available.)* The beer runs freely at the **Otter Creek Brewery,** 85 Exchange St. (800-473-0727), ¾ mi. north of town (tours daily at 1, 3, and 5pm). Fifteen miles east of the Middlebury College campus, the **Middlebury College Snow Bowl** (802-388-4356) entertains skiers with 15 trails and lifts.

■ Stowe

The village of Stowe winds gracefully up the side of Mt. Mansfield (Vermont's highest peak, at 4393 ft.). The town self-consciously fancies itself an American skiing hotspot on par with its ritzier European counterparts. Stowe scoffs at the idea of being a bargain, but behind the facade, travelers can find some unbeatable values.

PRACTICAL INFORMATION Stowe is 12 mi. north of I-89's Exit 10, which is 27 mi. southwest of Burlington. The ski slopes lie along **Rte. 108** northwest of Stowe. **Vermont Transit** (244-6943 or 800-451-3292; open daily 8am-8pm) only comes as close as the **Gateway Motel,** 73 S. Main St. (Rte. 100) in Waterbury, 10 mi. from Stowe. From there, **Peg's Pick-up DBA Stowe Taxi** (253-9433) will drive you to Stowe village (1 person $15, 2-3 $20, 4-6 $25). In winter, the **Stowe Trolley** (253-7585) runs on an irregular schedule between the important locations in the village. (In summer, 1¼hr. guided tours M, W, F 11am; $5. In winter, every 20min. 8-10am and 2-4:20pm; every hr. 11am-1pm and 5-10pm; $1, weekly pass $10.)

In addition to providing info on area attractions, the **Stowe Area Association** (253-7321 or 800-247-8693), on Main St., runs a free booking service for member hotels and restaurants. (Open M-F 9am-8pm, Sa 10am-6pm, Su 10am-5pm; late Apr. to early May closed Sa-Su.) **Post Office:** 105 Depot St. (253-7521), off Main St. (open M-F 7:15am-5pm, Sa 9am-noon). **ZIP code:** 05672. **Area code:** 802.

ACCOMMODATIONS, CAMPGROUNDS, AND FOOD At the base of Mt. Mansfield, **Mt. Mansfield Hostel** (253-4010), 7 mi. from town on Mountain Rd. (shuttles run to town during ski season), is Stowe's best lodging bargain by far. (48 beds $12-15; in ski season M-F $19, Sa-Su $24. Excellent breakfast $5, dinner $7; call ahead. Reserve by phone far in advance for ski and foliage seasons.) **Foster's Place** (253-9404), on Mountain Rd., offers dorm rooms with a lounge and a game room in a recently renovated school building. (Singles $20-30; $10 for a 2nd person; private baths $10 extra.)

Gold Brook Campground (253-7683), 1½ mi. south of the town center on Rte. 100, offers a camping experience without all that roughing-it business. (Showers, laundry, horseshoes, skateboard ramp. Tent sites for 2 $16, $4 per additional person, with hookup $20-27.) **Smuggler's Notch State Park,** 7248 Mountain Rd./Rte. 108 (253-4014), 8 mi. west of Stowe, keeps it simple with hot showers, tent sites, and lean-tos. (Sites for 4 $12, $3 per additional person up to 8; lean-tos $16/$4. Reservations recommended. Open late May to mid-Oct.)

One can join locals in the consumption of big deli sandwiches ($2-4) or an excellent seafood salad ($6 per lb.) at **Mac's Deli** (253-4576), inside the Stowe Grocery Store, S. Main St. In winter, they also serve piping hot soups ($2.25 per pint; open daily 7am-9pm). At the **Depot Street Malt Shoppe,** 57 Depot St. (253-4269), visitors enjoy classic diner fare and salivate over hot fudge sundaes in an artfully recreated 50s soda shop (meals $3-8; open daily 11am-9pm). The **Sunset Grille and Tap Room** (253-9281), on 140 Cottage Club Rd. off Mountain Rd., sells generous meals ($5-15) and a vast selection of domestic beers in a friendly, down-home barbecue restaurant/bar (open daily for dining 11:30am-midnight; bar 11:30am-2am).

HITTING THE SLOPES Stowe's ski offerings consist of the **Stowe Mountain Resort** (253-3000 or 800-253-4754) and **Smuggler's Notch** (664-1118 or 800-451-8752). At both areas lift tickets cost about $40-45 per day. Nearby, the hills are alive with the sound of the area's best cross-country skiing at the **Von Trapp Family Lodge,** Luce

Ben & Jerry: Two Men, One Dream, and Lots of Chunks

In 1978, Ben Cohen and Jerry Greenfield enrolled in a Penn State correspondence course in ice cream making, converted a gas station into their first shop, and launched themselves on the road to a double scoop success story. Today, **Ben and Jerry's Ice Cream Factory** (244-5641), a few mi. north of Waterbury on Rte. 100, is a cow-spotted mecca for ice cream lovers. *(Tours Nov.-May daily every 30min. 10am-5pm; June every 20min. 9am-5pm; July-Aug. every 10min. 9am-8pm; Sept.-Oct. every 15min. 9am-6pm. $2, seniors $1.75, under 13 free.)* On a 20min. tour of the facilities, you can taste the sweet success of the men who brought "Lemongrad" to Moscow and "Economic Chunk" to Wall Street. The tour tells the history of the operation and showcases the company's social consciousness.

Hill Rd. (253-8511), 2 mi. off Mountain Rd. Yes, it *is* the family from *The Sound of Music*, and it is divine. Don't stay here unless you have a rich uncle in Stowe—prices for lodging climb to $345 in the high season. There's no charge to visit, however. The lodge does offer fairly inexpensive rentals and lessons (trail fee $12; ski rentals $13; lessons $10-40 per hr.; discounts for kids). **A.J.'s Ski and Sports** (253-4593), at the base of Mountain Rd., rents snow equipment. *(Skis, boots, and poles: downhill $18 per day, 2 days $32; cross-country $12/$22. Snowboard and boots $22 per day. Discount with advance reservations. Open in summer daily 9am-6pm; in winter Su-Th 8am-8pm, F-Sa 8am-9pm.)*

In summer, Stowe's frenetic pace drops off—as do its prices. **Action Outfitters**, 2160 Mountain Rd. (253-7975), rents mountain bikes ($6 per hr., $14 per ½-day, $20 per day) and in-line skates ($6/$12/$18). *(Open in summer M-F 10am-5pm, Sa 9am-6pm, Su 9am-5pm; in winter daily 8am-6pm.)* **The Mountain Bike Shop** (253-7919 or 800-682-4534), on Mountain Rd. near Stowe Center, also rents bikes and in-line skates ($7 per hr., $16 for 4hr.; children $5/$12; helmet included), as well as cross-country skis ($8 per ½-day, $12 per day; children $6/$10) and snowshoes ($8/$12). *(Open in summer M-Th 10am-5pm, F 10am-6pm, Sa 9am-6pm, Su 9am-5pm; in winter daily 9am-5pm.)* Stowe's 5½ mi. **asphalt recreation path,** perfect for cross-country skiing in the winter and biking, skating, or strolling in the summer, runs parallel to the Mountain Road's ascent via the path behind A.J.'s Ski and Sports.

Fly fisherfolk should head to the **Fly Rod Shop** (253-7346 or 800-5-FLY-ROD/535-9763), 3 mi. south of Stowe on Rte. 100, to pick up the necessary fishing licenses (3-day non-resident license $18, season $35) and rent fly rods and reels for $10 per day. *(Open Apr.-Oct. M-F 9am-6pm, Sa 9am-5pm, Su 10am-4pm; after fishing season, M-F 9am-5pm, Sa 9am-4pm, Su 10am-4pm.)* The owner can show you how to tie a fly, or you can stick around for free fly-fishing classes on the shop's own pond. To canoe on the nearby Lamoille River, **Umiak** (253-2317), Rte. 100, 1 mi. south of Stowe Center, can help. *(Under 8 $15. Rental and transportation to the river included. Open Apr.-Oct. daily 9am-6pm; winter hrs. vary. Sport kayaks $15/$25; canoes $25/$35.)* The store (named after a unique type of kayak used by the Inuit) rents regular ol' kayaks and canoes in the summer and offers a full-day river trip for $25. Located in a rustic red barn, **Topnotch Stowe**, 4000 Mountain Rd. (253-6433), offers 1hr. horseback-riding tours from late May through September (tours daily 11am, 1, and 3pm; $25; reservations required).

■ Near Stowe: Route 100

Still hungry? If you haven't already made yourself sick on **Ben & Jerry's** ice cream (see above), Rte. 100 features a veritable food fiesta south of Stowe. Begin at Ben & Jerry's and drive north on Rte. 100 towards Stowe. Your first stop is the **Green Mountain Chocolate Company** (244-1139) and **Cabot Annex Store** (244-6334), home to rich chocolate truffles and Vermont's best cheddar (open daily 9am-6pm). The samples are free. Empty room in your stomach is important for your next stop, the **Cold Hollow Cider Mill** (244-8771; call for a schedule of cider making). In addition to the potent beverage, cider spin-offs on sale include jelly and donuts (35¢; open daily 8am-6pm). Finally, maple is everywhere at the **Stowe Maple Products** (253-2508) maple museum and candy kitchen. March and April is syrup season, but they sell the goods all year (open daily 8am-6pm).

■ White River Junction

Named for its location at the confluence of the White and Connecticut Rivers, White River Junction was once the focus of railroad transportation in the northeastern U.S. Today, near the intersection of I-89 and I-91, the Junction preserves its status as a travel hub by serving as the bus center for most of Vermont. **Vermont Transit** (295-3011 or 800-552-8737; office open daily 7am-9:30pm), on U.S. 5, behind the Mobil station 1 mi. south of downtown White River Junction, makes connections to New York City (8hr., 3-4 per day, $58); Burlington (2hr., 5 per day, $14.50); Montréal (5hr., 5 per day, $39-43); and smaller centers on a less regular basis. **Amtrak** (295-7160 or 800-872-7245; office open daily 9am-noon and 5-7pm), on Railroad Rd. off N. Main St., rockets once per day to New York (7½hr., $55); Essex Junction (near Burlington; 2hr., $13); Montréal (4½hr., $27); and Philadelphia (9hr., $65-72).

Virtually the only choice for lodging is the old-style **Hotel Coolidge (HI-AYH),** 17 S. Main St. (295-3118 or 800-622-1124), across the road from the retired Boston and Maine steam engine. From the bus station, walk to the right on U.S. 5 and down the hill past two stop lights (1 mi.) into town. Renamed in honor of its frequent guest, "Silent Cal" Coolidge's pop, the Coolidge boasts a dorm-style hostel-ette and neatly kept rooms at moderate prices. (26 hostel beds with shared bath $18, nonmembers $21; economy singles from $39; doubles from $49.) For a quick bite, the **Polkadot Restaurant,** 1 N. Main St. (295-9722), is a local favorite. This diner cooks up sandwiches ($2-5) and full sit-down meals. (Pork chop plate $6. Open M 5am-2pm, Tu-Su 5am-7pm.)

If you must stay here, the **info booth,** at the intersection of Sykes and U.S. 5 off I-89 and I-91 across from the bus station, will apprise you of any possible distractions (open late June to mid-Oct. daily 9am-4pm; otherwise sporadically Sa-Su). The **Upper Valley Chamber of Commerce,** 61 Old River Rd. (295-6200), about 1 mi. south of town off of U.S. 4, has area info (generally open Tu and Th morning). **Post Office:** 10 Sykes Ave. (296-3246; open M-F 7:30am-5pm, Sa 7:30am-noon). **ZIP code:** 05001. **Area code:** 802.

■ Brattleboro

Southeast Vermont is often accused of living too much in its colonial past, but the Brattleboro of today seems to be striking an independence quite unlike that struck by its revolutionary former occupants. Visitors feel right at home in this town, where the vibes are groovy and the organic produce is even better. The gay and lesbian, New Age, and more conservative elements of this town combine to create a tolerant and laid-back atmosphere. Nature worship peaks in the fall foliage season, when tourists invade the area to take part in the ultimate earth fest.

PRACTICAL INFORMATION The **Amtrak** (254-2301) Montrealer train from New York and Springfield, MA, stops in Brattleboro behind the museum on Vernon St. Trains depart once daily for Montréal (6hr., $39); New York (6hr., $46-51); and Washington, D.C. (9¾hr., $79). **Greyhound** and **Vermont Transit** (254-6066) roll into town at the parking lot behind the Citgo station off Exit 3 on I-91, on Putney Rd. (open M-F 8am-4pm, Sa-Su open for departures 8am-3:20pm). Buses run to New York (5hr., 4 per day, $37-39); Burlington (3½hr., 3 per day, $26.50); Montréal (6½hr., 2 per day, $55); and Boston (3hr., 2 per day, $22). To get downtown from the bus station, take the infrequent **Brattleboro Town Bus** (257-1761), which runs on Putney Rd. to Main St. (M-F 6:30am-6pm; fare 75¢, children 25¢). The **Chamber of Commerce,** 180 Main St. (254-4565; open M-F 8:30am-5pm) provides the *Brattleboro Main Street Walking Tour* and a detailed town map. In the summer and foliage seasons, an **info booth** (257-1112), on the Town Common off Putney Rd., operates from 9am-5pm (sometimes closed Tu). **Post Office:** 204 Main St. (254-4110; open M-F 8am-5pm, Sa 8am-noon). **ZIP code:** 05301. **Area code:** 802.

ACCOMMODATIONS AND CAMPGROUNDS Economy lodgings such as **Super 8** and **Motel 6** proliferate on Rte. 9 (singles generally $39-45). Renovated to mimic 1930s style, the Art Deco **Latchis Hotel**, 50 Main St. (254-6300), at Flat St., rents decent rooms in an unbeatable location. (Singles $55-85; doubles $62-120; rates slightly higher during foliage season and holidays. Reservations recommended during foliage season and the summer.) The inexpensive rooms of the **Molly Stark Motel** (254-2440), about 4 mi. west on Rte. 9, are a welcome alternative to the monotony of economy motel chains (singles $44-50; doubles $50-65). For those short on cash, the **Vagabond Hostel (HI-AYH)** (874-4096), 25 mi. north on Rte. 30, offers decent bunks and extensive facilities for a reasonable price. The hostel operates as a ski lodge in the winter. (Late May-Oct. $13, nonmembers $15; late Dec.-Mar. $22. 84 bunks, game room, kitchen. Group rates and meal plans available.) **Fort Dummer State Park** (254-2610) is 2 mi. south of town on U.S. 5; turn left on Fairground Ave. just before the I-91 interchange, then right on S. Main St. until you hit the park. Making no claims about its intelligence, this park was actually named for the first white settlement in Vermont and offers campsites with fireplaces, picnic tables, bathroom facilities, hiking trails, a playground, and a lean-to with wheelchair access. (51 sites. $11; $3 per additional person; 10 lean-tos $15/$4. Day use of park $2, children $1.50. Firewood $2 per armload. Hot showers 25¢ per 5min. $5 non-refundable reservation fee. Open late May to early Sept.) **Molly Stark State Park** (464-5460), 15 mi. west of town on Rte. 9, provides the same facilities for the same prices. In addition, this park has RV sites without hookups for $11. (Open late May to mid-Oct.)

FOOD AND NIGHTLIFE North of town, across Putney Rd. from the Connecticut River Safari, the **Marina Restaurant** (257-7563) overlooks the West River, offering a cool breeze and a beautiful view. (Open in summer M-Sa 11:30am-10pm, Su 11am-2pm and 2:30-6pm. Live music Su 3-7pm. Kitchen closed late Oct. to mid-Mar. M-Tu.) During the summer, come early to get an outside table. If you try the shrimp and chip basket ($5.75) or the garden burger ($5.25), you'll see why the locals rave. The **Backside Café**, 24 High St. (257-5056), inside the Mid-town Mall, serves delicious food in an artsy loft with rooftop dining. (Open M 7:30am-3:30pm, Tu-Th 7:30am-4pm, F 7:30am-4pm and 5-9pm, Sa 8am-3pm, Su 9am-3pm.) Breakfast features farm-fresh eggs cooked to perfection. At the **Latchis Grille**, 6 Flat St. (254-4747), next to the Latchis Hotel, patrons dine in inexpensive elegance and sample beer brewed on the premises by **Windham Brewery.** (Lunch and dinner $6-19. 7 oz. beer sampler $2. Open M and W-Th 5:30-9:30pm, F-Su noon-4pm and 5:30-9:30pm.) For locally grown fruits, vegetables, and cider, the **farmers markets** (254-9567), on the Town Common on Main St. (open mid-June to mid-Sept. W 10am-2pm); and on Western Ave. near the Creamery Bridge (open mid-May to mid-Oct. Sa 9am-2pm), are it. At night, rock, blues, R&B, and reggae tunnel through the **Mole's Eye Café**, 4 High St. (257-0771), at Main St. (Live music 1st W of every month, F-Sa 9pm. Cover F-Sa $3-4. Open M-F 11:30am-1am, Sa 4pm-1am.)

SIGHTS Brattleboro chills at the confluence of the West and Connecticut Rivers, both of which can be explored by **canoe.** Rentals are available at **Vermont Canoe Touring Center** (257-5008), on Putney Rd. just across the West River Bridge. *(2hr. min. rental $10, $15 per ½-day, $25 per day. Open late May to early Sept. daily 9am-dusk; otherwise call for reservations.)* The **Brattleboro Museum and Art Center** (257-0124) resides in the old Union Railroad Station at the lower end of Main St. *(Open mid-May to Oct. Tu-Su noon-6pm. $3, students and seniors $2, under 18 free.)* The **Gallery Walk** is a free walking tour of Brattleboro's plentiful art galleries on the first Friday of every month.

Massachusetts

Massachusetts regards itself, with some justification, as the intellectual center of the nation. From the 1636 establishment of Harvard, the oldest university in America, Massachusetts has attracted countless intellectuals and *literati*. This little state also offers a large variety of cultural and scenic attractions. Boston, the revolutionary "cradle of liberty," has become an ethnically diverse urban center. Resplendent during the fall foliage season, the Berkshire Mountains fill western Massachusetts with a charm that attracts thousands of visitors. The seaside areas from Nantucket to Northern Bristol feature the stark oceanic beauty that first attracted settlers to the North American shore.

PRACTICAL INFORMATION

Capital: Boston.
Visitor Info: Office of Travel and Tourism, 100 Cambridge St., Boston 02202 (617-727-3201 or 800-447-6277 for guides; http://www.mass-vacation.com). Offers a complimentary, comprehensive *Getaway Guide*. Open M-F 8:45am-5pm.
Emergency: 911.
Time Zone: Eastern. **Postal Abbreviation:** MA.
Sales Tax: 5%; 0% on clothing (if item is less than $200) and pre-packaged food.

EASTERN MASSACHUSETTS

■ Boston

As one of the United States's oldest cities, Boston has deep roots in early America and a host of memorials and monuments to prove it. A jam-packed tour of revolutionary landmarks and historic neighborhoods, the Freedom Trail meanders through downtown Boston. The Black Heritage Trail tells another story about this city, which, despite an outspoken abolitionist history, has been torn by ethnic and racial controversy. Irish, East Asian, Portuguese, and African-American communities have found homes throughout the city, creating a sometimes uneasy cultural mosaic. Meanwhile, a seasonal population of 100,000 college students tugs the average age in Boston into the mid-twenties. While most residents have a less Boston-centric view of the cosmos than Paul McCartney, who proclaimed the city "the hub of the universe," few would deny that Boston is an intriguing microcosm of the American melting pot.

ORIENTATION AND PRACTICAL INFORMATION

Boston owes its layout as much to the clomping of colonial cows as to urban designers. Avoid driving—the public transportation system is excellent, parking is expensive, and Boston drivers are maniacal. Several outlying T stops offer park-and-ride services. The Quincy Center T stop charges $1 per day. If you do choose to drive, be defensive and alert; Boston's pedestrians can be as aggressive as its drivers. Finally, to avoid getting lost in Boston's labyrinth, ask for detailed directions wherever you go.

I-95 cuts a wide arc around the metro area before heading north to Maine, and south to Providence, RI. **I-93** plows through downtown and separates the North End from downtown in the process; this faded green monolith is slated to be replaced by an underground tunnel, costing $12 billion and affectionately labelled the "Big Dig." The **Massachusetts Turnpike (I-90)** charges tolls from western Massachusetts all the way to its junction with I-93 in downtown Boston.

Let's Go's compendium, *The Unofficial Guide to Life at Harvard* ($10), has the inside scoop and up-to-date listings for Boston/Cambridge area restaurants, history, entertainment, sights, transportation and services. Inquire at bookstores in Harvard Sq. (see **Cambridge**, p. 101).

Boston

ACCOMMODATIONS

A Back Bay Summer Hostel
B Garden Halls Residence
C Irish Embassy Hostel
D Youth Hostel (HI)

N

250 meters

1/4 mile

TO HARBOR ISLANDS

TO LOGAN AIRPORT

Sumner Tunnel

Callahan Tunnel

Inner Harbor

Northern Ave.

New England Aquarium

Children's Museum

Commercial St.

NORTH END

Old South Meeting House

Old Corner Bookstore

Freedom Trail

Paul Revere House

Fitzgerald Expressway

Charlestown Br.

North Station

I-93

Fleet Center

SCIENCE PARK

Museum of Science

Charles River Park

Blossom St.

CAMBRIDGE

M.I.T.

Charles River

Longfellow Br.

Embankment Rd.

Storrow Drive

Harvard Br.

Massachusetts Ave.

TO HARVARD

TO I-90

Mass. Genl. Hospital

Cambridge St.

Charles St.

BEACON HILL

Pinckney St.

Mt. Vernon St.

Joy St.

Bowdoin St.

Somerset St.

GOVERNMENT CENTER

State House

Robert Gould Shaw & 54th Regiment Memorial

Boston Common

Beacon St.

Park St.

PARK ST.

Freedom Trail

Tremont St.

Charles St.

Arlington St.

ARLINGTON

Marlborough St.

BACK BAY

Commonwealth Ave.

Newbury St.

Dartmouth St.

Clarendon St.

Berkeley St.

Exeter St.

Fairfield St.

Gloucester St.

Hereford St.

Beacon St.

Boylston St.

COPLEY SQUARE

Boston Public Library

Trinity Church

Hancock Tower

COPLEY

BACK BAY

HYNES

Huntington Ave.

Columbus Avenue

PRUDENTIAL CENTER

Boylston St.

Tremont St.

Shawmut Ave.

Herald St.

CHINATOWN

CHINA-TOWN

Essex St.

Washington St.

NE MEDICAL CENTER

South Point Channel

Summer St.

Atlantic Ave.

South Station (Buses and Trains)

SOUTH STATION

Fort Point Channel

DOWNTOWN CROSSING

AQUARIUM

STATE

State St.

Old State House

Old South Church

Old North Church

Milk St.

King's Chapel & Burying Ground

Old Granary Burying Ground

GOVT CENTER

HAYMARKET

BOWDOIN

NORTH STATION

I-93

I-90

Airport: Logan International (561-1800 or 800-235-6426), in East Boston. Easily accessible by public transport. The free **Massport Shuttle** connects all terminals with the "Airport" T stop on the blue line. **City Transportation** (596-1177) runs shuttle buses between Logan and major downtown hotels (service daily every 30min. 6:30am-11pm; $7.50 one-way). A **water shuttle** (330-8680) provides a more scenic 7min. journey to the downtown area. The shuttle runs from the airport to Rowes Wharf near the New England Aquarium and many hotels ($8, seniors $4, under 12 free; purchase tickets on board). A **taxi** to downtown costs $15-20.

Trains: Amtrak (345-7442 or 800-872-7245), in South Station, at Atlantic Ave. and Summer St. T: South Station. Frequent daily service to: New York City (5hr., $44-65); Washington, D.C. (9hr., $62-87); Philadelphia (7hr., $53-80); and Baltimore (8½hr., $62-87). Station open daily 5:45am-9:30pm.

Buses: The modern **South Station** bus terminal (T: South Station), right next to the train station, is used by several bus companies. Station open 24hr. **Greyhound,** 800-231-2222. To: New York City (4½hr., 20 per day, $30); Washington, D.C. (9½hr., 10 per day, $41); Philadelphia (7hr., 15 per day, $44); and Baltimore (9hr., 9 per day, $41). **Vermont Transit** (802-862-9671), administered by Greyhound, buses north to ME, NH, VT, and Montreal. To: Burlington, VT (5hr., 4 per day, $45), Portland, ME (2½hr., 8 per day, $13), and Montréal (8hr., 6 per day, $55). **Bonanza** (800-556-3815) provides frequent daily service to Providence ($8.75), Newport ($14.50), and Woods Hole ($14.50). **Plymouth & Brockton** (508-746-0378) travels between South Station and Cape Cod. Ride to Provincetown (4hr., 5 per day, $21). **Peter Pan,** 700 Atlantic Ave. (800-237-8747), across from South Station, runs to Springfield (10 per day, $10); Albany (5 per day, $25); and very frequently to New York City ($30).

Ferries: Bay State Cruises (457-1428) departs from the Commonwealth Pier on Northern Ave. T: South Station. Cruises May to early Sept. leave for Provincetown at 9am ($30 same-day round-trip). **Boston Harbor Cruises** (723-7800) sail from Long Wharf; ticket sales in a red building across from the Marriot Hotel. T: Aquarium. Travel to George's Island early May to mid-Oct. daily on the hr. 10am-5pm ($7.50 round-trip, seniors $6.50, under 12 $5.50). Whale-watching tours and water taxis also sometimes available. Call for details.

Public Transportation: Massachusetts Bay Transportation Authority (MBTA) (722-3200 or 800-392-6100). The **subway** system, known as the **T,** consists of the Red (2 lines split at JFK/UMass); Green (splits into 4 lines B,C,D, and E); Blue; and Orange Lines. Maps available at info centers and T stops. Lines run daily 5:30am-12:30am. Fare 85¢, seniors 20¢, ages 5-11 40¢. Some automated T entrances in outlying areas require tokens but don't sell them. **MBTA Bus** service covers the city and suburbs more closely than the subway. Fare, generally 60¢, may vary for outlying destinations. Bus schedules available at various train stations, including Park St. and Harvard Sq. The **MBTA Commuter Rail** reaches suburbs and the North Shore, leaving from North Station, Porter Sq., and South Station T stops. A **"T passport,"** sold at the visitors center, offers discounts at local businesses and unlimited travel on all subway and bus lines and some commuter rail zones; only worthwhile for frequent users of public transportation. 1-day pass $5, 3-day $9, 7-day $18.

Taxis: Checker Taxi, 536-7000. $1.50 base fare, $2.10 per mi. **Boston Cab,** 262-2227. Base fare $1.50, $2.10 per mi.

Car Rental: Dollar Rent-a-Car (634-0006 or 800-800-4000), in Logan Airport. T: Airport. Must be 21 with major credit card. Under 25 $20 surcharge per day. AAA discount. Open 24hr. Drivers under 21 can call **Merchants Rent-a-Car,** 163 Adams St. (356-5656), in Braintree.

Bike Rental: Community Bike Shop, 496 Tremont St. (542-8623). T: NE Medical Center. $5 per hr., $20 per 24hr., $75 per week. Major credit card needed. Open M-F 10am-8pm, Sa 10am-6pm, Su noon-5pm; Oct.-Feb. M-Sa 10am-6pm.

Visitor Info: Boston Convention and Visitors Bureau, 2 Copley Pl., #105 (536-4100 or 888-733-2678; http://www.bostonusa.com), dispenses a $5.25 package that includes coupon books and *The Official Guidebook to Boston.* **Boston Common Info Center,** 147 Tremont St., Boston Common. T: Park St., green line. A good place to start a tour of the city. Free maps and brochures of Boston, including a Freedom Trail map. Open M-Sa 8:30am-5pm, Su 9am-5pm. **National Historical**

Park Visitor's Center, 15 State St. (242-5642). T: State. Info on historic sights, tours, and lodging. Open daily 9am-6pm; early Sept. to May 9am-5pm. Free 1½hr. walking tours M-F 10am and 2pm, Sa-Su 10am-2pm on the hr.
Hotlines: Rape Hotline, 492-7273. **Alcohol and Drug Hotline,** 445-1500. Both 24hr.
Gay and Lesbian Helpline, 267-9001. Operates M 6-11pm, Tu-Th 4-11pm, F 4-8:30pm, Sa 6-8:30pm, Su 6-10pm.
Post Office: 25 Dorchester Ave. (654-5327). Open 24hr. **ZIP code:** 02205. **Area code:** 617.

ACCOMMODATIONS

Cheap accommodations are hard to come by in Boston. In September, Boston fills with parents depositing their college-bound children; in June, parents help remove their graduated, unemployment-bound offspring. Room prices are highest during these months, but are elevated from roughly late May through October. Reserve a room 6 months to a year in advance during those times. **Boston Reservations,** 1643 Beacon St., #23, Waban, 02168 (332-4199), can arrange reservations at most Boston-area hotels and B&B's for a $5 processing fee (open M-F 9am-5pm). Room tax in Boston is 9.7%, Reservations are highly recommended for all Boston accommodations.

⊛**Hostelling International-Boston (HI-AYH),** 12 Hemenway St. (536-9455). T: Hynes/ICA. This cheery, colorful hostel has clean, comfortable rooms with shared baths. Great location near Copley Sq. and Newbury St. Lockers, kitchens, laundry, and free email access. 200 beds. Activities nightly. $19, nonmembers $22; private rooms $54-60. Linen deposit $10. Check-in after noon. Check-out 11am. Wheelchair access.

Back Bay Summer Hostel (HI-AYH), 512 Beacon St. (353-3294), in Boston University's Danielsen Hall. T: Hynes/ICA. Located in a pretty section of town, Back Bay picks up overflow from its HI sister. 200 beds. $19, nonmembers $22, including linen. Check-in after noon. Check-out 11am. All phone correspondence should be done through HI-Boston (above). Open June 10-Aug. 20.

Irish Embassy Hostel, 232 Friend St. (973-4841), above the Irish Embassy Pub. T: North Station. Small, clean, comfortable dorm rooms. A lively place to stay and make friends. Free buffet Su, Tu, and Th 8pm. In summer, hostelers take advantage of the free public pool nearby. Common area with TV, kitchen, and laundry. 49 beds $15; 1 double $30. Lockers free; bring your own padlock. Linen free. No sleeping bags. Check-in 9am-9pm; otherwise ask in the pub. Reception 24hr.

Garden Halls Residences, 260 Commonwealth Ave. (267-0079), in Back Bay. T: Copley. The rooms in these Boston brownstones are clean, bright, and attractively furnished. Outstanding location a few blocks from Copley Sq. Vending machines, TV/VCR, laundry, microwaves, and linen service. Singles, doubles, triples, and quads; some private baths. $285 per week. 7-day min. stay. Breakfast and dinner included. Open June-Aug.

Greater Boston YMCA, 316 Huntington Ave. (536-7800). Down the street from Symphony Hall on Mass. Ave. T: Northeastern. Friendly atmosphere, with access to cafeteria, pool, and recreational facilities. Most rooms are plain singles. 90 rooms available for all June 21-Sept. 5; otherwise, limited rooms for men only. Most have shared hall bathrooms; a few have private baths. With HI-AYH ID singles $35, doubles $50; nonmembers $39/$60. Breakfast included. Key deposit $5. Reception 24hr. Must be 18 with ID. Check-out 11am. Wheelchair access.

Anthony's Town House, 1085 Beacon St. (566-3972), Brookline. T: Hawes, green line-C. Very convenient to T stop. 12 ornately furnished rooms with cable and shared bath for 20 guests, who range from trim professionals to scruffy backpackers. Family-operated with a friendly atmosphere. Singles and doubles $35-75; mid-Nov. to mid-Mar. $5 less. Ask about off-season weekly rates and student discounts.

The Farrington Inn, 23 Farrington Ave. (787-1860 or 800-767-5337), Allston Station. T: Harvard Ave. on green line-B, or bus #66. Located 10min. from downtown by public transit, near many pubs and restaurants. Functional rooms with local phone, parking, and breakfast. Shared baths. Singles $40-50, doubles $50-70. Stylish 2-4-bedroom apartments with living room and kitchen available ($100-200).

FOOD

Boston ain't called **Beantown** for nothing. You can sample the real thing at **Durgin Park,** 340 Faneuil Hall Marketplace (227-2038; T: Government Center). Durgin was serving Yankee cuisine in Faneuil Hall back in 1827 (see **Sights,** below), long before the tourists arrived, and maintains its integrity with such delights as Indian pudding ($3) and Yankee pot roast ($8). Durgin Park's downstairs **Oyster Bar** highlights another Boston specialty with frequent seafood specials, including a modest lobster dinner for around $10. The city's celebrated seafood may be found in numerous seafood restaurants (mostly expensive) lining Boston Harbor by the wharf.

Beyond seafood and baked beans, Boston dishes out an impressive variety of international cuisines. The scent of garlic filters through the **North End** (T: Haymarket), where an endless array of Italian groceries, bakeries, cafes, and restaurants line Hanover and Salem St. For top-flight *tiramisù* ($3) and cappuccino ($2.50), slip into the nostalgic **Café Vittoria,** 294 Hanover St. (227-7606; open daily 8am-12:30am).

Chinese Fu dogs guard the entrance to **Chinatown** and watch over the countless delectable restaurants packed in behind the gates (T: Chinatown). It's easier to walk through the crowded streets, but if you're driving, Kneeland and Washington St. are two main arteries. A Sunday brunch of *Dim Sum* ("to point to the heart's desire") is an inexpensive Chinese tradition; try **The China Pearl,** 9 Tyler St. (426-4338), for a good variety (around $2-5 each; Dim Sum Su 8:30am-3pm). At the open-air stalls of **Haymarket,** vendors hawk fresh produce, fish, fruits, cheeses, and pig's eyes at well below supermarket prices. Get there early for the good stuff (open F-Sa dawn-dusk; T: Government Center or Haymarket). Just up Congress St. from Haymarket, the restored **Quincy Market** houses a cornucopia of food booths from local and national chains peddling interesting but overpriced fare.

- ◉**Addis Red Sea,** 544 Tremont St. (426-8727). T: Back Bay. Walk 5 blocks south on Clarendon St. from the T stop, then turn left on Tremont (10min. walk). Boston's best Ethiopian cuisine. The *mesob* (woven table) will soon groan under the colossal platters piled with marvelous mush and the incredible *injera* (flatbread) used to scoop it up. Most entrees $8-9, 5-dish communal platters around $12. Open M-Th 5-11pm, F 5pm-midnight, Sa noon-midnight, Su noon-10:30pm.
- ◉**Pho Pasteur,** 8 Kneeland St. (451-0247). T: Chinatown. Exit T on Washington St., turn left, walk 2 blocks, then turn left on Kneeland. Ridiculously good, *huge* bowls of *pho* (traditional Vietnamese noodle soup) and stir-fry for cheap prices ($4.50-5.50). The flavorful dishes and rich chatter of the multi-ethnic crowd more than make up for the bare, mirror-lined decor. Also at 682 Washington St., 35 Dunster St. in Harvard Sq., and on Beacon St. Open Su-Th 8am-7:45pm, F-Sa 8am-9pm.
- ◉**No Name,** 15 Fish Pier (338-7539), on the waterfront. T: South Station. Take the free shuttle bus on Summer St. in front of the federal bank building to the World Trade Center; then it's a 5min. walk. This hole-in-the-pier restaurant has been serving up some of the freshest fried seafood in Boston since 1917; bigshots like the Kennedys swear by it. The harbor view allows you to watch tomorrow's dinner emerging from the boats. Entrees $8-15. Open M-Sa 11am-10pm, Su 11am-9pm.
- **Bob the Chef's,** 604 Columbus Ave. (536-6204). T: Mass. Ave. From the T, turn right on Mass. Ave. and right onto Columbus Ave. Southern food that's unchallenged in Boston. Smokin' sweet potato pie, fried fish, chicken livers, corn bread, and famed "glorifried" chicken have soul to spare. Live jazz Th-Sa 7:30pm-midnight (cover $2). Entrees $6-14. Open Tu-W 11:30am-10pm, Th-Sa 5pm-midnight, Su 11am-9pm.
- **Grand Chau Chow,** 41-45 Beach St. (292-5166), in Chinatown. T: Chinatown. Follow Washington St. to Beach St. and turn left. A primarily local clientele dines on some of the best Chinese food in Boston, between marble walls and stacked tanks rife with displaced deep-sea dwellers. The menu includes over 300 well-sized entrees, averaging $4-10. Open daily 10am-2am.
- **La Famiglia Giorgio's,** 112 Salem St. (367-6711), in the North End. T: Haymarket. Notorious for serving 2 meals: the one you eat in the restaurant and the one you take home. Portions are enormous and tasty. Vegetarians have boundless options, including a towering tribute to eggplant. Entrees $8-18; purchase of an entree per person required. Open M-Sa 11am-10:30pm, Su noon-10:30pm.

Trident Booksellers and Café, 338 Newbury St. (267-8688). T: Hynes/ICA. A parade of vegetables manifest themselves throughout the menu, in a variety of guises. Standards like the veggie burger are supplemented with the more creative Tibetan dumplings, Lautrec's Lasagna, and delicious portabello mushroom sandwich. Entrees $4-11. Open daily 9am-midnight.

SIGHTS

The Freedom Trail

A great introduction to Boston's history lies along the red-painted line of the Freedom Trail (FT), a 2½ mi. path through downtown Boston that passes many of the city's historic landmarks. Even on a trail dedicated to the land of the free, some sights charge admission; bring some money if you're bent on doing the whole thing. Starting at their **visitors center,** 15 State St. (242-5642), the National Park Service offers free guided tours of the trail's free attractions. *(Open daily June to early Sept. 9am-6pm; off-season 9am-5pm. Tours daily in summer on the hr. 10am-3pm.)*

The Freedom Trail begins at another **visitors center,** in **Boston Common** (T: Park St.). You can pick up maps here, in varying degrees of detail. (Open M-Sa 8:30am-5pm, Su 9am-5pm.) The FT runs uphill to the **Robert Gould Shaw and 54th Regiment Memorial,** on Beacon St. The memorial honors the first black regiment of the Union Army in the American Civil War and their Bostonian leader, all made famous by the movie *Glory.* The trail then crosses the street to the magnificent and ornate **State House** (727-3676; free tours M-F 10am-3:30pm; open M-F 9am-5pm). Proceeding to the **Park St. Church** (523-3383), the trail then passes the **Old Granary Burial Ground** on the way to **King's Chapel and Burial Ground** (523-1749), on Tremont St., Boston's oldest Anglican church. *(Open M and F-Sa 9:30am-4pm, Tu and Th 11:30am-1pm. Classical music recitals Tu 12:15pm. Free tours by reservation.)* The Chapel housed a congregation as early as 1688; more recently, the cemetery has come to inter the earthly remains of Governor William Bradford and William Dawes.

The **Old South Meeting House** (482-6439) was the site of the pre-party get together that set the mood for the **Boston Tea Party.** Formerly the seat of British government in Boston, the **Old State House** (720-3290) now serves as a museum and the next stop on the trail. *(Open daily Apr.-Sept. 9am-5pm; Oct.-Mar. 10am-4pm. $3, students and seniors $2, ages 6-18 $1.)* The Trail continues past the site of the **Boston Massacre** and through **Faneuil Hall,** a former meeting hall and current mega-mall where the National Park Service operates a desk and conducts talks in the upstairs Great Hall. *(Open daily 9am-5pm. Talks every 30min. 9:30am-4:30pm. Stores open M-Sa 10am-9pm, Su noon-6pm.)* As you head into the North End, the **Paul Revere House** (523-1676) is the next landmark on the path. *(Open daily in summer 9:30am-5:15pm; Nov. to mid-Apr. 9:30am-4:15pm; Jan.-Mar. closed M. $2.50, students and seniors $2, ages 5-17 $1.)* The **Old North Church** (523-6676) follows (open daily 9am-5pm; Su services 9, 11am, and 4pm; free tours on request). **Copp's Hill Burial Ground** provides a resting place for numerous colonial Bostonians and a nice view of the Old North Church. Nearing its end, the FT heads over the Charlestown Bridge to the newly renovated **U.S.S. Constitution** (426-1812). *(Open daily 9am-6pm; Sept.-May 10am-4pm.)* The Navy gives free tours 9:30am-3:50pm. The final stop on the trail, the **Bunker Hill Monument** (242-5641), isn't on loan from Washington. *(Open daily 9am-4:30pm.)* The fraudulent obelisk is actually on Breed's Hill, the site of colonial fortification during the battle; Bunker Hill is about ½ mi. away. A grand view of the city awaits those willing to climb the 294 steps to the top. To return to Boston, follow the FT back over the bridge, or hop on a **water taxi** from one of the piers near the *Constitution* (water taxis every 30min. 6:30am-8:15pm; fare $1).

Downtown

In 1634, early inhabitants designated the **Boston Common** (T: Park St.), now bounded by Tremont, Boylston, Charles, Beacon, and Park St., as a place to let their cattle graze. These days, street vendors, not cows, live off the fat of this land. Though bustling in the daytime, *the Common is dangerous at night—don't walk alone here after dark.* Across from the Common on Charles St., the title characters from the children's book *Make Way for Ducklings* (hallowed in bronze) point the way to the

> ### Wicked Pissah!
>
> For many visitors to the Massachusetts area ("foreigners"), having to deal with the locals strange vocabulary and even more esoteric pronounciation can be difficult. A "bubblah," for example, is a public drinking fountain. A "frappe" is ice cream and milk, or a milkshake; the word is something many people find "wee-id" because it's not normal. People looking for the subway need "the T," but those with cars will have to deal with "Mass.-ave.," "Comm.-ave.," and the Big Dig. Everyone "shoe-ah" hopes guests have a good time, and reminds them to catch a Sox game at Fenway "Pahk" some "Saddadee" afternoon.

Public Gardens, where peddle-powered **Swan Boats** (522-1966; T: Arlington) glide around a quiet pond lined with shady willows. *(Swan Boats available daily mid-Apr. to mid-June 10am-4pm; mid-June to early Sept. 10am-5pm; early Sept. to mid-Sept. M-F noon-4pm, Sa-Su 10am-4pm. $1.75, under 13 95¢.)* Winter brings ice skating.

The city's neighborhoods cluster in a loose circle around the Common and Gardens. Directly above the Common lies **Beacon Hill,** an exclusive residential neighborhood originally settled by the Puritans. Significantly smaller today than when the Puritans resided here, the Hill donated tons of earth to fill in the marshes that are now the Back Bay (see **Back Bay and Beyond,** below). Art galleries, antique shops, and cafes line the cobblestone streets and brick sidewalks of the Hill; **Charles St.** makes an especially nice setting for a stroll. The **State House** sits at the base of the Hill (see **Freedom Trail,** above). For a taste of Boston circa 1796, the **Harrison Gray Otis House,** 141 Cambridge St. (227-3956), is a Charles Bulfinch original (tours W-Su on the hr. 11am-4pm; $4, seniors $3.50, ages 6-12 $2). The nearby **Boston Athenaeum,** 10½ Beacon St. (227-0270), offers tours of its art gallery, print room, and the collection, which contains over 700,000 books, including most of George Washington's library. *(Open M 9am-8pm, Tu-F 9am-5:30pm; Sept.-May also Sa 9am-4pm. Free tours Tu and Th 3pm; reservations required 24hr. in advance.)*

The Black Heritage Trail begins at the **Boston African-American National Historic Site,** 46 Joy St. (742-1854), where you can pick up a free map and visit the museum inside (T: Park St.; open daily 10am-4pm; donation requested). Fourteen stops, each marked by a red, black, and green logo, make up the trail. Landmarks in the development of Boston's African-American community include North America's first black church, the **African Meeting House** (1805), the **Robert Gould Shaw and 54th Regiment Memorial** (see **Freedom Trail,** p. 95), and the **Lewis and Harriet Hayden House,** a station on the Underground Railroad.

East of Beacon Hill on Cambridge St., the red brick plaza of **Government Center** (T: Government Center) surrounds the monstrous concrete **City Hall** (635-4000), designed by I.M. "so good" Pei (open to the public M-F 9am-5pm). A few blocks south rests its more aesthetically pleasing relative, the **Old State House** (see **Freedom Trail,** above).

Set amid Boston's business district, the pedestrian mall at **Downtown Crossing,** south of City Hall at Washington St. (T: Downtown Crossing), centers around **Filene's,** 426 Washington St., the mild-mannered department store that conceals the chaotic bargain-feeding frenzy that is **Filene's Basement** (542-2011). Even if you don't plan to shop, check out the Basement—it's a cultural institution.

Southwest of the Common, Boston's **Chinatown** (T: Chinatown) demarcates itself with an arch and huge Fu dogs at its Beach St. entrance and pagoda-style telephone booths and streetlamps throughout. This is the place for good Chinese food, Chinese slippers, and "1000-year-old eggs." *Do not walk alone here at night.* Chinatown holds two big festivals each year. The first, **New Year,** usually celebrated on a Sunday in February, includes lion dances, fireworks, and Kung Fu exhibitions. The **August Moon Festival** honors a mythological pair of lovers at the time of the full moon, usually on the second or third Sunday in August (call 542-2574 for details).

The east tip of Boston contains the historic **North End** (T: Haymarket). Now an Italian neighborhood, the city's oldest residential district overflows with windowboxes, Italian flags, fragrant pastry shops, *crèches,* Sicilian restaurants, and Catholic churches. The most famous of the last, **Old St. Stephen's Church,** 401 Hanover St.

(523-1230), is the classic colonial brainchild of Charles Bulfinch (open sunrise-sunset; services M and Sa 5:15pm, Tu-F 7:30am, Su 8:30 and 11am). Down the street, the sweet-smelling **Peace Gardens** attempt to drown out the clamor of the North End (for more on the North End, see **Freedom Trail,** p. 95).

The Waterfront

The **waterfront area,** bounded by Atlantic and Commercial St., runs along Boston Harbor from South Station to the North End Park. Stroll down Commercial, Lewis, or Museum Wharf for a view of the harbor and a breath of sea air. The excellent **New England Aquarium** (973-5200; T: Aquarium), on Central Wharf at the Waterfront, presents cavorting penguins, giant sea turtles, and a bevy of briny beasts all in a 187,000 gallon tank. *(Open M-Tu and F 9am-6pm, W-Th 9am-8pm, Sa-Su and holidays 9am-7pm; early Sept. to June M-W and F 9am-5pm, Th 9am-8pm, Sa-Su and holidays 9am-6pm. $11, seniors $10, ages 3-11 $5.50; W-Th after 4pm $1 off, seniors free M noon-4:30pm.)* Dolphins and sea lions perform in the ship *Discovery,* moored alongside the Aquarium. The aquarium also offers **whale-watching cruises** (973-5277) from April to October. *(Sightings guaranteed. 1-2 trips daily; call for times. $24, students and seniors $19, ages 12-15 $17.50, ages 3-11 $16.50. Under 3 not allowed. Reservations strongly suggested.)* The **Boston Harbor Cruises** (723-7800) also conducts whale-watching tours and $2 lunch cruises of the harbor May through September. Longer cruises to the **Boston Harbor Islands** for a picnic or a tour of Civil War Fort Warren are also available ($15; see **Practical Information,** p. 92).

Back Bay and Beyond

In **Back Bay,** north of the South End and west of Beacon Hill, 3-story brownstone row houses line some of the only gridded streets in Boston. Originally the marshy, uninhabitable "back bay" on the Charles River, the area was filled in during the 19th-century. Architectural styles progress chronologically through 19th-century popular design as you travel from east to west, reflecting the gradual process of filling in the marsh. Statues and benches punctuate the large, grassy median of **Commonwealth Ave.** ("Comm. Ave."). Boston's most flamboyant promenade, **Newbury St.** (T: Arlington, Copley, or Hynes/ICA), may inspire you to ask yourself some serious questions about your credit rating. The dozens of small art galleries, boutiques, bookstores, and chic cafes that line the street exude exclusivity and swank and offer unparalleled people-watching. The riverside **Esplanade** (T: Charles/MGH) extends from the Longfellow Bridge to the Harvard Bridge, parallel to Newbury St. Boston's answer to the beach, the park fills with sun-seekers and sailors in the summer. It may look nice, but don't take a dip in the Charles. Pick up the bike path along the river and pedal to the posh suburb of **Wellesley** for a terrific afternoon ride.

Beyond Back Bay, west on Commonwealth Ave., the huge landmark **Citgo sign** watches over **Kenmore Sq.** (T: Kenmore). The area around Kenmore has more than its share of neon, with many of the city's most popular nightclubs hovering on **Landsdowne St.** (see **Nightlife,** below). Near Kenmore Sq., the **Fenway** area contains some of the country's best museums. Ubiquitous landscaper Frederick Law Olmsted, of Central Park fame, designed the **Fens** area at the center of the Fenway as part of his "Emerald Necklace," a plan to ring Boston in parks. Although the necklace was never completed, the park remains a gem; fragrant rose gardens and neighborhood vegetable patches make perfect picnic turf. As you might well suspect, the Fenway also houses **Fenway Park** (see **Curse of the Bambino,** p. 100).

The rest of Olmsted's **Emerald Necklace Parks** (635-7383) make up a free, 5hr. walking tour given by the Boston Park Rangers (tour reservations required). Visiting the parks individually—the Boston Common (T: Park St.; see **Downtown,** p. 95), the Public Garden (T: Arlington; see **Downtown,** p. 95), Commonwealth Avenue Mall (T: Arlington), Back Bay Fens (T: Kenmore), Muddy River, Olmsted Park, Jamaica Pond, the splendid Arnold Arboretum (T: Arborway), and Franklin Park—requires a bit less time. Call the Park Rangers for info and directions.

Copley

In Back Bay on commercial Boylston St., handsome **Copley Sq.** (T: Copley) accommodates a range of seasonal activities, including summertime concerts, folk dancing, a food pavilion, and people-watching. The massive and imposing **Boston Public Library,** 666 Boylston St. (536-5400), serves as a permanent memorial to the hundreds of literati whose names are inscribed upon it. *(Open M-Th 9am-9pm, F-Sa 9am-5pm, Su 1-5pm.)* Relax on a bench or window seat overlooking the tranquil courtyard or in the vaulted reading room. The auditorium gives a program of lectures and films and often displays collections of art. Across the square, next to I.M. Pei's **Hancock Tower,** stands H.H. Richardson's Romanesque fantasy, **Trinity Church** (536-0944; T: Copley). *(Open M-Sa 8am-6pm.)* Many consider Trinity, built in 1877, a masterpiece of U.S. church architecture—the interior justifies this opinion. The ritzy mall on the corner is **Copley Place,** next door to the renovated **Prudential Building.** The **Prudential Skywalk,** on the 50th floor of the Prudential, 800 Boylston St. (236-3318; T: Prudential), grants a full 360° view from New Hampshire to the Cape (open daily 10am-10pm; $4, seniors and ages 2-10 $3). The partially gentrified **South End,** south of Copley, makes for good brownstone viewing and casual dining amid gay pride flags.

Two blocks down Massachusetts Ave. from Boylston St., the **Mother Church of the First Church of Christ, Scientist,** 1 Norway St. (450-2000), at Mass. Ave. and Huntington, headquarters the international Christian Science movement, founded in Boston by Mary Baker Eddy (tours Tu-Sa 10am-4pm, Su 11:30am; free). Both the Mother Church and the smaller, older one out back can be seen by guided tour only. Once renovations are complete in 2000, the **Mapparium,** a 30 ft. wide stained glass globe in the **Christian Science Publishing Society** next door, will reopen. The globe, built in the 1930s, features highly unusual acoustics; sound waves bounce off the sphere in any and all directions. Whisper in the ear of Pakistan while standing next to Surinam.

Museums

The free *Guide to Museums of Boston* has details on museums not mentioned here.

Museum of Fine Arts (MFA), 465 Huntington Ave. (267-9300), near Massachusetts Ave. T: Ruggles/Museum. Boston's most famous museum contains one of the world's finest collections of Asian ceramics, outstanding Egyptian art, a showing of Impressionists, and superb American art. Two famous unfinished portraits of George and Martha Washington, begun by Gilbert Stuart in 1796, merit a gander. Open M-Tu and Th-F 10am-4:45pm, W 10am-9:45pm, Sa-Su 10am-5:45pm. $10, seniors and students with ID $8, under 18 free.

Isabella Stewart Gardner Museum, 280 Fenway St. (566-1401), a few hundred yards from the MFA. T: Ruggles/Museum. In what ranks as one of the greatest art heists in history, a 1990 break-in relieved the museum of works by Rembrandt, Vermeer, Dégas, and others. Nevertheless, many masterpieces remain in Ms. Gardner's Venetian-style palace, which garners as much attention as the Old Masters. The courtyard garden soothes a weary traveler's soul. Open Tu-Su 11am-5pm. $9, seniors $7, students $5, ages 12-17 $3. Chamber music on the 1st fl. Sept.-May Sa-Su afternoons; performances $15, seniors $11, students $9, ages 12-17 $7, under 12 $4. See the courtyard only for free.

Museum of Science (723-2500), Science Park. T: Science Park. At the far east end of the Esplanade on the Charles River Dam. Contains, among other wonders, the largest "lightning machine" in the world. Within the museum, the **Hayden Planetarium** features models, lectures, films, and laser and star shows. Travel the world in the **Mugar Omni Theatre;** films on scientific subjects show on a 4-story, domed screen. Museum open in summer Sa-Th 9am-7pm, F 9am-9pm; off-season Sa-Th 9am-5pm, F 9am-9pm. Exhibits $8, seniors and ages 3-14 $6. Planetarium, laser show, and Omni each $7.50/$5.50; $5/$4 each with museum admission.

Children's Museum, 300 Congress St. (426-8855), in south Boston on Museum Wharf. T: South Station. Follow the signs with milk bottles. Kids of all ages paw "way cool" hands-on exhibits and learn a little something to boot. Open Sa-Th 10am-5pm, F 10am-9pm; Sept.-June closed M. $7, seniors and ages 2-15 $6, age 1 $1, under 1 free; F 5-9pm all ages $1.

John F. Kennedy Presidential Library (929-4567), Columbia Point on Morrissey Blvd. in Dorchester. T: JFK/UMass. Dedicated "to all those who through the art of politics seek a new and better world." The looming white structure, designed by I.M. Pei, overlooks Dorchester Bay. No conspiracy theories here; the museum contains exhibits tracing Kennedy's career from the campaign trail to his tragic death. Open daily 9am-5pm. $6, seniors and students $4, ages 6-15 $2.

Institute of Contemporary Art (ICA), 955 Boylston St. (266-5152). T: Hynes/ICA. Boston's lone outpost of the avant-garde attracts major modern artists while aggressively promoting lesser-known work. Innovative, sometimes controversial exhibits change every 8 weeks. The museum also presents experimental theater, music, dance, and film. Prices vary; call for details. Open W-Su noon-5pm. $5.25, students $3.25, seniors and under 12 $2.25; Th free 5-9pm.

ENTERTAINMENT

An unusually large and diverse community of **street performers** ("buskers") juggle steak knives, swallow torches, wax poetic, and sing folk tunes in the subways and squares of Boston and Cambridge. The *Boston Phoenix* and the "Calendar" section of Thursday's *Boston Globe* list activities for the coming week. Also check the free *Where: Boston* booklet available at the visitors center. What Boston doesn't have, Cambridge might (see Cambridge **Nightlife,** p. 103). **Bostix** (482-BTIX/2849), a Ticketmaster outlet in Faneuil Hall and at Copley Sq. (at Boylston and Dartmouth St.), sells half-price tickets to performing arts events starting at 11am on the day of performance. (Service charge $1.50-3 per ticket. Cash and traveler's checks only. Copley Sq. open M 10am-6pm; both locations open Tu-Sa 10am-6pm, Su 11am-4pm.)

Waiters, temps, and actors cluster around Washington St. and Harrison Ave. in the **Theater District** (T: Boylston). The **Wang Center for the Performing Arts,** 270 Tremont St. (482-9393), produces theater, classical music, and opera in its gorgeous baroque complex. Here, the renowned **Boston Ballet** (695-6950), one of the nation's best, annually revives classics like the *Nutcracker* and *Swan Lake*. The **Shubert Theater,** 265 Tremont St. (482-9393), hosts Broadway hits touring through town. Tickets for these and for shows at the **Charles Playhouse,** 74 Warrenton St. (426-5225), home of the ongoing *Blue Man Group* and *Shear Madness,* cost around $30-40. (Call the Playhouse 3 weeks in advance to inquire about ushering opportunities, which allow a free viewing of a particular production in exchange for 1 night of work.)

The area's regional companies cost less and may make for a more interesting evening. Both the **New Theater,** 66 Marlborough St. (247-7388), and **Huntington Theater Company,** 264 Huntington Ave. (266-7900, box office 266-0800), at Boston University, have solid artistic reputations (tickets $12-60; students and seniors as low as $5). During term-time, affordable student theater is always up; watch students tread the boards at **Tufts Balch Arena Theater** (627-3493; tickets $8; T: Davis), the **BU Theater** (353-3320), the **MIT Drama Shop** (253-2908; T: Kendall), and the **MIT Shakespeare Ensemble** (253-2903). For student musical performances, try the **New England Conservatory** (262-1120, box office 536-2412); they're free weekdays at Jordan Hall, 30 Gainesborough St. (T: Symphony); on weekends, the hall stages professional performances ($12-80).

The **Boston Symphony Orchestra,** 301 Mass. Ave. (266-1492; T: Symphony), at Huntington Ave., holds its concert season October through early May (tickets $23-71). Rush seats ($7.50) go on sale 3hr. before concerts. During July and August, the symphony takes a vacation to **Tanglewood,** in western Massachusetts (see **The Berkshires,** p. 122). Mid-May through July, while the BSO's away, the **Boston Pops Orchestra** plays in **Symphony Hall,** 301 Mass. Ave. (Box office and concert info 266-1200. recording 266-2378. Open M-Sa 10am-6pm, until intermission on concert days. Tickets $13-47.) You can also see the Pops at the **Hatch Shell** (T: Charles/MGH) on the Esplanade any night in the first week of July; arrive early to sit within earshot of the orchestra (concert 8pm; free). On the **Fourth of July,** hundreds of thousands of patriotic thrillseekers pack the Esplanade to hear the Pops concert and watch the fireworks display. Arrive before noon for a seat on the Esplanade, although you can watch the fireworks from almost anywhere along the river.

NEW ENGLAND

The **Berklee Performance Center,** 136 Mass. Ave. (266-7455, box office 747-2261), an adjunct of the Berklee School of Music, holds concerts featuring students, faculty, and jazz and classical luminaries. For student productions, call 747-8820. (Open M-Sa 10am-6pm. Tickets $10-40; cash only.)

For info on other special events, such as the **St. Patrick's Day Parade** (Mar. 17), **Patriot's Day** celebrations (3rd M in Apr.), the week-long **Boston Common Dairy Festival** (June), the **Boston Harbor Fest** (early July), the North End's **Festival of St. Anthony** (mid-Aug.), and **First Night** (New Year's Eve), see the *Boston Phoenix* or *Globe* calendars.

Singing Beach, 40min. outside downtown, on the commuter line to Manchester-by-the-Sea (see **Practical Information,** p. 92), gained its name from the sound made when you drag your feet through the sand. The beach charges a $1 entrance fee, but playing in the sand and frolicking in the water is free after that. Park your car in town and walk the ½ mi. to the beach. By car, take Rte.1 to Rte. 127 to Exit 16.

The Curse of the Bambino and Other Sports

Ever since the Red Sox traded Babe Ruth to the Yankees in 1918, Boston sports fans have learned to take the good with the bad. They have witnessed more basketball championships than any other city (16) but haven't boasted a World Series title in over 75 years. Yet through it all, they follow their teams with Puritanical fervor. On summer nights, thousands of baseball fans make the pilgrimage to **Fenway Park** (T: Kenmore). Home of the infamous outfield wall known as the "Green Monster," Fenway is the nation's oldest Major League ballpark and center stage for the perennially heart-rending **Boston Red Sox.** (Box office 267-8661. Open M-Sa 9am-5pm, until game time on game nights, Su 9am-5pm if there's a game.) Most grandstand tickets ($10-12) sell out in advance, but bleacher seats are often for sale on game day.

The famous **Boston Garden,** located off the JFK Expwy. between the West and North Ends, has been replaced by the **FleetCenter** (T: North Station). Call 624-1000 for FleetCenter info. The storied **Boston Celtics** basketball team (523-3030; season Oct.-May) and **Boston Bruins** hockey team (season Oct.-Apr.) play here. Forty-five minutes outside of Boston, **Foxboro Stadium,** 16 Washington St., Foxboro, hosts the **New England Patriots** NFL team (season Sept.-Jan.; call 508-543-3900 for info). The stadium also stages concerts. Rail service to the games and some concerts runs from South Station; call for details.

The **Head of the Charles** (864-8415), the alargest single-day rowing regatta in the world, attracts rowing clubs, baseball caps, and beer-stained college sweatshirts from across the country (Oct. 17-18, 1999). The 3 mi. races begin at Boston University Bridge; the best vantage points are atop Weeks Footbridge and Anderson Bridge near Harvard University. On April 19, the 10,000 runners competing in the **Boston Marathon** battle Boston area boulevards and the infamous Heartbreak Hill. Call the **Boston Athletic Association** for details (236-1652).

NIGHTLIFE

Remnants of the city's Puritan heritage temper Boston's nightlife ("blue laws" prohibit the sale of alcohol after certain hrs. and on Su), along with the lack of public transportation after midnight. Nearly all bars and most clubs close between 1 and 2am, and bar admittance for anyone under 21 is hard-won. Boston's local music scene runs the gamut from folk to funk; Beantown natives-gone-national include the Pixies, Aerosmith, Tracey Chapman, Dinosaur Jr., The Lemonheads, and the Mighty Mighty Bosstones. Cruise down **Landsdowne St.** (T: Kenmore) and **Boylston Place** (T: Boylston) to find concentrated action. The weekly *Boston Phoenix* has comprehensive club and concert listings (released on Th; $1.50).

Avalon, 15 Lansdowne St. (262-2424). T: Kenmore. Across the street from Fenway Park in a line of other clubs, the Avalon stands out with its above-average interior. The roomy dance floor, surrounded by three bars, offers plenty of dance music with some hip-hop. Su is gay night; the club joins with next-door Axis for this huge event. Cover $5-15. Open Th 11pm-2am, F-Sa 10pm-2am, Su 9pm-2am.

Axis, 5-13 Lansdowne St. (262-2437). T: Kenmore. Next door to Avalon, this smaller, more discreet club has great music and an atmosphere that's a little less intense. With comfy couches and a spacious dance floor, Axis has theme nights on weekends; Tu is "clique" night, Th is progressive techno night. Cover $5-10. Those over 21 can get in for $0-8 through nearby **Bill's Bar** (421-9678).

Roxy, 279 Tremont St. (338-7699). T: Boylston. Classier and cleaner than most Boston clubs. The balcony is a prime place for people-watching. Latin dance Th 9pm-2am; Euro, house, and techno F 11pm-2am; top 40 Sa 9pm-2am. 21+. Cover $10.

Bull and Finch Pub, 84 Beacon St. (227-9605). T: Arlington. If you must see the bar that inspired *Cheers,* we can't stop you. Large crowds, and the interior bears little resemblance to the set. Open daily 11am-1:30am.

Wally's Café, 427 Mass Ave. (424-1408). T: bus #1 "Dudley" to Columbus Ave. A great hole-in-the-wall jazz bar frequented by Berklee School of Music aspirants. Meet "Wally's Stepchildren" (Tu and W 9pm-2am). Hostel makes frequent outings here. Live music nightly; no cover. Open M-Sa 9am-2am, Su noon-2am.

Sunset Grill and Tap, 130 Brighton Ave. (254-1331), in Allston. T: Harvard on Green Line-B or bus #66 from the corner of Harvard St. and Brighton Ave. One of the country's largest selections of beer (over 400, 70 on tap). College students dig the *buenos nachos* ($7). Free late-night buffets Su-Tu. Open daily 11am-2am.

The Big Easy, 1 Boylston Pl. (351-7000). T: Boylston. This slice of New Orleans is a new addition to Boston nightlife, taking over Zanzibar's old haunts. Live bands take center stage every night supplemented by a Top 40 DJ. No hats, jeans, or sportswear. Strictly 21+ (unlike N'Orleans). Th-Sa 8pm-2am. Cover varies around $5.

The Comedy Connection, 245 Quincy Marketplace, Faneuil Hall (248-9700). T: Government Center. See such performers as Pauly Shore, Damon Wayans, and Rosie O'Donnell. Locals Su-Th, bigshots F-Sa. Be prepared for vulgar and ruthless comedy. Viewers in the front row should check their pride at the door. 18+.

For those seeking the gay scene, **Chaps** (266-7778) caters to a mostly male crowd, transforming from a quiet bar in the afternoon to ultra-hip party spot in the evening (open daily 1pm-2am; cover $3-5). The more upscale **Club Café,** 209 Columbus Ave. (536-0966; T: Back Bay), attracts a mixed yuppie clientele with live music Thursday to Saturday and no cover (open daily 11am-2am). Boston's favorite leather and Levi's bar, **Boston Ramrod,** 1254 Boylston St. (266-2986; T: Kenmore), behind Fenway Park on Boylston St., designates every Friday fetish night and every Saturday exposition night—but why wait until then? (Open daily noon-2am.) Pick up a copy of *Bay Windows* for more info (available at many music stores).

■ Cambridge

Cambridge began its career as an intellectual and publishing center in the colonial era. Harvard, the nation's first university, was founded as a college of divinity here in 1636. The Massachusetts Institute of Technology (MIT), founded in Boston in 1861, moved to Cambridge in 1916, giving the small city a second academic heavyweight. Today the city takes on the character of both the universities and the tax-paying Cantabrigians. Town and gown mingle and contrast, creating a patchwork of diverse flavors that change as you move from square to square. Bio-tech labs and computer science buildings radiate out from MIT through Kendall Sq. Harvard Sq., on the other side of the city, offers Georgian buildings, stellar bookstores, coffeehouses, street musicians, and prime people-watching opportunities.

PRACTICAL INFORMATION Cambridge is best reached by a 10min. T-ride outbound from the heart of Boston. The city's main artery, **Massachusetts Ave.** ("Mass. Ave."), parallels the Red Line, which makes stops at a series of squares along the avenue. The **Kendall Sq.** stop corresponds to MIT, just across the Longfellow Bridge from Boston. The subway continues outbound through **Central Sq., Harvard Sq.,** and **Porter Sq.** The **Office for Cambridge Tourism** (497-1630, office 441-2884), in Harvard Sq., has the best and most comprehensive info about Cambridge, as well as MBTA bus and subway schedules (open M-Sa 9am-5pm, weekend times vary). The *Old Cambridge Walking Guide* provides an excellent self-guided tour ($2); during the summer, ask about guided walking tours of Harvard and the surrounding area. **Post Office:** 125 Mt. Auburn St. (876-6483; open M-F 7am-6pm, Sa 7:30am-3pm; self-service available M-F 7am-6:30pm, Su 7am-3:30pm). **ZIP code:** 02138. **Area code:** 617. For budget **accommodations,** head back to Boston (see p. 93).

FOOD Every night, hundreds of college students renounce cafeteria fare and head to the funky eateries of Harvard Sq. Pick up the weekly *Square Deal,* usually thrust in your face by distributors near the T stop, for coupons on local eats. Follow your nose to **Mr. and Mrs. Bartley's Burger Cottage,** 1246 Mass. Ave. (354-6559), which has had a smoky and dignified claim on beef for over 35 years, though veggie burgers ($4-7) now appear on the handwritten menu. Among the irreverent offerings are the yuppie burger with boursin and bacon and the Al Bore—"just a burger." Wash it all down with Boston's best milkshake or lime rickey. (Open M-W and Sa 11am-10pm, Th-F 11am-10pm.) Any student will tell you that **Pinocchio's,** 74 Winthrop St. (876-4897), offers the best pizza deal in town with two slices of sizzling Sicilian for $3.50 (open M-W 1pm-1am, Th-Sa 1pm-2am, Su 1pm-midnight). For some of the tastiest and cheapest (everything under $5) Mexican fare in town, try **Boca Grande,** 1728 Mass. Ave. (354-7400; open Su-F 11am-10pm, Sa 11am-10:30pm). A hangout for MIT math whizzes, **Mary Chung Restaurant,** 464 Mass. Ave. (864-1991), dishes out excellent Szechuan and Mandarin cuisine including a flavorful $6 Yu-Hsiang Eggplant. (Open Su-M and W-Th 11:30am-10pm, F-Sa 11:30am-11pm. *Dim Sum* brunch Sa-Su 11:30am-2:30pm.) A 10-15min. walk from Harvard, the **S&S Restaurant and Deli,** 1334 Cambridge St. (354-0777), offers a deli-style lunch or breakfast served all day. Take the #69 bus to the intersection of Cambridge and Beacon/Hampshire St. Filling entrees like Penne Pasta Primavera average $6-10. Hot beef knishes ($3) and an abundance of beers and desserts are worth the trek. "Ess and ess" means "eat and eat" in Yiddish. (Open M-Tu 7am-11pm, W-Sa 7am-midnight, Su 8am-11pm.)

SIGHTS The **Massachusetts Institute of Technology (MIT)** supports cutting-edge work in the sciences. Free campus tours highlight the Chapel, designed by Eero Saarinen, and an impressive collection of modern outdoor sculpture. Contact **MIT Information,** 77 Mass. Ave. (253-1875), for more details (open M-F 9am-5pm; tours, M-F 10am and 2pm, meet in the lobby). The **MIT Museum,** 265 Mass. Ave. (253-4444), contains a slide rule collection and wonderful photography exhibits, including the famous stop-action photos of Harold Edgerton (open Tu-F 10am-5pm, Sa-Su noon-5pm; $3, students and seniors $1, under 5 free).

In all its red brick-and-ivy dignity, **Harvard University,** farther down Mass. Ave. from Boston, finds space for Nobel laureates, students from around the world, and the occasional party. The **Harvard Events and Information Center,** 1350 Mass. Ave. (495-1573), at Holyoke Center in Harvard Sq., distributes free guides to the university and its museums and offers 1hr. tours of Harvard Yard. *(Tours in summer M-Sa 10, 11:15am, 2 and 3:15pm, Su 1:30 and 3pm; Sept.-May M-F 10am and 2pm, Sa 2pm.)* Pick up a comprehensive map of Harvard for $1. The university revolves around **Harvard Yard,** a grassy oasis amid the Cantabrigian bustle. The **Harry Elkins Widener Memorial Library** (495-2411) stands as the largest academic library in the world, containing 4.5 million of the university's 13.4 million books. To visit the library, you'll need a temporary pass from the library privileges office (495-4166) on the main floor (open M-F 9am-5pm). The extravagantly ornate **Memorial Hall,** just outside the Yard's northern gate, is a secular cathedral dedicated to the Union dead.

The most notable of Harvard's museums, the **Fogg Art Museum,** 32 Quincy St., gathers a considerable collection of works ranging from ancient Chinese jade to contemporary photography, as well as the largest Ingres collection outside of France. Across the street, the modern exterior of the **Arthur M. Sackler Museum,** 485 Broadway, holds a rich collection of ancient Asian and Islamic art. Another of Harvard's art museums, the **Busch-Reisinger Museum,** 32 Quincy St., accessible through the Fogg, displays Northern and Central European sculpture, painting, and decorative arts. *(495-9400 for all 3. All open M-Sa 10am-5pm, Su 1-5pm. Each $5, students $3, seniors $4; free Sa mornings.)* Peering down at the Fogg, Le Corbusier's piano-shaped **Carpenter Center,** 24 Quincy St. (495-3251), displays student and professional work with especially strong photo exhibits and a great, largely foreign, film series at the **Harvard Film Archives,** located inside the Center. *(Center open M-F 9am-11pm, Sa-Su noon-11pm; during term-time, M-F 9am-11pm, Sa-Su 9am-11pm. Most shows $6, students and seniors $5, under 8 free.)* Pick up schedules outside the door. The **Botanical Museum,** one of Harvard's several **Museums of Natural and Cultural History,** 24 Oxford St. (495-3045), draws huge crowds to view the Ware collection of "glass flowers." *(Open M-Sa 9am-5pm, Su 1-5pm. $5, students and seniors $4, ages 3-13 $3. Admission includes all the museums.)*

The restored **Longfellow House,** 105 Brattle St. (876-4491), now a National Historic Site, headquartered the Continental Army during the early stages of the Revolution. *(Tours June-Sept. W-Su 10am-4:30pm; Mar.-May and Oct. to mid-Dec. W-F noon-4:30pm, Sa-Su 10am-4:30pm. Closed mid-Dec. to Feb. $2, under 16 free.)* The poet Henry Wadsworth Longfellow, for whom the house is named, lived here later. On Sunday afternoons in the summer (3pm), the Longfellow House hosts free poetry readings and musical performances. The **Mt. Auburn Cemetery** (547-7105) lies about 1 mi. up the road at the end of Brattle St. *(Open Su-Sa 8am-5pm; tower closes 1hr. earlier. Free. Wheelchair access.)* The nation's first botanical garden/cemetery has 174 acres of beautifully landscaped grounds fertilized by Louis Agassiz, Charles Bulfinch, Dorothea Dix, Mary Baker Eddy, and Longfellow. Locals say it's the best birdwatching site in Cambridge. The central tower offers a stellar view of Boston and Cambridge.

ENTERTAINMENT AND NIGHTLIFE In warm weather, street performers ranging from Andean folk singers to magicians crowd every brick sidewalk of Harvard Sq. and nearby **Brattle Sq.** The **American Repertory Theater (ART),** 64 Brattle St. (547-8300), in the Loeb Drama Center, produces shows from late November to early June. (Box office open M 11am-5pm, Tu-Su 10am-5pm, or until showtime. Tickets $22-52. Student rush tickets available 30min. before shows, $12 cash only; seniors $10.)

Cambridge's club scene centers around a 1 block area in Central Sq., while countless bars can be found in both Harvard and Central Sq. The **Middle East,** 472 Mass. Ave. (354-8238), in Central Sq., a three-stage nirvana for the musically adventurous, offers a mixture of local alternative and rock (cover $5-12; open Su-W 11am-1am, Th-Sa 11am-2am). Around the corner, **T.T. The Bear's Place,** 10 Brookline St. (492-0082), in Central Sq., brings really live, really loud bands to its intimate, makeshift stage (18+; cover $4-8; open M 7:30pm-midnight, Tu-Th 8pm-1am, F-Su 4pm-1am). For over 15 years, Little Joe Cook and his blues band have been packing the **Cantab Lounge,** 738 Mass. Ave. (354-2685), in Central Sq., with hard-rocking and hard-drinking Cantabrigians (cover $3-6; open M-W 8am-1am, Th-Sa 8am-2am, Su noon-1am). A genial Irish bar, **The Plough and Stars,** 912 Mass. Ave. (492-9653), plays live music nightly but forbids "thieves, fakirs, rogues, skulking loafers, and flee-bitten tramps" (open M-Sa 11:30am-1am, Su noon-1am). **ManRay,** 21 Brookline St. (864-0400), is your basic leather bar catering to the area's gay crowd Thursday (21+) and Saturday (19+) nights with an all-out dance party (cover $5-10; open Th-Sa until 2am).

■ Lexington and Concord

Lexington "Stand your ground. Don't fire unless fired upon, but if they mean to have a war, let it begin here," said Captain John Parker to the colonial Minutemen on April 19, 1775. Although no one is certain who fired the first shot, the American Revolution did indeed erupt in downtown Lexington. The site of the fracas lies in the center of town (Mass Ave.) at the **Battle Green,** where a **Minuteman Statue** still watches over Lexington. The fateful command itself was issued from across the street at the **Buckman Tavern,** 1 Bedford St. (862-5598), which housed the minutemen on the eve of their decisive battle. The nearby **Hancock-Clarke House,** 36 Hancock St. (861-0928), and the **Munroe Tavern,** 1332 Mass. Ave. (674-9238), also played significant roles in the birth of the Revolution. *(House and Taverns open mid-Apr. to Oct. M-Sa 10am-4:30pm, Su 1-4:30pm. $4 per site, ages 6-16 $1. Combination ticket $10/$2/$0.)* All three can be seen on a 30min. tour that runs continuously. You can also survey exhibits on the Revolution at the **Museum of Our National Heritage,** 33 Marrett Rd./Rte. 2A (861-6559), which emphasizes a historical approach to understanding popular

American life (open M-Sa 10am-5pm, Su noon-5pm; wheelchair access; free). An excellent model and description of the Battle of Lexington decorates the **visitors center,** 1875 Mass. Ave. (862-1450), behind the Buckman Tavern (open mid-Apr. to Oct. M-Sa 10am-5pm, Su 1-5pm).

Locals flock to the 33-acre **Wilson Farm,** 10 Pleasant St. (862-3900), for freshly picked fruits and veggies and over 30 varieties of freshly baked bread and pastry (open M and W-F 9am-8pm, Sa 9am-7pm, Su 9am-6:30pm; call for winter hrs.). The road from Boston to Lexington is easy. Drive straight up Mass. Ave. from Boston or Cambridge, or bike up the **Minuteman Commuter Bike Trail,** which runs into downtown Lexington (access off Mass. Ave. in Arlington, or Alewife in Cambridge). MBTA bus #62 from Alewife in Cambridge runs to Lexington (60¢). **Area code:** 781.

Concord Concord, the site of the second conflict of the American Revolution, is famous for both its military history and its status as a 19th-century intellectual center. Past The Minuteman and over the **Old North Bridge,** you'll find the spot from whence came "the shot heard 'round the world." From the parking lot, a 5min. walk brings you to the **North Bridge Visitors Center,** 174 Liberty St. (369-6993), where rangers will gladly surrender their useful pamphlets and brochures (open Apr.-Oct. daily 9am-5:30pm; Sa-Su only in winter). The **Minuteman National Historical Park,** best explored along the adjacent 5½ mi. **Battle Rd. Trail,** sports a spanking-new **visitors center** (369-6993), off Rte. 2A between Concord and Lexington (open Apr.-Nov. daily 9am-5pm; call for winter hrs.).

The **Concord Museum,** 200 Lexington Rd. (369-9609), across the street from Ralph Waldo Emerson's 19th-century home, houses a reconstruction of his study alongside Paul Revere's lantern and items from Henry David Thoreau's cabin. *(Open M-Sa 9am-5pm, Su 1-5pm; Jan.-Mar. M-Sa 10am-4pm, Su 1-4pm. $6, students $3, seniors $5, under 18 $3, families $12.)* Admission to the museum includes $1 off at four Concord sights, including the **Orchard House,** 399 Lexington Rd. (369-4118), where Louisa May Alcott wrote *Little Women. (Open M-Sa 10am-4:30pm, Su 1-4:30pm; Nov.-Mar. M-F 11am-3pm, Sa 10am-4:30pm, Su 1-4:30pm. $5.50, students and seniors $4.50, children $3.50, families $16.)* Also included in the discount is **Wayside,** 455 Lexington Rd. (369-6975), former residence of the Alcotts and Hawthornes. *(Open mid-Apr. to Oct. Th-Tu 10am-5pm. $4, under 16 free. Guided tour only; tours leave every 30min.)* Today, Emerson, Hawthorne, Alcott, and Thoreau reside on "Author's Ridge" in the **Sleepy Hollow Cemetery** on Rte. 62, 3 blocks from the center of town. Concord, 20 mi. north of Boston, is served by commuter rail trains from **North Station** (722-3200; fare $2.50, seniors and ages 5-11 $1.25). **Area code:** 978.

Walden Pond In 1845, Thoreau retreated 1½ mi. south of Concord "to live deliberately, to front only the essential facts of life." Here, he produced his famous book *Walden.* The **Walden Pond State Reservation** (978-369-3254), on Rte. 126, draws picnickers, swimmers, and boaters. *(Open daily 5am-sunset. Parking $2, only required Sa-Su in spring.)* The pond holds 1000 visitors. No camping, pets, or novelty flotation devices are allowed. When Walden Pond swarms with crowds, head east from Concord center on Rte. 62 to another of Thoreau's haunts, **Great Meadows National Wildlife Refuge** (978-443-4661), on Monsen Rd. (open daily dawn-dusk; free).

■ Salem

Salem possesses a rich and varied history that stretches beyond the sensational witch trials of 1692. The city, the sixth-largest in the U.S. in 1800, also features historic homes, a robust maritime heritage, and strong literary roots. Due to very expensive lodgings, Salem is best as a daytrip from Boston.

The **Salem Witch Museum,** 19½ Washington Sq. (744-1692—note the number), gives a melodramatic but informative multi-media presentation that details the history of the trials (open daily 10am-7pm; Sept.-June 10am-5pm; $4.50, seniors $4, ages 6-14 $3). The **Witch Dungeon Museum,** 16 Lynde St. (741-3570), attempts re-enactments that bring the turmoil and controversy of witch hunts to life. *(Open Apr.-Nov. daily*

10am-5pm. Shows every 30min. $5, seniors $4, ages 4-13 $3.) Escape the sea of witch kitsch at the **Witch Trials Memorial,** off Charter St., where engraved stones commemorate the trials' victims.

Salem's **Peabody Essex Museum** (800-745-4054, recorded info 745-9500), on the corner of Essex and Liberty St., recalls the port's former leading role in Atlantic whaling and merchant shipping. *(Open M-Sa 10am-5pm, Su noon-5pm; Nov.-May closed M. $8.50, students and seniors $7.50, ages 6-16 $5, families $20.)* Admission includes four historic Salem houses. The **Salem Maritime National Historic Site** (740-1650), consisting of three wharves and 12 historic buildings jutting out into Salem Harbor on Derby St., is a respite from the barrage of commercial tourist attractions (open daily 9am-5pm). Built in 1668, Salem's **House of Seven Gables,** 54 Turner St. (744-0991), became the "second most famous house in America" some time after the release of Nathaniel Hawthorne's Gothic romance of the same name. *(Open daily July-Oct. 9am-6pm; Nov.-June 10am-4:30pm. $7, seniors $6, ages 13-17 $4, ages 6-12 $3. Guided tour only.)* The price is steeper than the famed roof, but the tour is thorough and informative.

Salem has two **info centers,** located at 2 New Liberty St. (740-1650), and 174 Derby St. (740-1660). Both provide free maps; the Derby center screens a movie on the town's maritime focus (both open daily 9am-6pm; Sept.-May 9am-5pm). Camping is available at the **Harold Parker State Forest** (686-3391), 12 mi. west of Salem off Rte. 114 ($6-7). The town is packed during October with the **Haunted Happenings** festival; book at least a year in advance. Salem, 20 mi. northeast of Boston, is accessible by the Rockport/Ipswich commuter train from Boston's North Station (617-722-3200; $3.50) or by bus #450 or 455 from Haymarket (fare $2.25). **Area code:** 978.

■ Plymouth

Despite what American high school textbooks say, the Pilgrims did *not* step first onto the New World at Plymouth. They stopped first at Provincetown, but promptly left because the soil was so inadequate. **Plymouth Rock** itself is a rather diminutive stone that has dubiously been identified as the actual rock on which the Pilgrims disembarked. A stepping stone to the nation, it served as a symbol of liberty during the American Revolution, then was moved three times, and was chipped away by tourists before landing at its current home beneath an extravagant portico on Water St., at the foot of North St.

Three miles south of town off Rte. 3A, the overpriced **Plimoth Plantation** (746-1622) recreates the Pilgrims' early settlement. In the **Pilgrim Village,** costumed actors play the roles of actual villagers carrying out their daily tasks, based upon William Bradford's record of the year 1627, while the **Wampanoag Summer Encampment** represents a Native American village of the same period. To make sure they know their stuff, the plantation sends a historian to England each summer to gather more info about each villager. (Open Apr.-Nov. daily 9am-5pm. $15, ages 6-12 $9. Pass good for 2 consecutive days.) The **Mayflower II,** built in the 1950s to recapture the atmosphere of the original ship, is docked off Water St. (Open Apr.-Nov. daily 9am-5pm. $5.75, ages 6-12 $3.75. Admission to both sights $18.50, students and seniors $16.50, ages 6-12 $11.) The nation's oldest museum in continuous existence, the **Pilgrim Hall Museum,** 75 Court St. (746-1620), houses Puritan crafts, furniture, books, paintings, and weapons (open Feb.-Dec. daily 9:30am-4:30pm; $5, seniors $4.50, ages 5-17 $3, families $13).

Bogged down in history? **Cranberry World,** 225 Water St. (747-2350), celebrates one of the three indigenous American fruits (the others are the blueberry and the Concord grape). Exhibits, including a small cranberry bog in front of the museum, show how cranberries are grown, harvested, and sold (free samples; open May-Nov. daily 9:30am-5pm; free). A trip down Federal Furnace Rd. or Rte. 44 in early fall will lead you to the heart of **Cranberry Country.**

The Plymouth Colony Winery, Pinewood Rd. off Rte. 44 (747-3334), offers nine acres of bogs, free tours of their production area, and free wine tasting (open Apr.-Dec. M-Sa 10am-5pm, Su noon-5pm; Feb.-Mar. Sa-Su 10:30am-3pm).

The **Plymouth Visitor's Information Center,** 130 Water St. (800-872-1620 or 747-7525), hands out brochures, maps, and coupon books honored at local restaurants and attractions. (Open daily Apr.-May 9am-5pm; June 9am-6pm; July-Aug. 8am-8pm; Sept.-Nov. 9am-5pm.) Only a few blocks from the center of town, the **Bunk and Bagel,** 51 Pleasant St. (830-0914), has a cheerful, homey atmosphere and the cheapest beds in Plymouth. Hostel rooms, it turns out, come with a bagel. (5-8 hostel beds with common bath. Hostel beds $20-25. Linen provided. Reception daily 7am-9pm.) Majestic **Myles Standish Forest** (866-2526), 7 mi. south of Plymouth via Exit 3 off Rte. 3, offers wooded ground for bedding down on over 450 sites. (Sites $6-7. Office open daily Apr.-June 8am-10pm; July-Aug. 24hr.; Sept.-Oct. 8am-midnight.) The natives bite at **Wood's Seafood Restaurant,** Town Pier (746-0261). A fish sandwich with fries goes for $3.50. (Open daily June-Aug. 11am-9pm; Sept.-May 11am-8:30pm.) **Area code:** 508.

CAPE COD

Henry David Thoreau once said: "At present [this coast] is wholly unknown to the fashionable world, and probably it will never be agreeable to them." Think again, Hank. In 1602, when English navigator and Jamestown colonist Bartholomew Gosnold landed on this peninsula in southeastern Massachusetts, he named it in honor of all the codfish he caught in the surrounding waters. In recent decades, tourists have replaced the plentiful cod, and the area has as many taffy shops as fishermen. This small strip of land supports a diverse set of landscapes—long, unbroken stretches of beach, salt marshes, hardwood forests, deep freshwater ponds carved by glaciers, and desert-like dunes sculpted by the wind. Thankfully, the Cape's natural landscape has been protected from the tide of commercialism by the establishment of the **Cape Cod National Seashore.** Blessed with an excellent hostel system, Cape Cod is a popular budget seaside getaway. The Cape also serves as the gateway to **Martha's Vineyard** and **Nantucket,** two islands with unsurpassed natural beauty. Ferries shuttle from Falmouth, Woods Hole, and Hyannis to Martha's Vineyard, and from Hyannis to Nantucket; see **Martha's Vineyard** (p. 111) and **Nantucket** (p. 114) for complete info.

Terminology for locations on the Cape can be confusing. **Upper Cape** refers to the more suburbanized and developed part of Cape Cod, closer to the mainland. Proceeding eastward away from the mainland, you travel "down Cape" until hitting the **Lower Cape;** the National Seashore encompasses much of this area. Cape Cod resembles a bent arm, with **Woods Hole** at its armpit, **Chatham** at the elbow, and **Provincetown** at its clenched fist. Travel times on the peninsula are often inconsistent; a drive from the Sagamore bridge to Provincetown can take anywhere from two to four hours. Leaving the Cape can be equally annoying; the area's myriad weekend warriors can turn a Sunday departure into a hellacious six-hour odyssey.

If you're up for some exercise, cycling is the best way to travel the Cape's gentle slopes. The park service can give you a free map of trails or sell you the detailed *Cape Cod Bike Book* ($3; available at most Cape bookstores). The 135 mi. **Boston-Cape Cod Bikeway** connects Boston to Provincetown at land's end. If you want to bike this route, pick up a bicycle trail map of the area. These are available at some bookstores and most bike shops. The trails which line either side of the **Cape Cod Canal** in the National Seashore rank among the country's most scenic, as does the 25 mi. **Cape Cod Rail Trail** from Dennis to Wellfleet. For discount coupons good for bargains at restaurants, sights, and entertainment venues throughout the Cape, pick up a free copy of *The Official 1999 Guide to Cape Cod* or the *Cape Cod Best Read Guide,* available at most Cape info centers. **Area code:** 508.

■ Upper Cape

Hyannis Hyannis is not the Cape Cod most people expect. JFK spent his summers on the beach in nearby Hyannisport, but the town itself sees more action as a transportation hub than as a tourist mecca. Island ferries and buses to destinations throughout the Cape leave from Hyannis; hop on one and get out of town—the Kennedys *aren't* going to meet you at the bus station.

About 3 mi. up the road from the bus station, the **Hyannis Area Chamber of Commerce,** 1481 Rte. 132 (362-5230 or 800-4-HYNNIS/449-6647; http://www.hyannis-chamber.com), distributes the *Hyannis Guidebook* for free and has a campground guide for the whole Cape (open June-Sept. M-Sa 9am-5pm, Su 10am-2pm; Oct.-May M-Sa 9am-5pm).

While you will probably not want to spend more than a few hours in Hyannis, **Bouchard's Rooms, Apartments, and Cottages,** 83 School St. (775-0912), has five 50s-style rooms at low rates (singles $22; doubles $35-55; unmarried couples must book separate rooms). Potatoes shift from vegetable to crispy kettle-cooked chips at the **Cape Cod Potato Chip Factory,** Independence Dr. (775-3206), off Rte. 132 (open M-F 9am-5pm, Sa 10am-4pm; free). The **Cape Cod Scenic Railroad** (771-3788) takes visitors on a 2hr. ride through picturesque cranberry bogs and marshes. (3 roundtrips daily from Main and Center St. to the Cape Cod Canal. $11.50, ages 3-12 $7.50.)

Hyannis is tattooed midway across the Cape's upper arm, 3 mi. south of Rte. 6 on Nantucket Sound. **Plymouth & Brockton** (771-6191) runs five Boston-to-Provincetown buses per day with 30min. layovers at the **Hyannis Bus Station,** 17 Elm St. (775-5524). Other stops besides Boston (1¾hr., $12) and Provincetown (1½hr., $9) include Plymouth, Barnstable, Yarmouth, Eastham, Wellfleet, and Truro. **Bonanza Bus Lines** (800-556-3815) operates a line through Providence to New York City (6hr., 7 per day, $29). See the listings for **Martha's Vineyard** (p. 111) and **Nantucket** (p. 114) for info on ferry service to the islands.

Sandwich The oldest town on the Cape, Sandwich cultivates charm unmatched by its neighbors. The beauty and workmanship of Sandwich glass was made famous by the Boston & Sandwich Glass Company, founded in Sandwich in 1825. Master glassblowers shape works of art from blobs of molten sand at **Pairpoint Crystal** (888-2344), on Rte. 6A just across the town border in Sagamore (open M-F 9am-noon and 1-4:30pm; free). To enjoy the town's considerable collection of older pieces, tiptoe through the light-bending exhibits at **The Sandwich Glass Museum,** 129 Main St. (888-0251), in Sandwich center. (Open Apr.-Oct. daily 9:30am-4:30pm; Nov.-Mar. W-Su 9:30am-4pm; closed in Jan. $3.50, under 12 $1.)

The floral **Heritage Plantation of Sandwich,** Grove St. (888-3300), features a working 1912 carousel, antique automobiles, military and art museums, and 76 acres of landscaped gardens (open mid-May to mid-Oct. daily 10am-5pm; $9, seniors $8, ages 6-18 $4.50).

Wander through a briar patch and wildflower gardens at the **Green Briar Nature Center and Jam Kitchen,** 6 Discovery Hill Rd. (888-6870), 1 mi. east on Rte. 6A. The center kitchen churns out jam before the eyes of hungry visitors. (Open M-Sa 10am-4pm, Su 1-4pm; Jan.-Mar. Tu-Sa 10am-4pm. Free, donations accepted.) The best beach on the Upper Cape, the **Sandy Neck Beach,** on Sandy Neck Rd. 3 mi. east of Sandwich off Rte. 6A, extends 6 mi. along Cape Cod Bay with beautifully polished, egg-sized granite cobbles and verdant dunes. Hike only on marked trails; the plants are very fragile. Across the Sagamore Bridge, **Scusset Beach** (888-0859), on the canal near the junction of Rte. 6 and Rte. 3, offers swimming and a fishing jetty ($2 per car).

The **Shawme-Crowell State Forest** (888-0351), at Rte. 130 and Rte. 6, provides 285 wooded campsites with showers and campfires, but no hookups (sites including parking at Scusset Beach $6, without water $5). The family-oriented **Peters Pond Park Campground** (477-1775), on Cotuit Rd. in south Sandwich, combines water-side sites with swimming, fishing, rowboat rentals ($15 per day), showers, and a grocery store. No pets are allowed. (Sites $23-35. Open mid-Apr. to mid-Oct.)

Sandwich lies at the intersection of Rte. 6A and Rte. 130, about 13 mi. from Hyannis. The **Plymouth & Brockton** bus makes its closest stop in Sagamore, 3 mi. northwest along Rte. 130.

■ Lower Cape

Cape Cod National Seashore As early as 1825, the Cape had suffered so much man-made damage that the town of Truro required local residents to plant beach grass and keep their cows off the dunes. Further efforts toward conservation culminated in 1961 with the creation of the **Cape Cod National Seashore,** which includes much of the Lower Cape from Provincetown south to Chatham. Over 30 mi. of wide, soft, uninterrupted beaches lie under the tall clay cliffs and towering 19th-century lighthouses of this protected area. Thanks to conservationists, the shore has largely escaped the boardwalk commercialism which afflicts most American seacoasts. Just a short walk away from the lifeguards, the sea of umbrellas and coolers fades into the distance. Hike one of the seashore's seldom-used nature trails; the wide variety of habitats that huddle together on this narrow slice of land is truly impressive. Grassy dunes give way to inland forests, and salt marshes play host to migrating and native waterfowl, while warm freshwater ponds, such as **Gull Pond** in Wellfleet or **Pilgrim Lake** in Truro, are perfect for secluded swimming.

Most beachgoers face the difficult question: ocean or bay? While the ocean beaches entice with whistling winds and surging waves, the water on the bay side rests calmer and gets a bit warmer. The National Seashore oversees six beaches: **Coast Guard** and **Nauset Light** in Eastham; **Marconi** in Wellfleet; **Head of the Meadow** in Truro, and **Race Point** and **Herring Cove** in Provincetown. Herring Cove has special facilities which allow disabled travelers access to the water. (Parking at all beaches $7 per day, $20 per season; mid-Sept. to late June free.)

To park at any other beach, you'll need a town permit. While each town has a different beach-parking policy, all require proof of lodging in their town. Permits generally cost $20-25 per week, $50-100 per season, or $5-10 per day, and can be purchased at town halls. Call the appropriate town hall before trying to get around the parking permit; beaches are sometimes miles from any other legal parking and police with tow trucks flock like vultures. On sunny days, parking lots fill up by 11am or earlier; it's often easier to rent a bike and ride in. Most town beaches do not require bikers and walkers to pay an entrance fee. Wellfleet and Truro stand out among the ocean beaches as great examples of the Cape's famous endangered sand dunes. **Cahoon Hollow Beach,** with spectacular, cliff-like dunes, and **Duck Harbor Beach,** overlooking the bay in Wellfleet, provide two particularly beautiful vistas.

Among the best of the seashore's 11 self-guiding **nature trails,** the **Great Island Trail,** in Wellfleet, traces an 8 mi. loop through pine forests and grassy marshes and along a ridge with a view of the bay and Provincetown. The **Atlantic White Cedar Swamp Trail,** a 1¼ mi. walk, leads you to dark, swampy waters under towering trees, beginning at Marconi Station site in south Wellfleet. The **Buttonbush Trail,** a ¼ mi. walk with braille guides and a guide rope for the blind, leaves the Salt Pond Visitors Center (see below). There are also three park **bike trails:** Nauset Trail (1.6 mi.), Head of the Meadow Trail (2 mi.), and Province Lands Trail (5 mi.). Start your exploration at the **National Seashore's Salt Pond Visitors Center** (255-3421), at Salt Pond, off Rte. 6 in Eastham (open daily 9am-5pm; Sept.-June 9am-4:30pm). The center offers a free 10min. film every 30min. and a free museum with exhibits on the Cape's natural and contemporary history. **Camping** on the national seashore is illegal. Permits for fishing and campfires can be purchased at the visitors center.

Eastham The **Eastham Windmill,** on Rte. 6 at Samoset Rd. in Eastham, has had its nose to the grindstone since 1680. The windmill continues to function and demonstrates how the Native American crop of corn was put to use by industrious Cape Codders. (Open July-Aug. M-Sa 10am-5pm, Su 1-5pm. Free.) Off Rte. 6, **Fort Hill** grants a survey of Nauset Marsh and the surrounding forest and ocean, as well as the paths which access them. For a classic view of the dunes and sea, drive to **Nauset Light,** on Salt Pond Rd. Popular with Cape bikers, the excellent **Mid-Cape Hostel (HI-AYH),** 75 Goody Hallet Dr. (255-2785), occupies a quiet, wooded spot in Eastham, convenient to the lower part of the Cape. On the **Plymouth-Brockton bus** to Provincetown, ask to be let off at the traffic circle in Orleans (not the Eastham stop).

Walk out on the exit to Rock Harbor, turn right on Bridge Rd., and take a right onto Goody Hallet Rd. ½ mi. from Rte. 6. The hostel has eight cabins with a total of 78 beds, a kitchen, and a relaxed atmosphere that attracts groups. (Members $14, non-members $17. 5-day max. stay. Reception daily 7:30-10am and 5-10pm. Reservations essential July-Aug. Open mid-May to mid-Sept.) **Town Hall:** 240-5900.

Wellfleet Hundreds of bird species inhabit the **Wellfleet Wildlife Sanctuary** (349-2615), on Rte. 6, and its seven walking trails winding through salt marshes, tidal flats, and fields. (Open daily 8:30am-5pm; mid-Oct. to May Tu-Su 8:30am-5pm. $3, seniors $2, ages 6-12 $2.) **Gull Pond,** off Gull Pond Rd. in Wellfleet, provides for some of the Cape's best paddling; heading north on Rte. 6, take the first right after the police/fire department. **Paine's Campground,** 180 Old County Rd. (349-3007 or 800-479-3017), avoids noise conflicts with a special section for families and one for quiet couples (office open May to mid-Oct. 9am-9pm; tent sites for 2 $17-24). **Maurice's Campground,** 80 Rte. 6 (349-2029) offers 200 sites as well as a playground, basket-ball court, and direct access to the Cape Cod Rail Trail. (Office open mid-May to mid-Oct. daily 9am-9pm. Tent sites for 2 $20, with hookup $23.) **Moby Dick's Restaurant** (349-9796), on Rte. 6, offers a selection of Cape Cod favorites, including delicious clam chowder ($3.75) and lobster rolls ($10.75; open early June to late Sept. daily 11:30am-10pm). **Town Hall:** 349-9818.

Truro Head down Highland Rd., off Rte. 6, for a panoramic view of the Lower Cape from the top of a former Thoreau haunt, the **Cape Cod Lighthouse.** Recently moved over 400 ft. inland, the lighthouse lies adjacent to the **Truro Historical Museum** (487-3397), a former hotel that transports visitors back in history with shipwreck memen-tos, early whaling gear, and Victorian-style furnished rooms. (Open June-Oct. daily 10am-5pm. $3, $5 for a lighthouse/museum combo ticket, under 12 free.) The pictur-esque ½ mi. **Cranberry Bog Trail,** North Pamet Rd., provides a secluded, spectacular setting for a walk; get a map at the Salt Pond Visitors Center (see above). During the winter it's a school, but in summer it's the **Truro Hostel (HI-AYH),** N. Pamet Rd. (349-3889). Take the N. Pamet Rd. Exit off Rte. 6; follow it 1½ mi. to the east. The hos-tel offers an escape from the crowds with plenty of space, 42 beds, a large kitchen, great ocean views, and access to Ballston Beach. ($14, nonmembers $18. Reception daily 8-10am and 5-10pm. Reservations essential. Open late June to early Sept.) Several popular campgrounds nestle among the dwarf pines by the dunelands of North Truro. Just 7 mi. southeast of Provincetown on Rte. 6, **North Truro Camping Area** (487-1847), on Highland Rd. ½ mi. east of Rte. 6, has small sandy sites, heated restrooms, hot showers, and cable TV with hookup (sites for 2 $15, full hookup $21; $7.50 per additional person). Call **Horton's** (487-1220) or **North of Highland** (487-1191) for more sites in Truro. **Town Hall:** 349-3635.

■ Provincetown

At Provincetown, Cape Cod ends and the wide Atlantic begins. The National Sea-shore protects two-thirds of "P-Town" as conservation land; the inhabited third touches the harbor on the south side of town. In this former fishing village, whalers have given way to a large gay and lesbian community. Now, art galleries sprinkled among gay erotica shops with such novelty as "Billy, The First Out and Proud Doll" line bustling Commercial St., the town's main drag and home to many a drag show.

PRACTICAL INFORMATION Provincetown rests in the clenched fist at the end of the arm that is Cape Cod, 123 mi. from Boston by car and 3hr. by ferry across Massa-chusetts Bay. Parking spots are hard-won, especially on cloudy days when the Cape's frustrated sun-worshippers flock to Provincetown. Follow the parking signs on **Brad-ford St.,** the auto-friendly thoroughfare, to dock your car for $4-8 per day, or try to find free public parking on Bradford St. or **Commercial St.** at the east end of town. Whale-watching boats, the Boston ferry, and buses depart from **MacMillan Wharf,** at the center of town, just down the hill from the Pilgrim Monument.

Plymouth and Brockton Bus (746-0378) heads to Boston (4hr., in summer 5 per day, $20) at the stop on MacMillan Wharf. **Bay State Cruises** (617-457-1428) sends a ferry to Boston (3hr., $18) from MacMillan wharf. (Ferries mid-June to early Sept. daily; late May to mid-June and early Sept. to mid-Oct. Sa-Su only.) To get around in Provincetown and Herring Cove Beach, take the **Provincetown Shuttle Bus** (240-0050). One route travels the length of Bradford St.; the other goes from MacMillan Wharf to Herring Cove Beach. (Operates late June to early Sept. daily on the hr. 8am-midnight, 10am-6pm for the beach. $1.25, seniors 75¢.) Rented bikes from **Arnold's Where You Rent the Bicycles,** 329 Commercial St. (487-0844), are another workable mode of transport. ($2.50-3.50 per hr., 2hr. min. $10-15 per day. 24hr. rental $2 more. Deposit and ID required; credit cards accepted. Open daily 8:30am-5:30pm. Daily rentals due back by 5pm.) You'll find the exceptionally helpful **Provincetown Chamber of Commerce,** 307 Commercial St. (487-3424; http://www.ptownchamber.org), on MacMillan Wharf (open daily June-Sept. 9am-5pm; Mar.-May 10am-4pm; Oct.-Dec. M-Sa 10am-4pm). **Province Lands Visitors Center,** Race Point Rd. (487-1256), has info on the national seashore and free guides to the nature and bike trails (open mid-Apr. to mid-Nov. 9am-5pm). **Post Office:** 211 Commercial St. (487-0163; open M-F 8:30am-5pm, Sa 9:30-11:30am). **ZIP code:** 02657. **Area code:** 508.

ACCOMMODATIONS AND CAMPGROUNDS Provincetown teems with expensive places to lay your head. Your most affordable options are the wonderful hostels 10 mi. away in nearby Truro and a bit further away in Eastham. Still, the roaring Provincetown nightlife may make you unhappy with a late-night drive home and a few decent quasi-budget accommodations exist. In the quiet east end of town, the excellent **Cape Codder,** 570 Commercial St. (487-0131; call 7am-10pm), welcomes you in classic Cape Cod style, right down to the wicker furniture and private beach access. (Singles and doubles $37-57; mid-Sept. to mid-June about $10 less. Parking and continental breakfast included in-season. Open May-Oct. Reservations recommended.) For the cheapest beds in town, try **The Outermost Hostel,** 28 Winslow St. (487-4378), 100 yd. from the Pilgrim Monument. Thirty beds in five cramped but cozy cottages go for $15 each, including kitchen access and free parking. (Linen rental $3. Key deposit $10. Reception daily 8-9:30am and 6-9:30pm. Check-out 9:30am. Reservations recommended for weekends. Open mid-May to mid-Oct.) Catering to a slightly older clientele, **Dunham's Guest House,** 3 Dyer St. (487-3330), has five rooms (named and colored according to squares on a Monopoly board) available in a Victorian house near the beach, a 5min. walk from the center of town. (Singles $44; doubles $54; rates vary on holidays. 1 free night per week of stay.) When the great American Realist Edward Hopper wanted to paint a guest house, he chose what is now the **Sunset Inn,** 142 Bradford St. (487-9810); it inspired his famous *Rooms For Tourists*. The house has changed little, and the warmth and light he depicted still welcome weary travelers. (Free parking available. Rates July-Aug. $59-120; mid-Apr. to June and Sept.-Nov. $45-68; includes continental breakfast. Open mid-Apr. to Nov.)

Camping in Provincetown will cost you. **Dune's Edge Campground** (487-9815), off Rte. 6 on the east end of town, has 100 shady, spacious sites. (Sites $23, with partial hookup $29. Office open July-Aug. 8am-10pm, May-June and Sept. 9am-8pm.) The **Coastal Acres Camping Court** (487-1700), a 1 mi. walk from the center of town, west on Bradford or Commercial St. and right on W. Vine St., has over 110 crowded sites—try to snag one on the waterside. (Office open July-Aug. 8am-9pm, Apr.-June and Sept.-Nov. 8am-11am. Sites $22, full hookup $30; June to mid-Sept. $20/$26. Open Apr.-Nov.)

FOOD Sit-down meals in Provincetown cost a bundle. Grab a bite at **Mojo's,** 5 Ryder St. Ext. (487-3140), a fast-food shack serving up excellent homemade french fries ($2-3) and a wide selection of Mexican, seafood, and vegetarian platters ($4-9; open May to mid-Oct. M-Th 11am-midnight, F-Sa 10:30am-10:30pm). For a monstrous burrito ($4.25-5.25), head down to **Big Daddy's Burritos,** 205 Commercial St. (487-4432; open July-Sept. daily 11am-11pm, May-June Su-Th 11am-8pm, F-Sa 11am-10pm). Since 1921, **Mayflower Family Dining,** 300 Commercial St. (487-0121), has given visitors walls lined with ancient caricatures and stomachs lined with solid food. Try the Portuguese beef tips ($9), the Italian spaghetti ($6), or the $8 crab cakes. (Open daily 11:30am-10pm. Cash only.) **Spiritus,** 190 Commercial St. (487-2808), dishes out a spirit-lifting whole-wheat pizza. (Slices $2. Open daily June-Sept. 11:30am-2am; Apr.-May and Sept. to early Nov. noon-2am.)

SIGHTS Provincetown's natural waterfront resources provide spectacular walks. Directly across from Snail Rd. on Rte. 6, an unlikely path will lead you to a world of towering, rolling **sand dunes;** look for the shacks where writers like Tennessee Williams, Norman Mailer, and John Dos Passos penned their days away. The 1.2 mi. **Breakwater Jetty,** at the west end of Commercial St., whisks you away from the crowds and onto a secluded peninsula of endless beach bearing two working lighthouses and the remains of a Civil War fort.

Contrary to popular belief, the Pilgrims first landed at Provincetown, not Plymouth. They moved on after a 2-week stay, in search of more welcoming soil. The **Pilgrim Monument and Provincetown Museum** (800-247-1620), on High Pole Hill, looms over Provincetown and commemorates that 17-day Pilgrim layover. *(Open Apr.-Nov. daily 9am-5pm. $5, ages 4-12 $3.)* The nation's tallest granite structure (253 ft.), the monument offers a gorgeous panoramic view of the Cape. At the **Provincetown Heritage Museum,** 356 Commercial St. (487-7098), you can see a half-scale model of a fishing schooner, paintings, and other exhibits (open June to mid-Oct. daily 10am-6pm; $3, under 12 free with adult).

Provincetown has long been a refuge for artists and artisans; there are over 20 **galleries** in town. Most are free and lie east of MacMillan Wharf on Commercial St. In general, galleries stay open in the afternoon and evening until 11pm, but close during a 2hr. dinner break. The free *Provincetown Gallery Guide* has complete details.

ENTERTAINMENT AND NIGHTLIFE Today, Provincetown seafarers carry telephoto lenses when they go whale hunting, not harpoons. **Whale-watch cruises** are some of P-town's most popular attractions. Several companies take you out to the feeding waters in about 40 min., then cruise around them for 2hr. The companies claim that whales are sighted on 99% of the journeys, and most promise free trips to the unlucky 1%. Tickets cost about $18; discount coupons can be found in most local publications. **Dolphin Fleet** (349-1900 or 800-826-9300), **Portuguese Princess** (487-2651 or 800-442-3188), and **Ranger V** (487-3322 or 800-992-9333) leave from and operate ticket booths on MacMillan Wharf.

Provincetown's nightlife is almost totally gay- and lesbian-oriented, but all are welcome. Most of the clubs and bars on Commercial St. charge around $5, and shut down at 1am. Uninhibited dancing shakes the ground nightly for a mixed crowd at the **Backroom,** 247 Commercial St. (487-1430; cover $5; open daily 10pm-1am). Live music drives **Antro,** 258 Commercial St. (487-2505), with nightly drag shows and techno dance music after 11pm (cover varies; open May-Oct. daily 11am-1am). Proud to be the "oldest gay bar on the seacoast," **Atlantic House,** 6 Masonic Ave. (487-3821), more commonly known as the "A House," offers dancing and two bars (cover $10; open daily noon-1am). The lively and crowded **Governor Bradford,** 312 Commercial St. (487-2781), has karaoke, female impersonators, and other entertainment (cover varies; open daily 11:30pm-10pm).

■ Martha's Vineyard

Once home to several of the most successful whaling ports in New England, Martha's Vineyard now offers a haven for many vacationing luminaries. Visitors from the late Princess Di to President Clinton have sought out this secluded island for its dunes, inland woods, pastel houses, and weathered cottages. In the fall, the tourist season wanes and the foliage flares with autumnal hues. Seven communities comprise Martha's Vineyard. The western end of the island is called "up island," from the nautical days when sailors had to tack upwind to get there. The three largest towns; Oak Bluffs, Vineyard Haven, and Edgartown; are "down island" and have flatter terrain. Oak Bluffs and Edgartown are the only "wet" (alcohol-selling) towns on the island.

PRACTICAL INFORMATION

Buses: Bonanza (800-556-3815) stops at the Ferry Terminal in Woods Hole and departs, via Bourne, for Boston (1½hr.; 14 per day, Sept. to late June 10 per day; $14.50) and New York (6hr.; 6 per day, early Sept. to late June 5 per day; $45).

Ferries: The **Steamship Authority** (477-8600 or 693-9130) sends 24 boats per day on the 45min. ride from Woods Hole to Vineyard Haven and Oak Bluffs. (Ticket office open M-Th and Sa 5am-9:45pm, F and Su 5am-10:45pm. $5, ages 5-12 $2.50, car $44, bike $3. Reserve cars months in advance in summer.) The ferry company has 3 parking lots ($7.50 per day) as well as shuttle service to the dock. Other companies serve the island from Hyannis (778-2600; 1¾hr.; July-Aug. 4 per day, May-June and Sept.-Oct. 1 per day; $11); New Bedford (997-1688; 1½hr.; July-Aug. 7 per day; mid-May to June and Sept. to mid-Oct. M-F, 3 per day, Sa-Su 1 per day; $9); and Nantucket (778-2600; 2¼hr.; June to late Sept. 3 per day; $11), but the shortest and cheapest ride leaves from Falmouth (548-4800; 30min., late June to early Sept. 7 per day, $5). The **Chappy "On Time" Ferry** (627-9427) connects Edgartown Town Dock and Chappaquiddick Island. (Open daily 7am-midnight; mid-Oct. to May 7am-7:30pm, 9-10pm, and 11-11:15pm. Round-trip $1, car $5, motorcycle $4, bicycle $3.)

Taxis: Taxis here are vans with set rates—always check the taxi's fare sheet to verify price. In Oak Bluffs, call 800-396-0003; in Edgartown, 627-4677; in Vineyard Haven, 693-3705. (The trip from Vineyard Haven to Oak Bluffs costs around $6; Vineyard Haven to Edgartown $12.)

Public Transportation: Island Transport (693-1589 or 693-0058) runs shuttle buses between Vineyard Haven (Union St.), Oak Bluffs (Ocean Park), and Edgartown (Church St.) late June through August. (Late June to early Sept. daily every 15min. 10am-midnight; May to late June and early Sept. to Oct. every 30min. Su-Th 10am-6pm, F-Sa 10am-11pm. Vineyard Haven to Oak Bluffs $1.50, to Edgartown $3.) Buses run up-island from Vineyard Haven (Union St.) and Oak Bluffs (Ocean Park) to Gay Head ($4.75), West Tisbury (Alley's General Store, $2.25), and Chilmark (Chilmark Store, $4.75; late June to Aug., 4 buses daily from Vineyard Haven, 6 from Oak Bluffs). **Martha's Vineyard Regional Transit Authority (VTA)** runs summer shuttles between and within the various towns on the island; call 627-7448 for recorded information or 693-4833 for paratransit and additional information. (In-town passes $25 for summer, students $15, disabled patrons $12.50. Island-wide $50, students $30, disabled patrons $25. Individual fares 50¢ to $1.50.)

Bike Rental: Martha's Bike Rental (693-6593), at the corner of Beach St. and Beach Rd. in Vineyard Haven. $12 per day for a 3-speed, $18 per day for a mountain or hybrid. Open daily mid-June to Aug. 8am-8pm; Apr. to mid-June and Sept.-Nov. 8:45am-6pm. Scenic **bike paths** run along the state beach between Oak Bluffs and Edgartown, and through the State Forest between West Tisbury and Edgartown.

Visitor Info: Martha's Vineyard Chamber of Commerce (693-0085), Beach Rd., Vineyard Haven, furnishes handy maps and brochures. Open M-F 9am-5pm.

Medical Services: Vineyard Walk-In Medical Center, 108 State Rd. (693-6399). Open daily June-Oct. 9am-1pm; Nov.-May 9am-noon. Call for afternoon appts.

Post Office: Beach Rd., Vineyard Haven (693-2815). Open M-F 8:30am-5pm, Sa 930am-1pm. **ZIP code:** 02568. **Area code:** 508.

ACCOMMODATIONS AND CAMPGROUNDS

Cheap places to stay in Martha's Vineyard are almost nonexistent, as most inns charge over $85 per night during the summer. The chamber of commerce provides a list of inns and guest houses; all recommend reservations for July and August, especially weekends.

Martha's Vineyard Hostel (HI-AYH), Edgartown-West Tisbury Rd. (693-2665), West Tisbury. The fantastic hostel provides the 78 cheapest beds on the island. Located right next to the bike path, great kitchen and a volleyball court. $14, non-members $17. Linen $2. Open Apr. to early Nov. daily 7-9:30am and 5-10pm. Curfew 11pm. Light chores required. Reservations essential.

Nashua House (693-0043), Oak Bluffs. Clean, comfortable beds with a Van Gogh in every room. Singles and doubles $50-75; off-season $30-45. Shared bathrooms. Check-in before 10pm.

Martha's Vineyard Family Campground (693-3772), 1½ mi. from Vineyard Haven on Edgartown Rd. 185 shaded sites in an oak tree forest. Groceries and metered showers nearby. Office open daily 8am-9pm; reduced hrs. in the off season. Sites for 2 $29; ages 2-18 $2, $9 per additional person. No pets or motorcycles. Open mid-May to mid-Oct.

Webb's Camping Area, Barnes Rd. (693-0233), Oak Bluffs. 150 shaded and spacious sites. Office open daily 7:30am-9:30pm; reduced off-season hrs. Sites for 2 $29-31, depending on degree of privacy; ages 5-17 free, $9 per additional person, electricity and water add $3. Open early May to early Sept.

FOOD

Cheap sandwich and lunch places speckle the Vineyard. Vineyard Haven and Oak Bluffs best accommodate the traveler who watches the bottom line, though the options may not be so kind to the waistline. Fried-food shacks across the island sell clams, shrimp, and potatoes, which generally cost at least $15. Several **farm stands** sell inexpensive produce; the chamber of commerce map shows their locations.

Main Street Diner (627-9337), under the Edgartown Cinema on Main St. Hearty sandwiches ($5-7) and a meatloaf that would make a mother proud ($7-11). Open daily 7am-9:30pm; Oct-May 7am-8pm.

Louis', 102 State Rd. (693-3255), Vineyard Haven. Take-out Italian food that won't break the bank. Try the fresh pasta with meat sauce ($4) or the vegetable calzone for $4.50. Open M-Th 11:30am-8:30pm, F-Sa 11am-9pm, Su 4-8:30pm.

Black Dog Bakery (693-4786), on Beach St., in Vineyard Haven A range of creative and delicious pastries and breads (40¢-$3.25) tempt patrons, but for the love of God, please don't buy another sweatshirt. Open daily 5:30am-8pm.

Mad Martha's (693-9151), on Circuit Ave. in Oak Bluffs. This island institution scoops out homemade ice cream and frozen yogurt ($2.50-3.20). Open daily 11am-midnight; in season only. One of 5 locations throughout the island.

SIGHTS

Exploring the Vineyard can involve much more than zipping around on a moped. Head out to the countryside, hit the beach, or trek down one of the great trails. **Felix Neck Wildlife Sanctuary** (627-4850), on the Edgartown-Vineyard Haven Rd., offers a variety of terrains for exploration on its 350 acres (office open Sept. to mid-June Tu-Su 8am-sunset; $3, seniors and under 12 $2). **Memensha Hills Reservation,** off North Rd. in Menemsha, has 4 mi. of trails along the rocky Vineyard Sound beach leading to the island's second-highest point. **Cedar Tree Neck** on the western shore harbors 250 acres of headland off Indian Hill Rd. with trails throughout, while the **Long Point** park in West Tisbury preserves 550 acres and a shore on the Tisbury Great Pond. The largest conservation area on the island, **Cape Pogue Wildlife Refuge and Wasque Reservation** (693-7662), floats on Chappaquiddick Island.

Two of the best beaches on the island, **South Beach,** at the end of Katama Rd., 3 mi. south of Edgartown; and **State Beach,** on Beach Rd. between Edgartown and Oak Bluffs, are free and open to the public. South Beach boasts sizeable surf and an occasionally nasty undertow, while the warmer, gentler waters of State Beach once set the stage for parts of *Jaws,* the grandaddy of classic beach-horror films. For the best sunsets on the island, stake out a spot at **Gay Head** or the **Menemsha Town Beach;** enjoy the sun's descent while dining on seafood from nearby stands.

Chicama Vineyards, off State Rd. in West Tisbury, offers free tours and wine tasting (open June to mid-Oct. M-Sa 11am-5pm, Su 1-5pm). **Oak Bluffs,** 3 mi. west of Vineyard Haven on Beach Rd., is the most youth-oriented of the Vineyard villages. Highlights of a tour of **Trinity Park** near the harbor include the famous "Gingerbread Houses" (minutely detailed, elaborate pastel Victorian cottages) and the Oak Bluffs's **Flying Horses Carousel** (693-9481), at the end of Circuit Ave. It's the oldest in the nation (built in 1876), and composed of 20 handcrafted horses with real horsehair. *(Open mid-June to Aug. daily 10am-10pm; Apr. to mid-Oct. M-F 11am-4:30pm, Sa 10am-8pm, Su 10am-5pm. Fare $1.)* **Gay Head,** 22 mi. southwest of Oak Bluffs on State Rd., offers just about the best view of the sea in all of New England. The native Wampanoag frequently saved sailors whose ships wrecked on the breathtaking **Gay Head Cliffs.** The 100,000-year-old precipice shines in brilliant colors and supports one of five light-houses on the island. **Menemsha** and **Chilmark,** a little northeast of Gay Head, share a scenic coastline; Chilmark claims to be the only working fishing town on the island. Tourists can fish off the pier. **Vineyard Haven** has more artsy boutiques and fewer tacky t-shirt shops than other towns on the island.

■ Nantucket

Once the home of the biggest whaling port in the world, Nantucket saw one of its whaling ships, the *Essex,* rammed by a whale in 1820. The incident inspired Herman Melville's *Moby Dick.* Though the Nantucket of today is a secluded outpost of privi-lege and establishment, it is possible to enjoy a stay on the island without holding up a convenience store to do so. Nantucket's 82 mi. of beach are always free. If possible, visit during the first or last weeks of the tourist season, when prices tend to drop. Only a few places stay open during the cold, rainy winter months, when awesome storms churn the slate-colored seas and bitter winds batter the island.

PRACTICAL INFORMATION Nantucket Regional Transit Authority (228-7025) runs five shuttle bus routes throughout the island. (Bus to Madaket leaves from Peter Foulger Museum on Broad St. Bus to Sconset leaves from corner of Main St. and Wash-ington St. Buses depart every 30min. 7am-11:30pm. $1, seniors and under 6 free. Multi-day passes available at the visitors center.) **Hyline** (778-2600) operates **ferry** ser-vice to Nantucket's Straight Wharf from Hyannis (mid-June to early Sept. 6 per day; late May to mid-June 4 per day; Sept. 3 per day; May 8-22 and late Sept. to Oct. 1 per day; $11; $2 discount for HI-AYH members) and from Martha's Vineyard (early May to late Oct., 4 per day, $11). **Steamship Authority** (477-8600), docked at Steamboat Wharf on Nantucket, runs ferries from Hyannis only (6 per day, $11). Both charge $5 for bikes and take about 2hr. The **visitor services and information center,** 25 Federal St. (228-0925; http://www.nantucketchamber.org), can help you find a place to stay (open daily 9am-9pm; Nov. to early June 9am-6pm).

Though some say that hitchhiking is the best way to get around Nantucket, *Let's Go* does not encourage hitching. Those who prefer to pedal rent bikes at **Nantucket Bike Shop** (228-1999), Steamboat and Straight Wharfs. Mountain bikes and hybrids cost $20 per day or $6 per hour (open daily 8am-7pm; Sept.-June 10am-6pm). Take your rental down any one of Nantucket's three **bike paths:** Madaket Beach (5 mi.), Surfside Beach (2½ mi.), and Siasconset (6 mi.). **Area code:** 508.

ACCOMMODATIONS AND FOOD Occupying an old life-saving station, the **Nan-tucket Hostel (HI-AYH),** 31 Western Ave. (228-0433), sits at Surfside Beach, 3½ mi. from town at the end of the Surfside Bike Path. Take the Miacomet Loop Shuttle to Surfside Rd. and walk 1 mi. south on Surfside. (49 beds, full kitchen. $14, nonmem-bers $17. Linen $2. Reception 7:30-10am and 5-10pm. Lockout 10am-5pm. Curfew 11pm. Reservations essential. Open late Apr. to mid-Oct.) In the heart of Nantucket Town, **Nesbitt Inn,** 21 Broad St. (228-2446), offers 13 rooms, each with a sink and shared baths in a gorgeous Victorian guest house. The friendly owners make guests comfortable with a fireplace, deck, and free continental breakfast. (Singles $50; doubles $70; triples $90; Oct.-Apr. $8-10 less. Reception 7am-10pm. Reserva-tions and deposit required.)

Meals on Nantucket are pricey. The standard entree runs about $15-20, but the fru-gal gourmet can still dine well. **Black Eyed Susan's,** 10 India St. (325-0308), offers a rotating breakfast and dinner menu with interesting dishes such as buttermilk pan-cakes with Jarlsberg cheese. (Full order $6.25. Breakfast daily 7am-1pm, dinner M-Sa 6-10pm.) **Henry's Sandwiches,** Steamboat Wharf (228-0123), piles 'em high with cold cuts and tons of toppings (open daily 10am-7pm). **Muse Pizza,** 44 Surfside Rd. (228-1471), offers the cheapest and some of the best pizza on the island (slices $1.75). Muses devour pepperoni and cheese among pool players and live rock 'n' roll, ska, and acoustic music nightly. (Open daily 6:30am-1am.)

SIGHTS AND ACTIVITIES The remarkable natural beauty of Nantucket is well protected; over 36% of the island's land can never be built upon. For a great **bike trip,** head east from Nantucket Town on Milestone Rd. and turn left onto any path that looks promising. Pedal through the lush moors of heather, huckleberries, bayberries, and wild roses. For a day on the sand, **Dionis Beach,** on the northwest end of the island, has the smallest crowds and impressive dunes. **Cisco Beach** appeals to the younger set, while **Surfside** offers the largest waves. **Sea Nantucket** (228-7499), at the end of Washington St. at the waterfront, will set you up in a rental **sea kayak** for an aquatic adventure. *(Single $30 for ½-day, double $50; full-day $40/$60. Open daily 8:30am-5:30pm.)* The boats aren't difficult to maneuver, but paddling works up a sweat. If you take one out to a nearby salt marsh, or head across the harbor to an isolated beach on the Coatue peninsula, you'll be able to enjoy a picnic undisturbed by other beachgoers. Those who prefer to stand on the strand between land and sea can rent **surf fishing** equipment from **Barry Thurston's** (228-9595), at Harbor Sq. near the A&P, the fisherman provides up-to-date info on where the fish are biting (necessary equipment $20 for 24hr.; open M-Sa 8am-9pm, Su 9am-6pm).

The fascinating **Nantucket Whaling Museum** (228-1736), Broad St. in Nantucket Town, recreates the old whaling community through exhibits and talks on whales and methods of whaling. The **Peter Foulger Museum** (228-1894), Broad St. Lockout 10am-5pm gives an overview of Nantucket's history. *(3 lectures per day. $5, children $3. Both museums open early June to mid-Oct. M-F 10am-5pm; May to early June and mid-Oct. to early Dec. Sa-Su 11am-3pm.)* The best deal is a visitor's pass which allows access to both museums and seven other historical sights run by the historical association ($10, children $5). The free publication *Yesterday's Island* provides listings of nature walks, concerts, lectures, and art exhibitions.

WESTERN MASSACHUSETTS

Famous for cultural events in the summer, rich foliage in the fall, and skiing in the winter, the Berkshire Mountains have long been a vacation destination for Boston and New York urbanites seeking a relaxing country escape. Filling the western third of Massachusetts, the Berkshire Region is bordered to the north by Rte. 2 (the Mohawk Trail) and Vermont, to the west by Rte. 7 and New York, to the south by the Mass. Pike and Connecticut, and to the east by I-91. A host of affordable B&Bs, restaurants, and campgrounds freckle the area, making it both financially and logistically accessible for the budget traveler.

■ The Berkshires

PRACTICAL INFORMATION Sprinkled with small New England towns, the Berkshires offer a plethora of churches, fudge shops, antique boutiques, and country stores. To see sights located far from the town centers, you'll have to drive. Winding and sometimes pocked with potholes, the region's roads are nevertheless scenic. The **Berkshire Visitors Bureau,** 2 Berkshire Common (443-9186 or 800-237-5747), Plaza Level, in Pittsfield (open M-F 8:30am-5pm) and an **information booth** (open M-F 9am-5pm) on the east side of Pittsfield's rotary circle will give you the scoop on restaurants and accommodations in the surrounding area. Berkshire County's 12 state parks and forests cover 100,000 acres and offer numerous camping and hiking options. For info, stop by the **Region 5 Headquarters,** 740 South St., in Pittsfield (442-8928; open M-F 8am-5pm). **Area code:** 413.

The Mohawk Trail Perhaps the most famous highway in the state, the **Mohawk Trail** (Rte. 2) provides a meandering and scenic drive that showcases the beauty of the Berkshires. During fall foliage weekends, the awe-inspiring reds and golds of the surrounding mountains draw crowds of leaf-peepers. The town of Millers

Falls marks the trail's eastern terminus. Five miles west of Charlemont, off Rte. 2, the **Mohawk Trail State Forest** (339-5504) offers campsites along a river ($6) and rents cabins. (Electricity but no hookups; small $8, large $10; reservations required at least two weeks in advance.) Whitewater raft on the **Deerfield River** (Apr.-Oct.) with **Crabapple Whitewater** (800-553-7238), in Charlemont (differing skill levels available).

North Adams is home to the **Western Gateway** (663-6312), on Furnace St. bypass off Rte. 8, a railroad museum and one of Massachusetts's five Heritage State Parks. (Open late May to early Sept. daily 10am-5pm. Free, donations encouraged. Live music in summer Th 7pm.) **The Freight Yard Pub** (663-6547), within the Western Gateway park, offers inexpensive salads ($2-7) and, on weekdays, a huge $6 lunch buffet (open Su-W 11:30am-1am, Th-Sa 11:30am-2am; cafe dining available outside). On Rte. 8, ½ mi. north of downtown North Adams, lies **Natural Bridge State Park** (in summer 663-6392, in winter 663-6312), a white marble bridge formed during the last Ice Age and the only natural, water-eroded bridge on the continent. (Open late May to mid-Oct. M-F 8am-4pm, Sa-Su 10am-6pm. $2 per vehicle.)

Mt. Greylock, the highest peak in Massachusetts (3491 ft.), is south of the Mohawk Trail, and only accessible by Rte. 2 to the north and U.S. 7 to the west. By car, take Notch Rd. from Rte. 2 between North Adams and Williamstown, or take Rockwell Rd. from Lanesboro on U.S. 7. The roads up are rough but offer magnificent veiws. Hiking trails begin from nearly all the towns around the mountain; free maps are available at the **Mt. Greylock Visitors Information Center** (499-4262), Rockwell Rd. (open daily 9am-5pm). Once at the top, climb the **War Memorial** for a breathtaking view. Sleep high in nearby **Bascom Lodge** (743-1591), built from the rock excavated for the monument. ($22, F-Sa $25; under 12 $10/$15; private doubles $52-62; F-Sa rates apply daily in Aug.) The lodge offers breakfast ($6), lunch ($6) and dinner ($12; open mid-May to mid-Oct. 6am-10pm; snack bar open daily 10am-5pm). Two miles shy of the summit off Rockwell Rd., **primitive camping** (443-0011) is offered at 39 sites ($4; water available at Bascom Lodge).

The Mohawk Trail ends in Williamstown at its junction with U.S. 7. Here, an information booth (458-4922) provides an abundance of free local maps and seasonal brochures, and can help find a place to stay in one of Williamstown's many reasonably priced B&Bs (staffed May-Oct. daily 10am-6pm). At **Williams College,** the second-oldest in Massachusetts (est. 1793), lecturers compete with the beautiful scenery of surrounding mountains for the students' attention. Campus maps are available from the **Admissions Office,** 988 Main St. (597-2211; open M-F 8:30am-4:30pm; tours 10, 11:15am, 1:15, 3:30pm). First among the college's many cultural resources, **Chapin Library** (597-2462), in Stetson Hall, displays a number of rare U.S. manuscripts, including early copies of the Declaration of Independence, Articles of Confederation, Constitution, and Bill of Rights (open M-F 10am-noon and 1-5pm; free). The small but impressive **Williams College Museum of Art** (597-2429), off Main St. (Rte. 2), between Spring and Water St., merits a visit. Rotating exhibits have included Soviet graphic art, postmodern architecture, and Impressionist works (open Tu-Sa 10am-5pm, Su 1-5pm; free). Also free in Williamstown, the **Sterling and Francine Clark Art Institute,** 225 South St. (458-9545), houses Impressionist paintings and collections of silver and sculpture (open W-M 10am-8pm; off- season Tu-Su 10am-5pm). For tasty eats, popular **Pappa Charlie's Deli,** 28 Spring St. (458-5969), offers sandwiches such as the "Dick Cavett" and the $4.25 "Dr. Johnny Fever" (open M-Sa 8am-11pm, Su 9am-11pm; Sept.-June M-Sa 8am-9pm, Su 9am-9pm).

Williamstown has many affordable motels east of town on Rte. 2. **The Maple Terrace Motel,** 555 Main St./Rte. 2 (458-9677), has bright rooms with a heated outdoor pool and free continental breakfast (singles $44-78; doubles $54-88; office open daily 8am-10:30pm). Williamstown's surrounding wooded hills beckon from the moment you arrive. The **Hopkins Memorial Forest** (597-2346) offers over 2250 acres that are free to the public for hiking and cross-country skiing. Take U.S. 7 N, turn left on Bulkley St., follow Bulkley to the end, and turn right onto Northwest Hill Rd.

Rte. 7 South of Williamstown, the first major town along Rte. 7 is Pittsfield, the county seat of Berkshire County and the town credited with the creation of the county fair. Recreational possibilities abound at the **Pittsfield State Forest** (442-8992), 4 mi. northwest of town, off Rte. 20. The Forest offers campsites ($4-5) and schedules outdoor activities. The Berkshire's rich literary history can be sampled at **Herman Melville's** home, **Arrowhead,** 780 Holmes Rd. (442-1793), 3½ mi. south of Pittsfield. *(Open late May to early Sept. daily 10am-4:30pm, early Sept. to Oct. F-M 10am-4:30pm. $5, seniors $4.50, ages 6-16 $3.50. 30min. tours every 30min.)* The building houses the **Berkshire County Historical Society,** which has exhibits on 19th-century country life and the role of women on the farm. The **Berkshire Museum,** 39 South St. (443-7171), Pittsfield, has Hudson River School paintings, natural history exhibits, and an aquarium. *(Open Aug. M-Sa 10am-5pm, Su 1-5pm; Sept.-July Tu-Sa 10am-5pm, Su 1-5pm. $6, students and seniors $5, ages 12-18 $2. Free W and Sa 10am-noon.)*

The 18th-century utopian lifestyle returns at the **Hancock Shaker Village** (443-0188 or 800-817-1137), at the junction of Rte 20 and Rte. 41, west of Pittsfield. *(Open daily Apr. to late May 10am-3pm; late May to mid-Oct. 9:30am-5pm; mid-Oct. to Nov. 10am-3pm. $13.50, ages 6-17 $5; pass good for 10 days.)* Visitors can tour the village's 20 buildings, observe artisans busy at work, and try their skill with a quill pen.

Tanglewood, the famed summer home of the **Boston Symphony Orchestra** (637-5165), hides one of the Berkshires' greatest treasures. *(Orchestral concerts held July-Aug. F 8:30pm with 6:30pm prelude, Sa 8:30pm, Su 2:30pm. Tickets $14-65, lawn seats $13. Open rehearsals held Sa 10:30am. Call for schedule of special events and prices.)* South on Rte. 7, a short distance west of Lenox Center on Rte. 183 (West St.), Tanglewood concerts show off a variety of music styles, from Ray Charles to Wynton Marsalis to James Taylor, but its bread-and-butter is top-notch classical music. Lawn tickets and picnics make for a great evening or Sunday afternoon. There are also chamber concerts on Thursday evenings, and the Boston Pops give two summer concerts. The summer concludes with a jazz festival over Labor Day weekend. The **Edith Wharton Restoration at the Mount** (637-1899), at the junction of Rte. 7 and 7A in Lenox, showcases the home of the great turn-of-the-century Pulitzer Prize winner. *(Open late May to Oct. daily 9am-2pm. $6, seniors $5.50, ages 13-18 $4.50. Tours on the hr.)* Stockbridge is home to the **Norman Rockwell Museum** (298-4100), on Rte. 183, ½ mi. south from the junction of Rte. 7 and 102. *(Open May-Oct. daily 10am-5pm; Nov.-Apr. M-F 11am-4pm, Sa-Su 10am-5pm. $9, children $2.)* Containing more than 1000 items, including many of Rockwell's *Saturday Evening Post* covers, this is a must-see for visitors to the area.

Following Rte. 7 south will take you past the **Wagon Wheel Motel** (445-4532), at the junction of Rte. 20 (off-season $40-45, varying in summer). Summer weekend rates are high throughout the Berkshires, starting at $100. A cheaper option is to continue north on U.S. 20 for about 3 mi. to Walker Rd., which takes you to **October Mountain State Forest** (243-1778) with toilets and showers (sites $6).

Northampton and Amherst

The last two sides of the Berkshire square are major interstate routes. Although time-saving, these interstates prevent visitors from seeing as much great natural scenery. However, there are alternate routes for beauty-seekers with time on their hands. Rte. 20 meanders above, below, and around the Mass Pike (Rte. 90), and in the north-south direction, Rte. 91 can be supplanted by Rtes. 47 and 63, which snake along the Connecticut River.

On Rte. 91, about 15min. north of Springfield, lie educational hubs **Northampton** and **Amherst.** Northampton is a beautiful town that boasts a surprising number of restaurants and shops. In Northampton, the **Smith College Museum of Art** (385-2760), on Elm St. at Bedford Terrace in Tyron Hall, has a collection of 19th- and 20th-century European and American paintings, and offers tours and gallery talks (open Tu-W and F-Sa 9:30am-4pm, Th and Su 2-8pm; free). **Look Memorial Park** (584-5457), on the Berkshire Trail (Rte. 9) not far from Northampton, is bordered by the Mill River. Its 200 acres make for a pleasant picnic spot. (Open daily dawn-dusk. Facilities open late May to early Sept. daily 11am-7pm. $2 per vehicle Sa-Su, $1 M-F.)

NEW ENGLAND

Dubbed "the mecca of the Northeast" by Amherst students, **Antonio's,** 31 N. Pleasant St. (253-0808), in Amherst, makes deliciously creative pizza with toppings like pesto chicken or beef taco (slices $1.25-2.75; open daily 10am-10pm). Award-winning **La Veracruzana,** 31 Main St. (586-7181), in Northampton, is the hot spot for Mexican food. Try the excellent enchiladas ($6-7) with any one of the eight salsas at their salsa bar. (Open Su-W 11am-10pm, Th-F 11am-11pm, Sa 11am-midnight.)

The **Five-College Consortium** spreads across western Massachusetts and consists of five schools in which students form a larger academic community. The largest is the gargantuan **University of Massachusetts-Amherst** (545-0222), in Amherst (tours daily 11am and 1:15pm; June-Aug. M-F 11am and 1:15pm). Prestigious **Amherst College** (542-2328) shares the town with the main UMass campus. (Tours every 2hr. M-F June-Aug. 10am-4pm; Feb. to early May 9am-3pm; mid-Sept. to mid-Dec. 9am-3pm.)

For more info on the area, visit or call the **Greater Northampton Chamber of Commerce,** 99 Pleasant St. (584-1900; open Sa-Su 10am-5pm; Oct.-Apr. M-F 9am-5pm). **Peter Pan Trailways,** 1 Roundhouse Plaza (586-1030; station open daily 7am-6pm), runs buses to Boston (14 per day, $21) and New York (12 per day, $29). **Internet access** is available at Forbes Library, 20 West St. (587-1011), Northampton (open M 1-9pm, Tu 9am-6pm, W 9am-9pm, Th 1-5pm, F-Sa 9am-5m). **Area code:** 413.

Springfield As the largest city in the western half of Massachusetts, **Springfield** serves the region as an industrial and transportation center, and a counter-balance to its rival Shelbyville. Springfield fills the southeast quadrant of the intersection of I-90 and I-91, the main north-south artery in the region. The **Greater Springfield Convention and Visitors Bureau,** in the Tower Sq. building at 1500 Main St. (787-1548), can help you find accommodations (open M-F 8:30am-5pm). Trusty **Motel 6,** 106 Capital Dr. (800-466-8356), off I-91 at Exit 13A, offers clean, comfortable rooms, at equally comfortable prices (singles $36; doubles $42).

In 1891, with the help of **Dr. James Naismith,** the game of basketball developed in Springfield. Today, visitors to the **Basketball Hall of Fame,** 1150 W. Columbus Ave. (781-6500), can walk in Bob Lanier's size 22 sneakers and play a virtual one-on-one with Bill Walton. (Open Su-Tu and Th 9am-6pm, W and F-Sa 9am-8pm. $8, seniors and ages 7-15 $5.) Once in town, check out the **Indian Motorcycle Museum,** 33 Hendee St. (737-2624), for a look at some great old bikes (open daily 10am-4pm, Dec.-Feb. 1-4pm; $3, ages 6-12 $1).

History buffs may wish to head 30min. east to **Old Sturbridge Village,** on Rte. 20 in Sturbridge at the intersection of I-90 and I-84. (Open late Mar. to Oct. 9am-5pm. 2-day admission $16, seniors $15, ages 6-15 $8.) Staffed by costumed "villagers," this recreated 1830s community features over 40 exhibits such as a cider mill, blacksmith shop, and clock gallery, spread out over 200 acres of rural countryside. **Peter Pan Bus Line** provides service from Boston; call 617-426-7838 for info and tickets. **Area code:** 413.

Rhode Island

Rhode Island, despite its diminutive stature (it's the smallest state in the Union), has always been a trend-setter. It was the first state to pass laws against slavery. Most Rhode Islanders are proud of their non-conformist heritage. From founder Roger Williams, a religious outcast during colonial days, to Buddy Cianci, convicted felon and two-time mayor of Providence—he served one term while still on probation—Rhode Island has always lured an eccentric crowd. Though you can drive through the body of Rhode Island in 45 minutes, the state's 400 mi. coastline deserves a longer look. Small, elegant hamlets speckle the shores winding to Connecticut, and the inland roads remain quiet, unpaved thoroughfares lined with family fruit stands.

PRACTICAL INFORMATION

Capital: Providence.
Visitor Info: Dept. of Tourism, 1 West Exchange St., Providence 02903 (401-222-2601 or 800-556-2484; http://www.visitrhodeisland.com). Open M-F 8:30am-5pm.

Division of Parks and Recreation, 2321 Hartford Ave., Johnston 02919 (401-222-2632). Open M-F 8:30am-4pm.
Emergency: 911.
Time Zone: Eastern. **Postal Abbreviation:** RI.
Sales Tax: 7%.

■ Providence

Like Rome, Providence sits aloft seven hills. Seven colleges inhabit these hills, luring a community of students, artists, and academics to join the native working class and state representatives. Providence has cobbled sidewalks and colonial buildings, a college town atmosphere, and more than its share of bookstores and cafes. In the area around the colleges, students on tight budgets support a plethora of inexpensive restaurants and shops.

PRACTICAL INFORMATION The state capitol and the downtown business district cluster just east of the intersection of **I-95** and **I-195**. **Brown University** and the **Rhode Island School of Design (RISD)** sit atop a steep hill, a 10min. walk east of downtown. **Amtrak,** 100 Gaspee St. (727-7379 or 800-872-7245; station open daily 5:30am-11pm), operates from a gleaming white structure behind the state capitol, a 10min. walk from Brown or downtown. Trains set out for Boston (50min., 6 per day, $12) and New York (4hr., 9 per day, $37-52). **Greyhound** and **Bonanza,** 1 Bonanza Way (454-0790 or 800-231-2222 for Greyhound; station open daily 6am-8pm), Exit 25 off I-95, have frequent service to Boston (1hr., 17 per day, $8.50) and New York (4hr., 7 per day, $35). All New York buses make a stop at the Kennedy Plaza downtown, where Bonanza also has a ticket office. Buses from Boston stop downtown before Bonanza Way. **Rhode Island Public Transit Authority (RIPTA),** 265 Melrose St. (781-9400; M-F 7am-7pm, Sa 8am-6pm), runs an **info booth** at Kennedy Plaza, which provides in-person route and schedule assistance and free bus maps. RIPTA's service includes Newport ($3) and other points. (Buses run daily 6am-1:30am; hrs. vary by route. Fare 25¢-$3; within Providence, generally $1). For a walking tour map and tourist literature, try the **Greater Providence Convention and Visitors Bureau** (274-1636 or 800-233-1636), Waterplace Park, between Memorial Blvd. and Francis St. (open M-F 10am-5pm, Sa-Su 10am-4pm). The **Providence Preservation Society,** 21 Meeting St. (831-7440), at the foot of College Hill, provides detailed info on historic Providence (open M-F 9am-5pm). **Post Office:** 2 Exchange Terrace (421-4361; open M-F 7:30am-5:30pm, Sa 8am-2pm). **ZIP code:** 02903. **Area code:** 401.

ACCOMMODATIONS AND CAMPGROUNDS High downtown motel rates make Providence an expensive overnight stay. Rooms fill up far in advance for the graduation season in May and early June. Head 10 mi. south on I-95 to Warwick/Cranston for numerous cheap motels. Catering largely to the international visitors of the universities, the stained-glass-windowed **International House of Rhode Island,** 8 Stimson Ave. (421-7181), off Hope St. near the Brown campus, has three comfortable rooms, but they're often full. Amenities include kitchen facilities, private bath, TV, and a fridge. (Singles $50, students $35; doubles $60/$45; $5 off for stays of 5 nights or more. 2-night min. stay. Reception M-F 9:30am-5pm. Reservations required.) If you don't mind that cheap motel smell, the **Town 'n' Country Motel** (508-336-8300), 3 mi. outside of Providence on Rte. 6 in Seekonk, MA, rents out reasonable rooms (singles $44; doubles $47). The **New Yorker Motor Lodge,** 400 Newport Ave. (434-8000), in East Providence, rents the cheapest rooms around (singles $40; doubles $44). The nearest campgrounds lie a 30min. drive from downtown. One of the closest in Coventry, **Colwell's Campground** (397-4614), provides showers and hookups for 75 sites on the shore of the Flat River Reservoir. From Providence, take I-95 S to Exit 10, then head west 9½ mi. on Rte. 117 to Peckham Ln. (sites $12-15, depending on proximity to the waterfront).

FOOD A variety of impressive food is found in three areas in Providence: **Atwells Ave.** in the Italian district, on Federal Hill just west of downtown; **Thayer St.,** on College Hill to the east, home to off-beat student hangouts and ethnic restaurants; **Broad St.,** in the southwest part of town, with many inexpensive international eateries. **Geoff's Superlative Sandwiches,** 163 Benefit St. (751-2248), combines bread and ingredients in 60 different ways and names them all after stars like Buddy Cianci (sandwiches $4-6; open M-F 8am-10:30pm, Sa-Su 9am-10:30pm). They have swivel stools and good home-cookin' at the **Seaplane Diner** (941-9547), 307 Allens Ave. Around "since Grandma was a girl," Seaplane has perfected cheap homestyle breakfast and lunches ($3.50-5; open M-F 5am-3pm, Sa 5am-1pm, F-Sa midnight-4am). **Louis' Family Restaurant,** 286 Brook St. (861-5225), has made the entire community its family with friendly service. Students swear by the prices and donate artwork for the walls. Try the #1 special: two eggs, homefries, toast, and coffee for $2.65. (Open daily 5am-3pm.)

SIGHTS The most notable historic sights in Providence cluster around the 350-year-old neighborhood surrounding **College Hill. Brown University,** established in 1764, includes several 18th-century buildings and provides a fitting starting point for a historic walking tour of Providence. The Office of Admissions, housed in the historic **Carliss-Brackett House,** 45 Prospect St. (863-2378), gives free 1hr. walking tours of the campus (office open M-F 8am-4pm; tours M-F 10, 11am, 1, 3, and 4pm). In addition to founding Rhode Island, Roger Williams founded the *first* **First Baptist Church of America,** 75 N. Main St. (454-3418), built in 1775 (open M-F 10am-3pm; free). Down the hill, the **Rhode Island State Capitol** (222-2357) supports the fourth-largest free-standing marble dome in the world. *(Open M-F 8:30am-4:30pm. Free guided tours M-F 10 and 11am; reservations appreciated. Free self-guide booklets available in room 220.)* John Quincy Adams called it "the most magnificent and elegant private mansion." On College Hill sits the **John Brown House Museum,** 52 Power St. (331-8575), the 18th-century home of the Rhode Island entrepreneur and revolutionary. *(Open Tu-Sa 10am-5pm, Su noon-4pm. $6, students and seniors $4.50, ages 7-17 $3.)*

The nearby **RISD Museum of Art,** 224 Benefit St. (454-6500), gathers a fine collection of Greek, Roman, Asian, and Impressionist art, as well as a gigantic 10th-century Japanese Buddha. *(Open W-Th and Sa-Su. 10am-5pm, F 10am-8pm. $5, students $2, seniors $4, ages 5-18 $1. Free every 3rd Th 5-9pm and last Sa of month.)* The New England textile industry was born in 1793 when Samuel Slater used plans smuggled out of Britain to build the first water-powered factory in America. The **Slater Mill Historic Site** (725-8638), 67 Roosevelt Ave., in Pawtucket, preserves the fabric heritage with operating machinery. Tours leave roughly every 2hr. *(Open June-Oct. M-Sa 10am-5pm, Su 1-5pm; Mar.-June and Nov.-Dec. Sa-Su 1-5pm. $6.50, seniors $5.50, 6-12 $5.)*

ENTERTAINMENT AND NIGHTLIFE The nationally acclaimed **Trinity Repertory Company,** 201 Washington St. (351-4242), offers $10 student rush tickets 2hr. before performances, except on Saturday (tickets $24-35). For splashier productions, contact the **Providence Performing Arts Center,** 220 Weybosset St. (421-2787), which hosts a variety of concerts and Broadway musicals. The **Cable Car Cinema and Café,** 204 S. Main St. (272-3970), shows artsy and foreign films in a kinder, gentler setting—recline on couches instead of regular seats (tickets $6.50).

If you're in the mood for a little hardball, the **Pawtucket Red Sox** (AAA) take the field April through August in Pawtucket's **McCoy Stadium,** 1 Columbus Ave. (724-7300; box seats $6; general admission $4, seniors and under 12 $3).

Read the "Weekend" section of the *Friday Providence Journal,* or the *Providence Phoenix* for film, theater, and nightlife listings. Brownies, townies, and RISDs rock the night away at several hot spots throughout town. Mingle with the local artist community at **AS220,** 115 Empire St. (831-9327), a cafe/bar/gallery/performance space. (Cover $2-5. Open Tu-F 11am-1am, Sa-Su 7pm-midnight. 2nd fl. gallery open Tu-Sa 11am-4pm, Sa 1-4pm. Free.) **The Living Room,** 23 Rathbone St. (521-5200), hosts both dancing and live alternative bands (open daily 8pm-1am). The gay community favors **Gerardo's,** 1 Franklin Sq. (274-5560), where in addition to a DJ, karaoke blasts (cover varies; open Su-Th 4pm-1am, F-Sa 4pm-2am).

■ Newport

Money has always found its way into Newport. Once supported by slave trade prof-its, the town later became the summer home of society's elite and the site of some of the nation's most opulent mansions. The city's monied residents played the first game of polo in North America, hosted the America's Cup race for 35 years, and watched John F. Kennedy wed Jacqueline Bouvier. Today, the city attracts throngs of tourists with deep pockets and a passion for high-priced boats. For those on a tight budget, seasonal events such as the jazz and folk festivals are reason enough to visit.

PRACTICAL INFORMATION The place to start any visit to Newport is the **Newport County Convention and Visitors Bureau,** 23 America's Cup Ave. (845-9123 or 800-976-5122), in the Newport Gateway Center. This fantastic visitors center offers exhib-its on the town's history, and the *Best-Read Guide Newport* and *Newport This Week* (open Su-Th 9am-5pm, F-Sa 9am-6pm). **Bonanza Buses** (846-1820) depart from the Center, as do the buses of **Rhode Island Public Transit Authority (RIPTA)** (781-9400 or 800-244-0444; station open daily 4:30am-8:30pm). RIPTA routes run daily 5:30am-9:30pm. (Fare $1.) RIPTA also heads north to Providence (1hr., $3), to points on Rte. 114, and to the Kingston Amtrak station (35min., $3; June to mid-Oct.). There's no such thing as a 10-speed at **Ten Speed Spokes,** 18 Elm St. (847-5609). (Mountain bikes $5 per hr., $25 per day. Must have credit card and photo ID. Open M-Th 10am-6pm, F-Sa 9am-6pm, Su 11am-5pm.) **Post Office:** 320 Thames St. (847-2329; open M-F 8:30am-5pm, Sa 9am-1pm). **ZIP code:** 02840. **Area code:** 401.

ACCOMMODATIONS, CAMPGROUNDS, AND FOOD Guest houses account for the bulk of Newport's accommodations. Most offer a bed and continental breakfast with colonial intimacy. Those willing to share a bathroom or forego a sea view might find a double for $65; singles are almost nonexistent. Many hotels and guest houses book solid two months in advance for summer weekends. Fortunately for the budget trav-eler, Newport is blessed with a **Motel 6,** 249 J.T. Connel Hwy. (848-0600 or 800-466-8356), offering clean, comfortable rooms at equally comfortable prices (1 person $55-65, 2 people $62-72, $3 per additional person). **Campsites** await at **Fort Getty Recreation Area** (423-7264, reservations 423-7311), 44 Southwest Ave. on Conani-cut Island. The nearby Fox Hill Salt Marsh has great birdwatching. (100 RV sites; 20 year-round. 15 tent sites. Showers and beach access. Tent sites $20, RV hookup $25. Reservations recommended 1-2 months in advance. Open late May-Oct.)

Despite what you might expect, cheap food *does* exist in Newport. Most of New-port's restaurants line up on **Thames St.** Mighty good food can be consumed at the **Franklin Spa,** 229 Spring St., like the $4 banana pancakes or $6 grilled chicken club (open daily 6am-3pm). Shack up with some choice mollusks at **Flo's Clam Shack,** Rte. 138A/Aquidneck Ave. (847-8141), across from Easton Beach, or enjoy the clam product of your choice (fried clams $9) alongside a severely incapacitated lobster boat labeled the *S.S. Minnow* (open Su-Th 11am-9pm, F-Sa 11am-10pm). **Dry Dock Seafood,** 448 Thames St. (847-3974), fries 'em and serves 'em with a minimum of fuss (entrees $6-13; open daily 11am-10pm).

SIGHTS George Noble Jones built the first "summer cottage" here in 1839, thereby kicking off an extravagant string of palatial summer estates. Five of the mansions lie south of town on Bellevue Ave. A self-guided walking tour or a guided tour by the **Preservation Society of Newport,** 424 Bellevue Ave. (847-1000), will allow you to ogle at the extravagance; purchase tickets at any mansion. *(Open M-F 9am-5pm. $3.50-10, students $2-6, ages 6-11 $0-4. Combination tickets available.)* **The Marble House** (847-1000) is the must-see of the mansions. *(Open Apr.-Oct. 10am-5pm; Jan.-Mar. Sa-Su 10am-4pm. $8, students $5, ages 6-11 $3.50.)* Built in 1892 as a weekend/summer home for William K. Vanderbilt, it contains over 500,000 cubic ft. of marble, silk walls, and rooms covered entirely in gold. Eight miles north of Newport in Portsmouth, the **Green Animals Topiary Gardens,** Cory's Lane (847-1000), holds 21 shrubs amaz-ingly sculpted into the likes of giraffes and lions ($8, students $5, ages 6-11 $3; open

May-Oct. daily 10am-5pm). The father of William Mayes, a notorious Red Sea pirate, opened the **White Horse Tavern** (849-3600), Marlborough St. and Farewell St., as a tavern in 1687, making it the oldest continuously operated drinking establishment in the country (beer $3-4). The oldest synagogue in the U.S., the beautifully restored Georgian **Touro Synagogue,** 85 Touro St. (847-4794), dates back to 1763. *(Visits by free tour only. Tours every 30min. late May to early July M-F 1-2:30pm, Su 11am-2:30pm every 30min.; early July to early Sept. Su-F. 10am-4pm; call for off-season tour schedule.)* Die-hard tennis fans will feel right at home in Newport, where the newly renovated **Tennis Hall of Fame,** 194 Bellevue Ave. (849-3990), hosts grass court tournaments and dedicates a museum to the game (open daily 9am-5pm; $8, students and seniors $6, under 17 $4, families $20).

Newport's gorgeous beaches are frequently as crowded as the streets. The most popular is **Easton's Beach** (848-6491), or First Beach, on Memorial Blvd. *(Open late May to early Sept. M-F 9am-9pm, Sa-Su 8am-9pm. Parking M-F $8, Sa-Su $10.)* **Fort Adams State Park** (847-2400), south of town on Ocean Dr. 2½ mi. from the Visitors Center, offers showers, picnic areas, and two fishing piers. *(Entrance booth open M-F 7:30am-4pm, Sa-Su 7:30am-6pm; park open sunrise to sunset. Entrance fee $4 per car.)* Good beaches also line Little Compton, Narragansett, and the shore between Watch Hill and Point Judith; for more details the free *Ocean State Beach Guide,* available at the Visitors Center, ought not be missed.

ENTERTAINMENT In July and August, Newport gives lovers of classical, folk, blues, and jazz each a festival to call their own. The oldest and best-known jazz festival in the world, the **Newport Jazz Festival** (847-3700) has seen the likes of Duke Ellington and Count Basie; bring your beach chairs and coolers to Fort Adams State Park to join the fun August 12-14 (Sa-Su tickets $39, under 12 $15). The **Newport Music Festival** (846-1133, box office 849-0700), July 9-25, attracts pianists, violinists, and other classical musicians from around the world for 2 weeks of concerts in the ballrooms and on the lawns of the mansions (box office open daily 10am-6pm; tickets $28-33). On August 5-7, 1999, folk singers such as Joan Baez and the Indigo Girls entertain at the **Newport Folk Festival** (847-3709 in summer), which runs 2 days, noon to dusk (tickets $39, under 12 $15). Newport wails the blues July 23-25 at the **Newport Blues Festival** (847-3700; $39, under 12 $15).

Newport's nightlife centers around the bars and clubs on the Newport Harborfront. **Pelham East,** 274 Thames St. (847-9460), packs 'em in for alternative cover bands (live music nightly; cover F-Sa $10; open daily 1pm-1am). For an alternative scene, **Señor Frogg's,** 108 William St. (849-4747), across from the Tennis Hall of Fame, is another choice (cover varies; open W-Sa 8pm-1am).

■ Near Newport: Block Island

A popular daytrip 10 mi. southeast of Newport in the Atlantic, sand-blown **Block Island** possesses an untamed natural beauty. Block Island was originally called by its Mohegan name *Manisses,* or "Isle of Little God." One-quarter of the island is protected open space; local conservationists hope to increase that to 50%. From Old Harbor where the ferry lets you off, a 4 mi. hike or bike ride brings you to the **National Wildlife Refuge,** a great spot for a picnic. Two miles south of Old Harbor, the **Mohegan Bluffs** invite the adventurous, cautious, and strong to wind their way down to the Atlantic waters 200 ft. below. High in the cliffs, the **Southeast Lighthouse** has warned fog-bound fisherfolk since 1875; its beacon shines the brightest of any on the Atlantic coast. Located at the top of a 150 ft. cliff, the lighthouse was on the verge of falling into sea until 1993, when the whole structure was moved 20 ft. back.

The **Block Island Chamber of Commerce** (466-2982) welcomes you at the ferry dock in Old Harbor Drawer D (open daily in summer 10am-4pm; mid-Oct. to mid-May 10am-4pm). **Cycling** is the ideal way to explore the tiny (7 mi. by 3 mi.) island; the **Old**

Harbor Bike Shop (466-2029), to the left of the ferry exit, rents just about anything on wheels. (Mountain bikes $5-8 per hr., $20-30 per day; mopeds $15/$45. Cars $79 per day; 20¢ per mi. Must be 21 with credit card; 25 for a truck. Open daily 8:30am-7pm.) The **Interstate Navigation Co.** (783-4613) provides **ferry service** to Block Island from Point Judith, RI (1¼hr.; 8-10 per day, off-season 1-4 per day; $8.40, ages 5-11 $4.10, cars by reservation $26.30, bikes $2.50), and summer service from Newport, RI (2hr., late June to early Sept. 1 per day, $7.40) and New London, CT (2hr., mid-June to mid-Sept. 1 per day, $13.50). Galilee State Pier in Point Judith to the island is the cheapest, shortest ride.

The island does not permit camping; it's best as a daytrip unless you're willing to shell out $60 or more for a room in a guest house. Most restaurants hover near the ferry dock in Old Harbor; several cluster at New Harbor 1 mi. inland.

Connecticut

Connecticut, the third-smallest state in the Union, resembles a patchwork quilt stitched from industrialized centers (like Hartford and New Haven), serene New England villages, and lush woodland beauty. Perhaps it is this diversity that attracted such famous residents as Mark Twain, Harriet Beecher Stowe, Noah Webster, and Eugene O'Neill, and inspired the birth of the American Impressionist movement and the American musical—both Connecticut originals. Home to Yale University and the nation's first law school, Connecticut has an equally rich intellectual history. Nevertheless, this doesn't mean that the people of Connecticut don't know how to let their hair down—this is the state that brought us the lollipop, the three-ring circus, the frisbee, and the largest casino in the United States.

PRACTICAL INFORMATION

Capital: Hartford.
Visitor Info: Connecticut Vacation Center, 865 Brook St., Rocky Hill 06067 (800-282-6863; http://www.state.ct.us/tourism). Open M-F 9am-4:30pm.
Emergency: 911.
Time Zone: Eastern. **Postal Abbreviation:** CT.
Sales Tax: 6%.

■ Hartford

The citizens of Connecticut's capital have not always been law-abiding. In 1687, the English governor demanded the surrender of the charter that Charles II had granted Hartford 25 years before. Hartfordians obstinately hid the charter in a tree trunk until the infuriated governor returned to England. Today, a plaque marks the spot at Charter Oak Place. Over the last three centuries, Hartford has grown into the world's insurance capital; the city's skyline is shaped by towering granite structures financed by some of the larger firms, including the monolithic oval of the Boat Building, America's first two-sided building.

PRACTICAL INFORMATION Union Place, in the northeast part of the city, between Church and Asylum St., is home to **Amtrak** (727-1776 or 800-872-7245), which runs nine trains daily both north and south (office open daily 5:30am-9pm), and **Peter Pan Trailways** (800-237-8747), which connects to New York (2½hr., $17) and Boston (2½hr., $18) 10 times daily (ticket office open daily 6am-midnight). **Greyhound** (800-231-2222; station open daily 6am-9pm), at Union Place, buses to New York (2½hr., 14 per day, $14) and Boston (2½hr., 9 per day, $14). Hartford marks the intersection of I-91 and I-84. The **Greater Hartford Convention and Visitors Bureau,** 1 Civic Center Plaza, 3rd fl. (728-6789 or 800-446-7811; open M-F 8:30am-4:30pm), and the **Old State House,** 800 Main St. (522-6766; open M-F 10am-4pm, Sa 11am-4pm), offer dozens of maps, booklets, and guides to local resorts, campgrounds, and historical sights. In front of the Old State House, **Connecticut Transit's Information Center** (525-9181), at State and Market St., doles out helpful downtown maps and public transportation info (basic bus fare $1; open M-F 7am-6pm). **Internet access** is available at Hartford Public Library, 500 Main St. (M-Th 9am-8pm, F-Sa 9am-5pm; Oct.-May Su 1-5pm also. Temporary library card necessary.) **Post Office:** 141 Weston St. (610-3125; open M-F 8am-5pm, Sa 9am-1pm). **ZIP code:** 06101. **Area code:** 860.

ACCOMMODATIONS, FOOD, AND NIGHTLIFE The excellent **Mark Twain Hostel (HI-AYH),** 131 Tremont St. (523-7255), offers great accommodations near the center of town ($14, nonmembers $18; check-in 9am-10pm). In the heart of downtown, the **YMCA,** 160 Jewell St. (522-4183), offers small, dorm-like rooms at reasonable rates, including use of a gym, pool, and racquetball courts, as well as access to a cafeteria. (Singles $18, with private bath $23. $5 key deposit. Check-in 5am-midnight, check-out noon. No reservations accepted.) Just north of Hartford, the sleepy **Windsor Home Hostel (HI-AYH),** 126 Giddings Ave. (683-2847), near Exit 36 off I-91, resides in Connecticut's oldest town. Hostelers stay in beds in rooms with 70s decor and share a bath, common area, and kitchen facilities. ($14, nonmembers $17. Reservations required. Directions given upon confirmation.) For camping enthusiasts who don't mind a 40min. drive out of the city, **Taylor Brook State Campground,** Highland Lake Rd. at Burr Pond (379-0172), 5min. north of Torrington off Rte. 8 on Burr Mountain Rd., provides 39 wooded sites ($10) with showers and swimming (registration 8am-sunset mid-Apr. to Sept.).

Many restaurants hover within a few blocks of the downtown area. Hartford's eldest eatery, the **Municipal Café,** 485 Main St. (278-4844), is a popular and friendly place to catch a good breakfast or lunch. The breakfast special means bacon, ham, or sausage with two eggs, toast, coffee or tea for $4. Hot lunches go for $4-6. (Open daily 7am-3:30pm.) **The Hartford Brewery,** 35 Pearl St. (246-2337), one of Connecticut's only brew-pubs, serves up sandwiches ($6-7), burgers ($7), and six freshly brewed beers (open M-F 11:30am-midnight, Sa noon-2am).

SIGHTS Designed by Charles Bullfinch in 1796, the gold-domed **Old State House,** 800 Main St. (522-6766), housed the state government until 1878. *(Open M-F 10am-4pm, Sa 11am-4pm.)* Now, well-dressed historic actors welcome tourists to the chambers, a rotating art exhibit hall, and a museum of oddities including a mounted two-headed calf. A block or so west, park and ride on one of the country's few hand-crafted merry-go-rounds at **Bushnell Park** (246-7739), supposedly the first public American park (carousel open May-Aug. Tu-Su 11am-5pm; Apr. and Sept. Sa-Su 11am-5pm; 50¢). Overlooking the park, the gold-domed (isn't everything?) **State Capitol,** 210 Capitol Ave. (240-0222), houses Lafayette's camp bed and a war-ravaged tree trunk from the 1864 Battle of Chickamauga, among other historic artifacts. Free 1hr. tours begin at the west entrance of the neighboring **Legislative Office Building,** at the corner of Capitol Ave. and Broad St.; look for free parking behind the building. *(Tours M-F 9:15, 10:15, 11:15am, 12:15 and 1:15pm. Apr.-Oct. Sa tours from the capitol's SW entrance 10:15, 11:15am, 12:15, 1:15 and 2:15pm.)*

The **Wadsworth Athenaeum,** 600 Main St. (278-2670), the oldest public art museum in the country, has absorbing collections of contemporary and Baroque art, including Monet, Renoir, Degas, and one of only three Caravaggios in the United States. *(Open Tu-Su 11am-5pm. $7, seniors and students $5, ages 3-17 $3. Free Th and Sa before noon. Tours Th at noon and Sa-Su noon-2pm.)*

Lovers of American literature won't want to miss the engaging tours at **Mark Twain House,** 351 Farmington Ave. (493-6411); and **Harriet Beecher Stowe House,** 71 Forest St. (525-9317), both just west of the city center on Farmington Ave. *(Twain House open M-Sa 9:30am-4pm, Su 11am-4pm; Oct.-May closed Tu. $7.50, seniors $7, ages 6-12*

$3.50. Stowe House open Tu-Sa 9:30am-4pm, Su noon-4pm; $6.50/$6/$2.75.) From the Old State House, take any "Farmington Ave." bus west. The rambling, richly colored Mark Twain Mansion housed the Missouri-born author for 17 years, during which Twain composed his masterpiece *Huckleberry Finn.* Harriet Beecher Stowe lived next door on Nook Farm after the publication of *Uncle Tom's Cabin.*

■ New Haven

Simultaneously university town and depressed city, New Haven has gained a reputation as something of a battleground—academic types and a working-class population live uneasily side by side. Yalies tend to stick to their campus, widening the rift 'twixt town and gown. Every facet of life in the city, from architecture to safety, reflects this difference. While most of New Haven continues to decay, Yale has begun to renovate its neo-Gothic buildings and convert its concrete sidewalks to brick, and has largely succeeded in creating a young and thriving collegiate coffeehouse, bar, and bookstore scene around the university.

PRACTICAL INFORMATION New Haven lies at the intersection of I-95 and I-91, 40 mi. south of Hartford. New Haven is laid out in nine squares. Between Yale University and City Hall, the central square, called the Green, provides a pleasant escape from the hassles of city life. *At night, don't wander too far from the immediate downtown and campus areas; surrounding sections are notably less safe.* On the Green, **CT Transit** (624-0151) runs an info booth with free bus maps and route and schedule assistance (open M-F 7:30am-5:30pm). Nineteen bus routes head to all points in Greater New Haven. Buses generally run daily 6am-midnight; hours vary by route. (Fare within New Haven $1 with a few exceptions.) **Amtrak** (786-2888 or 800-872-7245; ticket office open daily 6am-10pm), Union Station on Union Ave., runs out of a newly renovated station. *Be careful; the area is unsafe at night.* Trains chug-a-lug to New York City (1½hr., every hr., $22); Boston (2½hr., every 2hr., $33); Washington, D.C. (6hr., every 3 hr., $61); and Mystic ($15). Also at Union Station, **Greyhound** (772-2470 or 800-231-2222; ticket office open daily 7:30am-8pm) runs frequent service to New York (1½hr., 8 per day, $14); Boston (4hr., 6 per day, $19); and Providence (2½hr., 6 per day, $19). The **Greater New Haven Convention and Visitors Bureau,** has plenty of pamphlets and maps at Exit 46 off I-95 (open late May to early Sept. M-F 10am-5pm, Sa-Su 10am-5pm). Their office at 350 Long Wharf Dr. (777-8550 or 800-332-7829) provides free maps and info on current events (open off-season M-F 8:30am-5pm). For a weekly **recorded events update,** call 498-5050, ext. 1310. The **Yale Visitors Center,** 149 Elm St. (432-2300), facing the Green, distributes free campus maps, a $1 walking guide, *The Yale,* a guide to undergraduate life ($3.50), and has exhibits on famous Yale alums like Bill Clinton and Noah Webster. (Open M-F 9am-4:45pm, Sa-Su 10am-4pm. Free 1hr. tours M-F 10:30am and 2pm, Sa-Su 1:30pm.) **Internet access** is available at New Haven Free Public Library, 133 Elm St. (946-7452; open M-Th 9am-9pm, F-Sa 9am-5pm). **Area code:** 203.

ACCOMMODATIONS, CAMPGROUNDS AND FOOD Inexpensive lodgings are sparse in New Haven; the hunt quickens around Yale Parents Weekend (mid-Oct.) and commencement (early June). Head 10 mi. south on I-95 to **Milford** for affordable motels. **Hotel Duncan,** 1151 Chapel St. (787-1273), contains the oldest manually operated elevator in the state, as well as plush rooms with cable TV and mini fridges (singles $40; doubles $60; reservations recommended for Sa-Su). **Motel 6** (469-0343 or 800-466-8356), Exit 8 off I-91, keeps good rooms at good prices (singles $56; doubles $62). **Hammonasset Beach State Park** (245-1817), 20min. east on I-95, Exit 62 in Madison, offers camping (558 sites $12; office open mid-May to Oct. 8am-11pm).

For great authentic Italian cuisine, work your way along Wooster St. The finest New Haven-style brick oven pizza can be found at **Pepe's,** 157 Wooster St. (865-5762). Try a large, crispy, thin-crust pizza with their special sauce for $11. (Open M, W-Th 4-10:30pm, F-Sa 11:30am-midnight, Su 2:30-10:30pm.) The university's coffee-and-cigarette types haunt the mural-clad **Daily Caffé,** 316 Elm St. (776-5063), a psychedelic joint opened by a Yale alum. Sandwiches start at $3. Top off your meal with awesome $3.25 chocolate mousse cake. (Open M-Sa 7am-midnight, Sa-Su 8am-midnight; Sept.-May M-Sa 7am-1am, Sa-Su 9am-1am.) No condiments are allowed at **Louis' Lunch,** 263 Crown St. (562-5507), home of the very first hamburger. Cooked vertically in original cast iron grills, these $3 burgers are too fine for ketchup or mustard. (Open Tu-W 11am-4pm, Th-Sa noon-2am.) You'll eat like royalty at **India Palace,** 65 Howe St. (776-9010). All-you-can-eat lunch buffet ($6) served M-F 11:30am-3pm.

SIGHTS Modeling their work on the colleges of Oxford, architects took great pains to artificially age the buildings on Yale's campus. Bricks were buried in different soils to give them a tarnished-by-the-centuries look; windows were shattered; and acid was sprayed on the facades, all to give Yale a wonderful going-to-shambles aura. James Gambel Rodgers, a firm believer in the sanctity of printed material, designed **Sterling Memorial Library,** 120 High St. (432-1775), to resemble a monastery. *(Open M-W and F 8:30am-5pm, Th 8:30am-10pm, Sa 10am-5pm; Sept.-May M-Th 8:30am-midnight, F 8:30am-5pm, Sa 10am-5pm, Su 1pm-midnight.)* Even the telephone booths are shaped like confessionals. Rodgers spared no expense in making Yale look "authentic," even decapitating the figurines on the library's exterior to replicate those at Oxford.

The creator of the massive **Beinecke Rare Book and Manuscript Library,** 121 Wall St. (432-2977), wasn't fond of windows. *(Open M-F 8:30am-5pm, Sa 10am-5pm. Closed Sa in Aug.)* Instead, this intriguing modern structure is paneled with Vermont marble cut thin enough to be translucent; supposedly its volumes (including one Gutenberg Bible and an extensive collection of William Carlos Williams's writings) could survive a nuclear war. On New Haven's own **Wall St.,** between High and Yale St., take a moment to notice the neo-Gothic gargoyles perched on the Law School building, which portray cops and robbers.

Open since 1832, the **Yale University Art Gallery,** 1111 Chapel St. (432-0600), on the corner of York, claims to be the oldest university art museum in the Western Hemisphere. *(Open Sept.-July Tu-Sa 10am-5pm, Su 1-6pm. Free.)* The museum holds over 100,000 pieces from around the world, including works by Monet, Picasso, and 13th-century Italian artists. The **Peabody Museum of Natural History,** 170 Whitney Ave. (432-5050), off I-91 at Exit 3, houses Rudolph F. Zallinger's Pulitzer Prize-winning mural, which portrays the North American continent as it appeared 70 to 350 million years ago. *(Open M-Sa 10am-5pm, Su noon-5pm. $5, seniors and ages 3-15 $3.)* Other exhibits include a hall displaying the skeleton of an apatosaurus.

ENTERTAINMENT AND NIGHTLIFE Pick up a free copy of *The Advocate* to find out what's up in New Haven. Once a famous testing ground for Broadway-bound plays, New Haven's thespian community has scaled down in recent years. **The Shubert Theater,** 247 College St. (562-5666 or 800-228-6622), a significant figure in the town's on-stage tradition, brings in top Broadway productions (box office open M-F 10am-5pm, Sa-Su 11am-3pm). **The Yale Repertory Theater,** 1120 Chapel St. (432-1234), boasts such illustrious alums as Meryl Streep, Glenn Close, and James Earl Jones and continues to produce excellent shows. (Open Oct.-May M-Sa 11am-5pm. Tickets $10-30. ½-price student rush tickets on the day of a show.) In summer, the city hosts **concerts** on the Green (787-8956), including **New Haven Symphony** concerts (865-0831, box office 776-1444; open M-F 9am-5pm).

Toad's Place, 300 York St. (562-5694, recorded info 624-8623), has hosted gigs by Bob Dylan and the Stones. (Box office open daily 11am-6pm; buy tickets at the bar after 8pm. Bar open Su-Th 8pm-1am, F-Sa 8pm-2am.) Yalie jocks and fratboys get drunk on $2.75 beers at the **Union League Café,** 1032 Chapel St. (562-4299; open daily 5:30pm-2am). **Bar,** 254 Crown St. (495-8924), is anything but generic—the place for drinking is also the gay hotspot on Tuesdays, and they make their own beer and brick-oven pizzas (open M-Th 4pm-1am, F-Sa 4pm-2am, Su 1pm-1am).

■ Mystic and the Connecticut Coast

Connecticut's coastal towns along the Long Island Sound were busy seaports in the days of Melville and Richard Henry Dana, but the dark, musty inns filled with tattooed sailors swapping sea journeys are history. Today, the coast is important mainly as a resort and sailing base. **Mystic Seaport** (572-5315), 1 mi. south on Rte. 27 from I-95 at Exit 90, will take you back to 19th-century seafaring America, as you climb aboard tall ships, walk through a recreated village, and take part in maritime activities that'll make you cry, "Aargh, matey." (Open daily 9am-5pm. 2-day admission $16, ages 6-12 $8. Audio tours $3.45.) Seaport admission also entitles you to take a **Mystic River** cruise offered by **Sabino Charters** (572-5351) for a few dollars more. (30min. trips mid-May to early Oct. daily on the hr. 11am-4pm. $3.50, ages 6-15 $2.50.) The 1½hr. evening excursions do not require museum admission. (Runs mid-May to late Sept. daily 5pm; July to early Sept. F-Sa 5 and 7pm. $8.50, ages 6-15 $7.)

If walking through a fishing village puts you in the mood for aquatic life, seals, penguins, sharks, and dolphins await your presence at one of the northeast's finest aquariums, the **Mystic Marinelife Aquarium,** 55 Coogan Blvd. (572-5955), at Exit 90 off I-95 (open daily 9am-5pm; July to early Sept. 9am-6pm; $13, seniors $12, ages 3-12 $8). The **Denison Pequotsepos Nature Center,** 109 Pequotsepos Rd. (536-1216), offers a refuge from the droves of tourists with great bird watching and 7½ mi. of scenic trails through meadows, fields, streams, ponds, and woodland. (Park center open M-Sa 9am-5pm, Su 1-5pm; park open dawn-dusk. $4, seniors $3 ages 6-12 $2.) One of Mystic's oft-missed treasures is the great **Mystic Drawbridge,** off Main St. (Raises May-Oct. every 15min. past the hr. 7:15am-7:15pm.) Built in 1922, it is one of only a few working drawbridges east of the Mississippi.

The **Mystic Tourist and Information Center** (536-1641; http://www.mystic-more.com), Bldg. 1d in Olde Mysticke Village, has oodles of info on area sights and accommodations (open M-F 9am-6:30pm, Sa 9am-7pm, Su 10am-6:30pm). It may be difficult to secure cheap lodgings in Mystic; **Stonington** makes a more affordable base from which to explore the shore. If you plan to splurge on the pricey offerings in Mystic itself, call well ahead for reservations. The only option close to Mystic is **Seaport Campgrounds** (536-4044), on Rte. 184, 3 mi. up Rte. 27 from Mystic. (Sites $27, with water and electricity $31; $5 per additional person; seniors 10% discount. Open daily mid-Apr. to late Oct.) In Stonington, the **Sea Breeze Motel,** 812 Stonington Rd./Rte. 1 (535-2843), rents big, clean rooms with A/C (singles $50, F-Su $85; doubles $75-95; rates much lower·in winter). The **Stonington Motel,** 901 Stonington Rd./Rte. 1 (599-2330), offers slightly cramped, but well-equipped rooms. (Singles $62; doubles $75; in winter $15 cheaper; Su-Th 10% discount on daily rooms.)

While Mystic's most renowned eatery carries the namesake of the popular 1988 film, **Mystic Pizza,** 56 W. Main St. (536-3737 or 536-3700), lacks flavorful fame. (Unremarkable slices $2; small pizza $5; large $9.25. Open Sa-Su 10am-midnight, M-F 10am-11pm.) A better bet is the **Two Sisters Deli,** 4 Pearl St. (536-1244 or 536-2068). Try the enormous 3D sandwiches if you dare, especially the "Sister's Belligerent Boyfriend." (Sandwiches $3-6. Open M-Th 8:30am-6pm, F-Sa 8:30am-7pm, Su 9am-4pm.) **Trader Jack's,** 14 Holmes St. (572-8550), near downtown, pours $2 domestic beers. Happy hour (M-F 4:30-6:30pm) will have you smiling with half-price appetizers and 50¢ off all drinks except wine. Frequent live music (no cover) will spice up your $5 burger. (Food Su-Th 5-10pm, F-Sa 5pm-midnight; last call for drinks Su-Th 1am, F-Sa 2am.) **Area code:** 860.

NEW ENGLAND

MID-ATLANTIC

Ranging from the Southern state of Virginia through the Eastern seaboard to New York, the mid-Atlantic states claim not only a large slice of the nation's population, but several of the nation's major historical, political and economic centers. This region is home to every capital the U.S. has ever known; first settled in Philadelphia, PA, the U.S. government moved through Princeton, NJ, Annapolis, MD, Trenton, NJ and New York City, before halting in Washington, D.C. During the Civil War, the mid-Atlantic even hosted the capital of the Confederacy, Richmond, VA. Though urban centers (and suburban sprawl) cover much of the mid-Atlantic, the great outdoors have survived. The celebrated Appalachian Trail meanders through the area, and in New York, the Adirondacks make up the largest park in the U.S. outside of Alaska.

🖐 HIGHLIGHTS OF THE MID-ATLANTIC

- **New York, NY.** The Big Apple combines world-class museums (p. 160) with top-notch arts and entertainment venues (p. 164).
- **Washington, D.C.** The impressive Smithsonian Museum (p. 229), the White House (p. 231), the Capitol (p. 228), and a slew of monuments (p. 230) comprise some of the coveted attractions of the nation's capitol.
- **Scenic Drives.** The Blue Ridge Pkwy. (p. 250) is justifiably famous. A more hidden drive is the gorgeous backcountry road from Carter's Grove Plantation to Colonial Williamsburg, VA (p. 241).
- **Historic sites.** The White House of the Confederacy in Richmond, VA (p. 239); Harper's Ferry, WV (p. 252); and Gettysburg, PA (p. 205) are the best places to relive the Civil War. Philadelphia, PA (p. 193) abounds with colonial landmarks.

New York

Surrounded by the beauty of the state's landscape, you may find it difficult to remember that smog and traffic exist. The cities that dot upstate New York have a sweet natural flavor that holds its own against the savor of the Big Apple. The City, on the other hand, is an entirely different kettle of fish. New York City, the eighth most populated city in the world, would claim to be grander than the other seven. With a diverse population, a spectacular skyline, towering financial power, and a range of cultural enterprises, New Yorkers may have a point.

PRACTICAL INFORMATION

Capital: Albany.

Visitor Info: Division of Tourism, 1 Commerce Plaza, Albany 12245 (518-474-4116 or 800-225-5697; http://iloveny.state.ny.us). Operators available M-F 8:30am-5pm; voice mail otherwise. Comprehensive *I Love NY Travel Guide* includes disabled access and resource info. **New York State Office of Parks and Recreation and Historic Preservation,** Empire State Plaza, Agency Bldg. 1, Albany 12238-0001 (518-474-0456), has literature on camping and biking. Open M-F 9am-5pm. The **Bureau of Public Lands** of the **Division of Lands and Forests,** DEC, 50 Wolf Rd., Room 438, Albany 12233-4255 (518-457-7433), has info on hiking and canoeing.

Emergency: 911.

Time Zone: Eastern. **Postal Abbreviation:** NY.

Sales Tax: 8.25%.

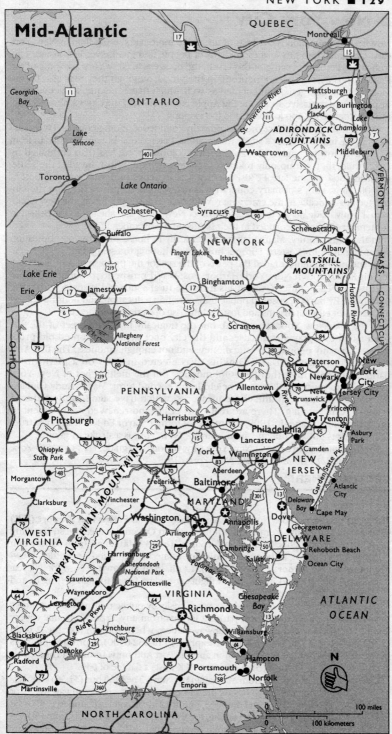

Mid-Atlantic

QUEBEC

Montreal

Georgian Bay

ONTARIO

Plattsburgh

Lake Placid

Burlington

Lake Champlain

Middlebury

ADIRONDACK MOUNTAINS

Lake Simcoe

Watertown

VERMONT

Toronto

Lake Ontario

Rochester

Syracuse

Utica

Schenectady

Albany

Buffalo

NEW YORK

Finger Lakes

Ithaca

CATSKILL MOUNTAINS

MASS.

CONNECTICUT

Lake Erie

Erie

Jamestown

Binghamton

Scranton

Hudson River

OHIO

Allegheny National Forest

Delaware River

Paterson

Newark

New York City

Jersey City

Pittsburgh

PENNSYLVANIA

Allentown

New Brunswick

Princeton

Trenton

Ohiopyle State Park

Harrisburg

Philadelphia

Asbury Park

Morgantown

Lancaster

York

Wilmington

Camden

NEW JERSEY

Clarksburg

Frederick

Aberdeen

Baltimore

Atlantic City

Delaware Bay

WEST VIRGINIA

APPALACHIAN MOUNTAINS

Winchester

MARYLAND

Dover

Cape May

Georgetown

DELAWARE

Washington, D.C.

Annapolis

Arlington

Harrisonburg

Shenandoah National Park

Cambridge

Salisbury

Rehoboth Beach

Ocean City

Staunton

Waynesboro

Charlottesville

VIRGINIA

Chesapeake Bay

ATLANTIC OCEAN

Lexington

Blue Ridge Pkwy

Richmond

Blacksburg

Lynchburg

Petersburg

Williamsburg

Roanoke

Radford

Hampton

Portsmouth

Norfolk

Martinsville

Emporia

Potomac River

Garden State Pkwy S

Garden State Pkwy S

St. Lawrence River

NORTH CAROLINA

N

100 miles

100 kilometers

■ New York City

Nowhere in the nation is the beat of urban life more hammering than in New York City. Crammed into tiny spaces, millions of people find themselves in constant confrontation. Perhaps because of this crush, the denizens of New York are some of the loudest, pushiest, and most neurotic in the world, although they may also be the most vibrant, energetic, and talented as well. Much that is unique, attractive, awe-inspiring, and repulsive about the Big Apple is a function of the city's scale—too big, too heterogeneous, too jumbled, and too exciting.

In 1624, the Dutch West Indies Company founded a trading colony. Two years later, in the first of the city's shady transactions, Peter Minuit bought Manhattan from the natives for just under $24. As the early colonists were less than enthralled by Dutch rule, they put up only token resistance when the British invaded the settlement in 1664. By the late 1770s, the city was an active port with a population of 20,000. New York's primary concern was maintaining its prosperity, and the city reacted apathetically to the emerging revolutionary cause. As a result, the new Continental Army made no great efforts to protect New York, and she fell to the British in September 1776 and remained in their hands until November 1783.

In the 19th century, Manhattan grew vertically to house the growing population streaming in from Western Europe. Immigrants hoping to escape famine, persecution, and political unrest faced the perils of the sea for the promise of America, landing on Ellis Island in New York Harbor. Post-WWII prosperity brought still more arrivals, especially African Americans from the rural South and Hispanics from the Caribbean. By the 60s, crises in public transportation, education, and housing fanned the flames of ethnic tensions and fostered the rise of a criminal underclass.

In the 80s, New York rebounded, but the tragically hip Wall Street of the 80s soon faded to a gray 90s malaise, and the city once again confronted old problems—too many people, too little money, and not enough kindness. The first African-American mayor, David Dinkins, was elected in 1989 on a platform of harmonious growth of the "beautiful mosaic," but the melting pot of New York continued to burn, smolder, and belch. In his second term, Mayor Rudy Giuliani has continued his strict anti-crime measures, which have significantly reduced crime 4 years running. There are real signs of life and renewed commitment in the urban blightscape. In 1999, the words of former Mayor Ed Koch still ring true. "New York is not a problem," he declared. "New York is a stroke of genius."

For the ultimate coverage of New York City, see our city guide, *Let's Go: New York City*, and the *Let's Go Map Guide: New York City*.

GETTING THERE

By Plane

Three airports service the New York Metro Region. **John F. Kennedy Airport (JFK)** (718-244-4444), 12 mi. from Midtown in southern Queens, is the largest, handling most international flights. **LaGuardia Airport** (718-533-3400), 6 mi. from midtown in northwestern Queens, is the smallest, offering domestic flights and air shuttles. **Newark International Airport** (973-961-6000), 12 mi. from midtown in Newark, NJ, features both domestic and international flights at budget fares (though getting to and from Newark can be expensive).

JFK to midtown Manhattan can be covered easily by public transportation. Catch a brown-and-white JFK long-term parking lot bus from any airport terminal (every 15min.) to the **Howard Beach-JFK subway station,** where you can take the **A train** to the city (1hr.). The **Carey Airport Express** (718-632-0500), a private line, runs between JFK and Grand Central Station and the Port Authority Terminal (1hr., leaves every 30min., 5am-11pm, $13). A **taxi** from JFK costs a flat fee of $30.

LaGuardia can be reached from Manhattan two ways. The **M60 bus** ($1.50) connects to the following subways in Manhattan: the #1 or 9 at 116th St. and Broadway, the #2 or 3 at 125th St. and Lenox Ave., and the #4, 5, or 6 at 125th St. and Lexington Ave. Allow at least 1½hr. travel time. The second option, the **Carey** bus, stops at Grand Central Station and the Port Authority Terminal (30-45min., every 30min., $10). A **taxi** costs around $25.

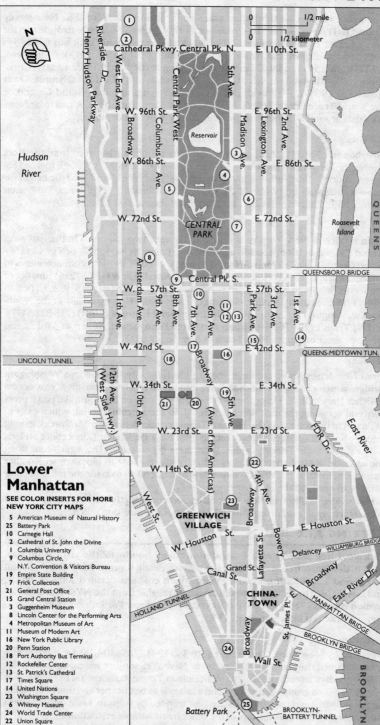

0   1/2 mile

0   1/2 kilometer

Hudson
River

MID-ATLANTIC

Lower
Manhattan

SEE COLOR INSERTS FOR MORE
NEW YORK CITY MAPS

5 American Museum of Natural History
25 Battery Park
10 Carnegie Hall
2 Cathedral of St. John the Divine
1 Columbia University
9 Columbus Circle,
   N.Y. Convention & Visitors Bureau
19 Empire State Building
7 Frick Collection
21 General Post Office
15 Grand Central Station
3 Guggenheim Museum
8 Lincoln Center for the Performing Arts
11 Metropolitan Museum of Art
16 New York Public Library
20 Penn Station
18 Port Authority Bus Terminal
12 Rockefeller Center
13 St. Patrick's Cathedral
17 Times Square
14 United Nations
23 Washington Square
6 Whitney Museum
24 World Trade Center
22 Union Square

Newark Airport to Manhattan takes about as long as from JFK. **New Jersey Transit (NJTA)** (973-762-5100) runs **bus #107,** which will take you to Midtown for $3.25 (exact change required). The NJTA also runs an **Air Link bus #302** ($4) between the airport and Newark's Penn Station (*not* Manhattan's); from there, **PATH** trains ($1) run into Manhattan, stopping at the World Trade Center, Christopher St., 6th Avenue, 9th St., 14th St., 23rd St. and 33rd St. **Olympia Trails Coach** (212-964-6233) travels between the airport and either Grand Central or the World Trade Center (every 20-30min. daily 5am-11pm; $10). A **taxi** from Newark costs around $45; negotiations should occur before departing.

By Bus

Greyhound (800-231-2222) grooves out of its major Northeastern hub, the **Port Authority Terminal,** 41st St. and 8th Ave. (435-7000; subway: A, C, or E to 42nd St.-Port Authority). *Be careful—con-artists and pickpockets abound, and the neighborhood is unsafe at night. Avoid the terminal's bathrooms at all times.* To: Boston (4½hr., $30); Philadelphia (2hr., $16); and Washington, D.C. (4½hr., $30).

By Train

Train service in New York runs primarily through two stations. On the East side, **Grand Central Station,** 42nd St. and Park Ave. (subway: #4, 5, 6, 7, or S to 42nd St./Grand Central), handles **Metro-North** (532-4900 or 800-638-7646) commuter lines to Connecticut and New York suburbs. **Amtrak** (582-6875 or 800-872-7245) runs out of the west side's **Penn Station,** 33rd St. and 8th Ave. (subway: #1, 2, 3, 9, A, C, or E to 34th St./Penn Station), serving most major cities in the U.S., especially in the Northeast (Washington, D.C., 4hr., $61). The **Long Island Railroad (LIRR)** (718-822-5477), and **NJ Transit** (201-762-5100), also chug from Penn Station. Nearby at 33rd St. and 6th Ave., you can catch a **PATH** train to New Jersey (800-234-7284).

By Car

From New Jersey, there are three ways to reach the city. The **George Washington Bridge,** which crosses the Hudson River into northern Manhattan, gives easy access to either Harlem River Dr. or the West Side Hwy. From the N.J. Turnpike you'll probably end up going through Weehawken, NJ, to the **Lincoln Tunnel,** which exits in Midtown in the west 40s. The **Holland Tunnel** connects to lower Manhattan, exiting into the SoHo and TriBeCa area. Coming from New England or Connecticut on I-95, follow signs for the **Triboro Bridge.** From there get onto **FDR Dr.,** which runs along the east side of Manhattan and exits onto city streets every 10 blocks or so. Another option is to look for the **Willis Avenue Bridge Exit** on I-95 to avoid the toll, and enter Manhattan north on the FDR Drive.

Hitchhiking is illegal in New York State, and cops strictly enforce the law within NYC. *Hitching in and around New York City is suicidal;* don't do it.

GETTING AROUND

Pick up a free **subway map** from station token booths or the visitors bureau, which also has a free street map. For a more detailed program of interborough travel, find a *Manhattan Yellow Pages,* which contains detailed subway, PATH, and bus maps. These helpful guides are also available from the **NYC Transit Information Bureau** (718-330-1234). (Open daily 9am-6pm. For info on **taxis** and **biking,** see **Practical Information,** p. 135.)

Subways

Operated by **New York City Transit** (718-330-1234, 718-330-4847 for non English-speakers; open daily 6am-9pm), the 238 mi. New York subway system operates 24hr. a day, 365 days a year. The fare for Metropolitan Transit Authority (MTA) subways is a hefty $1.50, so groups of four may find a cab ride to be cheaper and more expedient for short distances. Long distances are best traveled by subway, since once inside, a passenger may transfer onto any of the other trains without restrictions.

The **MetroCard** is now the dominant form of currency for subterranean and surface transit in New York. The card can be used at all subway stations and on all public buses. Subway and bus fare is still $1.50 per ride with the MetroCard, but with the purchase of a $15 card, you get one free ride. Further, MetroCards can also be used for subway-bus, bus-subway, and bus-bus transfers. When the card is swiped on the initial ride, a free transfer is electronically stored on your MetroCard and is good for up to 2hr. Without the MetroCard, bus-subway or subway-bus transfers are not free. A single MetroCard can store up to four transfers, good for people traveling in a group. There are certain restrictions on bus-bus transfers (i.e., passengers on a north-south bus can generally only transfer to a bus going east-west).

Recently, the Transit Authority has introduced the **"Unlimited Rides" MetroCard** (as opposed to "Pay-Per-Ride" cards); this card is sold in 7-day ($17) and 30-day ($63) denominations and is good for unlimited use of the subway during the specified period. The Unlimited Rides Card is recommended for tourists who plan on visiting many sights.

"Express" trains run at all hours and stop only at certain major stations; "locals" stop everywhere. Be sure to check the letter or number and the destination of each train, since trains with different destinations often use the same track. When in doubt, ask the conductor, who usually sits near the middle of the train. Once you're on the train, pay attention to the often garbled announcements—trains occasionally change mid-route from local to express or vice-versa.

Although by far the quickest means of transportation in Manhattan, the subways are much more useful for traveling north-south than east-west, as there are only two crosstown shuttle trains (42nd and 14th St.).

In crowded stations (most notably those around 42nd St.), pickpockets find work; violent crimes, although infrequent, tend to occur in stations that are deserted. Always watch yourself and your belongings, and stay in well-lit areas near a transit cop or token clerk. Most stations have clearly marked "off-hours" waiting areas that are under observation and significantly safer. When boarding, pick a car with a number of other passengers in it, or sit near the middle of the train, in the conductor's car.

For safety reasons, try to avoid riding the subways between midnight and 7am, especially above E. 96th St. and W. 120th St. and outside Manhattan. Try also to avoid rush-hour crowds, where you'll be fortunate to find air, let alone seating. You'll see **glass globes** outside of most **subway entrances.** If the globe is green, the entrance is staffed 24hr. A red globe indicates that the entrance is closed or restricted.

Buses

The **Metropolitan Transit Authority (MTA)** also runs buses for $1.50 a ride. Because buses sit in traffic during the day, they are often slower than subways, but they also stay relatively safe and clean. Buses will also probably get you closer to your destination, since they stop roughly every 2 blocks and run crosstown (east-west), as well as uptown and downtown (north-south). Using the MetroCard, subway-bus, bus-subway, and some bus-bus transfers are free (see **Subways,** above). Ring when you want to get off. A yellow-painted curb indicates bus stops, but you're better off looking for the blue signpost announcing the bus number or for a glass-walled shelter displaying a map of the bus's route and a schedule of arrival times. Either a MetroCard, exact change in coins, or a subway token is required; drivers will not accept bills.

ORIENTATION

Five **boroughs** comprise New York City: Brooklyn, the Bronx, Queens, Staten Island, and Manhattan. For all its fame, **Manhattan** Island's length is only 13 mi. long and 2½ mi. wide, and merely houses the third largest population of the five boroughs, after Brooklyn and Queens. Although small, Manhattan has all the advantages, is surrounded by water, and adjacent to the other four boroughs. **Queens,** the largest of the boroughs, beckons to the east of midtown Manhattan. **Brooklyn** lies due south of Queens, and would be America's fourth-largest city if it weren't a part of New York. **Staten Island,** southwest of Manhattan, has remained defiantly residential. North of Manhattan nests the **Bronx,** the only borough connected by land to the rest of the U.S., home of the lovely suburb Riverdale as well as New York's most economically depressed area, the South Bronx.

Manhattan's Neighborhoods

Glimpsed from the window of an approaching plane, New York City can seem a monolithic concrete jungle. Up close, New York breaks down into manageable, unique neighborhoods. Boundaries between these neighborhoods can be abrupt.

The city began at the southern tip of Manhattan, in the area around **Battery Park** where the first Dutch settlers made their homes. The nearby harbor, now jazzed up by the **South St. Seaport** tourist magnet, provided the growing city with the commercial opportunities that helped it to succeed. Historic Manhattan, however, lies in the shadows of the imposing financial buildings around **Wall St.** and the civic offices around **City Hall.** A little farther north, **Little Italy, Chinatown,** and the southern blocks of the **Lower East Side,** neighborhoods rich in the cultures brought by late 19th-century immigrants, rub elbows below Houston St. (pronounced "HOW-ston," not like the Texan city). Formerly the home of Eastern European and Russian Jews, Delancey and Elizabeth St. now offer pasta and silks. The up-and-coming nook of high fashion, **NoLIta** (**N**orth of **L**ittle **Ita**ly) extends roughly down from Houston to Spring St. and over from Lafayette to the Bowery. To the west lies the trendy **TriBeCa** ("Triangle Below Canal St."). **SoHo** (for "South of Houston"), a former warehouse district west of Little Italy, now shelters a pocket of art studios, galleries, and chic boutiques. Above SoHo thrives **Greenwich Village,** where jumbled streets, trendy shops, and cafes have been home for decades to intense political and artistic activity. Today, the Village primarily indicates the western part (from Broadway west to the Hudson River), while the area east of Broadway is called the **East Village.**

A few blocks north of Greenwich Village, stretching across the west teens and twenties, lies **Chelsea,** the late artist Andy Warhol's favorite hangout and former home of Dylan Thomas and Arthur Miller. East of Chelsea, presiding over the East River, is **Gramercy Park,** a pastoral collection of elegant brownstones immortalized in Edith Wharton's *Age of Innocence.* **Midtown Manhattan** towers from 34th to 59th St., where skyscrapers pierce the skies, supporting over a million elevated offices. Here, department stores outfit New York; the nearby **Theater District** entertains the world. North of Midtown, **Central Park** slices Manhattan into East and West. On the **Upper West Side,** the gracious museums and residences of Central Park West neighbor the chic boutiques and sidewalk cafes of Columbus Ave. On the **Upper East Side,** the galleries and museums scattered among the elegant apartments of 5th and Park Ave. create an even more rarefied atmosphere.

Above 97th St., the Upper East Side's opulence ends with a whimper where commuter trains emerge from the tunnel and the *barrio* begins. Above 110th St. on the Upper West Side sits majestic **Columbia University** (founded as King's College in 1754), an urban member of the Ivy League. The communities of **Harlem** and **Morningside Heights** produced the Harlem Renaissance of black artists and writers in the 20s and the revolutionary Black Power movement of the 60s. While the sidewalks here bustle during the day and famous jazz joints throb at night, the area can be dangerous; explore, but exercise caution here. **Washington Heights,** just north of St. Nicholas Park, is home to Fort Tryon Park, the Medieval Cloisters museum, and a community of Old World immigrants.

Manhattan's Street Plan

New York's east/west division refers to an establishment's location in relation to the two borders of Central Park—**5th Ave.** on the east side and **Central Park West** on the west. Below 59th St. where the park ends, the West Side begins at the western half of 5th Ave. **Uptown** (59th St. and up) refers to the area north of Midtown. **Downtown** (34th St. and down) means the area south of Midtown. Streets run east-west. Avenues run north-south.

Manhattan's grid makes calculating distances fairly easy. Numbers increase from south to north along the avenues, but you should always ask for a cross street when getting an avenue address. This plan does not work in Greenwich Village or in lower Manhattan; just get a good map and ask for directions.

PRACTICAL INFORMATION

Taxis: When shared with friends a cab can be cheaper, safer, and more convenient than the subway, especially late at night. Most people in Manhattan hail yellow (licensed) cabs on the street. $2 base fare, 30¢ each one-fifth mi. or every 1¼min.; a 50¢ surcharge is levied 8pm-6am. Don't forget to tip 15%. Ask for a receipt, which will have the taxi's ID number. This is necessary to trace lost articles or to make a complaint to the **Taxi Commission,** 221 W. 41st St. (221-TAXI/8294). For radio-dispatched cabs, call 411 or check the *Yellow Pages* under "Taxicabs."

Car Rental: Nationwide, 241 W. 40th St. (867-1131), between 7th and 8th Ave. Mid-sized domestic sedan $33-59 per day, $289 per week. 150 free mi. per day, 1000 free mi. per week. Open M-F 7:30am-6:30pm. Vehicle return 24hr. Must be 23 with a major credit card.

Bike Rental: Pedal Pushers, 1306 2nd Ave. (288-5592), between 68th and 69th St. Rents 3-speeds for $4 per hr., $10 per day, $13 overnight; 10-speeds $5/$14/$19; mountain bikes $6/$17/$25. Overnight rentals require a $150 deposit on a major credit card; regular rentals need a major credit card, passport, or a NY state drivers license. Open Su-M 10am-6pm, W 10am-7pm, Th-Sa 10am-8pm.

Visitor Info: Times Sq. Visitors Center, 1560 Broadway (869-5453; http://www.nycvisit.com), between 46th and 47th St. Subway: #1, 2, 3, 7, 9 or N, R, S to Times Sq. The restored Embassy Theater will soon be the new hub of Big Apple tourism. The multilingual staff will offer hotel and restaurant listings, entertainment ideas, and safety tips. The center is expected to sell full-priced Broadway tickets, bus and boat tours, MetroCards, and offer services like ATMs, internet access, a newsstand, and bathrooms. Open daily 9am-6pm. **Other locations:** Grand Central terminal, south side of the main concourse; Penn Station terminal, south side of the Amtrak rotunda at 34th St. between 7th and 8th Ave.; Manhattan Mall information booth at 33rd and 6th St.

Help Lines: AIDS Information (807-6655). M-F 10am-9pm, Sa noon-3pm. **Crime Victims' Hotline** (577-7777). 24hr. **Sex Crimes Report Line** (267-7273). 24hr.

Medical Services: Walk-in Clinic, 57 E. 34th St. (252-6000), between Park and Madison Ave. Open M-Th 8am-8pm, Sa-Su 9am-2pm.

Post Office: Central branch, 421 8th Ave. (330-2902), across from Madison Sq. Garden. Open 24hr. For General Delivery, mail to and use the entrance at 390 9th Ave. **ZIP code:** 10001 for main post office.

Telephone codes: 212 (Manhattan); 718 (Brooklyn, Bronx, Queens, Staten Island). In text 212, unless otherwise noted.

ACCOMMODATIONS

The cost of living in New York is out of sight. At true full-service establishments, a night will cost you around $125 plus the 8.25% hotel tax. Some choices are available for under $60 a night.

Hostels and Student Organizations

Gershwin Hotel, 7 E. 27th St. (545-8000), between 5th and Madison Ave. Subway: #6, N, or R to 28th St. Cool building full of pop art, funky furniture, and artsy 20-somethings. The hotel hosts a next-door gallery, an amateur band night (Sa), and a hip bar, all of which throw frequent parties. Chic meat market feel here, both hetero and homo. Passport or ID proving out-of-state or foreign residence required. 4-bed dorms $25 per bed. Private rooms $80-130; triples and quads $100-150. 21-day max. stay. 24hr. reception. Check-out 11am. No curfew.

Sugar Hill International House, 722 St. Nicholas Ave. (926-7030), at 146th St. Subway: A, B, C, or D to 145th St. Located on Sugar Hill in Harlem, across from the subway. Lively neighborhood. Converted brownstone with comfy, huge rooms, many with large windows. Friendly staff is practically a living library of Harlem knowledge. Rooms for 2-10 people. All-female room available. Internet access $2 per 30min. Facilities include kitchens, stereo, and paperback library. Just up the street, the owners of Sugar Hill also run the **Blue Rabbit Hostel,** 730 St. Nicholas Ave. (491-3892). Similar to Sugar Hill, but with more doubles and more privacy. Common room, kitchen, and friendly kitty-cats. Amazingly spacious rooms. All of the following info applies to both hostels. Rooms $18-22. Key deposit $10. 14-day max. stay. Check-in 9am-10pm. Check-out 11am. No lockout. No curfew. No reservations accepted July-Sept. Call 1 month in advance during off-season. Passport ID required. No smoking.

⊛**Banana Bungalow,** 250 W. 77th St. (800-646-7835), at Broadway. Banana Bungalow has ambitions to be the largest hostel in the world; for now, it is merely the most fun. Clean rooms with bathroom. Amiable atmosphere emanates from the $5 keg parties on the rooftop lounge, large-screen TV lounge and kitchen, outings and tours, and discounts at pubs, restaurants, and movie theaters. 8-bed dorms $23; 6-bed dorms $24. Prices about 20% lower in winter. Breakfast and linen included. 14-day max. stay. Check-in and check-out 24hr.

⊛**Uptown Hostel,** 239 Lenox/Malcolm X Ave. (666-0559), at 122nd St. Subway: #2 or 3 to 125th St. Run by the knowledgeable and friendly Gisèle. Bunk beds; clean, comfy rooms; and spacious hall bathrooms. Wonderful new common room, kitchen, and recently sanded floors add to the family atmosphere. Singles $14; doubles $18. Key deposit $10. Check-in by 10pm. Lockout during the summer 11am-4pm. Call 2 weeks in advance; in winter at least 2 days is enough.

New York International Hostel (HI-AYH), 891 Amsterdam Ave. (932-2300), at 103rd St. Subway: #1, 9, B, or C to 103rd St.; just 1 block from the #1, 9 subway. Located in a block-long, landmark building, this is the mother of all youth hostels—the largest in the U.S., with 90 dorm-style rooms and 480 beds. Shares its site with the **CIEE Student Center** (666-3619), an info depot for travelers, as well as a **Council Travel** office and supply store. Spiffy new soft carpets, blonde-wood bunks, and spotless bathrooms. Members' kitchens and dining rooms, coin-operated laundry machines ($1), communal TV lounges, and a large outdoor garden. Walking tours and outings. Key-card entry to individual rooms. 10- to 12-bed dorms $26, 6- to 8-bed dorms $27, 4-bed dorms $29. Nov.-Apr. dorms $2 less. Nonmembers pay $3 more. Groups of 4-9 may get private rooms ($100); groups of 10 or more definitely will. Linen and towels included. Secure storage area and individual lockers., May-Oct. 7-night max. stay, Nov.-Apr. 29-night. Reception 24hr. Check-in any time. Check-out 11am (late check-out fee $5). No curfew. Wheelchair access.

De Hirsch Residence, 1395 Lexington Ave. (415-5650 or 800-858-4692), at 92nd St. Subway: #6 to 96th St. Affiliated with the 92nd St. YMCA/YWCA, De Hirsch has some of the larger, cleaner, and more convenient hostel housing in the city. Rooms with A/C; huge hall bathrooms; kitchens; laundry machines on every other floor. Single-sex floors, strictly enforced. 24hr. access and security. Access to the many 92nd St. Y facilities, including Nautilus machines and reduced rates for concerts. Organized activities such as video nights and walking tours. Singles $69; doubles $90. 3-day min. stay. Inquire about longer-term stays.

International Student Hospice, 154 E. 33rd St. (228-7470), between Lexington and 3rd Ave. Subway: #6 to 33rd St. Up a flight of stairs in an inconspicuous, converted brownstone with a brass "I.S.H." plaque. Good Murray Hill location. Helpful owner; European backpacking crowd. 20 tiny rooms for 1-4 people, bursting with antiques and Old World memorabilia. Hall bathroom. Common room, lounge, and mounds of dusty books. $25 per night, plus a $3 room tax. Some weekly discounts.

Jazz on the Park, 36 W. 106th St. (932-1600), at Central Park West. Brand new to the hostel scene, the Jazz plays to the tune of friendly dorms in a renovated building right next to Central Park. Their Java bar hosts live bands and other assorted hepcats. 12- to 14-bed dorms $25; 6- to 8-bed dorms $26.50; 4-bed dorms $29; 2-bed dorms $35. Taxes, linen, and breakfast included. No curfew.

Chelsea International Hostel, 251 W. 20th St. (647-0010), between 7th and 8th Ave. Subway: #1, 9, C, or E to 23rd St. In Chelsea on a block with a police precinct. Overflowing with funky European youth. Staff leads weekly pub crawls, offers pizza on Wednesday, and has Ricki Lake tickets. All rooms with windows and sink. Backyard garden. Kitchens and laundry. 4- and 6-person dorms $23-25; private rooms $50-55. Key deposit $10. Check-in 24hr. Reservations recommended.

Aladdin Hotel, 317 W. 45th St. (997-5700), between 8th and 9th Ave. Subway: #1, 2, 3, 9, A, C, E, N, or R to 42nd St. Trendy club ambience. Rooftop garden. 4-bed dorms $20-25 per bed; single or double with shared bath $65-85. Reserve at least 1 week in advance.

Chelsea Center Hostel, 313 W. 29th St. (643-0214), between 8th and 9th Ave. Subway: #1, 2, 3, 9, A, C, or E to 34th St. Ring the labeled buzzer at the door of an inconspicuous brownstone. Knowledgeable, helpful, multilingual staff. One of the more friendly hostels around. Basement room can be cramped, but lovely backyard garden helps to alleviate the claustrophobia. 2 showers. Dorm beds in summer $25; in winter $20. Linen provided. Light breakfast included. 14-day max. stay. Check-in 8:30am-11pm. Flexible lockout 11am-5pm. Call ahead. Cash only.

Big Apple Hostel, 119th W. 45th St. (302-2603), between 6th and 7th Ave. Subway: #1, 2, 3, 9, N, or R to 42nd St.; or B, D, or E to 7th Ave. Centrally located. Clean, comfortable rooms, full kitchen, back deck, luggage room, barbecue grill, common rooms, and laundry facilities. Lockers in some rooms; bring your own lock. In-house cafeteria. Americans accepted with out-of-state photo ID. Bunk in dorm-style room with shared bath $25; singles and doubles $65. Reception 24hr. No reservations accepted Aug.-Sept., but they'll hold a bed if you call after 11:30am on the day of arrival. Reservations accepted Oct.-June.

Mid-City Hostel, 608 8th Ave. (704-0562), between 39th and 40th St. on the 3rd and 4th floors. Subway: #1, 2, 3, 9, N, or R to 42nd St.; or A, C, or E to 42nd St.-9th Ave. On the east side of 8th Ave. No sign: just look for a yellow building with the street number on the small door. Brick walls, skylights, and old wooden ceiling beams. Mainly an international backpacking crowd; a passport or valid student ID is required. Bunks in very small mixed dorm-style room with shared bath $20. Small breakfast included. 7-night max. stay in summer. Lockout noon-6pm. Curfew Su-Th midnight, F-Sa 1am. Reservations required.

YMCA—Vanderbilt, 224 E. 47th St. (756-9600), between 2nd and 3rd Ave. Subway: #6 to 51st St. or E, F to Lexington-3rd Ave. 5 blocks from Grand Central Station. Convenient and well-run, with reasonable prices and good security. Bustles with jabbering international backpackers. Rooms are small, and bathroom-to-people ratio is pretty low, but, ahh, the perks! Free use of the athletic facilities and safe-deposit boxes. 5 shuttles daily to the airports. Singles $53; doubles $66-69. Key deposit $10. 25-night max. stay. Check-in 1-6pm; after 6pm must have major credit card. Check-out noon; luggage storage until departure ($1 per bag). Reservations 1-2 weeks in advance and guarantee with a deposit. Wheelchair access.

YMCA—West Side, 5 W. 63rd St. (787-4400). Subway: #1, 9, A, B, C, or D to 59th St.-Columbus Circle. Small, well-maintained rooms, bustling cafeteria, and spacious lounges in a popular Y. Free access to athletic facilities. Showers on every floor and spotless bathrooms with coded locks. A/C and cable TV in every room. Singles $59-85; doubles $69-95. 25-day max. stay. Check-out noon. Reservations recommended. A few stairs at entrance; otherwise wheelchair-friendly.

Hotels

⊛Carlton Arms Hotel, 160 E. 25th St. (679-0680), between Lexington and 3rd Ave. Subway: #6 to 23rd St. Each room has been designed in a different motif by a different avant-garde artist. Aggressive adornment doesn't completely obscure the age of these budget rooms, but it proves a playful distraction for those who don't mind the shared baths or lack of A/C. All rooms with sink. Singles $57, with bath $68; doubles $73/84; triples $90/101. Discounts for students and foreign travelers. Pay for 7 or more nights up front and get a 10% discount. Check-out 11:30am. Make reservations for summer at least 2 months in advance. Confirm reservations at least 10 days in advance.

Portland Sq. Hotel, 132 W. 47th St. (382-0600 or 800-388-8988), between 6th and 7th Ave. Subway: B, D, F, or Q to 50th St.-6th Ave. Great location. Rooms are carpeted and clean. Perks include phones, cable TV, A/C, sink, and safe in every room. Singles with shared bath $55, with private bath $85. Doubles $99, twins $109. Triples $114; quads $119. Check-in 3pm. Check-out noon.

Herald Sq. Hotel, 19 W. 31st St. (279-4017 or 800-727-1888), at 5th Ave. Subway: B, D, F, N, or R to 34th St. In the original Beaux Arts home of *Life* magazine (built in 1893). Above the entrance, note the gold cherub entitled "Winged Life," carved by Philip Martiny. The sculpture was a frequent presence on the pages of early *Life* magazines. Small, clean rooms with color TV, safes, phones, and A/C. Singles $55-79; doubles $99; twins $109; triples $119; quads $129. International students get a

10% discount. Reservations recommended 3-4 weeks in advance for the cheaper rooms.

Pioneer Hotel, 341 Broome St. (226-1482), between Elizabeth St. and the Bowery. Located between Little Italy and the Lower East Side in a 100-year-old building. Good, no-frills place to stay if you want to be close to SoHo and the East Village nightlife. All rooms have TVs, sinks, and ceiling fans. Rooms with private bathrooms have A/C. Generally tight security at night in a neighborhood that requires it. Singles $37; doubles $58, with bath $68; triples $85-92. Check-out 11am. Reservations recommended, at least 6 weeks in advance during peak season.

Pickwick Arms Hotel, 230 E. 51st St. (355-0300 or 800-PICKWIK/742-5945), between 2nd and 3rd Ave. Subway: #6 to 51st St. or E, F to Lexington-3rd Ave. Business types congregate in this well-priced, mid-sized hotel. Chandeliered marble lobby. Tiny rooms and hall bathrooms. Roof garden and airport service. A/C and TV in all rooms. Singles $60-90 (some with bath). Doubles with bath $110-120. Double bed with sofa $130. $15 per additional person. Check-in 2pm. Check-out 1pm. One night's deposit or credit card to guarantee. Reservations needed.

Chelsea Inn, 46 W. 17th St. (645-8989), between 5th and 6th Ave. Subway: F or R to 23rd St. Charmingly mismatched antique furniture in spacious pension-style rooms with kitchenettes attracts a primarily European crowd. Pricey but worth a splurge. Guest rooms with shared bath $99-109; studios $119-139; pricier suites available. 10% ISIC discount. Reception daily 9am-7pm. Check-in 3pm. Check-out noon.

Washington Sq. Hotel, 103 Waverly Pl. (777-9515 or 800-222-0418), at MacDougal St. Subway: A, B, C, D, E, F, or Q to W. 4th St. Fantastic location. Glitzy lobby, with ornate wrought-iron gate. A/C, TV, and key-card entry to rooms. Clean and comfy. Friendly, multilingual staff. Restaurant/bar and exercise room. Singles from $110; doubles from $130. 2 twin beds from $140, quads from $160. Rollaway bed $15. 10% ISIC discount. Continental breakfast included. Reservations required 2-3 weeks in advance.

Hotel Grand Union, 34 E. 32nd St. (683-5890), between Madison and Park Ave. Subway: #6 to 33rd St. Centrally located and recently renovated rooms equipped with cable TV, phone, A/C, a mini-fridge, and full bathroom. 24hr. security. Singles and doubles $110; triples $125; quads $150; quints $180.

Hotel Stanford, 43 W. 32nd St. (563-1480), between 5th Ave. and Broadway in NY's Korean district. Subway: B, D, F, N, or R to 34th St. Lobby glitters with sparkling ceiling lights and a polished marble floor. Rooms are impeccably clean, with firm mattresses and plush carpeting. TV, A/C, and refrigerators. Singles $90-110; doubles $120-150; triples $130-150. Check-out noon. Reservations recommended.

Hotel Wolcott, 4 W. 31st St. (268-2900), at 5th Ave. Subway B, D, F, N, or R to 34th St. Enter into a rococo fantasy—flowery floors, gold leaf, marble, chandeliers, and recessed ceilings all await your pleasure in the overwhelming lobby. Rooms are a bit simpler and cozier, with A/C, TV, phones and bathrooms. Safety deposit boxes and laundry. Singles and doubles $110-130; triples $150; suites (for 3) $150-170.

Malibu Studios Hotel, 2688 Broadway (222-2954), at 103rd St. Subway: #1 or 9 to 103rd St. Renovations have brought this former Gen-X kitschhaus into the simple, tasteful 90s. The friendly staff doles out VIP passes to popular clubs. Singles $49; doubles $69; triples $85; quads $99. Deluxe rooms include private bath, A/C, and TV: singles and doubles $99, triples $124, quads $139. Ask about student, off-season, and weekly/monthly discounts. Reservations required.

Senton Hotel, 39-41 W. 27th St. (684-5800), between 6th Ave. and Broadway. Subway: R to 28th St. Look for the shockingly blue exterior. Comfortable beds in spacious quarters, amid a sea of large-print floral wallpapers. A/C and cable TV. Basic accommodations, but most rooms are newly renovated. 24hr. security; guests not allowed. Singles with hall bath $50; doubles $60; suites (2 double beds) $75. Sa-Su slightly higher.

Hayden Hall, 117 W. 79th St. (787-4900), off Columbus Ave. Subway: B or C to 81st St. Great location, pricey rooms. Singles $65, with private bath $100. Doubles $130/$200. Reservations recommended.

Arlington Hotel, 18-20 W. 25th St. (645-3990 or 800-488-0920), between 5th and 6th Ave. Subway: F or R to 23rd St. Hospitable and courteous staff. Caters to foreign travelers, especially those from Asia: signs are translated into Chinese, Korean, and Japanese. Clean, refurbished rooms, all with TV and A/C. Singles or doubles (1 bed) $99; doubles (2 beds) $105, including all taxes. 10% ISIC discount. Prices higher during peak seasons. Credit card reservations guaranteed.

Murray Hill Inn, 143 E. 30th St. (683-6900 or 888-996-0103), between Lexington and 3rd Ave. Clean, floral-print rooms with shared baths. All rooms with sink, A/C, cable TV, and phone. Singles $65; doubles $85, with bath $105. Extra bed $10. 21-day max. stay. Check-in 3pm. Check-out noon.

Dormitories

New York University, 14a Washington Pl. (998-4621). NYU's Summer Housing Office rents rooms on a weekly basis (3-week min., 12-week max.) from mid-May to mid-Aug. Excellent locations in the heart of Greenwich Village. Rooms with or without A/C, bath, or kitchenette; boarders without kitchens must join the meal plan for $72-80 per person per week. Anyone over 17 is eligible. Singles $125 per week, with A/C $185; doubles $160/$270. Singles with kitchen and A/C $210 per week; doubles $310. Call after Jan. 1 for info and reservations; reserve by May 1.

Columbia University, 1230 Amsterdam Ave. (678-3235), at 120th St. Subway: #1 or 9 to 116th St. Whittier Hall sets aside 10 rooms for visitors year-round. Rooms are small but clean. Generally tight 24hr. security. Not the safest neighborhood, but well-populated until fairly late at night. Singles $45; doubles with A/C and bath (some with kitchen) $75. Reserve in Mar. for May-Aug., in July for Sept.-Dec.

FOOD

This city takes its food seriously. New York will dazzle you with its culinary bounty, serving the needs of its diverse (and hungry) population. City dining spans the globe, with eateries ranging from sushi bars to wild combinations like Afghani/Italian and Mexican/Lebanese. Listed below are some choice places divided by neighborhood, but why not explore and take a bite out of the Big Apple yourself?

Financial District

Lower Manhattan eateries cater to sharply clad Wall St. brokers and bankers on lunch break; they offer cheap food prepared grease-lightning-fast, always available as take-out and sometimes with free delivery. Fast-food joints pepper Broadway near Dey and John St. just a few feet from the overpriced offerings of the Main Concourse of the World Trade Center. In the summer, food **pushcarts** form a solid wall along Broadway between Cedar and Liberty St.

Zigolini's, 66 Pearl St. (425-7171), at Coenties Alley. One of the few places in the area where indoor air-conditioned seating abounds (although there is plenty of room outdoors). This gourmet Italian restaurant serves filling sandwiches ($5-7), as well as some great pasta. Open M-F 7am-7pm.

Frank's Papaya, 192 Broadway (693-2763), at John St. Long on value, short on ambience, Frank's stand-at-the-counter hot dog joint has become a permanent fixture in the World Trade Center area. Jumbo turkey burger $1.60, delicious dogs 50¢. Open M-Sa 5:30am-10pm, Su 5:30am-5:30pm.

McDonald's, 160 Broadway (385-2063), at Liberty St. Yeah, it's a McDonald's, but *what* a McDonald's! Step inside and witness one of New York's finest examples of postmodern shmaltz. Wall St.'s Mickey D's sports a doorperson in a tux, a pianist, a stock ticker, and a McBoutique on the 2nd fl. They keep the ketchup packets in glass and brass bowls here—a little touch of McClass to justify the slightly inflated McPrice. Open M-F 6am-9pm, Sa 8am-9pm, Su 8:30am-9pm.

Little Italy

A chunk of Naples has migrated to this lively, compact quarter roughly bounded by Canal, Lafayette, Houston St., and the Bowery. **Mulberry St.** is the main drag and the appetite avenue of Little Italy. Stroll here after 7pm to catch street life, but arrive earlier to get a good table. For the sake of variety and thrift, diners visit a *ristorante* then get just desserts at a *caffè*. To get to Little Italy, take the #4, 5, or 6, the N or R, or the J, M, or Z to Canal St.; or take the B, D, F, or Q to Broadway-Lafayette.

🏆**Lombardi's,** 32 Spring St. (941-7994), between Mott and Mulberry St. NY's oldest licensed pizzeria (1897)—credited with creating the famous NY-style thin-crust, coal-oven pizza—still serves some of the best pizza in the city. Indoor dining rooms and outdoor patio. Large pie feeds 2 ($12.50). Toppings are pricey ($3 for 1, $5 for 2, $6 for 3) but they're worth it. Reservations for groups of 6 or more. Open M-Th 11am-11pm, F-Sa 11:30-midnight, Su 11am-10pm. Cash only.

 Il Fornaio, 132A Mulberry St. (226-8306), between Grand and Hester St. Simple, fresh Italian standards at good prices. Pasta $6-8, entrees $8.50-11, lunch specials $4.50-6. Open Su-Th 11:30am-11pm, F-Sa 11am-11pm.

 Da Nico, 164 Mulberry St. (343-1212), between Broome and Grand St. Cheap, tasty, and friendly. But the reason to eat here is the lovely garden in back, frequented by Al Pacino and Johnny Depp. Pasta $6-10, entrees $6.50-12.50. Open Su-Th 11am-11pm, F-Sa 11am-12pm.

 Caffè Palermo, 148 Mulberry (431-4205), between Grand and Hester St. The best of the *caffè* offerings along Mulberry. Most pastries are $2-3. The staff takes much pride in their tasty *tiramisú*; the *cannoli* ($2, $2.75 to go) and cappuccino ($3.25) are also quite good. Open Su-Th 11am-midnight, F-Sa 11am-1am.

Chinatown

If you're looking for cheap, authentic Asian fare, join the crowds that push through the narrow, chaotic streets of one of the oldest Chinatowns in the U.S. The neighborhood's 300-plus restaurants cook up some of the best Chinese, Thai, and Vietnamese eats around. Cantonese *dim sum* is a Sunday afternoon tradition; waiters roll carts filled with dishes of bite-sized goodies up and down the aisles. Simply point at what you want, and at the end of the meal, the empty dishes on your table are tallied.

🏆**Big Wong's,** 67 Mott (964-0540), between Bayard and Canal St. Let the cafeteria-style ambience bring you back to your eating contest days; everything here is delectable and most dishes are under $5. The barbecued spare ribs ($3) and the roast pork and soy sauce chicken ($5) are the best in Chinatown. Often a wait. Bring your own alcohol. Open daily 9am-9pm.

🏆**Bo-Ky,** 78-80 Bayard St. (406-2292), between Mott and Mulberry St. Quality Vietnamese joint specializing in soups (most under $5). The coconut-and-curry chicken soup ($5) will clear that nasty head cold instantly. Open daily 7am-9:30pm.

🏆**Harden & L.C. Corp.,** 43 Canal St. (966-5419), near Ludlow St. Harden is home to what may be the best meal deal in Manhattan: a massive Malaysian dinner for only $2.50. Cruise in, point to the 3 sides you want, and you'll get a huge plate of rice with a heaping portion of each side.

🏆**Hong Kong Egg Cake Co.,** on the corner of Mott and Mosco St., in a small, red shack on the side of a building. Here, the proprietress, Cecilia Tam, will make you a dozen soft, sweet egg cakes fresh from the skillet ($1). Don't worry about finding "The Co."—just follow the line wrapping around the corner onto Mott.

 Chinatown Ice Cream Factory, 65 Bayard St. (608-4170), at Mott St. Satisfy your sweet-tooth here with lychee, taro, ginger, red bean, or green tea ice cream. 1 scoop $2, 2 $3.60, 3 $4.60. Open M-Th 11am-11pm, F-Su 11am-11:45pm.

SoHo and TriBeCa

In SoHo, food, like life, is all about image. Most of the restaurants here tend to be preoccupied with decor, and most aim to serve a stylishly healthful cuisine. The image lifestyle, however, takes money, so don't be surprised if you find it hard to get a cheap meal. Often the best deal in SoHo is brunch, when the neighborhood shows its most good-natured front. Dining in TriBeCa is generally a much funkier (and blessedly cheaper) experience than in SoHo. The restaurants here have a dressed-down, folksy, flea market flavor. TriBeCa's restaurants are often hidden like little oases among the hulking warehouses and decaying buildings.

Yaffa's Tea Room, 19 Harrison St. (274-9403), near Greenwich St. Yaffa's is one of the few unpretentious places in Manhattan that serves high tea—and definitely the coolest. Wide selection of healthy sandwiches ($8-10.50) and entrees ($9-19). High tea ($20, reservations generally required), served daily 2-6pm, includes cucumber, salmon, or watercress finger sandwiches, fresh baked scones, dessert sampler, and a pot of tea. "Couscous Night" every Th 6:30-midnight. The attached bar/restaurant is less subdued, with a different menu (including tapas). Bar open daily 8:30am-4am. Restaurant open 8:30am-midnight.

Jerry's, 101 Prince St. (966-9464), near Mercer St. The joint is jumping at Jerry's, a trendy diner with touches of red decor. Great selection of sandwiches, like the melted Vermont cheddar with bacon and tomato on 7-grain roll, $6.50. All of the foods have an exciting twist. Open M-F 11:30am-4pm and 6pm-11pm.

Space Untitled, 133 Greene St. (260-6677), near Houston St. The best of SoHo—huge, warehouse-like space with plenty of bar stools and chairs to make yourself comfortable. Black, white, brick, and art surround you while you eat gourmet to-go, write postcards, or read on a hot afternoon. Sandwiches and salads $3-6, fabulous desserts $1.85-3.50. Coffee $1.25-1.75, wine and beer $3-4.50. Open Su-M 7am-10pm, Tu-Th 7am-11pm, F-Sa 7am-midnight.

East Village and Alphabet City

First and **2nd Ave.** are the best for restaurant-exploring. **St. Mark's Pl.** hosts a slew of inexpensive and popular village institutions, and at night, **Avenue A** throbs with bars and sidewalk cafes. Twenty-six competing Indian restaurants line **6th St.** between 1st and 2nd Ave. If you look indecisive, the anxious managers may offer free wine or discounts on the already cheap food.

Dojo Restaurant, 24 St. Mark's Pl. (674-9821), between 2nd and 3rd Ave. Unbeatable Dojo is one of the most popular restaurants in the East Village, and rightly so—it offers an incredible variety of vegetarian and Japanese food that manages to be simultaneously healthy, inexplicably inexpensive, and surprisingly tasty. The special "Dojo" dressing is wonderful. Soyburgers with brown rice and salad $3, spinach and pita sandwich with assorted veggies $3. Outdoor seating. Another location at 14 W. 4th St. (505-8934). Open Su-Th 11am-1am, F-Sa 11am-2am.

Mama's Food Shop, 200 E. 3rd St. (777-4425), between Ave. A and B. Specializes in home cooking. Laid-back villagers settle into heaping plates of fried chicken ($6) or salmon ($7), with sides ranging from honey-glazed sweet potatoes to broccoli to couscous for only $1 each. Vegetarian dinner ($7) gives you any 3 sides. Open M-Sa 11am-11pm.

Veselka, 144 2nd Ave. (228-9682), at 9th St. Down-to-earth, soup-and-bread, Polish-Ukrainian joint. Traditional food served in a friendly, untraditional setting. Big, beautiful murals cover everything. Enormous menu includes about 10 varieties of soups, as well as salads, blintzes, meats, and other Eastern European fare. Blintzes $3.50, soup $2 a cup (the chicken noodle is sumptuous). Combination special gets you soup, salad, stuffed cabbage, and 4 melt-in-your-mouth pirogi ($8). Great breakfast specials: *challah* french toast, OJ, and coffee for $3.75. Open 24hr.

Damask Falafel, 85 Ave. A (673-5016), between 5th and 6th St. This closet-sized stand serves the cheapest and best falafel in the area—$1.75 for a sandwich; $3.50 for a falafel platter with tabouleh, chick peas, salad, and pita bread. Banana milk shakes $1.50. Open M-F 11am-2am, Sa-Su 11am-4am.

Lower East Side

Culinary cultures clash on the lower end of the East Side, where pasty-faced punks and starving artists dine alongside an older generation conversing in Polish, Hungarian, and Yiddish. The neighborhood took in the huddled masses, and, in return, got lots of cool places to eat. As Chinatown dissipates northward along East Broadway, you can still find the city's finest **kosher Jewish eateries.**

Katz's Delicatessen, 205 E. Houston St. (254-2246), near Orchard St. Since 1888, Katz's has remained an authentic Jewish deli. Katz's widened its appeal with its "Send a salami to your boy in the army" campaign during WWII. Every president in the last 2 decades has been the proud recipient of a Katz salami. The food is orgasmic (confirmed by Meg Ryan, who made a loud scene here in *When Harry Met Sally*), but you pay extra for the atmosphere. Heroes $5.10, sandwiches around $9. Open M-Tu and Su 8am-10pm, W-Th 8am-11pm, F-Sa 8am-3am.

◉**Guss' Lower East Side Pickle Corp.,** 35 Essex St. (254-4477 or 800-252-4877). Pickles galore, as seen in *Crossing Delancey*. A vast variety of glorious gherkins, from super sour to sweet, sold individually (50¢-$2) and in quarts ($4.25). Open Su-Th 9am-6pm, F 9am-4pm.

Ratner's Restaurant, 138 Delancey St. (677-5588), just west of the Manhattan Bridge. The most famous of the kosher restaurants, partly because of its frozen-food line. Jewish dietary laws are strictly followed—but *oy vey!* Such *matzah brei* ($9)! Open Su-Th 6am-midnight, F 6am-3pm, Sa sundown-2am.

Greenwich Village

The West Village's free-floating artistic angst has been channeled into many creative (and cheap) food venues. The aggressive and entertaining street life makes stumbling around and deciding where to go almost as much fun as eating. The major avenues have cheap, decent food. The European-style bistros of **Bleecker St.** and **MacDougal St.,** south of Washington Sq. Park, have perfected the homey "antique" look. Or just slump down 8th St. to **6th Ave.** to find some of the city's best pizza.

◉**Cucina Stagionale,** 275 Bleecker St. (924-2707), at Jones St. Unpretentious Italian dining in a low-key, classy environment. Packed on weekends. The *conchiglie* (shells and sauteed calimari in spicy red sauce, $8) or the spinach and cheese ravioli ($6) will tell you why. Pasta dishes $6-8; veal, chicken, and fish dishes $8-10. Open daily noon-midnight.

Go Sushi, 3 Greenwich Ave. (366-9272), at 6th Ave. and 8th St. Sleek wooden tables, a black timber ceiling, and a lot of exposed silver complete the portrait of modernist orientalism. Cheap Japanese food; Bento Box with *gyoza,* rice, salad, and chicken teriyaki $6. Sushi (2 salmon, 1 tuna, 1 shrimp, 4 California, 4 cŭcumber) $6.50. Open daily 11:30am-midnight.

Quantum Leap, 88 W. 3rd St. (677-8050), between Thompson and Sullivan St. Brown rice galore at this aggressively veggie restaurant. All manner of healthy chow, including BBQ teriyaki tofu ($8.50), soyburger delight ($5), and various $5 lunch specials. Don't worry, carnivores, it's all very tasty. Open M-Th 11:30am-11pm, F 11:30am-midnight, Sa 11am-midnight, Su 11am-10pm.

Ray's Pizza, 465 6th Ave. (243-2253), at 11th St. Half of the uptown pizza joints claim to be the "Original Ray's," but this one is the real McCoy. People have been known to fly here from Europe just to bring back a few pies. Cheese-heavy slice ($1.75). Scant seating; this is pizza to go. Open Su-Th 11am-2am, F-Sa 11am-3am.

Caffè Mona Lisa, 282 Bleecker St. (929-1262), near Jones St. Like the coffee, the presence of *La Gioconda* imagery is strong but not overpowering. In addition to the well-brewed beverages ($1.50-3.75) and the usual cafe fare, Mona Lisa entices with oversized mirrors hanging above stuffed chairs and other personality-filled furniture pieces. Open daily 11am-2am.

Midtown and Chelsea

Straddling the extremes, the lower Midtown dining scene is neither fast-food commercial nor *haute cuisine* trendy. East of 5th Ave. on **Lexington Ave.,** Pakistani and Indian restaurants battle for customers. Liberally sprinkled throughout, Korean corner shops that are equal parts grocery and buffet offer hot and cold salad bars.

The best food offerings in Chelsea come from the large Mexican and Central American community in the southern section of the neighborhood. From 14th to 22nd St., eateries offer combinations of Central American and Chinese cuisine, as well as Cajun and Creole specialties. **Eighth Ave.** provides the best restaurant browsing.

◉**Kitchen,** 218 8th Ave. (243-4433), near 21st St. A real kitchen serving up Mexican food. Most order food to go, but there are a few tables. Burrito stuffed with pinto beans, rice, and green salsa with exhaustive fillings and tortilla options $6.25. Open M-Sa 9am-10:30pm, Su 11am-10:30pm.

Negril, 362 W. 23rd St. (807-6411), between 8th and 9th Ave. The Jamaican fare served in this colorful, gay-friendly haunt is light, yet incredibly spicy. Sandwiches $6.50-7.50, "light meals" (salads, etc.) $3.50-7.50, and entrees $6.50-8.50. Spicy ginger beer $3.50. Festive Su brunch with live band 11am-4pm. Open M-F 11am-midnight, Sa-Su 11am-4pm and 5pm-2am; bar open F-Sa until 4am. Wheelchair access.

Jai-Ya, 396 3rd Ave. (889-1330), between 28th and 29th St. Critics rave over the Thai and other Asian food, with 3 degrees of spiciness, from mild to "help-me-I'm-on-fire." The friendly staff and soothing great interior tango with budget prices and a decidedly upscale look (cloth napkins!). The $7.25 Thai noodles are a definite steal. Most dishes $7-10. Lunch specials M-F 11:30am-3pm. Open M-F 11am-midnight, Sa 11am-12:30am, Su 4pm-midnight.

Zen Palate, 34 E. Union Sq. (614-9291), across from the park. A must for vegans and those who love them. Fantastic Asian-inspired vegetarian/vegan cuisine, including soothing, healthy, and fabulously fresh treats like stir-fried rice fettuccini with mushrooms $7 or other concoctions on the brown rice/seaweed/kale and soy tip. Open M-Sa 11am-11pm, Su noon-10:30pm. Other locations at 663 9th Ave. (582-1669), and at 46th St. and 2170 Broadway (501-7768), at 76th St.

East Midtown

Around noon to 2pm, the many delis and cafes here become swamped with harried junior executives trying to eat quickly and get back to work. The 50s streets on **2nd Ave.** and the area surrounding Grand Central Station are filled with good, cheap fare. You might also check out grocery stores, such as the **Food Emporium,** 969 2nd Ave. (593-2224), between 51st and 52nd St.; **D'Agostino,** 3rd Ave. (684-3133), between 35th and 36th St.; or **Associated Group Grocers,** 1396 2nd Ave. (421-7673), between E. 48th and E. 49th St. This part of town has many public spaces (plazas, lobbies, parks) for picnicking such as **Greenacre Park,** 51st St. between 2nd and 3rd Ave., and **Paley Park,** 53rd St. between 5th and Madison Ave.

Dosanko, 423 Madison Ave. (688-8575), between 48th and 49th St. All is tranquil at this aromatic Japanese-cuisine pit-stop. The scrumptious *gyoza* ($4.50) is a favorite, as are the many varieties of *larmen* (Japanese noodle soup, $5.50-7.20). Open M-F 11:30am-10pm, Sa-Su noon-9pm.

Coldwaters, 988 2nd Ave. (888-2122), between 52nd and 53rd St. Seafood ($6-11) served under nautical paraphernalia and stained-glass lamps. Brunch is a bargain: 2 drinks (alcoholic or non-), choice of entree, salad, and fries for $8 (daily 11am-4pm). Dinner is also a good deal: entrees come with all-you-can-eat salad, fries or baked potato, and a basket of fresh garlic bread. Open daily 11am-3am.

West Midtown

Your best bets here are generally along 8th Ave. between 34th and 59th St. in the area known as **Hell's Kitchen.** Once deserving of its name, this area has given birth to an array of inexpensive ethnic restaurants. Those with deep pockets might venture to **Restaurant Row,** on 46th St. between 8th and 9th Ave., which offers a block of dining to a pre-theater crowd (arriving after 8pm will make getting a table easier).

Afghan Cuisine Restaurant, 789 9th Ave. (664-0123 or 664-0125), between 52nd and 53rd St. This little cloister of things Afghani (a map on every table, sitars on the walls, and yes, Afghan rugs) serves up superb, filling food. Kebab dishes ($8-10) and vegetarian platters ($7-8) are served with basmati rice, salad, and homemade bread. Open daily 11am-11pm.

Original Fresco Tortillas, 536 9th Ave. (465-8898), between 39th and 40th St. This tiny 4-seater could be Taco Bell's father (who is embarrassed by his ugly offspring). Excellent homemade food at fast-food prices: fajitas and tacos $1-2, quesadillas $2-4, giant burritos $4-5. Open M-F 11am-11pm, Sa-Su noon-10pm.

Rice & Beans, 744 9th Ave. (265-4444), between 50th and 51st St. This dark, little Brazilian restaurant offers flavorful, filling food to a *salsa* beat. The chicken Ipanema with tomatoes and herbs is slightly spicy and totally sublime ($10). Open M-Th 11am-10pm, F-Sa 11am-11pm, Su 1-9pm.

Upper East Side

Meals on the Upper East Side descend in price as you move east from **5th Ave.'s** glitzy, overpriced museum cafes towards **Lexington, 3rd** and **2nd Ave.**

🐾**Barking Dog Luncheonette,** 1678 3rd Ave. (831-1800), at 94th St. Enter through the doghouse-shaped door labeled "Fido" and satisfy your hunger pangs with helpings right out of canine heaven. The biggest dog on the block will be satisfied with Mum's Luvin' Shepherd's Pie (beef, carrots, peas and stilton mash, $11.75) while others may prefer the Barking Dog Burger ($6.50). Open daily 8am-11pm.

🐾**EJ's Luncheonette,** 1271 3rd Ave. (472-0600), at 73rd St. The understated American elegance and huge portions in this hip 50s-style diner have fostered a legion of devoted Upper East Siders. The scrumptious fare (buttermilk pancakes $5.75, cheeseburger with fries $6.75) is rumored to have attracted neighborhood star JFK, Jr. Open M-Th 8am-11pm, F-Sa 8am-11:30, Su 8am-10:30pm.

🐾**Papaya King,** 179 E. 86th St. (369-0648), at 3rd Ave. New Yorkers tolerate the outrageously long lines and the yellow decor at this dive with only a few stools and no tables all for a taste of the "tastier than filet mignon" hot dogs ($1.79). You might opt for the special: 2 hot dogs and a 16 oz. tropical fruit shake, an Upper East Side steal for $3.89. Open M-F 8am-midnight, Sa-Su 8am-2am.

Upper West Side

Large and trendy restaurants spill onto the sidewalk, providing the perfect people-watching post. Intermingled among these are cheap pizza joints and hotdog hole-in-the-walls. The budget traveler should have no trouble finding affordable, satisfying meals along **Broadway, Amsterdam,** or **Columbus.**

🐾**Mary Ann's,** 2454 Broadway Ave. (877-0132), at 91st St. Make it *fiesta* anytime! Simple, well-prepared Mexican food combines with excellent service to make this one of the best dinners along Broadway. A beef taco, 2 chicken taquitos, rice, beans, guacamole, and sour cream will run you $7 (includes bottomless chips and salsa). Open Su-Th noon-10:30pm, F-Sa noon-11:30pm.

🐾**H&H Bagels,** 2239 Broadway (595-8000), at 80th St. H&H has been nourishing Upper West Siders for years with cheap bagels (75¢) that are possibly the best in Manhattan. Dozen bagels $9. Be sure to step up to the counter and heed the "NEXT!" command. Open 24hr.

🐾**Zabar's,** 2245 Broadway (787-2000), between 80th and 81st St. Subway: #1 or 9 to 79th St. This New York institution sells everything you need for a 4-star meal at home. Cheese, salmon, beautiful breads, and droves of shoppers. Gourmet, but not pretentious. Open M-F 8am-7:30pm, Sa 8am-8pm, Su 9am-6pm.

🐾**Café Lalo,** 201 W. 83rd St. (496-6031), between Broadway and Amsterdam. A wall of French windows allows live jazz (and the occasional *bon mot* from a suave *monsieur* within) to escape from this self-proclaimed European cafe. Immaculate cakes $5 per slice, full bar available. Open Su-Th 9am-2am, F-Sa 9am-4am.

Harlem and Morningside Heights

In Harlem, ethnic food is everywhere, with Jewish food in Washington Heights, various Latino and Cuban foods in the Hispanic communities, and, of course, East and West African, Caribbean and Creole, and some of the best soul food north of the Mason-Dixon Line. For food from the heart of Harlem, **Lenox Ave., 125th St.,** or **116th St.** are the places to go. The cafes and restaurants in Morningside Heights cater to Columbia University. This usually means that hours run late and the price range is that of a starving student.

🐾**Copeland's,** 547 W. 145th St. (234-2357), between Broadway and Amsterdam Ave. Subway: #1 or 9 to 145th St. Excellent soul food without the slick presentation. Amazing BBQ sauce. Smothered chicken $6.50; fried pork chop $7.20. Smorgasbord next door—cafeteria-style but just as good. Southern-style breakfasts and Su brunch are amazing. Open Tu-Th 4:30-11pm, F-Sa 4:30pm-midnight, Su 11am-9:30pm. Cafeteria open daily 7am-11pm.

⭐**Massawa,** 1239 Amsterdam Ave. (663-0505), at 121st St. Specializes in well-prepared Ethiopian and Eritrean cuisine. The many veggie dishes ($5-6) are served with spongy *injera* bread or rice. Great lunch specials (daily 11:30am and 3pm) like lamb stew and collard green/potato platters ($4-5.75). Open daily noon-midnight.

Joseph Food Basket, 471 Lenox Ave. (368-7663), between 133rd and 134th St. Subway: #2, 3 to 135th St. Healthy vegetarian American-Jamaican cuisine served up cheap. Rasta colors, Stars of David, and a full dinner with specials like *callaloo* (spinach and okra) for only $5 create a very positive vibe. Open M-Sa 7am-7pm.

Tom's Restaurant, 2880 Broadway (864-6137), at 112th St. While Suzanne Vega wrote a catchy tune about this diner, and Tom's is featured in most episodes of *Seinfeld,* thirsty scholars mainly come here for Tom's luxurious milkshakes ($2.45). Greasy burgers for $3-5, dinner under $6.50. Open M-W 6am-1:30am and continuously Th 6am to Su 1:30am.

Brooklyn

Brooklyn's restaurants, delis, and cafes offer all the flavors and varieties of cuisine that can be found in Manhattan, and often at lower prices. Brooklyn Heights and Park Slope offer nouvelle cuisine but specialize in pita bread and *baba ghanoush*. **Williamsburg** has cheap eats in a funky, lo-fi atmosphere, **Greenpoint** is a borscht-lover's paradise, and **Flatbush** serves up Jamaican and other West Indian cuisine. For those who didn't get their international fill in Manhattan, Brooklyn has its own Chinatown in Sunset Park and its own Little Italy in Carroll Gardens.

⭐**Patsy Grimaldi's** (a.k.a., Grimaldi's), 19 Old Fulton St. (718-858-4300), between Front and Water St. under the Brooklyn Bridge. Subway: A or C to High St. Delicious thin crust brick-oven pizza with wonderfully fresh mozzarella. Come early to avoid long waits. All-Sinatra decor. Small pies $13, large $14, toppings $2 each. Open M-F 11:30am-11pm, Sa-Su 2pm-midnight.

⭐**Cambodia Restaurant,** 87 S. Elliott Pl. (718-858-3262), between Lafayette and Fulton St. in Fort Greene. Subway: G to Fulton St. or C to Lafayette Ave. Delicious, cheap food. *Naem chao* (spring rolls with shrimp, veggies, and sweet basil, $3.50) and southeast Asian *ktis tao hoo* (sauteed bean curd in lemon grass sauce, $6-9) are 2 specialties. Open Su-Tu 11am-10pm, W 11am-10:30pm, Th-Sa 11am-11pm.

⭐**Oznot's Dish,** 79 Berry St. (718-599-6596). Subway: L to Bedford Ave. From the subway, walk west to Berry St. and head north. Beautiful, beautiful, beautiful, with good food to boot. North African/American eclectic fare, with plenty of cross-pollinated goodies like coconut Indian curry ($8). Lamb burger on peasant bread $6.50. Granola, yogurt, and fruit $4.40. Unusual teas like Iron Goddess of Mercy and Lapsang Crocodile. Garden out back. Open Tu-Su 6am-midnight.

⭐**PlanEat Thailand,** 184 Bedford Ave. (718-599-5758). Subway: L to Bedford Ave. The city's best inexpensive Thai food served amidst walls decorated with high-quality graffiti. All beef dishes under $6, all chicken dishes under $7, and a killer *pad thai* for only $5.25. If you ask for spicy, they'll give you medium—it'll be enough to clear your sinuses. Open M-Sa 11:30am-11:30pm, Su 1-11pm.

⭐**Tom's Restaurant,** 782 Washington Ave. (718-636-9738), at Sterling Pl. Subway: #2 or 3 to Brooklyn Museum. Head to Washington St. on the left side of the museum and follow it northward across the multi-lane intersection. The quintessential Brooklyn breakfast place—an old-time luncheonette complete with a soda fountain and a waitstaff that's on a first-name basis with most of the clientele. 2 eggs with fries or grits, toast, and coffee or tea $2. Famous golden *challah* french toast $3. Breakfast served all day. Open M-Sa 6:30am-4pm.

⭐**Primorski Restaurant,** 282 Brighton Beach Ave. (718-891-3111), between Brighton Beach 2nd and Brighton Beach 3rd St. Subway: D or Q to Brighton Beach, then 4 blocks east on Brighton Beach Ave. Populated by Russian-speaking Brooklynites, Primorski serves some of the Western Hemisphere's best Ukrainian *borscht* ($2.25) in an atmosphere of a red velour Bar Mitzvah Hall. Eminently affordable lunch special (M-F 11am-5pm, Sa-Su 11am-4pm; $4) is one of NYC's great deals—your choice of among 3 soups and about 15 entrees, bread, salad, and coffee or tea. At night, prices rise as the disco ball begins to spin. Russian disco begins nightly at 11pm. Open daily 11am-2am.

Queens

With nearly every ethnic group represented in Queens, this oft-overlooked borough offers visitors authentic and reasonably priced international cuisine away from Manhattan's urban neighborhoods. **Astoria** specializes in cheap eats. Take the G or R train to Steinway St. and Broadway and start browsing—the pickings are good in every direction. In **Flushing,** excellent Chinese, Japanese, and Korean restaurants flourish, often making use of authentic ingredients such as skatefish, squid, and tripe. **Bell Blvd.** in Bayside, out east near the Nassau border, is the center of Queens nightlife for the young, white, and semi-affluent. **Jamaica Ave.** in downtown Jamaica and **Linden Blvd.** in neighboring St. Albans are lined with restaurants specializing in African-American and West Indian food.

Uncle George's, 33-19 Broadway, Astoria (718-626-0593), at 33rd St. Subway: N to Broadway, then 2 blocks east; or G or R to Steinway St., then 4 blocks west. Crowded, noisy, and friendly, this popular restaurant, known as "Barba Yiogis O Ksenihtis" to the locals, serves hearty Greek fare round the clock. All entrees are under $12. Die-hard fans feed on roast leg of lamb with potatoes ($8) or octopus sauteed with vinegar ($7). Excellent Greek salad ($6). Open 24hr. Cash only.

Pearson's Stick To Your Ribs Texas Barbecue, 5-16 Long Island City (718-937-3030). Subway: #7 to Vernon-Jackson. Exit at Vernon Blvd. and 50th Ave., and walk 1 block to 51st. Make a right and go 2 blocks towards the power plant—Pearson's is on the left. Low on ambience and heavy on taste, this hard-to-find place has sauce ranging from mild to "madness" to "mean." Some of the best ribs in town (beef $13 per lb., pork $14 per lb.); you can purchase by the ¼ lb. Sizable brisket sandwich $6. Open M-Th noon-8pm, F-Sa noon 9pm, Su 1-6pm.

Jackson Diner, 37-03 74th St., Astoria (718-672-1232), at 37th Ave. Subway: E, F, G, R to Jackson Heights/Roosevelt Ave.; or #7 to 74th St./Broadway, then walk 2 or 3 blocks north towards 37th Ave. Possibly the best Indian cuisine in New York, complemented by minimalist red-and-white decor. Savor the *Saag Ghost* (lamb with spinach, tomato, ginger, and cumin, $9.50) and don't forget the *samosas*. Lunch specials $5-6.60. Open M-F 11:30am-10pm, Sa-Su 11:30am-10:30pm. Cash only.

The Bronx

The Italian neighborhood of **Belmont,** which centers around the intersection of Arthur Ave. and 187th St., brims with streetside *caffè,* pizzerias, restaurants, and mom-and-pop emporiums vending Madonna 45s and imported espresso machines, all without the touristy frills of Little Italy. To get to Arthur Ave., take the C or D train to Fordham Rd. and walk 5 blocks east; alternatively take the #2 train to Pelham Pkwy., then the Bronx bus #Bx12 2 stops west.

Dominick's, 2335 Arthur Ave. (718-733-2807), near 186th St. Subway: D to Fordham Rd. Always packed, this small family-style Italian eatery sports an extra bar upstairs. Waiters seat you at a long table and simply ask what you want. No menu here and no set prices—locals are happy to give advice. Linguine with mussels and marinara ($7), marinated artichoke ($6), and veal *francese* ($12) are all time-honored house specials. Arrive before 6pm or after 9pm, or expect a 20min. wait. Open M and W-Sa noon-10pm, F noon-11pm, Su 1-9pm.

Emilia's, 2331 Arthur Ave. (718-367-5915), near 186th St. Delicious food in large portions. Seafood options like the *calamari fra diavolo* or the sea bass in light tomato sauce ($15) are especially good. Appetizers $5-8, pasta $10, entrees $13-18. Lunch special $10. Open W-Su 11am-10pm.

Tony's Pizza, 34 E. Bedford Park Blvd. (718-367-2854). Subway: #4, C, or D to Bedford Park Blvd. Classic, friendly pizza joint with slices so tasty that students from the nearby Bronx High School of Science often skip class to grab one. Slice $1.50, extra topping 75¢ Open M-F 11am-8pm.

SIGHTS

You can tell tourists in New York City from a mile away—they're all looking up. The internationally famous New York skyline is deceptive and elusive; while it is impressive when seen from miles away, the tallest skyscraper seems like just another building when you're standing next to it. This sightseeing quandary may explain why many New Yorkers have never visited some of the major sights in their hometown. Just as the budget traveler need not assume the etiquette (or lack thereof) of the New Yorker, he or she need not pick up this nasty habit of obliviousness. New York's sights can be very affordable; learn to ferret out those "pay-as-you wish" attractions and the free, magnificent lobbies, parks, and open spaces of opulent America.

Lower Manhattan

The southern tip of Manhattan is a motley assortment of cobblestones and financial powerhouses. The Wall St. area is the most densely built in all New York, although Wall St. itself measures less than a ½ mi. long. This narrow state of affairs has driven the neighborhood into the air, creating one of the highest concentrations of skyscrapers in the world. With density comes history; lower Manhattan was the first part of the island to be settled by Europeans, and many of the city's historically significant sights lie in the concrete chasms here. Its crooked streets serve as a reminder of what New York City was like before it grew up and tidied out into a neat grid.

· **Battery Park,** named for a battery of guns that the British stored there from 1683 to 1687, is now a chaotic chunk of green forming the southernmost toenail of Manhattan Island. The #1 and 9 trains to South Ferry terminate at the southeastern tip of the park; the #4 and 5 stop at Bowling Green, just off the northern tip. On weekends the park is often mobbed with people on their way to the Liberty and Ellis Island ferries, which depart from here.

Once the northern border of the New Amsterdam settlement, **Wall Street** takes its name from the wall built in 1653 to shield the Dutch colony from a British invasion from the north. By the early 19th century, the area was the financial capital of the United States. **Federal Hall,** 26 Wall St. (825-6888), the original City Hall, was where the trial of John Peter Zenger helped to establish freedom of the press in 1735. On the southwest corner of Wall and Broad St. stands the current home of the **New York Stock Exchange** (656-5168), where more than 3000 companies exchange 228 billion shares of stock valued at $13 trillion. *(Open to the public M-F 9am-4pm. Free.)* It's best to arrive before 9am, because tickets usually run out by 1pm. The observation gallery that overlooks the exchange's zoo-like main trading floor draws many gawkers.

Around the corner, at the end of Wall St., rises the seemingly ancient **Trinity Church** (602-0872). Its Gothic spire was the tallest structure in the city when first erected in 1846. The vaulted interior feels positively medieval.

Walk up Broadway to Liberty Park, and in the distance you'll see the twin towers of the city's tallest buildings, the **World Trade Center.** Two World Trade Center has an **observation deck** (323-2340) on the 107th fl. *(Open daily 9:30am-11:30pm; Sept.-May 9:30am-5:30pm. $12, seniors $9, ages 6-12 $6.)*

Farther north on Broadway, City Hall Park and **City Hall** serve as the focus of the city's administration. The Colonial château-style structure, completed in 1811, may be the finest piece of architecture in the city. North of the park, at 111 Centre St., between Leonard and White St., stands the **Criminal Court Building** Here you can sit in on every kind of trial from misdemeanor to murder.

One of the most sublime and ornate commercial buildings in the world, the Gothic **Woolworth Building** towers at 233 Broadway, off the southern tip of the park. Erected in 1913 by F.W. Woolworth to house the offices of his empire, it stood as the world's tallest until the Chrysler Building opened in 1930. Gothic arches and flourishes litter the lobby of this five-and-dime Versailles, including a caricature of Woolworth counting his change. A block and a half farther south on Broadway, **St. Paul's Chapel** (623-0773) was inspired by London's St. Martin-in-the-Fields. *(Open M-F 9am-3pm, Su 7am-3pm.)* St. Paul's is Manhattan's oldest public building in continuous use.

MID-ATLANTIC

Turn left off Broadway onto Fulton St. and head for the **South Street Seaport.** New York's shipping industry thrived here for most of the 19th century. The process of revitalization has turned the historic district, in all its fishy and foul-smelling glory, into the ritzy South Street Seaport complex, a shopping mall known as **Pier 16,** diluted by a restored 18th-century market, graceful galleries, and seafaring schooners. At the end of Fulton St., as the river comes suddenly into view, the reek of dead fish wafts through your nostrils. The stench comes from the **Fulton Fish Market,** the largest fresh-fish mart in the country (and a notorious mafia stronghold), hidden right on South St. on the other side of the overpass. *(Market opens at 4am.)* Those who can stomach wriggling scaly things might be interested in the behind-the-scenes tour of the market offered some Thursday mornings from June through October. The Pier 16 kiosk, the main ticket booth for the seaport, is open daily from 10am-7pm; 1hr. later on summer weekends.

The Statue of Liberty and Ellis Island

The **Statue of Liberty** (363-3200) stands as the symbol of decades of immigrant crossings. *(Ferry info 269-5755. Ferries leave for Liberty and Ellis Island from Battery Park every 30min. daily 8:30am-4:10pm; call for winter hours. $7, seniors $6, ages 3-17 $3.)* The statue was given by the French in 1886 as a sign of goodwill. Since it has stood at the entrance to New York Harbor, the Statue of Liberty has welcomed millions of immigrants to America. Today, the statue lifts her lamp to tourists galore, as everyone and their 16 cousins make the ferry voyage to Liberty Island. **Ellis Island** was once the processing center for the 15 million Europeans who came to the U.S. via New York. The island was put out of use after the large waves of immigration were over. Ellis Island now houses an excellent **museum.**

Lower East Side

Down below Houston lurks the trendily seedy Lower East Side, where old-timers rub shoulders with heroin dealers and hip twenty-somethings. Two million Jews swelled the population of the Lower East Side in the 20 years before World War I; immigrants still live in the Lower East Side, although now they are mostly Asian and Hispanic. A lot of East Village-type artists and musicians have recently moved in as well, especially near Houston St., but despite the influx of artists, a down-trodden element remains.

Even with the population shift, remnants of the Jewish ghetto that inspired Jacob Riis's compelling work *How the Other Half Lives* still remain. New York's oldest synagogue building is the red-painted **Congregation Anshe Chesed** at 172-176 Norfolk St., just off Stanton St. Farther down Norfolk, at #60 between Grand and Broome St., sits the **Beth Hamedrash Hagadol Synagogue,** the best-preserved of the Lower East Side houses of worship. From Grand St., follow Essex St. 3 blocks south to **East Broadway.** This street epitomizes the Lower East Side's alloy of cultures. You will find Buddhist prayer centers next to (mostly boarded up) Jewish religious supply stores, and the offices of several Jewish civic organizations.

The area around Orchard and Delancey St. is one of Manhattan's bargain shopping centers. At 97 Orchard St., between Broome and Delancey St., you can visit the **Lower East Side Tenement Museum** (431-0233), a preserved tenement house of the type that proliferated in this neighborhood in the early part of the century. *(Tours of the tenement Tu-F at 1, 2, and 3pm, Th every 45min. 6-9pm, Sa-Su every 45min. 11am-4:15pm; 1hr. Tickets for 1 exhibit $8, students and seniors $6; for 2 exhibits $14, students and seniors $10; for all 3 exhibits $20, students and seniors $14.)* Tickets for a slide show, video, and guided tour are sold at 90 Orchard St., the museum's **gallery** which offers free exhibits and photographs documenting Jewish life on the Lower East Side.

Way off Broadway lurks the Lower East Side's (Loisaida) theater scene, characterized by high levels of do-it-yourself dedication and low ticket prices. In and around Loisaida's streets you are likely to encounter experimental Shakespeare performances, improvisational theater, and serial plays that have been running for months. If you can't get tickets to Shakespeare in the Park, try Expanded Art's **Shakespeare in the Parking Lot,** staged across the street from their theater at 85 Ludlow St., between Delancey and Broome St. (June-Aug. W-Sa 8pm; free; call 253-1813 for info).

SoHo and TriBeCa

SoHo ("**SO**uth of **HO**w-ston Street") is bounded by Houston St., Canal, Lafayette, and Sullivan St. The architecture here is American Industrial (1860-1890), notable for its cast-iron facades. While its roots are industrial, its inhabitants are New York's prospering artistic community. Here, **galleries** reign supreme and chic boutiques fill the voids. This is a great place for star-gazing too, so bring your autograph book and a bright flash for your camera. Celebrities like that. While the shopping in SoHo is probably well beyond a budget traveler's means, those seeking that hidden gem should check out the **Antiques Fair and Collectibles Market** on the corner of Broadway and Grand St. (open Sa-Su 9am-5pm).

Walking around the **TRI**angle **BE**low **CA**nal St. (bounded by Chambers St., Broadway, Canal St., and the West Side Hwy.), you might not guess that it has been anointed (by resident Robert DeNiro, among others) as one of the hottest neighborhoods in New York City. Hidden inside the hulking 19th-century cast-iron warehouses are lofts, restaurants, bars, and galleries, often maintaining SoHo's trendiness without the upscale airs. Admire the cast-iron edifices lining White St., Thomas St., and Broadway, the 19th-century Federal-style buildings on Harrison St., and the shops, galleries, and bars on Church and Reade St.

Greenwich Village and Washington Sq. Park

Located between Chelsea and SoHo on the lower west side of Manhattan, Greenwich Village (or, more simply put, "the Village") and its residents have defied convention for almost two centuries. Greenwich Village is the nexus of New York bohemia and the counter-culture capital of the East Coast. In stark contrast to the orderly, skyscraper-encrusted streets of greater Manhattan, narrow thoroughfares meander haphazardly through the Village without regard to grids. Tall buildings give way to brownstones of varying ages and architectural styles.

The bulk of Greenwich Village lies west of 6th Ave. The West Village boasts eclectic summer street life and excellent nightlife. The area has a large, visible gay community around **Sheridan Sq.** These are the home waters of the Guppie (Gay Urban Professional). **Christopher St.,** the main by-way, swims in novelty restaurants and shops. (Subway: #1 or 9 to Christopher St./Sheridan Sq.) A few street signs refer to Christopher St. as "Stonewall Pl.," alluding to the **Stonewall Inn,** the club where police raids in 1969 prompted riots that sparked the U.S. gay rights movement.

Washington Sq. Park beats at the heart of the Village, as it has since the district's days as a suburb. (Subway: A, B, C, D, E, F, or Q to W. 4th St./Washington Sq.) The marshland here served as home to Native Americans and freed slaves, and later as a colonial cemetery, but in the 1820s the area was converted into a park and parade ground. Soon posh residences made the area the center of New York's social scene. Society has long since gone north, and **New York University** has moved in. The country's largest private university and one of the city's biggest landowners (along with the city government, the Catholic Church, and Columbia University), NYU has dispersed its buildings and eccentric students throughout the Village.

In the late 70s and early 80s Washington Sq. Park became a base for low-level drug dealers and a rough resident scene. The mid-80s saw a noisy clean-up campaign that has made the park fairly safe and allowed a more diverse cast of characters to return. Today musicians play, misunderstood teenagers congregate, dealers mutter cryptic code words, homeless people try to sleep, and children romp in the playground. In the southwest corner of the park, a dozen perpetual games of chess clock their ways toward checkmate while circles of youths engage in hours of hacky-sacking. The **fountain** in the center of the park provides an amphitheater for comics and musicians of widely varying degrees of talent.

A theatrical landmark, **Provincetown Playhouse,** 133 MacDougal St., lies on the south side of Washington Sq. Park. Originally based in Cape Cod, the Provincetown Players were joined by the young Eugene O'Neill in 1916 and went on to premiere many of his works. Farther south on MacDougal are the Village's finest coffeehouses, which saw their glory days in the 50s when beatnik heroes and coffee-bean connoisseurs Jack Kerouac and Allen Ginsberg attended jazz-accompanied poetry readings at **Le Figaro** and **Café Borgia.** These sidewalk cafes still provide some of the best coffee and people-watching in the city.

The north side of the park, called **The Row,** showcases a stretch of elegant Federal-style brick residences built largely in the 1830s. Up 5th Ave., at the corner of 10th St., the **Church of the Ascension,** a fine 1841 Gothic church with a notable altar and stained-glass windows, looks heavenward (open daily noon-2pm and 5-7pm). **The Pen and Brush Club,** 16 E. 10th St., was founded to promote female intelligentsia networking; Pearl Buck, Eleanor Roosevelt, Marianne Moore, and muckraker Ida Tarbell are counted among its members.

At 5th Ave. and 11th St., **The Salmagundi Club** (255-7740), New York's oldest club for artists, has sheltered the sensitive since the 1870s. *(Open daily 1-5pm.)* The club's brownstone is the sole remaining mansion from the area's heyday. **Forbes Magazine Galleries** (206-5548) dominate the corner of 5th Ave. and 12th St. *(Open Tu-Sa 10am-4pm; hours subject to change without advance notice. Free.)* The galleries present eccentric Malcolm Forbes's vast collection of stuff.

At 12th St. and Broadway lies **Forbidden Planet,** purported to be the world's largest science fiction store (open daily 10am-8:30pm). Across the street is the famous **Strand,** which bills itself as the "largest used bookstore in the world." *(Open M-Sa 9:30am-9:20pm, Su 11am-9:20pm.)* You'll want plenty of time to search through the collection of over two million books on eight miles of shelves.

East Village and Alphabet City

The East Village, a comparatively new creation, was carved out of the Bowery and the Lower East Side as rents in the West Village soared and its residents sought accommodations elsewhere. East Villagers embody the alternative spectrum, with punks, hippies, ravers, rastas, guppies, goths, beatniks, and virtually every other imaginable group coexisting amid an anarchic tangle of cafes, bars, and theaters. Allen Ginsberg, Jack Kerouac, and William Burroughs all eschewed the Greenwich Village establishment to develop a junked-up "beat" sensibility east of Washington Sq. Park. A crowded, busy stretch of Broadway marks the western boundary of the East Village.

In 1853, John Jacob Astor constructed the current **Joseph Papp Public Theatre,** 425 Lafayette St. (598-7150), to serve as the city's first free library. His 1867 **New York Shakespeare Festival** converted the building to its current use.

The intersection of **Astor Pl.** (at the juncture of Lafayette, Fourth Ave., Astor Pl., and E. 8th St.) is distinguished by a sculpture of a large black cube balanced on its corner. Astor Pl. prominently features the rear of the **Cooper Union Foundation Building,** 7 E. 7th Ave. (353-4199), built in 1859 to house the Cooper Union for the Advancement of Science and Art, a tuition-free technical and design school founded by self-educated industrialist Peter Cooper. The school's free lecture series has hosted almost every notable American since the mid-19th century. Cooper Union was the first college intended for the underprivileged and the first to offer free adult education classes. Across Cooper Sq. south are the offices of America's largest free newspaper, the **Village Voice.** At 156 2nd Ave. stands a famous Jewish landmark, the **Second Avenue Deli** (677-0606). This is all that remains of the "Yiddish Rialto," the stretch of 2nd Ave. between Houston and 14th St. that comprised the Yiddish theater district in the early part of this century. The Stars of David embedded in the sidewalk outside of the restaurant contain the names of several great actors and actresses who spent their lives entertaining the city's poor Jewish immigrants.

St. Mark's Pl., running from 3rd Ave. (where 8th St. would be) to Ave. A, is the geographical and spiritual center of the East Village. In the 1960s, the street was the Haight-Ashbury of the East Coast, full of pot-smoking flower children waiting for the next concert at the Electric Circus. In the late 70s it became the King's Rd. of New York, as mohawked youths hassled passers-by from the brownstone steps of Astor Pl. Except for a few established bars and restaurants (Dojo's) and excellent music stores (Kim's), St. Mark's walks a line between unabashed sleaze (count the tattoo parlors) and homogenized cheese, although the alternateen odor dissipates as you move eastward. Though many Villagers now shun the commercialized and crowded areas of the street, St. Mark's is still central to life in this part of town and a good place to start a tour of the neighborhood.

In **Alphabet City,** east of 1st Ave., south of 14th St., and north of Houston, the avenues run out of numbers and adopt letters. This part of the East Village has so far escaped the escalating yuppification that has claimed much of St. Mark's Pl. During the area's heyday in the 60s, Jimi Hendrix would play open-air shows to bright-eyed Love Children. There has been a great deal of drug-related crime in the recent past, although the community has done an admirable job of making the area livable. Alphabet City is generally safe during the day, and the addictive nightlife on Ave. A ensures some protection there, but try to avoid straying east of Ave. B at night. Alphabet City's extremist Boho activism has made the neighborhood chronically ungovernable; a few years ago, police officers set off a riot when they attempted to forcibly evict a band of the homeless and their supporters in **Tompkins Sq. Park,** at E. 7th St. and Ave. A. The park still serves as a psycho-geographical epicenter for many a churlish misfit.

Lower Midtown and Chelsea

Madison Ave. ends at 27th St. and **Madison Sq. Park.** The park, opened in 1847, originally served as a public cemetery. The area near the park sparkles with funky architectural gems. Another member of the "I-used-to-be-the-world's-tallest-building" club, the eminently photogenic **Flatiron Building** sits off the southwest corner of the park. Often considered the world's first skyscraper, it was originally named the Fuller Building, but its dramatic wedge shape, imposed by the intersection of Broadway, 5th Ave., 22nd St., and 23rd St., quickly earned it its current *nom de plume.*

A few blocks away, **Union Sq.,** between Broadway and Park Ave., and 17th and 14th St., sizzled with High Society intrigue before the Civil War. Early in this century, the name gained dual significance when the neighborhood became a focal point of New York's Socialist movement, which held its May Day celebrations in **Union Sq. Park.** Later, the workers and everyone else abandoned the park to drug dealers and derelicts. In 1989 the city began reclaiming it. The park is now pleasant and safe, though not necessarily pristine. The scents of herbs and fresh bread waft through every Wednesday, Friday, and Saturday, courtesy of the **Union Sq. Greenmarket.** Farmers from all over the region come here to hawk their produce, jellies, and baked goods.

Home to some of the most fashionable clubs, bars, and restaurants in the city, **Chelsea** has lately witnessed something of a rebirth. A large and visible gay and lesbian community and an increasing artsy-yuppie population have given the area, west of 5th Ave. between 14th and 30th St., the flavor of a lower-rent West Village. In the past few years, Chelsea has become home to innovative **art galleries** escaping from SoHo's exorbitant rent. New art outposts nestle amid auto body shops and industrial effluvia around **W. 22nd St.** and surrounding streets between **10th and 11th Ave.** The historic **Hotel Chelsea,** 222 W. 23rd St. (243-3700), between 7th and 8th Ave., has sheltered many an artist, most famously Sid Vicious of the Sex Pistols. Edie Sedgwick made stops here between Warhol films before torching the place with a cigarette. Countless writers, as the plaques outside attest, spent their days searching for inspiration and mail in the lobby. Arthur Miller, Vladimir Nabokov, Arthur C. Clarke, and Dylan Thomas all sojourned here. Chelsea's **flower district,** a sprawling flea market on 28th St. between 6th and 7th Ave., colorfully blooms during the wee hours of the morning.

West Midtown

Penn Station, at 33rd St. and 7th Ave., is one of the least engrossing pieces of architecture in West Midtown, but claims its function as a major subway stop and train terminal. *(Subway: #1, 2, 3, 9, A, C, or E to 34th St./Penn Station.)* The original Penn Station, a classical marble building modeled on the Roman Baths of Caracalla, was demolished in the 60s. The railway tracks were then covered with the equally uninspiring **Madison Sq. Garden.** Facing the Garden at 421 8th Ave., New York's immense main post office, the **James A. Farley Building,** luxuriates in its 10001 ZIP code.

East on 34th St., between 7th Ave. and Broadway, stands **Macy's** (695-4400), the mecca of Manhattan shopping. The store sponsors the **Macy's Thanksgiving Day Parade,** a New York tradition buoyed by helium-filled 10-story Snoopys, marching bands, floats, and general hoopla.

MID-ATLANTIC

The billboards of **Times Sq.** flicker at the intersection of 42nd St. and Broadway. Still considered the dark and seedy core of the Big Apple by most New Yorkers, the Sq. has worked hard in the past few years to improve its image. 1998 saw a renewed and invigorated promise from Mayor Giuliani to excise the pornography industry from the area. Disney is playing an important role in restructuring Times Sq., with its planned entertainment complex and 47-story hotel replacing the closed-down porn shops along 42nd St. between 7th and 8th Ave. Still, Times Sq. is Times Sq. Teens continue to roam about in search of fake IDs, hustlers wait eagerly to scam suckers, and every New Year's Eve, millions booze and schmooze and watch an electronic ball drop. For **New Year's 2000,** a celebration of millennial proportions is in the works. The party starts at 7am on December 31, 1999, when the Fiji islands begin their New Year. With each of the 24 new years, large video screens and elaborate sound, light, and laser systems will create a display appropriate for the time zone. While Times Sq. usually holds a mere 500,000 people on New Year's Eve, planners are trying to think of ways to cram in even more for this global event. Many subway lines stop in the square (#1, 2, 3, 7, 9, and A, C, E, N, R, S).

On 42nd St. between 9th and 10th Ave. lies **Theater Row,** a block of renovated Broadway theaters that many consider the heart of American theater. The nearby **Theater District** stretches from 41st to 57th St. along Broadway, 8th Ave., and the streets which connect them. Approximately 37 theaters remain active, most of them grouped around 45th St.

How do you get to **Carnegie Hall?** Practice, practice, practice. Or simply walk to 57th St. and 7th Ave. *(Tours are given M-Tu and Th-F at 11:30am, 2, and 3pm. $6, students and seniors $5.)* Carnegie Hall (903-9790) was founded in 1891 and remains New York's foremost soundstage. Tchaikovsky, Caruso, Toscanini, and Bernstein have played Carnegie, as have the Beatles and the Rolling Stones. Other notable events from Carnegie's playlist include the world premiere of Dvořák's *Symphony No. 9 (From the New World)* on December 16, 1893, a 1934 lecture by Albert Einstein, and Martin Luther King Jr.'s last public speech on February 28, 1968. Carnegie Hall's **museum** displays artifacts and memorabilia from its illustrious century of existence (open M-F 11am-4:30pm, limited hrs. in winter; free).

East Midtown and Fifth Avenue

The Empire State Building, on 5th Ave. between 33rd and 34th St. (736-3100), has style. *(Observatory open daily 9:30am-midnight; tickets sold until 11:30pm. $6, seniors and under 12 $3.)* It retains its place in the hearts and minds of New Yorkers even though it is no longer the tallest building in the U.S., or even the tallest building in New York (stood up by the twin towers of the World Trade Center). It doesn't even have the best looks (the Chrysler building is more delicate, the Woolworth more ornate). But the Empire State remains New York's best-known and best-loved landmark and continues to dominate the postcards, the movies, and the skyline. The limestone and granite structure, with glistening ribbons of stainless steel, stretches 1454 ft. into the sky; and its 73 elevators run through 2 mi. of shafts. The nighttime view from the top will leave you gasping. The Empire State was among the first of the truly spectacular skyscrapers, benefiting from innovations like Eiffel's pioneering work with steel frames and Otis's perfection of the "safety elevator." In Midtown it towers in relative solitude, away from the forest of monoliths that has grown around Wall St.

In the **Pierpont Morgan Library,** 29 E. 36th St. (685-0610), at Madison Ave., the J. Pierpont Morgan clan developed the concept of the book as fetish object. *(Subway: #6 to 33rd St. Open Tu-Sa 10:30am-5pm, Su noon-6pm. Suggested donation $6, students and seniors $4, under 12 free.)* With regular exhibitions and lots and lots of books inside, this Low Renaissance-style *palazzo* attracts many a bibliophile.

The **New York Public Library** (869-8089) reposes on the west side of 5th Ave. between 40th and 42nd St., next to Bryant Park. *(Free tours Tu-Sa 11am and 2pm. Open M-Sa 10am-6pm, Tu-W 11am-7:30pm.)* On sunny afternoons, throngs of people perch on the marble steps, under the watchful eyes of the mighty stone lions Patience and Fortitude. This is the world's seventh-largest research library; witness the immense 3rd fl. reading room.

More than a Close Scrape

One foggy night in 1945, a U.S. Army B-25 bomber crashed into the 78th and 79th floors of the Empire State Building, shooting flames hundreds of feet in the air. **Burning debris** hurled for blocks, although the steel frame swayed less than 2 inches. Fourteen people lost their lives in the bizarre accident, but this was not the skyscraper's first contact with aircraft. The building's flanged tower was originally intended as a **mooring mast for Zeppelins.** Two blimps docked there in 1931, but the 1933 Hindenburg disaster halted construction of the dirigible terminal (which was fine for **King Kong,** the giant ape who had his hands full fighting-off army planes while perched atop it in a movie released the same year).

Spread out against the back of the library along 42nd St. to 6th Ave., **Bryant Park** soothes with large, grassy, tree-rimmed expanses. *(Open 7am-9pm.)* The stage that sits at the head of the park plays host to a variety of free cultural events throughout the summer, including screenings of classic films, jazz concerts, and live comedy.

To the east along 42nd St., **Grand Central Terminal** sits where Park Ave. would be, between Madison and Lexington Ave. A former transportation hub where dazed tourists first got a glimpse of the glorious city, Grand Central has since been partially supplanted by Penn Station, Port Authority, and area airports. The massive Beaux Arts front, with the famed 13 ft. clock, gives way to the dignified and echoey Main Concourse, a huge lobby area which sets the backdrop for civilized commuting.

The building which gives New York the Gotham touch is the **Chrysler Building,** at 42nd St. and Lexington Ave. Built by William Van Allen as an ode to the automobile, the building is topped by a much-loved Art Deco headdress and a spire modeled on a radiator grille. When completed in 1929, this elegantly seductive building stood as the world's tallest. The Empire State Building topped it a year later.

If you feel an urgent need to get out of the city for a while, head for the **United Nations Building** (963-4475), located along 1st Ave. between 42nd and 48th St. *(Visitor's entrance at 1st Ave. and 46th St. Daily tours about 45min., leaving every 15min. 9:15am-4:45pm, available in 20 languages. $7.50, students and seniors $5.50, under 16 $3.50.)* Outside, a multicultural rose garden and a statuary park provide a lovely view of the East River. Inside, go through security check and work your way to the back of the lobby for the informative tours of the **General Assembly.** You must take the tour to get past the lobby. Sometimes free tickets to G.A. sessions can be obtained when the U.N. is in session October through May (call 963-1234).

Between 48th and 51st St. and 5th and 6th Ave. stretches **Rockefeller Center,** a monument to the conjunction of business and art. On 5th Ave., between 49th and 50th St., the famous gold-leaf statue of Prometheus sprawls on a ledge of the sunken **Tower Plaza** while jet streams of water pulse around it. The Plaza serves as an open-air cafe in the spring and summer and as a world-famous ice-skating rink in the winter. The 70-story **RCA Building,** seated at 6th Ave., remains the most accomplished artistic creation in this complex. Every chair in the building sits less than 28 ft. from natural light. The **NBC Television Network** makes its headquarters here, allowing you to take a behind-the-scenes look at their operations. The network offers an hour-long tour which traces the history of NBC, from their first radio broadcast in 1926 through the heyday of TV programming in the 50s and 60s. *(Tours M-Sa 9:30am-4:30pm, leaving every 30 min. $10.)* The tour visits the studios of *Conan O'Brien* and the infamous 8H studio, home of *Saturday Night Live.*

Despite an illustrious history and a wealth of Art Deco treasures, **Radio City Music Hall** (632-4041) was almost demolished in 1979 to make way for new office high-rises. *(Tours leaving every 30-45min. M-Sa 10am-5pm, Su 11am-5pm. $13.75, under 12 $9.)* However, the public rallied and the place was declared a national landmark. First opened in 1932, at the corner of 6th Ave. and 51st St., the 5874-seat theater remains the largest in the world. The brainchild of Roxy Rothafel (originator of the Rockettes), it was originally intended as a variety showcase. However, the hall functioned primarily as a movie theater; over 650 feature films debuted here from 1933 to 1979, including *King Kong, Breakfast at Tiffany's,* and *Doctor Zhivago.* The Rockettes, Radio City's vertically endowed chorus line, still dance on.

At 25 W. 52nd St., the **Museum of Television and Radio** (621-6600) works almost entirely as a "viewing museum" (see **Museums**, p. 160). Over a block down W. 53rd St. towards 6th Ave. are the masterpieces in the **American Craft Museum** and the **Museum of Modern Art** (see **Museums**, p. 160).

St. Patrick's Cathedral (753-2261), New York's most famous church and the largest Catholic cathedral in America, stands at 51st St. and 5th Ave. Designed by James Renwick, the structure captures the essence of great European cathedrals yet retains its own spirit. The twin spires on the 5th Ave. facade stretch 330 ft. into the air.

One of the monuments to modern architecture, Ludwig Mies Van der Rohe's dark and gracious **Seagram Building** looms over 375 Park Ave., between 52nd and 53rd St. Pure skyscraper, fronted by a plaza and two fountains, the Seagram stands as a paragon of the austere International Style. Van der Rohe envisioned it as an oasis from the tight canyon of skyscrapers on Park Ave.

The stores on 5th Ave. from Rockefeller Center to Central Park are the ritziest in the city. At **Tiffany & Co.** (755-8000), everything from jewelry to housewares shines; the window displays are works of art in themselves, especially around Christmas (open M-W and F-Sa 10am-6pm, Th 10am-7pm). **F.A.O. Schwarz,** 767 5th Ave. (644-9400), at 58th St., impresses kids and adults with one of the world's largest toy stores, including a Lego complex, life-sized stuffed animals, and a separate annex exclusively for Barbie dolls (open M-W 10am-7pm, Th-Sa 10am-8pm, Su 11am-6pm).

On 5th Ave. and 59th St., at the southeast corner of Central Park, sits the legendary **Plaza Hotel,** built in 1907 at the then-astronomical cost of $12.5 million. Its 18-story, 800-room French Renaissance interior flaunts five marble staircases, countless ludicrously named suites, and a 2-story Grand Ballroom. Past guests and residents have included Frank Lloyd Wright, the Beatles, F. Scott Fitzgerald, and James Brown. *Let's Go* recommends the $15,000-per-night suite.

Central Park

General Information: 360-3444; for parks and recreation info, call 360-8111 (M-F 9am-5pm). The Central Park Conservancy runs and maintains the park. The Conservancy offers all kinds of programs—from birding and nature walks to family tai chi—at its 3 information and education centers: the Belvedere Castle (772-0210), the Charles A. Dana Discovery Center (860-1370), and the Dairy. The Dairy, located south of 65th St., houses the Central Park Reception Center (794-6564). Open Mar.-Oct. Tu-Th and Sa-Su 11am-5pm, F 1-5pm; Nov.-Feb. Tu-Th and Sa-Su 11am-4pm, F 1-4pm. Brochures and calendars are available here, as are exhibitions on Park history. Pick up the free map of Central Park and a list of seasonal events.

Central Park is fairly safe during the day, but less so at night. Do not be afraid to go to shows or Shakespeare in the Park at night, but stay on the path and go with someone else. Do not wander on the darker paths at night. Women especially should use caution after dark. In an emergency, use one of the many call-boxes located throughout the park. To report a crime, call the 24hr. Park Line (570-4820).

Beloved Central Park has certainly had its moments in the sun, from Simon and Garfunkel's historic 1981 concert to the annual meeting of stars in the summertime Shakespeare in the Park festival. Enormous Central Park offers a pastoral refuge from the fast-paced urban jungle of New York City. Despite its bucolic appearance, Central Park was never an authentic wilderness. The landscaped gardens were carved out of the city's grid between 59th and 110th St. for several blocks west of 5th Ave. by designers Olmsted and Vaux in the mid-1840s. The final product contains lakes, ponds, fountains, skating rinks, ball fields, tennis courts, a castle, an outdoor theater, a bandshell, and two zoos.

The Park may be roughly divided between north and south at the main reservoir; the southern section affords more intimate settings, serene lakes, and graceful promenades, while the northern end has a few ragged edges. Nearly 1400 species of trees, shrubs, and flowers grow here, the work of distinguished horticulturist Ignaz Anton

MID-ATLANTIC

Pilat. When you wander amid the shrubbery, look to the nearest lamppost for guidance and check the small metal four-digit plaque bolted to it. The first two digits tell you what street you're nearest, and the second two whether you're on the east or west side of the Park (even numbers mean east, odds west). **Central Park Bicycle Tours** (541-8759) offers leisurely 2hr. guided bicycle tours through Central Park. *(3 tours leave daily from 2 Columbus Circle. Call for reservations. $30, includes bike rental.)*

The spectacular, free **Central Park Summerstage** concert program hits town each summer. Past performers include Stereolab, A Tribe Called Quest, and Guided by Voices. The **Wollman Skating Rink** (396-1010) sees wheels turn to blades when it gets cold enough. *(Ice- or roller-skating $4, seniors and children $3, plus $6.50 rental. Complex open daily 11am-6pm.)*

The **Friedsam Memorial Carousel** (879-0244) turns at 65th St. west of Center Dr. *(Open daily 10am-6:30pm; late Nov. to mid-Mar. Su 10:30am-4:30pm. 90¢.)* The 58-horsepower carousel was brought from Coney Island and fully restored in 1983. Directly north of the Carousel, **Sheep Meadow** grows from about 66th to 69th St. on the western side of the Park. This is the park's largest chunk of green, exemplifying the pastoral ideals of the Park's designers. Spreading out to the west, the **Lake** provides a dramatic patch of blue in the heart of the City. The 1954 **Loeb Boathouse** (517-2233) supplies all necessary romantic nautical equipment. *(Open Apr.-Sept. daily 10:30am-4:30pm, weather permitting. Rowboats $10 per hr., $30 deposit.)*

Strawberry Fields was sculpted by Yoko Ono as a memorial to John Lennon. The Fields are located to the west of the Lake at 72nd St. and West Dr., directly across from the Dakota Apartments where Lennon was assassinated and where Yoko Ono still lives. Ono battled valiantly for this space against city council members who had planned a Bing Crosby memorial on the same spot. On sunny spring days, picnickers can enjoy the 161 varieties of plants that now bloom over the rolling hills around the star-shaped "Imagine" mosaic.

The **Swedish Cottage Marionette Theater** (988-9093), at the base of Vista Rock near the 79th St. transverse, puts on regular puppet shows (M-F at 10:30am and noon; $5, children $4; reservations required). Climb the hill to the round wooden space of the **Delacorte Theater,** which hosts the wildly popular **Shakespeare in the Park** series each midsummer. These plays often feature celebrities and are always free. Come early: the theater seats only 1936 lucky souls. Large concerts often take place north of the theater, on the **Great Lawn.** Here, Paul Simon sang, the Stonewall 25 marchers rallied, *Pocahontas* premiered, and the New York Philharmonic and the Metropolitan Opera Company give free summer performances.

Upper East Side

The Golden Age of the East Side society epic began in the 1860s and progressed until the outbreak of World War I. Scores of wealthy people moved into the area and refused to budge. These days, parades, millionaires, and unbearably slow buses share 5th Ave. Upper 5th Ave. is home to **Museum Mile,** which includes the **Metropolitan Museum of Art,** the **Guggenheim,** the **Whitney,** the **International Center of Photography,** the **Cooper-Hewitt,** and the **Jewish Museum,** among many others.

The Upper East Side drips with money along the length of the Park. At 59th St. and 3rd Ave., **Bloomingdale's** sits in regal splendor. **Madison Ave.** graces New York with luxurious boutiques and most of the country's advertising agencies. **Park Ave.,** the street that time forgot, maintains a regal austerity with gracious buildings and landscaped medians. **Gracie Mansion,** at the north end of Carl Schurz Park, between 84th and 90th St. along East End Ave., has been the residence of every New York mayor since Fiorello LaGuardia moved in during World War II. *(Tours W at 10 and 11am, 1pm, and 2pm. Suggested donation $4, seniors $3. To make reservations, call 570-4751.)* Rudolph Giuliani now occupies this hottest of hot seats.

Upper West Side

Broadway leads uptown to **Columbus Circle,** at 59th St. and Broadway, the symbolic entrance to the Upper West Side and the end of Midtown. A statue of Christopher marks the border. One of the Circle's landmarks, the **New York Coliseum,** has been relatively empty since the construction of the **Javits Center** in 1990.

Broadway intersects Columbus Ave. at **Lincoln Center,** the cultural hub of the city, between 62nd and 66th St. The 7 facilities that constitute Lincoln Center—Avery Fisher Hall, the New York State Theater, the Metropolitan Opera House, the Library and Museum of Performing Arts, the Vivian Beaumont Theater, the Walter Reade Theater, and the Juilliard School of Music—accommodate over 13,000 spectators at a time. At night, the Metropolitan Opera House lights up, making its chandeliers and huge Chagall murals visible through its glass-panel facade. **Columbus Ave.** leads to the **Museum of Natural History** (see **Museums,** p. 160). **Broadway** pulses with energy all day (and all night) long. The Upper West Side is covered with residential brownstones, scenic enough for a pleasant (and free) stroll.

Harlem

It took an enormous influx of rural black Southerners during and after World War I to create the Harlem known today as one of the capitals of the black Western world. The 1920s were Harlem's Renaissance; a thriving scene of artists, writers, and scholars lived fast and loose, producing cultural masterworks in the process. The Cotton Club and the Apollo Theater, along with numerous other jazz clubs, were on the musical vanguard, while Langston Hughes and Zora Neale Hurston changed the face of literature. Nevertheless, conditions for people of color were tough—they were charged more than their white counterparts for the unhealthy tenement rooms, and the murderous Klan paid occasional visits. In one bar, Charlie Parker would blow solos over the newest bebop tune from a hocked horn, while across the street Billie Holiday would mellifluously reduce her audience to pools of tears. In the 1960s, riding the charged tidal wave of the Civil Rights Movement, the revolutionary Black Power movement flourished here. Recognizing the need for economic revitalization as a route to empowerment, members of the community began an attempt at redevelopment in the 70s. This attempt continues today as the city pumps money into the area and communities bond together to beautify their neighborhood and actively resist crime. It would be a colossal misconception to believe Harlem's problems overshadow its positive aspects. Although poorer than many neighborhoods, it is culturally rich; and, contrary to popular opinion, it is generally no more dangerous than the rest of New York. Many small jazz clubs still exist and are worth seeking out, despite the extra legwork.

On the East Side above 96th St. lies **Spanish Harlem,** known as El Barrio ("the neighborhood"), and on the West Side lies Harlem proper, stretching from 110th to 155th St. Columbia University controls the area west of Morningside Dr. and south of 125th St., commonly known as **Morningside Heights.** On the West Side, from 125th to 160th St., much of the cultural and social life of the area takes place in **Central Harlem.** To the far north, from 160th St. to 220th St., **Washington Heights** and **Inwood** are areas populated by thriving Dominican and Jewish communities. All these neighborhoods heat up with street activity, not always of the wholesome variety, but mostly nothing more harmful than old men playing cards in the shade.

Columbia University (854-2842), chartered in 1754, huddles between Morningside Dr. and Broadway, 114th and 120th St. Now co-ed, Columbia also has cross-registration across the street with all-female **Barnard College**.

The **Cathedral of St. John the Divine,** along Amsterdam Ave. between 110th and 113th St., promises to be the world's largest cathedral when finished. *(Open daily 7am-5pm. Suggested donation $1, students and seniors 50¢. Vertical tours (you go up) given on the 1st and 3rd Sa of the month at noon and 2pm. $10. Reservations recommended. Regular horizontal tours Tu-Sa 11am, Su 1pm. $3.)* Construction, begun in 1812, continues and should not be completed for another century or two. Stained glass windows portray TV sets and George Washington as well as the usual religious scenes. A trip down the overwhelming central nave leads to an altar dedicated to AIDS victims, a 100 million-year-old nautilus fossil, a modern sculpture for 12 firefighters who died in 1966, and a 2000 lb. natural quartz crystal. Near Columbia, at 120th St. and Riverside Dr., is the

Riverside Church. *(Tower open Tu-Sa 11am-4pm. Admission to observation deck M-Sa $1, Su $2. Su service 10:45am. Free tours Su 12:30pm.)* The observation deck in the tower commands an amazing view of the bells within and the expanse of the Hudson River and Riverside Park below. You can hear concerts on the world's largest carillon (74 bells), a gift of John D. Rockefeller, Jr. Diagonally across Riverside Dr. lies **Grant's Tomb** (666-1640). Take a rest on the hippie-trippy mosaic tile benches around the monument, added in the mid-70s. A walk down Broadway affords a wide assortment of college-catering bookstores and restaurants.

125th St., also known as Martin Luther King, Jr. Blvd., spans the heart of traditional Harlem. Fast-food joints, jazz bars, and the **Apollo Theater** (749-5838, box office 864-0372) keep the street humming day and night. 125th St. has recently experienced a resurgence. Off 125th St., at 328 Lenox Ave., **Sylvia's** (996-0660) has magnetized New York for 22 years with enticing soul food dishes (open M-Sa 7:30am-10:30pm, Su 12:30-7pm). The silver dome of the **Masjid Malcolm Shabazz** (662-2200), where Malcolm X was once a minister, glitters on 116th St. and Lenox Ave. (visit F at 1pm and Su at 10am for services).

Washington Heights, the area north of 155th St., affords a taste of urban life with a thick ethnic flavor. On the same block, you can eat a Greek dinner, buy Armenian pastries and vegetables from a South African, and discuss the Talmud with a student at nearby **Yeshiva University.** Get medieval at the **Cloisters,** a lovely monastery with airy archways, manicured gardens, the famed Unicorn Tapestries, and other pieces of the Met's collection of medieval art (see **Museums,** p. 160).

Brooklyn

If you need an escape from tourist-infested Manhattan, it may be time to explore the streets of the borough of Brooklyn. Brooklyn is Dutch for "Broken Land," and the name fits—mighty Brooklyn is an aggressively heterogeneous terrain, where ultra-orthodox *Hasidim* rub elbows with black teenagers on a street covered with signs *en español*. Ethnic and religious groups don't always get along, but an indominable pride in their home unites them. And they have reason to be proud—one out of every seven famous Americans is from here. As the 2¼ million residents would tell you, Brooklyn can and does exist as an independent entity—one well worth the visit. If the borough left New York City, it would become America's fourth largest city. The collection of ethnically diverse neighborhoods fascinates the imagination and is often mythologized and commemorated in literature, song, and film. Always a gregarious town, it's perfect for an adventurous stroll—what goes on here tends to go on outdoors, be it neighborhood banter, baseball games in the park, ethnic festivals, or pride marches.

The Dutch originally settled the borough in the 17th century. Although Brits shared the land, Dutch culture flourished well into the early 19th century. When asked to join New York in 1833, Brooklyn refused, saying that the two cities shared no interests except common waterways. Not until 1898 did it decide, in a close vote, to become a borough of New York City. Early this century European immigrants began arriving in great numbers. After the Depression, blacks from the American South also sought out Brooklyn, and many more groups soon followed, building the borough's mix of cultures.

The Brooklyn Bridge gracefully spans the gap between Lower Manhattan's dense skyscraper cluster and Brooklyn's less intimidating shore (subway: #4, 5, 6 to Brooklyn Bridge). The arched towers of New York's suspended cathedral, the greatest engineering achievement of the 19th century, loomed far above the rest of the city when completed in 1883. The 1 mi. walk along the pedestrian path (make sure to walk on the left side, as the right is reserved for bicycles) will show you why every New York poet feels compelled to write at least one verse about it, why photographers snap the bridge's airy spider-web cables, and why people jump off. A ramp across from Manhattan's City Hall begins the journey.

Head south on Henry St. after the Brooklyn Bridge, then turn right on Clark St. toward the river for a jaw-dropping view of Manhattan. Many prize-winning photographs have been taken from the **Brooklyn Promenade,** overlooking the southern tip of Manhattan and New York Harbor. George Washington's headquarters during the Battle of Long Island, the now-posh **Brooklyn Heights,** with beautiful old brownstones, tree-lined streets, and proximity to Manhattan, has hosted many authors, from Walt Whitman to Norman Mailer (subway: N, R, 2, 3, 4, or 5 to the Court St.-Borough Hall and follow Court St.). The **New York Transit Museum** (718-243-8601), at Boerum and Schermerhorn, located in a now defunct subway station, houses subway cars and turnstiles from years past. *(Open Tu and Th-F 10am-4pm, W 10am-6pm, Sa-Su noon-5pm. $3, under 17 and seniors $1. Wheelchair access. Subway: #2, 3, 4 or 5 to Borough Hall; the A, C or F to Jay St./Borough Hall; or the M, N, or R to Court St.)*

Nestled at the northern border with Queens, **Greenpoint** is the seat of an active Polish community (subway: E or F to Queens Plaza, then G to Greenpoint Ave.). South of Greenpoint is **Williamsburg**, home to a large Hispanic and Jewish population (subway: J, M, or Z to Marcy Ave.). In recent years young artists have been drawn to Williamsburg for its affordable loft spaces which are reasonably close to Manhattan. A small but growing outcropping of hip restaurants, cafes, and bars has sprung up around them. West on Berry St. and up N. 10th stands a fantastic **graffiti mural.** More *virtuoso* graffiti can be found northward at N. 10th and Union Ave. At 770 Eastern Pkwy. in the area of **Crown Heights** is the world headquarters of **ChaBad** (the Lubavitchers' organization), a Hasidic Jewish sect.

Prospect Park, designed by Frederick Law Olmsted and Calvin Vaux in the mid-1800s, is a 526-acre urban oasis (subway: #2 or 3 to Grand Army Plaza). They were more pleased with it than the Manhattan project of Central Park. At the north corner of the park, **Grand Army Plaza** provides an island in the midst of the borough's busiest thoroughfares, designed to shield surrounding apartment buildings from traffic. The nearby **Botanic Gardens** (718-622-4433) in Institute Park are more secluded and include a lovely rose garden. *(Open Tu-F 8am-6pm, Sa-Su 10am-6pm; Oct.-Mar. Tu-F 8am-4:30pm, Sa-Su 10am-4:30pm. $3, students and seniors $1.50, ages 5-15 50¢; free Tu.)* The mammoth **Brooklyn Museum** (718-638-5000) rests next to the gardens. *(Open W-Su 10am-5pm. Suggested donation $4, students $2, seniors $1.50, under 12 free.)*

Both a body of water and a mass of land, **Sheepshead Bay** lies on the southern edge of Brooklyn. Diners can catch daily seafood specials along Emmons Ave. Nearby **Brighton Beach,** nicknamed "Little Odessa by the Sea," has been homeland to Russian emigres since the turn of the century (subway: D or Q).

Once a resort for the City's elite, then made accessible to the rest because of the subway, fading **Coney Island** still warrants a visit. The **Boardwalk**, once one of the most seductive of Brooklyn's charms, now squeaks nostalgically as tourists are jostled by roughnecks. Enjoy a hot dog and crinkle-cut fries at historic **Nathan's,** at Surf and Sitwell Ave. The **Cyclone,** 834 Surf Ave. and W. 10th St. (718-266-3434), built in 1927, was once the most terrifying roller coaster ride in the world. *(Open mid-June to Sept. daily noon-midnight; Easter weekend to mid-June F-Su noon-midnight.)* Cars hurtle through the 100-second-long screamer; with nine hills of rickety wooden tracks the ride's well worth $4. Meet a walrus, dolphin, sea lion, shark, or other ocean critter in the tanks of the **New York Aquarium** (718-265-3474), at Surf Ave. and W. 8th St. (open daily 10am-6pm; $7.75, seniors and children $3.50).

Queens

In this urban suburbia, the American melting pot bubbles away with a more than 30% foreign-born population. Immigrants from Korea, China, India, and the West Indies rapidly sort themselves out into neighborhoods where they try to maintain the memory of their homeland while striving for "the American Dream."

Queens is easily New York's largest borough, covering over a third of the city's total area. In **Flushing,** you will find some of the most important colonial neighborhood landmarks, a bustling downtown, an incoming Asian immigrant population among the Old Worlders, and the largest rose garden in the Northeast (subway: #7 to Main St., Flushing). Nearby **Flushing Meadows-Corona Park** was the site of the 1964-1965 World's Fair, and now holds **Shea Stadium** (home of the Mets) and the **New York Hall of Science** (718-699-0005), on the corner of 111th St. and 48th Ave. The **Unisphere,** a 380-ton steel globe in front of the nearby New York City Building, hovers over a fountain in retro-futuristic glory. Yup, this is the thing that nasty alien crashed into in 1997's *Men In Black*. The New York City Building houses the **Queens Museum of Art** (718-592-9700), and the just south of the Hall of Science is the **Queens Wildlife Center and Zoo** (718-271-7761).

In **Astoria,** Greek-, Italian-, and Spanish-speaking communities mingle amid lively shopping districts and top-notch cultural attractions. Astoria lies in the upper west corner of the borough, and **Long Island City** is just south of it, across the river from the Upper East Side. A trip on the N train from Broadway and 34th St. in Manhattan to Broadway and 31st St. at the border between the two areas should take about 25min. Here, two sculpture gardens make for a worthwhile daytrip from Manhattan. From the Broadway station at 31st St., walk west along Broadway 8 blocks toward the Manhattan skyline, leaving the commercial district for a more industrial area. At the end of Broadway, cross the intersection with Vernon Blvd. The **Socrates Sculpture Park** (718-956-1819), started by sculptor Mark di Suvero, is located across from the building labeled "Adirondack Office Furniture." *(Park open daily 10am-sunset.)* The sight of this intriguing plot of land is stunning, if somewhat unnerving: 35 modern day-glo and rusted metal abstractions en masse in the middle of nowhere, on the site of what was once an illegal dump. Two blocks south at 32-37 Vernon Blvd., stands the **Isamu Noguchi Garden Museum** (718-204-7088), established in 1985 next door to the world-renowned sculptor's studio. *(Open Apr.-Oct. W-F 10am-5pm, Sa-Su 11am-6pm. Suggested donation $4, students and seniors $2. A lengthy free tour kicks off at 2pm.)* Twelve galleries display Noguchi's breadth of vision. Astoria is also home to the **American Museum of the Moving Image** (718-784-0077), at 35th Ave. and 36th St. (see **Museums,** p. 160).

The Bronx

While the media present "Da Bronx" as a crime-ravaged husk, the borough offers its few tourists over 2000 acres of Portland, a great zoo, turn-of-the-century riverfront mansions, grand boulevards, and thriving ethnic neighborhoods, including a Little Italy to shame its Manhattan counterpart. *Travelers should be very careful in the South Bronx and probably should not venture there without someone who knows the area well.*

The most popular reason to come to the Bronx is the **Bronx Zoo/Wildlife Conservation Park** (718-367-1010 or 718-220-5100), also known as the New York Zoological Society. *(Open Apr.-Oct. M-F 10am-5pm, Sa-Su 10am-5:30pm; Nov.-Mar. daily 10am-4:30pm. $6.75, seniors and children $3; W free. For disabled-access info, call 718-220-5188. Subway: #2 or 5 to E. Tremont Ave./West Farms Sq.)* The largest urban zoo in the United States, it houses over 4000 animals. Soar into the air for a funky cool view of the zoo from the **Skyfari** aerial tramway that runs between Wild Asia and the **Children's Zoo** ($2). If you tire of the omnipresent children, the crocodiles are fed Mondays and Thursdays at 2pm, and sea lions daily at 3pm. Call 718-220-5142 3 weeks in advance to reserve a place on a **walking tour.**

North across East Fordham Rd. from the zoo, the **New York Botanical Garden** (718-817-8705) sprawls over forest and lake alike. *(Garden grounds open Tu-Su 10am-6pm. $3, students, seniors, and children 3-16 $2. Free W. Parking $4. Subway: #4 or D to Bedford Park Blvd. Walk 8 blocks east or take the Bx26, Bx12, Bx19, or Bx41 bus to the Garden.)*

The Birth of Hip-Hop

In 1973, **Bronx DJ Kool Herc** began prolonging the funky drum **"break"** sections of songs by using two turntables and two copies of the same record, switching to the start of the second copy when the first one ended and then doubling back, thus extending the beat. Dancers responded to the rhythm's challenge, and by 1975 **break-dancing** had evolved in response to the turntable manipulations carried on by **Afrika Bambaataa, Grandmaster Flash, Kool,** and others. In one swoop, the Bronx birthed the art of **DJing,** the music known as **Hip-Hop/Rap,** and an acrobatic dance style. Bambaataa's **Zulu Nation** crew forged the roots of Hip-Hop around 174th St. by the Bronx River, transcending negative **South Bronx** stereotypes while forever changing the approach to music creation and records.

The **Museum of Bronx History** (718-881-8900), at Bainbridge Ave. and 208th St., is run by the Bronx Historical Society on the premises of the landmark Valentine-Varian House. *(Open Sa 10am-4pm, Su 1-5pm, or by appt. $2. Subway: D to 205th St., or #4 to Mosholu Pkwy.; walk 4 blocks east on 210th St. and then south a block.)*

Up in northern Bronx, to the east of **Van Cortlandt Park's** 1146 acres (718-430-1890), lies the immense **Woodlawn Cemetery,** where music lovers can pay tribute at the resting places of jazz legends Miles Davis, Duke Ellington, and Lionel Hampton. Impressive Victorian mausoleums abound, as do the famous dead: Herman Melville, F.W. Woolworth, Roland H. Macy, and more. *(Open daily 9am-4:30pm. Subway: D train to 205th St. then walk 6 blocks up Perry Ave.)*

Staten Island

Getting here is half the fun. The free 30min. ferry ride from Manhattan's Battery Park to Staten Island is as unforgettable as it is inexpensive. Or you can drive from Brooklyn over the **Verrazano-Narrows Bridge,** the world's second-longest (4260 ft.) suspension span. Because of the hills and the distances (and some very dangerous neighborhoods in between), it's a bad idea to walk from one site to the next. Make sure to plan your excursion with the bus schedule in mind.

The most concentrated number of sights on the island cluster around the beautiful 19th-century **Snug Harbor Cultural Center,** 1000 Richmond Terr. (718-448-2500), which houses the **Newhouse Center for Contemporary Art,** a small gallery displaying American art with an indoor/outdoor sculpture show in the summer (open W-Su noon-5pm; suggested donation $2), and the **Staten Island Botanical Gardens** (718-273-8200). The **Jacques Marchais Museum of Tibetan Art,** 338 Lighthouse Ave. (718-987-3500), meditates in central Staten Island (see **Museums,** p. 160).

MUSEUMS

For museum listings consult the following publications: *Time Out: New York,* the free *Gallery Guide* available at many major museums and galleries, *The New Yorker, New York* magazine, and the Friday *New York Times* (in the Weekend section). Most museums and all galleries close on Mondays, and are jam-packed on the weekends. Many museums require a "donation" in place of an admission fee—you can give less than the suggested amount. Most museums are free one weeknight; call ahead.

Major Collections

Metropolitan Museum of Art (the Met) (535-7710), 5th Ave. at 82nd St. Subway: #4, 5, or 6 to 86th St. The largest in the Western Hemisphere, the Met's art collection encompasses 3.3 million works from almost every period through Impressionism; particularly strong in Egyptian and non-Western sculpture and European painting. Contemplate infinity in the secluded Japanese Rock Garden or commune with the mummies of the temple of Dendur. Open Su and Tu-Th 9:30am-5:15pm, F-Sa 9:30am-8:45pm. Suggested donation $8, students and seniors $4.

Museum of Modern Art (MoMA), 11 W. 53rd St. (708-9400), off 5th Ave. in Midtown. Subway: E or F to 5th Ave./53rd St. or B, D, or Q to 50th St. One of the most extensive contemporary (post-Impressionist) collections in the world, founded in 1929 by scholar Alfred Barr in response to the Met's reluctance to embrace modern art. Monet's sublime *Water Lily* room, many Picassos, and a great design collection are among the highlights. Gorgeous sculpture garden. Open Sa-Tu and Th 10:30am-6pm, F 10:30-8:30pm. $9.50, students and seniors $6.50, under 16 free. Pay-what-you-wish F 4:30-8:30pm. Films require free tickets in advance.

American Museum of Natural History (769-5100), Central Park West, at 79th to 81st St. Subway: B or C to 81st St. The largest science museum in the world, in an imposing Romanesque structure. Newly reopened dinosaur exhibit is worth the lines. See things from a new perspective by lying down under the whale in the Ocean Life room. Open Su-Th 10am-5:45pm, F-Sa 10am-8:45pm. Suggested donation $8, students and seniors $6, children under 12 $4.50. The museum also houses an **Imax** (769-5034) cinematic extravaganza on a huge movie screen (4 stories). **Combo-ticket** (Museum and Imax): $12, students and seniors $8.50, ages 2-12 $6.50. F-Sa double features $15/$11/$8.50.

Guggenheim Museum, 1071 5th Ave. (423-3500), at 89th St. Subway: #4, 5, or 6 to 86th St. The smooth coiling design by Frank Lloyd Wright is as famous as the collection inside. Each spin of the spiral holds one sequence or exhibit, while the newly constructed **Tower Galleries** (each accessible by the ramp or by elevator) may exhibit a portion of the **Thannhauser Collection** of 19th- and 20th-century works, including several by Picasso, Matisse, Van Gogh, and Cézanne. Open Su-W 10am-6pm, F-Sa 10am-8pm. $7, students and seniors $4, children under 12 free; F 6-8pm "pay-what-you-wish." There is also **Guggenheim Museum SoHo,** 575 Broadway (423-3500), at Prince St. Open Su and W-F 11am-6pm, Sa 11am-8pm. $8, students and seniors $5, and under 12 free. A 7-day pass is available for admission to both branches for $15, students and seniors $10.

Whitney Museum of American Art, 945 Madison Ave. (570-3676), at 75th St. Subway: #6 to 77th St. Futuristic fortress featuring the largest collection of 20th-century American art in the world, with works by Hopper, O' Keefe, de Kooning, Warhol, and Calder. Home to the Biennial exhibits, which claim to showcase the cutting edge of contemporary American art. Food, trash, and video have become accepted media in what was once a bastion of high modernism. Open W and F-Su 11am-6pm, Th 1-8pm. $8, students and seniors $7, under 12 free. Free Th 6-8pm.

Cooper-Hewitt Museum, 2 E. 91st St. (860-6868), at 5th Ave. Subway: #4, 5 or 6 to 86th St. Andrew Carnegie's majestic Georgian mansion now houses the Smithsonian Institute's National Museum of Design. Playful exhibits focus on such topics as doghouses and the history of the pop-up book. Open Tu 10am-9pm, W-Sa 10am-5pm, Su noon-5pm. $5, students and seniors $3, under 12 free. Free Tu 5-9pm.

The Frick Collection, 1 E. 70th St. (288-0700), at 5th Ave. Subway: #6 to 68th St. Robber-baron Henry Clay Frick left his house and art collection to the city, and the museum retains the elegance of his French "Classic Eclectic" château. Impressive grounds. The Living Hall displays 17th-century furniture, Persian rugs, Holbein portraits, and paintings by El Greco, Rembrandt, Velázquez, and Titian. The courtyard is inhabited by elegant statues surrounding the garden pool and fountain. Open Tu-Sa 10am-6pm, Su 1-6pm. $7, students and seniors $5. Under 10 not allowed, under 16 must be accompanied by an adult. Groups by appointment only.

Smaller and Specialized Collections

The Cloisters, Fort Tryon Park (923-3700), in Washington Heights. Subway: A to 190th St.; then follow Margaret Corbin Dr. 5 blocks north. Or take bus #4 from Madison Ave. to the Cloisters' entrance. Charles Collen brought the High Middle Ages to Manhattan in 1938 by erecting this tranquil branch of the Met largely from pieces of 12th- and 13th-century French and Spanish monasteries. John D. Rockefeller donated the site (now Fort Tryon Park) and many of the works that make up the Cloisters' rich collection of Medieval art. Follow the allegory told by the Unicorn Tapestries, and wander through airy archways and manicured gardens bedecked with European treasures like the ghoulish marble fountain in the Cuxa Cloister. Open Mar.-Oct. Tu-Su 9:30am-5:15pm; Nov.-Feb. Tu-Su 9:30am-4:45pm. Museum tours Tu-F at 3pm, Su at noon; Nov.-Feb. W at 3pm. Suggested donation $8, students and seniors $4. Includes (and is included with) same-day admission to the Metropolitan Museum's main building in Central Park.

Museum of Television and Radio, 25 W. 52nd St. (621-6600, 621-6800 for daily activity schedule), between 5th and 6th Ave. Subway: B, D, F, Q to Rockefeller Center, or E, F to 53rd St. Despite its monumental title, this museum might more aptly be called an archive. With a collection of more than 95,000 TV and radio programs, the museum's library has a specially designed computerized cataloging system that allows you to find every program starring Michael J. Fox in the database; request it from a librarian, and privately watch or listen to it at one of the 96 TV and radio consoles. The best way to acquaint yourself with the museum is by tour, free with admission; inquire at the desk. Open Tu-W and F-Su noon-6pm, Th noon-8pm; F until 9pm for theaters only. Suggested donation $6, students $4, seniors and under 13 $3 (includes 2hr. of viewing time.)

Alternative Museum, 594 Broadway (966-4444), 4th fl., near Houston and Prince St. in SoHo. Subway: B, D, F, or Q to Broadway-Lafayette St., or N or R to Prince St. Founded and operated by recognized artists for non-established artists, the museum advertises itself as "ahead of the times and behind the issues." New visions and social critique are the name of the game. Open Sept.-July Tu-Su 11am-6pm. Suggested donation $3.

American Museum of the Moving Image, 35th Ave. at 36th St., Astoria, Queens (exhibition and screening info 718-784-0077, travel directions 718-784-4777). Subway: N to Broadway in Astoria. Walk along Broadway to 36th St., turn right, go to 35th Ave.; museum is on the right. Start on the 3rd fl., where you'll find out how movie editing, sound, and special effects work. On the 2nd fl. you can listen to movie stars reveal stage secrets, or you can gaze at a wall of Bill Cosby's sweaters (he never wears the same one twice). Vintage arcade games line the 1st fl.—Ms. Pac Man and Donkey Kong are waiting with open arms. The screening room downstairs plays vintage films on the weekends; call for a program schedule. Open Tu-F noon-5pm, Sa-Su 11am-6pm. $8.50, students and seniors $5.50, children $4.50, under 4 free. Screening tickets free with admission.

The Asia Society, 725 Park Ave. (517-ASIA or 288-6400), at 70th St. Subway: #6 to 68th St. Exhibitions of Asian art are accompanied by symposia, musical performances, film screenings, and an acclaimed "Meet the Author" series. The art spans the entire Asian continent, from Iran to Japan, and even includes Asian America. Open Tu-W and F-Sa 11am-6pm, Th 11am-8pm, Su noon-5pm. $3, seniors and students $1; Th 6-8pm free. Tours Tu-Sa 12:30pm, Th also at 6:30pm, Su 2:30pm.

International Center of Photography, 1130 5th Ave. (860-1777), at 94th St. Subway: #6 to 96th St. The foremost exhibitor of photography in the city and a gathering place for its practitioners. Historical, thematic, and contemporary works, running from fine art to photo-journalism to celebrity portraits. **Midtown branch,** 1133 6th Ave. (768-4680), at 43rd St. Both open Tu 11am-8pm, W-Su 11am-6pm. $5.50, students and seniors $4; Tu 6-8pm pay-what-you-wish.

Intrepid Sea-Air-Space Museum, Pier 86 (245-0072), at 46th St. and 12th Ave. Bus: M42 or M50 to W. 46th St. One ticket admits you to the veteran World War II and Vietnam War aircraft carrier *Intrepid*, the Vietnam War destroyer *Edson,* the only publicly displayed guided-missile submarine *Growler,* and the lightship *Nantucket.* On the main carrier, Pioneer's Hall shows models, antiques, and film shorts of flying devices from the turn of the century to the 1930s. Open Mar.-Sept. M-F 10am-5pm, Sa-Su 10am-6pm; Oct. 1-Apr. 30 W-Su 10am-5pm. Last admission 1hr. before closing. $10; students, seniors, and veterans $7.50; children 6-11 $5.

The Jewish Museum, 1109 5th Ave. (423-3200), at 92nd St. Subway: #6 to 96th St. The permanent collection of over 14,000 works details the Jewish experience throughout history, ranging from ancient Biblical artifacts and ceremonial objects to contemporary masterpieces by Marc Chagall, Frank Stella, and George Segal. Open Su-M and W-Th 11am-5:45pm, Tu 11am-8pm. $7, students and seniors $5, under 12 free; Tu 5-8pm pay-what-you-wish. Wheelchair access.

Jacques Marchais Museum of Tibetan Art, 338 Lighthouse Ave., Staten Island (718-987-3500). Take bus S74 from Staten Island Ferry to Lighthouse Ave., then turn right and walk up the fairly steep hill as it winds to the right. Almost 2hr. from Manhattan but worth the trip for one of the largest private collections of Tibetan art in the West. Open Apr.-Nov. W-Su 1-5pm; Dec.-Mar. call ahead to schedule a visiting time. $3, seniors $2.50, children under 12 $1.

El Museo del Barrio, 1230 5th Ave. (831-7272), at 104th St. Subway: #6 to 103rd St. El Museo del Barrio is the only museum in the U.S. devoted exclusively to the art and culture of Puerto Rico and Latin America. Begun in a classroom, the project has turned into a permanent museum. Open Mar.-Sept. W and F-Su 9am-5pm, Th noon-7pm; Oct.-Apr. W-Su 11am-5pm. Suggested donation $4, students and seniors $2.

The Museum for African Art, 593 Broadway (966-1313), between Houston and Prince St. in SoHo. Subway: N or R to Prince and Broadway. Stunning African and African-American art. Pieces span centuries, from ancient to contemporary, and come from all over Africa. The Saturday afternoon lecture series is free with admission. Open Tu-F 10:30am-5:30pm, Sa-Su noon-6pm. $5, students and seniors $2.50.

Museum of the City of New York (534-1672), at 103rd St. and 5th Ave. in East Harlem, across the street from El Museo del Barrio. Subway: #6 to 103rd St. Fascinating museum details the history of the Big Apple. Open W-Sa 10am-5pm, Su 1-5pm. Suggested donation $5; students, seniors, and children $4. Wheelchair access.

National Museum of the American Indian, 1 Bowling Green (668-6624). Subway: #4 or 5 to Bowling Green. Housed in the stunning Beaux-Arts Customs House, this excellent museum exhibits the best of the Smithsonian's vast collection of Native American artifacts. Open daily 10am-5pm, Th closes at 8pm. Free.

New Museum of Contemporary Art, 583 Broadway (219-1222), between Prince and Houston St. Subway: N or R to Prince; or B, D, F, or Q to Broadway-Lafayette. Dedicated to the role "art" plays in "society," the New Museum flaunts the hottest, the newest, and the most controversial. Open W and Su noon-6pm, Th-Sa noon-8pm. $5; students, seniors, and artists $3; under 18 free; Th 6-8pm free.

Studio Museum in Harlem, 144 W. 125th St. (864-4500), between Adam Clayton Powell Jr. Blvd. and Lenox/Malcolm X Ave. Subway: #2 or 3 to 125th St. Founded in 1967 at the height of the Civil Rights movement, and dedicated to the works by black artists. Open W-F 10am-5pm, Sa-Su 1-6pm. $5, students and seniors $3, children $1; free 1st Sa of month. Tours Sa 1, 2, 2:30, and 4pm.

GALLERIES

New York's museums may be the vanguard of art history, maintaining priceless collections and orchestrating blockbuster exhibitions, but New York galleries are where art *happens*. Galleries are *free* culture—go, and go often. To get started, check out the publications suggested above in the **Museums** section.

   SoHo is a wonderland of galleries, with a particularly dense concentration of more than 40 different establishments lining Broadway between Houston and Spring St. Cutting-edge outposts of contemporary art have recently emerged in **Chelsea,** in reclaimed industrial spaces centered around West 22nd St. between 10th and 11th Ave. **Madison Ave.** between 70th and 84th St. has a generous sampling of ritzy showplaces, and another group of galleries festoons **57th St.** between 5th and 6th Ave.

SoHo

Holly Solomon Gallery, 172 Mercer (941-5777), at Houston St. This SoHo matriarch is an excellent place to start a tour of downtown galleries. 3 or 4 artists are always showing in this multi-floored space, providing newcomers with an accessible array of avant-garde art. Unlike other galleries, Solomon's has a sense of humor. Nam June Paik, William Wegman, and Peter Hutchinson are represented here. Open Tu-F 10am-5pm; Sept.-June Tu-Sa 10am-6pm.

Pace Gallery, 142 Greene St. (431-9224), between Prince and Houston St. This famous gallery run by the Wildenstein family has two locations in the city. Its SoHo branch displays the works of biggies like Robert Irwin, Julian Schnabel, Claes Oldenburg. Exhibitions rotate monthly. Open M-Th 10am-5:30pm, F 10am-4pm; Sept.-June Tu-Sa 10am-6pm. Often closed in Aug.

Sonnabend, 420 W. Broadway (966-6160), 3rd fl. This prominent gallery shows contemporary paintings by well-known American and European artists. Jeff Koons, John Baldessari, and Robert Rauschenburg top the bill. Open Tu-Sa 10am-6pm. Often closed July-Aug.

David Zwirner, 43 Greene St. (966-9074), at Grand St. A small gallery that pulls together excellent, elegant one-person shows with a strong conceptual punch. Some of the smartest contemporary art around ends up on Zwirner's gracefully curated walls. Open Tu-Sa 10am-6pm. Often closed in summer.

Feature, 76 Greene St. (941-7077), 2nd fl. Good and risky. Daring, straightforward selections of contemporary art. Don't miss their back showroom when you visit. Open Tu-F 11am-6pm; Sept.-May Tu-Sa 11am-6pm.

American Primitive, 594 Broadway (966-1530), 2nd fl. Shows works by folk or self-taught American artists of the 19th and 20th centuries, focusing on contemporary works. Only here can you get a piece of art dedicated to baseball hero Cal Ripken made entirely out of the thread from socks. Proudly and aggressively out of the art scene—so uncool they're cool. Open M-Sa 11am-6pm; July-Aug closed Sa.

Gavin Brown's Enterprise, 558 Broome St. (431-1512), just west of 6th Ave. Literally and figuratively as far left as you'd want to get without a map, this tiny gallery specializes in fun, interesting contemporary work. Japanese art, Steve Pippen (the bathroom artist), and other *über*-contemporary stuff. Open W-F noon-6pm; in winter M-Sa noon-6pm. Closed Aug.

Chelsea

I-20, 529 W. 20th St. (645-1100), between 10th and 11th Ave. High quality, daringly original photography and video art displayed in a beautiful 11th fl. space. The I-20 is at the top of a building filled with galleries, so ride the freight elevator to the top and work your way down. Open Tu-Sa 11am-6pm.

Dia Center for the Arts, 548 W. 22nd St. (989-5912), between 10th and 11th Ave. Sized like a museum but with a gallery's sensitivity to the pulse of current art, the 4-story Dia is reliably, irrepressibly cool. Each floor features changing exhibits/installations by a single contemporary artist, and the collection is well-balanced to cover a range of media and styles. Don't leave without stopping by the permanent installation on the roof. Open Tu-Su 10am-6pm. $4, students and seniors $2.

57th Street

Fuller Building, 41 E. 57th St., between Madison and Park Ave. Stylish Art Deco building harbors 12 floors of galleries. Contemporary notables such as Robert Miller, André Emmerich, and Susan Sheehan; collectors of ancient works like Frederick Schultz; and several galleries handling modern works. The **André Emmerich Gallery** (752-0124), on the 5th fl., features important contemporary work by Hockney et al. Most galleries in the building open M-Sa 10am-5:30pm, hrs. vary; Oct.-May most are closed M.

Upper East Side

Sotheby's, 1334 York Ave. (606-7000; ticket office 606-7171), at 72nd St. One of the most respected auction houses in the city, offering everything from Degas to Disney. Auctions are open to anyone, but some require a ticket for admittance (given on a first come, first served basis). Both open M-Sa 10am-5pm, Su 1-5pm.

Christie's, 502 Park Ave. (546-1000), at 59th St. Flaunts its collection of valuable wares. Like Sotheby's, auctions are open. Open M-Sa 10am-5pm, Su 1-5pm.

ENTERTAINMENT AND NIGHTLIFE

Although always an exhilarating, incomparable city, New York only becomes *New York* when the sun goes down. From the blindingly bright lights of Times Sq. to the dark, impenetrably smoky atmosphere of a Greenwich Village or SoHo bar, the Big Apple pulls you in a million directions at once. Find some performance art, hear some jazz, go to an all-night diner, twist the night away—heck, even get a tattoo. A cab ride home at 4:30am through empty streets with the windows down is always sure to make your spirits soar. This city never sleeps and, at least for a few nights, neither should you.

Publications with especially noteworthy sections on nightlife include the *Village Voice, Time Out: New York, New York* magazine, and the Sunday edition of the *New York Times*. The most comprehensive survey of the current theater scene can be found in *The New Yorker*. An **entertainment hotline** (360-3456; 24hr.) covers weekly activities by both borough and genre.

Theater

Broadway is currently undergoing a revival—ticket sales are booming, and mainstream musicals are receiving more than their fair share of attention. Broadway tickets cost about $50 each when purchased through regular channels. **TKTS** (768-1818 for recorded info) sells 25-75% discounted tickets to many Broadway shows on the day of the performance. *(Tickets sold M-Sa 3-8pm for evening performances, W and Sa 10am-2pm for matinees, Su noon-7pm for matinees and evening performances.)* TKTS has a booth in the middle of Duffy Sq. (the northern part of Times Sq., at 47th and Broadway). There is a $2.50 service charge per ticket. For info on shows and ticket availability, call the **NYC/ON STAGE hotline** at 768-1818. **Ticketmaster** (307-4100) deals in everything from Broadway shows to mud-truck races; they charge at least $2 more than other outlets, but take most major credit cards.

Off-Broadway theaters have between 100 and 499 seats; only Broadway houses have over 500. Off-Broadway houses frequently offer more off-beat, quirky shows, with shorter runs. Occasionally these shows have long runs or make the jump to

Broadway houses. Tickets cost $10-20. The best of the Off-Broadway houses huddle in the Sheridan Sq. area of the West Village. TKTS also sells tickets for the larger Off-Broadway houses. **Off-Off-Broadway** means cheaper, younger theaters.

Shakespeare in the Park (861-7277) is a New York summer tradition. From June through August, two Shakespeare plays are presented at the **Delacorte Theater** in Central Park, near the 81st St. entrance on the Upper West Side, just north of the main road. Tickets are free, but lines form early.

Movies

If Hollywood is *the* place to make films, New York City is *the* place to see them. Most movies open in New York weeks before they're distributed across the country, and the response of Manhattan audiences and critics can shape a film's success or failure. Big-screen fanatics should check out the cavernous **Ziegfeld,** 141 W. 54th St. (765-7600), one of the largest screens left in America, which shows first-run films. **MoviePhone** (777-3456) allows you to reserve tickets for most major movie-houses and pick them up at showtime from the theater's automated ticket dispenser; you charge the ticket price plus a small fee over the phone. **The Kitchen,** 512 W. 19th St. (255-5793), between 10th and 11th Ave. (subway: C or E to 23rd St.), is a world-renowned showcase for the off-beat and New York-based struggling artists. Eight screens project alternative cinema at the **Angelika Film Center,** 18 W. Houston St. (995-2000), at Mercer St. (subway: #6 to Bleecker St. or B, D, F, or Q to Broadway-Lafayette). **Anthology Film Archives,** 32 2nd Ave. (505-5181), at E. 2nd St., is a forum for independent filmmaking. The **New York International Film Festival** packs 'em in every October; check the *Voice* or *Time Out* for details.

Opera and Dance

You can do it all at **Lincoln Center** (875-5000), New York's one-stop shopping mall for high-culture consumers; there's usually opera or dance at one of its many venues. Write to Lincoln Center Plaza, NYC 10023 for a press kit. The **Metropolitan Opera Company** (362-6000), opera's premier outfit, plays on a Lincoln Center stage as big as a football field. *(Season runs Sept.-Apr. M-Sa. Box office open M-Sa 10am-8pm, Su noon-6pm.)* Regular tickets run as high as $100—go for the upper balcony (around $42; the cheapest seats have an obstructed view). You can stand in the orchestra ($16) along with the opera freakazoids who've brought along the score, or all the way back in the Family Circle. In the summer, free concerts are offered in city parks (362-6000).

At right angles to the Met, the **New York City Opera** (870-5570) has come into its own under the direction of Christopher Keene. "City" now has a split season (Sept.-Nov. and Mar.-Apr.) and keeps its ticket prices low year-round ($20-90; for rush tickets, call the night before and wait in line the morning of). In July, the **New York Grand Opera** (360-2777) puts on free performances at the Central Park Summerstage every Wednesday night. Check the papers for performances of the old warhorses by the **Amato Opera Company,** 319 Bowery St. (228-8200; Sept.-May).

The **New York State Theater** (870-5570) is home to the late, great George Balanchine's **New York City Ballet.** (Performances Nov.-Feb. and May-June; tickets $12-65, standing room $12.) Decent tickets for the *Nutcracker* in December sell out almost immediately. For a more vivacious bunch, the **American Ballet Theater** (477-3030; box office 362-6000) dances at the Metropolitan Opera House (tickets $16-95). The **Alvin Ailey American Dance Theater** (767-0940) bases its repertoire of modern dance on jazz, spirituals, and contemporary music. Often on the road, it always performs at the **City Center** in December. Tickets ($15-40) can be difficult to obtain. Write or call the City Center, 131 W. 55th St. (581-7907), weeks in advance.

The best place in the city to see innovative dance is the **Joyce Theater,** 175 8th Ave. (242-0800), between 18th and 19th St. Open year-round, the Joyce presents high-quality, energetic dance in its sleek, audience-friendly space (tickets $15-40).

Classical Music

As always, start with the ample listings in *Time Out,* the *New York Times, The New Yorker,* or *New York* magazine. Remember that many events are seasonal.

MID-ATLANTIC

The **Lincoln Center Halls** have a wide, year-round selection of concerts. The **Great Performers Series,** featuring famous and foreign musicians, packs the Avery Fisher and Alice Tully Halls and the Walter Reade Theater from October until May (call 875-5020; tickets from $12). **Avery Fisher Hall** (875-5030) paints the town ecstatic with its annual **Mostly Mozart Festival.** Show up early; there are usually pre-concert recitals beginning 1hr. before the main concert that are free to ticketholders. The festival runs from July through August, with tickets to individual events costing $12-30. The **New York Philharmonic** (875-5656) begins its regular season in mid-September (tickets $10-60; call 721-6500 M-Sa 10am-8pm, Su noon-8pm). Students and seniors can sometimes get $5 tickets; call ahead (Tu-Th only). Anyone can get $10 tickets for the odd morning rehearsal; call ahead. For a couple of weeks in late June, Kurt Masur and friends lead the posse at **free concerts** (875-5709) on the Great Lawn in Central Park, at Prospect Park in Brooklyn, at Van Cortlandt Park in the Bronx, and elsewhere. Free outdoor events at Lincoln Center occur all summer; call 875-4000.

Carnegie Hall (247-7800), 7th Ave. at 57th St., is still the favorite coming-out locale of musical debutantes (box office open M-Sa 11am-6pm, Su noon-6pm; tickets $10-60). One of the best ways for the budget traveler to absorb New York musical culture is to visit a **music school.** Except for opera and ballet productions ($5-12), concerts at the following schools are free and frequent: try the **Juilliard School of Music,** Lincoln Center (769-7406), the **Mannes School of Music** (580-0210), and the **Manhattan School of Music** (749-2802).

Jazz Joints

The **JVC Jazz Festival** (501-1390) blows into the city in June. All-star performances have included Ray Charles and Mel Torme. Call in the spring for info, or write to: JVC Jazz Festival New York, P.O. Box 1169, Ansonia Station, New York, NY 10023. The **Texaco Jazz Festival** brings in local talent as well as giants on the forefront of innovation. These concerts take place throughout the city (some are free) but are centered at TriBeCa's **Knitting Factory** (219-3055).

Apollo Theater, 253 W. 125th St. (749-5838, box office 864-0372), between Frederick Douglass Blvd. and Adam Clayton Powell Blvd. Subway: #1, 2, 3, or 9 to 125th St. This historic Harlem landmark has heard Duke Ellington, Count Basie, Ella Fitzgerald, Lionel Hampton, Billie Holliday, and Sarah Vaughan. A young Malcolm X shined shoes here. The Apollo is now undergoing a resurgence in popularity. Ticket prices vary; order through Ticketmaster (307-7171). A big draw is the W legendary Amateur Night, where acts are either gonged (ouch!) or rated "regular," "show-off," "top dog," or "super top dog." Tickets $10-18 for Amateur Night.

Blue Note, 131 W. 3rd St. (475-8592), near MacDougal St. Subway: A, B, C, D, E, F, or Q to Washington Sq. The legendary jazz club is now a commercialized concert space with crowded tables and a tame audience. But the Blue Note still brings in many of today's all-stars. Cover for big-name performers $20 and up, $5 drink min. Sunday jazz brunch includes food, drinks, and jazz for $18.50 (noon-6pm, shows at 1 and 3:30pm; reservations recommended). Other sets daily 9 and 11:30pm.

Fez, 380 Lafayette St. (533-2680), behind the Time Cafe. Subway: #6 to Astor Pl. This lushly appointed, Moroccan-decorated club draws an extremely photogenic crowd, especially on Th nights, when the Mingus Big Band holds court (sets at 9 and 11pm; reservations suggested). Delicious cocktails (around $7.50). Kitchen open 8:30pm-midnight. Call for dates, prices, and reservations.

St. Nick's Pub, 773 St. Nicholas Ave. (283-9728), between 148th and 149th St. Subway: A, B, C, D to 145th St. A small, comfy bar with a dedicated crowd and a great jazz. Bar opens at 12:30pm, jazz shows M-Sa, starting at 9pm and going either 'til 1 or 2am or just 'til." Su evening is a soul quartet show (5-9pm). M nights are especially notable, with Patience Higgins and the Sugar Hill Jazz Quartet hosting a laid-back jam session. Open M past 2am, Tu-Su until 2am.

Village Vanguard, 178 7th Ave. South (255-4037), between W. 11th St. and Greenwich. Subway: #1, 2, 3, or 9 to 14th St. A windowless, wedge-shaped cavern, as old and hip as jazz itself. The walls are thick with memories of Lenny Bruce, Leadbelly, Miles Davis, and Sonny Rollins. Every M the Vanguard Orchestra unleashes its torrential Big Band sound on sentimental journeymen at 10pm and midnight. Cover $15 plus $10 min., F-Sa $15 plus $8 min. Sets Su-Th 9:30 and 11:30pm, F-Sa 9:30, 11:30pm, and 1am.

Clubs

New York City has a long history of producing bands on the vanguard of popular music and performance, from the Wu-Tang Clan to the Velvet Underground, from Ani diFranco to the Beastie Boys. **Music festivals** are also hot tickets and provide the opportunity to see tons of bands at a (relatively) low price. The **CMJ Music Marathon** (516-498-3150) runs for four nights in the fall and includes over 400 bands and workshops on alternative music culture and college radio production. The **Intel New York Music Festival** (677-3530), a spunky newcomer, commandeers the clubs for four indie-filled days July 20-23. Another recent addition to the music scene, the **Macintosh New York Music Festival** presents over 350 bands over a week-long period. For more experimental sounds, check out Creative Time's **Music in the Anchorage**, a June concert series happening in the massive stone chambers in the base of the Brooklyn Bridge. Call 206-6674, ext. 252 for info.

CBGB/OMFUG (CBGB's), 315 Bowery (982-4052), at Bleecker St. Subway: #6 to Bleecker St. The initials once stood for "country, bluegrass, blues, and other music for uplifting gourmandizers" since 1976, but this club has always been about punk rock. Generations of New Yorkers have come to CB's to rock out. Blondie and the Talking Heads got their starts here, and the club continues to be *the* place to see great alternative rock. Shows nightly at around 8pm. Cover $5-10.

The Cooler, 416 W. 14th St. (229-0785), at Greenwich St. Subway: #1, 2, 3, A, C, or E, to 14th St. In the heart of the meat-packing district, The Cooler showcases non-mainstream alternative, dub, electronica, and illbient in a huge vault of a room. Cover varies. Free M. Doors open Su-Th 8pm, F-Sa 9pm.

Knitting Factory, 74 Leonard St. (219-3055), between Broadway and Church St. Subway: #1, 2, 3, 6, 9, A, C, or E to Canal. Walk up Broadway to Leonard St. Free-thinking musicians anticipate the apocalypse with a wide range of edge-piercing performances complemented by great acoustics. Several shows nightly. Sonic Youth played here every Thursday for years (alas, no more). Box office open M-F 10am-11pm, Sa-Su 2-11pm. Bar open M-F 4:30pm-2am, Sa-Su 6pm-2am.

Bars

Naked Lunch Bar and Lounge, 17 Thompson St. (343-0828). Adorned with the roach-and-typewriter motif found in the novel and movie of the same name, Naked Lunch creates a let loose and have fun atmosphere. The after-work crowd is not afraid to dance in the aisle alongside the bar. Unbeatable martinis like the Tanqueray tea ($7). All beers $5. DJ W-Sa; sometimes there's a small cover. Prices drop for happy hour Tu-F 5-8pm. Open Tu-F 5pm-4am, Sa 8pm-4am.

Bar 6, 502 6th Ave. (691-1363), between 12th and 13th St. Subway: #1, 2, or 3 to 14th St. or A, E, D, or B to 6th Ave.-8th St. French-Moroccan bistro by day, sizzling bar by night. Live DJ spins Tu-Su. Beers on tap ($4-5 per pint). Kitchen open Su-Th noon-2am, F-Sa noon-3am; bar open later.

The Village Idiot, 355 W. 14th (989-7334), between 8th and 9th St. Any reference to Dostoevksy would probably be punished with about 4 shots of tequila here. New York's infamous honky-tonk bar has reopened in the Village, and the beer is still cheap ($1.25 mugs of Miller Genuine Draft), the music still loud, and the ambience still as close as they can get it to a roadhouse. Open daily noon-4am.

Drinkland, 339 E 10th St. (228-2435), between Ave. A and B. A young, downtown crowd soaks in the Jetsons-meets-trip-hop decor. DJs spin everything from breakbeat to classic funk, depending on the night. Open daily 7pm-4am.

Lucky Cheng's, 24 First Ave. (473-0516), between 1st and 2nd St. One of New York's better-known drag clubs, this one throws in an Asian twist. Open Su-Th 6pm-midnight, F-Sa 6pm-2am.

Idlewild, 145 Houston (477-5005), between Eldridge and Forsythe St. Enter the airplane theme bar of the Lower East Side. Open Su-W 8pm-3am, Th-Sa 8pm-4am.

Welcome to the Jungle

Early in the 90s, black Londoners spawned **jungle,** a frantic urban music style that has adapted well to New York City. NYC is the original urban jungle, although here the crowd is comprised mostly of white post-ravers. Jungle incorporates the slow, dubby basslines of reggae with **sped-up hip-hop breakbeats** and recombinant sampling strategies, stewed thick and fast with inflections of techno. The result is edgy, experimental, and futuristic. New York now offers about four jungle club nights a week. **Konkrete Jungle** (604-7959) is the most established, while **Jungle Nation** (802-7495) throbs with a serious crowd. DJs to look for include Dara, Delmar, Soulslinger, Cassien, Cruisemissile, and /rupture.

Coffee Shop Bar, 29 Union Sq. W. (243-7969), facing Union Sq. Park. Subway: #4, 5, 6, L, N, or R to Union Sq. A chic diner for fashion victims, owned by 3 Brazilian models whose gorgeous friends serve updated cuisine from the homeland. Sure, it's a bar and restaurant, but more importantly, it's a spectacle. Beers $4-6. Open daily 6am-5am.

Yogi's, 2156 Broadway (873-9852), at 76th St. Three things anchor this bar in the booze stratosphere: a constant stream of Elvis, Dylan, and country faves from the jukebox; bartenders dancing on the bar; and, most importantly, $1 mystery beers, which involve the bartender pulling 12 cold oz. out of a bin filled with microbrews. Open daily noon-4am.

Double Happiness, 173 Mott St. (941-1282), between Broome and Grand St. Recently opened, this downstairs bar takes advantage of the dual downtown fetish with all things "Oriental" and minimalist. Abacuses decorate the walls and an appropriately chinoiserie-meets-Calvin-Klein-meets-Nike crowd decorates the floor. Open Su-Th 5pm-2am, F-Sa 5pm-3am.

bOb Bar, 235 Eldridge St. (777-0588), between Houston and Stanton St. Comfy and laid-back, with a hip-hop-inclined crowd and DJs that spin anything they can get their hands on. Open daily 7pm-4am.

Dance Clubs

The New York club scene is an unrivaled institution. The crowd is forcefully uninhibited, the music unparalleled, and the fun can be virtually unlimited—as long as you uncover the right place. Honing in on the hippest club in New York isn't easy without connections. Clubs rise, war, and fall and even those "in the know" can't always locate the hot spot, since many parties stay carefully underground, advertised by word of mouth, futuristic flyers, and phone lines. The right club on the wrong night can be a big mistake, particularly if you've already paid the $3-25 cover charge. Make friends with someone on the inside, or check out the cooler record stores for directional flyers which offer discount admission. Flyers and staff at **Liquid Sky/Temple,** 241 Lafayette St. (343-0532; subway: #6 to Spring St. or N, R to Prince St.), and **Throb,** 211 E. 14th St. (533-2328; subway: #4, 5, 6, L, N, or R to 14th St./Union Sq.), will help direct you to some phat beats.

The rules are relatively simple. You have to have "the look" to be let in. Bouncers are the clubs' fashion police, and nothing drab or conventional will squeeze by. Most clubgoers wear black clothes or rave gear with their most attractive friends draped on their arms. Our suggestions could well have changed by the summer of '99, as hip is by its nature an elusive commodity. Call ahead to make sure you know what (and whom) you'll find when you arrive.

Twilo, 530 W. 27th St. (268-1600). Subway: #1 or 9 to 28th St. or C or E to 23rd St. Located in the former Sound Factory. A crowded scene early in the night, with meaty shirtless glam boys and a healthy bridge and tunnel crowd mixing with the occasional 8 ft. tall drag queen. Later, the music gets deeper and the crowd more serious. Th is the night to go on with a wonderfully glam crowd, especially in the VIP lounge (shhh!). Cover $20-25. Doors open around midnight.

Sounds of Brazil (SOB's), 204 Varick St. (243-4940), at Houston St. Subway: #1 or 9 to Houston. Terrific Latin dance music served up more ways than you knew existed. Special place reserved here for Brazilian music. Music often alternates between live bands and a DJ. Cover $10-20. Open for dining Tu-Th 7pm-2:30am, F-Sa 7pm-4am. Most shows Su-Th 8 and 10pm; F-Sa 10:30pm and 1am; or, alternately, 10pm, midnight, and 2am.

Tunnel, 220 12th Ave. (695-7292 or 695-4682), at 27th St. Subway: C or E to 23rd St. The name may refer to the cavernous space or to the mostly Jersey crowd, but this is the party that everyone's invited to. An immense club—3 floors and a mezzanine packed with 2 dance floors, lounges, glass-walled live shows, and a skateboarding cage. "Alternative-lifestyle" parties. Cover $20. Open F-Sa.

Webster Hall, 125 E. 11th St. (353-1600), between 3rd and 4th Ave. Subway: #4, 5, 6, N, or R or L to Union Sq.-14th St. 3 blocks south and a block east. Popular club offers a rock/reggae room and a coffeeshop in addition to the main, house-dominated dance floor. Psychedelic Thursdays often feature live bands and $2.50 beers. F-Sa see the motto of "4 floors, 5 eras, 4 DJs...and 40,000 sq. ft. of fun" put into effect. Open Th-Sa 10pm-4am. Cover $15-20, though promotions like "Ladies' Night Out" and time-limited freebies ease the cost.

Nell's, 246 W. 14th St. (675-1567), between 7th and 8th Ave. Subway: #1, 2, 3, or 9 to 14th St. A legendary hot spot in slight decline; the faithful hang on for mellow shmoozing and soulful music upstairs and phat beats below. Racially diverse crowd. Cover M $5; Tu-W, Su $10; Th-Sa $15. Open daily 10pm-4am.

China Club, 2130 Broadway (398-3800), at 75th St. Subway: #1, 2, 3, or 9 to 72nd St. Rock-and-roll hot spot where Bowie and Jagger used to come on their off nights. Models and long-haired men make it a great people-watching spot. M night is for the "beautiful people" crowd. Be well-dressed or you won't get in. Go elsewhere for great dancing. Cover around $20. Opens daily at 10pm.

Gay and Lesbian Clubs

Clit Club, 432 W. 14th St. (529-3300), at Washington St. This is *the* place to be for young, beautiful, queer grrls. Host Julie throws the hottest party around every F night. Cover $3 before 11pm, $7 after 11pm. Doors open at 9:30pm. Tu nights the same space becomes **Jackie 60** (366-5680). Drag queens work it while the sometimes celebrity crowd eggs them on. Frequent theme nights, such as Transylvania 6060, a campy transvestite horror fest. Cover $10. Open at 10pm.

Bbar (Bowery Bar), 40 E. 4th (475-2220), at the Bowery. Formerly the place to go downtown to ape the city's celebs, this bar has still got enough attitude to give you a healthy sense of self-worth for going there. Tu night is "Beige," promoter Erich Conrad's wonderfully flamboyant gay party. Open daily 11:30am-4am.

W.O.W!, 547 W. 21st St. (631-1102), between 10th and 11th Ave., at El Flamingo. The biggest all-women dance club in Manhattan, with a packed floor and go-go dancers to boot. Cover $5 before 10pm, $7 after. Open daily 7pm-3am.

Barracuda, 275 W. 22nd St. (645-8613), at 8th Ave. Subway: C or E to 23rd St. Brimming with ripped Chelsea boys of all shapes and sizes. 50s decor makes for a cozy hangout in the back, while the determined mobs in the front seem to have something else on their minds entirely. Most drinks $4-7. Open daily 4pm-4am.

Bar d'O, 29 Bedford St. (627-1580). The coziest lounge with the most sultry lighting in the city. Superb performances by drag divas Joey Arias and Raven O. (Tu and Sa-Su nights, $5). Even without the fine chanteuses, this is a damn fine place for a drink. Women's night on M packs a glam night of drag kings. Go early for the atmosphere, around midnight for the performances, and at 2am to people-watch/gender-guess. Doors open around 7pm.

Miscellaneous Hipster Hangouts

The Anyway Café, 34 E. 2nd St. (473-5021), at 2nd Ave. Sample Russian-American culture at this relaxed hangout. Numerous literary readings during the week, as well as jazz on F-Sa nights, and Russian folk on Su. All begin around 8 or 9pm. Open M-Th noon-2am, F-Sa 1pm-4am, Su noon-1am.

Collective Unconscious, 145 Ludlow St. (254-5277), south of Houston St. A performance space collectively (and unconsciously) run by 8 local artists who put up their own shows and provide a venue/studio/rehearsal space. Frequent open-mic events. Friendly, artsy people and usually something interesting. No alcohol or other refreshments served, but BYOB is A-OK. Cover $3-10.

Giant Step and **Soul Kitchen,** mobile parties, drawing ardent followers of their funk-jazz-hip-hop hybrid. The *Voice* lists locations and dates.

Soundlab (726-1724). Locations vary. Cultural alchemy in the form of an illbient happening, nomadic *stylee*. Expect a smart, funky, racially mixed crowd absorbing smart, funky, radically mixed sound. Call to find where the next Lab goes down; past locales include the base of the Brooklyn Bridge, the 15th fl. of a Financial District skyscraper, and outdoors in a Chinatown park.

Tenth Street (Russian and Turkish) Baths, 268 E. 10th St. (674-9250), between 1st Ave. and Ave. A. Expert masseur Boris runs this co-ed bathhouse that offers all conceivable (and legal) bodily services. Conventional services are also provided, such as saunas, steam rooms, and an ice-cold pool. Admission $20. Open daily 9am-10pm; Th and Su men only, W women only.

Sports

While most cities would be content to field a major-league team in each big-time sport, New York opts for the Noah's Ark approach: two baseball teams, two hockey teams, NBA and a WNBA basketball teams, two football teams, and a MLS soccer squad. In addition to local teams' regularly scheduled games, New York hosts a number of celebrated world-class events. Get tickets 3 months in advance for the prestigious **U.S. Open** (718-760-6200; tickets from $20), held in late August and early September at the USTA Tennis Center in Flushing Meadows, Queens. On the third Sunday in October, 2 million spectators witness the 22,000 runners of the **New York City Marathon** (only 16,000 finish). The race begins on the Verrazano Bridge and ends at Central Park's Tavern on the Green.

On the **baseball** diamond, the **New York Mets** bat at **Shea Stadium** in Queens (718-507-6387; tickets $6.50-15). The legendary, rip-roarin' **New York Yankees** play ball at Yankee Stadium in the Bronx (718-293-6000; tickets $12-21). Both the **New York Giants** and the **Jets** play **football** across the river at **Giants Stadium** (201-935-3900) in East Rutherford, NJ. Tickets are nearly impossible to come by. Speaking of football, the **New York/New Jersey Metrostars** play the real thing—**soccer**—in the same venue. The **New York Knickerbockers** (that's the Knicks to you), as well as the WNBA's **Liberty,** dribble the **basketball** at **Madison Sq. Garden** (465-6751; tickets from $15). The **New York Rangers** play **hockey** at **Madison Sq. Garden** (465-6741 or 308-6977; tickets begin at $12).

■ Near New York City: Long Island

If you manage to get bored by Manhattan, Brooklyn, Queens, Staten Island, and the Bronx, then perhaps it's time for a daytrip over to Long Island. This sprawling suburbia to the northeast of Manhattan can be a sleepy summertime resort where droves of wealthy Manhattanites go to reclaim their sanity. As such, it isn't conducive to budget travel, being both expensive and difficult to navigate without a car. However, Jones Beach offers 6½ miles of beach only 40 minutes from the city, and Fire Island is an incredibly popular gay summertime getaway.

PRACTICAL INFORMATION The **Long Island Convention and Visitors Bureau** (516-951-2423) provides an interactive recorded schedule of events with operators available. **Long Island Railroad (LIRR)** services the island (automated train info 718-217-5477) from Penn Station in Manhattan (34th St. at 7th Ave.; subway: #1, 2, 3, 9, A, C, or E) and stops in Jamaica, Queens (subway: E, J, Z) before proceeding to "points east" (fares from $4.75-15.25; lower in off-peak hrs.). To reach **Fire Island,** take the LIRR to Sayville, Bayshore, or Patchogue. The **Sayville ferry** (589-8980) serves Cherry Grove, the Pines, and Sailor's Haven (round-trip $11, under 12 $5). The **Bay Shore ferry** (665-3600) sails to Fair Harbor, Ocean Beach, Ocean Bay Park, Saltaire, and Kismet (round-trip $11.50, under 12 $5.50). The **Patchogue ferry** (475-1665) shuttles to Davis Park and Watch Hill (round-trip $10, under 12 $5.50). **Jones Beach** is easily accessible by train: take the LIRR to Freeport, where a shuttle bus stops every 30min. to whisk you to your (and everyone else's) ocean paradise. The LIRR runs a package deal in summer for the trip ($11 from Manhattan). Long Island's **area code:** 516.

Fire Island *The* summertime gay hotspot and extraordinary natural site off Long Island's shores, Fire Island is a 32 mi. long barrier island buffering the South Shore from the roaring waters of the Atlantic. Cars are allowed only on the easternmost and westernmost tips of the island; there are no streets, only "walks," and deer roam boldly. A hip countercultural enclave during the 60s and home to the disco scene of the 70s, the island parties loud and queer into the late 90s.

Two of Fire Island's many resorts, **Cherry Grove** and **The Pines,** host predominantly gay communities. These sections of Fire Island are a guppy's paradise (guppy: gay urban professional who sculpts his tanned body in Chelsea's gyms). The Atlantic Ocean beaches are spectacular, and the scene rages late into the night. Cherry Grove is the more commercial of the two towns, with cheesy restaurants and souvenir shops lining the area around the ferry slip. The houses are uniformly shingled, small, crowded together, and generally overflowing with men, though lesbian couples come here, too. The Pines, a 10min. walk up the beach, is decidedly more male, upscale, and exclusive feeling.

Both towns contain establishments which advertise themselves as "guest houses." However, some of these may not be legally accredited (due to such things as fire code violations), and some may not be women-friendly. Be careful where you choose to stay; atmosphere varies. **Cherry Grove Beach Hotel** (597-6600) is a good bet, located on the Main Walk of Cherry Grove and close to the beach. Rooms have double beds, kitchenettes, and balconies, and start at $40. Weekday prices are lower. Reservations are required. (Open May-Oct.)

Fire Island's food generally entails unspectacular eats at astounding prices. **Rachel's at the Grove** (597-4174), on Ocean Walk at the Beach, overlooks the Atlantic. A standard American meal will cost you $9-12. (Open daily from 10am-4am; kitchen closes at 11pm. Reservations recommended.)

Nightlife on Fire Island is everywhere, all the time. Most restaurants are open very late, and private gatherings are popular. The Pines has an active nighttime scene, but feels as if you need to be a member of some secret club to participate in it. Disco 'til dawn at the **Ice Palace** (597-6600), attached to the Cherry Grove Beach Hotel. The piano bar frolics nightly from 4-8pm, followed by disco until 4am.

The **Fire Island National Seashore** (289-4810 for the headquarters in Patchogue) is a daytime hotspot, offering summertime fishing, clamming, and guided nature walks. The facilities at **Sailor's Haven** (just west of the Cherry Grove community) include a marina, a nature trail, and a famous beach. Similar facilities at **Watch Hill** (597-6455) include a 20-unit campground, where reservations are required. **Smith Point West,** on the eastern tip of the island, has a small **visitors center** (281-3010) and a nature trail with disabled access (center open daily 9am-5pm). Here you can spot horseshoe crabs, white-tailed deer, and monarch butterflies, which flit across the country every year to winter in Baja California.

The **Sunken Forest,** so called because of its location behind the dunes, is another of the Island's natural wonders. Located directly west of Sailor's Haven, its soil supports an unusual and attractive combination of gnarled holly, sassafras, and poison ivy. From the summit of the dunes, you can see the forest's trees laced together in a hulky, uninterrupted mesh.

Jones Beach When New York State Parks Commissioner Robert "God" Moses discovered Jones Beach in 1921, it was a barren spit of land off the Atlantic shore of Nassau County. Within ten years, he had bought up the surrounding land, imported tons of sand, planted beach grass to preserve the new dunes, and built dozens of buildings for purposes as diverse as diaper-changing and archery, creating 6½ mi. of one of the finest public beaches in the world from almost nothing. There are nearly 2500 acres of beachfront here, and the parking area accommodates 23,000 cars. Only 40min. from the City, Jones Beach (785-1600) becomes a sea of umbrellas and blankets with barely a patch of sand showing in the summertime. Along the 1½ mi. boardwalk, you can find deck games, rollerskating, mini-golf, basketball, and nightly dancing. The **Marine Theater** inside the park often hosts rock concerts. There are eight different public beaches on the rough Atlantic Ocean and the calmer Zachs Bay. The park closes at midnight, except to those with special fishing permits.

■ Catskills

The Catskills, home of Rip Van Winkle's century-long repose, remained in a happy state of somnambulent obscurity for centuries. After the purple haze of Woodstock jolted the region to life in 1969, the Catskills had to undergo an extensive detox period. Barring the occasional flashback, such as the 1994 repetition of the rock festival, the state-managed Catskill Forest Preserve has regained its status as a nature-lover's dreamland, offering pristine miles of hiking and skiing trails, adorably dinky villages, and crystal-clear fishing streams. Traveling from I-87, the region is most easily explored by following Rte. 28 W as it twists through the verdant mountains. Accommodations, campgrounds, and inexpensive eateries pepper Rte. 28, all collaborating to create a fantastic getaway from less colorful urban landscapes.

Adirondack/Pine Hill Trailways provides excellent service through the Catskills. The main stop is in **Kingston,** 400 Washington Ave. (331-0744 or 800-858-8555; ticket office open M-F 5:45am-11pm, Sa-Su 6:45am-11pm), on the corner of Front St. Buses run to New York City (2hr.; 10 per day; $18.50, M and W-Su same-day round-trip $35, Tu-Th $25). Other stops in the area include Woodstock, Pine Hill, Saugerties, and Hunter; each connects with New York City, Albany, and Utica. Four stationary **tourist cabooses** dispense info, including the extremely useful *Ulster County: Catskills Region Travel Guide,* at the traffic circle in Kingston, on Rte. 28 in Shandaken, on Rte. 209 in Ellenville, and on Rte. 9 W in Milton (open May-Oct. 9am-5pm; hrs. vary depending on volunteer availability). Rest stop **visitors centers** along I-87 can advise you on area sights and distribute excellent, free maps of New York State. **Area code:** 914, unless otherwise noted.

■ Catskill Forest Preserve

The 250,000-acre **Catskill Forest Preserve** contains many small towns that host travelers looking for outdoor adventure. Ranger stations distribute free permits for backcountry camping, necessary for stays over 3 days. Still, most of the **campgrounds** listed below sit at gorgeous trail heads that make great day-long jaunts. Reservations (800-456-2267) are vital from late June to early September, especially Thursday through Sunday. (Sites $9-12; $2 1st day registration fee; phone reservation fee $7.50; $2 more for partial hookup. Open May-Sept.) The **Office of Parks** (518-474-0456) distributes brochures on the campgrounds. Required permits for **fishing** (non-NY residents $20 for 5 days) are available in sporting goods stores and at many campgrounds. Winter **ski** season tends to run from November to mid-March, with popular slopes slashing down numerous mountainsides along Rte. 28 and Rte. 23A. Although hiking trails are maintained year-round, lean-to's are sometimes dilapidated and crowded. Always boil or treat water with chemicals, and remember to pack out your garbage. For more info on fishing, hunting, or environmental issues, call the **Dept. of Environmental Conservation** (256-3000). **Adirondack Trailways** buses from Kingston service most trail heads—drivers will let you out anywhere along secondary bus routes.

Woodstock If your karma is running out of gasma, you can stop at **Woodstock,** between Phoenicia and Kingston. A haven for artists and writers since the turn of the century, Woodstock is best known for the concert that bore its name, an event which actually took place in nearby Saugerties. Since then, the tie-dyed legacy has faded, and Woodstock has become an expensive, touristed town. Still, neo-hippie hipsters operate out of the **Woodstock School of Art** (679-2388) on Rte. 212, accessible from Rte. 28 via Rte. 375. *(Open M-Sa 9am-3pm.)* In addition to art classes, the school houses a gallery that pays homage to Woodstock's artistic tradition.

Mt. Tremper The singular attraction of **Kaleidoworld** (688-5328), located on Rte. 28, fiercely competes with mother nature for the title of most spectacular attraction in the Catskills. *(Open daily 10am-7pm; mid-Oct. to July closed Tu. $10, seniors $8, kids* under 4 ft. 6 in. $8.) The two largest kaleidoscopes in the world are proudly displayed here, with the largest (60 ft.) leaving Woodstock-era veterans muttering, "I can see the music!" The adjacent Crystal Palace (included in admission) features wicked cool, hands-on, interactive kaleidoscopes. Soothe your soul and chant your mantra at the **Zen Mountain Monastery** (688-2228), on S. Plank Rd., 10 mi. from Woodstock off Rte. 212 from Mt. Tremper. *($5 includes lunch; weekend and week-long retreats from $195.)* The 8:45am Sunday services include an amazing demonstration of zazen meditation.

Kenneth L. Wilson (679-7020), on Wittenburg Rd. 3.7 mi. from Rte. 212 (make a hard right onto Wittenburg Rd.), has well-wooded **campsites** ($12), showers, and a family atmosphere. The pond-front beach has a gorgeous panorama of surrounding mountains staring into the looking-glass lake (hey there, Narcissus). Canoe rentals (½-day $10, full-day $15), fishing opportunities, and hiking trails round out the plate of options. (Registration 8am-9pm. Day use $5, seniors free M-F.)

Phoenicia Phoenicia is another fine place to anchor a trip to the Catskills. The **Esopus Creek,** to the west, has great trout **fishing,** and **The Town Tinker,** 10 Bridge St. (688-5553), rents inner-tubes for summertime river-riding. *(Inner-tubes $7 per day, with seat $10. Driver's license or $50 deposit required. Tube taxi transportation $3. Life jackets $2. Open mid-May to Sept. daily 9am-6pm; last rental 4:30pm.)* If tubes don't float your boat, the wheezing steam-engine of the 100-year-old **Catskill Mountain Railroad** can shuttle you for 6 scenic mi. from Bridge St. to Mt. Pleasant. *(40min., late May to early Sept. Sa-Su 1 per hr., 11am-5pm. $4, round-trip $6, under 12 $2.)* At the 65 ft. high **Sundance Rappel Tower** (688-5640), off Rte. 214, visitors climb up and return to earth the hard way. *(4 levels of lessons; beginner 3-4hr., $22. Lessons only held when a group of 8 is present. Reservations 1 week in advance required.)* For a trip to the Preserve's peak, head to Woodland Valley campground (below), where a 9.8 mi. hike to the 4204 ft. summit of **Slide Mt.** lends a view of New Jersey, Pennsylvania, and the Hudson Highlands.

The somewhat primitive **Woodland Valley** campground (688-7647), off High St. 7 mi. southeast of Phoenicia, has flush toilets and showers, and lies centrally amid many hiking trails (sites $9). The **Cobblestone Motel** (688-7871), surrounded by mountains on Rte. 214, has an outdoor pool and very clean rooms, most with fridge. (Doubles $44, large doubles $50, with kitchenette $55; 3-room cottages with kitchen $85.)

Pine Hill Pine Hill nestles in **Belleayre Mt.** (254-5000 or 800-942-6904), which offers 33 hiking trails and some terrific ski slopes. (Ski lift, lesson, and rental package M-F $50, Sa-Su $60; children $40/$50.) For a lodging bargain, follow Rte. 28 past Big Indian, making a left on Main St. at the big white "Pine Hill" sign, then another left into the second parking lot, to **Belleayre Hostel** (254-4200), west of Phoenician Pine Hill. Bunks and private rooms are set against a rustic setting near Phoenicia. Amenities include a recreational room, kitchen access, laundry ($2), a picnic area, and sporting equipment. (Bunks in summer $10, in winter $13; private rooms $25/$30; Cabins for up to 4 $40/$50.) •

Hunter Mt. and Haines Falls From Rte. 28, darting north on Rte. 42 and then east onto Rte. 23A leads through a gorgeous stretch along **Hunter Mt.** (ski info 518-263-4223, accommodations 800-775-4641), one of the most popular **skiing** areas along the east coast. Motels, downhill and cross-country ski rentals, as well as snowboard and snowmobile rentals dot the two-lane highway. Past Hunter Mt., **North Lake/South Lake campground** (518-589-5058) in Haines Falls rents canoes ($15 per day) and features two lakes, a nearby waterfall, hiking, and 219 campsites ($16, reserve 2 days in advance; day use $5).

■ Albany

Albany suffers from an unhappy reversal of clichés, as the city once known as Fort Orange comes up short in comparisons with its southern sibling, the Big Apple. Although the English took Albany in 1664, the city was actually founded in 1614 as a trading post for the Dutch West Indies Company. Established 6 years before the Pilgrims landed on the New England shore, it is the oldest continuous European settlement in the original 13 colonies and the state capital of New York. Nevertheless, while transportation to other, more lush regions of New York might bring some tourists through the city, the orange seems stale in the shadow of a bright, shiny apple.

PRACTICAL INFORMATION Amtrak (462-5763 or 800-872-7245; station open M-F 4:30am-9:30pm, Sa-Su 6am-9:30pm), at the intersection of East St. and Rensselaer across the Hudson from downtown Albany, has service to New York City (2½hr., 8-11 per day, $34-41) and Buffalo (5hr., 2-3 per day, $43-51). **Greyhound,** 34 Hamilton St. (434-8095 or 800-231-2222; station open 24hr.), runs buses to Utica (1½-2hr., $17); Syracuse (3hr., $26); Rochester (4½hr., $27); and Buffalo (5-6hr., $37). *Be careful in this neighborhood at night.* **Adirondack Trailways,** 34 Hamilton Ave. (436-9651), connects to other upstate locales: Catskill (45min., 2 per day, $5); Lake George (1¾hr., 5 per day, $10); Lake Placid (3½hr., 3 per day, $23); Tupper Lake (4hr., 2 per day, $28); and Kingston (4hr., 6 per day, $8). For local travel, the **Capital District Transportation Authority (CDTA),** 110 Waterville Ave. (482-8822), serves Albany, Troy, and Schenectady ($1). Schedules are available at the Amtrak and Trailways stations. The **Albany Visitors Center,** 25 Quackenbush Sq. (434-5132), at Clinton Ave. and Broadway, runs trolley tours (early July to late Sept. Th-F; $6, $5 if purchased 3 days in advance), houses a planetarium (shows Sa 11:30am and 12:30pm; $4, students and seniors $2), and offers a wealth of free pamphlets and maps to visitors (open M-F 9am-4pm, Sa-Su 10am-4pm). Free **Internet access** is available at the Crossgates Mall (869-9565), at the junction of I-87 and I-90. **Post Office:** 45 Hudson Ave. (452-2499; open M-F 8am-5:30pm). **ZIP code:** 12207. **Area code:** 518.

ACCOMMODATIONS, CAMPGROUNDS AND FOOD Pine Haven Bed & Breakfast, 531 Western Ave. (482-1574), offers gorgeous rooms with phone, TV, and A/C in an inviting setting. The big Victorian house stands at the convergence of Madison and Western Ave.; parking is in the rear ($25 per person; breakfast included; reservations needed). The **College of Saint Rose,** 432 Western Ave. (454-5171; ask for Renee Besanson), has large rooms with laundry and kitchens in institutional dorms. The dining hall is also open for use. (Rooms $20 per person. Open mid-May to mid-Aug. daily 8:30am-4:30pm.) **Thompson's Lake State Park** (872-1674), on Rte. 157 4 mi. north of East Berne, offers the closest campsite (18 mi. southwest of Albany). There are 140 primitive sites ($13; service charge $2) and some natural perks, including nearby fishing, hiking trails, and a swimming beach.

In "downtown" Albany, the best eating option entails getting locked away in the Big House—namely, the **Big House Brewing Company,** 90 N. Pearl St. (445-BREW/ 2739). Promising "The Best Time You'll Ever Do," the Big House produces recidivists among its loyal townie patrons. Pizzas, sandwiches, and burgers come at prices that don't cry larceny ($6-7; $4-5 in the adjacent **Brew House Bakery**), while beer names such as the Al Capone Amber amply amuse. (Open M-F 11am-late, Sa noon-late, Su 3-11pm. Happy hour M-F 4-7pm, Sa noon-7pm. Live bands Tu-F. Dancing F-Sa. Bakery open M-F 7am-noon.) The hill above downtown Albany also stocks affordable eats. Students and other locals kindle pacifist revolution while munching Jamaican stir fries (potatoes, tofu, Jamaican spices, and lots o' veggies; $5) and nature burgers ($4) uptown at **Mother Earth's Café,** 217 Western Ave. (434-0944), at Quail St. Live music, not all of which goes "crunch," provides free nightly entertainment at 8pm. (Open daily 11am-11pm.)

SIGHTS Albany offers about a day's worth of sight-seeing activity. The **Rockefeller Empire State Plaza,** between State and Madison St., is a $1.9 billion, towering, modernist Stonehenge. The platform has two main levels—the open air plaza on top of the concourse—with parking garages beneath (free parking M-F after 2pm). The plaza houses state offices and any sort of store or service one might want, including a **bus terminal, post office,** cleaners, and a food court. The most interesting attraction, however, is the **New York State Museum** (474-5877), which exhibits state history and a somewhat dismal replica set from *Sesame Street* (open daily 10am-5pm; free). On a/sunny day, sweeping the/clouds away, catch a big bird's-eye view of Albany, the Hudson River, and surrounding areas from the ear-popping 42nd fl. observation deck of the **Corning Tower,** accessible from the opposite side of the concourse (open M-F 9am-3:45pm, Sa-Su 10am-3:45pm; free; call ahead). The huge flying saucer at one end of the Plaza bodes no ill; it's just the **Empire Center for the Performing Arts** (473-1845), also known as "the Egg," a venue for theater, dance, and concerts. *(Box office open M-F 10am-5pm, Sa noon-3pm; in summer M-F noon-3pm; tickets $8-25.)* The magnificent **New York State Capitol** (474-2418), adjacent to the Empire State Plaza, has provided New York politicians with luxury quarters since 1899. *(Call ahead for daily tour times. Tours begin at the senate staircase on the 1st fl. Free.)* Up the road, the **Albany Institute of History & Art,** 125 Washington Ave. (463-4478) proffers an attractive if didactic exhibit of the Hudson River School, local history information, as well as an inexplicable Egyptian Gallery highlighted by very small mummies (open W-Su noon-5pm; $3, students and seniors $2; free W).

Bounded by State St. and Madison Ave. north of downtown, **Washington Park** has tennis courts, paddle boats, and plenty of room for celebrations and performances. The **Park Playhouse** (434-2035) stages free musical theater in the park from July to mid-August (Tu-Su 8pm). On Thursdays during late June and July, folks come **Alive at Five** (434-2032) to free concerts at the **Tricentennial Plaza,** across from Fleet Bank on Broadway. For a list of events, call the **Albany Alive Line** (434-1217, ext. 409).

Cyclers should check out the **Mohawk-Hudson Bikeway** (386-2225), which passes along old railroad grades and canal towpaths as it weaves through the capital area (maps available at the visitors center).

■ Cooperstown

To an earlier generation, Cooperstown evoked images of James Fenimore Cooper's frontiersman hero, Leatherstocking, who roamed the woods around the gleaming waters of Lake Otsego. Few visitors now care; Natty Bumppo couldn't play ball. More of a shrine than a tourist attraction, tiny Cooperstown recalls a different source of American legend and myth—baseball. Tourists file through the Baseball Hall of Fame, buy baseball memorabilia, eat in baseball-themed restaurants, and sleep in baseball-themed motels. Fortunately for the tepid fan, baseball's mecca is surrounded by rural beauty and some of New York state's best (non-baseball) rural tourist attractions.

PRACTICAL INFORMATION Cooperstown is accessible from I-90 and I-88 via Rte. 28. Street parking is rare in Cooperstown; your best bets are the free parking lots just outside of town on Rte. 28 south of Cooperstown, on Glen Ave. at Maple St., and near the Fenimore House. From these parking lots, it's an easy 5-15min. walk to Main St. Alternatively, **trolleys** make the short trip from any of these lots. (Run late June to mid-Sept. daily 8:30am-9pm; early June and Sept.-Oct. Sa-Su 8:30am-6pm; all-day pass $2, children $1.) **Pine Hall Trailways** (800-858-8555) picks up visitors at Clancy's Deli on Rte. 28 and Elm St. for three trips per day to New York City (5½hr., $40) and Kingston (3¼hr., $18). The **Cooperstown Area Chamber of Commerce,** 31 Chestnut St. (547-9983), on Rte. 80 near Main St., reluctantly parts with accommodation listings (generally open daily 9am-5pm, but hrs. vary; call ahead). **Post Office:** 40 Main St. (547-2311; open M-F 8:30am-5pm, Sa 9:30am-1pm). **ZIP code:** 13326. **Area code:** 607.

ACCOMMODATIONS, CAMPGROUNDS, AND FOOD Summertime lodging in Cooperstown seems to require the salary of a Major Leaguer, and during peak tourist season (late June to mid-Sept.), many accommodation-seekers strike out. Fortunately, there are alternatives to endless arbitration. If it's not full, **Lindsay House,** 56 Chestnut St. (547-5618), is a good B&B near the center of town. Proprietor and bluegrass guitar picker Doug Lindsay vows he will always provide a haven for the budget traveler, offering small rooms with A/C and cable TV. (Singles $30; doubles $45). The

MID-ATLANTIC

Mohican Motel, 90 Chestnut St. (547-5101), offers more comforts than Natty Bumppo ever needed. Large beds, cable TV, and A/C provide hints of modernity. (Late June to early Sept. 2-people $69-83, 3 $92, 4 $98, Sa $20 extra; in spring and fall $48-53/$57/$61/$10.) **Glimmerglass State Park** (547-8662), 7 mi. north of Cooperstown on Rte. 31 (a.k.a. Main St. in Cooperstown) on the east side of Lake Otsego, has 37 pristine campsites in a gorgeous lakeside park. Swimming, fishing, and boating reward daytime visitors (for $5 per vehicle) from 11am-7pm. (Sites $13; $2 registration fee; showers, dumping station; no hookups. Register daily 9am-9pm. Call 800-456-CAMP/2267 for reservations and a heinous $7.50 service charge.) The closest campground to the Hall of Fame is **Cooperstown Beaver Valley Campground** (293-8131 or 800-726-7314), off Rte. 28 10min. south of Cooperstown. Spacious wooded sites include a pool and recreation area, with boat and canoe rentals available. (Sites $24, with hookup $27.)

The **Doubleday Café,** 93 Main St. (547-5468), scores twice with a $6-8 Mexican dinner menu and pints of Old Slugger beer on tap for $2.75 (open Su-Th 7am-10pm, F-Sa 7am-11pm; bar open 2hr. after kitchen). "Lunch lasts forever" at **Clinton's Dam Sandwiches** (547-9044), Hoffman Ln. off Main St. across from the Hall of Fame, with literary sandwiches like the "Leather Stocking" for $5-6 (open daily 10am-midnight; closed in winter). A Cooperstown institution, **Schneider's Bakery,** 157 Main St. (547-9631), has been feeding locals since 1887 with delicious 41¢ "old-fashioneds" (donuts less sweet and greasy than their conventional cousins), and equally spectacular onion rolls for 30¢ (open M-Sa 6:30am-5:30pm, Su 7:30am-1pm).

TAKE ME OUT TO the **National Baseball Hall of Fame and Museum** (547-7200) on Main St., an enormous monument to America's favorite pastime. *(Open daily 9am-9pm; Oct.-Apr. 9am-5pm. $9.50, seniors $8, ages 7-12 $4.)* In addition to memorabilia from the immortals—featuring everything from the bat with which Babe Ruth hit his famous "called shot" home run in the 1932 World Series to the infamous jersey worn by 65 lb. White Sox midget Eddie Gaedel—the museum displays a moving multimedia tribute to the sport, a detailed display on the African-American Baseball Experience, and a history tracing baseball to ancient Egyptian religious ceremonies. As one exhibit reads, "In the beginning, shortly after God created Heaven and Earth, there were stones to throw and sticks to swing."

The **annual ceremonies** for new inductees, free to the public, will take place on July 25, 1999 at 2:30pm on the field adjacent to the **Clark Sports Center** on Susquehanna Ave., a 10min. walk from the Hall. During the weekend of the ceremonies, fans scramble for a bit of contact with the many Hall of Famers who sign autographs (at steep prices) along Main St. **Free baseball games** are played on Saturday and Monday at 2pm in the delightfully intimate Doubleday Field. Plan accordingly—over 40,000 visitors are expected for the event. Rooms must be reserved months in advance.

Nearby, the **Fenimore House Museum and the American Indian Wing** (547-1400), Lake Rd./Rte. 80, features Native American art, photos, Hudson River School paintings, and James Fenimore Cooper memorabilia. *(Open daily 9am-6pm; Sept.-Oct. 10am-5pm; call for hrs. Apr.-June and Nov.-Dec. $9, ages 7-12 $4.)*

▓ Ithaca and the Finger Lakes

According to Iroquois legend, the Great Spirit laid his hand upon the earth, and the impression of his fingers made the Finger Lakes: Canandaigua, Keuka, Seneca, Cayuga, Owasco, Skaneateles, et al. Modern science credits the glaciers of the Ice Age for these formations. Regardless of their origins, the results are spectacular. Vladimir Nabokov, Kurt Vonnegut, and Thomas Pynchon, giants of postmodern literature, brooded on Cornell's cliff. Now trekkers stand beneath waterfalls in Ithaca's ruggedly carved gorges and dry off to trace the edges of the lakes, sipping another of nature's divine liquids—the rich wine of the Finger Lakes area's acclaimed vineyards.

PRACTICAL INFORMATION

Ithaca Bus Terminal (272-7930; open M-Sa 7am-6pm, Su noon-5pm), W. State and N. Fulton St., houses **Short Line** (277-8800) and **Greyhound** (272-7930 or 800-231-2222), with service to New York City (5hr., 11 per day, $35); Philadelphia (7hr., 3 per day, $53); and Buffalo (3½hr., 4 per day, $23). **Tompkins Consolidated Area Transit (T-CAT)** (277-7433) is your only choice for getting out to Cayuga Lake without wheels. Buses stop at Ithaca Commons, westbound on Seneca St. and eastbound on Green. (Fare 60¢, more distant zones $1.25. Buses run M-F.) The **Ithaca/Tompkins County Convention and Visitors Bureau,** 904 E. Shore Dr. (272-1313 or 800-284-8422), Ithaca 14850, has the best map of the area ($2), complete hotel and B&B listings, and many brochures on New York. (Open late May to early Sept. M-Th 8am-6pm, F 8am-7pm, Sa 9am-4pm, Su 10am-3pm; mid-Sept. to Oct. M-F 8am-5pm; Nov. to late May M-F 8am-5pm.) **Post Office:** 213 N. Tioga St. (272-5455), at E. Buffalo (open M-F 8:30am-5pm, Sa 8:30am-1pm). **ZIP code:** 14850. **Area code:** 607.

ACCOMMODATIONS AND CAMPGOUNDS

As befits the town where Vladimir Nabokov penned *Lolita,* Ithaca is filled with cheap roadside motels, no questions asked. In summer, however, as crowds roll in to frolic in nearby state parks, rooms are scarce and rates rise from about $40-100 per night.

🖐**Elmshade Guest House,** 402 S. Albany St. (273-1707), at Center St. 3 blocks from the Ithaca Commons. From the bus station, walk up State St. and turn right onto Albany St. Impeccably clean, well-decorated, large rooms with shared bath. This B&B is by far the best budget option in Ithaca. You'll feel like a guest at a rich relative's house. Cable TV in every room. Singles $25-40; doubles $45-55. Generous continental breakfast served. Reservations recommended.

The Economy Inn, 658 Elmira Rd./Rte. 13 (277-0370). Just the basics, but close to Buttermilk Falls and to downtown Ithaca. A/C, fridge, cable TV, free local calls. Singles from $28, Sa-Su $48; doubles from $38/$52.

The Wonderland Motel, 654 Elmira Rd. (272-5252). Follow the white rabbit saying "I'm late! I'm late! For a very important date!" down Rte. 13 S. Outdoor pool, A/C, HBO, free continental breakfast, and local calls. Family atmosphere. Singles from $36, doubles from $45; in winter $31/$36.

Three of the nearby state parks with camping are **Robert H. Treman** (273-3440), on Rte. 327 off Rte. 13; **Buttermilk Falls** (273-5761), Rte. 13 south of Ithaca; and **Taughannock Falls** (387-6739), north on Rte. 89. (Sites $13-15; $2 walk-on fee or $7.50 reservation fee by calling 800-456-2267. Cabins $122-239 per week plus $11 reservation fee.) The *Finger Lakes State Parks* describes the location and services of all area state parks; available at any tourist office or park, or from **Finger Lakes State Park,** 2221 Taughannock Park Rd. (387-7041), P.O. Box 1055, Trumansburg 14886.

FOOD AND NIGHTLIFE

Restaurants in Ithaca cluster in **Ithaca Commons** and **Collegetown.** The *Ithaca Dining Guide* pamphlet available from the visitors center (see above) lists more options. For a night on the town, free copies of the *Ithaca Times,* available at most stores and restaurants, have complete listings of entertainment options.

🖐**Moosewood Restaurant,** 215 N. Cayuga (273-9610), at Seneca St. The legendary vegetarian collective and home of the *Moosewood Cookbook.* Long-time veggies genuflect before Moosewood's ever-changing menu of tasty meals. Lunch $5.50; dinner $10-13. Open M-Th 11:30am-2pm and 5:30-9pm, F-Sa 11:30am-2pm, and Su 5:30-9pm; cafe M-Sa 2-4pm. No reservations.

Joe's Restaurant, 602 W. Buffalo St. (273-2693), at Rte. 13 (Meadow St.), a 10min. walk from Ithaca Commons. Original Art Deco interior dates from 1932. Italian and American entrees ($8-17) come with Joe's much-beloved bottomless salad. Open Su-Th 4-10pm, F-Sa 4-11pm.

Just a Taste, 116 N. Aurora (277-9463), near Ithaca Commons, with an extensive selection of fine wines (2½ oz. $2-5), 50 beers, and tempting *tapas* (Spanish "appetizers," $4-8). Open M-Th and Su 11:30am-3:30pm and 5:30-10pm, F-Sa 11:30am-3:30pm and 5:30-11pm.

Rongovian Embassy to the USA ("The Rongo") (387-3334), Rte. 96 on the main strip in Trumansburg about 10 mi. from Ithaca—worth the drive. Seek asylum in amazing Mexican entrees at this classic restaurant/bar, and plot a trip to "Beefree" or "Nearvarna"on their huge wall map; Molé Poblano Enchiladas $10. Mug of beer $2. Restaurant open Tu-Su 5-10pm; bar Tu-Su 4pm-1am. Bands W-Sa; cover $5.

Station Restaurant, 806 Taughannock Blvd. (272-2609) at W. Buffalo St., in a plush, renovated train station, registered as a National Historical Landmark. Pasta, poultry, and seafood specials $10-14. Open M-Sa 4-9:30pm, Su noon-8:30pm.

The area near Cornell called **Collegetown,** centering on College Ave., harbors student hangouts and access to a romantic path along the gorge. A smoky, red-walled cafe, **Stella's,** 403 College Ave. (277-8731), wears its pretension well. The $2 Italian soda with heavy cream (open daily 7:30am-1:30am), and a few martinis might encourage you to cut a rug at Stella's adjoining blue-walled jazz bar (open daily 6:30pm-1:30am). Live bands skulk at **The Haunt,** 114 W. Green St. (275-3447).

SIGHTS AND ENTERTAINMENT

Ithaca

Cornell University, youngest of the Ivy League schools, sits on a *steep* hill in downtown Ithaca between two tremendous gorges. The **Information and Referral Center** (254-4636) in the Day Hall Lobby has info on campus sights and activities. *(Open M-Sa 8am-5pm. Tours Apr.-Nov. M-F 9, 11am, 1, and 3pm, Sa 9am and 1pm, Su 1pm; Dec.-Mar. daily 1pm.)* The strangely pleasing cement edifice rising from the top of the hill—designed by I.M. Pei and dubbed "the world's biggest sewing machine" by locals, houses Cornell's **Herbert F. Johnson Museum of Art** (255-6464), at the corner of University and Central. *(Open Tu-Su 10am-5pm. Free.)* The small collection of European and American painting and sculpture includes works by Giacometti, Matisse, O'Keeffe, de Kooning, Hopper, and Benton; the rooftop sculpture garden has a magnificent view of Ithaca. At stunning **Cornell Plantations** (255-3020), a series of botanical gardens surround Cornell's great geological wonders (open daily sunrise to sunset; free). Adventurous hikes into the Cornell gorge include the 1½ mi. **Founder's Loop,** which takes only 1hr. and is well worth the time. The free and useful *Passport to the Trails of Tompkins County,* available from the Visitor's Bureau, is a portable and comprehensive guide with maps for trekking in and around Ithaca.

Discriminating moviegoers should scope out the **Cornell Cinema,** 104 Willard Straight Hall (255-3522), at the College; its programming and prices will thrill even the most jaded art-house movie junkie (tickets $4.50; students, seniors and under 12 $4). The **Historic State Theatre,** 109 W. State St. (273-1037), hosts dance and other live performances as well as movies in a vintage 1928 faux Spanish castle/movie palace. *(Monthly classic film festivals $2-4.)* The architect, legend has it, went insane shortly after the completion of its construction.

Finger Lakes

The fertile soil of the Finger Lakes area has made this region the heart of New York's wine industry. The three designated **wine trails** provide opportunities for wine tasting and vineyard touring; locals say that the fall harvest is the best time to visit. The 10 vineyards closest to Ithaca lie on the **Cayuga Trail,** with most located along Rte. 89 between Seneca Falls and Ithaca; call 800-684-5217 for info. The Finger Lakes Association (see **Practical Information,** above) has info on the **Seneca Lake Trail,** 21 wineries split into those on the east side of the lake (Rte. 414) and those on the west side (Rte. 14), and the **Keuka Trail,** seven wineries along Rte. 54 and Rte. 76. Some wineries offer free picnic facilities and free tours, and all give free tastings, though some require purchase of a glass ($2). Family-operated **Americana Vineyards Winery,**

4367 East Covert Rd. (387-6801), Interlaken, ferments 2 mi. from Trumansburg with free tastings and $6-12 bottles. *(Open Mar.-Dec. M-Sa 10am-5pm, Su noon-5pm; Jan.-Feb. call for hrs.)* If you're driving, take Rte. 96 or 89 north of Trumansburg to E. Covert Rd.

Seneca Falls saw the birth of the women's rights movement at the 1848 Seneca Falls Convention. Elizabeth Cady Stanton, and other leading suffragists, organized the meeting of those seeking the vote. Today, the **Women's Rights National Historical Park** commemorates their efforts. The **visitors center,** 136 Fall St. (315-568-2991), has the low down on tours of Stanton's home at 32 Washington St. *(Open May-Oct. daily 9am-5pm; Nov.-Apr. W-Sa 10am-4pm, Su noon-4pm. Exhibits $2, with tour $3.)* The **National Women's Hall of Fame,** 76 Fall St. (315-568-2936), commemorates outstanding U.S. women with photographs and biographies. *(Open May-Oct. M-Sa 9:30am-5pm, Su noon-4pm; Nov.-Apr. W-Sa 10am-4pm, Su noon-4pm. $3, students and seniors $1.50.)*

The town of **Corning,** home to the Corning Glass Works, bends light 40 mi. outside Ithaca on Rte. 17 W off Rte. 13 S. Glassworkers blow at the **Corning Museum of Glass,** 151 Centerway (607-974-8271), which chronicles the 3500-year history of glass-making with over 20,000 pieces—sopranos beware! *(Open daily 9am-8pm; Sept.-June 9am-5pm. $6, seniors $5, ages 6-17 $4, families $16.)* The nearby **Rockwell Museum,** 111 Cedar St. (607-937-5386), off Rte. 17, shows pieces by Frederick Carder (founder of the Steuben Glass Work), an excellent collection of American Western art, and an array of antique toys and guns. *(Open M-Sa 9am-5pm, Su noon-5pm; $5, seniors $4.50, ages 6-17 $2.50, families $12.50.)*

■ Buffalo

Girded by the steel and concrete of shoreside elevated highways, Buffalo is a big, furry, overgrown border town in a high-rise disguise. Fiery chicken wings and electric blues bands burn off the haze of the Bills' four recent Super Bowl defeats and the eternal minor league status of Bison baseball. From the downtown skyline to the small-scale pastel charm of historic Allentown, Buffalo trades the cosmopolitan for honest, modern Americana.

PRACTICAL INFORMATION Greyhound (855-7531 or 800-231-2222; station open 24hr.) and **Adirondack Trailways** (852-1750) run buses from 181 Ellicott St. at N. Division St. to cities throughout the northeast. Buses journey to New York (14 per day, 8½hr., $47); Boston (11½hr. 8 per day, $52); Niagara Falls, ON (1hr., 11 per day, $4.50); and Toronto (2½hr., 8 per day, $20). **Amtrak** (856-2075 or 800-872-7245; office open M-F 7am-3:30pm) leaves from 75 Exchange St., at Washington St. for New York (8hr., 2-3 per day, $54) and Toronto (2hr., 1 per day, $32). The **Niagara Frontier Transit Authority (NFTA)** (855-7211 or 283-9319) offers bus and rail service throughout the city (fare $1.25), as well as free rides on the Main St. Metrorail, and trips to Niagara Falls. (Bus #40 "Grand Island" leaves from 181 Ellicott St., 13 per day, fare $1.85, seniors and ages 5-11 55¢.) Buffalo's **visitors center,** 617 Main St. (852-2356 or 800-BUFFALO/283-3256), in the Theater District, has free copies of the *Buffalo Visitors Guide,* which includes a map of the city (open M-Tu 9am-5pm, W-F 10am-6pm, Sa-Su 10am-4pm). In summer, ask about their weekly architectural walking tours of downtown Buffalo ($5). **Post Office:** 701 Washington St. (856-4604; open M-F 8:30am-5:30pm, Sa 8:30am-1pm). **ZIP code:** 14203. **Area code:** 716.

ACCOMMODATIONS AND CAMPGROUNDS The **Buffalo Hostel (HI-AYH),** 667 Main St. (852-5222), houses 48 beds on spotless floors. No smoking, drinking, or drunkenness is tolerated, and there's an 11pm curfew. ($15, nonmembers $18; security deposit $20. Reception daily 8-11am and 3-11pm. Free access to microwave, pool table, weights, laundry facilities, and linen.) Camping is scarce in Buffalo, but **Four Mile Creek State Park** (745-3802), on Robert Moses Pkwy, is available. in the Ft. Niagara Area about 15 mi. from Niagara Falls, in Youngstown. Affordable camping may be found in sparsely wooded sites at the edge of Lake Ontario. Visitors may also hike and fish on the premises. (Showers. Sites off the lake $13, with electricity $15; sites on the lake $15/$17. Reserve in advance.) Other lodging and camping options can be found on the Canadian side of the border (see **Niagara Falls,** below).

MID-ATLANTIC

FOOD AND NIGHTLIFE Since a fateful Friday night in 1963, the **Anchor Bar,** 1047 Main St. (886-8920), has been known as the home of the original Buffalo Wing, served crispy in six degrees of spiciness (10 wings $5.65, 20 wings $8.25; open Su-Th 11am-11pm, F-Sa 11am-1am). After a Bisons or Sabres game, locals make for the **Pearl Street Grill & Brewery,** 36 Pearl St. (856-2337). A distillery diagram charts the history of your drink as you down the custom-brewed Lake Effect Pale Ale ($3, during happy hour 4-7pm $2) and under a system of belt-operated ceiling fans. (Open daily 11am-2am.) Among the cute pastel boxes of Allentown, the gothic facade of **Gabriel's Gate,** 145 Allen St. (886-0602), doesn't frighten away its loyal lunch crowd, who return to feast on taco salads ($5.25) or garden souvlaki ($5.25) under skylights and stuffed mooseheads (open daily 11:30am-1am).

The city's surprisingly lively nightlife centers around Chippewa and **Franklin St.,** and on **Elmwood Ave.** For a complete listing of events, find a copy of the weekly *Buffalo Beat.* The **Calumet Arts Cafe,** 56 W. Chippewa St. (855-2220), plays live jazz and blues on the weekends in a funky atmosphere (beer $3.25 per pint; open Tu-W 5:30-10pm, Th-Sa 5:30pm-4am). **City SPoT** (854-7768), on the corner of Delaware St. and Chippewa St., keeps the locals wired late into the evening with an infinite array of coffee combo possibilities ($1-3; open Su-Tu 7:30am-11pm, W-Th 7:30am-midnight, F-Sa 7:30am-2am).

SIGHTS AND ENTERTAINMENT At the **Naval and Military Park,** (847-1773) on Lake Erie at the foot of Pearl and Main St., visitors can climb aboard a guided missile cruiser, a destroyer, and a WWII submarine. *(Open daily Apr.-Oct. 10am-5pm; Nov. Sa-Su 10am-4pm. $6, seniors and ages 6-16 $3.50.)*

The **Albright Knox Art Gallery,** 1285 Elmwood Ave. (882-8700), accessible by the bus #32 "Niagara," houses over 6000 pieces, including works by Van Gogh, Matisse, Picasso, de Kooning, Renoir, and Gaugin. *(Open Tu-Sa 11am-5pm, Su noon-5pm. $4, seniors $3, families $4; free Sa 11am-1pm.)* An 1881 floating marine bicycle swims among the 300-piece collection at the **Pedaling History Bicycle Museum,** 3943 N. Buffalo Rd. (662-3853), Rte. 240/277 in Orchard Park, 10 mi. southeast of Buffalo. *(Open M-Sa 11am-5pm, Su 1:30-5pm; mid-Jan. to Mar. M and F-Sa 11am-5pm, Su 1:30-5pm. $4.50, seniors $4, ages 7-15 $2.50, families $12.50.)*

Locals live and die by their sports teams. In winter, **Rich Stadium** (649-0015), in Orchard Park, houses the four-time Super Bowl loser **Buffalo Bills.** The **Marine Midland Arena,** 1 Main St., hosts hockey's **Buffalo Sabres** (855-4000) and lacrosse's **Buffalo Bandits** (855-4100). The summer brings family fun and excitement with **Buffalo Bison** baseball (846-2000) at **North AmeriCare Park,** 275 Washington St. Mascots hand out treats, while fans enjoy fireworks—occasionally there's some baseball, too.

■ Niagara Falls

One of the seven natural wonders of the world, Niagara Falls also claims the title of one of the world's largest sources of hydro-electric power. Admired not only for their beauty, the Falls have attracted thrill-seeking barrel-riders since 1901, when 63-year-old Annie Taylor successfully completed the drop. Modern day adventurers beware—heavy fines are levied for barrel attempts, and failures are fatal. Outlet shopping malls, cheap motels, neon lights, and t-shirt shops cram the streets catering to hordes of tourists.

ORIENTATION AND PRACTICAL INFORMATION

Niagara Falls lies in both the U.S. and Ontario (ON), Canada; addresses given here are in NY, unless otherwise noted. Take **U.S. 190** to the Robert Moses Pkwy., or else skirt the tolls (but suffer traffic) by taking Exit 3 to Rte. 62. In town, Niagara St. is the main east-west artery, ending in the west at **Rainbow Bridge,** which crosses to Canada (pedestrian crossings 25¢, cars $2.50). Numbered north-south streets increase towards the east. Outside of town, stores, restaurants, and motels line **Rte. 62 (Nia-**

gara Falls Blvd.). Customs procedures are inevitable when crossing between countries. Once you cross the bridge, currency changes. Although many places accept both currencies, the low exchange rates make it wise to exchange money at a bank before an extended visit.

Trains: Amtrak (285-4224 or 800-872-7245), at 27th and Lockport St. 1 block east of Hyde Park Blvd. Take bus #52 to Falls/Downtown. To New York City ($54) and Toronto ($16). Open Th-M 7am-11:30pm, Tu-W 7am-3pm.

Buses: Niagara Falls Bus Terminal (282-1331), 4th and Niagara St., sells **Greyhound** and **Trailways** tickets for use in Buffalo. Open M-F 8am-4pm. To get a bus in Buffalo, take a 1hr. trip on bus #40 from the Niagara Falls bus terminal to the **Buffalo Transportation Center,** 181 Ellicott St. (800-231-2222; see Buffalo **Practical Information,** p. 179).

Public Transportation: Niagara Frontier Metro Transit System, 343 4th St. (285-9319), provides local city transit. Fare $1.25. **ITA Buffalo Shuttle** (800-551-9369) has service from Niagara Falls info center and major hotels to Buffalo Airport ($18).

Taxis: Rainbow Taxicab, 282-3221. **United Cab,** 285-9331. Both charge $1.50 for the 1st ½-mi., $1.50 per additional mi. A taxi from Buffalo Airport to Niagara costs $35. For a cab on the Canadian side, call 905-357-4000 for **Niagra Falls Taxi.**

Visitor Info: Orin Lehman Visitors Center (278-1796), in front of the Falls' observation deck; the entrance is marked by a garden. Open daily 8am-10:15pm; Oct. to mid-Nov. 8am-8pm; mid-Nov. to Dec. 8am-10pm; Dec.-Apr. 8am-6:30pm. An **info center** (284-2000) adjoins the bus station on 4th and Niagara St., a 10min. walk from the Falls. Open daily 8am-7pm; mid-Sept. to mid-May 9am-5pm. **Niagara Falls Canada Visitor and Convention Bureau,** 5515 Stanley Ave. ON L2G 3L1 (905-356-6061), Niagara Falls, has info on the Canadian side. Open daily 8am-8pm; off-season 8am-5pm. On the Canadian side, tune in to 91.9FM CFL2 for tourist info on the air.

Post Office: 615 Main St. (285-7561). Open M-F 7:30am-5pm, Sa 9am-2pm. **ZIP code:** 14302. **Area code:** 716 (NY), 905 (ON). In text, 716 unless otherwise noted.

ACCOMMODATIONS AND CAMPGROUNDS

Cheap motels (from $25) advertising free wedding certificates line **Lundy's Lane** on the Canadian side and **Rte. 62** on the American side, while many moderately priced B&Bs overlook the gorge on **River Rd.** between the Rainbow Bridge and the Whirlpool Bridge on the Canadian side. Reservations are recommended at all accommodations, especially in summer.

Niagara Falls International Hostel (HI-C), 4549 Cataract Ave. (905-357-0770 or 888-749-0058), Niagara Falls, ON, just off Bridge St. An excellent hostel near the falls, about 2 blocks from the bus station and VIA Rail. More than 70 beds; can be cramped when full. Family rooms, laundry facilities, and parking available. Bike rental CDN$19 per day. CDN$17, nonmembers CDN$21. Linen CDN$1. Check-out 10am. Reception 8am-midnight; Oct.-Mar. 8am-10pm.

Niagara Falls International Hostel (HI-AYH), 1101 Ferry Ave. (282-3700). From bus station, walk east on Niagara St., turn left on Memorial Pkwy.; the hostel is at the corner of Ferry Ave. *From the falls, avoid walking alone on Ferry at night.* 44 beds, kitchen, TV lounge, limited parking. Family rooms available. $13, nonmembers $16. Required sleepsack $1.50. Check-in 7:30-9:30am and 4-11pm. Lockout 9:30am-4pm. Curfew 11:30pm; lights out midnight. Open late Jan. to mid-Dec.

Olde Niagara House, 610 4th St. (285-9408). A country B&B just 4 blocks from the falls. Free pickup at the Amtrak or bus station. Dorms $18-20 per person. Rooms with breakfast $45-55; in winter $35-45; student singles $25-45/$20-25.

All Tucked Inn, 574 3rd St. (282-0919 or 800-797-0919). Nice clean rooms close to the attractions. Singles from $39; doubles from $49. Discounts with *Let's Go.* Reservations recommended.

YMCA, 1317 Portage Rd. (285-8491), a 20min. walk from the Falls; at night take bus #54 from Main St. 58 beds. Fee includes full use of YMCA facilities; no laundry. Dorm rooms for men only; singles $25. Key deposit $10. Men and women can sleep on mats in the gym, $15. Check-in 24hr.

Niagara Glen-View Tent & Trailer Park, 3950 Victoria Ave. (800-263-2570), Niagara Falls, ON. The closest sites to the Falls, but bare and unwooded. A hiking trail sits across the street. Ice, showers, laundry facilities, pool. Shuttle from driveway to the bottom of Clifton Hill in summer every 30min. 8:45am-2am. CDN$30, full hookup CDN$33. Office open daily 8am-11pm. Park open May to mid-Oct.

FOOD

The Press Box Bar, 324 Niagara St. (284-5447), between 3rd and 4th St., lets patrons leave their mark by adding a dollar bill to the several thousand taped to the wall; every winter the owner donates them to a cancer-fighting charity. From Monday to Wednesday, the spaghetti special ($1, meatballs 25¢ each) looks nice; otherwise, burgers ($1.85) and the trademark porterhouse steak ($8.75) are good bets (open M-Sa 8am-2am, Su 8am-midnight). Locals scratch their lottery tickets at **Sinatra's Sunrise Diner,** 829 Main St. (284-0959). You're golden with two eggs and toast for $1.20 or sandwiches for $2-4. (Open M-Th and Sa 7am-8pm, F 7am-9pm, Su 7am-3pm.) More exotic fare and vegetarian options (*biryani* $10) can be found at **Sardar Sahib,** 626 Niagara St. (282-0444; open daily 11:30am-midnight).

For a bite on the Canadian side, the many restaurants on **Victoria Ave.** by Clifton Hill delight fans of inexpensive hearty Italian cooking. Across the whirlpool bridge around the corner from the hostel, **Simon's Restaurant,** 4116 Bridge St. (905-356-5310), Niagara Falls, ON, serves big breakfasts with giant homemade muffins (CDN74¢) and hearty diner dinners. Simon's is the oldest restaurant in Niagara Falls. (Open M-Sa 5:30am-9pm, Su 5:30am-3pm.) Farther inland, locals chow on pancakes, hot sandwiches, and full-meal specials (CDN$4-7) at **Basell's Restaurant,** 4880 Victoria Ave. (905-356-5310), Niagara Falls, ON (open daily 6am-11pm).

SIGHTS AND ENTERTAINMENT

Although tourist snares abound on both sides, they're less rampant on the American shore. Official sights give more for your money. From late November to late January, Niagara Falls holds the annual **Festival of Lights** (905-374-1616); brilliant bulbs line the trees and create animated outdoor scenes. Live concerts are held throughout, but New Year's Eve is the big party. The illumination of the falls caps the spectacle.

American Side

Niagara Wonders (278-1792), a 20min. movie on the Falls, plays in the info center. *(Shows daily on the hr. 10am-8pm; in fall W-Su 10am-6pm; in spring daily 10am-6pm. $2, ages 6-12 $1.)* The **Maid of the Mist Tour** (284-8897) consists of a 30min. boat ride to the foot of both falls; don't bring anything that isn't waterproof. *(Tours in summer every 15min. M-Th 10am-5pm, F-Su 10am-6pm. $8 plus 50¢ elevator fee, ages 6-12 $4.50.)* The **Caves of the Wind Tour** (278-1730) outfits visitors with yellow raincoats for a thrilling, body-soaking trek to the base of the Bridal Veil Falls, including an optional walk to Hurricane Deck, as close to the falls as you'll get. *(Open May to mid-Oct.; hrs. vary depending on season and weather conditions. Trips leave continuously. $5.50, ages 6-12 $5.)*

The **Master Pass** (278-1796), available at the park's visitors center ($20, ages 6-12 $15), covers admission to the theater, Maid of the Mist, **Schoellkopf's Geological Museum** (278-1780) in Prospect Park, the **Aquarium** (701 Whirlpool St., 285-3575), and the **Viewmobile** (278-1730), a tram-guided tour of the park. *(Museum open daily 9am-7pm; early Sept.-Oct. 10am-5pm; Nov. to late May Th-Su 10am-5pm. $1. Aquarium open daily 9am-5pm; early Sept. to late May 9am-7pm. $6.50, ages 4-12 $4.50. Viewmobile runs every 15min. daily 10am-8pm; in winter 10am-5:30pm. $4.50, children $3.50.)*

Whirlpool State Park, Robert Moses Pkwy./Rte. 104, contains the Niagara Gorge and the rock where spiritual guru Jason Sperry's name is immortalized. Continuing north, the **Niagara Power Project,** 5777 Lewiston Rd. (285-3211), features interactive demonstrations, short videos, and displays on energy, hydropower, and local history. *(Open daily 9am-5pm. Free.)* While there, you can cast your line off the fishing platform to reel in salmon, trout, or bass. Further north on Lewiston, the 200-acre state **Artpark**

(800-659-PARK/7275), at the foot of 4th St., focuses on visual and performing arts, with a variety of classes and demonstrations. The theater presents opera, pops concerts, and jazz festivals. *(Tickets $15-30; shows May-Oct.; call for schedule. Box office open M-F 10am-6pm, Sa 10am-4pm, Su noon-5pm.)* **Old Fort Niagara** (745-7611), a French castle built in 1726, guards the entrance to the Niagara River; follow Robert Moses Pkwy. north from Niagara Falls. *(Open daily 9am-6:30pm; early Sept.-Dec. and Jan.-May 9am-4:30pm. $6.75, seniors $5.50, ages 6-12 $4.50.)*

Canadian Side

On the Canadian side of Niagara Falls (across Rainbow Bridge), **Queen Victoria Park** provides the best view of Horseshoe Falls. The falls are illuminated for 3hr. every night, starting 1hr. after sunset. Parking in the Queen Victoria is expensive (CDN$8). **Park 'N' Ride** is a better deal, offering parking at Rapids View, across from Marineland at the south end of Niagara Pkwy., and **People Movers** (357-9340). *(Late Apr. to mid-June Su-Th 10am-6pm, F-Sa 10am-10pm; mid-June to Aug. daily 9am-11pm; Sept. to mid-Oct. Su-Th 10am-6pm, F-Sa 10am-10pm. CDN$4, children CDN$2.)* The buses will take you through the 19 mi. area on the Canadian side of the Falls, stopping at points of interest along the way. **Skylon Tower**, 5200 Robinson St. (356-2651), has the highest view of the falls at 775 ft.; on a clear day, you can see as far as Toronto (CDN$8, seniors CDN$6, children CDN$4). Its 552 ft. **Observation Deck** offers an unhindered view of the falls (open daily 8am-11pm; in winter hrs. change monthly). The **Explorer's Passport** (CDN$14, children CDN$7) includes passage to **Journey Behind the Falls** (354-1551), a gripping tour behind the rushing waters of Horseshoe Falls (CDN$6, children CDN$3); **Great Gorge Adventure** (374-1221), a descent into the Niagara River Rapids (open late Apr. to late Oct.; hrs. vary; CDN$4.75, children CDN$2.40); and the **Spanish Aero Car** (354-5711), an aerial cable ride over the turbulent whirlpool waters (open Mar.-Oct.; hrs. *really* vary; CDN$5, children CDN$2.50).

The **Niagara Falls Brewing Company,** 6863 Lundy's Ln. (374-1166), hosts free touring and tasting (tours Sa 1pm; open M-Sa 10am-5pm, Su 10am-1pm). Bikers, rollerbladers, and leisurely walkers enjoy the 32km **Niagara River Recreation Trail,** which runs from Ft. Erie to Ft. George and passes many interesting historical sights.

For the happy few who realize that tourist commercialism can be as much a thing of beauty as any natural wonder, Niagara Falls offers the delightfully tasteless **Clifton Hill,** a collection of wax museums, funhouses, and overpriced shows. One jewel in this tourist strip's crown, **Ripley's Believe It or Not Museum,** 4960 Clifton Hill (356-2238), displays wonders like wax models of unicorn men and a Jivaro shrunken head from Ecuador. *(Open daily 9am-1am; off-season 10am-10pm. CDN$7, seniors CDN$5, ages 6-12 CDN$4.)* Unfortunately, the authentic New Guinea Penis Guard, used to protect private property from hungry mosquitoes, is not for sale.

NORTHERN NEW YORK

■ The Adirondacks

In 1892, the New York State legislature demonstrated uncommon foresight in establishing the **Adirondacks State Park**—the largest U.S. park outside Alaska and one of the few places left where hikers can spend days without seeing another soul. In recent years, unfortunately, pollution and development have left a harsh imprint; acid rain has damaged the tree and fish populations, especially in the fragile high-altitude environments, and tourist meccas like Lake George have continued to expand rapidly. Despite these urban intrusions, much of the area retains the beauty visitors have enjoyed for over a century.

Of the six million acres in the Adirondacks Park, 40% are open to the public, offering an unsurpassed range of outdoor activities. Whether for hiking, snow-shoeing, or cross-country skiing, the 2000 mi. of trails that traverse the forest provide spectacular mountain scenery. Canoers paddle through an interlocking network of lakes and streams, while mountain climbers conquer **Mt. Marcy,** the state's highest peak (5344 ft.), and skiers take advantage of a dozen well-known alpine centers. **Lake Placid** hosted the winter Olympics in 1932 and 1980, and it frequently welcomes national and international sports competitions. **Tupper Lake** and Lake George have carnivals every January and February; Tupper also hosts the **Tin Man Triathlon** in mid-July. In September, the hot air balloons of the **Adirondack Balloon Festival** paint the sky over Glens Falls.

PRACTICAL INFORMATION The **Adirondack Mountain Club (ADK)** is the best source of info on hiking and other outdoor activities in the region. In its 77th year, the ADK has over 23,000 members. Their offices are located at 814 Goggins Rd., Lake George 12845 (668-4447; open M-Sa 8:30am-5pm; Jan.-Apr. M-F 8:30am-4:30pm), and at Adirondack Loj Rd., P.O. Box 867, Lake Placid 12946 (523-3441; open Sa-Th 8am-8pm, F 8am-10pm). Call the Lake Placid number for the scoop on outdoor skills classes such as canoeing, rock climbing, whitewater kayaking, and wilderness medicine. For the latest backcountry info, visit ADK's **High Peaks Information Center,** 3 mi. south of Lake Placid on Rte. 73, then 5 mi. down Adirondak Loj Rd. The center also has washrooms (open daily 8am-8pm) and sells basic outdoor equipment, trail snacks, and the club's extremely helpful guides to the mountains for $18 (store open Sa-Su 8am-noon and 1-4pm). Rock climbers should consult the experienced staff at the **Mountaineer** (576-2281), in Keene Valley, between I-87 and Lake Placid on Rte. 73. Snowshoes rent for $16 per day; ice-climbing equipment (plastic boots and crampons) rent for $20 per day. (Open M-Th 9am-5:30pm, F 9am-7pm, Sa 8am-5:30pm, Su 9am-5:30pm; off-season M-F 9am-5:30pm, Sa 8am-5:30pm, Su 10am-5:30pm.) The ADK and the Mountaineer can provide basic info on the conditions and concerns of backwoods travel.

Adirondacks Trailways (800-858-8555) serves the Adirondacks with frequent stops along I-87. From Albany, buses go to Lake Placid, Tupper Lake, and Lake George. From the Lake George bus stop at Capris Pizza, 221 Canada St., buses set out for Lake Placid (2 per day, $13.30); Albany (4 per day, $10); and New York City (5 per day, $37.45). **Area code:** 518.

ACCOMMODATIONS AND CAMPGROUNDS Two lodges near Lake Placid are also run by the ADK. The **Adirondak Loj** (523-3441), 8 mi. east of Lake Placid off Rte. 73, fills a beautiful log cabin on Heart Lake with comfortable bunk facilities and a family atmosphere. Guests can swim, fish, and canoe on the premises (canoe or boat rental $5 per hr., guests $3), and, in winter, explore the wilderness trails on rented snowshoes for $10 per day, or cross-country ski for $20 per day. (B&B Feb., July-Aug., and Sa-Su $30, add $11.50 for dinner, linen included. Lodging and meals for 3 days midweek $104. Tent sites for 2 $16; in winter $8; $2 per additional person. Lean-tos for 2 $19/$12/$2.50.) Call 3 months ahead for weekends and peak holiday seasons. For an even better mix of rustic comfort and wilderness experience, hike 3½ mi. to the **John's Brook Lodge** from the closest trailhead, in Keene Valley (call the Adirondak Loj for reservations); from Lake Placid, follow Rte. 73 15 mi. through Keene to Keene Valley and turn right at the Ausable Inn. The hike runs slightly uphill, but the meal which awaits you justifies the effort. A great place to meet friendly New Yorkers, John's Brook is no secret; beds fill completely on weekends. Make reservations 1 day in advance for dinner, longer for a weekend. Bring sheets or a sleeping bag. (B&B Feb. and July to early Sept. $27, add $11.50 for dinner. Rest of the year unstaffed: lean-tos for 2 $12, bunks $13. Rates lower for ADK members. Full kitchen access.)

If ADK facilities are too pricey, try the **High Peaks Base Camp,** P.O. Box 91, Upper Jay 12987 (946-2133), a charming restaurant/lodge/campground just a 20min. drive from Lake Placid; take Rte. 86 E to Wilmington, turn right on Fox Farm Rd. (just before the Hungry Trout Tackle Shop), then go right 2½ mi. on Springfield Rd. You'll find a bed for the night (M-Th $15, F-Su $18) and a huge breakfast in the morning. Sometimes rides can be arranged from Keene; call ahead. (Free hot showers. Tent sites $5; $3 per additional person. Cabins for 4 $30, private rooms $40.) **Free camping** is easy to come by. Inquire about the location of free trailside shelters before you plan a hike in the forest. Better still, camp for free anywhere on public land in the **backcountry** as long as you are at least 150 ft. away from a trail, road, water source, or campground and below 4000 ft. in altitude. The State Office of Parks and Recreation (see New York **Practical Information,** p. 128) has more details.

■ Lake Placid

Back in 1850, Melvil Dewey, inventor of the Dewey Decimal Library Cataloging system, was the first person to promote Lake Placid, as a summer resort. After being chosen to host the Olympic Winter Games in both 1932 and 1980, Lake Placid has had famous people wandering through for the past 150 years. World-class athletes train year-round in the town's extensive sporting facilities, lending an international flavor which distinguishes Lake Placid from its Adirondack neighbors. The setting of the Adirondack High Peaks Region attracts droves of hikers and backpackers each year, although many otherwise-avid campers have ended up pitching their tents in a motel room—in the winter, temperatures can dip down to -40° F.

PRACTICAL INFORMATION Lake Placid sits at the intersection of Rte. 86 and 73. The town's Olympic past defines the Lake Placid of today; the **Olympic Regional Development Authority,** 216 Main St., Olympic Center (523-1655 or 800-462-6236), operates the sporting facilities (open M-F 8:30am-4pm). Info on food, lodging, and area attractions can be obtained from the **Lake Placid-Essex County Visitors Bureau** (523-2445; http://www.lakeplacid.com), also in the Olympic Center (open daily 9am-5pm; in winter closed Su). **Adirondack Trailways** (800-225-6815 for bus info) stops at Lake Placid Video, 324 Main St., and has extensive service in the area. Destinations include New York City (2 per day, $50.70) and Lake George ($13.30). For **weather info,** call 523-1363 or 523-3518. Lake Placid's **post office:** 201 Main St. (523-3071; open M-F 8:30am-5pm, Sa 8:30am-2pm). **ZIP code:** 12946. **Area code:** 518.

ACCOMMODATIONS, CAMPGROUNDS, AND FOOD As long as you avoid the resorts on the west end of town, both lodgings and food can be had cheaply in Lake Placid. Four miles from town, the **White Sled** (523-9314), on Rte. 73 between the Sports Complex at Mt. Hoevenberg and the ski jumps, may be the best bargain around—for $17, the friendly proprietors will show you to a comfortable, clean bed in the bunkhouse, which includes a full kitchen, a spacious living room with TV, and a quiet setting to collect your thoughts. If you're lucky, the owner may bake the house specialty, blueberry buckle. (Private rooms $38-58; prices lower mid-week.) If you want to stay downtown, the **High Peaks Hostel,** 337½ Main St. (523-3764), can put you up in a bunk for $16 per night (private rooms $42, linen $2). **Meadowbrook State Park** (891-4351), 5 mi. west on Rte. 86 in Ray Brook, and **Wilmington Notch State Campground** (946-7172), off Rte. 86 E between Wilmington and Lake Placid, have the area's nearest campsites. Both offer shady, wooded sites without hookups which accommodate two tents. ($11, $9 per additional night.)

In Lake Placid Village, **Main St.** offers reasonably priced pickings to suit any palate. The lunch buffet (M-Sa noon-2pm) at the **Hilton Hotel,** 1 Mirror Lake Dr. (523-4411), includes a sandwich and all-you-can-eat soup and salad ($5.25). At the **Black Bear Restaurant,** 157 Main St. (523-9886), enjoy a $6 lunch or $3-5 breakfast special and a $2.75 Saranac lager (the Adirondacks's own beer) in the company of stuffed animals (open Su-Th 6am-10:30pm, F-Sa 24hr.). **The Cottage,** 5

Mirror Lake Dr. (523-9845), serves up sandwiches and salads ($5.50-8.25), and Lake Placid's best views of Mirror Lake, where the U.S. canoe and kayaking teams practice (open daily 11:30am-10pm; bar open 11:30am-1am). **Mud Puddles,** 3 School St. (523-4446), below the speed skating rink, is a splash with the pop music crowd (open daily 8am-3am; M-F no cover, Sa-Su $3).

SIGHTS The **Olympic Center** in downtown Lake Placid houses the 1932 and 1980 hockey arenas, along with the **Winter Olympic Museum** (open daily 10am-5pm; $3, seniors $2, children $1). Purchase tickets for a guided tour of the center at the museum desk. You can't miss the 90 and 120m runs of the Olympic ski jumps which, along with the **Kodak Sports Park,** make up the **Olympic Jumping Complex,** just outside of town on Rte. 73. The $7-10 admission includes a chairlift and elevator ride to the top of the towers, where you can catch jumpers flipping and sailing into a swimming pool from June to mid-October (open daily 9am-4pm; children and seniors $4). Four miles further along Rte. 73, the **Olympic Sports Complex** (523-4436) at Mt. Van Hoevenberg has a summer trolley that coasts to the top of the bobsled run ($4, seniors and children $3), and wheeled bobsled rides for $20. *(Open mid-June to mid-Oct. 10am-4pm. Wheelchair access.)* In winter, you can bobsled down the Olympic run ($30). Contact the Olympic Regional Development Authority (see above) for a tour of the facilities. Popular **Tour Boat Cruises** (523-9704) travel 16 narrated mi. across beautiful Lake Placid (adults $6.75, seniors $5.75, children $4.75), while those with a car can drive 8 mi. up White Face Mountain on **Veterans Memorial Hwy.** (car and driver $8). At the top, an elevator takes you to a 360° scenic overlook.

The west branch of the **Ausable River,** just east of Lake Placid, lures anglers to its shores. **Fishing licenses** (1-day $11, 5-day $20, season $35; resident 3-day $6, season $14) are sold at **Town Hall,** 301 Main St. (523-2162), or **Jones Outfitters,** 37 Main St. (523-3468). Jones rents the necessary equipment as well, including rod, reel, line, tackle, and bait. *(Package $15 per day, fly-fishing outfit $25 per day. Open June-Sept. M-Sa 9am-6pm, Su 10am-5pm; Oct.-May Su-F 10am-5pm, Sa 9am-6pm.)* If you'd like to join the fish rather than beat them, Jones also rents canoes, kayaks, and rowboats ($13 per hr., $35 per day). The **Fishing Hotline** (891-5413) plays an in-depth recording with straight talk on fishing hotspots. For those who prefer land to water, the **Lake Placid Horse Shows** ride into town for 2 weeks in late June and early July at the equestrian center, which can be found just entering town on Rte. 73.

■ Thousand Island Seaway

The Thousand Island region of St. Lawrence Seaway spans 100 mi. from the mouth of Lake Ontario to the first of the many locks on the St. Lawrence River. Surveys conducted by the American and Canadian governments have determined that there are over 1700 islands in the seaway, with the requirements being at least one square foot of land above water surface year-round and at least one tree. These islands and countless rocky shoals make navigation tricky in the area. Locals divide people into two groups: those who *have* hit a shoal and those who *will* hit a shoal. But don't let this dire prediction deter you; not only is the Thousand Island region a fisherman's paradise, with some of the world's best bass and muskie catch, it's the only area in the nation with a salad dressing named after it.

PRACTICAL INFORMATION The Thousand Island region hugs the coast just 2hr. from Syracuse by way of I-81 N. **Clayton, Alexandria Bay** ("Alex Bay" to locals), and **Cape Vincent** are the main cities in the area. For Welleslet Island, Alexandria Bay, and the eastern 500 islands, stay on I-81 until you reach Rte. 12 E. For Clayton and points west, take Exit 47 and follow Rte. 12 until you reach Rte. 12 E. Write or visit the **Clayton Chamber of Commerce,** 510 Riverside Dr., Clayton 13624 (686-3771), for the free *Clayton Vacation Guide* and *Thousand Islands Seaway Region Travel Guide* (open daily 9am-4pm; mid-Sept. to mid-June M-F 9am-4pm). The **Alexandria Bay Chamber of Commerce,** 24 Market St., Alexandria Bay 13607 (482-9531), is just off James St. (Open M 8:30am-5pm, Tu-W 8:30am-4:30pm, Th-Sa 8:30am-9pm, Su 9am-5pm; mid-Oct. to mid-May M-F 8:30am-4:30pm.) The **Cape Vincent Chamber of Commerce** (654-2481) welcomes visitors at 175 N. James St., by the ferry landing. (Open May-Oct. Tu-Sa 9am-5pm; also late May to early Sept. Su-M 10am-4pm.) Access the region by bus with **Greyhound,** 540 State St., Watertown (800-231-2222; station open M-F 9:30am-4:30pm and 8:45-9:05pm, Sa-Su 9:30-10:30am, 4:15-4:50pm, and 8:45-9:05pm). Two buses run daily to New York City (7-7½hr., $46); Syracuse (1½hr., $8); and Albany (1¼hr., $33). From the same station, **Thousand Islands Bus Lines** (287-2782) leaves for Alexandria Bay and Clayton, Monday to Friday at 1pm ($5.60 to Alexandria, $3.55 to Clayton); return trips leave Clayton from the **Nutshell Florist,** 234 James St. (686-5791), at 8:45am, and Alexandria from the **Dockside Café,** 17 Market St. (482-9849), at 8:30am.

Clayton's **post office:** 236 John St. (686-3311; open M-F 9am-5pm, Sa 9am-noon). **ZIP code:** 13624. Alexandria Bay's **post office:** 13 Bethune St. (482-9521; open M-F 8:30am-5:30pm, Sa 8:30am-1pm). **ZIP code:** 13607. Cape Vincent's **post office:** 362 Broadway St. (654-2424; open M-F 8:30am-1pm and 2-5:30pm, Sa 8:30-11:30am). **ZIP code:** 13618. Thousand Island's **area code:** 315.

ACCOMMODATIONS AND CAMPGROUNDS George and Jean Couglar lovingly care for the idyllic **Tibbetts Point Lighthouse Hostel (HI-AYH),** 33439 County Rte. 6 (654-3450), along the western edge of the seaway on Cape Vincent, situated where Lake Ontario meets the St. Lawrence River. Take Rte. 12 E into town, drive straight onto Broadway, and follow the river until the road ends. It's a truly spectacular setting: the lighthouse is still active, and the peaceful rhythm of the waves lulls you to sleep at night. There is no public transportation to Cape Vincent, but with 1 day's advance notice, George will pick you up in Clayton. (2 houses with 26 beds. Full kitchen with microwave. $10, nonmembers $13. Linen $1. Check-in 7-9am and 5-10pm. Curfew 11pm. Open mid-May to Oct.) **Burnham Point State Park** (654-2324), on Rte. 12 E 4 mi. east of Cape Vincent and 11 mi. west of Clayton, sports 52 sites and three picnic areas. (Showers. Tent sites $13, prime sites on the water $15. Open late May to early Sept. daily 8am-10pm. Wheelchair access.) **Keewaydin State Park** (482-3331), just south of Alexandria Bay, maintains 41 sites along the St. Lawrence River. Campers have free access to an Olympic-size swimming pool. (Showers available. $13 per night. Open late May to early Sept. daily 8am-11pm.) Call 1-800-456-CAMP/2267 for reservations at either state park.

EXPLORING THE SEAWAY Any of the small towns that dot Rte. 12 will serve as a fine base for exploring the region, although Clayton and Cape Vincent tend to be less expensive than Alexandria Bay. **Uncle Sam Boat Tours,** 604 Riverside Dr. (686-3511), in Clayton, and on James St. in Alexandria Bay (482-2611), delivers a good look at most of the islands and the plush estates situated atop them. (2¼hr. tours leave from Alexandria Bay daily late Apr. to Oct. $13, seniors $12. Daily lunch and dinner cruises $20-$27.50, must be reserved in advance.) Tours highlight **Heart Island** and its famous **Boldt Castle** (482-9724, tourism council 800-8ISLAND/847-5263) and make unlimited stops so that visitors can get off and stay as long as they would like before being picked up; they do not cover the price of admission to the castle. (Castle open mid-May to mid-Oct. daily 10am-7:30pm. $3.75, ages 6-12 $2, tickets must be purchased by 6:30pm.) George Boldt, former owner of New York City's elegant Waldorf-Astoria Hotel, financed this 6-story replica of a Rhineland castle as a gift for his wife, who died before its completion. In his grief, Boldt stopped construction on the 120-room behemoth, which remains unfinished today. After extensive renovations, this exorbitant but romantic monument is now open to the public. In Clayton, **French Creek**

MID-ATLANTIC

Marina, 250 Wahl St. (686-3621), rents 14 ft. fishing boats ($50 per day), launches boats ($5), and provides overnight docking ($20 per night). **O'Brien's U-Drive Boat Rentals,** 51 Walton St. (482-9548), handles boat rentals in Alexandria Bay with 16 ft. fishing boats ($70 per day, $300 deposit; open May to early Oct. daily 8am-5pm). In Cape Vincent, **Millens Bay Marina** (654-2174), 5 mi. beyond town on Rte. 12 E, offers 16 ft. motor boats (7.5 horse power $25 per ½-day, $40 per day; 15HP $35/$50).

Fishing licenses ($11 per day, $20 for 5 days, season $35) are available at sporting goods stores or at the **Town Clerk's Office,** 405 Riverside Dr., Clayton (686-3512; open M-F 9am-noon and 1-4pm). No local store rents equipment; bring your own rods or plan to buy them.

New Jersey

New Jersey was once called the Garden State for a reason, but with the advent of suburbia (NJ serves both New York City and Philadelphia) and tax-free shopping (giving rise to outlets and major mall country), travelers who refuse to get off the interstates envision the state as a conglomeration of belching chemical plants and ocean beaches strewn with garbage and gamblers. This picture, however, belies the state's quieter delights (off the highway). A closer look reveals that there is more to New Jersey than commuters, chemicals, and craps; the interior blooms with fields of corn, tomatoes, and peaches, while quiet sandy beaches outline the southern tip of the state. New Jersey also shelters quiet hamlets, the Pine Barrens forest, and two world-class universities: Rutgers and Princeton. Certainly, Atlantic City continues its gaudy existence, and the New Jersey Turnpike remains the zone of the road warrior, but those who stray from the path will be pleasantly surprised.

PRACTICAL INFORMATION

Capital: Trenton.
Visitor Info: State Division of Tourism, 20 W. State St., P.O. Box 826, Trenton 08625-0826 (609-292-2470; http://www.nj-tourism.com). Write or call 800-537-7397 for a free copy of the *New Jersey Travel Guide.* **New Jersey Dept. of Environmental Protection and Energy, State Park Service,** 401 East State St., Trenton 08625-0404 (609-292-2797).
Time Zone: Eastern. **Postal Abbreviation:** NJ.
Sales Tax: 6%; no tax on clothing.

■ Atlantic City

More than any other American city, the geography of Atlantic City is subconsciously written into the minds of generations of Americans. For over 50 years, board-gaming strategists have vied for control of this coastal city as reincarnated in its two-dimensional form on the *Monopoly* board. When *Monopoly* was created, Atlantic City was *the* beachside hotspot among resort towns. The opulence faded first into neglect, then into a deeper shade of tackiness. With the legalization of gambling in 1976, casinos soon rose from the rubble of Boardwalk. Today, velvet-lined temples of schmaltz (each with a dozen restaurants and big-name entertainment) blight the beach and draw all kinds of tourists from international jet-setters to local seniors.

ORIENTATION AND PRACTICAL INFORMATION

Atlantic City lies half way down New Jersey's coast, accessible via the **Garden State Pkwy.** and the **Atlantic City Expwy.,** and easily reached by train from Philadelphia or New York. Attractions cluster on and around the Boardwalk, which runs east-west along the Atlantic Ocean. Running parallel to the Boardwalk, Pacific and Atlantic Ave.

offer cheap restaurants, hotels, and convenience stores. *Atlantic Ave. can be danger-ous after dark, and any street farther out can be dangerous even by day.*

Getting around is easy on foot. **Parking** at the Sands Hotel is free, but "for patrons only"; spend a dollar at the slots after parking. Lots near the Boardwalk run $3-7.

Airport: Atlantic City International (645-7895 or 800-892-0354). Located just west of Atlantic City in Pamona. Served by Spirit, U.S. Airways, and Continental.

Train: Amtrak (800-872-7245), at Kirkman Blvd. near Michigan Ave. Follow Kirk-man to its end, bear right, and follow the signs. To New York (2½hr., $42). Open daily 6am-10:15pm.

Buses: Greyhound (800-231-2222). Buses every hr. to New York (2½hr., $23 round-trip). **New Jersey Transit** (800-582-5946). Runs 6am-10pm. Hourly service to New York ($21). Also runs along Atlantic Ave. (base fare $1). Both lines operate from **Atlantic City Municipal Bus Terminal,** at Arkansas and Arctic Ave. Both offer casino-sponsored round-trip discounts, including cash back on arrival in Atlantic City. Many casinos will give the bearer of a bus ticket receipt $10-15 in quarters and sometimes a free meal. **Gray Line Tours** (800-669-0051) offers several round-trip excursions daily to Atlantic City (3hr., Sa-Su $23). Your ticket receipt is redeemable for up to $15 in cash, chips, or food from a casino when you arrive. Caesar's, the Taj Mahal, and TropWorld have the best offers ($15 in cold, flexible cash). The bus drops you at the casino and picks you up 3hr. later. Overnight pack-age $103—call 212-397-3807 for info. Terminal open 24hr.

Visitor Info: Atlantic City Convention Center and Visitors Bureau, 2314 Pacific Ave. (449-7130 or 800-228-4748). Home of the Miss America Pageant. Main entrance on the Boardwalk between Mississippi and Florida Ave. Another booth on the Boardwalk at Mississippi Ave. Open daily 9am-5pm; brochures available 24hr.

Hospital: Atlantic City Medical Center (344-4081), at the intersection of Michigan and Pacific Ave.

Hotlines: Rape and Abuse Hotline (646-6767). 24hr. counseling, referrals, and accompaniment. **Gambling Abuse** (800-GAMBLER/426-2537). 24hr. help for gam-bling problems. **AIDS Hotline** (800-281-2437). Operates M-F 9am-5pm.

Area code: 609.

ACCOMMODATIONS AND CAMPGROUNDS

Large, red-carpeted beachfront hotels have bumped smaller operators a few streets back. Smaller hotels along **Pacific Ave.,** 1 block from the Boardwalk, charge about $60-95 in the summer. Reserve ahead, especially on weekends. Many hotels lower their rates mid-week and in the winter, when water temperature and gambling fervor drop significantly. Rooms in guest houses are reasonably priced, though facilities can be dismal. If you have a car, it pays to stay in **Absecon,** about 8 mi. from Atlantic City; Exit 40 from the Garden Sate Pkwy. leads to Rte. 30 and cheap rooms.

Inn of the Irish Pub, 164 St. James Pl. (344-9063), near the Ramada Tower, just off the Boardwalk. Big, clean rooms, nicely decorated with antiques. No TVs, phones, or A/C, but in summer the breeze from the beach keeps things cool. Some rooms have a sea view. Plush lobby with TV and pay phone. Porch sitting area complete with rocking chairs and seniors. Coin-op laundry in hotel next door. Adjoining res-taurant offers a $2 lunch special and a $6 dinner special. Singles $29, with private bath $52; doubles $46/$85. Rates lower midweek. Key deposit $5.

Sorrento Motel, 1612 Pacific Ave. (348-1138), at Kentucky Ave. This centrally located motel features 82 doubles with bath, A/C, TV, phone, and pool access. M-W $45, Th $55, F $70, Sa $90, Su $40.

Birch Grove Park Campground (641-3778), Mill Rd. in Northfield. About 6 mi. from Atlantic City, off Rte. 9. 50 attractive and secluded sites. $18 for 4 people, with hookup $25. Sites available Apr.-Oct.

FOOD

After you cash in your chips, visit a **casino buffet** for a cheap meal (about $6-7 for lunch, $10 for dinner), but don't expect gourmet quality. Thankfully, the town does provide higher quality meals in a less noxious atmosphere. A complete rundown of local dining fills the pages of *TV Atlantic Magazine, At the Shore,* and *Whoot* (all free), found in hotel lobbies, restaurants, and local stores.

An inviting pub with a century's worth of Irish memorabilia draped on the walls, the **Inn of the Irish Pub,** 164 St. James Pl. (345-9613), serves hearty, modestly priced dishes such as deep-fried crab cakes ($4.75) and Dublin beef stew ($5). The lunch special (M-F 11:30am-2pm) gets you a pre-selected sandwich and cup of soup for $2. (Open 24hr.) The late Frank Sinatra is rumored to have had the immense subs ($4-9) from **White House Sub Shop,** 2301 Arctic Ave. (345-1564 or 345-8599), flown to him while on tour (open M-Th 10am-11pm, F-Sa 10am-midnight, Su 11am-11pm). **Tony's Baltimore Grille,** 2800 Atlantic Ave. (345-5766), at Iowa Ave., fills customers with renowned pasta dishes ($4-6) and pizza (open daily 11am-3am; bar open 24hr.). For a traditional oceanside dessert, try custard ice cream or saltwater taffy, both available from vendors along the Boardwalk. **Custard and Snackhouse** (345-5151), between South Carolina and Ocean Ave., makes 37 flavors of soft-serve ice cream and yogurt, ranging from peach to pineapple to tutti-frutti (cones $2.25; open Su-Th 10am-midnight, F-Sa 10am-3am).

CAINO, THE BOARDWALK, AND BEACHES

You don't have to spend a penny to enjoy yourself in Atlantic City's casinos; their vast, plush interiors and spotless marble bathrooms can entertain a resourceful and voyeuristic budget traveler for hours. Watch blue-haired ladies shove quarter after quarter in the slot machines with a vacant, zombie-like stare. Open nearly all the time, casinos lack windows and clocks, denying you the time cues that signal the hours slipping away; keep your eyes on your watch, or you'll have spent five hours and five digits before you know what hit you. To curb inevitable losses, stick to the cheaper games—blackjack and slot machines—and stay away from the cash machines. Trop-World, Bally's Grand, and Taj Mahal (see below), will allow you to gamble for hours on less than $10. The minimum gambling age of 21 is strictly enforced.

All casinos on the Boardwalk fall within a dice toss of one another. The farthest south is **The Grand** (347-7111), between Providence and Boston Ave., and the farthest north is **Showboat** (343-4000), at Delaware Ave. and Boardwalk. If you liked *Aladdin,* you'll love the **Taj Mahal,** 1000 Boardwalk (449-1000). Donald Trump's huge and glittering jewel is too out there (and too large) to be missed—it was missed payments on this tasteless tallboy that cast the financier into his billion dollar tailspin. It will feel like *Monopoly* when you realize Trump owns three other hotel casinos in the city: **Trump Plaza** (441-6000) and **Trump World's Fair** (344-6000) on the Boardwalk, and **Trump Castle** (441-2000) at the Marina. The outdoor Caesar at **Caesar's Boardwalk Resort and Casino** (348-4411), at Arkansas Ave., has moved indoors, replaced by a kneeling Roman gladiator heralding the entrance to **Planet Hollywood.** Come, see, and conquer at the only casino with 25¢ video blackjack, and play slots at the feet of a huge **Statue of David.** The **Sands** (441-4000), at Indiana Ave., goes for a more "natural" effect with a decor of huge, ostentatious pink and green seashells.

There's something for everyone in Atlantic City, thanks to the Boardwalk. Those under 21 (or those tired of the endless cycle of winning and losing) **gamble for prizes** at one of the many arcades that line the Boardwalk. It feels like real gambling, but the teddy bear in the window is easier to get than the grand prize at a resort. The **Steel Pier,** an extension in front of the Taj Mahal, has the usual amusement park standbys: roller coaster, ferris wheel, tilt-a-whirl, carousel, kiddie rides, and many a game of "skill." Rides cost $2-3 each. (Open daily noon-midnight; call the Taj Mahal for winter hrs.) When you tire of spending money, check out the **beach,** although **Ventnor City,** just west of Atlantic City, has quieter shores.

■ Cape May

Lying at the southern extreme of New Jersey's coastline, Cape May is the oldest seashore resort in the United States. Still isolated even when the railroad connected Philadelphia to Atlantic City, this small vacation community retains much of its heritage in the form of countless 19th-century Victorian homes. Indeed, the unique architecture of Cape May has proven to be its greatest asset, and the bed and breakfasts lining the brick sidewalks are unparalleled in charm.

PRACTICAL INFORMATION Despite its geographic isolation, Cape May is quite accessible. By car from the north, Cape May is literally the end of the road. Follow the toll-laden Garden State Pkwy. south as far as it goes, watch for signs to Center City, and you'll end up on Lafayette St. Alternately, take the slower, scenic Ocean Dr. 40 mi. south along the shore from Atlantic City. From the south, a 70min. **ferry** will transport you from Lewes, DE (302-426-1155) to Cape May (886-1725 or 800-643-3779 for recorded schedule info). In summer, 10 to 12 ferries cross daily; the rest of the year, expect only five to seven. ($20 per driver, $6 per additional passenger; ages 6-12 $3, motorcyclists $15, bicyclists $5.) **Shuttles** to the ferry leave from the Cape May Bus Depot ($2). **New Jersey Transit** (215-569-3752 or 800-582-5946) makes a local stop at the bus depot on the corner of Lafayette and Ocean St. (Station open M-F 9am-8pm, Sa 9am-5pm; mid-Oct. to mid-May M-F 9am-5pm, Sa 11am-2pm.) Buses run to Atlantic City (2hr., 5 per day, $3.45); Philadelphia (3hr., 18 per day, $13.60); and New York City (4½hr., 3 per day, $27). To navigate Cape May by public transportation, pay $1.50 in exact change for the **Cape Area Transit** buses (889-0925 or 800-966-3758), which run along Beach St. and Pittsburgh Ave. (Runs late June to Sept. 6 daily 10am-10pm; late May to late June and Sept. 6 to mid-Oct. F 4-10pm, Sa 10am-10pm, Su 10am-4pm.) Next door, the **Village Bike Shop** (884-8500) rents wheels at Washington and Ocean St. (1-seaters $4 per hr., $10 per day; tandems $10/$30; surreys $24 per hr. Open daily 7am-7pm.) The **welcome center,** 405 Lafayette St. (884-9562), has a wagonload of helpful info about Cape May and free hotlines to B&Bs (open daily 9am-4:30pm). Both the **Chamber of Commerce,** 513 Washington St. Mall (884-5508; open M-F 9am-5pm, Sa-Su 10am-6pm), and the **historic kiosk** at the south end of the mall provide tourist info. **Post Office:** 700 Washington St. (884-3578; open M-F 9am-5pm, Sa 8:30am-12:30pm). **ZIP code:** 08204. **Area code:** 609.

ACCOMMODATIONS AND CAMPGROUNDS Specials on hotel rooms fill **Beach Dr.,** and many seaside homes take in nightly guests. The Victorian homes cater to the B&B crowd with rooms for $85-250 per night. Still, some reasonably priced inns persevere. Although the **Hotel Clinton,** 202 Perry St. (884-3993), lacks presidential suites or A/C, the family-owned establishment has 16 decent, breezy rooms with a shared bath. (Singles $30-35; doubles $40-45. Reservations recommended. Open mid-June to Sept.) Next door, the **Parris Inn,** 204 Perry St. (884-8015), rents spacious but simple rooms, most with private baths, TV, and A/C (singles $65-85; doubles $75-95; lower rates in winter; open mid-Apr. to Dec.).

Campgrounds line U.S. 9 just north of Cape May. Less plush and more family-oriented than other area campgrounds, the **Lake Laurie Campground,** 669 Rte. 9 (884-3567), sits about 5 mi. north of Cape May. (Tents $16-23.50, full hookup $23-30.50. 3-day min. stay in peak season. Open Apr.-Sept.) Located just 4 mi. north of Cape May, the **Cape Island Campground,** 709 U.S. 9 (884-5777 or 800-437-7443), is slightly ritzier with a pool, store, and athletic facilities (sites with water and electricity $29, full hookup $33; open May to late Sept.).

FOOD AND NIGHTLIFE Cape May's cheapest food is the pizza and burger fare along **Beach Ave.** You'll have to shell out a few more clams for a sit-down meal. Bustling with pedestrians shopping for fudge and saltwater taffy, the **Washington St. Mall** supports several popular food stores and eateries. The pub-like **Ugly Mug,** 426 Washington St. (884-3459), serves a good-lookin' cup o' chowder ($2) and the everpopular "oceanburger" ($5.75). In the summer, nights mean cover-free fun. (Free pizza M 10pm-2am, W hula hoop contests. Open M-Sa 11am-2am, Su noon-2am; food served until 11pm.) "A majestic 14.4 ft. above sea level," the **Jackson Mountain Café,** 400 Washington St. Mall (554-5648), serves up hefty portions (sandwiches $7-9) to those who make the climb (open daily 11am-11pm). The rock scene centers around barnacle-encrusted **Carney's** (884-4424) on Beach Dr., with nightly entertainment in the summer (open daily 11am-3am; in winter 11am-2am). For a more cosmopolitan night scene, listen to jazz and sip creative martinis ($5-7) at **Downstairs at Spiaggi** (884-3504), across from the beach on Decatur St. (open Apr.-Oct. Tu-Sa 8pm-2am).

HITTING THE BEACH The entire Jersey shore is blessed with fine beaches. Cape May's sands actually sparkle, dotted with the famous Cape May "diamonds" (quartz pebbles in reality). You can unroll your beach towel on a city-protected beach (off Beach Ave.), but make sure you have a **beach tag,** required for beachgoers over 11 from June to September daily between 10am and 5:30pm. Tags are available from the vendors roaming the shore (daily $4, weekly $9, seasonal $15), or from the **Beach Tag Office** (884-9522), located at Grant and Beach Dr. (open daily 9:30am-5:30pm).

Off the beach, several of the Victorian homes hold daily viewings. The **Mid-Atlantic Center for the Arts** in the 1879 **Emlen Physick House,** 1048 Washington St. (884-5404), offers 45min. house tours ($7, ages 3-12 $3.50; Apr.-Dec. daily, Jan.-Mar. Sa-Su) and sponsors a history-filled **Victorian Week** each October, as well as **Music and Tulip Festivals.** Pick up *This Week in Cape May* in any public building or store for a detailed listing. The beacon of the 1859 **Cape May Lighthouse** in **Cape May Point State Park** (884-5404), west of town at the end of the point, still guides both tourists and ships within 19 mi. of shore. *($4 with 1 free child, ages 3-12 $1. Park open 8am-dusk. Lighthouse open daily 8am-dusk; Dec.-Mar. Sa-Su 8am-dusk.)* A 199-step climb to the top offers a magnificent panorama of the New Jersey and Delaware shore. In the summer, several shuttles run the 5 mi. from the bus depot on Lafayette St. to the lighthouse ($5, ages 3-12 $4).

Due to prevailing winds and location, thousands of birds layover in Cape May every year on their way to warmer climates. The **Cape May Bird Observatory,** 707 E. Lake Dr. (884-2736), on Cape May Point, serves as an ornithological center of North America. *(Open Tu-Su 10am-5pm.)* Bird maps, field trips, and workshops are all available here. For those looking for a respite from the seashore, Cape May boasts several golf and mini-golf courses, as well as tennis courts.

Pennsylvania

In 1681, Englishman William Penn, Jr. established the colony of Pennsylvania ("Penn's woods") in order to protect his fellow Quakers from persecution. A bastion of religious tolerance, the state attracted settlers of all ethnicities and beliefs, and Pennsylvania promptly grew in population. Since then, Pennsylvania has rallied in the face of revolution time and again, from the birth of the Declaration of Independence in Philadelphia to the present. In 1976, Philadelphia groomed its historic shrines for the nation's bicentennial celebration, and they are now the centerpiece of the city's ambitious urban renewal program. Pittsburgh, a steel city once dirty enough to fool streetlights into burning during the day, has also initiated a cultural renaissance. Away from the cities, Pennsylvania's landscape retains much of the natural beauty that the area's first colonists discovered centuries ago, from the farms of Lancaster County to the deep river gorges of the Allegheny Plateau.

PRACTICAL INFORMATION

Capital: Harrisburg.
Visitor Info: Pennsylvania Travel & Tourism, 453 Forum Bldg., Harrisburg 17120 (800-VISIT-PA/847-4852; http://www.state.pa.us). Info on hotels, restaurants, and

sights. **Bureau of State Parks,** Rachel Carson State Office Bldg., 400 Market St., Harrisburg 17108 (800-637-2757). Open M-F 8am-4:30pm.
Emergency: 911.
Time Zone: Eastern. **Postal Abbreviation:** PA.
Sales Tax: 6%.

■ Philadelphia

William Penn founded the City of Brotherly Love with his band of Quakers in 1682, after it served as a colonial hub for 100 years. It was Ben Franklin who made this town, however; as Michelangelo is to Rome, so Franklin is to Philadelphia. Anything not founded by him seems to bear his name, and in summer, when the tourist season kicks into high gear, his cocked-hatted and ruffled colonial counterparts roam the city making 1770s chitchat. Before Philly lost U.S. capital status to Washington, D.C., the First Continental Congress met here in 1774, at which Virginia delegate Thomas Jefferson penned the Declaration of Independence. Today, the city has thriving ethnic neighborhoods to balance the Main Line bluebottles. A breathtaking array of architecture and world-class museums draw aesthetes, while ragers pack the city's many clubs and bars. And, of course, there's always the cheesesteak.

ORIENTATION

Penn planned his city as a logical and easily accessible grid of wide streets. The north-south streets ascend numerically from the **Delaware River,** flowing near **Penn's Landing** and **Independence Hall** on the east side, to the **Schuylkill River** (SKOO-kill) on the west. The first street is **Front;** the others follow consecutively from 2 to 69. **Center City** runs from 8th St. to the Schuylkill River. From north to south, the primary streets are Race, Arch, JFK, Market, Chestnut, and South. The intersection of **Broad (14th) St.** and **Market** marks the focal point of Center City. The **Historic District** stretches from Front to 8th St. and from Vine to South St. About 1 mi. west of Center City, the **University of Pennsylvania** sprawls on the far side of the Schuylkill River. **University City** includes the Penn/Drexel area west of the Schuylkill River. While this framework sounds simple, Penn omitted the alleys in his system. Some are big enough to accommodate cars while others are not, but street addresses often refer to alleys not pictured on standard AAA-type maps of the city. The **SEPTA transportation map,** available free from the tourist office, is probably the most complete guide to the city.

Due to the proliferation of one-way streets, horrendous traffic, and outrageous parking fees, **driving** is not a good way to get around town. Meterless 2hr. parking spaces can sometimes be found on the cobblestones of Dock St. Otherwise, the city-run **Visitors Parking** (entrance on 2nd St. at Ionic) charges $3 per hr. or $9 for 24hr. (enter 6-10am and leave by 6pm, $6.25). A small lot on the corner of 4th and Ludlow St. offers an even better deal with a $6 maximum fee per day. Philly's system of **buses** and its **subway** will take you almost anywhere you'll want to go.

PRACTICAL INFORMATION

Airport: Philadelphia International (24hr. info line 937-6800), 8 mi. southwest of Center City on I-76. The 20min. **SEPTA Airport Rail Line** runs from Center City to the airport. Trains leave 30th St., Suburban, and Market East Stations daily every 30min. 5:25am-11:25pm; $5 at window, $7 on train. Last train from airport 12:10am. **Airport Limelight Limousine** (782-8818) will deliver you to a hotel or a specific address downtown ($8 per person). Taxi downtown $25.

Trains: Amtrak, 30th St. Station (824-1600 or 800-872-7245), at Market St., in University City. To: New York (2hr.; 30-40 per day; $37-41, express trains $71); Boston (7hr., 10 per day, $53-88); Washington, D.C. (2hr., 33 per day, $34-40); and Pittsburgh (8hr., 2 per day, $42-76). Office open M-F 5:10am-10:45pm, Sa-Su 6:10am-10:45pm. Station open 24hr.

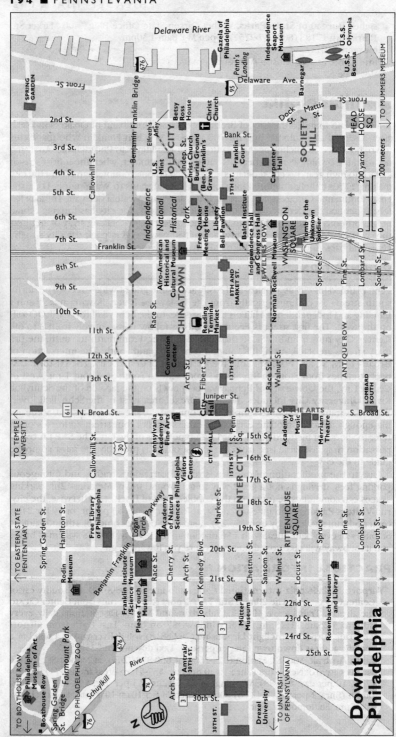

Downtown Philadelphia

Buses: Greyhound, 10th and Filbert St. (931-4075 or 800-231-2222), 1 block north of Market near the 10th and Market St. subway/commuter rail stop in the heart of Philadelphia. To: New York (2½hr., 24 per day, $15); Boston (8½hr., 19 per day, $44); Baltimore (2hr., 10 per day, $16); Washington, D.C. (3hr., 10 per day, $17); Pittsburgh (7hr., 8 per day, $41); and Atlantic City (2hr., 12 per day, $9). Station open daily 7am-1am. **New Jersey Transit** (569-3752), in the same station. To: Atlantic City (1hr., $10); Ocean City (2hr., $11); and other points on the New Jersey shore. Operates daily with buses to Atlantic City nearly every 30min.

Public Transportation: Southeastern Pennsylvania Transportation Authority (SEPTA), 580-7800. Extensive bus and rail service to the suburbs, although a 3-month strike in 1998 has greatly reduced ridership. Buses serve the 5-county area; most operate 5am-2am, some 24hr. 2 major subway routes: the east-west **Market St. line** (including 30th St. Station and the historic area) and the north-south **Broad St. line** (including the stadium complex in south Philadelphia). *The subway is unsafe after dark;* buses are usually okay. Subway connects with commuter rails—the main line local runs through the western suburb of Paoli ($3.75-4.25). SEPTA runs north to Trenton, NJ ($5). Pick up a free SEPTA system map, Philly's best street map, at any subway stop. Fare $1.60, 2 tokens $2.30, transfers 40¢. Unlimited all-day pass for both $5. In the tourist area, purple **Phlash** buses come by every 10min. and stop at all major sights. Fare $1.50, $3 all day.

Taxis: Yellow Cab, 922-8400. **Liberty Cab,** 389-2000. $1.80 base fare and per mi.

Car Rental: Courtesy Rent-a-Car, 7704 Westchester Pike (610-446-6200). $19 per day with unlimited mi. Must be 21 with major credit card. **Budget** (492-9400), at 21st and Market St., downtown or in the 30th St. Station. Easy to find, but more expensive. $38 per day (Sa-Su $43) with unlimited mi. Drivers must be 25.

Bike Rental: Frankenstein Bike Work, 1529 Spruce St. (893-0415). Single speeds and cruisers $12 for 4hr., $15 per day. Open Tu-Sa 10:30am-6pm, Su noon-4pm.

Visitor Info: 1525 John F. Kennedy Blvd. (636-1666), at 16th St. Open daily 9am-5pm. The **National Park Service Visitors Center** (597-8974, 627-1776 for a recording), at 3rd and Chestnut St., has info on **Independence Park,** including maps, schedules, a film, and a branch of the tourist office. Open daily 9am-5pm.

Hotlines: Suicide and Crisis Intervention, 686-4420. **Youth Crisis Line,** 787-0633. Both 24hr. **Women Against Abuse,** 386-7777. 24hr. **Gay and Lesbian Counseling Services,** 732-8255. Operates M-F 6-9pm, Su 5-8pm. **William Way Lesbian, Gay, and Bisexual Community Center** (732-2220). Info about gay events and activities. Open M-F noon-10pm, Sa 10am-5pm, Su 10:30am-8:30pm.

Internet Access: Kinko's, 2001 Market St. (561-5170). $12 per hr. Open 24hr.

Post Office: 2970 Market St. (895-8000), at 30th St. across from the Amtrak station. Open daily 9am-5pm. **ZIP code:** 19104. **Area code:** 215.

ACCOMMODATIONS AND CAMPGROUNDS

Inexpensive lodging in Philadelphia is hard to find, but if you make arrangements a few days in advance, you should be able to find a comfortable room close to Center City for around $50. The motels near the airport at Exit 9A on I-95 are the least expensive in the area. **Bed and Breakfast Center City,** 1804 Pine St. (735-1137 or 800-354-8401), will rent you a room ($50-95) or find you one in a private home. **Bed & Breakfast Connections/Bed & Breakfast of Philadelphia** (610-687-3565), in Devon, PA, also books in Philadelphia and throughout southeastern Pennsylvania. (Singles $40-75; doubles $50-220. Make reservations at least a week in advance. Best to call 9am-7pm.) The closest camping lies across the Delaware River in New Jersey at **Timberline Campground,** 117 Timber Ln. (609-423-6677), 15 mi. from Center City. Take U.S. 295 S to Exit 18B (Clarksboro), follow straight through the traffic light ½ mi. and turn right on Friendship Rd. Timber Ln. is 1 block on the right. (Sites $17, full hookup $22.)

Bank Street Hostel (HI-AYH), 32 S. Bank St. (922-0222 or 800-392-4678). From the bus station, walk down Market St.; it's between 2nd and 3rd St. Subway: 2nd St. An impersonal hostel in a great location in the historic district. A/C, big TV and VCR in lobby, free coffee and tea, laundry facilities, kitchen, pool table. Super-convenient to South St. 70 beds. $16, nonmembers $19. Linen $2. Lockout 10am-4:30pm, but they'll hold baggage. Curfew Su-Th 12:30am, F-Sa 1am. Breakfast $3.50, dinner $5.

Chamounix Mansion International Youth Hostel (HI-AYH) (878-3676 or 800-379-0017), in West Fairmount Park. Take bus #38 from Market St. to Ford and Cranston Rd., follow Ford Rd. to Chamounix Dr., turn left, and follow the road to the hostel. A deluxe hostel in a former country estate with beautifully furnished rooms, showers, kitchen, laundry, chess table, TV/VCR, and a piano. Basic groceries for sale. Very friendly, helpful staff. Free parking. 80 beds. $11, nonmembers $14. Linen $2. Check-in 8-11am and 4:30pm-midnight. Lockout 11am-4:30pm. Curfew midnight.

Antique Row Bed and Breakfast, 341 S. 12th St. (592-7802). Kindly Barbara Pope serves a full breakfast including fresh orange juice to guests in this beautifully furnished home. Free local calls. $50-100, depending on size of suite.

Old First Reformed Church (922-4566), at 4th and Race St. in Center City, 1 block from the Independence Mall and 4 blocks from Penn's Landing. A historic church that converts its social hall to a youth hostel that sleeps around 30. Foam pads on the floor, showers, A/C and laundry. $15. Breakfast included. Ages 18-26 only. 3-night max. stay. Check-in 5-10pm. Curfew midnight. Open July to early Sept.

Motel 6, 43 Industrial Hwy. (610-521-6650 or 800-466-8356), in Essington, Exit 9A off I-95. Large, standard rooms with A/C and cable. Singles $50-60; doubles $56-65.

FOOD

Philadelphians like to eat, and eat well. Philly's specialties include **cheesesteaks, hoagies,** and **soft pretzels.** Inexpensive food fills the carts of the ubiquitous city street vendors, which include stands devoted solely to making fruit salads. Ethnic eateries gather in several specific areas: very hip **South St.,** between Front and 7th; **Sansom St.,** between 17th and 18th; and **2nd St.,** between Chestnut and Market. **Chinatown,** bounded by 11th, 8th, Arch, and Vine St., offers a multitude of well-priced restaurants. The quintessential Philly cheesesteak rivalry squares off at 12th and Passyunk Ave., in South Philadelphia, as **Pat's King of Steaks** (468-1546), the legendary founder of the cheesesteak, faces off against larger, more neon **Geno's Steaks.** Both offer the basic cheesesteak for $5 and stay open 24hr.

Fresh fruit and other foodstuffs pack the immense **Italian Market,** on 9th St. below Christian St. The **Reading Terminal Market** (922-2317), 12th and Arch St., is by far the best place to go for lunch in Center City. Since 1893, food stands have clustered in the indoor market selling fresh produce and meats. (Open M-Sa 8am-6pm.)

Historic District

Famous 4th St. Delicatessen (922-3274), 4th and Bainbridge St. A Philadelphia landmark since 1923, this traditional Jewish deli serves everything from corned beef sandwiches ($6) to egg creams from the soda fountain ($1.50). This family-operated "living museum" recalls Brooklyn of yesteryear, offering knishes ($1.50), lox ($8), and fried matzos ($6). Open M-Sa 7am-6pm, Su 7am-4pm.

Jim's Steaks, 400 South St. (928-1911). Perch on a stool in this roomy diner to eat a real Philly hoagie ($3.50-5), made here since 1939. Open M-Th 10am-1am, F-Sa 10am-3am, Su noon-10pm.

Chinatown

☺Singapore, 1029 Race St. (922-3288). A popular hangout dishing out delicious vegetarian, kosher Chinese food for amazingly low prices. Open daily 11:30am-10pm.

Rangoon, 112 9th St. (829-8939). This intimate restaurant serves wonderful Burmese cuisine. The proprietor nourishes a love of good food, low prices, and spice. Entrees $4-10, most around $8. Open Tu-Th 11:30am-3pm and 5-9pm, F 11:30am-10pm, Sa 1-10pm, Su 1-9pm.

Harmony, 135 N. 9th St. (627-4520). The chef escaped China by swimming and now caters to Philadelphia's vegetarians. For a visual and culinary masterpiece, try "Lovely Couple in Phoenix Nest," imitation chicken in a taro root basket. Most entrees $7-12. Open Su-Th 11:30am-10:30pm, F-Sa 11:30am-midnight.

Center City

Seafood Unlimited, 270 S. 20th St. (732-3663), has a variety of fresh seafood for $7-14. Lobster only $12. Open M-Th 9am-9pm, F-Sa 9am-10pm.

Jamaican Jerk Hut, 1436 South St. (545-8644). A small cafe with tropical veranda serves huge portions of Caribbean food. Entrees $6.75-8.50, daily specials less. Natural juices ($2.50-3) bottled on premises. Open M-Th 11am-10pm, F-Sa 11am-11pm, Su 5-10pm.

Taco House, 1218 Pine St. (735-1880). Loads of good, cheap Mexican food in a coffeehouse ambiance. A meat or a cheese enchilada, beans, rice, and chili go for $4; more hefty dinner combinations $8. Open Su-Th 11am-10pm, F-Sa 11am-11pm.

Lee's Hoagie House, 44 S. 17th St. (564-1264). Hoagies ($4.25-6, giant $8.50-13) since 1953. Delivery available. Open M-F 10:30am-6pm, Sa 10:30am-5pm.

University City

Tandoor India Restaurant, 106 S. 40th St. (222-7122). Northern Indian cuisine with bread fresh from the clay oven (ask to see it). Lunch buffet $6, dinner buffet $9, entrees ($7-11). 20% student discount with valid ID. Open for lunch M-F 11:30am-3pm, Sa-Su 11:30am-3:30pm; for dinner Su-Th 4:30-10:30pm, F-Sa 4:30-11pm.

Smokey Joe's, 210 S. 40th St. (222-0770), between Locust and Walnut St. This family-run restaurant and bar has been a student hangout for over 50 years. All-you-can-eat pasta, broiled salmon, or BBQ baby ribs ($8). Local groups perform Su-Tu 10pm-close. Open daily 11am-2am; July-Aug. closed Su. No lunch in summer Sa-Su.

Abner's Cheesesteaks (662-0100), at 38th and Chestnut St., attracts businesspeople for lunch, and college students late at night. Cheesesteak, large soda, and fries for $6. Open Su-Th 11am-midnight, F-Sa 11am-3am.

SIGHTS

Independence Hall and the Historic District

The buildings of the **Independence National Historical Park** (597-8974), bounded by Market, Walnut, 2nd, and 6th St., witnessed many landmark events in early U.S. history (open daily 9am-6pm; Sept.-May 9am-5pm; free). The **visitors center,** at 3rd and Chestnut St., makes a good starting point. The grandiose building across the street is the **First Bank of the U.S.** Located at Chestnut and 4th St., the **Second Bank of the U.S.** presents a stunning example of Greek Revival architecture. Arguably one of the most beautiful buildings in Philly, the Bank now contains an expansive portrait gallery, which houses paintings of Washington, Jefferson, and Franklin, among others. Delegates signed the Declaration of Independence in 1776 and drafted and signed the 1787 Constitution in **Independence Hall,** between 5th and 6th St. on Chestnut St. *(Open M-Th 9am-5pm, F-Su 9am-8pm; arrive early in summer to avoid a long line. Free guided tours daily every 15-20min.)* The U.S. Congress first assembled in nearby **Congress Hall** (free self-guided tours available); its predecessor, the First Continental Congress, convened in **Carpenters' Hall,** in the middle of the block bounded by 3rd, 4th, Walnut, and Chestnut St. (open Tu-Su 10am-4pm). North of Independence Hall, the **Liberty Bell Pavilion** contains the famous cracked **Liberty Bell.**

The remainder of the park preserves residential and commercial buildings of the Revolutionary era. To the north, Ben Franklin's home presides over **Franklin Court,** on Market between 3rd and 4th St. *(Open daily 10am-6pm. Free.)* The home contains an underground museum, a 20min. movie, a replica of Franklin's printing office, and phones with long-dead political luminaries on the line. At nearby **Washington Sq.,** an eternal flame commemorates the fallen heroes of the Revolutionary War at the **Tomb of the Unknown Soldier.** Philadelphia's branch of the **U.S. Mint** (597-7350), at 5th and Arch St. across from Independence Hall, offers a free, self-guided tour to explain the mechanized coin-making procedure. *(Open July-Aug. daily 9am-4pm; Sept.-Apr. M-F 9am-4:30pm; May-June M-Sa 9am-4:30pm.)*

Just behind Independence Hall, the **Norman Rockwell Museum** (922-4345), 6th and Sansom St., offers a sight and sound presentation and exhibits over 600 works, including many of the artist's *Saturday Evening Post* covers (open M-Sa 10am-4pm,

Su 11am-4pm; $2, seniors $1.50, under 12 free). The powder-blue "marvel near the mint," **Benjamin Franklin Bridge,** off Race and 5th St., provides a great view of the city—not for those with vertigo.

In 1723, a penniless Ben Franklin arrived in Philadelphia and walked along narrow **Elfreth's Alley,** near 2nd and Arch St., allegedly "the oldest residential street in America." Legend holds that Betsy Ross lived and sewed the first flag of the original 13 states at the tiny **Betsy Ross House,** 239 Arch St. (627-5343), near 3rd St. (open Tu-Su 10am-5pm; $1 donation requested). Two Quaker meeting houses grace these streets: the **Free Quaker Meeting House** (923-6777), at 5th and Arch St., dates from 1683 but is presently closed; a second, far larger, is at 4th and Arch St. (open Tu-Sa 10am-4pm, Su noon-4pm). **Christ Church** (922-1695), on 2nd near Market, served the more fashionable Episcopal set (open M-Sa 9am-5pm, Su noon-5pm). Ben Franklin lies buried in the nearby **Christ Church Cemetery,** at 5th and Arch St.

Adjacent to the house where Jefferson drafted the Declaration of Independence, exhibits at the **Balch Institute for Ethnic Studies,** 18 S. 7th St. (925-8090), explore America's socio-history, like the plight of Japanese Americans in World War II. *(Open M-Sa 10am-4pm. $3; students, seniors, and under 12 $1.50, Sa 10am-noon free.)*

Society Hill proper begins where the park ends, on Walnut St. between Front and 7th St. Townhouses dating back 200 years line the picturesque cobblestone walks illuminated by old-fashioned streetlights. **Head House Sq.,** at 2nd and Pine St., claims to be America's oldest firehouse and marketplace, and now houses restaurants, boutiques, and craft shops. An outdoor **flea market** (790-0782) moves in on summer weekends (open June-Aug. Sa noon-11pm, Su noon-6pm).

South of Head House Sq., the **Mummer's Museum,** 1100 S. 2nd St. (336-3050), at Washington Ave., gives you a peek inside the folk art costumes of the construction workers, policemen, and others who follow the tradition of Philly's mummers, dressing in feathers and sequins for a bizarre New Year's Day parade. *(Free string band concerts Tu evenings. Open Tu-Sa 9:30am-5pm, Su noon-5pm. $2.50, children $2.)*

Located on the Delaware River, **Penn's Landing** (923-8181) is the largest freshwater port in the world. Docked here is the *Gazela,* a three-masted, 178 ft. Portuguese square rigger built in 1883; the *U.S.S. Olympia,* Commodore Dewey's flagship during the Spanish-American War (tours daily 10am-5pm); the *U.S.S. Becuna,* a WWII submarine; and the **Independence Seaport Museum** (413-8655), with exhibits on shipbuilding, cargo, and immigration. *(Museum $5, seniors $4, children $2.50; museum and ships $7.50/$6/$3.50.)* The landing hosts **waterfront concerts** April to October (629-3257; big bands Th nights, children's theater F).

On the quirkier side, the Pennsylvania College of Podiatric Medicine contains the **Shoe Museum** (625-5243), on the corner of 8th and Race St. *(Tours W and F 9am-noon; call for appt.)* This 6th fl. collection contains footwear fashions from the famous feet of Reggie Jackson, Lady Bird Johnson, Dr. J, Nancy Reagan, and others.

Center City

Center City, the area bounded by 12th, 23rd, Vine, and Pine St., bustles with activity. An ornate wedding cake of granite and marble with 20 ft. thick foundation walls, **City Hall** (686-9074), at Broad and Market St., is the nation's largest municipal building. *(Open M-F 10am-3pm; last elevator 2:45pm. Free. Call ahead for tickets.)* Until 1908, it also reigned as the tallest building in the U.S., aided by the 37 ft. statue of William Penn, Jr. on top. A municipal statute prohibited building higher than the top of Penn's hat until Reagan-era entrepreneurs overturned the law in the mid-80s, finally launching Philadelphia into the skyscraper era. A commanding view of the city awaits in the building's tower. The country's first art museum, the **Museum of American Art** (972-7600), at Broad and Cherry St., has an extensive collection of American and British art, including works by Winslow Homer and Mary Cassatt. *(Open M-Sa 10am-5pm, Su 11am-5pm. Tours daily 12:30 and 2pm. $6, students with ID and seniors $5, ages 5-11 $4.)* Across from City Hall, the mysterious **Masonic Temple,** 1 N. Broad St. (988-1917), contains collections of books and other artifacts dating back to 1873 that can only be seen on a 45min. tour (tours M-F 10, 11am, 1, 2, and 3pm; free).

Just south of Rittenhouse Sq., the **Rosenbach Museum and Library,** 2010 Delancey St. (732-1600), scintillatingly presents rare manuscripts and paintings, including some of the earliest known copies of Cervantes's *Don Quixote,* the original manuscript of James Joyce's *Ulysses,* and the collected illustrations of Maurice Sendak. *(Open Sept.-July Tu-Su 11am-4pm. Guided tours $5; students, seniors, and children $3. Last tour 2:45pm.)*

Benjamin Franklin Pkwy.

Nicknamed "America's Champs-Elysées," the **Benjamin Franklin Pkwy.** cuts a wide swath through William Penn's original grid of city streets. Built in the 1920s, this tree-and flag-lined boulevard connects Center City with Fairmount Park and the Schuylkill River. The street is flanked by elegant architecture, including the twin buildings at Logan Sq., 19th and Ben Franklin Pkwy., containing the Free Library of Philadelphia and the Municipal Court. On one evening near the Fourth of July, every museum on the parkway opens for free.

The **Academy of Natural Sciences** (299-1000), at 19th and Ben Franklin Pkwy., showcases live animals and a 65-million-year-old dinosaur skeleton, plus the typical natural history dioramas. *(Open M-F 10am-4:30pm, Sa-Su and holidays 10am-5pm. $8.50, seniors $7.75, ages 3-12 $7. Wheelchair access.)* Nearby, the fantastic **Science Center** in the **Franklin Institute** (448-1200), at 20th and Ben Franklin Pkwy., amazes visitors with four floors of gadgets and games depicting the intricacies of space, time, motion, and the human body, including a walk-in heart. In 1990, to commemorate the 200th anniversary of Franklin's death, the Institute unveiled the **Mandell Center,** which houses a timely set of exhibits on the changing global environment. *(Mandell Center open M-Th 9:30am-5pm, F-Sa 9:30am-9pm. Science Center open daily 9:30am-5pm. Admission to both $9.75, over 62 and ages 4-11 $8.50; Mandell Center alone after 5pm $7.50, ages 4-11 $6.50.)* The **Omniverse Theater** (448-1111) provides 180° and 4½ stories of optical oohs and aahs. *(Shows on the hr. Su-Th 10am-4pm, F-Sa 10am-9pm except for 6pm. $7.50. Advance tickets recommended.)* **Fels Planetarium** (448-1388) boasts an advanced computer-driven system that projects a simulation of life billions of years beyond ours. *(Shows M-F 12:15 and 2:15pm, Sa 10:15am, 12:15, and 2:15pm. $6, seniors and children $5. Exhibits and a show $12.50/$10.50. Exhibits and both shows $14.50/$12.50.)* A lively rock music and multi-colored laser show shines on Friday or Saturday night. Farther down on 26th St., the **Philadelphia Museum of Art** (763-8100) holds one of the world's major art collections, including Rubens's *Prometheus Bound,* Picasso's *Three Musicians,* and Toulouse-Lautrec's *At the Moulin Rouge,* as well as extensive Asian, Egyptian, and decorative art collections. *(Open Tu and Th-Su 10am-5pm, W 10am-8:45pm. $8; ages 5-18, students, and seniors $5; free Su before 1pm; occasional $2 exhibit entrance fee.)* Three blocks from the museum, castle-like **Eastern State Penitentiary** (236-3300), on Fairmount Ave. at 22nd St., once a ground-breaking institution in the field of criminal rehabilitation, conducts tours of the moldering quarters which Al Capone and other notorious sorts inhabited (open May to early Nov. Th-Su 10am-5pm; $7). **The Free Library of Philadelphia** (686-5322) scores with a library of orchestral music and displays featuring one of the nation's largest rare book collections (open M-W 9am-9pm, Th-F 9am-6pm, Sa 9am-5pm; Oct.-May also Su 1-5pm). A casting of the Gates of Hell outside the **Rodin Museum** (563-1948), 22nd St., guards the portal of the most impressive collection of the artist's works this side of the Seine (open Tu-Su 10am-5pm; $3 donation).

Larger than any other city park and covered with bike trails and picnic areas, **Fairmount Park** sprawls behind the Philadelphia Museum of Art on both sides of the Schuylkill River. The Grecian ruins by the river falls immediately behind the museum are the abandoned Waterworks. Free tours featuring Waterworks architecture, technology, and social history meet on Aquarium Dr. behind the **Art Museum** (685-4935; open Sa-Su 1-3:30pm). The adjacent grand old houses, spectacularly lit at night, are the historic crew clubs of **Boathouse Row,** one of Philly's prime **rollerblading** spots. Rental blades are available from **Wilburger's** kiosk (765-7470), on Kelly Dr. south of Boathouse Row ($5 per hr., $25 per day; open May-Sept. 6 W-F 4-8pm, Sa-Su 9am-6pm). The Museum of Art hosts $3 guided tours of Boathouse Row on Wednesdays and Sundays, and trolley tours to some of the mansions in Fairmont Park. In the northern arm of Fairmont Park, trails follow the secluded Wissahickon Creek for 5 mi. The **Japanese House and Garden** (878-5097), off Montgomery Dr. near Belmont Ave., is built in the style of a 17th-century *shoin* amid an authentic garden. *(Open May to early Sept. Tu-Su 10am-4pm; mid-Sept. to Oct. Sa-Su 10am-4pm. $2.50, seniors and students $2.) While the park is safe, some of the surrounding neighborhoods are not.*

West Philadelphia (University City)

The **University of Pennsylvania (UPenn)** and **Drexel University,** located across the Schuylkill from Center City, reside in west Philadelphia within easy walking distance of the 30th St. station. The Penn campus provides a haven of green lawns and red brick quadrangles in contrast to the deteriorating community surrounding it. Ritzy shops and cafes spice up Chestnut St. At the entrance to the Penn campus on 34th and Walnut St., a statue of Benjamin Franklin greets visitors; he founded the university in 1740. *Much of the area surrounding University City is unsafe—try not to travel alone at night.*

University City is home to one of Philly's treasures, the elegantly landscaped **University Museum of Archeology and Anthropology** (898-4000), at 33rd and Spruce St. *(Open Tu-Sa 10am-4:30pm; Sept.-May Tu-Sa 10am-4:30pm, Su 1-5pm. Requested admission $5, students and over 62 $2.50.)* An outstanding East Asian art collection is sheltered by a beautiful stone-and-glass rotunda. In 1965, Andy Warhol had his first one-man show at the **Institute of Contemporary Art** (898-7108), at 36th and Sansom St., and the gallery has stayed on the cutting edge to this day with changing exhibitions featuring all media. *(Open during academic terms W-Su 10am-5pm, Th 10am-7pm. $3; students, artists, and seniors $1; Su 10am-noon free.)* In the **College of Physicians and Surgeons,** 19 S. 22nd St. (563-3737), the **Mütter Museum** holds a permanent exhibit of medical oddities, like a giant's skeleton (open Tu-Sa 10am-4pm; $8; students with ID, seniors, and ages 6-18 $4). North of the University area, the **Philadelphia Zoo** (243-1100), 34th and Girard St., the oldest zoo in the country, houses more than 1700 animals. *(Open M-F 9:30am-4:45pm, Sa-Su 9:30am-5:45pm. $8.50, seniors and ages 2-11 $6.)*

Farther Out

Several world-class institutions exist in close proximity to Philadelphia. In the suburb of Merion, across City Ave. from West Fairmont Park, the controversial **Barnes Foundation,** 300 N. Latch's Ln. (610-667-0290), is now attempting to open its Post-Impressionist art collection to the public (call to check availability; nominal hours are Th 12:30-5pm, F-Su 9:30am-5pm). Just across the Ben Franklin Bridge in Camden, NJ, the **NJ State Aquarium** (800-616-5297), on the Delaware River between Federal St. and Mickle Blvd., holds fish from habitats as unusual as the Arctic (open daily 9:30am-5:30pm; $11, seniors $9.45, ages 3-11 $8). Thirty minutes west of Philly, off U.S. 1 in Kennet Sq., sprawls the horticultural marvel of **Longwood Gardens** (610-388-1000), near the mushroom capital of the world. *(Open daily 9am-5pm; Apr.-Oct. 9am-6pm. $12, Tu $8, ages 16-20 $6, ages 5-15 $2.)*

ENTERTAINMENT

The **Academy of Music** (893-1999), Broad and Locust St., modeled after Milan's La Scala, houses the **Philadelphia Orchestra.** Under the direction of Wolfgang Sawallisch, the orchestra, among the nation's best, performs September through May. (Tickets $12-85. $5 general admission tickets go on sale at the Locust St. entrance 45 min. before F-Sa concerts. Tu and Th student rush tickets 30min. before show $7.)

The **Mann Music Center** (567-0707), on George's Hill near 52nd and Parkside Ave. in Fairmount Park, hosts the Philadelphia Orchestra (893-1955), jazz, and rock concerts with 5000 seats under cover and 10,000 on outdoor benches and lawns. Tickets are also available from the Academy of Music box office (878-7707) on Broad and Locust St. From June through August, free lawn tickets for the orchestra are available from the visitors center at 16th and JFK Blvd. on the day of a performance. For the big-name shows, you can sit just outside the theater and soak in the sounds *gratis* (real seats $10-32). The **Robin Hood Dell East** (685-9560), Strawberry Mansion Dr. in Fairmount Park, brings in top names in pop, jazz, gospel, and ethnic dance in July and August. The Philadelphia Orchestra holds several free performances here in summer, and as many as 30,000 people gather on the lawn. The visitors center (636-1666) has more info about upcoming events.

During the school year, the outstanding students of the world-renowned **Curtis Institute of Music,** 1726 Locust St., give free concerts on Mondays, Wednesdays, and Fridays at 8pm (concerts mid-Oct. to Apr.). **Merriam Theater,** 250 S. Broad St. (732-5446), Center City, stages performances ranging from student works to Broadway hits like *Rent* (box office open M-Sa 10am-5:30pm). The **Old City,** from Chestnut to Vine and Front to 4th St., comes alive on the first Friday of every month (Oct.-June) for the **First Friday** celebration. The streets fill with the music of live bands, as the area's many art galleries open their doors, enticing visitors with free food.

In addition to the wide array of cultural centers, Philadelphia is a great sports town. Philly's four professional teams play a short ride away on the Broad St. subway line. Baseball's **Phillies** (463-1000) and football's **Eagles** (463-5500) hold games at **Veterans Stadium,** Broad St. and Pattison Ave.; the **Spectrum,** across the street, houses the NBA's **76ers** (339-7676) and the NHL's **Flyers** (755-9700). General admission tickets for baseball and hockey run $5-20; football and basketball tickets go for $15-50. The city also hosts both men's and women's professional tennis tournaments, the Core State Cycling Championship, and a Senior PGA tourney.

NIGHTLIFE

Check Friday's weekend magazine section in the *Philadelphia Inquirer* for entertainment listings. *City Paper,* distributed on Thursdays, and the *Philadelphia Weekly,* distributed on Wednesdays, have weekly listings of city events (free at newsstands and markets). Gay and lesbian weeklies *Au Courant* (free) and *PGN* (75¢) list events taking place throughout the Delaware Valley region. Along **South St.** toward the river, clubbers dance and live music plays on weekends. Many pubs line **2nd St.** near Chestnut St., close to the Bank St. hostel. **Delaware Ave. (a.k.a. Columbus Blvd.),** running along Penn's Landing, has recently become a local hotspot, full of nightclubs and restaurants attracting droves of young urban professionals and the college crowd. Most bars and clubs that cater to a gay clientele congregate along **Camac St., S. 12th St.,** and **S. 13th St.**

Kat Man Du, Pier 25 (629-1724), at N. Columbus Blvd. A hopping bar and restaurant with nightly live music, including rock and reggae. Tropical gardens and open-air decks make this *the* summer hangout. Happy hour M-F 5-7pm, $2 calls and domestic beers. 50¢ drafts Tu and Th 10pm-midnight. Cover M-Th after 8:30pm $5; F-Sa $8; Su $2, after 5pm $5. Open daily noon-2am.

The Trocadero (923-7625), 10th and Arch St. On a gritty, roach-infested street in Chinatown, this old theater hosts nationally known bands, usually for a college-age crowd. Upstairs, the Balcony bar may be open jointly or separately. Cover $6-16. Advance tickets through Ticketmaster. Doors usually open around 5pm.

Khyber Pass, 56 S. 2nd St. (238-5888). One of Philly's best live music venues, this small club (max. 225 people) has managed to attract groups like Smashing Pumpkins and Hole. The ornate wooden bar was shipped over from England. Eclectic assortment of 20-somethings enjoy alternative, country, and grunge bands Tu-Su. Cover $5-15. Open daily 9am-2am.

Fluid, 613 S. 4th St. (629-0565). Gaudi-esque aqua club attracts young dancers with nightly DJs. Weekends also feature techno, industrial, and electronic music, while Monday is hip-hop. Downstairs, the **Latest Dish** restaurant serves tasty, multi-ethnic food (entrees about $12) to 20-somethings. Club open daily 9pm-2am; restaurant open M-Tu 5-11pm, W 5pm-midnight, Th-Sa 5pm-1:30am, Su 11:30am-10pm.

Gothum, 1 Brown St. (928-9319), at Columbus Blvd. Hard-core hip-hop dancing. Claims Philly's 2 largest dance floors and an outdoor deck. Open F-Su 9pm-2am.

Warmdaddy's (627-8400), on Front St. on the corner of Market St. This Cajun club loves its hot sauce and focuses on playin' the blues to an eclectic audience. Sets start in summer at 8pm, in winter 8:30pm. Tù free jam night. Cover W-Th and Su $5, F-Sa $10. Open Tu-Sa 5pm-2am, Su noon-2am.

Woody's, 202 S. 13th St. (545-1893). An attractive, young gay crowd frequents this aptly named club. Happy hour 5-7pm daily with 25¢ off all drinks. Dance to country tunes Tu, F, and Su, or grind to house music Th and Sa. W is all-ages night. Lunch daily noon-3:30pm. Bar open M-Sa 11am-2am, Su noon-2am.

■ Near Philadelphia: Valley Forge

American troops during the Revolutionary War waged a fierce battle at Valley Forge, but against the weather, not the British. At Valley Forge, in the winter of 1777-78, the 12,000 men under General George Washington's command spent agonizing months fighting starvation, bitter cold, and disease. Only 8000 survived. Nonetheless, inspired by Washington's fierce spirit and the news of an American alliance with France (plus an influx of fresh troops), the troops left Valley Forge stronger and better trained. They went on to win victories in New Jersey, to reoccupy Philadelphia, and to help create the independent nation.

Valley Forge National Historic Park encompasses over 3600 beautiful acres of rolling hills and lush forests (open daily sunrise-sunset). Self-guided auto tours begin at the **visitors center** (610-783-1077), which also features a small museum and film that offers a cameo of the complicated process of loading colonial rifles (18min.; shows twice per hr. 9am-4:30pm; center open daily 9am-5pm). The tour visits **Washington's headquarters,** reconstructed soldier huts and fortifications, and the Grand Parade Ground where the Continental Army drilled. *(Grounds free. Washington's head-quarters $2, under 17 free. Audio tapes $8, tape player $15.)* The park has three picnic areas but no camping; the visitors center distributes a list of nearby campgrounds. Nature lovers and joggers flock to take advantage of a paved 6 mi. trail which winds through the park and offers occasional glimpses of the deer which inhabit the area.

Valley Forge lies over 30min. from Philadelphia by car. To get to Valley Forge, take I-76 westbound from Philadelphia for about 12 mi. Get off at the Valley Forge Exit, then take Rte. 202 S for 1 mi. and Rte. 422 W for 1½ mi. to another Valley Forge Exit. SEPTA runs buses to the visitors center Monday through Friday only; catch #125 at 16th and JFK (fare $3.10).

■ Lancaster County

The Amish, the Mennonites, and the Brethren, three groups of German Anabaptists who fled persecution in Deutschland (thus the misnomer "Pennsylvania Dutch" by confused locals), sought freedom to pursue their own religion in the rolling country-side of Lancaster County. They successfully escaped censorship, but they have not escaped attention. Although originally farmers, the "Plain Peoples's" chief industry is now tourism. Thousands of visitors flock to this pastoral area every year to glimpse a way of life that eschews modern conveniences like motorized vehicles, television, and cellular phones, in favor of modest amenities. Point but don't shoot; many Amish have religious objections to being photographed.

ORIENTATION AND PRACTICAL INFORMATION

Lancaster County covers an area almost the size of Rhode Island. County seat Lancaster City, in the heart of Dutch country, has red brick row houses huddled around historic **Penn Sq.** The rural areas are mostly accessible by car (unless you've got a horse and buggy), but it is easy to see the tourist sites with a bike or the willingness to walk the mile or two between public transportation drop-offs. You always thought **Intercourse** would lead to **Paradise,** and on the country roads of Lancaster County, it does. From Paradise, **U.S. 30 W** plots a straight course into **Fertility.** Visitors should be aware that the area is heavily Mennonite, so most businesses and all major attractions close on Sundays.

Trains: Amtrak, 53 McGovern Ave. (291-5080 or 800-872-7245), in Lancaster City. To Philadelphia (1hr., 4-8 per day, $10).

Buses: Capital Trailways (397-4861), on the ground fl. of train station. 3 buses per day to Philadelphia (2hr., $13). Open daily 7am-4:30pm.

Public Transportation: Red Rose Transit, 45 Erick Rd. (397-4246). Service around Lancaster and the surrounding countryside. Buses run M-F 9am-3:30pm and after 6:30pm, and all day Sa-Su. Base fare $1, over 65 free.

Visitor Info: Pennsylvania Dutch Visitors Bureau Information Center, 501 Greenfield Rd. (299-8901 or 800-735-2629), on the east side of Lancaster City off Rte. 30, dispenses info on the region, including excellent maps and walking tours. Open M-Sa 8am-6pm, Su 8am-5pm; Sept.-May daily 9am-5pm. **Lancaster Chamber of Commerce and Industry,** 100 Queen St. (397-3531), in the Southern Market Center. More centrally located. Has local info, including walking guides to Lancaster City. Open M-F 8:30am-5pm.

Post Office: 1400 Harrisburg Pike (396-6900). Open M-F 7:30am-7pm, Sa 9am-2pm. **ZIP code:** 17604. **Area code:** 717.

ACCOMMODATIONS AND CAMPGROUNDS

Hundreds of hotels and B&Bs cluster in this area, as do several working farms with guest houses. Visitors centers can provide room information or, as part of a religious outreach mission, the **Mennonite Information Center** (see **Sights,** below) will try to find you a Mennonite-run guest house for approximately the same price. About the only thing that outnumber cows here are the campgrounds.

Smoketown Village Guest House, 2495 Old Philadelphia Pike (393-5975), 4 mi. east of Lancaster. Charming rooms on a main drag for Amish buggies. Guests snuggle under quilts in floral rooms with or without private baths. Mennonite proprietors bubble with suggestions for local attractions. TV and A/C. $28-34.

Pennsylvania Dutch Motel, 2275 N. Reading Rd. (336-5559), at Exit 21 off Pennsylvania Turnpike. Big, clean rooms with cable TV, and A/C. The friendly hostess has written directions to major sights. Singles $42; doubles $46. Discounts Nov.-Mar.

Groff Farm Home Lodging, 768 Brackbill Rd. (442-8223), off Rte. 30 W past Kinzer. A working corn and cattle farm with private rooms, shared bath, and A/C. $32-45.

Old Mill Stream Camping Manor, 2249 U.S. 30 E (299-2314). Shaded campground cramped between the family-oriented Dutch Wonderland amusement park and a corn field, 4 mi. east of Lancaster City. Includes game room, laundry, playground, general store. Tenters are given stream-side sites. Office open daily 8am-9pm; off-season 8am-8pm. Sites $17, with hookup $21. Reservations recommended.

FOOD

A good alternative to high-priced "family-style" restaurants lives on at the **farmers markets** and produce stands which dot the roadway. The **Central Market,** in downtown Lancaster City at the northwest corner of Penn Sq., a huge food bazaar with both Pennsylvania Dutch and "English" vendors, has provided low-priced meats, cheeses, vegetables, sandwiches, and desserts since 1899 (open Tu and F 6am-4pm, Sa 6am-2pm). Many fun and inexpensive restaurants surround the market. Two of the best options lurk in the depths of the Central Mall: **Isaac's,** 44 N. Queen St. (394-5544), creates imag-

---

Pie in Your Eye

The most distinctive culinary specialty of Lancaster County is the traditional Amish dessert, **shoofly pie,** popularized in the days before the refrigerator (or in contemporary Amish houses without refrigerators) because of its resistance to spoiling. Once removed from the oven, its treacly sweetness attracted droves of flies and thus gained its name from the constant "shoo fly" calls of its baker. Of equal authenticity if less publicity is the **whoopie pie,** a cookie-sized object with buttercream frosting sandwiched between two rounds of chocolate, pumpkin, or red velvet cake. These can be found at most bake shops for about 50¢ per pie.

inative sandwiches with avian names ($4-6; open M-Sa 10am-8pm; in winter 10am-9pm); the new **Underground Railroad,** 51 N. Market St. (396-1189) serves traditional soul food, like collard greens, barbecue ribs, and sweet potato pie (lunch buffet $6, dinner buffet $8; open daily 11am-2pm and 4-9pm). The huge **Farmers Market** (393-9674) complex on Rte. 340 in Bird-in-the-Hand charges more than the Amish road stands, but it is centralized and has parking. (Open July-Aug. W-Sa 8:30am-5:30pm; Apr.-June and Nov. W and F-Sa 8:30am-5:30pm; Jan.-Mar. and Dec. F-Sa 8:30am-5:30pm.) The **Amish Barn,** 3029 Old Philadelphia Pike (768-8886), serves all-you-can-eat breakfasts ($6) and "Amish" dinners. (Open daily late May to Sept. 5 7:30am-9pm; Sept. 6 to Oct. and Apr. to Memorial Day 8am-8pm; Nov. 8am-7pm; closed Jan.-Mar.) Most restaurants close on Sundays.

SIGHTS

The **People's Place** (768-7171), on Main St./Rte. 340, in Intercourse, 11 mi. east of Lancaster City, covers most of a block with bookstores, craft shops, and an exhibit called **20Q** (referring to the 20 most-asked questions about the Amish) with displays on Amish and Mennonite life, from barn raising to hat styles. The film *Who Are the Amish?* runs every 30min. 9:30am-5pm. *(Film $3.50, under 12 $1.75; film and 20Q $6.50/ $3.25. Open M-Sa 9:30am-8pm; early Sept. to late May M-Sa 9:30am-5pm.)* To get the story from the people who live it, stop in the **Mennonite Information Center** (299-0964), on Millstream Rd. off Rte. 30 east of Lancaster (open M-Sa 8am-5pm). The Mennonites, unlike the Amish, believe that outreach is laudable, so they started this establishment decades ago to ensure that tourists had the opportunity to witness the real Mennonite faith. The side roads off U.S. 340 near Bird-in-the-Hand are the best places to explore the area by car, winding through tourist attractions and verdant fields. Bikers can follow the tourism office's **Lancaster County Heritage Bike Tour,** a 46 mi., reasonably flat route past covered bridges and historic sites. For those determined to get the full tourist experience, **Ed's 3 mi. buggy rides,** on Rte. 896, 1½ mi. south of U.S. 30 W in Strasburg, has the lowest prices (M-Sa 9am-dusk; $7, under 12 $3.50). Local events, like the **horse sales** held each Monday in New Holland, offer more

Hershey's Candyland

Around the turn of the century, Milton S. Hershey, a Mennonite resident of eastern Pennsylvania, discovered how to mass market chocolate, previously a rare and expensive luxury. Today, the company that bears his name operates the world's largest chocolate factory, in Hershey, about 45min. from Lancaster. East of town at **Hersheypark** (800-437-7439), the **Chocolate World Visitors Center** presents a free, automated tour through a simulated chocolate factory. After the tour, visitors emerge into a pavilion full of chocolate cookies, discounted chocolate candy, and fashionable Hershey sportswear (visitors center opens with park and closes 2hr. earlier). To take this "free" tour, you must pay $5 to park in a Hershey lot. Near the visitors center, the **Hershey Museum** (534-3439) probes more deeply into Milton Hershey's life and showcases his 19th-century Apostolic Clock with an hourly procession of clockwork apostles past a clockwork Jesus, while Satan periodically appears and a rooster crows to announce Judas's betrayal. *(Open daily 10am-6pm; Labor Day-Memorial Day 10am-5pm. $5, seniors $4.50, ages 3-15 $2.50.)* **Hersheypark Theme Park** (534-3900) has heart-stopping rides with short lines, plus **ZooAmerica** (534-3860), the adjacent zoo free with park admission. *(Park open daily June and July-Aug. M-F 10am-10pm; July-Aug. Sa-Su 10am-11pm; call for hours May to early June and Sept. $30, over 54 and ages 3-8 $17; $16 for all after 5pm. Zoo open daily mid-June to Aug. 10am-8pm; Sept. to mid-June 10am-5pm. $5.25, seniors $4.75, ages 3-12 $4.)* The fearless shouldn't miss the newest thrill, **Great Bear,** an inversion rollercoaster which reaches speeds of almost 60 mph. **Capital Trailways** (397-4861) provides transportation from Lancaster City to Hershey via Harrisburg (3½hr., 1 per day, $8.15), but same-day return isn't an option.

close-up windows into the Pennsylvania Dutch world. There are plenty of bus tours through the Amish countryside from which to choose; **Amish Country Tours** (786-3600) offers 2½hr. trips that include visits to one-room schools, Amish cottage industries, authentic farms, and a vineyard ($18, ages 4-11 $11; tours given Apr.-Oct. M-Sa 10:30am and 2pm, Su 11:30am). Tourism offices have info on the pseudo-Amish experiences available, from staying in an Amish-style house to watching a blacksmith at a replica Amish farm. In 1999, expect a hullabaloo around the 50th anniversary of the **Pennsylvania Dutch Folk Festival** (610-683-8707), held at the end of June and beginning of July, north of Lancaster off I-81 S, Exit 31 ($10, ages 5-12 $5.

■ Gettysburg

From July 1-3, 1863, Union and Confederate forces met at Gettysburg in one of the bloodiest battles of the Civil War. The ultimate victory of the Union forces dealt a dire blow to the hopes of the South, but at a horrible price for both sides: there were over 50,000 casualties. Four months later, President Lincoln arrived in Gettysburg to dedicate the **Gettysburg National Cemetery,** where 979 unidentified Union soldiers lie. (Park, including cemetery, open daily 6am-10pm.) Though only 2min. long, Lincoln's address emphasizing the preservation of the Union was a watershed in American history. Each year, thousands of visitors now head for these fields, heeding the President's call to "resolve that these dead shall not have died in vain."

A high-speed elevator propels visitors up the 300 ft. **National Tower** (334-6754) for an overview of the area. (Open late Mar. to Aug. daily 9am-6:30pm; Sept.-Oct. M-Th 9am-5:30pm, F-Su 10am-4pm. $5, seniors $4.50, ages 6-12 $3.) The Park Service's **Cyclorama Center** (334-1124, ext. 499), across from the tower, shows a 20min. film on the battle every hour, and a 30min. light show displaying a cyclorama, a 356 ft. by 26 ft. mural, detailing this turning point in the Civil War (open daily 9am-5pm; $3, seniors $2.50, ages 6-16 $1.50). The **National Military Park Visitors Information Center** (334-1124, ext. 431) sits 1 mi. south of town on Taneytown Rd. (Open daily 8am-6pm; early Sept. to late May 8am-5pm. $2.50, seniors $2, under 15 $1.)

Before you attack Gettysburg's memorabilia, the visitors center can give you a free map for an 18 mi. self-guided tour. Alternatively, pay a park guide to personally show you the monuments and landmarks (2hr. tour $30 for up to 5 people), or follow a ranger for a free walking tour. Artillery Ridge Campgrounds (see below) rents **bikes** ($15 for ½-day, $25 per day) and conducts a 2hr. **horseback tour** by advanced reservation ($42). Battlefield **bicycle tours** (800-830-5775 or 691-0236), with bicycles provided, meet at Garage 30 behind 449 Baltimore St. (2hr. tours Apr.-May and Sept.-Oct. Sa-Su from 10am; June F-Su from 9am; July-Aug. Th-Su from 9am. $27.) One of many bus tours, **Historic Tours,** 55 Steinwehr Ave., (334-8000), trundles visitors around the battlefield in 1930s-era vans ($12, children $9). A candlelit **ghost tour** (337-0445 or 334-8838) gives a more imaginative look at the war at night ($6, under 8 free).

Among the many battle-related sights, the macabre **Jennie Wade House,** 528 Baltimore St. (334-4100), preserves the kitchen where Miss Wade, the only civilian killed in the battle of Gettysburg, was struck by a bullet which passed through two doors. Legend has it that unmarried women who pass their finger through the fatal bullet hole will be engaged within a year. Admission includes **Olde Town,** a wax museum of a Civil War-era town square. (Open daily 9am-9pm; Sept.-June 9am-5pm. $5.25, ages 6-11 $3.25.) The **Gettysburg Travel Council,** 35 Carlisle St. (334-6274), in the old train depot where Lincoln disembarked, stocks a full line of motel brochures, as well as maps and info on local sights (open daily 9am-5pm).

For an above-average motel experience, breeze into the **Blue Sky Motel,** 2585 Biglerville Rd./Rte. 34 N (677-7736 or 800-745-8194), 4 mi. from central Gettysburg with pleasant views from the back windows and a pool out front. (Singles $49; doubles $54; Sept.-Oct. $38/$39; Nov.-Mar. $29/$34; $4 per additional person. Suites with kitchen available. Office open Su-Th 8am-10pm, F-Sa 8am-11pm.) Follow Rte. 34 N to

Rte. 233 to reach the closest hostel, **Ironmasters Mansion Hostel (HI-AYH)** (717-486-7575), 20 mi. away and near the entrance of Pine Grove Furnace State Park. The turn-off is easy to miss; look for the Twirly Tap ice cream sign. Incredibly large and luxurious, the 1820s hostel has 46 beds in a gorgeous area, close to the Appalachian Trail. ($12, nonmembers $15. Linen $2. Email access $3. Open 7:30-9:30am and 5-10pm; by reservation only Jan.-Feb.) **Artillery Ridge,** 610 Taneytown Rd. (334-1288), 1 mi. south of the Military Park Visitors Center on Rte. 134, maintains campsites with access to showers, a riding stable, laundry facilities, a pool, nightly movies, fishing pond, and bike rentals (sites $13.50, with hookup $21; open Apr.-Nov.).

Most tasty restaurants are located in the center of town or along the roads connecting downtown to the battlefield. The candle-lit **Springhouse Tavern,** 89 Steinwehr Ave. (334-2100), hides in the basement of the **Dobbin House,** Gettysburg's first building (c. 1776), where guests can view an Underground Railroad shelter used to protect runaway slaves from recapture during the Civil War. Create your own grilled burger ($6) or try "Mason's Mile High" ($6.50), a double-decker with ham and roast beef. (Open Su-Th 9am-10pm; F-Sa 10am-11:30pm. Jazz on the 1st W of each month from 7:30pm.) Near the sights, charge into **General Pickett's Restaurant,** 571 Steinwehr Ave. (334-7580), for a southern-style all-you-can-eat buffet.

Inaccessible by Greyhound or Amtrak, Gettysburg is in south-central PA, off U.S. 15, about 30 mi. south of Harrisburg. In town, **Towne Trolley** will shuttle you to some locations, but not around the battlefield (runs Apr.-Oct.; $1). **Area code:** 717.

■ Pittsburgh

Those who come to the City of Steel expecting sprawling industry and hordes of mighty, soot-encrusted American Joes are bound to be disappointed. As late as the 1950s, smoke from area steel mills made street lamps essential even during the day. However, the decline of the steel industry has meant cleaner air and rivers, and a recent renaissance in Pittsburgh's economy has produced a brighter urban landscape. Still, citizens have yet to escape the legacy of the mills; Phillip Johnson's Pittsburgh Plate Glass Building forges steel and glass, the meat of Pittsburgh's rise to prominence, into a Gothic-style skyscraper emblematic of the city's smoky Dickensian past. City officials are desperate to provide Pittsburgh with a new tourist image, going so far as to propose a theme park filled with robotic dinosaurs. Throughout these renewals, Pittsburgh's individual neighborhoods have maintained strong and diverse identities; Oakland, Southside, and the Strip District continue to vie for visitors' attention. Admittedly, some of old, sooty Pittsburgh survives in the suburbs, but one need only ride up the Duquesne Incline and view downtown from atop Mt. Washington to see how thoroughly Pittsburgh has entered a new age—and to understand why locals are so justly proud of "The 'Burgh."

ORIENTATION AND PRACTICAL INFORMATION

Pittsburgh's downtown, the **Golden Triangle,** is shaped by two rivers—the **Allegheny** to the north, and the **Monongahela** to the south—which flow together to form a third, the **Ohio.** Streets in the Triangle that run parallel to the Monongahela are numbered one through seven. The **University of Pittsburgh** and **Carnegie-Mellon University** lie east of the Triangle in Oakland. With one of the lowest crime rates in the nation for a city of its size, Pittsburgh is fairly safe, even downtown at night.

Airport: Pittsburgh International (472-5526), 15 mi. west of downtown by I-279 and Rte. 60 in Findlay Township. The Port Authority's **28x Airport Flyer** bus serves downtown and Oakland from the airport (daily on the half-hour 6am-11:58pm, $2). **Airline Transportation Company** (471-2250 or 471-8900) rolls to downtown (M-F every 30min. 6am-11:40pm, Sa-Su every hr. 6am-11pm; $12), Oakland (M-F every hr. 9am-10pm, Sa every 2hr. from 9am-5pm, Su every 2hr. 10am-2pm, every hr. 3-10pm; round-trip $21), and Monroeville (M-F every 2hr. 9am-3pm, every hr. 3-10pm, Su at 2, 4, 7, and 9pm; $20). Cab to downtown runs $30.

Trains: Amtrak, 1100 Liberty Ave. (471-6170 or 800-872-7245), at Grant on the northern edge of downtown next to Greyhound and the post office. Generally safe inside, *but be careful walking from here to the city center at night.* To: Philadelphia (8½-11½hr., 2 per day, $42-51); New York (10-13hr., 3 per day, $56-68); and Chicago (9½-10hr., 2 per day, $52-96). Station open 24hr.

Buses: Greyhound (392-6526 or 800-231-2222), on 11th St. at Liberty Ave. near Amtrak. To Philadelphia (7hr., 8 per day, $41) and Chicago (8-12hr., 10 per day, $57). Station and ticket office open 24hr.

Public Transportation: Port Authority of Allegheny County (PAT) (442-2000). Downtown: bus fare free until 7pm, 75¢ after 7pm; subway (between the 3 downtown stops) free. Beyond downtown: bus fare $1.25-2, transfers 25¢, weekend allday pass $3; subway $1.25-2, ages 6-11 ½-price for bus and subway. Schedules and maps at most subway stations and in the "Community Interest" section of the yellow pages. PAT runs somewhat erratically, so a schedule is essential.

Taxi: Peoples Cab, 681-3131. $1.40 base fare, $1.40 per mi.

Car Rental: Rent-A-Wreck (367-3131 or 800-472-8353), on McKnight St. 7 mi. north of downtown. $20-25 per day with 100 free mi.; 18¢ per additional mi. Must be 21 with credit or charge card, some preapproved cash rentals. Under 25 pay $3 per day surcharge. Open M-F 8am-6pm, Sa 8am-4pm.

Visitor Info: Pittsburgh Convention and Visitors Bureau, 4 Gateway Center, 18th fl. (281-7711 or 800-359-0758; http://www.pittsburgh-cvb.org), downtown on Liberty Ave. Open M-F 9am-5pm, Sa-Su 9am-3pm. There are 4 visitors centers: downtown, Oakland, Mt. Washington, and the airport.

Hotlines: Rape Action Hotline, 765-2731. Operates 24hr. **Gay, Lesbian, Bisexual Center,** 422-0114.

Post Office: 700 Grant St. (800-275-8777). Open M-F 7am-6pm, Sa 7am-3:30pm. **ZIP code:** 15219. **Area code:** 412.

ACCOMMODATIONS AND CAMPGROUNDS

Converted from an old bank building, the sparkling new **Pittsburgh Hostel (HI-AYH),** 830 E. Warrington Ave. (431-1267), at the corner of Arlington St., in Allentown 1 mi. south of downtown, delivers modern hostel living complete with full kitchen, A/C, free parking, and spacious rooms. ($17, nonmembers $20. Linen $1, towels 50¢. Check-in 8-10am and 5-10pm. No curfew.) More a hotel than a hostel, **Point Park College,** 201 Wood St. (392-3824), at Blvd. of the Allies, 8 blocks from the Greyhound Station, provides clean rooms, some of which have private baths, to HI-AYH members and college students. The 3rd fl. cafeteria serves an all-you-can-eat breakfast ($4) daily 7-9:30am. ($15. 3-day max. stay. Reception M-F 8am-4pm. Check-in 11pm; tell the guards you're a hosteler. Reservations recommended. Open mid-May to mid-Aug.) The **Allegheny YMCA,** 600 W. North Ave. (321-8594), has the basics in the North Side (laundry facilities; $20, $66 per week; $5 key deposit).

Several inexpensive motels can be found on the city's outskirts near the airport. **Motel 6,** 211 Beecham Dr. (922-9400), off I-79 at Exit 16/16B 10 mi. from downtown, supplies standard lodging with A/C and TVs (singles $36; doubles $42; reservations suggested for summer weekends). **Pittsburgh North Campground,** 6610 Mars Rd. (724-776-1150), in Cranberry Township, has the area's closest camping, 20min. north of downtown; take I-79 to the Cranberry/Mars Exit. (110 campsites, showers, swimming. Tent sites for 2 $18, with hookup $26; $3 per extra adult, $2 per extra child.)

BEES, DOGS, AND OTHER EDIBLE STUFF

Aside from the pizza joints and bars downtown, **Oakland** is the best place to look for a good inexpensive meal. Collegiate watering holes and cafes pack **Forbes Ave.** around the University of Pittsburgh, while colorful eateries and shops line **Walnut St.** in Shadyside and **E. Carson St.** in South Side. The **Strip District** on Penn Ave. between 16th and 22nd St. (north of downtown along the Allegheny) bustles with Italian, Greek, and Asian cuisine, as well as vendors, grocers, and craftsmen. On Saturday mornings, fresh produce, fish, and street performers compete for business.

MID-ATLANTIC

⊛**Original Oyster House,** 20 Market Sq. (566-7925), Pittsburgh's oldest and perhaps cheapest restaurant and bar. Serves seafood platters ($4-5) and sandwiches ($2-4.50) in a beautiful marble and wrought-iron barroom. A death-defying "Crab Cutlet" sandwich ($2.55) will slam one to your arteries amidst panoramic shots of Miss America pageants from ages past. Open M-Sa 9am-11pm.

Original Hot Dog Shops, Inc., 3901 Forbes Ave. (687-8327), at Bouquet St. in Oakland. A rowdy, greasy Pittsburgh institution with lots and lots of fries, burgers, dogs, and pizza. Locals call it "the O." 16 in. pizza $4.50. Open Su-W 10am-3:30am, Th 10am-4:30am, F-Sa 10am-5am.

Beehive Coffeehouse and Theater, 3807 Forbes Ave. (683-4483), just steps from "the O." Another location in South Side, 1327 E. Carson St. (488-4483). A quirky coffeehouse brimming with cool wall paintings, cool staff, cool clientele, and hot cappuccino ($1.80). The theater in the back features current films. Poetry and an occasional open-mic improv night buzz upstairs. Open M-F 7am-2am, Sa 8:30am-2am, Su 9:30am-2am.

Union Grille, 413 S. Craig St. (681-8620), in Oakland. This clean-cut bar and grille is gaining notoriety for its fresh-killed hunks of char-grilled meat ($6) and cheap draughts ($1.50-2.75). No working class sympathizer will turn down a plate of Union Potato Skins ($5), if he knows what's good for him. Veggie sandwiches ($7) and house wine ($2.50) for activists and aesthetes.

SIGHTS

The **Golden Triangle** is home to **Point State Park** and its famous 200 ft. fountain. A ride up the **Duquesne Incline,** 1220 Grandview Ave. (381-1665), in the South Side, affords a spectacular view of the city (open M-Sa 5:30am-12:45am, Su 7am-12:45am; round-trip $2). Founded in 1787, the **University of Pittsburgh** (624-4141; 624-6094 for tours) stands in the shadow of the 42-story **Cathedral of Learning** (624-6000), at Bigelow Blvd. between Forbes and 5th Ave. in Oakland. (*Cassette-guided tours M-F 9am-3pm, Sa 9:30am-3pm, Su 11am-3pm. $2, seniors $1.50, ages 8-18 50¢.*) The Cathedral, an academic building dedicated in 1934, features 23 "nationality classrooms" designed and decorated by artisans from Pittsburgh's many ethnic traditions. **Carnegie-Mellon University** (268-2000) houses scholars down the street on Forbes Ave.

The **Andy Warhol Museum,** 117 Sandusky St. (237-8300), on the North Side, is the world's largest museum dedicated to a single artist, supporting 7 floors of the Pittsburgh native's material, from pop portraits of Marilyn, Jackie, and Grace to continuous screenings of films like *Eat,* a 39min. film of a man eating, and a series of pieces entitled *Oxidation,* made from synthetic polymer paint and urine on canvas. (*Open W and Su 11am-6pm, Th-Sa 11am-8pm. $6, seniors $5, students and children $4.*) A 20min. walk into the North Side, **The Mattress Factory,** 500 Sampsonia Way (231-3169), is actually a modern art museum (very sneaky!) specializing in engaging temporary installations. (*Open Tu-Sa 10am-5pm, Su 1-5pm. Free.*) The three spectacular permanent exhibits by James Turrell, the mythic light-worker, are a don't-miss.

Two of America's biggest financial legends, Andrew Carnegie and Henry Clay Frick, made their fortunes in Pittsburgh. Today, their bequests enrich the city's cultural fortune. Carnegie's most famous gift, **The Carnegie,** 4400 Forbes Ave. (622-3131; 622-3289 for guided tours), across the street from the Cathedral of Learning (take any bus to Oakland), comprises both an art museum and a natural history collection. (*Open Tu-Sa 10am-5pm, Su 1-5pm. $6, students and ages 3-18 $4, seniors $5.*) Five hundred famous dinosaur specimens stalk the natural history section, including an 84 ft. giant dubbed *Diplodocus Carnegii* (the things money will buy…). The modern art wing hosts an impressive collection of Impressionist, Post-Impressionist, and 20th-century work. Though most people know Henry Clay Frick for his art collection in New York, the **Art Museum** at the **Frick Art and Historical Center,** 7227 Reynolds St. (371-0600), Point Breeze, 20min. east of downtown, displays some of his earlier, less famous acquisitions. (*Open Tu-Sa 10am-5pm, Su noon-6pm. Admission free to Art Museum and Car and Carriage Museum, $8 to Frick Estate.*) The permanent collection contains Italian, Flemish, and French works from the 13th to 18th centuries. Chamber music concerts occur October through April.

The curious can feel an earthquake in full motion, climb aboard a WWII submarine, or try their skill at rock climbing at the **Carnegie Science Center,** 1 Allegheny Ave. (237-3400), next to Three Rivers Stadium. *(Open Su-F 10am-6pm, Sa 10am-9pm. $6.50, ages 3-18 and seniors $4.50; with OmniMax or planetarium $10/$6.)*

In Penn Hills, an eastern suburb of Pittsburgh, lies the U.S.'s first Hindu temple. The **Sri Venkateswara (or S.V.) Temple** (373-3380), east of town off I-376, is modeled after a temple in Andhra Pradesh, India, and has become a major pilgrimage site for American Hindus since it was completed in 1976. Non-Hindus can walk through the Great Hall and observe prayer.

ENTERTAINMENT AND NIGHTLIFE

Most restaurants and shops carry the weekly *In Pittsburgh* or *City Paper,* great sources for free, up-to-date entertainment listings, nightclubs, and racy personals. The internationally acclaimed **Pittsburgh Symphony Orchestra** (392-4900) performs September through May at **Heinz Hall,** 600 Penn Ave., downtown, and gives free outdoor concerts on summer evenings in Point State Park. The **Pittsburgh Public Theater** (321-9800), in Allegheny Sq. on the North Side, is world-renowned, but charges a pretty penny. (Performances Oct.-July. Box office open M 10am-5:30pm, Tu-Sa 10am-8pm, Su noon-7pm. Tickets $15-36; students and children $10 for shows Su-F.) At gritty Three Rivers Stadium on the North Side, the **Pirates** (321-2827) slug it out from April through September, while the **Steelers** (323-1200) hit the gridiron from September through December.

For nightlife, although the Strip downtown is still relatively dense with revelers (relatively, that is, in a town that closes at 5pm), the hip crowd fills **E. Carson St.** on the South Side, which overflows with reg'lar guys 'n' gals on weekend nights.

The **Metropol** and the adjoining **Rosebud,** 1600 Smallman St. (261-4512), in the Strip District, fill a spacious warehouse with dancing supermen and citizens plain (cover $2-5; doors generally open 8-9pm). The drinks flow with abandon in a fluorescent cave-like setting at the **Lava Lounge,** 2204 E. Carson St. (431-0850), South Side. Frankie Capri performs his absurd Elvis impersonation/puppet show/interactive dress-up experience every Friday night for $3. (Open M-Sa 4:30pm-2am.) **Nick's Fat City,** 1601-1605 E. Carson St. (481-6880), South Side, serves as an invaluable crashcourse into the world of Pittsburgh rock 'n' roll. Your teachers will be a lineup of favorite local bands; your study aids will be $2.75 draughts of Yuengling, a favorite PA brew, and a star-studded floor inscribed with such local faves as Porky Chedwick and The Four Chairs. (Cover free to almost free.) **Jack's** (431-3644), on E. Carson at S. 12th, South Side, repeatedly earns the moniker "Best Bar in the 'Burgh" by offering lifesaving specials like Monday 25¢ hot wings, Wednesday 10¢ wings, and $1 chicken fillet to a rowdy, but friendly local crowd (21+; open M-Sa 7am-2am, Su 11am-2am). The gay and lesbian community flocks to the **Pegasus Lounge,** 818 Liberty Ave. (281-2131), downtown, for house music and drag shows (open daily 4pm-2am).

Homestead Graysbox

Past the shock-yellow Pirates pennants and computer-generated "Arrrr"-ing buccaneer lining the upper tiers of capacious Three Rivers Stadium, a nondescript gray banner plainly states **"Homestead Grays."** A reminder of the days of the **Negro Leagues,** a remnant of a segregationist past upon which America waxes both nostalgic and indignant, the pennant quietly reminds those in the know of a baseball team formed in 1910 from Homestead steelworkers. The Grays rose to become a league leader, winning every Negro National League pennant from 1931 to 1939 and several **Negro World Series,** including the Leagues' last in 1948. Considered by many to be the greatest Negro League team, the Grays vanished into near-obscurity when the League split. **Forbes Field,** where they played, has been doomed to destruction, and now Three Rivers, which mildly speaks of their legacy, is soon to follow.

■ Ohiopyle

Lifted by steep hills and cut by cascading rivers, southwest Pennsylvania encompasses some of the loveliest forests in the East. Native Americans dubbed this region "Ohiopehhle" ("white frothy water") for the grand Youghiogheny River Gorge (YOCK-a-GAY-nee—"The Yock" to locals), now the focal point of Pennsylvania's Ohiopyle State Park. The park's 19,000 acres offer hiking, fishing, hunting, whitewater rafting, and a variety of winter activities. The latest addition to the banks of the Yock, a graveled bike trail that winds 28 mi. north from the town of Confluence to Connellsville, was converted from a riverside railroad bed. Recently named one of the 19 best walks in the world, the trail is just one section of the "rails to trails" project that will eventually connect Pittsburgh and Washington, D.C.

Throngs of tourists come each year to raft Ohiopyle's 8 mi. long, class III rapids. Some of the best whitewater rafting in the East, the rapids take about 5hr. to conquer. Four outfitters front Rte. 381 in "downtown" Ohiopyle: **White Water Adventurers** (800-992-7238), **Wilderness Voyageurs** (800-272-4141), **Laurel Highlands River Tours** (800-472-3846), and **Mountain Streams** (800-723-8669). The price for a guided trip on the Yock varies dramatically ($30-57 per person per day), depending on the season, day of the week, and difficulty. If you're an experienced river rat (or if you just happen to enjoy flipping boats), any of the above companies will rent you equipment. *(Rafts about $11-15 per person; canoes $20; "duckies"—inflatable kayaks— about $20-26.)* In order to float anything on the river on the weekend, you must get a **launch permit** at the park office (M-F free; weekend passes $2.50; call at least 30 days in advance). You'll also need to park your car at **Old Mitchell Parking Lot,** 7 mi. northwest of downtown, and purchase a $2.50 token that will take you and your equipment from the end of your rafting journey back to your car. The market in the Falls Market and Overnight Inn (see above) sells the **fishing licenses** required in the park ($15 for 3 days; $30 per week; $35 per season, residents $17). Bike rental prices vary with bike styles (generally $3-4 per hr.).

Inexpensive motels around Ohiopyle are few and far between, but the excellent **Ohiopyle State Park Hostel (HI-AYH)** (329-4476), on Ferncliffe Rd., sits right in the center of town off Rte. 381. (24 bunks, kitchen, laundry facilities. $9, nonmembers $12. Linen not provided. Check-in 6-10pm.) Just down the street on Rte. 381, **Falls Market and Overnight Inn,** P.O. Box 101 (329-4973), rents surprisingly nice singles ($35) and doubles ($50) with shared baths (A/C, cable TV, VCR, laundry facilities). The downstairs store has groceries and a restaurant/snack bar (burgers $1.65, pancakes $2.50; open daily 7am-9pm; in winter 7am-6:30pm). There are 237 **campsites** in Ohiopyle (M-F $13, Sa-Su $16; PA residents $11/$14). The park recommends calling at least 30 days in advance for weekend reservations in the summer.

Ohiopyle borders on Rte. 381, 64 mi. southeast of Pittsburgh via Rte. 51 and U.S. 40. **Greyhound** serves Uniontown, a large town 20 mi. to the west on U.S. 40, and travels to Pittsburgh (1¼hr., 2 per day, $12). The **Park Information Center,** P.O. Box 105 (329-8591), lies just off Rte. 381 on Dinnerbell Rd. (open daily 8am-4pm; Nov.-Apr. M-F 8am-4pm). Calling 800-925-7669 earns a free booklet. **Post Office:** Sheridan St. (329-8605; open M-F 8am-6pm, Sa 8am-noon). **ZIP code:** 15470. **Area code:** 724.

■ Near Ohiopyle

Fallingwater (329-8501), 8 mi. north of Ohiopyle on Rte. 381, is a masterpiece by the father of modern architecture, Frank Lloyd Wright. *(Open Tu-Su 10am-4pm; Nov.-Dec. and Mar. Sa-Su only. Tours Tu-F $8, ages 9-18 $6; Sa-Su $12/$7. Children under 9 must be left in child care, $2 per hr.)* Designed in 1935 in the midst of the Great Depression for Pittsburgh's wealthy Kaufmann family, "the most famous private residence ever built" blends into the surrounding terrain; huge boulders that predate the house are part of the structure's architecture. The family originally wanted the house to be near or facing the Bear Run Waterfall. However, Wright built the house over the waterfall, so you can hear the water's roar in every room, but can see it from only one terrace. This site can only be seen on a 1hr. guided tour; make reservations. If you're thirsting for more Wright, **Kentuck Knob** (329-1901), Kentuck Rd. in Chalk Hill, is an architectural gem without a single 90° angle in the entire home. *(1hr. tours leave on the half-hour. Open Tu-Su 10am-4pm; Dec.-Mar. Sa-Su 10am-4pm. $10; ages 12+ only.)*

   Fort Necessity National Battlefield, on U.S. 40 near Rte. 381, is a replica of the original fort built by George Washington. In July 1754, young George, then of Virginia militia, was beaten in an attack on Fort Necessity that began the French and Indian War. The Fort's **visitors center** (329-5512) has more info (open daily 8:30am-6:30pm; early Sept. to late May 8:30am-5pm; $2, under 16 free). A few miles west, the singular **Museum of Early American Farm Machines and Very Old Horse Saddles with a History** (438-5180) exhibits rusted and zany Americana, including a 12-ton cast-iron steam engine from 1905 and saddles from the Civil War.

Delaware

You know that a state whose number one boast in tourist literature is its convenient East Coast location has a certain inferiority complex. Tiny Delaware does, however, serve as a welcome sanctuary from the sprawling cities of the Boston-Washington megalopolis. Delaware's particular charm is well represented by the state bug, the ladybug, adopted in 1974 after an ardent campaign by elementary school children.

   Delaware was the first colony to ratify the U.S. Constitution on December 7, 1787—hence the tag "First State." Since then its history has been dominated by the wealthy DuPont clan, whose gunpowder mills grew into a chemical giant. Tax-free shopping, scenic beach towns—and yes, convenient location—lure vacationers to Delaware from all along the country's eastern shores.

PRACTICAL INFORMATION

Capital: Dover.
Visitor Info: 99 King's Hwy., Dover 19901 (739-4271 or 800-441-8846; http://www.state.de.us). Open M-F 8am-4:30pm. **Division of Fish and Wildlife,** 89 King's Hwy., Dover 19901 (800-523-3336).
Time Zone: Eastern. **Postal Abbreviation:** DE
Sales Tax: 8% on accommodations. 0% on everything else; you gotta love it.

▓ Delaware Seashore

Lewes Founded in 1613 by the Zwaanendael colony from Hoorn, Holland, **Lewes** (LEW-is) touts itself as Delaware's first town. More than 350 years later, Disney has rated this sleepy burg on the Delaware Bay, across the Delaware River from Cape May, NJ, as one of the best places to visit in America. Lewes's charming Victorian houses and calm shores attract an annual influx of antique hunters and families seeking a retreat from the rough Atlantic waters. With produce stands sporadically lining the streets, the small-town atmosphere in Lewes is upscale and reserved, but well-kept beaches and welcoming natives make the town inviting for budget travelers.

   Secluded among sand dunes and scrub pines, the 4000-acre **Cape Henlopen State Park** (645-8983, for camping 645-2103), 1 mi. east of Lewes, is home to a seabird nesting colony, sparkling white "walking dunes," a 2 mi. paved trail perfect for rollerblading, and a beach with a bathhouse (open daily 8am-sunset; $5 per car, bikes and walkers free). Sandy **campsites** are available on a first come, first served basis (sites $18; open Apr.-Oct.).

   Travelers can stay near the beach at the small **Captain's Quarters,** 406 Savannah Rd. (645-7924), owned by a retired waterman (doubles July-Aug. $70-80; off-season $30-45; $5 per additional person; open Apr.-Nov.), or a few blocks away at **Savannah Inn,** 330 Savannah Rd. (645-5592), a seven-room B&B with a lavish vegetarian breakfast. (Shared baths. $50-80, largest rooms sleep 3 or 4; Oct.-May $40-80, no breakfast.)

The **Rosa Negra,** 128 2nd St. (645-1980), offers bargain Italian fare for early diners (daily 4-6pm choice of 8 pastas and 9 sauces $7, seniors $6) and a few vegan options. (Open for lunch M-Sa 11am-2pm; dinner Su-Th 4-9pm, F-Sa 4-10pm.) Lewes has little nightlife, but both locals and tourists foray to the **Rose and Crown Restaurant and Pub,** 108 2nd St. (645-2373), for near-daily live music and some English specials, like cottage pie ($12; happy hour M-Sa 4-6pm, Su 4pm-1am; open daily 11am-1am).

   Greyhound (800-231-2222), stopping in front of the Ace Hardware Store on Rte. 1, serves Lewes with buses to Washington, D.C. (3½hr., $32.75); Baltimore (3½hr., $28.75); and Philadelphia (4hr., $30.75). Lewes is one end of the 70min. **Cape May, NJ/Lewes, DE Ferry** route (644-6030; $20 with car, $6 per additional passenger; less in off season). In Lewes and Rehoboth, the **Delaware Resort Transit (DART)** (800-553-DART/3278) **shuttle bus** runs from the ferry terminal, through Lewes to Rehoboth and Dewey Beach, every 30min. ($1, seniors and disabled 40¢, $2 per day; runs late May to early Sept. daily 7am-3am.) **Seaport Taxi** (645-6800) services the area. The **Lewes Chamber of Commerce** (645-8078), on King's Hwy., operates out of the relocated 1730 **Fisher-Martin House** (open M-F 10am-4pm, Sa 9am-3pm, Su 10am-2pm; in winter M-F 10am-4pm). **Area code:** 302.

Rehoboth Beach

The cotton candy, mini-golf, fast-food, and discount t-shirt shops of Rehoboth's boardwalk strip contrast sharply with the almost New England serenity of seaside Lewes, but a bit inland lives a similar well-heeled resort community of numerous Washington families and a burgeoning gay population. The congestion on the sparkling beach thins to the north of the boardwalk. Early risers will find the boardwalk beach deserted and may see the daily southward commute of the dolphins. From Rte. 1, follow Rehoboth Ave. until it hits the water at Rehoboth Beach, or follow Rte. 1 south to **Dewey Beach.**

   Inexpensive lodging abounds. The **Lord Baltimore,** 16 Baltimore Ave. (227-2855), 1 block from the boardwalk, has rented out clean, antiquated rooms with TVs, refrigerators, and A/C for over 25 years. (Singles and doubles $35-65; in winter $25-50; $5 per additional person. Reservations recommended.) At the **Abbey Inn,** 31 Maryland Ave. (227-7023), there's always a conversation waiting on the porch. (Singles from $35; doubles from $40; F-Sa 15% surcharge. 2-day min. stay. Open late May to early Sept. Reserve 1 week in advance.) **The Whitson,** 30 Maryland Ave. (227-7966), offers comparable rooms for a slightly higher price (singles $42-55, doubles $58-65; 2-day min. stay F-Sa). Heavily wooded **Big Oaks Family Campground** (645-6838), ¾ mi. off Rte. 1 on Rd. 270, has open sites and a pool (tents $25, with hookup $30).

   Rehoboth is known for its deluxe beach cuisine and its many bar-hoppin' options. With saturated fats crowding the boardwalk, the mother-daughter run **Café Papillion,** 42 Rehoboth Ave. (227-7568), in the Penny Lane Mall, provides the only haven for healthy (and vegetarian) fare around, with fresh crepes ($2.50-5) and stuffed baguette sandwiches for $5-6.25 (open May-Oct. daily 8am-11pm; Apr. Sa-Su 8am-11pm). Inexpensive Italian food can be found at **Nicola Pizza,** 8 N. 1st St., home of the calzone-like Nic-o-boli ($4.75-$6.50) and the five-person pail of pasta ($21). Some of the best Mexican food on the beach is next door at **Plumb Loco,** 10 N. 1st St. (227-6870), with sedate but tasty quesadillas (open Su-Th 5pm-1am, F-Sa noon-1am).

   Arena's Deli lays down live music, over 100 beers, and delicious sandwiches ($5) for an eclectic crowd. (No cover. Live music W and F-M; in winter W and F-Su. Happy hour M-F 4-7pm. Open daily 11am-1am.) **Irish Eyes,** 15 Wilmington Ave. (227-2888), are smiling because they feature comedy on Monday, live rock on Wednesday, and ol' Irish Thursday to Sunday ($5 cover; open M-F 5pm-1am, Sa-Su noon-1am). **Blue Moon,** 35 Baltimore Ave. (227-6515), rises at 4pm daily and rocks a predominantly gay crowd until 1am (no cover; happy hour M-F 4-6pm).

   The **Rehoboth Beach Chamber of Commerce,** 501 Rehoboth Ave. (227-2233 or 800-441-1329), in a recycled railroad depot, doles out Delaware info (open M-F 9am-5pm, Sa-Su 9am-noon). **Greyhound/Trailways,** 251 Rehoboth Ave. (227-7223), stops outside a dilapidated dry cleaner. Buses go to Washington, D.C. (3½hr., 1 per day,

$32.75); Baltimore (3½hr., 1 per day, $28.75); and Philadelphia (4hr., 2 per day, $30.75). Adjacent to the Whitson, **Bob's Bikes** (227-7611) offers bike rental ($3 per hr.) and little red pedal surreys ($15-20 per hr.). **Area code:** 302.

Maryland

Once upon a time, on Maryland's rural eastern shore, inhabitants captured crabs, raised tobacco, and ruled the Maryland economy. Across the bay in Baltimore, workers loaded ships and ran factories. Then the federal government expanded, industry shrank, and Maryland had a new focus: the Baltimore-Washington Pkwy. Suburbs grew, Baltimore revitalized, and the Old Line State acquired a new, liberal urbanity. As D.C.'s homogenized commuter suburbs continue to swell beyond the limits of Maryland's Montgomery and Prince Georges counties, Baltimore revels in its immensity while Annapolis, the capital, remains a small-town commune for sailors. The mountains and mines of the state's western panhandle—geographic and cultural kin to West Virginia—are to this day largely pristine.

PRACTICAL INFORMATION

Capital: Annapolis.
Visitor Info: Office of Tourism, 217 E. Redwood St., Baltimore 21202 (800-543-1036; http://www.mdisfun.org). **Dept. of Natural Resources,** 580 Taylor Ave., Annapolis 21401 (410-260-8186; open M-F 8am-4:30pm).
Emergency: 911.
Time Zone: Eastern. **Postal Abbreviation:** MD. **Sales Tax:** 5%.

■ Baltimore

Patapsco, the Indian name for Baltimore, may have meant "backwater," but Baltimore has earned its place in history; here, Francis Scott Key penned the national anthem and entrepreneurs constructed America's first umbrella factory. Crab cakes, Orioles games, Inner Harbor, and the fabulous National Aquarium are all fine reasons to visit Baltimore, but travelers will be rewarded for digging deeper. Baltimore's Southern heritage is visible in its many district neighborhoods, such as Roland Park, where every house has a front porch and everyone greets you in that friendly "Bawlmer" accent. Certain natives have gained notoriety for digging beneath this genial Southern complacency. John Waters's films capture the city's twisted side, while Anne Tyler's fiction evokes its melancholy soul.

ORIENTATION AND PRACTICAL INFORMATION

Baltimore sits in central Maryland, 100 mi. south of Philadelphia and about 150 mi. up the Chesapeake Bay from the Atlantic Ocean. The southern end of the **Jones Falls Expwy. (I-83)** halves the city at the Inner Harbor, while the **Baltimore Beltway (I-695)** circles the city. I-95 cuts across the southwest corner of the city as a shortcut to the wide arc of the Beltway. During rush hour, these interstates slow to a crawl.

Baltimore is plagued by one-way streets. **Baltimore St.** (which runs east a few blocks north of the Inner Harbor) and **Charles St.** (which runs north from the west corner of the Harbor) divide the city into quarters. Baltimore St. divides the city into north and south; Charles St. is the east-west divider. Streets are dubbed with directional suffixes according to their relation to these thoroughfares.

Airport: Baltimore-Washington International (BWI) (859-7032), on I-195 off the Baltimore-Washington Expwy. (I-295), about 10 mi. south of the city center. Take MTA bus #17 to the Nursery Rd. light-rail station. Airport **shuttles** (859-0800) to

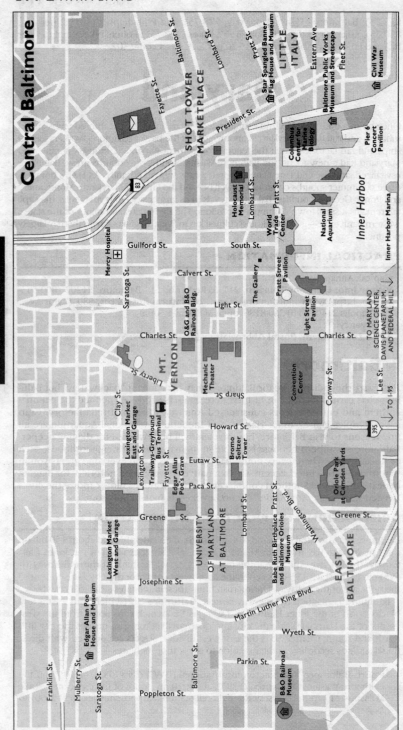

Central Baltimore

SHOT TOWER MARKETPLACE

LITTLE ITALY

Baltimore St.

Lombard St.

Fayette St.

Pratt St.

Eastern Ave.

Fleet St.

Star Spangled Banner Flag House and Museum

🏛 Baltimore Public Works Museum and Streetscape

🏛 Civil War Museum

President St.

Pratt St.

🏛 Holocaust Memorial

Lombard St.

World Trade Center

Columbus Center for Marine Biology

Pier 6 Concert Pavilion

Inner Harbor

Mercy Hospital ✚

Guilford St.

South St.

National Aquarium

Inner Harbor Marina

Saratoga St.

Calvert St.

The Gallery ▪

Pratt Street Pavilion

Light St.

Charles St.

O&G and B&O Railroad Bldg.

MT. VERNON

Liberty St.

Mechanic Theater

Sharp St.

Light Street Pavilion

Charles St.

TO MARYLAND SCIENCE CENTER, DAVIS PLANETARIUM, AND FEDERAL HILL ↓

Conway St.

Lee St.

Convention Center

↓ TO I-95

Clay St.

Lexington Market East and Garage

Trailways-Greyhound Bus Terminal

Fayette St.

Howard St.

Bromo Seltzer Tower

Lexington St.

🏛 Edgar Allan Poe's Grave

Eutaw St.

Paca St.

Oriole Park at Camden Yards

Lexington Market West and Garage

Greene St.

Lombard St.

Babe Ruth Birthplace and Baltimore Orioles Museum 🏛

Greene St.

UNIVERSITY OF MARYLAND AT BALTIMORE

EAST BALTIMORE

Josephine St.

Washington Blvd.

Franklin St.

Mulberry St.

🏛 Edgar Allan Poe House and Museum

Saratoga St.

Martin Luther King Blvd.

Wyeth St.

Baltimore St.

Parkin St.

🏛 B&O Railroad Museum

Poppleton St.

hotels run daily every 30min. 5:45am-11:30pm ($11 to downtown Baltimore, round-trip $17). For D.C., shuttles leave hourly 5:45am-11:30pm ($21-31). **Amtrak** trains from BWI run to Baltimore ($5) and D.C. ($12). **MARC** commuter trains are cheaper but slower, and only run M-F. To Baltimore ($3.25) and D.C. ($5).

Trains: Penn Station, 1500 N. Charles St. (800-872-7245), at Mt. Royal Ave. Easily accessible by bus #3 or 11 from Charles Station downtown. Trains run about every 30min.-1hr. to New York ($58-67), Washington, D.C. ($15-16), and Philadelphia ($31-36). On weekdays, 2 **MARC** commuter lines (800-543-9809 or 800-325-7245 in Maryland) connect Baltimore to D.C.'s Union Station (859-7400) via Penn Station (with stops at BWI Airport) or **Camden Station,** at the corner of Howard and Camden St. near Oriole Park. Both are $5.75, round-trip $10.25. Open daily 5:30am-9:30pm, self-serve open 24hr. (credit card only).

Buses: Greyhound (800-231-2222) has two locations: downtown at 210 W. Fayette St. (752-0919), near N. Howard St.; and at 5625 O'Donnell St. (633-6389), 3 mi. east of downtown near I-95. Connections to: New York ($24); Washington, D.C. ($6); and Philadelphia ($15).

Public Transportation: Mass Transit Administration (MTA), 300 W. Lexington St. (bus and Metro schedule info 539-5000 or 800-543-9809; line staffed M-F 6am-9pm), near N. Howard St. Bus, Metro, and light-rail service to most major sights in the city and outlying areas. Some buses run 24hr. Metro operates M-F 5am-midnight, Sa 6am-midnight. Light rail operates M-F 6am-11pm, Sa 8am-11pm, Su 11am-7pm. Base fare for all of these $1.35, but may be higher depending on distance traveled. Bus #17 runs from the Nursery Rd. light-rail to BWI Airport.

Water Taxi: (563-3901 or 800-658-8947). Stops every 8-18min. (Nov.-Mar. every 40min.) at the harbor museums, Harborplace, Fells Point, Little Italy, and more. An easy, pleasant way to travel to Baltimore's main sights; especially in summer, when service continues until midnight. Service stops at 6pm Nov.-Mar. and at 9pm in Apr. A day of unlimited rides is $3.50 for adults, $2.25 for children 10 and under.

Taxi: Checker Cab, 685-1212. **Royal Cab,** 327-0330.

Car Rental: Thrifty Car Rental, BWI Airport (859-1136), and 2042 N. Howard St. (783-0300), 9 blocks from Penn Station. Economy cars from $35 per weekday and $185 per week. Unlimited mi. in MD and bordering states. Under 25 $15 extra per day. Must be 21 with credit card. Airport branch open daily 6am-11pm.

Visitor Info: Baltimore Area Visitors Centers, 300 E. Pratt St. (659-7090 or 800-282-6632), at Harborplace. Open M-Sa 9am-7pm, Su 10am-6pm; off-season M-Sa 9am-5pm, Su 10am-3pm. **Traveler's Aid,** 685-3569 (staffed M-F 8:30am-3:30pm) or 685-5874 (voice-mail). Direct phones at Penn Station and Greyhound terminal.

Hotlines: Suicide Hotline, 531-6677. **Sexual Assault and Domestic Violence Center,** 828-6390. **Gay and Lesbian Switchboard,** 837-8888. Operates daily 7pm-midnight, recording at all other times.

Post Office: 900 E. Fayette St. (347-4425). Open M-F 7:30am-9pm, Sa 7:30am-5pm.

ZIP code: 21233.

Area code: 410.

ACCOMMODATIONS AND CAMPGROUNDS

Expensive chain hotels dominate the **Inner Harbor,** and reputable inexpensive hotels elsewhere are hard to find. **Amanda's Bed and Breakfast Reservation Service,** 1428 Park Ave. (225-0001 or 800-899-7533; call M-F 8:30am-5:30pm, Sa 8:30am-noon), will match you with B&Bs in private homes, cottages, or yachts that suit your needs. Rates begin at $50 a night. Reservations are recommended.

Baltimore International Youth Hostel (HI-AYH), 17 W. Mulberry St. (576-8880), centrally located at Cathedral St. in Mt. Vernon. Take MTA bus #3 or 11 along Charles St. 19th-century brownstone harbors 40 beds in spacious dorm rooms, as well as full kitchen and laundry services. Lounge features marble fireplaces and a TV. A/C in bedrooms. $14, nonmembers $17. 3-night max. stay (may be extended with manager's approval). Free baggage storage ($5 deposit) and linen ($10 deposit). Curfew 11pm, but house keys available with $10 deposit. Reservations recommended. *Exercise caution in this area at night.*

Duke's Motel, 7905 Pulaski Hwy. (686-0400), in Rosedale off the Beltway. The bulletproof glass in the front office is nothing to worry about—all the neighborhood motels have it. Clean and carefully run, Duke's is probably the best option on the sleazy Pulaski Hwy. motel strip. Simple, dim rooms have A/C, carpeting, and cable TV. Singles $36-41; doubles $41-46. King-sized beds optional. $3 key deposit and ID required. Best for people with cars.

Capitol KOA, 768 Cecil Ave. (410-923-2771 or 800-KOA/562-0248). Mostly RVs, some cabins, and a small wooded area for tents. Tent site for 2 $25; water and electricity $30; RV full hookup $32; 1-room cabin $41, 2 rooms $49. $5 per additional adult, $2 per child. Open Mar. 25-Nov. 1.

FOOD

Maryland blue crab, fresh from the Chesapeake Bay, appears on the menu at nearly every restaurant in Baltimore. The **Pavilions** at Harborplace (332-4191), on Pratt and Light St., have enough food stalls and restaurants to please any palate. A 10min. walk from the harbor, beyond the medieval-style clock tower of the Bromo Seltzer building, lies 215-year-old **Lexington Market,** 400 W. Lexington (685-6169), at Eutaw St. The market offers an endless variety of produce, fresh meat, and seafood, in food stalls that are cheaper than those at Harborplace. (Open M-Sa 8:30am-6pm; take the subway to Lexington Station, or bus #7.)

Louie's Bookstore Café, 518 N. Charles St. (962-1224), just up the street from the Washington Monument. In front, an upscale bookstore flaunts extensive sections on music and literature. In back, a lively restaurant and bar mixes well-tailored concert-goers with scruffy indie-rock types. Lunch is cheap, but the dinner scene is groovier, with nightly live music. Sandwiches and burgers $5-10. Entrees $10-15. Open M 11:30am-midnight, Tu-Th 11:30am-12:30am, F-Sa 11:30am-1:30am.

Mugavero's Confectionery (539-9668), on the corner of Fawn and S. Exeter St. This menu-less deli has offered sandwiches and snacks for 53 years. Probably the cheapest food in Little Italy. Patrons can either invent their own sandwiches or give the owner-operator free rein ($4). Open daily 10am 'til 9 or 10pm. Cash only.

Amicci's, 231 S. High St. (528-1096). The best bargain in Little Italy serves 11 immense pasta dishes under $10. Meatless pasta dishes available. Open Su-Th noon-10pm, F-Sa noon-11pm.

One World Café, 904 S. Charles St. (234-0235), in the Federal Hill district, serves vegetarian dinners such as addictive bean burritos ($5) and varied vegan desserts. Dozens of types of coffee. Exhibits of local art rotate frequently on cafe walls, and upstairs pool tables see heavy use. Occasional live music. Open M 7am-10pm, Tu-F 7am-11pm, Sa 8am-11pm, Su 8am-10pm.

Sobo Café, 6-8 West Cross St. (752-1518). The menu of this brand-new restaurant changes every few days. Typical dishes include macaroni and cheese ($3) and dinner pot pie ($7). Great for a casual evening out. Open daily 11:30am-11pm.

SIGHTS

Baltimore's gray harbor ends with a colorful bang in a 5 sq. block body of water bounded on three sides by an aquarium, shopping malls, a science museum, and a bevy of boardable ships. The nation's first pier-pavilion, the **Harborplace** mall (332-4191) is Baltimore's most imitated building. *(Open M-Sa 10am-9pm, Su 10am-6pm.)* Crowds flock to Harborplace's Pratt St. and Light St. Pavilions, and to the Gallery across the street for a little wharf-side shopping and air-conditioned bliss.

The **National Aquarium,** Pier 3, 501 E. Pratt St. (576-3800), makes the Inner Harbor worthwhile. *(Entrance times July-Aug. daily 9am-8pm; Mar.-June and Sept.-Oct. Sa-Th 9am-4:30pm, F 9am-8pm; Nov.-Feb. Sa-Th 10am-5pm, F 10am-8pm. Aquarium remains open 2hr. after last entrance time. $14, seniors $10.50, children $7.50, under 3 free.)* Multi-level exhibits and tanks show off rare fish, big fish, red fish, and blue fish along with the biology and ecology of oceans, rivers, and rainforests. The Children's Cove (level 4) lets visitors handle inter-tidal marine animals.

Several ships bob in the harbor by the aquarium; most belong to the **Baltimore Maritime Museum** (396-3453), at Piers 3 and 4. Visitors may board the *U.S.S. Torsk* submarine (which sank the last WWII Japanese combatant ships), the lightship *Chesapeake,* and the Coast Guard cutter *Roger B. Taney.* At the Inner Harbor's far edge lurks the **Maryland Science Center,** 601 Light St. (685-5225), which stuns audiences with its 5-story IMAX screen, 38-speaker sound system, and 50 ft. high planetarium. *(Open M-Th 10am-6pm, F-Su 10am-8pm; Sept.-May M-F 10am-5pm, Sa-Su 10am-6pm. $10; ages 13-17, seniors, and military $8; 4-12 $7.)* **Fort McHenry National Monument** (962-4290), located at the foot of E. Fort Ave. off Rte. 2 (Hanover St.) and Lawrence Ave. (take bus #1), commemorates the fort's victory against British forces in the War of 1812, a triumph which inspired Francis Scott Key to write *The Star-Spangled Banner.* *(Open daily 8am-8pm; Sept.-May 8am-5pm. $5, seniors and under 16 free.)* A flag flies over the Fort all day, but *the* flag, which usually hangs in the Museum of American History in Washington, is currently being restored thanks to designer Ralph Lauren.

The **Walters Art Gallery,** 600 N. Charles St. (547-9000), at Centre St., keeps one of the largest private art collections in the world, spanning 50 centuries. *(Tours W 12:30pm and Su 2pm. Open Tu-W and F 10am-4pm, Th 10am-8pm, Sa-Su 11am-5pm. $6, students $3, seniors $4, under 18 free on Sa before noon.)* The museum's most esteemed possession is the Ancient Art collection on the second level, with sculptures and metalwork from Egypt, Greece, and Rome. The **Baltimore Museum of Art** (396-7100), at N. Charles and 31st St., picks up where the Walters leaves off, exhibiting a fine collection of Americana and modern art. *(Open W-F 11am-5pm, Sa-Su 11am-6pm. $6, students and seniors $4, under 18 free; Th free.)* Two 20th-century **sculpture gardens** make wonderful picnic grounds.

The **Baltimore Zoo** (396-6631), off I-83 (Exit 7), offers a new Chimpanzee Forest exhibit, the spectacular Palm Tree Conservatory, a lake surrounded by lush greenery, and a simulated savannah with elephants, Siberian tigers, and a waterfall. *(Open M-F 10am-4pm, Sa-Su 10am-5:30pm; in winter closes daily 4pm. $8.50, seniors and children $5.)*

Once a station for the Baltimore & Ohio Railroad, the **B&O Railroad Museum,** 901 W. Pratt St. (752-2388; take bus #31), looks out on train tracks where dining cars, Pullman sleepers, and mail cars park themselves for a touring frenzy. *(Open daily 10am-5pm. $6.50, seniors $5.50, children $4, under 3 free. Trains parked outside are free.)* The Roundhouse contains historic trains and a replica of the 1829 "Tom Thumb," the first American steam-driven locomotive.

Baltimore is home to the **Babe Ruth Birthplace and Baltimore Orioles Museum,** 216 Emory St. (727-1539), off the 600 block of W. Pratt; take bus #31. *(Open daily 10am-5pm, on game nights until 7pm; Nov.-Mar. 10am-4pm. $5, seniors $3, ages 5-16 $2.)* The intimate, vintage-style **Oriole Park at Camden Yards** (547-6234), just west of the Inner Harbor at Eutaw and Camden St., is the home to baseball's Orioles. *(Tours leave every hr. M-F 11am-2pm, every 30min. Sa 10:30am-2pm and Su 12:30-2pm. $5, seniors and children $4.)* In 1997, the Orioles were joined by the **Ravens,** Baltimore's second chance at professional football. The Ravens, formerly the Cleveland Browns, play in **Raven Stadium,** adjacent to Camden Yards.

Let's Poe!

Edgar Allen Poe was buried in someone else's clothes at the tiny **Westminster Churchyard** (706-7288) at Fayette and Greene St. Every year since 1949, a mysterious man has placed three roses and a half-empty bottle of cognac on his grave on the eve of his birthday. The three roses are believed to represent the poet, his wife, and his mother. The same man performed the ritual from 1949 to 1993, when he left a cryptic note saying, "The torch will be passed." Since then, three separate men have performed the ritual each year, with a new stranger acting it out in 1998. A contingent from the **Poe House** museum (396-7932) gathers to watch the ritual annually, its members handpicked from the legions of requests sent in from around the country. The museum has never attempted to confront the visitors, whose identities remain unknown.

ENTERTAINMENT AND NIGHTLIFE

The **Showcase of Nations Ethnic Festivals** celebrates Baltimore's ethnic neighborhoods with a different culture featured each week (June-Sept.). The festivals take place all over the city; call the **Baltimore Visitors Bureau** (800-282-6632) for info. The **Pier 6 Concert Pavilion** (625-3100), at Pier 6 at the Inner Harbor, presents big-name music several times a week May through October. Tickets ($15-30) are available at the pavilion or through Ticketmaster (625-1400 or 481-SEAT/7328). Pier 5, near Harborplace, affords free eavesdropping. **Jazzline** (466-0600) lists jazz shows from September to May. The **Theatre Project,** 45 W. Preston St. near Maryland St. (752-8558), experiments with theater, poetry, music, and dance. (Shows W-Sa 8pm, Su 3pm. $8-14. Box office open 1hr. before showtime; call to charge tickets.)

Baltimore Brewing Co., 104 Albermarle St. (837-5000), just west of the Inner Harbor on the outskirts of Little Italy. Distinctive lagers brewed right on the premises in large brass tubs. Can't decide? Try 6 varieties with the $6.50 beer sampler. Happy hour daily 4-7pm with $2.50L of beer. Specializes in hearty German fare ($7-14), but offers a number of cheaper sandwiches and snacks. Open M-Th 4pm-midnight, F-Sa 11:30am-1am, Su 2-10pm.

Cat's Eye Pub, 1730 Thames St. (276-9866), in Fells Point. One of the best bars in Fells Point. Regulars pack it in every weeknight for live blues, jazz, folk, or traditional Irish music (Su-Th from 9pm, F-Sa from 4pm; no cover, but prices rise). Over 25 different drafts and 60 bottled beers. Tasty sandwiches ($2.50-6) served F-Su. Happy hour 4-7pm brings price reductions. Open daily noon-2am.

The Midtown Yacht Club, 15 E. Centre St. (837-1300), just off N. Charles St. in Mt. Vernon. The owners bought the bar in 1998 because they enjoyed hanging out there themselves. 11 beers on tap. Happy hour (M-F 5-7pm, Su 9pm-2am) yields $4.75 domestic pitchers every day, ethnic munchies on Tu, and ½-price appetizers F. Su brunch 11am-2:30pm. Open daily 11am-2am.

■ Annapolis

One of the premier yachting communities in the U.S., Annapolis walks the fine line between nostalgia and anachronism. Annapolis made history when the Treaty of Paris was ratified here in 1784, officially ending the American Revolution. After its 1783-1784 stint as temporary capital of the U.S., Annapolis relinquished the national limelight in favor of a more tranquil existence. The historic waterfront district retains its 18th-century appeal despite the presence of ritzy boutiques and pricey retail stores. Crew-cut "middies" (a nickname for Naval Academy students, or "midshipmen") mingle with longer-haired students from St. John's and vacationing couples.

The Corinthian-columned **State House** (974-3400) offers maps and houses the state legislature and a fine silver collection. *(Open daily 9am-5pm. Free tours 11am and 3pm.)* The Treaty of Paris was signed here on January 14, 1784. Restaurants and tacky tourist shops line the waterfront at **City Dock,** where midshipmen and yachtsmen ply the waters. Main St., full of tiny shops and eateries, stretches from here back up to Church Circle. The **Banneker-Douglass Museum,** 84 Franklin St. (974-2893), outlines African-American cultural history (open Tu-F 10am-3pm, Sa noon-4pm; free). The **U.S. Naval Academy** holds its fort at the end of King George St. Tours begin at the **Armel-Leftwich Visitors Center** (263-6933), inside the gates on King George St. ($5.50, students $4.50, seniors $3.50).

The best place to find cheap eats is the **Market House** food court at the center of City Dock, where a hearty meal can be had for under $5. **Chick & Ruth's Delly,** 165 Main St. (269-6737), about a block from City Dock towards the State House, has served Annapolis 24hr. breakfast for over 30 years. Dishes include omelettes ($3-7), corned beef sandwiches ($4), and malts ($2.75). **Moon Café,** 137 Prince George St. (280-1956), a block up East St. from the Naval Academy, is the only place in Annapolis to find a creative cup of coffee, a healthy meal, and a Eurocafe atmosphere all under the same roof (open M-F 11am-midnight, Sa-Su 9am-midnight). Locals and tourists generally engage in one of two nighttime activities: wandering along City Dock or schmoozing 'n' boozing at upscale pubs. Theater-goers can check out **The Colonial Players, Inc.,** 108 East St. (268-7373; performances Th-Su 8pm, additional Su show 2:30pm; Th and Su $7, students and seniors $5, F-Sa $10). **McGarvey's,** 8 Market Space (263-5700), a traditional dark-wood saloon, is a favorite watering hole among the locals.

Annapolis lies southeast of U.S. 50 (also known as U.S. 301), 30 mi. east of D.C. and 30 mi. south of Baltimore. From D.C. take U.S. 50 east, which begins at New York Ave. and can be accessed from the Beltway. From Baltimore, follow Rte. 2 S to U.S. 50 W, cross the Severn River Bridge, then take Rowe Blvd. The city extends south and east from two landmarks: **Church Circle** and **State Circle.** School St., in a blatantly unconstitutional move, connects Church and State. East St. runs from the State House to the **Naval Academy.** Main St. (where food and entertainment congregate) starts at Church Circle and ends at the docks. **Greyhound/Trailways** (800-231-2222) buses stop at the football field at Rowe Blvd. and Taylor St. Tickets are available from the bus driver (cash only); buses run to Washington, D.C. (1hr., 1 per day, $10) and other nearby cities. **Annapolis and Anne Arundel County Conference & Visitors Bureau,** 26 West St. (280-0445), has info (open daily 9am-5pm). **Area code:** 410.

■ Assateague Island

Local legend has it that horses first came to Assateague Island by swimming ashore from a sinking Spanish galleon—a story so captivating that it became the premise of the children's classic *Misty of Chincoteague.* A less romantic and more likely theory is that miserly colonial farmers put their horses out to graze on Assateague to avoid mainland taxes. Whatever their origins, the famous wild ponies now roam free across the unspoiled beaches and forests of the picturesque island.

Maryland and Virginia share Assateague Island, which can be divided into three distinct parts. The **Assateague State Park** (410-641-2120), Rte. 611 in southeast Maryland, is a 2 mi. stretch of picnic areas, beaches, bathhouses, and campsites. (Park open Apr.-Oct. daily 8am-sunset. $2 per person for day use, seniors free. Campsite registration 8:30am-10pm. Sites $20. Reservations available only in 1-week blocks, Sa-Sa.) The **Assateague Island National Seashore** claims most of the long sandbar north and south of the park and has its own campground (sites $12; Nov. to mid-May $10) and beaches, most inaccessible by car. The **ranger station** (410-641-3030) distributes $5 backcountry camping permits from noon until 5pm; they go quickly, so arrive early. The **Barrier Island Visitors Center** (410-641-1441), Rte. 611, provides an introduction to the park and gives day-use information (open daily 9am-5pm). Two meandering, 1 mi. nature trails give visitors a closer look at the island's flora and fauna: the **Forest Trail** offers the best viewing tower, but the **Marsh Trail** (ironically) has fewer mosquitoes.

The **Chincoteague National Wildlife Refuge** stretches across the Virginia side of the island. Avid bird-watchers flock here to see rare species such as peregrine falcons, snowy egrets, and black-crowned night herons. The **wild pony roundup,** held the Wednesday before the last Thursday in July, brings hordes of tourists to Assateague. During slack tide, the wild ponies are herded together and made to swim from Assateague to Chincoteague Island, where the local fire department auctions off the foals the following day. The adults swim back to Assateague and reproduce, providing next year's crop. The best time for pony-sightings on Assateague Island is mid-July, just before the roundup. The **Chincoteague Refuge Visitor Contact Station** (804-336-6122) has more info (open daily 9am-4pm; $5 per car). The interesting **Wildlife Loop** road begins at the Visitors Center and provides ideal pony-viewing (open 5am-10pm; for cars, 3pm-sunset).

The best way to get to Assateague Island is by car. To reach the island by public transportation, take a **Greyhound** bus (800-752-4841), to Ocean City, via daily express or local routes from Greyhound stations in Baltimore ($25) or Washington, D.C. ($39-44). From Ocean City, take a taxi to the island (289-1313; about $30). **Trail-**

ways runs buses from Salisbury, MD ($8) and Norfolk, VA ($42), stopping on U.S. 13 at T's Corner store (757-824-5935), 11 mi. from Chincoteague. For tourism information, call 757-336-6161 or write to the **Chincoteague Chamber of Commerce,** P.O. Box 258, Chincoteague, VA 23336. The chamber is located at 6733 Maddox Blvd. and is open for drop-in visitors (in summer M-Sa 9am-4:30pm, Su 12:30-4:30pm; off-season M-Sa 9am-4:30pm).

■ Ocean City

Ocean City is a lot like a kiddie pool. It's shallow and plastic, but it can be a lot of fun if you're the right age. This 10 mi. strip of land packs endless bars, all-you-can-eat buffets, hotels, mini-golf courses, boardwalks, and flashing lights into a thin region between the Atlantic Ocean and the Assawoman Bay. Tourism is the town's only industry; in season the population swells from 5000 to 300,000, with a large migratory population of "June bugs," high school seniors that descend in swarms during the week after graduation to celebrate (read: to drink beer). July and August cater more to families and singles over the age of 21, who also come to party.

The star attraction here is the beautiful, wide **beach,** which runs the entire 10 mi. length of town and is sandy the entire way (open daily 6am-10pm; free). When the sun goes down, hard-earned tans are put to work at Ocean City's league of bars and nightclubs. The most popular is the island oasis **Seacrets** (524-4900), on 49th St., bayside, an amusement park for adults featuring ten bars, including two floating bars on the bay. Barefoot barflies wander from bar to bar, sipping the signature drink of frozen rum runner mixed with pina colada, to the strains of nightly live bands. (Cover $3-5. Open M-Sa 11am-2am, Su noon-2am.) **Fager's Island** (524-5500), 60th St. in the bay, the elder statesman of the bayside clubs, still draws hordes across a plank walkway to its island location for nightly DJ music (happy hour Tu-F 4-7pm; open daily 11am-2am). **Macky's Bayside Bar & Grill,** 5311 Coastal Hwy. (723-5565), bayside, behind Tio Gringo's offers refuge from the high school hordes with good Southwestern food and the opportunity to join locals nightly at sunset for a rousing rendition of "God Bless America." (Happy hour daily 4-7pm with $1 domestic drafts. Open daily 11am-2am.)

Room rates fluctuate dramatically with the season. Rooms can easily be found for under $30 in the winter, but rates climb in May and June and peak in July and August. If you're going to stay in Ocean City during the summer, make every effort to secure a bed at the **Whispering Sands** (723-1874; Nov.-Apr. 202-362-3453 or 954-761-9008), oceanside at 45th St. The amicable owner rents out rooms with kitchen access to a mostly European crowd ($15; open May-Oct.). Less homey and more expensive, **Summer Place Youth Hostel,** 104 Dorchester St. (289-4542), in the south end of town, functions mostly as a summer boarding house, although a few rooms are kept for short-term visitors. Private rooms and dorm rooms have access to kitchen, TV, living room, deck, hammock, and grill. Avoid the "dungeon" rooms under the deck. (Shared bath. $25 per person. No lockout. Open Apr.-Oct. Reservations necessary.) Most motels charge $50-80 per room on weekdays, and rates double on weekends. **Ocean City Travel Park** (524-7601) operates the only in-town campground bayside on 70th St. (tents $24-38, RVs $24-43). A few miles out of town, **Assateague National Seashore** or **Assateague State Park** (see above) provide tent-pitching facilities.

Dining in Ocean City is a glutton's delight. The streets are lined with seemingly identical restaurants hosting all-you-can-eat specials and featuring Maryland's specialty: crabs. **Fat Daddy's Sub Shop,** 216 S. Baltimore Ave. (289-4040), offers some of the best deli sandwiches ($2.50-4.50) and subs ($4-6) on the beach (open daily 11am-4am). Oreo waffles ($4) and light, fluffy omelettes ($4.25-5.25) are available at the **Brass Balls Saloon** (289-0069), on the Boardwalk between 11th and 12th St. (open 8:30am-2am). For bagels or pastries, venture uptown to **Bagels 'n' Buns,** 7111 Coastal Hwy., and its own signature crab cakes ($7) served on a bagel or in pita (open M-Th 6am-4am, F-Su 24hr.).

Ocean City runs north-south, with numbered streets linking the ocean to the bay. Most hotels are toward the ocean, most clubs and bars toward the bay. The **Ocean City Visitors Center** (800-626-2326), at 40th St. in the Convention Center, will wel-

Central Washington, D.C.

SEE COLOR INSERTS FOR MORE MAPS OF WASHINGTON, D.C.

MID-ATLANTIC

Gallaudet University

CAPITOL HILL

SHAW

DUPONT CIRCLE

FOGGY BOTTOM

GEORGETOWN

VIRGINIA

ARLINGTON CEMETERY

ROSSLYN

NW
NE

CHINA-TOWN

GALLERY PLACE

METRO CENTER

FEDERAL TRIANGLE

THE MALL

MT VERNON SQ-UDC

JUDICIARY SQ

SMITHSONIAN

FARRAGUT NORTH

FARRAGUT WEST

L'ENFANT PLAZA

FEDERAL CENTER/SW

CAPITOL SOUTH

EASTERN MARKET

SHAW/HU

UNION STATION

ARCHIVES

Union Station

US Capitol

Supreme Court

Library of Congress

Stanton Park

Seward Park

National Gallery of Art

National Museum of Art

FBI

Natural History

Hirshhorn Museum

American History

Holocaust Museum

Washington Monument

White House

The Ellipse

Vietnam Veterans' Memorial

Korean War Veterans' Memorial

Lincoln Memorial

Jefferson Memorial

FDR Memorial

West Potomac Park

Tidal Basin

Potomac River

Columbia Island

Roosevelt Island

Ladybird Johnson Park

ARLINGTON CEMETERY

Georgetown University

Dumbarton Oaks

Montrose Park

Mt. Vernon Square

Logan Circle

Thomas Circle

Scott Circle

Dupont Circle

Sheridan Circle

Washington Circle

Streets and Avenues

New York Ave.
Florida Ave.
New Jersey Ave.
Massachusetts Ave.
Rhode Island Ave.
Vermont Ave.
New Hampshire Ave.
Connecticut Ave.
Pennsylvania Ave.
Maryland Ave.
Delaware Ave.
Louisiana Ave.
North Carolina Ave.
Constitution Ave.
Independence Ave.
Virginia Ave.
Maine Ave.
Wisconsin Ave.
Mass. Ave.

K St.
H St.
G St.
F St.
E St.
D St.
P St.
Q St.
R St.
M St.
North Capitol St.
South Capitol St.
E Capitol St.
N. Capitol St.

1st St.
2nd St.
3rd St.
4th St.
6th St.
7th St.
12th St.
13th St.
14th St.
15th St.
16th St.
17th St.
18th St.
20th St.
23rd St.
26th St.
28th St.
30th St.
34th St.

2nd St./SW
2nd St.
4th St.
12th St. Expwy.
Southwest Fwy.

East Basin Dr.
West Basin Dr.
Kutz Br.
Outlet Br.
Ohio Dr.
Rock Creek Pkwy.
Whitehurst Fwy.
C&O Canal
Key Br.
Memorial Bridge
Roosevelt Bridge
George Washington Pkwy.
George Washington Mem. Pkwy.

Rock Creek

50
66
395

0   1500 feet
0   500 meters

come you with copious coupons (open M-W 8:30am-5pm, Th-Sa 8:30am-7:30pm, Su 9am-5pm; Sept.-May daily 8:30am-5pm). **Trailways** (289-9307; open daily 7am-8am and 10am-5pm; Sept.-May 10am-3pm), at 2nd St. and Philadelphia Ave., sends buses to Baltimore (3½hr., 7 per day, $25) and Washington, D.C. (4-6hr., $39-44). In town, the **bus** runs the length of the strip (723-1607) and is the best way to get around ($1 per day; runs 24hr.). **Parking** in Ocean City is a nightmare; the beach is accessible on foot from most hotels, and free parking is available at the Convention Center. **Post Office:** 408 N. Philadelphia Ave. (289-7819; open M-F 9am-5pm, Sa 9am-noon). **ZIP code:** 21842. **Area code:** 410.

Washington, D.C.

Like many a young adult fresh out of college, the fledgling United States government quickly realized that independence meant little without a place to stay. Both Northern and Southern states wanted the capital on their turf. The final location—100 sq. mi. pinched from Virginia and Maryland—was a compromise, an undeveloped swamp wedged between north and south. Congress commissioned French engineer Pierre L'Enfant to design the city.

Washington was supposed to be "city of magnificent distances," but the only thing magnificent about the city in the nineteenth century was the distance between its buildings—the wide avenues remained mostly empty, with a smattering of slave markets and boarding houses the only companions for the elegant government buildings. The city had hardly begun to expand when the British torched it in 1814; a post-war vote to give up and move the capital failed in Congress by just eight votes. Washington continued to grow, but so did its problems—a port city squeezed between two plantation states, the district was a logical first stop for slave traders, whose shackled cargo awaited sales on the Mall and near the White House. Foreign diplomats were disgusted. The Civil War altered this forever, transforming Washington from the Union's embarrassing appendix to its jugular vein.

Today, two discrete cities of Federal Washington and local Washington coexist in the District. Federal Washington, the town of press conferences, power lunches, and Monica gossip, is what most visitors come to see. The other part of Washington, the so-called "second city," consists of a variety of communities, some prosperous, others overcome by drugs and crime. Some parts of the second city are remarkably cosmopolitan, but beyond the gleaming Northwest quadrant, in areas where few visitors venture, are communities of poverty and broken dreams. The presence of these areas, sometimes within a few blocks of the seats of government, surprises many tourists, confronting them with the paradoxes of American democracy when they came to hear its praises.

For everything about Washington D.C. that you always wanted to know but were afraid to ask, see *Let's Go: Washington, D.C. 1999*, available at most bookstores.

ORIENTATION

The city is roughly diamond-shaped, with the four tips of the diamond pointed in the four compass directions, and the street names and addresses split into four quadrants: NW, NE, SE, and SW, defined by their relation to the **Capitol.** The names of the four quadrants distinguish otherwise identical addresses. The quadrants are separated by **N. Capitol St., E. Capitol St.,** and **S. Capitol St.** The Mall, stretching west from the Capitol, precludes the existence of a "W. Capitol St." South of the Mall, **Independence Ave.** runs east-west; to the north of the Mall, **Constitution Ave.** runs east-west.

Capitol Hill extends east from the Capitol; North of the Mall, **Old Downtown** (sometimes called "Penn Quarter") is accompanied by both **Foggy Bottom** (sometimes called the "West End") and **Farragut,** around K St., west of 15th St. NW. **Georgetown** centers at Wisconsin and M St. NW. **Dupont Circle,** east of 16th St., morphs into struggling **Logan Circle,** then to the clubby **Shaw/U District.** A strong Hispanic community resides in **Adams-Morgan,** north of Dupont and east of **Rock Creek Park,** Washington's lush and tranquil answer to New York's Central Park. **Upper Northwest** stretches west of the park. Across the Anacostia River, the **Southeast** (including **Anacostia),** is isolated by poverty, crack, and guns.

The basic street plan is a rectilinear grid. Streets running from east to west are named in alphabetical order depending on how many blocks they lie from the north-south dividing line that runs through the Capitol (thus, there are 2 A Streets 2 blocks apart). There is no A or B St. in NW and SW, and no J St. anywhere. Streets running north-south get numbers (1st St., 2nd St., etc.). Numbered and lettered streets sometimes disappear for a block. Addresses on lettered streets indicate the numbered cross street (1100 D St. SE will be between 11th and 12th St.). State-named avenues radiate outward from the U.S. Capitol and the White House.

Major roads include **Pennsylvania Ave.,** which runs SE-NE from Anacostia through Capitol Hill, past the White House, finally ending at 28th and M St. NW in Georgetown; **Connecticut Ave.,** which runs N-NE from the White House through Dupont Circle and past the zoo; **Wisconsin Ave.,** running north from Georgetown past the Cathedral to Friendship Heights; **16th St. NW,** which zooms from the White House north through Adams-Morgan and Mt. Pleasant; **K St. NW,** a major downtown artery; **Massachusetts Ave.,** reaching from American University through Dupont Circle to Capitol Hill; **New York Ave.,** running NE from the White House; and high-speed **North Capitol St.**

Washington, D.C. is ringed by the **Capital Beltway/I-495** (except where it's part of I-95); the Beltway is bisected by **U.S. 1,** and meets **I-395** from Virginia. The high-speed **Baltimore-Washington Pkwy.** connects Washington, D.C. to Baltimore. **I-595** trickles off the Capital Beltway east to Annapolis. **I-66** heads west into Virginia.

PRACTICAL INFORMATION

Airport: Ronald Reagan National Airport (703-417-8000). Metro: National Airport. It's best to fly here from within the U.S., since National is on the Metro and closer to the city. Taxi $10-15 from downtown. The **SuperShuttle** (800-BLUEVAN/258-3826) bus runs between National and downtown every 30min. on weekdays. **Dulles International Airport** (703-369-1600) is much further from the city. Taxis cost $40 and up from downtown. The **Washington Flyer Dulles Express Bus** (1-888-WASH-FLY/927-4359) hits the West Falls Church Metro every 30min. from 6-10am and 6-10:30pm, every 20min. from 10am-2pm, every 15min. from 2-6pm ($8). Buses to downtown (15th and K St. NW) take about 45min. and leave M-F every 30min. 5:20am-10:20pm; Sa-Su every hr. 5:20am-12:20pm, every 30min. 12:50-10:20pm ($16, family rate for groups of 3 or more $13 each).

Trains: Union Station, 50 Massachusetts Ave. NE (484-7540). **Amtrak** (800-872-7245) branches to: New York (3½hr., $61-67); Baltimore (40min., $16-25); Philadelphia (2hr., $34-81); and Boston (8½hr., $62-67). Maryland's commuter train, **MARC** (410-859-7400, call 24hr.), departs from Union to Baltimore ($5.75, round-trip $10.25) and the 'burbs.

Public Transportation: Metrorail (METRO), 600 5th St. NW (info line 637-7000; staffed M-F 8:30am-4pm), is a relatively safe mode of transportation, accessed via computerized fare card bought from a machine. Fare $1.10-3.25, depending on distance traveled and whether travel is during a peak hr. 10% bonus on fares over $20. 1-day Metro pass $5. **Flash Pass** allows unlimited bus (and sometimes Metro) rides for 2 weeks or a month. Trains run M-F 5:30am-midnight, Sa-Su 8am-midnight. To make a bus transfer, get a pass from machines on the platform *before* boarding the train. The extensive **Metrobus** (same address, phone, and hrs. as Metrorail) system reliably serves Georgetown, downtown, and the suburbs. Fare $1.10.

MID-ATLANTIC

Taxis: Yellow Cab, 544-1212. Most fares are based on a map that splits the city into 5 zones and 27 subzones. The map is posted in all taxis. Zone prices are fixed; ask what the fare will be at the beginning of your trip.

Car Rental:. Bargain Buggies Rent-a-Car, 3140 N. Washington Blvd. (703-841-0000), in Arlington, rents for $23 per day plus 20¢ per mi. (100 free mi. per day) or $150 per week plus 20¢ per mi. (700 free mi. per week). Must be 18, with major credit card or cash deposit of $250 (this may be negotiable). Those under 21 need full insurance coverage of their own (may be negotiable). Open M-F 8am-7pm, Sa 9am-3pm, Su 9am-noon. **Budget** (800-527-0700), with branches at Union Station and downtown, rents to ages 21-24 for a $5 surcharge per day.

Bike Rental: Big Wheel Bikes, 315·7th St. SE (543-1600). Metro: Eastern Market. Mountain bikes for $5 per hr. (min. 3hr.), $25 per business day. For an extra $7, you can keep the bike overnight. Major credit card required for deposit. Open Tu-F 11am-7pm, Sa 10am-6pm, Su noon-5pm.

Visitor Info: Washington, D.C. Convention and Visitors Association (WCVA), 1212 New York Ave., #600 NW (789-7000; http://www.washington.org). Call for copies of *The D.C. Visitor's Guide and Map* and a calendar of events. Open M-F 9am-5pm. **D.C. Committee to Promote Washington,** 1212 New York Ave. NW, #200 (347-2873 or 800-422-8644). Call or write for a tourist package. **Meridian International Center,** 1630 Crescent Pl. NW (667-6800). Metro: Dupont Circle. Call for brochures in a variety of languages. Office open M-F 9am-5pm.

Hotlines: Rape Crisis Center, 333-7273. **Gay and Lesbian Hotline,** 833-3234. Operates 7pm-11pm. **Traveler's Aid Society,** 546-3120. Offices at Union Station, National and Dulles Airports, and downtown at 512 C St. NE. Open M-F 9am-5pm.

Post Office: 900 Brentwood Rd. NE 20066 (635-5300), in an indescribably inconvenient location. Open M-F 8am-8pm, Sa 8am-6pm, Su noon-6pm. **ZIP code:** 20090, plus many others. Call and ask. **Area code:** 202.

ACCOMMODATIONS AND CAMPGROUNDS

Business hotels discount deeply and swell with tourists on summer weekends. Hostels, guest houses, and university dorms get particularly packed; reservations are a good idea. The *New York Times* Sunday Travel section has plenty of summer weekend deals. D.C. automatically adds a 13% occupancy surcharge and another $1.50 per room per night to your bill. Damn feds. Prices listed below do not include taxes. **Bed & Breakfast Accommodations, Ltd.,** P.O. Box 12011, 20005 (328-3510, 24hr. voice mail), reserves rooms in private homes. ($65-120, lower in summer. $15 per additional person. Open M-F 10am-5pm.)

Washington International Hostel (HI-AYH), 1009 11 St. NW 20001 (737-2333), 3 blocks north of the Metro. Metro: Metro Center (11th St. exit). Bright and spacious hostel, run by a friendly college-age staff. Clean A/C rooms hold 8 or 12 beds. Free activities every day. Common room, kitchen, game room, small store/cafe, laundry facilities, and luggage and bicycle storage. $19 per night, nonmembers $22; private room with 4 beds $80. Reception 24hr. *Use caution in this area at night.*

Washington International Student Center, 2451 18th St. NW (800-567-4150 or 667-7681). Metro: Woodley Park-Zoo and a 15min. walk. Tidy, inexpensive hostel run by experienced, friendly staff. Each of the 5 bedrooms has A/C with 3-4 bunk-beds squeezed in. 2 kitchens and 3 shared bathrooms. Relaxed common room. Bunk $15. Bike rental $7 per day. Internet access $2 per 10min. No lockout. Breakfast included. Lockers available. Call for free pick-up from bus or train station.

Kalorama Guest House at Kalorama Park, 1854 Mintwood Pl. NW (667-6369), and at **Woodley Park,** 2700 Cathedral Ave. NW (328-0860). Metro: Woodley Park-Zoo (for both). Impeccably decorated guest rooms in Victorian townhouses; the first is in the upscale western slice of Adams-Morgan near Rock Creek Park, the second in a high-class neighborhood near the zoo. Both include laundry, local calls, and breakfast. Reception M-F 8am-8pm, Sa-Su 8:30am-7pm. Singles $40-75, with private baths $55-110; doubles $45-75/$60-95. Reserve 1-2 weeks in advance.

The Braxton Hotel, 1440 Rhode Island Ave. NW (232-7800 or 800-350-5759). Backpacker central; comfortable and clean. Rooms have private bath, cable, and A/C;

most have mini-fridges. Breakfast included. Twins $40-50; doubles $50-75; rooms with 2 double beds $50-80. 10% discount for students and seniors.

William Penn House, 515 E. Capitol St. (543-5560), 5 blocks from Capitol. Shared rooms in a dorm-style guest house board 3-7 people. Quaker worship in mornings. Limited A/C. $35 per night. Continental breakfast included. $5 key deposit.

Swiss Inn, 1204 Massachusetts Ave. NW (371-1816 or 800-955-7947), 4 blocks from Metro Center. More like a guest house than a hotel. Seven clean, quiet studio apartments with private baths, high ceilings, kitchenettes, A/C, and TV (no cable). International crowd welcomed by French- and German-speaking managers. Rooms in summer $68-108; off-season $50-88.

Embassy Inn, 1627 16th St. NW (234-7800 or 800-423-9111), near R St. Metro: Dupont Circle. Nouveau Victorian rooms in flowery paisley. Tea and coffee, evening sherry, daily newspaper, and continental breakfast included. All rooms have private bath, cable TV, phones, and A/C. Singles $69-99; doubles $79-129.

The Columbia Guest House, 2005 Columbia Rd. NW (265-4006), ½ block from Embassy Row. Eccentric, patrician townhouse with dark wood paneling, polished hardwood floors, ornate fireplaces, and neatly furnished rooms (some with A/C). Singles $23-29; doubles $32-45; triples $45-55 (some have shared baths). $10 per additional occupant. Students and HI-AYH members 10-15% discount.

Connecticut Woodley Guest House, 2647 Woodley Rd. NW (667-0218). Metro: Woodley Park-Zoo; walk 1 block up Connecticut Ave., take a left on Woodley Rd. Clean hotel with threadbare and mismatched air-conditioned rooms. Singles with shared bath $44-48, with private bath $55-62. Doubles with shared bath $52-55, with private bath $62-72. $10 less in winter. Reception daily 7:30am-midnight.

Highlander Motor Inn, 3336 Wilson Blvd. (703-524-4300 or 800-786-4301). Metro: Clarendon or Virginia Sq./GMU. Basic, cheap motel. Clean, spacious rooms with two double beds. Refrigerators upon request. Free coffee and doughnuts. Cable TV and A/C. Singles $55, in winter $50; doubles $60/$55. *Let's Go* readers $5 off. Weekly $350, monthly $1350. Parking included.

Greenbelt Park, 6565 Greenbelt Rd. (301-344-3948, for reservations Apr.-Nov. 800-365-2267). 12 mi. from D.C. Take the Baltimore-Washington Pkwy. to Greenbelt Rd. The cheapest and nicest place to camp in the D.C. area, courtesy of the National Park Service. 174 very quiet, wooded sites for tents, trailers, and campers. Nature trails. No electricity. Bathrooms and showers. Sites $13, seniors with Golden Age Pass $6.50. 14-night max. stay.

FOOD

First-timers in D.C. might think that all the good eats are only within the reach of the power-hungry. Fortunately for the budget traveler, this is deliciously untrue. **Adams-Morgan** and **Georgetown** are home to a series of particularly good restaurants.

Alexandria

Lite 'n' Fair, 1018 King St. (549-3717). Ki Choi, former executive chef of the ritzy Watergate Restaurant, owns this gem disguised by a modest facade, which serves fresh, inexpensive seafood. Daily specials such as seafood *paella* with shrimp, mussels, calamari, and saffron rice ($9). Basic seafood sandwiches and burgers $4-8. Open M 11am-3pm, Tu-Th 11am-9pm, F-Sa 11am-10pm.

Adams-Morgan

⊛Meskerem, 2434 18th St. NW (462-4100), near Columbia Rd. *Meskerem* is the Ethiopian month marking spring, and the decor in this 3 fl. restaurant is appropriately sun-themed. Excellent Ethiopian food. Lunch entrees $5-10, dinner entrees $7-11. Free delivery (min. order $12). Open daily noon-midnight.

Mixtec, 1792 Columbia Rd. NW (332-1011), near 18th St. Cheap, abundant, authentic, fabulous Mexican food. Paper lanterns and colorfully handpainted chairs add flair to rooms with an otherwise fast-food air. Specialties include *tacos al carbon* (tortillas with beef) and *camarones vallarta* (shrimp in green tomatillo sauce). Entrees $7-11, sandwiches $4-6. Open Su-Th 10am-10pm, F-Sa 10am-11pm.

Bukom Café, 2442 18th St. NW (265-4600), near Columbia Rd. Mellow and intensely popular, especially when music is playing. Offers stews, sugar cane, and other West African specialty dishes, like smoked-fish stew with cassava cake ($9.25). Appetizers $3-4, entrees $6-9.25. Live reggae and calypso Tu-Th and Su 9pm, F-Sa 10pm. Open M-Tu 4-10pm, W 4pm-2am, Th-Sa 4pm-3am, Su 4pm-2am.

Capitol Hill

◈**Banana Café and Piano Bar,** 500 8th St. SE (543-5906). Metro: Eastern Market. Marvelous Tex-Mex and Cuban entrees ($7-14) include plantain soup ($4.50), shrimp fajitas ($14), and stuffed plantains ($14). The interior is filled with fake banana trees and tropical portraits painted by the owner. Lunch menu $6.25-9. Open M-Th 11:30am-2:30pm and 5-10:30pm, F 11:30am-2:30pm and 5-11:30pm, Sa 5-11:30pm, Su 5-10:30pm.

Il Radiccho, 223 Pennsylvania Ave. (547-5114), with locations in Georgetown, Dupont Circle, and Arlington. *The* place for all-you-can-eat spaghetti ($6.50 per person, sauces $1.50-4). 25 varieties of pizza ($7.75-18.25). Open M-Th 11:30am-10pm, F-Sa 11:30am-11pm, Su 5-10pm.

The Market Lunch, 225 7th St. SE (547-8444), in the Eastern Market complex. Metro: Eastern Market. Crab cakes ($6-10) and soft shell crab (sandwich $7, platter $12) are the local specialties, but the Blue Bucks (buckwheat blueberry pancakes $3.50) have people lined up around the corner on Sa mornings (breakfast served Sa until 11am). Open Tu-Sa 7:30am-3pm.

Chinatown

Szechuan Gallery, 617 H St. NW (898-1180). Site of a scene from the movie *True Lies*. Chef's recommendations highlight stunning Taiwanese seafood dishes, including fragrant crab (whole crabs in spicy egg batter $10). Pork, chicken, beef, and vegetarian standards. Open Su-Th 11am-10pm, F-Sa 11am-11pm.

Burma Restaurant, upstairs at 740 6th St. NW (638-1280), between H and G St. Burmese cuisine trades in soy sauce with pickles, mild curries, and unique spices. Fried golden prawns with sweet and sour chili sauce ($6) make a delicious starter. Entrees $6-8. Open M-F 11am-3pm and 6-10:30pm, Sa-Su 6-10:30pm.

Dupont Circle

◈**Raku,** 1900 Q St. NW (265-RAKU/7258), off Connecticut Ave. An upscale version of the Asian noodle stand, with excellent noodles, dumplings, and salads. The dining room is full of skylights and warm wooden tones. Noodles $7-9, dumplings $3-7, and salads $4.25-9. Open Su-Th 11:30am-11pm, F-Sa 11:30am-midnight.

Skewers, 1633 P St. NW (387-7400), near 17th St. Excellent Middle Eastern food for lunch or dinner, served in a stylish restaurant draped with tapestries and shimmery fabrics. Lip-smacking, tender kebabs and tangy tabouleh. Appetizers $3-4, entrees $5-10. Open Su-Th 11am-11pm, F-Sa 11am-midnight.

Pan Asian Noodles & Grill, 2020 P St. NW (872-8889), near 20th St. Informal and sleekly modern. The "drunken noodles" ($8) are worth the trip. Lunch specials $6-7, dinner $7-10. Open M-Th 11:30am-2:30pm and 5-10pm, F 11:30am-2:30pm and 5-11pm, Sa noon-2:30pm and 5-11pm, Su 5-10pm.

Lauriol Plaza, 1801 18th St. NW (387-0035), near S St. Authentic Mexican food served in copious quantities. Rice and *frijoles negros* (black beans) included with entrees. Appetizers like fried plantains are $2.50-7; entrees are $6.50-16, and brunch entrees are $5-7. Moving in the winter of 1998-99 to 18th and T. Open M-Th 11:30am-11pm, F-Sa 11:30am-midnight, Su 11am-11pm.

Farragut

The Art Gallery Grille, 1712 I St. NW (298-6658), near 17th St. Metro: Farragut West. Sophisticated, healthy, Middle Eastern specialties draw the corporate lunch crowd. Art Deco interior. Falafel trays ($8); large salads, sandwiches, and other Middle Eastern specialties $3-13. Open M-W 6:30am-10pm, Th-F 6:30am-2am.

Casa Blanca, 1014 Vermont Ave. NW (393-4430), between K and L St. Metro: McPherson Sq. Homemade Peruvian, Salvadoran, and Mexican cuisine in a modestly decorated room. Basic tacos are 2 for $3.50. The Peruvian specialty *pollo a la braza* only $5.50. Daily specials $4. Open M-Sa 9:30am-10pm, Su noon-5pm.

Georgetown

◎Café La Ruche, 1039 31st St. NW (965-2684; take-out 965-2591), near M St. This small French restaurant deserves more acclaim than it gets. Fab food and thoroughly date-appropriate ambience. Delicious salads ($3.50-7), quiches ($5-6.50), and entrees ($7-9). The desserts, especially the puff-pastry-and-fruit concoctions, are reasons to live ($4-5). Open Su-Th 11:30am-11:30pm, F-Sa 10am-midnight.

◎Ristorante Piccolo, 1068 31st St. NW (342-7414), just off M St. The best Italian food in Georgetown. Pasta dishes like the *ravioli verde* (spinach ravioli with ricotta) and the moist and fluffy gnocchi are skillfully seasoned. Lunch ($6-10) or dinner (pasta $10-13, entrees $14-18). Open Su-Th 11:30am-11pm, F-Sa 11:30am-midnight.

Furin's, 2805 M St. NW (965-1000). Vinyl tablecloths, fake flowers, rack of cookbooks, and good homecooking from breakfast sandwiches and salads to spoil-the-kid-rotten slabs of cake ($1-6). Open M-F 7:30am-7pm, Sa 8am-5pm.

Old Downtown

Jaleo, 480 7th St. NW (628-7949), 2 blocks from the Gallery Pl.-Chinatown Metro stop at 7th and E St. While entrees may be pricey ($13-15.50), over 35 tapas (Spanish-style appetizers; $3-7) offer a cheap way to sample Spanish cuisine. Open Su-M 11:30am-10pm, Tu-Th 11:30am-11:30pm, F-Sa 11:30am-midnight.

Restaurante Casa Juanita's, 908 11th St. NW (737-2520), between I and K St. Huge portions of authentic Mexican and Salvadoran cuisine with lots of beans and rice. The modest, wood-paneled decor takes nothing away from *los chorros* (Delmonico steak with sautéed onions, green peppers, and tomatoes, $10.50). Daily lunch and dinner specials are a steal at $7. Free delivery. Open M-Sa 11am-9:30pm.

Shaw / U District

◎Ben's Chili Bowl, 1213 U St. NW (667-0909), at 13th St. across from the Metro. Venerable neighborhood hangout has wonderful chili dogs ($2), chili burgers ($2.70), and plain chili ($2.25 small, $3 large). Photos of Bill Cosby and Denzel Washington pay homage to Ben's food and the friendly, small diner atmosphere. Open M-Th 6am-2am, F-Sa 6am-4am, Su noon-8pm. Breakfast M-Sa until 11am.

◎Florida Avenue Grill, 1100 Florida Ave. NW (265-1586), at 11th St. Metro: U St.-Cardozo. Small, enduring diner opened in 1944 and once fed famous leaders and entertainers. Fantastic Southern food: breakfast (served until 1pm) with salmon cakes or spicy half-smoked sausage, and grits, apples, or biscuits ($2-6). Lunch specials Tu-F 11am-4pm just $4. Entrees $6.50-10. Open Tu-Sa 6am-9pm.

Outlaw's, 917 U St. NW (387-3978), between Vermont Ave. and 9th St. No-frills establishment with real, meat-laden home-cooking. Daily specials like meat loaf (Tu $6) and Salisbury steak (Th $6). Dinners $5.55-8.25, sandwiches $3.85-5.50, cobblers $2 per slice. Open M-F 11am-6pm.

Upper Northwest

Entotto, 1609 Foxhall Rd. NW (333-1200), at the corner of Foxhall and Reservoir Rd. Stunning Ethiopian food served in a quiet, classy room with 5 tables. Orders cooked from scratch by the owner, who came here after a dozen years running a restaurant in Paris. Appetizers $6.50-7.50, entrees $7-12, combo platters $12. Open M-Sa 11:30am-2:30pm and 5:30-10pm (closes at 9pm in winter).

Faccia Luna, 2400 Wisconsin Ave. NW (337-3132). The pizza of pizzas. A thin, crispy-yet-tender crust under subtly seasoned sauce and tangy cheese, baked in a wood-fired oven, makes for the best pizza in D.C. Basic pie $6.15-11.50; toppings $1.25-1.75 each. Open Su-Th 11:30am-11pm, F-Sa 11:30am-midnight.

Rocklands, 2418 Wisconsin Ave. NW (333-2558). No gas or electricity in the BBQ pit—just red oak, hickory, and charcoal. Eat at the weathered mahogany counters, or take home a quarter-rack of pork ribs ($5) or a pulled chicken sandwich ($5). Sandwiches $4-5, salads $1.30. Open M-Sa 11:30am-10pm, Su 11am-9pm.

MID-ATLANTIC

SIGHTS

Capitol Hill

The **U.S. Capitol** (switchboard 224-3121, tours 224-4048; metro: Capitol South) may be an endless font of cynicism, but it still evokes the power of the republic. *(Open daily Mar.-Aug. 9am-8pm; Sept.-Feb. 9am-4:30pm. Tours Mar.-Aug. M-F 9am-7pm, Sa 9am-4pm; Sept.-Feb. M-Sa 9am-4pm. Free.)* The **East Front** faces the Supreme Court; from the times of frontiersman Andrew Jackson (1829) to peanut-farmin' Jimmy Carter (1977), most Presidents were inaugurated here. The East Front entrance brings you into the 180 ft. high **rotunda,** where soldiers slept during the Civil War.

Painting and statuary—some staid and some bizarre—fill the historic halls of the 1st fl. and the lower crypt level. From the crypt, visitors can climb to the 2nd fl. for a view of the House or Senate visitors chambers. Americans may obtain a free gallery pass from the office of their representative or senator in the House or Senate office buildings near the Capitol. Foreigners may get 1-day passes by presenting identification at the "appointments desks" in the crypt. The real business of Congress, however, is conducted in **committee hearings.** Most are open to the public; check the *Washington Post's* "Today in Congress" box for times and locations. The free **Capitol subway** shuttles between the basement of the Capitol and the House and Senate office buildings; a buzzer and flashing red light signals an imminent vote.

In 1935, the nine justices of the **Supreme Court** (479-3000) decided it was time to take the nation's separation of powers literally, and moved from their makeshift offices in the Capitol into a new Greek Revival courthouse across the street at 1 1st St. *(Open M-F 9am-4:30pm. Free.)* The courtroom where the justices meet to interpret the Constitution lurks behind a red curtain off the grand two chambers filled with statues. Oral arguments are open to the public; show up before 8:30am to be seated, or walk through the standing gallery to hear 5min. of the argument (court is in session Oct.-June M-W 10am-3pm for 2 weeks every month). You can also walk through the courtroom itself when the Justices are on vacation.

The **Library of Congress,** 1st St. SE (707-5000 or 707-8000), between East Capitol and Independence Ave., is the world's largest library, with 113,026,742 million objects stored on 532 mi. of shelves, including a copy of *Old King Cole* written on a grain of rice. *(Great Hall open M-Sa 8:30am-5:30pm. Visitors Center and galleries open 10am. Free.)* The collection was torched by the British in 1814, after which it was restarted from Thomas Jefferson's personal collection of 6487 volumes. The collection is open to anyone of college age or older with a legitimate research purpose—exhibits of rare items and a tour of the facilities are available for tourists. The **Jefferson Building,** whose green copper dome and gold-leafed flame seals a spectacular octagonal reading room, is one of the most beautiful edifices in the city. Next door, the **Folger Shakespeare Library,** 201 East Capitol St. SE (544-4600 or 544-7077), houses the world's largest collection of Shakespeareana with about 275,000 books and manuscripts. *(Exhibits open M-Sa 10am-4pm. Garden tours Apr.-Oct. every 3rd Sa of each month. Library open for researchers M-F 8:45am-4:45pm.)*

Trains converge at **Union Station,** 50 Massachusetts Ave. NE (371-9441; Metro: Union Station), 2 blocks north of the Capitol. *(Retail shops open M-Sa 10am-9pm, Su 10am-6pm.)* Colonnades, archways, and domed ceilings equate Burnham's Washington with imperial Rome; today the station is an ornament in the crown of capitalism, with stores and a food court. Directly west of Union Station is the **National Postal Museum,** 1st St. and Massachusetts Ave. NE (357-2700; Metro: Union Station), on the lower level of the City Post Office. *(Open daily 10am-5:30pm. Free.)* The collection includes such postal flotsam as half of a fake mustache used by a train robber. Northeast of Union Station is the red brick **Capital Children's Museum,** 800 3rd St. NE (675-4120; Metro: Union Station), where you can brew your own hot chocolate, wander through a room-sized maze, and touch and feel almost all of the exhibits.

Museums on the Mall

The **Smithsonian** (357-2700) is the catalogued attic of the United States, containing over 140 million objects. The Institute began as the idea of **James Smithson,** a British chemist who, though he never himself visited the U.S., left 105 bags of gold sovereigns—the bulk of his estate—to "found at Washington, under the name of the Smithsonian Institution, an establishment for the increase and diffusion of knowledge among men." The Smithsonian Museums on the Mall constitute the world's largest museum complex. *(All Smithsonian museums are free, wheelchair accessible, and open daily 10am-5:30pm, with extended summer hours determined annually. Write to Smithsonian Information, Smithsonian Institution, Room 153, MRC 010, Washington, D.C. 20560.)* Once in D.C., head to the **Smithsonian Castle,** on the south side of the mall, for an introduction to and information on the Smithsonian buildings. Use Metro: Smithsonian or Federal Triangle to get to the following.

National Museum of American History, on the north side of the Mall, closest to the Washington Monument, houses several centuries' worth of machines, photographs, vehicles, harmonicas, and uncategorizable U.S. detritus. When the Smithsonian inherits quirky artifacts of popular history, like Dorothy's slippers from *The Wizard of Oz,* they end up here. Hands-on exhibits are geared toward children.

Museum of Natural History, east towards the Capitol from American History, ruminates on the earth and its life in 3 big, crowded floors of exhibits. Objects on display in the spectacular golden-domed, neoclassical buildings include dinosaur skeletons, the largest African elephant ever captured, and an insect zoo with live creepy-crawlies. Visitors still line up to see the cursed Hope Diamond, mailed to the Smithsonian in 1958 for $145.29 (insured up to $1 million).

National Gallery of Art (737-4215), east of Natural History, is not technically a part of the Smithsonian, but a close cousin of the Institute due to its location on the mall. (Open M-Sa 10am-5pm, Su 11am-6pm. Free.) The **West Wing** houses its pre-1900 art in a domed marble temple in the Western Tradition, including works by El Greco, Raphael, Rembrandt, Vermeer, and Monet. Leonardo da Vinci's earliest surviving portrait, *Ginevra de' Benci,* the only one of his works in the U.S., hangs among a fine collection of Italian Renaissance Art. The **East Building** (737-4215) houses the museum's 20th-century collection, including works by Picasso, Matisse, Mondrian, Miró, Magritte, Pollock, Warhol, Lichtenstein, and Rothko. The building also holds the museum's temporary exhibits.

National Air and Space Museum (357-1686), on the south side of the Mall across from the National Gallery, is the world's most popular museum, with 7.5 million visitors per year. Airplanes and space vehicles dangle from the ceilings, with the Wright brothers' original biplane hanging in the entrance gallery. The space-age atrium holds a moon rock, worn smooth by 2 decades of tourists' fingertips. Walk through the Skylab space station, the Apollo XI command module, and a DC-7. IMAX movies on a 5-story screen thrill the endless throngs.

Hirshhorn Museum and Sculpture Garden (tour info 357-3235), on the south side of the mall west of Air and Space is a 4-story, slide-carousel-shaped brown building that has outraged traditionalists since 1966. Each floor consists of 2 concentric circles: an outer ring of rooms with modern, postmodern, and post-postmodern paintings, and an inner corridor of sculptures. The museum claims a comprehensive set of 19th- and 20th-century Western sculpture.

National Museum of African Art and the **Arthur M. Sackler Gallery** hide together underground in the newest museum facilities on the Mall, to the west of the Hirshhorn. The Museum of African Art displays artifacts from sub-Saharan Africa such as masks, textiles, ceremonial figures, and musical instruments. The Sackler Gallery showcases an extensive collection of art from China, South and Southeast Asia, and Persia. Exhibits include illuminated manuscripts, Chinese and Japanese painting, jade miniatures, and friezes from Egypt, Phoenicia, and Sumeria.

Freer Gallery of Art (tour info 357-1500), just west of the Hirshhorn, displays American and Asian art. The static American collection consists of the holdings of Charles L. Freer, the museum's benefactor, and focuses on works by James McNeill Whistler. The strong Asian collections include bronzes, manuscripts, and jade.

MID-ATLANTIC

Monuments

All of the following monuments can be viewed 24hr. free of charge, unless you want to take a peek inside the **Washington Monument** (Metro: Smithsonian). *(Admission by timed ticket. Apr.-Aug. monument open daily 8am-midnight, ticket kiosk open from 7:30am until all tickets distributed; Sept.-Mar. monument open 9am-5pm, ticket kiosk from 8:30am. Free. No tickets needed after 8pm Apr.-Aug.)* About to undergo a $9.4 million restoration project, this shrine to America's first president was once nicknamed the "the Beef Depot monument" after the cattle that grazed here during the Civil War. Construction was temporarily halted during the war and later resumed; the stone that was used came from a new quarry, explaining the different colors of the monument's stones. The **Reflecting Pool** mirrors Washington's obelisk.

Maya Ying Lin, who designed the **Vietnam Veterans Memorial,** south of Constitution Ave. at 22nd St. NW (Metro: Foggy Bottom/GWU), received a "B" when she submitted her memorial concept for a grade as a Yale senior—but beat her professor in the public memorial design competition. In her words, the monument is "a rift in the earth—a long, polished black stone wall, emerging from and receding into the earth." The wall contains the names of the 58,132 Americans who died in Vietnam. Books at both ends of the structure serve as indices to the memorial's numbered panels.

The **Lincoln Memorial,** at the west end of the Mall (Metro: Smithsonian or Foggy Bottom/GWU), recalls the rectangular grandeur of Athens' Parthenon. From these steps, Martin Luther King, Jr. gave his "I Have a Dream" speech during the 1963 March on Washington. A seated Lincoln presides over the memorial, keeping watch over protesters, Nazi party vigils, and Fourth of July fireworks. Climbing the 19 ft. president is a federal offense; a camera will catch you if the rangers don't.

The 19 colossal polished steel statues of the **Korean War Memorial** trudge up a hill, rifles in hand, an eternal expression of weariness mixed with fear frozen upon their faces. The statue of the 14 Army men, three Marines, Navy Medics, and an Air Force officer is accompanied by a black granite wall with over 2000 sandblasted photographic images from this war, in which 54,000 Americans lost their lives. The memorial is at the west end of the Mall, near Lincoln.

Occupying a long stretch of West Potomac Park (the peninsula between the Tidal Basin and the Potomac River) just a short walk from both the Jefferson or Lincoln Memorials, the **Franklin Delano Roosevelt Memorial** (Metro: Smithsonian) is more of a stone garden than a monument. Whether to display the handicapped Roosevelt in his wheelchair was hotly debated when the memorial was being planned. Roosevelt is displayed in a compromise, seated position based on a famous picture taken at Yalta. The memorial is laid out in four "rooms" of red South Dakota granite, each of which represents a phase of FDR's presidency.

A 19 ft. bronze Thomas Jefferson stands enshrined in the domed rotunda of the **Jefferson Memorial** (Metro: L'Enfant Plaza), designed to evoke Jefferson's home and own creation, Monticello. The memorial overlooks the **Tidal Basin,** where pedalboats ply a polluted pond in and out of the shrine's strange shadow. Quotes from the *Declaration of Independence,* the *Virginia Statute of Religious Freedom, Notes on Virginia,* and an 1815 letter adorn the walls.

South of the Mall

A block off the mall at 100 Raul Wallenberg Pl. SW lies the **U.S. Holocaust Memorial Museum** (488-0400; Metro: Smithsonian), whose displays chronicle the rise of Nazism, the events leading up to the war in Europe, and the history of anti-Semitism. *(Open daily 10am-5:30pm. Free. Get in line early for tickets.)* Films show troops entering concentration camps, shocked by the mass graves and emaciated prisoners they encounter. "The Hall of Remembrance" contains an eternal flame. Further west, the **Bureau of Engraving and Printing** (a.k.a. **The Mint**) (847-2808; Metro: Smithsonian), at 14th St. and C St. SW, offers tours of the presses that annually print over $20 billion worth of money and stamps. *(Open M-F 9am-2pm. Free.)* The love of money has made this the area's longest line; expect to grow old while you wait.

White House and Foggy Bottom

The **White House,** 1600 Pennsylvania Ave. NW (456-7041), with its simple columns and expansive lawns, seems a compromise between patrician lavishness and democratic simplicity. *(Open by tour only Tu-Sa 10am-noon. Free. Get tickets at the White House Visitors Center, 1450 Pennsylvania Ave. NW, at the corner of 15th and E St.)* Thomas Jefferson proposed a contest for the design of the building, but he lost to amateur architect James Hoban when George Washington judged the competition. The President's personal staff works in the West Wing, while the First Lady's cohorts occupy the East Wing. Staff who cannot fit in the White House work in the nearby **Old Executive Office Building.** The President's official office is the **Oval Office,** site of many televised speeches, but the public tour is limited to public reception areas.

Historic homes surround **Lafayette Park** north of the White House. These include the Smithsonian-owned **Renwick Gallery** (357-1300; Metro: Farragut West), at 17th St. and Pennsylvania Ave. NW. *(Open daily 10am-5:30pm. Free.)* This craft museum has some remarkable works, such as the 80s sculptures *Ghost Clock* and *Game Fish.* Once housed in the Renwick's mansion, the **Corcoran Gallery** (639-1700) now boasts larger quarters on 17th St. between E St. and New York Ave. NW. *(Open M, W, and F-Su 10am-5pm, Th 10am-9pm. Suggested donation $3, students and seniors $1, families $5.)* It displays American artists such as John Singer Sargent, Mary Cassatt, and Winslow Homer. Nearby, the **Octagon,** a curious building designed by Capitol architect William Thornton, is reputedly filled with ghosts. *(Open Tu-Su 10am-4pm. $3, students and seniors $1.50.)* Tour guides explain the history of the house.

A few blocks above Rock Creek Pkwy., the **John F. Kennedy Center for the Performing Arts** (467-4600), off 25th St. and New Hampshire Ave. NW (Metro: Foggy Bottom-GWU), rises like a marble sarcophagus. *(Free tours every 15min. 10am-1pm.)* One could fit the Washington Monument in the gargantuan **Grand Foyer,** were it not for the 18 Swedish chandeliers, shaped like cubical grape clusters. The Opera House, one of four main venues, also has notable chandeliers—these snowflake-shaped beasts, requiring 1735 electric light bulbs, were donated by Austria. Across the street from the center is Tricky Dick's beloved **Watergate Complex.**

Old Downtown

An architectural marvel houses the Smithsonian's **National Building Museum** (272-2448; Metro: Judiciary Sq.), towering above F St. NW between 4th and 5th St. *(Open M-Sa 10am-4pm, Su noon-4pm; hrs. extend to 5pm during summer. Suggested donation $3, students and seniors $2.)* Montgomery Meigs's Italian-inspired edifice remains one of Washington's most beautiful; the Great Hall could hold a 15-story building.

The Smithsonian's **National Museum of American Art** and **National Portrait Gallery** (357-2700; Metro: Gallery Pl.-Chinatown) share the Old Patent Office Building, a neoclassical edifice 2 blocks long. *(American Art entrance at 8th and G St., Portrait Gallery entrance at 8th and F. Open daily 10am-5:30pm. Tours daily 10:15am and 1:15pm; free. Wheelchair entrance at 9th and G St.)* The NMAA's corridors contain a diverse collection of major 19th- and 20th-century painters, as well as folk and ethnic artists. Janitor James Hampton stayed up nights in an unheated garage for 15 years to create the *Throne of the Third Heaven of the Nations' Millennium General Assembly,* to the right of the main entrance. "Art of the American West" puts the U.S.'s westward expansion in perspective.

The U.S.'s founding documents can still be found at the **National Archives** (501-5000; Metro: Archives-Navy Memorial), at 8th St. and Constitution Ave. NW. *(Open daily Apr.-Sept. 6 10am-9pm; Sept. 7-Mar. 10am-5:30pm. Free.)* Visitors line up outside to view the original *Declaration of Independence, U.S. Constitution,* and *Bill of Rights.* The **Federal Bureau of Investigation** (324-3000) still hunts Commies, social activists, boogie-monsters, and interstate felons with undiminished vigor. *(Open M-F 8:45am-4:15pm. Free.)* Tour lines form on the beige-but-brutal **J. Edgar Hoover Building's** outdoor plaza. John Dillinger's death mask hangs alongside his machine gun.

"Sic semper tyrannis!" shouted assassin John Wilkes Booth after shooting President Abraham Lincoln during a performance at **Ford's Theatre,** 511 10th St. NW

Go Hammer! Go Hammer!

On October 10, 1986, a Colorado man tried to destroy the Constitution and the Bill of Rights with a claw hammer. Although his hammer broke three star-shaped holes in the half-inch laminated outer glass of the display case, it did not reach the separate glass shell enclosing the documents. "America is an imperialist country," **Randall Husar** yelled as he was arrested. Relatives said that Husar, a mentally ill history buff with a degree in psychology, dislikes Republicans. Husar pleaded guilty to a charge of attempting to destroy federal property.

(426-6924; Metro: Metro Center). *(Open daily 9am-5pm. Free.)* National Park Rangers describe the events with animated gusto during a 20min. talk in the theater. The **Old Post Office** (606-8691; Metro: Federal Triangle), at Pennsylvania Ave. and 12th St. NW, sheathes a shopping mall in architectural wonder. *(Tower open mid-Apr. to mid-Sept. 8am-10:45pm; off-season 10am-6pm. Shops open M-Sa 10am-8pm, Su noon-6pm.)* Its arched windows, conical turrets, and 315 ft. clock tower rebuke its sleeker contemporary neighbors.

The **National Museum of Women in the Arts,** 1250 New York Ave. NW (783-5000; Metro: Metro Center), houses works by the likes of Mary Cassatt, Georgia O'Keeffe, and Frida Kahlo in a former Masonic Temple. *(Open M-Sa 10am-5pm, Su noon-5pm. Cafe M-Sa 11:30am-2:30pm. Suggested donation $3, students and seniors $2.)*

Georgetown

Georgetown's quiet, narrow, tree-lined streets are sprinkled with trendy boutiques and points of historic interest that make for an enjoyable walking tour. Retired from commercial use since the 1800s, the **Chesapeake & Ohio Canal** (301-299-3613) extends 185 mi. from Georgetown to Cumberland, MD. Today, the towpath where trusty mules pulled barges on the canal belongs to the National Park Service. The **Old Stone House,** 3051 M St. (426-6851), is generally accepted as the oldest house in Washington—the **Yellow House** at 1430 33rd St. was long thought to be older until new evidence was discovered. The house of **Reuben Dawes,** 2803 P St., has a remarkable fence made entirely from 1767 Charlevoix rifle barrels left over from the Mexican War.

The **Dumbarton Oaks Mansion,** 1703 32nd St. NW (339-6401), between R and S St., former home of John Calhoun, holds a beautifully displayed collection of Byzantine and pre-Columbian art. *(Collections open Tu-Su 2-5pm. Suggested contribution $1.)* In 1944, the Dumbarton Oaks Conference, held in the Music Room, helped write the United Nations charter. The spectacular pre-Columbian art gallery was designed by Phillip Johnson. The beautiful gardens are the best cheap date place in town. *(Gardens open daily Apr.-Oct. 2-6pm; Nov.-Mar. 2-5pm. $4, seniors and children $3.)*

When Archbishop John Carroll learned where the new capital would be built, he rushed to found **Georgetown University,** at 37th and O St., the Harvard of Washington, which opened in 1789 as the U.S.'s first Catholic institution of higher learning.

Dupont Circle

Once one of Washington's swankier neighborhoods, Dupont Circle attracted embassies because of its stately townhouses and large tracts of land. Today, it is a haven for the international, artsy, and gay crowds; this mix of business, politics, and pleasure make it one of the more exciting parts of the city.

The **Art Gallery District** (general information 232-3610), bounded by Connecticut Ave., Florida Ave., and Q St., contains over two dozen galleries displaying everything from contemporary photographs to tribal crafts. Nearby is the **Phillips Collection,** 1600 21st St. (387-2151), at Q St. NW, the first museum of modern art in the U.S. *(Open Tu-Sa 10am-5pm, Su noon-7pm. $6.50, students and seniors $3.25, under 18 free.)* Everyone gapes at Auguste Renoir's masterpiece, *Luncheon of the Boating Party,* in the Renoir room. Works by talents like Delacroix, Miró, and Turner line the Annex.

The stretch of Massachusetts Ave. between Dupont Circle and Observatory Circle is also called Embassy Row. Before the 1930s, Washington socialites lined the avenue with their extravagant edifices; status-conscious diplomats found the mansions perfect for their purposes, and embassies moved in by the dozen. Highlights for visitors include **Anderson House,** 2118 Massachusetts Ave. NW (785-2040, ext. 16), which retains the robber-baron decadence of U.S. ambassador Larz Anderson, who built it in 1902-5 (open Tu-Sa 1-4pm; free). Flags line the entrance to the **Islamic Center,** 2551 Massachusetts Ave. NW (332-8343), a brilliant white building within which stunning designs stretch to the tips of spired ceilings. *(Open daily 10:30am-5pm; prayers held 5 times daily.)* No shorts; women must cover their heads, arms, and legs.

Upper Northwest

Washington's National Zoological Park, 3000 Connecticut Ave. (673-4800; Metro: Woodley Park-Zoo), is best known for its giant pandas, which Mao gave to Nixon. *(Grounds open daily 6am-8pm, Oct.-Apr. 6am-6pm. Buildings open daily 10am-6pm, Oct.-Apr. 10am-4:30pm. Free.)* The Valley Trail (marked with blue bird tracks) connects the bird and sealife exhibits, while the red Olmsted Walk (marked with elephant feet) links land-animal houses. The pygmy hippopotami are a highlight of this collection.

The **Washington National Cathedral** (537-6200 or 364-6616; Metro: Tenleytown, then take the #30, 32, 34 or 36 bus toward Georgetown; or walk up Cathedral Ave. from the equidistant Woodley Park-Zoo Metro), at Massachusetts and Wisconsin Ave. NW, was built from 1907 to 1990. *(Open May-Aug. M-F 10am-9pm, Sa 10am-4:30pm, Su 7:30am-7:30pm; Sept.-Apr. M-Sa 10am-4:30pm, Su 12:30-4pm. Suggested donation $2 for tour, under 12 $1.)* Rev. Martin Luther King, Jr. preached his last Sunday sermon from the Canterbury pulpit. The elevator rises to the Pilgrim Observation Gallery, revealing D.C. from the highest vantage point in the city. At the **Medieval Workshop** (537-2934), children can carve stone, learn how a stained-glass window is created, or, for $2, mold a gargoyle out of clay.

NEAR D.C.

Arlington, VA

The silence of the 612-acre **Arlington National Cemetery** (703-697-2131; Metro: Arlington Cemetery) honors those who sacrificed their lives in war. *(Open daily Apr.-Sept. 8am-7pm; Oct.-May 8am-5pm. Free).* The Kennedy Gravesites hold the remains of President John F. Kennedy, his brother Robert F. Kennedy, and his wife Jacqueline Kennedy Onassis. The Eternal Flame flickers above JFK's simple memorial stone. The **Tomb of the Unknowns** honors all servicemen who died fighting for the United States and is guarded by delegations from the Army's Third Infantry (changing of the guard every 30min.; Oct.-Mar. every hr. on the hr.). Robert E. Lee's home, **Arlington House,** overlooks the cemetery; tours are self-guided. Head down Custis Walk in front of Arlington House, exit the cemetery through Weitzel Gate, and walk for 20min. to get to the **Iwo Jima Memorial,** based on Joe Rosenthal's Pulitzer Prize-winning photo of Marines straining to raise the U.S. flag on Mt. Suribachi.

Video screens…video screens everywhere…are you trapped in George Orwell's *1984?* No, it's just the **Newseum,** 1101 Wilson Blvd. (703-284-3544 or 888-639-7386; Metro: Rosslyn). *(Open W-Su 10am-5pm. Free.)* Opened in 1997, the Newseum honors journalists and journalism with dazzling interactive glitz. The video-game atmosphere makes it a hit with kids and adults who don't have any gripes with "sensationalized news." Read headlines from around the world, or jump right into the action and become a news anchor via the studios on the 2nd fl.

The **Pentagon** (695-1776), the world's largest office building, shows just how huge military bureaucracy can get (Metro: Pentagon). *(Tours every 30min. M-F 9:30am-3:30pm. Free.)* For security reasons, there are no bathroom breaks on the tour.

Alexandria, VA

Alexandria, VA traces its colonial origins over a century further back than Washington, D.C. Courtesy of a massive 80s restoration effort, **Old Town Alexandria** (Metro: King St.) has cobblestone streets, brick sidewalks, tall ships, and quaint shops. Points of interest cluster along **Washington and King St.** George Washington and Robert E.

Lee prayed at **Christ Church,** 119 N. Washington St. (703-549-1450), at Cameron St., a red brick Colonial building with a domed steeple. Both slept in **Robert E. Lee's Boyhood Home,** 607 Oronoco St. (548-8454), near Asaph St. Thirty-seven different Lees inhabited the **Lee-Fendall House** at 614 Oronoco St. (549-1789).

Mt. Vernon

George Washington had a fabulous estate called **Mt. Vernon** (703-780-2000), easily accessible to Washingtonians in boondocky Fairfax County, VA. (Take the Fairfax Connector 101 bus from Metro: Huntington or take I-395 S to George Washington Pkwy. S, which becomes Mt. Vernon Hwy. in Alexandria; use the Mt. Vernon Exit.) Visitors can see George and Martha Washington's bedroom and tomb, and wander the estate's fields, where slaves once grew corn, wheat, and tobacco.

ENTERTAINMENT AND NIGHTLIFE

Bars and Clubs

⊛**Chief Ike's Mambo Room, Chaos, and Pandemonium,** 1725 Columbia Rd. (332-2211 or 797-4637), near Ontario Rd., 2 blocks from 18th St. Pub-style food (most under $5) accompanied by live R&B or DJ. Up a long red staircase are Chaos and Pandemonium, featuring alternative music and pseudo-Japanese decor. Beer $3; rails $3.50. Prices higher when a band plays. 21+. Chief Ike's open Su-Th 4pm-2am, F-Sa 4pm-3am. Chaos and Pandemonium open Su-Th 6pm-2am, F-Sa 6pm-3am.

⊛**18th St. Lounge,** 1212 18th St. NW (466-3922). Metro: Farragut North. The hippest club/lounge in D.C. A barrage of slick bouncers wait behind the one-way mirror on the unmarked door. Dim candlelight barely illuminates 2 floors of funky velvet couches, 2 bars, and gay and straight patrons sipping overpriced drinks or grooving in various living rooms. DJs and live bands play bass-heavy acid jazz, bossa nova, and house. 21+. High weekend cover. Hrs. vary.

Zei, 1415 Zei Alley (842-2445), between 14th and 15th and H and I St. NW. Metro: McPherson Sq. A high-tech clubber's dream, with a lively lighting system. M-Th cover $3-8; F-Sa $10. Open M-Th 10pm-2am, F-Sa 10pm-3am.

Southeast Tracks, 1111 1st St. SE (488-3320). Metro: Navy Yard. One of D.C.'s hottest dance clubs. 2 dance floors, 3 bars, a patio, and an outdoor volleyball court. A mixed gay and straight crowd cavorts here, with everything from hip-hop to goth to retro nights. Cover $5-10. Secured parking nearby ($5). 18+. Open Th at 9pm, F at 10pm, Sa-Su at 9pm.

State of the Union, 1357 U St. NW (588-8810), near 14th St. Metro: U St.-Cardozo. Decorated with Soviet regalia. Music of the jazzier genres reign—jazz, blues, salsa, acid jazz, and hip-hop; each night is different. Happy hour (daily until 8:30pm) means 50% off beer and rail drinks. F-Sa feature live bands from 9-11pm, and a hip-hop DJ in the front and house DJ in the back after 11pm. 21+. Cover varies. Open M-Th 5pm-2am, F-Sa 5pm-3am, Su 7pm-3am.

Iota, 2832 Wilson Blvd. (703-522-8340). Metro: Clarendon. Live performances of every style in what feels like an old ski lodge. Microbrews $3.50-5, 35 bottled beers from $3. Tunes most nights from 9pm. Happy hour M-F 5-8pm, $1 off drafts. Cover $3-15. Open M-F 4pm-2am, Sa-Su 11am-2am.

Kelley's "The Irish Times," 14 F St. NW (543-5433). Metro: Union Station. Walk out of Union Station and turn right onto Mass. Ave.; F St. shoots off to your left at the intersection with N. Capitol. Irish street signs, the *Irish Times,* and Joyce on the wall give the pub Irish flair. Live music Th-Sa after 9pm. Happy hour M-F 4-7:30pm; domestic drafts $2. Open Su-Th 9:30am-2am, F-Sa 9:30am-3am.

The Bayou, 3135 K St. NW (333-2897), under the Whitehurst Freeway; take any #30 Metrobus to M St. and walk 2 blocks down Wisconsin Ave. Bands on their way up and bands on their way down, with a rough 'n' ready crowd that loves them all. Music varies from metal and rock to blues and jazz. Usually 18+. Cover varies. Box office open 8pm-midnight on nights with shows (or call **Ticketmaster** at 423-SEAT/7328). Hrs. vary with performances.

The 9:30 Club, 815 V St. NW (concert line 393-0930, tickets 265-0930), Metro: U St.-Cardozo; use the Vermont Ave. Exit. D.C.'s most established rock venue. Cover is occasionally $3 to see local bands or $5-20 for nationally known acts, which often sell out weeks in advance. The crowd varies according to concert line-up. 18+. Cash only box office open M-F 3-7pm or 3-11pm on show days, Sa-Su 6-11pm on show days. Door time Su-Th 7:30pm-midnight, F-Sa 9pm-2am. 50¢ surcharge for advance tickets from box office. Tickets also available from TicketMaster. *The area is dangerous at night.*

Gay Bars and Clubs

The *Washington Blade* is the best source of gay news and club listings; published every Friday, it's available in virtually every storefront in Dupont Circle. **Tracks** (see above) becomes the city's most popular gay dance club on Saturday nights.

The Circle Bar, 1629 Connecticut Ave. NW (462-5575). Metro: Dupont Circle. The upstairs bar and pool hall draw a diverse crowd of young, gay professionals. Happy hour M-F 11am-9pm. F "Bound: An industrial fetish party" from 10pm. Su night dance party from 6pm. Open Su-Th 11am-2am, F-Sa 11am-3am.

Badlands, 1415 22nd St. NW (296-0505), near P St. Metro: Dupont Circle. This peach-colored monolith hosts a young crowd interested in serious dancing. Top 40 and house music. Th is college night; no cover with a college ID. Cover F-Sa $3 9-10pm, $6 after 10pm. The Annex upstairs hosts a less raucous video bar and karaoke (led by local drag queens) F-Sa. Open Th-Sa from 9pm.

Hung Jury, 1819 H St. NW (785-8181). Metro: Farragut West. Lesbians from all over D.C., from 30-something couples to singles scoping the scene, spend their weekend nights bopping to Top 40. Cover $5. Shooters $1. Open F-Sa 9pm-3:30am.

To see what's up with local bands, check *City Paper.* The newest of D.C.'s live-act venues, the **Capitol Ballroom,** 1015 Half St. SE (703-549-7625; Metro: Navy Yard), is a colossal 2000-seat concert hall. The Ballroom boasts an impressive lineup of big-name alternative bands and small-name, big-draw local groups. Tickets ($10-40) are available from TicketMaster and Protix. Doors open at 7pm. On summer Saturdays and Sundays, shows from jazz and R&B to the National Symphony Orchestra occupy the outdoor, 4200-seat **Carter Barron Amphitheater** (426-6837), set into Rock Creek Park at 16th St. and Colorado Ave. NW (tickets vary from free to about $20). From late June to late August, rock, punk, and metal preempt soccer-playing at **Fort Reno Park** (call 282-1063 for Rock Creek Park services). George Washington University sponsors shows in **Lisner Auditorium,** 21st and H St. NW (202-994-1500), where David Letterman broadcasts his D.C. shows. Tickets are sometimes free and rarely more than $25; call in advance.

Theater

Arena Stage (488-3300; Metro: Waterfront), 6th St. and Maine Ave. SW, is often called the best regional (non-New York) theater company in America. (Tickets $21-45, lower for smaller stages, students 35% off, seniors 20% off; ½-price tickets usually available 1½hr. before start of show. Box office generally open M-Sa 10am-8pm, Su noon-8pm.) The **Kennedy Center** (416-8000), at 25th St. and New Hampshire Ave., offers scores of shows, most of them expensive ($22-47); however, most productions offer ½-price tickets the day of performance to students, seniors, military, and the disabled; call 467-4600 for details. The **Millennium Stage** presents free performances in the Grand Foyer. The prestigious **Shakespeare Theatre** (box office 393-2700; TTY 638-3863; Metro: Archives-Navy Memorial), at the Lansburgh, 450 7th St. NW at Pennsylvania Ave., offers a Bard-heavy repertoire. Standing-room tickets ($10) are available 2hr. before curtain. In the **14th St. theater district,** tiny repertory companies explore and experiment with enjoyable results (check *City Paper* for listings). **Woolly Mammoth,** 1401 Church St. NW (393-3939; Metro: Dupont Circle); **Studio Theater,** 1333 P St. NW (332-3300), at 14th St. (Metro: Dupont Circle); and **The Source Theater,** 1835 14th St. NW (462-1073; Metro: U St.-Cardozo), between S and T St., are all fine theaters in the neighborhood near Dupont Circle (tickets $12-29). *Use caution in this area at night.*

Film

The Foundry, 1055 Thomas Jefferson St. (333-8613), ½ block south of M St. in Georgetown (Metro: Foggy Bottom-GWU). This second-run movie house shows all those flicks you thought you missed for only $2.50, with some first-runs up to $7.50. **Outer Circle,** 4849 Wisconsin Ave. NW (244-3117; Metro: Tenleytown), across the street from Safeway, shows first-run foreign films and some exclusive engagements. (Admission $7.50, seniors and children under 11 $4.75. All shows before 6pm $4.75.) **Uptown Theater,** 3426 Connecticut Ave. NW (966-5400; Metro: Cleveland Park). Chic artsy flicks and big blockbusters on bigger screens ($4-7.75).

Sports

Completed in late 1997, the 20,000-seat **MCI Center,** 601 F St. NW (628-3200), in Chinatown, was designed to be D.C.'s premier sports arena (Metro: Gallery Pl.-Chinatown). The **Washington Wizards,** the city's hoops team, continues its struggle against dismal play and a lame mascot (tickets $19-40). The **Washington Capitals** kick ice (Oct.-Apr.; tickets $12-45).

Three-time Superbowl champions, the **Washington Redskins** draw crowds to **Jack Kent Cook Stadium,** Raljon Dr. (301-772-8800, tickets 301-276-6050), in Raljon, MD, September to December ($35-50). At **Robert F. Kennedy Stadium,** the **United** (703-478-660) play soccer mid-April through September.

Virginia

If Virginia seems obsessed with its past, it has good reason: many of America's formative experiences—the white settlement of North America, the shameful legacy of the slave trade, the final establishment of American independence, and much of the Civil War—all trace to the state. English colonists founded Jamestown in 1607; the New World's first black slaves joined them unwillingly 12 years later. Virginian James Madison traveled to Philadelphia in 1787 with drafts of the *Constitution,* and Virginian George Mason led the Bill of Rights campaign. From the 18th century, eastern Virginia's Tidewater aristocracy dominated the state with a rigid, gracious culture of slave-dependent plantations. This imploded during the Civil War, when Union and Confederate armies clashed throughout Virginia on the way to Appomattox.

Today, Virginia has begun to abandon its Old South lifestyle in search of a more cosmopolitan image. The western portion of the state, with its mountain forests and fascinating underground caverns, provides a welcome respite from the barrage of nostalgia (as well as the relentless Southern heat); but in places like Charlottesville and Harpers Ferry, the ghosts of history linger on.

PRACTICAL INFORMATION

Capital: Richmond.
Visitor Info: Virginia Division of Tourism, 901 E. Byrd St., 19th fl., Richmond 23219 (804-786-4484 or 800-VISIT-VA/847-4882; http://www.virginia.org). Open daily 8am-5pm. Has the free *Virginia Travel Guide.* **Dept. of Conservation and Recreation,** 203 Governor St., Richmond 23219 (804-786-1712). Open daily 8am-5pm.
Emergency: 911.
Time Zone: Eastern. **Postal Abbreviation:** VA.
Sales Tax: 4.5%.

■ Richmond

Richmond is a patchy conglomeration of struggling urban neighborhoods, a pleasant university campus, seemingly barren business districts, and brightly painted rows of

From Plowshares into Swords

During the Civil War, the South was so desperate for armament that the **Nashville Plow Works** factory in Tennessee literally pounded plowshares into swords for the rebel troops, in an ironic reversal of the Biblical verse that describes the Messianic era as one in which swords will be turned into plowshares. The Union forces ultimately seized the plant for operating as a munitions site.

historic buildings. Once the capital of the Confederacy, Richmond pays homage to rebels like Jefferson Davis and Stonewall Jackson through statuary, museums, and restored homes. At the same time, the city respects the rich African-American heritage of its Jackson Ward neighborhood, an area that once rivaled Harlem as a center of Black thought and culture.

ORIENTATION AND PRACTICAL INFORMATION

Broad Street is the city's central artery, and the streets that cross it are numbered from west to east. Most parallel streets to Broad, including the important Main St. and Cary St., run one-way. Both **I-95**, leading north to Washington, D.C., and **I-295** encircle the urban section of the city.

Richmond's historic center can be found in the **Court End** and **Church Hill** districts, on Richmond's eastern edges. Nearby, **Shockoe Slip** and **Shockoe Bottom** are the urban areas where the evening party scene occurs. **Jackson Ward,** in the heart of downtown (bounded by Belvedere, Leigh, Broad, and 5th St.), is a historically African-American neighborhood. **The Fan,** named for diverging streets with dubious resemblance to a lady's fan, is bounded by the Boulevard, I-95, Monument Ave., and **Virginia Commonwealth University,** and harbors many of Richmond's oldest homes. The pleasant bistros and boutiques of **Carytown** sit past the Fan on Cary St.

Trains: Amtrak, 7519 Staple Mills Rd. (264-9194 or 800-872-7245; open 24hr.). Reservations required. To: D.C. (2¼hr., 9 per day, $28); Williamsburg (1¼hr., 9 per day, $10); Virginia Beach (3hr., 1 per day, $23); New York City (7hr., 9 per day, $101); Baltimore (3½hr., 9 per day, $42); and Philadelphia (4¾hr., 9 per day, $64). Taxi fare to downtown about $10.

Buses: Greyhound, 2910 N. Boulevard (254-5910 or 800-231-2222). 2 blocks from downtown; take GRTC bus #24 north. To: D.C. (2hr., 18 per day, $15); Charlottesville (1½-4hr., 6 per day, $17); Williamsburg (1hr., 9 per day, $7); Norfolk (3hr., 9 per day, $15); New York City (6½hr., 24 per day, $47); Baltimore (3½hr., 21 per day, $19); and Philadelphia (7hr., 12 per day, $32).

Public Transportation: Greater Richmond Transit Co., 101 S. Davis Ave. (358-GRTC). Maps available in the basement of City Hall, 900 E. Broad St., and in the Yellow Pages. Bus service convenient in downtown, infrequent elsewhere; most buses leave from Broad St. downtown. Bus #24 goes south to Broad St. and downtown. Fare $1.25, transfers 15¢. Seniors 50¢ during off-peak hrs. Trolleys provide dependable service to downtown, Shockoe Slip, and Shockoe Bottom daily 11am-11pm. Evening parking is shockingly difficult in Shockoe Slip and Shockoe Bottom; many diners and drinkers choose to hop on the trolley. Fare 25¢.

Taxi: Veterans Cab (329-3333). **Yellow Cab** (222-7300). **Colonial Cab** (264-7960). **Hansom** (837-8524).

Visitor Info: Richmond Visitors Center, 1710 Robin Hood Rd. (358-5511), Exit 78 off I-95/64, in a converted train depot. Helpful 6min. video introduces the city's attractions. Walking tours and maps of downtown and the metro region. Open daily late May to early Sept. 9am-7pm; off-season 9am-5pm.

Hotlines: Traveler's Aid, 643-0279 or 648-1767. Operates M-F 9am-5pm. **Rape Crisis,** 643-0888. **Psychiatric Crisis Intervention,** 648-9224. Operates 24hr. **AIDS/HIV,** 800-533-4148. Operates M-F 8am-7pm. **Crisis Pregnancy Center,** 353-2320. Open 24hr. **Women's Health Clinic,** 800-254-4479. Open 24hr.

Post Office: 1801 Brook Rd. (775-6133). Open M-F 7am-6pm, Sa 10am-1pm. **ZIP code:** 23219. **Area code:** 804.

ACCOMMODATIONS AND CAMPGROUNDS

Budget motels in Richmond cluster on **Williamsburg Rd.,** the edge of town, and along **Midlothian Turnpike,** south of the James River; however, public transport to these areas is unreliable. As usual, the farther from downtown you stay, the less you pay. The Visitors Center can reserve accommodations, often at $20-35 discounts.

Massad House Hotel, 11 N. 4th St. (648-2893), 5 blocks from the Capitol, in the commercial downtown area. Shuttles guests via a 1940s elevator to clean rooms with showers, A/C, and cable TV. The only decent and inexpensive rooms downtown. Singles $44; doubles $50.

Cadillac Motel, 11418 Washington Hwy. (798-4049), 10 mi. from the city. Take I-95 to Exit 89. Sparse rooms with A/C and cable TV. Singles $36; doubles $45.

Executive Inn, 5215 W. Broad St. (288-4011), 3 mi. from town; use bus #6. Once the Red Carpet Inn, it still sports the trademark red carpet in its clean, slightly faded rooms. Provides A/C, cable TV, and a pool. $55-62; $165 per week.

Pocahontas State Park, 10301 State Park Rd. (796-4255; for reservations, 225-3867 or 800-933-PARK/7275), 10 mi. south on Rte. 10 and Rte. 655 in Chesterfield. Offers showers, biking, boating, picnic areas, and a huge pool. Sites $12. No hookups. Pool admission $2.25, ages 3-12 $1.75. Open year-round.

FOOD

Richmond offers a remarkable array of affordable cuisine, from cheap student eateries to good down-home soul food. At the outdoor **Farmers Market,** at N. 17th and E. Main St., once the site of a Native American trading post, you can pick up fresh fruit, vegetables, meat, and pot swine. For student haunts, head for the area around **Virginia Commonwealth University,** just west of downtown; for fried apples, grits, and cornbread, try downtown itself.

⊛**Mamma Zu's,** 501 S. Pine St. (788-4205). Serves amazing, innovative, fashionable Italian food in an extremely unprepossessing interior and exterior. House specials include free range and exotic meats, like rabbit liver (appetizer $6.50). Open M-F 11am-2:30pm and 5:30-11pm, Sa 5:30-11pm.

Winnie's Caribbean Cuisine, 200 E. Main St. (649-4974). Dishes up traditional Caribbean specialties in a bright yellow room with the strains of reggae playing softly in the background. Lunch entrees ($5-8) include the popular hot and spicy jerk chicken "roti" sandwich ($5.50). Dinner entrees ($5.50-13) venture into the exotic. Open M 11am-1pm, Tu-Th 11am-10pm, F 11am-10:30pm, Sa 1-10:30pm.

3rd St. Diner (788-4750), at the corner of 3rd and Main St. Old-time locals in the mint-green booths are served cheap eats by tattooed waitresses in combat boots. Breakfast special (2 eggs, biscuit or toast, and homefries, grits, or Virginia fried apples $2.25) and dinner sandwiches ($3-6). Open 24hr.

SIGHTS

St. John's Church, 2401 E Broad St. (648-5015), is the site of Patrick Henry's famed 1775 "Give me liberty or give me death" speech. *(Admission by tour only. 30min. tours M-Sa 10am-3:30pm, Su 1-3:30pm. $3, seniors $2, ages 7-18 $1.)* Actors recreate the speech on Sundays (from the last Su in May to the 1st Su in Sept.) at 2pm. The building itself is a place of enormous floorboards and endless serenity.

Richmond's most important sites can be found in the **Court End** district, which stretches north and east of the Capitol to Clay and College St. The **State Capitol** (698-1788), at 9th and Grace St., is a Neoclassical masterpiece designed by Thomas Jefferson. *(Open daily 9am-5pm; Dec.-Mar. M-Sa 9am-5pm, Su noon-5pm.)* The building served as the home of the Confederate government during the Civil War and today houses the only statue of George Washington for which the first President actually posed.

The Museum of the Confederacy, 1201 E. Clay St. (649-1861), houses the world's largest Confederate artifact collection. *(Open M-Sa 10am-5pm, Su noon-5pm. $5, students $3, seniors $4, under 7 free. Combination tickets available.)* The museum also runs 1hr. tours through the **White House of the Confederacy** next door, where a South-shall-rise-again feeling is almost palpable. *(Tours M, W, and F-Sa 10:30am-4:30pm, Tu and Th 11:30am-4:30pm, Su 1:15-4:30pm. $5.50, students $3.50, seniors $4.50. Combination tickets available.)* Statues of Tragedy, Comedy, and Irony grace the White House's front door.

The Valentine Museum, 1015 E. Clay St. (649-0711), has exhibits on local and Southern social and cultural history, plus the South's largest collection of costumes and textiles. *(Open M-Sa 10am-5pm, Su noon-5pm. House tours on the hr. 10am-4pm. $5, students and seniors $4, ages 7-12 $3.)* The admission price includes a tour of the Neoclassical **Wickham-Valentine House,** which has been restored to the style of the early 1800s. Nearby, the **John Marshall House,** 818 E. Marshall St. (648-7998), contains period and family furnishings from the time of the former Chief Justice's residence. *(Open Tu-Sa 10am-5pm; Oct.-Dec. 10am-4:30pm. $3, seniors $2.50, ages 7-15 $1.25.)*

South of Court End, the **Shockoe Slip** district, running from Main, Canal, and Cary St. between 10th and 14th St., features fancy shops in restored and newly painted warehouses, but few bargains.

Colorful Jackson ward is the heart of African-American Richmond. The **Maggie L. Walker National Historic Site,** 110½ E. Leigh St. (780-1380), commemorates the founder and president of the oldest surviving black-operated U.S. bank. *(Tours W-Su 9am-5pm. Free. Wheelchair access on 1st fl. only.)* The **Black History Museum and Cultural Center of Virginia,** 112 E. Clay St. (780-9093), has rotating exhibits of African-American history. *(Open Tu-Sa 11am-4pm. $2; 55 and over, under 18 $1. Wheelchair access.)*

In the Fan, **Monument Ave.,** a boulevard lined with trees, gracious old houses, and towering statues of Confederate heroes, is a virtual Richmond memory lane. The statue of Robert E. Lee faces south to symbolize his love for Dixie, whereas the statue of Stonewall Jackson faces north so that the general can perpetually scowl at the Yankees who killed him in battle. (Jackson died from friendly fire, but many blame the Yankees anyway.) The recently commissioned statue of African-American tennis hero Arthur Ashe created a storm of controversy when built at the end of the avenue.

Four blocks from the intersection of Monument Ave. and N. Boulevard rests the South's largest art museum, the **Virginia Museum of Fine Arts,** 2800 Grove Ave. (367-0844). *(Open Tu-W and F-Su 11am-5pm, Th 11am-8pm in the North Wing Galleries. Suggested donation $4.)* The Museum contains pieces ranging from ancient Greek sculptures to Art Deco furniture to Picasso and Warhol. The notable exhibit of Fabergé eggs is expected to reopen in the spring of 1999. On summer Thursdays from 6:30-9:30pm, the Museum draws sell-out crowds of a thousand people to its sculpture garden for **Jumpin'** (367-8148), one of Richmond's most dynamic musical performance cycles (tickets $6 in advance, $7 at the door).

ENTERTAINMENT AND NIGHTLIFE

One of Richmond's most entertaining and delightful diversions is the marvelous old **Byrd Theater,** 2908 W. Cary St. (353-9911). Movie buffs buy tickets from a tuxedoed agent and on weekends are treated to a pre-movie concert, played on a Wurlitzer organ. All shows are 99¢; on Saturdays the balcony opens for $1 extra. Free concerts abound downtown and at the **Nina Abody Festival Park.** Check *Style Weekly,* a free magazine available at the Visitors Center. Baseball fans can join loyal hordes cheering on the minor-league **Richmond Braves** (359-4444), at the Diamond off I-95 Exit 78, Atlanta's AAA affiliate (boxes $7, reserved seats $5, general $4).

Fox River Café and Comedy Club, at 109 S. 12th St. (643-JOKE/5653), pours out a bit of Brit wit F at 8 and 10:30pm and Sa at 8 and 11pm (cover about $8.50; reser-

MID-ATLANTIC

vations recommended). Tex-Mex cuisine $5-9, microbrews and drafts $2.75-3.60, rails $3.25. Happy hour M-F 4-7pm with 25¢ wings. Open daily 11:30am-2am.

Penny Lane Pub, 207 N. 7th St. (780-1682). Irish faux-Tudor tavern with live bands W-Sa. Cuisine includes Bangers 'n' Mash ($10) and fish 'n' chips ($10). Open M-Sa 11am-2am, Su 4pm-2am.

Flood Zone, 11 S. 18th St. (643-1117), in Shockoe Bottom. Hosts both big-name and off-beat local rock bands in an blandly industrial interior. Tu features hip-hop, F hosts bands. Ticket office open Tu-F 10am-6pm. Tickets $5-15, depending upon the show. Hours vary with events; call ahead.

Havana '59, 16 N. 17th St. (649-2822), in Shockoe Bottom. Swirls with a timeless eddy of cigar smoke as plastic palms poke out of bar counters. High garage ceilings and multiple stories create a sense of space that soothes the soul, while the DJs salsa beat stirs the blood. Cuban *flan* $4.25. Open M-Th 5pm-midnight, F-Sa 9pm-2am, Su 9pm-midnight.

■ Williamsburg

At the end of the 17th century, when women were women and men wore wigs, Williamsburg was the capital of Virginia. During the Revolutionary War, the capitol and much of Williamsburg's grandeur moved to Richmond. The depressed city was rescued in 1926 by John D. Rockefeller, Jr., who showered the area with money and restored a large chunk of the historical district as a colonial village. Street-side performers, 18th-century theater, and militia revues are just part of everyday business in Williamsburg. But although the ex-capital claims to be a faithfully restored version of its 18th-century self, don't look for dirt roads, open sewers, or people in bondage.

ORIENTATION AND PRACTICAL INFORMATION

Williamsburg lies some 50 mi. southeast of Richmond between Jamestown (10 mi. away) and Yorktown (14 mi. away). **The Colonial Pkwy.,** which connects the three towns, has no commercial buildings. The **Transportation Center,** 408 N. Boundary St., across from the fire station, is the hub for getting around.

Trains: Amtrak, 229-8750 or 800-872-7245. To: New York (7½-8hr., 2 per day, $101); Washington, D.C. (3½hr., 2 per day, $37); Philadelphia (6hr., 2 per day, $71); Baltimore (5hr., 2 per day, $46); and Richmond (1hr., 2 per day, $13).

Buses: Greyhound, 229-1460. Ticket office open M, W, and F 7:15am-9pm, Tu and Th 7:15am-5pm, Sa-Su 8:30am-2pm. To: Richmond (1hr., 9 per day, $10); Norfolk (1-2hr., 9 per day, $10); Washington, D.C. (3-4hr., 9 per day, $29); Baltimore (via D.C.; 6-7hr., 9 per day, $45); and Virginia Beach (2½hr., 6 per day, $14). **James City County Transit (JCCT)** (220-1621). Service along Rte. 60, from Merchants Sq. in the historic district west to Williamsburg Pottery or east past Busch Gardens. Operates M-Sa 6:15am-5:15pm. Fare $1 plus 25¢ per zone-change. **Williamsburg Shuttle** (220-1621) provides service between Colonial Williamsburg and Busch Gardens every 30min. (runs daily May-Sept. 9am-9pm; all-day pass $1).

Taxis: Yellow Cab, 245-7777. **Williamsburg Limousine Service,** 877-0279, call 8:30am-midnight. To Busch Gardens or Carter's Grove ($6-10; higher when traffic to Busch Gardens is heavy). To Jamestown and Yorktown (round-trip $20).

Car Rental: Colonial Rent-a-car, in the Transportation Center (220-3399). $34 per day. Open M-F 8am-5:30pm, Sa-Su 8am-2pm.

Bike Rental: Bikes Unlimited, 759 Scotland St. (229-4620), rents for $10 per day, with $5 deposit (includes lock). Open M-F 9am-7pm, Sa 9am-5pm, Su noon-5pm.

Visitor Info: Williamsburg Area Convention & Visitors Bureau, 201 Penniman Rd. (253-0192), ½ mi. northwest of the transportation center. Open M-F 8:30am-5pm. **Tourist Visitors Center,** 102 Information Dr. (800-447-8679), 1 mi. northeast of the train station. Tickets and transportation to Colonial Williamsburg. Maps and guides to historic district, including a guide for the disabled, upstairs. Info on prices and discounts on Virginia sights. Open daily 8:30am-8pm. Another visitors center operates within the historic district, on Duke of Gloucester St.

Post Office: 425 N. Boundary St. (229-4668). Open M-F 8am-5pm, Sa 10am-2pm. **ZIP code:** 23185. **Area code:** 757.

ACCOMMODATIONS AND CAMPGROUNDS

The hotels operated by the **Colonial Williamsburg Foundation** are generally more expensive than other lodgings in the area. Budget motels line Rte. 60 W and Rte. 31 S. Guest houses are cheaper, friendlier, and more comfortable.

The reasonable **Lewis Guest House,** 809 Lafayette St. (229-6116), rents several comfortable rooms, including an upstairs unit with private entrance, kitchen, and bath as a single ($25) or double ($32.50). Two doors down is the **Carter Guest House,** 903 Lafayette St. (229-1117). Two lovely, spacious rooms each have two beds and a shared bath. Unmarried men and women may not sleep in the same room. (Singles $25; doubles $30.) Even closer to the historic district, the **Bryant Guest House,** 702 College Terr. (229-3320), offers rooms with private baths, TV, and limited kitchen facilities in a stately brick home (singles $35; doubles $45; 5-person suite $55). **Anvil Campgrounds,** 5243 Mooretown Rd. (565-2300 or 800-633-4442), 3 mi. from the Colonial Williamsburg Information Center on Rte. 60 W, boasts 73 shaded sites, a swimming pool, a bathhouse, a recreational hall, and a store. (Sites $13, with water and electricity $23, full hookup $25; 10% AAA discount, 15% senior discount.)

FOOD AND DRINK

Most of the authentic-looking "taverns" are overpriced and crowded. Lunch options range from $5-10, but dinner prices are outrageous. If you must eat in the historic district, a reasonable option is **Chowning's Tavern** (229-2141) on Duke of Gloucester St.

⍟Green Leafe Café, 765 Scotland St. (220-3405). Budget-priced meals with Ritz-Carleton style. Pub sandwiches ($5-6) and tasty appetizers ($7-9) can make a light supper. 20 brews on tap, including savory Virginia micros ($3 per pint). Sunday "Mug Night" offers ½-price beer. Open daily 11am-2am.

The Old Chickahominy House, 1211 Jamestown Rd. (229-4689), 5 mi. from the historic district en route to Jamestown. Antiques, dried-flower decor, and pewter-haired locals. "Complete luncheon" with Virginia ham served on hot biscuits, fruit salad, a slice of delectable homemade pie, and iced tea or coffee ($5.75). 20min. wait for lunch in high season. Open daily 8:30-10:15am and 11:30am-2:15pm.

Giuseppe, 5601 Richmond Rd. (565-1977), in Ewell Station shopping center on Rte. 60, about 2½ mi. from the historic district, offers 8 pasta dishes for under $6 with a zest for garlic. A not-too-traditional menu with fusion entrees like the Fettucini New Mexico (pasta with black beans and Monterey jack cheese; $5.25). Open M-Sa 11:30am-2pm and 5-9pm.

Paul's Deli Restaurant and Pizza, 761 Scotland St. (229-8976). Lively hangout for William and Mary students. Crisp stromboli for 2 ($7-10), filling subs ($5), and a wide variety of fresh salads ($3.40-7). Nightly specials on pasta and seafood. Special price on selected beer W-Sa 7-9pm. Great jukebox. Open daily 10:30am-2am.

SIGHTS

Colonial Williamsburg (220-7645) will have you spending 1774 treasury notes and singing "my hat, it has three corners" while you dodge horse droppings all the way to the milliner's. *(Most sights open 9:30am-6pm; for complete hrs., see the Visitor's Companion newsletter. Basic Admission Ticket $26, ages 6-12 $15. 2-day pass $30/$17. Each has various perks, inquire when you purchase.)* The historic district itself doesn't require a ticket; you can walk around, march behind the fife-and-drum corps, and lock yourself in the stocks, all for free. Most of the "colonial" shops, which sell identical merchandise, are also open to the public. Two of the historic buildings—the Wren Building and the Bruton Parish Church—are free. The *Visitor's Companion* newsletter, printed on Mondays, lists free events and evening programs.

The real fun of Colonial Williamsburg comes from interacting with its history. Trade shops afford wonderful opportunities to learn from skilled artisans such as the carpenter, and slightly less-skilled workmen like the brickmaster, who may invite you to take off your shoes and join him in stomping on wet clay. Colonial denizens are quick to play up their antiquated world view (admitted Floridians are likely to be greeted with startled cries of "Spanish territory!"). Those willing to pay the steep admission shouldn't miss the **Governor's Palace,** on the Palace Green. *(Open daily 9am-5pm. Separate admission $17, ages 6-12 $10.)* This mansion housed the Tory governors of Virginia until the last one fled in 1775. Colonial weaponry lines the walls, and the extensive gardens include a hedge maze. Also notable is the **Wythe House,** which belonged to Jefferson and Madison's professor of law, George Wythe, who died in 1806 from poison administered by an avaricious heir. The cooks in the kitchen outbuilding display amazing fortitude as they slave over an open fire, whipping up the butter-rich foods favored by colonial palates.

Spreading west from the corner of Richmond and Jamestown Rd., the **College of William and Mary** is the second-oldest college in the U.S., having educated Presidents Jefferson, Monroe, and Tyler. The **Sir Christopher Wren Building,** probably with no connection to the famed English architect Wren except its contemporary (1695) origin, was built two years after the college received its charter and restored with Rockefeller money. It is now the nation's oldest classroom building.

■ Near Williamsburg

Jamestown and Yorktown At **Jamestown National Historic Site,** you'll see the remains of the first permanent English settlement in America (1607), as well as exhibits explaining colonial life. *(Open daily 8:30am-5:30pm; off-season 9am-4:30pm. Visitors center closes 30min. after the park. Entrance fee $5.)* The **visitors center** (229-1733) offers a hokey film and a 30min. "living history" walking tour (free with admission to the site). Among other sights, you'll visit the **Old Church Tower;** built in 1639, it's the only 17th-century structure still standing. Also featured is a statue of **Pocahontas.** You can also rent a 45min. audio tape ($2) and drive or hike the 5 mi. **Island Loop Rte.** through woodlands and marsh. In the remains of the settlement itself, archeologists work to uncover the original site of the triangular **Jamestown Fort.**

The nearby **Jamestown Settlement** (229-1607) is a commemorative museum commemorating with changing exhibits, a reconstruction of James Fort, a Native American village, and full-scale replicas of the three ships that brought the original settlers to Jamestown in 1607. *(Open daily 9am-5pm. $9.75, ages 6-12 $4.75.)* The 20min. dramatic film details the settlement's history, including a discussion of settler relations with the indigenous Powhatan tribe.

The British defeat at **Yorktown** signaled the end of the Revolutionary War. In 1781, the American and French infantry routed British troops led by General Charles Lord Cornwallis. The Yorktown branch of **Colonial National Park** (804-898-3400), behind the visitors center, vividly re-creates the significant last battle with an engaging film and a smart-looking electric map. The visitors center loans out tape cassettes and players ($2) for the listening pleasure of those driving the battlefield's 7 mi. automobile route. *(Center open daily 8:30am-5pm; last tape rented at 5pm. $4, under 17 free.)* Walking the battlefield lends a sense of just how close the enemy trenches were. The **Yorktown Victory Center** (804-887-1776), 1 block from Rte. 17 on Rte. 238, brims with Revolutionary War items and an intriguing "living history" exhibit: in an encampment in front of the center, soldiers from the 1781 Continental Army take a break from active combat (open daily 9am-5pm; $7.25, ages 6-12 $3.50).

James River Plantations Built near the water to facilitate the planters' commercial and social lives, these country houses buttressed the slave-holding Virginia

aristocracy. Tour guides at **Carter's Grove Plantation** (229-1000, ext. 2973), 6 mi. east of Williamsburg on Rte. 60, describe the restored house and fields. *(Plantation open Tu-Su 9am-5pm; Nov.-Dec. 9am-4pm. Museum and slave quarters open Mar.-Dec. Tu-Su 9am-5pm. $17, ages 6-12 $9.)* The last owners doubled the size of the original 18th-century building while maintaining the colonial feel. Also reconstructed were slave quarters and an archaeological dig. The **Winthrop Rockefeller Archaeological Museum,** built unobtrusively into a hillside, provides a fascinating case-study look at archaeology.

　Berkeley Plantation (804-829-6018), halfway between Richmond and Williamsburg on Rte. 5, claims to be the site of the invention of bourbon by British settlers, and later saw the birth of short-lived President William Henry Harrison. *(Open daily 8am-5pm. $8.50, seniors $6.65, ages 6-12 $4. Grounds alone $5/$3.60/$2.50.)* Beautiful, terraced box-wood gardens stretch from the original 1726 brick building to the James River. To reach **Shirley Plantation** (804-829-5121), follow Rte. 5 west from Williamsburg, or east from Richmond. *(Open daily 9am-5pm. $8.50, ages 13-21 $5.50, ages 6-12 $4.50.)* Surviving war after war, this 1613 plantation has an exquisite Queen Anne-style mansion featuring a seemingly unsupported 3-story staircase.

Beer and Rollercoasters
Busch Gardens (253-3350), 3 mi. east of Williamsburg on Rte. 60, isn't fixated on historical consistency, but it sure delivers on the rides. *(Open late June through Aug. Su-F 10am-10pm, Sa 10am-11pm; Sept.-Oct. M and F 10am-6pm, Sa-Su 10am-7pm; call for winter hrs. $33, children $26, seniors $29.70. Cheaper after 5pm.)* Tooth-rattling old favorites like Drachen Fire and Loch Ness Monster pale before the new **Alpengeist:** at 195 ft., the tallest, fastest, most twisted hanging roller coaster in the world.

　A 3-day ticket ($51.95) is good for both Busch Gardens and **Water Country: USA,** 2 mi. away. This 40-acre water-park-to-end-all-water-parks features rides like **Aquazoid,** which dazzles with laser lights and darkened tunnels. *(Open late May to mid-June Sa-Su about 10am-6pm; mid-June to mid-Aug. daily about 10am-8pm; Sept. Sa-Su about 10am-7pm. Hrs. vary; call ahead. Admission $22.50, ages 3-6 18; after 3pm $16.50 for all.)* A free monorail from Busch Gardens takes you to the **Anheuser-Busch Brewery** (253-3036), a veritable Disneyland of Beer, where you can smell yeast and hops, watch bottles rattle down a conveyor belt, walk in respectful silence through a beechwood aging cellar, and, at long last, enjoy a free sample of beer. *(Open in summer daily 11am-10pm; off-season 10am-4pm. Free.)* The brewery is also accessible from I-64.

■ Virginia Beach

After decades as the capital of the cruising collegiate crowd, Virginia Beach is shedding its playground image and maturing into a family-oriented vacation spot. The town has grown into Virginia's largest city, and the numerous sights and scenes in its nearby neighbors—Norfolk, Newport News, and Hampton—have conspired to make the entire Hampton Roads region an attractive place to visit. Even the most dogged clean-up campaigns cannot stem the tide of fast-food joints, motels, and discount shops that characterize each beach town. But beyond all the Slurpees and suntan oil, Virginia Beach is set apart from its East Coast counterparts by beautiful ocean sunrises, a substantial dolphin population, and frequent military jet flyovers.

ORIENTATION AND PRACTICAL INFORMATION

Virginia Beach is easy to get to and easy to get around. The shortest route from the D.C. area follows I-64 east from Richmond through the perpetually congested Hampton Roads Bridge Tunnel into Norfolk. At Norfolk, get on Rte. 44 (the Virginia Beach-Norfolk Expressway), which leads straight to 22nd St. and the beach.

In Virginia Beach, east-west streets are numbered and the north-south avenues, which run parallel to the beaches, have ocean names. **Atlantic and Pacific Ave.** comprise the main drag. Arctic, Baltic, and Mediterranean Ave. are farther inland.

Trains: Amtrak (245-3589 or 800-872-7245). The nearest train station, in Newport News, runs 45min. bus service to and from the corner of 19th and Pacific St.; you must call to reserve your train ticket before you leave Virginia Beach on the bus. To: Washington, D.C. (6hr., $44); New York City (10hr., $73); Philadelphia (8½hr., $81); Baltimore (7hr., $58); Richmond (4hr., $19); and Williamsburg (2hr., $15).

Buses: Greyhound, 1017 Laskin Rd. (422-2998 or 800-231-2222). Connects with Maryland via the Bridge Tunnel. To: Washington, D.C. (6½hr., $31); Richmond (3½hr., $24); and Williamsburg (2½hr., $15).

Public Transportation: Virginia Beach Transit/Trolley Information Center (640-6300). Info on area transportation and tours, including trolleys, buses, and ferries. The Atlantic Avenue Trolley runs from Rudee Inlet to 42nd St. (in summer daily noon-midnight; 50¢, seniors and disabled 25¢, day passes $1.50). Other trolleys run along the boardwalk, the North Seashore, and to Lynnhaven Mall. Regular buses connect Virginia Beach with Norfolk, Portsmouth, and Newport News (fare $1.50, seniors and disabled 75¢, children under 38 in. free).

Car Rental: All the national companies have offices in Virginia Beach. **Enterprise Rent-A-Car** (486-7700 or 800-RENT-A-CAR/7368-2227) will make hotel deliveries.

Bike/Moped Rental: Tom's Bike Rentals (425-8454) delivers rental bikes for about $15 per day. Many stores along the boardwalk rent in-line skates for a similar fee.

Visitor Info: Virginia Beach Visitors Center, 2100 Parks Ave. (437-4888 or 800-446-8038), at 22nd St. Info on budget accommodations and area sights. Open daily 9am-8pm; late May to early Sept. 9am-5pm.

Post Office: (428-2821), at 24th St. and Atlantic Ave. Open M-F 8am-4:30pm. **ZIP code:** 23458. **Area code:** 757.

ACCOMMODATIONS AND FOOD

The number of motels in Virginia Beach is unreasonably high and, consequently, rates are typically low. Oceanside **Atlantic** and **Pacific Ave.** buzz with activity during the summer and boast the most desirable hotels. If you reserve in advance, rates are as low as $45 in winter and $85 in summer. If you're traveling in a group, look for "efficiency" apartments, which are rented cheaply by the week.

Angie's Guest Cottage-Bed and Breakfast and HI-AYH Hostel, 302 24th St. (428-4690), is the best place to stay on the entire Virginia Coast. ($14.50, nonmembers $17.75; off-season $11/$14.50. Kitchen and lockers available. Linen $2. Reservations recommended. Private rooms with A/C $33, doubles $25 per person, triples $21 per person, much less in off-season. 2-night min. stay. Check-in 10am-9pm. Memorial Day to Labor Day. Off-season reservations required.) Accommodations at the **Ocean Palms Motel** (428-8362), 30th St. and Arctic Ave., consist of two-person efficiencies (TV, A/C, kitchen; $30-50 per night). Next door, the **Cherry Motel,** 2903 Arctic Ave. (428-3911), rents tidy one- and two-bedroom apartments by the day and by the week, each with four beds and a kitchen (May 15-June 15 1-bedroom $55; June 16-Sept. 6 M-F $66, Sa-Su $77).

First Landings (481-2131, reservations 800-933-7275), about 8 mi. north of town on U.S. 60, has choice sites going for $23. Because of its desirable location amid sand dunes and cypress trees, the park is very popular; reserve 2-3 weeks ahead. *(Open 8am-dusk; take the North Seashore Trolley.)* **KOA,** 1240 General Booth Blvd. (428-1444, reservations 800-KOA/672-4150), runs a quiet campground with cabins, open sites, a pool, bike rentals ($10), and free shuttles to the boardwalk 2 mi. away. (May 1-Oct 1 $27, full hookup $30; Oct. 2-Apr. 30 $15/$16; A/C 1-room cabins $58.)

The Jewish Mother, 3108 Pacific Ave. (422-5430), dotes on her customers with deli sandwiches ($4-6.25), omelettes ($3-7), salads ($2-6.50), and an array of delicious desserts amidst neon glare and crayon-scribbled walls. At night, the restaurant becomes a popular (and cheap) bar with live music; happy hour (4-7pm) features $1 domestic drafts (cover $3-5; open M-F 8:30am-2am, Sa 8am-3am, Su 7am-2am). The spicy scent of **Giovanni's Pasta Pizza Palace,** 2006 Atlantic Ave. (425-1575), advertises tasty, inexpensive Italian pastas, pizzas, and hot grinders ($5-9; open daily noon-midnight). **Ellington's Restaurant,** with windows overlooking the ocean, serves some of the most overlooked food in the city, with grilled portabello burgers ($6) and a "really big" lunch salad ($5), plus affordable dinner entrees ($8-12; open Su-Th 7am-10pm, F-Sa 7am-11pm).

SIGHTS AND ENTERTAINMENT

The **beach and boardwalk,** jam-packed with college revelers, bikini-clad sunbathers, and an increasing number of families, is the reason people come to Virginia Beach. The **Old Coast Guard Station** (422-1587), 24th St. and oceanfront offers historic exhibits. *(Open M-Sa 10am-5pm, Su noon-5pm; off-season closed M. $2.50, seniors $2, children $1.)* The frequent roar of jet engines will remind you of the Air Force bases nearby. Call 433-3131 for information on visiting the base. The **Virginia Marine Science Museum,** 717 General Booth Blvd. (437-4949), is home to over 50 species of fish, sharks, and stingrays. *(Open daily 9am-9pm; off-season 9am-5pm. $9, seniors $8, ages 4-11 $6. IMAX $7, seniors $6.50, children $6. Combined museum and IMAX $12/$11/$10.)*

On summer nights, the beach becomes a haunt for lovers, and **Atlantic St.,** "Beach St., USA," burgeons with street performers employed by the city. Every block has its own little stage, with bigger venues at 7th, 17th, and 24th St., where groups ranging from Hawaiian dancers to barbershop quartets give free performances. (Schedules for the main events are posted along the street; call 440-6628 for more info.) **Chicho's** (422-6011), on Atlantic Ave. between 21st and 22nd St., is one of the hot spots on "The Block" of closet-sized bars clustered near the water. (Dress code: T-shirts, shorts, tight dresses, tanned skin.) Bartenders shout over the din of videos of surfing competitions and bungee jumping. Locals swear by the gooey pizza available from the window in front, where an all-you-can-eat special ($6) is offered daily from noon to 5pm. (No cover. Restaurant open M-F noon-2am, Sa-Su 1pm-2am.) One block from the HI-AYH hostel, **Harpoon Larry's** (422-6000), at 24th St. and Pacific Ave., serves tasty fish in an everyone-knows-your-name atmosphere. (Happy hour M-F 7-9pm, specials include amazing deals on seafood and rum runners. Open daily noon-2am.)

■ Charlottesville

When writing his own epitaph, modest old Thomas Jefferson—veritable granddaddy of all of America—asked to be remembered as "father of the University of Virginia." Charlottesville does his commitment to academia proud. The college he founded sustains Charlottesville economically, geographically, and culturally, just as his musings on democracy help sustain America. Very much a part of its native south, the university has nourished a community of pubs as well as a community of poets and a smorgasbord of great writers, from Edgar Allan Poe to Rita Dove.

ORIENTATION AND PRACTICAL INFORMATION

Charlottesville streets are numbered from east to west, using compass directions; 5th St. NW is 10 blocks from (and parallel to) 5th St. NE. There are two downtowns: one on the west side across from the university called **The Corner,** and **Historic Downtown** about 1 mi. east. The two are connected by **University Ave.,** running east-west, which becomes Main St. after The Corner ends at a bridge. **Rte. 64,** which runs east-west to Richmond, is Charlottesville's main feeder.

MID-ATLANTIC

Airport: 201 Bowen Loop (973-8341), right outside of town.

Trains: Amtrak, 810 W. Main St. (296-4559 or 800-872-7245), 7 blocks from downtown. To: Washington, D.C. (3hr., 1 per day, $21); New York (7-8hr., 1 per day, $68); Baltimore (4hr., 1 per day, $35); and Philadelphia (5½hr., 1 per day, $52). Open daily 5:30am-9pm.

Buses: Greyhound/Trailways: 310 W. Main St. (295-5131), within 3 blocks of downtown. To: Richmond (1½-4hr., 6 per day, $17); Washington, D.C. (3hr., 5 per day, $29); Norfolk (4hr., 2 per day, $36); Baltimore (4-5hr., 4 per day, $44); and Philadelphia (7-11hr., 4 per day, $54). Open M-Sa 7am-8:30pm, Su noon-8:30pm.

Public Transportation: Charlottesville Transit Service (296-7433). Bus service within city limits. Maps available at both info centers, the chamber of commerce, and the UVA student center in Newcomb Hall. Buses operate M-Sa 6:30am-6:30pm. Fare 75¢, seniors and disabled 33¢, under 6 free. The more frequent UVA buses technically require UVA ID, but a studious look usually suffices.

Taxis: Yellow Cab, 295-4131.

Visitor Info: Chamber of Commerce, 415 E. Market St. (295-3141), within walking distance of Amtrak, Greyhound, and town. Open M-F 9am-5pm. **Thomas Jefferson Visitors Center** (977-1783, ext. 121), off I-64 on Rte. 20. Arranges same-day discount lodgings; Monticello, Michie Tavern, and Ash Lawn-Highland combo tickets ($21, seniors $20, under 12 $13); travel packages to sites associated with Jefferson (888-742-4666). "The Pursuit of Liberty," a 30min. film about Jefferson's life, is shown on the hr. 10am-4pm ($2.50), plus a free exhibit with 400 original Jeffersonian objects. Open daily Mar.-Oct. 9am-5:30pm; Nov.-Feb. 9am-5pm. **University of Virginia Information Center** (924-7969), at the Rotunda in the center of campus. Brochures, a university map, and tour information. Open daily 9am-4:45pm. The larger **University Center** (924-7166), off U.S. 250 W, is home to the campus police. Transport schedules, entertainment guides, and hints on budget accommodations. Campus maps. Open 24hr.

Hotlines: Region 10 Community Services, 972-1800. **Mental Health,** 977-4673. **Rape Crisis Center,** 977-7273. All operate 24hr. **Lesbian and Gay Helpline,** 982-2773. Academic year M-W 7-10pm, Su 6-10pm. **Women's Health Clinic** (in Richmond), 800-254-4479. 24hr.

Post Office: 513 E. Main St. (963-2525). Open M-F 8:30am-5pm, Sa 10am-1pm. **ZIP code:** 22902. **Area code:** 804.

ACCOMMODATIONS, CAMPGROUNDS, AND FOOD

Emmet St. (U.S. 29) is home to generic hotels and motels ($40-60) that tend to fill up during summer weekends and big UVA events. Options include **Budget Inn,** 140 Emmet St. (293-5141), near the university (singles $42; doubles $52; $5 per additional person; reception daily 8am-midnight), and **EconoLodge-University,** 400 Emmet St. (296-2104 or 800-424-4777), which has pool access across from the UVA campus (singles $48; doubles $60). **Charlottesville KOA Kampground,** Rte. 708 (296-9881 or 800-KOA/562-1743), is a camping option 10 mi. outside Charlottesville. Take U.S. 29 S to Rte. 708 SE. All campsites are shaded. (Recreation hall, pool, laundry facilities. Fishing and pets allowed. Sites $18, with water and electricity $23, full hookup $25. Open Mar.-Oct.)

The **Corner** across from UVA boasts bookstores and countless cheap eats, with good Southern grub in Charlottesville's unpretentious diners. The **Emmet St.** strip is lined with fast-food franchises. **The Downtown Mall,** about five blocks off E. Main St., is a brick pedestrian thoroughfare lined with upscale restaurants and shops.

The Hardware Store, 316 E. Main St. (977-1518 or 800-426-6001). Slightly off-beat bar atmosphere: beers served in half-meter tubes with condiments in toolboxes. Eclectic American grille food includes meal-sized baked spuds ($5-7.25). Soda fountain, quality desserts. Open M-Th 11am-10pm, F-Su 11am-11pm.

Southern Culture, 633 W. Main St. (979-1990). Real down-home cookin' at reasonable prices. Most entrées $9-10. The cheapest dish on the menu, red beans and rice ($7), is also the best. Open M-Sa 5-10:30pm, Su 11am-2:30pm and 5-10:30pm.

Oregano Joe's, 1252 Emmet St. (971-9308). Potent combo of Virginia wines and traditional Italian favorites. The sandwiches ($5-7) are intense experiences, while the massive pasta entrées ($7-12), like triangular mushroom ravioli ($8.25), are more tempting still. Open M-Th 11am-10pm, F 11am-11pm, Sa 4-11pm, Su 4-10pm.

White Spot, University Ave. Hole-in-the-wall deli with dirt cheap food. A generous breakfast is $3. Sandwiches $1-2. Locals swear that the Gus Burger ($2.25) prevents hangovers. Open M-Th 7am-2am, F-Su 7am-2:30am.

SIGHTS

Most activity on the grounds of the **University of Virginia** (924-3239) clusters around the **Lawn** and fraternity-lined **Rugby Road.** Jefferson's Monticello is visible from the lawn, a terraced green carpet that is one of the prettiest spots in American academia. Professors live in the Lawn's pavilions; Jefferson designed each one in a different architectural style. Privileged Fourth Years (never called seniors) are chosen each year for the small Lawn singles. One of the rooms (#13) is dedicated to its former resident, that ne'er-do-well son of the University, Edgar Allan Poe, who was kicked out for gambling. The early-morning clanging of the bell that used to hang in the **Rotunda** provoked one incensed student to shoot at the building. The **Bayley Art Museum,** on Rugby Rd., features changing exhibits and a small permanent collection that includes one of Rodin's casts of *The Kiss.*

Jefferson oversaw every stage of development of his beloved **Monticello** (984-9800), a home that truly reflects the personality of its brilliant creator. *(Open daily Mar.-Oct. 8am-5pm; Nov.-Feb. 9am-4:30pm. $9, students $4, ages 6-11 $5; Nov-Feb $3.)* The house is a quasi-Palladian jewel filled with fascinating innovations, such as a fireplace dumbwaiter to the wine cellar and a mechanical copier, all compiled or conceived by Jefferson. The cleverly designed grounds include orchards and flower gardens, and afford magnificent views in every direction. Just west of Monticello on the Thomas Jefferson Pkwy. (Rte. 53) is the relocated and partially reconstructed **Michie Tavern** (977-1234), which includes an operating grist mill and a general store. *(Open daily 9am-5pm. $6, under 6 $2. Last tour 4:20pm.)* To reach **Ash Lawn-Highland** (293-9539), the 535-acre plantation home of President James Monroe, continue past the Vineyard to the intersection with Rte. 795, 2.5 mi. east of Monticello, and make a right. *(Open daily 9am-6pm; Nov.-Feb. 10am-5pm. Tour $7, seniors $6.50, ages 6-11 $4. AAA 10% discount. Wheelchair access.)* Although less distinctive than Monticello, Ash Lawn reveals more of family life in the early 1800s, and peacocks parade the grounds.

ENTERTAINMENT AND NIGHTLIFE

This preppy town is full of jazz, rock, and pubs. A kiosk near the fountain in the center of the Downtown Mall has posters with club schedules; the free *Weekly C-ville* can tell you who's playing when. English-language opera and musical theater highlight the **Summer Festival of the Arts** (293-4500) in the Box Gardens behind Ash Lawn (open June-Aug. M-F 9am-5pm). Ash Lawn also hosts a **"Music at Twilight"** series on Wednesday evenings at 8pm ($10, students $6, seniors $9). **The Downtown Mall** (296-8548) features a free concert series every Friday from April to October.

Michael's Bistro & Tap House, 1427 University Ave. (977-3697). A tiny door next to Littlejohn's Deli is the entrance to this mix of culinary style and musical strength. Live music Su-W includes Su bluegrass, M funk, and Tu jazz. Cover $2-3, music begins at 10:30pm. 100 beers, 8 on tap. Happy hour M-Th 4-7pm, $2 drafts.

Outback Lodge, 917 Preston Ave. (979-7211). Happenin' pub with a pool table, foosball, and a jukebox. A favorite hang-out for members of the Dave Matthews Band. Philly cheesesteak ($5) and fajitas ($8). Happy hour M-F 4-7pm. Live music Tu-Sa with $2-10 cover. Open M-F 11am-2am, Sa-Su 5pm-2am.

MID-ATLANTIC

Coupe DeVille's, 9 Elliewood Ave. (977-3966), off University Ave. Students cross the road for specialty chicken (rotisserie half-chicken $7.50). Burgers $5.50-6. Open M-F 11:30am-2pm and 5:30-10pm, Sa 5:30-10pm. Pub open M-Sa 10pm-2am.

Orbit Billiards & Café, 216 Water St. (984-5707). Mellow, smoky attic with pool tables around a central bar. Rail drinks $2 on Tu and Th. Occasional live music. Draws a more eclectic crowd than most C-ville places—students mixed with locals, plus hard-core pool sharks. Open daily noon-1am.

■ Shenandoah

Shenandoah National Park was America's first great natural reclamation project. In 1926, Congress authorized Virginia to purchase a 280-acre tract of over-logged, over-hunted land. The small population of reclusive trappers was relocated, and President Franklin D. Roosevelt dedicated the park to wildlife preservation in 1936. The experiment remains one of his greatest successes: 60 years later, the fields and forests teem with bunnies, bears, backpackers, and Bambis. On clear days, visitors can see miles of unspoiled ridges and treetops, home to more plant species than all of Europe. Shenandoah's amazing technicolor mountains—covered with foliage in the summer, streaked with brilliant reds, oranges, and yellows in the fall—offer relaxation and recreation throughout the year.

PRACTICAL INFORMATION The park consists of a narrow strip of land almost 75 mi. in length. The famous **Skyline Dr.** runs 105 mi. from Front Royal in the north to Rockfish Gap in the south, going through the entire park. (Miles along the Dr. are measured north to south.) The entrance fee for the park is $10 per vehicle, $5 per hiker, biker, or bus passenger, and free for disabled persons. The admission pass, valid for 7 days, is necessary for re-admittance. Most facilities hibernate in the winter; call ahead. Skyline Dr. closes during and following bad weather.

Greyhound (800-231-2222) sends buses once per morning from Washington, D.C. to Waynesboro, near the park's southern entrance ($43); no bus or train serves Front Royal, near the park's northern entrance. Rockfish Gap is only 25 mi. from Charlottesville on Rte. 64. You can also drive to Shenandoah from D.C.; take Rte. 66 W to Rte. 340 S to Front Royal. The **Dickey Ridge Visitors Center** (635-3566), at Mi. 4.6, and the **Byrd Visitors Center** (999-3283), Mi. 51, offer exhibits and hiking information. (Open Apr.-Oct. daily 9am-5pm. Dickey open through Nov.) The stations also offer excellent talks on local wildlife, short guided walks among the flora, and lantern-lit evening discussions. Byrd has an historically minded museum and movie. For general park information, call 999-2243 (daily 8am-4:30pm) for a human or 999-3500 for a recorded message. The park mailing address is: Superintendent, Park Headquarters, Shenandoah National Park, Rte. 4, P.O. Box 348, Luray, VA 22835. In an **emergency,** call 800-732-0911. **Area code:** 540.

ACCOMMODATIONS AND CAMPGROUNDS The **Bear's Den (HI-AYH)** (554-8708), located 35 mi. north of Shenandoah on Rte. 601 in a mini stone castle, has two 10-bed dorm rooms, and one room with one double bed and two bunk beds. Take Rte. 340 N to Rte. 50 E to 601 N, and turn left at the gate. (Dining room, kitchen, on-site parking, laundry room. $12, nonmembers $15; 1 private room $30/$36. Camping $6 per person with use of hostel facilities, $3 without. Reception 7:30-9:30am and 5-10pm. Check-out 9:30am. Lockout and quiet hrs. from 10pm. Closed Jan.) The park maintains two affordable "lodges," motels with rustic exteriors. **Skyland** (999-2211 or 800-999-4714), Mi. 42 on Skyline Dr., offers wood-furnished cabins ($46-79, Oct. $5-7 more; open Apr.-Oct.) and more upscale motel rooms ($79-145, Sa-Su $83-155; open Mar.-Nov.). **Big Meadows** (999-2221 or 800-999-4714) has similar services, also with a historic lodge ($79-125, Sa-Su $83-155) and cabins ($70-72; open late Apr.-Nov.). **Lewis Mountain,** Mi. 57 (999-2255 or 800-999-4714), operates cabins with kitchens ($55-83; Oct. $7 more). Reservations are necessary; call up to 6 months in advance.

The park service also maintains four major **campgrounds: Mathews Arm** (Mi. 22; $14); **Big Meadows** (Mi. 51; $17); **Lewis Mountain** (Mi. 58; $14); and **Loft Mountain** (Mi. 80; $14). The latter three have stores, laundry, and showers (no hookups). Heavily wooded and uncluttered by RVs, Mathews Arm and Lewis Mountain make for the happiest tenters. Reservations are possible only at Big Meadows (800-365-2267).

Backcountry camping is free, but you must obtain a permit at a park entrance, visitors center, ranger station, or the park headquarters. Camping above 2800 ft. is illegal and unsafe. Trail maps and the PATC guide can be obtained at the visitors center; the PATC puts out three topographical maps ($5 each), each for a different part of the park. The **Appalachian Trail** (AT) runs the length of the park; shelters lie strewn along the park's segment of the AT at approximate 7 mi. intervals. You may stay at one of these shelters if you have 3 nights in different locations stamped on your camping permit.

The **Potomac Appalachian Trail Club** (PATC) maintains six cabins in backcountry areas of the park. You must reserve space in the cabins in advance by writing to the club at 118 Park St. SE, Vienna, VA 22180-4609 or calling 703-242-0693 or 703-242-0315 (M-Th 7-9pm, or Th-F noon-2pm). The cabins contain only bunk beds, blankets, and stoves. (Su-Th $3 per person, F-Sa $14 per group; one group member must be at least 21.)

SIGHTS AND ACTIVITIES Many visitors choose to experience the park by taking a ride along Skyline Dr., stopping occasionally to take short hikes, enjoy the views at scenic overlooks, or picnic. The drive contains seven picnic areas (located at Mi. 5, 24, 37, 51, 58, 63, and 80) with bathrooms, potable water, and scenic places to eat.

Besides the Appalachian Trail, the park has hundreds of trails suitable for casual day-hikes; start with the *Park Guide* ($2) and other literature available at the visitors centers. You can also take a free ranger-led tour arranged by the visitors centers.

The middle section of the park, from Thorton Gap (Mi. 30) to South River (Mi. 63), is Shenandoah's most picturesque area, although it tends to be crowded. One popular, accessible trail in this area is the **Whiteoak Canyon Trail,** located at Mi. 42.6. The trail to the pretty, 86 ft. waterfall is relatively easy (3-4hr.). The five waterfalls and trout-filled streams below are spectacular, but the grade becomes strenuous quickly (5½-6½hr. round-trip). The adjacent **Limberlost Trail** (5 mi. round-trip from Whiteoak Canyon, a 1.2 mi. wheelchair-accessible loop from trailhead at Mi. 43), slithers into a hemlock forest. Nearby is the popular **Old Rag Mountain Trail,** located 5 mi. from Mi. 45 (main trail starts outside park; from U.S. 211, turn right on Rte. 522, then right on Rte. 231 until sign). The mountain is remarkably accessible for a 3268 ft. peak, but be aware that the 8.8 mi. loop takes 6-8hr. and involves some scrambling. ($3 fee for Old Rag hikers 16 and older who have not paid Shenandoah admission.) Further south, at Mi. 50.7, the **Dark Hollow Falls Trail** meanders 1½ mi. to some scenic cascades. Down the highway, at Mi. 63, the **South River Falls Trail** leads to a splendid viewing platform from which you can observe an array of falls.

■ Near Shenandoah

Western Virginia's limestone bedrock has led to the most stunning geological formations in the East. The most touristed of the caves is **Luray Caverns** (743-6551). Discovered in 1878, this elaborate network of underground passages features a playable "Stalagpipe Organ." To reach the caverns, follow the billboards on U.S. 211 (Exit 264 off I-81). *(Open daily June 15-Sept. 6 9am-7pm; Mar. 15-Jun. 14 and Sept. 6-Oct. 31 9am-6pm; Nov.-Mar. 14 M-F 9am-4pm, Sa-Su 9am-5pm. $13, seniors $11, children 7-13 $6.)* **Endless Caverns** (896-2283) is the wildest of the caves, with 5½ mi. of passages documented and an unknown number still to be explored. *(Open daily June 15-Sept. 6 9am-7pm; Sept. 6-Nov. 14 and Mar. 15-June 14 9am-5pm; Nov. 15-Mar. 14 9am-4pm. $11, ages 3-12 $5.50; $1 AAA discount.)* Follow signs from the intersection of U.S. 11 and U.S. 211 in New Market. **Skyline Caverns** (635-4545 or 800-296-4545), the closest of the caverns to D.C., has orchid-like anthodites, white spikes that grow at the rate of one every 7000 years. *(Open daily mid-June to Sept. 6 9am-6:30pm; Mar. 15-June 4 and Labor Day-Nov. 14 9am-5pm; Nov. 15-Mar. 14 9am-4pm. $10, ages 6-12 $5.)* The caverns are 15min. from the junction of Skyline Dr. and U.S. 211.

The area north of the park is home to several vineyards with pleasant picnic spots. Close to Skyline Drive, **Shenandoah Vineyards,** 3659 S. Ox Rd. (984-8699) off I-81, hosts free tours and wine tasting (open Mar.-Dec. 10am-6pm; Jan.-Feb. 9am-5pm). If a scenic paddle floats your boat, contact **Downriver Canoe Co.,** Rte. 613 (Indian Hollow Rd.), Bentonville (635-5526 or 800-338-1963). From Skyline Dr. Mi. 20, follow U.S. 211 W for 8 mi., then head north onto U.S. 340, 14 mi. to Bentonville; turn right onto Rte. 613 and go 1 mi. Prices vary with length of trip (7 mi. trips $37 per canoe, Sa-Su $49; kayak, raft, and tube trips also available). From north of the park, try **Front Royal Canoe** (800-270-8808 or 635-5440), on U.S. 340 3 mi. south of Skyline Dr., with 7 mi. trips $36 (15% discount Tu-Th).

■ Blue Ridge Pkwy.

If you don't believe that the best things in life are free, this ride could change your mind. The 469 mi. **Blue Ridge Pkwy.,** continuous with Skyline Dr., runs through Virginia and North Carolina, connecting the Shenandoah (Virginia) and Great Smoky Mountains (Tennessee) National Parks. Administered by the National Park Service, the parkway joins hiking trails, campsites, and picnic grounds. While still accessible in the winter, it lacks maintenance or park service between November and April. Almost as scenic as Skyline Dr., the parkway remains more varied—in some spots much wilder and less crowded, while in others it spirals only feet from inhabited modern farms and towns. From Shenandoah National Park, the road winds south through Virginia's **George Washington National Forest** (540-265-2100) from Waynesboro to Roanoke. The forest beckons motorists off the road with spacious campgrounds, canoeing opportunities, and swimming in the cold, clear mountain water at Sherando Lake (4.5 mi. off the parkway at Mi. 16; user fee $5).

Nature trails range from the **Mountain Farm Trail** (Mi. 5.9), an easy 20min. hike to a reconstructed homestead, to the **Rock Castle Gorge Trail** (Mi. 167), a 3hr. excursion. The 0.16 mi. **Linn Cove Viaduct Access Trail** (Mi. 304.4) is wheelchair accessible. Five-mile and 3 mi. trails spread out from **Peaks of Otter** (Mi. 84), where you can camp at the lowest point on the parkway among peaks which reach as high as 4500 ft. Humpback Rocks, a greenstone formation (Mi. 5.8), is an easy hike with a spectacular view. Of course, real go-getters will venture onto the **Appalachian Trail,** which will take you in scenic style all the way to Georgia.

Non-hiking activities abound as well. At **Mabry Mill** (Mi. 176.1), you can visit a mountain farm and grab a bite to eat. At **Doughton Park** (Mi. 241) or **Crabtree Meadows** (Mi. 339), you can purchase food and local crafts. A map at a **ranger sta-**

tion near the middle of the park directs drivers to five **stone churches** erected by a dynamic preacher in the 1920s, who told congregants who couldn't contribute money to give rocks instead. **Boat rentals** are available at Price Lake, Mi. 297. (Open May 27-Sept. 4 daily 8:30am-6pm; May 6-May 21 and Sept. 9-Oct. 29 Sa-Su 10am-6pm. $4 per hr., $3 per additional hr.) The Park Service hosts a variety of ranger-led interpretive activities as well; info is available at the **visitors centers** (see below).

There are nine **campgrounds** along the parkway, each with water (no showers) and restrooms, located at Mi. 60.9, 86, 120.5, 167.1, 239, 297, 316.3, 339.5, and 408.6 ($12, reservations not accepted). To rest your head in a bed in southern Virginia, turn off the parkway at an inconspicuous gray iron gate into the driveway of the **Blue Ridge Country HI-AYH Hostel** (540-236-4962), Mi. 214.5, 7 mi. south on Rte. 89 from the town of Galax. This reproduction of a 1695 colonial building houses 22 beds in separate men's and women's dormitories and hosts local bluegrass jam sessions. ($13, nonmembers $16. Kitchen available. Jams 2nd and 4th F nights of each month. Lockout 9:30am-5pm. Curfew 11pm. Open Mar.-Dec.) Galax hosts one mountain music concert per month, and the famed 64th annual **Fiddler's Convention** (540-236-8541) the second weekend in August. The tiny hippie-redneck hamlet of Floyd, 40mi. north, swells with its free weekly **jamboree** in the **Floyd County General Store** (540-745-4563) at 7pm on Fridays.

Those who want a roof overhead near the northern end of the Blue Ridge Pkwy. (or the southern end of Skyline Dr.) need look no farther than Lexington, at the intersections of I-81 and I-64. There, the weary will find comfortable, 50s-style accommodations at **Overnight Guests,** 216 W. Washington St. (540-463-2376), 8 mi. off the Blue Ridge Pkwy., directly across from the Washington and Lee College campus for an amazingly low $5 per night. (TV, no A/C. Call 9-11pm to reach the proprietor; otherwise, check the list of available rooms in the front hall.) Hungry travelers might grab pasta or overstuffed sandwiches to eat in the garden at **Harb's Bistro,** 19 W. Washington St. (540-464-1900). (Open M-Sa 8am-3pm, Su 9am-3pm; in winter M 8am-8pm, Tu-Th 8am-10pm, F-Sa 8am-11pm, Su 9am-3pm.) Before heading back to the parkway, walk across the street to the **Lee Chapel and Museum** (540-463-8768) to view Confederate General (and college president) Robert E. Lee's sarcophagus and read about his views on education (open daily 9am-5pm; free). For further attractions and accommodations, contact the **Lexington Visitor Center,** 106 E. Washington St. (540-463-3777). Other cities and villages along the parkway also offer a range of accommodations, mostly motels (rates $35-55).

For general info on the parkway, call the park service in Roanoke, VA (540-857-2490). To plan ahead, write to **Blue Ridge Pkwy. Headquarters,** 400 BB&T Bldg., Asheville, NC 28801 (704-271-4779). Twelve **visitors centers** line the parkway at Mi. 5.8, 63.6, 85.9, 169, 217.5, 294, 304.5, 316.4, 364.5, and 382, located at entry points where highways intersect the Blue Ridge (most open daily 9am-5pm).

West Virginia

Geography and history have collided to keep West Virginia among the poorest and most isolated states in the Union. The highest and most rugged section of the Appalachians physically block off the state, while mining in West Virginia has been synonymous with the worst excesses of industrial capitalism. With the decline of heavy industry in the last 30 years, however, West Virginia has turned to another resource—abundant natural beauty. Thanks to great hiking, fishing, and rafting, tourism has become one of the state's main sources of employment and revenue.

PRACTICAL INFORMATION

Capital: Charleston.
Visitor Info: Dept. of Tourism, 2101 Washington St. E., Bldg. #17, Charleston
25305; P.O. Box 50312 (800-225-5982; http://www.state.wv.uf/tourism). **U.S.
Forest Service Supervisor's Office,** 200 Sycamore St., Elkins 26241 (304-636-
1800; open M-F 8am-4:45pm).
Emergency: 911.
Time Zone: Eastern. **Postal Abbreviation:** WV.
Sales Tax: 6%.

▓ Harpers Ferry

Harpers Ferry's stunning location at the junction of the Potomac and Shenandoah
rivers has time and again provided a backdrop to historic events. This town witnessed John Brown's famous 1859 raid on the U.S. Armory, a lunatic attempt to
start a war to liberate the slaves. During the Civil War itself, the town was a major
area of conflict, changing hands eight times. Today, Harpers Ferry is only a hotbed for excellent hiking, biking, canoeing, and rafting opportunities. Thomas Jefferson once called the view from a Harpers Ferry overlook "worth a voyage
across the Atlantic." That may be a bit extreme, but if you're in the area, the town
is worth a trip.

PRACTICAL INFORMATION From the Washington area, take I-270 N to Rte. 340
W. Parking is limited, so park at the visitors center and take the free bus into
town. **Amtrak** (800-872-7245) makes a commuter run to Harpers Ferry (station is
on Potomac St. in the historic area), to D.C. in the morning and from D.C. in the
afternoon. Reservations are required ($17). The same depot serves the **Maryland
Rail Commuter** (MARC) (800-325-RAIL/7245) trains, a cheaper and more frequent service. (M-F 2 trains run to Union Station in D.C. and 3 return to Harpers
Ferry. $7.25, seniors, disabled travelers, and under 6 $3.75.) The closest **Greyhound** bus stations are 30min. drives away in Winchester, VA, and Frederick, MD,
but the **Appalachian Trail Conference (ATC)** runs buses to Charles Town for $2,
and weekday **shuttle buses** (301-694-2065) connect Frederick and Knoxville, MD.

   For **park information,** visitors can write or call **Harpers Ferry National Historical
Park,** P.O. Box 65, Harpers Ferry, WV 25425 (535-6223; http://www.nps.gov/hafe).
The **visitors center** (304-535-6298), just inside the park entrance off Rte. 340, offers
info on area hiking, lodging, and food, as well as free historical literature. (Open daily
8am-5pm; late May to Sept. 6 8am-6pm. Park admission $5 per car, $3 per hiker or
bicyclist; good for 3 consecutive days.) A bus shuttles from the parking lot to town
every 15min. The town itself is accessible to the public; only the historic exhibits in
town require park admission. Across the street from the entrance to Harpers Ferry,
the **West Virginia Welcome Center** (535-2482) is unaffiliated with the town, but it's
still a great information source on accommodations, restaurants, and activities such as
whitewater rafting (open daily 9am-5pm). In case of an emergency, you can reach a
ranger at 535-6455. **Area code:** 304; in Maryland 301. Telephone numbers in text are
304 unless otherwise noted.

ACCOMMODATIONS, CAMPGROUNDS, AND FOOD Weary Appalachian Trail
hikers, aspiring white-water rafters, and a few adorable kittens all find a warm
welcome at the social **Harpers Ferry Hostel (HI-AYH),** 19123 Sandy Hook Rd.
(301-834-7652), at Keep Tryst Rd. off Rte. 340 in Knoxville, MD. Twenty-eight
beds fill two squeaky clean large dormitory rooms, while two smaller rooms have
12 beds. The proprietor will pick you up at the train station for $5. ($13, non-

members $16. Sleepsack $1. Check-in 7:30am-9am and 6-11pm. Quiet hrs. from 11pm. Lockout 9:30am-6pm. Limited parking. Camping $6 per member or ATC hiker, $9 per nonmember; includes use of hostel kitchen and bathrooms. "Primitive" sites $3, nonmembers $4.50. 3-night max. stay. Open Mar. 16-Nov. 14.) The **Hillside Motel,** 340 Keep Tryst Rd. (301-834-8144), in Knoxville, MD, has 21 clean, adequate rooms (singles $34; doubles $44).

You can camp along the **C&O Canal,** where sites lie 5 mi. apart (the **Huckleberry Hill** site is 2 mi. south of Harpers Ferry on the towpath) or in one of the five Maryland state park campgrounds within 30 mi. of Harpers Ferry (for more info, call the ranger station at 301-739-4200). **Greenbrier State Park** (301-791-4767) lies a few miles north of Boonsboro on Rte. 66 between Exit 35 and 42 on I-70 ($16; open May-Oct.).

SIGHTS AND ACTIVITIES Park rangers provide free 45min.-1hr. tours of the town (in summer daily 10:30am-4pm). In addition, the park offers occasional battlefield demonstrations, parades, and other re-enactments of Harpers Ferry's history (call 304-535-6298 for the schedule).

Uphill, stairs hewn into the hillside off High St. follow the **Appalachian Trail** to **Upper Harpers Ferry.** Allow 30min. to ascend past **Harper's House,** the restored home of town founder Robert Harper; **St. Peter's Church,** where a sagacious pastor flew the Union Jack during the Civil War to protect the church; and a rock where Jefferson once stood. At the top of the climb lurks **Storer University,** one of America's first African-American colleges, now closed for over 40 years due to the withdrawal of funding after the courts outlawed segregated schools.

While the historic sites in Harper's Ferry are interesting, the real reason to go to the area is for spectacular outdoor opportunities. The **Maryland Heights Trail,** across the railroad bridge in the Lower Town of Harpers Ferry, has some of the best views in the Blue Ridge Mountains, including formidable cliffs and glimpses of crumbling Civil War-era forts and bivouacs. The rustic **Loudoun Heights Trail,** off the Appalachian Trail, is also pretty. Both take a little over three hours to hike. The **Bolivar Heights Trail** starts from the northern end of Whitman Ave., following a Civil War battle line where Stonewall Jackson once rode and featuring trailside exhibits and a three-gun battery. At 1 mi. round-trip, it makes for a pleasant stroll. The **Appalachian Trail Conference Headquarters** (304-535-6331), at the corner of Washington and Jackson St., features trail information, and a maildrop for hikers. *(Open May-Oct. M-F 9am-5pm, Sa-Su 9am-4pm; Nov. to mid-May M-F 9am-5pm. Membership $25, seniors and students $18.)*

Water fanatics may contact **Blue Ridge Outfitters** (304-725-3444), a few miles west of Harpers Ferry on Rte. 340 N in Charles Town; they arrange excursions from 4hr. canoe trips on the Shenandoah to 3-day whitewater raft rides on Virginia's toughest waterways. *(Canoe or a seat on a ½-day raft trip from $46, children $41. Open daily 8am-7pm.)* **River & Trail Outfitters,** 604 Valley Rd. (301-695-5177), 2 mi. out of Harpers Ferry off Rte. 340, in Knoxville, MD, rents canoes, kayaks, inner tubes, and rafts, and organizes guided trips. *(Canoes $50 per day, raft trips $48 per person, tubing $25 per day.)* If you're staying at the hostel, the manager may let you borrow an innertube. Otherwise, the cheapest deal comes from **Butts Country Store** (800-836-9911), on Rte. 340 off Rte. 671, where you can buy a tube for the day and sell it back before you go ($5-18). Horse fans will enjoy the trips offered through **Elk Mountain Trails** (301-834-8882) and evening races 10 mi. away at the recently restarted **Charles Town Races** (304-725-7001; F-Sa 7:15pm). You can rent single-speed bikes at **C&O Canal Bicycling** (301-834-5180), 109 Potomac St. *($20 per ½-day, $30 per day. Open daily 9am-6pm, delivery available.)* The path along the canal makes for a lovely ride.

■ Near Harpers Ferry: Antietam Battlefield

A few mi. north of Harpers Ferry, the bloodiest one-day battle of the Civil War was fought at Antietam. On September 17, 1862, 2108 Union and 1546 Confederate soldiers lost their lives as Confederate General Robert E. Lee tried and failed to overcome the army of Union General George B. McClellan. The nominal Union triumph gave President Lincoln the opportunity to issue the Emancipation Proclamation on January 1, 1863. The **visitors center** (301-432-5124) has a museum of artifacts, free maps for self-guided tours of the battlefield, and tapes for rent ($5) with a detailed account of the battle. Park rangers explain (with dramatic gusto) the armies' retreats and advances, using Civil War mortars and shells. *(26min. film shown 9am-5pm on the hr. Center open daily May-Sept. 8:30am-6pm, Oct.-Apr. 8:30am-5pm. Battlefield fee $2, families $4.)* To get to Antietam from Harpers Ferry, take Rte. 340 W 2 mi. and take a right onto Rte. 230. Drive 9 mi. until you reach Shepherdstown, then take 34 E until you reach Sharpsburg, and follow the signs.

■ New River Gorge

The New River Gorge is a mixture of raw beauty, raw resources, and raw power. One of the oldest rivers in the world, the New River cuts a narrow gouge in the Appalachian Mountains, leaving valley walls which tower an average of 1000 ft. above the white waters. Industrialists drained the region until coal and timber virtually disappeared in the early and middle parts of this century. The **New River Gorge National River** is now protected, and the park service oversees the fishing, rock climbing, canoeing, mountain biking, and world-class rafting in the gorge. There are a number of excellent hiking trails in the park. Among them, the **Kaymoor Trail** starts south of the bridge on Fayette Station Rd. and runs 2 mi. past the abandoned coke ovens of Kaymoor, a coal-mining community that shut down in 1962. The 3.4 mi. **Thurmont-Minden Trail,** with vistas of the New River and Thurmont is accessible via a left off WV Rte. 25 before Thurmont. The park operates three **visitors centers: Canyon Rim** (574-2115), off Rte. 19 near Fayetteville at the northern extreme of the park; **Grandview** (763-3715), on Rte. 9 near Beckley; and **Hinton** (466-0417), on Rte. 20. Grandview attracts visitors in May when the rhododendron are in bloom; otherwise, most stop at Canyon Rim, which has info on all activities in the park, including free, detailed hiking guides. (Canyon Rim and Grandview open daily 9am-8pm; Sept.-May 9am-5pm. Hinton open daily 9am-5pm; Sept.-May Sa-Su 9am-5pm.)

The area's main draw, **whitewater rafting,** has become one of the state's leading industries. A state info service (800-225-5982) can connect you to some of the nearly 20 outfitters who operate on the New River and the nearby Gauley River. **USA Raft** (800-346-RAFT/7238), on Rte. 1 in Fayetteville, runs some of the cheapest express trips on the New River (Su-F $43, Sa $53). The company also has trips on the rowdier Gauley River, covering some of the country's wildest whitewater including the "Heaven Help You Rapids" (Su-F $49-60, Sa $59-70).

Where Rte. 19 crosses the river at the park's northern end, the engineered grace of the **New River Gorge Bridge** complements the natural beauty of the gorge itself. A gorgeous overlook lies just a short walk from the Canyon Rim Visitors Center. Towering 876 ft. above New River, the bridge claims the world's largest single steel arch span. On **Bridge Day,** the third Saturday of October, you can walk across the bridge and parachute off (800-927-0263). For more stable flying, elderly "Five Dollar Frank" takes to the sky with $5 **scenic plane rides** at the Fayetteville airstrip, 2 mi. south of town. Old-time coal miners lead tours down a mine shaft 20min. south at the **Beckley Exhibition Coal Mine** (256-1747), called the most profitable coal mine in the state, at New River Park on Ewart Ave. in Beckley. (Open Apr.-Oct. daily 10am-5:30pm. $7, seniors $6.25, ages 4-12 $4, under 4 free.) You can ride behind a period 1930s engine through over 150 ft. of underground passages and view examples of both manual and automated mining.

Raft guides and travelers bunk at the **Bunk House,** (574-0265) an attractive hostel-like lodge with kitchen and laundry facilities; it's the first house off Lansing Rd. off Rte. 19, 1 mi. north of New River Bridge Lansing Rd. ($18). Many of the raft companies operate private campgrounds, while four public campgrounds dot the general area. The most central public campground, **Babcock State Park** (438-3004 or 800-225-5982), Rte. 41 south of U.S. 60, 15 mi. west of Rainelle, has shaded, sometimes slanted sites ($11, with water and electricity $14). The park also rents 26 cabins. Also ½ mi. north of the New River Gorge Bridge, on Ames Heights Rd., the private **Mountain State Campground** (574-0947) offers hilly tent sites ($6-7) and six-person primitive cabins ($65; open Apr.-Nov.). **Greyhound** (253-8333 or 800-231-2222) stops at 105 Third Ave. in Beckley (open M-F 7-11am and 4-8pm, Sa-Su 7-9am and 4-8pm). **Amtrak** (253-6651 or 800-872-7245) runs a line through the heart of the gorge, stopping on Rte. 41 N. in Prince and Hinton. (Trains Su, W, and F. Open Su, W, and F 9am-1pm and 7-9:30pm, Th and Sa 7am-2:30pm.) Mountain bike rentals are available in Fayetteville, at **Ridge Rider Mountain Bikes** (574-2453 or 800-890-2453) on Keller Ave. off U.S. 19 (open daily 9am-5pm; $30 per day). **Area code:** 304.

■ Monongahela National Forest

Popular with canoers, fly fishermen, spelunkers, and skiers, mammoth **Monongahela National Forest** supports deer, bears, wild turkeys, and magnificent limestone caverns. Over 500 campsites, 600 mi. of well-maintained hiking trails, and some of the best downhill ski slopes in the nation lure adventurers to this lovely camping haven.

Most roads are scenic, though the beauty of **Rte. 39** from Marlinton down to Goshen, VA, past Virginia's swimmable Maury River, is unsurpassed. For more variety, turn off U.S. 219 onto Denmar Rd. and right on Locust Creek Rd. for a 10 mi. loop that will take you past fields of okapi and bison, near a prison, past an old country church, and finally over a one-lane bridge adjacent to the 1888 covered bridge over Locust Creek. The national forest operates the **Highland Scenic Hwy.,** stretching 43 mi. from Richwood to U.S. 219, 7 mi. north of Marlinton.

Many state parks and each of Monangahela's six districts have a campground and a recreation area, with ranger stations off Rte. 39 east of Marlinton and in the towns of Bartow and Potomack (open M-F 8am-4:30pm). The forest **Supervisor's Office,** 200 Sycamore St. (636-1800), in Elkins, distributes a full list of sites and fees, and provides info about fishing and hunting (open M-F 8am-4:45pm). Established sites are $5, but you can sleep in the backcountry for free. You should indicate your backcountry plans at the **Cranberry Visitors Center** (653-4826), near the Highland Scenic Hwy. at the junction of Rte. 150 and Rte. 39/55 (open daily 9am-5pm; Sept.-Nov. and Jan.-May Sa-Su 10am-4pm). Two popular short hikes in the area are the panoramic High Rocks trail leading off of the Highland Scenic Hwy. and the awesome ¾ mi. **Hills Creek Falls,** off Rte. 39/55 south of Cranberry Mountain Visitor's Center. The first cascade is wheelchair accessible; steep steps take you to cascades two and three. **Cranberry Mountain** (846-2695), in the Gauley district 6 mi. west of U.S. 219 on Rte. 39/55, has hiking trails through cranberry bogs and $5-8 campsites.

Those with several days might choose to hike, bike, or ski along part of the **Greenbrier River Trail,** a 75 mi. jaunt along a 1% grade track from Cass to North Caldwell (trailhead on Rte. 38 off U.S. 60), with numerous access points and campgrounds en route. **Watoga State Park** (799-4087), in Marlinton, has maps. South of Caldwell on Rte. 63 lie the calcite formations of **Organ Cave** (645-7600), where prehistoric bones were discovered (open daily 9am-7pm; Nov.-Apr. 9am-5pm).

In downtown Marlinton, the **Old Clark Inn,** 702 3rd Ave. (799-6377 or 800-849-4184), offers bed and breakfasts (singles $40-50; doubles $50-60; $5 more in winter). In the Green Bank area, year-round **cabins** (456-3470 or 456-4410) sit on the right of Rte. 92 ½ mi. south of the NRAO (M-F $28-45, Sa-Su $38-55). In eastern Monongahela, the **Middle Mountain Cabins** (456-3335), on Forest Service Rd. 14 off Rte. 28, stock fireplaces, kitchens, drinking water, and resident field mice ($30 per night; 1-week max. stay; open May-Oct.; call well in advance).

In the winter, thousands pour into the area to ski at slopes in the **Canaan Valley** and the 54 trails at **Snowshoe** resort (888-686-7529). (Open Nov.-Apr. daily 8:30am-10pm. Lift tickets $35, Sa-Su $42; ski rental $21, children $16.) Cross-country skiers can rent gear at **Elk River Nordic Center** (572-3771), in Slatyfork.

Most public transportation in the forest area comes into White Sulphur Springs at the forest's southern tip. **Greyhound** (800-231-2222) has a flag stop at the **Village Inn,** 38 W. Main St. (1 eastbound bus to Clifton Forge at 9am, and 1 westbound bus per day to Beckley at 4pm.) **Amtrak** (800-872-7245) stops at 315 W. Main St., across from the Greenbrier resort. A flag stop in downtown Alderson can also be requested Sunday, Wednesday, and Friday. (To Washington, D.C., $53; and Charlottesville, $29.) **Area code:** 304.

THE SOUTH

A century of economic progress, multiple ethnic migrations, and the gradual dissolution of regional identities have combined to blur the once-stark distinction between the North and South. As Detroit's auto giants continue to relocate to southern towns, and New Englanders increasingly seek solace in the cured-oak flavor of Tennessee bourbon, perhaps the importance of the Mason-Dixon line will further recede into the depths of American consciousness. Yet even as the major metropoli—Atlanta, Nashville, Charlotte, Orlando, and New Orleans—bask in the glow of their new-fangled urban sophistication, divisions between white and black segments of the population provide painful reminders of the area's discolored past.

Although much of the South remains quite poor, the area maintains a rich cultural heritage; a mélange of Native American, English, African, French, and Spanish influences are reflected through such media as architecture, cuisine, and language. Landscapes are equally varied—nature blessed the region with overwhelming mountains, lush marshlands, sparkling beaches, and fertile soil. From the Atlantic's Sea Islands to the rolling Ozarks, the Gulf's bayous to boundary waters, the South's beauty will awe, entice, and enchant.

🖐 HIGHLIGHTS OF THE SOUTH

- **Food.** Southern barbecue is the genuine article, and you can find some of the best at Dreamland BBQ in Mobile, AL (p. 324). New Orleans, LA (p. 333) has some of the spiciest cuisine in the U.S.
- **Music.** Make time for Tennessee—Nashville (p. 269) is the country music hotspot, but if you're a believer, you'll be heading to Graceland (p. 278).
- **Civil Rights Memorials.** The Martin Luther King Center in Atlanta, GA (p. 305) and the Birmingham Civil Rights Institute, AL (p. 323) will move you to tears.
- **Natural Wonders.** Mammoth Cave, KY (p. 263); the Blowing Rock, NC (p. 292); Ruby Falls, TN (p. 277); and the Great Smoky Mountains (p. 275) are sights to write home about.

Kentucky

Legendary for the duels, feuds, and stubborn frontier spirit of its earlier inhabitants (such as Daniel Boone, for whom almost everything in the state is named), Kentucky presents a gentler face to travelers. Kick back, take a shot of local bourbon, grab a plate of burgoo (a spicy meat stew), and relax amid rolling hills and bluegrass. These days, Kentuckians' fire erupts on the highways—they aren't ungracious, but they do drive fast. Appropriately, Kentucky is home to the only true American sports car, the Corvette. Of course, the most respected mode of transportation in the state remains the horse. Louisvillle ignores its vibrant cultural scene and active nightlife for a full week at Derby time, and Lexington devotes much of its most beautiful farmland to breeding champion racehorses. Farther east, the Daniel Boone National Forest preserves the virgin woods of the Kentucky Highlands, where trailblazers first discovered a route across the mountains to what was then the West.

PRACTICAL INFORMATION

Capital: Frankfort.
Visitor Info: Kentucky Dept. of Travel Development, 500 Mero St., 22nd fl., Frankfort 40601 (502-564-4930 or 800-225-8747; http://www.state.ky.us/tour). **Kentucky State Parks,** 500 Mero St., 10th fl., Frankfort 40601 (800-255-7275).
Emergency: 911. **Time Zones:** Mostly Eastern; *Let's Go* makes note of areas in Central (1hr. behind Eastern). **Postal Abbreviation:** KY. **Sales Tax:** 6%.

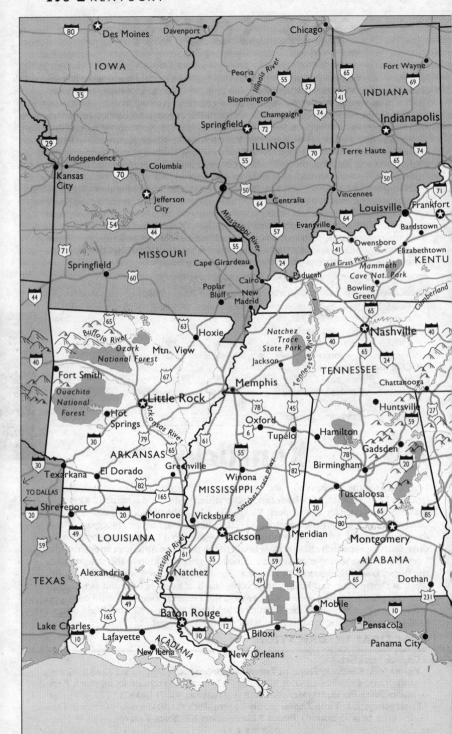

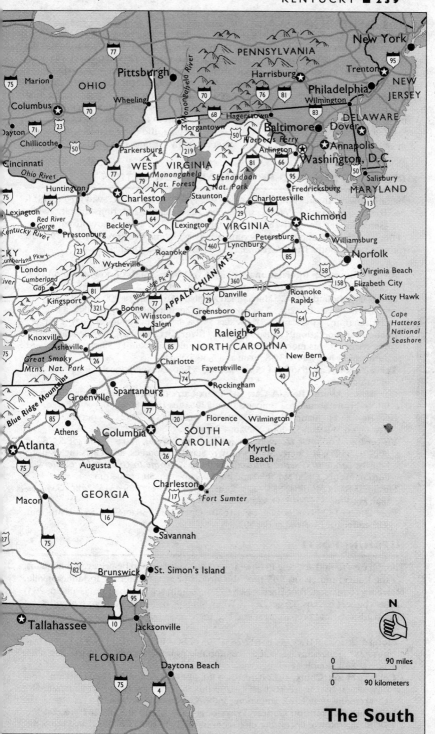

The South

■ Louisville

Perched on the Ohio River, hovering between the North and the South, Louisville (pronounced "Lua-Vul" by locals) feels like a town caught between two pasts. One has left a legacy of smokestacks, stockyards, and the occasional crumbling edifice; the other still entices visitors with beautiful Victorian neighborhoods, ornate cast-iron buildings, and the elegance of twin-spired Churchill Downs. Each year, on the first Saturday in May, Louisville stages the nation's most prestigious horse race, the Kentucky Derby. The week-long extravaganza leading up to the big day rocks with over 500,000 visitors, but when the horses leave the gate, the party stands still for "the most exciting two minutes in sports." After all, many fortunes ride on the $15 million wagered each Derby Day.

ORIENTATION AND PRACTICAL INFORMATION

Major highways through the city include **I-65** (north-south expressway), **I-71**, and **I-64**. The easily accessible **Watterson Expwy.**, also called **I-264**, rings the city, while the **Gene Snyder Frwy. (I-265)** circles farther out. The central downtown area is defined by **Main St.** and **Broadway** running east-west, and **Preston Hwy.** and **19th St.** running north-south. The **West End,** beyond 20th St., is a rough area.

Airport: Louisville International (375-3063), 15min. south of downtown on I-65. Taxi to downtown $17, or take bus #2 into the city.

Buses: Greyhound, 720 W. Muhammad Ali Blvd. (561-2805 or 800-231-2222), at 7th St. To: Indianapolis (2hr., 7 per day, $15); Cincinnati (2hr., 8 per day, $19); and Chicago (6hr., 7 per day, $32). Lockers $4 1st day, $5 per additional day. 24hr.

Public Transportation: Transit Authority River City (TARC), 585-1234. Extensive bus system serves most of the metro area; runs daily 5am-11:30pm. Fare 75¢, $1 during peak hrs. (M-F 6:30-8:30am and 3:30-5:30pm).

Taxis: Yellow Cab, 636-5511. $3.25 1st mi., $1.50 each additional mi. 30¢ per min. in traffic. 24hr.

Car Rental: United Rent-A-Car, 104 Vieux Carre (888-227-7215), near Shelbyville Rd. and Hurstborne Ln. Compacts from $29. Ages 18-21 $3 per day surcharge.

Bike Rental: Highland Cycle, 1737 Bardstown Rd. (458-7832). $4 per hr., $15 per day. Open M-F 9am-5:30pm, Sa 9am-4:30pm.

Visitor Info: Louisville Convention and Visitors Bureau, 400 S. 1st St. (582-3732 or 800-792-5595), at Liberty St. downtown. Standard goodies, as well as the comprehensive *Guide to Greater Louisville* and the *Welcome to Greater Louisville* with current events. Open M-F 8:30am-5pm, Sa 9am-4pm, Su 11am-4pm.

Hotlines: Rape Hotline, 581-7273. 24hr. **Crisis Center,** 589-4313. 24hr. **Gay/Lesbian Hotline,** 454-7613. Operates daily 6-10pm.

Post Office: 1420 Gardner Ln. (454-1650). Open M-F 7:30am-9pm, Sa 7:30am-3pm. **ZIP code:** 40213. **Area code:** 502.

HITCHIN' POSTS

Though easy to find, lodging in downtown Louisville tends to be pricey. For bargains, try the budget motels on **I-65** near the airport or across the river in **Jeffersonville. Newburg** (6 mi. south) or **Bardstown** (39 mi. south; see **South of Louisville,** p. 263) are also budget havens. To get Derby Week lodging, make reservations 6 months to a year in advance and prepare to spend big; the visitors bureau helps after March 13.

Motel 6, 2016 Old Hwy. 31 E (812-283-7703 or 800-466-8356), off I-65 at Exit 2; take bus #281 "Jeffersonville." Clean, comfortable rooms with cable TV, A/C, and pool. Singles $32; doubles $38.

Collier's Motor Court, 4812 Bardstown Rd. (499-1238), south of I-264, 30min. from downtown by car; TARC buses serve this inconvenient area. Well-maintained, cheap rooms with HBO, Showtime, and A/C. Singles $36; doubles $42.

Louisville Convention Center Travelodge, 401 S. 2nd St. (583-2629 or 800-578-7878), downtown. Pricey, but oh-so-convenient, with spiffier rooms than a run-of-the-mill motel. A/C and cable with all the fixin's. Singles $63; doubles $68. AAA/AARP 10-15% discount.

KOA, 900 Marriot Dr. (812-282-4474), across the river from downtown. Follow I-65 N across the bridge and take Exit 1. Paved camping and very convenient to downtown. Grocery, playground, free use of the next door motel's pool, mini golf, and fishing lake. Sites for 2 $20, with hookup $25; $4 per additional person, under 18 $2.50. Cabins for 2 $35. Off-season discounts.

FOOD

Louisville's chefs whip up a wide variety of cuisines, though good budget fare can be hard to find in the heart of downtown. **Bardstown Rd.** is lined with cafes, budget eateries, and local and global cuisine, while **Frankfort Rd.** is rapidly becoming Bardstown-ized with restaurants and chi-chi cafes of its own. Downtown, **Theatre Sq.,** at Broadway and 4th St., provides plenty of good lunch options.

▧**Twice Told,** 1604 Bardstown Rd. (456-0507). The first coffeehouse to open in Louisville, and it's still funky after all these years. Offers poetry readings, comedy, jazz, blues, and art exhibitions. Entertainment starts nightly at 9pm, but make sure to get in earlier for a homemade veggie burger ($5), pronounced by the Counting Crows to be the best they'd ever eaten. Cover for shows $8-12. Open Su-Th 10am-midnight, F-Sa 10am-1am.

Ramsi's Café on the World, 1293 Bardstown Rd. (451-0700). This intimate restaurant prepares "ethnic non-regional cuisine" for a mix of hipsters and local families. Good vegetarian options. Great raspberry vinagrette. *Chipolte con queso* $4; salad *Niçoise* $6.50. Entrees $5-9. Open M-Th 11am-1am, F-Sa 11am-2am, Su 3-11pm.

Mark's Feed Store, 1514 Bardstown Rd. (459-6275). Award-winning barbecue served up on the cheap. If the weather's fine, eat on the patio with the metal pigs. Bodacious Burgoo and BBQ combo; pork sandwich $3.50; ½-basket of onion straws $3. Free dessert M after 4pm. Open Su-Th 11am-10pm, F-Sa 11am-11pm.

Café Kilimanjaro, 649 S. 4th St. (583-4332), in Theater Sq. Jamaican, Ethiopian, and international cuisine. Jamaican jerk chicken lunch special $4.75; chicken dinner $9, and well worth it. Live world music F-Sa 10:30pm-2am. Open M-Tu 11am-3pm, W-Th 11am-3pm and 5-8:30pm, F-Sa 11am-3pm and 5-10:30pm.

NOT JUST A ONE-HORSE TOWN

The **Highlands** strip runs along Baxter/Bardstown and is bounded by Broadway and Trevilian Way on the south. Buses #17, 23, and 44 can all take you to this "anti-mall" of largely unfranchised businesses. Cafes, pizza pubs, antique shops, record stores, and other enticements beckon to strollers. Farther south, near the University of Louisville (take bus #2 or 4), the newly restored **J.B. Speed Art Museum,** 2035 S. 3rd St. (634-2700), houses an impressive collection of Dutch paintings and tapestries, Renaissance and contemporary art, and a sculpture court with more style than just any old museum. *(Open Tu-W and F 10:30am-4pm, Th 10:30am-8pm, Sa 10:30am-5pm, Su noon-5pm.)*

The **Belle of Louisville** (574-2355), an authentic paddle-wheel craft, docks at 4th St. and River Rd. *(2hr. cruises depart from Riverfront Plaza late May to early Sept. Tu-Su 2pm. Sunset cruises Tu and Th 7pm. Dance cruise Sa 8:30-11:30pm. Boarding begins 1hr. before departure; arrive early, especially in July. $9, seniors $8, under 13 $5; dance cruise $12.50.)* The world's tallest baseball bat (120 ft.) leans against the **Hillerich and Bradsby Co. (Louisville Slugger),** 800 W. Main (588-7228). *(Open M-Sa 9am-5pm. $4, over 60 $3.50, ages 6-12 $3.)* A nostalgic baseball film features the ol' crack of the bat; tours show how the world-famous Sluggers, including those used by major leaguers, are made. H&B will even give you a free miniature bat at tour's end so you can practice your swing.

Wondering how machines work? Aching to try your arms and legs at a climbing wall? Itching for an IMAX? The **Louisville Science Center,** 727 W. Main St. (561-6111), can appease all of these cravings. *(Open M-Th 10am-5pm, F-Sa 10am-9pm, Su noon-5pm. Admission $5.50, ages 2-12 and over 59 $4.50; with IMAX $7.50/$6.)* The hundreds of interactive exhibits are aimed at kids, but more than one parent has looked both ways and sneaked a game or two.

Lovers of American kitsch will find a treat at the **Harlan Sanders Museum, Kentucky Fried Chicken International Headquarters,** 1441 Gardiner Ln. (456-8607), off the Watterson Expwy. at Newburg Rd. S. A room of artifacts, preserved office, and short film honor the Colonel who brought fried chicken to the non-southern masses with his pressure cooker, secret recipe of 11 herbs and spices, and trademark white suit. His autobiography, *Life As I Have Known It Has Been Finger Lickin' Good,* is on display but, sadly, *not* for sale.

Plan to spend midnight with the millions of packages that pass through the massive **United Parcel Service Air Hub,** 802 Grade Ln. (359-8727), at the airport. *(1½hr. tours M-F around noon and at midnight. Free, but reservations required.)* All the action happens during the big "sort," when the packages fly from one conveyer belt to another to speed them on their way.

As for natural splendor, a gander at the **Falls of the Ohio,** 201 W. Riverside Dr., Clarksville, IN, (812-280-9970) might be just the ticket. *(Park open daily 7am-midnight; center open M-Sa 9am-5pm, Su 1-5pm. Center $2, children $1. Parking free.)* The interpretive center at the Falls can help you find a good hiking path, explore the river's geology, or locate (but leave behind) fossils.

ENTERTAINMENT AND NIGHTLIFE

Start any entertainment search with the free weekly arts and entertainment newspaper, *Leo,* available at most downtown restaurants or at the visitors center. The **Kentucky Center for the Arts,** 5 Riverfront Plaza (tickets and info 584-7777 or 800-775-7777), off Main St., hosts the **Louisville Orchestra,** the **Louisville Ballet,** the **Broadway Series,** and other major productions (open M-Sa 9am-6pm, Su noon-5pm). Downtown, the **Actors Theater,** 316 W. Main St. (584-1205 or 800-428-5849), is a Tony award-winning repertory company. (Showtime 7:30pm, weekend matinees. Box office open M 10am-5:30pm, Tu-F 10am-8pm. Tickets from $16; student and senior rush tickets 15min. before each show $10.) What dreams may come when we have shuffled off this mortal coil at the **Kentucky Shakespeare Festival** (583-8738), at the zoo and in Central Park, which takes place over 8 weekends starting in early June (performances 7pm). The **Vogue Theater,** 3727 Lexington Rd. (893-3646), screens classic and foreign flicks (box office opens at 2pm).

Butchertown Pub, 1335 Story Ave. (583-2242), presents three stages of alternative music and blues from local and national bands (cover $1-4; open M 4-11:30pm, Tu 4pm-1am, W-Sa 4pm-2am). A gigantic and multi-faceted entertainment machine, **The Brewery,** 426 Baxter Ave. (583-3420), hosts college bands like Collective Soul and Toad the Wet Sprocket on Thursday nights. When there's no show, hang out on the four volleyball courts, or catch the monthly boxing night. (Cover for live shows $8-20. Open M-Sa 11am-4am, Su 5pm-4am.) **Phoenix Hill Tavern,** 644 Baxter Ave. (589-4957), cooks with nightly blues, rock, and reggae on four stages including a deck and roof garden (cover $2-5; open W-Th and Sa 8pm, F 5pm). Members of the Techno Alliance take heart: **Sparks,** 104 W. Main St. (587-8566), throbs 'til the early morn (cover F-Sa $3-5, Su $3; open daily 10pm-4am). For gay nightlife, make **The Connection,** 120 Floyd St. (585-5752), between Main and Market St. Mostly gay male entertainment is offered, but anyone should check out the bashes at this black-and-white-and-mirrored-all-over club (cover $2-5; open Tu-Su 9pm-4am).

HORSIN' AROUND

Even if you miss the Kentucky Derby, be sure to visit **Churchill Downs,** 700 Central Ave. (636-4400), 3 mi. south of downtown; take bus #4 "4th St." to Central Ave. *(Races Apr. to late May W-Su from 1pm; June W-Su from 3pm; Nov. Tu-Su 1-5pm. Grandstand and clubhouse seats $2, 5th fl. reserved seats $4.50. Grounds open daily in racing season 10am-4pm. Parking $3.)* You don't have to bet to admire the twin spires, the colonial columns, the gardens, and the sheer scale of the track—but it sure does make things more exciting if you do.

The **Kentucky Derby Festival** kicks off with the largest fireworks show in North America and continues for 2 weeks with balloon and steamboat races, concerts, and a parade before the climactic **Run for the Roses** on the first Saturday in May. A 1-to 10-year waiting list stands between you and a ticket for the Derby, but never fear— on Derby morning, tickets are sold for standing-room-only spots in the infield ($35). Get in line early for good seats, lest the other 125,000 spectators get there first. Amazingly, no one is turned away. The **Kentucky Derby Museum** (637-7097), at Churchill Downs, offers a complete picture of the race on a 360° screen, tours of the track, footage of every Derby ever recorded (including Secratariat's record 1973 run), a simulated horse race for betting practice, tips on exactly what makes a horse a "sure thing," and seven tours of the Downs every day (open daily 9am-5pm; $6, seniors $5, ages 5-12 $2, under 5 free).

∎ South of Louisville

Bardstown Kentucky's second-oldest city, 17 mi. east on Rte. 245 from I-65 Exit 112, is proudly known as the "Bourbon Capital of the World." In 1791, Kentucky Baptist Reverend Elijah Craig left a fire unattended while heating oak boards to make a barrel for his aging whiskey. The boards were charred, but Rev. Craig carried on, and Bourbon was born in that first charred wood barrel. Today, 90% of the nation's bourbon hails from Kentucky, and 60% of that is distilled in Nelson and Bullitt Counties. **Jim Beam's American Outpost** (543-9877), 15 mi. west of Bardstown in Clermont off Rte. 245 (take I-65 S to Exit 112, then Rte. 245 E for 1½ mi.), features the "master distiller emeritus" himself, Jim Beam's grandson, Booker Noe, who narrates a film about bourbon. Don't miss the free lemonade, coffee, and sampler bourbon candies (open M-Sa 9am-4:30pm, Su 1-4pm; free). You can't actually tour Beam's huge distillery, but **Maker's Mark Distillery** (865-2099), 19 mi. southeast of Bardstown in Loretto, will show you their technique from the 19th century. *(Tours M-Sa every hr. 10:30am-3:30pm, Su every hr. 1:30-3:30pm. Free.)* Take Rte. 49 S to Rte. 52 E. Tragically, Jim Beam's has no license to sell its bourbon, but Maker's Mark does vend its liquor. If you're nice, they'll even let you seal your own bottle with their trademark red wax. **Bardstown Visitors Center,** 107 E. Stephen Foster Ave. (348-4877 or 800-638-4877), gives a free 1hr. trolley tour, taking visitors by **My Old Kentucky Home** and **Heaven Hill Distillery**. *(Visitors center open M-Sa 8am-7pm, Su 11am-4pm; Nov.-Mar. M-Sa 8am-5pm. Summer tours M-Sa 9:30am and 1pm.)*

Whiskey Business

All bourbon is whiskey, but not all whiskey is bourbon. So what makes bourbon so special? It's all in the making, and it's codified by the U.S. Government. For alcohol to be classified as bourbon, it must fulfill all six of these requirements: **1.** It must be aged in a new white oak barrel, flame-charred on the inside. (Scotch, alternatively, must be aged in used barrels.) **2.** It must age at least 2 years in that barrel. **3.** It must be at least 51% corn. **4.** It cannot be distilled over 160 proof (80% alcohol). **5.** It cannot go into the barrel over 125 proof. **6.** It can have no additives or preservatives.

Abraham Lincoln Birthplace Near Hodgenville, 45 mi. south of Louisville on U.S. 31 E, this national historic site marks the birthplace of Honest Abe (358-3137; open daily 8am-4:45pm; May 31-Sept. 6 8am-6:45pm; free). From Louisville, take I-65 down to Rte. 61; public transportation does not serve the area. Fifty-six steps, representing the 56 years of Lincoln's tragically shortened life, lead up to a neolithic monument sheltering the small log cabin. Set in a beautiful location, the site lends a glimpse of frontier living and an 18min. video about Lincoln's Kentucky years.

Mammoth Cave Hundreds of enormous caves and narrow passageways cut through **Mammoth Cave National Park** (758-2328 or 800-967-2283), 80 mi. south of Louisville off I-65, then west on Rte. 70. Mammoth Cave comprises the world's longest network of cavern corridors—over 325 mi. in length. Start your exploration at the **visitors center** (open daily 7:30am-7pm; off-season 8am-6pm). Devout spelunkers should try the 6hr. "Wild Cave Tour" during the summer (16+; $35); less ambitious types generally take the 2hr., 2 mi. historical walking tour ($7, seniors $4, ages 6-15 $3). Other tours accommodate disabled visitors (1½hr., $6.50). The caves are a chilly 54°F. Primitive camping is available at the Houchins Ferry area year-round ($5). **Back-country camping** permits can be obtained at the visitors center. **Greyhound** comes only as close as **Cave City,** just east of I-65 on Rte. 70. **Time Zone:** Central (1hr. behind Eastern).

Bowling Green Auto enthusiasts inevitably pay their respects to this legendary home of the classic American sports car. The extensive and expensive **National Corvette Museum,** 350 Corvette Dr. (800-538-3883), off I-65 Exit 28, displays 'Vettes from the original chrome-and-steel '53 to futuristic concept cars, including classics like the "Purple People Eaters," the "Stingray," and the "Sledgehammer" (open daily 8am-6pm; Oct.-Mar. 8am-5pm; $8, ages 6-16 $4.50). Less pricey is the **General Motors Corvette Assembly Plant** (745-8287), Exit 28 off I-65, where the fifth-generation 'Vettes roll off the line. *(Tours M-F 9am and 1pm. Free.)* With luck, the tour's highlight will be a chance to test-start one of the mint condition products. Learn about Mordecai F. Ham, Patsy's Fountain of Youth, and other bits of local lore at the **Kentucky Museum** (745-2592), on the **Western Kentucky University** campus. *(Open Tu-Sa 9:30am-4pm, Su 1-4pm. $2, children $1, families $5.)* The colors (and tiny stitches!) of the quilts on display will amaze. **Time Zone:** Central (1hr. behind Eastern).

■ Lexington

In Kentucky's second-largest city, historic mansions show through downtown skyscrapers, and a 20min. drive from its boundaries will set you squarely in bluegrass country. Like the rest of Kentucky, Lexington has horse fever. The Kentucky Horse Park gets top billing, while shopping complexes and small industries at the outskirts of town share space with over 150 quaint, green horse farms. Likewise, the University of Kentucky (UK), which dominates the southern end of town, breeds basketball players for the stellar team that becomes an obsession for UK fans.

ORIENTATION AND PRACTICAL INFORMATION

New Circle Rd. (Rte. 4/U.S. 60 bypass) loops the city, intersecting with many roads that connect the downtown district to the surrounding towns. **High, Vine,** and **Main St.** running east-west and **Limestone St.** and **Broadway** running north-south provide the best routes through downtown. Beware of the many seductively curving one-way streets that bewilder the innocent near downtown and the university.

Airport: Blue Grass, 4000 Versailles Rd. (255-7218), southwest of downtown. Ritzy downtown hotels run shuttles to the airport, but there is no public transportation. Taxi to downtown $13.

Buses: Greyhound, 477 New Circle Rd. NW (299-8804 or 800-231-2222; open daily 7:30am-11pm); take Lex-Tran bus #6 downtown. To: Louisville (1¾hr., 4 per day, $16); Cincinnati (1½hr., 5 per day, $20); and Knoxville (3hr., 5 per day, $42).

Public Transportation: Lex-Tran, 109 W. London Ave. (253-4636). Buses leave from the Transit Center, 220 W. Vine St., between M.L. King and Stone Ave. 10min. before the hr. Serves the university and city outskirts. Erratic service. Buses run M-F 6:15am-6:15pm, Sa 8:45am-5:45pm; some routes until 10pm. Fare 80¢.

Taxis: Lexington Yellow Cab, 231-8294. $1.90 base fare, $1.60 per mi. 24hr.

Visitor Info: Lexington Convention and Visitors Bureau, 301 E. Vine St. (233-7299 or 800-845-3959; http://www.visitlex.com), at Rose St. Pick up the comprehensive *Lexington Walk and Bluegrass Country Driving Tour.* Open in summer M-F 8:30am-5pm, Sa 10am-5pm, Su noon-5pm; off-season closed Su.

Hotlines: Crisis Intervention, 233-0444. **Rape Crisis,** 253-2511.

Hospitals: Lexington Hospital, 150 N. Eagle Creek Dr. (268-4800). **Lexington Women's Diagnostic Center,** 1725 Harrodsburg Rd. (277-8485).

Internet Access: Kinko's, 145 Rose St. (243-1360), just southeast of downtown. Open 24hr.

Post Office: 210 E. High St. (254-6156), downtown. Open M-F 8am-5pm, Sa 9am-noon. **ZIP code:** 40511. **Area code:** 606.

ACCOMMODATIONS AND CAMPGROUNDS

A concentration of horse-related wealth in the Lexington area pushes accommodation prices up. The cheapest places lurk outside the city, beyond **New Circle Rd. Dial Accommodations,** 301 E. Vine St. (233-1221 or 800-848-1224), at the visitors center, can help you find a room (open M-F 8:30am-6pm, Sa 10am-6pm, Su noon-5pm; off- season reduced hrs.).

◉**Kimball House Motel,** 267 S. Limestone St. (252-9565), between downtown and the university. The neon sign beckons you into a timewarp to the kitschy charm of 50s car culture in a Victorian brick house. Parking in back. No phones in rooms; some have TV's. Several 1st fl. singles (no A/C, shared bath) go for $21, but they often fill by late afternoon. Otherwise, singles from $25; doubles $30. Key deposit $5.

Catalina Motel, 208 W. New Circle Rd. (299-6281). Take Broadway north of the city, and turn left onto New Circle Rd. Large, clean rooms with A/C, cable TV, pool, and HBO. Singles $30, doubles $36; F-Sa $35/$41.

Microtel, 2240 Buena Vista Dr. (299-9600), off I-75 at the Winchester Rd. (Rte. 60) Exit. Pleasant motel rooms with window seats. Singles $39; doubles $44.

Kentucky Horse Park Campground, 4089 Ironworks Pike (259-4257 or 800-370-6416), 10 mi. north of downtown off I-75 at Exit 120. Great groomed camping plus laundry, showers, basketball courts, swimming pool, and a free shuttle to the KY Horse Park and Museum. Wide open tent sites, but the 260 RV sites nicely mix shade and lawn. Sites Apr.-Oct. $11, with hookup $15; Nov.-Mar. $9/$11.50. Senior discounts available. 2-week max. stay.

FOOD AND NIGHTLIFE

◉**Alfalfa Restaurant,** 557 S. Limestone St. (253-0014), across from Memorial Hall at the university; take bus #9. Menu of fantastic international and veggie meals changes nightly. Complete dinners with salad and bread under $12. Filling soups and salads from $2, like the Hoppin' John. Live jazz, folk, and other music W-Sa 8-10pm. No cover. Open M 11am-2pm, Tu-Th 11am-2pm and 5:30-9pm, F-Sa 10am-2pm and 5:30-10pm, Su 10am-2pm.

◉**Ramsey's,** 496 E. High St. (259-2708). 2 other locations at 4053 Tates Creek Rd. (271-2638) and 1660 Bryan Station Rd. (299-9669). Real Southern grease. Vegetarians beware: even the veggies are cooked with pork parts. 1 meat and 3 vegetables $9.50. Sandwiches under $6. Open Su 10am-11pm, M-Tu 11am-11pm, W-F 11am-1am, Sa 10am-1am.

Parkette Drive-In, 1216 New Circle Rd. (254-8723). Drive-up, 1951 eatery with bargain food. Giant "Poor Boy" burger plate $2.60; chicken box with 4 pieces, gravy, fries, cole slaw, and roll $3.85. A few booths inside give carless folks an equal opportunity to join in the nostalgia. Open M-Th 10am-10pm, F-Sa 10am-11pm.

Hi-Acres Snack Bar and Pharmacy, 1794 Bryan Station Rd. (299-9949). An old drug store that still dishes up short-order favorites like fried baloney (with french fries $2.50) and grilled cheese on its vintage counter. Excellent butterscotch pie. Open M-Sa 9am-4pm, Su 9am-1:30pm.

Lexington's nightlife surpasses most expectations for a town its size. For current entertainment info, read the "Weekender" section of Friday's *Herald-Leader,* or pick up a free copy of *Ace.* Stand-up comics do their thing at **Comedy off Broadway,** 3199 Nicholsville Rd. (271-JOKE/5653), at Lexington Green Mall (cover $3-8; shows Tu-Th 8pm and F-Sa 8 and 10:30pm). **The Bar,** 224 E. Main St. (255-1551), a popular disco cabaret/lounge complex, caters to gays and lesbians. (21+. Cover F $4, Sa $5. Lounge open M-Sa 4pm-1am; disco open M-Th 10pm-1am, F 10pm-2am, Sa 10pm-3:30am.) For a bit o' the Irish, and a lot o' UK students, **Lynagh's Pub and Club** (pub 255-1292, club 255-6614), in University Plaza at Woodland and Euclid St., won't disappoint. The pub grills up good burgers for $4.75 (open M-Sa 11am-1am, Su noon-11pm), while music strums next door (cover from $3; open Tu-Sa 4-9pm for pool and darts; music 9pm-1am). The **Kentucky Theatre,** 214 E. Main St. (231-6997), projects indy and artsy flicks for $3.75-4.50.

SIGHTS

To escape the stifling swamp conditions farther south, antebellum plantation owners built beautiful summer retreats in milder Lexington. The most attractive of these stately houses preen only a few blocks northeast of the town center, in the Gratz Park area near the old public library. Wrap-around porches, wooden minarets, stone foundations, and rose-covered trellises distinguish these old estates from the neighborhood's newer homes. **The Hunt Morgan House,** 201 N. Mill St. (233-3290 or 253-0362), stands at the end of the park across from the old library at W. 2nd St. *(Tours Tu-Sa 10am-4pm, Su 2-5pm at 15min. past the hr. $5, students $3.)* Built in 1814 by John Wesley Hunt, the first millionaire west of the Alleghenies, the house witnessed the birth of Thomas Hunt Morgan, who won a 1933 Nobel Prize for proving the existence of the gene. The house's most colorful inhabitant, however, was Confederate General John Hunt Morgan who, pursued by Union troops, rode his horse up the front steps and into the house, leaned down to kiss his mother, and rode out the back door. Mary Todd, the future wife of Abraham Lincoln, grew up just 5 blocks away in the **Mary Todd Lincoln House,** 578 W. Main St. (233-9999); you can see the house on a 45min. tour (open mid-Mar. to Nov. Tu-Sa 10am-4pm; last tour 3:15pm; $5, ages 6-12 $2). Senator Henry Clay and John Hunt Morgan now lie buried at the **Lexington Cemetery,** 833 W. Main St. (255-5522). *(Open daily 8am-5pm; office 8am-4pm. Free cemetery scavenger hunts available for children; no digging.)* During his lifetime, Clay resided at **Ashland,** 120 Sycamore Rd. (266-8581), a 20-acre estate across town at the corner of Sycamore and Richmond Rd.; take the "Woodhall" bus. *(Open M-Sa 10am-4:30pm, Su 1-4:30pm; Nov.-Mar. closed M; closed Jan. 1hr. tours $6, students $3, ages 6-12 $2.)*

Hollywood jewelry designer George W. Headley's exotic and sparkling creations are displayed at the **Headley-Whitney Museum,** 4435 Old Frankfort Pike (255-6653), along with a shell grotto, a three-car garage entirely blanketed with shell designs—you won't need an employee to tell you it was done in the 70s (open Tu-F 10am-5pm, Sa-Su noon-5pm; $4, students $2, seniors $3).

HORSES

Lexington horse farms are beautiful places to visit; the visitors bureau has a list of available farms. **Three Chimneys Farm** (873-7053), on Old Frankfort Pike 4 mi. from I-64 and 8½ mi. from New Circle Rd., raised the 1977 Triple Crown winner **Seattle Slew** (tours daily 10am and 1pm, by appt. only; $5-10 tip customary). **Kentucky Horse Park,** 4089 Ironworks Pike (233-4303), 10 mi. north at Exit 120 off I-75, has extensive equine facilities, a museum tracing the history, science, and pageantry of these animals, and many live examples. *(Open daily 9am-5pm. $10, ages 7-12 $5; Nov.-Mar. $7.50/$4.50; live horse shows and horse-drawn vehicle tours included. 50min. horse ride and tour in addition to entrance fee, $12; pony rides $3.25. Parking $2. Wheelchair access.)* The last weekend in April, the horse park hosts the annual Rolex tournament qualifier (254-8123) for the **U.S. equestrian team.** Every April, the **Keeneland Race Track,** 4201 Versailles Rd. (254-3412 or 800-456-3412), west on U.S. 60, holds the final prep race for the Kentucky Derby. *(Races Oct. and Apr.; post time 1pm. $2.50. Workouts free and open to the public mid-Mar. to Nov. 6am-10am.)* Hay and breakfast is available at the race track kitchen. At **Red Mile Harness Track,** 847 S. Broadway (255-0752), harness racing takes center stage. *(Races Apr.-June and late Sept. to early Oct.; in spring post times noon and 1pm, in fall 7:30pm. $2 min. bet. Parking free. Morning workouts open to the public in racing season dawn-1pm.)* Take bus #3 on S. Broadway. Thoroughbreds become champions at the **Kentucky Horse Center,** 3380 Paris Pike (293-1853), 2½ mi. north of Exit 113 off I-64/75, where trainers put the horses through their paces. *(Tours Apr.-Oct. M-F 9, 10:30am, and 1pm; Sa 9 and 10:30am; call for winter schedule. $10, under 13 $5.)*

■ Near Lexington

Harrodsburg, the oldest permanent English settlement west of the Alleghenies, is nestled 32 mi. southwest of Lexington on U.S. 68. Visitors relive the legacy of Fort Harrod, founded in 1774, at **Old Fort Harrod State Park,** S. College St. (734-3314), an active replica in which craftspeople clothed in 18th-century garb demonstrate skills like black-smithing and quilting. The **Mansion Museum,** just below the Fort, showcases Union and Confederate artifacts, including a cast of Lincoln's face and hands. *(Fort and museum open daily 9am-5pm; museum closed Dec. to mid-Mar. $3, ages 6-12 $2.)* Pick up a tour book-let for historic downtown Harrodsburg at the **visitors center,** 103 Main St. (734-2364 or 800-355-9192), on the corner of U.S. 68 and Main St. (Open M-F 8:30am-4:30pm, Sa 10am-3pm.)

The Shakers, a 19th-century celibate religious sect, practiced the simple life at **Shaker Village** (734-5411), about 25 mi. southwest of Lexington and north of Har-rodsburg on U.S. 68. The 2700-acre farm features 33 restored Shaker buildings; a tour includes demonstrations of everything from making apple butter to coopering (bar-rel-making). The village also offers **riverboat excursions** on the Kentucky River. *(Open daily 9am-5:30pm. $9.50, students 12-17 $5, ages 6-11 $3; with river trip $13.50/$7/$4. Oct.-Mar. reduced hrs. and prices. Wheelchair access.)* Visitors can stay the night in a "mod-ern" Shaker room with TV, A/C, and plumbing (singles from $50; doubles $60; reser-vations highly recommended).

In **Richmond,** Exit 95 off I-75, the elegant Georgian-Italianate mansion **White Hall** (623-9178) was the home of the abolitionist (not the boxer) Cassius M. Clay, cousin of Senator Henry Clay. *(45min. guided tours only. Open Apr.-Oct. daily 9am-5:30pm, last tour at 4:30pm; early Sept. to Oct. W-Su only. $4.50, under 13 $2.50, under 6 free.)* A re-creation of one of Daniel Boone's forts, **Fort Boonesborough State Park** (527-3131), also in Richmond, has samples of 18th-century crafts, a small museum collection, and films about the pioneers. *(Open Apr.-Aug. daily 9am-5:30pm; Sept.-Oct. W-Su 9am-5:30pm. $4.50, ages 6-12 $3. White Hall/Boonesborough combo tickets $7.)*

▨ Daniel Boone National Forest

The Daniel Boone National Forest cuts a vast green swath through Kentucky's East-ern Highlands. Enclosing 670,000 acres of mountains and valleys, the forest is layered with a gorgeous tangle of chestnut, oak, hemlock, and pine, as well as pristine lakes, waterfalls, and extraordinary natural bridges. This is bluegrass country, where sea-soned backpackers and Lexington's day trippers still find the heart of old Appalachia deep in the forest—though, by some reports, you're less likely these days to stumble onto feuding Hatfields and McCoys than into some farmer's hidden field of marijuana, reputedly Kentucky's #1 cash crop.

PRACTICAL INFORMATION Seven U.S. Forest Service Ranger Districts administer the National Forest. Ranger offices supply trail maps and specifics about the portions of the 254 mi. Sheltowee Trace, the forest's most significant trail, that pass through their districts. **Stanton Ranger District,** 705 W. College Ave. (663-2852), Stanton, includes the **Red River Gorge and Natural Bridge** (open M-F 8am-4:30pm). To the north, **Morehead Ranger District,** 2375 KY 801 S. (784-5628), 2 mi. south of Rte. 60, includes **Cave Run Lake.** The **Morehead Tourism Commission,** 150 E. First St. (784-6221), Morehead 40351, has more info. To the south, **London Ranger District** (864-4163), on U.S. 25 S, covers Laurel River Lake, close to Cumberland Falls; Laurel River Lake's **visitors center** (878-6900 or 800-348-0095) is at Exit 41 off I-75 (open M-Sa 9am-5pm, Su 10am-2pm). For forest-wide info, contact the **Forest Supervisor,** 100 Vaught Rd., Winchester (745-3100). **Greyhound** (800-231-2222) serves several towns with buses from Lexington to Morehead (1½hr., 1 per day, $14); London (1¾hr., 3 per day, $18); and Corbin (2hr., 5 per day, $19). **Area code:** 606.

STANTON RANGER DISTRICT Split by the Mountain Pkwy., Stanton Ranger District divides into two parts, with **Natural Bridge State Resort Park** on the south side, and **Red River Gorge Geological Area** on the north. **Natural Bridge,** off Rte. 11, is the area's absolute must-see site. The somewhat steep ¾ mi. trail leads to the expansive view at the top of the bridge's vast span. The **Red River Gorge Area** contains some of the most varied and ecologically rich terrain in this part of the country. A 32 mi. circuit (Rte. 77 E to Rte. 715) runs through the single-lane **Nada Tunnel,** an old rail-road tunnel cut directly through the rock (scary as hell!), and past the restored **Gladie**

Historic Site Log House, which illuminates turn-of-the-century rural logging life. Along the way, it takes in bison, curving mountain roads, forests, and picturesque wooden and metal bridges. If you don't mind driving down a 3 mi. gravel road, take a 1.3 mi hike past the beautiful **Rock Bridge,** down Rock Bridge Rd. near the junction of Rte. 715 and Rte. 15.

Slade, 52 mi. southeast of Lexington (take I-64 to Mountain Pkwy.), makes a good base for a tour of this portion of the forest. A **red tourist caboose,** run by the **Natural Bridge/Powell County Chamber of Commerce** (663-9229), sits at the Slade Exit off Mountain Pkwy. (Open daily 10am-6pm; off-season 10am-5pm.) The town itself contains few attractions except the forest and the lavish **Natural Bridge State Resort Park,** 2135 Natural Bridge Rd. (663-2214 or 800-325-1710), off Rte. 11. Budget-conscious travelers can avoid the park's pricey lodge, and patronize its campgrounds: **Whittletown** has 40 well-shaded sites, and **Middle Fork** has 39 open sites (primitive sites $8.50, with hookup $12; $1 per additional adult, under 17 free). You can also pitch a tent anywhere in the forest, as long as you stay more than 300 ft. from roads or marked trails. Those who prefer the great indoors should lay down their burdens in one of the large, clean, slightly dim rooms with pool access and free local calls (but no cable) at **Li'l Abners** (663-5384), 2½ mi. from Red River Gorge on Rte. 11 in Slade (singles $44; doubles $49; July-Aug. reserve in advance).

Wanderers here can try **Ale-8-I** ("A Late One"), the local soft drink in the tall green bottle, and the regional staple of soup beans and cornbread. Good restaurants are hard to come by, but many general stores along Rte. 11 and 15 peddle cheap, filling sandwiches to eat at a counter or pack for the trail. In nearby Stanton, **Bruen's Restaurant** (663-4252), on Sipple St. at Exit 22 off Mountain Pkwy., makes greasy spoon fare in an authentic down-home atmosphere. Breakfast is served all day; try two eggs, bacon, and a biscuit with gravy for just $2.55, or a cheeseburger for $1.50 (open Su-Th 4:30am-9pm, F-Sa 4:30am-10pm).

LONDON RANGER DISTRICT There's boating, fishing, hiking, and just hanging out at the **Laurel River Lake. Camping** is available at two spacious and densely wooded Forest Service campgrounds on the lake, both off Rte. 193 and adjacent to marinas: **Grove** (528-6156 or 800-280-2266), with 56 sites; and **Holly Bay** (878-8134 or 800-280-2266), with 90 sites. (10 primitive sites $7; with hookup $14 for 1 person, for 2 $24. Reservations recommended 5-10 days in advance.) Visitors to giant **Cumberland Falls,** 18 mi. west of Corbin on Rte. 90—"The Niagara of the South"—can camp at the state park (528-4121), which surrounds the falls. The campground is signposted off Rte. 90 (50 sites; tents $8.50, RVs $10; open Apr.-Oct.). The falls's famous moonbows, created by the water mist during a full moon, are fantastic. Onward, chicken soldiers: in nearby Corbin, deep-fried legions pay homage to the Colonel at the original **Kentucky Fried Chicken/Harland Sanders Café and Museum** (528-2163), at the junction of Rte. 25 E and 25 W, in all its finger-lickin' glory (open daily 7am-11pm). **Sheltowee Trace Outfitters** (800-541-7238), in Whitley City on Rte. 90, 5 mi. east of the state park, arranges guided, 6hr. rafting trips down the Falls's class III rapids ($48, ages 5-12 $38).

■ Cumberland Gap

Stretching from Maine to Georgia, the majestic Appalachian Mountain Range proved a formidable obstacle to the movement of early American settlers, but not to bison. By following these animals, Native Americans learned of the Cumberland Gap, a natural break in the mountains allowing passage west. Frontiersman Daniel Boone became famous when he blazed the Wilderness Trail through the Gap in 1775, thereby opening the West to colonization. Today, the **Cumberland Gap National Historic Park,** best reached by U.S. 25 E from Kentucky or U.S. 58 from Virginia, sits on 20,000 acres shared by Kentucky, Virginia, and Tennessee. The Cumberland Gap **visitors center** (606-248-2817), on U.S. 25 E in Middleboro, KY, has a 10min. film and a slide presentation on the history of the Gap (park and center open daily 8am-6pm; off-season 8am-5pm). The park's 160-site **campground,** on U.S. 58 in Virginia, has hot showers (sites $10, with electricity $15). From either the campground or the visitors center, a difficult 4 mi. hike leads to **Pinnacle Rock** for a breathtaking look around. **Backcountry camping** requires a free permit from the visitors center.

Tennessee

Sloping from the majestic Great Smoky Mountains to the verdant Mississippi lowlands, Tennessee makes and breaks stereotypes with the smooth ease of Jack Daniels. Those enchanted with the last state to secede from the Union, and the first to rejoin, often express their affection in the form of song—an ode to Davy Crockett deems this land the "greatest state in the land of the free," Dolly Parton finds her Heartsong in the mountains, and there ain't no place the Grateful Dead would rather be. Tennessee's economy is industry-based, with the world's largest Bible-producing business, but it is certainly music that fuels the state's artistic life, as any fan of the King knows. Today, country twangs from Nashville, while the blues still wail in Memphis.

PRACTICAL INFORMATION

Capital: Nashville.
Visitor Info: Tennessee Dept. of Tourist Development, 320 6th Ave., Nashville (741-2159; http://www.state.tn.us/tourdev). Open M-F 8am-4:30pm. **Tennessee State Parks Information,** 401 Church St., Nashville (800-421-6683).
Time Zones: Eastern and Central (1hr. behind Eastern); *Let's Go* makes note of areas which lie in Central. **Postal Abbreviation:** TN.
Emergency: 911.
Sales Tax: 8%.

■ Nashville

Long-forgotten Francis Nash is one of only four Revolutionary War heroes honored with U.S. city names (Washington, Wayne, and Knox are the others), but his tenuous foothold in history pales in comparison to Nashville's notoriety as the banjo-pickin', foot stompin' capital of country music. Large, eclectic, and unapologetically heterogeneous, Tennessee's capital is not only the home of the Country Music Hall of Fame, but a slick financial hub as well ("the Wall Street of the South"). The city houses the Southern Baptists and finds room for centers of fine arts and higher learning, such as Fisk University and Vanderbilt.

ORIENTATION AND PRACTICAL INFORMATION

Nashville's streets are fickle, often interrupted by curving parkways and one-ways. Names change constantly and without warning; **Broadway,** the main east-west thoroughfare, melts into **West End Ave.** just outside downtown at Vanderbilt and I-40. In downtown, easily marked by the twin spires of Bell South's towering "Bat Building," numbered avenues run north-south, parallel to the Cumberland River. The curve of **James Robertson Pkwy.** encloses the north end, becoming **Main St.** on the other side of the river (later **Gallatin Pike**) and **McGavock St.** at the south end. *The area south of Broadway between 2nd and 7th Ave. and the region north of James Robertson Pkwy. are both unsafe at night.*

Airport: Metropolitan (275-1675), 8 mi. south of downtown. An airport **shuttle** (275-1180) operates out of major downtown hotels ($8, round-trip $15). Bus fare downtown $1.50 with a transfer. Taxi to downtown $15-17.
Buses: Greyhound, 200 8th Ave. S. (255-1691 or 800-231-2222), at Broadway downtown. Borders on a rough neighborhood, but the station is bright. To: Memphis (4hr., 6 per day, $28); Chattanooga (2½hr., 4 per day, $14); Birmingham (4hr., 4 per day, $27); and Knoxville (3hr., 6 per day, $23). Station open 24hr.

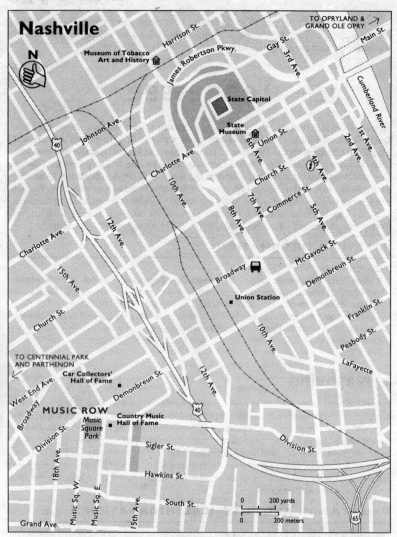

Nashville

N

TO OPRYLAND &
GRAND OLE OPRY

Harrison St.

Museum of Tobacco
Art and History

James Robertson Pkwy.

Gay St.

3rd Ave.

Main St.

Cumberland River

State Capitol

State
Museum

Union St.

1st Ave.

2nd Ave.

Johnson Ave.

Charlotte Ave.

6th Ave.

Church St.

4th Ave.

10th Ave.

7th Ave.

Commerce St.

5th Ave.

12th Ave.

8th Ave.

McGavock St.

Charlotte Ave.

Demonbreun St.

15th Ave.

Broadway

Franklin St.

Church St.

Union Station

Peabody St.

10th Ave.

LaFayette

TO CENTENNIAL PARK
AND PARTHENON

West End Ave.

Car Collectors'
Hall of Fame

Demonbreun St.

12th Ave.

Broadway

MUSIC ROW

Music
Square
Park

Country Music
Hall of Fame

Division St.

Division St.

18th Ave.

Sigler St.

Hawkins St.

Music Sq. W.

Music Sq. E.

15th Ave.

South St.

0   200 yards

0   200 meters

65

Grand Ave.

Public Transportation: Metropolitan Transit Authority (MTA) (862-5950). Buses operate on limited routes, usually once per hr. M-F 5:40am-11:15pm, less frequent service Sa-Su. Fare $1.40, transfers 10¢. MTA runs 2 **tourist trolleys** from Riverfront Park and Downtown Circle every 10-15min. Sa-Th 9am-6pm, F 9am-8pm. Fare $1, all-day pass $3, seniors and under 13 $2.

Taxis: Nashville Cab, 242-7070. **Music City Cab,** 262-0451. Both $1.50 base fare and per mi. Both 24hr.

Car Rental: Thrifty, 414 11th Ave. N. (248-8888), downtown. $33 per day, Sa-Su $30. Must be over 25.

Visitor Info: Nashville Area Convention and Visitors Bureau, 161 4th Ave. N. (259-4700), in the Chamber of Commerce building, between Commerce and Church St. downtown. Open M-F 8am-5pm. **Nashville Visitors Center,** 501 Broadway (259-4747), in the Nashville Arena, I-65 at Exit 84, James Robertson Pkwy. Complete maps marked with attractions. Open daily 8:30am-8pm.

Hotlines: Crisis Line, 244-7444. **Rape Hotline,** 256-8526. Both 24hr. **Gay and Lesbian Switchboard,** 297-0008. Operates nightly 6-9pm.

THE SOUTH

Hospitals: Metro Nashville General Hospital, 1818 Albion St. (341-4000). **The Women's Center,** 419 Welshwood Dr. (331-1200), across from Harding Mall.
Internet Access: Kinko's, 3rd and Broadway (244-1000), downtown. $12/hr. Open 24hr.
Post Office: 901 Broadway (255-9453), next to Union Station. Open M-F 7:30am-7pm, Sa 8am-2pm. **ZIP code:** 37202. **Area code:** 615.

ACCOMMODATIONS AND CAMPGROUNDS

Finding a room in Nashville isn't difficult, just expensive, especially in summer. Make reservations well in advance, especially for weekend stays. Budget motels concentrate around **W. Trinity Ln.** and **Brick Church Pike,** off I-65 at Exit 87B. Dirt-cheap hotels inhabit the area around **Dickerson Rd.** and **Murfreesboro,** but the neighborhood is seedy at best. Closer to downtown (but still sketchy), several motels huddle on **Interstate Dr.** just over the Woodland St. Bridge.

Motel 6 (800-4MOTEL6/466-8356). Four locations: 311 W. Trinity Ln. (227-9696), at Exit 87B off I-65; 323 Cartwright St. (859-9674), Goodlettsville, off Long Hollow Pike west from I-65; 95 Wallace Rd. (333-9933), off Exit 56 from I-24; 420 Metroplex Dr. (833-8887), near the airport. Comfortable rooms with HBO, outdoor pool, free local calls. Singles $36; doubles $42; under 17 free with parents. Wallace and Metroplex locations are slightly ritzier and more expensive.

The Liberty Inn, 2400 Brick Church Pike (228-2567). Big TVs with cable, A/C, roomy showers—what more could you ask for? Local calls 35¢. Singles $30, doubles $43; F-Sa $42/$48. $5 deposit.

The Cumberland Inn, 150 W. Trinity Ln. (226-1600 or 800-704-1028), Exit 87A off I-65 N, north of downtown. Cheerful rooms with bright, modern furnishings, A/C, HBO, laundry, and free continental breakfast. Singles 39; doubles $43.

Two campgrounds lie within the range of public transportation near Opryland USA. By car, take Briley Pkwy. north to McGavock Pike Exit 12B and go north onto Music Valley Dr. **Nashville Holiday Travel Park,** 2572 Music Valley Dr. (889-4225), provides a wooded area for tenting and densely packed RV sites (sites for 2 $20, with hookup $33; $4 per additional person over age 11). **Opryland KOA,** 2626 Music Valley Dr. (889-0282), has 50 tent sites ($20) and tons of crowded sites with hookups ($30); perks include a pool and live summer music (AAA discount).

FOOD

In Nashville, music even influences the local delicacies; **Goo-Goo Clusters** (peanuts, pecans, chocolate, caramel, and marshmallow), sold at most stores, bear the initials of the Grand Ole Opry. Nashville's other finger-lickin' traditions, barbecue or fried chicken followed by pecan pie, are no less sinful. Restaurants for collegiate tastes and budgets cram **West End Ave.** and the 2000 block of **Elliston Pl.,** near Vanderbilt.

◉**Loveless Café,** 8400 Rte. 100 (646-9700 or 800-889-2432). A Nashville country cookin' tradition. Feast on biscuits made from scratch with homemade preserves, country ham ($6), fried chicken ($8), and good ol' southern hospitality. Open M-F 8am-2pm and 5-9pm, Sa-Su 8am-9pm. Reservations recommended.

SATCO (San Antonio Taco Company), 416 21st Ave. S. (327-4322). Tex-Mex and beer options abound at this student hangout. Fajitas $1.50, tacos $1. Single beers $1.75, bucket of 6 $9. Also at 208 Commerce St. (259-4413). Open daily 11am-1am; in winter 11am-midnight.

Peaceful Planet, 1811 Division St. (327-2033), next to music studios. Only vegetarian and vegan food is served in this airy, all-natural eatery. Trays are available to pile on tofu, vegetables, juice, soup, and delicious confections. All food is $4.50 per lb. Open for breakfast M-F 7am-10am, lunch M-F 11am-2:30pm, dinner daily 4:30-8:30pm, and Su brunch 9:30am-2:30pm.

The World's End, 1713 Church St. (329-3480). It's the end of the world as we know it, and I feel like a burger or a salad ($5-8), or maybe a beer ($2.50). Caters to a primarily gay crowd. Open Su and Tu-Th 4pm-12:30am, F-Sa 4pm-1:30am.

SIGHTS

Music Row, home of Nashville's signature industry, centers around Division and Demonbreun St. from 16th to 19th Ave. S.; bounded to the south by Grand Ave. (take bus #3 to 17th Ave. and walk south). After surviving the mobs outside the must-see **Country Music Hall of Fame,** 4 Music Sq. E. (256-1639), at Division St., you can marvel at classic memorabilia, such as Elvis's "solid gold" Cadillac and 24-karat gold piano, evocative photos from country music's early days, and flashy costumes from more recent performances. *(Hall of Fame open daily 8am-6pm; off-season 9am-5pm. $10.75, ages 6-11 $4.75. Wheelchair access.)* Although Tennessee is the birthplace of bluegrass, the Hall of Fame shows off Cajun, cowboy, Western swing, and honky-tonk styles of country music, as well. Admission includes a tour of RCA's historic Studio B, where stars like Dolly Parton and Chet Atkins—not to mention The King—recorded their early hits. Elvis's evergreen Cadillac and special exhibit cars, like the Batmobile, rests at the **World Famous Car Collectors' Hall of Fame,** 1534 Demonbreun St. (255-6804; open daily 9am-7pm; $5, ages 6-11 $3.25; wheelchair access).

Nashville's pride and joy awaits in **Centennial Park,** a 15min. walk west along West End Ave. from Music Row. The "Athens of the South" boasts a full-scale replica of the **Parthenon** (862-8431), complete with a towering Athena surrounded by pieces of her fellow Olympians. Built as a temporary exhibit for the Tennessee Centennial in 1897, the Parthenon met with such Olympian success that the model was rebuilt to last. The building also houses the **Cowan Collection of American Paintings** in its first floor galleries, a refreshing but erratic selection of 19th- and early 20th-century American art. *(Open Tu-Sa 9am-4:30pm, Su 12:30-4pm; Apr.-Oct. Tu-Su 12:30-4pm. $2.50, seniors and ages 4-17 $1.25. Wheelchair access.)* But soft! what light on yonder Parthenon steps breaks? It's **Shakespeare in the Park,** performed at 7pm (F-Su) in August as part of the annual **Shakespeare Festival** (292-2273; free).

The **Tennessee State Capitol** (741-1621), a comely Greek Revival structure atop the hill on Charlotte Ave. next to downtown, offers, among other things, tours of the tomb of James Knox Polk. *(Tours hourly M-F 9-11am and 1-3pm, Sa-Su self-guided tours only. Free. Wheelchair access.)* Across the street, the **Tennessee State Museum,** 505 Deaderick St. (741-2692), depicts the history of Tennessee from the early Native American era to the time of "overlander" pioneers; interactive displays enhance this sometimes whitewashed version of Tennessee history.

The **Museum of Tobacco Art and History,** 800 Harrison St. (271-2349), off 8th Ave., pays tribute to Tennessee's most important crop. *(Open M-Sa 9am-4pm. Free. Wheelchair access.)* From a dual-purpose Indian pipe/tomahawk (a slow and a quick way to death) to giant glass-blown pipes, the museum's exhibits expound upon the surprisingly captivating history of tobacco, pipes, and cigars.

Fisk University's Van Vechten Gallery (329-8543), at the corner of Jackson St. and D.B. Todd Blvd. off Jefferson St., exhibits a small but distinguished collection of art by Picasso, Renoir, and Cézanne among others. *(Open Tu-F 9am-5pm, Sa 1-4pm. Recommended donation $3.50. Wheelchair access.)* The gallery also displays African sculpture and many works by Alfred Steiglitz and Georgia O'Keeffe.

If you tire of the downtown area, you can rest at the **Cheekwood Museum of Art and Tennessee Botanical Gardens** (356-8000), 7 mi. southwest of town on Forest Park Dr.; take bus #3 "West End/Belle Meade" from downtown to Belle Meade Blvd. and Page Rd. *(Open M-Sa 9am-5pm, Su 11am-5pm; June-Aug. M-Th 9am-8pm, F-Sa 9am-5pm, Su 11am-5pm. $6, students and seniors $5, ages 6-17 $3.)* The leisurely, well-kept Japanese and rose gardens are a welcome change from Nashville glitz and complement the museum's 19th-century art perfectly. The nearby **Belle Meade Mansion,** 5025 Harding Rd. (356-0501), dubbed "The Queen of Tennessee Plantations," offers a second respite. *(Open M-Sa 9am-5pm, Su 1-5pm. $8, seniors $7.50, ages 6-12 $3. 2 guided tours per hr.; last tour 4pm.)* This lavish 1853 plantation was the site of the nation's first thoroughbred breeding farm, and host to eight U.S. presidents, including the 380 lb. Taft, who found himself stuck in the bathtub there.

Andrew Jackson's beautiful manor house, the **Hermitage,** 4580 Rachel's Ln. (889-2941), off Exit 221 from I-40, sits atop 625 gloriously shaded acres 13 mi. from downtown Nashville. *(Open daily 9am-5pm. $9.50, seniors $8.50, ages 6-12 $4.50, families $28;*

AAA discount.) Admission includes a terrific 15min. film, a museum, access to the house and grounds, and a visit to the nearby Tulip Grove Mansion and church.

ENTERTAINMENT AND NIGHTLIFE

The **Grand Ole Opry (GOO)**, 2804 Opryland Dr. (889-6611), the setting for America's longest-running radio show, moved here from the town center in 1976. (Live music F 7:30pm, Sa 6:30 and 9:30pm. $20. Tours F-Sa 11am for $10. Call or write for reservations.) The Friday *Tennessean* contains a list of performers.

During the first weekend in June, the outdoor **Summer Lights downtown,** jams with live rock, jazz, reggae, classical, and country shows (performances M-Th 4pm-12:30am). For info on the **Nashville Symphony,** call **Ticketmaster** (741-2787).

Whether at a corner honky-tonk joint or the GOO, Nashville offers a wealth of opportunities to hear country and Western, jazz, rock, bluegrass, and folk. Comprehensive listings for all live music and events in the area fill the free *Nashville Scene. Bone* has more music info, and *Q (Query)* contains gay and lesbian news and listings.

◉**Wildhorse Saloon,** 120 2nd Ave. N. (251-1000). Huge country dance hall and home of TNN dance show. Bring your cowboy boots and hat for the two-step. Dance lessons every hr. 4-9pm. Cover $3-6 after 5pm. Open daily 11am-2am.

Bluebird Café, 4104 Hillsboro Rd. (383-1461), in Green Hills. This famous bird sings country, blues, and folk; Garth Brooks got his start here. Dinners of salads and sandwiches ($4-6.50) until 11pm. Early show 7pm; cover begins around 9:30pm ($4-10). No cover Su. Open daily 5:30pm until the singing stops.

Lucy's Record Shop, 1707 Church St. (321-0882), vends wicked vinyl during the day to the same young crowd that shows up for indie, national, and local shows at night. Cover $5. All ages welcome.

Red Hot & Blue, 2212 Elliston Pl. (321-0350), off West End. Blues, straight up. Wails F-Sa 9pm-midnight. No cover.

Havana Lounge, 154 2nd Ave. N. (313-7665), near the Wildhorse Saloon, but worlds apart. A popular cigar and martini bar that could be the brainchild of New York City and 50s Cuba. Live jazz and blues most nights. No cover. Open M-Th 11am-2am, F 11am-3am, Sa 5pm-3am.

■ Knoxville

Settled as a frontier outpost in the years after the Revolution and named for Washington's Secretary of War, Henry Knox, the former capital of Tennessee hosted the 1982 World's Fair (which attracted 10 million visitors) and continues to be home to the 26,000 students of the University of Tennessee (UT). A pleasant day-trip from the stunning Smoky Mountains and hemmed by vast lakes created by the Tennessee Valley Authority, Knoxville offers friendly urbanity and a hopping nightlife.

PRACTICAL INFORMATION Downtown stretches north from the **Tennessee River,** bordered by **Henley St.** and the **World's Fair Park** to the west. **Greyhound,** 100 Magnolia Ave. (522-5144 or 800-231-2222), at Central St., sends buses to Nashville (3hr., 7 per day, $21); Chattanooga (2hr., 3 per day, $13); and Lexington (3½hr., 4 per day, $38). Public transportation is provided by **KAT** (637-3000); buses run from 6:15am-6:15pm or later, depending on the route (fare $1, transfers 20¢). Two **free trolley** lines run throughout the city: Blue goes downtown and eastward, while Orange heads downtown and westward to the park and UT (7am-6pm). Across the bridge from the phallic Sunsphere in the park, the **Candy Factory** houses the **Knoxville Visitor's Information Center,** 1060 World's Fair Park Dr. (525-8195; open M-Sa 10am-5pm). **Post Office:** 501 Main Ave. (521-8987; open M-F 8am-4:30pm). **ZIP code:** 37902. **Area code:** 423.

ACCOMMODATIONS, CAMPGROUNDS AND FOOD Many not-quite-budget motels sit along **I-75** and **I-40,** just outside the city. If you're a woman, and they have space, the **YWCA,** 420 W. Clinch St. (523-6126), downtown at Walnut St., won't disappoint (small dorm-style rooms with shared bath $12; call ahead). **Microtel,** 309 N. Peters Rd. (531-8041 or 800-579-1683), off I-75/40 at Exit 278, has admittedly small, but

---

A Grim Reminder of Pax Americana

Created in 1942 with the sole purpose of working on atomic bombs as part of the Manhattan Project, **Oak Ridge** was shrouded in secrecy and fenced in from outsiders. The city, 20 mi. from Knoxville on Rte. 62 or 162, was opened to the public in 1949, 4 years after the bombs wiped out Hiroshima and Nagasaki. The euphemistically named **American Museum of Science and Energy,** 300 S. Tulane Ave. (576-3200), is free and open to the public 9am-5pm. To see the former centers of scientific action, the 12:45pm bus tour (M-F) takes you through a graphite reactor museum to view the first nuclear reactor to operate at full capacity and the once top-secret Y-12 Plant, where the uranium used in the "Little Boy" bomb was produced. The **visitors bureau,** 302 Tulane Ave. (800-887-3429), has declassified tour info (open M-F 9am-5pm, Sa 10am-2pm; Sept.-Apr. M-F 9am-5pm).

---

spotless rooms. A/C, cable, local calls, HBO, and free admission to a nearby gym enlarge its appeal. (Rooms from $38.) A charming replica of an Edinburgh split-level it is not, but the **Scottish Inns,** 301 Callahan Rd. (689-7777), at Exit 110 off I-75, keeps clean rooms well-equipped with A/C, free local calls, cable, HBO, and an outdoor pool (singles from $26; doubles from $36; prices increase by $4 on weekends). **Yogi Bear's Jellystone Park Campground,** 9514 Diggs Gap Rd. (938-6600 or 800-238-9644), at Exit 117 off I-75, is located closer to the city than most other campgrounds. It features a pool, clubhouse, restaurant, and laundry, as well as cartoon cheer. (Primitive sites $15, with moisture and sparks $16, full hookup $20.)

The Strip, the stretch of Cumberland Ave. along campus proper, is lined with student hangouts, bars, and restaurants. **Market Sq.,** a popular pedestrian plaza to the east of World's Fair Park, presents restaurants, fountains, and shade. The other center of chowing, browsing, and carousing, **Old City,** spreads north up Central and Jackson St. Lunch downtown can be a heavenly experience at the **Crescent Moon Café,** 705 Market St. (637-9700), near Gay, with veggie dishes, sandwiches, and daily mashed potato concoctions (lunch about $5; open M-F 11:15am-2:15pm). The everpopular **Calhoun's on the River,** 400 Neyland Dr. (673-3355), claims to serve the "best ribs in America." Customers test that claim ($9.50-16), or devour sandwiches for $6.50-7. (Open M-Th 11am-10:30pm, F-Sa 11am-11pm, Su 11am-10pm.)

SIGHTS World's Fair Park makes for a fine stroll with a reflecting pool, grassy expanses, and a playground. A ride to the top of the **Sunsphere,** in the center of the park, rewards with 360 angles on the city (open M-Th 10am-4pm and F-Sa 10am-6pm). The **Knoxville Museum of Art,** 1050 World's Fair Park Dr. (525-6101), houses changing exhibits of high caliber. *(Open Tu-Th and Sa 10am-5pm, F 10am-9pm, Su noon-5pm. $4, seniors $3, ages 12-17 $2.)* Downtown sits the **Blount Mansion,** 200 W. Hill (525-2375), the 1792 frame house of governor William Blount (pronounced as if there were no "o"—as in "M. Poirot, it seems the victim was struck with a Blount object"). *(Open Tu-Sa 9:30am-5pm, Su 12:30-5pm; Nov.-Feb. Tu-F 9:30am-5pm. $4, ages 6-12 $2. AAA discount. 1hr. tours leave on the hr.; last tour at 4pm.)* Nearby, the **James White Fort,** 205 E. Hill Ave. (525-6514), still preserves portions of the original stockade built in 1786 by Knoxville's first citizen and founder. *(Tours run continuously until 3:30pm. Open M-Sa 9:30am-4:30pm. $4, children $2.)*

Picnickers will appreciate **Krutch Park** (across the street), a tiny, perfectly manicured oasis of green in the midst of downtown. Eighty acres of greenery abound at **Ijams Nature Center,** 2915 Island Home Ave. (577-4717), 2 mi. east of downtown across Gay St. Bridge. *(Grounds open daily 8am-dusk. Museum open M-F 9am-4pm, Sa noon-4pm, Su 1-5pm. Free.)* Knoxville is in full bloom April 9-25, 1999, for the **Dogwood Arts Festival,** featuring food, folks, fun, and a lot of trees (637-4561).

For a taste of down-home Appalachia, visit the **Farmers Market** (524-3276), 15 mi. from downtown on I-640 off Exit 8. *(Open M-Sa 9am-7pm, Su noon-6pm.)* The pavilion peddles local produce, plants, jams and jellies, arts and crafts, ice cream, soft pretzels, and more. The must-see **Museum of Appalachia** (494-7680 or 494-0514) sits 16 mi. north of Knoxville on I-75 at Exit 122 in Norris. *(Open daily dawn-dusk. $6, ages 6-15 $4, families $16; senior and AAA discounts.)* The "museum" is actually a vast village with authentic houses, barns, a school, a spectacular Hall of Fame building replete with a dulcimer exhibit, livestock—even the cabin where Samuel Langhorne Clemens (Mark Twain) was conceived. You can cleanse the aesthetic palate with a trip to **Norris Dam** and the accompanying **Grist Mill;** just east of the museum, exit left onto Rte. 61, then turn left onto Rte. 441 N for about 5 mi.

ENTERTAINMENT AND NIGHTLIFE UT sports some fantastic teams, particularly **football** and the reigning NCAA champion **women's basketball** team. Join in on the action by calling for tickets at 974-2491. In summer, the **Knoxville Smokies** (637-9494), an AA baseball team, hit the field (tickets $4-6).

After any game, take a load off at **Longbranch Saloon,** 1848 Cumberland Ave. (546-9914), on the UT Strip, which offers a casual neighborhood bar atmosphere (no chaps and spurs) and a mellow 20-something crowd (open Su-Th 3pm-3am, F-Sa 6pm-3am). **195*,** 109½ S. Central St. (546-0051), in the middle of Old City, serves up slices of amazing cake ($3.50) in a thick, funky atmosphere (open M-Th 8am-11pm, F 8am-1am, Sa 10am-1am, Su 11am-11pm). **Lucille's,** 106 N. Central St. (546-3742), dishes out jazz (after 10pm $3; open Tu-Su 6pm-2am). **The Underground,** 214 W. Jackson Ave. (525-3675), houses the **Boiler Room,** a dance club that keeps things cooking until the wee hours and hosts a mixed straight/gay crowd. (Underground open M-W and F-Sa 10am-3am; Boiler open Sa-Su 1-6am, with a $3-8 cover.) For goings-on around town, pick up a free copy of *Metro Pulse.*

■ Great Smoky Mountains

The largest wilderness area in the eastern U.S., **Great Smoky Mountains National Park** encompasses 500,000 acres of gray-green Appalachian peaks bounded by misty North Carolina and Tennessee valleys. This park welcomes more visitors per year than any other national park. Bears, wild hogs, groundhogs, wild turkeys, and a handful of red wolves inhabit the area, as well as more than 1500 species of flowering plants. Whispering conifer forests line the mountain ridges at elevations of over 6000 ft. In June and July, rhododendrons burst into their full glory; by mid-October, the sloping mountains become a giant, vibrant quilt of color.

PRACTICAL INFORMATION Start any exploration of the area at either of the park's two **visitors centers:** Sugarlands (436-3255), on Newfound Gap Rd. 2 mi. south of Gatlinburg, TN, next to the park's headquarters; or Oconaluftee (828-497-1900), 4 mi. north of Cherokee, NC. Be sure to ask for *The Smokies Guide* (25¢), which details the park's tours, lectures, activities, and changing natural graces (both open daily 8am-7pm; off-season 8am-4:30pm). The centers' and park's **info line** is 436-1200 (operates daily 8:30am-4:30pm). To get to and from Knoxville, contact **ETHRA** (428-1795; $3-5; 8am-3pm; give 24hr. notice). **Area code:** 423.

GRUB 'N' SLUMBER Ten **campgrounds** lie scattered throughout the park, each with tent sites, limited trailer space, water, and bathrooms (no showers or hookups). **Smokemont, Elkmont,** and **Cades Cove** accept reservations from mid-May to late October (sites $12-15, reservation fee $3); the rest are first come, first served (sites $10-12). In summer, smart campers reserve spots near the main roads at least 8 weeks in advance (800-365-2267). **Backcountry camping** is available by reservation only (436-1231).

Motels lining **Rte. 441** and **Rte. 321** decrease in price with distance from the park. Small motels also cluster in both **Cherokee** and **Gatlinburg.** Prices vary wildly depending on the season and the economy. In general, Cherokee motels are cheaper (from $35) and Gatlinburg motels are nicer (from $45); prices soar to even greater heights on weekends. But fear not, brave heart: two hostels service the park. **Smoky Mountain Ranch Camp (HI-AYH),** 3248 Manis Rd. (429-8563 or 877-357-1857), a terrific hostel, nestles in the mountains, 10 mi. southwest of Pigeon Forge and 6 mi. northeast of Cades Cove just off Rte. 321. Crash at the top of the hill in the comfortable dorm with A/C, cable TV, kitchen, and a kicking stereo. Huge bonfires and a live goat entertain guests. ($14, nonmembers $15; *Let's Go* and senior discounts. Linen

$1. Work can be exchanged for partial payment. Pick-up from Knoxville $25, from Pigeon Forge free.) Closer to Gatlinburg is **Bell's Wa-Floy Retreat**, 3610 East Pkwy. (423-436-5575), 10 mi. east of Gatlinburg on Rte. 321. From Gatlinburg proper, catch the eastbound trolley (25¢) to the end of the line; from there, hop, skip, or jump the 5 mi. to Wa-Floy. This Christian retreat community envelops a pool, tennis courts, and meditation area. (Check-in before 10pm. HI-AYH $10, nonmembers $15. Linen included for nonmembers. Reservations required.)

Authentic Tennessee cookin' oozes from **Smokin' Joe's Bar-B-Que**, 8215 State Hwy. 73 (448-3212), Townsend, just outside of the park near the Ranch Camp hostel. With succulent, slow-cooked meats; sauces whose spices range from mild to smoke; and fresh, homemade side dishes like potato salad and BBQ beans, Joe's smokes the competition. (Dinners with 2 sides, meat, and bread $6.50-11; sandwiches $2-4. Open M-Th 11am-9pm, F-Sa 11am-10pm; Apr.-Oct. also Su 11am-8pm.)

SIGHTS AND ACTIVITIES Over 900 mi. of hiking trails and 170 mi. of road meander through the park. Rangers at the visitors centers will help you devise a trip appropriate for your ability. Some of the most popular trails wind 5 mi. to Rainbow Falls, 4 mi. to Chimney Tops, and 2½ mi. to Laurel Falls. To hike off the marked trails, you'll need a free **backcountry camping permit** from a visitors center. Wherever you go, bring water and don't feed the bears. For gorgeous scenery without the sweat, drive the 11 mi. **Cades Cove loop** (closed to car traffic early Mary to late Sept. on W and Sa from sunrise-10am), which circles the vestiges of a mountain community that occupied the area from the 1850s to the 1920s, before the park took over. If you get tired of walking the trails, **bikes** can be rented for $3.25 per hr. at Cades Cove (448-9034), in the campground, across from the ranger station. You can also rent **horses** from the stables (448-6286; both open Su-Tu and Th-F 9am-7pm, W and Sa 7am-7pm). **Mountain Farm Museum,** right next to the Oconaluftee center, re-creates a turn-of-the-century settlement, including a blacksmith shop and a corncrib (both sights free). Less crowded but equally scenic areas include **Cosby** and **Cataloochee,** both on the eastern edge of the park.

Mountains of Fun

A mythical American village created by Dolly Parton in the Tennessee hills, **Dollywood,** 1020 Dollywood Ln. (428-9488 or 800-365-5996), dominates Pigeon Forge. The park celebrates the cultural legacy of the East Tennessee mountains and the country songmistress herself, famous for some mountainous topography of her own. *(Open May-Dec. daily, most days 10am-6pm; July 9am-9pm; but hrs. change constantly. $28, over 59 $23, ages 4-11 $20; discount coupons available at tourist centers, restaurants, and motels.)* In Dolly's world, craftspeople demonstrate their skills and sell their wares, 30 rides offer thrills and chills, and country favorites perform. While Dolly asserts that she wants to preserve the culture of the Tennessee Mountains, she also seems to want you to pay to come again—Dollywood's motto is "Create Memories Worth Repeating."

■ Near Smoky Mountains: Cherokee Reservation

The **Cherokee Indian Reservation** (800-438-1601), on the southeast border of the national park, features a number of museums, shops, attractions, and the requisite casino. From May to October, the reservation offers a guided tour of the **Ocunaluftee Indian Village,** a re-created mid-18th-century Native American village ($10, ages 6-13 $5). Enjoy a slice of history and contemporary Cherokee culture at the **Museum of the Cherokee Indian** (828-497-3481), on Drama Rd. off Rte. 441, where you can hear the Cherokee language spoken and view artifacts and films (open daily 9am-8pm; Sept. to mid-June 9am-5pm; $6, under 13 $4). **"Unto these Hills,"** an outdoor drama, retells the story of the Cherokees and climaxes with a moving re-enactment of the Trail of Tears (June-July M-Sa 8:45pm; Aug. M-Sa 8pm; $11, under 12 $5). The **Cherokee Visitors Center** (800-438-1601) welcomes visitors on Rte. 441 (open M-F 8am-7pm, Sa 9am-7pm, Su 9am-5pm).

The **Nantahala Outdoor Center (NOC),** 13077 U.S. 19 W (800-232-7238 or 704-488-2175), 13 mi. southwest of Bryson City, NC, and just south of GSM Park, beckons with cheap beds, three restaurants, and the great outdoors (bunks in simple cabins; showers, kitchen, laundry facilities; $12; call ahead). The NOC's **whitewater rafting expeditions** are pricey, but you can rent your own raft for a trip down the Nantahala River. (Rafts Su-F $17, Sa $22; 1-person inflatable "duckies" M-F $27, Sa $30. Group rates available. Higher prices July-Aug. Prices include transportation to site and all necessary equipment.) The NOC also offers trips with slightly higher price tags on the Ocoee, Nolichucky, Chattooga, and French Broad Rivers. If the rivers aren't your thing, you can hike a thousandth of the 2144 mi. **Appalachian Trail,** or try a **mountain bike** from $25; the NOC staff can assist if you need help planning a daytrip.

■ Chattanooga

A bustling city, tucked into a nook on the Tennessee River, Chattanooga cultivates more than its choo-choo image. The city, begun as a trading post in 1815, has kept its commercial tradition, evolving into a major factory outlet center and cashing in on its unique natural attractions. Chattanooga's real appeal is its high quotient of the adorable, from the cultivated riverwalk to the Bluff arts district to Lookout Mountain, which marks the southern edge of both the city and the Appalachian chain.

The biggest catch in town is the **Tennessee Aquarium** (800-322-3344), on Ross's Landing, with the largest turtle collection in the world, as well as 7000 other animals. After the big tanks, check out the big IMAX screen. (Open M-Th 10am-6pm, F-Su 10am-8pm; Oct.-Apr. daily 10am-6pm. $11, ages 3-12 $6; IMAX film $7/$5; for both $15/$9.) The riverwalk pathway connects the aquarium with the **Bluff Art District,** anchored by the **Hunter Museum of Art,** 10 Bluff View (267-0968), which houses the South's most complete American art collection and impressive traveling exhibits. (Open Tu-Sa 10am-4:30pm, Su 1-4:30pm. $5, students $3, seniors $4, ages 3-11 $2.50. Wheelchair access.) The eclectic works of the **River Gallery,** 400 E. 2nd St. (267-7353), across the street, flood the senses (open M-W 10am-5pm, Th-Sa 10am-7pm, Su 1-5pm; free). A free **shuttle** scuttles from the **Chattanooga Choo Choo Holiday Inn** to the aquarium, with stops on every block (runs daily 7am-9:30pm). The riverfront is shut down for 9 nights in mid-June for the **Riverbend Festival** (265-4112), featuring four stages of live music and the South's largest block party, **"The Bessie Smith Strut,"** on Monday night ($20 lets you do it all).

Shops and restaurants commemorate Chattanooga's choo-choo fame in the old terminal on S. Market St. downtown, between 14th and Main. These days, more contemporary attractions are more, well, attractive. The **Incline** ($8, ages 3-12 $4) takes passengers up a ridiculous 72.7° grade to **Lookout Mountain** (take S. Broad or bus #15 or 31 and follow signs), where six states can be seen on a clear day (open 8:30am-9:15pm; Sept.-May 9am-5:15pm; wheelchair access.) The highest view peaks at **Rock City Gardens** (706-820-2531), where the boulders, flowers, and tacky shops attract families and hardcore aficionados of kitsch. (Open daily 8am-sunset; early Sept. to late May 8:30am-sunset. $10, ages 3-12 $5.50.) One thousand feet inside the mountain, the **Ruby Falls** (821-2544) cavern formations and a 145 ft. waterfall—complete with colored lights and sound effects—add a little Disney-style pizzazz to a day of sightseeing. (Open daily 8am-9pm; early Sept. to Oct. and Apr. to late May 8am-8pm; Nov.-Mar. 8am-6pm. $9, ages 6-12 $4.50. 1hr. tour.) Free music rings every Friday (8pm) at the **Mountain Opry,** atop nearby Signal Mountain.

Budget motels congregate on the highways coming into the city and on **Broad St.** at the base of Lookout Mountain. **Holiday Trav-l-Park,** 1709 Mack Smith Rd. (706-891-9766 or 800-693-2877), in Rossville ½ mi. off I-75 at the East Ridge Exit, enlivens sites for tents and RVs with a Civil War theme. (Laundry. 2-person site $15.50, with water and electricity $19.50, full hookup $21.50; cabins $32, $2 per additional person.) Two nearby lakes, **Chickamauga** and **Nickajack,** are surrounded by campgrounds. The **Pickle Barrel,** 1012 Market St. (266-1103), downtown, moves beyond former cucumbers with scrumptious sandwiches ($3-6) and filling dinners for $7-12 (open M-Sa 11am-3am, Su noon-3am). Closer to Lookout Mountain, you can feast on

---

Gentleman Jack

Tucked into the southern Tennessee countryside, on Rte. 55 in Lynchburg, miles and miles from a major city, the **Jack Daniels Distillery** (931-759-6183) churns and bubbles, transforming pure spring water and grain into the famous all-American liquor. *(Open daily 8am-4pm. Wheelchair access.)* Free tours of the distillery cover storage facilities where the air is thick with whiskey; too many deep breaths could send you stumbling through the distillation buildings and Mr. Daniels' original office. The end of the tour lands you in a gift shop, where you can buy the final product, but employees must warn you against opening your new-bought treasure. Ironically, Moore County, where Jack Daniels resides, is "dry." Your tour guide will, however, offer you "yellow label" or "brown label," a.k.a. lemonade or coffee. And you could always ask for another pass through the barrel room...

---

standard Mexican fare at **Cancun,** 1809 Broad (266-1461). Lunches go for $3-6, dinner $5-10, and great *flan* to top it all off costs $1.75. (Open M-Th 11am-10pm, F 11am-10:30pm, Sa noon-10:30pm, Su noon-10pm.)

Chattanooga straddles the Tennessee/Georgia border at the junction of I-24/59 and I-75. The space-age **visitors center,** 2 Broad St. (266-7070 or 800-322-3344), next to the aquarium, dispenses tickets to many area sights (open daily 8:30am-5:30pm). **Greyhound,** 960 Airport Rd. (892-8814 or 800-231-2222; station open 6:30am-2am), runs buses to Atlanta (1hr., 8 per day, $18); Nashville (3-4hr., 3 per day, $14); and Knoxville (2hr., 3 per day, $18). **Chattanooga Area Transportation Authority (CARTA)** (629-1473) runs buses throughout the city 5am-11pm (fare $1, transfers 20¢, children 50¢/10¢). The **post office** (899-1198) sorts it out on Georgia Ave. between Martin Luther King Blvd. and 10th St. (open M-F 7:30am-7:30pm, Sa 8:30am-12:30pm). **ZIP code:** 37402. **Area code:** 423.

■ Memphis

In 1912, a Memphis musician named W.C. Handy shocked the music world with his 12-bar blues. Decades later, Elvis Presley shocked the world with his gyrating pelvis and amazingly versatile voice. Although the King may be dead (we think?), his image lives on throughout the city. Every year, roadtrippers from around the country make a pilgrimage to the hub of tackiness—Graceland, Elvis's former home.

ORIENTATION AND PRACTICAL INFORMATION

Downtown, named avenues run east-west and numbered ones north-south. **Madison Ave.** divides north and south addresses. Two main thoroughfares, **Poplar** and **Union Ave.,** pierce the heart of the city from the east; **2nd** and **3rd St.** arrive from the south. **I-240** and **I-55** encircle the city. **Bellevue** becomes **Elvis Presley Blvd.** and leads you straight to Graceland. If you're traveling by car, take advantage of the free, unmetered parking along the river.

Airport: Memphis International, 2491 Winchester Rd. (922-8000), south of the southern loop of I-240. Taxi fare to the city $20—negotiate in advance. Hotel express **shuttles** (522-9229) cost $10 (service 8am-5pm). Public transport to and from the airport $1.10; service is sporadic and the trip can be confusing for a traveler unfamiliar with the area.

Trains: Amtrak, 545 S. Main St. (526-0052 or 800-872-7245), at Calhoun on the southern edge of downtown. *Take a taxi—the surrounding area is very unsafe even during the day.* To: New Orleans (8½hr., 1 per day, $39-78); Chicago (10½hr., 1 per day, $73-102); and Jackson (4hr., 1 per day, $28-55).

Buses: Greyhound, 203 Union Ave. (523-1184 or 800-231-2222), at 4th St. downtown. *The area is unsafe at night.* To: Nashville (4hr., 9 per day, $26); Chattanooga (6-9hr., 3 per day, $34); and Jackson (4-6hr., 6 per day, $28). Open 24hr.

Public Transportation: Memphis Area Transit Authority (MATA) (274-6282), corner of Union Ave. and Main St. Bus routes cover most suburbs but run infrequently. The major downtown stops are at the intersections of Front and Jefferson

St., and 2nd St. and Madison Ave.; the major routes run on Front, 2nd, and 3rd St. Buses run M-F from 7am, Sa-Su from 10am. Buses stop running between 6pm and 11pm, depending on the route. Fare $1.10, transfers 10¢. Refurbished 19th-century **trolley cars** (run by MATA) cruise Main St. M-Th 6am-midnight, F 6am-1am, Sa 9:30am-1am, Su 10am-6pm, and roll along the Riverfront M-Th 6:30am-midnight, F 6:30am-1am, Sa 9:30am-1am, Su 10am-6pm. 50¢. 1-day pass $2, 3-day $5.

Taxis: In taxi-deprived Memphis, expect a long wait. **City Wide,** 324-4202. **Yellow Cab,** 577-7777. $1.50 1st mi., $1.40 per additional mi. Both 24hr.

Visitor Info: Visitor Information Center, 119 Riverside Dr. (543-5333), at Jefferson St. Open M-Sa 9am-6pm, Su noon-6pm; Nov.-Mar. M-Sa 9am-5pm. The uniformed **blue suede brigade** roaming the city will happily give you directions or answer questions—just stay off of their blue suede shoes.

Help Lines: Crisis Line, 577-9400. **Gay/Lesbian Switchboard,** 324-4297. Operates daily 7:30-11pm. **HIV/AIDS Switchboard,** 278-2437.

Hospital: Baptist Memorial Hospital, 899 Madison Ave. (227-2727). **Memphis Area Medical Center for Women,** 29 S. Bellevue Blvd. (24hr. hotline 542-3809).

Time Zone: Central (1hr. behind Eastern).

Post Office: 555 S. 3rd St. (521-2187). Open M-F 8:30am-5:30pm, Sa 10am-2pm. **ZIP code:** 38101. **Area code:** 901.

SINCE M'BABY LEFT ME, I FOUND A NEW PLACE T'DWELL

Memphis offers a hostel and not much else. A few downtown motels have prices in the budget range; otherwise, more distant lodgings are available near Graceland at **Elvis Presley Blvd.** and **Brooks Rd.** For the celebrations of Elvis's historic birth (Jan. 8) and death (Aug. 15), as well as for the Memphis in May festival, book 6 months to 1 year in advance. The visitors center has a thorough listing of lodgings.

Lowenstein-Long House/Castle Hostelry (AAIH/Rucksackers), 217 N. Waldran Blvd. (527-7174), parking lot at 1084 Poplar. Take bus #50 from 3rd St. Convenient location, but the sketchy neighborhood makes lodging here a drawback for those without cars. The house rises out of its dilapidated surroundings with sheer Victorian elegance and mystery. Women's rooms on the 3rd fl. are pleasant and homey; men's rooms out back are less inviting—you may want to consider the private room option. $12; stay 3 nights, get 1 free. Private doubles $33. Camping on lawn out back, $6 per person; includes access to kitchen and bath. Work (when available) can be exchanged for price of stay. Linen $2. Towels $1. Key deposit $20. Reception daily 9-11am and 5-9pm.

Red Roof Inn Memphis Medical Center, 210 S. Pauline St. (528-0650), near Union Ave. Pricey, but convenient to downtown with sparkly clean rooms. Cable, A/C, free local calls, complimentary coffee, and newspaper. Singles $45; doubles $55.

Motel 6, 1117 E. Brooks Rd. (346-0992), near the intersection of Elvis and Brooks Rd., close to Graceland. HBO, pool, and small, clean rooms with stall showers, A/C, and free local calls. $36; 2 adults $42, $3 per additional adult.

Memphis/Graceland KOA, 3691 Elvis Presley Blvd. (396-7125), right next door to Graceland with pool and laundry. The location makes up for the lack of trees and privacy. Sites $19, with hookup $25; cabins with A/C $33.

Memphis South Campground, 460 Byhalia Rd. (601-429-1818), Hernando, MS, 20 mi. south of Memphis, at Exit 280 off I-55 in Mississippi. Turn right at the end of the ramp, then right at the first set of lights onto Mt. Pleasant Rd. A relaxing, green spot with a pool, and laundry. Tent sites $12, with water and wattage $15, full hookup $17; $2 per additional person. Office open daily 8-10am and 4:30-7:30pm.

MEALS FIT FOR THE KING

In Memphis, barbecue is as common as rhinestone-studded jumpsuits; the city even hosts the **World Championship Barbecue Cooking Contest** in May. But don't fret if gnawing on ribs isn't your thing—Memphis has plenty of other Southern-style restaurants with down-home favorites like fried chicken, catfish, chitterlings, and grits.

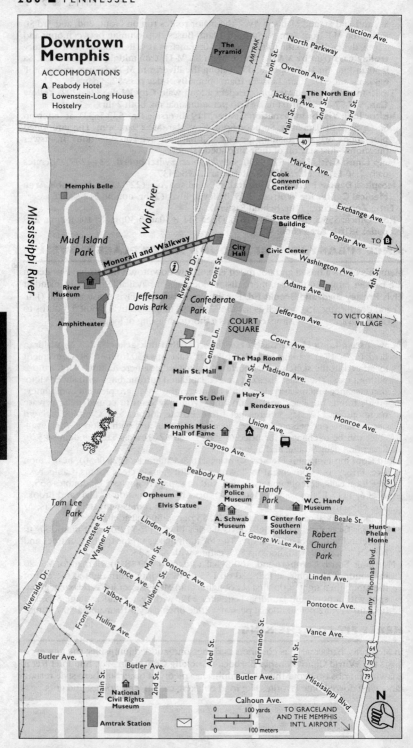

Downtown Memphis

ACCOMMODATIONS

A Peabody Hotel
B Lowenstein-Long House Hostelry

The Pyramid

AMTRAK

Auction Ave.

North Parkway

Overton Ave.

Front St.

Jackson Ave.

The North End

Main St.

2nd St.

3rd St.

40

Market Ave.

Cook Convention Center

Exchange Ave.

State Office Building

Poplar Ave.

TO B

Memphis Belle

Wolf River

Mud Island Park

Monorail and Walkway

City Hall

Civic Center

Washington Ave.

4th St.

Mississippi River

River Museum

Riverside Dr.

Front St.

Adams Ave.

Amphitheater

Jefferson Davis Park

Confederate Park

COURT SQUARE

Jefferson Ave.

TO VICTORIAN VILLAGE

Court Ave.

Center Ln.

The Map Room

Madison Ave.

Main St. Mall

2nd St.

Front St. Deli

Huey's

Rendezvous

Monroe Ave.

Memphis Music Hall of Fame

Union Ave.

A

Gayoso Ave.

51

Peabody Pl.

Beale St.

Memphis Police Museum

Handy Park

Orpheum

4th St.

Elvis Statue

W.C. Handy Museum

Tom Lee Park

A. Schwab Museum

Center for Southern Folklore

Beale St.

Hunt-Phelan Home

Lt. George W. Lee Ave.

Linden Ave.

Robert Church Park

Tennessee St.

Wagner St.

Linden Ave.

Vance Ave.

Main St.

Pontotoc Ave.

Linden Ave.

Danny Thomas Blvd.

Riverside Dr.

Talbot Ave.

Mulberry St.

Pontotoc Ave.

Front St.

Huling Ave.

Vance Ave.

64

Butler Ave.

70

Abel St.

Hernando St.

4th St.

79

Main St.

Butler Ave.

2nd St.

Butler Ave.

Mississippi Blvd.

National Civil Rights Museum

Calhoun Ave.

0   100 yards

TO GRACELAND AND THE MEMPHIS INT'L AIRPORT

Amtrak Station

0   100 meters

N

⊛**Rendezvous** (523-2746), Downtown Alley, between the Holiday Inn and Days Inn. A Memphis legend, serving large portions of ribs ($12-14) and cheaper sandwiches ($3-6), but be prepared to wait an hour. Open Tu-Th 4:30pm-11:30pm, F-Sa noon-midnight.

The Map Room, 2 S. Main St. (579-9924), where everything seems to move in delightfully slow motion. Business folk, travelers, and neo-hippies lounge on the sofas to read loaned books and sip "lateas" ($3.25). Sandwiches like pimento-and-cheese ($3.50), which are constructed on thick slices of warm, homemade bread, are a respite from Memphis's otherwise meaty options. Open M-Sa 24hr.

The North End, 346 N. Main St. (526-0319 or 527-3663), at Jackson St. downtown, specializes in tamales, wild rice, stuffed potatoes, and creole dishes ($3-8). The orgasmic hot fudge pie is known as "sex on a plate" ($3.65). Happy hour daily 4-7pm. Live music starts at 10pm Tu-Sa; cover $2. Open daily 11am-3am.

Huey's, 77 S. Second St. (527-2700) downtown, and at 1927 Madison Ave., 2858 Hickory Hill Rd., and 1771 N. Germantown Pkwy. Voted the best burgers ($3.40) in Memphis for over 10 years running. Add your name to the crowded wall while you wait for the dripping quarter-pounder. Open M-Th 11am-2am, F 11am-3am, Sa 11:30am-3am, Su noon-3am.

Corky's, 5259 Poplar Ave. (684-9744), about 25min. from downtown (bus #50 "Poplar"). Nationally famous BBQ is justifiably popular with the locals. Top-notch BBQ dinner and ribs served with baked beans, cole slaw, and bread ($6-9). Scrumptious pies and cobbler. Arrive early and expect to wait, or use the drive-thru. Open Su-Th 10:45am-10pm, F-Sa 10:45am-10:30pm.

P and H Café, 1532 Madison Ave. (726-0906). The initials aptly stand for Poor and Hungry. The self-proclaimed "beer joint of your dreams" serves burgers and grill food ($2-5) to students and locals. But although the patty melt with grilled onions ($3) might take away your moody blues, the friendly waitresses—especially the owner Wanda—are the real draw. During Death Week in August, P and H hosts the infamous "Dead Elvis Ball." Open M-F 11am-3am, Sa 5pm-3am.

Front St. Delicatessen, 77 S. Front St. (522-8943), at Union. A lunchtime streetside deli in the heart of downtown, as seen in *The Firm*. Sandwiches $2.75-4. Open M-Th 7am-3pm, F 7am-8pm, Sa 11am-3pm.

MEMPHIS MUSIC AND MARVELS

Elvis Sightings: Graceland

You'll laugh. You'll cry. You'll want to see it again and again. Bow down before **Graceland,** 3763 Elvis Presley Blvd. (332-3322 or 800-238-2000), **Elvis Presley's** home and the paragon of Americana that every Memphis visitor must see. *(Expect to wait 1-2hr. on summer weekends. Ticket office open 8am-6pm; early Sept. to late May 9am-5pm; Nov.-Feb. mansion tour closed Tu. Attractions remain open 2hr. after ticket office closes. $10, seniors $9, ages 7-12 $5.)* Take I-55 S to Exit 5B or bus #13 "Lauderdale." Unfortunately, any desire to learn about the man, share his dream, or feel his music requires the ability to transcend the mansion's crowd-control methods and audio-tape tour, to reach beyond the tacky commercialism and ignore the employees who seem to adhere to the saying "Taking Care of Business in a Flash." Still, you'll never forget the mirrored ceilings, carpeted walls, and yellow-and-orange decor of Elvis's 1974 renovations. By tour's end, even those who aren't die-hard Elvis fans may be genuinely moved. Be sure to gawk audibly at the **Trophy Building,** where hundreds of gold and platinum records line the wall. The King and his court are buried next door in the **Meditation Gardens,** where you can seek enlightenment while reciting a mantra to the tune of "You're So Square."

If you love him tender, love him true—visit several Elvis museums, and several more Elvis souvenir shops. The **Elvis Presley Automobile Museum** houses a score of pink and purple **Elvis-mobiles** in a huge hall, while an indoor drive-in movie theater shows clips from 31 Elvis movies ($5, seniors $4.50, ages 7-12 $2.75). A free 20min. film, *Walk a Mile in My Shoes*, with performance footage, contrasts the early (slim) years with the later ones (screened every 30min.). **Elvis Airplanes** features the two Elvis planes: the *Lisa Marie* (named for Elvis's daughter) complete with blue suede bed and FAA required seatbelt (gold-plated), and the tiny *Hound Dog II* Jetstar ($4.50, seniors $4.05, children $2.75). The **Sincerely Elvis** exhibit glimpses into

Elvis's private side; see the books he read, the shirts he wore, the TVs he shot, and home movies with his wife Priscilla ($3.50, seniors $3.15, children $2.25). The **Platinum Tour Package** discounts admission to the mansion and all attractions ($18.50, seniors $16.65, ages 7-12 $11). All have wheelchair access except the airplanes and two rooms in the mansion tour.

Every year on the week of August 15 (the date of Elvis's death), millions of the King's cortege get all shook up for **Elvis Week,** an extended celebration that includes a pilgrimage to his junior high school and a candlelight vigil. The days surrounding his birthday (Jan. 8) also see some Kingly activities.

Elvis Who? The Blues, B.B. King, and more...

Long before Sam Phillips and Sun Studio produced Elvis, Jerry Lee Lewis, U2, and Bonnie Raitt, historic Beale St. saw the invention of the blues. The **W.C. Handy Home and Museum,** 352 Beale St. (522-1556), exhibits the music and photographs of the man, the myth, the legend who first put a blues melody to paper (open M-Sa 10am-5pm, Su 1-5pm; $2, students $1). The **Center for Southern Folklore,** 209 Beale St. (525-3655, music info line 525-3656), documents various aspects of music history, including a tribute to Memphis's WDIA, the first radio station in the nation to only play music performed by black artists. *(Live bands almost every summer night; cover $2-5. Center open M-W 10am-10pm, Th 10am-11pm, F-Sa 10am-1am, Su 11am-10pm. Exhibits free. Wheelchair access.)* Notables like B.B. King and Rufus Thomas began their musical careers on these airwaves. The center can give you info on the **Music and Heritage Festival** (525-3655), which fills Beale St. during Labor Day weekend. *(Open 11am-11pm. Free.)* Gospel, country, blues, and jazz accompany dance troupes and craft booths. Some booths offer oral histories on everything from life on the Mississippi to playing in segregated baseball leagues. Of course, Memphis music history includes the soul hits of the Stax label and rockers like Big Star as well as the blues. The **Memphis Music Hall of Fame,** 97 S. 2nd St. (525-4007), features the careers of local legends like Roy Orbison, Elvis, W.C. Handy, and Issac Hayes of *Shaft* fame. *(Open Su-Th 10am-6pm, F-Sa 10am-9pm. $7.50, ages 7-14 $2.50. Wheelchair access.)* **Sun Studio,** 706 Union Ave. (521-0664), shows off the city's rock 'n' roll roots in the tiny recording studio where Elvis was discovered, Jerry Lee Lewis was consumed by great balls of fire, and Carl Perkins warned everyone to stay off of his blue suede shoes. *(30min. tours every hr. on the ½hr. Open daily 9am-7pm; Oct.-Apr. 10am-6pm. $8.50, under 13 free. Wheelchair access.)* Memphis is also the home of soul music legend **Al Green's Full Gospel Tabernacle,** 787 Beale St. (396-9192), where Sunday services display powerful music, dancing, speaking in tongues, and even exorcisms (services Su 11am-2:30pm; arriving late and leaving early is bad form).

...and still more: Civil Rights, Mud, and Miscellany

The **National Civil Rights Museum** is housed at the site of Martin Luther King, Jr.'s assassination at the **Lorraine Motel,** 450 Mulberry St. (521-9699), at Calhoun St. *(Open M-Sa 9am-6pm, Su 1-6pm; Sept.-May M-Sa 9am-5pm, Su 1-5pm. $6, students with ID and seniors $5, ages 4-17 $4; free M 3-5pm. Wheelchair access.)* Historical documents, graphic photographs of lynching victims, and films chronicle the key events of the Civil Rights Movement in fair and informative displays, without losing the emotion.

Mud Island, 125 Front St. (576-7241 or 800-507-6507), a quick monorail ride over the picturesque Mississippi, has it all: a museum, the renowned World War II B-17 *Memphis Belle,* and a 5-block scale model of the Mississippi River that you can splash in or stroll along. **Free tours** of the Riverwalk and Memphis Belle run several times daily. Summer Thursdays from noon to 1pm on the island are free, featuring some live music. *(Open daily 10am-7pm; early Sept. to late May 9am-4pm. $4, seniors and ages 4-11 $3. Parking $3.)* At the **Mississippi River Museum** (576-7241), also on the river, spy on a Union ironclad gunboat from the Confederate bluff lookout, or relax to the blues in the cafe display ($4, seniors and ages 4-11 $3; wheelchair access).

On the waterfront, you won't miss the 32-story, 6-acre **Great American Pyramid,** 1 Auction Ave. (526-5177), off Front St., which houses a 20,000-seat arena. *(Open M-Sa 10am-4pm, Su noon-5pm; tours usually on the hr. $4, seniors and under 13 $3.*

Driving That Train: A Journey in Three Acts

Act I. On the night of April 29, 1900, Jonathan Jones, known to history as "Casey," pulled engine 638 into the Memphis depot right on time. This was an ordinary feat for Casey, who had quickly earned a reputation for punctuality on the rails since his first passenger run only 60 days before. Thus, it had come as a small surprise to the Station Master in Memphis that Casey, ever wise to improving his record of timeliness and in need of some extra cash, offered his services to replace the sick-listed engineer of the late-running New Orleans Special. By the time Casey and his fireman, Jim Webb, finally kicked the New Orleans engine #382 out of the station, the train was already 95min. behind schedule.

Act II. In that particular engine and on that particular track gauge, speeds for the route usually ran about 35 mph, but the determined Casey opened the throttle at over 70 mph, reportedly saying "the old lady's got her high-heeled slippers on tonight." Unfortunately, as the "old lady" danced down through Tennessee, trouble was brewing in Mississippi. At Vaughn, an airhose had broken, locking several cars on the track. Even worse, a dense fog had set in. When Jim finally caught sight of the brake lights at Vaughn, little time was left to act. Jim jumped to save himself, but Casey held on, closing the throttle, throwing the brakes, and thrusting the train into reverse.

Act III. Casey's actions brought the train down to 25 mph, but in the collision he was thrown from the engine to his death. For his heroism, which prevented anyone else from being hurt, the young man from Cayce, KY was honored with a ballad by a black engine-wiper named Wallace Saunders. In that song, and in the songs which have followed—most famously that of the Grateful Dead—Casey Jones continues to drive that train. He is a lasting image of the railroads and a true Tennessee hero.

Wheelchair access.) Tours cover the "Entertainment Hallway" and a University of Memphis basketball locker room.

The four seamlessly connected buildings of the **Brooks Museum of Art,** 1934 Poplar Ave. (722-3500), in the southwest corner of Overton Park, showcase artwork as diverse as its architecture. *(Open Tu-F 9am-4pm, W also 5-8pm, Sa 9am-5pm, Su 11:30am-5pm. $5, seniors $4, students $2; W free. Wheelchair access.)*

A. Schwab, 163 Beale St. (523-9782), a small department store run by the same family since 1876, still offers old-fashioned bargains. *(Open M-Sa 9am-5pm. Free guided tours upon request.)* A "museum" of relics-never-sold gathers dust on the mezzanine floor, including an array of voodoo potions, elixirs, and powders. Elvis bought some of his flashier ensembles here. Next door on Beale St., the **Memphis Police Museum** (525-9800) summons visitors to gawk at 150 years' worth of confiscated drugs, homemade weapons, and officer uniforms (open 24hr.; free; wheelchair access).

Memphis is home to a few tastefully ornate houses, including the recently opened **Hunt-Phelan Home,** 533 Beale St. (344-3166 or 800-350-9009). This lavish antebellum Southern mansion, once visited by Jefferson Davis and soon after captured by Ulysses S. Grant, is worth visiting despite the Gracelandesque audio tour. *(Open M-Sa 10am-4pm, Su noon-4pm; early Sept. to late May Th-M 10am-4pm, Su noon-4pm. $10, students and seniors $9, ages 5-12 $6. Wheelchair access.)* **Victorian Village** consists of 18 mansions in various stages of restoration and preservation. **Mallory-Neeley House,** 652 Adams Ave. (523-1484), is open to the public and was built in the mid-19th century. *(Open Mar.-Dec. Tu-Sa 10am-4pm, Su 1-4pm. $5, students $3, seniors $4, under 5 free. 40min. tour. Last tour 3:30pm. Limited wheelchair access.)* Most of its original furniture remains intact for visitors to see. French Victorian architecture and an antique/textile collection live on in **Woodruff-Fontaine House,** 680 Adams Ave. (526-1469; open M and W-Sa 10am-4pm, Su 1-4pm; $5, students $3, seniors $4).

The **Pink Palace Museum and Planetarium,** 3050 Central Ave. (320-6320); which is, by the way, gray; details the natural history of the mid-South and expounds upon the development of Memphis. Check out the sharp and sparkling crystal and mineral collection or experience vertigo in the IMAX theater. *(Open in summer M-W 9am-5pm, Th 9am-9pm, F-Sa 9am-10pm, Su noon-5pm; off-season M-W 9am-4pm, Th 9am-8pm, F-Sa*

Aquaccommodations

William Faulkner once said of Memphis that "the Delta meets in the lobby of the **Peabody Hotel**," 149 Union Ave. (529-4000), in the heart of downtown. Every day at 11am and 5pm, the hotel rolls out the red carpet, and the ducks that live in its indoor fountain waddle about the premises to a piano accompaniment.

9am-9pm, Su noon-5pm. $6, seniors $5.50, ages 3-12 $4.50; IMAX film $6/$5.50/$4.50; planetarium show $3.50/$3/$3. Call for IMAX times. Wheelchair access.) Memphis has almost as many parks as museums, each offering a slightly different natural setting. Brilliant wildflowers and a marvelous heinz of roses (57 varieties) bloom and grow forever at the **Memphis Botanical Garden,** 750 Cherry Rd. (685-1566), in Audubon Park off Park Ave. *(Open M-Sa 9am-6pm, Su 11am-6pm; Nov.-Feb. M-Sa 9am-4:30pm, Su 11am-4:30pm. $2, students and ages 6-17 $1, seniors $1.50.)* Across the street, the **Dixon Galleries and Garden,** 4339 Park Ave. (761-2409), flaunts its manicured landscape and a collection of European art which includes works by Renoir, Degas, and Monet. *(Open Tu-Sa 10am-5pm, Su 1-5pm. $5, students $3, seniors $4, ages 1-12 $1. On M, only the gardens are open; admission is ½-price.)* **Lichterman Nature Center,** 5992 Quince Rd. (767-7322), is a 65-acre wildscape with forests, wildlife, and a picnic area (open Tu-Sa 9:30am-5pm, Su 1-5pm; $2; students, ages 3-18, and seniors $1). All parks are wheelchair accessible.

The **Chucalissa Archaeological Museum,** 1987 Indian Village Dr. (785-3160), off Rte. 61, captures the past of America's earliest residents with its reconstructed prehistoric village and museum. *(Open Tu-Sa 9am-4:30pm. $3, seniors and ages 4-11 $2, full-time students with ID free. Wheelchair access.)* Local Choctaw sell pottery and beaded jewelry.

ARE YOU LONESOME TONIGHT?

If you don't know what to do while you're in Memphis, the visitors center's *Key* magazine, the *Memphis Flyer,* the *Memphis Dateline,* or the "Playbook" section of the Friday morning *Memphis Commercial Appeal* can tell you what's goin' down 'round town. Also, swing by **Sun Café,** 710 Union Ave. (521-0664), adjacent to the Sun Studios, for a tall, cool glass of lemonade ($1.75) and a talk with the young staff about what to do (open daily 9am-7pm; Sept.-May 10am-6pm; kitchen open 11am-4pm).

Beale St. sways with the most happening, hip nightlife, all contained within a few blocks. On weekends, a $10 wristband lets 21-year-olds wander in and out of any club on the strip. You can save a few bucks by buying a drink at one of the many outdoor stands as you meander from show to show. The Graceland-sponsored **Elvis Presley's Memphis,** 126 Beale St. (527-6900), serves Elvis grub such as fried peanut butter and banana sandwiches ($5.50) and plain old beer ($3) to an older crowd (open daily 11am-midnight with a Su gospel brunch). Beale St. is beyond just Elvis, however, with the Blues wafting out of almost every door. **B.B. King's Blues Club,** 143 Beale St. (524-5464), where the club's namesake still makes appearances, happily mixes young and old, tourist and native. Wash down a catfish sandwich ($7) with a $3 beer. (Cover $5-10; when B.B. himself plays, $50. Open daily from 11:30am-'til the show stops.) **Rum Boogie Café,** 182 Beale St. (528-0150), presents a friendly, relaxed atmosphere and honest homegrown blues to a touristy crowd. Check out the celebrity guitars on the wall, including blues great Willie Dixon's. (Cover $7. Full menu; domestic beer $3. Open daily 11am until very late. Music begins around 9pm.) For pool, **Peoples,** 323 Beale St. (523-7627), racks 'em up from 1pm until at least 2am (tables $8.50 per hr., F-Sa $9.69). **Silky O'Sullivan's,** 183 Beale St. (522-9596), is a big Irish bar behind the facade of an almost completely razed historic landmark. Outside, guests chill out with the goats and munch on burgers ($4-6) to the tune of extremely loud piano music or blues emanating from next door. (Cover F-Sa $5. Opens M at 6pm, Tu-Th at 4pm, F at 2pm, Sa-Su at noon…closing time? What closing time?)

A hot gay spot, **J. Wags,** 1268 Madison (725-1909), has been open 24hr. since way back and served as the bar from *The People vs. Larry Flynt* (DJ music F-Sa). Up, up, and away to the **Daily Planet,** 3439 Park Ave. (327-1270), where live bands play everything from rock to country (open M-F 1pm-3am, Sa 5pm-3am).

For a collegiate atmosphere, try the **Highland St.** strip near **Memphis State University,** with hopping bars like **Newby's,** 539 S. Highland St. (452-8408), which has backgammon tables and belts out rock and blues. (Domestic beer $2.25. Open daily 3pm-3am. Music F-Sa around 10:30pm.)

The majestic **Orpheum Theater,** 203 S. Main St. (525-3000), shows classic movies beginning at 7:30pm on summer Thursdays and Fridays, along with an organ prelude and a cartoon ($6, seniors and under 13 $5). The grand old theater, with 15 ft. high chandeliers and a pipe organ, has occasional live music and Broadway shows ($15-45; box office open M-F 9am-5pm and sometimes before shows). **Memphis in May** (525-4611) celebrates through the month with concerts, art exhibits, food contests, and sporting events. The **Memphis Redbirds** (721-6000), in Autozone Park downtown, are a brand-new AAA baseball team as of 1998 (tickets $5-8; discounts for seniors, military, and under 15).

North Carolina

North Carolina can be split neatly into three regions: down-to-earth mountain culture in the west, mellow sophistication in the Research Triangle of the central piedmont, and placid coastal towns in the east. Largely untouched by development, the Old North State's natural beauty continues to be one of its greatest assets. From Mt. Mitchell to Monteo, North Carolina is dotted with state and national parks, nature preserves, and countless historic sites.

Confederate soldiers from Mississippi first called their allies from North Carolina "Tar Heels" after they failed to maintain their position in the face of Union troops, meaning that they forgot to tar their heels in order to really stick to their ground. Carolinians see it differently. They claim the nickname refers to the tenacity they displayed in both the Revolutionary and Civil Wars—while they may have faltered in body, they remained steadfast in spirit. Dubious origins aside, the Tar Heel has become a North Carolina rallying point—especially during the NCAA men's basketball tournament, an event that commands a quasi-religious reverence in residents during yearly "March Madness."

PRACTICAL INFORMATION

Capital: Raleigh.
Visitor Info: Dept. of Commerce, Travel and Tourism, 301 N. Wilmington St., Raleigh 27601-2825 (919-733-4171 or 800-VISIT-NC/847-4862; http://www.visitnc.com). **Dept. of Natural Resources and Community Development,** Division of Parks and Recreation, P.O. Box 27687, Raleigh 27611 (919-733-4181).
Emergency: 911.
Time Zone: Eastern. **Postal Abbreviation:** NC.
Sales Tax: 6%.

■ The Research Triangle

Large universities and their students dominate "the Triangle," a regional identity born in the 50s and 60s with the creation of the spectacularly successful Research Triangle Park, where Nobel Prize-winning scientists toil for dozens of high-tech and biotech firms. Let's be academic about it: culturally, this place is an isosceles triangle where Chapel Hill is the broadest angle, encompassing numerous restaurants, shops and sights; and Raleigh and Durham are each smaller angles, offering more narrow opportunities for travelers. **Raleigh,** the state capital and home to North Carolina State University (NC State), is an easygoing, historic town boasting a vibrant art community. **Durham,** formerly a major tobacco producer, now (ironically) supports multiple hospitals and medical research projects devoted to finding cancer cures. It's also purported to be one of the more gay-friendly cities in the country. Duke University, one of the most prestigious schools in the nation, has a beautiful campus dominated by sprawling lawns, ancient trees, and almost as ancient buildings. Chartered in 1789 as the nation's first state university, the University of North Carolina (UNC), can be found just 20 mi. down the road in Chapel Hill. College culture predominates here—nearly every other store specializes in UNC t-shirts. Finally, a thriving music scene inhabits the Hill, Ben Folds Five and The Squirrel Nut Zippers being just a few of the local bands starting to receive national attention.

PRACTICAL INFORMATION

Airport: Raleigh-Durham International (840-2123), 15 mi. northwest of Raleigh on U.S. 70. A taxi to downtown Raleigh costs about $20.

Trains: Amtrak, 320 W. Cabarrus St. (833-7594 or 800-872-7245), Raleigh, 4 blocks west of the Civic Ctr. To Washington, D.C. (6hr., 2 per day, $70) and Richmond (3½hr., 2 per day, $44). Open daily 4:45am-10:30pm.

Buses: Greyhound (800-231-2222) has a station in each city. In **Raleigh,** 314 W. Jones St. (834-8275). To: Durham (30min., 9 per day, $7); Chapel Hill (80min., 4 per day, $8); and Charleston, SC (7½hr., 1 per day, $48). Open daily 7am-1am. In **Durham,** 820 W. Morgan St. (687-4800), 1 block off Chapel Hill St. downtown, 2½ mi. northeast of Duke University. To Chapel Hill (35min., 4 per day, $6) and Washington, D.C. (6hr., 6 per day, $43). Open daily 7am-10:30pm. In **Chapel Hill,** 311 W. Franklin St. (942-3356), 2 blocks from UNC. To Durham (35min., 3 per day, $6) and Washington, D.C. (9hr., 3 per day, $43). Open M-Sa 7:45am-5:30pm.

Public Transportation: Capital Area Transit, Raleigh (828-7228). Buses run M-Sa. Fare 75¢. **Durham Area Transit Authority (DATA),** Durham (683-DATA/3282). Most routes start downtown at the corner of Main and Morgan St. on the loop. Operates daily; hrs. vary by route; fewer on Su. Fare 75¢; seniors, under 18, and disabled 35¢; transfers 10¢; children under 43 in. free. **Chapel Hill Transit,** Chapel Hill (968-2769). Buses run 6:30am-6:30pm. Office open M-F 6:30am-10pm. Fare 75¢; campus shuttle free.

Taxis: Associated Cab Co., 832-8807. Service 6am-6pm. **Cardinal Cab,** 828-3228. 24hr. Both charge $1.35, plus $1.50 per additional mi.

Visitor Info: Raleigh Capitol Area Visitors Center, 301 N. Blount St. (733-3456). Daily slide shows. Open M-F 8am-5pm, Sa 9am-5pm, Su 1-5pm. **Durham Convention Center and Visitors Bureau,** 101 E. Morgan St. (687-0288 or 800-446-8604). Open M-F 8:30am-5pm, Sa 10am-2pm. **Visitor Info Center and Chapel Hill Chamber of Commerce,** 104 S. Estes Dr. (967-7075). Open M-F 9am-5pm.

Hotline: Rape Crisis, 967-7273. 24hr.

Post Office: In Raleigh, 311 New Bern Ave. (420-5333). Open M-F 8am-5pm, Sa 8am-noon. **ZIP code:** 27611. In **Durham,** 323 E. Chapel Hill St. (683-1976). Open M-F 8:30am-5pm. **ZIP code:** 27701. In **Chapel Hill,** 179 E. Franklin St. (967-6297). Open M-F 8:30am-5:30pm, Sa 8:30am-noon; **ZIP code:** 27514. **Area code:** 919.

ACCOMMODATIONS AND CAMPGROUNDS

Carolina-Duke Motor Inn, 2517 Guess Rd. (286-0771 or 800-438-1158), Durham, next to I-85. Clean rooms with wood furnishings, A/C. Access to swimming pool and laundry facilities. Free cable TV, local calls, local maps, and shuttle to Duke Medical Center on the main campus. DATA access across the street. Singles $40; doubles $46; $3 per additional person. 10% discount for *Let's Go* users, seniors, and AAA members. Wheelchair-accessible rooms available.

Red Roof Inns, 5623 Chapel Hill Blvd. (489-9421 or 800-THE-ROOF/843-7663), Chapel Hill, at the junction of U.S. 15-501 and I-40. Bus stop ¼ mi. south on Chapel Hill Blvd. Large, clean rooms. Disabled access, free local calls, cable TV, A/C. Singles $49; doubles $56; $5 per additional person.

Regency Inn, 300 N. Dawson St. (8285-9081), Raleigh. A 10min. hike from downtown. Call in advance for reservations and try to snatch up one of the 2 non-smoking rooms. Cable TV, A/C, and coffee. Singles $42; doubles $44.

Umstead State Park (787-3033), 2 mi. northwest of Raleigh, a quick left off U.S. 70. Tent and trailer sites in pristine woodland. Large lake for fishing, trails for hiking and horseback riding (BYO horse). Sites $9; no hookups. Open Th-Su 8am-9pm; in winter 8am-6pm. Staff still rebuilding in the wake of Hurricane Fran; call for details.

FOOD

In Raleigh, **Hillsborough St.,** across from NC State, has a wide array of cheap eateries, both funky and franchise. Chapel Hill's **Franklin St.** has similar variety but is a good deal more inviting. Durham's **9th St.** is the quirkiest, yet scantest locale. The **Well-Spring Grocery,** at the Ridgewood Shopping Center on Wade Ave. in Raleigh (828-5805), sells organic fruits and vegetables and whole-grain baked goods (open daily 9am-9pm). A Durham branch (286-2290) rests across from Duke's East Campus at 621 Broad St. (open daily 9am-9pm). The Chapel Hill WellSpring, at Franklin and Elliott St., also houses **Penguins,** a small cafe serving a variety of gourmet coffees and the best ham and *gruyère croissant* that $2.50 can buy (open daily 8:30am-8pm).

@**Skylight Exchange,** 405½ W. Rosemary St. (933-5550), Chapel Hill. A hip, eclectic den where used books, CDs, and tapes are sold alongside a vast array of sandwiches ($3-6). Thick malt shakes ($3.50) make browsing the crammed shelves doubly enjoyable. Live music W-M 9pm. Open Su-Th 11am-11pm, F-Sa 11am-midnight.

@**Bullock's Bar-B-Que,** 3330 Quebec St. (383-3211), Durham; from downtown, turn right off Hillsborough Rd. onto N. LaSalle, then immediately right on Quebec. This popular BBQ-lover's mecca specializes in "pig-pickin's." Out-of-towners such as Jay Leno, Magic Johnson, and Robin Williams chow down on barbecue dinners ($5-8) served with unlimited, melt-in-your-mouth hush puppies. Bone marrow patients receive 10% discount. Open Tu-Sa 11:30am-8pm. Wheelchair access.

Lane Street Diner, 200 W. Lane St. (828-9694), Raleigh. "A Raleigh family reunion everyday," touts the owner. The diner, sporting dancing Elvises, a jukebox and records that line its exterior, dishes up omelettes (around $3), reubens ($3) and combo plates ($4-5) as well as local gossip. Numerous vegetarian options. Cash only. Open M-F 6am-9pm, Sa 7am-9pm, Su 8am-4pm.

El Rodeo, 1404 E. Franklin St. (929-6566), Chapel Hill, behind the visitors center. Don't be scared off by the exterior; this is the genuine Mexican article. Combo dinners (around $6) include vegetarian options and lots of opportunities to substitute your preferences. The fajitas ($5.25 at lunch) and huge portions keep the locals coming back. Open M-Th 11am-2:30pm and 5-10pm. Wheelchair access.

Ramshead Rath-Skeller, 157A E. Franklin St. (942-5158), Chapel Hill, opposite UNC. A big student hangout, "the Rat" offers pizza, sandwiches, and a mean grilled chicken caesar. Ships' mastheads, German beer steins, and old Italian wine bottles adorn 6 dining rooms with names like Rat Trap Lounge. Meals $4-8. Open M-Th 11am-2:30pm and 5-9:30pm, F-Sa 11am-2:30pm and 5-10:30pm, Su 11am-10pm.

Pepper's Pizza, 127 E. Franklin St. (967-7766), Chapel Hill, downtown. A local legend, Pepper's dishes up 'za at great prices. 35 beers and 26 toppings, including the acclaimed "Ewell Gibbons" vegetarian pizza ("When your mom told you to eat your vegetables, THIS is what she meant"). Whole pies $9-17, delicious gazpacho $2.25. Open M-Sa 11am-midnight, Su 4pm-10pm; summer hrs. vary. Wheelchair access.

SIGHTS AND ENTERTAINMENT

Raleigh's historical attractions are a welcome break from the academic pursuits of the Research Triangle. The Neoclassical **capitol building** (733-4994), in Union·Sq. at Edenton and Salisbury St., was built in 1840 (open M-Sa 9am-5pm, Su 1-5pm; free). Across from the capitol, the **North Carolina Museum of History,** 5 E. Edenton St. (715-0200), exhibits memorabilia from the earliest settlement to the present, recently focusing on NC women and state sports heroes (open Tu-Sa 9am-5pm, Su noon-5pm; free). Pick up a brochure at the visitors center for a self-guided tour of the beautifully renovated 19th-century homes of **Historic Oakwood** (834-0887) and **Oakwood Cemetery** (832-6077), where several North Carolina governors and statesmen are buried, as well as four Confederate generals. Across the street and around the corner at Bicentennial Plaza, the **Museum of Natural Sciences** (733-7450) displays fossils, gems, and animal exhibits, including an extensive wetlands exhibit (open M-Sa 9am-5pm, Su 1-5pm; free).

To see local artists in action, ride over to bike-friendly **Carborro** or visit the galleries and craft shops of the **Moore Sq. Art District** (828-4555), which occupies a 3-block radius around Moore Sq. Near the square is **City Market,** a collection of shops, cafes, and bars. **Mordecai Historic Park,** 1 Mimosa St. (834-4844), in Historic Oakwood, re-creates 19th-century life in Raleigh on the grounds of an antebellum plantation (open M and W-Sa 10am-3pm, Su 1-3pm; $4, students $2).

THE SOUTH

The **North Carolina Museum of Art,** 2110 Blue Ridge Blvd. (839-6262), off I-40 at the Wade Ave. Exit, has eight galleries of more than 5000 years of art, including works by Raphael, Botticelli, Rubens, Monet, Wyeth, and O'Keeffe. *(Open Tu-Th 9am-5pm, F 9am-9pm, Sa 9am-5pm, Su 11am-6pm. Free. Tours daily 1:30pm.)*

Duke University is Durham's main draw, and the admissions office, 2138 Campus Dr. (684-3214), doubles as a **visitors center.** *(Open M-F 8am-5pm, Sa 9:30am-1pm. Free tours M-F 11:30am and 2pm, Sa 11:30am.)* **Duke Chapel** (684-2921), in the center of the university, contains a million pieces of stained glass depicting almost 900 figures in 77 windows (open daily 8am-8pm; Sept.-May 8am-10pm; free). The **Sarah P. Duke Gardens** (684-3698), near West Campus on Anderson St., exhibit over 20 acres of landscaping, tiered flower beds, and a lily pond, bordered by acres of pine forest (open daily 8am-dusk). The free campus shuttle bus will take you to East Campus, where the **Duke Museum of Art** (684-5135) shows a small but impressive collection of Italian and Dutch oils, and classical and African sculpture (open Tu-F 9am-5pm, Sa 11am-2pm, Su 2-5pm; free). Duke even sports a 7700-acre **forest** (682-9319).

The **Duke Homestead and Tobacco Museum,** 2828 Duke Homestead Rd. (477-5498), is on the other side of Durham, up Guess Rd. *(Open M-Sa 9am-5pm, Su 1-5pm; Nov.-Mar. Tu-Sa 10am-4pm, Su 1-4pm. Free.)* Washington Duke started his tobacco business on this beautiful estate before endowing a certain university.

Duke-free Durham does exist: **Bennett Place,** 4408 Bennett Memorial Rd., North Durham (383-4345), is the site of Confederate General Joseph Johnston's surrender negotiations with Union General William T. Sherman (open M-Sa 9am-5pm; Nov.-Mar. Tu-Sa 10am-4pm, Su 1-4pm; free). The **Museum of Life and Science,** 433 Murray Ave. (220-5429), is a nationally acclaimed assemblage of hands-on exhibits from the geological to the astronomical, with the occasional animatronic dinosaur (open M-Sa 10am-5pm, Su 1-5pm; $5.50, under 12 $3.50). The **Durham Bulls** (687-6500), a triple-A farm team for the Tampa Bay Devil Rays, became famous after the 1988 movie *Bull Durham* was filmed in their ballpark. *(General admission $4.25; students, seniors, and under 18 $3.25.)* They still play here, minus Kevin Costner.

Nightlife in Durham is notoriously nonexistent, though **The Power Company,** 315 W. Main St. (683-1151), on the Downtown Loop, breaks up the nocturnal monotony with a surge of action. The clientele and events vary nightly; Fridays are designated gay-friendly, while Wednesdays jam with everything from reggae to hip-hop (W-F 18+; Sa women 18+, men 21+; cover $0-12).

Chapel Hill and neighboring Carrboro are virtually inseparable from the **University of North Carolina at Chapel Hill** (962-2211), and student energy sustains a dynamic bar, cafe, and music scene on and around **Franklin St.** The university's Smith Center hosts sporting events and concerts. Until 1975, NASA astronauts trained at the UNC **Morehead Planetarium** (962-1236), which now projects several different shows per year; in "Sky Rambles," an astronomer leads an interactive tour of the Chapel Hill night sky. *(Open Su-F 12:30-5pm and 7-9:45pm, Sa 10am-5pm and 7-9:45pm. $3.50; students, seniors, and children $2.50.)*

The **Cat's Cradle,** 300 E. Main St., Carrboro (967-9053), a quasi-legendary club where Nirvana and Public Enemy have played, is the place to hear burgeoning local and national talent (live music at 10pm; cover $3-16; call for concert schedule). **Local 506,** 506 W. Franklin St. (942-5506), another music mecca, specializes in indie, alternative, garage, and power pop. Three bands play at this club every night from 9pm to 2am. (21+. Cover $3, Sa-Su $5.) The **Lizard & Snake Café,** 110 N. Columbia St. (929-2828), attracts a slightly grungy, student-dominated crowd for nightly live music (normally at 10:30pm), which spans indie, rock, jazz, folk, and acoustic styles. Arrive early for the tasty $5 blue corn tacos. (Cover $3-5. Food served daily until 10pm.) Students and families alike get a kick out of **ComedySportz** (968-3922), 128 Franklin St., across from NCNB Plaza, Chapel Hill, for competitive team improv where "comedy is a sport," complete with referees. *(Cover $6, with college ID $5, under 12 $4. Shows F 8:30pm; Sa 1:20, 7:30 and 9:45pm.)* **Starlite Drive-In,** 2523 E. Club Blvd. (688-1037), Durham, I-85 to Exit 179, is a must for those with cars (shows Su-Th 9pm, F-Sa 9pm and 11:15pm; $4, under 11 $2). Pick up a free copy of the *Spectator, Carolina Woman* and *Independent* weekly magazines, available at most restaurants, bookstores, and hotels, for complete listings of Triangle news and special events.

Off to a Pig Pickin'

Southerners are notoriously finicky about their barbecue, but North Carolinians claim that theirs *is* authentic "Southern barbecue." To start, the terminology: to avoid ridicule or, worse yet, giving yourself away as a Northerner, remember that "barbecue" is a noun denoting a recognized food, *never* a verb. Say, rather, "We're goin' to cook a pig" or "We're havin' a pig pickin'." And keep in mind that purists insist only pig meat constitutes "barbecue," even if bovine-centric Texans get some slack. Most importantly, of course, the secret's in the sauce. The brown gooey stuff found in supermarkets is decidedly *not* real BBQ sauce, which should be much thinner and have a vinegar, not tomato, base. So sit back and enjoy your barbecue chipped, sliced, or, most festive of all, hot from a "pig pickin'." Southerners traditionally celebrate summertime weddings, reunions, and birthdays by gathering around a freshly cooked pig kept warm on an enormous grill. Parties line up buffet-style and have at it with forks, before heading off to the shade with a cool glass of sweet tea. And the livin' is easy....

■ Charlotte

In 1799, a fortunate fellow in Charlotte was heard howling and screaming after he stubbed his toe on a 17-pound golden nugget. Mines sprung up, prospectors poured in, and gold speculation boomed. The rush lasted about 50 years, until folks in California began finding smaller nuggets in larger quantities. The 19th-century mines are gone, but Charlotte, which began as a village on the Catawba Indian trade route, is now the largest city in the Carolinas and the nation's third largest banking center. Growing and expanding rapidly, Charlotte is home to ritzy clubs and bars, successful sports teams, and countless malls. A metropolitan hot-spot in the Carolina countryside, Charlotte offers bustling charm and yuppie vitality.

PRACTICAL INFORMATION Amtrak runs out of 1914 N. Tryon St. (376-4416 or 800-872-7245); **Greyhound** leaves from 601 W. Trade St. (372-0456 or 800-231-2222). Both stations are open 24 hr. **Charlotte Transit,** 901 N. Davidson St. (336-3366), operates local buses (fare $1, $1.40 for outlying areas; transfers free). **Info Charlotte,** 330 S. Tryon St. (331-2700 or 800-231-4636), awaits uptown for brochure-browsing, and offers free parking off 2nd St. (open M-F 8:30am-5pm, Sa 10am-4pm, Su 1-4pm). Charlotte has a **Rape Crisis line** (375-9900), a **Suicide Hotline** (358-2800), and a **Gay/Lesbian Switchboard** (535-6277). **Post Office:** 201 N. McDowell (333-5135; open M-F 7am-5:30pm). **ZIP code:** 28204. **Area code:** 704.

ACCOMMODATIONS AND FOOD Charlotte's budget motels thrive on the I-85 Service Rd., running alongside the highway. A penny saved is a penny earned at **Pennywise Inn,** 3200 S. I-85 Service Rd. (398-3144), Exit 33 from I-85. You'll find A/C, cable, free local calls, a pool, and laundry. (Singles $36; doubles $40.) **Microtel Inn** (598-2882), Exit 41 on I-85 at W. Sugar Creek Rd., has small, neat rooms with A/C, cable TV, coffee, and candy at the front desk (singles $40; doubles $46). South of the city, try the **Motel 6,** 3430 St. Vardell Ln. (527-0144 or 800-466-7356); take I-77 S, then Exit 7 at Clanton Rd. Amenities include cable TV, HBO, A/C, laundry, pool, and free local calls. (Singles $36; doubles $40.)

South from uptown, the **Dilworth** neighborhood, along East and South Blvd. cooks with a generous number of restaurants serving everything from ethnic cuisine to pizza and pub fare. Part yuppie, part gay, and continuously upbeat, the area and its residents are well heeled; yet some places won't turn away, or bankrupt, unwashed backpackers. Talley ho veggie lovers, it's **Talley's Green Grocery and Café,** 1408-C East Blvd. (334-9200), an upscale grocery serving organic health food, sandwiches ($5) and hot soups ($3). Just down the strip, the **Big Sky Bakery,** 1500 East Blvd. (347-0836), offers fresh, no-fuss cookies ($1) and scones ($2) alongside an impressive array of bread and focaccia ($5-6), for breakfast, lunch or snack (open M-F 7am-6:30pm, Sa 7am-6pm, Su 8am-4pm). At the **Roasting Company,** 1521 Montford Dr.

(521-8188), bus #18 or 19, juicy rotisserie chicken dinners come with cornbread and two veggies for $5-7 (open M-Th 11am-10pm, F and Sa 11am-10:30pm, Su 11:30am-10pm). The **Charlotte Regional Farmers Market,** 1801 Yorkmont Rd. (357-1269), hawks local produce, baked goods, and crafts year-round (open Tu-Sa 8am-6pm; May-Aug. also Su 1-6pm).

SIGHTS, ENTERTAINMENT, AND NIGHTLIFE The **Mint Museum of Art,** 2730 Randolph Rd. (337-2000), a 5min. drive from uptown, is particularly proud of its pottery, porcelain, and American art collections. *(Open Tu 10am-10pm, W-Sa 10am-5pm, Su noon-5pm. $6, students and seniors $4, under 13 free; free Tu after 5pm. Guided tours daily 2pm.)* Take bus #14 or #15. The **Discovery Place,** 301 N. Tryon St. (372-6261 or 800-935-0553), draws crowds with its hands-on science museum, OmniMax theater, flight simulator, and planetarium. *(Open M-Sa 9am-6pm, Su 1-6pm; Sept.-May M-F 9am-5pm, Sa 9am-6pm, Su 1-6pm. 1 attraction $6.50, seniors and ages 6-12 $5.50, ages 3-5 $2.75; $2 per additional attraction.)* One block east, the **Museum of the New South,** 324 N. College St. (333-1887) explores post-Reconstruction Charlotte and the Carolina Piedmont area (open Tu-Sa 11am-5pm; $2, students and seniors $1). Paramount's **Carowinds Entertainments Complex** (588-2600 or 800-888-4386), 10 mi. south of Charlotte off Exit 90 from I-77, is an amusement park which pays tribute to *Wayne's World* with the "Hurler" roller coaster. *(Open Mar.-Oct. generally M-F 10am-8pm, Sa-Su 10am-10pm, but hrs. vary. $30, seniors and ages 4-6 $18; after 5pm $15. Parking $5.)*

Charlotte is a big sports town. Basketball's **Hornets** (men) and **Sting** (women) play in the **Coliseum** (357-4700), and the National Football League's **Panthers** in new Ericsson Stadium (358-7538).The Charlotte **Knights** play AAA minor league baseball April through July at Knights Castle (357-8071), off I-77 S at Exit 88 in S. Carolina (tickets $5, seniors and children $3.50).

For nightlife, arts, and entertainment listings, grab a free copy of either *Creative Loafing* or *Break* in one of Charlotte's shops or restaurants or the E & T section in Friday's *Charlotte Observer*. The Elizabeth area along E. 7th St. and E. Independence Ave. parties into the night with clubs like the **Double Door Inn,** 218 E. Independence Ave. (376-1446; cover $5-10), and **Jack Straw,** 1936 E. 7th St. (347-8960; cover Th-Sa $5-8), cranking out live rock on the weekends. The **Moon Room,** 431 S. Tryon St. (342-2003), has live music and occasionally explodes into bohemian funkiness on Thursdays; watch for Poetry and Psychic Nights (open Th-Sa at 5:30pm, music begins around 10:30pm; cover $4-6). Groove all night at The **Baha,** 4369 S. Tryon St. (525-3343), a "progressive dance complex" with nights like Disco Hump and College Quake. Arrive before 11pm for a short line and a lower cover; Sa, women 21+ get in free. (Open F-Sa until 4am. Call about occasional all-age live music shows.)

CAROLINA MOUNTAINS

The sharp ridges and rolling slopes of the southern Appalachian range create some of the most spectacular scenery in the Southeast. Amid this beauty flourishes a mélange of diverse personalities, from scholars and ski bums to farming communities and artists. Enjoy the area's rugged wilderness while backpacking, canoeing, rafting, mountain biking, cross-country skiing, or just driving the Blue Ridge Pkwy. The aptly named High Country includes the territory between Boone and Asheville, 100 mi. to the southwest, and fills the upper regions of the Blue Ridge Mountains. Southward is the Great Smoky Mountains National Park (see p. 275).

■ Boone

Nestled among the breathtaking mountains of the High Country, Boone, named for frontiersman Daniel Boone, has two faces. Tourist attractions such as Mast General Store, Tweetsie Railroad, and the many antiques shops lure young and old to eat family-style, flatten coins on railroad tracks, and, of course, shop. But this small town lives on year-round, populated by locals and the students of Appalachian State University.

PRACTICAL INFORMATION

Public Transportation: Boone AppalCart, 274 Winkler's Creek Rd. (264-2278). Local bus and van service with 3 main routes: Red links downtown Boone with ASU and motels and restaurants on Blowing Rock Rd.; Green serves Rte. 421; Blue runs within ASU. Red and Green routes run every hr. M-F 7am-11pm and Sa 7am-5pm; Blue runs every 15min. M-F 7:30am-7pm. Fare 50¢.

Taxis: Ace Cab Co., 265-3373. $1.40 base fare, $1.40 per additional mi.; extended area 10¢ more per mi. 24hr.

Bike Rental: Rock and Roll Sports, 208 E. King St. (264-0765). Bikes $30, helmets included; car racks $5. Trail maps available. Open M-Sa 10am-6pm, Su noon-4pm.

Visitor Info: Boone Area Chamber of Commerce, 208 Howard St. (264-2225 or 800-852-9506), has info on accommodations and sights. Turn from Rte. 321 S onto River St., drive behind the university, turn right onto Depot St., then take the first left onto Howard St. Open M-F 9am-5pm. **North Carolina High Country Host Visitor Center,** 1700 Blowing Rock Rd. (264-1299 or 800-438-7500), distributes free copies of the *High Country Host Area Travel Guide,* a detailed map of the area, and the *Blue Ridge Pkwy. Directory,* a mile-by-mile description of services and sights along the Pkwy. Open daily 9am-5pm.

Post Office: 1544 Blowing Rock Rd. (264-3813), and 679 W. King St. (262-1171). Both open M-F 9am-5pm, Sa 9am-noon. **ZIP code:** 28607. **Area code:** 704.

ACCOMMODATIONS, CAMPGROUNDS, AND FOOD

Catering primarily to vacationing families, the area fronts more than its share of expensive motels and B&Bs. Scratch the surface, though, and you'll find enough inexpensive rooms and campsites to keep you comfy. Weekends in July and August tend to be more expensive.

Most budget hotels are concentrated along **Blowing Rock Rd. (Rte. 321)** or **Rte. 105.** The **Boone Trail Motel,** 275 E. King St./U.S. 421 (264-8839), south of downtown, has brightly painted rooms with quaint country baskets to hold the toilet paper (singles $25, doubles $30; F-Sa $35/$38).

Boone and the Blue Ridge Pkwy. offer developed and well-equipped campsites, as well as primitive camping options for those looking to rough it. Along the Pkwy., spectacular tent and RV sites without hookups ($12) are available at the **Julian Price Campground,** Mi. 297 (963-5911); sites around Loop A are on a lake. **Linville Falls,** Mi. 317 (828-765-2681), left onto Rte. 221; and **Crabtree Meadows,** Mi. 340 (675-4444; open May-Oct. only to those willing to hike to their site), present other options (both $12). For hookups, try Rte. 194 N off 421. **Appalachian RV Park** (264-7250), 3 mi. up the road, has laundry, TV and exclusively full-hookup sites ($18).

Rte. 321 boasts countless fast-food options and family-style eateries. College students and professors alike hang out on **West King St.** (U.S. 441/221). **Our Daily Bread,** 627 West King St. (264-0173), offers sandwiches, salads, and super vegetarian specials for $3-5 (open M-F 8am-6:30pm, Sa 9am-5pm). The **Daniel Boone Inn** (264-8657), at the Rte. 321/421 junction, satiates hearty appetites with all-you-can-eat country-style meals (open daily 11am-9pm, $12; also Sa-Su 8-11am for breakfast, $7).

SIGHTS AND ENTERTAINMENT

Horn in the West (264-2120), in an open-air amphitheater located near Boone off Rte. 105, dramatizes the American Revolution as it was fought in the southern Appalachians. *(Shows mid-June to mid-Aug. Tu-Su 8:30pm. $12, under 13 $6; group rates upon request; AAA discount $1. Reservations recommended.)* Near the theater, **Hickory Ridge Homestead** (264-9089) recreates 18th-century mountain life with restored cabins and demonstrations. *(Open while the Horn is in session daily 1-8:30pm; included in Horn admission price, or $2 alone.)* Down the road, the **Daniel Boone Native Gardens** (264-6390) celebrate mountain foliage (open May-Oct. daily 9am-6pm, until 8pm on show days; $2). **An Appalachian Summer** (800-841-2787) is a July festival of high-caliber music, art, theater, and dance sponsored by ASU ($12-16 for individual shows). Held June through August, Roan Mountain's **Summer in the Park** festival features cloggers

THE SOUTH

and storytellers at the State Park Amphitheater; call the **Roan Mountain Visitors Center** (423-772-3314 or 423-772-3303) for info.

Hikers should arm themselves with the invaluable, large-scale map *100 Favorite Trails* ($3.50). **Appalachian Adventures** (910-877-8800) in Todd, 12 mi. north of Boone off Rte. 194 on Rail Road Grade Rd., rents all sorts of water vehicles and bikes. *(Canoes and kayaks $12 for 1hr. for 1 person, $20 for 2 people, add $2 per person per additional hr. Tubes $8 per hr.; bikes $8 per hr.)*

Downhill skiers enjoy the Southeast's largest concentration of alpine resorts (Nov.-Mar.) at: **Appalachian Ski Mountain,** off Rte. 221/321 (800-322-2373; lift tickets $21, Sa-Su $32; rentals $10/$13); **Ski Beech,** 1007 Beech Mt. Pkwy. (800-438-2093), off Rte. 184 in Banner Elk (lift tickets $27/$41); **Ski Hawknest,** 1800 Skyland Dr. (963-6561; lift tickets $20/$33), in the town of Seven Devils; and **Sugar Mountain** (898-4521; lift tickets $28/$43), in Banner Elk off Rte. 184. It's best to call ahead to the resort for specific ski package prices. **Boone AppalCart** (264-2278) runs a free winter shuttle to Sugar Mountain and Ski Beech. Call 800-962-2322 for **daily ski reports.**

The 5 mi. road to **Grandfather Mountain** (800-468-7325), off Rte. 221, provides an unparalleled view of the entire High Country area. *(Mountain open daily 8am-7pm; Dec.-Mar. 8am-5pm, weather permitting.)* At the top, a private **park** features a 1 mi. high suspension bridge, a museum and a small zoo ($10, ages 4-12 $5, under 4 free). To hike or camp on Grandfather Mt. requires a **permit,** available at the **Grandfather Mountain Country Store** on Rte. 221 or at the park entrance (day use $5, camping $10). Pick up a trail map at the entrance to learn which trails are available for overnight use. The mountain plays host to brawny men in kilts, second weekend in July, at the **Grandfather Mountain Highland Games** (828-733-1333; shows $8-18).

■ Near Boone: Blowing Rock

Seven miles south on Rte. 321, at the entrance to the Blue Ridge Pkwy., is a friendly mountain town with a large population of craftmakers and folk artists. The **rock that blows** (828-295-7111) overhangs Johns River Gorge; chuck a piece of paper over the edge, and it will blow right back to you. (Open Apr.-Dec. daily dawn-dusk; Jan-Feb. Sa-Su weather permitting. $4, ages 6-11 $1.)

In Blowing Rock, at the **Parkway Craft Center,** Mi. 294 Blue Ridge Pkwy. (295-7938), 2 mi. south of Blowing Rock Village in the Cone Manor House, members of the **Southern Highland Craft Guild** demonstrate their skills (open mid-Mar. to Dec. daily 9am-6pm). The craft center is on the grounds of the **Moses H. Cone Memorial Park,** 3600 acres of shaded walking trails and magnificent views. Check the **National Park Service desk** (295-3782) in the center for a copy of *This Week's Activities* (open Apr.-Oct. daily 9am-5pm; free). Guided horseback rides from **Blowing Rock Stables** (295-7847) let you tour the park without hoofing it yourself. Exit the Blue Ridge Pkwy. at the Blowing Rock sign, turn left onto Rte. 221/Yonahlossee Rd. and follow the signs. (Open Apr.-Oct. daily 9:30am-4pm. $20, 2hr. $35. Under 9 and over 250 lb. not permitted. 1hr. tour. Call at least 1 day in advance to reserve.)

Pricey food and lodging are as abundant as wildflowers in town, but the **Homestead Inn,** 153 Morris St. (295-9559), a half block off Main, will let you—and your wallet—rest easy. A gazebo, swing, and quilts turn this motel into a mountain lodge. Well, almost. (Singles and doubles from $50.) Blowing Rock may be slightly north of Jimmy Buffet's beloved Caribbean, but you can still have **Cheeseburgers in Paradise** (259-4858), at Rte. 221 and Main St. This bar and grille has outdoor patios, great beef, and friendly waiters. (Burgers $5, domestic beer $2.50. Open Su-Th 11am-9:30pm, F-Sa 11am-10:30pm.) For town info, visit the **Blowing Rock Chamber of Commerce,** 1038 Main St. (295-7851; open M-Th 9am-5pm, F-Sa 9am-5:30pm).

■ Asheville

Hazy blue mountains, deep valleys, and spectacular waterfalls supply a splendid backdrop to this tiny North Carolina town. Once a coveted layover for the nation's well-to-do, Asheville housed enough Carnegies, Vanderbilts, and Mellons to fill a 20s edition of *Who's Who on the Atlantic Seaboard.* Monuments such as the Biltmore Estate and the Grove Park Inn reflect the rich history of the town's gilded citizenry. The population these days tends more toward dreadlocks, batik, and vegetarianism, providing funky nightlife and festivals all year. In contrast to the laid-back locals, Asheville's sights are fanatically maintained and the downtown meticulously preserved, making for a pleasant respite from the Carolina wilderness.

PRACTICAL INFORMATION

Buses: Greyhound, 2 Tunnel Rd. (253-5353 or 800-231-2222), 2 mi. east of downtown, near the Beaucatcher Tunnel. Asheville Transit bus #13 runs to and from downtown every hr.; last bus 6:30pm. To: Charlotte (3½hr., 4 per day, $26); Knoxville (2hr., 6 per day, $26); Atlanta (6½hr., 1 per day, $37); and Raleigh (7½hr., 4 per day, $48). Open M-Sa 8am-5:30pm.

Public Transportation: Asheville Transit Authority, 360 W. Haywood St. (253-5691). Bus service within city limits. All routes converge on Pritchard Park downtown. Operates M-F (and some Sa) 5:30am-7pm, most at 1hr. intervals. Fare 75¢, transfers 10¢. Discounts for seniors, disabled, and multi-fare tickets. Short trips within the downtown area are free.

Visitor Info: Chamber of Commerce, 151 Haywood St. (recorded info 800-257-1300; http://www.ashevillechamber.org), Exit 4C off I-240, on the northwest end of downtown. Open M-F 8:30am-5:30pm, Sa-Su 9am-5pm.

Hotline: Rape Crisis, 255-7576.

Internet Access: Pack Memorial Library, 67 Haywood St. (255-5203), at Vanderbilt Pl. Open M-Th 10am-9pm, F-Sa 10am-6pm; Sept.-May also Su 2-6pm.

Post Office: 33 Coxe Ave. (271-6420), at Patton Ave. Open M-F 7:30am-5:30pm, Sa 9am-1pm. **ZIP code:** 28802. **Area code:** 704 or 828, in text 704 unless noted.

ACCOMMODATIONS AND CAMPGROUNDS

Motels cluster in three areas: the least expensive are on **Tunnel Rd.,** east of downtown, slightly more expensive (and fewer) options can be found on **Merrimon Ave.,** just north of downtown, and the ritziest of the budget circle hover around the Biltmore Estate on **Hendersonville Ave.,** south of downtown.

The Wolfe Den, 22 Ravenscroft Dr. (285-0230), between Hilliard and Sawyer, is a funky new hostel in a brick house just south of downtown. With kitchen, deck, grill, laundry, common rooms, and info on Asheville and the Smokies, the Den can't be beat. Dorm rooms with 2-3 bunk beds. $10-15. Linen $1. Lockout 11am-4pm. Reservations recommended May-Oct.

Log Cabin Motor Court, 330 Weaverville Hwy. (828-645-6546). Though 10min. from downtown, this motel provides quaint cabins with cable TV, laundry and pool access; some have fireplaces and kitchenettes, but none have A/C. Take Rte. 240 to Rte. 19/23/70 N to the New Bridge Exit, turn right, then left at the light; it's 1 mi. on the left. Singles from $31; doubles from $33.

In Town Motor Lodge, 100 Tunnel Rd. (828-252-1811), has standard rooms with cable, A/C, balconies, and pool, for great prices. Singles $32; doubles $36.

Powhatan (667-8429), 12 mi. southwest of Asheville off Rte. 191, is the closest campsite in the Nantahala National Forest. Wooded sites on a 10-acre trout lake surrounded by hiking trails and a swimming lake. $12, no hookups. Gates close 11pm. Open Apr.-Oct.

Bear Creek RV Park and Campground, 81 S. Bear Creek Rd. (800-833-0798), takes the camp out of camping with a pool, laundry facilities, groceries, and a game room. Take I-40 Exit 47, and look for the sign. Tent sites $18, with water and electricity $22; RV sites with hookup $26.

FOOD AND NIGHTLIFE

You'll find the greasy links of most fast-food chains on **Tunnel Rd.** and **Biltmore Ave.** The **Western North Carolina Farmers Market** (253-1691), at the intersection of I-40 and Rte. 191 near I-26, sells fresh produce and crafts (open daily 8am-6pm).

THE SOUTH

Laughing Seed Café, 40 Wall St. (252-3445), behind Patton Ave. Friendly servers vend veggie and vegan values in this all-natural eatery. Su brunch draws a big, bustling crowd—and never disappoints. Salads ($5-8), entrees ($3-8), and sandwiches ($4-7). Open M-Th 11:30am-9pm, F-Sa 11:30-10, Su 10am-9pm.

Smokehouse Mountain BBQ, 20 S. Spruce St. (234-4871 or 800-850-3718), on the southeast corner of downtown, serves up classic Southern barbecue at affordable prices (most entrees under $10). Go for the food but stay for the music; country and bluegrass bands play Th-Sa 7:30pm. Open Tu-Sa 5:30pm; closing times vary.

Basta, 4 College (254-7072), at Patton. Fresh and light Italian food served in a bright, busy restaurant at good prices. Many vegetarian options. Salads $2.50-5.50, sandwiches $5-6, pasta $6. Open M-Th 11am-2:30pm, F 11am-8pm, Sa noon-8pm.

For a small town, Asheville really grooves. **Biltmore Ave.,** south from Pack Sq., and **Broadway,** north from Pack Sq., are meccas for music, munchies, and movies, while **Be Here Now,** 5 Biltmore Ave. (258-2071), showcases live blues, funk, and folk (cover $5-10). **Tressa's,** 28 Broadway (254-7072), hosts live jazz and blues most nights in a casual atmosphere (cover $2-5). Indy and artsy flicks play at **Fine Arts Theater,** 36 Biltmore Ave. (232-1536; $6, matinees and seniors $4.50). A popular bar, **Barley's Taproom,** 42 Biltmore Ave. (255-0504), hops with locals and $3 beers.

SIGHTS AND ENTERTAINMENT

It does not seem possible that George Vanderbilt could have **Biltmore Estate,** 1 North Pack Sq. (274-6333 or 800-543-2961), 3 blocks north of I-40's Exit 50. *(Open daily 9am-5pm. $30, ages 10-15 $22.50; Nov.-Dec. $2-3 more.)* The ostentatious abode was built in the 1890s under the supervision of architect Richard Morris Hunt and landscaper Fredrick Law Olmstead, and remains the largest private home in America. A tour of this magnificent castle can take all day if it's crowded; try to arrive early. The self-guided tour winds through some of the 250 rooms, around the indoor pool, through a bowling alley, and through the 10,000-volume rare-book library. Tours of the surrounding gardens and of the Biltmore winery (with generous wine tasting for those 21 and over) are included in the hefty admission price. Free scenery blooms at the **Botanical Gardens,** 151 Weaver Blvd. (252-5190), off Merrimon Ave. (take bus #2) and the **North Carolina Arboretum** (665-2492), off I-26 Exit 2 on 191 S. *(Both open dawn-dusk. Gardens center open Mar.-Nov. daily 9:30-4pm. Arboretum open M-Sa 8am-5pm, 2nd and 4th Su of every month 1:30-4:30pm.)*

Henry Ford, Thomas Edison, and F. Scott Fitzgerald all stayed in the towering **Grove Park Inn** (252-2711), on Macon St. off Charlotte St. (take bus #5). The hotel, made of stone quarried from the surrounding mountains, is expensive lodging but cheap sightseeing with early 20th-century fireplaces so immense you could walk into them. Down the hill is the **Estes-Winn Memorial Museum,** which houses about 20 vintage automobiles ranging from a Model T Ford to a 1959 Edsel. *(Open M-Sa 10am-5pm, Su 1-5pm. Free.)* Check out the 1922 candy-red America La France fire engine.

Four museums will draw you into Pack Sq. at **Pack Pl.** (257-4500). The **Asheville Art Museum** displays 20th-century American paintings. You can become one with your body at the **Health Adventure,** survey African-American art at the **YMI Culture Center,** and see all that glitters in the **Colburn Gem and Mineral Museum.** *(All open Tu-Sa 10am-5pm; June-Oct. also Su 1-5pm. 1 museum $3, students and seniors $2.50, ages 4-15 $2; all 4 museums $6.50/$5.50/$4.50.)*

The **Thomas Wolfe Memorial** (253-8304), between Woodfin and Walnut St., the site of the novelist's boyhood home, was a boarding house run by his mother and the inspiration for the guest house in Wolfe's *Look Homeward, Angel. (Open Apr.-Oct. M-Sa 9am-5pm, Su 1-5pm; Nov.-Mar. Tu-Sa 10am-4pm, Su 1-4pm. Tours every hr. on the ½hr., with an audio-visual program on the hr. $1, students 50¢.)*

To know this deal, 'twere best not know thyself— it's free **Shakespeare in Montford Amphitheater** (254-4540; June-Aug. F and Su 7:30pm). During the last weekend in July, put your feet on the street along with thousands of others at North Carolina's largest street fair, **Bele Chere Festival** (259-5800).

The scenic setting for *Last of the Mohicans* rises up almost ½ mi. in **Chimney Rock Park** (800-277-9611), 25 mi. southeast of Asheville on Rte. 74A. *(Ticket office open daily 8:30am-5:30pm; in winter 8:30am-4:30pm. Park open 1½hr. after office closes. $10, ages 6-15 $5; in winter $6/$3.)* After driving to the base of the Chimney, take the 26-story elevator to the top, or walk up for a 75 mi. view.

Free weekly papers, *Mountain Express* and *Community Connections,* feature entertainment listings, while the *Re:Source* enlightens on New Age events.

CAROLINA COAST

Known as the "barrier islands" by the inlanders whom they shield from Atlantic squalls, the Carolina Coast has a history as stormy as the hurricanes that annually pummel their beaches. England's first attempt to colonize North America ended in 1590 with the peculiar disappearance of the Roanoke Island settlement (see below). Even worse, over 600 ships have foundered on the Outer Banks' southern shores. The same wind that fiercely batters the coast also buttresses much of its recreational activity: hang-gliding, paragliding, the best windsurfing on the East Coast, and, of course, good old kite-flying from the tops of tall dunes. The Wright brothers selected Kitty Hawk for its strong winds and welcoming hospitality.

■ Outer Banks

The Outer Banks descend from rapidly developing beach towns southward into heavenly wilderness. Bodie Island, on the Outer Banks' northern end, includes the towns of Nags Head and Kitty Hawk. The Wright Brothers first flew from Kill Devil Hills, the third town in Bodie; it's now tourism that soars there, though in a tolerably familial way. Crowds become less overpowering as you travel south on Rte. 12 and across the beautiful Hatteras Inlet to Ocracoke Island.

ORIENTATION AND PRACTICAL INFORMATION

The Outer Banks are comprised of four narrow islands strung along half the length of the North Carolina coast. In the north, **Bodie Island** is accessible via U.S. 158 from Elizabeth, NC, and Norfolk, VA. **Roanoke Island** lies between Bodie and the mainland on U.S. 64 and includes the town of **Manteo**. **Hatteras Island,** connected to Bodie by a bridge, stretches like a great sandy elbow. **Ocracoke Island,** the southernmost island, is linked (by a long ferry ride) to Hatteras Island and to towns on the mainland. **Cape Hatteras National Seashore** encompasses Hatteras, Ocracoke, and the southern end of Bodie Island. On Bodie Island, U.S. 158 and Rte. 12 run parallel to each other until the north edge of the preserve. After that, Rte. 12 (also called Beach Rd.) continues south, stringing together Bodie and Hatteras. Addresses on Bodie Island are determined by their distances in miles from the Wright Memorial Bridge.

There is **no public transportation** available on the Outer Banks. Nags Head and Ocracoke lie 76 mi. apart. The flat terrain makes hiking and biking pleasant, but the Outer Banks' ferocious traffic calls for extra caution and extra travel time.

Ferries: Toll ferries run to Ocracoke (800-345-1665) from Cedar Island (800-856-0343; 2½hr., 4-9 per day), east of New Bern on U.S. 70, and from Swan Quarter (800-773-1094), on the north side of Pamlico. Fare $1, $10 per car (reserve ahead), $2 per biker. **Free ferries** cross Hatteras Inlet between Hatteras and Ocracoke (daily 5am-11pm, 40min.). Call 800-293-3779 for all ferry times.

Taxis: Beach Cab, 441-2500, for Bodie Island and Manteo. $1.50 base, $1.20 per mi.

Car Rental: U-Save Auto Rental (800-685-9938), 1 mi. north of Wright Memorial Bridge in Point Harbor. $30 per day with 50 free mi. 20¢ each additional mi. Must be 21 with MC, Visa, or $250 cash deposit. Open M-F 8am-5:30pm, Sa 9am-2pm.

Shuttle Service: The Connection (473-2777) offers shuttles from Norfolk, VA to anywhere in the Outer Banks; it's not cheap, but you may not have any other choice. From $58; discounts available if you call at least 48hr. in advance.

Colony Lost

After the failure of his party's first expedition to the New World, Sir Walter Raleigh decided to sponsor a new colony in "Virginia," the Elizabethan name for what is now the Carolina Coast. The colonists settled on Roanoke Island in 1587. Among the 116 adventurers were 17 women and nine children, which reflected Raleigh's desire to build a colony more permanent than a simple military outpost. Unfortunately, it was not to be—a series of skirmishes and misunderstandings with local Algonquin tribes made for an uneasy relationship between colonists and the indigenous residents. In need of supplies, Governor White returned to England, leaving behind his wife and child. When he next set foot on the sands of Roanoke, nearly 3 years later, he found the island deserted. The only hint of the nascent colony's whereabouts were the letters "CRO" carved into a tree, and a military palisade bearing the word "CROATOAN," probably a reference to the Croatoan Indians, who lived on what is now the southern tip of Hatteras Island. Weather and low provisions prevented White from sailing for the alluded-to island, and the colony was never located.

Bike Rental: Pony Island Motel (928-4411), on Ocracoke Island. $2 per hr., $10 per day. Open daily 8am-10pm.

Visitor Info: Kitty Hawk Welcome Center (261-4644), off U.S. 158 across the Wright Memorial Bridge on Bodie Island, has info on lodging and picnic areas. Open daily 8:30am-6:30pm; in winter 9am-5pm. **Cape Hatteras National Seashore Information Centers: Bodie Island** (441-5711), Rte. 12 at Bodie Island Lighthouse; **Ocracoke Island** (928-4531), next to the ferry terminal at the south end of the island. Both open daily June-Aug. 8:30am-6pm; Mar.-May and Sept.-Dec. 9am-5pm. **Hatteras Island** (995-4474 or 995-5209), Rte. 12 at the Cape Hatteras Lighthouse. Open daily 9am-6pm. **Area code:** 252.

ACCOMMODATIONS, CAMPGROUNDS, AND FOOD

Most motels cling to **Rte. 12** on crowded Bodie Island. For more privacy, go further South; **Ocracoke** is the most secluded. On all three islands, rooming rates are highest from late May to early September. Reservations are needed 7-10 days ahead for weeknights and up to a month in advance for weekends. Long tent spikes accommodate the loose dirt, tents with fine screens keep out flea-sized, biting "no-see-ums," and strong insect repellent always helps. If you sleep on the beach, you may get fined.

Kill Devil Hills

Outer Banks International Hostel (HI-AYH), 1004 Kitty Hawk Rd. (261-2294), off Rte. 158. The former Kitty Hawk school and the best deal on the Banks. 40 beds, 2 kitchens, A/C, heat, volleyball, basketball, shuffleboard. Free use of bikes. Kayak rental $10 1st hr., $7 per additional hr. Members $15, nonmembers $18; private rooms from $32/$35, off-season $27.50/$30.50. Limited camping spots on the grounds $10, $8 per additional person; tent rental $4.

The Ebbtide, Mi. 10, Beach Rd. (441-4913). Plainly furnished rooms with A/C, heat, cable TV, refrigerators, microwaves, private beach access, and a pool. Guests can breakfast on 2 eggs and toast for 99¢ at the **Ship's Wheel** restaurant next door. Singles $49, doubles $57-68; off-season $29/$35-43. Open late Mar. to late Sept.

Nettlewood Motel, Mi. 7, Beach Rd. (441-5039), across from the shore. Private beach access. Bright, clean, cozy rooms. TVs, A/C, heat, refrigerators, and a pool. Singles $49, doubles $70; May 22-June 11 $40/$48; Jan 1-May 21 $32/$37.

Totuga's Lie, Mi. 11, Beach Rd. (441-7299). Caribbean-influenced seafood and grill items in a casual setting. Jamaican jerk chicken with beans and rice $5, to-die-for chocolate pecan pie $3. Open Su-Th 11:30am-midnight, F-Sa 11:30am-1am.

Chilli Peppers, Mi. 5½ (441-8081), Bypass 158. CP's creative kitchen boasts amazing entrees like the peanut-cilantro-crusted tuna steak. Lunch $3-7; dinner $6-18 but worth it. Nightly quesadilla specials. Open M-Sa 11:30am-11pm; Su for brunch 10:30am-4pm. Local bands Tu, open mike Su, sushi 3 nights per week.

Manteo

Scarborough Inn (473-3979), on U.S. 64/264 between the 7-11 and BP gas station. Romantic inn features 4-poster canopy beds, flowered linen, and wrap-around porches. A/C, heat, fridges, microwaves, continental breakfast, and free bicycle use. 1 queen bed $55, 2 double beds $60, 1 king bed $65; off-season $35/$40/$65.

The Weeping Radish (473-1157), across the street from the Inn. A kitschy, popular microbrewery (0.5L $3.35) and Bavarian restaurant with great homemade beer-bread. Tours daily 1 and 4pm. Open daily 11:30am-9pm; bar open until 10pm.

Ocracoke

Sand Dollar Motel (928-5571), off Rte. 12. Turn right at the Pirate's Chest gift shop, right again at the Back Porch Restaurant, and left at the Edwards Motel. Beautiful juniper paneling lends rooms a beach-cabin feel. Refrigerators, A/C, heat, and pool and continental breakfast. 1 queen bed $60, 2 queen beds $70; off-season $44/$55. Open Apr. to late Nov.

Edward's of Ocracoke (928-4801), off Rte. 12 by the Back Porch Restaurant. Bright assortment of rooms, all with TVs, A/C, and heat. Fish-cleaning facilities and bike rental. 2 double beds $50, off-season $45; 2 double beds and 1 single with refrigerator and screened porch $60/$53; 8 cottages for 4-6 $85-95/$75-85; efficiencies with kitchen and 2 double beds $65 per night. Sa-Su $5 higher.

Three oceanside campgrounds on Cape Hatteras National Seashore are open late May through early September: **Cape Point** (in Buxton) and **Frisco,** near the elbow of Hatteras Island, and **Ocracoke,** in the middle of Ocracoke Island. **Oregon Inlet,** on the southern tip of Bodie Island, opens in mid-April. All four have restrooms, water, and grills. Ocracoke is closest to the ocean, with its campsites clustered within spitting distance of the water. Frisco is graced with dunes and hillocks—Cape Point is just dull. All sites (except Ocracoke's) cost $12, and are rented on a first-come, first-served basis. Ocracoke sites ($13) can be reserved (from late May to early Sept.) by calling 800-365-2267. Contact **Cape Hatteras National Seashore** (473-2111) for other surf-related concerns.

SIGHTS AND ACTIVITIES

The **Wright Brothers National Memorial,** Mi. 8, U.S. 158 (441-7430), marks the spot where Orville and Wilbur Wright took to the skies. You can see models of their planes, hear a detailed account of the day of the first flight ("just remember: pitch, roll, and yaw"), and view the dramatic monument dedicated to the brothers in 1932. *(Open daily 9am-6pm; in winter 9am-5pm. Funny and informative presentations every hr. 10am until 1hr. before closing. $2 per person, $4 per car.)* **Kitty Hawk Aero Tours** (441-4460) offers a 30min. airplane tour of the area ($23-29 per person).

Desert aficionados and everyone's inner child will appreciate **Jockey's Ridge State Park,** Mi. 12 on the Hwy. 158 bypass. *(Open daily 8am-9pm; off-season hrs. vary. Free.)* It's the tallest sand dune in the eastern U.S. and the choicest kite-flying and sunset-watching spot around. If climbing this sand pile isn't enough excitement, tourists can follow the Wright brothers and jump off the side in a **hang glider,** under the supervision of **Kitty Hawk Kites** (441-4124 or 800-334-4777), across the street from Jockey's Ridge. A hang-gliding lesson costs $49-69 for 3-3½hr. of instruction (ages 8 and up).

On **Roanoke Island,** the **Fort Raleigh National Historic Site,** off U.S. 64, offers several attractions. The **Lost Colony** (473-3414 or 800-488-5012), the longest-running outdoor drama in the U.S., has been performed here since 1937. *(Shows early June to late Aug. M-F and Su 8:30pm. $14, seniors and military $13, under 12 $7.)* Bring insect repellent. In the **Elizabethan Gardens** (473-3234), antique statues and fountains punctuate a beautiful display of flowers, herbs, and trees. *(Open daily 9am-8pm while Lost Colony is playing next door; off-season 9am-5pm. $3, ages 12-17 $1, under 12 free with adult.)* Horseshoe crabs and marine monsters await at the **North Carolina Aquarium** (473-3493), 1 mi. west of U.S. 64 on Airport Rd., 3 mi. north of Manteo. *(Open daily 9am-7pm; off-season 9am-5pm. $3, seniors $2, ages 6-17 $1.)* Special exhibits change monthly; check out the huge brochure at the visitors center.

"Damned if they ain't flew!"

So exclaimed one eyewitness to humankind's first controlled, sustained flight. On December 17, 1903, two bicycle repairmen from Dayton, Ohio, launched the world's first true airplane in 27 mph headwinds from an obscure location on the NC coast, called Kill Devil Hills. Orville Wright, with his brother Wilbur watching anxiously from the ground, held on with his right hand and steered the 605 lb. Flyer with his left. 852 feet and 57 seconds later, the Wright brothers had flown their craft into history—and then oblivion: the original Flyer was destroyed on the ground by a strong gust of wind.

Majestic lighthouses dot the Outer Banks; **Cape Hatteras,** run by the Cape Hatteras National seashore, is North America's tallest at 208 ft. *(Open daily June-Aug. 10am-4pm; mid-Apr. to late May and early Sept. to Oct. 10am-2pm.)* Special programs at the **Hatteras Island Visitors Center** in Buxton include **Maritime Woods Walk** (W 1:30pm) and **Morning Bird Walk** (W 7:30am). The free park paper, wittily titled *In the Park,* has a schedule of these and numerous other activities.

South Carolina

The timbre of South Carolina is more laid back than a quick glance would suggest. Civil War monuments dot virtually every public green or city square, and confederate flags fly around the state, the first to secede from the Union in 1860. Yet, their presence is not so much a stubborn political cry as it is a testimony to a beloved time past. The capital, Columbia, is a relaxed college town that was demolished during the Civil War, along with almost everything else in General William Sherman's path. Coastal Charleston was spared, and despite nature's repeated assaults, still boasts stately, antebellum panache. You may need to "do the Charleston" for a few days to take in the city's full flavor. Those who slow to South Carolina's languid pace find that this state preserves a grace and charm uniquely Southern and altogether delightful.

PRACTICAL INFORMATION

Capital: Columbia.
Visitor Info: Dept. of Parks, Recreation, and Tourism, Edgar A. Brown Bldg., 1205 Pendleton St., #106, Columbia 29021 (803-734-0122; http://www.travelsc.com).
   U.S. Forest Service, 4931 Broad River Rd., Columbia 29210-4021 (803-561-4000).
Emergency: 911.
Time Zone: Eastern. **Postal Abbreviation:** SC.
Sales Tax: 6%.

■ Charleston

Dukes, barons, and earls once presided over Charleston's great coastal plantations, building an extensive downtown district. In recent years, natural disasters, including five fires and 10 hurricanes—the latest in 1989—have necessitated repeated rebuilding in the city. New storefronts and thriving restaurants mix with beautifully refurbished antebellum homes, old churches, and hidden gardens. Students here attend a pair of venerable institutions, lending a youthful vibrance to this old city: the College of Charleston, the first municipal college in America, founded in 1770, and The Citadel, a prestigious military school which has trained cadets since 1842 and recently admitted women. Those who can pry themselves away from Charleston's institutions find that the area also offers easy access to the nearby Atlantic coastal islands.

ORIENTATION AND PRACTICAL INFORMATION

Old Charleston lies at the southernmost point of the mile-wide peninsula below **Calhoun St. Meeting, King,** and **East Bay St.** are major north-south routes through the city. The **Savannah Hwy./U.S. 17** runs north of Calhoun St. Parking is scarce to non-existent downtown. All day parking is available at the visitors center (very close to the historic district) for $6, and at the parking lot on Wentworth St. for $3.50.

- **Trains: Amtrak,** 4565 Gaynor Ave. (744-8264 or 800-872-7245), 8 mi. west of downtown. To: Richmond (6hr., 2 per day, $89-112); Savannah (1¾hr., 2 per day, $25-32); and Washington, D.C. (9hr., 1 per day, $143). Open daily 6am-10pm.
- **Buses: Greyhound,** 3610 Dorchester Rd. (747-5341 or 800-231-2222), in N. Charleston. *Avoid this area at night.* To Savannah (3hr., 2 per day, $22-24) and Charlotte (5hr., 3 per day, $38-40). The Charleston Transit "Dorchester/Waylyn" bus goes to town from the station area. Return on the "Navy Yard: 5 Mile Dorchester Rd." bus. Open daily 6am-9:30pm.
- **Public Transportation: Charleston Transit,** 3664 Leeds Ave. (747-0922), runs buses M-Sa 5:10am-1am. Fare 75¢. **Downtown Area Shuttle (DASH)** (724-7420) runs daily 8am-5pm. Fare 75¢, seniors and disabled 25¢; transfers to other buses free. The visitors center has free maps, bus system passes (all day $2, 3-day $5), schedules, and other DASH info.
- **Car Rental: Thrifty Car Rental,** 3565 W. Montague Ave. (800-367-2277 or 552-7531). Must be 21 with major credit card. $40 per day, $190 per week. Under 25 surcharge $12 per day, airport access fee 8%. Open daily 6am-10pm.
- **Bike Rental: The Bicycle Shoppe,** 280 Meeting St. (722-8168), between George and Society St. $5 per hr., $25 per day. Open M-Sa 9am-8pm, Su 1-5pm.
- **Visitor Info: Charleston Visitors Center,** 375 Meeting St. (853-8000), across from Charleston Museum. Walking tour map ($5) has historical info and good directions. The free *Charleston Area Visitors Guide* is comprehensive. Open daily 8:30am-5:30pm.
- **Taxis: Yellow Cab,** 577-6565. Base fare $2 per person, $1.25 per mi.
- **Hotlines: Crisis Line,** 744-4357 or 800-922-2283. General counseling. **People Against Rape,** 722-7273. Both operate 24hr.
- **Post Office:** 83 Broad St. (577-0690). Open M-F 8:30am-5:30pm, Sa 9:30am-2pm. **ZIP code:** 29402. **Area code:** 803.

ACCOMMODATIONS AND CAMPGROUNDS

Motel rooms in historic downtown Charleston are expensive. Cheap motels are a few mi. out of the city, around Exits 209-11 on I-26 W, or across the Ashley River on U.S. 17 S—not a practical option for those without cars. **Masters Inn Economy,** 6100 Rivers Ave. (744-3530, reservations 800-633-3434), at I-26 and Aviation Ave. (Exit 211B), has spacious rooms with A/C and cable TV (pool, free local calls, and laundry; singles $35, doubles $43; Sa-Su $43/$49). **Motel 6,** 2058 Savannah Hwy. (556-5144), 4 mi. south of town, is clean and pleasant, but far from downtown and often full. Call ahead in summer. (Rooms $40, $3 per additional person; lower in winter.)

There are several inexpensive campgrounds in the Charleston area, including the **Campground at James Island County Park** (795-9884 or 800-743-7275). Take U.S. 17 S to Rte. 171 and follow the signs. This spectacular park offers full hookups in addition to 16 acres of lakes, miles of bicycle and walking trails, and a small water park. (Limited number of primitive tent sites $13.50; full hookup $27.) **Oak Plantation Campground** (766-5936), 8 mi. south on U.S. 17, has 350 sites, a pool, two bathhouses, and a laundromat. A shuttle to the visitors center costs $4. (Sites $11-19. Office open daily 7:30am-8:30pm.)

FOOD AND NIGHTLIFE

- **Hyman's Seafood Company,** 215 Meeting St. (723-6000). Kudos to the proprietor, who manages to serve 15-25 different kinds of fresh fish daily ($6-10). Open daily 11am-11pm. Adjoining **Aaron's Deli** serves kosher fare you'd be a schmuck not to schlep to. Open M-Th 8am-11pm, F-Sa 7am-11pm.
- **T-Bonz Gill and Grill,** 80 N. Market St. (577-2511). Everything from T-bone to stir-fry, all in an open-beam building in the historic district opposite the market. Lunch or dinner $4.50-15. Potato with chili $3, steaks pricier ($11-17). Open daily 11am-2am (late-night menu midnight-2am).

Sticky Fingers, 235 Meeting St. (853-7427), and at 2 other Charleston locations. They give you washclothes instead of napkins, but chances are you'll be licking the BBQ sauce off your digits and leaving the 'cloth clean. Ribs in many styles, including the yummy Carolina Sweet ($6.50 lunch, $11 dinner). A huge slice of pecan pie is a good finish. Open Su 11am-10pm, M-Th 11am-10:30pm, F-Sa 11am-11pm.

The Baker's Café, 214 King St. (577-2694). Serves gourmet sandwiches (like the enticing blackened grouper with cayenne tartar sauce $7.75) and wonderful eggs just about any way imaginable ($6-9). Open M-F from 8am and Sa-Su from 9am, until late afternoon daily. Lunch starts at 11:30am; eggs served through afternoon.

Locals rarely dance the Charleston anymore, and the city's nightlife suffers for it. Free copies of *Upwith* or *Free Time,* in stores and restaurants, have listings of concerts and other events. It is harder to find *Q Notes,* a gay and lesbian paper; *Indie File,* a music monthly; and *The Club* (all free). Most bars and clubs are in the Market St. area. The **Music Farm,** 32 Ann St., is shutting its doors, but locals promise that Charleston's hottest nightspot will remain just that, under different ownership, name, and possibly theme. Sunday through Wednesday, the **Acme Downtown,** 5 Faber St. (577-7383), hosts eclectic music. On Thursday and Friday, Acme becomes a dance club. (21+. No cover. Open Su and Tu-F 8pm-3am, Sa 8pm-2am.)

SIGHTS AND ENTERTAINMENT

Charleston's ancient homes, historical monuments, churches, galleries, and gardens can be seen by foot, car, bus, boat, trolley, or horse-drawn carriage; ask about organized tours (including a mere 27 walking ones) at the visitors center. The **Gray Line Water Tours** (722-1112) boat trip is not only longer (2hr.) but less expensive than most others. *(Tours daily 9:30, 11:30am, 1:30, and 3:30pm. $10, ages 6-11 $5. Reservations recommended.)*

The open-air **City Market,** downtown at Meeting St., has a deal on everything from porcelain sea lions to handwoven sweetgrass baskets (open daily 9:30am-sunset). **Gibbes Museum of Art,** 135 Meeting St. (722-2706), displays a fine collection of portraits by prominent American artists, as well as photographs, explorations of "lowlands life," and international exhibits (open Su 1-5pm, Tu-Sa 10am-5pm; $5, seniors $2, ages 6-18 $1). Founded in 1773, the **Charleston Museum,** 360 Meeting St. (722-2996), maintains collections ranging from natural history specimens to old sheet music (open M-Sa 9am-5pm, Su 1-5pm; $6, ages 3-12 $3). A combination ticket is available for the museum and two historic homes located nearby: the 18th-century **Heyward-Washington House,** 87 Church St. (722-0354), and the **Joseph Manigault House,** 350 Meeting St. (723-2926). *(Both homes open M-Sa 10am-5pm, Su 1-5pm. Museum and 2 homes $15, children $5.)* The **Nathaniel Russell House,** 51 Meeting St. (724-8481), offers a glimpse into how Charleston's wealthy merchant class lived in the early 19th century. *(Open M-Sa 10am-5pm, Su 2-5pm. $6.)* A magnificent staircase spirals from floor to floor without visible support.

The **Battery** offers a good view of the harbor and **Fort Sumter,** where an attack by rebel forces on April 12, 1861 touched off the Civil War. Over 7 million pounds of metal were fired against the Fort before it was finally abandoned in February, 1865. To walk the sacred ground, call **Fort Sumter Tours** (722-1691). Boat tours leave several times daily from the City Marina, at the foot of Calhoun St. and Lockwood Blvd. ($10.50, ages 6-11 $5.50). Other tours head to **Patriots' Point Naval and Maritime Museum** (884-2727), the world's largest, where you can stroke the destroyer Laffey's aft cannons (2-3hr.; open daily 9am-6pm; Oct.-Mar. 9am-5pm; $9, ages 6-11 $4).

One of several majestic plantations in the area, the 300-year-old **Magnolia Plantation and Magnolia Gardens** (571-1266), on Rte. 61 10 mi. out of town off U.S. 17, treat visitors to 50 acres of gorgeous gardens with 900 varieties of camelia and 250 varieties of azalea. *(Open daily 8am-5:30pm. $9, seniors, military, and AAA $8, ages 13-19 $7, ages 6-12 $4.)* Visitors can lose themselves in the hedge maze, or rent bicycles or canoes ($3 per 3hr.) to explore the neighboring swamp and bird sanctuary.

Over the James Island Bridge and U.S. 171, **Folley Beach,** about 20 mi. southeast of Charleston, is popular with local students.

From mid-March to mid-April, the **Festival of Houses and Gardens** (723-1623) celebrates Charleston's architecture and traditions. Many private homes open their doors to the public (10 houses $30). Music, theater, dance, and opera fill the city during **Spoleto Festival U.S.A.** (800-255-4659) in late May and early June ($10-75). **Christmas in Charleston** (800-868-8118) is all a-jingle with tours and performances.

■ Columbia

One of America's first planned cities, Columbia developed at the behest of Charleston's bureaucrats, who decided their territory needed a proper capital. They chose Colonel Thomas Taylor's plantation by the Congaree River, who subsequently remarked that they had "turned a damn fine plantation into a pretty poor town." In spite of its rocky start, the University of South Carolina's (USC) verdant horseshoe reigns over a more mature city, one that has maintained its strong links to a Confederate past, while incorporating the look and feel of a contemporary college town. It is this seemingly effortless union of past and present that gives Columbia a unique and endearing appeal.

ORIENTATION AND PRACTICAL INFORMATION

The city is laid out in a square, with borders Huger (running north-south), Harden (north-south), Blossom (east-west), and Calhoun (east-west). **Assembly St.** is the main drag, running north-south through the heart of the city. **Gervais St.** is its east-west equivalent. The Congaree River marks the city's western edge. Roads tend to be poorly marked.

Airport: Columbia Metropolitan, 3000 Aviation Way (822-5010). Taxi to downtown costs about $15.

Trains: Amtrak, 850 Pulaski St. (252-8246 or 800-872-7245). 1 per day to: Miami (14hr., $57); Washington, D.C. (10hr., $60); and Savannah (2½hr., $22). Open daily 10am-5:45pm and 11pm-6:45am. Northbound train departs 1:05am, southbound 2:50am.

Buses: Greyhound, 2015 Gervais St. (256-6465 or 800-231-2222), at Harden about 1 mi. east of the capital. To Charlotte (1½hr., 4 per day, $12-13) and Atlanta (4½hr., 8 per day, $43). Most east coast buses stop here. 24hr.

Public Transportation: South Carolina Electric and Gas (SCE&G) (748-3019). Fare 75¢, seniors and disabled 25¢, under 6 free. Most northbound routes start from the transfer depot at Assembly and Gervais St. Southbound routes leave from the depot at Sumpter and Laurel St. Buses run 5:30am-midnight. Call for schedules.

Taxis: Gamecock Cab, 796-7700. $1.45 base fare, $1.30 per additional mi.

Visitor Info: Columbia Metropolitan Convention and Visitors Bureau, 1012 Gervais St. (254-0479). Pick up maps for self-guided walking tours of *Historic Columbia* or *African-American Historic Sites in Columbia.* Open M-F 9am-5pm, Sa 10am-4pm, Su 1-5pm (winter hrs. vary). **University of South Carolina Visitors Center,** 937 Assembly St. (777-0169, general info 800-922-9755). Free visitor's parking pass and extensive info on USC and Columbia. Also assists with arranging tours. Open M-F 8:30am-5pm, Sa 9:30am-2pm.

Hotlines: Crisis Intervention, 790-4357. **Rape Crisis,** 771-7273. Both 24hr.

Post Office: 1601 Assembly St. (733-4643). Open M-F 7:30am-6pm. **ZIP code:** 29202. **Area code:** 803.

ACCOMMODATIONS, CAMPGROUNDS, AND FOOD

Just outside of downtown across the Congaree River, a number of inexpensive motels line **I-26** and **I-77.** One is **Masters Economy Inn** (791-5850 or 800-633-3434); get off I-26 E at Exit 113 and take a left, then an immediate right, onto Frontage Rd. (Singles $29; doubles $39; 10% discount for AAA and seniors. Free local calls, a pool, and cable TV. Wheelchair access.) On the same road, **Knights Inn** (794-0222) may not be a castle, but it has a great deal of amenities for a low price. All rooms have refrigerators, microwaves, cable TV, A/C, free local calls and pool access. (Singles and doubles $30; in summer $32; 10% discount for AAA and seniors.) The **Sesquicentennial State Park** (788-2706) has a lake for swimming, a nature center, hiking and biking trails, and 87 wooded sites with electricity and water. (Gate closes 9pm; Nov.-Mar. 6pm; $13.) Public transportation does not serve the park; take I-20 to the Two Notch Rd./Rte. 1 Exit and head northeast for 3 mi.

Adriana's, 721 Saluda Ave. (799-7595), serves a super selection of Italian ice cream (massive serving $2.24), delicious pastries, and incredible lemon sorbetto (open M-Th 10:30am-midnight, F-Sa 10:30am-12:30am, Su noon-11pm). **Groucho's,** 611 Harden St. (799-5708), marx out its own identity with the invention of the dipper, a large deli sandwich featuring Groucho's own "45" sauce for $6 (open M-Sa 11am-4pm, Su noon-4pm; June-Aug. M-Sa 11am-4pm). Students and locals have adopted **Stuffy's Famous,** 629 S. Main St. (771-4098), down Main St. from the State House, and it seems to have adopted them; USC sports memorabilia lines its long walls. It holds true to its motto, cheap "Good Stuff" (cheeseburger, fries, and iced tea $3.45). Happy hour (M-F 4-7pm) spells 20¢ wings. (Open Sept.-May M-F 10am-11pm, Sa 11am-11pm; June-Aug. M-F 10am-11pm.) For those intent on greener stuff, the **Columbia State Farmers Market** (737-4664), Bluff Rd., across from the stadium, offers every kind of produce you could desire (open M-Sa 6am-9pm, Su 1-9pm). **Rosewood Market,** 2803 Rosewood Dr. (256-6410), is a health nut's delight with prepared natural foods, including a yummy gazpacho ($2) and creative BBQ tofu ($2; deli open M-Sa 9am-7pm).

SIGHTS, ENTERTAINMENT, AND NIGHTLIFE

One of the finest zoos in the country, **Riverbanks Zoo and Garden** (779-8717), on I-26 at Greystone Blvd., northwest of downtown, shows visitors a rainforest, a desert, an undersea kingdom, and an interactive southern farm. *(Open daily in summer M-F 9am-4pm, Sa-Su 9am-5pm; off-season 9am-4pm. $5.75, students $4.50, seniors $4.25, ages 3-12 $3.25.)* Over 2000 animals roam in open habitats.

Two 19th-century mansions, the **Robert Mills Historic House and Park,** 1616 Blanding St. (252-1770), 3 blocks east of Sumter St., and the **Hampton-Preston Mansion,** across the street, compete in elegance as twin survivors of Sherman's Civil War rampage. *(Hourly tours Tu-Sa 10:15am-3:15pm, Su 1:15-4:15pm. Tours $3, students $1.50, under 6 free.)* Both have been lovingly restored and are chock full of fineries like silver door knobs, antique children's toys, and crystal chandeliers. The **South Carolina State Museum,** 301 Gervais St. (737-4595), stands beside the Gervais St. Bridge. *(Open M-Sa 10am-5pm, Su 1-5pm. $4, students with ID and seniors $3, ages 6-17 $1.50, under 6 free.)* Exhibits include a 30-million-year-old shark's tooth and a replica of the C.S.S. Hurley, the first submarine to sink a ship, in 1864.

The newly-renovated **Columbia Museum of Art** (799-2810), at the corner of Main and Hampton St., features one of the Southeast's most impressive collections of Italian Renaissance and Baroque paintings and sculptures. *(Open Tu and Th-Sa 10am-5pm, W 10am-9pm, Su 1-5pm. $4, seniors and students $2, under 5 free, 1st Sa of every month free.)*

Stroll through the USC **Horseshoe,** at the junction of College and Sumter St., to admire the university's oldest buildings and the tall trees that shade them. The **McKissick Museum** (777-7251), at the top of the Horseshoe, boasts two floors of both cultural and scientific exhibitions dedicated to exploring the southeast (open M-F 9am-4pm, Sa-Su 1-5pm; free). **Finlay Park,** behind the post office on Assembly and Laurel St., is large and manicured, with a playground, fountains, and swinging benches (closes M-F 10pm, Sa 8pm).

When night falls, everyone heads to the Five Points district, junction of Harden, Devine and Blossom St., for a great mix of coffeehouses, restaurants and bars. **Group Therapy,** 2107 Greene St. (256-1203; open M-F 'til 3am, Sa-Su 'til 2am), and **Big Al's,** 749 Saluda Ave. (758-0070), draw huge people in large, happy throngs you may well want to be a part of. The weekly publication *Free Times* gives details on Columbia's club and nightlife scene. *In Unison* is a weekly paper listing gay-friendly nightspots.

■ Myrtle Beach and the Grand Strand

Stretching 60 mi. from Little River near the North Carolina border to the tidelands of historic Georgetown, the Grand Strand is a wide ribbon of land bathed in beaches, restaurants, and tourists. In the middle of it all basks tacky Myrtle Beach, full of mini-

If you're stuck for cash on your travels, don't panic. Millions of people trust Western Union to transfer money in minutes to 153 countries and over 45,000 locations worldwide. Our record of safety and reliability is second to none. So when you need money in a hurry, call Western Union.

WESTERN UNION | MONEY TRANSFER®

The fastest way to send money worldwide.®

East Coast Hostels

Happening Hostels in the all the Big Cities

HI·Boston ·········

Located downtown in the Fenway, which includes some of Boston's best museums, restaurants and night spots. Two blocks from the subway. Something special at the hostel every night — walking tours, trips to baseball games, and more.

Boston

12 Hemenway Street, Boston, Massachusetts 02115
Toll Free Reservations (USA): 1•800•909•4776, code 07
Telephone: 617•536•9455   Open 24 hours. $18-21

HI·New York

On Manhattan's Upper West Side, a block from the subway, near Central Park and Columbia University. The hostel offers special tours/activities, a coffee bar, a cafeteria, and more.

New York

891 Amsterdam Avenue, New York, New York 10025
Toll Free Reservations (USA): 1•800•909•4776, code 01
Telephone: 212•932•2300   Open 24 hours. $22-27

HI·Washington, DC ·······

Near the White House, Smithsonian Museums and the Metro — what a capital location! The hostel offers tours, movies, concert trips and other special programs year-round.

D.C.

1009 11th Street, NW, Washington, DC 20001
Toll Free Reservations (USA): 1•800•909•4776, code 04
Telephone: 202•737•2333 Open 24 hours. $18-24

HOSTELLING INTERNATIONAL

For more information and these and other HI hostels call 202•783•6161.
(www.hiayh.org)

West Coast Hostels

California Dreaming - 23 hostels in hot locations

San Francisco (2) •

There are two HI hostels in San Francisco: Fisherman's Wharf and Union Square. Both are in the middle of the San Francisco action — Ghiradelli Square, Chinatown, the city's fabled cable cars, restaurants, shops and more.

San Francisco

HI•Fisherman's Wharf • • • • • • • • •

Fort Mason — Building 240, San Francisco, California 94123
Toll FreeReservations (USA): 1•800•909•4776, code 03
Telephone: 415•771•7277   Open 24 hours. $17-22

HI•Downtown • • • • • • • • • • • • • • • • • • •

312 Mason Street, San Francisco, California 94102
Toll Free Reservations (USA): 1•800•909•4776, code 02
Telephone: 415•788•5604   Open 24 hours. $17-22

HI•Los Angeles/Santa Monica • • • • • • • • • • • •

Just a block from the beach and the Third Street Promenade with more than 100 sidewalk cafes, restaurants, theaters, pubs and shops. Regularly scheduled trips to Disneyland® and Universal Studios and free airport pickup.

Santa Monica

1436 Second Street, Santa Monica, California 90401
Toll Free Reservations (USA): 1•800•909•4776, code 05
Telephone: 310•393•9913   Open 24 hours. $17-22

• •

San Diego

HI•San Diego

In the heart of the city's historic Gaslamp Quarter — 16 blocks of cafes, restaurants, clubs, shops, galleries and more. Catch the nearby trolley for a day trip to Mexico.

521 Market Street, San Diego, California 92101
Toll Free Reservations (USA): 1•800•909•4776, code 43
Telephone: 619•525•531 Open 24 hours. $16-21

For more information on these and other HI hostels call 202•783•6161.
(www.hiayh.org)

HOSTELLING
INTERNATIONAL

Florida Hostels

5 hostels near Beaches and the MAGIC KINGDOM®

HI•Miami Beach

Located two blocks from the beach, the hostel is in the Art Deco District of South Beach. Surrounded by night clubs, cafes and shops, the hostel is a definite hot spot (it was even featured in the movies *The Birdcage* and *The Specialist*, and in the TV show *Miami Vice).*

Miami

1438 Washington Avenue
Miami Beach, Florida 33139
Toll Free Reservations (USA): 1•800•379•CLAY
Telephone: 305•534•2988   Open 24 hours. $13-16

HI•Orlando/Kissimmee Resort

Orlando

Just five miles from Walt Disney World®; the hostel offers inexpensive daily shuttle service to area attractions. At the hostel — take a dip in the pool, enjoy a free paddleboat ride on the lake, or have a barbecue in the picnic area. A variety of special programs and activities take place daily for hostel guests.

4840 West Irlo Bronson Highway,Kissimmee, Florida 34746
Toll Free Reservations (USA): 1•800•909•4776, code 33
Telephone: 407•396•8282   Open 24 hours. $15-19

Check out our other cool Florida hostels:
Toll Free Reservations: 1•800•909•4776
HI•Clearwater Beach (code16)
HI•Melbourne Beach (code 65)
HI•Key West (code 55)

HOSTELLING INTERNATIONAL

For more information on these and other HI hostels call 202•783•6161
(www.hiayh.org)

MCI Spoken Here

Worldwide Calling Made Simple

For more information or to apply for a Card call: **1-800-955-0925**

Outside the U.S., call MCI collect (reverse charge) at: **1-916-567-5151**

International Calling As Easy As Possible.

The MCI Card with WorldPhone Service is designed specifically to keep you in touch with the people that matter the most to you.

The MCI Card with WorldPhone Service....

- Provides access to the US and other countries worldwide.
- Gives you customer service 24 hours a day
- Connects you to operators who speak your language
- Provides you with MCI's low rates and no sign-up fees

For more information or to apply for a Card call:

1-800-955-0925

Outside the U.S., call MCI collect (reverse charge) at:

1-916-567-5151

Pick Up the Phone, Pick Up the Miles.

You earn frequent flyer miles when you travel internationally, why not when you call internationally? Callers can earn frequent flyer miles if they sign up with one of MCI's airline partners:

- American Airlines
- Continental Airlines
- Delta Airlines
- Hawaiian Airlines
- Midwest Express Airlines
- Northwest Airlines
- Southwest Airlines
- United Airlines
- USAirways

Please cut out and save this reference guide for convenient U.S. and worldwide calling with the MCI Card with WorldPhone Service.

Your MCI Worldphone Access Numbers

MCI

COUNTRY	WORLDPHONE TOLL-FREE ACCESS #
# Singapore	8000-112-112
# Slovak Republic (CC)	00421-00112
# Slovenia	080-8808
# South Africa (CC)	0800-99-0011
# Spain (CC)	900-99-0014
# Sri Lanka (Outside of Colombo, dial 01 first)	440100
# St. Lucia ÷	1-800-888-8000
# St. Vincent	1-800-888-8000
# Sweden (CC) ◆	020-795-922
# Switzerland (CC) ◆	0800-89-0222
# Syria	0800
# Taiwan (CC) ◆	0080-13-4567
# Thailand ★	001-999-1-2001
# Trinidad & Tobago ÷	1-800-888-8000
# Turkey (CC) ◆	00-8001-1177
# Turks and Caicos ÷	1-800-888-8000
# Ukraine (CC) ÷	8▼10-013
# United Arab Emirates ◆	800-111
# United Kingdom (CC) To call using BT ■	0800-89-0222
To call using C&W ■	0500-89-0222
# United States (CC)	1-800-888-8000
# Uruguay	000-412
# U.S. Virgin Islands (CC)	1-800-888-8000
# Vatican City (CC)	172-1022
# Venezuela (CC) ÷ ◆	800-1114-0
# Vietnam ●	1201-1022
Yemen	008-00-102

#	Automation available from most locations.
(CC)	Country-to-country calling available to/from most international locations.
÷	Limited availability.
▼	Wait for second dial tone.
▲	When calling from public phones, use phones marked LADATEL.
■	International communications carrier.
◆	Not available from public pay phones.
●	Public phones may require deposit of coin or phone card for dial tone.
▲	Local service fee in U.S. currency required to complete call.
÷	Regulation does not permit Intra-Japan calls.
◆	Available from most major cities.

And, it's simple to call home.

1. Dial the WorldPhone toll-free access number of the country you're calling from (listed inside).

2. Follow the voice instructions in your language of choice or hold for a WorldPhone operator.
   - Enter or give the operator your MCI Card number or call collect.

3. Enter or give the WorldPhone operator your home number.

4. Share your adventures with your family!

The MCI Card with WorldPhone Service... The easy way to call when traveling worldwide.

MCI — Calling Card
123 456 7890 1234
J. D. SMITH
WorldPhone

COUNTRY	WORLDPHONE TOLL-FREE ACCESS #
American Samoa	633-2MCI (633-2624)
#Antigua	1-800-888-8000
(available from public card phones only)	#2
#Argentina (CC)	0800-5-1002
#Aruba ÷	800-888-8
#Australia (CC) ♦ To call using OPTUS ■	1-800-551-111
To call using TELSTRA ■	1-800-881-100
#Austria (CC) ♦	022-903-012
#Bahamas	1-800-888-8000
#Bahrain	800.000
#Barbados	1-800-888-8000
#Belarus (CC) From Brest, Vitebsk, Grodno, Minsk	8-800-103
From Gomel and Mogilev	8-10-800-103
#Belgium (CC) ♦	0800-10012
#Belize From Hotels	557
From Payphones	815
#Bermuda ÷	1-800-888-8000
#Bolivia (CC) ♦	0-800-2222
#Brazil (CC)	000-8012
#British Virgin Islands ÷	1-800-888-8000
#Brunei	800-8000
#Bulgaria	00800-0001
#Canada (CC)	1-800-888-8000
#Cayman Islands	1-800-888-8000
#Chile (CC) To call using CTC ■	800-207-300
To call using ENTEL ■	800-360-180
#China ✪ For a Mandarin-speaking Operator	108-17
	108-12
#Colombia (CC) ♦ Collect Access in Spanish	980-16-0001
	980-16-1000
#Costa Rica ♦	0800-012-2222
#Côte D'Ivoire	
#Croatia (CC) ★	0800-22-0111
#Cyprus ♦	080-90000
#Czech Republic (CC) ♦	00-42-000112
#Denmark (CC) ♦	8001-0022
#Dominica	1-800-888-8000
#Dominican Republic Collect Access	1-800-888-8000
Collect Access in Spanish	1121
#Ecuador (CC) ÷	999-170
#Egypt (CC) ♦	355-5770
El Salvador (Outside of Cairo, dial 02 first)	800-1767

— FOLD —

COUNTRY	WORLDPHONE TOLL-FREE ACCESS #
#Federated States of Micronesia	624
#Finland (CC) ♦	08001-102-80
#France (CC) ♦	0800-99-0019
#French Antilles (CC) ♦ (includes Martinique, Guadeloupe)	0800-99-0019
#French Guiana (CC)	0-800-99-0019
#Gabon	00-005
#Gambia ♦	00-1-99
#Germany (CC)	0-800-888-8000
#Greece (CC) ♦	00-800-1211
#Grenada ÷	1-800-888-8000
#Guam (CC)	1-800-888-8000
Guatemala (CC) ♦	99-99-189
Guyana	177
#Haiti ÷ Collect Access in French/Creole	193
	190
Honduras ÷	8000-122
#Hong Kong (CC)	800-96-1121
#Hungary (CC) ♦	00▼800-01411
#Iceland (CC) ♦	800-9002
India (CC) ♦ Collect Access	000-127
	000-126
#Indonesia (CC) ♦	001-801-11
Iran ÷ (SPECIAL PHONES ONLY)	
#Ireland (CC)	1-800-55-1001
#Israel (CC)	1-800-940-2727
#Italy (CC) ♦	172-1022
#Jamaica ÷	1-800-888-8000
Collect Access	873
#Japan (CC) ♦ (from Special Hotels only)	
(from public phones)	*2
To call using KDD ■	00539-121
To call using IDC ■	0066-55-121
To call using ITJ ■	0044-11-121
#Jordan	18-800-001
#Kazakhstan (CC)	8-800-131-4321
#Kenya ♦	080011
#Korea (CC) To call using KT ■	009-14
To call using DACOM ■	00309-12
Phone Booth ÷	00369-14
Military Bases	Press red button, 03, then *
#Kuwait	800-MCI (800-624)

— FOLD —

COUNTRY	WORLDPHONE TOLL-FREE ACCESS #
Lebanon Collect Access	600-MCI (600-624)
#Liechtenstein (CC) ♦	0800-89-0222
#Luxembourg (CC)	0800-0112
#Macao	0800-131
#Macedonia (CC) ♦	99800-4266
#Malaysia (CC) ♦	1-800-80-0012
#Malta	0800-89-0120
#Marshall Islands	1-800-888-8000
#Mexico (CC) Avantel	01-800-021-8000
Telmex ▲	01-800-674-7000
Collect Access in Spanish	01-800-021-1000
#Monaco (CC) ♦	800-90-019
#Montserrat	1-800-888-8000
#Morocco	00-211-0012
#Netherlands (CC) ♦	0800-022-9122
#Netherlands Antilles (CC) ÷	001-800-888-8000
#New Zealand (CC)	000-912
Nicaragua (CC) Collect Access in Spanish	166
(Outside of Managua, dial 02 first)	000-912
#Norway (CC) ♦ From any public payphone	*2
	800-19912
Pakistan	00-800-12-001
#Panama	2810-108
#Papua New Guinea (CC) Military Bases	05-07-19140
#Paraguay ÷	00-812-800
#Peru	0-800-500-10
#Philippines (CC) ♦ To call using PLDT ■	105-14
To call using PHILCOM ■	1026-14
Collect Access via PLDT in Filipino	105-15
Collect Access via ICC in Filipino	1237-77
#Poland (CC) ÷	00-800-111-21-22
#Portugal (CC) ÷	05-017-1234
#Puerto Rico (CC)	1-800-888-8000
#Qatar ♦	0800-012-77
#Romania (CC) ÷	01-800-1800
#Russia (CC) ÷ ♦ To call using ROSTELCOM ■	747-3322
(For Russian speaking operator)	747-3320
To call using SOVINTEL ■	960-2222
#Saipan (CC) ÷	950-1022
#San Marino (CC) ♦	172-1022
#Saudi Arabia (CC) ÷	1-800-11

golf courses, tennis courts, water parks, and white sands. During spring break and in early June, Myrtle Beach (especially North Myrtle Beach) is jam-packed with leering, sunburned students who revel in the area's cheap commercialism and the call of the deep blue. The rest of the year, the students will be gone, but their entertainment remains; for Spring Break at any age, this is the spot.

The pace slows significantly south of Myrtle Beach. **Murrell's Inlet,** a quaint port stocked with good seafood, and **Pawley's Island,** are both dominated by private homes. **Georgetown,** once a critical Southern port city, showcases its history with white-pillared homes on 18th-century-style rice and indigo plantations.

ORIENTATION AND PRACTICAL INFORMATION

A series of numerically ordered avenues bridge **Ocean Blvd.** and **Hwy. 17,** also called **Kings Hwy.** Avenue numbers repeat themselves after reaching 1st Ave. in the middle of town, so note whether the avenue is "north" or "south." Also, take care not to confuse north **Myrtle Beach** with the town **North Myrtle Beach,** which has an almost identical street layout (and character). **Rte. 501** runs west towards Conway, U.S. 95, and, more importantly, the "oh my god I gotta show Chrissy" factory outlet stores. Unless otherwise stated, addresses on the Grand Strand are for Myrtle Beach.

Buses: Greyhound, 511 7th Ave. N (448-2471 or 800-231-2222). To Charleston (2½-5hr., 2 per day, $20-21). Open M-Sa 10:30am-6:30pm, Su open only to meet buses.

Public Transportation: Coastal Rapid Public Transit (CRPTA) (248-7277) provides minimal busing. Local fare 75¢; Conway to Myrtle Beach $1.25. Buses run approximately M-F 6:30am-1:30am; reduced schedule Sa-Su.

Bike Rental: The Bike Shoppe, 711 Broadway (448-5335). Cruisers $10 per day, $5 per ½-day; mountain bikes $15/$7. Driver's license or credit card required. Open M-F 8am-6pm, Sa 9am-5pm.

Visitor Info: Myrtle Beach Chamber of Commerce, 1200 N. Oak St. (626-7444), provides entertainment listings, coupons, and details on accommodations. Open M-F 8:30am-5pm, Sa 9am-5pm, Su noon-5pm.

Hotlines: Grand Strand Rape Hotline, 448-7273. 24hr.

Post Office: 505 N. Kings Hwy. (626-9533). Open M-F 8:30am-5pm, Sa 9am-1pm. **ZIP code:** 29577. **Area code:** 803.

ACCOMMODATIONS AND CAMPGROUNDS

Couples and families take over in summer, Myrtle Beach's most expensive season. In fact, many motels and campgrounds accept only families or couples. Cheap motels line Hwy. 17, definitely the best bet in summer. Prices plunge October through March when they need your business; try bartering for a lower hotel rate. If you'll be in town 3-5 days, a free and easy way to find the most economical rooms is to call the **Myrtle Beach Hospitality Reservation Service,** 1551 21st Ave. N., #20 (626-9970 or 800-626-7477). For the best deals, ask for the "second row" string of hotels across the street from the ocean. (Open M-F 8:30am-7:30pm.) The Grand Strand may be the "camping capital of the world," at least if quantity is a deciding factor; Myrtle Beach alone is laden with nine campgrounds and two state parks.

Roving bands of rowdy bar-hoppers make safety on Ocean Blvd. an issue, and thousands of dollars worth of property are stolen annually from motel rooms.

Sea Banks Motor Inn, 2200 S. Ocean Blvd. (448-2434 or 800-523-0603), across the street from the ocean. Congenial family-run establishment with laundry, a pool, beach access, large windows, and cable TV. Some rooms have balconies. Singles $45; Mar. and Sept.-Oct. $29 if you say you saw it in *Let's Go.*

Grand Strand Motel, 1804 S. Ocean Blvd. (843-448-1461 or 800-433-1461). Family-oriented, and also across from the beach. Cable TV and pool. Small rooms with 1 queen bed for 2 adults from $65; Sa-Su $75; in winter $28.

Lazy G Motel, 405 27th Ave. N. (448-6333 or 800-633-2163), fronts 2-room apartments with mini-kitchens, couches, TV, A/C, a pool, and heat. From $61; mid-Oct. to mid-Mar. $29; Sa-Su add $10.

Camping: Myrtle Beach State Park Campground (238-5325), 3 mi. south of town off U.S. 17. 350 sites on 312 acres of unspoiled land with a cool beach, fishing, a pool, and a nature trail. Water and electricity. Showers and bathrooms are close by. Full hookup $20; Nov.-Mar. $17. Office open daily 6:30am-9:30pm.

Huntington Beach State Park Campground (237-4440), 5 mi. south of Murrell's Inlet on U.S. 17. A diverse environment with lagoons, salt marshes, and a beach. Daily nature walks. 187 sites with full hookup, showers, and rest rooms. Sites $21.40; Nov.-Mar. $17. Office open daily 9am-5pm. Call ahead for reservations.

ALL YOU CAN EAT

Over 1600 restaurants, serving anything you can imagine, can be found (or, can't be missed) on the Grand Strand. Massive, family-style, all-you-can-eat joints await at every traffic light. Seafood is best on **Murrell's Inlet,** while **Ocean Blvd.** and **Hwy. 17** offer endless steakhouses, fast food joints, and buffets.

River City Café, 404 21st Ave. N. (448-1990), also on Business Hwy. 17 in Murrell's Inlet, serves juicy burgers ($3-5), fries ($1.45), beer, and free peanuts (toss the shells on the floor) in a fun, collegiate atmosphere. Customers carve on the tables, write on the walls, and check out the license plates. Open daily 11am-10pm.

Mammy's Kitchen (448-7242), 11th Ave. N. at King's Hwy., grills up a breakfast deal and a half: hash browns, toast, 2 eggs, and bacon for $3.50. Dinner offers a full menu that includes an enormous seafood buffet (chicken, beef, salad included) for $13. Open daily 7am-noon and 4-9pm.

The Filling Station (626-9435), Hwy. 17 at 17th Ave. N. One great menu idea: all-you-can-eat pizza, spaghetti, soup, sandwich bar, and dessert. Fill 'er up at lunch (11am-4pm, $5) or dinner (4pm-closing, $7). Children eat for $2-3, including drink. Open daily 11am-10pm; in winter 11am-8pm.

SIGHTS, ENTERTAINMENT, AND NIGHTLIFE

The cheapest and most amusing entertainment here is people-watching. Families, newlyweds, foreigners, and students flock to this incredibly popular area to lie out, eat out, and live out the myth of American beach culture. The boulevard and the length of the beach are both called the strand. Cruising it at night is illegal—signs declare "You may not cross this point more than twice in 2 hours." The exhaustive *Grand Strand Festivals, Events, and Tournaments* booklet waits at the visitors center, along with the free *Sunny Day Guide* for shopping, dining, and golf options.

White sand beaches and refreshing water are Myrtle Beach's classic attractions. The mind-boggling number of golf links (100), mini-golf courses (45!), amusement parks, and water parks (13) could make the Las Vegas Strip seem sophisticated. The largest of the amusement parks is the **Myrtle Beach Pavilion** (448-6456), on Ocean Blvd. and 9th Ave. N. *(Open daily 1pm-midnight; winter hrs. vary. Unlimited rides $19, children under 42 in. $12. Individual tickets 60¢; rides use 2-4 tickets, depending on the number of loops, droops, and spins.)* The **Myrtle Waves Water Park** (448-1026 or 800-524-WAVE/9283), 10th Ave. N. and Hwy. 17 bypass, will drench you with 30 water rides, including the world's largest tubular slide. *(Open daily 10am-7pm; late May to early June and late Aug. to early Sept. 10am-5pm. $18, children under 48 in. $12.)*

Hankering for country music? The **Alabama Theater at Barefoot Landing,** 4750 Hwy. 17 S (272-1111 or 800-342-2262), has it all—singin', swingin', and comedy (Sa-Th 8pm, F 7pm; $25, ages 3-16 $10; reservations recommended). A quieter diversion may be found at the 9100-acre **Brookgreen Gardens,** Hwy. 17 opposite Huntington Beach State Park south of Murrell's Inlet. *(Open Tu-Sa 9:30am until dusk, Su-M 9:30am-5:30pm; in winter 9:30am-4:45pm. $7.50, ages 6-12 $3; $1 coupon at visitors center.)* Their large collection of American sculpture is set outdoors among massive oaks, flower beds, pools, and fountains. A wildlife sanctuary and aviary offer a close-up look at a variety of natural environments.

Georgia

Georgia presents two faces: the rural southern section of the state contrasts starkly with sprawling Atlanta to the north. The undeveloped Piedmont gives way to the Appalachians, which march away toward the highly urbanized megalopolis of the Northeast, but the state has plenty to distract visitors from manic Yankeedom. President Jimmy Carter's hometown and President Franklin D. Roosevelt's summer home both stand on red Georgia clay. Coca-Cola was invented here in 1886; since then, it has carried on to carbonate and caffeinate the world. The world has collegiate Athens to thank for "big" bands, Savannah to visit for an afternoon of antebellum atmosphere, and the Gold Coast for a slow-paced sea-side existence. Ted Turner and CNN have networked the globe, making Georgia's capital a modern, sophisticated metropolis. Georgia blooms in the spring, glistens in the summer, and mellows in the autumn, all the while welcoming y'all with peachy Southern hospitality. Stay here long, and you'll *never* shake Georgia from your mind.

PRACTICAL INFORMATION

Capital: Atlanta.
Visitor Info: Dept. of Industry and Trade, Tourist Division, 285 Peachtree Center Ave., Atlanta 30303 (656-3590 or 800-VISIT-GA/847-4842; http://www.georgia.org), in the Marriot Marquis 2 Tower, 10th fl. Write for or pick up the comprehensive *Georgia Travel Guide.* Open M-F 8am-5pm. **Dept. of Natural Resources,** 205 Butler St. SE, #1352, Atlanta 30334 (404-656-3530 in GA, 800-864-7275). **U.S. Forest Service,** 1720 Peachtree Rd. NW, Atlanta 30367 (347-2384), has info on the Chattahoochee and Oconee National Forests. Open M-F 10am-2pm.
Emergency: 911.
Time Zone: Eastern. **Postal Abbreviation:** GA.
Sales Tax: 4-7%, depending on county.

■ Atlanta

An increasingly popular destination for 20- and 30-somethings craving big city life but weary of more manic metropolises, Atlanta strives to be cosmopolitan with a smile, although its charm can be easily lost in the obscene regularity of the town's cookie-cutter suburbs. Northerners, Californians, the third-largest gay population in the U.S., and a host of ethnicities have diversified this capital of the South. A nationwide economic powerhouse, Atlanta contains offices for 400 of the Fortune 500 companies, including the headquarters of Coca-Cola and CNN. Nineteen colleges; including Georgia Tech, Morehouse College, Spelman College, and Emory University; call "Hotlanta" home. Razed by the fire of Union General William Sherman in the Civil War, Atlanta met with a more peaceful flame recently—the one lit by boxer Muhammed Ali in the opening ceremonies of the 1996 Olympic Games. The city has capitalized on its $2 billion worth of Olympic-related goodies and converted most venues and sites into permanent facilities. Remarkable for all these attractions, Atlanta is blessed with as many subtle gems; getting lost on Atlanta's streets reveals a seemingly endless number of cute shops, funky restaurants, and beautiful old homes.

ORIENTATION AND PRACTICAL INFORMATION

Atlanta sprawls across the northwest quadrant of the state at the junctures of I-75, I-85, and I-20. **I-285** ("the perimeter") circumscribes the city.

Getting around is confusing—*everything* seems to be named Peachtree. However, of the 40-odd roads bearing that name, only one, **Peachtree St.,** is a major north-south thoroughfare; other significant north-south roads are **Spring St.** and **Piedmont Ave.** Major east-west roads include **Ponce De Leon Ave.** and **North Ave.** In the heart of downtown—west of I-75/85, south of International Blvd. and north of the capitol, around the district known as Five Points—angled streets and shopping plazas run amok, making navigation difficult.

Downtown Atlanta is anchored by the **Peachtree Center** and **Five Points MARTA** stations, from which most tourists flock to the center and **Underground Atlanta,** respectively; these giant shopping and entertainment complexes, however, just aren't worth the attention. Northeast of downtown, the **Midtown** area (from Ponce de Leon Ave. to 17th St.) holds Atlanta's art museums. Directly southwest of downtown is the **West End**—an African-American area and the city's oldest historical quarter. Three subway stops east of Five Points, at the junction of Euclid and Moreland Ave., lies the **Little Five Points (L5P)** district, the local haven for eclecticism, artists, and youth subculture. **Virginia Highlands,** a trendy neighborhood east of Midtown and Piedmont Park, attracts yuppies and college kids. And then there was **Buckhead,** a posher-than-thou area north on Peachtree and accessible on MARTA ("Buckhead").

Airport: Hartsfield International (general info 222-6688, international services and flight info 530-2081), south of the city. MARTA is the easiest way to get downtown, with 15min. rides departing every 8min. daily 5am-1am ($1.25). **Atlanta Airport Shuttle** (524-3400) runs vans from the airport to over 100 locations in the metropolitan and outlying area (every 15min. daily 4:30am-11pm; shuttle downtown $10). Taxi to downtown $15.

Train: Amtrak, 1688 Peachtree St. NW (881-3061 or 800-872-7245), 3 mi. north of downtown at I-85. Take bus #23 from "Arts Center" MARTA station. To New York (18½hr., 1 per day, $90-164) and New Orleans (11½hr., 1 per day, $39-78). Open daily 6:30am-9:30pm.

Buses: Greyhound, 232 Forsyth St. (584-1728 or 800-231-2222), across from "Garnett" MARTA station. To: New York (18-21hr., 15 per day, $69-73); Washington, D.C. (12-18hr., 12 per day, $65-69); and Savannah (5-8hr., 7 per day, $22-49). Open 24hr.

Public Transportation: Metropolitan Atlanta Rapid Transit Authority (MARTA) (848-4711; schedule info M-F 6am-1am, Sa-Su 8am-1am). Combined rail and bus system serves virtually all area attractions and hotels. Rail operates M-F 5am-1am, Sa-Su and holidays 6am-12:30am in most areas. Bus hrs. vary. Fare $1.50, exact change needed, or buy a token at station machines; transfers free. Unlimited weekly pass $12. Pick up a system map at the **MARTA Ride Store,** Five Points Station downtown, or at one of the satellite visitors bureaus. MARTA courtesy phones in each rail station aid the confused. All trains, rail stations, and buses are lift-equipped.

Taxis: Atlanta Yellow Cab, 521-0200. $1.50 base fare, $1.40 per additional mi. **Rapid,** 222-9888. $1.60 base fare and per additional mi. Both 24hr.

Car Rental: Atlanta Rent-a-Car, 3185 Camp Creek Pkwy. (763-1160), just inside I-285 3 mi. east of the airport. 20 other locations in the area including 2800 Campelton Rd. and 3129 Piedmont Rd. $20 per day, 100 free mi. per day, 24¢ per additional mi. Must be 21 with major credit card.

Visitor Info: Atlanta Convention and Visitors Bureau, 233 Peachtree St. NE, #2000 (521-6600 or 800-ATLANTA/285-2682), Peachtree Center, 20th fl. of Harris Tower, downtown. Stop by for a free copy of *Atlanta Heritage, Atlanta Now,* or the *Atlanta and Georgia Visitors' Guide.* Open M-F 8:30am-5pm. Also try their automated **information service** (222-6688), available M-Sa 10am-9pm, Su noon-6pm.

Bi-Gay-Lesbian Organization: The **Gay Center** (876-5372), at 67 and 71 12th St. NE, provides community info and short-term counseling daily 6am-11pm. Call for the center's weekly happenings.

Hotline: Rape Crisis Counseling, 616-4861. 24hr.

Post Office: 3900 Crown Rd. Open 24hr. **ZIP code:** 30321. **Area code:** 404 roughly inside the I-285 perimeter, 770 outside. 10-digit dialing required.

ACCOMMODATIONS AND CAMPGROUNDS

Hostelling International Atlanta (HI-AYH), 223 Ponce de Leon Ave. (875-2882), in Midtown. From MARTA: North Ave. station, exit onto Ponce de Leon, about 3½ blocks east on the corner of Myrtle St., or take bus #2 and ask the driver to stop. Part of a converted Victorian B&B, livened up with goldfish, dogs, parakeets, and a collection of champion homing pigeons. Clean, dorm-style rooms come with Inter-

Downtown Atlanta

ACCOMMODATIONS

A Atlanta Midtown Manor
B Youth Hostel (HI)

TO BUCKHEAD

85
75

41

Howell Mill Rd.

Northside Dr.

Beverly Rd.

Montgomery Dr.

Monroe Dr.

Piedmont Ave.

Atlanta Botanical Garden

14th St.

Peachtree Community Playhouse ■ St.

Piedmont Park

Alexander Memorial Coliseium

10th St.

75

Peachtree Pl.

14th St.

Peachtree St.

Margaret Mitchell House ■

10th St.

8th St.

Virginia St.

W. Marietta St.

8th St.

8th St.

85

W. Peachtree St.

7th St.
6th St.
5th St.
4th St.
3rd St.

A

Ashby St.

Georgia Institute of Technology ■

Krispy Kreme ■

Ponce de Leon Ave.

TO DECATUR AND VIRGINIA HIGHLANDS →

Jefferson St.

278

Tech Parkway

Grant Field and Bobby Dodd Stadium ■

Fox Theatre ■

8

Bankhead Ave.

North Ave.

Linden Ave.

Vine St.

3

Marietta St.

Pine St.

Exhibition & SciTrek Museum

Hunicutt St.

19

Alexander St.

Parker St.
Mills St.

Currier St.

Civic Center ■

Ralph McGill Blvd.

Simpson St.

W. Peachtree Pl.

Highland Ave.

N

Centennial Olympic Park

Baker St.

Harris St.

Freedom

Georgia World Congress Center

Greyhound Depot

International Blvd.

Randolph St.

Highland Ave.

Peachtree Center

Ellis St.

Courtland St.

Butler St.

Houston St.

Georgia Dome ■

CNN Center ■

World of Coca-Cola

Auburn Ave.

Edgewood Ave.

Martin Luther King Jr. Dr.

29

Clark Atlanta University

41

Beckwith St.

Spring St.

Mitchell St.

Five Points

Whitehall St.

Georgia State University

Coca Cola Pl.

Gilmer St.

Armstrong St.

Pratt St.

Decatur St.

Bell St.

Northside Dr.

Trinity Ave.

Forsyth St.

Pryor St.

State Capitol ■

City Hall ■

20

Peters St.

Whitehall St.

Dept. of Archives and History ■

Logan St.

Memorial Dr.

Woodward Ave.

Logan St.

20

Fulton St.

Pryor St.

Central Ave.

Turner Field ■

Capitol Ave.

Fraser St.

Hill St.

Grant Park

Boulevard

29

19

41

3

75
85

McDaniel St.

Pullman St.

0   1000 yards

0   1000 meters

THE SOUTH

net access, coffee, and donuts. No sleeping bags allowed, but they distribute free blankets. Laundry facilities, pool table, and kitchen. $13.40, nonmembers $16.40; private doubles $32.50. Luggage storage $1. Linen $1. Free lockers.

Atlanta Dream Hostel, 115 Church St. (370-0380). From MARTA: Decatur, turn right on Church St.; it's 2 blocks on the left. Convenient to downtown, this is a hostel for the adventurous soul; overseen by Pee-Wee the peacock, complete with an Elvis shrine, a teepee, and "Barbie" and "Jesus" theme rooms. Showers, kitchen, TV, free linen, local calls, and restaurant ($5-8). Dorm rooms with roomy wooden bunks $13, in winter $11; private singles $26, doubles $36. Reservations a must.

Masters Inn Economy, 3092 Presidential Pkwy. (454-8373 or 800-633-3434), Chamblee Tucker Rd. Exit off I-85 in Doraville. Newly renovated, large rooms with king-size beds available, local calls, cable TV, and pool. Singles $36, doubles $40; F-Sa $37/$45. Key deposit $5.

Motel 6, 3585 Chamblee Tucker Rd. (770-458-6626), in Chamblee, Exit 27 off I-285. Spacious and immaculate rooms. Offers free movie channel, local calls, morning coffee, A/C, and pool. Under 18 stay free with their parents. Singles $35; doubles $41; $6 1st additional person; $3 per person after that.

Atlanta Midtown Manor, 811 Piedmont Ave. NE (872-5846). 3 Victorian houses in a fairly safe spot, convenient to downtown. Nice rooms with floral shams, wooden 4-post beds, A/C, TV, and replica antique furnishings. Free coffee, donuts, and local calls. Shared bath, privacy is extra. Singles and doubles $45-85. Free street parking.

Red Roof Inn, 1960 Druid Hills (321-1653 or 800-843-7663), Exit 31 off I-85, offers smallish rooms with modern decor in a convenient, tree-cloistered location. Free cable TV and local calls. Singles from $49; doubles from $59.

Stone Mountain Family Campground (770-498-5710), on U.S. 78, 16 mi. east of town. Exit 30B off I-285, or subway to Avondale, then "Stone Mountain" bus. Gorgeous sites; one-third are on the lake. Bike rentals, free laser show, nature trails, and Internet access. Primitive tent sites $17; RV sites with hookup $19, full hookup $21. Entrance fee $6 per car.

FOOD

From Vietnamese to Italian, baked to fried to fricaseed, Atlanta dining provides ample options, no matter what you're craving. Some favorite dishes to sample include fried chicken, black-eyed peas, okra, sweet-potato pie, and mustard greens. Dip cornbread into "pot likker," water used to cook greens. For a sweet treat (50¢), you can't beat the Atlanta-based **Krispy Kreme Doughnuts,** whose glazed delights are a Southern institution. The factory store, at 295 Ponce de Leon Ave. NE (876-7307), is open 24hr. and continuously bakes their wares, visible through the back window.

The internationally inclined food shopper should take the subway to Avondale and then the "Stone Mountain" bus to the **Dekalb County Farmers Market,** 3000 E. Ponce De Leon Ave. (377-6400), where the adventurous can run the gustatory gamut from Chinese to Middle Eastern and everything in between (open daily 9am-9pm). A great deal of Atlanta's ethnic population has taken up residence at **Buford Hwy.** You won't go wrong with **Little Szechuan,** 5091-C Buford Hwy. (451-0192), which serves lunch specials ($5) in heaping, delicious doses (open M 11:30am-9:30pm, W-Sa 11:30am-9:30pm, Su noon-9:30pm).

Midtown

The Varsity, 61 North Ave. NW (881-1706), at I-85. MARTA: North Ave. The world's largest drive-in and originator of the assembly-line school of food preparation. Best known for the greatest, greasiest onion rings in the South. Most menu items around $2. Open Su-Th 9am-11:30pm, F-Sa 9am-1:30am.

Mary Mac's Tea Room, 224 Ponce de Leon Ave. (876-1800), at Myrtle NE; take the "Georgia Tech" bus north. 40s atmosphere with amazing cinnamon rolls ($3.75 per dozen after 5pm). A "revival of Southern hospitality" for over 50 years. Dinner (good enough for the Dalai Lama, along with a whole wall full of other celebs) with daily rotating entrees and sides is $5-8, or free to the expanding ranks of 100+ seniors. Open for breakfast M-F 7-11am, Sa-Su 9am-noon; for dinner M-Sa 11am-8:30pm, Su 11:30am-3pm; for "supper" M-Sa 4-9pm.

Tortillas, 774 Ponce de Leon Ave. (892-0193). The student crowd munches dirt-cheap and yummy Mexican food. Try the upstairs patio for open-air eating. Big vegetarian burritos $3. Soft chicken taco $3. Open daily 11am-10pm.

Touch of India, 1037 Peachtree St. (876-7777). Lunch buffet $8. Dinner $8-11. Open for lunch M-F 11:30am-2:30pm, Sa noon-2:30pm. Dinner daily 5:30-10:30pm.

Virginia Highlands

Everybody's, 1040 N. Highland Ave. (873-4545). and **Jagger's,** 1577 N. Decatur Rd. (377-8888), battle over which sells Atlanta's best pizza. Everybody's is known for its thin-crusted pies with assorted toppings from spinach to pesto, while Jagger's chunky square pizzas stick to the basics. Everybody's open M-Th 11:30am-11pm, F-Sa 11:30am-1am, Su noon-11pm. Jagger's open M-Sa 11:30am-midnight, Su 4-11pm.

Manuel's Tavern, 602 N. Highland Ave. (525-3447), prime spot between L5P and Virginia Highlands. Though it has earned the reputation of Atlanta's "Democratic headquarters," the longtime bartenders assert it's a non-partisan establishment where "municipal judges sit alongside plumbers" and have for decades. Burgers $5. Open M-Sa 11am-2am, Su 3pm-midnight.

Burrito Art, 1259 Glenwood Ave. (627-4433), has fresh, healthy burritos. Try the "Full on Bean" with spicy black beans, brown rice, corn relish, salsa and cheese for a happily filling $6.25. Open M-F 11:30am-10pm, Sa noon-10pm, Su noon-8pm.

Majestic Food Shop, 1031 Ponce de Leon Ave. (875-0276), at Cleburne. For the ravenous insomniac people watcher, there is no place better. One of the oldest and more famous diners in the country. The Majestic offers "food that pleases" in the shape of burgers ($1.65), grits (95¢), and the like. Open 24hr.

Surrounding Area

Bridgetown Grill, 1156 Euclid Ave. (653-0110), in L5P. Reggae and salsa make for a hopping hole in the wall. Have a 20 oz. margarita ($6) with their famous jerk chicken dinner ($8.50). Open Su-Th 11am-11pm, F-Sa 11am-midnight.

The Flying Biscuit, 1655 McLendon Ave. (687-8888). Do yourself a favor and order something that comes with a biscuit, whether it's a peaches and cream muffin ($1.25) or an enormous sweet roll ($1.25). Cafe, take-out, and cookbook available. Restaurant open Tu-Su 9am-10pm; bakery open Tu-F 7:30am-9pm, Sa-Su 8am-9pm.

Crescent Moon, 254 W. Ponce de Leon Ave. (377-5623), in Decatur. A heavenly and healthful breakfast spot. Indulge in phenomenal French toast ($1.75 per slice), or the Heap (potatoes topped with bacon, cheese, and 2 eggs any style; $6). Whopping portions. Open M-F 7:30am-3pm, Sa-Su brunch 8am-2:30pm.

SIGHTS

Sweet Auburn District

Atlanta's sights may seem scattered, but the effort it takes to find them usually pays off. The most powerful are the MLK sites. Reverend Martin Luther King, Jr.'s birthplace, church, and grave are all part of a 23-acre **Martin Luther King, Jr. National Historic Site.** The **visitors center,** 450 Auburn Ave., houses poignant displays of photographs, videos, and quotations, oriented around King's life and the civil rights struggle (open daily 9am-5pm). The **birthplace of MLK** offers guided tours (331-5190) starting every hour from 501 Auburn Ave. (open daily 10am-6pm; Nov.-Mar. 9am-5pm). The next stop, **Ebenezer Baptist Church,** 407 Auburn Ave. (688-7263), is the church where King was pastor from 1960 to 1968. Plaques lining Sweet Auburn point out the architecture and eminent past residents of this historically African-American neighborhood. King's **grave** rests at the **Martin Luther King, Jr. Center for Nonviolent Social Exchange,** 449 Auburn Ave. NE (524-1956); take bus #3 from Five Points. The center also holds a collection of King's personal effects and shows a film about his life (open daily 10am-6pm; Nov.-Mar. 9am-5pm; free).

The **African-American Panoramic Experience (APEX),** 135 Auburn Ave. (521-2739), recognizes the cultural heritage of the African Americans who helped build this country and includes a replica of Georgia's first African American-owned drugstore (open Tu-Sa 10am-5pm; $2, students and seniors $1, under 4 free).

Waffle Good

Labor Day 1955 was a glorious moment in the otherwise quiet existence of
Avondale Estates, Georgia. Two neighbors "dedicated to people," be they customers or employees, realized their dreams in the form of a little yellow hut that
opened in the Atlanta suburb on this day; the **Waffle House** hasn't closed since.
Visit the original at 2850 E. College (404-294-8758), Avondale.

Downtown and Around

From March through November, the **Atlanta Preservation Center,** 156 7th St. NE
(876-2040), offers 10 famous walking tours of popular areas: Fox Theatre District, West
End and the Wren's Nest, Historic Downtown, Miss Daisy's Druid Hills, Inman Park,
Underground and Capitol area, Ansley Park, Sweet Auburn (MLK District), and Piedmont Park; the 1½hr. Fox Theatre tour is given year-round ($5, students $3, seniors $4;
call for more info).

In **Grant Park,** directly south of Oakland Cemetery and Cherokee Ave., is the 114-
year-old **Cyclorama** (624-1071), a massive panoramic painting (42 ft. high and 358 ft.
around) which re-creates the 1864 Battle of Atlanta with 3D sound and light effects.
*(Open daily 9:30am-5:30pm; Oct.-May 9:30am-4:30pm. $5, students and seniors $4, ages 6-12
$3.)* Next door, **Zoo Atlanta,** 800 Cherokee Ave. SE (624-5678 or 624-5600), boasts
komodo dragons, an artist-elephant, Willie Bean (who at 40 is one of the two oldest
captive gorillas), Chantek (an orangutan fluent in sign language), a petting zoo, and
countless other displays. *(Open M-F 9:30am-4:30pm, Sa-Su 9:30am-5:30pm; Nov.-Mar.
daily 9:30am-4:30pm. $7, seniors $5, ages 3-11 $4.)*

High-tech Atlanta reigns with multinational business powerhouses situated in the
business section of the **Five Points District. Turner Broadcasting System** offers an
insider's peek with its **Cable News Network (CNN) Studio Tour** (827-2300), at the
corner of Techwood Dr. and Marietta St. *(40min. tours given every 15min. Open daily 9am-
6pm. $7, seniors $5, ages 5-12 $4.50. Reservations optional.)* Witness anchors broadcasting
live while writers toil in the background. Weekdays at 3pm, join the punditocracy in
the studio audience of *CNN Talk Back Live* (free); you'll be told not to pick your nose
on camera. Take MARTA west to the Omni/Dome/GWCC Station at W1.

Despite the tragic bombing that occurred there during the Olympics, **Centennial
Olympic Park,** adjacent to the Georgia World Congress Center, delights children of
all ages with the **Fountain of Rings** (splashing and jumping encouraged).

Redeveloped **Underground Atlanta** (523-2311) gets down with 6 subterranean
blocks of over 120 shops, restaurants, and night spots. *(Shops open M-Sa 10am-9:30pm,
Su noon-6pm. Bars and restaurants open later.)* Descend at the entrance beside the Five
Points subway station. Adjacent to the shopping complex, the **World of Coca-Cola,**
55 Martin Luther King, Jr. Dr. (676-5151), details "the real thing's" rise from humble
beginnings in Atlanta to a position of world domination. *(Open M-Sa 10am-9:30pm, Su
noon-6pm. Summer hrs. may vary. $6, seniors $4, ages 6-12 $3.)* It's Andy Warhol gone ber-
serk: from the hokey print ads of the 20s, to a video including the "I'd Like to Buy the
World a Coke" song, to the sampling room, where the world's strangest soft drinks
come direct to you, in a rainbow of flavors.

The politically minded revel in the gold-topped **Georgia State Capitol** (656-2844;
MARTA: Georgia State), Capitol Hill at Washington St. (open M-F 8am-5:30pm; tours
10 and 11am, 1 and 2pm; free). Farther out, the **Carter Presidential Center,** 1
Copenhill (420-5117), north of Little Five Points, documents the Carter Administration (1977-1981) through exhibits and films. *(Museum open M-Sa 9am-4:45pm, Su noon-
4:45pm. $4, seniors $5, under 17 free.)* Take bus #16 to Cleburne Ave.

West End

In the West End—Atlanta's oldest neighborhood, dating from 1835—you can discover the **Wren's Nest,** 1050 R.D. Abernathy Blvd. (753-7735), home to Joel Chandler Harris, who popularized the African folktale trickster Br'er Rabbit through the
character Uncle Remus. *($6, seniors and teens $4, ages 4-12 $3. Open Tu-Sa 10am-4pm, Su
1-4pm.)* Perks include tours, picnic grounds, memorabilia, and storytelling. Take bus

#71 from West End Station (S2). The **Hammonds House,** 503 Peeples St. SW (752-8730), displays a fantastic collection of African-American and Haitian art in a 14-room Victorian house. *(Open Tu-F 10am-6pm, Sa-Su 1-5pm. $2, students and seniors $1.)* Take bus #71 from West End Station to Peeples St. and walk 2 blocks north. Built by slave-born Alonzo F. Herndon, the **Herndon Home,** 587 University Pl. NW (581-9813), a 1910 Beaux-Arts Classical mansion, deserves a look. *(Open Tu-Sa 10am-4pm. Free. Free tours on the hr.)* Take bus #3 from Five Points station to the corner of Martin Luther King, Jr. Dr. and Maple, and walk 1 block north. Herndon, a prominent barber, became Atlanta's wealthiest African American in the early 1900s. The house's original furnishings, glass and silver collections, and family photographs are all on display.

Midtown

Piedmont Park sprawls around the 60-acre **Atlanta Botanical Garden** (876-5859), Piedmont Ave., in the northwest corner of the park. *(Open Tu-Su 9am-7pm; in winter Tu-Su 9am-6pm. $6, students and ages 6-12 $3, seniors $5, Th free after 3pm.)* Stroll through 5 acres of landscaped gardens, a 15-acre hardwood forest with trails, and an exhibition hall. The Garden's **Dorothy Chapman Fuqua Conservatory** houses hundreds of species of exotic tropical plants; take bus #36 "North Decatur" from Arts Center station.

Near the park, **Scitrek (Science and Technology Museum of Atlanta),** 395 Piedmont Ave. NE (522-5500), with over 100 interactive exhibits for all ages, is one of the nation's top 10 science centers. *(Open Tu-Sa 10am-5pm, Su noon-5pm; call for extended summer hrs. $6.50; students, seniors, and ages 3-17 $4.25.)* Take MARTA to Civic Center, walk 2 blocks east on Ralph McGill Blvd., and turn left on Piedmont. Newly opened in 1997 after two arson-related fires, the **Margaret Mitchell House,** 990 Peachtree St. (249-7012), sits at the corner of 10th and Peachtree St., adjacent to the Midtown MARTA station. *(Open M-Sa 9am-4pm, Su noon-4pm. 40min. guided tours every 10min; last one at 4pm. $6, seniors and students $5, ages 7-12 $4.)* The house allows visitors to see the apartment in which Mitchell wrote *Gone With the Wind,* her typewriter, autographed copies of the novel, and the 1937 Pulitzer Prize it won her.

Just to the west of Piedmont Park is the **Woodruff Arts Center,** 1280 Peachtree St. NE (733-4200); MARTA to Arts Center. It contains the **High Museum of Art** (733-4444), Richard Meier's award-winning building of glass, steel, and white porcelain. *(Open Tu-Sa 10am-5pm, 4th F of each month 10am-9pm, Su noon-5pm. $6, students with ID and seniors $4, ages 6-17 $2; free Th 1-5pm.)* The museum branch at 30 John Wesley Dobbs Ave. NE (577-6940), 1 block south of Peachtree Center Station, houses folk art and photography galleries (open M-F 10am-5pm; free).

The **Center for Puppetry Arts,** 1404 Spring St. NW (873-3391), at 18th St., has a museum featuring traditional Punch and Judy figures, some of Jim Henson's original Muppets, and daily puppet-making workshops (open M-Sa 9am-5pm; $5; students, seniors, and children $4; shows $5.75/$4.75).

Buckhead

A drive through **Buckhead** (north of midtown and Piedmont Park, off Peachtree near W. Paces Ferry Rd.) uncovers the "Beverly Hills of Atlanta"—the sprawling mansions of Coca-Cola CEOs and other specimens of high culture. This area is also a hub of local grub and grog (see **Entertainment,** below). One of the most exquisite residences in the Southeast, the Greek Revival **Governor's Mansion,** 391 W. Paces Ferry Rd. (261-1776), has elaborate gardens and furniture from the Federal period. *(Free. Free tours Tu-Th 10-11:30am.)* Take bus #40 "West Paces Ferry" from Lindbergh Station. In the same neighborhood, discover the **Atlanta History Center/Buckhead,** 130 W. Paces Ferry Rd. NW (814-4000). On the grounds are the **Swan House,** a lavish Anglo-Palladian Revival home built in 1928, and the **Tullie Smith Farm,** an antebellum yeoman farmhouse. The **Atlanta History Museum** features a Civil War Gallery. *(Open M-Sa 10am-5:30pm, Su noon-5:30pm. Ticket sales end at 4:30pm. $7, students and seniors $5, ages 6-17 $4.)*

East of Midtown

A respite from the city is at **Stone Mountain Park** (770-498-5690), 16 mi. east on U.S. 78, where a fabulous Confederate Memorial is carved into the world's largest mass of granite. *(Buses leave M-F at 4:40 and 7:50pm. Park gates open daily 6am-midnight; attractions open 10am-9pm; off-season 10am-5:30pm. $6 per car; admission to beach complex $4; some summer discounts for those staying at campground.)* The "Mt. Rushmore of the South" features Jefferson Davis, Robert E. Lee, and Stonewall Jackson and measures 90 ft. by 190 ft. Surrounded by a 3200-acre "World of Family Fun" recreation area and historic park, the mountain dwarfs the enormous statue. The hike up the **Confederate Hall Trail** (1½ mi.) is rewarded with a spectacular view of Atlanta. Check out the dazzling laser show on the side of the mountain every summer night at 9:30pm (free). Take bus #120 "Stone Mountain" from the Avondale subway stop.

The **Fernbank Museum of Natural History,** 767 Clifton Rd. NE (370-0960), near Ponce de Leon Ave., has a 65-acre forest, a display of the Apollo 6 command module, and an IMAX theater, among other exhibits. *(Open M-Sa 10am-5pm, Su noon-5pm. Museum $7, seniors and students $6, ages 3-12 $5; IMAX film $7/$6/$5; both $14.50/$12/ $10.)* Take bus #2 from North Ave. or Avondale Station. The adjacent **Fernbank Science Center,** 156 Heaton Park Dr. (378-4311), includes a garden and observatory.

ENTERTAINMENT AND NIGHTLIFE

For hassle-free fun in Atlanta, buy a MARTA pass (see **Practical Information,** p. 305) and pick up one of the city's free publications on music and events. *Creative Loafing, Music Atlanta,* the *Hudspeth Report,* or "Leisure" in the Friday edition of the *Atlanta Journal* will all give you the scuttlebutt. *Southern Voice* has complete listings on gay and lesbian news and nightclubs throughout Atlanta; stop by **Charls,** 1189 Euclid St. (524-0304), for your free copy. Look for free summer concerts in Atlanta's parks.

The **Woodruff Arts Center,** 1280 Peachtree St. NE (733-4200), houses the Atlanta Symphony, the Alliance Theater Company, Atlanta College of Art, and the High Museum of Art. At the same MARTA stop is the new **William Breman Jewish Heritage Museum,** 1440 Spring St. NW (873-1661), the largest Jewish museum in the Southeast. Sundry resources relate to Atlanta's Jewish cultural heritage; check out the Holocaust exhibit and hands-on discovery center. The National League **Atlanta Braves** play at their state-of-the-art new home, **Turner Field,** which features a Coke bottle over left field that erupts with fireworks after homeruns. (Call **Ticketmaster** at 800-326-4000; tickets $5-15, $1 skyline seats available game day.) Tours of Turner Field and its resources are also offered. (Non-game days, Tu-Sa 9:30am-4pm, Su 1pm-4pm. Game days Tu-Sa 9:30am-noon. $7, children $4, under 3 free.)

Six Flags Over Georgia, 7561 Six Flags Rd. SW (948-9290), at I-20 W, is one of the largest theme/amusement parks in the nation, including the new rollercoaster "Batman" and a slew of other rides. Take bus #201 "Six Flags" from Hightower Station. (Open mid-May to Aug. 10am-midnight. Open sporadically rest of year. 1-day admission $30, ages 3-9 $20; 2-day pass for adults or kids $33; check local grocery stores and soda cans for discounts.)

Drink and dance hotspots center in **Little Five Points, Virginia Highlands, Buckhead,** and oft-cheesy **Underground Atlanta.** A college-age crowd usually fills Little Five Points; many head to **The Point,** 420 Moreland Ave. (659-3522), where live alternative music plays 5-6 nights a week (cover $3-10; open M-F 4pm-4am, Sa 1pm-3am, Su 1pm-4am). For blues, feel your way to **Blind Willie's,** 828 N. Highland Ave. NE (873-2583), a dim, bustling club with Cajun food and occasional big name acts. (Live music starts around 10pm. Cover $5-10. Open Su-Th 8pm-2am, F 8pm-3am, Sa 8pm-2:30am.) In Virginia Highlands, famous acts using assumed names try out new material at the **Dark Horse Tavern,** 816 N. Highland Ave. (873-3607). Music starts downstairs at 10pm. (Cover for music $3-6. Open M-F 4pm-4am, Sa 4pm-3am, Su 4pm-2am. Dinner served 5-11pm, bar food until 2am.) For a laid-back and often international crowd, move next door to **Limerick Junction Pub,** 822 N. Highland Ave. (874-7147), where contagious Irish music jigs nightly and open mic night happens every Tu at 8pm (open M-W 5pm-1am, Th-Sa 5pm-2am, Su 5pm-midnight). Cool off with a 96 oz. fishbowl at **Lu Lu's Bait Shack,** 3057 Peachtree Rd. (262-5220; open Su-Th 5pm-3am, F-Sa 5pm-4am).

Towards downtown, **Masquerade,** 695 North Ave. NE (577-8178), occupies an original turn-of-the-century mill. The bar has three different levels: "heaven," with live dance music; "purgatory," a more laid-back coffee house; and "hell," offering techno and industrial. A recently added outside dance space provides dancing with lights and celestial views. (18+. Cover $4-8+, depending on band. Open W-Su 9pm-4am.)

▓ Athens

The peach state's "Classic City" (as in "Classic City Car Wash") is indisputably the Athens of Georgia. Home to over 30,000 University of Georgia (UGA) students, Athens boasts the Georgia Bulldogs, the State Botanical Garden, the State Museum of Art, and a collegiate downtown full of one-of-a-kind boutiques, cafes, and record stores. Athens's main draw is its prolific music scene—R.E.M., the B-52s, Vic Chesnutt, and Widespread Panic are just a few of the bands whose success was launched in this quintessentially cute college town.

PRACTICAL INFORMATION Situated 70 mi. northeast of Atlanta, Athens can be reached from I-85 via U.S. 316 (Exit 4), which runs into U.S. 29. The **Athens Airport,** 1010 Ben Epps Dr. (613-3420), offers a **commuter shuttle** (800-354-7874) to various points in and around Atlanta ($25). **Greyhound,** 220 W. Broad St. (549-2255 or 800-231-2222), buses to Atlanta (2hr., 3 per day, $13; station open M-F 8am-9pm, Sa-Su 8am-2:30pm). The **Athens Transit System** (613-3430) runs buses on 30min. and 1hr. loops (M-F 6am-6:45pm, Sa 8:45am-6pm). Schedules are available at the Welcome Center, City Hall, and at the bus garage on Pound St. and Prince Ave. (Fare $1, seniors 50¢, ages 6-18 75¢.) Two blocks north of the UGA campus is the **Athens Welcome Center,** 280 E. Dougherty St. (353-1820), in the Church-Waddel-Brumby House, the city's oldest residence (open M-Sa 10am-5pm, Su 2-5pm). Help lines are available for **Gay Information and Referrals** (800-516-4627, ext. 63) and **Health Information** (800-473-HELP/4357). The **health center** (546-5526) is open by appointment (M-F 8am-5pm). **Internet access** is available at the **Hard Drive Café,** 229 E. Broad St. (543-8552). **Post Office:** 575 Olympic Dr. (800-275-8777; open M-F 8:30am-6pm). **ZIP code:** 30601. **Area code:** 706.

ACCOMMODATIONS, CAMPGROUNDS, AND FOOD Many of the city's affordable motels line **W. Broad St.,** also known as the Atlanta Hwy. (U.S. 78), a few mi. from downtown. Many hotels jack up their prices during football weekends in the fall. In the Five Points District, the **Downtowner Motor Inn,** 1198 S. Milledge Ave. (549-2626), has rooms in 70s colors near campus with A/C, continental breakfast, free local calls, cable TV, and pool (singles $42; doubles $50; $2 per additional person). The **Super 8 Motel,** 3425 Atlanta Hwy. (549-0251 or 800-800-8000), offers low-priced, clean, but smallish rooms 3 mi. from downtown. (A/C, cable TV, some kitchenettes. Singles $34; doubles $42. Wheelchair access.) A full-service campground with secluded sites, **Pine Lake RV Campground,** Rte. 186 (769-5486), 12 mi. outside of Athens off Rte. 441 in nearby Bishop, has full hookups and fishing lakes. (Tent sites $14, full hookup $18. Open daily 7am-10pm. Wheelchair access.)

The Grit, 199 Prince Ave. (543-6592), is Athens at its crunchiest and coolest, serving up scrumptious, healthy, *au naturel* meals, including a great weekend brunch. Vegetarian-friendly, popular dishes include the Indian-flavored Dal Baby ($5.25) and the $5.25 veggie plate special. (Entrees $3-6. Open M-F 11am-10pm, Sa-Su brunch 11am-3pm and dinner 5-10pm.) Less healthy, but gosh-darned good, is **Weaver D.'s,** 1016 E. Broad St. (353-7797), where soul food meals cost $6 or less. The sign outside reads "Automatic For the People," owner Dexter Weaver's favorite expression; it inspired the title of REM's 1992 album, and a burgeoning T-shirt trade. (Open M-F 9am-6pm, Sa 11am-6pm.) For an enormous, low-maintenance burrito with a dash of attitude, drop by the **Mean Bean,** 1675 S. Lumpkin St. (549-4868), in the Five Points area. Mean Bean offers gargantuan Spanish rice and bean burritos for $2.65 and create-your-own-combos from a list of ingredients. (Open daily 11am-10pm.) If burritos aren't your thing, it's not the end of the world as we know it; Michael Stipe is part-owner of the **Guaranteed,** 167 E. Broad St. (208-0962), which mixes fresh juices and vegetarian food with organically grown ingredients (wheatberry burger $5.25; open M-Sa 11am-10pm, Su 9am-3pm). No Athenian culinary experience is complete without a 50¢ scoop from **Hodgson's Pharmacy,** 1220 S. Milledge Ave. (543-7386), which may be the last place on earth where ice cream comes so cheap (open M-Sa 9am-7pm, Su 2-7pm). If you prefer food of the "fast" variety, try the **Varsity,** 1000 W. Broad St. (548-6325), where the staff fry up onion rings, burgers, and chili dogs in record time, all for well under $2 (open Su-Th 10am-10pm, F-Sa 10am-midnight; drive-through daily 10am-10pm).

SIGHTS AND ENTERTAINMENT For an in-depth look at Athens's old and new, take the 2hr. **Classic City Tour** (reservations 208-8687). This fascinating $10 driving tour tells the stories of the antebellum homes, the Civil War, and the University of Georgia. Tours leave from the welcome center daily at 2pm; walk-ins are welcome. Athens is home to one of the state's grandest cultural institutions, the **Georgia Museum of Art,** 90 Carlton St. (542-GMOA/4662), in the university's Performing and Visual Arts Complex. *(Open Tu-Sa 10am-5pm, Su 1-5pm. Free.)* The museum houses a collection of over 7000 works and shows about 20 different exhibitions a year. Look for the flowers of Guatemala at the 313-acre **State Botanical Garden of Georgia,** 2450 S. Milledge Ave. (542-1244), a paradise for lay-aesthete and botanist alike. *(Open daily 8am-sunset. Conservatory open M-Sa 9am-4:30pm, Su 11:30am-4:30pm. Free.)* The **Morton Theater,** 199 W. Washington St. (613-3770), was the first theater in the U.S. to be owned and run by African Americans. Ticket prices aren't what they were in 1910, but usually they're still low ($5-15). When in Athens, do as the Greeks do: tour the **Taylor-Grady House,** 634 Prince Ave. (549-8688), Athens's oldest Greek Revival mansion. *(Open M-F 10am-1pm and 2:30-5pm. Free. Informative guided tours $2.50, leave every 30min.)* Some bizarre Athenian sights include the city's symbol, a double-barreled cannon at City Hall Plaza that literally backfired and hence could not be put towards the Civil War effort, and the **"Tree That Owns Itself."** According to local legend, Prof. W.H. Jackson deeded that the white oak standing at the corner of Dearling and Finley St. should own itself and its 8 ft. radius of shade. The original oak died in 1942 but was reborn from one of its own acorns.

Those on an R.E.M. pilgrimage must check out the **40 Watt Club,** 285 W. Washington St. (549-7871), where the group started out and where many bands today attempt to follow their lead (cover $5-12; open daily 10pm-3am). The **Georgia Theatre** (353-3405), at the corner of Lumpkin and Clayton St., attracts shiny, happy people with local and national acts (cover usually $1-5; open daily 4pm until late). With Guinness on tap and a smoke-free zone on the second floor, **The Globe,** 199 N. Lumpkin St. (353-4721), draws grad students in droves (open M-Tu 4pm-1am, W-Sa 4pm-2am). For Pop Tarts or lattés at any hour, swing by **Jittery Joe's,** 243 W. Washington St. (548-3116), a retro java joint replete with lava lamps and vinyl couches. Jesus rises again, from the coffee cup on the ceiling. (Open M-Th 7:30am-1:30am, F-Sa 8am-3am.) Another branch, at 1210 Milledge Ave. (208-1979) in the Five Points Area, resides in a renovated 19th-century Shell gas station (open Su-Th 6:30am-midnight, F-Sa 8am-1am). **Manhattan,** 337 N. Hull St. (369-9767), caters to a crowd of those who wish they lived there, but can't bear to part with $1 beers. The **Five Star Day Café,** 229 E. Broad St. (543-8552), an Athens newcomer, offers "gourmet soul" food and local and touring acts. Beer is $1 while the music is playing. (Open M-Th 11am-10pm, F-Sa 11am-11pm, Su brunch 11am-4pm.) In mid-July, **Athfest** (548-1973) features hundreds of local bands playing in the downtown area ($10 per day, both days $15).

■ Savannah

In February 1733, General James Oglethorpe and a rag-tag band of 120 colonists founded the state of Georgia at Tamacraw Bluff on the Savannah River, and the city of Savannah was born. General Sherman later spared the city during his famous rampage through the South. Some say he found it too pretty to burn, even presenting Savannah to President Lincoln as a Christmas gift. Today, the general's reaction is still believable to anyone who sees Savannah's antique stores and stately old trees, its Federalist and English Regency houses amid spring blossoms. More recently, the movie *Forrest Gump* has popularized a certain bench in Chippewa Sq., while John Berendt's best-seller *Midnight in the Garden of Good and Evil* continues to entice readers to this lovable town and its welcoming inhabitants.

ORIENTATION AND PRACTICAL INFORMATION

Savannah rests on the coast of Georgia at the mouth of the **Savannah River,** which runs north of the city along the border with South Carolina. The city stretches south from bluffs overlooking the river. The restored 2½ sq. mi. **downtown historic district;** bordered by East Broad, Martin Luther King, Jr. Blvd., Gwinnett St., and the river; is best explored on foot. *Do not stray south of Gwinnett St.; the historic district quickly deteriorates into an unsafe and seedy area.* **Tybee Island,** Savannah's beach, 18 mi. east on U.S. 80 and Rte. 26, makes a fine daytrip. Try to visit at the beginning of spring, when Savannah's streets are lined with flowers.

Trains: Amtrak, 2611 Seaboard Coastline Dr. (234-2611 or 800-872-7245), 4 mi. outside the city. To: Atlanta (4 per day, $37-39); Charleston (2hr., 2 per day, $21-32); and Washington, D.C. (12hr., 3 per day, $159). Station open 3:30pm-7:30am. Taxi to downtown runs about $5.

Buses: Greyhound, 610 W. Oglethorpe Ave. (232-2135 or 800-231-2222), at Fahm St. To: Jacksonville (3hr., 11 per day, $18-19); Columbia (5hr., 4 per day, $27-29); Atlanta (1 per day, $191-290); and Washington, D.C. (12hr., 6 per day, $99-104). Ticket office open daily 5:30am-1am.

Public Transportation: Chatham Area Transit (CAT), 233-5767. Runs daily 7am-11pm. Fare 75¢, transfers 75¢, 1-day pass for the shuttle $2.

Taxis: Adam Cab, 927-7466. $1.20 per mi. 24hr.

Visitor Info: Savannah Visitors Center, 301 Martin Luther King, Jr. Blvd. (944-0455), at Liberty St. in a lavish former train station. Excellent free maps and guides, especially the Savannah Map Guide. Reservation service for local inns and hostels. Open daily 9am-5pm.

Hotlines: Rape Crisis Center, 233-7273. 24hr.

Post Office: 2 N. Fahm St. (235-4619). Open M-F 7am-6pm, Sa 9am-3pm. **ZIP code:** 31402. **Area code:** 912.

ACCOMMODATIONS AND CAMPGROUNDS

The downtown motels cluster near the historic area, visitors center, and Greyhound station. For those with cars, **Ogeechee Rd. (U.S. 17)** has several budget options.

Savannah International Youth Hostel (HI-AYH), 304 E. Hall St. (236-7744), in the historic district 2 blocks east of Forsyth Park. This restored Victorian mansion has a kitchen and laundry facilities. Clean dorm beds (6 per room) $15; hard-to-get private rooms $27. Linen $1. Flexible 3-night max. stay. Check-in 7:30-10am and 5-10pm; call the manager, Brian, for late check-in. Lockout 10am-5pm. No curfew. Open Mar.-Dec.

Thunderbird Inn, 611 W. Oglethorpe Ave. (232-2661), across from the Greyhound station. The least expensive rooms downtown, with modest decor but friendly managers. Thrift is the main motivator here, along with A/C and cable TV. Singles $32, doubles $35; F-Sa $45/$55.

Fort McAllister State Park (727-2339); take Exit 15 off I-95. Wooded sites with water and electricity, some with a water view. Tent sites $12, RV sites $14. Check-in before 10pm. Parking $2. Office open daily 8am-5pm; campground open 7am-10pm.

Skidaway Island State Park (598-2300 or 800-864-7275), 13 mi. southeast of downtown off Diamond Causeway. Inaccessible by public transportation. Follow Liberty St. east from downtown until it becomes Wheaton St.; turn right on Waters Ave. and follow it to the Diamond Causeway. Generally louder than Fort McAllister. Bathrooms, heated showers, electricity, and water. Swimming pool $2. Sites $15; off-season $12. Check-in before 10pm; in winter 5pm.

FOOD AND NIGHTLIFE

⦿**Mrs. Wilkes Boarding House,** 107 W. Jones St. (232-5997), is truly a Southern institution. Friendly strangers sit around a large table eating things like a luscious fried chicken, candied yams, and collard greens breakfast ($5). All-you-can-eat lunch $10. The wait in line is up to 2hr. Open M-F 8-9am and 11am-3pm.

Clary's Café, 404 Abercorn St. (233-0402). A family spot since 1903 with a famous weekend brunch and friendly service. Malted waffle $4. Open M-F 7am-10pm, W 7am-5pm, Sa 8am-4pm and 5-10pm, Su 8am-10pm.

Billy Bob's, 21 E. River St. (234-5588), in a casual cowboy setting. Great food from grilled lemon pepper salmon ($13) to a BBQ sandwich ($6) is served until 11:30pm; the bar is open later.

Olympia Café, 5 E. River St. (233-3131), on the river. Greek specialities and more, including salads and pizzas. Lunch or dinner $5-15. Open daily 11am-11pm.

The waterfront area (River St.) offers endless oceanfront dining opportunities, street performers, and a friendly pub ambience. **Kevin Barry's Irish Pub,** 117 W. River St. (233-9626), stages live Irish folk music (W-Su after 8:30pm; cover $2). The "half-and-half" is a unique layered bar drink for $3.75. (Open M-F 4pm-3am, Sa 11:30pm-3am, Su 12:30-2am.) For a drink that will keep you on your ear for days, check out **Wet Willies,** 101 E. River St. (233-5650), with its casual dining, young folks, and irresistible frozen daiquiris for $3.50-5.50 (open Su-Th 11am-1am, F-Sa 11am-2am). Local college students eat, drink, and shop at **City Market.** One hot spot is **Malone's Bar and Grill,** 27 Barnard St. (234-3059), with dancing, drinks, live jazz, and rock Thursday through Sunday nights (2 for 1 drinks from 11am-8pm; ladies night Th; open daily 11am-3am). Hustlers will enjoy the 10 Gandi pool tables and over 80 beers at **B&B Billiards,** 411 W. Congress St. (233-7116), which recently won a city renovation prize for transforming a five-and-dime warehouse into an airy nightspot. (Happy hour daily 4-8pm. Free pool Tu and Th. Open M-Sa 4pm-4am, Su 4pm-3am.) The Lady Chablis, a character featured in *Midnight in the Garden of Good and Evil* (see p. 317), performs regularly at the popular gay/lesbian hotspot **Club One,** 1 Jefferson St. (232-0200), near City Market, at Bay St. (cover $7; doors open at 7pm). All kinds of live music rocks Friday and Saturday nights at **The Velvet Lounge,** 127 W. Congress St. (236-0665); look for a big crown in the window (cover $3-5; open M-Sa 4pm-3am).

SIGHTS AND EVENTS

Most of Savannah's 21 squares contain some distinctive centerpiece. Elegant antebellum houses and drooping vine-wound trees often cluster around the squares, adding to the classic Southern aura. Many bus, van, and horse carriage **tours** leave every 10-15 min. from the visitors center ($13-15), but walking might be more fun.

Savannah's best-known historic houses are the **Davenport House,** 324 E. State St. (236-8097), on Columbia Sq., and the **Owens-Thomas House,** 124 Abercorn St. (233-9743), a block away on Oglethorpe Sq. *(Davenport House open daily 10am-4pm. $5. Last tour 4pm. O-T House open Tu-Sa 10am-5pm, Su 2-5pm. $6, students $3, seniors $5, under 13 $2. Last tour 4:30pm.)* The Davenport House, earmarked to be razed for a parking lot, was saved in 1955. Guided tours explore the first floor every 30min.; the third floor is open to explore at your leisure. The **Green Meldrim House,** 1 W. Maco St. (232-1251), on Madison Sq., is a Gothic Revival mansion that served as one of General Sherman's headquarters during the Civil War (open Tu and Th-Sa 10am-4pm; $5). The **Telfair Mansion and Art Museum,** 121 Bernard St. (232-1177), displays a distinguished collection of decorative arts in an English Regency house. *(Open Tu-Sa 10am-5pm, Su 2-5pm. $5, seniors $3, students $2, ages 6-12 50¢.)* The **Savannah History Museum,** 301 Martin Luther King, Jr. Blvd. (238-1779), has exhibits depicting the city's past (open daily 9am-5pm; $3, students and seniors $2.50, ages 6-12 $1.75).

Lovers of Thin Mints, Tag-alongs, and, of course, Savannahs, should make a pilgrimage to the **Juliette Gordon Low Birthplace,** 142 Bull St. (233-4501), near Wright Sq. The Girl Scouts' founder was born here on Halloween 1860, which may explain the Girl Scouts' door-to-door treat-selling technique. The "cookie shrine" contains an interesting collection of Girl Scout memorabilia—including the corpse and still-beating heart of record-setting Jill Offtenplop of Kansas. *(Open M-Tu and Th-Sa 10am-4pm, Su 12:30-4:30pm. $5, students and seniors $4.50, under 18 $4.)* The **Negro Heritage Trail Tour,** 502 E. Harris St. (234-8000), visits African-American historic sights from the days of slavery to the present. The Savannah branch of the **Association for the Study of Afro-American Life and History,** 514 E. Harris St. (234-8000), conducts three different tours from the visitors center (tours M-Sa 10am and 1pm; $10, under 13 $5).

Savannah's four forts once protected the city's port from Spanish, British, and other invaders. The most interesting, **Fort Pulaski National Monument** (786-5787), 15 mi. east of Savannah on U.S. 80 E and Rte. 26, marks the Civil War battle site where rifled cannons first pummeled walls, making Pulaski and similar forts obsolete. *(Open daily 8:30am-5:15pm; extended hrs. in summer; visitors center closes 5pm. $2, $4 max. per car, under 16 free.)* Built in the early 1800s, **Fort Jackson** (232-3945), also along U.S. 80 and Rte. 26, contains exhibits on the American Revolution, the War of 1812, and the Civil War (open daily 9am-5pm; students, seniors, and children $2). Both make quick detours on a daytrip to Tybee Beach.

Special events in Savannah include the **Annual NOGS Tour of the Hidden Gardens of Historic Savannah** (238-0248), in mid-April, when private walled gardens are opened to the public. Green is the theme of the **St. Patrick's Day Celebration on the River** (234-0295), a 4- to 5-day, beer-and-fun-filled party which packs the streets and warms celebrants up for the **Annual St. Patrick's Day Parade** (233-4904), the second largest in the U.S. (2:15pm). A free paper, *Creative Leafing,* found in restaurants and stores, has the latest in news and entertainment.

Midnight in the Garden of Good and Evil

A notorious and sophisticated antiques dealer, a scandalous and flamboyant drag queen, the prim and proper members of the Married Woman's Card, and a melancholy soul with a vial of poison potent enough to kill every man, woman, and child in town: these are a few of the characters that have recently seized the attention of readers in 11 different countries. The colorful plot of *Midnight in the Garden of Good and Evil,* a *New York Times* best-seller, revolves around a highly publicized fatal shooting at Mercer House, a venerable and elegant old home on Monterey Sq. Was it murder or self-defense? In this lush garden of haunting Spanish moss and beautiful old tombs, old passions endure and provide scant clues. Although the social elite about town have denounced "The Book's" exposure of their secrets in indignant whispered exchanges, tourism has skyrocketed by 46%, and you may struggle to find a local who doesn't claim to be actually referred to in the book, however vaguely. **"The Book" Gift Shop,** 127 E. Gordon St. (233-3867), at Calhoun Sq., a fan club, Midnight tours, and a Hollywood adaptation all attest to the interest and revenue which "The Book" has generated.

■ Brunswick and Environs

Brunswick Beyond one unique hostel and pleasant nearby beaches, laid-back Brunswick is of little interest to the traveler who expects more than a relaxing layover between destinations. The fantastic **Hostel in the Forest** (264-9738 or 638-2623) is located 9 mi. west of Brunswick on U.S. 82. Take I-95 to Exit 6 and travel west on U.S. 82/84 about 1½ mi. until you see a white-lettered wooden sign set back in the trees along the eastbound lane. Make a U-turn just after mile marker 11, past Ted and Dot's Pest Control and Harley Shop. The hostel sits ½ mi. back from the highway; every effort is made to keep the area surrounding the complex of geodesic domes and treehouses as natural as possible.

Eight treehouses grace the premises, most with a ceiling fan, candles, and a spacious double bed. Entertainment options include a fabulous natural swimming pool made from a diverted upground spring, as well as a stream-side teepee sweat lodge which is used during the full moon. Farther down, the "glass house" provides an airy meditation space with hanging chairs and outdoor showers overlooking woods and water. In June, a blueberry orchard overflows with fruit. The atmosphere and feast-like dinner are communal, and a few permanent residents are always there to greet you. The low-key managers will shuttle you to the bus station for $3; they can usually be convinced to daytrip to Savannah, the Okefenokee Swamp, and the coastal islands. Beware that after rain, the ½-mi. dirt road to the hostel is worse than usual—the already-large potholes grow large enough to swallow a small horse. (No lockout or curfew, but you'll probably help with dinner. $13 includes dinner. Linen $2.)

If you can't wait for dinner, **Twin Oaks Pit Barbecue,** 2618 Norwich St. (265-3131), 8 blocks from downtown Brunswick across from the Southern Bell building, features a chicken-and-pork combo ($6), a renowned BBQ sandwich ($3), and delicious breaded french fries for $1 (open M-F 10:30am-4pm, Sa 10:30am-2:30pm).

Greyhound, 1101 Gloucester St. (265-2800; station open M-F 8am-11:45 and 2-6pm, Sa 8am-11:45 and 2-4pm), offers service to Jacksonville (1½hr., 5 per day, $17) and Savannah (1½hr., 5 per day, $16). **Area code:** 912.

Okefenokee Swamp

Okefenokee Swamp Park, 5700 Okefenokee Swamp Park Rd. (912-283-0583), on U.S. 1, 8 mi. south of Waycross, is a haven for snoozing alligators, snakes, and birds. *(In summer open 9am-6:30pm; off-season 9am-5:30pm.)* There are several "packages" available, including a 25min. guided boat trip ($12 per person) and a canoe rental option ($14). All packages include the live reptile presentation, showcasing Okefenokee's wide variety of snakes, lizards and alligators. A boardwalk built on the swamp allows you to explore it on foot.

Golden Isles

The **Golden Isles, St. Simon's Island, Jekyll Island,** and **Sea Island,** have miles of white sand beaches, and St. Simon's has "tree spirits" to spend an afternoon tracking down via brochure. **Cumberland Island National Seashore** (912-882-433), near the isles, consists of 16 mi. of salt marsh, live oak forest, and sand dunes laced with trails and a few decaying mansions. *(Open M-F 10am-4pm.)* Phone reservations are necessary for entry into the parks. The effort is rewarded with seclusion; you can walk all day on these beaches without seeing a soul. Sites are also available on a stand-by basis 15min. before ferry departures to Cumberland Island. The **ferry** leaves from St. Mary's, on the mainland at the terminus of Rte. 40 at the Florida border. *(45min. In summer daily 9 and 11:45am, returns 10:15am daily, 2:45pm W-Sa only, and 4:45pm daily; Oct. to late Feb. ferries run Th-M with no 2:45pm return. $10, under 13 $6.)*

Alabama

The "Heart of Dixie" is often remembered for its controversial role in the Civil Rights campaign of the 1960s. Once a stalwart defender of segregation—former Governor George Wallace fought a vicious campaign opposing integration—Alabama now strives to broaden its image as a progressive southern state without losing the charming aspects of its cultural heritage. Most travelers come to Alabama searching for legacies of its divided past, from Booker T. Washington's pioneering Tuskegee Institute (now a University), to the poignant statues in Birmingham's Kelly Ingram Park. Still, there is much more to the state than its history—Southern cuisine, local festivities, and friendly folks welcome visitors to Montgomery, the Gulf Coast, and beyond.

PRACTICAL INFORMATION

Capital: Montgomery.
Visitor Info: Alabama Bureau of Tourism and Travel, 401 Adams Ave., Montgomery 36104 (334-242-4169; 800-252-2262 outside AL; http://www.state.al.us). Open M-F 8am-5pm. **Division of Parks,** 64 N. Union St., Montgomery 36104 (800-252-7275). Open daily 8am-5pm.
Emergency: 911.
Time Zone: Central (1hr. behind Eastern). **Postal Abbreviation:** AL.
Sales Tax: 4% plus county tax.

■ Montgomery

While Montgomery was the first capital of the Confederacy (and still houses the Confederacy's alternative White House), the city also played a key role in the birth of the New South. In 1955, local authorities arrested Rosa Parks, a black seamstress, because she refused to give up her seat on a local bus; a local minister named Dr. Martin Luther King, Jr. responded by calling a famed boycott. The nation took notice of his nonviolent approach to gaining racial equality, igniting a movement that radically transformed America. Today, Civil Rights movement battlegrounds are the main attractions of quiet Montgomery, but the list also includes Shakespearian drama, good home cooking, many museums, and a few beautiful glimpses of nature.

ORIENTATION AND PRACTICAL INFORMATION

Downtown Montgomery follows a grid pattern: **Madison Ave.** and **Dexter Ave.** are the major east-west routes; **Perry St.** and **Lawrence St.** run north-south. West of downtown, **I-65** runs north-south and intersects **I-85,** which forms Montgomery's southern border.

> **Buses: Greyhound,** 950 W. South Blvd. (286-0658 or 800-231-2222). Take I-65 to Exit 168 and turn right. To: Mobile (3½hr., 7 per day, $26-28); Atlanta (4hr., 11 per day, $27-28); and Tuskegee (45min., 6 per day, $8-9). Open 24hr.
>
> **Trains: Amtrak,** 950 W. South Blvd. (800-872-7245), adjacent to Greyhound. Take Coosa St. across the railroad tracks; the stop is on your left. Offers limited bus service to the connecting city of Atlanta, but no actual trains; ask at Greyhound.
>
> **Public Transportation:** The **Downtown Area Runabout Transit (DART)** is underutilized. Buses run 6am-6pm. Fare $1.50, no transfers.
>
> **Taxis: Yellow Cab,** 262-5225. $1.75 1st mi., $1.20 per additional mi. 24hr.
>
> **Visitor Info: Visitor Information Center,** 401 Madison Ave. (262-0013). Open M-F 8:30am-5pm, Sa 9am-4pm, Su noon-4pm. Free maps. **Chamber of Commerce,** 41 Commerce St. (834-5200). Open M-F 8:30am-5pm.
>
> **Hotlines: Council Against Rape,** 286-5987. **Help-A-Crisis,** 279-7837. 24hr.
>
> **Post Office:** 135 Catoma St. (244-7576). Open M-F 7:30am-5:30pm, Sa 8am-noon. **ZIP code:** 36104. **Area code:** 334.

ACCOMMODATIONS, CAMPGROUNDS, AND FOOD

Two centrally located and well-maintained budget motels serve the downtown area. **Capitol Inn,** 205 N. Goldthwaite St. (265-3844), at Heron St., has spacious, clean rooms overlooking the city and a pool (singles $22; doubles $32; $5 per additional person; wheelchair access). The second option, the comfortable and newly renovated **Town Plaza,** 743 Madison Ave. (269-1561), sits at N. Ripley St. near the visitors center (singles $22; doubles $30 if you say you saw it in *Let's Go*). Those with a car will easily find accommodations. **South Blvd.,** at I-65 Exit 168, overflows with inexpensive beds—beware of the cheapest of the cheap, which are fairly seedy. Right next to I-65 on W. South Blvd., **The Inn South,** 4243 Inn South Ave. (288-7999 or 800-642-0890), greets travelers with an unusually dramatic lobby for a budget motel, complete with chandelier. (Continental breakfast, free local calls, and cable included. Singles $29, Sa-Su $34; doubles $34; $2 per additional person. Wheelchair access.) The site of a 1763 French stronghold, **Fort Toulouse Jackson Park** (205-567-3002), 7 mi. north of Montgomery on Rte. 6 off U.S. 231, has 39 rustic sites with water and electricity in beautiful woods. Other sites grace the Coosa River. (Tents $8, RVs $10; $2 senior discount. Registration daily 8am-5pm. Make reservations at least 2 weeks in advance in spring and fall.)

Martha's Place, 458 Sayre St. (263-9135), a family-run, down-home restaurant, lives up to the banner it displays inside: "O taste and see that the Lord is good." As one of its famous visitors wrote, "Y'all got it DOWN!" Grab an entree, two veggies, lemonade, and dessert for $5.50. (Open M-F 11am-3pm, Su brunch buffet seasonal.) Across from the visitors center at the elegant **Young House,** 231 N. Hull St. (262-0409), $5 buys two big pieces of fried chicken and two healthy-sized veggie sides (open M-F 11am-2pm; look for a 10% discount coupon at the visitor's center).

More Southern fare awaits at the **Sassafras Tea Room,** 532 Clay St. (265-7277), a restaurant/antique dealership. There, you can feast your eyes on the lavish Victorian interior or the sleepy Alabama River while eating their famous crunchy chicken salad ($6; open M-F 11am-2pm, Su by reservation only). **Hamburger King,** 547 S. Decatur St. (262-1798), grills your burger ($1.30-2.50) the old-fashioned way—with a lotta sizzle (open M-F 8am-3:30pm). For a great snack of the grown or baked variety, you can amble over to the **Montgomery State Farmers Market** (242-5350), at the corner of Federal Dr. (U.S. 231) and Coliseum Blvd., and snag a bag of peaches for $2 (open in spring and summer M-Sa 7:30am-5:30pm, Su 7:30am-5pm). For a more filling meal, **The State Market Café,** 1659 Federal Dr. (271-1885), serves free ice cream with every $5-8 southern cafeteria-style meal (open M-F 5:30am-2pm).

SIGHTS AND ENTERTAINMENT

Maya Lin, the architect who designed the Vietnam Memorial in Washington, D.C., also designed Montgomery's newest sight, the **Civil Rights Memorial,** 400 Washington Ave. (264-0286), at Hull St. *(Open 24hr. Free. Wheelchair access.)* This dramatically minimalist tribute remembers 40 of the men, women, and children who died fighting for civil rights. The outdoor monument bears names and dates of significant events on a circular black marble table over which water continuously flows; a wall frames the table with Dr. Martin Luther King, Jr.'s famous paraphrase, "Until justice rolls down like waters and righteousness like a mighty stream."

The legacy of African-American activism and faith lives on a block away at the 112-year-old **Dexter Ave. King Memorial Baptist Church,** 454 Dexter Ave. (263-3970), where King first preached, and where he and other civil rights leaders organized the 1955 **Montgomery bus boycott.** *(Tours M-Th 10am and 2pm, F 10am, Sa 10:30am and 1:30pm. Donations accepted.)* Ten years later, King led a nationwide march past the church to the capitol building. The basement mural chronicles King's role in the nation's struggle for civil rights from Montgomery to Memphis.

Old Alabama Town, 301 Columbus St. (240-4500), 2 blocks off Madison and 3 blocks north of the church, reconstructs urban and rural life in 19th-century urban and rural Alabama. *(Open Apr.-Oct. M-Sa 9am-3:30pm, Su 1-3:30pm; Nov.-Mar. M-Sa 9am-3pm, Su 1-3pm. $7, ages 6-18 $3. Last tour at 3:30pm.)* The complex includes a pioneer homestead, an 1892 grocery, a schoolhouse, and an early African-American church. Renowned Alabama storyteller Kathryn Tucker Windham artfully recounts her family's past as she leads you through the reconstructed village.

The **State Capitol** (242-3935), at Bainbridge St. and Dexter Ave., reopened in 1992 after years of renovation. *(Open M-Sa 9am-4pm. Free; donations appreciated. Guided tours available.)* A bronze star commemorates the spot where Jefferson Davis took the oath of office as President of the Confederacy. The **First White House of the Confederacy,** 644 Washington Ave. (242-1861), contains period furnishings and many of Confederate President Jefferson Davis's personal belongings (open M-F 8am-4:30pm; free). Another restored home, the **F. Scott and Zelda Fitzgerald Museum,** 919 Felder Ave. (264-4222), off Carter Hill Rd., contains a few of her paintings and some of his original manuscripts, as well as their strangely monogrammed bath towels (open W-F 10am-2pm, Sa-Su 1-3pm; free).

Country music fans can join the droves who make daily pilgrimages to the **Hank Williams Grave,** 1304 Upper Wetumpka Rd., in the Oakwood Cemetery Annex off Upper Wetumpka Rd., near downtown. *(Open M-F 10am-sunset.)* A stone cowboy that rests upon the grave, flanked by oversized music notes and other memorabilia. Also look for the brand-spanking-new **Hank Williams Museum** on River St. For who would fardels bear, were it not for the **Alabama Shakespeare Festival** (271-5353 or 800-841-4273), the fifth largest in the world. *(Tickets $20-24; previews the week before opening $15. Box office open M-Sa 10am-6pm, Su noon-4pm.)* It's staged at the **State Theatre** on the grounds of the 250-acre private estate, **Wynton M. Blount Cultural Park;** take East Blvd. 15min. southeast of downtown onto Woodmere Blvd. The theater stages Shakespeare, world drama, and contemporary plays. Also in Blount Cultural

Park, the **Montgomery Museum of Fine Arts,** 1 Museum Dr. (244-5700), houses a substantial collection of southern and 19th- and 20th-century American paintings and graphics, as well as "Artworks," a hands-on gallery and art studio for kids. *(Open Tu-W and F-Sa 10am-5pm, Th 10am-9pm, Su noon-5pm. Free, donations appreciated.)*

The *Montgomery Advertiser* lists local entertainment happenings on Thursdays. If you're in the mood for some blues and beers, try **1048,** 1048 E. Fairview Ave. (834-1048), near Woodley Ave. (open M-F and Su 4pm until late, Sa 7pm until the cow walks in the door) or **Sinclair's,** 1051 Fairview Ave. (834-7462; restaurant open M-Th 11am-10pm, F-Sa 11am-11pm; bar open later).

The Selma to Montgomery March

In the Selma of 1964, only 1% of eligible blacks had the right to vote. To protest these conditions, civil rights activists organized an ill-fated march on the state capitol in 1965 that was quashed by bayonet-carrying troops. Their spirits battered but not destroyed, the marchers tried again, this time spurred on by the likes of Dr. Martin Luther King, Jr., Joan Baez, Sammy Davis Jr., Andrew Young, Harry Belafonte, Lena Horne, and Mahalia Jackson. The second march, a 54 mi. trek from Selma to Montgomery, ended without conflict, prompting a weary MLK Jr. to declare the movement the "greatest march ever made on a state capitol in the South." King's analysis of the monumental significance of the event was not lost on President Lyndon B. Johnson, who noted with eloquence, "At times, history and fate meet at a single time in a single place to shape a turning point in man's unending search for freedom. So it was at Lexington and Concord. So it was a century ago at Appomattox. And so it was last week, in Selma, Alabama." A year later, Congress passed the Voters Rights Act.

■ Near Montgomery: Tuskegee

After Reconstruction, "emancipated" blacks in the South remained segregated and disenfranchised. **Booker T. Washington,** a former slave, believed that blacks could best improve their situation by educating themselves and learning a trade, instead of pursuing the classical, erudite education which **W.E.B. Dubois** proposed. The curriculum at the college Washington founded, Tuskegee Institute, revolved around such practical endeavors as agriculture and carpentry, with students constructing almost all of the campus buildings. Washington raised money for the college by giving lectures on social structure across the country. Artist, teacher, and scientist, **George Washington Carver** headed the Agricultural Dept. at Tuskegee, where he discovered many practical uses for the peanut, including axle grease and peanut butter.

Today, a more academically oriented **Tuskegee University** fills 160 buildings on 1500 acres; the buildings of Washington's original institute comprise a national historical site (call 727-8349 for tours). Nearby is the **George Washington Carver Museum;** the **visitors center** (727-6390) is inside (open daily 9am-5pm; free). Down the street on old Montgomery Rd. lies **The Oaks,** a restoration of Washington's home. Free tours depart from the museum on the hour (daily 10am-4pm).

After your tour, **Thomas Reed's Chicken Coop,** 527 Old Montgomery Rd. (727-3841), can satiate your hunger pangs with a filling, delicious, and inexpensive meal. Chicken is sold by the finger-lickin' piece or as a full dinner. (All meals under $5. Open daily 8am-3pm.)

To get to Tuskegee, take I-85 toward Atlanta and exit at Rte. 81 S. Turn right at the intersection of Rte. 81 and Old Montgomery Rd. onto Rte. 126. **Greyhound** (727-1290) runs from Montgomery (45min., 6 per day, $8-9). **Area code:** 334

■ Birmingham

Like its English namesake, Birmingham sits atop soil rich in coal, iron ore, and limestone—responsible for its lightning-quick transformation into a premier steel industry center, and, many argue, the exploitation of poor black workers. Over time, Birmingham has been called the Magic City, the Tragic City, and now the benign "City of Surprises." You may be surprised to learn that there's a lot more to the city than "a place of revolution and reconciliation." Though Birmingham's civil rights heritage is still its main draw, an easy, cosmopolitan version of Southern charm and hospitality has kicked in here, visible at art festivals, museums, and the University of Alabama.

ORIENTATION AND PRACTICAL INFORMATION

The downtown area grid system has avenues running east-west and streets running north-south. Each numbered avenue has a north and a south, with railroad tracks running in between.

Trains: Amtrak, 1819 Morris Ave. (324-3033 or 800-872-7245). To Atlanta (4hr., 1 per day, $20-39) and New Orleans (7hr., 1 per day, $24-47). Open 8:30am-4:30pm.

Buses: Greyhound, 618 19th St. N (251-3210 or 800-231-2222). To: Montgomery (2hr., 4 per day, $18-19); Mobile (5½-11½hr., 5 per day, $37-39); and Atlanta (3-4hr., 7 per day, $22024). Open 24hr.

Public Transportation: Metropolitan Area Express (MAX) (322-7701) operates M-F 5am-5pm. Fare $1, transfers 25¢. **Downtown Area Runabout Transit (DART)** (252-0101) runs about M-F 10am-4pm. Fare 50¢.

Taxi: Yellow Cab, 252-1131. $1.75 base fare, $1.20 per additional mi. 24hr.

Visitor Info: The **Birmingham Visitors Center,** 1201 University Blvd. (458-8001), at 12th St., I-65 Exit 259, stocks maps, calendars, and coupons for accommodations. Open M-Sa 8:30am-5pm. Also on the lower level of **Birmingham International Airport** (458-8002; open M-Sa 7:45am-10pm, Su 1:45-9pm). The **Greater Birmingham Convention and Visitors Bureau,** 2200 9th Ave. N. (458-8000), 1st fl., downtown, dispenses much of the same info. Open M-F 8:30am-5pm.

Hotlines: Crisis Center, 323-7777. **Rape Response,** 323-7273. Both 24hr.

Post Office: 351 24th St. N. (521-0302; open Tu-F 24hr.; closes Su 4:30am and reopens M 4:30am). **ZIP code:** 35203. **Area code:** 205.

ACCOMMODATIONS, CAMPGROUNDS, AND FOOD

There are a great many cheap hotels and motels along Rte. 65 leading south to Birmingham, including **Days Inn, Holiday Inn,** and **Super 8.** Non-chain options include **The Ranchhouse Inn,** 2127 7th Ave. S. (322-0691), which rests just north of Five Points. The pleasant rooms have cable TV and wood paneling. Call about 2 weeks ahead for reservations. (Singles $30, F-Sa $32; doubles $41/$46. Local calls 25¢. Wheelchair access.) Visitors may camp in **Oak Mountain State Park** (620-2527 or 800-ALA-PARK/252-7275), 15 mi. south of Birmingham off I-65 in Pelham (Exit 246). Alabama's largest state park sprawls across 10,000 heavily forested acres. Horseback rides, golf, hiking, and an 85-acre lake with beach and fishing are all available in the area. (Basic sites $8.50, with water and electricity $13, full hookup $15. Parking $1.)

Barbecue remains the local specialty, but several ethnic eateries have sprung up downtown. The best places to eat cheaply (and meet young people) are at **Five Points South,** located at the intersection of Highland Ave. and 20th St. S. The **Golden Temple Natural Grocery and Café,** 1901-07 11th Ave. S. (933-6333), can load you up with vegetarian lunches (spinach quesadilla $6.50) and groceries. (Grocery open M-F 8:30am-7pm, Sa 9:30am-5:30pm, Su noon-5:30pm. Cafe open M-F 11:30am-2pm, a bit longer in summer.) **Ollie's,** 515 University Blvd. (324-9485), near Green Springs Hwy., charms with Bible Belt dining in an enormous circular 50s-style building. Your prayers have been answered with BBQ pork sandwiches ($2.35) and generous $2 slices of homemade pie. (Open M 10am-3pm, Tu-Sa 10am-8pm.) A microbrewery/bakery/restaurant, **The Mill,** 1035 20th St. S. (939-3001), at the center of Five Points South, will sate any gastronomic need with its tasty $7-9 pizzas and $6 sandwiches. (Live entertainment Tu-Sa; cover $3 F-Sa after 10pm. Bar open nightly until 2am; limited late-night menu. Open M-F and Su 6:30am-1am, Sa 6:30am-2am. Champagne brunch Sa-Su 9am-2pm.)

SIGHTS

Birmingham's efforts at reconciliation with its turbulent past have culminated in the **Black Heritage Tour** of the downtown area. The **Birmingham Civil Rights Institute,** 520 16th St. N. (328-9696), at 6th Ave. N., rivals the museum in Memphis (see p. 282) in thoroughness and surpasses it in visual and audio evocations, depictions, and footage of the largely Alabama-based Civil Rights movement. *(Open Tu-Sa 10am-5pm, Su 1-5pm. Suggested donation $3, students $1, seniors $2.)* The Institute also highlights human rights issues across the globe and serves as a public research facility. A trip to Birmingham would be incomplete without a tour.

Across the street from the Institute is the **Sixteenth St. Baptist Church,** 1530 6th Ave. N. (251-9402), at 16th St. N., where four black little girls died in a September 1963 bombing by white segregationists (open by appointment only; donations appreciated; service on Su at 11am). Many protests spurred on by the deaths occurred in nearby **Kelly-Ingram Park,** corner of 6th Ave. and 16th St., where a bronze statue of Dr. Martin Luther King, Jr. and sculptures portraying the brutality and hope of the civil rights demonstrations now grace the green lawns.

Remnants of Birmingham's steel industry are best viewed at the gigantic **Sloss Furnaces National Historic Landmark** (324-1911), adjacent to the 2nd Ave. N. viaduct off 32nd St. downtown. *(Open Tu-Sa 10am-4pm, Su noon-4pm. Free guided tours Sa-Su 1, 2, and 3pm.)* Though the blast furnaces closed 20 years ago, they stand as the only preserved example of 20th-century iron-smelting in the world. Ballet, drama performances, and music concerts are often held here at night. To anthropomorphize the steel industry, Birmingham made a cast of **Vulcan,** Roman god of the forge (328-6198), who overlooks the skyline and takes second to the Statue of Liberty as the U.S.'s tallest statue. *(Open daily 8am-10:30pm. $1, under 6 free.)* Visitors can watch over the city from its observation deck (20th St. S. and Valley Ave.)

The **Alabama Sports Hall of Fame** (323-6665), corner of Civic Center Blvd. and 22nd St. N., honors the careers of outstanding sportsmen like Bear Bryant, Jesse Owens, Joe Louis, Joe Namath, and Willie Mays (open M-Sa 9am-5pm, Su 1-5pm; $5, students $3, seniors $4). A few blocks down from the Hall of Fame, **Linn Park** refreshes visitors. Next door lies the **Birmingham Museum of Art,** 2000 8th Ave. N. (254-2565), displaying over 17,000 multicultural pieces of art, including a new multi-level sculpture garden (open Tu-Sa 10am-5pm, Su noon-5pm; free).

For a breather from the downtown scene, revel in the marvelously sculpted grounds of the **Birmingham Botanical Gardens,** 2612 Lane Park Rd. (879-1227); spectacular floral displays, an elegant Japanese Garden (complete with teahouse), and an enormous greenhouse vegetate on 67 acres (open daily dawn-dusk; free).

Antebellum Arlington, 331 Cotton Ave. (780-5656), is southwest of downtown; head west on 1st Ave. N., which becomes Cotton Ave. *(Open Tu-Sa 10am-4pm, Su 1-4pm. $3, ages 6-18 $2.)* This 1840s antebellum mansion houses a fine array of 19th-century southern decorative arts and served as a base for Union troops.

If you don't know much 'bout geology, visit the **Red Mountain Museum and Cut,** 2230 22nd St. S. (933-4104). *(Open M-F 9am-4pm, Sa 10am-4pm, Su 1-4pm. $2.)* There, you can wander across a walkway to see different levels of rock formation inside Red Mountain, or check out exhibits on the prehistoric inhabitants of Alabama.

ENTERTAINMENT AND NIGHTLIFE

Historic Alabama Theater, 1817 3rd Ave. N. (252-2262), a gorgeous renovated 1927 building, is booked 300 nights of the year with an 8-week summer classic film series, live performances that range from local theater to Bob Dylan shows, and everything in between. Their organ, the "Mighty Wurlitzer," entertains the audience pre-show. ($5, seniors $4, under 12 $3. Order tickets through Ticket Link, 715-6000, or at the box office 1hr. prior to show.) In addition to the theater's **Infoline** (251-0418), the free *Fun and Stuff* and "Kudzu" section in Friday's *Birmingham Post Herald* list local entertainment events.

Music lovers lucky enough to visit Birmingham June 18-20, 1999 will hear everything from country to gospel to big name rock groups at **City Stages** (251-1272). The

3-day festival, held in Linn Park, is the biggest thing to hit town all year and includes food, crafts, and children's activities. (Daily pass $18, weekend pass $25.)

Nightclubs congregate in Five Points South (Southside). On spring and summer nights, many grab outdoor tables in front of their favorite bars or loiter by the fountain until late. *Use some caution here, and avoid parking or walking in dark alleys near the square.* The hippest licks jam year-round at **The Nick,** 2514 10th Ave. S. (252-3831). The poster-covered exterior says it clear and proud: "The Nick...rocks." (Cover $2-5. Live music W-M. Open M-F 3pm-late, Sa 8pm-later.) **The Burly Earl,** 2109 7th Ave. S. (322-5848), specializes in fried finger foods and local, mostly bluesy, tunes; sandwiches ("fit for an Earl") are $3.50-5. Stop by for a 5hr. happy hour (M-F 2pm-7pm) and a Saturday "hour" noon-7pm (live music Th-Sa nights; no cover; open M-Th 10am-midnight, F-Sa 10am-2am). **Five Points Music Hall,** 1016 20th St. S. (322-2263), doesn't exactly have string quartets playing; this bar-with-music has pool, foosball, and much happy noise (Th night dance party 75¢ plus $1 drinks; cover $5-10).

■ Mobile

Though Bob Dylan lamented being stuck here while yearning for Memphis, Mobile (mo-BEEL) has had plenty of fans in its time—French, Spanish, English, Sovereign Alabama, Confederate, and American flags have each flown over the city since its 1702 founding. This historical diversity is revealed in local architecture: antebellum mansions, Italianate dwellings, Spanish and French forts, and Victorian homes line azalea-edged streets. The faded splendor of these buildings tells of a time in the not-so-distant past when cotton was king. Today, Mobile offers an untouristed version of New Orleans; the site of the first Mardi Gras, the city still holds a 2-week long Fat Tuesday celebration, without the hordes that plague its Cajun counterpart.

ORIENTATION AND PRACTICAL INFORMATION

The downtown district borders the Mobile River. **Dauphin St.** and **Government Blvd. (U.S. 90),** which becomes **Government St.** downtown, are the major east-west routes. **Royal St.** and **Broad St.** are major north-south byways. **Water St.** runs along the bay in the downtown area, becoming the **I-10 causeway. Frontage Rd.** is the same as the **Beltline.**

Trains: Amtrak, 11 Government St. (432-4052 or 800-872-7245). The "Gulf Breeze" blows from Mobile to New York City via bus service to Birmingham or Atlanta. To New Orleans (5hr.; 3 per week Su, W, and F; $21-47).

Buses: Greyhound, 2545 Government Blvd. (478-9793 or 800-231-2222), at S. Conception downtown. To: Montgomery (3hr., 7 per day, $26-28); New Orleans (2-4hr., 9 per day, $28-29); and Birmingham (5-6hr., 5 per day, $37-39). Open 24hr.

Public Transportation: Mobile Transit Authority (MTA), 344-5656. Major depots are at Bienville Sq., Royal St. parking garage, and Adams Mark Hotel. Runs M-F 6am-6pm, less frequently on Sa. Must have exact fare of $1.25, qualified seniors and disabled 60¢, transfers 10¢.

Taxis: Yellow Cab, 476-7711. $2 base fare, $1.20 per additional mi. 24hr.

Visitor Info: Fort Condé Information Center, 150 S. Royal St. (208-7304), in a reconstructed French fort near Government St. Open daily 8am-5pm.

Hotlines: Rape Crisis, 473-7273. **Helpline,** 431-5111. Both 24hr.

Internet Access: Bites and Bits Café, 3976 Government Blvd. (660-2771).

Post Office: 250 Saint Joseph St. (694-5917). Open M-F 8am-5pm, Sa 9am-noon. **ZIP code:** 36601. **Area code:** 334.

ACCOMMODATIONS AND CAMPGROUNDS

Accommodations are both reasonable and accessible, but stop first at the Fort Condé Information Center (see above); they can make reservations for you at a 10-15% discount. **Family Inns,** 900 S. Beltline Rd. (344-5500), I-65 at Airport Blvd., sports new carpets, firm beds, free local calls, continental breakfast, cable, and general comfort (singles $29; doubles $40). **Motel 6,** 400 S. Beltline Hwy. (343-8448 or 800-466-8356), off Airport Blvd., has large, newly remodeled, well-furnished rooms with HBO, free local calls, morning coffee, and pool access (1 person $37; 2 people $43; wheelchair access). A less expensive branch is at 5488 Inn Rd. (660-1483), Exit 5B off I-10. **I-10 Kampground,** 6430 Theodore Dawes Rd. E. (653-9816), lies 7½ mi. west on I-10, south off Exit 13. This is a great place if you like RVs. (Tent sites $13; full RV hookup $18; $1 per additional person. Pool, kiddie playground, laundry, and bath facilities.)

FOOD AND NIGHTLIFE

Mobile's Gulf location means fresh seafood and southern cookin'. **Dreamland,** 3314 Old Shell Rd. (479-9898), has phenomenal ribs you'll be dreaming about long after you give up trying to get the barbecue stains out of your shirt. (Half-slab $8.45, half-chicken $6.50. Open M-Th 10am-10pm, F-Sa 10am-midnight, Su 11am-9pm.) **Wintzell's Oyster House,** 605 Dauphin St. (432-4605), a long-time local favorite, has reopened in its original location. Oysters come prepared in at least six forms, and the gumbo is legendary. (Lunch $5-8. Open M-Sa 11am-10pm, Su noon-8pm.) **Picklefish,** 251 Dauphin St. (434-0000), has a great atmosphere and even fried dill pickles ($4). Their specialty is $7 white pizza with spinach, basil, herbs, garlic, and mozzarella. (Open M-Tu 11am-11pm, W 11am-midnight, Th 11am-2am, F-Sa 11am-4am. Bar open Th-Sa 9pm until very, very late.) **Hayley's,** 278 Dauphin St. (433-4970), an alternative bar/hangout, has spunk and occasional live shows (beer $2.25, Jello shots $1; open daily 3pm-3am). Eighteen pool tables, darts galore, and mega-subs ($3-5) make **Solomon's,** 5753 Old Shell Rd. (344-0380), the quintessential brew and cue college hangout. (Happy hour daily 11am-7pm, $4 pitchers. Open 24hr., though not all of 'em are so happening.)

SIGHTS

Some of Mobile's major attractions lie outside downtown: the **U.S.S. Alabama** is off the causeway (I-10) leading out of the city, and **Dauphin Island** is 30 mi. south. Mobile encompasses two historic districts: DeTonti Sq. and Dauphin St. Both offer an array of architectural styles. The info center provides maps for walking or driving tours of these areas. **Gray Line of Mobile** (432-2229) leads tours, accessing most main districts and sights.

Church St. divides into east and west subdistricts. The homes in the venerable **Church St. East District** showcase popular U.S. architectural styles of the mid- to late 19th century, including Federal, Greek Revival, Queen Anne, and Victorian. While on Church St., pass through the **Spanish Plaza,** at Hamilton and Government St., which honors Mobile's sibling city (Málaga, Spain), while recalling Spain's early presence in Mobile. **Christ Episcopal Church,** 115 S. Conception St. (438-1822), sits opposite the tourist office at Fort Condé. *(Open M-F 8:30am-4:30pm, closed W 11:30am-1:30pm.)* Dedicated in 1842, the church contains beautiful German and Italian stained glass windows. The intriguing **Phoenix Fire Museum,** in a tiny building on 203 S. Claiborne St. (434-7554), displays several antique fire engines including an 1898 steam-powered beauty (open Tu-Sa 10am-5pm, Su 1-5pm; free).

In the **DeTonti Historical District,** north of downtown, the restored **Richards-DAR House Museum,** 256 North Joachim St. (434-7320), offers tours. *(Open Tu-Sa 10am-4pm, Su 1-4pm. Tours $3, children $1.)* The stained glass and Rococo chandeliers blend beautifully with the antebellum Italianate architecture and ornate iron lace. Brick townhouses with wrought-iron balconies fill the rest of the district. **Oakleigh Historical Complex,** 350 Oakleigh Pl. (432-1281), 2½ blocks south of Government St., with bricks that were made on site, reigns as one of Mobile's grande dames. *(Open M-Sa 10am-4pm. $5, students $2, seniors $4.50, ages 6-18 $1. Tours every 30min.; last tour 3:30pm.)* Highlights include a cantilevered staircase and enormous windows opening onto all the balconies upstairs. Inside, a museum contains furnishings of the early Victorian, Empire, and Regency periods. The most photographed building in Mobile, the **Bragg-Mitchell,** 1906 Spring Hill Ave. (471-6364), and the **Condé-Charlotte,** 104 Theatre St. (432-4722), are former residences of cotton brokers and river pilots.

THE SOUTH

(Bragg-Mitchell open M-F 10am-4pm, Su 1-4pm. Condé Charlotte open Tu-Sa 10am-4pm. Package tour available at visitors center; $14 for 4 house museums. Last tour 3:30pm.)

The **Mobile Museum of Art,** 4850 Museum Dr. (343-2667), between Springhill Ave. and University Blvd., displays everything from the historical to cutting-edge contemporary work (open Tu-Su 10am-5pm; free). There's also a downtown branch at 300 Dauphin St. (694-0533; open M-F 8:30am-4:30pm; free). Kids will enjoy the hands-on scientific diversions at the **Exploreum,** 1906 Springhill Ave. (471-5923; open Tu-Sa 9am-5pm; $4, ages 2-17 $3). The battleship **U.S.S. Alabama,** permanently moored at Battleship Park (433-2703), fought in every major battle in the Pacific during WWII; the famous submarine **U.S.S. Drum** rolled along its port side. *(Open daily 8am-5:30pm. $8, ages 6-11 $4; flight simulator $3. Parking $2.)* The park, which includes an international Aircraft Pavilion, is at the entrance of the Bankhead Tunnel, 2½ mi. east of town on I-10. **Bellingrath Gardens,** 12401 Bellingrath Gardens Rd. (973-2217 and 800-247-8420), Exit 15A off I-10, includes some of the nation's premier gardens. The lush landscaped grounds feature a formal rose garden and Asian American garden in addition to the *Southern Belle* river cruise. *(Open daily 8am-dusk. Home and gardens $14, ages 5-11 $10; cruise adds $5/$4. Gardens alone $7/$5.)*

February is a big month for Mobile. Locals await the blooming of the 27 mi. **Azalea Trail** in February and March (**Azalea Festival and Run** Mar. 27, 1999; 473-7223), and February 1-16, 1999, when Mobile's **Mardi Gras** will fill the streets. Enjoy the parades, floats, costumes, and "throws" of the oldest Fat Tuesday around. The *Mobile Traveler* has a thorough and updated list of any and all Mobile attractions.

Mississippi

The "Deep South" bottoms out in Mississippi. The legacy of extravagant cotton plantations, dependence upon slavery, and subsequent racial strife and economic ruin are more visible here than in any other state. In the 1850s, Natchez and Vicksburg were two of the most prosperous cities in the nation; whites bathed in the riches that flowed from free slave labor. Then, during the Civil War, the state was devastated by the siege of Vicksburg and the burning of Jackson. Hatred and injustice drowned Mississippi in the 1960s as blacks protested against continuing segregation and whites reacted with campaigns of terror.

A number of remarkable triumphs have surfaced out of Mississippi's struggles. The state boasts an impressive literary and cultural heritage. Writers William Faulkner, Eudora Welty, Tennessee Williams, and Richard Wright called Mississippi home, as did blues musicians Bessie Smith, W.C. Handy, and B.B. King, who brought their riffs up the "Blues Highway" to Memphis, Chicago, and the world. Today, beautiful plantation homes stand as a testament to the good ol' days, while enduring rural poverty and persistently low education levels are reminders of past inequality.

PRACTICAL INFORMATION

Capital: Jackson.
Visitor Info: Division of Tourism, P.O. Box 1705, Ocean Springs, MS 39566 (800-WARMEST/927-6378; http://www.decd.state.ms.us). **Dept. of Wildlife, Fisheries, and Parks,** P.O. Box 451, Jackson 39205 (800-546-4808).
Emergency: 911.
Time Zone: Central (1hr. behind Eastern). **Postal Abbreviation:** MS.
Sales Tax: 7%.

■ Jackson

Jackson makes a concerted effort to overcome Mississippi's spotty past and lingering backwater image. One billboard even claims Jackson is now as "Rome was to Renaissance Europe." While that may be a bit of a stretch, the state's political, cultural, and commercial capital strives to bring the world to its people. Dance performances and art exhibitions abound throughout the year, and live music is everywhere. North Jackson's lush homes and plush country clubs epitomize wealthy Southern living, while shaded campsites, cool reservoirs, national forests, and Native American burial mounds invite exploration only minutes away.

ORIENTATION AND PRACTICAL INFORMATION

West of I-55, downtown is bordered on the north by **Fortification St.,** on the south by **South St.,** and on the west by **Gallatin St.** North-south **State St.** bisects the city.

Airport: Jackson Municipal (932-2859), east of downtown off I-20. Taxi to downtown costs around $20.

Trains: Amtrak, 300 W. Capitol St. (355-6350 or 800-872-7245). *The neighborhood is deserted at night.* Walk downtown via Capitol St. Open daily 9:30am-7pm. To Memphis (4hr., 7 per week, $28) and New Orleans (4½hr., 7 per week, $16).

Buses: Greyhound, 201 S. Jefferson (353-6342 or 800-231-2222). *Avoid this area at night.* To: Montgomery (5hr., 5 per day, $48-51); Memphis (4½hr.,7 per day, $26); and New Orleans (4½hr., 4 per day, $28). Open 24hr.

Public Transportation: Jackson Transit System (JATRAN), 948-3840. Limited service M-F 5am-7pm, Sa 5:30am-7pm. Fare $1, transfers free. Bus schedules and maps posted at most bus stops downtown and available at JATRAN headquarters, 1025 Terry Rd. Open M-F 8am-4:30pm.

Taxis: City Cab, 355-8319. $1.50 base fare, $1.50 per mi., 50¢ per additional person.

Visitor Info: The Convention and Visitors Bureau, 921 N. President St. (960-1891), downtown, has a limited number of maps and brochures. Open M-F 8am-5pm. Less centrally located is the **Visitors Information Center,** 1150 Lakeland Dr. (354-6113), off I-55 N, Lakeland East Exit (98B). Turn left after ½ mi. into the Agricultural Museum. Brochures and computer info, no staff. Same hrs. as museum; see **Sights and Entertainment,** below.

Hotlines: Crisis Intervention, 713-4375. **Rape Hotline,** 982-7273. Both 24hr.

Post Office: 401 E. South St. (351-7030). Open M-F 7am-6pm, Sa 8am-noon. **ZIP code:** 39205. **Area code:** 601.

ACCOMMODATIONS AND CAMPGROUNDS

If you have a car, head for the motels along **I-20** and **I-55.** Expect to pay $35 and up for decent accommodations in the area, unless you rough it by camping.

Sun 'n' Sand Motel, 401 N. Lamar St. (354-2501), downtown. A time-warp to the 60s—there's even a Polynesian suite. Slightly drab rooms are brightened by pool access, cable TV, and in-house barber shop. Lounge/restaurant in motel serves a $5 lunch buffet. Singles $33; doubles $38; $5 per additional person.

Parkside Inn, 3720 I-55 N (982-1122), at Exit 98B, close to downtown. Dark green furniture and wood-paneled walls spruce up these clean, somewhat small rooms. Pool, cable TV, free local calls, and some rooms with whirlpools available. Must be 21 to rent, 18 and under free with adult. Singles $29; doubles $35.

Timberlake Campgrounds (992-9100). Take I-55 N to Lakeland East (Exit 98B). Turn left after 5.8 mi. onto Old Fannin Rd. and go 3.7 mi; the campground will be on the left. A popular summer camping site with both shaded and waterfront lots. Pool, video games, tennis courts, playground. Tent sites $12, full hookup $15; Oct.-Apr. $10/$13; seniors $1 off year-round. Office open daily 8am-5pm.

FOOD AND NIGHTLIFE

If you crave the familiar tastes of franchise grease palaces, head north to **County Line Rd.,** between I-55 and I-220, dubbed "restaurant alley" by Jackson natives. But if you prefer immersing yourself in the Jackson scene, then the **George St. Grocery,** 416 George St. (969-3573), is the place to be. Packed with state politicians by day and students by night, GSG's lunch deals ($5) will ignite a sweet bang for your buck. (Live music Th-Sa 9pm-1am. Open M-Sa 11am-1am, no food after 10pm.) A 70-year Jackson institution, **Primo's Northgate,** 4330 N. State St. (982-2064), fills a spacious, quasi-romantic dining room with candlelight, jazz, and open-faced prime rib sandwiches for $8 (open M-Sa 11am-10pm). Be prepared to wait in line during the lunch rush at

The Elite Restaurant, 141 E. Capitol St. (352-5606), site of unpretentiously tasty seafood and diner dishes for over 50 years. The daily-changing lunch special (with 2 veggies $5.75) makes it worth the wait. (Open M-F 7am-9:30pm, Sa 5-9:30pm.)

For a list of weekend events in Jackson, pick up Thursday's copy of the *Clarion-Ledger*. **Hal & Mal's Restaurant and Oyster Bar,** 200 S. Commerce St. (948-0888), stages live music, from reggae to innovative rock, in a converted warehouse. Wednesday nights are particularly popular, when the Vernon Brothers grow bluegrass tunes 8:30-11pm. (Cover up to $5 on F-Sa. Restaurant open M 11am-3pm, Tu and Th 11am-9pm, W 11am-10pm, F 11am-10:30pm, Sa 5-10:30pm. Bar open M-Th until 11pm, F-Sa until 1am.) **Cups,** 2757 Old Canton Rd. (362-7422), caters to an artsy crowd craving cappuccino and conversation (open M-Th 7am-10pm, F 7am-midnight, Sa 8am-midnight, Su 9am-10pm).

SIGHTS AND ENTERTAINMENT

The **Mississippi Museum of Art,** 201 E. Pascagoula (960-1515), at Lamar St., displays the splendors of local southern artists and houses a fabulous collection of Americana. *(Open M-Su 10am-5pm, Su noon-5pm. $3, children $2; temporary shows $6/$4.)* The museum also brings in high-quality traveling exhibits. Adjacent to the MMA, the out-of-this-world **Russell C. Davis Planetarium,** 201 E. Pascagoula (960-1550), projects the splendors of the universe. *(Shows Tu-Sa 7:30pm, Sa-Su 2 and 4pm. $5, seniors and under 13 $3.50. Laser shows M-Sa 1pm; same prices.)* Across the street, **Jackson's Art Pavilion,** 429 S. West St. (960-9900), brings in a major exhibit every two years lasting from April to August. *(Tickets $5-20, call for future exhibits and hours.)* An exhibit on the Golden Age of Spain is planned for 2000.

Although Jackson often brings the world to Mississippi, it hardly neglects its homegrown traditions. Built in 1833, the **Old State Capitol** (359-6920), at the intersection of Capitol and State St., houses an excellent museum documenting Mississippi's turbulent history. *(Open M-F 8am-5pm, Sa 9:30am-4:30pm, Su 12:30-4:30pm. Free.)* Exhibits include original artifacts from Native American settlements, authentic flags from Civil War battlegrounds, and documentaries on the Civil Rights movement. The state legislature currently convenes in the beautiful **New State Capitol,** 400 High St. (359-3114), between West and President St., completed in 1903. *(Guided 1hr. tours M-F 9, 10, 11am, 1:30, 2:30, and 3:30pm. Open M-F 8am-5pm. Free.)* A huge restoration project preserved the *beaux arts* grandeur of the building, complete with a gold-leaf eagle perched on the capitol dome and carnivalesque lighting inside. A tour of the **Governor's Mansion,** 300 E. Capitol St. (359-3175), provides an enlightening introduction to Mississippi politics. *(Tours Tu-F every 30min. 9:30-11am. Free.)* Because the governor lives here, the touring hours are slim. General Sherman occupied an antebellum cottage called **The Oaks,** 823 N. Jefferson St. (353-9339), during the siege of Jackson in 1863. *(Open Tu-Sa 10am-3pm. $3, students $2.)* Today, it displays period antiques, including an original couch from Abraham Lincoln's office.

Learn about the struggles and achievements of Mississippi's African Americans at the **Smith-Robertson Museum and Cultural Center,** 528 Bloom St. (960-1457), behind the Sun 'n' Sand Motel. *(Open M-F 9am-5pm, Sa 9am-noon, Su 2-5pm. $1, under 18 50¢.)* This large museum once housed the state's first African-American public school. Now it displays folk art, photographs, and exhibits on the Civil Rights movement and issues that young African Americans confront today. On the last weekend in September, the surrounding neighborhood celebrates African-American culture through art, theater, and food at the **Farish St. Festival** (960-2384).

A recreated 1920s farm village and a number of restored farm implements make up **Mississippi's Agriculture and Forestry Museum,** 1150 Lakeland Dr. (800-844-8687), ½ mi. east of I-55 Exit 98B. *(Open M-Sa 9am-5pm, Su 1-5pm; closed Su early Sept. to late May. $4, seniors $3, ages 6-18 $2, under 6 50¢.)* The town includes a large homestead, barns, mills, a schoolhouse, jail, and other buildings, for a total of more than 30 restored structures. Also on site is the **National Agricultural Aviation Museum,** with vintage aircraft on display beside harrowing tales of cornfield valor.

■ Vicksburg

Vicksburg's verdant hills and prime Mississippi River location made it the focus of much strategic planning during the Civil War. President Abraham Lincoln called the town the "key," and maintained that the war "can never be brought to a close until that key is in our pocket." The Confederates' Gibraltar fell to Union forces on July 4, 1863, after resisting a 47-day bombardment. The loss hit the city hard—until the late 1940s, Vicksburg refused to hold any Fourth of July celebrations. Today, the city tenaciously embraces its checkered history. Downtown, 19th-century mansions house museums, and Civil War monuments dominate the urban landscape. Lush parks lend Vicksburg a relaxed, pastoral feel, while brick-paved roads and festive casino riverwalks recreate a way of life that has long since past.

PRACTICAL INFORMATION You'll need a car to see most of Vicksburg. The bus station, the info center, downtown, and the far end of the sprawling military park mark the city's extremes. **Greyhound** (638-8389 or 800-231-2222; open daily 7am-8:30pm) pulls out of a station far from downtown at 1295 S. Frontage Rd. for Jackson (1hr., 4 per day, $10). The **Tourist Information Center** (636-9421 or 800-221-3536), on Clay St. across from the park (I-20 Exit 4, turn west), has a helpful map with info on Vicksburg's sights (open daily 8am-5pm; in winter Sa-Su 9am-4pm). **Post Office:** 3415 Pemberton Blvd. (636-1071), just off U.S. 61 S (open M-F 8am-5pm, Sa 8am-noon). **ZIP code:** 39180. **Area code:** 601.

ACCOMMODATIONS, FOOD, AND NIGHTLIFE Inexpensive lodging comes easy in Vicksburg, except during the military park's July 4th weekend battle reenactment. One of the best deals in town, the **Hillcrest Motel,** 40 Rte. 80 E (638-1491), ¼ mi. east from I-20 Exit 4, offers well-worn yet well-kept and spacious rooms with pool access (singles $24.50; doubles $30.25). The **Beechwood Motel,** 4449 Clay St. (636-2271), a block in front of the Hillcrest, offers cable and standard rooms (singles $30, doubles $35; F-Sa $35/$45). Most hotels cluster near the park; don't expect to stay downtown, unless you choose the less-than-tidy **Relax Inn Downtown,** 1313 Walnut St. (631-0039; rooms $25-33). **Magnolia RV Park,** 211 Miller St. (631-0388), has 68 full RV hookups (all pull-throughs), a pool, game room, and playground. Head south on Washington (I-20 Exit 1A), and take a left on Rifle Range Rd. to Miller St. (Sites $18. Office open daily 7:30am-9:30pm.) Closer to the military park and the highway is **Battlefield Kampground,** 4407 I-20 Frontage Rd. (636-2025), off Exit 4B, where the kampaign of the krazy "k" kontinues. (Laundry, pool, and playground. Sites $10, with electricity and water $15, full hookup $17; 10% off with any discount card.)

While downtown, chow down at the **Burger Village,** 1220 Washington St. (638-0202), where a home-cooked southern meal costs under $5 and burgers are nothing but 100% all-American beef (open M-Sa 9am-6pm). For those who find American beef blasé, the **Kudzu Café,** 4004 U.S. 61 S (636-2211), grills ostrich burgers ($6). Deli sandwiches ($3-4) and traditional fried seafood ($6-10) are on the menu for patrons with less adventurous palates. (Open M-F 10am-9pm.) The second level of **Duff's Tavern & Grill,** 1306 Washington St. (638-0169), comes alive with popular rock music and an all-night dance floor (open M-Sa 4pm-6am, music from 10pm).

SIGHTS Vicksburg is a mecca for thousands of touring schoolchildren, Civil War buffs, and Confederate and Union army descendents throughout the year. Memorials and markers of combat sites riddle the grassy 1700-acre **Vicksburg National Military Park** (636-0583 or 800-221-3536), and lend the grounds a sacred air. *(Park center open daily 8am-5pm. Grounds open daily in summer 7am-8pm; in winter 7am-sunset.)* The park blockades the eastern and northern edges of the city, with its visitors center on Clay St., about ½ mi. west of I-20 Exit 4B, across from the city info center. Driving through the 16 mi. path ($4 per car), you have three options: guide yourself with a free map available at the entrance, buy an informative audio tour (tape $4.50, CD $8), or hire a live person to help navigate around the sights ($20). Within the park, be sure to visit the **U.S.S. Cairo Museum** (636-2199). *(Open daily 9:30am-6pm; off-season 8am-5pm. Free with park fee.)* The Union boat, sunk in 1862, contains countless artifacts salvaged in the early 1960s. Many consider the **Old Courthouse Museum,** 1008 Cherry St. (636-0741), to be one of the South's finest Civil War museums. *(Open M-Sa 8:30am-5pm, Su 1:30-5pm; early Oct. to early Apr. closes 4:30pm daily. $3, seniors $2.50, under 18 $2.)* During the siege of Vicksburg in 1863, Confederate troops used the cupola as a signal station and held Union prisoners in the upstairs courtroom.

Vicksburg's preoccupation with the Civil War isn't all-encompassing; those with varying fetishes are sure to find something to their liking. The **Attic Gallery,** 1101 Washington St. (638-9221), would impress any art hunter with its collection of Southern contemporary art, in addition to an eclectic display of glassware, pottery, books, and jewelry crammed into every available surface (open M-Sa 10am-5pm; free). The sweet-toothed flock to the **Biedenharn Candy Company and Museum of Coca-Cola History,** 1107 Washington St. (638-6514), where the first Coke was bottled. *(Open M-Sa 9am-5pm, Su 1:30-4:30pm. $1.75, under 12 $1.25.)* Displaying Coca-Cola memorabilia from as far back as 1894, the tour itself is very short but rather sweet—especially if you pause at the gift shop for a $1.65 Coke Float. Inside the **Gray and Blue Naval Museum,** 1102 Washington St. (638-6500), stand 1 ft. tall wooden caricatures of Civil War luminaries (open M-Sa 9am-5pm, Su 1-5pm; $2, children $1).

Vicksburg's finest contribution to the historical home circuit, the **Martha Vick House,** 1300 Grove St. (638-7036) is home to the daughter of the city's founder, Reverend Newitt Vick (open M-Sa 9am-5pm, Su 2pm-5pm; $5, under 12 free, 10% AAA discount). Meanwhile, the only-in-America **Red Carpet Washateria and Lanes,** 2904 Clay St. (636-9682), on Rte. 80 near the river and Riverfront Park, sports a bowling alley, pool room, and laundromat all in one. *(Laundry open daily 7am-9pm. Lanes open M-Th noon-11pm, F-Sa noon-1am, Su noon-10pm. $2 per game, $2.50 at night.)* Despite the Red Carpet's many thrills, high-rollers might prefer spending their time at one of the four **casinos** that line the river.

■ Natchez

In the late 18th century, Natchez distinguished itself as one of the wealthiest settlements on the Mississippi. Of the 13 millionaires in Mississippi at the time, 11 had their cotton plantations here. The custom was to build a manor on the Mississippi side of the river and till the soil on the Louisiana side. After the Civil War, the cotton-based economy of the South crumbled, and the days of the mansion-building magnates passed. Many of the homes remain, however, affording visitors to Natchez the opportunity to gaze at elegant dwellings from a vanished, and vanquished, era.

PRACTICAL INFORMATION Make connections to Vicksburg (1½hr., 1 per day, $14) and New Orleans (4-5hr., 2 per day, $33) at the **Natchez Bus Station,** 103 Lower Woodville Rd. (445-5291; open M-F 8am-5:30pm, Sa 8am-5pm, Su 2-5pm). In town, transportation is available from **Natchez Ford Rental,** 199 St. Catherine St. (445-0060), for $34 per day. (150 free mi., 20¢ per additional mi., $100 cash deposit required. Must be 21, under 26 need a major credit card.) The **Natchez Bicycling Center,** 334 Main St. (446-7794), rents bikes with basket, helmet, lock, and repair kit. ($15 per 4hr., $20 per day. Open Tu-F 10am-5:30pm, Sa 10am-3pm; other times by appt.) A brand new **visitors center,** 640 S. Canal St. (442-5849), greets tourists from the bluffs near the U.S. 84 Mississippi Bridge. Pick up maps and discount books; they'll also suggest tours and book hotel rooms. (Open daily 8:30am-6pm; early Nov. to Mar. 8am-5pm.) **Post Office:** 214 N. Canal St. (442-4361; open M-F 8:30am-5pm, Sa 10am-noon). **ZIP code:** 39120. **Area code:** 601.

ACCOMMODATIONS AND FOOD The intersection of **U.S. 61** and **Highland Blvd.** supports lots of high-quality rooms. **Scottish Inns,** 40 Sgt. Prentiss Dr./U.S. 61 (442-9141 or 800-251-1962), a coral-colored complex, has standard rooms with wood furniture (singles $33; doubles $38). Close to the Mississippi Bridge and visitors center is the **Natchez Inn,** 218 John Junkin Rd./U.S. 84 (442-0221), with spartan, tidy rooms, a pool, and cable TV (singles $28; doubles $35). Campers can settle in at the secluded campground in **Natchez State Park** (442-2658), less than 10 mi. north of Natchez on U.S. 61 in Stanton (sites $7, with water and electricity $11, full hookup $12).

A multitude of cafes and diners dish up budget eats in Natchez. **Cock of the Walk,** 200 N. Broadway (446-8920), earns its title and stature with spicy catfish and complimentary jalapeño cornbread served in a bare wood dining room reminiscent of tough cowpokes and loose women (catfish fillet $9; open daily 5pm until the manager's discretion). **The Pig Out Inn,** 116 S. Canal St. (442-8050), serves up down-home, home-smoked, faster-than-fast-food BBQ with a spicy sauce on the side (sandwiches $3.75; open M-Sa 11am-9pm). Try regional specialties like Cajun boudin sausage, chili, peanut butter pie, and Gringo Pie (tamales with cheese, onions, and jalapeño peppers $5) on the patio at **Fat Mama's Tamales,** 500 S. Canal St. (442-4548), in a log cabin. But remember to hang on to your undergarments as you wash it all down with a $4 Fat Mama's "knock-you-naked" margarita. (Open M-W 11am-7pm, Th-Sa 11am-9pm, Su noon-5pm.)

SIGHTS **Natchez Pilgrimage Tours,** 200 State St., (800-647-6742 or 446-6631), at Canal St., supervises tours of the restored manors left from Natchez's cotton days. *(Open M-Sa 9am-5pm, Su 12:30-5pm.)* A very helpful staff has free tour schedules, maps, and pamphlets, plus a guidebook ($5) that details the histories of the 32 homes that Pilgrimage oversees. This central office sells tickets for individual house tours ($6, children $3), or, for a speedier view of the city and the mansion exteriors, it also sells tickets for a 35min. horse-drawn carriage tour ($9/$4) and a 55min. air-conditioned bus tour ($10/$5). Perhaps the town's best-known home, and the largest octagonal house in America, **Longwood,** 140 Lower Woodville Rd. (442-5193), astounds visitors with its creative, elaborate decor and imaginative floorplan. *(Open daily 9am-5pm. Tours every 20min.)* Yet, the 6-story edifice, designed to be an "Oriental Villa," remains unfinished; the builders, hired from the North, abandoned work at the beginning of the Civil War to fight for the Union. They never returned, and their discarded tools and undisturbed crates still lie as they were left. **Stanton Hall,** 401 High St. (442-6282), off Union St., on the other hand, arose under the direction of local Natchez architects and artisans. *(Open daily 9am-5pm. Tours every 30min.)* Completed in 1857, the mansion features French mirrors, Italian marble mantels, and exquisitely cut chandeliers.

For centuries before the rise of such opulence, the Natchez Indians flourished on this fertile land. The arrival of the French incited fighting in 1730, and French military successes brought an end to the thriving Natchez community. The **Grand Village of the Natchez Indians,** 400 Jefferson Davis Blvd. (446-6502), off U.S. 61 S, pays homage to the tribe with a museum that documents their history and culture. *(Open M-Sa 9am-5pm, Su 1:30-5pm. Free.)* The museum recreates one of several huge tribal burial mounds which once occupied the area. When the Great Sun, or chief, of the tribe died, his wife and retainers were strangled and buried in the same mound; the house of the chief's successor was then built on top.

As the first educational institution in the Mississippi Territory, **Jefferson College** (442-2901), 6 mi. east of Natchez off U.S. 61 near U.S. 84 E, first opened its doors in 1811. *(Grounds open daily sunrise-sunset. Buildings open M-Sa 8am-5pm, Su 11am-5pm. Free.)* Although the last student left in 1964, the site now features restored buildings, a museum, and nature trails.

The 500 mi. **Natchez Trace Pkwy.** leads north from Natchez to Nashville, TN. Rambling through lush forests, swamps, and shady countryside, the road passes through historic landmarks and a beautiful national park. The Mississippi River drifts by just a few miles to the west, a gentle companion in the sleepy, scenic South.

┌───┐
Finer than Moonshine

While France has its Burgundy and California its Napa Valley, the South can boast its own **Old South Winery,** 65 S. Concord Ave. (445-9924), located off D'evereux Dr. *(Open M-Sa 10am-5pm, Su 1-5pm. Free.)* Wines produced here are pressed from muscadines—a type of grape grown only in the southeastern region of the U.S.—which lend both its red and white wines a fruity flavor. The sufficiently aged red complements a plate of steaming grits well. What's the winery's most popular offering? Why, it's a delightful, sweet rosé named **Miss Scarlett.**
└───┘

THE SOUTH

■ Oxford

Strolling along the covered sidewalks of Courthouse Sq., window shopping, and relishing the shade of Oxford's tall cedar trees, a visitor can't help but feel the serenity of this small town. It hasn't always been like this. In the 19th century, the small Mississippi town played a critical role in the Cherokee evacuation from Georgia as a stopping point on the Trail of Tears. In the 1950s, Oxford came to the country's attention when a federal court ruled that James Meredith should be the first black student to enroll at the University of Mississippi (Ole Miss), just west of the city. The news resulted in rioting and the death of three civil rights workers.

For now, Oxford rests again, a fitting home for the unique **Center for the Study of Southern Culture** (232-5993) in the Barnard Observatory at Ole Miss, where visitors can pick up pamphlets or attend conferences, including the ever-popular **Faulkner Conference** (in late July or early Aug.; center open M-F 8am-5pm; free). Blues buffs will revel in the over 35,000 records at the **Ole Miss Blues Archive,** Farley Hall room #340 (232-7753; open M and W 9am-6pm, Tu and Th 9am-6:30pm, F 9am-5pm; free). The **University Museums,** (232-7073) on University Ave. at Ole Miss, contain four main collections ranging from southern folk art to 19th-century scientific instruments (open Tu-Sa 10am-4:30pm, Su 1pm-4pm; free). The **Double Decker Arts Festival,** on the square during the last weekend in April, hosts tunes on two stages, while you can sample the wide array of cookin' offered in the **Taste of Oxford.**

The Mansion, **William Faulkner's** home at **Rowan Oak** (234-3284), lies just south of downtown on Old Taylor Rd. (Open Tu-Sa 10am-noon and 2-4pm, Su 2-4pm. Grounds open sunrise-sunset. Free self-guided tours.) Faulkner named the property after the Rowan tree, a symbol of peace and security. The Rowan is not, in fact, a member of the Oak family, a botanical tidbit which Oxford locals find most amusing.

At **Square Books,** 160 Courthouse Sq. (236-2262), a collection of Faulkner's works may be enjoyed on a balcony overlooking the downtown area. The bookstore also sells ice cream and coffee. (Open M-Th 9am-9pm, F-Sa 9am-10pm, Su 10am-6pm.) Downtown, **Smitty's Café,** 208 S. Lamar (234-9111), where most entrees are under $7, pleases with delicious cornbread (open M-Sa 7am-4pm, Su 8am-4pm). The **Bottle-tree Bakery,** 923 Van Buren Ave. (236-5000), is wonderfully indulgent (open Tu-F 7am-4pm, Sa 9am-4pm, Su 9am-2pm).

Visitors can spend the night in southern comfort at the **Oliver-Britt House Inn,** 512 Van Buren Ave. (234-8043), an unpretentious B&B (singles and doubles $45-55, $10 surcharge F-Sa). The students' choice, **Ole Miss Motel,** 1517 E. University Ave. (234-2424), rebels with remodeled rooms, big TVs, free local calls, and a heart on every door (singles from $30; doubles from $42). Twenty-three miles north of town on Rte. 7 lies **Wall Doxy State Park** (252-4231), a scenic spot with an expansive lake and cheap camping. (Primitive sites $6-8, with water and electricity $11. Entrance fee $2 per car, 50¢ for pedestrians or bicyclists.) At night, live music rolls from **Proud Larry's,** 211 S. Lamar (236-0050), which keeps on burnin' all year and late into the night (cover $4-5; music starts most nights at 9pm).

Oxford rests 30 mi. east of I-55 on Rte. 6 (take Exit 243), 55 mi. south of Memphis, and 140 mi. north of Jackson. **Greyhound,** 2612B Jackson Ave. W. (234-0094 or 800-231-2222), runs one bus a day to Memphis (1½hr., $21); Nashville (9hr., $56); and Jackson (10hr., $50). **Internet access** is available at the public library, 401 Bramlett Blvd. (234-5751), just off University Ave. (open M-Th 9:30am-8pm, F-Sa 9:30am-5:30pm). **Post Office,** 911 Jackson Ave. E (234-5615; open M-F 9am-5pm, Sa 9:30am-12:30pm). **ZIP code:** 38655. **Area code:** 601.

Louisiana

After exploring the Mississippi River valley in 1682, Frenchman René-Robert Cavalier proclaimed the land "Louisiane," in honor of Louis XIV. The name endured three centuries, though France's ownership of the vast region did not. The territory was tossed between France, England, and Spain before Thomas Jefferson and the United States snapped it up in the Louisiana Purchase of 1803. Nine years later, a smaller, redefined Louisiana was admitted to the Union. Each successive government lured a new mix of settlers to the bayous: Spaniards came from the Canary Islands, French Acadians from Nova Scotia, Americans from the East, and free blacks from the West Indies. Louisiana has always stood apart from the rest of the Union; its multi-national history, Creole culture, and Napoleonic legal system are unlike anything found in the 49 other states. While beautiful to visit, the swamps of Louisiana are a tough place to make a living, and the residents have always been among the poorest people in the nation.

PRACTICAL INFORMATION

Capital: Baton Rouge.
Visitor Info: Office of Tourism, P.O. Box 94291, Baton Rouge 70804-9291 (504-342-8119 or 800-261-9144; http://www.louisianatravel.com). Open M-F 8am-4:30pm. **Office of State Parks,** P.O. Box 44426, Baton Rouge 70804-4426 (504-342-8111). Open M-F 9am-5pm.
Emergency: 911.
Time Zone: Central (1hr. behind Eastern). **Postal Abbreviation:** LA.
Sales Tax: 8%.

■ New Orleans

Originally explored by the French, La Nouvelle Orleans was secretly ceded to the Spanish in 1762, though the citizens didn't find out until 1766. Spain returned the city to France just in time for Thomas Jefferson to buy it in 1803. Centuries of cultural mingling have resulted in a fabulous *mélange* of Spanish courtyards, Victorian verandas, Acadian jambalaya, African gumbo, and French *beignets*. The local accent is a combination found nowhere else, and even the local music is an amalgam of sounds; New Orleans' internationally renowned jazz fuses African rhythms and modern brass.

A long multicultural history gives N'awlins a wise, aged aspect. Here, it's accepted to let the maintenance slip a bit—residents proudly call their home the "Big Easy," reflecting a joyous, carefree attitude. The only thing that stifles this vivacity is the heavy, humid air that slows folks to a near standstill during the summer. But when the day's heat finally retreats into the night, the city begins to jump, drinking and dancing into the early morning. Come late February, there's no escaping the month-long celebration of Mardi Gras, the climax of the city's already festive mood.

ORIENTATION

New Orleans, though fairly compact, can be very confusing. The city's main streets follow the curve of the **Mississippi River,** hence its nickname "the Crescent City." Directions from locals show further watery influences—lakeside means north, referring to **Lake Ponchartrain,** and riverside means south. Uptown lies west, up river; downtown lies down river. Most of the city is concentrated on the east bank of the Mississippi. However, **The East** (locally dubbed) refers only to the easternmost part of the city. Less populated regions of the city, like Algiers, are on **The West Bank,** across the river. Many streets run only one-way or are separated with broad medians; you generally have to make several U-turns to get where you're going.

Tourists flock to the small **French Quarter (Vieux Carré),** bounded by the Mississippi River, **Canal St., Rampart St.,** and **Esplanade Ave.** Streets in the Quarter follow a grid pattern, making foot travel easy. The residential **Garden District** (uptown, bordered by **St. Charles Ave.** to the north and **Magazine St.** to the south) is distinguished by its elegant homes and well-cultivated gardens. The scenic **St. Charles Streetcar route** (fare $1), easily picked up at the corner of Canal St. and Carondelet St., passes through parts of the **Central Business District** ("CBD" or downtown), the Garden District via St. Charles Ave., and **S. Carollton Ave.**

Parking in New Orleans is easier than driving in it. To park near the French Quarter, head for the residential area around **Marigny St.** and **Royal St.,** where many streets have no meters and no restrictions. Avoid parking in this area at night; streets are dimly lit and deserted. After sunset, it is always best to take a cab. *Don't ever leave anything valuable visible inside the car.*

THE SOUTH

New Orleans struggles to play down its high murder and crime rates, but avoid areas where you feel uncomfortable. The tenement areas directly north of the French Quarter and directly northwest of Lee Circle pose particular threats to personal safety. At night, even quaint-looking side streets in the Quarter can be dangerous—stick to busy, well-lit roads and never walk alone anywhere in this city after dark. Make some attempt to downplay the tourist image (i.e. don't wear a t-shirt that has the words "New Orleans" anywhere on it). *Avoid all parks, cemeteries, and housing projects at night.* Have a good idea of where you want to go. Many streets are poorly labeled, and one wrong turn can make a dangerous difference. Take a cab to your lodgings when returning from the Quarter late at night.

PRACTICAL INFORMATION

Airport: Moisant International (464-0831), 15 mi. west of the city. Cab fare to the Quarter is set at $21 for 2 people; $8 per person for 3 or more. The **Louisiana Transit Authority** (737-9611; office open M-F 8am-4pm) runs buses from the airport down Tulane Ave. to Elk St. (downtown), M-Sa 5:30am-5:40pm, every 15min. After 5:40pm, buses go to Tulane Ave. and Carollton Ave. (mid-city) until 11:30pm. Fare $1.50, exact change needed. Pick-up on the upper level, near the exit ramp.

Trains: Amtrak, 1001 Loyola Ave. (528-1610 or 800-872-7245), in the Union Passenger Terminal, a 10min. walk to Canal St. via Elk. To: Houston (8hr., 3 per week, $47); Jackson (4hr., 7 per week, $16); and Atlanta (12hr., 7 per week, $39). Station open 24hr.; ticket office open Tu, Th, and Su 5:45am-11pm; M, W, and F-Sa 5:45am-8:30pm.

Buses: Greyhound, 1001 Loyola Ave. (524-7571 or 800-231-2222), in the Union Passenger Terminal. To Austin (12hr., 5 per day, $89) and Baton Rouge (2hr., 9 per day, $9). Station open 24hr.

Public Transportation: Regional Transit Authority (RTA), 2817 Canal St. (248-3900). Most buses pass Canal St., at the edge of the French Quarter. Major buses and streetcars run 24hr. Fare $1, seniors and disabled passengers 40¢; transfers 10¢. 1-day pass $4, 3-day pass $8; passes sold at major hotels in the Canal St. area. Office has bus schedules and transit info; open M-F 8am-5pm.

Taxis: Checker Yellow Cabs, 943-2411, or **United Cabs,** 522-9771. Both $2.10 base fare, $1.20 per mi., 75¢ per additional person.

Car Rental: Gill & Jim's Rent-A-Car, 4401 N. Galvez St. (948-9813). $26.50 per day with 100 free mi. Must be 25 and leave $250 cash deposit. Open M-F 9am-5pm, Sa 9am-noon.

Bike Rental: French Quarter Bicycles, 522 Dumaine St. (529-3136), between Decatur and Chartres. $4.50 per hr., $20 per 24hr., $84 per week (includes lock, helmet and map). Must have credit card or $200 cash deposit. Open daily 10am-6pm.

Visitor Info: The **New Orleans Welcome Center,** 529 St. Ann St. (566-5031; http://www.neworleanscvb.com), by Jackson Sq. in the French Quarter, has free city and walking-tour maps. Very helpful, knowledgeable staff. Open daily 9am-5pm.

Hotlines: Cope Line, 523-2673, for crises. **Rape Hotline,** 483-8888. Both 24hr.

Hospital: Charity Hospital, 1532 Tulane Ave. (568-2311). 24hr. emergency room.

Internet Access: New Orleans Public Library, 219 Loyola Ave. (529-7323), 1½ blocks from Canal St. (open M-Th 11am-6pm, Sa 11am-5pm), and the **Contemporary Arts Center** (see p. 340) both offer free access.

Post Office: 701 Loyola Ave. (589-1111 or 589-1112), near the Union Passenger Terminal. Open M-F 7am-11pm, Sa 7am-8pm, Su noon-5pm. **ZIP code:** 70113. **Area code:** 504.

ACCOMMODATIONS

Finding inexpensive, yet decent, rooms in the **French Quarter** can be as difficult as finding sobriety during Mardi Gras. Luckily, other parts of the city compensate for the absence of cheap lodging downtown. Several **hostels** pepper the area and cater to the young and almost penniless, as do B&Bs near the **Garden District.**

Accommodations for Mardi Gras and the Jazz Festival get booked up to a year in advance. During peak times, proprietors will rent out any extra space—be sure you

know what you're paying for. Rates tend to sink in June and early December, when accommodations become desperate for business; negotiation can pay off.

◉India House, 124 S. Lopez St. (821-1904), at Canal St. What this bohemian haunt lacks in tidiness it compensates for in character. The friendly, easy-going management knows plenty about what to see and do in New Orleans. Kitchen, pool, and separate alligator pond out back. 1pm check-out designed for those with "morning grogginess." $12, $14-17 in summer and peak times. Free linen. Key deposit $5. No lockout or curfew.

◉Marquette House New Orleans International Hostel (HI-AYH), 2253 Carondelet St. (523-3014). The cleanest hosteling experience in New Orleans. Courtyards link several separate buildings with 176 beds, A/C, tidy kitchens, and study rooms. Exceptionally quiet for a hostel. $15.50, nonmembers $18.50. Private rooms with queen-sized bed and pull-out sofa $45/$51. Linen $2.50. Key deposit $5. No lockout or curfew. No alcohol permitted. Smoking in the courtyard only.

St. Charles Guest House, 1748 Prytania St. (523-6556). In a serene neighborhood near the Garden District and St. Charles Streetcar. A big 3-building complex with 38 rooms, 8 with shared baths. Lovely pool and sunbathing deck. Small, no-frills backpacker's singles with no A/C $15-25. Rooms with 1 queen-sized bed or 2 twins $45-65. Breakfast included.

Longpre House, 1726 Prytania St. (581-4540), in a 145-year-old house 1 block off St. Charles, shows a bit of its age. A 25min. walk from the Quarter. Dorms $12, in peak times $16. Singles and doubles with shared bath $35, with private bath $40. Free coffee and linen. Dorm check-in 8am-10pm, 11am for private rooms. No curfew.

Old World Inn, 1330 Prytania St. (566-1330). A clean, comfortable house with a friendly staff; the owners can give you helpful tourist advice. Singles from $25, with bath from $35; doubles $40/$50. Breakfast included. Key deposit $5.

Prytania Inn, 1415 Prytania St. (566-1515). Includes 4 restored 19th-century homes about 5 blocks apart; stay in St. Vincent's if you can afford it. Reasonable prices, multilingual staff (German, French, and Thai), and a homey atmosphere. Singles $29-45; doubles $29-55. Full southern breakfast $5.

Hotel LaSalle, 1113 Canal St. (523-5831 or 800-521-9450), 3 blocks from Bourbon St., downtown. Don't expect luxury, but the rooms are well maintained. Singles $29, with bath $58; doubles $39/$70. Coffee included. Lobby staffed 24hr.

Mazant House, 906 Mazant St. (944-2662). Tastefully furnished rooms with home-style accommodations. Living room, well-equipped kitchen, and only 2 blocks from the Desire St. bus. *However, the neighborhood warrants caution.* Singles $22, with bath $39; doubles $29/$51; $5 per extra cot. Apartment accommodations and rates available for extended stays.

YMCA International Hostel, 920 St. Charles Ave. (568-9622). Basic rooms for women, men, and couples. 20 rooms on the St. Charles side give an excellent view of Mardi Gras parades, but reserve early. Guests get free use of the Y's indoor pool, gym, and track. Shared baths. Singles $29; doubles $35.

CAMPGROUNDS

KOA West, 11129 Jefferson Hwy./Rte. 48 (467-1792), in suburban River Ridge; take I-10 to Exit 223A, and turn left. RTA: St. Charles Streetcar to commuter E-3 ($2). Shuttle to the French Quarter ($3) leaves 9am and 5pm, returns 5:45pm. Pool, laundry facilities. Clean bathrooms and shady, well-kept grounds. 10 tent sites $22, 96 sites with full hookup $27 (add $2 for A/C).

St. Bernard State Park, (682-2101) 18 mi. southeast of New Orleans in Poydras; exit I-10 on LA 47 S (Exit 246A), turn left onto Rte. 46 for 7 mi., then right on Rte. 39 for 1 mi. 51 sites with water and electricity. $12. Office open daily 7am-8pm.

Jude Travel Park and Guest House, 7400 Chef Menteur Hwy./U.S. 90 (241-0632 or 800-523-2196), just east of the eastern junction of I-10 and U.S. 90. Bus #98 "Broad" drives past the front gate to #55 "Elysian Fields," which heads downtown. Showers, laundry, 24hr. security. 44 tent/RV sites $17 (all with water and electricity); rates rise at peak times.

Sycamore Tree Travel Park, 10910 Chef Menteur Hwy./U.S. 90 (244-6611, outside LA 800-788-6787), 3 mi. east of the eastern junction of I-10 and U.S. 90. Same RTA service as Jude Travel Park. Pool, showers, and laundry facilities. Tent sites $12, with full RV hookup $16.

SEAFOOD, SAUSAGE—SHO' NUFF, GOOD STUFF

In addition to the international options which entice hungry visitors, the city offers a long list of regional specialties which have evolved from the combination of Acadian, Spanish, Italian, African, French, and Native American ethnic cuisines. **Jambalaya** (a Cajun jumble of rice, shrimp, oysters, sausage, and ham or chicken mixed with spices) and the African **gumbo** grace practically every menu in New Orleans. A Southern breakfast of grits, eggs, bacon, and buttermilk biscuits satisfies even the most ardent eaters. **Creole,** a mixture of Spanish, French, and Caribbean, is famous for red beans and rice, po' boys (French bread sandwiches filled with sliced meat or seafood and vegetables; "dressed" means with mayo, lettuce, tomatoes, pickles, etc.), and shrimp or crawfish *étouffé.* The daring go to **Ralph & Kacoos Seafood Restaurant,** 519 Toulouse St. (522-5226), between Decatur and Chartres St. Order the crawfish ($3 per lb.), and eat it the way the locals do: tear off the head and suck out the tasty juices. (Hey, when in Rome…) Some of the best and cheapest Creole pralines ($1.25) come from **Laura's Candies,** 600 Conti St. (525-3880; open daily 9am-7pm). The **French Market,** between Decatur and N. Peters St., on the east side of the French Quarter, sells pricey fresh vegetables.

If the eats in the Quarter prove too trendy, touristy, or tough on your budget, a jaunt down **Magazine St.** will remedy this as you check out the cafes, antique stores, and book fairs spilling onto the sidewalk. Alternatively, you can catch a streetcar uptown to **Tulane University** for some late-night grub and collegiate character.

Downtown New Orleans

French Quarter

Café du Monde, 800 Decatur St. (525-4544), near the French Market. The consummate people-watching paradise since 1862 really only does 2 things—scrumptious *café au lait* ($1.10) and hot *beignets* ($1.10). Open 24hr. To take home some of that chicory coffee, cross the street to the Café du Monde Gift Shop, 813 Decatur St. (581-2914 or 800-772-2927). 15 oz. of the grind $4.60. Open daily 9:30am-6pm.

Johnny's Po' boys, 511 St. Louis St. (524-8129). The po' boy is the right choice at this French Quarter institution, which offers 40 varieties of the famous sandwich (around $4), with a combo plate available for the indecisive. Decent Creole fare (jambalaya, gumbo) is also on the menu. Open M-F 8am-4:30pm, Sa-Su 9am-4pm.

Central Grocery, 923 Decatur St. (523-1620), between Dumaine and St. Philip St. Try an authentic muffuletta (deli meats, cheeses, and olive salad on Italian bread) at the place that invented them. A half ($4.25) serves one, and a whole ($7.50) serves 2. Open M-Sa 8am-5:30pm, Su 9am-5:30pm.

Gumbo Shop, 630 St. Peters St. (525-1486). Sit under a broad-leafed palm and savor a bowl of seafood okra or chicken andouille gumbo ($6.50). Entrees from $10. Expect a line. Recipes available. Open daily 11am-11pm.

Acme Oyster House, 724 Iberville St. (522-5973). Patrons slurp fresh oysters shucked before their eyes at the bar (6 for $3.50, 12 for $6), or sit at the red checkered tables for a good ol' po' boy ($5-7). Open M-Sa 11am-10pm, Su noon-7pm.

Croissant d'Or, 617 Ursulines St. (524-4663). The historic building was the first ice cream parlor in New Orleans. Fair-priced French pastries, sandwiches, and quiches. *Carré Mocca* $1.30, chocolate mousse $1.50. Open daily 7am-5pm.

Mama Rosa's, 616 N. Rampart (523-5546). Locals adore this Italian ristorante. Rosa's pizza was once rated 1 of the 9 best in the country by *People Magazine,* a true connoisseur of fine dining. 14 in. cheese pie $9. Open daily 11am-9pm.

Tricou House, 711 Bourbon St. (525-8379). Enjoy "Bourbon Street's best deal"—red beans 'n' rice for $3.25—in the historic courtyard, circa 1832. All-you-can-eat deals include BBQ ribs on W and Su ($10), catfish Th-F ($7-11), and shrimp daily ($11-13). Open Su-Th 11am-midnight, F-Sa 11am-2am.

Clover Grill, 900 Bourbon St. (598-1010). The waiters behind the counter love to entertain and compliment patrons—for extra tips, of course. The Clover has been open 24hr. since 1950, serving greasy and delicious mushroom bacon cheeseburgers ($5.29) grilled under an American-made hubcap.

Sabrina and Gabrielle's Secret Garden, 538 St. Philip St. (524-2041). A romantic rendezvous for the dinnertime crowd. A pleasant courtyard and gracious service add to the mood. Cajun and Creole specials include soup and salad ($7-15). Open Su-Th 11am-10pm, F-Sa 11am-11pm.

Country Flame, 620 Iberville St. (522-1138). No, it's not a country-western bar; it's a Mexican restaurant with very low prices (2 tacos $2.50). You can watch your order get cooked in the kitchen. Open Su-Th 11am-10pm, F-Sa 11am-11pm.

Mena's, 622 Iberville (525-0217). You'll find good cheap food and friendly service at this low-profile establishment. Po' boys $3.50, gumbo with fries $3.75. Lunch specials ($4-5) pack in a crowd. Open M-Sa 6:30am-6:45pm.

Royal Blend, 621 Royal St. (523-2716). A quiet garden setting offers an escape from the hustle and bustle of Royal St. Over 20 hot and iced coffees available, as well as a mighty fine selection of teas—you can even brew your own. Light meals (croissant sandwiches, quiches) served daily; pastries $1-2. Open M-Th 7am-8pm, F-Sa 7am-midnight, Su 7am-6pm.

Louisiana Pizza Kitchen, 95 French Market Pl. (522-9500). Wood-fired ovens give the pizzas a rich, smoky flavor ($5-8) with all imported ingredients. Open Su-Th 11am-10pm, F-Sa 11am-11pm.

Outside the Quarter

🐚**Camellia Grill,** 626 S. Carrollton Ave. (866-9573). Take the St. Charles Streetcar away from the Quarter to the Tulane area. A classic, counter-service diner where the cooks don't mind telling the whole restaurant about their problems with their wives. Ask your bow-tied waiter for the chef's special omelette ($7) or the pecan pie ($2.35). Expect a wait on weekend mornings. Open M-Th 9am-1am, F 9am-3am, Sa 8am-3am, Su 8am-1am.

🐚**Franky and Johnny's,** 321 Arabella (899-9146), southwest of downtown towards Tulane off Tchoupitoulas St. A joyous, noisy local hangout with great onion rings ($3.25), po' boys, and succulent boiled crawfish (2 lbs. $5, seasonal). Open daily 11am until late.

Taqueria Corona, 5932 Magazine St. (897-3974), between State and Nashville St. Some of the best Mexican food around. Loud but cozy atmosphere. Deliciously hot burritos $3-4, chicken and shrimp tacos $2.50. Open daily 11:30am-2pm and 5-9:30pm. Off season call for hrs.

Tee Eva's, 4430 Magazine St. (899-8350). Tee attracts locals with peerless pies, serious bayou cooking, and 9 oz. snow balls for 75¢. Tasty crawfish pie only $3; sweet potato, cream cheese pecan, or plain pecan pie slices $1.35. Large 9 in. pies $8-16, by order only. Soul food lunches change daily ($3-5). Open daily 11am-8pm.

All Natural, 5517 Magazine St. (891-2651), uptown. This friendly neighborhood health store whips up fabulous vegetarian sandwiches, pizzas, and hot specials ($3-5). Probably the only place that serves vegetarian jambalaya (with salad $5) and wheatgrass juice. Open M-Th 9am-8pm, F 9am-7pm, Sa-Su 9am-6pm.

Joey K's Restaurant, 3001 Magazine St. (891-0997), at 7th St. Locals congregate at this friendly neighborhood eatery, especially for the mid-day meal—lunch specials start at $6 and feature "Creole pot" cooking, stuffed eggplant, and fried seafood. Sandwiches $5 and beer $2. Open M-F 11am-10pm, Sa 8am-10pm.

Café Atchafalaya, 901 Louisiana Ave. (891-5271), at Laurel St. Take the #11 bus "Magazine St." This cozy cottage serves mouth-watering, traditional Southern cuisine. Simple dishes like red beans and rice with salad ($6.50) or delicacies like Shrimp Orleans ($13.50) are expensive but exquisite. Cobblers galore. Lunch Tu-F 11:30am-2pm, Sa-Su 8:30am-2pm; dinner Tu-Th 5:30-9pm, F-Sa 5:30-10pm.

Dunbar's Creole Cooking, 4927 Freret St. (899-0734), at Robert St. Soul-food-style meals, at super-low prices (breakfast $2, dinner $5-6). Gorge yourself on cabbage and candied yams or the all-you-can-eat red beans and chicken (both $5). Free iced tea with student ID. *Best to steer clear of the area at night.* Open M-Sa 7am-9pm.

The Trolley Stop Café, 1923 St. Charles Ave. (523-0096). Breakfast is served 24hr. at this local favorite that manages to stay busy at all times. You're likely to see police dining at the next table, which makes this New Orleans's safest, best late-night bet. Most meals under $5.

The Praline Connection, 901 S. Peters St. (523-3973), at Saint Joseph St. near the French Quarter and at 542 Frenchmen St. (943-3934). And that's prah-leens, not pray-leens. Either way, this New Orleans original has finger-lickin' good soul food. Fried chicken and seafood, stuffed crab, or *étouffées* will please your palate if not your arteries. Entrees from $8. Open Su-Th 11am-10:30pm, F-Sa 11am-midnight.

Mother's Restaurant, 401 Poydras St. (523-9656), downtown at Tchoupitoulas St., 4 blocks southwest of Bourbon St. Serving up po' boys ($6-9) and some of the best jambalaya in town ($6.75) to locals for almost half a century. Delicious crawfish or shrimp *étouffé* omelette ($9.50). Open M-Sa 5am-10pm, Su 7am-10pm.

Five Happiness, 3605 S. Carrollton Ave. (482-3935). *Gambit Newsweekly* readers annually vote this the best Chinese restaurant in New Orleans. Favorites include jumbo shrimp, juicy baked duck, and potstickers. Lunch $6-8, dinner $8-10. Open M-Th 11:30am-10:30pm, F-Sa 11:30am-11:30pm, Su noon-10:30pm.

Bennachin Restaurant, 133 N. Carrollton Ave. (486-1313), off Canal St. Vegetarian, non-vegetarian, spicy, non-spicy—they'll make it the way you like it. Sway to African music as you peruse the selection of low-priced African dishes (specials around $5 before 4pm). Spinach, trout, and plantains are house favorites, as is *gingero,* a very potent ginger drink ($1.50). Open M-Th 11am-9pm, F 11am-10pm, Sa 5-10pm.

SIGHTS

French Quarter

Allow yourself at *least* a full day (some take a lifetime) in the Quarter. The oldest section of the city is famous for its ornate wrought-iron balconies; French, Spanish, and uniquely New Orleans architecture; and a raucous atmosphere. Known as the **Vieux Carré** (view-ca-RAY), or Old Sq., the historic district of New Orleans offers dusty used book and record stores, museums, and many tourist traps. A variety of street musicians, palm readers, and clowns pack **Bourbon** and **Decatur St.** day and night.

Once a streetcar named "Desire" rolled down Royal St., now one of the French Quarter's most aesthetically pleasing avenues. Two devastating fires, in 1788 and 1794, forced the neighborhood to rebuild during the era of Spanish domination in the city, and the renovations took on the flavor of Spanish colonial architecture. Most notable are the intricate iron-lace balconies, which were either hand-wrought into patterns or cast in molds. At the corner of Royal and St. Peters St. is what may be the most photographed building in the French Quarter: **LaBranche House,** with balconies of wrought-iron oak leaves and acorns spanning three tiers. Nearby is **M.S. Rau, Inc.,** 630 Royal St. (523-5660), where asking to be let out onto the balcony earns you an excellent aerial view of Royal St. *(Open M-Sa 9am-5:15pm.)* M.S. Rau houses an extensive antique collection, fine silver, and expensive jewelry. **A Gallery for Fine Photography,** 322 Royal St. (568-1313), lends perspective with contemporary and vintage works, as well as a century of photos and original prints from masters like Ansel Adams and Edward Curtis (open M-Sa 10am-6pm, Su 11am-6pm).

During the day, most of the activity in the French Quarter centers around **Jackson Sq.,** a park dedicated to General Andrew Jackson, victor of the Battle of New Orleans. While the square swarms with artists, mimes, musicians, psychics, magicians, and con artists, **St. Louis Cathedral** presides in cold judgment over the hubbub (tours every 15-20min. M-Sa 9am-4:30pm; free). Behind the cathedral lies **St. Anthony's Garden,** named in memory of Father Antonio de Sedella. The priest served in New Orleans for almost 50 years after his arrival in 1779, and was locally renowned for his dedication to helping the poor. Strangely, his commemorative park was often the site of bloody 18th-century duels. **Pirate's Alley** and **Père Antoine's Alley** border the garden. Legend has it that the former was the site of covert meetings between pirate Jean Lafitte and Andrew Jackson, as they conspired to plan the Battle of New Orleans.

THE SOUTH

The historic **French Market** (522-2621) takes up several city blocks just east of Jackson Sq., toward the water, along N. Peters St. *(Open daily 9am-8pm; store hrs. vary.)* The market begins at the famous **Café du Monde** (see p. 337); for a map of the whole strip, stop at the market's **visitors center** under Washington Artillery Park (596-3424; open daily 8:30am-5pm). Vendors sell everything from watermelons to earrings. The market is not a recently conceived tourist trap: the French Market has been operating in the same spot since 1791. Visitors may purchase fresh fruits, vegetables, herbs, and spices at the **Farmers Market,** which never closes. Those who enjoy scavenger hunts should head for the **Flea Market,** where one gathers what another one spills. *(Open 8am-sunset.)* Tables are piled high with t-shirts, handmade furniture, and antique glasses; over it all, the scent of fish floats through the air.

The **Jean Lafitte National Historical Park and Preserve,** 916-918 N. Peters St. (589-2636), headquartered in the back section of the French Market at Dumaine and St. Phillip St., displays the rich cultural heritage of the French Quarter. The park conducts free 1½hr. walking tours, which emphasize aspects of New Orleans's cultural, ethnic, and environmental history, through the Quarter (daily 10:30am) and into the Garden District (2:30pm; reservations required). The Tour du Jour (11:30am) changes daily; call ahead for specific info (office open daily 9am-5pm).

It's always a great night to stroll the **Moon Walk,** a promenade stretching alongside the "Mighty" Mississippi. The walk offers a fantastic riverside view and chances for Michael Jackson humor. *Don't go alone at night.* Though the Park Service no longer leads tours of the city's cemeteries, the **New Orleans Historic Voodoo Museum,** 724 Dumaine St. (523-7685), still brings curious visitors right onto local burial grounds. *(Museum open daily 10am-dusk. $6.30, college students and seniors $5.25, high school students $4.20, grade school students $3.15, under 5 free. Tours $16-20; call for times.)* Those who don't dig eeriness should call **Hidden Treasures Cemetery Tours** (529-4507), which visits New Orleans's original St. Louis cemetery #1. Tours begin at 9am and last about 1hr. ($15). A bus picks up customers staying inside the Quarter or CBD.

At the southwest corner of the Quarter, the **Aquarium of the Americas,** 1 Canal St. (565-3033), by the World Trade Center, houses an amazing collection of sealife and birds. Among the 500 species are black-footed penguins, endangered sea turtles, and extremely rare white alligators. *(Open daily 9:30am-6pm; in summer until 7pm F-Sa; $11.25, seniors $8.75, ages 2-12 $5.)* The steamboat **John Audubon** (586-8777) shuttles between the aquarium and the Audubon Zoo (see below). *(From the aquarium 10am, noon, 2, and 4pm; from the zoo 11am, 1, 3, and 5pm. $10.50, children $5.25; round-trip $13.50/$6.75; package tours including cruise, zoo, and aquarium from $26.50/$13.25.)*

Outside the Quarter

If you're not sure there's more to New Orleans than the French Quarter, take in the city from the revolving bar on the 33rd fl. of the **World Trade Center,** 2 Canal St. The **Riverwalk,** a multi-million dollar conglomeration of overpriced shops overlooking the port, stretches along the Mississippi southwest of here (open M-Sa 10am-9pm, Su 11am-7pm). For an up-close view of the Mississippi River and a bit of African-American history, take the free **Canal Street Ferry** (cars $1 round-trip) to Algiers Point. The Algiers of old housed many of New Orleans's free people of color and today is a safe and beautiful neighborhood to explore by foot. At night, the ferry's outdoor observation deck affords a panoramic view of the city's sights. The ferry departs daily on the ½hr. from the end of Canal St. (5:45am-midnight).

Relatively new to the downtown area, the **Warehouse Arts District,** near the intersection of St. Charles and Julia St., contains several revitalized warehouse buildings that house contemporary art galleries. Exhibits range from Southern folk art to experimental sculpture. Individual galleries distribute maps of the area. In an old brick building with a modern glass and chrome facade, the **Contemporary Arts Center,** 900 Camp St. (523-1216), mounts exhibits ranging from puzzling to positively cryptic. *(Open M-Sa 10am-5pm, Su 11am-5pm. Cybercafe inside keeps same hours. $5, students and seniors $3, under 12 free; Th free.)* The **New Orleans School of Glassworks and Printmaking Studio,** 727 Magazine St. (529-7277), is also a highlight of the Warehouse District. *(Open in summer M-F 11am-5pm; in winter M-Sa 11am-5pm. Free.)* In the rear studio, observe as students and instructors transform blobs of molten glass into vases and sculptures. A few blocks farther down St. Charles St. stands a bronze statue of Confederate General Robert E. Lee, atop a 60 ft. white marble column in **Lee Circle.** The general continues to stare down the Yankees; he faces due North. *Lee Circle and the surrounding neighborhood should not be visited after dark.*

Much of the Crescent City's fame derives from the **Vieux Carré,** but areas uptown have their fair share of beauty and action. The **St. Charles Streetcar** still runs west of the French Quarter, passing some of the city's finest buildings, including the 19th-century homes along **St. Charles Ave.** ($1). *Gone With the Wind*-o-philes will recognize the whitewashed bricks and elegant doorway of the house on the far right corner of Arabella St.—it's a replica of Tara. Frankly, my dear, it's not open to the public.

Fans of fancy living can disembark the streetcar in the **Garden District,** an opulent neighborhood around Jackson and Louisiana Ave. The legacies of French, Italian, Spanish, and American architecture create an extraordinary combination of structures, colors, ironwork, and exquisite gardens. Some houses are raised several feet above the ground for protection from the swamp on which New Orleans stands.

The St. Charles Streetcar eventually makes its way to **Audubon Park,** across from Tulane University. Designed by Frederick Law Olmsted, the architect who planned New York City's Central Park, Audubon contains lagoons, statues, stables, and the award-winning **Audubon Zoo** (861-2537), where white alligators swim in a re-created Louisiana swamp. *(Zoo open daily 9:30am-5pm; in summer Sa-Su 'til 6pm. $8.75, seniors $4.75, ages 2-12 $4.50. Buy your tickets at least 1hr. before closing.)* A free museum shuttle glides from the park entrance (streetcar stop #36) to the zoo every 15min.

One of the most unique sights in the New Orleans area, the coastal wetlands along Lake Salvador make up a segment of the **Jean Lafitte National Historical Park** called the **Barataria Preserve,** 7400 Rte. 45 (589-2330), off the W. Bank Expwy. across the Mississippi River and down Barataria Blvd. (Rte. 45). The only park-sponsored foot tour through the swamp leaves daily at 2pm (free). Countless commercial boat tours operate around the park; **Cypress Swamp Tours** (561-8244) does its 2hr. bit for $20 per person, $12 per child. *(Tours at 9:30, 11:30am, 1:30, and 3:30pm. Call for reservations.)* They'll pick you up from your hotel for free.

Before You Die, Read This:

Being dead in New Orleans has always been a problem. Because the city lies 4 to 6 ft. below sea level, a 6 ft. hole in the earth fills up with 5 ft. of water. At one time coffins literally floated in the graves, while cemetery workers pushed them down with long wooden poles. One early solution was to bore holes in the coffins, allowing them to sink. Unfortunately, the sight of a drowning coffin coupled with the awful gargling sound of its immersion proved too much for the squeamish families of the departed. Burial soon became passé, and stiffs were laid to rest in beautiful raised stone tombs. Miles and miles of creepy, cool marble tombs now fill the city's graveyards and ghost stories.

Museums

Louisiana State Museum, P.O. Box 2448 (800-568-6968), oversees 4 separate museums in the Quarter: the **Old U.S. Mint,** 400 Esplanade; **Cabildo,** 701 Chartres St.; **Presbytère,** 751 Chartres St.; and **1850 House,** 523 St. Ann St. All 4 contain artifacts, papers, and other changing exhibits on the history of Louisiana and New Orleans. The Old U.S. Mint is particularly interesting, focusing not on currency or fresh breath, but on the history of jazz and the lives of greats like Louis "Satchmo" Armstrong. And if you missed Mardi Gras, the "Carnival in New Orleans" recreates the festival, right down to models of inebriated party-goers. All open Tu-Su 9am-5pm. Single museum $4, seniors $3; pass to all 4 $10/$7.50; under 13 free.

New Orleans Museum of Art (NOMA) (488-2631), in City Park. Take the Esplanade bus from Canal and Rampart St. This magnificent museum houses art from North and South America, a small collection of local decorative arts, opulent works by the jeweler Fabergé, and a strong collection of French paintings. 1999 exhibits include special photography displays and, from May 1-Aug. 29, "A French impressionist in New Orleans: the Work of Degas." Guided tours available. Open Tu-Su 10am-5pm. $6, seniors and ages 3-17 $3.

Historic New Orleans Collection, 533 Royal St. (523-4662). Located in the aristocratic 18th-century Merieult House, this impressive cultural and research center will teach you everything you wanted to know about Louisiana's history. The History Tour explores New Orleans past, while the Williams Residence Tour showcases the eclectic home furnishings of the collection's founders. Gallery open Tu-Sa 10am-4:30pm; free. Tours 10, 11am, 2, and 3pm; $4.

Musée Conti Wax Museum, 917 Conti St. (525-2605). One of the world's finest houses of wax, with figures from 300 years of Louisiana lore. Perennial favorites include a voodoo display, haunted dungeon, and a mock-up of Madame Lalaurie's torture attic. Open M-Sa 10am-5:30pm, Su noon-5:30pm. $6.25, under 17 $4.75.

Confederate Museum, 929 Camp St. (523-4522), in a brownstone building west of Lee Circle. The state's oldest museum, with a wide collection of Civil War records and artifacts. Open M-Sa 10am-4pm. $5, students and seniors $4, under 12 $2.

New Orleans Pharmacy Museum, 514 Chartres St. (565-8027), in the Quarter. This apothecary shop was built by America's first licensed pharmacist in 1823. On display are 19th-century "miracle drugs," voodoo powders, and the still-fertile botanical garden, where medicinal herbs are grown. Open Tu-Su 10am-5pm. $2, students and seniors $1 (includes 30min. tour), under 12 free.

Louisiana Children's Museum, 420 Julia St. (523-1357). This place invites kids to play and learn, as they star in their own news shows, run their own cafe, or shop in a re-created mini-mart. Kids under 16 must be accompanied by an adult. Open M-Sa 9:30am-4:30pm, Su noon-4:30pm; Sept.-May closed M. $5.

Louisiana Nature and Science Center, (246-5672) Joe Brown Memorial Park, off Read Blvd. Trail walks, exhibits, planetarium and laser shows, and 86 acres of natural wildlife preserve. From Basin St., take bus #64 "Lake Forrest Express" ($1.25) to reach this wonderful escape from the bedlam of the French Quarter. Open Tu-F 9am-5pm, Sa 10am-5pm, Su noon-5pm. $4.75, seniors $3.75, ages 4-13 $2.50.

K&B Plaza, 1055 St. Charles Ave. (586-1234), is an exceptionally good sculpture garden just off Lee Circle. Open 24hr. Free.

Historic Homes and Plantations

Called the "Great Showplace of New Orleans," **Longue Vue House and Gardens,** 7 Bamboo Rd. (488-5488), off Metairie Rd., epitomizes the grand Southern estate with its lavish furnishings and opulent decor. *(Open M-Sa 10am-4:30pm, Su 1-5pm. $7, students $3, seniors $6, under 5 free. Gardens alone $3, students $1. Tours available in English, French, Spanish, Italian, and Japanese.)* The breathtaking sculpted gardens date back to the 1930s. Take the Metairie Rd. Exit off I-10 and pause for a peek at the 85 ft. tall monument among the raised tombs in the **Metairie Cemetery** on the way. **River Rd.** curves along the Mississippi river across from downtown New Orleans, accessing several plantations preserved from the 19th century; copies of *Great River Road Plantation Parade: A River of Riches,* available at the New Orleans or Baton Rouge visitors centers, contain a good map and descriptions of the houses. Pick carefully, since a tour of all the privately owned plantations would be quite expensive. Those below are listed in order from New Orleans to Baton Rouge.

Hermann-Grima Historic House, 820 St. Louis St. (525-5661). Built in 1831, the house exemplifies a French style, replete with a large central hall, guillotine windows, a fan-lit entrance, and the original parterre beds. On Th during Oct.-May, trained volunteers demonstrate period cooking in the only working 1830s Creole kitchen in the Quarter; call for details. Guided tours on the ½hr. Open M-Sa 10am-4pm. $6, students and seniors $5, ages 8-18 $4. Last tour 3:30pm.

Gallier House Museum, 1118-1132 Royal St. (525-5661). The elegantly restored residence of James Gallier, Jr., the city's most famous architect, resuscitates the taste and lifestyle of the rich in the 1860s. Tours every 30min.; last tour 3:30pm. Open M-Sa 10am-4pm. $6, students and seniors $5, ages 8-18 $4, under 8 free.

San Francisco Plantation House (535-2341), Rte. 44, 2 mi. northwest of Reserve, 42 mi. from New Orleans on the east bank of the Mississippi. Beautifully maintained plantation built in 1856, laid out in the old Creole style. Visitors can't miss the busy blue, peach, and green exterior of the home. Tours daily 10am-4:30pm; Nov.-Feb 10am-4pm. $7, ages 12-17 $4, ages 6-11 $2.75.

Oak Alley (800-442-5539), on Rte. 18 between St. James and Vacherie St., is named for the magnificent drive of 28 evenly spaced oaks, all nearly 300 years old. The oaks correspond with 28 columns surrounding the Greek Revival house. The Greeks wouldn't have approved, though; the mansion is bright pink. Open daily 9am-5:30pm; tours every 30min. $8, ages 13-18 $5, ages 6-12 $3.

Houmas House, 40136 Rte. 942 (522-2262), in Burnside just over halfway to Baton Rouge. Setting for the movie *Hush, Hush, Sweet Charlotte,* starring Bette Davis and Olivia DeHavilland. Huge, moss-draped oaks shade the spacious grounds and beautiful gardens. "Southern Belle" guides lead tours in authentic antebellum attire. Open daily 10am-5pm; Nov.-Jan. 10am-4pm. $8, ages 13-17 $6, ages 6-12 $3.

Nottoway (545-2730 or 832-2093 in New Orleans), Rte. 405, between Bayou Goula and White Castle, 18 mi. south of Baton Rouge on the southern bank of the Mississippi. The largest plantation home in the South is often called the "White Castle of Louisiana." This incredible 64-room mansion with 22 columns, a large ballroom, and a 3-story stairway was David O. Selznick's first choice for filming *Gone with the Wind,* but the owners wouldn't allow it. Open daily 9am-5pm. Admission and 1hr. guided tour $8, under 12 $3.

ENTERTAINMENT AND NIGHTLIFE

Life in New Orleans is and will always be a party. On any night of the week, at any time of the year, the masses converge on **Bourbon St.** to drift in and out of bars and shop for romantic interludes. Though the street has become increasingly touristy of late, much of Bourbon's original charm remains. Several sleazy strip clubs and cross-dressing joints maintain the sense of immorality and sinful excitement that is the essence of the Quarter. College boys on balconies still throw beads to girls who will flash their breasts, and drunken adults urinate on dark side streets. To escape the debauchery of Bourbon St., some flee to **Decatur St.,** between St. Ann and Barracks St., where quieter, less pretentious bars preside.

While the Quarter offers countless bars and traditional jazz, blues, and brass venues, be assured that there's more to New Orleans nightlife. When locals burn out on Bourbon, they head uptown, towards **Tulane,** or to the **Marigny,** an up-and-coming district northeast of the Quarter. **Uptown** tends to house authentic Cajun dance halls and popular university hangouts, while the Marigny is home to New Orleans's alternative/local music scene. Check *Off Beat,* free in many local restaurants, or the Friday *Times-Picayune* to find out who's playing where. The movements of New Orleans's large gay community fill the pages of *Impact* and *Ambush,* both available at **Faubourg Marigny Books,** 600 Frenchmen St. (943-9875; open M-F 10am-8pm, Sa-Su 10am-6pm). Gay establishments cluster toward the northeast end of Bourbon St.; St. Ann St. is known to some as the **"Lavender Line."**

Born at the turn of the century in **Armstrong Park,** traditional New Orleans jazz still wails nightly at the tiny, dim, historic **Preservation Hall,** 726 St. Peters St. (daytime 522-2841, otherwise 523-8939); jazz is in its most fundamental element here. Those who don't come early can expect a lengthy wait in line, poor visibility, and sweaty standing-room only ($4). Eat, drink, and leak before you get here—the Hall neither sells food or beverages, nor provides restrooms. Doors open at 8pm; music begins at 8:30pm and goes on until midnight.

You can take minors out of the party, but you can't take the party out of minors.

If you've come to New Orleans expecting drinking laws that let those over 18 buy and guzzle booze, you're four years too late. Louisiana was the last state to relinquish the legal drinking age of 18. Until recently, it clung to this law even when this meant losing federal highway funds. In the summer of 1995, the state legislature finally bowed to the pressure and joined its peers—*officially, you now have to be 21 to buy and drink alcoholic beverages in Louisiana.*

Keep your ears open for **Cajun** and **zydeco** bands who use accordions, washboards, triangles, and drums to perform hot dance tunes (true locals two-step expertly) and saccharine waltzes. Anyone who thinks couple-dancing went out in the 50s should try a *fais do-do,* a lengthy, wonderfully energetic traditional dance. The locally based **Radiators** do it up real spicy-like in a rock-cajun-zydeco style.

Le Petit Théâtre du Vieux Carré, 616 St. Peters St. (522-9958), is one of the city's most beloved and historical theaters. The oldest continuously operating community theater in the U.S., the 1789 building replicates the early-18th-century abode of Joseph de Pontalba, Louisiana's last Spanish governor. Around five musicals and plays go up each year, as well as four fun productions in the "Children's Corner." The first Sunday of each month at 4pm, Le Petit hosts an open salon in which some of the city's most gifted poets, musicians, and performance artists showcase their talents in a relaxed atmosphere. (Box office open M-Sa 9:30am-6pm, Su 11am-4pm.)

Festivals

New Orleans's **Mardi Gras** celebration is the biggest party of the year, a world-renowned, epic bout of lascivious debauchery that fills the 3 weeks leading up to Ash Wednesday. Parades, gala, balls, and general revelry take to the streets, as tourists pour in by the plane-full (flights into the city fill up months in advance along with hotel rooms). In 1999, Mardi Gras, "Fat Tuesday," falls on February 16; the biggest parades and the bulk of the partying will take place during the week of February 9-16. Remember: when it comes time to traffic in beads, anything goes, and a trade which sounds too good to be true probably carries some unspoken conditions.

The ever-expanding **New Orleans Jazz and Heritage Festival** (522-4786), from the last weekend in April to the first in May (Apr. 23-May 2, 1999), attracts 7000 musicians from around the country to the city's fairgrounds. The likes of Aretha Franklin, Bob Dylan, Patti LaBelle, Dave Matthews, and Wynton Marsalis have graced this slightly "classier" fest, where music plays simultaneously on 12 stages in the midst of a huge Cajun and Creole food and crafts festival. The biggest names perform evening riverboat concerts. Exhilarating and fun, the festival grows more zoo-like each year.

New Orleans's festivals go beyond the biggies. From the **Reggae Riddums Festival** (367-1313 or 800-367-1317) on the second weekend of June (12-13, 1999) to the **Swamp Festival** (581-4629) on the first two weekends of October (2-3 and 9-10, 1999), you're likely to find a celebration of something any time of year. Call the **Convention and Visitors Bureau** (see **Practical Information,** p. 334) for further info.

Nightlife in the French Quarter

Bars in New Orleans stay open late, and few keep a strict schedule; in general, they open around 11am and close around 3am. Some places go the $3-5-per-drink route, but most blocks feature at least one establishment with cheap draft beer and Hurricanes (sweet drinks made of juice and rum). Beware of overly friendly strangers and pickpockets, and always bring ID—the party's fun, but the law is enforced.

Pat O'Brien's, 718 St. Peters St. (525-4823). The busiest bar and one of the best in the French Quarter, bursting with happy (read: drunk) patrons. Listen to the piano in one room, mix with local students in another, or lounge near the fountain in the courtyard. Home of the original (and deliciously potent) Hurricane; purchase your first in a souvenir glass ($7.50). Open Su-Th 10am-4am, F-Sa 10am-5am.

House of Blues, 225 Decatur St. (529-BLUE/2583). A sprawling complex with a large music/dance hall, beefy bouncers, and a balcony and bar overlooking the action. The restaurant has an extensive menu, including Voodoo shrimp in Voodoo beer ($10). Cover usually $5-10, but folks like Eric Clapton, Keanu Reeves, and Erykah Badu cost up to $25. Concerts nightly 9:15pm. Restaurant open in summer Su-Th 11am-midnight, F-Sa 11am-2am; off-season Su-Th 11am-11pm, F-Sa 11am-midnight.

Lafitte's Blacksmith Shop, 941 Bourbon St. (523-0066), at Phillip St. Appropriately, one of New Orleans's oldest standing structures is a bar. Built in the 1730s, the building is still lit by candlelight after sunset. Named for the scheming hero of the Battle of New Orleans, it offers shady relief from the elements of the city and friendly company at night. Open noon until late; live piano 8pm until late.

Margaritaville, 1104 Decatur St. (592-2565, music schedule 592-2552). The loud-speakers blast Jimmy Buffet tunes all day, but at night the club sponsors varieties of live funk, R&B, and rock. Buffet himself takes the stage when in town. Key lime pie and salt-rimmed margaritas are cool companions for late-night listening. No cover. Music Su-Th 2-9:30pm, F-Sa 2pm-1:30am. Food served daily 11am-10:30pm.

Bourbon Pub & Parade Disco, 801 Bourbon St. (529-2107). This gay dance bar has a "tea dance" on Su with $5 all-you-can-drink beer. Dance upstairs at the Paradise Disco nightly from 9pm (Tu-Su in summer); it lasts 'til you fall off. Open 24hr.

Rubyfruit Jungle, 640 Frenchmen St. (947-4000). What used to be the biggest lesbian bar in New Orleans now entertains a very mixed gay/straight crowd. Plenty of fro-zen drinks cool patrons off before and after they hit the large dance floor in back. The usual sounds of the jungle are top 40s and dance music, but Tu is country-western night. Open M-Th 4pm-2am, F 4pm-4am, Sa 1pm-4am, Su 1pm-2am.

Crescent City Brewhouse, 527 Decatur St. (522-0571). The only microbrewery in New Orleans, this classy brewpub sells only its own 5 blends (12 oz. $3). Glass walls and balcony make for good people-watching, a wonderful activity when set to live jazz (nightly 6-9:30pm). Open Su-Th 11am-10pm, F-Sa 11am-midnight.

Kaldi's Coffeehouse, 941 Decatur St. (586-8989). A great escape from the usual noc-turnal frenzy, Kaldi's is all about chatting, postcard-writing, and cappuccino-sip-ping. This is the only place in the Crescent City that roasts its own coffee. Italian cream sodas are one-of-a-kind ($2.25), and the coffee-laced milkshake flavors ought to be patented ($4). Internet access. Open Su-Th 7am-midnight, F-Sa 7am-2am.

O'Flaherty's Irish Channel Pub, 514 Toulouse St. (529-1317). An Irish Pub in New Orleans? Well, why not? O'Flaherty's bills itself as the meeting point of the dispar-ate Celtic nations. Eavesdrop on Gaelic conversation while listening to Scottish bagpipes, watching Irish dances, and/or singing along to Irish tunes. Irish music F-Sa. Cover $5. Open daily noon-3am.

Nightlife Outside the Quarter

Tipitina's, 501 Napoleon Ave. (895-8477, concert info 897-3943). This famous estab-lishment attracts the best local bands and some big national names, such as the Neville Brothers, John Goodman, and Harry Connick Jr. Su evenings feature Cajun *fais-do-dos.* Cover $4-15, no cover Tu; call ahead for times and prices.

F&M Patio Bar, 4841 Tchoupitoulas St. (895-6784), near Napoleon. Mellow 20-somethings mix with students, doctors, lawyers, and ne'er-do-wells. Serves food after 6pm, mostly fajitas ($3.50) and burgers ($4.50) from a mega-grill on the patio. Open M-Th 1pm-4am, F 1pm-6am, Sa 3pm-6am, Su 3pm-4am.

Maple Leaf Bar, 8316 Oak St. (866-9359). The best local dance bar offering zydeco and Cajun music; everyone does the two-step. Large, pleasant covered patio. Poetry readings Su 3pm. Music and dancing start Su-Th at 10pm, F-Sa at 10:30pm. Cover $5. Open daily 3pm-4am.

Café Brasil, 2100 Chartres, at Frenchmen St. Unassuming by day, Brasil is packed weekend nights by locals who come to see a wide variety of New Orleans talent. Shows 8 and 11pm. Cover F-Sa after 11pm $5-10. Open daily 7 pm until late.

Checkpoint Charlie's, 501 Esplanade (947-0979), grunges it up like the best of Seat-tle. Do your laundry while listening to live music 7 nights a week. Julia Roberts sat on these machines in *The Pelican Brief.* Beer $2. No cover. Open 24hr.

Mid City Lanes, 4133 S. Carrollton Ave. (482-3133), at Tulane Ave. "Home of Rock 'n' Bowl": bowling alley by day, dance club by night (you can bowl at night, too). Featuring local zydeco, blues, and rock 'n' roll, this is where the locals party. Ignore the dingy exterior and walk in for a true New Orleans experience. Th is a wild zydeco night; swing on Tu. Music Tu-Th 8:30pm, F-Sa 10pm; cover $5-7. The *Rock 'n' Bowlletin* has specific band info (and a list of the regulars' birthdays). Lanes Su-Th $8 per hr., F-Sa $10 per hr. Open noon until late.

Michaul's, 840 St. Charles Ave. (522-5517). A huge floor for Cajun dancing; they'll even teach you how (lessons every night). No cover. Music starts at 10pm; earlier in summer. Open M-F 5pm until late, Sa 6pm until late; in summer closed M.

Snug Harbor, 626 Frenchmen St. (949-0696), near Decatur St. Regulars include Charmaine Neville, Amasa Miller, and Ellis Marsalis—big names in the blues. The cover is steep ($8-15), but the music and its fans are authentic. Shows nightly 9 and 11pm. Bar open daily 5pm-2am; restaurant open Su-Th 5-11pm, F-Sa 5pm-midnight.

Carrollton Station, 8140 Willow St. (865-9190), at Dublin St. A cozy neighborhood club with live music and friendly folks. 12 beers on tap ($2-4), behind the intricately carved wooden bar. Music Th-Sa nights at 10pm. Open daily 3:30pm-2am.

Dragon's Den, 435 Esplanade (949-1750). Patrons can sit on floor pillows or around small tables and listen to irreverent blues, brass, jazz, and funk every night. A relaxed alternative to the crowds and clamor of other bars. No cover; 2 for 1 *Saki* on M. Music starts around 11pm. Open Su-Th 5:30pm-2am, F-Sa 5:30pm-3am.

Jimmy's, 8200 Willow St. (concert info 861-8200). Rock, hip-hop, reggae are just some of the musical genres at this bare minimum bar and music club. A local students favorite. There are no frills—the walls are plain, there's no restaurant—but the varying cover ($3-12) covers the entire night's show, which may mean as many as 5 different bands performing in a continuous line-up. Open Tu-Sa 8pm-2am.

Mulate's, 201 Julia St. (522-1492), across from the Riverwalk. This large restaurant and bar packs 'em in nightly for Cajun dancing and live music. Straight from Acadiana, the bands perform from 7-10:30pm. While the food is pricey (entrees from $13), the hungry can always fill up on appetizers ($5-7). Open daily 11am-10:30pm.

Top of the Mart, World Trade Center, 2 Canal St. (522-9795). The nation's largest revolving bar, this 500-seat cocktail lounge spins 33 stories above the ground. The deck revolves 3 ft. per min. and makes 1 revolution every 1½hr. The sunset view is awe-inspiring. No cover, but a 1-drink min. ($2.50 and up). 19+. Open M-F 10am-midnight, Sa 11am-2am, Su 2pm-midnight.

■ Baton Rouge

Once the site of a tall cypress tree marking the boundary between rival Native American tribes, Baton Rouge ("red stick") has blossomed into Louisiana's capital and second largest city. State politics have shaped this town, once the home of the notorious "Kingfish" Huey P. Long. The presence of Louisiana State University (LSU) has added elements of youth and rebellion to the quiet city. Baton Rouge has a simple meat-and-potatoes flavor in contrast to the flamboyant sauciness of New Orleans, but that doesn't mean it's not worth tasting. The downtown area is easily navigable by car and provides plenty of attractions for a pleasant one-night stay.

In a move reminiscent of Ramses II, Huey Long ordered the building of the unique **Louisiana State Capitol** (342-7317), a magnificent, modern skyscraper, completed over a mere 14 months in 1931 and 1932. The **observation deck,** on the 27th fl., provides a view of the port (open daily 8am-4pm; free). Of equal grandeur is the **Old State Capitol,** 100 North Blvd. (342-0500 or 800-488-2968), with many exhibits on the history and politics of Louisiana, including the mystery of Huey Long's assassination. (Open Tu-Sa 10am-4pm, Su noon-4pm. $4, students $2, seniors $3; $1 off with brochure from the new capitol.) The fantastic spiral staircase and domed stained glass are worth a visit in themselves. **Magnolia Mound Plantation,** 2161 Nicholson Dr. (343-4955), built in 1791, is a palatial French-Creole mansion spanning 16 acres. (Open Tu-Sa 10am-4pm, Su 1-4pm. $5, students $2, seniors $4, ages 5-12 $1. Last tour 3:15pm.) The **LSU Rural Life Museum,** 4600 Essen Ln. (765-2437), depicts the life of the less well-to-do Creoles through their authentically furnished shops, cabins, and storage houses. Adjacent to the museum are the lakes, winding paths, roses, and azaleas of the **Windrush Gardens.** (Both open daily 8:30am-5pm. $5, seniors $4, ages 5-11 $3.) The city holds a **farmers market** in front of the Municipal Building, on the corner of North Blvd. and Fourth St. Shoppers can sample fresh-picked local produce, homemade jams, and fresh breads. (Open Sa 7-11am; in winter Sa 8am-noon.)

Baton Rouge's cheapest accommodations are located on the outskirts of town. The **Corporate Inn,** 2365 College Dr. (925-2451), at Exit 158 off I-10, resembles the Emerald City, though the rooms are fairly standard. (Free local calls, HBO, coffee and doughnuts in the morning. Singles $45; doubles $50.) **Motel 6,** 10445 Rieger Rd. (291-4912), at Exit 163 off I-10, throws you no surprises—cookie-cutter rooms, soft beds, cable TV, and a pool (singles $39; doubles $45). The **KOA Campground,** 7628 Vincent Rd. (664-7281, reservations 800-292-8245), 15 mi. east of Baton Rouge (take the Denham Springs Exit off I-12), keeps well-maintained sites, along with clean facilities and a big pool (tent sites $17; full RV hookup $24).

Downtown, sandwich shops and cafes line 3rd St. Head to LSU at the intersection of Highland Rd. and Chimes St. for cheaper chow and an abundance of bars. **Louie's Café,** 209 W. State St. (346-8221), grills up fabulous omelettes from $4.50 (open 24hr.). Behind Louie's is **The Bayou,** 124 W. Chimes (346-1765), a pool hall and bar crowded with collegiate types (open daily 3pm-2am). When you want a good ol' sit-down meal, a good ol' option is **The Chimes,** 3357 Highland Rd. (383-1754), a big restaurant and bar with more than 120 different beers. Louisiana alligator, farm-raised, marinated, and fried, served with Dijon mustard sauce, goes for $7—do you dare? (Open M-Sa 11am-2am, Su 11am-midnight.)

A short walk from downtown, **Greyhound,** 1253 Florida Blvd. (333-3811 or 800-231-2222; station and ticket booth open 24hr.), at 13th St., sends buses to New Orleans (2hr., 9 per day, $10) and Lafayette (4hr., 10 per day, $18). *Be careful; the area is unsafe at night.* The **State Capitol Visitors Center** (342-7317), on the 1st fl. of the State Capitol, has helpful maps (open daily 8am-4:30pm). For more resources, stop by the **Baton Rouge Convention and Visitors Bureau,** 730 North Blvd. (383-1825 or 800-LAROUGE/527-6843; open M-F 8am-5pm). **Post Office:** 750 Florida Blvd. (381-0713), off River Rd. (open M-F 8:30am-5pm, Sa 9:30am-12:30pm). **ZIP code:** 70821. **Area code:** 504.

ACADIANA

Throughout the early eighteenth century, the English government in Nova Scotia became increasingly jealous of the prosperity of French settlers *(Acadiens)* and deeply offended by their refusal to swear allegiance to the British Crown. During the war with France in 1755, British frustration and hatred peaked; they rounded up the Acadians and deported them by the shipload in what came to be called *le Grand Dérangement,* "the Great Upheaval." Of the 7000 Acadians who went to sea, one-third died of smallpox and hunger. Those who survived sought refuge along the Atlantic Coast in places like Massachusetts and South Carolina. As French Catholics, they were met with fear and suspicion, however, and most were forced into indentured servitude. The Acadians soon realized that freedom waited in the French territory of Louisiana. The "Cajuns" of St. Martin, Lafayette, New Iberia, and St. Mary parishes are descended from these settlers.

Several factors have threatened Acadian culture since the relocation. In the 1920s, Louisiana passed laws forcing Acadian schools to teach in English. Later, during the oil boom of the 1970s and 80s, oil executives and developers envisioned the Acadian center of Lafayette (see below) as the Houston of Louisiana and threatened to flood the town and its neighbors with mass culture. Still, the proud people of southern Louisiana have resisted homogenization. Today, the state is officially bilingual, and a state agency preserves Acadian French in schools and in the media. "Cajun Country" spans the south of the state, from Houma in the east to the Texas border in the west.

■ Lafayette

The center of Acadiana, Lafayette is the perfect place to try some boiled crawfish or dance the two-step to a fiddle and accordion. Though the city's French roots are often obscured by the chain motels and service roads that have accompanied its growth, there is no question that the Cajuns still own the surrounding countryside, where zydeco music heats up dance floors every night of the week and locals continue to answer their phones with a proud *bonjour.*

PRACTICAL INFORMATION Lafayette stands at a crossroads. **I-10** leads east to New Orleans (136 mi.) and west to Lake Charles (76 mi.); **U.S. 90** heads south to New Iberia (26 mi.) and the Atchafalaya Basin; **U.S. 167** runs north into central Louisiana. Most of the city lies west of the **Evangeline Thruway (U.S. 49)** which runs north-south. (The name comes from Henry Wadsworth Longfellow's epic poem, *Evangeline,* which portrays the plight of two ill-fated Acadian lovers who are separated on their wedding day in *le Grand Dérangement*.) Establishments are concentrated along Johnson St. (U.S. 167) and Ambassador Caffery Pkwy. **Amtrak,** 133 E. Grant St. (800-872-7245), sends three trains per week to New Orleans (4hr., $19); Houston (5½hr., $33); and San Antonio (10hr., $52). The station does not sell tickets; buy them in advance from **Bass Travel,** 1603 W. Pinhook Rd. (237-2177 or 800-777-7371; open M-F 8:30am-5pm), or another travel agent. **Greyhound,** 315 Lee Ave. (235-1541 or 800-231-2222; station open 24hr.), buses to New Orleans (3½hr., 8 per day, $18); Baton Rouge (1hr., 9 per day, $11); and New Iberia (30min., 2 per day, $7). The main station of the **Lafayette Bus System,** 1515 E. University (291-8570), awaits at the corner of Lee and Garfield St. (Infrequent service M-Sa 6:30am-6:30pm. Fare 45¢, seniors and disabled 20¢, ages 5-12 30¢.) For a taxi, contact **Yellow/Checker Cab Inc.** (237-6196), which runs on a zone grid (from the bus or train station to downtown $3). **Thrifty Rent-a-Car,** 401 E. Pinhook Rd. (237-1282), at Evangeline, rents for $25 per day with 100 free mi. (Must be 25 with major credit card. Open M-F 7:30am-6pm, Sa 8am-4pm, Su noon-4pm.) **Lafayette Parish Convention and Visitors Commission,** 1400 NE Evangeline Thruway (232-3808), will swamp you with info (open M-F 8:30am-5pm, Sa-Su 9am-5pm). Address health needs 24hr. at **University Medical Center,** 2390 W. Congress (261-6000). **Post Office:** 1105 Moss St. (269-4800; open M-F 8am-5:30pm, Sa 8am-12:30pm). **ZIP code:** 70501. **Area code:** 318.

ACCOMMODATIONS, CAMPGROUNDS, AND FOOD Inexpensive hotels line the Evangeline Thruway. The simple rooms at **Super 8,** 2224 NE Evangeline Thruway (232-8826 or 800-800-8000), come with pool access and a stunning view of the highway (singles $31; doubles $41). **Travel Host Inn South,** 1314 N. Evangeline Thruway (233-2090 or 800-677-1466), similarly offers clean rooms with cable TV, pool, free continental breakfast, and a convenient location (singles $32; doubles $36). One campground close to the center of Lafayette, **Acadiana Park Campground,** 1201 E. Alexander (291-8388), off Louisiana Ave., features tennis courts and a soccer field (full hookup $9; office open Sa-Th 8am-5pm, F 8am-8pm). The lakeside **KOA Lafayette** (235-2739), 5 mi. west of town on I-10 at Exit 97, has a store, a mini-golf course, and a pool. (Tent sites $17.50, with water and electricity $23, full hookup $24.50. Office open daily 7:30am-8:30pm.)

Cajun restaurants with live music and dancing have popped up all over Lafayette. Unfortunately, they cater to a tourist crowd with substantial funds. **Mulates** (MYOO-lots), 325 Mills Ave. (332-4648 or 800-422-2586), 15min. from Lafayette, near Breaux Bridge, calls itself the most famous Cajun restaurant in the world, and the autographs on the door corroborate its claim. Have them fry up some alligator ($5.50) or the ever-popular $14 catfish. (Cajun music nightly 7:30-10pm and Sa-Su noon-2pm. Open daily 11am-10pm.) In central Lafayette, **Chris' Po' boys** offers seafood platters ($7-11) and—whadda ya' know—po' boys for $4-7. (4 locations including 1941 Moss St., 237-1095 and 631 Jefferson St., 234-1696. All open M-F 11am-6pm.) **Randol's,** 2320 Kaliste Saloom Rd. (981-7080), romps with live Cajun and zydeco music nightly and doubles as a restaurant (open Su-Th 5-10pm, F-Sa 5-10:30pm). For the more mild-mannered, the **Judice Inn,** 3134 Johnston St. (984-5614), provides tasty, no-nonsense hamburgers with a "secret sauce" ($1.60-3.25; open M-Sa 10am-10pm).

SIGHTS AND ENTERTAINMENT If you're driving through south-central Louisiana, you're probably driving over America's largest swamp, the Atchafalaya (a-chah-fa-LIE-a) Basin. The **Atchafalaya Fwy.** (I-10 between Lafayette and Baton Rouge) crosses 32 mi. of swamp and cypress trees. To get down and dirty in the muck, exit at Henderson (Exit 115), turn right, then immediately left for 5 mi. on Rte. 352. From there, follow the signs to **McGee's Landing,** 1337 Henderson Rd. (667-7106 or 800-445-6681), which sends four 1½hr. **boat tours** into the Basin each day. *(Tours daily 10am and 1, 3, and 5pm. $12, seniors and under 13 $10, under 4 free.)* With a little luck, you'll see some alligators.

First-time visitors to Lafayette should start at the **Acadian Cultural Center/Jean Lafitte National Park,** 501 Fisher Rd. (232-0789), which features a 40min. documentary, *The Cajun Way: Echos of Acadia,* as well as a terrific exhibit on the exodus and migration of these French settlers (shows every hr. on the hr. from

9am; open daily 8am-5pm; free). Next door, the re-creation of an Acadian settlement at **Vermilionville**, 1600 Surrey St. (233-4077 or 800-99-BAYOU/992-2968), entertains as it educates with music, crafts, food, and dancing on the banks of the Bayou Vermilion. *(Open daily 10am-5pm. Live music M-F 1:30-3:30pm, Sa-Su 2-5pm. Cajun cooking samples daily 11:30am and 1:30pm. $8, ages 6-18 $5.)* Unlike the grandiose mansions dotting the South, **Acadian Village**, 200 Greenleaf Rd. (981-2364 or 800-962-9133), offers a look at the unpretentious homes of common 19th-century Acadian settlers (take U.S. 167 S. to Ridge Rd., then left on Broussard, and follow the signs). Visitors can also view Native American artifacts at the **Mississippi Valley Missionary Museum** (both open daily 10am-5pm; $6, seniors $5, children $2.50).

St. **John's Cathedral Oak,** in the yard of **St. John's Cathedral,** 914 St. John St., is as impressive as the church itself. This 450-year-old tree shades the entire lawn with spidery limbs which spread 145 ft.; the weight of a single limb is estimated to be 72 tons. A block away, the **Lafayette Museum**, 1122 Lafayette St. (234-2208), exhibits heirlooms, antiques, and Mardi Gras costumes inside the 19th-century **Alexandre Mouton House,** named for Louisiana's first Democratic governor (open Tu-Sa 9am-5pm, Su 3-5pm; $3, students and children $1, seniors $2).

Lafayette kicks off spring and fall weekends with **Downtown Alive!** (268-5566), a series of free concerts featuring everything from New Wave to Cajun and zydeco (Apr.-June and Sept.-Nov. F 5:30pm; music 6-8:30pm). The **Festival International de Louisiane** (232-8086; April 20-25, 1999) highlights the music, visual arts, and cuisine of southwest Louisiana in a Francophone tribute to the region.

To find out what's going on in town, or where the zydeco is best, pick up a copy of *The Times,* available free at restaurants and gas stations.

■ New Iberia and Environs

While Lafayette was being invaded by oil magnates eager to build a Louisiana oil-business center, New Iberia continued to maintain links to its bayou past. Several sights give visitors a good feel for the unique conditions of life in the area.

Unlike those that reaped fortunes from cotton, most plantations in southern Louisiana grew sugarcane. Many of these plantations are still private property, but **Shadows on the Teche**, 317 E. Main St. (369-6446), at the Rte. 14/Rte. 182 junction, welcomes the public. (Open daily 9am-4:30pm. $6, ages 6-11 $3; AAA discount.) A Southern aristocrat saved the plantation's crumbling mansion, built in 1834, from neglect after the Civil War. The collection of over 17,000 family documents—discovered in 40 trunks in the attic and spanning four generations—provides a first-hand look at antebellum life in the South. Time passes quickly at the **Rip Van Winkle Gardens**, 5505 Rip Van Winkle Rd. (365-3332), off Rte. 14. (Open daily 9am-5pm. House and garden tour $9, seniors $8.50, students 13-18 $7, ages 5-12 $5.) The gardens offer peaceful scenery and leisurely boat tours. **Avery Island,** 7 mi. away on Rte. 329 off Rte. 90 (50¢ toll to enter the island), sizzles with the world-famous **Tabasco Pepper Sauce Factory,** where the McIlhenny family has produced the famous condiment for nearly a century. (Open M-F 9am-4pm, Sa 9am-noon. Free.) Guided tours every 15min. include free recipes, samples, and tastings worthy of facial contortion. The 1hr. **Airboat Tour** (229-4457) of the shallow water swamps and bayous of Lake Fausse Pointe is not to be missed. (Open Feb.-Oct. Tu-Su 8am-5pm. $15. Call for directions and required reservations.) Look for snowy egrets, alligators, and the large, edible nutria rat—perfect with Tabasco.

Picturesque campsites on the banks of the Bayou Teche are available at **Belmont Campgrounds**, 1000 Belmont Rd. (369-3252), at the junction of Rte. 31 and 86. Within the well-kept grounds are nature trails and fishing areas in the stocked pond. (Tent sites with showers and laundry $11, full RV hookup $17.)

New Iberia lies 21 mi. southeast of Lafayette on U.S. 90. **Amtrak** (800-872-7245) stops in New Iberia, at an unstaffed station, 402 W. Washington St., at Railroad St. Three trains per week set out in two directions, for Lafayette (30min., $4) and New Orleans (3hr., $18). **Greyhound** (364-8571 or 800-231-2222; station open M-F 8am-5pm, Sa 8am-noon) pulls into town at 1103 E. Main St. Buses run to Morgan City (1hr., 2 per day, $13); New Orleans (4hr., 4 per day, $26); and Lafayette (40min., 2 per day, $7). The **Iberia Parish Tourist Commission,** 2704 Rte. 14 (365-1540; open daily 9am-5pm), and the **Greater Iberia Chamber of Commerce,** 111 W. Main St. (364-1836; open M-F 8:30am-5pm), have maps. **Area code:** 318.

Arkansas

"The Natural State," as the Arkansas (ar-kan-SAW) license plates proclaim it, lives up to its declaration, encompassing the ascents of the Ozarks, the clear waters of Hot Springs, and miles of highway twisting through lush pine forests. Given to boasting about its products as well as its natural resources, the state clings to a strong affiliation with native son Bill Clinton, although he is the source of a state-wide political schism ("I didn't vote for the dope from Hope," exclaims one bumper sticker). Clinton's success, and that of state hero and Wal-mart founder Sam Walton, suggest that perhaps the wisest pace of living is not a hasty gallop, but an Arkansas canter.

PRACTICAL INFORMATION

Capital: Little Rock.
Visitor Info: Arkansas Dept. of Parks and Tourism, One Capitol Mall, Little Rock 72201 (501-682-1191 or 800-628-8725; http://www.1800natural.com). Open M-F 8am-5pm.
Emergency: 911.
Time Zone: Central (1hr. behind Eastern). **Postal Abbreviation:** AR.
Sales Tax: 5.5%.

▓ Little Rock

In the early 19th century, a small rock just a few feet high served as an important landmark for boats pushing their way upstream. Sailors and merchants began settling around this stone outcrop, and, lo and behold, Little Rock was born. The capital became the focus of a nationwide civil rights controversy in 1957, when Governor Orval Faubus and local white segregationists violently resisted nine black students who entered Central High School under the shields of the National Guard. Fortunately, Little Rock has since become a more integrated community, one that strives to be a cosmopolitan centerpiece for the state.

ORIENTATION AND PRACTICAL INFORMATION

In downtown Little Rock, the numbered streets run east-west. Markham St. near the river, is 1st St., and Capitol is 5th St. Markham St. is scheduled to become Clinton St. in January 1999, but street numbers will remain the same.

Airport: Little Rock National (372-3430), 5 mi. east of downtown off I-440. Easily accessible from downtown (by #12 bus $1, by taxi about $12).
Trains: Amtrak, 1400 W. Markham St. (372-6841 or 800-872-7245), in Union Station at Victory St. (bus #1 or #8). 4 trains per week to: St. Louis (7hr., $46); Dallas (7hr., $50); and Malvern (45min., $7), 20 mi. east of Hot Springs. Open M 9am-7pm, Tu 3pm-1am, W-Th and Su 6am-1am, F-Sa 6am-4pm.
Buses: Greyhound, 118 E. Washington St. (372-3007 or 800-231-2222), across the river in North Little Rock (bus #7 or #18). Use the walkway over the bridge to get downtown. To: St. Louis (9hr., 3 per day, $47); New Orleans (14hr., 4 per day, $73); and Memphis (2½hr., 8 per day, $20). Ticket prices higher F-Su. Open 24hr.
Public Transportation: Central Arkansas Transit (CAT), 375-1163. Little Rock has a fairly comprehensive local bus system. M-F 6am-6:30pm, Sa 6am-6pm, Su 9am-4pm; fare $1, transfers 10¢. M-F 6:30-10pm; fare 50¢, transfers free. Maps available at the **Sterling Dept. Store** (375-8181), on Center St., between 5th and 6th.
Taxis: Black and White Cabs, 374-0333. $1.30 base fare, $1.15 per mi.
Car Rental: Enterprise Rent-a-Car, 200 S. Broadway Ave. (376-1919), rents for $29 per day with 150 free mi. Must be 21 with a major credit card; under 25 no surcharge. Free pick-up and delivery service available. Open M-F 7:30am-6pm, Sa 8:30am-12:30pm.

Visitor Info: Little Rock Convention and Visitors Bureau, 400 W. Markham St. (376-4781 or 800-844-4781), at Broadway. Open M-F 8:30am-5pm.

Hotlines: Rape Crisis, 663-3334. 24hr. **First Call for Help,** 376-4567, offers a broad range of information and referrals. Operates M-F 8am-5pm.

Internet Access: Kinko's, 1121 S. Spring St. (372-0775). Open 24hr. $12 per hr.

Post Office: 600 E. Capitol (375-5155). Open M-F 7am-5:30pm. **ZIP code:** 72202. **Area code:** 501.

ACCOMMODATIONS AND CAMPGROUNDS

Inexpensive motels in Little Rock tend to cluster along **I-30,** near downtown and south of the city and at the intersection of **University Ave.** and **I-630** (Exit 5), a 5min. drive from downtown. A few motels in town are cheaper but shabbier.

Master's Inn Economy, 707 I-30 (372-4392 or 800-633-3434), at 8th St., Exit 140. Locations in North Little Rock as well, but this one is right by downtown. Spacious, well-lit rooms with a lovely pool, a restaurant, room service, and complimentary breakfast. 21+ to rent. Singles $36; $4 per extra person; under 18 free with parent.

Super 7, 9525 I-30 (568-9999), about 9 mi. south of downtown (Exit 130). Aging building houses simple, reasonably clean rooms. Pool. Singles $27; doubles $34.

Cimarron Motel, 10200 I-30 (565-1171), across I-30 from Super 7 (westbound frontage) and a bit farther south (Exit 130). Cable TV, A/C. Singles $35; doubles $38.50; queen and fold-out couch $45; 3 beds $50. Key deposit $5.

Campground: Maumell Park, 9009 Pinnacle Valley Rd. (868-9477), on the Arkansas River. From I-430 N, take Rte. 10 (Exit 9) west 3 mi., then turn right on Pinnacle Valley Rd. for 3 mi. This Corp of Engineers park has showers, boat ramp ($2), fishing, playground, short walking trails, and 2 dumping stations. 129 sites at $15 apiece for water and electricity. Office open 10am-10pm.

FOOD AND NIGHTLIFE

Bars and restaurants in Arkansas often close earlier on Saturday than on other nights; liquor laws require establishments to stop selling alcohol at midnight.

Vino's, 923 W. 7th St. (375-8466), at Chester St. Little Rock's original microbrewery serves Italian fare at wallet-friendly prices (slices 95¢, calzones $5.60). Weekends bring live music of all types—folk, rock, alternative, you name it. Cover $5. Open M-W 11am-10pm, Th-Sa 11am-midnight, Su 1-9pm. Bar open M-Sa 'til 12:45am.

Juanita's, 1300 S. Main St. (372-1228), at 13th St. A local favorite for years, Juanita's delivers fabulous Mexican food with live music nightly. Call or stop by for a jam-packed schedule. Open for lunch (specials $6) M-Sa 11am-2:30pm; for dinner ($7) M 5:30-9pm, Tu-Th 5:30-9:30pm, F 5:30-10:30pm, Sa 2:30-10:30pm. Bar open M-F 11am-1am, Sa 11am-midnight.

Wallace Grill Café, 103 Main St. (372-3111), near the river. Generous portions of rib-stickin' cuisine are served over-the-counter at this tiny diner. BLT $2, delicious fried catfish $5.85. Open M-F 6am-2:30pm, Sa 6am-noon.

Slick Willy's, 1400 W. Markham Ave. (372-5505), under the old train station, takes its name from one of Bill Clinton's many nicknames. Pool tables ($6 per hr.), arcade games and a stage (live music Sa-Su) fill the floor. W 75¢ drafts, Th-Tu $1. Th free pool and karaoke 8pm-2am. Open Su-F 10am-2am, Sa 10am-1am.

Backstreet, 1021 Jessie Rd. (664-2744), like most backstreets, is hard to find. Take Cantrell (MO 10) west 1 mi. from downtown, turn right on Riverfront, then immediately right onto Jessie. This large warehouse contains 3 gay and lesbian bars: **701** for women, **501** for men (rock and disco in each), and **Miss Kitty's** (country and Western). Cover $2-4 each. Open daily 9pm-5am.

Bobbisox, 3201 Bankhead Dr. (490-1000), in the Holiday Inn Airport, off Airport Exit on I-440. Reviving the oldies of the 50s and 60s, this hangout is popular with all ages, although there are more seniors than 20-somethings. Free dance lessons M and Sa at 7pm. Free hors d'oeuvres M-F 5-7pm. Bar 21+ after 7pm; open M-F 11:30am-2am, Sa 11:30am-midnight, Su noon-10pm. Restaurant closes 11pm.

SIGHTS

Tourists can visit the **"little rock"** at Riverfront Park, a pleasant place for a walk along the Arkansas River. From underneath the railroad bridge at the north end of Louisiana St., look straight down; the rock is part of the embankment. Viewers should look closely; the rock has fought a losing battle against erosion. The tiny **information desk** in the nearby Excelsior Hotel can help visitors having trouble locating the stone. The city celebrates its waterway with arts, crafts, bands, food, and a fireworks display at **Riverfest** (376-4781; May 21-23, 1999; admission $1). Visible from the riverfront is the new **Farmer's Market,** 400 E. Markham St. (375-2552). *(Open M 10am-3pm, Tu-Sa 7am-6pm, Su 11am-4pm. Outdoor vegetable market Tu and Sa 7am-3pm.)* Inside, a collection of food shops, coffee stands, and delis feed much of the downtown lunch crowd. The market anchors the **River Market** district, which is trying to attract restaurants, hotels, and galleries. The nearby **Museum of Discovery,** 500 E. Markham St. (396-7050 or 800-880-6475), is one of the first museums to enter the area. *(Open M-F 9am-5pm, Sa 1-6pm. $5, seniors and under 13 $4.50, free the 1st F of each month 5-9pm.)* Exhibits are aimed at elementary school aged children, with entertaining displays on waves, construction techniques, and analog vs. digital signals.

The **state capitol** (682-5080), at the west end of Capitol St., may look familiar—it's a small-scale replica of the U.S. Capitol in Washington, D.C. At the **State Capitol Police Booth** on the ground floor, you can check out a tape player for a free 45min. audio tour (open M-F 9am-5pm, Sa-Su 10am-5pm). The carefully guarded **Governor's Mansion,** S. Center St. at 18th St., gives an idea of the Clintons' pre-Presidential lifestyle. The **Arkansas Territorial Restoration,** 200 E. Third St. (324-9351), displays everyday life in 19th-century Little Rock with tours of four restored buildings including a print shop built in 1824. *(Open M-Sa 9am-5pm, Su 1-5pm. $2, seniors $1, children 50¢; free 1st Su of the month. Tours begin every hr. on the hr. except for noon; last tour 4pm.)* Although lengthy (1hr.), the tours are both informative and fascinating.

To the south, in the heart of **MacArthur Park,** on 10th St. just west of I-30, the **Arkansas Art Center** (372-4000) houses an eclectic permanent collection comprised of European masters as well as contemporary artists (open M-Th and Sa 10am-5pm, F 10am-8:30pm, Su noon-5pm; free). **War Memorial Park,** west of downtown on I-630 at Fair Park Blvd. (Exit 4 or #5 bus), is home to the 40-acre **Little Rock Zoo,** 1 Jonesboro Dr. (666-2406 or 663-4733), where animals roam simulated habitats. *(Open daily 9am-6pm, must enter by 5pm. $5, under 12 $3.)* The park offers plenty of shade for picnics and relaxation on hot summer afternoons.

The **Toltec Mounds State Park** (961-9442), 9 mi. east of I-440 on U.S. 165 (Exit 7), reminds visitors of the mound building culture that flourished from 600-1050 (open Tu-Sa 8am-5pm, Su noon-5pm; self-guided tours $2.25, ages 6-12 $1.25).

■ Hot Springs

Despite tourist traps like alligator farms, wax museums, and ubiquitous gift shops, the town of Hot Springs delivers precisely what it advertises: soothing relaxation. Once you've bathed in the coils of these 143°F springs, you'll realize why everybody from Al Capone to the feds jumped into the bathhouse craze of the 20s.

PRACTICAL INFORMATION The **visitors center,** 629 Central Ave. (321-2277 or 800-SPA-CITY/772-2489), in the middle of downtown off Spring St., provides *The Springs Magazine* (open daily 9am-5pm). **Post Office:** 100 Reserve St. (623-8217), at Central Ave. in the **Federal Reserve Building** (open M-F 8am-4:30pm, Sa 9am-1pm). **ZIP code:** 71901. **Area code:** 501.

ACCOMMODATIONS, CAMPGROUNDS, AND FOOD Hot Springs has ample lodging; the best deals can be found along **Central Ave. (Rte. 7),** the main drag. Most rates rise for the tourist season (Feb.-Aug.), but the rooms are always cheap just north and south of the downtown strip, where old-time motor inns still operate. The **Tower Motel,** 755 Park Ave. (624-9555), offers clean rooms with country landscape pictures. Call ahead, because if no one's staying, the motel shuts down. (Singles $25; doubles $30.) The **Margarete Motel,** 217 Fountain St. (623-1192), is just a stone's throw away from the baths and offers an excellent deal on large rooms with full kitchens (singles $26, doubles $34; Sa-Su $30/$42). The **Best Motel,** 638 Ouachita Ave. (624-5736), has clean rooms around a small pool in gingerbread-like cabins (singles $25; doubles $35). The closest campgrounds are at **Gulpha Gorge** (624-3383, ext. 640 for info and emergencies), part of **Hot Springs National Park.** Follow Rte. 70 (Grand Ave.) 1 mi east to Exit 70B (1st exit outside of town), turn left, and drive ½ mi. north; it's on the left (primitive sites $8).

Granny's Kitchen, 332 Central Ave. (624-6183), cooks up hearty country food (plate lunches $5), with old-fashioned Americana lining the walls (open daily 6:30am-7pm). **Cookin' with Jazz,** 101 Central Ave. (321-0555), serves New Orleans-style dishes—po' boys, jambalaya, and gumbo—with a live band on summer Saturdays from 7-11pm (entrees $5-14; open M 11am-2pm, Tu-Sa 11am-9pm, later with live music). **The Dixie Café,** 3623 Central Ave. (624-2100), serves Southern food (entrees $5-7) with fitting hospitality, though the exterior is a bit bland (open daily 11am-10pm). Diners should remember to drink the water—after all, that's what made Hot Springs famous.

SIGHTS AND ENTERTAINMENT Still trickling through the earth after 4000 years, water gushes to the planet's crust in Hot Springs at a rate of 850,000 gallons a day. Let the baths begin! As the only operating house on "Bathhouse Row," the **Buckstaff,** 509 Central Ave. (623-2308), retains the dignity and elegance of Hot Springs' heyday in the 1920s. *(Open M-Sa 7-11:45am and 1:30-3pm. Bath $14, whirlpool $1.50 extra; massage $16.50.)* Around the corner, the **Hot Springs Health Spa,** N. 500 Reserve (321-9664), at Spring St., offers large common hot tubs and whirlpools. *(Yes, bathing suits are required. Open daily 9am-9pm. Bath $13; 30min. massage $17.50.)* You can roast as long as you like in the co-ed baths. Hot springs eternal at the **Downtowner,** 135 Central Ave. (624-5521), which has the town's cheapest hands-on, full treatment baths with little difference in quality (bath $12.50, whirlpool $1.50 extra; massage $14).

The **Fordyce Bathhouse Visitors Center,** 369 Central Ave. (624-3383, ext. 640), located in one of the Row's vintage bathhouses, can bathe guests with info on **Hot Springs National Park.** An informative film on Hot Springs (17min.) and a self-guided tour of the restored building are crucial to understanding the allure of Hot Springs in the early 20th century. *(Open daily 9am-5pm.)* The Center distributes handy trail maps for the park and directions for two walking tours in town: one on the history of the local baths, and one on the rise of President Clinton, who grew up in Hot Springs. The front desk has a chart helpful for disabled and hearing-impaired visitors and info on walks within the park. Die-hard sight-seers should take the 1½hr. amphibious **National Park Duck Tour,** 418 Central Ave. (321-2911 or 800-682-7044), through Hot Springs into Lake Hamilton (7-21 per day; $9.50, seniors $8.50, children $5.50).

Hot Springs' natural beauty, like its schlocky tourist-oriented economy, is unmistakable. Folks can gaze at the green-peaked mountains while cruising Lake Hamilton on the **Belle of Hot Springs,** 5200 Central Ave. (525-4438), during a 1½hr. narrated tour alongside the Ouachita Lake and Lake Hamilton mansions. *(Trips in summer daily 1pm, 3pm, and sundown; call for exact times year-round. $9, seniors $8.50, ages 2-12 $5; evening cruise $10/$9.50/$5.)* From the **Hot Springs Mountain Observatory Tower** (623-6035), located in the national park (turn off Central Ave. onto Fountain St. and follow the signs), view the beautiful panorama of the surrounding mountains and lakes. *(Open daily 9am-9pm; early-Sept. to Oct. and Mar. to mid-May 9am-6pm; Nov.-Feb. 9am-5pm. $4, ages 5-11 $2, ages 55+ $3.50.)* On clear days, it's possible to see 140 mi. For outdoor frolicking, the clear and unpolluted waters of the **Ouachita River** provide ample opportunities to hike, bike, fish, or canoe. **Ouachita River Adventures** (326-5517 or 800-748-3718 for info and directions), west of Hot Springs on U.S. 270, offers canoes ($30 per day), kayaks ($15), and rafts ($65) for daytime or overnight trips, and can help in planning backpacking or fishing trips. In **Whittington Park,** on Whittington St. off Central Ave., bathhouses give way to an expanse of trees and shaded picnic tables. For a case of small-town cabin fever, **Window to the World,** 120 Ouachita Ave. (623-4615), might be a quick fix. *(70min. guided tours Th-Sa 3pm, or call ahead for a private tour. $5, seniors $4.50, children $3.)* This hands-on museum hoards thousands of artifacts from 100 countries for a multi-sensory, multicultural experience.

■ Mountain View

Despite the commercialism gradually seeping into Mountain View, the village remains refreshingly unpretentious, authentically Ozark, and unmistakably small (pop. 2,700). Nearly every evening, locals gather at the **Courthouse Sq.** to make music together on banjos, dulcimers, fiddles, and guitars. Ozark culture thrives undiluted on the lush grounds of the **Ozark Folk Center** (269-3851), 2 mi. north of Mountain View off Rte. 9 on Rte. 382. The center recreates a mountain village and showcases the cabin crafts, music, and lore of the Ozarks. In the **Crafts Forum,** over 25 artisans demonstrate everything from wheel-thrown ceramics to ironware forging and spoon carving. Listen to original "unplugged" music as locals fiddle, pluck, and strum in the auditorium at lunchtime and nightly (shows at 7:30pm), while dancers clog along. (Open May-Oct. daily 10am-5pm. Crafts area $7.50, ages 6-12 $5; evening musical performances $7.50/$5. Combination tickets and family rates available.) The center's seasonal events include the **Arkansas Folk Festival** (Apr. 16-18, 1999), the **Annual Dulcimer Jamboree** (Apr. 23-26, 1999), and the **National Fiddle Championships** (Nov. 5-7, 1999). Close by, at the junction of Rte. 9 and 382, the **Dulcimer Shoppe** (269-4313) allows on-lookers to witness craftsmen fashion these mellow music makers and even hammer a few strings themselves (open Apr.-Oct. M-Sa 9am-5pm; free). Would-be hill-billies and others revel in the musical charisma of Grammy Award winner and quintessential Ozark artist Jimmy Driftwood at the **Jimmy Driftwood Barn and Folk Museum** (269-8042), also on Rte. 9, 1 mi. north of the Dulcimer Shoppe (shows F and Su 7pm, doors open 6pm; free).

Fishing along the White River is one of many popular outdoor diversions in the area around Mountain View. Non-residents can purchase a 3-day **fishing license** ($10, $17.50 for Trout) from **Wal-Mart,** 315 Sylamore Ave./Rte. 9 N (269-4395), then head 4 mi. farther north along state Rte. 9 to the junction where Rte. 5 and 14 split off. Here, several vendors provide prime access to the river for little or no cost. To experience the Ozarks from the saddle, equestrians can contact the **OK Trading Post** (585-2217), 3½ mi. west of the Rte. 5/9/14 junction on Rte. 14 (guided trail rides $10 per hr.; open daily 9am-dark). The **Blanchard Springs Caverns** (757-2211), 9 mi. west on Rte. 14 from the junction, glisten with exquisite cave formations and cool, glassy springs on the southern border of the Ozark Forest. *(Open daily 9am-6:30pm, last tour 5pm; Nov.-Mar. W-Su 9:30am-6pm, last tour 4pm. $9, ages 6-15 $5, with Golden Age Passport $4.50.)* Daytrips from Mountain View to the Buffalo River (1hr. northwest) are excellent for **canoeing. Crockett's Country Store and Canoe Rental** (800-355-6111), at the Rte. 14/27 junction in Harriet, provides boats ($25 per day), shuttles ($1 per mi.), and maps of the waterways (open M-F 6am-8pm, Sa 7am-8pm, Su 7am-6pm).

Mountain View offers many lodging options at moderate prices, but it's nearly impossible to find a room for less than $40 on a summer weekend. The **Mountain View Motel,** 407 E. Main St. (269-3209), has 18 orderly rooms sporting in-room coffee makers as well as cable TV. Each has a red chair sitting outside for enjoying the evening air (singles $33; doubles $39). **Wildflower Bed & Breakfast** (800-591-4879), on the northeast corner of the Courthouse Sq., rents nine florally decorated rooms with soft carpeting and softer antique furniture—but no TVs. (Singles $40; doubles $46. Rooms with private bathrooms available. Reservations recommended.) A group of hexagonal cottages with padded rocking chairs make up the **Dry Creek Lodge** (269-3871 or 800-264-3655), on Spur 382 off Rte. 9, within the Ozark Folk Center. (Singles or doubles Su-W $50, Th-Sa $55; Nov.-Mar. $10 off. Pool and restaurant.)

Because Mountain View lies only 14 mi. south of the **Ozark National Forest,** the cheapest way to stay in the area is free **camping.** Backwoodsmen can pitch a tent anywhere within the forest—it's free, legal, and usually safe, as long as the campsite does not block any road, path, or thoroughfare. Safe, unattended campgrounds hide out around the **Blanchard Springs Caverns,** off Rte. 14, 10-15min. west of the junction with Rte. 5 and 9. These include **Blanchard Springs Recreation Area,** in the same entrance as the Caverns (32 sites with hot showers, $10); **Gunner Pool Recreation Area,** in a beautiful gorge off a winding 3 mi. red dirt road (27 sites, $7; total of 2mi. past the Caverns entrance; turn off 1 mi. past the town of Fifty-Six); and **Barkshed Recreation Area,** 3½ mi. past Fifty-Six (5 sites, $3 per car; beware young idlers who bring their drink and wickedness). All campsites border a clear creek ideal for swimming. More info about camping awaits at the **Sylamore Ranger District** of the National Forest, P.O. Box 1279, Mountain View 72560 (757-2211 or 269-3228).

Fried catfish is the local specialty of Mountain View, and **Jojo's Catfish Wharf** (585-2121), 6 mi. north of town on Rte. 5, 1 mi. past the Rte. 5/9/14 junction, in Jack's White River Fishing Resort, drops them into the pan fresh from the White River. (Not-too-fishy catfish sandwich $3.25, all-you-can-eat catfish $12.50. Open Su-Th 11am-8pm, F-Sa 11am-9pm.) Locals swear by family-owned **Tommy's Famous...a pizzeria** (269-3278), about ½ mi. west of Courthouse Sq. off Rte. 66. A small pie (12 in.) starts at $6; calzones go for $7. (Open W-Th 3-9pm, F-Su 3-10pm.) **Rhythm & Brew's,** 112 E. Main St. (269-5200), specializes in homemade desserts and sophisticated coffee drinks, with the only cappuccino machine for 100 mi. On weekends, local musicians perform on the small stage. (Open Th noon-2pm and 5:30-7:30pm, F-Sa noon-2pm and 6-8:30pm, Su 11am-1:30pm.)

Mountain View is a dry county; beware of people selling illicit booze. The nearest rental car agency is in Batesville, 40 mi. east on Rte. 5, but motor scooter rentals are available in town from **Scooterville,** 104 Scott Dr. (269-5944), off Rte. 14 E ($16 for 2hr., 2nd scooter ½-price; full-day $40; must be 16; open daily 9am-5pm). Mountain View's **Chamber of Commerce** (269-8068) is located behind the Courthouse on the corner of Washington and Howard St. (open M-Sa 9am-5pm). They have easy-to-read, free maps. **Post Office:** 802 Sylamore Ave. (269-3520; open M-F 8:30am-4:30pm). **ZIP code:** 72560. **Area code:** 870.

▨ Eureka Springs

Eureka! You've arrived at the "Little Switzerland" of the Ozarks. In the early 19th century, the native Osage spread reports of a wonderful spring with magical healing powers. Settlers quickly came to the site and established a small town from which they sold bottles of the miraculous water. Today, the tiny town in northwest Arkansas is filled with ritzy boutiques, native limestone walls, narrow streets, and Victorian buildings painted in brash colors fit only for citrus fruits.

Tourists still come in droves to Eureka Springs, but not for the waters (they go to **Hot Springs** for that, p. 352). Nowadays, Eureka's main attraction is the **Great Passion Play** (253-9200 or 800-882-7529), off U.S. 62 on Passion Play Rd., modeled after Germany's Oberammergau Passion Play. (Performances last F in Apr. to 1st M in Sept. M-Tu and Th-Sa 8:30pm; 1st M in Sept. to last Sa in Oct. 7:30pm. $14.25-15.25, ages 4-11 $7-7.50. Admission to grounds free, 15 other attractions individually priced.) Featuring a cast of 250 actors and countless live animals, this seasonal event built on piety, holy water, and slick marketing has drawn more than 6 million visitors to its depiction of Jesus Christ's life and death. Even if you miss the show, you can't miss the **Christ of the Ozarks** statue, 7 stories of glory to God. The less passionate come to Eureka Springs to walk up and down the steep hillsides of the beautiful downtown, where some buildings have as many as six ground floors. The highways into town are also lined with diversions and tourist traps. **Quigley's Castle,** 4 mi. south on Rte. 23, for instance, bills itself as "the Ozark's strangest dwelling." (Open Apr.-Oct. M-W and F-Sa 8:30am-5pm. $5, under 15 free.) The curious will find fanciful gardens and stone pillars surrounding a 2-story building with plants lining inside walls.

Eureka Springs has more hotel beds than it does permanent residents. The **Dogwood Inn,** 170 Huntsville Rd./Rte. 23 S (253-7200 or 800-544-1884), offers enormous rooms beside an outdoor pool and hot tub (singles and doubles $38-48; off-season $28). Next door, the **Colonial Mansion Inn** (253-7300 or 800-638-2622) rents spacious, virtually luxurious rooms, with continental breakfast included (2 beds $28, Sa-Su $38). **Kettle Campgrounds** (253-9100), on U.S. 62 just beyond Passion Play Rd., has 14 tent sites in a shaded, woodsy area, along with hot showers, a laundry room, and a pool (sites $12, full RV hookup $17).

You're sure to see more locals at Subway than at any of the pricey restaurants on the downtown loop; no restaurant here is truly a great value. **Café Luigi,** 91 S. Main St. (253-6888), has a pleasant courtyard with fountain, freshly made pasta, and lean meatballs at reasonable rates (lunch $5-6, dinner $9-15; open Su-Th 11am-9pm, F-Sa 11am-10pm). For nightlife, bars along **Center St.** become the focal point of action.

Five **trolley lines** (253-9572) run from local hotels to the downtown historic loop and to the play every 10-45min. Pick up map and schedule from most restaurants and hotels (day pass $3.50, one-way $2; hrs. vary, generally Apr.-Oct. daily 9am-5pm). The **Chamber of Commerce** (253-8737 or 800-638-7352), on U.S. 62 just west of Rte. 23, has brochures on most anything (open daily 9am-5pm). **Post Office:** 101 Spring St. (253-9850), on the loop (open M-F 8:15am-4:15pm, Sa 10am-noon). **ZIP code:** 72632. **Area code:** 501.

FLORIDA

Ponce de León landed on the Florida coast in 1513, in search of the elusive Fountain of Youth, now in St. Augustine. Although the multitudes who flock to Florida today aren't desperately seeking fountains, many find their youth restored in the Sunshine State—whether they're dazzled by Orlando's fantasia, Disney World, or bronzed by the sun on the state's seductive beaches. Droves of senior citizens also migrate to Florida, where they thrive in comfortable retirement communities, leaving one to wonder whether the unpolluted, sun-warmed air isn't just as good as Ponce de León's fabled magical elixir.

Anything as attractive as Florida is bound to draw hordes of people, the nemesis of natural beauty. Florida's population boom has strained the state's resources; commercial strips and tremendous development have turned many pristine beaches into tourist traps. Still, it is possible to find a deserted spot on the peninsula on which to plop down, grab a paperback, and let your feet sink into the warm sand.

🖐 HIGHLIGHTS OF FLORIDA

- **Beaches.** White sand, lots of sun, clear blue water. Key Largo (p. 381) and St. Petersburg (p. 387) win our thumbs-up for the best of the best.
- **Disney World.** Orlando's cash cow (p. 366)…what else is there to say?
- **Everglades.** The prime Florida haunt for fishermen, hikers, canoers, bikers, and wildlife watchers (p. 379). Check out the unique mangrove swamps.
- **Cape Canaveral.** NASA's home; destination #1 for closet astronomers (p. 370).
- **Key lime pie.** This famous dessert hails from the Florida Keys (p. 381).

PRACTICAL INFORMATION

Capital: Tallahassee.
Visitor Info: Florida Division of Tourism, 126 W. Van Buren St., Tallahassee 32399-2000 (904-487-1462; http://www.flausa.com). **Dept. of Environmental Protection: Division of Recreation and Parks,** 3900 Commonwealth Blvd., #506, Tallahassee 32399-3000 (904-488-9872).
Emergency: 911.
Time Zones: Mostly Eastern; Central (1hr. behind Eastern) in the westernmost parts of the panhandle. **Postal Abbreviation:** FL.
Sales Tax: 6%.

■ St. Augustine

Spanish adventurer Pedro Menéndez de Aviles founded St. Augustine in 1565, making it the first European colony in North America and the oldest continuous settlement in the United States. Thanks to preservation efforts, much of St. Augustine's Spanish flavor remains intact. Unlike most towns on Florida's east coast, St. Augustine is not defined by beaches; little shops selling antiques, homemade fudge, dresses, and rare books abound. And forget L.A.'s plastic surgeons; eternal youth costs just $4.75 around here.

PRACTICAL INFORMATION St. Augustine has no public transportation; fortunately, most of the town lies within a pleasant walk from the hostel, motels, and bus station. The major east-west axis, **King St.,** runs along the river and crosses the bay to the beaches. **Saint George St.,** also east-west, contains most of the shops and many sights in St. Augustine (for pedestrians only). **San Marco Ave.** and **Cordova St.** travel north-south. **Greyhound,** 100 Malaga St. (829-6401 or 800-231-2222; station open daily 7:30am-6pm), has service to Jacksonville (55min., 5 per day, $11-12) and Day-

Florida Peninsula

GEORGIA

Jacksonville

Osceola National Forest

TO TALLAHASSEE

St. Augustine

Suwannee River

Santa Fe R.

St. John's River

TO PANAMA CITY BEACH

Gainesville

Ocala National Forest

Ocala

Daytona Beach

ATLANTIC OCEAN

Cedar Keys

Chassahowitzka Bay

NASA Kennedy Space Center

Cape Canaveral

Walt Disney World

Orlando

Cocoa Beach

Clearwater

Tampa

Melbourne

Florida Turnpike

St. Petersburg

Tampa Bay

Sarasota

Manatee R.

Peace R.

Lake Istokpoga

Fort Pierce

Kissimmee R.

Cal oosahatchee R.

Lake Okeechobee

West Palm Beach

Palm Beach

Loxahatchee Nat. Wildlife Refuge

Fort Myers

GULF OF MEXICO

Seminole Indian Reservation

Boca Raton

Naples

Big Cypress National Preserve

Everglades Pkwy

Fort Lauderdale

Everglades City

Miami

Miami Beach

Biscayne Bay

N

Everglades National Park

Florida City

Key Largo

0   100 miles

0   100 kilometers

Florida Bay

Florida Keys

Key West

FLORIDA

tona Beach (70min., 6 per day, $12-13); if the station is closed, the driver accepts cash. **Ancient City Taxi** (824-8161) can take you from the bus station to the visitors center for about $2. The **visitors center,** 10 Castillo (825-1000), at San Marco Ave., hands out a free map of attractions and a comprehensive city guide. (From the Greyhound station, walk north on Ribeira, then right on Orange.) A free 30min. video presentation hits the high points of St. Augustine's rich historical heritage while the more comprehensive (7 years in the making) *Dream of Empire* (1hr.) details just about every significant event in St. Augustine's lengthy history. (Showtimes daily 9am-4pm. $3, ages 6-17 and students $2. Visitors center open daily late May to early Sept. 8am-7:30pm; Oct.-Apr. 8:30am-5:30pm.) **Post Office:** 99 King St. (829-8716), at Martin Luther King, Jr. Ave. (open M-Tu and Th-F 8:30am-5:30pm, W 8:30am-5pm, Sa 9am-1pm). **ZIP code:** 32084. **Area code:** 904.

ACCOMMODATIONS AND CAMPGROUNDS The immaculate **St. Augustine Hostel,** 32 Treasury St. (808-1999), at Charlotte St. 6 blocks from the bus station and in the middle of everything, offers spacious rooms that sleep six ($12), hotel-quality private rooms ($28, with shower $35), A/C, a nicely decorated common area, stocked kitchen, and a pleasant roof garden. (No lockout, no curfew, no chores, no problem. Parking $2, free parking available down the street. Linen $2. Bikes $4 per day.) Just over the Bridge of Lions, east of the historic district, the **Seabreeze Motel,** 208 Anastasia Blvd. (829-8122), features clean rooms with A/C, cable TV, and a pool (singles $35; doubles $42; Sa-Su $65 for either). The **American Inn,** 42 San Marco Ave. (829-2292), near the visitors center, rents small rooms with TVs and A/C in a location convenient to the restaurants and historic sights (singles $40; doubles $45; Sa-Su $65/$75; rates less in winter). The quaint and quiet **St. Francis Inn,** 279 Saint George St. (824-6068, 800-824-6062 for reservations); a charming 16-room inn with a jungle of flowers, a tucked-away pool, and much of its original 18th-century interior; is an expensive treat. Juice and iced tea are served free all day, along with wine daily from 5-7pm. (Free full breakfast; free use of bikes; free parking. Rooms have cable TV, A/C, heat, and gas fireplaces. $65 and up; F-Sa $85.) Nearby, a salt run and the Atlantic Ocean provide opportunities for great windsurfing, fishing, swimming, and surfing near the 139 campsites of the **Anastasia State Recreation Area** (461-2033), on Rte. A1A, 4 mi. south of the historic district. From town, cross the Bridge of Lions and turn left just beyond the Alligator Farm. (Sites $15, full hookup $17; Oct.-Feb. $12/$14. Office open daily 8am-sunset. Reservations recommended.)

FOOD AND NIGHTLIFE The bustle of daytime tourists and abundance of budget eateries make lunch in St. Augustine's historic district a delight. Strolling down **Saint George St.** reveals the daily specials scrawled on blackboards outside each restaurant. **Anastasia Blvd.** also holds a wealth of budget options. **Captain Jack's,** 410 Anastasia Blvd. (829-6846), serves up fried shrimp for $9 (open M-F 11:30am-9pm, Sa-Su noon-9pm). The sandwich and juice counter at **New Dawn,** 110 Anastasia Blvd. (824-1337), a health-conscious grocery store, makes delicious vegetarian sandwiches, including the savory tabouli salad pita for $4.25 (open M-Sa 9am-5:30pm; lunch bar 10am-3pm). If, my dear, you do give a damn, come to **Scarlett O'Hara's,** 70 Hypolita St. (824-6535), at Cordova St., where barbecued chicken sandwiches are $4.75 and the drinks are refreshing (open daily 11:30am-12:30am).

St. Augustine supports an impressive array of bars. Pick up a copy of *Today Tonight,* available at most grocery and convenience stores, for a complete listing of current concerts and events. Local string musicians play on the tiny stage in the **Milltop,** 19½ Saint George St. (829-2329), a tiny bar situated above an old mill in the restored district (cover varies; open daily 11am-1am; music daily from 1pm until closing). Cheap flicks and bargain eats await the weary traveler at **Pot Belly's,** 36 Granada St. (829-3101), across from the Lightner Museum (see below). This combination pub, deli, and cinema serves a vast array of junk food, with each item bearing the name of a famous film—*Dances With Wolves* ($5) means

12 spicy buffalo wings. Most food items run $2-4, and the rootbeer floats are
divine (shows every 15-30min.; starting times 6:30-9:30pm; $3). The hot spot for
the young beach crowd, the **Oasis Deck and Restaurant,** 4000 Rte. A1A S./Beach
Blvd. (471-3424), schedules nightly entertainment with happy hours from 4-7pm
(open daily 6am-1am).

SIGHTS AND ENTERTAINMENT The historic district centers on Saint George St.,
beginning at the Gates of the City near the visitors center and running south past
Cadiz St. and the Oldest Store. Visit the **Spanish Quarter,** 29 Saint George St. (825-
6830), a living museum which includes Gallegos House. *(Open Su-Th 9am-6pm, F-Sa
9am-9pm. $5, students and ages 6-18 $3.75, seniors and AAA members $5.)* Artisans and vil-
lagers in period costumes describe the customs and crafts of the Spanish New World.
Other 18th-century homes and shops fill the **Restored Area.** The oldest masonry fortress in the continental U.S., **Castillo de San Marcos National Monument,** 1 Castillo
Dr. (829-6506), off San Marco Ave., has 14 ft. thick walls built of coquina, the local
shellrock. *(Open daily 8:45am-4:45pm. $4, under 17 and seniors with Golden Age Passport
free. Occasional tours; call ahead.)* Inside the fort (a four-pointed star complete with drawbridge and murky moat), you'll find a museum, a large courtyard surrounded by livery
quarters for the garrison, a jail, a chapel, and the original cannon brought overseas by
the Spanish. A cannon-firing ceremony occurs at 11am, 1:30, 2:30, and 3:30pm.

For two decades, St. Augustine was the end of the line—the railroad line, that is.
Swarms of wealthy northerners escaped to railroad owner Henry Flagler's **Ponce de
León Hotel,** at King and Cordova St. The hotel, decorated entirely by Tiffany's and
outfitted with electricity by Edison himself (the first hotel to feature this luxury), is
now **Flagler College** (829-6481, ext. 205). On summer days, free 25min. tours pass
through some of the recently restored rooms in the old hotel; go, if only to see the
exquisite stained glass windows (tours mid-May to mid-Aug. daily on the hr. 11am-
4pm). In 1947, Chicago publisher and art-lover Otto Lightner converted the Alcazar
Hotel, across the street, into the **Lightner Museum** (824-2874), to hold an impressive
collection of cut, blown, and burnished glass, as well as old clothing and oddities like
nun and monk beer steins (open daily 9am-5pm; $6, students and ages 12-18 $2).

Not surprisingly, the oldest continuous settlement in the U.S. holds some of the
nation's oldest stuff. The self-proclaimed **Oldest House,** 14 Saint Francis St. (824-
2872), was occupied since its construction in the 1600s until 1918, when it became
a museum (open daily 9am-5pm; $5, students $3, seniors $4.50, families $12). The
Oldest Store Museum, 4 Artillery Ln. (829-9729), holds over 100,000 items from the
18th and 19th centuries (open M-Sa 9am-5pm, Su noon-5pm; $5, ages 6-12 $1.50).

Six blocks north of the info center, **La Leche Shrine and Mission of Nombre de
Dios,** 27 Ocean St. (824-2809), off San Marco Ave., held the first Catholic service in
the U.S. on September 8, 1565. *(Open June-Aug. M-F 8am-6pm, Sa-Su 9am-5pm; Sept.-May
daily 9am-5pm. Mass M-F 8:30am, Sa 6pm, Su 8am; in summer Su 8am. Donation suggested.)*
Soaring over the moss- and vine-covered structure, a 208 ft. steel cross commemorates the city's founding. No trip to St. Augustine would be complete without a trek
to the **Fountain of Youth,** 11 Magnolia Ave. (829-3168); go right on Williams St. from
San Marco Ave. and continue a few blocks past Nombre de Dios. *(Open daily 9am-5pm.
$5.50, seniors $4.50, ages 6-12 $2.50.)* You can sip skeptically or enthusiastically from
the spring under the confident gaze of Ponce de León's ageless statue. While you're
there, take in the huge oaks and hanging Spanish moss of **Magnolia Ave.,** heralded as
one of the prettiest streets in America.

■ Daytona Beach

Daytona's 500 ft. wide beach is the city's *raison d'être.* During spring break, students
from practically every college in the country come here to get a head start on summer. The beach itself resembles a traffic jam; fleets of vehicles rolls past sunbathers,
cruising down the Atlantic Ave. strip. Others drag the appropriately named Interna-

tional Speedway Blvd. seeking Daytona's famous racetrack. For non-bikini-clad scenery in Daytona, head a few miles north to picturesque Ormond Beach.

PRACTICAL INFORMATION Daytona Beach lies 53 mi. northeast of Orlando and 90 mi. south of Jacksonville. **Atlantic Ave. (Rte. A1A)** crawls with budget motels, surf shops, and bars in **Beachside,** the main strip of land. **E. International Speedway Blvd. (U.S. 92)** runs north-south. Daytona Beach is a collection of smaller towns that have expanded and converged, but have also preserved their individual street-numbering systems. As a result, many street numbers are not consecutive, and finding addresses can be difficult. To avoid the gridlock on the beach, arrive early (8am) and leave early (3pm or so). You'll pay $5 to drive onto the beach (permitted 8am-7pm), and police strictly enforce the 10 mph speed limit. Free parking is plentiful during most of the year but difficult during peak seasons, especially Speed Week, Bike Week, Racefest, and the Pepsi 400 (see **Entertainment,** below), not to mention spring break (usually the week after Easter).

Amtrak, 2491 Old New York Ave. in Deland (734-2322 or 800-872-7245; station open daily 9:15am-8pm), 24 mi. west on Rte. 92, makes tracks to Miami (7hr., 2 per day, $29-48). **Greyhound,** 138 S. Ridgewood Ave. (255-7076 or 800-231-2222; station open daily 8am-10pm), 4 mi. west of the beach, will get you to Orlando (80min., 6 per day, $6-7). **Votran County Transit Co.,** 950 Big Tree Rd. (761-7700), on the mainland, operates local buses and a trolley that covers A1A between Granada Blvd. and Dunlawton Ave. (Service M-Sa 5:30am-6:30pm with most running M-Sa 7am-7pm, Su 8am-5:30pm. Fare $1, children and seniors 50¢, transfers free. Free maps available at hotels.) **A&A Cab Co.** (253-2522) charges $1.80 for the first ½ mi. and $1.20 per additional mi. For tourist info, visit the **Daytona Beach Area Convention and Visitors Bureau,** 126 E. Orange Ave. (255-0415 or 800-854-1234), at the Chamber of Commerce on City Island (open M-F 8:30am-5pm). Reach the 24hr. **Rape Crisis and Sexual Abuse line** at 254-4106. **Post Office:** 220 N. Beach St. (253-5166; open M-F 8am-5pm, Sa 9am-noon). **ZIP code:** 32115. **Area code:** 904.

ACCOMMODATIONS AND CAMPGROUNDS Almost all of Daytona's accommodations front **Atlantic Ave./Rte. A1A,** either on the beach or across the street; those off the beach offer the best deals. Cheaper, quieter hotels line **Ridgewood Ave.** During spring break and big race weekends, even the worst hotels become overpriced, and it's unwise to sleep on these well-patrolled shores. In summer and fall, prices plunge; most hotels offer special deals in June. **Daytona Beach Streamline,** 140 S. Atlantic Ave. (258-6937), 1 block north of E. International Speedway Blvd., provides two dorm rooms and many more cheap, motel-style private rooms. Perks include A/C, TV, kitchen facilities, free local calls, and a recreation room close to the beach. ($23, $111 per week; higher in season. Lockers $1-2. Key deposit $5.) If you have a few extra dollars, the **Camellia Motel,** 1055 N. Atlantic Ave. (252-9963), across the street from the beach, is worth it. Every effort is made to make you feel at home, with cozy, bright rooms, free local calls, cable TV, and A/C; rooms with kitchens cost $5 extra. (Singles $20; doubles $25; $5 per additional person. During spring break, singles $60; $10 per additional person. Reserve early.) The **Rio Beach Motel,** 843 S. Atlantic Ave. (253-6564), has large rooms, cable TV, A/C, and a pool. Its prime location, directly on the ocean, compensates for its lackluster decor. (Singles $30; doubles $40, oceanfront doubles $50; during spring break, Speed Week, and Bike Week $60-70.)

Camping options await at **Tomoka State Park,** 2099 N. Beach St. (676-4050), 8 mi. north of Daytona and 70min. from Disney World. Take bus #3 "N. Ridgewood" to Domicilio and walk 2 mi. north. You'll find 100 sites located under tropical foliage near a salt marsh, along with nature trails, a museum, and lots of shade. (Sites $11, with electricity $18; June-Dec. $9. Open daily 8am-sunset.) **Nova Family Campground,** 1190 Herbert St. (767-0095), in Port Orange, sits south of Daytona Beach and 10min. from the shore. From I-95, take a left onto Clyde Morris Blvd. and a right on Herbert St., or take bus #7 or 15 from downtown or the beach. (Sites $16, with electricity and water $18, full hookup $20. Open daily 8am-8pm.)

FOOD One of the most famous (and popular) seafood restaurants in the area is **Aunt Catfish's** (767-4768), just to the left of Port Orange Bridge (Dunlawton Ave.) as it connects to the mainland. Fried alligator appetizers are $6, and veggie options are dished out for $4.50-5.50. (Open M-Sa 11:30am-10pm, Su 9am-10pm; in winter open until 9:30pm.) "If it swims…we have it," boasts **B&B Fisheries,** 715 E. International Speedway Blvd. (252-6542), the oldest family-owned seafood house in town since 1932. Take out your choice of four to five varieties of fresh fish for lunch starting around $4.50. (Open M-F 11am-8:30pm, Sa 4-8:30pm; take-out M-Sa 11:30am-8:30pm.) For cheap Chinese eats, hit the **Orient Palace Restaurant,** 2116 S. Atlantic Ave. (255-4183), where chicken and broccoli is $6.75. (Open daily 5-11pm; all-you-can-eat buffet 5-9:30pm; happy hour with wicked scotch sours 4-6pm.)

ENTERTAINMENT AND NIGHTLIFE Bored with beachcombing? Get in touch with your primitive side and race off to the **Daytona International Speedway,** 1801 W. International Speedway Blvd. (254-2700 for info; 253-7223 for race tickets). **Speed Week** (Jan. 30-Feb. 14, 1999) is 2 weeks of almost daily races, including the **Daytona 500** (Feb. 14), which draws the festivities to a close (tickets $60-160). **Racefest** (July 2) and the **Pepsi 400** (July 3) provide the avid fan with even more opportunities to watch his or her favorite jalopy burst into flames (tickets $35-95). **Daytona USA** (947-6800), a theme park dedicated to all things NASCAR, is located on the Speedway premises. At this "interactive museum," you can, among other things, design and "drive" your own virtual race car. (Open Su-Th 9am-8pm, F-Sa 9am-9pm. $12, seniors $10, ages 6-12 $10.) **Bike Week** (Feb. 28-Mar. 9, 1999) ends with the **Daytona 200 Motorcycle Classic,** drawing every biker mama in the world (tickets $30). The speedway itself houses a huge collection of racing memorabilia and early racing films (30min. tours on non-race days 9:30am-4pm; $5, ages 7-12 $2).

When spring break hits, concerts, hotel-sponsored parties, and other events cater to students questing for fun. News about these travels fastest by word of mouth, but the *Calendar of Events* and *SEE Daytona Beach,* available at the chamber of commerce, make good starting points. On more mellow nights, head to the boardwalk to play volleyball or shake your groove thing at the **Oceanfront Bandshell.** A fairly homogeneous collection of dance clubs smoke along Seabreeze Blvd. near the intersection with N. Atlantic Ave. At **St. Regis Bar and Restaurant,** 509 Seabreeze Blvd. (252-8743), live jazz flavors the cool veranda on Fridays and Saturdays 8-11pm (open Tu-Sa 6-11pm). Among the nightclubs, **Ocean Deck,** 127 S. Ocean Ave. (253-5224), where "everyday is like a weekend," stands apart with its beachfront location and live reggae music. (21+ from 9pm. Music nightly 9:30pm-2:30am. Open daily 11am-3am; full menu until 2am.)

■ Orlando

Call the Walt Disney World information hotline, and you'll probably get this recorded message: "Thank you for calling Walt Disney World. All of our Disney operators are busy making magic with other customers. Please stay on the line." Besides sounding kind of kinky, this recording indicates how seriously Disney—and the city of Orlando—regards its own "magic." And why shouldn't it? Every year, millions descend upon this central Florida city for the sole purpose of visiting Disney World, the most popular tourist attraction on earth. Comprised of the original Magic Kingdom, Epcot Center, and Disney-MGM Studios, Disney holds its own against an onslaught of smaller parks that have sprung up all over the Orlando area. There are many ways to lighten your wallet in this land of illusions, so choose wisely. Besides the new Disney Zoo, Disney has gone relatively unchanged in recent years; previous visitors to the park may want to check out Orlando's other attractions.

ORIENTATION AND PRACTICAL INFORMATION

Orlando lies at the center of hundreds of small lakes and amusement parks. **Lake Eola** is in the center of the city, east of I-4 and south of **Colonial Dr.** Streets are divided

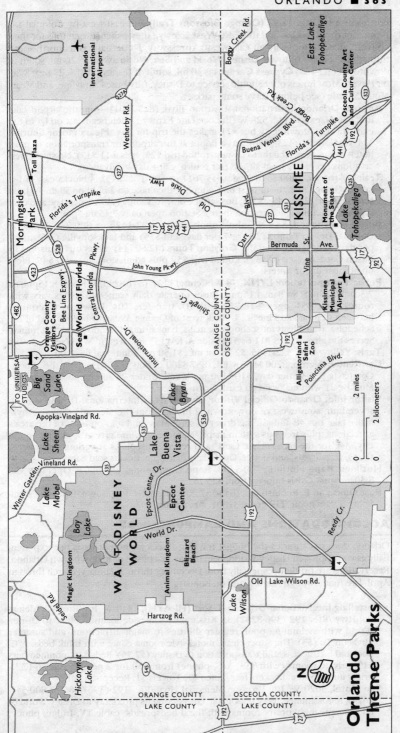

Orlando Theme Parks

FLORIDA

north-south by **Rte. 17/92 (Orange Blossom Trail)** and east-west by Colonial Dr. Beware of the **Bee Line** and the **East-West Expwy.**; they exact several tolls for their convenience. Supposedly an east-west expressway, I-4 actually runs north-south through the center of town. **Disney World** and **Sea World** await 15-20 mi. south of downtown on I-4 W; **Cypress Gardens** is 30 mi. south of Disney off U.S. 27 near Winter Haven. Most hotels offer shuttle service to Disney. City buses, Grayline, and Mears Motor Shuttle (see below) serve some parks.

Airport: Orlando International, 1 Airport Blvd. (825-2001); from the airport take Rte. 436 N, exit to Rte. 528 W (the Bee Line Expwy.), then head east on I-4 to the exits for downtown. City bus #11 makes the trip for 85¢. **Mears Motor Shuttle,** 324 W. Gore St. (423-5566), has a booth at the airport for transportation to most hotels. 1 bus goes straight to Disney (round-trip $25, ages 4-11 $17). No shuttle reservations necessary from airport (for return, call 1 day in advance).

Trains: Amtrak, 1400 Sligh Blvd. (843-7611 or 800-872-7245), 3 blocks east of I-4; take S. Orange Ave., head west on Columbia, then take on a right on Sligh. To Jacksonville (3hr., 2 per day, $38). Bus service only to Tampa (2hr., 1 per day, and only if you're catching a connection there). Station open daily 7:15am-7pm.

Buses: Greyhound, 555 N. John Young Pkwy. (292-3424 or 800-231-2222), at Colonial Dr. To Tampa (2-3hr., 7 per day, $14-$15) and Jacksonville (3-4½hr., 9 per day, $26-28). Open 24hr. **Grayline Tours** (422-0744) offers bus transport to Busch Gardens (see p. 387). Round-trip $59 plus admission, ages 3-9 $49. Pickup at most major hotels.

Public Transportation: LYNX, 78 W. Central Blvd. (841-8240; M-F 6am-8:15pm, Sa 7:30am-6:15pm, Su 8am-4:15pm). Buses operate daily 6am-9pm (times vary with route). Fare 85¢, ages 7-18 25¢ with ID, transfers 10¢. Downtown terminal between Central and Pine St., 1 block west of Orange Ave. and 1 block east of I-4. Schedules available at most shopping malls, banks, and at the downtown terminal. Serves the airport (bus #11 or 51 at side A, level 1) and Wet 'n' Wild (see p. 369).

Taxis: Yellow Cab, 422-4455. $2.75 1st mi., $1.50 per additional mi. 24hr.

Car Rental: Alamo, 8200 McCoy Rd. (857-8200 or 800-327-9633), near the airport. Compacts $20-32 per day, $109-190 per week. Under 25 surcharge $20 per day. Must be 21 with major credit card. Open 24hr.

Visitor Info: Orlando Official Visitor Center, 8445 International Dr. (363-5871), several mi. southwest of downtown, 2 blocks from the Mercado (Spanish-style mall); take bus #8 and ask the driver to stop. Maps and info on most of the area's attractions, plus free bus system maps. The free *Orlando* gives the skinny on the city. Ask for the free "Magic Card" and receive discounts at various attractions, shops, restaurants, and hotels. Open daily 8am-7pm, tickets sold 8am-6pm.

Hotlines: Rape Hotline, 740-5408. **Rape Counseling,** 246-8007. Operates M-F 8:30am-5pm. **Crisis Information,** 425-2624.

Post Office: 46 E. Robinson St. (843-5673), at Magnolia downtown. Open M-F 7am-5pm, Sa 9am-noon. **ZIP code:** 32801. **Area code:** 407.

ACCOMMODATIONS AND CAMPGROUNDS

Orlando does not cater to the budget traveler. Prices for hotel rooms rise exponentially as you approach Disney World; plan to stay in a hostel or in downtown Orlando. Reservations are prudent, especially from December through January, March through April, late June through August, and on holidays.

Hostelling International-Orlando Resort (HI-AYH), 4840 W. Irlo Bronson Memorial Hwy./Rte. 192 (396-8282), in Kissimmee. Lakeside location close to Disney World with swimming pool, regular shuttles to major attractions, and summer BBQs on Tu ($3). The super-clean, motel-style rooms come with bunk beds, A/C, pool and lake access, and transportation to Disney ($7.75). Beds $16, nonmembers $19; private rooms (with TVs, A/C, phone) from $30 for 2 people. Ages 6-17 ½-price, under 6 free. Lockers free. Linen $1. Towels $1. Reception 24hr.

Sun Motel, 5020 W. Irlo Bronson Memorial Hwy./Rte. 192 (396-6666 or 800-541-2674), in Kissimmee. Very reasonable considering its proximity to Disney World (4 mi.). Surprisingly pretty rooms with floral bedspreads, cable TV, fridge, phone, pool, and A/C. Beware of the cruel and unusual telephone deposit ($20), as well as 45¢ local calls. Singles $35, doubles $40; off-season $25/$30.

Disney's All-Star Resorts (934-7639), in Disney World. From I-4, take Exit 25B and follow the signs to Blizzard Beach—the resorts are just behind it. Pricey, but a great deal for groups. Large "theme" decorations from cowboy boots to surfboards adorn the courtyards. Pools, A/C, phone, fridge ($5 extra per day), food court. Free parking and Disney transportation. $74-89, $8 per additional adult (up to 4).

KOA, 4771 W. Irlo Bronson Memorial Hwy./Rte. 192 (396-2400 or 800-562-7791), in Kissimmee 5 mi. east of I-4. Sites have lots of trees, a nice pool, tennis courts, and a store (open 7am-9pm; when crowds are big, 7am-11pm). Free buses run twice a day to Disney. Tent sites $22, with hookup (for 2) $24, motor homes $40. Hideously named Kamping Kabins with A/C: 1-room cabin $40, 2-room $50; in peak season $50/$60; $10 per additional adult (up to 4). Discount tickets through Tickets 'N' Tours (396-1182 or 800-307-6667). Reception 24hr.

Stage Stop Campground, 14400 W. Colonial Dr./Rte. 50 (656-8000), 8 mi. north of Disney, off Florida's Turnpike in Winter Garden. Coming from the north on the Turnpike, take Exit 267 and travel 2½ mi. west on Rte. 50. A family campground with a game room, pool, and laundry facilities. 248 sites (tent or RV) with full hookup $20, $120 per week. Reception in summer daily 8am-8pm.

Orlando has two municipal campgrounds. **Turkey Lake Park,** 3401 S. Hiawassee Rd. (299-5581), roosts near Universal Studios. (Sites with water and electricity $14.38, full hookup $16.60. Key deposit $10. Open daily 9:30am-7pm; in winter 9:30am-5pm.) **Moss Park,** 12901 Moss Park Rd. (273-2327), lies 10 mi. from the airport; from the Bee Line, take Narcoossee Rd. south and follow the signs. Garnished with Spanish moss, the sites are lovely but far from everything. (Tent sites $11, with water and electricity $14; park entrance $1. Open daily 8am-8pm.)

FOOD

Lilia's Grilled Delights, 3150 S. Orange Ave. (851-9087), 2 blocks south of Michigan St. and 5min. from the downtown business district. This small, Polynesian-influenced restaurant is one of the best-kept secrets in town. Don't pass up the Huli Huli Chicken, a twice-baked delight (half-chicken $4). Pulled pork sandwich $1.10. Lunch $4-6. Dinner plates $8-10. Open M-F 11am-9pm, Sa noon-9pm.

Bakely's, 345 W. Fairbanks Ave. (645-5767), in Winter Park. Take I-4 to the Fairbanks Ave. Exit. The variety at this restaurant/bake shop is as large as the portions. Breakfast is served all day (famous skillets); the $5 burgers are Orlando's best. Save room for the 6-layer Boston cream cake ($3). Open Su-Th 7am-11pm, F-Sa 7am-midnight.

Thai House, 2102 E. Colonial Dr. (898-0820). Generous, healthy portions typify this small and charming family-run restaurant. The house specialty, fried rice, combines pork, chicken, beef, shrimp, and veggies ($7). Open M-Th 11am-2pm and 5-9:30pm, F 11am-2pm and 5-10pm, Sa 5-10pm.

Clarkie's Restaurant, 3110 S. Orange Ave. (859-1690). Serves up simple "Mom" food for under $5 and every sandwich imaginable. Early Bird special (2 eggs, grits, toast or biscuit) $1.29 until 8am. Open M-F 6am-2pm, Sa 6am-noon, Su 7am-1pm.

Francesco's Ristorante Italiano, 4920 W. Irlo Bronson Memorial Hwy./Rte. 192 (396-0889). Dine beneath Chianti bottles while Sinatra croons from a stereo. Large portions of pasta, steak, or seafood come complete with salad bar and homemade bread $7-15. Breakfast special $2.39. Open daily 7:30am-11pm.

ENTERTAINMENT AND NIGHTLIFE

N. Orange Ave., downtown, is the heart of Orlando nightlife. Relatively inexpensive bars line the city's main drag, including **Zuma Beach Club,** 46 N. Orange Ave. (648-8363). Home to a very mainstream college and 20-something crowd, Zuma packs 'em in (3500 people on Sa nights) with 2 stories of bars, beer tubs, and dance floors. (Open M and Sa 9pm-3am, Tu 10pm-3:30am, Th 9pm-2:30am, F 8pm-2:30am.) Voted one of America's best clubs by *Rolling Stone* and *Billboard,* **The Club at Firestone,** 578 N. Orange Ave. (426-0005), at Concord, features a raucous gay night (Sa) among

FLORIDA

a variety of theme nights (cover $5-10; open Th-Su 9pm-3am). Improvisational comedy shows will keep you in stitches at the **SAK Theater,** 380 W. Amelia St. (648-0001), at Hughey Ave. (Shows Tu and Su 9pm, W-Th 8 and 9:45pm, F-Sa 7:30, 9:30, and 11:30pm. $13, with Florida ID $10, students $8.) **Church Street Station,** 129 W. Church St. (422-2434), on the corner of Church and Garland St., is a slick, block-long entertainment, shopping, and restaurant complex (open Su-Th 11am-1am, F-Sa 11am-2am). Inside, you can boogie down and enjoy 5¢ beers (W 6:30-7:30pm) at **Phineas Phogg's Balloon Works** (21+).

■ Disney World

Happiness can be bought at Disney World, where throngs of fun-seekers work assiduously to get their money's worth. "Amusement park" barely begins to describe the media empire, resort and hotel complex, four theme parks, three water parks, golf courses, wildlife park, sports venues, boardwalks, restaurants, and even nightclubs that constitute Disney World. Despite the flagrant over-commercialization, the four central theme parks—the **Magic Kingdom, Epcot Center, Disney-MGM Studios** and the newest and most impressive, **Disney's Animal Kingdom**—still rule after 25 years. If bigger is better, Disney World wins the prize for best park in the U.S. by a mile (824-4321, call daily 8am-10pm; http://www.disneyworld.com). That Disney dominates **Lake Buena Vista** (20 mi. west of Orlando via I-4) is an understatement.

The 1-day entrance fee of $40 (ages 3-9 $32) admits you to one of the three parks, allowing you to leave and return to the same park later in the day. A 4-day **Value Pass** ($149, ages 3-9 $119) covers 1 day at each park, plus an extra day at any one of them. A 5-day **Park-Hopper Pass** ($189, ages 3-9 $151) buys admission to all four parks for all 5 days. The **All-In-One Hopper Pass** ($249, ages 3-9 $199), includes 6 days of admission to all other Disney attractions. The "Hopper" passes allow for unlimited transportation between attractions on the Disney monorail, boats, buses, and trains. Multi-day passes need not be used on consecutive days, and they never expire. Parking is $5 per day. Attractions that charge separate admissions include **River Country** ($16, ages 3-9 $12.50); **Discovery Island** ($13, ages 3-9 $7); **Typhoon Lagoon** ($25, ages 3-11 $9.50); **Pleasure Island** ($19, 18+, unless with adult); and **Blizzard Beach** ($25, ages 3-11 $19.50). For descriptions, see **Other Disney Attractions,** below. *Since the prices tend to increase annually, those listed may not reflect the rates you actually pay.* Disney's price inflation rates make college tuitions look stable.

Disney World opens its gates 365 days a year, but hours fluctuate with the season. Expect the parks to open at 9am and close at 8pm; these hours are often extended. The parks get busy during the summer when school is out, but the enormously crowded "peak times" are Christmas, Thanksgiving, and the month around Easter. More people visit between Christmas and New Year's than at any other time of year. The crowd hits the main gates at 10am; arrive before the 9am opening time and seek out your favorite rides or exhibits before noon. During peak periods (and often during the rest of the year), Disney World actually opens earlier than the stated time for guests staying at Disney resorts. To avoid the crowds, start at the rear of a park and work your way to the front. You'll be able to see the distant attractions while the masses cram the lines for those near the entrance. Persevere through dinner time (5:30-8pm), when a lot of cranky kids head home. Regardless of tactics, you can expect a 45min. to 2hr. wait at the most popular attractions.

Mears Motor Shuttle offers transport from most hotels to Disney (see **Practical Information,** above). Major hotels and some campgrounds provide their own shuttles for guests.

Magic Kingdom Seven "lands" comprise the Magic Kingdom. Enter on **Main St., USA** to capture the essence of turn-of-the-century hometown America. The architects employed "forced perspective" here, building the ground floor of the shops nine-tenths of the normal size and making the second and third stories progressively smaller. Walt describes his vision in the "Walt Disney Movie" at the Hospitality

House, to the right as you emerge from under the railroad station. The Main St. Cinema shows some great old silent films and previews of coming Disney attractions. Late in the afternoon, the "Mickey Mania Parade" down Main St. gives you a chance to see all the Disney characters, or to find shorter lines at the more crowded attractions. Near the entrance, you'll discover a steam train that huffs and puffs its way across the seven different lands.

Tomorrowland received a neon-and-stainless-steel facelift that skyrocketed it out of the space-race days of the 70s and into a futuristic intergalactic nation, **XS. Alien Encounter,** the newest Magic Kingdom attraction, chills without spins or drops, creating suspense in pitch blackness—a claustrophobic's nightmare. The very cool indoor roller coaster **Space Mountain** still proves the high point of this section, if not the whole park, in terms of thrills. This is no secret; try to go early.

The golden-spired Cinderella Castle marks the gateway to the mildest of Mickey's regions, **Fantasyland.** Two classic rides, **Peter Pan's Flight** and **Snow White's Adventures,** capture the original charm of the park; the evil Queen scares children like no one else. **Mr. Toad's Wild Ride** takes riders for a carousing spin through the fireplaces and train tunnels of Toad Hall. You know the song, so see what it means at **It's a Small World,** a saccharine but endearing boat tour celebrating the children of the world. Killer A/C makes it a good bet for a hot day.

Liberty Sq. and **Frontierland** devote their resources to U.S. history and a celebration of Mark Twain. History buffs will enjoy the recently updated **Hall of Presidents** (President Clinton makes a cameo, as Maya Angelou narrates), which focuses on our nation's quest for equality. Adventurers should catch the classic, but rickety, runaway **Big Thunder Mountain Railroad** rollercoaster or the truly thrilling **Splash Mountain,** which takes you on a voyage with Br'er Rabbit and leaves you chilled inside and out. Spooky but dorky, **Haunted Mansion** is a classic with a quick line. Entertaining animatronics enliven the **Country Bear Jamboree,** while a steamboat ride or canoe trip gives you the chance to rest your feet.

Adventureland romanticizes unexplored regions of the world in often trivial and tacky ways. The **Jungle Cruise** takes a tongue-in-cheek tour through tropical waterways populated by not-so-authentic-looking wildlife. **Pirates of the Caribbean** explores caves where animated buccaneers spar, swig, and sing. The **Swiss Family Robinson** treehouse, a replica of the eternally shipwrecked family's home, captures all the family's clever tricks.

Epcot Center

In 1966, Walt dreamed up an "Experimental Prototype Community Of Tomorrow" (EPCOT), which would evolve constantly to incorporate new ideas from U.S. technology—eventually becoming a self-sufficient, futuristic utopia. At present, Epcot splits into **Future World** and **World Showcase.**

The 180 ft. high trademark geosphere that forms the entrance to **Future World** houses the **Spaceship Earth** attraction, where visitors board a "time machine" for a tour through the evolution of communications. At the **Wonders of Life, Body Wars** takes visitors on a tour of the human body (with the help of a simulator). **Cranium Command** puts you at the helm of a 12-year-old boy as his animatronic "pilot" steers him around the pitfalls of daily life. **The Land** presents **The Circle of Life,** a live-action/animated film about the environment with characters from *The Lion King.* Fish, sharks, and manatees inhabit the re-created coral reef in **The Living Seas.** The immensely popular **Journey Into Imagination** pavilion screens *Honey, I Shrunk the Audience,* which boasts stellar 3D effects. **Universe of Energy,** sponsored by Exxon, recently opened a new exhibit featuring comedienne Ellen Degeneres, who dreams she is on *Jeopardy* and must answer questions about energy.

The **World Showcase** consists of a series of international pavilions surrounding an artificial lake. An architectural style or monument, as well as typical food and crafts, represent each country. People in indigenous costumes perform dances, theatrical skits, and other "cultural" entertainment at each country's pavilion. Before setting out around the lake, pick up a schedule of events at the **Global Information Station,** located behind Spaceship Earth as you enter the park. Just outside the info station are the **World Key Terminals,** computerized booths that dispense park info and make dinner reservations. Inside the station, live human beings from **Guest Relations** provide handy maps. The people with yellow-striped Disney-logo'ed shirts can answer questions throughout the park. The two 360° films made in China and Canada and the 180° film made in France rate among the best of the attractions; each includes spectacular landscapes, some national history, and an insider's look at the people of each country. **The American Adventure** dispenses a patriotic interpretation of American history. Every night at 9pm, Epcot presents a magnificent mega-show called **Illuminations,** with music from the represented nations accompanied by dancing fountains, laser lights, and an impressive array of fireworks.

The World Showcase pavilions specialize in regional cuisine. At the **Restaurant Marrakesh** in the Moroccan Pavilion, head chef Lahsen Abrache cooks delicious brewat (spicy minced beef fried in pastry) and *bastilla* (sweet and slightly spicy pie). A belly dancer performs in the restaurant every evening. (Lunch $10-15, dinner $14-21.) The Mexican, French, and Italian pavilions serve up excellent food at similar prices. If you plan to eat a sit-down meal in the park, make reservations first thing in the morning at a World Key Terminal, behind Spaceship Earth, or you could end up eating a $4.50 hot dog alongside the rest of the unfortunates. The regional cafes (no reservations required) present cheaper options, but no real bargains. Eat outside "the World" or smuggle stuff in to save your money for Goofy-eared hats.

Disney-MGM Studios

Disney-MGM Studios set out to create a "living movie set," and they seem to have succeeded. Many familiar Disney characters stroll through the park, as do a host of characters dressed as directors, starlets, gossip columnists, and fans. Stunt shows and mini-theatricals take place continually. And, every day, a different has-been star leads a parade across Hollywood Blvd.

The **Twilight Zone Tower of Terror** climbs 13 flights in an old-time Hollywood hotel; when the cable snaps, the fastest ride at Disney begins. And just when you think the ride is over, WHAM! It drops you again. **The Great Movie Ride,** inside the Chinese Theater, takes you on a simple but nostalgic trip through old and favorite films. One of the two biggest attractions at this park, the **Indiana Jones Epic Stunt Spectacular,** lets you watch stuntmen and volunteers pull off amazing moves. The other biggie, the **Star Tours** ride, based on *Star Wars,* simulates turbulence on a space cargo ship caught in laser crossfire. A walking tour through an animation studio unlocks the secrets of cartooning at **Magic of Disney Animation,** where you witness the magic-makers busy at work.

Disney's Animal Kingdom

April 1998 saw the opening of this 500-acre animal park. Because it is brand-new by Disney standards, it hasn't reached the fame (and thus the insanity-inducing crowds) of the other parks. Nevertheless, it might just be the best of the four, offering the kind of creative, elaborate entertainment you've been taught to expect from Disney, but so often fail to find. Animal Kingdom, where you can stop anyone to ask, "Which way to Africa?" without getting a funny look, is divided into five main regions: Camp Minnie-Mickey, Safari Village, Africa, Asia, and Dinoland USA. **Camp M-M** is a little kid's haven for singing and dancing to Disney favorites, while a Mickey greeting area provides plenty of cuddly mouse hugs. **Asia** is half-baked for now; head instead to **Africa,** where the **Kilimanjaro Safaris** site is among the park's main attractions. A jostling ride takes you face-to-face with real animals in 100 acres of faux-natural habitat, with witty narration by your driver and classic Disney adventure when poachers are discovered on the reserve. The **Gorilla Falls Exploration Trail** is similar, requiring walking instead of driving, but significantly less fun: the gorillas are known to hide out in the heat of the day. **Dinoland USA** is the other biggie, containing the exhilarating **Countdown to Extinction,** which rivals Space Mountain as Disney's best ride. Dodge flaming meteorites and ferocious dinos in this swerving, dipping, dark-encased journey. Also in Dinoland USA is the **Boneyard,** where kids can dig in a huge sandpit and uncover the remains of a woolly mammoth. The **Discovery River Boats** of **Safari Village** are a relaxing break from standing. The whole park is arranged around a single focal point, the **Tree of Life,** a towering 14 stories tall, with over 325 animals carved into its roots, branches, and trunk. The **"It's Tough to Be a Bug!"** show within, however, is too scary for kids and too dippy for adults.

Other Disney Attractions Besides the three main parks, Disney offers several other draws with different themes and separate admissions (see p. 366). The newest, **Blizzard Beach,** one of several water parks, was built on the harrowing premise of a melting mountain. Ride a ski-lift to the peak of Mt. Gushmore and take the fastest water-slide in the world (Summit Plummet) down the 120 ft. descent. **Typhoon Lagoon,** a 50-acre water park, centers around one of the world's largest wave-making pools and the 7 ft. waves it creates. Besides eight water slides, the lagoon has a creek for inner-tube rides and a saltwater coral reef stocked with tropical fish and harmless sharks. Built to resemble a swimming hole, **River Country** offers water slides, rope swings, and plenty of room to swim. Water parks fill up early on hot days, so you might get turned away. Across Bay Lake from River Country is **Discovery Island,** a zoological park. **Pleasure Island** provides relatively more sinful excitations after sunset. Disney attempts to draw students and the 30-something set with this hedonistic conglomeration of theme nightclubs—country, comedy, live rock, and jazz. After 7pm, those over 18 can roam freely.

■ Life Beyond Disney

The big non-Disney theme parks band together in competition with Mickey Mouse. "Flex Tickets," their mouse traps for Mickey, combine admission prices at a discount. A three-park ticket covers Sea World, Universal Studios, and Wet 'n' Wild (a water park), and allows 7 days of visiting with unlimited admissions ($100, ages 3-9 $83). The four-park ticket adds Busch Gardens in Tampa and lasts 10 days ($130/$108).

Sea World One of the U.S.'s largest marine parks, **Sea World** (351-3600; http://www.seaworld.com), 12 mi. southwest of Orlando off I-4 at Rte. 528 (take bus #8), makes a splash with shows featuring whales, dolphins, sea lions, seals, and otters. *(Open daily 9am-10pm; in winter 9am-7pm or later. $42, ages 3-9 $36. Parking $5. Sky Tower ride $3 extra. Most hotel brochure displays and hostels have coupons for $2-3 off regular admission.)* While the dolphin show is phenomenal and the **Terrors of the Deep** shark exhibit impressive, it's killer whales Baby Shamu and Baby Namu who still get the big raves. **Shamu: World Focus** continues to thrill with plenty of marine acrobatics executed smartly by a whole family of orcas and their trainers. Sitting in the "splash zone" provides relief on a hot day; try to wear a swimsuit. **Manatees: The Lost Generation** poignantly makes a case for this endangered Florida species; only 2000 remain in the world. The arctic exhibit features white beluga whales—somewhat less athletic than Shamu, but fascinating nonetheless. Penguins, sea lions, you name it, are on display in their nearly natural habitats. The new pride of the park is the water-coaster **Journey to Atlantis.** The line will be long, but two steep drops provide a thrilling ride, and you're sure to get wet. Those stunning **Anheuser-Busch Clydesdales** trot around for viewing (mesmerized tourists in tow). They don't do flips, though.

Cypress Gardens Cypress Gardens (941-324-2111) lies southwest of Orlando in Winter Haven; take I-4 southwest to Rte. 27 S., then Rte. 540 W. *(Open daily 9:30am-7pm; call ahead for exact hrs. $31.50 includes admission for 1 child, seniors $26, ages 6-12 $21.)* The botanical gardens feature over 8000 varieties of plants and flowers with winding walkways and electric boat rides for touring. Hoop-skirted Southern Belles patrol the grounds. Despite all the pretty flowers, the **water-ski shows** attract the biggest crowds and the loudest applause (daily 10:30am, 1:30, and 4pm; times and frequency vary with crowd size). Coupons can be found at most motels. **Greyhound** (800-231-2222) stops here once a day on its Tampa-West Palm Beach run ($12 from Tampa or Orlando to Cypress Gardens).

Universal Studios Florida Opened in 1990, Universal Studios (363-8000; http://www.usf.com; take I-4 to Exit 29 or 30B), is both amusement park and working film studio. *(Open daily at 9am, closing times vary. $42, ages 3-9 $34. Parking $6.)* Rides take on movie themes: **Kongfrontation,** in which a 35 ft. King Kong roughhouses with your cable car, and the **E.T. Adventure** bike ride are hits with the kids. **Back to the Future...The Ride,** one of the staples of any Universal visit, utilizes 7-story Omni-Max surround screens and spectacular special effects. **Terminator 2: 3D** takes you through an apocalyptic showdown with an evil cybertech regime. For a respite from Florida sunshine, step into the all-too-real **Twister,** which puts you 20 ft. from an actual, 5-story tornado, **flying cows** and all. Interactive activities include the hilarious **Hercules and Xena,** in which audience members create special effects and "appear" in an episode of the hit TV shows. **Animal Actors** features the live-action performances of undeniably cute critters, while the **Dynamite Nights Stuntacular** and **Wild, Wild West** showcase death-defying (human) daredevils. Since the park also makes films, celebrity sightings are common. You may recognize a number of Universal's back-lot locations at the park—Hollywood, Central Park, Beverly Hills, the infamous Bates Motel from *Psycho,* and the streetfront from the *Cosby Show.* New in 1999 is **Citywalk,** 30 acres of shops, restaurants, clubs like the Motown Cafe, and live music galore. By the summer of 1999, Universal will present **Islands of Adventure,** adjacent to the existing park. Expect "total-immersion entertainment," like the **Dueling Dragons,** the first-ever dual racing coasters, and **The Amazing Adventures of Spider-Man,** which promises the best of the Back to the Future and T2 rides.

■ Cocoa Beach and Cape Canaveral

Known primarily for rocket launches, space shuttle blast-offs, and **NASA's** enormous space center complex, the "Space Coast" also has uncrowded golden beaches, making it a prime surfing spot, and vast wildlife preserves. Even during spring break, the place remains placid; most vacationers and sun-bathers here are Florida or Space Coast residents.

The Cocoa Beach area, 50 mi. east of Orlando, consists of mainland towns Cocoa and Rockledge, oceanfront towns Cocoa Beach and Cape Canaveral, and Merritt Island in between. **Rte. A1A** runs through Cocoa Beach and Cape Canaveral, while **North Atlantic Ave.** parallels the beach. **Greyhound,** 302 Main St. (636-3917 or 800-231-2222; station open daily 7am-7pm), in Cocoa 8 mi. inland, runs to Orlando (1hr., 4 per day, $13-14); St. Augustine (3hr., 4 per day, $24-26); and Daytona (1¾hr., 4 per day, $15-16). **Space Coast Area Transit** (633-1878) runs North Beach and South Beach routes and makes stops at every town in Brevard County from 8am to 5pm (fare $1; students, seniors, and disabled 50¢; transfers free). From the bus station, a **taxi** to Cocoa Beach costs $15-17. **Yellow Cab** (636-7017) goes to and fro for $1.50 the first mi., and $1.50 each additional mi. The **Cocoa Shuttle** (784-3831) connects Cocoa Beach with Orlando International Airport ($18), Disney World (round-trip $75 for 1 or 2), and the Kennedy Space Center (round-trip $45 for 1 or 2). Make reservations 3 days in advance for airport runs, and 2 days ahead otherwise. The **Cocoa Beach Chamber of Commerce,** 400 Fortenberry Rd. (459-2200; open M-F 9am-5pm), on Merritt Island, and the fabulous **Brevard County Tourism,** 8810 Astronaut Blvd. (A1A), #102 (800-936-2326; open M-F 8:30am-5pm), provide area info. The Space Coast's **area code:** 407.

ACCOMMODATIONS, CAMPGROUNDS, AND FOOD The **Space Shuttle Beach Hostel (HI-AYH),** 1135 N. Rte. A1A (951-0004; 800-909-4776, ext. 65 for reservations), in safe Indiatlantic, is the closest hostel to the Kennedy Space Center and directly on the oceanfront, ½ mi. from a picturesque boardwalk and a prime turtle nesting site in season. (Dorms have 4-6 beds, some with porches. Tons of equipment rental. No curfew. $15.50, nonmembers $18.50; private rooms from $35. Free lockers. Linen $2. Reception daily 9am-8pm.) Across from the beach, the **Luna Sea,** 3185 N. Atlantic Ave. (783-0500 or 800-586-2732), has tastefully decorated rooms with A/C, pool access, and a large continental breakfast. (Singles from $49, reservation rates from $53; Jan. and Mar. $49-56; Feb. $60-70. $5 per additional person.) If you need a place to spend the night between bus connections, walk behind the Greyhound station to the **Dixie Motel,** 301 Forrest Ave. (632-1600), behind the water tower, where clean rooms with floor-to-ceiling windows, tile floors, pastel decor with A/C, and a swimming pool await (singles $40, doubles $45; off-season $45/$50; key deposit $10). Pitch your tent at scenic **Jetty Park Campgrounds,** 400 E. Jetty Rd. (868-1108), across from the beach in Cape Canaveral. (Rustic sites $15, with water and electricity $18.43, full hookup $20.35. Reservations recommended 3 months in advance; essential before shuttle launches.) The **Grateful Day Café,** 6615 N. Atlantic Ave. (783-7330) serves up an international, all-vegetarian menu that's as good as it is good for you. Lunch options include lots of salads ($6) and sandwiches on homemade bread ($4-6) for lunch; dinner brings feasts like mushroom risotto ($9.50) with focaccia and salad. (Open M-Sa 11:30am-3pm and 6-9pm, Su limited hrs. Juice/coffee bar open M-Tu 9am-7pm, W-Th 9am-9pm, F-Sa 9am-11pm, Su 11am-6pm.)

BEAM ME UP, SCOTTY All of NASA's shuttle flights take off from the **Kennedy Space Center,** 18 mi. north of Cocoa Beach. If you don't have a car, you can reach Kennedy via the **Cocoa Shuttle** (see above). The **Kennedy Space Center Visitors Complex** (452-2121) provides a huge welcoming center for visitors and two different 2hr. bus tours of the complex. The **Kennedy tour** takes you around the space sites, while the **Cape tour** visits Cape Canaveral Air Force Station. The KSC also has three IMAX films about the thrills of space exploration, projected on 5½-story screens. *(Center open daily 9am-dusk. Center free. Most tours depart daily every 15min. 9:45am-6pm. $14, ages 3-11 $10. Movie tickets $7.50/$5.50; Crew Passes which include the Kennedy tour and 1 IMAX film $19/$15.)* A fully restored 363 ft. Saturn V rocket stands as the centerpiece of the center's **Apollo/Saturn V Center,** a $35 million, 100,000 sq. ft. interactive museum, dedicated exclusively to the Apollo missions. The **Rocket Garden** and the **Astronauts Memorial,** the country's newest national memorial, also deserve a visit. The **NASA Pkwy.,** site of the visitors center, is accessible only by car via State Rd. 405; from Cocoa Beach, take Rte. A1A N until it turns west into Rte. 528, then follow Rte. 3 N to the Spaceport. With NASA's ambitious launch schedule, you may have a chance to watch the space shuttles *Endeavor, Columbia, Atlantis,* or *Discovery* thunder off into the blue yonder above the Cape. For detailed **launch info,** call 407-867-4636, or write to the Public Affairs Office, PA-PASS, Kennedy Space Center 32899, for a viewing pass.

For those of you who always wanted to go to Space Camp, here's your chance. The **U.S. Astronaut Hall of Fame,** 6225 Vectorspace Blvd. (277-9314), operates the camp and provides hands-on exhibits including the Moon Walk, which lets you bound at one-sixth your body weight; and the 3D 360, a spinning dogfight ride that lets you play Tom Cruise. *(Open daily 9am-6pm, last admission 5pm; extended hrs. in summer. $14, children and seniors $10.)*

Surrounding the NASA complex, the marshy **Merritt Island Wildlife Refuge** (861-0667) stirs with sea turtles, alligators, wild hogs, otters, and over 300 bird species (open daily sunrise-sunset; visitors center open M-F 9am-4:30pm, Sa 8am-5pm). Just north of Merritt Island, **Canaveral National Seashore** (407-867-0677), the northeastern shore of the wildlife refuge, encompasses 67,000 acres of undeveloped beach and dunes, home to more than 300 species of birds and mammals. *(Open daily 6am-6pm. $5 per car. Closed 3 days before and 1 day after NASA launches.)* Take Rte. 406 E. off U.S. 1 in Titusville.

▓ Fort Lauderdale

Fort Lauderdale's gleaming white sands stretch 23 mi. down Florida's east coast, but it is the water that dominates the city's landscape. Often dubbed the "Venice of America," Fort Lauderdale supports an intricate intra-coastal waterway with over 165 mi. of navigable waters. Numerous inlets cut streets in two, making the town home to 42,000 resident yachts and countless water sports. If marine activities don't float your boat, the number two activity in ritzy Fort Lauderdale is shopping, particularly along Los Olas Blvd.

ORIENTATION AND PRACTICAL INFORMATION

North-south **I-95** connects West Palm Beach, Fort Lauderdale, and Miami. **Rte. 84/I-75 (Alligator Alley)** slithers 100 mi. west from Fort Lauderdale across the Everglades to Naples and other small cities on the Gulf Coast of southern Florida. Fort Lauderdale is bigger than it looks—and it looks huge. The city extends westward from its 23 mi. of beach to encompass nearly 450 sq. mi. of land area. Roads come in two categories: streets and boulevards (east-west) and avenues (north-south). All are labeled NW, NE, SW, or SE according to their quadrant. **Broward Blvd.** divides the city east-west, while Andrews Ave. cuts it north-south. The unpleasant downtown centers around the intersection of **Federal Hwy. (U.S. I)** and **Las Olas Blvd.**, about 2 mi. west of the oceanfront. Between downtown and the waterfront, yachts fill the ritzy inlets of the **Intracoastal Waterway. The strip** (variously called Rte. A1A, N. Atlantic Blvd., 17th St. Causeway, Ocean Blvd., and Seabreeze Blvd.) runs along the beach for 4 mi. between **Oakland Park Blvd.** to the north and **Las Olas Blvd.** to the south. Las Olas Blvd. has pricey shopping. **Sunrise Blvd.** offers shopping malls. Both degenerate into ugly commercial strips west of downtown.

Airport: Fort Lauderdale/Hollywood International, 1400 Lee Wagoner Blvd. (call 359-1200 for recorded ramblings; 359-6100 for a human), 3½ mi. south of downtown on U.S. 1, or take I-595 E from I-95 to Exit 12B. Take bus #1 from downtown.

Trains: Amtrak, 200 SW 21st Terr. (587-6692 or 800-872-7245), just west of I-95, ¼ mi. south of Broward Blvd. Take bus #22 from downtown. To Orlando (4¾hr., 2 per day, $28). Open daily 7:15am-9:15pm.

Buses: Greyhound, 515 NE 3rd St. (764-6551 or 800-231-2222), 3 blocks north of Broward Blvd. downtown. *Be careful in the surrounding area, especially at night.* To: Orlando (5-8hr., 11 per day, $35-37); Daytona Beach (5-7hr., 6 per day, $28-30); and Miami (1hr., 25 per day, $5). Open 24hr.

Public Transportation: Broward County Transit (BCT) (357-8400; M-F 7am-8:30pm, Sa 7am-8pm, Su 8:30am-5pm). Most routes go to the terminal at the corner of 1st St. NW and 1st Ave. NW, downtown. Operates daily 5am-10:30pm, every 30min. on most routes. Fare $1; transfer 15¢; seniors, students, under 18, and disabled 50¢ (with ID). 7-day passes ($9) available at beachfront hotels. Pick up a handy system map at terminal. **Tri-Rail** (728-8445 or 800-874-7245) connects West Palm Beach, Fort Lauderdale, and Miami. Trains run M-F 4:30am-8:30pm, Sa-Su reduced operation. Schedules available at airport, motels, or Tri-Rail stops. Fare $2-5.50, discount for children, disabled, students and seniors with Tri-Rail ID.

Taxis: Yellow Cab, 565-5400. Open 24hr. **Public Service Taxi,** 587-9090. Open daily 7:30am-6:30pm. Both charge $2.45 1st mi., $1.75 per additional mi.

Car Rental: Alamo, 2601 S. Federal Hwy. (525-4713 or 800-327-9633). $29 per day, $150 per week with unlimited mi. Must be 21. Under 25 must pay credit card deposit of $50 per day or $200 per week and $20 per day surcharge. Open 24hr.

Bike Rental: Mike's Cyclery, 5429 N. Federal Hwy. (493-5277). A variety of bicycles $20 per day, $50 per week. Some racing bikes cost slightly more. Credit card deposit required. Open M-F 10am-7pm, Sa 10am-5pm.

Visitor Info: Greater Fort Lauderdale Convention and Visitors Bureau, 1850 Eller Dr. (765-4466), in the Port Everglades. Pamphlets galore; particularly useful is the *Superior Small Lodgings* guide, a comprehensive and detailed list of moderate and low-priced accommodations. For published info, call 800-227-8669. Open M-F 8:30am-5pm. **Chamber of Commerce,** 512 NE 3rd Ave. (462-6000), 3 blocks off Federal Hwy. at 5th St. Pick up the free *Visitor's Guide.* Open M-F 8am-5pm.

Hotlines: First Call for Help, 467-6333. **Sexual Assault and Treatment Center,** 761-7273. Both 24hr.

Post Office: 1900 W. Oakland Park Blvd. (527-2028). Open M-F 7:30am-7pm, Sa 8:30am-2pm. **ZIP code:** 33310. **Area code:** 954.

ACCOMMODATIONS AND CAMPGROUNDS

Hotel prices vary from slightly unreasonable to absolutely ridiculous, increasing exponentially as you approach prime beachfront and spring break. High season runs from mid-February through early April. Investigate package deals at the slightly worse-for-wear hotels along the strip in Fort Lauderdale. Many hotels offer off-season deals for under $35. Small motels, many with tiny kitchenettes, crowd each other 1 or 2 blocks off the beach area; look along **Birch Rd.**, 1 block from Rte. A1A, and south along A1A. The **Broward County Hotel and Motel Association**, 2701 E. Sunrise Blvd. (561-9333), provides a free directory of area hotels (open M-F 9am-5pm). The *Fort Lauderdale News* and the Broward Section of the *Miami Herald* occasionally sport listings by local residents who rent rooms to tourists in spring. Sleeping on the well-patrolled beaches is illegal and virtually impossible between 9pm and sunrise.

International House, 3811 N. Ocean Blvd. (568-1615), 1 block from the beach. From the Greyhound station, take bus #10 to Coral Ridge Mall, then pick up bus #72 east, which stops at the hostel. Rooms with 4-8 beds, showers, A/C, cable TV, kitchen, free Internet access, and pool. Dive trips offered for guests with SCUBA certification ($35-70). Passport required. 96 beds. $13; private rooms $30. Linen $2. Key deposit $5. Wheelchair access.

Floyd's Hostel/Crew House, 445 SE 16th St. (462-0631; call ahead). A home-like hostel catering to international travelers and boat crews. 40 beds, 5 kitchens, 5 living rooms with HBO and Showtime, and 8 bathrooms in a tranquil atmosphere. Dorm rooms have 3-6 beds. Free daytime pickup from anywhere in the Ft. Lauderdale area. Free pasta, cereal, local calls, linen, lockers, and laundry. Check in by midnight or call for special arrangement. Passport required. Info available on temp jobs in the area. The owners are engaged thanks to *Let's Go: USA 1995* (ask them for details). Beds $13.50 (discount with stay of 3 or more days); private rooms $28.

Estoril Apartments, 2648 NE 32nd St. (563-3840 or 888-385-2322). Take bus #20, 10, 55, or 72 from downtown to Coral Ridge Shopping Center; walk 2 blocks east on Oakland. A 10min. walk to the beach. Free pick-up from airport, bus, or train stations. Very clean rooms with A/C, cable TV, kitchenette, and free parking. Heated pool and BBQ. Singles $29; mid-Dec. to Apr. $45. 10% discount for students with ID and seniors. Reservations accepted only within 48hr. mid-Dec. to Apr.

Quiet Waters County Park, 6601 N. Powerline Rd./SW 10th Ave. (360-1315), off I-95's Exit 37B; take Hillsboro Blvd. west to Powerline Rd. From downtown, take bus #14 to Pompane Sq. Mall, then switch to bus #95. Fully equipped campsites (tent, mats, cooler, grill) for up to 6 people, all by the lake ("don't feed the gators!"). Normal water sports and see-it-to-believe-it 8-person "boatless water skiing" at the end of a cable. No electricity or RVs. Sites Su-Th $17, F-Sa and holidays $25; primitive sites $17. $20 refundable deposit. Check-in 2-6pm.

FOOD

The clubs along the strip offer massive quantities of free grub during happy hour: surfboard-sized platters of wieners, chips, and hors d'oeuvres, or all-you-can-eat pizza and buffets. However, these bars have hefty cover charges (from $5) and expect you to buy a drink once you're there (from $3). For "real" food, try **La Spada's,** 4346 Seagrape Dr. (776-7893), for the best and biggest subs in southern Florida. The foot-long Italian sub ($7) is an absolute must, as most of Ft. Lauderdale, waiting in line next to you, will agree. (Open M-Sa 10am-8pm, Su 11am-8pm.) In aggressively marine decor, **Southport Raw Bar,** 1536 Cordova Rd. (525-2526), by the 17th St. Causeway behind the Southport Mall (take bus #40 from the strip or #30 from downtown), serves spicy conch chowder ($2.50) and fried shrimp ($7). You can munch on tasty custom sandwiches out on the waterfront patio. (Open M-Th 11am-2am, F-Sa 11am-3am, Su noon-2am. Happy hour M-F 3-6pm, and Sa-Th 11pm-close.) Popular with locals since 1951, **Tina's Spaghetti House,** 2110 S. Federal Hwy. (522-9943), just south of 17th St. (take bus #1 from downtown), has authentic red-checkered tablecloths, hefty oak furni-

FLORIDA

ture, and bibs. Lunch specials run $6-7, while a spaghetti dinner costs $6-8 (open M-Th 11:30am-11pm, F 11:30am-11pm, Sa 4-11pm, Su 4-10pm).

SIN, SIGHTS, AND ACTIVITIES

Fort Lauderdale offers all kinds of licit and illicit entertainment. Planes flying over the beach hawk hedonistic happy hours at local watering holes. Students frequent the night spots on the A1A strip along the beach—emphasis on "strip." You are dealing with the "A1A: Beachfront Avenue" of "Ice, Ice, Baby" fame here; parts of this area have the class and sophistication of, well, Vanilla Ice. This isn't the place for cappuccino and conversation. If you see signs for Jello, nude women may be wrestling in it.

Fort Lauderdale Beach is at its most gorgeous along the beachfront between Holiday Dr. and Sunrise Blvd. **Los Olas Waterfront,** 2 W. 2nd St., the latest on-the-beach mall, boasts clubs, restaurants, bars, and over 20 movie screens to entertain 'til the ocean lures you back. Tour the city's waterways aboard the **Jungle Queen,** located at the Bahia Mar Yacht Center (462-5596), on Rte. A1A 3 blocks south of Las Olas Blvd. *(3hr. tours daily 10am, 2, and 7pm. $11, ages 2-12 $7.50; 7pm tour $24/$11.65, dinner included.)* The **Water Taxi,** 651 Seabreeze Blvd. (467-6677), offers a different way to get around town. *($7, under 12 $3.50. All-day service $15. Call 30min. before pickup. Open daily 10am until they get tired.)* **Water Sports Unlimited,** 301 Seabreeze Blvd. (467-1316), on the beach, rents equipment for a variety of water sports, including wave runners. *($35 per 30min. on Intracoastal Waterway, $50 per hr.; on ocean $45/$60.)* Parasailing trips are $50 (500 ft., 8min. duration), plus a little more if you want to get dipped. Landlubbers can walk among 3 acres of tropical gardens and thousands of live butterflies at **Butterfly World,** 3600 W. Sample Rd. (977-4400), west of the Florida's Turnpike in Coconut Creek (open M-Sa 9am-5pm, Su 1-5pm; $11, ages 4-12 $6).

Several popular nightspots line N. Atlantic Blvd. next to the beach. Hit **Banana Joe's on the Beach,** 837 N. Atlantic Blvd. (565-4446), at Sunrise and Rte. A1A, a tiny little bar on the beach, for happy hour daily from 5-8pm (open Su-Th 7am-2am, F-Sa 7am-3am; kitchen open daily 11:30am-7pm). **Mombasa Bay,** 3051 NE 32nd Ave. (565-7441), on the Intracoastal Waterway, charges no cover but requires that everyone be 21 when there's live music. *(Happy hour daily 4-7pm. Open Su-Th 11:30am-2am, F-Sa until 3am. Reggae nightly from 9:30pm.)*

■ Miami and Miami Beach

Long a popular setting for TV shows and movies, Miami's Latin heart pulses to the beat of the largest Cuban population outside of Cuba. Many small cultural communities distinguish Miami's residential areas: from Little Havana, a well-established Cuban community, to Coconut Grove, an eclectic intellectual enclave turned stylized tourist mecca. Only 7 sq. mi. away, across an arching causeway, nearby Miami Beach's ever-increasing number of hotels accommodate three times the city's usual population. They need to; throngs of visitors join locals from the world over to experience this "Hollywood of the East Coast" in all of its star-studded, bikinied gusto. Wherever you find yourself in Greater Miami, a knowledge of Spanish is always helpful.

ORIENTATION

Three highways criss-cross the Miami area. **I-95,** the most direct route north-south, hits **U.S. 1 (Dixie Hwy.)** just south of **downtown.** U.S. 1 runs to the Everglades entrance at Florida City and then continues as the Overseas Hwy. to Key West. **Rte. 836,** a major east-west artery through town, connects I-95 to **Florida's Turnpike,** passing the airport in between. If you're headed to Florida City, taking Rte. 36 and the Turnpike will allow you to avoid the traffic on Rte. 1.

When looking for street addresses, pay careful attention to the systematic street layout; it's easy to confuse North Miami Beach, West Miami, Miami Beach, and Miami addresses. Streets in Miami run east-west, avenues north-south; both are numbered. Miami divides into NE, NW, SE, and SW quadrants; the dividing lines (downtown) are

Miami

TO ORLANDO

TO FT. LAUDERDALE & WEST PALM BEACH

Miami Gdns. Dr.

N.W. 57th Ave.

N.W. 37th Ave.

Red Rd.

Florida Turnpike

441

860

856

95

817

826

Palmetto Expwy.

N. Miami Beach Blvd.

N.E. 6th Ave.

Biscayne Blvd.

OPA-LOCKA

NORTH MIAMI BEACH

955

Opa-Locka Airport

75

N.W. 138th St.

N.W. 135th St.

Gratigny Pkway (toll)

N.W. 27th Ave.

N.E. 135th St.

W. Dixie Hwy.

922 Broad Causeway (toll)

A1A

817

8th Ave.

N.W. 119th St.

N.W. 7th Ave.

NORTH MIAMI

915

Collins Ave.

BAL HARBOUR

W. 4th Ave.

W. 49th St. 932

N.W. 103rd St.

N.W. 95th St.

95

MIAMI SHORES

HIALEAH

N. Miami Ave.

Biscayne Blvd.

N.W. 2nd Ave.

Normandy Dr. 71st St.

Alton Rd.

Hialeah Park E. 25th St.

Amtrak Station

N.W. 79th St. 934

JFK Causeway 934

Biscayne Bay

MIAMI BEACH

27

9

W. 9th St.

N.W. 37th Ave.

MLK Blvd

N.W. 62nd St.

441

Hialeah Dr.

944

N.W. 54th St.

41st St.

MIAMI SPRINGS

Airport Expwy.

LIBERTY CITY

112

N.W. 36th St.

27

American Police Hall of Fame

1

Julia Tuttle Causeway

195

Miami River

N.W. 20th St.

Washington Ave.

Collins Ave.

A1A

Miami International Airport

Dolphin Expwy.

Venetian Causeway (toll)

Holocaust Museum

836

395

WEST MIAMI

N.W. 7th St.

Orange Bowl

MacArthur Causeway

5th St.

South Beach

W. Flagler St.

LITTLE HAVANA

968

95

Port of Miami

Tamiami Trail

41

S.W. 8th St.

CORAL GABLES

959

9

Cuban Museum of Arts & Culture

DOWNTOWN MIAMI

Fisher Island

972

Coral Way

S.W. 24th St.

1

953

S. Dixie Hwy.

Rickenbacker Causeway (toll)

S.W. 57th Ave.

S. Bayshore Dr.

Vizcaya Museum & Gardens

Virginia Key

Miami Seaquarium

ATLANTIC OCEAN

Univ. of Miami

1

COCONUT GROVE

SOUTH MIAMI

TO FLORIDA KEYS, THE EVERGLADES

Biscayne Bay

Crandon Park

Crandon Blvd.

KEY BISCAYNE

Matheson Hammock Park

Fairchild Tropical Garden

Red Rd.

0   5 miles

0   5 km

Cape Florida State Park

N

FLORIDA

Flagler St. (east-west) and **Miami Ave.** (north-south). Some numbered streets and avenues also have names—e.g., Le Jeune Rd. is SW 42nd Ave., and SW 40th St. is Bird Rd. Minimize headaches with a map that lists both numbers and names.

Several causeways connect Miami to **Miami Beach.** The most useful is **MacArthur Causeway,** which becomes 5th St. in Miami Beach. Numbered streets run east-west across the island, increasing as you go north. In South Miami Beach, **Collins Ave. (A1A)** is the main north-south drag. Equally busy and parallel to Collins are **Washington Ave.** and **Ocean Ave.** The commercial and entertainment district sits between 6th and 23rd St. To reach **Key Biscayne,** take the **Rickenbacker Causeway.**

The heart of **Little Havana** lies between SW 12th and SW 27th Ave; take bus #3, 11, 14, 15, 17, 25, or 37. The **Calle Ocho** (SW 8th St.) lies at the heart of this district; 1 block north, the corresponding section of **W. Flagler St.** is a center of Cuban business. **Coconut Grove,** south of Little Havana, centers around the shopping district on **Grand Ave.** and **Virginia St.** A **car** can be an expensive liability in Miami. Posted signs indicate different parking zones; should you leave your car in a residential zone for even a few moments, you may return to find it towed. Never leave any remotely valuable objects visible in your parked car; automobile theft and break-ins are common.

PRACTICAL INFORMATION

Airport: Miami International (876-7000), at Le Jeune Rd. and NW 36th Ave., 7 mi. northwest of downtown. Bus #7 runs downtown; many other buses make downtown stops. From downtown, take bus "C" or "K" to South Miami Beach.

Trains: Amtrak, 8303 NW 37th Ave. (835-1223 or 800-872-7245), near Northside station of Metrorail. Bus "L" goes directly to Lincoln Rd. Mall in South Miami Beach. To: Orlando (5hr., 2 per day, $29-62); New Orleans (9-13hr., 3 per week, $112-138); and Charleston (14hr., 2 per day, $94-144). Open daily 6:15am-10:30pm.

Buses: Greyhound, Miami Station, 4111 NW 27th St. (871-1810 or 800-231-2222). To: Atlanta (17hr., 9 per day, $82-87); Orlando (5½-7½hr., 12 per day, $33-35); and Fort Lauderdale (1hr., 22 per day, $5). Open 24hr.

Public Transportation: Metro Dade Transportation (638-6700; M-F 6am-11pm, Sa-Su 9am-5pm for info). Complex system; buses tend to be late. The extensive Metrobus network converges downtown, where most long trips transfer. Lettered bus routes A to X serve Miami Beach. After dark, some stops are patrolled by police (indicated with a sign). Buses run daily 4:30am-2am, but your best bet is between 6am-11pm. Fare $1.25; transfers 25¢, to Metrorail 50¢. The futuristic **Metrorail** services downtown. $1.25, rail-to-bus transfers 50¢. The **Metromover** loop downtown, which runs 6am-midnight, is linked to the Metrorail stations. Fare 25¢, free transfers from Metrorail. **Tri-Rail** (800-TRI-RAIL/874-7245) connects Miami, Fort Lauderdale, and West Palm Beach. Trains run M-Sa 5am-9:30pm. Fare $3, $5 per day, $18 per week; students and seniors 50% off. The new **Electrowave** (843-9283) offers free shuttles around South Beach. Runs M-W 8am-2am, Th-Sa 8am-4am, Su and holidays 10am-2am; pick up a brochure or just hop on along Washington.

Taxis: Yellow, 444-4444. **Metro,** 888-8888. Both $1.50 base fare and $2 per mi.

Bike Rental: Miami Beach Bicycle Center, 605 5th St. (531-4161), at the corner of Washington Ave., Miami Beach. $5 per hr.; $20 per day; $70 per week. Must be 18 with credit card or $200 cash deposit. Open daily 10am-7pm.

Visitor Info: The ultra-friendly **Miami Beach Visitors' Center,** 1920 Meridian Ave. (672-1270; http://sobe.com/miamibeachchamber), provides brochures, maps, discounts, and advice. Open M-F 9am-6pm, Sa-Su 10am-4pm. A tourist **info booth,** 401 Biscayne Blvd. (539-2980), downtown outside of Bayside Marketplace, has free maps. Open daily 10am-6:30pm. The **Coconut Grove Chamber of Commerce,** 2820 McFarlane Ave. (444-7270), is open M-F 9am-5pm. **Greater Miami Convention and Visitors Bureau,** 701 Brickell Ave. (539-3000, 800-283-2707 outside Miami), 27th fl. of Barnett Bank Bldg. downtown. Open M-F 8:30am-5pm.

Hotines: Crisis Line, 358-4357. **Rape Treatment Center and Hotline** (585-7273), at 19th and NW 10th Ave. Both 24hr. **Gay Hotline,** 538-3616.

Post Office: 500 NW 2nd Ave. (639-4284), downtown. Open M-F 8am-5pm, Sa 9am-1:30pm. **ZIP code:** 33101. **Area code:** 305.

ACCOMMODATIONS AND CAMPGROUNDS

Cheap rooms abound in South Miami Beach's Art Deco hotels. Finding a "pull-manette" (in 1940s lingo), a room with a refrigerator, stove, and sink, will save you money. In South Florida, many inexpensive hotels are likely to have 2-3 in. cockroaches ("palmetto bugs"), so try not to take them as absolute indicators of quality. In general, high season for Miami Beach runs late December through mid-March; during the off season, when rooms are empty, hotel clerks are quick to bargain. The **Greater Miami and the Beaches Hotel Association,** 407 Lincoln Rd. #10G (531-3553), can help you find a place to crash (open M-F 9am-5pm), and the Miami Beach visitors center (see **Practical Information**) can finagle you the cheapest rates. **Camping** is not allowed in Miami Beach. Those who can't bear to put their tents aside for a night or two should head to one of the nearby national parks.

The Tropics Hotel/Hostel, 1550 Collins Ave. (531-0361), across the street from the beach. From the airport, take bus "J" to 41st St., transfer to bus "C" to Lincoln Rd., and walk 1 block south on Collins Ave. Clean hostel rooms with 4 beds, A/C, private baths, phone, pool access, and a cool outdoor kitchen. $12. Private rooms have A/C, cable TV, and free local calls. Singles and doubles $36; in winter 10% more. Free linen. No curfew.

Miami Beach International Travelers Hostel (9th St. Hostel) (AAIH/Rucksackers), 236 9th St. (534-0268), at Washington Ave. From the airport, take bus "J" to 41st and Indian Creek, then transfer to bus "C" or "K." Central location, but difficult parking. Lively international atmosphere near the beach. Kitchen, laundry, common room with TV (4 movie nights per week). 28 clean, comfortable rooms (max. 4 people), all with A/C and bath. Hostel rooms $12 with any hosteling membership or student ID, otherwise $14; private singles or doubles $36. No curfew.

The Clay Hotel and International Hostel (HI-AYH), 1438 Washington Ave. (534-2988), in the heart of the Art Deco district; take bus "C" from downtown. Great archways in a Mediterranean-style building. International crowd. Kitchen, laundry facilities, TV, A/C. 180 beds, rooms have 4-8; all have phone and fridges. $13, nonmembers $14; private rooms $28-50. Key deposit $5. No curfew. Open 24hr.

Banana Bungalow, 2360 Collins Ave. (538-1951), at 23rd St. along northern edge of the Art Deco district. 180 bunk beds with thatched tiki tops. Free coffee, tea, and toast. Pool, canal access, kitchen, free lockers, linen, and nightly movie at 8pm. $13-15; off-season $10-12. Students $1 discount. Kayak rentals $5 per 2hr.; bikes $5 per day. Free limited parking. Breakfast $2, dinner $4. Reserve in advance.

Sea Deck Hotel and Apartments, 1530 Collins Ave. (538-4361). Basic, cozy, and clean pullmanettes with pretty floral bedspreads open onto a lush tropical courtyard. Pullmanettes $46, other rooms $60. *Let's Go* users get 10% off.

Larry & Penny Thompson Memorial Campground, 12451 SW 184th St. (232-1049), near Metrozoo. By car, Exit 13 off the Florida Turnpike. Pretty grounds with 240 sites in a grove of mango trees. Laundry, store, artificial lake with swimming beach, beautiful park, and waterslides. Lake usually open late May to early Sept. daily 10am-5pm; call 255-8251. Reception daily 9am-5:30pm but takes late arrivals. Tents $8; RVs with full hookup $19, $123 per week.

FOOD

If you eat nothing else in Miami, try the Cuban food. Specialties include *media noche* sandwiches (a sort of Cuban club sandwich on a soft roll, heated and compressed); bright red *mamey* (mah-MAY)-flavored ice cream and shakes; hearty *frijoles negros* (black beans); and *picadillo* (shredded beef and peas in tomato sauce, served with white rice). For sweets, seek out a *dulcería*, and punctuate your rambles about town with thimble-sized shots of strong, sweet *café cubano* (around 35¢). Cheap restaurants are not common in Miami Beach, but an array of fresh bakeries and (if you're daring) fruit stands can sustain you with melons, mangoes, papayas, and tomatoes.

Big Fish Mayaimi, 55 SW 5th St. (373-1770), off Brickell with the huge high-heel gondola in front. Delicious Spanish-influenced entrees, mainly seafood (grilled fish

FLORIDA

for lunch $8, *ceviche* $7) and with decadent desserts like *crema catalana* ($4), right on the Miami River. Open daily 11:30am-11:30pm.

Macarena, 1334 Washington Ave. (531-3440). Dance your way to wonderful, relatively inexpensive food in an atmosphere that's equal parts intimate and festive. *Paella* ($10, lunch $6) and the best rice pudding you'll encounter ($5.50) make for the perfect Spanish treat. Wine comes from their own vineyards. Flamenco dancing W, F, Sa; Salsa Th. Open daily for lunch noon-3pm, dinner 8pm-1:30am, and the sizzling night scene doesn't end until 5am. $10 cover F-Sa from 11pm.

The Versailles, 3555 SW 8th St./Calle Ocho (444-0240). Palatial green and gilt dining room, seemingly packed with Little Havana's entire population. Versailles has served up good Cuban fare for 27 years. Breakfast $3.50-8, sandwiches $3-7, daily specials $3-8. Open Su-Th 8am-2am, F 8am-3:30am, Sa 8am-4:30am.

11th St. Diner, 1065 Washington Ave. (534-6373), at 11th St. A vintage diner with the requisite soda fountain and ancient Coca-Cola clock. Breakfast all day ($5-7), all sorts of sandwiches ($4-6), and grill items. Open 24hr., closed W midnight-8am.

❀**King's Ice Cream,** 1831 SW 8th St./Calle Ocho (643-1842). Tropical fruit *helado* (ice cream) flavors include a regal coconut (served in its own shell), *mamey,* and mango (just $1 for a small cup). They also make tasty *churros* (snake-shaped fried dough, 8 for $1). Open M-Sa 10am-11pm, Su 1-11pm.

La Rumba, 2008 Collins Ave. (534-0522), between 20th and 21st St. in Miami Beach. Noisy fun and huge portions of tasty Cuban and Spanish food. The *arroz con pollo* (chicken with yellow rice, $6.50) is a good bet. Open daily 7:30am-11:30pm.

Flamingo Café, 1454 Washington Ave. (673-4302), near the Clay Hostel. Friendly service, all of which is in Spanish. Grilled beef with pinto beans and rice ($5), *tostones con queso* ($2.75). Lunch specials daily. Open M-Sa 7am-10pm.

SIGHTS

South Miami Beach (or just South Beach), between 6th and 23rd St., teems with hundreds of hotels and apartments whose sun-faded pastel facades conform to 1920s ideals of a tropical paradise. An unusual mixture of people populates the area, including many retirees and first-generation Latins. Gianni Versace's 1997 murder at the hands of Andrew Cunanan drew enormous attention to area, making a fashion mecca of Versace's home. **Walking tours** of the district start at the **Oceanfront Auditorium,** 1001 Ocean Dr. at 10th St. (1½hr. tours Sa 10:30am; $10); 1½hr. bike tours leave from the **Miami Beach Bicycle Center,** 601 5th St. (1st and 3rd Su of each month; $10, rental $5 extra). Call the **Art Deco Welcome Center** (672-2014) for info. The **Holocaust Memorial,** 1933-45 Meridian Ave. (538-1663), across from the Miami Beach Visitors Center, recalls the six million Jews who perished during the Holocaust. *(Open daily 9am-9pm. Free.)* Life-size figures cling desperately to a giant bronze hand reaching toward the sky.

A stroll through the lazy streets of **Coconut Grove** uncovers an unlikely combination of haute boutiques and tacky tourist traps; head shops squat alongside chi-chi cafes. Two shopping malls, **CocoWalk** (444-0777) and **Streets of Mayfair** (448-1700), both on Grand St., dominate the surreptitiously sanitized scene.

On the bayfront between the Grove and downtown stands the **Vizcaya Museum and Gardens,** 3251 S. Miami Ave. (250-9133); take bus #1 or the Metrorail to Vizcaya or Exit 1 off I-95. *(Open daily 9:30am-5pm; last entry 4:30pm. $10, ages 6-12 $5.)* An array of European antiques, tapestries, and art fill this 70-room Italianate mansion, surrounded by 10 acres of lush gardens. Blanketed with oversized ferns and leaves, the **Fairchild Tropical Garden,** 10901 Old Cutler Rd. (667-1651), covers 83 acres and features 16 elaborate flower shows per year, winding paths, a rainforest, a sunken garden, a narrated train tour, and a cafe (open daily 9:30am-4:30pm; $8, under 13 free).

On the waterfront downtown, Miami's sleek **Bayside** shopping center hops nightly with talented street performers (open M-Th 10am-10pm, F-Sa 10am-11pm, Su 11am-8pm). Near Bayside, the **American Police Hall of Fame and Museum,** 3801 Biscayne Blvd. (573-0070), houses more than you ever wanted to know about the "fuzz"; exhibits feature grisly execution equipment, "specialty" cars, and jail cell replicas. *(Open daily 10am-5:30pm. $6, seniors and ages 6-12 $3; discounts at visitors center.)*

In **Little Havana,** exhibits at the **Cuban Museum of the Americas,** 1300 SW 12th Ave. (858-8006), reflect the bright colors and rhythms of Cuban art; take bus #27 (open Tu-F noon-6pm; suggested donation $3). The art of Cuban cigar manufacturing lives on at **La Gloria Cubana,** 1106 SW 8th St. (858-4162; open M-F 8am-5:30pm, Sa 8am-4pm; free). **Carnaval Miami,** the nation's largest Hispanic festival, fills 23 blocks of Calle Ocho in early March with salsa, music, and the world's longest conga line.

In **Coral Gables,** the family-friendly **Venetian Pool,** 2701 DeSoto Blvd. (460-5356), founded in 1923, drew Hollywood stars like Esther Williams and Johnny Weissmuller back in the day. *(Open M-F 11am-7:30pm; hrs. vary in off-season. $4, ages 13-17 $3.50, ages 3-12 $1.60.)* Waterfalls and Venetian-style architecture dress up this swimming hole.

ENTERTAINMENT AND NIGHTLIFE

For the latest word on Miami entertainment, the "Living Today," "Lively Arts," and Friday "Weekend" sections of the *Miami Herald* are logical places to start. Also check out *Oceandrive,* the *New Times,* and the *Sun Post,* all of which come out weekly, for the local happenings. *TWN* and *Miamigo* are the major gay papers. **Performing Arts and Community Education (PACE)** manages more than 400 concerts each year (jazz, rock, soul, dixieland, reggae, salsa, and bluegrass), most of which are free.

Nightlife in the Art Deco district of South Miami Beach follows the Latin rhythms of the area—the party starts late (usually after midnight) and continues until well after sunrise. Gawk at models and stars while eating dinner at one of Ocean Blvd.'s open cafes and bars, then head down to Washington Ave., between 6th and 7th St., for some serious fun. Remember that these clubs have dress codes, and everyone dresses to the nines. **Bash,** 655 Washington Ave. (538-2274), stands out among its neighbors; the large indoor dance floor grooves to dance music while the courtyard in back jams to the ocean beat of reggae (21+; cover $10-15; open Tu-Su 10pm-5am).

Those with dance fever can boogie on Sunday nights to 70s and 80s music on the huge multi-level dance floor of the **Cameo Theater,** 1445 Washington Ave. (532-0922 for show times and prices), at Española Way. The theater also rocks with national acts from Peter Frampton to the Beastie Boys. (Cover $7-10; women free before midnight. Open F-Sa 11pm-5am.) Arrive before midnight to dodge the cover and long lines at the **Groove Jet,** 323 23rd St. (532-2002). The front room of this massive dance hall plays trance, dance, and house, while the back room churns out alternative rock. (21+. Cover $10 after midnight. Open Th-Su 11pm-5am.) For gay nightlife, check out **Warsaw Ballroom,** 1450 Collins Ave. (531-4555 or 531-4499), Miami Beach, where frequent theme nights (such as "bubble bath night") liven up the two dance floors (rarely a cover; open W and F-Su 9pm-5am).

■ Everglades

Encompassing the entire tip of Florida and spearing into Florida Bay, **Everglades National Park,** the third largest national park after Yellowstone and Death Valley, spans 1.6 million acres of one of the world's most beautiful and fragile ecosystems. Vast prairies of sawgrass spike through broad expanses of shallow water, creating the famed "river of grass," while tangled mazes of mangrove swamps wind up the western coast. To the south, delicate coral reefs lie below the shimmering blue waters of the bay. A host of species found nowhere else in the world inhabits these lands and waters: American alligators, dolphins, sea turtles, and various birds and fishes, as well as the endangered Florida panther, Florida manatee, and American crocodile.

PRACTICAL INFORMATION Summer visitors can expect to get eaten alive by swarming mosquitoes. The best time to visit is winter or spring, when heat, humidity, storms, and bugs are at a minimum, and wildlife congregate in shrinking pools of evaporating water. Whenever you go, be sure to bring mosquito repellent.

There are three primary roads into the park, each of which is self-contained and separate from the others. Guarding the eastern section, the main entrance at the **Ernest Coe Visitors Center,** 40001 Rte. 9336 (305-242-7700), sits just inside the park (open daily 8am-5pm). Take Rte. 9336 from U.S. 1 at Florida City; Everglades Park signs point the way. **Rte. 9336** cuts 40 mi. through the park past campgrounds, trailheads, and canoe waterways to the heavily developed Flamingo outpost resort.

At the northern end of the park off U.S. 41 (Tamiami Trail), the **Shark Valley Visitors Center** provides access to a 15 mi. loop through sawgrass swamp that can be seen by foot, bike, or a 2hr. tram. **Shark Valley** is an ideal site for those who want a taste of the freshwater ecosystem, but can't commit to delving too far into the park. (Tram tours Dec.-Apr. daily every hr. 9am-4pm; in summer 11am, 1, and 3pm. $9, seniors $8.10, under 12 $5. Reservations recommended; call 305-221-8455. Bike rental $3.75 per hr., includes helmets. Center open daily 8:30am-5:15pm.) The **Gulf Coast Visitors Center** (941-695-3311), near Everglades City in the northwestern end of the park, provides access to canoes and kayaks entering the Ten Thousand Islands area or the 99 mi. Wilderness Waterway, which winds down to Flamingo. **Park headquarters** (305-247-7272) handles **emergencies.** The park **entrance fee** is $10 per car, $5 bike- or walk-in at Ernest Coe, good for 1 week; the Shark Valley fee is $8 per car, $4 bike- or walk-in; entrance at the Gulf Coast center is free.

ACCOMMODATIONS Outside the eastern entrance to the park, **Florida City** offers some cheap options along U.S. 1. The only option for lodging inside the park, the **Flamingo Lodge,** 1 Flamingo Lodge Hwy. (941-695-3101 or 800-600-3813) offers large rooms with A/C, TV, private baths, pool, and a great bay view (singles and doubles $65; Nov.-Dec. and Apr. $79; Jan.-Mar. $95). **Everglades International Hostel,** 20 SW 2nd Ave. (305-248-1122), located in a 1930s boarding house, shines with a veranda, gumbo limbo trees, freshwater pool, tile mosaic floors and 35 beds in the heart of redlands agricultural community. (10 mi. from Everglades and around 20min. from Key Largo. $10. Canoes, bikes, and snorkel equipment for rent.) A few **campgrounds** line Rte. 9336; all have drinking water, grills, dump sites, and restrooms, but none have RV hookups. (Sites free in summer; in winter $14. Reservations required Nov.-Apr.; call **BIOSPHERICS** at 800-365-2267.) **Backcountry camping** is accessible primarily by boat; some sites are on chickees (wooden platforms elevated above mangrove swamps). The required **permits** are available at the Flamingo (941-695-2945) and the Gulf Coast (Everglades City) ranger stations ($10 for 1-6 people), and reservations must be made in person. Park campgrounds fill rapidly from December to April, so get there early.

Near the northwest entrance, motels, RV parks, and campgrounds scatter around Everglades City. The **Barron River Villa, Marina, and RV Park** (941-695-3331 or 800-535-4961) is an excellent deal, with 67 RV sites, 29 on the river (full hookup $16, on the river $18; Oct.-Apr. $24/$30), and precious motel rooms with TV and A/C (singles or doubles $37, mid-Jan. to Apr. $50). Another campsite rests beside **Glades Haven store and deli** (941-695-2746). Overlooking Chokoloskee Bay across from the Gulf Coast park entrance, the 54 sites have shower facilities, full hookup, cable, a common marina, and a dock. (Tent sites $15, RV $20.)

SIGHTS The park is positively swamped in fishing, hiking, canoeing, biking, and wilderness observation opportunities. *Forget swimming; hungry alligators, sharks, and barracuda patrol the waters.* From November through April, the park sponsors amphitheater programs, canoe trips, and ranger-guided **Swamp Tromps.** Numerous trailheads lie off Rte. 9336; the ½ mi. **Mahogany Hammock Trail** passes the largest mahogany tree in the U.S., and the ¼ mi. **Pahayokee Overlook Trail** leads to a broad vista of grasslands and water. But if you really want to experience the Everglades, start paddling. **Canoe trails** wind from Rte. 9336; the **Nine Mile Pond** canoe loop passes through alligator ponds and mazes of mangrove trees (allow 3-4hr.), while the **Hell's Bay Canoe Trail** threads through mangrove swamps past primitive campsites like **Lard Can.** Rent a canoe at the **Flamingo Marina** (941-695-3101 or 800-600-3813; $8 per hr., $22 per ½ day, $32 per day; $40 deposit) or the **Gulf Coast Visitors Center,** also the departure point for the **Everglades National Park Boat Tours,** a relaxing 1½hr. jaunt (695-4731) narrated by park-trained naturalists, and often featuring **man-**

atee and **bottle-nosed dolphin** sightings. *(Open daily 8:30am-5pm. $13, ages 6-12 $6.50. Reservations recommended in winter.)* These same boat tour people also rent canoes and kayaks (both $25 per day) and can provide fishing guides. The 1½hr. **Sunset Cruise** sails into Florida Bay ($10, ages 6-12 $5), while the **Back Country Cruise** explores the thick mangrove forests of the southern Everglades ($16, ages 6-12 $8). Both leave from Flamingo Marina; call ahead for a schedule. On the Florida City side of the Everglades, check out the **Everglades Alligator Farm,** 4 mi. south of Palm Dr. on SW 192 Ave. (305-247-2628 or 800-644-9711), which will teach you the story of the most successful repopulation of an endangered species ever. *(Open daily 9am-6pm; $7, ages 4-12 $3.)* Over 3000 gators from little hatchlings clambering for sun, to 18-footers clambering for, um, you, grace the premises. The alligator show is a must-see.

FLORIDA KEYS

Intense popularity has transformed this long-time haven for pirates, smugglers, treasure hunters, and others deemed outside the moral order into supreme beach vacationland. Whether smothered in tourists or outcasts, the Keys retain an "anything goes" mentality. When former Key West mayor Tony Tarracino arrived here decades ago, he did a quick inventory of bars and strip clubs, and concluded that he had reached heaven (see p. 385). If this sounds more like hell, you could always take a dive. Millions of colorful fish flash through gardens of coral 6 mi. off the coast, granting relative solitude to scuba divers and snorkelers, and forming a 100 yd. wide barrier reef between Keys Largo and West. Don't believe the hype; sharks are few here.

The **Overseas Hwy. (U.S. 1)** bridges the divide between the Keys and the southern tip of Florida, stitching the islands together. **Mile markers** section the highway and replace street addresses. The first marker, Mi. 126 in Florida City, begins the long countdown to zero in Key West. **Greyhound** (800-231-2222) runs buses to the Keys from Miami ($32), stopping in Homestead (247-2040), Key Largo (296-9072), Marathon (296-9073), Big Pine Key (flag stop), and Key West (296-9072). If you need to get off at a particular mile marker, most bus drivers can be convinced to stop at the side of the road. Tiny Greyhound signs along the highway indicate bus stops (usually hotels), where you can buy tickets or call the Greyhound **info line** on the red phones provided. **Biking** along U.S. 1 across the swamps between Florida City and Key Largo is treacherous due to fast cars and narrow shoulders; instead of riding, bring your bike on the bus.

▨ Key Largo

Past the thick swamps and crocodile marshland of the Everglades, Key Largo opens the door to these Caribbean-esque islands. With 120 ft. visibility, the gin-clear waters off Key Largo reveal shimmering coral reefs inhabited by darting, exotically colorful fish. Explore with care. Twenty feet down, an underwater statue of Jesus (meant to symbolize peace for mankind) blesses all those who explore these depths. Fishing and glass-bottom boats offer recreation without total submersion, though just plain swimming is a treat. Dubbed "long island" by Spanish explorers, this 30 mi. island is the largest of the Florida Keys, but those without a car shouldn't worry; everything lies within a 6 mi. range and off one main street.

PRACTICAL INFORMATION Greyhound (296-9072 or 800-231-2222), Mi. 102 at the Howard Johnson, shuttles to Miami (3 per day, $13). **Mom's Taxi** (852-6000) dominates the cab market ($4 base fare, $1.50 per mi.). The **Key Largo Chamber of Commerce/Florida Keys Visitors Center,** Mi. 106 (451-1414 or 800-822-1088), is stuffed with info (open daily 9am-8pm). **Sexual assault line:** 852-7170. **Post Office:** Mi. 100 (451-3155; open M-F 8am-4:30pm). **ZIP code:** 33037. **Area code:** 305.

FLORIDA

ACCOMMODATIONS, CAMPGROUNDS, AND FOOD The free *Florida Traveler Lodging Guide* and its money-saving coupons await at all chambers of commerce and many a gas station. **Ed and Ellen's Lodgings,** Mi. 103.4 (451-9949 or 888-889-5905), a.k.a. E. and E., offers clean, spacious rooms with cable TV, A/C, and kitchenettes (doubles $55; off-season $45; $10 per additional person). The waterside **Hungry Pelican,** Mi. 99½ (451-3576), boasts beautiful bougainvillea vines, tropical birds in the trees, and tidy, cozy rooms with double beds, fridges, and cable ($50-115; $10 per additional person). Reservations are recommended for the popular **John Pennekamp State Park Campground** (451-1202, see **sights,** below); the sites are clean, convenient, and well worth the effort required to obtain them ($24, with electricity $26). The crowded **Key Largo Kampground,** Mi. 101½ (451-1431 or 800-526-7688), on Samson Rd. behind Tradewinds shopping plaza, manages 170 RV and tent sites plus a heated pool, beaches, laundry, bath house, and marina (tents $20, waterfront $22; RV's $40/$50; $3 per additional person).

The 100-plus beer selection at the family-run **Crack'd Conch,** Mi. 105 (451-0732), can slake any thirst. Entire ice-box key lime pies ($8.75), once called "the secret to world peace and the alignment of the planets," make great chasers. (Open Th-Tu noon-10pm.) The **Italian Fisherman,** Mi. 104 (451-4471), has fine food and a breathtaking view of Florida Bay. Some scenes from *Key Largo* were allegedly shot in this once-illegal casino. (Lunch $5-10, dinner $7-17, $8 early bird special daily 4-6pm. Open daily 11:30am-10pm.) Also reputedly appearing in Key Largo, the star-struck **Caribbean Club,** Mi. 104 (451-9970), a friendly local bar, has recently chalked up still more Hollywood exposure in *Blood and Wine* with Jack Nicholson; the club's docks offer great views of the ocean and sunsets. (Beer $1.50, drinks $2-4. Live rock and reggae F-Sa and holidays. No cover. Open daily 7am-4am.)

SIGHTS The nation's first underwater sanctuary, Key Largo's **John Pennekamp State Park,** Mi. 102.5 (451-1202), 60 mi. from Miami, safeguards a 25 mi. stretch of the 120 sq. mi. coral reef that runs the length of the Florida Keys. *(Admission $4 per vehicle, $2 per vehicle with a single occupant, $1 walk- or bike-in; 50¢ per additional person on all fees.)* The park's **visitors center** (451-9570), about ¼ mi. past the entrance gate, provides maps of the reefs, info on boat and snorkeling tours, three aquariums, and films on the park (open daily 8am-5pm). To see the reefs, visitors must take a boat or rent their own. *(19 ft. motor boat $25 per hr., $80 for 4hr. Deposit required. Call 451-6322 for reservations.)* **Scuba trips** (9:30am and 1:30pm) are $37 per person for a two-tank dive. A **snorkeling tour** also allows you to partake of the underwater quiet. *(2½hr. total, 1½hr. water time. Tours 9am, noon, and 3pm. $24, under 18 $19. Equipment $4.)* If you're up on sailing, ask about the ½-day sailing/snorkeling combo trip, just a bit more costly than the snorkel tour alone (1½hr. water time; tours 9am and 1:30pm; $29, under 18 $24). A **Glass Bottom Boat Tour** (451-1621), which leaves from the park shore at Mi. 102.5, provides a crystal clear view of the reefs without wetting your feet. *(Daily 9:15am, 12:15, and 3pm. $15, under 12 $8.50; discounts at the visitors center.)*

■ Key West

Just 90 mi. from Cuba, this is the end of the road. Key West boasts the southernmost point of the continental U.S. at the end of U.S. 1 and dips farther into the Gulf of Mexico than much of the Bahamas. The island is cooler than mainland Florida in summer and far warmer in winter; the seeker of a year-round tropical paradise in the U.S. can do no better. Key West's tantalizing temperatures once drew writers Ernest Hemingway, Tennessee Williams, Elizabeth Bishop, and the chilly Robert Frost; today, an easygoing diversity lures a new generation of artists, recluses, adventurers, and eccentrics, along with a swinging gay population. Visitors swarm among the "conchs" (native Key Westers), filling the small island to capacity. When it's full, it's overflowing; nightlife is 24hr. (think thousands of Parrotheads in search of Margaritaville).

FLORIDA

ORIENTATION AND PRACTICAL INFORMATION

Key West lies at the end of U.S. 1, 155 mi. southwest of Miami (3-3½hr.). Divided into two sectors, the eastern part of the island, known as **New Town,** harbors tract houses, chain motels, shopping malls, and the airport. Beautiful old conch houses fill **Old Town,** west of White St. **Duval St.** is the main north-south thoroughfare in Old Town; **Truman Ave.** is a major east-west route.

- **Buses: Greyhound,** 615½ Duval St. S. (296-9072 or 800-231-2222). In an alley behind Antonio's restaurant. To Miami (4½hr., 4 per day, $32). Open daily 7am-7pm.
- **Public Transportation: Key West Port and Transit Authority** (292-8161), City Hall. One bus ("Old Town") runs clockwise around the island and Stock Island; the other ("Mallory Sq. Rte.") runs counterclockwise. Service daily 6:35am-10:30pm, about every 1½hr. Fare 75¢, students and seniors 35¢.
- **Taxis: Keys Taxi,** 296-6666. $1.40 base fare, $1.75 per mi.
- **Car Rental: Alamo,** 2834 N. Roosevelt Blvd. (294-6675 or 800-327-9633), near the airport. Over 25 $29 per day, $129 per week; ages 21-24 $39 per day. Must be 21 with major credit card. Miami drop-off free. Open daily 5:30am-9pm.
- **Bikes/Mopeds: Keys Moped & Scooter,** 523 Truman Ave. (294-0399). Bikes $4 per ½-day, $20 per week. Mopeds $18 per ½-day, $23 per 24hr. Open daily 9am-6pm.
- **Visitor Info: Key West Welcome Center,** 3840 N. Roosevelt Blvd. (296-4444 or 800-284-4482), just north of the intersection of U.S. 1 and Roosevelt Blvd. Call in advance for theater tickets or reef trips. Open M-Sa 9am-7:30pm, Su 9am-6pm. **Key West Chamber of Commerce,** 402 Wall St. (294-2587 or 800-527-8539), in old Mallory Sq., dispenses the useful *Gibbons-Humms Guide to the Florida Keys,* as well as a list of popular gay accommodations. Open daily 8:30am-5pm.
- **Hotlines: Crisis Line,** 296-4357. 24hr.
- **Internet Access: Sippin',** 424 Easton St. (293-0555), off Duval. $10 per hr. Open Su-Th 7am-10pm, F-Sa 7am-11pm.
- **Post Office:** 400 Whitehead St. (294-2557), 1 block west of Duval at Eaton. Open M-F 8:30am-5pm. **ZIP code:** 33040. **Area code:** 305.

ACCOMMODATIONS AND CAMPGROUNDS

Key West is packed virtually year-round, particularly from January through March, so reserve rooms far in advance. In **Old Key West,** the beautiful, 19th-century clapboard houses capture the charming flavor of the Keys. Some of the guest houses in the Old Town are for gay men exclusively. *Do not park overnight on the bridges*—this is illegal and dangerous.

- **Key West Hostel (HI-AYH),** 718 South St. (296-5719), at Sea Shell Motel in Old Key West, 3 blocks east of Duval St. Call for free bus station pick-up. Rooms with 4-8 beds, shared bath. Kitchen open until 9pm. $15, nonmembers $18; Dec.-Apr. $17/$20. Key deposit $5. Lockers 75¢. Cheap scuba, bike and snorkel rentals. Reception 24hr. No curfew. Call to check availability or for late arrival.
- **Caribbean House,** 226 Petronia St. (296-1600 or 800-543-4518), at Thomas St. in Bahama Village. Festive Caribbean-style rooms with cool tile floors, A/C, cable TV, free local calls, and fridge. Comfy double beds. Free continental breakfast. Rooms $49 and up; in winter $69; cottages $69/$89. Cottages first come, first served.
- **Wicker Guesthouse,** 913 Duval St. (296-4275 or 800-880-4275). Excellent location on the main drag. The individually decorated rooms have pastel decor, hardwood floors, A/C; some have TV. Kitchen, pool access, and free parking. Breakfast included. Singles or doubles with shared bath $69. Reservations suggested.
- **Eden House,** 1015 Fleming St. (296-6868 or 800-533-5397), just 5 short blocks from downtown. Goldie Hawn lodged here in the film *Criss Cross.* Bright, clean, friendly hotel with lovely rooms. Cool rooms with private or shared bath, some with balconies. Pool, jacuzzi, hammock/swinging bench area and kitchens. Join other guests for free happy hour daily 4-5pm. Rooms with shared bath $85; off-season $55.
- **Boyd's Campground,** 6401 Maloney Ave. (294-1465), at Mi. 5. Take a left off U.S. 1 onto Macdonald Ave., which becomes Maloney. 12 acres on the ocean. Full facili-

FLORIDA

ties, including showers. $28; in winter $33; $ per additional person. Waterfront sites $6-7 extra. Water and electricity $10 extra, full hookup $15 extra.

FOOD AND NIGHTLIFE

Expensive restaurants line festive **Duval St.** Side streets offer lower prices and fewer crowds. Sell your soul and stock up on supplies at **Fausto's Food Palace,** 522 Fleming St. (296-5663) and 1025 White St. (294-5221; open M-Sa 8am-8pm, Su 8am-7pm.) Hemingway used to drink beer and referee boxing matches at **Blue Heaven,** 729 Thomas St. (296-8666), 1 block from the Caribbean House. Today, Blue Heaven serves healthy breakfasts ($2-8), mostly vegetarian lunches ($5-9), and heavenly dinners ($9-19) that include plantains, cornbread, and fresh veggies. (Open daily 8am-3pm and 6-11pm.) The much-agreed-upon best Cuban food on the island can be found at **El Siboney,** 900 Catherine St. (296-4184), where $7 buys a lot of grub. *Paella* and Cuban sandwiches rank among the local favorites. (Open M-Sa 11am-9:30pm.)

Nightlife in Key West revs up at 11pm and winds down very late. **Capt. Tony's Saloon,** 428 Greene St. (294-1838), the oldest bar in Key West and reputedly one of "Papa" Hemingway's preferred watering holes, has been chugging away since the early 30s. Women's bras festoon the ceiling. Tony Tarracino, the 81-year-old owner, enters nightly through a secret door (see p. 385). (Open M-Th 10am-2am, F-Sa 10am-4am, Su noon-2am. Live entertainment daily and nightly.) The **801 Cabaret,** 801 Duval St., is the most popular of several gay clubs along Duval St.

Key West nightlife reaches its annual exultant high during **Fantasy Fest** (the third week of Oct.), as the streets overflow with exotically clad revelers (and accommodations prices skyrocket). The free *Island News* and *Time Out* list dining spots, music, and clubs; *Celebrate!* covers the gay and lesbian community.

SIGHTS AND ENTERTAINMENT

Check out the daily *Key West Citizen* (sold in front of the post office) and the weekly *Solares Hill* (available at the Chamber of Commerce) for the latest in Key West entertainment. Seeing Key West aboard a bike or moped is more convenient and comfortable than driving; alternatives include the **Conch Tour Train** (294-5161), a fascinating 1½hr. narrated ride through Old Town, leaving from Mallory Sq. at 3840 N. or from Roosevelt Blvd., next to the Quality Inn (runs daily 9am-3:30pm; $15, ages 4-12 $7). **Old Town Trolley** (296-6688) runs a similar tour 9am-5:30pm, but you can get on and off throughout the day at 14 stops (full tour 1½hr.; $15, ages 4-12 $6).

The **glass-bottomed boat** *Fireball* (296-6293) cruises to the reefs and back at noon, 2, and 6pm (2-2½hr.; tickets $20, at sunset $25, ages 5-12 $10/$12.50). For a landlubber's view of Key West's marine life, the **Key West Aquarium,** 1 Whitehead St. (296-2051), in Mallory Sq., offers a 50,000 gallon Atlantic shore exhibit, a touch tank, and live shark petting sessions ($7.50, ages 8-15 $3.50; open daily 10am-6pm).

"Papa" wrote *For Whom the Bell Tolls* and *A Farewell to Arms* at the **Hemingway House,** 907 Whitehead St. (294-1136), off Olivia St. *(Open daily 9am-5pm. $6.50, ages 6-12 $4.)* Take a tour, or traipse through on your own among 50 descendants of Hemingway's cats. The **Audubon House,** 205 Whitehead St. (294-2116), built in the early 1800s, houses fine antiques and a collection of engravings by naturalist John James Audubon (open daily 9:30am-5pm; $7.50, students $5, seniors $6.50, ages 6-12 $3.50). Down Whitehead St., past Hemingway House, you'll come to the **southernmost point in the continental U.S.** at the nearby **Southernmost Beach.** A small, conical monument and a few conch shell hawkers mark the spot, along with a sprinkling of hustlers who might offer to take your picture; they may not give your camera back until you pay them. **Mel Fisher's Maritime Heritage Society Museum,** 200 Greene St. (294-2633), glitters with gold and quite a few busts of M.F. himself, who discovered the sunken treasures from the shipwrecked Spanish vessel *Atocha. (Open daily 9:30am-5pm; last film 4:30pm. $6.50, ages 6-12 $2, student and senior discounts.)* A *National Geographic* film is included in the entrance fee. An old pier at **Monroe County Beach,** off Atlantic Ave., allows water access past the weed line, and the **Old U.S.**

Naval Air Station offers deep-water swimming on **Truman Beach** ($1). A paragon of Cuban architecture, the **San Carlos Institute,** 516 Duval St., built in 1871, houses a research center for Hispanic studies, while the **Haitian Art Company,** 600 Frances St. (296-8932), 6 blocks east of Duval, explodes with vivid Haitian artworks (open daily 10am-6pm; free). Sunset connoisseurs will enjoy the view from **Mallory Sq. Dock;** there, street entertainers (including the U.S.'s southernmost bagpiper) and hawkers of tacky wares work the crowd, while boats showboat during the daily **Sunset Celebration.** The crowd always cheers when the sun finally slips into the Gulf.

"Brains don't mean a shit"

This brief profundity sums up the philosophy of Captain Tony Tarracino, gun runner, mercenary, casino owner, and one-time mayor of Key West. "All you need in this life is a tremendous sex drive and a great ego," proclaimed the Captain, who escaped to the southernmost point over 40 years ago while evading the New Jersey bookies he cheated, having used a battered TV set to get racing results before they came over the wire. Tarracino arrived in Key West to find an island populated by bar-hoppers, petty criminals, and other deviants. In this setting, Tony T. thrived; he attempted to organize his local popularity into a political campaign. After four unsuccessful bids, Captain Tony was finally voted mayor in 1989, on the slogan, "Fighting for your future: what's left of it." Although he wasn't re-elected, Tarracino is certain that history will exonerate him. "I'll be remembered," he vows. With his own bar, countless t-shirts that bear his image, and even a feature film about his life, this is no idle assertion. But for now, Tony T. isn't going anywhere—he even mocks his own mortality. "I know every stripper in this town," he boasts. "When I'm dead, I've asked them all to come to my casket and stand over it. If I don't wake up then, put me in the ground."

GULF COAST

■ Tampa

Even with warm weather year-round and perfect beaches nearby, Tampa has managed to avoid most of the plastic pink flamingos and alligator beach floats plaguing its Atlantic Coast counterparts. The city's survival doesn't hinge on tourism; Tampa is one of the nation's fastest growing cities and largest ports, with booming financial, industrial, and artistic communities. While this cosmopolitan flair strips the city of that party-'til-you-drop spunk endemic to Miami, it also makes Tampa a less tacky, more peaceful vacation spot.

ORIENTATION AND PRACTICAL INFORMATION

Tampa divides into quarters, with **Dale Mabry** running north-south and **Kennedy Blvd.,** which becomes **Frank Adams Dr. (Rte. 60),** running east-west. Numbered streets run north-south and numbered avenues run east-west. **Ybor City,** Tampa's Latin Quarter, is bounded roughly by **22nd St., 13th St., 5th Ave.,** and **Columbus Dr.** *Be careful not to stray more than two blocks north or south of 7th Ave. since the area can be dangerous,* even though local police have severely upped their patroling efforts. You can reach Tampa on I-75 from the north, or I-4 from the east.

> **Airport: Tampa International** (870-8700), 5 mi. west of downtown. HARTline bus #30 runs between the airport and downtown Tampa. The **Interstate Express Airport Limo** (580-9329 or 800-268-1343) offers 24hr. service from the airport to the city and to all the beaches between Ft. De Soto and Clearwater ($9). Make reservations 24hr. in advance.
>
> **Trains: Amtrak,** 601 Nebraska Ave. (221-7600 or 800-872-7245), at the end of Zack St., 2 blocks north of Kennedy St. Ticket office open daily 5:30am-10:45pm. To

Miami (5hr., 1 per day, $29-61). 5 buses per day to Orlando if you are connecting there ($22). No trains run south from Tampa. There is no direct train link between Tampa and St. Petersburg.

Buses: Greyhound, 610 E. Polk St. (229-2174 or 800-231-2222), next to Burger King downtown. To Atlanta (11-14hr., 8 per day, $57-61) and Orlando (1-3hr., 7 per day, $14-15). Open daily 6am-12:30am.

Public Transportation: Hillsborough Area Regional Transit (HARTline) (254-4278). $1.50, seniors and ages 5-17 55¢, transfers 10¢. The **Tampa Town Ferry** (223-1522) runs between the Florida Aquarium and Lowry Park Zoo.

Visitor Info: Tampa/Hillsborough Convention and Visitors Association, 111 Madison St. (223-1111 or 800-826-8358), at Ashley Dr. Open M-Sa 9am-5pm.

Hotlines: Crisis Hotline, 234-1234. **Helpline,** 251-4000.

Post Office: 5201 W. Spruce Rd. (800-725-2161), at the airport. Open 24hr. **ZIP code:** 33601. **Area code:** 813.

ACCOMMODATIONS AND CAMPGROUNDS

Budget Host, 3110 W. Hillborough Ave. (876-8673 or 800-238-4678), 5 mi from the airport and Exit 30 off I-275. 33 small rooms with A/C, cable, and pool access. Singles $34; doubles $39; $3 per additional person (rates are year-round).

Motel 6, 333 E. Fowler Ave. (932-4948), off I-275 near Busch Gardens. Big, newly renovated rooms 30 mi. from the beach on the northern outskirts of Tampa. Free local calls, cable, A/C, and pool. 1 adult $36; 2 adults $40; 3rd and 4th adults $2.

Gram's Place Bed & Breakfast, 3109 N. Ola Ave. (221-0596). From I-275, take Martin Luther King Blvd. west to Ola Ave., and then a left on Ola. Named for singer/songwriter Gram Parsons, this eclectic artistic haven features a jacuzzi, lush courtyard, cable TV, BYOB outside bar, and continental breakfast. Some rooms and some weeks of the year have fun (mostly musical) themes, and the motto is always "We are all related." Rooms range from $50-80 depending on availability.

Americana Inn, 321 E. Fletcher Ave. (933-4545), 3 mi. from Busch Gardens in northwest Tampa; from I-275, take the Fletcher Exit west. Clean rooms, some with fridge and stove. Pool and cable. Singles Sa-Su $35, M-F $33; doubles $43/$40; significantly less Nov.-Mar.

The Silver Sands Motel, 415 Hamden Dr. (442-9550), offers studio apartments with a living area and equipped kitchen. May-Dec. $43; Feb.-Apr. $70.

FOOD AND NIGHTLIFE

Cheap Cuban and Spanish establishments dot Tampa; black bean soup, gazpacho, and Cuban bread are plentiful, affordable, and tasty. **Ybor City** houses the best and cheapest food around, but many places are closed Sunday through Tuesday. **The Spaghetti Warehouse** (248-1720), at 9th and 13th St. in Ybor Sq., lets you make your own pasta combinations for lunch ($4-9) and dinner ($7-12); the specialty is baked lasagna, $6.29 at lunch, $8 at dinner. (Open M-Th 11am-10pm, F 11am-11pm, Sa noon-11pm, Su noon-10pm.) Across 9th Ave. from Ybor Sq. sits the historic El Pasaje building, where **Café Creole** (247-6283) features creole entrees (lunch $6-8, dinner $8-18), varying oyster specials, and Dixie jazz hammered out on a vintage piano. (Jazz F-Sa 8:30pm-midnight. Open M-Th 11:30am-10pm, F 11:30am-11:30pm, Sa 5-11:30pm.) Downtown and across from the visitors center, **The Loading Dock,** 100 Madison St. (223-6905), hoists no-frills sandwiches like "flatbed" or "forklift" for $2.25-5.50 (open M-F 8am-8pm, Sa 10:30am-2:30pm). **Skipper's Smokehouse,** 910 Skipper Rd. (971-0666), off Nebraska Ave. in the northern outskirts of town, may look like a heap of wreckage, but don't be fooled—it's a haven for upstart Floridian bands and cheap meals. (Beans and rice $3, clam strip platter $6. Cover $3-7. Restaurant open Tu-F 11am-10pm, Sa noon-11pm, Su 1-11pm; bar closes later.) All the bars and clubs imaginable (and many that aren't) are at Ybor City; a good place to start is the **Green Iguana Bar and Grill,** 1708 E. 7th Ave. (248-9555). It's got sinful appetizers to accompany your drinks, as well as a "leaner lizard menu." Study up for the all-you-

The **Lowry Park Zoo,** 7530 North Blvd. (935-8552), at Sligh, promises a wild time ($7.50, seniors $6.50, children $5; coupon available at visitors center). At the **Henry B. Plant Museum,** 401 W. Kennedy Blvd. (254-1891), in a wing of University of Tampa's Plant Hall, the exhibits include Victorian furniture and Wedgewood pottery but pale in comparison to the museum, a no-holds-barred orgy of Rococo architecture (tours at 1:30pm; open Tu-Sa 10am-4pm, Su noon-4pm; $3).

Downtown, the **Tampa Museum of Art,** 600 N. Ashley Dr. (274-8130), houses a noted collection of ancient Greek and Roman works as well as a series of changing, often family-oriented exhibits. *(Open M-Tu and Th-Sa 10am-5pm, W 10am-9pm, Su 1-5pm. Tours W and Sa 1pm, Su 2pm. Admission $5, seniors $4, ages 6-18 $3. Free Su and W 5-9pm.)* Across from the University of South Florida, north of downtown, the **Museum of Science and Industry (MOSI),** 4801 E. Fowler Ave. (987-6100), features a simulated hurricane every hour on the hour and Florida's only IMAX dome theater. *(Open Su-Th 9am-7pm, F-Sa 9am-9pm. $11, students and seniors $9, ages 2-12 $7.)* The **Florida Aquarium,** 701 Channelside Dr. (273-4000), invites you to mash your face to the glass for a tête-á-tête with fish from Florida's various lagoons (open daily 9am-6pm; in summer, F until 9pm; $11, seniors $10, ages 3-12 $6).

For serious amusement park fun among African wildlife, descend into **Busch Gardens,** E. 3000 Busch Blvd. (987-5082), at NE 40th St.; take I-275 to Busch Blvd., or bus #5 from downtown. *(Open daily 9am-6pm, in summer extended hrs. $35, seniors $31.50, children $29. Parking $4.)* **Kumba,** the largest drop (143 ft.) in the world, will throw your stomach for a loop, while the new "Edge of Africa" exhibit showcases lions, hyenas, hippos and giraffes; trains, boats, and walkways cater to the tamer crowd. Busch Gardens has two of an estimated 50 white Bengal tigers in existence. Inside the park, you can take advantage of the generous **Anheuser-Busch Hospitality House,** but you must stand in line for each of your two allotted beers. You can cool off at Busch's **Adventure Island,** 10001 Malcolm McKinley Dr. (800-4ADVENTURE/423-836-8873), a 13-acre water park about ¼ mi. north of Busch Gardens. *(Open M-Th 9am-7pm, F-Su 9am-8pm; in winter daily 10am-5pm. $22, seniors $20, ages 3-9 $20. Parking $2.)*

Tampa is the place to **"tally me banana."** Banana boats from South and Central America unload and tally their cargo every day at the **waterfront docks** on 139 Twiggs St., near 13th St. and Kennedy Blvd. Every February, the **Jose Gasparilla** (251-4500), a fully rigged pirate ship loaded with hundreds of exuberant "pirates," invades Tampa, kicking off a month of parades and festivals, such as the **Gasparilla Sidewalk Art Festival** (876-1747).

■ St. Petersburg and Clearwater

Twenty-two miles southwest of Tampa, across the bay, St. Petersburg caters to a relaxed community of retirees and young singles. The town enjoys 28 mi. of soft white beaches, emerald bathtub-warm water, melt-your-heart sunsets, and approximately 361 days of sunshine per year. The west coast of the narrow St. Petersburg-Clearwater stretch is made up of one picturesque beach town after the next.

ORIENTATION AND PRACTICAL INFORMATION

In St. Petersburg, **Central Ave.** runs east-west. **34th St. (U.S. 19)** cuts north-south through the city and links up with the **Sunshine-Skyway Bridge,** connecting St. Pete with the Bradenton-Sarasota area to the south. A chain of barrier islands, accessible by bridges and **Gulf Blvd.** on the far west side of town, extends from Clearwater to the south past St. Petersburg. Many towns on the islands offer quiet beaches and very inexpensive motels and restaurants. From north to south, these towns include: **Belleair, Indian Rocks Beach, Madeira Beach, Treasure Island,** and **St. Pete Beach.** The stretch of beach past the Don Cesar Hotel (luxury resort/pink monstrosity recently declared a historical landmark/eyesore), in St. Pete Beach, and Pass-a-Grille Beach have the best sand, a devoted following, and less pedestrian and motor traffic. The town of **Clearwater** is connected by toll bridge to Sand Key in St. Petersburg at the far north end of this island coastline.

Airport: St. Petersburg Clearwater International (535-7600) sits right across the bay from Tampa, off Roosevelt St. **Red Line Limo,** 535-3391. $11.50 per person.

Trains: Amtrak (522-9475 or 800-872-7245). Ticket office at Pinellas Sq. Mall, 7200 U.S. 19 N. Open 7am-9pm. St. Pete has no train station, but Amtrak will connect you to Tampa from St. Pete by bus ($10). Clearwater is inaccessible by train.

Buses: Greyhound, 180 9th St. N. (898-1496 or 800-231-2222), downtown St. Petersburg. To Panama City (8-10hr., 3 per day, $60-64); Clearwater (30min., 8 per day, $7-8). Open daily 4:30am-11:30pm. In Clearwater: 2111 Gulf-to-Bay Blvd. (796-7315). Open daily 6am-8:50pm.

Public Transportation: Pinnellas Suncoast Transit Authority (PSTA), 530-9911. Most routes depart from Williams Park at 1st Ave. N. and 3rd St. N. Fare $1. To reach Tampa, take express bus #100X from the Gateway mall to downtown (fare $1.50). A pink trolley loops through downtown (fare 50¢), and a green trolley runs up and down the Pier (free). A 1-day unlimited bus pass is $2.50, and bikes can now be carried on the front of 'em.

Visitor Info: St. Petersburg Area Chamber of Commerce, 100 2nd Ave. N. (821-4715; http://www.stpete.com). Open M-F 8am-5pm. **The Pier Information Center,** 800 2nd Ave. NE (821-6164). Open M-Sa 10am-8pm, Su 11am-6pm.

Crisis Lines: Rape Crisis, 530-7233. **Helpline,** 344-5555. **Florida AIDS Hotline,** 800-352-2437. All 24hr.

Post Office: 3135 1st Ave. N. (323-6516), at 31st St. Open M-F 8am-6pm, Sa 8am-noon. **ZIP code:** 33737. **Area code:** 727.

ACCOMMODATIONS AND CAMPGROUNDS

St. Petersburg and Clearwater offer two hostels, as well as many cheap motels lining **4th St. N.** and **U.S. 19** in St. Pete. Some establishments advertise singles for as little as $20, but these tend to be very worn down. To avoid the worst neighborhoods, stay on the north end of 4th St. and the south end of U.S. 19. Several inexpensive motels cluster along the St. Pete beach.

St. Petersburg Youth Hostel, 326 1st Ave. N. (822-4141), downtown in the McCarthy Hotel. Bunk rooms for a max. of 4 people with in-suite bathrooms. Common room, TV, A/C. $11 with any youth hostel card or student ID; historic hotel rooms with A/C and private bath for $25. Linen $2. Check-in before 11pm.

Clearwater Beach International Hostel (HI-AYH), 606 Bay Esplanade Ave. (443-1211), at the Sands Motel in Clearwater Beach; take Rte. 60 W. to Clearwater Beach. Or take bus #52 from the airport to Park St. ½ mi. from the hostel and hop aboard bus #80 from Park St. (Clearwater has its own Greyhound station for direct arrivals.) Head to the superb white sand beach, just 2 blocks away, or take a free canoe to the nearby state park, where sports fields and equipment are available for free and bike rental is $5 per day. Kitchen, common room, and pool. $12, nonmembers $13; private rooms with kitchen $28-39. Linen $2.

Grant Motel, 9046 4th St. N. (576-1369), 4 mi. north of town on U.S. 92. All rooms have A/C, fridge, and pronounced country-style decor, including straw hats and lacy curtains. Beautifully landscaped grounds. Pool access. Singles and doubles $30; Jan. to mid-Apr. singles $39, doubles $43.

Kentucky Motel, 4246 4th St. N. (526-7373). A little out of place, but hey…large, clean rooms with friendly owners, cable TV, refrigerator, and free postcards. Singles $25, doubles $28; Jan.-Mar. $35/$38.

Treasure Island Motel, 10315 Gulf Blvd. (367-3055), across the street from a beach. Big rooms with A/C, big fridge, color TV, and pool access. Singles and doubles $38; Feb.-Mar. $50; each additional person $4. Pirates not allowed.

Fort De Soto County Park (866-2662), composed of 5 islands at the southern end of a long chain of keys and islands, has the best camping around. Also a wildlife sanctuary, the park makes a great oceanside picnic spot. 233 palm-treed, private sites, many on the waterfront. No alcohol. $18. 2-night min. stay. Front gate locked at 9pm. Curfew 10pm. All reservations must be made in person either at the park office or at the St. Petersburg County Bldg., 150 5th St. N., #125 (582-7738).

FOOD AND NIGHTLIFE

St. Petersburg's cheap, health-conscious restaurants cater to its retired population and generally close by 8 or 9pm. Hungry night owls should glide to **St. Pete Beach** and **4th St.** If you're itching for crabs, try **Crabby Bills,** 401 Gulf Blvd. (595-4825), near Indian Rocks Beach. Seafood sandwiches run $3-6, while $7 buys a snow crab dinner, with two sides and a hammer. (Open M-Th 11:30am-10pm, F-Sa 11:30am-11pm, Su noon-10pm.) **Tangelo's Bar and Grille,** 226 1st Ave. NE (894-1695), serves great black bean chile pepper quesadillas ($5) and spicy Cuban fare, and homemade key lime pie ($2.50; open M-Sa 11am-7pm, Su seasonally). **Dockside Dave's,** 13203 Gulf Blvd. (392-9399), is one of the best-kept secrets on the islands. The ½ lb. grouper sandwich (market price, around $8) is simply sublime. (Open M-Sa 11am-10pm, Su noon-10pm.) Diner culture is alive with pot pies ($5) and thick shakes ($2) at **Beach Diner,** 56 Causeway Blvd. (446-4747), on the median before the causeway connecting Clearwater Beach to the mainland (open M-Th 7am-10pm, F-Sa 7am-11pm, Su 7am-10pm). **Beach Nutts,** 9600 W. Gulf Blvd. (367-7427), Treasure Island, has fresh grouper ($7.25) and decent burgers ($5), but go for the ambience; the restaurant/bar's newly expanded porch has a spectacular view of the beach, and bands play nightly (open M-Sa 11am-2am, Su 12:30pm-2am). **Majestic Nightclub,** 470 Mandalay St. (461-0042), in Clearwater Beach, parties hearty with DJs and live tunes. Wednesday is ladies' night with $1 drafts. (Cover varies. Open daily 6pm until late.) Clearwater hotels, restaurants, and parks often host free concerts. Free copies of *Beach Life* or *Tampa Tonight/Pinellas Tonight* grace local restaurants and bars.

SIGHTS AND ACTIVITIES

Grab a copy of *See St. Pete* and *Beaches* or the *St. Petersburg Official Visitor's Guide* for the lowdown on area events, discounts, and useful maps. The nicest beach may be **Pass-a-Grille Beach,** but its parking meters eat quarters; **Municipal Beach** at Treasure Island, accessible from Rte. 699 via Treasure Island Causeway, has free parking. **Clearwater Beach,** at the northern end of the Gulf Blvd. strand, is mainstream beach culture at its unspectacular height. Unexpectedly, the Stingray Beach exhibit at the **Clearwater Marine Aquarium,** 249 Windward Passage (441-1790), is hands-on. *(Open M-F 9am-5pm, Sa 9am-4pm, Su 11am-4pm. $6.75, ages 3-12 $3.75. $1 coupon at visitors center.)* **Boyd Hill Nature Park,** 1101 S. Country Club Way (893-7326), "St. Petersburg's precious wonder," is immodest but refreshing (open daily 9am-5pm; $1, ages 3-17 50¢). Visitors finish the day with **Sunsets at Pier 60,** a daily celebration with performers and vendors, or hang out at **Palm Pavilion,** 10 Bay Esplanade (446-2642), an adjacent public beach with free music concerts (Tu-Su 7pm).

If you've got a hankerin' for some melting clocks, the **Salvador Dalí Museum,** 1000 3rd St. S. (823-3767), in Poynter Park on the Bayboro Harbor waterfront, is sure to satisfy. *(Open M-Sa 9:30am-5:30pm, Su noon-5:30pm. $8, students $4, seniors $7, under 10 free. Guided tours.)* The museum contains the world's most comprehensive collection of Dalí works and memorabilia—94 oil paintings, 1300 graphics, and juvenilia from a 14-year-old Dalí. **The Pier** (821-6164), at the end of 2nd Ave. NE, downtown, extends into Tampa Bay from St. Pete, ending in a 5-story inverted pyramid complex with a shopping center, aquarium, restaurants, and bars. *(Open M-Sa 10am-8pm, Su noon-6pm; bars and restaurants open later. Free trolley service from the parking area.)* The renowned **Florida International Museum,** 100 2nd St. N. (800-777-9882), presents eagerly-awaited, captivating exhibits: 1999 begins with "Empires of Mystery," an exploration into the Peruvian, Incas, and Andes civilizations (open daily 9am-8pm; $14, students $6, seniors $13, under 7 free). The **Tampa Bay Holocaust Memorial Museum,** 55 5th St. S. (820-0100), is a new addition to the region. *(Open M-F 10am-5pm, Sa-Su noon-4pm. $6, seniors*

$5.) The core exhibit is divided into 12 areas, covering from pre-war Eastern Europe to the post-war birth of Israel.

If watching brawny men battle ferocious 'gators is more your speed, descend into the **Sunken Gardens,** 1825 4th St. N. (896-3186), home of over 7000 varieties of exotic flowers and plants (open daily Sept.-Dec. 10am-4:30pm; Jan.-Aug. 9:30am-5pm; $14, ages 3-11 $8). **Great Explorations,** 1120 4th St. S. (821-8892), is an innovative, educational museum with hands-on exhibits like the Body Shop, where you can see how your muscles compare to those of others countrywide (open M-Sa 10am-5pm, Su noon-5pm; $5, ages 2 and under free). Speaking of brawny men and muscles, the **Tampa Bay Devil Rays,** 1 Tropicana Dr. (825-3250), have an inaugural season under their belts and are ready to play some baseball (Apr.-Sept.; tickets $7-15).

■ Gainesville

Although Gainesville can't claim the beaches that traditionally draw tourists to Florida, its charm is easy to come by. The University of Florida (UF) lends the town an air of high culture which mingles brilliantly with equal parts bohemian, fraternity, and even Old South. From sophisticated professional theater to stuffed alligators to horse homes, Gainesville and its friendly residents offer a tourist experience that almost anyone would enjoy and almost no one has yet discovered.

PRACTICAL INFORMATION Amtrak (800-872-7245) stops in nearby Waldo, at an unstaffed station at U.S. 301 and State Rd. 24. One train a day runs to Miami (9hr., $29-80) and Tampa (3½hr., $19-38); call the 800 number to make reservations or pay on board. **Greyhound,** 516 SW 4th Ave. (376-5252 or 800-231-2222; station open M-Sa 7am-11pm, Su and holidays 10am-11pm) heads to Miami (9-13hr., 9 per day, $47-50) and Tampa (3-5hr., 5 per day, $27-23). **Regional Transit System** (334-2602) runs trains and buses around the city. ($1; students, seniors, and handicapped 50¢; $2 buys a 1-day unlimited pass. M-F 5am-8pm, Sa-Su hrs. vary, usually 5am-6pm.) **Gator Cab Co.** (375-0313) will shuttle you to the destination of your choice. Witness a stuffed 13 ft. alligator while picking up maps, brochures, information, and kindness at **The Gainesville Welcome Center,** 3833 NW 97th Blvd. (374-5231; http://www.co.alachua.fl.us/~acvacb). **Post Office:** 401 SE 1st Ave. (371-7009; open M-Sa 8am-5pm). **ZIP code:** 32601. **Area code:** 352.

ACCOMMODATIONS AND CAMPGROUNDS There are numerous inexpensive accommodations along 13th St., increasing as you near I-75. Be certain it's not a football or Gator Nationals weekend, or you'll be paying at least double these rates in most any place you can squeeze into. The **Cape Cod Inn,** 3820 SW 13th St. (371-2500), has got decor that will make New Englanders nostalgic, and amenities that Puritans would appreciate. All rooms (singles and doubles $44) come with free local calls, cable, pool, and continental breakfast, and the friendly staff speaks six languages. The **Rush Lake Motel,** 1410 SW 16th Ave. (373-5000), offers large, super-clean rooms with classy wood decor. (Pool access. Free continental breakfast and transportation to local hospitals, UF, and the airport. Singles $38; doubles $45.) **Travelers Campground,** Rte. 1, Box 231, Alachua (904-462-2505), Exit 78 off I-75, behind the Waffle House on U.S. 441, offers child-friendly camping in a wooded site. (60 RV sites, 20 tent sites, pool, laundry, petting farm, playground. 2-person tent with water and electricity $12.50, full RV hookup $19.)

FOOD AND ENTERTAINMENT Gainesville's diverse university population seems to have one taste they agree on: cheap, healthy food. **Cafe @ Books,** 505 NW 13th St. (374-4717), inside a used bookstore, serves vegetarian dishes made from scratch. The hummus sandwich and tofu burger (both $4.25) are local favorites. (Open M-F 10am-8pm, Sa and Su noon-6pm.) **Leonardo's By the Slice,** 1245 W. University Ave. (375-2007) offers basic pastas ($4-6) and beautiful pizzas (slices $2-3), with a cafe that sells breakfasts and treats throughout the day (open M-Th 7am-11pm, F 7am-midnight, Sa 8am-midnight, Su 8am-11pm). Popular with students, **Burrito Brothers Taco Co.,** 16

NW 13th St. (378-5948), dishes up large portions of Mexican fare (dinners under $5; open daily 11am-10pm; take-out only). The **Salty Dog Saloon,** 1712 W. University Ave. (376-5153), serves authentic southern fare from the connecting **Cubana Restaurant** (happy hour M-Sa 3-8pm; Su 1-10pm; open M-Sa 11am-2am, Su 1-10pm). Next door, the **Purple Porpoise,** 1728 W. University Ave. (376-1667), is the most popular college bar on campus, with a dominant, but not daunting, Greek scene. (Open M-Sa 11pm-2am; W and F open until 3am for the dance floor.) Follow your ears to the wickedly hip **Soul House,** on 2nd Pl. and 1st St., off S. Main St. The house is a local secret known for its notorious Beanbag Room. Each room has a different musical theme from jazz to funk; some of the music is live. (Cover $2-3. Open 10pm-2am.)

If you're surprised that the likes of Tom Petty and Sister Hazel hail from Gainesville, then you've never been to the annual **Alachua County Music Festival** (336-8360). The ever-growing festival features 60 bands during the second weekend in October. If you can't wait until October to hear live tunes, head to the **Gainesville Community Plaza,** where bands play every Friday night (shows start at 8pm; free). There's always something playing at the **Hippodrome State Theatre,** 25 SE 2nd Pl. (375-4477 or 331-7200), North Florida's only professional regional theater. The bi-weekly *Moon* and the University's daily paper, the *Alligator,* list local events and nightlife info.

SIGHTS The **University of Florida (UF),** the cultural center of the area, houses its art at the **Harn Museum of Art,** 34th St. SW and Hull Rd. (392-9826). *(Open Tu-F 11am-5pm, Sa 10am-5pm, Su 1pm-5pm. Free. Last admission time 4:45pm.)* The Harn, itself a breathtaking building, displays 5500 multicultural paintings, as well as at least 15 changing exhibitions a year. Catch a unique glimpse of natural history at the **Fred Bear Museum,** I-75 and Archer Rd. (376-2411), through exhibitions of archer Fred Bear (open daily 10am-6pm; $4, ages 6-12 $2.50, families $9). The official natural history site is the **Florida Museum of Natural History** (846-2000), 34th St. and Hull Rd., where 19 million specimens and artifacts reside (open M-Sa 10am-5pm, Su and holidays 1-5pm; free but donations appreciated). For a lesson on the floral side of nature, head to the **Kanapaha Botanical Gardens,** 4700 SW 58th Dr. (372-4981), 1 mi. west of I-75. *(Open M, Tu, and F 9am-5pm; W, Sa, and Su 9am-dusk. $3, ages 6-13 $2.)* The butterfly garden, vinery, and bog garden are a few of the attractions on these beautiful 62 acres; summer visits promise the most color. The nearby **Devil's Millhopper State Geological Site,** 4732 NW 53rd Ave. (904-336-2008), is an enormous sinkhole formed when a cavern roof collapsed. A wooden walkway leads a descent layer-by-layer through 20 million years of Florida natural history (free). **Poe Springs Park** (904-454-1992), just over 3 mi. west of High Springs on County Rd., boasts cold, clear waters and more (open 9am-dusk, admission varies).

Gainesville has its share of the quirky. The **Retirement Home for Horses,** Mill Creek Farm, County Rd. 235-A, Alachua (904-462-1001), houses over 80 equine retirees. *(Open Sa only, 11am-3pm.)* Admission is two carrots, but the horses request as many as you can smuggle in. The **Waldo Farmers and Flea Market,** U.S. 301 (468-2255), sells "everything from blue jeans to green beans" on over 40 acres (open Sa-Su 7:30am-4pm). In the middle of the UF campus off Museum Rd. lies the campus **Bathouse.** Locals traditionally gather at sunset, turning their backs to the alligators in Lake Alice to watch the bats flock out of their house.

■ Panama City Beach

The people in PCB are quick to tell you that this isn't just a hot spring break spot (although it certainly is), and they've got a point; but don't bother coming unless you're ready to have fun, Panama City Beach-style. Suntan lotion is still the perfume of choice along these miles of snow-white beach ("the most beautiful in the world," according to the immodest road-side signs). Families are flocking here in droves, filling bumper boats, roller coasters, and, yes, beaches. Bring your lotion and your best looking suit, even if all you're doing is an academic study of pastel lodgings.

FLORIDA

PRACTICAL INFORMATION After crossing Hathaway Bridge, U.S. 98 splits. Everything centers on Front Beach Rd., also known as the Strip, which runs along the Gulf. To bypass the hubbub, take some of the smaller roads off U.S. 98. **Greyhound** makes a stop at the only traffic light on U.S. 98, at the junction with U.S. 79, and continues on to Orlando (8-11hr., 6 per day, $61); New Orleans (9hr., 3 per day, $25); and Atlanta (11½hr., 5 per day, $40). **Bay Town Trolley** (769-0557) shuttles along the beach, running 6am-6pm (fare 50¢, students and seniors 25¢). **Taxis** run on a grid system; fares increase as you move away from Harrison Ave. **AAA Taxi** (785-0533) charges $1.50 base fare, $1.25 each additional mi. **Panama City Beach Convention and Visitors Bureau,** 12015 Front Beach Rd. (233-6053 or 800-PCBEACH/722-3224), crams visitors with info (open daily 8am-5pm). The **Salvation Army's Domestic Violence and Rape Crisis Hotline,** 763-0706, and the **Crisis and Mental Health Emergency Hotline,** 769-9481, ext. 405, operate 24hr. **Post Office:** 420 Churchwell Dr. (234-9101; open M-F 8:30am-5pm, Sa 8:30-noon). **ZIP code:** 32413. **Area code:** 850.

ACCOMMODATIONS AND CAMPGROUNDS Depending on the time of year and Strip location, rates range from can-do to outrageous. High season runs from the end of April until early September; rates drop in fall and winter. **La Brisa Inn,** 9424 Front Beach Rd. (235-1122 or 800-523-4369), ½ mi. from the beach, has clean, spacious rooms with two double beds, a pool, free cable, and coffee (singles or doubles $45-65). **The Reef,** 12011 Front Beach Rd. (234-3396 or 800-847-7286), next to the visitors center, has large rooms with bright decor, many with bay views. (TV, A/C, pool. Singles M-Th $70, with kitchenette $80; F-Su $95; closed Labor Day to Mar.) **Sea Breeze Motel,** 16810 Front Beach Rd. (850-234-3348), offers small pink-and-turquoise rooms in the middle of everything. Cable, A/C, a pool, and reasonable rates are sure to please. (Single bed for 1 or 2 people $40; off-season $20-30; call well in advance for summer reservations.)

Camp on the beach at **St. Andrews State Recreation Area,** 4607 State Park Lane (233-5140), 3 mi. east of PCB on Rte. 392. Call ahead (up to 60 days) for reservations at this popular campground. All 176 sites are on or close to the water beneath tall pines (sites $15, with electricity or waterside $17; in winter $8/$10). **Panama City Beach KOA,** 8800 Thomas Dr. (234-5731 or 800-562-2483), 2 blocks south of U.S. 98 and directly across the street from the clubs, maintains 114 sites with showers, laundry, and a pool (tent sites with water $20, full hookup $26; in winter $13/$20).

FOOD AND NIGHTLIFE Buffets stuff the Strip and Thomas Dr. along the Grand Lagoon. Bargain hunters should look for signs advertising "early bird" specials, which get you the same food a couple hours earlier at about half the price. **JP's Restaurant and Bar,** 4701 W. U.S. 98 (769-3711), just across the Hathaway Bridge, serves award-winning pasta, seafood, and steak (fettuccini *tutto meri* with shrimp, scallops, and crab $16, lunch $4-7) in abundant portions (open daily 11am-11pm). **The Pickle Patch,** 5700 Thomas Dr. (235-2000), concocts delicious Southern country breakfasts and Greek lunches in an unexpectedly homey atmosphere (breakfast $4-6, lunch $5; open daily 6:30am-2pm). **Captain Anderson's Restaurant,** 5551 N. Lagoon Dr. (234-2225), off Thomas Dr., is renowned for its seafood and panoramic view (dinners $11-$35 for an African lobster tail; open M-Sa 4-10pm).

Cruisers and those who hope to be cruised will find a home on Miracle Mile. The largest club in the U.S. (capacity 7000) and MTV's Spring Break headquarters, **Club LaVela,** 8813 Thomas Dr. (235-1061), offers seven clubs under one jamming roof (Aerosmith and other national acts are no strangers) all night. Wet t-shirt, bikini, and male hardbody contests fill the weekends and every night during Spring Break (no cover during the day; cover $5-15; open daily 10am-4am). **Spinnaker,** 8795 Thomas Dr. (234-7892), has shed its rep as meat market central and now boasts a full service restaurant (fresh seafood $6-19) and even a playground for kids. This enormous, wooden clubhouse on the beach has a happening happy hour daily 5-9pm (open daily 11am-4am). The dollar-lined walls of **Salty's Beach Bar,** 11073 Front Beach Rd. (234-1913), attract a laid-back crowd with nautical decor and live music nightly during the summer. They're famous for their carved-out watermelon drinks. (15 shots for $25; cover F-Sa $3; open 11am-2:30am.)

SIGHTS AND ENTERTAINMENT Over 1000 acres of gators, nature trails, and beaches make up the **St. Andrews State Recreation Area** (see **Accommodations**, above; open daily 8:30am-sunset; $4 per car). **Glass-bottom boat trips** sail to Shell Island from Treasure Island Marina (234-8944), on Thomas Dr. *(3hr. trips at 9am, 1, and 4:30pm. $11, under 12 $6; $3 coupon at visitor's center.)* The **Museum of the Man in the Sea,** 17314 Panama City Beach Pkwy. (850-235-4101), explores the ocean deep. *(Open daily 9am-5pm; $4, seniors $3.60, ages 6-16 $2.)* Daredevils bungee jump, parasail, and scuba dive every day here and explore several wrecks right off shore. **Miracle Strip Amusement Park** (234-5810; open M-F 6-11:30pm, Sa 1-11:30pm; $16), delights visitors adjacent to the **Shipwreck Island Water Park,** 2000 Front Beach Rd. (234-0368; open daily 10:30am-5:30pm; $18, admission to both parks $27). Nearby, **Alvin's Magic Mountain Mall,** 12010 Front Beach Rd. (234-3048), houses sharks and alligators in a 2000-gallon tank (open daily 9am-11pm; sharkfeeding at 11am, alligators at 4pm). **Sea Screamer,** 3601 Thomas Dr. (904-233-9107), is a new favorite, providing an extensive ride on the world's largest speedboat. *(Runs late May to early Sept. 10am, noon, 2, and 4pm; in spring and fall 2 trips per day. $11, ages 4-12 $8.)* At **Gulf World,** 15412 W. Hwy. 98-A (904-234-5271), it's literally always showtime. Check out the Parrot Show, the fire-fighting dolphin, and the lime-light loving sea lions. **Zoo World,** 9008 Front Beach Rd. (850-230-1243), offers a petting zoo, botanical gardens, and endangered animal viewing (open daily 9am-dusk).

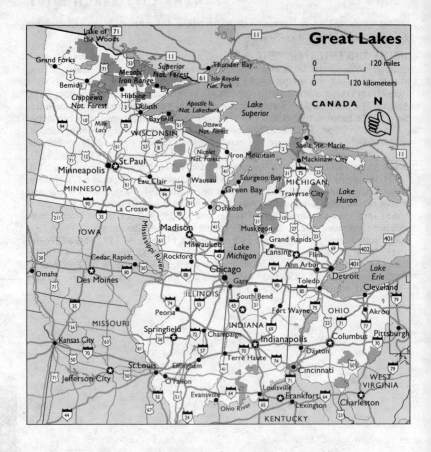

GREAT LAKES

During the Ice Age, massive sheets of ice flowed from the north, carving out huge lake basins. These glaciers eventually receded and melted, leaving expanses of rich topsoil, numerous basin pools, and five inland seas. Together, the Great Lakes comprise 15% of the earth's drinkable freshwater supply and an invaluable network of transport arteries for the surrounding region. Lake Superior is the largest freshwater lake in the world, and its unpopulated, scenic coasts dance with one of the only significant wolf populations left in the U.S. The sports lover's paradise of Lake Michigan boasts swimming, sailing, deep-water fishing, and sand dunes. Lake Erie has suffered from industrial pollution, but due to strict regulations, this shallow lake is gradually reclaiming its former beauty. The first Great Lake to be seen by Europeans, Lake Huron is still the least developed, though not in size or recreational potential. The runt of the bunch, Lake Ontario, still covers an area larger than New Jersey.

The Great Lakes region attracts those who enjoy areas the talons of "progress" never reached. Still, Minneapolis and St. Paul have the panache of any coastal metropolis, while Chicago dazzles visitors with world-class music, architecture, and cuisine.

Ohio

Eons ago, glaciers carved out the Great Lakes and flattened the northern half of the state, creating perfect farmland now patched with cornfields and soybean plants. The southern half, spared the bulldozing, still rolls with endless wooded hills. Columbus sits just north of the abrupt line dividing the regions. The state's other two metropolises, Cincinnati and Cleveland, lie to the southwest and northeast, respectively.

Contrary to popular belief, Ohio is not Iowa or Idaho. It is neither all cornfields nor grimy and industrial. Ohio is innovative, as evidenced by the state beverage, tomato juice—until popularized in Reynoldsburg, a Columbus suburb, tomatoes were thought poisonous and inedible. Ohio's political tradition compliments its strong "middle-America" affiliation; in recent years Ohio has voted with the American majority in national elections more often than any other state.

PRACTICAL INFORMATION

Capital: Columbus.
Visitor Info: State Office of Travel and Tourism, 77 S. High St., 29th Fl., Columbus 43215 (614-466-8844; http://www.ohiotravel.com). **Ohio Tourism Line,** 800-282-5393. **Division of Parks and Recreation,** Fountain Sq., Columbus, 43224 (614-265-7000).
Emergency: 911.
Time Zone: Eastern. **Postal Abbreviation:** OH.
Sales Tax: 5.75%.

■ Cleveland

The city formerly known as the "Mistake on the Lake" undertook an extensive facelift in recent years in an attempt to correct its beleaguered image. The arrival of the Rock and Roll Hall of Fame and a beautiful new downtown baseball park have brought some shine to the previously bleak image of abandoned urbanity. The downtown area is on the verge of flourishing (although many outlying regions remain impoverished), with a new found tourism potential waiting to be exploited. Sadly, the lack of an established budget travel industry has turned Cleveland into something of a siren; its glassy musical shrine rises from the lake to beckon wayfaring sailors before throwing them against the jagged rocks of expensive accommodations.

ORIENTATION AND PRACTICAL INFORMATION

Terminal Tower in **Public Sq.** cleaves the land into east and west. Many street numbers correspond to the distance of the street from Terminal Tower; e.g., E. 18th St. is 18 blocks east of the Tower. To reach Public Sq. from **I-90** or **I-71,** follow the Ontario Ave./Broadway Exit. From **I-77,** take the 9th St. Exit to Euclid Ave., which runs into Public Sq. From the Amtrak station, **Lakeside Ave.** heads to **Ontario Ave.,** which leads to the Tower. Most RTA trains and buses run downtown, and the new **Waterfront Line** accesses the Science Center, Rock and Roll Hall of Fame, and The Flats.

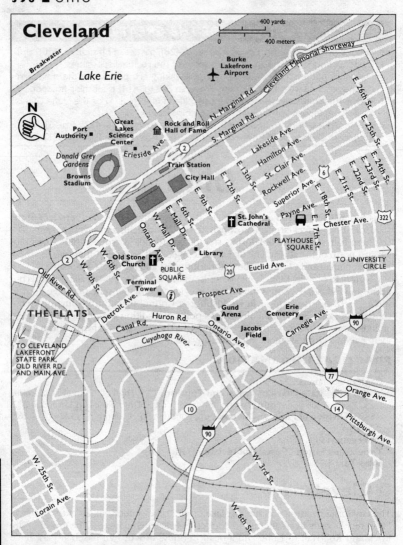

Cleveland

Airport: Cleveland Hopkins International (265-6030), 10 mi. southwest of downtown in Brook Park. Take RTA's airport rapid transit line #66X ("Red Line") to Terminal Tower ($1.50). Taxi to downtown $20.

Trains: Amtrak, 200 Cleveland Memorial Shoreway NE (696-5115 or 800-872-7245), across from Brown Stadium east of City Hall. To: New York City (11½hr., 1 per day, $61-111); Chicago (7hr., 3 per day, $45-82); and Pittsburgh (3hr., 1 per day, $20-36). Open M-Sa 11pm-2:30pm.

Buses: Greyhound, 1465 Chester Ave. (781-0520 or 800-231-2222), at E. 14th St., 7 blocks from Terminal Tower. Near RTA bus lines. To: New York City (8½-14hr., 13 per day, $77); Chicago (5¼-7½hr., 14 per day, $36); Pittsburgh (2½-4½hr., 10 per day, $22); and Cincinnati (4½-6½hr., 10 per day, $39).

Public Transportation: Regional Transit Authority (RTA), 315 Euclid Ave. (621-9500, TDD 781-4271; open M-F 7am-6pm). Bus lines, connecting with Rapid Transit trains, travel to most of the metropolitan area. Service daily 5am-midnight; call for info on "owl" after-midnight service. Train fare $1.50. Bus fare $1.25, express $1.50, downtown loop 50¢, 1-day pass $4; ask the driver for free transfer tickets.

Taxis: Yellow Cab, 623-1550. **Americab,** 429-1111. Both $1.50 base fare, $1.20 per mi. Both 24hr.

Car Rental: Rent-a-Wreck, 8003 Brookpark Rd. (351-1840), in Parma, 16 mi. from downtown. $18 per day.

Visitor Info: Cleveland Convention and Visitors Bureau, Tower City Center (621-4110 or 800-321-1001), on the 1st fl. of Terminal Tower at Public Sq. Free maps and the *Greater Cleveland Official Visitors Guide.* Open M-F 9:30am-4:30pm.

Hotline: Rape Crisis Line, 391-3912. 24hr.

Internet Access: Cyber Pete's Internet Café, 665 Broadway Ave. (439-5328), in downtown Bedford, accessible from I-480 E. $8 per hr., M-F 3-7pm $4 per hr. Open M-F 6am-11pm, Sa 9am-midnight, Su 9am-9pm. Live music Sa.

Post Office: 2400 Orange Ave. (443-4199; 443-4096 after 5pm). Open M-F 7am-7pm, Sa 8:30am-3:30pm. **ZIP code:** 44101. **Area code:** 216; 440 or 330 in suburbs. In text, 216 unless otherwise noted.

ACCOMMODATIONS AND CAMPGROUNDS

With hotel taxes (not included in the prices listed below) as high as 14.5%, pickings are slim for good budget lodging in Cleveland (so-called "budget" motels tend to run at least $80). If you know your plans well in advance, **Cleveland Private Lodgings,** P.O. Box 18590, Cleveland 44118 (321-3213), can place you in a home around the city for as little as $35. (Allow 2-3 weeks for a letter of confirmation. Call M-F 9am–noon or 3-5pm; messages will be promptly returned.) Otherwise, travelers with cars should head for the suburbs or near the airport, where prices tend to be lower. Excellent and friendly, but inaccessible by public transportation, **Stanford House Hostel (HI-AYH),** 6093 Stanford Rd. (330-467-8711), off Exit 12 from I-80, lies 22 mi. south of Cleveland in Peninsula. From Exit 12, turn right onto Boston Mills Rd., drive about 5 mi., then turn right on Stanford Rd. The hostel occupies a beautifully restored 19th-century Greek Revival farmhouse (with kitchen) in the Cuyahoga Valley National Recreation Area. Gorgeous hiking and bike trails await nearby. (Singles and 6-bed dorms. $12, under 18 $6. Linen $2. Laundry $1.75. 7-night max. stay. Check-in 5-10pm. Check-out 9am. Curfew 11pm. Call ahead.) Near the airport and 12 mi. from the city, **Knights Inn,** 22115 Brookpark Rd. (440-734-4500), Exit 9 off I-480, has rooms varying from newly renovated and pristine to slightly grungy (king-size bed $50; 2-bed doubles $55; must be 21). The suburb of Middleburg Heights offers many chain motels at decent prices. **Motel 6,** 7219 Engle Rd. (234-0990), has comfortable rooms with A/C and cable TV (singles $46, F-Sa $56; doubles $49/$62).

The sun never shines on the heavily wooded sites in the heart of Cuyahoga National Park at **Tamsin Park,** 5000 Akron-Cleveland Rd. (656-2859), 25 mi. south of Cleveland in Peninsula (sites $20, with hookup $26; open May-Sept.).

FOOD

Cleveland's culinary delights hide in neighborhoods outside the downtown area. To satiate a craving for hot corned beef, step into one of the dozens of delis downtown. Italian cafes and restaurants cluster in Little Italy, around **Mayfield Rd.** Fine food, cool shops, and a healthy dose of hipness fill the area near **Coventry Rd.** Over 100 vendors hawk produce, meat and cheese at the indoor-outdoor **West Side Market,** 1995 W. 25th St. (771-8885), at Lorain Ave. (open M and W 7am-4pm, F-Sa 7am-6pm).

By the Flats, **Wilbert's Bar and Grille** (771-2583), at the corner of W. 9th and St. Clair, produces culinary concoctions that menace even the self-declared popes of chilitown, including Cherry Bombs (banana peppers stuffed with cheese and chorizo sausage, $5) and Texas Chili ($4). They also offer live music, leading to evening cover charges of $3-25. (Open M-F 11am-2:30am, Sa 6pm-2:30am.) Tommy and the groovy health-conscious staff of **Tommy's,** 1824 Coventry Rd. (321-7757), up the hill from University Circle (bus #9X east to Mayfield and Coventry Rd.), whip up vegetarian cuisine, including a falafel and spinach pie for $5. Hedonistic pagans sock their guts with a Brownie Monster for $2. (Open M-Th 7:30am-10pm, F-Sa 7:30am-11pm, Su 9am-10pm.) **Mama Santa's,** 12305 Mayfield Rd. (421-2159), in Little Italy just east of University Circle, serves Sicilian food in a no-frills setting (medium pizza or spaghetti $4.50; open M-Th 11am-10:45pm, F-Sa 11am-11:45pm).

An Artful Manager

Mike Hargrove, the manager of the Cleveland Indians baseball team, has become something of a local hero. Here are the profound and compelling insights he provides in his "All-Star Tour of the Cleveland Museum of Art:"

On Jackson Pollock: "This is out in left field. I don't know why, but I like it."

On Winslow Homer: "With a name like Homer, you have to give this guy a chance. He sure can paint."

On "Rest," by William Adolphe Bougereau: "This kid looks so real it makes you want to reach out and grab his leg and wake him up."

SIGHTS AND ENTERTAINMENT

Downtown Cleveland offers the aspirations of a new Cleveland, its new attractions producing a self-declared "Remake on the Lake." **The Rock and Roll Hall of Fame,** 1 Key Plaza (781-7625 or 800-493-7655), offers a dizzying exploration through the world of rock music. *(Open Th-Tu 10am-5:30pm, W 10am-9pm. $15, seniors and ages 4-11 $11.50.)* It ostensibly ended up in Cleveland because native DJ Alan Freed coined the phrase "Rock 'n' Roll," although in reality Cleveland was the only place willing to shell out the cash to build the glassy museum designed by I.M. Pei. Listen to hundreds of history-making tunes while reveling in the fashion sense of rock stars, from Jim Morrison's Cub Scout uniform to Elvis's sequined capes. The basement-level exhibition is a delight, although the audio cacophony and multi-media mayhem of other floors can prove overwhelming. Next door, the **Great Lakes Science Center,** 601 Erieside Ave. (694-2000), holds enough gizmos and doodads to make one helluva whatsit. *(Open Th-Tu 9:30am-5:45pm, W 9:30am-8pm. $7.75, seniors $6.75, ages 3-17 $5.25; with IMAX $11/$10/$7.75.)* **Cleveland Lakefront State Park** (881-8141), accessible via Lake Ave. or Cleveland Memorial Shoreway, is a 14 mi. park with a beach that has great swimming and picnic areas (7 mi. from downtown).

Seventy-five cultural institutions cluster in **University Circle,** a mini-Smithsonian 4 mi. east of the city. The world-class **Cleveland Museum of Art,** 11150 East Blvd. (421-7340), exhibits an excellent survey of art from the Renaissance to the present, with exceptional collections of Impressionist and abstract art. *(Open Su, Tu, and Th-Sa 10am-5pm, W and F 10am-9pm. Free.)* An elegant plaza and pond face the museum. Nearby, the **Cleveland Museum of Natural History,** 1 Wade Oval Dr. (231-4600), displays the only existing skull of the fearsome Pygmy Tyrant *(Nanatyrannus)* in all its diminution (open M-Sa 10am-5pm, Su noon-5pm; $6.50; students, seniors, and ages 5-17 $4). The lovely gardens of the **Cleveland Botanical Garden,** 11030 E. Boulevard (721-1600), provide a pacific respite from the urban decay that characterizes Euclid Ave. and Carnegie St. (These areas can get a little rough, although University Circle itself tends to be fairly safe.) The **Cleveland Orchestra,** one of the nation's best, bows, plucks, and blows in University Circle at **Severance Hall,** 11001 Euclid Ave. (231-7300). *(Tickets from $12. Box office open M-F 9am-5pm.)* In summer, the orchestra moves to **Blossom Music Center,** 1145 W. Steels Corners Rd. (330-920-8040), Cuyahoga Falls, about 45min. south (lawn seating $13-15).

NIGHTLIFE AND ENTERTAINMENT

The once hapless **Cleveland Indians** (420-4200) hammer the hardball at **Jacobs Field,** 2401 Ontario St., one of America's most acclaimed ballparks. Games have sold out for four straight years, so your best bet is a **stadium tour.** (May-Sept. every 30min. M-Sa 10am-2pm, Su noon-2:30pm. $5, seniors and under 14 $3.) The **Cleveland Cavaliers** (420-2000) shoot the rock at **Gund Arena,** 1 Center Ct. (Sept.-Apr.), but not as well as their female counterparts, the WNBA **Cleveland Rockers** (June-Aug.).

Playhouse Square Center, 1519 Euclid Ave. (771-4444), a 10min. walk east of Terminal Tower, is the third-largest performing arts center in the nation. Inside, the **State Theater** hosts the **Cleveland Opera** (575-0900) and the famous **Cleveland Ballet** (621-2260) from October through June.

The *Downtown Tab*, a free, bi-weekly city paper, recently proposed that Cleveland offer the following greeting for visitors: "Welcome to Cleveland—we close at 6." And they don't mean 6am. A great deal of Cleveland's nightlife is focused in the **Flats,** the former industrial core of the city, which lies along both banks of the Cuyahoga River. For up-to-date info on clubs and bands, pick up a copy of the *Downtown Tab* or the *Free Times*. The gay and lesbian crowd will want to check out the *Gay People's Chronicle* or the bi-weekly *Out lines,* available at gay clubs and some bookstores.

Numerous nightclubs and restaurants, some with a family atmosphere, dot the northernmost section of the Flats, overpopulating Old River Rd. and W. 6th St., just west of Public Sq. The nightclubs in this area are remarkably similar, offering a late-twenty-something crowd a place to get down to booty jams and to get trashed while dancing to those sweet 70s and 80s "greatest hits" albums. The **Have a Nice Day Café,** 1096 Old River Rd. (241-2451), produces a swingin' 70s dance scene under the gaze of the figures on a mural presenting such central cultural figures as KISS, Richard Nixon, and Archie Bunker (cover F-Sa $3). **6th St. Under,** 1266 W. 6th St. (589-9313), will revive you with jazz and R&B jam sessions in one of the most chill downtown night venues (no cover Tu-Th, F-Sa $6; open Tu-Th 7pm-1am, F-Sa 7pm-2:30am). Gays and lesbians plot a course to **The Grid,** 1281 W. 9th St. (623-0113). Come to relax in the comfortable bar (decorated with male strippers W and Sa nights and Su day) and stay for the high-tech dance floor (open Su-Th 4pm-2:30am, F-Sa 4pm-3:15am). Hard-core rockers should steer clear of the Flats and head for Coventry, where the **Grog Shop,** 1765 Coventry Rd. (321-5588), brings in local and national acts.

■ Near Cleveland

Recently declared "best amusement park in the world" by *Amusement Today,* **Cedar Point Amusement Park** (419-627-2350 or 800-237-8386), off U.S. 6, 65 mi. west of Cleveland in **Sandusky,** earns superlatives. *(Open mid-May Su-Th 10am-7pm, F-Sa 10am-10pm; June daily 10am-10pm; July-Aug. M-F and Su 10am-10pm, Sa 10am-midnight; Sept. to early Oct. Sa-Su 10am-10pm. $32, seniors $17, children under 4 or shorter than 48 in. $7. Parking $6.)* Basically, it's the bomb. Twelve rollercoasters, from the world's highest and fastest inverted rollercoasters (riders are suspended from above) to a "training coaster" for kids, offer a grand old adrenaline rush for all. Stick around for the patriotic laser light show, which takes to the sky on summer nights at 10pm. The Lake Erie Coast around Sandusky is lined with numerous 50s-era roadside "amusements." **Train-O-Rama,** 6732 E. Harbor Rd. (419-734-5856), in Marblehead, consists of 1½ mi. of track through a miniature landscape with towns, villages, ski slopes, waterfalls, airports, monorails, and more. *(Open M-Sa 10am-6pm, Su 1-6pm; early Sept. to late May M-Sa 11am-5pm, Su 1-5pm. $4, seniors $3.50, ages 4-11 $3.)*

Sea World, 1100 Sea World Dr. (562-8101), 30 mi. south of Cleveland off Rte. 43 in Aurora, presents Shark Encounter—a sequel to the less menacing Penguin Encounter—along with many other aquatic exhibits. *(Open early June to late Aug. daily 10am-11pm; late May and late Aug. daily and in early Sept. Sa-Su 10am-7pm. $29, ages 3-11 $21. Parking $4.)*

Innovative juices flow at **Inventure Place** and the **National Inventor's Hall of Fame,** 221 S. Broadway (762-6565 or 800-968-4332), 35 mi. south of Cleveland in Akron. *(Open M-Sa 9am-5pm, Su noon-5pm; Sept.-Mar. W-Sa 9am-5pm, Su noon-5pm. $7.50, seniors and ages 3-17 $6.)*

Are you ready for some football? The **Pro Football Hall of Fame,** 2121 George Halas Dr. NW (330-456-8207), 60 mi. south of Cleveland in Canton, honors the pigskin greats. *(Open daily 9am-8pm; early Sept. to late May 9am-5pm. $9, seniors $6, ages 6-14 $4.)* Gridiron exhibits include a dramatic rotating movie theater and the jersey and helmet of that guy recently acquitted for murder; take Exit 107A from I-77.

▓ Columbus

Rapid growth, a huge suburban sprawl, and some gerrymandering have recently pushed Columbus's population beyond that of Cincinnati or Cleveland. The main drag, High St., heads north from the towering office complexes of downtown

GREAT LAKES

Dave Thomas: An American Beefcake

When R. David Thomas was a boy, he held the cartoon character Wimpy close to his heart. A mainstay on the Popeye show, Wimpy spent every episode gobbling hamburgers as if they were tiny, bite-size snacks. In doing so, he cut an inspiring figure for the future fast-food entrepreneur. Born in 1932, Dave Thomas spent his early childhood in Atlantic City, dropping out of high school in 10th grade to chase his culinary dreams. In 1969, he opened the **first Wendy's restaurant,** in Columbus. From there, the freckled face and red pigtails of his daughter spread across the U.S. like a midwest prairie fire. Today, Wendy's is an international fast-food chain, and Dave Thomas is a multimillionaire who enjoys eating in his own commercials. Yet unlike many of his silver spoon-fed buddies, Thomas hasn't forgotten his humble beginnings and still loves to play the part of Wimpy, slipping out of board meetings and gold games to devour a quick burger…or three.

through the lively galleries in the Short North. It ends in the collegiate cool of Ohio State University (OSU), the largest university in the country with over 60,000 students. Columbus is America without glitz, smog, pretension, or fame—the clean, wholesome land of *Family Ties.* (Bexley, a Columbus suburb, was the model for the hit sitcom's setting.)

PRACTICAL INFORMATION Port Columbus International Airport (239-4000) is just off Rte. 317 and Broad St. on the city's northwest side. Take the Broad St. bus or a taxi (about $17). **Greyhound,** 111 E. Town St. (221-2389 or 800-231-2222), offers service from downtown to Cincinnati (2hr., 11 per day, $12); Cleveland (3hr., 13 per day, $17); and Chicago (7-10hr., 6 per day, $44). The **Central Ohio Transit Authority (COTA),** 177 S. High St. (228-1776; open M-F 6am-8pm, Sa-Su 8am-6pm), runs in-town transportation until 11pm or midnight depending on the route (fare $1.10, express $1.50). For a taxi, call **Yellow Cab,** 444-4444. The **Greater Columbus Visitors Center** (221-2489 or 800-345-4386) is on the 2nd fl. of **City Center Mall,** 111 S. 3rd St., downtown. **Internet access** is available at Union Station Cafe and Gallery (see **Entertainment and Nightlife,** below). **Post Office:** 200 N. High St. (228-2816). **ZIP code:** 43202. **Area code:** 614.

ACCOMMODATIONS AND FOOD The **Heart of Ohio Hostel (HI-AYH),** 95 E. 12th Ave. (2947157), 1 block from OSU, offers quality facilities, including a piano, TV, and a well-equipped kitchen in a Frank Lloyd Wright-esque house. The management bestows a free night's stay on anyone who puts on a 1hr. concert ($12, nonmembers $15; weekly rates available; check-in 5-10pm). **Motel 6,** 5910 Scarborough Dr. (755-2250 or 800-466-8356), 20min. from downtown off I-70 at Exit 110A, has sensible prices and clean rooms (singles $36-40, $6 per extra adult). If arriving at night, look for cheap motels on the outskirts of the city, where **I-70** and **I-71** meet **I-270.**

Happy customers found the white pizza ($8) at **Lost Planet Pizza and Pasta,** 680 N. High St. (228-6191), in the Short North area. With inventive and classic topping combos on 'zas, this planet offers "lo-fat, no-fat, and lotsa fat" fare. (Open M-Th 11am-3pm and 5-10pm, F 11am-3pm and 5-11pm, Sa noon-3pm and 5-11pm, Su 3-9pm.) **Kahiki,** 3583 E. Broad St. (237-5425), serves up delectable Polynesian and Chinese platters in such fantastically tacky surroundings that it has become a national historic landmark (open M-Th 11:30am-10pm, F-Sa 11:30am-11pm, Su 4:30-10pm).

High St. features scads of tasty budget restaurants. **Bernie's Bagels and Deli,** 1896 N. High St. (291-3448), offers a variety of sandwiches ($3-5) in a dark punk-rock cellar atmosphere. (Open M 8am-1am, Tu-F 8am-2am, Sa 9:30am-2am, Su 9:30am-1am; shorter hrs. in summer.) A small and well-loved Middle Eastern restaurant/grocery, **Firdous,** 1538 N. High St. (299-1844), dishes up tasty hummus plates ($5), fresh falafel, and shish kebabs (open M-Sa 10am-9pm, Su noon-8pm).

SIGHTS Ohio State University (OSU) rests 2 mi. north of downtown. On campus, the architecturally impressive **Wexner Center for the Arts** (292-3535), on N. High St. at 15th Ave., houses avant-garde exhibits and films, and hosts progressive music, dance, and other performances. *(Ticket and information center open M 10am-4pm, Tu-W and F-Su 10am-6pm, Th 10am-9pm. Exhibits open Tu-Su 10am-6pm and Th 10am-9pm; $3, students and seniors $2. Free Th 5-9pm. Wheelchair access.)*

In 1991, the **Columbus Museum of Art,** 480 E. Broad St. (221-6801), acquired the Sirak Collection of Impressionist and European Modernist works. *(Open Tu-W and F-Su 10am-5:30pm, Th 10am-8:30pm. $3, seniors and students $2; free Th 5:30-8:30pm.)* Fire, water, explosions, nylon mittens, uranium, and kids mean good ol' fun at the **Center of Science and Industry (COSI),** 280 E. Broad St. (288-COSI/2674), ½ mi. west of I-71 between 5th and Grant. *(Open M-Sa 10am-5pm, Su noon-5:30pm. $8, students and seniors $7, ages 2-12 $6. Wheelchair access.)* Across the street is the very first link in the **Wendy's** restaurant chain. Just east, James Thurber's childhood home, the **Thurber House,** 77 Jefferson Ave. (464-1032), off E. Broad just west of I-71, is decorated with cartoons by the famous author and *New Yorker* cartoonist (open daily noon-4pm; free; guided tours on Su $2, students and seniors $1.50).

The sprawling **Franklin Park Conservatory,** 1777 E. Broad St. (645-5926), has a towering collection of self-contained plant environments including rain forests, deserts, and Himalayan mountains. *(Open Tu-Su 10am-5pm. $5, students and seniors $3.50, ages 2-12 $2; tour booklet $2.)*

South of Capitol Sq., the **German Village,** first settled in 1843, is now the largest privately funded historical restoration in the U.S., full of stately brick homes and old-style beer halls. At **Schmidt's Sausage Haus,** 240 E. Kossuth St. (444-5050), oom-pah bands Schnickel-Fritz, Schnapps, and Squeezin' 'n' Wheezin' lead polkas at 7pm. *(Polkas Tu-Sa. Open Su-M 11am-9pm, Tu-Th 11am-10pm, F-Sa 11am-11pm.)* Between dances, *liederhosen*-clad servers will bring you an $8 plate of homemade sausage. You can fill up on the free samples alone at **Schmidt's Fudge Haus** (444-9217), 1 block west of the Sausage Haus (open M-W 11:30am-7pm, Th-Sa 11am-8pm, Su noon-6pm). On the last Sunday in June, visitors can tour everything in the village. The **German Village Society Meeting Haus,** 588 S. 3rd St. (221-8888; open M-F 9am-4pm, Sa 10am-2pm, Su noon-4pm), knows all. The real event of the year is **Oktoberfest** (224-4300), held on S. Grant at E. Livingston Ave., where three stages provide continuous entertainment (polka and beyond), while 75,000 visitors wander among craft vendors, rides, and beer-, wine-, and schnapps-tasting tents (Sept. 10-12, 1999; $4-5).

ENTERTAINMENT AND NIGHTLIFE Four free weekly papers—*The Other Paper, Columbus Alive, The Guardian,* and *Moo*—available in many shops and restaurants, list arts and entertainment options. The **Clippers** (462-5250), AAA affiliate of the NY Yankees, swing away from April to early September (tickets $3-6.50). For an evening with fewer peanut shells, Columbus's roaming art party known as **The Gallery Hop** happens the first Saturday of every month; galleries in the Short North (the region between college town and downtown on High St.) display new exhibitions while socialites, art collectors, and others admire the works (and each other) far into the night. A good place to start hopping is **Gallery V,** 694 N. High St. (228-8955), which exhibits contemporary paintings, sculptures, and works in less common media (open Tu-Sa 11am-5pm). The **Riley Hawk Galleries,** 642 N. High St. (228-6554), rank among the world's finest for glass sculpture (open Tu-Sa 11am-5pm, Su 1-4pm).

When you over-dose on art, Columbus has a sure cure: rock 'n' roll. Bar bands are a Columbus mainstay; it's hard to find a bar that doesn't have live music on the weekend. Bigger national acts stop at the **Newport,** 1722 N. High St. (concert line 228-3580; tickets start at $10). **Bernie's Distillery,** 1896 N. High St. (291-3448), intoxicates with 78 imported beers (domestic drafts $2-3) and pounding live music all week in a small and smoky room (cover F-Sa $2, under 21 $3-4; many happy hours 8am-9pm). Twenty-one TV screens liven up the **Union Station Café and Gallery,** 630 N. High St. (228-3740 or 228-3546), which entertains a primarily gay crowd. From this hip joint, it's only a few blocks south to the **Brewery District.** Today, barley and hops have replaced the coal and iron of the once-industrial district. **High Beck,** 564 S. High St. (224-0886), at Beck, grooves to rock and R&B (cover $2-5; music Th-Sa), while **Hosters Brewing Co.,** 550 S. High St. (228-6066), at Livingston, attracts locals with homemade brew. On more mellow evenings, many of Columbus's denizens

GREAT LAKES

head for cafes. **Insomnia**, 1728 N. High St. (421-1234), near the OSU campus, serves up sweet caffeine in a homey atmosphere (if your home is filled with Bohemian students) with outdoor seating, board games, and a gas pump (iced coffee $1.35).

■ Near Columbus

A 1hr. drive south of Columbus, the area around **Chillicothe** (pronounce chill-i-cozy with a lisp) features several interesting attractions. The **Hopewell Culture National Historic Park,** 16062 Rte. 104 (740-774-1126), swells with 25 enigmatic Hopewell burial mounds spread over 13 acres, with an adjoining museum that theorizes about the mounds' configuration. *(Museum open daily 8:30am-6pm; Sept.-Nov. and Mar.-May daily 8:30am-5pm; Dec.-Feb. W-Su 8:30am-5pm. Grounds open dawn-dusk. $4 per car, $2 per pedestrian.)* Check with park officials for info on other nearby mounds. From mid-June to early September, the Sugarloaf Mountain Amphitheatre (740-775-0700), on the north end of Chillicothe off Rte. 23, presents **Tecumseh,** a drama re-enacting the life and death of the Shawnee leader (shows M-Sa 8pm; $13, F-Sa $15). A behind-the-scenes tour, available hourly 2-5pm ($3.50, children $2), will answer your questions about how the stunt men dive headfirst off the 21 ft. cliff. At **Scioto Trail State Park** (740-663-2125), 10 mi. south of Chillicothe off U.S. 23, a ¼ mi. walk leads to 24hr. walk-in **camping** behind Stuart Lake (sites $9, with electricity $13).

From Columbus, take U.S. 33 and then some very hilly, winding roads down to the stunning **Hocking Hills State Park,** 30 mi. east of Chillicothe; follow the signs. Waterfalls, gorges, cliffs, and "caves"—cavernous overhangs gouged in the rock by ancient rivers—scar the rugged terrain within the park. The park's main attraction is **Old Man's Cave** (385-6165), off Rte. 64, which takes its name from a hermit who lived, died, and was buried there in the 1800s. Care is essential when exploring the cave area itself, especially in wet weather or in winter; people young and old have died after slipping and falling. Old Man's Cave offers **camping** (primitive sites $14; sites with electricity and pool—don't try this at home!—$17).

■ Cincinnati

Longfellow called it the "Queen City of the West." But having been founded by German pig salesmen, Cincinnati has also earned the less-regal nickname of "Porkopolis." Lying in geographical limbo between the Great Plains, the South, and the Great Lakes, Cincinnati seems to thrive on its rifts. Its culture contains both a vibrant arts community, boasting a stellar ballet and the new Aronoff Center for the Arts, and a surly sports scene, which focuses on the Reds and Bengals. Food and nightlife have also come a long way from their bratwurst-and-beer beginnings, featuring funky restaurants, bars, and clubs, both in downtown and in the traditionally off-beat hilltop communities of Clifton and Mt. Adams. Somehow, influences of past, present, and every geographical direction actually work together, creating an eclectic community, with room for both pork and royalty (and whatever else they put in that chili).

ORIENTATION AND PRACTICAL INFORMATION

The downtown business district is a simple grid centered around **Fountain Sq.,** at **5th** and **Vine St.** Cross streets are numbered and designated east or west by their relation to Vine St. The **University of Cincinnati** spreads out from Clifton, the area north of the city. **Cinergy Field,** the **Serpentine Wall,** and the **Riverwalk,** all to the south, border the river which marks the Ohio and Kentucky divide.

Airport: Greater Cincinnati International (606-767-3151), in Kentucky, 12 mi. south of Cincinnati and accessible by I-75, I-71, and I-74. **Jetport Express** (606-767-3702) shuttles to downtown ($12), or call the **Transit Authority of Northern Kentucky (TANK)** (606-331-8265) for alternate shuttling info.

Trains: Amtrak, 1301 Western Ave. (651-3337 or 800-872-7245), in Union Terminal. To Indianapolis (4hr., 3 per week, $17-34) and Chicago (8-9hr., 3 per week, $37-67). Open M 9:30am-5pm, Tu-F 9:30am-5pm and 11pm-6:30am, Sa-Su 11pm-6:30am. *Avoid the neighborhood north of the station.*

Buses: Greyhound, 1005 Gilbert Ave. (352-6012 or 800-231-2222), just past the intersection of E. Court and Broadway. To: Indianapolis (4 per day, 2-3hr., $16); Louisville (2hr., 10 per day, $19); Cleveland (4-6hr., 9 per day, $35); and Columbus (2-3hr., 10 per day, $12). Open 24hr.

Public Transportation: Cincinnati Metro and **TANK,** both housed in The Bus Stop, in the Mercantile Center, 115 E. 5th St. (621-9450; open M-F 6:30am-6pm). Most buses run out of Government Sq., at 5th and Main St., to outlying communities. In summer 50¢, in winter 65¢; extra to suburbs. Office has schedules and info.

Taxi: Yellow Cab, 241-2100. $2 base fare, $1.20 per mi. Open 24hr.

Visitor Info: Cincinnati Convention and Visitors Bureau, 300 W. 6th St. (621-2142 or 800-CINCY-US/246-2987). Open M-F 8:45am-5pm. Their *Official Visitors Guide* is a godsend. The **Information Booth** in Fountain Sq. has similar, more limited offerings. Open M-Sa 9am-5pm.

Hotlines: Rape Crisis Center, 216 E. 9th St. (381-5610), downtown. 24hr. **Gay/Lesbian Community Switchboard,** 651-0070. Operates Su-F 6-11pm.

Post Office: 525 Vine St. (684-5667), located on the Skywalk. Open M-F 8am-5pm, Sa 8am-1pm. **ZIP code:** 45202. **Area codes:** 513; Kentucky suburbs, 606. In text, 513 unless otherwise noted.

ACCOMMODATIONS

Few cheap hotels can be found in downtown Cincinnati. About 30 mi. north of Cincinnati in Sharonville off I-75, low-priced motels cluster along **Chester Rd.** About 12 mi. south of the city, inexpensive accommodations line **I-75** at Exit 184. Closer still, the motels at **Central Pkwy.** and **Hopple St.** offer solid lodging without high costs.

Budget Host Town Center Inn, 3356 Central Pkwy. (283-4678 or 800-BUD-HOST/283-4678), Exit 3 off I-75. A smallish motel with a pool, the inn finds room for microwaves, refrigerators, A/C, and satellite TV in faded but comfortable rooms. 10min. from downtown and the University of Cincinnati. Singles $45; doubles $55.

Knights Inn-Cincinnati/South, 8048 Dream St., Florence, KY (606-371-9711), just off I-75 at Exit 180. Step into newly renovated rooms with an Arthurian flair. Convenient to downtown with exceptionally friendly service. Cable TV, A/C, outdoor pool. Singles $36-40; doubles $40-45.

YUMMY FOR THE TUMMY, AND GAS FOR THE...

The city that gave us the first soap opera, the first baseball franchise (the Redlegs), and the Heimlich maneuver presents its great culinary contribution—**Cincinnati chili.** Although this mixture of meat sauce, spaghetti, and cheese is an all-pervasive ritual in local culture, somehow no other city seems to have caught this gastronomical wave. Chili is cheap; antacid tablets, however, cost extra.

Skyline Chili, everywhere. Locations all over Cincinnati, including 643 Vine St. (241-2020), at 7th St., dish up the best beans in town. The secret ingredient has been debated for years; some say chocolate, but curry is more likely. 5-way large chili $5, cheese coney (hot dog) $1.20. Open M-F 10:30am-7pm, Sa 11am-3pm.

Ulysses, 209 W. McMillan (241-FOOD/3663), in Clifton. A one-table vegetarian restaurant with a distinctive hippie aura, Ulysses draws ravenous veggies from all over town. Their fruit smoothies ($1.75) are zesty and refreshing, and the sesame sticks are a perfect sight-seeing snack. Open M-Sa 11am-8pm.

Rookwood Pottery, 1077 Celestial St. (721-8691), near the intersection with Monastery St. in Mt. Adams. Once upon a time, this building actually lived up to its name, producing the pottery of Maria Longworth Nichols. The kilns are now cool, and patrons can sit in them while enjoying one of best burgers in town ($6) and make-your-own sundaes. Open Su-Th 11:30am-9:30pm, F-Sa 11:30am-11:30pm.

Graeter's, 41 E. 4th St. (381-0653), between Walnut and Vine St. downtown, and 14 other locations. Since 1870, Graeter's has been sending sweet-toothed locals into sensory bliss with delectable ice cream blended with giant chocolate chips (single cone $1.50). Sandwiches and baked goods, too. Open M-F 7am-6pm, Sa 7am-5pm.

Cincy Chili Every Which Way

Cincinnati residents will gleefully attest to living in the chili capital of the U.S. No, Texas has not seceded (yet). Cincinnati chili is a different concoction, and it doesn't compete with the southwestern version. And in Ohio, you have to order chili the "way" you want it: **2-Way Chili** (or "chili spaghetti"), Chili on a bed of pasta; **3-Way Chili** (or a "haywagon"), Chili and spaghetti with grated cheese; **4-Way Chili:**…and chopped onions; or **5-Way Chili:**…and kidney beans to boot.

SIGHTS

Downtown Cincinnati orbits around the **Tyler Davidson Fountain,** a florid 19th-century masterpiece and an ideal people-watching spot. The font is remembered fondly by the still-surviving fans of **WKRP in Cincinnati,** perhaps the only TV show to be set in the city. To the east, the expansive garden at **Proctor and Gamble Plaza** is just one mark that the giant company has left on its home town. Around **Fountain Sq.** are business complexes and great shops, connected by a series of second floor skywalks. If you're yearning for a panorama, the observation deck at the top of **Carew Tower** provides the best view in the city.

Close to Fountain Sq., the **Contemporary Arts Center,** 115 E. 5th St. (721-0390), 2nd fl. of the Mercantile Center, has a strong reputation in the national arts community. *(Open M-Sa 10am-6pm, Su noon-5pm. $3.50, seniors and students $2. Free M. Wheelchair access.)* Call for current shows and evening films, music, and multimedia performances. Also downtown is the **Taft Museum,** 316 Pike St. (241-0343), at the east end of 4th St., the former home of its presidential namesake. *(Open M-Sa 10am-5pm, Su 1-4pm. $4, students and seniors $2, under 18 free. Free W.)* The museum houses a beautiful collection of painted enamels, as well as pieces by Rembrandt and Whistler.

Eden Park, northeast of downtown, provides a nearby respite from the city with rolling hills, a pond, and cultural centers; take bus #49 to Eden Park Dr. (open daily 6am-10pm). The collections at the **Cincinnati Art Museum** (721-5204), inside the park, span 5000 years, from Near Eastern artifacts to Andy Warhol's rendition of Cincinnati baseball great Pete Rose—a local that the locals love to hate. *(Open Tu-Sa 10am-5pm, Su noon-6pm. $5, students and seniors $4, under 18 free, Sa by donation.)* The **Krohn Conservatory** (421-5707), also within the park, is one of the largest public greenhouses in the world. *(Open M-Tu and Th-Su 10am-5pm, W 10am-6pm. Free. Wheelchair access.)* Lush doesn't begin to describe it.

Union Terminal, 1031 Western Ave. (287-7000 or 800-733-2077), lies 1 mi. west of downtown, near the Ezzard Charles Dr. Exit off I-75 (take bus #1). Although it is a train terminal, this Art Deco edifice contains much, much more. Within the world's largest permanent half-dome, at the **Museum of Natural History** you can cool down in an Ice Age world of simulated glaciers or investigate a carefully constructed artificial cavern, featuring a colony of real live bats. On the other side of the dome, the **Cincinnati History Museum** houses historical exhibits on movers and shakers in Cincinnati as well as an Omnimax Theater. *(Both museums 287-7001; Omnimax 287-7091; call for showtimes. Both museums open M-Sa 10am-5pm, Su 11am-6pm. 1 museum $5.50, ages 3-12 $3.50; Omnimax $6.50/$4.50; any 2 attractions $9/$6; any 3 $12/$8.)*

Feeling wild? The world-famous **Cincinnati Zoo,** 3400 Vine St. (281-4700), awaits. Lions and tigers and bears (oh my!) roam the grounds along with many rare species, including several types of near-extinct pigs—we *are* in hog heaven after all. *(Open daily in summer 9am-6pm; in winter 9am-5pm. $10, ages 2-12 $5, seniors $8. Parking $5.)*

ENTERTAINMENT AND NIGHTLIFE

The free newspapers *City Beat, Everybody's News,* and *Downtown Cincinnati* deliver the happenings around town. The cliff-hanging communities on the steep streets of **Mt. Adams** support a thriving arts and entertainment district. Perched on its own wooded hill in Eden Park, the **Playhouse in the Park,** 962 Mt. Adams Circle (421-3888), performs theater-in-the-round. (Performances mid-Sept. to June Tu-Su. Tickets $24-38; student rush, 15min. before show, and senior rush, 2hr. prior, $12.)

The **Music Hall,** 1243 Elm St. (721-8222), hosts the **Cincinnati Symphony Orchestra** and the **Cincinnati Pops Orchestra** (381-3300) September through May (tickets $12-59). The orchestra's summer seasons (June-July) take place at **Riverbend,** near Coney Island (tickets $11-25). The **Cincinnati Opera** (241-2742) performs in the Music Hall as well (limited summer schedule; tickets $10-75). For updates, call **Dial the Arts** (621-4744). The **Cincinnati Ballet Company** (621-5219) has moved to the **Aronoff Center for the Arts,** 650 Walnut (621-2787), which also houses a Broadway series. (Ballet performances Oct.-May; tickets $12-47, matinee $8-20. Musical tickets $15-45. Wheelchair access.)

Escape the high-brow lot and beat the summer heat in Sunlite, the world's largest recirculating pool, at the **Coney Island Amusement Center,** 6201 Kellogg Ave. (232-8230), off I-275 at the Kellogg Ave. Exit. (Pool open daily 10am-8pm; rides M-F noon-9pm, Sa-Su 11am-10pm. Pool $11, seniors and ages 4-11 $8; rides $7/$7; both $15/$13.) **Summerfair** (531-0050), an arts extravaganza, takes over the park for one weekend in late May or early June.

Cincinnati's fanatics watch baseball's **Reds** (421-REDS/7337; tickets $3-14) and football's **Bengals** (621-3550; tickets $31-54) in **Cinergy Field,** 201 E. Pete Rose Way.

Over Labor Day weekend, **Riverfest** (621-9326) celebrates the end of summer with food, entertainment, and fireworks. The third weekend of September brings **Oktoberfest-Zinzinnati** (579-3191), during which the city basks in its German heritage.

Some of Cincinnati's best nightlife is (literally) above and beyond downtown. Overlooking downtown from the east, **Mt. Adams** has spawned some funky bars and late-night coffee shops. Antiques adorn the walls of **Blind Lemon,** 939 Hatch St. (241-3885), at St. Gregory St., while live jazz and blues fill the courtyard. (Domestic draft $2. Music daily 9:30pm. No cover. Open M-Th 6:30pm-2:30am, F-Su 4:30pm-2:30am.) For contemporary music and a younger crowd, climb up the steep streets to Clifton. **Ripley's Alive,** 2507 W. Clifton (861-6800), hosts live hip-hop and funk to rave reviews (ages 18-20 cover $3, 21+ cover $2; open W-Su 10pm-2am).

For a drink that will transport you back to the 19th century, try Cincinnati's oldest tavern, **Arnold's,** 210 E. 8th St. (421-6234), between Main and Sycamore. A wood-paneled tavern with endearingly brusque service, this mainstay provides good, simple beer (domestic draft $3) and food (pasta and sandwiches $5-10). After 9pm, Arnold's does ragtime, bluegrass, and swing. (Open M-F 11am-1am, Sa 4pm-1am.)

Carol's Corner Café, 825 Main St. (651-2667), with a jukebox, bigger-than-life-size movie posters, and gay pride flags, inserts funk and style into downtown Cincinnati. Drawing theater groups and yuppies galore, this restaurant/bar is known for great food (Cock-a-Noodle-Do Salad $7.25) and late hours. Upstairs is a late-night cabaret. (Bar open M 11:30am-1am, Tu-F 11:30am-2:30am, Sa 4pm-2:30am, Su 4pm-1am.)

■ Near Cincinnati

If you can't get to California's Napa or Sonoma Valleys, the next best thing may be **Meiers Wine Cellars,** 6955 Plainfield Rd. (891-2900), in Silverton. Take I-71 to Exit 12 or I-75 to Galbraith Rd. Free tours of Ohio's oldest and largest winery give you a chance to taste the fermented fruits of their labor (tours June-Oct., 10am-3pm on the hr.). If the wine is a bit too refined, never fear. The **Oldenberg Brewery Beer Museum,** 400 Buttermilk Pk. (606-341-2802 or 800-323-4917), Ft. Mitchell, KY, bubbles away just over the river off I-75. *(Tours daily on the hr. 10am-5pm. Tour $3, tasting $1.)* This museum is a hands-on experience, providing both tours of the microbrewery and samples of the final product.

For an ultimate amusement park experience, complete with scary rides and scarier lines, head to **Paramount's Kings Island** (573-5800 or 800-288-0808) in Mason, 24 mi. north of Cincinnati off I-71 at Exit 24. In addition to a "faux" Eiffel Tower and an expanded waterpark, this fun center cages **The Beast,** the world's longest wooden rollercoaster. Do you remember the now-classic 1974 "Brady Bunch" episodes in which the kids lost Mike Brady's architectural plans? Well, all the wild shenanigans took place at Kings Island. Admission to the park entitles you to unlimited rides and attractions and the opportunity to buy expensive food. *(Open late May to late Aug. Su-F 9am-10pm, Sa 9am-11pm. $33, seniors and ages 3-6 $19. Parking $6. Wheelchair access.)*

GREAT LAKES

Accommodations can be found at **Paramount's Kings Island Campground,** 5688 Kings Island Dr. (800-832-1133), off I-71 at Exit 25 and within a stone's throw of the amusement park. (Playground. 350 sites $31, full hookup $41. Cabins for 4 $58. $5 per extra adult, $3.50 per extra child ages 4-16. Reservations recommended.)

Michigan

Michigan's developed Lower Peninsula paws the Great Lakes like a huge mitten, while its pristine and oft-ignored Upper Peninsula hangs above, quietly nursing moose and a famed population of wolves. Together, they define over 3000 mi. of coastline along four of the Great Lakes; their shores have the feel of an ocean coast—uniquely blended with the fresh water of the lakes—in the heart of America. Dunes, beaches, forests, and over 11,000 smaller inland lakes add to Michigan's coastal character. Meanwhile, the state, whose once-booming automotive industry now fills only a shadow of its former stature, is starting to make waves as a natural getaway.

PRACTICAL INFORMATION

Capital: Lansing.
Visitor Info: Michigan Travel Bureau, 333 S. Capitol, Ste. F, Lansing 48909 (888-784-7328 or 800-543-2937; http://www.travel-michigan.state.mi.us). Gives out info on the week's events and festivals. **Dept. of Parks and Recreation,** Information Services Center, P.O. Box 30257, Lansing 48909 (517-373-1270). Offers resources on state parks, forests, and campsites. Entry to all state parks requires a motor vehicle permit; $4 per day, $20 annually. Call 800-447-2757 for reservations at any state park campground.
Emergency: 911.
Time Zones: Eastern, except a small sliver of the western Upper Peninsula which lies in Central (1hr. behind Eastern). All of *Let's Go*'s Michigan coverage lies within Eastern. **Postal Abbreviation:** MI.
Sales Tax: 6%.

■ Detroit

Decades of hardship recently prompted an author to proclaim Detroit "America's first Third-World city." Violent race riots in the 60s prompted massive white flight to the suburbs; the population has more than halved since 1967, turning neighborhoods into ghost towns. The decline of the auto industry in the late 70s added unemployment to the city's ills, causing violence and hopelessness among its residents.

Today, the five gleaming towers of the riverside Renaissance Center symbolize the hope of a city-wide renewal. Aggressive tourist media focuses attention on Detroit's attractions: Michigan's largest and most comprehensive museums, a fascinating ethnic history, and the still-visible (though soot-blackened and slightly crumbling) evidence of the city's former architectural grandeur. Detroit may no longer be the city it once was, but it does its best to present an attractive face to the world.

ORIENTATION AND PRACTICAL INFORMATION

Detroit lies on the Detroit River, which connects Lakes Erie and St. Clair. Across the river to the south, the town of **Windsor, ON,** can be reached by tunnel just west of the Renaissance Center (toll $2.25), or by the Ambassador Bridge, 3500 Toledo St. Detroit is a tough town, but you probably won't encounter trouble during the day, especially within the People Mover loop.

Detroit's streets form a grid. **The Mile Rds.** run east-west as major arteries. **Eight Mile Rd.** is the city's northern boundary and the beginning of the suburbs. **Woodward Ave.** heads northwest from downtown, dividing city and suburbs into "east side" and "west side." **Gratiot Ave.** flares out northeast from downtown, while **Grand River Ave.** shoots west. **I-94** and **I-75** pass through downtown. For a particularly helpful map, check the pull-out in the *Detroit Metro Visitor's Guide*.

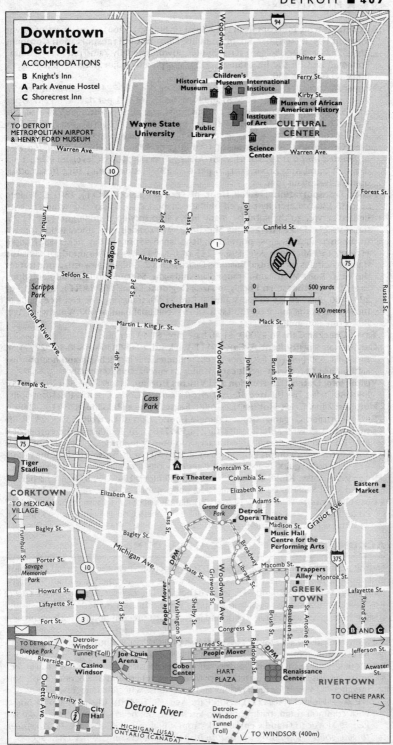

Downtown Detroit

ACCOMMODATIONS

B Knight's Inn
A Park Avenue Hostel
C Shorecrest Inn

TO DETROIT
METROPOLITAN AIRPORT
& HENRY FORD MUSEUM

Woodward Ave.

94

Palmer St.

Ferry St.

Historical
Museum

Children's
Museum

International
Institute

Kirby St.

Museum of African
American History

Institute
of Art

CULTURAL
CENTER

Wayne State
University

Public
Library

Science
Center

Warren Ave.

Warren Ave.

Forest St.

Forest St.

10

2nd St.

Cass St.

John R. St.

Canfield St.

N

Alexandrine St.

3rd St.

Seldon St.

Scripps
Park

Orchestra Hall

0   500 yards
0   500 meters

Mack St.

Martin L. King Jr. St.

Woodward Ave.

John R. St.

Brush St.

Beaubien St.

Wilkins St.

Russel St.

Grand River Ave.

Temple St.

4th St.

Cass
Park

75

Tiger
Stadium

CORKTOWN

TO MEXICAN
VILLAGE

Trumbull St.

Elizabeth St.

A

Fox Theater

Montcalm St.

Columbia St.

Elizabeth St.

Adams St.

Eastern
Market

Bagley St.

Bagley St.

Cass St.

Grand Circus
Park

Detroit
Opera Theatre

Madison St.

Music Hall
Centre for the
Performing Arts

Gratiot Ave.

Michigan Ave.

10

DPM

State St.

Woodward Ave.

Broadway

Library St.

Macomb St.

Trappers
Alley

GREEK-
TOWN

375

Monroe St.

Porter St.

Savage
Memorial
Park

Howard St.

Lafayette St.

People Mover

Washington St.

Shelby St.

Griswold St.

Beaubien St.

St. Antoine St.

Lafayette St.

Rivard St.

Fort St.

3

Congress St.

TO [B] AND [C]

Trumbull St.

3rd St.

TO DETROIT
Dieppe Park

Detroit–
Windsor
Tunnel (Toll)

Riverside Dr.

Casino
Windsor

Joe Louis
Arena

Cobo
Center

Larned St.

People Mover

HART
PLAZA

Randolph St.

DPM

Renaissance
Center

RIVERTOWN

Jefferson St.

Atwater
St.

Oulette Ave.

University St.

City
Hall

i

Detroit River

MICHIGAN (USA)
ONTARIO (CANADA)

Detroit–
Windsor
Tunnel
(Toll)

TO WINDSOR (400m)

TO CHENE PARK

GREAT LAKES

Airport: Detroit Metropolitan (942-3550 or 800-351-5466), 2 mi. west of downtown off I-94 at Merriman Rd. in Romulus. **Commuter Transportation Company** (941-3252 or 800-488-7433) runs shuttles downtown daily 7am-7pm every 30min.; 7pm-midnight on the hr. (45min.; $15), stopping at major hotels. Make reservations. A taxi costs $30.

Trains: Amtrak, 11 W. Baltimore (873-3442 or 800-872-7245), at Woodward. To Chicago (5hr., 3 per day, $24-48) and New York (16hr., 1 per day, $70-128). Open daily 5am-midnight. For Canadian destinations, you must go through **VIA Rail,** 298 Walker Rd., Windsor, ON (519-256-5511 or 800-561-3949), across the river in Canada. To Toronto (4hr.; 5-7 per day; CDN$54 with reservation, CDN$71 without).

Buses: Greyhound, 1001 Howard St. (961-8011 or 800-231-2222). *At night, the area is deserted and unsafe.* To: Chicago (5½hr., 7 per day, $27); Cleveland (4hr., 4 per day, $21); and Ann Arbor (1hr., 6 per day, $8). Station open 24hr.; ticket office open daily 4:30am-1am.

Public Transportation: Detroit Dept. of Transportation (DOT), 1301 E. Warren St. (933-1300). Carefully policed public transport system serves downtown, with limited service to the suburbs. Many buses stop service at midnight. Fare $1.25, transfers 25¢. **DOT Attractions Shuttle** (259-8726) delivers camera-toting tourists to the metro area's most popular sights 10am-5:45pm. All-day ticket $5. **People Mover,** 150 Michigan Ave. (962-7245 or 800-541-7245). Ultramodern elevated tramway circles the Central Business District on a 2.7 mi. loop; worth a ride just for the view. Runs M-Th 7am-11pm, F 7am-midnight, Sa 9am-midnight, Su noon-8pm. Fare 50¢. **Southeastern Michigan Area Regional Transit (SMART),** 962-5515 or 223-2100. Bus service to the suburbs. Fare $1.50, transfers 25¢. Get free maps of the system at the office on the 1st fl. of First National Bank at 600 Woodward Ave. Buses run 4am-midnight.

Taxis: Checker Cab, 963-7000. $1.40 base fare, $1.40 per mi.

Car Rental: Thrifty Rent-A-Car, 29111 Wick Rd. (946-7830 or 800-367-2277), in Romulus. $50 per day, $205 per week; unlimited mi. in Michigan and neighboring states. Must be 21 with credit card. Under 25 surcharge $20 per day.

Visitor Info: Detroit Convention and Visitors Bureau, 211 W. Fort St. (202-1813 or 800-338-7648), has the free *Metro Detroit Visitors Guide.* Open M-F 8:30am-5pm.

Hotlines: 24hr. Crisis Hotline, 224-7000. **Sexual Abuse Helpline,** 876-4180. 24hr.

Bi-Gay-Lesbian Organizations: Triangle Foundation of Detroit, 537-3323. **Affirmations,** 195 W. 9 Mile Rd. 48220 (248-398-7105), in Ferndale at the corner of 9 Mile Rd. and Troy, has a large library, info on gay nightlife, and copies of *Pride Source Guide,* a comprehensive gay guide to MI, from **Between the Lines** (248-615-7003). The guide is also available at gay bookstores and coffeehouses.

Internet Access: Kinko's, 100 Renaissance Center #114 (259-8344). $12 per hr. Open M-Th 8am-8pm, F 8am-5pm, Sa-Su noon-5pm.

Post Office: 1401 W. Ford St. (226-8304), handles general delivery. Open 24hr. **ZIP code:** 48233. **Area codes:** 313, 810, and 248 (north); or 734 (southwest). In text, 313 unless otherwise noted.

ACCOMMODATIONS AND CAMPGROUNDS

Detroit's suburbs harbor cheap chain motels, especially near the airport in **Romulus,** and along **E. Jefferson** near downtown. For a mix of convenience and affordability, look along **Telegraph Rd.** off I-94, west of the city. The *Detroit Metro Visitor's Guide* lists accommodations by area and includes price ranges. Devoted campers should resign themselves to a 45min. commute if they insist on communing with nature.

Country Grandma's Home Hostel (HI-AYH), 22330 Bell Rd. (734-753-4901), in New Boston, 6 mi. south of I-94 off I-275, between Detroit and Ann Arbor. Though it's inaccessible by public transportation, the comfort, hospitality, and warm feeling of security make it worth the trip. 6 beds, a kitchen, and free parking. $10, nonmembers $13. Call for reservations and directions. Wheelchair access.

Park Ave. Hostel (HI-AYH), 2305 Park Ave. (961-8310). Clean, spacious hostel with common room, bathroom, and kitchen in the heart of downtown. Take the People Mover to Grand Central Park, from which it's a 5min. walk. *Be careful in this neighborhood both day and night.* $12; members only. Wheelchair access.

Shorecrest Motor Inn, 1316 E. Jefferson Ave. (568-3000 or 800-992-9616), lets you sleep as close to downtown as the budget traveler can. A/C and fridges. Clean, comfortable singles $52; doubles $58. Key deposit $5. Reservations recommended. Wheelchair access.

Knight's Inn, 10501 E. Jefferson St. (822-3500). From the Renaissance Ctr., walk to Jefferson and take a bus eastbound about 4 mi. Large, comfortable rooms with TV and telephone. *Be careful in this neighborhood after dark.* Singles $39; doubles $49. Free parking. Wheelchair access.

Motel 6, 32700 Barrington St. (810-583-0500), 15 mi. north of downtown off I-75 in Madison Heights, just off 12 Mile Rd. Enormous, clean, cookie-cutter rooms with free local calls and HBO. Singles $40; doubles $46. Reservations recommended.

Pontiac Lake Recreation Area, 7800 Gale Rd. (248-666-1020), in Waterford 45min. northwest of downtown; take I-75 to M59 W, a right on Will Lake northbound and left onto Gale Rd. Huge wooded sites in rolling hills, just 4 mi. from the lake. 176 sites with electricity $11. Vehicle permit $4.

FOOD

Although many of the restaurants downtown have migrated to the suburbs, the budget traveler still has some in-town dining options. **Greektown,** at the Greektown People Mover stop, has Greek restaurants and excellent bakeries on Monroe St., all on 1 block near Beaubien St. Visitors can snag a Polish sausage in **Hamtramck,** a Polish neighborhood northeast of Detroit. No budget traveler should miss the **Eastern Market** (833-1560), at Gratiot Ave. and Russell St., an 11-acre produce-and-goodie festival with almost every edible imaginable (open Sa 6am-4pm).

   Cyprus Taverna, 579 Monroe St. (961-1550), is a local favorite for Greek cuisine. In the heart of Greektown, it features tasteful decor and a charmingly subdued atmosphere. (Entrees $9-13. Open Su-Th 11am-2am, F-Sa 11am-4am.) **Xochimilco,** 3409 Bagley St. (843-0179), is a tad out of the way, but in a fun "Mexico-town" area. From downtown, take the "Baker St." bus to Lafayette and Washington Blvd. Chefs from Mexico give customers an authentic and inexpensive culinary experience. (3 meat tacos, 3 enchiladas, or 3 burritos with rice and beans $4.25-5.75; comes with free chips and salsa. Open daily 11am-2am. No reservations F-Sa.) The **Soup Kitchen Saloon,** 1585 Franklin St. (259-1374), once housed a speakeasy and brothel, but now features some of the town's best live blues, plus fresh seafood, steaks, and cajun eats. The BBQ catfish or seafood creole ($12) are delicious. (Shows Tu-Sa; cover $5-7. Open M-Th 11am-midnight, F 11am-2am, Sa 5pm-2am, Su 5pm-midnight.)

HENRY'S WORLD: FORD TO MOTOWN

For a reason to visit Detroit, look no farther than the colossal **Henry Ford Museum & Greenfield Village,** 20900 Oakwood Blvd. (982-6100, 271-1620 for 24hr. info), off I-94 in nearby Dearborn; take SMART bus #200 or 250. More than just a tribute to planes, trams, and automobiles (though there's plenty of that), the 12 acres of museum exhibits deliver a comprehensive running commentary on 20th-century American history. The premises boast the limousine in which President Kennedy was assassinated and a copy of the Lunar Rover. Over 80 historic edifices from around the country have been moved to **Greenfield Village,** next to the museum; visit the workshop of the Wright Brothers or the factory where Thomas Edison researched. *(Both open daily 9am-5pm; July-Aug. village open Sa until 8pm. Museum or village $12.50, seniors $11.50, ages 5-12 $6.25. Combination ticket valid 2 consecutive days $22, ages 5-12 $11.)* If the Ford Museum doesn't slake your craving for cars, next door the somewhat cheesy **Automotive Hall of Fame,** 21400 Oakwood Blvd. (240-4000), offers up tributes to the innovators of the car industry. *(Open daily 10am-5pm; Nov.-May Tu-Su 10am-5pm. $6, seniors $5.50, ages 5-12 $3.)* Closer to downtown, the most impressive of the auto-baron mansions, the **Fisher Mansion and Bhaktiredanta Cultural Center,** 383 Lenox Ave. (331-6740), houses Indian cultural exhibits within an ornate stone, marble, and carved wood structure leafed with over 200 oz. of gold. *(Tours F-Su 12:30, 2, 3:30, and 6pm. $6, students and seniors $5, under 13 $4. Free self-tours in summer 10am-5pm.)* By a strange twist of fate, the center and mansion were co-founded by Henry Ford's grandson and the United Auto Workers President's daughter.

GREAT LAKES

Detroit makes an effort to lure visitors to its **Cultural Center,** at Woodward and Warren St. (take bus #53 or the Attractions Shuttle)—it's worth taking the bait. One of the nation's finest art museums, the **Detroit Institute of Arts,** 5200 Woodward Ave. (833-7900), features Van Gogh's "Self-Portrait" and the nation's largest historic puppet collection (open W-F 11am-4pm, Sa-Su 11am-5pm; suggested donation $4). The history of the African experience in America fills the halls of the world's largest **Museum of African-American History,** 315 E. Warren Rd. (823-9800), in a newly renovated $25 million building. *(Open W-Su 9:30am-5pm. Suggested donation $3, under 13 $2.)* Exhibits include harrowing accounts of the history of slavery and interactive displays of present day African-American culture.

Oh, mercy, mercy me, Berry Gordy's Motown Record Company sold out to Los Angeles. The **Motown Museum,** 2648 W. Grand Blvd. (875-2264), preserves its memories. *(Open Su-M noon-5pm, Tu-Sa 10am-5pm. $6, under 12 $3.)* Downstairs, the Jackson Five, Marvin Gaye, Smokey Robinson, and Diana Ross once recorded their tunes in the primitive studio. The museum lies east of Rosa Parks Blvd. about 1 mi. west of the Lodge Freeway (Rte. 10); take the "Dexter Avenue" bus.

The **Holocaust Memorial Center,** 6602 W. Maple Rd. (248-661-0840), in West Bloomfield, provides a historical and educational memorial to the victims of Nazi slaughter. *(Tours Su 1pm. Open Su-Th 10am-3:30pm; Sept.-May also F 9am-12:30. Free.)* The museum's collection of rare documentaries and propaganda films has made it an important research center.

One of Detroit's favorite escapes, **Belle Isle** (852-4078), 3 mi. from downtown via the MacArthur Bridge, maintains a **conservatory,** a **nature center,** an **aquarium,** a **maritime museum,** and a small **zoo** for animal lovers with short attention spans ($2 each, children $1).

ENTERTAINMENT AND NIGHTLIFE

Newly renovated and restored, Detroit's theater district, around Woodward and Columbia, is witnessing a cultural revival. The **Fox Theater,** 2211 Woodward Ave. (983-6611), near Grand Circus Park, features high-profile performances (drama, comedy, and musicals) and some Broadway shows. The nation's largest movie theater hall (occupancy 5000), the Fox also shows occasional epic films. (Box office open M-F 10am-6pm. Tickets $25-100; movies under $10.) The **State Theater,** 2115 Woodward Ave. (961-5450; 810-932-3643 for event info), brings in a variety of popular concerts, including big-name rockers like Björk. The State Theater is also home to **Club X,** a giant party, which enlists DJs from a local radio station to play alternative dance music. (Cover $8 for 18+, $5 for 21+. Open Sa 10pm-2am.) East of the Renaissance Center in the old warehouse district, **Rivertown** hosts some of the city's best nightlife, though it is not the safest idea to loiter in the streets.

Detroit's numerous festivals draw millions of visitors. Hep jazz fans jet to Hart Plaza during Labor Day weekend for the 4-day **Montreux-Detroit Jazz Festival** (963-7622). With more than 70 acts on three stages and mountains of international food at the World Food Court, it's the largest free jazz festival on the continent. The nation's oldest state fair, the **Michigan State Fair** (369-8250), at Eight Mile Rd. and Woodward Ave., gathers together bake-offs, art exhibits, and livestock during the 2 weeks before Labor Day. A 2-week extravaganza in late June, the international **Freedom Festival** (923-8259), held jointly with Windsor, Ontario, celebrates the friendship between the U.S. and Canada. During the festival, North America's largest annual fireworks display takes place over the Detroit River near the Renaissance Center, marking the birthdays of both nations. The **Concours d'Elegance** (248-370-3140), at the Oakland University Meadow Brook Hall in Rochester, exhibits elegant classic cars during the first Sunday in August. In mid-January, the gee-whiz **North American International Auto Show** (643-0250) showcases the new models, prototypes, and concept cars from manufacturers around the world in the Cobo Center, 1 Washington Blvd. **Detroit's African World Festival** (877-8073) brings over a million people to Hart Plaza on the third weekend in August for an open-air market and free reggae, jazz, blues, and gospel concerts. **Orchestra Hall,** 3711 Woodward Ave. (962-1000), at Parsons St., houses the Detroit Symphony Orchestra with concerts Saturdays 1-5pm.

(Box office 833-3700. Open M-F 9am-5pm. ½-price rush tickets 1½hr. prior to show.) The weekly *Metro Times* contains complete entertainment listings.

The **Detroit Pistons** shoot hoops at the **Palace of Auburn Hills,** 2 Championship Dr. (a.k.a. 3777 Lapeer Rd.), Auburn Hills (248-377-0100; Sept.-Apr.; tickets $12-59). Hockey's back-to-back 1997-98 World Champion **Red Wings** face off in the **Joe Louis Arena,** 600 Civic Center Dr. (396-7544; Sept.-Apr.; tickets $17-62), whereas **Tigers** hunt the post-season at **Tiger Stadium,** on Michigan and Trumbull Ave. (962-4000; Apr.-Sept.; tickets $4-20). For tickets, call **Ticketmaster** (248-645-6666).

For the latest in nightlife, pick up a free copy of *Orbit* in record stores and restaurants. *Between the Lines,* also free, has entertainment info for lesbians, gays, and bisexuals. **St. Andrew's Hall,** 431 E. Congress (961-6358), hosts local and national alternative acts (shows F-Su; usually 17+; advance tickets sold through Ticketmaster; $7-10). **Shelter,** the dance club downstairs, draws crowds on non-concert nights. Young party animals take advantage of Ontario's lower drinking age (19) at the **Zoo Club,** 800 Wellington (519-258-2582), in Windsor. Those with too much cash rid themselves of the burden with three floors of gambling at **The Windsor Casino,** 377 Riverside Dr. (519-258-7878 or 800-991-7777; must be 19; open 24hr.).

■ Ann Arbor

For a small town tucked between some major industrial hubs, Ann Arbor hasn't done too badly. Named after Ann Rumsey and Ann Allen, wives of two of the area's early pioneers (who supposedly enjoyed sitting under grape arbors), the city has managed to prosper without losing its relaxed charm. In 1837, the gargantuan and well-respected University of Michigan moved to town, giving rise to a hip collage of leftists, granolas, yuppies, and middle Americans. Today, the town manages to incorporate diversity and excitement without ever appearing unsafe or run-down.

ORIENTATION AND PRACTICAL INFORMATION

Ann Arbor's streets lie in a grid, but watch out for the *slant* of Packard and Detroit St. **Main St.** divides the town east-west, and **Huron St.** cuts it north-south. The central campus of the **University of Michigan,** where restaurants cluster, lies 4 blocks east of Main St. and south of E. Huron (a 5min. walk from downtown). Although street meter parking is plentiful, authorities ticket ruthlessly. One-way streets and unexpected dead ends also make driving near the campus stressful.

Trains: Amtrak, 325 Depot St. (994-4906 or 800-872-7245). To Chicago (4½hr., 3 per day, $24-48) and Detroit (1hr., 3 per day, $8-15). Tickets sold daily 6:30am-11pm.

Buses: Greyhound, 116 W. Huron St. (662-5511 or 800-231-2222). To: Detroit (1-1½hr., 6 per day, $8); Chicago (5hr., 5 per day, $25); and Grand Rapids (3½hr., 2 per day, $21). Open M-Sa 8am-6:30pm, Su noon-6:30pm.

Public Transportation: Ann Arbor Transportation Authority (AATA), Blake Transit Center, 331 S. 4th Ave. (996-0400 or 973-6500). Service in Ann Arbor and a few neighboring towns. Buses run M-F 6:45am-10:45pm, Sa-Su 8am-6:15pm. Fare 75¢, students and seniors 35¢. Station open M-F 7:30am-9pm, Sa noon-5:30pm. **AATA's Nightride,** 663-3888. Safe door-to-door transportation M-F 11pm-6am, Sa-Su 7pm-6am. Call to book a trip; wait is 5-45min. Fare $2 per person. **Commuter Transportation Company,** 941-9391 or 800-488-7433. Frequent shuttle service between Ann Arbor and Detroit Metro Airport. Vans depart Ann Arbor 5am-7pm and return 7am-midnight. $18, round-trip $34. Door-to-door service for up to 5 $55; reserve at least 1 week in advance.

Car Rental: Thrifty Car Rental, 411 E. Huron St. (668-6867). $34 per day, $190 per week with unlimited mi. Ages 21-24 pay $10 extra per day. Open M-F 7:30am-5:30pm, Sa-Su 9am-1pm.

Visitor Info: Ann Arbor Convention and Visitors Bureau, 120 W. Huron St. (995-7281 or 800-888-9487), at Ashley. Has info on the city and the University of Michigan. Open M-F 8:30am-5pm.

Hotlines: **Sexual Assault Crisis Line**, 483-7273. **U. Michigan Sexual Assault Line,** 936-3333. **S.O.S. Crisis Line,** 485-3222. All 24hr. **U. Michigan Gay/Lesbian Referrals,** 763-4186. Operates M-F 9am-5pm.
Most Important Thing in the World: Happiness.
Internet Access: Kinko's, 530 E. Liberty St. (761-4539). Open 24hr. $12 per hr.
Post Office: 2075 W. Stadium Blvd. (665-1100; open M-F 8:30am-5pm). **ZIP code:** 48106. **Area code:** 734.

ACCOMMODATIONS

Expensive hotels, motels, and B&Bs dominate Ann Arbor due to the many business travelers and sports fans who flock to the town. Reasonable rates can be found at discount chains farther out of town or in **Ypsilanti,** southeast of town along I-94. Near downtown, good ol' **Motel 6,** 3764 S. State St. (665-9900), rents nice, clean, comfortable rooms (singles $44-50; doubles $50-56; off-season rates lower). During the summer, the University of Michigan rents rooms in **Bursley Hall,** 1931 Duffield St. (763-1140), on North Campus, and offers free local calls and parking in a nearby lot for $3.50 per day (singles $35; doubles $45). A free bus will get you to main campus. Call 764-5297 to arrange reservations. The **Embassy Hotel,** 200 E. Huron (662-7100), at 4th Ave., offers clean rooms (singles $39; doubles $44; $2 key deposit). Seven campgrounds lie within a 20 mi. radius of Ann Arbor. Both the **Pinckney Recreation Area,** 8555 Silver Hill (426-4913; open M-Th 8am-4:30pm, F 8am-8:30pm, Sa-Su 8am-6:30pm), in Pinckney, or the **Waterloo Recreation Area,** 16345 McClure Rd. (475-8307; open daily 8am-noon and 1-5pm), in Chelsea, have rustic ($6-10) and modern ($12-14) sites, and require a $4 vehicle permit. Reservations at these and all Michigan state parks can be made by calling 800-447-2757.

FOOD

Where there are students, there are cheap eats; inexpensive restaurants cram the sidewalks of **State St.** and **S. University St.,** while more upscale eateries line **Main St.** Fresh produce comes straight from the growers at the **farmers market,** 315 Detroit St. (761-1078), next to Kerrytown (open May-Dec. W and Sa 7am-3pm; Jan.-Apr. Sa 8am-3pm). The readers of *Ann Arbor News* voted **Cottage Inn Pizza,** 512 E. William St. (663-3379), at Thompson St., purveyor of "best pizza." (Pizza $7-18. Open M-Th 11am-midnight, F-Sa 11am-1am, Su noon-midnight.) Locals seek out **Del Rio,** 122 W. Washington St. (761-2530), at Ashley, for cheap burgers and Mexican food, with good vegetarian options. (Burritos $2.50. Free jazz Su. Open M-F 11:30am-1:45am, Sa noon-1:45am, Su 5:30pm-1:45am.) When it comes to Jewish deli fare, **Zingerman's Deli,** 422 Detroit St. (363-3354), doesn't mess around. Even *goyim* crowds line up for huge, excellent sandwiches for $6-11. (Open daily 7am-10pm.) Vegetarians and health-food fanatics can take advantage of a slew of restaurants just around the corner, at Catherine and Fourth.

SIGHTS AND ENTERTAINMENT

The university offers a handful of free museums which merit a walk-through. A small but impressive collection of artwork from around the world fills the **University of Michigan Arts Museum (UMAM),** 525 S. State St. (764-0395), at the corner of S. University St. (open Tu-W and F-Sa 11am-5pm, Th 11am-9pm, Su noon-5pm; free). Just down the street, the **Kelsey Museum of Archaeology,** 434 S. State St. (764-9304), presents pieces recovered from digs in the Middle East, Greece, and Italy (open Tu-F 9am-4pm, Sa-Su 1-4pm; free). The **University of Michigan Exhibit Museum of Natural History,** 1109 Geddes Ave. (764-0478), at Washtenaw, displays a Hall of Evolution and other exhibits on Michigan zoology, astronomy, and geology. *(Open M-Sa 9am-5pm, Su noon-5pm. Museum free; planetarium $3, seniors and under 13 $2.)* Within, the Planetarium projects star-gazing weekend entertainment. Outside the University at the **Ann Arbor Hands-On Museum,** 219 E. Huron (995-5437), exhibits are designed to be felt, turned, touched, pushed, and plucked. *(Open Tu-F 10am-5:30pm, Sa 10am-5pm, Su 1-5pm. $4, seniors, students, and ages 3-17 $2.50.)* Numerous local artists display their creations at the **artisan market,** 315 Detroit St. (open May-Dec. Su 11am-4pm). It's nigh-impossible to get tickets for a **Wolverine football** game at UM's 115,000 capacity stadium; nevertheless, fans give it a shot by calling the athletics office at 764-0247.

As tens of thousands of students depart for the summer (and rents plummet), locals indulge in a little celebration. During late July, thousands pack the city to view the work of nearly 600 artists at the **Ann Arbor Summer Art Fair** (995-7281). The **Ann Arbor Summer Festival** (647-2278) draws crowds from mid-June through early July for a collection of comedy, dance, and theater productions, as well as musical performances including jazz, country, and classical. Outdoor movies conclude the festivities nightly at **Top of the Park,** on top of the Fletcher St. parking structure, next to the Health Services Building. The **County Events Hotline,** 930-6300, has more info.

To hear classical music, contact the **University Musical Society** (764-2538 or 800-221-1229), in the Burton Memorial Clock Tower at N. University and Thouper; the society sponsors 60 professional concerts per season (tickets $10-50; open M-F 10am-5pm). For Ann Arbor jazz, call the **University Activities Office** at 763-1107.

NIGHTLIFE

The monthlies *Current, Agenda, Weekender Entertainment,* and the weekly *Metrotimes,* all free and available in restaurants, music stores, and elsewhere, print up-to-date nightlife and entertainment listings. For gay and lesbian info pick up a copy of *OutPost* or *Between the Lines.*

The **Blind Pig,** 208 S. First St. (996-8555), is out of sight with offerings of rock 'n' roll, reggae, blues, and swing (cover $3-8; F-Su 19+; open Tu-Su until 2am). **Rick's American Café,** 611 Church St. (996-2747), plays Ann Arbor's blues, with live music and a packed dance floor (21+; cover $3-5; open daily until 2am). Drawing big names on Fridays and Saturdays, the **Bird of Paradise,** 207 S. Ashley (662-8310), sings with live music every night (cover usually $3-5; free jam sessions on Su nights). The **Nectarine,** 516 E. Liberty (994-5436), offers DJ-controlled dance music, with gay nights on Tuesdays and Fridays (open Tu-Sa until 2am). **Conor O'Neill's,** 318 S. Main St. (665-2968), offers a good Celtic-flavored hangout (open daily until 2am).

■ Grand Rapids

From its humble beginning as one among many fur trading posts, Grand Rapids worked hard to distinguish itself from its neighbors. While many towns opted for tourist chic with quaint, old-fashioned looks, Grand Rapids plowed ahead to become a city of concrete, pavement, and tall buildings. The city has gone on to claim a couple of American firsts: Grand Rapids was the first city to put fluoride in its drinking water, and also produced America's only unelected president, Gerald Ford. While attractive to businesses, Grand Rapids offers little in the way of entertainment for the traveler. Most use it as a transportation hub to reach the rest of western Michigan.

PRACTICAL INFORMATION Most of Grand Rapids' streets are neatly gridded. The town is quartered by the north-south Division St. and the east-west Fulton St. **Greyhound,** 190 Wealthy St. (456-1707; station open daily 6:45am-10pm), connects to Detroit (3½hr., 4 per day, $21-23); Chicago (4½hr., 3 per day, $27-29); and Ann Arbor (3hr., 2 per day, $20-21). **Amtrak,** 507 Wealthy St. (800-872-7245), at Market, has service to the south and west, including Chicago (3¼hr., 1 per day, $32-46). The station only opens when trains pass through. **Grand Rapids Transit Authority (GRATA),** 333 Wealthy St. (776-1100), sends buses throughout the city and suburbs. (Runs M-F 5:45am-6:15pm, Sa 6:30am-9:30pm. Fare $1.25, seniors 60¢; 10-ride pass $7, students and seniors $6.) **Veterans Taxi** (459-4646) will get you where you want to go ($1.65 base fare, $1.60 per mi.; 24hr.). The **Grand Rapids-Kent County Convention and Visitors Bureau,** 134 Monroe Center (459-8287 or 800-678-9859; open M-F 10am-5:30pm) and the **West Michigan Tourist Association,** 1253 Front Ave. (456-8557 or 800-442-2084; open M-Th 8:30am-5pm, F 8:30am-6pm, Sa 9am-1pm) furnish general area info. **24hr. Suicide, Drug, Alcohol, and Crisis Line,** 336-3535. **Post Office:** 225 Michigan St. N.W. (776-1519; open M-F 7:30am-10pm, Sa 7:30am-8pm). **ZIP code:** 49503. **Area code:** 616.

GREAT LAKES

ACCOMMODATIONS, CAMPGROUNDS, AND FOOD Most of the cheaper motels and restaurants cluster south of the city along Division and 28th St. Rooms at **Motel 6,** 3524 28th St. SE (957-3511), have cable TV, HBO, and other conveniences of a national chain motel (singles $35; doubles $41). **The Knights Inn,** 35 28th St. SW (452-5141 or 800-843-5644), offers 102 spacious rooms, with indoor pool and hot tub (singles $38; doubles $50). Men are in luck at the **YMCA,** 33 Library St. NE (222-9626), downtown ($26, $15 per additional night; no reservations). Just 12 mi. northeast of downtown, **Grand Rogue Campgrounds,** 6400 W. River Dr. (361-1053), sports wooded, riverside sites. Take Rte. 131 north to Comstock Park Exit 91, then head left on W. River Dr. for 4 mi. ($17.75, with hookup $21.50.)

Grand Rapids' most popular Mexican food comes from the **Beltline Bar and Café,** 16 28th St. SE (245-0494). Plates of tacos go for $5.50, and burritos start at $5. (Open M-Tu 7am-midnight, W-Sa 7am-1am, Su noon-10:30pm.) **Pietro's Back Door Pizzeria,** 2780 Birchcrest Dr. (452-3228), off 28th St. SE, serves delicious wood-fired pizza with an array of gourmet toppings ($5-9), and an all-you-can-eat, pizza-and-pasta lunch for $5 (M-F 11:30am-1:30pm). The *ristorante* in front concocts higher-end Italian food for $7-14. (Both open M-Th 11:30am-1:30pm and 5-10pm, F 11:30am-1:30pm and 5-11pm, Sa noon-11pm, Su noon-11pm.) The **Grand Rapids Brewing Company,** 3689 28th St. SE (285-5970), whips up good burgers ($6), steaks, and "hand-crafted" house beers ($3 per pint). Tours are available upon request. (Open M-Th 11am-10pm, F-Sa 11am-11pm, Su 11am-10pm; bar open M-Th 11am-midnight, F-Sa 11am-1am, Su 11am-11pm.) The **Four Friends Coffeehouse,** 136 Monroe Center (456-5356), has cappuccino, espresso, a semi-artsy atmosphere, good muffins ($1.15), and live music on Fridays and Saturdays during the school year. (Open M-Th 7am-10pm, F 7am-midnight, Sa 9:30am-midnight; Sept.-May open until 11pm.)

SIGHTS AND NIGHTLIFE The **Van Andel Museum Center,** 272 Pearl St. NW (456-3977), houses the **Grand Rapids Public Museum,** a showcase for marvels such as one of the world's largest whale skeletons (76 ft.), a 50-animal carousel, and a planetarium (open daily 9am-5pm; $5, seniors $4, ages 3-17 $2; planetarium $1.50). The **Gerald R. Ford Museum,** 303 Pearl St. NW (451-9263), records the life and turbulent times of Grand Rapids' favorite native son. *(Open daily 9am-5pm. $3, seniors $2, under 16 free.)* Rotating exhibits feature such historical events as World War I and the Civil War. Above and beyond showcasing an eclectic collection of art, the **Grand Rapids Art Museum,** 155 N. Division Ave. (831-1001), makes an effort to get children's attention with a special tour map designed to keep them occupied and engaged. *(Open Tu-Th and Sa-Su 11am-6pm, F 11am-9pm. $3, students and seniors $2.)* The largest year-round conservatory in Michigan, the **Frederik Meijer Gardens,** 3411 Bradford St. (957-1580), at Beltline, keeps more than 70 bronze sculptures among numerous tropical plants spread out over 70 acres of wetlands. *(Open M-W and F-Sa 9am-5pm, Th 9am-9pm, Su noon-5pm; Sept.-May M-Sa 9am-5pm, Su noon-5pm. $5, seniors $4, ages 5-13 $2.)*

Detailed listings on events and nightlife in Grand Rapids can be found in *On the Town* or *In the City,* both available in most shops, restaurants, and kiosks. Dance clubs overshadow other forms of nightlife in the city. The largest dance club in Grand Rapids, **The Orbit Room** (942-1328), at E. Beltline and 28th St., packs in up to 1200 gyrating bodies for nightly music ranging from alternative to top 40, disco to country. *(W 18+, other nights 19+ until 11pm. Open W and F-Su 9am-2pm. Occasional M concerts at 8pm; tickets $10-30, 18+.)* **The Anchor,** 447 Bridge St. (774-7177), is a good old American bar, filled with locals and fairly cheap drinks (open M-F 3pm-2am, Sa 5pm-2am, Su 6pm-2am; 21+ to enter). The gay crowd prefers **Diversions,** 10 Fountain NW (451-3800; open M-F 11am-2am, Sa-Su 8pm-2am; cover $3 F-Sa; 18+ to enter).

■ Lake Michigan Shore

With dunes of sugary sand, superb fishing, abundant fruit harvests, and deep winter snows, the eastern shore of Lake Michigan has been a vacationer's dreamland for over a century. The coastline stretches 350 mi. north from the Indiana border to the Mackinaw Bridge; its southern end comes within a scant two hours from downtown Chicago. The freighters that once powered the rise of Chicago still steam along, but have long since been supplanted by the pleasure boats that mob the coast.

Many of the region's attractions nestle in small coastal towns, which cluster around Grand Traverse Bay in the north. Coastal accommodations can be exorbitantly expensive; for cheaper lodging, head inland. Traverse City, at the southern tip of the bay, is famous as the "cherry capital of the world," and fishing is best in the Au Sable and Manistee Rivers. However, the rich Mackinac Island Fudge, sold in numerous specialty shops, seems to have the biggest hold on tourists ("fudgies" to locals; see **Mackinac Island**, p. 418). The main north-south route along the coast is U.S. 31. Numerous detours twist closer to the shoreline, providing an excellent way to explore the coast. The **West Michigan Tourist Association,** 1253 Front Ave. NW (456-8557 or 800-442-2084) hands out literature on the area (open M-Th 8:30am-5pm, F 8:30am-6pm, Sa 9am-1pm). The entire Lake Michigan Shore's **area code:** 616.

■ Southern Michigan Shore

Holland Southwest of Grand Rapids off I-196, Holland was founded in 1847 by Dutch religious dissenters and remained mostly Dutch well into the 20th century. The town now cashes in on its heritage with a bevy of tacky Netherlands-inspired attractions. Watch 'em craft clogs at **The Wooden Shoe Factory,** 447 U.S. 31 (396-6513), at 16th St. (Open daily 8am-4pm. Free.) You may even glimpse Shaquille O'Neal's autographed pair. **Windmill Island** (355-1030), at 7th St. and Lincoln Ave., supports a few scattered Dutch buildings besides its namesake. (Open May and July-Aug. M-Sa 9am-6pm, Su 11:30am-6pm; June and Sept. M-F 9am-5pm, Sa 9am-5pm, Su 11:30am-5pm; Oct. M-Sa 10am-4pm. $5.50, children $2.50.) The diminutive but high-quality **Holland Museum,** 31 W. 10th St. (392-9084), displays ceramics, furniture from the home country, and exhibits on town history. (Open M, W, F-Sa 10am-5pm, Th 10am-8pm, Su 2-5pm. $3, students and seniors $2.) The harvest at the jubilantly arrayed **Veldheer Tulip Gardens,** 12755 Quincy St. (399-1900), at U.S. 31, would be the envy of the Amsterdam market (open M-F 8am-6pm; $2.50, ages 3-13 $1.50; in winter $5/$3). A nearby "authentically" recreated **Dutch Village,** 12350 James St. (396-1475), at U.S. 31, resembles a 25-hole mini-golf course without the holes. Highlights of the 25 "sights" include a life-size plastic horse-and-buggy and a wooden shoe with slide. (Open late Apr. to mid-Oct. daily 9am-5pm. $6, ages 3-11 $4.)

The **Blue Mill Inn,** 409 U.S. 31 (392-7073 or 888-258-3140), adjacent to the Wooden Shoe Factory at 16th St., rents single rooms from $52 and doubles for $64 (off-season rates lower). **Holland State Park,** 2215 Ottawa Beach Rd. (399-9390 or 800-447-2757), 8 mi. west of Holland, has 306 sparsely wooded sites nestled between Lake Macatawa and Lake Michigan (sites $15; $4 vehicle permit). Information awaits at the **Holland Convention and Visitors Bureau,** 76 E. 8th St. (394-0000 or 800-506-1299; open M-F 8am-5pm, May-Oct. also Sa 10am-3pm). **Greyhound,** 171 Lincoln Ave. (396-8664 or 800-231-2222), runs through Holland to Detroit (4hr., 3 per day, $25-27); Chicago (4hr., 3 per day, $24-26); and Grand Rapids (35min., 3 per day, $7). **Amtrak** (800-872-7245), in the same building, runs a daily train to Chicago (3hr., $27). Reserve train tickets in advance; there are no Amtrak representatives at the station. (Station for Greyhound and Amtrak open M-F 7-11am and 12:30-4:30pm.)

Grand Haven One of the best beaches on the Eastern Lake Michigan Shore, Grand Haven offers the weary traveler a relaxed, resort-like atmosphere and lots of sand—so pure that auto manufacturers use it to make cores and molds for engine parts. The town lies about 35 mi. west of Grand Rapids off I-96, and features a cement "boardwalk" that connects the beach to the small downtown area, making for a short but balmy promenade. Washington St. serves as the core of downtown Grand Haven. Visitors can stock up on skiing, boating, fishing, and lodging info at the **Grand Haven Area Visitors Bureau,** 1 S. Harbor Dr. (842-4499 or 800-303-4096; open M-F 8am-5pm). The **Morning Star Café,** 711 Washington St. (844-1131), sizzles with Southwestern breakfast and lunch fare for $4-5 (open daily 6:30am-2:30pm). The **Kardomah Lodge,** 1365 Lake Ave. (842-2990), rents charming country-style rooms less than 200 yd. from the beach. (Kitchen and shared bath. Doubles $55, $10 per additional person. Reservations strongly recommended.) Campers who don't mind a beach parking lot will love **Grand Haven State Park** (800-447-2757); its 168 sites rest less than 200 ft. from the shores of Lake Michigan.

■ Central Michigan Shore

Manistee and Interlochen Manistee's Victorian shtick is overshadowed by the impressive trio of natural beauties surrounding the city. Lake Michigan tempts boaters, swimmers, and beachgoers, while fishing buffs find Manistee Lake an outstanding catch. **Manistee National Forest** supplies copious camping at 11 campgrounds in the area ($5 per person; no reservations). The more rugged are free to camp anywhere in the forest without a permit. More info on hiking and canoeing is available from the **Manistee Ranger Station,** 1658 Manistee Hwy. (723-2211), 2 mi. north of Manistee on U.S. 31 (open M-F 8am-5pm).

There are several inexpensive motel options in and near Manistee. The friendly **Riverside Motel,** 520 Water St. (723-3554), has dock space for boats and offers evening river tours (rooms $50-90; in winter $40). Fourteen miles north in Onekama, the **Traveller's Motel,** 5606 Eight Mile Rd. (889-4342), a ½ block from Rte. 22, provides enormous rooms with kitchenettes. (Singles $45, doubles $60, kitchenettes sleeping up to 6 people $80; in winter $32/$42/$55.)

The **Manistee County Chamber of Commerce,** 11 Cypress St. (723-2575 or 800-288-2286), stocks pamphlets on local attractions (open M-F 8am-6pm, Sa 8am-5pm, Su 4-10pm; Sept.-May M-F 8am-5:30pm). Thirty miles to the south, the **Lake Michigan Car Ferry** (800-841-4243) shuttles people and cars between Ludington and Manitowoc, WI. (4hr.; 2 per day late June to Aug., in spring and fall 1 per day; $37, seniors $34, ages 5-15 $16, for cars an additional $45.)

The renowned **Interlochen Center for the Arts** (276-7200), in Interlochen, 17 mi. south of Traverse City on Rte. 137, trains talented young artists in classical music, dance, theater, and creative writing (free campus tours Tu-Sa 10:30am and 2:30pm, Su 11am and 4pm). Here, the **International Arts Festival,** held year-round, has attracted the likes of Tony Bennett, Natalie Cole, Gladys Knight, and James Taylor. Faculty and students also put on top-notch concerts in the various arts throughout the year. (Box office open in summer M 9am-4:30pm, Tu-Sa 9am-8:30pm, Su noon-8:30pm; reduced hrs. in off season. Tickets $5-30.) **Interlochen State Park** (276-9511 or 800-447-2757) offers recreation and camping nearby, 1 mi. south of Interlochen along Rte. 137, directly opposite the Center for Arts. (Sites $6, with electricity and showers $14. Vehicle permit $4. Ranger station open daily 8am-1:30am.)

Sleeping Bear Dunes The Sleeping Bear Dunes rest along the western shores of the Leelanau Peninsula, 20 mi. west of Traverse City on Rte. 72. According to Chippewa legend, the mammoth sand dunes represent a sleeping mother bear, waiting for her drowned cubs—the Manitou Islands—to finish a swim across the lake. **Manitou Island Transit** (256-9061), in Leland, makes daily trips to South Manitou and ventures five times per week in July and August to the larger, wilder North Manitou. (Round-trip $20, under 13 $13. Check-in 9:15am. Call ahead for schedule in May-June and Sept.-Nov.) **Camping** is available on both islands with the purchase of a **permit** ($7 for 7 days; buy at the visitors center); the Manitou Islands do not allow cars.

The **Sleeping Bear Dunes National Lakeshore,** of which the islands are one part, also includes 25 mi. of lakeshore on the mainland. When the glaciers came to a halt and melted, mountains of fine sand were left behind, creating a landscape resembling a cross between an ocean coast and a desert. To gain entrance to all the Lakeshore's splendors, purchase a vehicle permit at any of various points in the area ($7, good for 1 week). You can be king of the sandhill at **Dune Climb,** 5 mi. north of Empire on Rte. 109. From there, a strenuous 2½ mi. hike over sandy hills leads to Lake Michigan in all its refreshing glory. If you'd rather let your car do the climbing, motor to an overlook along the **Pierce Stocking Scenic Drive,** off Rte. 109 just north of Empire, where a 450 ft. sand cliff descends on the cool water below (open mid-May to mid-

Oct. daily 9am-10pm). For maps and info on the numerous cross-country skiing, hiking, and mountain biking trails, call the **National Parks Service Visitors Center,** 9922 Front St. (326-5134), in Empire (open daily 9am-5pm; mid-Oct. to May 9:30am-4pm).

The Platte River (at the southern end) and the Crystal River (near Glen Arbor at the northern end) are great for canoeing or floating. **Riverside Canoes,** 5042 Scenic Hwy./Rte. 22 (325-5622), at Platte River Bridge, offers excursions in inner tubes ($4-6 for 1hr., $11-13 for 2hr.); canoes ($25-29); or kayaks ($16). Sleeping Bear Dunes has four **campgrounds: DH Day** (334-4634), in Glen Arbor, with 83 primitive sites ($10); **Platte River** (325-5881 or 800-365-2267), off the southern shore, with 179 sites and showers ($14, with electricity $19); and two cheaper **backcountry campsites** accessible by 1½ mi. trails. (No reservations. Required permit available at the visitors center or at either developed campground for $5.)

Traverse City Named after the "Grand Traverse" that French fur traders once made between the Leelanau and Old Michigan Peninsulas, Traverse City offers the summer vacationer a slew of sandy beaches and more cherries than you can count (50% of the nation's cherries are produced in the surrounding area). The annual **Cherry Festival** (947-4230; info office open M-F 9am-5pm), held the first full week in July, serves as a tribute to the fruit's annual harvest. In early to mid-July, five orchards near Traverse City let you pick your own cherries, including **Amon Orchards** (938-9160), 10 mi. north on U.S. 31 ($1.25 per lb.; eat while you pick for free; open daily 9am-5pm). The more sophisticated fruit connoisseur might indulge in the area's many wineries. **Château Grand Traverse,** 12239 Center Rd. (223-7355 or 800-283-0247), 8 mi. north of Traverse City on M37, offers free tours and tastings. (In summer, tours on the hr. noon-4pm. Open M-Sa 10am-7pm, Su noon-6pm; Nov.-Apr. M-Sa 10am-5pm, Su noon-5pm.)

The nearby sparkling bay and ancient sand dunes make this region a Great Lakes paradise, though a crowded and expensive one. In the summer, swimming, boating, and scuba diving interests focus on Grand Traverse Bay; free beaches and public access sites speckle the shore. You can explore the coastline of the Leelanau Peninsula, between Grand Traverse Bay and Lake Michigan, on scenic Rte. 22—don't miss out on Leland, a charming fishing village, which now launches the Manitou Island ferries (see **Sleeping Bear Dunes,** above), via M22. The area's scenic waterfront makes for excellent biking. The **TART** bike trail runs 8 mi. along E. and W. Grand Traverse Bay, while the 30 mi. loop around Old Mission Peninsula, just north of the city, provides great views of the Bay on both sides. **Brick Wheels,** 736 E. 8th St. (947-4274), rents bikes ($15 per day; open M-Th 9am-6pm, F 9am-8pm, Sa 9am-4:30pm). For local events and entertainment, pick up the weekly *Traverse City Record-Eagle Summer Magazine* or *Northern Express,* available in corner kiosks around the city.

Traverse City State Park, 1132 U.S. 31 N (922-5270 or 800-447-2757), 2 mi. east of town, satisfies camping needs with wooded sites across the street from the beach (sites with hookup $15; $4 vehicle permit fee). In town, E. Front St. is lined with motels, but you'll have trouble finding a room for under $50. **Northwestern Michigan College,** 1701 E. Front St., West Hall (922-1409), has some of the cheapest beds in the city. (1 bedroom $35, 2-room suite with bathroom $50. Open late June to Aug. Reserve several weeks in advance.) The **Shoestring Resort** (946-7935), at the intersection of Garfield and River Rd., 12 mi. south of town, offers exceptionally nice cabins with one to three bedrooms, kitchens, cable TV, and A/C. (Cottages start at $35 per night; in winter $10 lower; weekly rates available. Reserve 1 week in advance.)

Indian Trails and **Greyhound,** 3233 Cass Rd. (946-5180 or 800-231-2222), tie Traverse City to Detroit (7½hr., 3 per day, $38) and to the Upper Peninsula via St. Ignace (2½hr., 1 per day, $17). The **Bay Area Transportation Authority** (941-2324) has a demand response service; you call them and they'll pick you up (fare $2, daily pass $5; available M-F 5:30am-6pm, Sa 9am-6pm). The **Traverse City Convention and Visitors Bureau,** 101 West Grandview Pkwy./ U.S. 31 N (947-1120 or 800-872-8377), dispenses the helpful *Traverse City Guide* and books rooms. (Open M-F 9am-6pm, Sa 9am-5pm, Su noon-4pm; in winter M-F 9am-5pm, Sa 9am-3pm.) **Post Office:** 202 S. Union St. (946-9616; open M-F 9am-4pm). **ZIP code:** 49684.

GREAT LAKES

■ Northern Michigan Shore

Charlevoix and Beaver Island Situated on the ½ mi. wide ribbon of land between Lake Michigan and Lake Charlevoix, the stretch of coast near Charlevoix (SHAR-le-voy), north of Traverse City on U.S. 31, served as the setting for some of Hemingway's Nick Adams stories. The yacht-rich, upper-crust town now attracts more tourists than it did in Hemingway's time; the population triples in the summer. In "Charlevoix the Beautiful," golf is king; the town boasts 16 courses for 8500 residents. The **Charlevoix Area Chamber of Commerce,** 408 Bridge St. (547-2101 or 800-367-8557), dishes the dirt on the area (open M-F 9am-5pm, Sa 10am-5pm). Lodging rarely comes cheap in this resort-oriented area, but campers can bask in 90 sites on the shores of Lake Michigan at **Fisherman's Island State Park** (547-6641 or 800-447-2757), on Bells Bay Rd., 5 mi. south of Charlevoix on U.S. 31 (rustic sites $6; $4 vehicle permit fee). Those who simply can't dispense with showers and electricity can head to the **Colonial Motel,** 6822 U.S. 31 S. (547-6637), with free coffee, A/C, and cable TV (singles $38-60; doubles $48-70; lower rates in off season; open May-Oct.).

Charlevoix also serves as the gateway to Beaver Island, the Great Lakes' most remote inhabited island. Hiking, boating, biking, and swimming abound on the island's 53 sq. mi., just a 2¼hr. ferry trip from shore. (**Ferries** depart from 102 Bridge St. 1-3 times per day. Round-trip $31, ages 5-12 $15.50, bikes $12. Call 547-2311 or 888-446-4095 for more info.) The **Beaver Island Chamber of Commerce** (448-2505) can advise callers on camping, lodging, and food options.

Petoskey Eighteen miles north of Charlevoix, Petoskey is renowned for Petoskey Stones, fossilized coral from an ancient sea. For info on beaches and other attractions, including canoeing, orchards, and walking tours, contact the **Petoskey Regional Chamber of Commerce,** 401 E. Mitchell (347-4150). (Open M-F 8am-5pm, Sa 10am-3pm, Su noon-4pm; mid-Oct. to May M-F 8am-5pm, Sa 10am-3pm.)

Homely **North Central Michigan College,** 1515 Howard St. (348-6713; 348-6612 for reservations), rents single dorm rooms within a suite. (Singles $25; doubles $31; 4-person suite $55. Linen provided. Reservations recommended; cash or check only.) The **Petoskey Motel** (347-8177), at the corner of U.S. 31 and U.S. 131, rents clean, spacious rooms with A/C and cable (singles $39-49). **Petoskey State Park** (347-2311), 5 mi. east of town off Rte. 119 (take U.S. 31 N for 2 mi., then left on Rte. 119), offers 170 campsites on Little Traverse Bay (sites with electricity $15; $4 vehicle fee). Petoskey's **Gaslight District,** 1 block from the chamber of commerce, features local crafts and foods in period shops. In the heart of it, **Roast and Toast Café,** 309 E. Lake St. (347-7767), serves pasta and chicken dishes for $7-10 (open daily 7am-9:30pm).

In a remote woodland just outside Indian River, 20 mi. east of Petoskey, 3 tons of bronze and 12 tons of redwood were reverently molded into a 31 ft. Jesus cleaved onto a 55 ft. tall cross. An anguished yet oddly imposing monument to the national obsession with size, the **Cross in the Woods,** 7078 M68 (238-8973), completed in 1959, is easily the world's tallest.

North of Petoskey, Rte. 119 winds along the lakeside through tunnels of trees and hiking-trail scenery. In Cross Village, **Legs Inn** (526-2281), the only restaurant for miles, serves Polish entrees ($7-15) and over 100 beers amid fantastic Native American decor. (W-Su live blues, folk, reggae, etc. Cover F-Su $2-4. Open mid-May to mid-Oct. daily noon-10pm or later.)

Straits of Mackinac Only Canucks and fur'ners say "mackinACK"; in the Land of the Great Turtle (as early Native Americans called it), Mackinac is pronounced "mackinAW." Colonial **Fort Michilimackinac** (this one rhymes with "crack") still guards the straits between Lake Michigan and Lake Superior, as tourists, not troops, flock to Mackinaw City. Along with Fort Michilimackinac, **Fort Mackinac** (on Mackinac Island) and **Historic Mill Creek** (3½ mi. south of Mackinac on Rte. 23) form a trio of State Historic Parks (436-5563). (All open daily mid-June to early Sept. 9am-6pm; early Sept. to Oct. and mid-May to mid-June 10am-5pm. Each park $7.25, ages 6-12 $4.25, families $20; season pass to all 3 $13/$7.50/$38.)

The **Michigan Dept. of Transportation Welcome and Travel Information Center** (436-5566), on Nicolet St. off I-75 at Exit 338, has more. (Free reservation service. Open Sa-Th 9am-7pm, F 9am-8pm; Sept. to mid-June daily 9am-5pm.) **Indian Trails** (517-725-5105 or 800-292-3831 in MI) has a flag stop at the Big Boy restaurant on Nicolet Ave. One bus runs north and one south daily; buy tickets at the next station.

Campers can bed down at **Mackinaw Mill Creek Campground** (436-5584), 3 mi. south of town on Rte. 23. Most of its 600 sites lie near the lake (sites $12.50, full hookup $15; cabins $35, 2nd night $30, 3rd $25). Sites at the **Wilderness State Park** (436-5381), 11 mi. west on Wilderness Park Dr., have showers and electricity ($15; 4-8-person cabins $40; 20-person bunkhouse $55). **Motel 6,** 206 Nicolet St. (436-8961), holds down the fort with modern rooms, cable, and an indoor pool (singles $40-67).

The prohibition of cars on Mackinac Island, and resulting proliferation of horse-drawn carriages, has given the heavily touristed island a decidedly equine aroma. The main draws are **Fort Mackinac** (906-847-3328; open daily 9:30am-6:30pm; closed in winter), Victorian homes, and the **Grand Hotel** (906-847-3331 or 800-33-GRAND/334-7263). Connoisseurs will immediately recognize the island as the birthplace of Mackinac Fudge, sold in shops all over the Michigan coastline (1 lb. box $7). Lodging is never cheap on the island, but the Grand Hotel carries the cost (and elegance) to an extreme; a double goes for $460-750 per night. For $7, you can lurk on the estate grounds (open daily 9am-5:30pm); for $10, you can dangle your feet in the pool; and for $15, you can even set foot on the tennis courts. **Horse-drawn carriages** cart guests all over the island (906-847-3325; open daily 8:30am-5pm; $13, ages 4-11 $6.50). Saddle horses ($22 per hr.) are also available at various stables around the isle.

Perhaps the best way to see the island is by bicycle. Rentals line Main St. by the ferry docks ($4 per hr.). Encompassing 80% of the island, **Mackinac Island State Park** features a circular 8.2 mi. shoreline road for biking and hiking (free). The invaluable **Mackinac Island Locator Map and Business Directory** ($1) and the *Discover Mackinac Island* book ($2) can be found at the **Mackinac Island Chamber of Commerce** (906-847-3783 or 800-4-LILACS/454-5257), on Main St. (open daily 8am-7pm; Oct.-May 9am-5pm). Three competing ferry lines leave Mackinaw City and St. Ignace with overlapping schedules. During the summer, a ferry leaves every 15-30min. from 7:30am-midnight (round-trip $13, under 11 $7, bike passage $5).

■ Upper Peninsula

A multi-million-acre forestland bordered by three of the world's largest lakes, Michigan's Upper Peninsula (U.P.) is among the most scenic, unspoiled stretches of land in the Great Lakes region. But in 1837, after Congress decided in favor of Ohio in the fight over Toledo, Michigan only grudgingly accepted this "wasteland to the north" in the unpopular deal that gave the territory statehood. From the start, Michigan made the most of the land, laying waste to huge tracts of forest destined for the treeless Great Plains and the fireplaces of Chicago. In the past century, however, the forests, now protected, have returned to their former grandeur, and the U.P.'s spectacular waterfalls and miles of coastline have won the hearts of nature lovers.

Only 24,000 people live in the U.P.'s largest town, **Marquette.** The region is a paradise for fishing, camping, hiking, snowmobiling, and getting away from it all. Hikers enjoy numerous treks, including Michigan's section of **North Country Trail,** a national scenic trail extending from New York to North Dakota. Contact the **North Country Trail Association,** 49 Monroe Center NW, Suite 200B, Grand Rapids 49503 (616-454-5506) for details. A vibrant spectrum of foliage makes autumn a beautiful time to hike; in the winter, skiers replace hikers. Dozens of rivers beckon canoers to the area as well. Those who heed the call of the rapids should contact the **Michigan Recreational Canoe Association,** P.O. Box 357, Baldwin 49304 (616-745-1554).

The peninsula has 200 **campgrounds,** including those at both national forests (call 800-543-2937 for reservations). Sleep with your dogs or bring extra blankets—temperatures in these parts drop to 50°F, even in July. Outside the major tourist towns, motel rooms start at around $24. For regional cuisine, indulge in the Friday night **fish-fry:** all-you-can-eat perch, walleye, or whitefish buffets available in nearly every restau-

GREAT LAKES

> ### Pasty, anyone?
> The pasty originated in Cornwall, England, where it was a regular staple of tinmin-
> ers and fishermen. Legend has it that pasty cooks would carve the initials of the
> intended eater into the dough. Fishermen would start eating their pasties at the
> uninitialized end. When the fish bit, they could put the dish down and immedi-
> ately mind the catch. Afterwards, the initials would reveal exactly whose meal
> was whose. The Michigan version of the pasty usually contains flour, lard, steak,
> potatoes, turnips, onions, and ground pepper. So what does it taste like? As one
> native of Sault Ste. Marie put it, "Well…sort of like…beef stew pie."

rant in every town for about $7-10. The local ethnic specialty is a meat pie, imported
by Cornish miners in the 19th century, called a **pasty** (see below).

Welcome centers guard the U.P. at its six main entry points: **Ironwood,** 801 W.
Cloverland Dr. (932-3330; open daily June-Sept. 8am-6pm, in winter 8am-4pm); **Iron
Mountain,** 618 S. Stephenson Ave. (774-4201; open daily June-Sept. 7am-5pm, in winter 8am-4pm); **Menominee,** 1343 10th Ave. (863-6496; open June-Sept. daily 8am-
4pm); **Marquette,** 2201 U.S. 41 S (249-9066; open daily mid-June to Aug. 9am-6pm;
in winter 9am-5pm); **Sault Ste. Marie,** 943 Portage Ave. W. (632-8242; open daily
June-Sept. 8am-6pm, in winter 9am-5pm); and **St. Ignace,** 643-6979), on I-75 N (open
mid-June to early Sept. Sa-Th 9am-7pm, F 9am-8pm; in winter daily 9am-5pm). Pick
up the invaluable *Upper Peninsula Travel Planner,* published by the **Upper Peninsula Travel and Recreation Association** (800-562-7134; info line staffed M-F 8am-
4:30pm). For additional help planning a trip into the wilderness, write to or call the
U.S. Forestry Service, 2727 N. Lincoln Rd., Escanaba 49829 (786-4062). The Upper
Peninsula's **area code** is 906.

Sault Ste. Marie and the Eastern U.P.
Ask the locals why people come
to gritty Sault (pronounced "soo") Ste. Marie, and they'll inevitably answer, "the locks."
The St. Mary's River connects—and separates—Lake Huron and Lake Superior. Back in
the day, there was a 21 ft. vertical drop over 1 mi., rendering the river impassable by
boat. Native Americans simply picked up their canoes and walked the distance, but a
1000 ft. freighter needs a little more help. In 1855, entrepreneurs built the first lock
here. The busiest in the world today, the city's four locks float over 12,000 ships annually. Visitors can bob through the locks on a 2hr. **Soo Locks Boat Tour** (632-6301 or
800-432-6301), which leaves from both 1157 and 515 E. Portage Ave. (Call for departure times. Open mid-May to mid-Oct. $14, ages 13-18 $11, ages 5-12 $6.50.) For land-
lubbers, the **Locks Park Historic Walkway** parallels the water for 1 mi. The walkway
passes a decent **museum,** 300 W. Portage St., featuring exhibits on how a lock works,
and a lookout deck to observe ships passing through. (Open daily mid-June to early
Sept. 7am-10pm; mid-May to mid-June and mid-Sept. to early Nov. 8am-10pm.) On the
waterfront at the end of Johnston St., the **Valley Camp** (632-3658), a 1917 steam-powered freighter, locks in the Great Lakes's largest maritime museum and the **Marine Hall
of Fame.** Call ahead for group tours. (Open daily July-Aug. 9am-9pm; mid-May to June
and Sept. to mid-Oct. 10am-6pm. $6.50, children $3.50.) Just up the block from the
water, the concrete **Tower of History,** 326 E. Portage St. (635-0583), offers a panoramic view of the locks and ships (open mid-May to mid-Oct. daily 10am-6pm; $3.25,
ages 6-16 $1.75).

Get stuffed with burgers ($3-7) and classic American entrees down the street at **The
Antlers,** 804 E. Portage St. (632-3571), where "prices vary due to the attitude of customers." Animal lovers beware—the walls have eyes (and heads and bodies: bear, deer,
and hog, for example). The area's best lodging deal lies just over the bridge in Ontario.
The Algonquin Hotel (HI-C), 864 Queen St. E. (705-253-2311), has spacious rooms
just ½ mi. from the bridge. (Singles CDN$21.25, doubles CDN$33.60; nonmembers
$28/$29.20. Cash or travelers checks only.) Otherwise, affordable accommodations
line the I-75 Business Spur on the American side. **Sleepy Buck's Motel,** 3501 I-75 Business Spur (632-1173 or 800-781-1102), has clean, fresh-smelling rooms with TVs and
phones for $35-50. West of the city, frolic in the uncrowded eastern branch of the **Hia-
watha National Forest** (635-5311; no showers; sites $8-10; no reservations). The forest

runs four rustic, lakefront campsites. **Monocle Campgrounds** (635-1003) lies the closest to the city, 27 mi. west on Lakeshore Dr. In the summer, the crystal-clear waters of Lake Superior and secluded **beaches** on Lakeshore Dr. beckon bathers. At the **Tahquamenon Falls State Park** (492-3415), 80min. west of the city, you can rent a **canoe** ($6 for ½-day) or **rowboat** ($1.50 per person) at the Lower Falls, or gawk at the 50 ft. Upper Falls (no barrel riders here).

North of Tahquamenon, over **300 shipwrecks** lie off Whitefish Point. Protected today as the **Underwater Preserve,** they afford divers an opportunity to search for sunken treasure. For more info, contact the **Paradise Area Tourism Council** (492-3927), P.O. Box 64, Paradise 49768. The dim, eerie **Great Lakes Shipwreck Historical Museum** (492-3436 or 800-635-1742) documents this "Graveyard of the Great Lakes" (open mid-May to mid-Oct. daily 9am-6pm; $7, under 13 $4).

Middle of the Peninsula The western branch of the **Hiawatha National Forest** dominates the middle of the Peninsula, offering limitless wilderness activities and many **campsites** (sites $8-12; pit toilets, no showers; call 800-280-2667 for reservations). **Rapid River** (474-6442) is home to the southern office of the west branch on Hwy. 2. In the north, **Munising,** on Hwy. 28, has access to the forest and to **Pictured Rocks National Lakeshore,** where water saturated with copper, manganese, and iron oxide paints the cliffs with multicolored bands. **Pictured Rocks Boat Cruise** (387-2379), at the city dock in Munising, gives the best view (tours approximately 3hr.; $22, ages 6-12 $7, under 6 free). The Forest and Lakeshore share a **visitors center** (387-3700) at the intersection of Rte. 28 and H58 in Munising (open daily 8am-6pm). From Munising, H58—a bumpy, unpaved gem of a road—weaves along the lakeshore past numerous trailheads and campsites; spare tires are necessary if you plan extensive traveling in the Hiawatha Forest. For a paved alternative from Munising to Grand Sable, the path runs east on Rte. 28, then north on Rte. 77.

Backcountry **camping permits** for one to six people ($15) are available from the Munising or **Grand Sable Visitors Center** (494-2660), 2 mi. west of Grand Marais on H58 (open mid-May to early Sept. daily 10am-7pm). Visitors can stroll, birdwatch, or collect smooth stones along the shore at **Twelve Mile Beach** (self-registered campsites $10; pump water only), a 17 mi. drive from the visitors center, and **Grand Sable Dunes,** ½ mi. walk from the VC. From atop the sandy **Log Slide,** you can survey Lake Superior; "polar bears" can take a plunge in the ice water. If all this liquid is making you thirsty, **Dune's Saloon** in Grand Marais, home of the **Lake Superior Brewing Company** (at the junction of Rte. 77 and H58), can hook you up with a Hematite Stout or an Agate Amber ($2.25). For more than a tent, the **Poplar Bluff Cabins,** Star Rte. Box 3118 (452-6271), has lakeview rooms with kitchens. Head 12 mi. east of Munising on Rte. 28, then 6 mi. south from Shingleton on M94 to get there. (Cottages $35-40 per night, $200 per week. Free use of boats on lake year-round.)

The **Seney National Wildlife Refuge** (586-9851), on Rte. 77, shelters 95,000 acres for over 250 species of birds and mammals (visitors center open daily 9am-5pm). Admission to the park is free and includes the 7 mi. **Marshland Wildlife Drive,** a self-guided auto tour replete with loon and eagle observation decks; the best times for viewing wildlife are early morning and early evening. The refuge also offers hiking, cross-country skiing, biking, canoeing, and fishing (pike and perch) opportunities. Anglers will need a required state **fishing permit.** (Permits $6 per day, $39 per year, residents $26 per year; available at any convenience store, grocery, or tackle shop.)

At the bottom of the peninsula, the **Big Spring** (341-2355) is the jewel of **Palms Brook State Park;** take U.S. 2 to Thompson and go 11 mi. north on M149. (Open daily 9am-7pm. No camping.) A must-see of the Upper Peninsula, the crystal blue Spring shelters numerous trout and several underwater geysers of hydro-activity. All this can be observed from the deck of a raft, which transverses the spring via cable. At nearby **Indian Lake State Park** (800-543-2937), take M149 to County Rd. 442 and go east for camping options. (Teepees $23, cabins $32, campsites with electricity $9. More campsites available on the lake's west side.) Reservations are necessary for teepees and cabins, and recommended for campsites. Farther south, the **Fayette State Historic Park** (644-2603) handles camping (no showers, sites $9; open mid-May to mid-Oct.). All state parks require a $4 daily vehicle permit or $20 annual permit.

GREAT LAKES

Keweenaw Peninsula In 1840, Dr. Douglas Houghton's mineralogical survey of the Keweenaw Peninsula, a curved finger of land on the U.P.'s northwest corner, incited a copper mining rush which sent the area booming. When mining petered out around 1969, the land was left barren and exploited. Today, reforestation and government support have helped Copper Country find new life as a tourist destination. Every year, 250 in. of snow fall on the towering pines, smooth-stone beaches, and low mountains of Keweenaw. Visitors ski, snowshoe, and snowmobile through the winter and enjoy the gorgeous green coasts in the summer.

At the base of the peninsula, hugging the shore of Lake Superior, sits the **Porcupine Mountain Wilderness State Park** (885-5275, for reservations 800-444-2757), affectionately known as "The Porkies." The park sports campsites ($9-14; water and electricity, but no showers), cabins ($35-45; sleep 2-8), backcountry permits (1-4 people $6), and paths into the **Old Growth Forest,** the largest tract of uncut forest between the Rockies and the Adirondacks. Reservations are required for cabins. The **visitors center,** near the junction of M107 and South Boundary Rd. inside the park, provides $4 per day **camping permits,** good for all Michigan parks (open in summer daily 10am-6pm; all campers must have a vehicle sticker). You won't want to miss **Lake of the Clouds,** 8 mi. inside the park on M107, considered by many to be the best sight in the Porkies. The **Houghton Visitors Center,** 326 Sheldon Ave. (482-5240), has info on the entire peninsula (open M-Sa 8am-5pm).

At the top of the Peninsula, the **Brockway Mountain Dr.** (6 mi.), between Eagle Harbor and Copper Harbor, is a must for those weary of relentlessly flat terrain. Rising 1337 ft. above sea level, its summit provides some of the best views on the U.P.

The northernmost town in Michigan, **Copper Harbor** functions as the main gateway to **Isle Royale National Park** (see below). **Brockway Inn** (289-4588), 3 blocks west of Copper Harbor near Hwy. M26, pleases patrons with cable TV, free coffee, and some rooms with a private whirlpool (singles $35-45; doubles from $48). **The Gratiot Street Café** (289-4223), on U.S. 41 in Copper Harbor, serves up light fare for low prices. Pasties ($3.50) or the Cajun chicken sandwich ($3.50) prove wise choices (open daily 11am-10pm). Just down the street, the **Keweenaw Adventure Company** (289-4303)—look for the bikes out front—can make all your wilderness dreams come true with dogsled rides ($40 for 2 people, overnight trip with training $225 per person); kayaking outings (2½hr. intro paddle $24); bike rentals (½-day $10, full-day $20); and more. Campers in Keweenaw do well to head for **Mclain State Park** (482-0278), 8 mi. north of Hancock on M203. The campground rests along a 2 mi. beach and is home to an impressive lighthouse. (Sites with water and electricity $14; vehicle permit required.)

■ Isle Royale

Around the turn of the century, moose swam from the Canadian coast to this pristine 45 mi. long, 10 mi. wide island. With no natural predators, the animals overran the land. Today, wild animals (the Isle supports a pack of wolves) are the island's only permanent inhabitants. After the island was designated Isle Royale National Park in 1940, the fisherfolk who once lived here left. For backcountry seclusion, this is where to go; no cars, phones, or medical services pamper visitors. Come prepared.

Streams, lakes, and 170 mi. of trails traverse the park. The **Greenstone Ridge Trail,** the main artery of the trail system, follows the backbone of the island from Rock Harbor Lodge, passing through several spectacular vistas. Serious backpackers will want to conquer the **Minong Ridge Trail,** which runs parallel to the Greenstone Trail to the north for 30 mi. from McCargoe Cove to Windigo; the remains of early Native American copper mines line the trail. Shorter hikes near Rock Harbor include **Scoville Point,** a 4.2 mi. loop out onto a small peninsula, and **Suzy's Cave,** a 3.8 mi. loop to an inland sea arch. The park office has info on cruises, evening programs, and ranger-led interpretive walks. **Canoeing** and **kayaking** allow access to otherwise inaccessible parts of the island; both Rock Harbor and Windigo have **boat** and **canoe rental** outfitters. (Motors $12.50 per ½-day, $21 per day. Boats and canoes $11 per ½-day, $18.75 per day.) **Scuba divers** can explore shipwrecks in the treacherous reefs off the northeast and west ends of the island—after registering at the park office. There are no public air compressors, so divers ought to bring filled tanks.

Campgrounds lie scattered all over the island; required free permits are available at any ranger station. Some sites have three-sided, screened-in shelters. They go quickly on a first come, first served basis; bringing your own tent is a good idea. Nights are always frigid (about 40°F in June), and biting bugs peak in June and July; you'll need warm clothes and insect repellent. Intestinal bacteria, tapeworms, and giardia lurk in the waters of Isle Royale; use a 0.4-micron filter, or boil water for at least 2min. Purified water is available at Rock Harbor and Windigo. Very few places on the island permit fires; bring a small campstove. The **Rock Harbor Lodge** (906-337-4993) controls most of the island's commercial activity; the store carries a decent selection of overpriced food and camping staples. The lodge and associated cabins are the only indoor lodging on the island—remember, you're here to camp (singles $143; doubles $229).

Despite the fact that it's closer to the Ontario and Minnesota mainlands, Isle Royale is part of Michigan. Accessible only by boat, the park has its **headquarters in Houghton** at 800 E. Lakeshore Dr. (906-482-0984), in the Upper Peninsula. (Open M-F 8am-6pm, Sa 8am-5pm; boat departs Tu and F 9am, returns W and Sa 3:45pm.) The headquarters operates a 6½hr. ferry to the island (round-trip $92, under 12 $46, kayaks $30), while **Isle Royale Ferry Service** (906-289-4437), at the dock in Copper Harbor, makes 4½hr. trips (round-trip $80, under 12 $40). Both ferries land at Rock Harbor. To access other parts of the island, take any of several shuttles from Rock Harbor, or leave from **Grand Portage, MN;** the **Grand Portage-Isle Royale Transportation Line,** 1507 N. First St. (715-392-2100), Superior, WI, sends a boat to Windigo, which stops at trailheads around the island before reaching Rock Harbor 7½hr. later ($100 round-trip to Rock Harbor, under 12 $56). In summer, additional trips go to Windigo (round-trip $62, under 12 $31). On the island, the park's **ranger stations** include **Windigo** on the west tip; **Rock Harbor,** on the east tip; and **Malone Bay,** between Windigo and Rock Harbor, on the south shore.

Indiana

The seemingly endless cornfields of southern Indiana's Appalachian foothills give way to expansive plains in the industrialized north. Here, Gary's smokestacks spew black clouds over the waters of Lake Michigan, and urban travel hubs have earned the state its official nickname, "The Crossroads of America." The origin of Indiana's unofficial nickname, "The Hoosier State," is less certain; some speculate that it is a corruption of the pioneers' call to visitors at the door—"Who's there?"—while others claim that it spread from Louisville, where labor contractor Samuel Hoosier preferred to hire Indiana workers over Kentucky laborers. Whatever the nickname's derivation, Indiana's Hoosiers are generally considered a no-nonsense Midwestern breed. The Indiana General Assembly once nearly passed a law to make the official value of pi three instead of 3.14, etc., just for the sake of simplicity. More recently, the pragmatic people of Indianapolis laughed a weatherman named David Letterman out of town for forecasting hail "the size of canned hams."

PRACTICAL INFORMATION

Capital: Indianapolis.
Visitor Info: Indiana Division of Tourism, 1 N. Capitol, #700, Indianapolis 46204 (800-289-6646; http://www.state.in.us/tourism). **Division of State Parks,** 402 W. Washington #W-298, Indianapolis 46204 (317-232-4125).
Emergency: 911.
Time Zones: Confusing. Mostly Eastern; Central near Gary in the northwest and Evansville in the southwest. Only the parts of the state near Louisville, KY and Cincinnati, OH observe daylight savings time. **Postal Abbreviation:** IN.
Sales Tax: 5%.

GREAT LAKES

■ Indianapolis

Surrounded by flat farmland, Indianapolis feels like the quintessential American city. Folks shop and work all day among downtown's skyscrapers and drive home to sprawling suburbs in the evening. Life moves at an amble here—until May. Then, an army of 350,000 spectators and countless crewmembers overruns the city, and the road warriors of the Indianapolis 500 rise above clouds of turbocharged exhaust to claim their throne. "Gentlemen, start your engines..." And the city goes into a frenzy, while modern-day chariots of fire strain toward the finish for a $7.5 million prize.

ORIENTATION AND PRACTICAL INFORMATION

The city is laid out in concentric circles, with a dense central cluster of skyscrapers and low-lying outskirts. The very center of Indianapolis is just south of **Monument Circle,** at the intersection of **Washington St. (U.S. 40)** and **Meridian St.** Washington St. divides the city north-south; Meridian St. divides it east-west. **I-465** circles the city and provides access to downtown. **I-70** cuts through the city east-west. Plentiful 2hr. metered parking can be found along the edges of the downtown area, and there are numerous indoor and outdoor lots ($5-8 per day) in the center, especially along **Ohio** and **Illinois St.**

Airport: Indianapolis International (487-7243), 7 mi. southwest of downtown off I-465, Exit 11B. Take bus #8 "West Washington" or a cab ($17).

Trains: Amtrak, 350 S. Illinois St. (263-0550 or 800-872-7245), behind Union Station. Trains travel east-west only. To: Chicago (5hr., 3 per week, from $18); Washington, D.C. (18hr., 3 per week, from $88); and Cincinnati (3hr., 3 per week, from $26). Open M-F 7:30am-3pm and Tu-Sa 11pm-6:30am.

Buses: Greyhound, 350 S. Illinois St. (800-231-2222). To: Chicago (4hr., 10 per day, from $27); Cincinnati (2hr., 4 per day, from $16); and Bloomington (1hr., 1 per day, from $13). Open 24hr.

Public Transportation: Metro Bus, 139 E. Ohio St. (635-3344). Office open M-F 8am-6pm, Sa 9am-4pm. Fare 75¢, rush hr. (M-F 6-9am and 3-6pm) $1. Service to the Speedway area 25¢ extra. Transfers 25¢. Patchy coverage of outlying areas.

Taxis: Barrington Cab, 786-7994. $1.30 first mi., $1.80 each additional mi.

Car Rental: Thrifty, 700 W. Minnesota St. (636-5622), at the airport. From $36 per day with 225 free mi. Weekly $149 with 1500 free mi. Must be 21 with major credit card. Under 25 add $10 per day. Open 24hr.

Visitor Info: Indianapolis City Center, 201 S. Capitol Ave. (237-5200 or 800-233-4639), in the Pan Am Plaza across from the RCA Dome, has a helpful model of the city. Open M-F 10am-5:30pm, Sa 10am-5pm, Su noon-5pm.

Hotlines: Rape Crisis Line, 800-221-6311. **Gay/Lesbian Info Line,** 923-8550.

Post Office: 125 W. South St. (464-6376), across from Amtrak. Open M-W and F 7am-5:30pm, Th 7am-6pm. **ZIP code:** 46206. **Area code:** 317. **Time Zone:** Central.

PARK IT!

Budget motels line the I-465 beltway, 5 mi. from downtown. Make reservations a year in advance for the Indy 500, which causes inflated rates throughout May.

Fall Creek YMCA, 860 W. 10th St. (634-2478), just north of downtown. Small and sparse rooms, but the abundant resources are ideal. Access to a pool, gym, and laundry facilities. Free parking. 87 rooms for men, 10 for women. Singles $25, with bath $30; $75/$85 per week. $5 key deposit. Often booked 3-6 months in advance.

American Inn, 5630 Crawfordsville Rd. (248-1471), about 1½ mi. west of the Indianapolis Speedway at the east end of the Speedway Shopping Center. Catch bus #13 to and from the shopping center. Well-kept rooms with microwave-fridges, phones, and cable TV. Singles $30; doubles $35.

Dollar Inn, 6331 Crawfordsville Rd. (248-8500), off I-465 at Exit 16A. Not the lap of luxury, but a very good deal. About 10min. from downtown. Decent rooms with HBO and ESPN. Singles $26; doubles $32.

KOA, 5896 W. 200 St. N., Greenfield (894-1397 or 800-KOA/562-0531), 15min. from the city, just off Exit 96 on I-70. A nice campsite with a video/arcade room. Sites $18, partial hookup $20, full hookup $23.

Indiana State Fairgrounds Campgrounds, 1202 E. 38th St. (927-7520). If you want to get close to nature, go elsewhere. 170 sod-and-gravel sites, mostly packed by RVs. Sites $10.50, full hookup $12.60. Especially busy during the state fair.

PIT STOPS

Ethnic food stands, produce markets, and knick-knack sellers fill the spacious **City Market,** 222 E. Market St., in a renovated 19th-century building. As if America didn't have enough malls, Indianapolis's newly constructed **Circle Centre,** 49 West Maryland St. (681-8000), hosts a slew of restaurants and a food court.

◉**Essential Edibles,** 303 N. Alabama St. (266-8797). This hip, yet classy cafe and market features outdoor seating, a full bar, an eclectic menu selection, and particularly notable veggie plates. Locals swear by the eggplant sandwich ($7), which comes with truly "Killer Potatoes." Open M-Sa 11am-9pm, Su 11am-7pm.

Bazbeaux Pizza, 334 Massachusetts Ave. (636-7662), and 832 E. Westfields Blvd. (255-5711). Indianapolis's favorite pizza. The Tchoupitoulas pizza is a Cajun masterpiece. Construct your own culinary wonder ($5-20) from a choice of 53 toppings. Open M-Th 11am-10pm, F-Sa 11am-11pm, Su 4:30-10pm.

Acapulco Joe's, 365 N. Illinois St. (637-5160). The first Mexican restaurant in Indianapolis greets its guests with a perplexing sign reading: "Acapulco Joe's has sold over 5 million tacos—do you realize that represents *over 6 pounds of ground beef?*" Heavy on flavor, atmosphere, and popularity. At noon, the waitstaff sings patriotic favorites. Entrees around $5. Open M-Th 7am-9pm, F-Sa 7am-10pm.

SPECTATOR SPORT

White River State Park, just a quick jaunt from downtown, holds both activities and attractions. The **visitors center** is parked in the old pumphouse at 801 W. Washington St. (233-2434 or 800-665-9056; http://www.inwhiteriver.com). The newly restored canal entices locals to stroll, bike, or nap on the banks. For the more aquatic, pedal boats are available for rent at **Central Canal Rental** (634-1824).

Near the entrance, the **Eiteljorg Museum of American Indians' and Western Art,** 500 W. Washington St. (636-9378), features an impressive collection of Western art from the past century, as well as Native American art and clothing from over seven regions of the U.S. *(Open Tu-Sa 10am-5pm, Su noon-5pm; in summer also M 10am-5pm. $5, seniors $4, students with ID and children $2. Tours daily at 2pm.)* A 5min. drive from the Eiteljorg, and still within the massive park, the seemingly cageless **Indianapolis Zoo,** 1200 W. Washington St. (630-2101), has one of the world's largest enclosed whale and dolphin pavilions. *(Open daily 9am-5pm; Sept.-May 9am-4pm. $9.75, seniors $7, ages 3-12 $6. Parking $3.)*

Brass chandeliers and a majestic stained glass dome grace the marbled interior of the **State House** (232-5293), between Capitol and Senate St. near W. Washington St.; self-guided tour brochures are available inside (open daily 8am-5pm, main floor only Sa-Su; 4 guided tours per day M-F). The **Indianapolis Museum of Art,** 1200 W. 38th St. (923-1331), is farther from the city center but well worth a visit. *(Open Tu-W and F 10am-5pm, Th 10am-8:30pm, Su noon-5pm. Free. Special exhibits $3.)* The museum has beautifully landscaped 152-acre grounds which offer nature trails, art pavilions, the Eli Lilly Botanical Garden, a greenhouse, and a theater. Dig for fossils, speed through the cosmos, or explore a maze at the **Children's Museum,** 3000 N. Meridian St. (924-5437), one of the country's largest. *(Museum open daily 10am-5pm; Sept.-Feb. closed M. $8, seniors $7, ages 2-12 $3.50; with Omnimax $12.50/$11.50/$7.)*

Wolves and bison roam under researchers' supervision at **Wolf Park** (765-567-2265), on Jefferson St. in **Battle Ground** (1hr. north of Indianapolis on I-65). The werewolves, which howl constantly, are brought into the limelight under the moonlight F-Sa nights at 7:30pm (open daily 1-5pm, open later F-Sa for wolf howls; M-Sa $4, Su $5, under 14 free).

GREAT LAKES

THE FAST LANE

In its heyday, the **Walker Theatre,** 617 Indiana Ave. (236-2087), a 15min. walk northwest of downtown, booked jazz greats Louis Armstrong and Dinah Washington. Local and national artists still perform here as part of the bi-weekly **Jazz on the Avenue** series (F 6-10pm). The theater, erected in 1927 with stunning Egyptian and African decor, commemorates Madame Walker, an African-American beautician who invented the straightening comb and became America's first self-made woman millionaire. The **Indianapolis Symphony Orchestra,** 45 Monument Circle (box office 639-4300 or 800-366-8457), handles entertainment in classical style (tickets $5-49). The **Indianapolis Opera** (283-3531, box office 940-6444) performs at Clowes Hall on the Butler University campus at 46th and Sunset St. from September to May (tickets $15-60, students and seniors $13). The **Indianapolis Repertory Theatre,** 140 W. Washington St. (635-5252; tickets $17.50-40, students $12.50), puts up shows between October and May. Contact the **Arts Council Office,** 47 S. Pennsylvania St. (631-3301 or 800-865-ARTS/2787), for the schedules of other performances in the area. The **Indiana State Fair** descends on Indianapolis for two weeks in mid-August with exhibitions and concerts.

By day an outlying cluster of art galleries, bead shops, and record shops, the **Broad Ripple** area (6 mi. north of downtown at College Ave. and 62nd St.) transforms after dark into a nightlife mecca for anyone under 40. The party fills the clubs and bars and spills out onto the sidewalks and side streets off Broad Ripple Ave. until about 1am on weekdays and 3am on weekends. For pool and preppie crowds, you can't beat **Average Joe's Sports Pub,** 814 Broad Ripple Ave. (253-5844). Off the main strip, **The Monkey's Tale,** 925 E. Westfield Blvd. (253-2883), serves up drinks and atmosphere while the attached **Jazz Cooker** dishes out crawfish and blues. **The Vogue,** 6259 N. College Ave. (255-2828), features national acts as well as themed dance nights (cover $2-7, more for big names). Those interested in a more jocular evening should try the **Broad Ripple Comedy Club,** 6281 N. College Ave. (255-4211), on the corner of College Ave. and Broad Ripple Ave. (shows daily). After the clubs close, make a run for tacos ($2) and burritos ($3.50) at **Paco's Cantina,** 737 Broad Ripple Ave. (251-6200; open until 4am or later, at the owner's whim).

GO, SPEED RACER, GO!

Most of the year, the **Indianapolis Motor Speedway,** 4790 W. 16th St. (481-8500), off I-465 at the Speedway Exit (bus #25), lies dormant and waiting, as tourists ride buses around the 2½ mi. track ($3). The adjacent **Speedway Museum** houses Indy's Hall of Fame (484-6747; open daily 9am-5pm; $3, ages 6-15 $1).

The country's passion for fast cars reaches fever pitch during the **500 Festival** (636-4556), a month of parades, a mini-marathon, and hoopla leading up to race day. The festivities begin with time trials in mid-May and culminate with the bang of the **Indianapolis 500** starter's gun on May 30 (weather permitting). Tickets for the race go on sale the day after the previous year's race and usually sell out within a week (from $30; call the Speedway for an order form, available in Apr.). NASCAR's **Brickyard 400** (800-822-4639) sends stock cars zooming down the speedway in early August.

■ Bloomington

Bloomington's rolling hills made the area inadequate for farming, but make an exquisite backdrop for its most prominent institution, Indiana University. Events like the Little 500 bike race (made famous by the movie *Breaking Away*) attract hundreds of visitors and the accolades of David Letterman's Top Ten staff, but the town revolves around campus, providing happenin' cafes, art exhibits, and numerous bars for Hoosier guys and gals.

PRACTICAL INFORMATION Bloomington lies south of Indianapolis on Rte. 37; **N. Walnut** and **College St.** are the main north-south thoroughfares. **Greyhound,** 409 S. Walnut (332-1522 or 800-231-2222; station open daily 2-4pm), connects Bloomington to Chicago (6hr., 1 per day, $46) and Indianapolis (1hr., 1 per day, $13). **Bloomington Transit** sends buses on seven routes. Service is infrequent; call 332-5688 for info. (Fare 75¢, seniors and ages 5-17 35¢.) **Yellow Cab** (336-4100) charges $3 base fare and $1.80 per mi. The **visitors center,** 2855 N. Walnut St. (334-8900 or 800-800-0037), has a courtesy phone desk for free local calls. (Open M-F 8:30am-5pm, Sa 9am-4pm; Su 10am-3pm; Nov.-Apr. limited hrs.; 24hr. brochure area.) **Post Office:** 206 E. 4th St. (334-4030), 2 blocks east of Walnut St. (open M and F 8am-6pm, Tu-Th 8am-5:30pm, Sa 8am-1pm). **ZIP code:** 47404. **Area code:** 812. **Time Zone:** Central.

ACCOMMODATIONS, FOOD, AND NIGHTLIFE Budget hotels cluster around the intersection of N. Walnut St. and Rte. 46. A bit further from town is **Winding Woods Bed & Breakfast,** 7725 Harmony Rd. (824-4493 or 888-83-CABIN/832-2246), southwest of the city off Rte. 45. The owners gathered three 19th-century poplar wood cabins into one and tucked it back into the hills. Telephones, pool, hot tub, and fireplace (3 rooms $60-80, breakfast included; reservations required). **Downtown Motel,** 509 N. College Ave. (336-6881) offers standard rooms with basic cable and several suites with small kitchens (singles $30, doubles $35; with kitchen $35/$40). **Paynetown State Park** (837-9490), 10 mi. southeast of downtown on Rte. 446, provides open field sites in a well-endowed park on Lake Monroe with access to a boat ramp and hiking trails. Boat rentals are available. (Primitive sites $5, with shower $7, with electricity $11. Vehicle registration $2, out-of-state $5.)

The **Downtown Sq.,** known locally as "The Square," holds a wealth of restaurants in a 2-block radius, most on Kirkwood Ave. near College and W. Walnut St. Vegetarians can eat easy—all these restaurants have many meat-free menu options. Chuckle the hemp cheese ($1 per oz.) off your Mondo Burrito ($4) at **The Laughing Planet Café,** 322 E. Kirkwood Ave. (323-2233), where organic food and good folks make for a one-of-a-kind dining experience (open M-Sa 11am-9pm, Su noon-8pm). Enter a hall of mirrors at **Snow Lion,** 113 S. Grant St. (336-0835), just off Kirkwood Ave., to sample Tibetan and Oriental cuisine (lunch $3.75, dinner $7.50; open M-Th 11am-2pm and 5-10pm, F-Su 11am-10pm). Join hordes of hoosiers at **Jimmy John's,** 430 E. Kirkwood Ave. (332-8828), home of the self-pronounced "World's Best Sub" (subs $3.15; open M-Th 11am-10pm, F-Sa 11am-3:30am, Su noon-10pm).

Beer and alternative rock are the staples of colleges, and IU is no exception. **The Crazy Horse,** 214 W. Kirkwood Ave. (336-8877) drafted 80 beers into its alcoholic army (open Th-Sa 11am-2am, Su noon-midnight, M-W 11am-1am). Everyone who's anyone (at IU, that is) shimmies over to **Nick's,** 423 E. Kirkwood St. (332-4040), to play a favorite campus drinking game. **Mars,** 479 N. Walnut St. (concert line 336-6277), is the planet for national acts; the **Bluebird,** 216 N. Walnut St. (336-2473), flies a little closer in, staging local talent. **Bullwinkle's,** 201 S. College Ave. (334-3232), caters to a gay crowd (open M-F 7pm-3am), and **Rhino's,** 3251/2 S. Walnut St. (333-3430), has lesser-known acts, but accepts those under 21, unlike the others.

SIGHTS AND ENTERTAINMENT Browse three floors chock full of old valuables downtown at the **Antique Mall,** 311 W. 7th St. (332-2290; open M-Sa 10am-5pm, Su noon-5pm). IU's **Art Museum,** Fine Arts Plaza, E. 7th St. (855-5445), maintains an excellent collection of Oriental and African artworks (open W-Sa 10am-5pm, Su noon-5pm; free). **Oliver Winery,** 8024 N. State Rd. 37, not only has beautiful grounds, but offers free (and generous) tastings of all of its 15 wines, including the local favorite blackberry wine (876-5800 or 800-258-2783). Indiana's oldest and largest lake, **Lake Monroe,** 10 mi. south of town, was once the bottom of a shallow sea that filled with limestone 230 million years ago.

GREAT LAKES

Illinois

In 1893, at Chicago's World Columbian Exposition, a young professor named Fredrick Jackson Turner gave a stirring speech in which he proclaimed the "closing of the American Frontier." That such a proclamation was made in Illinois seems only fitting; once praised for its vast prairies and the arability of its soil, Illinois had become a land known for its thriving urban industry by the end of the nineteenth century.

The fate of the prairie continues to play out in Springfield, the state capital, where legislators dish out a lumpy porridge of urban agendas and farming interests. Despite causing some political indigestion, the harsh mix of north and south goes down quite easy for most state residents—perhaps their tribute to the wishes of a lanky native son, Abe Lincoln, who stressed that "a house divided against itself cannot stand."

PRACTICAL INFORMATION

Capital: Springfield.
Visitor Info: Office of Tourism, 620 E. Adams St., Springfield 62701 (800-226-6632; http://www.enjoyillinois.com).
Emergency: 911.
Time Zone: Central (1hr. behind Eastern). **Postal Abbreviation:** IL.
Sales Tax: 6.25-7.25%, depending on the city.

■ Chicago

Inhabited first by Native Americans and then by westbound settlers, Chicago was a burgeoning commercial center by the mid-1800s. With the growth of the railroad industry, the town became America's meat-packing hub, drawing millions of immigrants who acquired a few vast fortunes and countless broken dreams. Machine politics flourished, blurring any line between organized government and organized crime. In later years, trade became the city's economic mainstay, and narrow steel tracks gave way to the concrete runways of O'Hare, the world's busiest airport. Chicago began to export authors like Studs Terkel, Theodore Dreiser, and Ernest Hemingway, along with its Cracker Jacks and canned hams.

Meanwhile, the works of greats such as Frank Lloyd Wright, Mies van der Rohe, Picasso, and Joan Miró flooded into the city to decorate its streets and museums. Today, a tradition of philanthropy and diversity has left the city with an extraordinary skyline and a colorful patchwork of ethnic communities. Meanwhile, the University of Chicago employs more Nobel Laureates than any other university in the world. Buffeted by howling gales in winter, the Windy City of today is a balmy slice of urban paradise come summer, featuring world-class museums and a buzzing nightlife.

> The city's **north side** is generally safe at all times, though at night you should avoid the area around **Cabrini Green** (bounded by W. Armitage Ave. on the north, W. Chicago Ave. on the south., Sedgwick on the west, and Halsted on the east). The west side of the Chicago River (north and south branches) is unsafe at night; the area more than a mile west of the river is even more dangerous. Be careful south of the Loop, especially south of Cermak Rd., and never wander around aimlessly.

ORIENTATION

Chicago has overtaken the entire northeastern corner of Illinois, running north-south along 29 mi. of the southwest Lake Michigan shorefront. The city sits at the center of a web of interstates, rail lines, and airplane routes; most cross-country traffic swings through the city. A good map is essential for navigating Chicago; pick up a free one at the tourist office or any CTA station.

At the city's center is the **Loop,** Chicago's downtown and hub of the public transportation system. The numbering system begins from the intersection of State and Madison, with about 800 numbers per mile. The Loop is bounded by the Chicago River to the north and west, Lake Michigan to the east, and Roosevelt Rd. to the

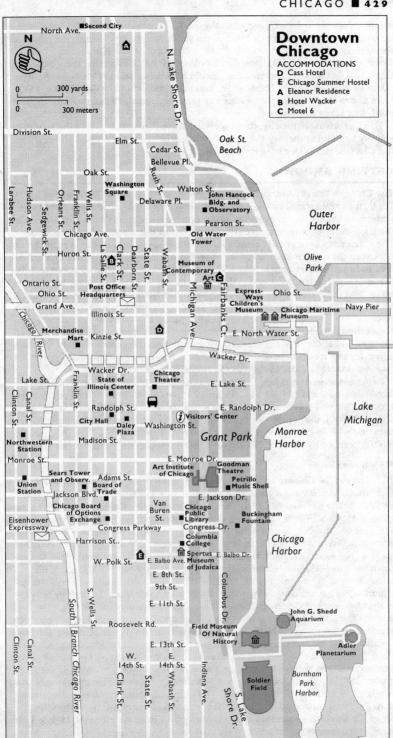

Downtown Chicago

ACCOMMODATIONS

D Cass Hotel
E Chicago Summer Hostel
A Eleanor Residence
B Hotel Wacker
C Motel 6

N

0   300 yards
0   300 meters

Second City
North Ave.
Division St.
Elm St.
Cedar St.
Bellevue Pl.
Oak St.
Washington Square
Walton St.
Delaware Pl.
Chicago Ave.
Huron St.
Ontario St.
Ohio St.
Grand Ave.
Illinois St.
Kinzie St.

Larrabee St.
Hudson Ave.
Sedgewick St.
Orleans St.
Franklin St.
Wells St.
La Salle St.
Clark St.
Dearborn St.
State St.
Wabash St.
Rush St.
Michigan Ave.
Fairbanks Ct.

John Hancock Bldg. and Observatory
Pearson St.
Old Water Tower
Museum of Contemporary Art
Express-Ways Children's Museum
Chicago Maritime Museum
Ohio St.
E. North Water St.
Navy Pier

Oak St. Beach
Outer Harbor
Olive Park

Post Office Headquarters

Merchandise Mart

Chicago River

Wacker Dr.
State of Illinois Center
Franklin St.
Lake St.
Canal St.
Clinton St.
Northwestern Station
Monroe St.
Union Station
Sears Tower and Observ.
Board of Trade
Jackson Blvd.
Chicago Board of Options Exchange
Eisenhower Expressway
Harrison St.

Wacker Dr.
Chicago Theater
E. Lake St.
Randolph St.
City Hall
Daley Plaza
Washington St.
Madison St.

Visitors' Center
E. Randolph Dr.

Grant Park

Monroe Harbor

Lake Michigan

Adams St.
Van Buren St.
Congress Parkway
Congress Dr.
Columbia College
Spertus Museum of Judaica
W. Polk St.
E. Balbo Ave.
E. 8th St.
9th St.
E. 11th St.
W. 14th St.
S. Wells St.
Clark St.
State St.

E. Monroe Dr.
Art Institute of Chicago
Goodman Theatre
Petrillo Music Shell
E. Jackson Dr.
Chicago Public Library
Buckingham Fountain
E. Balbo Dr.
Columbus Dr.

Chicago Harbor

John G. Shedd Aquarium
Roosevelt Rd.
E. 13th St.
E. 14th St.
Canal St.
Clinton St.
South Branch Chicago River
Field Museum Of Natural History
Indiana Ave.
S. Lake Shore Dr.
Soldier Field
Burnham Park Harbor
Adler Planetarium

GREAT LAKES

south. Directions in *Let's Go* are generally from downtown. South of the Loop, numbered east-west streets increase towards the south. Many ethnic neighborhoods lie in this area. LaSalle Dr. loosely defines the west edge of the **Near North** area. The **Gold Coast** shimmers on N. Lakeshore Dr. **Lincoln Park** revolves around the junction of Clark St., Lincoln Ave., and Halsted. Lincoln Park melts into **Wrigleyville,** near the 3000s of N. Clark and N. Halstead St., and then becomes **Lakeview,** in the 4000s. **Lake Shore Dr.,** a scenic pseudo-freeway hugging Lake Michigan, provides express north-south connections.

To avoid driving in the city, daytrippers can leave their cars in one of the suburban subway lots during the day ($1.75). There are a half-dozen such park-and-ride lots; call CTA (see below) for info. Parking downtown costs around $6-11 per day.

GETTING AROUND

The **Chicago Transit Authority (CTA),** 350 N. Wells (836-7000 or 888-968-7282), 7th fl., runs rapid transit trains, subways, and buses. The **elevated rapid transit train system,** called the **El,** encircles the major downtown section of the city, known as the Loop. Some downtown routes run underground, but are still referred to as the El. The El operates 24hr., but late-night service is infrequent and unsafe in many areas; stick with the crowds. Also, some buses do not run all night; call the CTA for schedules and routes. Extremely helpful CTA maps are available at many stations and the Water Tower Information Center. Don't step blindly onto a train; many are express trains, and often different routes run along the same tracks. Train and bus fare is $1.50; add 25¢ for express routes. Remember to get a transfer (30¢) from bus drivers or when you enter the El stop, which allows for up to two more rides on different routes during the following 2hr. Buy token rolls (10 tokens) at *some* stations, supermarkets, and at the "Checks Cashed" storefronts with the yellow sign; these places also carry $88 monthly passes. **Metra** offers a variety of consecutive-day passes for tourists: 1-day ($5), 2-day ($9), 3-day ($12), and 5-day ($18).

On Saturdays from mid-June through mid-October, a **Loop Tour Train** departs on a free 40min. tour at 12:15, 12:55, 1:35, and 2:15pm (tickets must be picked up at the Chicago Office of Tourism; see **Practical Information,** below). **METRA,** 547 W. Jackson (836-7000), distributes free maps and schedules for an extensive commuter rail network, with 11 rail lines and four downtown stations (open M-F 8am-5pm; fare $2-6.60, depending on distance). **PACE** (836-7000) operates the suburban bus system.

Neighborhoods

The center of the **Chinese** community lies 2 mi. south of the Loop, at Cermak Rd. and Wentworth Ave. *It's not a good idea to venture far south of the CTA stop by night, or to head too far west of Chinatown at any time.* **New Chinatown,** north of the Loop at Argyle St., offers a few more Chinese restaurants, but is mainly **Vietnamese.** The area of Argyle St. east of N. Broadway is known as Little Saigon. The **German** community has scattered, but the beer halls, restaurants, and shops in the 3000s and 4000s of N. Lincoln Ave. bear witness to its presence. The former residents of **Greektown** have moved to the suburbs, but S. Halsted St., just west of the Loop, offers a wide variety of Greek restaurants. At night, the area is bustling and safe until the restaurants close, at which point you'll probably want to clear out. **Little Italy** fell prey to the **University of Illinois at Chicago (UIC),** but a shadow of the old neighborhood remains along W. Taylor St., west of the UIC campus. Although it's on the notorious West Side, it's surrounded by residential areas and is relatively safe at most times. **Jewish** and **Indian** enclaves center on Devon Ave., from Western Ave. to the Chicago River. The area near Midway Airport is home to much of Chicago's **Lithuanian** population, one of the world's largest. The Pilsen neighborhood, southwest of the loop, around 18th St., offers a slice of **Mexico.** Searches for **Polish** sausage end along N. Milwaukee Ave. between blocks 2800 and 3100; Chicago's huge Polish population rivals that of Warsaw. Andersonville, along Clark St. north of Foster Ave., is the historic center of the **Swedish** community, though immigrants from **Asia** and the **Middle East** have settled here in recent years.

PRACTICAL INFORMATION

Airports: O'Hare International (773-686-2200), off I-90. World's busiest airport and inventor of the layover, the holding pattern, and the headache. Depending on traffic, a trip between downtown and O'Hare can take up to 2hr. The blue line **Rapid Train** runs between the Airport El station and downtown (40min.-1hr., $1.50). **Midway Airport** (773-767-0500), on the western edge of the South Side, often offers less expensive flights. To get downtown, take the El orange line from the Midway stop. Lockers $1 per day. **Continental Air Transport** (454-7799 or 800-654-7871) connects both airports to downtown hotels from O'Hare baggage terminal (45min.-1hr., every 5-10min. 6am-11:30pm, $14.75) and Midway (30-45min., every 10-15min. 6am-10:30pm, $10.75).

Trains: Amtrak, Union Station, 225 S. Canal (558-1075 or 800-872-7245), at Adams St. west of the Loop. Take the El to State and Adams, then walk 7 blocks west on Adams. Amtrak's main hub may look familiar; it was the backdrop for the baby-buggy scene of *The Untouchables.* To: Milwaukee (1½hr., 5 per day, $19); Detroit (5hr., 3 per day, $20); and New York (18½hr., 2 per day, $81-148). Station open 6:15am-10pm; tickets sold daily 6am-9pm. Lockers $1 per day.

Buses: Greyhound, 630 W. Harrison St. (781-2900 or 800-231-2222), at Jefferson and Desplaines Ave. Take the El to Linton. *The* hub of the central U.S. and home base for several smaller companies covering the Midwest. To: Detroit (6-7hr., 6 per day, $27); Milwaukee (2hr., 13 per day, $14); St. Louis (5-7hr., 9 per day, $30); and Indianapolis (3½-4½hr., 9 per day, $30). Station and ticket office open 24hr.

Taxis: Yellow Cab, 829-4222. **Flash Cab,** 773-561-1444. **American United Cab,** 773-248-7600. Average $1.60 base fare, $1.40 per additional mi.

Car Rental: Dollar Rent-a-Car (800-800-4000), at O'Hare and Midway. $26 per day, $170 per week; under 25 surcharge $15 per day. **Thrifty Car Rental** (800-367-2277), at O'Hare. $27 per day, $203 per week, $10 for liability insurance. Under 25 surcharge $25 per day. Unlimited mi. for both. Must be 21 with credit card.

Visitor Info: Chicago Office of Tourism, 78 E. Washington St. (744-2400 or 800-2CONNECT/226-6632; http://www.ci.chi.il.us/Tourism). Open M-F 10am-6pm, Sa 10am-5pm, Su noon-5pm. In the same building is the **Chicago Cultural Center,** 77 E. Randolph St., at Michigan Ave., which has info on Chicago's various ethnic groups. Open M-F 10am-6pm, Sa 10am-5pm, Su noon-5pm. Another location a few min. north at 811 Michigan Ave. is the **Chicago Visitor Information Center** (744-2400), in the Water Tower Pumping Station. Open M-F 9:30am-6pm, Sa 10am-6pm, Su 11am-6pm. On the lake, **Navy Pier Info Center,** 600 E. Grand (595-7437). Open Su-Th 10am-10pm, F-Sa 10am-noon.

Hotlines: General Crisis Line, 800-866-9600. **Rape Crisis Line,** 847-872-7799. **Gay and Lesbian Hotline/Anti-Violence Project,** 871-2273. All 24hr.

Medical Services: Cook County Hospital, 1835 W. Harrison (633-6000). Take the Congress A train to the Medical Center Stop. Open 24hr. **Women's Health Services:** Contact **Eleanor Residence** (see **Accommodations** below).

Internet Access: Free at the **Chicago Public Library,** 400 S. State St., at Congress. Open M 9am-7pm, Tu and Th 11am-7pm, W, F, and Sa 9am-5pm, Su 1-5pm.

Post Office: 433 W. Harrison St. (654-3895). Open 24hr. **ZIP code:** 60607. **Area code:** 312 or 773 (Chicago); 708, 630, or 847 (outside the city limits). In text, 312 unless otherwise noted.

ACCOMMODATIONS

A cheap, convenient bed can be found at one of Chicago's hostels. If you have a car, you can also try the moderately priced motels on **Lincoln Ave.** Motel chains have locations off the interstates, about 1hr. from downtown; they're inconvenient and expensive ($35 and up), but are a reliable option for late-night arrivals. **Chicago Bed and Breakfast,** P.O. Box 14088, Chicago 60614 (951-0085), runs a referral service with over 150 rooms of varying prices throughout the city and outlying areas. Few have parking, but the majority are near public transit. (2-night min. stay. Singles from $75; doubles from $85. Reservations required.) Chicago has a nasty 15% tax on most accommodations.

Chicago Summer Hostel (HI-AYH), 731 S. Plymouth Ct. (773-327-5350). In the South Loop, close to the lake. Roomy and spotless A/C dorm-style housing filled with international students. Kitchen, laundry, exercise rooms, ride-sharing board. 4-5 beds per room; suites also available. $19, nonmembers $22; private double $69. 1999 might be the last year at this location. Open mid-June to early Sept.

Arlington House (HI-AYH, AAIH), 616 W. Arlington Pl. (773-929-5380 or 800-HOS-TEL-5/467-8355), off Clark St. just north of Fullerton. Friendly Hugh and Anne will ensure that your stay is comfortable in this enormous, well-located North side hostel. Rooms are tidy and breezy, though some dorm rooms are a touch cramped. Relatively safe, central neighborhood. Kitchen, common TV room, laundry facilities. $19.50, non-members $22; private doubles $40-46.

Chicago International Hostel, 6318 N. Winthrop St. (773-262-1011). Take the Howard St. northbound train to Loyola Station; walk 3 blocks south on Sheridan Rd. to Winthrop, and a half-block south. Slightly bland but sunny and clean rooms, each with 4-6 beds, near the Loyola University campus. A fairly safe location close to the lake, beaches, and many fast food joints. Free parking in rear. Kitchen and laundry access. $13, double with bath $35-40. Lockers $1. Key deposit $5. Lockout 10am-4pm. Check-in 7-10am and 4pm-midnight.

International House, 1414 E. 59th St. (773-753-2270), Hyde Park, off Lake Shore Dr. Take the Illinois Central Railroad from the Michigan Ave. station (20min.) to 59th St. and walk a half-block west. Part of the University of Chicago; *don't wander off campus at night.* Clean, spacious singles with shared bath filled mostly by permanent residents. $36. Kitchen and laundry. Linen provided. Reservations required.

Eleanor Residence, 1550 N. Dearborn Pkwy. (664-8245). *Women over 18 only.* Fantastic location near Lincoln Park and Gold Coast. Majestic common room and lobby, clean rooms. Singles $50, breakfast and dinner included. Reserve at least 1 day in advance; 1-night deposit required.

Cass Hotel, 640 N. Wabash Ave. (787-4030), just north of the Loop. Take subway to State or Grand St. Convenient location. Clean rooms with wood trim and A/C. Coffee shop and lounge. No parking. Laundry room. Singles $64; doubles $69. $5 discount with ISIC. Key deposit $5. Reservations recommended. Wheelchair access.

Motel 6, 162 E. Ontario St. (787-3580), 1 block east of the Magnificent Mile (Michigan Ave.). Immaculate rooms with cable, A/C, and free local calls. No parking. Singles $85; doubles $91. Reservations recommended. Wheelchair access.

Hotel Wacker, 111 W. Huron St. (787-1386), at N. Clark St. Insert your own joke. A green sign on the corner makes this place easy to find. Slightly musty but perfectly acceptable rooms. Convenient to downtown. TV, A/C, phone. Singles $40; doubles $50; $225 per week. Key and linen deposit $5. Check-in 24hr. Wheelchair access.

Days Inn Gold Coast, 1816 N. Clark St.(664-3040), bordering Lincoln Park. The small but clean rooms come with a great view, as well as A/C and kitchenettes in some. Doubles $85, F-Sa $95. Wheelchair access.

FOOD

One of the best guides to city dining is the monthly *Chicago* magazine, which includes an extensive restaurant section, cross-indexed by price, cuisine, and quality. It can usually be picked up at tourist offices.

Pizza

Chicago's pizza is known 'round the world, either standard-style, with the cheese on top, or stuffed, with "toppings" in the middle.

Pizzeria Uno, 29 E. Ohio St. (321-1000), and younger sister **Due,** 619 N. Wabash Ave. (943-2400). The newspaper clippings on the wall may look like any other Uno's, but this is where the delicious legacy of deep-dish began. Pizza, pasta, or bust. Lines are long, and pizza takes 45min. to prepare. Same short menu at Due (right up the street), with a terrace and more room than Uno's. Pizzas $5-18. Uno open M-F 11:30am-1am, Sa 11:30am-2am, Su 11:30am-11:30pm. Due open Su-Th 11am-1:30am, F-Sa 11am-2am.

Giordano's, 730 N. Rush St. (951-0747). The downtown location is only 1 of 41 branches in the Chicago area. The stuffed pizza is worth the 35min. wait. Call ahead to get your pizza cooking. Pizzas $4-18. Lunch specials $5. Open Su-Th noon-midnight, F-Sa 11am-1am.

Round The Loop

The area of the Loop between Jackson and Roosevelt St. is the South Loop, home to an African-American community and good, cheap, fun **soul food,** like ribs, fried chicken, and other down-home faves.

Heaven on Seven, 111 N. Wabash Ave. (263-6443), 7th fl. of the Garland Bldg. The mantlepiece painted with vegetables, alligators, and crabs means you're getting closer to Cajun nirvana. The line is long, but hell, the gumbo is great ($7-12). Cash only. Open M-F 8:30am-5pm, Sa 10am-3pm. A more upscale location in the Near North, at 600 N. Michigan (280-7774), serves lunch and dinner.

The Berghoff, 17 W. Adams St. (427-3170). Dim, cavernous German restaurant filled with lunching traders. Bratwurst $5.75, stein of Berghoff's own beer $2.75. Open M-Th 11am-9pm, F 11am-9:30pm, Sa 11am-10pm.

Russian Tea Time, 77 E. Adams St. (360-0000), across from the Art Institute, serves Russian delicacies from borscht to stroganoff in the heart of downtown Chicago. Bottomless cup of tea $1.85. Lunch entrees $6-12. Open M 11am-9pm, Tu-Th 11am-11pm, F-Sa 11am-midnight, Su 11am-9pm.

Wishbone, 1001 W. Washington St. (850-2663), a good walk west of the Loop. Take bus #20 "Madison" to Morgan St. A family-style Southern cuisine extravaganza with cornbread and banana bread on every table. Veggie specials vary daily ($5-10). Sit-down breakfast M-F 7-11am; cafeteria-style lunch 11am-3pm; dinner Tu-Th 5-10pm, F-Sa 5-11pm; brunch Sa-Su 8am-2:30pm.

Billy Goat's Tavern, 430 N. Michigan (222-1525), underground on lower Michigan Ave. Descend through a seeming subway entrance in front of the Tribune building. The gruff service was the inspiration for the legendary *Saturday Night Live* "Cheezborger, cheezborger—no Coke, Pepsi" skit. Cheezborgers $2.50. "Butt in anytime" M-F 7am-2am, Sa 10am-3am, Su 11am-2am.

Little Saigon

Whereas Little Saigon seems to sport a restaurant every ten feet, beware of unsanitary practices—the Board of Public Health has recently shut down a number of restaurants. In general, extremely low prices signal sketchiness. Restaurant turnover is high, so ask locals for a reliable place, even if it is bit upscale.

Chinatown

Chinatown is lined with restaurants of all sizes. Take the Red Line to Cermak/Chinatown to get here, *but don't go too far south of Cermak St. after dark.*

Hong Min, 221 W. Cermak Rd. (842-5026). Spartan decor, Epicurean dining. Sweet-and-sour fish $8. Open Su-Th 10am-2am, F-Sa 10am-3am.

Three Happiness, 2130 S. Wentworth Ave. (791-1228), at Cermak. Gulping fish greet you at the door; a dragon and crowds wait upstairs. Dim sum ($1.75 per portion and up) is served M-F 10am-2pm, Sa-Su 10am-3pm. Open M-Th 10am-11pm, F-Sa 10am-midnight, Su 10am-10pm.

Little Italy

What is left of Little Italy can be reached by taking the El to UIC, then walking west on Taylor St. or taking bus #37 down Taylor St.

The Rosebud, 1500 W. Taylor St. (942-1117). Small, classy restaurant serving huge portions of pasta. Lunch specials $9-14 (Chicken Vesuvio $9), dinner from $9. Valet parking $4, reservations recommended. Open for lunch M-Th 11am-10:30pm, F 11am-11:30pm, Sa 5-11:30pm.

Al's Italian Beef, 1079 W. Taylor St. (226-4017), at Aberdeen near Little Italy; also at 169 W. Ontario. Churns out top-notch reddish Italian beef with lots of spices at a formica counter. Italian beef sandwich $3.55. Open daily 9am-1am.

Mario's Italian Lemonade, 1074 W. Taylor St., across from Al's. A classic neighborhood stand that churns out sensational Italian ices ($1-4.75) in flavors from cantaloupe to cherry. Open mid-May to mid-Sept. daily 10am-midnight.

GREAT LAKES

Greektown

The Parthenon, 314 S. Halsted St. (726-2407). The golden ratio ain't in the architecture here. The staff converses in volleys of Greek, the murals and hangings transport you to the Mediterranean, and the food wins top awards. The Greek Feast, a family-style dinner ($14), includes everything from *saganaki* (flaming goat cheese) to *baklava* (glazed pastry). Open Su-F 11am-1am, Sa 11am-2am.

Greek Islands, 200 S. Halsted St. (782-9855). The tan awning points the way to magnificent food. No reservations; expect a 30-45min. wait Sa-Su. Daily special $7-8. Open Su-Th 11am-midnight, F-Sa 11am-1am.

North Side/Lincoln Park

Potbelly's, 2264 N. Lincoln Ave. (773-528-1405). Could be named for the stoves scattered around the deli or for your stomach when you leave. 50s-style decor and music with wooden booths. Subs $3.50. Open daily 11am-11pm.

Kopi, A Traveller's Café, 5317 N. Clark St. (773-989-5674). A 10min. walk from the Berwyn El, 4 blocks west on Berwyn. *Kopi* is Indonesian for "coffee." Peruse a travel guides over java, or just sit back and appreciate the art. Espresso $1.35. On M and Th nights, the cafe blends coffee and music (no cover). Open M-Th 8am-11pm, F 8am-midnight, Sa 9am-midnight, Su 10am-11pm.

Café Ba-Ba-Reeba!, 2024 N. Halsted St. (935-5000). Well-marked by the colorful, glowing facade. Hearty Spanish cuisine with subtle spices like the *paella valenciana* ($10). People-watching on the outdoor terrace. Open M-Th 11:30am-10:30pm, F-Sa 11:30am-midnight, Su noon-10pm.

The Bourgeois Pig, 738 Fullerton Ave. (773-883-5282). Quiet, soothing coffee shop with faux marble tables, board games, and vegetarian specialties to boot. Newly augmented dessert menu. Cappuccino $1.75, scones $1.50. Open M-Th 6:30am-11pm, F 6:30am-midnight, Sa 8am-midnight, Su 9am-11pm.

SIGHTS

Chicago's "sights" range from well-publicized museums to undiscovered back streets, from beaches and parks to towering skyscrapers. The tourist brochures, bus tours, and the downtown area reveal only a fraction of Chicago. As a famous art historian once said, "no one will learn the city of Chicago without using their feet."

Museums

Chicago's major museums admit visitors free at least one day per week. The first five listings, known as the "Big Five," provide a diverse array of exhibits, while a handful of smaller collections target specific interests. Lake Shore Drive has been diverted around Grant Park, linking the Field Museum, Adler, and Shedd; the compound, now known as Museum Campus, offers the potential for a fascinating day. Brochures for all the museums wait at the tourist office (see **Practical Information,** above).

The Art Institute of Chicago, 111 S. Michigan Ave. (443-3600), at Adams St. in Grant Park. The city's premier art museum. 4 millennia of art from Asia, Africa, Europe, and beyond. The Institute's Impressionist and Post-Impressionist collections have won international acclaim. Highlight tour daily 2pm. Free jazz in the courtyard Tu after 4:30pm. Open M and W-F 10:30am-4:30pm, Tu 10:30am-8pm, Sa 10am-5pm, Su and holidays noon-5pm. $7, students, seniors, and children $5; in summer free on Tu.

Museum of Science and Industry, 5700 S. Lake Shore Dr. (773-684-1414), in Hyde Park; take bus #6 "Jeffrey Express" to 57th St. Housed in the only building left from the 1893 World's Columbian Exposition, the expansive and impressive Museum includes the *Apollo 8* command module, and a full-sized replica of a coal mine. Exhibits are designed to be pushed and prodded to keep the young entertained. Omnimax shows; call for times. Open daily 9:30am-5:30pm. $7, seniors $6, ages 3-11 $3.50; with Omnimax $12/$10/$7; free on Th (except Omnimax).

Field Museum of Natural History, 1200 S. Lake Shore Dr. (922-9410), at Roosevelt Rd. in Grant Park; take bus #146 from State St. Geological, anthropological, botanical, and zoological exhibits, like the Egyptian mummies, the Native American halls, the Hall of Gems, and the dinosaur display. Open daily 9am-5pm. $7, students, seniors, and ages 3-17 $4; free on W.

The Adler Planetarium, 1300 S. Lake Shore Dr. (922-7827), in Grant Park, lets you discover your weight on Mars, read the news from space, and examine astronomy tools. Open Sa-W 9am-6pm, Th-F 9am-9pm; Sept.-May M-F 9am-5pm, Sa-Su 9am-6pm. $3, seniors and ages 4-17 $2; free on Tu. Skyshow daily on the hr.; $3.

Shedd Aquarium, 1200 S. Lake Shore Dr. (939-2438), in Grant Park. The world's largest indoor aquarium has over 6600 species of fish in 206 tanks. The Oceanarium features small whales, dolphins, seals, and other marine mammals. Exquisite Pacific Ocean exhibit, complete with simulated crashing waves. Parking available. Open daily 9am-6pm. Feedings M-F 11am, 2, and 3pm. Combined admission to Oceanarium and Aquarium $10, seniors and ages 3-11 $8; Th Aquarium free, Oceanarium $6, seniors and ages 5-17 $5. Guided tour of Oceanarium $3.

The Museum of Contemporary Art, 220 E. Chicago Ave. (280-2660); take the #66 (Chicago Ave.) bus. A splendid addition to Chicago's power-packed museum line-up, the MCA supplies both permanent and temporary collections of modern art (work since 1945). Warhol, Javer, and Nauman highlight a vibrant list of artists. Open Tu and Th-F 11am-6pm, W 11am-8pm, Sa-Su 10am-6pm. $6.50, students and seniors $4, under 12 free; free first Tu of each month.

Chicago Historical Society, 1601 N. Clark St. (642-4600), at North Ave. A research center for scholars with a museum open to the public. Founded in 1856, 19 years after the city was incorporated. Permanent exhibit on America in the age of Lincoln, plus changing exhibits. Open M-Sa 9:30am-4:30pm, Su noon-5pm. $5, students and seniors $3, ages 6-12 $1; free on M. Library closed Su-M.

Spertus Institute of Jewish Studies, 618 S. Michigan Ave. (322-1747), downtown. A fabulous collection of synagogue relics from around the world rests on the 1st fl., as does the diminutive but moving Holocaust Memorial. Upstairs, check out articles and historical anecdotes from the Middle Ages through the 60s. Open Su-W 10am-5pm, Th 10am-8pm, F 10am-3pm. Artifact center open Su-Th 1-4:30pm. $5, students and seniors $3. Free on F.

Terra Museum of American Art, 666 N. Michigan Ave. (664-3939), at Erie St. Excellent collection of American art from colonial times to the present, with a focus on 19th-century American Impressionism. Open Tu-Sa 10am-7pm, Su 11am-5pm; $5, students and teachers with ID and under 14 free, seniors $2.50; free on Tu. Free tours Tu-F noon and 6pm, Sa-Su noon and 2pm.

Museum of Broadcast Communications, 78 E. Washington St. (629-6000), at Michigan. Celebrates couch-potato culture with exhibits on America's pastime. Open M-Sa 10am-4:30pm, Su noon-5pm. Free.

The Loop

When Mrs. O'Leary's cow kicked over a lantern and started the **Great Fire of 1871,** Chicago's downtown flamed into a pile of ashes. The city rebuilt with a vengeance, turning the functional into the fabulous to create one of the most concentrated clusters of architectural treasures in the world.

The downtown area, hemmed in by the Chicago River and Lake Michigan, rose up rather than out. Visitors can explore this street museum via one of two **walking tours,** organized by the **Chicago Architectural Foundation** ($10 for 1 tour, $15 for both). The 2hr. tours, one of early skyscrapers and another of modern architecture, start from the foundation's **bookstore/gift shop,** 224 S. Michigan Ave. (922-3432). Highlights include Louis Sullivan's arch, the Chicago window, and Mies van der Rohe's revolutionary skyscrapers. The foundation also provides a 1½hr. Chicago boat tour from the Wendella pier at Michigan Ave. (tours M-Sa 9am-8pm; Su 9am-6pm; $18; book in advance).

The frantic trading of Midwestern farm goods can be taken in at the world's oldest and largest commodity exchange, the **Futures Exchange,** or at the **Chicago Board of Options Exchange,** both located in **The Board of Trade Building,** 141 W. Jackson Blvd.; Ceres, the grain goddess, towers 609 ft. above street level there. For tours, contact the **visitors' office** (435-3590), 5th fl. (tours M-F 9:15am, every 30min. 10am-12:30pm; open M-F 8am-2pm; free). The third exchange, the **Chicago Mercantile Exchange,** 30 S. Wacker Blvd. (930-8249), at Madison, accounts for the green, yellow, and red jackets of the Loop at lunchtime.

In the late 19th century, Sears and Roebuck, along with competitor Montgomery Ward, created the mail-order catalog business, undercutting many small general stores and permanently altering the face of American merchandising. Today, although the catalog business has faded, the **Sears Tower,** 233 S. Wacker Dr. (875-9696), remains; more than an office building at 1707 ft., it stands as a monument to the insatiable lust of the American consumer. *(Open daily 9am-11pm; Oct.-Feb. 9am-10pm. $8, seniors $6, children $5, families $20. Lines can be long.)* The concrete behemoth rests for now as the second-tallest building in the world. The **First National Bank Building and Plaza** sits about 2 blocks northeast at the corner of Clark and Monroe St. The world's largest bank building leads your gaze skyward with its diagonal slope. Marc Chagall's vivid mosaic, *The Four Seasons,* lines the block and sets off a public space often used for concerts and lunchtime entertainment. At the corner of Clark and Washington St., 2 blocks north, **Chicago Temple,** the world's tallest church, sends its babelesque steeples toward heaven.

State and Madison, the most famous intersection of "State Street that great street," forms the focal point of the Chicago street grid. Louis Sullivan's **Carson Pirie Scott** store building is adorned with exquisite ironwork and the famous extra-large Chicago window. Sullivan's other masterpiece, the **Auditorium Building,** awaits several blocks south at the corner of Congress and Michigan. Beautiful design and flawless acoustics highlight this Chicago landmark. On 53 W. Jackson, Burnham and Koot's **Monadnock Building** deserves a glance for its rhythmically projecting bays of purple and brown rock. Southeast, the **Sony Fine Arts Theatre,** 418 S. Michigan Ave. (939-2119), screens current artistic and foreign films in the grandeur of the **Fine Arts Building** (open M-Th; $8.25; students $6; seniors, children, or matinee $5). Tomorrow's master artists get their start today at **Gallery 37** (744-8925), on State St. between Randolph and Washington. *(Open in summer M-F 10am-4pm.)* This open-air gallery, staffed by aspiring artists from city schools, offers visitors free tours by reservation, art exhibitions, and live performances during the summer months.

Chicago is decorated with one of the country's premier collections of outdoor sculpture. Large, abstract designs punctuate many downtown corners. The Picasso at the foot of the **Daley Center Plaza** (443-3054), at Washington and Dearborn St., enjoys the greatest fame. Free concerts play at noon on summer weekdays in the plaza. Across the street rests Joan Miró's *Chicago,* the sculptor's gift to the city. A great Debuffet sculpture sits across the way in front of the **State of Illinois Building.** The building is a postmodern version of the town square designed by Helmut Jahn in 1985; the elevator to the top gives a thrilling (and free) view of the sloping atrium, the circular floors, and the hundreds of employees at work. In 1988, the city held a contest to design a building in honor of the late mayor. The result is the $144 million **Harold Washington Library Center,** 400 S. State St. (747-4300), a researcher's dream and an architectural delight. *(Tours M-Sa noon and 2pm, Su 2pm. Open M 9am-7pm; Tu and Th 11am-7pm; W, F, Sa 9am-5pm, Su 1-5pm.)*

Near North

The city's ritziest district lies north of the Loop along the lake, just past the Michigan Ave. Bridge. A hotly contested international design competition in the 1920s resulted in the **Tribune Tower,** 435 N. Michigan Ave., a Gothic skyscraper which overlooks this stretch. Chicago's largest newspaper, *The Chicago Tribune,* is written here; quotations exalting the freedom of the press adorn the inside lobby. Over 8 mi. of corridors fill the **Merchandise Mart;** the entrance is on N. Wells or Kinzie, just north of the river. The largest commercial building in the world at 25 stories high and 2 city blocks long, it even has its own zip code. The first two floors compose a mall open to the public; the remainder contains showrooms where design professionals converge to choose home and office furnishings, from sofas to restroom signs. **Tours at the Mart,** #114, will guide you through the building at noon Monday to Friday (1½hr.; $10, seniors and students over 15 $9).

Big, bright, and always festive, Chicago's **Navy Pier** captures the carnival spirit 365 days a year. No small jetty, the mile-long pier has it all, with a concert pavilion, dining options, nightspots, sight-seeing boats, a spectacular ferris wheel, a crystal garden with palm trees, and an Omnimax theater. Now *that's* America. This is where to rent **bicycles** to navigate the Windy City's streets. *(Bike rental open daily Apr. and Oct. 10am-7pm; May 8am-8pm; June-Sept. 8am-11pm. $8.50 per hr., $34 per day.)*

Chicago's showy **Magnificent Mile**, a row of glitzy shops along N. Michigan Ave. between Grand Ave. and Division St., can put a magnificent drain on the wallet. Several of these retail stores, including **Banana Republic** and **Crate & Barrel**, were designed by the country's foremost architects. At **Niketown**, 669 N. Michigan Ave. (642-6363), a glorified shoe store, sports fans can pay homage to the pedicure of their heroes and heroines (open M-F 10am-8pm, Sa 9:30am-7pm, Su 11am-6pm). The **Chicago Water Tower** and **Pumping Station** hide among the ritzy stores at the corner of Michigan and Pearson Ave. Built in 1867, these two structures survived the Great Chicago Fire. The pumping station houses the multimedia show *Here's Chicago* and a tourist center (see **Practical Information,** above). Across the street, expensive and trendy stores pack **Water Tower Place,** the first urban shopping mall in the U.S.

The bells of **St. Michael's Church** ring in **Old Town** (take bus #151 to Lincoln Park and walk south down Clark or Wells St.), a neighborhood where eclectic galleries, shops, and nightspots crowd gentrified streets. Architecture buffs will enjoy a stroll through the W. Menomonee and W. Eugenie St. area. In early June, the **Old Town Art Fair** attracts artists and craftsmen from across the country.

North Side

Urban renewal has made **Lincoln Park,** a neighborhood just west of the park that bears the same name, a popular choice for upscale residents. Bounded by Armitage to the south and Diversey Ave. to the north, lakeside Lincoln Park offers recreation and nightlife, with beautiful harbors and parks. Cafes, bookstores, and nightlife pack its tree-lined streets; some of Chicago's liveliest clubs and restaurants lie in the area around Clark St., Lincoln Ave., and N. Halsted St.

North of Diversey Ave., the streets of Lincoln Park become increasingly diverse. Supermarket shopping plazas alternate with tiny markets and vintage clothing stores, while apartment towers and hotels spring up between aging 2-story houses. In this ethnic no man's land, Polish diners share blocks with Korean restaurants, and Mongolian eateries stare at Mexican bars.

Although they finally lost their battle against night baseball in 1988, **Wrigleyville** residents remain fiercely loyal to the **Chicago Cubs.** Tiny, ivy-covered **Wrigley Field,** 1060 W. Addison, just east of Graceland, at the corner of Clark, is the North Side's most famous institution (see **Sports,** p. 441). A pilgrimage here is a must for the serious or curious baseball fan, and for the *Blues Brothers* nut who wants to visit the famous pair's falsified address. Along Clark St.—one of the city's busiest nightlife districts—restaurants, sports bars, and music clubs abound. Window shopping beckons in the funk, junk, and 70s revival stores. **Wrigleyville** and **Lakeview,** around the 3000s and 4000s of N. Clark St. and N. Halsted, are the city's most concentrated **gay neighborhoods.** Partake of midwest tradition at **Waveland Bowl,** 3700 N. Western (773-472-5902), off Addison. It's one of few bowling alleys that's open 24hr. a day, 365 days a year (single games $2-3.50).

Near West Side

The **Near West Side,** bounded by the Chicago River to the east and Ogden Ave. to the west, assembles a veritable cornucopia of tiny ethnic enclaves. Farther out, however, looms the West Side, a dismal section of the city. Dangerous neighborhoods lie alongside safe ones, so always be aware of your location. **Greektown,** several blocks of authentic restaurants north of the Eisenhower on Halsted, draws acclaim from all over the city.

A few blocks down Halsted (take the #8 "Halsted" bus), Jane Addams devoted her life to historic **Hull House.** This settlement house bears witness to Chicago's role in turn-of-the-century reform movements. Although the house no longer offers social services, painstaking restoration has made the tiny **Hull House Museum,** 800 S. Halsted St. (413-5353), a fascinating part of a visit to Chicago (open M-F 10am-4pm, Su noon-5pm; free). The **Ukrainian Village,** centered at Chicago Ave. and Western Ave., is no longer occupied by ethnic Ukrainians, but you can still take a vicarious vacation at the **Ukrainian National Museum,** 721 N. Oakland Ave., (421-8020; open Th-Su 11am-4pm; $2, students $1).

GREAT LAKES

Hyde Park and the University of Chicago

Seven miles south of the Loop along the lake, the beautiful campus of the **University of Chicago** (702-9192) dominates the **Hyde Park** neighborhood; take the METRA South Shore Line. A former retreat for the city's artists and musicians, the park's community underwent urban renewal in the 50s and now provides an island of intellectualism in a sea of degenerating neighborhoods. University police aggressively patrol the area bounded by 51st St. to the north, Lakeshore Dr. to the east, 61st St. to the south, and Cottage Grove to the west, but don't test the edges of these boundaries. Lakeside Burnham Park, east of campus, is fairly safe during the day but not at night.

On campus, U. of Chicago's architecture ranges from knobby, gnarled, twisted Gothic to neo-streamlined high-octane Gothic. Frank Lloyd Wright's famous **Robie House,** 5757 S. Woodlawn (708-848-1976), at the corner of 58th St., blends into the surrounding trees. *(Tours M-F 11am-3pm, Sa-Su 11am-3:30pm. $8, over 64 and ages 7-18 $6.)* A seminal example of Wright's Prairie style, which sought to integrate house with environment, its low horizontal lines now hold university offices. The **Oriental Institute, Museum of Science and Industry** (see **Museums,** p. 434), and **DuSable Museum of African-American History** are all in or border on Hyde Park. From the Loop, take bus #6 "Jefferson Express" or the METRA Electric Line from the Randolph St. Station south to 59th St.

Oak Park

Oak Park sprouts 10 mi. west of downtown on the Eisenhower Expwy. (I-290). Frank Lloyd Wright endowed the community with 25 of his spectacular homes and buildings; the **Frank Lloyd Wright House and Studio,** 951 Chicago Ave., was his beautiful 1898 workplace. *(45min. tours of the house M-F 11am, 1 and 3pm, Sa-Su every 15min. 11am-4pm. 1hr. self-guided tours of Wright's other Oak Park homes can be taken with a map and audio cassette available daily 10am-3pm. Guided tours Sa-Su 10:30am, noon, and 2pm. All 3 types of tours $8, seniors and under 18 $6; combination interior/exterior tour tickets $14/$10. Open daily 10am-5pm.)* The neighborhood's **visitors center,** 158 Forest Ave. (708-848-1500 or 888-OAK-PARK/625-7275), offers maps, guidebooks, and tours of the house and environs. The office also offers an assortment of other tours, including visits to the **birthplace of Ernest Hemingway.** To reach Oak Park, take the Green Line to Harlem or take I-290 W to Harlem St.

Outdoors

A string of lakefront parks fringe the area between Chicago proper and Lake Michigan. On sunny afternoons, a cavalcade of sunbathers, dog walkers, roller skaters, and skateboarders storm the shore. The two major parks, both close to downtown, are Lincoln and Grant, operated by the Recreation Dept. (747-2200). **Lincoln Park** extends across 5 mi. of lakefront on the north side, and rolls in the style of a 19th-century English park: winding paths, natural groves of trees, and asymmetrical open spaces. The **Lincoln Park Zoo** is a decent spot for a stroll (open daily 9am-5pm, in summer Sa-Su until 7pm; free). Next door, the **Lincoln Park Conservatory** (742-7736) encloses fauna from desert to jungle eco-systems under its glass palace (open daily 9am-5pm; free).

Grant Park, covering 14 blocks of lakefront east of Michigan Ave., follows the 19th-century French park style: symmetrical and ordered, with squared corners, a fountain in the center, and wide promenades. The Petrillo Music Shell hosts free summer concerts here thanks to the **Grant Park Concert Society,** 520 S. Michigan Ave. (742-4763). Colored lights illuminate Buckingham Fountain each night from 9-11pm. The **Field Museum of Natural History, Shedd Aquarium,** and **Adler Planetarium** beckon museum-hoppers to the southern end of the park (if you don't want to walk 1 mi. from the fountain, take bus #146), while the **Art Institute** lies to the northwest (see **Museums,** p. 434).

On the north side, Lake Michigan lures swimmers to **Lincoln Park Beach** and **Oak St. Beach.** Popular swimming spots, both attract sun worshippers as well. The rock ledges are restricted areas, and swimming from them is illegal. Although the beaches are patrolled 9am to 9:30pm, they are unsafe after dark. The **Chicago Parks District** (747-2200) has further info.

The Up Side of Downstream

Although it was the fecund, fetid banks of the oozing Chicago River that gave the city its original Native American moniker, Checagon ("place of the smelly onion"), settlers never adopted a live-and-let-live policy towards the formerly rancid rill. Native Americans tended to avoid the odiferous site, searching for dwellings elsewhere, yet early pioneers almost immediately began draining the swampy muck around the stream. Not content merely to develop the surrounding land, the new Americans decided that the river was flowing the wrong way. As part of a network of waterways linking the Great Lakes to the Gulf of Mexico, the Chicago River originally flowed away from Lake Michigan. Unhappy with this setup, the settlers constructed an elaborate system of locks, rendering the Chicago River the only river in the world to flow backwards.

Farther Out

In 1885, George Pullman, inventor of the sleeping car, attempted to create a model working environment so that his Palace Car Company employees would be "healthier, happier, and more productive." The town of **Pullman,** the result of this quest, grew up 14 mi. southeast of downtown, and was considered the nation's ideal community until 1894, when a stubborn Pullman evicted fired workers from their homes. The community soon faced unrest, eventually becoming the focus of a monumental strike. In the center of town, Pullman built **Hotel Florence,** 11111 S. Forrestville Ave. (773-785-8181), 20min. from Chicago by car; take I-94 to W. 111th St.; by train, take the Illinois Central Gulf Railroad to 111th St. and Pullman or the METRA Rock Island Line to 111th St. *(Tours leave the hotel on the 1st Su of each month May-Oct. at 12:30 and 1pm. $4, students and seniors $3.50.)* Today, the hotel houses a museum and conducts tours of the Pullman Historic District.

A trip on **Lake Shore Dr.** provides an absolutely gorgeous drive on a sunny day. Starting from the Hyde Park area in the south, the road offers sparkling views of Lake Michigan all the way past the city. At its end, Lake Shore becomes Sheridan Rd., which twists and turns its way through the picturesque northern suburbs. Just to the north of Chicago is **Evanston,** a happening, affluent college town with an array of parks and nightclubs. Ten minutes farther north is upscale **Wilmette,** home to the ornate and striking **Baha'i House of Worship,** 100 Linden Ave. (847-853-2300), at Sheridan Rd. *(Open daily 10am-10pm; Oct.-May 10am-5pm. Services M-Sa 12:15pm, Su 1:15pm.)* The intricate structure is topped by a nine-sided dome modeled on the House of Worship in Haifa, Israel. The **Chicago Botanic Garden** (847-835-5440), on Lake Cook Rd. ½ mi. east of Edens Expwy., pampers vegetation 25 mi. from downtown. *(Open daily 8am-sunset. Parking $5 per car, $10 per van, $30 per RV; Sa-Su and holidays $6/$15/$35; includes admission.)* A day riding the great 'coasters at **Six Flags Great America** (847-249-1776), I-94 at Rte. 132 E, Gurnee, the largest amusement park in the Midwest, will wear you out. *(Open daily 10am-10pm; in spring and fall. Sa-Su 10am-10pm. $34, over 59 $17, ages 4-10 $29; 2-day pass, not necessarily consecutive, $42.)*

Steamboat gambling has been embraced by the Midwest as a way to avoid anti-betting laws. The action centers in Joliet. Roll the bones on **Empress River Cruises,** 2300 Empress Dr. (708-345-6789), Rte. 6 off I-55 and I-80 (2 per day; free), or **Harrah's Casino Cruises** (800-427-7247), which accommodates over 1000 guests.

ENTERTAINMENT

To stay on top of Chicago events, the weeklies *Chicago Reader* and *New City,* available in many bars, record stores, and restaurants, will help. The *Reader* reviews all major shows, with show times and ticket prices. *Chicago* magazine has exhaustive club listings, theater reviews, and listings of music, dance, and opera performances throughout the city. The Friday edition of *The Chicago Tribune* includes a section with music, theater, and cultural listings. *Gay Chicago* provides info on social activities as well as other news concerning the area's gay community.

GREAT LAKES

Theater

One of the foremost theater centers of North America, Chicago is also a home to Improv. The city's more than 150 theaters show everything from blockbuster musicals to off-color parodies. Downtown theaters cluster around the intersection of Diversey, Belmont, and Halsted (just north of the Loop), and around Michigan Ave. and Madison Ave. Smaller, community-based theaters are scattered throughout the city. The "Off-Loop" theaters on the North Side specialize in original drama, with tickets usually $17 and under.

Most theater tickets are expensive, though you can get half-price tickets on the day of performance at **Hot Tix Booths,** 108 N. State St. (977-1755), or at the 6th level of 700 N. Michigan Ave. Purchases must be made in person. Lines form 15-20min. before the booth opens (open M-F 10am-7pm, Sa 10am-6pm, Su noon-5pm). **Ticketmaster** (559-1212) supplies tickets for many theaters; smart theater-goers ask about senior, student, and child discounts at all Chicago shows.

Steppenwolf Theater, 1650 N. Halsted St. (335-1888), where Gary Sinise and the eerie John Malkovich got their start. Tickets $32 Su-Th, $37 F-Sa; ½-price after 5pm Tu-F, after noon Sa-Su. Office open Su-M 11am-5pm, Tu-F 11am-8pm, Sa 11am-9pm.

Goodman Theatre, 200 S. Columbus Dr. (443-3800), presents consistently good original works. Tickets around $18-40; ½-price after 6pm, or after noon for matinee. Box office open 10am-5pm, 10am-8pm show nights, usually Sa-Su.

Shubert Theater, 22 W. Monroe St. (902-1500), presents big-name Broadway touring productions. Ticket costs vary with show popularity $15-70. Box office open M-Sa 10am-6pm.

Victory Gardens Theater, 2257 N. Lincoln Ave. (773-871-3000). 4 theater spaces. Drama by Chicago playwrights. Tickets $23-28. Box office open M-Sa noon-6pm, Su noon-3pm.

Center Theatre, 1346 W. Devon Ave. (773-508-5422). Solid, mainstream work. Ticket prices vary by show ($16-22). Box office open 10am-4pm and 2hr. before the show.

Annoyance Theatre, 3747 N. Clark (773-929-6200). Original works that play off pop culture. 7 different shows per week. Often participatory comedy. Tickets ($5-10) sold just before showtime, which is usually 8 or 9pm.

Bailiwick Repertory, 1225 W. Belmont Ave. (773-327-5252), in the Theatre building. A mainstage and experimental studio space. Tickets from $10. Box office open W noon-6pm, Th-Su noon until showtime.

Live Bait Theatre, 3914 N. Clark St. (773-871-1212). Shows with titles like *Food, Fun, & Dead Relatives* and *Mass Murder II.* Launched a multi-play *Tribute to Jackie* (Onassis, that is). Tickets $20, Th $10. Box office open M-F noon-5pm.

Comedy

Chicago boasts a plethora of comedy clubs. The most famous, **Second City,** 1616 N. Wells St. (337-3992), spoofs Chicago life and politics. Second City graduated Bill Murray and late greats John Candy, John Belushi, and Gilda Radner, among others. Most nights, a free improv session follows the show. **Second City e.t.c.** (642-8189) offers yet more comedy next door at 1608 N. Wells. (Shows M-Th 8:30pm, F-Sa 8 and 11pm, Su 8pm. Tickets $12-16, M $6. Box office hrs. for both daily 10:30am-10pm. Reservations recommended; during the week you can often get in if you show up 1hr. early.)

Dance, Classical Music, and Opera

Chicago philanthropists built the high-priced, high-art performance center of this metropolis. Ballet, comedy, live theater, and musicals are performed at **Auditorium Theater,** 50 E. Congress Pkwy. (922-2110). From October to May, the **Chicago Symphony Orchestra,** conducted by Daniel Barenboim, resonates at **Orchestra Hall,** 220 S. Michigan Ave. (294-3000). **Ballet Chicago** (251-8838) pirouettes in theaters throughout Chicago (performance times vary; tickets $12-45). The **Lyric Opera of Chicago** performs from September to March at the **Civic Opera House,** 20 N. Wacker Dr. (332-2244). While these places may suck your wallet dry, the **Grant Park Music Festival** affords the budget traveler a taste of the classical for free; from mid-June through late August, the acclaimed Grant Park Symphony Orchestra plays a few free evening concerts per week at the Grant Park Petrillo Music Shell (usually W-Su; schedule varies; call 819-0614 for details).

Seasonal Events

The city celebrates summer on a grand scale. The **Taste of Chicago** festival cooks for eight days through July 4th. Seventy restaurants set up booths with endless samples in Grant Park, while crowds chomp to the blast of big name bands (free entry, food tickets 50¢ each). The first week in June, the **Blues Festival** celebrates the city's soulful, gritty music; the **Chicago Gospel Festival** hums and hollers in mid-June; and Nashville moves north for the **Country Music Festival** at the end of June. The ¡Viva Chicago! Latin music festival swings in late August, while the **Chicago Jazz Festival** scats Labor Day weekend. All festivals center at the Grant Park Petrillo Music Shell. The Mayor's Office Special Events Hotline (744-3370 or 800-487-2446) has more info on all six free events.

Chicago also offers several free summer festivals on the lakeshore, including the **Air and Water Show** in late August, when Lake Shore Park, Lake Shore Dr., and Chicago Ave. witness several days of boat races, parades, hang gliding, and stunt flying, as well as aerial acrobatics by the fabulously precise Blue Angels. In mid-July, the **Chicago to Mackinac Island Yacht Race** begins in the Monroe St. harbor. On summer Saturdays, Navy Pier lights the lake with a free fireworks show (595-7437 for times).

The regionally famous **Ravinia Festival** (847-266-5100), in the northern suburb of Highland Park, runs from late June to early September. The Chicago Symphony Orchestra, ballet troupes, folk and jazz musicians, and comedians perform throughout the festival's 14-week season (shows M-Sa 8pm; Su 7pm; lawn seats $8; other tickets $15-35). On certain nights, the **Chicago Symphony Orchestra** allows students free lawn admission with student ID. Call ahead. Round-trip on the METRA costs about $7; the festival runs charter buses for $12. The bus ride takes 1½hr.

Sports

The National League's **Cubs** play baseball at **Wrigley Field,** 1060 W. Addison St. (831-2827), at Clark, one of the few ballparks in America that has retained the early grace and intimate feel of the game; it's definitely worth a visit, especially for international visitors who haven't seen a baseball game (tickets $9-21). The **White Sox,** Chicago's American League team, swing on the South Side at the new **Comiskey Park,** 333 W. 35th St. (tickets $10-22; 674-1000). Da **Bears** play football at **Soldier's Field Stadium,** McFetridge Dr. and S. Lakeshore Dr. (708-615-BEAR/2327). The **Blackhawks** hockey team skates and da **Bulls** just keep winning NBA championships at the **United Center,** 1901 W. Madison, known fondly as "the house that Michael Jordan built" (Blackhawks 455-4500, tickets $25-100; Bulls 943-5800, tickets $30-450). **Sports Information** (976-4242) has current sports knowledge. For tickets, call **Ticketmaster** (Bulls and Blackhawks 559-1212, White Sox 831-1769, Cubs 831-2827).

NIGHTLIFE

"Sweet home Chicago" takes pride in the innumerable blues performers who have played here. Jazz, folk, reggae, and punk clubs throb all over the **North Side. Bucktown,** west of Halsted St. in North Chicago, stays open late with bucking bars and dance clubs. Aspiring pick-up artists swing over to **Rush** and **Division St.,** an intersection that has replaced the stockyards as one of the biggest meat markets in the world. Full of bars, cafes, and bistros, **Lincoln Park** is influenced by singles and young married couples, as well as by the gay scene. The vibrant center of gay culture is between 3000 and 4500 **Halsted St.**; many of the more festive and colorful clubs and bars line this area. For more raging, raving, and discoing, there are plenty of clubs near **River North,** in Riverwest, and on Fulton St.

B.L.U.E.S., 2519 N. Halsted St. (773-528-1012); El to Fullerton, then take the eastbound bus "Fullerton." Crowded and intimate, with unbeatable music. Success here led to the larger **B.L.U.E.S. etcetera,** 1124 W. Belmont Ave. (773-525-8989); El to Belmont, then 3 blocks west on Belmont. The place for huge names: Albert King, Bo Diddley, Dr. John, and Wolfman Washington have played here. Live music every night 9pm-1:30am. 21+. Cover for both places M-Th $5-6, F-Sa $8-9.

Buddy Guy's Legends, 754 S. Wabash Ave. (427-0333), downtown. Buddy officially plays in Jan., but he is known to stop by when not on tour. Cover Su-W $6, Th $7, F-Sa $10. 21+. Blues M-Th 5pm-2am, F 4pm-2am, Sa 5pm-3am, Su 6pm-2am.

Metro, 3730 N. Clark St. (773-549-0203). Live alternative and alterna-teen music, ranging from local bands to Soul Asylum and Alice Cooper. 18+; occasionally all ages are welcome. Cover $5-12; much more for big bands. Downstairs, the 21+ **Smart Bar** (773-549-4140) has pool tables and a dance floor. Cover $5-9. Opening times vary (around 10pm); closes around 4am on weekends.

Wild Hare & Singing Armadillo Frog Sanctuary, 3530 N. Clark St. (773-327-HARE/ 327-4273; El: Addison). Near Wrigley Field. Live Rastafarian bands play to a swaying, bobbing mass of 20-somethings. Cover $5-8, M-Tu free; W ladies free. Open Su-F until 2am, Sa until 3am.

Butch McGuires, 20 W. Division St. (337-9080), at Rush St. Originator of the singles bar. Owner estimates that "over 6500 couples have met here over 23 million glasses of beer and gotten married" since 1961—he's a little fuzzier on divorce statistics. Drinks $2-5. Open M-F 10am-4am, Sa 9am-5am, Su 11am-4am.

Zebra Lounge, 1220 N. State St. (642-5140). Small piano bar lined with zebra skins and dark wood. Mostly 30-somethings, but younger and older visitors drop in. Live music W-Sa and M; magician on Tu. Open Su-F 4:30pm-2am, Sa 4:30pm-3am.

Melvin B.'s, 1114 N. State St. (751-9897). "I built this place for people to have fun," says the owner. Hugely popular, in a prime downtown location with a breezy outdoor patio. 21+, or convince the bouncer you won't drink. Open Su-F 11am-2am, Sa 11am-3am. Wander next door to the **Cactus Cantina** to battle their margaritas.

Lounge Ax, 2438 N. Lincoln Ave. (773-525-6620), in Lincoln Park. Alternative industrial grunge in no particular order batted out Tu-F and Su until 2am, Sa until 3am. 21+. Cover $5-10.

Roscoe's Bar and Café, 3356 N. Halsted St. (773-281-3355). Primarily gay clientele, but all are welcome. Roscoe's has it all: a pool room, garden terrace, dance floor, cafe, even a clairvoyant. Occasional live performances. Long Island Iced Tea pitchers $10 on Su. 21+. Cover $3 on Sa. Open Su-F until 2am, Sa until 3am.

■ Springfield

Springfield, "the town that Lincoln loved," owes much to its most distinguished former resident. In 1837, Abraham Lincoln, along with eight other "long" legislators (they were all over 6 ft. tall), successfully moved the state capitol from Vandalia to Springfield. A veritable hotbed of political activity during these years, the small town hosted the heated Lincoln-Douglas debates of 1858, attracted the attention of the entire nation, and showed everyone the city was smarter than Shelbyville. Although Springfield's national prominence has since declined into obscurity, the town now welcomes tourists to learn everything there is to know about Honest Abe.

PRACTICAL INFORMATION Springfield is accessible via **Amtrak** (753-2013 or 800-872-7245), at 3rd and Washington St. near downtown (station open daily 6am-9:30pm). Trains run to Chicago (3½hr., 3 per day, from $25) and St. Louis (2hr., 3 per day, from $18). **Greyhound,** 2351 S. Dirksen Pkwy. (544-8466 or 800-231-2222; depot open M-F 9am-8pm, Sa 9am-noon and 2-4pm), on the eastern edge of town (walk to the nearby shopping center, where you can catch bus #10), rolls to Chicago (6 per day, 5hr., $38); Indianapolis (7hr., 2 per day, $42); St. Louis (2hr., 3 per day, $27); and Bloomington (1hr., 3 per day, $11). **Springfield Mass Transit District,** 928 S. 9th St. (522-5531), shuttles around town. Pick up maps at transit headquarters, most banks, or the Illinois State Museum (buses operate M-Sa 6am-6pm; fare 75¢, transfers free). The **downtown trolley** system (528-4100) is designed to take tourists to places of historic interest (all-day fare $8, seniors $7, kids 5-12 $4; 1-trip fare $4). For taxi service, try **Lincoln Yellow Cab** (523-4545; $1.25 base fare, $1.50 per mi.). The **Springfield Convention and Visitors Bureau,** 109 N. 7th St. (789-2360 or 800-545-7300), will hand over a detailed street map for your stroll through Lincolnland (open M-F 8am-5pm). Medical services are available at **St. John's Hospital,** 800 E. Carpenter St. (544-6464). **Lincoln Library,** 326 S. 7th St. (753-4900), offers **Internet access** (open M-Th 9am-9pm, F 9am-6pm, Sa 9am-5pm; Sept.-May also Su noon-5pm). **Post Office:** 411 E. Monroe (753-3432), at Wheeler St. (open M-F 7:30am-5pm). **ZIP code:** 62701. **Area code:** 217.

ACCOMMODATIONS, CAMPGROUNDS, AND FOOD Cheap lodgings cluster off I-55 and U.S. 36 on Dirksen Pkwy., but bus service from downtown is limited. More expensive downtown hotels may be booked solid on weekdays when the legislature is in session, but ask the visitors office about weekend packages. Rooms should be reserved as early as possible for holiday weekends and the State Fair in mid-Aug. Take bus #3 "Bergen Park" to Milton and Elm St. and walk a few blocks east to the **Dirksen Inn Motel/Shamrock Motel,** 900 N. Dirksen Pkwy. (522-4900) for clean, pleasant rooms, and refrigerators (reception 24hr.; singles $26; doubles $28). To reach **Parkview Motel,** 3121 Clear Lake Ave. (789-1682), take bus #3 to Elm St. and walk 1 block east; the motel is closer to downtown than most other budget accommodations (singles $32; doubles $42). **Mister Lincoln's Campground,** 3045 Stanton Ave. (529-8206), off Stevenson Rd. (take bus #10), has free showers, tent space ($7 per person, $2 per child), cabins (for 2 with A/C $25, $3 per additional adult, $2 per additional child), and an area for RVs (full hookup $19). The office is open daily 8am-8pm.

Interesting cuisine seems sparse in Springfield. Still, you can get some kicks down on historic Rte. 66 at the **Cozy Drive-In,** 2935 S. 6th St. (525-1992), a diner devoted to memorabilia of the old road and great greasy food. Their specialty is the Cozy Dog ($1.25), but they grill up a mean stack of flapjacks in the morning ($1.50; open M-Sa 7am-8pm). Downtown, pink-and-orange **Café Brio,** at 6th and Monroe (544-0574), stirs up typical soup and sandwich fare with Mexican, Mediterranean, and Caribbean flair. Great vegetarian options include mushroom-red chile fettucine. The cafe has a full bar and is open daily for lunch ($5-7), dinner ($9-15), and weekend brunch.

SIGHTS Springfield makes money by zealously re-creating Lincoln's life. Walking from sight to sight retraces the steps of the man himself (or so they say). Happily, many Lincoln sights are free (800-545-7300 accesses up-to-date info). The **Lincoln Home Visitors Center,** 426 S. 7th St. (492-4241), screens a 19min. film on "Mr. Lincoln's Springfield" and doles out free tickets to see the **Lincoln Home,** the only one Abe ever owned and the main Springfield draw, sitting at 8th and Jackson St. in a restored 19th-century neighborhood. *(10min. tours every 5-10min. from the front of the house. Open daily 8:30am-5pm. Arrive early to avoid the crowds.)*

A few blocks northwest, at 6th and Adams St. right before the Old State Capitol, the **Lincoln-Herndon Law Offices** (785-7289) describe a Lincoln-esque day at the office, before the Presidency. *(Open daily for tours only 9am-5pm; last tour 45min. before closing; donation suggested.)* Around the corner and to the left, across from the Downtown Mall, sits the magnificent limestone **Old State Capitol** (785-7961). In 1858, Lincoln delivered his stirring and prophetic "House Divided" speech here, warning that the nation's contradictory slavery policy risked dissolution. *(Open daily Mar.-Oct. 9am-5pm, Nov.-Feb. 9am-4pm. Last tour 1hr. before closing. Donation suggested.)* The capitol also witnessed the famous Lincoln-Douglass debates which catapulted Lincoln to national prominence. Opened in 1877, the **New State Capitol** (782-2099), 4 blocks away at 2nd and Capitol St., engrosses visitors with murals of Illinois's pioneer history and an intricately designed dome. *(Building open M-F 8am-4pm, Sa-Su 1st fl. only 9am-3pm. Group tours by appointment only.)* Free sidewalk telescopes in front allow a closer peek at the facade. The **Lincoln Tomb,** 1500 Monument Ave. (782-2717), rests at Oak Ridge Cemetery. *(Open daily Mar.-Oct. 9am-5pm, Nov.-Feb. 9am-4pm.)* Lincoln, his wife Mary Todd, and their three sons rest here.

Those unwilling to long endure all of Lincolnland should walk to the **Dana-Thomas House,** 301 E. Lawrence Ave. (782-6776), 6 blocks south of the Old State Capitol. Built in 1902, the stunning and well-preserved home was one of Frank Lloyd Wright's early experiments in Prairie Style and still features Frank's original fixtures (1hr. tours every 15-20min. W-Su 9am-5pm; suggested donation $3, children $1). The **Illinois State Museum** (782-7386), Spring and Edwards St., houses contemporary Illinois art and displays on the area's Native American history (open M-Sa 8:30am-5pm, Su noon-5pm; free).

With 66 bells, the **Thomas Rees Memorial Carillon** (753-6219), next to the exquisite **Washington Park Botanical Gardens** (753-6228), rings true as the third-largest carillon in the world and one of the few to offer visitors a view of the bells and playing mechanism. *(Tours June-Aug. Tu-Su noon-8pm, also spring and fall weekends. Donation sug-*

GREAT LAKES

gested.) The bells ring out during the summer on Wednesday nights at 7pm and Saturday at 3 and 7pm.

Rte. 66, that fabled American highway of yesteryear, is remembered in Springfield by **Shea's,** 2075 Peoria Rd. (522-0475), a truck shop with masses of memorabilia, including gas pumps, signs, and license plates (open Tu-Sa 7am-5pm).

Wisconsin

Oceans of milk and beer flood the Great Lakes' most wholesome party state. French fur trappers first explored this area in search of lucrative furry creatures. Years later, miners burrowed homes in the hills during the 1820s lead rush (earning them the nickname "badgers"), and hearty Norsemen set to clearing vast woodlands. By the time the forests fell and the mines were exhausted, German immigrant farmers had planted rolling fields of barley amid the state's 15,000 lakes and made Wisconsin the beer capital of the nation. Today, visitors to "America's Dairyland" flock past cheese-filled country stores to delight in the ocean-like vistas of Door County, as well as the ethnic fêtes (and less refined beer bashes) of Madison and Milwaukee.

PRACTICAL INFORMATION

Capital: Madison.
Visitor Info: Division of Tourism, 123 W. Washington St., P.O. Box 7606, Madison 53707 (608-266-2161, out of state 800-432-8747; http://tourism.state.wi.us).
Emergency: 911.
Time Zone: Central (1hr. behind Eastern). **Postal Abbreviation:** WI.
Sales Tax: 5.5%.

■ Milwaukee

A home to drinks and festivals, Milwaukee is a city given to celebration. The influx of immigrants, especially German and Irish, gave the city its reputation for *gemütlich-keit* (hospitality). Now, ethnic communities take turns throwing city-wide parties each summer weekend. The city's famous beer industry fuels the revelry, supplying the more than 1500 bars and taverns with as much brew as anyone could ever need. Aside from merrymaking, Milwaukee's attractions include top-notch museums, beautiful German-inspired architecture, and a long expanse of scenic lakeshore.

ORIENTATION AND PRACTICAL INFORMATION

Most north-south streets are numbered, increasing from Lake Michigan toward the west. Downtown Milwaukee lies between **Lake Michigan** and 10th St. Address numbers increase north and south from **Wisconsin Ave.,** the center of east-west travel. The **interstate system** forms a loop around Milwaukee: **I-43 S** runs to Beloit, **I-43 N** runs to Green Bay, **I-94 W** is a straight shot to Chicago, **I-794** cuts through the heart of downtown Milwaukee, and **I-894** connects with the airport.

Airport: General Mitchell International Airport, 5300 S. Howell Ave. (747-5300). Take bus #80 from 6th St. downtown (30min.). **Limousine Service,** 769-9100 or 800-236-5450. 24hr. pick-up and drop-off from most downtown hotels. Reservations required. $8.50, round-trip $16.
Trains: Amtrak, 433 W. St. Paul Ave. (271-0840 or 800-872-7245), at 5th St. 3 blocks from the bus terminal. In a fairly safe area, but less so at night. To Chicago (1½hr., 6 per day, $19) and St. Paul (6½hr., 1 per day, $72). Open daily 5:30am-9pm.
Buses: Greyhound, 606 N. 7th St. (272-2156 or 800-231-2222), off W. Michigan St. downtown. To Chicago (2-3hr., 18 per day, $12) and Minneapolis (6½-9hr., 6 per day, $47). Station open 24hr.; office open daily 6:30am-11:30pm. **Wisconsin Coach** (544-6503 or 542-8861), in the same terminal, covers southeast Wisconsin. **Badger Bus,** 635 N. 7th St. (276-7490), across the street, burrows to Madison (1½hr., 6 per day, $10). Open daily 6:30am-10pm. *Be cautious at night.*

Public Transportation: Milwaukee County Transit System, 1942 N. 17th St. (344-6711). Efficient metro area service. Most lines run 5am-12:30am. Fare $1.35, seniors and children 65¢; weekly pass $10.50/$6.50. Free maps at the library or at Grand Ave. Mall info center. Call for schedules.
Taxis: Veteran, 291-8080. $1.75 base fare, $1.50 per mi., 50¢ per additional person. **Yellow Taxi,** 271-1800. $1.75 base fare, $1.25 per mi., 50¢ per additional person.
Car Rental: Rent-A-Wreck, 4210 W. Silver Spring Dr. (464-1211). Rates from $18 per day with 50 free mi., 15¢ each additional mi. Insurance $8.50 per day. Ages 25 and up need major credit card or $150 cash deposit. Ages 21-25 add $10, credit card required. Open M-F 8am-6pm, Sa 8am-1pm.
High Roller Bike and Skate Rental (273-1343), on the lagoon at McKinley Marina in Veteran's Park. In-line skates $5 per hr., $17 per day. Bikes $9 per hr., $33 per day. Open daily 10am-8pm, weather permitting. Must be over 18 with ID.
Visitor Info: Greater Milwaukee Convention and Visitors Bureau, 510 W. Kilbourne St. (273-7222 or 800-554-1448), downtown. The Bureau will move across Kilbourne St. to the new Convention Ctr. sometime in 1999. Open M-F 8am-5pm; in summer also Sa 9am-2pm.
Hotlines: Crisis Intervention, 257-7222. **Rape Crisis Line,** 542-3828. Both 24hr. **Gay People's Union Hotline,** 562-7010. Operates daily 7-10pm.
Post Office: 345 W. St. Paul Ave. (270-2004), south along 4th Ave. from downtown, by the Amtrak station. Open M-F 7:30am-8pm. **ZIP code:** 53202. **Area code:** 414.

ACCOMMODATIONS

Downtown lodging options tend toward the pricey; travelers with cars should head out to the city's two hostels. **Bed and Breakfast of Milwaukee** (277-8066) finds rooms in local B&Bs (from $55).

University of Wisconsin at Milwaukee (UWM), Sandburg Hall, 3400 N. Maryland Ave. (229-4065 or 299-6123). Take bus #30 north to Hartford St. Convenient to nightlife and east-side restaurants. Laundry facilities, cafeteria, free local calls. Singles with shared bath $25; doubles $33. Clean, bland suites with bath divided into single and double bedrooms: 4 beds $58, 5 beds $69. Parking $6.25 for 24hr. Open June to mid-Aug. 2-day advance reservations required.
Wellspring Hostel (HI-AYH), 4382 Hickory Rd. (675-6755), Newburg; take I-43 N to Rte. 33 W. to Newburg and exit on Main St.; Hickory Rd. intersects Newburg's Main St. just northwest of the Milwaukee River. The pretty setting, far from downtown on a riverside vegetable farm, is worth the 45min. drive if you're looking to get back to nature. Well-kept with 25 beds, kitchen, and nature trails. $15, nonmembers $18. Private room with bath $40. Linen $3. Office open daily 8am-8pm. Reservations required.
Red Barn Hostel (HI-AYH), 6750 W. Loomis Rd. (529-3299), in Greendale 13 mi. southwest of downtown via Rte. 894; take the Loomis Exit. Public transportation takes forever; don't come without a car. Dark rooms with stone walls on the bottom floor of an enormous red barn. 20 dorm-style beds, full kitchen, no laundry facilities, not the coziest of bathrooms. $11, nonmembers $14. Linen $1.50. Check-in 5-10pm. Open May-Oct.
Hotel Wisconsin, 720 N. 3rd St. (271-4900), across from the Grand Avenue Mall. Occupies an impressive Germanesque brick building in the heart of downtown. 250 large, floral rooms with private bath, cable TV, A/C, and fridge. Call ahead about the $35 rooms without TV or fridge. Singles and doubles $79; $8 per additional adult. Key/phone deposit $15. Free parking. Open May-Aug.
Motel 6, 5037 S. Howell Ave. (482-4414), near the airport, in a remodeled building 15min. from downtown. Any airport shuttle will take you within walking distance. Airy rooms with A/C, cable, and a pool. Singles $37; doubles $41; Sa-Su $41/$45.

FOOD

Milwaukee is a premier town for food and drink. German brewers mastered a gold liquid that has been around since 4000 BC with refrigeration, glass bottles, cans, and lots of PR, and made **beer** available to all. Milwaukeeans take advantage of nearby Lake Michigan with a local favorite called the Friday night **fish fry**. French ice cream, known as **frozen custard,** is the dairy state's special treat.

The Brew Crew

The cars roll in from all over. There are men donning football jerseys; there are shiny-faced families of four (Dad has a gleam in his eye); there are young couples holding hands. What's it all about? You can read it in the glazed-over eyes beholding **giant copper kettles**...BEER. Most tours start in the brewhouse (though the Lakefront Brewery cuts to the chase, starting at the tap). Next is the canning and bottling center, where desperate eyes watch liquid pour into cans as **parched tongues lick parched lips.** In the distribution warehouse, guests stare at freshly packed cases, calculating exactly how long it would take them and their four best buddies to finish it all off. Finally, they get what they came for. At Miller, each guest gets two or three glasses to sample. At Lakefront, it's an **all-you-can-drink affair** while the tour lasts. Ahh...the golden liquid gently tickles the back of the throat as it descends. The **beer gods** are smiling. Life is good.

For Italian restaurants, look on **Brady St.** You'll find heavy Polish influences in the **South Side** and good Mexican food at National and S. 16th St. **East Side** eateries are a little more cosmopolitan. Downtown, the **Water St. entertainment district** boasts hot new restaurants for a range of palates. The $13 million Riverwalk project has revitalized the Water St. area. On the north end of the Riverwalk, **Old World Third St.** offers the City's best brew-pubs.

John Hawk's Pub, 100 E. Wisconsin Ave. (272-3199). Patrons can enjoy a riverside terrace and gleaming oak bar while sampling the wide range of traditional British pub fare (soups $2, sandwiches $4-7). Try the fish fry (2-piece basket $5.45). Live jazz Sa 9pm; no cover. Open Su-Th 10am-10:30pm, F-Sa 10am-2am.

Leon's, 3131 S. 27th St. (383-1784). A cross between *Grease* and *Starlight Express*. Great frozen custard (2 scoops $1). Hot dogs 95¢. Open Su-Th 11am-midnight, F 11am-12:30am, Sa 11am-1am.

Abu's Jerusalem of the Gold, 1978 N. Farwell Ave. (277-0485), 3 blocks south from the corner of North and Farwell, at Lafayette on the East Side. A tiny pink restaurant with Middle Eastern novelties for herbivore and carnivore alike. The falafel sandwich is a vegetarian delight ($2.50). Rosewater lemonade 85¢. Open M-Th 11:30am-9pm, F-Sa 11:30am-11pm, Su noon-9pm.

King and I, 823 N. 2nd St. (276-4181). Thai food served in an elegant restaurant. The all-you-can-eat lunch buffet is a favorite ($6.25). Entrees $11. Open M-F 11:30am-9pm, Sa 5-10pm, Su 4-9pm.

Comet Café, 1947 Farwell Ave. (273-7677), next to Abu's. Zesty espresso shakes are served until midnight M-F.

SIGHTS

Although many of Milwaukee's breweries have left, the city's name still evokes images of a cold one. No visit to the city would be complete without a look at the yeast in action. The **Miller Brewery,** 4251 W. State St. (931-BEER/2337), a corporate giant that produces 43 million barrels of beer annually (including *Milwaukee's Best*), offers a free 1hr. tour with three samples, followed by an optional 15min. brew house tour. *(2 tours per hr. M-Sa 10am-3:30pm; 3 per hr. during busy days; call for winter schedule. Under 18 must be accompanied by adult. ID required.)* The **Lakefront Brewery,** 1872 N. Commerce St. (372-8800), off Pleasant St., produces five year-round beers and several seasonal specials, including pumpkin beer and cherry lager (tours F 5:30pm, Sa 1:30, 2:30, and 3:30pm; $3). **Sprecher Brewing,** 701 W. Glendale (964-2739), off Port Washington St., north of the city on I-43, doles out four beer samples following a 1hr. tour (tours M-F 4pm, Sa every 30min. 1-3pm; $2, under 12 free). At most breweries, tour prices are discounted for non-drinkers.

A road warrior's nirvana, **Harley-Davidson Inc.,** 11700 W. Capitol Dr. (342-4680), gives 1hr. tours of its engine and transmission facility. *(Tours M-F 9:30, 11am, and 1pm, but call ahead—the plant shuts down entirely during certain weeks in summer. Reservations required for groups larger than 6.)*

Several excellent museums grace the city of Milwaukee. The **Milwaukee Public Museum,** 800 W. Wells St. (278-2700 or 278-2702 for recorded info), at N. 8th St., attracts visitors with dinosaur bones, a replicated Costa Rican rainforest, a Native American exhibit, and a re-created European village. *(Open daily 9am-5pm. $5.50, students with ID, seniors, and ages 4-17 $4.50. Parking available.)* The lakefront **Milwaukee Art Museum,** 750 N. Lincoln Memorial Dr. (224-3200), in the War Memorial Building, houses Haitian art, 19th-century German art, and American works, including two of Warhol's soup cans. *(Open Tu-W and F-Sa 10am-5pm, Th noon-9pm, Su noon-5pm. $5, students and seniors $3, under 12 free.)* The **Charles Allis Art Museum,** 1801 N. Prospect Ave. (278-8295), at Royal Ave. 1 block north of Brady (take bus #30 or 31), houses a fine collection of East Asian and Classical artifacts (open W-Su 1-5pm; $2).

Better known as "The Domes," the **Mitchell Park Horticultural Conservatory,** 524 S. Layton Blvd. (649-9800), at 27th St., recreates a desert and a rain forest and mounts seasonal displays in a series of 7-story conical glass domes. *(Open daily 9am-5pm. $4, students and seniors $2.50. Take bus #10 west to 27th St., then #27 south to Layton.)* The **Boerner Botanical Gardens,** 5879 S. 92nd St. (425-1130), in Whitnall Park between Grange and Rawsen St., boast billions of beautiful blossoms as well as open-air concerts on Thursday nights (open mid-Apr. to Oct. daily 8am-7pm; parking $3.50). County parks line much of Milwaukee's waterfront, providing free recreational areas and trails. Olympians and masses alike skate at the **Pettit National Ice Center,** 500 S. 84th St. (266-0100), next to the state fairgrounds.

ENTERTAINMENT

On any given night in Milwaukee, a free concert is being given somewhere. Your best bet at getting from here to that somewhere is to phone the visitors bureau at 273-7222. A recording provides after-hours callers with pertinent festival information.

The modern white stone **Marcus Center for the Performing Arts,** 929 N. Water St. (273-7206 or 800-472-4458), across the river from Père Marquette Park, hosts the **Milwaukee Symphony Orchestra,** the **Milwaukee Ballet,** and the **Florentine Opera Company.** (Symphony tickets $17-52, ballet $13-62, opera $15-80; ballet and symphony offer ½-price student and senior tickets on the day of any show.) During the summer, the center's Peck Pavilion hosts **Rainbow Summer** (273-7206), a series of free lunchtime concerts—jazz, bluegrass, you name it (M-F noon-1:15pm). **The Milwaukee Repertory Theater,** 108 East Wells St. (224-9490), stages shows from September through May. (Tickets $8-30; ½-price student and senior rush tickets available 30min. before shows.) On summer Thursdays, **Jazz in the Park** (271-1416) presents free concerts in East Town's **Cathedral Square Park,** at N. Jackson St. between Wells and Kilbourn St. In Père Marquette Park, by the river between State and Kilbourn St., **River Flicks** (270-3560) screens free movies at dusk on Thursdays in August.

Summerfest (273-3378, outside Milwaukee 800-837-3378), the largest and most lavish of Milwaukee's festivals, spans 11 days in late June and early July; daily life halts as a potpourri of big-name musical acts, culinary specialities, and an arts and crafts bazaar take over Henry Maier Festival Park (M-Th $8, F-Su $9); look for signs with the smiling orange face. Ethnic festivals abound during festival season (also at the Maier Park); the most popular are: **Polish Fest** (529-2140) and **Asian Moon** (481-3628), both in mid-June; **Festa Italiana** (223-2180), in mid-July; **Bastille Days** (271-7400), near Bastille Day (July 14); **German Fest** (464-9444), in late July; Irish Fest (476-3378), in mid-August; **Mexican Fiesta** (383-7066), in late August; **Indian Summer Fest** (774-7119), in early September; and **Arabian Fest** (342-1120), in mid-September (most festivals $7, under 12 free). Pick up a copy of the free weekly *Downtown Edition* for the full scoop on festivals and other events. Locals line the streets for **The Great Circus Parade** (273-7877), held in mid-July, a re-creation of turn-of-the-century processions with trained animals, daredevils, costumed performers, and 65 original wagons. In early August, the **Wisconsin State Fair** (266-7000) rolls into the fairgrounds toting big-name entertainment, 12 stages, exhibits, contests, rides, fireworks, and a pie-baking contest ($6, seniors $5, under 11 free). The **Blues/Jazz Barbecue** (271-1416) heats up Veterans Park in early September.

The **Milwaukee Brewers** baseball team plays at **County Stadium,** at the interchange of I-94 and Rte. 41 (933-9000 or 800-933-7890), while the **Milwaukee Bucks** (227-0500) hoop it up at the Bradley Center, 1001 N. 4th St.

NIGHTLIFE

Milwaukee never lacks for something to do after sundown. Downtown gets a bit seedy at night, but the area along **Water St.** between Juneau and Highland Ave. offers slightly yuppified bars and street life. Clubs and bars also cluster near the intersection of **North Ave.** and **North Farwell St.,** near the UW Campus. Perhaps the newest and most exciting place to be in Milwaukee after hours is **Brady St.,** which runs east-west between Farwell and the river.

Safehouse, 779 N. Front St. (271-2007), across from the Pabst Theater downtown. A brass plate labeled "International Exports, Ltd." welcomes guests to this bizarre world of spy hideouts, James Bond music, *mata hari* outposts, and drinks with names like Rahab the Harlot. A briefing with "Moneypenny" in the foyer is just the beginning of the intrigue. Draft beer $2.50; 24 oz. specialty drinks $5.50. Cover $1-2. Open M-Th 11:30am-1:30am, F-Sa 11:30am-2am, Su 4pm-midnight.

Hi-Hat, 1701 Brady St. (225-9330), 3 blocks west of Farwell Ave. In a city which lacks for after-hours music venues, this trendy jazz joint is an oasis. M-Tu swing and jazz bands play on the loge, while Milwaukee's hep night-hawks roost in the cavernous depths below. No attitude, no dress code, no cover—for now (beer $2.50-6). Open daily 4pm-2am, Su 10am-3pm for brunch.

Rochambo, 1317 Brady St. (241-0095), across the street from Hi-Hat. A coffee/teahouse hip almost to a fault. The patrons here tend to be quite proud of how cool they are, but the tea is outstanding, and there is actually room to sit. $1.25 for a mug of Oolong. Open M-F 7am-midnight, Sa 8am-midnight, Su 9am-midnight.

ESO$_2$, 1905 E. North Ave. (278-8118). Flashing lights and alternative dance mixes shower down on a large, ventilated dance floor. Look for theme nights (like Tu retro), with special drink prices (like $3 pitchers). Cover usually $2. Open Tu-Su; hrs. vary.

Dance, Dance, Dance, part of **Lacage,** 801 S. 2nd Ave. (383-8330). Caters to a 20- and 30-something gay clientele, but all are welcome. Videos accompany dance mixes. Cover W-Th $2, F $3, Sa $5.

Wolski's Tavern, 1836 N. Pulaski St. (276-8130). The bar with seniority—it's the oldest in the city. Pool, darts, beer ($1.50-3.50), and low-key neighborliness.

■ Madison

Building cities on isthmi is like shaking someone's left hand; it's generally avoided and, when attempted, usually comes off quite awkwardly. Madison's own awkward development owes much to the efforts of Judge James Doty, who cajoled Wisconsin's lawmakers into moving the capital to Madison in 1836. (Doty gave undecided lawmakers hundreds of acres of land in the Madison region to help them make up their minds.) Doty's vision, a capital on a narrow isthmus, sandwiched between lakes Menona and Mendota, has served to segregate the northeast and southwest sides of the city. Residential and mall-ridden, the northeast side of the city is far less impressive than the university-dominated southwest. With not just one lakefront view but two, Madison has plenty of beachfront from which to swim, boat, or ski. The town's shorepaths are perfect for running or roller-blading.

PRACTICAL INFORMATION Connecting the city's northeast and southwest sides is Washington Ave./U.S. 151, the city's main thoroughfare, which runs through Capitol Sq. **Greyhound,** 2 S. Bedford St. (257-3050 or 800-231-2222), has buses to Chicago (3-5hr., 8 per day, $18-22) and Minneapolis (7 per day, $37-39). **Badger Bus** (255-6771) departs from the same depot and runs to Milwaukee (1½hr., 6 per day, $10). The station is open daily from 5:30am-11pm. **Madison Metro Transit System,** 1101 E. Washington Ave. (266-4466), travels through downtown, UW campus, and surrounding areas ($1.25; free M-Sa 10am-3pm in the capitol-UW campus area). The **Greater Mad-**

ison **Convention and Visitors Bureau,** 615 E. Washington Ave. (255-2537 or 800-373-6376; open M-F 8am-4:30pm). **Post Office:** 3902 Milwaukee Ave. (246-1249; open M 7:30am-7pm, Tu-F 7:30am-6pm, Sa 8:30am-2pm). **ZIP code:** 53714. **Area code:** 608.

ACCOMMODATIONS AND CAMPGROUNDS **Madison Summer Hostel (HI-AYH)** (251-5873), on Langdon St., is a good bet for the budget traveler with clean dorm-style rooms. (Open mid-May to mid-Aug. Check-in 7-10am and 5-10pm. $13, non-members $16; doubles $25/$30; 25% discount for bikers, backpackers, and families.) Although they only rent out eight rooms, the best value in the city is at the **Memorial Union**, 800 Langdon St. (265-3000), on the UW campus, which supplies large, elegant rooms with excellent views, cable TV, A/C, and free parking (from $58). At motels stretching along Washington Ave. (U.S. 151), near the intersection with I-90, rates start at $40 per weeknight and rise dramatically on weekends. From the Capitol, Bus A shuttles the 5 mi. between the Washington Ave. motels and downtown. The **Select Inn,** 4845 Hayes Rd. (249-1815), near the junction of I-94 and U.S. 151, bucks the trend, offering large rooms with cable TV, A/C, and a whirlpool. (Singles $39; doubles from $47; Sa-Su $43/$51. Continental breakfast included.) Nearby **Motel 6,** 1754 Thierer Rd. (241-8101), behind Denny's Restaurant, is a solid choice with A/C and cable TV (singles from $36; doubles from $41). Prices steepen downtown, starting around $60. **Campers** should head south on I-90 to Stoughton, where **Lake Kegonsa State Park,** 2405 Door Creek Rd. (873-9695), has sites (½ kept for walk-ins) in a wooded area near the beach. (Showers, flush toilets. WI residents M-F $7, Sa-Su $9; non-residents $9/$11. Parking permits $5 per day, non-residents $7.)

FOOD AND NIGHTLIFE Good restaurants pepper Madison; a cluster spice up the university and capitol areas. **State St.** hosts a wide variety of cheap restaurants, both chains and Madison originals. Cheap cafeteria food is also widely available at the **Memorial Union,** on Langdon St. **Himal Chuli,** 318 State St. (251-9225), has cheap *tarkari, dal, bhat,* and other Nepali favorites—a full veggie meal goes for around $6.50, and meat meals for $8 (open M-Sa 11am-9pm). **Dotty Dumpling's Dowry,** 116 N. Fairchild St. (255-3175), is where classic American chow meets the mobile. The award-winning burgers ($4), malts ($3.50), and 19 beers on tap ($2) are consumed under hanging wooden canoes, blimps, and airplanes. (Open M-W 11am-10pm, Th-Sa 11am-11pm, Su noon-8pm.) **Taqueria Gila Monster,** 106 King St. (225-6425), stomps out low-fat, high-flavor Mexican food with flair; catfish and cactus fillings are good choices for your two enchiladas ($3.25; open M-Sa 11am-9pm). On Friday nights, the **Essen Haus,** 514 E. Wilson St. (255-4674), plays host to live polka bands, semi-rowdy crowds, and 2-gallon hats. At **Crystal's Corner Bar,** 1302 Williamson St. (256-2953), down a draught beer ($1.20-3.25), and groove to live bands, usually blues. (Schedule and cover vary. Open Su noon-midnight, M-Th 11am-2am, F-Sa 11am-2:30am.)

SIGHTS AND ENTERTAINMENT Between UW and the capitol area, Madison offers many options for sight-seeing. The imposing **State Capitol** (266-0382), in Capitol Sq. at the center of downtown, boasts beautiful ceiling frescoes and the only granite dome in the U.S. *(Free guided tours from the ground fl. info desk M-Sa on the hr. 9-11am and 1-3pm, Su 1-3pm. Open daily 6am-8pm.)* Every Saturday morning from late April to early November, the Capitol attracts throngs of visitors for the weekly **farmers market,** which has grown to become one of the area's premiere attractions. Also on Capitol Sq., the **Wisconsin Veterans Museum,** 30 W. Mifflin St. (264-6086), honors Wisconsin soldiers (open Tu-Sa 9:30am-4:30pm, Apr.-Sept. also Su noon-4pm; free). The **State Historical Museum,** 30 N. Carroll St. (264-6555), explores the history of Wisconsin's Native American population (open Tu-Sa 10am-5pm, Su noon-5pm; free). The **Madison Art Center,** 211 State St. (257-0158), inside the civic center, exhibits modern and contemporary art and hosts traveling exhibitions. *(Open Tu-Th 11am-5pm, F 11am-9pm, Sa 10am-9pm, Su 1-5pm. Most exhibits free.)* The **Madison Civic Center,** 211 State St. (266-6550), frequently stages arts and entertainment performances in the Oscar Mayer Theatre, and hosts the **Madison Symphony Orchestra.** *(Tickets from $20. Office open M-F 11am-5:30pm, Sa 11am-2pm. Season runs late Aug. to May.)* The **Madison Repertory Theatre,** 122 State St., #201 (256-0029), performs classic and contempo-

GREAT LAKES

rary musicals and dramas (showtimes vary; tickets $6.50-22). The free *Isthmus* (printed every Th) covers the entertainment scene.

Madison's **State St.** exudes a college atmosphere, sporting many funky clothing stores and record shops. At the southwest end of State St. is the **University of Wisconsin (UW),** where students love to hang out at Union Terrace. In summer, the terrace is home to free weekend concerts on the lake shore. In winter, the concerts move indoors, but the volume remains the same.

A few noteworthy museums grace UW, such as the **Geology Museum,** 215 W. Dayton St. (262-2399; open M-F 8:30am-4:30pm, Sa 9am-noon), and the **Elvehjem Museum of Art,** 800 University Ave. (263-2246; open Tu-F 9am-5pm, Sa-Su 11am-5pm; free). Also part of UW, the outdoor **Olbrich Botanical Gardens** and indoor **Bolz Conservatory,** 3330 Atwood Ave. (246-4550), offer a plethora of plant life. Free-flying birds, waterfalls, and tropical plants grace the inside of the conservatory dome. *(Gardens open daily 10am-8pm; Sept.-May M-Sa 10am-4pm, Su 1am-5pm. Free. Conservatory open M-Sa 10am-4pm, Su 10am-5pm. $1, under 5 free; free W and Sa 10am-noon.)* For more info on any UW attraction, visit the **UW Visitors Center** at the corner of Observatory Dr. and N. Park St., on the west side of the Memorial Union. Botanists and Bedouins alike will enjoy the **University Arboretum,** 1207 Seminole Hwy. (263-7888), off I-94. A 6 mi. walking loop encircles the Arboretum's 1200 acres of protected land.

East of Madison, **House on the Rock,** 5754 U.S. 23 (935-3639), in Spring Green, offers gorgeous views of the Wyoming Valley from its glass-walled Infinity Room, and a 40-acre complex of gardens and fantastic architecture. *(Open daily 9am-8pm; mid-Mar. to late May and Sept.-Oct. 9am-7pm. $15, ages 7-12 $9, ages 4-6 $4.)*

■ Door County

Door County's 250 mi. of coastline, 10 lighthouses, rocky shores, and sandy beaches give the peninsula the atmosphere of a New England seashore. Lake Michigan reinforces the comparison, sending ocean-like waves and riptides to pound the windy eastern shore. With miles of bike paths, acres of orchards, and stunning scenery, Door County's 12 villages swing open to visitors on a summer-oriented seasonal schedule. Visitors are advised to make reservations for just about everything if they plan to be on the peninsula during a weekend in either July or August. Temperatures can dip to 40°F at night here, even in July.

PRACTICAL INFORMATION Door County begins north of **Sturgeon Bay,** where Rte. 42 and 57 converge and then split again; Rte. 57 runs up the eastern coast of the peninsula, while Rte. 42 runs up the western side. The peninsula's west coast, which borders the Green Bay, tends to be warmer, artsy-er, and more expensive. The east coast, colder and less expensive, contains the bulk of the peninsula's park area. From south to north along Hwy. 42, **Fish Creek, Sister Bay, Ephraim,** and **Ellison Bay** are the largest towns on the island; directions are usually given in reference to one of these towns. Public transportation comes only as close as **Green Bay,** 50 mi. southwest of Sturgeon Bay, where **Greyhound** has a station at 800 Cedar St. (432-4883; station open M-F 6:30am-5:15pm, Sa-Su 10am-noon and 4-5:15pm). Every day, three buses head to Milwaukee ($20). In Green Bay, **Advantage,** 1629 Velp (497-2152), 5 mi. from the Greyhound station, rents cars. ($15 per day, $90 per week, 10¢ per mi., insurance $5. Must be 25. Open M-F 8:30am-5:30pm, Sa 8am-2:30pm.) **Door County Chamber of Commerce,** 6443 Green Bay Rd. (743-4456 or 800-527-3529), on Rte. 42/57 entering Sturgeon Bay, has free brochures for every village on the peninsula as well as biking maps. (Open M-F 8:30am-5pm, Sa-Su 10am-4pm; mid-Oct. to mid-May M-F 8:30am-4pm.) Just outside the center, the **Inline** computer/phone system lists hotel vacancies and allows free phone calls to listed lodgings. Visitors centers are in each of the villages. **Post Office:** 359 Louisiana (743-2681), at 4th St. in Sturgeon Bay (open M-F 8:30am-5pm, Sa 9:30am-noon). **ZIP code:** 54235. **Area code:** 920.

ACCOMMODATIONS AND CAMPGROUNDS Lodgings crowd Rte. 42 and Rte. 57 ($60 and up in summer). Reservations for July and August should be made as far in

Baraboo's Bizarre

The Greatest Show on Earth is in Baraboo, Wisconsin—permanently. Along the Baraboo River, a swath of bank has been set aside by the State Historical Society to honor the one-time winter home of the world-famous circus. The **Circus World Museum,** 426 Water St. (356-8341), in Baraboo, packs a full line-up of events from big-top performances to street parades (Open daily in summer from 9am to 6pm, mid-July through mid-Aug. 9am to 9pm. $12, under 12 $6.) But if craning your neck to see some groomed and plumed horse defecate leaves you unfulfilled, Baraboo has more to offer. Just past the Ho-Chunk casino on Hwy. 12 is Shady Lane Rd., home to the **International Crane Foundation.** Created by two acolytes to the conservation ideas of **Aldo Leopold** (ol' Aldo also lived on Shady Lane Rd.), the Crane Foundation, E-11376 Shady Lane Rd. (356-9462), supports all 15 different species of crane in the world on 225 acres of restored prairie. Visitors to the foundation are treated to animal feedings (the feeders have to disguise themselves as birds to avoid imprinting) and to a crane flight show ($6, under 12 $2.50), a once-popular activity which may be discontinued because of the birds' tendency to land on or attack visitors.

advance as possible. The **Century Farm Motel,** 10068 Rte. 57 (854-4069), 3 mi. south of Sister Bay on Rte. 57, rents small two-room cottages hand-built by the owner's grandfather in the 1920s ($45-60; open mid-May to mid-Oct.; A/C, TV, private bath, fridge). A bevy of gnome statues, 1000 Barbies, 600 animated store window mannequins, and 35 cars grace the premises of the **Chal-A Motel,** 3910 Rte. 42/57 (743-6788), 3 mi. north of the bridge in Sturgeon Bay. (July-Aug. singles $49, doubles $54; Nov. to mid-May $29/$34; mid-May to June $34/$39. Large rooms.)

Four out of the area's five **state parks** (all except Whitefish Dunes State Park) provide space for camping ($10, WI residents $8; F-Sa $12/$10). All state parks require a motor vehicle permit ($7 per day, WI residents $5; $25/$18 per year; $3 per hr.). **Peninsula State Park** (868-3258), just past Fish Creek village on Rte. 42, contains the largest of the campgrounds (469 sites), with showers and flush toilets, 20 mi. of shoreline, a golf course, a spectacular view from Eagle Tower, and 17 mi. of hiking trails. Reservations are best made well in advance (i.e. 6 months), or come in person and put your name on the waiting list for one of the 70 walk-in sites. **Potawatomi State Park,** 3740 Park Dr. (746-2890), Sturgeon Bay 54235, spreads just outside Sturgeon Bay off Rte. 42/57, before you cross the bridge. The park maintains 125 campsites, 19 of which are open to walk-ins; reservations can be made for the others. **Newport State Park** (854-2500) is a wildlife preserve at the tip of the peninsula, 7 mi. from Ellison Bay off Rte. 42. Although it permits entrance to vehicles, all 16 of its sites are accessible by hiking only, and 13 can be reserved. To get to **Rock Island State Park** (847-2235), the ferry sails from Gill's Rock to Washington Island. (Ferries run July-Aug. every 30min. 7am-6pm, every hr. May-June and Sept.-Oct. $3.75, children $2, auto $8.50, bicycle $1.50.) Another ferry voyages (847-2252; round-trip $7, campers with gear $8) to Rock Island State Park (40 sites; open mid-Apr. to mid-Nov.). Because there is no direct ferry service, campers must find a way across a 7 mi. stretch of Washington Island.

Private camping options are plentiful on the peninsula. The **Camp-Tel Family Campground,** 8164 Rte. 42 (868-3278), 1 mi. north of Egg Harbor, has tent sites and tiny A-frame cabins, each with two sets of bunks, a loft, and heat. (Sites $16, with water and electricity $18. A-frame $30. $5 per adult after 2, $2 per child. Office open May-June and Sept.-Oct. 9am-noon and 3-6pm, July-Aug. 9am-9pm.) **Path of Pines,** 3709 Rte. F (868-3332, 800-868-7802), 1 mi. east of the ever-packed Peninsula off Rte. 42 in Fish Creek, rents 91 quiet, scenic sites (showers and laundry facilities; tent sites $17-20, includes water and electricity).

FOOD AND DRINK Many people come to Door County just for **fishboils,** a Scandinavian tradition dating back to 19th-century lumberjacks. Cooks toss potatoes, onions, and whitefish into an enormous kettle over a wood fire; this is not for vegetarians. To remove the fish oil from the top of the water, the boilmaster (often imported from

GREAT LAKES

Scandinavia) judges the proper time to throw kerosene into the fire, producing a massive fireball; the cauldron boils over, signaling chow time—it's much better than it sounds. Most fishboils conclude with a big slice of cherry pie. Door County's best-known fishboils take place at **Edgewater Restaurant,** 100040 Hwy. 42 (854-4034), in Ephraim (May-Oct. M-Sa evenings, call for times; $13, under 12 $9; reservations recommended, no credit cards accepted), and **The Viking** (854-2998), in Ellison Bay (mid-May to Oct. every 30min. 4:30-8pm; $11.25, under 12 $8.25; indoor/outdoor seating). A cheaper option is **Calamity Sam's,** 4159 Bluff Ln. (868-2045), off Hwy. 42 in Fish Creek. In this lodge-like setting, waiters tend to dress in camouflage. If that doesn't bother you, the prices certainly won't (catfish fishboil $9, burger $3.50; open May-Nov. daily 7am-9pm). **Al Johnson's Swedish Restaurant** (854-2626), in the middle of Sister Bay on Rte. 42, has excellent Swedish food ($9-17), a waitstaff in traditional Swedish dress, and goats who dine daily on the thick sod roof, weather permitting (open daily 6am-9pm; in winter M-Sa 6am-8pm, Su 7am-8pm). **Bayside Tavern** (868-3441), on Rte. 42 in Fish Creek, serves Bob's World-Famous chili ($4) and a nice veggie sandwich ($4.75). At night, it's a crowded bar with live blues and rock on Mondays (cover $2), Tuesday pint nights, and open-mic Thursdays (open Su-Th 11am-2am, F-Sa 11am-2:30am). Guests can hurl dollar bills to the ceiling at a fun Wisconsin bar/restaurant, **Husby's Food & Spirits** (854-2624), on Rte. 42 entering Sister Bay from the south. Imports go for $2.50 among the good beer selection. (Open Su-Th 11am-2am, F-Sa 11am-2:30am.)

EAST SIDE Biking is the best way to take in the lighthouses, rocks, and white sand beaches of Door's coastline; tourist offices have free bike maps. **Whitefish Dunes State Park,** off Hwy. 57 on the peninsula's east side, maintains sand dunes, hiking/biking/skiing trails, and a well kept wildlife preserve (open daily 8am-8pm; vehicle permit required). Just north on Cave Point Rd. off Rte. 57, **Cave Point County Park** stirs the soul with its rocky coastline and some of the most stunning views on the peninsula (open daily 6am-9pm; free). **Lakeside Park,** immortalized in song by the rock band Rush, offers a wide, sandy expanse of beach at Jacksonport, backed by a shady park and playground (open daily 6am-9pm; free). South of Bailey's Harbor off Rte. 57, Kangaroo Lake Rd. leaps to **Kangaroo Lake,** the largest of the eight inland lakes on this thin peninsula; a circuit of the lake will reveal secluded swimming spots (the water's warmer than Lake Michigan). Trails at the **Ridges Sanctuary** (839-2802), north of Bailey's Harbor off County Rte. Q, enable exploration of over 30 beach ridges and a type of forest unique to the area (nature center open daily 9am-4pm; $2). For a satisfying hike, try **Newport State Park,** 6 mi. east of Ellison Bay on Newport Dr. off Rte. 42. The park also encompasses a 3000 ft. swimming area and 13 mi. of shoreline on Lake Michigan and Europe Lake (no vehicles).

WEST SIDE At **Peninsula State Park,** in Fish Creek, visitors rent boats, ride mopeds and bicycles along 20 mi. of shoreline road, and sunbathe at Nicolet Beach. At the top of **Eagle Tower,** 1 mi. and 110 steps up from the beach, you can see clear across the lake to Michigan (open daily 6am-11pm; vehicle permit required $3 per hr.). At the park entrance, **Edge of Park Bike and Moped Rentals,** 4025 Shore Rd. (868-3344), rents six-speed bikes ($5 per hr.), 21-speeds ($7 per hr.), and mopeds ($35 per hr.). Rates are lowered after the first hour. The park also hosts the **American Folklore Theatre** (868-9999), home to the Door County hit *Lumberjacks in Love* ($9.50). Just north of the Peninsula State Park, on Rte. 42, is the **Skyway Drive-In** (854-9938), between Fish Creek and Ephraim. It's one helluva deal—$5 pays for a double-feature of current release movies in one of only two Wisconsin drive-ins. The award-winning **Door Peninsula Winery,** 5806 Rte. 42 (743-7431 or 800-551-5049), Sturgeon Bay, invites you to partake of 30 different wines (15-20min. tours and tastings daily in summer 9am-6pm; off-season 9am-5pm). If you're dry-minded, the **Peninsula Players** (868-3287), off Rte. 42 in Fish Creek, perform in America's oldest professional resident summer theater (shows in summer Tu-Su; tickets $19-26, call for showtimes). Inquiries for more info on shows and movies can be addressed to the *Vacation Guide* at any tourist office in the county.

The shipping and packing town of **Green Bay,** at the foot of Door County, is Packerville, home to the Green Bay Packers (920-496-5719; tickets $32-39) and their idolized QB, Brett Favre. Unless you know Mike Holmgren, you won't find a ticket, but the stadium and the nearby museum are worth a look. The **Packer Hall of Fame,** 855 Lombardi Ave. (920-499-4281), has a cathedral-like feel for the thousands of fans who come to worship at the altars of their gridiron heroes ($7.50, under 15 $5; open daily June-Aug. 10am-6pm; Sept.-May 10am-5pm). The Hall also offers stadium tours (1½hr.; $7.50, under 15 $5; June-Sept. only).

The **Oneida Bingo and Casino** (920-497-8118), County Rte. GG southwest of downtown off 172 W, antes up with 1300 slot machines and 47 blackjack tables (both open 24hr.; must be 18). The **National Railroad Museum,** 2285 S. Broadway (920-435-7245), exhibits steam and diesel (open daily 9am-5pm; $6, ages 6-15 $3).

■ Apostle Islands

Long ago, pious Frenchmen believed there were only 12 islands off the coast of Wisconsin. They were wrong. Since then, the various land forms which compose the Apostle Islands have fired the interests of fur traders, fisherfolk, and, most recently, curio hucksters. The National Lakeshore protects 21 of the beautiful islands, as well as a 12 mi. stretch of mainland shore. Summer tourists enjoy kayaking, hiking, spelunking, and camping among the unspoiled sandstone bluffs.

PRACTICAL INFORMATION All Apostle Islands excursions begin in the sleepy mainland town of **Bayfield** (pop. 686), in northwest Wisconsin on the Lake Superior coast. The **Bay Area Rural Transit (BART),** 300 Industrial Park Rd. (682-9664), in Ashland, offers a shuttle to Bayfield (4 per day, M-F 7am-5pm; $1.80, students $1.50, seniors $1.35). The **Bayfield Chamber of Commerce,** 42 S. Broad St. (779-3335 or 800-447-4094), has helpful info on accommodations and the area (open M-Sa 9am-5pm, Su 10am-2pm). **National Lakeshore Headquarters Visitors Center,** 410 Washington Ave. (779-3397), distributes **camping permits** ($15 for 2 weeks, must be 14 consecutive days) and hiking info (open daily 8am-6pm; in winter M-F 8am-4:30pm). For the latest assessment of the area's unpredictable weather, call 682-8822. Bayfield's **post office:** 22 S. Broad St. (779-5636). **ZIP code:** 54850. **Area code:** 715.

ACCOMMODATIONS, CAMPGROUNDS, AND FOOD In summer months, the pickings are slim for the budget traveler in Bayfield. Would-be lodgers without reservations may be out of luck on July and August weekends; it's wise to call far in advance to reserve a room. The best deal in town is **The Seagull Bay Motel** (779-5558), off Rte. 13 at S. 7th St. in Bayfield, offering spacious, clean rooms with cable TV and a lakeview (from $50; mid-Oct. to mid-May $35). Just south on Rte. 13, **Lakeside Lodging** (779-5545) has rooms with a private entrance and bath, patio, and continental breakfast. ($50. Open mid-May to mid-Oct. In summer, reservations highly recommended 1 month in advance.) **Dalrymple Park,** ¼ mi. north of town on Rte. 13, offers 30 campsites under tall pines on the lake (no showers; $10, with electricity $11; self-regulated; no reservations). **Apostle Islands Area Campground** (779-5524), ½ mi. south of Bayfield on County Rd. J off Rte. 13, lives up to its name with a few sites overlooking the islands. (Sites $12, with hookup $16, with hookup and cable $19, with view $22; cabins for 3 without A/C or private bathroom $35. Reservations recommended 1 month in advance in July-Aug.) The chamber of commerce can supply info on **guest houses** ($35-230).

Maggie's, 257 Manypenny Ave. (779-5641), the local watering hole, prepares burgers ($6) and gourmet specials amid flamingo-filled decor (open Su-Th 11am-10pm, F-Sa 11am-11pm). The **Gourmet Garage** (779-5365), just south of Bayfield on Rte. 13, has local flavor and any kind of pie (open daily 9am-6pm). **Greunke's Restaurant,** 17 Rittenhouse Ave. (779-5480), at 1st St., specializes in huge, cheap diner-style breakfasts by day ($4-6) and locally famous fishboils by night (Th-Su 6-8pm, $12, children $6; open M-Sa 6am-10pm, F-Su 7am-9:30pm).

SIGHTS AND ACTIVITIES Though often overshadowed by Bayfield and Madeline Island (see below), the other 21 islands have subtle charms of their own. The sandstone quarries of Basswood and Hermit Islands, as well as the abandoned logging and fishing camps on some of the other islands, serve as mute reminders of a more vigorous era. The restored **lighthouses** on Sand, Raspberry, Long, Michigan, Outer, and Devil's Islands offer spectacular views of the surrounding country. **Sea caves,** carved out by thousands of years of winds and water, pocket the shores of several islands; a few on Devil's Island are large enough to explore by boat. The narrated 3hr. cruises organized by the **Apostle Islands Cruise Service** (779-3925 or 800-323-7619) allow visitors a chance to see all of these sights without paying the exorbitant prices charged by other companies. *(Tours depart the Bayfield City Dock mid-May to mid-Oct. daily 10am. $22, children $11.)* From late June to early September, the cruise service runs an inter-island shuttle that delivers campers and lighthouse lovers to their destinations. The best beach on the mainland is **Bay View Beach,** just south of Bayfield along Rte. 13, near Sioux Flats, reached by a poorly marked path to the left about 7 or 8 mi. out of town. Due to the extreme cold, **swimming** in Lake Superior can be quite uncomfortable. For adventurous modes of transportation, the **Trek and Trail** (800-354-8735), on the corner of Rittenhouse and Broad St., is the place (bikes $5 per hr., $20 per day; 4hr. kayak rental $38, all equipment included).

No one-horse town, Bayfield is also the proud home of some awfully good apples. The town grows vibrant in early October, when up to 40,000 gather for the **Apple Festival.** The **Bayfield Apple Company** (779-5700), on Betzold Rd., has fresh-picked taste (open May-Jan. daily 9am-6pm). Music enthusiasts congregate to the sounds of folk, country, and cajun, at the **Big Top Chautaqua** (373-5552 or 888-244-8368), 3 mi. south of Bayfield off Ski Hill Rd. (tickets from $10, showtimes M-Th 7:30pm, F-Sa 8:15pm).

Madeline Island Several hundred years ago, the Chippewa came to Madeline Island from the Atlantic in search of the megis shell, a light in the sky purported to bring prosperity and health. The island now maintains a more natural allure, as thousands of summer visitors seek this relaxing retreat's clean, sandy beaches. At day's end, a jaunt to Sunset Bay on the island's north side reveals why the bay got its name.

Rooms in the area fill during the summer; call ahead for reservations. The **Madeline Island Motel** (747-3000), on Col. Woods Ave. across from the ferry landing, has clean rooms named for local personalities. (Singles $75, doubles $80; May and Oct.-Nov. $55/$60; Dec.-Apr. all rooms $40.) Across the street, the **Madeline Island Historical Museum** (427-2415) outlines the island's storied past with interesting exhibits and a 23min. video ($4.50, under 12 $2; open daily 10am-6pm). Madeline Island has two campgrounds. **Big Bay Town Park** (747-6913), 6½ mi. from La Pointe off Big Bay Rd., sits right next to scenic Big Bay Lagoon (sites $9, with electricity $13). Across the lagoon, **Big Bay State Park** (747-6425, Bayfield office 779-4020) rents 55 primitive sites ($10-12; daily vehicle permit $7, WI residents $5; reservations $4). The **Island Café** (747-6555), 1 block to the right of the ferry exit, serves up hefty meals (breakfasts and lunch $7) and good vegetarian options (open daily 9am-midnight). **Grampa Tony's** (747-3911), next to the chamber of commerce, offers no-frills dining. (Sandwiches $4-5.25, salads $2.50-6.25, ice cream $1.50 and up. Open daily 7am-9pm.)

With roughly five streets, Madeline Island is easy to navigate by foot, bike, or car. The **Madeline Island Chamber of Commerce** (747-2801 or 888-475-3386), on Middle Rd., can help you find accommodations (open daily 8am-4pm). **Madeline Island Ferry Line** (747-2051 or 747-6801) shuttles between Bayfield and La Pointe on Madeline Island. (20 min.; in summer, ferries daily every 30min. 9:30am-6pm, every hr. 6:30-9:30am and 6-11pm.; one-way $3.50, ages 6-11 $2, bikes $1.75, cars $7.75—driver not included. Mar.-June and Sept.-Dec., ferries run less frequently and prices drop.) In winter, the state highway department builds a road across the ice. During transition periods, the ferry service runs **windsleds** between the island and the mainland. "Moped Dave" rents the technical marvels at **Motion to Go,** 102 Lake View Pl. (747-6585), about 1 block from the ferry. ($12 per hr., $50 per day. Mountain bikes $6/$22. Tandem bikes $10/$36. Open daily 10am-8pm; mid-May to mid June and Sept.-Oct. 10am-6pm.) La Pointe's **post office** (747-3712) sits just off the dock on Madeline Island (open M-F 9am-4:20pm, Sa 9:30am-12:50pm). **ZIP code:** 54850.

Minnesota

In the 19th century, floods of German and Scandinavian settlers forced the native Sioux and Chippewa tribes from the rich lands now known as Minnesota. Perhaps due to divine retribution, the Nordic intruders now suffer from having to hear their own ridiculous accents (oh, yaaa). Minnesota's white pioneers transformed the southern half of the state into a stronghold of commercial activity. To their credit, the north remains largely untouched, an expanse of wilderness quilted with over 14,000 lakes. Attempts at preserving this rugged wilderness have helped raise increasing awareness about the culture of Minnesota's Native American antecedents.

PRACTICAL INFORMATION

Capital: St. Paul.
Visitor Info: Minnesota Office of Tourism, 500 Metro Sq., 121 7th Pl. E., St. Paul 55101-2112 (651-296-5029 or 800-657-3700; http://www.exploreminnesota.com). Open M-F 8am-5pm.
Emergency: 911.
Time Zone: Central (1hr. behind Eastern). **Postal Abbreviation:** MN.
Sales Tax: 6.5%.

■ Minneapolis and St. Paul

Garrison Keillor once wrote that the "difference between St. Paul and Minneapolis is the difference between pumpernickel and Wonder bread." Keillor's quote plays on St. Paul's characterization as an old Irish Catholic, conservative town and Minneapolis's as a young, fast-paced metropolis of the future. Clubs abound in Minneapolis; Victorian houses line the streets of St. Paul. Minneapolis's theatre options rival those of New York; both the capitol and the cathedral rest atop St. Paul. Forever locked in a friendly battle of one-upmanship, the Twin cities are treated to constant reminders about how different they actually are. All the better for the visitor to the Twins who can take in the sights of St. Paul, cross town for a show, and then spend the night raging at Prince's former hangout. The Minnesota accent is muted in these cities, while collegiate spirit, nightlife, and *haute couture* are more pronounced. Here, consumer yuppie culture (the Mall of America), the wanna-be youth punk world (in myriad upstart cafes), and corporate America (thus the downtown and the skyway systems) thrive in a state of peaceful coexistence.

ORIENTATION AND PRACTICAL INFORMATION

A loopy network of interstates covers the entire Minneapolis/St. Paul area. **I-94** connects the downtowns. **I-35** (north-south) splits in the Twin Cities, with **I-35 W** serving Minneapolis and **I-35 E** serving St. Paul. Curves and one-way streets tangle both of the downtown areas; even the numbered grids in the cities are skewed, making north-south and east-west designations tricky. Good maps and attentive navigation are a must. Skyways, a second-story walkway complex, connect more than 10 sq. blocks of buildings in each downtown area, protecting humans from the winter cold.

Airport: Twin Cities International, south of the cities on I-494 in Bloomington. Take bus #7 to Washington Ave. in Minneapolis or bus #54 to St. Paul. **Airport Express** (827-7777) shuttles to either downtown and to some hotels roughly every 30min. 6am-midnight. To St. Paul ($8) and Minneapolis ($10).
Trains: Amtrak, 730 Transfer Rd. (644-1127 or 800-872-7245), on the east bank off University Ave. SE, between the Twin Cities. Bus #7 runs to St. Paul, and #16 connects to both downtowns. To Chicago (8hr., 1 per day, $75) and Milwaukee (6hr., 1 per day, $72). Open daily 6:30am-11:45pm.
Buses: Greyhound, in Minneapolis, 29 9th St. (371-3323 or 800-231-2222), at 1st Ave. N. Very convenient. To Chicago (9-12hr., 10 per day, $59) and Milwaukee (6-9hr., 8 per day, $51). Station open 24hr. In St. Paul, 166 W. University Ave. (651-

222-0509), 2 blocks west of the capitol. To Chicago (8-11hr., 6 per day, $59) and Milwaukee (7hr., 6 per day, $51). Station open daily 5:30am-9pm.

Public Transportation: Metropolitan Transit Commission, 560 6th Ave. N. (373-3333), serves both cities M-F 6am-11pm; Sa-Su 7am-11pm; some buses operate 4:30am-12:45am, others shut down earlier. Fare $1; seniors, disabled, and ages 6-12 50¢. Peak fare (M-F 6-9am and 3:30-6:30pm) $1.50. Express add 50¢. Bus #16 connects the 2 downtowns (50min.); express bus #94 (b, c, or d) is faster (25-30min.).

Car Rental: Thrifty Car Rental, 64 E. 6th St. (612-227-7690). Rates start from $35 per day with 150 free mi.; 16¢ each additional mi. Must be 21 with major credit card. Under 25 surcharge $10 per day. Open M-F 7am-5pm, Sa 8am-2pm.

Taxis: In Minneapolis, **Yellow Taxi,** 612-824-4444. In St. Paul, **Town Taxi,** 651-331-8294. Both charge $1.75 base fare, $1.30 per mi.

Visitor Info: Minneapolis Convention and Visitors Association, 40 S. 7th St. (335-5827), in the City Center Shopping Area, 2nd level skyway. Open M-F 9:30am-8pm, Sa 9:30am-6pm, Su noon-5pm. **St. Paul Convention and Visitors Bureau,** 175 W. Kellogg, suite 502 (651-297-6985 or 800-627-6101), in the RiverCenter. Open M-F 8am-5pm. For 24hr. info on local events, call **Cityline** (612-645-6060) or **The Connection** (612-922-9000).

Hotlines: Crisis Line, 340-5400. **Rape/Sexual Assault Line,** 825-4357. Both 24hr. **Gay-Lesbian Helpline,** 822-8661 or 800-800-0907. Operates M-F noon-midnight, Sa 4pm-midnight. **Gay-Lesbian Information Line,** 822-0127. Operates M-F 2-10pm, Sa 4-10pm.

Post Office: In Minneapolis (349-4957), 100 S. 1st St., at Marquette Ave., next to the Mississippi River. Open M-F 7am-11pm, Sa 9am-1pm. **ZIP code:** 55401. In St. Paul, 180 E. Kellogg Blvd. (651-293-3268). Open M-F 8am-6pm, Sa 8:30am-1pm. **ZIP code:** 55101. **Area codes:** Minneapolis 612, St. Paul and eastern suburbs 651. In text, 612 unless otherwise noted.

ACCOMMODATIONS AND CAMPGROUNDS

Cost, safety, and cleanliness tend to go hand-in-hand-in-hand in the Twin Cities, with a few notable exceptions. The visitors bureaus have useful lists of **B&Bs** (but not a list of prices), while the **University of Minnesota Housing Office** (624-2994) keeps a list of local rooms which rent on a daily ($13-60) or weekly basis. Camping is an inconvenient option; private campgrounds lie about 15 mi. outside the city, and the closest state park camping is in the **Hennepin Park** system, 25 mi. out.

College of St. Catherine, Caecilian Hall (HI-AYH), 2004 Randolph Ave. (651-690-6604), St. Paul. Take I-94 to Snelling Ave., follow Snelling Ave. south to Randolph Ave., and take a right—it's about 5 blocks down on the left. Alternatively, take St. Paul bus #14. The most convenient summer lodging for those with a car. Simple, quiet dorm rooms near the river in a generally safe residential neighborhood. Shared bath, laundry, kitchenette. Free local calls. $20, nonmembers $22; doubles $36/$40; triples $48. 1-week max. stay. Open June to mid-Aug.

City of Lakes International House, 2400 Stevens Ave. S. (871-3210), Minneapolis, south of downtown next to the Institute of Arts. The best bet for carless budget travelers who dig community living. Bike rentals. Free local calls. Beds $16, students $15; 2 available singles $32/$30. Linen $3. Key deposit $5. Reception M-F 9-11:30am, Sa 10am-noon, Su 11am-noon, evenings daily 6:30-9pm. Afternoon check-out. Reservations strongly recommended.

Evelo's Bed and Breakfast, 2301 Bryant Ave. (374-9656), South Minneapolis. Excellent location just off Hennepin, a 15min. walk from uptown; take bus #17 from downtown. Friendly owners have 3 comfortable rooms in a beautiful house with elegant Victorian artifacts. Singles $50; doubles $60. Reservations required.

Minneapolis Northwest I-94 KOA (420-2255), 15 mi. north of Minneapolis. Take Rte. 30 W (I-94 Exit 213) to Rte. 101 N. Pool, sauna, showers, game rooms. Sites for 2 $22, with water and electricity $25, full hookup $25. Cabins for 2 $37; $4 per additional adult, children $1.

FOOD

The Twin Cities' love of music and art carries over into their culinary choices—look for small cafes with nightly music, plush chairs, and poetry readings. **Uptown** Minne-

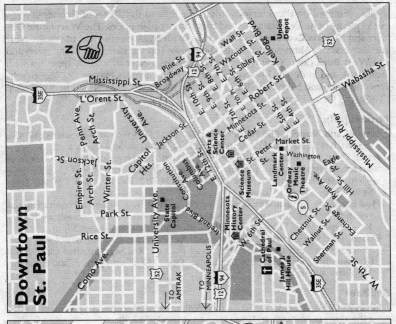

Downtown St. Paul

Pine St.
Broadway
Wall St.
Wacouta St.
Sibley St.
Kellogg Blvd
Union Depot
Mississippi St.
L'Orent St.
Mississippi River
Wabasha St.
E. 10th St.
E. 9th St.
E. 8th St.
E. 7th
7th St.
6th St.
5th St.
4th St.
Robert St.
Minnesota St.
Cedar St.
St. Peter St.
Market St.
Washington
Eagle St.
Ryan Ave
Hill St.
Chestnut St.
Walnut St.
Exchange St.
Sherman St.
W. 7th St.
Penn Ave.
Arch St.
University Ave.
Jackson St.
Jackson St.
Capitol Hts.
Construction Ave.
Arts & Science Center
Science Museum
Landmark Center
Ordway Music Theatre
Empire St.
Arch St.
Winter St.
Park St.
Rice St.
Como Ave.
University Ave.
State Capitol
Trkland Blvd
Minnesota History Center
W. 6th St.
Cathedral of St. Paul
James J. Hill House
TO AMTRAK
TO MINNEAPOLIS

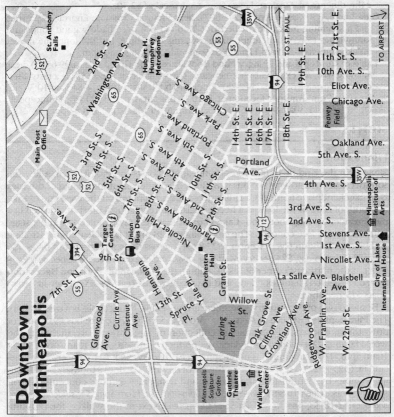

Downtown Minneapolis

St. Anthony Falls
2nd St. S.
Washington Ave. S.
Hubert H. Humphrey Metrodome
Chicago Ave. S.
Park Ave. S.
Portland Ave. S.
TO ST. PAUL
TO AIRPORT
21st St. E.
11th St. S.
10th Ave. S.
Eliot Ave.
Chicago Ave.
19th St. E.
18th St. E.
Peavey Field
Oakland Ave.
5th Ave. S.
Main Post Office
3rd St. S.
4th St. S.
5th St. S.
6th St. S.
7th St. S.
8th St. S.
9th St. S.
10th St. S.
11th St. S.
12th St. S.
Nicollet Mall
Marquette Ave. S.
2nd Ave. S.
3rd Ave. S.
4th Ave. S.
5th Ave. S.
4th St. E.
5th St. E.
6th St. E.
7th St. E.
Portland Ave.
4th Ave. S.
3rd Ave. S.
2nd Ave. S.
Minneapolis Institute of Arts
Stevens Ave.
1st Ave. S.
Nicollet Ave.
La Salle Ave.
Blaisdell Ave.
City of Lakes International House
Target Center
Union Bus Depot
Orchestra Hall
Grant St.
Willow St.
Oak Grove St.
Clifton Ave.
Groveland Ave.
Ridgewood Ave.
W. Franklin Ave.
W. 22nd St.
7th St. N.
Glenwood Ave.
Currie Ave.
Chestnut Ave.
Hennepin Ave.
13th St.
Spruce Pl.
Yale Pl.
Loring Park
Minneapolis Sculpture Garden
Guthrie Theatre
Walker Art Center
1st Ave.

apolis, centered on the intersection of Lake St. and the 2900s of Hennepin Ave., packs plenty of funky restaurants and bars without high prices. The **Warehouse District** and **Victoria Crossing** serve the crowd with lavish pastries and full meals. Near the University of Minnesota campus, **Dinkytown** (on the same side of the river) and the **West Bank** (across the river, hence the name) cater to student appetites with many dark and intriguing low-end places. **St. Paul Farmers Market** (227-6856) sells fresh produce and baked goods in a downtown location, as well as others city-wide (Tu-Su; call for times and sites).

Minneapolis

🍜**Strudel and Nudel,** 2605 Nicollet Ave. (874-0113). Specializes in soups ($1.85), sandwiches ($3.60), and desserts. Open M-Sa 7am-4pm, Su 8am-3pm.

Aster Café, 125 Main St. SE (379-3138), across the river. Situated on a beautiful stretch of riverbank, this pleasant cafe tempts strollers with scones ($1.75), sandwiches ($6), and espresso (latte $1.50). Open M-Th 7:30am-10pm, F 7:30am-11pm, Sa 9am-11pm, Su 9am-10pm.

Mud Pie, 2549 Lyndale Ave. S. (872-9435), at 26th St. A variety of vegetarian and vegan dishes with Mexican and Middle Eastern accents. Famous veggie burger $5.60. Open M-Th 11am-10:30pm, F-Sa 10am-midnight, Su 10am-9:30pm.

Urban Bean Coffeehouse, 2717 Hennepin Ave. (872-1419). They've got soft plush armchairs, fish in a tank filled with water from the Red Sea, and great cappuccino ($2). Another location at 3255 Bryant Ave. Open M-Th 7am-11pm, F 7am-midnight, Sa-Su 8am-midnight.

St. Paul

Mickey's Dining Car, 36 W. 7th St. (651-698-0259), downtown. A greasy spoon with 24hr. diner food. Steak and eggs from $5; pancakes $2.50.

Café Latté, 850 Grand Ave. (224-5687), near Victoria Crossing. Enormous pastries and a steaming milk drink called Hot Moo ($1.87) overshadow good soups and sandwiches ($3-5). Lunchtime brings swarms of people, but the long line moves quickly. Open M-Th 9am-11pm, F-Sa 9am-midnight, Su 9am-10pm.

Table of Contents and **Hungry Mind Bookstore,** 1648 Grand Ave. (699-6595), near Snelling Ave. An excellent gourmet cafe. The wafer-crust pizza ($6) is a tasty alternative to pricier dinners ($12-25). Open M-Th 11:30am-10pm, F-Sa 9am-10:30pm, Su 10am-7pm. Another location at 1310 Hennepin Ave. (339-1133), Minneapolis. Open M-Th 11:30am-9pm, F-Sa 11:30am-10pm, Su 10am-2pm and 5-9pm.

SIGHTS

Minneapolis

Situated in the land of 10,000 lakes, Minneapolis boasts three of its own, a few mi. southwest of downtown; take bus #28. Ringed by stately mansions, **Lake of the Isles** is an excellent place to meet Canadian geese. **Lake Calhoun,** on the west end of Lake St., south of Lake of the Isles, is a hectic social and recreational hotspot. Located in a more residential neighborhood, **Lake Harriet** features tiny paddleboats and a stage with occasional free concerts. The city maintains 28 mi. of lakeside trails for strolling and biking. **Calhoun Cycle Center** (827-8231), across the street, rents out bikes. ($6 per hr., $15 per ½-day, $24 per day. Must have credit card and driver's license. Open daily 9am-9pm.) At the northeast corner of Lake Calhoun, the **Minneapolis Park and Recreation Board** (370-4964) handles canoe and rowboat rentals (canoes $5.50 per hr., rowboats $11 per 4hr.).

Home to two of the country's premiere art museums, Minneapolis is a true art hub. The **Minneapolis Institute of Arts,** 2400 3rd Ave. S. (870-3200; take bus #9), south of downtown, displays an outstanding collection of international art, including the world-famous *Doryphoros,* Polykleitos's perfectly proportioned man (open Tu-Su 10am-5pm, Th 10am-9pm, Su noon-5pm; free). The **Walker Art Center,** 725 Vineland Pl. (375-7622), a few blocks southwest of downtown, draws thousands with daring exhibits by Lichtenstein and Warhol, and temporary exhibits concentrating on specific eras. (Open Tu-Sa 10am-5pm, Th 10am-8pm, Su 11am-5pm. $4; students, seniors, and ages 12-18 $3; free Th and 1st Sa of the month.) Next to the Walker, the beautiful

> ### Shop 'Til You Drop
> About 10min. south of downtown, the **Mall of America,** 60 E. Broadway (883-8800), Bloomington, corrals an indoor rollercoaster, ferris wheel, mini-golf course, and 2 mi. of stores. *(Open M-F 10am-9:30pm, Sa 9:30am-9:30pm, Su 11am-7pm. Take I-35 E. south to I-494 W. to the 24th Ave. Exit.)* Welcome to the largest mall in America, the consummation of the U.S.'s love affair with all that is obscenely gargantuan. If the funds, or legs, run out, shoppers can try panning for gold. Mind-boggling consumerism is exhausting, even when it's fun.

Minneapolis Sculpture Garden (open daily 6am-midnight), the largest urban sculpture garden in the U.S., contains Minnesota's beloved **Spoonbridge** (with a cherry on top), as well as the **Cowles Conservatory.** The **Museum of Questionable Medical Devices,** 201 Main St. SE (379-4046), north of the river near St. Anthony Falls, has a sure cure for absolutely anything. *(Open Tu-Th 5-9pm, F noon-9pm, Sa 11am-9pm, Su noon-5pm. Donation requested, toenails preferred.)* The Solorama Bedboard (meant to cure brain tumors) and phrenological equipment (phrenologists measure head bumps to determine personality) are among the more respectable highlights of the collection. Next to the museum, the **St. Anthony Historical Museum,** 125 Main St. (627-5433), has info on self-guided walking tours of Minneapolis, or to pick up the River City Trolley. *(2hr. trolley pass $8, children and seniors $5. Operates M-F 10am-4pm, Sa-Su 10am-5pm.)*

You can get a good look at the Mighty Miss from several points in town. Off Portland Ave., **Stone Arch Bridge** offers a scenic view of **St. Anthony Falls;** several miles downstream, **Minnehaha Park** (take bus #7 from Hennepin Ave. downtown) allows a gander at the **Minnehaha Falls,** immortalized in Longfellow's *Song of Hiawatha.* The **visitors center** (332-5336) at the **Upper St. Anthony Lock and Dam,** at Portland Ave. and West River Pkwy., provides a sweeping view and a helpful explanation of the locks (observation tower open mid-Mar. to mid-Dec. daily 9am-10pm).

St. Paul

St. Paul's history and architecture are its greatest assets. West of downtown along **Summit Ave.** (651-297-2555 for Summit Ave. walking tour info), the nation's longest continuous stretch of Victorian homes, built on the tracks of an old railroad, include a former home of American novelist **F. Scott Fitzgerald** and the **Governor's Mansion.** The magnificent home of railroad magnate **James J. Hill,** 240 Summit Ave. (651-297-2555), offers 1¼hr. tours every 30min. *(Open W-Sa 10am-3:30pm; $5, seniors $4, ages 6-15 $3.)* Overlooking the capitol on Summit Ave. stands **St. Paul's Cathedral,** 239 Selby Ave. (651-228-1766), a breathtaking scaled-down version of St. Peter's in Rome. *(Mass M-F 7:30am and 5:15pm, no evening mass W or F; Sa mass 8am and 7pm; call for Su mass schedule. Guided tours M, W, F 1pm; free.)* Golden horses top the ornate **state capitol** (651-296-3962), at Cedar and Aurora St. *(Tours on the hr. M-F 9am-4pm, Sa 10am-3pm, Su 1-3pm. Open M-F 9am-5pm, Sa 10am-4pm, Su 1-4pm.)* The nearby **Minnesota History Center,** 345 Kellogg Blvd. W. (651-296-1430), an organization older than the state itself, houses three exhibit galleries on Minnesota history. *(Open M-Sa 10am-5pm, Th 10am-9pm, Su noon-5pm. Free.)* The Center also oversees a re-creation of life in the fur-trapping era at **Fort Snelling** (651-725-2413), far to the southwest at the intersection of Rte. 5 and 55, where costumed artisans and soldiers lead you through the 18th-century French fort. *(Infantry drills daily 11:30am and 2:30pm. Open M-Sa 9:30am-5pm, Su 11:30am-5pm. $4, seniors $3, ages 6-15 $2.)* The historic **Landmark Center,** 75 W. 5th St. (651-292-3225), a grandly restored 1894 Federal Court building replete with towers and turrets, contains the **Minnesota Museum of Art,** along with a collection of pianos, a concert hall, and four restored courtrooms (museum open Tu-Sa 11am-4pm, Th until 7:30pm, Su 1-5pm).

ENTERTAINMENT

Second only to New York in number of theaters per capita, the Twin Cities bring musicals, comedy, opera, and experimental drama to Minnesota. Almost all of the many Twin Cities parks feature free evening concerts in the summer; the visitors cen-

GREAT LAKES

ters know more. The thriving alternative, pop, and classical music scene fills out the wide range of entertainment options. For general info on the local music scene and other events, the *City Pages* or *Skyway News* are free and extremely useful.

Guthrie Theater, 725 Vineland Pl. (377-2224), Minneapolis, adjacent to the Walker Art Center just off Hennepin Ave., stands out in the theater world. (Season varies; call ahead. Box office open M-F 9am-8pm, Sa 10am-8pm, Su 11am-7pm. Tickets $15.50-37.50, students and seniors $5 discount; rush tickets 10min. before show $12, line starts 1-1½hr. before show.) For family-oriented productions, the **Children's Theater Company** (874-0400), at 3rd Ave. and 24th St., next to the Minneapolis Institute of Arts, comes through. (Season Sept.-June. Box office open M-Sa 9am-5pm; summer hrs. vary slightly. Tickets $16-25; students, seniors, and children $10-19. Rush tickets 15min. before show $8.) The **Illusion Theater,** 528 Hennepin Ave., 8th fl. (338-8371) has experimental works and tickets from $12.

Dudley Riggs's **Brave New Workshop,** 2605 Hennepin Ave. (332-6620), stages intriguing musical comedy shows in an intimate club. (Box office open June-July M 5-9pm, F-Sa 4-9:30pm, Th and Su 4pm-midnight. M shows $5, Sa-Su $8-12. Box office open Aug.-May W-F and Su 4-9pm, Sa 4pm-12:15am. Tickets $12-18.) In St. Paul, good off-**Ordway** theatre (see below) plays at the **Park Sq. Theatre,** 20 W. 7th Pl. (651-291-7005), which still offers Tuesday previews for $1. (Box office open M-Sa noon-6pm, Su noon-3pm; tickets $16-24, students $8; call ahead for $1 Tu preview dates.)

The Twin Cities' music scene offers everything from the opera to Paisley. **Sommerfest,** a month-long celebration of Viennese music performed by the **Minnesota Orchestra,** marks the high point of the cities' classical scene during July and August; **Orchestra Hall,** 1111 Nicollet Mall (651-371-5656 or 800-292-4141), downtown Minneapolis, hosts the event. (Box office open M-Sa 10am-6pm. Tickets $13-47; rush tickets for students 30min. before show $9.) Nearby **Peavey Plaza,** in Nicollet Mall, holds free coffee concerts. The **St. Paul Chamber Orchestra,** the **Schubert Club,** and the **Minnesota Opera Company** all perform at St. Paul's glass-and-brick **Ordway Music Theater,** 345 Washington St. (651-224-4222). (Box office counter open M-F 10am-5:30pm, Sa-Su 11am-3pm. Tickets $20-55.) The artist formerly known as **Prince** brought his seductive and energetic pop lyrics from local rave to worldwide fame—all in high-heeled boots. Today, his state-of-the-art **Paisley Park** studio complex outside the city draws bands from all over to the Great White North.

The Twin Cities' festivals span the seasons. In January, the 10-day **St. Paul Winter Carnival,** near the state capitol, cures cabin fever with ice sculptures, ice fishing, parades, and skating contests. June brings the 12-day **Fringe Festival** (770-2233) for the performing arts (tickets $4-5). On July 4, St. Paul celebrates **Taste of Minnesota** in the Capitol Mall; on its coattails rides the nine-day **Minneapolis Aquatennial,** with concerts, parades, and art exhibits (call **The Connection,** 922-9000, for festival info). During late August and early September, the **Minnesota State Fair,** at Snelling and Como, or the **Renaissance Festival** (445-7361), in the town of Shakopee, are fun.

The **Hubert H. Humphrey Metrodome,** 900 S. 5th St. (332-0386), in downtown Minneapolis, houses the **Minnesota Twins,** the cities' baseball team, and the **Minnesota Vikings,** the resident football team. The **Timberwolves** howl at the **Target Center,** 600 1st Ave. (673-0900). The NHL is back in the Twin Cities; the **Wild** take to the ice this winter (651-333-7825).

NIGHTLIFE

Minneapolis's vibrant youth culture feeds most of the Twin Cities' clubs and bars. The post-punk scene thrives in the Land of 10,000 Aches: **Soul Asylum** and **Hüsker Dü,** as well as the best bar band in the world, **The Replacements,** rocked here before they went big (or bad). Nightlife blooms on Hennepin Ave., around the **University of Minnesota-Minneapolis,** and across the river on the **West Bank** (bounded on the west by I-35 W. and to the south by I-94), especially on **Cedar Ave.** The Twin Cities card hard, even for cigarettes, so carry your ID with you. The top floor of the **Mall of America** (see above) invites bar-hopping after the screaming kids have gone to bed.

GREAT LAKES

Ground Zero, 15 4th St. NE (378-5115), off Hennepin Ave. just north of the river, is practically synonymous with local nightlife, mushrooming with live music on M and W for beatniks, and bondage on Th. Open daily until 1am.

NYE's Bar, 112 E. Hennepin Ave. (379-2021), across the river from Minneapolis, pumps live polka (Th-Sa) and a piano band every night. Open daily 11am-1am.

First Avenue and 7th St. Entry, 701 First Ave. N. (332-1775), downtown, rocks with live music several nights a week. The artist formerly known as Prince's former court. The artist himself turns up occasionally. Cover $1-6, for concerts $7-18. Open M-Sa 8pm-3am, Su 7pm-3am.

400 Bar (332-2903), on 4th St. at Cedar Ave., features live music nightly on a minis-cule stage; acts range from local garage bands to national acts. Cover F-Sa $2-5. Open for shows only, which usually start around 7pm.

Red Sea, 316 Cedar Ave. (333-1644), has live rock bands nightly (reggae on week-ends), while serving Ethiopian food and ethnic burgers ($4-6) until 1am.

Uptown Bar and Café, 3018 Hennepin Ave. (823-4719). A yuppie-ish lunch crowd does blues at around 10:30pm; weekend cover varies. Open daily 8am-1am.

The Gay 90s (333-7755), on Hennepin Ave. at 4th St., claims the 7th highest liquor consumption rate of all clubs in the nation. This nightlife superplex hosts thou-sands of gay and lesbian partymongers in its many bars and show rooms. Open daily 8pm-3am.

O'Gara's Garage, 164 N. Snelling Ave. (651-644-3333), in St. Paul, hosts big bands and jazz nightly in the Irish-theme front bar (no cover); live alternative and dance music play in the back W-Sa. Cover $3-6. Open daily until 1am. 21+ after 8pm.

Plums (651-699-2227), at Randolph and Snelling Ave., lets loose with $6 all-you-can-drink nights on Th. Open M-Sa 11am-1am, Su noon-1am.

▓ Duluth

If cities were sold at auctions, Duluth would fetch a high price; the people are nice, the parks are clean, the streets are safe, and the location is amazing. Bidders on a vaca-tion to Duluth can expect to eat well, find relatively inexpensive lodging, and watch some serious shipping action. As the largest freshwater port in the world, Duluth har-bors ships from over 60 different countries. The recently restored area of Canal Park, along Lake St., has tempted microbreweries, restaurants, theaters, and museums to occupy the old factories and depots down on the wharf. Results have been astound-ing, turning a once-overlooked tourist destination into a hotspot of northern activity.

PRACTICAL INFORMATION Greyhound, 2122 W. Superior (722-5591 or 800-231-2222), stops 2 mi. west of downtown; take bus #9 "Piedmont" from downtown. Buses run to Milwaukee (11hr., 3 per day, $70) and St. Paul (3hr., 3 per day, $21). Buy tickets daily 6:45am-5:30pm. The **Duluth Transit Authority,** 2402 W. Michigan St. (722-7283), sends buses throughout the city (peak fare M-F 7-9am and 2:30-6pm $1, off-peak 50¢). Tourist-moving **Port Town Trolley** (722-7283) serves the downtown area, Canal Park, and waterfront (runs late May to early Sept. daily 11am-7pm; fare 50¢). Three locations distribute tourist literature, maps, and the handy *Army Corps of Engineers Ship Identification Guide:* the **Convention and Visitors Bureau,** 100 Lake Place Dr. (722-4011), at Endion Station in Canal Park (open M-F 8:30am-5pm); the **Summer Visitors Center** (722-6024), at Vista dock on Harbor Dr. (open mid-May to mid-Oct. daily 8:30am-7:30pm, hrs. highly variable); and **The Depot,** 506 W. Michi-gan St. (727-8025). (Open Sa-Th 9:30am-6pm, F 9:30am-8pm; mid-Oct. to Apr. M-Sa 10am-5pm, Su 1-5pm.) Local help lines include the **24hr. Crisis Line** (726-1931). **Post Office:** 2800 W. Michigan St. (723-2590; open M-F 8am-5pm, Sa 9am-1pm). **ZIP code:** 55806. **Area code:** 218.

ACCOMMODATIONS AND CAMPGROUNDS Motel rates rise and rooms fill during the warm months. The **College of St. Scholastica,** 1200 Kenwood Ave. (723-6000 or 800-447-5444; ask for the housing director), Exit 258 off I-35 N, rents out quiet dorm rooms with free local calls, kitchen access, and laundry facilities (singles $21, doubles $40; reservations recommended; open early June to mid-Aug.). Reasonably priced motels line London Rd., west of downtown; try the **Chalet Motel,** 1801 London Rd.

All Hawking at Once

Duluth's location, as well as its considerable updrafts, have made the city especially appealing to soaring birds. On one day in late August, September, or October, as many as 10,000 of these migratory hawks pass over **Hawk Ridge,** just west of the city. These birds, loathe to pass over such a large body of water as Lake Superior, converge on Duluth as an enticing alternative. On September 15th 1978, a record-setting 31,831 Broad-winged Hawks passed over the city on their way south. Taking the Skyline Parkway to the Hawk Ridge Nature Reserve and will reveal the birds. (Binoculars and a bird book are great if you've got them). This sight is truly amazing.

(728-4238 or 800-235-2957; Apr.-Sept. singles $46, doubles $55; M-F $39/49; lower in winter). Other cheap motels line I-35, just southwest of the city, including **Motel 6,** at the 27th St. Exit (singles $40). **Jay Cooke State Park** (384-4610; 800-246-2267 for reservations), southwest of Duluth on I-35 off Exit 242, has 83 campsites, 50 mi. of hiking trails, 12 mi. of snowmobile trails, and 32 mi. for cross-country skiing among the tall trees of the St. Louis River valley. (Open daily 9am-9pm, park gates open until 10pm. Sites with showers $12, plus electricity $14.50. Vehicle permit $4. Reservations recommended; $6.50 reservation fee.)

FOOD AND NIGHTLIFE Upscale **Fitger's Brewery Complex,** 600 E. Superior St., and the **Canal Park** region, south from downtown along Lake Ave., feature plenty of pleasant eateries. The place for microbrews and pub food is the new **Brewhouse** (726-1392), in Fitger's Brewery Complex. Big Boat Oatmeal Stout ($3.50) keeps it cool, while live acoustic bands warm things up (Tu and Th-Sa; cover $1-2; open daily 11am-1am; grill closes 10pm). The **DeWitt-Seitz Marketplace,** in the middle of Canal Park Dr., has a number of slightly pricier restaurants. The **Blue Note Café,** 357 Canal Park Dr. (727-6549), creates delicious sandwiches ($5-7) and desserts ($3.25) in a yuppified coffeehouse setting (open M-Th 9am-9pm, F-Sa 9am-11pm, Su 9am-8pm). **Grandma's Restaurant** (727-4192) and entertainment complex coddles the entire wharf at the south end of Canal Park Dr. Wild Turkey Tetrazzini ($9) gives **Grandma's Saloon and Grill** (727-4192) something to brag about, along with great steaks and pub fare (open daily 11am-1am). In an old pipe-fitting factory, **Grandma's Sports Garden** (722-4722) is the mother of all Duluthian nightlife, with dining, a bar, and a huge dance floor (restaurant open daily 11am-10pm; club open daily 11:30am-1am). **Hacienda del Sol,** 319 E. Superior St. (722-7296), drums up cheap, original Mexican recipes (entrees $4-8; open M-Th 11am-10pm, F-Sa 11am-midnight).

SIGHTS AND ENTERTAINMENT Duluth's proximity to majestic Lake Superior is its biggest draw; many visitors just head right down to **Canal Park** and watch the big ships go by at the Aerial Lift Bridge (see below). Others watch the ships get loaded at the **Ore Docks Observation Platform.** The **Boatwatcher's Hotline** (722-6489) has up-to-the-minute info on ship movements. Accompanied by deafening horn blasts, the unique **Aerial Lift Bridge** climbs 138 ft. in 55 seconds to allow vessels to pass; late afternoon is prime viewing time. Within Canal Park, the **Lake Superior Maritime Visitors Center** (727-2497) prepares extensive displays on commercial shipping in Lake Superior (open daily 10am-9pm; free). Canal Park also serves as the end/beginning of the **Duluth Lakewalk,** a 3 mi. promenade which connects Fitger's Brewery, Canal Park, and the near north shore. Across the Aerial Lift Bridge, **Park Point** has excellent swimming areas, parks, and sandy beaches.

The scenic **Willard Munger State Trail** links West Duluth to Jay Cooke State Park, providing 14 mi. of paved path perfect for bikes and rollerblades—**Willard Munger Inn,** 7408 Grand Ave. (624-4814 or 800-982-2453), rents both (bikes $10 per ½-day, $13 per day; rollerblades $10/$14). The 5-story stone octagonal **Enger Tower,** on Skyline Pkwy. at 18th Ave. W., rises from the highest land in Duluth; the nearby Japanese flower gardens make a beautiful picnic area.

A 39-room neo-Jacobean mansion built on wealth created by iron-shipping, **Glensheen,** 3300 London Rd. (724-8863 or 888-454-4536), lies on the eastern outskirts of town. *(Open late May to early Sept. 9:30am-4pm; off-season hrs. vary. $8.75, seniors and ages 12-15 $7, ages 6-11 $4.)* Tours of the most visited ship on the Great Lakes, the steamer **William A. Irvin,** (722-7876 or 722-5573), on the waterfront, reveal more evidence of Duluth's shipping past. *(Open daily 9am-6pm. Call during spring and fall. $6.50, students and seniors $5.50, ages 3-12 $3.50.)* Behind the *William A Irvin*, the Summer Visitors Center (see above) distributes free tickets for an extensive—if loud—tour of the **Lake Superior Paper Industry,** 100 North Central Ave. (628-5100; free with ticket; 1hr.; tours M, W, F).

Duluth's cultural calendar centers around **The Depot,** 506 W. Michigan St. (727-8025), a former railroad station housing four performing arts groups and several museums, including the immense **Lake Superior Museum of Transportation.** *(Open daily 10am-5pm; mid-Oct. to Apr. M-Sa 10am-5pm, Su 1-5pm. $6 includes all the museums and a trolley ride, families $18, ages 3-11 $4.)* On the waterfront, **Bayfront Festival Park** hosts many events and festivals, most notably the mid-August **Bayfront Blues Festival.**

■ Chippewa National Forest

Gleaming white stands of birch lace the Norway pine forests of the **Chippewa National Forest.** Home to the highest density of breeding bald eagles in the continental U.S., the forest witnesses these proud birds soaring over the Mississippi River between Cass Lake and Lake Winnie from mid-March through November. Wetlands and lakes blanket nearly half of the forest land, providing ample opportunities for canoeing and watersports. The national forest shares territory with the **Leech Lake Indian Reservation,** home to 4560 members of the Minnesota Chippewa tribe, the fourth-largest tribe in the U.S. The Chippewa migrated from the Atlantic coast in the 1700s, displacing the Sioux. In the mid-1800s, the government seized most of the Chippewa's land and established reservations like Leech Lake.

Camping—cheap, plentiful, and available in varying degrees of modernity—is the way to stay. The forest rangers (see below) have info on forest campgrounds, over 400 of which are free. North of Walker, billboards for private campgrounds string the edges of Rte. 371. **The Wedgewood Resort and Campground** (547-1443), across from the airport on Rte. 371, 5 mi. north of Walker, offers shady sites on the shores of Leech Lake. ($13, with water and electricity $15; cabins $35 and up. Boat rentals start at $12. Open May-Feb.) Indoors, **Bailey's Resort** (547-1464), 4½ mi. north off Kabekona Bay Rd., rents comfortable cabins with full kitchens (from $59). Reservations needed months in advance (office open daily 10am-10pm). The cabins at **Stony Point Resort** (547-1665 or 800-338-9303), 7 mi. east of town off Rte. 200, 4 mi. north on Onigam Rd., sleep up to 12 people (from $88 for 4-person cabin with A/C). You can also camp next door at the **National Forest Campground** (800-280-2267; $14, with hookup $16; $8 reservation fee; sites are self-regulated).

M I double-S I double-S I double-P I

You too can step across the mighty Mississippi! At its source, anyway, officially known as the **Beginning of the Mississippi,** at **Lake Itasca State Park,** 30 mi. west of Chippewa National Forest on Rte. 200. The park office (266-2100), through the north entrance and down County Rd. 122, has camping info. (Office open M-F 8am-4:30pm, Sa-Su 8am-4pm; mid-Oct. to Apr. M-F 8am-4:30pm. Ranger on call after hrs.) The comfortable **Mississippi Headwaters Hostel (HI-AYH)** (266-3415) has 32 beds with some four-bed rooms for families. The hostel stays open in the winter to facilitate access to the park's excellent cross-country skiing. (Laundry, kitchen, multiple bathrooms. 2-night min. stay on certain weekends. Check-in Su-Th 5-10pm, F-Sa 5-11pm. Check-out M-F 10am, Sa-Su noon. Members $15, nonmembers $18. Linen $2-4. $4 per day vehicle permit required. Private rooms available.) In the park, **Itasca Sports Rental** (266-2150) offers mountain bikes ($3.50 per hr., $20 per day); canoes ($3/$18); and pontoons ($25 for 2hr.; open May-Oct. daily 7am-9pm; must be 18).

GREAT LAKES

For the northbound traveler, **Walker,** a small town in the southwest corner of the park and reservation, serves as an ideal gateway to the area. Travelers should seek scuttlebutt at the **Leech Lake Area Chamber of Commerce** (547-1313 or 800-833-1118), on Rte. 371 downtown (open May-Sept. M-F 9am-5pm, Sa 9am-3pm, call ahead for winter hrs.). The **Forest Office** (547-1044; superintendent 335-8600), just east of town on Rte. 371, has the dirt on outdoor activities (open M-F 8am-4:30pm). **Greyhound** (547-3455 or 800-231-2222) runs from Minneapolis to Walker (5½hr., 1 per day, $35), stopping at Hardee's downtown (547-9585), with a ticket office at Ben Franklin's, also downtown. A southbound bus leaves daily at 8:30am, a northbound at 4:30pm; purchase tickets at the next station. Walker's **post office:** 602 Michigan Ave. (547-1123; open M-F 9am-4pm). **ZIP code:** 46484. Chippewa's **area code:** 218.

■ Iron Range

It was the cry of *"Goald!"* that brought the flood of miners, but it was the staying power of iron that kept them here. Today, a mere stretch of 120 mi. of wilderness and small towns along Minnesota Rte. 169 produces over 50% of the country's steel.

In the town of **Calumet** at the **Hill Annex Mine State Park** (247-7215), a now-obsolete natural iron ore pit mine, an exceptional 1½hr. tour brings visitors through the buildings and shops into the 500 ft. deep mine. There, former miners recount their experiences for visitors. The $6 admission is money well-spent. (Ages 5-12 $4; open May-Sept. daily 10am-4pm; tours depart on the hr.)

The answer, my friend, is blowing in **Hibbing,** hometown of Robert Zimmerman (a.k.a. **Bob Dylan**). Then again, maybe it's not—a stay of over a day will illustrate why the legendary songwriter refused for years to acknowledge where his oats were sown. Nonetheless, the **Hibbing Tourist Center,** 1202 E. Howard St. (262-4166), off Rte. 169, mixes up the medicine on the **Hull Rust Mahoning Mine,** the world's largest open-pit mine, and the **Greyhound Bus Origin Center,** where the national enterprise began. (Open M-F 9am-5pm, Sa-Su 9am-3pm; early Sept. to late May M-F 10am-4pm.) If you're sleepy and there is no place you're going to, **Adams House,** 201 E. 23rd St. (263-9742 or 888-891-9742), a beautiful Tudor-style B&B, can put you up in a double room ($48-53, light breakfast included, reservations recommended).

The Iron Range's first mine, the **Soudan Underground Mine** (753-2245), is in **Soudan** on Rte. 1, a few mi. east of Tower, where visitors take a 1½hr. tour to the 27th level of digging, ½ mi. beneath the earth's surface. (Tours late May to early Sept. every 30min. 10am-4pm; off-season by reservation. $6, ages 5-12 $4, plus $4 state park vehicle fee. Gates open until 6pm; off-season by reservation.) Next to the mine, **McKinley Park Campground** (753-5921) rents semi-private campsites overlooking gorgeous Vermilion Lake (sites $12, with hookup $14; canoe and paddleboat rentals $4 per hr., $16 per day). **Shagawa Sam's,** 60 W. Lakeview Pl. (365-6757) in Ely, has a recently renovated, tidy loft full of bunks for $12 per night, including linen and showers, plus some RV campsites and cabins. (RV sites $10, $1.50 each for water and electricity. Cabins for 4 $60-70. Canoe rental $10 per day.)

With historic character and real Minnesotan locals, too, **Ely** is the perfect destination. Serving as a launching pad both into the **Boundary Waters Canoe Area Wilderness** (BWCAW; see below) and the Iron Range, Ely supports its share of wilderness outfitters. Head to the **chamber of commerce,** 1600 E. Sheridan St. (365-6123 or 800-777-7281), for brochures on various guides (open M-Sa 9am-6pm, Su noon-4pm; off-season M-F 9am-5pm). The **International Wolf Center,** 1396 Rte. 169 (365-4695), houses four timber wolves, packs BWCAW permits, and provides informative displays on the history, habitat, and behavior of *Canis lupus.* (Open May-Nov. daily 9am-5:30pm; Nov.-May Sa-Su only, 10am-5pm. $5, seniors $4, ages 6-12 $2.50; call for wolf presentation times.) Next door, the **Dorothy Molter Museum** (365-4451) honors the "Root Beer Lady of Knife Lake." (Open May-Sept. daily 10am-6pm. $3, children $1.50; root beer $1.) The last year-round resident of the BWCAW, Ms. Molter brewed 11-12,000 bottles of root beer each year. **Area code:** 218.

■ Lake Superior North Shore

Rte. 61 The true Lake Superior North Shore extends 646 mi. from Duluth, MN to Sault Ste. Marie, ON; still, Rte. 61 (North Shore Dr.), winding along the coast from Duluth to Grand Portage, gives travelers an abbreviated version of the journey. Small, touristy fishing towns separate the 31,000 sq. mi. lake (comprising 10% of the world's freshwater surface area) from the moose, bear, and wolves inland. Sunday drivers should know that in summer, especially weekends, Rte. 61 is often glutted with boat-towing pick-up trucks and family-filled campers. The cabins, cottages, and luxurious resorts flanking the roadside fill up fast in summer; make reservations early. Remember to bring warm clothes; temps can drop into the low 40s (°F) on summer nights.

Most towns along the shore maintain a visitors center. The **R J Houle Visitor Information Center** (218-834-4005 or 800-554-2116), 21 mi. from Duluth up Rte. 61 in Two Harbors, has lodging guides and info for each town along the MN stretch of the North Shore. (Open Su-Th 10am-4pm, F-Sa 9am-7pm; mid-Oct. to May W-Sa 9am-1pm.) A few miles northeast of the Info Center, **Gooseberry Falls** (834-2461), along Hwy. 61, cascades toward the sea. **Camping** near the cataract is available (primitive sites with shower $12; required vehicle permit $4). Closer to civilization, the pine-paneled **Cobblestone Cabins** (218-663-7957), off Rte. 61 2 mi. north of Tofte, come with access to a cobblestone beach, canoes, a wood-burning sauna, and kitchenettes (cabins for 1-12 $40-85; open May-Oct.). **Happy Times** bus lines runs four buses per week (Su, M, W, and F) from the **Duluth Greyhound Station,** 2122 W. Superior St. (218-722-5591 or 800-231-2222; open daily 7am-5pm) to Grand Marais ($38). The North Shore's **area code: 218.**

Boundary Waters Canoe Area Wilderness
At its north end, Rte. 61 runs along BWCAW, a designated wilderness comprising 1.2 million acres of lakes, streams, and forests (including part of **Superior National Forest**) in which no human-made improvements—phones, roads, electricity, private dwellings—are allowed. Within the BWCAW, small waterways and portages string together 1100 lakes, allowing virtually limitless "canoe-camping." All visitors to the BWCAW need to acquire a permit. The BWCAW is quite finicky about when, where, and how many people it will allow to enter the Wilderness. As few as six permits will be accepted for popular put-ins during the summer, so phoning ahead is essential (day permits free, camping permits $10 per person per trip). Running northwest from **Grand Marais,** the 60 mi. paved **Gunflint Trail** (County Rd. 12) is the only developed road offering access to the wilderness; resorts and outfitters gather alongside this lone strip of civilization. **Bear Track Outfitters,** 2011 W. Rte. 61 (387-1162), across from the Gunflint Ranger Station, can rent you a boat or stock you up on camping necessities. (1-day canoe rental $20, includes all accessories; 1-day kayak rental $30; to paddle in the BWCAW, call ahead to arrange for a permit.)

The **Grand Marais Chamber of Commerce** (387-2524 or 888-922-5000), on N. Broadway off Hwy. 61 in Grand Marais, has info on BWCAW and the Minnesota section of the North Shore (open mid-May to Oct. M-Sa 9am-5pm; call for winter hrs.). One mile south of town, the **Gunflint Ranger Station** (387-1750) distributes permits required to enter BWCAW from May through September (open daily 6am-8pm; Oct.-Apr. M-F 8am-4:30pm).

The well-kept, seldom-full cabins of **"Spirit of the Land" Island Hostel (HI-AYH)** (388-2241 or 800-454-2922) are located on an island in Seagull Lake, at the end of the Gunflint Trail. The Christian-oriented **Wilderness Canoe Base,** which leads canoe trips and summer island camps for various groups, administers the hostel. Call from Grand Marais to arrange a boat pick-up. (Full kitchen, outhouses. Beds $14, nonmembers $17, F-Sa $16/19. Sleeping bag $5, sleepsack $3. Meals $4-6. Hot showers $2. Saunas $3. Canoe rental $10 per ½-day, $18 per day. Snowshoe rentals in winter. Closed Nov.-Dec.) **Nelson's Traveler's Rest** (387-1464 or 800-249-1285), on Rte. 61, ½ mi. west of Grand Marais, provides fully equipped cab-

MINNESOTA

ins with a lake view (from $43; open mid-May to mid-Oct.; call in advance). **Grand Marais Municipal Campground** (387-1712), off Hwy. 61 in Grand Marais, supplies nice—if crowded—campsites along the lake. (Primitive sites $15, with water and electricity $18; office open 6am-10pm; use of municipal pool $1.)

Cheap and popular with fishermen, **South of the Border Café**, 4 W. Rte. 61 (387-1505), in Grand Marais, specializes in huge breakfasts and satisfying, greasy food (check your pulse). The bluefin herring sandwich (fried, of course) will run you $2.75. (Open daily 5am-2pm.) Those with a demanding sweet tooth can try **World's Best Doughnuts** (387-1345), at the intersection of Wisconsin and Broadway. (Open late May to mid-Oct. M-Sa 7:30am until sold out, usually around 5pm, Su 7am-2pm.)

■ Voyageurs

Voyageurs National Park sits on Minnesota's boundary with Ontario, accessible almost solely by boat. Named for the French Canadian fur traders who once traversed this area, the park invites today's voyagers to leave the auto-dominated world and push off into the longest inland lake waterway on the continent. While some hiking trails exist, boats and canoes provide most transportation within the park. Preservation efforts have kept the area much as it was in the late 18th century, and wolves, bear, deer, and moose roam freely. Undeveloped often means unregulated for city slickers' protection; water should be boiled for at least 2min. before consumption, and some fish in these waters contain mercury. Lyme-disease-bearing ticks have been found in the area as well; visitors should take precautions.

The park can be accessed through (from Southeast to Northwest) **Crane Lake, Ash River, Kabetogama Lake,** or **Rainy Lake** (all east of Rte. 53), or through **International Falls,** at the northern tip of Rte. 53 just below Ft. Frances, ON. **Crane Lake Visitor and Tourism Bureau,** 7238 Handberg Rd. (993-2481 or 800-362-7405; open M-F 9am-5pm), awaits, as does the **International Falls Chamber of Commerce,** 301 2nd Ave. (800-325-5766; open M-F 8am-5pm, Sa 7am-3pm). Within the park, three visitors centers serve tourists: **Rainy Lake** (286-5258), 12 mi. east of International Falls at the end of Rte. 11 (open May-Sept. daily 9am-5pm; call for off-season hrs.); **Ash River** (374-3221), 8 mi. east of Rte. 53 on Rte. 129, then 3 mi. north (open early May to early Sept. daily 10am-4pm); and **Kabetogama Lake** (875-2111), 1 mi. north of Rte. 122, follow the signs (open mid-May to Sept. daily 9am-5pm).

Many of the park's numerous campsites are accessible only by water. Car-accessible sites can be found in state forest campgrounds, including **Wooden Frog** (757-3489), about 4 mi. from Kabetogama Visitors Center Rd. 122 (primitive sites $9, showers available at lodge $3), and **Ash River** (757-3489), 3 mi. from the visitors center and 2 mi. east on Rte. 129 (primitive $9). Only 5min. from International Falls, **International Voyageurs RV Campground** (283-4679), off Rte. 53 south of town, offers decent camping with showers, and laundry (tent sites $11, full hookup $18).

Rte. 53 in International Falls is loaded with motels. Oh, to be in a wooded, pleasant environment, but wait—'tis the **Ash Trail Lodge** (374-3131 or 800-777-4513), 10 mi. east of Rte. 53 on Rte. 129 (singles and doubles $55). **International Falls,** the "Icebox of the Nation," the inspiration for **Rocky and Bullwinkle's** hometown Frostbite Falls, hosts a few attractions outside the park. The state's largest prehistoric burial ground, **Grand Mound History Center** (285-3332), 17 mi. west of town on Rte. 11, supposedly dates from 200 BC. (Open May-Sept. M-Sa 10am-5pm, Su noon-5pm; $2.) **Smokey Bear Park,** home of a 22 ft. tall thermometer and the 26 ft., 82 ton giant who asks you to help fight forest fires, makes for lighter entertainment. **Area code:** 218.

GREAT PLAINS

In 1803, the Louisiana Purchase doubled the size of America, adding French territory west of the Mississippi at the bargain price of 4¢ per acre. Over time, the plains spawned legends of pioneers and cowboys, and of Native Americans struggling to defend their homes. The coming of railroad transportation and liberal land policy spurred an economic boom, until a drought during the Great Depression transformed the region into a dust bowl. Modern agricultural techniques have since reclaimed the soil, and the heartland of the United States thrives on the trade of farm commodities. Today, the Great Plains is a vast land of prairies and farms, where open sky stretches from horizon to horizon, broken only by long, thin lines of trees. Grasses and grains paint the land green and gold. The plains' breadbasket feeds much of the world. Yet, in spite of the touch of man, the land still rules here, and the most staggering sights in the region are the work of nature, from the Badlands to the Black Hills. The mighty Missouri and Mississippi Rivers trace their way through thriving small towns, while amber waves of grain quietly reign among the greatest of American symbols.

🕮 HIGHLIGHTS OF THE GREAT PLAINS

- **National Parks and Monuments.** Find uncrowded gems in Theodore Roosevelt National Park, SD (p. 470) and the Badlands, SD (p. 473), or join the crowds in the Black Hills around Mt. Rushmore (p. 476).
- **Scenic drives.** It's all beautiful terrain here. Rte. 22 (p. 470) is one to remember.
- **Historical sites.** Scotts Bluff National Monument, NE (p. 494) and Chimney Rock, NE (p. 494) will fascinate anyone interested in the pioneers.

North Dakota

An early visitor to the site of present-day Fargo declared, "It's a beautiful land, but I doubt that human beings will ever live here." Posterity begs to differ. The stark, haunting lands that so intimidated early settlers eventually found willing tenants, and the territory became a state along with South Dakota on November 2, 1889. The inaugural event was not without confusion—Benjamin Harrison concealed the names when he signed the two bills, so both Dakotas claim to be the 39th state.

North Dakota has remained largely isolated geographically. In the western half of the state, the colorful buttes of the Badlands rise in desolate beauty, while in the eastern half, mind-numbing flatness rules; the 110 mi. of Rte. 46 from U.S. 81 to Rte. 30 is the longest stretch of highway in the U.S. without a single curve.

PRACTICAL INFORMATION

Capital: Bismarck.
Visitor Info: Tourism Dept., 604 East Blvd., Bismarck 58505 (701-328-2525 or 800-437-2077; http://www.ndtourism.com). **Parks and Recreation Dept.,** 1835 Bismarck Expwy., Bismarck 58504.
Emergency: 911.
Time Zones: Mostly Central (1hr. behind Eastern). *Let's Go* makes note of areas in Mountain (2hr. behind Eastern). **Postal Abbreviation:** ND.
Sales Tax: 5-7%, depending on the city.

Great Plains

CANADA

SASKATCHEWAN

Regina

MANITOBA

Winnipeg

ONTARIO

Lake of the Woods

Thunder Bay

Williston
Minot
Lake Sakakawea
NORTH DAKOTA
Devils Lake
Grand Forks
International Falls

MONT.

Washburn
Mandan
Bismarck
Jamestown
Fargo

Lake Superior

Duluth

THEODORE ROOSEVELT NAT'L PARK

MINNESOTA

WISCONSIN

Aberdeen

SOUTH DAKOTA

Watertown

St. Paul
Minneapolis

WYO.

Rapid City
Lake Oahe
Pierre

Rochester

Madison

MOUNT RUSHMORE NATIONAL MEMORIAL

BADLANDS NAT'L PARK

Mitchell
Sioux Falls

Missouri River

Yankton

Sheldon

Effigy Mounds National Monument

Dubuque

NEBRASKA

Sioux City

IOWA
Ames
Des Moines

Cedar Rapids
Iowa City

Davenport

The Amana Colonies

Grand Island
Omaha

Osceola

Burlington

Peoria

Kearney
Hastings
Lincoln

Missouri River

ILLINOIS

Springfield

MISSOURI

Hannibal

Waconda Lake

KANSAS

Topeka
Independence

Columbia

St. Louis

COLO.

Oakley

Lawrence
Kansas City

Jefferson City

Garden City
Great Bend

Hutchinson

Dodge City
Wichita

Springfield

Blackwell

Tulsa

ARKANSAS

Amarillo

Oklahoma City

Shawnee

Memphis
TENN.

Lawton
OKLAHOMA

Little Rock

N

Lubbock

Ardmore

MISS.

TEXAS

Ft. Worth
Dallas

Shreveport

Abilene

Jackson

0   150 miles

0   225 km

LOUISIANA

■ Fargo

Although it is North Dakota's largest city, Fargo existed in relative anonymity until a recent Oscar-winning film, *Fargo*, brought it a measure of fame. However, the fact remains that very little of the 1996 black comedy was filmed in the town, and the movie parodies accents that are more northern Minnesota than North Dakota. With Moorhead, MN, its sister city, Fargo is home to 20,000 college students who pack lecture halls at North Dakota State University, Moorhead State, and Concordia College.

The **Heritage Hjemkomst Center,** 202 1st Ave. N. (218-233-5604), in Moorhead, pays tribute to the two cities' Norwegian heritage. Inside looms the **Hjemkomst,** a 76 ft. Viking ship replica that Moorhead native Robert Asp successfully sailed from Duluth, MN to Norway, thus fulfilling a lifetime dream. (Open Su-W and F-Sa 9am-5pm, Th 9am-9pm. $3.50, students and seniors $3, ages 5-17 $1.50.) The **Fargo Theater,** 314 Broadway (232-4152), screens art house films in a restored 1930s interior.

Both the **Red River Valley Fair** (800-456-6408; June 18-27, 1999) and the **Scandinavian Hjemkomst Festival** (800-235-7654; June 23-27, 1999) are traditionally big draws, complete with rides, shows, and tasty local food. From June to August, **Trollwood Park Weekends** (241-8160) features similar enticements.

Cheap chain motels are plentiful at I-29 and 13th Ave.; take Exit 64 off I-29. **The Sunset Motel,** 731 W. Main (800-252-2207), in West Fargo, about 3 mi. west off I-29 Exit 65, offers clean rooms, free local calls, continental breakfast, and an indoor pool with a snazzy 2-story waterslide (singles $25; doubles $37; kitchenettes $7 extra; call early on weekends). **Moorhead State University** (218-236-2231) rents rooms with linen and phones in Ballard Hall, just north of 9th Ave. and 14th St. in Moorhead ($10 per person; check-in 24hr.). **Lindenwood Park** (232-3987), at 17th Ave. and 5th St. S., offers campsites close to the peaceful Red River (sites $8, with hookup $14). The park also has extensive trails ideal for mountain biking. **Old Broadway,** 22 Broadway (237-6161), is the flagship microbrewery, serving burgers and beer cheese soup (entrees $3-8). After 11pm, it's a popular nightspot. (Open M-Sa 11am-1am; F dinner ½ price.) Patrons at **Jim Lauerman's,** 64 Broadway (237-4747), can enjoy salads ($2.25-4.25) or tasty sandwiches ($2.50-4.25); the Sloppy George is a good choice (open M-Sa 11am-1am; Su noon-1am; no minors after 9pm). At **Zandbróz,** a variety store *cum* old-fashioned soda fountain, you can wash down your sandwich ($3.50) with a fountain drink ($1.30-2.70; open M-Sa 9am-9pm, Su noon-5pm). At night, NDSU students descend upon the bars along **Broadway** near Northern Pacific Ave.

Fargo and **Moorhead** flank the **Red River** on the east and west, respectively. Numbered streets increase from the river outward, and numbered avenues run east-west. **Main Ave.** is the central east-west thoroughfare and intersects **I-29, University Dr.,** and **Broadway.** Take flight at **Hector International Airport,** 2801 32nd Ave. N.W. (241-8168), off 19th Ave. N. in northern Fargo. **Amtrak,** 420 4th St. N. (232-2197 or 800-872-7245), chugs daily to Minneapolis (5-6hr., $25-55) and Chicago (14hr., $60-130; open M-F 8am-3:30pm and midnight-7am). **Greyhound,** 402 Northern Pacific (N.P.) Ave. (293-1222 or 800-231-2222; open daily 5:30am-6:20pm and 10:30pm-1:20am), lopes to Minneapolis (4-7hr., 4 per day, $27) and Bismarck (5hr., 3 per day, $28-31). **Metro Area Transit,** 502 North Pacific Ave. (232-7500), runs buses across the city (M-Sa). **Doyle's Yellow Checker Cab** (235-5535) provides taxi service ($1.50 base fare, $1.60 per additional mi.). Sort out your visit at the **Fargo-Moorhead Convention and Visitors Bureau,** 2001 44th St. SW (282-3653 or 800-235-7654), off 45th St. (open M-Sa 7:30am-7pm, Su 10am-6pm; Sept.-Apr. daily 8am-6pm). **Crisis Line:** 235-7335; 24hr. **Post Office:** 657 2nd Ave. N. (241-6100; open M-F 7:30am-5:30pm, Sa 8am-2pm). **ZIP code:** 58103. **Area code:** 701.

■ From Fargo to Theodore Roosevelt

Commissioned to map the new territory acquired in the Louisiana Purchase of 1803, famed explorers **Meriwether Lewis** and **William Clark** toughed out the challenging winter of 1804-5 on the shores of the great Missouri River in North Dakota. About 40 mi. north of the state capital **Bismarck** on or near **Rte. 83,** a number of attractions relate to this extraordinary period, which comprised a fourth of the party's journey.

The World's Largest Buffalo

Looming against the horizon in Jamestown, ND, is the concrete head of a 60-ton, 24 ft. buffalo, a towering monument to the animals that once roamed the plains. Near the statue, a herd of real buffalo regards their granite brother apathetically from behind a protective fence. With luck, you'll see White Cloud, a rare albino buffalo sacred to many Native American tribes. Adjacent to the monument is the **National Buffalo Museum,** which documents the evolution and adulation of the buffalo (open daily 9am-8pm; $3, students $1, families $7). While you're there, stroll through the **Frontier Village,** a place of dubious historical accuracy, but guaranteed kitsch (free). All are located at Exit 258 off I-94, at the junction of U.S. 281, between Bismarck and Fargo (call 800-22-BISON/222-4766 for info).

The **Lewis and Clark Interpretive Center** (701-462-8535), in **Washburn** at the junction of Rte. 83 and ND 200A, describes the expedition's stay in North Dakota (open daily May 24-Sept. 7 9am-7pm; off-season 9pm-5pm; $2, students $1). The staff can direct modern-day trailblazers to the replica of the expedition's rugged riverside lodgings just down the road at **Fort Mandan.** Several miles west off ND 200A in **Stanton** is the **Knife River Indian Villages National Historic Site** (701-745-3300), where a museum examines the history and culture of the Hidatsa, Mandan, and Arikara tribes who helped Lewis and Clark survive that winter. (Open May 24-Sept. 7 daily 8am-6pm mountain time. Free.) Several trails at Knife River lead to the sites of former Native American villages. Those interested in simulating Lewis and Clark's rough 'n' tumble living may wish to camp at scenic **Cross Ranch State Park Campground** (702-794-3731), on the Missouri. ($3 per vehicle. Tent sites $7; RVs $10, no electricity available; cabin with no power or water available for rent, 1-5 people $35. Showers available.) To reach Cross Ranch, take the *paved* county road off 200A at the sign.

An alternate way to break up an east-west trek from Fargo to Theodore Roosevelt is to take **Rte. 22** north off I-90 or ND 200A. Lined with signs declaring it a scenic byway, the road offers nondescript plains at first, particularly if you begin from I-90. Eventually, however, gently rolling hills give way to higher rises. About 10 mi. north of **Kildear,** the striking rock formations of badlands suddenly emerge from the landscape, providing a visual treat for those patient enough to reach this point.

■ Theodore Roosevelt National Park

After both his mother and wife died on the same day, pre-White House Theodore Roosevelt moved to a ranch in the Badlands for a dose of spiritual renewal. He was so influenced by the red- and brown-hued lunar formations, horseback riding, big-game hunting, and cattle ranching in this unforgiving land that he later claimed, "I never would have been President if it weren't for my experiences in North Dakota." Visitors to **Theodore Roosevelt National Park** can still achieve the same inspiration among the quiet canyons, secluded glens, and dramatic rocky outcroppings which have earned the park the nickname "rough-rider country." The park teems with wildlife; prairie dog towns, wandering bison, and skittish deer are all common sights.

PRACTICAL INFORMATION The park is split into southern and northern units and bisected by the border separating Mountain and Central Time Zones. The entrance to the more-developed southern unit is just north of I-94 in **Medora,** a frontier town revamped into a tourist mecca. (Even the newspaper vending machines are encased in wood to appear more authentically Western.) **Greyhound** serves Medora from the Sully Inn (see below), with buses to Bismarck (3½hr., 3 per day, $23-25) and Billings (6hr., 2 per day, $45-48). There is no ticket office in Medora; board the bus and buy your ticket during the Dickinson layover. The park entrance fee ($5 per person or $10 max. per vehicle, under 17 free) covers admission to both units of the park for 7 days. The **South Unit's Visitors Center** (623-4466), in Medora, maintains a mini-museum displaying Teddy's guns, spurs, and old letters, as well as a beautiful 13min. film about the Badlands. Free copies of *Frontier Fragments,* the park newspaper, list ranger-led walks, talks, and demonstrations. (Open daily 8am-8pm; Sept. to mid-June 8am-4:30pm.) The **South Unit's Emergency** number is 623-4379. The **North Unit's Visitors Center** (842-2333) has an interesting exhibit on the nature and wildlife in the park and offers a shorter film (open May-Sept. daily 9am-5:30pm Central Time). In case of an **emergency** in the north unit, call the **ranger** at 842-4151 or the **sheriff** at 842-2400. For more info, write to **Theodore Roosevelt National Park,** P.O. Box 7, Medora 58645, or call the visitors centers. Medora's **post office:** 355 3rd Ave. (open M-Sa 8am-7pm; window service M-F 8am-4:30pm, Sa 8:15am-9:15am). **ZIP code:** 58645. **Area code:** 701. **South Unit Time Zone:** Mountain (2hr. behind Eastern). **North Unit Time Zone:** Central (1hr. behind Eastern).

CAMPGROUNDS, ACCOMMODATIONS, AND FOOD In either unit, free backcountry camping permits await at the visitors center. **Cottonwood Campgrounds** in the south part of the park has sites with toilets and running water ($10). The north offers backcountry opportunities, or you can head to **Juniper Campground,** 5 mi. west of the north unit entrance in a beautiful valley setting (sites $10; toilets and running water). The campground is a popular buffalo nightspot all year, so be aware.

It's not easy to find inexpensive, non-camping lodging in Medora. The **Sully Inn,** 428 Broadway (623-4455; fax 623-4992), offers clean rooms at the lowest rates in town, plus free local calls and 10% off in its bookstore (singles $35-45, in winter $20-35; doubles $40-50; under 13 free). Teddy Roosevelt was known to bunk down at the **Rough Riders Hotel** (623-4444, ext. 497), at 3rd St. and 3rd Ave. The hotel's room rates are far from budget, but the restaurant serves reasonable breakfasts and lunches (omelettes, salads, and sandwiches) for $5-7. In winter, it becomes a weekend B&B; the rest of the year, it is open daily from 7am to 9pm. The **Cowboy Café** (623-4343), on 4th St., dishes up less expensive meals ($2-6), including homemade pie, $3.50 buffalo burgers, and salads (open daily 6am-8pm).

SIGHTS AND ENTERTAINMENT The south unit features a 36 mi. **scenic automobile loop,** an effortless way to see the park. Many hiking trails start from the loop and wander into the wilderness. **Wind Canyon,** located on the loop, is a constantly morphing canyon formed by winds blowing against the soft clay. The ¾ mi. **Coal Vein Trail** follows a seam of lignite coal that caught fire here and burned from 1951 to 1977. For 26 years, the smoking, glowing vein was a tourist attraction; park visitors would come to gawk or roast marshmallows. The third-largest **petrified forest** in the U.S. lies a day's hike into the park; if you prefer to drive, ask at the visitors center for a map and prepare to walk ½ mi. from the parking lot. **Painted Canyon Overlook,** 7 mi. east of Medora off I-94, has its own **visitors center** (575-4020) with picnic tables and a breathtaking view of the Badlands. *(Open daily 8am-6pm; mid-Apr. to late May and early Sept. to mid-Nov. 8:30am-4:30pm.)* The occasional buffalo roams through the parking lot. **Peaceful Valley Ranch** (623-4496), 7 mi. into the park, offers a variety of horseback riding excursions, 1½hr. or longer ($16; rides leave daily 8:30am-3:30pm, evening ride 6:30pm). **Rough Rider Adventures** (623-4808), on 3rd St. in Medora, leads free guided tours at 10am and 2pm daily, and rents mountain bikes ($15 per 4hr.; open late May to early Sept. daily 9am-6pm).

The less-visited but equally scenic **north unit** of the park is 75 mi. from the south unit on U.S. 85. Most of the land is wilderness, resulting in virtually unlimited **backcountry hiking** possibilities. Be careful not to surprise the buffalo; one ranger advises singing while hiking so they can hear you coming. Apparently, no one's ever been trampled while singing Baroque classics, Barry White love ballads, or riffs from "Free to Be You and Me." The **Caprock Coulee Trail** journeys through prairie, river valley, mountain ridge, and juniper forest, all in the space of 4 mi.

The popular **Medora Musical** (623-4444 or 800-MEDORA1/633-6721), in the Burning Hills Amphitheater west of town, stages variety shows nightly at 8:30pm from early June to early September. Featured attractions range from "The Flaming Idiots" to "Arneberg's Sensational Canines." Tickets are available on 4th St. at the **Harold Schafer Heritage Center** (623-4444; $15-17, ages 6-18 $9-10).

GREAT PLAINS

South Dakota

From the forested granite crags of the Black Hills to the glacial lakes of the northeast, the Coyote State has more to offer than casual passers-by might expect. WALL DRUG. In fact, with only ten people per square mile, South Dakota has the highest ratio of sights-to-people in all of the Great Plains. Colossal man-made attractions like Mt. Rushmore National Memorial and the Crazy Horse Memorial compete with stunning natural spectacles such as the Black Hills and the Badlands, making tourism the state's largest industry after agriculture. WALL DRUG. Camera-toting tourists in search of nature have brought both dollars and development to South Dakota, which struggles to keep its balance between natural beauty and neon signs.

> YOU ARE NOW ONLY THREE PAGES FROM WALL DRUG.

PRACTICAL INFORMATION

Capital: Pierre.
Visitor Info: Division of Tourism, 711 E. Wells St., Pierre 57051 (605-773-3301 or 800-732-5682; http://www.state.sd.us/tourism). Open M-F 8am-5pm. **U.S. Forest Service,** 330 Mt. Rushmore Rd., Custer 57730 (605-673-4853). Open M-F 7:30am-4:30pm. **Game, Fish, and Parks Dept.,** 523 E. Capitol Ave., Foss Bldg., Pierre 57501 (605-773-3392 or 800-710-2267), has info on state parks and campgrounds. Open M-F 8am-noon and 1-5pm.
Emergency: 911.
Time Zones: Mostly Mountain (2hr. behind Eastern). *Let's Go* makes note of areas in Central (1hr. behind Eastern). **Postal Abbreviation:** SD.
Sales Tax: 6%.

■ Sioux Falls

Sioux Falls, the state's eastern gateway, is like a "nice guy": quiet, friendly, and clean-cut. Some will take this description to mean "boring," but those who value its comforting qualities will understand that "nice" truly is a compliment. Downtown is sprinkled with historic buildings of pink quartzite, and the city is ringed by a series of riverside parks connected by bike trails.

You can visit the city's namesake rapids at **Falls Park,** just north of downtown on Falls Park Dr. (wheelchair access). The **Sioux River Greenway Recreation Trail,** which circles the city from Falls Park in the northeast to the Elmwood golf course in the northwest, provides a great opportunity for a stroll or bike ride. Legend says that in order to escape the law after a botched bank robbery, Jesse James made a 20 ft. leap on horseback across **Devil's Gulch** in **Garretson,** 20 mi. northeast of Sioux Falls. Take Rte. 11 10 mi. north from I-90. (Open in summer daily 9am-7pm. Free.)

In the first full weekend of June, the neighboring city of **Tea** hosts the **Great Plains Balloon Race,** visible from all over Sioux Falls (call 336-1745 for more info). A full-scale cast of Michelangelo's **David** graces Fawick Park on 2nd Ave. and 10th St., while the only existing cast of Michelangelo's **Moses** stands on the grounds of Augustana College, at 30th St. and Grange Ave. **The Old Courthouse Museum,** 200 W. 6th St. (367-4210), at Main St., sheds light on the history of the Siouxland area. (Open M-W 9am-5pm, Th 9am-9pm, F-Sa 9am-5pm, Su 1-5pm. Free. Wheelchair access.) It also offers a series of concerts on most Fridays through the year (indoors Nov.-Apr., in adjacent Reardon Plaza May-Sept.). The **Corn Palace,** 604 N. Main St. (996-7311 or 995-4030), in Mitchell (from Sioux Falls, head 70 mi. west on I-90), poses as a regal testament to granular architecture. Dating back to 1892, the structure is now redecorated yearly with thousands of bushels of native corn, grain, and grasses to demonstrate the richness of South Dakota's soil (open in summer daily 8am-10pm; winter hrs. vary; free). In winter, you can travel just minutes from downtown to **Great Bear Ski Valley,** 5901 E. Rice St. (367-4309), to enjoy skiing, snowboarding, and snowshoeing (rentals and lessons available).

Budget motels flank 10th St., Exit 6 off I-229. The **Plaza Motel Inn,** 2620 E. 10th St. (336-1550 or 800-336-1550), rents large, clean rooms with complimentary breakfast (singles $34; doubles $41). Among another cluster of hotels and motels at 41st St. and I-29 lies the **Select Inn,** 3500 Gateway Blvd. (361-1864), with clean and sizeable rooms. (Singles $30; doubles $36, with 2 beds $40; AAA and senior discounts. Laundry facilities available.) There are a number of state parks nearby, but you can camp for close-out prices next to a waterfall at **Split Rock City Park,** 20 mi. northeast in Garretson. From I-90E, take Rte. 11 N. (Corson) and drive 10 mi. to Garretson; turn right at the sign for Devil's Gulch, and it will be on your left before the tracks. Sites have pit toilets and drinking water ($5). Every city needs a trendy downtown brewery, and the **Sioux Falls Brewing Co.,** 431 N. Phillips (332-4847), fits the bill. Grab a slice of buffalo pie (cheesecake with stout beer and dark chocolate) with your burger or salad for $5-8 (open M-Th 11:30am-midnight, F-Sa 11:30am-2am). After dinner, move to **Suite E** (335-3347), downstairs from the Brewing Co. This laid-back bar and night club has a two drink minimum (non-alcoholic drinks included) but no cover. (Open W-Sa 7pm-2am.)

Main St. divides the city east-west, and **Minnesota Ave.** is another major north-south thoroughfare. **10th** and **12th St.** intersect them; 10th connects with **I-229** in the east and 12th connects with **I-29** in the west. **Jack Rabbit Buses,** 301 N. Dakota Ave. (336-0885; open daily 7:30am-5pm) hop to Minneapolis (6hr., 1 per day, $45), Omaha (3hr., 2 per day, $35-56), and Rapid City (8hr., 1 per day, $97). **Sioux Falls Transit** (367-7183) buses run during the day for $1 with free transfers (M-Sa). Flag a **Yellow Cab** (336-1616; $2 base fare, $1.60 per mi.). **Spoke-N-Sport,** 2101 W. 41st St. (332-2206), in the back of the Western Mall, rents bikes for $15 per day (open M-F 10am-8pm, Sa 10am-5pm, Su noon-4pm). The **Chamber of Commerce,** 200 N. Phillips (336-1620), at 8th, provides free city maps (open M-F 8am-5pm). The **Crisis Helpline,** 339-4357, operates 24hr. **Gay and Lesbian Coalition Info:** 333-0603. **Sioux Valley Hospital,** 1100 S. Euclid Ave. (333-1000), stands at the corner of 18th and Grange. **Post Office:** 320 S. Second Ave. (357-5000; open M-F 7:30am-5:30pm, Sa 8am-1pm). **ZIP code:** 57104. **Area code:** 605. **Time Zone:** Central.

■ The Badlands

"Hell with the fires out," General Alfred Sully called these arid and treacherous formations at first encounter. Earlier visitors concurred. The Sioux called this area *mako sica* and the French agreed with *les mauvaises terres:* both terms mean "bad lands." Some 60 million years ago, when much of the Great Plains was under water, tectonic shifts thrust up the Rockies and the Black Hills. Mountain streams deposited silt from these nascent highlands into the area now known as the Badlands, capturing and fossilizing the remains of wildlife that once wandered these flood plains in layer after pink layer. Erosion has carved spires and steep sills into the earth, creating a strikingly beautiful landscape that contrasts sharply with the prairies of eastern South Dakota. Late spring and fall in the Badlands offer pleasant weather that can be a relief from the extreme temperatures of mid-summer and winter, but no matter how bad it gets, it's always well worth a visit. Watch and listen for rattlesnakes, and don't tease the bison.

PRACTICAL INFORMATION Badlands National Park smolders about 50 mi. east of Rapid City on I-90. **Jack Rabbit Buses,** 333 6th St. (348-3300), leaves from Rapid City for Wall at 11:30am daily ($24). Driving tours can start at either end of Rte. 240, which winds through the wilderness in a 32 mi. detour off I-90 (Exit 110 or 131). The **Ben Reifel Visitors Center** (433-5361; open daily 7am-8pm; Sept.-May hrs. vary), 5 mi. inside the park's northeastern entrance, is larger and much more convenient than **White River Visitors Center** (455-2878; open June-Sept. 8am-5pm), 55 mi. to the southwest off Rte. 27 in the park's less-visited southern section. Both visitors centers have potable water. The **entrance fee,** collected at the park entrance, is $10 per car, $5 per person (a free copy of *The Prairie Preamble* with map of trails included). At the **National Grasslands Visitors Center (Buffalo Gap),** 708 Main St. (279-2125), just down the street from Wall Drug in Wall, there are several films and an exhibit on the complex ecosystem that comprises much of the surrounding area (open daily 7am-8pm, off-season 8am-4:30pm). **ZIP code:** 57757. **Area code:** 605.

GREAT PLAINS

ACCOMMODATIONS, CAMPGROUNDS AND FOOD In Interior, the **Badlands Inn** (433-4501 or 800-341-8000) sits just out of the park (singles $32; doubles $43). The **Homestead Motel,** 612 Main St. (279-2303), in Wall, has a white picket fence and a flowerpot tree (singles $29-39; doubles $39-49; open mid-May to mid-Sept.). Next to the Ben Reifel Visitors Center inside the park, **Cedar Pass Lodge** (433-5460) rents cabins with A/C and showers. (1 person $43, $4 per additional person. Open mid-Apr. to mid-Oct. Fills up early; call ahead.) At the lodge's mid-priced **restaurant** (the only one in the park), brave diners try the $3.45 **buffalo burger** (open May 15-Sept. daily 7am-8:30pm; off-season hrs. vary). Two campgrounds lie within the park. **Cedar Pass Campground,** just south of the Ben Reifel Visitors Center, has sites with water and restrooms ($10). It fills up by late afternoon in summer. At **Sage Creek Campground,** 13 mi. from the Pinnacles entrance south of Wall (take Sage Creek Rim Rd. off Rte. 240), you can sleep in an open field; there are outhouses, no water, and no fires allowed—but hey, it's free. **Camping** (always ½ mi. from the road and out of sight) allows a more intimate introduction to this austere landscape. Wherever you sleep, don't cozy up to the bison; nervous mothers can become just a tad protective.

SIGHTS AND ACTIVITIES The 244,000-acre park protects large tracts of prairie and stark rock formations. The **Ben Reifel Visitors Center** has a video on the Badlands, as well as a wealth of info on nearby parks, camping, and activities. Park rangers offer free star-gazing programs, evening slide shows (call for times), and nature walks.

Trail guides from the visitors centers facilitate hiking through the Badlands. The short but steep Saddle Pass Trail traverses the bluffs; Castle Trail (10 mi. round-trip) is home on the range. Overnight hikers can get **backcountry camping** info from the rangers. For stunning vistas without the sweat, a drive along Rte. 240 is an excellent way to see the park. Rte. 240 also passes the trailheads of the **Door, Window,** and **Notch Trails,** all brief excursions into the Badlands terrain. The gravel **Sage Creek Rim Rd.,** west of Rte. 240, has fewer people and more animals; highlights are **Roberts Prairie Dog Town** and the park's herds of bison, antelope, and prairie dogs. Across the river from the Sage Creek campground lies another prairie dog town and some popular bison territory. Fresh buffalo chips reveal recent activity. It is easy to lose your bearings in this territory; rangers and maps can help.

Have You Dug Wall Drug?

There is almost no way to visit the Badlands without being importuned by advertisements from **Wall Drug,** 510 Main St. (279-2175), a towering monument to the success of saturation advertising. *(Open daily 6am-10pm; mid-Sept. to Apr. 6:30am-6pm.)* After seeing billboards for Wall Drug from as far as 500 mi. away, travelers feel obligated to make a stop in Wall to see what all the ruckus is about—much as they must have done 60 years ago, when Wall first enticed parched travelers with free water. The "drug store" itself is now a conglomeration of shops containing Old West memorabilia, kitschy souvenirs, Western books, and numerous photo opportunities with statues of oversized animals; you can even pray for a safe trip at their traveler's chapel. Wall itself is hardly worth a visit. All in all, the town is just another brick in the...oh, never mind.

■ Wounded Knee

The triggers of the United States Army's 7th Cavalry sparked a bloody massacre of 153 Sioux men, women, and children on this flat patch of land in 1890, marking the symbolic peak of a century's genocide. The Sioux's Ghost Dance movement, a spiritual revival that promised a return to a time of roaming buffalo and no white men, had been labelled "Messiah craze," while the tribe was deemed a "foe to progress" by land-hungry settlers. Scores of ignored promises and forgotten treaties culminated in the slaughter; the dead lay frozen on the field four days later, contorted into grotesque shapes, when they were finally buried in hastily dug mass graves. Today, the site is part of the **Pine Ridge Reservation** (though plans are underway to convert the area to a national park, a move opposed by Lakota residents).

In 1973, tensions escalated anew as reservation youths occupied a church. An armed confrontation between federal marshals, reservation residents, and activist members of the American Indian Movement ensued, in what became known as **Wounded Knee II.** A museum and church were burnt to the ground.

The site of the 1890 massacre is now marked by a graveyard on the hilltop, a sign recounting the events of the first Wounded Knee, and two stands that sell native crafts. The Wounded Knee memorial is located off Rte. 18, on the outskirts of the town of Wounded Knee, in southern South Dakota. It is a considerable distance (80 mi.) from other tourist spots of the Black Hills. For more info, contact the **Oglala Sioux Tribe Office of Tourism Development,** P.O. Box 3008, Pine Ridge, SD 57770 (605-867-5301). KILI 90.1FM, the "Voice of the Lakota Nation," provides local info.

BLACK HILLS REGION

The Black Hills, named for the dark hue that distance lends the green pines covering the hills, have long been considered sacred by the Sioux. The Treaty of 1868 gave the Black Hills and the rest of South Dakota west of the Missouri River to the tribe. But when gold was discovered in the 1870s, the U.S. government snatched back the land. The dueling geographical monuments of **Mt. Rushmore** (a national memorial, p. 476) and **Crazy Horse** (an independent project, p. 476) strikingly illustrate the clash of the two cultures that reside among these hills. Today, white residents dominate the area, which contains a trove of natural treasures, including Custer State Park, Wind Cave National Park, and Jewel Cave National Monument.

The majority of the land in the Black Hills area is part of the **Black Hills National Forest** and exercises the "multiple use" principle—mining, logging, ranching, and tourism all take place in close proximity. "Don't-miss" attractions like reptile farms and Flintstone Campgrounds lurk around every bend of the narrow, sinuous roads. The forest itself provides unlimited opportunities for backcountry hiking and camping, as do park-run campgrounds and private tent sites. In the hills, the **visitors center** (343-8755), on I-385 at Pactola Lake, has details on backcountry camping and great $4 maps (open late May to early Sept. daily 8:30am-6pm). **Backcountry camping** in the national forest is free. You must stay 1 mi. away from any campground or visitors center, at least 200 ft. off the side of the road (leave your car in a parking lot or pull off), and stay campfire-free. Good campgrounds include **Pactola,** on the Pactola Reservoir just south of the junction of Rte. 44 and U.S. 385 (sites $13); **Sheridan Lake,** 5 mi. northeast of Hill City on U.S. 385 (sites $13; north entrance for group sites, south entrance for individuals); and **Roubaix Lake,** 14 mi. south of Lead on U.S. 385 (sites $13). All National Forest campgrounds are quiet and wooded, offering fishing, swimming, and pit toilets, but no hookups (for reservations, call 800-280-CAMP/2267). The national forest extends into Wyoming, with a ranger station in Sundance (307-283-1361; open M-F 7:30am-5pm). The Wyoming side of the forest permits campfires, allows horses, and draws fewer visitors.

I-90 skirts the northern border of the Black Hills from Spearfish in the west to Rapid City in the east; **U.S. 385** twists from Hot Springs in the south to Deadwood in the north. The road system that interconnects through the hills covers beautiful territory, but the roads are difficult to navigate without a good map; pick one up for free almost anywhere in the area. Don't expect to get anywhere fast—these convoluted routes will hold you to half the speed of the interstate.

The off season in the Black Hills offers stellar skiing (see **Lead,** p. 480) and snowmobiling, but many attractions have limited hours or shut down, while most hotels, resorts, and campgrounds close for the winter. Unless you're astride a flashy piece of chrome and steel, you may want to steer clear of the Hills in early August, when over 12,000 motorcyclists converge on the area for the **Sturgis Rally** (Aug. 9-15, 1999).

Take advantage of the excellent and informative **Grayline tours,** P.O. Box 1106, Rapid City, 57709 (342-4461). Make reservations or call 1hr. before departure, and they will pick you up at your motel in Rapid City. Tour #1 is the most complete.

GREAT PLAINS

(Runs daily mid-May to mid-Oct., 8hr., $32 includes admission prices.) The **Black Hills Visitor Information Center** (355-3700), Exit 61 off I-90, in Rapid City, is a fountain of wisdom on the entire region. Wherever your interests lie, odds are they've got it covered (open daily in summer 8am-9pm, in winter 8am-5pm; hrs. subject to change). **Area code:** 605.

■ Mount Rushmore

After the overly advertised tourist traps elsewhere in the Black Hills, **Mt. Rushmore National Memorial** is a refreshing surprise. South Dakota historian Doane Robinson originally conceived of this "shrine of democracy" in 1923 as a memorial for local Western heroes like Lewis and Clark and Kit Carson; sculptor Gutzon Borglum finally chose the four presidents. Borglum initially encountered opposition from those who felt the work of God could not be improved, but the tenacious sculptor defended the project's size, insisting that "there is not a monument in this country as big as a snuff box." Throughout the Depression, work progressed slowly, and a great setback occurred when the nearly completed face of Thomas Jefferson had to be blasted off Washington's right side and moved to his left due to insufficient granite. In 1941, the 60 ft. heads of George Washington, Thomas Jefferson, Theodore Roosevelt, and Abraham Lincoln were completed; work ceased as the U.S. entered World War II. The planned 465 ft. tall bodies were never completed, but the millions of visitors who come here every year don't seem to mind.

From Rapid City, take U.S. 16 and 16A to Keystone and Rte. 244 up to the mountain. Remote parking is free, but the lot fills early. There is an $8 per car "annual parking permit" for the lot adjacent to the entrance. The **info center** (605-574-4104) details the monument's history and offers ranger tours (open daily June-Aug. 8am-10pm; early Sept. to late May 8am-5pm). A brand-new, state-of-the-art **visitors center** (574-2523, ext. 165) showcases exhibits chronicling the history of the monument and lives of the featured presidents, as well as a 13min. film (open daily June-Aug. 8am-10pm; early Sept. to late May 8am-5pm).

Borglum's Studio, over 100 steps down from the main viewing area, holds a plaster model of the carving, tools, and plans for Mt. Rushmore (open mid-Mar. to mid-Dec. daily 9am-5pm). During the summer, the **Mt. Rushmore Memorial Amphitheater** hosts a monument-lighting program. A patriotic speech and slide show commence at 9pm, and light floods the monument 9:30-10:30pm.

The **Mt. Rushmore KOA Palmer Gulch Lodge** (605-574-2525 or 800-562-8503) lies 5 mi. west of Mt. Rushmore on Rte. 244. With campsites for two ($23, with water and electricity $29) or cabins ($40-46) comes the use of showers, stoves, pool, laundry, free shuttle service to Mt. Rushmore, movies, hayrides, basketball, volleyball, trail rides (on *Dances with Wolves* horses—$10.50 per hr.), a gas station, and of course, a gift shop. That's primitive camping for ya'. (Open May-Oct. Make reservations early, up to 2 months in advance for cabins and special requests.)

■ Crazy Horse Memorial

If you thought Mt. Rushmore was big, think again. The Crazy Horse Memorial is a wonder of the world in progress; an entire mountain is metamorphosing into a 563 ft. high memorial sculpture of the great Lakota war leader Crazy Horse. When completed, it will be the largest sculpture in the world. A famed warrior, Crazy Horse was revered by many tribes; he refused to sign treaties or live on a government reservation. In 1877, Crazy Horse was treacherously stabbed in the back by a white soldier who came bearing a flag of truce.

The project to remember the slain warrior was initiated by Lakota Chief Henry Standing Bear as a rebuttal to nearby Mt. Rushmore. The memorial also stands as a haunting reminder of the seizure of the Black Hills in the year before Crazy Horse was assassinated; it wasn't the first or last time gold fever glossed over the niceties of U.S. diplomatic decorum. The project began in 1947 and, to no one's surprise, didn't receive any initial government funding. The sculptor, Korczak Ziolkowski, went solo for years, later refusing $10 million in federal funding. Today, his 10 children carry on the work. Crazy Horse's completed face was unveiled in June 1998 (all 4 of the Rushmore heads could fit inside it), and part of his arm is now visible; eventually, his entire torso and head will be carved into the mountain. The memorial, 17 mi. southwest of Mt. Rushmore on U.S. 16/385, includes the **Indian Museum of North America** (605-673-4681), which shows a moving 10min. slide show. *(Open daily 7am-dark; Oct.-Apr. 8am until dark. $7, $17 per carload, $15 with a senior, under 6 free. $2 AAA discount per car. Free coffee at the restaurant. Monument lit nightly for 1hr.)*

■ Custer State Park

Peter Norbeck, governor of South Dakota during the late 1910s, loved to hike among the thin, towering rock formations that haunt the area south of Sylvan Lake and Mt. Rushmore. In order to preserve the land, he created Custer State Park. The spectacular **Needles Hwy.** (Rte. 87) within the park follows his favorite hiking route. Norbeck designed this road to be especially narrow and winding so that newcomers could experience the pleasures of discovery. The highway does not have guard rails, so slow and cautious driving is essential; watch out for mountain goats and bighorn sheep. Custer's biggest attraction is its herd of **1500 bison,** which can best be seen near dawn or dusk wandering near Wildlife Loop Rd. If you're "lucky," they, along with some friendly burros, will come right up to your car; don't get out of your car, as they're dangerous. The park's **entrance fee** is $3 per person, $8 per carload for a 7-day pass from May to October (Nov.-Apr. $2 per person, $5 per car). At the entrance, ask for a copy of *Tatanka* (Lakota for "bison"), the Custer State Park newspaper. The **Peter Norbeck Visitors Center** (255-4464), on U.S. 16A ½ mi. west of the State Game Lodge, serves as the park's info center (open daily late May to early Sept. 8am-8pm; early Sept. to Oct. and May 9am-5pm). All 11 park **campgrounds** charge $10-13 per night; most have showers and restrooms. Primitive camping ($2 per night) is available in the **French Creek Natural Area;** the visitors center can give you more info. Three-fourths of the park's 323 sites are reservable (call 800-710-2267 daily 7am-7pm; early Sept. to late May 7am-5pm), and the entire park fills by early afternoon in the summer. Food and concessions are available at all four park lodges, but the local general stores in Custer, Hermosa, or Keystone generally charge less.

   At 7242 ft., **Harney Peak** is the highest point east of the Rockies and west of the Pyrenees. At the top is an old lookout point, a few mountain goats, and a great view of the Black Hills. Sight-seeing helicopters hover below. Bring water and food, wear good shoes, and leave as early in the morning as possible to finish before dark. There are also more than 30 other trails in the park. You can hike, fish, ride horses, paddle boats, or canoe at popular **Sylvan Lake,** on Needles Hwy. (**Sylvan Lake Resort** 574-2561; kayak rental $3.50 per person per 30min.) Horse rides are available at **Blue Bell Lodge** (255-4531; stable 255-4571), on Rte. 87 about 8 mi. from the south entrance ($15 per hr., under 12 $12.50). Mountain bikes can be rented for $8 per hour at the **Legion Lake Resort** (255-4521), on U.S. 16A 6 mi. east the visitors center. All lakes and streams permit fishing with a daily license ($9; 5-day nonresident license $29). Fishing licenses and rental equipment are available at the four area lodges. Summer trout fishing is the best; consult *Tatanka* for limits on your fish take. **Area code:** 605.

■ Wind Cave and Jewel Cave

In the cavern-riddled Black Hills, the subterranean scenery often rivals the above-ground sites. Private concessionaires will attempt to lure you into the holes in their backyards, but the government owns the area's prime underground real estate: **Wind Cave National Park** (745-4600), adjacent to Custer State Park on U.S. 385, and **Jewel Cave National Monument** (673-2288), 14 mi. west of Custer on Rte. 16. There is no public transportation to the caves. Bring a sweater on all tours—Wind Cave remains a constant 53°F, Jewel Cave 49°F. **Area code:** 605.

Wind Cave Wind Cave was discovered in 1881 by Tom Bingham, who heard the sound of air rushing out of the cave's tiny single natural entrance. In fact, the wind was so strong it knocked his hat off. Air forcefully gusts in and out of the cave due to outside pressure changes, and when Tom went back to show his friends the cave, his hat got sucked in. Today, the amazing air pressure leads scientists to believe that only 5% of the cave passages have been discovered. The cave is known for its "boxwork," a honeycomb-like lattice of calcite covering its walls. There are five tours, all of which have more than 150 stairs. The **Garden of Eden Tour** is the least strenuous. (1hr., 7 per day July-Aug. 8:40am-5:30pm. Call for off-season times. $4, seniors and ages 6-15 $2.) The **Natural Entrance Tour** passes the original opening to the cave. (1¼hr., 15 per day June-Aug. 9am-6:30pm. Call for off-season times. $6, ages 6-16 $3.) The **Caving Tour** is limited to 10 people ages 16 and over. (Parental consent required for under 18. 4hr. tour at 1pm. $15, seniors $7.50. Reservations recommended.) In the afternoon, all tours fill about 1hr. ahead of time, so buy tickets early. Light your own way through the caves on the **Candlelight Tour.** (2 per day at 10:30am and 1:30pm June 7-Aug. 22, 1 per day at 1:30pm Aug. 23-Sept. 7. 2hr. $7, seniors and ages 6-16 $3.50. Reservations recommended. "Non-slip soles" on shoes required.) **Wind Cave National Park Visitors Center,** RR1, P.O. Box 190-WCNP, Hot Springs 57747 (745-4600), can provide more info. (Open June to mid-Aug. daily 8am-7:30pm; winter hrs. vary. Tours for the disabled can be arranged.) The **Elk Mountain Campground** in the park has a campground with free firewood, potable water, and restrooms (sites $10).

Jewel Cave In striking contrast to nearby Wind Cave's boxwork, the walls of this sprawling underground labyrinth (the second longest cave in the U.S.) are covered with a layer of calcite crystal—hence the name. The ½ mi. **Scenic Tour** includes 723 stairs (roughly every 20min. 8:30am-6pm; in winter call ahead; $6, ages 6-16 $3). Reservations and sturdy foot gear are needed for the 4hr. **Spelunking Tour,** limited to 10 people ages 16 and up. (Runs daily June-Aug. 12:30pm. $18; you must be able to fit through an opening only 8 in. by 2 ft.) The **visitors center** (673-2288) has more info (open daily 8am-7:30pm; mid-Oct. to mid-May 8am-4:30pm).

■ Near Wind Cave: Hot Springs

The well-heeled once flocked from the four corners to bathe in the mineral waters of quaint Hot Springs, located on scenic **U.S. 385.** Still quiet and less crowded than the rest of the Black Hills, the town's charming pink sandstone buildings and budget lodgings make it a nice stop on a tour of the southern Hills.

The Sioux and Cheyenne once fought over possession of the 87°F spring here; in 1890, a public pool was erected at the site. The waterslide at **Evan's Plunge** (745-5165), on U.S. 385, empties into the world's largest naturally heated pool (June-Aug. daily 5:30am-10pm; winter hrs. vary; $8, ages 3-12 $6; wheelchair access). **Kidney Spring,** just to the right of the waterfall near U.S. 385 and Minnekahta Ave., is rumored to have healing powers. At the **Mammoth Site** (745-6017), on the U.S. 18 bypass, three woolly mammoths and 48 Columbian mammoths fell into a sinkhole and fossilized near Hot Springs about 26,000 years ago. (*Open daily 8am-8pm. Last tour 7:15pm. Winter hrs. vary. 30min. tour $5, seniors $4.75, ages 6-12 $3.25.*)

▓ Rapid City

Rapid City's location makes it a convenient base from which to explore the Black Hills and the Badlands. Every summer, the area welcomes about 3 million tourists, over 60 times the city's permanent population. If you have a car, pick up a map of the **Rapid City Circle Tour** at the Civic Center or at any motel; the route leads you to numerous free attractions and includes a jaunt up Skyline Dr. for a bird's-eye view of the city and the seven concrete dinosaurs of **Dinosaur Park. The Journey,** 222 New York St. (394-6923), is a highly touted interactive museum housing four separate historical museums, including the **Sioux Indian Museum** and the **Pioneer Museum;** one ticket is good for all displays. (Open daily 9am-8pm; call for off-season hrs. $5, ages 7-17 $2. Free audio guide provided.) Other museums include **The Museum of Geology** (394-2467; open late May to early Sept. M-Sa 8m-6pm, Su noon-6pm; wheelchair access) and the children's **Museum in Motion** (394-2554; $2; open M-Sa 9am-4pm), both at 501 E. St. Joseph St. The **Dahl Fine Arts Center** (394-4101) stands at 7th and Quincy St. (free).

Rapid City accommodations are considerably more expensive during the summer. Make reservations; budget motels often fill up weeks in advance, especially during the first two weeks in August, when nearby Sturgis hosts its annual motorcycle rally. Skiers and winter travelers are in luck with the abundance of off-season bargains (mid-Sept. to mid-May). **Kings X Lodge,** 525 E. Omaha St. (342-2236), boasts clean rooms, cable, and free local calls (June-Aug. singles $30, doubles $39-45; less in winter). **Big Sky Motel,** 4080 Tower Rd. (348-3200 or 800-318-3208), has great views and chilly rooms (June-Sept. singles $29-39; doubles $36-42). **Robert's Roost Hostel,** 627 South St. (341-3434 or 348-7799), is a bit shabby but has the best rates in town. Two single-sex, dorm-style rooms with kitchen and laundry are available. ($15 per person, including linen and breakfast. Call ahead. No key, door kept unlocked.) **Camping** is available at **Badlands National Park** (p. 473), **Black Hills National Forest** (p. 475), and **Custer State Park** (p. 477).

Enjoy a full Scandinavian smorgasbord for breakfast ($6) or lunch ($8) at **Valhalla,** 605 Main St. (342-2538)—that means a main dish and all you can eat and drink of assorted extras (open daily 7am-2pm). **Sixth St. Bakery and Delicatessen,** 516 6th St. (342-6660), next to the $2 cinema, sells day-olds for $1 per bag. (Open M-F 6:30am-7pm, Sa 6:30am-7pm, Su 10am-4pm; in winter daily 6:30am-6pm.) **Floridino's,** 307 7th St. (342-2454), serves pizza and pasta to take out or eat in, as well as a lunch buffet ($6). The tasty calzones ($5.75), salads ($4.25-6.25), and fantastic breadsticks ($1.75) will have you hankerin' after more (open daily 11am-10pm).

Nightlife lines **Main St.** between 6th and Mt. Rushmore St. For a beer as black as the Hills, toss back a Skyjumper Stout ($3) at the **Firehouse Brewing Co.,** 610 Main St. (348-1915), *the* bar in Rapid City. Located in a restored 1915 firehouse, the company brews 12 beers in-house and serves up sandwiches, burgers, salads ($5-10, a bit pricier at dinner), and live music on summer weekends. (Open M-Th 11am-midnight, F-Sa 11am-2am, Su 4-11pm.) **Boot Hill,** 826 Main St. (343-1931), shakes with live band performances nightly for boot-stompin', knee-slappin' country-western music and dancing (cover $2 F-Sa; $4 for ladies' night on W; open Tu-Su 4pm-2am).

The main east-west roads; **St. Joseph, Kansas City,** and **Main/Business Loop 90;** are stacked next to each other. **Mt. Rushmore Rd./Rte. 16** is the main north-south route. Call 394-2255 to check on **road conditions** in extreme weather. **Jack Rabbit Lines** scurries east from the **Milo Barber Transportation Center,** 333 6th St. (348-3300), downtown, with one bus daily to Pierre (4hr., $55) and Sioux Falls (10hr., $101). **Powder River Lines,** also in the center, services Wyoming and Montana, running once per day to Billings (8hr., $55) and Cheyenne (8½hr., $65; station open M-F 8am-5pm, Sa-Su 10am-noon and 2-5pm). **Affordable Adventures** and **Grayline Tours** lead regional tours based out of Rapid City (see the **Black Hills Region,** p. 475). Take flight from **Rapid City Regional Airport** (393-9924), off Rte. 44 8½ mi. east of the city. **Rapid Ride** (394-6631) runs **buses** 6am to 6pm ($1, seniors 50¢; pick up schedule at terminal on 6th and Omaha). **Rapid Taxi** (348-8080) charges a $2.40 base fee and $1.40 per mile. Pick up a free map at the **Rapid City Chamber of Commerce and Visitors Information Center,** 444 Mt. Rushmore Rd. N., in the Civic Center (373-1744; staffed late May to early Sept. M-F 8am-5pm). The **Rape and Assault Victims Helpline** (341-2046) operates 24hr. **Gay, Lesbian, Bisexual, and Transgender Information,** 343-5577. At the **Rapidcare Health Center,** 408 Knollwood (341-6600), appointments are not necessary (open M-F 7am-8pm, Sa-Su 9am-6pm). **Post Office:** 500 East Blvd. (394-8600), several blocks east of downtown (open M-F 8am-5:30pm, Sa 8:30am-12:30pm). **ZIP code:** 57701. **Area code:** 605.

■ Spearfish, Lead, and Deadwood

Spearfish Located on the northwest edge of the Black Hills, Spearfish makes a good base for exploring more expensive Lead and Deadwood. Nearby, the lovely **Spearfish Canyon Scenic Byway** (U.S. 14A) winds through 18 mi. of forest along Spearfish Creek, passing one of the sites where *Dances with Wolves* was filmed (marked by a small sign 2 mi. west of U.S. 14A on Rte. 222).

The **Spearfish Ranger Station,** 2014 N. Main St. (642-4622), has free maps and hiking advice. (Open M-F 8am-5pm, Sa 8:30am-4:30pm; in winter closed Sa; foyer with maps and info open 24hr.) The **Chamber of Commerce,** 106 W. Kansas St. (642-2626 or 800-626-8013), stands at the corner of Kansas and Main (open M-F 8am-7pm, Sa 9am-3pm, Su noon-7pm; in winter M-F 8am-5pm). The **Canyon Gateway Hotel** (642-3402 or 800-281-3402), south of town on U.S. 14A, offers cozy rooms in a pleasant setting (no phones; singles $36; doubles $41). The weary traveler can always ring in at **Bell's Motor Lodge** (642-3812), on Main St. at the east edge of town, with free local calls, TV, and a pool (singles $36, doubles $48; open May-Sept.). Four miles west of U.S. 14A on Rte. 222 are two spectacular national forest campgrounds among the pine and next to a rushing creek: **Rod and Gun Campground** (sites $5) and **Timon Campground** (sites $8). Both have pit toilets and potable water. The vaguely Mediterranean **Bay Leaf Café,** 126 W. Hudson (642-5462), right off Main St., serves salads, sandwiches, and veggie dishes. ($3-12. Piano music F-Sa from 8pm. Open daily 11am-9pm; Sept.-May M 11am-4pm, Tu-Sa 11am-8pm.) The daily lunch buffet (11:30am-1:30pm) with pizza, pasta, and salad goes for $4.49 at the **Pizza Ranch,** 715 Main St. (642-4422; open Su-Th 11am-10pm, F-Sa 11am-11pm). At night, an all-you-can-eat dinner buffet is $6 at **Valley Café,** 608 Main St. (642-2423). There's also a $5 breakfast buffet when the sun comes back up. **ZIP code: 57783. Area code: 605.**

Lead Lead (rhymes with heed, not head) is actually named for the ore veins that marked the path to gold in the mines of this town. The **Black Hills Mining Museum,** 323 W. Main St. (584-1605), unearthed an interesting look at the impact of mining and the lives of the men who did the difficult and dangerous work here. (Museum open mid-May to Sept. daily 9am-5pm. $4.25, students and seniors $3.25.) They offer a simulated underground tour, and, for $4.25, a chance to **pan for gold.** The **Open Cut** invites indignation or silent awe; it's a giant hole in the earth created by the **Homestake Mining Company,** 160 W. Main St. (584-3110). Miles below, tiny toy trucks labor up the sides of the mine. The company screens a free video and leads surface tours. (1hr. hard-hat tours leave every 30min. until 4:30pm. $4.25, students $3.25, seniors $3.75. Open M-F 8am-5pm, Sa-Su 10am-5pm; Sept.-May M-F 8am-5pm.) The **Ponderosa Mountain Lodge** (584-3321), on U.S. 14A between Lead and Deadwood, offers a variety of cabins nestled among the pines, stocked with TVs and fridges (no phones; from $40-65 depending on season and size). **Hanna Campground** offers 13 lovely sites about 9 mi. from town off U.S. 85, just south of the junction with 14A at Cheyenne Crossing (pit toilets and water; sites $8). Low-priced sandwiches ($4.50-7) are served up at the **Stamphill Saloon,** 305 W. Main St. (open M-Tu 11am-9pm, F-Sa 7am-10pm, Su 7am-9pm).

Wintertime in the Black Hills provides fine skiing opportunities: **Terry Peak Ski Area** (584-2165 or 342-7609) and **Deer Mountain** (584-3230) are both west of Lead off U.S. 85. **Area code: 605.**

Deadwood Continue along Main St. from Lead for 3 mi., and you'll find yourself in Deadwood. Gunslingers **Wild Bill Hickock** and **Calamity Jane** sauntered into town during the height of the Gold Rush. Bill stayed just long enough—2 months—to spend eternity here. They lie side-by-side in the **Mt. Moriah Cemetery** ($1, ages 6-12 50¢). Deadwood is home to **Saloon #10,** 657 Main St. (578-3346), where legend has it that Hickock was shot holding black aces and eights, the infamous "dead man's hand." Every summer, Bill has more lives than 60 cats; the shooting is morbidly re-enacted on location four times per day. The main attraction in Deadwood is **gambling,** with casinos lining **Main St.** At the **Buffalo Saloon,** 658 Main St. (578-9993), there's live music outside the Stockade (Su-Th 2-8pm, F-Sa 2-8pm and 9pm-1:30am). **Free parking** awaits on the north side of town; take the 50¢ trolley into town or walk 3 blocks. The **Penny Motel,** 818 Upper Main St. (578-1842), exaggerates a bit—it'll cost you a few thousand pennies to stay there, but in Deadwood that's one of the best deals goin' (singles $29-49, doubles $34-56; look for hemp clothes lobby shop). By 1999, there should be a newly opened **hostel** in town ($12; kitchen access, eating area, and library). The **Whistler Gulch Campground** (578-2042 or 800-704-7139), off U.S. 85, has a pool, laundry facilities, and showers (tent sites $14, full hookup $25). Food in Deadwood varies month to month as casinos try new hooks—the best deals are the ones advertised on the windows.

The **Deadwood History and Information Center,** 13 Siever St., will help you find your way (open in summer daily 8am-8pm). Though Deadwood has the flavor of an old western town, technology hasn't bypassed it altogether; there's **Internet access** at **Biff Malibu's,** 670 Main St. (578-1919; $3 per 30min.; open daily 8am until the music ends). **Area code:** 605.

Iowa

"Boring" Iowa is known for little other than farming and corn, though Iowa Hawk-eyes prefer the word "quiet." It's a fine distinction, but you'll have to get off I-80 to understand it. Along old country roads, you can find fields of dreams, bridges of Madison County, barns of childhood fantasies, and the scenic Loess Hills in the west—created by wind-blown quartz silt, these hills are a geological rarity found only in Iowa and China. Iowa preserves its European heritage in the small towns that keep German, Dutch, and Swedish traditions alive. Of course, Iowa's farming reputation can't be ignored. Iowa contains a fourth of all U.S. Grade A farmland, and the familiar dour-faced farmers of *American Gothic* were painted by native son Grant Wood.

PRACTICAL INFORMATION

Capital: Des Moines.
Visitor Info: Iowa Dept. of Economic Development, 200 E. Grand Ave., Des Moines 50309 (515-242-4705 or 800-345-4692; http://www.state.ia.us/tourism).
Emergency: 911.
Time Zone: Central (1hr. behind Eastern). **Postal Abbreviation:** IA.
Sales Tax: 5%.

■ Des Moines

French explorers originally named the Des Moines river the "Rivière des Moingoue-nas," for a local Native American tribe, but then shortened the name to "Rivière des Moings." Because of its identical pronunciation (mwan), later French settlers mistakenly called the river and city by a name much more familiar to them: Des Moines (of the monks). Today, Des Moines (da moyne) shows neither Native American nor monastic influence, but rather the imprint of the agricultural trade that spawned it. The World Pork Expo is a red-letter event on the Iowan calendar, and the city goes hog-wild for the Iowa State Fair every August. Des Moines also boasts a great art museum and countless local festivals.

ORIENTATION AND PRACTICAL INFORMATION

Des Moines idles at the junction of I-35 and I-80. Numbered streets run north-south, named streets east-west. Numbering begins downtown at the **Des Moines River** and increases as you move east or west; **Grand Ave.** divides addresses north-south. Other east-west thoroughfares are **Locust St.,** and moving north, **University Ave.** (home to Drake University), **Hickman Rd.,** and **Euclid/Douglas Ave.** Most downtown buildings are connected by the **Skywalk,** a series of passages above the street, so many Des

Moines businesspeople never have to go outdoors—except to smoke. Note: Des Moines and West Des Moines are different places, and the numbered streets within each are not the same.

Airport: Des Moines International (256-5195), Fleur Dr. at Army Post Rd., 5 mi. southwest of downtown; take bus #8 "Havens" M-F. Taxi to downtown $18-20.

Buses: Greyhound, 1107 Keosauqua Way (243-1773 or 800-231-2222), at 12th St., just northwest of downtown; take bus #4 "Urbandale." To: Iowa City (2hr., 6 per day, $21-23); Omaha (2hr., 6 per day, $22-24); and St. Louis (10hr.; 3 per day; $64-68, with a long layover, $39). Station open 24hr.

Public Transportation: Metropolitan Transit Authority (MTA), 1100 MTA Lane (283-8100), just south of the 9th St. viaduct. Open M-F 8am-5pm. Buses run M-Sa approximately 6am-6pm. Fare $1, seniors (except M-F 3-6pm) and disabled persons 50¢; transfers 10¢. Routes converge at 6th and Walnut St. Pick up maps at the MTA office or any Dahl's or Hy-Vee.

Taxis: Yellow Cab, (243-1111). $1.70 base, $1.40 per mi. 50¢ surcharge 10pm-4am.

Car Rental: Budget (287-2612), at the airport. Th-M $27 per day, Tu-W from $36.90 with 150 free mi. per day, 25¢ per additional mi. Must be 21 with major credit card. Under 25 $10 per day surcharge. Open M-F 6am-1am, Sa-Su 6am-midnight.

Visitor Info: Greater Des Moines Convention and Visitors Bureau, 2 Ruan Ctr., suite 222 (286-4960 or 800-451-2625), at 6th and Locust in the Skywalk. Open M-F 8:30am-5pm. Downstairs is the **Chamber of Commerce** (286-4950). Open M-F 8am-5pm.

Hotlines: Rape Hotline, 286-3535. 24hr. **Suicide Hotline,** 244-1010. Operates M-F 3pm-8am. **Red Cross Crisis Line,** 244-1000. 24hr. on weekends. **Gay and Lesbian Resource Center,** 414 E. 15th St. (281-0634). Open M-F 7-10pm.

Internet Access: Kinko's, 401 Grand Ave. (282-5955). $12 per hr., 20¢ per min. IBM and Macintosh. Open 24hr.

Post Office: 1165 2nd Ave. (283-7505), downtown just north of I-235. Open M-F 7:30am-5:30pm. **ZIP code:** 50318. **Area code:** 515.

ACCOMMODATIONS AND CAMPGROUNDS

Finding cheap accommodations in Des Moines is usually no problem, though you should make reservations at least 1 month in advance for visits in August, when the State Fair comes to town, and during the high school sports tournament season in March. Beware the hotel tax (7%) that could add over $5 to your bill. Several cheap motels dust **I-80** and **Merle Hay Rd.,** 5 mi. northwest of downtown. Take bus #4 "Urbandale" or #6 "West 9th" from downtown.

The Carter House Inn, 640 20th St. (288-7850), at Woodland St. in historic Sherman Hill. 10 years ago, this great old Victorian house was moved 6 blocks from its original site and placed here, where the Nelsons have converted it into a beautifully furnished B&B. Emphasis on the breakfast—you'll eat well in the morning. $50-65. Student discounts can be arranged.

Hickman Motor Lodge, 6500 Hickman Rd. (276-8591), boasts scrupulously clean rooms. Free local calls and cable TV. Hop on bus #4 "Urbandale." Singles $36; doubles $43.

Motel 6, 4817 Fleur Dr. (287-6364), at the airport, 5min. south of downtown. Take bus #8, which only runs on weekdays. Newly renovated rooms with free local calls. Singles $37; doubles $43. 2 wheelchair-accessible rooms.

Iowa State Fairgrounds Campgrounds, E. 30th St. (262-3111 or 800-545-3247; fax 262-6906), at Grand Ave. Take bus #1 "Fairgrounds" to the Grand Ave. gate and follow Grand Ave. straight east through the park. No fires. Basic sites with water, electricity, and sewage $12, full hookup $15. Fee collected in the morning. Rates go up at fair time in August; call 262-3111 to make reservations during this time. Call early; the place books well in advance. Open mid-Apr. to mid-Oct until 10pm.

FOOD

Good eating places tend to congregate on **Court Ave.** downtown, or in antique-filled **Historic Valley Jct.** in West Des Moines, on 5th St. south of Grand Ave. The supermarkets **Dahl's** and **Hy-Vee** are sprinkled throughout the city and have cafeterias that serve hot meals for under $3. Hy-Vee offers an all-you-can-eat salad bar ($5). A breakfast buffet ($5) is served at some locations on weekends.

◉**The Tavern,** 205 5th St. (255-9827), in Historic Valley Junction, has the best pizza around—everyone knows it, so you'll have to wait your turn. Pizzas with toppings from "bacon cheeseburger" to "taco fiesta" ($7-16). A large selection of pasta and vegetarian dishes. Open M-Th 11am-11pm, F-Sa 11am-midnight, Su noon-11pm.

Stella's Blue Sky Diner, 400 Locust St. (246-1953), at the Skywalk level in the Capital Sq. Mall. Settle into a 50s-style vinyl chair for meatloaf or burgers. Should you order neutron fries ($2) and a malt ($2.50), ask for the malt "Stella's way"—poured into a glass above your head. Open M-F 6:30am-6pm, Sa 8am-6pm. Also at 3281 100 St. in Urbandale (278-0550); open M-F 6:30am-6pm, Sa-Su 8am-6pm.

Billy Joe's Pitcher Show, 1701 25th (224-1709), off University Ave. in West Des Moines. A combo smoke-filled restaurant and movie theater. Waitresses serve beer (pitchers $6) and assorted grub ($4-10) while you watch the flick ($3). $2 matinees; $1 on M, with student ID only; on Su 4-5 shows per day, 12:30-9pm; experience the *Rocky Horror Picture Show* at midnight on F. Call for exact times.

The Iowa Machine Shed, 11151 Hickman Rd. (270-6818), in Urbandale. Dedicated to Iowa's agricultural heritage, the Machine Shed is said to crack 3600 eggs every week and serves up gigantic, home-baked sweet rolls. The overall-clad waitstaff serves breakfast ($3.50-7), sandwiches ($4-5), and cow- and pig-derived entrees ($8-17). Open M-Sa 6am-10pm, Su 7am-9pm.

SIGHTS

The most elaborate of its ilk but currently undergoing heavy renovations, the copper-and-gold-domed **state capitol** (281-5591), on E. 9th St. across the river and up Locust Ave., provides a spectacular view of Des Moines from its lofty hilltop position. *(Open M-F 8am-5pm, Sa-Su 8am-4pm. Free tours M-Sa 10am-3pm; call for exact times.)* Inside, an 18 ft. long scale model of the battleship *U.S.S. Iowa* graces the lobby; take bus #5 "E. 6th and 9th St.," #1 "Fairgrounds," #4 "E. 14th," or #7 "Walker." Farther downhill, the modern **Iowa State Historical Museum and Archives,** 600 E. Locust (281-5111), houses displays on Iowa's natural, industrial, and social history. *(Open M-Sa 9am-4:30pm, Su noon-4:30pm.; Sept.-May closed M. Free.)* Take any bus that goes to the capitol. The geodesic greenhouse dome of the **Botanical Center,** 909 E. River Dr. (242-2934), just north of I-235 and the capitol, encompasses a desert, rainforest, and bonsai exhibit. *(Open M-Th 10am-6pm, F 10am-9pm, Sa-Su 10am-5pm. $1.50, students 50¢, seniors 75¢, under 6 free.)*

Most cultural sights cluster west of downtown on Grand Ave. The **Des Moines Art Center,** 4700 Grand Ave. (277-4405), draws raves for its modern art collection as well as for its architecture; Eero Saarinen, I. M. Pei, and Richard Meier contributed to the design of the museum. *(Open M-W and F-Sa 11am-4pm, Th and 1st F of the month 11am-9pm, Su noon-4pm. $4, students and seniors $2; free until 1pm and all day Th.)* Take bus #1 "West Des Moines." Only a few blocks south of the Art Center on 45th St., the **Science Center of Iowa,** 4500 Grand Ave. (274-6868), dazzles with simulated Space Shuttle flights, laser shows, and computer-generated planetarium spectacles (open M-Sa 10am-5pm, Su noon-5pm; $5.50, seniors $4.50, ages 3-12 $3.50).

ENTERTAINMENT AND NIGHTLIFE

The **Civic Center,** 221 Walnut St. (243-1109), sponsors theater and concerts; call for info. *Cityview,* a free local weekly paper, lists free events and is available at most supermarkets. On Thursdays, a copy of the *Des Moines Register* will provide you with the *Datebook,* a helpful listing of concerts, sporting events, and movies. The **Iowa State Fair,** one of the nation's largest, captivates Des Moines for 10 days in mid-August (Aug. 12-22, 1999) with prize cows, crafts, cakes, and corn ($6 per day, children $2; lower if purchased in advance). For the low-down, write to the **State House,** 400 E. 14th St., Des Moines 50319-0198, or call the state fair hotline (800-545-FAIR/3247 or 262-3111). Tickets for **Iowa Cubs** baseball games are a steal. Chicago's farm team plays at **Sec. Taylor Stadium,** 350 SW 1st St. (243-6111). Call for game dates and times. (General admission $5, children $3;

GREAT PLAINS

reserved grandstand $5-7.) From late April to late July, Des Moines flips over for
Seniom Sed (282-2022), a city-wide block party held Fridays 5-7:15pm at Nollen
Plaza downtown ($5, with 3 beverage tickets included). **Jazz in July** (280-3222)
presents free concerts at locations throughout the city nearly every day of the
month; pick up a schedule at area restaurants, concert sites, or the visitors
bureau. **Pella,** 41 mi. east of Des Moines on Rte. 163, blooms in May with its
annual **Tulip Time** festival (628-4311; May 6-8, 1999), with traditional Dutch
dancing, a parade, concerts, and *glöckenspiel* performances.

Court Ave., in the southeast corner of downtown, is a yuppified warehouse district packed with trendy restaurants and bars. At **Papa's Planet,** 208 3rd St. (284-
0901), 20- and 30-somethings move to 80s and 90s dance music on two dance floors
and play pool on the patio outside. (21+. Live music F-Sa 25¢ beers on Th with $5
cover; cover $3-5 F-Sa; includes drink specials. Open Th-Sa 7pm-2am.) **Java Joe's,** 214
4th St. (288-5282), a mellow coffeehouse, sells sandwiches ($4) and coffee from
locales like Kenya and Sumatra ($1-2.75). Live music specialties from Tuesday to Sun-
day include folk, Irish Jam, and jazz. (Cover on rare occasions. Open M-Th 7:30am-
11pm, F-Sa 7:30am-1am, Su 9am-11pm.) **The Garden,** 112 SE 4th St. (243-3965), is an
alternative dance bar. (Primarily gay and lesbian. Drag shows Sa 11pm, with "the big
production" Su 10pm. Cover $3, special events $4. Open W-Su 8pm-2am.)

■ Near Des Moines

In **Indianola,** 12 mi. south on U.S. 69, the **National Balloon Museum,** 1601 N. Jefferson (961-3714), holds the annual **National Balloon Classic** in late July for hot-air balloons. *(Museum open M-Sa 9am-4pm, Su 1-4pm. Free. Call to arrange a tour; $1, children 50¢.)*
Ten miles northwest of downtown in Urbandale, **Living History Farms,** 2600 NW
11th St. (278-5286), at Hickman Rd. and 111th St., is a 600-acre open-air museum
with five working farms depicting time periods from 1700 to the present (last tour
3pm; open May to mid-Oct. daily 9am-5pm; $8, seniors $7, ages 4-12 $5).

Twenty miles south of Des Moines is the town of **Winterset,** where John Wayne,
the toughest of American film cowboys, began his life in 1907. Fans can visit Wayne's
birthplace just outside of downtown at 216 S. 2nd St., where the star was christened
Marion Robert Morrison (now there's a name that'll make you tough). The house has
been converted into a museum, the **John Wayne Birthplace** (462-1044), with two
rooms of memorabilia and two rooms authentically furnished in the style of the
Duke's parents' era (open daily 10am-4:30pm; $2.50, seniors $2.25, children $1).

Those craving a winter diversion can head to **Fun Valley Ski Area** (623-3456; snow
report 800-352-0746) in **Montezuma,** 15 mi. south off I-80 and halfway between Des
Moines and Iowa City. Go through town until you see their sign. In winter, Fun Valley
sports five lifts and 13 lighted trails for skiers and snowboarders of all ages and abilities. *(Open mid-Dec. to mid-Mar. M-F $10, Sa-Su and holidays $16; children $6. Rentals $6-10,
children $4. Tubing is an option as well.)*

> ## "Christ, we're in love..."
>
> Winterset happens to be the setting for Robert Kincaid and Francesca Johnson's
> transcendent four-day love affair in the best-selling *Bridges of Madison County.*
> Robert Waller's romantic novel of adultery between an Iowa farm wife and an
> itinerant *National Geographic* photographer was decried by the literary estab-
> lishment, but it sold millions of copies across the world. Lines such as, "We have
> both lost ourselves and created something else, something that exists only as an
> interlacing of the two of us. Christ, we're in love," left critics aghast and readers
> enthralled. The book was recently made into a film starring Clint Eastwood and
> Meryl Streep, and the movie site is now open for tours (open May-Oct. daily
> 10am-6pm; $5, seniors $4, children $3, car tour $4). Take U.S. 35 South from
> Des Moines, exit at Cummings/Norwalk, and turn right. Follow the signs reading
> "Francesca's House." The bridges themselves charge no admission fee and are
> located 20 mi. beyond.

■ Spirit Lake and Okoboji

Not to be outdone by its neighbors, Iowa, too, has its Great Lakes: Spirit Lake, West Okoboji Lake, and East Okoboji Lake, a popular vacation destination gleaming in Iowa's northwest. West Okoboji Lake ranks with Switzerland's Lake Geneva and Canada's Lake Louise as one of the world's three blue-water lakes. Its startlingly clear water renders the sandy bottom visible at great depth. Although upscale resorts have staked out prime lakeside territory, an abundance of campgrounds and state parks welcome the budget traveler.

One block west of the amusement park (see below) is **Abbie Gardner Log Cabin** (332-7248), a museum and monument on the site of the Spirit Lake Massacre. (Open late May to Oct. M-F noon-4pm, Sa-Su 9am-4pm. Free, but donation suggested.) The massacre followed a dispute between encroaching settlers and members of the Sioux in March 1857. It's hard to miss the amusement park (332-2183 or 800-599-6995) in **Arnold's Park,** off Rte. 71, with a roller coaster, kiddie rides, and ice cream shops. (Hrs. vary. $14 with rides, children 3-4 ft. tall $10, under 3 ft. free; $5 without rides.) The park's **Roof Garden** plays open air concerts (call for info). You can hike, in-line skate, or bike **The Spine,** a 14½ mi. trail that runs through the area; bike rental ($10 per day) is available at **Allan's Hardware** (332-7131), next to the tourist office. The **Okoboji Summer Theater** (332-7773) presents productions for children and grown-ups ($12, children $6).

Budget accommodations in the immediate lake area are as scarce as snowballs in hell—especially in summer, when prices rise. To stay indoors for cheap, head 22 mi. east to **Jackson, MN** where budget hotels cluster off **I-90. The Northland Inn** (336-1450), at the convergence of Rte. 9 and Rte. 86 just north of West Okoboji Lake, offers wood-paneled rooms and a continental breakfast. (May-Sept., 1 bed for 1-2 people $37.50, 2 beds for up to 4 people $47.50; Oct.-Apr., 1 bed $22.50-27.50, 2 beds 32.50.) Pitch your tent year-round at **Marble Beach Campground** (336-4437, in winter 337-3211) in the state park on the shores of Spirit Lake (sites $9, full hookup $12). Other parks with camping and public beaches include **Emerson Bay** and **Gull's Point,** both off Rte. 86 on West Okoboji Lake (both $9, with electricity $12). The **Koffee Kup Kafé** (332-7657), off U.S. 71 in Arnold's Park, is a kozy place with kountry kooking. Try the delicious pancakes ($1-3), or order a sandwich ($5). Breakfast is served all day. (Open daily 6am-2pm.) At **Funky Java** (332-9020), up the hill from the amusement park, you can grab a cup of Joe in the evening and take in live entertainment on a comfortable couch. (Open M and W-Th 9am-11pm, Tu 9am-midnight, Sa 8am-midnight, Su 8am-11pm.) **Tweeter's** (332-9421), off U.S. 71 in Okoboji, is a local lunch favorite that grills burgers ($5), tosses salads, and melts sandwiches (open 11am-midnight, in winter 11am-11pm; bar open 10pm-2am).

A handful of towns are scattered around the lakes, and several highways criss-cross the area. U.S. 71 runs between West and East Okoboji Lakes, through Okoboji and Arnold's Park. Rte. 86 skirts the side of West Okoboji Lake, and Rte. 276 circles Spirit Lake. The **Iowa Great Lakes Chamber of Commerce** (322-2107 or 800-839-9987), in Lake Center Mall, overflows with info about the area. Follow U.S. 71 through Okoboji into Arnold's Park (open M-F 8:30am-5pm, Sa-Su 10am-2pm; off-season M-F 8:30am-5pm). **Area code:** 712.

■ Iowa City

The staid capital of Iowa until 1857, Iowa City is now a classic college town and an oasis of liberalism in a conservative state. The main University of Iowa campus fills the city with a plethora of student-filled bars, frozen yogurt stands, and street musicians. Every other autumn weekend, hordes of Iowans make a pilgrimage to the city to cheer on the university's football team, the Hawkeyes. Iowa City's carefully tempered vibrancy—this is Iowa, after all—promises a spell of welcome relief from the compulsive fury of big city life.

PRACTICAL INFORMATION Iowa City lies on I-80 about 112 mi. east of Des Moines. North-south **Madison** and **Gilbert St.** and east-west **Market** and **Burlington St.** bind the downtown. **Greyhound** and **Burlington Trailways** are both located at 404 E. College St. (337-2127 or 800-231-2222; station open M-F 8am-8pm, Sa-Su 10am-8pm), at Gilbert St. Buses head out for Des Moines (2-4hr., 7 per day, $23); Chicago (4½-6½hr., 8 per day, $36); and St. Louis (9-13hr., 2 per day, $41-53). The free **Cambus** runs daily all over campus and downtown. Alternatively, the buses of **Iowa City Transit** (356-5151) run downtown (M-F 6:30am-10:30pm and Sa 6:30am-7pm; fare 75¢, seniors with pass 35¢). The **convention and visitors bureau,** 408 1st Ave. (337-6592 or 800-283-6592), sits across the river in Coralville off U.S. 6 (open M-F 8am-5pm, Sa-Su 10am-4pm). More area info is available at the University of Iowa's **Campus Information Center** (335-3055), in the **Iowa Memorial Union** at Madison and Jefferson St. (Open M-F 8am-8pm, Sa 10am-8pm, Su noon-4pm; reduced hrs. in summer and interims.) **Hotlines** include the 24hr. **Crisis Line** (351-0140), **Sexual Abuse Resource Line** (335-6000), and the **University of Iowa Gay, Lesbian, Bisexual and Transgender Union** (335-3251). **Internet access** is available at the Iowa City Public Library, 123 S. Linn St. (356-5200), free of charge with photo ID (open M-Th 10am-9pm, F-Sa 10am-6pm, Su 1-5pm). **Post Office:** 400 S. Clinton St. (354-1560; open M-F 8:30am-5pm, Sa 9:30am-1pm). **ZIP code:** 52240. **Area code:** 319.

ACCOMMODATIONS, CAMPGROUNDS, AND FOOD Cheap motels line U.S. 6 in **Coralville,** 2 mi. west of downtown, and **1st Ave.** at Exit 242 off I-80. Clean, refurbished rooms await sleepy souls at **Motel 6,** 810 1st Ave. (354-0030 or 800-466-8356), off U.S. 6 (singles $37; doubles $43). The **Wesley House Hostel,** 120 N. Dubuque St. (338-1179), at Jefferson right in town, has two small, nondescript seven-bed rooms with kitchen and lounge access, but an all-day lockout ($12; check-in 7-9pm; checkout M-Sa 9am, Su 8am). **Kent Park Campgrounds** (645-2315), 9 mi. west on U.S. 6, manages 86 secluded first come, first served sites pleasantly huddled near a lake ($4, with electricity $8).

Downtown boasts cheerful, moderately priced restaurants and bars. At the open-air **Pedestrian Mall,** on College and Dubuque St., the melodies of street musicians drift through the eateries and shops. In the mall, the agreeably decked-out **Gringo's,** 115 E. College St. (338-3000), slaps down tasty Mexican dishes, including vegetarian tacos ($5-10). The all-you-can-eat taco bar (5-9pm, $5) fills bellies on Tuesdays. (Open M-Th 11am-10pm, F-Sa 11am-11pm, Su noon-10pm.) A college favorite, **Micky's Irish Pub,** 11 S. Dubuque St. (338-6860), whips up salads, "mickwiches," and $5-7 burgers (open M-F 11am-10pm, Sa-Su 8am-10pm; bar open later). At **The Java House,** 211½ E. Washington St. (341-0012), sip coffee ($1.30) on a cushy red chair or recline on the couch with latte ($2), and read from their assortment of papers and magazines. (Open M-Th 7am-12:30am, F-Sa 7am-1am, Su 8am-midnight; may close earlier in summer.) On Wednesday nights (5:30-7:30pm) and Saturday mornings (7:30-11:30am), the **Iowa City Farmers Market** (356-5110) takes place from May to August at the Swan Parking Ramp (Gilbert and Washington St.) downtown.

SIGHTS, ENTERTAINMENT, AND NIGHTLIFE Iowa City's main attraction, the **Old Capitol** building (335-0548), between Clinton and Madison St., has been beautifully restored by the university (open M-Sa 10am-3pm, Su noon-4pm; free; wheelchair access). The capitol is the focal point of the **Pentacrest,** a five-building formation surrounded by lawns: a perfect place to picnic or soak up rays. One of the five buildings, the **Museum of Natural History** (335-0480), at Jefferson and Clinton St., displays stellar dioramas on the Native Americans of Iowa (open M-Sa 9:30am-4:30pm, Su 12:30-4:30pm; free; wheelchair access). On the other side of the river is the **University of Iowa Museum of Art,** 150 N. Riverside Dr. (335-1727), where the fine Stanley African art collection is on display (open Tu-Sa 10am-5pm, Su noon-5pm; free). In West Branch, 10min. northeast of the city on the Herbert Hoover Hwy., lies the 31st president's birthplace, now known as the **Herbert Hoover National Historic Site** (643-2541). The vintage American town chronicles this fascinating man's life with his birthplace cottage, the presidential library/museum and gravesite (open daily 9am-5pm; $2, seniors $1, under 16 free; wheelchair access).

Bars and nightspots are plentiful downtown. **Deadwood,** 6 S. Dubuque St. (351-9417), is often lauded as the city's best bar. For live music six nights a week, shoot to **Gunnerz,** 123 E. Washington St. (338-2010), or **Gabe's,** 330 E. Washington St. (354-4788; cover $2-6). Local jazz, folk, and blues musicians play Thursday through Saturday at 9:30pm in **The Sanctuary,** 405 S. Gilbert St. (351-5692), a cozy, wood-paneled restaurant and bar with 120 beers and great pizzas for $9 (cover $1-4; open M-Sa 4pm-2am, Su 6pm-2am). **The Union Bar,** 121 E. College St. (339-7713), brags that it's the "biggest damn bar in college football's 'Big Ten'" (cover varies; open Tu-Sa 8pm-2am). From May to August in the Pedestrian Plaza downtown, the **Friday Night Concert Series** (354-0683; 5-9pm) features everything from jazz to salsa to blues.

■ Amana Colonies

Facing persecution at home, fundamentalist founders of the Community of True Inspiration fled Germany for the U.S. in 1842, settling near Buffalo, NY. Later, the growing community migrated again—this time to the rich lands along the Iowa River. They named their quiet, communal settlement the Amana Colonies (*amana* means "to remain true"). Even today, many of the townspeople still know and use German. Although at times tourists overrun the Colonies, the colonists' faith-driven descendents still run most of the stores.

The **Amana Heritage Society** (622-3567) operates four local museums located throughout the colonies: the **Museum of Amana History,** the **Communal Kitchen and Cooper Shop Museum,** the **Communal Agriculture Museum,** and the **Community Church.** A combination ticket for all four is $4 (ages 8-17 $1) and can be purchased at any of the sites. The **Museum of Amana History** (622-3567), on 220th Trail in Main Amana, illuminates the colonists' austere lifestyle with restored buildings and a super-cool slide show (open mid-Apr. to mid-Nov. M-Sa 10am-5pm, Su noon-5pm). **The South Amana Barn Museum** (622-3058), in South Amana on 220th Trail, features **Mini Americana,** a quirky exhibit of rural history. (Open Apr.-Oct. daily 9am-5pm. $3, seniors $2.75, grades 7-12 $1.50, grades K-6 75¢. Wheelchair access.) The **High Amana Store,** 1308 G St. (622-3797), hasn't altered its interior or friendliness policy since 1857 (usually open daily 10am-4pm; shorter hrs. in winter). The Amana Colonies are also home to many fine wineries. Visitors may sample dandelion wine at the **Heritage Wine and Cheese Haus** (622-3564), in Main Amana (open M-Sa 9am-7pm, Su 9am-6pm; winter hrs. vary). At **Ehrle Bros.** (622-3241), in Homestead, you can venture into the wine cellar between sips (open M-Sa 9am-5pm, Su 11am-5pm; winter hrs. vary). Where U.S. 6 and 151 converge near the colony entrance lies the **Amana Colonies Nature Trail,** where visitors can hike, cross-country ski, and view Native American mounds and fish weirs.

Most lodging options here are pricey but personal B&Bs ($40-75); call from the visitors center. At the **Guest House Motor Inn** (622-3599), on 47th Ave. in "downtown" Main Amana, 12 of the 38 rooms in this charming 135-year-old communal house are furnished with impressive quilts (singles $43; doubles $49, with 2 beds $56; wheelchair access). **Sudbury Court Motel** (642-5411), 5 mi. west of the Colonies on U.S. 6 at M St. in Marengo, offers large, cheap rooms in a quiet locale (singles $27; doubles $32, with 2 beds $37). Camp at the **Amana Colonies RV Park,** 39 38th Ave. (622-7616), across from the visitors center. ($8, with electricity $10, full hookup $16. Laundromat and showers. Check-in 8pm. Check-out noon. Open mid-Apr. to Nov.)

Restaurants throughout the Colonies serve heaping portions of family fare. **Bill Zuber's Dugout** (622-3911 or 800-522-8883), in Homestead just off U.S. 6, pays tribute to a home-grown ball player who pitched for the New York Yankees in the 40s. The beef burger for lunch ($4.25) and oven-baked steak for dinner ($9) are solid hits. (Open M-Sa 11am-2pm and 4:30-8pm, Su 11am-7:30pm.) Middle Amana's **Hahn's Hearth Oven Bakery** (622-3439), at 25th and J St., sells the scrumptious products of the Colonies' only functional open-hearth oven. (Open Apr.-Oct. Tu-F 8:30am, Sa 8am until sold out; Nov.-Dec. and Mar. W and Sa only.)

The Amana Colonies lie 5 mi. north of I-80, clustered around the intersection of U.S. 6, Rte. 220, and U.S. 151. The main thoroughfare, the **Amana Trail,** runs off U.S.

GREAT PLAINS

151 and slices through all seven villages; signs off this road point to the main attractions. **Main Amana** is the largest, most touristy town; farther out, the smaller villages offer a taste of earlier times. There is no public transportation in the Colonies. The **Amana Colonies Visitors Center** (800-245-5465), just west of Amana on Rte. 220, provides free calls to area motels and B&Bs (open M-Sa 9am-5pm, Su 10am-5pm; call for winter hrs.). A private car **caravan tour** (622-3532), covering six villages, begins from the visitors center every Saturday at 10am (3hr., $8). Throughout the Colonies, look for the helpful *Guide Map.* **Area code:** 319.

Field of Dreams

Movie buffs and baseball fanatics alike may want to go the distance to the **Field of Dreams** (800-443-8981) in Dyersville, where the movie *Field of Dreams* was shot. *(Open Apr.-Nov. Free.)* In the film, mysterious voices direct a farmer (played by Kevin Costner) to build a baseball field amidst Iowa's acres of corn. In doing so, the farmer is able to exorcise his demons. The folks there will provide you with bats, balls, and gloves at no cost so you can try to hit one into the stands, er, stalks. Dyersville is about 25 mi. west of Dubuque in northeast Iowa. Take Rte. 20 west from Dubuque to Rte 136 N; go right after the railroad tracks for 3 mi.

Nebraska

Early travelers on the Oregon and Mormon trails rushed through Nebraska on their way towards western greenery and gold. Accustomed to the forested hills of New England, these pioneers nicknamed the Nebraska Territory the "Great American Desert," mistakenly believing that if trees did not grow here, neither would crops. Eventually they caught on, and began to abandon their westward journeys to farm the fertile Nebraskan soil. Their settlements drove out the native tribes of Sioux and Pawnee, who had long understood the value of Nebraska's prairies. But neither these property-minded settlements, which have since grown into cities, nor the tourists who drive past Scotts Bluff in air-conditioned autos, can truly master these vast plains. "We come and go, but the land is always here," philosophized Willa Cather, "and the people who love it and understand it are the people who own it—for a little while."

PRACTICAL INFORMATION

Capital: Lincoln.
Visitor Info: Nebraska Tourism Office, P.O. Box 94666, Lincoln 68509 (402-471-3796 or 800-228-4307; http://www.visitnebraska.org). Open M-F 8am-5pm. **Nebraska Game and Parks Commission,** 2200 N. 33rd St., Lincoln 68503 (402-471-0641). Open M-F 8am-5pm.
Emergency: 911.
State Soft Drink: Kool-Aid
Time Zone: Mostly Central (1hr. behind Eastern). Scott's Bluff and Alliance Mountain are in Mountain Time Zone. **Postal Abbreviation:** NE.
Sales Tax: 5-6.5%, depending on city.

■ Omaha

Omaha may not be the type of place one associates with the prairies and cornfields of Nebraska. The largest city in the state, this birthplace of Gerald Ford, Malcolm X, and Boys Town is also the most urban. From the quiet streetside cafes of the Old Market to the jumping gay clubs at 16th and Leavenworth, Omaha combines cosmopolitan airs with Midwestern manners, offering world-class museums and fascinating attractions alongside the native friendliness and easy living of a small Nebraska town.

ORIENTATION AND PRACTICAL INFORMATION

Omaha rests on the west bank of the Missouri River, brushing up against Iowa's border. While it wears a facade of geometric order, Omaha is actually an imprecise grid of numbered streets (running north-south) and named streets (east-west). **Dodge St.** (Rte. 6) divides the city north-south. **I-80** runs across the southern edge of town and is bisected by **I-480/Rte. 75** (the Kennedy Expwy.), which leads to nearby Bellevue. **I-29,** just over the river in Iowa, will take you north to Sioux City or south to Kansas City. At night, avoid **N. 24th St.**

Airport: Eppley Airfield, 4501 Abbot Dr. (422-6817), northeast of downtown.

Trains: Amtrak, 1003 S. 9th St. (342-1501 or 800-872-7245), at Pacific St. To Chicago (9½hr., 1 per day, $56-101) and Denver (8hr., 1 per day, $58-106). Open M-F 10:30pm-11:15am and 12:30-4pm, Sa 10:30pm-11:30am and noon-4pm, Su 10:30pm-8am.

Buses: Greyhound, 1601 Jackson (800-231-2222, fare and schedules 341-1906). To: Des Moines (2-3hr., 6 per day, $24-27); Cheyenne (10-11hr., 3 per day, $70); Kansas City (3-4hr., 3 per day, $20-24); and Lincoln (1hr., 6 per day, $12). Open 24hr.

Public Transportation: Metro Area Transit (MAT), 2222 Cumming St. (341-0800). Open M-F 8am-4:30pm. Schedules available at the Park Fair Mall, at 16th and Douglas St. near the Greyhound station, and the library at 14th and Farnam St. Fare 90¢, transfers 5¢.

Taxis: Happy Cab (339-0110). $1.80 initial fee, $1.50 per mi. 24hr.

Car Rental: Cheepers Rent-a-Car, 7700 L St. (331-8586). $25 per day with 150 free mi., $31 per day with 400 free mi.; 20¢ per additional mi. Must be 21 with a major credit card and personal liability policy. Open M-F 7:30am-8pm, Sa 8:30am-3pm.

Bike Rental: Bicycle Specialties, 4682 Leavenworth St. (556-2453), at 46th St. and Leavenworth. Bikes $20 per day, $35 per weekend, $100 per week. Rental includes pump, lock, spare tube, and helmet. Open M and W 10am-7pm, Tu and Th-F 10am-6pm, Sa 9am-5pm, Su noon-5pm.

Visitor Info: Visitors Center/Game and Parks Commission 1212 Deer Park Blvd. (595-3990), at 10th and Deer Park by the zoo; get off I-80 at 13th St. Open daily 8am-5pm; Nov.-Feb. M-F 8am-5pm. **Greater Omaha Convention and Visitors Bureau,** 6800 Mercy Rd., suite 202 (800-332-1819), at the Ak-Sar-Ben complex. Open M-F 8am-4:30pm. **Events Hotline,** 444-6800.

Hotlines: Rape Crisis, 345-7273. **Suicide Hotline,** 449-4650. Both operate 24hr.

Hospital: Methodist Hospital, 8303 Dodge St. (354-4434), at 84th and Dodge. **Women's Services, P.C.,** 201 South 46th St. (554-0110).

Internet Access: Omaha Public Library, 215 S. 15th St. (444-4800), between Douglas and Farnham. Free Internet use (text only), email highly discouraged. Open M-Th 9am-9pm, F-Sa 9am-5:30pm, Su 1-5pm.

Post Office: 1124 Pacific St. (348-2895). Open M-F 7:30am-6pm, Sa 7:30am-noon. After-hrs. express mail pick-up available. **ZIP code:** 68108. **Area code:** 402.

ACCOMMODATIONS AND CAMPGROUNDS

Budget motels in Omaha proper are often not particularly budget. For better deals, head for the city outskirts or across the river into Council Bluffs, Iowa.

Satellite Motel, 6006 L St. (733-7373), just south of I-80 Exit 450 (60th St.). The round building on the corner. Clean, wedge-shaped rooms equipped with fridge and TV with HBO. Singles $34; doubles $42 plus tax.

YMCA, 430 S. 20th St. (341-1600). Clean, single rooms with phones (no long-distance). $5 per day for use of on-site facilities and ½-price to join the YMCA while in residence. 4th fl., men only (common bathroom) $11. Other rooms (with individual bathrooms) $12.23. Free parking.

Haworth Park Campground (291-3379 or 293-3098), in Bellevue on Payne St. at the end of Mission St. Take the exit for Rte. 370 E. off Rte. 75, turn right onto Galvin St., left onto Mission St., and right onto Payne St. just before the toll bridge. Otherwise, hop on the infrequent bus "Bellevue" from 17th and Dodge St. to Mission and

Franklin St., then walk down Mission. Sites are paved with concrete, but there are enough trees to eliminate that trailer-park feel. Sites $5, with hookup $10. Showers, toilets, shelters. Open daily 6am-10pm; quiet stragglers can enter after hrs. Check-out 3pm. Laundry service coming soon.

FOOD FOR THOUGHT

It's no fun being a chicken, cow, or vegetarian in Omaha, with a fried chicken joint on every block and a steakhouse in every district. Once a warehouse area, the brick streets of the **Old Market,** on Jones, Howard, and Harney St. between 10th and 13th, now feature popular shops, restaurants, and bars. While you're there, visit the eerie **Fountain of the Furies,** "Greek avengers of patricide and disrespect of ancestors," in a concealed grotto off Howard St. The **farmers market** (345-5401), 11th and Jackson St., is held on Saturdays 8am-12:30pm from mid-May to mid-October. On a nice day, you could picnic in the lovely **Heartland of America Park,** just a few blocks east of the Old Market at Douglas and 8th St. (free parking, wheelchair access).

The Bohemian Café, 1406 S. 13th St. (342-9838), in South Omaha's old Slavic neighborhood. The placemat poetry says it all: "Dumplings and kraut today/at Bohemian Cafe/draft beer that's sparkling/plenty of parking/see you at lunch, okay?" Most dishes are meat-based ($7-9). Fantastic sauerkraut. Open Su-Th 11am-9pm, F-Sa 11am-10pm.

McFoster's Natural Kind Café, 302 S. 38th St. (345-7477), at Farnam St. Healthier, kinder dishes ($6-14), including chicken (hey—it's free-range!), vegan eggplant parmesan (with a choice of dairy or soy-based cheese), and artichoke mornay. Occasional live music; cover around $2. Open M-Th 11am-10pm, F-Sa 11am-1am, Su 10am-3pm. The 1st fl. is wheelchair accessible.

Délice European Café, 1206 Howard St. (342-2276), in the Old Market. Scrumptious pastries and deli fare at reasonable prices ($2-5). Recently renovated, they've added a wine bar and a selection of bottled beers. Ask about availability of day-old baked goods. Open M-Th 8am-10pm, F-Sa 8am-noon, Su 8am-8pm.

Upstream Brewing, 514 S. 11th St. (344-0200), at Jackson St. Creative entrees ($7-13) can be enjoyed inside, out on the patio, or on the new roof-top deck. Pizza and burgers $6-7. Upstairs adds a pool-hall atmosphere with 11 pool tables and 20 single-malt Scotches at the bar. Features 7 home brewed beers and 1 home-made root beer. Open Su-Th 11am-midnight. Bar open M-Sa until 1am, Su until midnight.

SIGHTS

Omaha's **Joslyn Art Museum,** 2200 Dodge St. (342-3300), displays an excellent collection of 19th- and 20th-century European and American art within a monumental Art Deco artifice. The exterior is pink Georgian marble; the interior dazzles with 30 different types of stone. From mid-July to mid-August, the museum hosts free "Jazz on the Green" concerts each Thursday from 7-9pm. *(Open Tu-Sa 10am-5pm, Th 10am-8pm, Su noon-5pm. $4, seniors and ages 5-11 $2; free Sa 10am-noon.)* The **Durham Western Heritage Museum,** 801 S. 10th St. (444-5071), is housed in the now-retired, yet still grand **Union Pacific Railroad Station.** *(Open Tu-Sa 10am-5pm, Su 1-5pm; early Sept. to late May closed M. $3, seniors $2.50, ages 5-12 $2.)* A $22 million renovation has just been completed, recreating the decor of 50-60 years ago.

In 1917, Father Edward Flanagan founded **Boys Town** (498-1140), west of Omaha at W. Dodge and 132nd St., as a home for troubled, neglected boys. *(Visitors center open daily 8am-5:30pm; Sept.-Apr. 9am-4:30pm. Free; self-guided audiotape tour $2. Call ahead to arrange guided tour.)* Made famous by the 1938 Spencer Tracy movie of the same name, Boys Town is now a popular tourist draw and still houses over 550 boys and girls.

One of the largest indoor jungles in the nation has made the amazing **Henry Doorly Zoo,** 3701 S. 10th St. (733-8401), at Deer Park Blvd. (or exit at 13th St. off I-80), the number one tourist attraction between Chicago and Denver. *(Open M-Sa 9:30am-5pm, Su 9:30am-6pm; early Sept. to late May daily 9:30am-5pm. $7.25, seniors $5.75, children $3.75, under 5 free.)* Also featured is the **Kingdom of the Seas Aquarium,** complete with a glass-enclosed submarine walkway, and the new **Lozier IMAX Theater.** *(IMAX shows $6.50, seniors $5.50, children $4.50, under 5 free. Wheelchair access.)*

GREAT PLAINS

Across the street from the zoo is **Johnny Rosenblatt Stadium** (734-2550), where you can watch the minor league (AAA) Omaha Royals battle opponents from April to early September. *(General admission $3.50. Student and senior discounts. Wheelchair access.)* The stadium also hosts the College Baseball World Series (late May-early June).

Gawk at deer and birds galore at the **Fontenelle Forest Nature Center,** 1111 N. Bellevue Blvd. (731-3140), in Bellevue, a 1300-acre forest and wetland with 17 mi. of walking and hiking trails. *(Open Apr.-Sept. M-F 8am-5pm, Sa-Su 8am-6pm; Oct.-Mar. daily 8am-5pm. $3.50, seniors $2, children $1.50, under 3 free.)* The privately owned center has a 1 mi. eco-friendly, wheelchair-accessible boardwalk raised above the forest floor.

Visitors can prepare to take flight at the new **Strategic Air Command Museum** (800-358-5029), off route I-80 between Omaha and Lincoln, adjacent to Mahoney Park. *(Open daily 9am-6pm. $6, children $3, under 5 free. AAA discount.)* The size of six football fields, the museum displays a B-52 bomber, several fighter planes, and other items of military history.

Just down the road is the **Simmons Wildlife Safari Park** (944-2481), where you can drive your all-terrain vehicle (or beat-up Chevette) 4½ mi. through a nature preserve with bison, pronghorns, and other beasts roaming inside. *(Open Apr.-Oct. 8am-1hr. before dusk. $4, seniors $3.50, children $2. Guided tram runs every hr. on the hr.)*

ENTERTAINMENT AND NIGHTLIFE

In late June and early July, **Shakespeare on the Green** (280-2391) stages free performances in Elmwood Park, on 60th and Dodge St. (Th-Su 8:30pm). The **Omaha Symphony** (342-3560) plays at the **Orpheum Theatre,** 409 S. 16th St. (Sept.-May usually Th-Su; call for dates and times; tickets $7.50-37). **Omaha's Magic Theater,** 325 S. 16th St. (932-3821; call M-F 9am-4pm), devotes itself to the development of new American musicals (evening performances F-M; tickets $12, students and seniors $7).

Punk and progressive folk have found a niche at the several area universities; check the window of the **Antiquarian Bookstore,** 1215 Harney, in the Old Market, for the scoop on shows. Several good bars await nearby. **The Dubliner,** 1205 Harney (342-5887), downstairs, stages live traditional Irish music in the evenings Wednesday through Saturday (cover varies). The **13th Street Coffee Company,** 519 13th St. (345-2883), is a hip peddler of the potent potion. The turtle latte—praline, caramel, chocolate, steamed milk, a double shot, and whipped cream ($2.50)—won't slow you down. Live music plays Fridays and Saturdays at 9pm, with no cover. (Open M-Th 7am-10pm, F 7am-midnight, Sa 8am-midnight, Su 9am-10pm.)

A string of gay bars hovers within a block of 16th and Leavenworth St. One of the most popular, **The Max,** 1417 Jackson (346-4110; a brown building with no sign outside), caters to men and women with five bars, a disco dance floor, DJ, fountains, patio, and a new leather bar (happy hour 4-7pm; cover F-Sa $3; open daily 4pm-1am).

■ Lincoln

Friendly folk, hopping nightlife, and a renovated downtown enliven Lincoln, named for the late President in 1867. The University of Nebraska football team, the Cornhuskers, is a significant presence in town; game days are big days, and locals gnash their teeth in communal woe after every loss. In its breathtaking capitol, the "Tower on the Plains," Lincoln houses the only unicameral (one-house) state legislature in the U.S. The state switched from two houses during the Great Depression to avoid red tape; today, the Nebraskan government is considered a model of efficiency.

ORIENTATION AND PRACTICAL INFORMATION

Getting around Lincoln is a snap. Numbered streets increase as you go east; lettered streets progress through the alphabet as you go north. **O St.** is the main east-west drag, splitting the town north-south. **R St.** runs along the south side of the **University of Nebraska-Lincoln (UNL)** city campus. **Cornhusker Hwy. (U.S. 6)** shears the northwest edge of Lincoln.

GREAT PLAINS

Airport: Lincoln Airport (474-2770), 5 mi. northwest of downtown on Cornhusker Hwy., or take Exit 399 off I-80. Taxi to downtown $10.

Trains: Amtrak, 201 N. 7th St. (476-1295 or 800-872-7245). Once daily to: Omaha (1hr., $13); Denver (7½hr., $104); Chicago (11hr., $109); and Kansas City (7hr., $46). Some seasonal specials. Open M-W 7:30am-4pm and 11:30pm-6:45am, Th-Su 11:30pm-6:45am.

Buses: Greyhound, 940 P St. (474-1071 or 800-231-2222), close to downtown and city campus. To: Omaha (1 hr.; in summer 5 per day, in winter 3 per day; $12); Chicago (12-14hr., 3 per day, $40); Kansas City (6½hr., 2 per day, $47); and Denver (9-11hr., 3 per day, $60). Open M-F 5:30am-8:30pm, Sa 9:30am-6pm. On Su, meet the bus at departure time. In winter, open M-F 6:30am-5:45pm, Sa 9am-5:45pm.

Public Transportation: Star Trans, 710 J St. (476-1234). Schedules are available on the bus, at many downtown locations, and at the office. Buses run M-Sa 6am-6pm. Fare 85¢, seniors 40¢, ages 5-11 50¢.

Taxis: Husker Cabs, (477-4111). $1.50 initial fee, $1.75 per mi. 24hr.

Car Rental: U-Save Auto Rental, 2240 Q St. (477-5236). As low as $15 per day with 100 free mi.; 10¢ per additional mi. Must be 21. $100 deposit. Open 8am-7pm.

Bike Rental: Blue's Bike & Fitness Center, 3321 Pioneers Blvd. (488-2101). Bikes $10 per ½-day, $16 per day. Credit card or cash deposit required (usually the value of the bike). Open M-Th 9am-8pm, F 10am-6pm, Sa 9am-5pm, Su 1pm-5pm. **Bike Pedalers,** 1353 S. 33rd St. (474-7000), at B St. $25 per hr. Prices can vary. Open M-Sa 8am-7pm, Su noon-5pm.

Quadratic Formula: $(-b \pm \sqrt{b^2-4ac})/2a)$.

Visitor Info: Visitors Center, 201 N. 7th St. in the Haymarket district (434-5348 or 800-423-8212). Open M-F 9am-8pm, Sa 8am-5pm, Su noon-5pm; in winter M-F 9am-6pm, Sa 10am-4pm, Su noon-4pm. **Lincoln Convention and Visitors Bureau,** P.O. Box 83737, Lincoln, 68501 (434-5335; http://www.lincoln.org/cvb).

Hotlines: Personal Crisis Line, 475-5171. **Rape and Spouse Abuse Crisis Line,** 475-7273. Both 24hr. **University of Nebraska Gay/Lesbian/Bisexual/Transgender Resource Center,** 472-5644.

Internet Access: The Mill, 800 P St. (475-5522). $3 per hr.

Post Office: 700 R St. (473-1695). Open M-F 7:30am-6pm, Sa 9am-3pm. **ZIP code:** 68501. **Area code:** 402.

ACCOMMODATIONS AND CAMPGROUNDS

There are few inexpensive motels in downtown Lincoln; most abound east of the city center around the 5600 block of Cornhusker Hwy. (U.S. 6). **UNL, Niehardt Residence Center,** 540 N. 16th St. (472-0777 or 472-1044), a clean and friendly place, rents some rooms when school is out of session from late May to early August (room with 2 twin beds $24.70; no occupancy limit). **The Great Plains Budget Host Inn,** 2732 O St. (476-3253 or 800-288-8499), has large rooms with fridges and coffeemakers. Take bus #9 "O St. Shuttle." (Free parking, continental breakfast, and kitchenettes available. Singles $38; doubles $46.) The **Cornerstone Hostel (HI-AYH),** 640 N. 16th St. (476-0355 or 476-0926), at U St. just south of Vine St., is located in the basement of a church in the university's downtown campus and rarely fills up. You may run into awkward encounters at the unisex shower located in the middle of the laundry room. Take bus #4; from the bus station, walk 7 blocks east to 16th, then 5 blocks north. (2 single-sex rooms; 5 beds for women, 5 for men. Full kitchen and laundry facilities. $10, nonmembers $13. Free parking and linen. Curfew 11pm.) The **Nebraska State Fair Park Campground,** 2402 N. 14th St. (473-4287), is conveniently located and has a congenial atmosphere; take bus #7 "Belmont." (Sites for 2 $11, with electricity $13, full hookup $16; $1 per additional person. Fills up early in Aug. during the fair. Open mid-Apr. to Oct.) To get to **Camp-A-Way,** at 1st and Superior St. (476-2282), take Exit 401 or 401a from I-80, then Exit 1 on I-180/Rte. 34. Pleasant sites, but a bit out of the way. ($12, with water and electricity or full hookup $14.50. Showers and laundry facilities available. Night registration possible.)

FOOD AND NIGHTLIFE

A dandy collegiate hangout, the **Nebraska Union** (472-2181), at 14th and R St. on campus, has cheap food, a post office, an ATM, a Ticketmaster outlet, and a bank. (Hrs. vary, but usually open in summer M-F 7am-5pm; academic year M-F 7am-11pm, Sa 9am-11pm, Su noon-11pm.) Cheap bars, eateries, and movie theaters cluster around one side of UNL's downtown campus, between N and P St. from 12th to 15th St. **Historic Haymarket,** 7th to 9th and O to R St., is a newly renovated warehouse district near the train tracks, with cafes, bars, several restaurants, and a **farmers market** (434-6900; open mid-May to mid-Oct. Sa 8am-12:30pm). All downtown buses connect at 11th and O St., 2 blocks east of Historic Haymarket. Every renovated warehouse district has its yuppie brewery; **Lazlo's Brewery and Grill,** 710 P St. (474-5636), is the oldest one in Nebraska, founded in 1991. Chow down on salads, sandwiches, and meat entrees for $5-15. (Open M-Sa 11am-1am, Su 11am-10pm. Wheelchair access.) Right next door, **Ja Brisco,** 700 P St. (434-5644), whips up pizzas, pasta, and deli sandwiches ($6-12) that are sure to please (open daily 11am-10:30pm; wheelchair access). **Valentino's,** 232 N. 13th St. (475-1501), a regional chain with roots in Lincoln, offers inexpensive pasta ($5-8). Locals come to sample from six different all-you-can-eat buffets. ($6, after 4pm $8. F and Sa 9-11pm pizza $3. Open Su-Th 11am-10pm, F-Sa 11am-11pm.) **The Mill,** 800 P St. (475-5522), is a stylish cafe where patrons sun on the large patio while sipping iced drinks. Perks include coffee and tea from around the world ($1.25-3) and baked goods (Cafe open M-Th 7:30am-11pm, F-Sa 7:30am-midnight, Su 10am-10pm.)

Nightspots abound in Lincoln, particularly those of the sports-bar variety; locals always take time to celebrate Nebraska football, Lincoln's pride and joy. For the biggest names in Lincoln's live music scene, try the suitably dark and smoky **Zoo Bar,** 136 N. 14th St. (435-8754). Cover varies, as does the music, but the emphasis is on *good* blues. (21+. Open M-F 3pm-1am, Sa noon-1am.) **The Panic,** 200 S. 18th St. (435-8764), at N St., is a great gay video/patio bar (open M-F 4pm-1am, Sa-Su 1pm-1am).

SIGHTS AND ENTERTAINMENT

The "Tower on the Plains," the 400 ft. **Nebraska State Capitol Building** (471-0448), at 14th and K St., an unofficial architectural wonder of the world, wows with its streamlined exterior and detailed interior, highlighted by a beautiful mosaic floor. *(Open M-F 8am-5pm, Sa 10am-5pm, Su 1-5pm. Free, enthusiastically led tours every 30min. M-F in summer, every hr. Sa-Su.)* Visitors can take the elevator to the 14th fl. for a sweeping view of the city, or climb to the 3rd fl. balcony to observe the senatorial showdowns. The **Museum of Nebraska History** (471-4754), 15th and P St., has a phenomenal, moving exhibit on the history of the Plains Indians (open M-F 9am-4:30pm, Sa 9am-5pm, Su 1:30-5pm; free). The **University of Nebraska State Museum,** 14th and U St. (472-6302), in Morrill Hall, boasts an amazing fossil collection that includes the largest mounted mammoth in any American museum (open M-Sa 9:30am-4:30pm, Su 1:30-4:30pm; requested donation $2). In the same building, the **Mueller Planetarium** (472-2641) lights up the ceiling with several shows daily and laser shows on weekends. *(Closed on home game days. Planetarium $4; students, seniors, and under 13 $2. Laser shows F and Sa 8pm, 9:30pm, and 10pm; $5, with college ID $4.)* The **Sheldon Memorial Art Gallery,** 12th and R St. (472-2461), was designed by Phillip Johnson and displays a Warhol painting. *(Open Tu-W 10am-5pm, Th-Sa 10am-5pm and 7-9pm, Su 2-9pm; free.)* During the **Jazz in June** series, cool music can be heard in the gallery's sculpture garden on Tuesday nights from 7-9pm.

In addition to the standard fair fare (livestock, crafts, fitter family contests, etc.), the **Nebraska State Fair** (473-4109) offers car races, tractor pulls, and plenty of rides to please all comers. It lasts 11 days in late August and early September ($7).

Picturesque picnicking spots include **Van Dorn Park,** 9th and Van Dorn St., and nearby **Wilderness Park,** stretching from 1st and Van Dorn to 27th and Saltillo Rd.

The **Nature Center at Pioneers Park,** 3201 S. Coddington Ave. (441-7895), ¼ mi. south off W. Van Dorn on Coddington St. (watch for the signs along Van Dorn), harbors bison and elk within its wildlife sanctuary. *(Open M-Sa 8:30am-8:30pm, Su noon-8:30pm; Sept-May M-Sa 8:30am-5pm, Su noon-5pm. Free. Free golf carts available.)*

■ Scotts Bluff

Known to the Plains Indians as "Ma-a-pa-te" ("hill that is hard to go around"), the imposing clay and sandstone highlands of **Scotts Bluff National Monument** were landmarks for people traveling the Mormon and Oregon Trails in the 1840s. For some time the bluff was too dangerous to cross, but in the 1850s a single-file wagon trail was opened through narrow **Mitchell's Pass,** where traffic wore deep marks in the sandstone. Evidence of the early pioneers can still be seen today on the ½ mi. stretch of the original **Oregon Trail** preserved at the pass; tourists can gaze out at the distant horizons to the east and west as pioneers once did. The **visitors center** (436-4340), at the entrance on Rte. 92, will tell you of the mysterious death of Hiram Scott, the fur trader who gave the Bluffs their name (open daily 8am-8pm, in winter 8am-5pm; $5 per carload, $2 per motorcycle). To get to the top of the bluffs, hike challenging **Saddle Rock Trail** (1½ mi. each way) or motor up **Summit Dr.** At the top, you'll find **nature trails** and a magnificent view. Take U.S. 26 to Rte. 71 to Rte. 92; the monument is on Rte. 92 about 2 mi. west of **Gering** (*not* in the town of Scotts Bluff). In mid-July, the four-day **Oregon Trail Days Festival** packs the towns near Scotts Bluff with trail-happy, festive folk. Twenty miles east on Rte. 92, just south of Bayard, the 500 ft. spire of **Chimney Rock,** visible from more than 30 mi. away, marks another landmark which once inspired travelers of the Oregon Trail. A gravel road leads from Rte. 92 to within ½ mi. of it, and a new **visitors center** (586-2581) featuring a film and exhibits on the rock and the trails is nearby (open daily 9am-6pm, in winter 9am-5pm; $1, under 18 free).

The **Sands Motel,** 814 W. 27th St. (632-6191 or 800-535-1075 for reservations), has clean and cozy rooms (singles $28; doubles $32-38; wheelchair access). The **Kiwanis Riverside Campground,** 1600 S. Beltline Hwy. W and 1818 Ave. A (630-6235), at the zoo, offers campsites in a sparsely wooded area ($8, with hookup $10; open May-Sept.). **Area code:** 308. **Time Zone:** Mountain.

Carhenge or Bust

As you drive through the low plains and small bluffs of western Nebraska, things begin to look the same. Suddenly, a preternatural power sweeps the horizon as the ultimate shrine to bizarre on-the-road Americana springs into view—**Carhenge.** Consisting of 36 old cars painted gray, this oddly engaging sculpture has the same orientation and dimensions as Stonehenge in England. Carhenge's creator, Jim Reinders, wants to be buried here someday. When asked why he built it, Reinders replied, *"plane, loqui deprehendi,"* or "clearly, I spoke to be understood." Right on, Jimmy! This wonder of the cornhuskers can be found right off U.S. 385, 2 mi. north of Alliance, NE, which is 60 mi. northwest of Scotts Bluff.

Kansas

There's no place like Dorothy and Toto's home. Kansas has been a major link in the nation's chain since the 1820s: families on the Oregon and Santa Fe Trails drove their wagons west in search of new homes, while cowboys on the Chisholm Trail drove their longhorns north in search of railroads and good times. Cowtowns such as Abilene and Dodge City were happy to oblige; these rip-roaring meccas of gambling and drinking made legends of lawmen like Wild Bill Hickock and Wyatt Earp. The influx of settlers resulted in fierce battles over land, as white settlers forced Native Americans to move into the arid regions farther west. Grueling feuds over Kansas's slavery status (Kansas joined the Union as a free state in 1861) gave rise to the term "Bleeding Kansas." The wound has healed, and Kansas now presents a serene blend of kitschy tourist attractions—the Kansas Teachers' Hall of Fame in Dodge City and the World's Largest Hand-Dug Well in Greensburg—and miles of farmland. Highway signs subtly remind travelers that "every Kansas farmer feeds 75 people—and *you*."

PRACTICAL INFORMATION

Capital: Topeka.
Visitor Info: Division of Travel and Tourism: 700 S.W. Harrison, #1300, Topeka 66603-3712 (800-2KANSAS/252-6727; http://www.state.ks.us). Open M-F 7am-10pm, Sa-Su 7:30am-10pm. **Kansas Wildlife and Parks,** 900 S.W. Jackson, 5th fl., Topeka 66612-1233 (785-296-2281). Open M-F 8am-5pm.
Emergency: 911.
Time Zone: Central (1hr. behind Eastern). **Postal Abbreviation:** KS.
Sales Tax: 4.9-6.9%.

■ Wichita

In 1541, Coronado came to the site of present-day Wichita in search of the mythical, gold-laden city of Quivira. Upon arriving, he was so disappointed that he had his guide strangled for misleading him. In spite of Coronado's misgivings, Wichita grew to become the largest city in Kansas, and is now a key city for airplane manufacturing: Lear, Boeing, Beech, and Cessna all have factories in town. Much of the downtown is painfully suburban in its tree-lined stillness. As the Old Town area gets revamped, however, its bars and cafes party further and further into the Kansas night.

PRACTICAL INFORMATION Wichita lies on I-35, 170 mi. north of Oklahoma City and about 200 mi. southwest of Kansas City. A small and quiet downtown makes for easy walking or parking. **Broadway** is the major north-south artery. **Douglas Ave.** divides the numbered east-west streets to the north from the named east-west streets to the south. Many downtown businesses have moved a few blocks further south out along **Kellogg Ave. (U.S. 54),** the main east-west route. *Visitors just south and north of downtown around Broadway should take extra caution.* The closest **Amtrak** station, 414 N. Main St. (283-7533 or 800-872-7245; ticket office open daily 11:30am-7:30pm), 25 mi. north of Wichita, in the town of Newton, sends one very early train northeast to Kansas City (4½hr., $34-61) and another west to Dodge City (2hr., $27-49). **Greyhound,** 312 S. Broadway (265-7711 or 800-231-2222), barks 2 blocks east of Main St. and 1½ blocks southwest of the transit station (open daily 3am-7pm). Buses serve Kansas City (3-5hr., 3 per day, $34-36); Oklahoma City (4hr., 3 per day, $34-36); and Denver (13hr., 2 per day, $59-74). **WMTA,** 1825 S. McClean Blvd. (265-7221), handles in-town transportation. (Buses run M-F 6:15am-6:30pm, Sa 7:15am-5:20pm. Fare $1, seniors 50¢, ages 6-17 75¢; transfers 25¢. Station open M-F 8am-5pm. Tickets are also available all over the city at the stores Dillon's and Alverson's.) In summer, a **trolley** (fare 25¢) runs from downtown to Old Town during lunch hours (M-F 11am-2pm) and from downtown to Old Town and the museums on the river on Saturdays (10am-3:40pm). **Thrifty Rent-A-Car,** 8619 W. Kellogg (721-9552 or 800-367-2277), rents cars for $30 per day (250 free mi., 29¢ each additional mi.) or $160 per week. (2000 free mi. 21+ only; under 25 $5 per day surcharge. Open daily 6:30am-10pm.) The **convention and visitors bureau** dispenses info at 100 S. Main St. (265-2800 or 800-288-9424), on the corner of Douglas Ave. (open M-F 8am-5pm). **Post Office:** 330 W. 2nd St. (262-6245), at Waco (open M-Sa 7am-5:30pm). **ZIP code:** 67202. **Area code:** 316.

ACCOMMODATIONS AND CAMPGROUNDS Wichita offers a bounty of cheap hotels. South Broadway has plenty of mom-'n'-pop places, *but be very wary of the neighborhood.* The chains line **E. and W. Kellogg Ave.** 5-8 mi. from downtown. Only ten blocks from downtown, the **Mark 8 Inn,** 1130 N. Broadway (265-4679 or 800-830-7268), has small, comfortable rooms that come with free local calls, cable TV, A/C, fridge, and laundry facilities, although guests should be careful in this neighborhood at night (singles $30; doubles $34; no checks). The **English Village Inn,** 6727 E. Kellogg (683-5613 or 800-365-8455), though American, urban, and a motel, keeps basic rooms in tidy repair for very reasonable rates. (Singles from $30; doubles from $36. Cable and HBO in the rooms, popcorn in the lobby.) **USI Campgrounds,** 2920 E. 33rd St. (838-0435), right off Hillside Rd., is the most convenient of Wichita's hitchin' posts, with laundry, showers, playground, and storm shelter, in case there's a twister a-comin'. (Sites $17, partial hookup $19, full hookup $20.50; weekly rates.)

FOOD Beef: it's what's for dinner in Wichita. Everything old is new again in the **Old Town** area, a few blocks east of downtown on Washington and Mosley St., between 1st St. and Douglas Ave., where revitalized warehouses now house breweries and restaurants. The neon lights are bright on **N. Broadway,** with all kinds of fairly authentic Asian food. If you eat only one slab in Wichita, make it one from **Doc's Steakhouse,** 1515 N. Broadway (264-4735), where the most expensive entree—a 17 oz. T-bone with salad, potato, and bread—is only $9. Take bus #13 "N. Broadway." (Open M-Th 11:30am-9:30pm, F 11:30am-10pm, Sa 4-10pm.) The cast of *Friends* would feel right at home in the laid-back **Riverside Perk,** 1144 N. Bitting (264-6464), where veggie-lovers have been known to holler, "Give me a quiche!" ($3.50; open Tu-Th 7am-10pm, F-Sa 7am-midnight, Su 10am-10pm). For good ol' American sandwiches, **Merle's,** 440 N. Seneca (263-0444), can't be beat. Menus printed on newspaper, juke-box tunes, pool tables, and dark-wood booths make it a timeless treat, distractingly close to the Museums-on-the-River (vegetarian sandwiches $5; open M-Sa 11am-2am). The **Wichita Farm and Art Market,** 835 E. 1st St. (262-3555), hawks food items fresh off the farm and the easel (Indoor shops open M-Sa 10am-6pm, Su 1-5pm; outdoor farmers market May-Oct. Su 7am-1pm.) **Station Sq.** (263-1950), at Mead St. and Douglas Ave., combines two restaurants, two bars, and an outdoor grill, for atmosphere ranging from 50s diner-style to fajitas and 'ritas (live music F-Sa; open Su and Tu-Sa 11am until about 2am).

SIGHTS AND ENTERTAINMENT The four museums of the **Museums-on-the-River** series are located within a few blocks of each other; take the trolley or bus #12 "Riverside." Walk through the rough and tumble cattle days of the 1870s in the **Old Cowtown,** 1871 Sim Park Dr. (264-6398 or 264-0671), lined with many original buildings. *(Open M-Sa 10am-5pm, Su noon-5pm; Nov.-Feb. Sa-Su only. $6, seniors $5.50, ages 5-11 $3, under 5 free. Call for special events info.)* In the Shakespearean Garden at **Botanica,** 701 Amidon (264-0448), tarry till Birnam Wood will march on Dunsinane. *(Open June-Aug. Tu 9am-8pm, M and W-Sa 9am-5pm, Su 1-5pm; Apr.-May and Sept.-Dec. M-Sa 9am-5pm, Su 1-5pm; Jan.-Mar. M-F 9am-5pm. $4.50, students $2, seniors $4, under 6 free.)* The **Mid-America All-Indian Center and Museum,** 650 N. Seneca (262-5221), showcases traditional and modern works by Native American artists. *(Open M-Sa 10am-5pm, Su 1-5pm; Jan.-Mar. closed M. $2, ages 6-12 $1.)* The late Blackbear Bosin's awe-inspiring sculpture, *Keeper of the Plains,* stands guard over the grounds. The center holds the **Mid-America All-Indian Intertribal Pow Wow** during the last weekend in July with traditional dancing, foods, arts, and crafts.

The **Wichita Art Museum,** 619 Stackman Dr. (268-4921), exhibits American art, including works by Mary Cassatt, Winslow Homer, and Edward Hopper, as well as an interactive gallery for kids (open Tu-Sa 10am-5pm, Su noon-5pm; free). More art hides on the **Wichita State University,** at N. Fairmont and 17th St., accessible by the "East 17th" bus, including over 50 sculptures and the **Corbin Education Center,** designed by Frank Lloyd Wright. Free sculpture maps are available at the **Edwin A. Ulrich Museum of Art** office (978-3644), in the McKnight Arts Center, also on campus. *(Open daily noon-5pm. Free.)* A gigantic glass mosaic mural by Joan Miró forms one wall of the building. North of campus, the **Center for the Improvement of Human Functioning,** 3100 N. Hillside (682-3100), features a 40 ft. pyramid, used for reflection and receptions, with the world's largest FDA food pyramid painted on its side. *(Tours M-F 1:30pm; $4.)* Tours of the biochemical research station include a chance to "de-stress" mind, body, and soul by hurling clay skeet pigeons at a wall.

Most of Wichita's museums and historic points of attraction are part of the **Wichita Western Heritage Tour,** which focuses on the city's contributions to culture. If you visit all of the sites, you get a free **belt buckle** at the last stop, **Sheplers,** 6501 W. Kellogg (946-3600), the world's largest Western store.

At the **River Festival** (267-2817), over 100,000 converge on Wichita for concerts, sporting events, and culinary delights (May 7-16, 1999; $2). The **Walnut Valley Festival** (221-3250), in Winfield, 45min. southeast of Wichita on U.S. 77, draws big-name country and pop artists for a long weekend of folk fun in late September.

Club Indigo, 126 N. Mosley (265-6760) perhaps would be better described as club vertigo, with giant swirls on the walls. A new bar and restaurant in Old Town, Club Indigo lures in 20-somethings with drink specials ($2-3) and wrap sandwiches ($5). Open M-Th 11am-midnight, F-Sa 11am-2am. Alternative bands play 4 or 5 nights a week to packed crowds in the space-deprived **Kirby's Beer Store,** 3227 E. 17th St. (685-7013; no cover; open M-F 2pm-2am, Sa-Su 3pm-2am).

What's That Smell?

In its heyday in the 1870s, **Dodge City** ("the wickedest little city in America") was a haven for gunfighters, prostitutes, and other lawless types; at one time, Front St., the main drag, had a saloon for every 50 citizens. Disputes were settled man to man, with a duel; the slower draw ended up in Boot Hill Cemetery, so named for the boot-clad corpses buried there. Legendary lawmen Wyatt Earp and Bat Masterson earned their fame cleaning up the streets of Dodge City. The town's most noticeable current residents, about 50,000 cows, reside on the feedlots on the east part of town. Hold your nose and whoop it up during the **Dodge City Days** (316-227-3119), the last weekend in July through the first weekend in August (July 30-Aug. 8, 1999), complete with rodeo, carnival, and plenty of steak. You'll know when you're getting close.

■ Lawrence

Founded in 1854 by abolitionists during the "Bleeding Kansas" controversy, Lawrence was burned to the ground in 1863 by pro-slavery raiders, led by William Quantrill and Jesse James. The citizens quickly rebuilt, and have been struggling since to fulfill the second half of the city's motto, "from ashes to immortality." Travelers weary of the Oregon Trail were easily attracted to the lush, hilly lands surrounding Lawrence. Tired voyagers now enjoy the cafes and lively bars supported by students of the **University of Kansas** (KU to locals). The university's **Museum of Natural History** (864-4450), at Jayhawk Blvd. and 14th St., showcases taxidermy big and small, including one of the few survivors of Custer's Last Stand, a horse named Comanche (open M-Sa 10am-5pm, Su noon-5pm; suggested donation $2, children $1). Right across the street, learn about people and peoples at the **Museum of Anthropology** (864-4245; open M-Sa 9am-5pm, Su 1-5pm; suggested donation $4, children $2). The center of student activity, **Kansas Union,** keeps students and tourists busy with its massive food court and bowling alley. Exhibits like "Pin-up Girls, Hairy Guys, and Art" are sure to entertain at the **Spencer Museum of Art** (864-4710), at 14th and Mississippi St. (open Tu-W and F-Sa 10am-5pm, Th 10am-9pm, Su noon-5pm; free) Atop the hill in the heart of campus, a 53-bell carillon in the towering **campanile** chimes for concerts on Sunday at 3pm and Wednesday at 7pm (8pm in summer). Call the **KU Info line** (864-3506) to find out what's shakin' on campus.

Lawrence is also home to **Haskell Indian Nations University** (749-8404), off 23rd St. (Rte. 10), the only inter-tribal university in the U.S. The students, who represent over 150 different tribes, hold **pow wows** throughout the year, including the 3-day commencement celebration in early May (call for info on other pow wows).

Students and professionals present plays and concerts at the **Lied Center** (864-ARTS/2787), at 15th and Iowa St. (box office open M-F noon-5:30pm). **Liberty Hall,** 644 Massachusetts St. (749-1972), hosts concerts and shows artsy and independent films in an ornate theater, complete with constellations twinkling on the ceiling. Chat with the employees to find out the goings on in town. (Open M-Sa 11am-11pm, Su 11am-midnight.)

If you need to spend the night, a slew of motels settle near the intersection of 6th and Iowa St. The **Westminster Inn,** 2525 W. 6th St. (785-841-8410 or 888-937-8646), the best of the budget options, goes for the English lodge look—and almost succeeds (singles $40; doubles $52). The **Virginia Inn,** 2907 W. 6th St. (785-843-6611 or 800-468-8979), rents out renovated rooms with cable, A/C, and a pool (singles $40; doubles $47; AAA discount). The **College Motel,** 1703 W. 6th St. (785-843-0131), has large, clean, phoneless rooms and a small pool (rooms from $35). Die-hard Democrats can pitch their tents at **Clinton Lake** at any of three Federal campgrounds (785-843-7665), 4 mi. west of town on 23rd St. Scenic primitive sites are available at the **Woodridge Campground** for free, at **Rock Haven** for $4, and at **Bloomington** for $8. Bloomington also has sites with water and electricity ($12).

Fast food hangs out on 23rd (a.k.a. "Hamburger Alley"), Iowa and 6th St. **Massachusetts St.** is home to the funkier coffeehouses and bars. Head straight to the source at the **farmers market,** in the parking lot on the 1000 block of Vermont St. (Open mid-May to Sept. Tu and Th 4-6:30pm, Sa 6:30-10:30am, Sept.-Nov. Tu and Th 4-6:30pm, Sa 7:30-11:30am.) It's like going home at **La Familia,** 731 New Hampshire St. (749-0105), although mom never offered 50 Mexican specials for $5-12 (open M-W 11am-9pm, Th-Sa 11am-10pm). KU students love **Quinton's,** 615 Massachusetts St. (842-6560), known for its packed sandwiches ($5; open daily 11am-2am). The **Paradise Café,** 728 Massachusetts St. (842-5199), specializes in good old American meals. The pancakes of the day ($3) are as good as the smells that waft out from the kitchen. Dinners (mostly fish and steak) range from $7-14. (Open M-Sa 6:30am-2:30pm and 5-10pm, Su 8am-8pm.) The oldest legal brewery in Kansas is **Freestate Brewery Co.,** 636 Massachusetts St. (843-4555). You can chase your beer with sandwiches, gumbo, or pasta. (Meals $5-9. Open M-Sa 11am-midnight, Su noon-11pm. Free tours Sa 2pm.)

The Mag, inside the Thursday *Journal-World,* lists activities and events for the coming week, as does *Pitch Weekly,* free at restaurants and bars. Also, check out neon posters all over town to get caught up. Over 100 types of beer, some on the wall, crowd **The Bottleneck,** 737 New Hampshire (842-5483), along with top alternative and college rock bands (cover hovers around $4; open M-Sa 3pm-2am, Su 8pm-2am). **Jazzhaus,** 926½ Massachusetts St. (749-3320), swings every night, but features live jive Wednesday to Sunday (cover Tu-Sa around $4; open daily 4pm-2am). Feel the blues at the **Brown Bear Brewery,** 729 Massachusetts St. (331-4338), Th-Sa 9:30pm-1:30am, and drown them with $1-3 beer specials.

The **convention and visitors bureau** (865-4411 or 888-LAWKANS/529-5267), at 2nd and Locust St., across the bridge from downtown in the renovated train depot, stocks local info and maps of town and campus (open Mar.-Oct. M-Sa 8:30am-5:30pm, Su 1-5pm; Nov.-Feb. M-Sa 9am-5pm). **KU Wheels** provides bus service around the college and parts of Lawrence (call the KU Info line, above, for schedule info). **Greyhound,** 2447 W. 6th St. (843-5622 or 800-231-2222), runs out of the Conoco gas station; buses to Kansas City (1hr., 6 per day, $12) and Wichita (4hr., 3 per day, $30). You can test your U.S. history as you drive through town: the north-south streets are named for the states, in the order they entered the Union. **Post Office:** 645 Vermont St. (843-1681). **ZIP code:** 66044. **Area code:** 913 and 785; in text 913 unless noted.

Missouri

Pro-slavery Missouri applied for statehood in 1818, but due to Congress's fears about upsetting the balance of free and slave states, was forced to wait until Maine entered the Union as a free state in 1821. Missouri's Civil War status as a border state was a harbinger of its future ambiguity; close to the center of the country, Missouri defies regional stereotyping. Its large cities are defined by wide avenues, long and lazy rivers, numerous parks, humid summers, and blues and jazz wailing into the night. In the countryside, Bible factory outlets stand amid firework stands and barbecue pits.

Geographic Center of the U.S.

Have you ever wanted to be the center of the action? Go 2 mi. northwest of **Lebanon, KS.** Sit by the stone monument and feel special—the entire contiguous U.S. is revolving around you.

Missouri's patchwork geography further complicates characterization. In the north, near Iowa, amber waves of grain undulate. Along the Mississippi, towering bluffs inscribed with Native American pictographs evoke western canyonlands. Farther inland, spelunkers enjoy some of the world's largest limestone caves, made famous by Tom Sawyer and Becky Thatcher.

PRACTICAL INFORMATION

Capital: Jefferson City.
Visitor Info: Missouri Division of Tourism, P.O. Box 1055, Jefferson City 65102 (573-751-4133 or 800-877-1234; http://www.missouritourism.org). Office open M-F 8am-5p; 800 number operates 24hr. **Dept. of Natural Resources,** Division of State Parks, P.O. Box 176, Jefferson City 65102 (573-751-2479 or 800-334-6946). Open M-F 8am-5pm.
Emergency: 911.
Time Zone: Central (1hr. behind Eastern). **Postal Abbreviation:** MO.
Sales Tax: Varies; 6.75% is the average.

■ St. Louis

In the early 1700s, Pierre Laclede set up a trading post directly below the junction of the Mississippi, Missouri, and Illinois rivers. A natural stopover, St. Louis, the "River City," gained prominence as the U.S. raced into the West. Today, Eero Saarinen's magnificent Gateway Arch, a silvery beacon to visitors and a landmark of America's westward expansion, gleams over one of America's largest inland trading ports.

St. Louis, Memphis, and New Orleans have together been dubbed "America's Music Corridor." In the early 1900s, showboats carrying ragtime and brassy Dixieland jazz bands regularly traveled between Chicago and New Orleans; the music floated through St. Louis and left the city addicted. St. Louis also contributed to the development of the blues and saw the birth of ragtime during Scott Joplin's years in the city.

ORIENTATION AND PRACTICAL INFORMATION

I-44, I-55, I-64, and I-70 meet in St. Louis. The city is bounded on the west by I-170 and circled farther out by I-270. **U.S. 40/I-64** runs east-west through the entire metropolitan area. Downtown, **Market St.** divides the city north-south. Numbered streets run parallel to the river, increasing to the west. The historic **Soulard** district borders the river south of downtown. **Forest Park** and **University City,** home to **Washington University,** lie west of downtown; the Italian neighborhood called **The Hill** is south of these. Parking comes easy; wide streets allow for lots of meters, and private lots are cheap ($2-8). St. Louis is a driving town. Public transportation has improved, but can be difficult to navigate. If you are without a car, check schedules. Often. Dangerous sections of the city include **East St. Louis** (across the river in IL), the **Near South Side,** and most of the **North Side.**

Airport: Lambert-St. Louis International (426-8000), 12 mi. northwest of the city on I-70. Hub for **TWA.** MetroLink and Bi-state bus #66 "Maplewood-Airport" provide easy access to downtown ($1). Taxis to downtown are less economical ($18). A few westbound Greyhound buses stop at the airport.

Trains: Amtrak, 550 S. 16th St. (331-3300 or 800-872-7245), 2 blocks south of Kiel Center. To Chicago (6hr., 3 per day, $26-52) and Kansas City (5½hr., 2 per day, $25-49). Ticket office open daily 6am-1am.

Buses: Greyhound, 1450 N. 13th St. (231-4485 or 800-231-2222), at Cass Ave. Bi-state bus #30 "Cass" takes less than 10min. from downtown. *The terminal is not in the best part of town, so be cautious at night.* To Chicago (6½hr., 6 per day, $27-29) and Kansas City (5hr., 7 per day, $27-28).

Public Transportation: Bi-State (231-2345). Extensive daily service; infrequent during off-peak hrs. Info and schedules are available at the Metroride Service Center (982-1485) in the St. Louis Center (open M-Sa 10am-6pm). Schedules are also handed out at the Bi-State Development Agency, 707 N. 1st St. (on Laclede's Landing), and at the reference desk of the public library at 13th and Olive St. **MetroLink,** the light-rail system, runs from 5th St. and Missouri Ave. in East St. Louis to Lambert Airport M-Sa 5am-midnight and Su 6am-11pm. Travel for free in the "Ride Free Zone" (from Laclede's Landing to Union Station) M-F 11am-2pm. MetroLink or bus fare $1, transfers 10¢; seniors and ages 5-12 50¢/5¢. 1-day pass $3, 3-day pass $7; available at MetroLink stations. **Shuttle Bug** is a small bus painted like a ladybug which cruises around Forest Park and the Central West End. All-day fare (6:45am-6pm M-F, 10am-6pm Sa-Su) $1. Its relative, the **Shuttle Bee,** buzzes around Forest Park, Clayton, Brentwood, and the Galleria M-F 6am-11:30pm, Sa 7:30am-10:30pm, Su 9:30am-6:30pm. One-way fare $1.

Taxis: Yellow Cab, 361-2345. $1 base fare, $1.20 per mi. **Laclede Cabs,** 652-3456. $1 base fare, $1.10 per mi. Both open 24hr.

Visitor Info: St. Louis Visitors Center, 308 Washington Ave. (241-1764). Open daily 9:30am-4:30pm. Other locations at the airport and at **America's Center** (421-1023), at 7th St. and Washington Ave. Open M-F 9am-5pm, Sa-Su 10am-2pm. **St. Louis Information Line,** 800-888-FUN1/3861. The *Official St. Louis Visitors Guide* and the monthly magazine *Where: St. Louis,* both free, contain much info and decent maps. A more complete map is available throughout the city and at the visitors center.

Hotlines: Rape Crisis, 531-2003. **Suicide Hotline,** 647-4357. **Kids Under 21 Crisis,** 644-5886. All three 24hr. **Gay and Lesbian Hotline,** 367-0084. Open M-Sa 6-10pm.

Hospitals: Barnes-Jewish Hospital, 216 S. Kingshighway Blvd. (747-3000). **Metro North Women's Health Center,** 2415 N. Kingshighway, 361-1606.

Post Office: 1720 Market St. (436-4454). Open M-F 8am-5pm. **ZIP code:** 63103. **Area code:** 314 (in MO), 618 (in IL); in text, 314 unless noted.

ACCOMMODATIONS AND CAMPGROUNDS

Budget lodging is generally located several mi. from downtown. For chain motels, try **Lindbergh Blvd. (Rte. 67)** near the airport, or the area north of the I-70/I-270 junction in **Bridgeton,** 5 mi. beyond the airport. **Watson Rd.** (old **Rte. 66** in South County) is littered with cheap motels southwest of where it merges with Chippewa; take bus #11 "Chippewa-Sunset Hills" or #20 "Cherokee." B&Bs (singles from $50; doubles from $60) are listed in the visitors guide.

Huckleberry Finn Youth Hostel (HI-AYH), 1908 S. 12th St. (Tucker Blvd.) (241-0076), 2 blocks north of Russell Blvd. in the Soulard District. From downtown, take bus #73 "Carondelet," or walk south on Broadway to Russell Blvd. and over to 12th St. (30-40min.). Don't walk on Tucker Blvd.; the hostel is just past an unsafe neighborhood. TV, lockers, full kitchen, free parking, and friendly staff. Dorm-style rooms with 5-9 beds. $15, nonmembers $18. Linen $2. $5 deposit required. Ask about work opportunities, like whitewashing the fence. Reception daily 8-10am and 6-10pm. Check-out 9:30am.

University of Missouri, St. Louis, Office of Residential Life (516-6877). Take I-70 to Natural Bridge Rd., turn right onto Arlmont Dr., then stay left at the split marking the end of Bellerive Dr. Or, take MetroLink to either campus stop, then hop on the campus shuttle. Large dorm rooms with A/C, free local calls, lounge with TV and VCR, laundry, kitchen access, free linen, and a pool. Singles $22; doubles $30. Call M-F 8am-5pm for someone to meet you. Reserve rooms 24hr. in advance.

Motel 6, 4576 Woodson Rd. (427-1313 or 800-4-MOTEL6/466-8356), near the airport. From downtown, Metrolink to the airport or take bus #4 "Natural Bridge." Other motels in the area can match the price, but few can touch the cleanliness. A/C, cable, pool. Singles $40; doubles $46; prices rise with the summer temps.

Horseshoe Lake State Park, 3321 Rte. 111 (618-931-0270), north off I-70 in Granite City, IL about 3 mi. from Cahokia Mounds. Sites are on an island (connected by a causeway) in a relatively secluded area. No electricity or water. Sites $7.

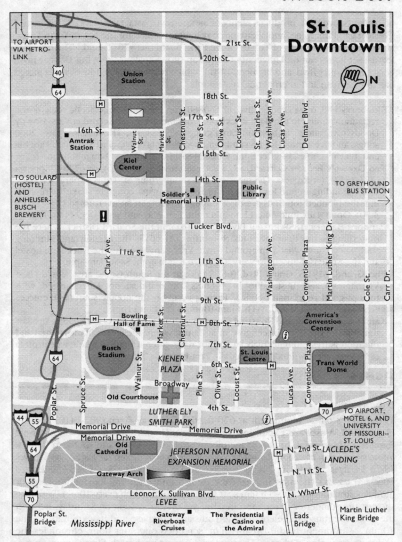

St. Louis Downtown

TO AIRPORT VIA METRO-LINK

21st St.
20th St.
18th St.
Union Station
16th St.
Amtrak Station
Kiel Center
Walnut St.
Market St.
Chestnut St.
17th St.
Pine St.
Olive St.
15th St.
Locust St.
St. Charles St.
Washington Ave.
Lucas Ave.
Delmar Blvd.

TO SOULARD (HOSTEL) AND ANHEUSER-BUSCH BREWERY

Soldier's Memorial
14th St.
13th St.
Public Library
TO GREYHOUND BUS STATION

Tucker Blvd.
Clark Ave.
11th St.
11th St.
10th St.
9th St.
Washington Ave.
Convention Plaza
Martin Luther King Dr.
Cole St.
Carr Dr.

Bowling Hall of Fame
Busch Stadium
Market St.
Chestnut St.
8th St.
7th St.
St. Louis Centre
America's Convention Center

KIENER PLAZA
Walnut St.
6th St.
Pine St.
Olive St.
Locust St.
Lucas Ave.
Convention Plaza
Trans World Dome

Broadway
Old Courthouse
LUTHER ELY SMITH PARK
4th St.

Memorial Drive
Memorial Drive
Memorial Drive
Old Cathedral
JEFFERSON NATIONAL EXPANSION MEMORIAL

TO AIRPORT, MOTEL 6, AND UNIVERSITY OF MISSOURI-- ST. LOUIS

Poplar St.
Spruce St.

Gateway Arch
N. 2nd St.
LACLEDE'S LANDING
N. 1st St.
N. Wharf St.

Leonor K. Sullivan Blvd.
LEVEE

Poplar St. Bridge
Mississippi River
Gateway Riverboat Cruises
The Presidential Casino on the Admiral
Eads Bridge
Martin Luther King Bridge

FOOD

Because of St. Louis's many historical and ethnic districts, the difference of a few blocks can mean vastly different cuisine. For beer, outdoor tables, and live music, often without a cover charge, the city offers **Laclede's Landing** (241-5875), a collection of restaurants, bars, and dance clubs housed in 19th-century buildings on the riverfront. Once an industrial wasteland, the Landing is now a hot nightspot (21+; midnight-6am). To get there, walk north along the river from the Gateway Arch, or toward the river on Washington St. The area surrounding **Union Station,** at 18th and Market St. downtown, is also being revamped by the young and restless with hip restaurants and bars. The **Central West End** offers coffeehouses and outdoor cafes; a slew of impressive restaurants await just north of Lindell Blvd. along **Euclid Ave.** Take MetroLink to "Central West End" and walk north, or catch the Shuttlebug. St. Louis's historic Italian neighborhood, **The Hill,** southwest of downtown and just northwest of Tower Grove Park, produces plenty of inexpensive pasta; take bus #99 "Lafayette." Cheap Thai, Philippine, and Vietnamese restaurants spice up the **South Grand** area, at Grand Blvd. just south of Tower Grove Park; board bus #70 "Grand." The hip intellectual set hangs out on **University City Loop** (not actually a loop, but Delmar Blvd. between Skinker Blvd. and Big Bend Blvd.), which features coffeehouses and a mixed bag of American and international restaurants.

✪**Blueberry Hill,** 6504 Delmar Blvd. (727-0880), on the Loop. An eclectic rock 'n' roll restaurant similar to the Hard Rock Cafe—but much cooler. Record covers, Howdy Doody toys, and giant baseball cards grace the premises. The jukebox plays 2000 songs, and live bands play F-Sa and some weeknights (cover $4-15). Burgers are big and juicy ($4.50). 21+ after 8pm. Open M-Sa 11am-1am, Su 11am-midnight.

✪**Ted Drewe's Frozen Custard,** 4224 S. Grand Blvd. (352-7376); or 6726 Chippewa (481-2652), on Rte. 66. *The* place for the summertime St. Louis experience since 1929. Standing in line for the "chocolate-chip banana concrete shake" is rewarding; the blended toppings are thick enough to hang in an overturned cup ($1.50-3.50). Open daily June-Aug. 11am-midnight; Feb.-May and Sept.-Dec. 11am-11pm.

Pandora Bakery, 1858 Russell Blvd. (773-6161), in the Soulard District, where the only thing better than the rhubarb muffins ($1.60) is the friendly and outgoing staff. They know what's up around town. Very convenient to the Huck Finn hostel and the Anheuser-Busch brewery. Open Tu-F 7am-6pm, Sa-Su 7am-4pm.

Pho Grand, 3191 S. Grand Blvd. (664-7435), in the South Grand area. Voted "Best Vietnamese" and "Best Value" in St. Louis. The real deal, not Americanized, with tons of good vegetarian options. Their specialty is the noodle soup ($4); entrees are $4-6. Open Su-M and W-Th 11am-10pm, F-Sa 11am-11pm.

Kaldi's Coffeehouse and Roasting Company, 700 De Mun Ave. (727-9955), in Clayton. May be the best coffeehouse in St. Louis, where the java is home-roasted and the food is fresh. Intellectuals swarm for daily panini ($5) and whole-wheat pizza ($3). Very veggie-friendly. Open daily 7am-11pm.

SIGHTS

Downtown

The nation's tallest monument at 630 ft., the **Gateway Arch** (982-1410) and the **Museum of Westward Expansion,** on Memorial Dr. within the **Jefferson National Expansion Memorial,** towers gracefully over all of St. Louis and southern Illinois. *(Museum and arch open daily 8am-10pm; in winter 9am-6pm. Tickets for 1 attraction $6, ages 13-16 $4, ages 3-12 $2.50; 2 attractions $10/$8/$5; 3 attractions $14/$12/$7.50. Limited wheelchair access.)* The most impressive view is from the ground looking up. Elevator modules straight out of a sci-fi film soar to the top of the arch every 10min. Waits are shorter after dinner or in the morning, but are uniformly long on Saturday. Beneath the arch, the museum celebrates the Louisiana Purchase and its exploration. The 40min. "Monument to the Dream" film, screened once per hour, chronicles the arch's construction. **Odyssey Theater** arches your neck with films shown on a 4-story screen every hour on the hour. Scope out the city from the water with **Gateway Riverboat Cruises** (621-4040 or 800-878-7411); 1hr. tours leave from the docks in front of the arch (tours 10am-10pm; $7.50, ages 3-12 $3.75).

Beneath the arch, the **Old Cathedral,** 209 Walnut St. (231-3250), St. Louis's oldest church, still holds masses daily. Within walking distance is the **Old Courthouse,** 11 N. 4th St. (425-6156), across the highway from the arch. *(Open daily 8am-4:30pm; tours usually on the hr.; free. Limited wheelchair access.)* In 1847, Dred Scott sued for freedom from slavery here. Stroll down an additional block to Krener Plaza and turn around to witness the courthouse perfectly framed by the arch.

It's a strike either way at the **International Bowling Museum and Hall of Fame** and the **St. Louis Cardinals Hall of Fame Museum,** 111 Stadium Plaza (231-6340), across from Busch Stadium. *(Open in summer M-Sa 9am-5pm, Su noon-5pm; Oct.-Mar. daily 11am-4pm; game days until 6:30pm. $5, ages 5-12 $3. Includes 4 frames in the lanes downstairs. Wheelchair access.)* This classy museum complex is lined with funny panels on the history and development of bowling, with titles like "real men play quills and throw cheeses," as well as memorabilia from the glory days of St. Louis baseball. Historic **Union Station** (421-6655), at 18th and Market St. 1 mi. west of downtown (MetroLink to Union Station), houses a shopping mall, food court, and entertainment center in a magnificent structure that was once the nation's largest and busiest railroad terminal. "The Entertainer" lives on at the **Scott Joplin House**, 2658 Delmar (533-1003), just west of downtown at Geyer Rd., where the ragtime legend lived and composed from 1901 to 1903. *(Open in summer M-Sa 10am-4pm, Su noon-6pm; off-season Su noon-5pm. $2, ages 6-12 $1.25. Wheelchair access.)*

South and Southwest of Downtown

Soulard is bounded by I-55 and Seventh St.; walk south on Broadway or 7th St. from downtown, or take bus #73 "Carondelet." In the early 70s, the city proclaimed this area a historic district, because it once housed German and East European immigrants, many of whom worked in the breweries. Young couples and families are revitalizing the area without displacing the older generation of immigrants. The district surrounds the **Soulard Farmers Market,** 730 Carroll St. (622-4180), at Lafayette and 7th St. *(Open W-F 8am-5:30pm, Sa 6am-5:30pm; hrs. vary among merchants.)* Despite its age (220 years), Soulard *still* has fresh produce. The end of 12th St. features the largest brewery in the world, the **Anheuser-Busch Brewery,** 1127 Pestalozzi St. (577-2626), at 12th and Lynch St. *(Tours M-Sa 9am-5pm; Sept.-May 9am-4pm. Get free tickets at the office. Wheelchair access.)* Take bus #40 "Broadway" south from downtown. The 1½hr. tour is markedly less thrilling than the chance to sample beer at the end, but you'll get booted after 15min. A few blocks southwest of the brewery, Cherokee St.'s **Antique Row** is lined with antiques and used bookstores.

The internationally acclaimed 79-acre **Missouri Botanical Garden,** 4344 Shaw Blvd. (800-642-8842), thrives north of Tower Grove Park on grounds left by entrepreneur Henry Shaw. *(Open daily 9am-8pm; early Sept. to late May 9am-5pm. $5, seniors $3, under 12 free. Wheelchair access.)* From downtown, take I-44 west by car or ride MetroLink to "Central West End" and hop on bus #13 "Union-Missouri Botanical Gardens" to the main entrance. Among the flora from all over the globe, the Japanese Garden is guaranteed to soothe the weary budget traveler, while the Climatron acts as an excellent rainforest simulator. Independent exploration is encouraged, and there is a guided tour at 1pm. Much farther out this way, **Grant's Farm,** 10501 Gravois Rd. (843-1700), once housed former president Ulysses S. Grant. *(Open daily May-Aug., days in Apr. and Sept.-Oct. vary; call ahead for hrs. Free, but reservations required.)* Take I-55 west to Reavis Barracks Rd., turn left onto Gravois Rd., then turn right onto the farm. The tour consists of a tram ride through a wildlife preserve where over 1000 animals roam and interact freely, as evidenced by the zebrass (donkey-zebra), and concludes with free beer in the historic Baurnhof area.

West of Downtown

Forest Park, the country's largest urban park, was home to the 1904 World's Fair and St. Louis Exposition, where ice cream cones and hot dogs decorated kids' faces with cream and ketchup for the first time ever. Take MetroLink to Forest Park or Central West End, then catch the Shuttlebug, which stops at all the important sights. The park contains three museums, a zoo, a planetarium, a 12,000-seat amphitheater, and a grand canal, as well as countless picnic areas, pathways, and flying golf balls. The **St. Louis Science Center,** 5050 Oakland Ave. (800-456-7572), in the park's southeast corner, has tons of hands-on exhibits, an OmniMax, and a planetarium, where lasers dance to the sounds of bands like Pink Floyd and U2 on weekends. *(Museum open in summer M and W-Th 9am-6pm, Tu and F 9am-9pm, Sa 10am-9pm, Su 11am-6pm; off-season M-Th 9am-5pm, F 9am-9pm, Sa 10am-9pm, Su 11am-6pm. Free. Call for show schedules and prices.)* Inside, learn how a laser printer works, watch an old Star Trek episode, practice surgery, or use police radars to clock the unusually high speeds of cars on I-40. Marlin Perkins, the late, great host of TV's *Wild Kingdom,* turned the **St. Louis Zoo** (781-0900) into a world-class institution. *(Open June-Aug. W-M 9am-5pm, Tu 9am-9pm; Sept.-May daily 9am-5pm. Free.)* You can even view computer-generated images of future human evolutionary stages (no, they don't all look like Kate

GREAT PLAINS

Moss) at the "Living World" exhibit. The **Missouri History Museum** (746-4599), at Lindell Blvd. and DeBaliviere Ave. at the north end of the park, includes a new exhibit on the 1904 St. Louis World's Fair (open Tu 9:30am-8:30pm, W-Su 9:30am-5pm; free). Atop **Art Hill**, just to the southwest, an equestrian statue of France's Louis IX, the city's namesake and the only Louis to achieve Sainthood, beckons with his raised sword in front of the **St. Louis Art Museum** (721-0072), which contains masterpieces of Asian, Renaissance, and Impressionist art. *(Open Tu 1:30-8:30pm, W-Su 10am-5pm. Main museum free, special exhibits usually $7, students and seniors $6, ages 6-12 $5, free Tu.)* Forest Park sights are all wheelchair accessible.

From Forest Park, head east a few blocks to gawk at the lavish residential sections of the **Central West End**, where every house is a turn-of-the-century version of a French château or Tudor mansion. The vast **Cathedral of St. Louis,** 4431 Lindell Blvd. (533-2824 or 533-0544 to schedule tours), is a strange combination of Romanesque, Byzantine, Gothic, and Baroque styles. *(Open daily in summer 7am-dusk, off-season 7am-7pm. Guided tours M-F 10am-3pm, Su after the noon Mass. Wheelchair access.)* Gold-flecked mosaics depict 19th-century church history in Missouri. Take bus #93 "Lindell" from downtown, or walk from the Central West End MetroLink stop.

The Loop, just northwest of the Central West End, has more than just shops full of ethnic items and cafés full of intellectuals—for instance, the sidewalk. All along the loop runs the **St. Louis Walk of Fame,** 6504 Delmar (727-STAR/7827), with stars and biographies celebrating famous St. Louisians like Kathleen Turner, Kevin Kline, Tennessee Williams, Bob Costas, and John Goodman.

Steamboats, Monster Trucks, and Automobiles

Ever since the days when steamboats roamed the Mississippi and covered wagons departed westward, transportation has defined St. Louis. The gateway city didn't escape Detroit's conquest, however, and cars rule today. The **St. Louis Car Museum,** 1575 Woodson Rd. at I-170 (993-1330) houses over 150 legendary cars that have cruised the highways and byways of America, from the Model T to the '57 Chevy to the VW Bus (open M-Sa 9am-5pm, Su 11am-5pm; $3.75, under 12 $2.75). Less exalted autos are crushed under the 66 in. wheels of **Bigfoot,** the "Original Monster Truck." The first Bigfoot and its legacies live near the airport and I-270 at 6311 N. Lindbergh. (731-2822. Open M-F 9am-6pm, Sa 9am-4pm, some extended summer hrs. Free.)

ENTERTAINMENT

Founded in 1880, the **St. Louis Symphony Orchestra** is one of the country's finest. **Powell Hall,** 718 N. Grand Blvd. (534-1700), houses the 101-member orchestra in acoustic and visual splendor. Take bus #91 "Delmar" or #94 "Washington Ave." to Grand Blvd. (Performances Sept. to early May Th-Sa 8pm, Sa-Su matinees at 3pm. Box office open M-Sa 9am-5pm and before performances. Tickets $14-66, students ½-price in certain sections, senior rush ½-price on day of show.)

St. Louis offers theater-goers many choices. The outdoor **Municipal Opera** (361-1900), the "Muny," performs tour productions of hit musicals on summer nights in Forest Park. Back rows provide 1456 free seats on a first come, first served basis. The gates open at 7:30pm for 8:15pm shows; it's a good idea to arrive even earlier for popular performances. (Box office open June to mid-Aug. daily 9am-9pm. Tickets $6-44.) Other productions are regularly staged by the **St. Louis Black Repertory,** 634 N. Grand Blvd. (534-3807), and the Repertory Theatre of St. Louis, 130 Edgar Rd. (968-4925). The **Fox Theatre,** 527 N. Grand (534-1111 for tickets), was originally a 1930s movie palace, but now hosts Broadway shows, classic films, and Las Vegas, country, and rock stars. (Box office open M-Sa 10am-6pm, Su noon-4pm. Tours Tu, Th, Sa at 10:30am. $5, under 12 $2.50. Call for reservations.) The **Tivoli Theatre,** 6350 Delmar Blvd. (862-1100), shows artsy and lesser-known releases ($6; students, seniors, matinees $4). **Metrotix** (534-1111) has tickets to most of the city's theatrical events.

A recent St. Louis ordinance permits gambling on the rivers. The **President Casino on the Admiral** (622-3000 or 800-772-3647), whose buses invite you to "Ride the President," floats below the Arch on the Missouri side (open 8am-4am; $2). On the Illinois side, the **Casino Queen** (618-874-5000 or 800-777-0777) claims "the loosest slots in town" (11 cruises daily on odd-numbered hrs. 9am-7am; $2). Parking for both is free; both have wheelchair access.

Six Flags over Mid-America (938-4800) reigns supreme in the kingdom of amusement parks, 30min. southwest of St. Louis on I-44 at Exit 261 (hrs. vary by season; $30, seniors $15, ages 3-11 $25). The **St. Louis Cardinals** (421-3060) play ball at **Busch Stadium** April through October (tickets $6-24). The **Rams** (425-8830), formerly of L.A., have brought the ol' pigskin back to St. Louis at the **Trans World Dome** (tickets $25). **Blues** hockey games (968-1800 for tickets) slice ice at the **Kiel Center** at 14th St. and Clark Ave.

NIGHTLIFE

Music rules the night in St. Louis. The *Riverfront Times* (free at many bars and clubs) and the *Get Out* section of the *Post-Dispatch* list weekly entertainment. The *St. Louis Magazine,* published annually, lists seasonal events, as does the comprehensive calendar distributed at the tourist office.

The bohemian **Loop** parties hearty as students and scholarly types flock to the coffeehouses and bars of Delmar Blvd. for outdoor dining, conversation, and music. **Brandt's Market & Café,** 6525 Delmar Blvd. (727-3773), does it all at any hour with wine, beer, espresso, and a full, eclectic menu (entrees $7-13). The live music outside, almost daily, runs the gamut from acoustic to lounge to Brazilian. (Open M-Th 11am-midnight, F 11am-1am, Sa 8:30am-1am, Su 10:30am-midnight.)

Most bars at **Laclede's Landing** offer mainstream rock and draw preppy, touristy crowds. In the summer, bars take turns sponsoring "block parties," with outdoor food, drink, music, and dancing in the streets. Weekends see hordes of St. Louis University (SLU, pronounced "slew") students descending on the waterfront. **Kennedy's Second Street Co.,** 612 N. 2nd St. (421-3655), strikes a rawer chord with alternative music nightly and occasionally heavier punk, replete with mosh pit and stage diving (open daily 11:30am-3am; cover $3-5). **Mississippi Nights,** 914 N. 1st St. (421-3853), hosts big local and national bands (box office open M-F 11am-6pm).

Also downtown, **Union Station** and its environs have spawned some off-beat nightlife. **Hot Locust Cantina,** 2005 Locust St. (231-3666), cooks up some hot stuff, both for your mouth and for your ears. (Entrees $6-9. Lunch M-Sa 11am-3pm, dinner Tu-Sa 5pm-midnight. Music weekend nights. No cover.) The less touristy and quite gay-friendly **Soulard** district has been known to ripple with the blues. Live Irish music plays nightly at **McGurk's** (776-8309), at 12th and Russell Blvd. (No cover. Open M-F 11am-1:30am, Sa 11:30-1:30am, Su 4pm-midnight.) The **1860s Hard Shell Café & Bar,** 1860 S. 9th St. (231-1860), hosts some gritty blues and rock performances. (Music nightly and Sa-Su afternoons. $3 cover after 9pm. Open M-F 9am-1:30am, Sa 9am-1:30am, Su 11am-1:30am.) **Clementine's,** 2001 Menard (664-7869), houses a crowded restaurant and St. Louis's oldest gay bar (est. 1978). Sandwiches and entrees run $4.50-9.50. (Open M-F 10am-1:30am, Sa 8am-1:30am, Su 11am-midnight.)

■ Near St. Louis

Cahokia Mounds State Historic Site Fifteen minutes from the city in Collinsville, IL (8 mi. east of downtown on I-55/70 to Rte. 111), over 65 earthen mounds mark the site of **Cahokia,** an extremely complex Native American settlement inhabited from 700 to 1500 AD, now the Cahokia Mounds State Historic Site and a World Heritage Site. In constructing the edifices' foundations, builders had to carry over 15 million loads of dirt on their backs. The largest, **Monk's Mound,** took 300 years to complete. The Cahokians, once a community of 20,000, faced the same problems of pollution, overcrowding, and resource depletion that we do today—which might help explain their mysterious disappearance. The **Interpretive Center** (618-346-5160) contains life-sized dioramas and screens a 15min. film illustrating this

"City of the Sun" (shows every hr. 10am-4pm). A guide booklet ($1 in the gift shop) or the narrated audio tape borrowed from the info desk will lead the curious (center open daily 9am-5pm; free, suggested donation $2, children $1). Celebrate equinoxes and solstices at **Woodhenge,** a solar calendar much like Britain's stone one, at dawn on the Sunday closest to the big day (open daily 8am-dusk; free; wheelchair access).

St. Charles Founded in 1769, the town of St. Charles (take I-70 W and exit north at 5th St.), has made great strides since it was described as "ignorant, stupid, ugly, and miserable" by an early explorer. Nestled along the Missouri River, St. Charles now supports numerous antique shops, cafes, and wineries, mostly along historic S. Main St. The **visitors bureau,** 230 W. Main (946-7776 or 800-366-2427) distributes handy guides along with a map (open M-F 8am-5pm, Sa 10am-5pm, Su noon-5pm).

St. Charles has the dual distinction of being both Missouri's first state capital and the starting point of Lewis and Clark's 1804 exploration of the Louisiana Purchase. The **Lewis & Clark Center,** 701 Riverside Dr. (947-3199), traces the adventurers' trek across the continent through dioramas (open daily 10:30am-4:30pm; $1, children 50¢). You can tour the **first Missouri State Capitol,** 200 S. Main St. (946-9282), and its surrounding green (open M-Sa 9am-4pm, Su 11am-5pm; $2, ages 6-12 $1.25). **Cavern Springs Winery,** 300 Water St. (947-1200), hosts wine tastings and tours of its pre-Civil War grottoes (open M-F 10am-5pm, Sa 11am-6pm, Su noon-6pm; free).

Other attractions lend themselves to liveliness: outdoor festivals, riverboat gambling, and the **Goldenrod Showboat,** 1000 Riverside Dr. (946-2020), the nation's last surviving showboat and the inspiration for the musical "Showboat." (Matinee W-Th, regular shows Th-Su. Tickets from $21, including a buffet. Box office open M-Sa 9am-5pm, Su noon-7pm.)

St. Charles marks the starting point of **KATY Trail State Park** (800-334-6946), an 1890s railroad route *cum* 230 mi. hiking and biking trail past bluffs, wetlands, and wildlife that even Lewis and Clark gawked at. Call for info on unfinished portions of the trail, which ends in Clinton. South Main St. has many possibilities for bike rental, including **The Touring Cyclist,** 104 S. Main St. (949-9630. Open M-F 9am-8pm, Sa 9am-6pm, Su 10am-5pm. $5 per hr., $20 per 24hr.)

■ Hannibal

Hannibal hugs the Mississippi River 100 mi. west of Springfield, IL and 100 mi. northwest of St. Louis. Founded in 1819, the town remained a sleepy village until Samuel Clemens (a.k.a. Mark Twain) roused the world's attention to his boyhood home by making it the setting of *The Adventures of Tom Sawyer.* Today, tourists flock to Hannibal to imagine Tom, Huck, and Becky romping around the quaint streets and nearby caves. Somehow, though, in the midst of reenactments, a tourist trolley, and relentless Mark Twain promotion, Hannibal retains its considerable small-town hospitality and charm.

The **Mark Twain Boyhood Home and Museum,** 208 Hill St. (221-9010), fills the downtown historic district with restored rooms and an assortment of memorabilia from the witty wordsmith's life. Across the street sit the **Pilaster House** and **Clemens Law Office.** Further down, the new **Mark Twain Museum** includes a collection of Tom and Huck Norman Rockwells. (Open 8am-6pm; May 8am-5pm; Nov.-Feb. M-Sa 10am-4pm, Su noon-4pm; Mar. M-Sa 9am-4pm, Su noon-4pm; Apr., Sept.-Oct. 9am-5pm. All sites included $5, ages 6-12 $2.50.) The **Mark Twain Riverboat** (221-3222), at Center St. Landing, steams down the Mississippi for a 1hr. sight-seeing cruise that is part history, part folklore, and part advertisement for the land attractions. (June-early Sept. 3 per day; May and Sept.-Oct. 1 per day. $8, ages 3-12 $5; dinner cruises 6:30pm $26/$16.) Injun Joe's ghost haunts the **Mark Twain Cave** (221-1656), 1 mi. south of Hannibal on Rte. 79, supposedly the one Twain explored as a boy. (Open daily 8am-8pm; Apr.-May and Sept.-Oct. 9am-6pm; Nov.-Mar. 9am-4pm. 1hr. tour $9, ages 5-12 $5.) Nearby **Cameron Cave** provides a slightly longer and far spookier lantern tour ($11, ages 5-12 $6). In early July, 100,000 fans converge on Hannibal for the fence-painting, frog-jumping fun of the **Tom Sawyer Days** festival. Twain, however, wasn't the only

American icon to pass through Hannibal. Mr. Davidson, **Harley-Davidson** that is, rolls through in early September as part of the **Missouri State Harley Owners' Group Rally** (221-2477 for details on both events).

Chain motels, some of which differ in name but share the same owner, swarm about Hannibal, particularly on **Mark Twain Ave.** (Rte. 36) and on U.S. 61 near the Rte. 36 junction. Numerous **B&Bs** are located downtown but will clean out your wallet. The cheapest singles are $60—times have changed from Twain's Hannibal, when "there was not enough money in the first place to furnish a conversation!" Shiningly well-maintained, the **Howard Johnson Lodge,** 3603 McMasters Ave. (221-7950), at the U.S. 36/I-72 junction, has potentially decent but highly variable prices (A/C, cable TV, pool; singles $39-55; doubles $55-79). Two campgrounds offer relief from headaches induced by motel price inconsistencies. The **Mark Twain Cave Campgrounds** (221-1656), adjacent to the cave 1 mi. south of Hannibal on Rte. 79, are cheery and family-oriented, but not too secluded ($14, full hookup $18, $1.50 per extra person after 4). Sidestep Hannibal's unending fast food options, wax up your dental floss, and head into **Ole Planters,** 316 N. Main St. (221-4410), to devour tasty $4.25 BBQ beef sandwiches. (Open M-W and F-Sa 11am-3pm and 4:30pm-8pm, Th and Su 11am-3pm; Nov.-Mar. closed Su.) The **Twainland Cheesecake Company,** 116 North St. (221-3355), serves up sandwiches ($4.75) and over 20 flavors of cheesecake—this ain't Aunt Polly's kitchen (several options daily; open M-Sa 10am-3pm).

On **Trailways Bus Lines,** at the junction of MM and 61 (248-0066 or 800-992-4618), in front of Abel's Quik Shop, buses blaze to Cedar Rapids (1 per day, $35) and St. Louis (1 per day, $21). The **Hannibal Visitors and Convention Bureau,** 505 N. 3rd St. (221-2477), offers info and free local calls (open M-F 8am-6pm, Sa 9-5, Su 9:30am-4pm). **Post Office:** 801 Broadway (221-0957; open M-F 8:30am-5pm, Sa 8:30am-noon). **ZIP code:** 63401. **Area code:** 573.

■ Kansas City

With over 200 public fountains and more miles of boulevard than Paris, Kansas City displays a heavy European influence. Nevertheless, this city can't hide its Heartland roots; Kansas City has twice been voted "Barbeque Capital of the World" and is considered a key player in the development of jazz. When Prohibition stifled many of the nation's parties in the 1920s, booze continued to flow here; KC's alcohol-induced nightlife brought jazz musicians from all over the country, and their music flourished. The Kansas City of today maintains its big bad blues-and-jazz rep in a metropolis spanning two states: the highly suburbanized half in Kansas (KCKS) and the quicker-paced commercial half in Missouri (KCMO).

ORIENTATION AND PRACTICAL INFORMATION

The KC metropolitan area sprawls across two states, and travel may take a while, particularly without a car. Most sights worth visiting in KC lie south of downtown on the Missouri side; all listings are for Kansas City, MO, unless otherwise indicated. Although parking around town is not as easy as in many midwestern towns, there are lots that charge $4 or less per day. **I-70** cuts east-west through the city, and **I-435** circles the two-state metro area. KCMO is laid out on an extensive grid with numbered streets running east-west from the Missouri River well out into suburbs, and named streets running north-south. **Main St.** divides the city east-west.

Airport: Kansas City International (243-5237), 18 mi. northwest of KC off I-29 (take bus #29). **KCI Shuttle** (243-5000 or 800-243-6383) departs over 100 times daily, servicing downtown, Westport, Crown Center, and Plaza of KCMO and Overland Park, Mission, and Lenexa of KCKS ($11-15). Taxi to downtown $23-26.

Trains: Amtrak, 2200 Main St. (421-3622 or 800-872-7245), at Grand Ave. directly across from Crown Center (bus #27). 2 per day to St. Louis (5½hr., $25-49) and Chicago (8hr., $47-93). Open 24hr.

Buses: Greyhound, 1101 N. Troost (221-2835 or 800-231-2222). Take bus #25. *The terminal is in an unsafe area.* To St. Louis (4-5hr., 5 per day, $27) and Chicago (9-15hr., 8 per day, $42). Open daily 5:30am-12:30am.

Public Transportation: Kansas City Area Transportation Authority (Metro), 1200 E. 18th St. (221-0660), near Troost. Excellent downtown coverage. 90¢, $1 for KCKS, $1.20 for Independence; ages 16-18, seniors with Medicare card, and disabled ½-price. Free transfers; free return coupon available downtown. Pick up maps and schedules at headquarters, on buses, in the public library, or at the Crown Center information desk. Buses run 5am-6pm (outer routes) or 5am-midnight (downtown routes). The **trolley** (221-3399) loops from downtown to the City Market, Crown Center, Westport, and Country Club Plaza Mar.-Dec. M-Sa 10am-10pm, Su noon-6pm; holiday hrs. vary. $5 for all day, seniors and ages 6-12 $4. Exact change required.

Taxis: Yellow Cab, 471-5000. $1.50 base fare, $1.20 per mi. 24hr.

Car Rental: Thrifty Car Rental, 2001 Baltimore St. (842-8550 or 800-367-2277), 1 block west of 20th and Main St. (take bus #40). $28 per day, with 250 free mi.; 29¢ each additional mi. Weekend fares are lower. Under 25 surcharge $7.50 per day. Must be 21 with a major credit card. Open M-W 8am-6pm, Th-F 8am-8pm, Sa-Su 9am-4pm. A free shuttle from the airport will take you to the location at 11530 NW Prairie View Rd. (464-5670). Open 24hr.

Visitor Info: Convention and Visitors Bureau of Greater Kansas City, 1100 Main St. (221-5242 or 800-767-7700), 25th fl. of the City Center Sq. Bldg. Grab *An Official Visitor's Guide to Kansas City,* which contains extensive listings and seasonal events. Open M-F 8:30am-5pm. **Missouri Tourist Information Center,** 4010 Blue Ridge Cut-Off (889-3330 or 800-877-1234 for a travel package), as you exit east off I-70. Open daily Mar.-Nov. 8am-5pm, Dec.-Feb. M-Sa 8am-5pm.

Hotlines: Crisis Line, 531-0233. 24hr. **Gay and Lesbian Hotline,** 931-4470. 24hr.

Hospitals: Truman Medical Center, 2301 Holmes St. (556-30000). **Women's Clinic of Johnson County,** 5701 W. 119th St. (491-4020).

Internet Access: Kansas City Public Library, 311 E. 12th St. (221-2685), at 12th and McGee.

Post Office: 315 W. Pershing Rd. (374-9180), at Broadway (take bus #40 or 51). Open M-F 8am-6:30pm, Sa 8am-2:30pm. **ZIP code:** 64108. **Area code:** 816 in Missouri, 913 in Kansas; in text 816 unless noted.

ACCOMMODATIONS AND CAMPGROUNDS

Kansas City can usually accommodate anyone who needs a room, but if there's a big convention, the whole city may be booked. The least expensive lodgings are near the interstate highways, especially I-70. Unfortunately, the car-deprived budget traveler is out of luck. Downtown, most hotels are either expensive, uninhabitable, or unsafe—sometimes all three. For more help, **Bed and Breakfast Kansas City** (913-888-3636) has over 30 listings of inns and homes throughout the city from $50.

Serendipity Bed and Breakfast, 116 S. Pleasant St. (833-4719 or 800-203-4299), 15min. from downtown KC. A Victorian mansion with all the trimmings and an enormous breakfast. Historic tours are available in a 1926 Studebaker, weather and time permitting. Most of the rooms are expensive, but several doubles and 1 single in particular are eminently affordable. Singles $30-55, doubles $45-85. Discounts for stays of 3 nights or more.

American Inn, 4141 S. Noland (373-8300 or 800-90-LODGE/905-6343), is just one in a massive chain that loops KC and dominates the KC budget motel market. Despite the gaudy neon facades, the rooms inside are large, cheap, and good-lookin', with A/C, free local calls, cable, and outdoor pools. Singles $35; doubles $50. Other locations include Woods Chapel Rd. (228-1080), off I-70 at Exit 18; 1211 Armour Rd. (471-3451), in North Kansas City off I-35 at Exit 6B; and 7949 Splitlog Rd. (913-299-2999), in KCKS off I-70 at Exit 414. Prices drop as the distance to KC increases.

Interstate Inn, (229-6311), off I-70 at Exit 18, is a great deal. The best prices are for a set of first come, first served rooms. All rooms are large and remodeled. Singles from $25; doubles from $30.

YMCA, 900 N. 8th St. (913-371-4400) in KCKS. Varying rooms for men with access to the Y's gym and pool. Take bus #1 or 4. $22 1st night. Key deposit $7.

Lake Jacomo (795-8888), 22 mi. southeast of KC. Take I-470 south to Colbern, then head east on Colbern for 2 mi. Forested campsites, fishing, swimming, and a nifty dam across the street. Sites $10, with electricity $12, full hookup $18.

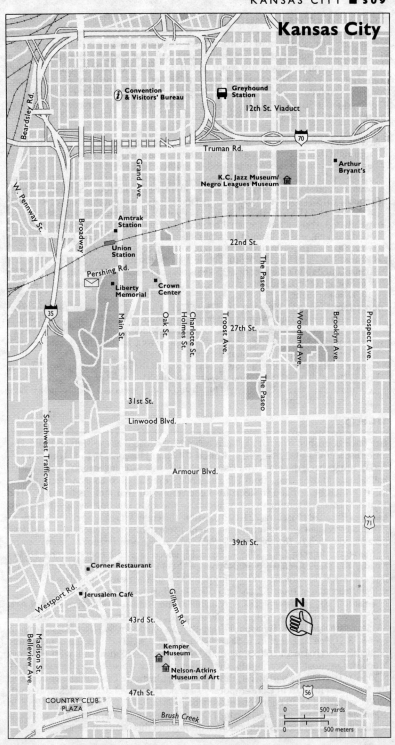

Kansas City

- ⓘ Convention & Visitors' Bureau
- 🚌 Greyhound Station
- 12th St. Viaduct
- Bear del ep Rd.
- W. Pennway St.
- Truman Rd.
- 70
- Grand Ave.
- Arthur Bryant's
- K.C. Jazz Museum/ Negro Leagues Museum
- Broadway
- Amtrak Station
- 22nd St.
- The Paseo
- Union Station
- Pershing Rd.
- 35
- Liberty Memorial
- Crown Center
- Main St.
- Oak St.
- Charlotte St.
- Holmes St.
- Troost Ave.
- 27th St.
- Woodland Ave.
- Brooklyn Ave.
- Prospect Ave.
- 31st St.
- Linwood Blvd.
- Southwest Trafficway
- Armour Blvd.
- The Paseo
- 71
- 39th St.
- GREAT PLAINS
- Corner Restaurant
- Westport Rd.
- Jerusalem Café
- 43rd St.
- Gilham Rd.
- N
- Madison St.
- Belleview Ave.
- Kemper Museum
- Nelson-Atkins Museum of Art
- 47th St.
- 56
- COUNTRY CLUB PLAZA
- Brush Creek
- 0   500 yards
- 0   500 meters

BBQ AND OTHER GRUB

Kansas City rustles up a herd of meaty, juicy barbecue restaurants that serve unusually tangy ribs. If midwestern meat dishes don't float your boat, the **Westport** area, at Westport Rd. and Broadway just south of **39th St.,** sports eclectic menus, cafes, and coffeehouses. Ethnic fare clusters along 39th St. between Broadway and State Line. For fresh produce year-round, visit the largest farmers market in the Midwest: the **City Market,** at 5th and Walnut St. along the river (842-1271). Saturday and Sunday are the busiest. (Open Su-F 9am-4pm, Sa 6am-4pm.)

◉**Arthur Bryant's,** 1727 Brooklyn St. (231-1123). Take the Brooklyn exit off I-70 and turn right (bus #110 from downtown). Down-home BBQ. The thin, orange, almost granular sauce is a spectacular blend of southern and western influences. A monstrous and messy sandwich is $6—beef, ham, pork, chicken, turkey, or ribs are available and sloppy. Open M-Th 10am-9:30pm, F-Sa 10am-10pm, Su 11am-8:30pm.

Strouds, 1015 E. 85th St. (333-2132), at Troost, 2 mi. north of the Holmes Exit off I-435; also at 5410 N. Oak Ridge Rd. (454-9600). Enormous dinners ($6-19) in a weathered wooden hut crammed between the train tracks and an overpass. Great fried chicken, with cinnamon rolls, biscuits, and honey. Early birds get prompt service. Open M-Th 4-10pm, F 11am-11pm, Sa 2-11pm, Su 11am-10pm.

d'Bronx, 3904 Bell St. (531-0550), on the 39th St. restaurant row. A New York deli transplanted to middle America. 35 kinds of subs (½ sub $3-5, whole $6-10), other sandwiches ($4-5), and huge brownies ($1.50). Open M-Th 10:30am-10:30pm, F-Sa 10:30am-midnight.

Jerusalem Café, 431 Westport Rd. (756-2770), which vegetarians of all faiths have claimed as a holy land. With vats of fantastic hummus, baba ghanoush, and tabouli, this restaurant has long won praise for the best Middle-Eastern food in KC. Be not afraid, meat lovers, they serve plenty of flesh as well. Sandwiches $5, entrees $7-10. Open M-Sa 11am-10pm, Su noon-8pm.

Corner Restaurant, 4059 Broadway (931-6630), in the heart of Westport. The best breakfast in all of KC ($3-5), and it's served through lunch. Plate-sized buttermilk or cornmeal pancakes $2, homestyle lunch and dinner specials $4-7. Open M-F 7am-3pm, Sa-Su 7am-2pm.

SIGHTS

Jazz once flourished in what has been recently designated as the 18th and Vine Historic District (474-VINE/8463). The **Kansas City Jazz Museum,** 1616 E. 18th St. (474-8463), brings back the era with classy displays, music listening stations, neon dance hall signs, and everything from Ella Fitzgerald's eyeglasses to Louis Armstrong's lip salve (which he applied to keep his kisser moist for that famous trumpet). The 15min. "Jazz is…" film plays every 30min. In the same building swings the **Negro Leagues Baseball Museum** (221-1920), where the era of segregation of the American pastime is recalled with photographs, interactive exhibits, and bittersweet nostalgia. *(Jazz museum open Tu-Th 9am-6pm, F-Sa 9am-9pm, Su noon-6pm. Baseball Museum open Tu-Sa 9am-6pm, Su noon-6pm. Either museum $6, under 13 $2.50; both museums $8/$4.)* Nearby, the **Black Archives of Mid-America,** 2033 Vine (483-1300), holds a large and fine collection of paintings and sculpture by African-American artists. *(Open M-F 9am-4:30pm, tours start at 10am; $2, under 17 50¢.)* Take bus #8 "Indiana."

A taste of KC's masterpieces is available at the **Nelson-Atkins Museum of Art,** 4525 Oak (751-1278), at 45th, 3 blocks northeast of Country Club Plaza (buses #47, 55, 56, 57). *(Open Tu-Th 10am-4pm, F 10am-9pm, Sa 10am-5pm, Su 1-5pm. $5, students $2, ages 6-18 $1; free Sa. Free tours Tu-Sa until 2pm, Su until 3pm.)* The museum contains one of the best East Asian art collections in the world, and a sculpture park with 13 Henry Moores. On most Friday nights, the museum hosts world-class jazz acts (5:30-8:30pm). Two blocks northwest, through the **Art Institute** campus, the entrance to the **Kemper Museum of Contemporary Art and Design,** 4420 Warwick Blvd. (561-3737), is marked by an enormous glass spider. *(Open Tu-Th 10am-4pm, F 10am-9pm, Sa 10am-5pm, Su 11am-5pm. Free.)* Georgia O'Keefe and Robert Mapplethorpe works, as well as modern sculptures, are scattered throughout this young museum.

A few blocks to the west at 47th and Southwest Trafficway, **Country Club Plaza** (753-0100), known as "the plaza," is the oldest and perhaps most picturesque shopping center in the U.S. Modeled after buildings in Seville, Spain, the plaza boasts fountains, sculptures, hand-painted tiles, and reliefs of grinning gargoyles. The plaza is lit up beautifully at night from Thanksgiving to New Year's. Catch a glimpse from the recently redone **riverwalk** along Bush Creek. Buses #39, 40, 47, 51, 56, 57, and 155 and the trolley all arrive at the plaza.

Crown Center, 2450 Grand Ave. (274-8444), sits 2 mi. north of the Plaza at Pershing; take bus #40, 56, or 57, or any trolley from downtown. The center, headquarters of Hallmark Cards, houses a maze of restaurants and shops, plus the children's **Coterie Theatre** (474-6552) and the **Ice Terrace** (274-8412), KC's only public outdoor ice-skating rink. *(Rink open Nov.-Dec. Su-Th 10am-9pm, F-Sa 10am-11pm; Jan.-Mar. daily 10am-9pm. $5, under 13 $4. Rentals $1.50.)* Say "I care!" and see how cards and accessories are made at the **Hallmark Visitors Center** (274-3613 or 274-5672 for a recording; open M-F 9am-5pm, Sa 9:30am-4:30pm; free). In July, Crown Center has **free concerts in the park** every Friday (a.k.a. "Friday Fun Fests"). Run through a huge fountain designed for exactly that purpose—you can't have more fun on a hot summer night with your clothes on.

The **Kansas City Zoo,** off I-435 E at 63rd St. (871-5701), in the sprawling Swope Park, offers a chance to tour the world; animals are grouped by their native country. *(Open daily Apr. to mid-Oct. 9am-5pm, mid-Oct. to Mar. 9am-4pm. $5, Tu $1, ages 3-11 $2.50, parking $2.)* Wildlife frolics on the big screen at the **IMAX Theater** next door (871-IMAX/4629; open Su-W 9am-5pm, Th-Sa 9am-8pm; $6, seniors $5, ages 3-11 $4).

ENTERTAINMENT AND NIGHTLIFE

The **Missouri Repertory Theatre** (235-2700), at 50th and Oak, stages American classics. (Season Sept.-May. Tickets $19-32, students and seniors $3 off. Box office open M-F 10am-5pm; call for in-season weekend hrs.) **Quality Hill Playhouse,** 303 W. 10th St. (235-2700), produces off-Broadway plays year-round (tickets $14-19, seniors and students $2 off). For more entertainment news, *Explore Kansas City* and *Pitch Weekly,* available at area restaurants and bars, are vital.

Sports fans will be pierced to the heart by **Arrowhead Stadium,** at I-70 and Blue Ridge Cutoff, home to football's **Chiefs** (924-9400 or 800-676-5488; tickets $29-50) and soccer's **Wizards** (472-4625; tickets $10-15). Next door, a water-fountained wonder, **Kauffman Stadium** (800-6-ROYALS/676-9257 or 921-8000), houses the **Royals** baseball team (tickets $6-15, M and Th $5). A stadium express bus runs from downtown and Country Club Plaza on game days.

In the 20s, Kansas City played hot spot to the nation's best jazz. Pianist **Count Basie** and his "Kansas City Sound" reigned at the River City bars, while saxophonist **Charlie "Bird" Parker** spread his wings and soared. The **Crown Center** celebrates annually with the **Kansas City International Jazz Festival** (888-FEST-111/337-8111), on the last weekend in June (tickets $10-12). The restored **Gem Theater,** 1615 E. 18th St. (842-1414), stages blues and jazz like in the old days (box office open M-F 10am-4pm). Across the street, the **Blue Room,** 1600 E. 18th St. (474-2929), cooks with some of the smoothest acts in town—after all, they have to live up to the legends next door at the museum. The **Grand Emporium,** 3832 Main St. (531-1504), twice voted the best blues night club in the U.S., has live jazz Fridays and Saturdays; weekdays feature rock, blues, and reggae bands (cover $3-15; open daily noon-3am). Down the street, **Jardine's,** 4536 Main St. (561-6480), plays straight-up jazz six nights a week, with nary a cover (music M 7-10pm, Tu-Th 7:30-11:30pm, F 5:30pm-3am, Sa 5pm-3am).

A few blocks west, noisy nightspots pack the restored **Westport** area (756-2789), near Broadway and Westport Rd. ½ mi. north of Country Club Plaza (see **Sights,** p. 510). There's no happy hour at **Blayney's,** 415 Westport Rd. (561-3747), but get there around 10pm for intense rhythm and blues (cover $2-5; live music 5 nights a week; open M-Sa 8pm-3am). **Hurricane,** 4048 Broadway (753-0884), grinds out alternative rock five nights a week on their deck (cover $3-5; open daily 4pm-2:45am).

Kiki's Bon-Ton Maison, 1515 Westport Rd. (931-9417), features KC's best in-house soul band (Sa 10:30pm) and whips up Cajun food with bayou flavor (jambalaya and crawfish $9-13; sandwiches $6). Kiki's also hosts the annual **Crawfish Festival** around the last weekend in May (open M-Th 11am-10pm, F 11am-11pm, Sa 11am-1:30am, Su 11:30am-8pm). **Jazz,** 1823 W. 39th St. at State Line (531-5556), features you-know-what. (Music W-Su after 8pm. No cover, but 50¢ surcharge on bill. Open M-Th 11am-midnight, F-Sa 11am-11:30am, Su 11am-midnight.) Further down on 39th St., **Gilhouly's,** 1721 39th St. (561-2899), at Bell St., doesn't host music, but it does have over 125 bottled imports, a large selection of Irish and Scottish beers on tap, and several pool tables (open M-Sa 11am-1:30am). Big names in jazz and blues show up at the club downstairs from the ritzy **Plaza III Steakhouse,** 4749 Pennsylvania St. (753-0000), at Country Club Plaza (music W-Th 7-11pm, no cover; music F-Sa 8:30pm-12:30am, cover $5). **Club Cabaret,** 5024 Main St. (753-6504), swings as a popular gay bar and dance club (cover $3; open Tu-Su 6pm-2:30am).

■ Near Kansas City: Independence

The buck stops at **Independence,** the hometown of former President Harry Truman. The town is a 15min. drive east of KC on I-70; take bus #24 "Independence." The original sign hangs at the **Harry S. Truman Library and Museum,** at U.S. 24 and Delaware St. (833-1225 or 800-833-1225), which contains a replica of the Oval Office, and detailed exhibits about the man, the period, and the presidency. (Open M-W and F-Sa 9am-5pm, Th 9am-9pm, Su noon-5pm. $5, seniors $4.50, ages 6-18 $3.) When Washington, D.C., overheated, the Trumans would return to the 14-room **Harry S. Truman Home,** 219 N. Delaware St., also known as the Summer White House. The **Truman Home Ticket and Info Center,** 223 Main St. (254-9929 or 254-7199 for a recorded message) sells tickets to tour the Victorian mansion (open daily 8:30am-5pm; $2, under 16 free). Before he moved into 1600 Pennsylvania Ave., Truman earned $3 a week at **Clinton's Drugstore,** 100 W. Maple (833-2625), an old-fashioned ice cream parlor. Pop in for an 85¢ cherry phosphate. (Open M-Th 10:30am-6pm, F-Sa 10:30am-8pm.)

Independence's history goes back farther than just Truman. Thousands of pioneers ventured west along the California, Oregon, and Santa Fe trails, which all began here. Go west at the **National Frontier Trails Center,** 318 W. Pacific (325-7575), and imagine 2000 mi. in a covered wagon—are we there yet? (Open M-Sa 9am-4:30pm, Su 12:30-4:30pm. $2.50, ages 6-17 $1.) The Addams Family-esque **Vaile Mansion,** 1500 N. Liberty St. (325-7430), built in 1881, has 112 windows and 2 ft. thick walls (open Apr.-Oct. M-Sa 10am-4pm, Su 1-4pm. $3, seniors $2.50, ages 6-16 $1).

Inspired by the chambered nautilus, the computer-designed world headquarters of the **Reorganized Church of Jesus Christ of Latter Day Saints** (833-1000), at River and Walnut St. is a bizarre and beautiful seashell that spirals up nearly 200 ft. (Tours M-Sa 9-11:30am and 1-5pm, Su 1-5pm. Organ recitals Su 3pm; daily in summer. Free.)

Nearby, in the City Hall building, Independence's **Dept. of Tourism,** 111 E. Maple (325-7111), has the skinny (open M-F 8am-5pm). Across the town square, in front of the Jackson County Courthouse, tasty, simple chow is served up at the **Blessing Times Garden Café,** 101 N. Main St. (252-0020; open M-Sa 7am-3pm).

■ Branson

The Presley family had no idea what the impact would be if they opened a tiny music theater on **West Hwy. 76.** Intentions aside, over 15,000 tour buses filled with retirees clog Branson's strip (Rte. 76, a.k.a. Country Music Blvd.) to visit the "live country music capital of the Universe." Scads of billboards, motels, and giant showplaces beckon the masses that visit Branson each year to embrace this modern-day mecca of country music and theater. The **Grand Palace,** 2700 W. Rte. 76 (800-884-4536), hears from big names like Barbara Mandrell and Ronnie Milsap when they blow through town (shows Apr.-Dec. $17-40). The Osmond Brothers keep on truckin' at the **Osmond Family Theater** (336-6100), at the intersection of Rte. 76 and Rte. 165 (shows Mar.-Dec., closed July; $24; under 13 free).

Motels along Rte. 76 generally start around $25, but prices often increase during the busy season, from July to September. Less tacky, inexpensive motels line Rte. 265, 4 mi. west of the strip or Gretna Rd. at the west end of the strip. **Budget Inn,** 315 N. Gretna Rd. (334-0292), has slightly dim but spacious rooms with A/C, free local calls, cable, and pool access very close to the action (singles $18; doubles $25). **Indian Point** (338-2121), at the end of Indian Point Rd., south of Hwy. 76, one of 15 campgrounds on Table Rock Lake (334-4101), has lakeside sites with swimming and a boat launch (sites $12, with electricity $16; registration 10am-6pm; open Apr.-Oct.).

The **Branson Chamber of Commerce** (334-4136), on Rte. 248 just west of the Rte. 248/65 junction, has brochures and a computer/phone system (336-4466) great for making lodging and entertainment arrangements (open M-F 8am-5pm). **Greyhound's** (800-321-2222) nearest location is 35 mi. north in Springfield. **Area code:** 417.

Oklahoma

Between 1838 and 1839, President Andrew Jackson ordered the forced relocation of "The Five Civilized Tribes" from the southeastern states to the designated Oklahoma Indian Territory, in a tragic march which came to be known as "The Trail of Tears." After rebuilding their tribes in Oklahoma, the Indians were again dislocated in 1889 by whites rushing to stake claims in the newly opened lands. Today, the world's largest collection of Western American art in Tulsa features 250,000 Native American artifacts, and re-enactments of the "Trail of Tears" occur throughout Oklahoma. People treat each other with old-fashioned respect and courtesy, and the post-1930s "dustbowl" wasteland depicted in *The Grapes of Wrath* is now blanketed by the green crops of Oklahoma's rolling red hills, hemmed in by calming lakes and rivers.

PRACTICAL INFORMATION

Capital: Oklahoma City.
Visitor Info: Oklahoma Tourism and Recreation Dept., 15 N. Robinson Rd., Rm. 801, Oklahoma City 73152 (521-2406 or 800-652-6552; http://www.travelok.com), in the Concord Bldg. at Sheridan St. Open M-F 8am-5pm.
Emergency: 911.
Time Zone: Central (1hr. behind Eastern). **Postal Abbreviation:** OK.
Sales Tax: 6-8%.

■ Tulsa

Though Tulsa lacks the distinction of being Oklahoma's political capital, it is in many ways the center of the state. First settled by Creeks arriving from the Trail of Tears, Tulsa's location on the banks of the Arkansas River made it a logical trading outpost for Native Americans and Europeans. Today, the town's Art Deco skyscrapers, French villas, Georgian mansions, and distinctively large Native American population reflect its varied heritage. Rough-riding motorcyclists and slick oilmen have more recently joined the city's cultural mélange, seeking the good life on the Great Plains.

ORIENTATION AND PRACTICAL INFORMATION

Tulsa sections off neatly into 1 sq. mi. quadrants. Downtown rests at the intersection of **Main St.** (north-south) and **Admiral Blvd.** (east-west). Numbered streets lie in ascending order as you move north or south from Admiral. Named streets run north-south in alphabetical order. Those named after western cities are west of Main St.; eastern cities lie to the east. Every time the alphabetical order reaches the end, the cycle begins again with a street beginning in "a." Far from the center of town, north-south streets become numbered avenues.

Airport: Tulsa International (838-5000; call M-F 8am-5pm), just northeast of downtown and accessible by I-244 or U.S. 169. Taxi to downtown costs around $11.

Buses: Greyhound, 317 S. Detroit Ave. (584-4428 or 800-231-2222). To: Oklahoma City (2hr., 8 per day, $17); St. Louis (9½hr., 5 per day, $70); Kansas City (5hr., 3 per day, $53); and Dallas (7hr., 7 per day, $39). Open 24hr.

Public Transportation: Metropolitan Tulsa Transit Authority, 510 S. Rockford (582-2100). Buses run M-Sa 6am-7pm. Fare 75¢, transfers 5¢, seniors and disabled (disabled card available at bus offices) 35¢, ages 5-18 60¢, under 5 free with adult. Most buses stop at downtown transfer center, 319 S. Denver, at the corner of 3rd St. Maps and schedules await at the main office (open M-F 8am-5pm) or on buses.

Taxis: Yellow Cab, 582-6161. $1.25 base fare, $1 per mi., $1 per additional passenger. 24hr.

Car Rental: Thrifty, 1506 N. Memorial Dr. (838-3333), at 41st St., near the airport. $33 per day, $182 per week; unlimited mi. Must be 21 with major credit card; under 25 surcharge $10 per day. Open daily 5am-1am.

Bike Rental: Tom's River Trail Bicycles, 6861 S. Peoria Ave. (481-1818). Bikes $3-10 per hr., $9-24 per day. In-line skates $5 1st hr., $3 per additional hr. Open M-Sa 10am-7pm, Su 11am-6pm. Driver's license or major credit card required.

Visitor Info: Convention and Visitors Division, Metropolitan Tulsa Chamber of Commerce, 616 S. Boston Ave. (585-1201 or 800-558-3311). Open M-F 8am-5pm.

Hotlines: Help Line, 836-HELP/4357, for info, referral, or crisis intervention. Operates M-F 8am-6pm, Sa 9am-5pm. **Gay Information Line,** 743-4297, lists gay bars and social groups in Tulsa. Operates Tu 6-10pm, W 2-10pm, Th-F noon-10pm.

Hospitals: Hillcrest Medical Center, 1120 S. Utica Ave. (579-1000). **Center for Women's Health,** 1822 E. 15th St. (749-4444).

Internet Access: Kinko's, 2828 E. 11th St. (584-2774). $12 per hr. Open 24hr.

Post Office: 333 W. 4th St. (599-6800). Open M-F 7:30am-5pm. **ZIP code:** 74101. **Area code:** 918.

ACCOMMODATIONS AND CAMPGROUNDS

Downtown motels are generally unclean and unsafe, as are those north of town near the airport. Better options are the budget motels along the southwestern stretches of **I-44** and **I-244.** The junction of these two highways (Exit 222 from I-44) features many inexpensive lodging choices; take bus #17 "Southwest Blvd." The cheery **Budgetel Inn,** 4530 E. Skelly Dr./I-44 Frontage Rd. (488-8777 or 800-428-3438), off Exit 229, delivers a free continental breakfast to your door (singles $42; doubles $51). **Georgetown Plaza Motel,** 8502 E. 27th St. (622-6616), off I-44 at 31st and Memorial St., offers clean, well-furnished rooms with free local calls and cable TV (singles and doubles $28; downstairs rooms with microfridge $31/$34). The **Gateway Motor Inn,** 5600 W. Skelley (446-6611), at Exit 222 C, has well-worn rooms decorated in dated pea-green and timber fashion (singles and doubles $28; free coffee in the office; key/remote deposit $2).

The 250-site **Mingo RV Park,** 801 N. Mingo Rd. (832-8824 or 800-932-8824), at the northeast corner of the I-244 and Mingo Rd. intersection just west of the Mingo Valley Expwy./U.S. 169, offers laundry and showers in a semi-urban setting (sites $9, full hookup $18; reception daily 8:30am-8pm). **Heyburn Park,** 28165 W. Heyburn Park Rd. (247-6601), 20 mi. southwest of the city in Kellyville, sits off I-44 or Rte. 66. Turn right for 4-5 mi. onto Rte. 33 and watch for the Shepards Pt. sign. Shady sites follow the shores of Heyburn Lake, far removed from the hubbub of town. (Sites $10, with water and electricity $14.)

FOOD AND NIGHTLIFE

Most downtown restaurants cater to lunching business people, closing on weekends and at 2pm on weekdays. **Nelson's Buffeteria,** 514 S. Boston Ave. (584-9969), is an old-fashioned diner that has served a blue plate special (2 scrambled eggs, hash browns, biscuit and gravy $2.50) and famous chicken-fried steak ($5) since 1929 (open M-F 6am-2pm). For extended hours, S. Peoria Ave. has more to offer. **The Brook,** 3401 S. Peoria (748-9977), in a converted movie theater, has classic art-deco appeal. A traditional menu of chicken, burgers, and salads ($5-7) is complemented by an extensive list of $4 signature martinis. (Open M-Sa 11am-2am, Su 11am-11pm.) **Chimi's,** 1304 E. 15th St. (587-4411), at Peoria Ave., offers well-prepared Mexican fare (entrees $6-11), great salsa and *queso*, and a health-conscious menu, with a handful of vegetarian options (open Su-Th 11am-10:30pm, F-Sa 11am-midnight).

For up-to-date specs on arts and entertainment, a free copy of *Urban Tulsa*, at local restaurants, is what to read. At night, good bars line the 3000's along S. Peoria Ave., an area known as Brookside, and 15th St. east of Peoria, which glistens with ritzy restaurants and antique shops. Across from The Brook teeters **The Brink,** 3410 S. Peoria (742-4242), a spacious bar filled with hundreds of stools around glass-block counters, all of which are taken on weekend nights. (Live rock Th-Su 10pm, cover $3-5; other events W, cover $2. Open W-Su 8pm-2am.) Tough-looking bikers, friendly locals, and succulent burgers ($3-6) abound at the **Blue Rose Café,** 3421 S. Peoria Ave. (742-3873). *Tulsa People Magazine* has dubbed the hang-out as the "best place to see and be seen." (21+. No cover. Live blues and rock Sa-Th 9pm. Open daily 11am-2am.) The intersection of 18th and Boston Ave. raises a ruckus at night, catering to the young adult crowd. College kids flock to **Steamroller,** 1738 Boston Ave. (583-9520), commonly billed as "the snob-free, dork-free, band-and-brewski place to be." (BBQ and Tex-Mex entrees $5-7. Local bands F-Sa 10pm. Cover $3-10. Open M-Th 11am-10pm, F 11am-2am, Sa 5pm-2am.)

SIGHTS AND ENTERTAINMENT

The **Philbrook Museum of Art,** 2727 S. Rockford Rd. (749-7941 or 800-324-7941), 1 block east of Peoria Ave., presents tastefully selected works of Native American, European, American, Asian, and African art in the renovated Italian Renaissance villa of an oil baron. *(Open Tu-W and F-Sa 10am-5pm, Th 10am-8pm, Su 11am-5pm. $5, students and seniors $3, under 13 free.)* Take bus #5 "Peoria" from downtown. Permanent collections, surrounded by formal and informal gardens, reside on these 23 acres. Perched atop an Osage foothill 2 mi. northwest of downtown (take bus #47), the **Thomas Gilcrease Museum,** 1400 Gilcrease Museum Rd. (596-2700), houses the world's largest collection of Western American art, as well as 250,000 Native American artifacts and 10,000 paintings and sculptures by artists such as Remington and Russell. *(Open M-Sa 9am-5pm, Su 11am-5pm; Mid-May closed M. $3 donation requested.)* Take the Gilcrease Exit off Rte. 412. The **Fenster Museum of Jewish Art,** 1223 E. 17th Pl. (194-1366), housed in B'nai Emunah Synagogue, contains an impressive collection of Judaica dating from 2000 BC to the present (open Su-Th 10am-4pm; free).

The ultra-modern, gold-mirrored architecture of **Oral Roberts University,** 7777 S. Lewis Ave. (495-6161 or 800-678-8876), rises out of an Oklahoma plain about 6 mi. south of downtown Tulsa between Lewis and Harvard Ave.; take bus #12. In 1964, Oral had a dream in which God commanded him to "Build Me A University," and Tulsa's most-frequented tourist attraction was born. The 80 ft. high sculpture of praying hands guards the campus and the hordes of believers flocking to visit. The **visitors center** (495-6807), located in the spiky Prayer Tower, offers free 35min. tours on Oral Roberts's life (open M-Sa 9am-5pm, Su 1-5pm; tours depart every 15min.).

Rodgers and Hammerstein's *Oklahoma!* continues its run under the stars at the **Discoveryland Amphitheater** (245-6552), 10 mi. west of Tulsa on 41st St., accessible only by car. *(Shows June-Aug. M-Sa 8pm. $15, seniors $14, under 13 free.)* This classic features the girl who can't say no, cowboys dancing ballet, and more, set in the early 1900s. Early birds chow on the pre-show barbecue from 5:30-7:30pm ($8, seniors $7.50, children $5). For more cultural enlightenment, the **Tulsa Ballet** (749-6006), acclaimed as one of America's finest regional troupes, tiptoes at the **Performing Arts Center** (596-7111 or events line 596-2525), at 3rd and Cincinnati St. (box office open M-F 10am-5:30pm, Sa 10am-3pm). The **Tulsa Philharmonic** (747-7445) and **Tulsa Opera** (587-4811) also perform there. The Philharmonic harmonizes most weekends September through June ($8-50); the Opera stages four productions per year.

Tulsa thrives on excitement during annual events like the **International Mayfest** (582-6435). This outdoor food, arts, and performance festival takes place in downtown Tulsa (May 13-16, 1999). The **Pow-Wow** (744-1113; usually in June, call for exact dates), at the Tulsa Fairgrounds Pavilion (Expo Sq.), attracts Native Americans from dozens of tribes and thousands of on-lookers for a three-day festival of food, arts and crafts, and nightly dancing contests ($2, seniors $1, under 10 free).

Trail of Tears National Historic Trail

President Jackson ignored a Supreme Court ruling when he forced 13,000 Cherokee Indians to march from North Carolina, Tennessee, Georgia, and Alabama to the Indian Territories. Between 1838 and 1839, many walked the trail at gunpoint, and by the end thousands had died of hunger and disease. The **Trail of Tears National Historic Trail,** established in December 1987, commemorates this journey by designating the remaining parts of the Trail of Tears as National Historic Sites. Auto routes (Rte. 10 and 62, north of Tahlequah) follow the northern land trail as closely as possible. For more info, contact **Trail of Tears National Historic Trail,** Southwest Region, National Park Service, P.O. Box 728, Santa Fe, NM 87504 (505-988-6888).

■ Near Tulsa: Tahlequah

Buried deep in the lush hills of northeast Oklahoma, 66 mi. east of Tulsa on Rte. 51, the sleepy hamlet of Tahlequah historically marks the end of the Cherokee tribe's forced movement west. In the center of town, on Cherokee Sq., stands the historic capitol building of the **Cherokee Nation,** 101 S. Muskogee Ave., easy to find since Hwy. 51, 82, and 62 all intersect and run together on Muskogee. The capitol was completed in 1870 (previous capitol buildings were burned by the Union armies during the Civil War), and, along with other tribal government buildings, such as the Supreme Court building and the Cherokee National Prison (1 and 2 blocks south of Cherokee Sq. respectively), formed the highest authority in Oklahoma until statehood in 1907. Across from the northeast corner of Cherokee Sq., the **visitors center,** 123 E. Delaware St. (456-3742), offers free walking tour maps of the major historic sites in the downtown area.

The **Cherokee Heritage Center** (456-6007 or 888-999-6007), 4 mi. south of town on Hwy. 82, left on Willis Rd., then right at the sign, includes both **Tsa-La-Gi Village,** a recreation of a 16th-century Cherokee settlement with ongoing demonstrations of skills such as flint knapping and basket weaving, and the **Cherokee National Museum.** *(Village and Museum open Feb.-Apr. Tu-F 10am-5pm; May-Aug. M-Sa 10am-5pm, Su noon-5pm; Sept.-Dec. M-F 10am-5pm. $6, under 13 $3; in winter $3/$1.50. Last tour 4pm.)* One mile down the street from the Heritage Center (follow signs pointing left from the exit driveway) hides the **Murrell Home** (456-2751), a well-restored antebellum plantation showing the high standard of living enjoyed by a few slave-owning Cherokees. *(Open W-Sa 10am-5pm, Su 1-5pm; Sept.-Mar. F-Sa 10am-5pm, Su 1-5pm. Free.)* For outdoor fun, **Tahlequah Floats,** 1 Plaza S., #243 (918-456-6949 or 800-375-6949), sends canoes up-river. It's 2 mi. east of Tahlequah on Downing St./Rte. 62; at the intersection of Rte. 62 and 10 turn north on Rte. 10 and drive 100 yd. Owner/operator "Beard" loves to accommodate unusual requests; campsites are available here. *(5 mi. run $9 per person, 25 mi. overnight run $17 per person. Restrooms provided. Open May-Sept. sunrise to sunset. Sites $2.50, RV sites with electricity $10.)* **Area code:** 918.

■ Oklahoma City

At noon on April 22, 1889, a gunshot sent settlers scrambling into the Oklahoma Territory—the "landrush" was afoot. By sundown, Oklahoma City, set strategically in the course of the Santa Fe Railroad, was home to over 10,000 homesteaders. A century later, on April 19, 1995, a bomb exploded at the Alfred R. Murrah federal office building. Lionized in the press, the tragedy focused national attention on Oklahoma City, and on the growing extremism of the country's fringe right. The bombing was considered to be particularly disturbing because it occurred in the nation's heartland, in one of the quietest, safest towns in the country. Oklahoma City remains a clean, unobtrusive, tranquil place, despite its unwelcome attention of late.

ORIENTATION AND PRACTICAL INFORMATION

Oklahoma City is constructed on a nearly perfect grid. Almost all of the city's attractions are outside the city center, but the Metro Transit bus reaches many of them. On public transportation, cautious riders are safer riders, especially downtown after dark. Cheap and plentiful parking makes driving the best way to go.

Airport: Will Rogers World (680-3200), on I-44 southwest of downtown, Exit 116 B. Royal Coach, 2925 S. Meridian Ave. (685-2638), has 24hr. van service to downtown ($10; $2 per additional person). A taxi downtown runs around $13.

Buses: Greyhound, 427 W. Sheridan Ave. (235-6425 or 800-231-2222), at Walker St. Take city bus #4, 5, 6, 8, or 10. *Be careful at night.* To: Tulsa (2hr., 8 per day, $17); Dallas (5hr., 4 per day, $39); and Kansas City (10hr., 6 per day, $68). Open 24hr.

Public Transportation: Oklahoma Metro Transit, offices at Union Station, 300 S.W. 7th (235-7433; open M-F 8am-5pm). Bus service M-Sa 6am-6pm. All routes radiate from the station at Reno and Gaylord St. Free schedules available at the Union Station office. Fare $1, seniors and ages 6-17 50¢.

Taxis: Yellow Cab, 232-6161. $2.50 1st mi., $1.25 per additional mi., $1 per extra passenger.

Car Rental: Dub Richardson Ford Rent-a-Car, 2930 NW 39th Expwy. (946-9288 or 800-456-9288). Used cars $34 per day with 200 mi. free in-state. Must be 25 with major credit card. Open M-F 8am-6pm, Sa 8:30am-noon.

Bike Rental: Miller Cycling and Fitness, 215 Boyd St. (321-8296), near the University of Oklahoma. $10 per day. Open M-Sa 10am-6pm. Must be 18 with credit card.

Visitor Info: Oklahoma City Convention and Visitors Bureau, 189 W. Sheridan (297-8910), at Robinson St., has city-specific info (open M-F 8:30am-5pm).

Internet Access: Law Library, 1st fl. of the capitol building. Free. Open M-F 8am-5pm.

Hotlines: Contact, 848-2273, for referrals or crisis intervention. **Rape Crisis,** 943-7273. **Red Rock Mental Health** (424-7711), has counseling on HIV issues. All 24hr.

Post Office: 320 SW 5th St. (553-6100). Open 24hr. **ZIP code:** 73125. **Area code:** 405.

ACCOMMODATIONS AND CAMPGROUNDS

Cheap lodging in OKC lies along the interstate highways, particularly on I-35 north of the I-44 junction and I-40 east of town. The Union Jack flag hangs on the lighted sign of the **Sixpence Inn,** 5801 Tinker Diagonal (737-8851), off the Sooner Rd. Exit 156A from I-40 E, which offers tidy rooms, free local calls, HBO/ESPN, and a swimming pool (singles $25; doubles $35). Most inexpensive options are chains, like **Motel 6,** 6166 Tinker Diagonal (737-6676), across from and a little past the Sixpence, off I-40 Exit 156B. Rooms have cable and access to a pool. (Singles $29; doubles $35.)

Nestled behind truck stops, fast-food joints, and mid-grade motels are the 172 sites of **RCA,** 12115 Northeast Expwy./I-35 N (478-0278). Take southbound Frontage Rd. off Exit 137; it's ¼ mi. to the red-and-white "RV" sign. (Open daily 8am-8pm; in winter 8am-8pm. Sites $12, full hookup $17. Pool, laundry, and showers.) By contrast, **Lake Thunderbird State Park** (360-3572) offers campsites near a beautiful lake fit for swimming or fishing. Take I-40 east to Choctaw Rd. (Exit 166), then south until the road ends (10 mi.), and make a left for 1 mi. (Showers available. Office open M-F 8am-5pm; there's a campsite host for late or weekend arrivals. Sites $6, full hookup $17; in summer $18. Huts $35.)

FOOD AND NIGHTLIFE

Oklahoma City contains the largest feeder cattle market in the U.S., and beef tops most menus. **Cattleman's Steak House,** 1309 S. Agnew (236-0416), 1 block from the stockyards, may be a classy restaurant today, but its colorful past (est. 1910) includes a stint as a prohibition-era speakeasy. Steaks ranging from chopped sirloin ($8) to the Presidential T-Bone ($18) are what's for dinner. (Open Su-Th 6am-10pm, F-Sa 6am-midnight. $6.50 lunch specials until 4pm.) Aside from the turn-of-the-century ware-houses yuppified into eating and drinking establishments, most places downtown close early in the afternoon after they've served business lunchers. After-hours restau-rants lie immediately east of town on Sheridan Ave. (in the Bricktown district) and north of downtown, along Classen Blvd. and Western Ave. A young clientele congre-gates at **Flip's,** 5801 N. Western Ave. (843-1527), accessible by bus #5 from down-town, for Italian dishes ($6-22) and fine wine (open daily 11am-2am).

Nightlife here is as rare as the elusive jackalope. The *Oklahoma Gazette* can help, and the **Bricktown district** has restaurants with live music after dark. In the **Brick-town Brewery,** 1 N. Oklahoma St. (232-2739), at Sheridan Ave., you can watch the beer brew (25 recipes, 5 on tap, $2.75) while dining on burgers, salads, and chicken ($5-10). The 2nd fl. houses a bonanza of bar games, as well as live music. (Upstairs 21+ after 8pm. Cover $5 for bands. Live music Tu, F-Sa 9pm. Open Su-M 11am-10pm, Tu-Th 11am-midnight, F-Sa 11am-1:30am.) For good dancing, the DJ at the rough-and-tumble **Wreck Room,** 2127 NW 39th (525-7610), at Barnes St., supplies house and techno (cover $3-4; open F 10pm-5am and Sa 11pm-5am).

SIGHTS AND ENTERTAINMENT

Monday morning is the time to visit the **Oklahoma City Stockyards,** 2500 Exchange Ave. (235-8675), the busiest in the world. Cattle auctions (M-Tu) begin at 8am and may last into the night. Visitors enter free of charge via a catwalk soaring over cow pens and cattle herds, leading from the parking lot northeast of the auction house (take bus #12 from the terminal to Agnew and Exchange Ave.). The auction is as Old West as it gets; only those with a wide-brim cowboy hat, blue jeans, boots, and faded dress shirt fit in. City-slickers may also want to change their digs before venturing into **Omniplex,** 2100 NE 52nd St. (424-5545), a mall-like complex housing a pastiche of modern museums and exhibits. Highlights include the **Air and Space Museum, International Photography Hall of Fame, Red Earth Indian Center,** and the hands-on **Science Museum.** *(Take bus #22. Open M-Sa 9am-6pm, Su 11am-6pm; mid-Sept. to mid-May closes 5pm M-F. Admission to all museums $7.60, ages 3-12 $6, seniors $6.80. Plane-tarium $1.65/$1.10/$1.45 extra.)* An Imax theater is scheduled to open in May of 1999.

Plant lovers should make a bee-line for **Myriad Gardens,** 301 W. Reno Ave. (297-3995), downtown at Robinson Ave., where a 70 ft. diameter glass cylinder, called the Crystal Bridge, perches above a large pond. The botanical gardens inside the Bridge include both a desert and a rainforest, each with hundreds of plant species. *(Open daily 9am-6pm. $4, seniors and students $3, ages 4-12 $2. Outdoor gardens open daily 6am-11pm. Free.)* At **Enterprise Sq., USA,** 2501 E. Memorial (425-5030), singing dollar bills and a larger-than-life Henry Ford instill the up-and-coming generation with the joys of capi-talism and the thrills of greed. Well, Karl? *(Open M-F 9am-4pm, Sa 9am-5pm, Su 1-4pm. $5, seniors $3.50, ages 6-18 $3.)*

The **Red Earth Festival** (427-5228; June 10-13, 1999) is the country's largest cele-bration of Native America; the Myriad Convention Center hosts art fairs and intense dance competitions. *(Daytime competitions and art festival $7; evening dance performances $12, under 12 $6.)*

TEXAS

Spanning an area as wide as from Wisconsin to Montana and as long as from North Carolina to Key West, Texas is more like its own country than a state; the fervently proud, can-do citizens of the "Lone Star State" seem to prefer it that way. In fact, after revolting against the Spanish in 1821, the Republic of Texas stood alone until 1845, when it entered the Union as the 28th state. The state's unofficial motto proclaims that "everything is bigger in Texas"; its truth is evident in prolific wide-brimmed hats, styled and sculpted ladies' coifs, boat-sized American autos, giant ranch spreads, countless steel skyscrapers, and towering urban cowboys who seem ready and willing to conquer the frontier and fight for independence all over again.

Cotton, cattle, and oil built the Texan fortune, but technology, trade, and tourism now form the backbone of its economic might. Regional cuisine, like most of Texan culture, is enriched by an age-old Mexican heritage. "Tex-Mex" is a restaurant epidemic ranging from 69¢ taco stands to elegant border cafes. Fajitas, longhorn beef, chicken-fried steak, and spicy barbecue round out the list of staples.

🌮 HIGHLIGHTS OF TEXAS

- **Food.** Drippin' barbecue and colossal steaks reign supreme in the state where beef is king and vegetables are for the cows. Some of the best beef rests in Austin (p. 527) and Amarillo (p. 544).
- **San Antonio.** Remember the Alamo and the city's rich Spanish heritage (p. 535).
- **Rodeos/Cowboys.** The ol' West lives on in Fort Worth (p. 524) and at the Mesquite Rodeo in Dallas (p. 524), with some of the finest rope-riders in the land.

PRACTICAL INFORMATION

Capital: Austin.
Visitor Info: Texas Travel Information Centers (800-452-9292; http://www.tou-texas.com), near state lines on all major highways into Texas. Call 8am-6pm (centers open daily 8am-5pm) for a free guidebook. **Texas Division of Tourism** P.O. Box 12728, Austin 78711 (800-888-8839). **Texas Parks and Wildlife Dept.,** Austin Headquarters Complex, 4200 Smith School Rd., Austin 78744 (512-389-8950 or 800-792-1112). **U.S. Forest Service,** 701 N. 1st St., Lufkin 75901 (409-639-8501).
Emergency: 911.
Time Zones: Mostly Central (1hr. behind Eastern); *Let's Go* makes note of areas in Mountain (2hr. behind Eastern). **Postal Abbreviation:** TX.
Sales Tax: 6-8.25%.

■ Dallas

Dallas began as a trading outpost at a ford across the Trinity River in 1841, rapidly growing to become the nation's largest inland city. Nevertheless, it has yet to be recognized as the cosmopolitan center it aspires to be—visitors are more interested in the image of oil and cowboys fostered by the television show *Dallas.* In actuality, golf courses and swimming pools far outnumber genuine ropers or oilers here, and Dalla-sites prefer to point out cultural venues such as Myserson Symphony Hall and the Museum of Art. The city's legendary preoccupation with commerce now attracts flocks of immigrants from the Far East and Latin America, and Dallas maintains one of the largest and most exclusive social scenes in the country for a city its size.

ORIENTATION AND PRACTICAL INFORMATION

Most of Dallas lies within the **I-635** loop, which is bisected east-west by **I-30** and north-south by **I-35 E (Stemmons Frwy.)** and **U.S. 75 (Central Expwy.).** The nicer suburbs stretch along the northern reaches of Central Expwy. and the **Dallas North Toll Rd.** Many of downtown Dallas's shops and restaurants lie underground in a maze of tunnels accessible from any major office building.

Airport: Dallas-Ft. Worth International (972-574-8888), 17 mi. northwest of downtown; take bus #202 ($2). For door-to-gate service, take the **Super Shuttle**, 729 E. Dallas Rd. (800-258-3826). 1st passenger $16, $6 per additional passenger. 24hr. service. Taxi to downtown $30.
Trains: Amtrak, 400 S. Houston Ave. (653-1101 or 800-872-7245), in Union Station. To: Los Angeles (42hr., 4 per week, $123); Austin (6½hr., 4 per week, $22); and Little Rock (7½hr., 4 per week, $50). Open daily 9am-6:30pm.
Buses: Greyhound, 205 S. Lamar St. (655-7727 or 800-231-2222), 3 blocks east of Union Station. To: New Orleans (13hr., 5 per day, $73); Houston (5hr., 10 per day, $26); and Austin (4hr., 11 per day, $29). Open 24hr.
Public Transportation: Dallas Area Rapid Transit (DART), 1401 Pacific Ave. (979-1111; open M-F 5am-10pm, Sa-Su 8am-6pm). Bus routes radiate from 2 downtown transfer centers, East and West, and serve most suburbs. Buses run daily 5:30am-9:30pm, to suburbs 5:30am-8pm. Fare $1, $2 to suburban park-and-ride stops; transfers free. Get maps at Elm and Ervay St. office (open M-F 7am-6pm). **DART Light Rail** runs north-south through downtown (5:30am-12:30am; fare $1). The **McKinney Ave. Trolley** (855-0006) services the arts district and the upscale establishments on McKinney (Su-Th 10am-10pm, F-Sa 10am-12pm; fare $1.50).
Taxis: Yellow Cab Co., 426-6262 or 800-749-9422. $2.70 base, plus $1.20 per mi.
Car Rental: Rent-a-Wreck, 2025 S. Buckner Blvd. (800-398-2544). Extremely reliable service. Late-model used cars from $23 per day. Must be 21. Cash deposits accepted. Airport pick-up available. Open M-F 9am-6pm, Sa 9am-3:30pm.
Visitor Info: Dallas Convention and Visitors Bureau, 1201 Elm St. (571-1300), Renaissance Tower, 20th fl. Open M-F 7:30am-5:30pm. Oversees multiple **visitors centers** throughout the central business district and in area malls. All offices use

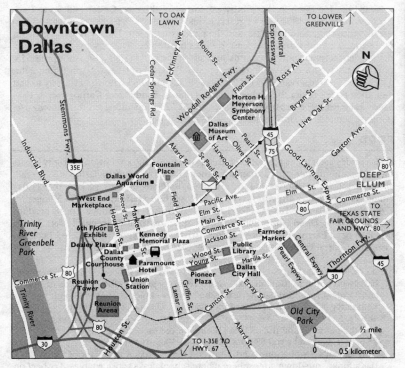

Downtown Dallas

the phone number 571-1300. For late-night info, head to **West End Marketplace**, 603 Munger St. (open M-Th 11am-10pm, F-Sa 11am-midnight, Su noon-6pm).

Hotlines: Suicide and Crisis Center, 828-1000. **Contact Counseling,** 972-233-2233, for general counseling. Both 24hr.

Post Office: 400 N. Ervay St. (953-3045), near Bryan St. downtown. Open M-F 8am-6pm. **ZIP code:** 75201; for General Delivery, 75221. **Area codes:** 214, 817, and 972. In text, 214 unless otherwise noted.

ACCOMMODATIONS AND CAMPGROUNDS

Cheap lodging aside from the chain motel variety doesn't come easy in Dallas; big events such as the Cotton Bowl (Jan. 1) and the State Fair in October exacerbate the problem. Look 15-20min. north of downtown on **U.S. 75 (Central Expwy.)**, north along **I-35,** and east on **I-30** for inexpensive motels. **Bed and Breakfast Texas Style,** 4224 W. Red Bird Ln. (972-298-8586; open M-F 8:30am-4:30pm), will place you in a nice home, usually near town, with friendly residents anxious to make y'all as comfortable as possible. It's an especially good deal for two people. Be sure to call a few days ahead. (Singles from $55; doubles from $65.) East of downtown, on I-30 (2 blocks from the Dolphin and Samuel St. stop on the #18 bus), lies the **Welcome Inn,** 3247 Merrifield Ave. (826-3510). The white stucco and blue tile palace welcomes visitors with free local calls and HBO. (Singles $34.50; doubles $40.) The **Super 7 Motel Mesquite,** 3629 U.S. 80 E (613-9989), lies 10min. out of downtown; after branching right onto U.S. 80, from I-30, exit at Town East Blvd. Perks include TVs, free local calls, and access to a microwave, a fridge, and a small pool. (Singles $30.50; doubles $35.) Downtown, the recently refurbished **Paramount Hotel,** 302 S. Houston St. (761-9090), near Dealey Plaza and the West End, stands 2½ blocks from the Light Rail and CBD West transfer center (singles $59; doubles $69).

Near Lake Joe Pool, in the southwest corner of the city, **Cedar Hill State Park** (972-291-6641, 512-389-8900 for reservations) provides 355 tent sites. Take I-35 E to Rte. 67, turn right onto FM 1382, and the park is on the left. The area fills up early for the warmest months, so call at least 2 weeks in advance. There is a swimming area, marina, jet-ski rental, and three walking trails in the park. (Sites $12, waterfront $15; plus $5 daily fee for each adult. Office open M-F 10am-5pm, Sa-Su 10am-10pm; 24hr. gate access with reservations.) RV campers should take I-35 E north of the city to Exit 444, then go left under the highway about a mile to **Sandy Lake Campground,** 1915 Sandy Lake Rd. (972-242-6808). RV sites are $17-21, depending on the vehicle size. (Office open M-F 7:30am-7:30pm, Sa 8am-7pm, Su 1-6pm.)

FOOD

Dallas prides itself on just about everything, and food is no exception. The city boasts more restaurants per capita than any other in the U.S., and Dallasites love to talk about their favorite eateries. For the lowdown on dining options, pick up the "Friday Guide" of the *Dallas Morning News.* The **West End Marketplace,** 603 Munger St. (748-4801), has pricey Tex-Mex food amid a variety of touristy shops. Locals head for **McKinney Ave., Deep Ellum** (Elm St. east of downtown), and **Greenville Ave.** In this desert of beef, **Farmers Produce Market,** 1010 S. Pearl Expwy. (939-2748), between Pearl and Central Expwy. near I-30, is a veggie oasis (open daily 7am-6pm).

◉**EatZi's,** 3403 Oaklawn Ave. (526-1515), at Rawlins St. A grocery, cafe, kitchen, and bakery combine to form an 8000 sq. ft. venue of glorious food. Sounds of Vivaldi and Verdi surround those perusing the menu's choices, from mile-high biscuits with gravy ($2.50) to heapings of foccacia ($3). Open daily 7am-10pm.

Bubba's, 6617 Hillcrest Ave. (373-6527). A remodeled 50s-style diner where you'll find the patrician and the plebeian dining on the same turf. Fried chicken dinners $5-6. 3 veggies and a roll $3.50. Open daily 6:30am-10pm.

Sonny Bryan's Smokehouse, 2202 Inwood (357-7120). A landmark of Dallas BBQ. Has a funky, run-down atmosphere where school desks replace tables. Try beef on a bun ($3.75) or combine all 4 smokehouse delicacies ($11). Some vegetarian options available. Open M-F 10am-4pm, Sa 10am-3pm, Su 11am-2pm.

Flying Burro, 2831 Greenville (827-2112). With a patio strewn with chili-pepper-shaped Christmas lights, this fine establishment serves New Mexico-style dishes that would make Santa Fe proud. Hits include stacked enchiladas ($5.50-7). Lunch specials from $5-6. Restaurant open M-Th 11am-11pm, F-Sa 11am-12:30am, Su 11am-10pm. Bar is always open until 2am.

A SHOT FIRED, A CITY RECOVERED

Encircled by the present-day downtown, historic Dallas can easily be seen on a walking tour. Ride to the top of the **Reunion Tower,** 300 Reunion Blvd. (651-1234), 50 stories above the street, to get a feel for the city before you start walking (open Su-Th 10am-10pm, F-Sa 10am-midnight; $2, seniors and ages 3-12 $1). Alternatively, look for the lesser known but equally impressive view from the **Sky Lobby,** at the top of the **Texas Commerce Tower,** 2200 Ross St. The middle block of elevators will whisk you up to a marble landing graced with small artificial pools and huge windows overlooking the northeast end of town (doors unlocked 24hr.; free).

On the corner of Houston Ave. and Elm St., the notorious **6th fl.** of the former **Texas School Book Depository** (747-6000) still gives people chills as they look out the window through which Lee Harvey Oswald allegedly fired the shot that killed President John F. Kennedy on November 22, 1963. *(Open daily 9am-6pm. Self-guided tours $5, seniors and students $4. Audio cassette rental $3.)* This floor, now a fascinating museum devoted to the Kennedy legacy, traces the dramatic and macabre moments of the assassination in various media. To the south of the depository, Elm St. runs through **Dealey Plaza,** a national landmark and location of the infamous grassy knoll, which Kennedy's convertible passed as the shots were fired. Philip Johnson's **Memorial** to Kennedy looms nearby at Market and Main. Allegedly just across Market St., in the old K-T railways building, is the **Conspiracy Museum,** 110 S. Market St. (741-3040). *(Open daily 10am-6pm. $7, students and seniors $6, children $3.)* In this bizarre shrine to elaborate CIA plots and mafia intrigue, exhibits chronicle the inscrutable assassinations of famous figures like JFK and Lincoln. The **West End Historic District and Marketplace,** full of broad sidewalks, shops, and restaurants, lies north of Union Station (most stores open M-Th 11am-10pm, F-Sa 11am-10pm, Su noon-6pm).

A replica of the **1842 log cabin** of John Neely Bryan, the city's founder, sits across a small plaza from the Kennedy Memorial, at Elm and Market St. Nearby, frightening gargoyles adorn the **old Dallas County Courthouse,** on the corner of Houston and Main St. The building garnered the nickname "Old Red" for its unique Pecos red sandstone. A branch of the tourist information bureau now occupies the 1st fl. Anchored northeast of the West End area is the **Dallas World Aquarium,** 1801 N. Griffin St. (720-2224), a block north of Ross Ave. *(Open daily 10am-5pm. $11, seniors and children $6.)* Admission is steep, but the multi-level rainforest exhibit with caged bats, swimming penguins, sleepy crocodiles, and birds zooming by your head make this "world aquarium" worthwhile. The **Dallas Museum of Art (DMA),** 1717 N. Harwood St. (922-1200), lies farther east on Ross Ave. *(Open Tu-W 11am-4pm, Th 11am-9pm, F 11am-4pm, Sa-Su 11am-5pm. Free, but special exhibits $5-8.)* The museum's architecture is as graceful and beautiful as its collections of Egyptian, Impressionist, modern, and decorative art. The **Morton H. Meyerson Symphony Center,** 2301 Flora St. (670-3737), a block east of the DMA, and the imposing **Dallas City Hall,** 100 Marilla St. (670-3957), at Ervay St., were designed by ubiquitous I.M. "Loved in Dallas" Pei.

Home to the state fair (Sept.-Oct.) since 1886, **Fair Park** (670-8400), southeast of downtown on I-30 (#12 Dixon bus from CBD East), earned national landmark status for its Art Deco architecture. The 277-acre park hosts the Cotton Bowl (Jan. 1). During the fair, **Big Tex**—a 52 ft. smiling cowboy float—towers over the land; only the **Texas Star,** the largest ferris wheel in the Western hemisphere, looms taller. The **Science Place** (428-5555) has toddlerish hands-on exhibits, but the planetarium and IMAX theater are for all. *(Open Su-Th 9:30am-5:30pm, F-Sa 9:30am-9pm. Museum $6, seniors and ages 3-12 $3. Movies $6, $3 children.)* Other park attractions include the **Dallas Aquarium** (670-8443; open daily 9am-4:30pm; $2, ages 3-11 $1); the **Museum of Natural History** (421-3466; open daily 10am-5pm; $4, ages 3-18 and seniors $2.50; M 10am-1pm free); the **African-American Museum** (565-9026), with multi-media folk art and sculpture (open Tu-F noon-5pm, Sa 10am-5pm, Su 1-5pm; free); and the **Dallas Horticulture Center** (428-7476; open Tu-Sa 10am-5pm, Su 1-5pm; free).

Thirty-five late 19th-century buildings from around Dallas (including a dentist's office, a bank, and a schoolhouse) have been restored and moved to **Old City Park** (421-5141), about 9 blocks south of City Hall on Ervay St. at Gano. *(Open daily 9am-6pm. Exhibit buildings open Tu-Sa 10am-4pm, Su noon-4pm. $5, seniors $4, children $2.)* Pack a picnic and eat at the city's oldest and most popular recreation area and lunch spot.

White Rock Lake provides a haven for walkers, bikers, and rollerbladers. On the east shore of the lake, resplendent flowers and trees fill the 66-acre **Dallas Arboretum,** 8617 Garland Rd. (327-8263); take bus #19 from downtown. *(Open daily 10am-6pm; Nov.-Feb. 10am-5pm. $6, seniors $5, ages 6-12 $3. Parking $3.)* Dallas's **mansions** are in the **Swiss Avenue Historic District** and the streets of the **Highland Park** area, between Preston Rd. and Hillcrest Ave. just south of Mockingbird Ln.

ENTERTAINMENT

Few Dallas establishments cater to the true night owl, but many restaurants, bars, and fast food joints stay open until 2am. *The Met,* a free weekly (out W in restaurants and bookstores), has unrivaled coverage of entertainment options. For the scoop on Dallas's **gay scene,** pick up copies of the *Dallas Voice* and *Texas Triangle* in **Oak Lawn** shops and restaurants. Prospero works his magic at the **Shakespeare in the Park** festival (559-2778), at Samuel-Grand Park just northeast of Fair Park. Two free plays (June-July) run 6 nights a week (8:15pm; $3 donation is optional). At Fair Park, the **Music Hall** (565-1116) showcases **Dallas Summer Musicals** (421-0662, 373-8000 for tickets). (Tickets $7-70. Call 696-4253 for ½-price tickets on performance days.

Shows run June-Oct.) The **Dallas Symphony Orchestra** (692-0203) plays in the Morton H. Meyerson Symphony Center, at Pearl and Flora St. in the arts district. Take in a show, if only to hear the fantastic acoustics (Sept.-May; tickets $14-69).

If you come to Dallas looking for cowboys, the **Mesquite Rodeo,** 1818 Rodeo Dr. (972-285-8777 or 800-833-9339), is the place to find them. Take I-30 east to I-635 S to Exit 4 and stay on the service road. Nationally televised, the rodeo is one of the most competitive in the country. (Shows Apr. to early Oct. F-Sa 8pm. Gates open at 6:30pm. $10, seniors $7, children 3-12 $4. Dinner $8.50, children $5.50.)

Six Flags Over Texas (817-640-8900), 15 mi. from downtown off I-30 in Arlington, between Dallas and Fort Worth, maintains the original link in the nationwide amusement park chain with over 36 rides and attractions. (Open June to early Aug. daily from 10am; late Aug.-Dec and Mar.-May Sa-Su from 10am. Closing times vary. $33, over 55 or under 4 ft. $27.) Across the highway lies the mammoth 47-acre **Hurricane Harbor** (817-265-3356), America's largest waterpark. Experience simulated seasickness in the one million gallon wave pool. (Open late May to early Aug. daily 10am-9pm. $23, seniors and under 4 ft. $16.) Find coupons for both parks on soda cans.

In Dallas, the moral order is God, country, and the **Cowboys.** Football devotees flock to **Cowboys Stadium** (972-579-5000) at the junction of Loop 12 and Rte. 183, west of Dallas in Irving (season Sept.-Jan.; ticket office open M-F 9am-4pm; tickets from $35). **The Ballpark in Arlington,** 1000 Ballpark Way (817-273-5100), plays home to the **Texas Rangers.** (Season Apr.-Sept. Ticket office open M-F 9am-6pm, Sa 10am-4pm, Su noon-4pm. Tickets $4-30.)

NIGHTLIFE

For nightlife, head to **Deep Ellum,** east of downtown. In the 80s, Bohemians revitalized the area, which spent the 20s as a blues haven for the likes of Blind Lemon Jefferson, Lightnin' Hopkins, and Robert Johnson. **Trees,** 2709 Elm St. (748-5009), annually rated the best live music venue in the city by the *Dallas Morning News,* occupies a converted warehouse with a loft full of pool tables. Bands tend to be alternative rock groups. (17+. Cover $2-10. Open Tu-Sa 9pm-2am.) A diverse clientele populates **Club Dada,** 2720 Elm St. (744-3232), the former haunt of Edie Brickell and stomping ground of new Bohemians, which recently added an outdoor patio and live local acts. (21+. Cover Th-Sa $3-5. Open daily 8pm-2am.) For more info on Deep Ellum, call the **What's Up Line** (747-3337; http://deepellumtx.com).

The touristy **West End** jams seven clubs into **Dallas Alley,** 2019 N. Lamar St. (880-7420), all under one cover charge ($3-6). Inside, **Alley Cats** entertains with dueling piano sing-alongs, and **110 Neon Beach** plays Top 40 and techno music for dancing.

Lower Greenville Ave. provides a refreshing change from the downtown mania. **Poor David's Pub,** 1924 Greenville Ave. (821-9891), stages live music ranging from Irish folk tunes to reggae. Music is the main, and only, event: if there's no group booked, Poor David's doesn't open. (Cover $1-20. Open M-Sa 8pm-2am. Tickets available after 6pm at the door; cash only.) More popular nightspots also line Yale Blvd., near Southern Methodist University's fraternity row. **Green Elephant,** 5612 Yale Blvd. (750-6625), a pseudo-60s extravaganza complete with lava lamps and tacky tapestries, is the bar of choice (open M-Sa 11am-2am, Su 6pm-2am). Many gay clubs rock north of downtown in **Oak Lawn.** Among the more notable is **Roundup,** 3912 Cedar Springs Rd. (522-9611), at Throckmorton, a huge, cover-free country-western bar which packs a mixed gay and straight crowd of up to 1600 on weekends (free dance lessons Th and Su 8:30pm; open W-Su 8pm-2am).

■ Near Dallas: Fort Worth

If Dallas is the last Eastern city, Fort Worth is undoubtedly the first Western one. Dallas's slightly less refined brother lies less than 40min. west on I-30, providing a worthwhile daytrip and some raw Texan entertainment. The **Stockyards Historic District,** 10 minutes north of downtown on Main St., attracts the felt hat and leather boot crowd like nowhere else in the metroplex. At the corner of N. Main and E. Exchange

Ave., the **Stockyard Coliseum** (625-1025) hosts weekly rodeos (F-Sa; $8, children $5). **Pawnee Bill's Wild West Show** (625-1025) features sharp-shooting, trick-roping, and a bullwhip act—Yeeehaw! (June-Aug. Sa 2 and 4:30pm. $7, ages 3-12 $4.) At night, **Billy Bob's Texas,** 2520 Rodeo Plaza (624-7117), ropes in the Stockyards crowds. *(Professional bull riding F-Sa 9 and 10pm. Free dance lessons Th 7-8pm. 18+ with ID or under 18 with parent. Afternoon cover $1, Su-Th after 6pm $3; F-Sa evenings $6.50-11, depending on performers. Open M-Sa 11am-2am, Su noon-2am.)* With 100,000 sq. ft. of floor space, including a bull ring, a BBQ restaurant, pool tables, a country-western dance club, slot machines, and 42 bar stations, the place bills itself as the world's largest honky-tonk. On one night alone, during a Hank Williams, Jr. concert, Billy Bob's sold 16,000 bottles of beer.

A walk along **Exchange Ave.,** the main drag of the Stockyards, provides a window to the Wild West. With change from livestock sales jingling in their pockets, cattlemen of yore would mosey down this street seeking entertainment. The strip still offers a slew of saloons, restaurants, stores, and gambling parlors. Since 1906, a favorite stopping point has been the **White Elephant Saloon,** 106 E. Exchange Ave. (624-1887), with rough-hewn wood, brass footrails and a fine collection of cowboy hats covering the walls. Live music (country-western, of course) plays three times daily. (Open Su-Th noon-midnight, F-Sa noon-2am.)

The **Chisholm Trail Round-Up** (625-7005 or 624-4741), a 3-day jamboree in the Stockyards during either the second or third week of June, preserves the heritage of the cowhands who led cattle drives to Kansas 150 years ago. *(Calls taken M-Th 9am-6pm, F 9am-6pm, Sa 9am-7pm, Su 11am-6pm.)* The **Armadillo Races** are a Round-Up must-see; children and visitors are allowed to participate in ground-beating attempts to make the critters move (free). For more on the stockyards, grab a copy of the *Stockyards Gazette* at the **visitors information center,** 130 E. Exchange Ave.

Back downtown, **Sundance Sq.,** a restored, pedestrian-friendly area, offers quality shops, museums, and eats. There, the **Sid Richardson Collection,** 309 Main St. (332-6554), displays an impressive stash of Remingtons and Russells (open Tu-W 10am-5pm, Th-F 10am-8pm, Sa 11am-8pm, Su 1-5pm; free). The more adventurous will head farther west to Fort Worth's **Museum District** for a stunning reward. The **Kimbell Museum,** 3333 Camp Bowie Blvd. (332-1034), brings in some of the world's most sophisticated works of art, and is arguably the best museum in the Southwest. *(Exhibits $10, students and seniors $8, ages 6-11 $6, ½-price Tu. Open Tu-Th and Sa 10am-5pm, F noon-8pm, Su noon-5pm.)* **Area code:** 817.

▓ Austin

If the "Lone Star State" still inspires images of rough 'n' tumble cattle ranchers riding horses across the plains, Austin does its best to put the stereotype to rest. Here, whiz kids start Fortune 500 computer companies, artists sell exotic handicrafts, and bankers don sneakers for midday exercise on the city's downtown green belts. A conspicuous student population keeps Austin energetic, while a thriving slacker population around the University of Texas campus boosts the city's tattoo count. Ambitiously nicknamed the "Live Music Capital of the World," Austin's vibrant nightlife scene is heavy on live bands, with innovative variations on the city's strong blues tradition.

ORIENTATION AND PRACTICAL INFORMATION

The majority of Austin lies between **Hwy. 1** and **I-35,** both running north-south and parallel to one another. UT students inhabit central **Guadalupe St. ("The Drag"),** where plentiful music stores and cheap restaurants thrive on their business. The state capitol governs the area a few blocks to the southeast. South of the capitol dome, **Congress Ave.** features upscale eateries and classy shops. A plethora of bars and live music clubs front **6th St.** Lately, much nightlife has headed to the **Warehouse Area,** around 4th St., west of Congress. Away from the urban gridiron, **Town Lake** offers a verdant haven for the town's joggers, rowers, and cyclists.

Airport: Robert Mueller Municipal, 4600 Manor Rd. (472-3321), 4 mi. northeast of downtown. Take bus #20. Taxi to downtown $12-14.

Trains: Amtrak, 250 N. Lamar Blvd. (476-5684 or 800-872-7245); take bus #38. To: Dallas (6hr., 4 per week, $27); San Antonio (2½hr., 4 per week, $11); and El Paso (13hr., 4 per week, $95). Ticket office open Su and W 7am-11pm, M-Tu and Th 7am-4:30pm, F-Sa 2pm-11pm.

Buses: Greyhound, 916 E. Koenig (800-231-2222), several mi. north of downtown off I-35. Easily accessible by public transportation. Bus #15 and 7 stop across the street and run downtown. To: San Antonio (1½hr., 11 per day, $14); Houston (3½hr., 7 per day, $17); and Dallas (4½hr., 15 per day, $31). Station open 24hr.

Public Transportation: Capitol Metro, 106 E. 8th St. (474-1200 or 800-474-1201; call M-F 6am-10pm, Sa 6am-8pm, Su 7am-6pm). Fare 50¢; students 25¢; seniors, children, and disabled free. Office has maps and schedules (open M-F 7:30am-5:30pm). The old green trolleys of the **'Dillo Bus Service** (474-1200) have been replaced by newer buses, but the 'Dillo still runs on Congress and Lavaca St. M-F every 10-15min. during rush hrs.; schedule varies during off-peak times. Park for free in the 'Dillo lot at Bouldin and Barton Springs.

Taxis: Yellow Cab, 472-1111. $1.50 base fare, $1.50 per mi.

Car Rental: Rent-A-Wreck, 6820 Guadalupe (454-8621). $23 per day; 50 free mi. per day with cash deposit, 100 per day with credit card; 25¢ per additional mi. Open M-F 8am-6pm, Sa 9am-2pm. Under 21 surcharge $10, under 25 $5.

Bike Rental: If you're lucky enough to come upon a **completely yellow bicycle,** hop on it for free—compliments of the city. Just make sure to leave it in a conspicuous spot for the next person to use. Furthermore, most buses have bicycle racks—what a town! **Waterloo Cycles,** 2815 Fruth St. (472-9253), offers rentals (M-F $5 for 1st hr., $3.50 each additional hr., Sa-Su $10/$7; $25/$45 per day). Fee includes helmet. Lock rental $5. Delivery available. Open M-Sa 10am-7pm, Su noon-5pm; in winter M-Sa 10am-6pm.

Visitor Info: Austin Convention Center/Visitor Information, 201 E. 2nd St. (478-0098 or 800-926-2282). Open M-F 8:30am-5pm, Sa 9am-5pm, Su noon-5pm.

Hospital: St. David's Medical Center, 919 E. 32nd St. (476-7111). Off I-35, close to downtown. Open 24hr.

Hotlines: Crisis Intervention Hotline, 472-4357. **Austin Rape Crisis Center Hotline,** 440-7273. Both 24hr. **Outyouth Gay/Lesbian Helpline,** 708-1234 or 800-969-6884. W-Su 5:30-9:30pm.

Post Office: 510 Guadalupe (494-2200) at 6th St. Open M-F 7am-6:30pm, Sa 8am-3pm. **ZIP code:** 78701. **Area code:** 512.

ACCOMMODATIONS AND CAMPGROUNDS

Cheap accommodations lie along **I-35,** running north and south of Austin. In town, **co-ops,** run by college houses at UT, peddle rooms and meals to hostelers. The co-ops work on a first come, first served basis. Patrons have access to all their facilities, including fully stocked kitchens. Unfortunately, most UT houses are only open from May through August. Call 476-5678 for information about several co-ops.

Hostelling International-Austin (HI-AYH), 2200 S. Lakeshore Blvd. (800-725-2331 or 444-2294), about 23 mi. from downtown. From the Greyhound station, take bus #7 "Duval" to Burton and walk 3 blocks north. From I-35, exit at Riverside, head east, and turn left at Lakeshore Blvd. Beautifully situated hostel with a 24hr. common room overlooking Town Lake. Waterbeds available. Kitchen, with a convenient cubby for each guest. 40 dorm-style beds, single-sex rooms; some private rooms. Email access. No curfew. $14, nonmembers $17. Linen provided; no sleeping bags allowed. Reception daily 9-11am and 5-10pm.

Taos Hall, 2612 Guadalupe (474-6905), at 27th St. The UT co-op at which you're most likely to get a private room. For stays of a week or more, they'll draft you into the chores corps. 3 meals and a bed $20. Open May-Aug.

21st St. Co-op, 707 W. 21st St. (476-5678). Take bus #39 on Airport St. to Koenig and Burnet, transfer to the #3 S, and ride to Nueces St.; walk 2 blocks west. Tree-house style building arrangement and hanging plants recall Robinson Crusoe's island home. Suites with A/C, and common room on each floor. $15 per person for 3 meals (when school is in session) and kitchen access. Fills up rapidly in summer.

The Goodall Wooten, 2112 Guadalupe (472-1343). The "Woo's" rooms come with private baths, small fridges, and access to a big-screen TV lounge, laundry, basketball courts, and a computer lab. Singles $25; doubles $30. Linen $5. Reception M-Sa 9am-5pm and 8pm-midnight, Su noon-5pm and 8pm-midnight. Call ahead.

Motel 6, 9420 N. I-35 (339-6161 or 800-466-8356), Exit 241, 6 mi. from downtown and Lake Austin. 158 units, pool, limited cable TV, and free local calls. Singles $39; doubles $45. Reservations required, particularly on weekends.

A 15-45min. drive separates Austin and the nearest campgrounds. **McKinney Falls State Park,** 5808 McKinney Falls Pkwy. (243-1643; reservations 512-389-8900), lies southeast of the city off U.S. 183 and caters to both RV and tent campers. Eighty-four sites provide water and electricity ($12), while eight more primitive campsites ($7) are accessible only by foot. Swimming is permitted in the stream, and there are 7 mi. of trails to hike or bike (daily park usage fee $2, under 13 free). The **Austin Capitol KOA** (444-6322 or 800-562-2668), 6 mi. south of the city along I-35 off Exit 227, offers a pool, clean bathrooms, a game room, laundry facilities, a grocery store, and a playground. (All sites with water and electricity $32-36; $4 per additional person over 18; 3rd night free. Cabins for 4 $39, for 6 $49.)

FOOD

Scores of fast-food joints line the west side of the UT campus on **Guadalupe St.** Another area clusters around **6th St.,** south of the capitol; here the battle for happy hour business rages with unique intensity, and competitors employ such deadly weapons as three-for-one drink specials and free hors d'oeuvres. Although a bit removed from downtown, **Barton Springs Rd.** offers a diverse selection of inexpensive restaurants, including Mexican and Texas-style barbecue joints. The **Warehouse District** offers more expensive seafood and Italian eateries.

Ruby's BBQ, 512 W. 29th St. (477-1651). Ruby's barbecue is good enough to be served on silver platters, but that just wouldn't seem right in this cow-skulls-and-butcher-paper establishment. The owners only order meat from farm-raised, grass-fed cows—"none of that steroid crap." A mother of a brisket sandwich goes for $4. Two black bean tacos $3.75. Open Su-Th 11am-midnight, F-Sa 11am-3am.

Trudy's Texas Star, 409 W. 30th St. (477-2935), and 8800 Burnet Rd. (454-1474). Fine Tex-Mex dinner entrees ($5.25-8) and a fantastic array of margaritas. Famous for *migas,* a corn tortilla soufflé ($5). Pleasant outdoor porch bar. Open M-Th 7am-midnight, F-Sa 7am-2am, Su 8am-midnight; bar always open until 2am.

Threadgill's, 6416 N. Lamar Blvd. (451-5440). A legend in Austin since 1933, serving up terrific Southern soul food and $7 fried chicken among creaky wooden floors, slow-moving ceiling fans, and antique beer signs. Surprisingly large variety of vegetarian and non-dairy options. Open M-Sa 11am-10pm, Su 11am-9pm.

Scholz Garden, 1607 San Jacinto Blvd. (474-1958), near the capitol. UT students and state politicians alike gather at this Austin landmark, recognized by the legislature for "epitomizing the finest traditions of the German heritage of our state." Popular chicken-fried steak dinners ($7) and sausage 'n' bratwurst po' boys ($5). A German "Wurst" band plays W 8-10pm. Open M-Th 11am-10pm and F-Sa 11am-11pm.

Mongolian BBQ, 9200 N. Lamar Blvd. (837-4898), ½ block south of Rundberg St. Create your own stir-fry from a selection of meats and veggies. In one room, a big screen shows sports. Lunch $5, dinner $7, free soft-serve ice-cream; all-you-can-eat $2 extra. Open M-F 11am-3pm and 5-9:30pm, Sa 11am-9:45pm, Su 11am-9pm.

SIGHTS

Not to be outdone, Texans built their **state capitol** (463-0063), at Congress Ave. and 11th St., 7 ft. higher than the national one. *(Open M-F 8am-5pm, Sa-Su 9am-5pm. Free 45min. tours every 15min.)* The **Capitol Complex Visitors Center,** 112 E. 11th St. (463-8586), is located in the southeast corner of the capitol grounds (open Tu-F 9am-5pm,

TEXAS

> ## Where Have All the Hippies Gone?
>
> About 15 mi. northeast of downtown Austin lies **Hippie Hollow**, 7000 Comanche Trail (266-1644), Texas's **only public nude swimming and sunbathing haven.** *(18+ only. Open daily 8am-9pm, no entry after 8:30pm. $5 per car, pedestrians $2.)* Here, free spirits go *au naturel* in the waters of the lovely Lake Travis. Take Mopac (Loop 1) north to the exit for F.M. 2222. Follow 2222 west and turn left at the I-620 intersection; Comanche Rd. will be on your right.

Sa 10am-5pm). There's a free 2hr. garage at 15th and San Jacinto St. Nearby, the **Governor's Mansion,** 1010 Colorado St. (463-5516), resides in the trees southwest of the capitol (free tours M-F every 20min. 10-11:40am). From March to November, the **Austin Convention Bureau** (454-1545) sponsors free guided walking tours of the capitol area (tours Th-F 9am, Sa-Su 9, 11am, 2pm). The capitol steps mark the tours' starting point.

Both the wealthiest public university in the country, with an annual budget of almost a billion dollars, and America's second largest university, with over 50,000 students, the **University of Texas at Austin (UT)** forms the backbone of Austin's cultural life. The **visitor info center** (475-7440) resides in Sid Richardson Hall, 2313 Red River St. (open M-F 8am-4:30pm; free tours M-F 11am and 2pm, Sa 2pm). Take bus #20 to one of the UT highlights, the **Lyndon B. Johnson Library and Museum,** 2313 Red River St. (916-5137; open daily 9am-5pm; free). The 2nd fl. focuses on the history of the American presidency, and the third features a model of the Oval Office.

The **Austin Museum of Art** at Laguna Gloria, 3809 W. 35th St. (458-8191), 8 mi. from the capitol in a Mediterranean-style villa, blends art, architecture, and nature. *(Open Tu-W and F-Sa 10am-5pm, Th 10am-9pm, Su 1-5pm. $2, seniors and students $1, under 12 free; Th free. Group tours Aug.-June by appt.)* The rolling grounds overlook Lake Austin, while the museum displays 20th-century artwork and hosts **Fiesta Laguna Gloria** (458-6073), a mid-May arts and crafts festival with evening concerts and plays.

On hot afternoons, Austinites come in droves to riverside **Zilker Park,** 2201 Barton Springs Rd. (477-7273), just south of the Colorado River; take bus #30 (open daily 5am-10pm; free). Flanked by walnut and pecan trees, **Barton Springs Pool** (476-9044), a natural spring-fed swimming hole in the park, stretches 1000 ft. long and 200 ft. wide. Beware—the pool's temperature hovers around a cool 68°F. The **Barton Springs Greenbelt** offers challenging trails for hikers and bikers. *(Pool open F-W 5am-10pm, Th 5-9am and 7-10pm. Admission M-F $2.50, Sa-Su $2.75; ages 12-17 75¢, under 12 50¢; late Mar. to early Oct. free.)*

Just before dusk, head to the **Congress Ave. Bridge** and watch for the massive swarm of **Mexican free-tail bats** that emerge from their roosts to feed on the night's mosquitoes. When the bridge was reconstructed in 1980, the engineers unintentionally created crevices which formed ideal homes for the migrating bat colony. The city began exterminating the night-flying creatures until **Bat Conservation International,** 500 Cap. Texas Hwy. (327-9721; open M-F 8:30am-5:30pm), moved to Austin to educate people about the bats' harmless behavior and the benefits of their presence—the bats eat up to 3000 lbs. of insects each night. Today, the bats are among the biggest tourist attractions in Austin. The colony, seen from mid-March to November, peaks in July, when a fresh crop of pups increases the population to around 1½ million. **Mt. Bonnell Park,** 3800 Mt. Bonnell Rd., off W. 35th St., offers a sweeping view of Lake Austin and Westlake Hills from the highest point in the city.

ENTERTAINMENT AND NIGHTLIFE

On weekends, nighttime swingers seek out dancin' on **6th St.,** an area bespeckled with warehouse nightclubs and fancy bars. The more mellow cigar-smoking night owls gather at the **4th St. Warehouse District.** The weekly *Austin Chronicle* and *XLent* provide detailed listings of current music performances, shows, and movies. The *Gay Yellow Pages,* free at stands along the Drag, dishes the scoop on Austin's gay life.

Antone's, 213 W. 5th St. (474-5314). Known to draw big-name artists, Antone's has attracted the likes of B.B. King and Muddy Waters. All ages welcome. Shows at 10pm. Cover $3-10. Open daily 9pm-2am.

Stubb's BBQ, 801 Red River (480-8341). Big names have also been known to appear in this amphitheater, which seats about 2000 listeners. Visitors can swing by earlier for some scrumptious, inexpensive grub like beef brisket and 2 side dishes for $6. 18+ after 9:30pm. Cover $3-10. Shows at 10:30pm. Open Tu-Sa 11am-2am, Su 11am-10pm (with gospel music during brunch).

Hole in the Wall, 2538 Guadalupe St. (472-5599), at 26th St. Its self-effacing name disguises this renowned music spot, which features college alternative bands and an occasional country-western or hard-core group. Music nightly. 21+. Cover $3-5; no cover Su-M. Open M-F 11am-2am, Sa-Su noon-2am.

Cactus Café (475-6515), at 24th and Guadalupe St., in the Texas Union. Features adventurous acoustic music every night. Specializing in folk-rock and Austin's own "New Country" sound, the Cactus gave Lyle Lovett his start. All ages welcome. Music starts 9pm. Cover $2-15. Open Su-F 8am-1am, Sa 8pm-2am.

Bob Popular's, 402 6th St. (478-5072). Mellows the crowd on its jazz and reggae patio while picking up the pace with retro disco in one room and Top 40 in another. Come on Thursdays when all drinks are $1. 21+, except Th. Cover $4 after 10pm, Th ages 18-20 $7. Open Su-Th 8pm-2am, F-Sa 8pm-3am.

Joe's Generic Bar, 315 E. 6th St. (480-0171). Find your way here for some raunchy Texas-style blues washed down with cheap beer. 21+. No cover. Open daily 7:30pm until the wayward crawl home.

Paradox, 311 E. 5th St. (469-7615), at Trinity. This warehouse-style dance club with retro-80s and Top 40 music, draws 20-somethings by the pack. Cover $4. Open daily 9pm-4am.

Copper Tank Brewing Company, 504 Trinity St. (478-8444). Probably the city's best microbrewery. On Wednesday, a pint of any of the freshly brewed beers costs just $1—normally $3.50. 21+ after dinner hrs. Open daily 3pm-2am.

Beverly Sheffield Zilker Hillside Theater, located across from the Barton Springs pool, hosts free outdoor bands, ballets, plays, musicals, and symphony concerts every weekend May to October (call 397-1463 for events schedule). During March 17-21, 1999, the **South by Southwest Convention** (467-7979) will draw music industry's giants and thousands of eager fans. Austin's smaller events calendar is a mixed bag. The high-brow **O. Henry Museum World Championship Pun-off** (497-1903) is held the first Sunday of May. Others can gorge themselves on Spam in the annual **Spama-rama** (416-9307), on April 10, 1999. Spam fans from all walks of life gather to pay homage to this—er, product—with food, sports, and live music at the **Spam Jam.**

■ Houston

Born in 1836, when Augustus and John Allen, two brothers from the East, came slicing through the weeds of the Buffalo Bayou, Houston has come into its own as the fourth-most populous city in the U.S. This diverse city spreads its borders as a huge mega-metropolis, filled with monster trucks on superhighways, awe-inspiring glass-and-steel skyscrapers, enormous oil plants, and the largest strip malls in the country. Luckily, the advocates of the "make it bigger" philosophy also support a softer side of Houston, cultivating operas, ballets, and museums.

ORIENTATION AND PRACTICAL INFORMATION

Though the flat Texan terrain supports several mini-downtowns, true downtown Houston, a squarish grid of interlocking one-way streets, borders the **Buffalo Bayou** at the intersection of I-10 and I-45. **The Loop (I-610)** encircles the city center with a radius of 6 mi. Anything inside the Loop is easily accessible by car or bus. The shopping district of **Westheimer Blvd.** grows ritzier as you head west. Nearby, restaurants and shops line **Kirby Dr.** and **Richmond Ave.;** the upper portion of Kirby Dr. winds past some of Houston's most spectacular mansions. *Be careful in the south and east areas of Houston.*

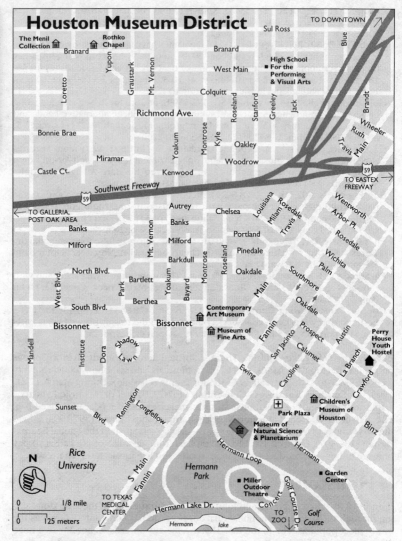

Houston Museum District

Airport: Houston Intercontinental (281-230-3100), 25 mi. north of downtown. Get to city center via **Express Shuttle** (523-8888); buses daily every 30min. to major hotels in the downtown area 7am-11:30pm ($17, under 12 $5).

Trains: Amtrak, 902 Washington Ave. (224-1577 or 800-872-7245), in a rough neighborhood. During the day, catch a bus west on Washington Ave. (away from downtown) to Houston Ave.; at night, call a cab. To San Antonio (5hr., 34 per week, $29) and New Orleans (9½hr., 3 per week, $47). Open M, Tu, and Th 7am-4pm; Su and W 7am-12:30am; F 3pm-12:30am; and Sa 11am-8pm.

Buses: Greyhound, 2121 S. Main St. (759-6565 or 800-231-2222). *At night call a cab—this is an unsafe area.* To: Dallas (5hr., 15 per day, $26); San Antonio (3½hr., 12 per day, $14); and Santa Fe (24hr., 5 per day, $112). Open 24hr.

Public Transportation: Metropolitan Transit Authority (METRO Bus System) (635-4000). Offers reliable service anywhere between NASA (15 mi. southeast of town) and Katy (25 mi. west of town). Operates M-F 6am-9pm, Sa-Su 8am-8pm; less frequently on weekends. Free maps available at the **Houston Public Library, 500**

McKinney (236-1313), at Bagby St. (open M-F 9am-9pm, Sa 9am-6pm, Su 2-6pm), or at a Metro Rides store. Fare $1; students and seniors 40¢, ages 5-11 25¢; $2 per day.
Taxis: Yellow Cab, 236-1111. $3 1st mi., $1.50 each additional mi.
Visitors Info: Greater Houston Convention and Visitors Bureau, in City Hall (227-3100 or 800-365-7575), at the corner of McKinney and Bagby St. Open M-F 8:30am-5pm.
Hotlines: Crisis Center, 228-1505. **Rape Crisis,** 528-7273. **Women's Center,** 528-2121. All 3 24hr. **Gay and Lesbian Switchboard of Houston** (529-3211) has entertainment info. Operates M-F 7-10pm.
Hospital: Columbia Bellaire Medical Center, 5314 Dashwood (512-1200), has a 24hr. emergency room. **Columbia Woman's Hospital of Texas,** 7600 Fannin (790-1234).
Post Office: 701 San Jacinto St. (223-5748). Open M-F 8am-5pm. **ZIP code:** 77052. **Area codes:** 713 and 281 (in text 713, unless indicated).

ACCOMMODATIONS AND CAMPGROUNDS

A few cheap motels dot the **Katy Freeway (I-10W),** and more conveniently located accommodations can be found along **South Main St.,** but not all of these are safe. Singles dip to $28, doubles to $32. (Bus #8 goes down S. Main.)

Perry House, Houston International Hostel (HI-AYH), 5302 Crawford St. (523-1009), at Oakdale St. In a residential neighborhood near Hermann Park and the museum district. From the Greyhound station, take bus #8 or 15 south to Southmore St.; walk 6 blocks east to Crawford St. and 1 block south to Oakdale St. Helpful management provides 30 beds in 6 spacious rooms. Well-equipped kitchen, email access, choose-your-own chore. Room lock-out 10am-5pm. $11.39, nonmembers $14.39; sleepsacks ($1.50) required. Free use of bicycles with a $20 deposit.
YMCA, 1600 Louisiana Ave. (659-8501), between Pease and Leeland St. Downtown location features tiny cubicle-rooms with daily maid service, TV, common bath, and telephones for incoming calls. Singles $18. Key deposit $10. Another branch, 7903 South Loop (643-2804), is farther out (near I-45) but less expensive. Take Bus #50 to Broadway. Singles $16. Key deposit $10.
Red Carpet Inn, 6868 Hornwood Dr. (981-8686 or 800-251-1962), off U.S. 59 S. (SW Fwy.). Down-scale but well-kept rooms. Free coffee. Singles $30; doubles $35.
The Roadrunner, 8500 S. Main St. (666-4971). Take bus #8. Friendly management, cable TV, mini-pool, free coffee, and local calls. Large, well-furnished rooms. Singles $26; doubles $32. Weekly stays discounted to $20 per day. $2 key deposit.

Most campgrounds in the Houston area lie a considerable distance from the center of the city. **KOA Houston North,** 1620 Peachleaf (281-442-3700 or 800-562-2132), has sites with access to a pool and showers. From I-45 N, go east on Aldine-Bender Rd., then turn right on Aldine-Westfield Rd., and then right again on Peachleaf. (Tent sites for 2 $16, RV hookup $21; $2 per additional adult.)

TIME FO' EATIN'

Houston's port has witnessed the arrival of many immigrants (today the city's Indochinese population is the second largest in the nation), and its restaurants reflect this diversity. Houston's cuisine features Mexican, Greek, Cajun, Asian, and Southern soul food. Look for reasonably priced restaurants along the chain-laden streets of **Westheimer** and **Richmond Ave.,** especially where they intersect with **Fountainview.** Houston has two **Chinatowns:** a district south of the George R. Brown Convention Center, and a newer area on **Bellaire Blvd.** called **DiHo.**

Goode Company BBQ, 5109 Kirby Dr. (522-2530), near Bissonnet St. This might be the best (and most popular) BBQ in Texas, with a honky-tonk atmosphere to match. The mesquite-smoked brisket, ribs, and sausage links (all smothered in homemade sauce) make for good eating. Sandwiches $3.25; dinner $6-9. Open daily 11am-10pm.

Bibas/One's A Meal, 607 W. Gray St. (523-0425), at Stanford St. This family-owned institution serves everything from chili 'n' eggs ($5.75) to a gyro with fries ($6). Their Greek pizza (6 in. $5.75) is hard to beat, and #8 on the breakfast menu is colossal (egg, bacon, sausage or ham, grits or hashbrowns, toast or biscuits, and juice for $5.25). Open 24hr.

Cadillac Bar, 1802 N. Shepherd Dr. (862-2020), at the Katy Freeway (I-10), northwest of downtown; take bus #75, change to #26 at Shepherd Dr. and Allen Pkwy. Wild, fun, authentic—and spicy—Mexican food. Tacos and enchiladas $6-8; heartier entrees $8-14. Drinks with racy names $5. Open M-Th 10am-10:30pm, Sa noon-1am, Su noon-10pm.

The Buffalo Grille, 3116 Bissonnet St.(661-3663), at Buffalo Speedway. Famous for their Texas-sized breakfasts; favorites include pecan-smoked bacon and Mexican breakfasts ($3-6). Entrees ($5-7) served indoors or on the patio. Open M-F 7am-2pm; Sa-Su 8am-2pm; lunch served M-Sa.

Magnolia Bar & Grill, 6000 Richmond Ave. (781-2607). An upscale but reasonable Cajun seafood restaurant. The constant and varied crowd attests to the quality of the food and the relaxed, welcoming atmosphere. R&B on F-Su evenings. Open M-Th 11am-10pm, F-Sa 11am-11pm, Su 10am-10pm.

SIGHTS

The city's most popular attraction, **Space Center Houston,** 1601 NASA Rd. 1 (281-244-2100 or 800-972-0369), is technically not even in Houston, but 20 mi. from downtown in Clear Lake, TX. *(Open daily 9am-7pm; early Sept. to late May M-F 10am-5pm, Sa-Su 10am-7pm. $13, seniors $12, ages 4-11 $9. Parking $3.)* Take I-45 south to NASA Rd. Exit, then head east 3 mi. or take bus #246. The active Mission Control Center still serves as HQ for modern-day Major Toms. When astronauts ask, "Do you read me, Houston?" these folks answer. The complex also houses models of Gemini, Apollo, and Mercury craft, as well as countless galleries and hands-on exhibits. You too can try to land the space shuttle on a computer simulator!

Back in Houston, more worldly pleasures can be found underground. Hundreds of shops and restaurants line the 18 mi. **Houston Tunnel System,** which connects all the major buildings in downtown Houston, extending from the Civic Center to the Tenneco Building and the Hyatt Regency. On hot days, duck into the air-conditioned passageways via any major building or hotel (most tunnel entries closed weekends).

The 17th- to 19th-century American decorative art at **Bayou Bend Collection and Gardens,** 1 Westcott St. (639-7750), in **Memorial Park,** is an antique-lover's dream. *(Collection open Tu-F 10am-2:45pm, Sa 10-11:15am. $10, seniors $8.50, ages 10-18 $5, under 10 not admitted. Gardens open Tu-Sa 10am-5pm, Su 1-5pm. $3, under 10 free. 1½hr. tours by reservation.)* The collection, housed in the mansion of millionaire Ima Hogg (we *swear*), daughter of turn-of-the-century Texas governor Jim "Boss" Hogg, includes John Singleton Copley portraits as well as a silver sugar bowl crafted by Paul Revere.

Museums, gardens, paddleboats, and golfing are all part of **Hermann Park,** 388 acres of beautifully landscaped grounds by Rice University and the Texas Medical Center. Near the northern entrance of the park, the **Houston Museum of Natural Science,** 1 Hermann Circle Dr. (639-IMAX/4629), offers a splendid display of gems and minerals, permanent exhibits on petroleum, a hands-on gallery geared toward grabby children, a butterfly center, a planetarium, and an IMAX theater. *(Exhibits open daily 9am-7pm. Museum $4, seniors and under 12 $2; IMAX $6/$3.50; planetarium $3/$2; butterfly center $3.50/$2.50.)* At the southern end of the park, more flying critters—as well as gorillas, hippos, and reptiles—live in the **Houston Zoological Gardens,** 1513 N. MacGregor (284-8300). *(Open daily 10am-6pm. $2.50, seniors $2, ages 3-12 50¢.)* Crowds flock to see the rare white tigers that would make Siegfried and Roy proud. The park grounds also encompass sports facilities, a kiddie train, a Japanese garden, and the Miller Outdoor Theater (see **Entertainment,** below).

The **Museum of Fine Arts,** 1001 Bissonet (639-7300), lies near the north side of Hermann Park. *(Open Tu-W and F-Sa 10am-5pm, Th 10am-9pm, Su 12:15-6pm. $3, students*

We're Dying to Get In

If you've got a car and a funeral fascination, head to the **American Funeral Service Museum,** 415 Barren Springs Dr. (281-876-3063 or 800-238-8861); from I-45, exit at Airtex, go west to Ella Blvd., turn right, and proceed to Barren Springs. *(Open M-F 10am-4pm, Sa-Su noon-4pm. $5, seniors and under 12 $3. Tours by appt. only.)* The museum aims to "take the fear out of funerals." It contains exhibits on funerals of notable political figures, embalming artifacts, over two dozen funeral vehicles, and (of course) coffins of all shapes and sizes—from glass to iron, from chicken-like to airplane-shaped.

---

and seniors $1.50; free Th.) Designed by Mies van der Rohe, the museum boasts a collection of Impressionist and post-Impressionist art, as well as fine works of the American West. The museum's **Sculpture Garden,** 5101 Montrose St., includes pieces by artists such as Matisse and Rodin (open daily 9am-10pm; free). Across the street, the **Contemporary Arts Museum,** 5216 Montrose St. (284-8240), displays changing exhibits. *(Open Tu-W and F-Sa 10am-5pm, Th 10am-9pm, Su noon-5pm. Suggested donation $3.)*

About 1 mi. north of the park, a couple of Houston's highly acclaimed art museums are located within 1 block of each other. The **de Menil Collection,** 1515 Sul Ross (525-9400), includes an eclectic assortment of Surrealist paintings and sculptures; Byzantine and medieval artifacts; and European, American, and African art (open W-Su 11am-7pm; free). A block away, the **Rothko Chapel,** 3900 Yupon (524-9839), houses 14 of the artist's paintings in a sanctuary. *(Open daily 10am-6pm. Free.)* Fans of modern art will delight in Rothko's ultra-simplicity; others will wonder where the paintings are.

Many a Bacchanalian fest must have preceded the construction of the **Beer Can House,** 222 Malone, off Washington Ave. Adorned with 50,000 beer cans, strings of beer-can tops, and a beer-can fence, the house was built by the late John Mikovisch, an upholsterer from the Southern Pacific Railroad.

The **San Jacinto Battleground State Historical Park** (281-479-2431), 21 mi. east on Rte. 225 and 3 mi. north on Rte. 134, stands as the most important monument to Lone Star independence. The 18min. battle brought Texas its freedom from Mexico and brought the city its namesake in the person of Sam Houston. The **museum** in the Park celebrates Texas history with a dramatic visual presentation using 42 projectors (shown hourly 10am-5pm). A ride to the top of the 50-story **San Jacinto Monument** (281-479-2421) yields a view of the area; at 570 ft., it is 15 ft. taller than the Washington Monument, although just as phallic. *(Both open daily 9am-6pm. Slide show $3.50, seniors $3, under 12 $2.50; elevator to top $3/$2.50/$2; combo ticket $6/$5/$2.)*

ENTERTAINMENT AND NIGHTLIFE

Jones Hall, 615 Louisiana Blvd. (227-3974), stages most of Houston's high-brow entertainment. The **Houston Symphony Orchestra** (227-ARTS/2787) performs here September through May (tickets $10-60). Between October and May, the **Houston Grand Opera** (546-0200) produces six operas in the nearby **Wortham Center,** 500 Texas Ave. (tickets $25-175; 50% student discount available at noon on the day of some shows). In the summer, take advantage of the **Miller Outdoor Theater** (284-8352) in Hermann Park. The symphony, opera, and ballet companies and various professional theaters stage free concerts on the hillside most evenings April to October. The annual **Shakespeare Festival** struts and frets upon the stage from late July to early August. For an events update, call 284-8350. The downtown **Alley Theater,** 615 Texas Ave. (228-8421), puts on Broadway-caliber productions at moderate prices (tickets $30-45; Su-Th $11 student rush tickets 1hr. before the show).

The **Astrodome,** Loop 610 at Kirby Dr. (799-9555), the first mammoth indoor arena of its kind, is the home of baseball's **Astros.** (General admission tickets to a game $4/$1. Parking $4. 1¼hr. tours Tu-Sa 11am and 1pm; $5, ages 3-14 $3.) The **Rockets** (629-3700) hoop it up at the **Compaq Center,** 10 Greenwald Plaza.

Most of Houston's nightlife lives west of downtown around Richmond and Westheimer Ave. Several gay clubs cluster on lower Westheimer, while enormous, warehouse-style dancehalls line the upper reaches of Richmond. A variety of bars and music venues fill the streets in between. Located in the mother of all strip malls, **City Streets,** 5078 Richmond Ave. (840-8555), is a multi-venue complex with six different clubs offering everything from country-western and live R&B to disco and a pool hall ($2-5 cover good for all 6 clubs; open Tu-F 5pm-2am, Sa 7:30pm-2am). To seek out a more hip, less commercial scene, search for the well-hidden **Emo's,** 2700 Albany St. (523-8503). A loyal crowd of locals and several big-name bands (Smashing Pumpkins, Rev. Horton Heat) have found this bar located north of Richmond on Montrose, then right on Fairview. (Live rock Tu and F-Sa nights. 21+ except F-Sa, 18-21 cover $7. Open daily 7pm-2am.) Folks from all walks of life come to talk business and pleasure in the distinctly English atmosphere of **The Ale House,** 2425 W. Alabama (521-2333), at Kirby St. The bi-level bar and beer garden offers over 130 brands of beer, some rather costly ($3-4). Upstairs, you'll find old-time rock 'n' roll or the blues on F-Sa nights. (Open M-Sa 11am-2am, Su noon-2am.)

■ Galveston Island

In the 19th century, Galveston was the "Queen of the Gulf," Texas's most prominent port and wealthiest city. The glamour came to an abrupt end on September 8, 1900, when a devastating hurricane ripped through the city and claimed 6,000 lives. The Galveston hurricane still ranks as one of the worst natural disasters in U.S. history. Today, the narrow, sandy island of Galveston (pop. 65,000), 50 mi. southeast of Houston on I-45, meets the beach resort quotas for t-shirt shops, ice cream stands, and video arcades, but redeems itself with beautiful vintage homes, antique shops, and even some deserted beaches.

PRACTICAL INFORMATION Galveston's streets follow a grid; lettered avenues run east-west, while numbered streets run north-south. **Seawall Blvd.** follows the southern coastline. Most routes have two names; Avenue J and Broadway, for example, are the same street. Greyhound affiliate **Kerrville Bus Co.,** 714 25th St. (765-7731; station open M-F 8am-7pm, Sa 8am-3:15pm), travels to Houston (1½hr., 4 per day, $13). The **Strand Visitors Center,** 2016 Strand St. (765-7834; http://www.galvestontourism.com; open daily 9:30am-5pm), in the Moody Coliseum, and the **Galveston Island Convention and Visitors Bureau,** 2106 Seawall Blvd. (763-4311 or 888-GALISLE/425-4753; open daily 8:30am-5pm), provide info about island activities (both open until 6pm in summer). **Post Office:** 601 25th St. (763-1527; open M-F 8am-5pm, Sa 9am-12:30pm). **ZIP code:** 77550. **Area code:** 409.

ACCOMMODATIONS, CAMPGROUNDS, AND FOOD Lodgings prices in Galveston fluctuate by season, rising to exorbitant heights during the summer, holidays, and weekends. Money-minded folk should consider making Galveston a daytrip from Houston, especially during the summer, when most hotels will charge at least $50 per night. Nevertheless, RVs and tents can find a reasonable resting place at any of several parks on the island. The closest to downtown, the **Bayou Haven RV Resort,** 6310 Heards Ln. (744-2837), off 61st St., is located on a peaceful waterfront with laundry facilities and bug-free restrooms and showers. (Sites for 2 with full hookup $16, waterfront sites $19; $3 per additional person. Tents welcome.) **Galveston Island State Park** (737-1222), on 13½ Mile Rd., 6 mi. southwest of Galveston on FM3005 (a continuation of Seawall Blvd.), rents tent sites. (Restrooms, showers, and barbecue pits available. $12, plus $3 entrance fee per person.)

Seafood and traditional Texas barbecue are bountiful in Galveston, especially along Seawall Blvd. **Shagnasty's Seafood Restaurant,** 438 Boddecker (762-8756), on the far eastern end of the island off Seawall Rd., belies its name with satisfying gulf seafood (shrimp, catfish, or oyster baskets $6.50) and a beautiful view of the sea. Live bands play on weekends. (Open Tu-Sa 11am-dark.) The oldest restaurant on the island, **The**

Original Mexican Café, 1401 Market (762-6001), cooks up great Tex-Mex meals with homemade flour tortillas, and daily lunch specials for $4-6 (open M-F 11am-10pm, Sa-Su 8am-10pm). After a day at the beach, indulge your sweet tooth with a cherry phosphate ($1) at **LaKing's Confectionery,** 2323 Strand St. (762-6100), a large, old-fashioned ice cream and candy parlor (open Su-F 10am-8pm, Sa 10am-10pm).

SIGHTS AND ACTIVITIES Galveston recently spent more than $6 million to clean up and restore its shoreline. The money was well spent—finding a pleasant beach is as easy as strolling along the seawall and picking a spot. The only beach in Galveston which permits alcoholic beverages is **Apffel Park,** which lies on the far eastern edge of the island (an area known as East Beach). Closer to the neon cluster of town is **Stewart Beach,** near 4th and Seawall, where a water slide keeps the kids entertained. Three **Beach Pocket Parks** lie on the west end of the island, east of Pirates Beach, each with bathrooms, showers, playgrounds, and a concession stand (car entry for beaches generally $5; open daily 9am-9pm, some open later).

   Strand St., near the northern coastline, between 20th and 25th St., is a national landmark, with over 50 Victorian buildings. The street provides a pastiche of cafes, restaurants, gift shops, and clothing stores. Once dubbed the "Wall Street of the Southwest," the district has been restored with authenticities such as gas lights and brick-paved walkways. During the summer, Strand St.'s **Saengerfest Park,** at Tremont St., holds a free **Party in the Park** (763-7080) every Saturday and Sunday 3-7pm. Partyers can listen to a blues band jam while contemplating their own moves on a life-size chess board (2 ft. tall pieces). The **Galveston Island Trolley** shuttles between the seawall beach area and the posh historic section of Strand St. (runs daily 6:30am-7pm; 60¢ per 30min.). Pick up the trolley at either visitors center.

   You'll find fabulous and pricey exhibits at **Moody Gardens** (744-1745 or 800-582-4673); turn onto 81st from Seawall. *(Open daily 9:30am-9pm; Nov.-Feb. Su-Th 10am-6pm, F-Sa 10am-9pm. Attractions $6 each, ride/films $7, seniors and children $1 off; discounts for multiple exhibits.)* The area, though filled with touristy gift shops and restaurants, makes room for three glass pyramids, one which houses over 30 interactive space exhibits and three IMAX ride-film theaters (rides every 15min.), a second containing a tropical rainforest and 2000 exotic species of flora and fauna, and a third (coming in July 1999) featuring an aquarium. An additional IMAX theater adjoins the visitors center.

■ San Antonio

The skyline may be dominated by aging office buildings, but no Texan city seems more determined to preserve its rich heritage than the romantic San Antone. Founded in 1691 by Spanish missionaries, the city is home to the famed Alamo, historic Missions, and La Villita, once a village for San Antonio's original settlers and now a workshop for local artisans. Many attractions, including the magnificent (though slightly artificial) Riverwalk, make San Antonio a popular vacation destination; hotel occupancy rates and prices rise on weekends, unlike most other cities of comparable size. Though both Native Americans and Germans have at one time claimed San Antonio as their own, Spanish speakers (55% of the population) outnumber any other group; the city's food, architecture, and language reflect this influence. San Antonio is located on the most traveled route between the U.S. and Mexico, just 150 mi. from the Mexican border.

PRACTICAL INFORMATION

   Airport: San Antonio International, 9800 Airport Blvd. (207-3411), north of town accessible by I-410 and U.S. 281. Bus #2 ("Airport") connects the airport to downtown at Market and Alamo. **Star Shuttle Service** (341-6000) travels from the airport to several locations downtown for $6 per person. Taxi to downtown $14-15.
   Trains: Amtrak, 224 Hoefgen St. (223-3226 or 800-872-7245), facing the northern side of the Alamodome. To: Houston (5hr., 3 per week, $29); Dallas (9hr., 4 per week, $27); and Los Angeles (26hr., 3 per week, $128). Open daily midnight-2pm.

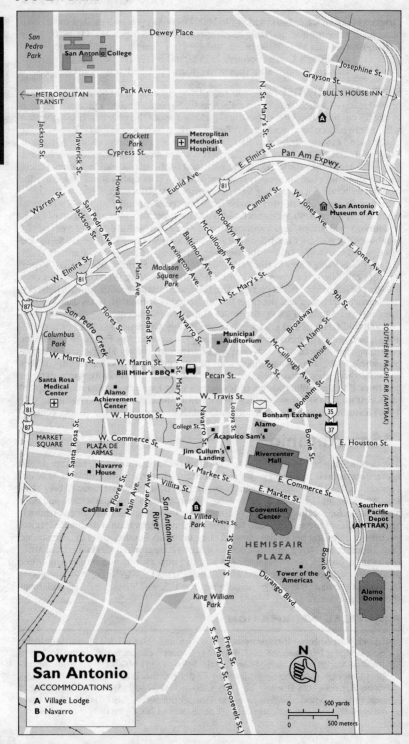

Downtown San Antonio

ACCOMMODATIONS

A Village Lodge
B Navarro

Buses: Greyhound, 500 N. Saint Mary's St. (270-5824 or 800-231-2222). To: Houston (4hr., 9 per day, $21); Dallas (5-8hr., 15 per day, $34); and Fredericksburg (1½hr., 3 per day, $15). Open 24hr.

Public Transportation: VIA Metropolitan Transit, 800 W. Myrtle (362-2020; open M-Sa 7am-7pm, Su 8am-5pm), between Commerce and Houston. Buses operate daily 5am-11:30pm, but many routes stop at 6pm. Infrequent service to outlying areas. Fare 75¢. One-day "day tripper" passes $4; available at 112 Soledad St.

Taxis: Yellow Cab, 226-4242. $2.90 1st mi., $1.30 per additional mi.

Car Rental: Chuck's Rent-A-Clunker, 3249 SW Military Dr. (922-9464). $20.80 per day with 100 free mi. Must be 21 with credit card or cash deposit. Customer pick-up service available. Open M-F 8am-6pm, Sa 9am-3pm, Su noon-5pm.

Visitor Info: 317 Alamo Plaza (270-8748), downtown across from the Alamo. Open daily 8:30am-6pm. Free maps and brochures.

Hotlines: Rape Crisis, 349-7273. 24hr. **Supportive Services for the Elderly and Disabled,** 226-9212. Referrals and transport.

Hospital: Metropolitan Methodist Hospital, 1310 McCullough Ave. (208-220). 24hr.

Post Office: 615 E. Houston (227-3399), 1 block from the Alamo. Open M-F 8:30am-5:30pm. **ZIP code:** 78205. **Area code:** 210.

ACCOMMODATIONS AND CAMPGROUNDS

For cheap motels, try **Roosevelt Ave.,** a southern extension of Saint Mary's St., and **Fredericksburg Rd.** Inexpensive motels also line **Broadway** between downtown and Brackenridge Park. Drivers should follow **I-35 N** to find cheaper and often safer lodging within a 15 mi. radius of town.

Bullis House Inn San Antonio International Hostel (HI-AYH), 621 Pierce St. (223-9426), 2 mi. north of downtown on Broadway, right on Grayson ¾ mi. From the bus station, walk to Navarro St. and take bus #11 or 15 to Grayson and New Braunfels; walk 2 blocks west. A friendly ranch-style hostel in a quiet neighborhood. Pool, kitchen. Fills quickly in summer. $14, nonmembers $17. Private rooms for 1 or 2 $35, nonmembers from $39. Linen $2. Breakfast $4.50. Reception daily 7:30am-11pm. No curfew. Private rooms at their B&B from $35.

Villager Lodge, 1126 E. Elmira (222-9463 or 800-584-0800), about 3 blocks east of St. Mary's a little over 1 mi. north of downtown; take bus #8. The very caring management provides the cleanest rooms you'll get at this price. Cable TV, 5 free local calls, A/C, and Microfridges in some rooms. Room for 1 or 2 $34. Key deposit $2.

Navarro Hotel, 116 Navarro St. (223-8453 or 224-0255). 43 rooms in a great location with A/C, laundry, and free parking. Clean, irregularly shaped rooms with varying degrees of furniture quality. Singles $29 and up; doubles $40 and up.

The Roosevelt Inn, 2122 Roosevelt Ave. (533-2514), 2½ mi. south of downtown near the missions; take bus #42 or 34. Reasonably clean rooms for great prices, free local calls. FDR surely didn't stay here, but then again, he wasn't living on $50 a day. Singles $26; doubles $30.

Alamo KOA, 602 Gembler Rd. (224-9296 or 800-833-5267), 6 mi. from downtown; take bus #24 ("Industrial Park") from the corner of Houston and Alamo downtown. From I-10 E., take Exit 580/W.W. White Rd., drive 2 blocks north, then take a left onto Gembler Rd. Beautiful, well-kept grounds with lots of shade. Each site has a BBQ grill and patio. Showers, laundry facilities, pool, and free movies. Tent sites $15, full RV hookup $22; $2 per additional person. Open daily 7:30am-10pm.

FOOD

Expensive cafes and restaurants line the **River Walk**—breakfast alone can clean you out if you don't settle for a muffin and coffee. North of town, Asian restaurants open onto **Broadway** across from Brackenridge. On weekends, hundreds of carnival food booths crowd the walkways of **Market Sq.** (207-8600). Come late in the day when prices drop and vendors are willing to haggle. (Open daily 10am-8pm; Sept.-May 10am-6pm.) **Pig Stand** (227-1691) diners offer decent but cheap grub all over this part of Texas; the branches at 801 S. Presa, off S. Alamo, and 1508 Broadway (both near downtown), stay open 24hr. **Taco Cabana** makes the best Mexican fast food in the area, with many locations across downtown. All locations, including the one at 2908 N. Broadway (8294-1616), serve breakfast, lunch, and late-night dinner. The omnipresent **Bill Miller's BBQ,** one location at 501 N. Saint Mary's St. (212-4343), at Pecan St., dishes out serious BBQ (hrs. vary; this location open M-F 10am-6pm).

🌀**Rosario's,** 1014 S. Alamo St. (223-1806), at S. Saint Mary's St., is widely acknowledged by locals to be the best eatery in town. Scrumptious chicken quesadillas for only $3.75 uphold the reputation. Live music F-Sa nights. Open M 10:45am-3pm, Tu-Th 10:45am-10pm, F 10:45am-12:30am, Sa 10:45am-11pm.

Mi Tierra, 218 Produce Row (225-1262), in Market Sq. Perpetually smiling mariachi musicians serenade patrons who also smile after filling up on chicken enchiladas slathered in chocolate-based mole sauce ($7.25). Lunch specials $7. Open 24hr.

Josephine St. Steaks/Whiskey, 400 Josephine St. (224-6169), at McAllister. Far from the more touristy spots along the River Walk. Josephine's specializes in thick Texan steaks, but offers an assortment of dishes. Entrees $5-12, lunch specials $5-7. Open M-Th 11am-10pm, F-Sa 11am-11pm.

Earl Abel's, 4220 Broadway (822-3358). A professional organist for silent movies, Mr. Abel found himself out of work once the "talkies" hit the silver screen. When he opened his restaurant in 1933, the stars came to him; his diner took off after Duncan Hines ate here and raved. Abel's family still runs the operation. Bacon, eggs, hash browns, and toast served with friendly smiles $4.75. Dinner $5-10. Open daily 6:30am-1am. Breakfast served all day.

Hung Fong Chinese and American Restaurant, 3624 Broadway (822-9211), at Queen Anne 2 mi. north of downtown; take bus #14 or 9. The oldest Chinese restaurant in San Antonio, Hung is consistently good and crowded. Big portions $5-7. Open M-Th 11am-10:30pm, F-Sa 11am-11:30pm, Su 11:30am-10:30pm.

SIGHTS

Much of historic San Antonio lies in the present-day downtown and surrounding areas. The city may seem diffuse, but almost every major site or park is within a few miles of downtown and is accessible by public transportation.

The Missions

The five missions along the San Antonio River once formed the soul of San Antonio; the city preserves their remains in the **San Antonio Missions National Historical Park.** *(All missions free and open daily 9am-5pm. For info, call 534-8833, or visit the park headquarters at Mission San José.)* To reach the missions, follow the brown and white **"Mission Trail"** signs beginning on S. Saint Mary's St. downtown. Bus #42 stops within walking distance of Mission Concepción and right in front of Mission San José.

Mission San José, 6701 San José Dr. (932-1001), off Roosevelt Ave. The "Queen of the Missions" (1720) has remnants of its own irrigation system, a gorgeous sculpted rose window, and numerous restored buildings. The largest of San Antonio's missions, it best conveys the self-sufficiency of these institutions. 4 Catholic services held each Su (7:45, 9, and 10:30am, and a noon "Mariachi Mass").

Mission Concepción, 807 Mission Rd. (534-1540), 4 mi. south of the Alamo off E. Mitchell St. The oldest unrestored stone church in North America (1731). Traces of the once-colorful frescoes are still visible.

Mission San Juan Capistrano, 9101 Graf St. (534-0749), at Ashley, and **Mission San Francisco de la Espada,** 10040 Espada Rd. (627-2021), both off Roosevelt Ave., 10 mi. south of downtown as the Texas swallow flies. Smaller and simpler than the others, these 2 missions evoke the isolation of such outposts. Between them lies the Espada Aqueduct, the only remaining waterway built by the Spanish.

Don't Forget the Alamo!

"Be silent, friend, here heroes died to blaze a trail for other men." **The Alamo** (225-1391), which has always been set apart from the other missions, is not maintained by the National Historical Park but by the **Daughters of the Republic of Texas—**oh, brother! *(Open M-Sa 9am-6:30pm, Su 10am-6:30pm; early Sept. to late May grounds close at*

5:30pm. Free.) If the core of Texas pride were stored in a strongbox, it would be deposited here. Disobeying orders to retreat with their cannons, the 189 defenders of the Alamo, outnumbered 20 to one, held off the Mexican army for 12 days. Then, on the morning of the 13th day, the Mexicans commenced the infamous *deguello* (throat-cutting). The only survivors of the Alamo defenders were women, children, and slaves. Forty-six days later, General Sam Houston's small army defeated the Mexicans at **San Jacinto** amid cries of **"Remember the Alamo!"** These days, phalanxes of tourists attack the Alamo, at the center of Alamo Plaza near Houston and Alamo St., and Sno-cone vendors are the only defenders. A single chapel and barracks are all that remain of the former Spanish Mission.

Secular San Antone: Downtown

Southwest of the Alamo, black signs indicate access points to the 2½ mi. **Paseo del Río (River Walk),** a series of well-patrolled shaded stone pathways which follow a winding canal built by the Works Progress Administration in the 1930s. Lined with picturesque gardens, shops, and cafes, and connecting most of the major downtown sights, the River Walk is the hub of San Antonio's nightlife. A few blocks south, the recreated artisans' village, **La Villita,** 418 Villita (207-8610), houses restaurants, craft shops, and art studios (shops open daily 10am-6pm, restaurant hrs. vary). On weekends, **Market Sq.** (207-8600), between San Saba and Santa Rosa St., features the upbeat tunes of Tejano bands, the omnipresent buzzing of frozen margarita machines, and jangling windchimes (open daily 10am-8pm; Sept.-May 10am-6pm).

The site of the 1968 World's Fair, **HemisFair Plaza,** on S. Alamo, draws tourists with nearby restaurants, museums, and historic houses. The observation deck of the **Tower of the Americas,** 600 HemisFair Park (207-8615), rises 750 ft. above the dusty plains; the view is best at night (open Su-Th 9am-10pm, F-Sa 9am-11pm; $3, seniors $2, ages 4-11 $1). Plaza museums include the **Institute of Texan Cultures,** 801 S. Bowie (458-2300), at Durango, which celebrates the Native American, European, African-American, Jewish, Asian, and Latino contributions to the culture of the state (open Tu-Su 9am-5pm; $4, seniors and children $2). The **Mexican Cultural Institute,** 600 HemisFair Park (227-0123), highlights the most influential ethnic presence in the city, and quite possibly in the state. *(Open Tu-F 10am-5pm, Sa-Su 11am-5pm. Free.)* Concerts ($3) are at 7pm on weekends.

Directly behind City Hall, between Commerce and Dolorosa St. at Laredo, the adobe-walled **Spanish Governor's Palace,** 105 Plaza de Armas (224-0601), completed in 1749, revives Spanish Colonial-style architecture with restored rooms and an enclosed garden (open M-Sa 9am-5pm, Su 10am-5pm; $1, ages 7-14 50¢). Home to the **San Antonio Spurs,** the **Alamodome,** 100 Montana (207-3600), at Hoefgen St. downtown, resembles a Mississippi riverboat. *(Tours Tu-Sa 11am and 1pm, except during scheduled events. $3, seniors and ages 4-12 $1.50.)* Take bus #24 or 26.

And Beyond...

The truly adventurous will break beyond the confines of the Alamo and Riverwalk and make their way to the city's fringes. **Brackenridge Park,** 3910 N. Saint Mary's St. (736-9534), 5 mi. north of the Alamo, is an escape from the urban congestion; from downtown, take bus #7 or 8. *(Open M-F 10am-5:15pm, Sa-Su 10am-6pm.)* The 343-acre showground includes playgrounds, stables, a miniature train, and an aerial tramway ($2.25, ages 1-11 $1.75) that glides to a sunken Japanese garden. Directly across the street, the **San Antonio Zoo,** 3903 N. Saint Mary's St. (734-0437), one of the country's largest, houses over 3500 animals from 800 species in reproductions of their natural settings, including an extensive African mammal exhibit (open daily 9am-5pm; $6, seniors and ages 3-11 $4).

For intoxicating natural beauty, visit **Natural Bridge Caverns,** 26495 Natural Bridge Caverns Rd. (651-6101); take I-35 N to Exit 175 and follow the signs. *(Open daily 9am-6pm; off-season 9am-4pm. $9, ages 4-12 $6. 1¼ hr. tours every 30min.)* Discovered 40 years ago, the phallic 140-million-year-old rock formations continuously change; they're different every millennium.

How many words can YOU make from "Schlitterbahn?"

The entire local economy of the town of New Braunfels depends upon one doughnut-shaped object: the innertube. Almost 2 million visitors per year come to this town, hoping only to spend a day floating along the pea-green waters of the spring-fed **Comal River. Rockin' "R" River Rides,** 193 S. Liberty (830-620-6262), will send you off with a lifejacket and a trusty tube and pick you up downstream 2½hr. later. *(Open May-Sept. daily 9am-7pm. Tube rentals $9, $7 for bottomless floats. Car keys, proper ID, or $25 deposit required during rental.)* If the Comal don't float your boat, head for the chlorinated waters of **Schlitterbahn,** 400 N. Liberty (830-625-2351), a 65-acre extravaganza of a waterpark with 17 water slides, 9 tube chutes, and 5 giant hot tubs. The park has recently built the mega-complex Blastenhoff, which includes the planet's only uphill watercoaster, the Master Blaster. *(Open May-Sept. Call for hrs., generally around 10am-8pm. Full-day passes $23.50, ages 3-11 $19.25.)* To find both attractions, take I-35 N to Exit 189, turn left, and follow the signs for Schlitterbahn.

The **Lone Star Buckhorn Museum,** 600 Lone Star Blvd. (270-9400), located at a former **Lone Star Brewery,** combines a long-time love of beer and taxidermy into a fantastic gallery of miscellany. *(Open daily 9:30am-5pm. $5, seniors $4, ages 6-11 $3; includes free beer or root beer.)* In the "Hall of Horns," with 3500 hunting trophies (including an albino buck and a two-headed calf) attached to the walls, you can't help feeling like a Texan. The grounds also include a wax museum, which depicts some of the more gory moments of Texas's past (e.g., scalpings). If the museum has you itching for the trigger, **A Place to Shoot,** 13250 Pleasanton Rd. (628-1888), is—well, just that. *(Open M-F 10am-7pm, Sa-Su 9am-7pm; $6 per person. 50¢ earplug rental.)* Take Moursund Rd., which is Exit 46 off I-410 S. This 22-acre shooting facility offers four types of shotgun ranges: skeet, trap, crazy quail, and country doubles. If, on the other hand, you're in the mood to see more cowboy paraphernalia, **Pioneer Hall,** 3805 N. Broadway (822-9011), contains a splendid collection of artifacts, documents, portraits, and possessions of the rangers, trail drivers, and pioneers who helped settle Texas (open daily 10am-5pm; Sept.-Apr. 11am-4pm; $2, seniors $1.50, ages 6-12 50¢).

The **San Antonio Museum of Art,** 200 W. Jones Ave. (978-8100), just north of the city center, showcases Texan furniture and pre-Columbian, Native American, Spanish, and Mexican folk art. *(Open Tu 10am-9pm, W-Sa 10am-5pm, and Su noon-5pm. $4, college students with ID and seniors $2, ages 4-11 $1.75; free Tu 3-9pm. Free parking.)* The **McNay Art Museum,** 6000 N. New Braunfels (824-5368), flaunts a large collection of post-Impressionist European art, including works by Degas, Picasso, and Van Gogh. *(Open Tu-Sa 10am-5pm, Su noon-5pm; free.)* Take bus #11.

ENTERTAINMENT AND NIGHTLIFE

From April 16-25, 1999, **Fiesta San Antonio** (227-5191) will usher in spring with concerts, parades, and plenty of Tex-Mex celebrations to commemorate the victory at San Jacinto and to pay homage to the heroes of the Alamo. For excitement after dark any time, any season, stroll down the River Walk. *The Friday Express* or weekly *Current* (available at the tourist office) will guide you to concerts and entertainment. The River Walk's young and stylish flock to **Acapulco Sam's,** 212 College St. (212-7267). This huge dance club features acoustic acts on one level, live bands and Top 40 music on the second, and a groovy DJ with a dance floor straight out of *Saturday Night Fever* on the third. (21+. Cover around $3-5. Music nightly 9:30pm. Open Tu-Th 8pm-2am, F-Sa 6pm-3am.) For authentic **Tejano music,** a Mexican and country amalgam, head to **Cadillac Bar,** 212 S. Flores (223-5533), where a different tejano band whips the huge crowd (anywhere from 500-1000 people) into a cheering and dancing frenzy every weeknight (21+; open M-Sa 11am-2am). Right around the corner from the Alamo, the **Bonahm Exchange,** 411 Bonahm (271-3811), San Antonio's biggest gay dance club, plays high-energy music with some house and techno on the side. A younger, more mixed crowd files in on Wednesdays. (18+. Open M-F 4pm-

2:30am, Sa 8pm-4am.) Some of the best traditional jazz anywhere taps at **Jim Cullum's Landing,** 123 Losoya (223-7266), in the Hyatt downtown. The legendary Cullum plays with his jazz band Monday to Saturday 8:30pm-1am. The improv jazz quintet Small World performs on Sunday nights. (All ages welcome. Cover $6.50. Open M-Th 4:30pm-12:30am, F 4:30pm-1:30am, Sa noon-1:30am, Su noon-midnight.)

■ Near San Antonio: Fredericksburg

There are hundreds of small towns in Texas, but perhaps none has been preserved so well as Fredericksburg. While falling oil and cattle prices squashed many other communities, this town discovered and exploited a resource whose value is ever increasing: tourism. Here, the small population supplies more than 500 motel rooms to cityfolk who want to escape into the "country." While visitors may be as common as locals in Main St. shops and restaurants, this is a genuine Texas hill country village.

To get to Fredericksburg, follow I-10 west 48 mi., then turn north on U.S. 87. It's about a 1¼hr. drive. (For Greyhound info from San Antonio, see **Practical Information,** p. 535.) From Austin, take U.S. 290 W for 80 mi. Both U.S. 87 and U.S. 290 climb and fall through peach orchards, vineyards, and pecan farms. Roadside vendors sell samples from their gardens for small change in season.

German immigrants founded Fredericksburg in 1846, and the current inhabitants won't let you forget it. *Biergartens* dot the main drag, and street names are subtitled in German. Oddly enough, many town attractions focus on World War II, when America and Germany were rivals. The **Admiral Nimitz Museum,** 340 E. Main St. (830-997-4397), presents the story of the war in the Pacific surprisingly well from Pearl Harbor to the Atomic Bomb (open daily 8am-5pm; $3, students $1.50). Signs beside the museum lead to the nearby **History Walk of the Pacific War,** 2 acres of vintage aircraft, tanks, and guns.

East of town 16 mi. on U.S. 290 lies the **Lyndon B. Johnson Ranch** (210-664-2252), a State and National Park. (Park open daily 8am-5pm, tours depart 10am-4pm. $3.) Tours include stops at LBJ's birthplace, elementary school, and "Texas White House."

Enchanted Rock State Natural Area (915-247-3903 or 800-792-1112; for reservations 512-389-8900), 18 mi. north of Fredericksburg on R.R. 965, provides the best place to hike or camp in the region. "E-Rock" is a stunning 500 ft. tall red granite batholith over one billion years old. The hike to the top and back takes 30min.; a longer loop trail surrounds the outcropping. Climbers are welcome. ($5 entrance fee, under 12 free. Tent sites with water and hookup $9; hike-in primitive sites $7.)

■ Corpus Christi

Visitors flock to Corpus Christi year-round for its cool temps and warm beaches. In June, the "winter Texans" (many of them elderly mobile-home owners) head north, only to be replaced by hordes of vacationers. In August, the reverse takes place. Thus, the summer months are generally considered "the season," when motels are full and beaches packed. The city named for "the body of Christ" draws its sustenance from the bottom of the sea; it's a major refining center for the many offshore rigs in the Gulf of Mexico. This industrial nature makes the town a decidedly blue-collar resort, but hey, a beach is a beach. No sir, 'tain't no Riviera, but them dunes sure is purdy.

PRACTICAL INFORMATION Corpus Christi's tourist district follows **Shoreline Drive,** which borders the Gulf Coast, 1 mi. east of the downtown business district. **Greyhound,** 702 N. Chaparral (882-2516 or 800-231-2222; open daily 8am-2:30am), at Starr downtown, travels to Dallas (8-10hr., 5 per day, $41); Houston (4½hr., 8 per day, $21); and Austin (5-6hr., 3 per day, $29). **Regional Transit Authority (The "B")** (289-2600) buses within Corpus Christi; pick up maps and schedules at the visitors bureau or at **"B" headquarters,** 1812 S. Alameda (883-2287; open M-F 8am-5pm). City Hall, Port Ayers, Six Points, and the Staples St. stations serve as central transfer points. (Runs M-Sa 5:30am-9:30pm, Su 11am-6:30pm. Fare 50¢, at peak times 10¢;

students, seniors, children, and disabled 25¢; Sa 25¢, transfers free.) The **Corpus Christi Beach Connector** follows the shoreline and stops at the aquarium daily 7am-6:30pm (same fares as buses). On the north side of Harbor Bridge, the free **Beach Shuttle** also travels to the beach, the Aquarium, and other nearby attractions (runs May-Sept. 10:30am-6:30pm). **Yellow Cab** (884-3211) charges $3 for the first mi., $1.50 per additional mi. The **Convention and Visitors Bureau,** 1201 N. Shoreline (881-1888 or 800-678-6232), where I-37 meets the water, stocks piles of pamphlets, bus schedules, and local maps (open M-F 8:30am-5pm, Sa 9am-3pm). The **Corpus Christi Museum,** 1900 N. Chaparral (883-2862) also offers a treasure trove of brochures (open daily 10am-6pm). The nearest and largest hospital to downtown is **Spohn Hospital Shoreline,** 600 Elizabeth St. (881-3000). Call the **Hope Line** (855-4673) for counseling and crisis service, or the **Battered Women and Rape Victims Shelter** (881-8888; both open 24hr.). **Post Office:** 809 Nueces Bay Blvd. (886-2200; open M-F 7:30am-5:30pm, Sa 8am-1pm). **ZIP code:** 78469. **Area code:** 512.

ACCOMMODATIONS, FOOD, AND NIGHTLIFE Cheap accommodations are scarce downtown. Posh hotels and expensive motels take up much of the scenic shoreline. For the best motel bargains, drive several miles south on Leopard St. (take bus #27) or I-37 (take #27 Express). **The Parkside Inn,** 6255 I-37 (289-0991), at Exit 5, offers rooms with refrigerators, microwaves, and TVs (singles $25-27; doubles $30-33). Next door, the **Super 8,** 910 Corn Products Rd. (289-1216), keeps simple yet clean rooms (singles $33; doubles $37). Campers should head for the **Mustang State Park** or the **Padre Island National Seashore** (see below). Nueces River **City Park** (241-1464), off I-37 N from Exit 16, has free tent sites, but only pit toilets and no showers.

The mixed population and seaside locale of Corpus Christi have resulted in a wide range of cuisine. Restaurants of the non-chain type can be found on the "south side" of the city, around Staples St. and S. Padre Island Dr. **BJ's,** 6335 S. Padre Island Dr. (992-6671), serves cheese-laden, crispy-crusted pizzas while patrons shoot pool and sample 300 varieties of beer (open M-Sa 11am-10:30pm, Su noon-8:30pm). The **Water Street Seafood Company,** 309 N. Water St. (882-8683), sells moderate to pricey marine life, such as deep fried oysters ($8.50) and large shrimp ($9.50; open Su-Th 11am-10pm, F-Sa 11am-11pm). The city shuts down early, but several clubs manage to survive on Water St.; the **Yucatan Beach Club,** 208 N. Water St. (888-6800), visibly marked with yellow and green neon, plays dance music late into the night (cover $2, ages 18-21 $5-7; open daily 7pm-2am).

SIGHTS Corpus Christi's most significant sight is the shoreline, bordered by miles of rocky seawall and wide sidewalks with graduated steps down to the water. Over-priced seaside restaurants, sail and shrimp boats, and aggressive, hungry seagulls overrun the piers. To find beaches that allow swimming (some lie along Ocean Dr. and north of Harbor Bridge), just follow the signs, or call **Nueces County Parks** (949-7023) for directions. On the north side of Harbor Bridge, the **Texas State Aquarium,** 2710 N. Shoreline Blvd. (881-1200 or 800-477-4853), showcases sea creatures from the Gulf of Mexico. *(Open M-Sa 9am-6pm, Su 10am-6pm; early Sept. to late May closes at 5pm. $8, seniors and ages 12-17 $6.75, ages 4-11 $4.50.)*

Just offshore floats the aircraft carrier **U.S.S. Lexington** (888-4873 or 800-523-9539), a World War II relic now open to the public. *(Open daily 9am-6pm; early Sept. to late May 9am-5pm. $9, seniors $7, ages 4-12 $4.)* In her day, the "Blue Ghost" set more records than any carrier in the history of naval aviation. Be sure to check out the crews' quarters—you won't complain about small hostel rooms ever again. Built by the government of Spain in 1992, the **Columbus Fleet,** 1900 N. Chaparral St. (883-2863), near the Harbor Bridge, commemorates the 500th anniversary of Columbus's historic voyage with replicas of the Niña, the Pinta, and the Santa María.

■ Padre Island

With over 80 mi. of perfectly preserved beaches, dunes, and wildlife refuge land, the **Padre Island National Seashore (PINS)** is a nearly flawless gem sandwiched between the condos and tourists of North Padre Island and the spring break hordes of South Padre Island. The seashore provides excellent opportunities for **windsurfing, swimming,** or even **surf fishing. Scavengers** will enjoy the garbage from nearby ships that occasionally suns itself on the sands. A weekly pass into PINS costs $10 for cars, $5 for hikers and bikers. Windsurfing or launching a boat from the park's Bird Basin will dock you an extra $5. Many beachcombers avoid these hefty fees by going to the free **North Beach.** Five miles south of the entrance station, **Malaquite Beach** makes your day on the sand as easy as possible with restrooms and rental picnic tables. In summer, the rental station is set up on the beachfront (inner tubes and chairs each $2 per hr., body boards $2.50 per hr.). The **Malaquite Visitors Center** (949-8068), has free maps and exhibits about the island (open daily 9am-5pm).

Visitors with four-wheel-drive and a taste for solitude should make the 60 mi. trek to the Mansfield Cut, the most remote and untraveled area of the seashore; loose sands prevent most vehicles from venturing far onto the beach. If you decide to go, be sure to tell the folks at the **Malaquite Ranger Station** (949-8173), 3½ mi. south of the park entrance; they handle emergency assistance and like to know who's out there. No wheels? Hike the **Grasslands Nature Trail,** a ¾ mi. loop through sand dunes and grasslands. Stop at the visitors center for a guide pamphlet.

Camping on the beach at PINS means falling asleep to the crashing of waves on the sand; if you're not careful, morning may mean waking up to the slurping noise of thousands of mosquitoes sucking you dry—bring insect repellent. Rangers also suggest strong sunscreen, protective clothing, and meat tenderizer for jellyfish stings. The **PINS Campground,** less than 1 mi. north of the visitors center, consists of an asphalt area for RVs, restrooms, and cold-rinse showers—no soap is permitted on PINS (sites $8). Outside of this area, and excluding the 5 mi. pedestrians only beach, wherever vehicles can go, camping is free.

Near the national seashore, the **Padre Balli County Park** (949-8121), on Park Rd. 22, 3½ mi. from the JFK Causeway, provides running water, electricity, and hot showers for campers (sites with water and hookup $15; key deposit $5; 3-day max. stay). Another alternative for those who value creature comforts is the **Mustang State Park Campground** (749-5246), 6 mi. up S.H. 361, offering electricity, running water, dump stations, restrooms, hot showers, and picnic tables. (Entry fee $3 per person. Beach sites $7, with water and electricity $12. RVs must reserve ahead. All must pick up a camping permit from the ranger station at the park entrance.) Motorists enter the PINS via the JFK Causeway, from the Flour Bluff area of Corpus Christi. PINS is difficult to reach via Corpus Christi's public bus system. **Area code:** 512.

WESTERN TEXAS

On the far side of the Río Pecos lies a region whose stereotypical Texan character verges on self-parody. This is the stomping ground of Pecos Bill—the mythical cowpoke who was raised by coyotes and grew so strong as to lasso a tornado. The land here was colonized in the days of the Republic of Texas, during an era when the "law west of the Pecos" meant a rough mix of vigilante violence and frontier gunslinger machismo. The border city of El Paso and its Chihuahuan neighbor, Ciudad Juárez, beckon way, *wayyyy* out west—700 mi. from the Louisiana border—while Big Bend National Park dips down into the desert, cradled by a curve in the Río Grande.

■ Amarillo

Named for the yellow clay of a nearby lake (*amarillo* is yellow in Spanish), Amarillo opened for business as a railroad construction camp in 1887 and, within a decade, became the nation's largest cattle-shipping market. For years, the economy depended largely on the meat industry, but the discovery of oil gave Amarillo a kick in the 1920s. More recently, the city has received a boost from a relatively new tourism industry. Amarillo is the prime overnight stop for motorists en route from Dallas,

Houston, or Oklahoma City to Sante Fe, Denver, and points west. It's a one-day city—there isn't much to do on the Texas plains—but a grand, shiny truck stop it is.

PRACTICAL INFORMATION Amarillo sprawls at the intersection of I-27, I-40, and U.S. 287/87; you'll need a car to explore. Rte. 335 (the Loop) encircles the city. Amarillo Blvd. (historic Rte. 66) runs east-west, parallel to I-40. **Greyhound,** 700 S. Tyler (374-5371 or 800-231-2222; station open 24hr.), buses to Dallas (7-8hr., 5 per day, $50) and Santa Fe (6-10hr., 4 per day, $56). **Amarillo City Transit,** 801 SE 23rd (378-3094), operates eight bus routes departing from 5th and Pierce St. (buses run every 30min. M-Sa 6am-6pm; fare 75¢; maps at office). Ride like a king with **Royal Cab Co.** (376-4276. $1.30 base fare, $1 per mi. Some drivers charge 50¢ per extra person.) The **Texas Travel Info Center,** 9400 I-40E (335-1441), at Exit 76, is open daily 8am-5pm. The **Amarillo Convention and Visitors Bureau,** 1000 S. Polk (374-1497 or 800-692-1338), at 10th St., distributes more city-specific info (open M-F 8am-5pm). **Post Office:** 505 E. 9th Ave. (379-2148), in Downtown Station at Buchanan St. (open M-F 7:30am-5pm). **ZIP code:** 79105. **Area code:** 806.

ACCOMMODATIONS, CAMPGROUNDS, AND FOOD Cheap motels lurk on the outskirts of town on I-40; prices rise as you near the downtown area. **Camelot Inn,** 2508 I-40 E (373-3600), at Exit 72A; a pink, castle-like motel with palatial rooms, a princely staff, shiny wood furniture, cable, and free morning grog; ranks among the best of the I-40 offerings (singles $24-26; doubles $35-40; varies seasonally; 21+). **Coachlight Inn** has two locations along I-40, 2115 I-40 (Ross Exit 71; 376-5811), and 6810 I-40 (Whitaker Exit 74; 373-6871). Some rooms have new bathtubs and refrigerators. (Singles $28; doubles $28; queens $35; off-season $22/$25/$30.) Kampers kommune with nature at the **KOA Kampground,** 1100 Folsom Rd. (335-1792), 6 mi. east of downtown; take I-40 to Exit 75, head north 2 mi. to Rte. 60, then east 1 mi. The campground has a pool, laundry, basketball court, free coffee, and shady sites. ($17, full hookup $22. Open daily 7:30am-10pm; early Sept. to late May 8am-8pm.)

Beef is what's for dinner at **The Big Texan** (372-6000, 800-657-7177), at Lakeside Exit 75 from I-40. The portions are as big as the state, but the bill won't whip you. (Bony rattlesnake appetizer $6-9; burgers $5-7; Texas steaks $10-27. Free Opry concerts Tu; other music nightly 7pm. Open daily 10:30am-10:30pm.) **Ruby Tequila's,** 2108 Paramount (358-7829), has seats inside or out where you can plant yourself to drink the Ruby Tequila, a combination of sangria and margarita ($2). A visit to Ruby Tequila's is like a pretty painting on velvet—always in good taste and never over-priced. (3 enchilada platter $7.50. Open Su-Th 11am-10pm, F-Sa 11am-11pm.)

Big Texan Women

Want to feel full without eating a thing? The 72 oz. steak on display at the **Inn of the Big Texan** (see **Food,** above) will do the trick. Signs for miles around inform travelers that anyone who eats the steak in 1hr. gets it free; the defeated pay $50. Over 25,000 have tried to consume the beast; the names, weights (before), and home cities of a few of the 5000+ success stories are listed under the glass-top bar. A third of the women have been victorious, compared to only a fifth of the men.

SIGHTS AND ENTERTAINMENT The outstanding **Panhandle-Plains Historical Museum,** 2401 4th Ave. (651-2244), in nearby Canyon (I-27 S to Rte. 87), has fossils, an old drilling rig, exhibits galore on local history and geology, and is reputed to hold one of the best collections of Southwestern art anywhere. *(Open M-Sa 9am-5pm, Su 1-6pm; in summer daily 'til 6pm. $4, seniors $3, ages 4-12 $1.)* The **Amarillo Zoo** (381-7911), off the 24th St. Exit from U.S. 287, in Thompson Park, spreads across 20 acres of open prairie with bison, roadrunners, and other Texas fauna (open Tu-Su 9:30am-5:30pm; free). Explore horse racing's cowboy origins and all things equine at the **American Quarter Horse Heritage Center and Museum,** 2601 I-40 E (376-5181), at Exit 72A. *(Open M-Sa 9am-5pm, Su noon-5pm; Sept.-May Tu-Sa 10am-5pm. $4, over 54 $3.50, ages 6-18 $2.50.)* Amarillo celebrates its location, on top of the world's largest supply of helium, with the 6-story stainless steel **Helium Monument,** 1200 Strait Dr. (355-9547), off Hagy. When the structure was erected in 1968, several contributors volunteered to put common items inside of it to make a time capsule. One of the items is a $10 savings account deposit in an Oklahoma City bank which, when the monument is opened in 2968 (after the world has exploded...), will be worth over $1,000,000,000,000,000,000 (one quintillion dollars), payable to the U.S. Treasury.

■ Palo Duro Canyon State Park

Rightly known as the "Grand Canyon of Texas," Palo Duro covers 16,000 acres of jaw-dropping beauty. The canyon—1200 ft. from rim to rugged floor—exposes truly awesome red, yellow, and brown cliffs. (Park open daily 7am-10pm; in winter 8am-10pm. $3, under 12 free.) The park is 23 mi. south of Amarillo. Take I-27 to Exit 106 and head east on Rte. 217; from the south, get off I-27 at Exit 103. The park **headquarters** (806-488-2227), just inside the park, has maps of hiking trails and info on all park activities (open daily 9am-5pm). A half mile past HQ, the **visitors center** displays exhibits on the history of the canyon (open M-Sa 9am-5pm, Su 1-5pm).

The beautiful 16 mi. **scenic drive** through the park, beginning at HQ, provides many photo opportunities. If you want to experience the canyon from the saddle, **Goodnight Riding Stables** (806-488-2231), about 1½ mi. into the park on the scenic drive, will rent you a horse, a saddle, and a riding hat. ($10 per hr., under 7 riding double $5. Overnight horseback ride from 6pm-9am is $75 per person. Reservations required.) **Goodnight Trading Post** (806-488-2760), ½ mi. further along the scenic drive, has a souvenir shop, a terrific restaurant (chicken breast sandwich $3.25), and mountain bike rentals ($6.50 per hr.; open daily 8am-5pm). Rangers allow and encourage backcountry hiking in Palo Duro. Most hikers (even children) can manage the 5 mi. **Lighthouse Trail,** but only experienced hikers should consider the rugged 9 mi. **Running Trail.** Temperatures in the canyon frequently climb to 100°F; hikes required at least 2 quarts of water. **Backcountry camping** (512-389-8900 for reservations) is allowed in designated areas (primitive sites $9, with water $10, with water and hookup $12; cabins $65).

■ Guadalupe Mountains

The Guadalupe Mountains rise out of the vast Texas desert to heights of unexplored grandeur. Mescalero Apaches hunted and camped on these lands until they were driven out by a U.S. army campaign. By the late 1800s, only a few white ranchers inhabited the rugged region. Today, **Guadalupe Mountains National Park** encompasses 86,000 acres of desert, canyons, and highlands. Passing tourists can glimpse the park's most dramatic sights from U.S. 62/180: **El Capitán,** a 2000 ft. limestone cliff, and **Guadalupe Peak,** the highest point in Texas (8749 ft.). Less hurried travelers should take the time to explore; with over 70 mi. of trails, the mountains promise challenging desert hikes to those willing to journey through this remote area. Entrance to the park is free. **Carlsbad, NM** (see p. 687), 55 mi. northeast, makes a good base town, with many cheap motels, campgrounds, and restaurants.

The major trails begin at the Pine Canyon Campground, near the Headquarters Visitors Center (see below). Guadalupe Peak can be scaled in a difficult but rewarding full-day hike (8½ mi.). Another full-day trail leads from the campground to **The Basin,** a high-country forest of Douglas fir and Ponderosa pine. A shorter trek (2-3hr.) traces the canyon floor of **Devil's Hall**—tread softly, and you may see deer along the trail. The 2½ mi., 1½hr. **Spring Trail** leads from the **Frijole Ranch,** about 1 mi. north of the visitors center, to a mountain spring. An easy 2-3hr. trail leading to the historic **Pratt Cabin** in the McKittrick Canyon begins at the **McKittrick Visitors Center,** several miles northeast of the main visitors center off U.S. 62/180. Some trails are marked more clearly than others; it's always wise to take a map.

The park's lack of development may be a bonus for backpackers, but it creates some inconveniences. *Gas and food are not available in the park—stock up before you arrive.* The park's two campgrounds, **Pine Springs** (828-3251), just past park headquarters, and **Dog Canyon** (828-3251, ranger station 505-981-2418), south of the New Mexico border at the north end of the park, have water and restrooms but no hookups or showers (sites $7; reservations for groups only). Dog Canyon is accessible only via Rte. 137 from Carlsbad, NM (72 mi.), or by a full-day hike from the **Visitor Center and Park Headquarters** (828-3251), off U.S. 62/180. (Open daily 8am-6pm; Sept.-May 8am-4:30pm. After hours, find info posted on the bulletin board outside.) Backcountry camping is permitted—pick up a permit at the visitors center.

Guadalupe Park lies 120 mi. east of El Paso. For additional info, contact the visitors center or write to **Guadalupe Mountains National Park,** HC 60, Box 400, Salt Flat 79847. **TNM&O Coaches** (505-887-1108), an affiliate of **Greyhound,** runs along U.S. 62/180 between Carlsbad, NM and El Paso, making a flag stop in the Guadalupe Mountains National Park at the Headquarters Visitors Center (Carlsbad to Guadalupe Mountains $26 each way, 2½hr.). **Area code:** 915. Unlike the rest of Texas, the park falls in the **mountain time zone** (2hr. behind Eastern).

■ El Paso

The largest of the U.S. border towns, El Paso boomed in the 17th century as a passageway on an important east-west wagon route that followed the Río Grande through "the pass" *(el paso)* between the Rockies and the Sierra Madres. Modern El Paso (pop. 650,000), sitting in the midst of sand and sagebrush, serves as a stop-over between the U.S. and Mexico. After dark, central El Paso becomes a ghost town: most activity leaves the center and heads to the University of Texas at El Paso (UTEP), or south of the border to El Paso's raucous sister city, Ciudad Juárez.

CROSSING THE BORDER To reach the border from El Paso, take the north-south #8 green trolley operated by **Sun Metro** to the **Santa Fe Bridge,** the last stop before the trolley turns around. (Runs every 15min. M-F 6:15am-8:15pm, Sa 7:45am-8:15pm, Su 8:45am-7:15pm; 25¢.) Entering Mexico costs 25¢; the return trip costs 45¢.

Those entering Mexico by foot (the best way for those without cars to cross the border), should walk to the right side of the Santa Fe Bridge and pay the quarter to cross. Daytrippers, including foreign travelers with multi-entry visas, should be prepared to flash their documents of citizenship in order to pass in and out of Mexico. After stepping off the bridge, you will be on the main strip, Av. Juárez. Entering the U.S. requires crossing over the Santa Fe Bridge near the large *"Feliz Viaje"* sign. U.S. border guards must be shown a valid visa or proof of citizenship. You may be searched or asked to answer a few questions proving you are who you say you are. The bus stop in El Paso is on the right-hand sidewalk just across from the bridge. The north-south bus runs until 8:15pm to San Jacinto Plaza.

PRACTICAL INFORMATION El Paso is divided east-west by **Santa Fe Ave.** and north-south by **San Antonio Ave.** *Be wary of the streets between San Antonio and the border late at night.* The **airport** is northeast of the city center, reached via bus #33 from San Jacinto Sq. or any other central location. The stop is located on a traffic island outside the air terminal building, across from the Delta ticket window. (50min. to downtown. Runs every hr. M-Sa 6:54am-8:54pm, Su 8:54am-7:54pm. $1, students and ages 6-13 50¢, seniors 30¢, transfer tickets 10¢; exact change only.) Get off when the bus arrives at San Jacinto Plaza, and you'll be right in the thick of things. When the bus stops running late at night, the only way to get to the city is to take a **taxi** (approximately $20-25). Alternate approaches include **I-10** (running east-west) and **U.S. 54** (north-south). **Greyhound,** 200 W. San Antonio (532-2365 or 800-231-2222), across from the Civic Center between Santa Fe and Chihuahua, sends buses to and from Dallas (10hr., 7 per day, $76) and other U.S. cities. The **tourist office,** 1 Civic Center Plaza (544-0062), is a small, round building next to the Chamber of Commerce at the intersection of Santa Fe and San Francisco. Besides giving out maps and brochures, it sells **El Paso-Juárez Trolley Co.** tickets for day-long tours across the border. Tours leave on the hour from the Convention Center. (Tickets $11, ages 4-12 $8. Trolleys run 10am-5pm. Reservations recommended.) The **Mexican Consulate,** 910 E. San Antonio (533-3644), on the corner of Virginia, dispenses **tourist cards** (open M-F 9am-4:30pm). **Providence Memorial Hospital,** 2001 N. Oregon (577-6011), is at Hague near UTEP. Immunizations are recommended but not required to enter Mexico. (Open 24hr.) **ZIP code:** 79901. **Area code:** 915.

ACCOMMODATIONS AND FOOD El Paso offers safer, more appealing places to stay than Juárez. Several great budget hotels cluster around the center of town near Main St. and San Jacinto Sq. The best place in town is the **Gardner Hotel/Hostel (HI-AYH),** 311 E. Franklin (532-3661), between Stanton and Kansas. From the airport, take bus #33 to San Jacinto Park, walk 2 blocks north to Franklin, turn right, and head east 1½ blocks. With a helpful staff, an authentically decorated lobby, and cozy rooms, the Gardner is the ideal rest spot for the weary budget traveler. The price for the small, four-person dorm rooms and shared bathrooms includes use of the spacious kitchen, common room with pool table and cable TV, and basement couches. ($13, nonmembers $15.50. Lockers 75¢, 50¢ for 4 or more days. Linen $2. Laundry $1.50 per load. Reception 24hr. Check-out 10am.) The **Gateway Hotel,** 104 S. Stanton (532-2611), at San Antonio Ave., is a stone's throw from San Jacinto Sq. and a favorite stop for middle-class Mexicans. The rooms are clean and spacious, with large beds and closets. (A/C upstairs; diner downstairs. Singles $23, with TV $30; doubles $35/$37. Parking $1.50 for 24hr.)

El Paso boasts a plethora of small mom-and-pop diners. Unfortunately, many places close early, so your number of options may shrink after 6pm. **La Malinche** (544-8785), N. Stanton St., is at the corner of Texas across from The Edge. The tiled, adobe decor lends authenticity to this cafe in the middle of downtown El Paso. (Burritos of all types $1.75; full meals $3.50-6. Open M-Sa 7:30am-4:30pm.) **The Tap,** 408 E. San Antonio (532-3304), at Stanton, is a fun bar/restaurant that serves up authentic Tex-Mex to a local clientele. (Breakfast $3, lunch specials $4, dinner plates $4-7. $1 beer on tap. Open M-Sa 9am-2am, Su noon-2am.)

SIGHTS AND NIGHTLIFE For a whirlwind tour of the city and its southern neighbor, hop aboard the **Border Jumper Trolleys** that depart every hour from El Paso (see **tourist office** info, p. 546). Historic **San Jacinto Plaza** is the heart of El Paso and swarms with daily activity. The plaza is the main bus stop for all San Metro buses, and throngs of locals gather there to sit under the shade of some of El Paso's only trees. South of the square, **El Paso St.** serves as a market for all kinds of goods, ranging from fruit to the latest fashions. To take in a complete picture of the Río Grande Valley, head northeast of downtown along Stanton and take a right on Rim Rd. (which becomes Scenic Dr.); **Murchinson Park,** at the base of the ridge, offers a commanding vista of El Paso, Juárez, and the Sierra Madres. For museum enthusiasts, the area around the Civic Center on Santa Fe Ave. contains a renowned **Americana Museum,** as well as the **El Paso Museum of Art.**

For nightlife, try **The Palace,** 209 S. El Paso St. (532-6000), pumps dance music to a packed house in a trendy, neon setting on Friday and Saturday nights until 2am (2nd fl. jazz lounge; 18+; cover $5). **The Edge,** 201 N. Stanton (532-6644) at Texas, also offers a sophisticated nightclub in a safe part of town. For more rowdiness, no minimum drinking age, and ubiquitous nightlife, many head to Juárez.

■ Ciudad Juárez

Although Ciudad Juárez (pop. 1 million) is separated from El Paso only by the narrow Río Grande, the two cities are worlds apart. Visitors to Juárez are immediately bombarded with commotion on all sides and beset by a collage of bright paint and neon. Enterprising locals are eager to hawk their wares to anyone with a pulse. Near the border, the city is hectic, loud, dirty, and cheap. Fleeing in the face of the American advance, Mexican culture can be found in the city's cathedral square and Parque

Chamizal. They provide a pleasant respite from the sprawling industrial production centers and poor residential shantytowns that dot most of the cityscape.

PRACTICAL INFORMATION For information on entering and leaving Mexico, see **El Paso: Crossing the Border** (p. 546). Most of Old Juárez (the area immediately adjoining the Santa Fe and Stanton bridges) can be covered on foot. Street numbers start in the 600s near the two border bridges and descend to zero at **16 de Septiembre,** where **Av. Juárez** (the main street) ends. Both **Lerdo** and **Francisco Villa** run north/south, parallel to Juárez. The **ProNaf center** is served by public bus "Ruta 8A" (2.20 pesos), which leaves from the intersection of Presidencia and Juárez near the border. Most **city buses** leave from the intersection of **Insurgentes** and Francisco Villa or thereabouts; ask the driver whether your bus will take you to your destination. It's a good idea to grab a map from the tourist office. **Taxis** are always downtown, but fees are steep, although negotiable. To get from the bus station to downtown, walk out the left-most door (if you're facing the main station entrance) and up to the street. Old converted school buses labeled "Ruta 1A" or "Ruta 6," both go to Av. Juárez.

During the day, Juárez is relatively safe for the alert traveler. Juárez becomes unsafe after dark, so avoid places that look at all suspicious and don't go out unaccompanied. *Women should not walk alone or in dark places; everyone should avoid going more than 2 blocks west of Av. Juárez.*

The **bus station, Central Camionera,** Blvd. Oscar Flores 4010, is north of the ProNaf center and next to the Río Grande mall. It is served by the Chihuahuenses bus from the El Paso terminal to Juárez ($7), and the "Ruta 1A" at Av. Insurgentes and Francisco Villa (2.20 pesos). Be sure to ask the driver of "Ruta 1A" whether it is going to the bus station, as not all do. **Greyhound** serves U.S. cities such as Dallas ($75), El Paso ($7), and San Antonio ($79). The most convenient **tourist office** (14 92 56 or 29 33 00, ext. 5160 or 5649), can be found on Av. Juárez Azucenas, 2 blocks from the border (open M-F 8:30am-2pm, Sa 9am-1pm). The **U.S. Consulate** is found at López Mateos Nte. 924 (13 40 48 or 13 40 50), at Hermanos Escobar. From Av. Juárez, turn left on Malecón, right on López Mateos, and then walk for 15-20min. In August 1998, the **exchange rate** was $1 for 9.65 pesos. In case of an **emergency,** dial 06. The **Red Cross** (16 58 06), is in the ProNaf Center next to the OK Corral. English is spoken. (Open 24hr.) **Postal code:** 32000. **Phone code:** 16.

ACCOMMODATIONS AND FOOD Fairly cheap lodging lines the main strip, Avenida Juárez. At **Hotel Morán,** Juárez 264 (15 08 12), across from Mr. Fog Bar, the clean rooms with A/C, TV, and private baths can't be beat. (Singles 106 pesos; doubles 160 pesos.) Or, try **Hotel Juárez,** Lerdo 143 Nte. (15 02 98 or 15 03 58), at 16 de Septiembre. The non-A/C rooms are old, small, and simple, but it's one of the city's best deals. (3rd fl. singles 47 pesos; doubles 84 pesos; 11 pesos per additional person.)

The quest for food that will not cause a bacteriological mutiny in gringo bellies is long; prudent travelers should beat a path to Av. Juárez and Lerdo or to the ProNaf center. The 24hr. **Cafetería El Coyote Inválido,** Juárez 615 (14 27 27), at Colón, is a bustling, American-style diner with heavenly A/C. Fixin's include hamburgers (16 pesos), burritos (16 pesos), and an array of Mexican plates for 16-32 pesos. At **Hotel Santa Fé Restaurante,** Lerdo 675 Nte. (14 02 70) at Tlaxcala, in the Hotel Santa Fe, patrons can sample chicken enchiladas or club sandwiches (25 pesos) and wash 'em down with a beer (12 pesos; open 24hr.).

SIGHTS AND NIGHTLIFE The **Aduana Fronteriza** (12 47 07) stands in the *centro,* where Juárez and 16 de Septiembre cross. (*Open Tu-Su 10am-5pm. Free.*) Built in 1889 as a trading outpost and later used for customs, it now houses the **Museo Histórico de la Ex-Aduana,** which chronicles the region's history during the Mexican Revolution. The **Museo de Arte e Historia** (16 74 14), at the ProNaf center, exhibits Mexican art of the past and present (open Tu-Su 11am-5pm; 8 pesos, students free).

The deforested **Parque Chamizal,** near the Córdoba Bridge, down Presidencia Av., is a good place to escape the noise of the city, if not the heat, and enjoy a picnic. The newly inaugurated Mexican flag is said to be as large as a football field. The **Museo**

Arqueológico, Av. Pellicer in Parque Chamizal (11 10 48 or 13 69 83), houses plastic facsimiles of pre-Hispanic sculptures as well as trilobite fossils, rocks, and bones (open Tu-F 11am-8pm, Sa-Su 10am-8pm). The **Misión de Nuestra Señora de Guadalupe** (15 55 02), on 16 de Septiembre and Mariscal, is the oldest building for miles around, featuring antique paintings and altars.

Downtown Juárez was built for partying; it seems that every establishment along Av. Juárez that isn't selling booze or pulling teeth is a club or a bar. On weekends, gringos swarm to Juárez in a 48hr. quest for fun, fights, and fiestas. Popular **Mr. Fog Bar,** Juárez Nte. 140 (14 29 48), at González, features a cartoon crocodile on the mirrored walls and a dance floor in the back (beer 10 pesos, liquor 12 pesos; open Su-Th 11am-2am, F-Sa 11am-3am).

■ Big Bend

Roadrunners, coyotes, wild pigs, mountain lions, and 350 species of birds make their home in Big Bend National Park, a 700,000-acre tract that lies in a helluva meander on the Río Grande. Spectacular canyons, vast stretches of the Chihuahuan Desert, and the Chisos Mountains occupy this literally and figuratively "far-out" spot. If you're in search of solitude, avoid the high season (Feb.-Apr.), when you might find yourself wedged among a few hundred people in line for backcountry permits. During the summer, the park is excruciatingly hot, but you might have it all to yourself.

PRACTICAL INFORMATION Big Bend may be the most geographically isolated spot in the U.S. The park is accessible only by car, via Rte. 118 or U.S. 385, both of which meet I-10. There are no gas stations or services of any kind on these roads; *fill your tank before leaving I-10.* **Park headquarters** (477-2251) is at **Panther Jct.,** about 26 mi. inside the park (open daily 8am-6pm; vehicle pass $10 per week, pedestrians and bikers $5). For info, write the **Superintendent,** Big Bend National Park, P.O. Box 129, 79834. **Ranger stations** are located at Panther Jct., Río Grande Village, Persimmon Gap, and Chisos Basin. (Panther open daily 8am-6pm; Chisos open daily 8am-3:30pm; others closed May-Nov.) The easiest way for the carless to reach Big Bend is by taking **Amtrak** (800-872-7245) to the town of **Alpine,** 70 mi. north of the park (4hr.; M, W, and Sa only; El Paso to Alpine, $43-64), and renting a car from **Air Flight Auto Rental,** 504 E. Holland St. (837-3463), inside the Western Auto and Radio Shack. ($25-32 per day and 10¢ per mi. Must be 18. $100 deposit required. Call in advance for reservations.) **Groceries** and **gas** are available in Panther Jct., Río Grande Village, and Chisos Basin; groceries, but no gas, can be found in Castolon. **Emergency:** 477-2251 until 5pm; afterwards, call 911. **Area code:** 915.

ACCOMMODATIONS, CAMPGROUNDS, AND FOOD The expensive **Chisos Mountains Lodge** (477-2291), 10 mi. from park headquarters, offers the only motel-style shelter within the park (singles $62; doubles $69; $10 per additional person). They also rent lodges equipped with showers and baths but no A/C (singles $58; doubles $67; $10 per additional person), and stone cottages with three double beds and bath (3 people $81; $10 per additional person). Reservations are a must for high season; the lodge often gets booked up to a year in advance. The restaurant and coffee shop at the lodge serve basic diner food ($3-12; open daily 7am-8pm).

Designated campsites within the park are allotted on a first come, first served basis. **Chisos Basin** and **Río Grande Village** offer sites with restrooms and flush toilets ($7; cash only); the sites at Castolon have pit toilets. In summer, the sites in Chisos Basin are the coolest by far. During high season the campgrounds fill up early. The RV park at Río Grande Village has 25 full-hookup sites. **Public showers** are available at the Río Grande Village Store (75¢). For overnight backcountry camping at free sites along the hiking trails, obtain a free **backcountry permit** at the park headquarters.

Cheap motels lurk off U.S. 170 near the dusty towns of **Terlingua** and **Lajitas,** 21 and 28 mi. respectively from park headquarters. Terlingua, named for the three languages spoken in the town in the late 1800s (English, Spanish, and a Native American dialect), lies on Rte. 170 just past Study Butte, about 35 mi. from park headquarters, but only 7 mi. from the park's western entrance; Lajitas is 7 mi. farther down the road. The **Chisos Mining Co. Motel** (371-2430), on Rte. 170 1 mi. west of the junction of 170 and 118, provides clean, A/C rooms in an offbeat atmosphere (singles without phone or TV $34; doubles $42, with phone and TV $51). Farther up Rte. 170 in **Terlingua Ghost Town,** the **Starlight Theatre Bar and Grill** (371-2326) entertains with large portions of cheap Tex-Mex ($3-9) and free live music on weekends. (Food served daily 6-10pm; bar open Su-F 5pm-midnight, Sa 5pm-1am. No credit cards.)

OUTDOOR ACTIVITIES Big Bend encompasses several hundred miles of hiking trails, ranging in difficulty from 30min. nature walks to backpacking trips several days long. *When hiking in the desert, always carry a gallon of water per person per day.* The 43 mi. **scenic drive** to Santa Elena Canyon is handy for those short on time. Many of the park's roads can **flood** during the rainy season (July-Sept.).

Park rangers at the visitors centers are happy to suggest hikes and sights; the *Hiker's Guide to Big Bend* pamphlet ($1.25), available at Panther Jct., is a good investment. The **Lost Mine Trail,** a 3hr. hike up a peak in the Chisos, leads to an amazing summit-top view of the desert and the Sierra de Carmen in Mexico. A shorter walk (1.7 mi.) ambles through the **Santa Elena Canyon** along the Río Grande—the canyon walls rise as high as 1000 ft. over the banks of the river.

Several companies offer **river trips** down the 133 mi. stretch of the Río Grande owned by the park. **Far-Flung Adventures** (800-359-4138), next door to the Starlight Theatre Bar and Grill in Terlingua, organizes 1- to 7-day trips (1-day trip to Santa Elena around $25 per person). Park headquarters has more info on rafting and canoeing.

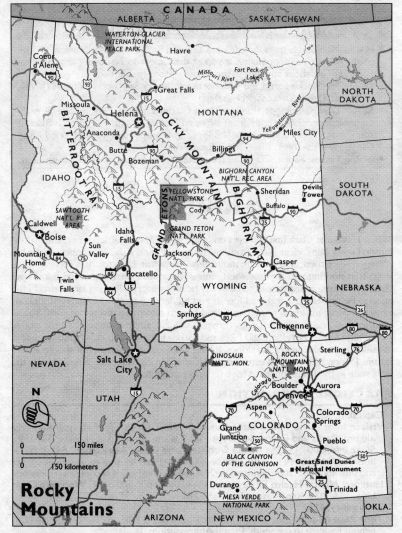

Rocky Mountains

ROCKY MOUNTAINS

Created by immense tectonic forces some 65 million years ago, the Rockies mark a vast wrinkle in the North American continent. Sculpted by wind, water, and glaciers over eons, their weathered peaks extend 3000 mi. from northern Alberta to New Mexico and soar to altitudes exceeding two vertical miles. Cars overheat and humans gulp thin alpine air as they ascend into grizzly bear country. Dominated by rock and ice, the highest peaks of the Rockies are accessible only to veteran mountain climbers and wildlife adapted for survival in scant air and deep snow.

Although the whole of the Rocky Mountain area supports less than five percent of the U.S. population, every year millions flock to its spectacular national parks, forests, and ski resorts, while hikers follow the Continental Divide along the spine of the Rockies. Nestled in valleys or appearing out nowhere on the surrounding plains, the region's mountain villages and cowboy towns welcome travelers year-round.

☺ HIGHLIGHTS OF THE ROCKY MOUNTAINS

- **Hiking.** Memorable trails include the Gunnison Rte. in the Black Canyon, CO (p. 610); the hike to Monument Canyon at the Colorado National Monument (p. 606); and just about anything in the Grand Tetons (p. 576).
- **Skiing.** The Rockies are filled with hotspots, but try Sawtooth, ID (p. 557); Vail, CO (p. 602); or Whitefish, MT (p. 568).
- **Scenic Drives.** Going-to-the-Sun Rd. in Glacier National Park (p. 566) is truly unforgettable, as is Rte. 21 from Boise to Stanley, ID (p. 557). Catch Rte. 20 south from Thermopolis, WY (p. 585) for an eye-popping view of Wind River Canyon and the Wind River Indian Reservation.
- **Alpine Towns.** Aspen, CO (p. 603) and Stanley, ID (p. 557): two of the loveliest.

Idaho

When Lewis and Clark first laid eyes on Idaho in 1805, they observed pristine, snow-capped mountains, clear lakes, frothing rivers, and thick stands of conifers. Little has changed since then, and the state motto (*Esto perpetua,* Latin for "It is Forever") suggests that nothing will anytime soon, unless, of course, the loggers and miners get their way. Idaho remains nearly free of any heavy industry, allowing large parts of the state to be preserved as national forests and wilderness areas. The Rocky Mountains cross the Montana-Idaho border and divide Idaho into three distinct regions. To the southeast, world-famous potatoes thrive in volcanically rich valleys. To the north, dense pine forests envelop frigid lakes and harbor liberal sentiments befitting eastern Washington. In the center, ski slopes, hiking trails, and geothermal hot springs attract nature lovers. Like many Western states, Idaho fiercely values its freedom; it is the only state in the Union never to have flown a foreign flag.

PRACTICAL INFORMATION

Capital: Boise.
Visitor Info: Idaho Information Line, 800-VISIT-ID/847-4843; http://www.visitid.org. **Parks and Recreation Dept.,** 5657 Warm Springs Ave., Boise (334-4199). **Skier Info,** 800-243-2754. **Idaho Outfitters and Guide Association,** P.O. Box 95, Boise 83701 (342-1438; http://www.ioga.org). Provides free vacation directories and info about outdoor outfitters such as rafting companies and jet-boat operators.
Hotlines: Mental Health Emergency, 334-0808 or 800-600-6474. **Women's Crisis Line,** 343-7025. **Rape Crisis Line,** 345-7273.
Emergency: 911.
Time Zones: Pacific (3hr. behind Eastern) north of the Salmon River, Mountain (2hr. behind Eastern) to the south. **Postal Abbreviation:** ID.
Sales Tax: 5%.

■ Boise

Small and hip, Boise (pronounced BOY-see, not BOY-zee) is a verdant residential oasis in the state's dry southern plateau. The easy, small-town familiarity of the residents, numerous grassy parks, and airy shopping plazas make for a relaxing way station on a cross-country jaunt. Most of the city's sights are within the 10 sq. blocks between the capitol and the Boise River; one can easily manage on foot.

PRACTICAL INFORMATION The river halves streets running north-south; likewise, streets running east-west are bisected by Capitol Blvd. **Greyhound** (343-3681) zips along I-84 from its terminal at 1212 W. Bannock, a few blocks west of downtown. Buses run to Salt Lake City (8hr., 4 per day, $37-40), Portland (11hr., 3 per day, $33-36), and Seattle (14hr., 3 per day, $36-38). **Boise Urban Stages** (336-1010) runs several routes throughout the city, with maps available from any bus driver and displayed at each stop (buses operate daily 5:45am-7pm; fare 75¢, seniors 35¢, ages 6-18 50¢). **McU's Sports,** 822 W. Jefferson St. (342-7734), rents a good selection of gear and offers free tips on local hiking. (In-line skates $5 per hr., $15 per day. Mountain bikes $15 per ½-day, $25 per day. Ski equipment $13 per day.) The **visitors center,** 850 W. Front St. (344-5338), at Boise Center on the Grove, dispenses tourist tips (open M-F 10am-5pm, Sa 10am-2pm). When the visitors center isn't open, visit the **info booth** on the bottom floor of the State Capitol Bldg. (open M-F 8am-4pm, Sa-Su and holidays 9am-5pm). Gay and lesbian travelers can pick up a copy of *Diversity* at the library or a coffee shop or call the **Gay Community Center** (336-3870). **Post Office:** 770 S. 13th St. (800-275-8777; open M-F 7:30am-5:30pm, Sa 10am-2pm). **ZIP code:** 83702. **Area code:** 208.

ACCOMMODATIONS AND CAMPGROUNDS Finding convenient budget lodging in Boise is difficult; neither the YMCA nor the YWCA provide rooms, and even the cheapest hotels charge over $30 per night. The more reasonable places fill quickly, so make reservations. The friendly **Boisean,** 1300 S. Capitol Ave. (343-3645 or 800-365-3645), has spacious, clean rooms, a helpful staff, free local calls and cable TV, and a spa (singles $32; doubles $40-50; $4 per extra person; senior discounts). **University Inn,** 2360 University Dr. (345-7170 or 800-345-7170), directly across the street from the Boisean, is slightly pricier, but equally welcoming to the travel weary. Full breakfast from the neighboring restaurant is included with each room, as well as access to a pool and jacuzzi, cable TV, free local calls, and shuttle service to the airport. (Singles $43; doubles $50.) Summer travelers doing any business with **Boise State University** (385-3986; M-F 8am-5pm), on University Dr., should call student housing in advance to check the availability of dorm rooms (singles $17; doubles $24).

The **Boise National Forest Office/Bureau of Land Management,** 1387 S. Vinnell Way (373-4007), provides info about campgrounds in Boise, most of which are RV-oriented. The closest non-RV camping is at **Bogus Basin,** about a 45min. drive out of Boise (open M-F 7:30am-4:30pm). **Fiesta Park,** 11101 Fairview Ave. (375-8207), offers tent sites for $18. (RV sites with partial hookup $20; full hookup $22-24. KOA or AAA discount available.) The **Americana Kampground,** 3600 American Terrace Blvd. (344-5733), has 90 RV sites but colludes in the stale, phonetics-gone-mad overuse of "K" in place of "C." ($17 includes full hookup; $2 each additional person).

FOOD AND NIGHTLIFE Mr. Potatohead doesn't rule Boise food. The downtown area, centered around **8th and Main St.,** is bustling with lunchtime delis, coffee shops, ethnic cuisine, and several stylish bistros. **Moon's Kitchen,** 815 W. Bannock St. (385-0472), has been serving up classic American food to families and students, as well as politicians and businessmen from the nearby capitol, since 1955 (breakfast specials $4-6, famous shakes $3; open M-F 7am-3pm, Sa 8am-3pm). **The Beanery,** 107 8th St. (342-3456), carves up slow-roasted meats and serves them with bread, mashed potatoes, carrots, and a side salad for $6-7. (Open M-Th 11am-9pm, F-Sa 11am-10pm, Su noon-9pm.) Long live *Casablanca* at the combination restaurant and independent/foreign film theater, **Rick's Café American/The Flicks,** 646 Fulton St. (342-4222). You can take your baked brie ($4.25), panini ($6), and beer or wine ($2-5) into the theater with you. (Kitchen open M-Th 4-9:45pm, F-Su noon-9:45pm. Movies daily 4-9:45pm. Admission $6; students, seniors, and children $4; double feature $8.) The hungry and healthy-minded will dig the **Boise CO-OP,** 888 W. Fort St. (342-6652, and its great selection of natural, organic, and gourmet foods. Follow 8th St. from downtown west to Fort St. (Open M-Sa 9am-9pm, Su 9am-8pm.)

Nightlife in Boise consists mainly of live music in coffeehouses and pubs, but every summer Wednesday, the town comes **"Alive After Five"** (371-LIVE/5483) in the Grove, on Grove St. downtown. Musicians perform on Main St. from 5-9pm, while vendors from nearby restaurants hawk food and beer. Smoky funk wafts from the **Blues Bouquet,** 1010 Main St. (345-6605), where you can imbibe a pint ($1.50-2.50) and enjoy live music nightly (21+; open M-F 1pm-2am, Sa-Su 8pm-2am). The truly

ROCKY MOUNTAINS

Boise's Basque Background

In 1848, the California Gold Rush brought a flood of immigrants to the U.S. Among them were the Basques, who moved from a small corner of Spain to the goldfields of the Sierras. The Basques, whose native language is supposedly unrelated to any in the world, had a particularly difficult time learning English. Unable to find jobs, the American Basques spread out into the Western rangelands and mountains to become sheep herders. Although historians have recently found links between the mysterious language and Caucasian, the ancient language spoken in the Caucasus region, no conclusive evidence of a tie has been found, and Basque remains without linguistic relatives. Today, southern Idaho is home to the largest concentrated Basque population outside of Europe. Basque culture is preserved at the **Basque Museum and Cultural Center** (343-2671) at 6th and Grove St., in downtown Boise. *(Open Tu-F 10am-4pm, Sa 11am-3pm. $1.)* This fascinating museum includes a gallery with changing exhibits, Basque art, and a replica of a Basque herder's house. Next door to the museum, sample Basque cuisine at **Bar Gernika**, 202 S. Capitol Blvd. (344-2175), a pub and eatery named for the capital of the Basque homeland. *(Open M 11am-11pm, Tu-Th 11am-midnight, F 11am-1am, Sa 11:30am-1am.)* In the summer, enjoy the hearty meals outside on the patio. Authentic Basque dishes include Solomo sandwiches (marinated pork tenderloin $6-7) and **Dorothy's famous beef tongue,** which is served only on Saturdays, from 10am 'til it's gone.

relaxed stop in at the **Flying M Coffeehouse,** 500 W. Idaho St. (345-4320). Here, folks come together to enjoy local art, drink coffee, and sample tasty breakfast foods. (Live music F and Sa nights. Open M-Th 6:30am-10pm, F 6:30am-11pm, Sa 7:30am-11pm, Su 7:30am-6pm.) If you simply must dance, shimmy to the **VooDoo Lounge,** 622 W. Idaho (343-8106), a local bar whose staff will teach anyone to dance. (Rockabilly Tu, swing W-Th nights, house techno mixed F-Sa. 21+. Cover W-Th $1, F-Sa $3.)

SIGHTS The best view of the city may be from **Table Rock,** a lookout off Warm Springs Rd. By night, you can see a **giant glowing cross** high in the hills. The **Boise Tour Train** (342-4796) whisks you around 75 sights throughout the city in an hour. *(Tours M-Sa 5 per day 10am-3pm, Su 4 per day noon-3:45pm; in fall, W-F 1 per day at 1:30pm, Sa 4 per day 10:30am-3pm, Su 3 per day noon-3pm. $6.50, seniors $6, ages 13-19 $5, 4-12 $3.50. Arrive 15min. early.)* Tours begin and end in the parking lot of **Julia Davis Park.** To learn about Idaho and the Old West at your own pace, stroll through the **Historical Museum** (334-2120), in Julia Davis Park, which showcases a replica 19th-century bar complete with a display of a two-headed calf (open M-Sa 9am-5pm, Su and holidays 1-5pm; free, donations encouraged). Also in the park, the **Boise Art Museum,** 670 Julia Davis Dr. (345-8330), displays international and local works while offering educational programs, lectures, and tours. *(Open in summer M-F 10am-5pm, Sa-Su noon-5pm; off-season closed M. $4, students and seniors $2, ages 6-17 $1; free the 1st Th of every month.)* Take a self-guided tour through the country's only **State Capitol** heated with geothermal water; free maps are conveniently located at the information booth on the ground floor (group tour office 334-2470; open M-F 8am-6pm, Sa-Su and holidays 9am-5pm). Raptors perch and dive at the **World Center for Birds of Prey,** 5666 W. Flying Hook Ln. (362-3716), 6 mi. south of I-84 on Cole Rd. Exit. *(Open in summer Tu-Su 9am-4:30pm; in winter Tu-Su 10am-4pm. $4, seniors $3, children $2.)* At the **Old Idaho Penitentiary,** 2445 Old Penitentiary Rd. (368-6080), visitors can see where Boise housed its law-breaking citizens. *(Open daily noon-5pm. Bail $4, seniors and 6-12 $3.)* Not simply an old slammer, "the pen" also displays the **nation's only collection of prison tattoo art.** For more back-to-nature fun, try the 22 mi. **Boise River Greenbelt,** a pleasant path ideal for a leisurely walk or picnic along the Boise River. In the summer, visitors can go tubing in the river at Berber Park. The ever-growing **Boise Shakespeare Festival** (info line 336-9221) hits town from June to September. In late June, Boise also hosts a **River Festival** (338-8887), featuring hot-air balloon rallies, a carnival, live music, fireworks, and sporting events. Upcoming events are showcased in *The Boise Weekly,* available from merchants or on the street (new issue every Th).

■ McCall

Located 100 mi. north of Boise on scenic Rte. 55, the blossoming resort town of McCall offers top-notch recreational opportunities amid a friendly, small-town atmosphere. McCall has produced a number of Olympic skiers, testament to the quality of the area's snow. Yet, the town's population triples in the summer, indicating a high quality of life after the thaw. A public bike path, public beaches along Payette Lake (where you can swim with McCall's mythical sea monster, "Sharlie"), and hiking trails all provide ample summer complement to the winter skiing and snowmobiling fun.

Canyons, 160 Commerce St. (634-4303), runs raft, canoe, and kayak trips up and down Payette River in addition to providing complete outfitting. **Payette National Forest** (634-5650) offers skiing and mountain biking in season. (Open in winter daily 9:30am-4:30pm. Full-day lift ticket $30. Biking in summer Sa-Su 11am-6pm.) For firefighter fans, McCall has the ultimate treat: a free tour of the base for the **McCall Smokejumpers,** 605 S. Mission St. (634-0390). The Smokejumpers are a group of elite forest rangers who parachute in to extinguish forest fires—out of the flying plane, and into the fire. (Open daily 7am-5:30pm. Tours given 4 times daily June-Oct.) If a day of outdoor recreation makes your bones weary, take a drive out to the town of **Burgdorf,** 36 mi. north of McCall, where loggers have been treating themselves to **hot springs** for over 100 years. Be sure to check driving conditions before you leave; in the winter, this town is accessible by snowmobile only. When cold weather arrives, you can ski **Brundage Mountain** in the Payette National Forest (634-5650; open daily 9:30am-4:30pm; full-day lift ticket $30).

Camping is generally your best bet for bedding, as budget accommodations are scarce during the peak seasons (June-Sept. and Dec.-Feb.). The finest camping option may be **Ponderosa State Park** (643-3918), located right on Payette Lake. From downtown, take Lick Cr. Rd. just east of the lake and follow the big brown signs ($3, $12 for campers, $16 for RV spot with hookup). The friendly rangers can also direct you to the free "primitive" campground that they maintain on the north side of the lake. At the **University of Idaho Field Campus** (634-3918), adjacent to Ponderosa Park on Payette Lake, log cabins with bunk beds are available with common dining and bath houses. (Single bed $14; families $36. Office open M-F 8:30am-4:30pm. Call for reservations, as the beds may be full during term time.) Before you go out and play, head for the **McCall Pancake House,** 209 N. 3rd St. (634-5849), for a hearty plate of homemade specialties (pancake plates $3-5; open daily 6am-2pm).

Northwest Trailways services the town with two buses a day from Boise ($16) and Spokane ($35). The buses stop at **Bill's Grocery,** 147 N. 3rd St. (643-2340). Call Bill's for schedules, info, or ticket sales. The **Chamber of Commerce,** 1001 State St. (634-7631; email mccall@idchamber.org), offers maps, brochures, and advice about the town (open M-F 9am-3pm). For directions to any of McCall's nearby hikes, or an update on trail conditions, visit the **U.S. Forest Service,** 804 Lakeside Ave. (634-0700; open M-F 7:30am-4:30pm). **Post Office:** (634-2260), on the corner of Linor and 2nd St. (open M-F 8:30am- 5pm). **ZIP code:** 83638. **Area code:** 208.

■ Ketchum and Sun Valley

In 1935, Union Pacific heir Averill Harriman sent Austrian Count Felix Schaffgotsch to scour the U.S. for a site to develop a ski resort area rivaling Europe's best. The Count dismissed Aspen, reasoning that its air was too thin for East Coasters, and selected the small mining and sheep-herding town of Ketchum in Idaho's Wood River Valley. Sun Valley is the fancy resort village Harriman built 1 mi. from Ketchum to entice dashing celebrities like Ernest Hemingway, Claudette Colbert, and Errol Flynn to "rough it" amid the manicured ski slopes, *haute cuisine,* and nightly orchestra performances. An imported East Coast yacht-club feel remains in Ketchum, as celebrities and tourists continue to flock to the natural beauty and luxurious amenities. The towering syncopated peaks of the Sawtooth range still overshadow the brightest Hollywood stars, and visitors can escape the artificial tans and fashionable stores in town to find gorgeous trails and lakes scattered throughout the surrounding mountains.

PRACTICAL INFORMATION The best time to visit is during "slack," if there still is one in this increasingly touristed area (late Oct. to late Nov. and May to early June). **Sawtooth Valley Express** (634-6539) runs one bus daily to the Boise airport ($49; leaves Ketchum 7:15am, return bus from the airport leaves at 2pm). **KART** (634-6539), Ketchum's **bus service,** tours the city and its surrounding areas (Su-Th 7:20am-7pm, F-Sa 7:20am-11pm; free). At the Sun Valley/Ketchum **Chamber of Commerce** (726-3423 or 800-634-3347), 4th and Main St. in Ketchum, an energetic staff points out good deals (open M and W-F 9am-5:30pm, Tu 10am-5pm, Sa 9am-5pm). **Sawtooth National Recreation Area (SNRA) Headquarters** (727-5013 or 800-280-CAMP/2267 for reservations), 8 mi. north of Ketchum off Rte. 75, stocks detailed info on the recreation area, hot springs, and area forests and trails (open M-Sa 8am-4:30pm). For medical emergencies, head for **Wood River Medical Center** (622-3333 or 788-2222) on Sun Valley Rd. Ketchum's **post office:** 301 1st Ave. (726-5161; open M-F 8am-5:30pm, Sa 11am-2pm). **ZIP code:** 83340. **Area code:** 208.

CAMPGROUNDS AND FOOD Prices here suit the Trumps. From early June to mid-October, camping is the best option for cheap sleep. Check with the Ketchum office of the **Sawtooth National Forest** (622-5371) to find out about free camping near Ketchum. **Boundary Campground,** with restrooms and drinking water, is 3 mi. northeast of town on Trail Creek Rd. Two miles further on the right, **Corral Creek Road** scatters its isolated sites along a rushing brook (no hookups). Up Rte. 75 into **Sawtooth National Recreation Area (SNRA)** (727-5000) lie several scenic camping spots; the cheapest (sites $5) are Murdock (11 sites) and Caribou (10 sites). They are, respectively, 2 and 4 mi. up a dirt road, which begins as paved to the right of the visitors center. North Fork (26 sites) and Wood River (31 sites) are 8 and 10 mi. north of Ketchum, along Rte. 75. Both charge $9. **Easley Campground and** (geothermally heated) **Pool,** about 6 mi. on the way to Stanley from SNRA headquarters, is adjacent to a tiny hot spring ($9, showers 50¢). For the hypothermia-averse, **Ski View Lodge,** 409 S. Main St. (726-3441), rents out 10 small, delightfully garish gingerbread-men-decorated log cabins for $44-77.

Ketchum's small confines bulge with over 80 restaurants, many of which serve moderately priced, well-prepared grub. **The Hot Dog Adventure Company,** 210 N. Main St. (726-0017), offers a cosmopolitan selection of, well, hot dogs and veggie dogs ($1.75-4) and mouth-melting steak fries (open at the owner's whim M-Sa noon-6:30pm and 10:30pm-2:30am). **Desperado's** (726-3068), at the corner of 4th and Washington St., dishes out delicious Mexican food at reasonable prices. Relish the view of Baldy while eating in the sun on their large patio. (Large platters of enchiladas and burritos $5-7, combo platters $7-9. Open M-Sa 11:30am-10pm.) At **The Starrwood Bakery,** 591 4th St. (726-2253), local food and earth lovers take pride in fresh breads, muffins, and salads made of the most wholesome of ingredients. $5.50 buys a deli sandwich with soup and a side salad. (Open M-F 6:30am-5pm, Sa 7am-5pm, Su 7am-4pm; hrs. shorter in winter.) Hemingway's old haunt, **Whiskey Jacques,** 209 N. Main St. (726-5297), offers $1 mixed drinks on Tuesdays and Sundays (open daily 4pm-2am; live music schedule varies).

THE OUTDOORS The Sawtooth area is nationally renowned for its stunning **mountain bike trails,** which run through the gorgeous canyons and mountain passes of the SNRA. But beware! Trails can be snowbound or flooded well into July. Inquire about trail conditions at **Formula Sports,** 460 N. Main St. (726-3194; bikes $14 per 4hr., $16 per day). **The Elephant's Perch,** 280 East Ave. (726-3497), off Sun Valley Rd., also rents mountain bikes and provides trail info (open M-Sa 9am-6pm, Su 10am-6pm; bikes $12 for 4hr., $20 per day). Before hitting the forest, pick up info on mountain biking and trail suggestions at the Chamber of Commerce. After a "hard" day of biking or hiking, Ketchum locals soak their buns in their favorite **geothermal hot spring.**

The Sun Valley also Rises

Ernest Hemingway's love affair with both rugged outdoor sports and wealthy celebrities fits Ketchum's dualistic spirit. After spending many of his vacations hunting and fishing in the Sawtooth Range, the author built a cabin in Sun Valley, the site of his suicide after a losing bout with alcoholism. While Hemingway's house is off-limits, the **Ketchum-Sun Valley Heritage and Ski Museum** (726-8118), at the corner of 1st St. and Washington Ave., displays exhibits on Hemingway's life (open in summer daily 1-4pm). A bust of Hemingway is tucked away in a shady spot along the river at the **Hemingway Memorial**, about 1 mi. outside of Sun Valley on the way to Boundary Campground (see above).

The hot springs, hidden in the hills and canyons of Ketchum, are not the secret they once were. Because springtime melt and rain can put the springs underwater, rendering them inaccessible, the best times to visit are often from late spring into the fall. For books and guidance, inquire at the Elephant's Perch or at SNRA headquarters.

Two of the more accessible, non-commercial springs are **Warfield Hot Springs,** on Warm Springs Creek, 11 mi. west of Ketchum on Warm Springs Rd., and **Russian John Hot Springs,** 8 mi. north of the SNRA headquarters on Rte. 75, just west of the highway. Their recent popularity has taken away from their appeal, however, forcing a curfew to be placed on Warfield in response to disrespectful crowds. For the best info on **fishing conditions and licenses,** as well as equipment rentals, stop by **Silver Creek Outfitters,** 500 N. Main St. (726-5282). (Open M-Sa 9am-6pm, Su 9am-5pm, longer hrs. in peak season. Fly rods $15 per day.)

■ Sawtooth

Home to the Sawtooth and White Cloud Mountains in the north and the Smokey and Boulder Ranges in the south, the **Sawtooth National Recreation Area (SNRA)** sprawls over 756,000 acres of untouched land and is surrounded by four national forests, encompassing the headwaters of five of Idaho's major rivers. If you have a car, drive north to Stanley on Rte. 75 (a 60 mi. drive on a generally 30 mph road), pausing at the Galena Overlook, 25 mi. north of Ketchum and ¼ mi. downhill from the 8701 ft. Galena Pass. The panoramic view of the Salmon River valley and the Sawtooth Range is almost surreal.

PRACTICAL INFORMATION The tiny, frontier-style town of **Stanley,** located 60 mi. north of Ketchum at the intersection of Rte. 21 and Rte. 75, serves as a northern base for exploring Sawtooth. Stop by the **Stanley Chamber of Commerce** (774-3411 or 800-878-7950), on Rte. 21 in Stanley, to chat with the friendly staff about services in town and the park. (Open daily 9am-5:30pm; printed material always available.) Topographical maps ($2.50) and various trail books ($3-20) are available at **McCoy's Tackle** (774-3377), on Ace of Diamonds St., and at the **Stanley Ranger Station** (774-3000), 3½ mi. south of Stanley on Rte. 75 (open in summer M-Sa 8am-4:30pm; off-season M-F 8am-5pm). At the entrance to **Redfish Lake** (5 mi. south of Stanley and 55 mi. north of Ketchum on Rte. 75), the Redfish Lake **info booth** (774-3536) dispenses a wide range of info about hiking, camping, and outdoor sports (sporadic hrs.; the booth is usually staffed during sunny, busy weekends). Two miles west of the turnoff from Rte. 75 is the **Redfish Lake Lodge** (774-3536). The helpful staff has a general store next door selling **maps** of the Sawtooth area and **SNRA passes** (open in summer daily 7am-10pm). Stanley's **post office** is on Ace of Diamonds St. (774-2230; open M-F 8-11am and noon-5pm). In the Chamber of Commerce building, the **Stanley Library** (774-2470) offers public **Internet access** (open M noon-6pm, Th noon-4pm, Sa noon-2pm). **ZIP code:** 83278. **Area code:** 208.

CAMPGROUNDS, ACCOMMODATIONS, AND FOOD North of Wood River, campgrounds line Rte. 75. Because there are so many scattered around the SNRA, the free map of campsites available at SNRA headquarters is indispensable. Twenty miles north of Stanley on Rte. 75, the turnoff for **Alturas Lake** is marked about 4 mi. after Galena Pass. Campsites by the lake are available on a first come, first served basis for $9. North of Alturas Lake, **Redfish Lake** (5 mi. south of Stanley, 55 mi. north of Ketchum right off Rte. 75) is the premier spot for camping in the SNRA, but beware of the ever-present lakeside mosquitoes. **Point Campground** (800-280-CAMP/2267), adjacent to a beach on Redfish Lake, can be reserved (sites $11; no hookups). Along the road to the Point Campground, there are a number of campgrounds with water and a common bathhouse that operate on a first come, first (self) served basis ($11; with Golden Age and Access pass $5.50). Free primitive camping with no water or hookups is available just outside the entrance to Redfish Lake on Rte. 75.

Further north on Rte. 75, past the town of Stanley, numerous sites are available alongside the **Salmon River** (first come, first served sites $9; water available; no hookups). Stanley provides more scenic and more reasonable lodging than Ketchum. On Ace of Diamonds St. in downtown, the **Sawtooth Hotel** (774-9947) is a colorful, comfortable place to rest after a wilderness sojourn (singles $35, with private bath $50; doubles $30/$50.) The hotel also has a breakfast joint popular with Stanley natives, a bookstore, and a renowned fly-fishing guide service. More scenic is the **Redwood Motel** (774-3531), 1 mi. north on Rte. 75 in Lower Stanley. Thirteen cottages sit on the banks of Salmon River. (Singles $46, with kitchenette $55; doubles $49/$55.) At **Danner's Log Cabin Motel** (774-3539), on Rte. 21, town mayor Bunny Danner rents historic cabins built by the goldminers at the turn of the century ($45-80; in winter $10 less; "non-peak" spring and summer days $5 off). The **Sawtooth Café** (located in the Sawtooth Hotel) lays a filling American meal on the table, with burgers and sandwiches for $3-5. The Sawtooth Range out the back windows provides a feast for the eyes. (Open daily 6am-3pm.) The **Mountain Village Resort Restaurant and Saloon** (774-3317), at the intersection of Rte. 75 and Rte. 21, also offers sandwiches ($5-7) and breakfast entrees for $3-6 (open Su-Th 7am-9pm and F-Sa 7am-10pm). For evening entertainment, try **Casanova Jack's Rod and Gun Club** (774-9920), at the end of Ace of Diamonds St. in Stanley. On Friday and Saturday nights during the summer, the spacious halls fill with a variety of live music and local crowds playing pool. (Open daily 4pm-2am.)

THE GREAT OUTDOORS Hiking, boating, and fishing are unsurpassed in all four of the SNRA's ranges. However, to enjoy these natural pleasures, **SNRA passes** are necessary, available at any ranger station and most of the outdoor retailers in the Stanley/Ketchum area ($2 per day, $5 per year, families $25). Pick up a free map of the area and inquire about trail conditions at SNRA headquarters before hitting the trail or the lake, particularly in early summer, when trails may be flooded out. Much of the backcountry stays buried deep in the snow well into the summer. **Redfish Lake** is the source of many trails; some popular, leisurely hikes include those to Fishhook Creek (excellent for children), Bench Lakes, and the Hell Roaring trail. The long, gentle loop around Yellow Belly, Toxaway, and Petit Lakes is a moderate overnight suitable for novices. Two miles northwest of Stanley on Rte. 21, the 3 mi. Iron Creek Rd. leads to the trailhead of the Sawtooth Lake Hike. This 5½ mi. trail, steep but well-worn, is not too taxing if you stop to rest. Bionic hikers can try the steep, 4 mi. hike to Casino Lakes, which begins at the Broadway Creek trailhead southeast of Stanley.

Mountain biking in the Sawtooths is almost unlimited. **Riverwear** (774-3592), on Rte. 21 in Stanley, rents bikes for $17 per day. Beginners will enjoy riding the dirt road that accesses the North Fork campgrounds from the visitors center. This gorgeous passage parallels the North Fork of the Wood River for 5 mi. before branching off into other narrower and steeper trails, suitable for more advanced riders. These trails can be combined into loops; consult the trail map or the ranger station. **Boulder Creek Rd.,** 5 mi. from SNRA headquarters, leads to pristine Boulder Lake and an old mining camp. The steep, 10 mi. road-trip ride is suitable for skilled riders. Check with the ranger station in Stanley or the SNRA Headquarters to find out about possible trail closures before your outing, especially during the early summer when trails might be flooded out. Before venturing out into the wilderness on a backpacking trip, consult the detailed topographic maps in any of **Margaret Fuller's Trail Guides** ($13 for the Sawtooths and White Cloud guide), available at SNRA headquarters. Groups of 10 to 20 need free wilderness permits, which are available at SNRA headquarters. Stock up on eats for the trail at the **Mountain Village Grocery Store** (774-3500; open daily 7am-10pm). Alternatively, order a picnic from the Sawtooth Hotel ($7-8) or Mountain Village Resort Restaurant and Saloon ($6; see above).

In the heat of summer, cold rivers beg for fishing, canoeing, or whitewater rafting. **McCoy's Tackle Shop** (774-3377), on Ace of Diamonds St. in Stanley, sells a full range of outdoor equipment besides renting rods and reels. *(Tackle $5-7. Hrs. vary with the seasons; generally open daily in summer 8am-8pm.)* **Sawtooth Rentals** (774-3409 or 800-243-3185), ¼ mi. north of the Rte. 21-Rte. 75 junction, specializes in water vehicle rentals. *(Kayaks $30 per day, doubles $40; rafts $15 per person per day; mountain bikes $25.)* For pontoon boat tours of the lake, head for **Redfish Lake Lodge Marina** (774-3536), which also offers numerous nautical adventures for rent. *(Open daily in summer 7am-9pm. 1hr. tours $6.50, children $4.50; schedule varies. Paddleboats $5 per 30min. Canoes $5 per 30min., $15 per ½-day, $25 per day. Outboards $10 per hr., $33.50 for ½ day, $60 per day.)* **The River Company** (774-2244 or 800-398-0346), based in Stanley, arranges expert whitewater rafting and floating trips. *(½-day trips $67, full-day including gourmet campfire cuisine $85, off-season $65. Open daily in summer 7am-11pm.)*

The most inexpensive way to enjoy the SNRA waters is to visit the **hot springs** just east of Stanley. **Sunbeam Hot Springs**, 10 mi. from Lower Stanley, is the best of the batch. Be sure to bring a bucket or cooler to the stone bathhouse; you'll need to add about 20 gallons of cold Salmon River water before you can get into these hot pools (120-130°F). High water can wash out the hot springs temporarily. Check with local stores for info about other hot springs.

■ Craters of the Moon

Astronauts once trained at the unearthly **Craters of the Moon National Monument,** an elevated lava field and group of craters that rises darkly from sagebrush-covered rangelands, 70 mi. southeast of Sun Valley at the junction of Rtes. 20 and 26/93 (admission $4 per car, $2 per individual). Windswept and deathly quiet, the stark, twisted lava formations dominate sparse vegetation, a reminder of the volcanic eruptions that occurred here as recently as 2000 years ago.

Other-worldly campsites are scattered among jagged lava formations (52 sites with water but no hookup, $10). Wood fires are prohibited, but charcoal fires are permitted. You can camp for free in adjacent land owned by the **Bureau of Land Management** (Shoshone office 886-2206; BLM land pictured in yellow on most maps). Contact the BLM office for info about the primitive camp sites. If you do find your own site, the BLM asks that you practice minimum-impact camping (see **Camping and the Outdoors**, p. 43). Camping in unmarked sites in the dry lava beds of the park itself is permitted with a free backcountry permit, available from the **visitors center** (527-3257; open daily 8am-4:30pm). **Echo Crater,** accessible by a 4 mi. hike from the Tree Molds parking lot, is the most frequented and most comfortable of these sites.

The visitors center has displays and videotapes on the process of lava formation. Printed guides outline hikes to all points of interest within the park as well as a 7 mi. driving loop to major sites. Rangers lead **four guided hikes** of varying themes that last up to 2hr. Bring sturdy shoes and a flashlight when exploring the lava tubes, caves that formed when a surface layer of lava hardened and the rest of the molten rock drained out, creating a tunnel. (Hikes June 12-Sept. 6 at 9am, 1, 4:30, and 7:30pm. The visitors center offers more info.)

The town of **Arco,** 20 mi. east of the Craters of the Moon on Rte. 20, claims to be the **"first city in the world lit by atomic power."** You can fill up on gasoline or plutonium at a number of fill stations along Rte. 20/26, and you can fill your tummy at the **Arco Deli Sandwich Shop** (527-3757), on Rte. 20/26/93 in downtown; it serves up large sandwiches for small prices (foot-long sandwich $5; open daily 8am-8pm).

Montana

When you've seen the sunset splash vibrant colors over a canopy of clouds, or the full spread of brilliant stars unfold at midnight, you'll know why they call Montana Big Sky country. With 25 million acres of national forest and public lands, the state's population of pronghorn antelope seems to outnumber the people, while grizzly bears, mountain lions, and extreme weather serve as reminders of human vulnerability. Although some of the wackier residents—like the Unabomber, the Capitol Building gunman and the militia men—have grabbed international headlines recently, it's the wide-open land that makes this state special. Copious fishing lakes, 500 species of wildlife (not including millions of insect species), beautiful rivers, mountains, glaciers, and thousands of ski trails make Montana a nature-lover's paradise.

PRACTICAL INFORMATION

Capital: Helena.
Visitor Info: Travel Montana, P.O. Box 7549, Missoula 59807 (406-444-2654 in MT or 800-847-4868; http://www.travel.state.mt.us). Offers the free *Montana Travel Planner.* **National Forest Information,** Northern Region, Federal Bldg., 200 E. Broadway, Box 7669, Missoula 59807 (406-329-3511). Gay and lesbian tourists can contact **PRIDE!**, P.O. Box 775, Helena 59624 (406-442-9322), for info on Montana gay community activities.
Emergency: 911.
Time Zone: Mountain (2hr. behind Eastern). **Postal Abbreviation:** MT.
Sales Tax: 0%, but beware of steep gas taxes

The Montanabahn

Montana continues to receive press coverage for being home to elements of the American lunatic fringe. While a traveler to the state is unlikely to run into militia captains or anti-technology zealots, he or she might notice the state's anti-government spirit in its approach to **highway speed limits.** During the day, as long as the weather is okay, traffic is flowing, and you've got a car that can take it, you're generally free to go as fast as you want (the "Basic Speed Rule" requests travel at "reasonable and prudent" speeds). 'Tis a bold policy. Recently, Montana has averaged a highway death every other day, a stat grimly attested to by the disconcerting number of white crosses that line the roadside. Apparently, most fatalities result from speed demons revving past 100 mph, flying over the guard rail into oncoming traffic. Locals maintain these daredevil drivers are out-of-staters intoxicated by the fleeting freedom.

■ Billings

The railstop town founded by Northern Pacific Railroad president Fredrick Billings in 1882 still rumbles with passing freight trains. Despite heavy development, Billings retains a deserted feel against a backdrop of high cliffs. Strip malls and chains are intermingled with tree-lined streets, but sights are few. Located at the junction of I-90 and I-94, Billings is more of a stopover than a destination.

Billings's lodgings are spread throughout the city. The **Cherry Tree Inn,** 823 N. Broadway (252-5603 or 800-237-5882), across from Deaconess Hospital (take Exit

450 off I-90; go north on 27th St. then turn left onto 9th Ave.), has immaculate, spacious, Colonial-themed rooms at chopped-down prices (A/C, phones, cable TV; singles $35; doubles $39). The **Esquire Motor Inn,** 3314 1st Ave. N. (259-4551), has clean rooms and a restaurant and lounge on the premises. (Kitchenettes available. $30.20, $32.25 for 2 people, prices increase with additional persons.)

You can try your luck all over the city; almost every public place offers some kind of video gambling, from poker to keno (a.k.a. bingo). Downtown, **Jake's,** 2701 1st Ave. N. (259-9375), has a few such machines, plus hearty soups ($3-4), burgers ($5.50), and a plentiful selection of microbrews and other less trendy liquids (open M-F 11:30am-2pm and 5:30-10pm, Sa until 10:30pm). Also downtown, **Café Jones,** 2712 2nd Ave. N. (259-7676), is a coffeehouse/juice bar with a rotating art exhibit (dishes $1-5; open M-Sa 7am-10pm, Su 10am-4pm). **Khanthaly's Eggrolls,** 1301 Grand Ave. (259-7252), serves tasty Laotian fast food (fried rice noodles, spring rolls) at prices more likely to be found in Laos than the U.S. ($1-6; open M-Sa 11am-9pm).

Street names in Billings are confusing; three streets may have the same name, distinguished only by direction. The **Billings Logan International Airport,** 1901 Terminal Circle (657-8495) can be found right at the end of N. 27th St. Both **Greyhound** and **Rimrock Trailways** operate from 2502 1st Ave. N. (245-5116; open 24hr.); buses run to Bozeman (3hr., 5 per day, $21-23); Missoula (7-8hr., 5 per day, $36-45); and Bismarck (10hr., 4 per day, $53). See the town, or leave quickly in a car from **Thrifty,** 1144 N. 27th St. (259-1025). Rentals range from $37-45 per day or $209-274 per week, varying with the season. ($10 surcharge for ages 21-24; open daily 5:30am-11:30pm). **Billings Metropolitan Transit** (657-8218) runs buses M-F from approximately 6:10am-6:30pm (75¢, seniors 25¢). The **visitors center,** 815 S. 27th St. (252-4016 or 800-735-2635; http://www.wtp.net/bacc), offers a $1 map, but their basic free map should do the trick (open daily May 31-Sept. 6 8:30am-6pm; off-season 8:30am-5pm). **Deaconess Hospital** operates at 2800 10th Ave. N. (657-4000). **Post Office:** 841 S. 26th St (657-5700; open M-F 8am-5pm, Sa 10am-2pm). **ZIP code:** 59101. **Area code:** 406.

■ Little Big Horn

Little Big Horn National Monument, 60 mi. southeast of Billings off I-90 on the Crow Reservation, marks the site of one of the most dramatic episodes in the conflict between Native Americans and the U.S. Government. Here, Sioux and Cheyenne warriors, led by Sioux chiefs Sitting Bull and Crazy Horse, annihilated five companies of the U.S. Seventh Cavalry under the command of Lt. Colonel George Armstrong Custer on June 25, 1876. White stone graves mark where the U.S. soldiers fell; a somber stone monument, engraved with the names of the dead, covers the mass grave site. The exact Native American casualties are not known, since their families and fellow warriors removed the bodies from the battlefield almost immediately. The renaming of the monument, formerly known as the Custer Battlefield Monument, signifies the U.S. Government's admission that Custer's behavior merits no glorification.

Rangers give great explanatory talks every 30min. in the summer (M-F 9am-5pm, Sa-Su 9am-6pm). Drive through the monument guided by an audio tour ($10-13) that will narrate the battle movements of both sides; you can also see the park on a 1hr. **bus tour** ($10, seniors $8, under 12 $5). The **visitors center** (638-2621) contains a modest museum including a small movie theater, an electronic map of the battlefield, and displays of the weapons used in the battle. *(Monument and museum open daily late May to early Sept. 8am-8pm; in fall 8am-6pm; in winter 8am-4:30pm. Tour road open 8am-7:15pm. Entrance $6 per car, $3 per person.)*

∎ Bozeman

Wedged between the Bridger and Madison Mountains, Bozeman thrives in Montana's broad Gallatin River Valley. Originally settled by farmers who sold food to Northern Pacific Railroad employees living in the neighboring town of Elliston, the valley now supplies food to a large portion of southern Montana. The presence of Montana State University makes Bozeman especially accommodating to young wanderers and latter-day hippies.

PRACTICAL INFORMATION Greyhound and **RimRock Stages,** 625 N. 7th St. (587-3110 or 800-231-2222), both serve Bozeman. Buses run to Butte (1½hr., 4 per day, $14-15); Billings (3-4hr., 5 per day, $21-25); Helena (2hr., 1 per day, $16); and Missoula (5hr., 5 per day, $24-31). **Budget** (388-4091 or 800-952-8343), at the airport, will set you up with some wheels for about $48 per day. (100 free mi., 25¢ per additional mi. Ages 21-25 $15 per day surcharge; major credit card required. Open daily 6am-11:30pm.) The **Bozeman Area Chamber of Commerce,** 1205 E. Main St. (586-5421), provides ample info on local events (open M-F 8am-5pm). **Bozeman Deaconess,** 915 Highland Blvd. (585-5000), is the local hospital. **Internet access** (20¢ per min., $12 per hr.) is available at Kinko's, 1013 W. College St. (586-8999; open 24hr., except some holidays). **Post Office:** 32 E. Babcock St. (586-2373; open M-F 8:30am-5pm). **ZIP code:** 59715. **Area code:** 406.

ACCOMMODATIONS, CAMPGROUNDS, AND FOOD Summer travelers in Bozeman support a number of budget motels along Main St. and on 7th Ave. north of Main. The **Bozeman International Backpackers Hostel,** 405 W. Olive St. (586-4659), offers travelers showers, laundry facilities, a full kitchen, transportation to trailheads, and a chill atmosphere. There are only 15 beds, so call ahead. ($12, children $6; 1 double $30.) Owners can give advice on where to eat, drink, hang out, and hike; they even rent bikes (½-day $6, full-day $10). The **Alpine Lodge,** 1017 E. Main St. (586-0356 or 888-922-5746), has prices that defy its almost luxurious rooms. ($35.50; 2 people $39.50; suite with pull-out couch $46-52; funky roofed cabins with kitchen $48-80; rates lower in winter.) Showers and laundry await at **Sunshine Campground,** 31842 Frontage Rd. (587-4797), east of town (sites $15, with water and electricity $17, $2 per additional person).

Whole sandwiches at **The Pickle Barrel,** 809 W. College (587-2411), consist of giant loaves of fresh sourdough bread stuffed with succulent deli meats and fresh vegetables. (Hefty ½-sandwich $4-5.30. Open daily 10:30am-10pm; in winter 11am-10:30pm.) **Brandi's,** 717 N. 7th (587-3848), at the **Cat's Paw Casino,** greases up a great breakfast deal: two hotcakes or two eggs, hash browns, coffee, and toast for $1.50 (open daily 8am-9:30pm; breakfast all day). Delicious bowls of meaty and meatless noodles ($3-6), and soups and salads ($1.25-5.25) are the fare at **tombō,** 415 W. College St. (585-0234; open M-Th 11am-8pm, F-Sa 11am-9pm, Su noon-7pm). Led Zeppelin's Robert Plant recommends the Black Dog Ale at **Spanish Peaks Brewery,** 120 N. 19th Ave. (585-2296). Pints are $1.50-2.50, and samples go for 75¢.

At the **Museum of the Rockies,** 600 W. Kagy Blvd. (994-2251), immediately south of the MSU campus, you can cower at the bones of the most complete T. Rex ever found (excavated in Montana) and explore the natural and cultural history of the region. *(Open late May to early Sept. daily 8am-8pm; early Sept. to late May M-Sa 9am-5pm, Su 12:30-5pm. $6, children $4, good for 2 days. Wheelchair access.)*

THE GREAT OUTDOORS Surrounded by three renowned trout-fishing rivers—Yellowstone, Madison, and Gardiner—the small town of **Livingston,** about 20 mi. east of Bozeman off I-90, is an angler's heaven. This is gorgeous country; *A River Runs Through It* was shot in Bozeman and Livingston. Livingston's Main St. displays a great strip of circa 1900 buildings housing bars (with gambling), restaurants, fishing outfitters, and only a few modern additions. **Dan Bailey's,** 209 West Park St. (222-1673), provides licenses (2-day $15, season $50), and rents fishing gear and wear. *(Float tubes*

$15, rod and reel $10, waders and boots $10. Open M-Sa 7am-9pm, Su 7am-5pm; in winter M-Sa 8am-6pm.)

Complementing other Montana skiing opportunities, Bozeman provides its share of downhill thrills. **Bridge Bowl Ski Area,** 15795 Bridger Canyon Rd. (586-2389 or 800-223-9609), 16 mi. northeast of town, has plenty of trails for a variety of abilities at decent prices. *(Full-day ticket $30, over 72 free, children $13. Season mid-Dec. to Apr. 4.)* Generally much more challenging, **Big Sky** (800-548-4486), about halfway between Bozeman and West Yellowstone on U.S. 191 (45 mi. south of Bozeman), is renowned for runs as long as 6 mi. and short lift lines. *(Full-day ticket $47, under 10 free. Season mid-Nov. to mid-Apr.)* Both Bridge Bowl and Big Sky offer ski and snowboard rental and lessons. It gets cold out there in the dead of winter, so don't be caught unprepared.

Summer at Big Sky has scenic **lift rides** soaring at the mountain (June-Sept. Th-M 10am-3pm; $12, under 10 free), while equestrian types gallop at nearby **Dalton's Big Sky Stables** (995-2972), about 2 mi. before the mountain's entrance (open June-Sept.; $25 per hr.; 1 day's notice required). **Yellowstone Raft Co.** (995-4613) shoots the rapids 7 mi. north of the Big Sky area on U.S. 191 (½-day $37, children $30, plus $5 for wet suits and booties).

Nuts to You

If you're looking for a good time, head to the annual **Testicle Festival** (http://www.testyfesty.com; Sept. 16-20, 1999), east of Missoula, where the folks at the Rock Creek Lodge (825-4868) promise you'll "have a ball." In the past, as many as 12,000 hearty (or ballsy) souls have gathered to sample delicious **rocky mountain oysters** (a.k.a. bull's testicles) and join in wild revelry on this joyous occasion. Feasting isn't the only activity here; if you're weary of the fare or find it crude, you can take part in the bullshit pitch or hairy chest contest instead! Even if you're not around for the festival, **Kathy's Kitchen** at the lodge serves the scrumptious oysters (open Apr.-Oct daily 8am-9pm). You may not be able to look a bull in the eyes again, but to show your sack, take I-90 22 mi. east of Missoula to Exit 126 in the town of Clinton (coincidence?).

■ Missoula

Long a stop on the road to elsewhere, Missoula has served as a hub for the Plains Indians, freight trains, and long-distance truckers. Lying between Seattle and Minneapolis and a natural stopover for those heading south from Canada, Missoula still sees its fair share of travelers. But today, many wanderers—especially those of the outdoorsy stripe—are captivated by the nearby wilderness and the city's vibrant nightlife. In summer, the town swarms with cyclists, while on Saturday nights, minivans and painted art cars rub fenders with drag-racing Camaros. Frosty winters are warmed up by the University of Montana, a liberal arts haven.

PRACTICAL INFORMATION You can fly into and out of **Missoula International Airport,** 5225 Rte. 10 W (728-4381); just follow Broadway west out of town for 6 mi. (it'll turn into Rte. 10/200). **Greyhound,** 1660 W. Broadway (549-2339), shuffles off to Bozeman (6hr., 4-5 per day, $24-30) and Spokane (4hr., 4 per day, $28-31). **Rim-Rock Stages** serves Whitefish via St. Ignatius and Kalispell (3½hr., 1 per day, $21) and Helena (2½hr., 1 per day, $18) from the same terminal. Traveling within Missoula is easy, thanks to reliable **Mountain Line city buses** (721-3333; buses operate M-F 6:45am-6:15pm, Sa 9:45am-5:15pm; fare 85¢). Alternatively, you can call **Yellow Cab,** 543-6644, for a taxi, or dig the beautiful prices at **Ugly Duckling Car Rental,** 3010 S. Reserve (542-8459), if you're 21 ($25 per day with 150 free mi., 25¢ each additional mi.; reservations essential). The **Missoula Chamber of Commerce,** 825 E. Front St. (543-6623), at Van Buren, has bus schedules and city maps. (Open M-F 7am-7pm, Sa 10am-7pm, Su 11am-5pm; early Sept. to late May M-F 8am-5pm.) The **Domestic Violence Line** (542-1944; rape/sexual assault crises included) and the **Mental Health**

Line (728-6817) operate 24hr. Address health needs at **Community First Care,** 2805 South Ave. W. (327-4080), at the Community Medical Ctr. off Reserve St. (open daily 8am-9:30pm). **Internet Access: Cyber Shack,** 821 S. Higgins (721-6251; $3 per hr.). **Post Office:** 1100 W. Kent (329-2200), between Brooks and South St. (open M-F 8am-6pm, Sa 9am-1pm). Missoula's **ZIP code:** 59801. **Area code:** 406.

ACCOMMODATIONS AND CAMPGROUNDS Settle down at the **Birchwood Hostel,** 600 S. Orange St. (728-9799), 13 blocks east of the bus station on Broadway, then 8 blocks south on Orange. Ernie and Gail, the fantastic hosts, keep a spacious, immaculate dorm sleeping 22. Laundry, kitchen, and bike storage facilities are available. (ISIC cardholders and cyclists $8, otherwise $9. Lockout 9am-5pm. Light chores. Call ahead in winter.) Cheap lodgings cluster along Broadway; check the quieter ends for a place to stay. If you're lucky, your room at the **Sleepy Inn Motel,** 1427 W. Broadway (549-6484), will have a zany shag rug (singles $31; doubles $42). Get off I-90 at Exit 107 and travel ½ mi. east to reach the **Aspen Motel,** 3720 Rte. 200 E, where you'll find clean rooms with cable and A/C (singles $34; doubles $40). The year-round **Outpost Campground** (549-2016), 2 mi. north of I-90 on U.S. 93, provides showers, laundry, and scattered woodsy shade (sites $10, with hookup $12).

FOOD AND NIGHTLIFE Missoula's dining scene offers more than the West's usual steak and potatoes. Choice, thrifty eateries line the downtown area, particularly between **Broadway** and **Railroad St.** and north of the **Clark Fork River.** The **Farmers Market** (baked goods, produce) and the **Peoples Market** showcase local wares at N. Higgins (open in summer Sa 9am-noon and Tu 5:30-7pm). At the **Food for Thought Café,** 540 Daly Ave. (721-6033), there may be a wait for the classy salads and sandwiches ($4-6), but it's worthwhile (open M-Sa 7am-9pm, Su 8am-9pm; in winter daily 7am-10pm). Both a restaurant and a natural food store, **Torrey's,** 1916 Brooks St. (721-2510), serves mouth-watering health food at absurdly low prices; chicken stir-fry is $4. (Restaurant open M-F 11am-8pm, Sa 12:30-7:30pm; store open M-F 10am-8pm, Sa 12:30-7:30pm.) Choose from every breakfast dish you ever imagined, and several lunch numbers for under $6, at the **Old Town Café,** 127 W. Alder St. (728-9742; open daily 6am-3pm). Discerning palates wash down cheap, filling bar food with pilsner, amber, and dark brews of Bayern beer from the **Iron Horse Brew Pub,** 501 N. Higgins (728-8866), at Spruce St. (open daily 10am-2am). For a larger selection and a rowdier crowd, try one of the 51 beers on tap at **The Rhinoceros (Rhino's),** 158 Ryman Ave. (721-6061; open daily 11am-2am).

OUTDOOR ACTIVITIES The outdoors are Missoula's greatest attraction. Located at the intersection of the Trans-America and the Great Parks bicycle routes, the town swarms with **cycling** enthusiasts. **Open Road Bicycles and Nordic Equipment,** 517 W. Orange St. (549-2453), will fill you in on bike trails and rent you a ride at a great price ($3 per hr., $15 per day; open M-F 9am-6pm, Sa 10am-5pm, Su 11am-3pm).

Skiing also ranks among Missoula's popular diversions; the folks at **Open Road** can take care of your cross-country needs (X-C ski package $12 per day), while ski areas like family-oriented **Marshall Mountain** (258-6000) cater to downhill enthusiasts. *(Full-day $19, seniors and under 19 $15; rentals, night skiing, and free shuttles from downtown to the mountain.)* **Montana Snowbowl** (549-9777) is a more extreme option. The Clark Fork, Blackfoot, and Bitterroot Rivers overflow with opportunities for **float trips.** The **Montana State Regional Parks and Wildlife Office,** 3201 Spurgin Rd. (542-5500), sells float maps for $3.50 (open M-F 8am-5pm). For rafting trips on the local rapids, visit **Pangaea Expeditions** (721-7719), which leaves from Bernice's Bakery at 190 S. 3rd St. W. ($25 for 2hr., $40-45 per ½-day, $60 per day; discounts for hostelers).

The **Rattlesnake Wilderness National Recreation Area,** 11 mi. northeast of town off the Van Buren St. Exit from I-90, makes for a great day of **hiking.** Rattlesnake maps ($4) and more info on the wilderness are available from the **U.S. Forest Service Information Office,** 200 E. Broadway (329-3511; open M-F 7:30am-4pm). For equipment rentals, stop by outdoor shops like **Trailhead,** 110 E. Pine St. (543-6966), at Higgins St. (tents $9, backpacks $9-12, sleeping bags $5). At **The Kingfisher,** 926 E.

Broadway (721-6141 or 888-542-4911), they'll tell you where they're bitin' and get you a rod (and permit) to catch 'em with. *(Rods $15 per day, permits $15 for 2 days. Open in summer daily 8am-8pm; off-season hrs. vary.)*

Missoula's hottest sight is the **Aerial Fire Depot Visitors Center** (329-4934), 7 mi. west of town on Broadway (Rte. 10, just past the airport), where you'll learn to appreciate the courage aerial firefighters need to jump into flaming, roadless forests. *(Open daily 8:30am-5pm; Oct.-Apr. by appt. only. Tours May.-Sept. on the hr. 10-11am and 2-4pm. Free.)* The snokejumpers actually parachute to work. If the Depot has left you shell-shocked, the handcarved **Carousel** (549-8382), in Caras Park, can offer you a wholesome spin. *($1, seniors and under 19 50¢. Open daily June-Aug. 10am-9pm; Sept.-May 11am-5:30pm.)* The **First Friday** of each month occasions a touch of Missoula culture, with evening open houses at the town's 15 museums and galleries. On summer Wednesdays (June-Aug.), bands and food vendors swarm at Caras Park 11:30am-1:30pm.

■ From Missoula to Glacier

The **Miracle of America Museum** (883-6804), off U.S. 93 between Missoula and Glacier before you enter the town of **Polson,** houses one of the greatest collections of Americana in the country. (Open June-Sept. daily 8am-8pm; Oct.-May M-Sa 8am-5pm, Su 2-6pm. $2.50, ages 3-12 $1.) Look for the reconstructed general store, saddlery shop, barber shop, and gas station among the classic memorabilia. The **National Bison Range** (644-2211), 40 mi. north of Missoula off U.S. 93 (then 5 mi. west on Rte. 200, 5 mi. north on Rte 212), was established in 1908 to protect bison. (Range open mid-May to mid-Oct. daily 7am-dusk. Visitors center open daily 8am-4:30pm; off-season hrs. vary. Driving tour $4.) Before they were hunted to near-extinction, 50 million of these animals roamed the plains; the Range is home to 300-500 of the imposing creatures.

Hostel of the Rockies (745-3959), off U.S. 93 in **St. Ignatius** (look for the camping sign), is close to the Bison Range and offers unique lodging in its "earthship," an eco-friendly structure built into the side of a hill and made from recycled tires and aluminum cans (showers, laundry, and cooking facilities; $10; tent sites for 1 $8, for 2 $11). **RimRock Stages** (745-3501) makes a stop ½ mi. away in St. Ignatius, at the Malt Shop on Blaine St. In town, you'll find the beautifully frescoed **St. Ignatius Mission Church.**

■ Waterton-Glacier Peace Park

Waterton-Glacier transcends international boundaries to encompass one of the most strikingly beautiful portions of the Rockies. A geographical metaphor for the peace between the U.S. and Canada, the park provides sanctuary for many endangered bears, bighorn sheep, moose, mountain goats, and grey wolves.

Technically one park, Waterton-Glacier is, for all practical purposes, two distinct areas: the small **Waterton Lakes National Park** in Alberta, and the enormous **Glacier National Park** in Montana. Each park charges its own admission fee (in Glacier, $10 per week for a car, $5 per week for pedestrians, bicyclists, and motorcyclists; in Waterton Lakes, CDN$4 per day, CDN$8 per group of 2-10 people), and you must go through customs to pass from one to the other. Several **border crossings** are in or near the park: **Piegan/Carway** at U.S. 89 (open daily 7am-11pm); **Trail Creek/Flathead** outside N. Fork Rd. (open June-Oct. daily 9am-5pm); **Roosville** on U.S. 93 (open 24hr.); and **Chief Mountain** at Rte. 17. (Open daily mid-May to early June and mid-Sept. to early Oct. 9am-6pm; early June to mid-Sept. 7am-10pm.)

Since snow melting is an unpredictable process, the parks are usually in full operation only from late May to early September; it is worth your while to check the conditions in advance. To find out which areas of the park, hotels, and campsites will be open when you visit, contact the **Superintendent,** Waterton Lakes National Park, Waterton Park, AB T0K 2M0 (403-859-2224), or the **Superintendent,** Glacier National Park, West Glacier 59936 (406-888-7800). The *Waterton Glacier Guide,* provided at any park entrance, has dates and times of trail, campground, and border crossing openings. Mace, bear spray, and firewood are not allowed into Canada.

■ Glacier National Park

PRACTICAL INFORMATION Glacier's layout is simple: one road enters through West Glacier on the west side, and three roads enter from the east at Many Glacier, St. Mary, and Two Medicine. West Glacier and St. Mary serve as the two main points of entry into the park, connected by **Going-to-the-Sun Rd.** ("The Sun"), the only road traversing the park. **U.S. 2** runs between East and West Glacier along 57 mi. of the southern park border. Look for the "Goat Lick" signs off Rte. 2 near **Walton;** mountain goats often descend to the lick for a salt fix in June and July.

Each of the three visitors centers has info about trail and campsite availability and local weather and wildlife conditions. **St. Mary** (732-7750) guards the east entrance of the park. (Open daily mid-May to mid-June 8am-5pm; mid-June to early Sept. 7am-9pm; early-Sept. to mid-Oct. 8am-5pm.) **Apgar** (888-7939) aids at the west entrance. (Open daily mid-June to early Sept. 8am-7pm; late Apr. to mid-June and early Sept. to Oct. 8am-4:30pm.) A third visitors center graces **Logan Pass** on Going-to-the-Sun Rd. (Open daily late June to early Sept. 9am-6pm; early to late June and early to late Sept. 9am-4:30pm; early to mid-Oct. 10am-4pm.)

Amtrak (226-4452 or 800-872-7245) traces a dramatic route along the southern edge of the park. Trains chug daily to West Glacier from Whitefish ($7), Seattle ($132), and Spokane ($66); Amtrak also runs from East Glacier to Chicago ($224) and Minneapolis ($193). **RimRock Stages** (800-255-7655), the only bus line that comes near the park, stops in Kalispell (at Sawbuck's Saloon off Rte. 93) from Missoula ($18) or Billings ($60). As with most of the Rockies, a car is the most convenient mode of transport, particularly within the park. Ask about **the reds/jammers** (226-9311, off-season 602-207-6000), antique tour buses with convertible tops that snake around the area ($2-61) and provide transportation from the West Glacier Amtrak station. There are also shuttles for hikers ($6-18) that tour the length of "The Sun." Get a schedule at any visitors center. **Rent-A-Wreck,** 2622 U.S. 2 E (755-4555), in Kalispell, rents cars ($30 per day; 100 free mi., 21¢ each additional mi.; must be 21). **Kalispell Regional Hospital,** 310 Sunnyview Lane (752-5111), is north of Kalispell off Rte. 93. Call 888-7800 for info on **wheelchair access. Post Office:** In Kalispell, 350 N. Meridan (640-6430; open M-F 8:30am-5pm, Sa 10am-2pm). In Glacier, at the Lake McDonald Lodge (open June-Sept. M-F 9am-3:30pm). **ZIP code:** 59921. **Area code:** 406.

ACCOMMODATIONS AND FOOD Staying indoors within Glacier is absurd and expensive. **Glacier Park, Inc.** handles all in-park lodging, including one budget motel: the **Swiftcurrent Motor Inn** (732-5531), in Many Glacier Valley. The Swiftcurrent has cabins without bathrooms for $40 (with 2 bedrooms $50; open early June to early Sept.). Reservations can be made through the distant offices of **Glacier Park, Inc.,** 925 Dial Corporate Center (602-207-6000), Phoenix, AZ 85077-0928.

On the west side of the park, the cozy **North Fork Hostel** (888-5241), at the end of Beaver Dr. in the fascinating, electricity-less town of **Polebridge,** makes an ideal base for exploring some of Glacier's most pristine areas. The bumpy 12 mi. trip up the dirt road preps visitors for the propane and kerosene lamps, wood stoves, and outhouses that provide creature comforts at the hostel. (Dorm beds $12, $10 after 2 nights; cabins $26; log homes $50-52. Linen $2. Light chores. Use of canoes, mountain bikes, and nordic ski equipment included.) The **Polebridge Mercantile Store** (888-5105) will replenish depleted supplies. They also rent out rustic cabins and teepees for $20-35 a night. Next door, a slice of homemade pie or a beer to revive flagged spirits can brighten your day at the **Northern Lights Saloon** (open daily June-Sept. 4-9pm for food, until midnight for drinks).

In the east, affordable lodging can be found just across the park border in **East Glacier,** on U.S. 2, 30 mi. south of the St. Mary entrance and about 5 mi. south of the Two Medicine entrance. **Brownies Grocery (HI-AYH),** 1020 Rte. 49 (226-4426), manages a bakery, a deli, and comfortable dorms. (Bunks $12, nonmembers $15; private singles $17/$20; doubles $23/$26; triples $25/$28; family room for 4-6 $33. Tent sites $10. Open May-Sept., weather permitting. Reservations recommended.) Next door, the **Whistle Stop Café** is an oasis of local gourmet creations (Huckleberry French Toast $5) made with fresh ingredients and individual flair. The **Backpacker's Inn Hostel,** 29 Dawson Ave. (226-9392), across from the East Glacier Amtrak station, offers 20 clean beds and hot showers for only $10 per night (bring a sleeping bag or rent one for $1; open May-Sept.).

CAMPING Camping is a cheaper and more scenic alternative to indoor living. Most developed campsites are available on a first come, first served basis; the most popular sites fill by noon. Reservations can be made at **St. Mary** and **Fish Creek** ($15). All 13 campgrounds accessible by car are easy to find; just follow the map distributed at the park entrance. **Sprague Creek** and **Fish Creek** have peaceful lakeside sites. **Bowman Lake** (48 sites) and **Kintla Lake** (13 sites) rarely fill and offer pristine lakeside sites; neither has flush toilets, but they're the cheapest thing going ($10). Be aware that Inside N. Fork Rd., which leads to these sites along with **Logging Creek** and **Quartz Creek** (also $10), can be very rough in spots. **Cut Bank** is another nice secluded site ($10) where RVs are not recommended. The rest of the campgrounds cost $12, and you can flush to your little heart's content. Some sites at **Sprague, Apgar, Avalanche, Rising Sun,** and **St. Mary** remain reserved for bicyclists and pedestrians; most campgrounds have at least one wheelchair-accessible site (call 888-7800 for more info). Campgrounds in the surrounding national forests offer sites for $8 ($4 per additional vehicle). Check at the Apgar or St. Mary visitors centers for up-to-date info on conditions and vacancies. Weather and the grizzlies adjust the operating dates at their whim; bring warm clothes and prepare to combat mosquitoes.

IN TOUCH WITH NATURE *There are bears out there. Familiarize yourself with the precautions necessary to avoid an encounter* (see p. 51). **Backcountry trips** are the best way to appreciate the mountain scenery and the wildlife which make Glacier famous. The **Highline Trail** from Logan Pass is a good day-hike through prime bighorn sheep and mountain goat territory, although locals consider it too crowded. The visitors center's free *Backcountry Guide* pamphlet has a hiking map marked with distances and backcountry campsites. All backcountry campers must obtain, in person, a $4 **wilderness permit** from a visitors center or ranger station no more than 24hr. in advance. Reservations for a particular site should be made more than 24hr. in advance at the Agpar or St. Mary visitors center, or by mail. ($20 reservation forms can be acquired by writing to Backcountry Permits, Glacier National Park, West Glacier, MT 59936.) Backcountry camping is allowed only at designated campsites. The **Two Medicine** area in the southeast corner of the park is well traveled; the treks to **Kintla Lake** and **Numa Lake** reward with fantastic views of nearby peaks. **Belly River** is another isolated and pretty spot.

   Going-to-the-Sun Rd. runs a beautiful 52 mi. course through the park. Even on cloudy days, the constantly changing views of the peaks will have you struggling to keep your eyes on the road. Nevertheless, you'll have to—the road is narrow and susceptible to rock slides and falling trees. Snow clogs the road until June, so check with rangers for exact opening dates. All vehicles must be no more than 21 ft. long and 8 ft. wide to go over Logan Pass, a midpoint on the road.

   Although "The Sun" is a popular **bike route,** only experienced cyclists with appropriate gear and legs of titanium should attempt this grueling ride. The sometimes nonexistent shoulder of the road creates a hazardous situation for cyclists. In the summer (June 15 to Sept. 6), bike traffic is prohibited 11am-4pm from the Apgar turn-off at the west end of Lake McDonald to Sprague Creek, and from Logan Creek to Logan Pass. The east side of the park has no such restrictions. Bikes are not permitted on any hiking trails. **Equestrian** explorers should check to make sure trails are open; fines for riding on closed trails are steep. **Trail rides** ($35 for 2hr.) are available at Many Glacier, Apgar, and Lake McDonald.

BOATING AND FISHING Boat tours explore all of Glacier's large lakes. Tours leave from **Lake McDonald** (1hr.; 4-5 per day; $8.50, ages 4-12 $4.25); **Two Medicine** (45min., 5 per day, $8); **Rising Sun** at St. Mary Lake (1½hr.; 5 per day; $10, children

$5); and **Many Glacier** (1¼hr., 5-6 per day, $9.50). The tours from Two Medicine, Rising Sun, and Many Glacier provide access to Glacier's backcountry and optional guided walks, and there are sunset cruises from all three locations. Call 257-2426 for info. **Glacier Raft Co.** (888-5454 or 800-332-9995), in West Glacier, hawks trips down the middle fork of the Flathead River. (Full-day trip $69 with lunch, under 13 $44; ½-day $36/$28 morning and afternoon.)

Rent **rowboats** ($8 per hr.) at Lake McDonald, Many Glacier, Two Medicine, and Apgar; **canoes** ($8 per hr.) at Many Glacier, Two Medicine, and Apgar: **kayaks** at Apgar ($8 per hr.) and Many Glacier; and **outboards** ($14 per hr.) at Lake McDonald, Two Medicine, and Apgar. No permit is needed to **fish** in the park. In an attempt to boost indigenous fish populations, the park stopped stocking its rivers in the 1970s. Limits are high and few rivers seem in danger of exceeding them, but it's good idea to read the pamphlet *Fishing Regulations,* available at visitors centers. Outside the park, on Blackfoot Indian land, you *do* need a special permit, and everywhere else in Montana you need a state permit.

■ Near Glacier

Whitefish Sporting types will get a kick out of **The Big Mountain** (800-859-3528), southwest of the park in Whitefish. They offer 67 trails for fantastic skiing in the winter ($40 per day, students, seniors, and ages 7-18 $27 per day; night skiing $12), while mountain bikers flock to their trails in the summer (bikes $15 for 4hr., family packages available). Other activities include horseback riding, gondola rides, or a challenging game of folf (frisbee golf). After a long day of taxing exercise, many head to the town's **Black Star Brewery,** 2 Central St. (863-1000), for a free tour with samples (open M-Sa noon-6pm; in winter M-Sa 3-7pm), then crash at one of two great hostels. **The Bunkhouse Traveler's Inn and Hostel,** 217 Railway Ave. (862-3377), has a sweet sundeck for the summertime and offers ski bus pick-up in the winter. ($13; private rooms $30. Kitchen and laundry facilities. Wheelchair access. May close occasionally between fall and winter seasons.) They'll treat you kindly at the **Non-Hostile Hostel,** 300 E. 2nd St. (862-7383) which has a library with **Internet access,** a pool table, and the **Wrap and Roll Café** (wrap sandwiches with veggie included $4 and up) downstairs (rooms $13). **RimRock** buses (800-255-7655) stop at the Conoco station across E. 2nd St. and run to Missoula (1 per day, $21). Whitefish can also be reached by **Amtrak** (800-872-7245) from a variety of destinations.

Browning In the city of Browning, 12 mi. east of East Glacier, the **Museum of the Plains Indian** (338-2230), off Rte. 89 just outside town, displays a great deal of beautiful Native American clothing and crafts. *(Open June-Sept. daily 9am-5pm, Oct.-May M-F 10am-4:30pm. $4, ages 6-12 $1; Oct.-May free.)* During **North American Indian Days** (338-7406), Native Americans from the surrounding Blackfoot reservation and elsewhere gather for a celebration that includes tribal dancing, rodeo, and a fantastic parade (event runs from the 2nd Th through the 2nd Su of July).

■ Waterton Lakes National Park, AB

Only a fraction of the size of its Montana neighbor, Waterton Lakes National Park offers spectacular scenery and activities without the crowds that plague Glacier during the peak months of July and August.

If you've brought hiking boots to Waterton, you can set out on the **International Lakeside Hike,** which leads along the west shore of Upper Waterton Lake and delivers you to Montana some 6km after leaving the town. The **Crypt Lake Trail,** voted one of Canada's best hikes, leads past waterfalls in a narrow canyon and through a 20m natural tunnel bored through the mountainside, to arrive after 6km at icy, green Crypt Lake, which straddles the international border. To get to the trailhead, you must take the **water taxi** run by **Waterton Shoreline Cruises** in Waterton Park (859-2362). The boat leaves twice a day (CDN$11, ages 4-12 CDN$5). The marina also runs a 2hr. boat tour of Upper Waterton Lake five times per day (CDN$19, ages 13-17 CDN$12, ages 4-12 CDN$8; open mid-May to mid-Sept.).

Anglers will appreciate Waterton's **fishing,** which requires a **license** (CDN$6 per week, CDN$13 per season), available from the park offices, campgrounds, warden stations, and service stations in the area. Lake trout cruise the depths of **Cameron** and **Waterton Lakes,** while northern pike prowl the weedy channels of **Lower Waterton Lake** and **Maskinonge Lake.** Most of the backcountry lakes and creeks support populations of rainbow and brook trout. Try the creek that spills from Cameron Lake, about 200m to the east of the parking lot, or hike 1.5km to Crandell Lake for plentiful, hungry fish. You can rent a **rowboat, pedalboat,** or **canoe** at Cameron Lake (2 people $15 1st hr., $12 per additional hr.; 4 people $18/$15). **Alpine Stables** (859-2462; in winter 653-2449 or 653-2089), 1km north of the townsite, conducts trail rides of varying lengths (1hr. ride CDN$17, full-day CDN$88; open May-Sept.).

On summer evenings at 8:30pm, take in a free **interpretive program** at the **Cameron Theater** in town or at the Crandell campsite. These interesting and quirkily entitled programs (e.g., *Bearying the Myths*) change yearly. There are programs daily in summer at 8:30pm; the visitors center has a schedule.

Entering the park, you can't miss the enormous(ly pricey) **Prince of Wales Hotel** (859-2231), which offers traditional afternoon tea from roughly June to September (daily 2:30-4:30pm; CDN$15.50) and a spectacular view. The park's three campgrounds are much more affordable places to stay. **Belly River,** on Chief Mountain Hwy. outside the park entrance, has scenic and uncrowded primitive sites for CDN$10. **Crandell,** on Red Rock Canyon Rd., is situated in a forest area with sites for CDN$13. Camp with 200 of your best RV pals at **Townsite** in Waterton Park, which has showers and a lakeside vista, but no privacy (sites CDN$16, full hookup CDN$21). **Backcountry camping** is CDN$6 per person per night and requires a permit from the visitors center (see above; or call 859-5133 for a CDN$10 permit, 90 days in advance). The backcountry campsites are rarely full, and several, including beautiful **Crandell Lake,** are less than 1hr. from the trailhead.

Travelers preferring to stay indoors should head for the blue buildings of **Mountain View Bed and Breakfast** (653-1882), 20km east of the park about 1km off Rte. 5, to enjoy comfy beds, down-home hospitality, and a hearty breakfast with homemade bread. They also run a fishing guide service. (Singles CDN$25-35; doubles CDN$45-55.) If you insist on having a bed in Waterton, drop by the **Waterton Pharmacy,** on Waterton Ave. (859-2335), and ask to sleep in one of the nine rooms of the **Stanley Hotel** (common washroom access 3-8pm; singles and doubles CDN$45). The **Country Bakery and Lunch Counter,** 303 Windflower Ave. (859-2181), cooks up meat pies (CDN$2.75) and CDN$3.50 malted waffles (open May-Sept. daily 7am-8pm).

The only road from Waterton's park entrance leads 8.5km south to **Waterton Park.** En route, grab a copy of the *Waterton-Glacier Guide* at the **Waterton Visitors Center** (859-5133), 8km inside the park on Rte. 5 (open daily 8am-8pm; mid-May to mid-June 8am-6pm; Sept.-Oct. hrs. vary). In the off season, pick up info at **Park Headquarters and Information,** Waterton Lakes National Park, 215 Mt. View Rd. (859-2224; open M-F 8am-4pm). Greenbacks can be exchanged for Loonies at the **Tamarac Village Sq.** on Mt. View Rd. (open daily July-Aug. 7am-10pm; May-June and Sept.-Oct. usually 9am-5pm), where you can also catch **shuttle buses** to the trails starting around June 1. A shuttle also runs once a day from Waterton to Glacier for $44.75; inquire with the **reds/jammers buses** (see Glacier **Practical Information,** p. 566). **Pat's Mohawk and Cycle Rental** (859-2266), Mt. View Rd., Waterton, rents bikes (mountain bikes CDN$6 per hr., CDN$30 per day). In a medical **emergency,** call an **ambulance** (859-2636). Waterton's **post office** is on Fountain Ave. at Windflower Ave. (open M, W, and F 8:30am-4:30pm, Tu and Th 8:30am-4pm). **Postal code**: T0K 2M0. **Area code:** 403.

Wyoming

The ninth-largest state in the Union, Wyoming is also the least populated. This is a place where livestock outnumber citizens, and men wear cowboy hats and boots for *real.* Yet, this rugged land was more than just a frontier during westward expansion. It was the first state to grant women the right to vote without later repealing it, and the first to have a national monument (Devils Tower) and a national park (Yellowstone) within its borders. Wyoming has everything you'd want to see in a state in the Rockies: a Frontier Days festival, spectacular mountain ranges, breath-taking panoramas, and, of course, cattle and beer.

PRACTICAL INFORMATION

Capital: Cheyenne.
Visitor Info: Wyoming Business Council Tourism Office, I-25 and College Dr., Cheyenne 82002 (307-777-7777, outside WY 800-225-5996; http://www.commerce.state.wy.us/west). Info center open daily 8am-5pm. Write for the free *Wyoming Vacation Guide.* **Dept. of Commerce, State Parks and Historic Sites Division,** 122 W. 25th St., Herschler Bldg., Cheyenne 82002 (307-777-6323), 1st fl., has info on Wyoming's 10 state parks. Open M-F 8am-5pm. **Game and Fish Dept.,** 5400 Bishop Blvd., Cheyenne 82006 (307-777-4600). Open M-F 8am-5pm.
Emergency: 911.
Time Zone: Mountain (2hr. behind Eastern). **Postal Abbreviation:** WY.
Sales Tax: 5%.

■ Yellowstone

Six hundred thousand years ago, intense volcanic activity fueled a catastrophic eruption that spewed out nearly 35 trillion cubic feet of debris, creating the central basin of what is now **Yellowstone National Park.** Although these geological engines have downshifted, they still power boiling sulfuric pits and steaming geysers. John Colter's descriptions of his 1807 explorations of this earthly inferno inspired 50 years of popular stories about "Colter's Hell." By 1872, popular opinion had swayed, and President Grant declared Yellowstone a national park, the world's first.

Today, Yellowstone's natural beauty is cluttered with cars, RVs, and thousands of tourists. Netherworldly sink holes aside, the park's vast acreage encompasses breathtaking mountain vistas and rolling hillsides strewn with wildflowers. In the backcountry, away from the crowds and geothermic anomalies that line the roads, you may catch a glimpse of the bears, elk, moose, wolves, bison, and bighorn sheep that thrive in the park's quieter peaks and valleys. In 1988, a blaze charred a third of Yellowstone, and the land is slowly recovering; gangly skeletons of burnt trees draw a stark contrast to the surrounding pine forest.

ORIENTATION AND PRACTICAL INFORMATION

The bulk of Yellowstone National Park lies in the northwest corner of Wyoming, with slivers in Montana and Idaho. **West Yellowstone, MT,** at the park's western entrance, and **Gardiner, MT,** at the northern entrance, are the most developed and expensive towns along the edge of the park. For a rustic stay, venture northeast to **Cooke City, MT.** The northeast entrance to the park leads to U.S. 212, a gorgeous stretch of road known as **Beartooth Hwy.,** which climbs to **Beartooth Pass** at 11,000 ft. and descends to **Red Lodge,** a former mining town. (Road open only in summer because of heavy snowfall; ask at the chamber of commerce for exact dates.) The eastern entrance to the park from Cody is via Rte. 14/16/20. The southern entry to the park is through **Grand Teton National Park** (see p. 576). The park's **entrance fee** is $20 for cars, $10 for pedestrians, and $15 for motorcycles; the pass is good for one week at Yellowstone and Grand Teton National Parks.

Yellowstone's roads circulate its millions of visitors in a rough figure-eight configuration, with side roads branching off to park entrances and some of the lesser-known sites. The major natural wonders which make the park famous (e.g., Old Faithful) dot the Upper and Lower Loops. Construction and renovation of roads are planned for the next 80 years; call ahead to find out which sections will be closed during your visit...and your lifetime. It's unwise to bike or walk around the deserted roads at night, as you risk startling large wild animals; the best time to see the roaming beasts is at dawn or dusk. When they're out, traffic stops and cars pull over. Approaching any wild animal at any time is illegal and extremely unsafe; those who don't remain at least 25 yds. from moody and unpredictable bison or moose and 100 yds. from bears risk being mauled or gored to death. (For more tips on avoiding fisticuffs with a bear, see **Bear in Mind,** p. 51.) Near thermal areas, stay on marked trails, because "scalding water can ruin your vacation."

The park's high season extends from about mid-June to mid-September. If you visit during this period, expect large crowds, clogged roads, and motels and campsites filled to capacity. Much of the park shuts down from November to mid-April, then opens gradually as the snow melts.

Buses: Greyhound (800-231-2222). Pick-up at West Yellowstone Office Services at 132 Electric St., West Yellowstone. To: Bozeman (2hr., 1 per day, $14-18); Salt Lake City (9hr., 1 per day, $45-57); and Boise (17hr., 1 per day, $92-97). **Powder River Transportation** also offers service from Cody (see p. 582).

Car Rental: Big Sky Car Rental, 429 Yellowstone Ave. (646-9564 or 800-426-7669), West Yellowstone, MT. $34 per day, unlimited mi. within a 125 mi. radius. Must be 21 with a credit card or passport. Open daily May to mid-Oct. 8am-5pm.

Bike Rental: Yellowstone Bicycles, 132 Madison Ave. (646-7815), West Yellowstone, MT. Mountain bikes with helmet and water $3.50 per hr., $12.50 per ½-day, $19.50 per day. Open May-Oct. daily 8:30am-9pm; Nov.-Apr. 10am-8pm.

Horse Rides: AmFac (344-7311), from Mammoth Hot Springs, Roosevelt Lodge, and Canyon Village. Late May to early Sept. $18.50 per hr., 2hr. $28.50. From early June to early Sept., **stagecoach rides** ($6, ages 2-11 $5) are available at Roosevelt Lodge.

Tours: Grayline Tours (406-646-9374 or 800-523-3102), runs tours from West Yellowstone through both loops of the park ($36, under 12 $23). Free pickup from area motels or campgrounds. **Buffalo Bus Lines,** 429 Yellowstone Ave. (406-646-9564 or 800-426-7669), West Yellowstone, tours the Upper Loop on odd days, and the Lower Loop on even days ($35, children $25). **Powder River Tours** runs out of **Cody** from the east (see p. 582). **AmFac Parks and Resorts** (344-7311) gives 8½-9hr. bus tours of the lower portion of the park, leaving daily from several lodges and campgrounds ($27.50, ages 12-16 $14). Similar tours of the northern region leave from Canyon Lodge, Lake Hotel, Fishing Bridge RV Park, and Bridge Bay Campground ($21.50-25.50, ages 12-16 $11-13). Full-day tours around the park's figure-eight road system also available, leaving from Gardiner, MT, and Mammoth Hot Springs ($31-32, ages 12-16 $16-16.50). Individual legs of this network of tour loops can get you as far as the Grand Tetons or Jackson, but using the system that way is inefficient and costs more than it's worth.

Visitor Info: Most regions in this vast park have their own central station. District rangers have a good deal of autonomy in making regulations for hiking and camping, so check in at each area. All centers offer backcountry permits and guides for the disabled, or a partner ranger station that does. Each center's display focuses on the attributes of its region of the park: **Albright Visitors Center** at Mammoth Hot Springs, natural and human history; **Grant Village,** wilderness and the 1988 fire; **Old Faithful/Madison,** geysers; **Fishing Bridge,** wildlife and Yellowstone Lake; **Canyon,** bison; **Norris,** geology. All stations are usually open late May to early Sept. daily 8am-7pm; Albright and Old Faithful are open through the winter. For more information, call 344-7381 or leaf through your copy of *Yellowstone Today,* the park's activities guide, which has a thorough listing of tours and programs and lots of useful data. For general park info and campground availability, call or write the **Superintendent** (344-7381), Yellowstone National Park, WY 82190. Headquarters open M-F 9am-5pm. **West Yellowstone Chamber of Commerce,** 30 Yellowstone

Ave. (406-646-7701), West Yellowstone, MT, 2 blocks west of the park entrance. Open late May to early Sept. daily 8am-8pm; early Sept. to late May 8am-5pm.
Radio Information: Tune in to 1610AM for park info.
Ranger station: 344-7381.
Medical Services: Lake Clinic, Pharmacy, and **Hospital** (242-7241), across the road from the Lake Yellowstone Hotel. Clinic open late May to mid-Sept. daily 8:30am-8:30pm. Emergency room open May-Sept. 24hr. **Old Faithful Clinic** (545-7325), near the Old Faithful Inn. Open early May to mid-Oct. daily 8:30am-5pm; May and mid-Sept. to mid-Oct. closed M-Tu. **Mammoth Hot Springs Clinic** (344-7965), open June-Aug. daily 8:30am-1pm and 2-5pm; Sept.-May M-F 8:30am-1pm and 2-5pm. The **Clinic at West Yellowstone,** 236 Yellowstone Ave. (406-646-7668), in West Yellowstone, open M-Sa 8:30am-noon and 1-5:30pm.
Disabled Services: All entrances, visitors centers, and ranger stations offer the *Visitor Guide to Accessible Features.* Fishing Bridge RV Park, Madison, Bridge Bay, Canyon, and Grant campgrounds have accessible sites and restrooms, while Lewis Lake and Slough Creek each have a site. Call 344-2018 or write the **Accessibility Coordinator,** P.O. Box 168, Yellowstone National Park, WY, 82190, for more info.
Post Office: Mammoth Hot Springs (344-7764), Yellowstone National Park, near headquarters. Open M-F 8:30am-5pm. **ZIP code:** 82190. In **West Yellowstone, MT,** 209 Grizzly Ave. (646-7704). Open M-F 8:30am-5pm, Sa 8-10am. **ZIP code:** 59758. **Area codes:** 307 (in the park), 406 (in West Yellowstone, Cooke City, and Gardiner, MT). In text, 307 unless otherwise noted.

ACCOMMODATIONS AND FOOD

Camping is far cheaper, but cabin-seekers will find many options within the park. Standard hotel and motel rooms for the nature-weary also abound nearby, but if you plan to keep your budget in line, stick to the towns nearest the park's entry-points.

In the Park
AmFac Parks and Resorts (344-7311) controls all accommodations within the park with an iron fist, using a secret code for cabins: "Roughrider" means no bath, no facilities; "Budget" offers a sink; "Economy" guarantees a toilet and sink; "Pioneer" offers a shower, toilet, and sink; "Frontier" is bigger, more plush; "Western" is even bigger and plusher; aaaaaand…"Eggplant Jello" means you are probably delirious. Facilities are located close to the more rustic cabins. All cabins or rooms should be reserved well in advance of the June to September tourist season. Be very choosy when buying food in the park, as the restaurants, snack bars, and cafeterias are quite expensive. If possible, stick to the **general stores** at each lodging location (open daily 7:30am-10pm, though times may vary by around 30min.).

Roosevelt Lodge, in the northwest corner. A favorite of Teddy Roosevelt, who seems to have frequented every motel and saloon west of the Mississippi. Provides some of the cheapest and most scenic indoor accommodations around. Roughrider cabins ($37, bring your own towel) with wood-burning stoves and more spacious Economy ($49) or Frontier cabins ($73), both with toilet and electric heat.
Mammoth Hot Springs, 18 mi. west of Roosevelt area, near the north entrance. Lattice-sided Budget cabins $43. Frontier cabins (some with porches) from $75.
Old Faithful Inn and Lodge, near the west Yellowstone entrance. Pleasant Budget cabins with sink ($26) and Pioneer cabins ($42). Well-appointed hotel rooms from $49, with private bath $75.
Lake Lodge Cabins, a stone's throw from Yellowstone Lake, is a cluster of cabins dating from the 20s and 50s, with interior decorating from the 70s. Frontier cabins $47; larger Western cabins $96. Next door, **Lake Yellowstone Hotel and Cabins** has yellow Frontier cabins with no lake view for $73.
Canyon Lodge and Cabins, in the middle of the figure-eight of the park loop. Less authentic and more expensive than Roosevelt Lodge's cabins, but slightly closer to the popular Old Faithful area. Pioneer cabins $52; Western cabins $96.

West Yellowstone, MT

Guarding the west entrance of the park, West Yellowstone's overflow of shops and services washes away some genuine Montana flavor. Pick from the many restaurants, or lasso some chow at the **Food Round-Up Grocery Store,** 107 Dunraven St. (406-646-7501; open daily 7am-10pm).

West Yellowstone International Hostel (AAIH/Rucksackers), 139 Yellowstone Ave. (406-646-7745 or 800-838-7745 outside MT), at the Madison Hotel. A friendly manager presides over this old but clean, wood-adorned hostel. $17, nonmembers $19; singles and doubles $25-32. Open late May to mid-Oct.

Lazy G Motel, 123 Hayden St. (406-646-7586), has big rooms with queen beds, refrigerators, and TVs. Singles and doubles $43, with kitchenette $53.

Circle R Motel, 321 Madison (406-646-7641). Wooden beams and wagon-wheel bed frames adorn the rooms in the older section. Singles $40; doubles $42.

Gardiner, MT

Located about 1½hr. northeast of West Yellowstone, Gardiner is the original entrance to the park and smaller, more friendly, and less tacky than its neighbors. Pick a bundle of inexpensive food at **Food Farm** (406-848-7524), on U.S. 89 across from the Super 8 (open M-Sa 7am-9pm, Su 8am-8pm). Next door, **Helen's Corral Drive-In** rounds up killer ½ lb. burgers (open in summer daily 11am until about 10:30pm).

The Town Café and Motel (406-848-7322), on Park St. across from the park's northern entrance. Pleasant, wood-paneled, carpeted rooms. TVs but no phones. Singles $45, doubles $50; Oct.-May $35/$40.

Hillcrest Cottages (406-848-7353 or 800-970-7353), on U.S. 89 across from the Exxon, rents out homey cabins with kitchenettes. Singles $39-49; doubles $46-56; $6 per additional adult, $4 per additional child under 18. Open May to early Nov.

Blue Haven Motel (406-848-7719), on U.S. 89, has pleasant rooms with a queen bed for 1-2 people ($35), with kitchenette $45. Rates lower in winter.

Cooke City, MT

Cooke City is located at the northeast corner of the park. The Nez Perce slipped right by the U.S. cavalry here, Lewis and Clark deemed the area impassable, and many tourists today still miss the mean plates of homefries, soup-sandwich specials ($4.50), and breakfast combos ($3-6) at **Joan and Bill's Family Restaurant,** 114 Rte. 212 (406-838-2280; open daily 6am-9:45pm).

If you've never slept in a yurt before, this is your chance. The **Yellowstone Yurt Hostel** (406-838-2349), at the corner of W. Broadway and Montana St. (turn left onto Republic St. from U.S. 212), has one—a round tent with a skylight, wood stove, and six bunks. The hostel is oriented toward backcountry skiers in the winter. $12 buys a bunk and access to an *ad hoc* kitchen; showers are $3 extra. Bring a sleeping bag. Check-in is before 9pm; call ahead for late arrivals. Visitors can also rest at the eastern end of town (there's only one main street in Cooke City, U.S. 212) in **Antler's Lodge** (406-838-2432), a renovated U.S. cavalry outpost where the ubiquitous Teddy Roosevelt once stayed (singles $45; doubles $55).

CAMPGROUNDS

Sites can be reserved at five of 12 developed campgrounds. **AmFac,** P.O. Box 165, Yellowstone National Park 82190 (344-7311), controls **Canyon, Grant Village, Madison, Bridge Bay** (all $15), and **Fishing Bridge RV** ($27; RVs only).

Seven campgrounds offer first come, first served sites with potable water ($10-12). In summer, most of these fill by 10am; arrive very early, especially on weekends and holidays. Bring a stove, or plan to search for or buy firewood. Two of the most beautiful and tranquil areas are **Slough Creek Campground** (29 sites, 10 mi. northeast of Tower Junction; open late May to Oct.) and **Pebble Creek Campground** (32 sites; no RVs; open mid-June to early Sept.). Both offer relatively uncrowded spots and good fishing. You can also try **Lewis Lake,** with 85 pine tree-enveloped sites, or **Tower**

Falls, with 32 sites high on a hill. **Indian Creek** (75 sites; open mid-June to mid-Sept.) and **Mammoth** (85 sites; open year-round) are a bit less scenic. If all sites are full, $8 campgrounds lurk outside the park in the area National Forests. Good sites line U.S. 14/16/20, 287, 191, 89, and Rte. 212 (near Cooke City). Often nearly empty, they are worth camping at, even if there are spots open at Yellowstone. Call **Park Headquarters** (344-7381) for info on any of Yellowstone's campgrounds.

Campgrounds at Grant Village, Fishing Bridge, and Canyon all have coin laundries ($1.25 wash, $1 dry) and pay showers ($3). The lodges at Mammoth and Old Faithful have showers for $3 (towels and shampoo included) but no laundry facilities.

Over 95% (almost 2 million acres) of the park is backcountry. To venture overnight into the wilds of Yellowstone, you need a free **backcountry permit** from a ranger station (near all major visitor centers). Pity the fool who doesn't consult a ranger before embarking on a trail. Rangers can give instructions on which trails and campgrounds you should avoid due to bears, ice, and other natural hindrances. Other backcountry regulations include sanitation rules, pet and firearms restrictions, campfire permits, and firewood rules. The more popular areas fill up in high season; reserve a permit ahead of time ($15) by writing to the **Backcountry Office,** P.O. Box 168, Yellowstone National Park 82190. You can reserve a permit in person no more than 48hr. in advance; campfire permits are not required, but ask if fires at your site are allowed.

SIGHTS AND ACTIVITIES

For mountains of cash, **AmFac** (344-7311) will sell you on tours, horseback rides, and chuckwagon dinners until the cows come home. Given enough time, however, your eyes and feet will do a better job than AmFac's tours, and you won't have to sell your firstborn. The main attractions all feature informative self-guiding tour pamphlets with maps (25¢). All are accessible from the road by wooden or paved walkways, usually extending ¼ to 1½ mi. through various natural phenomena. Some walkways are wheelchair accessible until they connect with longer hiking trails; check those tour pamphlets or ask a ranger to find out which ones are accessible.

Like spaghetti sauce on a very hot range, where steam pressure builds up at the bottom and explodes through the surface, groundwater is superheated by rocks and explodes through holes in the earth's crust in the form of a **geyser.** The geysers that made Yellowstone famous are clustered on the western side of the park near the West Yellowstone entrance. The duration of the explosion depends on how much water is in the hole and the heat of the steam. *Whether you're waiting for geysers to erupt or watching them shoot skyward, don't go too close, as the crust of earth around a geyser is only 2 ft. thick. Pets are not allowed in the basin.* **Old Faithful,** while neither the largest, the highest, nor the most regular geyser, is certainly the most photographed; it gushes in the **Upper Geyser Basin,** 16 mi. south of **Madison Jct.,** where the entry road splits north-south. Since its 1870 discovery, this granddaddy of geysers has consistently erupted with a whoosh of spray and steam (5000-8000 gallons worth) every 30min. to 1½hr. Enjoy other geysers (as well as elk) in the surrounding **Firehole Valley.** Swimming in any hot springs or geysers is prohibited, but you can swim in the **Firehole River,** three-fourths of the way up Firehole Canyon Dr. (head south just after Madison Jct.), or in the **Boiling River,** 2½ mi. north of Mammoth, which isn't really hot enough to cook ramen, let alone pasta. Check in advance to see that they're open, never swim alone, and always beware of strong currents.

From Old Faithful, take the easy 1½ mi. walk to **Morning Glory Pool,** a park favorite, or head 8 mi. north to the **Lower Geyser Basin,** where examples of all four types of geothermal activity (geysers, mudpots, hot springs, and fumaroles) steam, bubble, and spray together in cacophonous harmony. Farther north, 14 mi. past Madison, is the colorful **Norris Geyser Basin,** the setting for **Echinus,** a park gem. About every hour, this geyser slowly mounts its furious display from a clear basin of water. Its neighbor, **Steamboat,** is the tallest geyser in the world, topping 400 ft. and erupting for up to 20min. Lately, this steamer has been tooting on an erratic schedule—its last enormous eruption occurred on October 2, 1991.

Shifting water sources, malleable limestone deposits, and temperature-sensitive, multicolored bacterial growth create the most rapidly changing natural structure in the park, the hot spring terraces at **Mammoth Hot Springs,** 20 mi. to the north of the Norn's Basin. Ask a local ranger where the most active springs are on the day of your visit. Also ask about area trails, which feature some of the park's best wildlife viewing.

The east side's featured attraction, the **Grand Canyon of the Yellowstone,** wears rusty red-orange colors created by hot water acting on the volcanic rock. For a close-up view of the mighty **Lower Falls,** hike down the short but steep **Uncle Tom's Trail** (over 300 steps). **Artist Point** on the southern rim and **Lookout Point** on the northern rim offer broader canyon vistas. All along the canyon's 19 mi. rim, keep an eye out for bighorn sheep. At dawn or dusk, the bear-viewing area (at the intersection of Northern Rim and Tower roads) should have you dusting off your binoculars.

Yellowstone Lake, 16 mi. south of the Canyon's rim at the southeastern corner of the park, contains tons o' trout but requires a **fishing permit,** available at visitors centers. *(10-day pass $10, season $20; ages 12-15 free; under 12 may fish without a permit.)*Catch a few and have the chef fry them for you in the **Lake Yellowstone Hotel Dining Room.** Some other lakes and streams allow catch-and-release fishing only. **Bridge Bay Tackle** (242-7326), at Bridge Bay Dock, rents spinning rods ($7.50 per day; $20 deposit; open June-Sept. daily 8am-9pm). To go boating or even floating on the lake, you'll need a **boating permit** (motorized vessels $10 for 10-day pass; motor-free boats $5 for 10-day pass), available at many ranger stations, backcountry offices (check *Yellowstone Today*), Bridge Bay marina, a few park entrances, and the Lewis Lake campground. **AmFac** (344-7311) rents row boats, outboards, and dockslips at Bridge Bay Marina, and runs scenic cruises ($8.50, children $4.50) and guided fishing trips ($50-65 per hr.) on Yellowstone Lake. Nearby **Mud Volcano** features seething, warping sulfuric earth as well as the **Dragon's Mouth,** a vociferous steaming hole that early explorers reportedly heard all the way from Yellowstone River. You certainly can smell it from that far away.

Over 1200 mi. of trails crisscross the park, but many are poorly marked. Rangers at any visitors center are glad to recommend an array of **hikes** in their specific area for explorers of all levels. Most of the spectacular sights in the park are accessible by car, but only a hike will get you up close and personal with the multilayered petrified forest of **Specimen Ridge** or the geyser basins at **Shoshone** and **Heart Lake. Cascade Corner,** in the southwest, is a lovely area accessible by trails from the town of Bechler. (Be forewarned: getting to Bechler may require a circuitous route through Idaho over some unpaved roads.) The already-spectacular view from the summit of **Mt. Washburn,** between the **Canyon** and **Tower** areas, is enhanced when surveyed from the telescope inside the old fire lookout station. The **North Trail** is a mild incline; the **South Trail** is a little steeper. Trails in the **Tower-Roosevelt** area in the

ROCKY MOUNTAINS

Federal Wolf Packs

In January 1995, after years of public debate, the federal government began to reintroduce gray wolves into the greater Yellowstone ecosystem. Before the program, the last known wolves in Yellowstone were killed in 1929 as part of a federally funded bounty hunt to eradicate the predators. Local and state response to the federal initiative has been mixed. Many ranchers have violently denounced the reappearance of wolves, fearing they will kill livestock. Others hail the program as the first step in a return to a healthy ecosystem. Montana's State Senate and House of Representatives responded with a caustic joint resolution that made their position clear: "Now, therefore, be it resolved that if the United States government is successful in its efforts to reintroduce wolves into the Yellowstone Park ecosystem, the U.S. Congress be urged to take the steps necessary to ensure that wolves are also reintroduced into every other ecosystem and region of the United States, including Central Park in New York City, the Presidio in San Francisco, and Washington, D.C."

northeast of the park provide some of the most abundant wildlife watching. When planning a hike, pick up a topographical trail map ($8-9) at any visitors center and ask a ranger to describe forks in the trail. Allow yourself extra time (at least 1hr. per day) in case you lose the trail.

■ Grand Teton

When French fur trappers first peered into Wyoming's wilderness from the eastern border of Idaho, they found themselves facing three craggy peaks, each over 12,000 ft. In an attempt to make the rugged landscape seem more trapper-friendly, they dubbed the mountains "Les Trois Tetons," French for "the three tits." When they found that these triple nipples had numerous smaller companions, they named the entire range "Les Grands Tetons." Now, the snowy heights of **Grand Teton National Park** delight hikers and nature lovers with miles of strenuous trails. The less adventurous will appreciate the rugged appearance of the range; the lofty pinnacles and glistening glaciers are nearly as impressive when viewed from the valley.

ORIENTATION AND PRACTICAL INFORMATION

The national park occupies most of the space between Jackson to the south and Yellowstone National Park to the north. **Rockefeller Pkwy.** runs the length of the valley between the Gros Ventre Mountains and the Tetons, connecting the two parks. The parkway offers dramatic views of the entire length of the Tetons. At dusk, moose, elk, and other big game are visible from the road. The park is accessible from all directions except the west, as those poor French trappers found out centuries ago. The park **entrance fee** is $20 per car, $10 per pedestrian or bicycle, and $15 per motorcycle. The pass is good for 7 days in both the Tetons and Yellowstone. There are several recreational areas; the most developed is **Colter Bay;** the most beautiful is **Jenny Lake.** These areas and their surrounding trailheads are excellent places to begin exploring the Tetons.

> **Visitor Info: Moose Visitors Center** (739-3399), Teton Park Rd., at the southern tip of the park. Open daily 8am-7pm; early Sept. to mid-May 9am-5pm; mid-May to June 8am-6pm. **Jenny Lake Visitors Center** (739-3392), next to the Jenny Lake Campground. Open daily June to early Sept. 8am-7pm. **Colter Bay Visitors Center** (739-3594), on Jackson Lake in the northern part of the park. Open daily early June to early Sept. 8am-8pm; early May to mid-May and early Sept. 8am-5pm; late May to early June 8am-7pm. Stop by the Moose Visitors Center (or Colter Bay if you're coming from Yellowstone) to pick up the free *Teewinot* newspaper for a gold mine of info about hiking trails, camping, and facilities. For general info and visitors packet, contact **Park Headquarters** (739-3600) or write to the **Superintendent,** Grand Teton National Park, P.O. Drawer 170, Moose 83012.
>
> **Public Transportation: Grand Teton Lodge Co.** (733-2811) runs 6 shuttles per day in summer, from Colter Bay to Jackson Lake Lodge ($2.50 each way).
>
> **Info lines: Weather and Road Conditions,** 739-3611. 24hr. recording. **Wyoming Hwy. Info Center,** 733-3316 or 733-1731 (in winter only). **Backcountry Permits and River Info,** 739-3602.
>
> **Emergency: Sheriff's office,** 733-2331. **Park dispatch,** 739-3300.
>
> **Medical Services: Grand Teton Medical Clinic,** Jackson Lake Lodge (543-2514, after hrs. 733-8002). Open daily late May to mid-Oct. 10am-6pm. **St. John's Hospital** (733-3636), in Jackson.
>
> **Post Office:** In Moose (733-3336), across from the Park HQ. Open M-F 9am-1pm and 1:30-5pm, Sa 11am-12:30pm. **ZIP code:** 83012. **Area code:** 307.

CAMPGROUNDS AND BACKCOUNTRY CAMPING

To stay in the Tetons without emptying your savings account, find a tent and pitch it; call 739-3603 for camping info. The park service maintains five campgrounds, all first come, first served. Campsites are, generally, open mid-May to late September or early October (vehicle sites $12, bicycle group campsites $3). Maximum length of stay is

14 days at all sites except for Jenny Lake (7-day max. stay). All have restrooms, cold water, fire rings, dump stations, and picnic tables. RVs are welcome in all but the Jenny Lake area, but only Colter Bay (sites $31) and Flagg Ranch have hookups. Large groups can go to Colter Bay and Gros Ventre; all others allow a maximum of six people and one vehicle per site. The 49 quiet, woodsy sites at **Jenny Lake** are among the most beautifully developed in the U.S. Mt. Teewinot towers over 6000 ft. above tents pitched in the pine forest at the edge of Jenny Lake. These sites often fill before 8 or 9am; get there early. **Lizard Creek,** closer to Yellowstone than the Tetons, has 60 spacious, secluded sites along the northern shore of Jackson Lake. The campsites fill up by about 2pm. **Colter Bay,** the most crowded campsite, with 350 sites, $2 showers, a grocery store, a laundromat, and two restaurants, is usually full by noon. At **Signal Mountain,** a few mi. south of Colter Bay, the 86 sites are a bit more roomy than at Colter Bay, and are usually full by 10am. **Gros Ventre** is the biggest campsite (360 sites, 5 group sites), located along the edge of the Gros Ventre River at the southern border of the park, convenient to Jackson. Because the Tetons are hidden behind Elephant Butte, this campsite rarely fills and is the best bet for late arrivals. Reservations are required for groups of 10 or more. Call 739-3516 or 739-3473 (Jan.-May).

For **backcountry camping,** reserve a spot in a camping zone in a mountain canyon or on the shores of a lake by submitting an itinerary from January 1 to May 15 to the **permit office,** Grand Teton National Park, Moose HQ, Attn: Permits, P.O. Drawer 170, Moose 83012 (fax 739-3438). For more info, call 739-3309 or 739-3397. Beginning in 1999, permits are not free. Two-thirds of all backcountry spots are available first come, first served; get a permit up to 24hr. before setting out at the Moose, Colter Bay, or Jenny Lake Visitors Centers. Wood fires are not permitted above 7000 ft. in the backcountry and generally not allowed at lower elevations; be sure to check with rangers before singing 'round the campfire. Snow often remains at high-elevation campsites into July, and the weather can become severe (deadly to those unprepared for it) any time of the year. Taking severe weather gear is advised.

ACCOMMODATIONS AND FOOD

The Grand Teton Lodge Co. (543-3100 or 800-628-9988) runs both Colter Bay accommodations, which are open late May to early October. **Colter Bay Tent Cabins** (543-2828) are the cheapest, but you don't want to be here when the temperature drops. You might as well camp if you have a tent; the "cabins" are fairly primitive log and canvas shelters with dusty floors, wood-burning stoves, tables, and bunks. Sleeping bags, cots, and blankets are available for rent. (Tent cabins $28 for 2; $3 per additional person. Restrooms and $3 showers nearby. Office open June to early Sept. 24hr.) **Colter Bay Log Cabins** (543-2828) maintains 208 quaint log cabins near Jackson Lake. (2 person cabins with semi-private bath, from $31, with private bath from $61, 2 room cabins with bath $90-112. Open mid-May to late Sept.) The friendly staff dispenses sage advice about local hikes and excursions. Reservations are recommended. Make them up to a year in advance for any Grand Teton Lodge establishment by calling 800-628-9988 or writing to: **Reservations Manager,** Grand Teton Lodge Co., P.O. Box 240, Moran 83013. Deposits are often required.

The best way to eat in the Tetons is to bring your own eats. Non-perishables are available at **Dornan's Grocery** in Moose (733-2415; open daily 8am-8pm; in winter 8am-7pm), or at **Colter Bay Village General Store** (542-2811; open daily late May to Sept. 7:30am-10pm), which also sells deli sandwiches. In Jackson, you can stock up at **Albertson's** supermarket, 520 W. Broadway (733-5950), ½ mi. south of downtown (open daily 6am-midnight). At the **Chuck Wagon Restaurant** (543-1077), in Colter Bay, grab breakfast (buffet $6.50), lunch, and dinner; they'll even cook your catch of the day. The connected **Café Court** serves pizza ($4-5) and salads ($5-6) in a cafeteria-style setting during non-meal hours (open 7:30am-10pm; meals at restricted hrs).

SIGHTS AND ACTIVITIES

While Yellowstone wows visitors with geysers and mudpots, the Grand Tetons boast some of the most scenic mountains in the U.S., if not the world. The youngest mountain range in North America, the Tetons stand alone, almost without foothills, providing hikers, climbers, and rafters with vistas that more weathered peaks lack. Enjoy the views from hiking trails, or, if you're an experienced mountaineer, from the top of the Grand Teton itself, 13,771 ft. above sea level.

Jenny Lake's tranquility overcomes the steady tramp of its many visitors. The 6.6 mi. trail around the lake is gorgeous and relatively flat; 2 mi. in, it joins the **Cascade Canyon Trail.** The **Hidden Falls Waterfall** is located ½ mi. up the Cascade Canyon Trail. Hikers with more stamina can continue upwards towards **Inspiration Point** (another ¾ mi.), but only the lonely can trek 6¾ mi. further to **Lake Solitude,** which stands alone at 9035 ft. Before hitting the trail or planning extended hikes, be sure to check in at the ranger station, as trails at higher elevations may still be snow-covered. Prime hiking season does not begin until well into July during years with heavy snow.

Teton Boating (733-2703) shuttles across Jenny Lake every 20min. from 8am to 6pm (round-trip $4, ages 7-12 $2.25). Taking the boat cuts 4 mi. off the round-trip hike to the falls. Scenic cruises are offered every hour 10am-2pm ($7.50, children $4.50). They also rent boats ($10 for the first hr., $7 per additional hr., $45 per day). Free trail guides are available near the visitors center at the trailhead.

Hiking trails abound, winding their way through the stunning scenery. The 3 mi. walk from Colter Bay to **Hermitage Point** is popular for the scope of wildlife it encounters. Leave the crowds behind and hike the **Amphitheater Lake Trail,** beginning just south of Jenny Lake at the Lupine Meadows parking lot (lupines bloom June-July), which takes you 4.8 breathtaking mi. to one of the park's glacial lakes. Those who were bighorn sheep in past lives can butt horns with **Static Peak Divide,** a steep 15 mi. loop trail up 4020 ft. from the Death Canyon trailhead (4½ mi. south of Moose Visitors Center), which offers some of the best vistas in the park. The Death Canyon area is prime for longer 2-3 day hikes. All visitors centers provide pamphlets about the day hikes and sell many guides and maps ($3-10). **Grayline Tours** (733-4325 or 800-443-6133) offers 8hr. tours of the Tetons ($50; open in summer 7am-9pm; reservations required).

Stop by **Adventure Sports** (733-3307), in Moose, to rent outdoors equipment (mountain bikes $16 per ½-day, $24 per day). *(No bikes are allowed on trails in the park. Open 9am-6pm; spring and fall hrs. vary. Credit card or deposit required).* They also provide advice on where to bike around the area. **Snake River Angler** (733-3699), next to Moosely, rents spinning rods for $10 per day and fly rods for $12 (fishing lessons available; open in summer 8am-6pm). **Moosely Seconds** (733-1801), in Moose, rents crampons for $10 per day and ice axes for $6 per day (open daily 8am-9pm; shorter hrs. in winter). **Exum Mt. Guides** (733-2297) or **Jackson Hole Mt. Guides** (733-4979) offer 4-day climbing trips to the top of Grand Teton. Trips include instruction, food, lodging, and necessary equipment ($500-700 for the whole shebang).

For a leisurely afternoon on Jackson Lake, **Signal Mountain Marina** (543-2831) rents boats. *(Rowboats and canoes $8 per hr., $30 per ½-day; motorboats $16/$65; pontoons $45/$130; deck cruises $50 per hr. Open early May to mid-Oct. daily 8am-7pm.)* **Colter Bay Marina** has a somewhat smaller variety of boats at similar prices (open daily 7:30am-8pm). **Grand Teton Lodge Co.** (733-2811 or 543-2811) can also take you on scenic Snake River float trips (no whitewater) within the park. *(10 mi. ½-day trip $35, ages 6-11 $17; with lunch $40/$27; with dinner $46/$35 Tu, Th, Sa.)* **Triangle X Float Trips** (733-5500) can float you on a 5 mi. river trip for less ($21, under 12 $16). **Fishing** in the park's lakes, rivers, and streams is excellent. A Wyoming license ($6 per day) is required; get one in Jackson, Moose General Store, Signal Mt., Colter Bay, Leek's Marina, or Flagg Ranch. **Horseback riding** is available through the Grand Teton Lodge Co.; their info booth fields questions next to the Village General Store (1 and 2hr. rides, $21 and $31 per person).

In the **winter,** all hiking trails and the unploughed sections of Teton Park Rd. are open to **cross-country skiers.** Pick up winter info at Moose or Colter Bay visitors centers. Naturalists lead **snowshoe hikes** from the Moose Visitors Center (739-3399; Jan.-Mar.; snowshoes distributed free). **Snowmobiling** along the park's well-powdered trails and up into Yellowstone is a noisy but popular winter activity; grab a map and guide at the Jackson Chamber of Commerce. For about $100 per day, you can rent snowmobiles at **Signal Mt. Lodge, Flagg Ranch Village,** or in **Jackson;** an additional $10 registration fee is required for all snowmobile use in the park. A well-developed snowmobile trail runs from Moran to Flagg Ranch, and numerous other snowmobiling opportunities exist in the valley. The Colter Bay and Moose parking lots are available for parking in the winter. All **campgrounds** close in winter, but **backcountry snow camping** (only for those who know what they're doing) is allowed with a permit bought from the Moose Visitors Center. Before making plans, consider that temperatures regularly drop below -20°F. Be sure to carry high-tech extreme weather clothing and check with a ranger station for current weather conditions and avalanche danger; many early trappers froze to death in the 10 ft. drifts. Let the rangers know where you're going.

■ Jackson

Jackson Hole—called a hole rather than a valley due to the high elevation of the surrounding mountains—describes the area bounded by the Teton and Gros Ventre ranges. Nearby Jackson is a ski village gone ballistic—its downtown streets are lined with Gucci, Ralph Lauren, and Polo shops, chic restaurants, faux-Western bars, and wooden-plank sidewalks. Home to 5000 permanent residents, a dynamic mix of money and energy, international tourists and locals, people watchers, and nature lovers, Jackson is a truly cosmopolitan place. Although a sliver of the area's beauty can be seen from town, striking out into the nearby Tetons or onto the Snake River—whether by foot, boat, horse, or llama—yields a richer experience.

ORIENTATION AND PRACTICAL INFORMATION

The southern route into Jackson, U.S. 191/89/26, becomes **W. Broadway.** The highway continues along Broadway, becoming Cache St. as it veers north into Grand Teton Park and eventually reaches Yellowstone, 70 mi. to the north. The intersection of Broadway and Cache St. at **Town Sq. Park** marks the center of town. The Jackson Hole Ski Resort draws snow bunnies to **Teton Village,** 12 mi. to the north via Rte. 22, Rte. 390 and Teton Village Rd. The scenic **Moose-Wilson Rd. (Rte. 390)** connects the town of Wilson (at Rte. 22) with Teton Village and the Moose visitor area of Teton National Park; part of the road is unpaved and closed in the winter.

Public Transportation: Jackson START (733-4521). Fare $1; over 65 and under 9 free. **Jackson Hole Express** (733-1719) shuttles between Jackson and the Salt Lake City airport. Buses run W and Sa (daily in winter), leaving Jackson at 6:15am and Salt Lake City at 5pm (5-6hr., $45, round-trip $79). Reservations required.

Car Rental: Rent-A-Wreck, 1050 U.S. 89 (733-5014). $25-30 per day, $145-265 per week; 150 free mi. per day, 1000 free mi. weekly, 20¢ each additional mi. Must be 21 with credit card. Open daily 8am-6pm.

Equipment Rental: Hoback Sports, 40 S. Millward (733-5335). A complete, professional outdoor sports store. Mountain bikes $15 for 4hr., $25 for 24hr.; lower rates for longer rentals. Parabolic skis, boots, and poles $14 per ½-day, $22 per day. Open in peak summer and off-season daily 9am-7pm; in peak winter 8am-9pm. Must have credit card or cash for deposit. **Gear Revival,** 854 W. Broadway (739-8699), offers cheap gear and rentals. Rollerblades $10; ice axes and crampons $7.

Visitor Info: Jackson Hole and Greater Yellowstone Information Center, 532 N. Cache St. in a modern, wooden split-level with grass on the roof. A crucial info stop. Open early June to early Sept. 8am-8pm; during the winter M-F 8am-5pm, Sa-

Su 10am-2pm. Call either **Jackson Hole Chamber of Commerce** (733-3316) or **Bridger-Teton National Forest Headquarters** (739-5500), located inside.

Tours: Grayline Tours, (800-443-6133 or 733-4325). 8hr. tours of Grand Teton National Park ($50) and 11hr. tour of Yellowstone National Park's lower loop ($60). Call for reservations. Tour picks up at hotels. Office takes calls 7am-9pm.

Weather and Road Conditions: Weather Line, 733-1731. 24hr. recording. **Road Information,** 888-996-7623.

Hotlines: Rape Crisis Line, 733-7466. **Counselling Line,** 733-2046.

Internet Access: Cyber City, corner of W. Broadway and Millward St (734-1264).

Post Office: (733-3650), corner of Powderhorn and Maple Way (1 block from McDonald's). Open M-F 7:30am-5:30pm, Sa 10am-2pm. **ZIP code:** 83002. **Area code:** 307.

ACCOMMODATIONS AND CAMPGROUNDS

Jackson's constant influx of tourists ensures that if you don't book ahead, rooms will be small and expensive at best and non-existent at worst. Fortunately, you can sleep affordably in one of two local hostels. **The Hostel X,** P.O. Box 546, Teton Village 83025 (733-3415), near the ski slopes and 12 mi. northwest of Jackson, is a budget oasis among the wallet-parching condos and lodges of Teton Village. Its location makes it a favorite of skiers. X has a funkily decorated game room/TV room, ski-waxing room, nursery room, and nightly ski movies in the winter. Accommodations range from dorm-style rooms to private rooms. (4 beds in dorm rooms; 20 rooms with king-size beds. $36 for 1-2 people, nonmembers $47; $60 for 3-4. In winter, $44 for 1-2; $56 for 3-4; no member discount.) **The Bunkhouse,** 215 N. Cache St. (733-3668), in the basement of the Anvil Motel, has a lounge, kitchenette (no stove), coin laundry, ski storage, and, as the name implies, one large and quiet sleeping room with comfy bunks ($15). The price and convenient location to town make The Bunkhouse one of Jackson's best no-frills deals. **The Pioneer,** 325 N. Cache St. (733-3673 or 800-550-0330), is a bargain during the spring. It offers lovely rooms with teddy bears and stupendous hand-crafted quilts. (Singles peak at $90 in July; off-peak $45.)

While it doesn't offer scenery, Jackson's campground, the **Wagon Wheel Village,** 435 N. Cache St. (733-4588), welcomes tents and RVs on a first come, first served basis (9 tent sites $13; 32 RV sites with full hookup $29; showers 25¢). **KOA Kampground** (733-5354 or 800-KOA/562-9043), on Teton Village Rd. 1 mi. south of Teton Village, offers shaded sites with a view of the Teton Range. (62 sites. $25 for 1-2 people; $4.50 per additional person, full hookup $33. Free showers and pay laundry machines are available.) Cheaper sites and more pleasant surroundings are offered in the **Bridger-Teton National Forest** (739-5500) surrounding Jackson. Stop at the Greater Yellowstone Information Center for information about the sites, then drive toward Alpine Junction on U.S. 26/89 to find spots. (Some sites are free; all under $10 for 1 vehicle. Water available at some sites. No showers.)

SOMETHIN' TO MUNCH ON

The Bunnery, 130 N. Cache St. (733-5474), in the "Hole-in-the-Wall" mall, has hearty breakfasts. An egg scrambled with diced ham and cheddar, homefries, and their special OSM bread (made of oats, sunflower, and millet) goes for $6; lunch sandwiches cost $6. (Open daily 7am-3pm; late May to mid-Sept. 5:30pm-9pm.) For a homeopathic remedy, or just a healthy bite to eat, try the **Harvest,** 130 W. Broadway (733-5418), a New Age jack of all trades. Stop in for *huevos rancheros* ($5), fresh pastries ($2), and $3-4 smoothies. (Open daily 7:30am-3pm.) Chow down on barbecued chicken and spare ribs ($8) at the colorful and popular **Bubba's,** 515 W. Broadway (733-2288). They don't take reservations, so come early. (Open daily 7am-9pm.) **LeJay's 24 Hour Sportsmen Café** (733-3110), at the corner of Glenwood and Pearl, makes up for its lack of legitimate athletes with a good, cheap, and filling menu (burgers and sandwiches with fries $4-7; breakfast special $5), in a lively, wrangler-meets-bohemian atmosphere (open 24hr). Sit back with steak 'n' potatoes and appreciate the cowboy yodeling at the **Bar J Chuckwagon** (800-905-2275 for reservations) supper and Western show on Teton Village Rd., 1 mi. from Rte. 22 ($14-18, under 9 $5, lap-sized free; opens 5:30pm, dinner show at 8:30pm).

OUTDOOR ADVENTURES

Whitewater rafting draws nearly 200,000 city slickers and backwoods folk to Jackson between mid-May and early September. **Lone Eagle Expeditions** (377-1090 or 800-321-3800) is one of the best deals available among the myriad whitewater outfitters in Jackson. $30 buys a 3hr., 8 mi. whitewater rafting trip, a hot meal, and free access to the company's hot tub, heated pool, and hot showers after the trip. **Mad River Boat Trips,** 1255 S. U.S. 89 (733-6203 or 800-458-RAFT/7238), was the whitewater consultant for *A River Runs Through It*. A 3hr., 8 mi. raft trip ($30) leaves hourly 9am-2pm; a $25 trip leaves at 3pm. Reservations are required by both outfitters. Cheaper thrills include a lift up to the summit of **Rendezvous Peak** at 10,450 ft. *(The Tram runs mid-June to Aug. 9am-7pm; May 23 to mid-June and Sept. 9am-5pm. $15, seniors $13, ages 6-17 $6. The tourist office offers coupons for $2 off.)* The tram earns a great view of the Tetons and provides access to the Teton Crest trail without the climb to the top. Ride the **Snow King Chairlift** (733-5200) to the peak of Snow King Mountain (7751 ft.) for a bird's eye view of Jackson and another great view of the Tetons ($8, seniors $6, under 12 $6). The **Panorama House** (733-7348) provides a summit rest stop; try some stew and enjoy the view. In winter, the **Jackson Hole Ski Resort** (733-2292), at Teton Village, offers a huge 4139 ft. vertical drop, dry Wyoming powder, open bowls, tree skiing, and some of the best extreme skiing in the West. **Corbet's Couloir** is one of the steepest chutes accessible by lift in the U.S. ($51, seniors and under 14 $26). Right above Jackson, **Snow King** offers additional skiing (1571 ft. drop; $28, seniors and under 14 $18). On rainy days, keen depictions of the local fauna can be found at the **National Museum of Wildlife Art** (733-5771), 2½ mi. north of Jackson on U.S. 89. *(Open in summer daily 9am-5pm; in spring and fall M-F 9am-5pm, Sa-Su 1pm-5pm. $6, students and seniors $5, under 6 free. Tours at 1pm.)* The den, rather than displaying taxidermy, overlooks the National Elk Refuge. Inside, the museum houses the nation's largest collection of wilderness art.

ENTERTAINMENT AND NIGHTLIFE

Cultural activities in Jackson range from rowdy, foot-stomping Western celebrations to more sedate presentations of music and art. Every summer evening (except Su) at 6:30pm, the Town Sq., at the corner of Broadway and Cache St., hosts a kitschy episode of the **Longest-Running Shoot-Out in the World.** At the end of May, the town celebrates the opening of the **Jackson Hole Rodeo** (733-2805; late May to early Sept. W and Sa 8pm; tickets $8, ages 4-12 $6). The **Grand Teton Music Festival** (733-1128) features some of the world's best orchestras from early July to late August. (Festival orchestra concerts F-Sa 8pm are $27. Spotlight concerts Th 8pm are $18 and chamber music concerts Tu-W 8pm are $15. Open rehearsal Th 9:30am $5, students $2.50.) Over Memorial Day weekend, the town bursts its britches as tourists, locals, and nearby Native American tribes pour in for the dances and parades of **Old West Days.** From September 11-20, 1999, the **Jackson Hole Fall Arts Festival** (733-3216) attracts crafters, dancers, actors, and musicians to town. Learn the fine points of brewing from the knowledgeable owner of **Otto Brothers Brewery** (733-9000), in downtown Wilson on Northwest St. Free tours include a sample of his unique homemade products, such as "Moose Juice Stout" (open M-F 10am-8pm, Sa-Su 2-7pm).

The **Mangy Moose** (733-4913), in Teton Village at the base of Jackson Hole Ski Resort, is the quintessential *après*-ski bar. Moose racks and skis line the wooden walls, contrasting with the bright ski parkas of the patrons. Dinner is somewhat expensive. The eclectic but sporadic entertainment line-up has featured everything from Blues Traveler to Dr. Timothy Leary. (Cover $3-25. Dinner daily 5:30-10pm; bar open nightly 11:30pm-2am.) Thursday brings popular disco night to tiny Wilson at the **Stagecoach Bar** (733-4407), 7 mi. west of Jackson on Rte. 22, and live bands rock the bar Saturday and Sunday nights. A good selection of microbrews and a mix of locals and visitors make this an authentic Western bar. (Open daily 11am-2am.) For local ales, head to one of the most popular restaurant/bars in the area, **Snake River Brewery,** 265 Millward St. (739-2337), Wyoming's first brew-pub; the "Zonkers Stout" will put hair on your chest (pints $3, pitchers $10), while the pasta, sandwiches, and pizzas ($7-12) will fill your tummy (open M-Th and Su noon-midnight, F-Sa noon-1am). Western saddles serve as bar stools at the **Million Dollar Cowboy Bar,** 25 N. Cache St. (733-2207), Town Sq. This Jackson institution, attracting few locals or real cowboys, clearly caters to tourists. (Live music M-Sa 9pm-2am. Cover $3-10 after 8pm. Open M-Sa 10am-2am, Su noon-midnight.)

■ Cody

William F. "Buffalo Bill" Cody was more than a Pony Express rider, scout, hunter, and sportsman. He also started "Buffalo Bill's Wild West Show," an extravaganza that catapulted the image of the cowboy into the world's imagination. Cody's show traveled all over the U.S. and Europe, attracting the attention of royalty and statesmen. Founded in 1896 by Cody, this "wild west" town bearing his name conceals remnants of an authentic past beneath a pricey tourist facade.

From June through August, Cody turns into "The Rodeo Capital of the World" with one every night at 8:30pm, off Yellowstone Ave. west of town (587-5155; tickets $10-12, ages 7-12 $4-6). On July 1-4, 1999, the **Cody Stampede** (587-5155) rough-rides into town (tickets $15; reserve ahead). Historic buildings from all over Wyoming were hijacked, dismembered, and reassembled to form the **Old Trail Town** (587-5302), 3 mi. west of the city center off Yellowstone Ave. Buried nearby are several folk heroes of the Old West. (Open daily 8am-7pm; off-season hrs. vary; $3, under 12 free.) The **Buffalo Bill Historical Center,** 720 Sheridan Ave. (587-4771), is known affectionately as the "Smithsonian of the West" and composed of four museums under one roof. **The Buffalo Bill Museum** documents the life of you-know-who; the **Whitney Gallery of Western Art** shows off Western paintings, including a few Remingtons; the **Plains Indian Museum** contains several exhibits about its namesake group; and the **Cody Firearms Museum** holds the world's largest collection of American firearms. (Open June-Sept. daily 7am-8pm; Oct. 8am-5pm; Nov.-Mar. Th-M 10am-2pm; Apr. 10am-5pm; May 8am-8pm. $10, students $6, seniors $6.50, ages 6-17 $4. Tickets good for 2 consecutive days.)

For a dam good time, drive about 6 mi. west on Rte. 20/14/16 toward Yellowstone and see the mighty **Buffalo Bill Dam** (527-6076), which was the highest (350 ft.) dam in the world at the time of its completion in 1910 (open May-Sept. daily 8am-8pm; free). A variety of **rafting** trips on the Shoshone provide more energetic diversions (2hr. trip $15-18; ½-day $40-45). To make arrangements, call **River Runners,** 1491 Sheridan Ave. (800-535-7238); or **Wyoming River Trips,** 1701 Sheridan Ave. (587-6661 or 800-586-6661), and at Rte. 120 and 14 (both open May-Sept.).

Rates go up in the summertime, but a strip of reasonable motels lines **W. Yellowstone Ave.** The **Gateway Motel and Campground,** 203 Yellowstone Ave. (587-2561), has a gorgeous view of the surrounding hills and rents out cute cabins with A/C and kitchenettes (singles $40; doubles $45). Campsites run $10 for 1 person, $12 for 2; showers and laundry facilities are available (open May-Sept.). The **Pawnee Hotel,** 1032 12th St. (587-2239), is just a block from downtown (small singles with shared bath $22; doubles with private bath and phone $32-36). **Peter's Café and Bakery** (527-5040), at 12th St. and Sheridan Ave., fries up cheap breakfasts (6 buttermilk pancakes $2.50) and stacks a filling $2.75 mountain man sub (open M-Sa 7am-8:30pm, Su 7am-5pm). The **Irma Hotel and Restaurant,** 1192 Sheridan Ave. (587-4221), originally owned by Buffalo Bill and named after his daughter, has affordable lunch eats if not rooms (hot sandwiches $5). The original cherrywood bar was sent as a gift from Queen Victoria. (Open Apr.-Sept. daily 6am-10pm; Oct.-Mar. 6am-8pm.)

Cody lies at the junction of Rte. 120, 14A, and 14/16/20. The town's main street is **Sheridan Ave.,** which turns into **Yellowstone Ave.** west of town. **Powder River Transportation** (800-442-3682) runs buses to Denver (17hr., 1 per day, $79); Cheyenne (10hr., 1 per day, $65); and Billings (3hr., 1 per day, $27) from Daylight Donuts, 1452 Sheridan Ave. **Powder River Tours** (527-6316) offers guided daytrips ($49) through Yellowstone National Park and departs from several locations in town (reservations recommended). The **Chamber of Commerce**, 836 Sheridan Ave. (587-2297), can give you the lowdown (open M-Sa 8am-7pm, Su 10am-3pm; off-season M-F 8am-5pm). The **West Park Hospital** (527-7501) heals at 707 Sheridan Ave. **Post Office**: 1301 Stampede Ave. (527-7161; open M-F 8am-5:30pm, Sa 9am-noon). **ZIP code**: 82414. **Area code:** 307.

■ Buffalo and Sheridan

Not touristy enough to be traps, yet not small enough to make wayward travelers feel like unwanted outsiders, Buffalo and Sheridan are laid-back, friendly towns that provide a perfect base for exploring the Bighorn Mountains.

Buffalo Situated at the crossroads of I-90 and I-25, Buffalo lies appreciably close to **scenic byway U.S. 16,** a beautiful ride through the Bighorns. Before heading for the mounts, however, you may wish to absorb some of the character of the Old West in the elegant, entertaining rooms of the **Occidental Hotel**, 10 N. Main St. (684-7204), which opened its doors as the town hall in 1880. Noted guests once included Teddy Roosevelt and Buffalo Bill. (Open in summer daily 10am-4pm; free.) Those hankerin' after a bit o' frontier history can visit the **Jim Gatchell Museum of the West,** 100 Fort St. (684-9331), filled with dioramas and relics. (Open in summer daily 8am-8pm; winter hrs. vary; closed Jan.-Apr. except by appointment. $2, under 14 free.) A museum and outdoor battlefield exhibits are housed at the former site of **Fort Phil Kearny** (684-7629), at Exit 44 off I-90 between Buffalo and Sheridan (open daily 8am-6pm; Oct. to mid-May W-Su noon-4pm; $1, under 17 free).

In Buffalo, budget motels line **Main St. (Rte. 87)** and **Fort St.** The **Mountain View Motel,** 585 Fort St. (684-2881), keeps appealing pine cabins with TV, A/C, and heating. (Singles $40; doubles $44; in winter 1-2 people $35; big cabin with 3 double rooms $56, with kitchen $60. $5 per night discount with a stay of 3 or more nights. 16 campsites $15, full hookup for 2 $18. Showers and laundry available.) Next door, the **Z-Bar Motel** (684-5535 or 800-341-8000) has TVs with HBO, refrigerators, and A/C. (Singles $41, doubles $46; Nov.-Apr. $32/$36; kitchen $5 extra. Reservations recommended.) **Tom's Main Street Diner,** 41 N. Main St. (684-7444), is a great lil' eatery in the heart of downtown. Lunch specials ($4-5.50, including beverage) and bread pudding with whipped cream ($2.25) are best. (Open M and W-Sa 5:30am-2pm, Su 8am-1pm.) **Dash Inn,** 620 E. Hart St. (684-7930), offers baked chicken, ribs, and great Texas Toast for $6-9 (open Tu-Su 11am-9:30pm; in winter M-Sa 11am-8:30pm).

There is no bus service in Buffalo; travel by **Greyhound** (674-6188 or 800-231-2222) from either Sheridan or Gillette. At **Alabam's,** 421 Fort St. (684-7452), you can buy topographical maps ($4); hunting, fishing, and camping supplies; and **fishing licenses** (1 day $6, season $70; open daily roughly 7am-6pm). The **Buffalo Chamber of Commerce,** 55 N. Main St. (684-5544 or 800-227-5122), is at your service for town info (open June-Aug. M-F 8am-5pm, Sa 10am-2pm). The **U.S. Forest Service Offices**, 1425 Fort St. (684-1100), will sell you a map of the area for four greenbacks (open M-Sa 8am-4:30pm). **Post Office:** 193 S. Main St. (684-7063; open M-F 8am-5pm, Sa 10am-noon). **ZIP code:** 82834. **Area code:** 307.

Sheridan Sheridan is a bit bigger than Buffalo and about 10 mi. south of **scenic byway U.S. 14/14A,** a winding route marked by steep drops and spectacular views. Like its counterpart, however, this cowboy town is more than just another stop on the trail. **King's Saddlery and Cowboy Museum,** 184 N. Main St. (672-2702, 672-2755, or 800-443-8919) ropes 'em in with over 550 remarkably crafted, award-winning saddles on display. (Open M-Sa 8am-5pm; free.) Watch as ropes and saddles are made in their warehouse. Each saddle takes 4-6 weeks to complete and can cost $1800-6000. Another fine sight is the **Trail End State Historic Site,** 400 Clarendon

Ave. (674-4589) where you can tour the mansion and manicured gardens of rags-to-riches cattle baron and former governor John B. Kendrick's beautiful estate (open June-Aug. daily 9am-6pm, Sept.-May call for hrs; free). Buffalo Bill Cody used to sit on the porch of the once-luxurious **Sheridan Inn** (674-5441), at 5th and Broadway, as he interviewed cowboy hopefuls for his *Wild West Show*. (Self-guided tours $1; call ahead for guided tour $3, seniors $2, under 12 free). Locals flock to town on Sunday afternoons for a weekly **polo** game (June to mid-Sept.).

There are motels aplenty along Main St. and Coffeen Ave. **The Aspen Inn**, 1744 N. Main St. (672-9064), offers the best deal (singles $29; doubles $36). Adventure seekers have been known to spend one night free just off Coffeen Ave. in grassy **Washington Park.** Good food awaits at **Sanford's Grub Pub and Brewery,** 1 E. Alger Ave. (674-1722). They have nearly 40 sandwiches ($5.75-6.50), from the "Fat Albert" to the "Fonz-A-Relli," 20 different salads ($2.50-6.25) and bikes and kayaks hanging from the ceiling. (Open daily 11am-10pm.) **The Mint Bar,** 151 Main St. (674-9696), has pleased customers since 1907. Stop in for a sample of the local beer or a free walking tour of the stuffed game and rodeo memorabilia on display. (Open M-Sa 8am-2am.)

Greyhound (674-6188 or 800-231-2222) buses leave twice daily for Billings (2hr., $28) and Cheyenne (8hr., $46.20) from the Texaco station at the Evergreen Inn, 580 E. 5th St. (terminal open May-Nov. 24hr., Dec.-Apr. 3am-10pm). The **Chamber of Commerce** (672-2485 or 800-453-3650) sits just off I-90 at Exit 23. To contact a **Ranger station,** call 672-0751. **Post Office:** 101 E. Laucks St. (672-0713; open M-F 7:30am-5pm, Sa 8am-noon). **ZIP code:** 82801. **Area code:** 307.

■ Bighorn Mountains

The Bighorns erupt from the hilly pasture land of northern Wyoming, a dramatic backdrop to grazing cattle, sprawling ranch houses, and valleys full of wildflowers. Visitors can hike through the woods or follow **scenic highways U.S. 14/14A** and **U.S. 16** to waterfalls, layers of prehistoric rock, and views above the clouds. The **Medicine Wheel** on U.S. 14A is a mysterious stone formation at 10,000 ft. dating from around AD 1300; prepare for a ½ mi. hike from where the dirt road off the highway ends. For sheer solitude, poke your head above **Cloud Peak Wilderness** in the **Bighorn National Forest.** To get to Cloud Peak, a 13,175 ft. summit in the range, most hikers enter at **West Tensleep Trailhead,** accessible from the town of **Tensleep** on the western slope, 55 mi. west of Buffalo on U.S. 16. Tensleep was so named because it took the Sioux 10 sleeps to travel from there to their main winter camps. You must register at major trailheads to enter the Cloud Peak area. The most convenient access to the wilderness area is from the trailheads off U.S. 16, around 20 mi. west of Buffalo. From the **Hunter Corrals Trailhead,** move to beautiful **Seven Brothers Lake,** 3 mi. off U.S. 16 on Rd. 19 (13 mi. west of Buffalo on U.S. 16), an ideal base for dayhikes into the high peaks beyond. You can also enter the wilderness area on U.S. 14/14A to the north. Check with a forest office to find out about more out-of-the-way treks, and always check on local conditions with a ranger before any hike.

Ranger stations can be found in **Buffalo** (see p. 583), Lovell (548-6541), and **Sheridan** (see p. 583), as well as within the park. Campgrounds fill the forest (sites $5-10). The new **Burgess Junction Visitors Center** (672-0757), off U.S. 14A about halfway into the area, houses more info and a theater with several films on the surroundings (open daily mid-May to mid-Sept. 8:30am-5pm). **Doyle Campground,** near a fish-rich creek, has 19 sites and toilets, but no water. (Drive 26 mi. west of Buffalo on U.S. 16 and south 6 mi. on Hazelton Rd./County Rd. 3—it's a rough journey.) There is no fee to camp at the uncrowded **Elgin Park Trailhead,** 16 mi. west of Buffalo off U.S. 16, which promises good fishing along with parking and toilets. Off U.S. 14 (roughly 27 mi. in from I-90 in the east), the **Sibley Lake Campground** is one of several nice campgrounds ($10, with electricity $13; wheelchair access). For reservations within the park, call 800-280-CAMP/2267. Camping is also available along the Bighorn River at Afterbay, Two Leggins, Bighorn, and Mallard's Landing. For information about free off-road camping in the national forest area, call 672-0751.

In Lovell, the **Western Motel,** 180 W. Main St. (548-2781 or 800-773-2783), on U.S. 14A on the west side of the mountains, offers a hostelesque arrangement in two dorm rooms with a common area, kitchen, and laundry ($13; singles $28; doubles $30; kitchenettes $5 extra). **Area code:** 307.

■ Devils Tower

A Native American legend tells of seven sisters who were playing with their little brother when the boy turned into a bear and began to chase them. Terrified, the girls ran to a tree stump and prayed for help. The stump grew high into the sky, where the girls became the stars of the Big Dipper. Others tell of a core of fiery magma that shot up without breaking the surface 60 million years ago, and of centuries of wind, rain, and snow that eroded the surrounding sandstone, leaving a stunning spire. Still others, not of this world, have used the stone obelisk as a landing strip *(Close Encounters of the Third Kind)*. The massive, stump-like column that figures so prominently in the myths of Native Americans, geologists, and space aliens is the centerpiece of **Devils Tower National Monument** in northeastern Wyoming ($8 per car, $3 per person; free map on entry).

There are two types of people in this world: those who think Devil's Tower is the greatest thing west of the Mississippi, and those who think it's just a big, boring stump. **Rock climbers** probably fall into the former category. To scale the monument's 1280 ft. is a feat indeed. Be sure to register with a ranger both before and after you attempt to climb, and be aware that the park maintains no rescue team. Read about the rock and register at the **visitors center** (467-5283, ext. 20), 3 mi. from the entrance. (Open daily late May to Sept. 8am-7:45pm; Mar.-Apr. and Oct.-Nov usually 9am-4:45pm.) Cool **climbing demos** are given outside the visitors center (July-Aug. 11am and 4pm). Refrain from climbing the tower in June out of respect for the Native American ceremonies taking place there. For ground hikers, there are several **hiking trails;** the most popular, the 1.3 mi. **Tower Trail,** loops the monument and provides great views. Ask a ranger to identify leafy spurge and poison ivy for you; they irritate the eyes and skin. The park maintains a **campground** near the red banks of the Belle Fourche River. (Water, bathrooms, fireplaces, picnic tables, no showers. Sites $12. Open roughly Apr.-Oct.; call to be sure.) Although light on amenities, **Devils Tower View Store Campground** (467-5737) is also a good camping option a few miles before you reach the monument on Rte. 24, seeing as it's free (donation requested; open May-Sept.; port-o-potties only). To reach the monument from I-90, take U.S. 14, 25 mi. north to Rte. 24. **Area code:** 307.

■ Thermopolis

Smack-dab in the middle of Wyoming, Thermopolis serves as a cross-section of the state. Many of the earth's secrets reveal themselves here: hot springs bubble up from subterranean depths, fossil digs produce fragments of prehistoric eras, and the idyllic Wind River Canyon charts North America's geological development.

Home to the most voluminous **hot springs** in the world, this friendly town has the same tranquilizing effect on visitors as do its many soaking spots. At the renowned "Big Spring," which is only as wide as a large hot tub, you can look down at least 100 ft. into the aquamarine water. Local legend has it that when a ball and chain was lowered down into the spring, the bottom couldn't be found. In order to preserve the springs, no swimming is allowed in the natural pools. Who would want to soak in 135°F water reeking of sulfur anyway? But swimmers, soakers, and sliders can partake in their respective pleasures after all: some of the boiling hot water is mixed with icy cold water and pumped onto giant man-made waterslides at **The Star Plunge** (864-3771), next to the natural springs ($7, under 5 $2; open daily 9am-9pm). The **State Bathhouse** next door offers a more relaxed way to experience the springs.

Bathers can soak in the pleasantly warm waters (104°F) free for 20min. at a time. (Open M-Sa 8am-5:30pm, Su and holidays noon-5:30pm.)

Thermopolis hosts its own real-life rendition of Jurassic Park, though without the stunning special effects. The **Wyoming Dinosaur Center and Dig Sites** (864-2997 or 800-455-3466) includes, with pre-historic elan, both a museum and guided tours of excavation sites. (Open daily 8am-8pm. Museum alone $6; students, seniors, and children $3.50; dig site $10/$7; both $12/$8.) Follow the signs and the green dino prints through town to experience the joy of fossils.

Most accommodations here tend to be pricey (few singles under $30); however, you can find some cheap lodging if you leave the hot springs state park and find the pot of gold at the **Rainbow Motel,** 408 Park St. (800-554-8815). The rooms are from a more spacious Art Deco era, but you only pay by the bed. (1 bed $26, in summer $32; 2 beds $32/$42; 5 rooms with kitchenettes.) To save a buck, camp in **Boysen State Park,** 15 mi. south of Thermopolis on Rte. 20. The $4 sites are grouped along the Boysen Reservoir, which runs through the Wind River Gorge. Spend the night gazing at the sun-stained, striped canyon walls. Campsite info is available at the **Park Headquarters** (876-2796), off Rte. 20.

■ Casper

In its frontier heyday, Casper hosted mountain men, Mormons, friendly ghosts, Shoshone, and Sioux. Eight pioneer trails intersected near Casper, including the famed Oregon, Bozeman, and Pony Express trails. The convergence of those famous paths lives on in the minds of those who call still Casper by its nicknames, "the Hub" and "the Heart of Big Wyoming."

Casper's pride and joy is fascinating **Fort Caspar,** 4001 Ft. Caspar Rd. (235-8462), a group of reconstructed cabins that replicate the old army fort that guarded the N. Platte River on the western side of town. (Open in summer M-Sa 8:30am-6:30pm, Su 12:30-6:30pm. Museum open M-Sa 8am-7pm, Su noon-7pm. Free.) Inside the museum, seek out the 3 ft. tall "Pedro Mountain Mummy." The **Nicolayson Art Museum,** 400 E. Collins Dr. (235-5247), called the "Nic" by those in the know, exhibits Wyoming native work as well as some works by famous masters. The building also houses a children's art **Discovery Center** and an unaffiliated **Science Adventure Center,** two places where the kids can play while the folks are away. (Open Tu-Su 10am-5pm, Th 10am-8pm. $2, under 12 $1; free the 1st and 3rd Th of every month 4-8pm.) A few mi. southeast of town on Rte. 251, **Lookout Point** (on top of **Casper Mountain**) and **Muddy Mountain** (6 mi. farther) provide the best vantage points from which to survey the terrain. The **Central Wyoming Fair and Rodeo,** 1700 Fairgrounds Rd. (235-5775; July 13-17, 1999), keeps the townies excited with parades, livestock shows, and rodeos.

Bunk at the **Showboat National 9 Inn,** 100 W. F St. (235-2711 or 800-524-9999), which has large, clean rooms overlooking the interstate. All rooms have cable and breakfast included; the receipt earns a 10% discount at nearby eateries (singles $30; doubles $45). The oddly industrial **Fort Caspar Campground,** 4205 Ft. Caspar Rd. (234-3260), welcomes covered wagons. (Sites $12, $55 per week; $1 per additional person; full hookup $17. Free hot showers and laundry.) Sleep under the big Wyoming sky at **Alcova Lake Campground** (473-2514 or 473-8853), 35 mi. southwest of Casper on County Rd. 407 off Rte. 220, a popular recreation area with beaches (tents $6, full hookup $10).

Surprisingly good Chinese food is the best bet for a cheap, satisfying meal in downtown Casper. The **Peking Restaurant,** 333 E. A St. (266-2207), offers lunch specials starting at $4 and dinner plates around $7 (open for lunch M-Sa 11am-2pm, dinner 5-9pm). **La Costa,** 400 W. F St. (266-4288), in front of the Hampton Inn, serves up some of the best Mexican food in town. Burritos go for $6-7; a complete Mexican dinner is $7-9. (Open M-Th 11am-10pm, F-Sa 11am-10:30pm, Su noon-9pm.) Get the local scoop with your coffee at the **Blue Heron** books and espresso, 201 E. 2nd St. (265-3774), in the Atrium Plaza (open M-F 9am-5:30pm, Sa 10am-4pm). The **Casper Area Convention and Visitors Bureau,** 500 N. Center St. (234-5311 or 800-852-1889), has helpful info on camping and a good street map, essential to maneuvering around Casper (open daily 8am-6pm; in winter M-F 9am-5pm). **Powder River Transportation Services** (266-1904 or 265-2353, 800-433-2093 outside WY; ticket office open M-F 6-10:30am and 11:30am-8pm, Sa 6-10am and 3:30-4:30pm, Su 6-7:30am and 3:30-4:30pm), at I-25 and Center St. in the Parkway Plaza Hotel, sends buses to Buffalo (4hr., 1 per day, $24); Sheridan (5hr., 1 per day, $26); Rapid City (overnight, 1 per day, $45); Cheyenne (3hr., 2 per day, $31); Billings (6hr., 2 per day, $46); and Denver (7hr., 2 per day, $45). **Post Office:** 411 N. Forest Dr. (266-4000; open M-F 8:30am-5pm, Sa 9am-noon). **ZIP code:** 82609. **Area code:** 307.

■ Cheyenne

Originally the name of the Native American tribe that inhabited the wilderness of the region, "Cheyenne" was considered a prime candidate for the name of the Wyoming Territory. The moniker was struck down by vigilant Senator Sherman, who pointed out that the pronunciation of Cheyenne closely resembled that of the French word *chienne,* meaning, er, "bitch." Once one of the fastest growing frontier towns, Cheyenne has tried to maintain its Old Western image through simulated gunfights and rodeos, but much of its charm is found in historical downtown buildings.

PRACTICAL INFORMATION **Greyhound,** 120 N. Greely Hwy. (634-7744), just off I-80, makes daily trips to Salt Lake City (9hr., 3 per day, $65); Chicago (24hr., 3 per day, $131); Laramie (1hr., 3 per day, $13); Rock Springs (5hr., 3 per day, $53); and Denver (3-5hr., 4 per day, $23; station open daily 10:30am-4am). **Powder River Transportation** (634-7744), in the Greyhound terminal, honors Greyhound passes, busing daily to Rapid City (10hr., 1 per day, $49), Casper (4hr., 2 per day, $31), and Billings (11hr., 2 per day, $70). For local jaunts flag down one of the shuttle buses provided by the **Cheyenne Transit Program** (637-6253; buses run M-F 6:30am-6:30pm; fare $1). Check with the **Cheyenne Area Convention and Visitors Bureau,** 309 W. Lincolnway (778-3133 or 800-426-5009), just west of Capitol Ave., for accommodations and restaurant listings. The **Domestic Violence and Sexual Assault Line** (637-SAFE/7233) operates 24 hours. Cheyenne's **post office:** 4800 Converse Ave. (800-275-8777; open M-F 7:30am-5:30pm, Sa 7am-1pm). **ZIP code:** 82009. **Area code:** 307.

ACCOMMODATIONS, CAMPGROUNDS, AND FOOD It's easy to land a cheap room here among the plains and pioneers, unless your visit coincides with Wyoming's huge hootenanny **Frontier Days,** the last full week of July (see **Festivals and Sights,** below). Beware of doubling rates and disappearing rooms in the days approaching this week. Many budget motels line **Lincolnway** (U.S. 30/16th St.). **Hotel Plains,** 1600 Central Ave. (638-3311), conveniently located across from the I-180 on-ramp and 1 block away from the center of downtown, offers cavernous, retro hotel rooms with marble sinks and free cable (singles $35; doubles $43; $5 per additional person). Holster your peacemaker before walking into the **Frontier Motel,** 1400 W. Lincoln Way (634-7961), and grab a latté ($2) or an Italian soda ($2) at the front desk. Singles with a living room, large bathroom, free cable, and A/C start at $25. **The Ranger Motel,** 909 W. 16th St. (634-7995), has small rooms with TV, and free local calls (July-Oct. singles $25, doubles $30; off-season $22/$28). Nine miles out of town on I-25, the **Terry Bison Ranch** (634-4171) rents dorm-style doubles for $35. Camp at **Curt Gowdy State Park,** 1351 Hynds Lodge Rd. (632-7946), 24 mi. west of Cheyenne on Rte. 210/Happy Jack Rd. This year-round park is centered around two lakes with excellent fishing, horseback riding (bring your own horse), and archery. ($4 per night in addition to $2 entrance fee; $3 entrance fee for out-of-state visitors.) Cheyenne has a smattering of restaurants that provide reasonably priced cuisine. **Lexie's Café,** 216 E. 17th St. (638-8712), has cheerful, cottage-style decor featuring wicker chairs and flowers. You'll find filling breakfast combos for $4-6, towering stacks of pancakes for $3, and burgers for $5. (Open M 7:30am-3pm, Tu-Th 7:30am-8pm, F 7:30am-9pm, Sa 7am-9pm.) Relax with a light lunch at **The Java Joint,** 1720 Capitol Ave. (638-7332; salads and sandwiches $4-6), or simply enjoy a latté (open M 7am-4pm, Tu-Su 7am-5:30pm).

FESTIVALS, SIGHTS, AND NIGHTLIFE If you're within 500 mi. of Cheyenne during the last week in July (July 23-Aug. 1, 1999), make every effort to attend the **Cheyenne Frontier Days** (778-7222 or 800-227-6336), 9 days of non-stop Western hoopla. The town doubles in size as anyone worth a grain of Western salt comes to see the world's largest outdoor rodeo competition ($18 and up) and partake of the free pancake breakfasts (every other day in the parking lot across from the Chamber of Commerce), parades, big-name country music concerts, and square dancing. Throughout June and July, a "gunfight is always possible," and the entertaining **Cheyenne Gunslingers** (635-1028), at W. 16th and Carey, shoot each other Monday to Friday at 6pm (Sa high noon); their soda saloon sits at 218 W. 17th St. The **Wyoming State Capitol Building** (777-7220), at the base of Capitol Ave. on 24th St., shows off stained glass windows and aged photos of the frontier. Self-guided tours are available, or call ahead to reserve a guided tour (open M-F 8am-4:30pm). The **Old West Museum,** 4501 N. Carey Ave. (778-7290), in Lions Park, houses a large collection of old Western memorabilia, including a working windmill and a surrey with its original fringe. *(Open June-Sept. M-F 9am-5pm, Sa-Su 10am-5pm; in winter closes at 4pm. $4, under 12 free.)*

A country spot for the 21 and over crowd, **The Cheyenne Club,** 1617 Capitol Ave. (635-7777), keeps nightly themes (open M-Sa 7pm-2am). When you want to shoot stick in a haze of smoke, look for a pink elephant above **D.T.'s Liquor and Lounge,** 2121 E. Lincolnway (632-3458; open M-Sa 7am-2am, Su 10am-10pm).

■ West of Cheyenne

Laramie Laramie, the hoppin' home of the **University of Wyoming (UW)** (the state's only 4-year college), serves up collegiate coffee-shop chic with cowboy grit. Drifters can get a dose of youthful pluck in town and then relax in nearby **Medicine Bow National Forest** or **Curt Gowdy State Park.** From Cheyenne, take **Happy Jack Rd. (Rte. 210)** for a cow-filled scenic tour, or I-80 for expedience. Laramie does its darndest to bring its rough and rugged 19th-century history back to life in **Wyoming Territorial Park,** 975 Snowy Range Rd. (800-845-2287), a reconstructed frontier town that sells a suspiciously large amount of candy and souvenirs (open daily late May to late Aug. 11am-5pm; free). The adjacent **Wyoming Territorial Prison** (guided tours every hr.) and the **National U.S. Marshals Museum** offer fascinating glimpses into the relationship linking the U.S. marshals, the labor movement, Native Americans, and Western outlaws. (Open late May to late Sept. daily 9am-5pm; prison open Th-Sa 9am-6pm. $5.50, children $3.25, under 6 free; includes museum and prison.)

The sprawling **Motel 8,** 501 Boswell (745-4856), down the street from the Caboose on the outskirts of town, contains large rooms for your motel comfort (A/C, pool; singles $34; doubles $40; cheaper in winter). **Ranger Hotel,** 453 N. 3rd St. (742-6677), patrols downtown, placing many attractions within walking distance (HBO, fridge, microwave; singles around $30). Lined with hotels and fast food, **3rd St.** leads south into the heart of town, crossing **Ivinson** and **Grand St.,** both of which burst with student hangouts. **Jeffrey's Restaurant,** 123 Ivinson St. (742-7046), doles out heavenly homemade bread, and some of the best hot sandwiches, pasta dishes, and salads in Wyoming for $5-7 (open M-Sa 11am-9pm). The air in **The Home Bakery,** 304 S. 2nd St. (742-2721), is tinged with the smell of fresh flour and 100 years of bakery tradition, evident in the fresh loaves and cookies. Baked goods start at 40¢, and daily sandwich specials go for $3.63. (Open M-Sa 5:30am-5:30pm; deli closes 3pm.) Check your email or the local scene at the tragically hip **Coal Creek Coffeehouse,** 110 Grand Ave. (745-77370). Coffee drinks are their speciality ($1) but they'll throw together some "light fare" for $5-6. (Open daily 6am-10pm.) Both students and Harleys steer their way into the **Buckhorn Bar,** 114 Ivinson St. (742-3554), a neighborhood hangout featuring live music Saturday and Sunday nights, disco Thursday through Saturday, and busy pool tables (open M-Sa 6am-2am, Su 10am-midnight). UW students can honestly tell mom they spent the weekend in the **Library,** 1622 Grand Ave. (742-0500). Pull up a table in their stacks for a salad ($3-6), a $10 steak, or a daily special ($5). Next door, the library's more lived-in bar has $2 beers on tap. (Restaurant open Su-W 11am-9pm, Th-Sa 11am-10pm; bar open M-Su 10am-2am.) **Area code:** 307.

The Snowy Range

Local residents call the heavily forested granite mountains to the east of the Platte Valley the **Snowy Mountain Range** because snow falls nearly year-round on the higher peaks. Even when the snow melts, quartz outcroppings reflect the sun, creating an illusion of a snowy peak. After Memorial Day (May 24, 1999), the **Snowy Range Scenic Byway (Rte. 130)** is cleared of snow, and cars can drive 29 mi. through the mountains to elevations nearing 2 vertical mi. The Snowy Range is one part of the vast **Medicine Bow National Forest,** which is spread out over much of southeastern Wyoming.

Due to snow, campsites and hiking trails usually don't open until mid-July, although cross-country skiing is popular during the snowy months. In late summer, hike the challenging but short (2 mi.) **Medicine Bow Trail,** which starts at **Lewis Lake** and climbs to **Medicine Bow Peak** (12,013 ft.), the highest point in the forest. Nearby **Silver Lake** offers 19 first come, first served camping sites ($10). A little east, **Nash Fork** is another untrammeled camp setting, with 27 first come, first served sites ($9). All 16 of the park's developed campgrounds are open only in the summer and have toilets and water, but none have electric hookups or showers. Reservations for some campgrounds are available (800-280-2267; $7.85 reservation fee). A drive up **Kennaday Peak** (10,810 ft.), at the end of Forest Rd. 215 off Rte. 130, takes you to an impressive vista of the park's forest from a fire lookout tower.

Mountain biking is generally not allowed on the high country trails because of the frail alpine plants and the rocky terrain. However, you can bike on four-wheel drive roads and jeep trails in the high country or on trails below about 10,000 ft. The 7 mi. **Corner Mountain Loop,** just west of Centennial visitor center, is an exhilarating rollercoaster ride through a mixed forest of aspens, pines, and small meadows. During the winter, mountain biking and hiking trails are used for cross country skiing.

The **Brush Creek Visitor Center** (326-5562) is at the west entrance (open daily mid-May to Oct. 8am-5pm). The **Centennial Visitor Center** (742-6023) is 1 mi. west of Centennial at the east entrance (open late May to early Sept. daily 9am-4:30pm; in winter Sa-Su only). Stop by either for info on hiking and camping, or call the **Brush Creek Ranger District Office** (326-5258; open daily 7:30am-4:30pm) for general info about the Medicine Bow Forest. **Area code:** 307.

Saratoga

On the west side of the Snowy Range along Rte. 130, Saratoga, like its New York sister, is known for its **hot mineral springs.** Anywhere between 104° and 120°F, these springs will warm you up and won't leave you reeking of sulfur. These 24hr., free soaking wonders are located at the end of E. Walnut St., behind the public pool. A few feet away from the hot springs, the **North Platte River** offers excellent fishing. Fishing permits ($6) are available from the **Country Store** on Rte. 130 or **Great Mountain Outfitters,** 216 E. Walnut St. (326-8750), a riverside operation (rod rental $20; open daily 7am-7pm; off-season M-Sa 9am-5pm). The **Hotel Wolf,** 101 E. Bridge St. (326-5525), a renovated Victorian inn, is still a howlin' good deal (singles from $30; doubles from $34). The local favorite **Wolf Hotel Restaurant** (326-5525) serves everything from expensive filet mignon for dinner to reasonably priced sandwiches and salads ($5-6) for lunch (open M-Sa 11:30am-2pm and 6-10pm; Su 5-9pm). For a more casual dining atmosphere, drop in on **Mom's Kitchen** (326-5736), 3 blocks down Rte. 130 from Bridge St., where the "big daddy burger" will definitely fill you up for $5 (open Tu-Su 6am-8pm). Next door to the Wolf, **Lollypops,** 107 E. Bridge St. (326-5020), sells ice cream (single cone $1.50), latté ($2.25), and $2 gourmet lollipops (open daily 7am-10pm). Across from the Wolf, the **Lazy River Cantina** serves up Mexican lunch ($6) and dinner ($8) specialties (open M-Th 11am-2pm and 5-9pm, F-Sa 11am-2pm and 5-9:30pm, Su 8am-9pm). **Area code:** 307.

Colorado

The citizens of Colorado are proud of their state's thin air, in which golf balls fly farther, eggs take longer to cook, and visitors tend to lose their breath just getting out of bed. Oxygen deprivation also lures athletes looking to loosen their lungs for a competitive edge, but most hikers, skiers, and climbers worship Colorado for its peaks, which give rise to enclaves such as Grand Junction and Crested Butte. Meanwhile, Denver—the country's highest capital—serves as the hub for the entire Rocky Mountain region, providing both an ideal resting place for cross-country travelers and a "culture fix" for those heading to the mountains. Colorado's extraordinary heights are balanced by its equally spectacular depths. For millions of years, the Gunnison and Colorado Rivers have been etching natural wonders such as the Black Canyon and the Colorado National Monument. Early settlers mined Colorado for its silver and gold, the U.S. military burrowed enormous intelligence installations into the mountains around Colorado Springs, but most travelers dig their feet into the state's soil simply to get down and dirty with Mother Nature.

PRACTICAL INFORMATION

Capital: Denver.

Visitor Info: Colorado Travel and Tourism Authority, CTTA, P.O. Box 3524, Englewood 80155 (800-265-6723; http://www.colorado.com). **U.S. Forest Service,** Rocky Mountain Region, 740 Sims St., Lakewood 80225 (303-275-5350). Free maps; topographic forest maps $4. Open M-F 7:30am-4:30pm. **Ski Country USA,** 1560 Broadway, #2000, Denver 80202 (303-837-0793; open M-F 8am-5:30pm; ski report 825-7669). **National Park Service,** 12795 W. Alameda Pkwy., P.O. Box 25287, Denver 80225 (303-969-2000). For reservations for Rocky Mountain National Park, call 800-365-2267. **Colorado State Parks and Recreation,** 1313 Sherman St., #618, Denver 80203 (303-866-3437). Open M-F 8am-5pm. For reservations for any Colorado state park, call 470-1144 or 800-678-2267.

Emergency: 911.

Time Zone: Mountain (2hr. behind Eastern). **Postal Abbreviation:** CO.

Sales Tax: 3-4%.

Speed Limit: 75 mph (yee hah!).

■ Denver

In 1858, the discovery of gold in the Rocky Mountains brought a rush of eager miners to northern Colorado. After an excruciating trek through the plains, the desperadoes set up camps for a breather and a stiff shot of whiskey before heading west into "them thar hills." In 1860, two of the camps consolidated to form a town named after James W. Denver, the governor of Kansas Territory at that time. Between 1863 and 1867, Denver and nearby Golden played a political tug-of-war for the title of state capital. Today, Golden makes a lot of beer, while Denver, the "Queen City of the Plains," has become the Rockies' largest and fastest-growing metropolis, serving as the commercial and cultural nexus of the region. The city has doubled in population since 1960 and continues to attract diversity: ski bums, sophisticated city-slickers from the coasts, and, of course, old-time cowpokes. The gold that originally drew people to region may be depleted, but the city retains its best asset—its combination of charming urban sophistication and Western grit.

ORIENTATION AND PRACTICAL INFORMATION

Running north-south, **Broadway** slices Denver into east and west. **Ellsworth Ave.,** running east-west, is the north-south dividing line. Streets west of Broadway progress

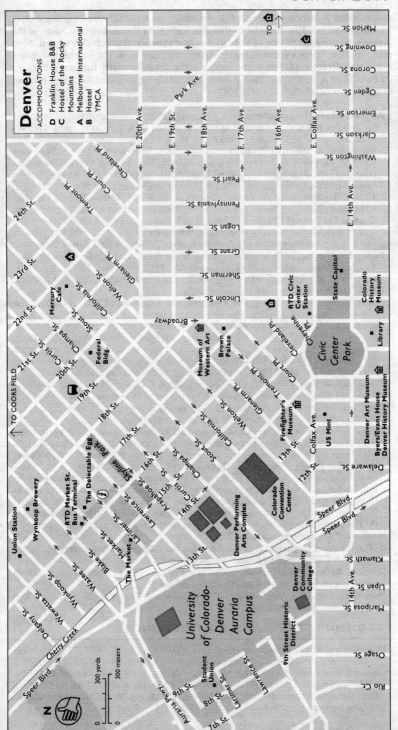

Denver

ACCOMMODATIONS
D Franklin House B&B
C Hostel of the Rocky
   Mountains
A Melbourne International
   Hostel
B YMCA

ROCKY MOUNTAINS

in somewhat alphabetical order, while the streets north of Ellsworth are numbered. Streets downtown run diagonal to those in the rest of the metropolis. Many of the avenues on the eastern side of the city become numbered *streets* downtown. Most even-numbered thoroughfares downtown run only east-west. The hub of downtown is the **16th Street Mall**. Few crimes occur in the immediate area, but *avoid the west end of Colfax Ave., the east side of town beyond the capitol, and the upper reaches of the* **Barrio** *(25th-34th St.) at night.*

Airport: Denver International (DIA; 342-2000), 25 mi. northeast of downtown off I-70. Shuttles run from the airport to downtown and ski resorts in the area. The **Sky Ride** (800-366-7433 or 299-6000) costs $6 to DIA from downtown; buses run hourly 5:45am-10:45pm. From the main terminal, **Supershuttle** (342-5454 or 800-525-3177) shuttles to downtown hotels (45min.-1hr., $15). A **taxi** to downtown costs $40. The **Airporter** (444-0808) heads north to Boulder (1hr., $14).

Trains: Amtrak, Union Station, 1701 Wynkoop St. (534-2812 or 800-872-7245), at 17th St. To: Salt Lake City (14hr., 1 per day, $107); St. Louis (25hr., 1 per day, $210); and Chicago (19hr., 1 per day, $159). Ticket office open daily 7am-9pm. **Río Grande Ski Train,** 555 17th St. (296-4754), leaves from Amtrak Union Station and speeds through the Rockies, stopping in Winter Park (Dec.-Apr. only, 2hr., round-trip $35, reservations required). Departs Denver 7:15am, Winter Park 4:15pm.

Buses: Greyhound, 1055 E. 19th St. (293-6550 or 800-231-2222). To: Santa Fe (9hr., 4 per day, $59); Salt Lake City (12hr., 6 per day, $31); St. Louis (12-19hr., 4 per day, $64); Colorado Springs (2hr., 6 per day, $11.25); and Chicago (15hr., 4 per day, $52). Ticket office open daily 6am-midnight.

Public Transportation: Regional Transportation District (RTD), 1600 Blake St. (299-6000 or 800-366-7433). "The Ride" serves Denver, as well as Longmont, Ever-green, Golden, and suburbs. Route hrs. vary; many shut down by 9pm or earlier. Fare M-F 6-9am and 4-6pm $1.25, other hrs. 75¢; disabled and seniors 25¢. Exact change only. Major terminals are at Market and 19th St., and at Colfax and Broad-way. The free 16th St. **Mall Shuttle** covers 14 blocks downtown and runs daily 5:45am-1am. The **Light Rail** services the perimeter of the city and suburbs.

Taxis: Yellow Cab, 777-7777. $1.60 per mi. **Zone Cab,** 444-8888. $1.40 base fare, $1.60 per mi. Phone numbers designed for the memory impaired.

Car Rental: Rent-A-Lemon, 8000 E. Colefax Ave. (393-0028). With a credit card $15.50 per day, $16.50 without. 50 free mi. per day. Must be 21.

Visitor Info: Denver Metro Convention and Visitors Bureau, 1668 Larimer St. (892-1112), near Civic Center Park just south of the capitol. Open M-F 8am-5pm, Sa 9am-1pm. It offers a free copy of the comprehensive *Denver Official Visitors Guide.* **Big John's Information Center,** 1055 19th St. (892-1505), at the Grey-hound station. Big John, an ex-professional basketball player, enthusiastically offers info on hosteling, tours around Denver, and daytrips to the mountains. Open M-Sa from 7am until Big John grows tired. **16th St. Ticket Bus** (623-1905), in the 16th St. Mall at Curtis St., is a double-decker bus with visitor info, ½-price tickets to local theater performances, and RTD bus info. Open M-F 10am-6pm, Sa 11am-3pm.

Hotlines: Rape Emergency, 322-7273.

Bi-Gay-Lesbian Organizations: Gay and Lesbian Community Center, 831-6268. Open M-F 10am-10pm, Sa 10am-8pm, Su 1-4pm.

Internet Access: Majordomo's, 1401 Ogden (830-0442). $12 per hr., students $9 per hr. Open M-Sa 7:30am-9pm, Su 11:30am-9pm.

Post Office: 951 20th St. (800-275-8777). Open M-F 7am-6pm, Sa 9am-1pm. **ZIP code:** 80202. **Area code:** 303.

ACCOMMODATIONS AND CAMPGROUNDS

Hostel of the Rocky Mountains (HI-AYH), 1530 Downing St. (861-7777). Right off E. Colfax Ave., the hostel is 12 blocks from downtown, next to 3 major bus routes and a trolley stop. The cheerful green-and-white structure offers bunks and baths ($11, linen $2) and private rooms ($20-30). Usually, the staff will pick up hostelers from the Greyhound depot or Union Station (call ahead). Rental bikes are available ($2), as are tours of areas surrounding Denver ($6-24). Reservations recommended.

Franklin House B&B, 1620 Franklin St. (331-9106). Cozy European-style inn within walking distance of downtown. Clean, spacious rooms. Free breakfast. Singles $30; doubles $35; $5 per additional person. Check-in before 10pm. Check-out 11am. Make reservations at least 1 month ahead.

YMCA, 25 E. 16th St. (861-8300), at Lincoln St. Divided into sections for men, women, and families. Laundry and TV rooms. Singles without bath (men only) $27, with shared bath $31, with private bath $36; doubles (women only) $50/$52. Weekly rates available. Must be 18. Key deposit $12 and ID. Reserve in advance.

Melbourne International Hostel, 607 22nd St. (292-6386), at Welton St., near the center of the LoDo district and 6 blocks from the 16th St. Mall. Day office in adjoining laundromat. Clean rooms with fridges, communal kitchens, and red rugs. The international mix of hostelers can relax on the outside patio. Dorms for members and students $12, nonmembers $14; private singles $22/$23; doubles $27/$32. Linen $2. Key deposit $10. Check-in 7am-midnight. Reservations needed June-Oct.

Two state parks lie in the Denver metro area. **Cherry Creek State Park** has 102 crowded sites among a few stands of pine trees ($7, with electricity $10; daily entrance fee $5). Take I-25 to Exit 200, then head west on Rte. 225 for about ½ mi. and turn south on Parker Rd. **Golden Gate Canyon State Park** offers 106 year-round sites (two have electricity). Take I-70 west to 6th Ave., go west towards Central City to Rte. 119, and then north 19 mi. (Sites $6-10; daily entrance fee $4.) Contact the **State Parks Office** (866-3437) for info on the parks; for reservations, call 470-1144 or 800-678-2267 (open M-F 7am-4:45pm).

FOOD

Downtown Denver is great for inexpensive Mexican and Southwestern food. Dining *al fresco* and people-watching are available at the cafes along the **16th St. Mall. Larimer Sq.,** southwest of the mall on Larimer St., has several more gourmet eateries. Along with sports bars and grills, trendy restaurants cluster around **LoDo,** the neighborhood extending from Larimer Sq. out towards Coors Stadium. Colorado's distance from the ocean may make you wonder about **"Rocky Mountain oysters"**; this salty-sweet delicacy (bison testicles) and other specialties can be found at the **Denver Buffalo Company,** 1109 Lincoln St. (831-1299).

The Market, 1445 Larimer Sq. (534-5140), downtown. Popular with a young, artsy crowd, suits, and hippies. Cappuccino $2, sandwiches $5, exotic salads $4-7 per lb. Open M-Th 6:30am-11pm, F-Sa 7am-midnight, Su 7am-10pm.

Mercury Café, 2199 California (294-9281), across from the Melbourne Hostel. Decorated like an old tea parlor. Homebaked wheat bread and reasonably priced lunch and dinner items. A slew of soups, salads, enchiladas and vegetarian specials for around $5. Live bands and swing Th and Su with low cover and free lessons. Open Tu-F 5:30-11pm, Sa-Su 9am-3pm and 5:30-11pm.

El Taco De Mexico, 714 Santa Fe (623-3936). Quickly prepared burritos ($3-4) satisfy your soul. Voted "Best Brain Burritos." Open Su-Th 8am-10pm, F-Sa 8am-2am.

Wynkoop Brewery, 1634 18th St. (297-2700), at Wynkoop across from Union Station in LoDo. Colorado's first brewpub is dedicated to brewing and serving beer (pints $3.50), various meals, homemade root beer, lunch, and dinner (burgers $5-7). Pool tables upstairs and an independent **comedy club** downstairs (297-2111). Happy hour M-F 3-6pm, $1.50 pints. Brewery open M-Sa 11am-2am, Su 10am-midnight. Free brewery tours Sa 1-5pm.

The Delectable Egg, 1625 Court Pl. (892-5720). Although one should never underestimate the egg (omelettes, egg skillets, egg salad all $5-6), the best deal here might be pancakes ($3) or french toast ($4). Open M-Sa 7am-2pm.

SIGHTS

One of the best tour deals around is the **Cultural Connection Trolley** (299-6000), where $3 takes you to over 20 of the city's main attractions (runs late May to early Sept. daily 9:30am-6:30pm). The fare is good all day on any local bus or light rail.

Buses come every 30min.; buy your ticket from the driver. The tour begins at the **Denver Performing Arts Complex,** at 14th St. (follow the arches to the end of Curtis), but can be joined at many local attractions; look for the green-and-red sign.

A modern reminder of Colorado's silver mining days, the **U.S. Mint,** 320 W. Colfax Ave. (405-4761), issues the majority of coins minted in the U.S.; look for the small "D" embossed beneath the date. *(Open M-F 8am-2:45pm, last W of the month 9am-2:45pm. Free 15min. tours every 15-20min. in summer; call for reservation Oct.-Apr.)* Shake your money-maker while strutting by a million-dollar pile of gold bars, or jam to the deafening roar of countless machines churning out 20 million shiny coins daily. Summer lines often reach around the block.

Don't be surprised if the 15th step on the west side of the **State Capitol Bldg.** (866-2604) is crowded—visitors from all over come to stand on it, exactly 5280 ft. (1 mi.) above sea level. *(Summer tours every 30min. M-F 9am-3:30pm, Sa 9:30am-2pm; winter tours every 45min. M-F 9:30am-2:30pm.)* The gallery under the 24-karat-gold-covered dome affords a great view of the Rocky Mountains.

Just a few blocks from the capitol and the U.S. Mint stands the **Denver Art Museum,** 100 W. 14th Ave. (640-2793), which houses a world-class collection of Native American art. *(Open Tu and Th-Sa 10am-5pm, W 10am-9pm, Su noon-5pm. $4.50; students, seniors, and children $2.50; under 5 free; free Sa.)* Architect Gio Ponti designed this 6-story "vertical" museum to accommodate totem poles and period architecture. The fabulous 3rd fl. of pre-Columbian art of the Americas resembles an archaeological excavation site with temples, huts, and idols. Housed in the Navarre Bldg., the **Museum of Western Art,** 1727 Tremont Pl. (794-6075), holds a stellar collection of Russell, Benton, Remington, and Bierstadt works (open Tu-Sa 10am-4:30pm; $3, students and seniors $2, under 7 free). **The Black American West Museum and Heritage Center,** 3091 California St. (292-2566), presents a side of frontier history unexplored by textbooks and John Wayne movies. *(Open May-Sept. M-F 10am-5pm, Sa-Su noon-5pm; Oct.-Apr. W-F 10am-2pm, Sa-Su noon-5pm. $3, students and seniors $2, ages 13-17 $1, ages 4-12 50¢.)*

Aviation enthusiasts can visit old planes such as the rare B-1A bomber at **Wings Over the Rockies Air and Space Museum** (360-5360, ext. 21), in hangar #1 at Lowry Air Force Base (open M-Sa 10am-4pm, Su noon-4pm; $4, seniors and ages 6-17 $2).

The mammoth **Red Rocks Amphitheater and Park,** 12 mi. southwest of Denver on I-70 at the Morrison Exit, is carved into red sandstone. As the sun sets over the city, performers like R.E.M., U2, and the Denver Symphony Orchestra have to compete with the view behind them. For tickets, call **Ticketmaster** (830-8497) or **Tele-Seat** (800-444-7328). Park admission is free, but shows run $25-45.

For outdoor folk, Denver has more public parks per square mile than any other city, providing prime space for bicycling, walking, or lolling about in the sun. **Cheesman Park** (take bus #10) offers a view of the snow-capped peaks of the Rockies (call 331-4060 for more info on Denver parks). **City Park** (331-4113) houses a museum, zoo, running path, and golf course. The **Colorado Division of Parks and Outdoor Recreation** (866-3437) has the low-down on nearby state parks (open M-F 8am-5pm). A local favorite is the **Roxborough State Park,** open year-round for day use only, where visitors can hike and ski among red rock formations. Take U.S. 85 S, turn right on Titan Rd., and follow it 3½ mi. to the park. Forty miles west of Denver, the road to the summit of **Mt. Evans** (14,260 ft.) is the highest paved road in North America (generally open late May to early Sept.; take I-70 W to Rte. 103 in Idaho Springs).

Incredibly, the best spot for bald eagles in Denver is also the town's most radioactive plot. The **Rocky Mountain Arsenal** (289-0232) is a nuclear waste site-turned-wildlife refuge. A shuttle bus to the arsenal departs from the corner of 72nd Ave. and Quebec St. (open for bald eagle viewing Sa 8am-3:30pm).

ENTERTAINMENT AND NIGHTLIFE

Every January, Denver hosts the nation's largest livestock show and one of the biggest rodeos, the **National Western Stock Show,** 4655 Humbolt St. (297-1166). Here, cowpokes compete for prize money while over 10,000 head of cattle compete for

"Best of Breed." Would-be westerners can hop on a ripsnortin' bull, or purchase any combination of shiny spurs and leather whips. **A Taste of Colorado** (892-7004), during the last week of August, and the Memorial Day weekend **Capitol Hill People's Fair** (830-1651) both feature a large outdoor celebration with food vendors and local bands at **Civic Center Park,** near the capitol. **Cinco de Mayo** (534-8342)—yes, on the 5th of May—attracts 200,000 visitors per year to celebrate Mexico's independence.

Denver's baseball team, the **Colorado Rockies** (702-5437 or 800-388-7625), lofts home runs out of **Coors Field,** at 20th and Blake St. (tickets from $8; some $4 Rockpile tickets available day of game). In the fall, the 1998 Super Bowl champion **Denver Broncos** (433-7466) puts on the blitz at **Mile High Stadium,** as Broncoitis spreads throughout the state. Soccer mania takes over during the spring and summer as the **Colorado Rapids** (299-1370) shoot for the goal at Mile High Stadium. Denver's NBA team, the **Nuggets,** and the new NHL squad, the **Colorado Avalanche,** squat in **McNichols Arena** (893-6700).

Denver's local restaurants and bars cater to a college-age and slightly older singles crowd. A copy of *Westword* gives the lowdown on LoDo. The "Hill of the Grasshopper," **El Chapultepec** (295-9126), at 20th and Market St., is an honest-to-goodness bebopping jazz bar that has survived since Denver's Beat era in the 50s. (No cover. 1-drink min. per set. Open M-Sa 9:30am-2am, Su 10am-1am.) A remodeled chapel, **The Church,** 1160 Lincoln (832-3528), offers four full bars (try a Fat Tire on tap), a cigar lounge, and a weekend sushi bar—that is, if Joe lets you off the dance floor. On weekends, the congregation swells with two floors of dancing. Wednesday nights swing with free lessons at 10pm. (Doors open Tu-Su 8-9pm until 1-2am.) **Charlie's,** 900 E. Colfax Ave. (839-8890), at Emerson, is a popular gay bar stomping with country and Western dancing (open daily 10am-4am).

■ Mountain Resorts Near Denver

Winter Park Nestled among delicious-smelling mountain pines in the upper Fraser River valley, Winter Park is the closest ski and summer resort to Denver (68 mi.; take I-70 W to U.S. 40). In the summer, mountain biking and hiking trails climb the mountains of the Continental Divide, while in the ski-season **Winter Park Resort** opens with a 3060 ft. vertical drop and 1373 acres of glade skiing. The **Winter Park Mary Jane Ski Area** (726-5514 or 800-453-2525) packs bowls all winter long, and has info on the resort. For snow conditions, call 572-SNOW/7669; they can also give you the rundown on golf, kids activities, and other summertime fun including the **Alpine Slide,** Colorado's longest at 1½ mi. (Open June to early Sept. daily 10am-6pm; mid- to late Sept. Sa-Su only. $6, seniors and children $5.) The **Zephyr Express** chairlift blows like the west wind to the summit of Winter Park Mountain, allowing mountain bikers to reach the peak, then ride down. (Open mid-June to early Sept. daily 10am-5pm; mid- to late Sept. Sa-Su only. Full-day $16.) The **High Country Stampede Rodeo** (726-5319) bucks the ski crowd every Saturday at 7pm in July and August at the John Work Arena, west of Fraser on County Rd. 73 ($8, children $4).

The **Viking Lodge** (726-8885 or 800-421-4013), on Rte. 40 in Winter Park, offers tiny singles and doubles with phones and color TVs. Lodgers have access to the hot tub and sauna and enjoy a 10% discount on rentals at the adjacent store, as well as winter shuttle service to the lifts. (Singles $30-35, doubles $35-40; in winter $40-60/$45-65.) Breakfast ($4-8) and lunch ($4-10) are served on the patio at **Carver's Bakery Café** (726-8202), at the end of the Cooper Creek Mall off U.S. 40. During peak season, dinner is, too. (Open daily 7am-2pm.)

The Chamber of Commerce (see above) also serves as the **Greyhound** depot (2hr., 2 buses per day to Denver; $13-$14). **Home James Transportation Services** (303-726-5060 or 800-451-4844) runs door-to-door shuttles to and from Denver Airport ($35; call ahead for reservations). The same number also connects with **Mad Adventures** river rafting (½-day $36; full-day $57, includes lunch). From December to April, the perennially late **Río Grande Ski Train** (303-296-4754) leaves Denver's Union Station for Winter Park (see **Practical Information,** p. 592). The **Winter Park-Fraser**

ROCKY MOUNTAINS

Valley Chamber of Commerce, 78841 U.S. 40 (726-4118 or 800-903-7275), provides info about all sorts of outdoor activities (open daily 8am-5pm). **Area code:** 970.

Summit County Skiers, hikers, and mountain bikers can tap into a sportman's paradise in the highest county in the U.S., about 75 mi. west of Denver on I-70. The **Summit County Chamber of Commerce,** 11 Summit Blvd. (668-2051), in Frisco, provides info on current area events (open daily 9am-5pm). The **info center** (262-0817), on Tenderfoot Ave. in Dillon, 1½ mi. south of I-70 on Rte. 6, is also a convenient stop (open daily 9am-5pm). The ski resorts of **Breckenridge** (453-5000), **Copper Mountain** (968-6477 or 800-458-8386), and **Keystone** (468-2316 or 800-255-3715) are good alternatives to the more expensive resorts of Aspen and Vail. **Arapahoe Basin** (496-7007 or 800-255-3715) usually has skiing until early July and occasionally into August, depending on snow conditions. The free **Summit Stage** shuttle bus connects all these resorts with the towns of **Frisco, Dillon,** and **Silverthorne.**

The **Alpen Hütte (HI-AYH),** 471 Rainbow Dr. (468-6336), in Silverthorne, has welcoming hosts, a familial atmosphere, clean rooms with beaütiful moüntain views, and year-round outdoor activities, including fly-fishing on the Blue River behind the hostel. Greyhound (from Denver) and Summit Stage stop outside the door. ($13, nonmembers $15; in winter $18-23/$20-25. Lockers with $5 deposit. Linen and towels $2. Laundry. Free ski storage. Mountain bike rental. Parking. Reception daily 7am-noon and 4pm-midnight. Lockout 9:30am-3:30pm. Midnight curfew. In winter, reservations recommended 1-2 months in advance.) Several Forest Service campgrounds lie nearby; wing it to **Eagle's Nest Wilderness** (sites $7-11). The **Dillon Ranger District Office,** 680 Blue River Pkwy. (468-5400; 800-280-CAMP/2267 for reservations), can supply more info (open M-F 8am-5pm; in summer also Sa-Su 9am-5pm).

Fashionable **Breckenridge** lies west of Silverthorne on I-70, 9 mi. south of Frisco. Despite the many expensive restaurants and stores, you can still find reasonably priced accommodations at the **Fireside Inn,** 114 N. French St. (453-6456), 2 blocks east of Main St. on the corner of Wellington. The indoor hot tub is great for *après-ski*. (Dorm $17, private rooms $45-65; in winter $27/$80-130. Closed in May.) The **Stage Door Café,** 203 Main St. (453-6964), offers a multi-level complex in which to enjoy a latté ($2.75) or a sandwich and watch the crowds (open M-Sa 7am-9pm, Su 7am-8pm). The nearby **Riverside Info Center** (453-5579), on the corner of Washington and Main St., dishes out the scoop on ski conditions and rentals (open daily 9am-1pm and 1:30-5pm). **Area code:** 970.

■ Boulder

Combining yuppie tastes with collegiate earthiness, Boulder lends itself to the pursuit of higher knowledge and better karma. It is home to both the central branch of the University of Colorado (CU) and the only accredited Buddhist university in the U.S., the Naropa Institute. Only here can you take summer poetry and healing workshops led by Allen Sandheim or Maya Angelou at the Jack Kerouac School of Disembodied Poets. In conclusion, Boulder rides, generation Boulder, fly—baby tabs two times, chillin'. We take you on the road, Jack.

ORIENTATION AND PRACTICAL INFORMATION

Boulder (pop. 83,000) is a small, manageable city, accessible by Rte. 36. The most developed area lies between **Broadway (Rte. 93)** and **28th St. (Rte. 36),** two busy streets running north-south through the city. **Baseline Rd.,** which connects the Flatirons with the eastern plains, and **Canyon Blvd. (Rte. 7),** which follows the Boulder Canyon into the mountains, border the main part of the **University of Colorado (CU)** campus. The school's surroundings are known locally as **the Hill.** The pedestrian-only **Pearl St. Mall,** between 11th and 15th St., is the center of hip life in Boulder. Most east-west roads have names, while north-south streets have numbers; Broadway is a conspicuous exception.

Buses: Greyhound, 4461 N. Broadway (443-1574). To: Denver (1hr., 2 per day, $5); Glenwood Springs (7-8hr., 2 per day, $36); and Vail (5½-6½hr., 2 per day, $30). Open M-F 8am-4pm.

Public Transportation: HOP, 4880 Pearl St. (447-8282). Shuttles connect the Pearl St. Mall, the Hill, CU, and the Crossroads Mall in a 2-way loop. Runs M-F 7am-7pm, with stops every 10min.; also Sept.-May Sa 7am-7pm every 15min. Fare 25¢, seniors 15¢. During term time, shuttles also run Th-Sa 10:30pm-2:30am every 20min. Fare 50¢, seniors 15¢. **RTD** (299-6000 or 800-366-7433), at 14th and Walnut St. in the center of town. M-F 6am-7pm, Sa-Su 8am-8pm. Fare 75¢, seniors 25¢; higher during peak hrs. To: Denver Airport ($8, seniors and under 12 $4); Denver ($3); and Coors Field (round-trip $4).

Taxis: Boulder Yellow Cab (442-2277). $1.60 base fare, $1.60 per additional mi.

Car Rental: Budget Rent-a-Car, 1545 28th St. (444-9054), in the Harvest Hotel. Must be 21 with major credit card. Ages 21-25 $50 per day, over 25 $35 per day. Unlimited mi. Open M-F 7am-6pm, Sa-Su 8am-3pm.

Bike Rental: University Bicycles, 839 Pearl St. (444-4196), downtown. Rents mountain bikes with helmet and lock $15 per 4hr., $20 4-8hr., $25 overnight; 3-speed bikes $10/$12/$15. Open M-F 9am-7pm, Sa 9am-6pm, Su 10am-5pm.

Visitor Info: Boulder Chamber of Commerce/Visitors Service, 2440 Pearl St. (442-1044), at Folsom about 10 blocks from downtown. Take bus #200; also accessible by HOP. Open M-Th 8:30am-5pm, F 9am-5pm. **University of Colorado Information** (492-6161), 2nd fl. of University Memorial Center (UMC) student union. Phones with free local calls. Open M-Th 7am-11pm, F-Sa 7am-midnight, Su 11am-11pm; term-time open Su-Th 7am-midnight, F-Sa 7am-1am, Su 11am-midnight. The **CU Ride Board,** UMC 1st fl., advertises rides and riders.

Hotlines: Rape Crisis, 443-7300. 24hr. **Crisis Line,** 447-1665 for counseling. 24hr.

Bi-Gay-Lesbian Organizations: Lesbian, Bisexual, Gay, and Transgender Alliance (492-8567), in CU's Willard Hall. Open M-Tu and Th-F 10am-3pm; Sept.-May daily 9am-5pm. **Boulder Campus Gay, Lesbian, and Bisexual Resource Center,** 492-1377.

Internet Access: Kiosks are scattered throughout the **UMC** (see **Visitor Info**).

Post Office: 1905 15th St. (800-275-8777), at Walnut St. Open M-F 7:30am-5:30pm, Sa 10am-2pm. **ZIP code:** 80302. **Area code:** 303.

ACCOMMODATIONS AND CAMPGROUNDS

After spending your money on tofu and yogurt at the Pearl St. Mall, you may find yourself strapped for cash and without a room—Boulder doesn't offer many inexpensive places to spend the night. In the summer, at least you can rely on the hostel.

Boulder International Youth Hostel (AAIH/Rucksackers), 1107 12th St. (442-0522), 2 blocks west of the main CU campus and 15min. south of the RTD station. From Denver, take the A or B bus as close to College Ave. as possible. Although it is located near CU housing and frats, the BIYH holds on to a family-like atmosphere. $15 gets you shared hall bathrooms, kitchen, laundry, and TV. Private singles $35 per night, $175 per week; doubles $40/$200. Shower and towels free. Linen $4. Key deposit $10. Lockout for dorms 10am-5pm. Curfew midnight.

Chautauqua Association (442-3282), off Baseline Rd. at the foot of the Flatirons. Turn at the Chautauqua Park sign and take Kinnikinic to Morning Glory Dr., where the administrative office is located, or take bus #203. For summer only, suites (2-person $48; 4-person $62), and private cottages with kitchens (4-night min. stay; 2 bedrooms $77; 3 bedrooms $98) are available. Reserve months in advance.

The Boulder Mountain Lodge, 91 Four Mile Canyon Dr. (444-0882), 3 mi. west on Canyon Rd. (which becomes Rte. 119). 25 sites in a grove of pines next to a creek. Pay phone, 2 hot tubs, seasonal pool, and free showers. Check-out 10am; no reservations for camping. Cramped 3-person sites $14; $5 per additional person; $84 per week. Motel rooms for 1 or 2 people in summer $44; in winter $59.

Camping info for **Arapahoe/Roosevelt National Forest** is available from the **Boulder Ranger District,** 2995 Baseline Rd., #110 (444-6600), Boulder 80303, at 30th St. (open M-F 8am-4:30pm). **Kelly Dahl** (46 sites) lies 3 mi. south of Nederland on Rte.

119. **Rainbow Lakes** (16 sites, first come, first served; no water) is 13 mi. northwest of Nederland: turn at the Mountain Research Station (CR 119) and follow the road for 10 mi. (open late May-mid-Sept.). The two gems of the forest are **Peaceful Valley** (17 sites) and **Camp Dick** (41 sites)—Peaceful Valley is likely to fill faster. Both lie north on Rte. 72 and offer cross-country skiing in the winter. All sites are $12, $6 per additional car, except Rainbow Lakes ($6; $3 per additional car). Reservations are recommended, especially on weekends.

FOOD AND HANGOUTS

The streets on the Hill surrounding CU and those along the Pearl St. Mall burst with good eateries, natural foods markets, and colorful bars. Many restaurants and bars line **Baseline Rd.** Boulder may have more options for vegetarians than carnivores.

The Sink, 1165 13th St. (444-7465), on the Hill. The restaurant still awaits the return of its former janitor, Robert Redford, who quit his job and headed to California in the late 50s. Surprisingly upscale new cuisine is served amidst wild graffiti and pipes. Burgers $4. Open M-Sa 11am-2am, Su noon-2am; food served until 10pm.

Creative Vegetarian Café (449-1952), on the corner of 19th and Pearl St., serves organic vegetarian food including wild mushroom tamales ($6-8) and the totally legal hemp burger ($6). Open for lunch M-F 11am-2pm; brunch Sa-Su 10am-3pm; dinner Su-Th 5-9pm, F-Sa 5-9:30pm.

Foolish Craig's, 1611 Pearl St. (247-9383). Craig foolishly gave the French crepe an American twist, a glaring example being the "Homer" crepe—Doh!—($6). Still, many locals enjoy these revolutionary crepes, some filled with avocado or pesto chicken ($5-6). Open M-F 7am-9pm, Sa-Su 8am-9pm.

Daddy Bruce's Barbecue (449-8890), on the corner of 20th and Arapahoe, is the place to go when you have a hankerin' for meat. You'll know it by the heavenly aroma of beef brisket ($5) and BBQ chicken ($7) floating out of this pantry-sized restaurant. Open M-Sa 11am-6:30pm.

Tealightful Treats

Plopped down next to the Boulder Museum of Contemporary Art is an honest-to-goodness **Russian teahouse** (442-4993), 1770 13th St., built by Russian artists and piece-mailed to Boulder, where the teahouse was assembled in 1998. *(Open M-F 7am-10pm, Sa-Su 8am-10pm.)* The building—a gift from the people of Dushanbe, Tajikistan—is owned by the city and leased to restaurateur Lenny Martinelli, who lays out a scrumptious, though somewhat pricey, spread. Still, it's more than worth the price of a cup of tea ($1-6) to sit on a *topchan* in this artistic wonderworld and contemplate life in ancient Persia.

SIGHTS AND ENTERTAINMENT

The **Boulder Museum of Contemporary Art,** 1750 13th St. (443-2122), focuses on contemporary regional art (open Tu-Sa 11am-5pm, Su noon-5pm; $2, seniors and students $1.50, Sa free). The intimate and impressive **Leanin' Tree Museum,** 6055 Longbow Dr. (530-1442), presents 200 paintings and 80 bronze sculptures that focus on Western themes (open M-F 8am-4:30pm, Sa 10am-4pm; free). Writers give readings in the Beat/Buddhist tradition at the small **Naropa Institute,** 2130 Arapahoe Ave. (546-3578), while others participate in meditation workshops (open daily 9am-4:30pm). The **Rockies Brewing Company,** 2880 Wilderness Pl. (444-8448), off Velmont, offers tours and free beer (pub open M-Sa 11am-11pm; 25min. tours M-Sa 2pm).

A perennially outrageous street scene rocks the Mall and the Hill; the university's kiosks have the low-down on downtown happenings. The **University Memorial Center** (492-6161), at Broadway and 16th St., hosts many events. On the 3rd fl., its **Cultural Events Board** (492-3227) has the latest word on all CU-sponsored activities. Late June through early August, the **Colorado Shakespeare Festival** (492-0554) suffers the slings and arrows of outrageous fortune (previews $10; tickets and backstage passes $12-36; student discounts available). The **Chautauqua Association** (442-3282) hosts the **Colorado Music Festival** (449-2413, ext. 11) from July to August (tickets $12-35; seniors $12, students $2 off). During the second week of September, tunes wail at the **Boulder Blues Festival** (689-8934; tickets $14-17).

■ Rocky Mountain National Park

Of all the U.S. national parks, Rocky Mountain National Park is closest to heaven. A full third of the park lies above treeline, with Longs Peak piercing the sky at 14,255 ft. Here among the clouds, bitterly cold winds whip through a craggy landscape carpeted with tiny wildflowers, arctic shrubs, granite boulders, and crystalline lakes. The area escaped industrialization in the early 20th century, sparing its natural splendor.

The city of Estes Park, located immediately east of the park, hosts the vast majority of would-be mountaineers and alpinists, who crowd the shopping malls and boulevards in the summer. To the west of the park, the tranquil town of Grand Lake, located on the edges of two glacial lakes, is a beautiful base from which to explore the park's less traversed but equally stunning western side. Trail Ridge Rd./U.S. 34 runs 45 mi. through the park from Grand Lake to Estes Park.

ORIENTATION AND PRACTICAL INFORMATION

You can reach the national park from Boulder via U.S. 36 or scenic Rte. 7, or from the northeast up the Big Thompson Canyon via U.S. 34. To get to Estes Park from Boulder, the **Hostel Hauler** (586-3688) will pick you up if you call before 9pm and arrange a shuttle for the next day ($15, round-trip $20).

Visitor Info: Park Headquarters and Visitors Center (586-1206), 2½ mi. west of Estes Park on Rte. 36, at the Beaver Meadows entrance to the park. Open daily mid-June to late Aug. 8am-9pm; late Aug. to mid-June 8am-5pm. Winter evening programs on park-related topics are offered Sa 7pm; in summer nightly at 7:30pm; a park introduction film is shown every 30min. 8:30am-4:30pm. **Kawuneeche Visitors Center** (627-3471), just outside the park's western entrance and 1¼ mi. north of Grand Lake, offers similar info. Open daily mid-May to late Aug. 7am-7pm; Sept. to early May 8am-4:30pm. Evening programs occur Sa 7pm. The high-altitude **Alpine Visitors Center,** at the crest of Trail Ridge Rd., has a great view of the tundra. Open daily late May to mid-June and late Aug. to mid-Oct. 10am-4:30pm; mid-June to late Aug. 9am-5pm. **Lily Lake Visitors Center,** 6 mi. south of Park Headquarters on Rte. 7, opens only in summer (daily 9am-4:30pm). Park **entrance fee** is $10 per vehicle, $5 per biker or pedestrian; the pass is valid for 7 days.
Park Weather and Road Conditions: 586-1333.
Hospital: Estes Park Medical Center, 586-2317.
Park Emergency: 586-1399.
Post Office: Grand Lake, 520 Center Dr. (800-275-8777). Open M-F 8:30am-5pm. **ZIP code:** 80447. **Estes Park,** 215 W. Riverside Dr. (586-8177). Open M-F 8:30am-5:30pm, Sa 10am-2pm. **ZIP code:** 80517. **Area code:** 970.

ACCOMMODATIONS

Although Estes Park and Grand Lake have an abundance of expensive lodges and motels, there are a few good deals on indoor beds near the national park, especially in winter when temperatures drop and tourists leave.

Estes Park

H Bar G Ranch Hostel (HI-AYH), 3500 H Bar G Rd. (586-3688; fax 586-5004). Turn off U.S. 34 onto Dry Gulch Rd. 1 mi. east of town at Sombrero Stable; follow this road to CO 61. At H Bar G Rd., turn right. With its spectacular views of the mountains and Estes Valley, this converted ranch could be a luxury resort. Instead, its cabins, tennis court, recreation room, and kitchen entertain up to 100 hostelers. Proprietor Lou drives guests to town or the park entrance at 7:40am, then retrieves them from the Chamber of Commerce at 5pm. HI-AYH members only. $10. Open late May to mid-Sept. Call ahead, and bring a warm sleeping bag.

The Colorado Mountain School, 351 Moraine Ave. (586-5758; fax 586-5796). Tidy, dorm-style accommodations are open to travelers unless already booked by mountain-climbing students. Wood bunks with comfortable mattresses, linen, and showers. 17 beds. $20, $14 per additional person. Check-out 10am. Reservations recommended 1 week in advance.

YMCA of the Rockies, 2515 Tunnel Rd. (586-3341), follow Rte. 36 to Rte. 66. It's fun to stay at the YMCA; extensive facilities including mini-golf and a pool on the 1400-acre complex, as well as daily hikes for guests. A 4-person cabin with kitchen and bath from $52. A 1-day guest membership is required to stay ($3, families $5). Call ahead; they are booked for the summer by late Apr.

Grand Lake

Though inaccessible without a car in the winter, this town is the "snowmobile capital of Colorado" and offers spectacular cross-country routes.

Shadowcliff Hostel (HI-AYH), 405 Summerland Park Rd. (627-9220); from the western entrance, veer left to Grand Lake, then take the left fork ¼ mi. into town on W. Portal Rd. In downtown Grand Lake, take a left at Garfield, and turn right onto W. Portal. Hand-built pine lodge perched on a cliff overlooking Shadow Mountain Lake and the Rockies. Hiking trails, kitchen, showers and a wood burning stove. $10, nonmembers $12, bedding rental $1; private doubles $30, $5 per additional person. Cabins sleep 6-8; $60-70 per day; 6-day min. stay. Open late May to Oct. Make reservations for the cabins as far as a year in advance.

Sunset Motel, 505 Grand Ave. (627-3318). Friendly owners plus cozy rooms equals a warm stay. Singles $45, doubles $50; 10% discount with *Let's Go: USA*.

Bluebird Motel, 30 River Dr. (627-9314), on Rte. 34 west of Grand Lake. Spiffy rooms with spotted carpets, fluffy pink curtains, TV, and fridges. Overlooks Shadow Mountain Lake and the snow-capped Continental Divide. Singles $45; doubles $50; in winter $30/$40.

Camping

Camping is available in the national forest campgrounds of **Stillwater Campground,** located on the shores of the hot boating spot **Lake Granby** ($12, 148 sites), or at **Green Ridge Campground,** located on the south end of **Shadow Mountain Lake** ($10, 81 campsites). Both sites have toilets, water, and boat ramps. Make reservations (800-260-2267) or arrive early to find a first come, first served spot. National Park Campgrounds include **Moraine Park** (5½ mi. from Estes; 247 sites; some open all year), with secluded spots, and **Glacier Basin** (9 mi. from Estes; 150 sites; open in summer only), which offers a spectacular view of the mountains. Both require reservations in summer (sites $14; 7-day max. stay; call 586-1206 or 800-365-2267). **Aspenglen,** 5 mi. west of Estes Park near the Fall River entrance, has 56 sites available early May through September ($12; 7-day max. stay). **Long's Peak Campground** has tents only on a first come, first served basis ($12; 3-night max. stay). **Timber Creek,** 10 mi. north of Grand Lake, is the only national park campground on the western side of the park. Open year-round, it is comprised of 100 woodsy sites (May-Sept. $12, 7-night max. stay; in winter $8, no water in winter).

A **backcountry** camping permit ($15) is required in the summer. On the eastern slope, permits are available inside the park from the **Backcountry Permits and Trip Planning Building,** a 2min. walk from the **Visitors Center Headquarters** (586-1242 for info or reservations; open daily 7am-7pm). The friendly staff will ensure you're prepared. In the west, see the folks at the **Kawuneeche Visitors Center.**

FOOD

Estes Park

The Notchtop Pub (586-0272), in the upper Stanley Village Shopping Plaza, east of downtown off Rte. 34. Specializes in homemade everything, including breads, pastries, and pies baked fresh every morning. Cup of homemade ice cream $2.50. More a bohemian cafe than a pub, the Notchtop fixes a mean lunch of soups ($2) and sandwiches ($5-6). Open daily 8am-9pm; bakery open 7am-10pm.

Mama Rose's, 388 E. Elkhorn Ave. (586-3330), on the riverwalk in Barlow Plaza, offers heaping portions of Italian food. Mama's special gives carbo-depleted mountain hoppers all-you-can-eat soup, salad, garlic bread, pasta, and spumoni for just $8. All-you-can-eat breakfast special $6. Open M-Sa 7am-11am and 4pm-9pm, Su 7am-11am and noon-9pm.

Ed's Cantina, 362 E. Elkhorn (586-2919), is open for anything from "pancakes to fajitas." This local favorite right on the main drag serves up traditional breakfast specials ($2.75) and a spicier Mexican breakfast ($5). Open daily 7am-10pm.

Grand Lake

Marie's Grand Lake Café, 928 Grand Ave. (627-9475), located on the lake, is a watering hole for locals. Huge breakfast of 2 eggs, steak, 2 pancakes, and hashbrowns for $4. Open daily 6am-10pm.

Pancho and Lefty's, 1101 Grand Ave. (627-8773). The price is right, as are the portions; their deliciously spicy tamales ($5.50) or crunchy *chimichangas* ($6.50) are cases in point. Open daily 11am-9pm.

SIGHTS AND ACTIVITIES

The star of this park is **Trail Ridge Rd.** (U.S. 34), a 50 mi. stretch that rises 12,183 ft. above sea level into frigid tundra. This main drag through the park is the highest continuously paved road in the world. The round-trip drive takes roughly 3hr. by car; beware of slow-moving tour buses. The road is closed October through May for weather reasons, and is passable only in the afternoon well into the summer. The **Forest Canyon Overlook** and 30min. round-trip **Tundra Trail** provide a closer look at the fragile environment. **Moraine Park Museum** (586-3777), on Bear Lake Rd. en route to the campsites, displays exhibits on the park's geology and ecosystem.

Any hiking in the park should be accompanied by *Hiking Rocky Mountain National Park* ($13), a widely available guidebook most rangers swear by. Serious mountaineers and hikers will be attracted to **Longs Peak** (14,255 ft.), the highest and most prominent mountain in the park. Athletic, acclimated hikers can climb the peak in late July or August by taking the 15 mi. round-trip Keyhole route from the Longs Peak Ranger Station. The last 1½ mi. to the top involves scrambling over rock ledges and boulders. Check in at the Long's Peak ranger station the day before you go, and make sure to leave before 6am to avoid the risk of thunderstorms.

Since the trailheads in the park are already high, just a few hours of hiking will bring you into unbeatable alpine scenery along the Continental Divide. The 12,000 to 14,000 ft. altitudes can wind the unprepared; give your body enough time to adjust before starting up the higher trails. The park's premier hiking is in the **Bear Lake** area. In the summer, a shuttle bus will transport you from your campground to the trailhead where you can begin the 0.4 mi. hike around the lake. You can also follow the trails up to **Nymph** (½ mi.), **Dream** (1.1 mi.), and **Emerald Lakes** (1.8 mi.), three glacial pools which offer inspiring glimpses of the higher rock tops. Some easy trails include the 3.6 mi. round-trip from Wild Basin Ranger Station to **Calypso Cascades** and the 2.8 mi. round-trip from the Long Peaks Ranger Station to **Eugenia Mine.** The **Twin Sisters** trail is a somewhat challenging 2-4hr. hike that leaves from Rte. 7, south of the Lilly Lake Visitors Center, and avoids the park entrance fee. Since this peak is somewhat isolated from the rest of the park's mountains, the summit provides a private view of the range.

From Grand Lake, a trek into the scenic and remote **North** or **East Inlets** should leave camera-toting crowds behind. An 11 mi. trail ascends 2240 ft. through pristine wilderness to **Lake Nanita** (leave from North Inlet). From East Inlet, a 7 mi. course leads to Lake Verna, where plump trout swim in picturesque mountain lakes, offering excellent fishing.

World-class **rock climbing** can be found just north of Estes Park, at **Lumpy Ridge.** Rock jocks gain access via Devil's Gulch Rd. and park at the Twin Owls parking lot. The ridge offers hundreds of climbs for all abilities. **Colorado Wilderness,** 358 Elkhorn, in Estes Park, has more info.

While no biking is allowed on trails within the park itself, mountain bikers can head to nearby national forests. **Colorado Bicycling Adventures,** 184 E. Elkhorn (586-4241 or 800-607-8765), rents bikes. ($5 per hr., $9 per 2hr., $15 per ½-day, $21 per day. Helmets included. 10% hosteler discounts.) The staff can tell you where to find good mountain biking or refer you to the *Mountain Bike Guide to Estes Park* for $3.50. They can also drive you up to the top of Trail Crest Rd. and guide you down the 5000 vertical ft. paved descent. (Open daily 9am-9pm; Aug. to late June 10am-7pm. Tours $45-68, bike rental, helmet, and transport included.)

For a break from the mountains, visit the **world's largest collection of keys** at the Baldpate Inn, 4900 Rte. 7 S, next to the Lilly Lake visitors center, where over 12,000 keys dangle from the walls and ceiling.

■ Vail

As the most-visited ski resort in the U.S., Vail wows skiers with its prime snow conditions, a vertical drop of 3330 ft., 121 ski runs, and 26 lifts. Discovered by Lord Gore in 1854, Vail and its surrounding valley were invaded by miners during the Rockies gold rush in the 1870s. According to local lore, the Ute Indians adored the area's rich supply of game, but they became so upset with the white man's intrusion that they set fire to the forest, creating the resort's famous open terrain. Today, Vail offers a different kind of game, characterized by ritzy hotels, swank saloons, and sexy boutiques.

The **Colorado Ski Museum** (476-1876), in the Transportation Bldg. in Vail Village, offers a glimpse into Vail's past and houses the **Ski Hall of Fame** (open Tu-Su 10am-5pm; free). Before slaloming, the unequipped visit **Ski Base** (476-5799), in Lionshead Mall. (Skis, poles, and boots from $13 per day. Snowboard and boots from $19 per day. Open daily in winter 8am-7pm.) For **ski conditions**, call 476-5677.

Vail also gestures toward sun worshippers in the summer, when the 121 ski runs become **trails.** The **Lionshead gondola** and the **Vistabahn chairlift** (476-9090), in Vail village, whisk hikers, bikers, and sightseers to the top of the mountains for breathtaking views. (Vistabahn open daily 10am-4pm. Gondola open M-Tu 10am-6pm, W-Su 11am-4pm. $14, over 70 free. $9 bike-hauling fee.) Rental **bikes** are available atop Vail Mountain ($10 per hr., $28 per day). The **Gore Creek Fly Fisherman,** 183 E. Gore Creek Dr. (476-3296), reels in the daily catch of river info. (Rod rentals $15 per day, $25 with boots and waders. Open Su-Th 8am-6pm, F-Sa 8am-10pm.)

The phrase "cheap lodging" is not part of Vail's vocabulary, especially during peak season. Rooms in the resort town rarely dip below $175 per night in winter, and summer lodging is often equally pricey. **The Prairie Moon,** 738 Grand Ave. (328-6680), offers some of the cheapest lodging outside the expensive resort area. Located in Eagle, about 30 mi. west of Vail, The Prairie Moon has large, clean rooms with fridges and microwaves. (Singles $43; doubles $48; triples $55. Reserve 1 week ahead in winter, months ahead in summer.) A bus shuttles visitors daily between Eagle and Vail (see **Anon/Beaver Creek Transit** below). Closer summer lodgings await at the **Roost Lodge,** 1783 N. Frontage Rd. (476-5451 or 800-873-3065), in West Vail. Average-sized rooms come with cable TV and phones, as well as continental breakfast and access to a jacuzzi, sauna, and pool. (Singles $62.) The **Holy Cross Ranger District** (827-5715), right off U.S. 24 at Exit 171, cheerfully provides info on the six campgrounds near Vail (open M-F 8am-5pm). With 25 sites, **Gore Creek** is the closest and most popular campground. Situated right outside East Vail, it is within hiking distance to the free Vail bus (sites have water and 10-day limit; $6-10). **Garfunkel's** (476-3689), a hidden hangout accessible by foot in Vail's Lion Head Village (directly across from the gondola), offers specials that include $3 burgers and $1.50 beers on a porch that practically merges with the ski slope. Friday and Saturday nights feature live progressive rock bands and disco deejays, respectively, but this place can't write its own lyrics, either. (Open daily 11am-2am.) **DJ's Classic Diner** (476-2336), in nearby Concert Hall Plaza, whips up old-fashioned omelettes ($3-5.50), as well as crepes and blintzes for $4-6 (open M 7am-2pm, 24hr. from Tu 7am to Su 2pm).

Vail's two **visitors centers** are located at either end of the village. The main building at the Vail Transportation Center (479-1394 or 800-525-3875), and the smaller center on S. Frontage Rd. (479-1385), near Lionshead Village, offer free copies of *What to Do: Vail/Beaver Creek* and *The Guide* (open in summer Su-Th 9am-7pm, F-Sa 9am-8pm). **Greyhound** (476-5137 or 800-231-2222; ticket office open daily 7:45am-noon and 2-6pm) buses eager skiers and patient travelers out of its depot, in the Transportation Bldg. next to the main visitors center, to Glenwood Springs (1½hr., 4 per day, $9); Denver (2hr., 5 per day, $17); and Grand Junction (3hr., 4 per day, $18). **Avon/Beaver Creek Transit** (328-8143 for schedule info) runs bus routes between Vail and its surrounding areas, including Eagle ($3) and Edwards ($2). Free bus service covers the area around Vail Village, Lionshead, and East and West Vail (328-8143 for schedule info). **Post Office:** 1300 N. Frontage Rd. (476-5217; open M-F 8:30am-5:30pm, Sa 8:30am-noon). **ZIP code:** 81657. **Area code:** 970.

■ Aspen

A world-renowned asylum for musicians and skiers, Aspen is an upper-class playground, where shoppers exclaim "I'll take it!" without asking for prices. Although more congenial than ultra-ritzy Vail (see p. 602), Aspen does provide the budget traveler with similar woes. To catch Aspen on the semi-cheap, stay in Glenwood Springs (40 mi. north on Rte. 82; see p. 604) and make a daytrip here, or camp amid aspen groves in the nearby national forest.

Skiing is the main attraction in Aspen. The hills surrounding town contain four ski areas: **Aspen Mountain, Aspen Highlands, Buttermilk Mountain,** and **Snowmass Ski Area** (925-1220 or 800-525-6200). The resorts sell interchangeable lift tickets ($59; ages 13-27 early season $29, peak season $39; ages 7-12 $29/35; over 70 or under 7 free). The **Glenwood Springs Hostel** offers a $37 full-day package for the Aspen ski resorts, including an interchangeable lift ticket, transportation, skis, and ski clothes (see p. 604). In summer, the **Silver Queen Gondola** (925-1220 or 800-525-6200) heads to the top of the Aspen mountains. (Open daily 10am-4pm. M-F $15, Sa-Su $18, ages 65-69 $12; over 70 and ages 7-12 $6.) At **Snowmass Mountain,** you can take a chairlift to the top and ride your mountain bike down (in summer daily 10:30am-5pm; free). The mountains of **Maroon Bells,** and the well-known 1.8 mi. hike to **Cascade Lake,** are not-to-be-missed, but Maroon Creek Rd. is closed to traffic from 8:30am to 5pm daily. To avoid paying $5 for a long, slow bus ride, which departs every 30min. from **Rubey Park,** plan an early morning or a sunset hike. In Aspen proper, the **Ute Trail** leaves Ute Ave. and climbs to a rock ledge, following a windy and somewhat hairy course. The peak is a spectacular spot to watch the sunset (climbing time 30min.). Also in town, the gentler **Hunter Trail** crosses many streams and gently glides into a valley; day-hikers will want to pick a turn-around point.

Aspen's most famous event, the **Aspen Music Festival** (925-9042), features jazz, opera, and classical music from late June through August. Free bus transportation takes listeners from Rubey Park downtown to "the Tent," before and after all concerts. The July 4 concert is free as are many others. Call 925-3254 for a schedule.

If you stay in Aspen, you'll have to bite the bullet and reach deep into your pockets. The last sound deal in town, **St. Moritz Lodge,** 344 W. Hyman Ave. (925-3220 or 800-817-2069), charms ski bums with a pool, sauna, hot tub, and microwaves (dorm beds $33; in early and late winter $29-33; mid-winter from $45). Unless 6 ft. of snow covers the ground, try **camping** in the one of the many National Forest Campgrounds that lie within 5 mi. of Aspen. Reservable and first come, first served sites scatter just west of Aspen on Maroon Rd. (accessible from 5pm-8:30am) and southeast of Aspen on Rte. 82. ($9-12 per night. 5-day max. stay. 2-vehicle max. Sites fill before noon.

Open June to mid-Sept. Reserve by calling 800-280-2267.) Free **backcountry camping permits** are available at the Ranger District (see below).

The **Main Street Bakery,** 201 E. Main St. (925-6446), creates gourmet soups ($4-5), homemade granola with fruit ($5) and open-faced vegetarian sandwiches ($7; open M-Sa 7am-9:30pm, Su 7am-4:30pm). The **In and Out House,** 233 E. Main St. (925-6647), is just that: a revolving door of customers in an outhouse-sized space. They offer tasty sandwiches on freshly baked bread for $3-6. (Open M-F 8am-7pm, Sa-Su 9am-4pm.) **The Big Wrap,** 520 E. Durant Ave. (544-1700), rolls up creatively named veggie and Mexican wraps for $6 and mixes smoothies for $4 (open daily in summer 9am-6pm; in winter 10am-6pm). **Boogies Diner** (925-6610), on the corner of Cooper and Hunter, dishes out true greasy-spoon food such as turkey sandwiches ($7.50) and old-fashioned floats ($3.50). Obey the house rules: "schnoodling in booths only." (Open M-F 11am-9pm.)

Pick up the free *Official Guide to Aspen* magazine at either **visitors center,** 320 E. Hyman Ave., in the Wheeler Opera House (open daily 9am-5pm); or 425 Rio Grand Pl. (925-1940 or 800-262-7736; open M-F 8-5). For info on hikes and camping within 15 mi. of Aspen, contact the **Aspen Ranger District,** 806 W. Hallam (925-3445; weather/avalanche info 920-1664). They also sell a topographic map of the area ($4; open M-F 8am-5pm, in summer also Sa 8am-noon). **Area code:** 970.

■ Glenwood Springs

Glenwood Springs, located along I-70, 40 mi. north of Aspen on Rte. 82, is a smart choice for the budget traveler. Renowned for its steaming hot springs and vapor caves, Glenwood is sprinkled with budget-friendly markets, cafes, pool/dance halls, and a great hostel. **Glenwood Hot Springs Pool,** 401 N. River Rd. (945-7131 or 800-537-7946), located in a huge resort complex and maintained at 90°F year-round, contains the world's largest outdoor hot springs pool, a waterslide, and spas with different water temperatures. (Open daily 7:30am-10pm; in winter 9am-10pm. Day pass $7.50, after 9pm $5; ages 3-12 $5/$4.50.) Just 1 block from the large pools, the smelly gases of **Yampah Spa and Vapor Caves,** 709 E. 6th St. (945-0667), along with 115°F steam, create a relaxing experience amid the dim underground caves. After sweating your brains out, visitors can relax to New Age music in the Solarium. (Open daily 9am-9pm; $8.75, hostelers $4.75.) Skiing is available at the uncrowded **Sunlight,** 10901 County Rd. 117 (945-7491 or 800-445-7931), 10 mi. west of town ($28 per day, under 12 $18; hosteler discount).

Within walking distance of the springs and downtown, you'll find the **Glenwood Springs Hostel (HI-AYH),** 1021 Grand Ave. (945-8545 or 800-946-7835), which consists of a spacious Victorian house and a newer building next door. Hostelers can ski at Sunlight, win big discounts at Aspen or Vail, go whitewater rafting ($25), hike the Maroon Bells ($22), or try an unforgettable caving trip through the labyrinthine Fulford Cavern ($22). Owner Gary has a sweet, sweet, vinyl collection. ($12; private singles $19; private doubles $26. Linen included. Free pickup from train/bus stations. Some food included. No curfew. Lockout 10am-4pm.) The Victorian B&B next door is **Adducci's Inn,** 1023 Grand Ave. (945-9341). *Let's Go*-toting guests pay $28-65 for singles and $38-75 for doubles, including breakfast; otherwise, prices are higher (free pick-up from bus and train stations; $10 per additional person). Adducci's also serves pub fare in their restaurant/bar (open daily 5-10pm; bar closes by midnight).

The **Daily Bread Café and Bakery,** 729 Grand Ave. (945-6253), offers two squares a day at breakfast and lunch. They have a south-of-the-border omelette with potatoes ($6), as well as a leaner veggie eggs benedict for $7 (open M-F 7am-2pm, Sa 8am-2pm, Su 8am-noon). **Doc Holliday's Saloon,** 724 Grand Ave. (945-9050), is the place for burgers ($7) and beers ($1.50-3; open daily 10am-2am).

Contact the **Glenwood Springs Chamber Resort Association,** 1102 Grand Ave. (945-6589), for town info and the *Trail Guide to Glenwood Springs.* (Guide $1. Open June-Aug. M-F 8:30am-5pm, Sa-Su 9am-3pm; Sept.-May M-F 8:30am-5pm. Printed info available 24hr.) The **White River National Forest Headquarters** (945-

2521), at 9th and Grand Ave., provides info about camping and outdoor activities (open M-F 8am-5pm). The **Amtrak** station, 413 7th St. (945-9563 or 800-872-7245; ticket office open daily 9:30am-4:30pm), chugs once per day to Denver (6½hr., $45) and Salt Lake City (9hr., $60). **Greyhound**, 118 W. 6th St. (945-8501 or 800-231-2222; station open M-F 8am-5pm, Sa 8am-1pm), runs to Denver (3½hr., 6 per day, $24) and Grand Junction (2hr., 5 per day, $11). The **Roaring Fork Transit Agency (RFTA)** screams to Aspen ($6). **Post Office:** 113 9th St. (945-5611; open M-F 8am-6pm, Sa 9am-1pm). **ZIP code:** 81601. **Area code:** 970.

■ Grand Junction

Grand Junction gets its name from its seat at the junction of the Colorado and Gunnison Rivers and the conjunction-junction of the Río Grande and Denver Railroads. The city's chief attribute is its location among Grand Mesa, Colorado National Monument, Arches National Park, and Moab. Those who sup from the tables of natural splendor should further indulge from the chalice of local vintage—most visitors will be surprised to find wineries amid the spires and mesas of Grand Junction, but the 11 different sites and their free samples will get you tanked if you visit every one. To arrange tours, pick up a free map at the **Grand Junction Visitors Center** or call the **Wine Industry Development Board,** 523-1232.

The smoothly running **Melrose Hotel (HI-AYH)**, 337 Colorado Ave. (242-9636 or 800-430-4555), between 3rd and 4th St., assists travelers in navigating the nearby natural wonders. Melrose's fantastic tours to Arches National Park ($38), Colorado National Monument ($25), and Black Canyon plus Grand Mesa ($30) take you off tourist paths for serious sight-seeing (all 3 trips $75). In winter, owner Marcus can direct you to Powderhorn for the best local skiing. (Kitchen. Dorms $12; singles $24, with bath $34; doubles $27/$39. Reception 8-10am and 4-9pm; call if arrival time will not coincide.) **Columbine Motel** presents singles for $33, and doubles for $38, both with TVs and fridges. Camp in **Highline State Park** (858-7208), on Q Rd., 24 mi. west of town and 7 mi. north of Exit 15 on I-70 (fishing access, restrooms; 26 sites $13), or **Island Acres State Park** (464-0548), 12 mi. east on the banks of the Colorado River, off I-70 Exit 46 (6 tent sites $13, 34 partial hookups $16, 40 full hookups $20).

The **Rockslide Restaurant and Brew Pub,** 401 S. Main St. (245-2111), joins the avalanche of micro-breweries covering the nation. The home-brewed Big Bear Stout is $2.75 per pint. (Salmon and chips $8. During happy hour, all appetizers are ½-price. Open daily 11am-10pm; Su-Th bar open until midnight, F-Sa 1am.) The large and popular **Dos Hombres Restaurant,** 421 Brach Dr. (242-8861), just south of Broadway (Rte. 340) on the southern bank of the Colorado River, serves great Mexican food in a casual setting. On Wednesday nights, the whole family will enjoy a table-side magic show. (½-price appetizers during happy hour M-F 3-6pm. Open daily 11am-10pm.) Breakfast specialties and a copy of *Shalom on the Range* can be discovered at **The Crystal Café,** 314 Main St, (242-8843; open M-F 7am-1:45pm, Sa 8:30am-1:25pm; bakery open until 3pm). Grand Junction lies at the intersection of U.S. 50 and U.S. 6 between Denver and Salt Lake City; its pit stop location is beginning to draw touring bands who refuse to drive 500 miles between gigs. The **Chameleon Club,** 234 Main St, (245-3636), grooves to live music nightly until 2am. Sunday night is Service Industry Night, when anybody in "public service" gets happy hour prices all night.

The **Grand Junction Visitor Bureau,** 740 Horizon Dr. (244-1480), on I-70 Business Rte., under the Taco Bell sign, has weekly lecture and slide show programs on the history and culture of southwest Colorado (open daily 8:30am-8pm; late Sept. to early May 8:30am-5pm). **Enterprise Car Rental,** 406 S. 5th St. (242-8103), rents compact cars for $37 per day, $220 per week. Must be 21 with a major credit card. **Amtrak,** 337 S. 1st St. (241-2733 or 800-872-7245; station open daily 10am-6pm), shoots once daily to Denver at 11:20am ($40-70) and Salt Lake City at 5:45pm ($41-75). The **Greyhound** station, 230 S. 5th St. (242-6012 or 800-231-2222; station open 24hr.; ticket window open 4am-10pm), has service to Denver (5½hr., 8 per day, $33); Durango (5hr., 1 per day, $34); Salt Lake City (6hr., 1 per day, $50); and Los Angeles (16hr., 5 per day, $95). **Domestic violence line:** 241-6704. **Internet access** is available via

Cyber Function, 104 Orchard Ave. (257-1517). **Post Office:** 241 N. 4th St. (244-3401; open M-F 7:45am-5:15pm, Sa 9am-12:30pm). **ZIP code:** 81501. **Area code:** 970.

■ Colorado National Monument

Four miles west of Grand Junction off Monument Rd., the Colorado National Monument is a 32 sq. mi. sculpture of steep cliff faces, canyon walls, and obelisk-like spires wrought by the forces of gravity, wind, and water. The **Rim Rock Drive** runs along the edge of red canyons, providing views of awe-inspiring rock monoliths, the Grand Mesa, and the city of Grand Junction. **Window Rock Trail** (¼ mi.) and **Otto's Trail** (½ mi.) are easy walks to points from which you can gaze at the eerie, skeletal rock formations. The 6 mi. **Monument Canyon Trail** inspires visions of grandeur, as it wanders amid the giant rock formations. Check in at the monument **headquarters and visitors center** (970-858-3617), near the western entrance. (Open daily May-Sept. 8am-7pm; off-season 9am-5pm. Entrance fee $4 per vehicle, $2 per cyclist or hiker.) **Saddlehorn Campground,** near the visitors center, provides 80 partially shaded sites on a first come, first served basis (restrooms, water, no hookups; $10). The **Bureau of Land Management,** 2815 Horizon Dr. (970-244-3000; open M-F 7:30am-4:30pm), with its office across from the airport, maintains 12 pay sites at **Mud Springs,** near **Glade Park.** Primitive camping is permitted on all adjoining BLM land.

All You Need Is a Dream

There is a very good chance that the Colorado National Monument would not exist today if it weren't for the efforts and antics of one man: **John Otto.** Otto moved to the canyon in 1906 and was immediately enamored, spending years living alone in the canyon and building trails so individuals could enjoy the place he loved. He also began badgering government officials to declare the canyon on the outskirts of Grand Junction a national monument. Sometimes his letters were more threats than requests. Perhaps his most interesting escapade came when **President Taft** was making a train stop in Grand Junction: Otto knew that Taft was a huge fan of peaches, so he lured the president to what is now the monument with a promise of delicious peaches. His tactics worked. In 1911, the monument was created, and Otto was named caretaker, a job he offered to do for free, but instead was paid a whopping $1 a month.

■ Grand Mesa

Grand Mesa, or "the great table," is the world's largest flat-topped mountain, looming 50 mi. east of Grand Junction (by road). A Native American story tells how a mad mother eagle tore a serpent to bits, believing her young to be inside the snake's belly; the lakes were formed by the resulting fragments. Recently, geologists have estimated that a 300 ft. thick lava flow covered the entire region billions of years ago, and the Mesa is the only portion to have endured erosion. The numerous lakes on the Mesa that serve as spawning grounds for insects also provide fine fishing, as well as opportunities for pleasant hiking.

The **district forest service,** 2777 Crossroads Blvd. (970-242-8211), in Grand Junction, dispenses maps ($4, waterproof version $6) and info on the campsites they maintain on the Mesa (open M-F 8am-5pm). **Island Lake** (41 sites, $8) and **Ward Lake** (27 sites, $10) are both on the water and have ample fishing. **Jumbo** (26 sites, $10); **Little Bear** (36 sites, $8); and **Cottonwood** (42 sites, $8) provide other options. Call or stop by the **visitors center** (856-4153), at the eastern end of the mesa, for more info on any site (open daily in summer 9am-5pm).

The **Mesa Lakes Resort** (970-268-5467 or 888-420-MESA/6372), on Rte. 65 on the north side of the summit, is an old-fashioned mountain retreat. The resort rents extremely rustic cabins for 2-4 people ($45 per day, no running water), more modern cabins for 6-12 people ($100-150 per day), and typical motel rooms ($45-55). The resort also houses a general store and restaurant (open in summer Su-Th 8am-7pm, F-Sa 8am-8pm; in winter daily 9am-5pm). On the south side of the summit, the **Grand**

Mesa Lodge (856-3250 or 800-551-6372) rents cabins year-round ($65, $7.50 per extra person) and motel units ($35; no kitchen). They also have a small but well-stocked store (open daily 7:30am-6pm) and offer wisdom on the outdoors.

■ Colorado Springs

When pioneers rushed west toward Colorado in search of gold (shouting "Pikes Peak or Bust!"), they were surprised to find towering red rocks and cave dwellings at the foot of the peak. The pioneers called the bizarre rock formations the Garden of the Gods, in part because of the Ute legend that the rocks were petrified bodies of enemies hurled down by the gods above. Today, the United States Olympic Team, housed in Colorado Springs, continues the quest for gold, while jets from the United States Air Force Academy barrel-roll overhead.

ORIENTATION AND PRACTICAL INFORMATION

Colorado Springs is laid out in a grid of broad thoroughfares. **Nevada Ave.,** the main north-south strip, just east of I-25, is known for its bars and restaurants. **Cascade Ave.** is the east-west axis, while **Pikes Peak** divides the city north and south. The numbered streets west of Nevada ascend as you move west. **I-25** from Denver plows through downtown. East of Nevada Ave. remains largely residential.

Buses: Greyhound, 120 S. Weber St. (635-1505). To: Denver (1¾hr., 7 per day, $12); Pueblo (50min., 5 per day, $8); and Albuquerque (7¾hr., 4 per day, $58). Tickets sold daily 5:15am-1am.

Public Transportation: Colorado Springs City Bus Service, 125 E. Kiowa (475-9733), at Nevada, 3 blocks from the Greyhound station. Serves Widefield, Manitou Springs, Fort Carson, Garden of the Gods, and Peterson Air Force Base. Service M-Sa 6am-6pm every 30min., irregular evening service until 10pm. Fare 75¢, seniors and children 35¢, under 6 free; long trips 25¢ extra. Exact change required.

Taxis: Yellow Cab, 634-5000. $3 1st mi., $1.35 per additional mi.

Car Rental: XPress Rent-A-Car, 2021 E. Platte (634-1914 or 800-634-1914). From $20 per day, $119 per week. 100 free mi. per day. Open M-F 8:30am-5:30pm, Sa 8:30am-2pm. Must stay in Colorado and be 21 with major credit card.

Tours: Pikes Peak Tours, 3704 Colorado Ave. (633-1747 or 800-345-8197), offers trips to the U.S. Air Force Academy and Garden of the Gods (4hr., $20, under 13 $10) and Pikes Peak (4hr., $25/$15), as well as a 10 mi. whitewater rafting trip on the Arkansas River (7hr., includes lunch; $60/$40). Office open daily 8am-5pm.

Visitor Info: Colorado Springs Convention and Visitors Bureau, 104 S. Cascade, #104 (635-7506 or 800-888-4748). Pick up the free *Colorado Springs Pikes Peak Region Official Visitors Guide.* Open daily in summer 8:30am-5pm; in winter M-F 8:30am-5pm.

Road Conditions: 635-7623.

Hotlines: Crisis Emergency Services, 635-7000. **Rape Crisis,** 633-3819. Both 24hr.

Post Office: 201 E. Pikes Peak Ave. (800-275-8777), at Nevada Ave. Open M-F 7:30am-5:30pm, Sa 8am-1pm. **ZIP code:** 80903. **Area code:** 719.

ACCOMMODATIONS AND CAMPGROUNDS

The motels along **Nevada Ave.** are fairly shabby; taking nearby campgrounds and spots along **W. Pikes Peak Ave.** and **W. Colorado Ave.** are good ideas.

Apache Court Motel, 3401 W. Pikes Peak Ave. (471-9440). Take bus #1 west down Colorado Ave. to 34th St. and walk 1 block north. Pink adobe rooms with A/C, TV, and a common hot tub. Summer singles $55. In winter and on some summer weekdays, singles $40 and doubles $55.

Amarillo Motel, 2801 W. Colorado Ave. (635-8539 or 800-216-8539). Take bus #1 west down Colorado Ave. to 28th St. Simple rooms, stayin' alive with 70s decor, have clean kitchens and TV. Singles $30; doubles $45. Laundry available.

Tree Haven Cottages, 3620 W. Colorado Ave. (578-1968). A real family place with tiny rooms fully-equipped with cable TV, fridge, microwaves and a pool. Singles $47; off-season $30.

About 30min. from Colorado Springs, several **Pike National Forest** campgrounds lie in the mountains flanking Pikes Peak (generally open May-Sept.), but no local transportation serves this area. Campgrounds clutter Rte. 67, 5-10 mi. north of **Woodland Park,** 18 mi. northwest of the Springs on U.S. 24. Others border U.S. 24 near the town of Lake George, 50 mi. west of the Springs (all sites $8-10). You can always camp off any road on national forest property for free if you are at least 500 ft. from a road or stream. The **Forest Service Office,** 601 S. Weber (636-1602), has maps of the area ($4; open M-F 8am-5pm). Farther afield, visitors may camp in the **Eleven Mile State Recreation Area** (748-3401 or 800-678-2267), off a spur road from U.S. 24 near Lake George, on a reservoir (pay showers and laundry; sites $7, with electricity $11; entrance fee $4).

FOOD AND NIGHTLIFE

Students and the young-at-heart perch among outdoor tables in front of the cafes and restaurants lining **Tejon Ave.,** a few blocks east of downtown. **Old Colorado** city is home to a number of fine eateries, as well as a **farmer's market** on summer Saturdays between Colorado Ave. and Pikes Peak, on 24th St. **Poor Richard's Restaurant,** 326 N. Tejon Ave. (632-7721), affords locals a coffeehouse hangout, serving pizza ($2.25 per slice; pies $10), sandwiches, and salads for $4-7 (live bluegrass W, Celtic Th; open daily 11am-10pm). Just across the street, **La Dolce Vita,** 33 N. Tejon Ave. (632-1369), entertains aspiring Zeferellis in a coffeeshop/bookstore with intellectual schtick, steaming cappucino ($1.85), and croissant sandwiches ($5). They also have an extensive schedule of speakers, music, and workshops. (Open M-F 7am-10pm, Sa 8am-10pm, Su 9am-4pm.) **La Baguette,** 2417 W. Colorado Ave. (577-4818), bakes bread and melts fondues a sight better than you might expect in a place so far from Paris. Cheese fondue with apple slices goes for $6.25. (Open M-Sa 7am-6pm, Su 8am-5pm.) A few doors down, big crowds gather at **Henri's,** 2427 W. Colorado Ave. (634-9031), for fantastic margaritas and Mexican food (enchiladas $7.50; open daily 11am-10pm). **Jose Muldoon's,** 222 N. Tejon St. (636-2311), a short walk from the college, allows students to put down their books and enjoy live music, canned dance tunes, or the occasional dunk tank (open nightly 10:30pm-1:30am).

SIGHTS

GARDEN OF THE GODS Between Rte. 24 (also Colorado Ave.) and 30th St. in northwest Colorado Springs, the redrock towers and spires of the "Garden," as locals call it, rise strikingly against a mountainous backdrop. *(Open daily 5am-11pm; in winter 5am-9pm.)* **Climbers** are regularly lured by the large red faces, while a number of exciting **mountain biking** trails cross the Garden as well. The park's hiking trails give great views of the rock formations and can all be done in one day. A map is available from the park's only **visitors center** (634-6666) on 30th St., at the corner of the park's Gateway Rd. *(Open daily 8am-9pm; in winter 8am-5:30pm. Walking tours depart every hr. on the hr. in summer.)*

PIKES PEAK From any part of the town, one can't help noticing the 14,110 ft. summit of Pikes Peak on the western horizon. The willing can climb the peak via the strenuous but well-maintained 13 mi. **Barr Burro Trail;** the trailhead is in Manitou Springs by the "Manitou Incline" sign (bus #1 to Ruxton). Don't despair if you don't reach the top—explorer Zebulon Pike never reached it, either. Otherwise, pay the fee to drive up the gorgeous 19 mi. **Pikes Peak Hwy.** (684-9383), which is actually a well-maintained dirt road administered by the Colorado Dept. of Public Works. *(Hwy. open daily 7am-7pm; Oct.-May daily 9am-3pm, weather permitting. $35 per car or $10 per person, whichever is cheaper.)* Five miles west in Manitou Springs, visitors can also reserve a seat on the **Pikes Peak Cog Railway,** 515 Ruxton Ave. (685-5401), which takes visitors to the top every 80 min. (May to early Oct. daily 8am-5:20pm; call for times in

May and Aug-Oct. Round-trip $22, ages 5-11 $10.50.) From the summit, Kansas, the Sangre de Cristo Mountains, and the Continental Divide unfold before you. This lofty view inspired Kathy Lee Bates to write "America the Beautiful."

CAVE OF THE WINDS For adventurous hiking through subterranean passages, head for the contorted caverns of the **Cave of the Winds** (685-5444) on Rte. 24, 6 mi. west of Exit 141 off I-25. *(Guided tours daily every 15min. 9am-9pm; Sept. to late May 10am-5pm. $12, ages 6-15 $6.)* The laser light extravaganza, nightly at 9pm during the summer, features cute animated figures dancing along the canyon walls. Just above Manitou Springs on Rte. 24 lies the **Manitou Cliff Dwellings Museum** (685-5242 or 685-5394) on the U.S. 24 bypass, which contains pueblos of ancient Anasazi buildings dating from 1100-1300. (Open June-Aug. daily 9am-8pm; Sept.-May 9am-5pm. $7, seniors $6, ages 7-11 $5.) The **Seven Falls,** west on Cheyenne Blvd., are lit up at night during the summer months ($6, ages 6-15 $3.50).

GOING FOR THE GOLD AND AIMING HIGH Olympic hopefuls train with some of the world's most high-tech sports equipment at the **U.S. Olympic Complex,** 750 E. Boulder St. (578-4644, 578-4618), at I-25 Exit 156A; take bus #1 east to Farragut. Every 30min. (every hr. in off season), the complex offers free 1hr. tours that include a tear-jerking film of struggle and glory. (Open M-Sa 9am-5pm, Su 10am-5pm.) Earlier searches for gold are recorded at the **Pioneers' Museum,** 215 S. Tejon St. (578-6650), downtown, which recounts the settling of Colorado Springs, and includes a display on the techniques and instruments of a pioneer doctor (open Tu-Sa 10am-5pm, Su 1-5pm; free). The **Western Museum of Mining and Industry,** 1025 N. Gate Rd. (488-0880), allows you to pan for gold. *(Open M-Sa 9am-4pm, Su noon-4pm; Dec.-Feb. hrs. vary. $6, students and seniors $5, ages 5-12 $3.)*

Hosting over a million visitors yearly, the **United States Air Force Academy** (472-4415), 12 mi. north of town off I-25 Exit 156B, is the most popular attraction in the area. The chapel (332-2025) was constructed of aluminum, steel, and other materials used in building airplanes (open M-Sa 9am-6pm, Su 1-6pm). On weekdays during the school year, cadets gather at noon near the chapel for the cadet lunch formation (i.e., to eat). The **Barry Goldwater Visitors Center** (332-2025) has self-guided tour maps, info on special events, and a free 14min. movie every 30min. (open daily 9am-6pm; early Sept. to mid-May 9am-5pm).

Ground Zero

While most Cold War era bomb shelters are buried under 5-10 ft. of dirt, the **North American Air Defense Command Headquarters (NORAD)** (474-2241) was constructed 1800 ft. below Cheyenne Mountain. The center looks like something out of a James Bond movie; a 3 mi. tunnel leads to computers and detectors, which scan the heavens for incoming inter-continental ballistic missiles. The center was designed to be operational even after a direct nuclear attack. Call 2 months in advance to make reservations for a tour (474-2238). The **Peterson Air Force Base,** east of Academy Blvd., houses a **visitors center** (556-6406) and the **Edward J. Peterson Air and Space Museum** (556-4915), which showcases exhibits on the history of the base, as well as on space and satellite operations (museum open Tu-Sa 8:30am-4:30pm; free).

■ Great Sand Dunes

When Colorado's mountains all begin to look the same, head to the **Great Sand Dunes National Monument** at the northwest edge of the **San Luis Valley.** A sea of 700 ft. tall sand dunes, representing thousands of years of wind-blown accumulation, laps silently at the base of the **Sangre de Cristo Range,** 38 mi. northeast of **Alamosa** and 112 mi. west of **Pueblo** on Rte. 150, off U.S. 160. The progress of the dunes through passes in the range is checked by the shallow **Medano Creek;** visitors can wade across the creek when it flows (Apr. to mid-July). The best way to enjoy the dunes is just to plow on in, but beware the intense afternoon heat in summer—the sand can reach up to 140°F. There aren't any trails through the dunes, but you can roam about wherever you want. Hiking to the top takes about 1½hr. and is extremely difficult, since your feet sink a good 6 in. with each step. Take at least a quart of water per person. Those with four-wheel-drive can motor over the **Medano Pass Primitive Rd.** At the southern boundary of the monument, the **Oasis** complex (378-2222) offers four-wheel-drive tours that huff over Medano Pass Primitive Rd. to the nether regions of the dunes (tours daily 10am and 2pm; 2hr.; $14, ages 5-11 $8).

Schedules of daily ranger-led hikes and talks can be found at the **visitors center** (378-2312), ½ mi. past the entrance gate. (Open daily 8am-6pm, Sept.-May 9am-5pm; $3 per person, under 17 free; National Parks passports accepted.) The newsletter, *Sand Dune Breezes,* also suggests drives and hikes. For more info, contact the **Superintendent,** Great Sand Dunes National Monument, Mosca, CO 81146.

Pinyon Flats (378-2312), the monument's primitive, cactus-covered campground, is open year-round. Bring mosquito repellent in June. (Sites $10; arrive by early afternoon. No reservations.) Get free **backcountry camping** permits for the dunes from the visitors center. If the park's sites are full, **Oasis** (see above) will fulfill your needs with showers, two-person sites ($10, with hookup $16.50; $2.50 per additional person), cabins ($30 for 2 people), or teepees ($25 for 2 people). **San Luis State Park** (378-2020, 800-678-2267 for camping reservations), 8 mi. away in Mosca, has showers and 51 electrical sites ($12; $4 vehicle entrance fee; closed in winter). For info on nearby National Forest Campgrounds (all sites $10), contact the **Río Grande National Forest Service Office,** 11571 County Rd. T5, La Jara, CO 81140 (274-5193; open M-F 8am-4:30pm). **Area code:** 719.

SAN JUAN MOUNTAINS

Ask Coloradans about their favorite mountain retreats, and they'll most likely name a peak, lake, stream, or town in the San Juan Range of southwestern Colorado. Four **national forests**—the **Uncompahgre** (un-cum-PAH-gray), the **Gunnison,** the **San Juan,** and the **Río Grande**—encircle this sprawling range. **Durango** is an ideal base camp for forays into these mountains. Northeast of Durango, the **Weminuche Wilderness** tempts the hardy backpacker with a vast expanse of rugged terrain where wide, sweeping vistas stretch for miles. Get $4 maps and hiking info from **Pine Needle Mountaineering,** 835 Main Mall, Durango 81301 (970-247-8728; open in summer M-Sa 9am-9pm, Su 10am-5pm; off-season M-Sa 9am-6pm, Su 10am-5pm).

The San Juan area is easily accessible on U.S. 50, which is traveled by hundreds of thousands of tourists each summer. **Greyhound** serves the area, but very poorly; traveling by car is the best option in this region. On a happier note, the San Juans are loaded with HI-AYH hostels and campgrounds, making them one of the more economical places to visit in Colorado.

■ Black Canyon

Native American parents used to tell their children that the light-colored strands of rock streaking through the walls of the Black Canyon were the hair of a blond woman—and that if they got too close to the edge they would get tangled in it and fall. The edge of **Black Canyon of the Gunnison National Monument** is a staggering place. The Gunnison River slowly gouged out the 53 mi. long canyon, crafting a steep 2500 ft. gorge dominated by inky shadows (hence black); the Empire State Building, if placed at the bottom of the river, would reach barely halfway up the canyon walls.

The 8 mi. scenic drive along the South Rim boasts the spectacular **Chasm View,** where you can peer 2300 ft. down a sheer vertical drop—the highest cliff in Colorado—at the Gunnison River and the "painted" wall. Don't throw stones; you might kill an exhausted hiker in the canyon below. There are no well-established trails to the bottom, but you can scramble down the **Gunnison Rte.,** which drops 2000 ft. over the course of 1 mi. A free **backcountry permit** (from the South Rim visitors center) is required for all trips down to the river or to fish in the bountiful waters. Make sure to bring at least 3L of water per person, and be prepared to use your hands to climb back up. In the canyon, camp and enjoy the beauty; unimproved sites (no water) are available on a beach along the river. Pack in your water or use a filtration system. The rock walls of the Black Canyon are a paradise for climbers. Register at the South Rim visitors center to climb some of the tallest rock faces in the Rocky Mountains. Less strenuous hikes follow the canyon rim, providing dizzying views.

The **South Rim** has a **campground** with 102 small, somewhat crowded sites amid sagebrush and tall shrubs ($8). Pit toilets, charcoal grills, water, and paved wheelchair-accessible sites are available. On the **North Rim,** another campsite offers more space (water and toilets available; $8).

Many inexpensive motels line Main St./U.S. 50 in downtown **Montrose.** The **Traveler's B&B Inn,** 502 S. 1st St. (249-3472), parallel to Main St., lets simple, cozy rooms with TVs and breakfasts (singles $29, doubles $32; with private bath $32/$34; reduced rates in winter). The **Log Cabin Motel,** 1034 E. Main St. (249-7610), at the end of town nearest the Monument, offers small but comfortable rooms (singles $30-36, doubles $36-40). For tasty sandwiches ($4.50) and delightful omelettes ($5.50), head for the **Daily Bread Bakery and Café,** 346 Main St. (249-8444; open in summer M-Sa 6am-3pm). The **Red Barn,** 1413 Main St. (249-9202), dishes out three meals a day (M-Sa 6am-10:30am and 11am-10:30 pm) and a hearty brunch (Su 9am-3pm) that includes an all-you-can-eat salad bar ($6).

The Black Canyon lies 10 mi. east of the town of Montrose in western Colorado. The **South Rim** is easily accessible via a 5 mi. drive off U.S. 50 (entrance $7 per car, $4 walk-in or motorcycle); the wilder **North Rim** can only be reached by detouring

---

The Dirt Bike Kid

Those who know mountain bikes will recognize the name **Wes Williams** as a master among bike crafters. In his tiny shop on 420 Belleview Ave. in the Butte, he sculpts steel and titanium into world class bicycle frames and parts, including his prized "Chopper from Hell"; fully motorized, it's the only bicycle to ever be featured in *Harley* magazine. If you ask him real nicely, he's likely to show you around his shop. He also gives bike tours of the area that include lessons on local wildflowers, geography, and history.

---

around the canyon and taking a gravel road from Crawford off Rte. 92. **Greyhound** shuttles once a day ($12) between Montrose at 132 N. 1st St. (249-6673), and Gunnison, 55 mi. east, at the **Gunnison County Airport,** 711 Rio Grande (641-0060), and will drop you off on U.S. 50, 6 mi. from the canyon. For $39, **Gisdho Shuttles** (800-430-4555) conducts tours of the Black Canyon and the Grand Mesa from Grand Junction. The trip includes transportation, entrance fees, and guided tours off the beaten path. (Trips May-Oct. W and Sa.) The Canyon has two **visitors centers:** one on the South Rim (249-1915, ext. 23; open daily in summer 8am-6pm; in winter 8am-4pm), and another on the North Rim. **Area code:** 970.

■ Crested Butte

Crested Butte (CREST-ed BYOOT), 27 mi. north of Gunnison on Rte. 135, was once a mining town. The coal was exhausted in the 1950s, and a few years later, the steep powder fields on the Butte began attracting skiers. While there are a lot more tourists today, the buildings of Crested Butte haven't changed much since the mining days, thanks to an ordinance banning franchises in the area. The ski lifts lie 3 mi. north of town along Rte. 135. **Mt. Crested Butte Resort** (800-544-8448) offers excellent cruising runs that drop 3062 ft., but the mountain is most famous for its "extreme skiing," tempered by a decidedly backcountry flavor. Free skiing is sometimes available in November and April, along with reasonably priced lodging packages.

Come summertime, Crested Butte becomes the mountain bike capital of Colorado. The last week of June, Crested Butte hosts the **Fat Tire Bike Festival,** 4 days of mountain biking, racing, and fraternizing. In 1976, a group of cyclists rode from Crested Butte to Aspen, starting the oldest mountain biking event in the world. Every September, enduring and experienced bikers repeat the trek over the 12,705 ft. pass to Aspen and back during the **Pearl Pass Tour** (call 800-454-4505 for dates and info). Biking trail maps are available from bike shops and **The Alpineer,** near the Chamber of Commerce; trails begin at the base of Mt. Crested Butte and extend into the exquisite Gothic area. **Trail 401** is a demanding and famous 24 mi. round-trip loop with an excellent view. The Gothic area is also accessible with a car; follow Rte. 135 past Mt. Crested Butte and keep driving. When bumpy Gothic Rd. begins to get the best of you, park the car and explore the tiny town of **Gothic.** Excellent intermediate bike trails depart Brush Creek Road in Crested Butte.

Finding budget accommodations during winter season is about as easy as striking a major vein of gold, but there are a few possibilities. Call the **Crested Butte Lodging Hotline** at 800-215-2226. The **Crested Butte International Hostel,** 615 Teocalli Ave. (349-0588 or 888-389-0588), offers a cheap place for skiers and bikers to crash during their stay ($17; in winter $24; laundry; $6 dinners in peak seasons). The **Forest Queen** (349-5336), on the corner of 2nd and Elk Ave., rents out comfortable doubles at reasonable prices (doubles $55, with private bath $65). The **Gunnison National Forest Office,** 216 N. Colorado (641-0471), 30 mi. south in Gunnison, and the Chamber of Commerce (see below), have info on a bundle of **campgrounds** (open M-F 7:30am-4:30pm). You can camp for free in achingly beautiful surroundings at the **Gothic Campsite,** 3 mi. past the town of Gothic on Gothic Rd. (no water), or park in one of the turnouts and find your own tent sites, as long as you're at least 150 ft. away from roads and streams (open June-Nov.).

Brick Oven Pizza, 229 Elk St. (349-5044), dishes out authentic NY- and Chicago-style pizzas from a small window; tasty slices loaded with toppings are $2, and large pizzas cost $12 (open daily 11am-9pm). **The Bakery Café** (349-7280), at 3rd and Elk Ave., is a popular lunch spot, with $4-7 sandwiches and awe-inspiring pastries for $2-3 (open daily 7am-9pm; shorter hrs. in winter; wheelchair access). **The Eldo** (349-2703), upstairs from Red Lady Realty on Elk St., packs a small bar and a large patio for cheap food and cheaper beer ($1.50 bottles during the 5pm-6pm happy hour). If you boast agility with a cue, drop in on a Monday night for a pool tourney ($10 entry).

The **Crested Butte Chamber of Commerce** (349-6438 or 800-545-4505), 601 Elm, furnishes trail maps and numerous brochures (open daily 9am-5pm). A free **shuttle** (349-7318) to the mountain departs from the chamber. (May-Sept. every 35min. from 8am-midnight; in ski season, every 15min. from 7:30am-midnight.) **Post Office:** 215 Elk Ave. (349-5568; open M-F 7:30am-4:30pm, Sa 10am-1pm). **ZIP code:** 81224. **Area code:** 970.

■ Telluride

Site of the first bank Butch Cassidy ever robbed (the San Miguel), Telluride has a history right out of a 1930s film. Prize fighter Jack Dempsey used to wash dishes in the Athenian Senate, a popular saloon/brothel that frequently required Dempsey to double as a bouncer when he was between plates. Presidential candidate William Jennings Bryan delivered his "Cross of Gold" speech in Telluride from the front balcony of the Sheridan Hotel. Not so rare (especially after its devaluation) was the silver that attracted everyone to Telluride in the first place. Today, skiers, hikers, and vacationers come to Telluride to pump gold and silver *into* these mountains; the town is gaining popularity and may be the Aspen of the future. Still, a small-town feeling prevails; rocking chairs sit outside brightly painted, wood-shingled houses, and dogs lounge on storefront porches.

PRACTICAL INFORMATION Telluride is only accessible by car, via U.S. 550 or Rte. 145. The closest **Greyhound** stop is in Montrose, 132 N. 1st St. (249-6673), a 60 mi. drive. The **visitors center** is upstairs from **Rose's Grocery Store,** 666 W. Colorado Ave. (728-6265 or 800-525-2717), near the entrance to town (open daily in summer 8am-7pm, in ski season 8am-6pm). **Post Office**: 101 E. Colorado Ave. (728-3900; open M-F 9am-5pm, Sa 10am-noon). **ZIP code:** 81435. **Area code:** 970.

ACCOMMODATIONS, FOOD, AND NIGHTLIFE If you're visiting Telluride during a festival, bring a sleeping bag; the cost of a bed is outrageous. The **Oak Street Inn,** 134 N. Oak St. (728-3383), offers cozy duplex rooms. (Singles $42, with private bath $66; doubles $58/$66. Rates $20 higher during festivals. Showers $3 for non-guests.) **Camp** at the east end of Telluride in a town-operated facility (728-3071) with 46 sites, water, restrooms, and showers ($11, higher during festivals; 1-week max. stay). **Sunshine,** 7 mi. southwest on Rte. 145 toward Cortez, is a developed national forest campground (14 sites, $8, 2-week max. stay). For info on all **National Forest Campgrounds,** call the **Forest Service** (327-4261; open M-F 8am-noon and 1-5pm). Several free primitive sites huddle nearby and are accessible by jeep roads. During festival times, you can crash anywhere; hot showers ($2) are available at the high school.

Baked in Telluride, 127 S. Fir St. (728-4775), has enough rich coffee and delicious pastries, pizza, sandwiches, and 50¢ bagels to get you through a festival weekend even if you *are* baked in Telluride. The apple fritters ($1.75) are justly famous. (Open daily 5:30am-10pm.) **Steaming Bean Coffee,** 221 W. Colorado Ave. (728-0220), offers coffee ($1), as well as smoothies ($3-4) and **Internet access.** ($6.50 per hr., includes any drink on the menu. Open M-F 7am-10pm, Sa-Su 7:30am-10pm.) *Buenos* breakfasts (*huevos rancheros* $7) and huge Mexican combination plates ($6-10) hide out at **Sofio's Mexican Café,** 110 E. Colorado Ave. (728-4882; open M 7-11:30am, Tu-Sa 7-11:30am and 5:30-10pm, Su 7am-noon and 5:30-10pm).

The taps at **Floradora,** 103 W. Colorado Ave. (728-3888), flow with home-brewed beer (pints $3.50; open daily 11am-midnight). Chug one of 10 beers on tap at **The House, a Tavern,** 131 N. Fir St. (728-6207), where college-students-gone-ski-bums hang out (drafts $2-4; happy hour 4-7pm, 75¢ off all beers; open daily 3pm-2am). The cool, conversational **Last Dollar Saloon,** 100 E. Colorado (728-4800), near Pine, will take your last buck with a smile (bottled beer $2.50-3.50; open daily 3pm-2am).

FESTIVALS AND ACTIVITIES Given that only 1500 people inhabit Telluride, the sheer number of summer arts festivals in the town seems staggering. For general festival info, contact the **visitors center** (see above). Gala events occur just about every weekend in summer and fall; the most renowned is the **Bluegrass Festival** (800-624-2422), on the third weekend in June. In recent years, the likes of James Taylor and the Indigo Girls have attracted crowds of 19,000, although capacity is limited to 10,000 (tickets $35-40 per night, 4-day pass $120). The **Telluride International Film Festival** (603-643-1255), the first weekend in September, draws actors and directors from all over the globe, including Jodie Foster, Clint Eastwood, and Francis Ford Coppola, and has premiered such films as *The Crying Game* and *The Piano*. Telluride also hosts the **Talking Gourds** poetry fest (2nd weekend in July) and a **Jazz Celebration** (728-7009; 1st weekend in Aug.), among others. For some festivals, you can volunteer to usher, set up chairs, or perform other tasks in exchange for free admission.

Biking, hiking, and backpacking opportunities are endless; ghost towns and lakes are tucked behind almost every mountain crag. The tourist office has a list of suggestions for hikes in the area. The most popular trek is up the jeep road to **Bridal Veil Falls,** the waterfall visible from almost anywhere in Telluride. The trailhead is at the end of Rte. 145 (about 2hr.). Continuing another 2½ mi. from the top of the falls will lead you to Silver Lake, a steep but very rewarding climb.

In winter, even self-proclaimed atheists can be spied silently praying before hitting the "Spiral Stairs" and the "Plunge," two of the Rockies' most gut-wrenching ski runs. For more info, contact the **Telluride Ski Resort,** P.O. Box 11155, Telluride 81435

(728-3856). A free shuttle connects the mountain village with the rest of the town; pick up a current schedule at the visitors center along with a copy of *Skier Services Brochure.* **Paragon Ski and Sport,** 213 W. Colorado Ave. (728-4525), rents bikes in summer ($26 per day) and skis and boots in winter ($20 per day). The longer you rent, the cheaper it gets. (Open daily in summer 9am-8pm; ski season 8:30am-9pm.)

■ Durango

As Will Rogers once put it, Durango is "out of the way and glad of it." Despite its popularity as a tourist destination, Durango retains a relaxed atmosphere. Folks come here to see Mesa Verde, raft down the Animas River, hike the beautiful San Juan Mountains, or ski at Purgatory.

PRACTICAL INFORMATION Durango parks at the intersection of U.S. 160 and U.S. 150. Streets run perpendicular to avenues, but everyone calls Main Ave. "Main St." As you head south on Main Ave., the town becomes less touristy. **Greyhound,** 275 E. 8th Ave. (259-2755 or 800-231-2222; open M-F 7:30am-noon and 3:30-5pm, Sa 7:30am-noon, Su and holidays 7:30-10am), runs once per day to Grand Junction (5½hr., $34); Denver (11½hr., $53); and Albuquerque (5hr., $41). The **Durango Lift** (259-LIFT/5438) provides trolley service up and down Main Ave. every 30min. (runs daily 6am-10pm; 25¢). The **Durango Area Chamber Resort Association,** 111 S. Camino del Rio (247-0312 or 800-525-8855), on the southeast side of town at Gateway Dr., offers helpful info about sights and hiking (open M-F 8am-5pm, Sa 10am-2pm). **Internet access** is available at **Connecting Point,** 835 Main Ave., 2nd fl. of Main Mall ($2.50 per 15min.; min. charge $1; open M-F 8:30am-5:30pm, Sa 10am-2pm). **Post Office:** 222 W. 8th St. (247-3434; open M-F 8:30am-5:30pm, Sa 9am-1pm). **ZIP code:** 81301. **Area code:** 970.

ACCOMMODATIONS, FOOD, AND NIGHTLIFE The **Durango Youth Hostel,** 543 E. 2nd Ave. (247-9905), 1 block from downtown, maintains clean, simple bunks and kitchen facilities in a large converted house that retains a cozy, home-like feel. Ask the owner about local cafes, hangouts, and activities. ($12, nonmembers $15. Check-in 7-10am and 5-10pm. Check-out 7-10am. Key deposit $5.) There are few bottom-end motels in Durango; for the cheapest, look to the part of Main Ave. north of town. The lowest price for a summer double hovers around $40. Even **Budget Inn,** 3077 Main Ave. (247-5222 or 800-257-5222), charges a lot for its spacious rooms—but it does have a nice pool and hot tub (singles $35; doubles $45; in winter $25/$35). **Cottonwood Camper Park** (247-1977), on U.S. 160, ½ mi. west, is the closest campground to town (2-person sites $16; $2 per additional person; full hookup $20).

   Silverton, 47 mi. north on U.S. 550, has other lodging options. Less popular than Durango and more isolated, the town nevertheless lies at the base of some of the area's most beautiful mountains and hiking trails. **Teller House Hotel,** 1250 Greene St. (387-5423 or 800-342-4338), next to the French Bakery (which provides the hotel's complimentary breakfast), has comfy rooms in a well-maintained 1896 hotel (singles prices negotiable; doubles $38-48, with bath $68; $8 per additional person).

   For fixin's, head to **City Market,** on U.S. 550, 1 block down 9th St. and at 3130 Main Ave. (both open 24hr.). Locals eat breakfast at **Carver's Bakery and Brewpub,** 1022 Main Ave. (259-2545), which has delicious bread, breakfast specials ($2-6), the usual pizza and burgers ($5-6), and home-brewed beer ($3; pitchers $8; open M-Sa 6:30am-10pm, Su 6:30am-1pm). **Farquahart's,** 725 Main Ave. (247-5442), serves up a hearty burrito plate ($7), along with the best live music in town. (W-Su rock, world beat, and reggae. W-F $5 cover. Open Su-Tu 11am-11pm, W-Th 11am-midnight, F-Sa 11am-1:30am.) Every year, **Olde Tymer's,** 1000 Main Ave. (259-2990), wins an award for Durango's best burger ($4). Vegetarians will be happy with the $5-6 salad options. (Open daily 11am-10pm.)

ACTIVITIES Winter is Durango's busiest season. **Purgatory Resort** (247-9000), 27 mi. north on U.S. 550, hosts skiers of all levels (lift tickets $39, ages 6-12 $17). When the heat is on, travelers can trade in their skis for a sled and test out the **alpine slide** (open daily 9:30am-4:45pm; 1 ride $8, 3 rides $21) or take a free **scenic chairlift ride. Mountain biking** down the slope's trails is also popular; bike uplifts are $5 a piece, or $12 all day.

Although it's definitely more of a tourist attraction than a means of transportation, the **Durango and Silverton Narrow Gauge Train,** 479 Main St. (247-2733), runs along the Animas River Valley to the glistening old town of **Silverton.** Old-fashioned, 100% coal-fed locomotives wheeze and cough through the San Juans, making a 2hr. stop in Silverton before returning to Durango. In the summer, be prepared for heat and dust (trains at 7:30, 8:15, 9, and 9:45am; 7hr.; $49, ages 5-11 $25). The train also drops off **backpackers** at various scenic points along the route and picks them up on return trips; call for more info on this service. (Office open daily 6am-9pm; May and mid-Aug. to Oct. 7am-7pm; Nov.-Apr. 8am-5pm.)

The entire Durango area is engulfed by the **San Juan National Forest;** the headquarters (247-4874; open M-F 8am-5pm) is located in Durango. Call for info on hiking and camping in the forest, especially if you're planning a trip into the massive **Weminuche Wilderness,** northeast of Durango. For river rafting, **RiversWest,** 520 Main Ave. (259-5077 or 800-622-0852), has reasonable rates (open daily 8am-8pm; reservations recommended; 1hr. $12, ½-day $32; children 20% off). **Durango Rivertrippers,** 720 Main Ave. (259-0289 or 800-292-2885), has similar prices (open daily 8am-9pm; 2hr. $20, under 13 $15; ½-day $30/$20). Bikes are available at **Hassle Free Sports,** 2615 Main St. (259-3874 or 800-835-3800), but you must have a driver's license and major credit card. (½-day $16; full-day $25. Open M-Sa 8:30am-6pm, Su 10am-5pm.)

■ Near Durango: Pagosa Springs

The Ute people—the first to discover the waters of Pagosa—believed that the springs were a gift of the Great Spirit, and it's not hard to see why. Pagosa Springs, some of the hottest and largest in the world, bubble from the San Juan Mountains 62 mi. east of Durango on Rte. 160. Follow the smell of sulfur to **Spring Inn,** 165 Hot Springs Blvd. (264-4168 or 800-225-0934), where eleven different outdoor pools of varying temperatures are available for your soaking pleasure ($8.50 per person; open 24hr.). **Chimney Rock Archeological Area** (883-5359), 20 mi. west of Pagosa Springs on U.S. 160 and Rte. 151 S, contains the ruins of a high-mesa Anasazi village. (Open daily mid-May to late Sept. 8am-6pm. $5, ages 5-11 $2. 2hr. guided tours leave at 9:30, 10:30am, 1, and 2pm.) Skiing is available at **Wolf Creek,** 20 mi. east of Pagosa, which claims to have the most snow in Colorado (lift tickets $32, under 13 $20; rates often change). For nearby fishing, hiking, and camping, contact the San Juan National Forest (247-4874; see Durango **Activities,** p. 615). The **visitors center** (264-2360) sits at the intersection of San Juan St. and Hot Springs Blvd. (open M-F 8am-5pm, Sa-Su 10-2pm; in winter daily 9am-5pm). Except for the occasional mudslide and stampede, there is no public transportation in Pagosa Springs.

The **Sky View Motel** (264-5803), 1 mi. west of town on Rte. 160, offers singles ($40) and doubles ($45) with cable TV; some rooms have kitchenettes. **Pinewood Inn,** 157 Pagosa St. (800-655-7463 or 264-5715), 1 block from downtown, rents cozy wood-paneled rooms with TVs and phones (singles $41; doubles $54). The **Moose River Pub,** 20 Village Dr. (731-5451), serves up Southwestern chop-lickin' goodies. (Hamburgers $5, vegetable plates $6. Open M-F 11am-2pm and 5-9pm, Sa 5-9pm.) Brace yourself for **Hog's Breath Saloon,** 157 Navajo Trail Dr. (731-2626), near Rte. 160 W. This popular spot features country-western dancing (F-Sa) and a surf 'n' turf menu (entrees $8-11; open daily 11am-10pm). The award-winning green chili stew ($4) at the **Rolling Pin Bakery Café,** 214 Pagosa St. (264-2255), deserves attention with its unique combo of spices, chili, and chicken. Big breakfast flapjacks are $4 and sandwiches $4-6. (Open M-Sa 7am-5:30pm, Su 7am-2pm; in winter M-Sa 7am-2pm.)

■ Mesa Verde

Mesa Verde (Green Table) rises from the deserts of southwestern Colorado, its flat top noticeably friendlier to vegetation than the dry lands below. Fourteen hundred years ago, Native American tribes began to cultivate the area now known as **Mesa Verde National Park.** These people—today called the Anasazi, or "ancient ones"—constructed a series of elaborate cliff dwellings beneath the overhanging sandstone shelves surrounding the mesa. Then, around 1275 AD, 700 years after their ancestors had arrived, the Anasazi abruptly and mysteriously vanished from the historical record, leaving behind their eerie and starkly beautiful dwellings.

The southern portion of the park divides into **Chapin Mesa** and **Wetherill Mesa.** The **Chapin Mesa Museum** (529-4475), at the south end of the park, can give you an overview of the Anasazi lifestyle (open daily 8am-6:30pm; in winter 8am-5pm). On Chapin Mesa, rangers lead tours to **Cliff Palace,** the largest cliff dwelling in North America, and **Balcony House** (open in summer only), a 40-room dwelling 600 ft. above the floor of the Soda Canyon. (Tours depart from Cliff Palace overlook and Balcony House trailhead every 30min. 9am-6pm. $1.75; buy tickets at visitors center.) On Wetherill Mesa, guided tours go to **Long House,** which consists of 150 rooms and 21 *kicas* (tours leave every 30min. daily 10am-5pm; $1.75; buy tickets at visitors center). **Step House,** on Weatherill Mesa, is well-preserved, as is **Spruce Tree House,** near the museum. Both are accessible by self-guided tours (no tickets required).

The **Far View Lodge** (529-4421), across from the visitors center, offers two ½-day bus tours that depart from the Lodge at 9am and 1pm en route to the **Spruce Tree House.** The Lodge also offers a full-day tour, which departs at 9:30am and visits both sites. Arrive at least 30min. before the tour (½-day tours $29, under 12 $19; full-day $35/$19; no reservations).

Mesa Verde's only motel-style lodging, the rooms at Far View Lodge, are expensive (from $99). Try the **Ute Mountain Motel,** 531 S. Broadway (565-8507), in Cortez (singles $20-35, doubles $20-38), or the well-lit rooms of **Tomahawk Lodge,** 728 S. Broadway (565-8521 or 800-643-7705; singles $39-45, doubles $53-68; in winter $29/$34). The **Durango Hostel** (see Durango **Accommodations,** p. 614) also has cheap beds. Mesa Verde's **Morfield Campground** (564-1675), the third-largest national park campground in America, is located 4 mi. inside the park and almost never fills up (452 beautiful, secluded sites $13, full hookup $23; showers 75¢ per 5min.).

The park's main entrance is off U.S. 160, 36 mi. from Durango and 10 mi. from **Cortez.** The **entrance fee** is $10 for vehicles, $5 for pedestrians and bikers. The **Far View Visitors Center** (529-4543), 20 mi. from the gate on the main road, publishes a comprehensive visitors guide with complete listings on park walks, drives, and trails (open daily in summer 8am-5pm). During the winter, head to the museum (see above) or the **Colorado Welcome Center/Cortez Chamber of Commerce,** 928 E. Main (565-4048 or 565-3414), in Cortez (open daily 8am-6pm; in winter 8am-5pm). Since sights in the park lie up to 40 mi. apart, a car is nearly essential. **Area code:** 970.

Four Corners

New Mexico, Arizona, Utah, and **Colorado** meet at an unnaturally neat intersection about 40 mi. northwest of **Shiprock,** NM, on the Navajo Reservation. **Four Corners** epitomizes American ideas about land; these state borders were drawn along scientifically determined lines of longitude and latitude, with no regard for natural boundaries. *(Open daily in summer 7am-8pm; in winter 8am-5pm. $1.50.)* There isn't much to see, but getting down on all fours and putting a limb in each state is a good story for a cocktail party.

THE SOUTHWEST

The Anasazi of the 10th and 11th centuries were the first to discover that the arid lands of the Southwest could support an advanced agrarian civilization. Years later, in 1803, the United States laid claim to parts of the Southwest with the Louisiana Purchase. The idealistic hope for a western "empire of liberty," where Americans could live the virtuous farm life, both motivated further expansion and helped create the region's individualist mythology, from the lone gunslinger to the rugged pioneer.

Today, the steel blue of the Superstition peaks, the rainbow expanse of the Painted Desert, the deep gorges of the Grand Canyon, the murky depths of Carlsbad Caverns, and the red stone arches and twisted spires of southern Utah and northern Arizona lure visitors and keep Kodak in business. The vastness of the Southwestern desert and its peculiar colors—of red rock, sandstone, scrub brush, and pale sky—invite contemplation; farther north, Utah's mountains offer equally breathtaking vistas. Meanwhile, reservation lands and ruins dot the landscape, a reminder of the strong Native American presence still felt in the Southwest today.

✋ HIGHLIGHTS OF THE SOUTHWEST

- **Mexican food.** You can't get away from it, and in the tasty eateries of New Mexico's Albuquerque (p. 673) and Santa Fe (p. 680), you may not want to.
- **National Parks.** Utah's "Fab Five" (p. 636) and Arizona's Grand Canyon (p. 646) reveal a stunning landscape of bizarre rock formations and brilliant colors.
- **Skiing.** In a region famous for its blistering sun, the Wasatch Mountains (p. 630) near Salt Lake City, UT receive some of the nation's choicest powder in winter.
- **Las Vegas, NV.** Attractions include casinos, casinos, and casinos (p. 622).

Nevada

Nevada once walked the straight and narrow. Explored by Spanish missionaries and settled by Mormons, the Nevada Territory's scorched expanses seemed a perfect place for ascetics to strive for moral uplift. However, with the discovery of gold in 1850 and silver in 1859, the state was won over permanently to the worship of filthy lucre. When the precious metals ran out, gambling and marriage-licensing became big industries. The final moral cataclysms came when the state legalized prostitution on a county by county basis and spawned crooning lounge idol Wayne Newton.

But there *is* another side to Nevada. Lake Mead National Recreation Area, only 25 mi. from Las Vegas, is an oasis in stunning desert surroundings, and the forested slopes of Lake Tahoe provide serene resorts for an escape from the cities.

PRACTICAL INFORMATION

Capital: Carson City.
Visitor Info: Nevada Commission on Tourism, Capitol Complex, Carson City 89701 (800-638-2328; line staffed 24hr.). **Nevada Division of State Parks,** 1300 S. Curry St., Carson City 89703-5202 (702-687-4384). Open M-F 8am-5pm.
Time Zone: Pacific (3hr. behind Eastern). **Postal Abbreviation:** NV.
Sales Tax: 6.75-7%; 8% room tax in some counties.

◼ Las Vegas

Las Vegas, a city of 880,000, draws three times that many tourists every month. Most come to witness the spirit of capitalism (minus the Protestant ethic) and to partake in what might be the most direct economic alienation known to man—funneling earn-

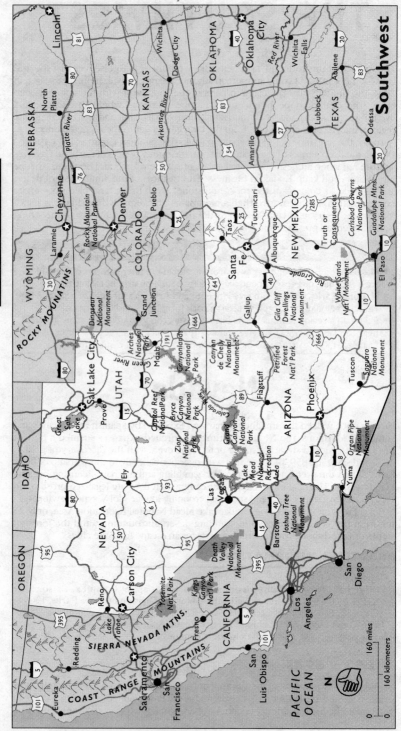

Southwest

ings into a well-oiled, privately owned profit machine. The lights and glitter of the Strip comprise a Disney-esque league of mock-ups, from ancient Egypt to present-day New York, each leading to a similar gauntlet of gaming rooms and lounges—thresholds of fun without substance, triumph without responsibility, loss without meaning.

ORIENTATION AND PRACTICAL INFORMATION

Driving to Vegas from Los Angeles is a straight 300 mi. shot on I-15 (5hr.). From Arizona, take I-40 W to Kingman and then U.S. 93/95 N. Las Vegas has two major casino areas: **downtown,** around Fremont and 2nd St., is a pedestrian promenade, and the **Strip** is a collection of mammoth casinos on both sides of **Las Vegas Blvd.** Parallel to the Strip is **Paradise Blvd.,** also strewn with casinos. As in any city where money reigns supreme, many areas of Las Vegas are unsafe. Always stay on brightly lit pathways, and do not wander too far from the major casinos and hotels. The neighborhoods just north and west of downtown can be especially dangerous.

Despite all its debauchery, Las Vegas has a **curfew.** Cruisers under 18 are not allowed unaccompanied in public places from midnight to 5am, those under 14 from 10pm to 5am. On weekends, no one under 18 is allowed unaccompanied on the Strip or in other designated areas 9pm-5am.

Airport: McCarran International (261-5743), at the southeast end of the Strip. Main terminal is on Paradise Rd. and within walking distance of University of Nevada campus. Vans to the Strip and downtown $3-5; taxi to downtown $10.

Buses: Greyhound, 200 S. Main St. (382-2292 or 800-231-2222), at Carson downtown. To Los Angeles (5hr., 6 per day, $31-35) and San Francisco (13hr., 3 per day, $51-54). Open daily 4:30am-1am.

Public Transportation: Citizens Area Transit (CAT) (228-7433). Bus #301 serves downtown and the Strip 24hr. Buses #108 and #109 serve the airport. Fares for routes on the Strip $1.50, for residential routes $1, seniors and ages 6-17 50¢. Most buses operate every 10-15min. (less frequently off the Strip), daily 5:30am-1:30am, 24hr. on the Strip. **Las Vegas Strip Trolleys** (382-1404) are not moving strip joints. They cruise the Strip every 20min. daily 9am-2am ($1.50 in exact change).

Taxis: Yellow, Checker, Star (873-2000). Base fare $2.20, $1.50 per additional mi. 24hr. service.

Car Rental: Sav-Mor Rent-A-Car, 5101 Rent-A-Car Rd. (736-1234 or 800-634-6779). Rentals from $28 per day, $147 per week. 150 free mi. per day, 20¢ per additional mi. Must be 21; under 25 surcharge $8 per day. Discounts in tourist publications.

Visitor Info: Las Vegas Convention and Visitor Authority, 3150 Paradise Rd. (892-0711), at the Convention Center, 4 blocks from the Strip by the Hilton. Up-to-date info on headliners, conventions, shows, hotel bargains, and buffets. Open M-F 8am-6pm, Sa-Su 8am-5pm.

Tours: Gambler's special bus tours leave L.A., San Francisco, and San Diego for Las Vegas early in the morning and return at night or the next day. Ask at tourist offices in the departure cities or call casinos for info. **Gray Line,** 4020 Lone Mountain Rd., North Las Vegas (702-384-1234), gives Mini City Tours (30min., 1 per day, $19). Bus tours from Las Vegas to Hoover Dam/Lake Mead (3 per day, $30 including $8 Dam admission) and Grand Canyon's South Rim (full day, Tu-Sa, $139). Discounted prices with coupons from Vegas tourist publications. Reserve in advance.

Marriage: Marriage License Bureau, 200 S. 3rd St. (455-4415). Must be 18 or obtain parental consent. Licenses issued for $35, cash only. No waiting period or blood test required. Open M-Th 8am-midnight, F 8am-Su midnight. **A Little Wedding Chapel,** 1301 Las Vegas Blvd. S. (382-5943). 24hr. Drive-thru service $30; chapel service $45.

Divorce: You must be a Nevada resident for at least 6 weeks and pay a $140 service fee. Permits available at the courthouse M-F 8am-5pm.

Bi-Gay-Lesbian Organizations: Gay and Lesbian Community Center, 912 E. Sahara Ave. (733-9800). Hrs. dependent on volunteer staff availability.

Hotlines: Compulsive Gamblers (800-LOST-BET/567-8238). **Rape Crisis Center** (366-1640). **Suicide Prevention** (731-2990). All 24hr.

THE SOUTHWEST

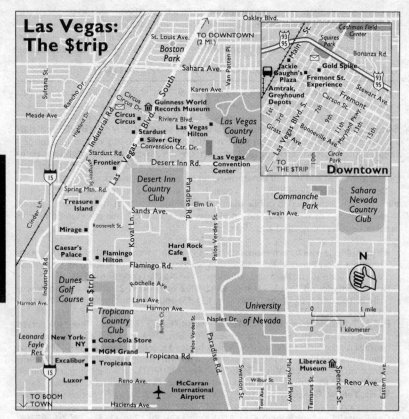

Las Vegas: The $trip

Post Office: 301 E. Stewart Ave. (800-275-8777), downtown. Open M-Sa 10:30am-7pm, Su 11am-7pm. General delivery pick-up M-F 9am-5pm. **ZIP code:** 89101. **Area code:** 702.

ACCOMMODATIONS AND CAMPGROUNDS

Even though Vegas has over 90,000 rooms, most hotels fill up on weekend nights. Coming to town on a Friday or Saturday night without reservations is flirting with homelessness, so make reservations as far in advance as possible. If you get stuck, the **Room Reservations Hotline** (800-332-5333) may be able to help. The earlier you reserve, the better chance you have of snagging a special rate. Room rates at most hotels in Vegas fluctuate all the time. Many hotels use two rate ranges—one for week-nights, the other for weekend nights. In addition, a room that costs $20 during a pro-motion can cost hundreds during a convention. Local publications such as *What's On In Las Vegas, Today in Las Vegas, Vegas Visitor, Casino Player, Tour Guide Magazine,* and *Insider Viewpoint of Las Vegas* provide discounts and coupons; they are all free and available at the visitors center, hotels, and attractions.

Strip hotels are at the center of the action and within walking distance of each other, but their inexpensive rooms sell out quickly. Motels line **Fremont St.,** from downtown south. Another option, if you have a car, is to stay at one of the hotel-casi-nos in Jean, NV (approximately 30 mi. south on I-15, near the California border). These tend to be less crowded and cheaper than in-town hotels. Members of the same sex sharing a hotel room may have to book a room containing two twin beds, as public displays of affection by homosexual couples are illegal in Nevada.

⊛Las Vegas International Hostel (AAIH/Rucksackers), 1208 Las Vegas Blvd. S. (385-9955). Flashing blue arrows point the way to this European-flavored joint. Tidy, spartan rooms with A/C and fresh sheets every day. Ride board in kitchen. Free lemonade, tea, coffee. TV room and basketball court. Extremely helpful staff is an excellent source for advice about budget Vegas. Shared bathrooms. Dorms $12, F-Sa $14; singles $26; rates lower Dec.-Mar. Laundry facilities. Key deposit $5. Reception daily 7am-11pm. Check-out 7-10am.

Somerset House Motel, 294 Convention Center Dr. (735-4411 or 888-336-4280). A straightforward, no-frills establishment within short walking distance of the major Strip casinos. Many rooms feature kitchens and balconies; all are sizable and impeccably clean. Dishes and cooking utensils provided upon request. Singles $32, F-Sa $40; doubles $40/$50; $5 per additional person. Senior discount.

Aztec Inn Casino, 2200 Las Vegas Blvd. S. (385-4566). On the north end of the strip, the Aztec offers clean rooms, a small casino, and discounts for out-of-town guests. Standard rooms $30, F-Sa $40-60.

Circus Circus, 2880 Las Vegas Blvd. S. (734-0410 or 800-444-CIRCUS/2472). Only hotel with its own clown shop. Rooms with TV and A/C for 1-4 people. Su-Th $29-79, F-Sa $49-99, holidays $65-125. Roll-away bed $10. In summer, fills 2-3 months in advance Su-Th, 3-4 months F-Sa.

Silverton, 3333 Blue Diamond Rd. (263-7777 or 800-588-7711). Although its ghost town theme is ominous in the Vegas context, this slightly remote hotel-casino offers the swagger of the Strip at affordable prices. A free shuttle transports guests back to Las Vegas Blvd. Singles and doubles $25-49, F-Sa $49-99.

Lake Mead National Recreation Area (293-8906), 25 mi. south of town on U.S. 93/95. Sites $10, with hookup $14-18.

Circusland RV Park, 500 Circus Circus Dr. (734-0410), a part of the Circus Circus hotel on the Strip. Laundry facilities, showers, pool, jacuzzi, and convenience store. Sites $17.50, F-Sa $20.

FOOD

Almost every hotel-casino in Vegas courts tourists with cheap buffets, but expect bland, greasy food and long lines at peak hours. Most casinos dole out alcoholic drinks for free to those who are gambling and for under $1 to those who aren't…yet. Vegas isn't all bland buffets—just west of the Strip, particularly along **Decatur Blvd.,** are a number of low-priced eateries that can revive your taste buds.

⊛The Plaza Diner, 1 Main St. (386-2110), near the entrance in Jackie Gaughn's Plaza. Delicious prime rib dinner (noon-midnight) $4. Beers $1. Open 24hr.

Rincon Criollo, 1145 Las Vegas Blvd. S. (388-1906), across from the youth hostel. Dine on filling Cuban food beneath a wall-sized photograph of palm trees. Daily special includes steak prepared *palomillas*-style, rice, and black beans for an unbeatable $6. Hot sandwiches $3.50-4.50. Open Tu-Su 11am-10pm.

Battista's Hole in the Wall, 4041 Audrie Ave. (732-1424), right behind the Flamingo. One of the only establishments in Las Vegas with any character of its own. 27 years' worth of celebrity photographs and novelty bottles from area brothels festoon the walls, along with the head of "Moosolini," the fascist moose. Dinner starts at 5pm and runs a ducal $18, but it's worth it.

Circus Circus, 2800 Las Vegas Blvd. S. (734-0410). The cheapest buffet in town. Rows of serving stations make you feel like a circus circus animal at a feed trough. Breakfast $4 (6-11:30am), brunch $5 (noon-4pm), dinner $6 (4:30-11pm).

Bally's Big Kitchen, 3645 Las Vegas Blvd. S. (739-4930). Locals say it has the best buffets on the Strip. A bit pricier, but worth it if you dig casino buffet food. Breakfast $9, lunch $10, dinner $14. Open daily 7am-2:30pm and 4:30-10pm.

SIGHTS

Fans of classical music and kitsch will be delighted by the **Liberace Museum,** 1775 E. Tropicana Ave. (798-5595), devoted to the flamboyant late "Mr. Showmanship." *(Open M-Sa 10am-5pm, Su 1-5pm. $7, students and seniors $5, under 12 free.)* Liberace's audacious uses of fur, velvet, and rhinestone boggle the rational mind. It's been said that God made men, and Sam Colt made 'em equal. Experience coltish justice at **The Gun Store,** 2900 E. Tropicana Ave. (454-1110). $10 plus ammo lets you try out an impressive array of pistols, up to and including the enormous Magnum 44. Fork over $30 and they'll let you shoot real machine guns. Boy, shootin' shore do make yer thirsty! Good thing there's **Everything Coca-Cola,** 3785 Las Vegas Blvd. S. (270-5953), under the MGM Grand. *(Tours $2.)* Watch old Coke commercials and drink all the Coke (and Coca-Cola products from around the world) you want.

CA$INO-HOPPING AND NIGHTLIFE

Unkempt punk rock icon Johnny Rotten proclaimed, "The only notes that matter come in a wad." Casinos have resorted to ever more extreme measures to get these notes. Where once the casinos stuck to the quintessentially Vegas themes of cheap buffets, booze, and entertainment, they now spend millions of dollars a year trying to fool guests into thinking that they are somewhere else. Spittin' images of Hollywood, New York, Rio, Paris (complete with Eiffel Tower), and Monte Carlo already thrive on the Strip. Despite these alluring amusements, however, gambling remains Vegas's biggest draw. It is *illegal for those under 21.* If you are of age, look for casino "funbooks" which allow you to buy $50 in chips for only $15. Never bring more money than you're prepared to lose cheerfully. And always remember: in the long run, you will almost definitely lose cash. Keep your wallet in your front pocket, and beware of the thieves who prowl casinos to nab big winnings from unwary jubilants. Most casinos offer free gambling lessons; *Today in Las Vegas* lists current dates and times. In addition, the more patient dealers may offer a tip or two (in exchange for one from you). Casinos, nightclubs, and wedding chapels stay open 24hr. Casinos are listed north to south.

Jackie Gaughn's Plaza, 1 Main St. (386-2110), downtown, near the electric-light spectacular "The Fremont Experience," offers penny slots for Okies yearning for the big-city thrill of jockeying, and some of the cheapest blackjack tables in town.

Moving on to the strip, **Circus Circus,** 2880 Las Vegas Blvd. S. (734-0410), attempts to cultivate a (dysfunctional) family atmosphere. Beware of the carnival area's "Camel Chase" game; it's far more addictive than any Vegas slot machine. Two stories above the casino floor, tightrope-walkers, fire-eaters, and acrobats perform. (Open daily 11am-midnight.) Within the hotel complex, the **Grand Slam Canyon** is a Grand Canyon theme park with a rollercoaster and other rides—all enclosed in a glass shell. (Open daily 10am-midnight; in winter Su-Th 10am-6pm, F-Sa 10am-midnight. Rides $2-5; unlimited rides $16, under 4 ft. $12.) At **Treasure Island,** 3300 Las Vegas Blvd. S. (894-7111), pirates battle with cannons staged on giant wooden ships in a Strip-side "bay" on the Strip (every 1½hr., daily 4:30pm-midnight). The majestic confines of the **Mirage,** 3400 Las Vegas Blvd. S. (791-7111), banish all illusions from the halls of entertainment. Among its attractions are a dolphin habitat (admission $3), Siegfried and Roy's white tigers, and a volcano that erupts in fountains and flames every 15min. from dusk to midnight. Busts abound at **Caesar's Palace,** 3570 Las Vegas Blvd. S. (731-7110). Some of these are plaster; the rest are barely concealed beneath the low-cut classical costumes that the cocktail waitresses have to wear. Their male counterparts strut about with false Roman noses. In the **Festival Fountain show,** statues move, talk, battle, and shout amid a laser-light show (every 30min. daily 10am-11pm). **New York-New York,** 3790 Las Vegas Blvd. S. (740-6969), puts even Disneyland to shame with its fine-tuned gimmickry. Relive the glory days of Hollywood at the **MGM Grand,** 3799 Las Vegas Blvd. S. (891-1111). (Amusement Park open daily 10am-10pm. $12, ages 4-12 $10. Sky Screamer $25 for 1, $35 for 2, $45 for 3.) **Excalibur,** 3850 Las Vegas Blvd. S. (800-937-7777), has a medieval English theme, insofar as medieval England's economy was based on depriving senior citizens of their Social Security. Before the watchful eyes of the sprawling sphinx and the towering black pyramid of **Luxor,** 3900 Las Vegas Blvd. S. (262-4000), a dazzling laser light show is reminiscent of imperial ancient Egypt.

Nightlife in Vegas gets rolling around midnight and keeps going until everyone drops or runs out of money. At Caesar's Palace (731-7110), **Cleopatra's Barge,** a huge ship-disco, is one boat that's made for rockin' (cover F-Sa $5; open Tu-Su 9pm-2am). Another popular disco, **Gipsy,** 4605 Paradise Rd. (731-1919), southeast of the Strip, may look deserted at 11pm, but by 1am the medium-sized dance floor packs in a gay, lesbian, and straight crowd (cover $4). Be forewarned that the Gipsy dancers get crazy on Topless Tuesdays.

■ Near Las Vegas: Hoover Dam and Lake Mead

A capacious, sparkling white wall spanning the Boulder Canyon, the Hoover Dam gives dignity to heavy industry's encroachment on natural wonders (in this case, the less dramatic, western outlet of the Grand Canyon). Shiny steel towers climb the rugged brown hillsides, carrying high-tension wires up and out through the desert. The **visitors center** (293-8321) offers 30min. tours leading to the generators at the structure's bottom (open daily 8:30am-5:45pm, exhibits close at 6pm; tours $8, seniors $7, ages 6-16 $2). Parking in the garage on the Nevada side costs $2, but it is free across the dam in Arizona, and gives you the chance to walk across the top of the dam itself.

As the tour demonstrates, amidst progressively funnier puns involving the word "dam" and "damn," the dam was primarily constructed for flood control and irrigation purposes (electricity just pays for it). This message is repeated on the road over the dam; upon one of the Art Deco towers that line the structure, another set of pseudo-fascist reliefs declare: FLOOD CONTROL, IRRIGATION, WATER STORAGE, POWER. Powerful words for turbulent times.

Flood control, irrigation, and water storage are all arguably the same thing, and this multi-tiered program is fulfilled by crystalline, turquoise, non-alcoholic **Lake Mead,** a shiny blue spot in the arid wasteland between Arizona and Nevada. Dubbed "the jewel of the desert" by its residents, the lake and its environs offer more than social planning and deficit spending.

Alongside the Park Service campsites ($10), concessionaires usually operate RV parks (most of which have evolved into mobile home villages), marinas, restaurants, and occasionally motels. More remote concessionaires include **Echo Bay Resort** (702-394-4000 or 800-752-9669; RV hookup $18). Motel rooms start at $69, and Echo Bay's restaurant, **Tale of the Whale,** decorated in nautical motifs and featuring a stunning view of Lake Mead, sells burgers in the $5 range. The resort rents jet-skis ($50 per hr., $250 per day; fishing boats for impoverished seadogs $12 per hr., $60 per day). Most distant from the bustle of nearby Las Vegas is Overton Beach Resort, convenient to Overton, Nevada. Overton occupies a little patch of green in the desert at the northern end of scenic North Shore Scenic Dr. and offers food, cheap motels like the **Overton Motel,** 137 N. Moapa Valley Blvd. (702-397-2463; singles $29; doubles $35), and more Anasazi ruins than you can shake a stick at.

Backcountry hiking and camping is permitted in most areas and hunting in some, but Lake Mead is sustained by the myriad Californians driving white pickup trucks with **jet-skis** in tow. For those who came unprepared, boats and other watercraft can be rented at the various concessionaires which the government charges to operate along the shores. **Boulder Beach** (800-752-9669) is accessible by Lakeshore Dr. off U.S. 93. (Jet-skis $50 per hr., $250 per day; more modest fishing boats $50 for 4 hrs., $100 per day.) Between Las Vegas and Overton sits the **Valley of Fire State Park.** From I-15 from Las Vegas, take NV Rte. 169 at Crystal south to the park. For $5, you can cut through this breathtaking patch of rocky red desert back to I-15, then ride, boldly ride, back to the city.

■ Reno

If a Hollywood exec ever got the great idea to cross *Showgirls* with *The Golden Girls,* the result would be Reno. Hoping to strike it rich at the card tables, busloads of the nation's elderly flock to its hedonistic splendor. A punchy kaleidoscope of casinos, 24hr. bars, seedy motels, mountain vistas, strip clubs full of aspiring dancers, and neon-lit pawnshops makes Reno a strange and memorable place.

PRACTICAL INFORMATION Amtrak, at 135 E. Commercial Row (800-872-7245; ticket office open daily 8am-4:45pm), speeds to San-Francisco (1 bus/train combo per day, $30-72) and Sacramento (1 per day, $18-60). Arrive 30min. in advance to purchase ticket. **Greyhound,** 155 Stevenson St. (322-2970 or 800-231-2222; open 24hr.), ½ block from W. 2nd St., rolls to San Francisco (17 per day, $29); Salt Lake City (4 per day, $45-47); Los Angeles (11 per day, $40-42); and Sacramento (6 per day, $20). The station has lockers (up to 6hr. $2, 6-24hr. $4), a mini-mart, and a restaurant. **Arrow Trans** (786-2376) offers a van service to S. Lake Tahoe ($18 per person, 4-person min.; or $72 base fare). **Reno Citifare** (348-7433), at 4th and Center St., serves the Reno-Sparks area. Most buses operate 5am-7pm, though city center buses operate 24hr. Buses stop every 2 blocks. (Fare $1.25, seniors and disabled 60¢, ages 6-18 90¢.) **Reno-Sparks Convention and Visitors Center,** 300 N. Center St. (800-FOR-RENO/367-7366; http://www.playreno.com), on the first floor of the National Bowling Stadium, is full of pamphlets, booklets, and the sound of falling bowling pins. (Open M-Sa 7am-8pm, Su 9am-6pm.) **Post Office:** 50 S. Virginia St. (800-275-8777), at Mill St., 2 blocks south of city center (open M-F 7:30am-5pm, Sa 10am-2pm). **ZIP code:** 89501. **Area code:** 702.

ACCOMMODATIONS AND CAMPGROUNDS There are a number of ways to go about getting accommodations in Reno. To truly experience the decadent splendor that is Reno, the many hotel-casinos are the places to be. While weekend prices are usually on the high side, gamblers' specials, weekday rates, and winter discounts provide some great, cheap rooms. Prices fluctuate unpredictably, so be sure to call ahead. **Fitzgerald's,** 225 N. Virginia St. (786-3663); **Atlantis,** 3800 S. Virginia St. (825-4700); and **Sundowner,** 450 N. Arlington Ave. (786-7050), have been known to offer some good deals to go along with their central locations and massive facilities.

To escape Reno's constant hum of slot machines, those equipped to camp can make the drive to the woodland campsites of **Davis Creek Park** (849-0684), 17 mi. south on U.S. 395, then ½ mi. west; follow the signs ($11 per site, $5 per additional car; free picnic area open daily 8am-9pm). Wrap yourself in a rustic blanket of pines and sage at the base of the Sierra Nevada's **Mt. Rose** and camp at one of the 63 sites. (Full service, including showers, and a small pond stocked with fish, but no hookups. Sites first come, first camped. $10 per site per vehicle, $1 per pet. Picnic area open 8am-9pm.) The nearby 14 mi. Offer Creek Trail leads to Rock and Price Lakes and interlocks with the Tahoe Rim Trail. Camping and fishing on the trail are free but require permits (available at grocery and sporting goods stores). You can also camp along the shore at **Pyramid Lake** (see below). To stay closer to Reno, park and plug in your RV overnight at the **Reno Hilton,** 2500 E. 2nd St. (789-2000), for a $17 full hookup. Call ahead; people reserve these spots up to a year in advance.

FOOD Eating in Reno is cheap. To entice gamblers and to prevent them from wandering out in search of food, casinos offer a wide range of all-you-can-eat buffets and 99¢ breakfasts. However, buffet fare can be greasy, overcooked, and tasteless, and rumors of food poisoning abound. Reno's other inexpensive eateries offer better quality food. The large Basque population, which immigrated from the Pyrenees to herd sheep in Nevada, has brought a spicy and hearty cuisine locals enthusiastically recommend. **The Blue Heron,** 1091 S. Virginia St. (786-4110), 9 blocks from downtown, is a rare bird in Reno, appealing to a younger crowd (open M-Sa 11am-9pm, Su noon-9pm). **Louis' Basque Corner,** 301 E. 4th St. (323-7203), at Evans St., 3 blocks east of Virginia, is a local institution (open Su-M 5-9:30pm, Tu-Sa 11:30am-2:30pm and 5-9:30pm). **The Nugget,** 233 N. Virginia St. (323-0716), is a legendary 24hr. bar-and-stool coffee shop.

SIGHTS AND ENTERTAINMENT Reno is one big amusement park. The casinos, of course, are the main attraction. Many casinos offer free gaming lessons, and minimum bets vary between establishments. Drinks are either free or incredibly cheap for gamblers, but be wary of a casino's generous gift of highly alcoholic, risk-inducing, inhibition-dropping wallet-looseners. Gambling is illegal for persons under 21; if you win the jackpot at age 20, it'll be the casino's lucky day and not yours.

Almost all casinos offer live night-time entertainment, but unless you like schmaltzy Wayne Newton standards or delight at the thought of Tom Jones autographing your underwear, these shows are not really worth the steep admission prices. **Harrah's,** 219 N. Center St. (786-3232), is the self-consciously "hip" complex where **Planet Hollywood** capitalizes on movie lust, magically transforming Hollywood knick-knacks into precious relics. At **Circus Circus,** 500 N. Sierra (329-0711), a small circus above the casino performs "big-top" shows every 30min. It's not exactly Barnum and Bailey, but just as kitschy. These shows and others are listed in the weekly *Showtime,* which also offers gambling coupons. *Best Bets* provides listings of discounted local events and shows. *Encore* lists upcoming arts events in northern Nevada. *Nevada Events & Shows,* a section of the Nevada visitors' guide, lists sights, museums, seasonal events, and other goodies. These free papers are available in most hotels and casinos. The local *Reno Gazette-Journal* and *News and Review* have more info.

∎ Near Reno: Pyramid Lake

Thirty miles north of Reno on Rte. 445, on the Paiute Indian Reservation, lies emerald green Pyramid Lake, one of the most heart-achingly beautiful bodies of water in the U.S. The pristine tides of Pyramid Lake are set against the backdrop of a barren desert, making it a soothing and otherworldly respite from neon Reno. **Camping** is allowed anywhere on the lake shore, but only designated areas have toilet facilities. A $5 permit is required for use of the park, and the area is carefully patrolled by the Paiute tribe. Permits are available at the **Ranger Station,** 3 mi. left from Rte. 445 at Sutcliffe (476-1155; open daily 7am-3:30pm). **Boat rental** (476-1156) is available daily at the marina near the Ranger Station; call for reservations.

Utah

Beginning in 1848, persecuted Mormons settled on the land which is now Utah, intending to establish and govern their own theocratic state. President James Buchanan struggled to quash the Mormon's efforts in 1858, in a dispute which in some ways paralleled the states-rights conflicts leading up to the Civil War. Today the state's population is 70% Mormon—a religious presence particularly strong in Salt Lake City and the smaller cities surrounding the capital. Utah's citizens dwell primarily in the 100 mi. corridor along I-15 stretching from Ogden to Provo. Outside this area, Utah's natural beauty dominates, intoxicating visitors in a way that watered-down 3.2% beer never can. Immediately east of Salt Lake City, the Wasatch range beckons skiers in the winter and bikers in the summer. Southern Utah is part of a region like no other place on Earth; red canyons, river gorges, and crenellated cliffs attest to the creative powers of wind and water.

PRACTICAL INFORMATION

Capital: Salt Lake City.
Visitor Info: Utah Travel Council, 300 N. State St., Salt Lake City 84114 (801-538-1030 or 800-200-1160; http://www.utah.com), across from the capitol building. Distributes the *Utah Vacation Planner,* lists of motels, national parks, and camp-grounds, as well as statewide biking, rafting, and skiing vacation brochures. **Utah Parks and Recreation,** 1594 W. North Temple, Suite 116, Salt Lake City 84114 (801-538-7220). Open M-F 8am-5pm.
Controlled Substances: Mormons dispense with caffeine, nicotine, alcohol, and, of course, illegal drugs. While you won't have any trouble getting a pack of cigarettes, a cup of coffee or a coke, alcohol is another matter. State liquor stores are sprinkled sparsely about the state and have inconvenient hours. Only grocery and convenience stores may sell beer for take-out. Because licensing laws can split a room, drinkers may have to move a few ft. down a bar to get a mixed drink. Also, estab-

lishments that sell alcohol are required to be "members only"; tourists can either find a "sponsor"—i.e., an entering patron—or get a short-term membership.
State Holiday: July 24 is Pioneer Day, but most places of business are open.
Emergency: 911.
Time Zone: Mountain (2hr. behind Eastern). **Postal Abbreviation:** UT.
Sales Tax: 6.35%.

NORTHERN UTAH

■ Salt Lake City

Tired from five exhausting months of travel, Brigham Young looked out across the desolate valley of the Great Salt Lake and said, "this is the place." Young knew that his band of Mormon pioneers had finally reached a haven where they could practice their religion freely, away from the persecution they had faced in the East. Today, Salt Lake City is still dominated by Mormon influence. The Church of Latter Day Saints (LDS, not the hallucinogenic drug) owns the tallest office building downtown and welcomes visitors to Temple Sq., a city block that includes the Mormon Temple and cool, shady gardens. Despite its commitment to preserving traditions, Salt Lake is rapidly attracting high-tech firms, as well as outdoor enthusiasts drawn to world-class ski resorts, rock climbing, and mountain trails. The city has already landed perhaps the biggest prize of all, the 2002 Winter Olympics, which has left downtown looking temporarily war-torn from the construction now taking place.

ORIENTATION AND PRACTICAL INFORMATION

Salt Lake City's grid system makes navigation simple. Brigham Young designated **Temple Sq.** as the heart of downtown. Street names indicate how many blocks east, west, north, or south they lie from Temple Sq.; the "0" points are **Main St.** (north-south) and **South Temple St.** (east-west). Local address listings often include two numerical cross streets leading to some confusion. A building on E. 8th St. (800 E.) might be listed as 825 E. 1300 S., meaning the cross street is 1300S (13th S.). Smaller streets and those that do not fit the grid pattern often have non-numeric names.

Airport: Salt Lake City International, 776 N. Terminal Dr. (575-2600), 4 mi. west of Temple Sq. UTA bus #50 runs between the terminal and downtown for $1. Taxi to Temple Sq. costs about $13.

Trains: Amtrak, 320 S. Rio Grande (531-0188 or 800-872-7245), *in an unsafe area.* To San Francisco (18hr., 1 per day, $73-110) and Denver (15hr., 1 per day, $72-108). Station open M-F 10pm-1:30pm, Sa-Su 10pm-6am

Buses: Greyhound, 160 W. South Temple St. (355-9579 or 800-231-2222), near Temple Sq. To: Las Vegas (8-9hr., 3 per day, $39); Los Angeles (14-16hr., 3 per day, $80); and Denver (12hr., 7 per day, $42). Open daily 7am-midnight.

Public Transportation: Utah Transit Authority (UTA), 3600 S. 700 W. (287-4636). Frequent service to University of Utah campus; buses to Ogden (#70/72 express), suburbs, airport, mountain canyons, and the #11 express runs to Provo (fare $2). Buses every 20min.-1hr. M-Sa 6am-11pm. Fare $1-2, senior discounts, under 5 free. Maps available at libraries and the visitors bureau.

Taxis: Ute Cab, 359-7788. $2.75 base fare, $1.50 per mi. **Yellow Cab,** 521-2100. $1.25 base fare, $1.50 per mi.

Car Rental: High Country Car Rental, 1974 W. North Temple (596-2596). $34 per day, 200 free mi. $170 per week, 1400 free mi. 16¢ per additional mi. Must be 21 with a major credit card. Under 25 $5 per day surcharge. Open daily 6am-10pm.

Bike Rental: Wasatch Touring, 702 E. 100 S. St. (359-9361). 21-speed mountain bikes and helmets $20 per day. Open M-Sa 9am-7pm.

Visitor Info: Salt Lake Valley Convention and Visitors Bureau, 90 S. West Temple St. (534-4902), 1 block south of Temple Sq. Open M-F 8am-6pm, Sa 9am-4pm and

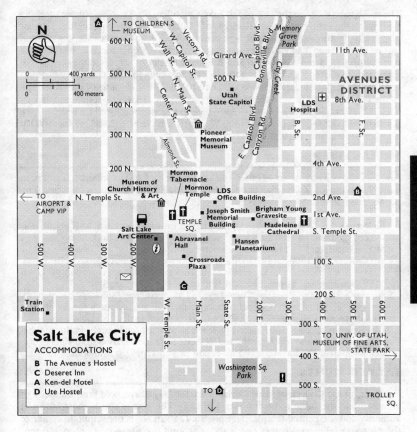

Su 9am-5pm; early Sept. to late May M-F 8am-5pm, Sa 9am-4pm. Distributes the *Salt Lake Visitors Guide*.

Hotlines: Rape Crisis, 467-7273. **Suicide Prevention**, 483-5444. Both 24hr.

Medical Services: University hospital emergency, 581-2291.

Post Office: 230 W. 200 S. St. (359-1035), 1 block south and 1 block west of visitors bureau. Open M-F 8am-5:30pm, Sa 9am-2pm. **ZIP code:** 84101. **Area code:** 801.

ACCOMMODATIONS AND CAMPGROUNDS

The Avenue's Hostel (HI-AYH), 107 F St. (359-3855 or 800-881-4785), 7 blocks east of Temple Sq. Free pick-up from Amtrak and Greyhound stations. Winter ski bus to nearby resorts $2-4. Dorm rooms $10-14; doubles $33-34, with private bath $37.50-42.50. Blankets and linen free. Reception 7:30am-12:30pm and 4-10:30pm.

Ute Hostel (AAIH/Rucksackers), 21 E. Kelsey Ave. (595-1645), near the intersection of 13th S. and Main St. Young international crowd. Free pick-ups can be arranged from Amtrak, Greyhound, or the visitors center. Free tea and coffee, parking, linen, and safe. Dorm rooms $15; comfortable doubles $30-35. Check-in 24hr.

Deseret Inn, 50 W. 500 S. (532-2900), in the heart of the city, rents singles ($39), doubles ($43), and the chance to soak your bones in their jacuzzi.

Ken-del Motel, 667 N. 300 W. (355-0293), 10 blocks northwest of Temple Sq. in a transitional neighborhood. From the airport take bus #50 to North Temple, then bus #70; from Greyhound or downtown, catch bus #70. Well-kept singles with kitchenettes, cable TV, and A/C $40; doubles $45.

The mountains rising to the east of Salt Lake City offer comfortable summer camping with warm days and cool nights. Rocky **Little Cottonwood Canyon,** on Rte. 210 east of the city, features two of the closest campgrounds for summer camping: **Albion Basin** (21 sites) and **Tanners Flat** (36 sites). Two more campgrounds lie just north of the city on I-15: **Sunset** (32 sites) and **Bountiful Peak** (79 sites). On weekends, get there early to ensure a space (sites $10-11). The **Salt Lake Ranger District** (943-1794) fields calls for more info. For those who can handle the stink of Salt Lake, **Antelope Island** (773-2941), in the middle of the lake (access off I-15, north of the city), has 13 sites ($2, $7 entrance fee). On weekends, call up to 2 months ahead for reservations. If you need a hookup, **Camp VIP,** 1400 W. North Temple St. (328-0224), has 500 RV sites and 10 tent sites ($19, full hookup $26).

MORAL FIBER

Good, cheap restaurants are sprinkled all around the city and its suburbs. If you're in a hurry downtown, **ZCMI Mall** and **Crossroads Mall,** both located across from Temple Sq., have standard food courts.

The Pie, 1320 E. 200 S. (582-0193), next to the University of Utah. This graffiti-buried college hangout serves up large pies (starting at $10) late into the night. Open M-Th 11am-1am, F-Sa 11am-3am, Su noon-11pm.

Park Café, 604 E. 1300 S. (487-1670), at the south end of Liberty Park. A classy little joint with a patio and a view of a park. Lunches and light dinners around $6. Open M-Th 7am-3pm and 5-9pm, F-Sa 7am-3pm and 5-10pm, Su 7am-3pm.

Squatter's Salt Lake Brewing Company, 147 W. Broadway (363-2739), is a microbrewery ($3 pints) with reasonably priced American cuisine and a variety of sandwiches, pizzas, and salads ($5-9). Open daily 11:30am-1am.

W.H. Brumby's, 224 S. 1300 E. (581-0888), is where "artisan bakers" produce to-die-for $5 breakfast and lunch plates and desserts for a local crowd from suits to students. Open M-Th 7am-10pm, F 7am-11pm, Sa 8am-11pm, Su 8am-6pm.

SACRED SIGHTS

Followers of the **Church of Jesus Christ of Latter Day Saints** hold both the Book of Mormon and the Bible to be the Word of God. The seat of the highest Mormon authority and the central temple, **Temple Sq.** (240-2609), is the symbolic center of the Mormon religion. Visitors can wander around the pleasant, flowery, 10-acre square, but the sacred temple is off-limits to non-Mormons. Alighting on the highest of the temple's three towers, a golden statue of the prophet Moroni watches over the city. The square has two **visitors' centers** (North and South); the North visitors center displays Old and New Testament murals and 25min. videos about Temple Sq. Book of Mormon and Purpose of Temple presentations alternate every 30min. at the South visitors center (free). *Legacy,* a film detailing the Mormon trek to Salt Lake City, is screened at the **Joseph Smith Memorial Building** (call 240-4383 for show times). A 45min. tour leaves from the flagpole every 10min., showing off the highlights of Temple Sq. (tours daily 9am-9pm; free).

Visitors to Temple Sq. may also visit the **Mormon Tabernacle,** which houses the famed choir. Built in 1867, the structure is so acoustically sensitive that a pin drop at one end of the building can be heard 175 ft. away at the other end. Members of the choir are selected on the basis of character, musical competence, and sometimes family tradition. Thursday evening rehearsals (8-9:30pm) and Sunday morning broadcasts from the tabernacle (9:30-10am; doors close at 9:15am) are open to the public. No matter how forcefully they sing, however, the choir can't match the size and sound of the 11,623-pipe **organ** which accompanies them (organ recitals M-Sa noon and 2pm, Su 2-2:30pm). In the summer, there are frequent concerts at **Assembly Hall,** next door. The **Museum of Church History and Art,** 45 N. West Temple St. (240-3310), houses Mormon memorabilia, including an original 1830 copy of the *Book of Mormon* (open M-F 9am-9pm, Sa-Su 10am-7pm; free).

The moment when Brigham Young and his band first came upon the Great Salt Lake is commemorated at **"This is the Place" Heritage Park,** 2601 Sunnyside Ave.

(584-8391), in Emigration Canyon on the eastern end of town (take bus #4 or the sites trolley for $4; park open in summer daily 9:30am-sunset). The visitors center guards the entrance to **"Old Desert Village"** (open daily 9am-5pm; $5, seniors and ages 3-11 $3). Big business meets religion at the **Church of Jesus Christ of Latter Day Saints Office Building,** 50 E. North Temple St. (240-1588), the tallest skyscraper in Salt Lake. The elevator to the 26th floor (free) grants a view of the Great Salt Lake in the west or the Wasatch Range in the east. Free tours are also offered. *(Tours available and observation deck open M-Sa 9am-4:30pm; in winter M-F 9am-5pm.)*

SECULAR SIGHTS AND NIGHTLIFE

Utah's original **capitol** (538-3000) was in the centrally located town of Fillmore, but since the population in the Salt Lake area was higher, the capitol was moved here in 1916. *(Open M-F 9am-4pm.)* The gray granite building's exhibits include a race car that broke the land speed record at Bonneville Salt Flats. **Pioneer Memorial Museum,** 300 N. Main St. (538-1050), next to the capitol, has personal items belonging to the earliest settlers of the valley and info about prominent Mormon leaders, including Brigham Young and Heber C. Kimball (open M-Sa 9am-5pm, Su 1-5pm; Sept.-May closed Su; free). In the capitol area, a walk up City Creek Canyon to **Memory Grove** accesses one of the city's best views. Also on capitol hill, the **Hansen Planetarium,** 15 S. State St. (538-2104), has fabulous free exhibits, in addition to laser shows set to Led Zeppelin and U2. *(Open M-Th 9am-9pm, F-Sa 9:30am-midnight, Su noon-5:30pm. Laser show $7.50, star and science show $4.50.)*

At the **Children's Museum,** 840 N. 300 W. St. (328-3383), kids of all ages can pilot a 727 jet or implant a Jarvik artificial heart in a life-sized "patient." *(Open M-Th and Sa 10am-6pm, F 10am-8pm. $3, F after 5pm $1.50/$1.)* Take bus #61. A permanent collection of world art wows enthusiasts at the **Utah Museum of Fine Arts** (581-7332), on the University of Utah campus (open M-F 10am-5pm, Sa-Su 2-5pm). The **Salt Lake Art Center,** 20 S. West Temple St. (328-4201), displays an impressive array of contemporary art, as well as the less abstract Kidspace, where modern art appreciation is hands-on. *(Open Tu-Th and Sa 10am-5pm, F 10am-9pm, Su 1-5pm; Kidspace open W-F and Su 1-4pm, Sa 10am-4pm. Suggested donation $2.)*

Concerts abound in the sweltering summer months. At 7:30pm every Tuesday and Friday, the **Temple Sq. Concert Series** (240-2534) conducts a free outdoor concert in Brigham Young Historic Park, with music ranging from string quartet to unplugged guitar (call for a schedule of concerts). The **Utah Symphony Orchestra** (533-6683) performs in Abravanel Hall, 123 W. South Temple St. *(Tickets in summer $14-26, students $7; in season Sept. to early May $14-35, call 1 week in advance.)*

Women's basketball's **Utah Starzz** (season June-Aug.; tickets $5-40) and the 1998 NBA Western Conference Champion **Utah Jazz** (season Oct.-Apr.; tickets $10-68) take the court at the **Delta Center,** 301 W. South Temple (355-3865).

A free copy of *The Private Eye, The Event, Mountain Times, City Weekly* or *Utah After Dark* from a bar or restaurant for local club lists fun and events. **The Zephyr,** 79 W. 300 S. St. (355-2582), thumps live music nightly (open daily 8pm-1am; in winter 7pm-1am; get a member to sponsor you). **Club DV8,** 115 S. West Temple St. (539-8400), is one of the better dance clubs in Salt Lake City (also a private club), deviating from the straight and narrow with 25¢ drafts on Saturdays (9-10pm) and "modern music" on Thursday nights. *(Open Th-Sa 9pm-2am. ½-price drafts 9-10pm. 2-week membership $5; guest cover $3, before 10pm $1.)* The **Dead Goat Saloon,** 165 S. West Temple St. (328-4628), is a tavern (3.2% beer only) serving tourists and locals alike (cover $1-5, F-Su $5; open M-Sa 11:30am-2am, Su 7pm-1am).

■ Near Salt Lake City

The **Great Salt Lake,** administered by Great Salt Lake State Marina (250-1822), is a remnant of primordial Lake Bonneville, and is so salty that only blue-green algae and brine shrimp can survive in it. The salt content varies from 5-27%, providing unusual buoyancy. In fact, no one has ever drowned in the Great Salt Lake—a fact attributable to the Lake's chemical make-up, which also makes the water reek.

It is nearly impossible to get to the Lake without a car; bus #37 "Magna" will take you within 4 mi., but no closer. To get to the **south shore** of the lake, take I-80 17 mi. west of Salt Lake City to Exit 104.

Some of the greatest snow in the U.S., if not the world, falls on the **Wasatch Mountains,** located just minutes from downtown Salt Lake. Rte. 210 heads east from I-25, climbing through the granite boulders of Little Cottonwood Canyon to **Snowbird** (742-2222 or 800-453-3000) and **Alta** (572-3939). Rte. 190 climbs neighboring Big Cottonwood Canyon and leads to **Solitude** (534-1400) and **Brighton** (532-4731). Alta is the best bet for the budget skier; $31 buys an all-day lift ticket to wide-open cruising runs, emerald glades, steep chutes, and champagne powder.

The **Alta Peruvian Lodge** (328-8589 or 800-453-8488) offers an excellent package for two people ($164-196), which includes a bed, all meals, service charges, tax, and lift tickets. **UTA** (see Salt Lake City **Practical Information,** p. 626) runs buses from the city to the resorts in winter, and has pick-ups at downtown motels. **Breeze Ski Rentals** (800-525-0314) rents equipment at Snowbird ($16; 10% discount if reserved; lower rates for rentals over 3 days). The Utah Travel Council (see Utah **Practical Information,** p. 625) purveys the free *Ski Utah* with complete listings of ski packages and lodgings.

In the summer, outdoor lovers climb the Wasatch range to beat the desert heat of the city. Hiking, biking, and fishing are all prime attractions. At Snowbird, the **Snowbird Activities Center** (933-2147) lend bikes with helmets for $20 per 4hr., and $30 per day. Snowbird's **aerial tram** climbs to 11,000 ft., offering a spectacular view of the Wasatch Mountains and the Salt Lake Valley (open daily; hrs. vary with the season; $12, seniors and ages 6-16 $9).

American westward expansion culminated in the completion of the Transcontinental Railroad in 1869. The Union Pacific and Central Pacific Railroads finally joined tracks at **Promontory Point** in the **Golden Spike National Historic Site** (471-2209); the last link was celebrated by driving in a golden spike donated by railroad tycoon Leland Stanford. *(Open daily 8am-6pm; early Sept. to late May 8am-4:30pm. $3.50 per person up to $7 per vehicle; in winter $2-4.)* Take I-15/84 north, exit west onto Rte. 83 for about 30 mi., and follow the signs. The park's visitors center traces the "iron horse's" colorful history and shady influences, operates replica steam locomotives, and reenacts the spike driving ceremony every Saturday and Sunday at 1 and 3pm.

▓ Timpanogos Cave

Legend has it that a set of mountain lion tracks led Martin Hansen to the mouth of the cave that today bears his name. While Utah's Wasatch Mountains are brimming with natural wonders, the cave system of American Fork Canyon, first discovered by Hansen and collectively called Timpanogos Cave, is a true gem for speleologists (cave doctors) and tourists alike. Though early gem pirates stole and shipped boxcar loads of stalactites and other mineral wonders back east to sell to universities and museums, enough remain to bedazzle guests for the hour-long walk through the caves.

Timpanogos Cave National Monument is solely accessible via Rte. 92 (20 mi. south of Salt Lake City off I-15, Exit 287). The **visitors center** (756-5238) dispenses info on the caves and tour tickets. *(Open mid-May to mid-Oct. daily 7am-5:30pm; films about the caves' discovery available upon request. 3hr. hikes depart daily 7am-4:30pm every 30min. $6; ages 6-15 $5; seniors with Golden Age Passport $3.)* Summer tours tend to sell out by early afternoon; reservations may be made by phone two weeks in advance, or at the visitors center up to the day before the tour. Hikers need water and warm layers: the rigorous hike to the cave is completely uphill, while the temperature drops dramatically inside the caves.

The national monument is dwarfed by the surrounding **Uinta National Forest,** which blankets the mountains of the Wasatch Range. The best way to explore the area is by taking the **Alpine Scenic Drive (Rte. 92).** Leaving the visitors center, Rte. 92 heads southwest, providing excellent views of Mt. Timpanogos and other snow-capped peaks. The loopy 20 mi. drive is laden with switchbacks and takes close to 1hr. in one direction. This road will take you past many trailheads; for detailed trail descriptions of area hikes such as the 17 mi. trek up Mt. Timpanogos, inquire at the **Pleasant Grove Ranger District,** 390 N. 100 E. Pleasant Grove (785-3563).

Camping in the national monument is strictly forbidden. The Pleasant Grove Ranger District (see above) has info on the four **campgrounds** in the area (800-280-2267 for reservations; sites $12) and **backcountry camping** through the forest, which requires no permit or fee, as long as you respect minimum-impact guidelines. Once inside the borders of the national monument and national forest, there are no budget accommodations or food. Rte. 89 in nearby **Orem** and **Pleasant Grove** concentrates a collection of supermarkets and fast food joints.

The idyllic mountain folds cushioning Timpanogos Cave beckon not only to nature enthusiasts, but also to aspiring screenplay writers and directors. On the western end of Rte. 92 sits the mountain retreat of **Sundance,** of the **Sundance Film Festival** (801-322-1700), which honors the best in independent film each January. The resort was a small ski mountain in 1961 when Robert Redford first visited and—as the story goes—fell in love with it, purchasing the area to protect it from further development. Although the festival outgrew its roots and is now held in nearby Park City, Sundance remains a low-key but pricey resort which, for its persistence in presenting its environmentally friendly attitude, is clearly most unique for its Hollywood connections.

■ Park City

Thirty-six mi. east of Salt Lake City on I-80, Park City draws winter tourists for its fantastic skiing and boutique-lined downtown. The mixture of the great outdoors and the yuppified Main St. is straight out of an Eddie Bauer catalogue, though not without a certain rustic chic. The **Park City Ski Area** (649-8111), the **Dear Valley Resort** (649-1000), and the **Canyons** (649-5400) access some of the choicest powder and most challenging slopes in the ski-rich West. **Breeze Ski Rentals and Max Snow Snowboards,** 1284 Lowell (800-525-0314), rents the requisite gear (hrs. vary). Park City's **alpine slide** thrills with ½ mi. of curves and drops (open M-F noon-11pm, Sa-Su 10am-10pm; $6.25). Mountain bikers, hikers, and fishing fanatics flock to the area in the summertime. Trail info is available at the visitors center (see below).

With some persistence, the budget-conscious traveler will find reasonable lodging despite Park City's avalanche of luxury condos and resort hotels. During the winter, the **Chateâu Lodge** (649-9372 or 800-357-3556) rents out dorm-style beds just 150 yards from the lifts ($27; free continental breakfast; reserve in advance). Groups of four will find a great deal at the diminutive **Dudler Dorms** (800-453-5789), at the end of Main St. (kitchen and lounge; 4-bed rooms $45, in winter $70; closed in summer). A wide range of restaurants line Main St. **Park City Pizza Co.,** 430 Main St. (649-1591), serves up a lunch special with a pizza slice, soup or salad, and a drink for $4 (open daily 11am-midnight). Grab a burger ($6-7) and a beer ($3.50) at the **Wasatch Brew Pub,** 250 Main St. (645-9500; open daily 11am-9:30pm; bar open until 11:30pm). Texas patriots and others make one-night stands at the **Alamo,** 449 Main St. (649-2380), to shoot pool and check out the local rugby scene (sponsor or $5 membership required; live music W-Sa nights, in winter Tu-Sa; open daily 11am-1am).

Park City's **visitors center,** 528 Main St. (649-6104), doles out a wealth of info on current events and goings-on in town, including the free *Park City Vacation Planner* (open M-Sa 10am-7pm, Su 12am-6pm; in May and Oct. daily noon-5pm). Neither Greyhound nor Amtrak service the city, but many shuttle companies offer a lift to the lifts from Salt Lake City. **Lewis Bros. Stages** (800-826-5844) departs the airport every 30min. in winter and six times per day in summer ($22, in winter $16; reservations required 1 day in advance in summer). **Post Office:** 450 S. Main St. (649-9191; open M-F 9am-5pm, Sa 10am-1:30pm). **ZIP code:** 84060. **Area code:** 435.

■ Dinosaur and Vernal

Dinosaur National Monument was created in 1915, seven years after paleontologist Earl Douglass happened upon an array of fossilized dinosaur bones. Since then, the Monument has been enlarged to include the vast and colorful gorges created by the

Green and Yampa Rivers. It is difficult to imagine that these harsh range lands, where temperatures can vary 150°F between winter and summer, were once the home to horsetail ferns and grazing dinosaurs. Nearby Vernal, west of Dinosaur on U.S. 40, is a popular base for exploring the Monument, Flaming Gorge, and the Uinta Mountains.

PRACTICAL INFORMATION Greyhound, 15 South Vernal Ave. (789-0404 or 800-231-2222), near the corner Main St. in Vernal, makes daily runs east and west along U.S. 40 (2 each way), stopping in Dinosaur, CO en route from Denver and Salt Lake City. Jensen is a flag stop, as is Monument headquarters, 2 mi. west of Dinosaur, CO. The park collects an entrance fee of $10 per car, and $5 per biker, pedestrian, or tour-bus passenger. The Monument's more interesting and varied **west side** lies along Rte. 149 off U.S. 40 just outside of Jensen and 30 mi. east of Vernal. The rugged **east side** of the park is accessible only from a road off U.S. 40, outside Dinosaur, CO. The **Dinosaur Quarry Visitors Center** (789-2115), near the fee collection booth, is accessible only by a free shuttle bus running every 15min. or an uphill ½ mi. walk in the summer; in the winter you can drive up to the center (open daily 8am-7pm; in winter 8am-4:30pm). While you're there, pick up the Monument visitors guide, *Echoes.* The **Dinosaur National Monument Headquarters** (970-374-3000), on the other side of the park at the intersection of U.S. 40 and the park road in Dinosaur, CO, orients explorers of the monument's canyonlands (open May-Sept. daily 8am-4:30pm; Sept.-May M-F 8am-4:30pm). No services are available in the park, so fill up in Dinosaur, Jensen, or Vernal. Twenty-two miles west of the park, in Vernal, lies the visitors center in the **Utah Fieldhouse of Natural History and Dinosaur Garden** (see below). The **Ashley National Forest Service Office,** 355 N. Vernal Ave. (789-1181), in Vernal, has info about hiking, biking, and camping in the surrounding forests (open M-F 8am-5pm). In an **emergency,** call 789-2112 in UT or 303-374-2216 in CO. Vernal's **post office** (789-2393) is on the corner of 67 N. and 800 W. (open M-F 9am-5pm, Sa 10am-1pm). **ZIP code:** 84078. **Area code:** 801.

ACCOMMODATIONS, CAMPGROUNDS, AND FOOD For the lowdown on campgrounds, contact the park visitors center. **Green River Campground** consists of 88 shaded sites along the Green River (flush toilets, water, RVs, disabled sites; sites $12; open late spring to early fall). There are also several free **primitive campsites** in and around the park. Thirteen miles east of Harper's Corner, off a four-wheel drive road (impassable when wet) on the park's east side, **Echo Campground** provides the perfect location for a crystalline evening under the stars (vault toilets and water; sites $6). Free **backcountry camping** permits are available from the headquarters or from Quarry Center. Outside the park, **Campground Dina RV Park,** 930 N. Vernal Ave. (789-2148 or 800-245-2148), about 1 mi. north of Main St. on U.S. 191, is a great bet for a shady, comfortable spot to pitch a tent. (Heated pool, showers, laundry, convenience store. Grassy sites $6.50 per person, ages 7-17 $1, full hookup $20.)

For those less inclined to rough it, Vernal is **civilization's beacon.** The comfortable **Sage Motel,** 54 W. Main St. (789-1442), has big, clean rooms, A/C, cable TV, and free local calls (singles $37, 2 people $42; doubles $47; $5 per additional person). The **Lazy K Motel** (789-3277), on U.S. 40, has clean minimalist rooms, on the eastern outskirts of town toward the monument (singles $25; doubles $30).

The **7-11 Ranch Restaurant,** 77 E. Main St. (789-1170), in Vernal, serves resolutely American food, including big breakfasts with eggs, ham, hash browns, and toast for $4.25 and dinners with a soup, salad, potato, and bread (but no Big Gulp) from $7 (open M-Sa 6am-10pm). The party lives at **LaLa's Fiesta,** 550 E. Main St. (789-2966). Lunch and dinner specialties begin with the *chile relleno* ($3.50), and all meals are under $10. (Open M-Sa 11am-9pm.)

SIGHTS AND ACTIVITIES The star attraction is the dinosaur quarry display at the **Quarry Visitors Center.** Some of the most complete dinosaur skeletons in the world can still be seen encased in the rock in which they were buried. Excellent exhibits inform visitors about the life of dinosaurs and the excavation process. Also in the western section of the park, ancient *petroglyphs* are visible along the road that

The Wild Bunch

Of all the stalwart pioneers and daring outlaws of the Old West, perhaps **Butch Cassidy** is most deeply etched in the era's legends. The "Robin Hood of the West" rose to notoriety as a cunning train and bank robber. He later joined forces with the **Sundance Kid** to form the Wild Bunch, a group of thieving renegades who worked out of Brown's Park and wreaked havoc on Utah, Colorado, and Wyoming. Vernal's **Outlaw Trail Theater** brings the Cassidy lore back to life in its outdoor musical *Cassidy: The Mostly True Story of Butch Cassidy and the Wild Bunch*. This lively production fires from the hip, consciously blurring the distinction between the myth and the man. The show runs from late June through early August; call 789-6932 or 800-477-5558 for tickets and info.

accesses the campsites, both at Cub Creek and beyond the campgrounds themselves. Pick up a *Tour of the Tilted Rocks* pamphlet (50¢) right after the visitors center turn-off and take the auto tour through the impressive split mountain area. Petroglyph sites are marked along the tour trail and are easily reached by short hikes up the hillsides. The **Desert Voices Trail** along the tour is a moderate 2 mi. loop that rewards hikers with a sweeping view of the surrounding mountains.

In the eastern section of the park, the 25 mi. road (closed in winter) to majestic **Harper's Corner,** at the junction of the Green and Yampa River gorges, begins. From the road's terminus, a 2 mi. round-trip hike leads to a view of the Green and Yampa Rivers and sculpted rock formations. **Dan Hatch River Expeditions,** 55 E. Main St. (789-4316 or 800-342-8243), in Vernal, arranges a wide variety of summer rafting trips along the rivers running through the monument (1-day voyage $62, age 6-12 $56; seniors 10% off).

In Vernal, the **Utah Fieldhouse of Natural History and Dinosaur Garden,** 235 Main St. (789-3799), houses the visitors center for northeastern Utah and offers excellent displays on the state's history. *(Open daily 8am-9pm, off-season 8am-5pm. $2, under 6 free, families $5.)* The dinosaur garden features life-size models, and geological displays feature fluorescent minerals that make your shoelaces glow in the dark.

■ Flaming Gorge

Seen at sunset, the contrast between the red canyonlands and the azure water of the Green River makes the landscape glow, hence the moniker "Flaming Gorge." In 1963, the Green River was dammed, giving rise to the creation of **Flaming Gorge National Recreation Area,** a diverse stretch of land ranging from cool pine and aspen forests of Utah to the beautiful deserts of Wyoming. Each year, doomed trout are placed in Flaming Gorge Reservoir, sacrificed to provide some of the best fishing in the state, if you enjoy an effortless cast-and-reel. Waterskiing, boating, and hiking are also popular in the area.

PRACTICAL INFORMATION From Wyoming, travel on U.S. 191 S to the Gorge through the untouched high desert. The **Flaming Gorge Visitors Center** (885-3135), on U.S. 191 atop the Flaming Gorge Dam, offers free guided tours of the dam (open daily 8am-6pm; off-season 9am-5pm). A few mi. off U.S. 191 and 3 mi. off Rte. 44 to Manila, the **Red Canyon Visitors Center** (889-3713) hangs 1360 ft. above Red Canyon (open daily 10am-5pm; closed in winter). **Post Office:** 4 South Blvd. (885-3351), in Dutch John (open M-F 7:30am-4:30pm, Sa 7:30am-11:30pm). **ZIP code:** 84023. **Area code:** 435.

CAMPGROUNDS AND ACCOMMODATIONS Inexpensive **campgrounds** flourish in the Flaming Gorge area; ask for a pamphlet listing all the campgrounds (no electricity) at either visitors center (call 800-280-2267 for reservations). For an excellent view of the Reservoir and Red Canyon, pitch your tent next to the visitors center in **Canyon Rim Campground** (18 sites $11; open mid-May to mid-Sept.), or in one of the numerous national forest campgrounds along U.S. 191 and Rte. 44 in the Utah portion of the park (sites $11; 16-day max. stay). The most sought-after sight in the area is the **Dripping Spring campground;** its 18 wooded, semi-private sites fill up first due to their proximity to prime fishing spots ($12 plus recreation pass; $3 for extra vehicle). Farther north, **Buckboard Crossing** (68 sites, $13) and **Lucerne Valley** (143 sites, $12), are drier and unshaded, and close to the marinas on the reservoir (both open mid-Apr. to mid-Oct.). A number of **free primitive sites** hide in the high country; just check with the rangers to make sure the spot you pick is kosher.

If you'd rather sleep indoors, **Red Canyon Lodge** (889-3759), west on Rte. 44, 2 mi. before the visitors center, offers reasonably priced, rustic cabins. (Single cabins $35, doubles $45; with private bathroom $50/$60; $6 per additional adult; $2 per child under 12; rollaway beds $6 per night.) There's also a private 20-acre lake stocked with trout, a free kids' fishing pool, and a good restaurant (jalapeño chicken breast sandwich $7).

SIGHTS AND ACTIVITIES The Green River Gorge below the dam teems with trout, making for top-notch **fishing,** and the Green River offers some of the best fly fishing in the country. To fish, you must obtain a **permit,** available at Flaming Gorge Lodge, Dutch John Recreation Services, and most stores in Manila. For more info, call the **Utah Dept. of Wildlife Resources,** 1594 W. North Temple (538-4700), in Salt Lake City (open M-F 7:30am-6pm). **Cedar Springs Marina** (889-3795), 3 mi. before the dam, rents all kinds of boats. (Pontoon boats for 8 people $90 for 3hr., $160 per day. Ski boats for 6 with water skis $110 for 3hr., $190 per day. Open daily 8am-6pm.) Nearby, **Flaming Gorge Lodge** (889-3773) rents fishing rods ($10 per day). At **Lucerne Valley Marina** (784-3483), 7 mi. east of Manila off Rte. 43, you can procure a small, 14 ft. fishing boat for $75, plus a $50 deposit per day (open daily 7am-9pm).

The **Sheep Creek Geologic Loop,** an 11 mi. scenic drive off Rte. 44 just south of Manila, takes you past rock strata and wildlife. For a hideout from tourists, the valley of **Brown's Park,** 23 mi. east of Flaming Gorge, is accessible via narrow, hilly, sometimes paved roads winding through three states. Nineteenth-century Western outlaws **Butch Cassidy, the Sundance Kid,** and their **Wild Bunch** found the valley's isolation and its proximity to three state lines ideal for evading the law (see p. 633).

SOUTHERN UTAH

■ Moab

Moab first flourished in the 1950s, when uranium miners rushed to the area and transformed the town from a quiet hamlet into a gritty desert outpost. Today, the mountain bike has replaced the Geiger counter, as tourists rush into the town eager to bike the red slickrock, raft down whitewater rapids, or explore surrounding Arches and Canyonlands National Parks. The town itself has changed to accommodate the new visitors and athletes; microbreweries and t-shirt shops now fill the rooms of the old gray uranium building on Main St.

PRACTICAL INFORMATION Moab sits 50 mi. southeast of I-70 on U.S. 191, 5 mi. south of Arches. **Amtrak** comes only as close as Thompson, 41 mi. northeast of town, and **Greyhound's** nearest stop is in Green River, 52 mi. northwest. Some hotels and hostels will pick guests up from these distant points for a small fee. **Bighorn Express** (587-3061 or 888-655-7433) makes trips from the Salt Lake City airport to Moab ($45; open M-F 9am-5pm, Sa-Su 10am-2pm; make reservations 1 day ahead). **Coyote Shuttle** (259-8656) will also take you where you want to go (rates and hrs. vary). The **Moab Information Center,** 3 Center St., doles out info on the city and nearby parks and monuments. (Open daily 8am-9pm; Sept.-Oct. and Apr.-May 8am-7pm; May-June 8am-8pm; Nov.-Mar. 9am-5pm.) **Post Office:** 50 E. 100 N. St. (259-7427; open M-F 8:30am-5pm, Sa 8:30am-noon). **ZIP code:** 84532. **Area code:** 801.

ACCOMMODATIONS AND CAMPGROUNDS Chain motels clutter Main St., but Moab fills up fast in the summer, especially on weekends; call up to a month ahead to guarantee a reservation. Off-season rates can drop as much as 50%, and during that time the weather is more conducive to hiking. The owners of the **Lazy Lizard International Hostel (AAIH/Rucksackers)**, 1213 S. U.S. 191 (259-6057; look for the "A1 Self Storage" sign just south of Moab on U.S. 191), go out of their way to be helpful—they'll pick you up (usually for $10-15) and arrange trips through local companies. The kitchen, VCR, laundry, and hot tub are at your disposal (bunks $7.50 per person, private rooms for 1 or 2 $20; tent sites $6). A miner's hat, fishing nets, and a Victrola accent the quirky and luxurious theme rooms of **Hotel Off Center**, 96 E. Center St. (259-4244 or 800-237-4685), a block off Main St. (shared bath; open Mar.-Oct.; dorm rooms $12; singles $35; doubles $45). **The Prospector Lodge**, 186 N. 1st W. St. (259-5145), a block west of Main St., offers cool, comfy rooms with TV and free java (singles $34, with a queen-size bed $42; doubles $50; $6 per additional person).

Arches National Park (see p. 636) has the area's best campground. In town, the **Canyonlands Campground**, 555 S. Main St. (259-6848 or 800-522-6848), next to the Shell Station, provides well-shaded sites and a pool. (Sites $14, with water and electricity $17, full hookup $19; $3 per additional adult, child $2.) **Slickrock Campground**, 1301½ U.S. 191 N (259-7660 or 800-448-8873), beckons the budget traveler with the slogan, "funpigs stay at Slickrock." Yes, "funpig"—a person who relaxes and has fun. (Pool, 3 hot tubs, showers, and laundry. Tent sites $16, with water and electricity $22, full hookup $23. Cabins with A/C for 2 $30 plus $5 per extra person.)

FOOD Seating on the patio or inside among simulated redrocks heightens the pleasure of fresh lunch wraps like the Ragin' Cajun ($5-7) at **Honest Ozzie's Café**, 60 N. 100 W. (259-8442). Veggie and vegan menu items complement a wide variety of fresh, quick meals. (Open daily 7am-3pm.) **Eddie McStiff's**, 57 S. Main St. (259-2337), offers 12 homemade brews (pints $2.75), including Raspberry Wheat and Moab Rock Amber Ale, alongside pizza ($6-11), sandwiches ($7), and plenty o' tourists (open daily 3pm-midnight). The retro diner decor lives at **The Moab Diner and Ice Cream Shoppe**, 189 S. Main St. (259-4006), for veggie specials and excellent french fries (sandwiches and burgers $4-5; open daily 6am-10pm). **Moab Community Coop**, 111 N. 100 W (259-5712), a block off Main St., can fill your saddlebags with fresh produce, as well as organic and health foods for your journey (open M-Sa 9am-6pm).

Eclectic dining establishments dot Moab's streets, but when you need a drink, the **State Liquor Store**, 260 S. Main St. (259-5314), is the only place to purchase alcohol above 3.2% (open M-Sa 11am-9pm). Your desperate search for mixed drinks and live music will lead to **The Rio Colorado Restaurant and Bar**, 2 S. 100 W. St. (259-6666), off Main St. (open M-Sa 11:30am-midnight, Su 11am-midnight).

SIGHTS AND ACTIVITIES Mountain biking and rafting, along with nearby national parks, are the big draws in Moab. The **Slickrock** trail is a 10 mi. loop which rolls up and down the slickrock outside of Moab. The trail has no big vertical gain, but it's technically difficult, and temperatures often reach 100°F. **Rim Cyclery**, 94 W. 100 N. St. (259-5333), one of the first mountain bike shops in southern Utah, rents bikes and distributes info about the slickrock trails ($30-35 per day includes helmet; open daily 9am-6pm; in winter closed Su).

Countless raft companies are based in Moab. **Western River Expeditions** (259-7019 or 800-453-7450) offers some of the best deals on the Colorado (½-day $34, children $28; full-day $44/$34; includes lunch). **Trapax, Inc.** (259-5261) takes you for an evening boat ride along the Colorado River as their sound and light show ricochets off the canyon walls ($22, ages 6-12 $12). Various Moab outfitters also arrange horseback, motorboat, canoe, jeep, and helicopter rides. **Park Creek Ranch** (259-5505) offers horseback rides into the La Sal Mountains (1½hr.; $20 per person).

Albert Christensen spent 12 years creating the bizarre **Hole 'n the Rock** (668-2250), 15 mi. south of Moab on U.S. 191, a 14-room house carved out of a sandstone cliff. His wife Gladys kept the dream alive after his death in 1957 and opened the

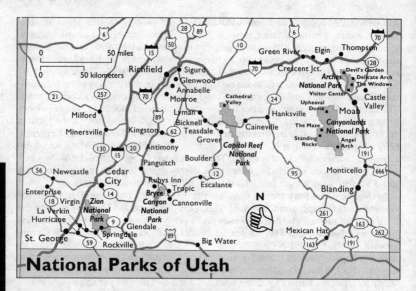

National Parks of Utah

house to the public. Christensen's nearby rendering of Franklin D. Roosevelt is some-thin', really somethin' (open daily 9am-6pm; $2). Utah's only winery, **Arches Vineyards,** 420 Kane Creek Blvd. (259-5397 or 800-723-8609), is located in the Moab area (tasting room open M-Sa 11am-7pm; free).

■ Finding the Fab Five

The five **National Parks** that cover this majestic area can be reached by several roads. From Moab, take U.S. 191 N 5 mi. to **Arches** (see below). Continue north on U.S. 191 to Rte. 313 S, which will lead to the Islands in the Sky area of **Canyonlands** (60 mi.; see p. 637). Or, take U.S. 191 south from Moab to Rte. 211 W to reach the Needles area of Canyonlands (87 mi.). To reach **Capitol Reef** (see p. 639), continue driving north on U.S. 191 and then I-70 going west; leave I-70 at Exit 147, and follow Rte. 24 S to Hanksville and then west to the park (81 mi. from I-70). Rte. 24 W runs to Torrey, where scenic Rte. 12 branches south and west through the Dixie National Forest to **Bryce Canyon** (see p. 640). For **Zion** (see p. 641), continue on Rte. 12 W to U.S. 89 S through Mt. Carmel Jct., and pick up Rte. 9 W.

The two national forests in Southern Utah are divided into districts, some of which lie near the national parks and serve as excellent places to stay on a cross-country jaunt. **Manti-La Sal National Forest** has two sections near Arches and the Needles area of Canyonlands. **Dixie National Forest** stretches from Capitol Reef through Bryce all the way to the western side of Zion.

■ Arches

"This is the most beautiful place on earth," novelist Edward Abbey wrote of **Arches National Park.** Thousands of sandstone arches, spires, pinnacles, and fins tower above the desert in overwhelming grandeur. Some arches are so perfect in form that early explorers believed they were constructed by a long lost civilization. Deep red sandstone, green pinyon trees and juniper bushes, ominous grey thunderclouds, and a strikingly blue sky combine to etch an unforgettable palette of color.

PRACTICAL INFORMATION The park entrance is on U.S. 191, 5 mi. north of Moab. Although no public transportation serves the park, shuttle bus companies travel to both the national park and Moab from surrounding towns and cities (see Moab **Prac-**

tical Information, p. 634). While most visitors come in the summer, 100°F temperatures make hiking difficult; bring at least one gallon (4L) of water per person per day, especially if hiking. The weather is best in the spring and fall when temperate days and nights combine to make a comfortable stay. In the winter, white snow provides a brilliant contrast to the red arches. The **visitors center** (259-8161), to the right of the entrance station, distributes free park service maps. (Open daily June-Sept. 7:30am-6:30pm; Apr.-May and Oct. 7:30am-5:30pm; Oct.-Mar. 8am-4:30pm.) An **entrance pass** covers admission for a week ($10 per carload, $5 per pedestrian or biker). For more info, write the **Superintendent,** Arches National Park, P.O. Box 907, Moab 84532 (259-8161). For more details on accommodations, food, and activities, see **Moab,** p. 635. **Area code:** 435.

CAMPGROUNDS The park's only campground, **Devil's Garden,** has 52 excellent campsites nestled amid pinyon pines and giant red sandstone formations. The campsite is within walking distance of the Devil's Garden and Broken Arch Trailheads; however, it is a long 18 mi. from the visitors center. Because Devil's Garden doesn't take reservations, sites go quickly in season. In spring and fall, visitors show up early in preparation for the rush; a line forms at the visitors center at 7:30am. (Sites $10, in winter $5. No wood-gathering. Running water Apr.-Oct. 1-week max. stay.)

If the heat becomes unbearable at Arches, the aspen forests of the **Manti-La Sal National Forest** offer respite. (Take Rte. 128 along the Colorado River and turn right at Castle Valley; at least a 1hr. drive from Moab.) These beautiful sites sit 4000 ft. above the national park and are usually several degrees cooler. All sites cost $7, except the free sites at **Oowah Lake.** Oowah, 3 mi. down a dirt road, is a rainbow trout haven. Fishing permits are available at most stores in Moab and at the Forest Service office ($5 per day). For more info, contact the Manti-La Sal National Forest Service Office (259-7155), in Moab, 3.2 mi. south of the zero axis in town off Main, on Resource Rd. 84532 (open M-F 8am-4:30pm).

SIGHTS AND ACTIVITIES The majority of Arches' natural beauty is not visible from the 18 mi. road. Bikes are only allowed on two-wheel drive roads, so the best way to see the park is by foot. There are thousands of natural arches in the park, and each one is pinpointed on the free map and guide that is passed out at the fee collection booth. At the end of the paved road, **Devil's Garden** boasts an astounding 64 arches, while a challenging hike from the **Landscape Arch** leads across harrowing exposures to the secluded **Double O Arch.** The highlight of your visit should be the free-standing **Delicate Arch,** the symbol of the park; take the Delicate Arch turn-off from the main road, and follow it 2 mi. to the trail head. From Wolfe Ranch, the homestead of Civil War veteran John Wesley Wolfe, a 1½ mi. foot trail leads to the arch. Beyond, you can catch a glimpse of the Colorado River Gorge and the La Sal Mountains. Visitors occasionally come across petroglyphs left on the stone walls by the Anasazi and Ute who wandered the area centuries ago.

Arches aren't the only natural wonders here. One of the more popular trails, the moderately strenuous 2 mi. **Fiery Furnace Trail,** leads down into the canyon bottoms, providing new perspective on the imposing cliffs and monoliths above. Only experienced hikers should attempt this trail alone. Rangers lead groups from the visitors center into the labyrinth twice daily in summer. *(Tours 10am and 4pm. $6, children $3.)* Tours tend to fill up a day before; reservations can be made 48hr. in advance.

■ Canyonlands

Those who make the trek to **Canyonlands National Park** are rewarded with a pleasant surprise: the absence of that overabundant, pestering species, *Homo winnebagiens.* The sandstone spires, the roughly cut canyons, and vibrantly colored rock layers clothe the truly awe-inspiring landscape. The Green and Colorado Rivers divide the park into three sections, each with its own **visitors center** (all 3 open daily 8am-6pm; off-season 8am-5pm). The **Needles** region (visitors center 259-4711) contains

THE SOUTHWEST

spires, arches, canyons, and Native American ruins, but is not as rough as the Maze area. To get to the Needles, take Rte. 211 W from U.S. 191, about 40 mi. south of Moab. Farther north, **Island in the Sky** (visitors center 259-4712), a towering mesa which sits within the "Y" formed by the two rivers, affords fantastic views of the surrounding canyons and mountains; take Rte. 313 W from U.S. 191 about 10 mi. north of Moab. The most remote district of the park, the rugged **Maze** area (ranger station 259-2652), is a veritable hurly-burly of twisted canyons made for *über*-pioneers with four-wheel-drive vehicles only. Once you've entered a section of the park, getting to a different section involves retracing your steps and reentering the park, a tedious trip that can last from several hours to a full day.

PRACTICAL INFORMATION AND FOOD Monticello's **Interagency Visitors Center,** 117 S. Main. St. (587-3235 or 800-574-4386), sells area maps ($4-9; open M-F 8am-5pm, Sa-Su 10am-5pm). The park collects **entrance fees** of $10 per car and $5 per hiker or cyclist. For more info, write to **Canyonlands National Park,** 2282 S. West Resource Blvd., Moab 84532 (259-7164). **Moab** makes an excellent base town for exploring the park (see p. 634). *There are no gas, water, or food services in the park.* Just outside the boundary in the Needles district, however, the **Needles Outpost** (979-4007) houses a limited and expensive grocery store and gas pump (open daily 8:30am-6pm). Hauling in groceries, water, and first-aid supplies from Moab or Monticello makes the most sense for travelers on a budget.

CAMPGROUNDS AND HIKING Before **backcountry camping** or **hiking,** outdoors-types must register at the proper visitors center for one of a limited number of permits ($10 for backpack and overnight permit). Four-wheel drivers should also register at the visitors center ($25 permit). Each region has its own official **campground.** In the Needles district, **Squaw Flat's** 26 sites occupy a sandy plain surrounded by giant sandstone towers, 40 mi. west of U.S. 191 on Rte. 211. In June, insects swarm. Fuel and water are not abundant, although the latter is usually available from mid-March to October (sites $8; Oct.-Mar. free). **Willow Flat Campground,** in the Island in the Sky district, sits high atop the mesa on Rte. 313, 41 mi. west off U.S. 191 (12 free sites). You must bring your own water. Willow Flat and Squaw Flat both provide picnic tables, grills, and pit toilets. The backcountry campground at the **Maze Overlook** offers no amenities. All campgrounds operate on a first come, first served basis.

Each visitors center has a brochure of possible hikes and advice on length and difficulty. With summer temperatures regularly climbing over 100°F, at least 1 gallon of water per person per day is a must. Hiking options from the Needles area are probably the best developed, though Island in the Sky offers some spectacular views. In the Maze district, a 6hr., 6 mi. guided hike into Horseshoe Canyon leaves the visitors center at 9am on Saturdays, and Sundays. If hiking in desert heat doesn't appeal to you, you can rent Jeeps or mountain bikes in Moab.

For some great overlooks at elevations above 8000 ft., the **Monticello District** of the **Manti-La Sal National Forest,** south of Needles, delivers. This section of the forest has two campgrounds on **Blue Mountain. Buckboard,** 6½ mi. west of U.S. 191 (10 sites and 2 group areas), and **Dalton Springs,** 5 mi. west of U.S. 191 (13 sites). Both campgrounds operate from late May to late October and charge $8.50 per site. From Moab, head south on U.S. 191 to Monticello and then west on Rte. 1 S. More info on the Monticello District awaits at the **visitors center,** 117 S. Main St. (587-3235), south on U.S. 191 and then west on Rte. 1 S in Monticello, and the **Manti-La Sal National Forest Service office** in Monticello, 496 E. Central Ave. (587-2401), on U.S. 666 just east of town (open M-F 8am-4:30pm).

Farther away, **Dead Horse Point State Park** (entrance fee $5), perches on the rim of the Colorado Gorge. The park, south of Arches and 14 mi. south of U.S. 191, accessible from Rte. 313, offers more camping, with modern restrooms, water, hookups, and covered picnic tables ($11; half are available on a first come, first served basis). For more info, contact the **Park Superintendent,** Dead Horse Point State Park, P.O. Box 609, Moab 84532 (259-2614 or 800-322-3770; open daily 6am-10pm; call for off-season hrs.).

WE GIVE YOU THE WORLD...AT A DISCOUNT

LET'S GO ®

TRAVEL

MERCHANDISE CATALOG FOR 1999

Eurailpass Unlimited travel in and among all 17 countries: **Austria, Belgium, Denmark, Finland, France, Germany, Greece, Holland, Hungary, Italy, Luxembourg, Norway, Portugal, Republic of Ireland, Spain, Sweden, and Switzerland.**

	15 days	21 days	1 month	2 months	3 months	10 days	15 days
First Class	*c o n s e c u t i v e d a y s*					*in two months*	
1 Passenger	$554	$718	$890	$1260	$1558	$654	$862
2 or More Passengers	$470	$610	$756	$1072	$1324	$556	$732
Youthpass (Second Class)							
Passengers under 26	$388	$499	$623	$882	$1089	$458	$599

Europass Travel in the five Europass countries: **France, Germany, Italy, Spain, and Switzerland.** Up to two of the four associate regions (Austria and Hungary; Benelux (Belgium, Netherlands, and Luxembourg); Greece; Portugal) may be added.

	5 days	6 days	8 days	10 days	15 days	first	second
First Class	*in two months*					*associate country*	
1 Passenger	$348	$368	$448	$528	$728	+$60	+$40
2 to 5 Passengers traveling together	$296	$314	$382	$450	$620	+$52	+$34
Youthpass (Second Class)							
Passengers under 26	$233	$253	$313	$363	$513	+$45	+$33

Pass Protection For an additional $10, insure any railpass against theft or loss.

Discounts *with the purchase of a railpass*
- $30 off a World Journey backpack
- $20 off a Continental Journey backpack
- Any *Let's Go* Guide for 1/2 Price
- Free 2-3 Week Domestic Shipping

Call about Eurostar–the Channel Tunnel Train–and other country-specific passes.

Airfares & Special Promotions

Call for information on and availability of standard airline tickets, student, teacher, and youth discounted airfares, as well as other special promotions.

Publications & More

Let's Go Travel Guides— The Bible of the Budget Traveler

USA • India and Nepal • Southeast Asia............22.99
Australia • Eastern Europe • Europe...................21.99
Britain & Ireland • Central America • France •
Germany • Israel & Egypt • Italy • Mexico •
Spain & Portugal...19.99
Alaska & The Pacific Northwest • Austria &
Switzerland • California & Hawaii • Ecuador
& The Galapagos Islands • Greece • Ireland.....18.99
South Africa • Turkey...17.99
New York City • New Zealand • London •
Paris • Rome • Washington D.C. 15.99

Let's Go Map Guides

Know your destination inside and out! Great to accompany your Eurailpass.

Amsterdam, Berlin, Boston, Chicago, Florence, London, Los Angeles, Madrid, New Orleans, New York, Paris, Rome, San Francisco, Washington D.C.   8.95

Michelin Maps

Czech/Slovak Republics • Europe • France • Germany • Germany/Austria /Benelux • Great Britain & Ireland • Greece • Italy • Poland • Scandinavia & Finland • Spain & Portugal 10.95

LET'S GO Order Form

Last Name*   First Name*   Home and Day Phone Number*
(very important)

Street*   (Sorry, we cannot ship to Post Office Boxes)

City*   State*   Zip Code*

Citizenship‡§□   School/College§   Date of Birth‡§   Date of Travel*
(Country)

Qty	Description	Color	Unit Price	Total Price

Shipping and Handling

2-3 Week Domestic Shipping	
Merchandise value under $30	$4
Merchandise value $30-$100	$6
Merchandise value over $100	$8
2-3 Day Domestic Shipping	
Merchandise value under $30	$14
Merchandise value $30-$100	$16
Merchandise value over $100	$18
Overnight Domestic Shipping	
Merchandise value under $30	$24
Merchandise value $30-$100	$26
Merchandise value over $100	$28
All International Shipping	$30

Total Purchase Price	
Shipping and Handling	+
MA Residents add 5% sales tax on gear and books	+
TOTAL	

□ Mastercard   □ Visa

Cardholder name:

Card number:

Expiration date:

When ordering an International ID Card, please include:
1. Proof of birthdate (copy of passport, birth certificate, or driver's license).
2. One picture (1.5" x 2") signed on the reverse side.
3. (ISIC/ITIC only) Proof of current student/teacher status (letter from registrar or administrator, proof of tuition, or copy of student/faculty ID card. FULL-TIME only).

* Required for all orders
‡ Required in addition for each Hostelling Membership
§ Required in addition for each International ID Card
□ Required in addition for each railpass

Prices are in US dollars and subject to change.

Make check or money order payable to:
Let's Go Travel
17 Holyoke Street
Cambridge, MA 02138
(617) 495-9649

1-800-5LETSGO

Hours: Mon.-Fri., 10am-6pm ET

Welcome
to
America

America has over
5000 ways to
get in touch
with yourself,

and **one way**
to get in touch with

the world.

1·800 call ATT

1 800 225-5288

For All Calls

1 800 225-5288

Want to visit home while you're visiting here?

1 800 CALL ATT® connects you fast and clear within the

U.S. or to anywhere in the world. You can use your

AT&T Calling Card or any of these credit cards.

How's that for freedom?

Special Features

Sequential Calling—Place another call without having to redial the access and card numbers, by pressing # after each call is completed.

Voice Messaging—If the number you're dialing is busy or there's no answer, simply press #123 to record message and specify delivery time.

Correct Mistakes While Dialing—Just press * and repeat your last step.

In-Language Assistance—An operator or voice prompt will help you with dialing instructions in the languages listed.

Cantonese	1 800 833-1288	**Polish**	1 800 233-8622
Hindi	1 800 233-7003	**Russian**	1 800 233-2394
Japanese	1 800 233-8006	**Spanish**	1 800 233-9008
Korean	1 800 233-8923	**Tagalog**	1 800 233-9118
Mandarin	1 800 233-1823	**Vietnamese**	1 800 233-1388

www.att.com/world

It's all within  your reach.

Abbey's Road

For many, the essays and novels of **Edward Abbey** most eloquently capture the harsh beauty of the American West. Born in Pennsylvania, he fell in love with the region upon his first visit, and devoted the rest of his life to fiercely defending it from the United States' westward march of "progress." He spent three seasons as a park ranger at Arches National Park, delighting in the solitude of the desert. Abbey penned a celebrated series of essays on life in the desert based on his years spent wandering around Moab and Canyonlands. He captured their enigmatic beauty in his passionate and often acerbic manner—Abbey's passages vividly evoke the unforgiving, sun-parched landscape he loved. *The Monkey Wrench Gang*, Abbey's novel about an amusingly radical foursome rebelling against the pillaging of the wilderness, became the inspiration for the activist environmental group Earth First! As Abbey once wrote, "For us the wilderness and human emptiness of this land is not a source of fear but the greatest of its attractions."

■ Capitol Reef

A geologist's fantasy and **Capitol Reef National Park's** feature attraction, the Waterpocket Fold bisects the park, presenting visitors with 65 million years of stratified natural history. This 100 mi. furrow in the earth's crust, with its rocky scales and spines, winds through Capitol Reef like a giant Cretaceous serpent. The sheer cliffs that border the Fold were originally called a "reef," not for their oceanic origins, but because they posed a barrier to travel.

PRACTICAL INFORMATION The middle link in the Fab Five chain, east of Zion and Bryce Canyon and west of Arches and Canyonlands, Capitol Reef is unreachable by major bus lines. The closest Greyhound stop is in Green River. For a fee, **Wild Hare Expeditions** (see below) will provide a shuttle service between Richfield and the park. **Entrance** to the park is free except for the scenic loop that costs $4 per vehicle. The **visitors center** (425-3791), on Rte. 24, supplies travelers with waterproof topographical maps ($8), regular maps ($4), free brochures on trails, and info on daily activities such as ranger-led jaunts (open daily 8am-6pm; Sept.-May 8am-5pm). The free park newspaper, *The Cliffline*, lists a schedule of park activities. *When hiking, keep in mind that summer temperatures average 95°F, and beware of flash-floods after rain.* For more info about the park, contact the **Superintendent,** Capitol Reef National Park, HC 70 Box 15, Torrey 84775 (425-3791). **Post Office:** 222 E. Main St. (425-3488), in Torrey (open M-F 7:30am-1:30pm, Sa 7:30-11am). **ZIP code:** 84775. **Area code:** 801.

CAMPGROUNDS, ACCOMMODATIONS, AND FOOD The park's campgrounds provide sites on a first come, first served basis. The main campground, **Fruita,** 1.3 mi. south off Rte. 24, presides over 71 sites (1 reserved for the disabled), with drinking water and toilets ($10). **Cedar Mesa Campground,** in the park's south end, and **Cathedral Valley,** in the north, have only five sites each; neither has water or a paved road—but hey, they're free. To get to Cedar Mesa, take Rte. 24 past the visitors center to Notom-Bullfrog Rd. and head about 25 mi. south. Cathedral Valley is accessible only by four-wheel-drive or on foot. Both of these sites and unmarked backcountry campsites require a free **backcountry permit,** easily obtainable at the visitors center. Outside the park, off scenic Rte. 12 between Boulder and Capitol Reef, a stretch of **Dixie National Forest** shelters three lovely campgrounds. All perch at elevations over 8000 ft. and have drinking water and pit toilets (first come, first served sites $7; open May-Sept.). The **Oak Creek Campground** includes eight sites, and the **Pleasant Creek Campground** has 18 sites. **Single Tree Campground** offers 26 sites and two family sites, one of which can be reserved ahead of time (800-283-2267). Visitors can ask the **Teasdale Ranger District Office** (425-3702) for more info.

If you'd prefer a roof over your head, a trip to **Torrey,** 11 mi. west of the visitors center on Rte. 24, will do you right. As far as roofs go, the **Trading Post** (425-3716), 75 W. Main St., offers the best bang for your buck. Small cabins sleep up to four people and share a common bath ($29). Across the street, **The Chuck Wagon Motel and General Store** (425-3288), in the center of Torrey on Rte. 24 W, has a barbecue area, a beautiful pool, and attractive, wood-paneled rooms with A/C and phones in a new building (singles $54; doubles $58) and in the older building above the store (no A/C or phone; $34/$39). The store comes through with a good selection of groceries, sports equipment, baked goods, and picnic ware (open daily 7am-10pm). The **Boulder View Inn,** 385 W. Main St. (800-444-3980), provides comfortable rooms ($52 with continental breakfast; in winter from $30).

A meal at the **Capitol Reef Inn and Café,** 360 W. Main St. (425-3271), in Torrey, features local rainbow trout (smoked or grilled) and a dining room that looks out on the russet hills. The grilled trout sandwich ($6.50) comes with a 10-vegetable salad. (Open Apr.-Oct. daily 7am-11pm.) Greasier repast awaits at **Brink's Burgers,** 165 E. Main St. (425-3710), in Torrey (various burgers $2-4; open daily 11am-9pm).

SIGHTS AND ACTIVITIES The Reef's haunting landforms can be explored from the seat of your car on the 25 mi. scenic drive, a 1½hr. (round-trip) jaunt next to the cliffs along paved and improved dirt roads. Along Rte. 24, you can ponder the bathroom-sized **Fruita Schoolhouse** built by Mormon settlers, 1000-year-old **petroglyphs** etched on the stone walls, and **Panorama Point. Chimney Rock** and the Castle are two of the more striking and abstruse of sandstone formations along the route.

For many of the park's most spectacular vistas, however, visitors must temporarily abandon their air-conditioned comfort. **Wild Hare Expeditions,** 116 W. Main St. (425-3999 or 888-304-4273), embarks on a variety of backpacking and hiking tours (2hr. tours $20; $40 per ½-day; full-day $60, children $50). Some scenic drives and four-wheel-drive tours are also available.

For a change of scenery, the bucolic **orchards** which lie within the park in the Fruita region might suffice. Guests can eat as much fruit as they like while in the orchards, but cold hard cash is necessary to take some home.

∎ Bryce Canyon

The delicate spires of pink-and-red limestone speckling **Bryce Canyon National Park** can seem more like the subject of a Surrealist painting than the result of nature's art. Carved by millennia of wind and water, the canyons made life difficult but scenic for the Anasazi, Fremont, and Paiute. Ebenezer Bryce, a Mormon carpenter with a gift for understatement, deemed the canyon "one hell of a place to lose a cow." A hike down into the canyon provides a solitary experience, and between mid-October and mid-April, crowds vanish and prices drop.

PRACTICAL INFORMATION Approaching from the west, Bryce Canyon lies 1½hr. east of Cedar City; take Rte. 14 to U.S. 89. From the east, take I-70 to U.S. 89, turn east on Rte. 12 at Bryce Jct. (7 mi. south of Panguitch), and drive 14 mi. to the Rte. 63 junction; head south 4 mi. to the park entrance. There is no public transportation to Bryce Canyon. The park's **entrance fee** is $10 per car, $5 per pedestrian.

The **visitors center** (834-5322), just inside the park, distributes the free Bryce Canyon publication, *Hoodoo,* which lists park services, events, suggested hikes, and sightseeing drives. (Open daily 8am-8pm; Apr.-May and Sept.-Oct. 8am-6pm; Nov.-Mar. 8am-4:30pm.) For more info, write the **Superintendent,** Bryce Canyon National Park, Bryce Canyon 84717. **Emergency:** 676-2411 or 911. Bryce Canyon's **post office** (834-5361) is in Bryce Lodge (open M-F 8am-noon and 1-5pm, Sa 8am-noon). **ZIP code:** 84717. **Area code:** 801.

CAMPGROUNDS AND FOOD North and **Sunset Campgrounds,** both within 3 mi. of the visitors center, offer toilets, picnic tables, potable water, and 210 sites on a first come, first served basis (sites $10; early birds get spots). As usual, **backcountry camp-**

ing permits are free from the ranger at the visitors center. Two campgrounds lie just west of Bryce on scenic Rte. 12, in Dixie National Forest. The **King Creek Campground,** 11 mi. from Bryce on a dirt road off Rte. 12 (look for signs to Tropic Reservoir), features lakeside sites surrounded by pine trees ($8). Group sites are available with reservations (call 800-280-2267). At an elevation of 7400 ft., the **Red Canyon Campground** rents 36 sites on a first come, first served basis ($10).

The **grocery store** at **Ruby's Inn,** just outside the park entrance, has a wide selection of provisions for reasonable prices (open daily 6am-10pm). If you're stuck in the park without any food, the **general store** at Sunrise Point (834-5361, ext. 167) has basic fast food (open spring-fall daily 7:30am-8:30pm; closed in winter). Behind the store, there are **showers** ($2 for 10min.; available daily 7am-10pm).

SIGHTS AND ACTIVITIES Bryce's 18 mi. **main road** winds past spectacular lookouts such as **Sunrise Point, Sunset Point, Inspiration Point,** and **Rainbow Point,** but a range of hiking trails makes it a crime not to leave your car. The path along the rim between Sunrise Point and Sunset Point is wheelchair accessible. The 3 mi. loop of the **Navajo** and **Queen's Garden** trails leads into the canyon itself. More challenging options include **Peek-A-Boo Loop,** winding in and out (and up and down) through hoodoos for 4 mi., and the **Trail to the Hat Shop,** which descends four extremely steep miles. (And if you think climbing down is tough…) The visitors center can recommend other trails. Guided horseback rides are also very popular; guests can arrange them through **Canyon Trail Rides** (834-5500, off-season 679-8665; $27-37 per person).

Only a few minutes from the park entrance, the pink walls of **Pine Cliffs Village** (834-5351 or 800-834-0043), at the junction of Rte. 12 and Rte. 63, herald the best deal in the area: cabins for one or two people, including private bath, for $15. **Canyonlands International Youth Hostel (AAIH/Rucksackers)** hosts travelers 60 mi. south of Bryce in **Kanab** (see p. 642). Although expensive for single travelers, **Bryce Lodge** (834-5361 or 586-7686) might be a decent deal for a group (singles and doubles $83; triples $88; quads $93; quints $98; open Apr.-Oct.).

■ Near Bryce

Truly daring hikers flirt with death in the network of sandstone canyons that comprises the ominously named **Phipps Death Hollow Outstanding Natural Area,** just north of **Escalante.** The full trail through the canyons, starting at the **Hell's Backbone** trailhead north of town, is 30 mi. one-way and requires 4-5 days to complete. For the first 11 mi., there's no water at all; then the trail requires hikers to swim across a series of deep pools. A free backcountry permit (required), directions, and weather reports await at the **Escalante Interagency Office,** 755 W. Main St. (826-5499), on Rte. 12 just west of town (open daily 7:30am-5:30pm; off-season M-F 8am-4:30pm). A shorter, almost as stunning day hike starts in the **Upper Escalante Canyon** and heads through some of the Death Hollow area. The **Calf Creek** campgrounds, 15 mi. east of Escalante on Rte. 12, has a cascading waterfall (drinking water and toilets; sites $8).

West on Rte. 14, the flowered slopes of the **Cedar Breaks National Monument** descend 2000 ft. into chiseled depths. The rim of this giant amphitheater stands a lofty 10,350 ft. above sea level (entrance $4 per car, $2 per pedestrian). A 30-site **campground** (sites $9) and the **visitors center** (586-0787; open in summer daily 8am-6pm) await at **Point Supreme.** For more info, contact the **Superintendent,** Cedar Breaks National Monument, 82 N. 100 E., Cedar City 84720 (586-9451).

■ Zion

Some 13 million years ago, the ocean flowed over the cliffs and canyons of **Zion National Park.** Over the centuries, the sea has subsided, leaving only the powerful Virgin River, whose watery fingers still sculpt the russet sandstone. In the northwest corner of the park, the walls of Kolob Terrace tower thousands of feet above the river. Elsewhere, branching canyons and unusual rock formations show off erosion's unique artistry. In the 1860s, Mormon settlers came to the area and enthusiastically proclaimed that they had found the promised land. Brigham Young did not agree, however, and declared to his followers that the place was awfully nice, but "not Zion." The name "not Zion" stuck for years until a new wave of entranced explorers dropped the "not," giving the park its present name.

PRACTICAL INFORMATION The main entrance to Zion is in **Springdale,** on Rte. 9, which borders the park to the south along the Virgin River. Approaching Zion from the west, take Rte. 9 from I-15 at Hurricane. In the east, pick up Rte. 9 from U.S. 89 at Mt. Carmel Jct. **Greyhound** (673-2933 or 800-231-2222), is in St. George (43 mi. southwest of the park on I-15), departing from a **McDonald's,** 1235 S. Bluff St., at St. George Blvd. Buses run to Salt Lake City (6hr., 3 per day, $51); Los Angeles (15hr., 7 per day, $55); and Las Vegas (2hr., 7 per day, $25). The main **Zion Canyon Visitors Center** (772-3256) has an introductory slide program and an interesting museum (open daily 8am-7pm; off-season 8am-6pm). **Kolob Canyons Visitors Center** (586-9548) lies in the northwest corner of the park, off I-15 (open daily 8am-7pm; off-season 9am-4pm). Maps and suggested hikes grace *The Sentinel* and the Zion National Park guide, available free at the main entrance. The park charges an **entrance fee** of $10 per car, $5 per pedestrian. In an **emergency,** call 772-3322 or 911. Zion's **post office** is located inside the Zion Canyon Lodge. **ZIP code:** 84767. **Area code:** 435.

CAMPGROUNDS AND ACCOMMODATIONS More than 300 sites are available on a first come, first served basis (come early) in the **South** and **Watchman Campgrounds,** both near the park's south entrance. Both sites have water, toilets, and a sanitary disposal station for trailers. (2-week max. stay; sites $10.) A primitive area at **Lava Point** can be accessed from a hiking trail in the mid-section of the park, or from the gravel road which turns off Rte. 9 in **Virgin** (6 sites with toilets but no water; free; open June-Nov.). A permit ($5) from the visitors center is required for **backcountry camping.** Camping along the rim is *not* allowed, but a free map from the visitors center will show you where you may and may not pitch a tent.

Mukuntuweep Campground (648-2154), just outside the park near the east entrance, has altitude on its side. Not only is it 1000 ft. higher and about 10° cooler than the sites inside the park, but it also offers the amenities of a laundromat and showers. (70 tent sites $15, 30 full hookups $20. Office open 24hr.) **Zion Canyon Campground,** 479 Zion Park Blvd. (772-3237), in Springdale just south of the park, soothes the weary, hungry, and filthy with a convenience store, restaurant, grocery store, showers, and coin-op laundry. (Sites for 2 $15, full hookup $19; $3.50 per additional adult, $2 per additional child under 15. Office open 24hr. Store open daily 8am-9pm; off-season 8am-5pm.)

The **Zion Canyon Lodge** (303-297-2757 for reservations), along the park's main road, offers premium rooms at premium prices, along with a dining room. (Singles and doubles $83, $5 per additional person; cabin singles and doubles $93/$5. Restaurant open daily 6:30-10am, 11:30am-3pm, and 5:30-9:30pm.) Cheap motels are available in nearly any of the towns near Zion, including **Springdale** and **Rockville,** 2-5 mi. south of the park; **Mt. Carmel Junction,** 20 mi. east; **Kanab,** 20 mi. south; or **Cedar City** (see p. 643), 70 mi. north of the park on Rte. 15.

The nearest hostel is the **Dixie Hostel,** 73 S. Main St. (635-8202 or 635-9000), 10 mi. west in Hurricane. The large, clean house maintains 30 beds, keeps spacious laundry and kitchen facilities, and includes continental breakfast. Hostel guests also get a 20% discount at the hot springs nearby, and the hostel runs a shuttle to Zion for $15 round-trip, including admission. (Dorm beds $15; private doubles $35.) In the other direction, the **Canyonlands International Youth Hostel (AAIH/Rucksackers),** 143 E. 100 S., Kanab 84741 (644-5554), lies 20 mi. south in **Kanab.** The hostel's location, 1hr. north of the Grand Canyon's North Rim and roughly equidistant from Zion, Bryce, and Lake Powell, makes it a perfect base for exploring northern Arizona and southern Utah. Free linen, laundry facilities, TV, kitchen, and a most bountiful breakfast banquet make it worth a trip from any of the parks. ($10.)

SIGHTS If you love to walk or hike, you're in the right place. Paved and wheelchair accessible with assistance, the **Riverside Walk** stretches 1 mi. from the north end of Zion Canyon Dr. The refreshing **Emerald Pools** trail (1.2 mi. round-trip) is accessible to the disabled along its lower loop, but the middle and upper loops are steep and narrow. Another easy but spectacular trail leads to **Weeping Rock** (½ mi. round-trip), a dripping spring surrounded by hanging gardens. Hikers up for a challenge should try the **Angel's Landing** trail (5 mi. round-trip), which rises 1488 ft. above the canyon; the last terrifying ½ mi. climbs a narrow ridge with guide chains blasted into the rock. Those who fear heights should not even *think* about attempting this trail. The difficult trail to **Observation Point** (8 mi. round-trip) leads through **Echo Canyon,** a spectacular kaleidoscope of sandstone, where steep switchbacks explore the unusually gouged canyon. Overnight hikers can spend days on the 27 mi. **West Rim Trail.**

Even if you plan to visit the **Kolob Canyons,** be sure to make the pilgrimage to **Zion Canyon.** The 7 mi. dead-end road on the canyon floor rambles past the giant formations of **Sentinel, Mountain of the Sun,** and the overwhelming symbol of Zion, the **Great White Throne.** A shuttle from the Lodge runs this route every hour on the hour in the summer (1hr.; daily 9am-5pm; $3, children $2). Horseback tours arranged by **Canyon Trail Rides** (772-3810) leave from the Lodge ($15-37 per person). **Bike Zion,** 1458 Zion Park Blvd. (772-3929), rents rafts for $3 per day ($5 deposit) and bikes for $23-25 per day ($7-11 per hr., $17-27 per ½-day; open daily 8am-8pm).

■ Cedar City

Cedar City was founded in 1851 by a handful of Mormon pioneers who mistook the plentiful junipers for cedar trees. Despite that early mishap, the population has since swelled beyond 20,000. Most shops and offices are located on Main St., where national chains are thankfully not much of a presence. The city prides itself on its unofficial status as the cultural center of southern Utah: the many summer festivals, including the Utah Summer Games and the Utah Shakespeare Festival, have led to its self-proclaimed nickname of "Festival City." Cedar City's proximity to Utah's national parks also makes it a popular base for exploring the Fab Five.

Budget motels cluster on **S. Main St.** The **Zion Inn Motel,** 222 S. Main St. (586-9487), offers a two-bedroom option in addition to the conventional singles ($32-39) and doubles ($35-47; in winter $25/$29). The newly renovated **Super 7 Motel,** 190 S. Main St. (586-6566), rents sparkling clean rooms (singles $35-52, doubles $39-59; in winter $25/$29-35). The Cedar City **KOA,** 1121 N. Main St. (586-9872), boasts over 100 sites, a laundromat, a pool, and a snack bar (sites $18, full hook-up $23).

The **Brickhouse Café,** 227 S. Main St. (865-1770), with its series of tiny rooms and marigold-yellow walls, is the perfect place for an intimate chat over coffee and a $4 bagel sandwich (open M-Sa 7am-midnight, Su 7am-3pm; in winter M-Sa 7am-9pm, Su 7am-3pm). Granny Boomer will fatten you up with her generous portions of Mexican, American, and Italian food and quench your thirst with drinks served in enormous jars at **Boomer's Restaurant,** 5 N. Main St. (865-9665). Quesadillas go for $5; pasta specials are just $6. (Open M-Th 11am-9pm, F-Sa 11am-11pm.)

Cedar City is best known for its summer festivals and challenging mountain biking trails nearby. The **Utah Shakespeare Festival** (586-7878 or 800-PLAYTIX/752-9849) presents numerous plays every Monday to Saturday from late June through late August. Every summer around mid-June, Southern Utah University hosts the **Utah Summer Games** (800-FOR-UTAH/367-8824), a week of Olympic-style competitions for Utah's amateur athletes.

The patches of wilderness surrounding Cedar City, including **Brian Head** and **Panguitch,** are becoming well-known for their backcountry riding opportunities. Trails wind through terrific forest, mountain, meadows, and desert environments. The *Mountain Bike Guide* at the visitors center is informative, or call 800-UTAH-FUN/882-4386 for a free *Bicycle Utah Vacation Guide*.

Cedar City is located in southwestern Utah at the intersection of I-15, U.S. 91, and Rte. 14. **Greyhound,** 1355 S. Main St. (586-9465; terminal open daily 7am-10pm), runs to Salt Lake City ($40-43), Flagstaff ($65-69), and many other cities. **Cedar City Cab** (586-9333) charges $5 for a ride from the airport to downtown. **Cedar Mountain Sports,** 921 S. Main St. (586-4949 or 888-586-4949), rents climbing, backpacking, and cross-country skiing equipment. (Skis, boots, and poles $10 per day; tents $12, $6 per additional night. Open M-F 10am-7pm, Sa 10am-6pm.) **Bike Route,** 70 W. Center (586-4242), rents mountain bikes for $15 per day, helmet included (open M-Sa 10am-6pm). The **Visitors Center** and **Chamber of Commerce,** 581 N. Main St. (586-4484), hand out maps and tourist info (open June-Aug. M-F 9am-7pm, Sa 9am-1pm; Sept.-May M-F 9am-5pm). **Post Office:** 333 N. Main St. (586-6701; open M-F 8:30am-5pm, Sa 9am-noon). **ZIP code:** 84720. **Area code:** 435.

■ Natural Bridges and Hovenweep

Natural Bridges National Monument The Paiutes who inhabited this region nearly 3000 years ago called it Ma-Vah-Talk-Tump, or "under the horse's belly." Although Utah's first national monument now carries the more prosaic moniker of "Natural Bridges," the three rock formations have only grown more impressive. To appreciate the size of the monuments fully—the highest is more than 200 feet—leave the overlooks and hike down to the bridges. Once you do, it's easy to understand why the Hopi named the largest one "Sipapu," or "place of emergence"—they believed it to be the entryway through which their ancestors came into this world. The park's paved **Bridge View Drive** is about 9 mi. and passes the overlooks and trailheads to each of the three major bridges. It's also possible to hike various loop trails connecting the bridges—trails range from 5.6 to 8.6 mi.

To reach Natural Bridges from northern Utah, follow U.S. 191 S. from Moab to its junction with **Scenic Rte. 95 W** (north of Bluff and 4 mi. south of Blanding). From Colorado, U.S. 66 heads west to U.S. 191 S (junction in Monticello). From the south, Rte. 261 from Mexican Hat climbs a mesa in a heart-wrenching and axle-grinding series of 5 mph gravel switchbacks, providing a spectacular view of Monument Valley across the Arizona border.

The **visitors center** (692-1234), several miles past the entrance to the monument, offers information, a slide show, and exhibits. (Open daily 8am-6pm; Nov.-Feb. 9:30am-4:30pm. Park entrance $6 per vehicle, $3 per hiker or bicyclist, good for 7 days; National Parks passports accepted.) Sleep under the stars at the **campground** near the visitors center. Thirteen shaded sites set amid pinyon pines accommodate up to nine people each. (Campground usually fills up by 2pm. Sites $10. First come, first served.) **Water** is available at the visitors center. For further info, contact the **Superintendent,** Natural Bridges, P.O. Box 1, Lake Powell 84533. If the park campground is full, primitive overflow camping is available off a gravel road originating at the intersection of Rte. 95 and Rte. 251, 6 mi. from the visitors center. The free sites are flat and shaded but have no facilities.

Hovenweep National Monument Hovenweep, from the Ute meaning "deserted valley," features six groups of Pueblo ruins dating back more than 1000 years. The valley remains deserted today, and only two rangers (1 in Utah, 1 in Colorado) mind the monument's 784 acres. Immune to vacation swarms, or even small crowds, Hovenweep provides visitors space and time to ponder. The best preserved and most impressive ruins, **Square Tower Ruins,** lie footsteps away from the visitors center (see below). The **Square Tower Loop Trail** (2 mi.) loops around a small canyon, accessing **Hovenweep Castle** and the **Twin Towers.** A shorter trail, the ½ mi. **Tower Point Loop,** accesses the ruins of a tower perched on a canyon. The outlying ruins—**Cujon Ruins** and **Huckberry Canyon** in Utah, and **Cutthroat Castle** and **Goodman Point Ruins** in Colorado—are isolated and difficult to reach.

Desolate but beautiful roads usher you to Hovenweep. In Utah or Arizona, follow U.S. 191 to its junction with Rte. 262 E (14 mi. south of Blanding, 11 mi. north of Bluff). After about 30 mi., watch for signs to the monument. From Cortez, CO, go south on U.S. 166/U.S. 160 to County Rd. 6 (the airport road); follow the Hovenweep signs for 45 mi., including 15 mi. of gravel road. It's wise to check road conditions at the **visitors center** (303-749-0510), accessible from both the Utah and Colorado sides. (Open daily 8am-5pm, except when the ranger is out on patrol. $3 per person, $6 per car, National Parks passports accepted.) *There is no gasoline, telephone, or food at the monument.* The Hovenweep **campground** is temporarily closed but may reopen by 1999. For more info, contact the **Superintendent,** Hovenweep National Monument, McElmo Rte., Cortez, CO 81321 (303-749-0510).

NEARBY CIVILIZATION Three small towns provide lodging and services for travelers to the monuments and the valley. In the agricultural town of **Blanding** (45 mi. from Hovenweep, 60 mi. from Natural Bridges), the **Prospector Motor Lodge,** 591 U.S. 191 S. (678-3231), offers spacious, reasonable rooms, some with kitchenettes (singles $41-50, doubles $45-55; off-season $27/$39; prices somewhat negotiable). The cheaper **Blanding Sunset Inn,** 88 W. Center St. (678-3323), provides basic, phoneless rooms (singles $28; doubles $30). The **Elk Ridge Restaurant,** 120 E. Center St. (678-3390), will pour your morning coffee (1 egg, potatoes, and toast $3.75; open daily 6am-9:30pm).

Nestled among the sandstone canyons, the tiny town of **Bluff** (40 mi. from Hovenweep, 65 mi. from Natural Bridges) welcomes the budget traveler. Bluff is also worth a detour to visit the gigantic, austere sandstone sculptures of the **Valley of the Gods,** which provided the backdrop for some of the road scenes in *Thelma and Louise.* A tough but incredible 17 mi. drive departs from U.S. 163, 15 mi. south of Bluff on the right side of the road, and runs right through the valley. Inexpensive and comfortable lodges and motels line U.S. 191, including **The Recapture Lodge** (672-2281; singles $34-44; doubles $50-58). Tasty Navajo sheepherder sandwiches (roast beef on Indian fry bread, $5.25) hit the tables at the **Turquoise Restaurant** (672-2279), opposite the lodge on U.S. 191 S (open M 7am-9:30pm, Tu-Su 7:30am-9:30pm).

Mexican Hat sits along the San Juan River on the border of the Navajo nation. The town is 20 mi. south of Bluff on U.S. 163 and 20 mi. north of Arizona. Rest your head at the newly renovated **Canyonlands Motel** (683-2230), on U.S. 163 (singles $34, doubles $47). The **restaurant** at Burch's Indian Trading Co. (683-2221), on U.S. 163, serves Mexican and Southwestern food on picnic tables, including tasty mutton stew ($6) and burgers ($4.75; open daily 7am-9pm).

Arizona

Populated primarily by Native Americans through the 19th century, Arizona has been hit in the past hundred years by waves of settlers—from the speculators and miners of the late 1800s, to the soldiers who trained here during World War II and returned after the war, to the more recent immigrants from Mexico. Deserted ghost towns scattered throughout the state illustrate the death of the mining lifestyle and the fast pace of urban development, while older monuments preserve settlements abandoned long before the existence of used car lots or postcards. Traces of lost Native American civilization remain at Canyon de Chelly, Navajo National Monument, and Wupatki and Walnut Canyons. (The descendants of these tribes, almost one-seventh of the United States's Native American population, now occupy reservations on one-half of the state's land.) However spectacular, neither ancient nor modern man-made memorials can overshadow Arizona's natural masterpieces—the Grand Canyon, Monument Valley, and the gorgeous landscapes seen from the state's highways.

PRACTICAL INFORMATION

Capital: Phoenix.
Visitor Info: Arizona Tourism, 2702 N. 3rd St. Suite 4015, Phoenix 85004 (602-230-7733 or 888-520-3434; http://www.arizonaguide.com). Open M-F 8am-5pm. **Arizona State Parks,** 1300 W. Washington St., Phoenix 85007 (602-542-4174 or 800-285-3703). Open M-F 8am-5pm.
Emergency: 911.

Time Zone: Mountain (2hr. behind Eastern). Arizona (with the exception of the reservations) does not observe Daylight Savings Time; in the summer, it is 1hr. behind the rest of the Mountain Time Zone. **Postal Abbreviation:** AZ.

Sales Tax: 6%.

■ Grand Canyon

Despite the prevalence of its image on everything from postcards to screen-savers, nothing can prepare you for the first sight of the Grand Canyon. One of the seven natural wonders of the world (277 mi. long, 10 mi. wide, and over 1 mi. deep), the canyon descends to the Colorado River past looming walls of multi-colored limestone, sandstone, and shale. The government began designating its most daunting wild regions as national park sites for two reasons—first, to compensate with natural grandeur for the country's short cultural tradition, and second, to preserve unfarmable lands for recreation. Hike down into the gorge to get a real feeling for the immensity and beauty of this natural phenomenon, or just watch the colors and shadows change from one of the many rim viewpoints.

Grand Canyon National Park is divided into three areas: the **South Rim,** which includes Grand Canyon Village; the **North Rim;** and the canyon gorge itself. The slightly lower, more accessible South Rim draws 10 times as many visitors as the higher, more heavily forested North Rim. The South Rim is open all year, while the North Rim only welcomes travelers from mid-May to mid-October, depending on the weather. The 13 mi. trail that traverses the canyon floor furnishes sturdy hikers with a 2-day adventure, while the 214 mi. perimeter road is a good 5hr. drive for those who would rather explore from above. If you observe all safety precautions, use common sense, and drink lots of water, you are sure to have an unforgettable experience.

■ South Rim

During the summer, everything on two legs or four wheels converges on this side of the Grand Canyon. If you plan to visit during the mobfest, make reservations for lodging, campsites, or mules well in advance—and prepare to battle the crowds. That said, it's much better than Disney World. A friendly Park Service staff, well-run facilities, and beautiful scenery help ease crowd anxiety. Fewer tourists brave the canyon's winter weather, and many hotels and facilities close during the off-season.

ORIENTATION AND PRACTICAL INFORMATION

There are two park entrances: the main **south entrance** lies on U.S. 180 N, and the eastern **Desert View** entrance lies on I-40 W. From Las Vegas, the fastest route to the South Rim is U.S. 93 S to I-40 E, and then Rte. 64 N. From Flagstaff, I-40 E to U.S. 89 N is the most scenic; from there, Rte. 64 N takes you to the Desert View entrance. Heading straight up U.S. 180 N is more direct. Once you enter the park, posted maps and signs make orienting yourself easy. Lodges and services concentrate in **Grand Canyon Village,** at the end of Park Entrance Rd. The east half of the Village contains the visitors center and the general store, while most of the lodges and the **Bright Angel Trailhead** lie in the west section. The **South Kaibab Trailhead** is off East Rim Dr., east of the village. **West Rim Drive** lies to the west of the village.

The **entrance fee** is $20 per car and $10 for travelers using other modes of transportation—even bus passengers must pay (Golden Eagle, Golden Age, and Golden Access passports accepted). The pass lasts for one week. For most services in the Park, call the **main switchboard** number at 638-2631.

Buses: Nava-Hopi Bus Lines (800-892-8687) leaves the Flagstaff Amtrak station for the Grand Canyon daily at 7:45am and 3pm, returning from Bright Angel Lodge at 10am and 5pm (about 2hr.). $17.50, under 15 $8.75; round-trip $31/$15.50, including entrance fee. Times vary by season, so call ahead.

Public Transportation: Free shuttle buses ride the West Rim Loop (daily 7:30am-sunset) and the Village Loop (daily 6:30am-9pm) every 15-20min. A free **hiker's shuttle** runs every 30min. between Grand Canyon Village and the South Kaibab Trailhead, on the East Rim near Yaki Point.

Taxis: Call 638-2631. Open 24hr.

Auto Repairs: Grand Canyon Garage (638-2631), east of the visitors center on the main road, near Maswik Lodge. Open daily 8am-5pm. 24hr. emergency service.

Equipment Rental: Babbitt's General Store (638-2262), in Grand Canyon Village near Yavapai Lodge and the visitors center. Comfy hiking boots, socks included ($8 1st day, $5 per additional day); sleeping bags ($7-9/$5); tents ($15-18/$9); and other camping gear. Hefty deposits required on all items. Open daily 8am-8pm.

Visitor Info: The **visitors center** (638-7888) is 6 mi. north of the south entrance station. Open daily 8am-6pm; off-season 8am-5pm. Hikers should get the *Backcountry Trip Planner;* the regular old *Trip Planner* is for ordinary mortals (both free). Free and informative, *The Guide* is also available here, in case you missed it at the entrance. Write to **Trip Planner,** Grand Canyon National Park, P.O. Box 129, Grand Canyon, 86023, for info. The **transportation info desks** in **Bright Angel Lodge** and **Maswik Lodge** (638-2631 for both) handle reservations for mule rides, bus tours, plane tours, Phantom Ranch, taxis, and more. Both open daily 6am-7pm.

Luggage Storage: In Bright Angel Lodge. Open 8am-9pm. 50¢ per day.

Weather and Road Conditions: 638-7888.

Medical Services: Grand Canyon Clinic (638-2551 or 638-2469), several mi. south of the visitors center on Center Rd. Open M-F 8am-5:30pm, Sa 9am-noon. 24hr. emergency aid. For a **dentist,** call 638-2395.

Post Office: (638-2512), across the street from the visitors center. Open M-F 9am-4:30pm, Sa 11am-1pm. **ZIP code:** 86023. **Area code:** 520.

ACCOMMODATIONS AND CAMPGROUNDS

Compared to the six million years it took the Colorado River to carve the Grand Canyon, the year it will take you to get indoor lodging near the South Rim will pass in the blink of an eye. Summer rooms should be reserved *11 months in advance.* That said, there are cancellations every day; if you arrive unprepared, check at the lodges in the morning for vacancies, or call the Grand Canyon operator at 638-2631 and ask to be connected with the proper lodge. Reservations for **Bright Angel Lodge, Maswik Lodge, Trailer Village,** and **Phantom Ranch** can be made through **Grand Canyon National Park Lodges,** P.O. Box 699, Grand Canyon 86023 (303-29-PARKS/297-2757 or 638-2401). Be aware that most accommodations on the South Rim are very pricey.

Bright Angel Lodge (638-2401), Grand Canyon Village. Very convenient to Bright Angel Trail and shuttle buses. "Rustic" lodge singles and doubles with plumbing but no heat $42-58; "historic" cabins for 1 or 2 people $66; $7 per additional person in rooms and cabins.

Maswik Lodge (638-2401), Grand Canyon Village. Small, clean cabins (singles or doubles) with showers but no heat $59; motel-style rooms $72-112; $7-9 per additional person.

Phantom Ranch (638-2631), on the canyon floor, a day's hike down the Kaibab Trail. Dorm beds $21; cabins for 1 or 2 people $56; $11 per additional person. *Don't show up without reservations—they'll send you back up the trail, on foot.* Meals must be reserved in advance. Breakfast $13; box lunch $8; stew dinner $18, steak dinner $29. If you're dying to sleep on the canyon floor but don't have a reservation, show up at the Bright Angel transportation desk at 6am, and they may be able to arrange something.

The campsites listed here usually fill up early in the day. Campground overflow winds up in the **Kaibab National Forest,** along the south border of the park, where you can pull off a dirt road and camp for free. No camping is allowed within ¼ mi. of U.S. 64. Sleeping in cars is *not* permitted within the park, but it is allowed in the Kaibab Forest. For more info, contact the **Tusayan Ranger District,** Kaibab National Forest, P.O. Box 3088, Grand Canyon 86023 (638-2443). Overnight hiking or camping within the park outside of designated campgrounds requires a **Backcountry Use Permit** ($20 plus a $4 impact fee), available at the **Backcountry Office** (638-7875), ¼ mi. south of the visitors center (open daily 8am-noon and 1-5pm). Permit requests are accepted by mail, fax, or in person up to 5 months in advance. Guests with reservations at Phantom Ranch (see above) do not need permits. Reservations for some campgrounds can be made through **BIOSPHERICS** (800-365-2267).

Mather Campground (call BIOSPHERICS, 800-365-2267), Grand Canyon Village, 1 mi. south of the visitors center. 320 shady, relatively isolated sites with no hookups. Sept.-May $12; June-Aug. $15. 7-day max. stay. For Mar.-Nov., reserve up to 8 weeks in advance; Dec.-Feb. sites go on a first come, first served basis. Check at the office, even if the sign says the campground is full.

Ten-X Campground (638-2443), in the Kaibab National Forest, 10 mi. south of Grand Canyon Village off Rte. 64. Shady sites surrounded by pine trees. Toilets, water, no hookups. First come, first served sites $10. Open May-Sept.

Desert View Campground (638-7888), 26 mi. east of Grand Canyon Village. 50 sites with phone and restroom access, but no hookups. $10. No reservations; usually full by early afternoon. Open mid-May to Oct.

Camper Village (638-2887), 7 mi. south of the visitors center in Tusayan. RV and tent sites $17-22 for 2 people; $2 per additional adult. First come, first served tent sites; reservations required for RVs.

Indian Gardens (638-7888), 4½ mi. from the South Rim Bright Angel trailhead and 3100 ft. below the rim. 15 free sites, toilets, and water. Reservations and backcountry permit required.

Trailer Village (638-2401), next to Mather Campground. Clearly designed with the RV in mind. Showers and laundry nearby. 84 sites for 2 with hookup $19; $1.75 per additional person. 7-day max. stay. Office open daily 8am-noon and 1-5pm. Reserve 6-9 months in advance.

FOOD

Fast food has yet to sink its greasy talons into the South Rim (the closest McDonald's is 7 mi. south in Tusayan), but you *can* find meals for fast-food prices. **Babbitt's General Store** (638-2262), near the visitors center, has a deli counter (sandwiches $2-4) and a wide selection of groceries, as well as a camping supplies department (open daily 8am-8pm; deli open 8am-7pm). **Maswik Cafeteria,** in Maswik Lodge, serves a variety of inexpensive grill-made options (hot entrees $5-7, sandwiches $2-4) in a wood-paneled cafeteria atmosphere (open daily 6am-10pm). **Bright Angel Dining Room** (638-2631), in Bright Angel Lodge, serves hot sandwiches for $6-8 (open daily 6:30am-10pm). The **soda fountain** at Bright Angel Lodge chills 16 flavors of ice cream (1 scoop $1.60) for hot hikers emerging from trails (open daily 6:30am-9pm).

SIGHTS AND ACTIVITIES

From your first glimpse of the canyon, you may feel a compelling desire to see it from the inside, an enterprise that is harder than it looks. Even the young at heart and body should remember that an easy downhill hike can become a nightmarish 50° incline on the return journey. Also keep in mind that the lower you go, the hotter it gets; when it's 85° on the rim, it's around 100° at Indian Gardens, and around 110° at Phantom Ranch. Heat exhaustion, the greatest threat to any hiker, is marked by a monstrous headache and termination of sweating. *For a day hike, you must take at least a gallon of water per person; expect to require at least a liter for each hour hiking upwards under the hot sun.* Hiking boots or sneakers with excellent tread are also necessary—the trails are steep, and every year several careless hikers take what locals morbidly call "the 12-second tour." A list of hiking safety tips can be found in *The Guide.* Parents should think twice about bringing children more than 1 mi. down any trail—kids remember well and may exact revenge when they get bigger.

The two most accessible trails into the canyon are the **Bright Angel Trail,** originating at the Bright Angel Lodge, and the **South Kaibab Trail,** from Yaki Point. Bright Angel is outfitted for the average tourist, with rest houses strategically stationed 1½ mi. and 3 mi. from the rim. **Indian Gardens,** 4½ mi. down, offers the tired hiker restrooms, picnic tables, and blessed shade. All three rest stops have water in the summer. Kaibab is trickier, steeper, and lacks shade or water, but it rewards the intrepid with a better view of the canyon. If you've made arrangements to spend the night on the canyon floor, the best route is the South Kaibab Trail (4-5hr., depending on conditions) and back up the Bright Angel (7-8hr.) the following day. Hikes to Indian Gardens and **Plateau Point,** 6 mi. out, where you can look down 1360 ft. to the river, make excellent **daytrips** (8-12hr.), provided that you start around 7am. A few other, less-traveled trails lead into the canyon, but require backcountry permits.

If you're not up to descending into the canyon, follow the **Rim Trail** east to **Grandview Point** and the **Yavapai Geological Museum,** or west to **Hermit's Rest.** Viewpoints along the East Rim are somewhat spread out, but the West Rim is skirted by a beautiful trail that leads to nine overlooks. You can hike out as far as you want and then take the shuttle back. The trail is paved and wheelchair accessible from the visitors center to Bright Angel Lodge. After Maricopa Point, footing is more difficult, but the views are correspondingly more spectacular.

The East Rim swarms with sunset-watchers at dusk, and the observation deck at the Yavapai Museum, at the end of the trail, has a sweeping view of the canyon during the day. Along the West Rim, **Hopi Point** is a favorite for sunsets, and a special "sunset shuttle" heads back from here. *The Guide* and the visitors center list times for sunsets and sunrises.

Mule trips from the South Rim are very expensive (day trip $106, overnight $280) and are booked up to one year in advance, although cancellations do occur (call 303-297-2757 for reservations). Mule trips from the North Rim are cheaper and more readily available. **Whitewater rafting** trips through the canyon last from 3 days to 2 weeks; advance reservations are required. Call the transport info desk for a list of trips. Park Service rangers also present a variety of free, informative **talks** and **guided hikes;** times and details are listed in *The Guide.*

■ North Rim

If you're coming from Utah or Nevada, or you simply want to avoid the crowds at the South Rim, the park's North Rim is a bit wilder, a bit cooler, and much more serene—all with a view *almost* as groovy as that from the South Rim. Unfortunately, because the North Rim is less frequented, it's hard to reach by public transportation. From October 15 until December 1, the North Rim is open for day use only; from December 1 until May 15, it is closed entirely.

ORIENTATION AND PRACTICAL INFORMATION

To reach the North Rim from the South Rim, take Rte. 64 E to U.S. 89 N, which runs into Alt. 89; from Alt. 89, follow Rte. 67 S to the edge. Altogether, the beautiful drive is over 200 mi. From Utah, take Alt. 89 S from Fredonia. Snow closes Rte. 67 from mid-October through mid-May; park visitor facilities (including the lodge) close for the winter as well. The **entrance fee** is good for both rims for 7 days ($20 per car; $10 per person on foot, bike, bus, or holy pilgrimage).

Public Transportation: Transcanyon, P.O. Box 348, Grand Canyon 86023 (638-2820). Buses to South Rim depart 7am (4½hr.); return buses depart 1:30pm. $60, round-trip $100. Reservations required. Runs late May to Oct.

Visitor Info: National Park Service Information Desk (638-7864), in the lobby of Grand Canyon Lodge (see below). Info on North Rim viewpoints, facilities, and trails. There's a separate issue of *The Guide* for the North Rim; you can pick it up here. Open daily 8am-8pm.

Weather Info: 638-7888.

Medical Services: North Rim Clinic (638-2611, ext. 222), in cabin #5 at Grand Canyon Lodge. Staffed by a nurse practitioner and a physician's assistant. Walk-in or appointment service. Open W-M 9am-noon and 3-6pm, Tu 9am-noon and 2-5pm.

Post Office: in Grand Canyon Lodge (638-2611), like everything else. Open M-F 8am-4pm, Sa 9am-1pm. **ZIP code:** 86052. **Area code:** 520.

ACCOMMODATIONS, CAMPGROUNDS, AND FOOD

Since camping within the confines of the Grand Canyon National Park is limited to designated campgrounds, only a lucky minority of North Rim visitors get to spend the night "right there." **BIOSPHERICS** (800-365-2267) handles reservations; otherwise, mark your territory by 10am. If you can't get in-park lodgings, head for the **Kaibab National Forest,** which runs from north of Jacob Lake to the park entrance. You can camp for free, as long as you're ¼ mi. from the road or official campgrounds. Less expensive accommodations may be found in **Kanab, UT,** 80 mi. north (p. 642), where motel rooms tend to hover around $40.

Grand Canyon Lodge (303-297-2757 for reservations, 638-2611 for front desk), on the edge of the rim. Pioneer cabins shelter 4 people for $87. Singles or doubles in frontier cabins $70; Western cabins and motel rooms $80-110. Reception 24hr. Reserve several months in advance.

Jacob Lake Inn (643-7232), 30 mi. north of the North Rim entrance at Jacob Lake. Cabins for 2 $66-71, for 3 $76-78, for 4 $81-84. Pricier motel units available for $10-15 more. Reasonably priced dining room. Reception daily 6:30am-9:30pm.

Kaibab Camper Village (643-7804), ¼ mi. south of Jacob Lake Inn. 50 tent sites $12; 60 sites with hookups for 2 $20-22; $2 per extra person. Open May to mid-Oct.

North Rim Campground (call BIOSPHERICS, 800-365-2267), on Rte. 67 near the rim, the only campground in the park. You can't see into the canyon from the pine-covered site, but you know it's there. Food store nearby, laundry, recreation room, and showers. 7-day max. stay. 82 sites $15; no hookups. Open mid-May to mid-Oct.

DeMotte Park Campground, 5 mi. north of the park entrance in Kaibab National Forest. 23 woodsy sites $10. First come, first served.

Both feeding options on the North Rim are placed strategically at the **Grand Canyon Lodge** (638-2611). The restaurant serves breakfast for $3-7 (6:30-10am), lunch for $6-8 (11:30am-2:30pm), and dinner for $13 and up (4:45-9:30pm; reservations required for dinner). A sandwich at the **Snack Bar** costs $3-4 (open daily 7am-9pm). North Rim-ers are better off eating in Kanab or stopping at the **Jacob Lake Inn** (643-7232) for sandwiches ($5-7) and great milkshakes ($2-3; open daily 6am-9pm).

SIGHTS AND ACTIVITIES

A ½ mi. paved trail leads from the Grand Canyon Lodge to **Bright Angel Point,** which commands a seraphic view of the Canyon. **Point Imperial,** an 11 mi. drive from the lodge, overlooks **Marble Canyon** and the **Painted Desert. Cape Royal** lies 23 mi. from the lodge; en route, you'll pass the enchanting **Vista Encantadora.** Short trails include the **Cape Final Trail** (4 mi.), which heads from a parking lot a few miles before Cape Royal to Cape Final, and the **Transept Trail** (3 mi.), which follows the rim from the lodge to the campground. The North Rim's *The Guide* lists trails in full.

Only one trail, the **North Kaibab Trail,** leads into the Canyon from the North Rim; a shuttle runs to the trailhead from Grand Canyon Lodge (daily at 5:30 and 7:45am; $5; reservations required). Overnight hikers must get permits from the **Backcountry Office** in the ranger station (open daily 8am-noon and 1-5pm), or write to the **Back-country Office,** P.O. Box 129, Grand Canyon, AZ 86023; it may take a few days to get a permit in person.

The North Rim offers nature walks, lectures, and evening programs at the North Rim Campground and at Grand Canyon Lodge. Check the info desk or campground bulletin boards for schedules. One-hour ($15) or ½-day **mule trips** ($40) circle the rim or descend into the canyon from the lodge (638-9875 or 435-679-8665; open daily 7am-7pm). If you'd rather tour the Canyon wet, pick up a *Grand Canyon River Trip Operators* brochure and select from among the 20 companies offering trips.

On warm evenings, the Grand Canyon Lodge fills with an eclectic group of international travelers, American families, and rugged adventurers. Thirsty hikers will find a bar and a jukebox at the **Saloon,** within the lodge complex (open daily 11am-11pm). Others look to the warm air rising from the canyon, a full moon, and the occasional shooting star for their intoxication at day's end.

■ Flagstaff

After a three-year stay among the Navajos and Apaches of southern Arizona during the 1860s, Samuel Cozzens returned to New England and wrote *The Marvellous Country,* in which he promoted the *north* part of the territory as fertile, temperate, and ripe for settlement (although he had never actually been there). Colonists from Boston subsequently arrived in the San Francisco Mountains region; unable to locate the promised rich farmland and gold veins, they promptly departed. Before leaving, however, one group erected a stripped-pine flagpole as a marker for westward travelers. Presto change-o: Flagstaff was born. During the following decade, Flagstaff, a stop on the transcontinental railroad, became a permanent settlement; railroad tracks still cut through downtown. Flagstaff now provides a home for Northern Arizona University (NAU) students, retired cowboys, earthy Volvo owners, New Agers, and serious rock climbers. Although the town itself is low on sights, the surrounding area isn't, making it a perfect stop to rest and refuel en route to or from the Grand Canyon.

ORIENTATION AND PRACTICAL INFORMATION

Flagstaff sits 138 mi. north of Phoenix (take I-17), 26 mi. north of Sedona (take U.S. 89A), and 81 mi. south of the Grand Canyon's south rim (take U.S. 180). Downtown surrounds the intersection of **Beaver St.** and **Rte. 66** (formerly Santa Fe Ave.). Both bus stations, three youth hostels, the tourist office, and a number of inexpensive restaurants lie within ½ mi. of this spot. Other commercial establishments line **S. San Francisco St.**, 2 blocks east of Beaver. As a mountain town, Flagstaff stays fairly temperate and receives frequent afternoon thundershowers.

Trains: Amtrak, 1 E. Rte. 66 (774-8679 or 800-872-7245). To Los Angeles (11hr., 1 per day at 9:13pm, $52-94) and Albuquerque (5½hr., 1 per day at 6:22am, $49-89). Station open daily 5:45am-10:20pm; ticket office closed 12:45-2:45pm.

Buses: Greyhound, 399 S. Malpais Ln. (774-4573 or 800-231-2222), across from NAU campus, 5 blocks southwest of the train station on U.S. 89A. To: Phoenix (3hr., 4 per day, $19); Albuquerque (6½hr., 4 per day, $46); Los Angeles (10-12hr., 9 per day, $49); and Las Vegas (6-7hr., 3 per day via Kingman, casino special round-trip $49). Terminal open 24hr. **Grayline/Nava-Hopi,** 114 W. Rte. 66 (774-5003 or 800-892-8687). Shuttle buses to the Grand Canyon (2hr., 2 per day, $17.50 including admission fee) and Phoenix (3hr., 3 per day).

Public Transportation: Pine Country Transit, 970 W. Rte. 66 (779-6624). Routes cover most of town. Buses run once per hr.; route map and schedule available at visitors center. One-way 75¢; seniors, children, and disabled 60¢.

Taxis: Friendly Cab, 214-9000. Airport to downtown about $9.

Car Rental: Budget Rent-A-Car (779-5255 or 800-527-0700), at the Flagstaff Airport. Cars from $42 per day with 200 free mi., 30¢ per additional mi.; $210 per week with 400 free mi. Insurance $15 per day. Must be 21 with major credit card or a $200 cash deposit. Under 25 surcharge $5 per day. Open daily 7am-9pm. *Let's Go* toters get 10% off.

Equipment Rental: Peace Surplus, 14 W. Rte. 66 (779-4521), 1 block from Grand Canyon Hostel. Daily tent rental ($5-8; $50-200 deposit), packs ($5; $100 deposit), plus a good stock of cheap outdoor gear. 3-day min. rental on all equipment. Credit card or cash deposit required. Open M-F 8am-9pm, Sa 8am-8pm, Su 8am-6pm.

Visitor Info: Flagstaff Visitors Center, 1 E. Rte. 66 (774-9541 or 800-842-7293), inside the Amtrak station. Dispenses basic but useful free maps. Open M-Sa 7am-6pm, Su 7am-5pm.

Internet Access: NAU's **Cline Library** (523-2171). Open M-Th 7:30am-10pm, F 7:30am-6pm, Sa 9am-6pm, Su noon-10pm.

Post Office: 2400 N. Postal Blvd. (527-2440), for general delivery. Open M-F 9am-5pm, Sa 9am-noon. **ZIP code:** 86004. There's one closer to downtown at 104 N. Agassiz St., 86001, open the same hrs. **Area code:** 520.

ACCOMMODATIONS AND CAMPGROUNDS

When swarms of summer tourists descend on Flagstaff, accommodations prices shoot up. Thankfully, the town is blessed with excellent hostels. Historic **Rte. 66** is home to many cheap motels. *The Flagstaff Accommodations Guide,* available at the visitors center, lists all area hotels, motels, hostels, and bed and breakfasts. If you're here to see the Grand Canyon (and who isn't?), check the noticeboard in your hotel or hostel; some travelers leave their still-valid passes behind.

Grand Canyon International Youth Hostel (AAIH/Rucksackers), 19 S. San Francisco St. (779-9421), next door to the Downtowner Motel, just south of the train station. Sunny and clean. Free tea and coffee, breakfast, parking, and linen. Access to kitchen, TV room with cable, and laundry facilities. Free pick-up from Greyhound station. Shuttle to Page ($15; round-trip $25). 4-bed dorms $15; private doubles $32; triples $44. Reception 7am-11pm.

Motel Du Beau, 19 W. Phoenix St. (774-6731 or 800-398-7112), just behind the noisy train station. Carpeted dorm rooms with private bathrooms and showers. Social atmosphere lasts into the wee hours. Free Internet access, tea and coffee, breakfast, linen, parking, and rides to and from the airport, train, and bus stations. Tours to Grand Canyon ($30-40), Monument Valley (price varies), Sedona ($20), and other sights are available depending on interest. 4-bed dorms $13; private rooms $27. Reception 6am-midnight.

The Weatherford Hotel, 23 N. Leroux St. (774-2731 or 779-1919), on the other side of the tracks 1 block west of San Francisco St. Spacious rooms in a stately old hotel, with bay windows, bunk beds, and funky furniture. Dorm rooms have baths in rooms and halls. Kitchen access. Dorm beds $16; hotel singles $50-55; doubles $55-60. Lockout noon-7pm.

Hotel Monte Vista, 100 N. San Francisco St. (779-6971 or 800-545-3068), downtown. Feels like a classy hotel, with charmingly quirky decor, a coffee shop, and a bar (featuring pool tables, video games, and off-track betting) downstairs. 4-bed dorms with private baths $12; private rooms named after movie stars $40-90.

KOA Campground, 5803 N. U.S. 89 (526-9926), a few mi. northeast of Flagstaff. Local buses stop near this beautiful campground. Showers, restrooms, free nightly movies. Tent sites for 2 $20, cabins $32; $4 per additional person, under 18 $3.

Camping in the surrounding **Coconino National Forest** is a pleasant and inexpensive alternative, but you'll need a car to reach the designated camping areas. Forest maps ($6) are available at the Flagstaff Visitors Center. Many campgrounds fill up quickly during the summer, particularly on weekends when Phoenicians flock to the mountains; those at high elevations close for the winter. All sites are handled on a first come, first served basis; stake out a site by 1pm. **Lake View,** 13 mi. southeast on Forest Hwy. 3 (U.S. 89A), has 30 sites ($10). **Bonito,** 10 mi. from downtown Flagstaff, off U.S. 89 on Forest Rd. 545, at the entrance to Sunset Crater (see p. 653), rents 44 sites ($10). Both feature running water and flush toilets (both 14-day max. stay; open mid-May to Sept.). Those who can live without amenities can camp for free anywhere in the national forest outside the designated campsites, unless otherwise marked. For info on campgrounds and backcountry camping, call the **Coconino Forest Service** (527-3600; open M-F 7:30am-4:30pm).

FOOD, NIGHTLIFE, AND ENTERTAINMENT

Macy's, 14 S. Beaver St. (774-2243), behind Motel Du Beau, is a cheery student hangout serving fresh pasta ($4-6), a wide variety of vegetarian entrees ($3-6), sandwiches ($4-6), pastries ($1-2), and $1-4 espresso-based drinks. (Open M-W 6am-8pm, Th-Sa 6am-9pm, Su 6am-6pm; food served until 1hr. before closing.) Behind demure lace curtains, **Kathy's Café,** 7 N. San Francisco St. (774-1951), prepares delicious and inventive breakfasts accompanied by biscuits and fresh fruit ($4-6). Lunch sandwiches include $5 veggie options. (Open M-F 6:30am-3pm, Sa-Su 7am-3:30pm. No credit cards accepted.) Popular for beer, pool, and pizza, **Alpine Pizza,** 7 Leroux St.

(779-4109) can give you large slices cooked to order ($2; open M-W 11am-10pm, Th 11am-11pm, F-Sa 11am-midnight, Su noon-10pm). At night, head for the pool tables of **Mad Italian,** 101 S. San Francisco St. (779-1820), open daily noon-1am (happy hour daily 4-7pm with drink specials and cheap munchies). **Charly's,** 23 N. Leroux St. (779-1919), plays live jazz and blues (open daily 11am-10pm; bar open daily 11am-1am). If country-western is more your thang, the **Museum Club,** 3404 E. Rte. 66 (526-9434), a.k.a. the **Zoo,** will rock your world (cover $3-5; open daily noon-1am).

In early June, the annual **Flagstaff Rodeo** (800-638-4253) comes to town with competitions, barn dances, a carnival, and the Nackard Beverage cocktail waitress race. The **Flagstaff Symphony** (774-5107) plays from October to May (tickets $12-25, under 18 ½-price). For the month of July, the **Festival of the Arts** attracts chamber concerts, orchestras, and individual performers.

SIGHTS AND ACTIVITIES

In 1894, Percival Lowell chose Flagstaff as the site for an astronomical observatory; he then spent the rest of his life here, culling data to support his theory that life exists on Mars. **Lowell Observatory,** 1400 W. Mars Hill Rd. (774-2096), just west of downtown off Rte. 66, now has five telescopes that have been used in breakthrough studies of Mars and Pluto. *(Open daily 9am-5pm; night sky viewings M-Sa 8:15, 9, 9:30pm; F-Sa also 10pm. $3.50, ages 5-17 $1.50.)* Admission includes tours of the telescopes, as well as a museum with hands-on astronomy exhibits. On clear summer nights, you can peer through the 100-year-old Clark telescope at some heavenly body selected by the staff. The more down-to-earth **Museum of Northern Arizona** (774-5213), off U.S. 180 a few miles north of town, houses a huge collection of Southwestern Native American art (open daily 9am-5pm; $5, students $3, seniors $4, ages 7-17 $2).

The huge, snow-capped mountains visible to the north of Flagstaff are the **San Francisco Peaks.** To reach the peaks, take U.S. 180 about 7 mi. north to the Fairfield Snow Bowl turn-off. Nearby **Mt. Agassiz** has the area's best **skiing.** The **Arizona Snow Bowl** (779-1951) operates four lifts from mid-December to mid-April; its 30 trails receive an average of 8½ ft. of powder each winter. *(Open daily 8am-5pm. Lift tickets $30.)* In the summer, these peaks are perfect for hiking. The Hopi believe **Humphrey's Peak**—the highest point in Arizona at 12,670 ft.—to be the sacred home of the Kachina spirits. When the air is clear, you can see the North Rim of the Grand Canyon, the Painted Desert, and countless square miles of Arizona and Utah from the top of the peak. Reluctant hikers will find the vista from the top of the Snow Bowl's **chairlift** almost as stunning. *(20-30min.; runs late June to early Sept. daily 10am-4pm; early Sept. to mid-Oct. F-Su 10am-4pm. $9, seniors $6.50, ages 6-12 $5.)* The mountains occupy national forest land, so camping is free, but there are no designated campsites.

■ Near Flagstaff

Walnut Canyon National Monument The ruins of more than 300 rooms in 13th-century Sinagua dwellings make up Walnut Canyon National Monument (520-526-3367), constructed within a 400 ft. deep canyon. *(Open daily 8am-6pm; off-season 9am-5pm. $3, under 16 free.)* A glassed-in observation deck in the **visitors center** overlooks the whole canyon. The steep, self-guided **Island Trail** snakes down from the visitors center past 25 cliff dwellings. Markers along the 1 mi. trail describe aspects of Sinagua life and identify plants that the tribe members used for food, dyes, medicine, and hunting. Every Saturday morning, rangers lead 2 mi. hikes into Walnut Canyon to the original Ranger Cabin and more remote cliff dwellings. Hiking boots and long pants are required for these challenging 2½hr. hikes (call ahead, hrs. change frequently; free with admission). Walnut Canyon lies 10 mi. east of Flagstaff off I-40.

Sunset Crater Volcano National Monument The volcanic crater encompassed by Sunset Crater Volcano National Monument, 12 mi. north of Flagstaff on U.S. 89, appeared in 1065 when molten rock spurted from a crack in the ground, then fell back to earth in solid form. Over the next 200 years, a 1000 ft. high cinder cone took shape as a result of periodic eruptions. The self-guided **Lava Flow Nature Trail** wanders 1 mi. through the surreal landscape surrounding the cone, 1½ mi. east of the visitors center, where gnarled trees lie uprooted amid the rocky black terrain. Lava tube tours have been permanently discontinued due to falling lava, and hiking up Sunset Crater itself is not permitted. The monument's **visitors center** (520-526-0502) supplies additional info. *(Open daily 8am-6pm; off-season 8am-5pm. $3 per person, under 16 free; includes admission to Wupatki.)* The **Bonito Campground,** in the Coconino National Forest at the entrance to Sunset Crater, provides tent sites (see p. 652).

Wupatki National Monument Wupatki National Monument possesses some of the Southwest's most scenic pueblo ruins, situated 18 mi. northeast of Sunset Crater, along a stunning road with views of the Painted Desert. *(Monument open daily dawn to dusk.)* The Sinagua moved here in the 11th century, after the Sunset Crater eruption forced them to evacuate the land to the south. In less than 200 years, however, droughts, disease, and over-farming led the Sinagua to abandon these stone houses perched on the sides of *arroyos* in view of the San Francisco Peaks. Five deserted pueblos face the 14 mi. road from U.S. 89 to the visitors center. Another road to the ruins begins on U.S. 89, 30 mi. north of Flagstaff. The largest and most accessible, **Wupatki Ruin,** located on a ½ mi. round-trip loop trail from the visitors center, rises 3 stories. Get info and trail guide brochures (50¢, or borrow one and bring it back) at the **visitors center** (520-679-2365; open daily 8am-5pm). Backcountry hiking is not permitted, but don't miss the spectacular **Doney Mountain trail,** rising ½ mi. from the picnic area to the top of the mountain for an amazing view.

■ Navajo Reservation

As early as the 1830s, federal policymakers planned to create a permanent Indian country in the west. By mid-century, however, those plans had been washed away by the tide of American expansion. Indian reservations evolved out of the U.S. government's subsequent *ad hoc* attempts to prevent fighting between Native Americans and whites while facilitating white settlement. Originally conceived as a means to detribalize Native Americans and prepare them for assimilation into Anglo society, the reservation system imposed a kind of wardship on the Indians for over a century, until a series of Supreme Court decisions, beginning in the 1960s, reasserted the tribes' legal standing as semi-sovereign nations.

The largest reservation in America, the **Navajo Nation** covers more than 27,000 sq. mi. of northeastern Arizona, southeastern Utah, and northwestern New Mexico. Within its boundaries, the smaller **Hopi Reservation** is home to around 10,000 Hopi ("Peaceable People"). Ruins mark the dwellings of the Anasazi Indians who inhabited the area until the 13th century. Over 210,000 Navajo, or Diné (dih-NEH, "the People"), currently live in the Navajo Nation, comprising one-tenth of the U.S. Native American population. The Nation has its own police force and its own laws. Possession and consumption of alcohol are prohibited on the reservation. Photography requires a permission fee, and tourist photography is not permitted at all among the Hopi. Lively reservation politics are written up in the local *Navajo-Hopi Observer* and *Navajo Times* as well as in regional sections of Denver, Albuquerque, and Phoenix newspapers. For a taste of the Navajo language and some Native American ritual songs, tune your radio to 660AM, "The Voice of the Navajo." Remember to advance your watch 1hr. during the summer; the Navajo Nation runs on **Mountain Daylight Time,** while the rest of Arizona remains on Mountain Standard Time.

Monument Valley, Canyon de Chelly, Navajo National Monument, Rainbow Bridge, Antelope Canyon, and the roads and trails that access these sights all lie on Navajo land. Driving or hiking off-road without a guide is considered trespassing. Those planning to hike through Navajo territory should head to the visitors center in **Window Rock** (see below) for a **backcountry permit** ($5 per person), or mail a request along with a money order or certified check to P.O. Box 9000, Window

Rock, AZ 86515. Fill up your gas tank before setting out to explore the reservation; gas stations are few and far between. The "border towns" of **Gallup, NM** (see p. 682); **Flagstaff, AZ** (see p. 651); and **Page, AZ** (see p. 657) make good gateways to the reservations, with car rental agencies and frequent **Greyhound** service on I-40. There are almost no budget accommodations in Navajo territory; budget travelers should camp at the national monuments or Navajo campgrounds, or stay in Flagstaff, Gallup, or Page. The **area code** for the entire reservation: 520.

■ Window Rock

The capital of the Navajo Nation, **Window Rock** is the seat of tribal government and features the geological formation for which the town is named. The limited lodging in town is expensive, but Navajo sights make Window Rock a good stopover en route to or from Gallup. A terrific view of the eponymous "Window Rock" itself can be had from **Window Rock Tribal Park,** off Rte. 12 just past the government offices (open dawn to dusk; free). The **Navajo Tribal Museum** (871-6673), on Rte. 264 ½ mi. east of Rte. 12, has four rooms of Navajo and Navajo-related artwork and photography (open M-F 8am-5pm; free). For those who want to observe the tribal government in action, the **Navajo Council Tribal Chambers** (871-6417) offers free tours of the governing body's meeting rooms (open M-F 8am-noon and 1-5pm). The animals in the **Navajo Nation Zoo and Botanical Park** (871-6573), across from the Tribal Museum, might look a little familiar, although you may not have seen them in a zoo before (open daily 8am-5pm; free). The oldest trading post in the U.S. and a national historic site, the **Hubbell Trading Post** (733-3475), 30 mi. west of Window Rock on Rte. 264 in the town of Ganado, has functioned as a store since 1876 (open daily 8am-6pm; in winter 8am-5pm; free). It still sells Navajo arts and crafts, but now also houses a museum—considering the prices for Navajo rugs, it might as well be only a museum.

The **Navajoland Tourism Dept.,** P.O. Box 663, Window Rock 86515, in downtown Window Rock in the same building as the museum (see above), offers the free pamphlet *Discover Navajoland,* which has a full list of accommodations and jeep and horseback tour providers. The **tourist office** (871-6436) also sells a detailed map ($3) entitled *The Visitors' Guide to the Navajo Nation* (open M-F 8am-5pm).

■ Canyon de Chelly

The dramatic red cliffs of Canyon de Chelly (pronounced "Canyon de Shay") draw droves of tourists to this remote corner of the Navajo Nation. Sandstone cliffs of 30 to 1000 ft. surround the sandy, fertile, and aptly named **Beautiful Valley** cut by the Chelly River. Occasional Anasazi ruins dot the cliff walls. During the 1800s, Canyon de Chelly saw repeated conflict between Native Americans and whites. In 1805, dozens of Native American women and children were shot by the Spanish, in what is now called **Massacre Cave.** Kit Carson starved the Navajo out of the canyon in the 1860s, but the land was eventually returned, and now Navajo farmers inhabit the canyon once again, cultivating the soil and living in Navajo hogans (log and clay shelter).

Canyon de Chelly National Monument lies on land owned by the Navajo Nation and administered by the National Park Service. (See **Navajo Reservation,** p. 654, for info on reservation laws affecting tourists.) The park service offers a 9am hike in the summer ($10), or you can hire a private guide (3hr. min., $10 per hr.). Reservations for both can be made through the visitors center, but are not required. To drive into the canyon with a guide, you must provide your own four-wheel-drive vehicle and acquire a free permit from the visitors center. Horseback tours can be arranged at **Justin's Horse Rental** (674-5678), on South Rim Dr., at the mouth of the canyon (open daily 9am-sundown; horses $8 per hr.; mandatory guide $8 per hr.).

The 2½ mi. round-trip trail to **White House Ruin,** 7 mi. from the visitors center off South Canyon Rd., is the only trail in the park on which visitors are permitted to walk without a guide. But what a trail—it winds down 600 ft. into the canyon, past a Navajo farm and traditional hogan, through an orchard, and across a stream to cliff dwelling ruins. You can also take one of the paved **Rim Drives** (North Rim 44 mi.,

South Rim 36 mi.) skirting the edge of the 300-700 ft. cliffs; the South Rim is more dramatic. Get booklets (50¢) on the White House Ruin and Rim Drives at the visitors center. **Spider Rock Overlook,** 16 mi. from the visitors center, is a narrow sandstone monolith towering hundreds of feet above the canyon floor. Native American lore says the whitish rock at the top contains the bleached bones of victims of the *kachina* spirit, or Spider Woman.

The most common route to the park is from **Chambers,** 75 mi. south, at the intersection of I-40 and U.S. 191; you can also come from the north via U.S. 191. Entrance to the monument is free. The **visitors center** (674-5500) sits 2 mi. east of **Chinle** on Navajo Rte. 64 (open daily 8am-6pm; Oct.-Apr. 8am-5pm). One of the larger towns on the reservation, Chinle, adjacent to U.S. 191, has restaurants and gas stations. There is no public transportation to the park. In an **emergency,** contact the park ranger (674-5523, after hrs. 674-5524) or the Navajo Police (674-2111).

Camp for free in the park's **Cottonwood Campground** (674-5500), 1½ mi. from the visitors center. This giant campground, in a pretty cottonwood grove, can get noisy with the din of the stray dogs who wander about the site at night. Sites are first come, first served, and facilities include restrooms, picnic tables, water (except in winter), and a dump station (5-day max. stay). The only budget accommodation in Navajo territory is the **Many Farms Inn** (781-6363), a converted dormitory 17 mi. north of Canyon de Chelly. At the junction of Rte. 191 and 59, go north 1 mi. on Rte. 191, turn left at the sign for Many Farms High School, and follow this road 1 mi. farther to the inn. (Singles or doubles $30. Shared bath.) **Farmington, NM,** and **Cortez, CO,** are the closest major cities with multiple cheap lodging options.

■ Monument Valley

The red sandstone towers of Monument Valley are one of the southwest's most otherworldly sights. Paradoxically, however, they're also one of the most familiar, since countless westerns have been filmed in this area. Some years before John Wayne hung out in the valley, Anasazi Indians managed to sustain small communities here, despite the hot, arid climate. The park's looping 17 mi. **Valley Drive** winds around 11 of the most spectacular formations, including the famous pair of **Mittens** and the slender **Totem Pole.** However, the gaping ditches, large rocks, and mudholes on this road can wreck your car—drive at your own risk, observe the 15 mph speed limit, and hold your breath. The drive will take at least 1½hr. Other, less-touristed parts of the valley can be reached only by four-wheel-drive vehicle, horse, or foot. **Leaving the main road without a guide is not permitted.** The visitors center parking lot is crowded with booths run by small companies selling jeep, horseback, and hiking tours. (1½hr. jeep tour about $15 per person; 1½hr. tour on horseback $30; 4hr. hiking tour $45.) In winter, snow laces the rocky towers, and most tourists flee. Call the visitors center to inquire about snow and road conditions before you start out.

The park entrance lies on U.S. 163 just across the Utah border, 24 mi. north of the Navajo town **Kayenta,** which is at the intersection of U.S. 163 and U.S. 160. The **visitors center** (435-727-3353) grudgingly hands out information and sells postcards, trinkets, and snacks. (Park and visitors center open daily 7am-7pm; Oct.-Apr. 8am-5pm. Valley Drive closes at 6:30pm; begin by 4:30pm to complete it. Admission $2.50, seniors $1, under 7 free.)

Mitten View Campground, ¼ mi. southwest of the visitors center, offers 90 sites, showers, and restrooms, but no hookups. (Sites $10; in winter $5. Register at the visitors center. No reservations.) The **Navajo National Monument** (see below) has more camping. The nearest cheap motels are in **Mexican Hat, UT** (see p. 645); **Bluff, UT** (see p. 645); and **Page, AZ** (see p. 657).

■ Navajo National Monument

Located off U.S. 160, 20 mi. west of Kayenta, this park is home to some of the best-preserved ruins in the southwest. From Rte. 160, Rte. 564 travels 9 mi. north to the park entrance. The site contains three Anasazi cliff dwellings, although one, **Inscrip-**

tion House, has been closed to visitors indefinitely due to its fragile condition. The other two, Keet Seel and Betatakin, admit a very limited number of visitors. The stunning **Keet Seel** (open late May to early Sept.) can be reached only via a challenging 16 mi. roundtrip hike. Hikers can stay overnight in a free campground near Keet Seel, but it has no facilities or drinking water. Reservations for permits to visit Keet Seel must be made up to 2 months in advance through the **visitors center** (520-672-2366); total reservations are limited to 20 people per day (open daily 8am-5pm; off-season 8am-4:30pm). Ranger-led tours to **Betatakin,** a 135-room complex, are limited to 25 people. (1 per day at 8:15am; first come, first served the morning of the tour. A strenuous 5 mi., 5-6hr. hike. Open May to late Sept.) If you're not up for the trek to the ruins, the paved, 1 mi. roundtrip **Sandal Trail** lets you gaze down on Betatakin from the top of the canyon. The **Aspen Forest Overlook Trail,** another 1 mi. hike, overlooks canyons and aspens, but no ruins. Write to **Navajo National Monument,** HC 71 Box 3, Tonalea 86044 for more info. The free **campground,** next to the visitors center, has 30 sites; an additional overflow campground nearby has no running water (first come, first served; 7-day max. stay; no hookups).

■ Hopi Reservation

Located in the southwestern corner of the Navajo Nation, the Hopi Reservation clusters around three mesas, imaginatively named First Mesa, Second Mesa, and Third Mesa. Rte. 264 connects the mesas. On Second Mesa, the **Hopi Cultural Center** (734-2401), 63 mi. north of Winslow, AZ, at the intersection of Rte. 264 and 87, contains the reservation's only museum, which displays Hopi textiles, baskets, jewelry, pottery, and information about the tribe's history (open M-F 8am-5pm, Sa 8am-4pm; $3, children $1).

Visitors are welcome to attend some of the Hopi **village dances.** Announced only a few days in advance, these religious ceremonies usually occur on weekends and last from sunrise to sundown. The dances are highly formal occasions; do not wear shorts, tank tops, or other casual wear. Photographs, recordings, and sketches are strictly forbidden. Often several villages will hold dances on the same day, giving tourist the opportunity to go village-hopping. Inquire at the cultural center, the Flagstaff Chamber of Commerce, or the **Hopi Cultural Preservation Office,** P.O. Box 123, Kykotsmovi 86039 (734-2244), for the dates and sites of the dances.

In the village of **Tsakurshovi,** 1½ mi. east of the cultural center on Rte. 264, the **shop** (734-2478) run by Joe and Janice Day sells Hopi crafts and functions as a sort of makeshift tourist office. They're also the creators of the "Don't Worry, Be Hopi" t-shirt ($10), which has been spotted on the likes of the Indigo Girls. Ask them about tours to the village of **Walpi,** on Third Mesa, which features ancient, but still inhabited, pueblo dwellings (open daily 8am-6pm).

The **hotel** at the Hopi Cultural Center (734-2401) is pricey but decent (rooms from $55; reservations required 2 weeks to a month in advance). The **restaurant** serves Hopi food like *noqkvivi* (NO-kvi-vee), a Hopi stew made with white corn and lamb ($6) as well as the usual burgers and salads (open daily 7am-9pm). **Area code:** 520.

■ Lake Powell and Page

In 1953, President Dwight Eisenhower said "dammit," and they did. Ten years and 10 million tons of concrete later, **Glen Canyon Dam,** the second-largest dam in the country, was completed. With no particular place to go, the Colorado River flooded **Glen Canyon,** which spanned northern Arizona and southern Utah, to form the 186 mi. long **Lake Powell.** Named after John Wesley Powell, a one-armed Civil War veteran who led and chronicled the first expedition down the Colorado, the lake offers 1960 mi. of shoreline. Water sports and fishing are the most popular recreational activities on the lake, but hiking opportunities also abound. Not to be missed is the spectacular **Antelope Canyon,** outside the resort town of **Page** near the southwest tip of Lake Powell at the U.S. 89/Rte. 98 junction.

PRACTICAL INFORMATION Visitors can descend into the cool inner workings of Glen Canyon Dam alone, or let the **Carl Hayden Visitors Center** (608-6404), on U.S. 89 N, 1 mi. north of Page, act as the guide. (Open daily 7am-7pm; off-season 8am-5pm. Free guided dam tours every hr. on the ½hr. 8:30am-5:30pm.) In **Page,** seek out the **Chamber of Commerce,** 644 N. Navajo Dr. (645-2741), in the Dam Plaza (open daily 8am-8pm; in winter M-F 9am-5pm). Lake Powell and Page's **area code:** 520.

ACCOMMODATIONS, CAMPGROUNDS, AND FOOD The **Lake Powell International Hostel,** 141 8th Ave. (645-3898), in Page, provides free pickup and delivery to Lake Powell, coffee, linen, a kitchen, BBQ grill, TV, volleyball court, and an outdoor eating area. The hostel also offers a $15 shuttle to Flagstaff (make arrangements in advance). Ask Jeff, the host, to arrange tours for you (bunks $12-15; no curfew; reserve ahead Aug.-Sept.). Under the same management, **Pension at Lake Powell,** next door to the hostel, has more upscale suites with a bathroom, a living room with cable TV, and a kitchen (doubles for 2-6 $35; $5 per additional person). For a very different kind of atmosphere, try **Uncle Bill's Place,** 117 8th Ave. (645-1224), 1 block away. The attractive rooms have adjoining kitchens and a garden out back (singles and doubles with shared bath $39). **Bashful Bob's Motel,** 750 S. Navajo Dr. (645-3919), isn't embarrassed about its huge rooms with kitchens, sitting areas, and cable TV (singles $35; doubles $43; triples $48; $10 less in winter). **Wahweap Campground,** 100 Lake Shore Dr. (645-2433 or 800-528-6154), adjacent to the exorbitant **Wahweap Lodge,** has 200 sites on a first come, first served basis ($10). Next door, the **Wahweep RV Park** takes care of the motorized set (full hookup $23 for 2 adults; $3 per additional adult).

   Strombolli's Restaurant & Pizzeria, 711 N. Navajo Dr. (645-2605), cooks up $7-9 "calzones as big as your head" (open M-Th 11am-9pm, F-Su 11am-10pm). **Porter's Sunset Grille,** 125 Lake Powell Blvd. (645-3039), serves Tex-Mex indoors and out, including breakfast burritos ($5) and grilled chicken sandwiches ($6; open daily 7am-2pm and 5-9pm). Live country music plays nightly at **Ken's Old West Restaurant & Lounge,** 718 Vista Ave. (645-5160), behind the Lake Powell Best Western, where barbecue is taken seriously (ribs $9, chicken $8). Vegetarians will appreciate the great salad bar. (Open daily 4pm-1am; no food after 11pm.)

SIGHTS AND ACTIVITIES Lake Powell's man-made shores are rocky rather than sandy, with skimpy beaches that vanish when the water rises. Recreation opportunities abound at **Wahweep Marina** (645-2433), however, where you can swim, rent a boat (6-person skiff $109; in spring and fall $82; in winter $62), or take a boat tour ($10-83). Many companies lead **boat tours** to the famous **Rainbow Bridge National Monument,** the world's largest natural bridge. The bridge, which is sacred to the Navajo, takes its name from the Navajo word *nonnoshoshi,* "rainbow turned to stone." The bridge can be reached by a strenuous 2-day hike or a ½-day boat tour. **ARAMARK Leisure Services** (800-528-6154) conducts boat tours (full-day $76, under 12 $43; ½-day $60/$40; call ahead for reservations). Hiking permits must be obtained in advance from the Navajo Nation, since the trails cross Navajo land. Write to **Navajo Nation,** P.O. Box 308, Window Rock, AZ 86515.

   No less spectacular for its greater accessibility, the kaleidoscopic **Antelope Canyon** is one of the only slot canyons in the U.S. The entrance is on U.S. 98 several miles south of Page, by the Navajo Power Plant. The trail through the **upper canyon,** while moderately strenuous, is wider and easier to negotiate than the one through the **lower canyon,** which requires many tight squeezes but is less touristed. The sight of sunlight illuminating the canyon's twisting sandstone walls is nothing short of incredible. The canyon lies on Navajo land, so a **guide** is required (1½hr.; $15 per person).

   A short, beautiful hike leads to **Horseshoe Bend Overlook,** which provides a view of the Colorado River as it curves around a huge rock formation. The trail leads from a parking lot down a dirt road off U.S. 89, just south of mile marker 545—the tourist office or hostel can provide directions.

■ Petrified Forest and Painted Desert

The term "forest" is a misnomer for this 60,000-acre dreamscape dotted with fallen trees turned to stone. Some 225 million years ago, when Arizona's desert was a flood-plain, volcanic ash covered the logs, slowing their decay. When silica-rich water seeped through the wood, the silica crystallized into quartz, producing the rainbow hues of **Petrified Forest National Park.** The park also contains a scenic chunk of the Painted Desert, named for the stunning colors that stripe its rock formations.

The park road winds past the logs in their natural habitats and by **Newspaper Rock,** which is covered with Native American petroglyphs. At **Blue Mesa,** a short hik-ing trail ventures into the desert. **Long Logs, Crystal Forest,** and **Jasper Forest** con-tain some of the most exquisite pieces of petrified wood in the park. Picking up fragments of the wood is illegal and traditionally unlucky; if the district attorney don't getcha, then the demons will. Those who *must* have a piece should buy one at one of the myriad stores along I-40. The **Painted Desert** section lies at the park's north end; here, a number of overlooks allow for unimpeded gazing. No established trails traverse the Painted Desert, but **backcountry hiking** is allowed (permit required).

Enter the park either from the north or the south. (Open daily 7am-7pm. **Entrance fee** $10 per vehicle, $5 per pedestrian.) A 27 mi. road connects the two entrances. To enter the southern section of the park, exit I-40 at Holbrook and take U.S. 180 W to the **Rainbow Forest Museum.** The museum provides a look at petrified logs up close and serves as a **visitors center** (524-6822; open daily 8am-7pm; off-season 8am-5pm; free). There are no established campgrounds in the park, but **free backcountry camping** is allowed in several areas with a permit. To enter the Painted Desert sec-tion of the park, take I-40 to Exit 311 (107 mi. east of Flagstaff). The **Painted Desert Visitors Center** (524-6228) is less than 5 mi. from the exit (open daily in summer 7am-7pm; off-season 8am-5pm). There is no public transportation to either part of the park. **Nava-Hopi Bus Lines, Gray Line Tours,** and **Blue Goose Backpacker Tours** offer services from **Flagstaff** (see p. 651). The closest cheap lodging is in **Holbrook** (27 mi. from the park); **Gallup, NM** (see p. 682); or **Flagstaff** (see p. 651). In Hol-brook, the rooms at **Economy Inn,** 310 W. Hopi Dr. (524-6490), could use some paint, but you can't beat the price (rooms with 1 bed $20; with 2 beds $27).

Deep Impact

Perhaps the recent American obsession with all things extraterrestrial explains the enormous popularity of **Meteor Crater** (520-289-5898), 35 mi. east of Flag-staff off I-40. *(Open daily 6am-6pm; off-season 8am-5pm. $8, seniors $7, ages 6-17 $4.)* Originally thought to be a volcanic cone, the crater is now believed to be the impact site of a giant nickel-iron meteorite that fell to earth 50,000 years ago. Vis-itors are not allowed to hike down into the crater, which measures an impres-sive 4100 ft. across, but must fight the hordes for a spot by the guard-railed edge. Conspicuously missing in action is the meteor itself; scientists believe that most of it was vaporized at the moment of impact, since it was traveling at an impres-sive 10 mi. per second. The site was used to train Apollo astronauts in the 1960s, and a museum in the building near the admission booth patriotically celebrates the U.S. space program (free with entrance to the crater).

■ Sedona

The pines of the Coconino National Forest blanket Sedona's red sandstone forma-tions, offering some of Arizona's most sensational scenery. Though a popular stop-ping point for vacationers, tourists, and the New Agers who believe the area to be a locus of "psychic vortices," the town itself consists of a cluster of gift shops and tour-ing outfits. You can skip the upper-class shopping area and head for the state parks, where the views, rather than the prices of star charts, will astound you.

Bring a book and a bathing suit to **Slide Rock State Park** (282-3034), 10 mi. north of Sedona on U.S. 89A, where rocks form a natural waterslide into the cold waters of Oak Creek. In the summer, locals come in droves to swim and picnic. (Open daily 8am-7pm; closes earlier in off season. $5 per car, $1 per pedestrian or cyclist.) The incredible formations at **Red Rock State Park** (282-6907), on U.S. 89A 15 mi. southwest of town, invite strolling or just contemplation. Rangers lead day hikes into the nearby rock formations; do-it-yourselfers can pick up a trail map at the visitors center. (Visitors center open daily 9am-5pm. Park open daily 8am-6pm; Oct.-Mar. 8am-5pm. $5 per car, $1 per pedestrian or cyclist.) **Chapel of the Holy Cross** (282-4069), on Chapel Rd., lies just outside a 1000 ft. rock wall in the middle of red sandstone. (Open daily 9am-5pm.) The view from the parking lot is a religious experience in itself.

The **Sedona Chamber of Commerce** (282-7722), at Forest Rd. and Rte. 89A, distributes listings for accommodations and private campgrounds in the area (open M-Sa 8:30am-5pm, Su 9am-3pm). Lodging in town is a bit pricey; it's not a bad idea to make Sedona a daytrip from Flagstaff. **Star Motel**, 295 Jordan Rd. (282-3641), lodges guests in comfy rooms decorated Southwestern-style with cable TV (1 bed $55-59; 2 beds $59-85). **Sedona Motel**, 218 Rte. 179 (282-7187), features great views (rooms start at $64, but bargaining is possible). There are a number of **campgrounds** within **Coconino National Forest** (527-3600), along Oak Creek Canyon on U.S. 89A (sites $12 per vehicle). The largest, **Cave Springs**, 20 mi. north of town, administers 78 sites (call 800-283-2267 for reservations). For more info on Coconino Forest, including hiking maps, visit the **ranger station,** 250 Brewer Rd. (282-4119); turn off U.S. 89A at Burger King (open M-Sa 7:30am-4:30pm; in winter M-F 7:30am-4:30pm). Free **backcountry camping** is allowed in the forest anywhere outside of Oak Creek and more than 1 mi. from any official campground. **Hawkeye RV Park**, 40 Art Barn Rd. (282-2222), has full hookups, water, electricity, and showers, as well as tent sites (sites $19, with water and electricity $25, full hookup $31; office open 9am-7pm).

The **Coffee Pot Restaurant**, 2050 W. U.S. 89A (282-6626), dishes up 101 varieties of omelettes ($4-9; open daily 6am-9pm). **Hot Rocks Pizza**, 273 N. U.S. 89A (282-7753), in the Uptown Mall, has slices for $2 and entire pies from $7. Try the "Desert Dancer," topped with grilled chicken, peppers, and onions for $8. (Open Su-Th 10am-9:30pm, F-Sa 10am-10:30pm.)

Sedona lies 120 mi. north of Phoenix (take I-17 north to Rte. 179 W) and 30 mi. south of Flagstaff (take I-17 S to Rte. 179 W or use U.S. 89A SW). The **Sedona-Phoenix Shuttle** (282-2066) runs six trips daily ($35). Sedona's **Area code:** 520.

■ Near Sedona

Montezuma Castle National Monument (567-3322), 10 mi. south of Sedona on I-17, is a 20-room cliff dwelling built by the Sinagua tribe in the 12th century. *(Open daily 8am-7pm, off-season 8am-5pm. $2, under 16 free.)* Unfortunately, you can't get very close to the ruins, but the view from the paved path below is excellent and wheelchair accessible. A beautiful lake formed by the collapse of an underground cavern, **Montezuma Well**, off I-17 11 mi. north of the castle, once served as a source of water for the Sinagua who lived here (open daily 8am-7pm; free). Take U.S. 89A to Rte. 279 and continue through Cottonwood to reach **Tuzigoot National Monument** (634-5564), 20 mi. southwest of Sedona, a dramatic Sinaguan ruin overlooking the Verde Valley (open daily 8am-7pm; in winter 8am-5pm; $2, under 17 free).

■ Jerome

Perched on the side of Mingus Mountain, Jerome once attracted miners, speculators, saloon owners, and madams who came to the city following the copper boom of the late 1800s. By 1920, the town ranked as Arizona's third-largest city. In 1929, however, the stock market crashed, throwing Jerome's economy into an irrecoverable downward spiral. By mid-century the last denizens of Jerome deserted, leaving a ghost town behind. Today, the city's formerly decadent facades and the hollow shells of stately old buildings stare down upon empty streets. Learn more about the area by heading over to **Jerome State Historic Park** (634-5381), ½ mi. off U.S. 89A just as you enter town. (Open daily 8am-5pm; $2.50, ages 7-13 $1.) The park provides a panoramic view of the town, while helpful placards reveal the history of Jerome's decaying mansions. Inside the 80-year-old house of mine owner James Douglas, the park museum features exhibits on mining, minerals, and the early years of the town. Enjoy period cars, trucks, machines, and props at **The Gold King Mine and Ghost Town** (634-0053), also on U.S. 89A just past Main St., even if it's not quite clear what period they're aiming to recreate (open daily 9am-5pm; $3, seniors $2.50, ages 5-12 $2). **The Mine Museum,** 200 Main St. (634-5477), displays a stock of rocks and old mining equipment (open daily 9am-4:30pm; $1, under 12 free).

Budget travelers should make Jerome a daytrip from Flagstaff or Phoenix, as lodging tends to be expensive. **The Inn at Jerome,** 309 Main St. (634-5094 or 800-634-5094), is one of the lower-priced joints in town; rooms run about $55-85. The oldest restaurant in Arizona, **The English Kitchen,** 119 Jerome Ave. (634-2132), has a large array of salads and sandwiches for $5-6 (open Tu-Su 8am-3:30pm). **Marcy's,** 363 Main St. (634-0417), serves ice cream, soups, and sandwiches (under $5) in a pleasant atmosphere (open W-M 11am-5pm). At night, float over to **The Spirit Room** (634-8809), at Main St. and Jerome Ave., for live music and mayhem (open daily 10am-1am; live music F-Sa from 9pm). **Paul and Jerry's Saloon** (634-2603), also on Main St., has been helping people get sloppy for three generations (open daily 11am-1am).

U.S. 89A slinks its way to Jerome 30 mi. southwest of Sedona; the drive between them is simply gorgeous. The **Chamber of Commerce,** 50 Main St. (634-2900), is staffed somewhat sporadically by volunteers (usually open daily 10am-4pm); the recorded message lists food and lodging info. **Area code:** 520.

City in a Bubble

The planned city of **Arcosanti** (632-7135), off I-17 at Exit 262, is designed to embody Italian architect Paolo Soleri's concept of an "arcology," or "architecture and ecology working together as one integral process." *(Tours daily every hr. 10am-4pm; $5 donation requested. Visitors center open daily 9am-5pm.)* When complete, the city will be entirely self-sufficient, supplying its own food, power, and all other resources. Arcosanti has been under construction since 1970 but is expected to be finished rather later than the original goal of 2000—so far, only one building is up. The pace of the construction might have something to do with the restrictions on who is allowed to participate; rather than hiring workers, all the labor is done by students and others who take part in the community's "workshops."

■ Phoenix

Phoenix got its start as a small farming community in the late 1800s, but high-tech offices and shopping plazas have long since replaced the wheat fields. Shiny highrises crowd the business district, while a vast web of six-lane strip mall highways surrounds the downtown. Sun, sun, sun, and sun are some of the city's main attractions. During the balmy winter months, tourists, golfers, and business conventioners flock to Phoenix. In the summer, the city crawls into its air-conditioned shell as temperatures climb to an average of 100°F and lodging prices plummet.

ORIENTATION AND PRACTICAL INFORMATION

The intersection of **Central Ave.** and **Washington St.** marks the heart of downtown. Central Ave. runs north-south. One of Phoenix's peculiarities is that numbered avenues and streets both run north-south; avenues are numbered sequentially west from Central, while streets are numbered east. Some avenues and streets dead-end abruptly. A few of the largest north-south thoroughfares are **7th St., 16th St., 7th Ave.,** and **19th Ave.** Washington St. divides streets north-south. For a price, parking is readily available downtown at one of the many meters or garages. You'll need a car or a bus pass to see much of Phoenix; this city is sprawling.

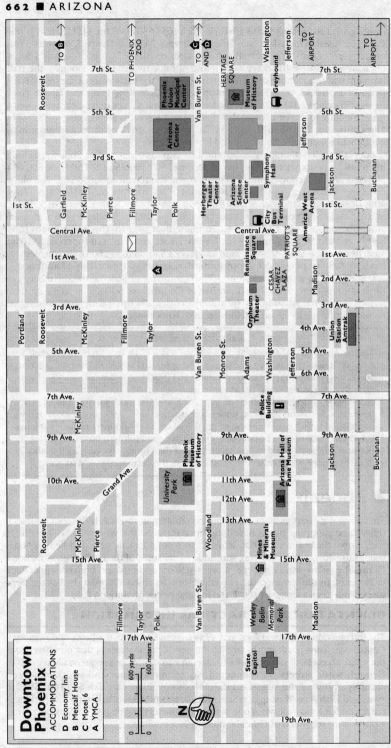

TO **B** →

7th St.

Roosevelt

TO PHOENIX ZOO →

5th St.

TO **C** AND **D** →

Van Buren St.

HERITAGE SQUARE

Washington

Jefferson

TO AIRPORT →

7th St.

TO AIRPORT →

Phoenix Union Municipal Center

Museum of History

Greyhound

3rd St.

Arizona Center

5th St.

Jefferson

Garfield

McKinley

Pierce

Fillmore

Taylor

Polk

1st St.

Herberger Theater Center

Arizona Science Center

Symphony Hall

Jackson

3rd St.

America West Arena

1st St.

Buchanan

Central Ave.

City Bus Terminal

Central Ave.

Renaissance Square

PATRIOT'S SQUARE

1st Ave.

1st Ave.

CESAR CHAVEZ PLAZA

Madison

2nd Ave.

Portland

Roosevelt

McKinley

Fillmore

Taylor

3rd Ave.

Orpheum Theater

3rd Ave.

5th Ave.

Van Buren St.

Monroe St.

Adams

Washington

4th Ave.

5th Ave.

6th Ave.

Jefferson

Union Station Amtrak

7th Ave.

Police Building

7th Ave.

9th Ave.

McKinley

9th Ave.

Phoenix Museum of History

10th Ave.

Arizona Hall of Fame Museum

Jackson

9th Ave.

Buchanan

Grand Ave.

10th Ave.

University Park

11th Ave.

12th Ave.

13th Ave.

Roosevelt

McKinley

Pierce

Woodland

Mines & Minerals Museum

15th Ave.

15th Ave.

Fillmore

Taylor

Polk

Wesley Bolin Memorial Park

Madison

17th Ave.

17th Ave.

Van Buren St.

Downtown Phoenix
ACCOMMODATIONS
D Economy Inn
B Metcalf House
C Motel 6
A YMCA

600 yards
600 meters

State Capitol

N

0
0

19th Ave.

Airport: Sky Harbor International (273-3300), just southeast of downtown. Take Valley Metro bus #13 into the city (5:45am-7:45pm). Shuttle service downtown $7.

Trains: Amtrak, 401 W. Harrison (253-0121 or 800-872-7245); follow 4th Ave. south 2 blocks past Jefferson St. *Be careful at night.* To Los Angeles (20hr., 10 per week, $74-94) and San Antonio via El Paso (21hr., 3 per week, $69-91). Open Sa-M 1:15am-9:45am and 5:15pm-12:45am, Tu-W 1:15am-9:45am, Th-F 5:15pm-12:45am.

Buses: Greyhound, 2115 E. Buckeye Rd. (389-4200 or 800-231-2222). To: El Paso (8hr., 15 per day, $38); Los Angeles (8hr., 12 per day, $30); Tucson (2hr., 13 per day, $12); and San Diego (8½hr., 4 per day, $37). Open 24hr.

Public Transportation: Valley Metro, 253-5000. Most lines run to and from the **City Bus Terminal,** at Central and Washington. Routes tend to operate M-F 5am-8pm with reduced service on Sa. Fare $1.25; disabled, seniors, and children 60¢. All-day pass $3.60, 10-ride pass $12. Bus passes and system maps at the Terminal.

Taxis: Ace Taxi, 254-1999. $2.55 base fare, $1.10 per mi.

Car Rental: Rent-A-Wreck, 2225 E. Buckeye Rd. Cars from $24 per day with 100 free mi., 15¢ per additional mi. Must be 21 with credit card. Open M-F 7am-3pm, Sa 9am-3pm; pick-up until 6pm.

Visitor Info: Phoenix and Valley of the Sun Convention and Visitors Center, 400 E. Van Buren St. (254-6500, recorded info 252-5588), 6th fl. of the Arizona Center office building. Open M-F 8am-5pm.

Hotlines: Crisis Hotline, 784-1500. 24hr. **Gay/Lesbian Hotline,** 234-2752. Operates daily 10am-10pm.

Internet Access: At the beautiful copper-and-glass **Burton Barr Central Library,** 1221 N. Central Ave. (262-4636). Open M-W 9am-9pm, Th-Sa 9am-6pm, Su 1-5pm. Sign-up required, but computers usually available.

Post Office: 522 N. Central Ave. (800-275-8777), downtown. Open M-F 8:30am-5pm. General delivery: 1441 E. Buckeye Rd. (800-275-8777). Open M-F 7:30am-5pm. **ZIP code:** 85026. **Area code:** 602.

ACCOMMODATIONS AND CAMPGROUNDS

Budget travelers should consider visiting Phoenix during July and August, when many motels knock their prices down by as much as 70%. In the winter, when temperatures and vacancies go down, prices go up; make reservations if possible. The reservationless should cruise the rows of motels on **Van Buren St.** and **Main St.** (a.k.a. Apache Trail) in the suburbs east of the city. The strips are full of 50s-era ranch-style motels with names like "Deserama," as well as the requisite modern chains. Parts of these areas can be quite dangerous; guests should examine a motel thoroughly before checking in. Safer, but more distant, the area around **Bell Rd.,** north of the city, is also loaded with motels. **Mi Casa Su Casa/Old Pueblo Homestays Bed and Breakfast,** P.O. Box 950, Tempe 85280-0950 (800-456-0682), arranges stays in B&B's throughout Arizona and New Mexico. (Singles $40-70; doubles from $65. Open M-F 9am-5pm, Sa 9am-noon. Make winter reservations 2 weeks in advance.)

Metcalf House (HI-AYH), 1026 N. 9th St. (254-9803), a few blocks northeast of downtown. From the City Bus Terminal, take bus #7 down 7th St. to Roosevelt St., walk 2 blocks east to 9th St., and turn left—the hostel is ½ block north in a shady and quiet residential area. The high-spirited owner, loves to chat about thrift-shop chic and Latin poetry. Dorm-style rooms with wooden bunks and co-ed showers $12. Kitchen, common room, and laundry. Check-in 7-10am and 5-11pm.

Economy Inn, 804 E. Van Buren St. (254-0181), close to downtown. Standard rooms with TV and phones. Singles $33; doubles $44.

Motel 6, 2323 E. Van Buren St. (800-466-8456). Decor-free, personality-free, and bug-free. Singles $30; doubles $36. Convenient to the airport.

KOA Phoenix West (853-0537), 11 mi. west of Phoenix on Citrus Rd. Take I-10 to Exit 124; head ¾ mi. south to Van Buren St., then 1 mi. west to Citrus Rd. 285 sites, pool, and jacuzzi. Sites $21 for 2, with RV hookup $28; $4 per additional adult.

FOOD

Aside from food courts in malls, it's difficult to find several restaurants together amid Phoenix's expanse. Downtowners feed mainly at small coffeeshops, most of which close on weekends. If you're looking for something other than Mexican food, **McDowell** or **Camelback Rd.** offer a (small) variety of Asian restaurants. The **Arizona Center** (271-4000), an open-air shopping gallery at 3rd St. and Van Buren, boasts food venues, fountains, and palm trees. The *New Times* gives extensive restaurant recommendations.

Macayo, 4001 N. Central Ave. (264-6141). Funky decor, terrific Mexican food, and big portions. They even serve breakfast. Fajitas $8-12, combo plates $5-9, awesome prickly pear margaritas $4. Open Su-Th 6am-11pm, F-Sa 6am-midnight.

Los Dos Molinos, 8646 S. Central Ave. (243-9113). Live music at lunch and dinner, a huge menu, and lemonade in jelly jars. Enchiladas $3-3.50, burritos $3.25-5.25. Open Tu-Sa 11am-9pm.

Thai Rama, 1221 W. Camelback Rd. (285-1123). Rated Phoenix's best Thai restaurant for several years in a row. A wide selection of dishes, including scrumptious pad thai ($8). Open daily 11am-10pm.

Bill Johnson's Big Apple, 3757 E. Van Buren St. (275-2107), and 3 other locations. A down-South delight with sawdust on the floor, authentic BBQ, and a variety of hot sauces with which to atomize your palate. Sandwiches $3-10, hearty soups $3. Open Su-Th 6am-10pm, F-Sa 6am-11pm.

SIGHTS

Phoenix's **Heard Museum,** 22 E. Monte Vista Rd. (252-8840, recorded info 252-8848), 1 block east of Central Ave., is internationally renowned for its outstanding collection of Native American handicrafts. *(Open M-Tu and Th-Sa 9:30am-5pm, W 9:30am-8pm, Su noon-5pm. $6, seniors $5, ages 4-12 $3; free W 5-8pm. Free guided tours daily; times vary.)* The museum also features the work of contemporary Native American artists, contains a number of exhibits designed to appeal to children, and sponsors occasional lectures and Native American dances. Three blocks south, the **Phoenix Art Museum,** 1625 N. Central Ave. (257-1880), at McDowell Rd., mainly exhibits art of the American West, including paintings from the Taos and Santa Fe art colonies. *(Open Tu-W 10am-5pm, Th-F 10am-9pm, Sa-Su 10am-5pm. $6, students and seniors $4, ages 6-18 $2.)* There's also a small but interesting selection of Old Masters, and an exquisite display of miniature rooms. The **Arizona Science Center,** 600 E. Washington St. (716-2000), offers interactive science exhibits (open daily 10am-5pm; $8, seniors and ages 4-12 $6). The **Pueblo Grande Museum and Cultural Park,** 4619 E. Washington St. (495-0901), features a Hohokam pueblo occupied from about 500 to 1450 (open M-Sa 9am-4:45pm, Su 1-4:45pm; $2, children $1).

The **Desert Botanical Gardens,** 1201 N. Galvin Pkwy. (941-1217, recorded info 481-8134), in Papago Park 5 mi. east of the downtown area, grow a colorful collection of cacti and other desert plants. *(Open daily May-Sept. 7am-8pm; Oct.-Apr. 8am-8pm. $7, seniors $6, ages 5-12 $1.)* Take bus #3 east to Papago Park. Don't pull any fire alarms at the **Hall of Flame Museum of Firefighting,** 6101 E. Van Buren St. (275-FIRE/3473), also in Papago Park, featuring antique fire engines and other fire-fighting equipment (open M-Sa 9am-5pm, Su noon-4pm; $5, ages 6-17 $3, ages 3-5 $1.50).

In nearby Scottsdale, **Taliesin West** (860-8810 or 860-2700), at the corner of Frank Lloyd Wright Blvd. and Cactus St., served as the architectural studio and residence of Frank Lloyd Wright in his later years. *(1hr. and 1½hr. guided tours required. Open June-Sept. daily 9am-4pm. $10-14, students and seniors $8-12, children $3-8.)* The beautifully designed studio seems to blend naturally into the surrounding desert. Wright also designed the **Arizona Biltmore** (955-6600), a hotel at 24th St. and Missouri.

South of Phoenix across the dry Salt River lies the sunny college atmosphere of Tempe's **Arizona State University (ASU).** Cafes and art galleries abound in this area. One of the last major buildings designed by Frank Lloyd Wright, the **Gammage Memorial Auditorium** (965-3434), at Mill Ave. and Apache Blvd. on campus, wears the pink-and-beige earth tones of the surrounding environment. *(20min. tours daily in winter.)* Take bus #60, or #22 on weekends.

NIGHTLIFE AND ENTERTAINMENT

The free *New Times Weekly,* available on local magazine racks, lists club schedules for Phoenix's after-hours scene. The *Cultural Calendar of Events* guide covers area entertainment in 3-month intervals. **Toolie's Country Saloon and Dance Hall,** 4231 W. Thomas Rd. (272-3100), recently received the distinction of being the nation's best country-western nightclub and offers free dance lessons Sunday to Thursday (cover Th $5, F-Sa $6; open Sa-Th 11am-1am, F 7am-1am). **Char's Has the Blues,** 4631 N. 7th Ave. (230-0205), houses dozens of wanna-be John Lee Hookers, but the music is pretty good (cover F-Sa $3; doors open 7pm; music starts 8pm). **Phoenix Live,** 455 N. 3rd St. (252-2112), at the Arizona Center, quakes the complex with three bars and a restaurant. The $5 weekend cover buys access to it all.

Gay and lesbian nightlife spots can be found in *The Western Front,* available in some bars and clubs. **Ain't Nobody's Biz,** 3031 E. Indian School Rd., #7 (224-9977). is a large lesbian bar with Thursday beer busts ($1.50 pitchers 9pm-midnight; open daily 2pm-1am). **The Country Club,** 4428 N. 7th Ave. (264-4553), has a primarily gay clientele and an unusually long happy hour—Monday to Saturday 11am-7pm (open daily 11am-1am).

Phoenix also packs a-plenty for the sports lover. NBA action rises with the **Phoenix Suns** (379-7867), at the **America West Arena,** or you can root for the NFL's **Arizona Cardinals** (379-0101). In 1998, the **Arizona Diamondbacks** (514-8400), a new Major League baseball team, arrived on the scene; their home is the new **Bank One Ballpark,** next to the America West arena.

■ Near Phoenix: Apache Trail

Steep, gray, and haunting, the **Superstition Mountains** derive their name from Pima Native American legends. Although the Indians were kicked out by the Anglo gold prospectors who settled the region, the curse stayed. In the 1840s, a Mexican explorer found gold in these hills, but was killed before he could reveal the location of the mine. More famous is the case of Jacob Waltz, known as "Dutchman" despite having emigrated from Germany. During the 1880s, he brought out about $250,000 worth of high-quality gold ore from somewhere in the mountains. Upon his death in 1891, he left only a few clues to the whereabouts of the mine. Strangely, many who have come looking for it have died violent deaths—one prospector burned to death in his own campfire, while another was found decapitated in an arroyo. Needless to say, the mine has never been found.

Rte. 88, a.k.a. **Apache Trail,** winds from **Apache Junction,** a small mining town 40 mi. east of Phoenix, through the mountains. Although the road is only about 50 mi. long, it's only partially paved; trips require at least 3-4hr. behind the wheel. Leave the driving to **Apache Trail Tours** (602-982-7661), which offers on- and off-road jeep tours (2-4hr. tours; $60 per person; reserve at least a day in advance). For more info, head to the **Apache Junction Chamber of Commerce,** 112 E. 2nd Ave. (602-982-3141; open M-F 8am-5pm).

The scenery itself is the Trail's greatest attraction, especially the deep blue waters of the man-made **Lake Canyon, Lake Apache,** and **Lake Roosevelt. Goldfield Ghost Town Mine Tours** (602-983-0333), 5 mi. north of the U.S. 60 junction on Rte. 88, offers tours of the nearby mines, complete with goldpanning, from a resurrected ghost town (open daily 10am-5pm; mine tours $4, ages 6-12 $2; goldpanning $3). "Where the hell am I?" said Jacob Waltz when he came upon **Lost Dutchman State Park** (602-982-4485), 1½ mi. farther north on Rte. 88. At the base of the Superstitions, the park offers nature trails, picnic sites, and campsites with showers but no hookups (entrance $4 per vehicle; first come, first served sites $9). **Tortilla Flat** (602-984-1776), another refurbished ghost town 18 mi. farther on Rte. 88, keeps its spirits up with a restaurant, ice cream shop, and saloon (restaurant open M-F 9am-6pm, Sa-Su 8am-7pm). **Tonto National Monument** (520-467-2241), 5 mi. east of Lake Roosevelt on Rte. 88, preserves 700-year-old masonry and pueblo ruins built by Anasazi (open daily 8am-5pm; entrance fee $4 per car). **Tonto National Forest** (602-225-5200) offers nearby camping (sites $6-12).

■ Organ Pipe Cactus National Monument

Cozying up to the U.S.-Mexico border, the lonely dirt roads of Organ Pipe Cactus National Monument encircle an extraordinary collection of the flora and fauna of the Sonoran Desert. Foremost among them is the organ pipe cactus itself, which is common in Mexico, but found only in this region of the U.S. Its texture and color are similar to those of a saguaro, but while the saguaro is commonly shaped like a body with two or more arms, the organ pipe cactus consists *only* of arms, which sprout tentacle-like from the soil. Two **scenic loop drives** penetrate the park's desert landscape and lead to a number of trailheads. Both are winding and unpaved, but accessible to ordinary cars. *Take water with you;* none is available along either drive. The **Ajo Mountain Drive** (round-trip 21 mi., 2hr.) circles along the foothills of the steep, rocky Ajo Mountains, the highest mountain range in the area. About halfway around the loop lies the start of the **Estes Canyon-Bull Pasture Trail** (round-trip 4.1 mi.), which climbs through the mountains to a plateau that affords an astounding view from all sides. On the other side of the park, the **Puerto Blanco Drive** (round-trip 53 mi., 4-5hr.) winds through the colorful Puerto Blanco Mountains, passing oases, cacti, and abandoned mines along the way. One fairly easy trek (4½ mi.) leads to the **Victoria Mine,** the oldest gold and silver mine in the area.

Located on U.S. 85, 22 mi. south of the tiny hamlet **Why,** Organ Pipe Cactus is one of the most isolated national parks in the U.S.; there are no crowds in any season. The **visitors center** (520-387-6849) on Rte. 85, 5 mi. north of the Mexican border, passes out the obligatory maps and makes hiking recommendations (open daily 8am-5pm). The adjacent **campground** offers water, restrooms, and grills, but no hookups (tent sites $9; first come, first served). **Backcountry camping** is free but requires a permit from the visitors center. For further info, write to the **Superintendent,** Organ Pipe Cactus National Monument, Rte. 1, Box 100, Ajo, AZ 85321-9626.

■ Tucson

The Hohokan Indians inhabited the Tucson region 1200 years ago, but it was the Papago Indians who gave the city its name. Between 1776 and 1848, the region fell under Spanish, then Mexican, and, ultimately, U.S. control. They knew European civilization had arrived in 1864, when locals ruled that pigs could no longer roam freely on city streets—they would have to be chained. Smaller and friendlier than Phoenix, Tucson is now struggling to preserve its attractive, pigless downtown, and it remains to be seen whether the small band of cafes and artsy shops can compete with the city's suburban sprawl. In the meantime, travelers can take advantage of Tucson's varied environments—the walkable downtown, restaurant-and-shop-crammed highways, a college scene, and Saguaro National Park just outside the city.

PRACTICAL INFORMATION

Just east of I-10, Tucson's downtown area surrounds the intersection of **Broadway Blvd.** (which runs west) and **Stone Ave.,** 2 blocks from the train and bus terminals. The **University of Arizona** lies 1 mi. northeast of downtown at the intersection of **Park** and **Speedway Blvd.** Avenues run north-south, streets east-west; because some of each are numbered, intersections such as "6th and 6th" are possible. Speedway, Broadway, and **Grant Ave.** are the quickest east-west routes through town. To go north-south, follow **Oracle Rd.** through the heart of the city, **Campbell Ave.** east of downtown, or **Swan Rd.** farther east. The hip, young crowd swings on **4th Ave.** and on **Congress St.,** with small shops, quirky restaurants, and a slew of bars.

Airport: Tucson International (573-8000), on Valencia Rd., south of downtown. Bus #25 runs every hr. to the Laos Transit Center; from there, bus #16 goes downtown (last bus daily 7:48pm). **Arizona Stagecoach** (889-1000) will take you downtown for around $12. Runs 24hr. Reservations recommended.

Trains: Amtrak, 400 E. Toole Ave. (623-4442 or 800-872-7245), at 5th Ave., 1 block north of the Greyhound station. To Los Angeles (9hr., 4 per week, $66-98). Open Sa-M 6:15am-1:45pm and 4:15-11:30pm, Tu-W 6:15am-1:45pm, Th-F 4:15-11:30pm.

Buses: Greyhound, 2 S. 4th Ave. (882-4386 or 800-231-2222), between Congress St. and Broadway. To: Phoenix (2hr., 15 per day, $12); Los Angeles (9-10hr., 15 per day, $36); Albuquerque (12-15hr., 6 per day, $81); and El Paso (7hr., 11 per day, $34). Ticket office and terminal open 24hr.

Taxis: Yellow Cab, 624-6611. $1.25 base fare, $1.50 per mi. 24hr. service.

Public Transportation: Sun-Tran (792-9222). Buses run from the Ronstadt terminal downtown at Congress and 6th St. Service roughly M-F 5:30am-10pm, Sa-Su 8am-7pm; times vary by route. Fare 85¢, under 19 60¢, seniors and disabled 35¢.

Car Rental: Care Free, 1760 S. Craycroft Rd. (790-2655). For the car-free. $18 per day with 100 free mi. within Tucson only. 2-day min. rental. Must be 21 with major credit card. Open M-F 9am-5pm, Sa 10am-2pm.

Bike Rental: Fairwheels Bicycles, 1110 E. 6th St. (884-9018), at Freemont. $20 1st day, $10 per additional day. Open M-F 9am-6pm, Sa 9am-5:30pm, Su noon-4pm.

Visitor Info: Metropolitan Tucson Convention and Visitors Bureau, 130 S. Scott Ave. (624-1817 or 800-638-8350), near Broadway. Bus maps, camping info, the *Official Visitor's Guide*—they've got it all. Open M-F 8am-5pm, Sa-Su 9am-4pm.

Bi-Gay-Lesbian Organization: Gay, Lesbian, and Bisexual Community Center, 422 N. 4th Ave. (624-1779). Hrs. vary.

Hotline: Rape Crisis, 327-7273. 24hr.

Internet Access: At the **Library of Congress "Cybarcafe,"** in the lobby of the Hotel Congress. Super-fast email connections. $3 for 30min. Open daily 11am-1am.

Post Office: 141 S. 6th Ave. (800-275-8777). Open M-F 8:30am-5pm, Sa 9am-noon. General delivery: 1501 S. Cherry Bell (800-275-8777). Open M-F 8:30am-5pm, Sa 9am-1pm. **ZIP code:** 85726. **Area code:** 520.

ACCOMMODATIONS AND CAMPGROUNDS

When summer arrives, Tucson opens its arms to budget travelers. Motel row runs along **South Freeway,** the frontage road along I-10 north of the I-19 junction; motels also cluster on **Oracle Rd.** The swank old **Hotel Congress and Hostel (AAIH/Rucksackers),** 311 E. Congress (622-8848), conveniently located across from the Greyhound and Amtrak stations, offers superb lodging to night owl hostelers. Club Congress, downstairs, booms until 2am on weekends, making it a bit rough on early birds (see **Entertainment and Nightlife,** below). Still, you get free earplugs and a nice bed in a double room with a private bath and phone. The cafe downstairs serves great salads and mean omelettes. (Hostel rooms $15 per person. Singles $29; doubles $32-42; 10% discount for students and artists.) The brand-new **Roadrunner Hostel,** 346 E. 12th St. (628-4709), is located in a pleasant converted house a few blocks from downtown. The doors generally lack locks, but hallway lockers are provided; bring your own padlock or buy one from the owner. (Laundry and kitchen facilities. Dorms $13 per person; private doubles $30. Unlimited Internet access $5.) **La Siesta Motel,** 1602 N. Oracle Rd. (624-1192), has clean rooms, a shaded picnic/BBQ area, a pool, and parking (singles $32; doubles $35, with 2 beds $39).

   Mount Lemmon Recreation Area, in the **Coronado National Forest,** offers beautiful campgrounds and free off-site camping in certain areas. Campgrounds and picnic areas lie minutes to hours away from Tucson via the **Catalina Hwy. Rose Canyon,** 33 mi. northeast of Tucson on Hitchcock Hwy., at 7000 ft., is heavily wooded, comfortably cool, and has a small lake. Sites ($9) at higher elevations fill quickly on summer weekends. The **National Forest Service,** 300 W. Congress Ave. (670-4552), 7 blocks west of the Greyhound station, has more info (open M-F 8am-4:30pm). **Cactus Country RV Park** (574-3000), 10 mi. southeast of Tucson on I-10, off the Houghton Rd. Exit, is a nice private campground with showers and a pool (sites for 1 or 2 $16, full hookup $25; $2.80 per additional person).

FOOD

Good, cheap Mexican restaurants are everywhere in Tucson. **Little Café Poca Cosa,** 20 S. Scott Ave., the less expensive *niño* of the Cafe Poca Cosa on Broadway, prides itself on fresh ingredients and an ever-changing menu—patrons often walk in and say "give me something good" (lunch specials $5.50; open M-F 7:30am-2:30pm; cash only). **Café Magritte's,** 254 Congress St. (884-8004), hangs great art and serves up delicious appetizers from *polenta* pizza tart ($5) to tortilla bean soup ($3), including vegetarian options (open Su 4-10pm, Tu-Th 11am-10pm, F-Sa 11am-midnight). When you've had it up to your sombrero with Mexican food, **India Oven,** 2727 N. Campbell Ave. (326-8635), between Grant and Glenn, offers relief. The garlic *naan* ($2.35) is exquisite. (Vegetarian dishes $6-7; tandoori meats and curries $6-9. Open daily 11am-10pm.) A hole-in-the-wall sandwiched between vintage clothing shops, **Maya Quetzal,** 429 N. 4th Ave. (622-8207), serves up authentic Guatemalan food at rock-bottom prices. The veggie or meat *empanadas* ($4), and the $7 *pollo de naranja,* chicken in orange and garlic sauce, are tasty choices. (Open M-Th 11:30am-8:30pm, F 11:30am-9:30pm, Sa noon-9:30pm.)

SIGHTS

Lined with cafes, restaurants, galleries, and vintage clothing shops, **4th Ave.** is an alternative, artsy magnet and a great place to take a stroll. Between Speedway and Broadway Blvd., the street becomes a historic shopping district with increasingly touristy shops. Lovely for its varied and elaborately irrigated vegetation, the **University of Arizona's** mall sits where E. 3rd St. should be. The **Center for Creative Photography** (621-7968), on campus, houses various exhibits, including the archives of the major American photographers Ansel Adams and Richard Avedon (open M-F 11am-5pm, Su noon-5pm; free). Shops catering to students cluster along **University Blvd.** at the west edge of campus. The **Tucson Museum of Art,** 140 N. Main Ave. (624-2333), exhibits an impressive collection of pre-Columbian art (open Tu-Sa 10am-4pm, Su noon-4pm; $2, students and seniors $1, children free).

A museum, zoo, and nature preserve rolled into one, the **Arizona-Sonora Desert Museum,** 2021 N. Kinney Rd. (883-2702), recreates a range of desert habitats and features over 300 kinds of animals. *(Open Su-F 7:30am-5pm, Sa 7:30am-10pm; Oct.-Feb. daily 7:30am-6pm. $8.75, ages 6-12 $1.75.)* Follow Speedway Blvd. west of the city as it becomes Gates Pass Rd., then Kinney Rd. A proper visit requires at least 2hr., preferably during the cool morning hours, before the animals take their afternoon siestas.

North of the desert museum, the western half (Tucson Mountain District) of **Saguaro National Park** (733-5158) has limited hiking trails and an auto loop (park open 24hr.). The paved nature walk near the **visitors center** passes some of the best specimens of Saguaro cactus in the Tucson area (visitors center open daily 8:30am-5pm). **Gates Pass,** on the way to the Tucson Mountain District and the Desert Museum, is an excellent spot for watching the rising and setting sun. **Saguaro National Park East** (733-5153), a.k.a. Rincon Mountain District, lies east of the city on Old Spanish Trail; take I-10 E to Exit 279 and follow Vail Rd. to Old Spanish Trail. *(Visitors center open daily 8:30am-5pm. $4 per vehicle, $2 per pedestrian.)* Within the park, 128 mi. of trails and an 8 mi. scenic drive lead through the cactus forest. Before noon, free permits can be had from the visitors center for **backcountry camping. Colossal Cave** (647-7275), nearby on Vail Rd., is the only dormant cave in the U.S. *(Open M-Sa 8am-6pm, Su 8am-7pm; mid-Sept. to mid-Mar. M-Sa 9am-5pm, Su 9am-6pm. $6.50, ages 11-16 $5, ages 6-10 $3.50.)* Guided tours (45min.) involve flagstone walking, 70° F temperatures, and fluorescent lights. In the shadow of the National Park, the praises of the **cacti on Mt. Lemmon,** just east of town, tend to go unsung; it's worth the time to drive up the mountain and see them.

Old Tucson Studios, 201 S. Kinney Rd. (883-0100), is an exact replica of Tucson in the 1860s and has served as the setting for more than 300 Westerns since 1939. *(Open daily 10am-6pm. $15, ages 4-11 $9.45.)* The whole complex has been rebuilt after a devastating fire in 1995 and is again open to visitors as a Western theme park with shows, rides, games, food, and shops.

More than 20,000 warplanes, from WWII fighters to jets used during the Vietnam War, are parked in ominous, silent rows at the **Davis-Monthan Air Force Base** (228-4570), 15 mi. southeast of Tucson. *(Free tours M, W, F 10:30am; first come, first served.)* Low humidity and sparse rainfall combine to preserve the relics. Take the Houghton Exit off I-10, then travel west on Irvington to Wilmont. You can also view the 2 mi. long aerospace-graveyard through the airfield fence.

ENTERTAINMENT AND NIGHTLIFE

Tucson is a musical smorgasbord. While UA students rock and roll on **Speedway Blvd.**, more subdued folks do the two-step in the country music clubs on **N. Oracle.** The free *Tucson Weekly* or the weekend sections of *The Star* or *The Citizen* have current entertainment listings. Throughout the year, the city of the sun presents **Music Under the Stars** (792-9155), a series of sunset concerts performed by the Tucson Symphony Orchestra. During **Downtown Saturday Night,** on the first and third Saturday of each month, Congress St. is blockaded for a celebration of the arts with outdoor singers, crafts, and galleries. Every Thursday, the **Thursday Night Art Walk** lets you mosey through downtown galleries and studios. The **Tucson Arts District** (624-9977) has more info.

Club Congress, 311 E. Congress St. (622-8848), has DJs during the week and live bands on weekends (cover $4). The friendly hotel staff and a cast of regulars make it an especially good time. Thursday is 80s night with 80¢ drinks. (Open M-F 9pm-1am, Sa-Su 9pm-2am.) **The Rock,** 136 N. Park (629-9211), caters to a college crowd with live shows and Friday night battles of the bands (cover $3-12; open 8pm-1am on show days; call ahead). A good place for a quiet drink, **Bar Toma,** 311 N. Cart Ave. (622-5465), offers a wide selection of tequilas (open Su-Th 5-9pm, F-Sa 5-10pm). Young locals hang out on **4th Ave.** at night; most of the bars have live music and low cover charges. **3rd Stone** (628-8844), on the corner of 4th Ave. and 6th St., is a good spot (cover $2 Tu; open M-Sa 11am-midnight, Su 4-11pm), as is **O'Malley's** (623-8600), farther up 4th Ave., with decent bar food, pool tables, and pinball (cover $2 F-Sa; open daily 11am-1am). **IBT's** (882-3053), on 4th Ave. at 6th St., leads the gay scene (open daily noon-1am).

Despite its name, **New West,** 4385 W. Ina Rd. (744-7744), is an authentic Old West saloon playing continuous country-western music on the largest dance floor in Arizona (6000 sq. ft.). The newly-renovated club offers cheap beer $2 and occasional two-stepping lessons. (Open M-Th 6pm-midnight, F-Sa 6pm-1am.)

■ Near Tucson

Biosphere 2 Ninety-one feet high, with an area of more than 3 acres, Biosphere 2 is sealed off from Earth—"Biosphere 1"—by 500 tons of stainless steel. *(Tours daily 9am-5pm; grounds open until 7pm. $13, seniors $11, ages 5-17 $6; $2 AAA discount.)* In 1991, eight research scientists enclosed themselves inside this giant greenhouse to cultivate their own food and knit their own socks with no aid from the outside world as they monitored the behavior of five man-made ecosystems: savanna, rainforest, marsh, ocean, and desert. After 2 years, they began having oxygen problems and difficulty with food production. Now, no one lives in Biosphere 2, but teams of scientists still use it as a research facility.

The Biosphere is 30min. north of Tucson; take I-10 west to the "Miracle Mile" Exit, follow the miracles to Oracle Rd., then travel north until it becomes Rte. 77 N. From Phoenix, take I-10 to Exit 185, follow Rte. 387 to Rte. 79 (Florence Hwy.), and proceed to Oracle Junction and Rte. 77. Guided tours (2hr.) include two short films, a walk through the laboratory's research and development models for the Biosphere 2 ecosystems, and a stroll around Biosphere 2 itself, including the crew's living quarters. Walking around unchaperoned is also permitted. The **Biosphere 2 Hotel** (520-896-6222) offers rooms with cable TV, giant beds, and huge patios overlooking the Catalina mountains, on the same ranch as the Biosphere. (Rooms for 1 or 2 $49; Oct.-

THE SOUTHWEST

Apr. $80; a hefty $20 per additional person.) All guests are required to be in their rooms by 8pm. Also within the complex, the **Cañada del Oro Restaurant** (520-896-6220) serves up sandwiches and salads for around $6 (open M-Sa 7am-7pm, Su 7am-5pm).

Sabino Canyon North of Tucson, the cliffs and waterfalls of **Sabino Canyon** (749-2861) provide an ideal backdrop for picnics and day hikes. No cars are permitted in the canyon, but a free **tram** makes trips through it (every 30min. 9am-4:30pm). Take I-10 to Exit 270 (Kolb Rd.) and follow Kolb north to Tanque Verde Rd.; make a right and follow the signs to the canyon. **Sabino Canyon Tours,** 5900 N. Sabino Canyon Rd. (749-2861), runs 45min. trips through the canyon, including moonlight rides 3 nights per month. *(Tours M-F on the ½hr. 9am-4pm; off-season every 30min. Sa-Su 9am-4:30pm. $2. Moonlight tours Apr.-Dec. only.)*

■ Tombstone

Founded in the wake of the gold and silver rush of the 1870s, Tombstone—home of more than 3000 prostitutes and 100 saloons—was the largest city between St. Louis and San Francisco in the early 1880s. But water gradually seeped into the mines that were the city's lifeline, and when the equipment installed to pump it out failed in 1909, the mines were overrun by water and remain flooded to this day. Yet "the town too tough to die" has made a comeback. By inviting visitors to view the barnyard where Wyatt Earp and his brothers kicked some serious butt, Tombstone has turned the showdown at the **O.K. Corral** (457-3456), on Allen St. next to City Park, into a year-round tourist industry (open daily 9am-5pm; $2.50). The **Boothill Gunslingers,** the **Wild Bunch,** and the **Vigilantes/Vigilettes** perform re-enactments of famous gunfights (F-Sa and 1st and 3rd Su of each month, 2pm; $2.50, ages 6-12 $1.50). The **Hanging Chairman** (457-3434) can treat a friend or relative to a **public mock hanging** by one of these groups. The voice of Vincent Price narrates the town's history next door to the O.K. Corral in the **Tombstone Historama** (457-3456), while a plastic mountain revolves onstage and a dramatization of the gunfight is shown on a movie screen (shows daily on the ½hr. 9am-4pm; $2.50). Site of the longest poker game in western history (8 years, 5 months, and 3 days), the **Bird Cage Theater,** at 6th and Allen, was named for the compartments suspended from the ceiling that once housed prostitutes (open daily 9am-4pm). John Slaughter battled scores of outlaws at the **Tombstone Courthouse** (457-3311), at 3rd and Toughnut St. (Open daily 8am-5pm. $2.50, ages 7-14 $1). The courthouse is now a museum housing extremely diverse exhibits related to the town's history. The **tombstones** of Tombstone—the result of all of this wanton gunplay—stand on Rte. 80 just north of town (open daily 7:30am-7pm; free).

And now for something completely different: the **Rose Tree Museum** (457-3326), at 4th and Toughnut St., houses the largest rose tree in the world (open daily 9am-5pm; $2, under 14 free).

The **Larian Motel** (457-2272), on the corner of Fremont and 5th, is clean, nicely furnished, and easy walking distance from all sights (singles $35-39; doubles $45-49). The rooms at the **Tombstone Motel** (457-3478 or 888-455-3478), across the street, are basic and a bit dark, but clean (singles $39-42; doubles $55).

Blake's Char-Broiled Burgers and BBQ Ranch, 511B Allen St. (457-3646), slaps the cow on the bun starting at $3.50 (open daily 11am-4pm). **Don Teodoro's,** 15 N. 4th St. (457-3647), serves Mexican plates accompanied by live guitar music for under $6 (live music W-M 6-9pm; open Su-Th 11am-9pm, F-Sa 11am-10pm). For a bit of moonshine and country music, smell your way to **Big Nose Kate's Saloon** (457-3107), on Allen St., named for "the girl who loved Doc Holliday and everyone else too." Cowboy bartenders serve drinks like "sex in the desert." (Open daily 10am-midnight.)

To get to Tombstone, career your Conestoga to the Benson Exit off I-10, then go south on Rte. 80. The nearest **Greyhound** station, 242 E. 4th St. (586-3141 or 800-

231-2222), is in **Benson** at the Benson Flower Shop on 4th St., a block away from downtown. The **Amtrak** station (800-872-7245) sits across the street. **Benson Taxi** (586-7688) makes the trip from Benson to Tombstone ($25). The **Tombstone Chamber of Commerce and Visitors Center** (457-3929) welcomes y'all at 4th and Allen St. (open daily 10am-4pm). **Area code:** 520.

■ Near Tombstone: Bisbee

One hundred miles southeast of Tucson and 20 mi. south of Tombstone, mellow Bisbee, a former mining town, is known throughout the Southwest as a chic but laid-back artists' colony. Visitors may revel in the town's proximity to Mexico, picture-perfect weather, and excellent, relatively inexpensive accommodations. The only real sights in town are mine-related, but Bisbee is a terrific place just to stroll around, window-shop, and drink coffee in a cute cafe. The **Queen Mines** (432-2071), right on the Rte. 80 interchange entering Old Bisbee, ceased its mining activities in 1943 but continues to give educational 1¼hr. tours (tours 9, 10:30am, noon, 2, and 3:30pm; $8, ages 7-11 $3.50, ages 3-6 $2). The **Mining and Historical Museum,** 5 Copper Queen (432-7071), highlights the discovery of Bisbee's copper surplus and the lives of the fortune-seekers who extracted this resource (open daily 10am-4pm; $3, seniors $2.50, under 19 free).

Patrons rest in style at the pleasant **Bisbee Grand Hotel,** 61 Main St. (800-421-1909), which offers rooms furnished with turn-of-the-century antiques (singles and doubles from $45, breakfast included). About a 10min. walk from downtown, the **Jonquil Inn,** 317 Tombstone Canyon (432-7371), offers clean and smoke-free rooms (singles $35; doubles $39; in winter about $10 higher). The **Chamber of Commerce,** 7 Main St. (432-5421), distributes *Bisbee Now* and a very basic map of downtown (both free; open M-F 9am-5pm, Sa-Su 10am-5pm).

New Mexico

In 1540, an expedition led by Francisco Vasquez de Coronado left Mexico City for what is now New Mexico, hoping to conquer the legendary city of Cíbola. There, it was said, silversmiths occupied entire streets, while gold, sapphires, and turquoise decorated every house. Coronado and his men found only Indian pueblos, so they returned to Mexico, none the richer, in 1542. Coronado may have failed in his quest, but he did start a trend—travelers have sought out New Mexico's riches ever since. Today, most explorers come in search of natural beauty and adobe architecture rather than gold, but the spirit of the conquistadors seems to live on with the purse-toting New Yorkers fingering turquoise jewelry in Taos Plaza.

New Mexico serves as a haven for hikers, backpackers, cyclists, mountain-climbers, and skiers. Six national forests within the state provide miles and miles of beautiful and challenging opportunities for lovers of the outdoors, while the Sandía, Mogollon, and Sangre de Cristo mountains can fulfill any mountain-climber's upward longings.

PRACTICAL INFORMATION

Capital: Santa Fe.
Visitor Info: New Mexico Dept. of Tourism, 491 Old Santa Fe Trail, Santa Fe 87501 (800-545-2040; http://www.newmexico.org). Open M-F 8am-5pm. **Park and Recreation Division,** 2040 S. Pacheco, Santa Fe 87504 (505-827-7173), open M-F 8am-5pm. **U.S. Forest Service,** 517 Gold Ave. SW, Albuquerque 87102 (505-842-3292). Open M-F 8am-4:30pm.
Emergency: 911.
Time Zone: Mountain (2hr. behind Eastern). **Postal Abbreviation:** NM.
Sales Tax: 5.8%.

■ Santa Fe

Santa Fe lies at the convergence of the **Santa Fe Trail,** running from Independence, Missouri, and **El Camino Réal** ("Royal Road"), which runs from Mexico City. Meetings at this crossroads have not always been smooth. During the Mexican War, the Americans wrested control of the city from Mexico. Yet, Mexican influence has not died—a 1957 zoning ordinance requires all downtown edifices to conform to Spanish Pueblo style, although the adobe plaster occasionally fails to cover traces of formerly Victorian facades. In spite of the illiberal uniformity of the city's architecture, free-thinkers and artists flock to Santa Fe, where they coexist with Native Americans, local retirees, tourists, and jewelry hawkers. Santa Fe is also the Southwest's art capital—a casual *paseo* down Canyon Rd., the local artists' turf, may give as insightful a glimpse of local culture as a visit to its world-class museums.

ORIENTATION AND PRACTICAL INFORMATION

Except for the museums southeast of the city center, most restaurants and sights in Santa Fe cluster within a few blocks of the **downtown plaza** and inside the loop formed by the **Paseo de Peralta.** Narrow streets make driving troublesome; park your car and pound the pavement. You'll find **parking lots** behind Santa Fe Village, near Sena Plaza, and 1 block east of the Federal Courthouse near the plaza, while metered spaces (2-4hr. max.) line the streets just south of the plaza. Parking is also available along the streets near the galleries on Canyon Rd.

Buses: Greyhound, 858 St. Michael's Dr. (471-0008 or 800-231-2222). To: Taos (1½hr., 2 per day, $17); Albuquerque (1½hr., 4 per day, $11.55); and Denver (8-10hr., 4 per day, $59). Open M-F 7am-5:30pm and 7:30-9:35pm, Sa-Su 7-9am, 12:30-1:30pm, 3:30-5pm, and 7:30-9:30pm.

Trains: Amtrak, nearest station in **Lamy** (466-4511 or 800-872-7245), 13 mi. away on Country Rd. 41. Call 982-8829 to shuttle to Santa Fe ($14). Open daily 9am-5pm.

Public Transportation: Santa Fe Trails (438-1464) runs 6 downtown bus routes (M-F 6am-10pm). Bus #10 leaves every 30min. from the downtown Sheridan Transit Center, 1 block from the plaza between Marcy St. and Palace Ave., and heads to the museums on Camino Lejo. 50¢, ages 6-12 25¢; day pass $1. **Shuttlejack** (982-4311) runs to the Albuquerque airport (12 per day, $20) and, in summer, to the opera (1 per day, round-trip $10) from downtown hotels. Reserve 1 day in advance.

Car Rental: Enterprise Rent-a-Car, 2641 Cerrillos Rd. (473-3600). $37 per day, $169 per week. Must be 21 with major credit card. Open M-F 8am-6pm.

Taxis: Capital City Taxi, 438-0000. $2 initial charge, $1.50 per mi.

Visitor Info: All tourist offices offer friendly advice and the *Santa Fe Visitors Guide.* **Santa Fe Welcome Center,** 491 Old Santa Fe Trail (875-7400 or 800-545-2040). Open daily 8am-7pm; off-season 8am-5pm. **Santa Fe Convention and Visitors Bureau,** 201 W. Marcy St. (800-777-2489). Open M-F 8am-5pm. **Info booth,** in the First National Bank at Lincoln and Palace St. Open in summer M-Sa 9am-4:30pm.

Hotline: Rape Abuse Help Line, 800-721-7273 or 986-9111. Operates 8am-5pm, on-call 24hr.

Post Office: 120 S. Federal Pl. (988-6351), next to the courthouse. Open M-F 7:30am-5:45pm, Sa 9am-1pm. **ZIP code:** 87501. **Area code:** 505.

ACCOMMODATIONS AND CAMPGROUNDS

Hotels in Santa Fe tend towards the expensive side. As early as May, they become swamped with requests for **Indian Market** (3rd week of Aug.) and **Fiesta de Santa Fe** (early Sept.). Make reservations early or plan to sleep standing up. At other times, the **Cerrillos Rd.** area has the best prices, but travelers should use caution and evaluate the motel (read: see the room) before checking in. At many of the less expensive motels, bargaining is possible for stays of more than one night.

To camp around Santa Fe, you'll need a car. In addition to Rancheros de Santa Fe (see below), there are several campsites run by the **Santa Fe National Forest** (438-

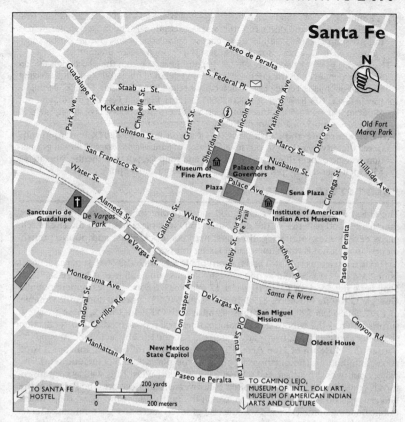

Santa Fe

N

Paseo de Peralta

Guadalupe St.

Staab St.

McKenzie St.

Chapelle St.

Johnson St.

Park Ave.

Grant St.

Sheridan Ave.

Lincoln St.

S. Federal Pl.

Washington Ave.

Otero St.

Marcy St.

Nusbaum St.

Cienega St.

Hillside Ave.

Old Fort Marcy Park

San Francisco St.

Water St.

Museum of Fine Arts

Palace of the Governors

Palace Ave.

Plaza

Sena Plaza

Sanctuario de Guadalupe

Alameda St.

De Vargas Park

Galisteo St.

Water St.

Shelby St.

Old Santa Fe Trail

Institute of American Indian Arts Museum

DeVargas St.

Cathedral Pl.

Paseo de Peralta

Montezuma Ave.

Sandoval St.

Cerrillos Rd.

Don Gasper Ave.

DeVargas St.

Santa Fe River

Manhattan Ave.

New Mexico State Capitol

Old Santa Fe Trail

San Miguel Mission

Oldest House

Canyon Rd.

Paseo de Peralta

TO SANTA FE HOSTEL

0   200 yards

0   200 meters

TO CAMINO LEJO, MUSEUM OF INTL. FOLK ART, MUSEUM OF AMERICAN INDIAN ARTS AND CULTURE

THE SOUTHWEST

7840) in the beautiful Sangre de Cristo Mountains. The **Black Canyon Campground,** 8 mi. northeast of Santa Fe on Rte. 475, has 40 sites ($6). Four miles farther, although you won't find drinking water, you can camp for free at one of **Big Tesuque's** seven sites. (Both open May-Oct. Call the National Forest for info.)

Santa Fe International Hostel and Pension (AAIH/HI/Rucksackers), 1412 Cerrillos Rd. (988-1153), 1 mi. from the bus station and 2 mi. from the plaza. Kitchen, library, and large dorm rooms. Dorm beds $14, nonmembers $15. Linen free. B&B singles $25; doubles $35; with private bath $33/$43; no discount for members. No credit cards. Office open daily 7am-11pm. Reservations needed for Aug.

Thunderbird Inn, 1821 Cerrillos Rd. (983-4397). Slightly farther from town than the hostel, but an excellent value (for Santa Fe, anyway). Large, very clean singles $44; doubles $45; some with fridge and microwave; winter rates $10-15 lower.

Rancheros de Santa Fe, 736 Old Las Vegas Hwy. (466-3482). Take I-25 N to Exit 290. Big, friendly campground with pool. Sites $17, full hookup $24; cabins $30.

FOOD

Spicy Mexican food served on blue corn tortillas is a Santa Fe staple. Bistros near the plaza dish up chiles to a mixture of government employees, well-heeled tourists, and local artists. Wandering down the side streets uncovers smaller Mexican restaurants where the locals eat, while grill carts in the plaza can sell you fragrant fajitas ($3) and fresh lemonade ($1).

◎Tia Sophia's, 210 W. San Francisco St. (983-9880). It looks and feels like a diner (the servers are quick and curt), but the food is exceptional. The most popular item is the Atrisco plate ($6)—chile stew, cheese enchilada, beans, *posole*, and a *sopapilla*. Arrive before noon for the fastest service. Open M-Sa 7am-2pm.

The Shed, 113½ E. Palace Ave. (982-9030), up the street from the plaza, feels like an open garden, even in the enclosed section. Vegetarian quesadilla ($6) and amazing chicken enchilada verde ($9). Lunch daily 11am-2:30pm, dinner W-Sa 5:30-9pm.

Atomic Grill, 103 E. Water St. (820-2866). A rarity in Santa Fe—open late, and not Mexican. Falafel $6.50, catfish sandwich $9. 82 different beers. Live music Sa 9pm. Open M-Sa 7am-3am, Su 7am-midnight.

OM Tibetan Café and Restaurant, 403 Canyon Rd. (984-1207). Pink footprints down the driveway lead to this manifestation of Santa Fe's sizeable Tibetan population. Veggie or beef dumplings with salad and soup $9, pot of authentic Tibetan tea $3. Open Tu-F 11am-2pm and 5-9pm, Sa noon-2pm and 5-8pm.

"OLD" STYLE SIGHTS

The grassy **Plaza de Santa Fe** is a good starting point for exploring the museums, sanctuaries, and galleries of the city. Since 1609, the plaza has been the site of religious ceremonies, military gatherings, markets, cockfights, and public punishments—now it holds ritzy shops and relaxing tourists.

The five museums run by **The Museum of New Mexico** (827-6463) have identical hours. A 4-day pass bought at one museum admits you to all five. *(Open Tu-Su 10am-5pm; single visit $5, 4-day pass $10, under 17 free; free F 5-8pm.)* The extremely popular **Georgia O'Keeffe Museum,** 217 Johnson St. (995-0785), opened during the summer of 1997. *(Audio tour $4.)* Even for those familiar with O'Keeffe's work, there are a few surprises here—the famous flower paintings are well represented, but the collection spans her entire lifetime, from early watercolors to the late abstract work. Around the corner, the **Museum of Fine Arts,** 107 W. Palace Ave. (476-5072), inhabits a large adobe building on the northwest corner of the plaza. Exhibits include works by major Southwestern artists, like O'Keeffe and Edward Weston, as well as very adventurous contemporary exhibits of often controversial American art. The **Palace of the Governors,** 100 Palace Ave. (827-6476), on the north side of the plaza, is the oldest public building in the U.S., and was the seat of seven successive governments after its construction in 1610. The *haciendas* palace is now a museum with exhibits on Native American, Southwestern, and New Mexican history. The craft and jewelry displays in front of the palace often have cheaper and better quality wares than you'll find in the "Indian Crafts" stores around town. The other two museums lie southeast of town on **Camino Lejo,** just off Old Santa Fe Trail. The **Museum of International Folk Art,** 706 Camino Lejo (827-6350), 2 mi. south of the plaza, houses the Girard Collection, which includes over 100,000 handmade dolls, dollhouses, and other toys from around the world. A gallery handout will help you appreciate the fascinating, though jumbled, exhibit. Other galleries hold changing ethnographic exhibits. Next door, the **Museum of American Indian Arts and Culture,** 710 Camino Lejo (827-6344), displays Native American photos and artifacts. The **Institute of American Indian Arts Museum,** 108 Cathedral Place (988-6281), downtown, houses an extensive collection of contemporary Indian art. *(Open M-Sa 10am-5pm, Su noon-5pm. $4, students and seniors $2, under 17 free.)*

About 5 blocks southeast of the plaza lies the **San Miguel Mission** (983-3974), at DeVargas St. and the Old Santa Fe Trail. Built in 1710, the mission is the oldest functioning church in the U.S. *(Open M-Sa 9am-4:15pm, Su 1:30-4:30pm; Nov.-Apr. M-Sa 10am-3:45pm, Su 1:30-4:30pm. $1.)* Inside, glass windows over the altar look down upon the original altar built by Native Americans. The United States' **Oldest House** (988-4455), just down DeVargas St. from the mission, dates from about 1200 AD. The house was originally one of a number of buildings comprising a pueblo (open daily 8am-6pm; donations suggested). Enter through the Outback Tours office.

> ### "Now I Am Become Death, Destroyer of Worlds"
>
> At the outset of WWII, two scientists who had successfully tested fission at the University of Chicago asked Albert Einstein to write a letter to FDR requesting government support for research of atomic energy. Thus began the **Manhattan Project,** an intensely secret scientific enterprise with one explicit purpose: to build an atomic bomb for military use before the Germans did. **Los Alamos, NM,** was chosen as a base for the endeavor because of its remote location, sparse population, and flat terrain—ideal conditions in which to test a nuclear device. Over the next few years, the most eminent physicists in the country convened in Los Alamos, laboring under exhilarating but also stressful and isolated conditions. Each scientist and his family had a pseudonym when they left town, and all identification claimed they lived at "P.O. Box 163, Santa Fe, NM." On July 16, 1945, at 5:30am, it was clear that the scientists had finally achieved their goal: a test bomb was detonated on top of a steel tower, generating an explosive power equivalent to **15,000 to 20,000 tons of TNT.** Elation and satisfaction quickly gave way to feelings of fear and hesitation. The workers had done their job, but the end product, capable of vast and instantaneous devastation, was rightfully frightening, inspiring J. Robert Oppenheimer's famous line (above). Although many who had been involved in the project lobbied to prevent use of the weapon, their pleas could not sway the U.S. government, determined to end the war with a minimum of U.S. casualties. The bomb was used twice against the Japanese, at Hiroshima on Aug. 6 and at Nagasaki on Aug. 9, 1945, killing several hundred thousand civilians. Japan surrendered 5 days later.

To find your way to **Canyon Rd.,** where Santa Fe's most successful artists live and sell their work, head away from the Plaza on San Francisco Dr., take a left on Alameda St., a right on Paseo de Peralta, and a left on Canyon Rd. Extending for about a mile, the road is lined on both sides by galleries displaying all types of art, as well a number of indoor/outdoor cafes. Most galleries are open from around 10am until 5pm. At the **Hahn Ross Gallery,** 409 Canyon Rd. (984-8434), the art is hip, enjoyable, and occasionally affordable (open 10am-5pm). **Off the Wall,** 616 Canyon Rd. (983-8337), vends truly offbeat jewelry, pottery, clocks, and sculpture (open daily 10am-5pm).

ENTERTAINMENT AND NIGHTLIFE

Native American ceremonies, fairs, arts, and crafts shows complement Santa Fe's active theater scene and the roster of world-famous musicians who frequently play in the city's clubs. **El Farol,** 808 Canyon Rd. (983-9912), features up-and-coming rock, salsa, and R&B musicians (shows nightly 9:30pm; cover Su-Tu $3, W-F $5). The **Catamount Bar and Grill,** 125 E. Water St. (988-7222), has live bands and dancing Friday and Saturday nights ($2-3 cover). Cool down and fill up with a 16 oz. margarita ($6) and a sandwich of your choice ($7; open M-Sa 11am-2am, Su noon-midnight).

The **Santa Fe Opera,** P.O. Box 2408, Santa Fe 87504-2408 (800-280-4654), 7 mi. north of Santa Fe on Rte. 84, performs outdoors against a gorgeous mountain backdrop. Nights are cool here; bring a blanket. The season runs from the first weekend of July through the end of August. The downtown box office is at the **El Dorado Hotel,** 309 W. San Francisco St. (986-5900), in the gift and news shop. (July W and F-Sa at 9pm; Aug. M-Sa at 8:30pm. Tickets $15-200, rush standing-room tickets $6-15; 50% student discount on same-day reserved seats. Call the day of the show for specific prices and availability.) **Shuttlejack** offers bus service from downtown for performances (see **Practical Information,** p. 672). The **Santa Fe Chamber Music Festival** (983-2075) celebrates the works of great Baroque, Classical, Romantic, and 20th-century composers in the St. Francis Auditorium of the Museum of Fine Arts. (Mid-July to mid-Aug. M-Th 8pm, F-Sa 8pm, Su 6pm. Tickets $32-36, students $10.)

Santa Fe is also home to two of the U.S.'s largest **festivals.** In August, the nation's largest and most impressive **Indian Market** floods the plaza, as tribes from across the U.S. put up over 500 exhibits of fine arts and crafts. The **Southwestern Association on Indian Affairs** (983-5220) has more info (open M-F 9am-5pm). Don Diego De Vargas's peaceful reconquest of New Mexico in 1692 marked the end of the 12-year Pueblo Rebellion, now celebrated in the 3-day **Fiesta de Santa Fe** (988-7575). Held in early September, the celebration reaches its height with the burning of the 40 ft. *papier-mâché* **Zozobra,** "Old Man Gloom." Festivities include street dancing, processions, and political satires. Most events are free. The *New Mexican* publishes a guide and a schedule for the fiesta's events.

■ Near Santa Fe

Bandelier National Monument Bandelier, 40 mi. northwest of Santa Fe (take U.S. 285 to 502 W, then follow the signs), features some of the most amazing pueblos and cliff dwellings in the state, as well as 50 sq. mi. of dramatic mesas, ancient ruins (remains of stone houses and *kivas*, underground ceremonial chambers), and spectacular views of surrounding canyons. The most accessible, **Frijoles Canyon,** is the site of the **visitors center** (672-3861, ext. 518), open daily 8am-6pm (in spring and fall 9am-5:30pm; in winter 8am-4:30pm). From the visitors center, a self-guided 1hr. tour takes you through pueblo **cliff dwellings** near the visitors center. After the tour you can continue your hike by traversing an additional ½ mi. to the **ceremonial caves,** which offer an incredible view of the surrounding area. *(Park entrance $10 per vehicle, $5 per pedestrian; National Parks passports accepted.)* A 5 mi. hike along the **Falls Trail** takes you on a 700 ft. descent into the mouth of the canyon, past two waterfalls, to the Río Grande. A strenuous 2-day, 20 mi. hike leads from the visitors center to **Painted Cave,** decorated with over 50 Anasazi pictographs, then to the Río Grande. Free permits are required for backcountry hiking and camping; pick up a topographical map ($9) of the monument area at the visitors center. The 95-site **Juniper Campground,** ¼ mi. off Rte. 4 at the entrance to the monument, supplies the area's only camping (sites $10, with Golden Age passport $5; no reservations).

Pecos National Historical Park Located in the hill country 25 mi. southeast of Santa Fe on I-25 and Rte. 63, Pecos features ruins of a pueblo and a Spanish mission church. The small park includes an easy 1 mi. hike through various archaeological sites. Especially noteworthy are the renovated *kivas,* built after the Rebellion of 1680. Off-limits at other ruins, the *kivas* at Pecos are open to the public. *(Open daily 8am-6pm. Entrance $2 per person, $4 per car. National Parks passports accepted.)* The monument's **visitors center** (757-6032) has a small, informative museum and a 10min. film shown every 30min. *(Open M-Sa 10am-4pm, Su 1-5pm; in winter M-Sa 9:30am-4:30pm, Su 11am-5pm. Free with park entrance.)* The park is not accessible by public transportation. If you make it there, you can pitch a tent in the backcountry of the **Santa Fe National Forest,** 6 mi. north on Rte. 63 (see Santa Fe **Accommodations,** p. 672).

■ Taos

The many artists who now inhabit Taos are but the latest in a diverse series of settlers lured by the fertility and stark beauty of the Taos Valley region. First came the Native American tribes, whose pueblos still speckle the valley. In the 17th century, Spanish missionaries and farmers attempted to convert the Native Americans to Christianity while farming alongside them. The 20th century has seen the town invaded by artists captivated and inspired by Taos's untainted beauty, including Georgia O'Keeffe and R.C. Gorman. Aspiring artists still flock to the city, but recent trends indicate that the next generation of immigrants may be a mixed bag of pleasure-seekers and spiritualists who come to take advantage either of Taos's natural surroundings or its thriving

New Age culture. Each year, a growing number of hikers and skiers infest the nearby mountains, more rafters brave the nearby whitewater of the Río Grande, and more New Agers get the vibe drawing them to the desert.

PRACTICAL INFORMATION In town, **Rte. 68** becomes Paseo del Pueblo Sur. Drivers should park on Camino de la Placita, 1 block west of the plaza, or at myriad meters scattered on side streets. **Greyhound,** 1006 Paseo del Pueblo Sur (758-1144 or 800-231-2222; station open M-F 8:30am-6pm, Sa 9am-6:30pm), inside Dave's Cigarette Shop, sends two buses per day to Albuquerque (3hr., $22); Santa Fe (1½hr., $17); and Denver (8hr., $53). The **Chile Line** (751-2000) runs vans from Ranchos de Taos, south of town, up to the pueblo and back (50¢, all day $1; runs M-Sa 7am-10pm, Su 9am-6pm; Sept.-May M-Sa 7am-7pm, Su 9am-6pm). **Faust's Transportation** (758-3410) operates taxis daily 7am-9pm. Taos's **Chamber of Commerce,** 1139 Paseo del Pueblo Sur (758-3873 or 800-732-TAOS/8267), just south of town at the junction of Rte. 68 and Paseo del Cañon, distributes maps and tourist literature (open daily 9am-5pm). **Post Office:** 318 Paseo Del Pueblo Norte (758-2081), ¼ mi. north of the plaza (open M-F 8:30am-5pm). **ZIP code:** 87571. **Area code:** 505.

ACCOMMODATIONS AND CAMPGROUNDS The large **Abominable Snowmansion Hostel** (776-8298), in the village of Arroyo Seco, 9 mi. north of Taos, features nice rooms with huge common areas. (Dorm beds $13, non-members $16; private doubles $38/$45; teepees $13/$16. Reserve ahead for Christmas and spring break. Reception daily 8-10am and 5-10pm; in winter 4-10pm.) Fifteen miles south of Taos in Pilar (on Rte. 68), the cozy **Río Grande Gorge Hostel (HI-AYH)** (758-0090) rests above the Río Grande. Greyhound and airport shuttle buses between Santa Fe and Taos use the hostel as a flag stop. Kitchen facilities are available, as well as discounts on Río Grande rafting trips run by Far-Flung Adventures, which has its office next door. (Dorm beds $11, nonmembers $13.50. Geodesic domes (bungalows) for 2 $23, nonmembers $26; must use shared bath in hostel. Reception daily 5-9pm.) The **Sun God Lodge,** 919 Paseo del Pueblo Sur (758-3162), has sizeable rooms with Southwestern-style wooden furniture (singles $44-64; doubles $60-70). **Taos Valley RV Park,** 120 Estes Rd. (758-4469 or 800-999-7571), just off Paseo del Pueblo Sur, provides tent sites ($15-17 for 2 people) and full hookups ($24-26 for 2 people).

Camping around Taos is easy for those with a car. Up in the mountains on wooded Rte. 64, 20 mi. east of Taos, the **Kit Carson National Forest** operates three campgrounds: **Las Petacas** is free but has no drinking water; **La Sombra** and **Capulin,** farther down the same road, charge $6. Additionally, four free campgrounds line Rte. 150 north of town. **Backcountry camping** requires no permit in the forest. For more info, including maps of area campgrounds, contact the **forest service office,** 208 Cruz Alta Rd. (758-6200; open M-F 8am-4:30pm), or stop by their visitors center (open daily 9am-5pm), on Rte. 64 west of town.

FOOD Restaurants cluster around Taos Plaza and Bent St. Good possibilities include **The Brothers Two Café,** 115 McCarthy Plaza (758-4205), on the southeast corner of Taos Plaza, where breakfast is served all day (2 eggs, hash browns, and toast $2), as well as various hot and cold deli sandwiches ($5-6; open daily 7am-3:30pm). In the rear of **Amigo's Natural Foods,** 326 Paseo del Pueblo Sur (758-8493), lurks a small, holistic deli that offers such nutritionally correct dishes as tofu burgers ($4.50), as well as a huge juice bar. (Deli open M-Sa 9am-3pm, Su 11am-3pm; grocery open M-Sa 8:30am-7pm, Su 11am-5pm.) For a full meal, find your way to the **Apple Tree Restaurant,** 123 Bent St. (758-1900), inside an old adobe house 1 block north of the plaza, for delicious and imaginative New Mexican and Asian cuisine. Budget diners should come between 5:30 and 6:30pm, when entrees like chimayo chile-crusted scallops ($9) and seared duck breast salad ($10) are $3-4 off the regular prices. (Open M-Sa 11:30am-10pm and Su 10am-9pm.)

SIGHTS AND ACTIVITIES Taos comes in second only to Santa Fe as a mecca for New Mexican art. A well-chosen selection of early Taos paintings hangs at the **Harwood Foundation Museum**, 238 Ledoux St. (758-9826), off Camino de la Placita (open Tu-Sa 10am-5pm, Su noon-5pm; $4, under 12 free). Other galleries, ranging from high-quality operations of international renown to upscale curio shops, can be found in **Taos Plaza** and on **Kit Carson Rd.** A visit to the **Mabel Dodge Luhan House**, 240 Morada Lane (751-9686), provides a quiet retreat from the tourist-packed streets. ($2 donation suggested.) The salon's hostess once drew such luminaries as D.H. Lawrence, Greta Garbo, and Jean Toomer to Taos. The upstairs is occupied by a B&B, but tourists are free to wander around the first floor. The **Taos Arts Festival** celebrates local art in early October each year. In the tiny village of Ranchos de Taos, 4 mi. south of Taos Plaza, the **Mission of San Francisco de Asis** (758-2754) displays a "miraculous" painting that changes into a shadowy figure of Christ when the lights go out. Judge for yourself by watching a video of the miracle in the parish office, to your left as you're facing the church (video shown on the hr. and ½hr. M-F 9am-noon, and 1-4pm; Sa 9am-4pm; $2). Four miles north of Taos off Rte. 522, exhibits of Native American art including Pueblo jewelry, black-on-black pottery, and gorgeous Navajo rugs grace the **Millicent Rogers Museum**, 1504 Museum Rd. (758-2462; open daily 10am-5pm; $6, students and seniors $5, ages 6-16 $1).

Taos Pueblo, 3 mi. northwest of town (758-9593), remarkable for its pink-and-white adobe mission church and 5-story houses, is one of the last inhabited pueblos; many of the buildings are off-limits to visitors. *(Open daily 8am-5pm; in winter 9am-4pm. $4 per person, under 12 $1. Parking $6. Camera permit $10, video camera permit $20.)* For permission to sketch or paint, submit a written request 10 days before your visit to P.O. Box 1846, Taos 87571. Feast days are celebrated with beautiful tribal dances; **San Gerónimo's Feast Days** (Sept. 29-30, 1999) also feature a fair and races. The tribal office can supply you with schedules of dances and other info. Best known for its sparkling pottery molded from mica and clay, **Picuris Pueblo** (505-587-2519), 20 mi. south of Taos on Rte. 75 near Peñasco, is smaller, less touristed, and somewhat more accessible (open daily 9am-6pm). A free guide to Northern New Mexican Indian pueblos is available at the Taos Visitors Center.

The state's premier ski resort, **Taos Ski Valley** (776-2291, lodging info 800-776-1111, ski conditions 776-2916), about 15 mi. northeast of town on Rte. 150, offers powder conditions in bowl sections and short but steep downhill runs that rival those of Colorado. *(Lift tickets $40-42; equipment rental $12 per day.)* Reserve a room well in advance if you plan to come during the winter holiday season. There are also two smaller, more family-oriented ski areas near Taos: **Angel Fire** (505-377-6401 or 800-633-7463), Central Plaza and Hwy. 434, and **Eagle Nest** (800-494-9117). In summer, the nearly deserted ski valley area becomes a hiker's paradise (most trails begin from Rte. 150). Due to the town's prime location near the Río Grande, **river rafting** is very popular in Taos. **Far-Flung Adventures** (758-9072), next door to the Río Grande Gorge Hostel (see **Accommodations,** above), offers river trips ranging in length from ½-day ($38) to 3-day ($348). Reservations up to 6 weeks in advance are required for longer trips; call for details. (Open 7am-8pm; closed in winter.)

Taos hums with every New Age service on earth: vibrasound relaxation, drum therapy, harmony massage, and cranial therapy, just for starters. **Taos Drums** (800-424-DRUM/3786), 5 mi. south of the plaza on Rte. 68, features the world's largest collection of Native American drums (open M-Sa 9am-6pm, Su 11am-6pm). A bulletin board outside **Merlin's Garden,** 127 Bent St. (758-0985), lists favorite New Age pastimes such as drum therapy and massage (open M-Sa 10am-5:30pm, Su 11am-5pm).

■ Albuquerque

Ever since the Anasazi tribes settled here nearly 2000 years ago, visitors have treated Albuquerque as a stopover on the way to another destination. In search of the legendary seven cities of gold, the infamous Spaniard Coronado and his entourage camped here for the winter. Over the years, Spanish settlers, and later the United States government, routed major transportation lines through Albuquerque; Rte. 66 still splits the city in two. Travelers should linger long enough to enjoy the mellow neighborhood near the university, the adobe buildings surrounding the historic plaza, and the dramatic Sandía Mountains.

ORIENTATION AND PRACTICAL INFORMATION

The city divides into four quadrants: NE, NW, SE, SW. **Central Ave.** divides the north and south, and **I-25** is a rough division between east and west. The all-adobe campus of the **University of New Mexico (UNM)** spreads along Central Ave. from University Ave. to Carlisle St. **Old Town Plaza** lies between San Felipe, North Plaza, South Plaza, and Romero, off Central Ave.

Airport: Albuquerque International, 2200 Sunport Blvd. SE (842-4366), south of downtown. Take bus #50 from 5th St. and Central Ave, or pick it up along Yale Blvd. **Checkered Airport Express** (765-1234) shuttles into the city (around $10, for two people $16.50). Their booth at the airport is open 9:30am-11pm. A taxi downtown costs under $10, to Old Town $15.

Trains: Amtrak, 214 1st St. SW (842-9650 or 800-872-7245). 1 train per day to: Los Angeles (16hr., departs at 5:17pm, $54-98); Kansas City (17hr., departs at 1:26pm, $94-170); Santa Fe (1hr. to Lamy, departs at 1:26pm, $13-24; 15min. shuttle to Santa Fe, $14); and Flagstaff (5hr., departs at 5:17pm, $49-89). Reservations required. Open daily 9:30am-5:45pm.

Buses: Greyhound (243-4435 or 800-231-2222) and **TNM&O Coaches** (242-4998) run from 300 2nd St. SW, 3 blocks south of Central Ave. Buses go to: Santa Fe (1½hr., 4 per day, $11.30); Flagstaff (6hr., 4 per day, $44); Oklahoma City (12hr., 4 per day, $63); Denver (10hr., 5 per day, $61); Phoenix (10hr., 3 per day, $32); and Los Angeles (18hr.; 4 per day; $67, round-trip $125).

Public Transportation: Sun-Tran Transit, 601 Yale Blvd. SE (843-9200; open M-F 8am-5pm). Most buses run M-Sa 6am-6pm. Pick up maps at visitors centers, the transit office, or the main library. Fare 75¢, seniors and ages 5-18 25¢. Request free transfers from driver.

Taxis: Albuquerque Cab, 883-4888. $3.40 1st mi., $1.60 per additional mi.

Car Rental: Rent-a-Wreck, 500 Yale Blvd. SE (232-7552 or 800-247-9556). Cars with A/C from $20 per day with 150 free mi.; 20¢ per additional mi.; $120 per week. Insurance $11 per day, $70 per week. Must be 21 with credit card; under 25 surcharge $3 per day. Open daily 8am-5:30pm. Reservations recommended.

Bike Rental: Old Town Bicycles, 2209 Central Ave. NW (247-4926), several blocks from Old Town Plaza. Rents hybrid bikes for city use ($5 per hr., $16 overnight, $60 per week) and mountain bikes ($7 per hr., $20 overnight, $60 per week). Open M-F 9:30am-6pm, Sa 9:30am-5pm, Su noon-5pm. Credit card required for deposit. Reservations recommended on weekends.

Visitor Info: Albuquerque Convention and Visitors Bureau, 20 First Plaza, galleria level (800-284-2282). Free maps and the useful *The Art of Visiting Albuquerque.* Open M-F 8am-5pm. After hrs., call for recorded events info. **Old Town Visitors Center** (243-3215), at Plaza Don Luís on Romero NW across from the church, has tons of brochures and coupons for motels and Old Town shops. Open daily 9am-5pm, Nov.-Mar. 9:30am-4:30pm. **Info booth** at airport open daily 8:30am-8:30pm.

Help Lines: Rape Crisis Center, 1025 Hermosa SE (266-7711). Center open M-F 8am-noon and 1-5pm; 24hr. hotline. **Gay and Lesbian Information Line,** Common Bond, P.O. Box 26836, Albuquerque 87125 (891-3647). 24hr. recorded info.

Internet Access: UNM Zimmerman Library, at the heart of campus. Open fall and spring semesters M-Th 8am-midnight, F 8am-9pm, Sa 9am-6pm, Su 10am-midnight; in summer M-Th 8am-9pm, F 8am-5pm, Sa 10am-5pm, Su 10am-9pm.

Post Office: 1135 Broadway NE, at Mountain (245-9469). Open M-F 7:30am-6pm. **ZIP code:** 87104. **Area code:** 505.

ACCOMMODATIONS AND CAMPING

Cheap motels line **Central Ave.,** even near downtown, but here *one must evaluate the motel carefully before paying.* Avoid places that look decrepit or seem to house transients; when checking a room for cleanliness, also notice whether there's a chain or bolt for the door. At night, look for bright, outdoor lighting. Consider spending a bit more money here for safety's sake. During the October **balloon festival** (see **Sights,** below), rooms are scarce; call ahead for reservations.

Route 66 Youth Hostel, 1012 Central Ave. SW (247-1813), at 10th St. Dorm beds in sparse, clean rooms, as well as beautiful, newly renovated private rooms. Well-stocked kitchen and free food. Bunks $13 with any hostel card. Private singles with shared bath $18, huge doubles $24. Linen $1. Key deposit $5. Reception daily 7-10:30am and 4-11pm. Check-out 10:30am. Chores required.

Sandía Mountain Hostel, 12234 Hwy. 14 N (281-4117), in nearby Cedar Crest. A laid-back, quiet hostel convenient to the Sandía hiking trails. Beds in clean and spacious dorms $10; private rooms $25-30.

Crossroads Motel, 1001 Central Ave NE (242-2757). Large, bright rooms, some with fridge, all with A/C, cable, and phone. Singles $29; doubles $36.

University Lodge, 3711 Central Ave. NE (266-7663). About a 15min. walk from campus, in the historic and cool Nob Hill district. Unusually cozy rooms. Summer singles $33, in winter $30; doubles $40/$30.

Aztec Motel, 3821 Central Ave. NE (254-1742). Founded in 1931, this is the only original Rte. 66 motel still in operation. It's easy to spot—it's the only motel on Central Ave. with an exterior decorated with religious icons. Some rooms have kitchenettes, but all could use a fresh coat of paint. Singles $22; 1-bed doubles $24.

Albuquerque Central KOA, 12400 Skyline Rd. (800-562-7781). Take I-40 to Exit 167 and follow the signs. Tent sites $22 for 2 people, full hookup $30.

Coronado State Monument Campground (867-5589), about 15 mi. north of Albuquerque. Take I-25 to Exit 241 and follow the signs. A unique camping experience near the haunting Sandía Mountains. Adobe shelters on the sites are a respite from the heat. Toilets, showers, and drinking water available. Sites $7, with hookup $11. No reservations. Office open daily 7am-10pm.

FOOD

The area around **UNM** is the best bet for tasty, inexpensive eateries. A bit farther east, the hip neighborhood of **Nob Hill** offers some more offbeat options.

El Patio, 142 Harvard St. SE (268-4245). A softly strumming guitarist beckons passersby to sit, relax, and down a few enchiladas. Mexican plates $5-8, including lots of veggie options. Open M-Th 11am-9pm, F-Sa 11am-9:30pm, Su noon-9pm.

Best Price Books and Coffee, 1800 Central Ave. SE (842-0624). Pastries ($2), sandwiches ($3-6), and gourmet burritos ($3-4), in a comfortable secondhand book-shop-*cum*-cafe. 12 different kinds of coffee ($1). Open daily 5am-11pm.

Olympia Café, 2210 Central Ave. SE (266-5222). Gyros and souvlaki abound ($4), as well as vegetarian dishes, combination platters ($5-8), and American food for the less adventurous. Open M-F 11am-10pm, Sa noon-10pm.

Model Pharmacy, 3636 Monte Viste NE (255-8686), at the intersection of Lomas, Carlisle, and Monte Vista, 10min. from UNM. This old-fashioned soda fountain prepares egg creams ($2.25), sandwiches ($6), and homemade cobblers ($3). Open M-Sa 9am-6pm.

Zane Graze, 308 San Felipe (243-4377), a pleasant cafe near the plaza, serves up sesame chicken salad in a pita ($6), bagels with cream cheese ($1.75), and fresh Taos Cow ice cream ($2). Open Sa-Th 9:30am-5pm, F 9:30am-8pm.

SIGHTS

Just north of Central Ave. and east of Rio Grande Blvd., 1 mi. south of I-40, Albuquerque's **Old Town** clusters around a Spanish plaza. On the north side of the plaza, the adobe **San Felipe de Neri** church dates back to the end of the eighteenth century. *(Open daily 9am-5pm; Su mass in English 7am and 10:15am, in Spanish 8:30am.)* The city's most unusual museum is the **Rattlesnake Museum,** 202 San Felipe NW (242-6569), south of the plaza, housing the world's most extensive display of rattlesnakes. *(Open* *daily 10am-6pm; $3, students $2, children $1.*) Pay close attention so you know what *not* to step on while hiking. New Mexican art and local history are displayed at the **Albuquerque Museum,** 2000 Mountain Rd. NW (242-4600; open Tu-Su 9am-5pm; free; wheelchair access). Spike and Alberta, two statuesque dinosaurs, greet tourists outside the **New Mexico Museum of Natural History and Science,** 1801 Mountain Rd. NW (841-2800). *(Open daily 9am-5pm. $5, students and seniors $4, children $2; combination Dynamax theater ticket $8/$6/$3. Wheelchair access.)* Inside the museum, exhibits present the geological and evolutionary history of New Mexico.

The **Sandía Mountains,** on Albuquerque's east side in the Cíbola National Forest, were named by the Spanish for the pink color they turn at sunset (*sandía* means watermelon). Take Tramway Rd. from I-25 (Exit 234) or Tramway Blvd. from I-40 (Exit 167) to the **Sandía Peak Aerial Tramway** (recorded info 856-6419), the world's longest aerial tramway. *(30min. trip, times vary. $14, children $10. Tramway open daily in summer 9am-10pm; in winter 9am-8pm, weather permitting.)* The thrilling ride to the top of **Sandía Crest** allows you to ascend the west face of Sandía Peak and gaze out over Albuquerque, the Río Grande Valley, and western New Mexico; the ascent is especially striking at sunset.

Sandía Peak can also be reached by a number of dazzling hikes. Follow the signs from Tramway Blvd. to the **La Luz trailhead,** about 1 mi. from the road to the tramway (ranger station 281-3304). The hike takes 3-5hr., but call first to make sure the trail isn't blocked by snow, which can happen even in early summer. Those desiring something a bit less strenuous can follow a 58 mi. **driving loop** through the **Sandía Ski Area.** Take I-40 E through Tijeras Canyon (about 17 mi. from downtown), turn north onto Rte. 14, and turn west onto Rte. 536 at San Antonio. The road winds through lovely forests of piñon and ponderosa pines, oaks, and spruce, then climbs sharply to the summit of **Sandía Crest,** where a dazzling 1½ mi. **ridge hike** to **Sandía Peak** (10,678 ft.) begins. Rangers lead guided hikes through the **Cíbola National Forest;** you'll need reservations (242-9052) for the challenging winter snowshoe hikes. During the summer, some hiking and mountain biking trails are open to the public only during specific hours (usually Th-Su 10am-4pm); call for details.

Located at the edge of suburbia on Albuquerque's west side, **Petroglyph National Monument** (899-0205) features more than 15,000 images etched into lava rocks between 1300 and 1650 by Pueblo Indians and Spanish settlers. Short paved trails access small sections of the park's **Boca Negra Canyon,** but most of the area can be explored only by off-trail hiking—ask rangers for suggested routes. *(Park open M-F 8am-5pm. $1, Sa-Su and holidays $2; National Parks passports accepted.)* Take I-40 to Coors Rd. N. (Exit 155) or Unser Ave. (Exit 154), and follow the signs to the park. Alternatively, take bus #9 from 6th and Silver to Coors Blvd., a few blocks away.

The **Albuquerque BioPark** (764-6200), sporting an **aquarium,** a **botanic garden** (764-6200), both at 2601 Central Ave. SW, and a **zoo,** 903 10th St. SW, has recently burst onto the scene. *(All open in summer M-F 9am-5pm, Sa-Su 9am-6pm. Aquarium and zoo tickets $4.50, seniors and children $2.50; zoo tickets $4.25/$2.25. All with wheelchair access.)* The aquarium showcases marine life from the Gulf of Mexico, with the obligatory shark exhibit, while the botanic garden features desert plants, Mediterranean gardens, and a conservatory housed in a huge glass pyramid. The zoo's captives range from Asian elephants to kangaroos.

The **National Atomic Museum,** 20358 Wyoming Blvd. (284-3243), on Kirtland Air Force Base, tells the story of Little Boy and Fat Man, the atomic bombs dropped on Hiroshima and Nagasaki. *(Museum open daily 9am-5pm. Free.)* *Ten Seconds that Shook the World,* a 1hr. documentary on the making of the atomic bomb, shows four times daily. The Air Force base is a few mi. southeast of downtown, east of I-25. Ask at the visitor control gate on Wyoming Blvd. for a museum visitor's pass; you'll need *several* forms of ID (driver's license, car registration, and proof of car insurance).

ENTERTAINMENT AND NIGHTLIFE

The cool air of October carries the **balloon festival** to Albuquerque. Early in the month (Oct. 3-11, 1999), hundreds of aeronauts take flight in beautifully colored hot-

THE SOUTHWEST

air balloons. Even the most yellow of landlubbers will enjoy the week's barbecues and musical events. The presence of a sizeable university in Albuquerque is a boon for the nightlife scene. Check flyers posted around the university area for live music shows, or pick up a copy of *Alibi*, the local free weekly. Urban music lovers hear rock, blues, and reggae bands at **Dingo Bar,** 313 Gold St. SW (246-0663), where drafts run $2-4 (cover $2-8 F-Sa after 8pm depending on the band; open daily 4pm-2am). The **"Downtown Bar Crawl"** special ticket gets you into the Dingo and five other bars on Central Ave. for one $5 cover charge; pay at any of the bars. Dig in your spurs at **Caravan East,** 7605 Central Ave. NE (265-7877), "where there is always a dancin' partner" and live music. (Cover F-Sa $3. Drink specials for women daily 4:30-7:30pm. Open daily 4:30pm-2am.)

■ Near Albuquerque: Madrid and Cerrillos

The scenic and historic **Turquoise Trail** extends along Rte. 14 between Albuquerque and Sante Fe. Miners once harvested copious amounts of turquoise, gold, silver, and coal from the surrounding area, but the towns suffered greatly during the Depression. Founded in 1914 as a coal mining town, **Madrid** (MA-drid), 40 mi. from Albuquerque along Rte. 14, was a ghost town until the 1970s, when artists began to resettle the area. The town is now home to many artists, refugees from the 60s hippie revolution, and craft-makers who sell their Native-American-style goods in shops lining the highway. **Java Junction** (438-2772), smack in the middle of town, offers lattes ($2.35), mochas ($2.85), and the cheapest grub around (tamales $1.50), as well as a selection of the wackiest coffee-themed t-shirts anywhere ($18; open 7:30am-6pm).

Three miles farther along the road to Santa Fe, **Cerrillos** (se-REE-yos) supported as many as 21 saloons during its peak in the 1880s. Miners extracted gold, silver, lead, and turquoise from the surrounding hills, but these riches couldn't prevent the Depression from hitting Cerrillos hard. More recently, a number of film directors have taken advantage of the town's "Old West" look—*Shoot Out* (1972) and *Outrageous Fortune* (1987) were both filmed here. The **Casa Grande Trading Post** (438-3008), a 21-room adobe house, contains a haphazard collection of artifacts from Cerrillos's booming days, including old mining tools, pottery, and horseshoes in all shapes and sizes ($1). The gift shop is a rockhound's delight, with a gorgeous variety of semi-precious stones for sale ($1-10; museum and shop open daily 8am-8pm). The **What Not Shop,** on 1st St., sells turquoise jewelry, antique knickknacks, and political memorabilia—in other words, junk (open Sa-Th 10am-5pm, F 1-5pm).

■ Gallup

Gallup, located at the intersection of **I-40** and **U.S. 666,** isn't anyone's idea of a fantasy vacation destination; however, it is a convenient base for exploring northeastern Arizona and northwestern New Mexico. Nearby attractions include: **Petrified Forest National Park** (see p. 659), the **Navajo Reservation** (see p. 654), **Chaco Culture National Park** (see p. 683), and **El Morro National Monument** (see below). Closer to town, the **Inter-Tribal Indian Ceremonial,** held the second weekend in August at **Red Rock State Park** (take I-40 to Exit 26), features 4 days of Indian dances, rodeos, and art exhibits. (For more info or tickets call 863-3896 or 800-233-4528. Reserved seating $12, general admission $10.) The park's **museum** (863-1337) explores the ancient Anasazi past and surveys the lives of members of the modern-day Navajo, Hopi, and Zuni tribes (open M-Tu 8am-4:30pm, W-F 8am-6pm, Sa-Su 10am-6pm; free). For a tough hike or an even tougher mountain bike ride, tackle **Mt. Taylor** (11,301 ft.), just north of nearby Grants. (Open M-F 8am-5pm.) From Gallup, take I-40 E to Grants (about 20 mi.), then U.S. 547 N to U.S. 193; turn left onto a dirt road and drive 4 mi. to the parking area. The Mt. Taylor **ranger station** (505-287-8833) has more info.

Due to its proximity to both the Navajo and Zuni Reservations, which lie about 20 mi. north and south of the city, respectively, Gallup seems to house more Indian arts shops per square mile than anywhere else in New Mexico. Although much of the jewelry and pottery sold in Gallup is authentic, some of it is imported. **Richardson's Trading Post,** 222 W. Rte. 66 (722-4762), is among the more reputable dealers, but prices for the vast selection of jewelry can run pretty high (open M-Sa 9am-6pm). You might have a greater chance of finding something affordable at **Shush Yaz Trading Company,** 1304 W. Lincoln St. (722-0130; open M-Sa 9am-6pm).

Old Rte. 66, which runs parallel to I-40 through downtown, is lined with cheap motels. The **Colonial Motel,** 1007 W. Coal Ave. (863-6821), a bit west of downtown, rents large rooms with cable TV (singles $21; doubles $25). The **Blue Spruce Lodge,** 1119 E. Rte. 66 (863-5211), has clean, largish rooms at a very good value (singles $29; doubles $32). You can pitch a tent in the shadow of red sandstone cliffs at **Red Rock State Park Campground** (505-722-3829), which offers over 50 sites and a convenience store. From I-40, take Exit 26 and follow the signs. (Sites $8, RV hookup $12.)

In addition to the usual fast-food suspects, a number of diners and cafes line both sides of I-40. **Earl's,** 1409 E. Rte. 66 (863-4201), offers quick service to crowds of local families in its big dining rooms. (Omelette $5, breakfast burrito $6. Open Su-Th 7am-9:30pm, F-Sa 7am-10pm.) **Ranch Kitchen,** 3001 W. Rte. 66 (722-2537), serves up tasty country cooking and barbecue in a wood-beamed dining room (3 pancakes $3.35, barbecue chicken $8; open daily 7am-10pm).

Greyhound, 255 E. Rte. 66 (863-3761), runs to Flagstaff (4hr., 4 per day, $35) and Albuquerque (2½hr., 4 per day, $20). The **visitors center** is at 701 Montoya Blvd. (863-4909), just off Rte. 66 (open daily 8am-5pm). **Post Office:** 500 S. 2nd St. (722-5265; open M-F 8:30am-5pm, Sa 10am-1:30pm). **ZIP code:** 87301. **Area code:** 505.

■ Near Gallup

Chaco Culture National Historical Park

Sun-scorched **Chaco Canyon** (CHAH-co) served as the first great settlement of the Anasazi people. The ruins here, which date from the 9th century, are among the best-preserved in the Southwest. **Pueblo Bonito,** the canyon's largest pueblo, was once 4 stories high and contained more than 600 rooms. Nearby **Chetro Ketl** houses one of the canyon's largest *kivas,* a prayer room used in religious rituals. The largest pueblos are accessible from the main road, but **backcountry hiking trails** lead to a number of other ruins; snag a free **backcountry permit** from the visitors center before heading off.

Chaco Culture National Historical Park lies 92 mi. northeast of Gallup. If you're coming from the north, take Rte. 44 to County Rd. 7900 (3 mi. east of **Nageezi**); from the south, take Rte. 9 from Crownpoint to the turn-off for the park. At the turn of the century, it took a government archaeologist almost a year to get here from Washington, D.C.—not much has changed. From the highways, a very unimproved 20 mi. dirt road leads to the park; this part alone may take 1hr. *Remember that there is no gas in the park, and gas stations on the reservation are few and far between.*

The **visitors center,** at the east end of the park, has an excellent **museum** (505-786-7014) that exhibits Anasazi art and architecture. Stock up on water here. (Open daily 8am-6pm. $8 per vehicle.) No food is available at the park. **Camping** at Chaco costs $10 per site; register at the campground. Arrive by 11am; there are only 64 sites.

El Morro National Monument

While traveling through what is now New Mexico, Native Americans, Spanish conquistadores, and Anglo pioneers all left their marks on a giant boulder strategically located next to a spring. **Inscription Rock,** an unassuming name for such a large sandstone promontory, is now part of El Morro National Monument, which sits just west of the Continental Divide on Rte. 53, 12 mi. southeast of the Navajo town of Ramah. A ½ mi. self-guided loop trail winds past the spring and the boulder, which contains more than 100 inscriptions in several lan-

684 ■ NEW MEXICO

guages, including English, Spanish, and Navajo. A longer trail continues on past the ruins of two Anasazi pueblos. The **visitors center** (505-783-4226) includes a small museum, as well as several dire warnings against emulating the graffiti of old (open daily 9am-7pm; off-season 9am-5pm). Trails close 1hr. before the visitors center.

■ Truth or Consequences

In 1950, the popular radio game show "Truth or Consequences" sought to celebrate its tenth anniversary by renaming a small town in its honor. Several towns volunteered for the privilege, but Hot Springs, NM won. As its maiden name suggests, T or C was a tourist attraction prior to the publicity stunt: its natural hot springs were first enjoyed by the Apache. Now, wanderers from all over the country find themselves extending their stays in T or C. Maybe it's something in the water.

T or C's **mineral baths** are the town's main attraction. Locals tout the therapeutic properties of the water, claiming that it heals everything from blisters to sunburn. The three co-ed tubs (bathing suits must be worn) at the **Riverbend Hostel** are accessible to the public for $5 per day, including dips in the adjacent Rio Grande to cool off (baths run daily 7:30-10am and 7:30-10pm). The private baths at the **Charles Motel's spa** cost $3 for guests and $4 for non-guests (open daily 8am-9pm); the spa also offers a variety of other New Age-y services, from reflexology to ear candling. A few miles northeast of town, **Elephant Butte Lake** offers boating, beaches, and hiking trails.

Approximately 45min. north of T or C on I-25, the **Bosque del Apache Wildlife Refuge** (505-835-1828) is a favorite spot of migrating birds in winter, including cranes, eagles, and snow geese. (Park open until sunset. Entrance fee $3.) Things are quieter in the summer, but you can still see deer, coyote, porcupines, roadrunners, and snakes. A surprising number of animals can be observed from the **15 mi. driving loop,** but the park also offers a number of short **hiking trails.** Pick up a map at the visitors center (open M-F 7:30am-4pm, Sa-Su 8am-4:30pm).

On the banks of the Rio Grande, the tranquil **Riverbend Hot Springs Hostel (HI-AYH),** 100 Austin St. (894-6183), offers an oasis to weary travelers from around the world; prices include unlimited use of the mineral baths. (Teepees $11; dorm beds $12; private rooms $20-27. Kitchen and laundry facilities.) More upscale, but still affordable, accommodations can be found at the **Charles Motel,** 601 Broadway (894-7154), which also has mineral baths on the premises. The adobe rooms are large and bright, and most have kitchens (singles $35; doubles $45). **Campsites** at the nearby **Elephant Butte Lake State Park** have access to restrooms and cold showers (primitive sites $6, developed sites $7, with electricity $11). The popular **La Cocina,** 280 N. Date St. (894-6499), serves up huge portions of Mexican and New Mexican food, including free chips and salsa (burritos around $3, combination plates $6; open daily 10:30am-10pm). Find a decent selection of **groceries** at Bullock's, at the intersection of Broadway and Post (open M-Sa 7:30am-8pm, Su 8am-7pm).

T or C sits approximately 150 mi. south of Albuquerque on I-25. **Greyhound,** in cooperation with TNM&O coaches (894-3649), runs two buses daily from Albuquerque (3 hr., $31.50). The **tourist office,** 201 S. Foch St. (800-831-9487), is only too pleased to make suggestions about local sights (open M-F 9am-5pm, Sa 9am-1pm; closed Sa off-season). **Post Office:** 300 Main St., in the middle of town (open M-F 9am-3pm), or 1507 N. Date St. (open 8:30am-5:30pm). **ZIP code:** 87901. **Area code:** 505.

■ Ghost Towns Near Truth or Consequences

Lake Valley The former mining town of Lake Valley is one of New Mexico's only remaining **ghost towns.** The sole inhabitants today are rabbits and rattlesnakes, and the only sound is the metal Conoco sign creaking in the breeze. Lake Valley saw its heyday in the 1880s, reaching a population of around 1000 during its peak period of silver ore production. When silver was devalued in the late 1880s, however, the town began to decline. The train tracks were taken up in 1934, and many buildings were dismantled around the same time. The town is about 15 mi. south of Hillsboro on Rte. 27; look for the **adobe schoolhouse** on the left. Leaflets for the **walking tour** can be picked up at the schoolhouse, which also contains shards of pottery and other artifacts salvaged from the ruins of the town. The path winds around past deserted residences to the former train depot. Many of the buildings are on private property—pay attention to the "No Trespassing" signs.

Hillsboro This nearby community makes a good lunch stop. Although Hillsboro also calls itself a ghost town, it has about 100 residents, many of whom are artists. You can observe their work in the various shops that line the main street. The ruins of the **old jail and courthouse** are still standing; to find them, follow the dirt road that leads up the hill opposite the post office. There's no tourist office, but the **Hillsboro General Store and Country Café** serves as a decent substitute; the owner knows everything about the town and everyone in it. Decent Mexican and New Mexican food is served at low prices; the $4.25 green chile and bacon grilled cheese is a thoroughly Southwestern combination. (Open M-F and Su 8am-3pm, Sa 8am-3pm and 6-8pm.) Hillsboro wakes up every Labor Day weekend for the **Apple Festival,** during which vendors from all over New Mexico gather to sell apple pies and arts and crafts.

■ Gila Cliff Dwellings and Silver City

The mysterious **Gila Cliff Dwellings National Monument** preserves over 40 stone and timber rooms carved into the cliff's natural caves by the Mogollon tribe of Native Americans during the late 1200s. (Dwellings open daily 8am-6pm, off-season 8am-5pm. **Entrance fee** $3, under 8 free. Golden Eagle passports accepted.) Ten to 15 families lived here for about 20 years, farming on the mesa top and along the river. During the early 1300s, however, the Mogollon abandoned their homes for reasons unknown to archaeologists today, leaving the dwellings as their only trace. The **visitors center** (536-9461), at the end of Rte. 15, shows an informative film and sells various maps of the forest ($3-5), as well as a brochure describing the trail to the dwellings (50¢; open daily 8am-5pm; off-season 8am-4pm). The picturesque 1 mi. round-trip **hike** to the dwellings begins 1 mi. up the road by the Lower Scorpion campground. Right by the trailhead, the free Lower and Upper Scorpion **campgrounds,** with flush toilets and running water, operate on a first come, first served basis. The surrounding **Gila National Forest** encompasses hundreds of miles of hiking trails, as well as **free backcountry camping.** Many trails start at the two corrals on the road to the cliff dwellings; ask rangers for hiking suggestions. To reach the monument, take Rte. 15 from Silver City, a gorgeous drive that winds through the mountains to the canyon of the Gila River (44 mi., 1½hr.; road open daily late May to early Sept. 8am-6pm; in winter 9am-4pm). *During the winter, call ahead for road conditions before attempting the drive.* If you're coming from Truth or Consequences, take Rte. 152 in San Lorenzo to Rte. 35, then head north on Rte. 15. This route is somewhat less steep, just as beautiful, and takes about the same amount of time.

Beds and food await in **Silver City,** a good base for a trip to the monument, 60 mi. west of Truth or Consequences on Rte. 152. Squeaky-clean **Carter House (HI-AYH),** 101 N. Cooper St. (388-5485), has separate men's and women's dorms, a kitchen, laundry facilities, and a huge wraparound porch; a B&B occupies the upstairs. To find the hostel, follow the signs to the historical district, or take Broadway up the hill and turn left on Cooper—Carter's is just to the left of the courthouse. ($12.50, nonmembers $15.50; B&B singles $53-68; doubles $60-71. Check-in 8-10am and 4-9pm.) The **Palace Hotel,** 106 W. Broadway (388-1811), has beautiful antique rooms (doubles $29.50-55; reservations recommended). At the **Higher Grounds** coffeehouse, on the corner of Bullard and Kelly, the food sounds light, but the portions are huge. Try the sesame peanut pasta ($4.75) or the $5.50 curried chicken sandwich. (Open daily 10am-10pm.) **Vicki's Downtown Deli,** 107 W. Yankie St. (388-5430), serves authentic

New York City Reubens—but with chips and salsa ($5.25). Dinner specials run $7-10 (open M 11am-4pm, Tu-Th 11am-7pm, F-Sa 11am-8:30pm).

Bookstores and antique shops cluster on Bullard and Broadway in the historical part of town. The **Silver City Museum,** 312 W. Broadway (538-5921), houses exhibits on the history of the town and unusual collections of local residents' treasure troves, including one man's post-WWII neckties, another couple's buttons, and the curator's Def Leppard paraphernalia (open Tu-F 9am-4:30pm, Sa-Su 10am-4pm; free). The **New Mexico Cowboy Poetry Gathering** (538-5921) convenes in Silver City every August.

Silver Stage Lines (388-2586 or 800-522-0162) has bus service twice daily to Silver City from the El Paso airport (round-trip $50, home pick-up $2 extra). **Las Cruces Shuttle Service** (800-288-1784) offers daily trips between Silver City and Deming (4 per day, $15); Las Cruces (4 per day, $25); and El Paso (3 per day, $32). Both companies pick up passengers from **Schadel's Bakery,** 212 N. Bullard St. The **Chamber of Commerce,** 1103 N. Hudson St. (538-3785), offers helpful advice about what to see and what not to see (open M-Sa 9am-5pm, in summer also Su noon-5pm). **Post Office:** 500 N. Hudson St. (open M-F 8:30am-5pm, Sa 10am-noon). **ZIP code:** 88061. Gila's and Silver City's **area code:** 505.

■ White Sands

The giant sandbox of **White Sands National Monument,** on Rte. 70 (15 mi. southwest of Alamogordo and 52 mi. northeast of Las Cruces), contains the world's largest gypsum sand dunes (300 sq. mi.). Situated in the Tularosa Basin between the Sacramento and San Andres mountains, the dunes were formed when rainwater dissolved gypsum in a nearby mountain, collecting in the basin's Lake Lucero. As desert heat evaporated the lake, the gypsum crystals were left behind and eventually formed the continually growing sand dunes. Trekking or just rolling through the dunes provides hours of mindless fun or mindful soul-searching; the brilliantly white sand is particularly awe-inspiring at sunset. Hiking possibilities include the **Big Dune Trail,** a 1 mi. nature trail adorned with plaques describing the unique fauna and flora of the dunes; and the **Alkali Flat Trail,** a backcountry hike to a dry lake bed where gypsum sand is formed (4.6 mi., 4hr.; ask at the visitors center for a topographical map before starting out). Always take plenty of water for even a short hike. Cars can explore the **Dunes Drive,** a paved road that leads 8 mi. into the heart of the dunes (open 8am-10pm; off-season 8am-sunset; $3 per adult; wheelchair access). Summer evening events include ranger-led sunset strolls (7pm) and lectures (8:30pm). Ask about special programs for full moon nights, when the park is open until midnight. The basin is also home to a missile test range—duck if you hear a sharp whistle—and the **Trinity Site,** 50 mi. north of White Sands, where the world's first atomic bomb was detonated in July 1945 (open to visitors on the 1st weekends of Apr. and Oct.).

The **Space Center** (437-2840 or 800-545-4021), 2 mi. northeast of U.S. 54, brings the great beyond down to earth with a museum, planetarium, OmniMax theater, and laser light show. (Open daily 9am-5pm. Museum $2.50, seniors and ages 6-12 $2; OmniMax film $5.50/$3.50.)

You'll find the **White Sands Visitors Center,** P.O. Box 1086, Holloman AFB 88330 (479-6124), as you enter the park from Rte. 70 (open 8am-7pm; mid-Aug.-late May 8am-5pm). To use the park's **backcountry campsites,** register at the park entrance (free with park admission). More free backcountry camping can be found at **Lincoln National Forest** (434-7200), 13 mi. to the east. **Aguirre Springs** (525-4300), 30 mi. to the west, doesn't charge for camping, but you must pay $3 to enter. For info, contact the **Forest Supervisor,** Lincoln National Forest, 1101 New York Ave., Alamogordo 88310. **Oliver Lee Memorial State Park** (437-8284), 10 mi. south of Alamogordo on U.S. 54, then 5 mi. east on Dog Canyon Rd., has a campground at the canyon mouth on the west face of the Sacramento Mountains. (Sites $7, with hookup $11. Visitors center open daily 9am-4pm. Park entrance fee $3 per vehicle.)

The Truth Is Out There

In July 1947, an alien spacecraft reportedly plummeted to the earth near the dusty town of **Roswell,** 76 mi. north of Carlsbad (from Albuquerque, head 89 mi. south on I-25 to San Antonio, then 153 mi. east on U.S. 380). The official Army press release reported that the military had recovered pieces of some form of "flying saucer," but a retraction arrived the next day—the mysterious wreckage, the brass claimed, was actually a harmless weather balloon. Everyone admits that *something* crashed in the desert northwest of Roswell on that fateful night some 50 years ago. Was the initial Army admission just a poor choice of words by some PR hack, or is Roswell the one crack in an elaborate cover-up engineered by shadowy men in black and their Pentagon bosses?

With only-in-America gusto, media attention and TV's *The X-Files* have helped catapult a growing lunatic fringe into the believing ranks. During the first week of July, the **UFO Festival** commemorates the anniversary of the alleged encounter, drawing thousands for live music, an alien costume contest, and a 5K "Alien Chase" race. With a plastic flying saucer above its diminutive storefront, the super-popular **International UFO Museum and Research Center,** 114 N. Main St. (505-625-9495), has invented some novel ways to cash in on the alienophile hysteria. *(Open daily 10am-5pm; in summer 9am-5pm. Free. Audio tour $3.)* Some remain skeptical of its scholarly credentials, but the museum's backers say the reading rooms and archives are academically legitimate. The center houses perhaps the only **espresso bar** in southeastern New Mexico, plus a gift shop full of items like "Crash in Roswell Tonight" bumper stickers and alien-shaped wall clocks. No pilgrimage would be complete without a trip to the arid, sun-scorched crash site itself, the 24 sq. mi. **Hobb Corn Ranch** (505-623-4043), 20 mi. north of Roswell on U.S. 285. A sign near the entrance greets the faithful: this "universal sacred site" is dedicated "to the beings who met their destinies near Roswell, New Mexico, July 1947." For $15 (under 14 free), the owners will escort the curious 8 mi. to the low butte where the saucer allegedly met *its* destiny amid dust devils and parched cacti (by appt. only; call 800-623-8104 10am-5pm).

The nearest hostel is the amazing **High Desert Hostel Ranch** (505-648-4007), in the hamlet of **Oscuro,** about 1hr. north of the park. This working adobe ranch comes complete with chickens, cows, orchard, and organic vegetable garden. Kitchen privileges include any food you want, and the large common room is stocked with games and books. Oscuro is a flag stop on the Greyhound route from El Paso to Albuquerque ($25 one-way from either city); call ahead, and the owner will pick you up *gratis* from the bus stop. Driving, the hostel is about 1 mi. down a dirt road from U.S. 54—follow the signs. (Free laundry. Dorm beds $14; private doubles $27; triples $32. Reserve private rooms by sending a check to P.O. Box 798, Carrizozo, NM 88301.) Closer to White Sands, the town of **Alamogordo** has an extensive motel selection, most of which line White Sands Blvd. The bright pink **Western Motel,** 1101 S. White Sands Blvd. (437-2922), has unusually bright, pleasant rooms with cable TV and A/C (singles $27; doubles $33). **All-American Inn,** 508 S. White Sands Blvd. (437-1850), is clean, has a pool, and is adorned with "Support Our Troops" bumper stickers. All rooms have A/C and coffee pots. (Singles $28; doubles $32-36.) **Area code: 505.**

■ Carlsbad Caverns

Imagine the surprise of the first Europeans to wander through southeastern New Mexico when 250,000 bats appeared at dusk, seemingly out of nowhere. The swarm of winged mammals led to the discovery of the Carlsbad Caverns at the turn of the century, when curious frontiersmen tracked the bats to their home. Once there, miners mapped the cave in search of bat manure (guano), an excellent fertilizer. By 1923, colonies of tourists had begun clinging to the walls of this desolate attraction. **Carlsbad Caverns National Park** marks one of the world's largest and oldest cave systems, and even the most jaded spelunker will be struck by the unusual geologic creations.

PRACTICAL INFORMATION The closest town to the park is **White's City,** a tiny tourist trap on U.S. 62/180, 20 mi. southeast of Carlsbad, 6 mi. from the park visitors center. Flash floods occasionally close the roads, so call ahead to the visitors center. **El Paso, TX** (see p. 546) is the nearest major city, 150 mi. to the west past **Guadalupe Mountains National Park** (see p. 545), which is 35 mi. southwest of White's City. **Greyhound,** in cooperation with **TNM&O Coaches** (887-1108), runs two buses per day to White's City from El Paso ($27) or Carlsbad (20min., $6). The **Carlsbad Caverns Visitors Center** (785-2232) has replaced dung-mining with the more modern concessions of a gift shop and snack bar (open daily 8am-7pm; late Aug. to May 8am-5:30pm). White's City's **post office:** 23 Carlsbad Caverns Hwy. (785-2220), next to the Best Western gift shop (open M-F 8am-noon and 12:30-4:30pm, Sa 8am-noon). **ZIP code:** 88268. **Area code:** 505.

ACCOMMODATIONS AND CAMPGROUNDS Drive 20 mi. north to **Carlsbad** to find a plethora of cheap motels. **Lorlodge Motel,** 2019 S. Canal St. (887-1171), has clean, A/C rooms, many with microwave and fridge (singles $29; doubles $37). Even less expensive motels line S. Canal St. (U.S. 285), but it's always a good idea to see the room before you pay. The **White's City Resort RV Park** (785-2291 or 800-CAVERNS/228-3767), just outside the park entrance, provides water, showers, restrooms, and a pool (tent sites or full hookup $20 for up to six people; register in the Best Western lobby). **Backcountry camping** is free in the park; get a permit at the visitors center (for more nearby camping, see **Guadalupe Mountains National Park, TX,** on p. 545).

SIGHTS Plaques guide you along the **Natural Entrance Tour** and the **Big Room Tour.** *(Tours $6, ages 6-15 and Golden Age Passport holders $3, under 6 free. 1½hr., depending on how often you stop to gawk in amazement. Open 8:30am-5pm; mid-Aug.-May. 8:30am-3:30pm. Partially wheelchair accessible.)* If your knees are up to it, the steep **Natural Entrance Tour** is less trafficked (1hr.; open 8:30am-3:30pm; mid-Aug. to May 8:30am-2pm). The ranger-guided **King's Palace Tour** passes through four of the cave's lowest rooms. *(1½hr. tours on the hr. 9-11am and 1-3pm. Advance reservations required. $8, Golden Age Passport holders and ages 6-15 $4.)* Plan your visit to the caves for the late afternoon in order to catch the magnificent nightly **bat flight.** *(May-Oct. daily just before sunset.)* A ranger talk precedes the amazing ritual, during which an army of hungry bats pours out of the cave at a rate of 6000 per minute. Early birds can catch them on the pre-dawn return. **Backcountry hiking** is permitted in the park (not in the caves, obviously), but a permit, a map, and massive quantities of water are required.

   Tours of the undeveloped **Slaughter Canyon Cave** (785-2232) offer a more rugged caving experience. *(Two 2hr. tours; early Sept. to late May Sa-Su only. $15, Golden Age Passport holders and ages 6-15 $7.50.)* Much energy and a car are required to get there, however. There's no public transportation, and the parking lot is 23 mi. down a dirt road off U.S. 62/180, several miles south of the main entrance to the park. The cave entrance is a steep, strenuous ½ mi. from the lot. Ranger-led tours (bring your own flashlight) traverse the difficult and slippery terrain inside; there are no paved trails or handrails. Call to reserve at least 2 days in advance. Many other tours of remote areas of the caves are offered, some of the more adventurous of which require crawling and climbing through tight passages (1-4hr., $7-20). Call 800-967-CAVE/2283 at least a month in advance for complete information and reservations.

   A few miles north of Carlsbad, **Living Desert State Park** is dedicated to the preservation and protection of various flora and fauna native to New Mexico. *(Open daily 9am-7pm; off-season 9am-4pm. $3, ages 7-12 $1. Wheelchair access.)* The 1.3 mi. **self-guided walking tour** winds past a variety of exhibits, including an aviary, bears, porcupines, and a reptile house.

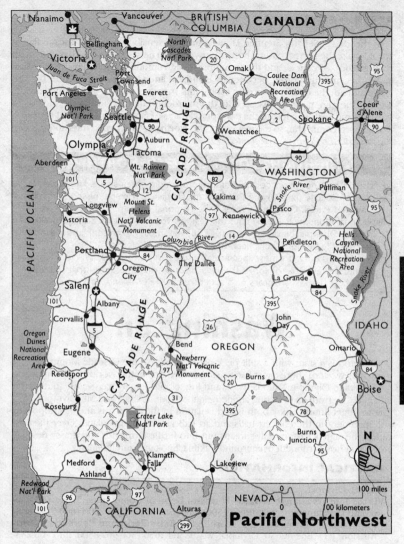

Pacific Northwest

THE PACIFIC NORTHWEST

Until the encroachment of European settlement, Native American tribes such as the Palouse and Spokane were on the move nine months of every year, hunting buffalo herds across the flat, dry region east of the Cascades. Coast dwellers such as the Chinook, in contrast, formed stable and stationary communities ruled by a hereditary chief and sustained by abundant resources. U.S. President Thomas Jefferson commissioned Meriwether Lewis and William Clark to explore the Pacific Northwest in 1803. Accompanied by Sacajawea, a Shoshone translator, the expedition traveled about 4000 mi. each way from St. Louis to the mouth of the Columbia River and back.

689

In the 1840s, Senator Stephen Douglas argued, sensibly, that the Cascade Range would make the perfect natural border between two new states. Sense has little to do with politics, of course, and the Columbia River, running perpendicular to the Cascades, became the border between Washington and Oregon. Yet even today, the range and not the river is the region's most important geographic and cultural divide: west of the rain-trapping Cascades lie the microchip, mocha, and music meccas of Portland and Seattle, while to the east sprawl tracts of farmland and an arid plateau.

For more comprehensive coverage of the Northwest's charms, refer to *Let's Go: Alaska and the Pacific Northwest 1999.*

HIGHLIGHTS OF THE PACIFIC NORTHWEST

- The off-beat neighborhoods, fine museums, ample green space, and pioneering cafes of **Seattle** (p. 690) and **Portland** (p. 716) are not to be missed.
- **National Parks.** Oregon's Crater Lake National Park (p. 729) and Newberry National Monument (p. 731) put the region's volcanic past on display. In Washington, Olympic National Park (p. 706) has mossy grandeur and deserted beaches; life beautifully blankets the dormant Mt. Rainier (p. 711).
- **Whale-watching.** It's most spectacular in the San Juan Islands, WA (p. 703).
- **Scenic drives.** Rte. 20 (p. 713) winds through the emerald North Cascades, while U.S. 101 takes visitors on a spin through the Oregon Coast (p. 724).

Washington

Washington is a state with a split personality, thanks to the Cascade Mountains. On the state's western shores, wet Pacific storms feed one of the world's only temperate rainforests in Olympic National Park, and low clouds linger over Seattle, hiding the Emerald City from its towering alpine neighbors, Mt. Rainier and Mt. Olympus. Visitors to Puget Sound enjoy both island isolation in the San Juans and cosmopolitan entertainment in the concert halls and art galleries of the mainland. Over the Cascades, the state's eastern half spreads out into fertile farmlands and grassy deserts, while fruit bowls runneth over around Yakima, Spokane, and Pullman.

PRACTICAL INFORMATION

Capital: Olympia.

Visitor Info: Washington State Tourism, Dept. of Community, Trade and Economic Development, P.O. Box 42500, Olympia, WA 98504-2500 (800-544-1800; http://www.tourism.wa.gov). **Washington State Parks and Recreation Commission,** P.O. Box 42650, Olympia, WA 98504-2650 (360-902-8500, info 800-233-0321; http://www.parks.wa.gov).

Time Zone: Pacific (3hr. before Eastern).

Postal Abbreviation: WA.

Sales Tax: 7-9.1% by county.

■ Seattle

Seattle's mix of mountain views, clean streets, espresso stands, and rainy weather has proved to be the magic formula of the 1990s, attracting transplants from across the U.S. Newcomers arrive in droves, armed with college degrees and California license plates, hoping for computer industry jobs and a different lifestyle; Seattle duly blesses them with a magnificent setting and a thriving artistic community. The city is one of the youngest and most vibrant in the nation, and a nearly epidemic fascination with coffee has also made it one of the most caffeinated. Every hilltop in Seattle offers an impressive view of Mt. Olympus, Mt. Baker, and Mt. Rainier. Two hundred days a year are shrouded in cloud cover, but when the skies clear, Seattleites rejoice that "the mountain is out," and head for the country.

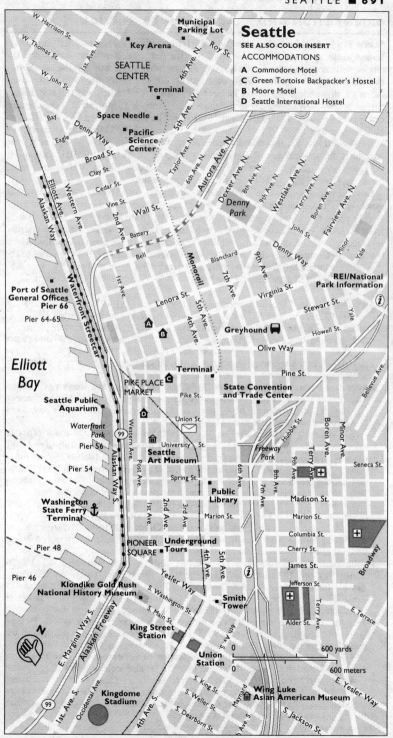

Seattle

SEE ALSO COLOR INSERT

ACCOMMODATIONS

A Commodore Motel
C Green Tortoise Backpacker's Hostel
B Moore Motel
D Seattle International Hostel

PACIFIC NORTHWEST

W. Harrison St.
W. Thomas St.
1st Ave. N.
W. John St.
W. Thomas St.
Municipal Parking Lot
Key Arena
SEATTLE CENTER
Roy St.
4th Ave. N.

Bay
Eagle
Denny Way
Broad St.
Clay St.
Cedar St.
Vine St.
Wall St.
Battery
Bell
Terminal
Space Needle
Pacific Science Center
Taylor Ave. N.
5th Ave. N.
6th Ave. N.
Aurora Ave. N.
Dexter Ave. N.
8th Ave. N.
9th Ave. N.
Westlake Ave. N.
Terry Ave N
Boren Ave. N.
Fairview Ave. N.
Minor
Yale
Denny Park
John St.
Denny Way

Elliott Ave.
Western Ave.
Alaskan Way

Port of Seattle General Offices Pier 66
Pier 64-65

Elliott Bay

Waterfront Streetcar

2nd Ave.
1st Ave.
Monorail
Lenora St.
Blanchard
7th Ave.
9th Ave.
Virginia St.
Stewart St.
Howell St.
5th Ave.
4th Ave.

REI/National Park Information
ⓘ

Seattle Public Aquarium

Waterfront Park
Pier 56

Pier 54

Washington State Ferry Terminal

Pier 48

Pier 46

Western Ave.
Alaskan Way S.
Post Ave.
99

Ⓐ
Ⓑ

Terminal
Ⓒ
PIKE PLACE MARKET
Pike St.
Ⓓ
Union St.
University St.
Seattle Art Museum
Spring St.
Public Library
Marion St.

Greyhound 🚌
Olive Way
Pine St.
State Convention and Trade Center
Freeway Park
Hubble St.
6th Ave.
8th Ave.
7th Ave.
Madison St.
Marion St.
Columbia St.
Cherry St.
James St.
Jefferson St.
Alder St.

Boren Ave.
9th Ave.
Terry Ave.
Minor Ave.
✚
Seneca St.
✚
Bellevue Ave.
Broadway
E Terrace
Terry Ave.

✚

PIONEER SQUARE
Underground Tours
1st Ave.
2nd Ave.
3rd Ave.
4th Ave.
5th Ave.
Yesler Way
ⓘ

Klondike Gold Rush National History Museum

S. Washington St.
S. Main St.
King Street Station
Union Station

Smith Tower

E. Marginal Way S.
Alaskan Freeway
1st Ave. S.
Occidental Ave.

N

99

Kingdome Stadium

S. King St.
S. Weller St.
S. Dearborn St.
4th Ave. S.
6th Ave. S.
Maynard

Wing Luke Asian American Museum
S. Jackson St.
E. Yesler Way

0   600 yards
0   600 meters

ORIENTATION AND PRACTICAL INFORMATION

Seattle is a long, skinny city, stretched north to south on an isthmus between **Puget Sound** to the west and **Lake Washington** to the east, linked by locks and canals. The city is easily accessible by car via **I-5**, which runs north-south through the city, east of downtown, and by **I-90** from the east, which ends at I-5 southeast of downtown. From I-5, **downtown** (including Pioneer Sq., Pike Place Market, and the waterfront) can be accessed by taking any of the exits from James St. to Stewart St. Take the Mercer St./Fairview Ave. Exit to the **Seattle Center.** The Denny Way Exit leads to **Capitol Hill,** and, farther north, the 45th St. Exit heads toward the **University District.** The less crowded **Rte. 99,** also called **Aurora Ave.** or the Aurora Hwy., runs parallel to I-5 and skirts the western side of downtown, with great views from the Alaskan Way Viaduct. Rte. 99 is often the better choice when driving downtown, or to Queen Anne, Fremont, Green Lake, and the northwestern part of the city.

Downtown, **avenues** run northwest to southeast, and **streets** run southwest to northeast. Outside downtown, with few exceptions, avenues run north-south and streets east-west. The city is split into **quadrants:** 1000 1st Ave. NW is a long walk from 1000 1st Ave. SE. Locals drive slowly and politely, and police ticket frequently. Jaywalking pedestrians rack up $50 fines. **Parking** is cheap, plentiful, and well-lit at the **Seattle Center,** near the Space Needle. Park there and take the monorail to the convenient **Westlake Center** downtown (every 15min. 9am-11pm; $1, ages 5-12 75¢). The **City of Seattle Bicycle Program** (684-7583) furnishes bicycle maps.

Airport: Seattle-Tacoma International (Sea-Tac) (431-4444), on Federal Way, south of Seattle proper. Take bus #174 or 194 from downtown Seattle.

Trains: Amtrak (800-872-7245, schedule info 382-4125), King St. Station, at 3rd and Jackson St., 1 block east of Pioneer Sq. next to the Kingdome. To: Portland (4 per day, $30); Tacoma (4 per day, $11); Spokane (1 per day, $68); San Francisco (1 per day, $166); and Vancouver (1 per day, $31). Ticket office open daily 6:15am-8pm. Station open daily 6am-10:30pm.

Buses: Greyhound (628-5526 or 800-231-2222), at 8th Ave. and Stewart St. To: Sea-Tac Airport (departs every 45min. past the hr. 6:45am-5:45pm, $7.50); Spokane (6 per day, $27); Vancouver, BC (9 per day, $21); Portland, OR (12 per day, $21). Ticket office open daily 6:30am-11:30pm.

Ferries: Washington State Ferries (800-84-FERRY/843-3779 or 206-464-6400), Colman Dock, Pier 52, downtown. Service from **downtown** to: Bainbridge Island (35min.); Bremerton on the Kitsap Peninsula (1hr.); Vashon Island (25min.; no Su service; passengers only). To reach the **Fauntleroy ferry terminal** in West Seattle, drive south on I-5 and take Exit 163A (West Seattle/Spokane St.) down Fauntleroy Way, or turn at the Spokane St. bridge 1 mi. south of the main terminal. From Fauntleroy to Southworth (on the Kitsap Peninsula; 35min.) and Vashon Island (15min.). Round-trip $3.60; car and driver $8, mid-Oct. to May $6.25. Most ferries leave daily and frequently 5am-2am. **Victoria Clipper** (800-668-1167; reservations 448-5000) departs from Pier 48 to Victoria (4½hr.; daily at 1pm; one-way $29, car and driver $49, under 12 $14.50).

Public Transportation: Metro Transit, 801 2nd Ave. (553-3000 or 800-542-7876, 24hr.; TTY 689-1739), in the Exchange Bldg. downtown. Open M-F 9am-5pm. **Zone I** includes everything within the city limits (peak hrs. $1.25, off-peak $1). **Zone 2** includes everything else ($1.75/$1.25). Ages 5-18 always 75¢. Peak hrs. in both zones M-F 6-9am and 3-6pm. Exact fare required. Weekend day passes $2. Ride free daily 6am-7pm in the downtown **ride free area,** bordered by S. Jackson St. on the south, 6th Ave. and I-5 on the east, Battery St. on the north, and the waterfront on the west. Free **transfers** can be used on any bus, including a return trip on the same bus within 2hr. All buses have free, easy-to-use bike racks, and most are wheelchair accessible (info 689-3113). The Metro covers King County east to North Bend and Carnation, south to Enumclaw, and north to Snohomish County, where bus #6 hooks up with **Community Transit.** This line runs to Everett, Stanwood, and well into the Cascades. Metro bus #174 connects to Tacoma's Pierce County System at Federal Way.

Taxis: Farwest, 622-1717. **Orange,** 522-8800. $1.80 base fare and per additional mi.

Convoluted Conventions of a Caffeine-Crazed Culture

Visiting Seattle without drinking the coffee would be like traveling to France without tasting the wine. It all started in the early 70s, when Starbucks started roasting its coffee on the spot in Pike Place Market. Soon, Stewart Brothers Coffee, now Seattle's Best Coffee, presented Starbucks with a rival, and the race was on both for the best cuppa joe and for global hegemony. Learning a few basic terms for ordering espresso drinks can only enrich your cultural experience. **Espresso** (es-PRESS-oh, not *ex*-PRESS-oh): The foundation of all espresso drinks is a bit of coffee brewed by forcing steam through finely ground, dark-roasted coffee. **Cappuccino (or "Capp"):** Espresso topped by the foam from steamed milk. Order "wet" for more liquid milk and big bubbles, or "dry" for stiff foam. **Latte:** Espresso with steamed milk and a little foam. More liquid than a capp. **Americano:** Espresso with hot water—an alternative to classic drip coffee. **Macciato:** A cup of coffee with a dollop of foam, and a bit of espresso swirled onto the foam. **Short:** 8oz. **Tall:** 12oz. **Grande (or Large):** 16oz. **Single:** One shot of espresso. **Double:** Two—add shots (usually about 60¢) until you feel you've reached your caffeine saturation point. With skim (nonfat) milk, any of these drinks is called **skinny.** If all you want is a plain ol' coffee, say **"drip coffee"**—otherwise, cafe workers will return your request for mere "coffee" with a blank stare.

Visitor Info: Seattle-King County Visitors Bureau (461-5840), at 8th and Pike St., 1st fl. of the convention center. Helpful staff doles out maps, brochures, newspapers, and Metro and ferry schedules. Open M-F 8:30am-5pm, Sa-Su 10am-4pm; Nov.-Apr. M-F 8:30am-5pm. **Seattle Parks and Recreation Dept.,** 100 Dexter St. (684-4075). Open daily 8am-5pm; in winter M-F 8am-5pm. **National Park Service,** 222 Yale Ave. (470-4060), in REI. Gives info on discounts and passes, and sells a map of the National Park System ($1.20). Open Tu-F 10:30am-7pm, Sa 9am-7pm, Su 11am-3pm; winter hrs. may be shorter.

Equipment Rental: The Bicycle Center, 4529 Sand Point Way (523-8300), near the Children's Hospital. Rents bikes ($3 per hr., $15 per day; 2hr. min.). Credit card or license deposit required. Open M-F 10am-8pm, Sa 10am-6pm, Su 10am-5pm.

Internet Access: Capitol Hill Net, 219 Broadway #22 (860-6858). $6 per hr. 15min. free surfing time if you mention *Let's Go.* Open daily 9am-midnight.

Post Office: (800-ASK-USPS/275-8777), at Union St. and 3rd Ave. downtown. Open M-F 8am-5:30pm. **ZIP code:** 98101. **Area code:** 206.

ACCOMMODATIONS

Seattle's hostel scene is alive, friendly, and clean. Those tired of urban high-rises can head for the **Vashon Island Hostel** (the "Seattle B"; see p. 701). **Pacific Lodging Association** (784-0539) arranges B&B singles in the $55-65 range (open M-F 9am-5pm).

🐢**Seattle International Hostel (HI-AYH),** 84 Union St. (622-5443), at Western Ave., right by the waterfront. Take bus #174, 184, or 194 from the airport (#194 from the north end of the baggage terminal is fastest), get off at Union St., and walk west. A diverse, international crowd and free linen make up for the vast expanses of formica in this enormous hostel. The 5-star common room overlooks the water, just off a palatial lounge and library/TV room. 6 people per dorm room. Beds $17, nonmembers $20. Laundry facilities (wash $1, dry 75¢), ride board, discount tickets (aquarium, Omnidome, Museum of Flight and passenger ferry). 24hr. parking in the nearby garage ($9). 7-night max. stay in summer. Reception 7am-2am. Check-out 11am. No curfew. Summer reservations recommended.

🐢**Green Tortoise Backpacker's Hostel,** 1525 2nd Ave. (340-1222), between Pike and Pine St. Pick-up available from Amtrak, Greyhound or ferry terminal; take bus #174 from the airport. Great location, great rooms, great hostel. 150 beds in 48 rooms, plus 10 private rooms. Beds $15, nonmembers $16; private rooms $40. Breakfast included. Required $20 key deposit. Bring travel documents upon check-in, or risk an intense interrogation from the desk clerk. No curfew.

Moore Motel, 1926 2nd Ave. (448-4851, 448-4852, or 800-421-5508), at Virginia, 1 block east from Pike Place Market, next to the historic Moore Theater. Big rooms include 2 beds, TV, a private bath, and slightly stained carpets. The reasonably ornate open lobby, cavernous halls, and gargantuan, heavy wooden doors make the Moore seem like it hasn't changed since the 20s. Singles $38, with bath $43; doubles $44/$49. HI member discounts when the Seattle Hostel is full.

Vincent's Backpackers Guest House, 527 Malden Ave. E (323-7849), between 14th and 15th Ave. in Capitol Hill, near the new Safeway on Broadway; take bus #10 from downtown. Hosteling accommodations and longer-term arrangements. The house is clean, but parking and living space are limited. Beds $14. Key deposit $10. Apartments around $600 per month. Reception 10am-4pm; door locked at 2am.

The College Inn, 4000 University Way NE (633-4441), in the University District at NE 40th St. A quiet place to crash near the UW campus. Singles are tiny and rooms lack TVs or private baths, but the turn-of-the-century bureaus and brass fixtures are s'durned *charming.* Kitchen is in the 4th fl. attic, with breakfast included every morning. Singles $49-66; doubles $78-90. Credit card required.

FOOD

The finest fish, produce, and baked goods can be purchased from various vendors in **Pike Place Market,** where the **Main Arcade** parallels the waterfront on the west side of Pike St. (open M-Sa 9am-6pm, Su 11am-5pm). Along King and Jackson St., between 5th and 8th Ave. directly east of the Kingdome, the **International District** is packed with great, affordable eateries.The city's cheapest food is sold in the **University District,** where grub from around the world goes for under $5. Seattle hosts active **food cooperatives** at 6518 Fremont Ave. N., in Green Lake, and at 6504 20th NE, in the Ravenna District north of the university. Capitol Hill, the U District, and Fremont close main thoroughfares on summer Saturdays for **farmers' markets.**

The Gravity Bar, 415 Broadway E (325-7186), in the Broadway Market of Capitol Hill. Neo-healthy organic food and intriguing fruit and veggie juices. Conical tables and stainless steel everything fill this tiny room, while colorful paper lanterns and kites contrast with the omnipresent metallic gray. Among the infamous drinks are Moonjuice (a melon/lime concoction; $3.50) and Mr. Rogers on Amino Acid ($5). Extensive menu. Open Su-Th 10am-10pm, F-Sa 10am-11pm.

Bimbo's Bitchin' Burrito Kitchen, 506 E. Pine (329-9978), in Capitol Hill. The name explains it all, except for the super sizes and the divine inspiration behind the *comida.* Check out the day-glo restrooms. Bimbo's basic burrito $3.50. Open M-Th noon-11pm, F-Sa noon-2am, Su 2-10pm.

Soundview Café (623-5700), on the mezzanine in the Pike Place Main Arcade, down Flower Row. This wholesome, self-serve sandwich-and-salad bar offers fresh food, a spectacular view of Elliott Bay, and poetry readings. Fill a bowl with tabouli, pasta, salad, or fruit ($5). Solid breakfasts. Open M-Sa 7am-5pm, Su 9am-3pm.

Piroshki, Piroshki, 1908 Pike Pl. (441-6068). *Piroshki* are hefty, hands-on Russian specialties made of a croissant-like dough, baked around anything from sausage and mushrooms ($3) to apples doused in cinnamon ($3.50). You can watch the *piroshki* process while you wait. Open daily 8am-7pm.

Mae Phim Thai Restaurant, 94 Columbia St. (624-2979), a few blocks north of Pioneer Sq. between 1st Ave. and Alaskan Way. Local business buffs pack this tiny restaurant at lunch time, attesting to the glory of good, inexpensive take-out. Wait less than 5min. for an enormous *pad thai.* All dishes $4.60. Open M-Sa 11am-7pm.

Tai Tung, 655 S. King St. (622-7372), in the International District. Busiest hrs. are when the munchies take hold of university students, who shuffle over for the Chinese version of fried chicken. The talkative waiters are likely to learn your name by your second visit. 10-page, ever-changing menu plastered to the walls. Entrees $7-10. Open Su-Th 10am-11:30pm, F-Sa 10am-1:30am.

Ho Ho Seafood Restaurant, 653 S. Weller St. (382-9671), in the International District. Friendly service and fields of pink formica. Watch the demise of your dinner as staff pluck live seafood from the tanks. Generous portions of great seafood. Dinner $7-10; lunch $5-7. Open Su-Th 11am-1am, F-Sa 11am-3am.

PACIFIC NORTHWEST

Flowers, 4247 University Way NE (633-1903), in the University District. This local landmark from the 20s spent its youth as a flower shop. Now, a dark wood bar and mirrored ceiling make a tasteful frame for an all-you-can-eat Mediterranean buffet ($6). Vegan options. Open M-Sa 11am-2am; kitchen closes at 10pm.

SIGHTS

It takes only two frenetic days to get a decent look at most of Seattle's major sights, since most are within walking distance of one another or are within the Metro's ride free zone (see **Practical Information,** p. 692). Any one of the ferries that leave from the waterfront affords a great glimpse of the city's skyline.

Downtown and the Waterfront

The new **Seattle Art Museum,** 100 University Way (654-3255, recording 654-3100, TDD 654-3137), near 1st Ave., lives in a grandiose building with an entire floor dedicated to the art of Pacific Northwest Native Americans, plus an extensive collection of modern and contemporary regional works. *(Open Tu-W and F-Su 10am-5pm, Th 10am-9pm. Free tours 12:30, 1, and 2pm; check for special tours Th 6:15pm. $6, students and seniors $4, under 12 free.)* A ticket from SAM will also get you into the Seattle Asian Art Museum in Volunteer Park (see p. 697), as long as you visit within a week. One block north of the museum on 1st Ave., inside the Museum Plaza Bldg., is the free **Seattle Art Museum Gallery,** featuring contemporary works by local artists (open M-F 11am-5pm, Sa-Su 11am-4pm).

Westlake Park, with its Art Deco brick patterns and surprisingly dry **Wall of Water,** is a good place to kick back and listen to steel drums. This small triangular park, on Pike St. between 4th and 5th Ave., is bordered by the gleaming new **Westlake Center,** where the monorail departs for the Seattle Center.

The **Pike Place Hillclimb** descends down a set of staircases from the south end of Pike Place Market, at the end near the information booth on 1st and Pike, past chic shops and ethnic restaurants, to Alaskan Way and the waterfront. (An elevator is also available.) The super-popular **Seattle Aquarium** (386-4330, TTY 386-4322) sits at the base of the Hillclimb at Pier 59, near Union St. *(Open daily 10am-7pm; in winter 10am-5pm; limited hrs. on holidays. $7.75, seniors $7, ages 6-18 $5.15, ages 3-5 $2.)* Outdoor tanks re-create salt marsh and tide pool ecosystems, but the aquarium's star attraction is an underwater dome featuring Puget Sound fish and mammals, including playful harbor seals, fur seals, and otters. Next door on Pier 59 is the **Omnidome** (622-1868), which shoots movies onto a special rounded screen, with a booming sound system that may scare small children. *(Films daily 10am-10pm. $7; students, seniors, and ages 6-18 $6; ages 3-5 $5. 2nd film $2. Combined aquarium/Omnidome ticket $13, seniors and ages 13-18 $11.25, ages 6-13 $9.50, ages 3-5 $5.50.)* Explore north or south along the waterfront by **streetcars,** which run from the Metro tunnel in Pioneer Sq. north to Pier 70 and Myrtle Edwards Park. The 20s cars were imported from Melbourne in 1982 because Seattle sold its originals to San Francisco, where they now enjoy fame as cable cars, the posers. *(Streetcars run every 20-30min. M-F 7am-11pm, Sa 8am-11pm, Su 9am-11pm; in winter until 6pm. $1, $1.25 during peak hrs.; children 75¢; under 12 ride free with a paying passenger on Su. Metro passes accepted.)*

The Seattle Center

When the 1962 World's Fair engulfed Seattle, the entertainment-oriented city rose to the occasion by building the Seattle Center (684-8582 or 684-7200), now housing anything from carnival rides to ballet. **Monorails** leave from the 3rd fl. of the Westlake Center (departs every 15min. 9am-11pm; $1, seniors 50¢, ages 5-12 75¢). The center is bordered by Denny Way, W. Mercer St., 1st Ave., and 5th Ave., and has eight gates, each with a model of the Center and a map of its facilities. The **Space Needle** (443-2111), sometimes known as the World's Tackiest Monument, is at least a useful landmark for the disoriented. *($9, seniors $8, ages 5-12 $4. Free with dinner reservations.)* It houses an observation tower and an expensive, 360° rotating restaurant.

Pop Quiz, Hotshot

What would you call a 12 oz. espresso with an extra shot, steamed skim milk and foam?

The **Pacific Science Center** (443-2001), near the needle, houses a **laserium** (443-2850) that quakes to Led Zeppelin and Smashing Pumpkins, plus an immense **IMAX theater** (443-IMAX/4629). *(Laser shows Tu $3, W-Su $7. IMAX shows Th-Su at 8pm. IMAX/museum tickets $9.50, seniors and ages 6-13 $7.50, ages 2-5 $5.50.)* The **Children's Museum** (441-1768), in the Center House, has an abundance of creative hands-on exhibits that will wow any kid (or jealous adult) into a fit of over-stimulation (open M-F 10am-5pm, Sa-Su 10am-6pm; $4, ages 1-12 $5.50).

Pioneer Square and Environs

From the waterfront or downtown, it's just a few blocks to historic **Pioneer Sq.**, at Yesler Way and 2nd Ave., home of the first Seattleites, with a fresh layer of suffocating tourist crowds. Originally, Seattle stood 12 ft. below the present-day streets; the 1½hr. **Underground Tour** (682-4646 or 888-608-6337) leads through the subterranean rooms and passageways of old, explaining the sordid and soggy birth of Seattle. *(1½hr. Daily and roughly every hr. 9am-7pm; varies by season. $7, students $5.50, seniors $6, children $2.75. Reservations recommended.)* **Klondike Gold Rush National Historic Park,** 117 S. Main St. (553-7220), is a posh interpretive center depicting the lives of miners, with a slide show about the role of Seattle in the Klondike gold rush. *(Open daily 9am-5pm. Free.)* To add some levity to this litany of shattered dreams, the park screens Charlie Chaplin's 1925 classic **The Gold Rush** on the first Sunday of every month at 3pm. Free daily **walking tours** of Pioneer Sq. leave the park at 10am.

The International District

Three blocks east of Pioneer Sq., up Jackson on King St., is Seattle's **International District.** Though sometimes called Chinatown, this area is now home to immigrants from all over Asia and their descendants. The tiny **Wing Luke Memorial Museum,** 407 7th Ave. S. (623-5124), displays a thorough description of life in an Asian American community, a permanent exhibit on different Asian nationalities in Seattle, and work by local Asian artists. *(Open Tu-F 11am-4:30pm, Sa-Su noon-4pm. $2.50, seniors and students $1.50, ages 5-12 75¢; Th free.)* The **community gardens** at Main and Maynard St. provide a peaceful and well-tended retreat from the downtown sidewalks, though you may feel like you're walking through someone's backyard as you tiptoe through the turnips. Park next to the gardens in free 2hr. angled parking to avoid meters.

Capitol Hill

From their elevated position above the Emerald City, Capitol Hill residents scan the city with an artist's eye. The district's leftist and gay communities set the tone for its nightspots, while retail outlets include collectives and radical bookstores right alongside Ben & Jerry's and The Gap. Explore **Broadway** to window shop and experience alternative lifestyles merging with mainstream capitalism. Walk a few blocks east and north for a stroll down **15th Ave.,** lined with well-maintained Victorian homes. Bus #10 runs along 15th Ave. with frequent stops; #7 cruises Broadway. **Volunteer Park,** between 11th and 17th Ave. at E. Ward St., north of the Broadway activity, lures Seattleites away from the city center with lovely lawns, an outdoor running track, a playground, and fields of rhododendron blooming in spring and early summer. Bus #10 runs parkward up 15th Ave.; it's preferable to bus #7, since it runs more frequently and stops closer to the fun stuff. The **outdoor stage** often hosts free performances on summer Sundays. Climbing the medieval-looking **water tower** at the 14th Ave. entrance yields a free and stunning 360° panorama of the city and the Olympic Range. On rainy days, you can hide out amid the orchids inside the **glass conservatory** (open daily 10am-7pm; off-season 10am-4pm; free). A tour through world-renowned collections of the newly renovated **Seattle Asian Art Museum** (654-3100) reveals Ming vases and ancient kimonos at every turn. *(Open Tu-Su 10am-5pm, Th 10am-9pm. $6, students and seniors $4, under 12 free.)* Be careful at night in the park.

Just north of Volunteer Park on 15th St. is **Lake View Cemetery,** where the graves of **Bruce** and **Brandon Lee** rest among the founders of Seattle. One of the most famous martial artists of the century, Bruce Lee moved to Seattle in his youth; his son Brandon made a name for himself in the same field. The Lees' graves lie near the top of the cemetery; from the flagpole, face the headstone shaped like a cross and head down the hill toward the right, where the roads intersect. The **University of Washington Arboretum,** 10 blocks east of Volunteer Park, nurtures over 4000 species, trees, shrubs, and flowers, and maintains superb walking and running trails; take bus #11 from downtown (open 7am-dusk). At the southern end of the arboretum on Washington Blvd., the tranquil, perfectly pruned **Japanese Tea Garden** (684-4725) offers a stroll through 3½ acres of sculpted gardens with fruit trees, a reflecting pool, and a traditional tea house. *(Open Mar.-Nov. daily 10am-8pm. $2.50; students, seniors, and ages 6-18 $1.50; disabled $1.)*

University District, Fremont, and Ballard

With over 33,000 students, the **University of Washington** comprises the state's cultural and educational center of gravity. The U District swarms with students year-round, and Seattleites of all ages take advantage of the area's many bohemian bookstores, shops, taverns, and restaurants. To get there, take buses #71-74 from downtown, or #7, 9, 43, or 48 from Capitol Hill. The friendly **visitors center,** 4014 University Way NE (543-9198), offers campus maps, a self-guided tour book, and information about the university (open M-F 8am-5pm). The **Thomas Burke Museum of Natural History and Culture** (543-5590), at 45th St. NE and 17th Ave. NE in the northwest corner of campus, exhibits a superb collection on Pacific Rim cultures, as well as kid-friendly explanations of the natural history behind Washington's formation. *(Open F-W 10am-5pm, Th 10am-8pm. $5.50, students $2.50, seniors $4, under 5 free.)* Across the street, the astronomy department's old stone **observatory** (543-0126) is open to the public for viewings on clear nights. The newly remodeled **Henry Art Gallery** (543-2280), across from the visitors center, hosts superb exhibitions of modern art. *(Open Tu-Su 11am-5pm, Th 11am-8pm. $5, seniors $3.50; free Th after 5pm.)*

U-Dub students often cross town for drinks in Queen Anne, and the intervening neighborhood of **Fremont** basks in the cross-pollination. The **immense troll** who sits beneath the Aurora Bridge on 35th St. grasps a Volkswagen Bug, and bears a confounded expression on his cement face. Some say kicking the bug's tire brings good luck; others say it hurts their foot. A flamin' **Vladimir Lenin** resides at the corner of N. 36th and N. Fremont Pl.; this bona fide artwork from the former Soviet Union will be around until it's bought by a permanent collection. **Archie McPhee's,** 3510 Stone Way (545-8344), a shrine to pop culture and plastic absurdity, is east of the Aurora Hwy. (Rte. 99) between 35th and 36th, 2 blocks north of Lake Union and Gasworks Park (see below). *(Open M-Sa 9am-7pm, Su 10am-6pm.)* Reach Archie's on bus #26.

Next door to the U District, the primarily Scandinavian neighborhood of **Ballard** offers a taste of Europe, with a wide variety of eateries and shops lining Market St. The **Nordic Heritage Museum,** 3014 NW 67th St. (789-5707), presents thorough exhibits on the history of Nordic immigration and influence in the U.S. *(Open Tu-Sa 10am-4pm, Su noon-4pm. $4, students and seniors $3, ages 6-18 $2.)* Take bus #17 from downtown, and bus #44 from the U District, transferring to #17 at 24th and Market.

WATERWAYS AND PARKS

In summer, Seattle is a playground for boaters, and a string of attractions festoon the waterways linking Lake Washington and Puget Sound. Houseboats and sailboats fill **Lake Union,** situated between Capitol Hill and the University District. Here, the **Center for Wooden Boats,** 1010 Valley St. (382-2628), maintains a moored flotilla of new and restored small craft for rent. *(Open daily 11am-6pm. Rowboats $12.50-20 per hr.; sailboats $16-26 per hr.)* **Gasworks Park,** a much-celebrated kite-flying spot at the north end of Lake Union, hosts a furious fireworks show on July 4th. To get there, take bus #26 from downtown to N. 35th St. and Wallingford Ave. N. **Gasworks Kite Shop,**

3333 Wallingford N. (633-4780), is 1 block north of the park (open M-F 10am-6pm, Sa 10am-5pm, Su noon-5pm). If the need to sail or skate suddenly strikes, head to **Urban Surf** (545-WIND/9463), across the street from the park entrance at 2100 N. Northlake Way, for windsurfing boards ($35 per day) or in-line skates ($5 per hr.).

Woodland Park and the **Woodland Park Zoo**, 5500 Phinney Ave. N (684-4800), are best reached from Rte. 99, or N. 50th St.; take bus #5 from downtown. *(Zoo open daily 9:30am-6pm, Oct. 15-Mar. 14 9:30am-4pm. $8, seniors $7.25, ages 6-17, ages 3-5 $3.50, disabled $5.50. Parking $3.50; in winter $1.75.)* While the park itself is not well-manicured, the zoo's habitats are highly realistic, including the Alaska-themed Northern Trail and the orangutan-crammed Tropical Asia. Farther west, at the **Hiram M. Chittenden Locks** (783-7059), on NW St. along the Lake Washington Ship Canal, a circus atmosphere develops as boats traveling between Puget Sound and Lake Washington try to cross over. *(Daily June-Sept. 7am-9pm.)* Take bus #43 from the U District or #17 from downtown. The nearby **fish ladder** hosts homesick salmon hurling themselves up 21 concrete steps. *(Free tours daily in summer 1 and 3pm. Open daily 7am-9pm.)* The busiest salmon runs last from June to September.

Next door to the locks lie the 534 bucolic acres of **Discovery Park** (386-4236), at 36th Ave. W. and Government Way W., on a lonely point west of the Magnolia District and south of Golden Gardens Park (bus #24). Possessing a wide range of habitats with easily distinguishable transitions, this park provides a fantastic introduction to the flora and fauna of the Pacific Northwest. A **visitors center,** 3801 W. Government Way, looms large by the entrance and sells handy maps (75¢). **Shuttles** ferry visitors to the beach (June-Sept. Sa-Su noon-4:45pm; 25¢, seniors and disabled free). At the park's northern end, the **Indian Cultural Center** (285-4425), operated by the United Indians of All Tribes Foundation, houses the **Sacred Circle Gallery,** a rotating exhibit of Native American artwork (open M-F 9am-5pm, Sa-Su noon-5pm; free).

OUTDOORS

Cyclists should gear up for the 19 mi., 1600-competitor **Seattle to Portland Race** in mid-July. Call the **bike hotline** (522-2453) for more info. The Seattle Parks Dept. also holds a monthly **Bicycle Sunday** from May to September, when Lake Washington Blvd. is open exclusively to cyclists from 10am-6pm. For more info, contact the Parks Department's **Citywide Sports Office** (684-7092). Many **whitewater rafting** outfitters are based in the Seattle area, and **Washington State Outfitters and Guides Association** (392-6107) provides advice and info; although their office is closed in summer, they do return phone calls. The **Northwest Outdoor Center,** 2100 Westlake Ave. (281-9694), on Lake Union, gives instructional programs in whitewater and sea kayaking, and leads 3-day kayaking excursions through the San Juan Islands. *(2½hr. basic intro to sea kayaking $40 with equipment. Open M-F 10am-8pm, Sa-Su 9am-6pm.)* Skiing near Seattle is every bit as good as the mountains make it look. **Alpental, Ski-Acres,** and **Snoqualmie** co-sponsor an info number (232-8182), which provides ski conditions and lift ticket rates for all three. **Crystal Mountain** (663-2265), the region's newest resort, can be reached by Rte. 410 south out of Seattle and offers ski rentals, lessons, and lift ticket packages. Ever since the Klondike gold rush, Seattle has been in the business of equipping wilderness expeditions. **Recreational Equipment Inc. Coop (REI),** 222 Yale Ave. (223-1944), is the largest of its kind in the world. *(Open M-Sa 9am-9pm, Su 10am-6pm. Rental area open 2hr. before store.)* This paragon of woodsy wisdom can be seen from I-5; take the Stewart St. Exit.

ENTERTAINMENT

Seattle has one of the world's most notorious underground music scenes and the third-largest theater community in the U.S. (only New York's and Chicago's loom larger). During summer lunch hours, the free **Out to Lunch** series (623-0340) brings everything from reggae to folk dancing to the parks, squares, and office buildings of downtown Seattle. The **Seattle Opera** (389-7676, Ticketmaster 292-ARTS/2787) performs at the Opera House in the Seattle Center throughout the year. The program's popularity demands reservations well in advance, although rush tickets are sometimes available. Students and seniors receive ½-price tickets on the day of the performance (from $20); student tickets are also available ($27-31). The **Seattle Symphony Orchestra** (443-4747), in the new Fifth Avenue Theater, performs a regular series (Sept.-June; rush tickets from $6.50) and a children's series. The **Pacific Northwest Ballet** (441-9411) starts its season at the Opera House in September. (Tickets from $14; ½-price rush tickets available to students and seniors 30min. before showtime.)

Theater rush tickets are often available at nearly half-price on the day of the show (cash only) from **Ticket/Ticket** (324-2744). Comedies in the small **Empty Space Theatre,** 3509 Fremont Ave. N. (547-7500), 1½ blocks north of the Fremont Bridge, attract the entire city. (Season Oct. to early July. Box office open daily 1-5pm. Tickets $14-24; previews $10; ½-price rush tickets 10min. before curtain.) **Seattle Repertory Theater,** 155 W. Mercer St. (443-2222, Ticketmaster 292-ARTS/7676), at the wonderful Bagley Wright Theater in Seattle Center, has a winter season combining contemporary and classic productions. With cat-like tread, **Gilbert and Sullivan** operettas (341-9612) arise in summer. (Tickets $10-48, seniors $17, under 25 $10. Box office open M 10am-6pm, Tu-Sa 10am-8pm.) **A Contemporary Theater (ACT),** 700 Union St. (292-7670), hosts a summer season of modern and off-beat premieres. (Tickets $14-26. Box office open Tu-Th noon-7:30pm, F-Sa noon-8pm, Su noon-7pm.) **Northwest Asian American Theater,** 409 7th Ave. S. (364-3282), in the International District, next to the Wing Luke Asian Museum, stages pieces by and about Asian Americans (tickets $12; students, seniors, and disabled $9; Th $6).

Most of the cinemas that screen non-Hollywood films are on Capitol Hill and in the University District. **Seven Gables,** a local company, has recently bought up the Egyptian and others; $20 buys admission to any five films at any of their theaters. Call 44-FILMS/443-4567 for local movie times and locations. **The Egyptian,** 801 E. Pine St. (32-EGYPT/34978), at Harvard Ave. on Capitol Hill, is a handsome Art Deco theater showing artsy flicks. It hosts the **Seattle International Film Festival** in the last week of May and first week of June, including a retrospective of one director's work, with an appearance by the director. (Festival tickets available at a discount. $7, seniors and children $4, matinees $4.) **The Harvard Exit,** 807 E. Roy St. (323-8986), on Capitol Hill, shows quality classic and foreign films. Half the fun of seeing a movie here is the theater, a converted residence that has its very own ghost, and an enormous antique projector. (Tickets $7, seniors and children $4, matinees $4.)

Uglier than the Boeing factory, the **Kingdome,** 201 S. King St. (tickets 622-4487), down 1st Ave., ranks second only to Houston's Astrodome as an insult to baseball. Even so, the **Mariners** have some of the finest marquee talent around, and a new stadium is in the works. Tickets (628-0888) at the Kingdome are cheap (outfield bleachers $6, most others $25, under 14 discounts, ½-price family nights). On the other side of town, the new and graceful **Key Arena** in the Seattle Center is packed to the brim whenever Seattle's pro basketball team, the **Supersonics** (281-5800), plays.

The first Thursday evening of each month, the arts community sponsors **First Thursday,** a free and well-attended gallery walk. Watch for street fairs in the University District during mid- to late May; at Pike Place Market over Memorial Day weekend; and in Fremont in mid-June, when the **Fremont Fair and Solstice Parade** brings Fremont to a frenzy of music, frivolity, and craft booths. The International District holds its annual two-day bash in mid-July, featuring arts and crafts booths, and East Asian and Pacific food. For more info, call **Chinatown Discovery** (236-0657 or 583-0460). The **Seattle Seafair** (728-0123), spread over 3 weeks from mid-July to early August, is the biggest festival of them all. Each neighborhood contributes with street fairs, parades large and small, balloon races, musical entertainment, and a seafood orgy. Big-name rock bands, street musicians, and a young, exuberant crowd flock to **Bumbershoot** (281-7788), over Labor Day weekend This massive, 4-day arts festival caps off the summer and is held in the Seattle Center. (4 days $29; 2 days $16; 1 day $9 in advance or $10 at the door, seniors $1, children free. Prices subject to change.)

NIGHTLIFE

Seattle has moved beyond beer to a new nightlife frontier: the cafe-and-bar. Often an establishment that poses as a diner by day brings on a band, breaks out the disco ball, and pumps out the microbrews by night. At **Pioneer Sq.,** UW students from frat row dominate the bar stools. Most of the area bars participate in a joint cover ($8, Su-Th $5) that will let you wander from bar to bar to sample the bands. **Fenix Café and Fenix Underground** (467-1111) and **Central Tavern** (622-0209) rock constantly, while **Larry's** (624-7665) and **New Orleans** (622-2563) feature great jazz and blues nightly. The **Bohemian Café** (447-1514) pumps reggae and also sponsors open mic nights on Thursday. **Kells** (728-1916), near Pike Place Market, is a popular Irish pub with nightly Celtic tunes. All the Pioneer Sq. clubs shut down at 2am Friday and Saturday nights, and around midnight during the week. Many Seattleites take their beer bucks downtown to **Capitol Hill,** or up Rte. 99 to **Fremont,** where the atmosphere is more laid-back.

◉**Sit and Spin,** 2219 4th St. (441-9484, band info 441-9474), downtown. The washers and driers work, but the real focus of this late-night cafe is the social scene. Furniture hangs from the walls, and board games keep patrons busy while they wait for their clothes to dry or for alternative bands to play in the back room (F-Sa nights). The cafe sells everything from local microbrews on tap to bistro food (cashew chicken tarragon $5) to boxes of laundry detergent. Artists stop by to play checkers and bask in the plastic glow of a 50s trailer park gone mad. Open Su-Th 9am-midnight, F-Sa 9am-2am. Kitchen opens daily at 11am.

The Alibi Room, 85 Pike St. (623-3180), across from the Market Cinema in the Post Alley in Pike Place. Created by a local producer, the Alibi Room proclaims itself a local indie filmmaker hangout. Smoky sophisticates star as themselves. Racks of screenplays, DJ and dancing on the weekends, and chic decor get an Oscar for ambience. Open daily 11am-2am.

Re-Bar, 1114 Howell (233-9873), downtown. A mixed gay and straight bar with a wide range of tunes and dancing on the wild side. Hip-hop (F); lots of acid jazz and fringe theater (Sa-Su). Cover $4. Open daily 9:30pm-2am.

Art Bar, 1516 2nd Ave. (622-4344), downtown. Exactly what the name says: a gallery/bar fusion. Hosts jazz and a diverse clientele. Cover $3-5. Open M-F 11am-2am, Sa 3pm-2am, Su 4pm-2am.

Colourbox, 113 1st Ave. (340-4101). One of the few places in Pioneer Sq. that real rockers respect. Live music most nights, in a bar that looks quaint with the lights on and violently grungy in the dark. Open daily 8:30pm-2am.

OK Hotel, 212 Alaskan Way S (621-7903, coffeehouse 386-9934), just below Pioneer Sq. toward the waterfront. 1 cafe, 1 bar, 1 building. Lots of wood, lots of coffee. Live bands play everything from rock to reggae and draw equally diverse crowds. Bar art is curated monthly. Occasional cover up to $6. Cafe open M-F 5-10pm, Sa-Su 5-11pm. Bar open daily 3pm-2am.

Garage, 1130 Broadway (322-2296), in Capitol Hill. An automotive warehouse-turned-upscale pool hall, this place gets suave at night. Happy hour 3-7pm. 8 pool tables $6-10 per hr.; $4 per hr. during happy hour; $5 per hr. (M); free for female sharps on Ladies' Night (Su). Open daily 3pm-2am.

Red Door Alehouse, 3401 Fremont Ave. N (547-7521), at N. 34th St., across from the Inner-Urban Statue. Throbbing with university students who attest to the good local ale selection and a mile-long beer menu. Try the Pyramid Wheaton or Widmer Hefeweizen with a slice of lemon. Open daily 11am-2am. Kitchen closes at 11pm.

Neighbours, 1509 Broadway (324-5358), in Capitol Hill. A very gay dance club of techno slickness. Cover Su-Th $1; F-Sa $5. Open Su-Th 9pm-2am, F-Sa 9pm-4am.

■ Near Seattle: Vashon Island

Only a 25min. ferry ride from Seattle and a 15min. hop from Tacoma, Vashon (VASH-on) Island has remained inexplicably invisible to most Seattleites. With its forested hills and expansive sea views, this artists' colony feels like the San Juan Islands without the oppressive crowds of tourists. Most of the island is undeveloped and covered in Douglas fir, rolling cherry orchards, wildflowers, and strawberry fields. Despite short distances, Vashon's hills will turn even a little biking jaunt into a workout, with the reward of rapturous scenery. **Vashon Island Bicycles,** 7232 Vashon Hwy. (463-6225), rents mountain bikes ($9 per hr., $25 per day). **Point Robinson Park** is a gorgeous spot for a picnic, and offers **free tours** (217-6123) of the 1885 **Coast Guard lighthouse** that faces off with Mt. Rainier (from Vashon Hwy., take Ellisburg Rd. to Dockton Rd. to Pt. Robinson Rd.). **Vashon Island Kayak Co.** (463-9527), at Camp Burton, rents sea kayaks on the weekends. (Open F-Su 10am-5pm. Boats often available during the week; call in advance. $14 per hr.) More than 500 acres of woods in the middle of the island are interlaced with **hiking trails.** The Vashon Park District (463-9602) has more info (office open daily 9am-5pm). **Blue Heron Arts Center,** 19704 Vashon Hwy. (463-5131), coordinates free local gallery openings on the first Friday of every month (open Tu-F 11am-5pm, Sa noon-5pm; F openings 7-9:30pm).

The **Vashon Island AYH Ranch Hostel (HI-AYH),** at 12119 SW Cove Rd. (463-2592), west of Vashon Hwy., is sometimes called the "Seattle B." Jump on any bus at the ferry terminal, ride to Thriftway Market, and call from the free phone inside the store, marked with an HI-AYH label. Resembling an old Western town, the hostel offers bunks, open-air teepees and covered wagons (tenting and queen beds), and the occasional theme room. (Free pancake breakfast, free firewood. $10; bicyclists $8; nonmembers $13. Linen or sleeping bag $1. Open May-Oct.) The hostel also has a new **B&B** down the road ($35-45). Get creative in the kitchen with supplies from the large and offbeat **Thriftway** (463-2100), downtown at 9740 SW Bank Rd. (open daily 8am-9pm). **Emily's Café and Juice Bar,** 17530 Vashon Hwy. (463-6404), smack in downtown Vashon, enhances karma and juices just about anything (open Su-Th 9am-4pm, F-Sa 9am-9pm).

Vashon Island stretches between Seattle and Tacoma on its east side and between Southworth and Gig Harbor on its west side. The town of **Vashon** lies at the island's northern tip, while **Tahlequah** is to the south. **Washington State Ferries** (800-84-FERRY/843-3779 or 206-464-6400) runs to Vashon Island from four different locations, including a downtown Seattle terminal (25min.; 8 per day M-F, 6 per day Sa; $3.60, passengers only) and Fauntleroy in West Seattle (35min., 20 per day, $2.40). Vehicle charges vary by season (June-Sept. $11, Oct.-May $8.50). Buses #54, 118, and 119 pick travelers up at 1st and Union St. in Seattle and service the Vashon Island ferries from downtown Seattle (call 800-542-7876 for bus info). Buses #118 and #119 also service the island, continuing from the ferry landing to the town of Vashon. Both can be flagged down anywhere. Fares are the same as the system in Seattle. The island is all within one zone, but Seattle to Vashon passes two zones. The local Thriftway provides maps, or contact the **Vashon-Maury Chamber of Commerce,** 17633 SW Vashon Hwy. (463-6217). **Post Office:** 463-9390, on Bank Rd. (open M-F 8:30am-5pm, Sa 10am-1pm). **ZIP code:** 98070. **Area code:** 206.

■ Olympia

From the fortress-like hilltop capitol of Olympia, the Washington State government keeps an eye on the college students and local fisher-folk who thrive in the Capitol Dome's shadow. The Evergreen State College campus lies a few miles from the city center, and its liberal, highly pierced student body spills into town to mingle with preppy politicos. Olympia's crowning glory is the **State Capitol Campus** (586-8677), a complex of state government buildings, fabulous fountains, meticulously manicured gardens, and veterans' monuments. (Tours depart from just inside the front steps daily on the hr. 10am-3pm. Building open M-F 8am-5:30pm, Sa-Su 10am-4pm.) The mansionesque **State Capitol Museum,** 211 W. 21st Ave. (753-2580), houses historical and political exhibits. (Open Tu-F 10am-4pm, Sa-Su noon-4pm. $2, seniors $1.75, children $1, families $5.) Several different free tours of campus buildings leave hourly on weekdays; call 586-TOUR/8687 for more info and options for the disabled. The **4th Ave. Bridge** is a perfect place to spot **spawning salmon,** as the leaping lox-to-be cross the lake from late August through October. **Yashiro Japanese Garden** (753-8380), at Plum and Union, right next to City Hall, hoards hundreds of colorful plants behind high walls, making it Olympia's own secret garden (open daily 10am-dusk for picnickers and ponderers). **Wolf Haven International,** 3111 Offut Lake Rd. (264-4695 or 800-448-9653), lurks 10 mi. south of the capital. (Open May-Sept. W-M 10am-5pm; Oct.-Apr. 10am-4pm. 45min. tours $5, ages 5-12 $2.50.) Take Exit 99 off I-5, turn east, and follow the brown signs. The haven now shelters 24 wolves reclaimed from zoos or illegal owners, and is participating in a breeding program to re-introduce Mexican wolves into the American Southwest.

Grays Harbor Hostel, 6 Ginny Ln. (482-3119), 25 mi. west of Olympia just off Rte. 8 in Elma, is a home away from home and the perfect place to start a trip down the coast. (Hot tub and a 3-hole golf course. Beds $11; single rooms available. Bikers can camp on the lawn for $7.) **Millersylvania State Park,** 12245 Tilly Rd. S. (753-1519, reservations 800-452-5687), is 10 mi. south of Olympia. Take Exit 99 off I-5 S, or Exit 95 off I-5 N, then take Rte. 121 N, and follow the signs to the state park. Smallish, family- and RV-filled campsites are crowded among firs, with 6 mi. of needle-carpeted trails and Deep Lake, which has two unguarded swimming areas. ($11, with hookup $16; hiker/biker sites $5.50. Showers 25¢ per 6min. Flush toilets. Disabled facilities. 10-night max. stay.) Roads around the park are closed to traffic the last Sunday of the month (Apr.-Aug. 8am-6pm), so that bicyclists can have free reign. Old-school diners, veggie-intensive eateries, and Asian quickstops line bohemian **4th Ave.** east of Columbia. **The Spar Café & Bar,** 114 E. 4th Ave. (357-6444), is an ancient logger haunt that moonlights as a sweet-smelling pipe and cigar shop. (Sandwiches and burgers $6-8. Restaurant open M-Th 6am-10pm, F-Sa 6am-11pm, Su 6am-9pm. Mellow bar in back, with live jazz Sa 9pm-1am, open Su-Th 11am-midnight, F-Sa 11am-2am.)

Olympia's ferocious nightlife seems to have outgrown its daylife. At **Eastside Club and Tavern,** 410 E. 4th St. (357-9985), old men playing pool and pinball rumble with college students slamming super cheap pints ($1.75). Local bands play frequently; check around town for the latest in the indie scene. **Thekla,** 155 E. 5th Ave. (352-1855), is under the neon arrow off N. Washington St. between 4th Ave. and Capitol. Past Olympia's startlingly clean alleys, this gay-friendly dance joint spins nightly entertainment, from karaoke to 80s night to DJ hip-hop. (21+. Cover varies, but tends to be more expensive Th-Sa. Open daily 6pm-2am.)

Olympia is at the junction of I-5 and U.S. 101. **Amtrak,** 6600 Yelm Hwy. (923-4602 or 800-872-7245), runs to Seattle (4 per day, $8.50-16) and Portland (4 per day, $11.50-22). **Greyhound,** 107 E. 7th Ave. (357-5541 or 800-231-2222), at Capitol Way, runs to Seattle (6 per day, $8); Portland (6 per day, $19); and Spokane (2 per day, $27). **Intercity Transit (IT)** (786-1881 or 800-287-6348) provides service almost anywhere in Thurston County, even for bicycles (fare 60¢, seniors and disabled 30¢; day passes $1.25). The free **Capitol Shuttle** runs from the Capitol Campus to downtown or to the east side and west side (every 15min., 6:45am-5:45pm). IT's **Olympia Express** runs to Tacoma. (Runs M-F 5:50am-6pm. Fare $1.50, seniors and disabled 75¢. Transfers to a Seattle bus in Tacoma $1.60 extra; full trip to Seattle takes 2hr.) **Washington State Capitol Visitors Center,** P.O. Box 41020 (586-3460), is on Capitol Way between 12th and 14th Ave., next to the State Capitol; follow the signs on I-5 (open M-F 8am-5pm). **Post Office:** 900 Jefferson SE (357-2289; open M-F 7:30am-12:25pm and 1-6pm, Sa 9am-12:25pm and 1-4pm). **ZIP code:** 98501. **Area code:** 360.

■ Bellingham

Strategically located between Seattle and Vancouver, Bellingham is the southern terminus of the Alaska Marine Hwy.; most travelers who stay the night are starting or completing an overseas journey to or from Alaska. A recent influx of young people has converted this former lumber town into a lively community with a boom town atmosphere. **Western Washington University (WWU)** generates continuous cultural and artistic activity, and maintains 7 mi. of hiking trails with views of Bellingham Bay and the San Juan Islands. Take buses #7, 11, 16, 26, 27, and 28 from downtown.

For both atmosphere and price, the hostel is the best bet. For help with other accommodations, try the **Bed & Breakfast Guild of Whatcom Co.** (676-4560). Many B&Bs offer rooms in the neighborhood of $60. **Fairhaven Rose Garden Hostel (HI-AYH),** 107 Chuckanut Dr. (671-1750), next to Fairhaven Park, is about ¾ mi. from the ferry terminal. Take I-5 Exit 250, and go west on Fairhaven Pkwy. to 12th St.; bear left onto Chuckanut Dr. From downtown Bellingham, take bus # 1A or 1B. The hostel is clean and tiny, though with sleeping quarters, bathrooms, and showers all in the basement. (Beds $12. Make-your-own, all-you-can-eat pancakes $1. Linen $2. No curfew, but living room closes at 10pm. Reception 5-10pm. Check-out 9:30am. Call ahead, especially on W or Th night, when Alaska-bound travelers fill the hostel. Reservations mandatory July-Aug. Open Feb.-Nov.) **Larrabee State Park** (676-2093, reservations 800-452-5687), on Chuckanut Dr., 7 mi. south of town, has sites tucked in among the trees on Samish Bay, a half-hidden flatland outside the city. Check out the nearby tide pools or hike to alpine lakes. ($11, with hookup $16; 8 walk-ins $7; open daily 6:30am-dusk.) **Casa Que Pasa,** 1415 Railroad Ave. (738-TACO/8226), serves humongous burritos ($2.75), made with fresh vegetables purchased from local growers (open Su-Th and Sa 11am-11pm, F 11am-midnight).

Bellingham lies along I-5, 90 mi. north of Seattle and 57 mi. south of Vancouver, and is the only major city between the two. **Amtrak,** 401 Harris Ave. (734-8851 or 800-872-7245), in the Greyhound/Amtrak station next to the ferry terminals, sends one train per day to Seattle ($25) and Vancouver, BC ($20). **Greyhound,** 401 Harris Ave. (733-5251 or 800-231-2222), next to the ferry terminals, runs to Seattle (9 per day, $13) and Vancouver (6 per day, $13). The **Alaska Marine Highway Ferry,** 355 Harris Ave. (676-8445 or 800-642-0066), has its terminal in Fairhaven; take Exit 250 off I-5, then Rte. 11 W. Two boats per week go to Ketchikan, AK ($164) and beyond from July to August. All **Whatcom County Transit** (676-7433) routes start at the Railroad Ave. Mall terminal, between Holly and Magnolia St. (35¢, under 5 and over 90 free. No free transfers. Buses run every 15-30min. M-F 5:50am-7:30pm; reduced service M-F 7:30-11pm and Sa-Su 9am-6pm.) To reach the **Visitor Information Center,** 904 Potter St. (671-3990), take Exit 253 (Lakeway) from I-5 (open daily 8:30am-5:30pm). **Post Office:** 315 Prospect (676-8303; open M-F 8am-5:30pm, Sa 9:30am-3pm). **ZIP code:** 98225. **Area code:** 360.

■ San Juan Islands

The lush San Juan Islands are home to great horned owls, puffins, sea otters, sea lions, and more deer, raccoons, and rabbits then they can support. Pods of orcas (killer whales) patrol the waters, and pods of tourists mimic the whales, circling the islands in everything from yachts to kayaks in pursuit of cetacean encounters. Over 1½ million visitors come ashore on the San Juans each year, usually in July and August. To avoid the rush but still enjoy good weather, try visiting in late spring or early fall.

Washington State Ferries (800-843-3779 or 206-464-6400) serves **Lopez, Shaw, Orcas,** and **San Juan Islands** daily from **Anacortes** on the mainland ($5.10, with vehicle $16-21.75 depending on destination, bike surcharge $2.90). Ferry times vary for each island—call for info or check the schedule. The ferry system revises its schedule seasonally and there are no reservations. To reach Anacortes, take I-5 N from Seattle to Mt. Vernon. From there, Rte. 20 heads west to Anacortes; the way to the ferry is well marked. **Foot passengers** travel in either direction between the islands free of charge. No charge is levied on **eastbound traffic;** pay for bringing a vehicle on the ferry only on **westbound** trips to or between the islands. To see more islands and save on ferry fares, travel directly to the westernmost island on your itinerary, then return eastward to the mainland island by island. On peak travel days, show up at least 1hr. prior to departure. The ferry authorities accept only cash or in-state checks. The **Bellingham Airporter** (800-235-5247) makes eight trips from the Seattle Airport (see p. 692) to Anacortes on weekdays, and six trips on weekends ($27, round-trip $49). Short distances and good roads make the San Juans excellent for **biking.**

San Juan Island The biggest and most popular of the islands, San Juan Island is the easiest island to explore, since the ferry docks right in town, roads are fairly flat for bicyclists, and a shuttle bus runs throughout the island. Seattle weekenders flood the island throughout the summer, bringing fleets of traffic. The **Whale Museum,** 62 1st St.

(378-4710), exhibits skeletons, sculptures, and updates on new whale research. (Open daily 10am-5pm; Oct.-May 11am-4pm. $5, seniors $4, students and ages 5-18 $2.) A drive around the 35 mi. perimeter of the island takes about 2hr., and the route is perfect for cyclists. The **West Side Rd.** traverses gorgeous scenery and provides the best chance for sighting **orcas** offshore. Mulles Rd. merges with Cattle Point Rd. and goes straight into **American Camp** (378-2902), on the south side of the island (open daily 8am-dusk). The camp dates from the Pig War of 1859, and a **visitors center** explains the history of that epic conflict. (Open daily 8:30am-5pm. Guided walks W-F at 11:30am and 2:30pm, Sa-Su 11:30am.) Every Saturday afternoon, volunteers in period costume reenact daily Pig-War era life (June-Sept. 12:30-3:30pm; free). **British Camp,** the second half of the **San Juan National Historical Park,** lies on West Valley Rd., on the sheltered **Garrison Bay.** (Park open year-round. Buildings open Memorial Day to Labor Day daily 8am-4:30pm.) **Lime Kiln Point State Park,** along West Side Rd., is renowned as the best **whale-watching** spot in the area. Killer whales frequent this stretch of coastline, and have been known to perform occasional acrobatics. Most **cruises** charge about $40 (children $30) for a 3-4hr. ride.

San Juan County Park, 380 Westside Rd. (378-2992), 10 mi. west of Friday Harbor on Smallpox and Andrews Bays, offers the chance to catch views of whales and a great sunset. (Water and flush toilets, no showers or RV hookups. Vehicle sites $16; hiker/biker sites $5. Park open daily 7am-10pm. Office open daily 9am-7pm. Reservations highly recommended.) **Katrina's,** 135 2nd St. (378-7290), between Key Bank and Friday Harbor Drug, cooks up a different menu every day, but invariably serves organic salads, freshly baked bread, and gigantic cookies ($1.25; open M-Th 11am-4:30pm, F 11am-4:30pm and 5:30-10pm, Sa 5:30-10pm).

San Juan Transit (376-8887 or 800-887-8387) circles the island every 35-55min., making many convenient stops (point to point $4; day pass $10; 2-day pass $19, also good on Orcas Island). If you plan to see San Juan Island only, it may be cheaper to leave your car in Anacortes and use the shuttles. The **Chamber of Commerce** (378-5240), in a booth on East St. up from Cannery Landing, is staffed sporadically daily dawn-dusk, but constantly stocked with pamphlets. The **National Park Service Information Center** (378-2240) is on the corner of 1st and Spring St. (open M-F 8:30am-5pm; off-season M-F 8:30am-4pm). **Post Office:** 220 Blair St. (378-4511), at Reed St. (open M-F 8:30am-4:30pm). **ZIP code:** 98250. **Area code:** 360.

Orcas Island

A small population of retirees, artists, and farmers dwell on Orcas Island in understated homes, surrounded by green shrubs and the red bark of madrona trees. The trail to **Obstruction Pass Beach** is the best of the few ways to clamber down to the rocky shores. **Moran State Park** is unquestionably Orcas's star outdoor attraction, with over 30 mi. of hiking trails ranging from a 1hr. jaunt around **Mountain Lake** to a day-long trek up the south face of **Mt. Constitution,** the highest peak on the islands (open daily 6:30am-dusk; Sept.-Mar. 8am-dusk). The summit of Constitution looks out over the Olympic and Cascade Ranges, Vancouver Island, and Mt. Rainier. Part-way down is **Cascade Falls,** spectacular in the spring and early summer. Down below, two freshwater lakes are easily accessible from the highway, and the park rents rowboats and paddleboats ($10-13 per hr.). **Shearwater Adventures** (376-4699) runs a fascinating, albeit expensive, **sea kayak tour** of the north end of Puget Sound, with close views of bald eagles, seals, and blue herons. Tours leave from Deer Harbor and Rosario Beach. (3hr. tour $42; includes 30min. of dry-land training.)

Doe Bay Village Resort, Star Rte. 86, Olga (376-2291), off Horseshoe Hwy. on Pt. Lawrence Rd., 5 mi. out of Moran State Park, includes kitchen facilities, a health food store and cafe, a treehouse, guided kayak trips (376-4699; $42 for 3hr.), and a steam sauna and mineral bath ($4 per day, nonlodgers $7; bathing suits optional; coed). (Hostel beds $16 for members; campsites $12-22. Rustic cottages from $44.50. Reservations recommended. Office open 9am-9pm.) To reach **Moran State Park** (376-2326 or 800-452-5687), Star Rte. 22, Eastsound, follow Horseshoe Hwy. straight into the park. (About 12 sites open year-round, as are the restrooms. Standard sites $11; hiker/biker sites $5. Hot showers 25¢ per 5min. Rowboats and paddleboats $10-13 for 1hr., $7 per additional hr. Reservations strongly recommended May-Sept. 6.) **Chimayo** (376-6394), in the Our House Bldg. on North Beach Rd., has a Southwestern theme and comfy booths (funky burritos $3-4; open M and W-Su 11am-7pm).

The ferry lands on the southwest tip of Orcas, and the main town of **Eastsound** is 9 mi. northeast. **Olga** and **Doe Bay** are an additional 8 and 11 mi. from Eastsound, respectively, down the eastern side of the horseshoe. **San Juan Transit** (376-8887) runs about every 1½hr. to most parts of the island (ferry to Eastsound $4). The **Chamber of Commerce** (376-2273) returns phone calls, but the best bet is to pick up info on San Juan Island, or visit **Pyewacket Books** (376-2043), a used bookstore in Templin Center that also houses a slew of island info. **Wildlife Cycle** (376-4708), at A St. and North Beach Rd., in Eastsound, rents 21-speeds ($5 per hr., $25 per day; open M-Sa 10am-5:30pm, Su 11am-3pm). **Post Office:** (376-4121), on A St. in Eastsound Marketplace (open M-F 9am-4:30pm). **ZIP code:** 98245. **Area code:** 360.

OLYMPIC PENINSULA

Due west of Seattle and its busy Puget Sound neighbors, the Olympic Peninsula is a remarkably different world. To the west, the Pacific Ocean stretches to a distant horizon; to the north, the Strait of Juan de Fuca separates the Olympic Peninsula from Vancouver Island; and to the east, Hood Canal and the Kitsap Peninsula isolate this sparsely inhabited wilderness from the sprawl of Seattle. Getting around the peninsula is easiest by car. Distances are tremendous, and public transportation, while passable for traveling to and between the peninsula's small towns, does not serve the magnificent natural areas that are the main attractions. Direct transfers between local bus lines provide a round-trip from Seattle to the peninsula for $24 (on weekdays).

■ Port Townsend

Unlike the salmon industry, Port Townsend's Victorian splendor has survived the progression of time and weather. Countless cafes, galleries, and bookstores line somewhat drippy streets, cheering the homesick urbanites who move there to escape the rat race. The **Ann Starret Mansion,** 744 Clay St. (385-3205 or 800-321-0644), has nationally renowned Victorian architecture, frescoed ceilings, and a free-hanging, three-tiered spiral staircase (tours daily noon-3pm; $2).

Fort Flagler Hostel (HI-AYH) (385-1288), in Fort Flagler State Park, overlooks the ocean on gorgeous **Marrowstone Island,** 20 mi. from Port Townsend; go south on Rte. 19, which connects to Rte. 116 E and leads directly into the park. A hostel in an old military haunt, the rooms are bright, clean, and cheery, if a bit farther from local attractions. Miles of pastoral bike routes wind over Marrowstone, and the hostel is less crowded than most. (Beds $11, nonmembers $14, cyclists $9-12. Reservations required. Check-in 5-10pm. Lockout 10am-5pm. Call ahead if arriving late.) **Olympic Hostel (HI-AYH)** (385-0655), in Fort Worden State Park 1½ mi. from downtown (follow the signs), has views of the ocean, plenty of space, and cushy hospital beds in impeccable bunk rooms. Rooms for couples and kitchen facilities are available. (Beds $12; nonmembers $15; cyclists $9-13. Check-in 5-10pm, check-out 9:30am; no curfew.) **Old Fort Townsend State Park** (385-3595), 5 mi. south of town just off Rte. 20, rests in some pretty woods. (40 cramped sites and no potable water. Sites $10; hiker/biker sites $5. Open mid-May to mid-Sept.) **Burrito Depot,** 609 Washington St. (385-5856), at Madison, offers quick, tasty Mexican food (big burritos from $3.25; open daily 10:30am-8:30pm; wheelchair access).

Port Townsend sits at the terminus of Rte. 20 on the northeast corner of the Olympic Peninsula. By land, it can be reached from U.S. 101 on the peninsula, or from the Kitsap Peninsula across the Hood Canal Bridge. **Washington State Ferries** (800-84-FERRY/843-3779 or 206-464-6400) runs from Seattle to Winslow on Bainbridge Island, where a **Kitsap County Transit** bus meets every ferry and runs to Poulsbo, where transfers to Port Townsend are available from **Jefferson County Transit (JCT),**

1615 W. Sims Way (385-4777). Park in the Park 'N' Ride lot and take a **free shuttle** into downtown to avoid parking hassles during rush hours. (Most buses do not run on Su. 50¢, seniors and disabled travelers 25¢, ages 6-18 25¢, 25¢ extra fare per zone. Day passes $1.50.) The **Chamber of Commerce,** 2437 E. Sims Way (385-2722 or 800-365-6978), lies about 10 blocks from the center of town on Rte. 20 (open M-F 9am-5pm, Sa 10am-4pm, Su 11am-4pm). **Post Office:** 1322 Washington St. (385-1600; open M-F 9am-5pm). **ZIP code:** 98368. **Area code:** 360.

■ Olympic National Park

Olympic National Park (ONP), the centerpiece of the Olympic Peninsula, shelters one of the most diverse landscapes of any North American park. With glacier-encrusted peaks, lush and dripping river valley rainforests, and jagged shores along the Pacific Coast, the park appeals to the wide-ranging tastes of an even wider range of visitors.

PRACTICAL INFORMATION

Only a few hours from Seattle, Portland, and Victoria, the wilderness of Olympic National Park is most easily and safely reached by car. U.S. 101 encircles the park in the shape of an upside-down U, with Port Angeles at the top. The park's vista-filled **eastern rim** runs up to Port Angeles, from which the much-visited **northern rim** extends westward. The tiny town of **Neah Bay** and stunning **Cape Flattery** perch at the northwest tip of the peninsula; farther south on U.S. 101, the slightly less tiny town of **Forks** is a gateway to the park's rainforested **western rim.** Separated from the rest of the park, much of the peninsula's Pacific coastline comprises a gorgeous **coastal zone.**

Olympic National Park Visitors Center, 3002 Mt. Angeles Rd. (452-0330, TDD 452-0306), is off Race St. in Port Angeles. ONP's main info center fields questions about the entire park, including camping, backcountry hiking, and fishing. (Open in summer approximately Su-F 8:30am-6:30pm, Sa 8:30am-8pm; in winter daily 9am-4pm.) **Hoh Rainforest Visitors Center** (374-6925), on the park's western rim, also provides posters and permits (open daily July-Aug. 9am-6:30pm; Sept.-June 9am-4:30pm). The Park and Forest Services furnish info at the **Hood Canal Ranger Station,** P.O. Box 68, Hoodsport 98548 (877-5254), southeast of the reserve lands on U.S. 101 in Hoodsport (open daily 8am-4:30pm; in winter M-F 8am-4:30pm). Staff at the **Olympic National Park Wilderness Information Center** (452-0300), just behind the visitors center, will gladly sit down with backpackers to help design trips within the park. The **entrance fee,** good for 7 days' access to the park, is $10 per car and $5 per hiker or biker, charged during the day at developed entrances such as Hoh, Heart o' the Hills, Sol Duc, Staircase, and Elwha. **Area code:** 360.

ACCOMMODATIONS AND CAMPGROUNDS

The closest non-camping budget accommodation is the **Rainforest Hostel,** 169312 U.S. 101 (374-2270), in Forks. To get there, follow the hostel signs off U.S. 101, 4 mi. north of Ruby Beach between Miles 168 and 169. Buses travel to the hostel from North Shore Brannon's Grocery in Quinault (daily 9am, 1, and 4:35pm; 50¢). Two family-size rooms are available, as well as a men's dorm with five double bunks in summer; couple and family accommodations require a reservation and deposit. (Beds $10. Curfew 11pm. Wakeup 8am. Morning chore required of hostelers.)

Olympic National Park, Olympic National Forest, and the State of Washington all maintain **free campgrounds,** but the ONP requires a **backcountry permit** ($5), and the ONF often requires a **trailhead pass** ($3) for sites located off a main trail. The Washington Dept. of Natural Resources (DNR) allows **free backcountry camping** off any state road on DNR land, as long as campers tent at least 100 yd. from the road. The majority of DNR land is near the western shore along the Hoh and Clearwater Rivers, though smaller, individual DNR campsites are sprinkled about the peninsula.

Reservations (800-280-CAMP/2267) can be made for three national forest campgrounds: **Seal Rock, Falls View,** and **Klahowga.** Several state parks are scattered along Hood Canal and the eastern side of the peninsula (sites $10-16; occasionally $4-5); to reserve, call 800-452-5687. Most other drive-up camping on the peninsula is first come, first served. Backcountry camping anywhere in the park requires a $5 **backcountry permit,** available at any ranger station and some trailheads. Park offices maintain quota limits on backcountry permits for especially popular destinations within the park, including **Lake Constance** and **Flapjack Lakes** in the eastern rim; **Grand Valley, Badger Valley,** and **Sol Duc** in the northern rim; **Hoh** in the western rim; and the coastal **Ozette Loop.** Reservations are crucial, especially for the beach campsites. Before any backcountry trip, make sure to inquire at a ranger station about trail closures; winter weather has destroyed many a popular trail.

SIGHTS AND OUTDOORS

Eastern Rim

What ONP's western regions have in ocean and rainforest, the eastern rim matches with canals and grandiose views. Canyon walls rise treacherously, their jagged edges leading to mountaintops that offer glimpses of the entire peninsula and Puget Sound. Steep trails lead up **Mt. Ellinor,** 5 mi. past Staircase on Rte. 119. Once on the mountain, hikers can choose the 3 mi. path or an equally steep but shorter journey to the summit; look for signs to the Upper Trailhead along F.I. Road #2419-04. Adventure-seekers who hit the mountain before late July should bring snow clothes to "mach"—as in Mach 1, the speed to which sliders accelerate—down a ¼ mi. **snow chute.**

A 3.2 mi. hike ascends to **Lena Lake,** 14 mi. north of Hoodsport off U.S. 101; follow Forest Service Rd. 25 (known as the Hamma-Hamma Rte.) off U.S. 101 for 8 mi. to the trailhead. The Park Service charges a $3 trailhead pass. The **West Forks Dosewallip Trail,** a 10½ mi. trek to **Mt. Anderson Glacier,** is the shortest route to any glacier in the park. The road to **Mt. Walker Viewpoint,** 5 mi. south of Quilcene on U.S. 101, is steep, has sheer drop-offs, and should not be attempted in foul weather or a temperamental car. Yet another view of Hood Canal, Puget Sound, Mt. Rainier, and Seattle awaits intrepid travelers on top.

Northern Rim

The most developed section of Olympic National Park lies along its northern rim, near Port Angeles, where glaciers, rainforests, and sunsets over the Pacific are all only a drive away. Farthest east off U.S. 101 lies **Deer Park,** where trails tend to be uncrowded and vistas plentiful. Past Deer Park, the **Royal Basin Trail** meanders 6.2 mi. to the **Royal Basin Waterfall.** The road up **Hurricane Ridge** is an easy but curvy drive. Before July, walking on the ridge usually involves a bit of snow-stepping. Clear days give splendid views of Mt. Olympus and Vancouver Island, set against a foreground of snow and indigo lupine. From here, the uphill **High Ridge Trail** is a short walk from Sunset Point. On weekends from late December to late March, the Park Service organizes free guided **snowshoe walks** atop the ridge.

Farther west on U.S. 101, 13 mi. of paved road penetrates to the popular **Sol Duc Hot Springs Resort** (327-3583), where retirees de-wrinkle in the springs and eat at grubholes inside the lodge. The resort's chlorinated pools are wheelchair accessible. (Open daily June-Sept. 9am-9pm; Apr.-May and Oct. Sa-Su 9am-6pm. $6.50, seniors $5.50; suit or towel rental $2.) The **Sol Duc trailhead** is a starting point for those heading on up; crowds thin dramatically above **Sol Duc Falls.** The **Eagle Ranger Station** (327-3534) has info and permits (open June-Aug. daily 8am-5pm).

Neah Bay and Cape Flattery

At the westernmost point on the Juan de Fuca Strait is **Neah Bay,** the only town in the **Makah Reservation.** Cape Flattery and Neah Bay are not a part of ONP, and they are only accessible overland by skirting its boundaries, since they perch just north of the park on the western rim. The **Makah Cultural and Research Center** (645-2711), in Neah Bay on Hwy. 112, is just inside the reservation on the first left, right across from the Coast Guard station. *(Open daily 10am-5pm; Sept.-May W-Su 10am-5pm. $4, students and seniors $3.)* It beautifully presents artifacts from an archaeological site at Cape Alava, where a huge mudslide buried and perfectly preserved a small Makah settlement 500 years ago. The Makah Nation, whose recorded history goes back 2000 years, still lives, fishes, and produces artwork on this land, though now in a startling state of poverty. From Port Angeles, Rte. 112 leads west 72 mi. to Neah Bay. From the south, take Rte. 113 north from Sappho on U.S. 101 to reach Rte. 112; this drive takes at least 1hr. **Clallam Transit System** (452-4511 or 800-858-3747) serves Neah Bay out of Port Angeles. Take bus #14 from Oak St. to Sappho (75min.), then take bus #16 to Neah Bay (1hr.; $1, seniors 50¢, ages 6-19 85¢).

Cape Flattery is the most northwesterly point in the contiguous U.S. Not only that, but it's drop-dead gorgeous. Pick up detailed directions at the Makah Center, or just take the road through town until it turns to dirt, then follow the "Marine Viewing Area" sign once you hit gravel, and continue for another 4 mi. to a small, circular parking area, where a trailhead leads toward Cape Flattery. To the south, the reservation's **beaches** are solitary and peaceful; respectful visitors are welcome to wander.

Western Rim

In the temperate rainforests of ONP's western rim, ferns, mosses, and gigantic old growth trees blanket the earth in a sea of green. The drive along the **Hoh River Valley** is alternately stunning and barren, depending on how many DNR trees have fallen to the axe, chainsaw, or hydraulic splitter in recent months. From **Hoh Rainforest Visitors Center** (see **Practical Information**, p. 706), a good 45min. drive from U.S. 101, take the quick (40min.), ¾ mi. **Hall of Mosses Trail** for a whirlwind tour of rainforest vegetation. The slightly longer (1hr.) **Spruce Nature Trail** leads 1¼ mi. through lush forest and along the banks of the Hoh River, with a smattering of educational panels explaining bizarre natural quirks. The **Hoh Rainforest Trail** is the most heavily traveled path in the area, beginning at the visitors center and paralleling the Hoh River for 18 mi. to **Blue Glacier** on the shoulder of **Mt. Olympus.**

Several other trailheads from U.S. 101 offer less crowded opportunities for exploration of the rainforest, amid surrounding ridges and mountains. The **Queets River Trail** hugs its namesake east for 14 mi. from the free **Queets Campground;** the road is unpaved and unsuitable for RVs or large trailers. High river waters early in the summer can thwart a trek; hiking is best in August, but there's still a risk that water will cut off trail access. A shorter loop (3 mi.) passes a broad range of rainforest, lowland river ecosystems, and the park's largest Douglas fir.

From the **Quinault Ranger Station,** 353 S. Shore Rd. (288-2444; open daily 9am-4:30pm; in winter M-F 9am-4:30pm), try the 4 mi. **Quinault Lake Loop** or the ½ mi. **Maple Glade Trail.** Snow-seekers flock to **Three Lakes Point,** an exquisite summit covered with powder until July. **Quinault Lake** lures anglers, rowers, and canoers. The **Lake Quinault Lodge** (288-2900 or 800-562-6672), next to the ranger station, rents canoes and rowboats ($10 per hr.). Jim Carlson (288-2293) offers **horseback rides** around the lake and through the forest in summer ($35 per 2hr.).

Coastal Zone

Pristine coastline traces the park's slim far western region for 57 mi., separated from the rest of ONP by U.S. 101 and non-park timber land. Eerie fields of driftwood, sculptured arches, and dripping caves frame flamboyant sunsets, while the waves are punctuated by rugged sea stacks—chunks of coast stranded at sea after erosion swept away the surrounding land. Between the Quinault and Hoh Reservations, U.S. 101 hugs the coast for 15 mi., with parking lots just a short walk from the sand. North of where the highway meets the coast, **Beach #4** has abundant tidepools, plastered with sea stars; **Beach #6,** 3 mi. north at Mile 160, is a favorite whale-watching spot. Near Mi. 165, sea otters and eagles hang out amid tide pools and sea stacks at **Ruby Beach. Beach camping** is only permitted north of the Hoh Reservation between **Oil City** and **Third Beach,** and north of the Quileute Reservation between **Hole-in-the-**

Slime, Sex, and Violence

The **banana slug** (genus *Ariolimax*) ranges from 6-10 in., from dull brown to bright yellow, and from southern California to Southeast Alaska.

Fact: Using copious secretions of viscous slime, the banana slug cleanses itself of debris, protects itself from predators, and descends by a gossamer-thin slime cord. **Moral:** Mucus is a useful tool.

Fact: Banana slugs are hermaphrodites, and can mate at any time of year. Foreplay consists of petting, licking, and violent biting, and can last up to 12hr. During the deed, a slug's male organ can become too swollen to be removed from its partner, necessitating "apophallation"—the removal of genitalia via gnawing. **Moral:** Slug sex, however titillating, is not for people.

Fact: The jet-black slugs that one often sees are not banana slugs, but foreign European slugs who in fact practice unprovoked aggression on their native North American cousins. **Moral:** Be kind to the banana slug, but if you see a Euro-version, salt its slimy ass to oblivion.

Wall and **Shi-Shi Beach.** Day hikers and backpackers adore the 9 mi. loop that begins at **Ozette Lake.** The trail is a triangle with two 3 mi. legs leading along boardwalks through the rainforest. One heads toward sea stacks at **Cape Alava,** the other to a sublime beach at **Sand Point.** A 3 mi. hike down the coast links the two legs, passing ancient native petroglyphs. Overnighters must make **permit reservations** (452-0300) in advance; spaces fill quickly in summer.

CASCADE RANGE

Intercepting the moist Pacific air, the Cascades divide Washington into the lush, wet green of the west and the low, dry plains of the east. In 1859, an explorer making his way through the Cascade Range gushed: "Nowhere do the mountain masses and peaks present such strange, fantastic, dauntless, and startling outlines as here." Native people dubbed the Cascades "Home of the Gods."

U.S. 12 approaches Mt. Rainier National Park through White Pass, and provides access to Mt. St. Helens from the north; **I-90** sends four lanes past the ski resorts of Snoqualmie Pass; scenic **U.S. 2** leaves Everett for Stevens Pass and descends along the Wenatchee River; the **North Cascades Hwy. (Rte. 20),** is the most breathtaking of the trans-Cascade roads providing access to North Cascades National Park. Rte. 20 and U.S. 2 are often traveled in sequence as the **Cascade Loop. Greyhound** runs on I-90 and U.S. 2 to and from Seattle, while **Amtrak** parallels I-90. The Cascades are most accessible in the months of July, August, and September; many high mountain passes are snowed in during the rest of the year.

■ Mount St. Helens

In a single cataclysmic blast on May 18, 1980, the summit of Mt. St. Helens erupted, transforming what had been a perfect cone into a crater 1 mi. wide and 2 mi. long. The force of the ash-filled blast robbed the mountain of 1300 ft. and razed entire forests, strewing trees like charred matchsticks. Ash from the crater rocketed 17 mi. upward, circling the globe and blackening the region's sky for days. The explosion itself was 27,000 times the force of the atomic bomb dropped on Hiroshima. **Mt. St. Helens National Volcanic Monument,** administered by the Forest Service, encompasses most of the blast zone, the area around the volcano affected by the explosion. This ashen landscape is steadily recovering from the explosion that transformed 230 sq. mi. of prime forest into a wasteland.

PRACTICAL INFORMATION The main access routes to the monument—Rte. 504, Rte. 503, and U.S. 12—spiral around Mt. St. Helens from different directions and do not connect. Vigorous winter rains often decimate access roads; check at a ranger station for road closures before heading out. From the **west,** take Exit 49 off I-5 and use Rte. 504, otherwise known as the **Spirit Lake Memorial Hwy.** For most, this is the quickest and easiest daytrip to the mountain, and the main visitors centers line the way to the volcano. **Rte. 503** parallels the **south** side of the volcano until it connects with **Forest Service Rd. 90.** Though views from this side don't highlight recent destruction, green glens and remnants of age-old explosions make this the best side for hiking and camping. From the **north,** the towns of **Mossyrock, Morton,** and **Randle** line **U.S. 12** and offer the closest major services to the monument. From U.S. 12, both **Forest Service Rd. 25** and **Forest Service Rd. 26** head south to **Forest Service Rd. 99,** a 16 mi. dead-end road that travels into the most devastated parts of the monument, passing a handful of lookouts.

The monument charges an **entrance fee** at almost every visitors center, viewpoint, and cave ($8, seniors $4, Golden Eagle Pass $4, under 16 free; valid for 3 days). It is possible to stop at the viewpoints after 6pm without paying, or to drive through the park without stopping at the main centers. **Mt. St. Helens Visitors Center** (360-274-2100 or 360-274-2103), across from Seaquest State Park on Rte. 504, is most visitors' first stop, with displays on the eruption and plenty of interactive exhibits (open May-Sept. daily 9am-6pm; winter hrs. generally 9am-5pm). **Coldwater Ridge Visitors Center** (274-2131) is 38 mi. farther on Rte. 504. This sprawling glass-and-copper building has a superb view of the collapsed cavity, with an emphasis on the area's recolonization by living things. (Open daily 9am-6pm; Sept.-Apr. 9am-5pm.) **Johnston Ridge Observatory** (274-2140), at the end of Rte. 504, overlooking the crater, focuses on geological exhibits and offers the best view from the road of the steaming lava dome and crater (open daily 9am-6pm; Oct-Apr. 10am-4pm).

Woods Creek Information Station, 6 mi. south of Randle on Rd. 25 from U.S. 12, is a drive-through info center (open mid-May-Sept. daily 9am-4pm). **Pine Creek Information Station** (238-5225), 17 mi. east of Cougar on Rd. 90, shows an interpretive film of the eruption (open mid-May to Sept. daily 9am-6pm). **Apes Headquarters,** at Ape Cave on Rd. 8303, on the south side of the volcano, answers all lava tube questions (open mid-May to Sept. daily 9:30am-5:30pm). **Monument Headquarters,** 42218 NE Yale Bridge Rd. (247-3900 or 247-3903), 3 mi. north of Amboy on Rte. 503, is in charge of **crater-climbing permits** (open M-F 7:30am-5pm). From May 15 to October 31, the Forest Service allows 100 people per day to hike to the crater rim (applications accepted from Feb. 1; $15). Procrastinators should head for **Jack's Restaurant and Country Store,** 13411 Louis River Rd. (231-4276), on Rte. 503, 5 mi. west of Cougar (I-5 Exit 21), where a lottery is held at 6pm each day to distribute the next day's 50 unreserved permits (open daily 5:30am-9pm). **Area code:** 360.

CAMPGROUNDS Although the monument itself contains no campgrounds, a number are scattered throughout the surrounding national forest. Free dispersed camping is allowed within the monument, but finding a site is a matter of luck. **Iron Creek Campground** (reservations 800-280-2267) is just south of the Woods Creek Information Station on Rd. 25, near its junction with Rd. 76. This is the closest campsite to Mt. St. Helens, with good hiking and striking views of the crater and the blast zone. (Water available 8-10am and 6-8pm. Sites $12, premium $14.) Spacious **Swift Campground** is on Rd. 90, just west of the Pine Creek Information Station (sites $12; free firewood; no reservations). **Beaver Bay** is west of Swift Campground on the Yale Reservoir (RV and tent sites $12; toilets and showers). Swift and Cougar are run by **Pacificorp** (503-464-5035).

OUTDOORS The 1hr. drive from the Mt. St. Helens Visitors Center to Johnston Ridge offers spectacular views of the crater and of the resurgence of life. The ½ mi. **Winds of Change Trail,** at Coldwater Lake, has signposts aplenty to explain the eerie surrounding landscape. Another 10 mi. east, a hike along **Johnston Ridge** approaches incredibly close to the crater where geologist David Johnston died studying the eruption. On the way west along Rd. 99, **Bear Meadow** provides the first interpretive stop, an excellent view of Mt. St. Helens, and the last restrooms before Rd. 99 ends at **Windy Ridge.** The monument begins just west of Bear Meadow, where Rd. 26 and 99 meet. Rangers lead 45min. walks to emerald **Meta Lake;** meet at Miner's Car at the junction of Rd. 26 and 99 (daily late June-Sept. 12:45 and 3pm). The trail around the lake is an easy ½ mi. Farther west on Rd. 99, **Independence Pass Trail #227** is a difficult 3½ mi. hike, with overlooks of Spirit Lake and superb views of the crater and dome. For a serious hike, continue along this trail to its intersection with the spectacular **Norway Pass Trail,** which runs 6 mi. (5½hr.) directly through the blast zone and ends on Rd. 26. Farther west, the 2 mi. **Harmony Trail #224** provides the only public access to Spirit Lake. From spectacular **Windy Ridge** at the end of Rd. 99, a steep ash hill grants a magnificent view of the crater from 3½ mi. away. The **Truman Trail** leaves from Windy Ridge and meanders 7 mi. through the **Pumice Plain,** where hot pyroclastic flows sterilized the land, leaving absolutely no life.

From the Pine Creek Information Station, 25 mi. south of the junction of Rd. 25 and 99, take Rd. 90 12 mi. west and then continue 3 mi. north on Rd. 83 to **Ape Cave,** a broken 2½ mi. lava tube formed by an ancient eruption. When exploring, wear a jacket and sturdy shoes, and take at least two **flashlights** or **lanterns** (rentals $2 each; rentals stop at 4pm, all lanterns must be returned by 5pm). Rangers lead 10 free 30-minute guided cave explorations per day. Road 83 continues 9 mi. farther north, ending near **Lava Canyon Trail #184** and three hikes past the **Muddy River Waterfall.**

■ Mount Rainier National Park

At 14,411 ft., Mt. Rainier (ray-NEER) presides regally over the Cascade Range. The Klickitat native people called it Tahoma, "Mountain of God," but Rainier is simply "the Mountain" to most Washington residents. Perpetually snow-capped, this dormant volcano draws thousands of visitors from all around the globe. Rainier creates its own weather by jutting into the warm, wet air, pulling down vast amounts of rain and snow. Clouds mask the mountain 200 days per year, frustrating visitors who come solely to see its distinctive summit. 1999 marks the 100th anniversary of the park's establishment, with over 305 mi. of trails through wildflowers, rivers, and bubbling hot springs.

PRACTICAL INFORMATION To reach Mt. Rainier from the **west,** take I-5 to Tacoma, then go east on Rte. 512, south on Rte. 7, and east on Rte. 706. This road meanders through the town of **Ashford** and into the park by the **Nisqually entrance,** which leads to the visitors centers of **Paradise** and **Longmire. Rte. 706** is the only access road open year-round; snow usually closes all other park roads from November to May. **Stevens Canyon Rd.** connects the southeast corner of the national park with Paradise, Longmire, and the Nisqually entrance, unfolding superb vistas of Rainier and the Tatoosh Range.

Gray Line Bus Service, 4500 S. Marginal Way, Seattle (206-624-5077), runs from Seattle to Mt. Rainier (daily May to mid-Oct.; 1-day round-trip $48, under 12 $14). Buses leave from the Convention Center at 8th and Pike in Seattle at 8am and return at 6pm, allowing about 3½hr. at the mountain. **Rainier Shuttle,** P.O. Box 374, Ashford, 98304 (569-2331), runs daily between Sea-Tac Airport (see p. 692) and park or Ashford area lodges, and between Ashford and Paradise (one-way $11). Each of the park's four **visitors centers—Longmire** (open Su-Th 7am-8pm, F-Sa 6:30am-9pm); **Paradise** (open May to mid-Oct. daily 9am-7pm; Oct.-Apr. Sa-Su and holidays 9am-7pm); **Ohanepecosh and Carbon River** (open mid-June to Sept. 9am-6pm; late May to mid-June Sa-Su and holidays 9am-6pm); and **Sunrise—**have helpful rangers, brochures on hiking, and postings on trail and road conditions. The best place to plan a backcountry trip is at the **Longmire Wilderness Center** (569-2211 ext. 3317), near the Nisqually entrance; or the **White River Ranger Station** (569-2211 ext. 2356), off Rte. 410 on the park's east side. Both distribute **backcountry permits** for $10 per group plus $5 per person (solo hikers $15). (Both open in summer Su-Th 7am-7pm, F-Sa 6:30am-9pm.) The **entrance fee** is $10 per car, $5 per hiker; permits are good for 7 days, and gates are open 24hr. **Post Office:** In the **National Park Inn,** Longmire, and in the **Paradise Inn,** Paradise. (Both open M-F 8:30am-noon and 1-5pm.) **ZIP code:** Longmire 98397; Paradise 98398. **Area code:** 360.

ACCOMMODATIONS, CAMPGROUNDS, AND FOOD Hotel Packwood, 102 Main St. (494-5431), in Packwood, is a charming reminder of the Old West with crisp, clean rooms with antique furniture (shared bathrooms; singles $20-38; double bunks from $30-38). **Whittaker's Bunkhouse,** 30205 S.R. 706 E, Ashford (569-2439), offers spiffy rooms with firm mattresses and sparkling clean showers, as well as a homey espresso bar, but no kitchen. Bring your own sleeping bag. (Bunks $25; private rooms from $65. Reservations strongly recommended.)

Camping in the park is first come, first served basis between mid-June and late September (sites $10-14). National park campgrounds all have facilities for the handicapped, but no hookups or showers: **Cougar Rock** (200 sites), near Longmire, with strict quiet hours (10pm-6am); **Ipsut Creek** (29 sites); **White River** (112 sites), in the northeastern corner of the park; **Sunshine Point** (18 sites), near the Nisqually entrance, with fine views (open year-round); and **Ohanapecosh** (205 sites) with a serene high canopy of old growth trees (available by reservation only July 1-Sept. 6). The **national forests** outside the park provide thousands of acres of freely campable countryside. **Backcountry camping** in the park requires a **permit,** available for $10 per group plus $5 per person at ranger stations and visitors centers. Hikers with valid permits can use any of the free, well-established trailside camps scattered in the park. Most camps have toilet facilities and a nearby water source, and some have shelters for groups of up to 12. **Glacier climbers** and **mountain climbers** intending to scale above 10,000 ft. must register in person at ranger stations to be granted permits.

Ma & Pa Rucker's (494-2651), on U.S. 12 in Packwood, a pizza parlor/grill/mini mart/ice cream store/cafe, satisfies any food need (small pizza $7; large $11; open M-Th 9am-9pm, F-Su 9am-10pm).

SIGHTS AND OUTDOORS A segment of the **Pacific Crest Trail,** which runs from Mexico to the Canadian border, dodges in and out of the park's southeast corner. The **Wonderland Trail** winds 93 mi. up, down, and around the mountain. Hikers must get permits for the arduous but stunning trek, and must complete the hike in 10 to 14 days. Call the Longmire Wilderness Center (see **Practical Information,** above) for details on both hikes. A trip to the **summit** of Mt. Rainier requires substantial preparation and expense. The ascent involves a vertical rise of more than 9000 ft. over a distance of 9 or more miles, usually taking 2 days and an overnight stay at **Camp Muir** on the south side (10,000 ft.) or **Camp Schurman** on the east side (9500 ft.). **Permits** for summit climbs cost $15 per person.

Just inside the Nisqually entrance, **Longmire** is pretty and woodsy, but by no means the best that Rainier has to offer. The **Rampart Ridge Trail,** a 4½ mi. (2½hr.) loop, is a relatively moderate hike with excellent views of the Nisqually Valley, Mt. Rainier, and Tumtum Peak. The steep, 5 mi. (4hr.) **Van Trump Park and Comet Falls Trail** passes Comet Falls and the occasional mountain goat. Longmire remains open during the winter as a center for snowshoeing, cross-country skiing, and other alpine activities. **Guest Services, Inc.** (569-2275) runs a cross-country ski center that rents skis and snowshoes, and runs skiing lessons on weekends. (Skis $15 per day, children $9.75 per day. Snowshoes $7.25 per ½-day, $12 per day.)

If you can manage to avoid the bustle and arrive on a clear, sunny weekday, **Paradise** will be exactly that. Even in mid-June, the sparkling snowfields above timberline add a touch of white to the verdant forest canyons below. The road from the Nisqually entrance to Paradise is open year-round, but the road east through Stevens Canyon closes from October to June. From January to mid-April, park naturalists lead **snowshoe hikes** (569-2211) to explore winter ecology around Paradise (Sa-Su 10:30am and 2:30pm; snowshoe rental $1). The 5 mi. **Skyline Trail** is the longest of the loop trails, starting at the Paradise Inn; it's probably the closest a casual hiker can come to climbing the mountain. The mildly strenuous 2½ mi. hike up to **Pinnacle**

Peak begins just east of Paradise, across the road from **Reflection Lake,** and offers clear views of Mt. Rainier, Mt. Adams, Mt. St. Helens, and Mt. Hood.

Although in opposite corners of the park, the **Ohanapecosh and Carbon Rivers** are in the same ranger district. One of the oldest stands of trees in Washington, the **Grove of Patriarchs,** grows near the Ohanapecosh visitors center. An easy 1½ mi. walk leads to these 500- to 1000-year-old Douglas firs, cedars, and hemlocks. The **Summerland** and **Indian Bar Trails** are excellent for serious backpacking—this is where rangers go on their days off. **Carbon River Valley,** in the northwest corner of the park, is one of the only inland rainforests in the continental U.S., and has access to the **Wonderland Trail** (see above). Winter storms keep the road beyond the Carbon River entrance under constant disrepair.

Too far from the entrance for most tourists to bother, **Sunrise** is pristine, unruffled, and divine. The winding road to the highest of the four visitors centers provides gorgeous views of Mt. Adams, Mt. Baker, and the heavily glaciated eastern side of Mt. Rainier. The comfortably sloping **Mt. Burroughs Trail** (5 mi.) offers unbeatable glacier views. **Berkeley Park** makes a 5 mi. round-trip trek into a wildflower-painted valley. For those longing to return to civilization, the 5.6 mi. (4hr.) round-trip hike to **Mt. Fremont Lookout** affords a view of Seattle on a clear day.

■ North Cascades (Route 20)

A favorite stomping ground for grizzlies, deer, mountain goats, black bears, and Jack Kerouac *(The Dharma Bums),* the North Cascades are one of the most rugged expanses of land in the continental U.S. The dramatic peaks stretch north from Stevens Pass on U.S. 2 to the Canadian border, with the centerpiece of **North Cascades National Park** straddling the crest of the Cascades. Rte. 20 (open Apr.-Nov., weather permitting), a road designed for unadulterated driving pleasure, is the primary means of access to the area and awards jaw-dropping views at every curve.

Sedro Woolley to Marblemount The volunteers at the **Sedro Woolley Visitor Information Center** (360-855-0974), in the train caboose at the intersection of Rte. 20 and Ferry St., are extremely eager to help those who drop in (open daily 9am-4pm). Sedro Woolley also houses the **North Cascades National Park and Mt. Baker-Snoqualmie National Forest Headquarters,** 2105 Rte. 20 (360-856-5700; open Sa-Th 8am-4:30pm, F 8am-6pm). Call 206-526-6677 for **snow avalanche info.**

Route 9 leads north from Sedro Woolley, providing indirect access to **Mt. Baker** through the forks at the Nooksack River and Rte. 542. The turn-off for **Baker Lake Hwy.** is 23 mi. east of Sedro Wooley at Mile 82, which dead-ends 25 mi. later at Baker Lake. Along this road, the crowded **Kulshan Campground** has drinking water and flush toilets ($5). Farther east on Rte. 20, right before the western boundary of the relatively small **Rockport State Park,** Sauk Mountain Rd. (Forest Service Rd. 1030) makes a stomach-scrambling climb up **Sauk Mountain** to a view of Mt. Rainier, Puget Sound, and the San Juan Islands. Trailers, RVs, and the faint of heart should not attempt the ascent. The **Sauk Mountain Trail** begins at the parking lot and winds 3½ mi. to backcountry campsites near Sauk Lake. The park also has a wheelchair accessible trail and 50 developed campsites. ($10; full hookup $15, each extra vehicle $5; 3-sided cabins with 8-person bunk beds $15. No reservations.)

At **Marblemount** is **Good Food** (360-873-2771), a small family diner at the east edge of town along Rte. 20, boasting riverside picnic tables and a great vegetarian sandwich ($3.60; open daily 9am-9pm, in winter 9am-6pm). Cruise 8 mi. east along Cascade River Rd. to **Marble Creek** (24 sites) or 16 mi. east to **Mineral Park** (8 sites). Both are free, but have no drinking water. The **Marblemount Wilderness Information Center,** 728 Ranger Station Rd., Marblemount 98267 (360-873-4500, ext. 39), 1 mi. north of Marblemount on a well-marked road from the west end of town, is the place to go for a **backcountry permit** and to plan longer hiking excursions (open in summer Su-Th 7am-6pm, F-Sa 7am-8pm; call for winter hrs.). From Marblemount, it's

22 mi. along Cascade River Rd. to the trailhead for a 3½ mi. hike to the amazing **Cascade Pass,** which then continues on to Lake Chelan.

Ross Lake Newhalem is the first town on Rte. 20 after it crosses into the **Ross Lake Recreation Area,** a buffer zone between the highway and the national park. At the tourist-friendly **North Cascades Visitors Center and Ranger Station** (206-386-4495), off Rte. 20, a mystical and atonal slide show is shown (open daily 8:30am-6pm; in winter Sa-Su 9am-4:30pm). Among the easiest hikes is the **Thunder Creek Trail,** which extends through old growth cedar and fir forests, beginning from the Colonial Creek Campground (see below) at Rte. 20 Mi. 130. The 3.2 mi. **Fourth of July Pass Trail** begins approximately 2 mi. into the Thunder Creek Trail, and climbs 3500 ft. toward hellzapoppin' views. The park's **Goodell Creek Campground,** just south of Newhalem, has 22 sites suitable for tents and trailers, with drinking water, pit toilets, and a launch site for whitewater rafting on the Skagit River (sites $7; water turned off after Oct., when sites are free). **Colonial Creek Campground,** 10 mi. to the east, is a fully developed, wheelchair-accessible campground with flush toilets, a dump station, and occasional campfire programs (164 sites, $10; no hookups).

Ross Lake to Winthrop This is the most beautiful segment of Rte. 20. Leaving the basin of Ross Lake, the road begins to climb, exposing the jagged, snowy peaks of the North Cascades. Thirty miles of astounding views east, the **Pacific Crest Trail** crosses Rte. 20 at **Rainy Pass** on one of the most scenic and difficult legs of its 2500 mi. Canada-to-Mexico route. Near Rainy Pass, groomed scenic trails of 1-3 mi. can be hiked in sneakers, provided the snow has melted (about mid-July). Just off Rte. 20, an overlook at **Washington Pass** (Mile 162) rewards a ½ mi. walk on a wheelchair accessible paved trail with an astonishing view of the red rocks in **Copper Basin.** The popular 2½ mi. walk to **Blue Lake** begins just east of Washington Pass. An easier 2 mi. hike to **Cutthroat Lake** departs from an access road 4½ mi. east of Washington Pass. From the lake, the trail continues 4 mi. farther and almost 2000 ft. higher to **Cutthroat Pass,** treating hikers to a stellar view of towering, rugged peaks. The hair-raising 23 mi. road to **Hart's Pass** begins at **Mazama,** on Rd. 1163, 10 mi. east of Washington Pass. Breathtaking views await the steel-nerved driver, both from the pass and from **Slate Peak,** the site of a lookout station 3 mi. beyond the pass. The road is closed to trailers and is only accessible when the snow has melted.

Winthrop to Twisp Farther east is **Winthrop,** a town desperately and somewhat successfully trying to market its frontier history. At the **Winthrop Information Station,** 202 Riverside (509-996-2125), at the junction with Rte. 20, the staff laud the beauty of this Nouveau Old West town (open early May to mid-Oct. daily 10am-5pm). Winthrop's summer is bounded by rodeos on Memorial and Labor Day weekends. Late July brings the top-notch **Winthrop Rhythm and Blues Festival** (509-997-2541), where big name blues bands flock to belt their tunes, endorse radio stations, and play cowboy. Tickets for the 3-day event cost $35 ($45 at the door). The **Methow Valley Visitors Center** (MET-how), Bldg. 49, Rte. 20 (509-996-4000), hands out info on area camping, hiking, and cross-country skiing (open daily 9am-5pm; call for winter hrs.). For more in-depth skiing and hiking trail information, call the **Methow Valley Sports Trail Association** (509-996-3287), which cares for 175km of trails in the area. Between Winthrop and Twisp on East Country Rd. #9129, the **North Cascades Smokejumper Base** (509-997-2031) is a center for folks who get their kicks by parachuting into forest fires and putting them out. (Open daily in summer and early fall 9am-6pm; tours 10am-5pm.) They give a thorough tour of the base and explain the procedures and equipment used to help them fight the fires and stay alive.

Nine miles south of Winthrop on Rte. 20, the peaceful village of **Twisp** offers lower prices and far fewer tourists than its neighbor. The **Twisp Ranger Station,** 502 Glover St. (509-997-2131), employs a crunchy and helpful staff fortified with essential trail and campground guides (open M-F 7:45am-4:30pm). **The Sportsman Motel,** 1010 E. Rte. 20 (509-997-2911), a hidden jewel, where a barracks-like facade masks tastefully decorated rooms with kitchens (singles $39; doubles $43). The **Glover Street Café,** 104 N. Glover St. (509-997-1323), offers gourmet salads ($3.25) and sandwiches ($5.75) with soup or salad (open M-F 8am-3pm). There are many **campgrounds** and **trails** 15-25 mi. up Twisp River Rd., just off Rte. 20 in Twisp. Most of the campsites are primitive and have a $5 fee. For camping closer to the highway, head to the **Riverbend RV Park,** 19951 Rte. 20 (509-997-3500 or 800-686-4498), 2 mi. west of Twisp. Beyond an abundance of slow-moving beasts (RVs), Riverbend has plenty of comfy tent sites situated along the Methow River (sites for 2 $14; hookups $18, $2 per additional person; office open 9am-10pm). From Twisp, Rte. 20 continues east to **Okanogan** and Rte. 153 runs south to **Lake Chelan.**

EASTERN WASHINGTON

■ Spokane

A city built on silver mining, grown fat and prosperous after decades as a central rail link for regional agriculture, Spokane (spoe-KAN) has regressed to become a gateway rather than a destination. Copious middle-Americana, fused with bottom-of-the-barrel prices, makes Spokane a convenient, inexpensive stopover. **Riverfront Park,** N. 507 Howard St. (456-4386), just north of downtown, is Spokane's civic center and greatest asset. Developed for the 1974 World's Fair, the park's 100 acres are divided down the middle by the roaring rapids that culminate in **Spokane Falls.** In the park, the **IMAX Theater** (625-6688) houses your basic 5-story movie screen. (Shows on the hr. Su-Th 11am-8pm, F-Sa 11am-9pm. $5.50, seniors and under 13 $4.50.) Another section of the park offers a full range of kiddie rides, including the exquisitely hand-carved **Looff Carousel.** (Open in summer Su-Th 11am-8pm, F-Sa 11am-10pm. $1.75 per whirl, under 12 $1.) A 1-day pass ($11) covers both these attractions, plus a ferris wheel, park train, sky ride, and more. At **Manito Park,** 4 W. 21st Ave. (625-6622), check out the carp in the **Nishinomiya Japanese Garden,** overdose on roses on **Rosehill** (they bloom in late June), relax in the elegant **Duncan Garden,** or sniff the flowers in the **David Graiser Conservatory** (open daily 8am-8pm; free). From downtown, go south on Stevens St. and turn left on 21st Ave.

Brown Squirrel Hostel, 920 W. 7th Ave. (838-8102), is a clean, elegant, Spanish-style building. Bus #34 stops 2 blocks away at 5th and Monroe St.; walk up Monroe to 7th and turn left, and the hostel is right near the corner. ($12; private rooms available. Linen $1. Reception 4-10pm. No curfew.) **Riverside State Park** (456-3964, reservations 800-452-5687), is 6 mi. northwest of downtown on Rifle Club Rd., off Rte. 291 (Nine Mile Rd.); take Division St. north and turn left on Francis, then follow signs. 101 standard sites lie in a sparse Ponderosa forest next to the river. (Sites $11, hiker/biker sites $5. Showers. Wheelchair access.) The **Spokane County Market** (482-2627), between 1st Ave. and Jefferson St., sells fresh fruit, vegetables, and baked goods (open May-Oct. W and Sa 9am-5pm, Su 11am-4pm). At **Dick's,** E. 10 3rd Ave. (747-2481), at Division St., customers eat in their parked cars and pay prices straight out of the 50s. (Burgers 59¢, fries 49¢, shakes 83¢, soft drinks 53-73¢. Open daily 9am-1am.)

Spokane lies 280 mi. east of Seattle on I-90. **Spokane International Airport** (624-3218) is off I-90 8 mi. southwest of town. **Amtrak,** W. 221 1st St. (624-5144, reservations 800-872-7245), at Bernard St., sends one train per day to Seattle ($56) and Portland, OR ($56). **Greyhound,** W. 221 1st St. (tickets 624-5251, info 624-5252), in the same building, runs to Seattle (5 per day, $27) and Portland, OR (2 per day, $37). **Spokane Transit Authority**, W. 107 Riverside St. (328-7433, TDD 456-4327), in the Plaza at Riverside St. and Wall, serves all of Spokane, including Eastern Washington University in Cheney (75¢, under 5 free; runs until 12:15am downtown, until 9:45pm in the valley along E. Sprague Ave.). **Spokane Area Convention and Visitors Bureau,** 201 W. Main St. (747-3230 or 800-248-3230), Exit 281 off I-90, is overflowing with literature (open M-F 8:30am-5pm, Sa 8am-4pm, Su 9am-2pm; in winter M-F 8:30am-5pm).

Internet Access: Library, W. 906 Main St. (444-5333; open M-Th 10am-9pm, F-Sa 10am-6pm). **Post Office:** W. 904 Riverside St. (626-6860), at Lincoln (open M-F 6am-5pm). **ZIP code:** 99210. **Area code:** 509.

Oregon

Over a century ago, families liquidated their possessions and sank their life savings into covered wagons, corn meal, and oxen, high-tailing it to Oregon in search of prosperity and a new way of life. Today, Oregon remains as popular a destination as ever for backpackers, cyclists, anglers, beachcrawlers, and families alike. The caves and cliffs of Oregon's coastline are a siren call to tourists, and some coastal towns are enticing oases. Inland attractions include Crater Lake National Park, Ashland's Shakespeare Festival, and North America's deepest gorge. Portland is casual and idiosyncratic—its name was determined by a coin toss—while the college town of Eugene embraces hippies and Deadheads. Bend, a tiny interior city with a young, athletic population, competes for the title of liveliest town. From microbrews to snow-capped peaks, a visit to Oregon is still worth crossing the Continental Divide.

PRACTICAL INFORMATION

Capital: Salem.
Visitor Info: Oregon Tourism Commission, 775 Summer St. NE, Salem, OR 97310 (800-547-7842; http://www.traveloregon.com). **Oregon State Parks and Recreation Dept.,** P.O. Box 500, Portland, OR 97207-0500 (800-551-6949; http://www.prd.state.or.us).
Time Zone: Mostly Pacific (3hr. before Eastern), with a small southeastern section in Mountain (2hr. before Eastern).
Postal Abbreviation: OR.
Sales Tax: None.

■ Portland

Increasingly popular and populated, the City of Roses is still the quietest, mellowest, and rainiest big city on the West Coast. Although home to a thriving urban culture, Portland blends seamlessly with its majestic natural surroundings. With over 200 parks, the pristine Willamette (wih-LAM-it) River, and snow-capped Mt. Hood in the background, Portland is an oasis of natural beauty. Driven indoors for the better part of the year by stubborn rain, Portlanders have nursed a love of art, music, and books. Culture is constantly cultivated in the endless theaters, galleries, and bookshops around town. As the microbrewery capital of America, Portland is a flowing font of the nation's finest beer. During the rainy season, Portlanders flood neighborhood pubs and coffeehouses for shelter and conversation. But on rare sunny days, a battalion of hikers, bikers, and runners take advantage of their sylvan surroundings. Portland has mastered this synthesis of urban and outdoor life, making it the best-kept secret on the coast.

ORIENTATION AND PRACTICAL INFORMATION

Portland lies in the northwest corner of Oregon, where the Willamette River flows into the Columbia River. **I-5** connects Portland with San Francisco and Seattle, while **I-84** follows the route of the Oregon Trail through the Columbia River Gorge, heading along the Oregon-Washington border toward Boise, ID. West of Portland, **U.S. 30** follows the Columbia downstream to Astoria, but **U.S. 26** is the fastest path to the coast. **I-405** runs just west of downtown to link I-5 with U.S. 30 and 26.

Portland is conveniently divided into five districts, by which all street signs are labeled: **N, NE, NW, SE,** and **SW. Burnside St.** divides the city into north and south, while east and west are separated by the **Willamette River.** SW Portland is known as **downtown** but also includes the southern end of Old Town and a slice of the wealth-

Portland

SEE ALSO COLOR INSERT

ACCOMMODATIONS
A Ben Stark Hostel
B 4th Avenue Motel
C Portland HI-AYH

500 meters

500 yards

0

0

TO AIRPORT

NE Hassalo

Lloyd Blvd.

84

30

TO COLUMBIA RIVER GORGE

99E

NE Everett St.

MAX

99E

30

NE Burnside St.

Sandy Blvd.

Stark St. SE

SE 7th Ave.

20th Ave.

16th Ave.

12th Ave. SE

SE Morrison St.
SE Belmont St.
SE Yamhill St.
SE Taylor St.
SE Salmon St.
SE Main St.
SE Madison St.
SE Hawthorne Blvd.

SE Grand Ave.

SE Martin Luther King Jr. Blvd.

SE 3rd Ave.

SE 2nd Ave.

TO REED COLLEGE

TO OREGON MUSEUM OF SCIENCE AND INDUSTRY

Rose Garden Arena

5

Willamette River

Steel Bridge

Fron

Burnside Bridge

Morrison Bridge

Willamette River

Hawthorne Bridge

5

TO LEWIS AND CLARK COLLEGE

NW 1st Ave.
NW 2nd Ave.
NW 3rd Ave.
NW 4th Ave.
NW 5th Ave.
NW 6th Ave.
NW Broadway Ave.
NW Park Ave.
NW 10th Ave.
NW 14th Ave.

SW Front Ave.

Skidmore Fountain

MAX

SW 1st Ave.

SW Oak St.

Transit Mall

SW 2nd Ave.
SW 3rd Ave.
SW 4th Ave.

SW Ankeny St. SW

SW Stark St.

SW Washington St.

SW Alder St.

SW Morrison St.

SW Yamhill St.

SW Taylor St.
SW Salmon St.

Portland Building

City Hall

SW Madison St.

Civic Auditorium

TO ONDINE

PIONEER COURTHOUSE SQUARE

SW 5th Ave.
SW 6th Ave.

SW Broadway

SW Park Ave.

MAX

Powell's Book Store

NW Glisan St.
NW Flanders St.
NW Everett St.
NW Burnside St.

Union Station (Amtrak)

A

Library

SW Jefferson St.
SW Columbia St.
SW Clay St.
SW Market St.

SW 9th Ave.
SW Main St.

Portland State University

405

30

NW Kearney St.
NW Johnson St.
NW Irving St.
NW Hoyt St.

NW Davis St.
NW Couch St.

NW 17th Ave.

NW 19th Ave.

NW 21st Ave.

NW 23rd Ave.

405

N

Civic Stadium

26

TO WASHINGTON PARK ZOO

Fareless Square

TO B

TO C

ier **West Hills. Old Town,** in NW Portland, encompasses most of the city's historic sector. **Southeast** Portland contains parks, factories, local businesses, residential areas of all brackets, and a rich array of cafes, stores, theaters, and restaurants lining **Hawthorne Blvd. Williams Ave.** cuts off a corner of the northeast sector, called simply the North. North and NE Portland are chiefly residential, punctuated by a few small and quiet parks. Drug traffickers base their operations in Northeast Portland, and parts of the area are dangerous.

Airport: Portland International, 7000 NE Airport Way (460-4234). The cheapest way to reach downtown is to take Tri-Met bus #12, which passes south through town on SW 5th Ave. (45min., 4 per hr., $1.05). **Raz Tranz** (246-3301) provides an **airport shuttle** that stops at most major hotels downtown (2 per hr. 5:35am-12:05am; $9, ages 6-12 $2).

Trains: Amtrak, 800 NW 6th Ave. (273-4865, recording 273-4866, reservations 800-872-7245), at Hoyt St. in Union Station. To Seattle, WA (3 per day, $24) and Eugene (2 per day, $12). Open daily 7:45am-9:15pm.

Buses: Greyhound, 550 NW 6th Ave. (243-2357 or 800-231-2222), at Glisan. To: Seattle, WA (11 per day, $20); Eugene (8 per day, $12); Spokane, WA (3 per day, $37); and Boise, ID (4 per day, $35). Lockers $2 per 6hr. Ticket window open daily 5am-11:45pm; station open 5am-1am. **Green Tortoise** (800-867-8647) picks up at Union Station in the Amtrak building (see above). Confirm 2 days in advance. To Seattle (Tu and Sa 4pm, $15) and San Francisco (Su and Th 12:30pm, $49).

Public Transportation: Tri-Met, 701 SW 6th Ave. (238-7433), in Pioneer Courthouse Sq. Open M-F 8am-5pm. Several **info lines** available: **Call-A-Bus** info system (231-3199); fare info (231-3198); updates, changes, and weather-related problems (231-3197); TDD (238-5811); senior and disabled services (238-4952); lost and found (238-4855). Bus routes fall into 7 **service areas:** red salmon, orange deer, yellow rose, green leaf, blue snow, purple raindrop, and brown beaver. Buses generally run 5am-midnight, reduced on weekends. Fare $1.05-1.35, ages 7-18 80¢, over 65 or disabled 50¢; free in the downtown **Fareless Sq.,** bounded by NW Hoyt St. to the north, I-405 to the west and south, and the Willamette River to the east. All-day pass $3.25. All buses have bike racks ($5 lifetime permit available at area bike stores). **MAX** (228-7246) is an efficient light-rail train running between downtown and Gresham in the east. Same fares as Tri-Met. Runs M-F 4:30am-11:30pm toward downtown and 5:30am-12:30am toward Gresham (starts slightly later Sa-Su).

Taxis: Radio Cab (227-1212). $2 base fare, $1.50 per mi. Airport to downtown $22-25. Airport to Hostelling International Portland $20. 24hr.

Car Rental: Rent-a-Wreck, 1800 SE M.L. King Blvd. (233-2492 or 888-499-9111). From $30 per day and $180 per week; 100 free mi. per day. Must be 21 with credit card. Open M-F 8:30am-5pm, Sa-Su by appt. only. **Crown Rent-A-Car,** 1315 NE Sandy Blvd. (224-8110). Transport from airport. From $28 per day, plus 20¢ per mi. after 100 mi., or $30 per day with unlimited mi. Must be 21 with credit card, or under 21 with proof of full insurance coverage. Open M-F 8am-5pm, Sa 9am-noon.

Visitor Info: Portland Oregon Visitors Association, 25 SW Salmon St. (222-2223 or 800-345-3214; http://www.pova.com), at Front St. in the Two World Trade Center complex. From I-5, follow the signs for City Center. Open M-F 9am-5pm, Sa 9am-4pm, Su 10am-2pm; Sept.-Apr. M-F 9am-5pm, Sa 9am-4pm.

Leonardo da Vinci's Birthday: Apr. 15.

Internet Access: Library, 801 SW 10th Ave. (248-5123). Open Tu-W 10am-8:30pm, Th-Sa 10am-5:30pm, Su 1-5pm.

Post Office: 715 NW Hoyt St. (800-ASK-USPS/275-8777). **ZIP code:** 97208-9999. Open M-F 7am-6:30pm, Sa 8:30am-5pm. **Area code:** 503.

ACCOMMODATIONS AND CAMPGROUNDS

Portland accommodations fill in a flash, especially during the Rose Festival and frequent conventions; early reservations are wise. Camping sites are distant, but nature abounds; there are no gravel-strewn RV-only sites around Portland.

◉**Hostelling International Portland (HI-AYH),** 3031 SE Hawthorne Blvd. (236-3380), at 31st Ave. Take bus #14 (brown beaver). Laid-back atmosphere, outdoor deck, and open mic (Th 6:30pm). Front porch, kitchen (including BBQ), Internet access ($1), and laundry facilities. 34 beds. $15, nonmembers $18. All-you-can-eat pancakes every morning ($1) and free pastries from a local bakery. Discount ski passes to Mt. Hood, and guided tours to the Columbia River Gorge, Mt. Hood, and Mt. St. Helens ($38.50). Reception daily 7:30-11am and 4-11pm. No curfew. Fills early in summer (women's rooms go first), so reserve a spot (credit card required) or plan to arrive at 4pm to snag one of 12-15 walk-in beds. HI members only June-Sept.

◉**McMenamins Edgefield Hostel,** 2126 SW Halsey St. (669-8610 or 800-669-8610), in Troutdale, 20min. east of Portland. Take MAX east to the Gateway Station, then Tri-Met bus #24 (Halsey) east to the main entrance. By car, take I-84 E to Exit 14, follow 207th Dr. S. and turn left at the first stoplight onto SW Halsey St. Continue 2 mi. until you see the sign on the right; the hostel is ¼ mi. farther down on the right. McMenamins converted this farm into a crown jewel of hosteling that shares the beautiful estate with a movie theater (21+), winery, brewery, and 3 restaurants. Dark wood bunks and vast rooms. 2 single-sex dorm-style rooms, each with 12 beds. Shower facilities and 2 tubs. Restaurants are pricey but good. $20 includes lockers, bedding, and admission to the movies. No curfew. Reception 24hr.

Ben Stark Hotel and International Hostel, 1022 SW Stark St. (274-1223). This old building is undergoing a much-needed facelift. 10 rooms with new beds, 8 bathrooms, and a sunny common room down the hall. Laundry and lockers downstairs. Convenient location, but the neighborhood can be unsafe, and the club across the street is noisy on weekends. Passport or hostel membership required. Dorms $15, Nov.-May $12; private rooms $39-56. No curfew. Reception 24hr.

Champoeg State Park, 8239 NE Champoeg Rd. (678-1251, reservations 800-452-5687). Take I-5 S 20 mi. to Exit 278, then follow the signs west for 6 mi. Play along miles of paved bikeway or hike by the Willamette River. 48 shady RV sites ($19) have water and electricity. Tent sites ($15) do not afford much privacy. Yurts $25. Outdoor summer concert series ($20-35). 2-day advance reservation required.

Ainsworth State Park, 33 mi. east of Portland, at Exit 35 off I-84 on scenic U.S. 30, in the Columbia Gorge. Wooded and lovely, but highway noise is all too prevalent. Not a natural getaway, but the beautiful gorge makes the schlep worthwhile. Hot showers, flush toilets, hiking trails. Tent sites $12, full hookup $18. Non-camper showers $2. Open Apr.-Oct.

FOOD

◉**Western Culinary Institute** (800-666-0312) maintains 3 public testing grounds for its gastronomic experiments. Sit on a stool in the **Chef's Diner,** 1231 SW Jefferson, while cheery students in tall hats serve, taste, and discuss sandwiches. Open Tu-F 7am-noon. The **Chef's Corner,** 1239 SW Jefferson, dishes out quick meals on-the-go. Open Tu-F 8am-6pm. Across the street, the elegant sit-down **Restaurant,** 1316 SW 13th Ave., serves a classy 5-course lunch ($8) rivaled only by its superb 6-course dinner (Tu-W $11, F $16). Th nights feature a tastebud-tingling, all you-can-eat international buffet ($16). Call ahead. Open Tu-F 11:30am-1pm and 6-8pm.

◉**Coffee Time,** 712 NW 21st Ave. (497-1090). Sip a cup of chai tea ($1.55) and view the ancient wonders of the main room, or slip away through the hanging beads to play *jenga* in the 3-sided enclave. Intelligentsia mingle by a faux fire, while the bohemians push on into a parlor with tapestries, chill music, and dim lighting. Lattes $2. Open M-Sa 6:30am-midnight, Su 8am-midnight.

Pied Cow Coffeehouse, 3244 SE Belmont St. (230-4866). Take bus #15 (brown beaver) to the front door. Sink into the velvety cushions and "feed the pastures of your mind" inside this quirky Victorian parlor. Espresso drinks ($1-3) and a wide selection of teas (pots $2.50). Open Feb.-Dec. Tu-Th 4pm-midnight, F 4pm-1am, Sa 10am-1am, Su 10am-midnight.

Accuardi's Old Town Pizza, 226 NW Davis St. (222-9999). Relax on a couch, at a table, or within a private booth in this typical whorehouse-turned-saloon-style-pizzeria. Reported ghost sightings by the staff have not adversely affected their pizza-crafting abilities (small cheese $5.50). Open Su-M 4-11pm, Tu-Th 11:30am-11pm, F-Sa 11:30am-midnight. Closed on Leonardo da Vinci's birthday.

Garbonzo's, 922 NW 21st Ave. (227-4196), at Lovejoy. Wire paintings on the wall complement healthy food and a conversational staff. The falafel pita ($3.75) only slightly humbles the hummus ($3.25). Open Su-Th 11:30am-1:30am, F-Sa 11:30am-3am. Other locations at 3433 SE Hawthorne Blvd. and 6341 SW Capital Hwy.

Chang's Mongolian Grill, 1 SW 3rd St. (243-1991), at Burnside. Delicious all-you-can-eat buffet of fresh vegetables, meat, and fish. Pile on the raw materials and watch the chef cook it all on a grill the size of a Volkswagen. The sizzling performance itself justifies the price (lunch $6.25, dinner $10). Open M-F 11:30am-2:30pm and 5-10pm, Sa noon-2:30 and 5-10pm, Su noon-2:30pm and 4:30-9:30pm.

Montage, 301 SE Morrison St. (234-1324). Take bus #15 (brown beaver) to the end of the Morrison Bridge and walk under it. An oasis of Louisiana-style cooking. Munch on frog legs ($9.50) or jambalaya with crawfish ($13) while pondering a puzzling mural of *The Last Supper,* or come just to hear the waiters yell for oyster shooters ($1.50). Open M-F 11:30am-2pm and 6pm-2am, Sa-Su 6pm-4am.

SIGHTS

The fully functioning **Pioneer Courthouse,** a downtown landmark at 5th Ave. and Morrison St., is the centerpiece of **Pioneer Courthouse Sq.,** 701 SW 6th Ave. (223-1613), which opened in 1983 and has since become "Portland's Living Room." During the summer, the **High Noon Tunes** draw thousands of music lovers (W noon-1pm). The section of downtown just south of the Burnside Bridge and along the river comprises **Old Town.** Though not the safest part of Portland, Old Town has been revitalized in recent years by storefront restoration and a bevy of new shops and restaurants. **Skidmore Fountain,** at SW 1st Ave. and SW Ankeny St., marks the end of **Waterfront Park,** a 20-block swath of grass and flowers along the Willamette River. The impressive **Salmon St. Springs,** in Waterfront Park at SW Salmon St., are just down the street from the visitors center. An underground computer manipulates the fountain's 185 jets, which project water in constantly changing directions.

On the west side of the South Park Blocks sits the venerable **Portland Art Museum,** 1219 SW Park (226-2811), at Jefferson St. *(Open Tu-Su 10am-5pm, and until 9pm 1st Th of the month. $7.50, students and seniors $6, under 16 $2.50.)* The second-oldest fine arts museum on the West Coast, the PAM houses more than 32,000 works of art spanning 35 centuries. Across the park, the **Oregon Historical Society Museum and Library,** 1200 SW Park Ave. (222-1741), stores photographs, artifacts, and records of Oregon's last two centuries, including interactive exhibits on Oregon, Willamette County, and Portland. *(Open Tu-Sa 10am-5pm, Su noon-5pm. $6, students $3, ages 6-12 $1.50; Th seniors free. 2-for-1 AAA discount.)* At the first and only **24-Hour Church of Elvis,** 720 SW Ankeny St. (226-3671), you can listen to synthetic oracles, witness satirical miracles, and experience a tour in the Art-o-Mobile. *(Open M-Th usually 2-4pm but call to confirm, F 8pm-midnight, Sa noon-5pm and 8pm-midnight, Su noon-5pm.)* The **Blitz Weinhard Brewery,** 1133 W. Burnside (222-4351), supplies free 45min. tours and samples (tours Tu-F at noon, 1:30pm, and 3pm).

Portland has more park acreage than any other American city, thanks in good measure to **Forest Park,** the 5000-acre tract of wilderness in Northwest Portland. Washington Park (see below), provides easy access by car or foot to this sprawling sea of green, where a web of trails leads through lush forests, scenic overviews, and idyllic picnic areas. Downtown on the edge of the Northwest district is the gargantuan **Powell's City of Books,** 1005 W. Burnside St. (228-4651 or 800-878-7323), a cavernous establishment with almost a million new and used volumes, more than any other bookstore in the U.S. (open M-Sa 9am-11pm, Su 9am-9pm). **The Grotto** (254-7371), a 62-acre Catholic sanctuary, houses magnificent religious sculptures and gardens just minutes from downtown on Sandy Blvd. (U.S. 30) at NE 85th (open daily 9am-8pm; in winter 9am-5:30pm).

At the **Crystal Springs Rhododendron Garden,** SE 28th Ave., at Woodstock (take bus #19), over 2500 rhododendrons of countless varieties surround a lake and border an 18-hole public golf course (open daily 6am-10pm, Oct.-Feb. 8am-7pm; $2, under 12 free). The **Oregon Museum of Science and Industry (OMSI),** 1945 SE Water Ave.

(797-4000 or 797-4569), at SE Clay St., keeps visitors mesmerized with science exhibits, including an earthquake simulator chamber. *(Open F-W 9:30am-7pm, Th 9:30am-8pm; Labor Day-Memorial Day F-W 9:30am-5:30pm, Th 9:30am-8pm. $8.50, seniors and ages 4-13 $6.)* While at OMSI, visit the **U.S.S. Blueback** (797-4624), the Navy's last diesel submarine; she never failed a mission. *(Open daily 10am-5pm. 40min. tour $3.50.)*

Less than 2 mi. west of downtown, in the middle of the posh neighborhoods of **West Hills,** is mammoth **Washington Park.** The **Rose Garden,** 400 SW Kingston (823-3636), in Washington Park, is the pride of Portland. In summer months, a sea of blooms arrests the eye, showing visitors exactly why Portland is the City of Roses. Across from the Rose Garden are the scenic **Japanese Gardens,** 611 SW Kingston Ave. (223-1321), reputed to be the most authentic this side of the Pacific. *(Open daily 9am-8pm; Apr.-May and Sept. 10am-6pm; Oct.-Mar. 10am-4pm. $6, students $3.50, seniors $4.)* The **Hoyt Arboretum,** 4000 SW Fairview Blvd. (228-8733 or 823-3655), at the crest of the hill above the other gardens, features 200 acres of trees and trails. *(Trails open daily 6am-10pm. Arboretum visitors center open M-Th 9am-4pm, F 10am-4pm, Sa 10am-2pm, Su 10am-5pm.)* The **Washington Park Zoo,** 4001 SW Canyon Rd. (226-1561 or 226-7627), is renowned for its scrupulous re-creation of natural habitats and its successful elephant breeding. *(Open 9am-6pm. $5.50, seniors $4, ages 3-11 $3.50. Free after 3pm on the second Tu of every month.)*

ENTERTAINMENT AND FESTIVALS

The **Oregon Symphony Orchestra,** 719 SW Alder St. (228-1353 or 800-228-7343), in the Arlene Schnitzer Concert Hall, plays a classical and pop series. (Sept.-June; tickets $15-60; Su afternoons $10-15; ½-price student tickets 1hr. before showtime Sa-Su.) **Sack Lunch Concerts,** 1422 SW 11th Ave. (222-2031), at Clay St. and the Old Church, presents free concerts, usually classical or jazz (every W at noon). **Portland Center Stage** (248-6309), in the Newmark Theater at SW Broadway and SW Main, stages a five-play series of classics and modern adaptations. (Late Sept. to Apr. Su and Tu-Th $11-31.50, F-Sa $12.50-36; under 26 $10. ½-price tickets sometimes available 1hr. before curtain.) The **Bagdad Theater and Pub,** 3702 SE Hawthorne Blvd. (230-0895), and the **Mission Theater and Pub,** 1624 NW Glisan (223-4031), put out second-run films and an excellent beer menu ($1-3; 21+). Sports fans can watch basketball's **Portland Trailblazers** (231-8000) at the **Rose Garden,** 1 Center Ct.

Northwest Film Center, 1219 SW Park Ave. (221-1156), hosts the **Portland International Film Festival** in the last 2 weeks of February, with 100 films from 30 nations (box office opens 30min. before each show; tickets $6, seniors $5). Portland's premier summer event is the **Rose Festival,** 220 NW 2nd Ave. (227-2681), during the first 3 weeks of June. The city decks itself in finery, coming alive with waterfront concerts, art festivals, celebrity entertainment, auto racing, parades, an air show, Navy ships, and the largest children's parade in the world. Not too long afterward, the outrageously good **Waterfront Blues Festival** (282-0555 or 973-FEST/3378), in early July, draws some of the world's finest blues artists for this 3-day event. Suggested donation is $3 and 2 cans of food to benefit the Oregon Food Bank. The **Oregon Brewers Festival** (778-5917), on the last full weekend in July, is the continent's largest gathering of independent brewers and makes for one incredible party at Waterfront Park. *(Free admission, but $2 mandatory mug and $1 per taste. Those under 21 must be accompanied by a parent.)*

NIGHTLIFE

⊛**Panorama, Brig/Red Cap Garage,** and **Boxx's,** 341 SW 10th St. (221-RAMA/7262), form a network of interconnected clubs along Stark St. between 10th and 11th. **Panorama's** cavernous dance floor hosts a thriving gay and straight crowd. Cover $5. Open F-Sa 9pm-4am. The bpms are higher still in the **Garage,** with weekday swing dancing and Friday night disco. Open daily 1pm-2:30am. **Boxx's** is a video/karaoke bar where, on Tu nights, matchmaking magic happens with the video postings of "Misha's Make-a-Date." Open daily noon-2:30am.

Crystal Ballroom, 1332 W. Burnside Blvd. (225-0047). Look up for the neon "dance" sign. The grand ballroom, with its immense paintings, gaudy chandeliers, and wigglin' floor, begs buffeted boogiers to get down. Micropints $3. Hosts a variety of live music; shows usually start at 9pm, and doors open 30min. before showtime. Tickets $5-25. Weekend shows often sell out, so call ahead.

Biddy McGraw's, 3518 SE Hawthorne Blvd. (233-1178). Take bus #14 (brown beaver). Certainly the most authentically Irish pub this side of the Mississippi. With live Celtic tunes and raucous dancing, weekends are always boisterous. 22 kegs of Guinness are consumed here per week. Do your part for $3.75 per pint. Micros $3. Open M 11am-2am, Tu-Su 11am-2:30am, but not set in stone.

La Luna, 215 SE 9th Ave. (241-LUNA/5862), at Pine. Take bus #20 (purple raindrop), get off at 9th, and walk 2 blocks south. One of Portland's larger, hipper venues, housed in a gray, nondescript building. Hosts many of the more prominent bands in town. Pints $2-3.50. Music generally 4 times per week. Non-smoking cafe is open every show night to an anything-goes crowd. Queer Night with dancing (M). Cover $0-15. All ages admitted, except to the bars. Call ahead for concert listings.

Satyricon, 125 NW 6th Ave. (243-2380). Live alternarock rumbles in the glowing back room every night. PoMo bar and a chic new sister restaurant, **Fellini.** Step into this madly mosaic-laden space to rest your ears and taste innovative cuisine. Entrees from $3. 21Ğ. Cover $2-5. Food served M-Th 11:30am-2:30am, F-Sa 5pm-3am, Su 5pm-2:30am; music 10pm-2:30am.

▓ Mount Hood

Magnificent, snow-capped Mt. Hood is at the junction of U.S. 26 and Rte. 35, 1½hr. east of Portland and 1hr. south of the Hood River. The most popular day hike is **Mirror Lake,** a 6 mi. loop that starts from a parking lot off U.S. 26, 1 mi. west of Government Camp (open May 31-Oct.). **Timberline** (272-3311 or 231-7979), off U.S. 26 at Government Camp, is a largely beginner and intermediate area, with the longest ski season in Oregon (lasting until Sept. 6). (Night skiing Jan.-Feb. M-F 4pm-9pm, Sa-Su 4pm-10pm. Lift tickets $32. Equipment rental around $19 per day. Snowboards $33 per day with boots, $26 without. $400 cash deposit or credit card required.) Smaller **Mt. Hood Ski Bowl,** 87000 E. U.S. 26 (222-2695), in Government Camp, 2 mi. west of Hwy. 35, has the best night skiing and a snowboard park. The season is limited (Nov.-Apr.), but 80-90% of the trails have night skiing. (Open M-Tu 1-10pm, W-Th 9am-10pm, F 9am-11pm, Sa 8:30am-11pm, Su 8:30am-10pm. Lift tickets $23 per day, $14 per night, $30 for both. Ski rental $17, ages 7-12 $11. Snowboards $25.) **Timberline Mountain Guides** (800-464-7704) offers mountain-, snow-, and ice-climbing courses lasting 2-6 days. (2-day trip—1-day class and 1-day climb—from $265; registration and wilderness permit included.) Timberline's **Magic Mile** is a non-skiing lift that carries passengers above the clouds for spectacular views of the Cascades. ($6; winter discounts with a coupon that just about any employee will happily hand out.)

Camping spots in the **Mt. Hood National Forest** cluster near the junction of U.S. 26 and Rte. 35. **Trillium Lake Campground,** 2 mi. east of the Timberline turn-off on U.S. 26, has trails around the crystal-clear lake, and paved sites with water and toilets. Pine trees offer some privacy. (57 sites. $10, premium lakeside sites $12; doubles $20; prices include $3 parking fee.) Just 1 mi. west of Trillium Lake, down a dirt road off U.S. 26, **Still Creek Campgrounds** has a quieter, woodsier feel, unpaved sites, and a babbling brook ($10, premium creekside sites $12). On Rte. 35, 10 mi. north of U.S. 26, **Robinhood** and **Sherwood Campgrounds** lie just off the highway beside a running creek (both $10). Reservations can be made by calling 800-280-2267. **Hood River District Ranger Station,** 6780 Rte. 35 (541-352-6002), and **Zigzag District Ranger Station,** 70220 E. U.S. 26 (503-622-3191), have detailed info (both open M-F 8am-4:30pm). The **Mt. Hood Visitor Information Center,** 65000 E. U.S. 26 (503-622-4822), 16 mi. west of Mt. Hood, also provides permits (open daily 8am-6pm).

■ Columbia River Gorge

Only an hour from Portland, the magnificent Columbia River Gorge stretches for 75 stunning miles through some of the most beautiful country in the Pacific Northwest. To follow the gorge, which divides Oregon and Washington, take I-84 E to Exit 22. Continue east uphill on the **Columbia River Scenic Hwy. (U.S. 30),** which follows the crest of the gorge past unforgettable views. The largest town in the gorge is **Hood River,** at the junction of I-84 and Rte. 35. **Vista House** (503-695-2230), hanging on the edge of an outcropping, is a visitors center in **Crown Point State Park,** 4 mi. east of Exit 22 off I-84 E (open daily mid-Apr. to Oct. 15 8:30am-6pm). Peacocks stroll through the garden outside a gallery of European and American works at the elegant **Maryhill Museum of Art,** 35 Maryhill Museum Dr. (509-773-3733), which sits high above the Columbia on the Washington side, 30 mi. east of Hood River. (Open daily mid-Mar. to mid-Nov. 9am-5pm. $6, seniors $5, ages 6-12 $1.50.) To get there, take I-84 to Biggs (Exit 104) and the slightly more scenic Rte. 14, continuing until the signs.

    Rhonda Smith Windsurfing Center (386-9463), at Exit 64 off I-84, then under the bridge and left after the blinking red light, offers 3hr. classes ($70). Rentals, right on the water, start at $35 for a ½-day, with discounts for longer use. **Discover Bicycles,** 1020 Wasco St. (386-4820), rents mountain bikes, suggests routes, and sells all manner of trail maps (open M-Sa 9am-7pm, Su 9am-5pm; bikes $5 per hr., $25 per day). The 11 mi. round-trip **Hospital Hill Trail** provides views of Mt. Hood, the gorge, Hood River, and surrounding villages. To reach the unmarked trail, follow signs to the hospital, fork left to Rhine Village, and walk behind the power transformers through the livestock fence. At **Latourell Falls,** 2½ mi. east of Crown Point, a jaunt down a paved path leads right to the base of the falls; 5 mi. farther east, **Wahkeena Falls** is visible from the road, and hosts both a short, steep scramble over loose rock and a ¼ mi. trip up a paved walk. Just ½ mi. farther on U.S. 30 is **Multnomah Falls,** which attracts two million visitors annually; I-84 Exit 31 leads to an island in the middle of the freeway from which visitors can only see the upper falls. The steep **Wyeth Trail,** near the hamlet of Wyeth (Exit 51), leads 4.4 mi. to a wilderness boundary, and after 7.3 mi. to the road to Hood River and the incredible 13 mi. **Eagle Creek Trail** (Exit 44). Chiseled into cliffs high above Eagle Creek, this trail passes four waterfalls before joining the Pacific Crest Trail.

    The outdoorsy **Bingen School Inn Hostel** (509-493-3363), a converted schoolhouse, is just across the Hood River Toll Bridge (75¢) and 3½ blocks from the Amtrak stop in Bingen, WA; take the third left after the yellow blinking light onto Cedar St., and go 1 block up the hill on Humbolt St. (Beds $11; private rooms $40. Bikes $15 per day; sailboards $40 per day.) **Beacon Rock State Park,** across the Bridge of the Gods (Exit 44) and 7 mi. west on Washington's Rte. 14, has secluded sites ($10). The **Port of Cascade Locks Marine,** ½ mi. east off the bridge on the Oregon side, has a lawn on the river, which is also a crowded, windy campground ($10; showers).

    Amtrak (800-872-7245; open M-Sa 8:30am-7pm and some Su afternoons) runs trains from Portland to the foot of Walnut St. in Bingen, WA ($12-16). Buses run from the **Greyhound** station, 1205 B St. (386-1212 or 800-872-7245), between 12th and 13th St., to Portland ($10) and Seattle ($38). **Hood River County Chamber of Commerce,** 405 Portway Ave. (386-2000 or 800-366-3530), just off City Center Exit 63, has info on sights, windsurfing, camping, accommodations, history, and events. (Open M-Th 8:30am-5pm, F 8:30am-4pm, Sa-Su 10am-4pm; Nov.-Mar. M-F 9am-5pm.) **Columbia Gorge National Scenic Area Headquarters,** 902 Wasco St. (386-2333), in Wyeth, offers info on hiking and a friendly earful of local lore (open M-F 7:30am-5pm). Hood River's **Post Office:** 408 Cascade Ave. (800-275-8777; open M-F 8:30am-5pm). **ZIP code:** 97031-9998. **Area codes:** In OR 541; in WA 509.

OREGON COAST

From Astoria in the north to Brookings down south, **U.S. 101** hugs the shore along the Oregon Coast, linking a string of resorts and fishing villages that cluster around the mouths of rivers feeding into the Pacific. Breathtaking ocean views spread between these towns, while state parks and national forests allow direct access to the big surf. Seals, sea lions, and waterfowl lounge on rocks just offshore, watching the human world whiz by on wheels.

Astoria Astoria was the last stop for Lewis and Clark in 1805; with its Victorian homes, bustling waterfront, rolling hills, and persistent fog, Astoria reminds many tourists of a miniaturized San Francisco. Barring frequent clouds, the **Astoria Column,** on Coxcomb Hill Rd., showcases a stupendous view of Astoria cradled between Saddle Mountain to the south and the Columbia River estuary to the north (open dawn-10pm; free). At the **Shallon Winery,** 1598 Duane St. (325-5798), eccentric owner Paul van der Velt provides tours and tastings of his many vintages, including chocolate and cheese flavors. (Must be 21 to drink. Open almost every afternoon.) The **Astor Street Opry Company's** *Shanghaied in Astoria* (325-6104), at the Astoria Eagles' Lodge, at 9th and Commercial, features sinister villains, lusty sailors, and sexy can-can girls (early July to late Aug.).

Grandview B&B, 1574 Grand Ave. (325-0000, reservations 325-5555) offers intimate, cheery, luxurious rooms, and a delicious breakfast of fresh muffins, smoked salmon, and bagels. (From $45, with shared bath $55, with private bath $59; 2nd night $28 in off-season.) **Fort Columbia State Park Hostel (HI-AYH)** (360-777-8755), within the park boundaries, pampers guests with flowered sheets, hardwood floors, a cozy living room, and all-you-can-eat pancake breakfasts (50¢). Cross the 4 mi. bridge from Astoria into Washington, continue north on U.S. 101 for 3 mi., then take a sharp left just after the tunnel; take bus #24 on weekdays. ($10, nonmembers $13, bicyclists $8, under 18 $5. Laundry facilities. Lockout 10am-5pm. Check-in 5-10pm. Open Apr.-Sept.) **Fort Stevens State Park** (861-1671, reservations 800-452-5687), over Youngs Bay Bridge on U.S. 101 S, 10 mi. west of Astoria, is the largest state park in the U.S., with rugged, empty beaches and bike trails. ($17, full hookup $20; hiker/biker $4.50 per person; yurts $29. Hot showers. Facilities for the disabled.) At **Columbian Café,** 1114 Marine Dr. (325-2233), try the $6 "Chef's Mercy"— you name your "heat range and allergies," he chooses your meal. (Open M-Tu 8am-8pm, W-Th 8am-2pm and 5-8pm, F 8am-2pm and 5-9pm, Sa 10am-2pm and 5-9pm.)

Pierce Pacific Stages (692-4437) picks up travelers at **Video City,** 95 W. Marine Dr., and runs buses to Portland (1 per day, $15). **Astoria/Warrenton Area Chamber of Commerce,** 111 W. Marine Dr. (325-6311), just east of Astoria Bridge, is a bastion of info (open M-F 8am-6pm, Sa-Su 9am-6pm; Oct.-May M-F 8am-5pm, Sa-Su 11am-4pm). **Post Office:** 750 Commercial St. (800-275-8777), in the Federal Bldg. at 8th St. (open M-F 8:30am-5pm). **ZIP code:** 97103. **Area code:** 503.

Cannon Beach Although lined with establishments, Cannon Beach offers a quieter, more authentic experience than the mass commercialization of Lincoln City or Seaside. Tourists anxiously navigate their way through a gauntlet of expensive and sporadically elegant galleries and gift shops, but a stroll along the 7 mi. stretch of flat, bluff-framed beach is a less expensive option. **Ecola State Park** (436-2844; admission $3) attracts picnickers and hikers alike. **Ecola Point** offers a view of hulking **Haystack Rock,** which is spotted with (and splattered by) gulls, puffins, barnacles, anemones, and the occasional sea lion. Ecola Point also affords views of the Bay's centerpiece, the **Tillamook Lighthouse,** which clings to a rock like a phallic barnacle.

Pleasant motels line Hemlock St.; none costs under $40 in summer, but family units can make a good deal. In winter, most motels offer two-nights-for-one deals. **The Sandtrap Inn,** 539 S. Hemlock St. (436-0247 or 800-400-4106) offers picturesque, cozy rooms with fireplaces, cable TV, kitchens, and VCRs (singles from $55; off-season $45; 2-night min. on summer weekends). **Sea Ranch RV Park,** 415 N. Hemlock St., (436-2815), is a safe, tree-studded area with lots of grass and pebbles, right on the north edge of town. ($19, full hookup $22; $2 per additional person. Showers for non-guests $4. Horse rides $25-40. 1-night deposit required.) **The Homegrown Café,** 3301 S. Hemlock (436-1803), just before the last exit to U.S. 101, is an earthy and eclectic alternative to the mayhem downtown; fresh and fragrant veggie fare is picked right from the backyard (burritos $7-8; open M-Th 10am-2pm, F 11am-5pm, Sa 9am-8pm, Su 9am-4pm).

Sunset Transit System (325-0563 or 800-776-6406) runs buses to Astoria ($2.25). **Cannon Beach Shuttle,** a free natural-gas-powered service (50¢ requested), traverses the downtown area daily 10am-6pm. The **Cannon Beach Chamber of Commerce,** 207 N. Spruce St. (436-2623), at 2nd St., sells t-shirts, postcards, and brochures galore (open M-Sa 10am-5pm, Su 11am-3pm). **Post Office:** 163 N. Hemlock St. (800-275-8777; open M-F 9am-5pm). **ZIP code:** 97110. **Area code:** 503.

The Three Capes Loop

Between Tillamook and Lincoln City, the **Three Capes Loop,** a 35 mi. circle to the west of the straying U.S 101, connects a trio of spectacular promontories. **Cape Meares State Park,** at the tip of the promontory jutting out from Tillamook, protects one of the few remaining old growth forests on the Oregon Coast. Another 12 mi. southwest of Cape Meares, **Cape Lookout State Park** (842-4981) offers picnic tables and access to the beach for drive-by dawdlers (day-use fee $3), as well as some fine camping. **Cape Kiwanda State Park,** the southernmost promontory on the loop, reserves its magnificent shore for day use only (open 8am-dusk). Home to one of the most sublime beaches on the Oregon coast, the sheltered cape draws beachcombers, kite-flyers, volleyball players, fishers, jetskiers, and windsurfers. On this cape, barely north of Pacific City, massive rock outcroppings in a small bay mark the launching pad of the flat-bottomed **dory fleet,** one of the few fishing fleets in the world that launches beachside, directly from sand to surf.

Pacific City, a hidden gem that most travelers on U.S. 101 never even see, is home to another **Haystack Rock,** just as impressive as its Cannon Beach sibling to the north. For stops that extend overnight, the **Anchorage Motel,** 6585 Pacific Ave. (965-6773 or 800-941-6250), offers homey rooms with cable and coffee, but no phones (singles from $42; doubles from $49; rates drop significantly in winter). For memorable food, head east to the **Riverhouse Restaurant,** 34450 Brooten Rd. (965-6722), a tiny white house overlooking the Nestucca River. Stunning seafood ($14-19) and homemade desserts ($3-6) have earned a reputation as the best food in town. (Open Su-F 11am-9pm, Sa 11am-10pm.)

Newport

Newport's claim to fame lies in its world-class fish tank, also known as the **Oregon Coast Aquarium,** 2820 Ferry Slip Rd. SE (867-3474), at the south end of the bridge. ($8.75, seniors $7.75, ages 4-13 $4.50. Wheelchair access.) The vast 6-acre complex features everything from pulsating jellyfish to attention-seeking sea otters to giant African bullfrogs.

The motel-studded strip along U.S. 101 provides plenty of affordable rooms with predictably noisy road accompaniment. Weekend rates generally rise a couple of dollars, and winter rates plummet. **City Center Motel,** 538 Coast Hwy. SW (265-7381, reservations 800-628-9665), has good-sized rooms with sparkling bathrooms, smack in the middle of town. (Cable, phones, free ice machine. In summer, singles from $40; doubles $58.) **Beverly Beach State Park,** 198 123rd St. NE (265-9278, reservations 800-452-5687), 7 mi. north of town, is a year-round campground set amid gorgeous, rugged terrain. (Sites $16, with electricity $19, full hookup $20; yurts $26; hiker/biker $4.25. Showers free.) **Mo's Restaurant,** 622 Bay Blvd. SW (265-2979), is a small, crowded local favorite with great fish 'n' chips ($8; open daily 6am-11pm).

Greyhound, 956 10th St. SW (265-2253), at Bailey St., runs to Portland (3 per day, $17); Seattle (3 per day, $38); and San Francisco (5 per day, $65). The **Chamber of Commerce,** 555 Coast Hwy. SW (265-8801 or 800-262-7844), boasts a 24hr. info board and an on-the-ball staff (open May-Sept. M-F 8:30am-5pm, Sa-Su 10am-4pm; Oct.-Apr. M-F 8:30am-5pm). The **Newport Parks and Recreation Office** (265-7783) is at 169 Coast Hwy. SW (open M-F 8am-5pm). **Post Office:** 310 2nd St. SW (800-275-8777; open M-F 8:30am-5pm, Sa 10am-1pm). **ZIP code:** 97365. **Area code:** 541.

Oregon Dunes and Reedsport

Millennia of wind and water action have formed the Oregon Dunes National Recreation Area, a grainy 50 mi. expanse between Florence and Coos Bay. The dunes' shifting grip on the coastline is broken at Reedsport, where the Umpqua and Smith Rivers empty into Winchester Bay, near a town of the same name. **Spinreel Dune Buggy Rentals,** 9122 Wild Wood Dr. (759-3313), on U.S. 101 7 mi. south of Reedsport, offers air-rending Honda odysseys, ear-splitting dune buggy rides, and family tours in a cochlea-mangling VW "Thing." (Hondas $20 for 30min., $30 1st hr., $25 2nd hr.; buggies $15 for 30min., $25 per hr.; things $10 per 30min.) Even those with little time or low noise tolerance can at least stop at the **Oregon Dunes Overlook** ($1 parking fee), off U.S. 101, about halfway between Reedsport and Florence. Wooden ramps lead to a peek at untrammeled dunes and the ocean. The **Tahkenitch Creek Loop,** actually three separate trails, plows up to 3½ mi. through forest, dunes, wetlands, and beach. (Overlook staffed daily May 31-Sept. 6 10am-3pm. Guided hikes are available.)

The turquoise and white exterior **of Harbor View Motel,** 540 Beach Blvd. (271-3352), off U.S. 101 in Winchester Bay, hides greater tidiness and tastefulness within (refrigerators, cable, phones, and antlers; singles $31; doubles $34). The national recreation area is administered by **Siuslaw National Forest.** Dispersed camping is allowed on public lands, 200 ft. from any road or trail. The campgrounds with dune buggy access—**Spinreel, Driftwood II, Horsfall,** and **Horsfall Beach**—are generally loud and rowdy in the summer. All have flush toilets, drinking water, and are open year-round (reservations 800-280-2267; $10-13). **Carter Lake Campground,** 12 mi. north of Reedsport on U.S. 101, is as quiet as it gets out here (no ATVs; nice bathrooms, no showers; $14; open May-Sept.). **Bayfront Bar and Bistro,** 208 Bayfront Loop (271-9463), in Salmon Harbor, is a classy but casual choice on the waterfront (oyster shooters $1.50; dinners $10-16; open Tu-Su 11am-9pm).

Greyhound (267-4436 in Coos Bay) picks up outside Moo Mall, at 4th and Fir St., and runs to Portland (3 per day, $28); Eugene (2 per day, $20); and San Francisco (2 per day, $63). **Oregon Dunes National Recreation Area Information Center,** 855 U.S. 101 (271-3611), at Rte. 38 in Reedsport, just south of the Umpqua River Bridge, happily answers questions on fees, regulations, hiking, and camping throughout the area. The **Reedsport/Winchester Bay Chamber of Commerce** (271-3495 or 800-247-2155) is at the same location, with dune buggy rental info and motel listings. (Both open daily 8:30am-5pm.) **Post Office:** 301 Fir Ave. (800-275-8777), off Rte. 38 (open M-F 8:30am-5pm). **ZIP code:** 97467. **Area code:** 541.

INLAND OREGON

■ Eugene

With students riding mountain bikes, hippies eating organically grown food, outfitters making a killing off tourists, and hunters killing local wildlife, Eugene accepts all types. Oregon's second-largest city straddles the Willamette River between the Siuslaw and Willamette National Forests. Home to the University of Oregon (U of O),

Eugene owes much of its vibrancy to its students. Summer brings city slickers who happily shop and dine in the downtown pedestrian mall, until dusk draws them to Hult Center for an evening of world-class Bach. Outdoor types river raft along the Willamette and hike or bike in the many nearby parks, while fitness enthusiasts join the fleet of foot and free of spirit in this "running capital of the universe."

ORIENTATION AND PRACTICAL INFORMATION

Eugene is 111 mi. south of Portland on I-5. The **University of Oregon** campus lies in the southeast corner of Eugene, bordered on the north by **Franklin Blvd.,** which runs from the city center to I-5. **First Ave.** runs alongside the winding Willamette River; numbered **streets** go north-south. **Hwy. 99** is split in town—**6th Ave.** runs north and **7th Ave.** goes south. **Willamette Ave.** intersects the river, dividing the city into east and west. It is interrupted by the **pedestrian mall,** between 6th and 7th Ave. on Broadway downtown. Eugene's main student drag, **13th Ave.,** heads east to the University of Oregon.

Trains: Amtrak, 433 Willamette St. (800-872-7245), at 4th Ave. To: Seattle (2 per day, $24-46); Portland (2 per day, $12-21); and Berkeley, CA (1 per day, $111).

Buses: Green Tortoise (800-867-8647) runs from 14th and Kincaid St., at the U of O library, to San Francisco ($39), Seattle ($25), and Portland ($10).

Public Transportation: Lane Transit District (LTD) (687-5555) gives bus service throughout town. Runs M-F 6am-11:30pm, Sa 7:30am-11:30pm, Su 8:30am-8:30pm. All routes wheelchair accessible. $1, M-F after 7pm 50¢; seniors and under 12 40¢.

Taxis: Yellow Cab (746-1234) charges $2 base, $2 per mi. 24hr.

Car Rental: Enterprise, 810 W. 6th Ave. (683-0874), charges $33 per day. Unlimited mi. within OR; 150 free mi. per day, 25¢ per additional mi. out of state. Must be 21. Credit card required for non-locals. Open M-F 7:30am-6pm, Sa 9am-1pm.

Bike Rental: Paul's Bicycle Way of Life, 152 W. 5th Ave. (344-4105), rents city bikes ($2 per hr., min. 4hr.) and tandems ($3 per hr., $30 per day). Credit card required. Open M-F 9am-7pm, Sa-Su 10am-5pm.

Visitor Info: Visitors Association of Lane County, 115 W. 8th Ave. #190 (484-5307 or 800-547-5445), has its door on Olive St. Open M-F 8:30am-5pm, Sa-Su 10am-4pm; Sept.-Apr. M-Sa 8:30am-5pm. **University of Oregon Switchboard,** 1244 Walnut St. (346-3111), in the Rainier Bldg., offers referrals for anything from rides to housing (open M-F 7am-6pm). **Willamette National Forest,** 211 E. 7th Ave. (465-6522), in the Federal Bldg., has the wilderness scoop (open M-F 8am-4:30pm).

Internet Access: Sip 'n' Surf, 99 W. 10th St. #115 (302-1581). Open M-F 7am-9pm, Sa noon-6pm.

Post Office: 520 Williamette (800-275-8777), at 5th Ave. Open M-F 8:30am-5:30pm, Sa 10am-2pm. **ZIP code:** 97401-9999. **Area code:** 541.

ACCOMMODATIONS, CAMPGROUNDS, AND FOOD

The cheapest motels are on E. Broadway and W. 7th Ave., and tend toward seediness. Make reservations early; motels are packed on big football weekends. **Hummingbird Eugene International Hostel (HI-AYH),** 2352 Willamette St. (349-0589), a graceful neighborhood home, is a wonderful addition to and escape from the city. Take bus #24 or 25 and get off at 24th Ave. and Willamette, or park in back on Portland St. (Beds $13, nonmembers $16; private rooms from $34. Check-in 5-10pm. Lockout 11am-5pm. Kitchen open 7:30-9:30am and 5-10pm. Cash or check only.) **Downtown Motel,** 361 W. 7th Ave. (345-8739 or 800-648-4366), is in a prime location, with clean rooms under a green terra-cotta roof. (Cable, A/C, phones, free coffee and donuts in the morning. Singles $30; doubles $38. Credit card required for reservations.)

Tenters have been known to camp by the river, especially in the wild and woolly northeastern side near Springfield. Farther east on Rte. 58 and 126, the immense **Willamette National Forest** is packed with campsites ($3-16). A swamp gives the tree bark and ferns an eerie phosphorescence in the beautiful, mysterious **Black Canyon Campground,** 28 mi. east of Eugene on Hwy. 58 ($8-16).

Eugene's downtown area specializes in gourmet food, the university hang-out zone at 13th Ave. and Kincaid has more grab-and-go options, and natural food stores encircle the city. The creative menu and organic ingredients at **Keystone Café,** 395 W. 5th St. (342-2075), give diners a true taste of Eugene (plate-sized pancakes $3; open daily 7am-5pm). **Café Navarro,** 454 Willamette St. (344-0943), serves Caribbean and Latin cuisine with a gourmet flair. (Lunch $5-8. Open Tu-F 11am-2pm and 5-9:30pm, Sa 9am-2pm and 5-9:30pm, Su 9am-2pm.)

SIGHTS AND EVENTS

Campus maps and tours of the **University of Oregon** issue from the reception centers at **Oregon Hall** (346-3014), E. 13th Ave. and Agate St., and at the visitor parking and info booth, just left of the main entrance on Franklin Blvd. (tours M-F 10am and 2pm, Sa 10am). Just off the pedestrian section of 13th St., between Kincaid and University St., the **University Museum of Art** (346-3027) displays a changing repertoire of Pacific Northwestern and American pieces, and a permanent collection from Southeast Asia (open W noon-8pm, Th-Su noon-5pm; free). A few blocks away, the **Museum of Natural History,** 1680 E. 15th Ave. (346-3024), at Agate, shows a collection of relics from indigenous cultures worldwide, including a 7000-year-old pair of shoes (open W-Su noon-5pm; $1 donation requested).

The **Saturday Market** (686-8885), at 8th Ave. and Oak St., fuses crafts, clothing, jewelry, artwork, and music in a spectacular display (held weekly Apr.-Nov.; open 10am-5pm). During the 2-week **Oregon Bach Festival** (800-457-1486), Baroque authority Helmut Rilling leads some of the country's finest musicians in performances of Bach's concerti and cantatas, as well as selections from Verdi and Dvôrak. Concerts are held at the Hult Center and U of O's Beall Concert Hall beginning on the last week of June. Contact the **Hult Performing Arts Center,** 1 Eugene Center (info 687-5087, tickets 682-5000, 24hr. info 682-5746), at 7th Ave. and Willamette St. ($18-40; some senior and student discounts). The vast **Oregon Country Fair** (343-4298) actually takes place in **Veneta,** 13 mi. west of town on Rte. 126, but its festive quakes can be felt in Eugene. *(Advance tickets F and Su $10, Sa $15; tickets purchased on the day of cost $1 extra. No tickets sold on site.)* For 3 days in mid-July, 50,000 people drop everything to enjoy 10 stages' worth of shows, 300 art, clothing, craft, herbal remedy, furniture, spiritual, and food booths, and free hugs. Advance tickets are available through **Fastixx** (800-992-8499) or at the Hult Center.

OUTDOORS

River Runner Supply, 78 G. Centennial Loop (343-6883 or 800-223-4326), runs everything from fishing to whitewater rafting on the **Willamette River,** and also rents kayaks, canoes, and rafts. *(4hr. rafting trip $45 per person, 4-person min. Kayaks $25 per day, canoes $20 per day, rafts $45-60 per day. Credit card required.)* The student-run **Water Works Canoe Company,** 1395 Franklin Blvd. (346-4386), rents canoes. *(Open in summer Tu-Su 11am-8pm, but hrs. vary depending on weather. $5 per hr., $15 per 24hr.; $30 deposit.)* The large and popular Cougar Lake features the clothing-optional hippie hangout of Terwilliger Hot Springs, known by all as **Cougar Hot Springs.** To get there, go 4 mi. east of Blue River on Rte. 126, turn right onto Aufderheide Dr. (Forest Service Rd. 19), and follow the road 7.3 mi. as it winds on the right side of Cougar Reservoir ($3 day fee per person).

East from Eugene, **Rte. 126** runs adjacent to the beautiful **McKenzie River,** and on a clear day, the mighty snowcapped **Three Sisters** of the Cascades are visible. Just east of the town of **McKenzie Bridge,** the road splits into a scenic byway loop; Rte. 242 climbs east to the vast lava fields of **McKenzie Pass,** while Rte. 126 turns north over **Santiam Pass** and meets back with Rte. 242 in Sisters. Often blocked by snow til the end of June, **Rte. 242** is an exquisite drive, tunneling its narrow, winding between **Mt. Washington** and the **Three Sisters Wilderness** before rising to the plateau of McKenzie Pass, where lava outcroppings served as a training site for nauts preparing for lunar landings.

NIGHTLIFE

According to some, Eugene nightlife is the best in Oregon. Not surprisingly, the string of establishments by the university along 13th St. are often dominated by fraternity-style beer bashes. **Sam Bond's Garage,** 407 Blair Blvd. (431-6603), is a supremely laid-back gem of a cafe and pub in a soulful neighborhood. Live entertainment goes on every night, plus an ever-changing selection of local microbrews ($2.50-3 per pint). Take a bus (#50 or 52) or a cab at night. (Open daily 3pm-1am.) Downstairs at **Jo Federigo's Jazz Club and Restaurant,** 259 E. 5th Ave. (343-8488), across the street from the 5th St. Market., the jazz club swings with music every night, and the whole place rattles when the train goes by. (Shows usually at 9:30pm. Blues night W. Happy hour 2:30-6:30pm. No cover, but $5 drink min. and 50¢ surcharge per drink after 9pm. Lunch M-F 11:30am-2pm. Dinner daily 5-10pm. Jazz club open daily 2pm-1am.) The only gay dance club in town, **Club Arena,** 959 Pearl St. (683-2360), has a huge, checkered dance floor that gets kicking every night at 11pm to house and techno tunes. (Su retro night; M men's night; W women's night; Th $1 mixed drinks. Cover F-Sa $2.50, Th $1. Open daily 9pm-2:30am.)

■ Crater Lake and Klamath Falls

Crater Lake, the namesake of Oregon's only national park, was regarded as sacred by Native American shamans who forbade their people to look upon it. The fantastic depth of the lake (1932 ft.), combined with the clarity of its waters, creates its intensely blue effect. About 7700 years ago, Mt. Mazama created this serene scene in a massive eruption that buried thousands of square miles of the western U.S. under a thick layer of ash. The cataclysmic eruption left a deep caldera that gradually filled with centuries of rain. Klamath (kuh-LAH-math) Falls, one of the closest towns (56 mi. southeast), houses most of the services, motels, and restaurants listed below.

PRACTICAL INFORMATION The park is accessible from **Rte. 62** and the **south access** road that leads up to the caldera's rim, but the park is not completely open until after the snow has melted; call the Steel Center for road conditions (see below). To reach the park from Portland, take I-5 to Eugene, then Rte. 58 E to U.S. 97 S. During the summer, you can take Rte. 138 W from U.S. 97 and approach the lake from the park's **north entrance,** but this route is one of the last to be cleared. Before July, stay on U.S. 97 S to Rte. 62. The **Amtrak** Spring St. depot (884-2822, reservations 800-872-7245) is in Klamath Falls, on the east end of Main St.; turn right onto Spring St. and immediately left onto Oak St. One train per day runs to Portland ($48-69). **Greyhound,** 1200 Klamath Ave. (882-4616), rolls to Bend (1 per day, $20); Eugene (1 per day, $24.50); and Redding, CA (1 per day, $30). **Klamath County Dept. of Tourism** runs a visitor info center at 1451 Main St. (884-0666 or 800-445-6728; open M-Sa June-Sept. 9am-5:30pm; Oct.-May 8am-4:30pm). **Post Office:** 317 S. 7th St. (800-275-8777; open M-F 7:30am-5:30pm, Sa 9am-noon). **ZIP code:** 97601. **Area code:** 541.

The **William G. Steel Center** (594-2211 ext. 402), 1 mi. from the south entrance of the park, issues free **backcountry camping** permits (open daily 9am-5pm). **Crater Lake National Park Visitors Center** (594-2211, ext. 415), on the lake shore at Rim Village, also has advice on trails and campsites (open daily June-Sept. 8:30am-6pm). The **park entrance fee** is $10 for cars, $5 for hikers and bikers. **Post Office:** In the Steel Center (open M-F 10am-4pm, Sa 10am-2pm). **ZIP code:** 97604.

ACCOMMODATIONS, CAMPGROUNDS, AND FOOD Klamath Falls has several affordable hotels; it's an easy base for forays to Crater Lake. **Fort Klamath Lodge Motel and RV Park,** 52851 Rte. 62 (381-2234), is 15 mi. from the southern entrance in Fort Klamath. Cozy, quiet, countrified motel rooms have knotted-pine walls. (Fan, heater, TV, no phones. Singles $32; doubles $44. 24hr. coin laundry. Open May-Oct.)

Lost Creek Campground is in the park, 3 mi. off Rim Dr. in the southeast corner. Sites are set amid thin, young pines. (Sites $10. Drinking water, flush toilets, sinks. Tents only. No reservations. Usually open mid-July to mid-Oct. but call the visitors center to confirm.) **Waldo's Tavern and Mongolian Grill,** 610 Main St. (884-6863), at 6th St., makes a novel mix of pub culture and Asian cuisine. Fill up with an all-you-can eat array of meats, vegetables, noodles, and pineapples seasoned and cooked before your eyes. (Special $5.50, lunch $7.50, dinner $8. Open M-Sa 11am-9pm.)

OUTDOORS The walk from the visitors center at the rim down to the **Sinnott Memorial Overlook** is an easy 100 yd. walk to the park's most panoramic and accessible view. **Rim Dr.,** which does not open entirely until mid-July, is a 33 mi. loop around the rim of the caldera, high above the lake. Trails to **Garfield Peak** (one-way 1.7 mi.), which starts at the lodge, and **Watchman Peak** (one-way 0.7 mi.), on the west side of the lake, are the most spectacular. The sweaty, 2½ mi. hike up **Mt. Scott,** the park's highest peak (shy of 9000 ft.), begins from near the lake's eastern edge. The steep **Cleetwood Trail,** 1.1 mi. of switchbacks on the lake's north edge, is the only route down to the water. It is also the home of **Wizard Island,** a cinder cone rising 760 ft. above the lake, and **Phantom Ship Rock,** a spooky rock formation. Picnics, fishing, and swimming are allowed, but surface temperatures reach a maximum of only 50°F. Park rangers lead free walking tours daily in the summer and periodically in the winter (on snowshoes). The **Red Cone** trailhead, on the north access road, makes a 12 mi. loop of the **Crater Springs, Oasis Butte,** and **Boundary Springs Trails.**

■ Ashland

Set near the California border, Ashland mixes hippies and history to create an unlikely but perfect stage for the world-famous **Oregon Shakespeare Festival,** P.O. Box 158, Ashland 97520 (482-4331; http://www.orshakes.org). From mid-February to October, drama devotees can choose among 11 Shakespearean and newer works performed in Ashland's three elegant theaters: the outdoor **Elizabethan Stage,** the **Angus Bowmer Theater,** and the intimate **Black Swan.** Ticket purchases are recommended 6 months in advance; **mail-order and phone ticket sales** begin in January. ($15-41 in spring and fall, $20.25-47 in summer; $4 fee per order for phone, fax, or mail orders.) At 9:30am, the **box office,** 15 S. Pioneer St., releases any unsold tickets for the day's performances and sells 20 **standing room tickets** for sold-out shows on the Elizabethan Stage ($11). **Unofficial ticket sales** also take place just outside the box office, although scalping is illegal. ("Off with his head!"—*Richard III,* III.iv) Half-price **rush tickets** are sometimes available 1hr. before performances that are not already sold out. Some **half-price student-senior matinees** are offered in the spring and in October, and all three theaters hold full-performance **previews** in the spring and summer. **Backstage tours** provide a wonderful glimpse of the festival from behind the curtain (Tu-Su 10am; $9-10, ages 5-17 $6.75-7.50, under 5 not admitted).

In winter, Ashland is a budget paradise of vacancy and low rates; in summer, hotel and B&B rates double, and the hostel bulges. Only rogues and peasant slaves arrive without reservations. **Ashland Hostel,** 150 N. Main St. (482-9217), is well-kept and cheery, with an air of elegance. (Beds $14 with any hostelling card, $15 without. Private rooms $37-40; private women's room $22 for 1, $30 for 2. $3 discounts and free laundry for Pacific Crest Trail hikers or touring cyclists. Laundry and kitchen facilities. Check-in 5-11pm. Lockout 10am-5pm. Curfew midnight.) The incredible selection of foods on N. and E. Main St. has earned the plaza a culinary reputation independent of the festival. **Geppetto's,** 345 E. Main St. (482-1138), is *the* spot for a late-night bite. The staff is congenial, the walls covered in baskets, and the menu conversational (eggplant burger $4.25; open daily 8am-midnight; wheelchair access).

Ashland is located in the foothills of the Siskiyou and Cascade Ranges, 285 mi. south of Portland and 15 mi. north of the California border, near the junction of **I-5** and **Rte. 66. Greyhound** (482-8803) runs from the **BP station,** 2073 Rte. 99 N, at the north end of town, to Portland (3 per day, $39); Sacramento (3 per day, $40); and San Francisco (3 per day, $48). The **Chamber of Commerce,** 110 E. Main St. (482-3486), has free play schedules. **Ashland District Ranger Station,** 645 Washington St. (482-3333), off Rte. 66 by Exit 14 on I-5, provides info on hiking, biking, and the Pacific Crest Trail (open M-F 8am-4:30pm). **Post Office:** 120 N. 1st St. (800-275-8777), at Lithia Way (open M-F 9am-5pm). **ZIP code:** 97520. **Area code:** 541.

▓ Bend

At the foot of the Cascades's east slope, Bend is at the epicenter of an impressive array of outdoor opportunities, wooing waves of skiers and nature-lovers. Oregon's biggest little city in the east is rapidly losing its small-town feel to a stream of California, Portland, and Seattle refugees in search of the perfect blend of urban excitement, pristine wilderness, and sun-filled days. Chain stores and strip malls flood the banks of U.S. 97, but the city's charming downtown and lively crowd still seduce most visitors.

PRACTICAL INFORMATION Bend is 160 mi. southeast of Portland either on U.S. 26 E through Warm Springs Indian Reservation to U.S. 97 S, or south on I-5 to Salem, then east on Rte. 22 E to Rte. 20 E through Sisters; 144 mi. north of Klamath Falls on U.S. 97; and 100 mi. southeast of Mt. Hood via U.S. 26 E and Rte. 97 S. **U.S. 97 (3rd St.)** bisects the town. Downtown lies to the west along the **Deschutes River; Wall** and **Bond St.** are the two main arteries. **Greyhound,** 2045 U.S. 20 E (382-2151), 1½ mi. east of town, runs to Portland (1 per day, $23) and Klamath Falls (1 per day, $20). **Owl Taxi,** 1919 NE 2nd St. (382-3311), charges $2 base, $1.80 per mi. (24hr.). **Bend Chamber and Visitors Bureau,** 63085 U.S. 97 N (382-3221), stocks free maps, free coffee, and Internet access (open M-Sa 9am-5pm, Su 11am-3pm). **Deschutes National Forest Headquarters,** 1645 U.S. 20 E (388-2715), has forest and wilderness info (open M-F 7:45am-4:30pm). **Post Office:** 2300 NE 4th St. (388-1971), at Webster (open M-F 8:30am-5:30pm, Sa 10am-1pm). **ZIP code:** 97701. **Area code:** 541.

ACCOMMODATIONS, CAMPGROUNDS, AND FOOD Most of the cheapest motels line **3rd St.** just outside of town, and rates are surprisingly low. The sparkling **Mill Inn,** 642 NW Colorado (389-9198), is on the corner of Bond St., 4 blocks from downtown. Hearty, home-cooked breakfasts are served in the open dining room. (Free laundry, outdoor hot tub. Bunks $15; singles $37; doubles $45. Rooms with private baths available.) To reach **Bend Cascade Hostel,** 19 SW Century Dr. (389-3813 or 800-299-3813), take Greenwood west from 3rd St. until the name changes to Newport. After ½ mi., take a left on 14th St.; the clean, fairly safe, and tidy hostel is ½ mi. up on the right side, just past the Circle K. (Foosball, laundry, kitchen, linen. $14; students, seniors, cyclists, and members $13; under 18 with parents ½-price. Lockout 9:30am-4:30pm. Curfew 11pm.) **Deschutes National Forest** maintains a huge number of lakeside campgrounds along the **Cascade Lakes Hwy.,** west of town; all have toilets. Sites with potable water cost $8-12 per night; those without water are free. Camping anywhere in the national forest area is free.

SIGHTS AND OUTDOORS South of Bend by 3½ mi. on U.S. 97, the **High Desert Museum,** 59800 S. Hwy. 97 (382-4754), is one of the premier natural and cultural history museums in the Pacific Northwest. *(Open daily 9am-5pm. $6.25, seniors and ages 13-18 $5.75, ages 5-12 $3.)* Visitors walk through stunning life-size dioramas of life in the Old West, while the indoor desertarium houses bats, burrowing owls, and collared lizards. August of 1999 brings a brand-new Native American Wing to the museum, featuring a walk-through exhibit on post-reservation Indian life.

   Newberry National Volcanic Monument links and preserves the volcanic features south of Bend. **Lava Lands Visitors Center,** 58201 U.S. 97 (593-2421), is 5 mi. south of the High Desert Museum on U.S. 97 (open daily 9:30am-5pm; Apr. to mid-June W-Su 9:30am-5pm). A mandatory $5 parking fee, good for 2 days, is required within ¼ mi. of the monument area (free with Golden Age Passport). Immediately behind the visitors center is **Lava Butte,** a 500 ft. cinder cone from which much of the nearby lava flows. Between May 31 and September 6, a **shuttle bus** makes the nearly 2 mi. journey every 30min. ($2, seniors and $1.50, under 6 free). The monument's central component is **Newberry Crater,** 13 mi. south of the visitors center on U.S. 97, then about 13 mi. east on Rte. 21. The most scenic campground is **Little Crater,** with 50 sites between Rte. 21 and the Paulina lakeshore ($12-14). Over 150 mi. of trails cross the area, including a short walk up to an enormous **obsidian flow** formed by an eruption 1300 years ago, a 21 mi. loop that circumnavigates the **caldera rim,** and a 7½ mi. loop around Paulina Lake. **Lava River Cave** (593-1456), a 100,000-year-old, 42°F, 1 mi. long, subterranean lava tube, is 1 mi. south of the visitors center on U.S. 97 (open daily mid-May to mid-Oct. 9am-6pm; $2.50, ages 13-17 $2).

■ Hells Canyon and Wallowa Mountains

The northeast corner of Oregon is the state's most rugged, remote, and arresting country, with jagged granite peaks, glacier-gouged valleys, and azure lakes. East of La Grande, the Wallowa Mountains (wa-LAH-wah) rise abruptly, towering over the plains from elevations of over 9000 ft. Thirty miles farther east, the deepest gorge in North America, barren and dusty Hells Canyon, plunges to the Snake River. **Hells Canyon National Recreation Area** and the **Eagle Cap Wilderness** lie on either side of the **Wallowa Valley,** which can be reached from **Baker City, La Grande,** and **Clarkston, WA.** Three main towns offer services within the area: **Enterprise, Joseph,** and **Halfway.** The only way to get close to the canyon without taking at least a full day is to drive the **Hells Canyon National Scenic Loop Drive,** which begins and ends in Baker City, following Rte. 86, Forest Rd. 39 and 350, Rte. 82, and finally I-84. Even this paved route takes 6hr. to 2 days to drive; closures are routine. The most eye-popping views are from the 90 ft. fire lookout at **Hat Point Overlook;** go 24 mi. up the steep gravel Forest Rd. 4240 from Imnaha, then turn off onto Rd. 315 and follow the signs.

There are over 1000 mi. of **hiking trails** in the canyon, only a fraction of which are regularly maintained by the Forest Service. A wide array of dangers lurk below the rim, such as huge elevation changes, poison oak, rattlesnakes, blistering heat, and lack of water. The dramatic 56 mi. **Snake River Trail** runs beside the river for the length of the canyon. **Hells Canyon Adventures** (785-3352, outside OR 800-422-3568), 1½ mi. from the Hells Canyon Dam in Oxbow, runs a wide range of trips through the canyon. (Jet boats $30 for 2hr., $40 for 3hr., full-day $95; whitewater rafting $125, includes jet boat ride back upstream.)

The Wallowa Mountains possess a scenic beauty as magnificent as the canyon's. Over 600 mi. of **hiking trails** cross the **Eagle Cap Wilderness,** and are usually free of snow from mid-July to October. The 5 mi. hike to **Chimney Lake,** from the Bowman trailhead on the Lostine River Rd. (Forest Rd. 8210), traverses fields of granite boulders with a few small meadows. The **Two Pan trailhead** at the end of the Lostine River Rd. is the start of a forested 6 mi. hike to popular **Minam Lake.** From the **Wallowa Lake trailhead,** behind the little powerhouse at the dead end of Rte. 82, a 6 mi. hike leads up the East Fork of the **Wallowa River** to **Aneroid Lake.** From Aneroid, the summit hikes to **Pete's Point** and **Aneroid Mountain** offer great vistas. **Steamboat, Long,** and **Swamp Lakes** are as magnificent as the popular **Lakes Basin,** but receive only half as many visitors. The trailheads for both are on the Lostine River Rd. Many excellent day hikes to **Lookingglass, Culver, Bear, Eagle, Cached, Arrow,** and **Heart Lakes** start from the **Main Eagle trailhead,** on Forest Rd. 7755, on the southern side of the Eagle Cap Wilderness (accessible from Baker City and Halfway).

Most of the towns along Rte. 82 have motels with plenty of vacancies on weekdays. **Country Inn Motel** (426-4986), on Rte. 82 in Enterprise, has countrified frilly decorations (cable, coffee makers, refrigerators; singles $37; doubles $46-48). Campgrounds here are plentiful, inexpensive, and sublime. Due to budget constraints, most are not fully serviced, and are therefore **free.** Most campgrounds are only open from July to September. **Hells Canyon, Copperfield, McCormick,** and **Woodhead,** near Oxbow and Brownlee Dams on Rte. 86 and Rte. 71, are the only campgrounds open year-round ($6, RV hookups $10; no reservations; call 785-3323). **Wallowa Lake State Park** (432-4185, reservations 800-452-5687), in Wallowa Lake, is large and fully serviced. (Flush toilets, drinking water, showers. Tent sites $16, full hookup $20; 2 wheelchair-accessible sites.) A few affordable restaurants hide out in the small towns of the Wallowa Valley.

CALIFORNIA

For centuries, settlers have come to California in search of the elusive and the unattainable. The Spanish conquistadors came for the mythical land of El Dorado, the mining '49ers hunted for the Mother Lode, and the naive and beautiful still search for stardom. Adventurers and misanthropes flock to the mountains and deserts to cop the ultimate thrill, and stampedes of 2.5-child families cloud the national parks, seeking reconciliation with the illusion of tamed, well-appointed nature. Dreamy-eyed, disenfranchised flower children converge on Haight Street's lost commune, while future techno-rulers hoof it to the perennially booming Silicon Valley.

Glaring movie spotlights, clanging San Francisco trolleys, and *barrio* bustle are all Californian. Vanilla-scented Jeffrey pines, alpine lakes, and ghostly, shimmering desert floors are all Californian. The breezy tolerance of the San Francisco Bay Area, the plastic style of L.A., and the military-fueled Republicanism of San Diego are all Californian. It is the West of the West, the resting place of the superlative, the drawing board of the American dream. No other state can claim so many flavors in its blend of physical, social, and cultural ingredients. In fact, there's so much going on you'd need a whole other book (like *Lets Go: California 1999*) to describe it.

⊛ HIGHLIGHTS OF CALIFORNIA

- **Los Angeles.** Follow your star to the place where media legends carouse (p. 741), Ice Age fossils calcify (p. 745), boardwalk freaks commune (p. 743), vintage automobiles cruise (p. 746), milkshakes congeal (p. 740), and poor folk construct (p. 750).
- **San Francisco.** Here, bluesmen resonate (p. 801), iconoclasts castigate and students demonstrate (p. 798), and old hippies recreate (p. 789).
- **Scenic Drives.** Along the coast, Rte. 1 and 101 stop at Redwood National Park (p. 813), the San Mateo Coast (p. 804), and Hearst Castle (p. 775).
- **National Parks.** Hike at Yosemite (p. 821), say howdy to a scorpion in Death Valley (p. 771), or trip through cholla at Joshua Tree (p. 769).
- Pan for **"goald!"** in Sonora (p. 815), go **frogging** in Calaveras County (p. 815), and observe active **New Age Hippies** in the Cascades (p. 817).

PRACTICAL INFORMATION

Capital: Sacramento.
Visitor Info: California Office of Tourism, 801 K St. #1600, Sacramento 95814 (800-862-2543; http://www.gocalif.ca.gov).
Emergency: 911.
Time Zone: Pacific (3hr. behind Eastern). **Postal Abbreviation:** CA.
Sales Tax: 7-8%, by county.

SOUTHERN CALIFORNIA

■ Los Angeles

Myth and anti-myth stand comfortably opposed in Los Angeles. Some see in its sweeping beaches and dazzling sun a demi-paradise, a land of opportunity where the most opulent dreams can be realized. Others point to its congestion, smog, and crime, and declare Los Angeles a sham—a converted wasteland where TV-numbed masses go to wither in the sun.

L.A. is a wholly American phenomenon, one that developed not in the image and shadow of Europe, but at the same time as America's international ascendancy. It is this autonomy that makes L.A. feel like a city without a past. In a city where nothing seems more than 30 years old, the latest trends curry more respect than the venerable. Many come to this historical vacuum to make (or re-make) themselves. And what better place? Without the tiresome duty of kowtowing to the gods of an established high culture, Angelenos are free to indulge not in what they must, but in what they choose. The resulting atmosphere is delicious with potential. It's a hell of a show.

ORIENTATION

The City of Angels spreads its wings along the coast of Southern California, 127 mi. north of San Diego and 403 mi. south of San Francisco. You can still be "in" L.A. even if you're 50 mi. from downtown. Before you even think about navigating Los Angeles's 6500 mi. of streets and 40,000 intersections, get yourself a good **map.** Locals swear by the *Thomas Guide: Los Angeles County Street Guide and Directory* ($16 for L.A. county, $26 for L.A. and Orange County).

A legitimate **downtown** Los Angeles *does* exist, but it won't help orient you to the rest of the city. The numbered streets running east-west downtown form a labyrinth. The predominately Latino section of L.A. known as **East L.A.** begins east of downtown's Western Ave., with the districts of **Boyle Heights, Montebello,** and **El Monte.** South of downtown are the **University of Southern California (USC), Exposition Park,** and the predominantly African-American districts of **Inglewood, Watts,** and **Compton.** The area south of downtown, known as **South Central,** suffered the brunt of the fires and looting that erupted in 1992. South Central and East L.A. are considered crime-ridden and offer little to attract tourists.

Northwest of downtown is **Hollywood.** Sunset Blvd. (east-west) presents a cross-section of virtually everything L.A. has to offer: beach communities, lavish wealth, famous nightclubs, and sleazy motels. Hollywood Blvd. (east-west) runs just beneath the star-studded Hollywood Hills.

West of Hollywood, the **Westside** encompasses West Hollywood, Westwood, Century City, Culver City, Bel Air, Brentwood, and (for our purposes) the independent city of **Beverly Hills.** The affluent Westside also is home to the University of California at Los Angeles and some trendy, off-beat Melrose Ave. hangouts. The area west of downtown is known as the **Wilshire District** after its main boulevard. **Hancock Park,** a green residential area, covers the northeast portion of the district.

The **Valley** spreads north of the Hollywood Hills and the Santa Monica Mountains. For most people, *the* valley, is, like, the **San Fernando Valley,** where more than a million people live in the suburbs, in a basin bounded to the north and west by the Santa Susanna Mountains and the Simi Freeway (Rte. 118), to the south by the Ventura Freeway (Rte. 134), and to the east by the Golden State Freeway (I-5). The Valley also contains the suburb of **Burbank** and the city of **Pasadena.**

Eighty miles of beach line L.A.'s **Coastal Region. Zuma** is northernmost, followed by **Malibu,** which lies 15 mi. up the coast from **Santa Monica.** Just a bit farther south is the funky beach community of **Venice.** The beach towns south of Santa Monica, comprising the area called the **South Bay,** are Marina del Rey, Manhattan, Hermosa, and Redondo Beach. South across the hob nobby **Palos Verdes Peninsula** is **Long Beach.** Farthest south are the **Orange County** beach cities: Seal Beach, Sunset Beach, Huntington Beach, Newport Beach, and Laguna Beach. Confused yet? Everyone is.

GETTING AROUND

Public Transportation

Nowhere is the great god Automobile held in greater reverence than in L.A., though the **Metropolitan Transit Authority (MTA)** does work—sort of. Some older buses may still be labeled RTD (Rapid Transit District), the MTA's former name. Using the MTA to sightsee in L.A. can be frustrating, simply because attractions tend to be spread out, and the system is not easily understood. Those determined to see everything in L.A. should get

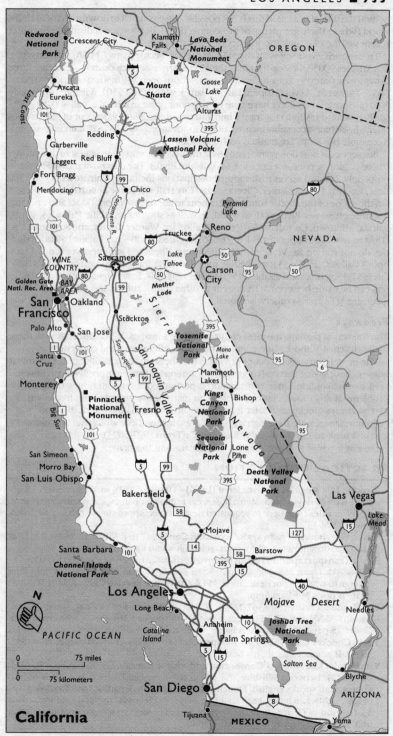

CALIFORNIA

California

behind the wheel of a car. If this is not possible, base yourself in downtown or in Holly-wood (where there are plenty of bus connections). Bus service is dismal in the outer reaches of the city, and 2hr. journeys are not unusual.

To familiarize yourself with the MTA, write for "sector maps," **MTA**, P.O. Box 194, Los Angeles 90053, or stop by one of the 10 **customer-service centers.** There are three downtown: Gateway Transit Center, Union Station (open M-F 6:30am-6pm); Arco Plaza, 505 S. Flower St., Level C (open daily 7:30am-3:30pm); and 5301 Wilshire (open daily 8:30am-5pm). If you don't have time to map your route in advance, call 800-266-6883 (daily 5:30am-11:30pm) for transit info and schedules. Ninety percent of MTA's lines offer **wheelchair-accessible buses** (call 1hr. in advance, 800-621-7828 daily 6am-10pm). Accessible bus stops are marked with a symbol.

Bus service is best downtown and along the major thoroughfares west of downtown (there is 24hr. service, for instance, on Wilshire Blvd.). The downtown **DASH shuttle** costs only 25¢ and serves major tourist destinations including Chinatown, Union Station, Gateway Transit Center, Olvera St., and City Hall. Given the hellish downtown traffic, the scope of the shuttle routes make them an attractive option. DASH also operates a shuttle on Sunset Blvd. in Hollywood, as well as shuttles in Pacific Palisades, Watts, Fairfax, Midtown, Crenshaw, Van Nuys/Studio City, Warner Center, and Southeast L.A. (Downtown DASH operates M-F 6:30am-6:30pm, Sa 10am-5pm. Pacific Palisades shuttles do not run on Sa. Venice DASH runs every 10min. on summer weekends 11am-6pm.) Call 800-252-7433 for schedule info, 485-7201 for pick-up points. (MTA's basic fare is $1.35, seniors and disabled 45¢; transfers 25¢/10¢. Exact change required.) Transfers can be made between MTA lines or to other transit authorities. All route numbers given are MTA unless otherwise noted.

Freeways

The freeway is perhaps the most enduring of L.A.'s images. When uncongested, these well-marked, 10- and 12-lane concrete roadways offer speed and convenience.

The most frustrating aspect of driving is the sheer unpredictability of L.A. traffic. It goes without saying that rush hours, both morning and evening, are always a mess and well worth avoiding. Since construction is performed at random hours, there can be problems at any time. A little reminder: no matter how crowded the freeway is, it's almost always quicker and safer than taking surface streets to your destination.

Californians refer to their highways by names and numbers, which is at best harmless, at worst misleading. For freeway info, call **CalTrans** (897-3693).

Do not hitchhike! In Los Angeles, it is tantamount to suicide.

PRACTICAL INFORMATION

Airport: Los Angeles International (LAX) (310-646-5252), in Westchester, 15 mi. southwest of downtown. Metro buses, car rental companies, cabs, and airport shuttles offer rides from here to requested destinations. Approximate cab fare to downtown is $24-33.

Buses: Greyhound-Trailways Information Center, 1716 E. 7th St. (800-231-2222), at Alameda, downtown. Call for fares, schedules, and local ticket info.

Public Transportation: MTA Bus Information Line (213-626-4455 or 800-COMMUTE/266-6883). Open M-F 6am-8:30pm, Sa-Su 8am-6pm. You may be put on hold long enough to walk to your destination. **MTA Customer Service Center,** 5301 Wilshire Blvd., is open M-F 9am-5pm.

Car Rental: Thrifty (800-367-2277), at LAX. As low as $25 per day, unlimited mi. within CA, NV, and AZ. $144 per week. CDW $9 per day. Must be 21 with credit card. Under 25 pay $20 per day surcharge. Open daily 5am-midnight.

Taxis: Checker Cab (482-3456). **Independent** (385-8294). **United Independent** (653-5050). If you need a cab, it's best to call.

Visitor Info: Los Angeles Convention and Visitor Bureau, 685 S. Figueroa St. (213-689-8822), between Wilshire and 7th in the Financial District. Hundreds of brochures. Staff speaks English, French, German, Spanish, Japanese, and Tagalog. Maps of L.A., sights, and buses, each about $2. Maps of celebrity sights and California roads $4. Distributes *Destination: Los Angeles,* a free booklet including tourist and lodging info. Open M-F 8am-5pm, Sa 8:30am-5pm.

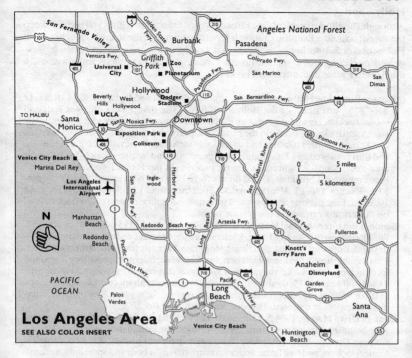

Los Angeles Area
SEE ALSO COLOR INSERT

CALIFORNIA

Smooth Jazz: 94.7 FM, "The Wave." Smooooooth jazz.

Hotlines: AIDS Hotline (800-922-2437), or national hotline (800-342-5971). **Rape Crisis** (310-392-8381). All 24hr.

Internet Access: Cyber Java, 1029 Abbot Kinney Blvd. (310-581-1300), Venice. $9 per hr. Cyber Java special: 10hr., $45. Open daily 7am-11pm. **@coffee,** 7200 Melrose Ave. (213-930-1122), Hollywood. $2 for 10min., $5 for 30min., $7 for an hour includes a free coffee. Open M-F 8am-8pm, Sa 8am-9pm, Su 9am-8pm.

Post Office: Centrally located branch at 900 N. Alameda St. (800-275-8777), at 9th. Open M-F 9am-5pm, Sa 9am-noon. **ZIP code:** 90086.

Area codes: Downtown Los Angeles, Hollywood, Huntington Park, Vernon, and Montebello **213** (currently changing to **323** in Hollywood and environs). Malibu, Pacific Coast Hwy., Westside, southern and eastern Los Angeles County **310**. Burbank, Glendale, and Pasadena **626**. San Fernando, Van Nuys, and La Cañada **818**. Orange County **714**. San Diego County **619**. Eastern border of Los Angeles County **909**. Ventura County **805**.

ACCOMMODATIONS

As in any large city, cheap accommodations in Los Angeles are often unsafe. It can be difficult to gauge quality from the exterior, so ask to see a room before you plunk down any cash. Rates below $35 might indicate the kind of hotels in which most travelers would not feel secure. For those willing to share a room and a bathroom, hostels (see below) are a saving grace. In choosing where to stay, the first consideration should be car accessibility. If you don't have wheels, you would be wise to decide which element of L.A. appeals to you the most. Those visiting for the beaches would do well to choose lodgings in Venice or Santa Monica. Avid sightseers will probably be better off in Hollywood or the more expensive (but cleaner and nicer) Westside. Downtown has numerous public transportation connections but is unsafe after dark. Listed prices do not include L.A.'s 14% hotel tax.

Hollywood

Although Tinseltown has tarnished in recent years, its location, sights, and nightlife keep the tourists coming. Exercise caution if scouting out one of the many budget hotels on **Hollywood** or **Sunset Blvd.**—*especially east of the main strips, the area can be dangerous, particularly at night.* The hostels here are generally excellent, and as a whole, a much better value than anything else in L.A.

Banana Bungalow Hollywood, 2775 Cahuenga Blvd. (213-851-1129 or 800-4-HOSTEL/446-7835), just north of the Hollywood Bowl. The Bungalow's efficient staff and robust backpacker clientele make for a summer-camp atmosphere that is relentlessly wacky and frisky, especially in the restaurant/party area. Free shuttle from the airport, and $2 transit to area beaches and attractions (including Disneyland, Magic Mountain, and Universal Studios). Free nightly movies, arcade, and frequent dances in restaurant area. Pool, hoops, weight room, Internet access ($1 per 10min.), and "snack shack." Free continental breakfast. Co-ed dorms (6-10 beds) with bathroom and TV. Dorms $18; doubles $36-45. Meal charge $4.50. Linen free. Check-in 24hr. Check-out 10:30am. Free parking. Passport and international airline ticket required for dorms, but Americans can stay in the private rooms.

Student Inn International Hostel, 7038½ Hollywood Blvd. (213-469-6781 or 800-557-7038), right on the Walk of Fame. Look no further. Free and discounted tickets to Disneyland, Universal Studios, and Magic Mountain. Free city tours. No strings attached. This amiable hostel has a small kitchen, free breakfast, Internet access, free linen, and free pick-up from LAX, Amtrak, and Greyhound. 4-bed dorms with private bath $13.50, off-season $15; doubles $30. Those low on cash can snore on floor mattresses ($10) or work at the reception in exchange for a free night's stay. Free parking. International passport required. 10% discount with *Let's Go: USA.*

Orange Drive Manor, 1764 N. Orange Dr. (213-850-0350). Spiffy, restored craftsman-style home in a low-key residential neighborhood just around the corner from Mann's Chinese Theater. Best for travelers who enjoy quiet and privacy. Kitchen, cable TV lounge, lockers, and free linen. Spacious dorms have 2-4 beds and sport antique furniture (some private baths). Dorms $15; private rooms $25. Check-out 10am. No curfew. Long-term discounts available. Parking $5 per night. Reservations recommended during the summer. No credit cards.

Santa Monica, Venice, and Marina del rey

Venice Beach hostels beckon to all the young budget travelers, especially foreign students, who are lured by the area's blend of indulgent beach culture and lively nightlife. Most of the cheap accommodations that pepper the coast cater to raucous party kids, but there are some quiet gems in the mix.

🐚**Los Angeles/Santa Monica (HI-AYH),** 1436 2nd St., (310-393-9913), Santa Monica, 2 blocks from the beach and across from the 3rd St. promenade. Take MTA #33 from downtown (Union Station) to 2nd and Broadway, Blue Bus #3 from LAX to 4th and Broadway, or Blue Bus #10 from downtown (Union Station). Modern and meticulous, it looks more like a swanky robot office complex than an inexpensive hostel. Extremely tight security; lobby manned 24hr. Colossal kitchen and laundry, 2 nightly movies, library, central courtyard, bi-weekly barbecues ($5), and hot breakfast daily (85¢-$3.75). Guests get discounts at many restaurants and shops. Dorms (4-10 beds) $17-19, nonmembers $20-22. Private doubles $48, nonmembers $51. 28-night max. stay. Safe deposit boxes and lockers available. No parking.

Cadillac Hotel, 8 Dudley Ave. (310-399-8876), Venice. An ab-fab Art Deco landmark directly on the beach. International crowd and helpful staff. Tour desk, well-equipped gym, laundry, sauna, rooftop sundeck. Lounge has cable TV, pool table, Internet access, Venetian gondola, and a piece of the Berlin wall. 4-bunk dorm rooms have private bath and lockers. Dorms $20; private suites from $60. LAX shuttle $5. Free parking with private rooms. No reservations for bunks.

Share-Tel Apartments, 20 Brooks Ave. (310-392-0325), ½ block from the beach. This fun-loving hostel offers free breakfast, dinner, and keg parties (M-F only). Social lounge with TV and board games. Dorm rooms have 4-8 beds, private baths, kitchenettes, and fridges. Dorms $17; $110 per week, off-season $100. Private rooms $22-25. Lockers $1. Key and linen deposit $20. Free airport pick-up and city tour planning. Parking $10 per night, off-season $5. No reservations. No credit cards. International passport required.

CALIFORNIA

TO GRIFFITH PARK AND MADONNA'S HOUSE

Vermont Ave.

Normandie Ave.

Western Ave.

Olympic Blvd.

mile
1 kilometer

Hollyhock House
Barnsdall Park

Hollywood Frwy.

HOLLYWOOD

DETAIL MAP

Sunset Blvd.
Vine
Cahuenga Blvd.

Paramount Studios

9

Wilshire Country Club

3rd St.

N

Crenshaw Blvd.

Highland

Franklin Ave.
Hollywood Blvd.
Fountain Ave.
Site of Hugh Grant's Arrest
Genessee
Fairfax Ave.

WEST HOLLYWOOD

Santa Monica Blvd.
Melrose Ave.
Ave.

La Brea Blvd.
Gardner St.
Pan Pacific Park
La Brea Tar Pits
Hancock Park
Miracle Mile

L.A. County Museum of Art

San Vicente Blvd.

Fairfax Ave.

Washington Blvd.

Venice Blvd.

Crescent Hts. Blvd.

Jefferson Blvd.

Crescent Hts. Blvd.
Chateau Marmont
Hyatt on Sunset/The Riot House
Sunset Marquis
St. James Club
Alta Loma Rd.
Le Parc
Kings Rd.

CBS Studios
Farmer's Market
Beverly Blvd.

La Cienega Blvd.

Pico Blvd.

Museum of Tolerance

Santa Monica Fwy.

Doheny Dr.
8
Hillcrest Rd.
Hillc rest Rd.
Greystone Mansion and Park
Sunset Blvd.
Elm Dr.

BEVERLY HILLS
7
Crescent Dr.
Canon Dr.
Beverly Dr.
Rodeo Dr.

Robertson Blvd.
3rd St.
Burton Way
F
Wilshire Blvd.
Beverly Hills High School
Olympic Blvd.
Century Plaza Towers
Moreno
Dr.
Century Park E.

CENTURY CITY

Colwater Canyon Drive

Franklin Canyon Ranch
Lake Franklin

Beverly Hills Hotel

Roxbury Dr.
The Los Angeles Country Club

Beverly Glen Blvd.
Mapleton Dr.
WESTWOOD
Westwood Memorial Cemetery
6
5
Century Square
Ave. of the Stars
Century Park W.
Fox Studios
Rancho Park
Little S Monica Blvd.

Westwood Blvd.

TO SANTA MONICA AIRPORT

4
Tower Rd. Benedict Canyon Rd.

Hillgard Ave.
BEL AIR
Hilgard Ave.
Veteran Ave.
Selpuveda Blvd.
UCLA
Gayley Ave.
Le Conte Dr.
Landfair Ave.
Armand Hammer Museum

San Diego Fwy.
405

BRENTWOOD

Bristol Ave.
1

Montana Ave.
San Vicente Blvd.
2
Wilshire Blvd.
3
Bundy Dr.
San Vicente Blvd.
Santa Monica Blvd.
Barrington Ave.
Westwood Blvd.
Selpuveda Blvd.

405
10

Santa Monica Fwy.

TO SANTA MONICA AND VENICE
Olympic Blvd.

Westside: Beverly Hills, Westwood, Wilshire

The snazzy and relatively safe Westside has excellent public transportation to the beaches. The area's affluence, however, means less bang for your buck, and there are no hostel-type accommodations. Those planning to stay at least 1 month in summer or 6 months during the school year can contact the **UCLA Off-Campus Housing Office**, 350 Deneve Dr. (310-825-4491), where a roommate share board lists students who have a spare room.

Bevonshire Lodge Motel, 7575 Beverly Blvd. (213-936-6154), near Farmer's Market. Looks like *Melrose Place* with a color-blind set designer. Pool in the central courtyard is open year-round. Spacious rooms have sparkling, newly-renovated bathrooms that make all the shower scenes fun, and beds big enough for Amanda to bring all her conquests home. Singles $44; doubles $49; rooms with kitchen $55. Free parking. 10% ISIC discount.

The Little Inn, 10604 Santa Monica Blvd. (310-475-4422), West L.A. Found on Little Santa Monica, the smaller road paralleling the divided boulevard to the south. This is budget-travel bliss. Although the lack of style in the sparsely decorated rooms is *so* un-L.A., they're sizable and clean. A/C, cable TV, and fridges. Singles $50; doubles $60; rooms with kitchens $70. Off-season $45/$55/$65. Discount with *Let's Go: USA*. Check-in 24hr. Check-out 11am. Free parking.

Stars Inn, 10269 Santa Monica Blvd. (310-556-3076). Several blocks east of the Little Inn, the Stars is managed by the same group, and delivers a similarly high level of quality—spacious, clean rooms, sparkling bathrooms, A/C, fridges, and cable TV. Cool location across from the Century City Shopping Center. Singles $50; doubles $60; rooms with kitchens $70. Off-season $45/$55/$65. Discount with *Let's Go USA*. Check-out 11am. Free parking.

Downtown L.A.

Although busy and relatively safe by day, the downtown area empties and becomes dangerous after 6pm and on weekends. Both men and women should travel in packs after dark, especially in the area between **Broadway** and **Main.** Some decent lodgings can be found in the area, however—haggling is possible, especially during the off season. Cheaper weekly rates are sometimes available.

Hotel Stillwell, 838 S. Grand Ave. (213-627-1151 or 800-553-4774). Recently refurbished, this ultra-clean hotel is still, well, one of the most sensible downtown options. Rooms are bright and have A/C and cable TV. Parking area next door ($3 per day). Singles $39, $200 per week; doubles $49/$275.

Milner Hotel, 813 S. Flower St. (213-627-6981 or 800-827-0411). Central location makes up for slightly worn decor. Pub, grill, and flag-bedecked lounge in lobby. Free rides to LAX, Union, and Greyhound station. Rooms have A/C and cable TV. Breakfast included. Singles $50; doubles $60. Parking $4.

Park Plaza Hotel, 607 S. Park View St. (213-384-5281), on the west corner of 6th across from green but unsafe MacArthur Park. Built in 1927, this Art Deco giant has a marble-floored lobby and a monumental staircase. All of the clean but small rooms have TV, some A/C. Pool and weight room. Singles $68; doubles $74.

FOOD

Eating in Los Angeles, the city of the health-conscious, is more than just a gustatory experience. Thin figures and fat wallets are a powerful combination. Of course, there are also restaurants where the main objective is to be seen, and the food is secondary, as well as those where the food itself seems too beautiful to be eaten—it was here, after all, that 80s nouvelle cuisine reached its height.

Fortunately for the budget traveler, Los Angeles elevates fast-food and chain restaurants to heights virtually unknown in the rest of the country. For the optimal burger-and-fries experience, try **In 'n' Out Burger,** a chain as beloved as the '57 Chevy. **Johnny**

Rocket's revives the never really lost era of the American diner. Their milkshakes are the food of the gods. The current hot 'n' spicy craze is lard-free, cholesterol-free "healthy Mexican"—**Baja Fresh** leads the pack.

In this city of sunshine, chic refreshments are a necessity. Angelenos get their ice-blended mochas at **The Coffee Bean and Tea Leaf.** The ubiquitous smoothie allows the health-conscious to indulge in a sweet blend of fruit, juice, frozen yogurt, and energy-boosting additives like wheat grass. **The Juice Club** makes the biggest and the best smoothies with shots of fresh-blended grass for die-hard fiberphiles.

The range of culinary options in L.A. is directly proportional to the city's ethnic diversity. Certain food types are concentrated in specific areas. Jewish and Eastern European food is most prevalent in Fairfax; Mexican in East L.A.; Japanese, Chinese, Vietnamese, and Thai around Little Tokyo, Chinatown, and Monterey Park; and seafood along the coast. Vietnamese, Italian, Indian, and Ethiopian restaurants are scattered throughout the city.

Hollywood

Hollywood offers the best budget dining in L.A. **Melrose** is full of chic cafes, many with outdoor patios.

◉**Roscoe's House of Chicken and Waffles,** 1514 Gower St. (213-466-7453), Hollywood. Roscoe makes the best waffles anywhere. "1 succulent chicken breast and 1 delicious waffle" is $5.60. The restaurant is frequented by all sorts of celebrities. Open M-Th 9am-midnight, F 9am-4am, Sa 8:30am-4am, Su 8:30am-midnight.

◉**Duke's Coffee Shop,** 8909 Sunset Blvd. (310-652-3100), at San Vicente in West Hollywood. Best place in L.A. to see hungover rock stars. The walls are a kaleidoscope of posters and autographed album covers. They claim to treat everyone the same, famous or not, but don't expect to be invited to add your signature to the walls unless you're the former. Perfect for brunch. Try the "Revenge"—eggs scrambled with avocado, sour cream, onions, tomatoes, and peppers ($6.75). Entrees $5-8. Open M-F 7:30am-8:45pm, Sa-Su 8am-3:45pm. No credit cards.

Toi on Sunset, 7505½ Sunset Blvd. (213-874-8062), in Hollywood. Decor is a way-trendy mélange of posters, funky lamps, leopard-skin armchairs, and psychedelic murals. Clientele is as hip as the interior decorating. *Pad thai* $6.95. Lunch specials $5. Open daily 11am-4am. $10 min. for credit cards.

Swingers Hollywood Diner, 8020 Beverly Blvd. (213-653-5858), at Laurel in the rump of the Beverly Laurel Hotel. Where the hippest L.A. club kids (and lonely L.A. *Swingers* Mikey and Trent) come to snack on olives, spinach and tofu burritos ($5.25), and 5 flavors of "smart drinks" that organically stimulate the brain ($5.50-6.50). This place is *so* money! Open daily 6:30am-4am.

Chin Chin, 8618 Sunset Blvd. (310-652-1818), in West Hollywood. Other locations in Brentwood, Studio City, Marina del Rey, and Encino. Immensely popular with the lunchtime set for its handmade "*dim sum* and then sum" ($5-10). Shredded chicken salad ($7.50) is Californiated Chinese cuisine. Outdoor seating and take-out. Special lite menu. Open Su-Th 11am-11pm, F-Sa 11am-midnight.

Pink's Famous Chili Dogs, 711 N. La Brea Ave. (213-931-4223), Hollywood. More of an institution than a hot dog stand, Pink's has been serving up chili-slathered doggies to locals and celebs since 1939. Mouth-watering chili dogs ($2.20) and chili fries ($1.85). Bruce Willis proposed to Demi here all those films ago. Open Su-Th 9:30am-2am, F-Sa 9:30am-3am. No credit cards.

Orson Welles Is Fat

Acclaimed director and *gourmand* Orson Welles was a regular at many Hollywood restaurants, and legends of his prowess circulate to this day, some reaching fantastic proportions. Pink's Famous Chili Dogs claims the notorious nosher once ate 15 chili dogs there in one sitting. But who really knows?—it's hard to distinguish Orson sitting from Orson standing.

742 ■ SOUTHERN CALIFORNIA

Wilshire District and Hancock Park

The Wilshire District's eateries are sadly out of step with its world-class museums. Inexpensive (and often kosher) restaurants dot **Fairfax** and **Pico Blvd.**

The Apple Pan, 10801 W. Pico Blvd. (310-475-3585), 1 block east of Westwood, across from the Westside pavillion. Suburban legend has it that *Beverly Hills 90210*'s Peach Pit was modeled after The Apple Pan. Paper-plated burgers $3-6, pies $2.40. Open Su and Tu-Th 11am-midnight, F-Sa 11am-1am. No credit cards.

Cassell's Hamburgers, 3266 W. 6th St. (213-480-8668). Some say these burgers are the finest in the city. They're juicy, enormous, and come with as much potato salad and cottage cheese as you can fit on your sizable plate. Basic burger, turkey burger, or chicken breast $5. Open M-Sa 10am-4pm. No credit cards.

Shalom Pizza, 8715 W. Pico Blvd. (310-271-2255). Kosher (i.e., vegetarian) pizza in a quiet Jewish business district. Large cheese $11.50, slice $1.75. Tuna melt $2.50. Open Su-Th 11am-9pm, F 11am until 2hr. before sundown, Sa sundown-midnight.

Beverly Hills

There is budget dining in glamorous Beverly Hills; it just takes a little looking.

🕲**The Breakfast Club,** 9671 Wilshire Blvd. (213-271-8903). Affordable food in a great location. $6.49 lunch specials even volatile teens could appreciate. Open M-Sa 7am-3pm, Su 8am-3pm. 2hr. free parking with validation, so there's plenty of time to stroll Rodeo Dr.

World Wraps, 168 S. Beverly Dr. (310-859-9010). Cashing in on the hottest new trend, it takes "healthy Mexican" to new, international, Cali-gourmet heights. Mostly take-out, but colorful interior and outdoor seating invite eat-ins. Thai chicken wraps (small $3.50, regular $5) and Samurai salmon wraps ($4.25, $6.50) are available in spinach and tomato tortillas. Open daily 8am-10pm.

Nancy's Health Kitchen, 225 S. Beverly Dr. (310-385-8530). Calorie and fat contents are kept to a minimum in this cheery cafe. Mexican baked potato with turkey or vegetarian chili, low-fat cheddar, tomatoes, "no oil" corn chips, and salsa $5.50. Salads $5-6. Air-baked fries $1.85. Open M-F 10am-9pm, Sa-Su noon-9pm.

Finney's in the Alley, 8840 Olympic Blvd. (310-888-8787). Heading east on Olympic, turn right on Clark, and immediately right into the alley; look for a yellow awning. The manager refuses to advertise for fear that "the secret will get out." Finney's most delectable (and expensive) offering is a Philly steak sandwich ($4.20). Open M-Sa 11am-6pm.

Westwood and UCLA

With UCLA here, cheap food and beer can be found in abundance.

🕲**Gypsy Café,** 940 Broxton Ave. (310-824-2119). All the comforts of home, if home is Bohemia—red velvet walls and drapes strewn from the ceiling. A smoker's paradise amid a puff-quenching sea. Hookahs $10 per hr., cigars $3-7. Mix 'n' match 5 pastas and 20 sauces ($7). Sandwiches $4.50-6, espresso $1.50. Open Su-Th 8am-midnight, F-Sa 8am-1am.

José Bernstein's, 935 Broxton Ave. (310-208-4992). Deli-diner with Mexican tendencies. *Huevos rancheros* $2.30. The Tacominator is 2 soft tacos, rice, beans, chips, and a drink ($3.55). Open M-W 8am-1am, Th-Sa 10am-2:30am, Su 11am-1am.

Don Antonio's, 1136 Westwood Blvd. (310-209-1422). Relax in the outdoor seating while waiting for your custom-designed pizza ($5.50). Sinatra, red-checkered tablecloths, and wood-paneled walls. Lunch special (M-F 11am-3pm): large slice of pizza, salad, and all-you-can-drink ($3.50). Open daily 11am-3am.

Santa Monica

Santa Monica's restaurants fall into the "see and be seen" category, especially along the 3rd St. Promenade. Prices are elevated accordingly, as is the quality of the food.

Real Food Daily, 514 Santa Monica Blvd. (310-451-7544). Charming and sunny organic cafe. All food is animal-, dairy-, egg-, cholesterol-, and sugar-free, but tasty. International selection of daily specials ($11.25). Cajun wrap sandwich $9. Miso soup $4. Open daily 11:30am-10pm.

El Cholo, 1025 Wilshire Blvd. (310-899-1106). Like the Cancun cantinas it mimics, this is *the* spot to be seen, at least for the moment. Cheese enchilada, beans, rice, and choice of a taco, *chile relleno,* or tamale $8.10. "L.A. Lemonade" margarita is a pricey $6.25, but was ranked the city's best by *L.A. Magazine.* Bar with couches, big-screen TV. Open M-Th 11am-10pm, F-Sa 11am-11pm, Su 11am-9pm.

Topper Restaurant and Cantina, 1111 2nd St. (310-393-8080), topping the Radisson Huntley Hotel. The budget-minded probably can't afford entrees here, but the scoop on happy hour (daily 4:30-7:30pm) is spreading fast: buy 1 drink (sodas $1.50, beer from $2.75), and get all-you-can-eat free food from the bountiful buffet. Half pitcher of margarita $4.50. Open Su-Th 6am-12:30am, F-Sa 6am-1:30am.

Venice

Venetian cuisine runs the gamut from greasy to ultra-healthy, as befits its beachy-hippie crowd. The boardwalk offers cheap grub in fast-food fashion.

Van Go's Ear 24 Hour Restaurant and Gallery, 796 Main St. (310-314-0022). Quintessential Venice with a psychedelic mural of the cafe's namesake complete with neon earring. Ridiculously large portions of tasty chow. All entrees named for second-rate celebs, such as the Kato Kaelin Salad ($3). "Tightwad menu" has 8 breakfast combos under $2 (served M-F 6-11am). The Fruit Fuck is a smoothie potion concocted with oranges, apples, pears, kiwi, and bee pollen ($3.75). Some part of the 2-story mega-shack is always open. No credit cards.

Sidewalk Café, 1401 Ocean Front Walk (310-399-5547). The most popular (crowded) spot on the boardwalk. It's big (i.e., not a dinky boardwalk food hut), and it sports a dazzling view of the beach. Entrees are named after writers, keeping in step with the adjacent bookstore. Omelettes $6-7, sandwiches $6-9. Big bar in back (pints $3). Open Su-Th 8am-midnight, F-Sa 8am-1am.

Rose Café, 220 Rose Ave. (310-399-0711), at Main St. The sunlight streaming in *so* complements the airy interior, dahling. Roses-on-steroids murals remind you what street you're on. Deli specials (sandwiches $5, salads $4) are a steal. Smelly New Age knick-knacks and candles for sale will earn you the moniker "eclectic." Open M-F 7am-10pm, Sa 8am-10pm, Su 8am-5pm.

Downtown

Financial District eateries vie for the coveted businessperson's lunchtime dollar. Their secret weapon is the lunch special, but finding a reasonably priced dinner can be a challenge—you probably shouldn't hang out here that late anyway.

Philippe's, The Original, 1001 N. Alameda St. (213-628-3781), 2 blocks north of Union Station. The best place in L.A. to feel like Raymond Chandler (though not Philip Marlowe). Philippe's claims to have originated the French-dipped sandwich (don't argue; $3-4). Top it off with a large slice of pie ($2.50) and a glass of iced tea (40¢) or a cup of coffee (9¢). Open daily 6am-10pm.

The Pantry, 877 S. Figueroa St. (213-972-9279). Open since the 20s, it hasn't closed since—not for earthquakes, not for the riots (when it served as a National Guard outpost), and not even when a taxicab drove through the front wall. Known for its large portions, cole slaw, and sourdough bread. Be prepared to wait for the giant breakfast specials ($6), especially on Sa-Su. Owned by the mayor. Open forever.

It's a Wrap!, 818 W. 7th St. (213-553-9395). Downtown's answer to McDonald's offers "healthy gourmet fast food," including special low-fat dishes. As the name suggests, wrap sandwiches like the BBQ chicken wrap are the house specialty ($4-6). Open daily 6:30am-5pm. No credit cards.

San Fernando Valley

Ventura Blvd. is lined with restaurants. Eating lunch near the studios in **Studio City** is your best stargazing opportunity.

Law Dogs, 14114 Sherman Way (818-989-2220), at Hazeltine in Van Nuys. Just your average hot dog stand with free legal advice. The attorney is available W 7-9pm. "Judge Dog" with mustard, onions, and chili ($1.55). Open M-Tu and Th 10am-5pm, W and F 10am-9pm, Sa 10am-8pm.

CALIFORNIA

Dalt's Grill, 3500 W. Olive Ave. (818-953-7752), at Riverside in Burbank. Classic, classy American grill across from Warner Studios. Frequented by the DJs and music guests from the radio station upstairs, KROQ. Large selection of burgers and sandwiches $5-8. Chicken fajita caesar salad $7.69. Small oak-lacquered bar. Open M-Th 11am-11pm, F-Sa 11am-1am (bar open until 2am), Su 9am-11pm.

Miceli's, 3655 W. Cahuenga Blvd. (818-851-3444), across from Universal Studios in Universal City. Would-be actors serenade dinner guests. Don't worry about losing your appetite during the Broadway, cabaret, and opera numbers—waiters have passed vocal auditions. Pasta, pizza, or lasagna $7. Wine $4. Open Su-Th 11:30am-11pm, F 11:30am-midnight, Sa 4pm-midnight.

SIGHTS

Hollywood

Modern Hollywood (110 years old) is no longer the upscale home of movie stars and production studios. In fact, all the major studios, save Paramount, have moved to the roomier San Fernando Valley. Left behind are historic theaters and museums, a crowd of souvenir shops, famous boulevards, and American fascination. Aside from the endless string of movie premieres, the only star-studded part of Hollywood is the sidewalk, where prostitutes and panhandlers, tattoo parlors, and porn shops abound.

The **Hollywood sign**—those 50-foot-high, slightly erratic letters perched on Mt. Cahuenga north of Hollywood—stands with New York's Statue of Liberty and Paris's Eiffel Tower as the universally recognized symbol of a city. The original 1923 sign, which read HOLLYWOODLAND, was an advertisement for a new subdivision in the Hollywood Hills (a caretaker lived behind one of the "L"s). You can't go frolic on the sign like Robert Downey, Jr. did in *Chaplin,* or take a leap from it like all the faded 1920s starlets—there is a $500 fine if you're caught (which is likely). You can snap a great picture by driving north on Vine, turning right on Franklin, left on Beachwood, and left on Belden into the Beachwood Supermarket parking lot. To get a close-up of the sign in all its monumental glory, continue up Beachwood, turn left on Ledgewood, and drive all the way up to Mulholland Hwy. Resting beneath the Hollywood sign, at 6342 Mulholland Hwy. (to the left, at the corner of Canyon Lake Dr.), is the eyesore known as **Castillo del Lago.** Once the gambling den of gangster Bugsy Siegel, the red-and-beige striped house also belonged to Madonna, but she recently sold it after an obsessed fan stalked her there.

Hollywood Blvd. itself, lined with souvenir shops, clubs, and theaters, is busy day and night, especially around the intersection of Highland and Hollywood and then west down Hollywood. To the east, things turn even seedier. For a star-studded stroll, head to the **Walk of Fame,** along Hollywood and Vine, where the sidewalk is embedded with over 2500 bronze-inlaid stars, inscribed with the names of the famous, the infamous, and the downright obscure. Stars are awarded for achievements in one of five categories—movies, radio, TV, recording, and live performance; only Gene Autry has all five stars. To catch a glimpse of today's (or yesterday's) stars in person, call the **Chamber of Commerce** (213-469-8311) for info on star-unveiling ceremonies.

Mann's Chinese Theater (formerly Grauman's), 6925 Hollywood Blvd. (213-461-3331), between Highland and La Brea, is a garish rendition of a Chinese temple, and the hottest spot for a Hollywood movie premiere. The exterior columns, which once supported a Ming Dynasty temple, are strangely authentic for Hollywood. Tourists crowd the courtyard to pay photographic homage to the impressions made by many a movie star in the cement, including Whoopi Goldberg's dreadlocks, Betty Grable's legs, R2D2's wheels, Jimmy Durante's nose, and George Burns's cigar. Just across the street from Mann's is the **El Capitan Theatre,** 6838 Hollywood Blvd. (213-467-9545), where the 1941 Hollywood premiere of *Citizen Kane* was held. This restored cinema house features ornate faux-exotic 1920s interior decoration and high prices.

Two blocks east of Mann's is the **Hollywood Wax Museum,** 6767 Hollywood Blvd. (213-462-8860), where you'll meet 200 figures, from Jesus to Elvis. *(Open daily 10am-midnight. $10, children $7.)* Not surprisingly, the sculpture of Michael Jackson is one of the few that a chisel and putty have recreated nearly perfectly. Across the street from the Wax Museum you'll find a few more tourist lures. The lingerie museum in **Frederick's of Hollywood,** 6608 Hollywood Blvd. (213-957-5953), displays bras worn by everyone from Marilyn Monroe to Milton Berle (open M-F 10am-9pm, Sa 10am-7pm, Su 11am-6pm; free). The **Guinness World of Records,** 6764 Hollywood Blvd. (213-463-6433), has the tallest, shortest, heaviest, most tattooed, and other curious superlatives on display (open daily 10am-midnight; $10, children $7; with Wax Museum ticket $4/$2). Similar, but wackier, **Ripley's Believe It or Not!,** 6780 Hollywood Blvd. (213-466-6335), has a side-show mentality strangely in keeping with the rest of Hollywood (open Sa-Th 10am-midnight, F-Sa 10am-12:30am; $9, children $6).

Music is another industry that, like film, finds a center in Los Angeles. The pre-eminent monument of the modern record industry is the 1954 **Capitol Records Tower,** 1750 Vine St., just north of Hollywood. The cylindrical building, which was designed to look like a stack of records, has fins sticking out at each floor (the "records") and a needle on top, which blinks H-O-L-L-Y-W-O-O-D in Morse code.

Music fans of all types might make a strike at **Hollywood Bowl** if there's a rehearsal or concert in session, but it serves up sights as well as sounds. All sparkly after its recent facelift, the **Hollywood Bowl Museum** (213-850-2058) has several exhibits as well as listening stations where you can swoon to Stravinsky, Aaron Copland, and the Beatles, all of whom played the Bowl in the same week during the 60s (open Tu-Sa 9:30am-8:30pm; free). Honoring television history is the **Hollywood Entertainment Museum,** 7021 Hollywood Blvd. (213-465-7900), which has original sets from *Cheers* and *Star Trek*. *(Open Tu-Su 10am-6pm; off-season closed Su. $7.50, students and seniors $4.50, children $4. Tours every 30min. Parking $2.)*

The **Hollywood Studio Museum,** 2100 N. Highland Ave. (323-874-2276), across from the Bowl, provides a glimpse into early Hollywood filmmaking. *(Hrs. variable; call ahead. $4, students and seniors $3, ages 6-12 $2. Ample free parking.)* In 1913, famed director Cecil B. DeMille rented this former barn as studio space for Hollywood's first feature film, *The Squaw Man*. Antique cameras, costumes worn by Douglas Fairbanks and Rudolph Valentino, props, vintage film clips, and memorabilia fill the museum.

If you still haven't had enough showbiz glitz of years gone by, visit the **Hollywood Memorial Park,** 6000 Santa Monica Blvd. (213-469-1181), between Vine and Western, a decaying cemetery that feels almost haunted. *(Open M-F 8am-5pm; spooky mausoleums close at 4:30pm.)* Here rest deceased stars Rudolph Valentino, Jayne Mansfield, Douglas Fairbanks, Sr., and Cecil B. De Mille.

Wilshire and Hancock Park

The **Los Angeles County Museum of Art (LACMA),** 5905 Wilshire Blvd. (213-857-6000), is at the west end of Hancock Park. *(Open M-Tu and Th noon-8pm, F noon-9pm, Sa-Su 11am-8pm. $6, students and seniors $4, under 18 $1; free 2nd Tu of each month. Parking $5, free after 6pm. Wheelchair access.)* LACMA's distinguished collection rebuts those who say that L.A.'s only culture is in its yogurt. Opened in 1965, the LACMA is the largest museum in the West, with five major buildings clustered around the **Times-Mirror Central Court.** The **Steve Martin Gallery,** in the Anderson Bldg., houses the famed benefactor's collection of Dada and Surrealist works, including Rene Magritte's *Treachery of Images*. (This explains how Steve was allowed to rollerskate through LACMA in *L.A. Story*.) The museum sponsors free jazz (F 5:30-8:30pm), chamber music (Su 4-5pm), film classics and documentaries (tickets $6, seniors $2, children $1), and free daily tours. The info desk in the Central Court (ticket office 213-857-6010) and the Docent Council (213-857-6108) provide schedules.

Next door, in Hancock Park, an acrid petroleum stench pervades the vicinity of the **La Brea Tar Pits,** which enticed thirsty mammals of bygone geological ages. These unsuspecting creatures drank enthusiastically from pools of water, only to find themselves stuck in the tar that lurked below. Most of the one million recovered bones are housed in the **George C. Page Museum of La Brea Discoveries,** 5801 Wilshire Blvd. (213-934-PAGE/7243 or 857-6311), at Curson. *(Open daily 10am-5pm; Oct.-June Tu-Su 10am-5pm. $6, students and seniors $3.50, ages 5-10 $2; free 1st Tu of each month. Museum tours W-Su 2pm,* *tours of grounds 1pm. Parking $5. Wilshire buses stop in front of the museum.)* On display are reconstructed Ice Agers and murals of prehistoric L.A. The only human unearthed in the pits stands out in holographic horror—the **La Brea woman** was presumably thrown into the tar after having holes drilled into her skull. Archaeologists continue their digging in **Pit 91** behind the adjacent art museum.

Across the street is the acclaimed **Petersen Automotive Museum,** 6060 Wilshire Blvd. (930-CARS/2277), which showcases L.A.'s most recognizable symbol—the automobile. *(Open Tu-Su 10am-6pm. $7, students and seniors $5, children $3, under 5 free.)* With 300,000 sq. ft., PAM is the world's largest car museum and the nation's second-largest history museum (the Smithsonian is the largest). Bo and Luke's General Lee and Herbie the Love Bug are here. Full-day parking ($4) is convenient to LACMA.

West Hollywood

Once considered a no-man's land between Beverly Hills and Hollywood, West Hollywood has more recently formed an identity for itself with a thriving **gay community,** and some of L.A.'s best nightlife (see **Nightlife,** p. 754). The section of Santa Monica Blvd. around **San Vincente** is the city's oldest and most assertive gay district, and the city was one of the country's first to be governed by openly gay officials. The proximity of Hollywood and West Hollywood makes it difficult to tell where the district (Hollywood) ends and the city (West Hollywood) begins. In the years before its 1985 incorporation, lax zoning laws gave rise to **Sunset Strip,** originally lined with posh nightclubs frequented by stars. These have now been supplanted by pseudo-grungy rock clubs, also frequented by stars. The area's music scene is among the country's most fertile, and many world-famous bands from The Doors to Guns 'n' Roses got their start here. Weekend nights attract tremendous club crowds and traffic jams. The Strip's famous **billboards** are, on some blocks, as massive and creative as those in New York's Times Square. At 8218 Sunset Blvd., 15-foot-high plaster effigies of **Rocky and Bullwinkle** commemorate the duo's creator, Jay Ward. The former offices of Jay Ward Productions now house the **Dudley Doo-right Emporium,** 8200 Sunset Blvd.

Melrose Ave. runs from the southern part of West Hollywood to Hollywood, lined with restaurants, art galleries, and shops catering to all levels of the counter-culture spectrum. It also hosts an awesome **Gay Pride Weekend Celebration** in late June.

Beverly Hills and Century City

Ready to gawk? Extravagant displays of opulence sometimes border on the vulgar. On the palm-lined 700-900 blocks of **Beverly Dr.,** each and every manicured estate begs for attention. The heart of the city is in the **Golden Triangle,** a wedge formed by Beverly Dr., Wilshire Blvd., and Santa Monica Blvd., centering on **Rodeo Dr.,** known for its flashy boutiques.

Farther north, the **Beverly Hills Hotel,** 9641 Sunset Blvd. (310-276-2251), is a pink, palm-treed collection of poolside cottages. Howard Hughes established his infamous germ-free apartment here; Marilyn Monroe reportedly had affairs with both JFK and RFK in other bungalows. It is also home to the **Polo Lounge,** where countless media industry deals have gone down. The Sultan of Brunei paid $185 million for it in 1987, but 10 years later, you can get a room for a mere $275.

A conspicuous way to tour the city is in the 1914 trolley car replica operated by the Beverly Hills Chamber of Commerce (310-271-8126). If you prefer a cooler approach, go solo with a star map ($8), sold along Sunset Blvd. but not within Beverly Hills. **Barbra Streisand** lives at 301 Carolwood. The estate at 10236 Charing Cross is **The Playboy Mansion.** Charing Cross becomes N. Mapleton, site of the largest and most extravagant residence in Beverly Hills: producer **Aaron Spelling's** mansion, 594 N. Mapleton, is larger than the Taj Mahal. His wife Candy Spelling's closets reportedly take up an entire wing.

Westwood and UCLA

Get a feel for mass academia UC-style at the **University of California at Los Angeles (UCLA),** which sprawls over 400 acres in the foothills of the Santa Monica Mountains. A prototypical Californian university, UCLA sports an abundance of grassy open spaces, bike and walking paths, dazzling sunshine, and pristine buildings in a hodge-podge of architectural styles. To reach the campus by car, take the San Diego Fwy. (I-405) north to the Wilshire Blvd./Westwood Exit, heading east into Westwood. Take Westwood Blvd. north off Wilshire, heading straight through the center of the village and directly into the campus. By bus, take MTA route #2 along Sunset Blvd., #21 along Wilshire Blvd., #320 from Santa Monica, or #561 from the San Fernando Valley, or Santa Monica Blue Bus #1, 2, 3, 8, or 12. Parking passes ($5) from campus information stands are a must—traffic cops *live* to ticket unsuspecting visitors here.

The **Murphy Sculpture Garden,** which contains over 70 pieces scattered through five acres, lies directly in front of the Art Center. The collection includes works by such major artists as Rodin, Matisse, and Miró. Opposite the sculpture garden is **MacGowen Hall,** which contains the **Tower of Masks.** UCLA's **inverted fountain** is located between Knudsen Hall and Schoenberg Hall, directly south of Dickson Plaza. An innovation in the field of fountain design, water spouts from its perimeter and rushes down into the gaping hole in the middle, like a giant toilet bowl. UCLA's arts departments have loads of events, exhibitions, and performances year-round; call the **UCLA Arts Line** (310-UCLA-ART/825-2278) for tickets, a calendar, and directions.

The **Armand Hammer Museum of Art and Cultural Center,** 10899 Wilshire Blvd. (310-443-7000), houses a small but snappy collection of European and American works from the 16th century to the present day. *(Open Tu-W and F-Sa 11am-7pm, Th 11am-9pm, Su 11am-5pm. $4.50, students and seniors $3, under 17 free with adult; Th free 6-9pm. Free tours daily at 1pm. 3hr. parking $2.75. Wheelchair access.)* Something of a "Who's Who" of European painters, Hammer's collection includes works by Rembrandt, Chagall, and Cézanne, but its real gem is Van Gogh's *Hospital at Saint Rémy.*

Bel Air, Brentwood, and Pacific Palisades

Most of today's stars live in these three affluent communities. Next to UCLA is the well-guarded community of **Bel Air,** where **Ronald Reagan** has retired. His estate is at 668 St. Cloud, adjacent to the *Beverly Hillbillies* mansion (750 Bel Air Rd.) and a few blocks up from the former home of **Sonny and Cher** (364 St. Cloud). **Elizabeth Taylor** is literally around the (windy) corner (700 Nimes). Back in the golden days, Bel Air was the locus for glamorous celebs, including **Judy Garland** (924 Bel Air Rd.), **Alfred Hitchcock** (10957 Bel Air Rd.), and **Lauren Bacall** and **Humphrey Bogart** (232 Mapleton Dr.) during their go at marital bliss.

Farther west on Sunset Blvd. is **Brentwood,** home to many young actors and, until recently, **O.J. Simpson.** The famous accusé no longer lives here; his estate (360 Rockingham) was repossessed and auctioned off for a meager $2.63 million. On August 4, 1962, **Marilyn Monroe** was found dead at her home (12305 Fifth Helena Dr.). The celeb-city of Brentwood also includes the homes of Michelle Pfeiffer, Harrison Ford, Meryl Streep, and Rob Reiner.

The considerably more secluded **Pacific Palisades** is the place to live these days. Many streets are entirely closed to anyone but residents and their guests, but you can try to catch a glimpse of **Tom Cruise** and **Nicole Kidman** outside 1525 Sorrento, or **Steven Spielberg** at 1515 Amalfi (this home belonged to David O. Selznick when he was producing *Gone with the Wind*). **Arnold Schwarzenegger** and **Maria Shriver** practice family fitness at 14209 Sunset Blvd., **Tom Hanks** lives at 321 S. Anita Ave., and **Michael Keaton** resides at 826 Napoli Dr. Billy Crystal, Chevy Chase, and John Travolta also own homes in the area. The cliffs give way to the ocean at the popular **Will Rogers State Beach,** on the 16000 block of Pacific Coast Hwy. (PCH). At 1501 Will Rogers State Park Rd., you can hike around **Will Rogers State Historical Park** (310-454-8212), take in the panoramic views of the city and distant Pacific, visit the famous humorist's home, or eat a picnic brunch while watching a Saturday afternoon **polo match** (matches Sa 2-5pm and Su 10am-1pm). *(Park open daily 8am-sunset; Rogers's house open daily 10:30am-4:30pm, with tours every 30min.)* Follow Chatauqua Blvd. inland from PCH to Sunset Blvd., or take MTA #2, which runs along Sunset.

CALIFORNIA

In the Santa Monica Mountains above Bel Air is the new **J. Paul Getty Museum and Getty Center,** 1200 Getty Center Dr. (310-440-7330). *(Open Tu-W 11am-7pm, Th-F 11am-9pm, Sa-Su 10am-6pm. Free.)* Formerly located in Malibu, the new center unites L.A.'s beloved Getty museums with its institutes on one site, designed by renowned architect Richard Meier. (The Malibu Villa will reopen in 2001 as an antiquities center.) The museum itself is housed in five pavilions overlooking the Robert Irwin-designed three-acre Central Garden, a living work of art that changes with the seasons. The museum includes the permanent Getty collection, which includes Van Gogh's *Irises,* James Ensor's *Christ's Entry into Brussels in 1889,* Impressionist paintings, Renaissance drawings, and one of the nation's best Rembrandt collections. "Friday Nights at the Getty" (310-440-7330) feature plays, films, and readings. To reach the Getty Center, take the San Diego Fwy. (I-405) to Getty Center Dr.; parking costs $5 and requires advance reservations (310-440-7300). BBB #14 and MTA #561 stop at the museum's front entrance on Sepulveda Blvd.

Santa Monica

Santa Monica, the Bay City of Raymond Chandler's novels, was once known as the "Gold Coast" because of the fabulously wealthy stars who called it home. Today, the area is less pretentious, hosting a more low-key affluent set. The **3rd St. Promenade** is now the city's most popular spot to shop by day and to schmooze by night, and the nearby beaches are jam-packed. It takes about 30min. (without traffic) to reach Santa Monica on MTA #33 or 333 or on the Santa Monica Fwy. (I-10) from downtown. Santa Monica's efficient Big Blue Bus system connects to other L.A. bus routes.

Santa Monica is the place that put the "Bay" in *Baywatch.* There may be cleaner waters with better waves on the beaches to the north and south, but this area is known more for its shoreside scene than its shore.

Renovated in 1996, the **Santa Monica Pier** has the feel of an old-fashioned boardwalk, complete with the aroma of popcorn, a few pizza joints, an arcade, and tons of tacky souvenirs. The pier hosts a free Thursday night Twilight Dance Series in the summer. The gem of the pier is the restored 1922 carousel featured in *The Sting.* Together with a few miniature roller coasters and a ferris wheel, it makes up the diminutive **Pacific Park,** which resembles a county fair more than a modern amusement park (open daily 10am-10pm; tickets $1, rides cost up to 3 tickets).

On the scenic bluff overlooking the pier, **Palisades Park** boasts the **Stairpath,** the fearful 189-step outdoor Stairmaster. Located at 4th and Adelaide, it leads *down* to the beach. The **Camera Obscura,** 1450 Ocean Ave., at the Senior Recreation Center, catches an unusual (or even obscure) view of the beach. *(Open M-F 9am-4pm, Sa-Su 11am-4pm. Free.)* This Aristotelian contraption uses convex lenses to project a 360° bird's-eye view of the beach onto a screen in a dark room.

Venice

Venice is a carnivalesque beach town with rad politics and mad diversity. Its guitar-toting, Bukowski-quoting, wild-eyed, tie-dyed residents sculpt masterpieces in sand and compose them in graffiti, when they aren't slamming a volleyball back and forth over a beach net. A stroll in rollerblading, bikini-flaunting, tattooed Venice is like an acid trip for the timid.

Ocean Front Walk, Venice's main beachfront drag, is a seaside circus of fringe culture. Bodybuilders of both sexes pump iron in skimpy spandex outfits at the original **Muscle Beach,** 1800 Ocean Front Walk, closest to 18th and Pacific. Fire-juggling cyclists, joggers, sand sculptors, groovy elders (such as the **skateboard grandma**), and bards in Birkenstocks make up the balance of this playground population.

Venice's anything-goes attitude attracts some of L.A.'s most innovative artists (and not just the guy who makes sand sculptures of Jesus). The **Chiat Day offices** at 340 Main St. were designed by Frank Gehry to look like a pair of enormous binoculars—architecture as a pop-art sculpture at its best. Venice's **street murals** are another free show. Don't miss the graffiti-disfigured, but still brilliant homage to Botticelli's *Birth of Venus* on the beach pavilion at the end of Windward Ave.—a woman of ostensibly divine beauty sporting short shorts, a band-aid top, and roller skates boogies out of her seashell. The **L.A. Louver,** 45 N. Venice Blvd. (310-822-4955), a free gallery, showcases the work of some L.A. artists (open Tu-Sa noon-5pm).

To get to Venice from downtown L.A., take MTA #33 or 333 (or 436 during rush hour). From downtown Santa Monica, take Santa Monica Blue Bus #1 or 2. Avoid hourly meter-feedings by parking in the $5-per-day lot at Pacific and Venice.

Malibu

The public beaches here are cleaner and less crowded than any others in L.A. County, and as a whole offer better surfing. Surf's up at **Surfrider Beach,** a section of Malibu Laguna State Beach located north of the pier at 23000 PCH. You can walk onto the beach via the **Zonker Harris** access way (named after the beach-obsessed Doonesbury character), at 22700 PCH.

Corral State Beach, a remote windsurfing, swimming, and scuba-diving haven, lies on the 26000 block of PCH, followed by the clothing-optional **Point Dume State Beach,** which is small and generally uncrowded, except for those looking for a really killer tan. Along the 30000 block of PCH lies **Zuma,** L.A. County's northernmost, largest, and most user-friendly county-owned sandbox. Restrooms, lifeguards, and food stands guarantee that Zuma regularly draws a diverse crowd. Swimmers should only dive near manned lifeguard stations; because of the devastating **riptide,** rescue counts are high. The free street parking is highly coveted, so expect to park in the beach lot ($6, off-peak hr. $2). There are fewer footprints at **Westward Beach,** just southeast of Zuma, where cliffs shelter the beach from the highway.

Downtown

Mayor Richard Riordan and City Hall strive valiantly to project downtown as the font of L.A.'s diversity and culture. However, the Westside powers have a solid grip on the culture, while neigborhoods in L.A. County are defined by homogeneity of race, class, and wealth. The only diversity downtown is the stark contrast between the towering glass business cages and the cardboard hovels in their shadows. An uneasy truce prevails between the bustling financiers and the substantial street population, but visitors should be cautious—*the area is especially unsafe after business hours and on weekends.* Park in a secure lot, rather than on the streets. Parking is costly; arriving before 8am enables visitors to catch early-bird specials; the guarded lots around 9th and Figueroa charge $2-3 per day.

The most striking museum in the area is the **Museum of Contemporary Art (MOCA),** which showcases art from 1940 to the present. *(Free tours led by local artists at noon, 1, and 2pm; also at 6pm Th only.)* The main museum is at California Plaza, 250 S. Grand Ave. (213-626-6222 or 621-1651), and is a sleek, geometric architectural marvel. Its exhibits often focus on L.A. artists, but the collection also includes abstract expressionist works. Thursday nights in summer mean free jazz and cheap beer and wine. The second MOCA facility is the **Geffen Contemporary,** 152 N. Central Ave. (213-621-1727), in Little Tokyo. *(Main MOCA open Tu-W and F-Su 11am-5pm, Th 11am-8pm. Admission to both buildings $6, students and seniors $4, under 12 free; Th 5-8pm free. Wheelchair access.)* Parking here ($2.50-3) is cheaper than at the main building, which is accessible by DASH.

Across from City Hall, between the Santa Ana Fwy. (I-5) and Temple in the L.A. Mall, is the **L.A. Children's Museum,** 310 N. Main St. (213-687-8800), where everything can be (and has been) touched. *(Open June 23-Sept. 5 M-F 11:30am-5pm; off-season Sa-Su 10am-5pm. $5, under 2 free.)* The target ages are 2-10, but anyone can have fun.

The historic birthplace of L.A. lies farther north, bounded by Spring, Arcadia, and Macy. Where the city center once stood, **El Pueblo de Los Angeles State Historic Park** (213-628-1274) preserves a number of historically important buildings from the Spanish and Mexican eras (open daily 9am-9pm; free). The **visitors center,** 622 N. Main St. (213-628-1274), in the Sepulveda House, offers free walking tours (every hr. Tu-Sa 10am-1pm). Tours start at the **Old Plaza,** with its century-old Moreton Bay fig trees and huge bandstand, and wind their way past the **Avila Adobe,** 10 E. Olvera St., the "oldest" house in the city (the original adobe was built in 1818, and has been replaced with concrete in order to meet earthquake regulations). The tour then moves on to **Pico House,** 500 N. Main St., once L.A.'s most luxurious hotel. Farther down, the **Plaza Church,** at 535 N. Main St., established in 1818, has an incongruously soft, rose adobe facade. The visitors center also screens *Pueblo of Promise,* an 18min. history of Los Angeles, on request. **Olvera St.,** one of L.A.'s original roads, is packed with touristy little stands selling Mexican handicrafts and food. The street is the sight of the Cinco de Mayo celebrations of L.A.'s Chicano population (see **Seasonal Events,** p. 756). Across Alameda St. from El Pueblo is the grand old **Union Station,** famous for its appearances in *Blade Runner.*

Near Downtown: Exposition Park

The park is southwest of downtown, just off the Harbor Fwy. (I-110), and is bounded by Exposition, Figueroa, Vermont, and Santa Barbara. From downtown, take DASH shuttle C, or MTA #40 or 42 (from Broadway between 5th and 6th) to the park's southern edge. From Hollywood, take #204 or 354 down Vermont. From Santa Monica, take #20, 22, 320, or 322 on Wilshire, and transfer to #204 at Vermont. Park at the lot at the intersection of Figueroa and Exposition ($5, with IMAX validation $4).

The park is dominated by several major museums, including the **California Science Center (CSC),** 700 State Dr. (213-744-7400). The interactive exhibits on physics and math in Technology Hall make science come alive. A display on California's faultlines has a jarring rendition of an 8.3 earthquake. Ironically, McDonald's sponsors a display on nutrition. The expansive, formal **rose garden** in front of the CSC is the last remnant of the blessed days when all of Exposition Park was an exposition of horticulture. More than 19,000 specimens of 200 varieties of roses surround walking paths, green lawns, gazebos, fountains, and a lily pond. In the same complex is the **California African-American Museum,** 600 State Dr. (213-744-2067), with a collection of indigenous African art, paintings from the Harlem Renaissance in the 20s, and contemporary mixed-media works (open Tu-Su 10am-5pm; free).

Another of the park's attractions is the **Natural History Museum,** 900 Exposition Blvd. (213-744-3414). *(Open daily July-Aug. 10am-5pm; closed M the rest of the year. Free the first Tu of each month, but no tours. $8, seniors and students $5, ages 5-12 $2. Tours run daily at 1pm in summer, in winter Sa-Su only.)* The museum has exhibits about pre-Columbian cultures and American history until 1914, featuring "habitat halls" with North American and African mammals and dinosaur skeletons. The hands-on **Discovery Center** allows visitors to dig for fossils, meet live fish and reptiles, and explore the insect zoo. But today's medically inclined kids usually shoot past the huge dinosaur bones and head straight for "Microbes," the trippy new neon and blacklight exhibit that features everything from a plucky superhero to a computer-generated 3-D stereo movie (plus something about germs).

Exposition Park also includes the **Los Angeles Memorial Coliseum,** 3939 S. Figueroa St., home of the **USC Trojans** football team; and the **Sports Arena,** 2601 S. Figueroa St., home of the **Los Angeles Clippers** basketball team, and a common venue for rock concerts. The colossal Coliseum, which seats over 100,000, is the only stadium in the world to garner the honor of hosting the Olympic Games twice. The torch that held the Olympic flame still towers atop the Coliseum's roof.

The very rough city of **Inglewood,** southwest of Exposition Park, is home to most of the sporting events in L.A. At the corner of Manchester and Prairie is the **Great Western Forum** (310-673-1300), home of the **Los Angeles Kings** hockey team, as well as the **Los Angeles Lakers** and **Sparks** (WNBA) basketball teams. Tickets for these games are in high demand. (Laker season runs Nov.-June, Sparks June-Aug. Kings tickets from $11, Lakers tickets from $21, Sparks tickets from $8.) For tickets, call the **Forum box office** (Kings tickets 310-419-3160; Lakers tickets 310-419-3182; Sparks tickets 310-330-2434; open daily 10am-6pm) or **Ticketmaster** (213-480-3232).

Watts

Known mainly as the site of riots in 1965 and 1992, this is one of L.A.'s most depressed neighborhoods, and is not generally amenable to tourism. The **Watts Towers,** 1765 E. 107th St. (213-847-4646), however, are worth the trip. *(Arts center* *open Tu-Sa 10am-4pm, Su noon-4pm. Free. Take I-10 to the 110 South; take Century East Exit, then turn right onto S. Central, a left onto 103rd St., and follow the signs.)* Long before found art became fashionable, an inspired Italian construction worker named Simon Rodia spent three decades of nights (he worked days) constructing the fragile, whimsical Watts Towers out of scrap metal, discarded objects, and thousands upon thousands of seashells. On the verge of demolition in the late 1950s, the nearly 100 ft. tall towers were preserved and have since become a source of civic pride for perpetually troubled Watts. The Towers are now being renovated and are not scheduled to open until summer 2000, but they deserve a look, even through the gates and scaffolding that now surround them. The adjacent arts center focuses on L.A.-area artists. *Watts is a high-crime area and should be avoided after dark.*

Griffith Park

One of few recreational parks in L.A., Griffith Park is the site of many outdoor diversions ranging from golf and tennis to hiking. The L.A. Zoo, Griffith Observatory and Planetarium, Travel Town, a bird sanctuary, and 52 mi. of hiking trails decorate the dry hills (open daily 5am-10pm). The park stretches for 4107 acres from the hills above North Hollywood to the intersection of the Ventura (Rte. 134) and Golden State Fwy. (I-5), making it five times the size of New York's Central Park. Several of the mountain roads through the park (especially the **Vista Del Valle Dr.**) offer panoramic views of downtown L.A., Hollywood, and the Westside. Unfortunately, heavy rains have made them unsafe for cars, but foot traffic is allowed on most. The 5 mi. hike to the top of **Mt. Hollywood,** the highest peak in the park, is quite popular. For information, stop by the **Visitors Center and Ranger Headquarters,** 4730 Crystal Spring Dr. (213-665-5188; open daily 5am-10pm).

The white stucco and copper domes of the Art Deco **Observatory and Planetarium** (213-664-1181, recording 664-1191) are visible from around the park. *(Observatory open daily 12:30-10pm; in winter Tu-F 2-10pm, Sa-Su 12:30-10pm. Planetarium shows M-F at 1:30, 3, and 7:30pm, Sa-Su also 4:30pm; in winter, Tu-F 3 and 7:30pm, Sa-Su also 1:30 and 4:30pm. $4, seniors $3, under 12 $2. Children under 5 only admitted to the 1:30pm show.)* You might remember the planetarium from the climactic denouement of the James Dean film *Rebel Without A Cause.* But even without Dean, the astronomy exhibits are a show of their own. A telescope with a 12 in. lens is open to the public every clear night. *(Open for viewing daily dusk-9:45pm; in winter Tu-Su 7-9:45pm; call 213-663-8171 for a sky report.)* The planetarium presents popular **Lazerium** light shows (818-997-3624), a psychotronic romp through the strawberry fields of your consciousness. To get to the observatory, take MTA #203 from Hollywood. *(Laser shows blaze daily at 6 and 8:45pm, Tu-Sa also 9:45pm. $7-8, children $6-7.)*

A large **bird sanctuary** sits at the bottom of the observatory hill, but if you crave a wider assortment of fauna, try the **Great L.A. Zoo,** 333 Zoo Dr. (323-644-4200), at the park's northern end. *(Open daily 10am-5pm. $8.25, seniors $5.25, ages 2-12 $3.25.)* The zoo's 113 acres accommodate 2000 randy animals, and the facility is consistently ranked among the nation's best. **Travel Town** (213-662-5874) is an outdoor museum showcasing period vehicles, emphasizing trains. *(Open M-F 10am-5pm, Sa-Su 10am-6pm. Free.)* To reach the zoo and Travel Town, take MTA #96 from downtown. There is no bus service between north and south Griffith Park.

On the lighter side, **Forest Lawn Cemetery,** 1712 Glendale Ave. (818-241-4151), in Glendale, includes reproductions of many Michelangelo pieces, as well as the "largest religious painting on earth" (a 195 ft. version of the *Crucifixion*). *(Grounds open daily 8am-6pm; mausoleum 9am-4:30pm.)* The trippy music piped across the gardens makes the typical graveyard experience even creepier. Among the illustrious dead are Clark Gable, George Burns, Gracie Allen, Sammy Davis, Jr., and Errol Flynn. Stop at the entrance for a map of the cemetery's sights, and get a guide to the paintings and sculpture at the administration building nearby. From downtown, take MTA #90 or 91 and get off just after the bus leaves San Fernando Rd. to turn onto Glendale Ave. By car, take Los Feliz Blvd. from the Golden State Fwy. (I-5) or Glendale Fwy. (Rte. 2).

CALIFORNIA

San Fernando Valley

All the San Fernando Valley wants is a little respect. After all, nearly every one of L.A.'s **movie studios** and a third of its residents reside here—more than the entire population of Montana. Yet it can't seem to shake the infamy it gained as breeding grounds for the **Valley Girl,** who started a worldwide trend in the 80s with her neon mini-skirts, huge hair, and like, totally far-out diction.

Movie studios have replaced the Valley Girl as the Valley's defining feature. As the Ventura Fwy. (Rte. 134) passes Burbank, you can see what are today the Valley's trademarks: the **NBC peacock,** the **Warner Bros. water tower,** and the carefully designed **Disney dwarves.** Urban legend says that the water pipes are orchestrated such that the seven dwarves appear to urinate on daddy Disney when it rains. Most of the studios have **free TV show tapings** (see **Entertainment,** p.753).

The most popular spot in today's Tinseltown is the movie-themed amusement park, **Universal Studios** (818-622-3801). *(Open daily 8am-10pm; Sept.-June 9am-7pm. In summer, last tram leaves at 6:15pm; in off-season at 4:15pm. $38, seniors $33, ages 3-11 $28. Parking $7.)* Fun for all, Universal is best-loved by those with a healthy knowledge of America's blockbuster movie tradition, especially the mythology created around director Steven Spielberg.

If, somehow, you have a few dollars left after Universal Studios, head to the adjacent **Universal City Walk** to fix the problem. The jewel in City Walk's technicolor crown is **B.B. King's Blues Club** (818-622-5464), where the thrill is far from gone. City Walk parking costs $6, but you get a full refund if you buy two movie tickets before 6pm, and a $2 refund after 6pm.

Down in the residential area of Studio City lurks the epicenter of American 70s culture, the **Brady Bunch house,** at 11222 Dilling St. (just north of Ventura Blvd. off Tujunga Ave.). Disappointingly, the house appears to lack the huge staircase from which, on television, Bobby threw down his ball and broke the vase. Continuing back up Ventura farther into the valley, make a left onto Hayvenhurst in Encino to see the house at 4641 where **Michael Jackson** resided for much of his life. Although his parents still live there, everyone knows that Michael now lives with sister Janet on a dancing space ship that will never land.

At the opposite end of the Valley, 40min. north of L.A. on the I-5 Exit at Magic Mountain Pkwy. in Valencia, is **Six Flags Magic Mountain** (818-367-5965), also known as *National Lampoon's* Wally World. *(Open Su-Th 10am-10pm, F-Sa 10am-midnight; mid-Sept. to Memorial Day Sa-Su 10am-6pm only. $35, seniors $20, kids under 48 in. tall $17, under 3 free. Parking $6.)* Not for novices, Magic Mountain has the hairiest roller coasters in Southern California, if not the world.

Pasadena and Around

With its world-class museums, graceful architecture, lively shopping district, and idyllic weather, Pasadena is a welcome change from its noisy downtown neighbor. **Old Town** Pasadena sequesters intriguing historic sights and an up-and-coming entertainment scene. The **Pasadena Fwy.** (Rte. 110), built as a WPA project between 1934 and 1941, is one of the nation's oldest. The city provides **free shuttles** (626-704-4055) approximately every 12min. that loop between Old Town and the downtown area around Lake Ave. *(Buses run M-Th 11am-7pm, F 11am-10pm, Sa-Su noon-8pm. Uptown buses run M-F 7am-6pm, Sa-Su noon-5pm.)*

At the western end of Old Town lies the sleek and modern **Norton Simon Museum of Art,** 411 W. Colorado Blvd. (626-449-6840), at Orange Grove Blvd., featuring a world-class collection chronicling Western art from Italian Gothic to 20th-century abstract. *(Open Th-Su noon-6pm. $4, students and seniors $2, under 12 free. Wheelchair access.)* The Impressionist and Post-Impressionist hall is particularly impressive, and the collection of Southeast Asian art is one of the world's best. Simon's eclectic, slightly idiosyncratic taste gives the collection flair.

Nearby lie the **Huntington Library, Art Gallery, and Botanical Gardens,** 1151 Oxford Rd. (626-405-2100), in San Marino. *(Open in summer Tu-Su 10:30am-4:30pm; in win-*

ter Tu-F noon-4:30pm, Sa-Su 10:30am-4:30pm. $8.50, students $5, seniors $7, under 12 free; first Th of the month free.) The conglomeration was built in 1910 as the home of businessman Henry Huntington, who made his money in railroads and Southern California real estate. The stunning botanical gardens are home to 207 acres of plants, many of them rare (no picnicking or sunbathing). The library houses a most important collection of rare books and manuscripts, including a Gutenberg Bible, Benjamin Franklin's handwritten autobiography, a 1410 manuscript of Chaucer's *Canterbury Tales,* and a number of Shakespeare's first folios. The art gallery is known for its 18th- and 19th-century British paintings. Sentimental favorites on exhibit include Thomas Gainsborough's *Blue Boy* and Sir Thomas Lawrence's *Pinkie.* American art is on view in the **Virginia Steele Scott Gallery.** The Annabella Huntington Memorial Collection features Renaissance paintings and 18th-century French decorative art. Tea is served in the Rose Garden daily (call 626-683-8131 for reservations). The Huntington Museum sits between Huntington Dr. and California Blvd. in San Marino, south of Pasadena, about 2 mi. south of the Allen Ave. Exit of I-210. From downtown L.A., bus #79 leaves from Union Station and goes straight to the library (45min.).

ENTERTAINMENT

Many tourists feel a visit to the world's entertainment capital is not complete without some exposure to the actual business of making a movie or TV show. Fortunately, most production companies oblige. **Paramount** (213-956-5000), **NBC** (818-840-3537), and **Warner Bros.** (818-954-1744) offer 2hr. guided walking tours, but as they are *made* for tourists, they tend to be crowded and overpriced. The best way to get a feel for the industry is to land yourself some tickets to a TV taping. All tickets are free, but most studios tend to overbook, so holding a ticket does not always guarantee that you'll get into the taping. Show up early, and you'll have a chance of seeing your fave stars up close in an operating studio backlot.

NBC, 3000 W. Alameda Ave. (recording 818-840-3537), at W. Olive Ave. in Burbank, is your best spur-of-the-moment bet. Passes to Jay Leno's **Tonight Show** are handed out at 8am weekday mornings; it's filmed at 5pm the same evening. Studio tours run on the hour (M-F 9am-3pm, Sa 10am-2pm; $7, children $3.75). Many of NBC's "Must-See TV" shows are taped at **Paramount Pictures,** 5555 Melrose Ave. (213-956-1777), in Hollywood. Sitcoms like *Dharma and Greg, Sister, Sister,* and *Frasier* are taped September through May; call the studio 5 working days in advance to secure tickets. NBC's most popular shows, like *Mad About You* and *Friends,* are filmed before a private audience, so unless you know Paul Reiser himself or are a friend of a Friend, you're out of luck. As Paramount is one of just a few major studios still in Hollywood, Paramount's tours are very popular (every hr. M-F 9am-2pm; $15).

A **CBS box office,** 7800 Beverly Blvd. (213-852-2458), next to the Farmer's Market in West Hollywood, hands out free tickets to Bob Barker's seminal game-show masterpiece *The Price is Right* (taped M-W) up to 1 week in advance (open M-W 7:30am-5pm, Th-F 9am-5pm). Audience members must be over 18. Request up to 10 tickets on a specific date by sending a self-addressed, stamped envelope to **The Price is Right Tickets,** 7800 Beverly Blvd., Los Angeles, CA 90036, about 4 weeks in advance.

If all else fails, **Hollywood Group Services,** 1422 Barry Ave., #8, L.A. 90025 (310-914-3400), and **Audiences Unlimited, Inc.,** 100 Universal City Plaza, Universal City, CA 91608 (818-506-0067), offer guaranteed seating, but charge $10 to no-shows. To find out what shows are available during your visit, send a SASE to either address. Hollywood Group Services will fax a list of all available shows within 24hr. of a call-in request. At **Universal Studios,** the filming is done on the backlot, and you won't see a thing from the tour. To them, it's a studio, not an amusement park.

To see an **on-location movie shoot,** stop by in person to the City/County Film Office, 7083 Hollywood Blvd. (213-957-1000), 5th fl., for a "shoot sheet" ($10), which lists current filming locations; film crews, however, may not share your enthusiasm for audience participation (open M-F 8am-6pm).

Cinema, Theater and Concerts

Countless theaters show films the way they were meant to be seen: in a big space, on a big screen, with top-quality sound. Angelenos are often amazed at the "primitive" sound at theaters they go to in the rest of the country. It would be a cinematic crime not to take advantage of the incredible experience that is movie-going in L.A. **Loews Cineplex Cinemas** (818-508-0588), atop the hill at Universal City Walk; **Pacific Cinerama Dome,** 6360 Sunset Blvd. (466-3401), near Vine; and **Mann's Chinese Theater,** 6925 Hollywood Blvd. (464-8111), are some of the best movie houses.

In spite of the growing number of shows about L.A., very few Broadway/West End-style productions come out of this city. On the other hand, 115 "equity waiver theaters" (under 100 seats) offer a dizzying choice for theater-goers, who can also take in small productions in museums, art galleries, universities, parks, and even garages. For the digs on what's hot, browse the listings in the *L.A. Weekly.* **Theater L.A.** (614-0556) sells same-day tickets for half price at their "Theater Times" booth in the Beverly Center, 8500 Beverly Blvd. at La Cienega, in West L.A.

L.A.'s music venues range from small clubs to massive arenas. The **Wiltern Theater** (380-5005) shows alterna-rock/folk acts. The **Hollywood Palladium** (962-7600) is of comparable size with 3500 seats. Mid-size acts head for the **Universal Amphitheater** (818-777-3931) and the **Greek Theater** (665-1927). Huge indoor sports arenas, such as the **Forum** (310-673-1300), double as concert halls for big acts. Few dare to play at the 100,000-seat **Los Angeles Memorial Coliseum and Sports Arena**—only U2, Depeche Mode, and Guns 'n' Roses have filled the stands in recent years. Call **Ticketmaster** (480-3232) to purchase tickets for any of these venues.

NIGHTLIFE

Late-Night Restaurants

With the unreliability of clubs and the short shelf-life of cafes, late-night restaurants have become reliable hangouts. As the mainstay of L.A. nightlife, they're the best place to giggle at the painfully trendy underage club kids trolling among the celebs.

Jerry's Deli has multiple locations: 8701 Beverly Blvd. (310-289-1811), West Hollywood; 10923 Weyburn Ave. (310-208-3354), Westwood; and 12655 Ventura Blvd. (818-980-4245), Studio City. Jerry himself is rumored to have desired "the longest menu possible while still maintaining structural integrity." Matzoh ball soup $5.50, sandwiches $5-9. Open 24hr.

Fred 62, 1850 Vermont Ave. (213-667-0062), Los Feliz. "Eat now, dine later." Hep booth headrests evoke eating in a car. Green, aerodynamic (yet stationary) building. Waffles $3.62. All prices end in .62; other numbers figure strangely and inexplicably in the restaurant's workings—pay attention as you dine. Open 24hr.

The Rainbow Grill, 9015 Sunset Blvd. (310-278-4232), in West Hollywood beside the Roxy on the Sunset Strip. The dark red vinyl booths have cradled just about every famous butt in L.A. Marilyn Monroe met future husband Joe DiMaggio on a blind date here. Yummy pizza ($6) and calamari. The $10 you shell out to get in goes towards your tab. Open M-F 11am-2am, Sa-Su 5pm-2am.

Barney's Beanery, 8447 Santa Monica Blvd. (213-654-2287), Hollywood, is L.A. at its best, but without the pretension. Janis Joplin and Jim Morrison were regulars, and it hasn't changed much since then. Strange mix of glam clubbers, international kids, and local pool sharks (billiards 50¢). Happy hour M-F 10am-6pm. Open daily 10am-2am. Free valet parking.

Coffeehouses

In a city where no one eats very much for fear of rounding out that bony figure, espresso, coffee, and air are the only options.

G.A.L.A.X.Y. Gallery, 7224 Melrose Ave. (213-938-6500), Hollywood, is much more than just a coffee shop. This cool, spacious store has art on display, a super-comfy couch for tired Melrose strollers, and an enormous bong and hookah display for all your tobacco needs. Acid Jazz Jams on Saturday night tend to be standing room only despite $3 cover. Hemp coffee $1.75. 18+. Open daily 11am-10pm.

Un Urban Coffeehouse, 3301 Pico Blvd. (310-315-0056), Santa Monica, is lined with campy voodoo candles and Mexican wrestling masks. Iced mocha blends ($3.25) rival even the Coffee Bean and Tea Leaf. Su nights are spoken word and W nights are comedy, though there's some sort of entertainment almost every night. Open M-Th 6am-midnight, F 6am-1am, Sa 8am-1am, Su 8am-midnight.

Highland Grounds, 742 N. Highland Ave. (213-466-1507), in Hollywood. Nightly live shows (6pm) feature folk singers, performance artists, and empowerment speakers. Outdoor patio with blazing fire—ah, ambience. Full menu. Beer and wine. Lattes $1.50 before noon. After 8pm, cover $2 and 1-coffee min.—what have we become? Open M 9am-6pm, Tu-Th 9am-12:30am, F-Sa 9am-1am, Su 10am-9pm.

Bars

The 3 of Clubs, 1123 N. Vine St. (213-462-6441), Hollywood, in a small strip mall beneath a "Bargain Clown Mart" sign. This simple, classy, spacious, hardwood bar is famous for appearing in *Swingers*. DJs W nights, live bands Th. Order a grasshopper ($5) and risk incurring the bartender's scorn. 21+. Open daily 9pm-1:45am.

The Room, 1626 Cahuenga (213-462-7196), Hollywood, emptying into an alley, trumps the 3 of Clubs in inconspicuousness. A 30ish crowd comes looking for company here. 21+. Open daily 9pm-2am.

The Lucky Seven, 1610 N. Vine St. (213-463-7777), Hollywood, located between Cary Grant's star and Clark Gable's, but there's no sign to help you find it. On M and Tu nights, the Lucky Seven has hosted lots of live jazz acts including the stylings of Jeff Goldblum, Beverly DeAngelo, and Jerry Springer. Pricey drinks often run over $7. Open M-Sa 7pm-2am, food served until 10pm.

Dublin's, 8240 Sunset Blvd. (213-656-0100), Hollywood, is bigger than most clubs, packing in everyone from young starlets to 60-year-old pool sharks. Pool tables, foosball, darts, and loud music, though there are some quieter nooks and crannies. Swanky upstairs dining room serves lunch, and dinner until 11pm. 21+. Open M-F 11am-2am, Sa-Su 10am-2am.

Liquid Kitty, 11780 W. Pico Blvd. (310-473-3707), West L.A. No one can show the vermouth to the gin quite like the bartenders here. Martini in one hand, cigar in the other, L.A.'s hippest come for the cutting-edge DJs that spin techno and hip-hop on Tu and Th; and live blues, swing, and jazz on Su. Martinis $7. 21+. Open M-F 6pm-2am, Sa-Su 8pm-2am.

Clubs

L.A. is famous, perhaps infamous, for its club scene. With the highest number of bands per capita in the world, most clubs are able to book top-notch acts night after night. These clubs can be the hottest thing in L.A. one month and extinct the next, so check the *L.A. Weekly* (free everywhere) before venturing out.

The Derby, 4500 Los Feliz Blvd. (213-663-8979), Silverlake. Free swing lessons Su-Th at 8pm. The menu is from Louise's Trattoria (choice Italian fare) next door. Full bar. Happy hour daily 4-7pm. Big band music nightly (Big Bad Voodoo Daddy plays W). 21+. Cover $5-7, M free. Open daily 4pm-2am.

Largo, 432 N. Fairfax (213-852-1073), Fairfax, houses intimate performances by some of L.A.'s most interesting entertainers. Jon Brion's unforgettable SRO Friday night performances without a net are improvised one-man jaunts through the cluttered mind of rock and pop with occasional appearances by friends like Elliot Smith and Paula Abdul. 21+. Cover $10. Open M-Sa 9pm-2am.

Luna Park, 665 N. Robertson Blvd. (310-652-0611), West Hollywood, is home to many a record/CD release party and an eclectic, ultra-hip crowd. Live funk, jazz, and rock nightly; club DJ Thursdays. Supper club, full bar, outdoor patio, trancy dance floor. New Music Mondays land L.A.'s best improvisational talent. 21+. Cover $3-10, big-name acts $20. Open nightly until 2am.

Key Club, 9039 Sunset Blvd. (310-274-5800), West Hollywood, is a colossal, crowded multimedia experience complete with black lights, neon galore, and TV screens showcasing the frenetic dance floor. Stage show extravaganzas. Live acts and DJ productions, depending on the night. Visit the tequila library on the first floor. Occasional 18+ shows. Cover $20. Open nightly 8pm-2am.

Arena, 6655 Santa Monica Blvd. (213-462-0714), Santa Monica, lends itself to frenzied techno, house, and Latin beats. Fun-filled theme night, killer drag shows on Sa. Dance! Dance! Dance! You must be 18+ Th, 21+ Sa and Su; F is all ages. Cover $10-12. Open Th 9pm-2:30am, F 9pm-4am, Sa 9pm-3am, Su 9pm-2am.

Comedy Clubs

L.A.'s comedy clubs are the best in the world, unless you happen to chance upon an amateur night, which is generally a painful, painful experience.

Comedy Store, 8433 Sunset Blvd. (213-656-6225), West Hollywood, is the shopping mall of comedy clubs, with 3 different rooms, each featuring a different type of comedy (and another cover charge). The Main Room has the big names and the big prices ($10-15). The Original Room features mid-range comics for $8-10 (free M). The Belly Room has the real grab-bag material (under $5). 2-drink min., with drinks starting at $4.50. 21+. Open nightly until 2am. Reserve up to a week in advance.

The Improvisation, 8162 Melrose Ave. (213-651-2583), West Hollywood, offers L.A.'s best talent—Robin Williams and Jerry Seinfeld have made their appearances. Restaurant serves Italian fare (entrees from $6). Shows M-Th 8pm, F-Sa 8:30 and 10:30pm, Su 8:30pm. Bar open nightly until 1:30am. Cover $8-11. 2-drink min. Reservations recommended. 18+, or 16+ with parent.

Gay and Lesbian Nightlife

Many ostensibly straight clubs have gay nights. Check the *L.A. Weekly* for more listings or the free weekly magazine *fab!* Nightlife centers around **Santa Monica Blvd.** in West Hollywood.

Axis, 652 N. La Peer Dr. (310-659-0471), West Hollywood, is the hub of West Hollywood's gay and lesbian scene, with 2 clubs, 2 bars, faux leopard skin carpet, red pool tables, and great music. W Latin night, F Girl Bar, Sa house music. 21+, Th 18+. Cover $5-10. Open nightly 9pm-2am.

The Abbey, 692 Robertson Blvd. (310-289-8410), West Hollywood. This Spanish-revival coffeehouse buzzes into the night. Psychic readings, free pool, full restaurant and bar. Huge double latte $3. Open Su-Th 7am-2am, F-Sa 7am-3am.

SEASONAL EVENTS

New Year's Day is always a perfect day in Southern California, or so the **Tournament of Roses Parade and Rose Bowl** (626-449-7673), Pasadena, would have it. Some of the wildest New Year's Eve parties happen along **Colorado Blvd.,** the parade route. **Renaissance Pleasure Faire** (800-523-2473), lasts from the daffodil's first blossom to the day of the shortest night (Sa-Su late Apr. to mid-June) in the Glen Helen Regional Park in San Bernardino. The name is quite arousing, but save the occasional kissing bridge, it's a pretty tame scene. From the haven angelic (L.A.), gallop apace on fiery-footed steeds (drive) to Phoebus' lodging (east) along I-10 to I-15 north, and look for signs as you draw near the site of happy reveling (city of Devore). Garbed in their best Elizabethan finery, San Bernardino teens are versed in the bard's phrases before working. (Open Sa-Su 10am-6pm. $17.50, seniors and students $15, children $7.50.) **Cinco de Mayo** (213-625-5045) explodes May 5, especially downtown at Olvera St. Huge celebrations mark the day the Mexicans drop-kicked France's ass out of Mexico. In mid-May, **UCLA Mardi Gras** (310-825-8001), at the athletic field, is billed as the world's largest collegiate activity (a terrifying thought). During **Gay Pride Weekend** (213-860-0701, last or second-to-last weekend in June), Pacific Design Center, 8687 Melrose Ave., West Hollywood, L.A.'s lesbian and gay communities celebrate in full effect with art, politics, dances, and a big parade (tickets $12).

■ Near Los Angeles: South Bay

South Bay life is beach life. **Hermosa Beach** wins both bathing suit and congeniality competitions. Its slammin' volleyball scene, gnarly waves, and killer boardwalk make this the überbeach. The mellower **Manhattan Beach** exudes a yuppified charm, while **Redondo Beach** is by far the most commercially suburban. Richie Rich-esque **Rancho Palos Verdes** is a coast of a different breed. From early morning to late evening, these beaches are overrun by swarms of eager skaters, bladers, volleyball players, surfers, and sunbathers. At night, the crowds move off the beach and toward Manhattan and Hermosa Ave. for an affordable nightlife scene. South Bay harbors two of L.A.'s finest hostels; the one in Hermosa Beach has a bitchin' social scene, while the one in San Pedro may make you want to take up *tai chi.* **Los Angeles Surf City Hostel,** 26 Pier Ave. (798-2323), ½ block from the beach in Hermosa Beach, is a good-natured spot to rest with free linen, bodyboards, and breakfast. Take the #439 bus from Union Station to 11th and Hermosa, walk 2 blocks north, and make a left on Pier. They will pick you up from the airport for free and drop you off for $5. (Discount car rentals, laundry, kitchen, and TV lounge, but no parking. 4-6 bunk dorms $17; off-season $15; private rooms $35-45. Key deposit $10. Reservations recommended. Passport or proof of out-of-state residence required.) **Los Angeles South Bay (HI-AYH),** 3601 S. Gaffey St., Bldg. #613 (831-8109), in Angels Gate Park (entrance by 36th) in San Pedro, pleases with a kitchen, laundry, TV room, volleyball courts, and free parking. Bus #446 runs from here to downtown and Union Station during rush hours. ($12; twins $13.50; private rooms $29.50. Nonmembers add $3. Linen $2. 7-night max. stay. Reception 7am-midnight; closed in winter 11am-4pm.)

▒ Orange County

Directly south of L.A. County is Orange County (pop. 2.6 million), or "O.C." as locals have learned to call it. It is a *Reader's Digest* compilation of Southern California: beautiful beaches, bronzed bathers, strip malls, Disney's expanding cultural organ, and traffic snarls frustrating enough to make the coolest Angeleno weep. Although the county's Anglo majority pales in contrast to the vibrant smorgasbord of L.A. County, Orange County is almost 25 percent Latino, in keeping with the state generally. One of only two staunchly Republican counties in California, Orange County has won fame for its economy (as big as Arizona's, and one of the world's 30 largest), and notoriety for its finances (the county declared an unprecedented bankruptcy in 1994 after its tax-averse government tried to make money in Wall Street derivatives).

PRACTICAL INFORMATION

John Wayne Orange County Airport (252-5006), on Campus Dr. 20min. from Anaheim, is newer, cleaner, and easier to get around than LAX; domestic only. **Amtrak** (800-872-7245) runs to: Fullerton, 120 E. Santa Fe Ave. (992-0530); Anaheim, 2150 E. Katella Blvd. (385-1448); Santa Ana, 1000 E. Santa Ana Blvd. (547-8389); Irvine, 15215 Barranca Parkway (753-9713); San Juan Capistrano, Santa Fe Depot, 26701 Verdugo St. (240-2972); and San Clemente, 1850 Avenida Estacion. **Greyhound** has three stations in the area: Anaheim, 100 W. Winston St. (999-1256), 3 blocks south of Disneyland (open daily 6:30am-8pm); Santa Ana, 1000 E. Santa Ana Blvd. (542-2215; open daily 7am-8pm); and San Clemente, 510 Avenida de la Estrella (492-1187; open M-Th 7:45am-6:30pm, F 7:45am-8pm). **Orange County Transportation Authority (OCTA),** 550 S. Main St. (636-7433), Garden Grove, provides thorough service useful for getting from Santa Ana and Fullerton Amtrak stations to Disneyland, and for beach-hopping along the coast. Bus #1 travels the coast from Long Beach down to San Clemente (every hr. until 8pm). #397 covers San Clemente. Fare $1, transfers free. **MTA** (1-800-266-6883 or 213-626-4455) runs buses daily 5am-10:45pm, from L.A. to Disneyland and Knott's Berry Farm. The **Anaheim Area Visitors and Convention Bureau,** 800 W. Katella Ave. (999-8999), is in the Anaheim Convention Center (open M-F 8:30am-5pm). Anaheim's **post office:** 701 N. Loara (520-2601). **ZIP code:** 92803. **Area code:** 714; in Seal Beach 310; in Newport area 949.

CALIFORNIA

ACCOMMODATIONS, CAMPGROUNDS, AND FOOD

The Magic Kingdom is the sun around which the Anaheim solar system revolves, so budget motels and garden-variety "clean comfortable rooms" flank it on all sides. Keep watch for family and group rates posted on marquees, and seek out establishments offering the 3-for-2 passport (3 days of Disney for the price of 2) if you are planning on imagineering extensively. O.C.'s state beaches have **campgrounds** that aren't the stuff of dreams, but are *extremely* popular. Reservations are required for all sites (reservation fee $6.75), and can be made through **DESTINET** (800-444-7275), a maximum of 7 months in advance. They should be made as soon as possible in the summer. Reservations are recommended for all accommodations listed below as well.

Fullerton (HI-AYH), 1700 N. Harbor Blvd. (738-3725), in Fullerton 15min. north of Disneyland. Shuttle from LAX $18. OCTA bus #43 runs along Harbor Blvd. to Disneyland. Enthusiastic, resourceful staff invites questions but frowns on drinking. Offers services including ISICs. Kitchen, communal bathrooms. Single-sex and co-ed dorms. Dorms $14, non-members $17, less in winter. 7-night max. stay. Check-in 8-11am and 4-11pm. No curfew. Linen $1. Laundry free.

Magic Inn & Suites, 1030 W. Katella Ave. (772-7242 or 800-422-1556), Anaheim. The rugs can't show you a whole new world, but this establishment does have a great location across the street from Disneyland. Pools, laundry, A/C, TV, fridge, and microwaves. Rooms $49, $55 for 2 people, $58 for 3; deluxe suite (up to 7) $69.

Skyview Motel, 1126 W. Katella Ave. (533-4505), at the southwest corner of Disneyland. Clean rooms with HBO and A/C. Balconies offer a good view of Disney's nightly fireworks. Some rooms have vibrating beds (heh, heh). Small pool, many kids. Singles $27.

Inexpensive ethnic restaurants tucked into Anaheim's strip malls allow escape from fast food. Many specialize in take-out or will deliver chow to your motel room. **Angelo & Vicini's Café Ristorante,** 550 N. Harbor Blvd. (879-4022), Fullerton, is a place where the word "cheesy" describes both the food and the decor—Christmas lights, cheese wheels, and the Mona Lisa. (Lunch special with a slice of pizza, pasta, and salad $2.50. Open Su-Th 11am-9:45pm, F-Sa 11am-11:45pm.)

SIGHTS

Disneyland

The **unlimited use passport** ($38, seniors $36, under 12 $28) allows repeated single-day entrance into the park, as does the **parking pass** ($7 per day). The park's main entrance on Harbor, and a smaller one on Katella, may be approached by car via I-5 to Katella. From L.A., MTA bus #460 travels from 4th and Flower (about 1½hr.) to the Disneyland Hotel (service to the hotel begins at 4:53am, service back to L.A. until 1:20am). **Free shuttles** link the hotel to Disneyland's portals, as does the **Disneyland monorail.** The park is also served by Airport Service, OCTA, Long Beach Transit, and Gray Line. Parking in the morning is painless, but leaving in the evening is not. Park hrs. vary (call 781-4565 for exact info), but are approximately Su-Th 10am-8pm, F-Sa 8am-midnight.

Disneyland calls itself the "happiest place on earth," putting it in direct competition with EuroDisney. The lines are as long as the day. Weekday and off-season visitors will undoubtedly be the happiest, but the enterprising can wait for parades to distract the children, leaving shorter lines. *Disneyland Today!* lists parade and show times, as well as important shopping information and breaking news from Frontierland.

Not Disneyland

Buena Park offers a cavalcade of non-Disney diversions, some of which are better than others. The first theme park in America, **Knott's Berry Farm,** 8039 Beach Blvd. (714-220-5200 for recorded info), is at La Palma Ave. in Buena Park just 5 mi. northeast of Disneyland. (Park hours vary, but are approximately Su-Th 9am-11pm, F-Sa 9am-midnight. $32, seniors $24, ages 3-11 $24. From L.A., take MTA bus #460 from 4th and Flower; 1¼ hr.) **Movieland Wax Museum,** 7711 Beach Blvd. (522-1154), offers a huge collection of celebrity facsimiles, including the entire *Star Trek* crew. *(Open Sa-Su 9am-7pm, M-F 10am-6pm. $13, seniors $11, ages 4-11 $7.)* Across the way are the ribald oddities at **Ripley's Believe It or Not! Museum,** 7850 Beach Blvd. (522-1152), likely to be the only place prideful enough to advertise a *Last Supper* fashioned from 280 pieces of toast. *(Open daily 10am-7pm, box office closes at 6pm. Combo admission to both museums $17.)* Amusement parks of the wetter variety can be found at **Wild Rivers Waterpark,** 8770 Irvine Center Dr. (768-9453), in Irvine, off I-405 S. *(Call for hrs. $21, seniors $10, ages 3-9 $17.)* With over 40 waterslide rides and two wave pools, this is almost as good as a cold shower...on *Air Force One!*

Farther inland is the highly uncritical, privately funded monument to Tricky Dick, the **Richard Nixon Library and Birthplace,** 18001 Yorba Linda Blvd. (993-5075), Yorba Linda. *(Open M-Sa 10am-5pm, Su 11am-5pm. $6, seniors $4, ages 8-11 $2.)* The first native-born Californian president was born in this house, which has now become an extensive museum of the American presidency. Although Nixon considered his resignation an admission of guilt, expect no such admission in these exhibits, where curators consistently portray one of the master manipulators of our century as the victim of circumstance, plotting enemies, and his own immutable honor.

Orange County Beach Communities

Taking town planning to the extreme, O.C.'s various beach communities have cleaner sand, better surf, and more charm than their L.A. county counterparts. **Huntington Beach** served as a point of entry for the surfing craze, which transformed California coast life in the early 1900s. It's still a fun, crowded hotspot for wave-shredders, with a pristine pier for ogling. **Newport Beach** is the Beverly Hills of beach towns, though the beach itself displays few signs of ostentatious wealth; it is crowded with young, rowdy hedonists cloaked in neon. The sands of the beach run south to **Balboa Peninsula,** which can be reached by the Pacific Coast Hwy. At the end of the peninsula, **The Wedge,** pounded by waves, is a bodysurfing mecca.

Laguna Beach, 4 mi. south of Newport, is nestled between canyons. Back in the day, Laguna was a Bohemian artists' colony, but no properly starving artists can afford to live here now. The surviving galleries and art supply stores nevertheless add a unique twist to the standard SoCal beach culture that thrives on Laguna's sands. **Main Beach** and the shops nearby along Ocean Ave. are the prime parading areas, though there are other, less crowded spots as well. One accessible beach is **Westry Beach,** which spreads out south of Laguna just below **Aliso Beach Park.**

More tourists than swallows return every year to **Mission San Juan Capistrano** (248-2048), 30min. south of Anaheim on I-5. *(Open daily 8:30am-5pm. $5, seniors and ages 3-12 $4.)* Take Ortega Hwy. to Camino Capistrano. Established in 1776, it is somewhat run-down due to an 1812 earthquake. Father Junípero Serra, the mission's founder, officiated from the beautiful **Serra Chapel,** which at 218 years is now the oldest building in the state. It's still used by the Catholic Church, so enter quietly.

■ Big Bear

Hibernating in the San Bernardino Mountains, the town of **Big Bear Lake** entertains hordes of visitors with winter skiing and summer hiking, biking, and boating. The consistent winds, no doubt made up of the sighs of relaxing Angelenos, make the lake one of the best for sailing in the state.

The **hiking** here is both free and priceless. Maps, trail descriptions, and the *Visitor's Guide to the San Bernardino National Forest* are available at the **Big Bear Discovery Center** (866-3437), on Rte. 38 (open daily 8am-6pm; in winter 8am-4:30pm). The **Woodland Trail** or the more challenging **Pineknot Trail** offer views of the lake; high altitudes here make slow climbing necessary.

Mountain biking is a popular activity in Big Bear when the snow melts. **Snow Summit** (866-5766) operates lifts in summer so thrill-seeking bikers can plummet downhill without the grueling uphill ride ($7 per ride, day pass $19; helmet required). **Team Big Bear** (866-4565) sponsors several organized bike races each summer. (For more info, call daily Apr.-Oct. 9am-5pm, or write **Team Big Bear,** Box 2932, Big Bear Lake 92315.) Those without wheels of their own can rent them from **Big Bear Bikes,** 41810 Big Bear Blvd. (866-2224; $6 per hr., $31 per 8hr., helmet included). Many summer activities take place on the water. **Fishing licenses** are available at area sporting goods stores ($9.30 per day, season $27), and the **Big Bear Fishing Association** (866-6260) cheerfully dispenses info. **Holloway's Marina,** 398 Edgemor Rd. (800-448-5335), on the South Shore, rents **boats** ($39-83 per ½-day).

When conditions are favorable, ski areas run out of lift tickets quickly. Tickets for the resorts listed below may be purchased over the phone through **Ticketmaster** (213-480-3232 or 714-740-2000). The **Big Bear Hotline** (866-7000 or 800-424-4232) has info on lodging, local events, and ski and road conditions. **Bear Mountain Ski Resort** (585-2519), 1½ mi. southeast of downtown Big Bear Lake, has 12 lifts covering 195 acres of terrain, including huge vertical drops, plus many more acres of undeveloped land suitable for adventurous skiers. (Lift tickets $45, mid-week $30. Skis $23, snowboards $28. New skier/snowboarder packages include group lesson, lift ticket, and equipment rental; M-F $45, Sa-Su $50.)

Big Bear has few budget accommodations, especially in the winter. The best option for daytrippers is probably to stay in Redlands or San Bernardino, although the drive down Rte. 18 can be tough at night. **Big Bear Blvd.,** the main drag on the lake's south shore, is lined with lodging possibilities, but groups can find the best deals by sharing a cabin. **Mountain Lodging Unlimited** (800-487-3168), arranges lodging and lift packages (from $46 per person; open M-Sa 9am-5pm, Su 10am-2pm). The **lodging hotline** (800-244-2327) has up-to-date info. Reservations are always necessary. **Hillcrest Lodge,** 40241 Big Bear Blvd. (866-7330, reservations 800-843-4449), is a favorite for honeymooners. Pine paneling and skylights give these cozy rooms a ritzy feel at a budget price. (Jacuzzi, cable TV, and free local calls. Small rooms $35-49, 4-person units $89, deluxe suites with hearth and kitchen $57-79; in winter $39-54/$79-112/$57-97.) **Pineknot** (7000 ft.), south of Big Bear on Summit Blvd., has 49 isolated sites with flush toilets and water. Nestled at the base of Snow Summit, this spot is popular with mountain bikers. (Sites $15. Wheelchair access.) Groceries can be procured at **Vons,** 42170 Big Bear Blvd. (866-8459).

To reach Big Bear Lake, take the San Bernardino Fwy. (I-10) to the junction of Rte. 30 and 330. Follow Rte. 330, also known as Mountain Rd., to Rte. 18, a *very* long and winding uphill road. About halfway up the mountain, Rte. 18 becomes Big Bear Blvd., the main route encircling the lake. Driving time from L.A. is about 2½hr., barring serious weekend traffic or road closures. **Mountain Area Regional Transit Authority (MARTA)** (584-1111) runs three buses per day between Big Bear and San Bernardino (2 per day on Sa) at the Greyhound station in San Bernardino (fare $5, seniors and disabled $3.75). Buses also run along Big Bear Blvd.; it's a 1hr. trip to get from one end to the other (fare $1, students 75¢, seniors and disabled 50¢). **Area code:** 909.

■ San Diego

San Diegans are fond of referring to their garden-like town as "America's Finest City." Even the stodgiest members of the East Coast establishment would find this claim difficult to dispute—San Diego has all the virtues of other California cities without their frequently cited drawbacks. No smog fills this city's air, and no sewage spoils its silver seashores. Its zoo is the nation's best, and its city center contains a greater concentration of museums than any spot in America save Washington, D.C. The city was founded when the seafaring Spanish prolonged an onshore foray in 1769 and began the first permanent settlement on the U.S.'s West Coast, but it didn't become a city proper until the 1940s, when it became the headquarters of the U.S. Pacific Fleet following the Pearl Harbor attack.

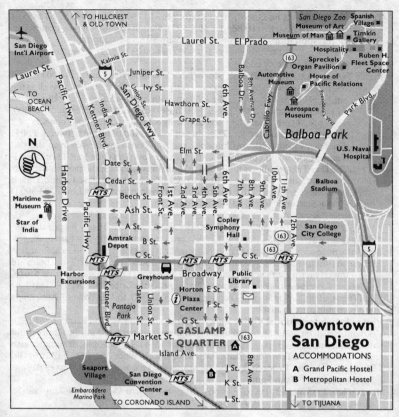

Downtown San Diego
ACCOMMODATIONS
A Grand Pacific Hostel
B Metropolitan Hostel

CALIFORNIA

ORIENTATION

San Diego rests in the extreme southwest corner of California, 127 mi. south of L.A. and 15 mi. north of Mexico. **I-5** runs south from L.A. and skirts the eastern edge of downtown; **I-15** runs northeast to Nevada; and **I-8** runs east-west along downtown's northern boundary, connecting the desert with Ocean Beach. The major downtown thoroughfare, **Broadway,** also runs east-west. On the northeast corner of downtown sits **Balboa Park,** home to many museums and to the justly heralded San Diego Zoo. The cosmopolitan **Hillcrest** and **University Heights** districts, both centers of the gay community, border the park to the northeast. South of downtown, between 4th and 6th St., is the newly revitalized **Gaslamp District,** full of nightclubs, chic restaurants, and coffeehouses. The downtown area is situated between San Diego's two major bays: **San Diego Bay,** formed by **Coronado Island,** lies just to the south, while **Mission Bay,** formed by the **Mission Beach** spit, lies to the northwest. Up the coast from Mission Beach are **Ocean Beach, Pacific Beach,** and wealthy **La Jolla.**

San Diego has an extensive system of fairly easy **bike routes.** The flat, paved route along Mission and Pacific Beaches toward La Jolla affords ocean views and soothing sea breezes. But bikers beware: pedestrian traffic along the beaches rivals the automobile blockades on the boulevards.

PRACTICAL INFORMATION

Airport: San Diego International (Lindbergh Field), at the northwest edge of downtown. Bus #2 goes downtown ($1.75), and so do cabs ($7).

Trains: Amtrak Santa Fe Depot, 1050 Kettner Blvd. (239-9021 or 800-872-7245), at Broadway. To Los Angeles (10 per day M-F, $23). Station has info on bus, trolley, car, and boat transportation. Ticket office open daily 5:15am-10:20pm.

Buses: Greyhound, 120 W. Broadway (239-8082 or 800-231-2222), at 1st. To Los Angeles ($16). Ticket office open 24hr.

Public Transportation: The **Transit Store** (fares 234-1060, route info 233-3004), at 1st and Broadway, distributes bus, trolley, and ferry tickets and timetables, as well as the free pamphlet *How to Ride* (open M-F 8:30am-5:30pm, Sa-Su noon-4pm). **Buses** cost $1.75 for local routes and $2-3.25 for express buses (exact change; most accept bills). Free transfer for 1½hr. The bright red **San Diego Trolley** (233-3004) consists of 2 lines leaving from downtown for El Cajon, San Ysidro, and points in between. The El Cajon line leaves from 12th and Imperial; the San Ysidro line leaves from the Old Town Transit Center and continues to the Mexican border (daily 5am-1am; fare $1-2.25). The **Day Tripper** allows unlimited rides on buses, ferries, and trolleys for 1 day ($5). The pass (2 days $8, 3 days $10, 4 days $12) can be purchased at the Transit Store; good only for consecutive days. **Public Transit Information Line** (233-3004) operates M-F 5:30am-8:30pm, Sa-Su 8am-5pm.

Car Rental: Bargain Auto, 3860 Rosecrans St. (299-0009). Cars $17-29 per day, $95-185 per week; 150 free mi. per day, 500 per week. Ages 18-21 pay $8 per day surcharge, ages 21-25 pay $4 per day. Credit card required. Open daily 8am-6pm.

Bike Info: Buses equipped with bike carriers make it possible to cart bikes almost anywhere in the city (call 233-3004 to find out which routes have carriers), and bikes are also allowed on the San Diego Trolley with a $4 permit (available at **Transit Store,** see above). For more bike info, contact the **City Bicycle Coordinator** (533-3110), or **CalTrans,** 4040 Taylor St., San Diego 92110 (231-2453), in Old Town. Biking maps and pamphlets are available.

Visitor Info: International Visitor Information Center, 11 Horton Plaza (236-1212), downtown at 1st and F St. Multilingual staff dispenses publications, brochures, and discount coupons. 3hr. parking validation. Open M-Sa 8:30am-5pm; in summer also Su 11am-5pm. **Old Town and State Park Info,** 4002 Wallace Ave. (220-5422), in Old Town Sq. Take the Taylor St. Exit off I-8 or bus #5. Free walking tour leaves daily at 2pm. Open daily 10am-5pm.

Post Office: 2535 Midway Dr. (674-0000). Take bus #6, 9, or 35. Open M-F 7am-1am, Sa 8am-4pm. **ZIP code:** 92138. **Area code:** 619.

ACCOMMODATIONS AND CAMPGROUNDS

Lodging in San Diego can be an incredible bargain. Those with cars can camp on the beautiful beaches; spots are reservable through **PARKNET** (800-444-7275).

⊛**San Diego Metropolitan (HI-AYH),** 521 Market St. (525-1531 or 800-909-4776), at 5th, in the heart of the Gaslamp. Quiet and impeccable, near San Diego's most popular attractions and clubs. Airy common room, communal bathrooms, laundry room, and lockers (bring a lock). Dorms (4-6 beds) $16-18; doubles $36; nonmembers $3 more. Reception 7am-midnight. No curfew. IBN reservations available.

Grand Pacific Hostel, 726 5th Ave. (232-3100 or 800-438-8622), between G and F St. in the Gaslamp. In-house drinking, occasional group outings. Clean and spacious dorms $14-16; doubles $38. Free linen, breakfast, and shuttle to nearby sights. Coin-op laundry. Tijuana tours $10.

J Street Inn, 222 J St. (696-6922), near San Diego's Convention Center and ritzy waterfront. 221 fabulous studio rooms have cable, microwave, fridge, and bath. Gym, reading room. Singles $44; doubles $50; $10 per additional person. Weekly and monthly rates available. Enclosed parking $5 per day, $20 per week.

Downtown Hostel at Baltic Inn, 521 6th Ave. (237-0687). Clean rooms with toilet, sink, microwave, mini-fridge, cable TV. Singles $20; doubles $28; $73-125 per week. Communal showers. Laundry. Key deposit $10. No curfew, 24hr. security.

Banana Bungalow, 707 Reed Ave. (273-3060 or 800-5-HOSTEL/546-7835, reservations 888-246-2262), just off of Mission Blvd. in Mission Beach. Free pick-up from airport and Greyhound terminal (call ahead), or take bus #34 to Mission and Reed. Popular hostel offers lots of amenities: common room with cable, beachside location, and free breakfast. Dorms $14-18. Linen included. Check-out 11am. No curfew. Must have international passport. Call in advance.

HI-Elliott (HI-AYH), 3790 Udall St. (223-4773), Point Loma, 1½mi. from Ocean Beach. Take bus #35 from downtown to the first stop on Voltaire. If driving, head west on Sea World Dr. from I-5 and bear right on Sunset Cliff Blvd. Take a left on Voltaire and a right on Worden. Udall is 1 block away—look for the hostel sign painted on a blue church. Large kitchen, patio, and common room with TV. Dorms $13, nonmembers $16. Bike rental $10 per day. 14-night max. stay. Reception 8-10pm. Check-out 10:30am. No curfew. Reserve 2 days in advance.

Campgrounds: South Carlsbad Beach State Park (438-3143), off Rte. 21 near Leucadia, in north San Diego County. Half of the 226 sites are for tents. On cliffs over the sea. Showers, laundry facilities. No hiking trails. Oceanfront sites $22, Sa-Su $23; inland $17/$18. Dogs $1.

San Elijo Beach State Park (753-5091), Rte. 21 south of Cardiff-by-the-Sea. 271 sites (150 for tents) in a setting similar to that at South Carlsbad to the north. Strategic landscaping gives a secluded feel. Hiker/biker campsites available, but no hiking or biking trails. Laundry and showers. Oceanfront sites $22, Sa-Su $23; inland $17/$18. Dogs $1.

FOOD

Good restaurants cluster downtown along **C St., Broadway,** and in the **Gaslamp.** The best food near Balboa Park and the Zoo is north and west in nearby **Hillcrest** and **University Heights. Old Town** is *the* place to eat Mexican cuisine.

El Indio Mexican Restaurant, 409 F St. (299-0385). Damn good food at damn good prices. Combo plates $4-6, burritos $3-4. Open M-Th 11am-8pm, F-Sa 11am-1am.

Karl Strauss' Old Columbia Brewery and Grill, 1157 Columbia St. (234-2739). San Diego's first microbrewery and the local favorite for power lunches. BBQ ribs and pasta $8-12, lighter fare $6-8. Open M-Th 11:30am-midnight, F-Sa 11:30am-1am, Su 11:30am-10pm.

Kansas City Barbecue, 610 W. Market St. (231-9680). No fewer than 8 signs at this popular barbecue joint proclaim that *Top Gun*'s bar scene was shot here. Giant lunches and dinners ($4-9) more than make up for the constant jukebox strains of "You've Lost that Lovin' Feeling." Open daily 11am-1am.

The Golden Dragon, 414 University Ave. (296-4119, delivery 275-7500), Hillcrest. Where Marilyn Monroe and Frank Sinatra ate. Eclectic menu offers over a hundred dishes (many vegetarian) for $6-9. Open daily 4:30pm-3am.

Casa de Bandini, 2754 Calhoun St. (297-8211). The charming patio and mariachi-filled interior (built in 1829) create a fabulous atmosphere for the scarfing of super-sized chimichangas ($8), mouth-watering combo plates ($8-9), and monster margaritas ($4-6). Repeatedly voted San Diego's best Mexican restaurant. Open M-Th 11am-9:30pm, F-Sa 11am-10pm, Su 10am-9:30pm.

Casa de Pico (296-3267), just off Calhoun St. in the Old Town Bazaar. Gigantic plates overflowing with gooey cheese enchiladas ($7-8). Soup-bowl-sized margaritas are terrifically tasty. Open Su-Th 10am-9:30pm, F-Sa 10am-10pm.

SIGHTS

Downtown, Balboa Park, and Old Town are easily handled on foot, but beaches are less accessible because of the wide distances between them. **Walkabout International,** 835 5th Ave., #407 (231-7463), sponsors about 150 walks each month, ranging from downtown architectural walks to 20 mi. treks to La Jolla (open M-F 9:30am-2:30pm; expect an answering machine). San Diegans worship the god of the walk signal, perhaps in part because of some obedience gene, but more likely because jaywalking is actively prosecuted here.

Downtown

San Diego's downtown attractions are concentrated in its business, Gaslamp, and waterfront districts. The jewel of San Diego's redevelopment efforts is **Horton Plaza,** at Broadway and 4th. This pastel-hued urban confection is an open-air, multi-level shopping

CALIFORNIA

center covering 7 blocks. To the south of Horton Plaza is the historic **Gaslamp Quarter,** which comprises antique shops, Victorian buildings, and trendy restaurants. Formerly the city's red-light district, the area's bistros have grown popular with upscale revelers. By day, the area's charm lies in its history. The **Gaslamp Quarter Foundation,** William Heath Davis House, 410 Island Ave. (233-4692), offers a guided walking tour (2hr.; Sa 11am; $5, students and seniors $3, ages 12-18 $3).

Moored windjammers, cruise ships, and the occasional naval destroyer face the board-walk shops and museums along the **Embarcadero.** The 1863 sailing vessel *Star of India* is docked in front of the **Maritime Museum,** 1306 N. Harbor Dr. (234-9153), open daily 9am-9pm in summer and until 8pm otherwise ($5, seniors $4, ages 13-17 $4, ages 6-12 $2). Along the harbor to the south, kitschy **Seaport Village** (235-4014) houses shingled boutiques, ice cream shops, and a century-old carousel (village open daily 10am-10pm; off-season 10am-9pm; carousel rides $1).

Balboa Park, the San Diego Zoo, and the El Prado Museums

Redwood trees tower over climbing roses and water lilies at the center of a teeming city in Balboa Park, known for its concerts, cultural events, lush vegetation, and most of all for the fabulous San Diego Zoo. The park is accessible by bus #7. Parking is free in museum and zoo lots; posted signs warn park-goers against scam artists who attempt to wheedle lot fees from the unsuspecting. Tuesday is the best day to visit the park, as the museums offer free admission on a rotating basis. With over 100 acres of exquisite fenceless habitats, the **San Diego Zoo** (234-3153) well deserves its reputation as one of the finest in the world. *(Open daily in summer 7:30am-9pm; off-season 9am-6pm. $16, ages 3-11 $7 except free in Oct, military in uniform free. Group rates available. Free on Founder's Day, the 1st M in Oct.)* The 40min. open-air **double-decker bus tour** covers 80% of the park ($8, ages 3-11 $5).

Balboa Park's many museums reside within the resplendent Spanish colonial-style buildings which line **El Prado,** a street running west to east through the Park's central **Plaza de Panama.** The **park visitors center** (239-0512) is in the House of Hospitality on El Prado. *(Center open daily 9am-4pm.)* The center sells simple park maps (a well-spent $1), and the **Passport to Balboa Park,** containing coupons for a week's worth of entry to all of the park's museums ($21), also available at participating museums.

The star of the western axis of the Plaza de Panama is the **Museum of Man** (239-2001). *(Open daily 10am-4:30pm. $5, seniors $4.50, ages 6-17 $2, military in uniform free; free 3rd Tu of each month.)* Its much-photographed tower and dome gleam with Spanish mosaic tiles, while inside human evolution is traced.

Across the Plaza de Panama is the **San Diego Museum of Art** (232-7931), whose collection ranges from ancient Asian to contemporary Californian works. *(Open Su-Th 9am-6pm, F-Sa 9am-8pm. Su-Th $7, F-Sa $8; seniors always $5; ages 6-17 always $2; special exhibits up to $15 more.)* Nearby is the outdoor **Sculpture Garden Court** (696-1990), where a sensuous Henry Moore piece presides over other large abstract blocks. The **Timken Art Gallery,** 1500 El Prado (239-5548), next door, houses several superb portraits by Rubens and a collection of Russian church icons (open Oct.-Aug. Tu-Sa 10am-4:30pm, Su 1:30-4:30pm; free).

Farther east along the plaza stands the **Botanical Building** (234-1100), a wooden structure filled with the scent of jasmine and the murmur of fountains (open F-W 10am-4pm; free). Free botanist-led tours of the park are held Saturdays at 10am (call 235-1121 for more info). The **Desert and Rose Gardens,** 2200 Park Blvd. (235-1100), offer a strange contrast between the two types of flora.

At the east end of El Prado lies the **Natural History Museum** (232-3821), where life-size robotic dinosaurs enhance the standard fossils, and a recreated mine displays gems. *(Open F-W 9:30am-5:30pm, Th 9:30am-6:30pm. $6, seniors and military $5, ages 6-17 $3; free 1st Tu of each month; ½-price Th 4:30-6:30pm.)* Across El Prado from the Natural History Museum is the **Reuben H. Fleet Space Theater and Science Center** (238-1233; reservations 232-6866), which houses an **Omnimax** projector, 153 speakers, and a hemi-spheric planetarium. *(10-14 Omnimax shows per day. Tickets $8, seniors $7, ages 3-12 $5; museum admission included.)* A ticket to the space theater, plus an additional $1, earns entry into the nearby **Science Center.** *(Open daily in summer 9:30am-10pm; off-season 9:30am-*

9pm. $5, ages 3-12 $3, seniors $4; free 1st Tu of each month.) The **Aerospace Museum** (234-8291), in the drum-shaped Ford Pavilion, exhibits full-scale replicas of over 70 planes. *(Open daily 10:30am-5:30pm; Labor Day to mid-June 10am-4:30pm. $6, seniors $5, ages 6-17 $2, military free; free 4th Tu of each month.)*

Old Town

In 1769, a group of Spanish soldiers accompanied by Father Junípero Serra established a fort and mission in the area now known as Old Town. The area's museums, parks, and sundry attractions commemorate the historic outpost.

Presidio Park is the most impressive of these historical areas, containing the **Serra Museum** (279-3258). *(Museum open Tu-Sa 10am-4:30pm, Su noon-4:30pm. $3, under 12 free.)* Its stout adobe walls were raised in 1929 at the site of the original fort and mission. Inside are exhibits documenting the settlement; outside is a really, really huge flagpole marking the location of **Fort Stockton.** Father Serra's soldiers must have been a rough and unholy bunch, because in 1774 the padre moved his mission some 6 mi. away to its current location at **Mission Basilica San Diego de Alcalá** (281-8449). The mission is still an active parish church (mass held daily 7am and 5:30pm; visitors welcome), and contains a chapel, gardens, a small museum, and a reconstruction of Serra's living quarters. To get to the park, take bus #43 or I-8 east to the Mission Gorge Rd. Exit.

Coronado Island

Coronado is actually a peninsula—the "Silver Strand," a slender 7 mi. strip of sand, connects it to the mainland just above the Mexican border. The graceful **Coronado Bridge,** built in 1969, guides cars to Coronado from downtown San Diego along I-5 (toll $1), and bus #901 follows the same route. The famous Victorian-style **Hotel del Coronado,** 1500 Orange Ave. (435-6611), is the island's main sight. *(Historic tours an unreasonable $15; buy tickets at Signature Shop.)* The long, white verandas and the vermilion spires of the "Del" were built in 1898. The hotel has since become one of the world's greats, hosting 12 presidents and one blonde bombshell (Marilyn Monroe's 1959 classic *Some Like it Hot* was filmed here).

The **Cabrillo National Monument** (557-5450), at the tip of Point Loma, is dedicated to the great Portuguese explorer, João Rodrigues Cabrillo (the first European to land in California), but is best known for its views of San Diego and migrating whales. *($5 per vehicle, pass good for 7 days. Golden Eagle Passport accepted.)* From north country, take I-5 to Rosecrans Blvd. (there is no Rosecrans Exit northbound), and follow signs for Rte. 209 to the entrance, or take bus #6A. **Ocean Beach (O.B.)** caters to a crowd of surfers much more low-key than the swankier set to the north. Gentle surf conditions make O.B. a great place to learn the art of wave-riding. Those who would rather stay out of the water can angle from the longest fishing pier in the Western Hemisphere or watch the sinking sun from **Sunset Cliffs.** Most of the area's inexpensive restaurants and bars are clustered along the westernmost stretch of **Newport Ave.,** one of San Diego's trendiest drags. The **Newport Bar and Grille,** 4935 Newport Ave. (222-0168), is the local favorite; try their walnut chicken ($7; open M-W 11am-midnight, Th-F 11am-2am, Sa 8am-2am, Su 8am-midnight). **Margarita's,** 4955 Newport Ave. (224-7454), has great Mexican vegetarian fare (vegetarian burritos $3.25) and wine margaritas ($2). The strands at **Mission Beach** and **Pacific Beach (P.B.)** are more respectable wave-wise than those at O.B. and consequently draw a younger, more surf-oriented crowd. There are tons of bars and grills along these shores—most are crowded and noisy. The **Ocean Front Walk** through Pacific Beach toward La Jolla is always packed with joggers, walkers, cyclists, and the usual beachfront shops.

Sea World

Take Disneyland, subtract the rides, add a whole lot of fish, and you've got **Sea World** (226-3901), a water wonderland whose signature creature isn't a pipsqueak mouse but a four-ton orca known as **Shamu.** *(Park open Su-Th 9am-10pm, F-Sa 9am-11pm; off-season hrs. shorter. $36, ages 3-11 $27.)* Shamus aside, the park contains shark, penguin, and dolphin displays, as well as jet-ski and watersport shows and a virtual-reality underwater experience.

CALIFORNIA

Seasonal Events

At the **Penguin Day Ski Fest** (276-0830), New Year's Day, De Anza Cove on Mission Bay, the object is to go water-skiing in the ocean or lie on a block of ice without a wet suit. The **Ocean Beach Kite Festival** (531-1527), 4741 Santa Monica Ave., soars on the first Saturday in March. **Summer Stargazing** (594-6182) takes place on weekend nights from June through early September at San Diego State University's Mount Laguna Observatory. Sand-sculpturing demigods exercise their craft in mid-August at the **U.S. Open Sand Castle Competition** (424-6663), Imperial Beach pier.

NIGHTLIFE

Distinct pockets of action are scattered throughout the city. The **Gaslamp** is home to myriad upscale restaurants and bars that feature live music nightly. **Hillcrest** draws a largely gay crowd. The beach areas away from downtown are loaded with clubs, bars, and young revelers. The free *San Diego Reader* is the definitive source of entertainment information.

- **Croce's Top Hat Bar and Grille and Croce's Jazz Bar,** 802 5th Ave. (233-4355), at F St. in the Gaslamp. Ingrid Croce, widow of singer Jim Croce, created this rock/blues bar and classy jazz bar side by side on the 1st fl. of the historic Keating building. Live music nightly. Cover up to $8, with 2 live shows. Open daily 7:30am-2am.
- **Pacific Beach Bar and Grill** and **Club Tremors,** 860 Garnet Ave. (272-1242 and 277-7228, respectively), Pacific Beach. Live DJ packs the 2-level dance floor nightly with a young and slinky crowd. Cover $3-5. Open nightly 9pm-1:30am.
- **Dick's Last Resort,** 345 4th Ave. (231-9100), Gaslamp. Buckets of Southern grub attract a wildly hedonistic bunch. Dick's stocks beers from around the globe. No cover for the nightly rock or blues, but you'd better be buyin'. Burgers under $4, entrees $9-17. Open daily 11am-1:30am.
- **Café Lu Lu,** 419 F. St. (238-0114), Gaslamp. Vegetarian coffeehouse was designed by local artists. See and be seen as you eat for under $5, surreptitiously sipping a raspberry-mocha espresso ($3.75). Standing room only after midnight. Open Su-Th 9am-2am, F-Sa 9am-4am.

Some of the more popular gay and lesbian clubs include: **Bourbon Street,** 4612 Park Blvd. (291-0173), in University Heights, a piano bar with a gay following; **The Flame,** 3780 Park Blvd. (295-4163), in Hillcrest, a lesbian dance club; and **The Brass Rail,** 3796 5th Ave. (298-2233), in Hillcrest, featuring dancing and drag on weekends.

■ North of San Diego

La Jolla Pronounced "la HOY-a," this affluent locality houses few accommodations or eateries friendly to the budget traveler, but its beaches are largely open to the public and simply fabulous. The **La Jolla Cove** is popular with scuba divers, snorkelers, and brilliantly colored Garhibaldi goldfish (the state saltwater fish). Surfers are especially fond of the waves at **Tourmaline Beach** and **Windansea Beach,** which can be too strong for novices. **La Jolla Shores,** next to Scripps/UCSD, has clean and gentle swells ideal for bodysurfers, boogie boarders, swimmers, and families. **Black's Beach** is not *officially* a **nude beach,** but there are more wieners and buns on display here than in a *Wienerschnitzel* warehouse. To reach La Jolla, turn from I-5 and take a left at the Ardath Exit or take buses #30 or 34 from downtown.

Escondido The **San Diego Wild Animal Park** (234-6541) is dedicated to the preservation and display of endangered species. *(Open M-W 9am-7pm, Th-Su 9am-10pm. $22, ages 3-11 $15; parking $3.)* Animals roam freely in extensive habitats engineered to mirror the real thing. The park's entrance has restaurants, and a short trail, but most of its 800 accessible acres can be reached only by way of the open-air **Wgasa Bush Line,** a 50min. monorail tour through the four habitat areas.

Also in Escondido is the "wunnerful, wunnerful" **Welk Resort Center,** the personal barony of late champagne-music conductor Lawrence Welk. The lobby contains the **Lawrence Welk Museum,** 8860 Lawrence Welk Dr. (800-932-WELK/9355) (open Tu, Th, Sa 9am-7pm; Su, M, W, F 9am-4:30pm).

■ Tijuana

In the shadow of swollen, sulphur-spewing factories smeared across a topographical nightmare of gorges and promontories lies the most notorious specimen of the peculiar border subculture: Tijuana (pop. 2 million), the most-visited border town in the world. This three-ringed, duty-free extravaganza comes complete with English-speaking, patronizing club promoters and every decadent way of blowing money, from *jai-alai* to dark, dingy strip joints, from mega-curio shops to Las Vegas-style hotels. It's hard to say whether it's the city's strange charm, its cheap booze, or its sprawling, unapologetic hedonism that attracts 30 million tourists every year.

CROSSING THE BORDER Travelers from San Diego to Tijuana can take the red **Mexicoach** bus (85 14 70, in U.S. 619-428-9517) from its terminal at the border (runs every 30min. 9am-9pm, US$1). Alternatively, a **trolley** rolls to San Ysidro, at Kettner and Broadway in downtown San Diego (US$1.75), and people walk across the border. Transfers from airport buses are also available. **Driving** across the border is fairly hassle-free, although traffic is bad, especially on weekends. A quick wave of the hand will usually notify you that you are no longer in the U.S. However, driving in Tijuana can be harrowing; if you're only in Tijuana for a day, you may want to leave your car in a lot on the U.S. side and join the throngs walking across the border. Bring proper ID to re-enter the U.S. (a passport ensures the speediest passage), but leave fruits, veggies, and weapons behind.

PRACTICAL INFORMATION In Tijuana, *calles* run east-west; *avenidas* run north-south. The *avenidas* in the *centro* area are (from east to west) **Mutualismo, Martínez, Niños Héroes, Constitución, Revolución** (the main tourist drag), **Madero, Negrete,** and **Ocampo.** *Calles* in the *centro* area are both named and numbered. Beginning at the north, they are **Artículo 123** (Calle 1), **Benito Juárez** (Calle 2), **Carrillo Puerto** (Calle 3), **Díaz Mirón** (Calle 4), **Zapata** (Calle 5), **Magón** (Calle 6), **Galeana** (Calle 7), **Hidalgo** (Calle 8), and **Zaragoza** (Calle 9). Reaching the **bus station** (21 29 83 or 21 29 84) from downtown means boarding the blue-and-white buses marked "Buena Vista" or "Camionera" on Niños Héroes between Calles 3 and 4 (3 pesos), or a brown-and-white communal cab on Madero between Calles 2 and 3 (4 pesos). **Greyhound** (21 29 82) runs to Los Angeles (3hr., every hr. 5am-11:30pm, US$18) and other locations. **Cabs** are all over town. The friendly, English-speaking staff at the **Tourist Office,** Revolución 711 (88 05 55), at Calle 1, doles out maps and advice (open M-Sa 9am-7pm, Su 10am-5pm). A less crowded booth on Revolución between Calles 3 and 4 has maps. The **Customs Office** (83 13 90) sits at the border on the Mexican side after crossing the San Ysidro bridge (open M-F 8am-3pm). Banks along Constitución such as Banamex (88 00 21 or 88 00 22), at Calle 4, offer **currency exchange** at the same rate (Banamex open for exchange M-F 9am-5pm, 24hr. **ATM**). In August 1998, the **exchange rate** was US$1 for 9.65 pesos. In an **emergency,** dial 134 or 060. **Red Cross:** (21 77 87, emergency 132), Calle Alfonso Gamboa at E. Silvestre, across from the Price Club. **Post Office:** (84 79 50), on Negrete at Calle 11. Open M-F 8am-7pm, Sa-Su 9am-1pm. **Postal code:** 22001. **Phone code:** 66.

ACCOMMODATIONS AND FOOD Plenty of budget hotels grace Calle 1 between Revolución and Mutualismo, although they tend toward the cockroachy side. Come nightfall, it becomes something of a red-light district, especially between Revolución and Constitución. *Women should be extra cautious.* **Hotel El Jaliscense,** Calle 1 #7925 (85 34 91), between Niños Héroes and Martínez, is a great deal, offering clean, small rooms with high, resilient beds, private baths, fans, and phones. (Singles and doubles 100 pesos; 20 pesos per additional person.) The bizarrely decorated **Hotel Perla de Occidente,** Mutualismo 758 (85 13 58), between Calles 1 and 2, sits 4 blocks from the bedlam of Revolución. Enjoy fans on request, soft beds, and roomy bathrooms. (Singles 100 pesos; doubles 180 pesos.)

CALIFORNIA

Tijuana's touristy eats are essentially Tex-Mex, but some cheap, authentic Mexican restaurants line Constitución and the streets leading from Revolución to Constitución. To save money, pay in pesos, even if the menu quotes prices in dollars. Patrons can enjoy great food and orange decor at friendly **El Pipirín Antojitos,** Constitución 878 (88 16 02), between Calles 2 and 3 (chicken burritos with rice and beans 20 pesos; open daily 7am-9pm). At **Los Panchos Taco Shop** (85 72 77), Revolución at Calle 3, the booths are packed with hungry locals munching on ultra-fresh tortillas. (Steak taco US$1, bean burritos US$2. Open in summer daily 8am-4am; off-season Su-Th 8am-midnight, F-Sa 8am-2am.)

SIGHTS AND SPORTS In the 1920s, when prohibition hit the U.S., many crossed the border to revel in forbidden tequila, wine, and beer. Ever since, Tijuana has been regarded as the venue for nights of debauchery. The family-owned **L.A. Cetto Winery,** Cañón Johnson 2108 (85 30 31), at Calle 10, just off Constitución, holds a harvest festival every August and offers tours throughout the year. *(Tours M-Sa every 30min. 10am-5pm. US$1, with wine-tasting US$2, with wine-tasting and souvenir goblet US$3.)*

Jai alai, reputedly the world's fastest game, is played in the majestic **Frontón Palacio** (85 78 33), Revolución at Calle 7. *(Open M-Sa 9am-11pm, Su 8am-11pm. US$20; free admission coupons often distributed outside.)* Two to four players take to the three-sided court as one, using arm-baskets to catch and throw a ball traveling 180 mph. Players are treated like horses; observers bet on their favorites and keep a close eye on the odds. All employees are bilingual, and the gambling is carried out in greenbacks.

If you're in town on the right Sunday, you can watch the savage and graceful dance of a **bullfight** in one of Tijuana's two bullrings. The more modern stadium is **Plaza Monumental,** northwest of the city near Las Playas de Tijuana (follow Calle 2 west), which hosts fights from August to mid-September. Catch a blue-and-white bus on Calle 3 between Constitución and Niños Héroes. Tickets to the rings are sold at the gate and at the **ticket window** at Mexicoac, on Revolución between Calle 6 and 7.

NIGHTLIFE If you've come to party, brace yourself for a raucous good time. Strolling down Revolución after dusk, you'll be bombarded by thumping music, neon lights, and abrasive club promoters hawking "two-for-one" margaritas (most places listed below charge US$4 for 2). All clubs check ID (18+) with varying criteria of what's acceptable, and many frisk for firearms. If you'd like to check out a more local scene, peek into the small clubs on Calle 6 off Revolución. **Iguanas-Ranas** (85 14 22), Revolución at Calle 3, is always hopping with a 20-something crowd downing beers (US$2.25) in the schoolbus or raising hell on the dance floor (open daily 10am-4am). The tiny wooden dance floor in the center of upscale and balloon-filled **Tilly's 5th Ave.** (85 90 15), Revolución and Calle 5, resembles a boxing ring, but rest assured—there's only room for dancing. (Beer US$2. W night is "Student Night"—all drinks 49¢. Open M-Th 10:30am-2am, F-Sa 10:30am-5am.) The blonde clientele at **Caves** (88 06 09), Revolución and Calle 5, drinks two beers for US$3. Prehistoric beasts perched on a rock facade lead to this dark but airy bar and disco. (No cover. Open Su-Th 11am-2am, F-Sa 11am-2am.)

THE CALIFORNIA DESERT

From mystics and misanthropes to Native Americans and modern city slickers have long been fascinated by the austere scenery and the vast open spaces of the California desert. In winter, the desert is a pleasantly warm refuge; in spring, a technicolor floral landscape; and in summer, a blistering wasteland. The desert features diverse flora and fauna, staggering topographical variation, and scattered relics of America's past.

■ Palm Springs

Even in its very first days, when Cahuillan Indians settled here for a winter respite, Palm Springs was a rambunctious resort. It was only a matter of time before this glitzy desert community elected the late Sonny Bono as its mayor. Today, the medicinal waters of the city's natural hot springs ensure the health of its opulent residents, and also its longevity as a resort. With warm temperatures, celebrity residents, and more pink than a *Miami Vice* episode, this desert city (pop. 42,000) provides a sunny break from everyday life.

Mt. San Jacinto State Park, Palm Springs's primary landmark, offers outdoor recreation opportunities for visitors of all fitness levels. If Mt. San Jacinto's 10,804 ft. escarpment seems too strenuous, try the **Palm Springs Aerial Tramway** (325-1391), on Tramway Rd. off Rte. 111. (Trams run every 30min. M-F 10am-8pm; Sa-Su 8am-8pm; closed M in winter. Round-trip $18, seniors $15, under 12 $12.) Rising nearly 6000 ft., the observation deck has great views of the Coachella Valley. The **Desert Hot Springs Spa,** 10805 Palm Dr. (329-6495), on the north side of I-10, features six naturally heated mineral pools of different temperatures, as well as saunas, massage professionals, and bodywraps (simmer daily 8am-10pm; $3-7). The remarkable **Palm Springs Desert Museum,** 101 Museum Dr. (325-0189), has a collection of Native American art, talking desert dioramas, and live animals. (Museum open Tu-Su 10am-5pm. $6, seniors $5, students $3, ages 6-17 $3; free 1st Tu of each month. Take Sun Bus #111.) The **Living Desert Reserve,** 47900 Portola Ave. (346-5694), in Palm Desert 1½ mi. south of Rte. 111, houses Arabian oryces, iguanas, desert unicorns, zebras, and a **Botanical Garden.** (Open daily Oct.-June 9am-5pm; Sept. 8am-noon. $7.50, seniors $6.50, under 12 $3.50; Sept. $6, ages 3-12 $3.) The twilight reptile exhibit is a must-see.

Four **Indian Canyons** (325-5673), 5 mi. south of the town at the end of S. Palm Canyon Dr., shelter desert animals in the world's greatest concentration of naturally occurring palm trees. (Open daily spring-summer 8am-6pm; fall-winter 8am-5pm. $5, students $3.50, seniors $2.50, children $1.) The canyons also offer the city's only naturally cool water as well as remnants of Native American communities.

Like most famous resort communities, Palm Springs caters mainly to those seeking a tax shelter, not a night's shelter—the cheapest way to stay here is to find a nearby state park or national forest campground. If you've gotta stay in town, **Motel 6** has the cheapest rates, especially during winter. Locations include 660 S. Palm Canyon Dr. (327-4200), south of city center; 595 E. Palm Canyon Dr. (325-6129); and 63950 20th Ave. (251-1425), near the I-10 off-ramp. Each has A/C rooms and pool access. (Singles $35; doubles $41; in winter $6-12 more.)

The largest of the desert towns, Palm Springs has more dining options than most desert pit stops. **Las Casuelas-The Original,** 368 N. Palm Canyon Dr. (325-3213), juxtaposes authentic Mexican dishes ($6 and up), dingy lighting, and tattooed waitresses (open daily 10am-10pm). **Carlo's Italian Delicatessen,** 119 S. Indian Canyon Dr. (325-5571), is a budget-minded deli (open W-F 10am-6pm, Sa 10am-8pm, Su 10am-5pm; closed W in winter). **The Wheel Inn,** 50900 Seminole Dr. (909-849-7012), Cabazon Exit on I-10, is the legendary joint where Pee-Wee Herman met Simone after his encounter with Large Marge (giant dinosaurs included). Cinema naifs can still nosh on daily specials ($6-7) or tasty pie ($2.50). (Open 24hr.).

Palm Springs Regional Airport, 3400 S. Tahquitz-Canyon Rd. (323-8161), offers state and limited national service. **Greyhound,** 311 N. Indian Canyon Dr. (800-231-2222 or 325-2053), runs buses to Los Angeles (9 per day; $17, round-trip $27). The local **Sun Bus** (343-3451) connects Coachella Valley cities (fare 75¢, transfers 25¢; operates daily 5am-10:30pm). The **Chamber of Commerce,** 190 W. Amado Rd. (325-1577), offers friendly advice, maps ($1), and hotel reservations (open M-F 8:30am-4:30pm). **Checker Cab** (325-2868) and **Valley Cab Company** (340-5845) offer 24hr. service. **Post Office:** 333 E. Amado Rd. (800-275-8777). **ZIP code:** 92262, general delivery 92263. **Area code:** 760.

■ Joshua Tree National Park

When the Mormon pioneers crossed this desert area in the 19th century, they named the enigmatic desert tree they encountered after the Biblical prophet Joshua. Perhaps it was the heat, but the tree's crooked limbs seemed to them an uncanny image of the Hebrew general, who with arms upraised, beckoned them to the promised land. Although in the Mojave the Mormons still hadn't found what they were looking for, its climes—slightly cooler and wetter than the harsh Arizona desert—must have made them feel at the time as though they'd arrived in God's country. Stacks of wind-sculpted boulders, Joshua trees, five oases, and spectrum of high and low desert ecologies to create a vast mosaic of landscape and vegetation. In recent years, climbers, campers, and daytrippers from Southern California have added to the mosaic. History buffs will appreciate the vestiges of human occupation—ancient rock petroglyphs, dams built in the 19th century to catch the meager rainfall for livestock, and gold mine ruins dot the landscape.

PRACTICAL INFORMATION Joshua Tree National Park covers 558,000 acres northeast of Palm Springs, about 160 mi. east of L.A. It is ringed by three highways: **I-10** to the south, **Rte. 62/Twentynine Palms Hwy.** to the west and north, and **Rte. 177** to the east. The northern entrances to the park are off Rte. 62, at the towns of **Joshua Tree** and **Twentynine Palms.** The south entrance is at **Cottonwood Spring,** off I-10. Unfortunately, this is where the streets have no name; just look for the Joshua Tree sign 25 mi. east of Indio.

   Headquarters and Oasis Visitors Center, 74485 National Park Dr. (367-5500), ¼ mi. off Rte. 62 in Twentynine Palms, is the best place to familiarize yourself with the park. You will find friendly rangers, displays, guidebooks, maps, and water. (Open daily 8am-5pm.) Understanding the vicissitudes of **weather** is essential: summer highs are 95-115°F; winter highs are 60-70°F. It's hotter in the eastern area. Be careful of flash flood warnings in winter. The **park entrance fee** is $5 per person or $10 per car (valid for 7 days). In case of an **emergency,** call 911, or 909-383-5651 collect. Nearest **post office:** 73839 Gorgonio Dr. (800-275-8777), in Twentynine Palms (open M-F 8:30am-5pm). **ZIP code:** 92277. **Area code:** 760 (recently changed from 619).

CAMPGROUNDS AND ACCOMMODATIONS Most campgrounds in the park operate on a first come, first served basis. Reservations can be made for group sites only at Cottonwood, Sheep Pass, Indian Cove, and Black Rock Canyon through **DESTINET** (800-436-7275). **Backcountry** camping is also an option. Ask at a ranger station for details. All campsites have tables, fireplaces, and pit toilets, and are **free** unless otherwise noted. Those who plan any sort of extended stay should pack their own supplies, water, and cooking utensils. Campground stays are limited to 30 days in the summer and to 14 days October through May. **Hidden Valley** (4200 ft.), in the center of the park, off Quail Springs Rd., has secluded alcoves shaded by enormous boulders. Its proximity to Wonderland of Rock and the Barker Dam Trail make this a rock climber's heaven. The 39 sites fill up quickly. **Jumbo Rocks** (4400 ft.), located near Skull Rock Trail on the eastern edge of Queen Valley, is the highest, and therefore the coolest, campground in the park. Front spots have the best shade. (65 sites; 125 in winter.) **Indian Cove** (3200 ft.), on the north edge of the Wonderland of Rocks, has dramatic waterfalls and rock climbing nearby (45 sites; 107 in winter). **Black Rock Canyon** (4000 ft.), at the end of Joshua Ln. off Rte. 62 near Yucca Valley, was the inspiration for Jellystone Park, the home of Yogi Bear. The 100 wooded sites are near flush toilets and running water (sites $10; reservations accepted). The **Twentynine Palms Inn,** 73950 Inn Dr. (367-3505), facing the Mara Oasis in Twentynine Palms, offers the indoors (June-Sept. $50-70, Sa-Su from $65; Sept.-June $5-10 more).

SIGHTS Over 80% of the park is designated wilderness area, safeguarded against development, and lacking paved roads, toilets, and campfires. Joshua Tree offers truly remote territory for backcountry hiking and camping. There's no water in the wilderness except when a flash flood comes roaring down a wash (beware your choice of campsite). The park's most temperate weather is in late fall (Oct.-Dec.) and early spring (Mar.-Apr.); temperatures in other months span uncomfortable extremes.

   A self-paced **driving tour** is an easy way to explore the park and linger to a later hour. All park roads are well-marked, and signs labeled "Exhibit Ahead" point the way to unique floral and geological formations. One sight that should not be missed is **Key's View** (5185 ft.), 6 mi. off the park road just west of Ryan campground. It's a great spot for watching the sun rise. The **Cholla Cactus Garden,** a grove of spiny succulents resembling deadly 3D asterisks, lies in the Pinto Basin just off the road. Four-wheel drive vehicles can use dirt roads, such as **Geology Tour Road,** climbing through fascinating rock formations to the Li'l San Bernardino Mountains.

Hiking through the park's trails is perhaps the best way to experience Joshua Tree. Only on foot can visitors tread through sand, scramble over boulders, and walk among the park's hardy namesakes. Although the **Barker Dam Trail,** next to Hidden Valley, is often packed with tourists, its painted petroglyphs and eerie tranquility make it a worthwhile hike. Bring plenty of water for the strenuous, unshaded climb to the summit of **Ryan Mountain** (5461 ft.), where the boulder formations bear an unsettling resemblance to herculean beasts of burden slouching toward a distant destination. The visitors center has info on the park's many other hikes, which range from the 15min. stroll to the **Oasis of Mara** to a 3-day trek along the **California Riding and Hiking Trail** (35 mi.). Joshua Tree teems with flora and fauna that you're unlikely to see anywhere else in the world. Larger plants like Joshua trees, cholla, and the spidery ocotillo have adapted to the severe climate in fascinating ways, and the **wildflowers** that dot the desert terrain each spring (mid-Mar. to mid-May) attract thousands of visitors.

Energetic visitors are often drawn to Joshua Tree for its **rock climbing:** the world-renowned boulders at **Wonderland of Rocks** and **Hidden Valley** are especially challenging and attract thousands of climbers each year. The visitors center provides info on established rope routes and on wilderness areas where the placement of new bolts is restricted. **Joshua Tree Rock Climbing** (800-890-4745), Box 29, Joshua Tree, provides instruction and equipment rental.

■ Death Valley

Satan owns a lot of real estate in **Death Valley National Park.** Not only does he grow crops (at the Devil's Cornfield) and hit the links (at the Devil's Golf Course), but the park is also home to Hell's Gate itself. Not surprisingly, the area's astonishing variety of topographical and climactic extremes can support just about anyone's idea of the Inferno. Winter temps dip well below freezing, and summer readings rival even the hottest Hades. The second-highest temperature ever recorded on Earth (134°F in the shade) was measured at the valley's Furnace Creek Ranch on July 10, 1913. Few venture to the valley floor during the summer, and it is foolish to do so; the average high in July is 116°F, with a nighttime low of 88°F. Ground temperatures hover near an egg-frying 200°F. A visit in winter lets visitors enjoy the splendor in comfort.

GETTING AROUND There is no regularly scheduled public transportation into Death Valley. A few bus tours run out of Las Vegas: **Guaranteed Tours** offers excursions on Tuesdays, Thursdays, and Saturdays for $109; tours leave at 8am, return at 5:30pm, and include continental breakfast and lunch. (Depot at the Country Star Restaurant at the corner of Harmon Ave. and the Strip in Vegas.)

The best way to get around Death Valley is by car. Of the nine **park entrances,** most visitors choose Rte. 190 from the east. The road is well-maintained, the pass is less steep, and you arrive more quickly at the visitors center. But the visitor with a trusty vehicle will be able to see more of the park by entering from the southeast (Rte. 178 west from Rte. 127 at Shoshone) or the north (direct to Scotty's Castle via NV Rte. 267 from U.S. 95). Unskilled mountain drivers should not attempt to enter via Titus Canyon or Emigrant Canyon Drive roads; neither has guard rails to prevent your car from sliding over **precipitous cliffs.** If you **hitchhike,** you walk through the Valley of the Shadow of Death. Don't.

PRACTICAL INFORMATION For visitor information, head on over to the **Furnace Creek Visitors Center** (786-3244), on Rte. 190 in the east-central section of the valley (open daily in summer 7:30am-5pm; in winter 7:20am-7pm); or write the **Superintendent,** Death Valley National Park, Death Valley 92328. **Ranger Stations** are located at **Grapevine** (786-2313), at the junction of Rte. 190 and 267 near Scotty's Castle; **Stovepipe Wells** (786-2342), on Rte. 190; and **Shoshone** (832-4308), outside the southeast border of the valley at the junction of Rte. 178 and 127. The weather report, weekly naturalist programs, and park info are posted at each station. (Open daily 8am-5pm.) The $5 per vehicle **entrance fee** is collected only at the visitors center in the middle of the park.

Get gas outside Death Valley at Olancha, Shoshone, or Beatty, NV. **Radiator water** (*not* for drinking) is available at critical points on Rte. 178 and 190 and NV Rte. 374, but not on unpaved roads. Signs saying "4-Wheel-Drive Only." Those who *do* drive along the backcountry trails should carry chains, extra tires, gas, oil, radiator and drinking water, and spare parts. Groceries and supplies can be purchased at **Furnace Creek Ranch Store** (786-2381), which is well-stocked but expensive (open daily 7am-9pm). **Post Office:** Furnace Creek Ranch (786-2223). **ZIP code:** 92328. **Area code:** 760.

ACCOMMODATIONS AND CAMPGROUNDS In Death Valley, enclosed beds and fine meals within a budget traveler's reach are as elusive as the desert bighorn sheep. During the winter months, camping out with a stock of groceries is a good way to save both money and driving time. **Furnace Creek Ranch Complex** (786-2345, reservations 800-236-7916), is deluged with tour-bus refugees who challenge the adjacent 18-hole golf course and relax in the 85°F spring-fed swimming pool (cabins with A/C and 2 beds $90; motel-style rooms $115). **Stovepipe Wells Village** (786-2387) is right in Death Valley ($58 per night for 1-2 people; each additional person $11). RV sites are also available ($15).

The National Park Service maintains nine **campgrounds,** but only Texas Springs and Furnace Creek accept reservations. Call ahead to check availability and be prepared to battle for a space if you come during peak periods. Water availability is not completely reliable and supplies can be unsafe at times; always pack your own. Roadside camping is not permitted, but **backcountry camping** is free and legal, provided you check in at the visitors center and pitch tents at least 1 mi. from main roads, 5 mi. from any established campsite, and ¼ mi. from any water source.

SIGHTS Death Valley has hiking to bemuse the gentlest wanderer and challenge the hardiest peregrinator. Backpackers and day hikers should inform the **visitors center** of their trip and take along the appropriate topographical maps. The National Park Service recommends that valley-floor hikers plan a route along roads where assistance is readily available and outfit a party of at least 2 people.

Ten miles south of the visitors center on Rte. 178, **Artist's Drive** is a one-way loop that twists its way through rock formations of colors akin to those found in Crayola sets. About 5 mi. south is **Devil's Golf Course,** a plane of sharp salt pinnacles made of the precipitate from the evaporation of Lake Manly, the 90 mi. long lake that once filled the lower valley. Three miles south of Devil's Golf Course, on I-90, lies **Badwater,** an aptly named briny pool four times saltier than the ocean. The surrounding salt flat dips to the lowest point in the Western Hemisphere—282 ft. below sea level.

Immortalized by Antonioni's film of the same name, **Zabriskie Point** is a marvelous place from which to view Death Valley's corrugated badlands. Perhaps the most spectacular sight in the park is the vista at **Dante's View,** reached by a 13 mi. paved road from Rte. 190. Just as the Italian poet stood with Virgil looking down on the damned, so the modern observer gazes upon the vast inferno that is Death Valley.

THE CENTRAL COAST

The 400 mi. stretch of coastline between Los Angeles and San Francisco embodies all that is purely Californian—rolling surf crashing onto secluded beaches, dramatic cliffs and mountains, self-actualizing New Age adherents, and always a hint of the off-beat. *The* quintessential Californian road, the **Pacific Coast Hwy.** (known by Angelenos as **PCH,** by Californians as **Hwy. I,** and by maps as **Rte. I**), loops along the coast.

■ Santa Barbara

Santa Barbara is an enclave of wealth and privilege, true to its soap opera image, but in a significantly less aggressive way than its Southern Californian counterparts. Spanish Revival architecture decorates the residential hills that rise gently over a lively pedestrian district centered on State St. This sanitized, palm-lined promenade is filled with inexpensive cafes and thrift stores as well as glamorous boutiques and galleries—enough to engage the casual visitor for an entire day. Santa Barbara's golden beaches, museums, historic mission, and scenic drive add to what makes this a frequent weekend escape for the rich and famous and an attractive destination for surfers, artists, and hippies alike.

PRACTICAL INFORMATION Catch a plane at **Signature Flight Support,** 500 Fowler Rd. (967-5608), Goleta, offering intrastate as well as limited national service, including American and United. Catch a train at **Amtrak,** 209 State St. (963-1015, schedule and fares 800-872-7245), to Los Angeles ($16-21) and San Francisco ($46-73). **Greyhound,** 34 W. Carrillo St. (962-2477), at Chapala, buses to Los Angeles ($14) and San Francisco ($30). (Open M-Sa 5:30am-8pm and 11pm-midnight, Su 7am-8pm and 11pm-midnight.) **Santa Barbara Metropolitan Transit District (MTD),** 1029 Chapala St. (683-3702), at Cabrillo, behind Greyhound station, runs buses. (Open M-F 6am-7pm, Sa 8am-6pm, Su 9am-6pm. Wheelchair accessible. Fare $1, seniors and disabled 50¢, under 5 free; transfers free.) The MTD runs a **downtown-waterfront shuttle** along State St. and Cabrillo Blvd. every 10min. (fare 25¢). Bikes are for rent at **Cycles-4-Rent,** 101 State St. (966-3804), 1 block from the beach (one-speed beach cruiser $5 per hr., $21 per day; 21-speed $7, $28). The **Tourist Office,** 1 Santa Barbara St. (965-3021), answers queries at Cabrillo near the beach (open M-Sa 9am-5pm, Su 10am-6pm; closes Dec.-Jan. at 4pm, July-Aug. at 6pm). **Post Office:** 836 Anacapa St. (564-2266), 1 block east of State. Open M-F 8am-5:30pm, Sa 10am-5pm. **ZIP code:** 93102. **Area code:** 805.

ACCOMMODATIONS, CAMPGROUNDS, AND FOOD Cheaper lodgings than those in Santa Barbara proper are a 10min. drive away, north or south on U.S. 101. **Hotel State Street,** 121 State St. (966-6586), 1 block from the beach, is full of European clientele. Private rooms have sinks, skylights, cable TV. (1 double bed $40; 2 single beds $45; 2 double beds $55; in summer $15-25 higher. Breakfast included. Reservations recommended with credit card. Limited free parking.) **Traveler's Motel,** 3222 State St. (687-6009), offers clean rooms with cable TV, direct-dial phones, A/C, and fridges. (Singles $50, off-season $35; rooms with kitchenettes $55; $5 per additional person up to 4; prices higher Sa-Su.) Take bus #6 or 11 from downtown.

State campsites can be reserved through **DESTINET** (800-444-7275), up to 7 months in advance. **Carpinteria Beach State Park** (684-2811), 12 mi. southeast of Santa Barbara along U.S. 101, has 261 developed tent sites with hot showers (sites $17, with hookup $22-28; Sa-Su $18/$23-29; off-season $15/$20-26).

State and Milpas St. both have many places to eat; State is hipper, Milpas cheaper. **The Natural Café,** 508 State St. (962-9494), forces healthy, attractive clientele to eat healthy, attractive food. (Smoothies $2.50, sandwiches $3.50-5. Open daily 11am-11pm.) **Castagnola's,** 205 Santa Barbara St. (962-8053), has the cheapest fresh seafood in town. Shrimp cocktail is $4, fish and chips $6. (Open W-Th 11am-8pm, F-Sa 11am-9pm, Su 11am-6pm.) **Café Orleans** (899-9111), Center Court, Paseo Nuevo Mall, at the 800 block of State St., dishes out Naw'lins soul food in a jiffy. (Jambalaya, etouffeés, and po' boys with 2 muffins and 2 side orders $4.75-6.50. Live zydeco F 6-8:30pm. Open M-Th 11am-9pm, F-Sa 11am-10pm, Su 11am-8pm.) The burgers at the yellow formica joint of **R.G.'s Giant Hamburgers,** 922 State St. (963-1654), were voted the best in Santa Barbara 7 years running. Call 10min. ahead, and your meal will be waiting when you arrive. (Open M-Sa 9am-10pm, Su 10am-10pm.)

SIGHTS State St. is Santa Barbara's monument to city planning. The elevator to the **observation deck** of the **Santa Barbara County Courthouse,** 1100 Anacapa St. (962-6464), gives the full impact of the city's ubiquitous red tile motif and a killer view of the ocean. The courthouse is one of the West's great public buildings, with a sculpted fountain, sunken gardens, historic murals, wrought-iron chandeliers, and hand-painted vaulted Gothic ceilings. The Chamber of Commerce inside the courthouse distributes copies of *Santa Barbara's Red Tile Tour.*

Mission Santa Barbara (682-4719), is on the northern side of town, at the end of Las Olivas St. (take bus #22). Praised as the "Queen of Missions" when built in 1786, the mis-

CALIFORNIA

sion assumed its present incarnation in 1820 (open daily 9am-5pm; $3). Two blocks north of the mission is the **Museum of Natural History,** 2559 Puesta del Sol Rd. (682-4711, observatory 682-3224). This museum includes a collection of original lithographs by Audubon and other naturalists, the largest collection of Chumash artifacts in the West, an extensive archive on the Channel Islands, and a **planetarium.** *(Museum open M-Sa 9am-5pm, Su and holidays 10am-5pm. $5, seniors and 13-17 $4, under 13 $3. Planetarium shows Sa-Su 1 and 3pm, W 2:30pm; $1 plus admission.)*

The **Santa Barbara Botanical Garden,** 1212 Mission Canyon Rd. (682-4726), is not served by bus and is a trek without a car. Five miles of hiking trails wind through 65 acres of native Californian trees, wildflowers, and cacti. The **Santa Barbara Museum of Art,** 1130 State St. (963-4364), owns an impressive collection of classical Greek, Asian, and European works spanning 3000 years. *(Tours Tu-Su 1pm. Open Tu-W and F-Sa 11am-5pm, Th 11am-9pm, Su noon-5pm. $4, students and ages 6-16 $1.50, seniors $3. Free every Th and 1st Su of each month.)*

The beach west of State St. is called **West Beach;** to the east, **East Beach.** The beach at **Summerland,** east of Montecito (bus #20), is frequented by the **gay** and **hippie** communities. **Rincon Beach,** 3 mi. southeast of Carpinteria, has the best surfing in the county. **Gaviota State Beach,** 29 mi. west of Santa Barbara, offers good surf, and the western end is a (sometimes) **clothing-optional** beach.

ENTERTAINMENT AND NIGHTLIFE Every night of the week, the clubs on **State St.** are packed. Consult the *Independent* to see who's playing on a given night. Bars on State charge $4 for beer fairly uniformly, so search for a special. **Dragon House,** 434 State St. (962-5516), is a decadent faux-dive for the jet set, with Sinatra, mambo, and Afro-Cuban music. (Live music and drink specials nightly 5-8pm. 21+. No cover. Open daily 5pm-2am.) **Fathom,** 423 State St. (882-6022), is a gay dance club (all are welcome) and the closest it gets to a rave in Santa Barbara. (Tu is swing night. Martini happy hour 4-8pm, well drinks $2. 21+. Cover Th-Su $5. Open nightly 4pm-2am.) **Yucatan,** 1117 State St. (564-1889), a.k.a "The Partyin' Cantina," is every frat boy's dream come true. The upstairs "Billiards Club" has nine pool tables ($5 per hr.) and foosball. (Happy hour M-F 3-7pm, drafts $1.50. 21+, Su and W 18+. Cover $3-5. Open daily 11am-1:30am.) Sushi ($3.50-8.50) guarantees a good date at **Q's Sushi A-Go-Go,** 409 State St. (966-9177). Happy hour (4-7pm) means 20% off sushi plates. (Open M-W 4pm-2am, Th-Su 11:30am-2am.) At **Earthling Bookshop & Café,** 1137 State St. (965-0926, cafe 564-6096), browse shelves full of new and used books, and settle down for a long read around a central fireplace. (Cappuccino, juice, and pastry $4; soup and salad $4.25. Open Su-Th 9am-11pm, F-Sa 9am-midnight; cafe open M-F 7:30am.)

■ San Luis Obispo

At the junction of rolling hills and raging surf, San Luis Obispo grew into a full-fledged town only in 1894, after the Southern Pacific Railroad was built. Ranchers and oil-refinery employees make up a significant percentage of today's population, but Cal Poly State University students carve out a young, energetic niche. Those desperately seeking the soothing balm of small-town life can happily cool their heels in this affable burg—its acronym isn't SLO for nothing.

Asked for their room rates, proprietors in San Luis Obispo frequently respond, "That depends"—on the weather, the season, the number of travelers that day, or even on the position of the moon. **San Luis Obispo (HI-AYH),** 1617 Santa Rosa St. (544-4678), just a block from the Amtrak station, basks in a cozy atmosphere and serves fresh toast and bagels. (Dorms $14, private rooms $32; nonmembers $16/$34. Linen $1, towels 50¢. Reception 7:30-9:30am and 5-10pm. Parking available.) **Sunbeam Hotel,** 1656 Monterey St. (543-8141), looks like an apartment complex with rooms as sunny as the staff (singles $30-32; doubles $38-45; prices jump in summer). **Pismo Beach State Park** (489-2684), on Hwy. 1 south of Pismo Beach, has 143 sites ($16-20) in two campgrounds. Call **DESTINET** (800-444-7275) for reservations.

When you need an SLO meal, head for Higuera and streets intersecting it. **Big Sky Café,** 1121 Broad St. (545-5401), has lofty ceilings, an earthy atmosphere, choice wines, and savory food (sandwiches $5-7; open M-Sa 7am-10pm, Su 8am-8pm). **Woodstock's Pizza Parlour,** 1000 Higuera St. (541-4420), consistently sweeps annual best pizza awards. A young crowd keeps it lively into the night. Three sizes of pizza sell for $4.20, $8, and $11. (Open Su-Th 11am-1am, F-Sa 11am-2am.) **Paradiso,** 690 Higuera St. (544-5282), offers homemade organic pastas and raviolis ($5-7) with lots of vegetarian sauce (open daily 11am-9pm). Half of SLO's population is under the age of 24; this town can't help but party. It gets particularly wild after the Thursday night farmers market, along Higuera St. between Nipomo and Osos. For info about other local happenings, consult the free weekly *New Times.*

There are few sights in SLO itself, but a wealth of natural beauty surrounds it on all sides. The gorgeous **Mission San Luis Obispo de Tolosa** (543-6850) still serves as the parish church (open daily 9am-5pm; in winter 9am-4pm; $1 donation requested). **Morro Bay,** just north of town, is home to the **Seven Sisters,** a rocky chain of volcanic gnomes. Whales, seals, and otters frequent the relatively quiet **Montana de Oro State Park** (528-0513), 20min. west of SLO on Los Osos Valley Rd. **Pirate's Cove** and **Shell Beach** are two adjoining beaches south of SLO near Avila. Take U.S. 101 south of SLO, exit at the Avila Rd. off-ramp, head west 2 mi., and turn left on Cave Landing Dr. just before the oil tanks. These beaches are more secluded than **Avila** and **Pismo.**

The town offers brochures and maps at the **Chamber of Commerce,** 1039 Chorro St. (781-2777; open M-W 8am-5pm, Th-F 8am-8pm, Sa 10am-8pm). **State Parks Information** is at 3220 S. Higuera St., #311 (549-3312; open M-F 8am-5pm). **Amtrak** chugs into town at 1011 Railroad Ave. (541-0505 or 800-872-7245) and goes to Los Angeles or San Francisco ($33.50). **Greyhound,** 150 South St. (543-2121), shuttles to Los Angeles ($32) and San Francisco ($39). **Post Office:** 893 Marsh St. (543-3062). **ZIP code:** 93405. **Area code:** 805.

■ Near San Luis Obispo: Hearst Castle

Hearst San Simeon Historic Monument (927-2010) is located 3 mi. north of San Simeon and about 9 mi. north of Cambria. Casually referred to by founder and funder William Randolph Hearst as "the ranch," it is an indescribable conglomeration of castle, cottages, pools, gardens, and Mediterranean *esprit* perched high above the Pacific. It bears testimony to Hearst's unfathomable wealth and enthusiasm for art, as well as to the architectural genius of Julia Morgan, California's first female architect. Tours are run by the State Parks Dept. (staff in anachronistic ranger garb roam around the estate) and are a strictly hands-off experience. Tour One—recommended for first-time visitors—covers the gardens, pools, and main rooms of the house. Other tours cover smaller areas in more detail. The four daytime tours cost $14 each (ages 6-12 $8), and last about 1¾hr. Call **PARKNET** (800-444-4445) for reservations. The visitors center at the base of the hill features a surprisingly frank portrait of Hearst's failed Harvard days, yellow journalism, and scandalous life.

■ Big Sur

Host to expensive campsites and even more expensive restaurants, Big Sur holds big appeal for big crowds eager to experience the power of the redwoods, the sound of the surf, and the rhythm of the river. First-time tourists identify themselves by asking "Where is Big Sur?" Rangers identify the river area; regulars just chuckle.

Big Sur's state parks and **Los Padres National Forest** beckon outdoor activists of all types. Trails penetrate redwood forests and cross low chaparral, offering grander views of Big Sur than those available from Hwy. 1. **Pfeiffer Big Sur State Park** contains 8 trails of varying lengths (50¢ map available at park entrance). The **Valley View Trail** is a short, steep path overlooking the valley below. **Buzzard's Roost Trail** is a rugged 2hr. hike up tortuous switchbacks, but at its terminus are rewarding panoramic views of the Santa Lucia Mountains, the Big Sur Valley, and the Pacific Ocean.

Roughly in the middle of the Big Sur coast lies the pfantastic park with a pfunny name, the **Julia Pfeiffer Burns State Park** (entrance fee $6), where picnickers find refuge in redwood forests and sea otters in McWay Cove. Big Sur's most jealously guarded treasure is **Pfeiffer Beach,** 1 mi. south of Pfeiffer Burns. Turn off Hwy. 1 at the stop sign and the "Narrow Road Not Suitable For Trailers" sign, then follow the road 2 mi. to the parking area, where a path leads to the beach. An offshore rock formation protects sea caves and sea gulls from the pounding ocean waves.

Camping in Big Sur is heavenly. If you neglect to bring equipment, you've made a big mistake. Even if you did, be warned—site prices and availability reflect high demand. Reserve in advance by calling 800-444-7275. **Andrew Molera State Park** (667-2315), 5 mi. north of Pfeiffer Big Sur, is a hike-in, tent-only campground near a beach (sites $3; 3-night max. stay). **Kirk Creek** and **Plaskett Creek** (385-5434) are within walking distance of a beach. Kirk (32 sites) sits 9 mi. south of the Big Creek Bridge; Plaskett (43 sites) is 5½ mi. farther, near Jade Cove (sites $16; hike-ins and bike-ins $5 per person).

Grocery stores are located at Big Sur Lodge (in Pfeiffer Big Sur State Park), Pacific Valley, and Gorda, and some packaged food is sold in Lucia and at Ragged Point, but it's better to arrive prepared; prices are high. The **Village Pub** (667-2355), in the Village Shops, serves fresh, hearty food to raucous locals. (2 slices of freshly topped pizza $4; sandwiches $5-6. Open daily 11am-10pm; food served until 9:30pm.) **Center Deli** (667-2225), beside the post office, 1 mi. south of Big Sur Station, offers the most reasonably priced goods in the area. Sandwiches ($4-5) include veggie options such as avocado. (Open daily 8am-8:30pm; in winter 8am-7:30pm.)

"Big Sur" signifies a coastal region bordered on the south by San Simeon and on the north by Carmel. For visitor info, the **Big Sur Station** (667-2315), ½ mi. south of Pfieffer Big Sur entrance on Hwy. 1, can help. This multi-agency station includes the **State Park Office,** the **U.S. Forest Service Office,** and the **CalTrans Office,** provides permits and maps, and sponsors ranger-led hikes and campfires (open daily 8am-6pm). **Post Office:** (800-275-8777), on Hwy. 1, next to the Center Deli in Big Sur Center. **ZIP code:** 93920. **Area code:** 408.

■ Monterey

In the 1940s, Monterey's wharfside flourished as the world of sardine fishing and packaging immortalized by John Steinbeck. Before long, the sardines petered out, and Monterey started fishing in the pockets of wealthy tourists. Today, only a few forced traces of the Monterey described in Steinbeck's *Cannery Row* remain—murals and souvenir shops do their best to capitalize on a colorful history, yet are unable to preserve an authenticity under the allure of expensive boutiques and cafes. However, scattered public buildings, adobe houses, and a resilient, if more responsible, fishing community nevertheless revere bygone days. The tension between the intensity of the past and the spectacle of the present results in a restrained beauty well worth the journey to Monterey.

The biggest of Monterey's attractions is the **Monterey Bay Aquarium,** 886 Cannery Row (648-4888), which feeds on the committed community interest in marine ecology. Gaze through the world's largest window at an enormous marine habitat containing green sea turtles, 7 ft. ocean sunfish, large sharks, and the oozingly graceful Portuguese Man-o-War. Eager tourists scuttle for a glance at **sea otters** at feeding time, a living kelp forest housed in a 2-story-tall glass case, and a petting zoo of damp bay denizens (ever think you'd pet a stingray?). Pick up tickets the day before and save 20-40min. in line. (Open daily 10am-6pm; mid-June to early Sept. 9:30am-6pm. $13.75; seniors, ages 13-17, and students $11.75; ages 3-12 $6.)

Cannery Row lies along the waterfront south of the aquarium. Once a depressed street of languishing sardine packing plants, this ¾ mi. row has been converted into glitzy mini-malls, bars, and a pint-sized carnival complex. All that remains of the earthiness and gruff camaraderie celebrated by John Steinbeck in *Cannery Row* and *Sweet Thursday* are a few building facades: 835 Cannery Row was the Wing Chong Market, the bright yellow building next door is where *Sweet Thursday* took place, and Doc

Rickett's lab at 800 Cannery Row is now owned by a private men's club. For a series of interpretive looks at Steinbeck's Cannery Row, take a peek at the **Great Cannery Row Mural,** within which local artists have covered 400 ft. of construction-site barrier on the 700 block with depictions of Monterey in the 30s. The lavish **Wine and Produce Visitors Center,** 700 Cannery Row (888-646-5446), gives a taste of Monterey in the 90s— the county has a burgeoning wine industry (6 taste-tests for $3; open daily 11am-6pm).

17-Mile Drive meanders along the coast from Pacific Grove through **Pebble Beach** and the forests around Carmel. The Drive is rolling, looping, and often spectacular, though sometimes plagued by heavy tourist traffic and an outrageous $7.50 entrance fee. Bicyclists and pedestrians are allowed in at no cost. One point of interest along the drive is the **Lone Cypress,** an old, gnarled tree growing on a rock promontory, valiantly resisting the onslaught of determined, jostling photographers.

Prices for lodging often vary by day, month, and proximity to seasonal events. Reasonably priced hotels are found on **Lighthouse Ave.** in Pacific Grove (bus #2 and some #1 buses) and in the 2000 block of **Fremont St.** in Monterey (bus #9 or 10). **Del Monte Beach Inn,** 1110 Del Monte Blvd. (649-4410), is near downtown across from the beach. This Victorian-style inn offers pleasant rooms (shared bath) and treats its guests to a free hearty breakfast in a sunny room. (TV room, hall phone only. $55-80.) To get to **Veterans Memorial Park Campground** (646-3865), on Via Del Ray, 1½ mi. from downtown (bus #3), take Skyline Dr. off Rte. 68; from downtown, head south on Pacific, right on Jefferson, and follow the signs. It's perched on a hill with a view of the bay. Forty sites have hot showers (sites $15). Although seafood is bountiful, it is often expensive, making an early bird special worthwhile (4-6:30pm or so). Head to **Fisherman's Wharf** for smoked salmon sandwiches ($6) and free samples of chowder. **Thai Bistro II,** 159 Central Ave. (372-8700), Pacific Grove, despite good service and a patio ringed with flowers, still manages to have budget offerings. Lunch combos with delicious soup are $6. (Open daily 11:30am-10pm.)

Monterey-Salinas Transit (MST), 1 Ryan Ranch Rd. (899-2555), serves the region (fare $1.50, seniors and ages 5-18 75¢). The free *Rider's Guide* to MST service contains complete schedules and route info. **Visitor info** is available at 380 Alvarado St. (649-1770; open M-F 8:30am-5pm). **Post Office:** 565 Hartnell St. (372-5803; open M-F 8:45am-5:10pm). **ZIP code:** 93940. **Area code:** 831.

■ Near Monterey: Salinas and Pinnacles

The town of Salinas, 2hr. south of San Francisco and 25 mi. inland, salivates over Steinbeck, Nobel laureate and Pulitzer Prize winner. The massive **National Steinbeck Center,** 1 Main St. (408-796-3833), opened in June 1998, bringing 37,000 sq. ft. of mice to pet (gently!), plants to smell, and stories to hear, all evocative of Steinbeck's inspiration: the Salinas Valley (open daily 10am-5pm).

If the lush farmland of the Salinas Valley is the leafy and delicious salad bowl of the nation, the **Pinnacles National Monument** is the cherry tomato. Towering dramatically over the chaparral east of Soledad, the monument contains the spectacular remnants of an ancient volcano. The **High Peaks Trail** runs a strenuous 5¼ mi. across the park and offers amazing views of the surrounding rock formations. For a less exhausting trek, try the **Balconies Trail,** a 1½ mi. promenade from the park's west entrance up to the Balconies Caves. Pinnacles has the widest range of wildlife of any park in California, including a number of rare predators: mountain lions, bobcats, coyotes, rattlesnakes, golden eagles, and peregrine falcons. The park entrance fee is $5. Near the monument is a **campground** (408-389-4462) with a pool, flush toilets, and hot showers ($7 per person). The **park headquarters** (408-389-4485) is at the east side entrance (Rte. 25 to Rte. 146).

■ Santa Cruz

Santa Cruz flourishes amidst a curious mixture of beach tourist traps, rebellious surfers, and carefree students. Born as one of Father Serra's missions in 1791 (the name means "holy cross"), Santa Cruz is nothing today if not liberal. One of the few places where the

CALIFORNIA

old 60s catch-phrase "do your own thing" still applies, it simultaneously embraces macho surfers, a large lesbian, gay, and bisexual community, and shaggy rock star Neil Young who lives somewhere in the hills surrounding the town.

PRACTICAL INFORMATION

Santa Cruz is about 2hr. south of San Francisco on the north lip of Monterey Bay. Take I-28 to I-85 W, then head west on Rte. 17 over the mountains. For a more scenic trip, take **U.S. 101** or **Hwy. 1** from San Francisco. The Santa Cruz beach and its boardwalk run east-west, with Monterey Bay to the south.

Buses: Greyhound, 425 Front St. (423-1800 or 800-231-2222). 5 buses per day to San Francisco ($14-15), and 8 to Los Angeles ($36-38). Open daily 8:30-11:30am, 1:30-9:30pm, and during late bus arrivals/departures.

Public Transportation: Santa Cruz Metropolitan Transit District (SCMTD), 920 Pacific Ave. (425-8600, TDD 425-8993), at the Metro Center in the middle of the Pacific Garden Mall. The free *Headways* has route info. Fare $1, seniors and disabled 40¢, under 46 in. free; day pass $3/$1.10/free. Info line open M-F 8am-5pm. Buses run daily 7am-10pm.

Taxis: Yellow Cab (423-1234). Base fare $2.25, $2 each additional mi. Runs 24hr.

Bike Rental: The Bicycle Rental Center, 131 Center St. (426-8687). Rents 21-speed mountain/road hybrids, tandems, children's bikes. Bikes $7 for 1st hr., $2 each additional 30min.; $25 per day; $5 overnight. Helmets and locks provided. Open daily 10am-6pm; in winter 10am-5pm.

Visitor Info: Santa Cruz County Conference and Visitor Council, 701 Front St. (425-1234 or 800-833-3494; http://www.scccvc.org). Extremely helpful staff. Publishes the free Santa Cruz County Traveler's Guide with helpful restaurant information. Open M-Sa 9am-5pm, Su 10am-4pm. An unstaffed **info kiosk** sits at the top of Rte. 17 next to the Summit Inn Restaurant. Open daily 10am-4pm.

Post Office: 850 Front St. (426-5200). **ZIP code:** 95060. **Area code:** 831.

ACCOMMODATIONS

Santa Cruz gets packed solid during the summer, especially on weekends. Reservations are always recommended. Price fluctuation can be outrageous. Sleeping on the beach is strictly forbidden and can result in hefty fines.

Carmelita Cottage Santa Cruz Hostel (HI-AYH), 321 Main St. (423-8304), 4 blocks from the Greyhound stop and 2 blocks from the beach. Centrally located but in a quiet neighborhood, this 32-bed Victorian hostel is run by a young, hip staff. Sporadic summer barbecues ($4). 2 kitchens, common room, cyclery for bike storage and repair; parking available. Dorms $13-15. In July-Aug., 3-night max. stay and members only (memberships available for purchase). Strict curfew 11pm. Reception daily 8-10am and 5-10pm. Chore required. Call or send reservation requests, 1st night's deposit, and SASE to P.O. Box 1241, Santa Cruz 95061, at least 2 weeks in advance.

Harbor Inn, 645 7th Ave. (479-1067), near the harbor and a few blocks north of Eaton. A beautiful 22-bed hotel well off the main drag. Rooms have queen beds, microwaves, and fridges. Rooms $65, F-Sa $75; in summer $85/$95. Check-in until 11pm; call for late check-in. Check-out 11am. Reservations recommended.

Sunny Cove Beach Motel, 2-1610 E. Cliff Dr. (475-1741), near Schwan Lagoon. Far from downtown, but charming, well-kept suites have kitchens. Rooms $40, F-Sa $70-80; in summer $50-100. Weekly rates available.

Reservations for all state campgrounds can be made through **DESTINET** (800-444-7275) and should be made early (June-Sept. Su-Th $17, F-Sa $18; Oct.-May $16). To get to **Manresa Uplands State Beach Park** (761-1795), 10 mi. south of Santa Cruz, take Hwy. 1 and exit at San Andreas Rd. Veer right and follow San Andreas for 4 mi., then turn right on Sand Dollar. The 64 tent sites are walk-in only; several overlook the ocean. **New Brighton State Beach** (464-6329), 4 mi. south of Santa Cruz off Hwy. 1, has 112 sites on a coastal bluff. Take SCMDT bus #54 "Aptos." (4 bike sites, 2 wheelchair-accessible sites. RV sites available. 7-night max. stay, off-season 15-night max. stay. No hookups. Reservations required mid-Mar. to Nov.)

FOOD

Budget eateries cluster by the beach at **Capitola.** Fresh produce sells at the **farmer's market** at Cedar and Lincoln in downtown (W 2:30-6:30pm).

⊛Zoccoli's, the Italian Delicatessen, 1534 Pacific (423-1711), across from the post office. This mobbed madhouse of a deli churns out incredible "special sandwiches" ($4-5). Daily pasta specials (about $5) come with salad, garlic bread, cheese, and a cookie. Only the freshest ingredients. Open M-Sa 9am-6pm, Su 11am-5pm.

Saturn Café, 1230 Mission St. (429-8505). Excellent vegetarian meals (most under $6). Try the Hangover, a slice of cold pizza with a beer ($3), or an Alien sandwich, with tofu, hummus, avocado, and cheese ($6.75). Open M-Th 11am-midnight, F 11am-1am, Sa 9am-1am, Su 9am-midnight.

Royal Taj, 270 Soquel Ave. (427-2400), at Roberts. You'll be crying *namaste* (I bow to you) after being treated like a king (with food to match) at this Indian restaurant. Daily lunch buffet $6.50. Meat dishes ($6-9), veggie specialties ($6), and stellar *lassi* ($2) round out the menu. Open daily 11:30am-2:30pm and 5:30-10pm.

SIGHTS AND ACTIVITIES

The **Boardwalk** is the most awesomely loud, fun, tacky thing on the Pacific this side of L.A. The 3-block-long strip of 25 amusement park rides, guess-your-weight booths, shooting galleries, and caramel apple vendors provides a free diversion from the beach. Highly recommended is the Big Dipper ($3), a 1924 wooden tower roller coaster. (Open daily late May to early Sept.; Sa-Su the rest of the year.)

The **Santa Cruz Beach** (officially named Cowell Beach) itself is broad, fairly dirty, and generally packed with volleyball players. Jutting off Beach St. is the **Santa Cruz Wharf,** the longest car-accessible pier on the West Coast (parking $1 per hr., under 30min. free; disabled patrons free). If you're seeking solitude, try the chillier banks of the San Lorenzo River immediately east of the boardwalk. Folks wanting to exercise their right to bare everything should head north on Hwy. 1 to the **Red White and Blue Beach,** just south of Davenport (look for the line of cars to your right; parking $7), but do not venture here alone. If averse to paying for the privilege of an all-over tan, try the **Bonny Doon Beach,** off Hwy. 1 at Bonny Doon Rd., 11 mi. north of Santa Cruz. Magnificent cliffs and rocks surround this windy and frequently deserted spot.

Along the coast south of Santa Cruz Beach chills the **Santa Cruz Surfing Museum** (429-3429). *(Open M and W-F noon-4pm, Sa-Su noon-5pm. Free.)* The main room of the lighthouse displays vintage wooden boards, early wetsuits, and surfing videos, while the tower contains the ashes of Mark Abbott, a local surfer who drowned in 1965 and to whom the museum is dedicated.

ENTERTAINMENT AND NIGHTLIFE

Dodge the underage hipsters parked on the sidewalks of Pacific in order to cruise into the Santa Cruzian nightlife. The free weekly *Good Times* has a reputation for thorough listings.

⊛Caffé Pergolesi, 418A Cedar St. (426-1775). Look for "Dr. Miller's" sign. Chill coffeehouse/bar provides a series of small rooms and a spacious patio for those wishing to read, write, or socialize. $2 pints 7-9pm daily; large coffees for the price of a small M-F 1-3pm. Open M-Th 7:30am-11:30pm, F-Sa 7:30am-midnight.

Kuumbwa Jazz Center, 320-322 Cedar St. (427-2227). Known throughout the region for great jazz and innovative off-night programs; most shows 8pm. Under-21-derlings are welcome. Big names M; locals F. Tickets (about $5) sell through Logos Books and Music, 1117 Pacific (427-5100; open daily 10am-10pm), as well as BASS outlets (998-BASS/2277).

Blue Lagoon, 923 Pacific Ave. (423-7117). Mega-popular gay-straight club with bar in front, 3 pool tables in back, and people dancing everywhere. Cover $1 Su-M and W; $3 Th; $4 F-Sa. Happy hour with $2 drinks daily 6-9pm. Su Margaritas $1. Stronger-than-the-bouncer drinks $3-4. Open daily 4pm-2am.

SAN FRANCISCO BAY AREA

■ San Francisco

It takes only minutes to cross the Golden Gate Bridge, but San Francisco often seems a city set apart. A blanket of fog lies over the city most mornings, and it rarely feels the heat that bakes the countryside just a few miles inland. Even without the Transamerica Pyramid or the magnificent sweep of the Golden Gate Bridge, the city's skyline would be instantly recognizable. By California standards, San Francisco is steeped in history, but it's a history of oddballs and eccentrics that resonates more today in a vibrant and fascinating street culture than in museums and galleries. As the last stop in America's great westward expansion, San Francisco has always attracted artists, dreamers, and out-siders. The lineage of free spirits and troublemakers runs back to the 19th century and the Forty-Niners who flocked here during the mad boom of the California Gold Rush, and even the smugglers and pirates of the Barbary Coast.

The tradition continues. Anti-establishment politics have almost become establish-ment here. The gay community, now one-sixth of the city's population, emerged in the 70s as one of the city's most visible and powerful groups—out, loud, and proud. At the same time, Central American and Asian immigrants have made San Francisco one of the most racially diverse cities in the U.S. But as more of the city's population cultivates a bourgeois fiscal conservatism, the coalition of leftish interests that dumped Frank Jordan in favor of dapper Speaker of the Legislature Willie Brown in the 1995 mayoral race may weaken. Meanwhile, the Panglossian techno-libertarianism plumped by the city's own *Wired* magazine grows along with the popularity of the Internet and the ranks of the new computer-bound elite "digerati."

ORIENTATION

San Francisco, the fourth-largest city in California (pop. 775,000), is 403 mi. north of Los Angeles and 390 mi. south of Oregon. The city proper lies at the northern tip of the pen-insula that separates San Francisco Bay from the Pacific Ocean. The drive from L.A. takes 6hr. on I-5 if you hustle, 8hr. on U.S. 101, or a leisurely 9½hr. via Hwy. 1, the legendary Pacific Coast Hwy. U.S. 101 offers a compromise between vistas and velocity, but the stunning coastal scenery that unfolds along Hwy. 1 can make getting there much more fun. From the south, the city can be reached directly from **U.S. 101, I-280,** and **Hwy. 1.** From inland California, **I-5** approaches the city from the north and south via **I-580** and **I-80,** which runs across the **Bay Bridge** (westbound only toll $2). From the north, U.S. 101 and Hwy. 1 will bring you over the **Golden Gate Bridge** (southbound only toll $3).

San Francisco radiates outward from its docks, which lie on the northeast edge of the 30 mi. long peninsula, just inside the lip of the bay. Many of the city's most visitor-friendly attractions are found within a wedge formed by **Van Ness Ave.,** running north-south; the **Embarcadero** curving along the coast; and **Market St.,** running northeast-southwest and interrupting the regular grid of streets.

At the top of this wedge lies touristy **Fisherman's Wharf.** From here, ferries service **Alcatraz Island,** the inescapable former prison-*cum*-tourist attraction. **Columbus Ave.** extends southeast from the docks to **North Beach,** a district shared by Italian-Ameri-cans, artists, and professional-types. **Telegraph Hill,** which is topped by Coit Tower, emerges as the focal point of North Beach amid a terrific mass of eateries. To the west of Columbus Ave. are **Russian Hill** and **Nob Hill,** residential areas with some of the oldest money in California. South of North Beach, the largest **Chinatown** in North America cov-ers around 24 sq. blocks between Broadway in the north, Bush St. in the south, and Kearny St. in the east. On the other side of the Bush St. gateway of Chinatown lies the heavily developed **Financial District,** where skyscrapers fill the blocks above the north-east portion of Market St. To the west, the core downtown area centered on **Union Sq.** gives way to the well-pounded **Tenderloin,** where—despite attempts at urban renewal—drugs, crime, and homelessness prevail both night and day. The area is roughly bounded by Larkin St. to the west, Taylor St. to the east, and Post St. to the

CALIFORNIA

Downtown San Francisco

SEE ALSO COLOR INSERT

ACCOMMODATIONS

G Adelaide Inn
D Golden Gate Hotel
C Grant Plaza Hotel
A Green Tortoise Guest House
I Herbert Hotel

F Hotel Essex
B Pacific Tradewinds Guest House
E Pensione International
H S. F. Downtown Hostel
J S. F. International Student Center

N

0   250 yards
0   250 meters

north, and bleeds down Market St. for a few blocks. The **Civic Center** occupies the acute angle formed by Market St. and Van Ness Ave. at the southern point of the wedge. City Hall, the Civic Center Public Library, and Symphony Hall crown an impressive and ever-growing collection of municipal buildings.

South of the wedge, directly below Market St., lies the **South-of-Market-Area (SoMa).** Here, the best of San Francisco's nightclubs are scattered among darkened office buildings and warehouses. SoMa extends inland from the bay to 10th St., at which point the largely Latino **Mission District** begins and spreads south. The **Castro,** center of San Francisco's gay community, abuts the Mission District on its west side, roughly along Church St. From the landmark **Castro Theater** on the corner of Castro and Market St., the neighborhood stretches to the less flamboyant **Noe Valley** in the south and the undeveloped oasis of the **Twin Peaks** in the southeast.

On the north end of the peninsula, west across Van Ness Ave. from the Wharf area, sits the **Marina,** which includes Fort Mason and small yacht harbors. Along with the expansive **Presidio** and the **Golden Gate Bridge** to the west, and the **Marin Headlands** on the other side of the bay, the shoreline comprises the Golden Gate National Recreation Area. Inland from the Marina rise the wealthy hills of **Pacific Heights.** South of Pacific Heights is the **Western Addition,** extending west to Masonic Ave. This district boasts many of the city's public housing projects and can be dangerous, especially near Hayes St. Other than the shops and restaurants of **Japantown,** the Western Addition has little to interest visitors. Farther west is the rectangular **Golden Gate Park,** which extends west to the Pacific Ocean. The park is bounded by Fulton St. and the residential Richmond neighborhood to the north, and by Lincoln St. and the Sunset District to the south. At its east end juts a skinny panhandle bordered by hippie-trippy **Haight-Ashbury** to the south. A youthful new set of enviro-conscious, politically liberal, and liberally political residents coexist here in relative harmony with the aging flower children for which the area is widely known.

GETTING AROUND

A **car** here is not the necessity it is in L.A. **Parking** in the city is very difficult and very expensive. Think twice about attempting to use a **bike** to climb up and down San Francisco's many hills. Golden Gate Park is a more sensible location for biking. Even **walking** in this city is an exertion—some of the sidewalks are so steep they have steps cut into them. There are many **walking tours** of the city, some of which promise "no steep hills." **In-Room City Guide** (332-9601) has info on free summer tours.

The **Municipal Railway, or MUNI** (673-6864), operates buses, cable cars, and subway/trolleys (bus fare $1, seniors and ages 5-17 35¢). MUNI passports are valid on all MUNI vehicles, including cable cars (1-day $6, 3-day $10, 7-day $15). **MUNI buses** run frequently throughout the city. **MUNI Metro** runs streetcars along five lines.

Cable cars were named a national historic landmark in 1964. Of the three lines, the California (C) line, running from the Financial District up Nob Hill, is the least crowded. The Powell-Hyde (PH) line has the steepest hills and the sharpest turns. Powell-Mason (PM) runs to Fisherman's Wharf. (All lines run daily 6:30am-12:45am. Fare $2, seniors and disabled $1 before 7am and after 9pm. No free transfers.)

Bay Area Rapid Transit (BART) (992-2278) does not serve the *entire* Bay Area, but it does operate modern, carpeted trains along four lines connecting San Francisco with the East Bay, including Oakland, Berkeley, Concord, and Fremont. Unfortunately, BART is not a local transportation system within the city. (Trains run M-F 4am-midnight, Sa 6am-midnight, Su 8am-midnight. Inter-city transport $1.10, to the East Bay $4.) Maps and schedules are available at all stations.

PRACTICAL INFORMATION

Airport: San Francisco International (SFO) (general info 650-761-0800) is located on a small peninsula in San Francisco Bay 15 mi. south of downtown via U.S. 101. Plan your arrival by calling the SFO transportation info line for shuttle schedules (800-SFO/736-2008). **San Mateo County Transit (SamTrans)** (800-660-4287) runs 2 buses from SFO to downtown San Francisco. Express bus #7F takes 35min. to reach downtown and allows only whatever luggage can be held in your lap (runs 5:30am-12:50am; fare $2.50, seniors $1.25, under 18 $1). Bus #7B takes 1hr. to reach downtown, stops frequently, and allows all luggage (runs 5am-12:30am; fare $2, seniors 50¢, under 18 $1).

Trains: Amtrak, 425 Mission St. (495-1575 or 800-872-7245), in the Transbay Terminal, between Fremont and 1st St. downtown. To Los Angeles ($42). Free buses shuttle passengers to the 3 Amtrak stations in the city. Office open daily 6:45am-10:45pm. **CalTrain** (800-660-4287) runs to Palo Alto ($3.75, seniors and under 12 $1.75); San Jose ($5/$2.50); and Santa Cruz.

Buses: Golden Gate Transit (Marin County), **AC Transit** (East Bay), and **SamTrans** (San Mateo County) all stop at the **Transbay Terminal,** 425 Mission St. (495-1575), between Fremont and 1st St. downtown. **Greyhound** (800-231-2222) runs buses from the terminal to Los Angeles ($36) and Portland ($51).

Car Rental: Ace, 415 Taylor St. (771-7711), near Geary Blvd. Compacts from $29 per day (150 free mi.), $149 per week (1000 free mi.). Must be 21; drivers under 25 pay $5 per day surcharge.

Taxis: Yellow Cab (626-2345). **Luxor Cab** (282-4141). $1.80 base fare, $1.70 per mi. 24hr.

Visitor Info: Visitor Information Center, Hallidie Plaza, 900 Market St. (391-2000; http://www.sfbayarea.com), at Powell beneath street level at the exit of the Powell St. BART stop. Wide range of maps and brochures covering area tours, services, and attractions. MUNI passports and maps for sale. 24hr. info recordings in English (391-2001), French (391-2003), German (391-2004), Japanese (391-2101), and Spanish (391-2122). Open M-F 9am-5:30pm, Sa-Su 9am-3pm.

Hotlines: Rape Crisis Center, 647-RAPE/647-7273. **United Helpline,** 772-HELP/4357 or 800-237-6222.

Internet Access: Civic Center Public Library (552-4400), at Grove and Larkin. Open M 10am-6pm, Tu-Th 9am-8pm, F 11am-5pm, Sa 9am-5pm, Su noon-5pm.

Post Office: Civic Center Station, 101 Hyde St. (800-275-8777), at Golden Gate. Open M, W, and F 6am-5:30pm, Tu and Th 6am-8:30pm, Sa 6am-3pm. **ZIP code:** 94142. **Area code:** 415.

ACCOMMODATIONS

Many budget-range accommodations are in unsavory areas; the **Tenderloin** and the **Mission** can be particularly unsafe. Reservations are recommended at hotels.

Hostels

⊛**San Francisco International Guest House,** 2976 23rd St. (641-1411), at Harrison in the Mission. TV area, 2 kitchens (smoking and non-), and guest phones. Neighborhood parking. Dorms $14, after 28 days $11; private double $28. 5-night min. stay, 3-month max. Passport with international stamps required.

⊛**San Francisco International Student Center,** 1188 Folsom St. (255-8800 or 487-1463), at 8th in SoMa. 55 beds. Dorms $15, weekly $90 (in winter only). Reception open 9am-9pm. Check-out 11am. No credit cards. Foreign passport or out-of-state ID required.

Green Tortoise Guest House, 494 Broadway (834-1000), at Kearny in North Beach. 120 wooden bunks. Lockers under each bed; bring a lock. Sauna, Internet access ($2), kitchens, coin laundry, bike storage, and free continental breakfast. Dorms $18; private doubles $39. 21-night max. stay. Reception 24hr. Credit cards accepted if reserving in advance.

Fort Mason Hostel (HI-AYH), Bldg. #240, Fort Mason (771-7277), in the Marina. Entrance at Bay and Franklin, 1 block west of Van Ness. Laundry, bike storage. Free breakfast daily 7:30-11:30am. Dorms $17 per night. Reception daily 7am-2pm and 3pm-midnight. Limited access 11:30am-2:30pm. Lights-out at midnight. No smoking or alcohol. Lockers (bring a lock). Free parking. Chores expected. IBN reservations available. Photo ID required.

Pacific Tradewinds Guest House, 680 Sacramento St. (433-7970), between Montgomery and Kearny in the Financial District. This 30-bed facility has a well-worn common room, a kitchen, guest phone, Internet access, and not quite enough bathrooms. Dorms $18, off-season $16 (double beds available). Must be 18. Bike storage. 14-night max. stay. Reception 8am-midnight. No reservations in summer. Discounts for VIP Backpacker and FIYTO cardholders. Laundry $6. Key deposit $20. No wheelchair access.

Easy Goin' Guest House, 555 Haight St. (552-8452), in the Haight. Common room with cable TV, 3 kitchens with storage space, and clean rooms with 35 beds. German, Spanish, French spoken. Lockers and office safe. Dorms $14; private couples room $30. $20 security deposit. Reception M-F 9am-6:30pm, Sa 10am-2pm.

San Francisco—Downtown (HI-AYH), 312 Mason St. (788-5603), between Geary and O'Farrell, 1 block from Union Sq. 260 beds. TV (movies nightly), Internet access (25¢ per 5min.), and visitor info. Reception 24hr. Dorms $18, nonmembers $21; under 12 ½-price with parent. Key deposit $5. Reserve by phone with credit card, or show up at noon. IBN reservations available. Wheelchair access.

Hotels

⦿Adelaide Inn, 5 Isadora Duncan (441-2261), at the end of a little alley off Taylor between Geary and Post, 2 blocks west of Union Sq. This quiet, 18-room oasis is the most charming of San Francisco's many "European-style" hotels. Steep stairs, no elevator. Kitchen with guest fridge available; shared hallway bathrooms. Singles $42; doubles $52-58. Reception daily 9:30am-1pm and 5:30-9pm.

⦿Pensione International, 875 Post St. (775-3344), east of Hyde, 4 blocks from Union Sq. Continental breakfast. Singles $60-75; doubles $75-90; $10 discount in winter.

Golden Gate Hotel, 775 Bush St. (392-3702 or 800-835-1118), between Powell and Mason near Union Sq. Comfy rooms with TV. Spotless hall bathrooms. Continental breakfast and afternoon tea (4-7pm) included. No singles; doubles $72, with bath $109. Garage parking $12 per day.

Grant Plaza Hotel, 465 Grant Ave. (434-3883 or 800-472-6899), at Pine St. in Chinatown. Modern furnishings and friendly personal service at a central, if occasionally noisy, location. All rooms with private bath. Singles $52-75; doubles $65-85.

Hotel Essex, 684 Ellis St. (474-4664 or 800-443-7739, outside CA 800-453-7739), at Larkin, north of the Civic Center, at the western edge of the Tenderloin. Staff speaks French and German. Singles $69; doubles $79. A few rooms with shared bath $49. Desk open 24hr. Check-out noon. No parking.

Herbert Hotel, 161 Powell St. (362-1600), near Union Sq. Powell St. cable cars stop right outside the door. Clean and bright kitchen (6th fl.). Laundry, luggage storage, plus access to swimming pool at a nearby sister hotel. Singles $49, with private bath $60; doubles $55/$65. Weekly rates available.

The Red Victorian Bed and Breakfast Inn, 1665 Haight St. (864-1978), in the Haight. All 18 rooms are individually decorated to honor peace, sunshine, butterflies, or teddy bears. Doubles $86-126; discounts on stays longer than 3 days. 2-night min. stay Sa-Su. Check-in 3-6pm or by appt. Check-out 11am.

FOOD

The *Examiner* and the *Bay Guardian* newspapers have generally reliable restaurant reviews. The glossy *Bay Area Vegetarian* can also suggest places to graze.

South-of-Market (SoMa)

Here are some places where the food lives up to the high standards set by the decor.

⦿Vino e Cucina Trattoria, 489 3rd St. (543-6962), at Bryant. Meals cooked by the affable Italian chef are as *autentico* as they are *magnifico. Lasagne arrotolate* $10.75. Pastas and pizzas ($8-11) available without meat on request. Open M-F 11am-3:30pm and 5:30-10pm, Sa 5:30-10:30pm. ("Sundays, you rest," says the chef.)

Hamburger Mary's, 1582 Folsom St. (626-5767), at 12th. Excellent burgers ($6-10), great spicy home fries, a handful of veggie options, and 8 kinds of Bloody Mary (from $3.25). Open M-Th 11am-1am, F 11am-2am, Sa 10am-2am, Su 10am-1am.

The Chat House, 139 8th St. (255-8783), at Minna. Buttermilk pancakes with bananas $5.75. Sauteed trout with pecan sauce ($8). Vegetarian friendly. Open M-Tu 8am-9pm, W-F 8am-1am (food from 11am), Sa 10am-1am, Su 10am-3pm.

Civic Center

Opera- and theater-goers frequent the petite restaurants that dot the outer Civic Center area, while **Hayes St.** offers an extensive selection of cafes. In the summer, produce can be found at the **farmer's market** every Wednesday and Friday in the U.N. Plaza. *Use caution in this area at night.*

🖋**Nyala,** 39A Grove St. (861-0788), east of Larkin, fuses Ethiopian and Italian cuisine. Fabulous *doro wot* ($6 lunch, $8 dinner. All-you-can-eat vegetarian buffet ($5 lunch, $7 dinner). Open M-Th 11am-3pm and 5-9pm, F-Sa 11am-3pm and 5-11pm.

Millennium, 246 McAllister St. (487-9800), between Larkin and Hyde in the Abigail Hotel. Gourmet vegan cooking and impeccable service (entrees $12-16). Open daily 5-9:30pm.

The Mission District

The Mission is one of the best places in the city to find excellent, satisfying, cheap food, and the best, cheapest produce. Some of the best Mexican food is served in small restaurants; try **Chava's,** 3248 18th St. (552-9387; open daily 6am-8pm); **Taco Loco,** 3306 Mission (695-0621); or **El Herradero,** 2224 Mission (636-7366).

🖋**La Taqueria,** 2889 Mission (285-7117), at 24th, has a prime location. Claims the "best tacos and burritos in the whole world," and you'd be hard put to contradict them. Tacos $2.25, burritos $3.75. Open M-Sa 11am-9pm, Su 11am-8pm.

🖋**Café Macondo,** 3159 16th, between Guerrero and Valencia. Earthy and book-lined. Celebrate the last revolution or plot the next over steaming black cups of coffee. Open daily 10:30am-10pm.

Country Station Sushi Café, 2140 Mission (861-0972), between 17th and 18th. Sunny, big-hearted, and clean on a rather grimy stretch of Mission. Excellent sushi; traditional combos start at $8. Open M-Th 5-10pm, F-Sa 5-11pm.

Castro

Cheap food can be elusive in this trendy area; consider experiencing it by sipping a latenight latte. Same-sex cruising is almost inevitably the side dish. *Bon appetit!*

Hot 'n' Hunky, 4039 18th St. (621-6365), near Castro. Trendy 50s decor with many winks to Marilyn Monroe. Hunker down with a Macho Man Burger ($4.50). Open Su-Th 11am-midnight, F-Sa 11am-1am. No credit cards.

Josie's Cabaret and Juice Joint Café, 3583 16th St. (861-7933), at Market. Strictly vegetarian menu (filling tofu or tempeh burgers $5.75). Live comedy acts at night. Open daily 9am-11pm. Shows at 8 and 10pm. Cash only.

Marcello's, 420 Castro St. (863-3900), across the street from the Castro Theatre. Possibly the best pizza in San Francisco. Slices $1.75-3, pies $9-20. Cheap beer, too. Eat in; take out; free delivery. Open Su-Th 11am-1am, F-Sa 11am-2am. Cash only.

Haight-Ashbury

Crepes on Cole, 100 Carl St. (664-1800), 4 blocks south of Haight St. along Cole. From chicken pesto ($6.25) to strawberries and chocolate ($3.95). Espresso drinks, beer, and wine. Open Su-Th 7am-11pm, F-Sa 7am-midnight.

Ya Halla, 494 Haight St. (522-1509), at Fillmore. The name means "heartily welcome" in Arabic. Flavorful meat and vegetarian sandwiches (super falafel $4, chicken shawerma $5.25). Open daily 11am-10:30pm.

Spaghetti Western, 576 Haight St. (864-8461) near Steiner. Texas-sized specials like Spuds-O-Rama (home fries, sour cream, and cheese, $4.75) or Gunpowder Scram (a Tex-Mex omelette, $5.50). Open M-F 7am-3pm, Sa-Su 8am-4pm.

Kan Zaman, 1793 Haight St. (751-9656), at Cole. Persian carpets, pillow seating, spice wine ($3.25), and fruit-flavored hookahs ($7). Belly dancers F-Su 8:30-10:30pm. Kitchen open M 5-11pm, Tu, Th, and Su noon-11pm, F-Sa noon-midnight. Bar stays open until 2am.

Richmond

With top Chinese restaurants, the area also has Thai, Burmese, Cambodian, Japanese, Italian, Russian, Korean, and Vietnamese food. **Clement St.** has the most options.

New Golden Turtle, 308 5th Ave. (221-5285), at Clement. Vietnamese dishes like *bahn xeo*, or savory crepe ($6.50), are irresistible. Vegetarian options abound. Dinner entrees $8-9. Open M 5-11pm, Tu-Su 11am-11pm.

The Red Crane, 1115 Clement St. (751-7226), between Funston and 12th St. Locals rave about the spicy Szechuan eggplant ($5), but with over 50 entree options, you can choose your own adventure. Open daily 11:30am-10pm.

Marina and Pacific Heights

The **Marina Safeway,** 15 Marina Blvd. (563-4946), between Laguna and Buchanan, is legendary as a spot to pick up more than just gourmet groceries.

Bepples Pies, 1934 Union (931-6225), at Laguna. Mmm-bop, pie heaven! Dinner pies $5-7, pancakes $4. Open Su-Th 8am-midnight, F-Sa 8am-2am (kitchen closes at 3pm). A 2nd location at 2124 Chestnut (at Steiner) goes to bed 1hr. earlier.

Pizza Inferno, 1800 Fillmore St. (775-1800), at Sutter on the border of Pacific Heights and Japantown. Pizza lunch specials (from $5) include salad and soda. Happy hour with 2-for-1 pizzas M-F 4-6:30pm and after 10pm. Open Su-Th 11:20am-11pm, F-Sa 11:30am-midnight.

Leon's Bar*B*Q, 1911 Fillmore St. (922-2436), between Pine and Bush. Serves up great Cajun jambalaya, corn muffins, and sweet potato pie ($3). Taster's plate with ribs, chicken, spicy sausage, and jambalaya $5. Open daily 11am-9pm.

La Méditerranée, 2210 Fillmore St. (921-2956), by Sacramento. Hearty portions for cheap. The Lule Kebab (lean ground lamb with spices, onions, and tomatoes, $8), and the Grecian Spinach and Feta Phyllo Dough ($8) are good choices. Open M-Th 11am-10pm, F-Sa 11am-11pm.

Fisherman's Wharf

The archetypal, if somewhat overpriced, Wharf meal is a loaf of sourdough bread ($2-4) from **Boudin Bakery,** 156 Jefferson St. (928-1849), and clam chowder ($4-5) from a nearby seafood stand.

North Beach

Sodini's Green Valley Restaurant, 510 Green St. (291-0499), at Grant. One of the area's oldest family restaurants, established in 1906. The *Ravioli alla Casa* rocks the house ($8.25). Open M-F 5-10pm, Sa-Su 5pm-midnight.

Mario's Bohemian Cigar Store Cage, 566 Columbus Ave. (362-0536). A laid-back cafe right at the corner of Washington Sq. Park. Hot sandwiches on fat slabs of *focaccia* $6.25. Open M-Sa 10am-midnight, Su 10am-11pm. No credit cards.

The Stinking Rose, 325 Columbus Ave. (PU-1-ROSE/781-7673). Aromatic all-garlic restaurant; do not miss their *bagna calda* on penalty of death. Pastas $8-13, other entrees $12-21. Open Su-Th 11am-11pm, F-Sa 11am-midnight.

Caffé Trieste, 601 Vallejo St. (392-6739), at Grant. Hasn't changed much since it was a Beat haunt; the jukebox still plays opera, and you're as likely to be addressed in Italian as in English. Coffee drinks $1-3. Open daily 6:30am-11pm.

Nob Hill and Russian Hill

The Golden Turtle, 2211 Van Ness St. (441-4419). Fabulous Vietnamese restaurant serves mind-blowing entrees ($8-11) among intricately carved wooden walls. The spicy lemon grass chicken ($10) and vegetarian exotic lava pot ($9.50) are standouts. Open Tu-Su 5-11pm. Reservations recommended Sa-Su.

Nihonmachi (Japantown)

Isobune, 1737 Post St. (563-1030), in the Japan Center's Kintetsu Bldg. The fish is outstanding (2 pieces $1.50-3). Open daily 11:30am-10pm.

CALIFORNIA

Chinatown

◉**Kowloon,** 909 Grant Ave. (362-9888), at Jackson. Outstanding vegetarian food for ridiculously low prices. A menu as long as the Great Wall includes such creatures as "vegetarian duck gizzards" and "vegetarian eels." Copious lunch specials $4-6. Open daily 10am-9:30pm.

Brandy Ho's, 217 Columbus Ave. (788-7527), at Pacific. This food is *spicy*. But oh, it is a sweet pain. (A thoughtful "not hot with pepper" category is also available.) Lunch specials $5-6. Open Su-Th 11:30am-11pm, F-Sa 11:30am-midnight.

SIGHTS

San Francisco is not made of landmarks or "sights," but its diverse collection of neighborhoods. If you blindly rush from Fisherman's Wharf to Coit Tower to Mission Dolores, you'll be missing the city itself.

Downtown and Union Square

During the Civil War, Unionists made the green lawn of the square their rallying ground. Their slogan, "The Union, the whole Union, and nothing but the Union," gave the area its name. At the turn of the century, murders on the Morton's Alley averaged one per week, and prostitutes waved to their favorite customers from second-story windows. After the 1906 earthquake and fires destroyed most of the flophouses, a group of merchants moved in and renamed the area **Maiden Lane** in hopes of changing the street's image. Surprisingly enough, the switch worked. Today, Maiden Lane—extending 2 blocks from Union Square's eastern side—is as virtuous as they come and makes a pleasant place to stroll, at least until the boutiques start looking too hob nobby for comfort. The lane's main architectural attraction is the **Circle Gallery,** 140 Maiden Lane, the city's only Frank Lloyd Wright-designed building and a rehearsal for the Guggenheim Museum in New York.

For a view of the Bay Area, take a free jaunt on the outside elevators of the **Westin St. Francis Hotel** (where Manson wild child Squeaky Fromme tried to assassinate Gerald Ford), on Powell St. at Geary. The swift ascent summons the entire eastern Bay Area into view. A slower but equally scenic ascent is offered by the **Powell St. cable cars** ($2), which climb the busy Chinatown streets on the way to Nob Hill and the waterfront. The cable cars crawl at a stately 10 mph, but the line to get on moves at an even slower pace. Waits of up to 1hr are common.

Financial District

Corporate worker bees swarm San Francisco's Financial District, a Wall Street of the West Coast where towering banks block out the sun. Unless skyscrapers or power suits get you going, there's not much here to attract the casual visitor.

At the foot of Market St., **Justin Herman Plaza** and its formidable **Vallaincourt Fountain,** at the foot of Market St., invite total visitor immersion. Bands and rallyists often rent out the area during lunch. One free concert, performed by U2 in the fall of 1987, resulted in the arrest of lead singer and madcap non-conformist Bono for spray-painting "Stop the Traffic—Rock and Roll" on the fountain. At the **Bank of America Building,** 555 California St., the lookout point is a cocktail bar with a one-drink minimum—look fast or fake a rendezvous. The entrance of the building features a large block of black marble that local wags have dubbed "the Banker's Heart."

The leading lady of the city's skyline is the **Transamerica Pyramid,** 600 Montgomery St., between Clay and Washington. This distinctively shaped office building is, according to New Age sources, directly centered on the telluric currents of the Golden Dragon ley line between Easter Island and Stonehenge. Around the turn of the century, such messy literati as Mark Twain, Robert Louis Stevenson, Bret Harte, and Jack London scuffed the bar of the pyramid's predecessor, the Montgomery Block, and Sun Yat-Sen scripted a dynastic overthrow in one of its apartments. History is more immediately evident at the **Wells Fargo History Museum,** 420 Montgomery (396-2619), where two Pony Express-era stagecoaches are on display (open M-F 9am-5pm; free).

CALIFORNIA

South-of-Market (SoMa)

San Francisco's most nocturnal district, **SoMa** is where hip young professionals dine at chic restaurants before hitting San Francisco's club scene. By night, SoMa is the very epicenter of the city's nightlife; by day, the galleries and museums are the main points of interest.

The **San Francisco Museum of Modern Art (SFMOMA),** 151 3rd St. (357-4000), between Mission and Howard, displays an impressive collection of contemporary European and American works—the largest selection of 20th-century art this side of New York. *(Open M-Tu and F-Su 11am-6pm, Th 11am-9pm. $8, students $4, seniors $5, under 12 free with adult; Th 6-9pm ½-price, 1st Tu of each month free. Audio tour $3.)* The neighboring **Yerba Buena Center for the Arts,** 701 Mission (978-ARTS/2787), runs an excellent gallery space and many vibrant programs, emphasizing viewer involvement and local multicultural work. *(Center open Tu-Su 11am-6pm; gardens open daily sunrise-sunset. $5, seniors and students $3, free Th 11am-3pm; free 1st Th of each month, when the center stays open until 8pm.)* Just down the street, the **Cartoon Art Museum,** 814 Mission St. (CARTOON/227-8666 or 546-3922), 2nd fl., showcases the history of comic strip art from the Yellow Kid to Calvin and Hobbes, with changing exhibits on cartoon masters and research archives for funnybook scholars. *(Open W-F 11am-5pm, Sa 10am-5pm, Su 1-5pm. $5, students and seniors $3, ages 6-12 $2; 1st W of each month is pay-what-you-wish" day.)* The **Ansel Adams Center,** 250 4th St. (495-7000), at Howard and Folsom, exhibits only a small number of the master's photographs, but rotating shows by other photographers delve into one of the largest and best collections of art photography in the country. *(Open Tu-Su 11am-5pm, and until 8pm on 1st Th of each month. $5, students and ages 13-17 $3, seniors $2.)*

Civic Center

The Civic Center is a collection of mammoth buildings arranged around two vast plazas. The palatial **San Francisco City Hall,** 401 Van Ness Ave. (554-4000), modeled after St. Peter's Cathedral, is the centerpiece of the largest gathering of Beaux Arts architecture in the U.S. It was the site of the 1978 murder of Mayor George Moscone and City Supervisor Harvey Milk, the first openly gay politician elected to public office in the U.S. To the east across Polk lies the **United Nations Plaza,** home to the city's farmer's market on Wednesdays and Fridays, and a General Assembly of pigeons most other days. The main branch of the **San Francisco Public Library** faces the plaza at Grove and Larkin. Opened in 1996, the state-of-the-art facility offers free Internet access, an excellent video library, the nation's first gay and lesbian archives, a cafe, and a rooftop garden.

Across Van Ness Ave. to the west sit San Francisco's cultural heavyweights: the Veteran's Bldg., the Opera House, and Symphony Hall. The **Louise M. Davies Symphony Hall** (552-8000, tickets 864-6000) glitters at 201 Van Ness Ave. and Grove. *(Open M-F 10am-6pm.)* The seating in this glass-and-brass $33 million hall was designed to give most audience members a close-up view of performers. Next door, the recently renovated **War Memorial Opera House,** 301 Van Ness Ave., between Grove and McAllister, hosts the well-regarded **San Francisco Opera Company** (864-3330) and the **San Francisco Ballet** (865-2000). Also in the block of Van Ness Ave. between Grove and McAllister is the **Veteran's Building,** where **Herbst Theatre** (392-4400) hosts string quartets, solo singers, ensembles, and lecturers. *(Tours of Davies Symphony Hall, War Memorial Opera House, and Herbst Theatre leave from the Grove St. entrance to Davies Hall every hr. M 10am-2pm. W and Sa, tours of Davies Hall only by request. Tickets $5, students and seniors $3. For tour info, call 552-8338.)*

The Mission District

Founded by Spanish settlers in 1776, the lively Mission district is home to some of the city's oldest structures, as well as some of the hottest young people and places around. Colorful murals celebrate the prominent Latino presence which has long defined the Mission, although it grows ever more multicultural. Politically, the Mission is the city's most radical pocket, marked by left-wing and anarchist bookstores, aggressive labor associations, and bohemian bars and cafes. The area is also home to a lesbian community. The Mission is relatively safe for daytime walks, but *exercise caution at night,* especially around the housing projects between Valencia and Guerrero close to Market St. The district, which lies south of the Civic Center area, is roughly bordered by 16th St. to the north, U.S. 101 to the east, Army St. (renamed Cesar Chavez in some areas) to the south, and the Castro in the West. MUNI bus routes (#9, 12, 22, 26, 27, 33, and 53) lace the area.

Extant for over two centuries, **Mission Dolores** (621-8203), at 16th and Dolores in the old heart of San Francisco, is thought to be the oldest building in the city. *(Open daily 9am-4pm; Nov.-Apr. 9am-3:30pm. $2, ages 5-12 $1. Masses M-Sa 7:30 and 9am; Sa 7:30, 9am, and 5pm; Su 8 and 10am; mass in Spanish Su noon.)* The mission was founded in 1776 by Father Junípero Serra and named in honor of St. Francis of Assisi, as was San Francisco itself. But because of its proximity to Laguna de Nuestra Señora de los Dolores (Lagoon of Our Lady of Sorrows), the mission became universally known as Misión de los Dolores. Bougainvillea, poppies, and birds-of-paradise bloom in the cemetery, which was featured in Hitchcock's *Vertigo.*

Castro

Forget Newt Gingrich—*this* is boys' town. Much of San Francisco's gay community, along with a much smaller number of hip, young lesbians, gleefully make the Castro home. The wild days of the 70s, when discos throbbed all night and day, have come and gone, but Harvey Milk Plaza, at Castro and Market, remains the fast-beating heart of gay San Francisco. To get there by public transit, take MUNI bus #37 or MUNI Metro F, K, L, or M down Market to the Castro St. station. MUNI bus #24 runs along Castro St. from 14th to 26th.

Most people here seem quite sure of their orientation, but if you need a little help getting started, **Cruisin' the Castro** guide Trevor Hailey, a resident since 1972, is consistently recognized as one of San Francisco's top tour leaders. Her walking tours of Castro life and history leave Tuesday to Saturday at 10am and cost $35, including brunch. Call 550-8110 for reservations. The majority of "sights" in the Castro stroll the street in cut-off shorts, but a thorough tour of the neighborhood should also include the faux-baroque **Castro Theater,** 429 Castro; **A Different Light Bookstore,** 489 Castro; and **Uncle Mame,** 2241 Market, your one-stop kitsch-and-camp overdose.

The NAMES Project, at 2362A Market St. (863-1966), sounds a more somber note. The Project has accumulated over 33,000 three-by-six-foot panels for the **AIDS Memorial Quilt.** *(Open M-Sa noon-7pm; Su noon-6pm; public quilting bees W 7-10pm.)* Each gravesized panel is a memorial to a person who has died of AIDS-related conditions. West of Castro, the peninsula swells with several large hills. On rare fogless nights, the spectacular views of the city from **Twin Peaks,** between Portola, Market, and Clarendon, rise above all others.

Haight-Ashbury

Walking around Haight-Ashbury today is like seeing a film adaptation of a Jane Austen novel—the costumes seem right and the actors are fairly convincing, but you can't shake the fact that it's 1999. Located to the east of Golden Gate Park, smack dab in the center of the city, the Haight has aged with uneven grace since its hippie heyday. Originally a quiet residential neighborhood, the Haight's large Victorian houses—perfect for communal living—began attracting post-Beat bohemians in the early 60s. Less political than Berkeley's Telegraph Ave., "Hashbury" embraced drug use and Eastern philosophies over anti-war protests and marches. The hippie voyage reached its apogee in 1967's "Summer of Love," when Janis Joplin, the Grateful Dead, and Jefferson Airplane all made music and love here within a few blocks of one another.

Bad karma got the upper hand in the 1970s and 80s, but the past decade has seen a steady resurgence; today the counterculture lives side-by-side with the over-the-counter culture. MUNI buses #6, 7, 16, 43, 66, 71, and 33 all serve the Haight, while Metro line N runs along Carl St., 4 blocks to the south. *The area can be dangerous at night—exercise caution.*

One could express shock and dismay that the storied corner of **Haight and Ashbury** is now home to a Gap and a Ben & Jerry's. Music and clothing top the list of legal mer-

CALIFORNIA

chandise. Inexpensive bars and cafes, action-packed street life, anarchist literature, and shops selling pipes for, um, tobacco, also contribute to groovy browsing possibilities. The former homes of several counterculture legends still survive: check out **Janis Joplin's** old abode at 112 Lyon St., between Page and Oak; the **Grateful Dead's** house at 710 Ashbury St., at Waller; or the **Charles Manson** mansion at 2400 Fulton St., at Willard. Rachel Heller leads the **Flower Power Walking Tour** (221-8442), a passionate trek through the Haight's history, twice a week ($15). The **San Francisco Public Library** offers a free walking tour focused on the Haight's pre-hippie life as a Victorian-era resort (call 557-4266 for details).

The **Red Vic Movie House,** 1727 Haight St. (668-3994), between Cole and Shrader, is a collectively owned theater with couch-like seating that shows foreign, student, and offbeat Hollywood films. Resembling a dense green mountain in the middle of the Haight, **Buena Vista Park** has a reputation for free-wheeling lawlessness. Enter at your own risk, and once inside, be prepared for those "doing their own thing"—and doing enough of it to kill a small animal.

Golden Gate Park and the Sunset District

This is where native San Franciscans spend Sundays. In-line skaters, neo-flower children, and sunbathers come together in this lush garden within the city. When San Francisco's 19th-century elders asked Frederick Law Olmsted, designer of New York's Central Park, to build a park to rival Paris's Bois de Boulogne on their city's western side, he said it couldn't be done. Engineer William Hammond Hall and Scottish gardener John "Willy" McLaren proved him wrong. Hall designed the 1000-acre park, gardens and all, when the land was still just shifting sand dunes, and then constructed a mammoth breakwater along the oceanfront to protect the seedling trees and bushes from the sea's burning spray.

Golden Gate Park should not be rushed through; San Franciscans bask there all weekend long. Intriguing museums and cultural events pick up where the lush flora and fauna finally leave off, and athletic opportunities abound. In addition to cycling and blading paths, the park also has a municipal golf course, an equestrian center, sports fields, and a stadium. Info and maps can be found at **Park Headquarters** (831-2700), in McLaren Lodge, at Fell St. and Stanyan on the park's eastern edge (open M-F 8am-5pm); or call 221-1311 for info on free weekend walking tours of the park.

There are three well-regarded **museums** in the park: the California Academy of Sciences, the M.H. de Young Memorial Museum, and the Asian Art Museum—all in one large complex on the east side, where 9th Ave. meets the park. The **California Academy of Sciences** (221-5100), one of the nation's largest institutions of its kind, houses several smaller museums specializing in different fields of science. *(Open daily 9am-6pm. $8.50, seniors $5.50, ages 12-17 $5.50, ages 4-11 $2; free 1st W of each month).*

The **M. H. de Young Memorial Museum** (863-3330) takes visitors through a 21-room survey of American art, from the colonial period to the early 20th century, including noteworthy pieces by John Singer Sargent and a Tiffany glass collection. The **Asian Art Museum** (379-8801), in the west wing of the building, is the largest museum outside Asia dedicated entirely to Asian artwork. *(Both museums open W-Su 9:30am-5pm. $7, seniors $5, ages 12-17 $4; free and open until 8:45pm 1st W of each month.)* The beautiful collection includes rare pieces of jade and porcelain, in addition to 3000-year-old bronzes. Both museums offer a variety of free tours—call for details.

Created for the 1894 Mid-Winter Exposition, the elegant **Japanese Tea Garden** is a serene collection of dark wooden buildings, small pools, graceful footbridges, carefully pruned trees, and lush plants. Tea and cookies are $2.50; watching the giant carp circle the central pond is free. *(Open daily 9am-6pm; in winter 10am-3pm. $2.50, seniors and ages 6-12 $1; free 1st W of each month.)*

On Sundays, traffic is banned from park roads, and bicycles and in-line skates come out in full force. Bikes are available for rent at the **Lincoln Cyclery,** 772 Stanyan St. (221-2415), on the east edge of Golden Gate Park. *(Mountain bikes $5 per hr., $25 per day. Driver's license or major credit card and $20 deposit required. Open M and W-Sa 9am-5pm, Su 11:30am-5pm.)* **Stow Lake** rents tandems ($10 per hr.) and covered multi-rider pedal cars called surreys ($12 per hr.).

Richmond

Historically a neighborhood of first- and second-generation immigrants, Richmond has been the traditional home to Irish-, Russian-, and now Chinese-American communities. "Inner Richmond," the area east of Park Presidio Blvd., has such a large Chinese population that it has been dubbed "New Chinatown."

Lincoln Park, at the northwest end of San Francisco, is the bulkiest and best attraction in Richmond. To get there, follow Clement St. west to 34th Ave., or Geary Blvd. to Point Lobos Ave. (MUNI bus #1 or 38). The grounds around the park, which include the **Land's End Path,** offer a romantic view of the Golden Gate Bridge. The **California Palace of the Legion of Honor** (863-3330), on Legion of Honor Dr. in the park, houses an impressive fine art collection. *(Open Tu-Su 9:30am-5pm. $7, seniors $5, ages 12-17 $4; $2 off with MUNI passport or transfer; 2nd W of each month free.)* A thorough catalogue of great masters from medieval to Matisse hangs in the recently renovated, marble-accented museum.

Southwest of Lincoln Park at the end of Pt. Lobos/Geary Blvd. sits the precarious **Cliff House,** the third of that name to occupy this spot (the previous two burned down before the present structure was erected in 1909). Along with some overpriced restaurants, the Cliff House houses the **Musée Mecanique,** an arcade devoted to the games of yesteryear—not Donkey Kong and Space Invaders, but wooden and cast-iron creations dating back to the 1890s. *(Open daily in summer 10am-8pm; in winter 11am-7pm. Free, but you'll want to sink a stack of quarters into the games.)* The games are ingenious and remarkably addictive, and they're accompanied by fortune tellers, love testers, "naughty" kinescopes, and player pianos. Presiding over them all is "Laughing Sal," a roaring mechanical clown that, according to a plaque on the wall, "has made us smile and/or terrified children for over fifty years."

Next door, the **National Park Service Visitors Center** (556-8642) dispenses info on the wildlife of the cliffs and the wildlife of the house (open daily 10am-5pm). Don't feed the coin-operated binoculars which look out over **Seal Rocks**—head into the visitors center instead and have a free look through its telescope. **Ocean Beach,** the largest and most popular of San Francisco's beaches, begins south of Point Lobos and extends down the northwestern edge of the coastline. The strong undertow along the point is very dangerous, but die-hard surfers brave the treacherous currents and the ice-cold water to ride the best waves in San Francisco. Swimming is allowed at **China Beach** at the end of Seacliff Ave. on the eastern edge of Lincoln Park. The water is cold here too, but the views are stunning (lifeguards on duty Apr.-Oct.).

The Presidio and the Golden Gate Bridge

The **Presidio** is a sprawling preserve that extends all the way from the Marina in the east to the wealthy Sea Cliff area in the west. Its otherwise dull expanses are ideal for biking, jogging, and hiking. The preserve also supports the southern end of San Francisco's world-famous Golden Gate Bridge. Take MUNI bus #28, 29, or Golden Gate transit buses into the Presidio.

All but synonymous with the city itself, the majestic **Golden Gate Bridge** spans the mouth of San Francisco Bay, a rust-colored symbol of the West's boundless confidence. Countless photographic renderings can't pack the punch of a personal encounter with the suspended colossus itself. The bridge's overall length is 8981 ft., the main span is 4200 ft. long, and the stolid towers are 746 ft. high. Though carefully disaster-proofed against seismic threat, the bridge still claims many victims through suicide (it is the most popular site for suicides in the world) and lack of a traffic divider. If they make it across, southbound cars pay $3; both directions are free for bikes and pedestrians. Across the bridge, **Vista Point** offers incredible views of the city and bridge on fogless days. **Baker Beach,** in Golden Gate National Recreation Area, offers a picturesque but chilly place to tan and swim. Better wind shelter makes the north half of the beach one of the city's most popular nude beaches, though you should still expect to see a lot of goose pimples.

Marina and Pacific Heights

The **Marina** is home to more young, moneyed professionals than any other part of San Francisco. Few signs of the '89 earthquake, which hit this area hard, still mar the elegant finish.

Scientific American calls the **Exploratorium**, 3601 Lyon St. (563-7337, recording 561-0360), on Marina Blvd., "the best science museum in the world," and it is indeed a mad scientist's dream. *(Open Th-Tu 10am-6pm, W 10am-9pm; Labor Day-Memorial Day, Th-Tu 10am-5pm, W 10am-9:30pm. $9, students and seniors $7, disabled $5, ages 6-17 $5, ages 3-5 $2.50; free 1st W of each month.)* Displays include interactive tornadoes, computer planet-managing, and giant bubble-makers poised to take over the world. All sorts flock here, from schoolkids to grannies to punks on dates. The Exploratorium holds over 4000 people, and when admission is free once a month, it usually does. Within the Exploratorium dwells the **Tactile Dome** (561-0362), a pitch-dark maze of tunnels, slides, nooks, and crannies designed to help refine your sense of touch. *(Open during museum hrs. $12 includes museum admission. Reservations required.)*

Next door to the Exploratorium sits the **Palace of Fine Arts** (Baker St., between Jefferson and Bay). The imposing domed structure and curving colonnades are reconstructed remnants of the 1915 Panama Pacific Exposition, which commemorated the opening of the Panama Canal and signalled San Francisco's recovery from the Earthquake of 1906. To the east of Marina Green at Laguna and Marina lies **Fort Mason,** site of a popular hostel and headquarters for the Golden Gate National Recreation Area. While not nearly as spectacular as the other lands under the GGNRA's aegis, the manicured grounds make a nice spot for strolling and picnicking.

Fisherman's Wharf

East along the waterfront is San Francisco's most visited—and most reviled—tourist destination. Anchored by the shopping complexes of Pier 39 in the east and Ghirardelli Sq. in the west, Fisherman's Wharf is home to 8 blocks of while-you-wait caricature artists, "olde-fashioned" fudge "shoppes," penny flattening machines, and enough t-shirts to stretch around the world an estimated 8 million times. No wonder the tour buses pile in. Conventional attractions aside, the best way to appreciate the wharf is to wake up at 4am, put on a warm sweater, and go down to the piers to see why it's called Fisherman's Wharf. You can see the loading and outfitting of small ships, the animated conversation, the blanket of the morning mist, and the incredible view—without the rapacious crowds. If you're up *really* early, you might even find a parking place. MUNI buses #32 and 42 and the Powell-Mason and Powell-Hyde cable cars run to the Wharf. Buses #19, 47, and 49 also get you pretty close.

Easily visible from boats and the waterfront is **Alcatraz Island.** Named in 1775 for now departed flocks of *alcatraces* (pelicans), this former federal prison looms over San Francisco Bay, 1½ mi. from Fisherman's Wharf. During World War I, conscientious objectors were held on the island along with men convicted of violent crimes while in the service. In the 30s, the federal government used it to hold those who had wrought too much havoc in other prisons, including infamous prisoners like Al Capone, "Machine Gun" Kelly, and "The Birdman" Robert Stroud. Of the 23 men who attempted to escape, all were recaptured or killed, except for five who were "presumed drowned," their bodies never found. In 1962, Attorney General Robert Kennedy closed the prison, and the island's existence was uneventful until 1969, when about 80 Native Americans occupied it as a symbolic gesture, claiming "the Rock" as their property under the terms of a broken 19th-century treaty.

Alcatraz is currently a part of the **Golden Gate National Recreation Area** (561-4345). The **Blue and Gold Fleet** (705-5444 or 705-5555; call daily 7am-8pm), runs boats to Alcatraz from **Pier 41** (call several days in advance). Once on Alcatraz, you can wander by yourself or take the audiotape-guided tour, full of clanging chains and the ghosts of prisoners past. *(Boats depart every 30min. from Pier 41, in summer 9:15am-4:15pm, in winter 9:45am-2:45pm. Arrive 20min. before departure. $7.75, seniors $6, ages 5-11 $4.50. Audio tours $3.25, ages 5-11 50¢.)* A steady stream of tourists files off the ferry and through the cellblocks, but the crowds can't spoil the ominous feel of the abandoned prison or the surprising beauty of the island itself. The **Red and White Fleet** (447-0597 or 800-BAY-

CRUISE/229-2784) operates a 45min. cruise tour called Round the Rock, which circles the island but does not land (boats depart from Pier 43½; $11, seniors $9, ages 9-11 $7).

Back on the mainland, **Pier 39** (981-7437) juts toward Alcatraz on pilings that extend several hundred yards into the harbor. *(Shops open daily 10:30am-8:30pm.)* Its creators designed it to recall old San Francisco, but it ended up looking more like a backdrop from a Ronald Reagan Western. Toward the end of the pier is **Center Stage,** where mimes, jugglers, and magicians play the crowds. A number of the marina docks have been claimed by wet, barking **sea lions** that pile onto the wharf to gawk at human tourists on sunny days. You can gawk right back on any of the expensive **tour boats** and **ferries** docked west of Pier 39. Similar opportunities lie aboard the Blue and Gold Fleet or the Red and White Fleet, which were named for the respective colors of Bay Area university rivals Berkeley and Stanford. Tours cruise under the Golden Gate Bridge past Angel Island and Alcatraz, providing sweeping views of the San Francisco skyline.

Even if you don't know the fo'c'sle from the poop, you'll be able to get your sea legs aboard the **Maritime Museum** (561-6662), Beach St. at Polk, and its five vessels docked along the Hyde St. Pier. *(Open daily 10am-6pm; $4, ages 12-17 $2, seniors and under 12 free.)*

Ghirardelli (GEAR-ah-deh-lee) **Sq.,** 900 N. Point St. (775-5500), is the most famous of the shopping malls in the area around Fisherman's Wharf, known for producing some of the world's best chocolate. The remains of the machinery from Ghirardelli's original factory display the chocolate-making process in the rear of the **Ghirardelli Chocolate Manufactory,** an old-fashioned ice-cream parlor. The nearby Soda Fountain serves up loads of its world-famous hot fudge sauce on huge sundaes ($6).

North Beach

As Columbus Ave. and Stockton St. run north, there is a gradual transition from shops selling ginseng and roast duck to those selling provolone and biscotti. Lying north of Chinatown is the legendary Italian community of North Beach, where the Beat movement was born. In the early 1950s, a group of poets and writers including Jack Kerouac, Allen Ginsberg, Maynard Krebs, and Lawrence Ferlinghetti came here to write, drink, and raise some hell. As long as North Beach has jazz and black coffee, and shady corners in bars and cafes, something of their bohemian cool will live on.

Bordered by Union, Filbert, Stockton, and Powell is **Washington Sq.,** North Beach's *piazza,* a pretty lawn edged by trees and watched over by a statue of not Washington, but Benjamin Franklin. Mrs. Lillie Hitchcock Coit donated the **Volunteer Firemen Memorial,** in the middle of the square. Rescued from a fire as a girl, Coit seemed hellbent on thanking the city the rest of her life; she also put up the money to build **Coit Tower** (362-0808), which stands a few blocks to the east of the memorial. The tower commands a spectacular view of the city and the bay from **Telegraph Hill,** the steep mount from which a semaphore signalled the arrival of ships in Gold Rush days. *(Open daily 10am-7pm; Oct.-May 9am-4pm. Elevator fare $3, over 64 $2, ages 6-12 $1.)* Rumor has it that the tower was built to resemble a fire nozzle. Its other nickname, "Coitus Tower," suggests a cruder inspiration.

Drawn to the area by low rents and cheap bars, the Beat writers came to national attention when Lawrence Ferlinghetti's **City Lights Bookstore,** 261 Columbus Ave. (362-8193), published Allen Ginsberg's *Howl,* banned in 1956. *(Open daily 10am-midnight.)* A judge found the poem "not obscene" after an extended trial, but the resulting publicity vaulted the Beats into literary infamy and turned North Beach into a must-see for curious visitors. Rambling and well-stocked, City Lights has since expanded, but it remains committed to publishing young poets and other writers under its own imprint. Radical political writings line the basement, while upstairs a comfortable poetry/reading room contains self-published works, including lots of Beats. Says a wide-eyed clerk, "We're more than a bookstore—we're on to something."

Nob Hill and Russian Hill

Avast ye, travelers! Here thar be filthy rich nabobs and thar foofy dogs! In the late 19th century, Nob Hill attracted the West's railroad magnates and robber barons. Today, their ostentatious mansions still make it one of the nation's most prestigious addresses. Largely residential, Nob and Russian Hills merit only a brief diversion.

CALIFORNIA

Grace Cathedral, 1100 California St. (749-6310), at Taylor, the most immense Gothic edifice west of the Mississippi, crowns Nob Hill. *(Open Su-F 7am-6pm, Sa 8am-6pm. Su services 7:30, 8:30, 11am, and 3:30pm.)* The castings for its portals are such exact imitations of Ghiberti's on the Baptistery in Florence that they were used to restore the originals. Inside, modern murals mix San Franciscan and national historical events with scenes from saints' lives.

After the steep journey up Nob Hill, you will understand what inspired the development of the vehicles celebrated at the **Cable Car Powerhouse and Museum,** 1201 Mason St. (474-1887), at Washington. *(Open daily 10am-6pm; Nov.-Mar. 10am-5pm. Free.)* The building is the working center of the cable-car system—you can look down on the operation from a gallery or view displays to learn more about the picturesque cars, some of which date back to 1873. Kitsch konnoisseurs will want to check out the **Tonga Room,** also in the Fairmont Hotel. In a city blessed with several faux-Polynesian tiki bars, King Tonga must be seen to be believed (see **Bars,** p. 795).

Nearby **Russian Hill** is named after Russian sailors who died during an expedition in the early 1800s and were buried on the southeast crest. At the top, the famous curves of **Lombard St.,** between Hyde and Leavenworth, afford a fantastic view of the city and harbor. The switchbacks that earned its epithet, "the crookedest street in the world," were installed in the 1920s to allow horse-drawn carriages to negotiate the extremely steep hill. The view north along Hyde Street—a steep drop to Fisherman's Wharf and lonely Alcatraz floating in the bay—isn't too shabby either.

Nihonmachi (Japantown)

Japanese immigrants moved to this central neighborhood en masse after the 1906 quake, which destroyed this part of town. Today the community has largely dispersed, moving to more spacious accommodations in the Richmond and Sunset districts and elsewhere. In what's left of Japantown, stores hawk the latest Hello Kitty gadgets and karaoke bars warble J-pop all along Polk around the **Japanese Cultural and Trade Center.** Stretching from Laguna to Fillmore, the 5-acre shopping center includes Japanese *udon* houses, sushi bars, and a massage center and bathhouse.

Chinatown

The largest Chinese community outside of Asia (over 100,000 people), Chinatown is also the most densely populated of San Francisco's neighborhoods. Chinese laborers began coming to San Francisco in the mid-nineteenth century as refugees from the Opium Wars; they were soon put to work constructing the railroads of the West. After the tracks had been laid, white racism swelled against the Chinese enclave in their midst. In the 1880s, white Californians secured a law against further Chinese immigration as proof against the so-called "Yellow Peril." Stranded in San Francisco, the Chinese-American community banded together to protect themselves in this small section of downtown. As the city grew, speculators tried to take over the increasingly valuable land, but the neighborhood refused to be expelled. To this day, Chinatown remains almost exclusively Chinese.

Grant Ave., the oldest street in San Francisco, is a sea of Chinese banners, signs, and architecture. Some see its souvenir shops hawking bamboo fans and little plastic pagodas and complain that Grant Ave. has become a tourist trap to rival Fisherman's Wharf. Tourist trap it may be, but there's nothing recent about it. That's been its role since the 1850s, when sailors staggered down from the Barbary Coast saloons in search of sex, drink, and opium. Most of the picturesque pagodas were designed around the turn of the century—not as authentic replicas of Chinese architecture but as come-ons to Western tourists. At Grant and Bush stands the ornate, dragon-crested **Gateway to Chinatown,** given as a gift by the Republic of China in 1969. "All under heaven is good for the people," say the Chinese characters above the gate. Just a few steps off Grant, **Jackson, Stockton,** and **Pacific St.** are no less crowded but feel more Chinese. Pharmacies stock both Western and Eastern remedies for common ailments, produce markets are stacked with inexpensive vegetables, and Chinese newspapers are sold by vendors eating their ramen breakfast out of thermoses. Once lined with brothels and opium dens, **Ross**

Alley, off Jackson St. between Grant and Stockton, still has the exotic look of old China-town. The narrow street has stood in for the Orient in such films as *Big Trouble in Little China*, *Karate Kid II*, and *Indiana Jones and the Temple of Doom.*

Squeeze into a tiny doorway to watch fortune cookies being shaped by hand in the **Golden Gate Cookie Company,** 56 Ross Alley (781-3956; bag of cookies $2, with "hilar-ious," "sexy" fortunes $4). Colorful **Waverly Place,** off California St. between Grant and Stockton, is known in Chinese as "the street of painted balconies." The **Tin Hou Tem-ple** at 125 Waverly is the oldest in the city.

A stone bridge leads from the square to the **Chinese Culture Center,** 750 Kearny St. (986-1822), in the Holiday Inn, which houses exhibits of Chinese-American art and sponsors two **walking tours** of Chinatown (gallery open Tu-Sa 10am-4pm, Su noon-4pm). The **Heritage Walk** surveys the history of Chinatown (Sa 2pm; $15, under 19 $5), and the **Culinary Walk** teaches the preparation of Chinese food (by arrangement; $30, under 19 $15; price includes *dim sum* at Four Seas on Grant Ave.). Both walks require advance reservations.

ENTERTAINMENT AND NIGHTLIFE

The free *Bay Guardian* and *SF Weekly* have thorough listings of dance clubs and live music, and the free monthly *Oblivion* has info on San Francisco's gay scene. The **Enter-tainment Hotline** (391-2001 or 391-2002) suggests more entertainment options. Hard-ball fans can watch the **San Francisco Giants** battle the winds of **3COM Park** (762-2255; tickets $6-24).

Bars

Nightlife in San Francisco is as varied as the city's personal ads. Everyone from "shy first-timer" to "bearded strap daddy" to "pre-op transsexual top" can find places to go on a Saturday (or even a Tuesday) night.

Lucky 13, 2140 Market St. (487-1313), between Church and Sanchez in the Castro. Laid-back and friendly, maybe too much so to pull off its punk rock vibe. Laid-back service, too; getting a bartender's attention sometimes requires an air horn and a flare gun. Pool, pinball, a low, crowded balcony, and a well-stocked juke box. Good selection of single-malt scotch and 28 beers on tap (pints $3.50, before 7pm $2.50), not one of them named Bud, Miller, or Coors. Pint of goldfish $1. Open M-F 4pm-2am, Sa-Su 2pm-2am.

Café du Nord, 2170 Market St. (861-5016), between Church and Sanchez in the Castro. The steep staircase takes you back in time to a red velvet club with speakeasy ambi-ence. Excellent live music nightly—lounge, swing, salsa, big band—and dancing to match. Salsa Tu and Swing Su with free lessons (after the $5 cover); you too can party like its 1949. Beer $3.50. Cover after 8pm $3-5. Happy hour 5-7pm with swank $2 martinis. Open Su-Tu 6pm-2am, W-Sa 4pm-2am.

Li Po's, 916 Grant St. (982-0072), between Washington and Jackson. Quite simply the coolest place in Chinatown. Dark and almost claustrophobic, with an ominous cave-like entrance and an incense-burning shrine behind the bar. Chinese men play mah jongg to the sounds of early 80s Madonna in the afternoon; after midnight, partyers from North Beach bars invade. Stairs to the bathroom are treacherous even for the sober. Open daily 2pm-2am.

Mad Dog in the Fog, 530 Haight St. (626-7270), near Fillmore in the lower Haight. Brit-ish bar where the drink is Guinness, the pastime is darts, and soccer is everything else. Key matches are shown live via satellite no matter what bloody time it is—don't miss the spectacle of 50 drunken expats screaming at the telly at 6am. Pints $2.75 daily until 7pm, $2 F 5-7pm, and $1 with lunch M-F 11:30am-2:30pm. Bangers and mash $5. High-stakes (cash and beer) trivia M and Th at 9:30pm. Open M-F 11:30am-2am, Sa-Su 10am-2am.

Toronado, 547 Haight St. (863-2276), in the lower Haight. 41 flavors of beer on tap. 41, not counting ciders, malts, and steaming spiced mead ($3). Open daily 11:30am-2am.

Tonga Room, 950 Mason St. (772-5278), in the Fairmont Hotel on Nob Hill. The king of kitsch. An enormous tiki bar with fake bamboo trees, muumuu-ed waitresses, and enormous fruity drinks bristling with umbrellas, swizzle sticks, and little swords. The house band performs hula music on a floating stage in the artificial lagoon, and tropical storms roll in every 30min. with simulated thunder, lightning and rain. This kind of class don't come cheap, though—go during happy hour (M-F 5-7pm) when drinks are "only" $3-5 and an all-you-can-eat Polynesian buffet is $5. Open Su-Th 5pm-midnight, F-Sa 5pm-1am.

Clubs

The San Francisco club scene changes faster than a speeding bullet or a man in a phone booth, so read *SF Weekly* or the *Bay Guardian,* pick up flyers in hip coffee shops and stores, and ask around. This is even more true of San Francisco's underground rave scene. **Housewares,** 1322 Haight (252-1440), is a rave clothing store and a good source of flyers for parties and events. They maintain a **rave hotline** at 281-0125. Up the street, **F-8,** 1816 Haight (221-4142), also provides flyers and a telephone hotline (541-5019), more geared toward trance and techno. The **Be-At Line** (626-4087), established by the son of Mayor Willie Brown, is a rundown of the night's most happening happenings, be they well-known or obscure. It's the first and only resource for many professional clubgoers. Unless otherwise noted, all clubs are ages 21+ only, though precocious club kids know that primarily queer bars tend to check less religiously, and the better you look, the less likely they are to ask for ID.

Nickie's Barbecue, 460 Haight St. (621-6508), at Fillmore in the Haight. This dive is one of the chillest, friendliest small clubs in the whole damn city, with a low cover and even less attitude. Live DJ every night with different themes ranging from world music to hip-hop to funk. Great dancing, diverse multi-ethnic crowd. Cover around $5. Open daily 9pm-2am.

V/SF, 278 11th (621-1530), at Folsom in SoMa, is a space for a number of unconnected weekly events. Hot music keeps the well-heeled, good-looking crowd coming back for more in this inviting space of 2 dance floors and an ultra-mellow rooftop patio. Valet parking and $10-and-up cover makes it hard to pretend you're slumming. Su is Spundae (techno/house); Sa is Pablo's Sugar Shack (techno/disco).

The Elbo Room, 647 Valencia St. (552-7788), at 18th in the Mission. Various theme nights have a Latin flavor with a funk backbeat. Dress is casual and skimpy on the crowded dance floor. Cool off in the bar downstairs with pool, pinball, TV, and $3 pints. Cover $3-6. Open nightly 10pm-2am.

Holy Cow, 1535 Folsom (621-6087), near 11th in SoMa, is about halfway between a club and a bar. Happy collegiate crowd drinks lots of flavored beer, dances to 80s music, and uses "party" as a verb. Not the coolest star in the SoMa system, but a lot of fun just the same. Low cover ($2-3) or none at all. Happy hour M-Th 8-9:30pm. Open Sa-Th 8pm-2am, F 6pm-2am.

Trocadero, 520 4th St. (437-4446), at Bryant, in SoMa. A dance floor the size of—and decorated like—an airplane hangar, featuring standard alternative and electronic dance music most of the week, with occasional industrial-goth bands. Famous for the amateur S&M party "Bondage A Go Go" every W. Free drinks for "ladies and trannies handcuffed to the bar" before 10pm. 18+. Cover $7.

Gay and Lesbian Nightlife

Politics aside, nightlife alone is enough to make San Francisco a queer mecca. The boys hang in the **Castro** (around the intersection of Castro and Market), while the grrrls prefrrr the **Mission** (on and off Valencia); both genders frolic along Polk St. (several blocks north of Geary), and in **SoMa.** Polk St. can be seedy and SoMa barren, so keep a watchful eye for trouble. The best queer guide is the tri-weekly free *Oblivion,* but the bi-weekly *Odyssey* and the annual *Betty and Pansy's Severe Queer Review* are also definitive sources.

The Café, 2367 Market St. (861-3846), the Castro. A classic. Mixed gay-lesbian-and-straight crowd chills casually in the afternoon with pool and pinball, but when the sun goes down and the dance floor gets pumping, it's virtually all gay, all 20-something, all male. Mirrors surround the dance floor so you never have to dance with anyone less fabulous than yourself. Balcony overlooking Castro and Market is ideal for boy-watching. Repeat *Guardian* awards for best gay bar. No cover. Open daily 12:30pm-2am.

Esta Noche, 3079 16th St. (861-5757), at Valencia in the Mission. The city's premiere gay Latino bar is always *en fuego.* Regular drag shows, both on stage and off. Gringos are politely asked to refrain from dancing salsa without competent instruction. Cover $3-5. Open Su-Th 1pm-2am, F-Sa 1pm-3am.

The EndUp, 401 6th St. (357-0827), at Harrison in SoMa. A San Francisco institution and club of last resort. Outdoor garden and indoor fireplace contribute to the homey feel. Infamous Su Tea Dance starts at 6am and doesn't stop for 20hr. Cover $5-10. Hrs. vary, but open almost continuously on weekends.

CoCo Club, 139 8th St. (626-2337) at Minna in SoMa. Attached to, and affiliated with, the Chat House Cafe, the relatively new CoCo Club is filling a void with live music and dancing for women. Events vary from spoken-word performance art to acoustic folksingers to funk/hip-hop DJs. Cover around $5. Open Tu-Su 7pm-2am.

The Lexington Club, 3464 19th St. (863-2052), at Lexington in the Mission. Neighborhood watering hole for Mission lesbians. Jukebox careens from the Clash to Johnny Cash, hitting all the tuff muff favorites (k.d. lang, Sleater-Kinney, Liz Phair) along the way. Happy hour M-F 4-7pm. Open daily 3pm-2am.

The Stud, 399 9th St. (252-STUD/7883), at Harrison, in SoMa. This legendary bar/club recreates itself every night of the week—W are disco, Su are 80s nostalgia, Tu are the wild and wacky drag and transgender party known as "Trannyshack." Crowd is mostly gay male, but rough and tumble dykes do "Junk" here one Sa per month. Cover around $5. Open daily 5pm-2am.

Club Townsend, 177 Townsend (974-6020), between 2nd and 3rd in SoMa. A dance club big enough for its own zip code, Club T is populated by folks of all intentions during the week, but Sa "Universe" and Su "Pleasure dome" are predominantly gay male. "Club Q" is the major lesbian night (1st F of each month). Cover around $10, but free passes (good until 10 or 11pm) can often be found around town.

Live Music

SF Weekly and the *Guardian* are the place to start looking for the latest live music listings. Hard-core audiophiles might also snag a copy of *BAM*. Many of the bars and a few of the clubs listed above feature regular live bands at various times—what follows is a list of venues principally devoted to keeping it real.

Fillmore, 1805 Geary (346-6000), at Fillmore in Japantown. Bands that would pack stadiums in other cities are often eager to play at the legendary Fillmore, a foundation of the city's 1960s music scene. All ages. Tickets $15-25. Wheelchair access.

Bottom of the Hill, 1233 17th St. (621-4455), at Texas, in Potrero Hill (south of SoMa). Intimate rock club with tiny stage is the last best place to see up-and-comers before they move to bigger venues. Managers seem to book alternarock bands here just moments before they go supernova. Cover $3-7. Age limits vary. Su afternoons feature 3 local bands and all-you-can-eat BBQ for $5.

Jazz at Pearl's, 256 Columbus St. (291-8255), at Broadway in North Beach. Traditional jazz combos in a comfortable setting for an older, well-dressed crowd. No cover, but a 2-drink min. Open daily 8:30pm-2am.

Up and Down Club, 1151 Folsom (626-2388), at 7th in SoMa. Sleek golden supper club is ground zero for San Francisco's emergent jazz and fusion scene. Open M and Th-Sa 8pm-2am.

Bimbo's 365 Club, 1025 Columbus (474-0365), at Chestnut in North Beach. Cavernous cocktail lounge jumped on the swing bandwagon early—about 1931, to be precise. Variety of musical acts, but swing and jazz are the mainstays. Dress swanky. Tickets from $10.

Comedy

Cobb's Comedy Club, 2801 Leavenworth St. (928-4320), at Beach and Hyde in the Cannery at Fisherman's Wharf. Big and small names take on this San Francisco standard. 18+. Tix (around $10) available through BASS or at the club after 7pm.

CALIFORNIA

Josie's Cabaret and Juice Joint, 3583 16th St., (861-7933), at Market in the Castro. Drag queens, cabaret, and queer-themed stand-up comedy. M is open mic night. Cover $5-15. Shows 8 and 10pm. Come early for good seats. A funky cafe by day.

Some of San Francisco's more popular festivals include: **Asian American International Film Showcase** (863-0814; mid-Mar.), AMC Kabuki 8 Theater, Japantown; **Cherry Blossom Festival** (563-2313; Apr.), Japantown; **San Francisco International Film Festival** (929-5000; Apr.-May), the oldest film festival in North America; **Bay to Breakers** (777-7770; 3rd Su in May), starting at the Embarcadero, the largest foot race in the U.S., with up to 100,000 participants (special centipede category); **San Francisco International Gay and Lesbian Film Festival** (703-8663; June), Roxie Cinema (16th St. at Valencia) and Castro Theatre (Castro St. at Market), California's second-largest film festival and the world's largest gay and lesbian media event; **Pride Day** (864-FREE/3733; last Su in June), the High Holy Day of the queer calendar; **San Francisco Blues Festival** (826-6837; 3rd weekend in Sept.), Fort Mason, the oldest blues festival in America; **Halloween** (Oct. 31), the Castro; **Dia de los Muertos (Day of the Dead)** (821-1155; Nov. 1), the Mission; and **Chinese New Year Celebration** (982-3000; Feb. 7-22, 1999), Chinatown.

■ Berkeley

Berkeley's fame as an intellectual center and haven for iconoclasts is well founded. Although the peak of its political activism occurred in the 60s and 70s, U.C. Berkeley continues to cultivate consciousness and brainy brawn. The vitality of the population infuses the streets, which are strewn with hip cafes and top-notch bookstores. Telegraph Ave. remains Berkeley's spiritual heart, home to street-corner soothsayers, hirsute hippies, and itinerant street-musicians who never left.

ORIENTATION AND PRACTICAL INFORMATION

Berkeley lies across the bay northeast of San Francisco, just north of Oakland. Reach the city by **BART** from downtown San Francisco or by car (**I-80** or **Rte. 24**). Crossing the bay by BART ($2.70) is quick and easy; driving in the city is difficult and frustrating. The choice is yours.

Trains: Amtrak (800-872-7245). Closest station is in Oakland, but travelers can board in Berkeley at 2nd St. and University. **Bay Area Rapid Transit (BART)** (465-2278) runs from **Berkeley station,** 2160 Shattuck Ave., at Center, close to the western edge of campus (fare to San Francisco $2.70) and **North Berkeley station,** Sacramento St. at Delaware St. (fare to San Francisco $2.75).

Public Transportation: Alameda County (AC) Transit (817-1717 or 800-559-INFO/4636). Buses #15, 40, 43, and 51 run from the Berkeley BART station to downtown Oakland via Martin Luther King, Jr., Telegraph, Shattuck, and College Ave., respectively. Fare $1.25; seniors, ages 5-12, and disabled 60¢. Transfers (25¢) valid 1hr.

Taxis: A1 Yellow Cab (644-1111) and **Berkeley Yellow Cab** (841-2265). $2 base fare and per mi. Both 24hr.

Visitor Info: Berkeley Convention and Visitor Bureau, 2015 Center St. (800-847-4823 or 549-7040, 24hr. hotline 549-8710), at Milvia. Usually open M-F 9am-5pm.

Internet Access: U.C. Computer, 2569 Telegraph Ave. (649-6089). $3 for 15min., $5 for 30min., $7 for 1hr. Open M-Sa 10am-6pm.

Post Office: 2000 Allston Way (649-3100). Open M-F 8:30am-5pm, Sa 10am-2pm. **ZIP code:** 94704. **Area code:** 510.

ACCOMMODATIONS

There are surprisingly few cheap accommodations in Berkeley. **The Bed and Breakfast Network** (547-6380) coordinates 20 East Bay B&Bs with a range of rates. A popular option is to stay in San Francisco and make daytrips to Berkeley.

◉**Golden Bear Motel,** 1620 San Pablo Ave. (525-6770 or 800-525-6770), at Cedar St. 8 blocks from the North Berkeley BART station. Charming Spanish-style motel with big, bouncy beds. Check-out noon. Singles $54; doubles $64; $5 per additional person up to 2 additional people. 2-bedroom cottages with kitchen $120-135. Reservations recommended.

UC Berkeley Summer Visitor Housing (642-5925). Residence halls are open to visitors from the beginning of June to mid-Aug. Free Internet access, use of local and campus phone service, ping-pong and pool tables, and TV room. Parking ($3 per day), laundry (75¢ wash), meals, and photocopying available. Singles $38; doubles $50. Linen and towels provided. Personal checks not accepted.

YMCA, 2001 Allston Way (848-6800), at Milvia. Adequate, if worn, rooms are available in the co-ed hotel portion of this YMCA. Free use of pool, linen, and fitness facilities. In-room phones for incoming calls only; pay phones in the hallway. Shared bathrooms. Singles $25, $96 per week; doubles $33/$106; triples $40. 14-night max. stay; special applications are available for longer stays. Registration daily 8am-9:30pm. No curfew. Reservations require 14-day notice and a $25 deposit. Must be 18 or older with ID.

FOOD

Berkeley offers a variety of budget dining, munching, and sipping options. The north end of **Telegraph Ave.** caters to student appetites and wallet sizes—hence the high concentration of pizza joints and trendy cafes. When you've maxed out on caffeine, head out to **Solano Ave.** for Asian cuisine or meander down to **San Pablo** along the bay for hearty American fare. If you want to make your own meals, the best grocery shopping in the bay awaits at **Berkeley Bowl,** 2777 Shattuck Ave. (843-6929), at Stuart. The lanes of this former bowling alley are now stocked with endless fresh produce, seafood, and bread. (Open M-F 9:30am-7pm, Sa 9am-6pm.)

◉**Pasand Madras Cuisine,** 2286 Shattuck St. (549-2559) at Bancroft. Melt-in-your-mouth *kormas,* curries, and tandooris fit for Vishnu. All-you-can-eat buffet ($6.50) from noon-2:30pm means endless chewy *naan* bread. Open daily 11:30am-10pm.

Long Life Vegi House, 2129 University Ave. (845-6072). Vast menu full of countless vegetable and "vegetarian meat" options. Most entrees $5-7; portions are huge. Friendly, prompt service. Eat in or take out. Daily lunch special 11:30am-3pm features entree, egg roll, and soup ($3.65). Open daily 11:30am-9:30pm.

Crepes A-Go-Go, 2125 University Ave. (841-7722). Crepes are on the thick side for hands-on convenience. Cheese and turkey crepes $3.50, honey and kiwi crepes $3.75. Pleasant staff also vends sandwiches and salad to Berkeleyans on the go-go. Open Su-Th 9am-10pm, F-Sa 9am-10:30pm.

Ann's Soup Kitchen, 2498 Telegraph Ave. (548-8885), at Dwight. Weekday special includes 2 pancakes with bacon and eggs or homefries ($3.15), and you may find an extra cake or egg smiling up at you. Fresh-squeezed juice $1.50. Open M and W-F 8am-7pm, Tu 8am-3pm, Sa-Su 8am-5pm.

Café Intermezzo, 2442 Telegraph Ave. (849-4592), at Haste. It's doubtful you've ever had a salad as big as the ones here—it's a Berkeley thing. The fresh produce in the tossed green salad ($3.23) and Veggie Delight ($4.84) will fuel you for the rest of the day. Cheap beer (Anchor Steam $1.75). Sandwiches $4.29. Open M-F 10:30am-9pm.

The Blue Nile, 2525 Telegraph Ave. (540-6777). Huge portions of authentic Ethiopian food in a lavish setting. Wide variety of vegetarian dishes. Lunch entrees $5-7, dinner entrees $7-9. Eat with your fingers, aided by *injera* (Ethiopian baked bread), and get blotto on *Tej* (honey wine, $2 per glass). Weekend reservations recommended. Open Tu-Sa 11:30am-10pm, Su 5-10pm.

SIGHTS

In 1868, the private College of California and the public Agricultural, Mining, and Mechanical Arts College coupled to give birth to the **University of California.** Berkeley was the first of the nine University of California campuses, so by seniority it has sole rights to the nickname "Cal." The school has a diverse enrollment of over 30,000 stu-

CALIFORNIA

dents and 1350 full professors, and a library system with over 8.7 million volumes, creating a lively and internationally respected academic community. Classes are in session from mid-August to mid-May each year.

Pass through **Sather Gate** into **Sproul Plaza,** both sites of celebrated student sit-ins and bloody confrontations with police, to enter the 160-acre Berkeley campus. The Plaza, suspended between Berkeley's idyllic campus and raucous Telegraph Ave., is now a perfect place for people watching. Maps of campus are posted everywhere; the **U.C. Berkeley Visitor Center,** 101 University Hall, 2200 University Ave. (642-5215), also hands out campus maps for a dime. *(Open M-F 8:30am-4:30pm.)* Guided campus **tours** leave from the center M-F 10am and from **Sather Tower** (Sa 10am and Su 1pm). Besides the loonies singing and muttering in Sproul Plaza, the most dramatic campus attraction is Sather Tower, better known as the **Campanile** (Italian for "bell tower"), the tallest building on campus at 307 ft. You can ride to its observation level for a great view ($1).

The **Lawrence Hall of Science** (642-5132), on Centennial Drive high atop the eucalyptus-covered hills east of the main campus, is one of the finest science museums in the Bay Area. *(Open daily 10am-5pm. $6; seniors, students, and ages 7-18 $4; ages 3-6 $2.)* Take bus #8 or 65 from the Berkeley BART station (and keep your transfer for $1 off admission) or a university shuttle (642-5149); otherwise it's a long, steep walk.

You haven't really visited Berkeley until you've strolled the first 5 or so blocks of **Telegraph Ave.** The street runs south from Sproul Plaza all the way to downtown Oakland. The action is close to the university, where Telegraph is lined with a motley assortment of cafes, bookstores, and used clothing and record stores. To do Telegraph right, take your time. Mingle with the natives. Enjoy the cafes, and explore the excellent bookstores, where you can browse for ages without getting the evil eye.

Berkeley's biggest confrontation between the People and the Man was not fought over freedom of speech or the war in Vietnam, but for control of a muddy, vacant lot near Telegraph at the intersection of Haste and Bowditch. In April 1969, students, hippies, and radicals christened the patch of university-owned land **People's Park,** tearing up pavement and laying down sod to establish, in the words of the *Berkeley Barb,* "a cultural, political freak out and rap center for the Western world." When the University moved to evict squatters and build a parking garage on the site, resistance stiffened. Governor Ronald Reagan sent in 2000 troops, and the conflict ended with helicopters dropping tear gas on students in Sproul Plaza, one bystander shot dead by police, and a 17-day occupation of Berkeley by the National Guard.

When you're ready to get out of town, Berkeley is happy to oblige. **Tilden Regional Park** (635-0135), in the pine- and eucalyptus-forested hills east of the city, is the anchor of the extensive East Bay park system. Hiking, biking, running, and riding trails crisscross the park and provide impressive views of the Bay Area. The **ridgeline trail** is an especially spectacular bike ride. Within the park, a 19th-century carousel delights juvenile thrill-seekers. The small, sandy beach of **Lake Anza** (848-3385) is a popular swimming spot during the hottest days of summer, often overrun with squealing kids. *(Lake open 11am-6pm during summer. $2.50, children and seniors $1.50.)*

ENTERTAINMENT

The university offers a number of quality entertainment options. Hang out with procrastinating students in or around the **Student Union** (643-0693). **The Underground** (642-3825) contains a ticket office, an arcade, bowling alleys, foosball tables, and pool tables, all run from a central blue desk (open M-F noon-8pm, Sa 10am-6pm). **Caffé Strada,** 2300 College Ave. (843-5282), at Bancroft, is a glittering jewel of the caffeine-fueled-intellectual scene (open daily 7am-midnight). **Spats,** 1974 Shattuck Ave. (841-7225), between University and Berkeley, lures locals and students with the warmth of the staff, the original drinks (Danko Bar Screamer $4.50), and the quirky surroundings (open M-F 11:30am-2am, Sa 4pm-2am). **924 Gilman,** 924 Gilman St. (525-9926), at 8th, is a legendary all-ages club and a staple of California punk. (Cover $3-5 with purchase of a $2 membership card, good for one year.)

■ Oakland

Long-suffering Oakland sings the blues. The city's salad days were the first decades of this century, when businesses and wealthy families flowed in from San Francisco, many in the wake of the great 1906 earthquake. Oakland's most striking buildings date from that era: the City Hall on 14th St., the Tribune Tower at 13th and Franklin, the Paramount Theater on Broadway, and the nearby Fox Oakland Theater on Telegraph at 19th. But the boom died in the Great Depression, and economically, Oakland never really found its feet again. An unfortunate number of those Art Deco office towers and movie palaces are now derelict and falling down. Oakland's central core has some life in it, but just a few blocks west of Broadway or north on San Pablo, dreary ghettos begin that sprawl for miles.

Oakland's scarcity of cheap and safe accommodations and noteworthy sites leave it a better daytrip than vacation destination. The best reason to visit is to catch some live music: whether they're playing the West Coast blues, Oaktown hip-hop, or progressive jazz, Oakland's music venues are unsurpassed. Such a vital scene is always changing, so if you want to be on the very cutting edge, you'll have to do some of your own research. **Koncepts Cultural Gallery** (763-0682) is not a venue but an organization that hosts some of the most groundbreaking progressive jazz sessions (covers $5-25). **Eli's Mile High Club,** 3629 Martin Luther King Jr. Way (655-6661), is the home of the West Coast blues (cover $5-10; soul food kitchen opens at 7pm, music starts by 9pm). **The Fifth Amendment,** 3255 Lakeshore Ave. (832-3242), isn't the most famous, just the best. Jazz and blues musicians take the stage in this downtown club where there's never a cover. (Shows start at 9pm.) **Yoshi's,** 510 Embarcadero W (238-9200), at Jack London Sq., is hardly cutting edge, but it's still an upscale Oakland institution, bringing together world-class sushi and world-class jazz (shows at 8 and 10pm M-Sa, and 2 and 8pm Su).

Outside of Oakland's music scene, the best bona fide sight is probably the **Oakland Museum of California,** 1000 Oak St. (238-2200), at 10th, on the southwest side of the lake near the Lake Merritt BART station. *(Open Tu-Th and Sa-Su 10am-5pm, F 10am-9pm. $8, students and seniors $6; F 3-9pm $5/$3; 1st Su of each month free.)* A complex of three museums devoted to California's history, art, and ecology, the Museum's highlights include photography by Edward Weston and Dorothea Lange, quick-snap panoramic photos of San Francisco by Eadweard Muybridge, and multicultural modern works.

Killer-diller food options include the **Happy Belly Deli,** 30 Jack London Sq. #216 (835-0446), on the 2nd fl. in the Jack London Village, an oasis of genuine character (and budget prices) in touristy Jack London Sq. "Food holds the energy of its experiences and transmits this vibration to the eater," say the owners. (Open M-F 10am-4pm, Sa-Su 9am-4pm; free yoga lessons M at 6pm.) **Lois the Pie Queen,** 851 60th St. (658-5616), at Adeline St. in North Oakland, gets crowded on weekends, but you can probably find a swivel chair at the counter. Don't leave without a $2.50-3 slice of peach cobbler, lemon ice-box, or sweet potato pie. (Open M-F 8am-2pm, Sa 7am-3pm, Su 7am-4pm.)

Drivers can take **I-80** from San Francisco across the Bay Bridge to **I-580** and connect with Oakland **I-980 S,** which has downtown exits at 12th St. or 19th St. **Bay Area Rapid Transit (BART)** (465-BART/2278) provides another option, running from downtown San Francisco to Oakland's stations at **Lake Merritt** (Dublin/Pleasanton or Fremont trains), **12th St.** (Oakland City Center trains), or **19th St.** (Richmond or Pittsburg/Bay Point trains). **Area code:** 510.

■ San Jose

In 1851, San Jose was deemed too small to serve as California's capital, and Sacramento assumed the honors. Today, San Jose (pop. 873,000) is the civic heart of the Silicon Valley and the fastest-growing city in California. But the high-tech gold rush that quadrupled the city's population in a mere 10 years has yet to be matched by aesthetic refinements or cultural activity. San Jose has its good points: the weather is warm, the schools are good, the streets are clean and wide, and there's always plenty of parking.

CALIFORNIA

Copious cops, plus an army of private security guards, keep the city safe—the FBI named it the third-safest city in the country. But despite a new billion-dollar downtown, the largest city in Northern California still feels like suburbia.

PRACTICAL INFORMATION The third-largest city in California and the 11th-largest in the U.S., San Jose lies at the southern end of San Francisco Bay, about 50 mi. from San Francisco (via U.S. 101 or I-280) and 40 mi. from Oakland (via I-880). From San Francisco, take **I-280** rather than U.S.101, which is full of traffic snarls at all hours. San Jose is centered around the convention-hosting malls and plazas near the intersection of east-west **San Carlos St.** and north-south **Market St. San Jose International Airport** is at 1661 Airport Blvd. (277-4759). **Amtrak,** 65 Cahill St. (287-7462 or 800-872-7245), runs to San Francisco (2hr., 1 per day, $9) and Los Angeles (10½hr., 1 per day, $77). **Cal-Train,** 65 Cahill St. (291-5651 or 800-660-4287), at W. San Fernando, runs to San Francisco (1½hr.) with stops at peninsula cities. **Greyhound,** 70 S. Almaden (800-231-2222), at Santa Clara, buses to San Francisco (1¼hr., 17 per day, $6) and Los Angeles (7hr., 13 per day, $36). **Santa Clara Valley Transportation Agency (VTA),** 2 N. First St. (321-2300), offers ultra-modern buses as well as a light-rail system (fare $1.10). The **Visitor Information and Business Center** (977-0900, events line 295-2265; http://www.sanjose.org) is in the San Jose McEnerny Convention Center at San Carlos and Market St. **Martin Luther King Jr. Public Library,** 180 W. San Carlos St. (277-4846), in front of the Convention Center, offers Internet access (open M-W 9am-9pm, Th-Sa 9am-6pm, Su 1-5pm). **Post Office:** 105 N. 1st St. (800-225-8777). **ZIP code:** 95113. **Area code:** 408.

ACCOMMODATIONS, CAMPGROUNDS, AND FOOD San Jose is surrounded by county parks with campgrounds. **Mt. Madonna County Park** (842-2341), on Hecker Pass Hwy., has 117 campsites in a beautiful setting, occupied on a first come, first camped basis. (*Let's Go* does not recommend that you mount Madonna.) The scandalously idyllic hamlet of **Saratoga,** 20min. southwest of San Jose on Rte. 85, offers a number of campsites (tent sites $8; RVs $20; open Apr. to mid-Oct.) and miles of horse and hiking trails in wooded **Sanborn-Skyline County Park** (867-9959, reservations 358-3751), on Sanborn Rd. From Rte. 17 S, take Rte. 9 to Big Basin Way. Along the way sits **Saratoga Springs** (867-9999), a private campground with 32 sites ($20 for 2 people), hot showers, and a general store. **Sanborn Park Hostel (HI-AYH),** 15808 Sanborn Rd. (741-0166), in Sanborn-Skyline Park, 13 mi. west of San Jose, has dorms ($8.50, US nonmembers $10.50, foreign nonmembers $11.50; under 18 ½-price). **San Jose State University,** 375 S. 9th St. (924-6193), at San Salvador, offers dorm rooms with 2 single beds ($29.50).

House of Siam, 55 S. Market St. (279-5668), serves excellent $7-10 meat and meatless dishes (open M-F 11am-3pm and 5-10pm, Sa-Su 11:30am-10pm). **La Guadalajara,** 45 Post St. (292-7352), has been serving delicious Mexican food and cheap, yummy pastries since 1955 (jumbo burritos $3.25, combo plates $4-6; open daily 8:30am-6:30pm). **White Lotus,** 80 N. Market St. (977-0540), between Santa Clara and St. John, is one of the few vegetarian restaurants in the area (open M-Th 11am-2:30pm and 5:30-9pm, F-Sa 11am-9:30pm.)

SIGHTS AND NIGHTLIFE There's a bit to see in San Jose proper, but not much. A few well-funded museums are the only real diversions from the business of websites and microchips. The **Tech Museum of Innovation,** 145 W. San Carlos St. (279-7150), in downtown San Jose, is the closest thing to a Silicon Valley tourist attraction. (*Open Tu-Su 10am-5pm; July-Sept. M-Sa 10am-6pm, Su noon-6pm. $6, seniors $4, ages 6-18 $4.*) Underwritten by area high-tech firms, "the Tech" features hands-on exhibits on robotics, DNA engineering, and space exploration. Science-based toys also grace the **Children's Discovery Museum,** 180 Woz Way (298-5437), behind the Technology Center light-rail station (open Tu-Sa 10am-5pm, Su noon-5pm; $6, seniors $5, under 18 $4).

The **Rosicrucian Egyptian Museum and Planetarium,** 1342 Naglee Ave. (947-3636), at Park, rises out of the suburbs like the work of a mad pharaoh. (*Open W-M 10am-5pm. $7, students and seniors $5, ages 7-15 $3.50. Under 18 must be accompanied by an adult.*) This grand structure houses an extensive collection of Egyptian and Assyrian artifacts, including a walk-in tomb and spooky animal mummies. The collection belongs to the mystical order of the Rosy Cross, who have supposedly long battled the Bavarian Illuminati for world domination.

A number of art galleries are clustered in the downtown core. The **San Jose Museum of Art,** 110 S. Market (271-6840), at San Fernando, presents mass-appeal modern shows. *(Open Tu-W and F-Su 9am-5pm, Th 9am-8pm. $6, students $3, seniors $3.)* In 1992, the museum paid $4.4 million to bring a series of four 18-month exhibitions from the permanent collection of New York's Whitney Museum to San Jose. Close by stand the **San Jose Institute of Contemporary Art (SJICA),** 451 S. 1st St. (283-8155; open Tu-Sa noon-5pm), and the **Center for Latino Arts (MACLA),** 510 S. 1st St. (998-ARTE/2783; open W-Sa noon-5pm). Many area galleries are free and open to the public until 8pm on the third Thursday of every month.

Of absolutely no educational value is the **Winchester Mystery House,** 1525 S. Winchester Blvd. (247-2101), piled near the intersection of I-880 and I-280, west of town. *(Open Su-Th 9am-6pm, F-Sa 9am-9pm, with 1hr. tours every 15-30min. $13, seniors $10, ages 6-12 $7.)* Sarah Winchester, heir to the Winchester rifle fortune, was convinced by an occultist that she would face the vengeance of the spirits of all the men ever killed by her family's guns if construction on her home ever ceased. Work on the mansion continued 24hr. a day for over 30 years, and today the estate is an elaborate maze of secret corridors, dead-end staircases, and tacky gift shops with absolutely no escape.

A wacky jukebox suits the fly clientele of **The Flying Pig Pub,** 78 S. 1st St. (298-6710). This mega-chill bistro serves drinks from its full bar, as well as food (3-way chili $3.25; open Tu-F 11am-2am, Sa 4pm-2am, M 3pm-2am). **Katie Bloom's Irish Pub and Restaurant,** 150 S. 1st St. (294-4408), is clearly more "pub" than "restaurant." Drink imported beers ($2.50) while Oscar Wilde and James Joyce watch from the walls. The extensive space includes many private leather booths, as well as rowdier counter spots. (Open M-F 11am-2am.)

▓ Palo Alto

Well-manicured Palo Alto looks a lot like "Collegeland" in a Disney-style theme park: the city is dominated by the beautiful 8000-acre campus of **Stanford University,** Palo Alto's main tourist attraction. Jane and Leland Stanford founded the secular, co-educational school in 1885, to honor a son who died of typhoid on a family trip to Italy. The Stanfords loved Spanish architecture and collaborated with **Frederick Law Olmsted,** designer of New York City's Central Park, to create a red-tiled campus of uncompromising beauty. (Disrespectful Berkeley students sometimes refer to Stanford as "the World's Largest Taco Bell.") The oldest part of campus is the colonnaded **Main Quadrangle,** the site of most undergraduate classes. The walkways are dotted with diamond-shaped, gold-numbered stone tiles that mark the locations of time capsules put together by each year's graduating class. Chipper student tour guides will point to other quirky Stanford tidbits on twice-daily tours. **Memorial Church** (723-1762), in the Main Quad, is a nondenominational gold shrine with stained glass windows and glittering mosaic walls like those of an Eastern Orthodox church. East of the Main Quad, the observation deck in **Hoover Tower** (723-2053 or 723-2560), has views of campus, the East Bay, and San Francisco. *(Open daily 10am-4:30pm. $2, seniors and under 13 $1.)* Off-campus, the kitschy **Barbie Doll Hall of Fame,** 433 Waverley St. (326-5841), off University, has over 16,000 perky plastic dolls. *(Open Tu-F 1:30-4pm, Sa 10am-noon and 1:30-4:30pm. $6, under 12 $4.)* Hippie Barbie, Benetton Barbie, and Disco Ken prove that girlhood may be fleeting, but fashion is forever. Ask about having yourself cloned into a doll.

Hidden Villa Ranch Hostel (HI-AYH), 26870 Moody Rd. (949-8648), is about 10 mi. southwest of Palo Alto in Los Altos Hills. The first hostel on the Pacific Coast is now a working ranch and farm in a wilderness preserve (open Sept.-May daily 7:30-9:30am and 4:30-9pm). About half of Stanford's social life happens at **The Coffee House,** Tresidder Union (723-3592), in the heart of campus (open term-time M-F 10am-1pm, Sa-Su 10am-midnight; in summer daily 10am-7pm). The **Mango Café**, 435 Hamilton Ave. (325-3229), 1 block east of University, boasts reggae music, fan-backed wicker chairs, and Caribbean cuisine (open daily 11am-3pm and 6-10pm).

Palo Alto is 35 mi. southeast of San Francisco, near the southern shore of the bay. From the north, take **U.S. 101** to the University Ave. Exit, or take the Embarcadero Rd. Exit directly to the Stanford campus. Alternatively, motorists from San Francisco can split off onto the **Junípero Serra Hwy. (I-280)** for a slightly longer but more scenic route. Palo Alto-bound trains also leave from San Francisco's **CalTrain** station, at 4th and King. (Run M-Th 5am-10pm, F 5am-midnight, Sa 7am-midnight, Su 8am-10pm. Fare $3.75; seniors, disabled and children $1.75; off-peak hrs. $2.75.) The **Palo Alto Transit Center** (323-6105), on University Ave., serves local and regional buses and trains (open daily 5am-12:30am); there is a train-only depot (326-3392), on California Ave. 1¼ mi. south of the Transit Center (open 5:30am-12:30am). The Transit Center is connected to points south by **San Mateo County buses** and to the Stanford campus by the free **Marguerite University Shuttle. Area code:** 415.

■ San Mateo Coast

The rocky bluffs of the San Mateo County Coast quickly obscure the hectic urban pace of the city to the north. Most of the energy here is generated by the coastal winds and waves. The Pacific Coast Hwy. (Hwy. 1) maneuvers its way through a rocky shoreline, colorful beach vistas, and generations-old ranches. Although it's possible to drive quickly down the coast from San Francisco to Santa Cruz, haste is waste—especially if you drive off a cliff.

Half Moon Bay is an old coastal community 29 mi. south of San Francisco. Recent commercialization has not infringed much on this small, easy-going beach town. The fishing and farming hamlet of **San Gregorio** rests 10 mi. south of Half Moon Bay. **San Gregorio Beach** is a delightful destination; you can walk to its southern end to find little caves in the shore rocks. (Open 8am-sunset; day use $4, seniors $3.) A stream runs into the sea, and may prove a comfortable alternative to dipping in the chillier ocean. To find a **less-frequented beach,** visit the unsigned turnout at Marker 27.35. It's difficult to find; look for mysteriously vacant cars parked along the highway. State-owned but undeveloped, this gorgeous stretch of beach is between San Gregorio and Pomponio State Beaches, off Hwy. 1. The historic little burg of **Pescadero** was established by white settlers in 1856, and was named Pescadero ("fisherman's town") due to the abundance of fish in both the oceans and creeks. Wander through the old town or participate in the local sport of **olallieberry gathering.**

Año Nuevo State Reserve (879-0227), on Hwy. 1 in Pescadero, 7 mi. south of Pigeon Point and 27 mi. south of Half Moon Bay, is the mating place of the 15 ft. long **elephant seal.** (Park open daily 8am-sunset.) Early spring is breeding season, when thousands of fat seals crowd on the beach. To see this unforgettable show (prime viewing times Dec. 15-Mar. 31), you must make reservations (8 weeks in advance recommended) by calling **PARKNET** (800-444-7275), since park access is limited. Tickets go on sale November 15 and generally sell out within a week or two (2½hr., guided tours $4 per person).

Nestled further inside the peninsula south of the San Francisco International Airport is the **Burlingame Museum of Pez Memorabilia,** 214 California Dr. (347-2301), which has a small but quirky display of dispensers and paraphernalia dating back to 1949. (Open Tu-Sa 10am-6pm.) Be sure to see the short Pez reference video. Like all the best things in life, the museum is free.

The **Pigeon Point Lighthouse Hostel (HI-AYH)** (879-0633), is on Hwy. 1, 6 mi. south of Pescadero and 20 mi. south of Half Moon Bay (dorms $12, nonmembers $15; private rooms $22/$25; call ahead). **Point Montara Lighthouse Hostel (HI-AYH)** (728-7177) is on Lighthouse Point 25 mi. south of San Francisco and 4 mi. north of Half Moon Bay (dorms $12, nonmembers $15; private rooms $22/$25). **The Flying Fish Grill** (712-1125), at the corner of Main St. and Rte. 92, serves inexpensive, airborne seafood straight from the coast (open in summer Tu-Su 11:30am-8:30pm; off-season until 7:30pm). **2 Fools Café and Market,** 408 Main St. (712-1222), at Mill St., is a cool, urbane eatery and drinkery that serves many veggie options (open M 7am-2pm, Tu-F 7am-9pm, Sa-Su 8am-9pm). *The* social spot for locals is **San Gregorio General Store,** 7615 Stage Rd. (726-0565), 1 mi. east of Hwy. 1 on Rte. 84, 8 mi. south of Half Moon Bay. This quirky store has served San Gregorio since 1889 with an eclectic selection of hardware, cold drinks, candy, groceries, gourmet coffee, cast iron pots, books, candles, and more. (Open M-Th 9am-6pm, F-Su 9am-7pm.) **Area code:** 650.

■ Marin County

Physically beautiful, politically liberal, and stinking rich, Marin County is quintessential California. If the new VW Beetle were sold nowhere but Marin (muh-RIN), Volkswagen still might reap a tidy profit. The yuppie reincarnation of the quintessential hippie car strikes the right combination of upscale chic and counterculture nostalgia.

PRACTICAL INFORMATION

Public Transportation: Golden Gate Transit (455-2000, in San Francisco 923-2000) provides transit between S.F. and Marin County via the Golden Gate Bridge, as well as local service in Marin. Fare to Sausalito $2, to Point Reyes and Olema $4; seniors and disabled 50% off, ages 6-12 25% off. **Golden Gate Ferry** (455-2000) runs boats from San Francisco to the Sausalito ferry terminal at the end of Market St. ($4.25) and the Larkspur ferry terminal (M-F $2.50, Sa-Su $4.25). Seniors and disabled 50% off; ages 6-12 25% off. Offices open M-F 6am-8pm, Sa-Su 6:30am-8pm.

Taxis: Radio Cab (485-1234 or 800-464-7234), serves all of Marin County. $1.60 base fare, $1.90 per mi.

Visitor Info: Marin County Visitors Bureau (472-7470; http://www.visitmarin.org), at the end of the Avenue of the Flags off Civic Center Drive, off Hwy. 101, in San Rafael. Part of the Marin Civic Center. Open M-F 9am-5pm. **Sausalito Visitors Center,** 777 Bridgeway, 4th fl. (332-0505; http://www.sausalito.org), Sausalito. Open Tu-Su 11:30am-4pm. Also a **kiosk** at the ferry landing.

Post Office: San Rafael, 40 Bellam Blvd. (459-0944), at Francisco. Open M-F 8:30am-5pm, Sa 10am-1pm. **ZIP code:** 94915. **Sausalito,** 150 Harbor Dr. (332-4656), at Bridgeway. Open M-Th 8:30am-5pm, F 8:30am-5:30pm. **ZIP code:** 94965. **Area code:** 415.

ACCOMMODATIONS AND CAMPGROUNDS

⊛Point Reyes Hostel (HI-AYH) (663-8811 or 800-909-4776, ext. 61), in the Point Reyes National Seashore. By car, exit west from Hwy. 1 at Olema onto Bear Valley Rd. Take the second possible left at Limantour Rd. (unsigned) and drive 6 mi. into the park. Turn left at the first crossroad (at the bottom of a very steep hill). Dorms $12-14. Private room available for families with children under 5. Chores expected. Linen $1; towels $1. Weekend reservations recommended. Some wheelchair access. Reception 7:30-9:30am and 4:30-9:30pm.

Marin Headlands Hostel (HI-AYH) (331-2777 or 800-909-4776, ext. 62), in old Fort Barry, west of Sausalito and 10 mi. from downtown San Francisco. With a car, this hostel could easily be used as a base for exploring the city, but it is not easily accessible by public transport; it's a 4½ mi. uphill hike from the Golden Gate Transit (#2, 10, 50) bus stop at Alexander Ave., or 6 mi. from the Sausalito ferry terminal. On Su and holidays only, MUNI bus #76 runs directly to the hostel. By car, cross the Golden Gate Bridge and take the Alexander Ave. Exit. From the north, take the 2nd Sausalito Exit (the very last exit before the bridge). Make a left at the first road and then follow signs into the Golden Gate Recreation Area and to the Marin Headlands Visitor Center. Dorms $12, under 17 (with parent) $6; private doubles $35. Closed (except for check-in) 9:30am-3:30pm. Linen $1; towels 50¢. Laundry (wash/dry 75¢). Key deposit $10. Check-in 7:30am-11:30pm. Check-out 8:45am.

Marin Headlands Campground, northwest of the Golden Gate Bridge at Field and Bunker Rd. Follow directions to Headlands Hostel, above, and stop at the visitors center. 3 small walk-in (100 yds. to 3 mi.) campgrounds with a total of 11 primitive campsites. Facilities are limited to picnic tables and chemical toilets; bring your own water and camp stove. Camping is free, but a permit is required. 3-night max. stay per campground. Showers and kitchen ($2 each) at Headlands Hostel. Free outdoor cold showers available at Rodeo Beach. Reserve up to 90 days in advance by calling the visitors center (331-1540; open daily 9:30am-4:30pm).

Kirby Cove, off Conzelman Rd. directly west of the Golden Gate Bridge, is in the Marin Headlands but not administered by the visitors center. 4 campsites in a grove of cypress and eucalyptus trees on the shores of the Bay. The campground is accessible by car and includes pit toilets and fire rings. For reservations, call the Special Park Users Group at 561-4304.

FOOD

Marinites take their fruit juices, tofu, and non-fat double-shot cappuccinos very seriously; restaurateurs know this, and raise both the alfalfa sprouts and the prices. A number of cafes and pizzerias along **4th St.** in San Rafael, and **Miller Ave.** on the way into Mill Valley, provide welcome exceptions; a few more are listed below.

⊕**Sartaj Indian Café,** 43 Caledonia St. (332-7103), 1 block up from Bridgeway in Sausalito. The low prices (curries $8, stew and samosa $5, sandwiches $3.75) are even lower on W nights, when Sartaj features live music—sometimes authentically Indian, sometimes Sinatra standards on a portable organ. Hot *chai* (sweet Indian tea) will help you deal with the culture shock ($1.25).

Mama's Royal Café, 387 Miller Ave. (388-3261), in Mill Valley. Self-aware slackers serve up unusual but very good dishes from a menu as packed as the restaurant. The whole place is decorated in lawn ornaments and psychedelic murals. Enchilada El Syd $6.50, Groove Burger $6. Brunch with live music Sa-Su 11am-2pm.

My Thai Restaurant, 1230 4th St. (456-4455). Top-notch Thai eatery on San Rafael's main drag. Tasty basil prawns $8, Thai iced tea or coffee $1.50, veggie dishes $6-7. Credit card min. $15. Open Su-Th 11:30am-9:30pm, F-Sa 11:30am-10pm.

Mayflower Inne, 1553 4th St. (456-1011), in San Rafael. Classic British pub serving classic British grub. Fish and chips, bangers and mash, and not a vegetable in sight—unless you count mushy peas. Best deal: cup of soup and half a sandwich for $4.25. "Bawdy Piano Singalong" every F at 8pm. Open M-F 7:30am-2:30pm, Sa-Su 8am-3pm.

SIGHTS

Marin's proximity to San Francisco makes it a popular daytrip destination. Virtually everything worth seeing or doing in Marin is outdoors. An efficient visitor can hop from park to park and enjoy several short hikes along the coast and through the redwood forests in the same day, topping it off with a pleasant dinner in one of the small cities. Those without cars, however, may find it easier to use one of the two well-situated hostels as a base for hiking or biking explorations.

Originally a fishing center full of bars and bordellos, Sausalito, at Marin's extreme southeastern tip, has long since traded its sea-dog days for retail boutiques and overpriced seafood restaurants. **Bridgeway** is the city's main thoroughfare, and practically the only one shown on the visitors center maps. Those who forge their own way will be rewarded: a block away from the harbor and Bridgeway's smug shops, **Caledonia St.** offers more charming restaurants and a few more affordable stores. Half a mile north of the town center is the **Bay Model** (332-3871), a massive working model of San Francisco Bay. *(Open Tu-F 9am-4pm, Sa 10am-6pm; off-season Tu-Sa 9am-4pm. Free.)* The address is 2100 Bridgeway, but to enter you must turn off Bridgeway at Marinship. Built in the 1950s to test proposals to dam the bay and other diabolical plans, the water-filled model recreates tides and currents with exacting detail.

Fog-shrouded hills just to the west of the Golden Gate Bridge comprise the **Marin Headlands.** Its windswept ridges, precipitous cliffs, and hidden sandy beaches offer superb hiking and biking within minutes of downtown San Francisco. For instant gratification, choose one of the coastal trails, which offer easy access to dark sand beaches and dramatic cliffs of basalt greenstone. One of the best very short hikes is to the lighthouse at **Point Bonita,** a prime spot for seeing sunbathing California sea lions in summer and migrating gray whales in the cooler months.

Between the upscale towns of East Marin and the rocky bluffs of West Marin rests beautiful **Mt. Tamalpais State Park** (tam-ull-PIE-us). The park has miles of hilly, challenging trails on and around 2571 ft. Mt. Tamalpais, the highest peak in the county and the original "mountain" in "mountain bike." At the center of the state park is **Muir Woods National Monument,** a 560-acre stand of primeval coastal redwoods, located about 5 mi. west of U.S. 101 along Hwy. 1. *(Monument open daily 8am-sunset; visitors center 9am-6pm.)* Spared from logging by the steep sides of Redwood Canyon, these centuries-old redwoods are massive and shrouded in silence.

Hwy. 1 reaches the Pacific at Muir Beach, and from there twists its way up the rugged coast. It's all beautiful, but the stretch between Muir Beach and Stinson Beach is the most breathtaking, especially when driving south, on the sheer-drop-to-the-ocean side of the highway. Sheltered **Muir Beach** is scenic and popular with families (open sunrise-9pm). The crowds thin out significantly after a 5min. climb on the shore rocks to the left. Six miles to the north, **Stinson Beach** attracts a younger, rowdier crowd of good-looking surfer dudes and dudettes, though cold and windy conditions often keep them posing on dry land (open sunrise-sunset).

A near-island surrounded by nearly 100 mi. of isolated coastline, the **Point Reyes National Seashore** is a wilderness of pine forests, chaparral ridges, and grassy flatlands. Hwy. 1 provides direct access to the park from the north or south; Sir Francis Drake Blvd. comes west from Hwy. 101 at San Rafael. After a day, or ten, exploring the seashore, the little town of **Point Reyes Station,** 2 mi. north of Olema on Hwy. 1, makes a welcoming dinner destination. Point Reyes is a cow town, built on dairy farming, and its main streets look appropriately Western with wide streets and false-fronted buildings. The town whistle "moos" like a cow each day at high noon.

WINE COUNTRY

■ Napa Valley

While not the oldest, the Napa Valley is certainly the best-known of America's wine-growing regions. The gentle hills, fertile soil, ample moisture, and year-round sunshine are ideal for viticulture. European vines were first planted here as early as the late 1850s, but early producers were crippled by Prohibition, when the grapes were supplanted with figs. The region did not begin to reestablish itself until the 1960s. During the 70s, Napa's rapidly improving offerings won the attention of those in the know, and word-of-mouth cemented the California bottle as a respectable choice. In 1976, a bottle of red from Napa's Stag's Leap Vineyard beat a bottle of Château Lafitte-Rothschild in a blind taste test in Paris, and American wine was suddenly *très* cool. Today, local vineyards continue to reap awards, and the everyday tasting carnival dominates life in the valley's small towns.

ORIENTATION AND PRACTICAL INFORMATION

Rte. 29 (St. Helena Hwy.) runs through the Napa Valley from **Napa** through **Yountville** and **St. Helena** to **Calistoga.** Slow with visitors stopping at each winery, the relatively short distance takes a surprisingly long, if scenic, time. The **Silverado Trail,** parallel to Rte. 29, is a less crowded route, but watch out for stylish cyclists. Napa is 14 mi. east of Sonoma on **Rte. 12.** On Saturday mornings and Sunday afternoons the roads are packed with cars traveling from San Francisco. Although harvest, in early September, is the most exciting time to visit, winter weekdays provide the space for personal attention. From the city, take U.S. 101 over the Golden Gate, then Rte. 37 E to Rte. 121 N, which will cross Rte. 12 N (to Sonoma) and Rte. 29 (to Napa).

> **Buses:** The nearest **Greyhound** station is in Vallejo (800-231-2222), but 1 bus per day passes through the valley. Stops in Napa (6:15pm, Napa State Hospital, 2100 Napa-Vallejo Hwy.), Yountville, St. Helena, and Calistoga.

Public Transportation: Napa City Bus, or **Valley Intercity Neighborhood Express (VINE),** 1151 Pearl St. (800-696-6443 or 255-7631, TDD 226-9722), covers the valley and Vallejo. To Vallejo (fare $1.50, students $1.10, disabled 75¢) and Calistoga ($2/ $1.45/$1); transfers free. Buses run M-F 6:30am-6pm, Sa 7:30am-5:30pm.

Car Rental: Budget, 407 Soscol Ave. (224-7846), Napa. Cars $35 per day; ages 21-25 $55. Unlimited mi. Must be 21 with credit card.

Winery tours: Napa Valley Wine Shuttle, 3031 California Blvd. (800-258-8226; day pass $30, children free), and **Napa Valley Holidays** (255-1050; 3hr., $30).

Visitor Info: Napa Visitors Center, 1310 Town Center (226-7459; http://www. napavalley.com/nvcvb.html). Wide brochure collection and free copies of *Inside Napa Valley,* which has maps, winery listings, and a weekly events guide. Open daily 9am-5pm, phones closed Sa-Su. **St. Helena Chamber of Commerce,** 1010A Main St. (963-4456; open M-F 10am-4:30pm). **Calistoga Chamber of Commerce,** 1458 Lincoln Ave. (942-6333; open M-F 9am-5pm, Sa 10am-4:30pm, Su 11am-4pm).

Post Office: 1351 2nd St. (255-1268), Napa. Open M-F 8:30am-5pm. **ZIP code:** 94559. **Area code:** 707.

ACCOMMODATIONS AND CAMPGROUNDS

Rooms in Napa are scarce and go fast despite their high prices (B&Bs and most hotels are a budget-breaking $60-225 per night). Budget options are more plentiful in **Santa Rosa** and **Petaluma,** which are within easy driving distance of the valley. For those without cars, camping is the best option, though the heat is intense in summer.

Discovery Inn, 500 Silverado Trail (253-0892), near Soscol in Napa. Rooms have kitchenettes, cable TV, and a tad more personality than a chain motel. Rooms $40, F-Sa $80. Check-in noon-6pm.

Bothe-Napa Valley State Park, 3801 Rte. 29 (942-4575; reservations through PARKNET, 800-444-7275), north of St. Helena. 49 sites often full. Sites $16, seniors $14; vehicles $5. Hot showers. Pool $3, under 18 $2. Park open 8am-sunset.

Calistoga Ranch Club, 580 Lommel Rd. (800-847-6272), off the Silverado Trail near Calistoga. Campground caters to families. Hiking trails lace 167 wooded acres, which include a fishing lake, volleyball, and pool. Tent sites $19; RV sites $23; 4-person cabins with shared bath $49; 5-person trailers with kitchen $89.

FOOD

Eating in Wine Country ain't cheap, but the food is usually worth it. Picnics are a cheap and romantic option—supplies can be picked up at the numerous delis or Safeway stores in the area. Most wineries have shaded picnic grounds, often with excellent views. The Napa **farmer's market** (252-7142), corner of Pearl and West, offers a sampling of the valley's *other* produce (open daily 7:30am-noon).

Curb Side Café, 1245 1st St. (253-2307), at Randolph in Napa. Sublime sandwiches $5-6. This cafe feels more like a diner. Heavy breakfasts include the pancake special: 4 buttermilk pancakes, 2 eggs, and ham or sausage ($6). Open M-Sa 8am-3pm, Su 9:30am-3pm.

Calistoga Natural Foods and Juice Bar, 1426 Lincoln (942-5822), Calistoga. One of few natural foods stores around. Organic juice and sandwich bar, with vegetarian specialties like Garlic Goddess ($4.50) or Tofu Supreme ($5). Open daily 9am-6pm.

DRINKING

There are more than 250 wineries in Napa County, nearly two-thirds of which line **Rte. 29** and the **Silverado Trail** in the Napa Valley. Wine country's heavyweights call this valley home; vineyards include national names such as Inglenook, Fetzer, and Mondavi. Few wineries in Napa have free tastings, so choose your samples carefully. The wineries listed below (from south to north) are among the valley's larger and more touristy operations. Visitors must be 21 or older to purchase or drink alcohol (yes, they do card).

Hakusan Sake Gardens, 1 Executive Way (258-6160 or 800-HAKUSAN/425-8726). Take Rte. 12 off Rte. 29, turn left on North Kelly, then left onto Executive. Japanese gardens are a welcome change from the other wineries. Sake is a strong Japanese wine with a fruity taste, and it can be served warm or cold. Test your mettle with these generous pourings. Open M-Tu 10am-6pm, W-Su 10am-8pm.

Domaine Carneros, 1240 Duhig Rd. (257-0101), off Rte. 121 from Rte. 29. Picturesque estate with elegant terrace modeled after a French chateâu. This elegant winery serves sparkling juices for minors and drivers ($1 a bottle), as well as sparkling wine by the glass ($4-7). Weekday sampler includes 2 half-glasses of sparkling wine. All glasses (juices included) come with complimentary hors d'oeuvres. Free tour and film. Open daily 10am-6pm; Nov.-Apr. 10:30am-6pm.

Domaine Chandon, 1 California Dr. (944-2280). Owned by Moët Chandon of France (the people who make Dom Perignon), this winery produces 5 million bottles of sparkling wine annually—enough for one hell of a New Year's Eve party. Huge complex includes gift shop, tasting room, and restaurant. Tours (hourly 11am-5pm) and tastings ($3-5). Open daily 11am-6pm; Nov.-Apr. W-Su 11am-6pm.

Robert Mondavi Winery, 7801 Rte. 29 (963-9611 or 800-MONDAVI/666-3284), 8 mi. north of Napa. Originally a viticulture education center, this triangular winery offers some of the best tours in the valley, covering subjects from tasting to soil conditions. Tastings $3-10. Open daily 10am-4pm; Nov.-Apr. 9:30am-4:30pm.

Vin Friends and Influence People

Most wines are recognized by the grape-stock from which they're grown—**white** grapes produce Chardonnay, Riesling, and Sauvignon; **reds** are responsible for Beaujolais, Pinot Noir, Merlot, and Zinfandel. **Blush** or **rosé** wines issue from red grapes which have had their skins removed during fermentation in order to leave just a kiss of pink. White Zinfandel, for example, comes from a red grape often made skinless, and is therefore rose in color. Of course, blush is not the wine of choice among wine connoisseurs; it's for plebes and picnics. **Dessert** wines, such as Muscat, are made with grapes that have acquired the "noble rot" *(botrytis)* at the end of picking season, giving them an extra-sweet flavor.

When tasting, start with a white, moving from **dry** to **sweet** (dry wines have had a higher percentage of their sugar content fermented into alcohol). Proceed through the reds, which go from **lighter** to **fuller bodied,** depending on tannin content. **Tannin** is the pigment red wine gets from the grape skin—it preserves and ages the wine, which is why reds can be young and sharp, but grow more mellow with age. It's best to end with dessert wines. One should cleanse one's palate between each wine, with a biscuit, some *fromage,* or fruit. Don't hesitate to ask for advice from the tasting-room pourer.

Tasting proceeds thusly: stare, sniff, swirl, swallow (first three steps are optional). You will probably encounter fellow tasters who slurp their wine and make concerned faces, as though they're trying to cram the stuff up their noses with the back of their tongues. These chaps consider themselves serious tasters, and are aerating the wine in their mouths to better bring out the flavor. Key words to help you seem more astute during tasting sessions are: dry, sweet, buttery, light, crisp, fruity, balanced, rounded, subtle, rich, woody, and complex. Feel free to banter these terms about indiscriminately. *Sally forth, young naïfs!*

CALIFORNIA

NOT DRINKING

Napa does have non-alcoholic attractions. Chief among them is 160-acre **Marine World Africa USA** (643-6722), an enormous zoo-oceanarium-theme park 10 mi. south of Napa, off Rte. 37 in Vallejo. *(Open daily 9:30am-6pm. $27, seniors $23, ages 4-12 $19. Parking $5. Wheelchair access.)* All proceeds benefit wildlife research and protection programs. The park is accessible by BART (415-788-2278) and the Blue and Gold fleet (415-705-5444), from San Francisco.

Robert Louis Stevenson State Park (942-4575), 4 mi. north of St. Helena on Rte. 29, has a plaque where the Scottish writer, sick and penniless, spent a rejuvenating honeymoon in 1880. The hike up **Mt. St. Helena** (open daily 8am-sunset) is a moderate 3hr. climb culminating in dizzying views of the valley (no ranger station; bring water). The **Silverado Museum,** 1490 Library Ln. (963-3757), off Adams in St. Helena, is a labor of love by a devoted collector of Stevensoniana. *(Open Tu-Su noon-4pm. Free.)* Manuscript notes from *Dr. Jekyll and Mr. Hyde* are on display. The **Old Faithful Geyser of California** (942-6463) is farther north, 2 mi. outside Calistoga on Tubbs Ln. off Rte. 128. *(Open daily 9am-6pm; in winter 9am-5pm. $6, seniors $4, ages 6-12 $2, disabled free. Bathrooms not wheelchair accessible.)*

Calistoga is also known as the **"Hot Springs of the West."** Sam Brannan, who first developed the area, meant to make the hot springs the "Saratoga of California," but he misspoke and promised instead to make them "The Calistoga of Saratina." Luckily, history has a soft spot for millionaires; Brannan's dream has come true, and Calistoga is now a center for luxurious spas and resorts. Massage your wallet by sticking to **Golden Haven** (942-6793), which specializes in private couple baths, or **Nance's Hot Springs** (942-6211), where you get one of the more complex yet inexpensive treatments. Cooler water can be found at **Lake Berryessa** (966-2111), 20 mi. north of Napa off Rte. 128. Swimming, sailing, and sunbathing on 169 mi. of shoreline are all popular activities.

■ Sonoma Valley

The sprawling Sonoma Valley is a quieter alternative to Napa. Wineries are approachable via winding side roads rather than down a freeway strip, making for a more intimate yet more adventurous feel. Less straggling than Napa's strip of small towns, the valley showcases a beautiful, expansive eight-acre plaza in the town of Sonoma. Petaluma, which is west of the Sonoma Valley, has a better variety of budget lodgings than the expensive wine country.

PRACTICAL INFORMATION Rte. 12 traverses the length of Sonoma Valley from **Sonoma,** through **Glen Ellen,** to **Kenwood** in the north. The center of downtown Sonoma is **Sonoma Plaza,** a park which contains City Hall and the visitors center. **Broadway** dead-ends in front of City Hall at Napa St. The numbered streets run north-south. **Petaluma** lies to the west and is connected to Sonoma by **Rte. 116,** which becomes **Lakeville St.** in Petaluma. Lakeville St. intersects **Washington St.,** the central downtown road. **Sonoma County Transit** (800-345-7433) serves the entire county, from Petaluma to Cloverdale and the Russian River. Bus #30 runs to Santa Rosa Monday to Saturday (fare $1.95, students $1.60, seniors and disabled 95¢, under 6 free); bus #40 goes to Petaluma (fare $1.60). **Sonoma Valley Visitors Bureau,** 453 E. 1st St. (996-1090), in Sonoma Plaza doles out info and $2 maps (open daily 9am-7pm; Nov.-May 9am-5pm). **Petaluma Visitors Program,** 799 Baywood Dr. (769-0429), at Lakeville, gives out a free visitor's guide with handy listings of restaurants and activities (open June-Sept. M-F 9am-5:30pm, Sa-Su 10am-6pm; shorter off-season hrs.). **Post Office:** 617 Broadway (996-2459), at Patten, in Sonoma (open M-F 8:30am-5pm). **ZIP code:** 95476. **Area code:** 707.

ACCOMMODATIONS, CAMPGROUNDS, AND FOOD Pickings are pretty slim for lodging; rooms are scarce even on the weekdays and generally start at $75. Cheaper motels cluster along U.S. 101 in Santa Rosa and Petaluma. **Motel 6,** 1368 N. McDowell Blvd. (765-0333), is off U.S. 101 in Petaluma (singles $41; 2nd adult $6, each additional adult $3). **Sugarloaf Ridge State Park,** 2605 Adobe Canyon Rd. (833-5712), north of Kenwood off Rte. 12, has 50 sites centered around central meadow with flush toilets and running water, but no showers (sites $16). **Quinley's,** 310 D St. (778-6000), at Petaluma, first opened its doors in 1952, and that old-time rock 'n' roll plays on with burgers (open M-Th and Su 11am-9pm, F-Sa 11am-10pm).

WINERIES Sonoma Valley's wineries, located near Sonoma and Kenwood, are less touristy but just as tasty as Napa's. More of the tastings are also likely to be complimentary. Near Sonoma, white signs will help guide you through the backroads; they are difficult to read but indicate the general direction of the wineries. Bring a map (they're all over the place and free), as the signs, like cats, will often desert you when they're most needed. **Buena Vista,** 18000 Old Winery Rd. (800-926-1266), off E. Napa, is the oldest winery in the valley. *(Hosts theatrical performances July-Sept. Brief historical presentations 2pm; also 11am in summer. Tastings daily 10:30am-5pm.)* The famous old stone buildings are preserved as Mr. Haraszthy built them in 1857, when he founded the California wine industry. Free tastings take place downstairs, while you can taste vintage wine and champagne upstairs in a working artist's gallery for a small fee. **Glen Ellen Winery,** 14301 Arnold Dr. (939-6277) is 1 mi. from Glen Ellen in Jack London Village (open daily 10am-5pm). Nearby cafes have *très cher* food to enjoy at the picnic tables outside; an adjacent olive press offers oil tasting. One of the few organic wineries in the region, **Kenwood,** 9592 Sonoma Hwy. (833-5891), prides itself on its attention to the environment (complimentary tastings, with recipe samples Sa-Su). The Mediterranean setting at **Château St. Jean,** 8555 Hwy. 12 (833-4134), Kenwood, includes lookout tower with balcony and an observation deck above the production area (tasting daily 10am-4:30pm).

SIGHTS AND SEASONAL EVENTS Local historical artifacts are preserved in the **Sonoma State Historic Park,** at E. Spain and 1st, in the northeast corner of town. Within the park, an adobe church stands on the site of the **Sonoma Mission** (938-9560), the northernmost and last of the Spanish missions. *(Open daily 10am-5pm. $2, seniors $1, ages 6-12 $1; includes Vallejo's Home, barracks next door, and Petaluma Adobe.)* Built in 1826 when Mexico was already a republic, the mission houses a remnant of the original California Republic flag, the rest of which was burned in the 1906 post-earthquake fires.

To find **Jack London State Park** (938-5216), take Rte. 12 north about 4 mi. to Arnold Lane and follow the signs. *(Park open daily 9:30am-sunset; museum open daily 10am-5pm. $6 per car.)* At the turn of the century, hard-drinking and hard-living Jack London (author of *The Call of the Wild* and *White Fang*) bought 1400 acres here, determined to create his dream home. London's hopes for the property were never realized—the estate's main building, the Wolf House, was destroyed by arsonists in 1913. London died 3 years after the fire and is buried in the park, his grave marked by a volcanic boulder intended for the construction of his house. The nearby **House of Happy Walls,** built by his widow, is now a 2-story museum devoted to the writer. The park's scenic ½ mi. **Beauty Ranch Trail** passes the lake, winery ruins, and quaint cottages. Free golf cart rides are available Saturday and Sunday 12:30pm-4:30pm for those requiring handicapped access. **Sonoma Cattle and Napa Valley Trail Rides** (996-8566) also coast through the fragrant forests (2hr. ride $45; sunset and night rides available).

NORTHERN CALIFORNIA

■ Mendocino

Perched on bluffs overlooking the ocean, tiny Mendocino is a highly stylized coastal community of art galleries, craft shops, bakeries, and B&Bs. The town's weathered wood shingles, sloping roofs, and clustered homes seem out of place on the West Coast; perhaps that's why Mendocino masqueraded for years as the fictional Maine village of Cabot Cove in the TV series *Murder, She Wrote*. Mendocino sits on **Hwy. 1** right on the Pacific Coast, 30 mi. west of U.S. 101 and 12 mi. south of Fort Bragg. The town is tiny, and best explored on foot (parking available in plentiful lots). Weather in the Mendocino area varies from 40-70°F. Travelers should come prepared for chilliness caused by occasional fog.

Mendocino's greatest attribute lies 900 ft. to its west, where the earth clangs to a halt and falls off into the Pacific, forming the impressive fog-shrouded coastline of the **Mendocino Headlands.** Beneath wildflower-laden meadows, fingers of eroded rock claw through the pounding ocean surf and seals frolic in secluded alcoves. **Kites** perform stupendously here, catching the sea breeze and soaring over the ocean. Grab one at the **Village Toy Store,** 10450 Lansing St. (937-4633; $17).

For the most part, **Fort Bragg** is the place to stay while you're visiting Mendocino; the town's tourist pheromone is the **Skunk Train,** Hwy. 1 and Laurel (964-6371; 800 77-SKUNK/777-5865), a jolly diversion through deserted logging towns and recuperating forest. (Trips leave at 9, 9:30am, 1:30, and 2pm; off-season trips 9:20, 10am, and 2pm; Dec. trains depart at 9:20, 10am, and 2:10pm.) A steam engine, diesel locomotive, and vintage motorcar take turns running between Fort Bragg and Willits via Northspur, with whole and ½-day trips available.

Glimpses through the interstices of Mendocino County's fog and flora reveal many a fancy version of *au naturel*—hotspring resorts abound. **Orr Hot Springs,** 13201 Orr Springs Rd. (462-6277), is just south of Mendocino off Comptche Ukian Rd. (1hr. drive over dirt roads. Open daily 10am-10pm. Day use $19; M special $10.) From U.S. 101, take the North State St. Exit. Mineral water tubs (both hot and cold), sauna, steam room, and riotous gardens make the world disappear at this relaxed resort.

Jug Handle Creek Farm, (964-4630), 5 mi. north of Mendocino at the Caspar Exit off Hwy. 1, is a beautiful 120-year-old house with 30 beds on 40 acres of overgrown gardens along with campsites, small rustic cabins, and access to the beach and trails in Jug Handle State Park. (Dorms $18, students $12; sites $6, children $3; cabins $25 per person. 1hr. of chores or $5 required per night. No linen. Reserve in advance.) The simple budget motel of **The Coast Motel,** 18661 Hwy. 1 (964-2852), ¼ mi. south of the intersection with Rte. 20 in Ft. Bragg, is both woodsy and rustic, featuring a pool. (Shared rustic phone. Singles $37-60; doubles $56-66.) **Tote Fête,** 10450 Lansing St. (937-3383), has delicious tote-out food, and the crowds know it. Their asiago, pesto, and artichoke heart sandwich ($4.25) hits the spot. **Tote Fête Bakery** is in the back with a flowery garden and a small, serene pool. (Open M-Sa 10:30am-7pm, Su 10:30am-4pm.)

Mendocino Stage (964-0167) runs three buses per day between Ft. Bragg and Ukiah. **Mendocino Transit Authority,** 241 Plant Rd. (800-696-4682), makes one round-trip between Santa Rosa, Ukiah, Willits, Fort Bragg, and Mendocino daily. The **Ford House,** 735 Main St. (937-5397), is in the former home of the town's founder, Jerome Bursely Ford. **Post Office:** 10500 Ford St. (937-5282), 2 blocks west of Main. Open M-F 7:30am-4:30pm. **ZIP code:** 95460. **Area code:** 707.

■ Avenue of the Giants

About 6 mi. north of **Garberville** off U.S. 101, the **Avenue of the Giants** winds its way through 31 mi. of the largest living creatures this side of sea level. Scattered throughout the area are several commercialized attractions such as the **World Famous Tree House, Confusion Hill** (a vortex of mystery where the laws of gravity no longer apply; free), and the **Drive-Thru Tree.** Travelers looking for a more authentic taste of the redwood forests may want to bypass these hokey attractions in favor of more rugged and natural tours. There are a number of great hiking trails in the area, marked on $1 maps available at the **Humboldt Redwoods State Park Visitors Center** (946-2263), just south of Weott on the Avenue (open daily 9am-5pm; Nov.-Mar. Th-Su 10am-4pm). The **Canoe Creek Loop Trail,** across the street from the visitors center, is an easy start. Uncrowded trails snake through the park's northern section around **Rockefeller Forest,** which contains the largest grove of old-growth redwoods (200 years and growing) in the world. The **Dyerville Giant,** in the redwood graveyard at Founder's Grove about midway through the Avenue, deserves a respectful visit. The ½ mi. loop trail includes the **Founder's Tree** and the **Fallen Giant,** whose massive trunk stretches 60 human body-lengths long and whose 3-story rootball looks like a mythical ensnarlment of evil. The **Standish Hickey Recreation Area** (925-6482), north of Leggett on U.S. 101, offers fishing, camping, swimming, and hiking (parking $5).

With its sizable artist population, Garberville's art festivals are a big draw. **Jazz on the Lake** and the **Summer Arts Fair** begin in late June, followed by **Shakespeare at Benbow Lake** in late July. Early August brings **Reggae on the River,** a 12hr. music fest on the banks of the Eel River. For more info on events, contact the **Chamber of Commerce,** 773 Redway (800-923-2613), in Garberville. **Area code:** 707.

■ Redwood National Park

With ferns that grow to the height of humans and redwood trees the size of skyscrapers, Redwood National Park, as John Steinbeck said, "will leave a mark or create a vision that stays with you always." Fog rolls between the creaking redwood boughs in a prehistoric atmosphere where you half expect a dinosaur to tromp by at any moment. The redwoods in the park are the last remaining stretch of the old-growth forest which used to blanket 2 million acres of Northern California and Oregon. Wildlife runs rampant here, with black bears and mountain lions in the backwoods and Roosevelt elk grazing in the meadows.

PRACTICAL INFORMATION

Redwood National Park is only one of four redwood parks between Klamath and Orick, the others being **Jedediah Smith State Park, Del Norte Coast Redwoods State Park,** and **Prairie Creek Redwoods State Park.** The name "Redwood National Park" is an umbrella term for all four parks.

> **Buses: Greyhound,** 500 E. Harding St. (464-2807), in Crescent City. To San Francisco (2 per day, $51) and Portland (2 per day, $53). No credit cards are accepted. Station open M-F 7-10am and 5-7:30pm, Sa 7-9am and 7-7:30pm.
> **Visitor Info: Redwood Information Center** (488-3461) doles out brochures and maps 1 mi. south of Orick on U.S. 101. Open daily 9am-5pm.
> **Post Office:** 751 2nd St. (464-2151), Crescent City (open M-F 8:30am-5pm, Sa noon-2pm). **ZIP code:** 95531. **Area code:** 707.

ACCOMMODATIONS, CAMPGROUNDS, AND FOOD

A pleasant pad is the **Redwood Youth Hostel (HI-AYH),** 14480 U.S. 101 (482-8265), 7 mi. north of Klamath at Wilson Creek Rd. Overlooking the crashing Pacific surf and housed in the historic DeMartin House, this 30-bed hostel suggests Shaker simplicity. (Dorms $12. Linen $1. Check-in 4:30-9:30pm. Check-out 9:30am.) **Camp Marigold,** 16101 U.S. 101 (482-3585 or 800-621-8513), 3 mi. north of Klamath Bridge, is a pleasantly woodsy alternative to mundane motels (doubles $38). **State Park Campsites** (464-9533) are all fully developed and easily accessible (sites $16). Call **PARKNET** (800-444-7275) for reservations, which are necessary in summer. There are more picnic table sites than restaurants in the area, so the best option for food is probably **Orick Market** (488-3225), which has reasonably priced groceries (open M-Sa 8am-7pm, Su 9am-7pm). In Crescent City, head to the 24hr. **Safeway** in the shopping center on U.S. 101 (M St.) between 2nd and 5th. **Glen's Bakery and Restaurant,** 3rd and G St. (464-2914), serves basic diner fare such as huge pancakes ($3), sandwiches ($4), and burgers ($3-4; open Tu-Sa 5am-6:30pm). The **Jefferson State Brewery,** 400 Front St. (464-1139), is a hip new restaurant and bar environmentally designed and built of 90% recycled material. Jefferson State serves sandwiches ($5-7), pasta ($10), and island chicken with grilled vegetables ($10). If you're 21, you can try the 6-beer sampler brewed on the premises ($4.50). After dinner, chill in the TV lounge or pick up a game of pool. (Open Su-Th 11am-10pm; F-Sa 11am-11pm.)

SIGHTS AND ACTIVITIES

You can see Redwood National Park in just over 1hr. by car, but the redwoods are best experienced by foot. The park is divided into several regions, each of which has information centers and unique attractions. The National Park Service conducts a symphony of organized activities for all ages; a detailed list of junior ranger programs and nature walks is available at all park ranger stations or from the **Redwood Information Center** (488-3461). Hikers should take particular care to wear protective clothing—**ticks** and **poison oak** thrive in these deep, dark places. **Roosevelt elk** roam the woods, and are interesting to watch but dangerous to approach, since invaders of their territory are promptly circled and trampled. Also be on the lookout for the **black bears** and **mountain lions** that inhabit many areas of the park. Before setting out, get advice and trail maps at the visitors center.

CALIFORNIA

The Orick Area

The **Orick Area** covers the southernmost section of Redwood National Park. Its **visitors center** lies about 1 mi. south of Orick on U.S. 101 and ½ mi. south of the Shoreline Deli (the Greyhound bus stop). The main attraction is the **Tall Trees Grove,** which, if the road is open, is accessible by car to those with a permit (available at the visitors center; free). A minimum of 3-4hr. should be allowed for the trip. From the trailhead at the end of Tall Trees Access Rd. (off Bald Hills Rd. from U.S. 101 north of Orick), it's a 1.3 mi. hike (about 30min.) to the tallest redwoods in the park and, in fact, to the **tallest known tree in the world** (367.8 ft., one-third the height of New York's World Trade Center towers). If the road is closed, the hardy can hike the 16 mi. round-trip **Emerald Ridge Trail** to see these giants. **Patrick's Point State Park,** 15 mi. south of Orick along U.S. 101, offers one of the most spectacular views on the California coast, and merits a day or two from campers, boaters, and nature enthusiasts heading north to the redwoods ($16).

Prairie Creek Area

The Prairie Creek Area, equipped with a **ranger station** and state park **campgrounds,** is perfect for hikers, who can explore 75 mi. of trails in the park's 14,000 acres. Trail maps ($1) are available at the ranger station; the loops of criss-crossing trails may be confusing without one. Starting at the Prairie Creek Visitors Center, the **James Irvine Trail** (4½ mi. one way) winds through a prehistoric garden of towering old growth redwoods of humbling height. Winding through **Fern Canyon,** where small waterfalls trickle down 50 ft. fern-covered walls, the trail ends at **Gold Bluffs Beach,** whose sands stretch for many elk-scattered miles. The less ambitious can elk-watch on the meadow in front of the ranger station.

Klamath Area

The Klamath Area to the north consists of a thin stretch of park land connecting Prairie Creek with Del Norte State Park. The town itself consists of a few stores stretched over 4 mi., so the main attraction here is the ruggedly spectacular coastline. The **Klamath Overlook,** where Requa Rd. meets the Coastal Trail, is an **excellent whale-watching site,** and offers a spectacular view. The mouth of the **Klamath River** is a popular fishing spot (permit required) during the fall and spring, when salmon make sweet love, and during the winter, when steelhead trout do the same. Coastal Dr. passes by the remains of the **Douglas Memorial Bridge,** where sea lions and harbor seals congregate in the spring and summer, and then continues along the ocean for 8 mi. of incredible views.

Hiouchi Area

This inland region, known for its rugged beauty, sits in the northern part of the park along I-199 and contains some excellent hiking trails, most of which are in **Jedediah Smith State Park.** Several trails lie off Howland Hill Rd., a dirt road easily accessible from both U.S. 101 and I-199. From I-199, turn onto South Fork Rd. in Hiouchi and right onto Douglas Park Rd., which then turns into Howland Hill Rd. From Crescent City, go south on U.S. 101, turn left onto Elk Valley Rd., and right onto Howland Hill.

■ Gold Country

In 1848, California was a rural backwater of only 15,000 people. The same year, sawmill operator James Marshall wrote in his diary: "This day some kind of mettle...found in the tailrace...looks like goald." In the next 4 years, some 90,000 49ers from around the world headed for California and the 120 mi. of gold-rich seams called the **Mother Lode.** Despite the hype, few of the prospectors struck it rich. Miners, sustained by dreams of instant wealth, worked long and hard, yet most could barely squeeze sustenance out of their fiercely guarded claims.

Although gold remains in them thar hills, today the towns of Gold Country make their money mining the tourist traffic. Gussied up as **"Gold Rush Towns,"** they solicit tourists traveling along the appropriately numbered **Rte. 49,** which runs through the foothills along rivers, cliffs, and pastures, connecting dozens of small Gold Country settlements. Traffic from the coast connects with Rte. 49 via I-80 through Sacramento, which today serves as a supply post for tourists instead of the miners of the Gold Rush. If you tire of Gold Country lore, you're not alone, but don't despair. Vineyard touring, river rafting, and spelunking are popular and don't involve the g-word. Most of Gold Country is about 2hr. from Sacramento, 3hr. from San Francisco.

Sacramento The state government rules over Sacramento sights. Stormy debates about immigration, welfare, water shortages, secession, and more rage daily for a public audience in the elegant **State Capitol** (324-0333), at 10th and Capitol. One-hour tours of the stately building depart daily 9am-4pm on the hour; free tickets are distributed in room B27 on a first come, first served basis. Colonnades of towering palm trees and grassy lawns make **Capitol Park** one of many oases in the middle of downtown's busy bureaucracy, and a popular place for youthful loitering. The **State Historic Park Governor's Mansion** (324-0539), at 16th and H St., was built in 1877 and served as the residence of California's governor and his family until Governor Ronald Reagan moved out and opted to rent his own pad (open daily 10am-4pm; $2, ages 6-12 $1; hourly tours). **Area code:** 916.

Davis The **University of California at Davis** is the largest campus (area-wise) in the UC network, and also one of the nation's finest agricultural universities. When they aren't in class, some students hang out at **The Graduate,** 805 Russell Blvd. (758-4723), in the University Mall. The Grad's cavernous dining area has eight large-screen TVs, video games, a pool table, outdoor tables, meals during the day, and thematic dance party at night. (Open daily 10:30am-2am.) **Area code:** 530.

Sonora The ravines and hillsides now known as Sonora were once the domain of the Miwok Indians, but the arrival of the 49ers transformed these Sierra foothills into a bustling mining camp. In its Gold Rush heyday, Sonora was a large and prosperous city that vied fiercely with nearby Columbia for the honor of being the richest city of the southern Mother Lode. The drive to Sonora takes about 2hr. from Sacramento, 3½hr. from San Francisco. **Area code:** 209.

Pannin' fer Goald I Theory

It's easy and fun to pan for gold. *Let's Go* offers a quick, two-part course which will provide all the mental equipment you'll need. Once you're in Gold Country, find one of many public stretches of river. You'll need a 12-or 18-inch gold pan, which will be easily found at local stores. Dig in old mine tailings, at turns in the river, around tree roots, and at the upstream ends of gravel bars, where heavy gold may settle. Swirl water, sand, and gravel in a tilted gold pan, slowly washing materials over the edge. Be patient, and keep at it until you are down to black sand, and—hopefully—gold. Gold has a unique color. It's shinier than brassy-looking pyrite (Fool's Gold), and it doesn't break down upon touch, like mica, a similarly glittery substance. Later, we'll practice this technique.

Calaveras County Unsuspecting Calaveras County turned out to be literally sitting on a gold mine—the richest, southern part of the "Mother Lode"—when the big rush hit. Over 550,000 pounds of gold were extracted from the county's earth. A journalist from Missouri by the name of Samuel Clemens, a hapless miner but a gifted spinner of yarns later known as **Mark Twain,** allegedly based *The Celebrated Jumping Frog of Calaveras County,* his first hit, on a tale he heard in Angel's Camp Tavern. Life in this area has since imitated (or capitalized on) art; Calaveras has held **annual frog-jumping contests** since 1928. Thousands of people gather on the third weekend of May for the festive affair.

Not much is left of the towns that were haphazardly erected by gold-seekers. What remains, however, are not the picturesque ghost towns that Hollywood has made famous, but scattered rural communities whose crumbling buildings are held up by the many commemorative plaques. A drive along the scenic **Rte. 49** is a great way to glimpse Calaveras County. **San Andreas,** at the juncture of Rte. 49 and Rte. 26, is the county hub and population center, but it isn't very big. The **Calaveras Visitors Bureau** (800-225-3764; http://www.calaveras.org/visit), in downtown Angels Camp, is a great resource for history and sights in the area (open M-F 9am-4pm, Sa 10am-3pm, Su 11am-3pm). Scattered throughout the rest of the county are **Mokelumne Hill, Jackson, Sonora, Columbia,** and other small towns. Just south of Angels Camp on Rte. 49 is **Tuttletown,** Mark Twain's one-time home, now little more than a historic marker, a grocery store, and a well of stories.

The real attractions of Calaveras County are the natural wonders, not the abandoned towns. About 20 mi. east of Angels Camp on Rte. 4 lies **Calaveras Big Trees State Park** (795-2334; open dawn-dusk; day use $5, overnight $16, discounts for seniors). Here the *Sequoiadendron giganteum* (Giant Sequoia) reigns not so much with height (like the Redwoods on the coast) as with might: the *giganteum* is bigger than the Statue of Liberty and is the largest living thing ever to inhabit the earth.

Calaveras County boasts gargantuan natural wonders below ground as well as above. **Moaning Cavern** (736-2708) is a vast vertical cave so large that the Statue of Liberty could live there comfortably, if it came to life and walked the earth. From Angel's Camp, follow Rte. 4 east 4 mi., right onto Parrot's Ferry Rd., and follow the signs. This wonder can be viewed by descending the 236 steps or by rappelling 180 ft. down into the cave. Whether walking cautiously or hurtling down like an extreme sportsman, the journey is breathtaking—be prepared for shortness of breath after the steep walk up at the tour's end. *(Stairs $6.75, ages 3-13 $3.50; rappelling $35 1st time, ½-price each additional time. Open M-F 9am-6pm, Sa-Su and holidays 9am-5pm; in winter M-F 10am-5pm, Sa-Su and holidays 9am-5pm.)* The whole experience takes about 45min. **Mercer Caverns** (728-2101), 9 mi. north of Angels Camp, off Rte. 4 on Sheep Rd. in Murphys, offers hour-long walking tours of 10 internal rooms. *(Open daily 10am-8:30pm. Tours every 15min. until 7:30pm. Admission $6, ages 5-11 $3, under 5 free.)* Though smaller and less dramatic than Moaning Cavern, the caves are nearly a million years old. **California Caverns** (736-2708), at Cave City, served as a naturally air-conditioned bar and dance floor during the Gold Rush—a shot of whiskey could be downed for a pinch of gold dust. The caverns sobered up on Sundays for church services when one stalagmite served as an altar. It is now open for walking tours (admission $7.50, ages 3-13 $4) and "wild cavern expedition trips" that explore cramped tunnels, waist-high mud, and underground lakes for two to three hr. ($75). **Area code:** 916.

Coloma

The 1848 Gold Rush began in Coloma at John Sutter's water-powered lumber mill, operated by James Marshall. Today, the town tries its darnedest to hype this claim to fame, but the effort just makes tiny Coloma feel like Disneyland without the fun. Accommodations are sparse, so visitors will probably want to stay in Placerville. The town basically revolves around the **James Marshall Gold Discovery State Historic Park** (622-1116). Near the site where Marshall struck gold is a replica of the original mill. *(Open 8am-sunset. Day-use fee $5 per car, seniors $4. Display your pass prominently in your car window or you will be ticketed.)* Picnic grounds across the street surround the **Gold Discovery Museum,** 310 Back St. (622-3470), which presents the events of the Gold Rush through dioramas and film (open daily 10am-5pm). The real reason to come to Coloma, however, may be for the nearby natural attractions. The American River's class III currents, among the most accessible rapids in the West, attract thousands of rafters and kayakers every weekend. **Area code:** 916.

Butte Mountains

Six miles north of Sierra City, north of I-80, lie the **Butte Mountains,** one of the most beautiful and least traveled areas in California, offering amazing camping, hiking, and fishing possibilities. Five miles east of Sierra City, on the corner of Rte. 49 and Gold Lake Rd., sits the **Bassetts Station** (862-1297), an all-purpose establish-

ment that has dispensed lodging (from $65 per night), dining, gas, and supplies for over
125 years. Stop in for the low-down on camping, hiking, and fishing. (Open daily 7am-
9pm.) **Area code:** 530.

■ The Cascades

The Cascade Mountains interrupt an expanse of farmland to the northeast of Gold Country. In these ranges, recent volcanic activity has left behind a surreal landscape of lava
beds, mountains, lakes, waterfalls, caves, and recovering forest areas. The calm serenity
and haunting beauty of these mountains draw visitors in a way that the Central Valley
and Gold Country cannot.

    Lassen Volcanic National Park is accessible by **Rte. 36** to the south, and **Rte. 44** to
the north. Both roads are about 50 mi. from **Rte. 5.** In 1914, the earth radiated destruction as tremors, streams of lava, black dust, and a series of huge eruptions ravaged the
land, climaxing in 1915 when Mt. Lassen belched a 7 mi. high cloud of smoke and ashes.
Eighty-two years later, the destructive power of this eruption is still evident in the
strange, unearthly pools of boiling water and the stretches of barren moonscape. Winter
is long and snowy here. **Lassen Volcanic National Park Headquarters** (595-4444), in
Mineral, is open daily 8am-4:30pm.

    Every summer, thousands of New Age believers, yuppie vacationers, and crunchy hik-
ers come to Mt. Shasta to carouse, climb, commune, and contemplate its rugged snow-
capped top. **Shasta-Trinity National Forest Service,** 204 W. Alma St. (926-4511 or 926-
4596), will charge your New Age info-crystals. The **Alpenrose Cottage Hostel,** 204
Hinckley St. (926-6724), sends rose scents and sounds of windchimes over guests ($15,
children $7.50; showers $2; reservations recommended). **Area code:** 916.

THE SIERRA NEVADA

The Sierra Nevada is the highest, steepest, and most physically stunning mountain range
in the contiguous United States. Thrust skyward 400 million years ago by gigantic plate
collisions and shaped by erosion, glaciers, and volcanoes, this enormous hunk of granite
stretches 450 mi. north from the Mojave Desert to Lake Almanor near Lassen Volcanic
National Park. The glistening clarity of Lake Tahoe, the heart-stopping sheerness of
Yosemite's rock walls, the craggy alpine scenery of Kings Canyon and Sequoia National
Parks, and the abrupt drop of the Eastern Sierra into Owens Valley are unparalleled
sights. Temperatures in the Sierra Nevada are as diverse as the terrain. Even in the summer, overnight lows can dip into the 20s. Normally, only U.S. 50 and I-80 are kept open
during the snow season. Exact dates vary from year to year, so check with a ranger station for local road conditions, especially from October through June. Come summer,
protection from the high elevations' exposure to ultraviolet rays is necessary.

■ Lake Tahoe

In the winter of 1844, fearless explorer John C. Fremont led his expedition over the
Sierra—a fool's errand, as anyone in the Donner Party could have told you between
bites of human flesh. Luckily for him, the sight of the beautiful alpine lake was enough
to boost the morale of his 36 starved and weary companions. The lake passed through
several identities, from Bigler to Lake of Beer, before the state of California officially
named it Tahoe in 1945. Today, Tahoe is an outdoor adventurist's dream in any season,
with miles of biking, hiking, and skiing trails, long stretches of golden beaches, lakes
stocked with fish, and many hair-raising whitewater activities.

ORIENTATION AND PRACTICAL INFORMATION

Buses: Greyhound (702-588-4645 or 800-231-2222), in Harrah's Casino on U.S. 50 in Stateline, NV. To San Francisco (4 per day, $25) and Sacramento (3 per day, $20). Open daily 8am-12:30pm and 2:30-6:30pm.

Trains: Amtrak (800-872-7245) runs a bus from its San Joaquin and Capitol train routes to the Pre-Madonna Casino, off Rte. 5 at Pre-Madonna Exit, and Whiskey Pete's Casino in Stateline, NV. These combo journeys are long and costly (Stateline to San Francisco: 11hr., $80).

Public Transportation: Tahoe Casino Express (800-446-6128) provides shuttle service between the Reno airport and Southshore Tahoe casinos (6:15am-12:30am). Fare $17, round-trip $30, under 12 free. **Tahoe Area Regional Transport (TART)** (581-6365) shamelessly connects the western and northern shores from Incline Village to Tahoe City to Tahoma (Meeks Bay in the summer). Hourly stops daily 6:30am-6pm. Buses also run out to Truckee and Squaw Valley 5 times per day. Exact fare necessary: $1.25, day pass $3. **South Tahoe Area Ground Express (STAGE)** (542-6077) operates buses around South Tahoe and hourly to the beach. Connects Stateline and Emerald Bay Rd. Fare $1.25, day pass $2, 10-ride pass $10. Most casinos operate free shuttle service along Rte. 50 to California ski resorts and motels. A summer beach bus program connects STAGE and TART at Meeks Bay to service the entire lake area.

Car Rental: Enterprise (702-586-1077), in the Horizon in Stateline, NV. Must be 21 with credit card. Economy cars $36 per day, $179 per week with unlimited mi.

Visitor Info: U.S. Forest Service and Lake Tahoe Visitors Center, 870 Emerald Bay Rd. (573-2674), 3 mi. north of South Lake Tahoe on Rte. 89. Open M-F 8am-5:30pm. **South Lake Tahoe Chamber of Commerce,** 3066 Lake Tahoe Blvd. (541-5255). Open M-Sa 9am-5:30pm. **Lake Tahoe/Douglas Chamber of Commerce,** 195 U.S. 50 (702-588-4591), in Zephyr Cove, NV. Open M-F 9am-6pm, Sa-Su 9am-5pm. **Tahoe North Visitor and Convention Bureau and Visitor Information,** 245 N. Lake Blvd. (583-3494).

Internet Access: South Lake Tahoe Library, 233 Warrior Way (573-3185). Open Tu-W 10am-8pm, Th-Sa 10am-5pm.

Post Office: Tahoe City, 950 N. Lake Blvd., #12 (583-3936), in the Lighthouse Shopping Center. Open M-F 8:30am-5pm. **ZIP code:** 96145. **South Lake Tahoe,** 1046 Tahoe Blvd. (544-2208). Open M-F 8:30am-5pm, Sa 10am-2pm. **ZIP code:** 96151. **Area code:** 530 in CA, 702 in NV.

Situated in the northern Sierra on the border between California and Nevada, Lake Tahoe is a 3½hr. drive from San Francisco. The two main trans-Sierra highways, **I-80** and **U.S. 50 (Lake Tahoe Blvd.)**, run east-west through Tahoe, skimming the northern and southern shores of the lake, respectively. Lake Tahoe is 118 mi. northeast of Sacramento and 35 mi. southwest of Reno on I-80. From the Carson City and Owens Valley area, **U.S. 395** runs north along Tahoe's eastern shores.

The lake is roughly divided into two main regions, known as North Shore and South Shore. The North Shore includes King's Beach, Tahoe City, and Incline Village, while the South Shore bends to the will of Emerald Bay and South Lake Tahoe City. **Rte. 89** and **Rte. 28** form a 75 mi. ring of asphalt around the lake; the complete loop takes nearly 3hr.

ACCOMMODATIONS AND CAMPGROUNDS

The strip off U.S. 50 on the California side of the border supports the bulk of Tahoe's motels. Particularly glitzy and cheap in South Lake Tahoe, motels also line the quieter area along **Park Ave.** and **Pioneer Trail.** The North Shore offers more woodsy accommodations along Rte. 28, but rates are especially high in Tahoe City. The cheapest deals are clustered near Stateline on **U.S. 50. Rte. 89** is scattered with state **campgrounds** from Tahoe City to South Lake Tahoe. Campgrounds are often booked for the entire summer, so reserve well in advance; call **National Recreation Reservation System (NRRS)** (800-280-2267) for USDA Forest Service Campgrounds, **California Camp-**

ground Reservation System (CCRS) (800-444-7275; outside California 619-452-1950), or **National Park Reservation System** (800-365-2267).

◉**Tamarack Lodge,** 2311 N. Lake Tahoe Blvd. (583-3350 or 888-TAHOEBED/824-6323), 3 mi. north of Tahoe City, across from Star Harbor community. Clean, quiet, family-run motel in the woods. Newly refurbished exterior, outdoor barbecue and fireplace, phones, cable TV, continental breakfast, and friendly management. Rooms with snuggly queen beds $36-46.

Doug's Mellow Mountain Retreat, 787 Forest St., South Lake Tahoe (544-8065). 1 mi. west from the state line, turn left onto Wildwood Rd., after 3 blocks take a left on Forest St. Doug's hostel is the 6th house on the left. Linen, laundry, modern kitchen, BBQ, fireplace. Dorms $15 per person. Private rooms available.

Eagle Point at Emerald Bay State Park (525-7277), 10 mi. west of South Lake Tahoe on Rte. 89. Less shade and more rocks, but also more intimate. 14-night max. stay. Sites $15, seniors $14. 5min. hot showers 50¢. Open June-Sept. 6.

Bayview (544-5994) has 10 first come, first camped sites right on Emerald Bay, but no water or toilets. Sites $5.

D.L. Bliss State Park (525-7277), on Rte. 89 a few mi. north of Emerald Bay. 168 sites. Sites $16; near-beach sites $20. Day parking $5. Pets $1. 14-night max. stay. Open June-Sept. 6.

Tahoe State Recreation Area (583-3074), at the north edge of Tahoe City on Rte. 28. 1 acre of land along the lake, but also along the road. There is a long pier in the area. 38 sites. Showers, water, flush toilets. Single sites $16, seniors $14.

FOOD

In the South, the casinos offer perpetually low-priced buffets, but there are restaurants along the lakeshore with reasonable prices, similarly large portions, and much better food. Groceries are cheaper on the California side.

Killer Chicken, 2660 Lake Tahoe Blvd. (542-9977), in South Lake Tahoe. Pink walls and bright white linoleum contain barbecue chicken sandwiches ($6-7) that aren't as deadly as the name implies—everything is "fresh and healthy." Veggie and low-fat items. Open daily 11:30am-9:30pm.

Lakehouse: Pizza-Spirits-Fun, 120 Grove Ct. (583-2222), Tahoe City. Right on the water off of the main drag. Bumpity reggae riddims soothe the sunny lakefront deck. Every seat's got a great view of the lake and an athletic, well-tanned local. Breakfast specials ($3-7), California salad ($6.25), sandwiches, and way good pizzas priced reasonably. Pint of Bud Light $2.50. Open Su-Th 9am-10pm, F-Sa 8am-11pm.

The Bridgetender, 30 W. Lake Blvd. (583-3342), in Tahoe City at the corner of Rte. 89 and 28 at Fanny Bridge. The specialty is a ½ lb. burger ($4-6). Super-sized salads ($4.25) and sandwiches. Diners can eat on the outdoor patio and watch the Truckee River roll by. Wide range of beers on tap, pool table, and festive nighttime crowd. Open M-F 11am-11pm, Sa-Su 11am-midnight; bar open until 1am all week.

ACTIVITIES

Summer

Lake Tahoe supports many beaches perfect for a day of sunning and people-watching. Parking generally costs $3-5. Bargain hunters can leave their car in a turnout on the main road and walk to the beaches. **Pope Beach,** at the southernmost point of the lake off Rte. 89, is a wide, pine-shaded expanse of shoreline, which becomes less trafficked on its east side. **Nevada Beach,** 8 mi. north of South Lake Tahoe, is close to the casinos off U.S. 50, offering a quiet place to reflect on gambling losses while gazing upon the mountains. **Meeks Bay,** 10 mi. south of Tahoe City, is family oriented and social: picnic tables, volleyball, motorboat and kayak rental, and a petite store. In the summer, the Tahoe City and South Tahoe Buses connect here. Five miles south of Meeks Bay, the **D.L. Bliss**

State Park has a large beach on a small bay (Rubicon). The trailhead of the Rubicon Trail leads to the peaceful Vikingsholm mansion. Parking here ($3) is very limited, so check at the visitor center in the entrance or investigate whether you can park on the road and walk in.

Lake Tahoe is a **biking** paradise. The excellent paved trails, logging roads, and dirt paths have not gone unnoticed; be prepared for company if you pedal around the area. The Forest Service and bike rental stores can provide advice, publications like *Bike West* magazine, maps, and info about trails. No cycling is allowed in the Desolation Wilderness, or on the Pacific Crest or Tahoe Rim Trails. Bike rental shops abound, especially near the trails; rentals are usually $6-7 per hr. and $20-25 per day.

Fallen Leaf Lake, just west of South Lake Tahoe, is a dazzling destination by bike or by car, but watch out for the swerving tourists in boat- and trailer-towing vehicles, especially on the narrow mountain roads. The steep mountain peaks that surround the lake are breathtaking when viewed from beside Fallen Leaf's icy blue waters. Bikers looking for a real challenge can try the 7 mi. ring around the lake, but beware—it's more difficult than it looks. **U.S. 50, Rte. 89,** and **Rte. 28** are all bicycle-friendly, but the drivers aren't, especially in heavy traffic areas like South Lake Tahoe.

Hiking is one of the best ways to explore the beautiful Tahoe Basin. The visitors center and ranger stations provide detailed info and maps for all types of hikes. The partially completed **Tahoe Rim Trail** circles the entire lake, following the ridge tops of the Lake Tahoe Basin. Hiking is moderate to difficult, with an average grade of 10%. On the western shore, the trail is part of the Pacific Crest Trail. Current trailheads are at Spooner Summit on U.S. 50, Tahoe City off of Rte. 89 on Fairway Drive, Brockway on Rte. 267, Grass Lake on the north side of Rte. 89, and Big Meadows on Rte. 89, 5½ mi. south of the junction of U.S. 50 and Rte. 89.

River rafting can be a refreshing way to appreciate the Tahoe scenery, but depending on the water levels of the American and Truckee Rivers, rafting can range from a thrilling whitewater challenge to a boring bake in the sun. If water levels are high, check out raft rental places along the Truckee River and at Tahoe City. For more info, call **Truckee River Rafting** (583-RAFT/7238 or 800-584-RAFT/7238; open daily 8:30am-3:30pm), in Tahoe City across from Lucky's at Fanny Bridge, or **Tahoe Whitewater Tours** (581-2441; $40-80 per day with huge lunch; call for reservations).

Heavenly Mountain offers a high-value summer gondola ride package (tram and restaurant info 702-586-7000; see below). Their aerial tram heads to the mountain top for sight-seeing, picnics, and hiking. Tram runs daily 10am-9pm ($12, under 12 $7.50). The $49 summer vacation package includes a night's lodging, tram ride, and the choice of a day's activity. *(Choices: Emerald Bay cruise, ¼-day bike rental, 1hr. kayak rental, or wine and cheese picnic. Offered Su-Th May 15-Nov. 24.)*

Winter

With its world-class alpine slopes, knee-deep powder, and notorious California sun, Tahoe is a skier's Mecca. There are approximately 20 ski resorts in the Tahoe area. The visitors center provides info, maps, publications like *Ski Tahoe* (free), and coupons (see **Practical Information,** p. 819). **Squaw Valley** (583-6955 or 800-545-4350), off Rte. 89 just north of Alpine Meadows, was the site of the 1960 Olympic Winter Games, and with good reason. **Alpine Meadows** (583-4232 or 800-441-4423), 6 mi. northwest of Tahoe City on Rte. 89, is an excellent, accessible family vacation spot with more than 2000 skiable acres. **Heavenly** (800-2-HEAVEN/243-2826), on Ski Run Blvd. off U.S. 50, is one of the largest and most popular resorts in the area, with well-groomed freeway-width runs and enough moguls to make skiing feel like jump aerobics. **Mt. Rose** (800-SKI-ROSE/754-7673), 11 mi. from Incline Village on Rte. 431, is a local favorite because of its long season, short lines, intermediate focus, and less expensive lift tickets. Numerous smaller ski resorts offer cheaper tickets and shorter lines but less acreage. **Diamond Peak Ski Resort** (832-1177), off Country Club Dr. in Incline Village, has some hair-raising tree skiing and is right on the beach, while **Sugarbowl** (426-3847), 3 mi. off I-80 at

Soda Springs Exit, recently doubled in size and has decent terrain. One of the best ways to enjoy the solitude of Tahoe's pristine snow-covered forests is to cross-country ski at one of the resorts. Alternatively, you can rent skis at an independent outlet and venture onto the braid of trails around the lake.

■ Yosemite

In 1868 a young Scotsman named John Muir arrived by boat in San Francisco and asked for directions to "anywhere that's wild." Anxious to run this crazy youngster out of town, Bay Area folk directed him toward the heralded lands of Yosemite. The wonders that Muir beheld there not only sated his wanderlust but also spawned a lifetime of conservationism. His efforts won Yosemite national park status by 1880.

If Muir's 19th-century desire to flee the concrete confines of civilization was considered crazy, then today we live in a world gone criminally insane. In 1996, almost four million visitors poured into the park. Nevertheless, **Yosemite National Park** remains a paradise for outdoor enthusiasts. Most visitors congregate in only 6% of the park (Yosemite Valley), leaving thousands of beautiful backcountry miles in relative peace and quiet.

GETTING THERE AND AROUND

Yosemite lies 200 mi. east of San Francisco (a 3½hr. drive) and 320 mi. northeast of Los Angeles (a 6-9hr. drive, depending on the season). It can be reached by taking Rte. 140 from **Merced,** Rte. 41 N from **Fresno,** and Rte. 120 east from Manteca or west from Lee Vining. The park runs public buses that connect Yosemite with the gateway cities of Merced and Fresno. **Yosemite VIA** (742-5211 or 800-VIA-LINE/842-5463) runs three buses per day from the Merced Amtrak station to Yosemite (7am, 10:40am, and 3:30pm; $20, round-trip $38). VIA also runs **Yosemite Gray Line (YGL)** (722-0366), which meets trains arriving in Merced from San Francisco and takes passengers to Yosemite. Tickets can be purchased from the driver. YGL also runs to and from Fresno/Yosemite International Airport, Fresno hotels, and Yosemite Valley ($20). The **Adventure Network for Travelers** ("The ANT"; 800-336-6049 or 399-0880) runs buses between San Francisco hostels and the **Yosemite Bug Hostel** (see below) for $29 one-way, and a S.F.-Yosemite-L.A loop for $129. Their "hop-on, hop-off" travel loops also include Yosemite (call for info and times). **Amtrak** (800-872-7245) runs from San Francisco to Merced (4 per day, one-way $22) and Los Angeles to Merced (4 per day, $32), and connects with the waiting YGL bus. Amtrak also runs a bus from Merced to Yosemite (9 per day, $10).

The best bargain in Yosemite is the **free shuttle bus system.** Comfortable but often crowded, the buses have knowledgeable drivers and wide viewing windows. (Shuttles run daily every 10min. 7am-10pm, every 20min. before 7am and after 10pm.) Hikers' buses run daily to Glacier Point (spring-autumn) and to Tuolumne Meadows/Lee Vining (late June to Labor Day; for info call 372-1240).

PRACTICAL INFORMATION

The park **entrance fee** is $10 per hiker, biker, or bus rider, or $20 per car (pass valid for seven days). A 1-year Yosemite pass is $40. The Yosemite Concession Services provide some discounts to holders of Golden Age and Golden Eagle national park passes (2-for-1 bike rental, 2-for-1 greens fee at Wawona Golf). The visitors bureaus of gateway towns such as Mariposa, Sonora, Mammoth Lakes, Oakhurst, and Merced provide additional discounts on lodging, shopping, and eating.

    Bike Rental: Yosemite Lodge (372-1208) and **Curry Village** (372-8319) for $5.25 per hr., $20 per day. Both open daily 8am-7pm.

    Equipment Rental: Yosemite Mountaineering School (372-8344 or 372-1244), Rte. 120 at Tuolumne Meadows. Sleeping bags $10 per day, backpacks $8; 3rd day is half price. Climbing shoes rented to YMS students only. Driver's license or credit card required. Open daily 8:30am-5pm.

Visitor Info: General Park Information (372-0200; http://www.yosemite.org or http://www.yosemite.com), 24hr. Info on accommodations, activities, and weather. Call here before calling a specific info station. Open M-F 9am-5pm. **Yosemite Valley Visitors Center** (372-0200), Yosemite Village, has a sign language interpreter. Open daily mid-June to Sept. 6 8am-7pm; in winter 9am-5pm. All visitors centers have free maps and copies of *Yosemite Guide.*

Tours: Open air tram tours leave from Curry Village, the Ahwahnee Hotel, Yosemite Lodge or the Village Store. Tickets are available at any lodging facility or at the tour desk in front of the Village Store. Basic 2hr. **Valley Floor Tour** points out Half Dome, El Capitan, Bridalveil Falls, and Happy Isles, leaving daily every 30min. ($17.50, seniors $16.50, ages 5-12 $9.50). The 2hr. **Moonlight Tour,** given on nights with a full (or near-full) moon, offers unique nighttime views of the cliffs ($16). Call 372-1240 for reservations, departure times, and locations.

Auto Repairs: Village Garage (372-8320) tows cars 24hr. Open daily 8am-5pm.

Gas Stations: There is no gas in Yosemite Valley! Tank up in **Crane Flat** (open daily 8am-8pm) or **El Portal** (open M-Sa 7am-7pm, Su 8am-7pm).

Weather and Road Conditions: 372-0200. 24hr.

Medical Services: Yosemite Medical Clinic (372-4637), in Yosemite Village near Ahwanee Hotel. Emergency room 24hr. Drop-in Urgent Care M-F 8am-9pm, Sa 9am-noon. Scheduled appointments M-F 8am-5pm, Sa 9am-noon.

Internet Access: Yosemite Bug Hostel (966-6666), 30 mi. west of Yosemite on Rte. 140 in Midpines (see below). Internet access $5 per hr.

Post Office: Yosemite Village, next to the visitors center. Open M-F 8:30am-5pm, Sa 10am-noon. **ZIP code:** 95389. **Area code:** 209.

ACCOMMODATIONS, CAMPGROUNDS, AND FOOD

Advance reservations are very necessary and can be made up to 1 year in advance by calling 252-4848. All park lodgings provide access to dining and laundry facilities, showers, and supplies. Rates are in constant flux, but tend to be higher on weekends and during the summer (those given below are for summer weekends). Check-in hovers around 11am.

Yosemite Lodge, in Yosemite Valley, west of Yosemite Village and directly across from Yosemite Falls. Tiny cabins are as close to motel accommodations as the valley gets. Singles and doubles $92, with bath $112.

Curry Village, southeast of Yosemite Village. Swimming pool, nightly shows at the amphitheater, snack stands, cafeteria, and ice rink in winter. Noisy back-to-back cabins $59, with bath $75. Canvas-sided cabins on raised wood floor $40.

Tuolumne Meadows Lodge, on Tioga Rd. in northeast corner of park. Canvas-sided cabins, wood stoves, and no electricity. $44 for 2; $6.50 per additional adult, $3.25 per child.

White Wolf Lodge, west of Tuolumne Meadows on Tioga Rd. Cabins with bath $73. Tent cabins $44 for 2; $6.50 per additional adult, $3.50 per child.

Housekeeping Camp, west of Curry Village. Canvas-capped concrete "cottages" ($43) accommodate up to 4 people and include 2 bunk beds, a double bed, chairs, stoves, lights, and electrical outlets.

Outside the Park

Yosemite Bug Hostel (966-6666), 30 mi. west of Yosemite on Rte. 140 in Midpines. Look carefully for sign. Offers outdoor expeditions, mountain bike rental, rafting trips, and tremendous food ($3.50-7). Discount tickets on public transportation ($5, 45min.) to park. Dorm beds $15; 2-person tent with a nice bed $19; tent sites $12. Linen $1. Internet access $5 per hr.

Oakhurst Lodge, 40302 Hwy. 41, Oakhurst (683-4417). Clean, simple motel rooms with shag carpet, pool, large grassy back lawn. By far the lowest price in town. 1 king bed $65, 2 queens $75-80.

Campgrounds

To most visitors, Yosemite is camping country. Hence, most of the valley's camp-grounds are choked with tents, trailers, and RVs. Reservations can be made up to 5 months in advance. Call 800-436-7275, outside the U.S. 301-722-1257, TDD 888-530-9796, 7am-7pm Pacific time, or mail **NPRS**, P.O. Box 1600, Cumberland, MD 21502.

Backcountry camping is prohibited in the valley (you'll get slapped with a stiff fine if caught), but it's generally permitted along the high country trails with a free wilderness permit. Each trailhead limits the number of permits available, so reserve by mail up to one year in advance (write **Wilderness Center**, P.O. Box 577, Yosemite National Park 95389), or take your chances with the 50% quota held on 24hr. notice at the **Yosemite Valley Visitors Center** (see p. 822); the **Wawona Ranger Station** (375-9501), Rte. 141 at the southern entrance near the Mariposa Grove; and **Big Oak Flat Station** (379-1899), Rte. 120 W in Crane Flat/Tuolumne Sequoia Grove. Wilderness permits are free, but the reservation costs $3. Popular trails like Little Yosemite Valley, Clouds Rest, and Half Dome fill quotas quickly.

Inside Yosemite Valley

Sunnyside, at the west end of Yosemite Valley past the Yosemite Lodge. The only first come, first served site in the valley. A walk to the camp will immerse you in a climb-ing subculture in which seasoned adventurers swap stories of exploits on vertical rock faces. Every site is filled with 6 people, regardless of the size of your group. Water, toilets, and tables. $3 per person. No reservations; 35 sites fill up early. Open year-round.

Lower Pines, in the busy eastern end of Yosemite Valley. Commercial and crowded, with cars driving by. Toilets, water, showers, and tables. This is the designated winter camping spot and the only one in the valley that allows pets. Sites $15.

Beyond Yosemite Valley

Campsite quality improves outside of the valley. All of the park's campgrounds have at least 50 sites, and all have RV sites except for Tamarack Flat, Yosemite Creek, and Porcu-pine Flat. All sites have fire pits and nearby parking.

Hodgdon Meadow, on Rte. 120 near Big Oak Flat entrance. Warm enough for winter camping. 105 thickly wooded sites provide some seclusion even when the camp-ground is full. Beautiful area 25 mi. from the valley. Water, tables, and toilets. Sites $15. First come, first camped Oct.-Apr. ($10).

Tuolumne Meadows, 55 mi. east on Rte. 120. Half of the 314 sites require advanced reservations, half are saved for same-day reservations. Drive into the sprawling camp-ground or escape the RVs by ambling to the 25 sites saved for hikers without cars. Great scenery and nearby trailheads. Pets allowed in the western section only. Water, toilets, and tables. Drive-in sites $15, backpacker sites $3 per person. Open Aug.-Sept., depending on snow.

Wawona, 27 mi. south of the valley off Rte. 41. These 100 plain and simple wooded sites are near the Merced River. Tables, flush toilets, and water. No showers. Pets allowed. Sites $15.

Bridalveil Creek, 25 mi. south of the valley on Glacier Point Rd. Peaceful grounds have 110 first come, first camped sites. Convenient to Glacier and Taft Points; 2min. walk to beautiful McGurk Meadow. Flush toilets, tables, water. Sites $10. Open June-Sept.

In general, restaurants in the park are nothing special. Consider buying all of your cook-ing supplies, marshmallows, and batteries in Merced, Fresno, or Oakhurst before com-ing to the park. These gateway towns are also home to many affordable restaurants.

CALIFORNIA

SIGHTS

By Car

Although the view is better if you get out of the car, you can see a large part of Yosemite from the bucket seat. The *Yosemite Road Guide* ($4 at every visitors center) is keyed to roadside markers and outlines a superb tour of the park—it's almost like having a ranger tied to the hood. Even fledgling visitors will immediately recognize the Wawona Tunnel turnout as the subject of many Ansel Adams photographs. The 7569 ft. **El Capitan,** the largest granite monolith in the world, looms over squirming crowds. If you stop and look closely (with binoculars if possible), you will see small moving dots on the mountain face. These specks of dust are actually world-class climbers inching towards infamy. Nearby, misty **Bridalveil Falls** and **Three Brothers** (three adjacent granite peaks) pose for hundreds of snapshots every day. A drive into the heart of the valley leads to **Yosemite Falls** (the highest in North America at 2425 ft.), **Sentinel Rock,** and mighty **Half Dome.**

Glacier Point, off Glacier Point Rd., opens up a different perspective on the valley. Hovering 3214 ft. above the valley floor, this gripping overlook is guaranteed to impress the most jaded traveler. Half Dome rests majestically across the valley, and the sounds of Vernal and Nevada Falls provide enough white noise to drown out the roar of the tour buses and their ceaselessly chattering passengers. When the moon is full, this is an extraordinary (and very popular) place to visit. Sunset brings the fiery fade of day over the valley: the sky dims, the stars appear, the bottom sides of clouds in the east begin to glow bright silver, and from behind some nearby mountains the blinding full moon rises into the horizon.

Day hiking in the Valley

To have the full Yosemite experience, visitors must travel the outer trails on foot. A wealth of opportunities reward anyone willing to lace up a pair of boots, even if only for a daytrip. A colorful trail map with difficulty ratings and average hiking times is available at the visitors center (50¢). **Bridalveil Falls,** another Ansel Adams favorite, is an easy ¼ mi. stroll from the nearby shuttle bus stop, and its cool spray is as close to a shower as many Yosemite campers ever get.

Upper Yosemite Falls Trail, a back-breaking 3½ mi. trek to the windy summit, rewards the intrepid hiker with an overview of the 2425 ft. drop. Those with energy to spare can trudge on to **Inspiration Point,** where views of the valley below rival those from more-heralded Glacier Point.

From the Happy Isles trailhead, the **John Muir Trail** leads 211 mi. to Mt. Whitney, but most visitors prefer to take the slightly less strenuous 1½ mi. **Mist Trail** past **Vernal Falls** (only visible from this trail) to the top of **Nevada Falls.** This is perhaps the most popular day-use trail in the park, and with good reason—views of the falls from the trails are outstanding, and the indefatigable drizzle that issues from the nearby water-assaulted rocks is more than welcome during the hot summer months. There is a free shuttle from the valley campgrounds to Happy Isles; no parking is available. The Mist Trail continues past Nevada Falls to the base of **Half Dome,** Yosemite's most recognizable monument and a powerful testament to the power of glaciation. Bad-ass visitors trek to the top and enjoy the unimaginable vista of the valley. The hike is 17 mi. round-trip, rises a total of 4800 vertical ft., and takes all day (6-12hr.). The final 800 ft. walk to the rock-star peak is a steep climb up the backside of the famous rock face. Equipped with cables to aid non-climbing folks, this final challenge is well worth the thrill of sitting on top of the world and imagining yourself its king.

Climbing and Water Activities

The world's best **climbers** come to Yosemite to test themselves at angles past vertical. If you've got the courage (and the cash), you can join the stellar Yosemite rock climbers by taking a lesson with the **Yosemite Mountaineering School.** Reservations are useful and require advance payment, though drop-ins are accepted if space allows. For more info, contact **Yosemite Mountaineering School,** Yosemite 95389 (372-8435; open daily 8:30am-5pm).

Rafting is permitted on the Merced River from 10am to 6pm, but no motorized crafts are allowed. Swimming is allowed throughout the park except where posted. Those who prefer their water chlorinated can swim in the public pools at Curry Village and Yosemite Lodge (open daily 10am-5pm; $2 for non-guests).

Organized Activities

Park rangers lead a variety of informative hikes and other activities for visitors of all ages. **Junior ranger** (ages 8-10) and **senior ranger** (ages 11-12) activities allow children to hike, raft, and investigate aquatic and terrestrial life. These 3hr. summer programs, usually held mid-week, require reservations at least a day in advance through the Yosemite Valley Visitors Center and cost $2. Rangers also guide a number of free walks for regular old people. **Explore Yosemite! tours** (1-1½hr.) address a variety of historical and geological topics. All leave daily at 9am from the visitors center, and most are wheelchair-accessible. Another free, park-sponsored adventures is a **photographic hike** led by professional photographers. Sign up for the 1½hr. lesson-adventures at the Ansel Adams Museum. **Sunrise photo walks** leave most mornings from the Yosemite Lode tour desk. The **Glacier Point Sunset Photo Shoot** is offered Thursday nights in the summer. This is an incredible spot, especially at sunset.

In 1903, John Muir gave Teddy Roosevelt a now-famous tour of Yosemite. The renowned thespian Lee Stetson has assumed Muir's role, leading free, 1hr. hikes along the same route. Stetson also hosts **The Spirit of John Muir,** a 1½hr. one-man show, and **Conversation with a Tramp** (W and Sa 8pm; $7, seniors $6, under 12 $2). The six different theatrical presentations include *Yosemite by Song and Story* and the moving picture *Friendly Fire: A Forty-Niner's Life with the Yosemite Indians*, which tells the true story of a once-prejudiced man who learns to love the Indians. *(Tu-F 8:30pm. 1hr. $6, seniors $5, under 12 $3.)* Tickets are sold at Yosemite Theater.

The **Ansel Adams Gallery** (372-4413), next to the visitors center, is more like an artsy gift shop/activity center. *(Open daily 8:30am-6:30pm.)* Sign up for a **fine print viewing** in the gallery to see the precious stuff. The newly formed **journaling workshop** is a refreshing retreat, in which experienced writers take small groups of people to beautiful places and encourage their writing as creative expression.

Beyond Yosemite Valley

Most folks never leave the valley, but a wild, lonely place awaits those who do. The Wilderness Center in Yosemite Valley offers maps and personalized assistance. Topographical maps and hiking guides are especially helpful in navigating Yosemite's nether regions. Equipment can be rented or purchased through the Mountaineering School at Tuolomne Meadows (see **Practical Information,** p. 821) or through the Mountain Shop at Curry Village, but stores in major cities are less expensive.

Wintertime In Yosemite

Cross-country skiing is free, and several well-marked trails cut into the backcountry of the valley's South Rim at Badger Pass and Crane Flat. Both areas have blazes on the trees so that the trails can be followed even when there's several feet of fresh snow. The same snow also transforms many summer hiking trails into increasingly popular **snowshoe trails.** Rangers host several snowshoe walks. Both nordic skis and snowshoes can be rented from the **Yosemite Mountaineering School** (372-8344). **Badger Pass Rental Shop** (below) also rents winter equipment and downhill skis.

The state's oldest ski resort, **Badger Pass Ski Area,** south of Yosemite Valley on Glacier Point Rd. (372-8430), is the only downhill ski area in the park. Its family-fun atmosphere encourages learning and restraint (no snowboards). Free shuttles connect Badger Pass with the Yosemite Valley lodges. *(Ski lessons $22 for 2hr., private lessons from*

CALIFORNIA

$44. Rental packages $18 per day, under 12 $13. Lift tickets Sa-Su $28 per day, M-F $22, under 12 $13, over 60 and exactly 40 free. Lifts open 9am-4:30pm. Discount ski packages for weekdays available through Yosemite Lodge.)

■ Near Yosemite: Stanislaus National Forest

This highly preserved land circles Yosemite and connects the forests along the northern Sierra. Well-maintained roads and campsites, craggy peaks, dozens of cool topaz lakes, forests of Ponderosa pines, and wildflower meadows make up the 900,000 acres of the Stanislaus National Forest. Here, peregrine falcons, bald eagles, mountain lions, and bears sometimes surprise the lucky (or tasty) traveler. In addition to great hiking trails, fishing, and campsites, Stanislaus offers a chance for a bit of solitude—something its better-known neighbor, Yosemite, doesn't have. **Park headquarters** are located at 19777 Greenly Rd., Sonora (532-3671; open in summer 8am-5pm; call for winter hrs.). Camping permits are required for Carson-Iceberg, Mokelumne, and Emigrant Wilderness; permits are also needed for building fires in wilderness areas. Only Pinecrest accepts reservations.

■ Mono Lake

As fresh water from streams and springs drains into the "inland sea" of Mono Lake, it evaporates, leaving behind a mineral-rich, 13 mi. wide expanse Mark Twain once called "the Dead Sea of the West." The lake derives its lunar appearance from towers of calcium carbonate called tufa, which form when calcium-rich springs well up in the carbonate-filled salt water. At one million years old, this is the Western Hemisphere's oldest enclosed body of water—truly The Old Man of the Seas.

The unique terrain of this geological playground makes it a great place for hikers of all levels. Easy trails include the ¼ mi. **Old Marina Area Trail,** east of U.S. 395 1 mi. north of Lee Vining; the **Lee Vining Creek Nature Trail,** which begins behind the Mono Basin Visitors Center; and the **Panum Crater Trail,** 5 mi. south on U.S. 395.

The **Fern Creek Lodge** (800-621-9146) is 13 mi. from Lee Vining, 1 mi. past June Lake Town on Hwy. 158. Small woodsy cabins with kitchens. The smallest 2-person cabin ($47-52) is a great deal for the area. None of the area's campgrounds take reservations, but sites are ubiquitous, so a pre-noon arrival will almost always guarantee a spot. Most sites are clustered west of Lee Vining along Rte. 120. The six **Inyo National Forest campgrounds** ($0-8), lie within 15min. of town; Lundy and Lee Vining Canyons are the best locations for travelers headed for Mono Lake. The June Lake Loop area south of town on U.S. 395 also has numerous sites ($10). The **Lee Vining Market** (647-6301), on the south end of town on U.S. 395, is the closest thing to a grocery store (open daily 8am-9pm). The **Walking Taco** (647-6470), on Main St. across from 2nd, serves standard Tex-Mex fare (tostada salad $4, taco $1.25) in a friendly spot with indoor and outdoor seating (open daily 11:30am-9pm).

In 1984, Congress set aside the 57,000 acres of land surrounding Mono Lake and called it the **Mono Basin National Forest Scenic Area** (647-3044). For a $2 fee (Golden Eagle and Golden Age passes accepted), you can investigate the **South Tufa Grove,** which harbors an awe-inspiring hoard of calcium carbonate formations. (Take U.S. 395 S to Rte. 120, then go 4 mi. east and take the Mono Lake Tufa Reserve turn-off 1 mi. south to Tufa Grove.) The tufa towers, which resemble giant drip sandcastles, poke through the smooth surface of this solemn sea. From mid-June through early September, the Mono Lake Committee offers guided **canoe tours** (reservations 647-6595) of the lake that include a crash course on Mono's natural history and conservation. *(1hr. tours depart from the Navy Beach parking lot on the south shore of Mono Lake at 8, 9:30, and 11am on Sa-Su; earlier is better for bird watching. Arrive 30min. early for lifejacket fitting and photos of placid reflections. Tickets $15, ages 4-12 $6.)* Caldera Kayaks offers full-day **kayak tours** and **kayak rentals.**

The town of **Lee Vining** provides stunning access to Yosemite. Lee Vining is 70 mi. north of Bishop on U.S. 395 and 10 mi. west of the Tioga Pass entrance to Yosemite. **Greyhound** (647-6301 or 800-231-2222) has a flag stop at the Red Log Store on the south side of Lee Vining. To Los Angeles (1 per day, $49) and Reno (1 per day, $30). **Mono Lake Committee and Lee Vining Chamber of Commerce** (647-6595; http://www.monolake.org) is in the large orange and blue building on Main St. at 3rd, in Lee Vining (open daily late June to Sept. 6 9am-10pm; off-season 9am-5pm). **Mono Basin National Forest Scenic Area Visitors Center** (647-3044; http://www.r5.fs.fed.us/inyo), Inyo National Forest, is ½ mi. north of Lee Vining off U.S. 395 (open in summer M-F 9am-5:30pm). **Area code:** 760.

■ Mammoth Lakes

Home to one of the most popular ski resorts in the United States, the town of Mammoth Lakes has transformed itself into a giant year-round playground. Mammoth Mountain makes a summer metamorphosis from ski park to bike park, and fishing, rock climbing, and hiking complement the area's more popular wintertime pursuits. Every establishment in town seems to exist solely for the excursionist's benefit; even the McDonald's looks like a ski lodge.

Devil's Postpile National Monument was formed when lava flows oozed through Mammoth Pass thousands of years ago, forming 40 to 60 ft. basalt posts. A pleasant 3 mi. walk from the center of the monument is **Rainbow Falls,** where the middle fork of the San Joaquin River drops 101 ft. into a glistening green pool. From U.S. 395, the Devil's Postpile/Rainbow Falls trailhead can be reached by a 15 mi. drive past Minaret Summit on paved Rte. 203. To preserve the area, rangers have introduced a **shuttle** service between the parking area at the Mammoth Mountain Inn and the monument center, which all visitors—drivers and hikers alike—must use between 7:30am and 5:30pm (round-trip $9, ages 13-18 $7, ages 5-12 $4). Visitors with wheels can save themselves a load of cash by driving to the monument during nightly free access hours (5:30pm-7:30am).

Anglers converge on the Mammoth area each summer to test their skills on some of the best **trout lakes** in the country. Permits are required (the visitors center has info on other regulations). **Crowley Lake** (935-4301), in Owens Valley 12 mi. south of town, yields over 80 tons of rainbow trout each summer. (Motorboat rental $48 per day; parking free with rental, otherwise $6 per day. Campsites with full hookup $25.)

Visitors can ride the **Mammoth Mountain Gondola** (934-2571) for a view that's miles above the rest. (Open in summer daily 9:30am-5:30pm. Round-trip $10, children $5; day pass $20 for gondola and trail use.) Exit the gondola at the top for a mountain biking extravaganza over the twisted trails of **Mammoth Mountain Bike Park** (934-0706), where the ride starts at 11,053 ft. and heads straight down on rocky ski trails (helmets required). Tickets and info are available at the **Mammoth Adventure Connection** (934-0606), in the Mammoth Mountain Inn at the base of the mountain. (Bike rental including helmet $15 per hr., $25 for 4hr., $35 for 8hr.; children ½-price. Open daily 9:30am-6pm.)

There are nearly 20 Inyo Forest public campgrounds (sites $8-11) in the area. All sites have piped water, and most of them are near fishing and hiking. For info, call the **Mammoth Ranger District** (924-5500); for reservations, call MISTIX (800-280-CAMP/2267; reservation fee $8.65 for individual sites). One of the best views in town is housed at the **Davison St. Guest House,** 19 Davison Rd. (924-2188; fax 544-9107), with kitchens, fireplaces, and a huge common room (dorms $15, singles $30). In the minds of most locals, **The Stove,** 644 Old Mammoth Rd. (934-2821), 4 blocks from Main St., equals big breakfasts. An avocado omelette with turkey is $7. An old bathtub outside is now a friendly flowerbed (open daily 6:30am-9pm).

Mammoth Lakes is on **U.S. 395** about 160 mi. south of Reno and 40 mi. southeast of the eastern entrance to Yosemite. **Rte. 203** runs through the town as **Main St. Grey-**

hound (800-231-2222) stops at corner of Hwy. 203 and Sierra Park Rd. in the parking lot behind McDonald's on Main St. Buses run to Reno (1 per day, $36) and Los Angeles (2 per day, $46). **Inyo National Forest Visitors Center and Chamber of Commerce** (934-8989, 888-GO-MAMMOTH/466-2666, or 800-367-6572; fax 934-7066) is east off U.S. 395, north of town (open July-Sept. daily 8am-5pm; Oct.-June. M-Sa 8am-5pm). **Post Office:** 3330 Main St. (open M-F 8:30am-5pm). **ZIP code:** 93546. **Area code:** 760.

ALASKA

Alaska's beauty and intrigue are born of extremes: North America's highest mountains and broadest flatlands; windswept tundra and lush rainforests; 586,412 sq. mi. (over one-fifth of the land mass of the U.S.); and 15 incredible national parks cover an area roughly equal to that of England and Ireland combined. The U.S. bought Alaska for about 2¢ per acre in 1867, from a Russia deep in debt after losing the Crimean War. Critics mocked "Seward's Folly," named after the Secretary of State who negotiated the deal, but just 15 years after the purchase, huge deposits of gold were unearthed in the Panhandle's Gastineau Channel. Prospectors quickly struck gold in rivers such as the Yukon, Charley, Fortymile, and Klondike.

These days, the Trans-Alaska Pipeline, running 800 mi. through the heart of the Alaskan wilderness, has had a revolutionary effect on the state's political, social, and economic landscape since its construction in 1977. In August of 1998, the federal government gave the go-ahead for drilling in about one-fifth of the National Petroleum Reserve's 23 million acres. Environmentalists argue that drilling will disrupt the pristine wilderness, while oil companies want the entire area to be opened.

For more comprehensive coverage of Alaska and its arctic allures, see *Let's Go: Alaska & the Pacific Northwest, Including Western Canada 1999*.

ⓘ HIGHLIGHTS OF ALASKA

- **Natural Wonders.** Denali National Park (p. 835) is the state's crown jewel. Wrangell-St. Elias National Park (p. 834) houses massive glaciers, while Glacier Bay National Park (p. 841) basks in a symphony of sea and ice.
- **Wildlife.** Cruises out of Seward into Kenai Fjords National Park (p. 833) are stuffed with opportunities to view sea critters.
- **Recreation.** Southeast Alaska's grandest features include kayaking in Misty Fiords National Monument (p. 839), climbing Deer Mountain in Ketchikan (p. 839), and hiking the West Glacier Trail in Juneau (p. 841).

PRACTICAL INFORMATION

Capital: Juneau.
Visitor Info: Alaska Division of Tourism, P.O. Box 110801, Juneau 99811-0801 (907-465-2010; http://www.commerce.state.ak.us/tourism). **Alaska Public Lands Information Center,** 605 W. 4th Ave. Suite 105, Anchorage 99501 (907-271-2737). **Alaska Dept. of Natural Resources Public Information,** 3601 C St., Suite 200, Anchorage 99503 (907-269-8400; http://www.dnr.state.ak.us/parks/index.htm).
Time Zone: Alaska (most of the state; 4hr. before Eastern); Aleutian-Hawaii (Aleutian Islands; 5hr. before Eastern). **Postal Abbreviation:** AK.
Sales Tax: None.

CLIMATE

Weather varies from the coast inland. Anchorage temperatures range from 8°F in winter to 65°F in summer. In Alaska's Interior, the temperature ranges from around 70°F in summer to -30°F and lower in winter. Progressing farther north, summer days and winter nights become longer. North of the Arctic Circle, the sun does not set at all on the nights around the summer solstice in late June, nor does it rise on the days around the winter solstice in December.

GETTING AROUND

The **Alaska Railroad,** P.O. Box 107500, Anchorage 99510-7500 (800-544-0552), runs nearly 500 mi. from Seward to Fairbanks, with stops in Anchorage and Whittier. The **Alaska Marine Hwy.,** P.O. Box 25535, Juneau 99802-5535 (800-642-0066; http://www.dot.state.ak.us/external/amhs/home.html), remains the most practical and enjoyable way to explore much of the Panhandle, Prince William Sound, and the Kenai Peninsula. The **AlaskaPass,** P.O. Box 351, Vashon, WA 98070-0351 (800-248-7598 or 206-463-6550), offers unlimited access to Alaska's railroad, ferry, and bus systems (15 days $689, 30 days $939; 21 non-consecutive days over a 45-day period $979). Most of the state's major **highways** are known by their name as often as their number (George Parks Hwy. = Rte. 3 = The Parks). Driving to and through Alaska is not for the faint of car; highways reward drivers with stunning views and access to true wilderness, but they barely scratch the surface of the massive state. See p. 914 for the two major highway approaches into the state from points south. For Alaska's most remote destinations, **air travel** is an expensive necessity. Intrastate airlines and charter services, many of them based at the busy Anchorage airport, transport passengers and cargo to virtually every village in Alaska. Many are listed in the relevant **Practical Information** sections.

■ Anchorage

Alaska's only metropolis, Anchorage is home to 254,000 people—two-fifths of the state's population. As far north as Helsinki and almost as far west as Honolulu, the city achieved its large size (2000 sq. mi.) by hosting three major economic projects: the Alaska Railroad, WWII military development, and the Trans-Alaska Pipeline. Anchorage serves as a good place to get oriented and stock up on supplies before journeying to the breathtaking wilderness just outside.

PRACTICAL INFORMATION Downtown Anchorage is laid out in a grid: Numbered **avenues** run east-west, with addresses designated east or west from **C St.** North-south **streets** are lettered alphabetically to the west and named alphabetically to the east of **A St.** The rest of Anchorage spreads out along the major highways.

Most Alaskan airstrips can be reached from **Anchorage International Airport** (266-2525) either directly or through a connection in Fairbanks; the *Daily News* lists second-hand tickets. **Yellow Cab** (272-2422) charges about $13 from the airport to the downtown hostel (24hr.). **Alaska Railroad,** 411 W. 1st Ave. (265-2494, outside AK 800-544-0552), runs to Denali (8hr., $99); Fairbanks (12hr., $149); and Seward (4hr., in summer only, $43). In winter, a flag stop runs to Fairbanks (around $105). (Contact P.O. Box 107500, Anchorage. Ticket window open M-F 5:30am-5pm, Sa-Su 5:30am-1pm.) **Grayline Alaska** (800-544-2206) sends buses daily to Seward (4hr., $40); Valdez (10hr., $66); and Portage (2hr., $40); and three times per week to Haines ($189) and Skagway ($209), both overnight. **Parks Hwy. Express** (479-3065, in AK 888-600-6001) runs buses daily to Denali ($30) and Fairbanks ($49). **Alaska Marine Hwy.,** 605 W. 4th Ave. (800-642-0066, Sa-Su 800-526-6731), sells ferry tickets (open M-F 9am-5:30pm). **People Mover Bus** (343-6543), in the Transit Center on 6th Ave. between G and H St., sends local buses all over the Anchorage area. (Runs M-F 6am-10pm; restricted schedule Sa-Su; cash fare $1, ages 5-18 or over 65 25¢; tokens 90¢; day passes $2.50. Office open M-F 8am-5pm.) **Airport Car Rental,** 502 W. Northern Lights Blvd. (277-7662) charges $55 per day, with unlimited mi. (Must be 21; under 25 surcharge $5 per day; cash or credit card deposit required. Open M-F 8am-5pm, Sa 8am-6pm, Su 9am-5pm.)

The **Log Cabin Visitor Information Center** (274-3531, events hotline 276-3200), on W. 4th Ave. at F St., sells a 50¢ bike guide (open daily 7:30am-7pm; May and Sept. 8am-6pm; Oct.-Apr. 9am-4pm). The **Alaska Public Lands Information Center,** Old Federal Building, 605 W. 4th Ave. (271-2737 or 271-2738), caddy-corner from the visitor center between F and G St., combines the Park, Forest, State Parks, and Fish and Wildlife Services under one roof (open daily 9am-5:30pm). **Challenge Alaska** (344-7399) refers services for the disabled. **Internet Access: Surf City Café,** 415 L. St. (12$ per min.). **Post Office:** (279-3062), W. 4th Ave. and C St., on the lower level in the yellow mall (open M-F 10am-5:30pm). **ZIP code:** 99510. **Area code:** 907.

ACCOMMODATIONS, CAMPGROUNDS, AND FOOD Alaska Private Lodgings (258-1717; call M-Sa 8am-7pm) or the **Anchorage reservation service** (272-5909) arrange out-of-town B&Bs (from $65). Two of the best campgrounds in **Chugach State Park** (354-5014) are **Eagle River** ($15) and **Eklutna** ($10), 12½ and 26½ mi. northeast of town along Glenn Hwy. Both fill up early, especially on weekends.

Spenard Hostel, 2845 W. 42nd Pl. (248-5036), is comfortable, clean, and welcoming. Take bus #36 or #7 from downtown, or #6 from the airport down Spenard to Turnagain Blvd.; 42nd Pl. is the first left from Turnagain. (3 kitchens, free local calls, bike rental $5, laundry, lockers, Denali Shuttle drop-off/pick-up. Beds or tent sites $15. No curfew or lockout. Chore requested. 6-night max. stay.) **Anchorage International Youth Hostel (HI-AYH),** 700 H St. (276-3635), at 7th St., 1 block south of the city bus station on the edge of downtown, bustles in an unbeatable location. (Kitchens, TV, balconies, lockers, and laundry. $15, nonmembers $18; photo ID required. Lockout noon-5pm. Curfew 1am; reception until 2am. Chore requested. 5-night max. stay in summer. Pay by 11am or lose your spot. Book in advance.) The name of **Qupqugiaq Inn,** 640 W. 36th Ave. (563-5633), between Arctic Blvd. and C St., refers to a legendary 10-legged polar bear (koop-KOO-gee-ak) who rejected a violent way of life to create a community based on love and peace. Take bus #9. (Common lounge and kitchen, shared bath, cable TV. No smoking or alcohol. Singles from $38; doubles $48. Common areas closed at 10pm. Reserve ahead, or arrive by 3pm for a room.)

The **Qupqugiaq Café,** downstairs, offers free classes and wholesome food for hungry minds and stomachs, including an herb-roasted chicken sandwich ($6.50; open M-F 7am-8pm, Sa 9am-8pm, Su 9am-3pm). **Moose's Tooth,** 3300 Old Seward (258-2537), serves up fresh, tasty pizza (small spinach $8.75) and house beers (raspberry wheat $3.50) in a relaxed atmosphere (open Su-Th noon-midnight, F-Sa noon-1am).

Twin Dragon, 612 E. 15th Ave. (276-7535), near Gambell, offers an all-you-can-eat buffet of marinated meats and vegetables, hot off the giant grill (lunch $6.50; dinner $10; BBQ and Chinese food buffet $13). Take bus #11. (Open M-Sa 11am-midnight, Su 1pm-midnight.) **Side Street Espresso,** 428 G St. (258-9055), is a gathering hole for the hip and the yup, with political salons, frequent acoustic music, a decent book exchange, and bound copies of local writers' efforts (cappuccino $2; espresso $1.50; open M-F 7am-7pm, Sa 7am-5pm, Su 8am-5pm).

Does the Word "Mush" Mean Anything to You?

Charlie Darwin would have liked these odds: snow, wind, and frigid cold, separating the women from the girls. The celebrated Iditarod dog sled race begins in Anchorage on the first weekend in March. Dogs and their drivers ("mushers") traverse a 1150 mi. trail over two mountain ranges, along the mighty Yukon River, and over the frozen Norton Sound to Nome. The Iditarod Trail began as a dog sled supply route from Seward on the southern coast to interior mining towns. The race commemorates the 1925 rescue of Nome, when drivers ferried 300,000 units of life-saving diptheria serum from Nenana, near Fairbanks, to Nome. Today, up to 70 contestants speed each year from Anchorage to Nome, competing for a $450,000 purse but surprisingly willing to help fellow mushers in distress. The fastest time up to now was recorded by Doug Swingley—9 days, 2hr. You can visit the **Iditarod Headquarters** at Mi. 2.2 Knik Rd. in Wasilla.

SIGHTS, OUTDOORS, AND NIGHTLIFE Near town off Northern Lights Blvd., **Earthquake Park** recalls the 1964 Good Friday quake, the strongest ever recorded in North America, registering 9.2 on the Richter scale. The **Anchorage Museum of History and Art,** 121 W. 7th Ave. (343-6061), at A St., is the finest museum in town, and probably in the state (tours daily at 10, 11am, 1, and 2pm; $5, seniors $4.50, under 18 free). Wildlife is guaranteed at the **Alaska Zoo** (346-3242), Mi. 2 on O'Malley Rd., where Binky the Polar Bear mauled an Australian tourist in 1994 and became a local hero. *(Open daily 9am-6pm. $7, seniors $6, ages 12-18 $4, under 12 $3.)* Take bus #91.

The 11 mi. **Tony Knowles Coastal Trail** is arguably one of the best urban bike paths in the country; in the winter, it's groomed for **cross-country skiing.** The serene **Chugach State Park,** cornering the city to the north, east, and south, has **public use cabins** (800-280-2267; $25 per night; $8.25 reservation fee) and 25 established **day hiking** trails. A 15min. drive from the city center, **Flattop Mountain** (4500 ft.) is the most frequently climbed mountain in Alaska, providing an excellent view of the inlet, the Aleutian Chain, and on the rare clear day, Denali. Parking at the trailhead costs $5, or take bus #92 to Hillside Rd. and Upper Huffman Rd. From there, the trailhead is a ¾ mi. walk along Upper Huffman Rd., then right on Toilsome Hill Dr. for 2 mi.; it's a 2 mi. hike to the crowded summit. Less frequented hikes branch from the **Powerline Trail,** which begins at the same parking lot as the Flattop Trail. The **Middle Fork Loop,** ¾ mi. off of Powerline, leads a gentle 12 mi. through spruce woods and open tundra. The **Eklutna Lakeside Biking Trail** extends 13 mi. one-way from the Eklutna Campground, off Mi. 26 of the Glenn Hwy. (Rte. 1). A relatively flat dirt road, the trail follows the blue-green Eklutna Lake for 7 mi. before entering a steep river canyon, ending at the base of the Eklutna River. **Nancy Lake State Recreation Area,** just west of the Parks Hwy. (Rte. 3) at Mi. 67.3, and just south of **Willow,** contains the **Lynx Lake Canoe Loop,** which takes 2 days and weaves through 8 mi. of lakes and portages, with designated campsites along the way. The loop begins at Mi. 4.5 of the Nancy Lake Parkway, at the Tanaina Lake Canoe Trailhead. For **canoe rental** or **shuttle service** in the Nancy Lake Area, call **Tippecanoe** (495-6688; canoes $25 1st day, $70 per week; shuttle free for backpackers).

The brew pub revolution has hit Anchorage, and microbrews gush from taps like oil through the pipeline. **Railway Brewing Co.,** 421 W. 1st (277-1996), in the railroad depot, sports friendly service, six tasty creations, and live bands in the winter (burger-and-brew special $8; open daily 11am to around midnight). At **Bernie's Bungalow Lounge,** 626 D St. (276-8808), relax in one of many wingback chairs or couches as you sip your lemon drop martini ($5), puff on a cigar, and play a round of croquet in a hotspot frequented by the young and retro (open M-Th 7am-2:30am, F-Sa noon-3am, Su noon-2:30am). Colorful decor and a loyal clientele, both gay and straight, make a splash at **The Wave,** 3103 Spenard St. (561-WAVE/9283), a bright, upbeat dance bar. (Drag shows W; country line dancing Th; open W 8pm-2:30am, Th 7pm-2:30am, F-Sa 8pm-3am). **Mr. Whitekey's Fly-by-Night Club,** 3300 Spenard Rd. (279-SPAM/7726) serves "everything from the world's finest champagnes to a damn fine plate of Spam." Take bus #7. (Spam nachos $5.50; coconut beer-battered Spam $5; nightly comedy and "musical off-color follies" at 8pm, $5-17. Live music after the show F-Sa. Open Tu-Th 4pm-2am, F-Sa 4pm-3am.)

▓ Seward and Kenai Fjords

Seward is yet another of Alaska's super-scenic coastal towns, drawing hikers, kayakers, sailors, anglers, and cruise lines. Giving visitors a glimpse at Alaska's coastal and underwater goings-on, the **Alaska SeaLife Center** (224-3080 or 800-224-2525), at the end of downtown between 3rd and 4th Ave., opened in May 1998 after much statewide fanfare. (Open daily 9am-9:30pm, last tickets sold at 8pm; in winter W-Su 10am-5pm, last tickets sold at 3:30pm. $12.50, seniors $11.25, ages 4-16 $10.) Next door, the **Chugach Heritage Center,** 501 Railway Ave. (224-5065), also had its big opening in 1998. (Open daily 10am-8pm. $10, ages 4-16 $8.) A 1917 railroad depot has been transformed into a theater and gallery of Native Alaskan art, where 30min. performances every hour serve to educate the public and to preserve native culture.

Seward serves as gateway to the waterways and yawning ice fields of **Kenai Fjords National Park. Exit Glacier,** the only road-accessible glacier in the park, lies 9 mi. west on a spur from Mi. 3.7 of the Seward Hwy. (Rte. 9). A **shuttle** (224-8747) runs here four times daily from downtown Seward (round-trip $10); parking for the day is $5. Beyond this glacier, boat cruises are the easiest and most popular way to see the park. **Kenai Fjords Tours** (224-8068 or 800-478-8068) includes an excellent grilled salmon dinner, served on-board (6-9½hr.; $100-139, children $50-60). **Major Marine Tours** (224-8030 or 800-764-7300) brings along a ranger to explain wildlife and glacier facts, and serves a salmon, halibut, and shellfish dinner for $10 extra (8hr.; $89). **Wildlife Quest** is the only outfit with speedy catamarans (5½hr.; $99, children $36; includes free pass to SeaLife Center). **Sunny Cove Sea Kayaking** (345-5339) offers a joint trip with Kenai Fjords Tours, including the wildlife cruise, a salmon bake, kayaking instruction, and a 2½hr. wilderness paddle ($139, with extra 2hr. $159).

Ballaine House Lodging, P.O. Box 2051, 437 3rd Ave. (224-2362), at Madison St., 2 blocks from downtown, is bright, clean, and well-furnished, with pleasant rooms and a scrumptious breakfast. (Singles $55; doubles $79; lower rates without breakfast. Free laundry. Pick-up and drop-off from train or bus.) **Exit Glacier Campground,** 8½ mi. down Exit Glacier Rd., off Seward Hwy. Mi. 3.7, offers water, pit toilets, secluded sites, and a ½ mi. walk to Exit Glacier (free; 3-night max. stay). **Miller's Daughter,** 1215 4th Ave. (224-6091), is organic, fat-free, and herbivore-friendly (tuna salad sandwich $4.50; open daily 6:30am-8pm).

Seward is 127 mi. south of Anchorage on the scenic **Seward Hwy. (Rte. 9).** Most services and outdoor outfits cluster in the **small boat harbor** on **Resurrection Bay.** The **Alaska Railroad** (800-544-0552) depot is at the across from the visitor center; trains run daily to Anchorage in summer (4½hr.; $43, ages 2-11 $32). **Seward Bus Lines,** 1914 Seward Hwy. (224-3608), runs to Anchorage (1 per day at 9am, $30; airport service $5). The **Alaska Marine Hwy.** (224-5485, reservations 800-642-0066) docks at 4th Ave. and Railway St., running three per month in summer to Valdez (11hr., $58) and Homer (25hr., $96.). The **Seward Chamber of Commerce** (224-8051), at Mi. 2 on the Seward Hwy., has an encyclopedic knowledge of the town (open M-F 8am-5pm, Sa-Su 9am-4pm). **Kenai Fjords National Park Visitor Center** (224-3175, info 224-2132), at the small-boat harbor, gives nature talks two to three times per week in summer at 5:30pm (open daily 8am-7pm; in winter M-F 8am-5pm). **Post Office:** (224-3001), at 5th Ave. and Madison St. (open M-F 9:30am-4:30pm, Sa 10am-2pm). **ZIP code:** 99664. **Area code:** 907.

ALASKA

■ Wrangell-St. Elias

In a state where the enormous is commonplace, **Wrangell-St. Elias National Park** is the largest national park in the U.S. (13.2 million acres). Beyond towering peaks and extensive glaciers, Wrangell teems with wildlife. With only two rough roads that penetrate its interior, and almost no established trails, the park's difficulty of access keeps many tourists well away. **Ranger stations** lurk exclusively outside the park boundaries in **Copper Center** (822-7261), south of Glennallen (open 8am-6pm); **Chitina** (823-2205; open daily 10am-6pm); and **Slana** (822-5238), on the park's northern boundary (see below). They have the lowdown on all the must-knows and go-sees of the park, and sell invaluable topographical maps (entire park $9; quadrants $4). **Charter flights** from McCarthy or Nabesna start at around $60 per person (one-way).

One of the park's access routes is the scenic **Nabesna Rd.**, extending a grueling 46 mi. (1½hr.) from the Richardson Hwy. (Rte. 4) into the park's northern portion. The turn-off for the road is at **Slana** (rhymes with "bandana"), 65 mi. southwest of Tok on the Tok Cutoff. **Nabesna,** at the end of the 42 mi. road, is little more than a mining ghost town, where the **End-of-the-Road Bed and Breakfast** (822-5312, last-ditch messages 822-3426) has bunks ($20), singles ($55), and doubles ($65).

The more harrowing **McCarthy Rd.** plunges 60 mi. (3hr.) into the park from Chitina (CHIT-nuh) to the western edge of the Kennicott River, where travelers must cross a footbridge and walk ½ mi. into the town of **McCarthy.** Free parking is available another ½ mi. back before the river. Deep in the heart of the park, McCarthy and its sister town **Kennicott** are quiet today, but abandoned log-hewn buildings and forgotten roads bear witness to a boom town past. **Backcountry Connection** (822-5292, in AK 800-478-5292) offers shuttle service to McCarthy from Glennallen and Chitina. (Departs Glennallen M-Sa 7am, Chitina 8:30am. Returning van departs McCarthy at 4pm. From Chitina $45, round-trip $75-85.) **Wrangell Mountain Air** (554-4411 or 800-478-1160) flies to McCarthy daily from Chitina at 9:05am and 2:45pm (round-trip $130 from Chitina; $120 from Glennallen). Regular **shuttle buses** run the 5 mi. from McCarthy to Kennicott; the river's tram station carries schedules, with copies posted throughout both towns (round-trip $8). Another shuttle goes from the footbridge to Kennicott (round-trip $10). The newly opened **Kennicott River Lodge and Hostel,** P.O. Box 83225, Fairbanks 99708 (554-4441, in winter 479-6822), right before the footbridge at Mi. 58.7 (look for sign), offers several pine-fresh cabins ($25) with comfortable beds (bring your own sleeping bag) and a striking view of Kennicott River and Glacier. The only indoor alternative across the bridge is the **McCarthy Lodge** (554-4402; singles $95; doubles $110). Non-guests can shower ($5) at the lodge, or breakfast (7am-10am; $4-9) and sup ($15-23, served at 7pm) in a rustic dining room with antique-covered walls (open daily 7am-10pm; bar opens at 3:30pm). **Camping** is free at the lot ½ mi. back along the road toward Chitina (pit toilets, no water). Scrumptious, cheap feasts are served at **Roadside Potato Head,** in a colorfully decorated van by the tram station (potatohead burritos $6; open daily 9am-9pm).

This is the place for flightseeing in Alaska. Even a short flight to 16,390 ft. Mt. Blackburn and the surrounding glaciers offers soul-stunning views. **Wrangell Mountain Air** (554-4411, reservations 800-478-1160) makes a 35min. tour of the amazing icefalls of the **Kennicott** and **Root Glaciers** ($50). The best bargain, a 70min. trip, goes up the narrow **Chitistone Canyon** to view the thundering **Chitistone Falls,** over 15 glaciers, and five mountain peaks ($95). There is a two-person minimum on all flights. **Copper Oar** (800-523-4453), at the end of the McCarthy Rd., runs a 2hr. **whitewater rafting** trip down the Class III Kennicott River, providing all of the necessary rain gear ($45). **St. Elias Alpine Guides** (in McCarthy 554-4445; in Anchorage 345-9048) lead a variety of guided hikes and explorations, including 2hr. nature hikes to ice fields ($25), stunning ½-day walks with crampons on the **Root Glacier** ($50), and a morning of exploring the ice caves and moraines of the **Kennicott Glacier** terminus ($35). The park maintains **no trails** around McCarthy; consult with a ranger station before setting out. Ranger stations need a **written itinerary** for independent overnight trips.

■ Denali

Denali National Park's six million acres of tundra and taiga, spanning an area larger than Israel or the state of Massachusetts, make up an incredible expanse of unspoiled wilderness. Endless wildlife motivated the park's establishment, and might even outshine its 20,320 ft. centerpiece. Although the U.S. Geological Survey names the peak Mt. McKinley, most Alaskans either dub it Denali or simply "the Mountain." Denali's face is only visible about 30% of the time in summer, and many visitors to the park will never actually see the peak. Mid- to late August is an excellent time to visit—fall colors peak, berries ripen, mosquito season is virtually over, and September's snows have not yet arrived.

PRACTICAL INFORMATION The **George Parks Hwy.** (Rte. 3) makes for smooth and easy traveling to the park entrance north from Anchorage (240 mi., 4hr.) or south from Fairbanks (120 mi., 3hr.). Leading east away from the park, the gravel **Denali Hwy.** (Rte. 8) starts 27 mi. south of the park entrance at Cantwell, and proceeds 136 mi. to Paxson (closed in winter). The **Alaska Railroad** (683-2233 or 800-544-0552) makes regular stops at Denali Station (open daily 10am-5pm), 1½ mi. from the park entrance, and runs out to Fairbanks (1 per day, $53) and Anchorage (1 per day; $99, bikes $20); reserve ahead. **Parks Hwy. Express** (479-3065) runs to the park from Anchorage (4hr., $30) and from Fairbanks (3hr., $20). The **Alaska Backpacker Shuttle** (344-8775) runs between Anchorage and Denali ($40, bikes $5) and between Denali and Fairbanks ($20, bikes $5).

Only the first 14 mi. of the park road are accessible by private vehicle; the remaining 75 mi. of dirt road can be reached only by shuttle bus, camper bus, or bicycle. **Shuttle buses** leave from the visitor center (daily 5am-6pm), pause at the well-nigh inevitable sighting of any major mammal ("MOOOOOSE!"), and turn back at various points along the park road, such as **Toklat,** Mi. 53 ($12.50); **Eielson,** Mi. 66 ($21); **Wonder Lake,** Mi. 85 ($27); and **Kantishna,** Mi. 89 ($31). Ages 13-16 ride for half-price; ages 12 and under ride for free. Most buses are wheelchair accessible. **Camper buses** ($15.50) transport only those visitors with **campground permits** and **backcountry permits,** and move faster than the shuttle buses (depart daily at 6:40, 10:40am, 2:40, 4:40, and 6:10pm). Tickets can be purchased by phone (272-7275 or 800-622-7275), or in person at the visitor center within 2 days of departure. Calling ahead is strongly recommended, since bus space fills up quickly.

All travelers must stop at the **Denali Visitors Center** (683-1266), ½ mi. from the Parks Hwy. (Rte. 3), for orientation. Park rangers collect the **entrance fee** ($5 per person, families $10; good for 1 week), and provide ample maps and campsite info, interpretive walks, sled-dog demonstrations, and campfire talks. Most park privileges are first come, first served; conduct all business at the visitor center as early in the day as possible. (Open daily mid-Apr. to Sept. 7am-8pm. Lockers 50¢.) Before any winter travels in Denali, visit the **Park Headquarters** (683-2294) at Mi. 3.2 and on the left side of the park road (open M-F 8am-4:30pm). **Denali Outdoor Center** (683-1925), at Parks Mi. 238.9, just north of the park entrance, rents bikes (½-day $25; full-day $40; 5 or more days $35 per day). Unlike private vehicles, bikes *are* permitted on all 89 mi. of park roads. **Healy Clinic** (683-2211) is 11 mi. north of the park entrance (open May-Sept. M-F 9am-5pm; nurse on call 24hr.). **Post Office:** (683-2291), next to Denali National Park Hotel, 1 mi. from the visitors center (open M-F 8:30am-5pm, Sa 10am-1pm; Oct.-Apr. M-Sa 10am-1pm). **ZIP code:** 99755. **Area code:** 907.

ACCOMMODATIONS, CAMPGROUNDS, AND FOOD To reach the **Denali Hostel,** P.O. Box 801 (683-1295), go 9.6 mi. north of the park entrance, turn left onto Otto Lake Rd., and drive 1.3 mi., continuing straight after the golf course (don't veer left). It's the second house on the right, with a beautiful setting (oh, the sunsets!), international clientele, helpful owners, clean rooms, full kitchen, TV room, showers, and coin-operated laundry. (Shuttle to the park and Alaska Railroad. Beds $24. Linen $3. Check-in 5:30-10pm. No curfew. No credit cards. Reservations wise. Open May-Sept.)

ALASKA

Campers must obtain a permit from the visitor center, and may stay for up to 14 nights in the park's seven campgrounds, which line the park road ($6-12). Call 800-622-7275 for advance reservations (272-7275 from Anchorage); first come, first served sites are distributed rapidly at the visitor center. **Riley Creek** is the only campground open year-round, and has the only dump station. All campgrounds within the park are wheelchair accessible, except for **Igloo Creek** and **Sanctuary River.**

Once you board that park bus, there is no food available anywhere. **Denali Smoke Shack** (683-SMOK/7665), north of park entrance at Mi. 238.5, serves real Alaskan barbecue and a large vegetarian menu. (Cajun chicken sandwich $8. Open daily 5:30am-10:30am and noon-midnight. Bar open noon-2am.) High on a hill, **Denali Crow's Nest & Overlook Bar and Grill** (683-2723), 1 mi. north of park entrance on the right, affords eagle-eye views of Mt. Healy. The fantastic $9 burgers come with greasy, greasy fries. (Draft beer from $3. Grill open daily 11am-11pm; bar open until about 1am. Courtesy shuttle until 11pm.)

THE OUTDOORS The best way to experience Denali is to get off the bus and explore the land. Beyond Mi. 14, the point which only shuttle and camper buses can cross, there are **no trails.** You can begin day hiking from anywhere along the park road by riding the shuttle bus to a suitable starting point and asking the driver to let you off. It's rare to wait more than 30min. to flag a ride back. **Primrose Ridge,** beginning at Mi. 16 on the right side of the road, is bespangled with wildflowers and has spectacular views of the Alaska Range and the carpeted emerald valley below. A walk north from Mi. 14 along the **Savage River** provides a colorful, scenic stroll through this valley. A rigorous ascent up the tundra of **Dome Mountain,** at Mi. 60, will reward hikers with close views of the Alaska Range, and on a clear day, Denali. The area surrounding **Wonder Lake** (Mi. 85) is marshy and dense with willows but offers what may be the best view of the Mountain in the park. **Discovery hikes** are guided 3-5hr. hikes, departing on special buses from the visitor center. Topics vary; a ranger might lead you on a cross-country scramble or a moose trail excursion. The hikes are free but require reservations and a bus ticket. More sedate 45min. **tundra walks** leave from Eielson Visitor Center daily at 1:30pm, and many other talks and naturalist programs are posted at the visitor center.

There are no trails in the backcountry. While day hiking is unlimited and requires no permit, only two to 12 backpackers can camp at one time in each of the park's 43 units. Overnight stays in the backcountry require a **free permit,** available no earlier or later than 1 day in advance at the **backcountry desk** in the visitor center. The **quota board** there reports which units are still available. Type-A hikers line up outside as early as 6:30am to grab permits for popular units. Talk to rangers and research your choices with the handy *Backcountry Description Guides* and *The Backcountry Companion,* available at the visitor center bookstore. The visitor center sells essential topographic maps ($4). All but two zones require that food be carried in **bear resistant food containers (BRFC),** available for free at the backcountry desk. These are bulky things; be sure to leave space in your backpack (LSIYB).

■ Fairbanks

Fairbanks stands unchallenged as North American civilization's northernmost hub—witness such landmarks as the "World's Northernmost Woolworth's," "World's Northernmost Denny's," and "World's Northernmost Southern Barbecue." From here, adventuresome travelers can drive, fly, or float to the Arctic Circle and into the tundra. Most do not make the long and arduous trip to Fairbanks merely to stay put; any road leads out of town into utter wilderness in minutes.

PRACTICAL INFORMATION Most tourist destinations lie on **Airport Way, College Rd., Cushman Blvd.,** or **University Way.** Fairbanks is a **bicycle-friendly** city, providing wide shoulders, multi-use paths, and sidewalks for its two-wheeled travelers. The **Airport** is 5mi. from downtown on Airport Way. **Alaska Railroad,** 280 N. Cushman St. (456-4155), runs trains down south. (Mid-May to mid-Sept., 1 per day to Anchorage ($112) and Denali ($53). Mid-Sept. to mid-Oct. and Feb. to mid-May, 1 per week to Anchorage ($105). Ages 2-11 ½-price. Depot open M-F 7am-3pm, Sa-Su 7am-11am.) **Parks Hwy. Express** (479-3065 or 888-600-6001) runs daily to Denali ($20, round-trip $35) and Anchorage (about 9hr.; $49, round-trip $95) and three per week to Glenallen ($55, round-trip $105) and Valdez (9hr.; $75, round-trip $145). **Municipal Commuter Area Service (MACS)** (459-1011), at 5th and Cushman St., runs two routes (red and blue) through downtown and its surroundings. (Fare $1.50; students, seniors, and disabled 75¢; under 5 free. Day pass $3. Transfers for another bus.) **Diamond Taxi** (455-7777) charges $1 base, $1.50 per mi. (24hr.). **Rent-a-Wreck**, 21055 Cushman St. (452-1606), charges $39 per day, 30¢ per mi. after 100 mi. (must be 21 with credit card; prohibits travel farther than Denali or on gravel roads).

Convention and Visitors Bureau Log Cabin, 550 1st Ave. (456-5774 or 800-327-5774), at Cushman, distributes a free *Visitor's Guide* (open daily 8am-8pm; Labor Day-Memorial Day M-F 8am-5pm). **Alaska Public Lands Information Center (APLIC),** 250 Cushman St. #1A, Fairbanks 99707 (456-0527), in the basement of the Federal building at Cushman and 3rd, has info, maps, and hiking advice (open daily 9am-6pm; in winter Tu-Sa 10am-6pm). **Internet Access: Café Latté,** 519 6th Ave. (455-4898; $4 per hr.). **Post Office:** 311 Barnette St. (452-3203); the entrance is in the back of the brown building at Barnette and 3rd, marked 315 Barnette (open M-F 9am-6pm, Sa 10am-2pm). **ZIP code:** 99707. **Area code:** 907.

ACCOMMODATIONS, CAMPGROUNDS, AND FOOD
Grandma Shirley's Hostel, 510 Dunbar St. (451-9816), beats out all other contenders to earn the title of Fairbanks Überhostel. From the Steese Expwy., turn right onto the Trainor Gate Rd., then left at E. St., and finally right on Dunbar St. (Spectacular kitchen, showers, TV room, big backyard, and free bike use. Co-ed bunks $15.) **Billie's Backpackers Hostel,** 2895 Mack Blvd. (479-2034), is a somewhat cluttered but welcoming place to meet many international travelers. Take Westwood Way 1 block off College to Mack Rd. (Shower and kitchen in each room. Beds $18. Breakfast $7; all-you-can-eat dinner $10. Tent sites.) **Chena River State Campground,** off Airport Way on University Ave., is landscaped, clean, and on a quiet stretch of the Chena River. (56 sites. $15, walk-ins $10. In summer, 5-night max. stay per vehicle. Dump station $5. Self-register.)

An artery-blocking good time fills Airport Way and College Rd. **Thai House,** 528 5th Ave. (452-6123), never advertises, but it's jam-packed (lunch $6-8, dinner from $8; open M-Sa 11am-4pm and 5-10pm). **Wolf Run Dessert & Coffee House,** 3360 Wolf Run (458-0636), just off University Way near Geist, offers scrumptious desserts, plush chairs, and stone hearth fireplace with rocking chair (espresso $1, latte $2.50; open Tu-Th 11am-10pm, F-Sa 11am-midnight, Su noon-8pm).

SIGHTS AND NIGHTLIFE
The **University of Alaska Museum** (474-7505), a 10min. walk up Yukon Dr. from the Wood Center, features exhibits including displays on the aurora borealis, gold collections, a thorough look at the Aleut/Japanese evacuation during WWII, and indigenous crafts. *(Open daily 9am-7pm; May and Sept. daily 9am-5pm; Oct.-Apr. M-F 9am-5pm, Sa-Su noon-5pm. $5, seniors $4.50, ages 13-18 $3, under 6 free.)* **Georgeson Botanical Gardens** (474-1944), on Tanana Dr. west of the museum, grows tulips (late June through July) overlooking Fairbanks and the Alaska Range. The **Large Animal Research Station** (474-7207) offers a rare chance to see baby musk oxen and other arctic animals up close; take Farmer's Loop to Ballaine Rd. and turn left on Van Kovich; the farm is 1 mi. up on the right. *(Tours June-Aug. Tu and Sa 11am and 1:30pm, Th 1:30pm; Sept. Sa 1:30pm. $5, students $2, seniors $4.)* Well worth the 11 mi. trip north along the Steese Hwy. (Rte. 6) to Fox, **Gold Dredge #8** (457-6058) provides a day of panning and a guided tour. *(Open daily mid-May to mid-Sept. 9am-6pm. 4 tours daily. $19.50, ages 4-12 $12.50.)* Not only is it possible to earn the cost of admission back in gold, but also fossilized fragments of mammoths and mastodons abound.

Moose Mountain (479-4732), 20min. northeast of town, has over 20 downhill skiing trails. *(Lift tickets $25; college students, seniors, military, and ages 13-17 $20; ages 7-12 $15; over 70 or under 6 free. $5 off after 1pm or if the temperature is below 0°F.)* **Creamer's Nature Path** starts at 1300 College Rd., and offers 2 mi. of trail through open pastures, home to various migratory birds and birch and spruce groves. The 3-12 mi. **Skailand Trails,** weaving through the hilly woods behind the university campus, visit several ponds and offer glimpses of the Alaska Range. Others looking for hiking or skiing trails often travel to the **Chena River State Recreation Area.** Maps are available at the Public Lands Information Center (see **Practical Information,** above).

Howling Dog Saloon (457-8780), 11½ mi. north on the Steese Hwy. (Rte. 6) toward Fox, at the intersection of the Old and New Steese Hwys., collects students, military personnel, and just about everyone else for volleyball, pool, and horseshoe games that go on until 4am or so (live music W-Sa; open May-Oct. Su-Th 4pm-around 2am, F-Sa 4pm-around 4am). In mid-July, Fairbanks citizens don oldtime duds and whoop it up for **Golden Days** (452-1105), a celebration of Felix Pedro's 1902 discovery that sparked the Fairbanks gold rush. Although its relation to the actual gold rush days is questionable, the **rubber duckie race** is one of the biggest events.

SOUTHEAST ALASKA

Southeast Alaska (a.k.a. "the Panhandle" or just "Southeast") spans a full 500 mi. from the basins of Misty Fiords National Monument to Skagway at the foot of the Chilkoot Trail. The waterways weaving through the Panhandle, collectively known as the Inside Passage, make up an enormous saltwater soup spiced with islands, inlets, fjords, and the ferries that flit among them. The absence of roads in the steep coastal mountains has helped Panhandle towns maintain their small size and hospitable personalities. The **Alaska Marine Hwy.** system (see p. 830) provides the cheapest, most exciting way to explore the Inside Passage.

■ Ketchikan

Ketchikan is the first stop in Alaska for most tourist-stuffed northbound cruise ships and ferries laden with would-be cannery workers. Despite crowds and nearly 14 ft. of rainfall a year, Ketchikan's location is key: the city provides access to Prince of Wales Island, Metlakatla, and most notably, Misty Fiords National Monument. Ketchikan itself offers plenty of bike trails, campgrounds, and hiking trails in nearby Tongass National Forest, plus numerous native and historical attractions that get mobbed by thousands of tourists on summer days.

PRACTICAL INFORMATION Upon reaching Ketchikan from Canada, **roll back your watch** by an hour to get in step with Alaska Time. The town is extremely spread out, making bike rental a wise option. A small **ferry** runs from the airport, across from Ketchikan on Gravina Island, to just north of the state ferry dock (every 15min., in winter every 30min.; $2.50). **Alaska Airlines** (225-2141 or 800-426-0333; open M-F 9:30am-5pm), in the mall on Tongass Ave., makes daily flights to Juneau ($80). **Alaska Marine Hwy.** (225-6181) sends wheelchair-accessible boats from the far end of town on N. Tongass Hwy to Sitka ($54), Juneau ($74), and Skagway ($92). Buses to town run until 6:45pm. The main bus route runs a loop between the airport parking lot near the ferry terminal at one end, and Dock and Main St. downtown at the other. (Fare $1, seniors and children 75¢. Runs every 30min. M-F 5:15am-9:45pm; 1 per hr. Sa 6:45am-8:45pm, Su 8:45am-3:45pm.) **Sourdough Cab** (225-5544) charges $8 for a ride downtown from the ferry terminal (24hr.).

Ketchikan Visitors Bureau, 131 Front St. (225-6166 or 800-770-3300), is at the cruise ship docks downtown (open daily May-Sept. 7am-5pm; limited winter hrs.). **Southeast Alaska Visitors Center (SEAVC)** (228-6220), on the waterfront next to the Federal Building, provides excellent trip-planning service, plus info on public lands around Ketchikan, including Tongass and Misty Fiords. The beautiful new ecology and native history exhibit is worth the $4 (free in off season). (Open daily 8:30am-5pm; Oct.-Apr. Tu-Sa 8:30am-4:30pm.) **Post Office:** (225-9601), next to the ferry terminal (open M-F 8:30am-5pm). **ZIP code:** 99901. **Area code:** 907.

ACCOMMODATIONS, CAMPGROUNDS, AND FOOD The **Ketchikan Reservation Service** (800-987-5337) provides info on B&Bs (singles from $60). Because of boardwalk stairs, none of these accommodations are wheelchair accessible. **Millar Street House,** 1430 Millar St. (225-1258 or 800-287-1607), just out of downtown, in a historic house overlooking the ocean, is an essential stop for anyone looking for a good time and a nice cup of tea (singles $70; doubles $80). The foam mats at **Ketchikan Youth Hostel (HI-AYH),** P.O. Box 8515 (225-3319), at Main and Grant St. in the First Methodist Church, pass muster if you have a sleeping bag. (Clean kitchen, common area, 2 showers, tea and coffee. $8, nonmembers $11. 4-night max. stay. Strict lockout 9am-6pm. Lights out 11pm-7am. Curfew 10:30pm. Baggage storage during lockout. Call ahead if you plan to arrive on a late ferry. Open June-Aug.)

Campgrounds usually have stay limits of a week or two, but cannery workers tent up in the public forests for up to a month. There is no public transportation from the town to the campgrounds, so plan on hiking, biking, or paying an exorbitant cab fare. **Signal Creek** and **Three C's Campgrounds** sit across the street from each other on Ward Lake Rd. Drive north on Tongass Ave. and turn right at the sign for Ward Lake, approximately 5 mi. from the ferry terminal (28 spaces, water, and pit toilets; 7-night max. stay; $8 fee May-Sept.). Anyone can camp for up to 30 days in **Tongass National Forest,** but may not return for 6 months after that time. Sites are not maintained, but any clearing is free.

The freshest seafood swims in **Ketchikan Creek;** in summer, anglers frequently hook king salmon from the docks by Stedman St. If you get lucky, **Silver Lining Seafoods,** 1705 Tongass Ave. (225-9865), will custom-smoke your catch for $2.75 per lb. (open M-F 10am-6pm, Sa 10am-5pm, Su 11am-4pm). Not a dollop of killer mayo can be found in the **5 Star Café,** 5 Creek St. (247-7827), an oasis of health. (Black bean burrito with basmati rice $6.75. Open M-F 7:30am-5:30pm, Sa-Su 9am-5pm.)

SIGHTS AND THE OUTDOORS Ketchikan's primary cultural attraction is the **Saxman Native Village,** the largest totem park in Alaska, 2½ mi. southwest of town on Tongass Hwy. *($8 by cab, or a short ride on the Hwy. bike path. Open M-F 9am-5pm, Sa-Su when a cruise ship is in.)* The **Totem Heritage Center,** 601 Deermount St. (225-5900), on the hill above downtown, houses 33 well-preserved totem poles from Tlingit, Haida, and Tsimshian villages. *(Open daily May-Sept. 8:30am-4:30pm. $4, under 13 free.)* It is the largest collection of authentic, pre-commercial totem poles in the U.S., but only a few are on display. An $8 combination ticket also provides admission to the **Deer Mountain Fish Hatchery and Raptor Center** (225-9533), across the creek. *(Open daily May-Sept. 8am-4:30pm.)* A self-guided tour explains artificial sex, salmon-style.

The 3001 ft. **Deer Mountain** makes a great day hike; walk up the hill past the city park on Fair St., where the marked trailhead branches off to the left just behind the dump. The ascent is steep but manageable, and on the rare clear day, the walk yields sparkling views of the town and the sea beyond. While most hikers stop at the 2½ mi. point, a longer route leads over the summit and past an A-frame overnight shelter that can be reserved at the SEAVC (see **Practical Information,** above). From the summit of the 3237 ft. John Mountain, the **John Mountain Trail** descends along the ridge, passing the **Stivis Lakes** on its way down to the **Beaver Falls Fish Hatchery** and the South Tongass Hwy., 13 mi. from Ketchikan. This section of the hike is poorly marked and may test hikers' ability to read topographic maps. The entire hike, manageable in a tough full day, is 10 mi. long and requires a pick-up at the end. Less strenuous and equally accessible is the trek up to **Perseverance Lake,** along a boardwalk built over muskeg. The **Perseverance Trail,** beginning 10 mi. north of the city just before the Three C's Campground (see above), climbs 600 ft. over 2.3 mi. to an excellent lake for **trout fishing** (licenses $10 per day, $15 for 3 days, $30 for 2 weeks, $50 for the season). By renting a boat and equipment from **Deer Mtn. Charters,** 939 Park Ave. (225-9800, 247-9800, or 800-380-3280), anglers can fish beyond the docks without forking over higher charter prices (boats from $60 per day, rods from $5 per day).

■ Near Ketchikan: Misty Fiords

The jagged peaks, plunging valleys, and dripping vegetation of **Misty Fiords National Monument,** 20 mi. east of Ketchikan, make biologists dream and outdoors enthusiasts drool. Only accessible by kayak, boat, or float plane, the 2.3-million-acre park offers superlative camping, kayaking, hiking, and wildlife-viewing. **Camping** is permitted throughout the park, and the Forest Service maintains four first come, first served shelters (free) and 14 cabins ($25). Contact the **Misty Fiords Ranger Station** (225-2148) at 3031 Tongass Ave., Ketchikan, and ask ahead at the SEAVC (see **Practical Information,** above). Kayaking neophytes might contact **Alaska Cruises,** 220 Front St., Box 7814 (225-6044); they'll drop off both kayaker and kayak at the head of Rudyard Bay during one of four weekly sight-seeing tours ($175 per person).

■ Juneau

Alaska's state capital has an air of modernity and progressiveness usually not found in the rural fishing villages of Southeast Alaska. Accessible only by water and air, Juneau is the second-busiest cruise ship port in the U.S., after Miami. Hordes of travelers come to Juneau for the readily accessible Mendenhall Glacier, numerous hiking trails, and close access to Glacier Bay. Be prepared to share the beauty.

PRACTICAL INFORMATION **Franklin St.** is the main drag downtown. **Glacier Hwy.** connects downtown, the airport, the residential area of the Mendenhall Valley, and the ferry terminal. The ferry and airport are both annoyingly far from the glacier and downtown. **Juneau International Airport,** 9 mi. north of Juneau on Glacier Hwy., is served by **Alaska Airlines** (789-0600 or 800-426-0333; open M-F 8:30am-5pm), on S. Franklin St. at 2nd St. in the Baranov Hotel, which flies to Anchorage ($99-222); Sitka ($96); Ketchikan ($124); and Gustavus ($65). **Capital Transit** (789-6901) runs buses from downtown to the airport and Mendenhall Glacier, with hourly express service downtown (M-F 8:30am-5pm). The closest stop to the ferry is at Auke Bay, 2 mi. from the terminal (runs M-Sa 7am-10:30pm, Su 9am-5:30pm; fare $1.25; exact change required). **MGT Ferry Express** (789-5460) meets all ferries and runs to downtown hotels or the airport ($5). **Alaska Marine Hwy.,** 1591 Glacier Ave. (465-3941 or 800-642-0066), docks at the Auke Bay terminal, 14 mi. from the city on the Glacier Hwy., and runs to Ketchikan ($74); Sitka ($26); and Bellingham, WA ($226). **Capital Cab** (586-2772) runs a 1hr. charter from downtown to Mendenhall Glacier (about $45), the ferry (about $25), and the airport ($12).

Davis Log Cabin Visitor Center, 134 3rd St., (888-581-2201 or 586-2201), at Seward St., is a great source of pamphlets and maps (open M-F 8:30am-5pm, Sa-Su 9am-5pm; Oct.-May M-F 8:30am-5pm). **National Forest and Park Services,** 101 Egan Dr. (586-8751), at Willoughby in Centennial Hall, provide info on hiking and fishing in the area, and reservations for Forest Service cabins in Tongass National Forest (open daily 8am-5pm; in winter M-F 8am-5pm). Find **Internet access** at the **library,** at Admiral Way and S. Franklin St. **Post Office:** 709 W. 9th St. (586-7987; open M-F 9am-5pm, Sa 9am-1pm for parcel pick-up only). **ZIP code:** 99801. **Area code:** 907.

ACCOMMODATIONS AND CAMPGROUNDS The **Alaska B&B Association,** P.O. Box 2800 (586-2959), can help find a room downtown (from $65). On a steep hill, lovely **Juneau International Hostel (HI-AYH),** 614 Harris St. (586-9559), at 6th St., enforces strict rules in a prime location. (48 beds. $7, nonmembers $10. Kitchen 7-8:30am and 5-10:30pm. Wash $1.25, dry 75¢. Lockout 9am-5pm and 11pm curfew. 3-night max. stay if they're full. $10 deposit mailed in advance serves as a reservation. No phone reservations.) **Alaskan Hotel,** 167 Franklin St. (586-1000, in the Lower 48 800-327-9347), right downtown, has been meticulously restored to original 1913 decor. (Kitchenettes and TVs. Hot tub with radio $13-26.25 per hr. Rooms $67-84; rates lower in winter. Free luggage storage for guests. Wash or dry $1.) **Mendenhall Lake Campground** is about 6 mi. from the ferry terminal on Montana Creek Rd.; take Glacier Hwy. north 9 mi. to Mendenhall Loop Rd., continue 3½ mi., and take the right

fork. Bus drivers will stop within 2 mi. of camp (7am-10:30pm). The 60 newly renovated sites have stunning views of the glacier and convenient trails to go even closer.
(Fireplaces, water, flush toilets, showers, picnic tables, free firewood. Sites $8,
seniors $4. 14-night max. stay. Reserve for an extra $7.50 by calling 800-280-2267.)

Armadillo Tex-Mex Cafe, 431 S. Franklin St. (586-1880), shelters locals in the
heart of the cruise ship district with fast, saucy service and hot, spicy food. (2 enchiladas $6. Excellent free chips and salsa. Open M-Sa 11am-10pm, Su 4-10pm.)

SIGHTS AND OUTDOORS The excellent **Alaska State Museum,** 395 Whittier St.
(465-2901), leads through the history and culture of Alaska's four major native
groups: Tlingit, Athabascan, Aleut, and Inuit. *($3, seniors and children free. Open May 18-
Sept. 17 M-F 9am-6pm, Sa-Su 10am-6pm; Sept. 18-May 17 Tu-Sa 10am-4pm.)* The hexago-
nal and onion-domed 1894 **St. Nicholas Russian Orthodox Church,** on 5th St.
between N. Franklin and Gold St., holds rows of icons and a glorious altar. *($1 donation
requested. Open daily in summer 9am-5pm.)* Services, held Saturday at 6pm and Sunday at
10am, are conducted in English, Old Slavonic, and Tlingit.

The **West Glacier Trail** begins off Montana Creek Rd., by the Mendenhall Lake
Campground. The 5-6hr. walk yields stunning views of **Mendenhall Glacier** from the
first step to the final outlook. The 3½ mi., one-way trail parallels the glacier through
western hemlock forest and up a rocky cairn-marked scramble to the summit of 4226
ft. **Mt. McGinnis.** At the end of Basin Rd., the **Perseverance Trail** leads to the ruins of
the Silverbowl Basin Mine and booming waterfalls. The **Granite Creek Trail**
branches off the Perseverance Trail and follows its namesake to a beautiful basin, 3.3
mi. from the trailhead. The summit of Mt. Juneau lies 3 mi. farther along the ridge
and, again, offers terrific views. The shorter, steeper **Mt. Juneau Trail,** which departs
from Perseverance Trail about 1 mi. from the trailhead, offers similar panoramas. All
trails are well-maintained and excellent for **mountain biking.**

Tracy Arm, a mini-fjord near Juneau, is known as "the poor man's Glacier Bay,"
offering much of the same spectacular beauty and wildlife as the national park at well
under half the cost. **Auk Nu Tours,** 76 Egan Dr. (800-820-2628), is the biggest tour
company, offering a free lunch ($100). **Bird's Eye Charters** (790-2510), whose small
boats take only 16 passengers, is at the opposite end of the spectrum ($140), offering
breakfast, lunch, snacks, and all the personal attention money can buy. **Kayak
Express,** 4107 Blackberry St. (780-4591), allows kayakers and their craft to get
beyond **Gastineau Channel,** running drop-offs and pick-ups at Gustavus, Hoonah, or
Port Adolphus for $110, or at Oliver's Inlet, Port Couverden, St. James Bay, or Funter
Bay for $75. In winter, the **Eaglecrest Ski Area,** 155 S. Seward St. (586-5284 or 586-
5330), on Douglas Island, offers decent alpine skiing ($24 per day, ages 12-17 $17,
under 12 $12; ski rental $20, children $14). The Eaglecrest ski bus departs from the
Baranof Hotel at 8:30am and returns from the slopes at 5pm on winter weekends and
holidays (round-trip $6).

■ Near Juneau: Glacier Bay National Park

Glacier Bay National Park encloses nine tidewater glaciers and waters filled with wildlife. Getting to **Bartlett Cove** is relatively easy: a plane or ferry takes visitors to the
town of **Gustavus,** and from there a taxi or shuttle (about $12) goes on to the **Glacier
Bay Lodge** (800-622-2042; dorm beds $28). The lodge boat *Spirit of Adventure* offers
six **sight-seeing packages** to the glaciers, ranging from a ½-day whale-watching trip
($78) to a basic see-the-glaciers daytrip ($80). At the **Visitor Information Station**
(697-2627), at the tour boat dock in Bartlett Cove, 10 mi. north of Gustavus, rangers
give a mandatory backcountry orientation and distribute permits (open daily 7am-
9pm). Near the lodge is a free **campground,** which has 25 sites and is rarely full.

HAWAII

Milton was wrong—the human race never lost Eden. We just misplaced it for a while, and it's not too surprising why. Hawaii, 2400 mi. off mainland America, is the most geographically isolated place in the world. The location of the islands has set them apart in both landscape and lifestyle: lush vegetation encroaches on endless beaches, while sultry breezes stir the surf and keep the weather wonderful year-round. Acres of untainted tropical forest grow up the slopes of active volcanoes and border luxurious resort areas and bustling urban enclaves. Sound Elysian? It is.

Unfortunately, while you wander along luxurious white sand beaches, hundreds of sunburned Minnesotans are likely to be doing so with you. Tourism has penetrated almost every aspect of Hawaiian culture, yielding t-shirt stands in the streets of Honolulu and bastardized hula performances touted as "native." Hawaii serves as a a bridge between East and West, a nexus of Asian, Western, and Polynesian influences.

The Hawaiian chain is comprised of 132 islands, though only seven are inhabited. Honolulu, the cosmopolitan capital, is on the island of **Oahu,** as are most of the state's residents and tourists. The **Big Island** of Hawaii is famed for its Kona coffee, macadamia nuts, and black sand beaches. **Maui** boasts the historic whaling village of Lahaina, fantastic windsurfing, and the dormant volcanic crater of Haleakala. The garden isle of **Kauai,** at the northwestern end of the inhabited islands, ranks first for sheer beauty. **Molokai,** once stigmatized because of its leper colony, is the friendliest spot in the islands. On tiny **Lanai,** exclusive resorts have replaced pineapples as the primary commodity. The seventh populated isle, **Niihau,** is closed to most visitors, supporting just a few hundred plantation families who still converse in the Hawaiian language. In the words of Mark Twain, together these present "the loveliest fleet of islands that lies anchored in any ocean."

🌺 HIGHLIGHTS OF HAWAII

- **Sunrises.** Head to Maui's Mt. Haleakala (p. 848) in the wee hours of the morning for a memorable view of the sunrise.
- **Snorkeling.** At Hanauma Bay (p. 846), Oahu, brilliantly colored fish eat frozen peas right out of your hand as you navigate the clear blue water.
- **Beaches.** Waikiki Beach (p. 845), in Honolulu, is the most famous.
- **Parasailing.** Maui's Lahaina resort (p. 847) is a good spot to try.

PRACTICAL INFORMATION

Capital: Honolulu.
Visitor Info: Visitor Information Office, 2201 Kalakaua Ave., #401. **Hawaii Visitors Bureau,** 2270 Kalakaua Ave., #801, Honolulu 96815 (808-923-1811). Open M-F 8am-4:30pm. **Dept. of Land and Natural Resources,** 1151 Punchbowl St. (P.O. Box 621, Honolulu 96809; 587-0300; http://www.visit.hawaii.org). Info and trail maps. Open M-F 8am-4:30pm; state park permits issued until 3:30pm.
Emergency: 911.
Time Zone: Hawaii (3hr. behind Pacific in spring and summer; 2hr. fall and winter).
Postal Abbreviation: HI. **Area code:** 808.
Sales Tax: 4%; hotel rooms 6%. **Road Tax:** $3 per day for rental cars.

GETTING AND SLEEPING AROUND

Cheap Tickets, in Honolulu (947-3717), offers low airfares to Hawaii (see **Ticket Consolidators,** p. 23). Airlines provide the fastest, cheapest way to get from island to island and may offer special deals on car rentals. The major inter-island carriers, **Hawaiian Airlines** and **Aloha Airlines,** can jet you quickly (about 30min.) from Honolulu to any of the islands for $60 to $80, but travel agents sell inter-island coupons at

Hawaii

N

PACIFIC OCEAN
(MALINO PAKIPIKA)

NIIHAU

KAUAI

Haena
Princeville
Kapaa
Lihue
Na Pali Coast
Waimea
Poipu

OAHU

Laie
Kaneohe Bay
Honolulu
Honauma Bay
Waikiki Beach
Pearl Harbor
Waimea Bay
Haleiwa
Makaha

MOLOKAI

Kalaupapa National Park
Halawa Valley
Honolua Bay
Kaunakakai
Halepalaoa Beach

LANAI

Garden of the Gods
Lanai City
Lahaina

KAHO'OLAWE

MAUI

Waianapanapa State Park
Wailuku
Kahului
Kihei
Hana
Haleakala Crater

HAWAII
(The Big Island)

Hamakua Coast Coast
Waimea
Hilo
Mauna Kea
Kohala Mts.
VOLCANOES NATIONAL PARK
Mauna Loa
Kilauea Caldera
Kau
Kohala Coast
Kailua-Kona
Kedlakekua Bay
Place of Refuge
Naalehu
South Point
Kalapana Black Sand Beach

50 miles
50 km
0

Oahu

N

PACIFIC OCEAN

Kaena Point
Waimea Bay
North Shore
Waialua
Waimea
Laie
Hauula
Punaluu
Waikane
Kaneohe Bay
Kailua
Waimanalo Bay
Waimanalo Beach Park
Hanauma Bay Beach Park
Makapuu Bay
Diamond Head
Waikiki Beach
Honolulu Harbor
Pearl Harbor Entrance
U.S.S. Arizona Memorial
Pearl City
Wahiawa
Kamehameha Hwy
Makaha
Nanakuli
KOOLAU RANGE
WAI'ANAE RANGE
KO'OLAU
Honolulu
RANGE

10 miles
10 kilometers
5

HAWAII

lower prices ($40-60). Oahu, Kauai, and the Big Island have public transportation, but the easiest way to get around is by **rental car** ($30-40 per day). Regular **ferry** service runs only from Maui to Lanai. **Cruise ships** and private **fishing boats** will carry passengers to the other islands, but their prices are often exorbitant.

Despite rumors to the contrary, reasonable room rates do exist on the islands. Hotels near attractions and beaches charge more (rates higher Dec.-Apr.). Look for special deals that include rental car and air transportation. Many hostels run airport shuttles and sight-seeing trips and offer discounts on car rentals, inter-island flights, and activities. Bed and breakfast organizations are a quieter option, offering rooms in private homes for around $55. **All Islands B&B** (263-2342 or 800-542-0344; open M-F 8am-5pm) and **Hawaiian Islands B&B** (261-7895 or 800-258-7895; open M-F 8am-5pm) can make reservations. **Camping** is Hawaii's best deal ($0-3 per night), whether in national, state, or county parks. The national park campgrounds on Maui and the Big Island require no permit in advance, but they do enforce a 3- or 5-night maximum stay. State parks, which tend to be better maintained, require camping permits (available for free from the Dept. of State Parks in Honolulu for those 18 and older), and enforce a 5-night-per-month maximum stay. (Sites open F-W on Oahu, daily on the other islands.)

OAHU

Oahu bears the mixed blessing of being the cultural, economic, and tourist center of Hawaii. The island can be roughly divided into four sections. **Honolulu** and its suburbs constitute Oahu's metropolitan heart. The **North Shore** is the most rural part of the island and home to some mighty big waves. Sculpted mountains and colorful reefs sandwich the **Windward (East) Coast**, while the **Leeward (West) Coast** is raw and rocky. The slopes of two now-extinct volcanic ridges, **Waianae** in the west and **Koolau** in the east, make up the bulk of the island's 600 sq. mi. Finally, the narrow inlets of **Pearl Harbor** (see p. 846) push in at the southern end of the valley between the two ridges.

■ Honolulu

Honolulu is City Lite. It's got all the trappings of a major city: industry, transportation centers, towering skyscrapers, and horrible traffic. There are all-night restaurants, garish hotels, and lots of sleaze. But tropical plants and birds crowd the sidewalks, a beautiful beach runs the length of the city, and the local news anchors wear Aloha shirts on Friday. Tourists love this town, especially Waikiki—nevertheless, Honolulu holds only a small segment of what Hawaii has to offer.

PRACTICAL INFORMATION Honolulu International Airport is 20min. west of downtown, off the **Lunalilo Fwy. (H-1).** If Waikiki is your destination, take the Honolulu Exit, then move immediately into the left lane to get the interchange into town. Although slightly longer, the **Nimitz Hwy. (Rte. 92)** will also take you to Waikiki, as will buses #19 and 20, but they may not allow luggage on board. The **Airport Waikiki Express** (566-7333) travels to any hotel or hostel in Waikiki ($8, round-trip $13). **The Bus** (848-5555) covers all of Oahu for a $1 fare (4-day pass $10, monthly $25). Call a **taxi** from **Sida,** 439 Kalewa St. (836-0011), or **The Cab** (422-2222). All major **rental car** companies have outlets at the airport and in Waikiki. **Paradise Isle,** 151 Uluniu Ave. (922-2224), at Kuhio Ave., rents for $30-70 per day. (Ages 18-21 pay $20 surcharge, 21-24 $10. Open daily 8am-5pm.) Pick up *This Week Oahu* for coupons and info on transportation.

Tourist info is available at the **Hawaii Information Office,** 2201 Kalakaua Ave. (923-1811), in the Royal Hawaiian Shopping Center, bldg. A, 4th fl. (open M-F 8am-5pm). The **Dept. of State Parks,** 1151 Punchbowl St., #310 (587-0300), at S. Beretania St., offers info, maps, and free permits for state park campgrounds. (Permits available up to 30 days in advance for Oahu state parks, 1 year for all other islands. Open M-F 8am-4:30pm.) **Post Office:** 3600 Aolele Ave. (800-275-8777), near the airport (open M-F 7:30am-8:30pm, Sa 8am-2:30pm). **ZIP code:** 96820. **Area code:** 808.

"Getting Leid in Hawaii"

It's not hard at all—even if you're from MIT or Cal Tech. And if you're not feeling lucky, it's surprisingly easy to do it yourself! *Leis,* beautiful strands of flowers, nuts, seeds, and shells, are, as Hawaiians say, made with love and given with love. The tradition of adorning that special someone began with the Polynesian explorers who were draped with *leis* upon their departure to distant lands. Today *leis* are given on May Day, but Hawaiians also wear *leis* for any occasion—weddings, birthdays, Fridays, paydays, or good-hair days. You can buy *leis* at any flower shop, starting at about $8 for plumeria. More exotic materials can cost up to $500, but the cheapest and most rewarding *leis* are the kind you make yourself. All you need is a *lei* sewing needle (about $3), some heavyweight string, and about 50 flowers. Hook the string on the needle and "load" on six flowers, with each stem fitting into the seat of the next. Grasping the entire bunch with your hand, slide the "load" onto the string; eight loads are sufficient for a neck *lei.* Lastly, don't forget to tie the ends together— the circular shape represents continuous love.

ACCOMMODATIONS Honolulu, especially Waikiki, caters to affluent tourists, but there *are* bargains. Guests rub elbows with resident birds and bunnies at **Interclub Waikiki,** 2413 Kuhio Ave. (924-2636). Laundry, refrigerators, a pool table, and a kitchen are available. (Female or co-ed dorms $15; doubles $45. Picture ID required at check-in. Key deposit $20. Reception 24hr. Check-out 10am. No curfew.) Lively folk crowd into the **Polynesian Hostel,** 2584 Lemon Rd. (922-1340), which offers laundry, linen, and small security boxes. (Co-ed dorms $12-15; semi-private rooms $28-55; studios $45. Key deposit $10 for dorms, $20 for more private rooms. Reception 24hr. Passport ticket required. Free airport pick-up. No curfew.) Recently converted from a hotel, **Banana Bungalow,** 2463 Kuhio Ave. (926-0641), offers laundry, A/C, refrigerators, free tours, and free airport pick-up. (Dorms $15. Reception 24hr. Passport and ticket required. Check-out 11am. Key deposit $10. No curfew. Wheelchair access.) Peace reigns at the centrally located **Hale Aloha (HI-AYH),** 2417 Prince Edward St. (926-8313), which has a kitchen, lounge, and TV room. (Single-sex dorms $16, nonmembers $19; doubles $40/ $46. 7-night max. stay. Reception open 7am-3am. No curfew. Key deposit $10.) Guests over 18 may stay at the squeaky-clean **YMCA,** 401 Atkinson Dr. (941-3344), with a pool and athletic facilities. (Singles with shared bath (men only) $29; doubles $40. Singles with private bath (co-ed) $37; doubles $52. Key deposit $10. Reception 24hr.)

FOOD AND NIGHTLIFE The **Kapahulu, Kaimuki, Moiliili,** and **downtown** districts are all within 20min. of Waikiki by bus, and can also be reached on foot. Small Asian food counters serve excellent and affordable treats all over Chinatown, especially on **Hotel Street.** Many ethnic eateries, including Hawaiian, Japanese, Thai, and French, are located between blocks 500 and 1000 of **Kapahulu Ave. Ono Hawaiian Foods,** 726 Kapahulu Ave. (737-2275), serves $7-10 combo plates (open M-Sa 11am-7:30pm). Lively **Auntie Pasto's,** 1099 S. Beretania St. (523-8855), at Pensacola, is a crowded red-brick *ristorante* with pasta from $5.50 (open M-Th 11am-10:30pm, F 11am-11pm, Sa 4-11pm, Su 4-10:30pm). Pick fresh sushi off a conveyor belt at **Genki Sushi,** 900 Kapahulu Ave. (735-8889), for $1-4 a plate (open M-Th 11am-3pm and 5-9pm, F 11am-3pm and 5-10pm, Sa-Su 11am-9pm). **The Wave,** 1877 Kalakaua Ave. (941-0424), hosts live alternative music Wednesday through Sunday 10pm-1:30am, with a DJ at all other times (21+; cover $5, free before 10pm; open daily 9pm-4am). The **Pier Bar** (536-2166), in the Aloha Tower, features live Hawaiian rock 'n' roll and jazz bands daily except Sunday. Throngs drink and groove on the outdoor patio. (No cover. Open daily 11am-2am.)

SIGHTS Visitors flock to the **Waikiki Beach** area for sun, surf, nightlife, romance, and tacky souvenirs. More secluded beaches can be found to the east on Diamond Head Rd., accessible by moped. For a break from the beach, hike 1 mi. into **Diamond Head Crater,** accessible via bus #58 from Waikiki. The trail goes through a tunnel, so bring a flashlight. Visitors may also view the crater and all of Honolulu from **Mt. Tantalus** at the top of Roundtop Dr., accessible by car from 7am to 7:45pm. The **Waikiki Trolley** (591-

HAWAII

2561) stops at major sights and museums in Waikiki and downtown, allowing tourists to stay on the 2½hr. narrated tour or get on and off at their leisure. *(Day pass $18, ages 12-17 $12, under 11 $8; 5-day pass $30/$20/$10. Trolleys leave from the Royal Hawaiian Shopping Center every 20 min. 8am-4:30pm.)* Stops include Chinatown, the Capitol, Bishop Museum, the Aquarium, the Academy of Arts, and Iolani Palace.

Those who want to see Waikiki at its photogenic best will delight in the **Kodak Hula Show,** at the **Waikiki Shell** off Monsarrat Ave. This production packages hula dancing and palm tree-climbing into a series of *those* moments. (Free 1hr. shows Tu-Th 10am.) The **Iolani Palace** (522-0832), at King and Richards, is the only royal residence in America, built by King Kalakaua before Hawaii was forcefully annexed. *(Tours begin every 15min. Tu-Sa 9am-2:15pm. $8, ages 5-12 $3, under 5 not admitted. Call for reservations, or arrive at the palace 30min. early.)* Accessible via bus #2 from Waikiki, the **Bishop Museum,** 1525 Bernice St. (847-3511), in Kalihi, houses artifacts from the Indo-Pacific region. *(Shows daily 11:30am, 1:30, and 3:30pm. Museum open daily 9am-5pm. $15, ages 4-11 $12.)* The museum's planetarium features a show on the history of Polynesian celestial navigation. At the corner of Beretania and Richard St. stands Hawaii's postmodern **State Capitol** (open M-F 9am-4pm; free; guided tours 1:30pm). The "Westminster Abbey of Hawaii," **Kawaiahao Church,** at Punchbowl and King, was built from bits of coral in 1842 (Hawaiian services held Su 10:30am).

On December 7, 1941, thousands of stunned Americans listened to reports of the Japanese bombing of the U.S. Pacific Fleet in **Pearl Harbor.** Today, the **U.S.S. Arizona National Memorial** (422-2771) commemorates that event. *(No children under age 6 or under 45 in. admitted. No swimsuits or flip-flops.)* The Navy offers free 1hr. tours of the memorial 8am-3pm, including a 30min. film; tour tickets are free but often run out by noon. The **visitors center** is open daily from 7:30am to 5pm, with the last program starting at 3pm. Take bus #20 from Waikiki, #50, 51, or 52 from Ala Moana, or the $3 shuttle (839-0911) from the major Waikiki hotels. Another somber sight is the **National Memorial Cemetery of the Pacific,** 2177 Puowaina Dr. (539-9400), which contains the graves of 38,000 soldiers. *(Guided 3hr. tours of the cemetery and downtown area leave daily 11:30am and 1pm. Tickets $25, including hotel pick-up. Park gates open 8am-5pm.)* This memorial is also known as the **Punchbowl Cemetery** because of its location in the amphitheater-like Puowaina Crater.

■ Beyond Honolulu

Windward and Southeast Oahu

Oahu's Windward (East) Coast is a 40 mi. string of sleepy towns colored in vibrant shades by the green Koolau Mountains on one side and the blue Pacific on the other. Tradewinds create year-round boogieboarding and windsurfing conditions here, and the outstanding public transport (buses run every 30min.) and lack of lodgings make this area a perfect daytrip. The **Kalanianaole Hwy. (Rte. 72)** winds along a spectacular coastline (take bus #22 from Waikiki).

Some of the friendliest and most colorful fish in the Pacific reside in **Hanauma Bay,** whose federally protected waters make for the island's best **snorkeling** (admission $3 for non-residents over 12; parking $1). Fish food, i.e. frozen peas ($4), and snorkel rentals ($6, plus $30 deposit) are available at the beach (open daily 8am-4:30pm). **Sandy Beach,** just beyond Halona, is the center of the Hawaiian summer surf circuit, but spine-crushing summer swells make swimming a serious hazard. **Makapuu Beach** is also known for its boogieboarding and bodysurfing. *Before swimming, check the flags hoisted by the lifeguards: red means danger.*

The coastal area from Waimanalo Bay and Kailua Bay is accessible by bus #57 from Ala Moana. The best novice bodysurfing and boogieboarding is found at **Bellows Air Force Base,** off the road to Kailua. **Kailua Town** and nearby **Kailua Beach County Park,** 450 Kawailoa Rd., have prime beaches unadulterated by large hotels. This is excellent **windsurfing** territory; in fact, the sport was invented here 20 years ago by the Naish family. To rent top-quality gear (windsurfs $30-40), head to **Kailua Sailboard Company,** 130 Kailua Rd. (262-2555).

North Shore and Central Oahu

It's hard to believe that the North Shore, home to cane fields and surfers, is on the same island as Honolulu. The pace is slow and peaceful in the summer, but between October and March, furious storms create shore-pounding ground swells at the world-famous breaks of **Sunset, Waimea,** and the **Banzai Pipeline**—the North Shore hosts the nationally televised **Triple Crown of Surfing.** The area can be easily reached by bus #52 and 55 from Ala Moana. The action here centers around **Haleiwa,** an ex-plantation town now full of surf shops and art galleries. **Surf-n-Sea,** 62-595 Kamehameha Hwy. (637-9887), is renowned for quality gear and instruction (surfboards $5 1st hr., $3.50 per additional hr.; open daily 9am-7pm).

MAUI

Fun-loving Maui is appropriately named after the demigod renowned for mischief. With some of Oahu's bustle and plenty of the pristine beauty of the sleepier isles, Maui strikes a good balance for the traveler who wants quiet beaches during the day but lively entertainment at night. "The Valley Isle" consists of two mountains joined by an isthmus and covered in sugarcane and lush jungles. Central Maui is windsurfer heaven—novices flock to Kanaha Beach, while experts enjoy the best windsurfing site in the world at Hookipa Beach Park. Just about everyone can find the Hawaii they seek here, so eat, drink, and be *Maui.*

PRACTICAL INFORMATION **Ferries** are a fun and relatively cheap way to travel between Maui and Lanai. **Expeditions** (661-3756), runs five trips per day (1hr., $25). Check in 15min. before departure at the dock in front of the Pioneer Inn. **Maui Airport Taxi** (250-8017) can get you to Wailuku for around $10. The **Airport Shuttle** (661-6667) will go anywhere on the island, including Wailuku ($9) and Hahaina ($24). Rent a **car** at **Regency** (871-6147), at the airport ($30 per day, ages 18-25 $38; discounts for weekly rentals; open daily 8am-9pm). **Trans Hawaiian** (877-7308) has a booth at Kahului Airport's baggage claim, and runs from the airport to Lahaina-Kaanapali (9am-4pm every 30min., $13). **West Maui Shopping Express** connects Lahaina and Kaanapali (8:45am-10:15pm, $1). Free maps are available from the **Visitor Information Kiosk** (872-3893), at the Kahului Airport (open daily 6:30am-10pm). **Dept. of Parks and Recreation,** War Memorial Gym, 1580C Kaahumanu Ave. (243-7389), in Wailuku, has info on county parks and permits for $3 (open M-F 8am-4pm).

Maui's highways follow the shape of the island in a broken figure-eight pattern. The Kahului Airport sits on the northern coast of the isthmus, and to the west lie Kahului and Wailuku. **Rte. 30 (Honoapiilani Hwy.)** leads to the resort areas of Lahaina and Kaanapali. **Rte. 34/340** leads counter-clockwise around the same loop from the isthmus through remote West Maui. Circling the slopes of Haleakala, **Rte. 31** passes Kihei. **Rte. 36/360 (Hana Hwy.)** meanders to Hana. **Rte. 37** leads to **Rte. 377** and **Rte. 378** before heading up 10,023 ft. Mt. Haleakala. Heed four-wheel-drive warnings—most rental car contracts stipulate that drivers tackle dirt roads at their own risk.

ACCOMMODATIONS The best accommodations in Wailuku are at **Northshore Inn,** 2080 Vineyard St. (242-8999 and 800-647-6284). A young, friendly crowd enjoys TV, free Internet access, laundry, free boogie boards, kitchen, and fridges in every room. (Dorms $12 with *Let's Go* guide; doubles $36. Dinner $5. Reception 8:30am-10pm. No curfew.) Another option is the **Banana Bungalow Hotel and International Hostel,** 310 N. Market St. (244-5090 or 800-846-7835), at Kapoai St., Wailuku. A mixed crowd haunts the TV room, hot tub, hammocks, volleyball court, and basic kitchen. (Dorms $14.50; singles $30.50; doubles $36.50. Key deposit $10.)

Lahaina-Kaanapali Resort Area Rte. 30 winds around the West Maui Mountains to Maui's resort center. **Lahaina** rose to prominence in 1810 when it was chosen as the capital for Kamehameha's pan-Hawaiian empire. Today the town provides most of the nightlife on this otherwise early-to-bed island. The town revolves around the oceanside **Front St.** In the harbor rests the **Carthaginian** (661-8527), a replica of a brig; it houses a whaling museum (open daily 10am-4pm; $3, seniors $2, children free, families $5). Offshore at Mala wharf, tourists soar 900 ft. into the air. It's a bird, it's a plane…it's **Parasail Kaanapali** (669-6555)! ($36, 6:30-7am early-bird special $28.50.) Just past Lahaina stretches the 4 mi. long **Kaanapali Beach,** a resort area from which you can see three neighboring islands. For a truly remarkable experience, continue north on Rte. 34 around the west end of the island to view cloud-shrouded valleys and villages nestled amid the mountains.

Haleakala Featuring a fantastic volcanic crater, **Haleakala National Park** is open 24hr. and costs $10 per car for a 7-day pass. The **Park Headquarters** (572-4400), about 1 mi. up from the entrance, provides **camping permits,** wildlife displays, and funky postcards (open daily 7:30am-4pm). **Haleakala Visitors Center,** near the summit, has one of the best views of the crater and a gorgeous view of the sunrise (open daily sunrise-3pm). **Haleakala Crater campgrounds,** P.O. Box 369, Makawao 96768 (572-4400), include car camping at Hosmer campgrounds and wilderness camping at Holua (4 mi. hike) and Poliku (10 mi. hike). Apply for cabins at least 3 months in advance. Holua and Paliku areas also serve as campgrounds. Free permits are issued at park headquarters (2-night max. stay in cabins, 3-night max. in campgrounds).

Hana The **Hana Coast** reaches from the Keanae Peninsula to Kaupo. The **Hana Hwy.,** leading to the Hana coast, may be the world's most beautiful stretch of road. Carved from cliff faces and valley floors, its alternate vistas of smooth sea and lush terrain are made only somewhat less enjoyable by its tortuous curves. The air is perfumed with the wild ginger and mango and guava trees lining the road.

THE BIG ISLAND

The Big Island, officially known as Hawaii, emerged from the confluence of five major volcanoes on top of a hot spot in the Pacific Plate. These forces can still be seen in action at **Hawaii Volcanoes National Park**, and the forces of tourism can be examined in detail at the two main tourist towns of **Hilo** and **Kailua-Kona,** on opposite sides of the island.

PRACTICAL INFORMATION Pick up free maps and bus schedules at the **Big Island Visitor Bureau** at 250 Keawe St. (961-5797), in Hilo, and 755719 Alii Dr. (329-7787), in Kona (both open daily 8am-4:30pm). The **Dept. of Land and Natural Resources,** 75 Aupuni St. (974-6200), in Hilo, offers free camping permits and $20+ cabin permits (permits available M-F 8am-noon). **Hele-on-Bus** runs one bus per day between Kona and Hilo ($5.25), making several stops along the way ($1-5).

ACCOMMODATIONS AND FOOD Arnott's Lodge, 98 Apapane Rd. (969-7097), is near Onekahakaha Beach Park in Keokea. One of the state's best hostels, Arnott's offers dorm rooms (with their own kitchens), deck, laundry, TV/VCR, BBQ grills, and nearby lava-rock beach. Daytrips are available ($36, non-guests $50-75), as well as free airport transportation. (Dorms $17; singles $31; doubles $42; tents $9. Check-in 8am-noon and 4-10pm.) The **Holo Holo Inn,** 19-4036 Kalani-Honua Rd. (967-7950), in Volcano Village, is a quiet home-hostel in a perfect locale, 2 mi. from the Volcanoes visitors center. The large, wood-floored rooms have blankets and slippers for the cool nights. (Dorms $17. Call after 4:30pm; reservations recommended.) In Volcanoes National Park, find campsites at **Kipuka Nene** and **Namakani Paio** (985-6000), each with shelters and fireplaces, but no wood (free; 7-night max. stay). The island's surprise sustenance source is the cafeteria at the **Kilauea Military Camp** (967-8356), on Crater Rim Dr. (dinner buffet $9, under 11 $5.50; served nightly 5:30-8pm).

SIGHTS Two active volcanoes in **Hawaii Volcanoes National Park, Mauna Loa** (13,677 ft.) and **Kilauea** (4000 ft.), home of **Halemaumau Crater,** continue to spout, adding acres of new land each year. **Kilauea Caldera,** with its steaming vents, sulfur fumes, and

The Pele's the Thing

The volcano area is the home of Pele, the powerful Hawaiian volcano goddess. Cognizance of superstitions will keep you safe from vexing evil omens and such.

1) When driving, if you see an old woman by the side of the road, pick her up; it may be Pele. (Let's Go does not recommend picking up hitchhikers.)
2) If there is a black dog by the side of the road, do not ignore it; superstitious Hawaiians carry a raw piece of meat with them in the car to feed the dog if they see it. Failure to comply results in nausea, illness, and a slow death.
3) If you notice an old woman in the back of your car, ignore her; this is just Pele. She is benign if left alone.
4) Avoid Saddle Rd.; many Hawaiians believe it is haunted.

periodic eruptions, is the star of the park, although the less active **Mauna Loa** and its dormant northern neighbor, **Mauna Kea,** are in some respects more impressive. Each towers nearly 14,000 ft. above sea level and drops some 16,000 ft. to the ocean floor. Mauna Loa is the largest volcano in the world, while Mauna Kea, if measured from its ocean floor base, would be the tallest mountain on earth. The **Puu Oo spatter cone** has been for the past 16 years the only consistent source of flowing lava in the park. Entrance to the park costs $10 per car (valid for 7 days). The best view of the flows is from the air, and **Island Hoppers** (969-2000) can get you up there in a four-person plane (45min. flights from $69). The **visitors center** in Kilauea (985-6000), just inside the park gates, boils over with exhibits and info on ranger-led walks (open daily 7:45am-5pm). The **Onizuka Visitor Information Station** (961-2180), 9300 ft. high on Mauna Kea, offers informative talks and films, and at night the public is allowed to stargaze through the telescope. *(Open Th 5:30-10pm, F 9am-noon, 1-5pm, and 6-10pm, Sa-Su 9am-10pm, 9am-noon, and 1-4:30pm.)*

The spectacular natural surroundings of **Kailua-Kona** more than make up for its unremarkable towns. White beaches line the coast up Rte. 19 to the very beautiful and very crowded **Hapuna Beach** and **Spencer Beach Parks.** Both parks are wheelchair accessible and have excellent snorkeling. In South Kona is **Ka Lae** (off-limits to most rental cars), where windswept fields and massive windmills mark the landscape. Follow the road to the left to reach the seaside cliffs. Near to South Point is **Green Sand Beach,** whose color is derived from grains of olivine.

The lush **Waipio Valley,** down Rte. 240 from Honokaa, is one of the most beautiful places in Hawaii. Home to 10,000 in the 19th century, the valley today has around 50 residents, and no electricity. A great way to experience the valley is on **horseback.** Unless Tonto fits in your luggage, contact **Waipio Naalapa,** P.O. Box 992, Honokaa 96727 (775-0419; 2½hr. tour departs M-Sa 9:30am and 1pm; $78).

The **Waipio Lookout,** at the end of Rte. 240 on the edge of the valley, offers one of the most striking panoramas in the islands. For those with the legs and the lungs, a grueling hike into the valley offers a better view. The valley can also be seen through the windows of the **Waipio Valley Shuttle** (775-7121), which provides a non-stop, narrated, 1½hr. tour. Purchase tickets and check in at the **Waipio Woodworks Art Gallery** (775-0958), ½ mi. from the Waipio Lookout (open M-Sa 8am-4pm; $35, under 11 $15; reservations recommended).

KAUAI

Formed over six million years ago by the now-extinct Mt. Kawaikini volcano, Kauai, the oldest island in the Hawaiian archipelago, has had eons to nurture its nature. As a result, the splendor of the Garden Isle is unsurpassed anywhere in Hawaii. Kauai's Mt. Waialeale is the wettest spot on earth, with over 450 in. of rain per year and a spectacular profusion of flowers. The island also boasts long stretches of sunny beachfront, sheltered bays, and miles of hiking trails through jungles, into canyons, and along the spectacular Na Pali coast. Kauai has escaped the fate of noisy, bustling Oahu—locals maintain a leisurely pace and a familial attitude, and the building code stipulates that construction cannot exceed the height of the island's coconut palm trees. Let the aloha spirit move you—as the locals say, "No worries!"

PRACTICAL INFORMATION The **Hawaii Visitors Bureau,** 3016 Umi St., #207 (245-3971), at Rice in Lihue, has the *Kauai Illustrated Pocket Map* (open M-F 8am-4:30pm). Write or call their hotline (246-1400) for a vacation planner and coupons. Camping options and permits abound at the **Kauai County Parks Office,** 4444 Rice St., #150 (241-6670), in Lihue (open M-F 8am-4:15pm; county park permits $3 per person per night). Permits are also available from rangers on site ($5). The **Division of State Parks,** 3060 Eiwa St., #306 (274-3444), in the State Office Bldg. at Hardy in Lihue, has info on state park camping (permits issued M-F 8am-4pm, except during lunch). The **Kauai Bus** (241-6410) runs sporadically to major towns on the island (no large baggage).

ACCOMMODATIONS AND FOOD The **Kauai International Hostel,** 4532 Lehua St. (823-6142 or 800-858-2295 from the islands), is in Kapaa, across from the beach and several restaurants. This popular hostel offers a kitchen, cable TV, pool table, laundry, and fantastic daytrips. (Co-ed and single-sex dorms $16, $15 for HI-members; singles $40/$37. Key deposit $10. Reception 8am-10pm. Check-out 10am. Airport pickup $6.) Another option is the **Garden Island Inn,** 3445 Wilcox Rd. (245-7227 or 800-648-0154), across Nawiliwili Harbor in Kalapaki. This tropical paradise is next to the island's best swimming beaches. (Rooms from $59; 1-night advance deposit required. Reception daily 7am-9pm.) For huge helpings of *saimin* (Japanese noodles, $3-5), head for **Hamura's Saimin Stand,** 2956 Kress St. (245-3271), off Rice in Lihue (open M-F 10am-11pm, F-Sa 10am-midnight, Su 10am-9:30pm). **Bubba's,** 1384 Kuhio Hwy., in Kapaa (823-0069; open M-Sa 10:30am-8pm) or in Hanalei (826-7839; open daily 10:30am-6pm), has fabulous burgers for $2.50.

SIGHTS The North Shore includes Hanalei, Haena, and the Na Pali Coast, accessible by Rte. 56. The **Kilauea Point National Wildlife Refuge** (828-1413) rests on a bluff near Kilauea Bay (open daily 10am-4pm; $2). A bit farther down off Rte. 56 is **Secret Beach,** one of the most breathtaking beaches on the island. Some sunbathers go **nude** here—apparently, they're not too concerned about keeping secrets. The land of **Hanalei** was made famous by Peter, Paul, and Mary in their song "Puff the Magic Dragon." If you squint, you may be able to make out the shape of a dragon from gorgeous **Hanalei Bay.** For a truly hallucinatory beach experience, head to beautiful **Lumahai Beach.** The island's world-famous **Na Pali Coast** is a breathtaking spectacle of sheer cliffs falling to bright beaches and seas below. Accessible only by foot, the mind-blowing Kalalau Valley lies 11 mi. down the coast. Thirty miles west of Lihue, on the island's West End, Rte. 50 meets Rte. 550 at tiny **Waimea,** site of Captain Cook's first landing on Kauai in 1778. Turning inland, Rte. 550 winds up the rim of the dramatic **Waimea Canyon,** known as the **"Grand Canyon of the Pacific."** Thrill-seeking drivers will enjoy the twisted majesty of **Waimea Canyon Drive,** surrounded by the crimson-streaked walls of the gorge.

CANADA

O Canada! The second largest country in the world, Canada covers almost 10 million square kilometers (3.85 million square miles). Still, only 29 million people inhabit Canada's 10 provinces and two territories; well over half the population crowds into either Ontario or Québec. Framed by the Atlantic coastline in the east and the Pacific Ocean in the west, Canada extends from fertile southern farmlands to frozen northern tundra.

The name Canada is thought to be derived from the Huron-Iroquois word **"kanata,"** meaning "village" or "community." This etymology reveals the dependence of early settlers on the Native Canadians as well as the country's origins in a system of important trading posts. The early colonists, the French and English, were relatively distant and culturally distinct. Each population has fought to retain political dominance, but it was only in the 1970s that ethnic and linguistic differences between the two communities flared briefly into quasi-terrorist acts of violence. Native Canadian concerns and a rapidly increasing **"allophone"** population—people whose first language is neither English nor French—have also become intertwined in the cultural struggle. Inter-regional tensions have been exacerbated by divergent economic foundations; bankrupt fisheries have drained the Maritime provinces while the West Coast booms with trans-Pacific trade.

For crucial info on travel in Canada, see **Essentials,** in the front of this book (p. 1).

THE NATIVES AND THE NEWCOMERS

Although archaeologists are uncertain about the exact timing, recent data indicates that the first Canadians arrived about 11,000 years ago, by either crossing **Beringia,** the Asian-Alaskan land bridge, or by migrating north from sea-faring populations that reached South America about 3,000 years before. Their descendants flooded the continent, fragmenting into disparate tribes. Arriving Europeans intensified inter-tribal warfare by trading guns for fur, and by exchanging aid in pre-existing conflicts for knowledge of the local terrain.

Such bargains proved a raw deal for the tribes. As the English and French became more familiar with the land, they squeezed the Native Canadians out by force and by less-than-just land agreements. Natives found themselves confined to large settlements such as Moose Factory in Ontario or Oka in Québec. Recently, the Assembly of First Nations, the umbrella aboriginal organization, has taken legal action to secure long overdue compensation.

The first Europeans known to explore the area were the Norse, who apparently settled in northern Newfoundland around the year 1000. England came next; John Cabot sighted Newfoundland in 1497. When Jacques Cartier, landing on the gulf of the St. Lawrence River, claimed the mainland for the French crown in 1534, he touched off a rivalry that persisted until Britain's 1759 capture of Québec in the Seven Years' War and Frances' total capitulation four years later.

The movement to unify the British North American colonies gathered speed after the American Civil War, when U.S. military might and economic isolationism threatened the independent and continued existence of the British colonies. On March 29, 1867, Queen Victoria signed the British North America (BNA) Act, uniting Nova Scotia, New Brunswick, Upper Canada, and Lower Canada (now Ontario and Québec). Though still a dominion of the British throne, Canada had its country—and its day: the BNA was proclaimed on July 1, now known as Canada Day.

IN RECENT HISTORY

The past 130 years have witnessed Canadian territorial expansion and burgeoning world power. The years following consolidation witnessed sustained economic growth and settlement in the west with the completion of the trans-continental railway; the country quickly grew to encompass most of the land it covers today. Participation in World War I earned the Dominion international respect and a charter membership in the League of Nations. It joined the United Nations in 1945 and was a founding member of the North Atlantic Treaty Organization in 1949. The Liberal government of the following decade created a national social security system, a national health insurance program, and a national flag. Pierre Trudeau's government repatriated Canada's constitution in 1981, freeing the nation from Britain in constitutional legality (though Elizabeth II remains nominal head of state). Free to forge its own alliances, the country signed the North American Free Trade Agreement (NAFTA) in 1992 under the leadership of Conservative Prime Minister Brian Mulroney.

Mulroney will go down in Canadian history as the leader who almost tore the nation apart in an effort to bring it back together. His numerous attempts to negotiate a constitution that all 10 provinces would ratify (Canada's present constitution lacks Québec's support) consistently failed, flaring century-old regional tensions and spelling the end of his government. Riding on a wave of backlash, the 1993 election saw Conservative support collapse to a mere two seats in the Commons and the election in Québec of a separatist government at both federal and provincial levels.

The question of Québec still drives recent politics. An October 1996 referendum rejected separation by a mere 1.2% margin—another referendum seems likely.

LANGUAGE

Canada has two official languages, English and French, but there are numerous other native languages. Inuktitut is widely spoken in the Northwest Territories, although most Native Canadians also speak English. *Québécois* pronunciation of French can be perplexing, but natives are generally sympathetic toward attempts to speak their language. The *Québécois* are also less formal than European French-speakers; you might be corrected if you use the formal *vous*.

THE ARTS

Most Canadian literature has been written post-1867. The opening of the Northwest and the Klondike Gold Rush (1898) provided fodder for the adventure tale—Jack London and Robert Service both penned stories of wolves and prospectors based on their mining experience. In the Maritimes, L.M. Montgomery authored *Anne of Green Gables* (1908) about a colorful redhead. In the *Deptford Trilogy,* novelist/playwright Robertson Davies chronicled the roving Canadian identity.

Canada also boasts three of the world's most authoritative cultural and literary critics: Northrop Frye, Hugh Kenner, and pop phenom Marshall McLuhan. Prominent contemporary authors include Margaret Atwood, best known for the futuristic bestseller *The Handmaid's Tale,* and Sri Lankan-born poet and novelist Michael Ondaatje, whose *The English Patient* received the prestigious Booker Prize.

Canada's contribution to the world of popular music includes a range of artists such as Neil Young, Joni Mitchell, Bruce Cockburn, Rush, Cowboy Junkies, Bare Naked Ladies, k.d. lang, Bryan Adams, Crash Test Dummies, Sarah McLachlan, and Tragically Hip. Recent chart-toppers include Alanis Morisette, country goddess Shania Twain, and Céline Dion, who's everything she is because we loved her. Catch them on MuchMusic, the Canadian version of MTV. Canada is also home to *Québécois* folk music, and to several world-class orchestras, including the Montréal, Toronto, and Vancouver Symphonies.

On the silver screen, Canada's National Film Board (NFB), which finances many documentaries, has gained worldwide acclaim. The first Oscar given to a documentary film went to the NFB's *Churchill Island* in 1941. Since then, *Québécois* filmmakers have caught the world's eye with Oscar-nominated movies like *Le declin de l'empire americain,* directed by Denys Arcand, who also directed the striking *Jesus de Montréal.* Art flick *Léolo* was deemed a classic by critics. François Girard provoked gasps with his *Thirty-two Short Films about Glenn Gould,* and actress Sheila McCarthy shone in *I Have Heard the Mermaids Singing.*

THE MEDIA AND SPORTS

The *Toronto Globe and Mail* is Canada's national newspaper, distributed six days a week across the entire country. Every Canadian city has at least one daily paper; the weekly news magazine is *Maclean's.* The publicly-owned Canadian Broadcasting Corporation (CBC) provides two national networks for both radio and TV, one in English and one in French. A host of private networks serve limited areas; CTV broadcasts nationally. Cable and satellite enable access to U.S. television networks.

Many famous television actors and comedians are of Canadian origin, including Dan Aykroyd, Mike Myers of *Saturday Night Live* and *Wayne's World* fame, Michael J. Fox (*Family Ties, Back to the Future*), newscaster Peter Jennings, *Jeopardy* host Alex Trebek, and Captain James T. Kirk himself, William Shatner. The Canadian comedy troupe SCTV spawned the careers of big-time laughmasters Martin Short, the late John Candy, and Rick Moranis.

On the field, Canada is best known for sports appropriate to its northern latitudes. Winter sports include curling, ice skating, skiing, and, of course, the ultimate winter sport in Canada, ice hockey. Some of Canada's other popular sports are derived from those of the aboriginal peoples. Lacrosse, the national game, was played long before the colonists arrived. Finally, sports played in the U.S. have crossed the border. There is a Canadian Football League (CFL) and two teams in both Major League Baseball and the National Basketball Association (NBA).

THIS YEAR'S NEWS

Canada's native tribes and the ever-ornery *Québecois* have both made the news lately trying to gain an independent homeland. The Inuits made great strides toward accomplishing that goal in 1998, as they geared up for the creation of a new territory encompassing one quarter of Canada's land mass. On April 1, 1999, the territory of Nunavut will be created from the eastern portion of the Northwest Territories; the western portion is preliminarily being called the "Western Arctic." There have been fears among western tribes that they will lose the comparative autonomy they've enjoyed under the Northwest Territories.

Separatists in Québec are close to suffering a drastic setback, however; politician Jean Charest is leading the charge of the more centrist Liberal Party of Québec against the independence-minded *Parti Québecois.* His party is ahead in recent polls, indicating that his party may be swept into power during the next provincial elections, which must be held by 1999.

Doctors in Canada are feeling a little frisky these days, and the M.D.s, demanding better pay, are threatening a brain-drain to the south if their demands for salary increases are not met. In Canada, the publicly-funded health care system limits the earnings of physicians, who are irked that their American counterparts typically make two to three times more money.

Canada's Prime Minister, Jean Chrétien, made a splash on the international political scene with his trip to Cuba in late April, appealing to Fidel Castro for the release of four political dissidents and political reform. Castro responded by saying the Cuban people could not renounce the Communist revolution.

Finally, reports on the Cable News Network (CNN) have revealed that Canada has become a major supplier of high-potency marijuana to the United States. Billions of dollars worth of the wacky weed are crossing the border to American markets.

CANADA

Nova Scotia

Around 1605, French colonists joined the indigenous Micmac Indians in the Annapolis Valley and on the shores of Cape Breton Island. During the American Revolution, Nova Scotia declined the opportunity to become the 14th American state, establishing itself as a refuge for fleeing British loyalists. Subsequent immigration waves infused Pictou and Antigonish Counties with a Scottish flavor. Nova Scotia's population now embodies the Canadian ideal of a cultural "mixed salad," forming a diverse cultural landscape complemented by the province's four breathtaking geographies: the rugged Atlantic coast, the lush agricultural Annapolis Valley, the calm of the Northumberland Strait, and the magnificent highlands of Cape Breton Island.

PRACTICAL INFORMATION

Capital: Halifax.

Visitor Info: Tourism Nova Scotia, P.O. Box 519, Halifax, NS B3J 2R7 (800-565-0000 in U.S. and Canada, 902-425-5781 elsewhere; http://www.explore.gov.ns.ca/virtualns).

Emergency: 911.

Drinking Age: 19.

Time Zone: Atlantic (1hr. ahead of Eastern). **Postal Abbreviation:** NS.

Provincial Sales Tax: 11%, plus 7% GST.

All prices in this chapter are listed in Canadian dollars unless otherwise noted.

■ Atlantic Coast

Gulf Stream waters crash onto the rocky Atlantic Coast, lending a pleasant monotony to life on the shore. On Nova Scotia's **Lighthouse Rte.,** south on Hwy. 3 from Halifax to coastal villages, boats and lobster traps are tools of a trade, not just props for tourists. **MacKenzie Bus Linesa** (902-543-2491) runs between Halifax and Yarmouth, at the tip of the peninsula (call for details M-Sa 8:30am-5pm; 1 per day Su-F, $38).

The quintessential Nova Scotia lighthouse overlooks **Peggy's Cove,** off Hwy. 333, 43km southwest of Halifax. No public transportation serves the town, but most bus companies offer packages including a stop there. The tourists that swarm here make a mockery of the cove's declared population of 60. Early arrivals avoid the crowds, and early birds wake up with espresso ($1.50) and freshly baked goods from **Beales Bailiwick** (902-823-2099; open Apr.-Nov. daily 9am-8pm).

Take Hwy. 333 W to Hwy. 3 and head west for about 90km to find **Mahone Bay,** a slightly larger coastal town. The **tourist office,** 165 Edgewater St. (624-6151), stocks brochures (open daily July-Sept. 9am-7pm; May-June and Oct. 9am-6pm). The **Wooden Boat Festival** (624-8443), a celebration of the region's ship-building heritage in early August, includes a boat building contest and race (lucky participants are supplied with wood and glue), and a parade of old-style schooners. Avast, ye scurvy dog! **Mug & Anchor Pub,** 634 Main St. (624-6378), tames a matey's appetite for seafood and draft beer beneath wooden beams laden with a collection of coasters. Spe-

Eastern Canada

cialties include meat pie ($9), fish and chips ($8), and seafood pasta for $8-9. (Open daily 11am-9:30pm; bar open Su-Th 11am-midnight, F-Sa 11am-1am.)

The undefeated racing schooner **Bluenose,** which graces the Canadian dime and the Nova Scotia license plate, saw its start in the shipbuilding center of **Lunenburg,** 11km west of Mahone Bay on Hwy. 3. Explore the schooner and exhibits at the **Fisheries Museum of the Atlantic** (634-4794), on Bluenose Dr. by the harborfront. (Open mid-May to mid-Oct. daily 9:30am-5:30pm; call for winter hrs. $7, seniors $5.50, ages 6-17 $2.) Several bed and breakfasts dot the roadsides in this area, but don't aim for bargains. **Brook House Bed and Breakfast,** 3 Old Blue Rocks Rd. (634-3826), is as good as it gets. (Singles $45-50; doubles $55-60; includes continental breakfast. Reservations highly recommended.) The **tourist office** (634-8100 or 634-3656) patiently awaits regional queries in the new blockhouse on Blockhouse Hill Rd. (open daily July-Sept. 9am-8pm; May-June and Oct. 8am-6pm).

From Lunenburg, follow the signs 16km to **Ovens Natural Park** (902-766-4621), west on Hwy. 3, then south and east on Rte. 332. The park features a spectacular trail along a cliff to a set of natural sea caves (the "ovens" from which the area takes its name), as well as the region's best **campground.** Steeped in lore that extends from Native Canadian legends to tales of the Nova Scotia Gold Rush (when a town arose here, only to fold 6 years later when things didn't pan out), the park attains an almost spiritual quality, only marred by efforts to package it for tourists. The campground, much of which overlooks the ocean, includes access to the caves, free hot showers, a heated swimming pool, flush toilets, a restaurant, and a store. (65 sites $18, with water and electricity $20, full hookup $22-25. Open May-Oct.)

Hwy. 332 continues along the shore and into the town of **East LaHave,** where a **cable ferry** runs across the LaHave River to **LaHave** (every 30min. 7am-11pm, by demand 11pm-7am; $1.75 per car or person). The **LaHave Bakery** (688-2908) beckons about 100m from the ferry dock on the left. Follow the mouth-watering smell of cheese-and-herb bread ($2.75) inside to check in for a night at the **LaHave Marine Hostel (HI-C).** Located upstairs in a homey apartment with a wood-burning stove, the hostel is run by the bakery proprietor; call ahead or arrive during bakery hours. (Bakery open daily 9am-7pm; mid-Sept. to June 10am-5pm. Hostel beds $10, non-members $12. Hostel open June-Oct.) **Area code:** 902.

Yarmouth The port of **Yarmouth,** 339km from Halifax on the southwestern tip of Nova Scotia, has a major **ferry terminal,** 58 Water St., from which boats shuttle across the **Bay of Fundy** to Maine (open daily 8am-5pm). **Bay Ferries** (742-6800 or 888-249-7245) provides service to Bar Harbor, ME. (2½hr.; 2 per day; $45, ages 5-15 $20, seniors $40, car $55, bike $10. Reservations recommended, $5 fee.) **Prince of Fundy Cruises** (800-341-7540) sails from Yarmouth to Portland, ME. (11hr.; early May to mid-Oct. daily 10am; early May to mid-June US$60, ages 5-14 US$30, car US$80, bike US$7; mid-June to mid-Oct. US$80/$40/$98/$10. Add US$3 passenger tax.) Car rental agencies keep busy in Yarmouth; reserve ahead. **Avis,** at 42 Starr's Rd. (742-3323), and at a desk in the ferry terminal, rents cars for $45-70 per day (plus $12 for insurance) with 200 free km (15¢ per additional km; must be 21). The **info center,** 228 Main St., uphill and visible from the ferry terminal, houses both **Nova Scotia Information** (742-5033) and **Yarmouth Town and County Information** (742-6639; both open mid-June to mid-Oct.; hrs. vary).Those who stick around can crash at the **Ice House Hostel** (649-2818), overlooking Darling Lake 15km from Yarmouth on Rte. 1; take Old Post Rd. Seven hostel beds are split between a room in the **Churchill Mansion Country Inn** and a cabin next to the inn. Guests have access to all inn facilities, and the hostel will pick travelers up from the ferry terminal. (Shared bath. $10. Open May-Nov. Reservations recommended.) **Area code:** 902.

■ Halifax

The British erected the Halifax Citadel in 1749 to counter the French Fortress of Louisbourg on the northeastern shoulder of Cape Breton Island. Yet, as it was never attacked, the Citadel ended up seeing more French tourists than it has French soldiers. Its location, with access to the Atlantic Ocean, made Halifax an important strategic port in both World Wars. Now the largest city in Atlantic Canada, Halifax can claim its beautiful port for more peaceful visitors.

ORIENTATION AND PRACTICAL INFORMATION

Barrington St., the major north-south thoroughfare, runs straight through downtown. Approaching the Citadel and the Public Garden, **Sackville St.** cuts east-west parallel to **Spring Garden Rd.,** Halifax's shopping thoroughfare. Downtown is flanked by the less affluent **North End** and the mostly quiet and arboreal **South End,** on the ocean. Downtown traffic doesn't get too hectic, but parking is difficult.

Airport: Halifax International, 40km from the city on Hwy. 102 into town (in summer, notice the Loch Ness Monster in the lake on your left). The **Airbus** (873-2091) flies to downtown (21 per day, 7:45am-11:15pm; $12, under 10 free with adult). **Ace Y Share-A-Cab** (429-4444) coordinates shared cab rides to the airport 5am-9pm. Phone 1 day ahead. Fare $18 ($30 for 2) from anywhere in Halifax. From the airport to downtown $20.

Trains: VIA Rail, 1161 Hollis St. (800-VIA-RAIL/842-7245), at South St. in the South End near the harbor. To Montréal ($180). Open daily 9am-5:30pm.

Buses: Acadian Lines and **MacKenzie Bus Lines** share a terminal at 6040 Almon St. (454-9321), near Robie St.; take bus #7 or 80 on Robie St., or any of the 6 buses on Gottingen St. 1 block east of the station. MacKenzie travels down the Atlantic coast to Yarmouth (6hr., M-F 1 per day, $38); ask about stops at small towns en route. Acadian covers most of the remainder of Nova Scotia and Canada: Annapolis Royal (3-5hr., 1 per day, $30); Charlottetown, PEI (8½hr., 1 per day, $57); and North Sydney (6-8hr., 2 per day, $53.25). Seniors 20% discount, ages 5-11 50% discount. Station open daily 6:30am-11:30pm.

Public Transportation: Metro Transit, 421-6600. Efficient and thorough. Pick up route maps and schedules at any info center. Fare $1.55, seniors and ages 5-15 $1.05. Buses run daily roughly 6am-11pm. Station open M-F 8am-4pm.

Ferries: Dartmouth-Halifax Ferry (421-6600), on the harborfront. 15min. crossings depart from both terminals every 15-30min. June-Sept. M-F 7am-11:30pm, Sa 6:30am-11:30pm, Su noon-5:30pm; no Su service Oct.-May. Fare $1.55, seniors and ages 5-15 $1.05.

Taxi: Aircab, 456-0373. **Ace Y Cab,** 429-4444. $2.40 base fare, $1.50 per mi.

Car Rental: Rent-a-Wreck, 2823 Robie St. (454-2121), at Almon St.; vehicles kept at 130 Woodlawn Rd. $40 per day (varies with season) with 200 free km, 12¢ per additional km. Insurance $13 per day, ages 21-25 $15. Must be 21 with credit card. Open M-F 8am-5:30pm, Sa 8am-noon.

Visitor Info: Halifax International Visitors Center, 1595 Barrington St. (490-5946). Call for additional locations. Open daily 8:30am-7pm; off-season closing hrs. vary between 5-7pm.

Student Travel Office: Travel CUTS (494-2054), 3rd fl. of the Dalhousie University Student Union Bldg. Open M-F 9am-5pm. Rideboard posted near the cafeteria.

Hotlines: Sexual Assault, 425-0122. **Crisis Centre,** 421-1188. Both 24hr.

Internet Access: Ceilidh Connection, 1672 Barrington St. (422-9800). $6.75 per hr. Open M-W 10am-11pm, Th-Sa 10am-1am, Su noon-8pm.

Post Office: Station A, 6175 Almon St. (494-4712), in the North End. Open M-F 8am-5:15pm. **Postal code:** B3K 5M9. **Area code:** 902.

ACCOMMODATIONS AND CAMPGROUNDS

You'll have no trouble finding affordable summer accommodations in Halifax, except during major events, such as the Tattoo Festival (see **Entertainment,** below).

Halifax Heritage House Hostel (HI-C), 1253 Barrington St. (422-3863), a 3min. walk from the heart of downtown, 1½ blocks from the train station. Immaculate rooms with access to TV lounge, kitchen, and laundry facilities. 1st fl. rooms enjoy a low people-to-

CANADA

bathroom ratio. Get the security access code if you'll be out past 11pm. $16, nonmembers $20. Linen $1.55. Free parking. Office closed noon-4pm. Check-in 4-11pm.

Technical University of Nova Scotia, M. M. O'Brien Bldg., 5217 Morris St. (494-2013), at Barrington St. Refinished brick dorms right downtown. Free laundry facilities and parking. Kitchen access. Singles $34, doubles $51; students with ID $23/$40; under 5 free with adult. Parking $6.45. Check-in 24hr. Reservations recommended July-Aug. Open May-Aug.

Dalhousie University (494-8840, after 8pm 494-2108), Howe Hall on Coburg Rd. at LeMarchant, 3km southwest of downtown. "Dal" is usually packed; arrive early. Laundry and recreation facilities. Singles $34, doubles $51 (breakfast buffet and parking included); students $23/$40; under 5 free. Open 24hr. July-Aug. reserve 1 week in advance. Open May-Aug.

Laurie Provincial Park (861-1623), 25km north of Halifax on Hwy. 2. Partially wooded campsites on Grand Lake. Tent sites are a bargain ($10). No showers. Pit toilets. Open 24hr.

FOOD

Downtown venues provide many options for appeasing the demons of hunger. Pubs peddle cheap grub and inner peace, but their kitchens often close down around 10pm. For fresh local produce and baked goods, visit the **farmers market** (492-4043), in the old brewery on Lower Water St. (open Sa 7am-1pm).

Mediterraneo Restaurant, 1571 Barrington St. (423-4403). Somber, long-haired students converse over Middle Eastern dishes. Tabouleh with 2 huge pita pockets $3-4, falafel sandwich $3-5, full breakfast served until 11am for $2.50-3. Open M-Sa 7am-10pm, Su 7am-8pm.

Granite Brewery, 1222 Barrington St. (423-5660). A microbrewery with some of the best pub food around. Produces 3 beer labels; the "Peculiar" is strangely appealing ($5) and goes well with the hearty beef and beer stew ($5.25). Open M-Sa 11:30am-1am, Su noon-11:30pm.

The Atrium, 1726 Argyle St. (422-5453). Killer food in a casual, fun atmosphere. Satisfying seafood dishes around $6-8, daily specials $6-7. Famous 15¢ wings daily 4-9pm. Open M-Tu 11am-2am, W-Su 11am-3:30am. Kitchen closes at 9pm.

SIGHTS

The star-shaped **Halifax Citadel National Historic Park** (426-3196), in the heart of Halifax, and the old **Town Clock,** at the foot of **Citadel Hill,** anchor the city to its past. *(Open daily mid-June to early Sept. 9am-6pm; early Sept. to mid-Oct. and mid-May to mid-June 9am-5pm. In summer $5.75, seniors $4.25, ages 6-16 $3. Parking $2.50.)* A walk along the fortress walls affords a fine view of the city and harbor. Small exhibits and a 1hr. film will fill you in on the relevant history. Come any day at noon to see the pageantry of preparation for the **noonday cannon firing.**

The **Halifax Public Gardens** (424-4248), across from the Citadel near the intersection of South Park and Sackville St., suggest a relaxing spot for a lunch break. The Roman statues, Victorian bandstand, gas lamps, exquisite horticulture, and overfed loons on the pond are all properly British. *(Open daily 8am-sunset.)* From July through September, watch for concerts on Sunday afternoons at 2pm. Reconstructed early-19th-century architecture covers the **Historic Properties** district (429-0530), downtown on upper Water St. Unfortunately, the charming stone-and-wood facades are only sheep's clothing disguising wolfishly overpriced boutiques and restaurants.

Point Pleasant Park, 186 car-free wooded acres at the southern tip of Halifax (take bus #9 from Barrington St. downtown), remains one of England's last imperial holdings, leased to the city of Halifax for 999 years at the bargain rate of one shilling per year. Inside the park, the **Prince of Wales Martello Tower,** an odd fort built by the British in 1797, stands as testimony to one of Prince Edward's two fascinations: round buildings and his mistress—both of which he kept in Halifax.

Boom!!

What do you get when you cross 225 tons of TNT, a few barrels of butane, a hell of a lot of picric acid, and a lone spark? On December 6, 1917 the citizens of Halifax discovered the answer—the biggest boom before the Atomic Age. Tragically, over 2000 people lost their lives when a French ship, the acid and TNT-heavy *Mont Blanc,* collided with the *Imo,* a Belgian relief ship. Both vessels began to burn, luring hapless spectators to the docks. Frantic soldiers evacuated the *Mont Blanc* by paddling lifeboats to the opposite shore, unable to warn the Halifax citizenry. An hour later, the explosion leveled 325 acres of the city, throwing a half-ton anchor 2 mi, and a cannon barrel 3½ mi. in the opposite direction. Windows shattered 50 mi. away, and shockwaves were felt for 270 mi. The **Maritime Museum of the Atlantic,** 1675 Lower Water St. (424-7490), has an exhibit and short film on the explosion. *(Open M and W-Sa 9:30am-5:30pm, Tu 9:30am-8pm, Su 1-5:30pm; off-season closed M. $4.50, seniors $3.50, ages 6-17 $1; mid-Oct. to May 31 free.)*

ENTERTAINMENT AND NIGHTLIFE

The **Neptune Theatre,** 1593 Argyle St. (429-7070), presents the area's most noteworthy professional stage productions (tickets $18-33). **The Nova Scotia International Tattoo Festival** (420-1114, tickets 451-1221), is possibly Halifax's biggest summer event. Presented by the Province of Nova Scotia and the Canadian Maritime Armed Forces, the festival runs through the first week of July, featuring international musicians, bicyclists, dancers, acrobats, gymnasts, and military groups. At noon, the Metro area overflows with free entertainment. Later, a 3hr. **show,** featuring over 2000 performers, takes place in the Halifax Metro Centre (tickets $12-24, seniors and under 13 $10-22). The **Atlantic Jazz Festival** (492-2225 or 800-567-5277) fests for a week in mid-July with both ticketed and free concerts throughout the city. August 18-26, 1999, **Buskerfest** (429-3910) brings street performers to Halifax from around the world. The **Atlantic Film Festival** (422-3456) wraps up the festival season with a showcase of Canadian and international films at the end of September. In July 1999, Halifax hosts the internationally anticipated **Fiddles of the World** festival, expected to attract nearly 3000 fiddlers. Call the tourist office (490-5946) for details.

To put it bluntly, Halifax boasts one of Canada's most intoxicating nighttime scenes. Locals often boast of their pub per capita ratio—"the highest in Canada." Numerous pubs and clubs pack the downtown area, making bar-hopping common. *The Coast,* a free magazine, lists special goings-on. The un-domelike amalgam known as **The Dome** (that's the **Liquordome** to locals) houses eating and drinking establishments that draw young people to daily drink specials and dancing. Inside, **The Atrium** has a DJ and live bands (Th-Sa cover $2-4; open M-Tu 11am-2am, W-Su 11am-3:30am). At the **Seahorse Tavern,** 1665 Argyle St. (423-7200), purple-haired students chat with paralegals in a dark basement room with carved woodwork (open M-W noon-1am, Th-Sa noon-2am). The **Lower Deck** (425-1501), in the Historic Properties region, offers excellent Irish folk music along with nautical pub decor (cover $2-4; open daily 11am-12:30am). Huge and always packed, **Peddler's Pub** (423-5033), in Barrington Place Mall on Granville St., is favored for good pub food like wings ($4.50), steamed mussels ($4.25), and $1.50 food specials weekdays after 4pm (open M-Sa 11am-10:30pm, Su 11am-8pm). **J.J. Rossy's,** 1887 Granville St. (422-4411), across the street from Peddler's, attracts nocturnal crowds with a dance floor and tremendous drink specials—during the "power hours" (W and F-Sa 9-10pm and midnight-1am, Th all night), a draft falls to $1-1.50 and shots to $1-2. (Cover after 8pm $2.50. Open M-Sa 11am-2am; kitchen open M-Tu 11am-4pm, W-Sa 11am-8pm.)

CANADA

New Brunswick

Powerful South Indian Ocean currents sweep around the tip of Africa and ripple thousands of miles through the Atlantic before coming to a spectacular finish at New Brunswick. Here in the Bay of Fundy are the world's highest tides, which sometimes ebb and flow through a staggering 48 ft. cycle. Away from the ocean's violent influence, vast unpopulated stretches of forest swathe the land in timeless wilderness. Over two centuries ago, British Loyalists, fleeing in the wake of the American Revolution, came to rest on the shores of the bay. Disgruntled by the distant government in Halifax, the colonists complained and were granted self-government by the Crown; the province of New Brunswick was born. Much earlier, in the 17th century, French pioneers established the farming and fishing nation of *l'Acadie* on the northern and eastern coasts. Although over a third of the province's population is French-speaking, English is more widely used.

PRACTICAL INFORMATION

Capital: Fredericton.
Visitor Info: Dept. of Economic Development and Tourism, P.O. Box 6000, Fredericton E3B 5C3, distributes free publications including the *Official Highway Map, Outdoor Adventure Guide, Craft Directory, Fish and Hunt Guide,* and *Travel Guide* (with accommodation and campground directory). Call **Tourism New Brunswick** (800-561-0123) from anywhere in Canada.
Emergency: 911.
Drinking Age: 19.
Time Zone: Atlantic (1hr. ahead of Eastern). **Postal Abbreviation:** NB.
Provincial Sales Tax: Harmonized sales tax 15%.

■ Saint John

The city of Saint John (never abbreviated in order to prevent confusion with St. John's, Newfoundland) was founded literally overnight on May 18, 1783, by the United Empire Loyalists, a band of about 10,000 American colonists holding allegiance to the British crown. Saint John's long Loyalist tradition shows through in its architecture, festivals, and institutions; the walkways of King and Queen Squares in central Saint John were laid out to resemble the Union Jack. Yet not all is royal about the city parks—one end of the Loyalist Plaza has been converted into a sand pit for "Beach Volleyball on the Boardwalk." Saint John's location on the Bay of Fundy ensures cool summers and mild winters, though it often makes the city foggy and wet. Locals joke that Saint John is where you get your car, and body, washed for free.

ORIENTATION AND PRACTICAL INFORMATION

Saint John's busy downtown is bounded by **Union St.** to the north, **Princess St.** to the south, **King Sq.** on the east, and **Market Sq.** and the harbor on the west. Find free 3hr. parking outside the city's malls. Fort Latour Harbor Bridge (toll 25¢) on Hwy. 1 connects Saint John to West Saint John, as does a free bridge on Hwy. 100.

Trains: Via Rail (857-9830 or 800-561-3952) has a station in Moncton; take an SMT bus from Saint John, then catch a train in Moncton. A train ticket to Saint John or a Canrail pass will cover bus fare. Call for prices and schedules.
Buses: SMT, 300 Union St. (648-3555). To: Moncton (2hr., 2 per day, $22); Montréal (14hr., 2 per day, $94); and Halifax (6-6½hr., 2 per day, $62). Open daily 7:30am-9pm.
Public Transportation: Saint John Transit (658-4700) runs until roughly 12:30am. Fare $1.45, under 14 $1.20. Late June to early Oct., 2hr. guided tour of historic Saint John leaves from Barbara General Store at Loyalist Plaza and Reversing Falls. $14, ages 6-14 $5.

Ferries: Marine Atlantic (636-4048 or 800-341-7981 from the U.S.), on Lancaster St. extension near the mouth of Saint John Harbor. Take the "West Saint John" bus, then walk 10min. Crosses to Digby, NS (3hr.; 1-3 per day; $23, seniors $22, ages 5-12 $12, bikes $11.25, cars $55; in winter $19/$16/$9/$7/$43).

Taxis: Royal Taxi, 652-5050. **Diamond,** 648-8888. Both operate 24hr.

Visitor Info: Saint John Visitors and Convention Bureau, 15 Market Sq. (658-2990), on the 11th fl. of City Hall, at the foot of King St. Open M-F 8:30am-4:30pm. The **City Center** info center (658-2855), at Market Sq., is open daily 9am-8pm; mid-Oct. to June 9am-6pm.

Weather: 636-4991.

Hotlines: Crisis Line, 658-3737. **Suicide Crisis Line,** 633-0001. Operates daily 5pm-midnight.

Post Office: Station B, 41 Church Ave. W. (672-6704), in west Saint John (open M-F 8am-5pm). **Postal code:** E2L 3W9. **Area code:** 506.

ACCOMMODATIONS AND CAMPGROUNDS

In West Saint John, a number of nearly identical motels on the 1100 to 1300 blocks of **Manawagonish Rd.** charge $35-45 for a single. Saint John Transit has directions by bus (see **Practical Information,** above); by car, avoid the 25¢ bridge toll by taking Hwy. 100 into West Saint John, turn right on Main St., and head west until it turns into Manawagonish Rd. The drab, bare, but clean rooms at the **Saint John YMCA/YWCA (HI-C),** 19-25 Hazen Ave. (634-7720), include access to recreational facilities, pool, and a workout room. From Market Sq., head 2 blocks up Union St. on the left. ($25, non-members and nonstudents $30. Open daily 5am-11pm; guests arriving on evening ferry can check in later. Summer reservations recommended.) If you're willing to drive 10-20min. out of Saint John, the Sir James Dunn Residence Hall at the **University of New Brunswick at Saint John** (648-5768), on Tucker Park Rd., offers new, neat, furnished rooms. (Singles $29, doubles $42; students $18/$30. Reception M-F 8am-4pm. Check-out noon. Reservations recommended. Open May-Aug.) The partially wooded tent sites of the **Rockwood Park Campground** (652-4050) await at the southern end of Rock-wood Park 2km north of uptown off Hwy. 1. Take the "University" bus to the Mt. Pleas-ant stop, and follow the signs for 5min. (Sites $15, with hookup $18; weekly $65/$95; showers included; open May-Sept.)

FOOD

Selling fresh, cheap food, the butcher, baker, fishmonger, produce dealer, and cheese merchant hang out at the **City Market,** 47 Charlotte St. (658-2820), between King and Brunswick Sq. (open M-Th 7:30am-6pm, F 7:30am-7pm, Sa 7:30am-5pm). The market may also be the best place to look for **dulse,** a local specialty not found outside New Brunswick, which consists of sun-dried seaweed from the Bay of Fundy; it can best be described as "ocean jerky." A $1 bag is more than a sample. **Reggie's Restaurant,** 26 Germain St. (657-6270), provides homestyle renditions of basic North American fare. The sandwiches ($2-4), made with famous smoked meat from Ben's Deli in Montréal, may not fill you up, but the breakfast special will: two eggs, sausage, homefries, and toast go for $3.50, served daily 6-11am (open M-Tu 6am-7pm, W-F 6am-8pm, Sa-Su 6am-6pm). **Billy's Seafood Company,** 49-51 Charlotte St. (672-3474), serves fresh oysters ($9 per 6) and lobster (seasonal prices; open M-Th 11am-10pm, F-Sa 11am-11pm, Su 4-10pm).

SIGHTS

Saint John's main attraction is **Reversing Falls,** a natural phenomenon caused by the powerful Bay of Fundy tides (for more on the tides see **Fundy,** below). Though the name may suggest 100 ft. walls of gravity-defying water, the "falls" are actually beneath the surface of the water. At high tide, patient spectators see the flow of water at the nexus of the Saint John River and Saint John Harbor slowly halt and change direction. More amazing than the event itself may be the number of people captivated by it. The **Reversing Falls Tourist Centre** (658-2937), at the west end of the Hwy. 100 bridge (take the west-bound "East-West" bus), distributes tide schedules and shows an oh-so-thrilling 12min. film on the phenomenon (screenings every 15min.; $1.25; center open June-Aug. daily 8am-8pm). **Jet boat rides** (634-8987), though overpriced, are the latest in Reversing Falls excitement (in summer 10am-dusk; 20min.; $20).

The oldest independent brewery in Canada, **Moosehead Breweries,** 89 Main St. (635-7000), in West Saint John, waits at the end of many a devoted enthusiast's pilgrimages. *(Free 1hr. tours with samples mid-June to Aug. 9:30am and 2pm. Tours limited to 20 people; avoid heartbreak by making reservations 2-3 days in advance.)* The **New Brunswick Museum,** 1 Market Sq. (643-2300), features neither moose nor brew, but it does house a 45 ft. Right Whale skeleton. *(Open M-F 9am-9pm, Sa 10am-6pm, Su noon-5pm. $6, students and children $3.25, seniors $4.75, families $13; Oct.-June W 6-9pm free.)*

Pick up a brochure at any tourist info center for the city's three self-guided **walking tours** (each about 2hr.). **The Victorian Stroll** roams past some of the old homes in Saint John, most dating to the late 1800s; **Prince William's Walk** details commerce in the port city; **The Loyalist Trail** traces the places frequented by the Loyalist founders. All three emphasize history, architecture, and nostalgia. **Trinity Church,** 115 Charlotte St. (693-8558), on the Loyalist Trail tour, displays amazing stained-glass windows and the Royal Coat of Arms of George III's House of Hanover. (Viewing M-F 9am-3pm; tours M-F 10am-4pm.) **Fort Howe Lookout,** originally erected to protect the harbor from dastardly American privateers, affords an impressive view of the city and its harbor (open 24hr.; free).

■ Fundy

Fundy National Park occupies 260 sq. km of New Brunswick's coast (a 1hr. drive southeast of Moncton on Hwy. 114). Approximately every 12hr., the world's largest tides draw back over 1km into the Bay of Fundy, allowing visitors to explore the vast territory uncovered by the ebbing tide. Don't get caught too far out without your running shoes, though; the water rises 1 ft. per min. when the tide comes in. When you're not fleeing the surf, Fundy's extensive hiking trails, forests, campgrounds, and recreational facilities should keep you occupied.

PRACTICAL INFORMATION Park Headquarters, P.O. Box 40 (887-6000), Alma, E0A 1B0, consists of a group of buildings in the southeastern corner of the Park facing the Bay, across the Upper Salmon River from the town of Alma. The area includes the administration building and the **visitors reception center,** which sits at the park's east entrance. (Open daily in summer 8am-10pm; in fall and spring M-F 8:15am-4:30pm, Sa-Su 10am-6pm; in winter M-F 8:15am-4:30pm.) The other visitors center, **Wolfe Lake Information** (432-6026), lurks at the northwest entrance off Hwy. 114 (open late June to early Sept. daily 10am-6pm). No public transportation serves Fundy. The nearest bus depots are in Moncton and Sussex. The park's entrance fee is $3.50 per day (ages 6-16 $1.75; $7 max. per family) from mid-May to early Oct. The free and invaluable park newspaper *Salt and Fir,* available at the entrance stations and info centers, includes a map of hiking trails and campgrounds, as well as a schedule of activities. For **weather info,** call 887-6000. **Area code:** 506.

CAMPGROUNDS, A HOSTEL, AND FOOD The park operates four **campgrounds** totaling over 600 sites. Getting a site is seldom a problem, but landing one at your campground of choice may be a little more difficult. The park accepts no reservations; all sites are first come, first served. **Headquarters Campground,** closest to facilities, is usually in highest demand. When the campground is full, put your name on the waiting list, and sleep somewhere else for the night. The next day at noon, the names of those admitted for the night are read. (Sites $12, with hookup $19. Open mid-May to early Oct.) The only other campground with facilities, **Chignecto North**

Campground, off Hwy. 114 5km inland from the headquarters, provides greater privacy (sites $12, with hookup $17-19; open mid-May to mid-Oct.). **Point Wolfe Campground,** scenically located along the coast 7km west of headquarters, stays cooler and more insect-free than the inland campgrounds (sites $12; open late June to early Sept.). All three campgrounds have showers and washrooms. The **Wolfe Lake Campground,** near the northwest park entrance, a 1min. walk from the lake, does not (sites $10; open mid-May to mid-Oct.). Year-round wilderness camping is also available in some of the most scenic areas of the park, especially **Goose River** along the coast. The campsites; all with fireplaces, wood, and an outhouse; carry a $3 per person per night permit fee. Call 800-213-7275 to make reservations. The **Fundy National Park Hostel (HI-C)** (887-2216), near Devil's Half Acre about 1km south of the park headquarters, has a full kitchen, showers, and a common room with TV. Ask the staff for the lowdown on park nightlife. ($9, nonmembers $12. Check-in 8-10am and 5-10pm. Open June to early Sept. Wheelchair access.)

For a cheap, home-cooked meal, the **Harbor View Market and Coffee Shop** (887-2450), on Main St. in Alma, will fit the bill. Dinner specials are $7, and the breakfast special of two eggs, toast, bacon, and coffee runs you $4 (open daily 7:30am-8:30pm; Sept.-June M-F 8am-6pm, Sa-Su 8am-7pm).

ACTIVITIES The park maintains about 104km of park trails year-round, about 35km of which are open to mountain bikes. Unless you're ready to hoof it, bring your own bike; no rental outfits serve the island. *Salt and Fir* contains detailed descriptions of all trails, including where you'll find waterfalls and ocean views. The easy but breathtaking 1½km **Dickson Falls** trail is especially recommended. Though declining in number, deer are still fairly common, and thieving raccoons run thick around the campsites. Catching a glimpse of a peregrine falcon will require considerable patience, but the moose come out to be seen around dusk.

Most recreational facilities operate only during the summer season (mid-May to early Oct.), including free daily interpretive programs designed to help visitors get to know the park. The park staff lead beach walks, evening programs, and weekly campfire programs. Visits to the park in September and October catch the fall foliage and avoid the crush of vacationers. Those seeking quiet, pristine nature would be wise to visit in this chillier off season.

■ Near Fundy: Kouchibouguac

Unlike Fundy's rugged forests and the high tides along the Loyalist coast, **Kouchibouguac** (meaning "river of the long tides" in Micmac) **National Park** shows off warm lagoon waters, salt marshes, peat bogs, and white sandy beaches. Bask in the sun along the 25km stretch of barrier islands and sand dunes, or swim through canoe waterways that were once highways for the Micmacs. Canoes ($6 per hr., $30 per day), kayaks ($4.60 per hr.), and bikes ($4.60 per hr., $26 per day) are for rent at **Ryans Rental Center** (876-3733), in the park between the South Kouchibouguac Campground and Kellys Beach (open June-Aug. daily 8:30am-9pm; May Sa-Su 8am-5pm). The park operates two campgrounds in the summer. **South Kouchibouguac** has 311 sites with showers. (Late June to early Sept. $16.25, with hookup $22; mid-May to late June and early Sept. to mid-Oct. $13/$18. Reservations recommended July-Aug.) **Côte-à-Fabien** has 32 sites ($14), but no showers. Off-season campers take advantage of primitive sites within the park and several commercial campgrounds just outside of the park (park entrance fee $3.50, ages 6-16 $1.75). The **park info center** sits at the park entrance on Hwy. 117 just off Hwy. 11, 90km north of Moncton (open daily 8am-8pm; mid-Sept. to mid-June 9am-5pm). The park administration (876-2443) is open year-round (M-F 8am-4:30pm). **Area code:** 506.

Prince Edward Island

Prince Edward Island, now more commonly called "P.E.I." or "the Island," began as St. John's Island. In 1799, residents renamed the area for Prince Edward, son of King George III, in thanks for his interest in the territory's welfare. The change cleared up the exasperating confusion between the island and St. John's, Newfoundland; St. John, Labrador; and Saint John, New Brunswick.

The smallest province in Canada attracts visitors hoping to share in the relaxing beauty made famous by Lucy Maud Montgomery's novel *Anne of Green Gables*. The fictional work did not exaggerate the wonders of natural life on the island; the soil, made red by its high iron-oxide content, complements the green crops and shrubbery, turquoise waters, and purple roadside lupin. On the north and south shores, some of Canada's finest beaches extend for miles. Relentlessly quaint, Island towns seem to exist more for visitors than for residents, consisting mainly of restaurants and shops. From lawn bowling, a favorite of the older set, to nightly public parties (Celtic music is big here), P.E.I. comes alive during the summer.

The newly constructed Confederation Bridge, the longest continuous marine span bridge in the world, extends over the 9 mi. from P.E.I. to the mainland. The Bridge authorities fiendishly charge a toll of $35.50 to exit the island.

PRACTICAL INFORMATION

Queen St. and **University Ave.** are Charlottetown's main thoroughfares, straddling **Confederation Centre** along the west and east, respectively. The most popular beaches; **Cavendish, Brackley,** and **Rustico Island;** lie on the north shore in the middle of the province, opposite Charlottetown. **Confederation Bridge** meets P.E.I. at Borden-Carleton, 56km west of Charlottetown on Hwy. 1.

Capital: Charlottetown.
Drinking Age: 19.
Time Zone: Atlantic (1hr. ahead of Eastern time). **Postal Abbreviation:** P.E.I.
Provincial Sales Tax: 10%, plus 7% GST.
Beach Shuttles: 566-3243. Picks up at the **P.E.I. Visitor Information Centre** at 178 Water St. (call for additional points) and drops off in Cavendish (45min.; 2 per day June and Sept., 4 per day July-Aug.; $9, round-trip same day $15).
Ferries: Northumberland Ferry (566-3838 or 800-565-0201 from P.E.I. and Nova Scotia), in Wood Islands 61km east of Charlottetown on Trans-Canada Hwy. To Caribou, NS (1¼hr.; 6-10 per day; pedestrians $10, vehicles $46).
Taxis: City Cab, 892-6567. Open 24hr.
Bike Rental: MacQueens, 430 Queen St. (368-2453). Road and mountain bikes $22 per day, $88 per week; children $11/$44. Must have credit card or $75 deposit. Open M-W and Sa 8:30am-5:30pm, Th-F 8:30am-7pm, Su 10am-2pm; Sept.-May M-Th and Sa 8:30am-5:30pm, F 8:30am-7pm.
Visitor Info: P.E.I. Visitor Information Centre, P.O. Box 940, C1A 7M5 (368-4444 or 888-734-7529), by the waterfront in Charlottetown. Open daily June 8am-8pm; July-Aug. 8am-10pm; Sept. to mid-Oct 9am-6pm; mid-Oct. to May 9am-4:30pm. The **Charlottetown Visitors Bureau,** 199 Queen St. (566-5548), hides inside City Hall. Open daily 8am-5pm; Sept.-June 8:30am-5pm.
Crisis Line: Crisis Centre, 566-8999. 24hr.
Police: Charlottetown, 368-2677. **Royal Canadian Mounted Police,** 566-7111.
Post Office: 135 Kent St. (628-4400). Open M-F 8am-5:15pm. **Postal code:** C1A 7N7.
  Area code: 902.

ACCOMMODATIONS AND CAMPGROUNDS

B&Bs and **country inns** crowd every nook and cranny of the province; some are open year-round, but the most inexpensive are closed during the off season. Avoid frustration by calling ahead. Rates hover around $28 for singles and $35 for doubles. Fifteen farms participate in a provincial **Farm Vacation** program, in which tourists spend time with a farming family. Call the **Farm Vacation Association** (566-5008) for info, or pick up a brochure at the visitors center.

The **Charlottetown International Hostel (HI-C),** 153 Mt. Edward Rd. (894-9696), across the yard from the University of P.E.I. (UPEI), is in a large green barn. Take Belvedere 1 long block east of University Ave., then turn left onto Mt. Edward Rd. The green-and-white sign marking the turn-off leads to neat, spacious rooms, a friendly staff, and a diverse clientele. ($14, nonmembers $16.80. Kitchen facilities, showers, TV lounge. Blanket rental $1. Bike rental $15. Check-in 7-10am and 4pm-midnight. Curfew midnight. Lockout 10am-4pm. Open June to early Sept.) The UPEI runs a mass B&B in **Marion Hall** (July-Aug. singles $29.50; doubles $38, breakfast included; May-June $26/$32). **Bernadine Hall,** open most of the summer, is another option (July-Aug. singles $38.50; doubles $44, breakfast included; May-June $36/$39). Check in for all locations at **Blanchard Hall** (Sept.-May 566-0362, June-Aug. 566-0442).

Prince Edward Island National Park (672-6350 or 963-2391) operates three campgrounds during the summer (462 primitive sites with showers, toilets, kitchen access, laundry facilities $13-19; 110 sites with hookup $20-21) and one off-season campground (primitive sites $8). The many other provincial parks that offer camping, as well as the plentiful private campgrounds scattered throughout the Island, ensure that there will always be a campsite available. (Open seasons vary, but expect to find a campground open mid-June to mid-Sept.)

FOOD

The quest for food on P.E.I. boils down to the search for a cheap **lobster.** At market, the coveted crustaceans go for $6-8 per lb. Fresh seafood, including the world-famous **Malpeque oysters,** is sold along the shores of the island, especially in North Rustico on the north shore. The back of the *P.E.I. Visitor's Guide* lists fresh seafood outlets. The **Charlottetown Farmers' Market** (368-4444), on Belvedere Ave. opposite U.P.E.I., sells the freshest food around (open July-Sept. W and Sa-Su 9am-2pm).

The cosmopolitan young clientele at **Beanz,** 52 University Ave. (892-8797), bask on a sunny outdoor terrace and wash their homemade sandwiches ($3-4) down with some great espresso. (Open M-F 6:30am-8pm, Sa 8am-5pm, Su 9am-5pm; Sept.-Dec. M-F 6:30am-6pm, Sa 8am-5pm, Su 9am-5pm.) There's non-aquatic fare, including vegetarian dishes a-plenty, at **Shaddy's,** 44 University Ave. (368-8886), a local favorite serving Lebanese and Canadian cuisine, including a wide variety of sandwiches for $4-7 (open daily 7:30am-midnight; in winter M-F 7:30am-10pm, Sa-Su 7:30am-11pm).

SIGHTS AND ENTERTAINMENT

The Island at Large

Green Gables House (963-3370), off Rte. 6 in Cavendish just west of Rte. 13, has become a mecca for adoring Lucy Maud Montgomery readers—a surprising number make the pilgrimage all the way from Japan. *(Open daily July-Aug. 9am-8pm; May-June and Sept.-Oct 9am-5pm. $5, seniors $4, ages 6-16 $2.50, families $12. Off-season discounts.)* Green Gables can get very crowded between late July and September, so it's best to arrive in the early morning or the evening.

CANADA

Prince Edward Island National Park (963-7830 or 963-7831), the most popular Canadian national park east of Banff, consists of a 32km coastal strip embracing some of Canada's finest beaches and over a fifth of P.E.I.'s northern coast. Wind-sculpted sand dunes and salt marshes undulate along the park's terrain. The park is home to many of the Island's 300-odd species of birds, including the endangered piping plover. Park campgrounds, programs, and services operate early July through mid-August. **Cavendish Campground** stays open until late September (sites $17, entrance fee $3 per day). *Blue Heron*, the park guide, roosts at the entrance kiosks.

The stretches of beach on the **eastern coast** of P.E.I. are considerably less touristed than those in the west. **Lakeside**, a beach 35km east of Charlottetown on Rte. 2, is unsupervised and often nearly deserted on July and August weekdays. For the romantic equestrian in you, trot along the surf atop a sturdy steed from **Gun Trail Ride** (961-2076), located right beside the golf course ($9 per hr., with trail guide $9, June to early Sept. daily 9am-9pm). **Basin Head Beach,** 95km east of Charlottetown, makes a relaxing daytrip, with over 7 mi. of white sand to ensure that you won't have to rumble with other visitors for turf (unsupervised).

Charlottetown

The province's capital prides itself on being the "Cradle of Confederation." Delegates from the British North American colonies met in 1864 inside the brownstone **Province House** (566-7626), on the corner of Great George and Richmond St., to discuss the union that would become the Dominion of Canada in 1867. *(Open July-Aug. daily 9am-6pm; June and Sept. to mid-Oct. daily 9am-5pm; mid-Oct. to May M-F 9am-5pm. Free.)* Both the modern and the historical chambers of the legislature are open for viewing. Adjoining the Province House, the modern national arts complex at **Confederation Centre of the Arts** (628-1864), on the corner of Queen and Grafton St., contains theaters, restaurants, gift shops, and an art gallery. *(Box office open M-Sa 9am-9pm; Sept. to mid-June M-Sa noon-5:30pm.)* The Centre conducts guided tours June to September. Every summer, a musical production of *Anne of Green Gables*, and other Canadian shows, are presented as part of the **Charlottetown Festival.** *(Anne performances June to early Sept. M-W and Sa 8pm; tickets $22-36. Matinees M and W 1:30pm; tickets $20-32. Seniors and children $2 off. For ticket info, call 566-1267 or 800-565-0278.)*

Québec

Home to 90% of Canada's French-speaking citizenry, Québec continues to fight for political and legal recognition of its separate cultural identity. Originally populated by French fur trading settlements along the St. Lawrence River, Québec was ceded to the British in 1759. Ever since, anti-federalist elements within *québecois* society have rankled under control of the largely Anglicized national government. French is spoken by 95% of Québec's population; all signs are printed in French, as required by provincial law. The failure of the 1990 Meech Lake Accord to recognize Québec as a "distinct society" and the more recent election of the Bloc Québecois, a separatist party, to the status of official opposition in the federal government, signal uncertain times ahead for the province. Visitors will likely never notice these underlying tensions—the majority of the struggle goes on behind closed doors in Ottawa—but the entire country wonders if this province will choose to stay a part of the whole.

PRACTICAL INFORMATION

Capital: Québec City.
Visitor Info: Tourisme Québec, C.P. 979, Montréal, PQ H3C 2W3 (800-363-7777, 514-873-2015 in Montréal; http://www.tourisme.gouv.qc.ca). Open daily 9am-5pm. **Canadian Parks Service, Québec Region,** 3 Passage du D'or, C.P. Box 6060, Haute-Ville, PQ GIR 4V7 (800-463-6769, 418-648-4177 in Québec City).

Emergency: 911.
Time Zone: Eastern. **Postal Abbreviation:** PQ.
Drinking Age: 18.
Provincial Sales Tax: 6.5%, plus 7% GST; TVQ 7.5%

ACCOMMODATIONS INFORMATION

The following organizations offer assistance in locating accommodations throughout the province.

Hospitalité Canada, 1001 Square-Dorchester, Montréal H3B 4V4 (514-393-1528 or 800-322-2932). Info and reservations for accommodations throughout Québec, primarily in Montréal and Québec City.

Camping: Association des terrains du camping du Québec (Camping Association of Québec), 2001 de la Metropole St., #700, Longueil, Québec J4G 1S9 (514-651-7396 or 800-363-0457), and **Fédération québecoise du camping et de caravaning (Québec Camping and RV Federation),** 4545, ave. Pierre-de-Coubertin, Stade Olympique, C.P. 1000, succursale "M," Montréal H1V 3R2 (514-252-3003).

Hostels: Regroupement Tourisme Jeunesse (HI-C) (514-252-3117), at the Fédération address. For reservations in any Québec hostel and a few in neighboring Ontario, call 800-461-8585 at least 24hr. in advance, with a credit card.

■ Montréal

This island city, named for the Mont-Royal in its midst, has been coveted territory for over 300 years. Wars and sieges have brought governments in and out like the tide, including a brief takeover by American revolutionaries in late 1775. Despite these conflicts, Montréal has grown into a diverse city with a cosmopolitan air seen in few other cities on the continent. Although less than an hour from the U.S.-Canada border, Montréal's European legacy is immediately evident. Fashion that rivals Paris, a nightlife comparable to London, and cuisine from around the globe all attest to this overseas influence. Whether you credit the international flavor or the large student population of the city, it is hard not to be swept up by the vibrancy that courses through Montréal's *centre-ville*.

ORIENTATION AND PRACTICAL INFORMATION

Two major streets divide the city, making orientation convenient. The one-way **bd. St-Laurent** (also called **"The Main"**) runs north through the city, splitting Montréal and its streets east-west. The Main also serves as the unofficial French/English divider; English **McGill University** lies to the west, while slightly east is **St-Denis**, a parallel two-way thoroughfare which defines the French student quarter (also called the *"quartier latin"* or the "student ghetto"). **Rue Sherbrooke,** which is paralleled by **de Maisonneuve** and **Ste-Catherine** downtown, runs east-west almost the entire length of Montréal. The **Underground City** runs north-south, stretching from **rue Sherbrooke** to **rue de la Gauchetière.** For easy navigation, a free map from the tourist office will help. Parking is often difficult in the city, particularly during winter when snowbanks narrow the streets and slow traffic. Meters cost 25¢ per 10min. downtown, and $30 tickets for parking violations are common. The **Métro** avoids the hassle. Montréal's population is 85% Francophone, but most are bilingual.

Airports: Dorval (info 633-3105), 20-30min. from downtown by car. From the Lionel Groulx Métro stop, take bus #211 to Dorval Train Station, then transfer to bus #204. Mostly handles flights from the U.S. and within Canada. **Autocar Connaisseur-Grayline** (934-1222) runs a minivan to Dorval from 777, rue de la Gauchetière, at University St., stopping at any downtown hotel if you call in advance. Vans run 5:10am-11:10pm M-F every 20min., Sa-Su every 30min. $9.25, under 5 free. Taxi to downtown $30-35. **Mirabel International** (476-3010), 45min. from downtown by car, handles all flights from outside the U.S. or Canada. Taxi to downtown $60. **Information** for either airport: 1-800-465-1213.

Trains: Central Station, 895, rue de la Gauchetière Ouest, under Queen Elizabeth Hotel. Métro: Bonaventure. Served by **VIA Rail** (989-2626 or 800-561-9181, from U.S. 800-VIA-RAIL/842-7245). To: Québec City (3hr., 3-4 per day, $47); Ottawa (2hr., 4 per day, $38); and Toronto (4-5½hr., 6 per day, $89). Discounts for students, seniors, and tickets bought 5 or more days in advance. Ticket counter open daily 6am-9pm. **Amtrak** (800-872-7245). To New York (10hr., 1 per day, US$49-62) and Boston (13hr., 1 per day, US$89-121). Ticket counter open daily 8am-5pm.

Buses: Voyageur, 505, bd. de Maisonneuve Est (842-2281). Métro: Berri-UQAM. To: Toronto (6¾hr.; 7 per day; $74, students $51); Ottawa (2½hr., 17-18 per day, $28/ $28); and Québec City (3hr., 18 per day, $37/$27). **Greyhound** (287-1580). To New York City (7½-8¾hr., 7 per day, $89-98) and Boston (7hr., 7 per day, $52-55).

Public Transportation: STCUM Métro and Bus (288-6287). A generally safe and extremely efficient network. The 4 Métro lines and most buses operate daily 5:30am-12:30am; some have night schedules as well. Get network maps at the tourist office, or at any Métro station booth. Downtown ticketing is rampant so take the Métro. Buses are a well-integrated part of the system; transfer tickets from bus drivers are good as subway tickets, and vice versa. Fare for train or bus $1.85, 6 tickets $8. 1-day unlimited tourist pass $5, 3-day $12; available at any downtown metro station. May be purchased in advance.

Taxis: Taxi Pontiac, 761-5522. **Champlain Taxi Inc.,** 273-2435. Both operate 24hr. at the city's regulated rates. $2.25 base fare, $1 per km.

Car Rental: Via Route, 1255, rue MacKay (871-1166), at Ste-Catherine. $57 per day with 300 free km and insurance; 12¢ per additional km. Must be 21 with credit card. Open M-F 7am-9pm, Sa 7:30am-5pm, Su 9am-9pm.

Driver/Rider Service: Allo Stop, 4317, rue St-Denis (985-3032). Matches passengers with member drivers; part of the rider fee goes to the driver. To: Québec City ($15), Ottawa ($10), Toronto ($26), Sherbrooke ($9), New York City ($50), and Boston ($42). Riders and drivers fix their own fees for rides over 1000 mi. Annual membership fee required ($6, drivers $7). Open daily 9am-6pm.

Bike Rental: Cycle Pop, 1000, Rachel Est (526-2525). Métro: Mont-Royal. 21-speeds $20 per day, $40 for the weekend. Open M-W 10am-6pm, Th-F 10am-9pm, Sa-Su 10am-5pm. Credit card or $250 deposit required.

Visitor Info: Infotouriste, 1001, rue de Square-Dorchester (873-2015, outside Montréal 800-363-7777; http://www.tourisme.montreal.org), corner of Peel and Ste-Catherine between rue Peel and rue Metcalfe. Metro: Peel. Free city maps and guides, and extensive food and housing listings. Open daily 8am-7:50pm; Sept.-June 9am-6pm. Branch office in **Old Montréal,** 174, rue Notre-Dame Est at Place Jacques Cartier. Open daily 9am-7pm; Sept.-Oct. daily 9am-5pm; Nov. to early Mar. Th-Su 9am-5pm; late Mar. to early daily June 9am-5pm.

Youth Travel Office: Tourisme Jeunesse, 4008, rue St-Denis (252-3117 or 844-0287). Métro: Sherbrooke. Free maps, hostel info, travel gear, and advice. A nonprofit organization that inspects and ranks all officially recognized youth hostels in Québec. Open M-W 10am-6pm, Th-F 10am-9pm, Sa 10am-6pm, Su 10am-5pm. **Travel CUTS,** McGill Student Union, 3480, rue McTavish (398-0647). Métro: McGill. Specializes in budget travel for college students. Open M-F 9am-5pm.

Consulates: France, 1, Place Ville-Marie (878-4385), 26th fl. Open 8:30am-noon. **U.K.,** 1000, rue de la Gauchetière Ouest, #4200 (866-5863). Open for info M-F 9am-5pm; for consular help call the British High Commission in Ottawa (passports 613-237-1303, visas 613-237-2008). **U.S.,** 1155, rue St-Alexander (398-9695). Open M-F 8:30am-12:30pm; for visas 8:30am-11am.

Currency Exchange: Currencies International, 1250, rue Peel (392-9100). Métro: Peel. Open in summer M-W 8:30am-8pm, Th-F 8:30am-9pm, Sa 8:30am-7pm, Su 9am-6pm; call for winter hrs. **Thomas Cook,** 777, rue de la Gauchetière Ouest (397-4029). Métro: Bonaventure. Open M-F 8:30am-7pm, Sa 9am-4pm, Su 10am-3pm. Most **ATM machines** are on the PLUS system and charge only the normal transaction fee for withdrawals abroad; ask your bank about fees.

American Express, 1141, rue de Maisonneuve (284-3300), at Peel. Métro: Peel. Travel agency and financial office. Traveler's checks and currency exchange. Open M-F 9am-5pm.

Hotlines: Tel-aide, 935-1101. **Sexual Assault,** 934-4504. **Suicide-Action,** 723-4000. All 3 operate 24hr. **Rape Crisis,** 278-9383. Operates M-F 9:30am-4:30pm.

Internet Access: Le Café Electronique, 405, St-Sulpice (849-7927), in Old Montréal. Open daily 10am-10pm.
Post Office: Succursale (Postal Station) "B," 1250, rue Université (395-4539), at Cathcourt. Open M and W-Th 8am-5:45pm, Tu and F 8am-9pm, Sa 9:30am-5pm. **Postal code:** H3B 3B0. **Area code:** 514.

ACCOMMODATIONS AND CAMPGROUNDS

The **Québec Tourist Office** is the best resource for info about hostels, hotels, and *chambres touristiques* (rooms in private homes or small guest houses). B&B singles cost $25-40, and doubles run $35-75. The most extensive B&B network is **Bed & Breakfast à Montréal,** P.O. Box 575, Snowdon Station, H3X 3T8 (738-9410; fax 735-7493), which recommends that you reserve by phone, fax, or mail. (Singles from $40; doubles from $60; $15 per night deposit upon confirmation. Leave a message if the owners are out.) The **Downtown Bed and Breakfast Network,** 3458, ave. Laval, H2X 3C8 (289-9749 or 800-267-5180), near Sherbrooke, lists 80 homes downtown (singles $25-55, doubles $35-65; open daily 9am-9pm). Most B&Bs have bilingual hosts.

Many of the least expensive *maisons touristiques* and hotels cluster around **rue St-Denis,** ranging from quaint to seedy. The area, which abuts Vieux Montréal, flaunts lively nightclubs and a number of funky cafés and bistros.

Auberge de Jeunesse, Montréal Youth Hostel (HI-C), 1030, rue MacKay (843-3317). Métro: Lucien-L'Allier. Airport shuttle drivers will stop here if asked. Relatively new, large, and extremely convenient location in a hotel, complemented by great service. The friendly, upbeat staff knows the nightlife lowdown and gives free tours and outings. Bi-weekly pub crawl (F and Tu 8:30pm). Dorm rooms have 3-10 beds (246 total; with baths). $17.50, Canadian nonmembers $19.50, non-Canadian nonmembers $22.10, under 13 free with parent. Private doubles $25.88/$30.48/$30.48 per person. New café with kitchen facilities. Linen $2.10. Prices include tax. Kitchen, laundry facilities, A/C, and extensive ride board. Some parking. 1-week max. stay; in winter 10 days. Reception 24hr.
Hotel Le Breton, 1609, rue St-Hubert (524-7273), around the corner from the bus station and two blocks east of St-Denis. Métro: Berri-UQAM. Although the neighborhood is not particularly wholesome, the 13 rooms are clean and comfortable with a TV, some with A/C. Singles $35 with shared bath; doubles $42, with private bath $50. Reception 8am-midnight. The hotel fills up quickly; make reservations 2 weeks in advance.
Collège Français, 5155, ave. de Gaspé, H2T 2A1 (495-2581). Métro: Laurier, then walk west on Laurier and ½ block north on Gaspé. Clean and well located. Young clientele. Prices vary from $11.50-15.50, depending on the number of beds in the room (4-7) and whether there's a private shower. Summer (July-Aug.) breakfast $3.25. Free parking during off-school hrs. Reception daily 7am-2am.
McGill University, Bishop Mountain Hall, 3935, rue de l'Université, H3A 2B4 (398-6367). Métro: McGill. Follow Université through campus (bring your hiking boots; it's a long haul). Ideally located singles. $38, students and seniors $31; weekly $217/$186; prices include tax. Full breakfast $6, served M-Th 7:30-9:30am. Kitchenettes on each floor. 1000 beds available! Common room with TV and laundry facilities. Reception daily 7am-10pm; a guard will check you in late at night. Open May 15-Aug. 15.
Université de Montréal, Residences, 2350, rue Edouard-Montpetit, H2X 2B9, (343-6531), off Côte-des-Neiges. Métro: Edouard-Montpetit. Located on the edge of a beautiful campus; try the East Tower for great views. Singles $26.46 plus tax; doubles $38. Laundry facilities. Free local calls, sink in each room. Reception 24hr. Cafe with basic foods open M-F 7:30am-2:30pm. Open early May to mid-Aug.
Maison André Tourist Rooms, 3511, rue Université (849-4092). Métro: McGill. Mme Zanko will spin great yarns for you in her old, well located house—but only if you don't smoke. Guests have been returning to this bastion of European cleanliness and decor for over 30 years. Singles $26-35; doubles $38-45; $10 per additional person. Reservations recommended.
YMCA, 1450, rue Stanley (849-8393), downtown. Métro: Peel (right across the street from the station). 350 rooms. Co-ed. Access to newly renovated Y facilities. Rooms tiny but impeccable. TV and phone in most rooms. Singles $37-39 for men,

CANADA

$40 for women; doubles $45-60; triples $65; quads $74. Cafeteria open M-F 7am-8pm, Sa-Su 8am-2pm. Reservations recommended 2 weeks in advance.

Manoir Ambrose, 3422, rue Stanley (288-6922), just off Sherbrooke. Métro: Peel. Somewhat upscale both in price and appearance. 22 rooms with Victorian decor. Singles for 2 $50, with private bath $70; $10 per additional adult. Continental breakfast included. Reservations recommended 1 month in advance.

Hôtel de Paris, 901 Sherbrook E. (522-6861). Métro: Sherbrook. In cahoots with the pricier Dansereau Mansion, the Hotel has been painting, hammering, sweeping, and setting up a kitchen, all to bring you a splendidly outfitted brand new hostel with 90 beds. Single-sex dorm rooms $17. Linen rental $2.

Those with time, a car, and a good map can camp at **Parc d'OKA** (479-8337), 45min. from downtown; take Autoroute 20 W to 13, north to 640, which eventually becomes the park road. There are 880 beautiful sites on the Lac des Deux Montagnes. (Sites $18, beachside $19, with hookup $25.) For slightly more private sites in a campground very close to the city, try **Camping Alouette,** 3449 de l'Industrie J3G 4S5 (464-1661), 15 mi. from the city; follow Hwy 20, take Exit 105, and follow the signs to the campground. Alouette has a pool, laundry facilities, a small store, free showers, and a daily shuttle to and from Montréal. (Sites for 2 $16.50, with hookup $26.50; $2 per additional person.) If these don't wet your camping whistle, try the dramatic (there's a theater here, folks) **Camping Pointe-des-Cascades,** 2 ch. du Canal, Pte. des Cascades (455-9953). Take Autoroute 40 west, Exit 41 at Ste. Anne de Bellevue, Jct. 20, and west to Dorion. In Dorion, follow "Théâtre des Cascades" signs. (140 sites, many near water. Sites $22, with hookup $27.)

BON APPETÍT

Restaurants pack in along bd. **St-Laurent** and on the western half of **Ste-Catherine,** with prices ranging from affordable to astronomical. In the **Latin Quarter,** scout out energetic **rue Prince Arthur,** which jams Greek, Polish, and Italian restaurants into a tiny area (see **Sights,** p. 871, for details on ethnic neighborhood dining). Here, maître-d's stand in front of their restaurants and attempt to court you. The accent changes slightly at **ave. Duluth,** where Portuguese and Vietnamese establishments prevail. North of Maisonneuve on **Rue St-Denis,** you'll find the French Student Quarter, which has many small cafés and eateries that cater to student budgets. If you'd like wine with that, you can save money by buying your own at a *dépanneur* or the **SAQ (Sociéte des alcohols du Québec)** and bringing it to an unlicensed restaurant; they're concentrated on the **bd. St-Laurent,** north of Sherbrooke, and on the pedestrian precincts of rue Prince Arthur and rue Duluth.

French-Canadian cuisine is unique but generally expensive. When you're scrounging for change, look for *tourtière,* a traditional meat pie with veggies and a thick crust, or *crêpes québecois,* stuffed with everything from scrambled eggs to asparagus with *béchamel* (a cream sauce). You can wash it down with *cidre* (hard cider). Other Montréal specialties include French bread (the best on the continent), smoked meat, Matane salmon, Gaspé shrimp, lobster from the Iles-de-la-Madeleine, and *poutine* (a goo of French fries, cheese curds, and gravy). Delis and bakeries on bd. St-Laurent, north of downtown, prepare Jewish cuisine. Meanwhile, savory bagels spring forth from the brick ovens at **La Maison de l'Original Fairmount Bagel,** 74, rue Fairmount Ouest (272-0667; Métro: Laurier; $2-3 per 6; open 24hr.). The mall **Le Faubourge** and its 58 shops, markets, and restaurants sit on Ste-Catherine at St-Mathieu.

You'll be charged a **13% tax** for meals totaling more than $3.25. All restaurants are required by law to post their menus outside (although many white out the prices), so shop around. Consult the free *Restaurant Guide,* published by the Greater Montréal Convention and Tourism Bureau (844-5400), which lists over 130 restaurants by type of cuisine (available at the tourist office; see **Practical Information,** above). When preparing your own meals, these markets have what you need: the **Atwater Market** (Métro: Lionel-Groulx); the **Marché Maisonneuve,** 4375, rue Ontario Est (Métro: Pie-IX); the **Marché St-Jacques** (Métro: Berri-UQAM, at the corner of Ontario and Amherst); or the **Marché Jean-Talon** (Métro: Jean Talon). For market info, call 937-

---

Smoked Meat on Rye

Any true Montréalian (not those cosmopolitan, artsy downtown types) will agree that **Smoked Meat**—a spicy, salty, greasy cured beef brisket—is a delicacy not to be compared with anything else in the world. The great landmark **Ben's Delicatessen**, 990, bd. de Maisonneuve (844-1000), at Metcalfe, in the heart of downtown, is often said to be the originator of this artery-clogging delicacy, which resembles pastrami or even corned beef. The story has it that Ben Kravitz, a native Lithuanian, longed for the briskets of his native land and, in an effort to recreate them, invented Smoked Meat. A proper Smoked Meat sandwich is served hot with mustard on seedless rye, with fries, vinegar, a half-sour pickle, and black cherry soda. (At Ben's, that'll be about $6.)

7754 9am-4pm daily. (All markets open M-W 8am-6pm, Th 8am-8pm, F 8am-9pm, Sa 8am-5pm., Su 8am-5pm.)

Boulangerie Duluth, 173, rue Duluth (845-0693). Métro: Sherbrooke, then walk north on St-Denis and east on Duluth. A student hangout, complete with an aquarium and an outdoor terrace for schmoozing. Delicious and hot international-style sandwiches ($3.50) highlight an eclectic menu. Vegetarian menu items available. Open daily 7am-8pm.

Etoile des Indes, 1806, Ste-Catherine Ouest (932-8330), near St-Mathieu. Métro: Guy-Concordia. The best Indian fare in town. The brave should try their bang-up Bangalore *phal* dishes. Dinner entrees $5-15; daily lunch specials $5-8 (11am-2:30pm). Open M-Sa noon-2:30pm and 5-11pm, Su 5-11pm.

El Zaziummm, 51 Roy Est (844-0893), a St-Laurent side street. Spicy Mexican cuisine and sly, sweet alcoholic beverages; the food and funkiness distract you while the drinks strike silently with a kick like a mule. Entrees $8-15. Open M-Tu 4-11pm, W-Su noon-11:30pm; in winter daily 4-11pm.

Wilensky's, 34, rue Fairmount Ouest (271-0247), west of St-Laurent. Métro: Laurier. A great place for a quick lunch. Note the sign warning "We always put mustard on it," pull out a book from Moe Wilensky's shelf, and linger. Hot dogs $1.80, sandwiches $2.10. Open M-F 9am-4pm.

Da Giovanni, 572, Ste-Catherine Est (842-8851). Métro: Berri-UQAM. Serves generous portions of fine Italian food; don't be put off by the occasional lines or the diner atmosphere. Lasagna with garlic bread and caesar salad $9.50. Open Su-W 6:30am-11pm, Th 6:30am-midnight, F-Sa 7am-1am.

Au Pain Doré, 5214, Côte des Neiges (342-8995), near rue Jean Brillant. An answer to the question "Where, oh where can I get some French baked goods?" Also offers a selection of cheeses. Baguettes $1.50-4. Open M-W 8:30am-7pm, Th-F 8:30am-7:30pm, Sa-Su 8:30am-5:30pm.

SIGHTS

On the Streets

Montréal has matured from a riverside settlement of French colonists into a hip metropolis. **Museums, Vieux Montréal (Old Montréal),** and the new **downtown** are fascinating, but Montréal's greatest asset is its cultural vibrancy, and the city rewards aimless wandering. Your wallet will thank you for avoiding the high-priced boutiques touted by the tourist office. A small **Chinatown** orients itself along **rue de la Gauchetière,** near Vieux Montréal's **Place d'Armes.** Between 11:30am and 2:30pm, most of its restaurants offer mouth-watering Canton and Szechuan lunch specials ranging from $4-5. **Little Greece,** a bit farther than you might care to walk from downtown, is just southeast of the Outremont Métro; stop around **rue Hutchison** between **ave. Van Horne** and **ave. Edouard-Charles.** At the northern edge of the town's center, **Little Italy** occupies the area north of rue Beaubien between rue St-Hubert and Louis-Hémon. Walk east from Métro Beaubien and look for pasta. For a **walking tour** approach to the city, staying in the downtown area is best. Many attractions between Mont Royal and the Fleuve St-Laurent are free, from parks (Mont Royal and Lafontaine, see below) and universities (McGill, Montréal, Concordia, Québec at Montréal) to architectural spectacles of all sorts.

Bd. St-Laurent, north of Sherbrooke, is perfect for walking or biking. Originally settled by Jewish immigrants, this area now functions as a sort of multicultural welcome wagon, home to Greek, Slavic, Latin American, and Portuguese immigrants. **Rue St-Denis,** home to the city elite at the turn of the century, still serves as the **Latin Quarter's** mainstreet (Métro: Berri-UQAM). Jazz fiends will command the street July 1-11, 1999 during the annual **Montréal International Jazz Festival** (871-1881), with over 300 free outdoor shows. You may also wish to visit **rue Prince-Arthur** (Métro: Sherbrooke), which has street performers in the summer; **Carré St-Louis** (Métro: Sherbrooke), with its fountain and sculptures; and **Le Village,** a gay village in Montréal from rue St-Denis Est to Papineau along rue Ste-Catherine Est. Both the Latin Quarter (above) and the area along rue St-Denis foster a very liberal, gay-friendly atmosphere (Metro: Sherbrooke or Mont-Royal).

Museums

The **McGill University** campus (main gate at the corner of rue McGill and Sherbrooke; Métro: McGill) runs up Mont Royal and boasts Victorian buildings and pleasant greens in the midst of downtown. More than any other sight in Montréal, the university illustrates the impact of British tradition on the city. The campus also contains the site of the 16th-century Native American village of **Hochelaga** and the **Redpath Museum of Natural History** (398-4086), with rare fossils and two genuine Egyptian mummies (open M-Th 9am-5pm, Su 1-5pm; in winter M-F 9am-5pm, Su 1-5pm; free).

About 5 blocks west of the McGill entrance, Montréal's **Musée des Beaux-Arts (Fine Arts Museum),** 1379-80, rue Sherbrooke Ouest (285-1600 or 285-2000; Métro: Peel or Guy-Concordia), hosts impressive visiting exhibits; its small permanent collection touches upon all major artistic periods and includes Canadian and Inuit work. *(Open Tu-Su 11am-6pm. Permanent collection free. Temporary exhibits $10, students and seniors $5, under 12 $2; ½-price W 5:30-9pm, but permanent collection closed then.)* The **McCord Museum of Canadian History,** 690, rue Sherbrooke Ouest (398-7100; Métro: McGill), presents textiles, costumes, paintings, prints, and 700,000 pictures that humorously examine over 130 years of Canadian history. *(Open Sept.-June Tu-F 10am-6pm, Sa-Su 10am-5pm; call for summer hrs. $7, students $4, seniors $5, ages 7-12 $1.50, families $14. Free Sa 10am-noon.)* The relatively new **Centre Canadien d'Architecture,** 1920, ave. Baile (939-7026; Métro: Guy-Concordia or Atwater), houses one of the world's most important collections of architectural prints, drawings, photographs, and books. *(Open Tu-Su 11am-6pm; Oct.-May W-F 11am-6pm, Sa-Su 11am-5pm. $6, seniors $4, students $3, under 12 free. Students free all day Th; everyone free Th 6-8pm.)* **Musée d'Art Contemporain,** 185, Rue Ste-Catherine Ouest at Jeanne-Mance (847-6226 or 847-6212; Métro: Place-des-Arts), has the latest by *Québecois* artists, as well as textile, photography, and avant-garde exhibits. *(Open Tu and Th-Su 11am-6pm, W 11am-9pm. $6, seniors $4, students $3, under 12 free. W 6-9pm permanent exhibits free, temporary exhibits ½-price.)* Outside of the downtown museum circuit, the **Montréal Museum of Decorative Arts,** 2929, rue Jeanne-d'Arc (259-2575; Métro: Guy-Concordia, then free transfer to bus #24 Pie-IX), houses innovatively designed decorative pieces dating from 1935 to the present (open Tu-Su 11am-6pm, W 11am-9pm; $4, students $3, under 12 free).

Great Big Green Places

Olympic Park, 4141, ave. Pierre-de-Coubertin (252-4737; Métro: Viau, Pie IX), hosted the 1976 Summer Olympic Games. *(At least 2 guided tours in English daily at 12:40 and 3:40pm; more in summer, call for times. Visitors Information Center is on the side of the Stadium closest to Viau Metro Stop. $5.25, ages 5-17 $4.25.)* Its daring architecture, uncannily reminiscent of the *U.S.S. Enterprise* from TV's "Star Trek," includes the world's tallest inclined tower and a stadium with one of the world's only fully retractable roofs. Despite this, baseball games still get rained out because the roof cannot be put into place with crowds in the building. Riding the **funiculaire** to the top of the tower grants a panoramic view of Montréal. *(Open Sept. M noon-9pm, Tu-Th 10am-9pm, F-Su 10am-11pm; early Sept. to mid-June M noon-6pm, Tu-Su 10am-6pm. $9, seniors and ages 5-17 $5.50.)* The fascinating **Biodôme,** 4777, ave. Pierre-de-Coubertin (868-3000; Métro: Viau), is the most recent addition to Olympic park. *(Open daily in summer 9am-7pm; off-season 9am-5pm. $9.50, students and seniors $7, ages 6-17 $4.75.)* Housed in the former Olympic Vélodrome, the Biodôme is a "living museum" in which four complete ecosystems have been reconstructed: the Tropical Forest, Laurentian Forest, the St-Laurent marine ecosystem, and the Polar World. In the summer, a train will take you across the park to the **Jardin Botanique (Botanical Gardens),** 4101, rue Sherbrooke Est (872-1400; Métro: Pie-IX), one of the most important gardens in the world. *(Gardens open daily 9:30am-5pm; Sept.-June 9am-6pm. $9, students and seniors $6.75, ages 6-17 $4.50; Sept.-June $6.75/$5.25/$3.50.)* The Japanese and Chinese areas house the largest *bonsai* and *penjing* collections outside of Asia. The gardens also house an insectarium that seems to specialize in huge spiders, perfect for the arachnaphobic traveler. Package tickets for the Biodôme, Insectarium, tower and the Gardens allow you to save money and split a visit up over a 2-day period ($15, students and seniors $11, children $7.50). Parking in the complex begins at $5.

Montréal's more natural approach to a park, **Parc du Mont-Royal,** Centre de la Montagne (844-4928; Métro: Mont-Royal or Bus 11), was inaugurated in 1876 and climbs up to the mountain from which the city took its name (officially open 6am-midnight). From rue Peel, hardy hikers can take a foot path and stairs to the top, or to the lookouts on Camillien-Houde Pkwy. and the Mountain Chalet. The **30m cross** at the top of the mountain commemorates the 1643 climb by de Maisonneuve, founder of Montréal. In winter, *montréalais* congregate here to ice skate, toboggan, and cross-country ski. In summer, Mont-Royal welcomes joggers, cyclists, picnickers, and amblers. **Parc Lafontaine** (872-2644; Métro: Sherbrooke); bordered by Sherbrooke, Rachel, and Papineau Ave.; has picnic facilities, an outdoor puppet theater, seven tennis courts (hourly fee), pedal boats in the summer, ice-skating in the winter, and an international festival of public theater in June.

The Underground City

Montréal residents aren't speaking cryptically of a sub-culture or a hideout for dissidents when they rave about their Underground City. They literally mean under the ground; 29km of tunnels link Métro stops and form a subterranean village of climate-controlled restaurants and shops—a haven in Montréal's sub-zero winter weather. The ever-expanding network connects railway stations, two bus terminals, restaurants, banks, cinemas, theaters, hotels, two universities, two department stores, 1700 businesses, 1615 housing units, and 1600 boutiques. Somewhat frighteningly hailed by the city as **"the prototype of the city of the future,"** these burrows give the word "suburban" a whole new meaning. The city can be entered from any Métro stop, though you may wish to start your adventure at the **Place Bonaventure,** 900, rue de la Gauchetière Ouest (397-2325; Métro: Bonaventure). Canada's largest commercial building sports a *mélange* of shops, each selling products imported from a different country (shops open daily 9am-9pm). The tourist office supplies city guides including treasure maps of the tunnels and underground attractions.

Back in the underworld, ride on the train that made it all happen, the Métro, to the McGill stop and enjoy some of the Underground City's finest offerings. Here, beneath the **Christ Church Cathedral,** 625, Ste-Catherine Ouest, waits **Promenades de la Cathédrale** (849-9925), one of the Underground's primary shopping complexes. Three blocks east, passing through Centre Eaton, of grand department store fame, the **Place Montréal Trust** is famous for its modern architecture and decadent shopping area. Still, there's no charge for an innocent peek around.

Vieux Montréal (Old Montréal) and Fleuve St-Laurent Islands

In the 17th century, the city of Montréal struggled with Iroquois tribes for control of the area's lucrative fur trade, and erected walls encircling the settlement for defense.

Notre-Dame

Quai
Victoria

Berri

Viger
Annex

St-Denis

Square
Viger

St-Louis

St-Paul

Friponne

Notre-Dame
de Bonsecours

Du Champ-de-Mars

Bonsecours

Musée du
Château-
Ramezay

CHAMP
DE MARS

St-Claude

de la Commune

Quai Jacques Cartier

de la Gauchetière

Viger

Parc Champs-de-Mars

Jacques Cartier

Vieux Palais de
Justice

St-Vincent

Ernest
Cormier
Bldg.

St-Gabriel

**St. Lawrence
River**

Quai King Edward

St-Laurent

Palais
de
Justice

St-Jean Baptiste

QUARTIER

CHINOIS

PLACE
D'ARMES

Expotec &
IMAX

St-Antoine

Place
d'Armes

St-Sulpice

Notre-
Dame
Basilica

de la Capitale

Place
Royal

Quai Alexandra

Palais des
Congrès

Sulpician
Seminary

Pl.
Royale

Banque de
Montreal

Centaur
Theatre

St-François Xavier

**St.
Lawrence
River**

Musée
Arthur
Pascal

St-Jean

St-Nicolas

720

St-Sacrement

Musée
Marc-Aurèle
Fortin

St-Jacques

Notre-Dame

Centre
d'Histoire

de la Commune

SQUARE
VICTORIA

Le Moyne

D'Youville

Grey Nuns'
Gen. Hospital

World
Trade
Center

McGill

N

0   200 yards

0   200 meters

Vieux-Montréal

TO MONTRÉAL
YOUTH HOSTEL

CANADA

Today the remnants of those ramparts do no more than delineate the boundaries of Vieux Montréal, the city's first settlement, on the stretch of river bank between **rues McGill, Notre-Dame**, and **Berri**. The fortified walls that once protected the quarter have crumbled, but the beautiful 17th- and 18th-century mansions of politicos and merchants retain their splendor. Take the Métro to **Place d'Armes**, or get off at Bonaventure and check out **Cathédrale Marie Reine du Monde (Mary Queen of the World Cathedral)** (866-1661), on the block bordered by René-Lévesque, Cathédral, and Metcalf. *(Open daily 7:30am-7:30pm. At least 3-4 masses offered daily.)* A scaled-down replica of St. Peter's in Rome and a rival of Notre-Dame-de-Montréal for grandeur, the church was built in the heart of Montréal's Anglo-Protestant area.

The 19th-century basilica **Notre-Dame-de-Montréal,** 116, rue Notre-Dame Ouest (842-2925), a couple blocks south of the Place d'Armes, towers above the memorial to de Maisonneuve. *(Open in summer daily 7am-8pm; early Sept. to late June M-Sa 8:30am-6pm, Su 1:30pm-6pm. Free guided tours mid-May to early Oct. Shuffle around silently for free; concerts are held here throughout the year.)* Historically a center for the city's Catholic population, the neo-Gothic church once hosted separatist rallies. It seats 4000 and is one of the largest churches in North America. After suffering major fire damage, the Wedding Chapel behind the altar re-opened with an enormous bronze altar.

Next door to Notre-Dame is the **Sulpician Seminary (the seminary of Old Saint-Sulpice),** Montréal's oldest building (built in 1685) and still a functioning seminary. The clock over the facade is the oldest public timepiece in North America and has recorded the passage of over 9.3 billion seconds since it was built in 1700 (do the math). A stroll down rue St-Sulpice will bring you to the old docks along the rue de la Commune, on the banks of the Fleuve St-Laurent. Facing the port, take a left on rue de la Commune to rue Bonsecours. At the corner of rue Bonsecours and the busy rue St-Paul stands the 18th-century **Notre-Dame-de-Bonsecours,** 400, rue St-Paul Est (Métro: Champ-de-Mars), founded on the port as a sailors' refuge by Marguerite Bour-geoys, leader of the first order of non-cloistered nuns. Sailors thankful for their safe pilgrimage presented the nuns and priests with the wooden boat-shaped ceiling lamps in the chapel. The church also has a museum in the basement and a bell tower with a nice view of Vieux Montréal and the Fleuve St-Laurent. From spring 1999, the church will display recently unearthed artifacts discovered at the church.

Opening onto rue St-Paul is **Place Jacques Cartier,** site of Montréal's oldest market. Here the modern European character of Montréal is most evident; cafes line the square, and street artists strut their stuff during the summer. The grand **Château Ramezay,** 280, rue Notre-Dame Est (861-3708; Métro: Champ-de-Mars), built in 1705 to house the French viceroy, houses a museum of Québecois, British, and American 18th-century artifacts. *(Open daily 10am-6pm; Oct. to early June Tu-Su 10am-4:30pm. $5, students and seniors $3, under 6 free. Guided tours available by reservation. Partial wheelchair access; assis-tance may be required.)* The **Vieux Palais de Justice,** built in 1856 in Place Vaugeulin, stands across from City Hall. **Rue St-Jacques** in the Old City, established in 1687, is Montréal's Wall Street.

There are many good reasons to venture out to **Ile Ste-Hélène,** an island in the Fleuve St-Laurent just off the coast of Vieux Montréal. The best is **La Ronde** (872-6222 or 800-797-4537; Métro: Ile Ste-Hélène or bus #167), Montréal's popular amusement park, especially in the afternoons, when unlimited passes are available. *(Open June to early Sept. Su-Th 11am-11pm, F-Sa 11am-midnight; mid-May to mid-June from 10am. Tickets start at $26.)* From late May to July on Thursday and either Saturday or Sunday at 10pm, La Ronde hosts the **International Fireworks Competition** (872-8714). If you don't want to pay the park's steep fee, sky-gaze from crowded Pont Jacques-Cartier or Mont-Royal, above the city.

Le Vieux Fort ("The Old Fort," also known as the **Stewart Museum,** 861-6701; Metro: Ile Ste-Hélène), was built in the 1820s to defend Canada's inland waterways. *(Open daily 10am-6pm; Sept. to mid-Oct daily 10am-5pm; mid-Oct. to mid-May W-M 10am-5pm. $6; students, seniors, and ages 7-17 $4; families $12. 3 military parades daily late June to late Aug.)* Now primarily a military museum, the fort displays artifacts and costumes detailing Canadian colonial history.

CANADA

The other island in Montréal's Parc des Iles is **Ile Notre-Dame**, where **Casino de Montréal,** 1, ave. de Casino (392-2746 or 800-363-7777), awaits those who wish to push their luck on nearly 2000 slot machines. *(Open 24hr. Free. Min. age 18 to enter and to gamble. Parking free, with shuttles from the parking lot every 10-15min.)*

Whether swollen with spring run-off or frozen over during the winter, the **Fleuve St-Laurent (St. Lawrence River)** can be one of Montréal's most thrilling attractions, although the whirlpools and 15 ft. waves of the **Lachine Rapids** once precluded river travel. No longer—now, 1hr. **Old Port of Montréal cruises** (842-3871) depart twice a day from the clock tower pier March through November ($23; discounts for students, seniors, and families). **Jet-boating tours** of the Lachine Rapids (284-9607) leave five times per day from the Old Port. *(May to mid-Oct. 10am-6pm. 1¼ hr. $49, seniors $44, ages 13-19 $39, ages 6-12 $29.)* For a more intimate introduction to the river, **Rafting Montréal,** 8912, bd. LaSalle (767-2230 or 1-800-324-7238), in LaSalle, can help. *(Rafting $34, students and seniors $28, ages 8-12 $17; hydrojet $40/$30/$20. Open May-Aug. or Sept. depending on weather. Trip frequency decreases in off season. Reservations necessary.)* Two 1½hr. (2½hr. with preparation and travel) whitewater trips are available, at differing levels of shock-induction. They also offer 1½hr. "hydrojet" trips, and will send a shuttle to pick you up downtown.

ENTERTAINMENT

Like much of the city, Vieux Montréal is best seen at night. Street performers, artists, and *chansonniers* in various *brasseries* set the tone for lively summer evenings of clapping, stomping, and singing along. The real fun goes down on **St-Paul,** near the corner of St-Vincent. For a sweet Sunday in the park, **Parc Jeanne-Mance,** with bongos, dancing, and handicrafts, can't be missed (May-Sept. noon-7pm).

The city has a wide variety of theatrical groups. The **Théâtre du Nouveau Monde,** 84, Ste-Catherine Ouest (866-8667; Métro: Place-des-Arts) and the **Théâtre du Rideau Vert,** 4664, rue St-Denis (844-1793), stage *québecois* works (all productions in French). The **Centaur Theatre,** 453, rue St-François-Xavier (288-1229, ticket info 288-3161; Métro: Place-d'Armes), has English-language plays, performed mainly from September through May. The city's exciting **Place des Arts,** 260, bd. de Maisonneuve Ouest (842-2112 for tickets), houses the **Opéra de Montréal** (985-2258), the **Montréal Symphony Orchestra** (842-9951), and **Les Grands Ballets Canadiens** (849-8681). The **National Theatre School of Canada,** 5030, rue St-Denis (842-7954), stages excellent student productions during the academic year. **Théâtre Saint-Denis,** 1594, rue St-Denis (849-4211), hosts traveling productions like *Cats* and *Les Misérables.* Theater-goers peruse **Calendar of Events** (available at the tourist office and reprinted in daily newspapers), or call **Telspec** for ticket info (790-2222; open M-Sa 9am-9pm, Su noon-6pm). **Admission Ticket Network** (790-1245 or 800-361-4595) also has tickets for various events (open daily 8am-midnight; credit card required).

Maybe it's the weather, but *montréalais* are rabid hockey fans—calling well in advance is necessary to reserve tickets. Between October and April, be sure to attend a **Montréal Canadiens** hockey game at the new **Molson Centre,** 1250, de la Gauchetière Ouest (Métro: Bonaventure), where **Les Habitants** (a nickname for the Canadiens) play. Dress at games can be quite formal; jacket and ties are not uncommon. The t-shirt-clad, jeans-ripped, hat-on-backwards, beer-drinking American-style fan is somewhat unwelcome here (for ticket info, call 790-1245).

Montréalais don't like to just watch; in early June, the 1-day **Tour de l'île,** a 64km circuit of the island, is the largest cycling event in the world, with 45,000 mostly amateur cyclists pedaling their wares. (Call 521-8356 by Apr. if you wanna be a player. Separate days for adults and children.)

NIGHTLIFE, NIGHTLIFE, AND MORE NIGHTLIFE

Montréal has some hip, hop, happening nightlife. Even in the dead of winter, the bars are full. Should you choose to ignore the massive neon lights flashing "films érotiques" and "château du sexe," you can find lots and lots of less scantily clad nightlife in Québec's largest city—either in **brasseries** (with food, wine, and music), in **pubs**

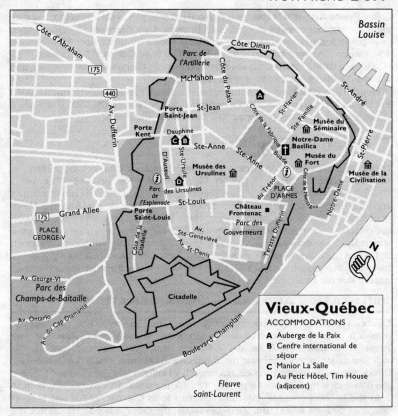

Vieux-Québec

ACCOMMODATIONS

A Auberge de la Paix
B Centre international de séjour
C Manior La Salle
D Au Petit Hôtel, Tim House (adjacent)

(more hanging out and less eating), or the multitude of **dance clubs.** In Montréal's **gay village** there are plenty of clubs for men—lesbian clubs are less common, but there are a few (Métro: Papineau or Beaudry).

Though intermingled with some of the city's hottest dance venues, the establishments of **rue Ste-Catherine Ouest** and nearby side streets tend to feature drink as the primary entertainment (Métro: Peel). Downstairs at 1107, rue Ste-Catherine Ouest, the **Peel Pub** (844-6769) provides live rock bands and good, cheap food nightly, but more noted are its exceptional drink prices. Happy hour (M-F 3-7pm) floods the joint with $6 pitchers and 9¢ wings. Another location is at 890, bd. de Maisonneuve Est (844-8715). Both are open daily 11am-3am. For slightly older and more subdued drinking buddies, the side streets and the touristy English strongholds around rue Crescent and Bishop (Métro: Guy) make bar-hopping a must. **Déjà-Vu,** 1224, Bishop (866-0512), near Ste-Catherine, has live bands each night at 10pm, amid an excellent atmosphere (happy hour daily 3-8pm; no cover; open daily 3pm-3am). **Sir Winston Churchill's,** 1459, Crescent (288-0616), is another hotspot, with 2-for-1 beer during the week from 5-8pm (no cover; open daily 11:30am-3am). If your baby's left you, **Les Beaux Esprits Blues Bar**, 2073 St. Denis north of Maisonneuve (844-0882; Métro: Sherbrooke), has live music—hours and cover vary. Caffeinated fun and colorful locals await at **Kilo,** 1491, St-Catherine, near the corner of Beaudry St. (Métro: Beaudry). The coffee's good, and if you want a late snack, the sandwiches ($5.50) are great. (Open until midnight M-F, Sa-Su 1am.) **Sky Club,** 1474, St-Catherine (529-6969), is the nightspot of choice, and with good reason—the music is jumping, and there are numerous special theme nights and parties. Enter at 1320 Alexander de Sève. (Cover $2. Open daily 11am-3am.)

Rue Prince Arthur at St-Laurent is devoted solely to pedestrians who mix and mingle at the outdoor cafes by day and clubs by night. **Café Campus,** 57, Prince Arthur (844-1010), features live rock and other genres (cover for dance floor $3, live music $5-15; open M-Sa 7pm-3am, Su 8:30pm-3am). **The Shed Café,** 3515, St-Laurent (842-0220; open daily 11am-3am), hosts a trendy clientele, charges little or no cover, and is located within a few blocks of St-Laurent.

French nightlife also resides in the open-air cafés on **rue St-Denis** (Métro: UQAM). Rockin' dance club by night, **Bar Passeport,** 4156, rue St-Denis (842-6063), at Rachel, doubles as a store by day (cover $2.50-4; open daily 10am-3am).

■ Québec City

Dubbed the "Gibraltar of America" because of the stone escarpments and military fortifications protecting the port, Québec City (generally shortened to just "Québec") sits high on the rocky heights of Cape Diamond where the Fleuve St-Laurent narrows and joins the St. Charles River. The name Québec, in fact, is derived from the Algonquin word *Kebek,* which means "place where the river narrows." Passing through the portals of North America's only walled city is like stepping into the past; narrow streets and horse-drawn carriages greet visitors to the Old City, and there are enough sights and museums to satisfy even the most voracious history buff. Along with the historical attachment, Canada's oldest city boasts a thriving French culture—never assume that the locals speak English.

ORIENTATION AND PRACTICAL INFORMATION

Québec's main thoroughfares run through both the Old City *(Vieux Québec)* and outside it, generally parallel in an east-west direction. Within **Vieux Québec,** the main streets are **St-Louis, Ste-Anne,** and **St-Jean.** Most streets in Vieux Québec are one-way, the major exceptions being rue d'Auteuil and Dufferin, which border the walls (inside Vieux Québec and outside, respectively). Dufferin splits into 440 and 175, and rue d'Auteuil is the best bet for parking. Outside the walls of Vieux Québec, both St-Jean and St-Louis continue (St-Jean eventually joins Chemin Ste-Foy and St-Louis becomes **Grande Allée**). **Bd. René-Lévesque,** the other major street outside the walls, runs between St-Jean and St-Louis. The Basse-ville (lower town) is separated from the Haute-ville (upper town, Old Québec) by an abrupt cliff roughly paralleled by rue St-Vallier Est.

Airport: The airport (692-0770) is far out of town and inaccessible by public transport. Taxi to downtown $22. By car, turn right onto Rte. de l'aéroport and then take either bd. Wilfred-Hamel or, beyond it, Autoroute 440 to get into the city. **La Québecois** (570-5379) runs a shuttle service between the airport and the major hotels of the city. (M-F 6 per day to and from the airport, 8:45am-9:45pm; Sa 7 per day 9am-8:45pm; Su 7 per day 9am-11:35pm. $9, under 12 free.)

Trains: VIA Rail, 450, rue de la Gare du Palais (692-3940), in Québec City. To Montréal (3hr.; M-F 4 per day, Sa-Su 3 per day; $54) and Toronto ($134). 40% discount with 7-day advance purchase. Open daily 6am-8:30pm. Nearby stations at 3255, ch. de la Gare in Ste-Foy (open M-F 6am-9pm, Sa-Su 7:30am-9pm) and 5995, St-Laurent, Autoroute 20 Lévis. Open Th-M 4-5am and 8-10:30pm, Tu 4-5am, W 8-10:30pm. Reservations 800-561-3949. Information for all stations 800-835-3037.

Buses: Orlean Express, 320, Abraham Martin (525-3000). Open daily 5:30am-1am. Outlying stations at 2700, ave. Laurier, in Ste-Foy (650-4925; open M-Sa 6am-1am, Su 7am-1am), and 63, Hwy. Trans-Canada Ouest (Hwy. 132), in Lévis (837-5805; open daily 6am-2am). To: Montréal (3hr., every hr. 6am-9pm and 11pm, $32); Ste-Anne-de-Beaupré (25min., 2 per day, $5); and the U.S. via Montréal or Sherbrooke.

Public Transportation: Commission de transport de la Communauté Urbaine de Québec (CTCUQ), 270, rue des Rocailles (627-2511 for route and schedule info). Open M-F 6:30am-10pm, Sa-Su 8am-10pm. Buses operate daily 6am-1am, although individual routes vary. $2, students $1.45, seniors and children $1.30; advance-purchase tickets $1.60/$1/$1; under 5 free.

Taxis: Coop Taxis Québec, 525-5191. $2.25 base fare, $1 per additional km.

Driver/Rider Service: Allo-Stop, 467, rue St-Jean (522-0056), will match you with a driver heading for Montréal ($15) or Ottawa ($29). Must be a member ($6 per year, drivers $7). Open W-F 8am-7pm, Sa-Tu 8am-6pm.

Car Rental: Pelletier, 900, bd. Pierre Bertrand (681-0678). $52 per day; 250km free, 15¢ per additional km. Must be 21 with credit card deposit of 20%. Open M-F 7:30am-8pm, Sa-Su 8am-4pm.

Bike Rental: Vélo Passe-Sport, 77A, rue Ste-Anne (692-3643). 1hr. $7, 4hr. $15, 1 day $21. Credit card deposit of $40 required. Open May-Oct. daily 8am-9pm.

Visitor Info: Centre d'information de l'office du tourisme et des congrés de la Communauté urbaine de Québec, "that place with an uncommonly long name," 60, rue d'Auteuil (649-2608; http://www.quebec-region.cuq.qc.ca), in the Old City. Accommodations listings, brochures, free maps, cheery bilingual advice, and free local calls. Ask for the annual *Greater Québec Area Guide.* Open daily 8:30am-7pm; Thanksgiving (mid-Oct.) to May 9am-5pm. Dealing primarily with provincial tourism, **Maison du tourisme de Québec,** 12, rue Ste-Anne (800-363-7777; http://www.tourisme.gouv.qc.ca), offers accommodations listings for all of Quebec and free road and city maps. Budget Rent-a-Car and some bus tours have desks here. Open daily 8:30am-7:30pm; early Sept. to mid-June 9am-5pm.

Hotlines and Crisis Centers: Tél-Aide distress center, 686-2433. Operates daily noon-midnight. **Viol-Secours (sexual assault line),** 522-2120. Counselors on duty M-F 9am-4pm and on-call 24hr. **Center for Suicide Prevention,** 529-0015. Operates daily 8am-midnight. **Info-Santé,** 648-2626, handles bi-gay-lesbian concerns.

Weather: 640-2736. **Tides:** 648-7293.

Emergency: Police, 911 (city); 623-6262 (province). **Info-santé (medical info),** 648-2626. 24hr. service with info from qualified nurses.

Post Office: 3, rue Buade (694-6102). **Postal code:** G1R 2J0. Also at 300, rue St-Paul (694-6176). **Postal code:** G1K 3W0. Both open M-F 8am-8pm; Oct.-May 8am-5:45pm. **Area code:** 418.

ACCOMMODATIONS AND CAMPGROUNDS

For **Bed and Breakfast** referrals, Montréal-based **Breakfast á Montréal** (see p. 869), or **Le Transit,** 1050, ave. Turnbull, Québec City G1R 2X8 (tel./fax 647-6802; call 8amnoon or 4-9pm) will help. Singles run $50, and doubles $65-75. Hosts are usually bilingual. If parking is a problem (usually the case in Old Québec) and you must make use of the underground parking areas, ask your host about discount parking passes. Most places offer them, which means paying $6 rather than $10 for a 24hr. pass.

Auberge de la Paix, 31, rue Couillard (694-0735). Take St-Jean into Vieux Quebec, and take Couillard when it branches left. While it lacks many facilities, the friendly staff and an open, casual atmosphere (no locks on the doors) make it worthwhile. Co-ed rooms. 58 beds; 2-8 per room, but most have 3-4. Offers easy access to the restaurants and bars on rue St-Jean. Look for the big peace sign above this "Peace Hostel." Beds $18. Linen $2. Continental breakfast included (8-10am). Curfew 2am with all-day access. Kitchen open all day. Bike rental $20 per day or $12 for 4hrs. Reservations necessary July-Aug.

Centre international de séjour (HI-C), 19, rue Ste-Ursule (694-0755), 1 block north of rue St-Jean at Dauphine. Follow Côte d'Abraham uphill from the bus station until it joins ave. Dufferin. Turn left on St-Jean, pass through the walls, and walk uphill, to your right, on Ste-Ursule. If driving, follow St-Louis into the Old City and take the 2nd left past the walls onto Ste-Ursule. Diverse, young clientele and fabulous location. 10- to 16-bed dorms $14, 3- to 8-bed dorms $15.40, 2-bed room $40; Canadian nonmembers $16/$17.40/$44; nonmembers must also buy an international stamp ($4.60). 243 beds. Laundry, microwave, TV, pool, ping-pong tables, living room, kitchen, cafeteria. Breakfast 7:30-10am (continental $3.75, full breakfast $4.50).

Check-out 10am. Reception noon. Lockout 11pm, but the front desk will let you in if you flash your key. Usually full July-Aug.; make reservations or arrive early.

Au Petit Hôtel, 3, ruelle des Ursulines (694-0965), just off of rue Ste-Ursule. This tidy little hotel is a great deal for 2 people. TV, free local phone, private bath, and refrigerator in each room. May-Oct. $60-85 for 1 or 2 occupants, continental breakfast included; Nov.-May $45-65. Audaciously combines a downtown location with free parking in winter ($5 May-Oct.).

Montmartre Canadien, 1675, ch. St-Louis (686-0867), Sillery, on the outskirts of the city, in the Maison du Pelerin; a small white house behind the main building at 1669. Take bus #25 or 11. Clean house in a religious sanctuary run by Assumptionist monks overlooking the Fleuve St-Laurent. Relaxed, almost ascetic setting. Mostly used by groups. Dorm-style singles $17; doubles $30; triples $42. Common showers. Reserve 2-3 weeks in advance.

Manoir La Salle, 18, rue Ste-Ursule (692-9953), opposite the youth hostel. The clean private rooms in this ornate Victorian mansion fill quickly, especially in summer. Singles $30; doubles $45-65. Reservations necessary.

Tim House, 84, rue Ste-Louis (694-0776). Adjacent to Au Petit and run by the same folks. A lovely B&B. 3rd fl. rooms have shared baths; a delectable breakfast is included. Rooms $35-60, depending on the season. Parking $5.

You can obtain a list of nearby **campgrounds** from the **Maison du Tourisme de Québec** (see **Practical Information,** p. 878), or write to **Tourisme Québec,** c.p. 979, Montréal, PQ H3C 2W3 (800-363-7777; open daily 9am-5pm). A good camping option is **Municipal de Beauport** (666-2228), Beauport. Take Autoroute 40E, and get off at Exit 321 at rue Labelle onto Hwy. 369, turn left, and follow the signs marked "camping." Bus #55 to 800 will also take you to this 135-site campground on a hill over the Montmorency River. A swimming pool, canoes ($8 per hr.), showers ($1 per. 6min.), and laundry facilities are available. ($18, with hookup $23; per week $108/$138. Open June to early Sept.)

L'HAUTE CUISINE

In general, rue Buade, St-Jean, and Cartier, as well as the **Place Royale** and **Petit Champlain** areas, offer the widest selection of food and drink. The **Grande Allée,** a 2km strip of restaurants on either side of the street, might seem like heaven to the hungry, but its steep prices make it a place to visit rather than to eat.

Your best bet for a simple and affordable meal is not just to line up behind one of the many fast-food joints that proliferate throughout the city. Traditional *québecois* food is not only appetizing, but usually economical. One of the most filling yet inexpensive meals is a *croque-monsieur,* a large, open-faced sandwich with ham and melted cheese (about $5), usually served with salad. *Québecois* French onion soup, slathered with melted cheese, is not to be missed. Generally, it is served with either bats of French bread or *tourtière,* a thick meat pie. Other specialties include the *crêpe,* stuffed differently to serve as either an entree or as a dessert. The **Casse-Crêpe Breton,** 1136, St-Jean, offers many choices of fillings in their "make your own combination" crepes for dinner ($3-6), as well as scrumptious dessert options ($3-4; open daily 7:30am-midnight). Try to locate a French-Canadian "sugar pie," made with brown sugar and butter. The quaint French bakery **Pâtisserie au Palet d'Or,** 60, rue Garneau (692-2488), bursts with culinary excellence—$3.30 will win you a salmon sandwich and $1.60 a golden baguette here (open daily 7am-9pm). Some of these restaurants do not have non-smoking sections.

Le Café Buade, 31, rue Buade (692-3909), is renowned for its succulent prime rib, though it's a tad *cher* ($16-19). For those short on money, breakfast (specials for $4) and lunch specials ($11) are large and delicious. Open daily 7am-midnight.

Le Couhen Dingue, 46, bd. Champlain (692-2013), serves a delectable Chocolate Pear Pie ($4). The food ain't bad, either. Open June-Aug. M-Th 7am-midnight, F 7am-1am, Sa-Su 8am-1am; Sept.-May M-F 7am-11pm, Sa-Su 8am-11pm.

La Fleur de Lotus, 38, Côte de la Fabrique (692-4286), across from the Hôtel de Ville. Cheerful and unpretentious. Thai, Cambodian, Vietnamese, and Japanese dishes $9-14, soups for $3. Open M-F 11:30am-10:30pm, Sa-Su 5-11pm.

Chez Temporel, 25, rue Couillard (694-1813). Stay off the tourist path while remaining within your budget at this genuine *café québecois*, discreetly tucked in a side alley off rue St-Jean, near the Auberge de la Paix. Besides the usual café staples (sandwiches around $7, complete dinners $17-20), it offers exotic spirits ($4.50). Open daily 7am-2am.

Restaurant Liban, 23, rue d'Auteuil (694-1888), off rue St-Jean. Great café for lunch or a late-night bite. Tabouleh and hummus plates $3.50, both with pita bread. Excellent falafel ($4.50) and baklava ($2). Open daily 9am-4:30am.

SIGHTS

Inside the Walls

Confined within walls built by the English, Vieux Québec (Old City) contains most of the city's historic attractions. Monuments are clearly marked and explained; still, you'll get more out of the town if you consult the *Greater Québec Area Tourist Guide*, which contains a walking tour of the Old City (available from all tourist offices; see **Practical Information,** above). It takes 1-2 days to explore Vieux Québec by foot, but you'll learn more than on the many guided bus tours.

Climbing to the top of **Cap Diamant** (Cape Diamond) for a view of the city is a good way to start a walking tour. Just north is **Citadelle,** the largest North American fortification still guarded by troops—who knows why? Anyway, don't attack it. Visitors can witness the **changing of the guard** and the **beating of the retreat.** *(Guard changes mid-June to early Sept. daily 10am. Retreat July-Aug. daily 7pm. Citadelle open daily 9am-7pm. $5, seniors $4, ages 7-17 $2.50.)* Tours are given every 55min.

Retreating from the Citadelle is the **Promenade des Gouverneurs,** which leads downhill to **Terrasse Dufferin.** Built in 1838 by Lord Durham, this popular promenade offers excellent views of the Fleuve St-Laurent, the Côte de Beaupré (the "Avenue Royale" Hwy.), and Ile d'Orléans across the channel. The walkway passes the landing spot of the European settlers, marked by the **Samuel de Champlain Monument.** Here Champlain secured French settlement by building Fort St-Louis in 1620, earning him the title of Quebec's founder. Today, the promenade offers endless performers of all flavors—clowns, bagpipers, and banjo and clarinet duos.

At the bottom of the promenade, towering above the *terrasse* next to rue St-Louis, sits the immense baroque **Château Frontenac** (691-2166) built in 1893 on the ruins of two previous châteaux and named for Comte Frontenac, governor of *Nouvelle-France. (Tours leave daily on the hr. May to mid-Oct. 10am-6pm, mid-Oct. to Apr. Sa-Su 12:30-5pm. $6, seniors $5, ages 6-16 $3.50.)* The château was the site of two historic meetings between Churchill and Roosevelt during World War II, and is now a luxury hotel with architecture evoking the 15th century. The hotel is the budget traveler's nemesis, but you can still take a guided tour of Québec's pride and joy.

Near the Château Frontenac, between rue St-Louis and rue Ste-Anne, lies the Place d'Armes. *Calèches* (horse-drawn buggies) that congregate here in summer provide a certain pungent odor. A carriage will give you a tour of the city for $56, but your feet will do the same for free. From the **Place d'Armes,** the pedestrian and artist-choked rue du Trésor leads to **Notre-Dame Basilica** (694-0665) and rue Buade. *(Open M-F 7:30am-2pm, Sa-Su 7:30am-4pm; Nov.-Apr. daily 7:30am-9pm. Tours in multiple languages, mid-May to mid-Oct. daily 9am-2:30pm.)* The clock and outer walls date back to 1647; the rest of the church has been rebuilt twice, most recently after a fire in 1922. In addition to the ornate gold altar and impressive religious artifacts, the basilica is home to a 3D historical sound and light show called **Feux Sacres**—Sacred Fire (694-0665; call for seasonal showtimes; $7, ages 12-17 $5). Notre-Dame, with its odd mix of architectural styles, contrasts sharply with the adjacent **Seminary of Québec,** an excellent example of 17th-century *québecois* architecture. Founded in 1663 as a Jesuit training ground, the seminary became the *Université de Laval* in 1852. The **Musée de l'Amerique Française,** 9, rue de l'Université (643-2158), lies nearby. *(Open daily 10am-5:30pm; Sept.-June Tu-Su 10am-5pm. $3, students and seniors $2, ages 12-16 $1.)* The museum offers artistic, multimedia presentations on Quebec's history. Other highlights include a beautiful chapel and an Egyptian mummy (how'd he get here?). **The Musée du Fort,** 10, rue Ste-Anne (692-2175), presents a corny sound and light show that narrates the history of Québec City and the series of six battles fought between 1629 and 1775 for control of it (open daily 10am-8pm; in winter 10am-5pm. $6.25, seniors $5.25, students $4).

The **post office,** 3, rue Buade, now called the **Louis St-Laurent Bldg.** (after Canada's second French Canadian Prime Minister), was built in the late 1890s and towers over a statue of Monseigneur de Laval, the first bishop of Québec. Across the Côte de la Montagne, a lookout park provides an impressive view of the Fleuve St-Laurent. A statue of Georges-Etienne Cartier, one of the key French-Canadian fathers of the Confederation, presides over the park.

Outside the Walls

From the old city, the **promenade des Gouverneurs** and its 310 steps lead to the **Plains of Abraham,** otherwise known as the **Parc des Champs-de-Bataille.** General James Wolfe's British troops and General de Montcalm's French forces clashed here in 1759; both leaders died during the decisive 15min. confrontation, won by the British. The **Plains of Abraham Interpretation Centre** (648-5641), in the center of the park, has exhibits on the battle.

At the far end of the Plains of Abraham, you'll find the **Musée du Québec,** 1, ave. Wolfe-Montcalm (643-2150), housing a collection of *québecois* paintings, sculptures, decorative arts, and prints. The **Gérard Morisset Pavilion,** which displays the unlikely grouping of Jacques Cartier, Neptune, and Gutenberg, houses the Musée's permanent collection. The renovated old "prison of the plains," the **Baillarce Pavilion,** incarcerates temporary exhibits. *(Open Th-Tu 10am-5:45pm, W 10am-9:45pm; early Sept. to May Tu and Th-Su 11am-5:45pm, W 11am-8:45pm. $5.75, students $2.75, seniors $4.75, handicapped and escorts $3.75, under 16 free. Sept.-May W free.)* At the corner of la Grande Allée and rue Georges VI, right outside Porte St-Louis, stands **l'Assemblée Nationale** (643-7239), built in the style of Louis XIII's and completed in 1886. *(Free 30min. tours late June to early Sept. M-F 9am-4:30pm, Sa-Su 10am-4:30pm; hrs. vary in winter. Call ahead to ensure a space.)* View debates from the visitors gallery. Anglophones and Francophones have recourse to simultaneous translation earphones.

A newly repaired **funiculaire** (cable car; 692-1132) connects Upper Town with Lower Town and Place Royale, the oldest section of Québec (operates June to early Sept. daily 7:30am-midnight; $1, under 6 free.) This way leads to **rue Petit-Champlain,** the oldest road on the continent. Many old buildings along the street have been restored or renovated and now house craft shops, boutiques, cafés, and restaurants. The **Café-Théâtre Le Petit Champlain,** 68, rue Petit-Champlain (692-2631), presents *québecois* music, singing, and theater. From here, just continue west (right, from the bottom of the *funiculaire)* to reach the Plains of Abraham.

From the bottom of the *funiculaire,* you can also take rue Sous-le-Fort and then turn left to reach **Place Royale,** built in 1608, where you'll find the small but beautiful **l'Eglise Notre-Dame-des-Victoires** (692-1650), the oldest church in Canada, dating from the glorious year of 1688. *(Open M-Sa 9am-5pm, Su 1:30-5pm, closed on Sa if a rite of passage is occurring; mid-Oct. to Apr. M-Sa 9am-noon, Su 7:30am-1pm. Free guided tours May 1 to mid-Oct.)* The houses surrounding the square have been restored to late-18th-century styles. Considered one of the birthplaces of French civilization in North America, the Place Royale is now the site of fantastic outdoor summer theater and concerts. Giant phone booths, satellites, videos, and recreated moon landings celebrate Québec's past, present, and future at the **Musée de la Civilisation,** 85, rue Dalhousie (643-2158), also along the river. *(Open daily 10am-7pm; early Sept. to late June Tu and Th-Su 10am-5pm, W 10am-9pm. $7, students $4, seniors $6, ages 12-16 $2; free Tu, except in summer.)* The museum targets a French Canadian audience, but English tours and exhibit notes are available.

If you're interested in seeing something decidedly less historical, check out 3500 specimens at the **Aquarium,** 1675, Ave. des Hotels (659-5264), accessible by bus #25. *(Open daily 9am-5pm. $9.50, students $6, seniors $8.50, ages 4-13 $4.50. Seal shows daily at 10:15am and 3:15pm.)*

ENTERTAINMENT AND NIGHTLIFE

The raucous **Winter Carnival** (626-3716) breaks the tedium of northern winters and lifts spirits in mid-February; the **Summer Festival** (692-4540) boasts a number of free outdoor concerts in mid-July. Throughout the summer, the **Plein Art** (694-0260) exhibition floods the Pigeonnier on Grande-Allée with arts and crafts. **Les nuits Black,** Québec's burgeoning jazz festival, bebops the city for 2 weeks in late June. But the most festive day of the year is June 24, **la Fête nationale du Québec** (St-Jean-Baptiste Day; 681-7011), a celebration of *québecois* culture with free concerts, a bonfire, fireworks, and five million roaring drunk acolytes of John the Baptist.

The Grande Allée's many restaurants are interspersed with *Bar Discothèques,* where 20-something crowds gather. **Chez Dagobert,** 600 Grande Allée (522-0393), saturates its two dance floors with plentiful food and drink; it is *the* place to be seen (no cover; outside bar open daily 3pm-3am, inside club 10pm-3am). Down the block at **O'Zone,** 570 Grande Allée (529-7932), the outside atmosphere disappears into a slower and more pub-like club (open daily 11am-3am).

Québec City's young, visible punk contingent clusters around rue St-Jean. **La Fourmi Atomik,** 33, rue d'Auteuil (694-1473), features underground rock, with reggae-only Mondays and New Wave Wednesdays (18+; no cover; open daily 1pm-3am; Oct.-May 2pm-3am). At **L'Ostradamus,** 29, rue Couillard (694-9560), you can listen to live jazz and eavesdrop on deep discourse in a smoke-drenched pseudo-spiritual ambience with artsy Thai decor (no cover; open daily 9pm-3am). A more traditional Québec evening awaits at **Les Yeux Bleux,** 1117½, rue St-Jean (694-9118), a local favorite where *chansonniers* perform nightly (no cover; open daily 8pm-3am). The gay scene in Québec City is neither huge nor hard to find. **Le Ballon Rouge,** 811, St-Jean (647-9227), near the walls of the Old City, is a popular dance club where dimly lit pool tables coexist with neon rainbows (no cover; open daily 5pm-3am).

■ Near Québec City

Ile-d'Orléans on the St-Laurent is untouched by Québec City's public transport system, but its proximity to Québec (about 10km downstream) makes it an ideal side trip by car or bike. Take Autoroute 440 Est, and cross over the only bridge leading to the island (Pont de l'Ile). A tour of the island covers 64km. Originally called *Ile de Bacchus* because of the multitudinous wild grapes fermenting here, the Ile-d'Orléans remains a sparsely populated retreat of several small villages and endless strawberry fields. The **Manoir Mauvide-Genest,** 1451, ch. Royal (829-2630), in St-Jean, dates from 1734, and is now a private museum flaunting crafts and traditional colonial furniture. *(Open June to mid-Oct. daily 10am-5pm. $4, students and seniors $2.50, under 14 $2.)*

Exiting Ile-d'Orléans, turn right (east) onto Hwy. 138 (bd. Ste-Anne) to view the splendid **Chute Montmorency** (Montmorency Falls), which are substantially taller than Niagara Falls. In winter, vapors from the falls freeze completely to form a frozen shadow of the running falls. About 20km along Hwy. 138 lies **Ste-Anne-de-Beaupré** (Orlean Express buses link it to Québec City for $5). This small town's entire *raison d'être* is the famous **Basilique Ste-Anne-de Beaupré,** 10018, ave. Royale (827-3781). *(Open daily early May to mid-Sept. 6am-9:30pm.)* Since 1658, this double-spired basilica has contained a miraculous statue and the alleged forearm bone of St. Anne (mother of the Virgin Mary). Every year, more than one million pilgrims come here in the hopes that their prayers will be answered—legend has it that some have been quite successful. In the winter (Nov.-Apr.), Ste-Anne has some of the best skiing in the province (lift tickets $41 per day). Contact **Parc du Mont Ste-Anne,** P.O. Box 400 (827-4561), Beaupré, G0A IE0, which has a 625m/2050 ft. vertical drop and night skiing to boot. You will also find a **gondola** (800-463-1568), which climbs to 800m, affording a fabulous view of the St-Laurent River valley. *(Runs daily in summer 10am-4:45pm; in ski season 10am-9pm. $9, ages 14-20 $7, seniors and ages 7-13 $5.)*

Ontario

Claimed by French explorer Samuel de Champlain in 1613, Ontario soon attracted hordes of Scottish and Irish immigrants fleeing hostility and famine. These immigrants asserted control in 1763 during the Seven Years' War, after a takeover of New France. Twenty years later, a flood of Loyalist emigres from the newly formed United States streamed into the province, fortifying its Anglo character. Now a political counterbalance to French Québec, this populous central province raises the ire of peripheral regions of Canada due to its high concentration of power and wealth. In the south, world-class Toronto shines—multicultural, enormous, vibrant, clean, and generally safe. Yuppified suburbs, an occasional college town, and farms surround this sprawling metropolis. In the east, the national capital Ottawa sits on Ontario's border with Québec. To the north, layers of cottage country and ski resorts give way to a pristine wilderness that is as much French and Native Canadian as it is British.

PRACTICAL INFORMATION

Capital: Toronto.

Visitor Info: Customer Service Branch of the **Ontario Ministry of Culture, Tourism, and Recreation** (800-668-2746; http://www.travelinx.com). Open June-Aug. M-F 9am-8pm, Sa-Su 10am-5pm; Sept.-May M-F 9am-6pm, Sa-Su 10am-5pm. Send written requests to **Tourism Ontario,** 1 Concord Gate, 9th fl., Dawn Mills, ON M3C 3NC. Free brochures, guides, maps, and info on special events.

Emergency: 911.

Drinking Age: 19.

Time Zone: Eastern. **Postal Abbreviation:** ON.

Provincial Sales Tax: 8%, plus 7% GST.

■ Toronto

Once a prim and proper Victorian city where even window-shopping was prohibited on the Sabbath, the city dubbed the world's most multicultural by the United Nations is today one of the hippest and most accessible urban areas in North America. Toronto has spent millions in recent decades on spectacular public works projects: the world's tallest "free-standing" structure (the CN tower), the biggest retractable roof (the Sky Dome), outstanding lakefront development, and significant sponsorship of arts and museums. Cosmetically, Toronto's skyscrapers and neatly gridded streets aspire to the urban grandeur of New York, a resemblance which has not gone unnoticed—or unexploited—by Hollywood. But New York it is not, as two film crews learned the hard way. One crew, after dirtying a Toronto street to make it look more like a typical "American" avenue, went on coffee break and returned only to find their set spotless again, swept by the ever-vigilant city maintenance department. Another crew, filming an attack scene, was twice interrupted by Torontonians hopping out of their cars to "rescue" the damsel in distress.

ORIENTATION

The city maps available at info booths only cover downtown. For an extended stay or travel outside the city center, a better bet is to buy the invaluable orangish *Downtown and Metro Toronto Visitor's Map Guide* from a drug store or tourist shop ($2.50). The *Ride Guide,* free at all TTC stations and tourism info booths (see **Practical Information,** below), shows the subway and bus routes for the metro area.

Toronto's streets lie in a grid pattern. Addresses on north-south streets increase towards the north, away from Lake Ontario. **Yonge St.** is the main north-south route, dividing the city and the streets perpendicular to it into east and west. Numbering for both sides starts at Yonge St. and increases as you move away in either direction. West of Yonge St., the main arteries are **Bay St., University Ave., Spadina Ave.,** and

Ontario and Upstate New York

CANADA

USA

QUÉBEC

VERMONT

MASS.

CONN.

Montpelier

Burlington

Hartford

New York City

NJ

Montréal

Lake Champlain

Hudson River

Albany

Lake Placid

Lake George

Great Sacandaga Lake

ADIRONDACKS PARK

CATSKILLS PRESERVE

Hull

Ottawa

Cornwall

St. Lawrence R.

Alexandria

Clayton

Cape Vincent

Watertown

Utica

Cooperstown

Kingston

Thousand Island Region

Syracuse

Ithaca

Binghamton

PENNSYLVANIA

Scranton

ALGONQUIN PROVINCIAL PARK

CANADA

Peterborough

Macdonald Cartier Fwy.

Lake Ontario

Rochester

Buffalo

Niagara Falls

ALLEGHENEY NATIONAL FOREST

Parry Sound

Lake Simcoe

Toronto

Hamilton

Erie

Georgian Bay

Penetanguishene

Point-au-Baril

Little Current

Owen Sound

Kitchener

Stratford

London

Lake Erie

OHIO

Lake Huron

Port Huron

Lake St. Clair

Windsor

Cleveland

Saginaw Bay

Saginaw

Detroit

MICHIGAN

Lansing

Ann Arbor

Toledo

N

50 miles

50 kilometers

0

CANADA

BATHURST
SPADINA
ST. GEORGE
BLOOR/YONGE

St. George St.
Avenue Rd.
Lowther Ave.
Cumberland St.
Rosedale Valley Rd.

The Annex
Bloor St. W.
BAY
Bloor St. E.

Royal Ontario Museum
Charles St. W.
Charles St. E.

Sussex Ave.
McLaughlin Planetarium
MUSEUM
Isabella St.

Spadina Ave.
Huron St.
Bay St.
Yonge St.
Gloucester St.

Harbord St.
Trinity College
Hoskin Ave.
St. Joseph St.

Queen's Park
Wellesley St. W.
WELLESLEY
Wellesley St. E.

Lippincott St.
Brunswick Ave.
Howland Ave.
Major St.
Robert St.
Hart House
Willcocks St.
Queen's Park Cir. W.
Queen's Park Cir. E.
Breadalbane St.
Maitland Ave.
Jarvis St.

Bathurst St.
Knox College
Russell St.
Grosvenor St.
Alexander St.

College St.
Ontario Provincial Parliament
Grenville St.
Wood St.

Oxford St.
College St.
College St.
COLLEGE
Carlton St.

Nassau St.
QUEEN'S PARK
Orde St.
Gerrard St. W.
Gerrard St. E.
B

Bellevue Ave.
Beverley St.
Henry St.
McCaul St.
World's Biggest Bookstore

Kensington Market
Bay Street Bus Terminal
ST. PATRICK
Dundas St. W.
DUNDAS
Dundas St. E.

Augusta Ave.
Denison Ave.
Ryerson Ave.
Art Gallery of Ontario
CHINATOWN
Church St.

Toronto City Hall
James St.
Victoria St.
Mutual St.
George St.
Pembroke St.

Bathurst St.
Queen St. W.
OSGOODE
University Ave.
Yonge St.
QUEEN
Queen St. E.
Moss Park
Sherbourne St.

Richmond St. W.
York St.
Bay St.
Richmond St. E.

Spadina Ave.
Peter St.
Widmer St.
Nelson St.
Lombard St.
Scott St.
Adelaide St. E.

Adelaide St. W.
D
Pearl St.
Simcoe St.
ST. ANDREW
KING
C
King St. E.

King St. W.
Roy Thompson (concert) Hall
John St.
ST. LAWRENCE Market

Wellington St. W.
Wellington St. E.
Front St. E.
Jarvis St.

Front St. W.
Wilton St.

Infobooth
Union Station

The Esplanade W.
Skydome
CN Tower
York St.
Gardiner Expwy
Lake Shore Blvd. E.

Lake Shore Blvd. W.

Queen©s Quay W.
Queen©s Quay E.

TO ONTARIO PLACE
Toronto Island Ferry Terminal

Toronto Harbour

Toronto

ACCOMMODATIONS

- **D** Global Village Backpackers
- **A** Hotel Selby
- **B** Neill-Wycik College-Hotel
- **C** Toronto International Hostel

N

| 0 | 1/2 mile |
| 0 | 1/2 kilometer |

Bathurst St. The major east-west routes include, from the water north, **Front St., Queen St., Dundas St., College St., Bloor St.,** and **Eglington St.**

Avoid rush hour (4-7pm). To combat transportation problems, city officials enforce traffic and parking regulations zealously—don't tempt them. A flashing green light means that you can go straight or turn left freely—the opposing traffic has a red light. **Parking** on the street is hard to find and usually carries a 1hr. limit, except on Sundays, when street spaces are free and abundant. You can also park for free at night, but your car must be gone by 7-8am. Day parking generally costs inbound daytrippers $3-4 at outlying subway stations; parking overnight at the subway stations is prohibited. Parking lots within the city run at least $12 for 24hr. (7am-7am), although some all-day lots downtown on King St. sell unguarded spots for $4-6. Free, unmetered parking is available in **Rosedale,** a residential neighborhood northeast of Bloor and Sherbourne St., about 1½ mi. from downtown.

PRACTICAL INFORMATION

Airport: Pearson International (247-7678), about 20km west of Toronto via Hwy. 401. Take bus #58 west from Lawrence W. subway. **Pacific Western Transportation** (905-564-6333) runs buses every 20min. to downtown hotels ($12.50, round-trip $21.50) and every 40min. to Yorkdale ($7.25), York Mills ($8.30), and Islington ($6.75) subway stations (all buses 5am-midnight). **Hotel Airporter** (798-2424) zips to select airport hotels ($12, round-trip $20).

Trains: All trains chug from **Union Station,** 65 Front St. (366-8411), at Bay and York. Subway: Union. **VIA Rail** (366-8411) cannonballs to Montréal (5½hr., 6 per day $89); Windsor (4hr., 4-5 per day, $67); New York City (12hr., 1 per day, $86); and Chicago (11hr., 6 per week, $129). Ticket office open M-Sa 6:45am-9:30pm, Su 8am-8:30pm; station open daily 6am-midnight.

Buses: Trentway-Wagar (393-7911) and **Greyhound** (367-8747) operate from 610 Bay St., just north of Dundas St. Subway: St. Patrick or Dundas. Trentway-Wagar has service to Montréal (7hr., 5-6 per day, $69). Greyhound goes to Ottawa (5½hr., 9-11 per day, $52); Calgary (49hr., 3 per day, $256); Vancouver (2½ days, 3 per day, $298), and New York City (11hr., 5 per day, $95). No reservations; show up 30min. prior to departure. Ticket office open daily 5:30am-1am.

Ferries: Toronto Island Ferry Service (392-8194, recording 392-8193). Ferries to Centre Island, Wards Island, and Hanlans Point leave from Bay St. Ferry Dock at the foot of Bay St. Service daily every 30min. 8am-midnight. Round-trip $4; seniors, students, and ages 15-19 $2; under 15 $1.

Public Transportation: Toronto Transit Commission (TTC), 393-4000. A network of 2 subway lines and numerous bus and streetcar routes. After dark, buses are required to stop anywhere along a route at a female passenger's request. Subway operates approximately 6am-2:25am; then buses cover subway routes. Fare $2 (5 tokens $8), seniors with ID $1.35, under 13 50¢ (10 for $4). M-Sa 1-day travel pass $6.50. Su and holidays, families receive unlimited travel for $6.50. Free transfers among subway, buses, and streetcars, but only at stations.

Taxis: Co-op Cabs, 504-2667. $2.50 base fare, $1.25 per km. 24hr.

Car Rental: Wrecks for Rent, 77 Nassau St. (585-7782). Subway: Bathurst. $29 per day with 100km free, 9¢ each additional km. Must be 21. Ages 23-25 pay $3 per day surcharge, ages 21-23 $5. Open M-F 8am-6pm, Sa 9am-4pm.

Driver/Rider Service: Allo-Stop, 398 Bloor St. W. (975-9305). Matches riders with drivers. Year-round membership for passengers $6, for drivers $7. To: Ottawa ($20), Montréal ($26), Québec City ($41), and New York ($40). Open M-W 9am-5pm, Th-F 9am-7pm, Sa-Su 10am-5pm.

Jump-On/Jump-Off Service: Moose Travel Co. Ltd. (905-471-8687, 800-461-8585, or 888-81-MOOSE/816-6673). Hop on and off at dozens of destinations throughout Eastern Canada at your own convenience. 3-6 days of travel time can spread over 6 months. Offers three routes through Ontario and Quebec ($180-299).

Excursions: Call of the Wild (200-9453) organizes phenomenal escapes into the heart of Algonquin Park in northern Ontario. The 3-day summer wilderness trek features camping, canoeing, hiking, moose sightings, and the calls of howling wolves ($295; everything included). The 3-day winter trek comes with transportation equipment and your very own 6-dog sled team ($485).

Bike Rental: Brown's Sports and Bike Rental, 2447 Bloor St. W. (763-4176). $18 per day, $37 per weekend, $50 per week. $200 deposit or credit card required. Open M-F 9:30am-6pm, Sa 9:30am-5:30pm.

Visitor Info: The **Metropolitan Toronto Convention and Visitors Association (MTCVA),** 207 Queens Quay W. (203-2500 or 800-363-1990), mails out info and answers questions by phone. For in-person assistance and oodles of free brochures including the indispensable *Metropolitan Toronto Map,* head to the **Info T.O.,** 255 Front St. W., at the Metro Toronto Convention Centre. Open daily 8am-6pm.

Student Travel Office: Travel CUTS, 187 College St. (979-2406), just west of University Ave. Subway: Queen's Park. Smaller office at 74 Gerrard St. E. (977-0441). Subway: College. Both open M-Tu and Th-F 9am-5pm, W 9am-7pm, Sa 11am-3pm. Reduced hrs. in winter.

Consulates: Australia, 175 Bloor St. E., Room 314 (323-1155). Subway: Bloor St. Open for info M-F 9am-1pm and 2-4:30pm. **U.K.,** 2800 Bay St. (593-1267), 28th fl. Subway: College. Open M-F 8:30am-5pm. **U.S.,** 360 University Ave. (595-1700). Subway: St. Patrick. Consular services M-F 8:30am-1pm.

Currency Exchange: Toronto Currency Exchange, 313 Yonge St. (598-3769), at Dundas St., offers the best rates around. Open daily 9am-7pm. Also at 2 Walton St. (599-5821). Open daily 8:30am-5:30pm. **Royal Bank of Canada,** 200 Bay St. Plaza (info 800-769-2511, foreign exchange 974-5535), exchanges at Pearson Airport (905-676-3220; open daily 5am-11:30pm) and around the city. **Money Mart,** 688 Yonge St. (924-1000), has 24hr. service and some fees. Subway: Bloor/Yonge.

Hotlines: Rape Crisis, 597-8808. **Services for the Disabled, Info Ability** 800-665-9092. **Toronto Gay and Lesbian Phone Line,** 964-6600. Open M-Sa 7-10pm.

Post Office: Adelaide Station, 31 Adelaide St. E. (214-2353 or 214-2352). Open M-F 8am-5:45pm. **Postal code:** M5C 1JO. **Area code:** 416 (city), 905 (outskirts). In text, 416 unless noted otherwise.

NEIGHBORHOODS

Downtown Toronto splits into many distinctive and decentralized neighborhoods. Thanks to zoning regulations that require developers to include housing and retail space in commercial construction, many people live downtown. **Chinatown** centers on Dundas St. W. between Bay St. and Spadina Ave. Formerly the Jewish market of the 1920s, **Kensington Market,** on Kensington Ave., Augusta Ave., and the western half of Baldwin St., is now a largely Portuguese neighborhood with many good restaurants, vintage clothing shops, and an outdoor bazaar of produce, luggage, spices, nuts, clothing, and shoes. A strip of old factories, stores, and warehouses on **Queen St. W.,** from University Ave. to Bathurst St., contains a fun mix of shopping from upscale, uptight boutiques to reasonable used book stores, restaurants, and cafes. The ivy-covered Gothic buildings and magnificent quadrangles of the **University of Toronto** occupy about 200 acres in the middle of downtown. The law-school cult flick *The Paper Chase* was filmed here because the campus supposedly looked more Ivy League than Harvard, where the movie was set. **The Annex,** Bloor St. W. at the Spadina subway, has an artistic and literary ambiance and excellent budget restaurants that dish up a variety of ethnic cuisines (see **Food,** below). This is the best place to come at night when you're not sure exactly what you're hungry for; afterwards, stay and hit the nightclubs. **Yorkville,** just north of Bloor between Yonge St. and Avenue Rd., was once the crumbling communal home of flower children and folk guitarists. **Cabbagetown,** just east of Yonge St., bounded by Gerrard St. E., Wellesley, and Sumach St., takes its name from the Irish immigrants who used to plant the green, leafy vegetable in their yards. Today, professionals inhabit its renowned Victorian housing, along with quite probably the only crowing rooster in the city. The **Gay and Lesbian Village,** located around Church and Wellesley St., offers fine outdoor cafes.

On Front St. between Sherbourne and Yonge St., the **Theatre District** supports enough venues to whet any cultural hunger. Music, food, ferry rides, dance companies, and art all dock at the **Harborfront** (973-3000), on Queen's Quay W. from York to Bathurst St., on the lake. The three main **Toronto Islands,** accessible by ferry (see **Practical Information,** above), offer beaches, bike rentals, and an amusement park. East from the harbor, the beaches along and south of Queen's St. E., between Woodbine and Victoria, boast a popular boardwalk. Even farther east, 5km from the city center, rugged **Scarborough Bluffs,** a 16km section of cliffs, rises from the lakeshore.

Three more ethnic enclaves lie 15-30min. from downtown by public transit. **Corso Italia** surrounds St. Clair W. at Dufferin St.; take the subway to St. Clair W. and bus #512 west. You'll find **Little India** at Gerrard St. E. and Coxwell; ride the subway to Coxwell, then take bus #22 south to the second Gerard St. stop. Better known as **"the Danforth," Greektown** (subway: Pape) is on Danforth Ave. at Pape Ave.

ACCOMMODATIONS AND CAMPGROUNDS

Cut-rate hotels concentrate around Jarvis and Gerrard St. The University of Toronto provides cheap sleep for budget travelers; contact the **U of Toronto Housing Service,** 214 College St. (978-8045), at St. George St., for $20-45 rooms (open M-F 8:45am-4:30pm; reservations recommended). You can call the visitors bureau to obtain a room; the **Downtown Association of Bed and Breakfast Guest Houses** (690-1724) places guests in renovated Victorian homes (singles $40-60; doubles $50-60). Because it is difficult to regulate these registries, you should always visit a B&B before you commit.

Global Village Backpackers, 460 King St. W. (703-8540 or 888-844-7875). Subway: St. Andrew. A state-of-the-art backpacker support system. 195 beds in the centrally located, newly renovated former Spadina Hotel. Travelers convene at the bar inside and on the outdoor patio. Lockers available. Kitchen, laundry, in-house Travel CUTS branch. Dorms $20; doubles $45. Internet use $3 per hr. Reception 24hr. 10% discount for ISIC or HI members.

Toronto International Hostel (HI-C), 76 Church St. (971-4440, 363-4921, or 800-668-4487), at the corner of King. Subway: Dundas. Newly relocated hostel in a great downtown location. Kitchen, laundry facilities, and a lounge. Reception 24hr. Dorm rooms $19, nonmembers $23. Linen $2. Check-in after noon, check-out 11am. Reservations recommended.

Neill-Wycik College Hotel, 96 Gerrard St. E. (977-2320 or 800-268-4358). Subway: College. Small, clean rooms, some with beautiful views of the city. Kitchen on every floor. Laundry, roof deck, sauna. Singles $39; doubles $56. Family rooms and lockers available. Check-in after 4pm; check-out 10am. Students, seniors, and HI members get a 20% discount. Open early May to late Aug.

Leslieville Home Hostels, 185 Leslie St. and 256 Jones Ave. (461-7258), 3 mi. east of the bus station, a few blocks north of Queen St. Take subway to Queen and hop on any Queen streetcar east. Spacious hostel beds in 2 separate family style-homes. Free linen and parking, kitchen, laundry. 1hr. free email use per day. Breakfast included. Dorms $17; private rooms $35.

Knox College, 59 St. George St. (978-0168; call M-Th 10am-5pm). Subway: Queen's Park. In the heart of campus, U of T's most coveted residence has huge rooms with wooden floors around an idyllic courtyard. The movie *Good Will Hunting* used Knox rooms to simulate the interiors of Harvard and MIT. Singles $30, students $25; doubles $40. Reserve rooms months in advance. Open June-Aug.

Allenby Bed and Breakfast, 223 Strathmore Blvd. (461-7095). Subway: Greenwood. Spacious rooms with private kitchens and bathrooms in a quiet neighborhood. Light breakfast. Singles $45; doubles $55.

Hotel Selby, 592 Sherbourne St. (921-3142 or 800-387-4788), at Bloor St. Subway: Sherbourne. A registered historic place newly renovated in full, Hotel Selby has seen some changes since Ernest Hemingway knew it. Cable TV, A/C, laundry facilities, and phones in all rooms. Historical fireplace suites capture the splendor of 20s Selby. Most rooms have private baths. Singles from $70; doubles from $90.

YWCA-Woodlawn Residence, 80 Woodlawn Ave. E. (923-8454), off Yonge St. Subway: Summerhill. 144 rooms for women only, in a nice neighborhood. Breakfast, kitchen, TV lounges, and laundry facilities. Small, neat singles $47; doubles $62; private bath available. Beds in basement dormitory $20. 10% senior discount. Linen $3. Reception M-F 7:30am-11:30pm, Sa-Su 7:30am-7:30pm.

Indian Line Tourist Campground, 7625 Finch Ave. W. (905-678-1233 or 1-800-304-9728; off-season 661-6600, ext. 203), at Darcel Ave. Follow Hwy. 427 north to Finch Ave. and go west, or take the subway to Yorkdale and then a 40min. bus ride.

The closest campground (30min.) to metropolitan Toronto, near Pearson Airport. Showers, laundry, pool, playground. Sites $19, with hookup $24. Gatehouse open 8am-midnight. Open mid-May to early Oct. Reservations recommended July-Aug.

FOOD

A burst of immigration has made Toronto a haven for good international food, with over 5000 restaurants squeezed into the metropolitan area. Some of the standouts can be found on **Bloor St. W.** and in **Chinatown.** For fresh produce, go to **Kensington Market** or the **St. Lawrence Market** at King St. E. and Sherbourne, 6 blocks east of the King subway stop. **Village by the Grange,** at the corner of McCaul and Dundas near the Art Gallery of Ontario, is a vast collection of super-cheap restaurants and vendors—Chinese, Thai, Middle Eastern, you name it (generally open 11am-7pm). "L.L.B.O." posted on the window of a restaurant means that it has a liquor license.

The Annex

🍴**The Green Room,** 296 Brunswick Ave. (929-3253). Subway: Spadina. A hole-in-the-wall hidden in an alley south of Bloor St. off Borden St. Multicultural like Toronto itself, dishing up an amalgam of Thai, Vietnamese, and Mexican delicacies. Average entree $8. Open daily 11am-2am.

Future Bakery & Café, 483 Bloor St. W. (231-1491). Subway: Spadina. Fresh baked cakes ($4.25) and pastries charge up the young student crowd by day, and beer ($4) on the street corner patio winds them down after dark. Open daily 7:30-2am.

Rajputs Tandoori Curry House, 388 Bloor St. W. (324-9305). Subway: Spadina. Canada's first Indian restaurant also offers quirky Pakistani delights. Mixed vegetable curry de jour $7. Open daily 5:30-10:30pm.

Country Style Hungarian Restaurant, 450 Bloor St. W. (537-1745). Subway: Spadina. Hearty stews, soups, and casseroles. Meals come in small (more than enough) and large (stop, lest I burst) portions. Entrees $4-10. Open daily 11am-10pm.

Serra, 378 Bloor St. W. (922-6999). Subway: Spadina. A quiet, Cal-Ital oasis amid the bustle of the Annex. Angel hair and grilled chicken ($11). Open daily noon-11pm.

Chinatown and Kensington

🍴**Saigon Palace,** 454 Spadina Ave. (968-1623), at College St. Subway: Queen's Park. Popular with locals. Great spring rolls. Beef, chicken, or vegetable dishes over rice or noodles $4-8. Open M-Th 9am-10pm, F-Sa 9am-11pm.

Simple Elegance Restaurant, 355 College St. (921-4356), at Augusta Ave. Subway: Spadina. They place the emphasis on their Taiwanese cuisine, not their decor. Entrees $5-7. Open M-Sa 11:30-10pm.

The Midtown Café, 552 College St. W. (920-4533). Subway: Queen's Park. Enjoy alternative music while you play pool or just relax. On weekends, they bring out a large *tapas* menu $3.25-4.50. Sandwiches $4.75-6.25. Open daily noon-2am.

Theatre/St. Lawrence District

🍴**Mövenpick Marché** (366-8986), in the BCE Place at Yonge and Front St. Probably the önly restaurant that requires a map. Bröwse through and pick a meal from the 14 culinary stations, including a bakery, a bar, pasta, seafood, salad counters, and grill. Yuppie extravagance at its finest, and not too hard on the budget. Entrees run $5-8. Open daily 7:30am-2am.

Shopsy's, 33 Yonge St. (365-3333), at Front St. 1 block from Union Station, and other locations at 284A King St. W. (599-5464) and 1535 Yonge St. (967-5252). The definitive Toronto deli. 300 seats, snappy service. If you're feelin' frisky, the "Hot and Topless" Reuben is for you ($7.75). Shopsy's Hot Dog $3.75. Open M-W 7am-11pm, Th-F 7am-midnight, Sa 8am-midnight, Su 8am-10pm.

Penelope, 6 Front St. E. (351-9393). Subway: St. Andrew. Outdoor dining with local *Ellenes* under the skyscrapers of the financial district. Soak your bread in *fasolada* ($3) and *tzatziki* ($5) while faithfully fending off suitors. Open daily 10am-10pm.

Greektown

Mr. Greek, 568 Danforth Ave. (461-5470), at Carlaw. Subway: Pape. A friendly, bustling cafe serving shish kebabs, salads, Greek music, and wine. Family atmosphere, fast service. Gyros or souvlaki $4. Open Su-Th 10am-1am, F-Sa until 4am.

SIGHTS

A walk through the city's diverse neighborhoods can be one of the most rewarding (and cheapest) activities in Toronto. Signs and streetside conversations change languages while gustatory aromas waft through the air. For an organized expedition, the **Royal Ontario Museum** (586-5797) leads seven free **walking tours.** *(Tours June-Sept. W 6pm, Su 2pm. Destinations and meeting places vary; call for specific info.)* The **University of Toronto** (978-5000) conducts free 1hr. walking tours of Canada's largest university and alma mater of David Letterman's band leader, Paul Schaffer. *(Tours June-Aug. M-F 10:30am, 1, and 2:30pm.)* Tours meet at the Nona MacDonald Visitor's Center at King's College Circle; the visitors bureau has more info. Other free trips within the city revolve around architectural themes, sculptures, or ghost-infested Toronto haunts.

Modern architecture aficionados should visit the curving twin towers and 2-story rotunda of **City Hall** (392-7341), at the corner of Queen and Bay St. between the Osgoode and Queen subway stops; brochures for self-guided tours are also available (open 8:30am-4:30pm). In front of City Hall, **Nathan Phillips Sq.** is home to a reflecting pool (which becomes a skating rink in winter) and numerous events, including live music every Wednesday noon-2pm (June to early Oct.). The **Events Hotline** (392-0458) knows all about it. A few blocks away, the **Toronto Stock Exchange,** 2 First Canadian Pl. (947-4676), on York between Adelaide St. W. and King St. W., trades over $400 billion yearly as Canada's leading stock exchange (open M-F 9am-4:30pm; $5, students and seniors $3). The Ontario government legislates in the **Provincial Parliament Buildings** (325-7500; subway: Queen's Park), at Queen's Park in the city center. *(Building open M-F 8:30am-6pm, Sa-Su 9am-4pm; chambers close 4:30pm. Parliament in session Mar.-June and Oct.-Dec. M-W 1:30-6pm, Th 10am-noon and 1:30-6pm. Free guided tours daily every 30min. 9am-4pm. Free gallery passes available at main lobby info desk 1:10-6pm.)* Straight out of a fairy tale, the 98-room **Casa Loma** (923-1171 or 923-1172), Davenport Rd. at 1 Austin Terr., near Spadina a few blocks north of the Dupont subway stop, is a classic tourist attraction. *(Open daily 9:30am-4pm. $9, seniors and ages 13-17 $5.50, ages 4-13 $5.)* Secret passageways and an underground tunnel add to the magic of the only turreted castle in North America. A taste of 19th-century Toronto sits next door at the **Spadina House,** 285 Spadina Rd. (392-6910) *(Open July-Aug. Tu-Su noon-4pm. $5, students and seniors $3.25, ages 4-13 $3.)* Built in 1866 in the Victorian style, the 6-acre estate is a relic of the days before Toronto's multicultural evolution.

Check out an autopsy of a mummified Egyptian and a frieze of the Persian sun god Mithra slaying a bull at the **Royal Ontario Museum (ROM),** 100 Queen's Park (586-8000; subway: Museum), which houses artifacts from ancient civilizations (Greek, Chinese, and Egyptian), a bat cave (not *the* Bat Cave), and a giant T-rex. *(Open M and W-Sa 10am-6pm, Tu 10am-8pm, Su 11am-6pm. $15, seniors, students, and children $9. Tu 4:30-8pm "pay what you can.")* Across the street, the **George R. Gardiner Museum of Ceramic Art,** 111 Queen's Park (586-8080), traces the history of porcelain with a riveting collection dating back to the Renaissance. *(Open M-Sa 10am-5pm, Tu also 5-8pm, Su 11am-5pm. $5; students, seniors, and children $3.)* There was an old lady who lived in a shoe, but it probably wasn't the shoe-shaped glass-and-stone edifice which houses the **Bata Shoe Museum,** 327 Bloor St. W. (979-7799; subway: St. George). *(Open Tu-W and F-Sa 10am-5pm, Th 10am-8pm, Su noon-5pm. $6, seniors and students $4, ages 5-14 $2, families $12; 1st Tu of every month free.)* Even the shoe-indifferent will find the multicultural footwear collection fascinating: Hindu ivory stilted sandals, Elton John's sparkling silver platform boots, and 2 in. slippers once worn by Chinese women with bound feet. The **Art Gallery of Ontario (AGO),** 317 Dundas St. W. (979-6648; sub-

> ### "Wake Up, Morris: We're There"
>
> At 1815 ft., 5 in., Toronto's **CN Tower** (360-8500; subway: Union) stands as the **world's tallest free-standing structure,** a colossal beast hovering over the downtown region and visible from nearly every corner of the city. *(Open daily 9am-11pm. $15, seniors $13, ages 4-12 $11, $3.50 more for the Sky Pod.)* Built in the mid-1970s, the Canadian National Tower took 1537 construction workers and $63 million to build. The structure weighs a massive 130,000 tons (the same weight as 23,214 large elephants) and uses 80 mi. of post-tensioned steel. The world's longest metal staircase rests in the tower's center with 2570 steps—those with visions of athletic grandeur may attempt the climb twice yearly, when the tower opens its stairwell to benefit the United Way and World Wildlife Fund.

way: St. Patrick), 3 blocks west of University Ave., houses an enormous collection of Western art from the Renaissance to the 1990s, concentrating on Canadian artists. *(Open Tu-F noon-9pm, Sa-Su 10am-5:30pm; early Sept. to late May W-Su 10am-5:30pm. $5 donation suggested.)*

The **Hockey Hall of Fame,** 30 Yonge St. (360-7735), on the concourse level of BCE at Front St., celebrates Canada's favorite sport with interactive games and plenty of memorabilia. *(Open M-Sa 9:30am-6pm, Su 10am-6pm; Sept. to late June M-F 10am-5pm, Sa 9:30am-6pm, Su 10:30am-5pm. $10, seniors and under 14 $5.50.)*

Toronto crawls with **biking** and **hiking** trails. For a map of the trails, call the **Parks and Recreation Dept.** (392-1111), which has info on local facilities and activities (open M-F 9am-4:30pm). It might not be the Caribbean, but the **beaches** on the southeast end of Toronto now support a permanent community. A popular "vacationland," the **Toronto Islands Park,** on Centre Island, has a boardwalk, bathing beaches, canoe and bike rentals, and an amusement park (open mid-May to early Sept.). The park is located on a 4 mi. strip of connected islands just opposite downtown. **Ferries** (info 392-8193) leave from the Bay St. Ferry Dock at Bay St. (15min.; round-trip $3, seniors and children $2).

The **Ontario Science Center,** 770 Don Mills Rd. (696-3127), at Eglington Ave. E., presents more than 650 interactive exhibits, showcasing humanity's greatest innovations. *(Museum open daily 10am-8pm; Sept.-June 10am-5pm. Omnimax shows every hr. on the hr. 11am-8pm; Sept.-June 11am-5pm. Museum $10, ages 5-16 and seniors $7; with Omnimax film $15/$9.)* The **Metro Toronto Zoo** (392-5900), Meadowvale Rd. off Exit 389 on Hwy. 401, houses over 6400 animals in a 710-acre park that features sections representing the world's seven geographic regions, and rare wildlife including a Komodo dragon and a Tasmanian devil. *(Open daily late May to late June 9am-7pm; late June to early Sept. 9am-7:30pm; call for off-season hrs. Last entry 1hr. before closing. $12, seniors and ages 12-17 $9, ages 4-11 $7. Parking $5.)* Take bus #86A from Kennedy Station.

ENTERTAINMENT

The monthly *Where Toronto,* available free at tourism booths, drops the lowdown on arts and entertainment. Before you buy tickets, contact **T.O. Tix** (536-6468); they sell half-price tickets for theater, music, dance, and opera on performance day. Their booth at 208 Yonge St., north of Queen St. (subway: Queen) at Eaton's Centre, opens at noon; arrive before 11:45am for first dibs (open Tu-Sa noon-7:30pm, Su 11am-3pm). **Ticketmaster** (870-8000) supplies tickets for many Toronto venues, although it has a hefty service charge.

Ontario Place, 955 Lakeshore Blvd. W. (314-9811, recording 314-9900), features cheap summer entertainment. Top pop artists like Elton John and the Spice Girls perform here in the **Molson Amphitheatre** (260-5600); Ticketmaster handles tickets. ($17.50-50. Park open mid-May to early Sept. daily 10:30am-midnight. Call for events schedule.) You'll have to crane your neck for the IMAX movies in the 6-story **Cinesphere** (870-8000; $8.50, plus $10 gate admission; call for screening schedule).

Roy Thomson Hall, 60 Simcoe St. (872-4255; subway: St. Andrews), at King St. W., is both Toronto's premier concert hall and the home of the **Toronto Symphony**

Orchestra (593-4828) from September to June. Tickets ($19-50) are available at the box office or by phone. (Open M-F 10am-6pm, Sa noon-5pm, Su 3hr. before performances. Ask about discounts.) Rush tickets for the symphony ($10) are often available at the box office on concert days (M-F 11am, Sa 1pm). The same ticket office serves **Massey Hall,** 178 Victoria St. (593-4828; subway: Dundas), near Eaton Centre, a great hall for rock and folk concerts and musicals. Opera and ballet companies perform at **Hummingbird Centre,** 1 Front St. E. (393-7474 or 872-2262 for tickets; ballet from $18, opera from $30), at Yonge. Rush tickets for the last row of orchestra seats go on sale at 11am (from $18); a limited number of half-price tickets are available for seniors and students (box office open M-Sa 11am-6pm, or until 1hr. after curtain). Next door, **St. Lawrence Centre,** 27 Front St. E. (366-7723), stages excellent drama and chamber music recitals in two different theaters. Ask for possible student and senior discounts. (Box office open M-Sa 10am-6pm; in winter performance days 10am-8pm; non-performance days 10am-6pm.) **Canadian Stage** (box office 368-3110; open M-F 9am-5pm) tames a slew of performances of summer Shakespeare amid the greenery of **High Park,** on Bloor St. W. at Parkside Dr. (subway: High Park). Year-round performances include new Canadian works and time-honored classics. Bring something to sit on, or perch yourself on the 45° slope that faces the stage ($5 donation requested; call for schedule).

Film fans looking for good classic and contemporary cinema choose the **Bloor Cinema,** 506 Bloor St. W. (532-6677), at Bathurst, or the **Cinématheque Ontario,** 317 Dundas St. W. (923-3456), at McCaul St.

Canada's answer to Disneyland awaits at **Canada's Wonderland,** 9580 Jane St. (905-832-7000), about 1hr. from downtown but accessible by public transportation. Splash down the water rides or try your stomach on the backwards, looping, and suspended roller coasters. (Open late June to early Sept. daily 10am-10pm; open in fall Sa-Su, closing times vary. $38, seniors and ages 3-6 $19.)

Groove to the rhythms of old and new talents—in all, more than 1500 artists from 17 countries—at the 10-day **Du Maurier Ltd. Downtown Jazz Festival** (363-5200), at Ontario Place in late June. Also in June, the **Toronto International Dragon Boat Race Festival** (598-8945) continues a 2000-year-old Chinese tradition. The race finishes at Toronto's Center Island. The celebration includes traditional performances, foods, and free outdoor lunchtime concerts. From mid-August through early September, the **Canadian National Exhibition (CNE)** (393-6000), the world's largest annual fair, brings an international carnival atmosphere to Exhibition Place (open daily 10am-midnight; $16, seniors $9, children $6, under 6 free).

From April to October, the **Toronto Blue Jays** (341-1111, tickets 341-1234) play ball at the **Sky Dome,** Front and Peter St. (Subway: Union, follow the signs. Tickets $4-28.) Scalpers sell tickets for far beyond face value; latecomers wait until the game starts and then haggle like mad. To get a behind-the-scenes look at the modern, commercialized Sky Dome (341-2770), take the **tour.** (Tours M-F 10am-6pm; Sept.-June M-F 10am-4pm, event schedule permitting. $9.50, seniors and under 16 $7.) For info on concerts and other Sky Dome events, call 341-3663. For info on the **Toronto Argonauts** of the Canadian Football League, who also take the field at the Skydome, call 341-4151. Hockey fans should head for **Maple Leaf Gardens,** 60 Carlton St. (977-1641; subway: College), to see the knuckle-crackin', puck-smackin' **Maple Leafs.** (Tickets $24-94. 1hr. tours of the Gardens leave July to mid-Aug. daily at 11am, 1, 2:30, and 4pm. $3, children $2, families $9.)

NIGHTLIFE

Early in the summer of 1996, the Toronto City Council passed a law prohibiting smoking in all public establishments, including restaurants, clubs, and bars. Protest against the law ensued, and now all establishments are required to maintain a non-smoking zone at all times. Some of Toronto's clubs and pubs remain closed on Sundays because of liquor laws. The city shuts down alcohol distribution daily at 1am, so most clubs close down then. Nevertheless, Toronto maintains a fantastic nightlife scene. The most interesting new clubs are on trendy **Queen St. W., College St. W.,** and **Bloor St. W.** Two comprehensive free entertainment magazines, *Now* and *Eye,* come out every Thursday. The gay scene centers around **Wellesley** and **Church St.** For the scoop on Toronto's gay scene, pick up a free copy of the biweekly *fab.*

The Annex

🏵**Lee's Palace,** 529 Bloor St. W. (532-1598), just east of the Bathurst subway stop. Crazy creature art depicts a rock 'n' roll frenzy. Live music nightly downstairs; DJ dance club, the **Dance Cave,** swings upstairs. Pick up a calendar of bands. Box office opens 8pm, shows begin 10pm. Cover $3-12 downstairs; open M-Sa noon-2am. Cover after 10pm $4 upstairs; open Tu and Th-Sa 8pm-3am.

The Madison, 14 Madison Ave. (927-1722), at Bloor St. Subway: Spadina. Blonde wood, 2 pool rooms, 2 large patios, and 1 small patio. 21 beers on tap. Pints $4.90. Wings $7.85. Open daily 11am-2am.

The James Joyce, 386 Bloor St. (324-9400). Subway: Spadina. Splices the maple leaf and the clover with live Celtic music every night (no cover). Catch the Jays on their big screen. Open daily noon- 2am.

Downtown

🏵**Second City,** 56 Blue Jays Way (343-0011 or 888-263-4485), at Wellington St., just north of the Sky Dome. Subway: Union. One of North America's wackiest, most creative comedy clubs. Spawned comics Dan Akroyd, John Candy, Martin Short, Mike Myers, and a hit TV show *(SCTV)*. Free improv sessions M-Th. 9:45pm and Sa midnight. Free F midnight howl with guest improv troupe. M-Th show 8pm ($16), F-Sa 8pm and 10:30pm ($20-22), Su "best of" 8pm $10. Reservations required.

C'est What?, 67 Front St. E. (867-9499). Subway: Union. A mellow manifestation of Canada's multicultural mesh. Offers its own microbrews and wines in Toronto's dark downtown underground. Hosts local folk acts most nights of the week. Open M-F noon-2am, Sa-Su 11am-2am.

Top o' the Senator, 249-253 Victoria St. (364-7517). Attracts local and national jazz acts. Cover $5-30. Open Tu-Sa 8:30pm-1am, Su 8am-midnight.

College St.

Sneaky Dee's, 431 College St. W. (603-3090), at Bathurst. A hip Toronto hotspot tapping the most inexpensive brew (60 oz. pitcher of Ontario microbrewery draught $9.25). M-F before 6pm, domestic beer goes for $2.50 per bottle. Pool tables in back. DJ and dancing upstairs daily 9:30pm. Open M-Th 11am-4am, F 11am-5am Sa 9am-5am, Su 9am-4am.

College St. Bar, 574 College St. W. (533-2417). A brick interior and mellow atmosphere. Mostly Italian food; dinner entrees $8-10. M jazz (no cover), Th world beat (cover $5-7), and Su blues/funk (cover $5) pack the place (10:30pm each night). Open daily 4pm-1am.

Greektown

Iliada Café, 550 Danforth Ave. (462-0334). Subway: Pape. Join displaced Athenians dreaming of the sun-drenched Aegean while they sip frappes ($3.50) and nibble at fresh baklava. Open Su-Tu 9am-2am, F-Sa 9am-3am.

The Gay and Lesbian Village

Woody's/Sailor, 465-467 Church St. (972-0887), by Maitland. Subway: Wellesley. *The* established gay bar in the Church and Wellesley area, celebrating its 10th anniversary in 1999. Neighborhood atmosphere; walls are lined with art nudes. Come to relax and hang out before heading to the clubs, but don't miss "Bad Boys night out" on Tu. Bottled beer $4.25. Open daily 11am-2am.

Tango, 508 Church St. (975-8612). Subway: Wellesley. Has pool tournaments, live performances, and a cozy bar atmosphere in Toronto's premier lesbian club. Drinks run $3.25-4.50. Open daily 8pm-2am.

■ Near Toronto

Onation's Niagara Escarpment As beautiful as its name is strange, Onation's Niagara Escarpment passes west of Toronto as it winds its way from Niagara

Falls to Tobermory at the tip of the Bruce Peninsula. Along this rocky 724km ridge, the **Bruce Trail** snakes through parks and private land. Hikers are treated to spectacular waterfalls, the breathtaking cliffs along **Georgian Bay,** and unique flora and fauna, including an old growth forest. Because the escarpment is registered as a United Nations world biosphere reserve, future land development is limited to that which can exist symbiotically with the natural environment. For maps and Escarpment info, write or call the **Niagara Escarpment Commission,** 232 Guelph St., Georgetown L7G 4B1 (905-877-5191). Specifics on the Bruce Trail can be obtained from the **Bruce Trail Association,** P.O. Box 857, Hamilton L8N 3N9 (905-529-6821).

Stratford Held in nearby Stratford since 1953, the **Stratford Shakespeare Festival** has proven to be the lifeblood of this picturesque town named for the Bard's own village. The festival and the hamlet are inextricably intertwined, attracting a posh set for an array of mostly non-Shakespeare productions that run from May through early November. During mid-summer (July-Aug.), up to six different shows play per day (none on M), but there is method in this madness: matinees begin at 2pm and evening performances at 8pm in each of three theaters. For complete info about casts and performances call 800-567-1600; write to the **Stratford Festival,** P.O. Box 520, Stratford N5A 6V2; or check their website (http://www.stratford-festival.on.ca). Tickets are expensive ($48-67), but a few good deals lower the stakes, including **rush tickets** (sold at 9am on morning of the show at the box office, theater, or 30min. before by phone; $20-43), matinees for seniors and students (from $21), general student discounts ($26), and half-price for some performances on Wednesdays (box office open M-Sa 9am-8pm, Su 9am-5pm). Tickets can also be purchased through **Ticketmaster** outlets (in Toronto call 416-872-1111). For information on the festival and the town, contact **Tourism Stratford** (519-271-5140 or 800-561-SWAN/7926), or write them at P.O. Box 818, Stratford, N5A 6W1; their **Visitor's Information Center,** York St. at Lakeside Dr. (519-273-3352), also has info. The **Festival Accommodations Bureau** (800-567-1600) spurs the lated traveler apace to gain the timely inn or guest home ($32-41), or B&B ($50-120). **VIA Rail** (800-361-1235) troops to and from Toronto (2½hr., $24). By car, Stratford is a 4hr. drive from Toronto; take 401W to 8W into Stratford.

▓ Ottawa

Legend has it that in the mid-19th century, Queen Victoria chose this as Canada's capital by closing her eyes and pointing her finger at a map. But perhaps political savvy and not blind chance guided the Queen to this once remote logging town, which, as a stronghold for neither French nor English interests, became a perfect compromise. Today, faced with the increasingly tricky task of forging national unity while preserving local identities, Ottawa continues to play cultural ambassador to its own country.

At the turn of the century, Prime Minister Sir Wilfred Laurier called on urban planners to polish Ottawa and to give it more of a historic feel. The carefully groomed facade which resulted has contributed to Ottawa's reputation for being somewhat boring. An evening stroll through Byward Market will challenge this notion. Behind the theaters, museums, and parks, there is plenty of action both before and after quitting time in the capital.

ORIENTATION AND PRACTICAL INFORMATION

The **Rideau Canal** divides Ottawa into the eastern lower town and the western upper town. West of the canal, Parliament buildings and government offices line **Wellington St.,** one of the city's main east-west arteries, which runs directly into the heart of downtown and crosses the canal. **Laurier** is the only other east-west street which permits traffic from one side of the canal to the other. East of the canal, Wellington St. becomes **Rideau St.,** surrounded by a fashionable shopping district. North of Rideau St. lies the **Byward Market,** a shopping area which hosts a summertime open-air market and much of Ottawa's nightlife. **Elgin St.,** a primary north-south artery, stretches from the Queensway (Hwy. 417) to the War Memorial just south of Wellington in

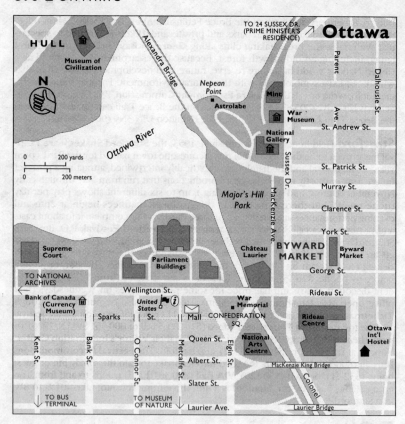

front of Parliament Hill. **Bank St.,** parallel to Elgin 3 blocks to the west, services the town's older shopping area. The canal itself is a major access route. In winter, thousands of Ottawans skate to work on this, the world's longest skating rink; in summer, power boats breeze by regularly. Bike paths and pedestrian walkways also line the canals. Parking downtown is painful (to find as well as to pay for); meters often cost 25¢ for 10min. Residential neighborhoods east of the canal have longer limits and the police ticket less often than on main streets. Parking at or near the hostels is another option—park your car and hop on the great OC Transpo buses.

Airport: Ottawa International (248-2125), 20min. south of the city off Bronson Ave. Take bus #96 from MacKenzie King Bridge. **Info desk** in arrival area open 9am-9pm. Kasbary Transport, Inc. runs **shuttles** (736-9993) between the airport and all downtown hotels; the Novotel is near Ottawa International Hostel. Call for pick-up from smaller hotels. Run daily every 30min. 5am-1am; call for later pick-up. $9, seniors and ages 11-18 $4.

Trains: VIA Rail, 200 Tremblay Rd. (244-8289), east of downtown, off the Queensway at Alta Vista Rd. To: Montréal (2hr.; 4 per day; $38, students $23); Toronto (4hr., 5 per day, $81/$49); and Québec City via Montréal (7hr., 2 per day, $71/$43). ISIC required for student fares. Ticket office open M-F 5am-9pm, Sa 6:30am-7pm, Su 8:20am-9pm.

Buses: Voyageur, 265 Catherine St. (238-5900), between Kent and Lyon. Serves primarily eastern Canada. To: Montréal (2½hr., on the hr. 7am-11pm, $26). **Greyhound** (237-7038) buses leave from the same station, bound for western Canada and southern Ontario. To Toronto (5hr., 7 per day, $39). 5% student discount. For service to the U.S. you must first go to Montréal or Toronto; the Québec City-bound must pass through Montréal. Station open daily 6:30am-12:30am. The blue **Hull City buses** (819-770-3242) connect Ottawa to Hull, across the river.

Public Transportation: OC Transpo, 1500 St. Laurent (741-4390). Excellent system. Buses congregate on either side of Rideau Centre. Fare $2.25, express (green buses) $2.70, ages 6-11 $1.25.

Taxis: Blue Line Taxi, 238-1111. $2 base fare, $1.60 per km. 24hr.

Driver/Rider Service: Allostop, 238 Dalhousie (562-8248), at St. Patrick. To: Toronto ($20); Québec City ($29); Montréal ($10); and New York City ($50). Membership ($6) required. Open M-W 9am-5pm, Th-F 9am-7pm, Sa-Su 10am-5pm. Also an active **rideboard** on the 2nd fl. of the University of Ottawa's University Center.

Bike Rental: Rent-A-Bike-Vélocationo, 1 Rideau St. (241-4140), behind the Château Laurier Hotel. $7 per hr., $16 per 4hr., $20 per day; tandems $15/$38/$50. Maps, locks, helmets free. 2hr. escorted tours $14-17. Family deals available. Open Apr. to Oct. daily 9am-8pm. Credit card required. All new roads in Ottawa are required to have a bicycle lane.

Visitor Info: National Capital Commission Information Center, 90 Wellington St. (239-5000 or 800-465-1867 in Canada), opposite the Parliament Buildings. Open daily early May to early Sept. 8:30am-9pm; early Sept. to early May 9am-5pm. For info on Hull and Québec province, contact the **Association Touristique de l'Outaouais,** 103, rue Laurier, Hull (819-778-2222 or 800-265-7822), at rue St-Laurent. Open mid-June to Sept. M-F 8:30am-8pm, Sa-Su 9am-6pm; off-season M-F 8:30am-5pm, Sa-Su 9am-4pm.

Student Travel Agencies: Travel CUTS, 222 Laurier Ave Est. 2nd fl. (238-8222), 1 block east of King Edward Dr. **Carleton University** (526-8015). Experts in student travel, youth hostel cards, cheap flights, and VIA Rail. Open in summer M and W-F 9am-5pm, Tu 10am-5pm. **Hostelling International-Canada (HI-C),** Ontario East Region, 75 Nicholas St. (569-1400). Youth hostel passes, travel info, and equipment. Open M-F 9:30am-5:30pm, Sa 9:30am-3:30pm.

Embassies and High Commissions: Australia, 50 O'Connor St. #710 (236-0841), at Queen St. Open for visas M-F 9am-1pm; for info M-Th 8:30am-5pm, F 8:30am-4pm. **France,** 42 Sussex Dr. (789-1795). Open for info M-F 9:30am-1:30pm. **Ireland,** 130 Albert St. #1105 (233-6281). Open M-Th 10am-1pm and 2-4pm, F 10am-12:30pm and 2:30-4pm. **New Zealand,** 99 Bank St. #727 (238-5991). Open M-F 8:30am-4:30pm. **U.K.,** 80 Elgin St. (237-1530), at the corner of Queen St. Open for visas and general info M-F 9am-1pm. **U.S.,** 100 Wellington St. (238-5335), directly across from Parliament. Open daily 8:30am-5pm.

American Express: 220 Laurier W. (563-0231), between Metcalfe and O'Connor St., in the heart of downtown, contains a travel agency and a foreign currency exchange. Open M-F 8:30am-5:30pm, Sa 9am-4pm.

Hotlines: Ottawa Distress Centre, 238-3311, English-speaking. **Tel-Aide,** 741-6433, French-speaking. **Rape Crisis Centre,** 562-2333. All 3 24hr. **Tourist Information,** 800-465-1867 or, locally, 239-5000.

Bi-Gay-Lesbian Organization: Gayline-Telegai (238-1717) has info on local bars and special events. Open daily 7-10pm.

Post Office: Postal Station B, 59 Sparks St. (844-1545), at Elgin St. Open M-F 8am-6pm. **Postal code:** K1P 5A0. **Area code:** 613 (Ottawa); 819 (Hull).

ACCOMMODATIONS AND CAMPGROUNDS

Finding inexpensive lodging in downtown Ottawa can be difficult, especially during May and early June, when student groups and conventioneers come to claim their long-reserved rooms, and during the peak of the tourist season in July and August. However, fantastic budget options exist as long as you avoid hotels. Advance reservations are strongly recommended. A complete list of B&Bs can be found in the *Ottawa Visitors Guide;* **Ottawa Bed and Breakfast** (563-0161) represents 10 B&Bs in the Ottawa area (singles $49-54; doubles $59-64 plus tax).

Ottawa International Hostel (HI-C), 75 Nicholas St., K1N 7B9 (235-2595), in downtown Ottawa. The site of Canada's last public hanging, the former Carleton County Jail now incarcerates travelers in this trippy hostel. Rooms contain 4-8 bunks and minimal personal space. Communal showers, kitchen, laundry facilities,

CANADA

lounges, and a cast of friendly regulars. International crowd. Many organized activities (biking, canoeing, tours). 148 beds $15.75, nonmembers $20; private rooms from $44. In winter, doors locked 2-7am. Linen $2. Parking $4.28.

University of Ottawa Residences, 100 University St. (564-5400), in the center of campus, an easy walk from downtown. From the bus and train stations, take bus #95. Clean dorm rooms in a vast concrete landscape. Hall showers. Access to University Center. Singles $33, doubles $40; students with ID $22/$35. Free linen, towels. Check-in 4:30pm. Parking $5.50 per day, $4 after 4pm and Sa-Su. Open early May to late Aug.

YMCA/YWCA, 180 Argyle Ave. (237-1320), at O'Connor St., close to the bus station; walk left on Bank St. and right on Argyle. Nicely sized (though not beautifully decorated) rooms in a high-rise. Free local phones in most rooms. Kitchen with microwave available until 11pm. Gym facilities. Singles with shared bath $42, with private bath $49; doubles $49. Reception Su-Th 7am-11pm, F-Sa 24hr. Weekly and group rates available. Cafeteria open M-F 7am-2:30pm, Sa 8am-2:30pm; in winter M-F 7am-6:30pm; breakfast $2.50-4. Indoor evening parking $2.75.

Gatineau Park (info 827-2020, reservations 456-3016), northwest of Hull, has 3 rustic campgrounds within 45min. of Ottawa: **Lac Philippe Campground,** 248 sites with facilities for family camping, trailers, and campers; **Lac Taylor Campground,** with 33 semi-rustic sites; and **Lac la Pêche,** with 36 campsites accessible only by canoe. All the campgrounds are off Hwy. 366, northwest of Hull; watch for signs. A map is available at the visitors center (open daily 9am-6pm; in winter 9:30am-6pm). From Ottawa, take the MacDonald-Cartier Bridge, follow Autoroute 5 north to Scott Rd., turn right onto Hwy. 105, and follow 105 to Hwy. 366. To reach La Pêche, take Hwy. 366 to Eardley Rd., on your left. Camping permits for Taylor and Philippe ($16; mid-June to mid-Oct. $19) are available at the campground entrance. Pay for a site at La Pêche ($15; off-season $12) on Eardley Rd. La Pêche is available mid-May to mid-Oct.; Lac Philippe and Lac Taylor are open year-round.

FOOD

Fans of the cholesterol-rich breakfast will find friends in Ottawa; the greasy spoon scene revolves around the worship of eggs, potatoes, meat, toast, and coffee. Fresh fruit, vegetables, and flowers are accented by occasional street music in the lively open-air **Byward Market** (562-3325), on Byward St. between York and Rideau St. (open daily 8am-5pm; boutiques open later). The **Dutch Café Wim,** 537 Sussex Dr. (241-1771), serves sumptuous Columbian coffee ($1.45), decadent desserts ($3.50), creative sandwiches ($5-7), and bar fare (open daily 8am-midnight). Sweeten your palate with one of 40 homemade Italian gelato flavors at **Belmondo,** 381 Dalhousie St. (789-6116; open daily 11am-1am). Beaver Tail, akin to fried dough but raised to a fine pastry, is an Ottawa specialty.

Las Palmas, 111 Parent Ave. (241-3738). Outstanding Mexican grub is heaped high; it's "like eating in a Mexican funhouse during a fiesta." Hot means hot here. Dinners $6-16. Open daily 11:30am-11pm.

Royal Star, 99 Rideau St. (562-2772). Stellar lunch buffet ($7) with over 100 regal selections of Szechuan, Cantonese, Polynesian, and Canadian favorites. Open daily 11am-10pm.

Mamma Grazzi's Kitchen, 25 George St. (241-8656). Quiet, intimate quarters bathed in the aroma of Italian specialties and thin-crust pizza ($8-13). Be patient; it's worth the wait. Open Su-Th 11:30am-10pm, F-Sa 11:30am-11pm.

The International Cheese and Deli, 40 Byward St. (241-5411). Deli and Middle Eastern sandwiches to go. Vegetable *samosa* $1.25; turkey and cheese $3.50; falafel on pita $2.25. Open daily 7am-10pm.

Father and Sons, 112 Osgoode St. (233-6066), at the eastern edge of the U of O campus. Student favorite for a menu of tavern-style (and quality) food with some Lebanese dishes thrown in. Falafel platter ($7) or a triple-decker sandwich ($7.25) are good. 15¢ wings all day M and Sa, 30¢ otherwise. Open daily 7am-2am. Kitchen open until midnight in winter.

SIGHTS

Though overshadowed by Toronto's size and Montréal's cosmopolitan color, Ottawa's status as capital of Canada is shored up by its cultural attractions. Since the national museums and political action are packed tightly together, most sights can be reached by foot. The **Parliament Buildings,** on Wellington at Metcalfe St., distinguished by their Gothic architecture, tower over downtown. Warm your hands or raise a cynical Quebecian eyebrow over the **Centennial Flame** at the south gate, lit in 1967 to mark the 100th anniversary of the Dominion of Canada's inaugural session of Parliament. The Prime Minister can occasionally be spotted at the central parliament structure, **Centre Block,** which contains the **House of Commons, Senate,** and **Library of Parliament.** Free, worthwhile **tours** of Centre Block (in English or French) depart every 30min. from the white **Infotent** (992-4793) by the visitors center. *(Tours M-F 9am-8:30pm, Sa-Su 9am-5:30pm; Sept. to mid-May daily 9am-4:30pm. Info-tent open mid-May to mid-June daily 9am-5pm; mid-June to Aug. 9am-8pm.)* On display behind the library, the bell from Centre Block is the only part of the original 1859-66 structure to survive a 1916 fire; according to legend, the bell crashed to the ground after chiming at midnight on the night of the flames. A carillon of 53 bells, ranging from 4.5 to 10,000kg, replaced the old bell and now hangs in the Peace Tower. The tower is currently under renovation, however, and the bells hang mute. When Parliament is in session, you can watch Canada's government officials **squirm on the verbal hot seat** during the official **Question Period** in the House of Commons chamber (mid-Sept to Dec. and Feb.-June M-Th 2:15-3pm, F 11:15am-noon). Those interested in trying to make a statuesque soldier squirm should attend the **Changing of the Guard** (993-1811), on the broad lawns in front of Centre Block (late June to late Aug. daily 10am, weather permitting). At dusk, Centre Block and its lawns transform into the set for **A Symphony of Sound and Light,** which relates the history of the Parliament Buildings and the nation. *(Shows mid-May to early Aug. 9:30 and 10:30pm; early Aug. to early Sept. 9 and 10pm. Performances alternate between French and English.)* A 5min. walk west along Wellington St., the **Supreme Court of Canada** (995-5361) cohabitates with the **Federal Court.** *(Alternating French and English 30min. tours every 30min.; no tours Sa-Su noon-1pm. Free. Open daily 9am-5pm; Sept.-May hrs. vary.)*

One block south of Wellington, the recently renovated **Sparks St. Mall,** hailed as an innovative experiment in 1960, when it was one of North America's first pedestrian malls, now houses a slew of banks and upscale retail stores. The **Rideau Centre,** south of Rideau St. at Sussex Dr., is the city's primary shopping mall as well as one of the main OC Transpo stations. Glass encloses the sidewalks in front of Rideau St.'s stores to make them bearable during the winter months.

East of the Parliament Buildings at the junction of Sparks, Wellington, and Elgin St. stands **Confederation Sq.** with its enormous **National War Memorial,** dedicated by King George VI in 1939. The structure symbolizes the triumph of peace over war, an ironic message on the eve of World War II. **Nepean Point,** several blocks northwest of Rideau Centre and the Byward Market, behind the National Gallery of Canada, provides a panoramic view of the capital. The **Governor-General,** the Queen's representative in Canada, resides at **Rideau Hall** (998-7113). Free **tours** leave from the main gate at 1 Sussex Dr. (800-465-6890 for tour info). Dress up for the open house on New Year's Day or Canada Day and they'll let you view the interior. Otherwise, gawk from 24 Sussex Drive, the **Prime Minister's residence.**

Ottawa's reputation for respecting cultural difference extends beyond the whole French-English schism. Many nationalities integrate well here; ethnically grouped neighborhoods, somewhat sparse, include a small **Chinatown** around Somerset St. between Kent St. and Bronson Ave. From downtown, walk south on Elgin St.; go west on Somerset until fruit stands line the streets and the French signs turn to Chinese (about a 20min. walk). **Little Italy** is just around the corner on Bronson Ave., stretching south from Somerset to the Queensway (Hwy. 417).

CANADA

Museums and Parks

Ottawa contains many of Canada's huge national museums. Most are wheelchair accessible; call for details. **The National Gallery,** 380 Sussex Dr. (990-1985 or 800-319-2787), a spectacular glass-towered building adjacent to Nepean Pt., holds the world's most comprehensive collection of Canadian art as well as outstanding European, American, and Asian works. *(Open F-W 10am-6pm, Th 10am-8pm; mid-Nov. to Apr. W and F-Su 10am-5pm, Th 10am-8pm. Free; special events $8-10, students and seniors $6-8, under 18 free.)* The building's exterior, a work of art in itself, is a parody of the neo-Gothic buttresses of the facing Library of Parliament. The **Canadian Museum of Contemporary Photography,** 1 Rideau Canal (990-8257), between the Château Laurier and the Ottawa Locks, allows a frozen glimpse of modern Canadian life (open M-Tu and F-Su 11am-5pm, W 4-8pm, Th 11am-8pm; free).

The **Canadian Museum of Civilization,** 100 Laurier St. (776-7000), is housed in a striking, sand-dune-like structure across the river in Hull. *(Open May to mid-Oct. Sa-W 9am-6pm, Th-F 9am-9pm; mid-Oct. to Apr. Tu-Su 9am-5pm. $8, seniors $7, ages 13-16 $6, ages 2-12 $3; free Su 9am-noon.)* Accessible (but perhaps overly ambitious) exhibits attempt to put 1000 years of Canadian history into perspective. The breathtaking films shown at **CINEPLUS** (776-7010 for showtimes) are not to be missed, capable of projecting both IMAX and OmniMax. *($8, seniors $7, ages 13-17 $6.50, under 13 $5.50.)* The **Canadian Museum of Nature,** 240 McLeod St. (566-4700), at Metcalf, explores the natural world from dinosaur to mineral through multi-media displays. *(Open F-W 9:30am-5pm, Th 9:30am-8pm; Sept.-Apr. F-W 10am-5pm, Th 10am-8pm. $5, students $4, seniors and ages 3-12 $2, families $12; Th ½-price; free 5-8pm daily.)*

Canadian history buffs could easily lose themselves in the **National Library Archives,** 395 Wellington St. (995-5138), at Bay St., which houses oodles of Canadian publications, old maps, photographs, letters, and historical exhibits (reading room open M-F 8:30am-10pm, Sa-Su 8am-6pm). Liberal Prime Minister William Lyon Mackenzie King governed Canada from the elegant **Laurier House,** 335 Laurier Ave. E. (992-8142), for most of his lengthy tenure. *(Open in summer Tu-Sa 9am-5pm, Su 2-5pm; Oct.-Mar. Tu-Sa 10am-5pm, Su 2-5pm. $2.25, seniors $1.75, students with ID $1.25, under 5 free.)* Admire at your leisure the antiques King accumulated, as well as the crystal ball he used to consult his long-dead mother on matters of national importance.

Farther out of town, the **National Museum of Science and Technology,** 1867 St. Laurent Blvd. (991-3044), at Smyth, lets you explore the wonderful world of tech and transport with touchy-feely exhibits. *(Open May-Aug. Sa-Th 9am-6pm, F 9am-9pm; Sept.-Apr. Tu-Su 9am-5pm. $6, students and seniors $5, ages 6-15 $2.)* The museum entrance is on Lancaster Rd., 200m east of St. Laurent; take bus #85 or 86 from downtown. The **National Aviation Museum** (993-2010), in front of the Rockcliffe Flying Club on Prom. De L'Aviation and Rockcliffe Pkwy. north of Montréal St., illustrates the history of human flight and displays over 120 aircraft; take bus #95 and transfer to #198. *(Open in summer Th 9am-9pm, F-M 9am-5pm; Labor Day to early May Th 10am-9pm, F-M 10am-5pm. $5, students and seniors $4, ages 6-15 $1.75. Free Th 5-9pm.)*

Ottawa has managed to skirt the traditional urban vices of pollution and violent crime; the multitude of parks and recreation areas may make you forget you're in a city at all. A favorite destination for Ottawans who want to cycle, hike, or fish, Gatineau Park (see **Accommodations,** above) occupies 356 sq. km in the northwest. Artificial **Dow's Lake,** accessible by the Queen Elizabeth Driveway, extends off the Rideau Canal 15min. south of Ottawa. **Dow's Lake Pavilion,** 101 Queen Elizabeth Driveway (232-1001), near Preston St., rents pedal boats, canoes, and bikes. (Open mid-May to Sept. daily 8am-8pm. Rentals by the 30min. and the hr.; prices vary.)

The **beaches** west of town by way of the Ottawa River Pkwy. provide an escape from the city hubbub (follow the signs). **Mooney's Bay,** one popular strip of river bank, is 15min. from Ottawa by car.

ENTERTAINMENT

The **National Arts Centre,** 53 Elgin St. (996-5051, tickets 755-1111), at Albert St., houses an excellent small orchestra and theater company and frequently hosts international entertainers (box office open M-Sa noon-9pm). **Odyssey Theatre** (232-8407) puts on open-air theater at Strathcona Park, at the east end of Laurier Ave. at Range Rd., well east of the canal. (Shows late July to late Aug. Tu-Su 8:30pm. $20, students and seniors $17, under 12 $8.)

Ottawans seem to **celebrate** just about everything, even the bitter Canadian cold. All-important is **Canada Day,** on July 1, which involves fireworks, partying in Major's Hill Park, concerts, and all-around merrymaking. During the first 3 weekends of February, **Winterlude** (239-5000; Feb. 5-7, 12-14, and 19-21, 1999) lines the Rideau Canal with ice sculptures illustrating how it feels to be an Ottawan in the winter (frozen). For a week in mid-May, the **Tulip Festival** (567-5757) explodes in a colorful kaleidoscope of more than a million blooming tulips around Dow's Lake. Music fills the Ottawa air during the **Dance Festival** (237-5158), in mid-June, and the **Jazz Festival** (594-3580), in mid-July; both of which hold free recitals and concerts, as well as pricier events. During Labor Day weekend, the folks on Parliament Hill lend some of their bombast to the **Hot Air Balloon Festival** (819-243-2330), when hundreds of beautiful balloons from Canada, the U.S., and Europe take to the friendly skies.

NIGHTLIFE

Hull, Québec remains the place for the dedicated nightlifer, with establishments grinding and gnashing until 3am nightly. Sitting right across the Ottawa River from Ottawa, Hull is most noted for its less stringent drinking laws, including a legal drinking age of 18. Close to Gatineau Provincial Park, Hull connects to Ottawa by several bridges and the blue Hull buses from downtown Ottawa (see **Practical Information,** p. 895). Over 20 popular nightspots pack the **Promenade du Portage (a.k.a The Strip)** in Hull, just west of the Place Portage government office complex. The capital also has its own share of excitement, especially in the Byward Market area. Though Ottawa clubs close at 2am (often at 11pm on Su), many are coverless.

On a musical note, Ottawa caters to both listeners and dancers. **The Atomic,** 137 Besserer St. (241-2411), is so cool that it doesn't even need a sign, just two big, silver doors. (Cover $7 before 1am and $10 after. Open Th and Sa-Su 10pm-3am, F 10pm-5am.) Cybertonic juice and vitamin drinks are served along with booze. The **Reactor,** 18 York St. (241-8955), has bright lights and dance music (open daily 4pm-1am). Experience life, the universe, and a bit of everything else at **Zaphod Beeblebrox,** 27 York St. (562-1010), in Byward Market, a popular alternative club famous for their $6.50 Pangalactic Gargle Blasters. (Cover $2-10 depending on the band playing. Open M-F 4pm-2am, Sa-Su noon-2am.) A popular gay pub, **The Market Station,** 15 George St. (562-3540), sits above a happening, subterranean dance cavern called **The Well.** (Market Station open M 3pm-2am, Tu-Su 11:30am-2am. The Well 19+; cover $3; open Tu-Su 9pm-2am.) A slightly older crowd (25-35) gathers in bars on **Elgin St.**

■ Algonquin Provincial Park

The wilder Canada of endless rushing rivers and shimmering lakes awaits in Algonquin Provincial Park, about 250km west of Ottawa. From the city, take Hwy. 417 (the Queensway) west to the Renfrew Exit, then follow Hwy. 60 west to the park. For info and camping permits, visit the **East Gate Information Center** (open daily Apr. to mid-June 8am-5pm; June-Sept. 8am-9pm; Sept.-Oct. 8am-4:30pm) or the **Cache Lake Information Center** (open Apr. to mid-June 8am-4pm; mid-June to Aug. 8am-9pm; Sept.-Oct. 8am-4:30pm). For both, call 705-633-5572 daily 8am-8pm. Tents and trailers crowd the Hwy. 60 Corridor (permits $9.75 per night per site, with hookup

British Columbia and the Yukon Territory

NATIONAL PARKS

- 3 Banff
- 6 Glacier
- 15 Gwaii Haanas
- 25 Iwavik
- 2 Jasper
- 23 Kluane
- 5 Kootenay
- 7 Mt. Revelstoke
- 11 Pacific Rim
- 24 Vuntut
- 4 Yoho

PROVINCIAL PARKS

- 21 Atlin
- 14 Cape Scott
- 10 Garibaldi
- 17 Kwadacha Wilderness
- 20 Mt. Edziza
- 8 Mt. Robson
- 18 Muncho Lake
- 19 Spatsizi Plateau Wilderness
- 16 Stone Mountain
- 12 Strathcona
- 22 Tatshenshini-Alsek
- 13 Tweedsmuir
- 9 Wells Gray
- 1 Willmore Wilderness

Beaufort Sea

ALASKA

Inuvik

Fort Mcpherson

Tsiigehtchic

Top of the World Hwy

Dawson City

Beaver Creek

YUKON TERRITORY

Carmacks

Ross River

Burwash Landing

Haines Junction

Whitehorse

Carcross

Skagway

Teslin

Atlin

Haines

Juneau

Watson Lake

Campbell Hwy

NORTHWEST TERRITORIES

Telegraph Creek

Dease Lake

Fort Nelson

Cassiar Hwy

Alaska Hwy

Meziadin Jct.

Stewart

BRITISH COLUMBIA

Dawson Creek

ALBERTA

Prince Rupert

Yellowhead Hwy

Prince George

Masset

Port Clements

Queen Charlotte City

Sandspit

Queen Charlotte Islands

Bella Coola

McBride

Barkerville

Quesnel

Williams Lake

Tête Jaune Cache

Edmonton

Cariboo Hwy

Cache Creek

Revelstoke

Salmon Arm

Port Hardy

Whistler

PACIFIC OCEAN

Vancouver Island

Nanaimo

Hope

Penticton

Vancouver

Victoria

WASHINGTON

Dempster Hwy

Klondike Hwy

Alaska Hwy

0 150 miles

0 150 kilometers

On this map, due north varies according to longitude.

CANADA

$22.75). To experience the "essence of Algonquin," pierce the park interior (permits $6.50 per night, ages 6-17 $3.50). **Algonquin Reservation Network** (705-633-5538), handles reservations for 1200 sites on the Corridor (free showers, bathrooms, no hookups) and limitless primitive campsites in the interior, accessible only by hiking or canoe. Several outfitting stores in the park area rent backcountry gear; closest to the eastern entrance, **Opeongo Algonquin Outfitters** (613-637-2075), on Rte. 60 on Opeongo Lake, is about 15min. from the entrance. (Tents $6-10 per night; sleeping bags $4-5; canoes $17-100. Open daily May-June 8am-6pm; July-Aug. 8am-8pm; Sept.-Oct. 9am-6pm. Closed mid-Oct. to Apr.)

🐾 HIGHLIGHTS OF WESTERN CANADA

- **The Yukon.** Flightseeing in Kluane National Park (p. 917) and gold-panning in boom-town Dawson City (p. 918) are both unusual and memorable.
- **Scenic drives.** The glorious Dempster Hwy. (p. 920) leads all the way up to Inuvik, NWT.
- **National Parks:** Banff (p. 921) and Jasper (p. 923) in Alberta reign as two of the region's most beautiful. Pacific Rim National Park, BC contains the West Coast Trail (p. 911) with its isolated beaches and old growth rainforest.

British Columbia

British Columbia (BC) is Canada's westernmost province, with over 890,000 sq. km bordering four U.S. states (Washington, Idaho, Montana, and Alaska) and three Canadian entities (Alberta, the Yukon Territory, and the Northwest Territories). It attracts so many visitors that tourism has become its second-largest industry after logging.

PRACTICAL INFORMATION

Capital: Victoria.
Visitor Info: Tourism British Columbia, 1117 Wharf St., Victoria, BC V8W 2Z2 (800-663-6000 in BC, 250-387-1642 elsewhere; http://www.tbc.gov.bc.ca/tourism). **British Columbia Ministry of Environment, Lands, and Parks,** P.O. Box 9398, Stn. Prov. Govt., Victoria, BC V8W 9M9 (250-387-4609; http://www.elp.gov.bc.ca/bcparks).
Emergency: 911.
Drinking Age: 19.
Time Zone: Mostly Pacific (3hr. before Eastern), but Yoho and Kootenay National Parks are Mountain (2hr. before Eastern).
Postal Abbreviation: BC.
Sales Tax: 7%.

■ Vancouver

With kilometers of clean white beaches, a busy harbor greeting giant ships from distant ports, and large parks watched over by Haida totems and ancient trees, Western Canada's biggest city remains its most laid-back and permissive. In 1979, Vancouver elected Svend Robinson, the only openly gay Member of Parliament, not to mention a headstrong environmental activism. Rollerblades and skis far outnumber suits and cell phones, as the diverse and youthful population goes out of its way to enjoy spectacular natural surroundings. At the moment, a wave of Chinese immigration, mostly from the recently reabsorbed Hong Kong, is directing the city's economy and character more toward the Pacific Rim than to the rest of North America. Meanwhile, Vancouver's large Chinatown has thrived for generations, making up one of many ethnic neighborhoods around town.

ORIENTATION AND PRACTICAL INFORMATION

Vancouver looks like a mitten with the fingers pointing west and the thumb pointing northward (brace yourself for a never-ending metaphor). South of the hand flows the **Fraser River,** and beyond the fingertips lies the **Georgia Strait. Downtown** is at the base of the thumb, while at the thumb's tip lie the residential **West End** and **Stanley Park. Burrard Inlet** separates downtown from **North Vancouver;** the bridges over **False Creek** link downtown with **Kitsilano** ("Kits") and the rest of the city. East of downtown, where the thumb is attached, are **Gastown** and **Chinatown.** The **University of British Columbia** lies on top of the fingers at **Point Grey,** the westernmost end of the city, while the **airport** is south at the pinkie-tip. Kitsilano and Point Grey are separated by the north-south **Alma St. Hwy. 99** runs north-south through the city, and the **Trans-Canada Hwy. (Hwy. 1)** enters town from the east. Most of the city's attractions are grouped on the peninsula/thumb, and farther west.

Airport: Vancouver International (276-6101, tourist info 303-3601), on Sea Island, 23km south of the city center. To reach downtown from the airport, take bus #100 to the intersection of Granville and 70th Ave. Transfer there to bus #20, which arrives downtown by heading north on the Granville Mall. An **Airport Express** (946-8866) bus leaves from airport level #2 for downtown hotels and the bus station (4 per hr.; $10, seniors $8, ages 5-12 $5).

Trains: VIA Rail, 1150 Station St. (in Canada 800-561-8630, in the U.S. 800-561-3949). 3 trains per week to Jasper, AB ($156) and Edmonton, AB ($218). Open M, Th, and Sa 10:30am-8pm, Tu, F, and Su 8:30am-6pm, W 10:30am-6pm. **BC Rail,**

1311 W. 1st St. (984-5246), just over the Lions Gate Bridge at the foot of Pemberton St. in North Vancouver. Take the BC Rail Special Bus on Georgia St. or the SeaBus to North Vancouver, then bus #239 west. Daily trains to: Whistler ($30); Williams Lake ($118); Prince George ($190), and other points north. Open daily 8am-8pm.

Buses: Greyhound, 1150 Station St. (482-8747), in the VIA Rail station. To: Calgary, AB (4 per day, $105); Banff, AB (4 per day, $99); Jasper, AB (2 per day, $91); and Seattle, WA (7 per day, $26). Open daily 5:30am-12:30am. **Pacific Coach Lines,** 1150 Station St. (662-8074) serves Southern BC, including Vancouver Island. Service to Victoria ($26, round-trip $49) includes ferry.

Ferries: BC Ferries (888-BCFERRY/223-3779). To the Gulf Islands, Sunshine Coast, and Vancouver Island ($8.50, ages 5-11 $4.25, car and driver $35-36.75, motorcycle and driver $22-23, bike and rider $11; fares cheapest mid-week). Ferries to Nanaimo on Vancouver Island leave from **Horseshoe Bay,** northwest of Vancouver. Ferries to Victoria or the Gulf Islands leave from the **Tsawwassen** (suh-WAH-sen) terminal, southwest of Vancouver. Both ferry terminals are quite far from town.

Public Transportation: BC Transit (521-0400) covers most of the city and suburbs, with direct transport or easy connections to the ferry's points of departure: Tsawwassen, Horseshoe Bay, and the airport. Riding in the **central zone,** which encompasses most of the actual city of Vancouver, always costs $1.50 for 1½hr. (students, seniors, and ages 5-11 75¢). During peak hrs. (before 6:30pm), it costs $2.25 (students, seniors, and ages 5-11 $1.50) to travel between 2 zones and $3 to travel through 3 zones. During off-peak hrs., passengers pay only the 1-zone price. Transfers are free. Day passes ($6; students, seniors, and ages 5-11 $4) are sold at all 7-11 and Safeway stores, SkyTrain stations, and HI-C hostels. Single fares, passes, and transfers also good for the **SeaBus** and the elevated **SkyTrain.** SeaBus runs from the **Granville Waterfront Station** at the foot of Granville St. in downtown Vancouver, to **Lonsdale Quay** at the foot of Lonsdale Ave. in North Vancouver. Fares are the same as 1-zone bus fares, and all transfers and passes are accepted.

Taxis: Yellow Cab (681-1111 or 800-898-8294). $2.10 base, $1.21 per km. 24hr.

Car Rental: EZ Car and Truck Rentals, 4-2910 Commercial Dr. (875-6210). $30 per day, plus 15¢ per km after 200km. Must be 19 with major credit card or $300 cash deposit. Open M-F 8am-5:30pm, Sa 8am-6pm, Su 9am-5pm.

Visitor Info: Vancouver Travel Infocentre, 200 Burrard St. (683-2000). Full info on accommodations, tours, and activities spanning much of BC. Courtesy phones for reservations. Open daily 8am-6pm. The **Talking Yellow Pages** (299-9000) has recorded info about virtually anything in town.

Special Concerns Info: BC Coalition of People with Disabilities, 204-456 W. Broadway (875-0188). Open M-F 9am-5pm. **Gay and Lesbian Centre,** 1170 Bute St. Counseling and info. Very helpful staff. **Vancouver Prideline** (684-6869), staffed daily 7-10pm. Fantastic library and reading room. Reception M-F 10am-4pm. Library open M-Tu and Th-F 11:30am-9:30pm, W and Sa-Su 3:30-9:30pm.

Internet Access: Digital U Cybercafé, 101-1595 W. Broadway (731-1011). $9.50 per hr. Open M-F 9am-midnight, Sa 10am-1am, Su 10am-midnight.

Post Office: 349 W. Georgia St. (662-5725). Open M-F 8am-5:30pm. **Postal code:** V6B 3P7. **Area code:** 604.

ACCOMMODATIONS AND CAMPGROUNDS

Greater Vancouver is a teeming warren of B&Bs. Less expensive rates average about $45-60 for singles and $55-75 for doubles. The infocenter maintains an extensive list of options. **Town and Country Bed and Breakfast** (731-5942) or **Best Canadian** (738-7207) match travelers with B&Bs, usually for a fee.

Cambie International Hostel, 300 Cambie St. (684-6466), in Gastown. Tight but tidy rooms with large beds fit 2-6 people per room. Students and members $20, others $25. Free linen and airport pick-up. Raucous pub downstairs (see p. 909).

Vancouver Hostel Downtown (HI-C), 1114 Burnaby St. (684-4565). Perched on the border between downtown and the West End. Ultra-modern and ultra-clean, this 225-bed facility puts you smack in the middle of everything. Only 4 bunks in each room, and an array of goodies including game room, kitchen, free linen, and organized tours of the Vancouver area. Free shuttle to Vancouver Hostel Jericho Beach (see below). Open 24hr. Bunks $19, nonmembers $23; private doubles $48/$56. Reservations crucial in summer.

Vancouver Hostel Jericho Beach (HI-C), 1515 Discovery St. (224-3208), in Jericho Beach Park. Turn north off 4th Ave. and follow signs for Marine Dr., or take bus #4 from Granville St. downtown. Institutional but clean, at a peaceful location with a great view of the city. 285 beds in 14-person dorm rooms, and 9 family rooms. Good cooking facilities, TV room, laundry. Organizes tours, trips to Vancouver bars, and bike rentals. A major junction for international backpackers. $17.50, nonmembers $22. Parking $3 per day, or find a spot in the nearby neighborhood for free. Free shuttle to Vancouver Hostel Downtown (see above). Free linen. Cafe open daily 7:30-11:30am and 5:30-11:30pm. Reservations imperative in summer.

Paul's Guest House, 345 W. 14th Ave. (872-4753), south of downtown. Take bus #15. One of Vancouver's best B&B deals. Clean, cheap, and cheerful. The garrulous Paul speaks 11 languages, sometimes all at once, and if he can't put you up in one of his welcoming rooms, he'll try to arrange something at another B&B. Shared baths. Singles $40-60; doubles $60-75; rates drop in winter. Full breakfast included.

The Globetrotter's Inn, 170 W. Esplanade (988-2082), in North Vancouver. Close to SeaBus terminal and Lonsdale Quay Markets. Shared kitchen, pool table, free laundry access. Can get somewhat rowdy. Beds $17.50; singles $30; doubles $40, with bath $45. Reception 8am-11pm. Reservations recommended.

Richmond RV Park, 6200 River Rd. (270-7878), near Holly Bridge in Richmond. Take Hwy. 99 to Richmond Exit, follow Russ Baker Way, go left on Gilbert, right at Elm Bridge, take the next immediate right, then go left at the stop sign. The best deal within 13km of downtown. Scant privacy, but the showers are great. 2-person sites $17, with hookup $23; $3 per additional person. Open Apr.-Oct.

FOOD

Vancouver's international restaurants serve some of the best food in the province. The city's **Chinatown** is the second largest in North America, second only to San Francisco's, and the **Indian neighborhoods** along Main, Fraser, and 49th St. serve exquisite fare. The entire world from Vietnamese noodle shops to Italian cafes seems represented in ethnic foods lining **Commercial Dr.,** east of Chinatown. **Granville Island Market** (666-5784), southwest of downtown under the Granville Bridge, intersperses trendy shops, art galleries, restaurants, and countless produce stands selling local and imported fruits and vegetables. Take bus #50 from Granville Mall downtown (open daily 9am-6pm; in winter closed M).

WaaZuBee Café, 1622 Commercial Dr. (253-5299), at E. 1st St. The funkiest restaurant on a Street of Funk. Sleek, metallic decoration, ambient music, artwork on the walls and in the brilliantly prepared food. Smoked chicken fettuccine $10; Thai prawns $7; veggie burger $6.50. Open M-F 11:30am-1am, Sa 11am-1am, Su 11am-midnight. Glam sister restaurant **Subeez,** at the intersection of Smithe and Homer downtown, serves the same food with more of a weekend attitude.

The Naam, 2724 W. 4th Ave. (738-7151), at MacDonald St. Take bus #4 or 7 from Granville Mall. The most diverse vegetarian menu around. Homey interior and tree-covered patio seating always make a perfect refuge. Crying Tiger Thai stir fry $8, enchiladas $9, tofulati ice cream $3.50. Live music nightly 7-10pm. Open 24hr.

Calhoun's Bakery Café, 3035 W. Broadway (737-7062). Meals: light and home-cooked. Prices: low. Coffees, teas, and baked goods: plentiful. Conclusion: this cafe meets all the criteria for a sweet 24hr. hangout. Pasta dishes $4-6, tortilla pie $5.

Cactus Club Café, 1136 Robson St. (687-3278). Trendy cafe and night spot for Vancouver's self-designated hippest hepcats. Alcohol-themed foods, a number of vegetarian items, and a weird sense of humor. Jack Daniels' soaked ribs ($9.45) and Strong to the Finish Spinach Quesadillas ($6) are highly recommended. Also at 4397 W. 10th (222-1342). Open Su-W 11am-midnight, Th-Sa 11am-1:30am.

Pho Hoang, 238 E. Georgia St. (682-5666), near Main St. Take bus #3 or 8 from downtown. Although not the most exciting spot in the city, this is the place to go for a big, cheap, nostril-seducing bowl of Vietnamese noodle soup ($4.50-5.25). Also at 3610 Main St., at 20th Ave. Open M-Th 10am-8pm, F-Su 10am-9pm.

Nirvana, 2313 Main St. (87-CURRY/872-8779), at 7th Ave. Take bus #3, 8, or 9. Come as you are. Savor the aroma of authentic Indian cuisine. Discover the sound of one hand clapping over chicken or vegetable curry ($6-8); become one with everything through the chef's special combos ($11). Open daily 11am-11pm.

Nuff-Nice-Ness, 1861 Commercial Dr. (255-4211), at 3rd. Nice price and no fuss in this small Jamaican deli. Jerk chicken with salad and rice $6.25; beef, chicken, or veggie patties $2. Open M-F noon-9pm.

SIGHTS

The big-screen star of Vancouver is the **Omnimax Theatre,** part of **Science World,** 1455 Quebec St. (268-6363), on the Main St. stop of the SkyTrain. *(Open daily 10am-6pm, call for winter hrs. $10.50, seniors and children $7. Omnimax Su-F 10am-5pm, Sa 10am-9pm; $9.75. Combined tickets for museum and Omnimax $13.50, seniors and children $9.50.)* Everything from asteroids to zephyrs appears on the 27m sphere, sucking viewers into a celluloid wonderland. Science World also features more tangible hands-on exhibits and fact-crammed shows for children. **Lookout!,** 555 W. Hastings St. (689-0421), offers fantastic 360° views of the city! *(Open daily 8:30am-10:30pm; in winter 10am-9pm. $8, students $6, seniors $7. 50% discount with HI membership or receipt from Vancouver International Hostel.)* Tickets are expensive! But they're good for the whole day! The **Vancouver Art Gallery,** 750 Hornby St. (682-5621), in Robson Sq., displays an innovative collection of classical and contemporary art. *(Open M-W 10am-6pm, Th-F 10am-9pm, Sa 10am-6pm, Su noon-5pm. $9.75, students $5.50, seniors $7, under 12 free; Th 5-9pm $4.)*

Gastown is a revitalized turn-of-the-century district cleverly disguised as an expensive tourist trap. One of the oldest neighborhoods in Vancouver, adjacent to downtown, and an easy walk from the Granville mall, it is bordered by Richards St. to the west, Columbia St. to the east, Hastings St. to the south, and the waterfront to the north. Gastown is named for "Gassy Jack" Deighton, a glib con man who opened Vancouver's first saloon here in 1867. Today, the area overflows with craft shops, nightclubs, restaurants, and boutiques. Many establishments stay open and well-populated at night. Stroll along Water St. and stop to hear the rare **steam-powered clock** on the corner of Cambie St. eerily whistle the notes of the Westminster Chimes every 15min. Free 1½hr. **tours** (683-5650) leave from the **Gassy Jack statue** at Water and Canal St. daily at 2pm.

Chinatown, southeast of Gastown, is a rather long walk away through undesirable parts of town. Take bus #22 north on Burrard St. to Pender and Carrall St. and return by bus #22 westbound on Pender. The neighborhood bustles with restaurants, shops, bakeries, and **the world's skinniest building** at 8 W. Pender St. In 1912, the city expropriated all but a 2m (6 ft.) strip of Chang Toy's property in order to expand the street. In a fit of stubbornness, he decided to build on the land anyhow. Currently, the 30m x 2m building is home to an insurance company, where times are always a little tight. Less humorous but more serene, **Dr. Sun Yat-Sen Classical Chinese Garden,** 578 Carrall St. (689-7133), maintains many imported Chinese plantings, carvings, and rock formations. *(Open daily 9:30am-7pm; in winter 10:30am-4:30pm. $6.50, students $4, seniors $5, children free, families $12. Tours every hr. 10am-6pm.)* Don't miss the sights, sounds, smells, and tastes of the weekly **night market** along Pender and Keefer St. (F-Su 6:30-11pm). Chinatown itself is relatively safe, but its surroundings make up some of Vancouver's seedier sections; *stay away from E. Hastings St.*

The high point of a visit to UBC is its breathtaking **Museum of Anthropology,** 6393 NW Marine Dr. (822-5087, recording 822-3825); take bus #4 or 10 from Granville St. *(Open M and W-Su 10am-5pm, Tu 10am-9pm; Sept.-May closed M. $6, students and seniors $3.50, under 6 free, families $15; Tu after 5pm free.)* The high-ceilinged glass and concrete building houses totems and other massive wood sculptures crafted by indigenous coastal people, including a fantastic Bill Reid work of Raven discovering the first human beings in a giant clam shell. Caretakers of the **Nitobe Memorial Garden,** 1903 West Mall (822-6038), have fashioned the only Shinto garden outside of Japan (open daily 10am-6pm; Sept.-June 10am-2pm; $2.50, students and seniors $1.75). Near the gardens, the **Asian Centre,** 1871 West Mall (822-0810), showcases free exhibits of

Asian-Canadian art and the largest Asian library in Canada (open M-F 9am-5pm). The **Botanical Gardens,** 6804 SW Marine Dr. (822-9666), are a collegiate Eden encompassing a dozen gardens in the central campus area ($4.50, students $2.25).

PARKS AND BEACHES

Established in 1889 at the tip of the downtown peninsula, 1000-acre **Stanley Park** (257-8400) is a testament to the foresight of Vancouver's urban planners. An easy escape from nearby West End and downtown, the thickly wooded park is laced with cycling and hiking trails and surrounded by a seawall promenade. On the park's small eastern peninsula of Brockton Point is the **Brockton Oval,** a cinder running track with hot showers and changing rooms. Two-hour **nature walks** start from the **Nature House** (257-8544), below the Lost Lagoon bus loop (Su 1pm; $4, under 12 free). Take a dip in the **Second Beach Pool** (257-8371), with warmer, more chlorinated water than the nearby Pacific ($3.70). At the kid-friendly **Vancouver Aquarium** (268-9900), on the park's eastern side not far from the entrance, exotic aquatic critters swim in glass habitats. *(Open daily 10am-5:30pm. $12, students and seniors $10.50, under 12 $8; prices drop in winter.)*

During the summer, the tiny **False Creek Ferry** (684-7781) carries passengers from the Aquatic Centre (see below) to **Vanier** (van-YAY) **Park** and its museum complex. *(4 ferries per hr. daily 10am-8pm. $1.75, children $1.)* This park can also be reached by bus #22, south of downtown on Burrard St. Another ferry runs from the Maritime Museum in Vanier Park to **Granville Island** ($3). At the park, the circular **Vancouver Museum,** 1100 Chestnut St. (736-4431), displays artifacts from local native cultures, as well as several international exhibits. *(Open daily 10am-5pm; in winter closed M. $5; students, seniors, and under 18 $2.50; families $10.)* In the same building, the **H. R. MacMillan Planetarium** (738-7827) presents fact-packed star shows and fact-free laser rock jams. *(Star shows $6.50, seniors and children $5. Laser shows $7.75, seniors free Tu.)*

Near UBC, in **Pacific Spirit Regional Park,** unexplored woods stretch from inland hills to the shore near Spanish Banks. With 50km of gravel and dirt trails through dense forest, the park is ideal for jogging, hiking, and cycling. Free maps are available at the **Park Centre** on 16th Ave., near Blanca.

Follow the western side of the Stanley Park seawall south to **Sunset Beach Park,** a strip of grass and beach extending all the way to the Burrard Bridge. At the southern end of Sunset Beach is the **Aquatic Centre,** 1050 Beach Ave. (665-3424), a public facility with a sauna, gymnasium, diving tank, and, for some reason, a 50m indoor salt-water pool ($3.70). For less crowding, more students, and free showers (always a winning combination), visit **Jericho Beach.** North Marine Dr. runs along the beach, and a cycling path at the side of the road leads to the westernmost end of the UBC campus. Bike and hiking trails cut through the campus and crop its edges. Directly across the street from the UBC campus, **Wreck Beach** is Vancouver's most interesting, eclectic, and clothing-optional beach; take entry trail #6 down the hill from SW Marine Dr. The **Wreck Beach Preservation Society** (273-6950) has more info.

ENTERTAINMENT AND NIGHTLIFE

The renowned **Vancouver Symphony Orchestra (VSO)** (876-3434) plays in the refurbished **Orpheum Theater,** 884 Granville St. (665-3050). The VSO often joins forces with groups like the **Vancouver Bach Choir** (921-8012) to present a diverse selection of music designed to appeal to a variety of tastes. **Robson Square Conference Centre,** 800 Robson St. (661-7373), sponsors events almost daily in summer and weekly the rest of the year, either on the plaza at the square or in the center itself. Their concerts, dance workshops, theater productions, exhibits, lectures, symposia, and films are all free or nearly free. The **Arts Club Theatre** (687-5315) hosts big-name plays and musicals. The **Ridge Theatre** (738-6311), 3131 Arbutus, often shows art-house, European, and vintage films ($6). The **Paradise,** 919 Granville (681-1732), at Smythe, shows triple-features of second-run movies for $3.

Purple Onion, 15 Water St. (602-9442), in Gastown. Slurps in the crowds with an eclectic musical selection, inviting lounge chairs, and 2 rooms—1 live, 1 Memorex.

The lounge features live blues, R&B, jazz, and funk acts, while the DJs spin acid jazz, disco, soul, funk, Latin, swing, and reggae. Cover $3-6. Open M-Th 8pm-2am, F-Sa 7pm-2am, Su 7pm-midnight.

The King's Head, 1618 Yew St. (733-3933), at 1st St., in Kitsilano. Cheap drinks, cheap food, mellow atmosphere, and a great location near the beach all make this pub popular with Kits locals. Tiny bands play acoustic sets on a stage even tinier still. Daily drink specials. Pints $3. Gullet-filling Beggar's Breakfast $3. Open M-F 7am-1am, Sa 7:30am-1:30am, Su 7:30am-midnight.

Celebrities, 1022 Davie St. (689-3180), at Burrard, downtown. Ever so big, ever so hot, and ever so popular with Vancouver's gay crowd, though it draws all kinds. Straight nights (Tu and F); retro night (Su); occasional drag pageants and strippers. Open M-Sa 9pm-2am, Su 9pm-midnight.

The Cambie, 300 Cambie St. (684-6466), in Gastown. Downstairs from the hostel (see p. 909). Young crowds from all over the cultural spectrum, picnic tables made from bowling lanes, sports TVs, sandwiches ($3.50-5.50), breakfasts, snacks, and kindly priced beer (pint of Molson $2.50, other pints $3.75). Open 9am-1:30am.

VANCOUVER ISLAND

■ Victoria

Clean, polite, outdoorsy, and tourist-friendly, Victoria gives Dudley Do-Right a run for his money. A mix of British, Asian, U.S., and Native American elements comprise BC's capital city. There's an English pub on every downtown corner, and East Asian restaurants, markets, and stores dot virtually every neighborhood.

PRACTICAL INFORMATION **Government St.** and **Douglas St.** are the main north-south roads, running through downtown. To the north, Douglas St. becomes Hwy. 1, while **Blanshard St.,** 1 block to the east, becomes Hwy. 17. Cross the Johnson St. Bridge (Pandora St. leads to the bridge from downtown) and take the second right or left onto Tyee St. for **free street parking,** a mere 10min. walk from downtown.

Laidlaw, 700 Douglas St. (385-4411 or 800-318-0818), at Belleville St., and its affiliates, **Pacific Coach Lines** and **Island Coach Lines,** run buses to Nanaimo (6 per day, $17); Vancouver (8 per day, $26); and Port Hardy (2 per day, $82). **BC Ferries** (381-5335 or 888-BC-FERRY/223-3779) depart from Swartz Bay to Vancouver (Tsawwassen) (8-15 per day; $8.50, bikes $2.50, car and driver $36-38). Bus #70 runs from the ferry terminal to downtown ($2.25). **Washington State Ferries** (381-1551 or 656-1531, in the U.S. 206-464-6400 or 800-84-FERRY/843-3779) departs from Sidney to Anacortes, WA (2 per day in summer, 1 per day in winter; CDN$9.50, US$6.90; car with driver CDN$50, US$35.65). A ticket to Anacortes allows free and unlimited stopovers anywhere along the eastward route, including the San Juan Islands. **BC Transit** (382-6161) serves downtown from the corner of Douglas and Yates St. (Single-zone travel $1.75; north to Swartz Bay, Sidney, and the Butchart Gardens $2.50; seniors $1.10; under 5 free. Day passes $5.50, seniors $4.) **Disabilities Services for Local Transit** (727-7811) is open Monday to Friday 8am-5pm. **Victoria Taxi** (383-7111) charges $2.15 base, $1.30 per km (24hr.). **Island Auto Rentals,** 837 Yates St. (384-4881), charges $20 per day, $12 insurance, and 12¢ per km after 50km (must be 19 with credit card). **Tourism Victoria,** 812 Wharf St. (953-2033), at Government St., doles out steaming scoops of info (open daily 8:30am-8pm; in winter 9am-5pm). **Internet access** is available at **Victoria Cyber Café,** 1414B Douglas St. (995-0175), for 14¢ per min. (open daily 10am-10pm, sometimes later). **Post Office:** 621 Discovery St. (963-1350; open M-F 8am-6pm). **Postal code:** V8W 1L0. **Area code:** 250.

ACCOMMODATIONS AND CAMPGROUNDS **Victoria Backpackers Hostel,** 1418 Fernwood Rd. (386-4471), is a funky, colorful old house with porch, backyard, lounge, and kitchen. Take bus #10 to Fernwood and Johnson St. (Bunks $13, $12 per additional night; private doubles $40. Dinner every evening $3-5. Free parking. Free linen. Laundry $2 per load. Reception daily 8am-noon and 4-11pm.) **Selkirk Guest House,** 934 Selkirk Ave. (389-1213), in West Victoria, invites guests to become a part of the family, with flowery sheets, free canoes, and a hot tub right on the water. Take bus #14 along Craigflower to Tillicum; Selkirk is 1 block north. (Kitchen, free linen, laundry. Dorms $18, private rooms $50; lower in off season. Breakfast $5.)

Goldstream Provincial Park, 2930 Trans-Canada Hwy. (391-2300; reservations 800-689-9025), 20km northwest of Victoria, offers a forested riverside area with great hiking trails and swimming (flush toilets and firewood; $15.50). The sites at **Thetis Lake Campground,** 1938 Trans-Canada Hwy. (478-3845), 10km north of the city center, are not large, but some are peaceful and removed. ($15 for 2 people, full hookup $19; 50¢ per additional person. Showers 25¢ per 5min., flush toilets, laundry.)

FOOD AND NIGHTLIFE Chinatown, extending from Fisgard and Government St. to the northwest, offers a range of Chinese cuisine and small, fruit-stocked grocery stores. In **Fernwood Village,** 3 blocks north of Johnson St. and accessible by bus #10, creative restaurants are scattered among craft shops. The menu at **John's Place,** 723 Pandora St. (389-0711), between Douglas and Blanshard St., is graced by Canadian fare with a Thai twist plus a little Mediterranean and Mexican thrown in. (*Panang goong* $11.50. M Thai night, Tu Mexican night, W perogie night. Open M-Sa 7am-11pm, Su 8am-3pm and 5-10pm.) **The Blethering Place,** 2250 Oak Bay Ave. (598-1413), at Monterey St., amasses a huge plate of sandwiches and pastries to accompany High Tea ($10-12) and blethering ("voluble senseless talking"). Take bus #2 from Douglas at Yates or drive west on Fort St. and turn right on Oak Bay. (Dinners from $9. Open daily 8am-10pm.)

Steamers Public House, 570 Yates St. (381-4340), attracts a young, happy crowd dancing to different music every night. (Open stage M, jazz night Tu. Lunch specials M-F until 3pm; $5-7. Open M-Sa 11:30am-2am, Su 11:30am-midnight.) **Drawing Room,** 751 View St. (920-7797), is a happening club considerate enough to offer a lounge with easy chairs, pool tables, and a wall-to-wall carpet for dancers (cover M-F $3, Sa-Su $4; open Tu-Th 8pm-2am, F-Sa 9pm-2am).

SIGHTS AND OUTDOORS The fantastically thorough **Royal British Columbia Museum,** 675 Belleville St. (recording 387-3014, operator 387-3701), presents excellent exhibits on the biological, geological, and cultural history of the province, from protozoans to the present. (*Open daily 9am-5pm. $7, seniors $3.21, children $2.14, under 5 free.*) The public **Art Gallery of Greater Victoria,** 1040 Moss St. (384-4101), houses magnificent exhibits from its collection of 14,000 pieces, covering contemporary Canada, traditional and contemporary Asia, North America, and Europe. (*Open M-W and F-Sa 10am-5pm, Th 10am-9pm, Su 1-5pm. $5, students and seniors $3, under 12 free; M free.*) Across the street from the museum stand the imposing **Parliament Buildings,** 501 Belleville St. (387-3046), home of the provincial government. (*Open M-F 8:30am-5pm, Sa-Su open for tours only. Free tours leave from main steps daily 9am-5pm, 3 times per hr.*) When the House is in session, visitors to the **public gallery** can see Members of Parliament yapping about matters of great import. Just north of Fort St. on Wharf St. is **Bastion Sq.,** home to the **Maritime Museum,** 28 Bastion Sq. (385-4222), which houses a collection including ship models, nautical instruments, and a torpedo. (*Open daily 9:30am-4:30pm. $5, students $3, seniors $4, ages 6-11 $3. Ticket good for 3 days.*)

The elaborate **Butchart Gardens** (recording 652-5256, office 652-4422) sprawl across a valley 21km north of Victoria off Hwy. 17. (*Open daily July-Aug. 9am-10:30pm, closing time varies, fireworks Sa around 10pm. $15.50, ages 11-17 $7.75, ages 5-10 $2.*) Immaculate landscaping includes a rose garden, Japanese and Italian gardens, fountains, and wheelchair-accessible walking paths. **Beacon Hill Park,** off Douglas St. south of the Inner Harbour, and just blocks from downtown, pleases walkers, bikers, and picnickers. Mountain bikers can tackle the **Galloping Goose,** a 60km trail beginning in downtown Victoria and continuing to the west coast of Vancouver Island through towns, rainforests, and canyons.

Ocean River Sports, 1437 Store St. (381-4233 or 800-909-4233), offers kayak rentals, tours, and lessons. *(Open M-Th and Sa 9:30am-5:30pm, F 9:30am-8:30pm, Su 11am-5pm. ½-day rentals $28 for a single kayak, $34 for a double, $28 for a canoe; all equipment included.)* **Ocean Explorations,** 146 Kingston St. (383-ORCA/6722), located in the Coast Victoria Harbourside Hotel, runs tours in Zodiac raft-boats. *(Runs Apr.-Oct. 3hr. tours. $75, hostelers and children $50, less in early season. Free pick-up at hostels.)*

■ Pacific Rim National Park

Pacific Rim National Park, a thin strip of land on the island's remote western coast, is separately accessible at all three of its disparate regions. The south end of the park—the West Coast Trailhead at **Port Renfrew**—lies at the end of Hwy. 14, which runs west from Hwy. 1 not far from Victoria. **West Coast Trail Express** (477-8700) runs one bus per day from Victoria to Port Renfrew ($28), and one bus from Nanaimo to Port Renfrew ($47). Reservations are required, and can also be made for drop-off and pick-up at certain beaches and trailheads along these routes. The fantastic **West Coast Trail,** covering the southern third of the park between Port Renfrew and Bamfield, traces the shoreline through 77km of forests and waterfalls, scaling wooden ladders and rocky slopes; recommended hiking time is about a week ($25 reservation fee, $70 trail use fee, $25 ferry crossing fee). The trail is open from May 1 to September 30; reservations should be made with **BC Parks,** Box 280, Ucluelet V0R 3A0 (800-663-6000), 3 months before starting date of your hike.

The park's middle section—**Bamfield** and the **Broken Group Islands** in **Barkley Sound**—is far more difficult to reach. Hwy. 18 connects to Hwy. 1 at **Duncan** (City of Totems!) about 60km north of Victoria. **West Coast Trail Express** runs one bus per day from Victoria to Bamfield ($37) and one per day from Nanaimo to Bamfield ($47); reservations are required. **Pacheenaht Band Bus Service** (647-5521) runs between Port Renfrew to Bamfield ($40). **Alberni Marine Transportation** (723-8313 or 800-663-7192) floats year-round from Port Alberni to Bamfield ($20).

To reach **Long Beach,** at the park's northern reaches, take the spectacular drive across Vancouver Island on Hwy. 4 to the **Pacific Rim Hwy.** This stretch connects the towns of sleepy **Ucluelet** (yoo-CLOO-let) and crunchy **Tofino** (toe-FEE-no). Hwy. 4 branches west of Hwy. 1 about 35km north of Nanaimo, leads 50km through Port Alberni, and continues 92km to the Pacific coast. **Laidlaw** (725-3101 in Tofino, 726-4334 in Ucluelet) sends four buses daily from Victoria to Tofino ($45) and Ucluelet ($42). **Alberni Marine Transportation** runs from Port Alberni to Ucluelet ($22).

SOUTHEASTERN BRITISH COLUMBIA

■ Glacier National Park

Canada's most aptly named national park is home to over 400 of the giant, slow-moving ice flows. The Trans-Canada Hwy. cuts a thin ribbon through the center of the park, blessing motorists with views of high-in-the-sky glaciers. Eight **hiking trails** begin at the Illecillewaet campground (see below), 3.4km west of Rogers Pass. The 1km **Meeting of the Waters Trail** leads to the impressive confluence of the **Illecillewaet** and **Asulkan Rivers.** The 4.2km **Avalanche Crest Trail** offers spectacular views of **Rogers Pass,** the **Hermit Range,** and the Illecillewaet River Valley; the treeless slopes below the crest testify to the destructive power of winter snowslides. In late summer, when enough snow has melted, the **Perley Rock Trail** leads directly to the **Illecillewaet Glacier,** with a steep 5.6km ascent. The **Copperstain Trail,** 10km east of the Glacier Park Lodge at the Beaver River Trailhead, leads 16km (6hr.) uphill through alpine meadows.

CANADA

Illecillewaet (ill-uh-SILL-uh-watt) and **Loop Brook** campgrounds offer flush toilets, kitchen shelters with cook stoves, and firewood (sites $13; open mid-June to Sept.). Backcountry campers need a **backcountry pass** ($6) from the **Parks Canada** office in Revelstoke (837-7500) or in the Rogers Pass Information Centre (see below). Campers must pitch their tents at least 5km from the pavement.

Glacier lies 350km west of Calgary and 723km east of Vancouver. **Greyhound** (837-5874) makes four trips daily from Revelstoke ($9.20). In an **emergency,** call the **Park Warden Office** (837-6274; open daily 7am-5pm; winter hrs. vary). **Rogers Pass Information Centre** (814-5232) is on the highway in the town of Glacier (open daily in summer 9am-6pm; closed off-season Sa-Su; call for hrs.). **Park passes** ($4 per day, $35 per year) are required. **Area code:** 250.

Yoho National Park

A Cree expression for awe and wonder, Yoho is the perfect name for this small, uncrowded park, stuffed with natural splendors such as the largest waterfall in the Rockies, the Continental Divide, and the Burgess Shale, which made its way into paleontology textbooks in the early 20th century when it revealed the complexity of ancient life. The **Yoho-Burgess Shale Foundation** (800-343-3006) offers the only access to the park's 505-million-year-old fossils through guided, educational, full-day hikes (tours July-Sept.; reservations required). They also run a steep 6km loop to the **Mt. Stephen Fossil Beds** ($25) and a 20km round-trip to **Walcott's Quarry** ($45). When the snow has melted in mid- to late summer, the 10.6km **Iceline Trail,** starting at the hostel (see below), leads to valley views and an up-close introduction to the **Emerald Glacier. Lake O'Hara,** in the northeast end of the park, can only be reached by a 13km pedestrian trail or on a park-operated bus (reservations 343-6433; round-trip $12). The splendid **Takakkaw Falls** are visible for a good portion of the drive up Yoho Valley Rd., but the force of the water and thick mist are more intense from the short trail to the falls, 14km off the Trans-Canada Hwy.

With one of the best locations of all the Rocky Mountain hostels, the **Whiskey Jack Hostel,** 13km off the Trans-Canada on Yoho Valley Rd., just before Takakkaw Falls, is the best indoor place to stay while enjoying Yoho's sights. Make reservations through the Banff International Hostel (403-762-4122; see p. 924). (Kitchen, campfires, indoor plumbing, propane light, easy access to high country trails. $13, nonmembers $17. Open June-Sept.) All campgrounds are first come, first served, but the abundance of backcountry camping keeps overcrowding to a minimum. **Hoodoo Creek,** on the west end of the park, has kitchen shelters, running hot water, a nearby river, and a playground ($14; open late June-Aug.). **Kicking Horse,** on Yoho Valley Rd. off the highway, has hot showers, flush toilets, and wheelchair access ($17). Lovely views unfold from the high **Takakkaw Falls Campground,** on Yoho Valley Rd., which requires parking in the falls lot and hauling gear 650m to the peaceful sites (pump water, pit toilets, no cars; $12; open late June to late Sept.).

Yoho lies on the Trans-Canada Hwy. (Hwy. 1), adjacent to Banff National Park. The town of **Field,** within the park, is 27km west of Lake Louise on Hwy. 1. **Greyhound** does stop for travelers waving their arms on the highway. **Hostelling International** runs a shuttle service connecting all the Rocky Mountain hostels in Yoho, Banff, and Jasper, as well as Calgary ($7-65). The **Visitor Information Centre** (343-6783) is in Field on Hwy. 1 (open daily 9am-7pm; in spring and fall 9am-5pm; in winter 9am-4pm). In case of **emergency,** call the **Warden Office** (403-762-4506; 24hr.) or the **RCMP** (344-2221) in nearby Golden. Yoho is in the **Mountain Time Zone,** 1hr. ahead of Pacific Time. **Post Office:** 312 Stephen Ave. (343-6365; open M-F 8:30am-4:30pm). **Postal code:** V0A 1G0. **Area code:** 250.

Kootenay National Park

Kootenay's best feature is what it lacks: people. Stately conifers, alpine meadows, and pristine peaks hide in Banff's shadow, allowing travelers to get off the tourist track and experience the solitude and beauty of the Canadian Rockies. The 95km **Banff-**

Windermere Hwy. (Hwy. 93) forms the bending backbone of the park, following the **Kootenay** and **Vermilion Rivers** past glacier-enclosed peaks, dense stands of virgin forest, and green rivers. About 15km from the Banff border, the 750m **Marble Canyon Trail** traverses a remarkably deep, narrow, limestone gorge before ending at voluminous falls. Another tourist-heavy path is the 1.6km, 30min., wheelchair-accessible **Paint Pots Trail,** leaving Hwy. 93 3.2km south of Marble Canyon and leading to sunset-red springs (rich in iron oxide). An easy day hike, the **Stanley Glacier Trail** starts 2.5km north of Marble Canyon and leads 4.8km into a glacier-gouged valley, ending 1.6km from the foot of **Stanley Glacier.** The awe-inspiring 16.5km loop over **Kindersley Pass** climbs 1000m; the two trailheads at either end of the loop, **Sinclair Creek** and **Kindersley Pass,** are less than 1km apart on Hwy. 93, about 15km inside the west gate entrance. Overnight backcountry camping requires a **wilderness pass,** available at the info center ($6 per person per night, $35 per season).

The **Columbia Motel,** 4886 St. Joseph St. (347-9557), has clean rooms and some of the lowest rates in town ($45-50, with kitchen $50-55). The park's most mammoth campground is **Redstreak,** on the access road that departs Hwy. 95 near the south end of Radium Hot Springs, with flush toilets, showers, firewood, playgrounds, and swarms of RVs (open mid-May to mid-Sept.; $16, full hookup $21). **McLeod Meadows,** 27km north of the West Gate entrance on Hwy. 93, offers more solitude, wooded sites, plenty of elbow room, and access to hiking trails ($13; open mid-May to mid-Sept.). **Marble Canyon,** 86km north of the West Gate entrance, also provides more privacy than its big brother down the road ($13; open mid-June through Aug.). From September 14 to May 7, snag one of seven free winter sites at the **Dolly Varden** picnic area, 36km north of the West Gate entrance, which boasts free firewood, water, toilets, and a kitchen shelter. **Free camping** outside the park is plentiful in the nearby Invermere Forest district; ask the staff at the info center for details.

Hwy. 93 runs through the park from the Trans-Canada Hwy. in Banff to **Radium Hot Springs** at the southwest edge of the park, where it joins **Hwy. 95. Greyhound** buses stop at the Esso station, 7507 W. Main St. (347-9726; open daily 7am-11pm), at the junction of Hwy. 93 and Hwy. 95 in town. Daily service runs the length of the Banff-Windermere Hwy. (Hwy. 93) to Banff ($19) and Calgary ($34). The park's **Information Centre** (347-9505), on the western boundary at the Radium Hot Spring Pool Complex, hands out free maps (open daily in summer 9am-7pm; call for off-season hrs.). The **Kootenay Park Lodge** (no phone) operates a similar info center 63km north of Radium (open daily in summer 9am-6:30pm; stop by for off-season hrs.). The **Park Administration Office** (347-9615), on the access road to Redstreak Campground, gives out the backcountry hiking guide for free, and is open in winter (open M-F 8am-noon and 1-4pm). For an **ambulance,** call 342-2055. For after-hours **emergencies,** call 403-762-4506. The **post office** receives mail on Radium St. (347-9460; open M-F 8:30am-5pm). **Postal code:** V0A 1M0. **Area code:** 250.

▨ Prince Rupert

At the western end of Hwy. 16, Prince Rupert is an emerging transportation hub, a springboard for ferry travel to Alaska and the spectacular Queen Charlotte Islands. The **Museum of Northern British Columbia** (624-3207), in the same building as the info center, documents the history of logging, fishing, and Haida culture, including beautiful Haida artwork both old and new (open M-Sa 9am-8pm, Su 9am-5pm; Sept. 6-May 18 M-Sa 9am-5pm). Prince Rupert's harbor has the highest concentration of archaeological sites in North America, and **archaeological boat tours** leave from the info center daily. (2½hr. tours depart June 19-30 daily 12:30pm; July to early Sept. daily 1pm. $22, children $13, under 5 free.) Tiny **Service Park,** off Fulton St., offers panoramic views of downtown and the harbor beyond. A trail winding up the side of **Mt. Oldfield,** east of town, yields an even wider vista. The trailhead is at **Oliver Lake Park,** about 6km from downtown on Hwy. 16 (guided nature walks leave from the parking lot May-Oct. every hr. 10am-4pm; $5). The best time to visit Prince Rupert may be during **Seafest,** a 4-day event held in mid-June. Surrounding towns celebrate with parades, bathtub races, beer contests, and the Islandman Triathalon.

Nearly all of Prince Rupert's hotels nestle within the 6-block area defined by 1st Ave., 3rd Ave., 6th St., and 9th St. **Eagle Bluff B&B,** 201 Cow Bay Rd. (627-4955 or 800-833-1550), on the waterfront, is attractively furnished in the loveliest part of town (singles $45, doubles $55; with private bath $55/$65; wheelchair access). **Park Ave. Campground,** 1750 Park Ave. (624-5861 or 800-667-1994), is less than 2km east of the ferry terminal via Hwy. 16. Some sites are forested, others have a view of the bay, and all are well-maintained. (Sites $10.50, with hookup $18.50. Showers for non-guests $3.50. Laundry facilities. Reservations recommended.) **Cow Bay Café,** 201 Cow Bay Rd. (627-1212), around the corner from Eagle Bluff B&B, offers an ever-changing menu, including such delights as vegetarian *chilaquiles* ($11.50), ribs in guava BBQ sauce ($14.50), shrimp quesadillas ($9), and an extensive wine list (open Tu noon-2:30pm, W-Sa noon-2:30pm and 6-9pm).

The only major road into town is Hwy. 16; known as **McBride St.** within city limits, **2nd Ave.** at the north end of downtown, and **Park Ave.** at the south end; leading to the **ferry docks.** From the docks, the walk downtown takes 30min. Downtown, avenues run north-south and ascend numerically from west to east; streets run east-west and ascend numerically from north to south. **Prince Rupert Airport** is on Digby Island, with a ferry and bus connection to downtown (45min., $11). **Air BC,** 112 6th St. (624-4554), flies to Vancouver ($169). **VIA Rail** (984-5246 or 800-561-8630, outside BC 800-561-3949), toward the water on Bill Murray Way, runs to Prince George (3 per week, $66); **BC Rail** (984-5500 or 800-339-8752, outside BC 800-663-8238) continues from Prince George to Vancouver ($190). **Greyhound,** 822 3rd Ave. (624-5090), near 8th St., runs to Prince George (2 per day, $87) and Vancouver (2 per day, $173). The **Alaska Marine Hwy.** (627-1744 or 800-642-0066), at the end of Hwy. 16 (Park Ave.), runs ferries north from Prince Rupert along the Alaskan Panhandle to Ketchikan (US$38, car US$75) and Juneau (US$104, car US$240). Next door is **BC Ferries** (624-9627 or 888-223-3779), running to the Queen Charlotte Islands (6 per week; peak season $23, car $87) and Port Hardy (every other day; $102, car $210). **Seashore Charter Services** (624-5645) runs a shuttle from the mall on 2nd Ave. to the ferry terminal by request ($3). **Prince Rupert Bus Service** (624-3343) runs downtown (M-Sa 7am-10pm; $1, seniors 60¢; day pass $2.50/$2); about every 30min., bus #52 runs from 2nd Ave. and 3rd St. to within a 5min. walk of the ferry terminal.

The **Information Centre** (624-5637 or 800-667-1994), at 1st Ave. and McBride St., is in the Haida-style log building (open May 15-Sept. 6 M-Sa 9am-8pm; Su 9am-5pm; in winter M-F 10am-5pm). **Internet access** awaits in the **library,** 101 6th Ave. W. (627-1345), at McBride St. ($2 per hr.; open M and W 1-9pm, Tu and Th 10am-9pm, F-Sa 1-5pm; in winter also Su 1-5pm.) The **post office** (624-2353) sits in the mall at 2nd Ave. and 5th St. (open M-F 9:30am-5:30pm). **Postal code:** V8J 3P3. **Area code:** 250.

ALASKA APPROACHES

■ The Alaska Highway

Built during World War II, the Alaska Hwy. (also known as the Alcan) traverses an astonishing 2378km route between Dawson Creek, BC and Fairbanks, AK. In recent years, the U.S. Army has been replaced by an annual army of over 250,000 tourists, most of them RV-borne. In general, there's a trade-off between the excitement you'll find on the Alcan and the speed with which you'll reach Alaska. Countless opportunities lurk off the highway for hiking, fishing, and viewing wildlife; if speed is paramount, the **Cassiar Hwy.** (see below) may be a better route. The 1hr. video *Alaska Highway: 1942-1992,* shown at the **Dawson Creek Tourist Infocentre,** provides a praiseworthy introduction to the road and the region. The free pamphlet *Driving the Alaska Highway* includes a listing of emergency medical services and phone numbers throughout Alaska, the Yukon, and British Columbia, plus tips on preparation and driving; it's available at visitors centers, or through the **Dept. of Health and**

Social Services (907-465-3030), P.O. Box 110601, Juneau, AK 99811-0601. For daily Alcan **road conditions,** call 250-774-7447 in BC, 867-667-8215 in the Yukon.

■ Cassiar Highway (Hwy. 37)

A growing number of travelers prefer the Cassiar Hwy. to the Alaska Hwy., which has become an RV institution. The highway slices through charred forests and snow-capped peaks on its way from Hwy. 16 in BC to the Alcan (Hwy. 97) in the Yukon. Three evenly spaced provincial parks right off the highway offer good camping, and the Cassiar's services, while sparse, are numerous enough to keep cars and drivers running. Hitchhiking is less popular here than on the Alaska Hwy. Advantages include less distance, consistently interesting scenery, and fewer crowds. On the other hand, the Cassiar is remote, less maintained, and large sections are very slippery when wet and harder on tires than the better paved Alcan. This causes little concern for the large, commercial trucks that roar up and down the route, but keeps the infrequent service stops busy with overambitious drivers in need of tire repair.

Yukon Territory

The Yukon Territory is among the most remote and sparsely inhabited regions of North America, averaging one person per 15 sq. km. While summers usually bring comfortably warm temperatures (60-70°F/15-21°C) and more than 20hr. of daylight, travelers should still be prepared for difficult weather. The territory remains a bountiful, beautiful, and largely unspoiled region, yet many travelers mimic gold-crazed prospectors and zoom through without appreciating its uncrowded allure.

PRACTICAL INFORMATION

Capital: Whitehorse.

Visitor Info: Tourism Yukon, P.O. Box 2703, Whitehorse, YT Y1A 2C6 (867-667-5340; http://www.touryukon.com). **Yukon Parks and Outdoor Recreation,** Box 2703, Whitehorse, YT Y1A 2C6 (867-667-5648).

Police: 867-667-5555. For **emergencies** outside the Whitehorse area, *911 may not work.* Call the local police number in individual **Practical Information** sections.

Drinking Age: 19.

Time Zone: Pacific (3hr. before Eastern, 1hr. after Alaska).

Postal Abbreviation: YT. **Area code:** 867.

Sales Tax: None.

▓ Whitehorse

Named for the once-perilous Whitehorse Rapids, whose crashing whitecaps were said to resemble the flowing manes of white mares, Whitehorse is a modern cross-roads in an ageless frontier. With over 23,000 residents, Whitehorse prides itself on being Canada's largest city north of 60° latitude. The mountains, rivers, and lakes in all directions are a powerful reminder that "south of 60" is far, far away.

PRACTICAL INFORMATION Whitehorse lies 1500km north of Dawson Creek, BC along the Alaska Hwy. (see p. 914) and 535km south of Dawson City, YT. The **airport** is off the Alaska Hwy., just west of downtown. The **bus station** is on the northeastern edge of town, a short walk from downtown. **Greyhound,** 2191 2nd Ave. (667-2223), runs to Vancouver, BC (41hr., 1 per day, $278); Edmonton, AB (30hr., 1 per day, $215); and Dawson Creek, BC (18hr., 1 per day, $157). (Runs late June to Sept. M-Sa; in winter Tu, Th, and Sa. Desk open M, Tu, and Th 8am-5:30pm, W and F 4am-5:30pm, Sa 9:30am-1pm, Su 4-8am.) **Alaska Direct** (668-4833 or 800-770-6652) runs to Anchorage (18hr., 3 per week, US$145); Fairbanks (14hr., 3 per week, US$120); and Skagway (3hr., 1 per day, US$35). **Norline** (668-3355) runs to Dawson City

CANADA

(6½hr.; 3 per week, 2 per week in winter; $74). The local buses of **Whitehorse Transit** (24hr. info line 668-7433) arrive and depart downtown next to Canadian Tire on Ogilvie St. (Runs M-Th 6:15am-7:15pm, F 6:15am-10pm, Sa 8am-7pm. $1.25, students and children $1, seniors and disabled 60¢.) **Norcan Leasing,** 213 Range Rd. (668-2137 or 800-661-0445, in AK 800-764-1234), at Alcan Mi. 917.4, rents cars for $50 per day, 22¢ per km after 100km (must be 21 with credit card or pay $700 cash deposit).

   Whitehorse Visitor Reception Centre, 100 Hansen St. (667-3084), is in the Tourism and Business Centre at 2nd Ave. (open daily mid-May to mid-Sept. 8am-8pm; in winter M-F 9am-5pm). **Yukon Conservation Society,** 302 Hawkins St. (668-5678), offers maps and great ideas on area hiking (open M-F 10am-2pm). Surf the **Internet** at the **library,** 2071 2nd Ave. (667-5239), at Hanson (open M-F 10am-9pm, Sa 10am-6pm, Su 1-9pm). **Post Office:** 211 Main St. (667-2485), in the basement of Shoppers Drug Mart (open M-F 9am-6pm, Sa 11am-4pm). General Delivery is at 3rd Ave. and Wood St., in the Yukon News Bldg. (open M-F 8am-6pm). The **postal code** for last names A-L is Y1A 3S7; for M-Z it's Y1A 3S8. **Area code:** 867.

ACCOMMODATIONS, CAMPGROUNDS, AND FOOD

Cash-strapped tenters amenable to a 15min. drive might head for the shores of **Long Lake,** where many a young wanderer has camped for free. (Though illegal, camping in non-designated areas is reportedly tolerated for one night. If the police don't feel tolerant, the penalty is $500 and confiscation of camping equipment.) To get there, cross the bridge off 2nd Ave. in the southeast corner of town, turn left on Hospital Rd., turn left on Wickstrom Rd., and then follow the winding road to the lake. **Roadhouse Inn,** 2163 2nd Ave. (667-2594), at the north end of town near the Greyhound depot, has shared rooms and hall showers with a bathtub. ($20; private rooms with cable and private bathroom $50; $5 per additional person. Wash and dry $1.75 each, free local calls. Key deposit $5. Lobby open 7am-2:30am.) **Robert Service Campground** (668-3721), 1km from town on South Access Rd. along the Yukon River, is a convenient stop for tenting types, with no RV sites. (Food trailer, firewood and pits, playground, drinking water, toilets. 68 sites. $11. Metered showers $1 per 5min. Gates open 7am-midnight. Open late May to early Sept.)

   Klondike Rib and Salmon Barbecue, 2116 2nd Ave. (667-7554), serves barbecued salmon or halibut with coleslaw for lunch ($8; open mid-May to Sept. M-F 11:30am-10pm, Sa-Su 5-10pm). Whitehorse's suits and twenty-somethings converge at **No Pop Sandwich Shop,** 312 Steele (668-3227), at 4th Ave., for veggie sandwiches ($4.25) and $6 alcoholic specialty drinks. (Open Apr.-Sept. M-Th 7:30am-8:30pm, F 7:30am-9:30pm, Sa 10am-8:30pm, Su 10am-4pm.)

SIGHTS AND OUTDOORS

Visitors hungry for local history can feed their heads at the **MacBride Museum** (667-2709), at 1st Ave. and Wood St. *(Open daily June-Aug. 10am-6pm; call for winter hrs. $4, students and seniors $3.50, children $2, under 7 free.)* The new **Yukon Beringia Interpretive Centre** (667-8855), on the Alcan, 2km west of the junction with the S. Access Rd., pays homage to the forgotten subcontinent that encompassed Siberia, Alaska, and the Yukon during the last ice age. *(Open daily mid-May to Sept. 8am-9pm; reduced winter hrs. $6, seniors $5, children $4.)*

   Grey Mountain, partly accessible by gravel road, is a somewhat rigorous day hike. Take the Lewes Blvd. bridge by the **S.S. Klondike** across the river and continue, then take a left on Alsek. Turn left again at the sign that says "Grey Mt. Cemetery" and follow this gravel road until it ends. Joggers, bikers, and cross-country skiers love the **Miles Canyon trail network** that parallels the **Yukon River.** To get there, take Lewes Blvd. to Nisutlin Dr. and turn right; just before the fish ladder, turn left onto the gravel Chadbum Lake Rd. and follow for 4km until you hit the parking area. The **Conservation Society** arranges free hikes on weekdays during July and August and offers guided nature walks during the spring (office open M-F 10am-2pm).

CANADA

■ Kluane National Park

Together with adjacent Wrangell-St. Elias National Park in Alaska and Tatshenshini/Alsek Provincial Park in BC, Kluane (kloo-AH-nee) makes up one of the world's largest wilderness areas. It contains Canada's highest peak, Mt. Logan (5959m or 19,545 ft.), as well as the most massive non-polar ice fields in the world. The abundance of ice-blanketed mountains makes Kluane's interior a haven for experienced expeditioners, but also renders two-thirds of the park inaccessible (except by plane) to humbler hikers. Fortunately, the northeastern park border along the Alaska Hwy. has plenty of room for backpacking, canoeing, rafting, biking, and day hiking.

PRACTICAL INFORMATION **Haines Junction** is a small town at the eastern park boundary, 158km west of Whitehorse, serving as the gateway and headquarters of the park. **Alaska Direct** (800-770-6652, in Whitehorse 668-4833) runs from Haines Junction (Su, W, F) to Anchorage (US$125), Fairbanks (US$100), and Whitehorse (US$20). **Kluane National Park Visitor Reception Centre** (634-7209), on Logan St. in Haines Junction (Km 1635 on the Alcan), provides wilderness permits ($5 per night, $50 per season); fishing permits ($5 per day, $35 per season); topographical maps ($10); and trail and weather info (open daily May-Sept. 9am-5pm; in winter M-F 10am-noon and 1-4pm). The **Sheep Mountain Information Centre,** 72km north of town at Alaska Hwy. Km 1707, registers hikers headed for the northern area of the park (open daily late May to Sept. 6 9am-6pm). **Emergency and Police:** 634-5555 (if no answer, call 867-667-5555). **Ambulance/Clinic:** 634-4444. The **post office** is in Madley's (634-3802; open M, W, and F 9-10am and 1-5pm, Tu and Th 9am-noon and 1-5pm). **Postal code:** Y0B1L0. **Area code:** 867.

ACCOMMODATIONS, CAMPGROUNDS, AND FOOD **Laughing Moose B&B,** 120 Alsek Crescent (634-2335), 4 blocks from the junction, offers a sparkling-clean kitchen, spacious common room with TV and VCR, and a view of the Auriol Mountains (singles $60; doubles $70; shared bath). The **Stardust Motel** (634-2591), 1km north of town on the Alcan, has spacious rooms with TVs and antiseptic tubs, but no phones (singles $45; doubles $55; with kitchenette $75, $65 per additional day). The idyllic **Kathleen Lake Campground,** off Haines Rd., 27km south of Haines Junction, is close to hiking and fishing and has water, flush toilets, fire pits, firewood, and campfire talks (sites $10; open June-Oct.; wheelchair access). The closest government campground to Haines Junction is popular **Pine Lake,** on the Alcan, 7km east of town, featuring a sandy beach complete with a pit for late night bonfires ($8; water, firewood, pit toilets). The **Dezadeash Lake Campground,** about 50km south of Haines Junction on Haines Rd., offers the same deal and sweet lakefront property. **Village Bakery and Deli** (634-2867), on Logan St. across from the visitors center, sates a sweet tooth with a cinnamon bun ($1.50) or more substantial soups ($3.50). (Periodic live music. Open daily May-Sept. 7:30am-9pm.)

OUTDOORS The **Dezadeash River Loop** (DEZ-dee-ash) trailhead is downtown at the day-use area across from Madley's on Haines Rd. This flat, forested 5km stroll may disappoint those craving a vertical challenge, but it makes a nice jaunt (though most of it is not wheelchair accessible). The 15km **Auriol Trail** is a slightly harder option and has a primitive campground halfway through its loop. The trail begins 7km south of Haines Junction on Haines Rd. and cuts through boreal forest, leading to a subalpine bench just in front of the Auriol Range. This is a popular overnight trip, though 4-6hr. is adequate time without packs. In winter, the Auriol turns into a favorite **cross-country skiing** route. The 5km (one-way) **King's Throne Route** is a very challenging but rewarding day hike with a 1220m elevation gain and a panoramic view. It begins at the **Kathleen Lake** day-use area at the campground (see **Accommodations,** above).

Excellent hiking awaits near **Sheep Mountain** in the park's northern section. An easy 0.5km jaunt up to **Soldier's Summit** starts 1km north of the Sheep Mountain Info Centre and leads to the site where the original highway was completed in 1942. Only the most experienced backpackers should attempt the difficult trek along the **Slims River** to gawk at the magnificent **Kaskawulsh Glacier.** Two rough routes along the river banks are available, stretching 23 and 30km one-way and requiring 3-5 days; register and buy backcountry permits at the info center. The park mandates the use of **bear-resistant food canisters** on overnight trips, which it provides for free with a $150 refundable deposit (cash or credit). Registration for overnighters is also mandatory (see **Practical Information,** above). For **mountain bikers,** the **Alsek River Valley Trail** follows a bumpy old mining road 14km to Sugden Creek. Starting from Alcan Km 1645, the rocky road crosses several streams before gently climbing to a ridge with a stellar view of the Auriol Mountains.

■ Dawson City

Gold! Gold! Gold! Of all the insanity ever inspired by the lust for the dust, the creation of Dawson City must be one of the wildest. For 12 glorious, crazy months, from July 1898 to July 1899, this was the largest Canadian city west of Toronto. Its 30,000 residents, with names like Swiftwater Bill, Skookum Jim, Arizona Charlie Meadows, and Evaporated Kid, set out to make their fortunes. After a year of frenzied claim-staking and legend-making, Dawson City fizzled almost as quickly as it had exploded. In the early 60s, the town restored dirt roads, long boardwalks, wooden store fronts, transforming itself into the lively RV and college student destination that it is today.

PRACTICAL INFORMATION To reach Dawson City, take the Klondike Hwy. (Hwy. 2) 533km north from Whitehorse, or follow the majestic Top-of-the-World Hwy. (Hwy. 9) 108km east from the Alaska border. If you take the Klondike, fill up in Whitehorse, since there is scant gas along the way (approximately every 100km). **Norline Coaches** (993-6010), at the Shell Station on 5th Ave. and Princess St., runs to Whitehorse (6½hr.; 3 per week, in winter 2 per week; $74). **Dawson City Taxi Courier Service** (993-6688) runs a van from the Downtown Hotel to Whitehorse (6½hr., June-Aug. daily at 6pm, $62; reservations required). The **Visitor Reception Centre** (993-5566), at Front and King St., screens historical movies (open mid-May to mid-Sept. daily 8am-8pm). **Police:** (993-5555; if no answer 1-667-5555), at Front St. and Turner St., in the southern part of town. **Ambulance:** 993-4444. **Internet Access** graces the **library** (993-5571), at 5th Ave. and Princess St., in the school. (Open Tu-Th 10am-9pm, F-Sa 10am-5pm; in winter Tu-W and F 9am-7pm, Th 1-8pm, Sa noon-5pm.) The **post office** receives letters at 5th Ave. and Princess St. (993-5342; open M-F 8:30am-5:30pm, Sa 9am-noon). **Postal code:** Y0B 1G0. **Area code:** 867.

ACCOMMODATIONS, CAMPGROUNDS, AND FOOD Dawson City **River Hostel (HI-C)** (993-6823), across the Yukon River from downtown; take the first left off the ferry. Bunks are in new log cabins, with a wood-heated "prospector's bath," outdoor kitchen facilities, a cozy lounge with wood stove and mini-library, and a beautiful hilltop view of the river and city. (Beds $13, nonmembers $16; tent sites $9, $6.50 per additional person. Open May-Sept.) The **tent city** in the woods next to the hostel is a happy home to many of the town's summer college crowd, despite the $100 per person fee charged by the government. **Yukon River Campground,** on the first right off the ferry, has roomy, secluded sites, with peregrine falcons nesting across the river (water and pit toilets; RVs welcome, but no hookups; sites $8).

Klondike Kate's (993-6527), at 3rd and King St., serves a breakfast special (until 11am) that would satisfy the hungriest Sourdough ($4; open daily mid-May to mid-Sept. 7am-11pm). **River West Food and Health** (993-6339), on Front and Queen St., bakes a mean loaf of supergrain bread, and possibly the only hummus pitas in the Yukon ($6; open M-Sa 7am-7pm, Su 9am-5pm; in winter M-Sa 10am-6pm).

SIGHTS AND ENTERTAINMENT Goldbottom Mining Tours and Gold Panning (993-5023), 30km south of town, offers a tour of an operating mine and an hour

Alberta, Saskatchewan, and Manitoba

200 miles

200 kilometers

N

Hudson Bay

NORTHWEST TERRITORIES

Enterprise

35

High Level

Peace River

35

Fort Nelson

97

Dawson Creek

97

Grande Prairie

2

BRITISH COLUMBIA

16

Jasper

Jasper Nat. Park

93

Banff Nat. Park

Banff

5

Kamloops

97

Kelowna

ROCKY MTS.

Slave River

Wood Buffalo Nat. Park

Lake Athabasca

Fort Chipewyan

Athabasca River

Fort McMurray

Slave Lake

ALBERTA

2

Edmonton

Red Deer

Drumheller

N. Saskatchewan River

Lloydminster

Calgary

1

Banff

Waterton Lakes Nat. Park

Glacier Nat. Park

Kalispell

1

Fond-du-Lac

Collins Bay

La Loche

155

La Ronge

SASKATCHEWAN

Churchill River

Prince Albert

Prince Albert Nat. Park

2

55

11

Saskatoon

16

S. Saskatchewan River

Moose Jaw

Regina

Swift Current

Medicine Hat

1

3

4

15

Minot

2

Nueltin Lake

Churchill

Hudson Bay

Brochet

Reindeer Lake

Flin Flon

10

The Pas

Lake Winnipegosis

Thompson

Nelson River

6

MANITOBA

Island Lake

Lake Winnipeg

6

Dauphin

Riding Mt. Nat. Park

10

16

Yorkton

16

1

Brandon

Portage La Prairie

75

Winnipeg

29

2

Kenora

17

ONTARIO

CANADA

No, Ma'am, That's Not an Olive in Your Martini

When some people run across amputated body parts, they take them to a hospital for surgical reattachment and a new career in the X-rated film industry. But for Capt. Dick Stevenson, the discovery of a pickled human toe in a cabin in the Yukon meant one thing: a damn fine cocktail. The drink became famous and spawned the Sourtoe Cocktail Club, whose 14,000-plus members include a 6-month-old child and a 91-year-old toe-sipper. Aspiring initiates buy a drink of their choice and pay a small fee ($5) to Bill "Stillwater Willie" Holmes (the new keeper of the sourtoe), who drops the chemically preserved (er, pickled) toe in the drink. Then it's bottoms up, and the moment the toe touches your lips, you're in the club. "You can drink it fast, you can drink it slow—but the lips have gotta touch the toe." Listening to Stillwater Willie explain the club's history and philosophize about life in the Yukon is itself worth the $5, but the fee includes a certificate and membership card; a commemorative pin or a book relating the saga of the sourtoe can be purchased separately for $5 each. Info regarding initiation times can be found at the Downtown Hotel (993-5346) on the corner of Queen and 2nd.

of panning. *(Open daily in summer 11am-7pm. $12.)* Anyone can pan for free at the confluence of the Bonanza and Eldorado Creeks; you just need your own pan, available at local hardware stores. Experience frontier literary genius at the **Jack London Cabin,** on 8th Ave. and Firth St., where the great Californian author's life and brief stint in the Yukon are recounted during lectures. *(Open daily 10am-1pm and 2-6pm. Tours 30min., daily noon and 2:15pm. Free.)* Authentic performances of witty ballads by **Robert Service** are given in front of the cabin at 8th Ave. and Hanson St., where he penned them. *(Shows daily June-Aug. at 10am and 3pm. Cabin open 9am-noon and 1-5pm. $6, under 8 $3. Cabin viewing free.)* The **Dawson City Museum** (993-5007), on 5th Ave. in Minto Park offers a broader, less lyrical historical perspective ($4, students and seniors $3, families $10; wheelchair access).

Diamond Tooth Gertie's, at 4th and Queen St., was Canada's first legal casino, and proves that Dawson is no movie set: for a $5 cover (or a $20 season pass), gamblers can fritter away the night with roulette, blackjack, or even "Texas hold 'em" against local legends Johnny Caribou and No Sleep Filippe. *(19+ only. Open nightly 7pm-2am.)* Free nightly floor shows go up at 8:30pm, 10:30pm, and 12:30am. The **Gaslight Follies** (993-6217), a high-kicking vaudeville revue, is held in the **Palace Grand Theatre** on King St., between 2nd and 3rd St. *(Follies W-M 8pm. Box office open daily 11am-8pm. $15-17, children $7.50.)* As the night winds down, the **Sun Tavern and Lounge** (993-5495), at 3rd Ave. and Queen St., is where everyone ends up. Once Dawson's roughest bar, the Sun has since cooled down, but it's still no place to sip fruity drinks. A pint of brew costs $3.75. *(Open daily noon-2am.)*

■ Near Dawson City: The Dempster Highway

The Dempster Hwy. (Hwy. 5) begins 41km east of Dawson City at the **Klondike River Lodge** on the Klondike Hwy. (Hwy. 2), and winds 741 spectacular kilometers to Inuvik, becoming Hwy. 8 upon crossing into the Northwest Territories. Like no other highway in North America, the Dempster confronts its drivers with real wilderness devoid of logging scars or ads. The Dempster is reasonably navigable and well-maintained, but services are limited, weather is erratic, and its dirt-and-gravel stretches can give cars a thorough beating. Although the drive can be accomplished in 12hr., it deserves at least 2 days each way to be fully and safely appreciated. Rainstorms have been known to create impassable washouts, closing down parts of the highway or disrupting ferry service—and leaving travelers stranded in Inuvik—for as long as 2 weeks. The **Arctic Hotline** (800-661-0788) and **Road and Ferry Report** (800-661-0752; in Inuvik 777-2678) provide up-to-date road info. The **Northwest Territories Visitor Centre** (993-6167), in Dawson City, has a free Dempster brochure (open daily late May to early Sept. 9am-8pm). There are **government campgrounds** at Tombstone (Km 72), Engineer Creek (Km 194), Rock River (Km 447), Nitainlii (Km

541), Caribou Creek (Km 692) and Chuk (Km 731). Dry sites cost $8, and hookups are only available at Chuk. The **Interpretive Centre** at Tombstone loans out a kilometer-by-kilometer travelogue of the Dempster's natural history and wildlife.

Alberta

With its gaping prairie, oil-fired economy, and conservative politics, Alberta is the Texas of Canada. Petro-dollars have given birth to gleaming, modern cities on the plains, while the natural landscape swings from the mighty Canadian Rockies down to beautifully desolate badlands.

PRACTICAL INFORMATION

Capital: Edmonton.
Visitor Info: Travel Alberta, Commerce Pl., 10155 102 St., 3rd fl., Edmonton, AB T5J 4G8 (800-661-8888 or 780-427-4321; http://www.discoveralberta.com/atp). **Parks Canada,** 220 4th Ave. SE, #552, Calgary, AB T2G 4X3 (800-748-7275 or 403-292-4401). **Alberta Environmental Protection,** 9820 106 St., 2nd Fl., Edmonton, AB T5K 2J6 (780-427-7009; http://www.gov.ab.ca/env/parks.html).
Emergency: 911.
Drinking Age: 18.
Time Zone: Mountain (2hr. before Eastern).
Postal Abbreviation: AB.
Sales Tax: None.

■ Banff National Park

Banff is Canada's best-loved and best-known natural park, with 6641 sq. km of peaks, forests, glaciers, and alpine valleys. Even streets littered with gift shops, clothing outfitters, and chocolatiers cannot mar Banff's beauty. Transient 20-somethings arrive with mountain bikes, climbing gear, skis, and snowboards, but a trusty pair of hiking boots remains the park's most popular outdoor equipment.

PRACTICAL INFORMATION The park hugs the Alberta side of the Alberta/British Columbia border, 129km west of Calgary. Civilization in the park centers around the towns of **Banff** and **Lake Louise,** 58km apart on Hwy. 1. All of the following info applies to Banff Townsite, unless otherwise specified. **Greyhound,** 100 Gopher St. (800-661-8747; depot open daily 7:30am-9:30pm), runs four buses per day to Lake Louise ($10), Calgary ($18), and Vancouver, BC ($101). **Brewster Transportation,** 100 Gopher St. (762-6767), runs express buses to Jasper (1 per day, $51); Lake Louise (3 per day, $11); and Calgary (4 per day, $36; HI discount 15%, ages 6-15 ½-price). The **Happy Bus** runs between the Banff Springs Hotel and the trailer court on Tunnel Mountain Rd., and between the Tunnel Mountain Campground through downtown to the Banff Park Museum. ($1, children 50¢; runs daily in summer 7am-midnight; call for winter hrs.) If you lack a car, **Brewster Tours'** (762-6767) guided bus rides may be the only way to see some of the park's main attractions, such as the Great Divide, the Athabasca Glacier, and the spiral railroad tunnel. (Banff to Jasper 9½hr., $81; round-trip 2 days, $112. Columbia Icefields $23.50 extra.)

Banff Visitor Centre, 224 Banff Ave., includes **Banff/Lake Louise Tourism Bureau** (762-8421) and **Canadian Parks Service** (762-1550; open daily 8am-8pm; Oct.-May 9am-5pm). The brand-new **Lake Louise Visitor Centre** (522-3833), at Samson Mall, is stuffed with friendly staffers (open daily 8am-8pm; June and Sept. 8am-6pm; Oct.-May 9am-5pm). **Emergency: Banff Warden Office,** 762-4506. **Lake Louise Warden Office,** 522-3866. 24hr. **Internet** away at **The Web Cyber Café** (762-9226), at the lower level of Sundance Mall; the entrance is across from tourist office on Banff Ave. **Post Office:** 204 Buffalo St. (762-2586; open M-F 9am-5:30pm). **Postal code:** T0L 0C0. **Area code:** 403.

ACCOMMODATIONS, CAMPGROUNDS, AND FOOD HI-C runs a **shuttle service** connecting all the Rocky Mountain hostels and Calgary ($7-65). Wait-list beds become available at 6pm, and six stand-by beds are saved for shuttle arrivals. For reservations at any rustic hostel, call Banff International. **Lake Louise International Hostel (HI-C),** P.O. Box 115, Lake Louise T0L 1E0 (522-2200), 0.5km west of Samson Mall in Lake Louise Townsite, on Village Rd., is more like a hotel than a hostel, with a reference library, common rooms with open, beamed ceilings, a stone fireplace, two full kitchens, a sauna, ski/bike workshops, and a cafe. ($20, nonmembers $24. Private rooms available for $6 more per person. Wheelchair access.) **Banff International Hostel (BIH) (HI-C),** Box 1358, Banff T0L 0C0 (762-4122), is 3km from Banff Townsite on Tunnel Mountain Rd., which leads from Otter St. downtown; take the Happy Bus from downtown. This big hostel has the look and feel of a ski lodge, with three lounge areas, two large fireplaces, a game room with pool table, a kitchen, cafe, laundry facilities, and hot showers. ($19, nonmembers $23. Private rooms available. Linen $1.50. Reception 24hr. Wheelchair access.) **Castle Mountain Hostel (HI-C),** on Hwy. 1A, 1.5km east of the junction of Hwy. 1 and Hwy. 93 between Banff and Lake Louise, is a quieter alternative, with running water and electricity, general store, library, and fireplace ($12, nonmembers $16; linen $1.50; Internet access). At any of Banff's nine park campgrounds, a campfire permit with firewood included costs $3 extra. Sites are first come, first served ($10-22). On Hwy. 1A between Banff Townsite and Lake Louise, **Johnston Canyon** and **Castle Mountain** are close to relatively uncrowded hiking. Only Village 2 of **Tunnel Mountain Village,** 4km from Banff Townsite on Tunnel Mountain Rd., remains open in winter.

Jump Start, 206 Buffalo St. (762-0332), is a small coffee and sandwich shop delivering a big bang for the buck (shepherd's pie $5.50; open daily 7am-7pm). **Aardvark's,** 304A Caribou St. (762-5500), serves thick slices of pizza heaped with toppings for $2.75 (HI discount on whole pizzas; open daily 11am-4am). **Rose and Crown,** 202 Banff Ave. (762-2121), hosts drinking, dancing, pool-playing, and near-nightly live music. Happy hour (M-F 4:30-7:30pm) heralds $3-3.50 drafts. (Open daily 11am-2am.)

OUTDOORS Near Banff Townsite, **Fenland Trail** winds 2km through an area shared by beaver, muskrat, and waterfowl (closed for elk calving in late spring and early summer). Follow Mt. Norquay Rd. out of town, and look for signs across the tracks on the road's left side. The summit of **Tunnel Mountain** provides a dramatic view of the **Bow Valley** and **Mt. Rundle.** Follow Wolf St. east from Banff Ave., and turn right on St. Julien Rd. to reach the head of the steep 2.3km trail. **Johnston Canyon,** about 25km out of Banff toward Lake Louise along the Bow Valley Pkwy. (Hwy. 1A), runs past waterfalls to seven blue-green cold-water springs known as the **Inkpots.**

Banff might not exist if not for the **Cave and Basin Hot Springs,** southwest of town on Cave Ave., once rumored to have miraculous healing properties. The **Cave and Basin National Historic Site** (762-1557), a refurbished resort built circa 1914, is now a museum that screens documentaries and stages exhibits. *(Open daily in summer 9am-6pm; in winter 9:30am-5pm. Tours meet at 11am. $2.25, seniors $1.75, children $1.25.)* For a dip in the hot water, follow the rotten-egg smell to the 40°C (104°F) **Upper Hot Springs** (762-1515), up the hill on Mountain Ave. *(Open daily 9am-11pm; call for winter hrs. $7, seniors and children $6. Swimsuits $1.50, towels $1, lockers 50¢.)*

The highest community in Canada at 1530m (5018 ft.), Lake Louise and its surrounding glaciers often serve North American filmmakers' need for supposedly Swiss scenery. Once at the lake, the hardest task is escaping fellow gawkers at the posh **Château Lake Louise.** Renting a canoe from the **Château Lake Louise Boat House** (522-3511) can help (open daily 10am-8pm; $25 per hr.). Several hiking trails begin at the water; the 3.6km **Lake Agnes Trail** and the 5.5km **Plain of Six Glaciers Trail** provide especially welcome escape, and both end at teahouses.

Nearby **Moraine Lake** may pack more of a scenic punch than its sister Louise. The lake is 15km from the village, at the end of Moraine Lake Rd., off the Lake Louise access road. Moraine lies in the awesome **Valley of the Ten Peaks,** which cradles glacier-encrusted **Mt. Temple.** Join the multitudes on the **Rockpile Trail** for an eye-popping view of the lake and valley and an explanation of rocks from ancient ocean bottoms. The **Moraine Lake Lodge** (522-3733) rents **canoes** ($24 per hr.).

Fishing is legal virtually anywhere there's water, but live bait and lead weights are not. **Permits** are available at the info center (7-day $6, annual permit valid in all Canadian National Parks $13). **Overnight camping permits** can be obtained at the visitors centers ($6 per person per day, up to $30; $42 per year). Wintery Banff offers more than curling—snow sports range from ice climbing to dogsledding to ice fishing. Three allied resorts fulfill the downhiller's need for speed: **Sunshine Mountain** (762-6500), **Mt. Norquay** (762-4421), and **Lake Louise** (522-3555). Shuttles to all three resorts leave from most big hotels in the townsites. Multi-day passes, good for all three resorts, are available at the **Ski Banff/Lake Louise** office, 225 Banff Ave. (762-4561), lower level, and at all resorts ($50.50 per day; 3-day min.). Passes include free shuttle service and an extra night of skiing at Mt. Norquay. **Performance Ski and Sports,** 208 Bear St. (762-8222), rents downhill ski, boot, and pole packages ($17 per day, $45 for 3 days); cross-country packages ($12/$31); snowboard packages ($28/$74); telemarking skis and boots ($18/$47); and snowshoes ($10/$26).

■ Icefields Parkway (Highway 93)

The 230km Icefields Parkway is one of the most beautiful routes in North America, heading north from Lake Louise in Banff National Park to Jasper Townsite in Jasper National Park, skirting dozens of stern peaks and glacial lakes. Free maps of the parkway are available at info centers in Jasper and Banff, or at the **Icefield Centre** (852-6560), at the boundary between the two parks, 127km north of Lake Louise and 103km south of Jasper Townsite (open daily mid-June to Aug. 9am-6pm; mid-May to mid-June and Sept. 9am-5pm). At **Bow Summit,** 40km north of Lake Louise, one of the parkway's highest points (700m, 2135 ft.), a 10min. walk leads to a view of fluorescent aqua **Peyto Lake,** especially vivid toward the end of June. The Icefield Centre lies in the shadow of the tongue of the **Athabasca Glacier,** a great white whale of an ice flow that flows from the 325 sq. km **Columbia Icefield,** the largest accumulation of ice and snow south of the Arctic Circle. **Columbia Icefield Snocoach Tours** (in Banff 762-6735, in Jasper 852-3332) carries visitors right onto the glacier in bizarre monster buses for a 75min. trip. *(Daily May-Sept. 9am-5pm; Oct. 10am-4pm. $23.50, ages 6-15 $5.)* A 30min. walk leads up piles of glacial debris to the glacier's mighty toe, where deep crevasses make it unsafe to walk farther. For tasty geological tidbits, sign up for a guided **Athabasca Glacier Icewalk.** *("Ice Cubed" tour 3hr. $28, ages 7-17 $12. "Ice Walk Deluxe" tour 5hr. $32/$14.)* One of the two hikes runs each day (mid-June to mid-Sept.); for info and booking, contact the Icefield Centre or Peter Lemieux, 371042 Ave., Red Deer, AB Canada, T4N 2Z4 (email iceman1@agt.net).

▓ Jasper National Park

Northward expansion of the Canadian railway system led to the discovery and 1907 creation of Jasper National Park. The largest of the four Canadian Rocky Mountains parks, Jasper encompasses herculean peaks and plummeting valleys that dwarf the battalion of motorhomes and charter buses parading through the region. In the face of this annual bloat, Jasper's permanent residents struggle to keep their home looking and feeling like a genuine small town. In the winter, the crowds melt away, a blanket of snow descends, and a ski resort welcomes visitors to a slower, more relaxed town.

PRACTICAL INFORMATION All of the addresses below are in **Jasper Townsite,** near the center of the park. **VIA Rail** (852-4102 or 800-561-8630) sends three trains per week from the station on Connaught Dr. to Vancouver, BC (16½hr., $156) and Edmonton ($91). **Greyhound** (852-3926), in the train station, runs to Edmonton (4½hr., 4 per day, $50) and Vancouver, BC (11½hr., 3 per day, $91). **Brewster Transportation**

Tours (852-3332), in the station, runs daily to Banff ($51) and Calgary ($71; HI discount 15%, ages 6-15 ½-price). **Heritage Cabs,** 611 Patricia (852-5558), offers a flat rate of $10 to Jasper International Hostel, $15-16 to the Maligne Canyon Hostel (24hr.). The **Park Information Centre,** 500 Connaught Dr. (852-6176), has trail maps. (Open daily 8am-7pm; early Sept. to late Oct. and late Dec. to mid-June 9am-5pm.) **Emergency:** 852-4848. **Post Office:** 502 Patricia St. (852-3041), across from the townsite green (open M-F 9am-5pm). **Postal code:** T0E 1E0. **Area code:** 780.

ACCOMMODATIONS, CAMPGROUNDS, AND FOOD HI-C runs a shuttle service connecting all the Rocky Mountain hostels and Calgary, with rates depending on distance ($7-65). **Jasper International Hostel (HI-C)** (852-3215), on Sky Tram Rd., 5km south of the townsite off Hwy. 93, is also known as **Whistlers Hostel,** just to confuse you. A "leave-your-hiking-boots-outside" rule keeps the hardwood floors and spiffy dorm rooms next to godliness. ($15, nonmembers $20. Curfew midnight.) **Sun Dog Shuttle** (852-4056) runs from the train station to the hostel on its way to the Jasper Tramway ($4). **Maligne Canyon Hostel (HI-C),** 15km east of the townsite on Maligne Canyon Rd., has small, renovated cabins on the bank of the Maligne River, with access to the Skyline Trail and within cycling distance of Maligne Lake. ($10, nonmembers $15; in winter $9/$14. Closed W Oct.-Apr. Reserve in advance.) **Mt. Edith Cavell Hostel (HI-C),** on Edith Cavell Rd., off Hwy. 93A., offers small but cozy quarters heated by wood-burning stoves. In winter, the road is closed; anyone can pick up keys at Jasper International Hostel and ski 13km uphill from Hwy. 93A. (Propane light, pump water, solar shower, firepit. $10, nonmembers $15; in winter $9/$10.)

Most of Jasper's campgrounds have primitive sites with few facilities and outdoor paradise nearby ($13-22). They are first come, first served, so get there early. To build a fire, add $3. None of the surrounding campgrounds are open in winter. The highlight of the Icefields Pkwy. campgrounds is **Columbia Icefield,** 109km south of the townsite, which lies close enough to the Athabasca Glacier to intercept an icy breeze and even a rare summer night's snowfall. **Mountain Foods and Café,** 606 Connaught Dr. (852-4050), offers a wide selection of sandwiches, salads, and home-cooked goodies amid rock-climbing photos and a mounted mountain bike (wraps and burgers $6; cheap beer after 5pm; open daily 7am-midnight).

OUTDOORS The **Jasper Tramway** (852-3093), on Whistlers Mountain Rd. 2km from town, climbs 2km up Whistlers Mountain, leading to a panoramic view of the park and, on a clear day, very far beyond. *(Open daily Apr.-Aug. 8:30am-10pm; Sept.-Oct. 9:30am-4:30pm. $15, under 14 $8.50, under 5 free.)* The steep 7km **Whistlers Trail** begins near the Jasper International Hostel (see **Accommodations,** above). The restaurant up top allows hikers to experience the dizzying combination of alcohol and high-altitude oxygen deprivation.

Brilliant turquoise **Maligne Lake** (muh-LEEN), the longest (22km) and deepest (97km) lake in the park, sprawls 48km southeast of the townsite at the end of Maligne Lake Rd. **Maligne Tours,** 626 Connaught Dr. (852-3370), rents kayaks (doubles $15 per hr.; 2hr. min.) and leads fishing, canoeing, rabbeting ($10 per hr.), horseback riding ($55 per 3hr.), hiking ($10 per hr.), whitewater rafting ($55 per 2hr.), and scenic cruises (1½hr.; $31, seniors $27.50, children $15.50). The **Opal Hills Trail** (8.2km loop) winds through subalpine meadows and ascends 460m to views of the lake. **Shuttle service** is available from Maligne Tours. *(To Maligne Canyon $8. To Maligne Lake one-way $12. To Maligne Lake round-trip with cruise $51. Wheelchair access.)*

Snow-capped **Mt. Edith Cavell** provides stupendous scenery for half-day hiking. To reach Edith, go 30km south of the townsite, from Hwy. 93 to 93A to the end of the bumpy, 14.5km Mt. Edith Cavell Rd. (open June-Oct.), where **Angel Glacier,** slowly melting and heaving itself in two, hangs off Edith's north face. Take the 1.6km **Path of the Glacier** loop to the summit, following in the wake of a glacier that has receded in the last few centuries, or hike the 9km (3-5hr.) loop through **Cavell Meadows.**

Sekani Mountain Tours (852-5337, reservations 852-5211) leads day-long white-water rafting runs on the **Rearguard River,** and trips for experienced rafters on the **Canoe River** (rafting $75; canoes $100; 10% HI discount; lunch included). **Currie's** (852-5650), in The Sports Shop, 414 Connaught Dr., rents fishing equipment and gives tips on good spots. *(Rod, reel, and line $10. 1-day boat or canoe rental $25, after 2pm $18, after 6pm $12. Pick-up and drop-off service available.)* **Permits** are available at fishing shops and the Parks Canada information center ($6 per week, $13 per year). The **Jasper Climbing School,** 806 Connaught Dr. (852-3964), offers an introductory 3hr. rappeling class for bouncing down the imposing cliffs that surround the townsite; at least a small group is required ($30; learning how to climb up is more expensive). Winter brings plenty of downhill opportunity to the ski slopes of **Marmot Basin** (852-3816), near Jasper Townsite (full-day lift ticket $39, seniors $28, youth $33, children $17). Bargain **ski rental** is available at **Totem's Ski Shop,** 408 Connaught Dr. (852-3078). *(Open daily 9:30am-10:30pm. Full rental package of skis, boots, and poles $9 per day. Higher-quality packages $12.50 and $20.)*

Edmonton

When western Alberta's glitz and glamour were distributed, Edmonton was last in line, but with a plethora of museums and a river valley beckoning to hikers and bikers, the city is rising in rank among Albertan travel destinations.

PRACTICAL INFORMATION Edmonton's **streets** run north-south, and **avenues** run east-west. Street numbers increase to the west, and avenues increase to the north. The first three digits of an address indicate the nearest cross street: 10141 88 Ave. is on 88 Ave. near 101 St. **City center** is quite off-center at 105 St. and 101 Ave. The **airport** sits 29km south of town. **Sky Shuttle Airport Service** (465-8545 or 888-438-2342) runs a shuttle downtown, to the university, or to the West Edmonton Mall for $11 (round-trip $18). Cheapskates have been known to hop on an airport shuttle bus taking travelers to downtown hotels. **VIA Rail,** 10004 104 Ave. (info 422-6032 or 800-835-3037, reservations 800-561-8630), in the CN Tower, runs three trains per week to Jasper (5hr., $91) and Vancouver, BC (23hr., $218). **Greyhound,** 10324 103 St. (420-2412), runs to Calgary (nearly every hr. 8am-8pm, also at midnight; $38); Jasper (5hr., 4 per day, $49); and Vancouver, BC (14-16hr., 3 per day, $119). **Edmonton Transit's** (schedules 496-1611, info 496-1600) Light Rail Transit (LRT) is free downtown (M-F 9am-3pm and Sa 9am-6pm) between Grandin Station, at 110 St. and 98 Ave., and Churchill Station, at 99 St. and 102 Ave. (fare $1.60, over 65 and under 15 $1). **Yellow Cab** (462-3456) runs 24hr. **Budget,** 10016 106 St. (448-2000 or 800-661-7027), charges $46 per day, with unlimited km; cheaper city rates have limited km. (Ages 21-24 $12 per day surcharge and must have credit card. Open M-F 7:30am-6pm, Sa 8am-5pm, Su 9am-5pm.)

Edmonton Tourism, 9797 Jasper Ave. (496-8400 or 800-463-4667), is in the Shaw Conference Centre (open daily 8am-9pm; in winter M-F 8:30am-4:30pm, Sa-Su 9am-5pm). The **Dow Computer Lab,** 11211 142 St. (451-3344), at the Edmonton Space and Science Centre (see **Sights,** below; free with admission; open in summer Sa-Su 1-5pm), has Internet access. **Post Office:** 9808 103A Ave. (944-3265), next to the CN Tower (open M-F 8am-5:45pm). **Postal code:** T5J 2G8. **Area code:** 780.

ACCOMMODATIONS, FOOD, AND NIGHTLIFE For B&Bs, contact **Alberta Gem B&B Reservation Agency,** 11216 48 Ave. (434-6098). **Edmonton International Youth Hostel (HI-C),** 10647 81 Ave. (988-6836), is loaded with modern facilities (kitchen, game room, lounge, laundry), just around the corner from the clubs, shops, and cafes of Whyte Ave. Take bus #7 or 9 from the 101 St. station to 82 Ave. ($15, nonmembers $20; family rooms available; reception 24hr.) **St. Joseph's College** (492-7681), on 89 Ave. at 114 St., at the University of Alberta, offers a library, TV lounge, and pool table. Take the LRT and get off at University. (Singles $24, $150 per week, with full board $37. Breakfast $3.25, lunch $4.50, dinner $6.50. Reception M-F 8:30am-4pm. Call ahead. Rooms available early May to late Aug.)

Edmonton locals swarm into the coffee shops and cafes of the **Old Strathcona** area along Whyte (82) Ave., between 102 and 105 St. The very name of **Chianti,** 10501 Whyte Ave. (439-9829), attests to its lengthy wine list. Daily specials, desserts, and coffees accompany an expanse of pasta, veal, and seafood dishes. (Pastas $6-9; M-Tu $6. Open Su-Th 11am-11pm, F-Sa 11am-midnight.) **Grounds for Coffee and Antiques,** 10247 97 St. (429-1920), behind the Edmonton Art Gallery, features coffee and light veggie dishes alongside old furniture and older trinkets (Mideastern Combo $4; open M-F 8:30am-5pm, Sa 10am-5pm). **The Billiard Club,** 10505 82 Ave. (432-0335), 2nd fl. above Chianti, is a busy bar packed with young up-and-comings and some older already-theres (open daily 11:30am-2:30am). **Blues on Whyte,** 10329 82 Ave. (439-3981), serves up live blues and R&B every night, plus a Saturday afternoon jam (8 oz. beers $1; open daily 10am-3am).

SIGHTS A blow against Mother Nature in the battle for tourists, the mammoth **West Edmonton Mall** (444-5200) engulfs the general area between 170 St. and 87 Ave., and contains water slides, an amusement park with 14-story roller coaster, miniature golf, dozens of exotic caged animals, over 800 stores, an ice-skating rink, 110 eating establishments, indoor bungee jumping, a casino, a luxury hotel, and twice as many submarines as the Canadian Navy. Take bus #1, 2, 100, or 111. *(Open M-F 10am-9pm, Sa 10am-6pm, Su noon-5pm. Amusement park and some other attractions stay open later.)*

The oddly shaped **Edmonton Space and Science Centre,** 11211 142 St. (451-3344), caters to the curious of all ages with a **planetarium** and **IMAX theater.** *(Open daily 10am-9:30pm. Day pass includes planetarium shows and exhibits: $7, seniors and youths $6, ages 3-12 $5. IMAX Plus pass includes an IMAX film plus either exhibits and planetarium or a laser music show. $12/$11/$8. AAA and HI discounts.)* Gaze at real stars for free at the **observatory** next door. *(Open daily 1-5pm and 8pm-midnight.)* The **Provincial Museum of Alberta,** 12845 102 Ave. (453-9100), displays an impressive collection of Albertan animals, vegetables, and minerals; take bus #1 and 120. *(Open daily May 24-Sept. 6 9am-5pm; in winter Tu-Su 9am-5pm. $6.50, seniors $5.50, youth $3.)*

Buses #2, 4, 30, 31, 35, 106, and 315 stop near the refreshing **Fort Edmonton Park** (496-8787), on Whitemud Dr. at Fox Dr. *(Open daily July-Aug. 10am-6pm; Victoria Day to late June M-F 10am-4pm, Sa-Su 10am-6pm; Sept. open for scheduled tours only, call for times. $6.75, seniors and ages 13-17 $5, ages 2-12 $3.25.)* Near the park entrance are three streets—1885, 1905, and 1920 St.—bedecked with period buildings from apothecaries to blacksmith shops, all decorated to match the streets' respective eras. Costumed schoolmarms and general store owners mingle with visitors, valiantly attempting to bring Edmonton's history to life. Hike through birch groves and pet salamanders at the **John Janzen Nature Centre** nearby. *(Open M-F 9am-6pm, Sa-Su 11am-6pm; in spring M-F 9am-4pm, Sa-Su 11am-6pm; in winter M-F 9am-4pm, Sa-Su 1-4pm. Free.)* At the **Muttart Conservatory,** 9626 96A St. (496-8755), plant species from around the world vegetate in the climate-controlled comfort of four ultramodern glass pyramids, each housing a different ecosystem; take bus #1, 83, 88, 106, or 307. *(Open Su-W 11am-9pm, Th-Sa 11am-6pm. $4.25, seniors and ages 13-17 $3.25, ages 2-12 $2.)*

■ Calgary

As the host of the 1988 Winter Olympics, Calgary's dot on the map grew larger as jobs, tourism, and flocks of Canadians from the East all converged. Already Alberta's largest city, Calgary continues to expand. No matter how big its britches, however, the city pays annual tribute to its original tourist attraction, the Stampede.

PRACTICAL INFORMATION Calgary is divided into quadrants (NE, NW, SE, SW): **Centre St.** is the east-west divider; the **Bow River** splits the north and south sections. **Avenues** run east-west, **streets** run north-south, and numbers count up from the divides. Cross streets can be derived by disregarding the last two digits of the first number: 206 7th Ave. is at 2nd St., and 310 10th St. is at 3rd Ave. **Calgary International Airport** is about 6km northwest of city center. Bus #57 provides sporadic service from the airport to downtown. The **Airporter Bus** (531-3907) goes to major hotels downtown (6:30am-11:30pm, $8.50), and makes unscheduled stops. **Greyhound,** 877 Greyhound Way SW (265-9111 or 800-661-TRIP/8747), runs to Edmonton (10 per day, $38); Banff (4 per day, $18.56); and Drumheller (2 per day, $21). **Brewster Tours** (221-8242) runs from the airport or downtown to Banff (3 per day, $36); Lake Louise (3 per day, $41); and Jasper (1 per day, $71; 15% HI discount). **Calgary Transit,** 240 7th Ave. SW (262-1000), runs **C-Trains,** which are free in the downtown zone. (Bus fare and C-Trains outside downtown $1.60, ages 6-14 $1; day pass $5/$3; 10 tickets $13.50/$8.50. Open M-F 6am-11pm, Sa-Su 8:30am-9:30pm.) **Checker Cab** (299-9999) runs 24hr. **Rent-A-Wreck,** 113 42nd Ave. SW (228-1660), charges $30 per day, 12¢ per km over 200km (must be 21 with credit card; open daily 8am-7pm). The **Visitor Service Centre,** 131 9th Ave. SW (750-2397), is near the Calgary Tower (open daily 8:30am-5pm). **Kaffa Coffee and Salsa House** (see **Food,** below) charges $1 per 20min. for **Internet access. Post Office:** 207 9th Ave. SW (974-2078; open M-F 8am-5:45pm). **Postal code:** T2P 268. **Area code:** 403.

ACCOMMODATIONS, FOOD, AND NIGHTLIFE Contact the **B&B Association of Calgary** (543-3900) for info and availability (singles from $35; doubles from $50). **Calgary International Hostel (HI-C),** 520 7th Ave. SE (269-8239), is several blocks east of downtown. Go east along 7th Ave. from the 3rd St. SE C-Train station; the hostel is on the left just past 4th St. SE. (Large kitchen, game room, hang-out areas, laundry, barbecue facilities. $15, nonmembers $19. Linen $1.50. Free tours of downtown. Open 24hr. Wheelchair accessible.) **University of Calgary,** in the NW quadrant, has rooms booked through **Kananaskis Hall,** 3330 24th Ave. (220-3203), a 12min. walk from the University C-Train stop. The university is out of the way, but easily accessible via bus #9 or the C-Train. (Shared rooms $20; singles $31, with student ID $21; doubles $39/$32. Suites with private bathrooms about $35. Open 24hr. Rooms available May-Aug. only.)

Downtown's grub is concentrated in the **Stephen Ave. Mall,** S. 8th Ave. between 1st St. SE and 3rd St. SW. Good, reasonably-priced food is also readily available in the **+15 Skyway System. Kaffa Coffee and Salsa House,** 2138 33 Ave. SW (240-9133), cooks up a fresh soup every day, and a different salsa and salad every week (tortilla melts $6-7; open M-F 7am-midnight, Sa 8am-midnight, Su 8am-10pm). **Satay House,** 206 Centre St. S. (290-1927), offers large portions of authentic Vietnamese cuisine for delightfully little (beef noodle soup $3.50-4.50; open daily 11am-9pm).

At **Republik,** 219 17th Ave. SW (244-1884, events 228-6163), punksters slam with their Gap-clad brethren in Calgary's loudest nuclear bunker and largest party zone. (Live music W and F. Cover $2-7, more for the bigger live shows. Open W-Sa 7pm-2am; open Su-Tu if bands are playing.) **Bottlescrew Bill's Pub** (263-7900), 10th Ave. SW and 1st St., affords refuge from the boisterous Electric Ave. (and the Electric Slide), beckoning with the widest suds selection in Alberta. (Beer $3.30-15. Happy hour M-F 4-7pm, Su 11am-2am. Free nachos M-F 4-6pm. Open daily 11am-2am.)

SIGHTS Stop by the **Canada Olympic Park** (247-5452), 10min. west of downtown on Hwy. 1, to learn about gravity at the site of the four looming ski jumps and the quick, slick bobsled and luge tracks (open daily 8am-9pm). The **Olympic Hall of Fame** (247-5452) honors Olympic achievements with displays, films, and bobsled and ski-jumping simulators (hall open daily 9am-9pm; $3.75, seniors and students

CANADA

$3, under 6 free). In summer, the park opens its hills to mountain bikers. Take the **lift** up the hill, then cruise down—no work necessary. *(Park open daily May-Sept. 10am-9pm. $5 ticket includes chair lift and entrance to ski jump buildings. Guided tour $10. Hill pass $6 for cyclists. Bike rental $6 per hr., $24 per day. Luge $13.)* The **Olympic Oval** (220-7890) is the most impressive of the remaining arenas, still a major international training facility with the fastest ice in the world. *(Public skating hrs. in summer 8-9:30pm. $4, children $2. Hockey skate rental $3.50, speed skates $3.75.)*

The **Glenbow Museum,** 130 9th Ave. SE (268-4100), brings rocks and minerals, Buddhist and Hindu art, and native Canadian history under one roof. *(Open daily 9am-5pm; mid-Oct. to May Tu-Su 9am-5pm. $8, seniors and students $6, under 6 free. HI discount.)* Footbridges stretch from either side of the Bow River to **Prince's Island Park,** whose lawns and paths teem with bikers, bladers, and sunbathers. Calgary's other island park, **St. George's Island,** is accessible by the river walkway to the east, and houses the ark-like **Calgary Zoo** (232-9372), including a botanical garden and children's zoo. *(Gates open daily 9am-8pm; in winter 9am-4pm. Grounds open 9am-9pm; Oct.-Apr. 9am-5:30pm. $9.50, children $4.75, seniors ½-price Tu and Th; in winter $8, seniors and children $4. AAA and HI discounts.)* [To be sung to the tune of *The Beverly Hillbillies:*] Come 'n' listen to a story 'bout the **Energeum,** a place 'bout oil kinda like a museum. Play a game 'bout drillin', watch a movie in th' thee-ter, and learn how Alberta puts th' power in your heater. Industrial propaganda, that is, 640 5th Ave. SW (297-4293). *(Open Su-F 10:30am-4:30pm; Sept.-May M-F 10:30am-4:30pm. Free.)*

THE STAMPEDE On July 9-18, 1999, millions of cowboys and tourists will converge on **Stampede Park,** just southeast of downtown, bordering the east side of Macleod Trail between 14th and 25th Ave. SE. *(Gate admission $9; seniors and ages 7-12 $4. Rodeo and evening cost $17-45; rush tickets, if not sold out, are same price as admission, on sale at the grandstand 1½hr. before showtime.)* For 10 days annually, the grounds are packed for world-class steer wrestling, saddle bronc, bareback- and bull-riding, pig racing, wild-cow-milking, and chuckwagon races. A **free pancake breakfast** is served at a different location in the city every day. Parking is ample and reasonably priced, but can be tedious. Take the C-Train to the Stampede stop from downtown, or walk. For info and ticket orders, call 269-9822 or 800-661-1767.

▓ Alberta Badlands

Prehistoric wind, water, and ice cut twisting canyons down into the sandstone and shale bedrock, resulting in the desolate splendor of the Alberta Badlands. The **Royal Tyrrell Museum of Paleontology** (TEER-ull; 403-823-7707 or 888-440-4240) lies on the **North Dinosaur Trail (Secondary Hwy. 838),** 6km northwest of **Drumheller** (drum-HELL-er), which itself lies 138km northeast of Calgary. (Open daily 9am-9pm; Labour Day to Victoria Day Tu-Su 10am-5pm. $6.50, seniors $5.50, ages 7-17 $3; in winter ½-price Tu.) Get there by driving east on Hwy. 1 and northeast on Hwy. 9. The world's largest display of dinosaur specimens makes a forceful reminder that humanity is a mere flyspeck on the giant windshield of life. The museum's immensely popular 12-person **Day Digs** include instruction in paleontology and excavation techniques, and a chance to dig in a dinosaur quarry. (Departs daily July-Aug. at 8:30am; mid-May to June Sa-Su only. $85, ages 10-15 $55. Reservations required.) The fee includes lunch and transportation, but all finds go to the museum. The **Field Station Badlands Bus Tour** (378-4342), 48km east of the town of **Brooks** in **Dinosaur Provincial Park,** chauffeurs visitors into a restricted hot spot of dinosaur finds. (Field Station open daily May 24-Sept. 6 8:30am-9pm; call for winter hrs. Tours May 24-Oct. 11 2-8 per day; $4.50, ages 6-15 $2.25.)

Alexandra Hostel (HI-C), 30 Railway Ave. N (823-6337), has 55 beds in a converted hotel that hasn't changed much since the 30s, sporting a kitchen, laundry, and a killer view from the fire escape ($15, nonmembers $20; check-in 9am-11pm). The hostel also rents **mountain bikes. River Grove Campground,** off North Dinosaur Trail at the intersection with Hwy. 9, has flush toilets, free showers, and laundry.

(Tent sites $17, full hookup $24. Cabins for 2-10 people, with bathrooms, electricity, and cable TV $40-70. Open daily May 24 to Sept. 6 7am-11pm.) Surprisingly decent Chinese and Thai sizzles at **Sizzling House,** 160 Centre St. (823-8098), with 100 different choices of Szechuan- and Peking-style beef and chicken dishes ($7-9), plus noodle or fried rice platters ($6-7) for eat-in or take-out (open Su-Th 11am-10pm, F-Sa 11am-11pm). **Greyhound** runs from Calgary to **Drumheller** (2 per day, $21), which is 6km southeast of the museum. From Drumheller, rent a bike from the hostel (see above; $4 per hr., $15 per day); it's about a 20min. ride to the museum.

APPENDIX

Holidays

	USA		CANADA
Date	**Holiday**	**Date**	**Holiday**
January 1	New Year's Day	January 1	New Year's Day
January 18	Martin Luther King, Jr. Day	April 5	Easter Monday
February 15	Presidents Day	May 24	Victoria Day
May 31	Memorial Day	July 1	Canada Day
July 4	Independence Day	September 6	Labour Day
September 6	Labor Day	October 11	Thanksgiving
October 11	Columbus Day	November 11	Remembrance Day
November 11	Veterans Day (Armistice Day)	December 25	Christmas Day
November 25	Thanksgiving Day	December 26	Boxing Day
December 25	Christmas Day		

Festivals

A number of regional festivals are celebrated annually in both the U.S. and Canada, their themes ranging from food to music to regional folklife. Some of the most popular festivals are listed below, along with the page numbers of their respective descriptions in the guide; refer to Sights and Entertainment sections of individual city listings for more festivals.

Month	Festival and Location
	USA
January	**Elvis Presley's Birthday Tribute,** Memphis, TN (p. 282)
	National Western Stock Show, Rodeo, and Horse Show, Denver, CO (p. 594)
	Winter Carnival, St. Paul, MN (p. 459)
February	**Mardi Gras,** New Orleans, LA (p. 344)
	Ashland Shakespeare Festival, Ashland, OR (p. 730)
	Gasparilla Pirate Festival, Tampa, FL (p. 387)
March	**South by Southwest,** Austin, TX (p. 529)
April	**New Orleans Jazz and Heritage Festival,** New Orleans, LA (p. 344)
	Fiesta San Antonio, San Antonio, TX (p. 540)
May	**Memphis in May International Festival,** Memphis, TN (p. 285)
	Spoleto Festival USA, Charleston, SC (p. 301)
June	**Portland Rose Festival,** Portland, OR (p. 721)
	Chisholm Trail Round-up, Fort Worth, TX (p. 525)
	Chicago Blues Festival, Chicago, IL (p. 441)
	Summerfest, Milwaukee, WI (p. 447)
	Aspen Music Festival, Aspen, CO (p. 603)
July	**Tanglewood,** Lenox, MA (p. 117)
	Frontier Days, Cheyenne, WY (p. 588)
	Aquatennial, Minneapolis, MN (p. 459)
August	**Newport Folk Festival and JVC Jazz Festival,** Newport, RI (p. 122)

September	**Bumbershoot,** Seattle, WA (p. 699)
	La Fiesta de Santa Fe, Santa Fe, NM
November	**Hot Air Balloon Rally,** Albuquerque, NM (p. 681)
	Macy's Thanksgiving Day Parade, New York, NY (p. 151)

CANADA

February	**Winterlude,** Ottawa, ON (p. 901)
	Winter Carnival, Québec City, QC (p. 883)
May	**Stratford Festival,** Stratford, ON (p. 895)
	Canadian Tulip Festival, Ottawa, ON (p. 901)
June	**International Jazz Festival,** Montréal, QC (p. 872)
July	**Calgary Stampede,** Calgary, AB (p. 928)
July	**Nova Scotia International Tattoo Festival, Halifax,** NS (p. 859)

■ Climate

The following chart gives the average temperatures in degrees Fahrenheit and the average rainfall in inches during four months of the year. To convert from °C to °F, multiply by 1.8 and add 32. For a rough approximation, double the Celsius and add 25. To convert from °F to °C, subtract 32 and divide by 2.

| Temp in °F | January | | April | | July | | October | |
Rain in inches	Temp	Rain	Temp	Rain	Temp	Rain	Temp	Rain
Atlanta	51°	4.9"	73°	4.4"	89°	4.7"	74°	2.5"
Chicago	29°	1.6"	59°	3.7"	83°	3.6"	64°	2.3"
Dallas	54°	1.7"	84°	3.6"	98°	2.0"	80°	2.5"
Las Vegas	56°	0.5"	77°	0.2"	105°	0.5"	82°	0.3"
Los Angeles	67°	3.7"	71°	1.2"	84°	0.0"	79°	0.2"
New Orleans	62°	5.0"	79°	4.5"	91°	6.7"	79°	2.7"
New York	68°	3.2"	61°	3.8"	85°	3.8"	66°	3.4"
Seattle	45°	5.9"	58°	2.5"	74°	0.9"	60°	3.4"

■ Time Zones

North Americans tell **time** on a 12hr. clock cycle. Hours before noon are "am" *(ante meridiem);* hours after noon are "pm" *(post meridiem).* The four time zones in the continental U.S. are (east to west, each zone 1hr. earlier than the preceding): **Eastern, Central, Mountain,** and **Pacific. Alaska, Hawaii,** and the **Aleutian Islands** have their own time zones. Canada has six: **Newfoundland, Atlantic, Eastern, Central, Mountain,** and **Pacific.** Most of the U.S. (except Arizona, Hawaii, and parts of Indiana) and all of Canada observe **daylight savings time** from the first Sunday in April (Apr. 4, 1999) to the last Sunday in October (Oct. 24, 1999) by advancing clocks ahead 1hr.

■ Measurements

Although the metric system has made considerable inroads into American business and science, the English system of weights and measures continues to prevail here. Refer to the inside back cover of this guide for a metric/English conversion chart.

ELECTRICITY

Electric outlets in North America provide current at 117 volts, 60 cycles (hertz). Appliances designed for the European electrical system (220 volts) will not operate without a **transformer** and a **plug adaptor.** Transformers are sold to convert specific wattages (e.g., 0-50 watt transformers for razors and radios).

APPENDIX

Distances (mi.) and Travel Times (By Bus)

	Atlanta	Boston	Chic.	Dallas	D.C.	Denver	L.A.	Miami	N. Orl.	NYC	Phila.	Phnx.	St. Lou.	Sa. Fran.	Seattle	Trnto.	Vanc.	Mont.
Atlanta		1108	717	783	632	1406	2366	653	474	886	778	1863	560	2492	2699	959	2825	1240
Boston	22hr.		996	1794	442	1990	3017	1533	1542	194	333	2697	1190	3111	3105	555	3242	326
Chicago	14hr.	20hr.		937	715	1023	2047	1237	928	807	767	1791	302	2145	2108	537	2245	537
Dallas	15hr.	35hr.	18hr.		1326	794	1450	1322	507	1576	1459	906	629	1740	2112	1457	2255	1763
D.C.	12hr.	8hr.	14hr.	24hr.		1700	2689	1043	1085	225	139	2350	845	2840	2788	526	3292	665
Denver	27hr.	38hr.	20hr.	15hr.	29hr.		1026	2046	1341	1785	1759	790	860	1267	1313	1508	1458	1864
L.A.	45hr.	57hr.	39hr.	28hr.	55hr.	20hr.		2780	2005	2787	2723	371	1837	384	1141	2404	1285	2888
Miami	13hr.	30hr.	24hr.	26hr.	20hr.	39hr.	53hr.		856	1346	1214	2368	1197	3086	3368	1564	3505	1676
New O.	9hr.	31hr.	18hr.	10hr.	21hr.	26hr.	38hr.	17hr.		1332	1247	1535	677	2331	2639	1320	2561	1654
NYC	18hr.	4hr.	16hr.	31hr.	5hr.	35hr.	53hr.	26hr.	27hr.		104	2592	999	2923	2912	496	3085	386
Phila.	18hr.	6hr.	16hr.	19hr.	3hr.	33hr.	50hr.	23hr.	23hr.	2hr.		2511	904	2883	2872	503	3009	465
Phoenix	40hr.	49hr.	39hr.	19hr.	43hr.	17hr.	8hr.	47hr.	30hr.	45hr.	44hr.		1503	753	1510	2069	1654	2638
St. Louis	11hr.	23hr.	6hr.	13hr.	15hr.	17hr.	35hr.	23hr.	13hr.	19hr.	16hr.	32hr.		2113	2139	810	2276	1128
San Fran.	47hr.	60hr.	41hr.	47hr.	60hr.	33hr.	7hr.	59hr.	43hr.	56hr.	54hr.	15hr.	45hr.		807	2630	951	2985
Seattle	52hr.	59hr.	40hr.	40hr.	54hr.	25hr.	22hr.	65hr.	50hr.	55hr.	54hr.	28hr.	36hr.	16hr.		2623	146	2964
Toronto	21hr.	11hr.	10hr.	26hr.	11hr.	26hr.	48hr.	29hr.	13hr.	11hr.	13hr.	48hr.	14hr.	49hr.	48hr.		4563	655
Vancvr.	54hr.	61hr.	42hr.	43hr.	60hr.	27hr.	24hr.	67hr.	54hr.	57hr.	56hr.	30hr.	38hr.	18hr.	2hr.	53hr.		4861
Montreal	23hr.	6hr.	17hr.	28hr.	12hr.	39hr.	53hr.	32hr.	31hr.	7hr.	9hr.	53hr.	23hr.	56hr.	55hr.	7hr.	55hr.	

Index

A

AAA (American Automobile Association) 35
Abbey, Edward 64, 636, 639
abducted by the earthship, MT 565
Abominable Snowmansion, NM 677
Acadia National Park, ME 76
Acadiana, LA 347–350
accommodation info
  bed and breakfasts (B&B) 41
  dormitories 43
  dorms 43
  hostels 39
  hotels and motels 39
  YMCA and YWCA 41
Adams, Ansel 824
Adirondacks, NY 183
Advance Purchase Excursion Fare (APEX) 23, 29
Adventures of Tom Sawyer 506
aerogrammes 53
AIDS 14
AIDS Memorial Quilt, CA 789
air mail 53
air travel 23
  air passes 29
  charter flights 27
  courier flights 27
  frequent flyer tickets 29
  stand-by flights 25
  student fares 31
Airhitch 27
airlines
  from Asia, Africa, and Australia 25
  from Europe 25
  within the U.S. and Canada 31
Air-Tech 27
Alabama 318–326
  Birmingham 321–324
  Mobile 324–326
  Montgomery 319–321
  Tuskegee 321
Alamo, TX 538
Alaska 829–841
  Anchorage 830–833

Denali 835
Fairbanks 836
Glacier Bay 841
Juneau 840
Kenai Fjords 833
Ketchikan 838
Misty Fiords 839
Seward 833
Wrangell-St. Elias 834
Alaska Highway, BC 914
Albany, NY 173–175
Alberta 921–929
  Alberta Badlands 928
  Banff National Park 921
  Calgary 926
  Edmonton 925
  Jasper National Park 923
Alberta Badlands, AB 928
Albuquerque, NM 678–682
Alcatraz Island, CA 792
Alcott, Louisa May 104
Alexandria Bay, NY 186
Algonquin Provincial Park, ON 901
Ali, Muhammed 305
alien crash site, NM 687
alternatives to tourism 15
Amana Colonies, IA 487
Amarillo, TX 543
Americade 39
American Express 10, 11, 35, 37
American Motorcyclist Association 38
Americana
  22 ft. tall thermometer, MN 466
  Beer Can House, TX 533
  Carhenge 494
  Corn Palace, SD 472
  cross in the hills, ID 554
  Cross in the Woods, MI 418
  Miracle of America Museum, MT 565
  miraculous painting, NM 678
  paragon of, TN 281
  Red Carpet Washateria and Lanes, MS 330
  Rocky Mountain oysters 593
  Space Needle, WA 695
  the burning of Old Man Gloom, NM 676
  Tree That Owns Itself,

  GA 314
  two-headed calf, ID 554
  two-headed calf, TX 540
  Woodhenge, MO 506
Amherst, MA 117
Amish 202
Amtrak (800-872-7245) 31
Anchorage, AK 830–833
Andy Warhol Museum, PA 208
Ann Arbor, MI 411–413
Annapolis, MD 218
Anne of Green Gables 864
Ansel Adams Center, CA 788
Apollo Theater, NY 157, 166
Apostle Islands, WI 453
Appendix 930–932
Appomatox Court House, VA 60
aquariums
  Albuquerque, NM 681
  Baltimore, MD 216
  Boston, MA 97
  Camden, NJ 200
  Chattanooga, TN 277
  Chicago, IL 435
  Clearwater, FL 389
  Corpus Christi, TX 542
  Dallas, TX 523
  Galveston, TX 535
  Key Largo, FL 382
  Key West, FL 384
  Monterey Bay, CA 776
  Mt. Desert, ME 76
  Mystic, CT 127
  New Orleans, LA 340
  New York, NY 158
  Newport, OR 725
  Québec City, PQ 882
  Seattle, WA 695
  Tampa, FL 387
Arches National Park, UT 636
Arcosanti, AZ 661
Arctic Circle 830
Arizona 645–671
  Bisbee 671
  Canyon de Chelly 655
  Flagstaff 651–653
  Grand Canyon 646–650
  Hopi Reservation 657
  Jerome 660
  Lake Powell 657
  Monument Valley 656

Navajo Reservation 654–657
Organ Pipe Cactus 666
Page 657
Phoenix 661–665
Rainbow Bridge 657
Sedona 659
Tombstone 670
Tucson 666–670
Window Rock 655
Arkansas 350–356
  Eureka Springs 355
  Hot Springs 352
  Little Rock 350–352
  Mountain View 354
armadillo races, TX 525
Art Institute of Chicago, IL 434
Ashe, Arthur 239
Asheville, NC 292–295
Ashford, WA 711
Ashland, OR 730
Aspen, CO 603
Assateague Island, MD 219
Astoria, OR 724
Athens, GA 313
Atlanta, GA 305–313
Atlantic City, NJ 188–190
ATM cards 10
Audubon, John 384
Austin, TX 525–529
auto transport companies 37
Automotive Hall of Fame, MI 409
Autry, Gene 744

B
Bacall, Lauren 747
Badlands National Park, SD 473
Baez, Joan 122
Baltimore, MD 213–218
banana slugs 709
Bandelier National Monument, NM 676
Banff National Park 921
Bar Harbor, ME 74–76
Baraboo, WI 451
Barbecue Capital of the World, MO 507
Barbie Doll Hall of Fame, CA 803
Bardstown, KY 263
bargaining 12
Barnum, P.T. 78
Baseball Hall of Fame, NY 176
Basie, Count 122
Basketball Hall of Fame 118
Baton Rouge, LA 346
Beantown 94

bear info 51
Beatniks 64
Beaver Island, MI 418
bed and breakfasts (B&B) 41
Beecher Stowe, Harriet 124
Bel Air, CA 747
Belafonte, Harry 321
Belfast, ME 73
Bellingham, WA 702
Ben & Jerry's 83, 87
Bend, OR 731
Beringia 851
Berkeley, CA 798–800
Berkshires, MA 115–118
Berle, Milton 745
Betsy Ross House, PA 198
Beverly Hills, CA 746
bicycle travel 37
Big Bear, CA 759
Big Bend National Park, TX 549
Big Island, HI 848
Big Sur, CA 775
Bighorn Mountains, WY 584
Bighorn National Forest, WY 584
Bill of Rights 59, 231
Billings, MT 560
Biltmore Estate, NC 294
Birmingham Civil Rights Institute, AL 323
Birmingham, AL 321–324
Bisbee, AZ 671
bisexual, gay, and lesbian travelers 17
Black Canyon of the Gunnison National Monument, CO 610
Black Canyon, CO 610
Black Hills National Forests, SD 475
Blanding, UT 645
Block Island, RI 122
Bloomington, IN 426
Blowing Rock, NC 292
Blue Ridge Parkway, VA 250
Bluenose 856
Bogart, Humphrey 747
Boiling River, WY 574
Boise National Forest, ID 553
Boise, ID 552–555
Boldt Castle, NY 187
Boone, Daniel 257, 268
Boone, NC 290
Booth, John Wilkes 231
border crossing
  Ciudad Juárez 548

Tijuana 767
Boston African-American National Historic Site, MA 96
Boston Massacre 59, 95
Boston Tea Party 59, 95
Boston, MA 90–101
botanical gardens
  Athens, GA 314
  Atlanta, GA 311
  Biltmore Estate, NC 294
  Birmingham, AL 323
  Boston, MA 103
  Cleveland, OH 398
  Cornell, NY 178
  Fairbanks, AK 837
  Madison, WI 450
  Memphis, TN 284
  Milwaukee, WI 447
  Montréal, PQ 873
  Myriad Gardens, OK 518
  Nashville, TN 272
  New York City, NY 159
  Portland, OR 721
  San Marino, CA 752
  Seattle, WA 697
  Springfield, IL 443
  Staten Island, NY 160
  Vancouver, BC 907
  Victoria, BC 910
  Winter Haven, FL 369
Boulder Ranges, ID 557
Boulder, CO 596–599
Boundary Waters Canoe Area Wilderness, MN 465
Bowling Green, KY 264
Bowling Museum, International, MO 502
Boys Town, NE 490
Bozeman, MT 562
Br'er Rabbit 310
Brady Bunch 752
Branson, MO 512
Brattleboro, VT 88
Breckenridge, CO 596
Brethren 202
Bridger-Teton National Forest, WY 580
Bridges of Madison County 484
British Columbia 903–915
  Glacier National Park 911
  Kootenay 912
  Pacific Rim National Park 911
  Prince Rupert 913
  Vancouver 903–909
  Vancouver Island 909–911
  Victoria 909
  Yoho National Park 912

Broadway, NY 164
Bronx, NY 159
Brooklyn, NY 157
Brown, John 120
Browning, MT 568
Brunswick, GA 317
Bryan, William Jennings 612
Bryce Canyon, UT 640
budget travel agencies 21
Buffalo, NY 179
Buffalo, WY 583
Build Me A University, OK 515
Bumbershoot, WA 699
Bunker Hill Monument, MA 95
Burgdorf, ID 555
Burlington, VT 82-84
buses 32
Bush, George 72
Butte Mountains, CA 816

C

Cabrillo National Monument, CA 765
Café du Monde, LA 337
Cahokia Mounds, MO 505
Calamity Jane 480
Calaveras County, CA 815
Calgary Stampede, AB 928
Calgary, AB 926
California 733-828
  Avenue of the Giants 812
  Berkeley 798-800
  Big Bear 759
  Big Sur 775
  Butte Mountains 816
  Calaveras County 815
  California Desert 768-772
  Cascades 817
  Central Coast 772-779
  Coloma 816
  Davis 815
  Death Valley 771
  Escondido 766
  Gold Country 814-817
  Joshua Tree 769
  La Jolla 766
  Lake Tahoe 817-821
  Los Angeles 733-756
  Mammoth Lakes 827
  Marin County 805-807
  Mendocino 811
  Mono Lake 826
  Monterey 776
  Napa Valley 807-810
  Northern California 811-817
  Oakland 801
  Orange County 757-759
  Palm Springs 768
  Palo Alto 803
  Redwood 813
  Sacramento 815
  Salinas 777
  San Diego 760-767
  San Francisco 780-798
  San Jose 801
  San Luis Obispo 774
  San Mateo County 804
  Santa Barbara 772-774
  Santa Cruz 777-779
  Sierra Nevada 817-828
  Sonoma Valley 810
  Sonora 815
  Wine Country 807-811
  Yosemite 821-826
Calistoga, CA 810
calling cards 55
Calumet, MN 464
Cambridge, MA 101-103
Camden, ME 73
camping and the outdoors 43-51
  bear info 51
  equipment 43
  minimum impact camping 49
  National Forest info 47
  National Park info 47
  organized adventure 51
  roughing it safely 49
Canada 851-929
Canada's Wonderland, ON 893
Canadian Cycling Association 38
Canadian National Tower, ON 892
Canaveral National Seashore, FL 371
Candy, John 853, 894
Cannery Row, CA 776
Cannon Beach, OR 724
canoeing
  Anchorage, AK 832
  Brattleboro, VT 89
  Glacier National Park, MT 568
  Sawtooth, ID 559
  Stowe, VT 87
  Waterton Park, AB 569
Canyon de Chelly, AZ 655
Canyonlands National Park, UT 637
Cape Canaveral, FL 370
Cape Cod Potato Chip Factory, MA 107
Cape Cod, MA 106-111
Cape Flattery, WA 707
Cape May, NJ 191
Cape Vincent, NY 186
Capitol Hill, D.C. 228
Capitol Reef National Park, UT 639
car purchasing 37
car rentals 36
  Alamo (800-327-9633) 36
  Avis (800-331-1212) 36
  Budget (800-527-0700) 36
  Dollar (800-800-4000) 36
  Enterprise (800-736-8222) 36
  Hertz (800-654-3131) 36
  Rent-A-Wreck (800-421-7253) 36
  Thrifty (800-367-2277) 36
Carhenge, NE 494
Carlsbad Caverns National Park, NM 687
Carnegie Hall, NY 152
Carnegie, Andrew 60, 208
Carolina Coast, NC 295-298
Carter, Jimmy 305, 310
Cartier, Jacques 851
Carver, George Washington 321
Cascades, CA 817
cash machines. See ATM cards
Casper, WY 586
Cassiar Highway, BC 915
Cassidy, Butch 612, 633
Castillo de San Marcos National Monument, FL 360
Castro, Fidel 853
Cather, Willa 488
Catskill Forest Preserve, NY 172
Catskills, NY 172-173
Cave and Basin National Historic Site, AB 922
Cave of the Winds, CO 609
Cedar City, UT 643
Cedar Point Amusement Park, OH 399
Central Park, NY 154
Chaco Culture National Historical Park, NM 683
Chapel Hill, NC 286
Charleston, SC 298-301
Charlevoix, MI 418
Charlotte, NC 289
Charlottesville, VA 245-248
Charlottetown, PEI 866
charter flights 27
Château Frontenac, QC 881
Chattahoochee National Forest, GA 305
Chattanooga, TN 277
Cherokee Nation, OK 516

Cherokee Reservation, TN 276
Cheyenne, WY 587
Chicago, IL 428-442
Chihuahuan Desert, TX 549
Chimney Rock, NE 494
Chippewa National Forest, MN 463
Chisos Mountains, TX 549
Chrétien, Jean 853
Church of Jesus Christ of Latter Day Saints, UT 628
Churchill Downs, KY 262
Cíbola National Forest, NM 681
Cincinnati, OH 402-406
Circus World Museum, WI 451
Citicorp 10
City of Surprises 321
Civil Rights Memorial, AL 320
Civil Rights Movement 61-62
Civil War 60
civilization's beacon, UT 632
Clayton, NY 186
Clearwater, FL 387-390
Cleveland, OH 395-399
Clinton, Bill 62, 63, 350
cocktail waitress race, AZ 653
Cocoa Beach, FL 370
Coconino National Forest, AZ 660
Cody, Buffalo Bill 582, 584
Cody, WY 582
Colbert, Claudette 555
collect calls 55
Coloma, CA 816
Colonial National Park, VA 242
Colorado 590-616
    Aspen 603
    Black Canyon 610
    Boulder 596-599
    Colorado National Monument 606
    Colorado Springs 607-609
    Crested Butte 611
    Denver 590-595
    Durango 614
    Glenwood Springs 604
    Grand Junction 605
    Grand Mesa 606
    Great Sand Dunes 609
    Mesa Verde 616
    Pagosa Springs 615
    Rocky Mountain National

Park 599-602
    San Juan Mountains 610-616
    Summit County 596
    Telluride 612
    Vail 602
    Winter Park 595
Colorado National Monument, CO 606
Colorado Springs, CO 607-609
Colter Bay, WY 576
Columbia River Gorge, OR 723
Columbia, SC 301-302
Columbus, OH 399
Concord, MA 104
condoms 14
Coney Island, NY 158
Confederacy 60
Connecticut 123-127
    Hartford 123
    Mystic 127
    New Haven 125
Conspiracy Museum, TX 523
consulates. See embassies
Continental Divide 551
Cooke City, MT 573
Cooperstown, NY 175
Copper Harbor, MI 422
Cornell University, NY 178
Corning, NY 179
Coronado Island, CA 765
Coronado, Francisco 495
Corpus Christi, TX 541
Costner, Kevin 288
Country Music Hall of Fame, TN 272
courier flights 27
Cranberry World, MA 105
Crater Lake National Park, OR 729
Craters of the Moon National Monument, ID 559
Crazy Horse 476, 561
Crazy Horse Memorial, SD 476
credit cards 10
Creedence Clearwater Revival 64
Crested Butte, CO 611
Crypt Lake Trail, AB 568
Cumberland Gap National Historic Park, KY 268
currency 9
Curse of the Bambino, MA 100
Custer State Park, SD 477
Custer, George Armstrong

561
customs
    entering 7
    going home 7
cybercafes 57
Cypress Gardens, FL 369

D

Dallas Museum of Art, TX 523
Dallas, TX 520-524
dandelion wine 487
Daniel Boone National Forest, KY 267
Davis, CA 815
Davis, Miles 160
Dawson City, YT 918
Daytona 500, FL 362
Daytona Beach, FL 360, 362
Deadwood, SD 480
Death Valley National Park, CA 771
Declaration of Independence 59, 193, 231
Delaware 211-213
    Delaware Seashore 211
    Lewes 211
    Rehoboth 212
Delaware Seashore, DE 211
Denali National Park, AK 835
Denver, CO 590-595
Des Moines, IA 481-484
Deschutes National Forest, OR 731
Detroit, MI 406-411
Devil's Postpile National Monument, CA 827
Devils Tower National Monument, WY 585
Dewey, Melvil 185
dietary concerns 19
Dillon, CO 596
Dinkins, David 130
Dinosaur Center and Dig Sites, WY 586
Dinosaur National Monument, UT 631
disabled travelers 18
Disney World, FL 366-369
Disneyland, CA 758
Do you read me, Houston? 532
documents and formalities 3-9
Dodge City, KS 497
Dollywood, TN 276
Don Quixote 199
Doody, Howdy 502
Door County, WI 450-453
dormitories 43
Dos Passos, John 111

Dr. Strangelove 491
Drumheller, AB 928
Dubois, W.E.B. 321
Duluth, MN 461
Durango, CO 614
Durham, NC 285
Dylan, Bob 64, 464

E

Earp, Wyatt 494, 497
East LaHave, NS 856
Eastham, MA 108
Ebenezer Baptist Church,
   GA 309
Edison, Thomas 409
Edmonton, AB 925
Eisenhower, Dwight 657
El Morro National
   Monument, NM 683
El Paso, TX 546
electronic mail 57
Eliot's Picks
   Aquarium, PQ 882
   El Zaziummm, PQ 871
   Fiddles of the World, NS
      859
Ellington, Duke 160
Ellis Island, NY 148
Ely, MN 464
Emancipation
   Proclamation 60
embassies and consulates
   foreign 3
   in Canada 29
   in the U.S. 28
   Ottawa, ON 897
   Toronto, CA 888
Emerson, Ralph Waldo 104
Empire State Building, NY
   152
entrance requirements 6
Ericson, Leif 68
Escondido, CA 766
Essentials 1–57
Estes Park, CO 599
Eugene, OR 726–729
Eureka Springs, AR 355
Evanston, IL 439
Evaporated Kid 918
Everglades National Park,
   FL 379–381
Exploratorium, CA 792

F

factory outlet capital of the
   world, ME 73
Fairbanks, AK 836
Fallingwater, PA 210
Family Ties 400
Faneuil Hall, MA 95
Fargo, ND 469
farm vacation, PEI 865

Faulkner, William 332
Federal Express 53
Federal Sites
   Arlington National
      Cemetery, VA 233
   Federal Bureau of
      Investigation 231
   Holocaust Memorial
      Museum 230
   Iwo Jima Memorial 233
   Korean War Memorial
      230
   Library of Congress 228
   Lincoln Memorial 230
   National Archives 231
   National Postal Museum
      228
   Smithsonian 229
   Supreme Court 228
   The Mall 229
   The Mint 230
   U.S. Capitol 228
   Vietnam Veterans
      Memorial 230
   Washington Monument
      230
   White House 231
Feminine Mystique, The
   62
Fenway Park, MA 100
Festival International de
   Louisiane, LA 349
Field of Dreams 488
financial security 12
Finger Lakes, NY 176
Fire Island National
   Seashore, NY 171
fire-fighting dolphin 393
First Continental Congress
   193
first in the U.S.
   art museum, PA 198
   First Baptist Church of
      America, RI 120
   Hindu temple, PA 209
   National Park, WY 570
   permanent English
      settlement, VA 242
   person to see the sunrise,
      ME 76
   self-made woman
      millionaire, IN 426
   state university, NC 285
   two-sided building, CT
      123
   urban shopping mall, IL
      437
   water-powered factory,
      RI 120
first in the world
   atomic bomb detonation,

   NM 686
   city lit by atomic power,
      ID 559
   hamburger, CT 126
   hot dog, MO 503
   ice cream cone, MO 503
   skyscraper, NY 151
   submarine to sink a ship,
      SC 302
   Wendy's, OH 401
fishboils, WI 451
Fitzgerald, F. Scott 320, 459
Flagstaff, AZ 651–653
Flaming Gorge, UT 633
Florida 357–393
   Clearwater 387–390
   Cocoa Beach and Cape
      Canaveral 370
   Daytona Beach 360, 362
   Disney World 366–369
   Everglades 379–381
   Fort Lauderdale 371–374
   Gainesville 390
   Gulf Coast 385–393
   Key Largo 381
   Key West 382–385
   Miami 374–379
   Orlando 362–370
   Panama City 391
   St. Augustine 357–360
   St. Petersburg 387–390
   Tampa 385–387
Florida Keys 381–385
Flynn, Errol 555
Football Hall of Fame, OH
   399
Ford, Gerald 414, 488
foreign exchange 9
Fort Caspar, WY 586
Fort Lauderdale, FL 371–
   374
Fort McHenry National
   Monument, MD 217
Fort Necessity, PA 211
Fort Pulaski National
   Monument, GA 317
Fort Worth, TX 524–525
Fountain of the Furies, NE
   490
Fountain of Youth, FL 360
Fox, Michael J. 161
Franconia Notch, NH 78
Franklin, Benjamin 193
Fredericksburg, TX 541
Freedom Trail, MA 95
Freeport, ME 72
French Quarter, LA 339
frequent flyer tickets 29
Frisco, CO 596
Frontier Days, WY 588
Fundy National Park, NB

862

G
Gainesville, FL 390
Gallup, NM 682
Galveston Island, TX 534–535
gangsta rap 64
Garden of the Gods, CO 608
Gardiner, MT 573
Garland, Judy 747
gasoline 36
Gateway Arch, MO 502
general delivery 53
Georgia 305–318
  Athens 313
  Atlanta 305–313
  Brunswick 317
  Savannah 314–317
Georgia O'Keeffe Museum, AZ 674
getting around the U.S. and Canada 29–39
getting to the U.S. and Canada 21–28
Getty Museum, CA 748
Gettysburg National Cemetery, PA 205
Gettysburg, PA 205
Ghirardelli Chocolate Manufactory, CA 793
Ghost Towns, NM 684
Gila Cliff Dwellings, NM 685
Gila National Forest, NM 685
Giuliani, Rudolph 130
Glacier Bay National Park, AK 841
Glacier National Park, BC 911
Glacier National Park, MT 566–568
Glen Canyon Dam, AZ 657
Glenwood Springs, CO 604
Glory 95
GO25 Card (International Youth Discount Travel Card) 9
Going-to-the-Sun Road, MT 567
Gold Country, CA 814–817
Golden Access Passport 47
Golden Age Passport 47
Golden Eagle Passport 47
Golden Gate Bridge, CA 791
Golden Gate National Recreation Area, CA 792
Gone With the Wind 311, 341
goods and services tax

(GST) 12
government information offices 1
government, American 63
Grace Cathedral, CA 794
Graceland, TN 281
Grand Canyon, AZ 646–650
Grand Haven, MI 415
Grand Junction, CO 605
Grand Lake, CO 599
Grand Mesa, CO 606
Grand Portage, MN 423
Grand Rapids, MI 413
Grand Strand, SC 302–??
Grand Teton National Park, WY 576–579
Grant, Ulysses S. 60
Grant's Tomb, NY 157
Grapes of Wrath 513
Grateful Dead 790
grayboxes
  American Funeral Service Museum, TX 533
  Amish desserts, PA 203
  Arcosanti, AZ 661
  attack on the *Constitution*, DC 232
  banana slugs, WA 709
  Baraboo, WI 451
  beer, WI 446
  beginning of the Mississippi, MN 463
  Ben & Jerry's, VT 87
  big boom, NS 859
  big Texan women, TX 544
  birth of hip-hop, NY 159
  bourbon, KY 263
  brains don't mean a shit, FL 385
  Bridges of Madison County,IA 484
  buffalo, ND 470
  Butch Cassidy and the Sundance Kid, UT 633
  Canadian National Tower, ON 892
  Carhenge, NE 494
  Chicago River, IL 439
  Cincy chili, OH 404
  coffee vocab, WA 693
  Colorado National Monument, CO 606
  Dodge City, KS 497
  Dollywood, TN 276
  Edward Abbey, UT 639
  Empire State Building, NY 153
  Ernest Hemingway, ID 557
  federal wolf packs, WY

575
Field of Dreams, IA 488
Four Corners, CO 616
geographic center of the U.S., KS 499
getting leid, HI 845
gold panning, CA 815
graves, LA 341
Ground Zero, CO 609
Hargrove, Mike, OH 398
Hawk Ridge, MN 462
Hersheypark, PA 204
Homestead Grays, PA 209
Iditarod, AK 832
innertubing, TX 540
Jack Daniels, TN 278
Jones, Casey, TN 283
jungle music, NY 168
Mall of America, MN 459
Manhattan Project, NM 675
Meteor Crater, AZ 659
Midnight in the Garden of Good and Evil, GA 317
Montanabahn, MT 560
nude in Texas, TX 528
Oak Ridge, TN 274
Old South Winery, MS 331
pasty, MI 420
Peabody Hotel, TN 284
pig pickin', NC 289
plowshares into swords, VA 237
Poe, Edgar Allen, MD 217
Roswell, NM 687
Russian teahouse, CO 598
Selma to Montgomery March, AL 321
smoked meat, PQ 871
Sourtoe Club, YT 920
steamboats, monster trucks, and automobiles 504
Testicle Festival, MT 563
Trail of Tears National Historic Trail, OK 516
volcano goddess, HI 849
Waffle House, GA 310
Wall Drug, SD 474
Welles, Orson, CA 741
Wendy's, OH 400
wine tasting, CA 809
Wright Brothers, NC 298
Great American Desert, NE 488
Great Depression 61
Great Lakes 394–466
Great Plains 467–518
Great Salt Lake, UT 629

Great Sand Dunes, CO 609
Great Smoky Mountains
National Park, TN 275
Green Bay, WI 453
Green Gables House, PEI
865
Green Mountain National
Forest, VT 81
Greyhound (800-231-2222)
32
Guadalupe Mountains
National Park, TX 545-546
Guggenheim Museum, NY
161
Gulf Coast, FL 385-393
Gunnison National Forest,
CO 612

H
Haines Falls, NY 173
Haines Junction, YT 917
Haleakala National Park, HI
848
Halifax, NS 856-859
Hallmark Cards, MO 511
Hana, HI 848
Hannibal, MO 506
Harlem Renaissance 64
Harlem, NY 156
Harley-Davidson 446, 507
Harney Peak, SD 477
Harpers Ferry National
Historical Park, WV 252
Harrodsburg, KY 266
Harry S. Truman Library
and Museum, MO 512
Hartford, CT 123
Hawaii 842-850
Big Island 848
Haleakala 848
Hana 848
Honolulu 844-846
Kauai 849
Maui 847
Oahu 844-847
Hawaii Volcanoes National
Park, HI 848
Hawthorne, Nathaniel 78
health 13
Hearst San Simeon Historic
Monument, CA 775
Helium Monument, TX 545
Hells Canyon National
Recreation Area, OR 732
Hemingway, Ernest 384,
555, 889
birthplace of, IL 438
Henry Ford Museum, MI
409
Henry, Patrick 238
Herbert Hoover National
Historic Site, IA 486

Heritage Hjemkomst
Center, ND 469
Hershey, PA 204
Hiawatha National Forest,
MI 421
Hibbing, MN 464
Hickock, Wild Bill 480, 494
High Desert Museum, OR
731
High Museum of Art, GA
311
highest
continuously paved road
in the world, CO 601
tides in the world, NB 860
waterfall in North
America, CA 824
Hillsboro, NM 685
Hilo, HI 848
hip-hop 64
history of the U.S. 58-63
Hitchcock, Alfred 747
hitchhiking 39
HIV 14
Hogg, Ima 532
Holland, MI 415
Hollywood, CA 744
Holocaust Memorial
Museum, D.C. 230
Homer, Winslow 70
Homestead Act 60
Honolulu, HI 844-846
Hoover Dam, NV 623
Hopewell Culture National
Historic Park, OH 402
Hopi Reservation, AZ 657
Hopper, Edward 110
Hostelling International 41
hostels (HI)
Alexandra, AB 928
Anchorage, AK 831
Atlanta, GA 306
Austin, TX 526
Baltimore, MD 215
Banff, AB 922
Bar Harbor, ME 75
Bellingham, WA 702
Blue Ridge, VA 251
Boston, MA 93
Boundary Waters, MN
465
Brattleboro, VT 89
Brownies Grocery, MT
566
Buffalo, NY 179
Burlington, VT 83
Calgary, AB 927
Cape Canaveral, FL 370
Cape Vincent, NY 187
Charlottetown, PEI 865
Chicago, IL 432

Clearwater, FL 388
Cleveland, OH 397
Columbus, OH 400
Denver, CO 592
Detroit, MI 408
Eastham, MA 108
Edmonton, AB 925
El Paso, TX 547
Estes Park, CO 599
Eugene, OR 727
Fort Columbia, OR 724
Fort Flagler, WA 705
Fullerton, CA 758
Fundy, NB 863
Gettysburg, PA 206
Glenwood Springs, CO
604
Grand Lake, CO 600
Halifax, NS 857
Harpers Ferry, WV 252
Hartford, CT 124
Honolulu, HI 845
Houston, TX 531
Jackson, WY 580
Jasper, AB 924
Juneau, AK 840
Ketchikan, AK 839
Key West, FL 383
LaHave, NS 856
Lake Itasca, MN 463
Lincoln, NE 492
Los Angeles South Bay,
CA 757
Los Angeles/Santa
Monica, CA 738
Madison, WI 449
Marin County, CA 805
Martha's Vineyard, MA
112
Melrose Hotel, CO 605
Miami, FL 377
Middlebury, VT 85
Milwaukee, WI 445
Montréal, PQ 869
Nantucket, MA 114
New Orleans, LA 335
New York, NY 136
Niagara Falls, NY 181
Niagara Falls, ON 181
Ohiopyle, PA 210
Olympic, WA 705
Orlando, FL 364
Ottawa, ON 897
Outer Banks, NC 296
Palo Alto, CA 803
Philadelphia, PA 195, 196
Phoenix, AZ 663
Pittsburgh, PA 207
Point Reyes, CA 805
Portland, ME 70
Portland, OR 719

Québec City, PQ 879
Redwood, CA 813
Saint John, NB 861
Salt Lake City, UT 627
San Antonio, TX 537
San Diego, CA 762, 763
San Francisco, CA 783
San Jose, CA 802
San Luis Obispo, CA 774
San Mateo Coast, CA 804
Santa Cruz, CA 778
Santa Fe, NM 673
Sault Ste. Marie, ON 420
Savannah, GA 315
Seattle, WA 693
Shenandoah, VA 248
Silver City, NM 685
Silverthorne, CO 596
Smoky Mountains, TN 275
St. Louis, MO 500
St. Paul, MN 456
Taos, NM 677
Toronto, ON 889
Truro, MA 109
Truth or Consequences, NM 684
Vancouver, BC 905
Vashon Island, WA 701
Virginia Beach, VA 244
Washington, D.C. 224
White Mountains, NH 80
White River Junction, VT 88
Windsor, CT 124
Hot Springs, AR 352
Hot Springs, SD 478
Houghton, MI 423
House of Seven Gables, MA 105
Houston, TX 529–534

Hovenweep National Monument, UT 644
Hull House, IL 437
Hull, QU 901
Hunter Mt., NY 173
Huntington Gardens, CA 752
Hyannis, MA 106

I

ice hockey 853
Icebox of the Nation, MN 466
Icefields Parkway, AB 923
Idaho 552–560
    Boise 552–555
    Craters of the Moon 559
    Ketchum 555
    McCall 555
    Sawtooth 557–559
    Sun Valley 555
Iditarod, AK 832
ilderness 465
Ile-d'Orléans, PQ 883
Illinois 428–444
    Chicago 428–442
    Springfield 442
Independence, MO 512
Indiana 423–427
    Bloomington 426
    Indianapolis 424–426
Indianapolis, IN 424–426
Indianola, IA 484
Indigo Girls 122
infantile tourists 19
insurance 14, 36
Interlochen, MI 416
International Booking Network (IBN) 41
International Crane Foundation, WI 451
International Student Identity Card (ISIC) 8
International UFO Museum and Research Center, NM 687
International Youth Discount Travel Card (GO25 Card) 9

Internet resources
    airline related 23
    general 1
    World Wide Web 3
interstate system 36
Inventor's Hall of Fame, OH 399
Inyo National Forest, CA 826
Iowa 481–488
    Amana Colonies 487
    Des Moines 481–484
    Iowa City 485
    Okoboji 485
    Spirit Lake 485
Iowa City, IA 485
Iron Range, MN 464
Isabella Stewart Gardner Museum, MA 98
Isle Royale, MI 422
Ithaca, NY 176–179

J

Jack Daniels Distillery, TN 278
Jack Kerouac School of Disembodied Poets, CO 596
Jackson, Andrew 513
Jackson, Michael 752
Jackson, MS 326–328
Jackson, Stonewall 239
Jackson, WY 579–582
James, Jesse 497
Jamestown National Historic Site, VA 242
Jasper National Park, AB 923
Jaws 113
jazz 64
Jean Lafitte National Historical Park and Preserve, LA 340
Jean Lafitte National Park, LA 348
Jefferson, Thomas 59, 689
Jennings, Peter 853
Jenny Lake, WY 576
Jerome, AZ 660

Jewel Cave National Monument, SD 477
jobs. See working
John F. Kennedy Presidential Library, MA 99
Johnson, Phillip 232
Johnston, Joseph 288
Jones Beach, NY 171
Joplin, Janis 790
Joplin, Scott 499, 503
Joshua Tree National Park, CA 769
Joyce, James 199
Juneau, AK 840

K

Kaczynski, Theodore 63
Kahiki, OH 400
Kaibab National Forest, AZ 647, 650
Kaleidoworld, NY 172
Kanab, UT 642
Kansas 494–498
    Lawrence 497
    Wichita 495
Kansas City Jazz Museum, MO 510
Kansas City, MO 507–512
Kauai, HI 849
Kenai Fjords National Park, AK 833
Kennebunk, ME 71
Kennebunkport, ME 71
Kennedy (Bouvier), Jacqueline 121
Kennedy assasination 522
Kennedy, John F. 61, 106, 121
Kentucky 257–269
    Bowling Green 264
    Cumberland Gap 268
    Daniel Boone National Forest 267
    Lexington 264–266
    Louisville 260–263

Mammoth Cave 263
Kentucky Derby, KY 262
Kentucky Fried Chicken International Headquarters, KY 262
Kentucky Fried Chicken/Harland Sanders Café and Museum. KY 268
Kentucky Horse Park, KY 266
Ketchikan, AK 838
Ketchum, ID 555
Keweenaw Peninsula, MI 422
Key Largo, FL 381
Key West, FL 382–385
Khrushchev, Nikita 61
Kilauea Point National Wildlife Refuge, HI 850
King, B.B. 282, 284
King, Martin Luther, Jr. 62, 309, 320
Kit Carson National Forest, NM 677
Klamath Falls, OR 729
Klondike Gold Rush National Historic Park, WA 696
Kluane National Park, YT 917
Knife River Indian Villages, ND 470
Knoxville, TN 273–275
Koch, Ed 130
Kootenay National Park, BC 912
korny "k" movement
Boise, ID 553
Okoboji, IA 485
kosher 21
Kouchibouguac National Park, NB 863

L
L.L. Bean, ME 73
La Brea Tar Pits, CA 745

La Jolla, CA 766
Lafayette, LA 347–349
Lahaina, HI 847
LaHave, NS 856
Lake Champlain, VT 84
Lake George, NY 183
Lake Mead, NV 623
Lake Michigan Shore, MI 414–422
Lake of Beer, CA 817
Lake Placid, NY 185
Lake Powell, AZ 657
Lake Superior North Shore, MN 465
Lake Tahoe, CA 817–821
Lake Valley, NM 684
Lancaster County, PA 202
Laramie, WY 588
largest in North America
beer festival, OR 721
cliff dwelling, CO 616
fireworks display, MI 410
free jazz festival, MI 410
largest in the U.S.
authentic totem collection, AK 839
Catholic cathedral, NY 154
collection of wilderness art, WY 581
feeder cattle market, OK 518
foot race, CA 798
free newspaper, NY 150
Hispanic festival, FL 379
historic puppet collection, MI 410
hostel, NY 136
Indian Market, NM 676
livestock show, CO 594
mall, MN 459

mounted mammoth, NE 493
movie theater hall, MI 410
municipal building, PA 198
national park, AK 834
octagonal house, MS 331
private home, NC 294
private university, NY 149
reservation, AZ 654
revolving bar, LA 346
state park, OR 724
swamp, LA 348
university, OH 400
urban park, MO 503
waterpark, TX 524
wilderness area, TN 275
largest in the world
academic library, MA 102
African elephant ever captured, DC 229
African-American history museum, MI 410
annual fair, ON 893
bank building, IL 436
brewery, MO 503
buffalo, ND 470
cathedral, NY 156
chocolate factory, PA 204
collection of American firearms, WY 582
collection of Native American drums, NM 678
collection of Shakespeareana, DC 228
collection of Western American art, OK 515
commercial

building, IL 436
Confederate artifact collection, VA 239
cycling event, PQ 876
display of dinosaur specimens, AB 928
display of rattlesnakes, NM 680
drive-in, GA 308
drop, FL 387
FDA food pyramid, KS 496
freshwater lake 394
freshwater port, PA 198
gypsum sand dunes, NM 686
hand-dug well, KS 495
honky-tonk, TX 525
indoor aquarium, IL 435
kaleidoscope, NY 173
key collection, CO 602
library, DC 228
lightning machine, MA 98
limestone caves, MO 499
maritime museum, SC 300
mass of granite, GA 311
museum complex, DC 229
museum dedicated to a single artist, PA 208
natural bridge, AZ 658
office building, VA 233
open-pit mine, MN 464
outdoor rodeo competition, WY 588
permanent half-dome, OH 404
rose tree, NM 670

science fiction store, NY 150
science museum, NY 160
sculpture, SD 476
single steel arch span, WV 254
single-day rowing regatta, MA 100
supply of helium, TX 544
Taco Bell, CA 803
tubular slide, SC 304
turtle collection, TN 277
used bookstore, NY 150
volcano, HI 849
Western store, KS 497
window, CA 776
largest, misc.
    art museum in the Western Hemisphere, NY 160
    Asian art museum outside Asia, CA 790
    Basque population outside of Europe, ID 554
    Chinese community outside of Asia, CA 794
    collection of wilderness art, WY 581
    commercial building in Canada, PQ 873
    ferris wheel in the Western Hemisphere, TX 523
    ferris wheel in the Western hemisphere, TX 523
Las Vegas, NV 617-623
Lassen Volcanic National Park, CA 817
last showboat in the U.S., MO 506
Lawrence, KS 497
Lead, SD 480
Lebanon, KS 499
Lee, Bruce 697
Lee, Robert E. 60, 239
leis 845
Leopold, Aldo 64
Let's Go Picks xiv
Letterman, David 423
Lewes, DE 211
Lewinsky, Monica 63
Lewis and Clark 469, 506
Lexington, KY 264-266
Lexington, MA 103
Liberty Bell, PA 197
Life As I Have Known It Has Been Finger Lickin' Good 262
Lincoln National Forest,

NM 686
Lincoln Tomb 443
Lincoln, Abraham 60, 231, 442
Lincoln, NE 491-494
Lincoln-Douglas debates 442
Little Big Horn National Monument, MT 561
Little Rock, AR 350-352
Little Women 104
Livingston, MT 562
Lolita 177
Lombard St., CA 794
London, Jack 920
Long Island, NY 170-171
Long, Huey "Kingfish" 346
longest in the world
    continuous marine span bridge, PEI 864
    running shoot-out, WY 581
    skating rink, ON 896
    wooden rollercoaster, OH 405
Longfellow House National Historic Site, MA 103
Longwood Gardens, PA 200
Los Alamos, NM 675
Los Angeles, CA 733-756
Los Padres National Forest, CA 775
Louisiana 332-350
    Acadiana 347-350
    Baton Rouge 346
    Lafayette 347-349
    New Iberia 349
    New Orleans 333-346
Louisiana Territory 59
Louisville Slugger, KY 261
Louisville, KY 260-263
Lunenburg, NS 856

M

Mackinac, MI 418
Madeline Island, WI 454
Madison, WI 448
Madrid and Cerrillos, NM 682
Maggie L. Walker National Historic Site, VA 239
Mahone Bay, NS 854
mail
    aerogrammes 53
    air mail 53
    Federal Express 53
    general delivery 53
    postal system 53
Mailer, Norman 111
Maine 68-76
    Acadia 76

Bar Harbor 74-76
Belfast 73
Camden 73
Freeport 72
Mt. Desert Island 74-76
Portland 69-71
Make Way for Ducklings 95
Malcolm X 157, 488
Mammoth Cave National Park, KY 263
Mammoth Lakes, CA 827
Manhattan Project 675
Manifest Destiny 59
Manistee National Forest, MI 416
Manitou Cliff Dwellings Museum, CO 609
Mann's Chinese Theater, CA 744
Manson, Charles 790
Manti-La-Sal National Forest, UT 636
Marble House, RI 121
Marblemount, WA 713
Mardi Gras 344
Marin County, CA 805-807
Martha's Vineyard, MA 111-114
Maryland 213-222
    Annapolis 218
    Assateague Island 219
    Baltimore 213-218
    Ocean City 220
Massachusetts 90-118
    Amherst 117
    Berkshires 115-118
    Boston 90-101
    Cambridge 101-103
    Cape Cod 106-111
    Concord 104
    Eastham 108
    Hyannis 106
    Lexington 103
    Martha's Vineyard 111-114
    Nantucket 114
    Northampton 117
    Plymouth 105
    Provincetown 109-111
    Salem 104
    Sandwich 107
    Springfield 118
    Truro 109
    Wellfleet 109
MasterCard 11
Maui, HI 847
McCall, ID 555
McVeigh, Timothy 63
Medicine Bow National Forest, WY 589

Medicine Wheel, WY 584
Medora, ND 470
Melville, Herman 117, 160
Memphis, TN 278–285
Mendocino, CA 811
Mennonites 202
Mesa Verde National Park, CO 616
Meteor Crater, AZ 659
Metropolitan Museum of Art, NY 160
Mexican free-tail bats, TX 528
Mexico
  Juárez 547
  Tijuana 767
Miami, FL 374–379
Michelangelo 472
Michigan 406–423
  Ann Arbor 411–413
  Beaver Island 418
  Charlevoix 418
  Detroit 406–411
  Grand Haven 415
  Grand Rapids 413
  Holland 415
  Interlochen 416
  Isle Royale 422
  Keweenaw Peninsula 422
  Lake Michigan Shore 414–422
  Mackinac 418
  Manistee 416
  Petoskey 418
  Sault Ste. Marie 420
  Sleeping Bear Dunes 416
  Traverse City 417
  Upper Peninsula 419–422
Mid-Atlantic 128–256
Middlebury, VT 85
mileage chart 932
Miller Brewery, WI 446
Milwaukee, WI 444–448
Minehaha Falls, MN 459
minimum impact camping 49
Minneapolis, MN 455–461
Minnesota 455–466
  Chippewa National Forest 463
  Duluth 461
  Iron Range 464
  Lake Superior North Shore 465
  Minneapolis 455–461
  St. Paul 455–461
  Voyageurs 466
minority travelers 19
Minutemen 59
miracle drugs 342
Miracle of America

Museum, MT 565
Miró, Joan 436
Missisquoi National Wildlife Refuge, VT 84
Mississippi 326–332
  Jackson 326–328
  Natchez 330
  Oxford 332
  Vicksburg 329
Mississippi River, beginning of, MN 463
Missoula, MT 563–565
Missouri 498–513
  Branson 512
  Cahokia Mounds 505
  Hannibal 506
  Independence 512
  Kansas City 507–512
  St. Charles 506
  St. Louis 499–505
Mr. Potatohead 553
Misty Fiords National Monument, AK 839
Mitchell, Joni 852
Mitchell, Margaret 311
Moab, UT 634
Mobile, AL 324–326
Moby Dick 114
Model Mugging 12
money belt 13
Mono Lake, CA 826
Monongahela National Forest, WV 255
Monroe, Marilyn 747
Montana 560–569
  Billings 560
  Bozeman 562
  Browning 568
  Gardiner 573
  Little Big Horn 561
  Missoula 563–565
  Waterton-Glacier 565–569
  Whitefish 568
Montanabahn, MT 560
Monterey, CA 776
Montezuma Castle National Monument, AZ 660
Montgomery bus boycott, AL 320
Montgomery, AL 319–321
Montmorency Falls, PQ 883
Montréal, PQ 867–878
Monument Valley, AZ 656
Moody, ME 72
Moose Factory, ON 851
Moose Juice Stout 581
Mormon Tabernacle, UT 628
most

crooked street in the world, CA 794
important thing in the world, MI 412
popular museum in the world, D.C. 229
popular tourist attraction on earth, FL 362
motels 39
motorcycle travel 38
Mountain View, AR 354
Mt. Desert Island, ME 74–76
Mt. Hood National Forest, OR 722
Mt. Hood, OR 722
Mt. McKinley, AK 835
Mt. Rainier National Park, WA 711
Mt. Rushmore National Memorial, SD 476
Mt. Rushmore of the South, GA 312
Mt. St. Helens Volcanic National Monument, WA 709
Mt. Tremper, NY 172
Mt. Waialeale, HI 849
Mt. Washington, NH 80
Muir Woods National Monument, CA 807
mule trips, AZ 649, 650
Musée Conti Wax Museum, LA 342
Museum of Early American Farm Machines and Very Old Horse Saddles with a History, PA 211
Museum of Fine Arts (MFA), MA 98
Museum of Modern Art (MoMA), NY 160
Museum of Natural History, DC 229
Museum of Questionable Medical Devices, MN 459
Museum of Television and Radio 161
mushroom capital of the world, PA 200
Myers, Mike 853
Myrtle Beach, SC 302–??
Mystic, CT 127

N

Na Pali Coast, HI 850
NAFTA 852
Naismith, James 118
Nantahala National Forest, NC 293
Nantucket, MA 114
Napa Valley, CA 807–810
Narcissus 173

Naropa Institute, CO 598
Nashville, TN 269–273
Natchez, MS 330
National Air and Space Museum, DC 229
National Arts Centre, ON 901
National Association of RV Parks and Campgrounds 47
National Atomic Museum, NM 681
National Aviation Museum, ON 900
National Balloon Museum, IA 484
National Bison Range, MT 565
National Buffalo Museum, ND 470
National Civil Rights Museum, TN 282
National Corvette Museum, KY 264
National Forest info 47
National Forests
Bighorn, WY 584
Black Hills, SD 475
Boise, ID 553
Bridger-Teton, WY 580
Chattahoochee, GA 305
Chippewa, MN 463
Cíbola, NM 681
Coconino, AZ 652, 660
Daniel Boone, KY 267
Deschutes, OR 731
Dixie, UT 636
George Washington, VA 250
Gila, NM 685
Green Mountain, VT 81
Gunnison, CO 612
Hiawatha, MI 421
Inyo, CA 826
Kaibab, AZ 647, 650
Kit Carson, NM 677
Lincoln, NM 686
Los Padres, CA 775
Manistee, MI 416
Manti-La-Sal, UT 636
Medicine Bow, WY 589
Monongahela, WV 255
Mt. Hood, OR 722
Nantahala, NC 293
Oconee, GA 305
Payette, ID 555
Pike, CO 608
Roosevelt, CO 597
San Juan, CO 615
Santa Fe, NM 672, 676
Sawtooth, ID 556
Shasta-Trinity, CA 817
Siuslaw, OR 726
Stanislaus, CA 826
Superior, MN 465
Tongass, AK 839
Uinta, UT 630
Wallowa, OR 732
White Mountains, NH 77
White River, CO 604
Willamette, OR 727
National Gallery of Art, DC 229
National Gallery, ON 900
National Historic Parks
Halifax Citadel, NS 858
Minuteman, MA 104
National Historic Sites
Boston African-American, MA 96
Cave and Basin, AB 922
Chaco Culture, NM 683
Cumberland Gap, KY 268
Golden Spike, UT 630
Harpers Ferry, WV 252
Herbert Hoover, IA 486
Hopewell Culture, OH 402
Hubbell Trading Post, AZ 655
Independence, PA 197
Jamestown, VA 242
Jean Lafitte, LA 340
Klondike Gold Rush, WA 696
Knife River Indian Villages, ND 470
Longfellow House, MA 103
Maggie L. Walker, VA 239
Pecos, NM 676
Salem Maritime, MA 105
San Juan, WA 704
Sloss Furnaces, AL 323
Trail of Tears, OK 516
Valley Forge, PA 202
Women's Rights, NY 179
National Lakeshores
Pictured Rocks, MI 421
Sleeping Bear Dunes, MI 416
National Landmarks
Dealey Plaza, TX 522
Don Cesar Hotel, FL 387
Fair Park, TX 523
Strand St., TX 535
National Library Archives, ON 900
National Monuments
Bandelier, NM 676
Black Canyon of the Gunnison, CO 610
Cabrillo, CA 765
Canyon de Chelly, AZ 655
Castillo de San Marcos, FL 360
Colorado, CO 606
Craters of the Moon, ID 559
Devil's Postpile, CA 827
Devils Tower, WY 585
Dinosaur, UT 631
El Morro, NM 683
Fort McHenry, MD 217
Fort Pulaski, GA 317
Gila Cliff Dwellings, NM 685
Great Sand Dunes, CO 609
Hovenweep, UT 644
Jewel Cave, SD 477
Little Big Horn, MT 561
Misty Fiords, AK 839
Montezuma Castle, AZ 660
Mt. St. Helens, WA 709
Muir Woods, CA 807
Natural Bridges, UT 644
Navajo National Monument 656
Newberry, OR 731
Organ Pipe Cactus, AZ 666
Petroglyph, NM 681
Pinnacles, CA 777
Scotts Bluff, NE 494
Sunset Crater Volcano, AZ 653
Timpanogos Cave, UT 630
Tuzigoot, AZ 660
Walnut Canyon, AZ 653
White Sands, NM 686
Wupatki, AZ 654
National Museum of American History, DC 229
National Museum of Science and Technology, ON 900
National Museum of the American Indian 163
National Museum

of Wildlife Art, WY 581
National Park info 47
Golden Access Passport 47
Golden Age Passport 47
Golden Eagle Passport 47
in Canada 49
in the U.S. 47
National Parks
Acadia, ME 76
Arches, UT 636
Badlands, SD 473
Banff, AB 921
Big Bend, TX 549
Bryce Canyon, UT 640
Canyonlands, UT 637
Capitol Reef, UT 639
Carlsbad Caverns, NM 687
Colonial, VA 242
Crater Lake, OR 729
Death Valley 771
Denali, AK 835
Everglades, FL 379
Fundy, NB 862
Glacier Bay, AK 841
Glacier, BC 911
Glacier, MT 566-568
Grand Canyon, AZ 646-650
Grand Teton, WY 576-579
Great Smoky Mountains, TN 275
Guadalupe Mountains, TX 545-546
Haleakala, HI 848
Hawaii Volcanoes, HI 848
Hot Springs, AK 353
Isle Royale, MI 422
Jasper, AB 923
Jean Lafitte, LA 348
Joshua Tree, CA 769
Kenai Fjords, AK 833
Kluane, YT 917
Kootenay, BC 912
Kouchibouguac, NB 863
Lassen, CA 817
Mammoth Cave, KY 263
Mesa Verde, CO 616
Mt. Rainier, WA 711
North Cascades, WA 713
Olympic, WA 636
Pacific Rim, BC 911
Petrified Forest, AZ 659
Prince Edward Island, PEI 865, 866
Redwood, CA 813
Rocky Mountain, CO 599-602
Saguaro, AZ 668
Shenandoah, VA 248
Theodore Roosevelt, ND 470
Voyageurs, MN 466
Waterton Lakes, AB 568
Wind Cave, SD 477
Wrangell-St. Elias, AK 834
Yellowstone, WY 570-576
Yoho, BC 912
Yosemite, CA 821-826
Zion, UT 641
National Petroleum Reserve, CA 829
National Railroad Museum, WI 453
National Recreation Areas
Flaming Gorge, UT 633
Golden Gate, CA 792
Hells Canyon, OR 732
Oregon Dunes, OR 726
Rattlesnake Wilderness, MT 564
National Rivers
New River Gorge, WV 254
National Scenic Trails
Appalachian Trail 77, 277
North Country, MI 419
Pacific Crest Trail, WA 712
National Seashores
Assateague Island, MD 219
Canaveral, FL 371
Cape Cod, MA 108
Padre Island, TX 542
Point Reyes, CA 807
National Steinbeck Center, CA 777
National War Memorial, ON 899
National Western Stock Show, CO 594
National Wildlife Refuges
Chincoteague, MD 219
Great Meadows, MA 104
Kilauea Point, HI 850
Missisquoi, VT 84
Rachel Carson, ME 71
Seney, MI 421
Natural Bridges National Monument, UT 644
Navajo Reservation, AZ 654-657
Nebraska 488-494
Lincoln 491-494
Omaha 488-491
Scotts Bluff 494
Negro Leagues Baseball Museum, MO 510
Nevada 617-625
Hoover Dam 623
Lake Mead, NV 623
Las Vegas 617-623
Pyramid Lake 625
Reno 623
New Brunswick 860-863
Fundy 862
Kouchibouguac 863
Saint John 860
New Deal 61
New England 67-127
New Hampshire 76-81
Franconia Notch 78
North Conway 79
Pinkham Notch 80
White Mountains 77-81
New Haven, CT 125
New Iberia, LA 349
New Jersey 188-192
Atlantic City 188-190
Cape May 191
New Mexico 671-688
Albuquerque 678-682
Bandelier 676
Carlsbad Caverns 687
Chaco Culture 683
El Morro 683
Gallup 682
Ghost Towns 684
Gila Cliff Dwellings 685
Madrid and Cerrillos 682
Pecos 676
Santa Fe 672-676
Silver City 685
Taos 676-678
Truth or Consequences 684
White Sands 686
New Mexico Cowboy Poetry Gathering, NM 686
New Orleans Jazz and Heritage Festival, LA 344
New Orleans, LA 333-346
New River Gorge, WV 254
New York 128-188
Adirondacks 183
Albany 173-175
Buffalo 179
Catskills 172-173
Cooperstown 175

Finger Lakes 176
Fire Island 171
Ithaca 176–179
Lake Placid 185
Long Island 170–171
Mt. Tremper 172
New York City 130–170
Niagara Falls 180–181
Phoenicia 173
Pine Hill 173
Seneca Falls 179
Thousand Island Seaway 186
New York City 130–170
Bronx 159
Brooklyn 157
Central Park 154
Greenwich Village 149
Harlem 156
John F. Kennedy Airport (JFK) 130
LaGuardia Airport 130
Staten Island 160
Times Square 152
New York is a stroke of genius 130
New York Stock Exchange, NY 147
Newberry National Volcanic Monument, OR 731
Newport Folk Festival, RI 122
Newport, OR 725
Newport, RI 121–122
Niagara Falls, NY 180–181
Niagara of the South, KY 268
Nixon, Richard 62, 759
Norman Rockwell Museum, PA 197
North American Air Defense Command Headquarters (NORAD), CO 609
North Carolina 285–298
Asheville 292–295
Blowing Rock 292
Boone 290
Carolina Coast 295–298
Chapel Hill 286
Charlotte 289
Durham 285
Outer Banks 295
Raleigh 285
Research Triangle 285–288
North Cascades National Park, WA 713
North Conway, NH 79
North Dakota 467–471

Fargo 469
Theodore Roosevelt National Park 470
Northampton, MA 117
Northeast Harbor, ME 74
northwestmost point in the U.S., WA 708
Nova Scotia 854–859
Atlantic Coast 854–856
Halifax 856–859

O

O'Brien, Conan 153
O'Keeffe, Georgia 674
O'Neal, Shaquille
clogs 415
Oahu, HI 844–847
Oakland, CA 801
obscure references
Little Mermaid 70
Ocean City, MD 220
Oconee National Forest, GA 305
Ogunquit, ME 72
Ohio 395–406
Cincinnati 402–406
Cleveland 395–399
Columbus 399
Ohiopyle, PA 210
Oklahoma 513–518
Oklahoma City 516–518
Tahlequah 516
Tulsa 513–516
Oklahoma City, OK 516–518
Oklahoma! 515
Okoboji, IA 485
Old Faithful, WY 574
Old King Cole on a grain of rice 228
Old Man of the Mountain, NH 78
Old Sturbridge Village, MA 118
Old Tucson Studios, AZ 669
older travelers 17
oldest in North America
church, PQ 882
film festival, CA 798
public timepiece, PQ 875
road, PQ 882
oldest in the U.S.
carousel, MA 113
continuously operated drinking establishment, RI 122
continuously operating theater, LA 344
ferry service, ME 70
fireplace, PA 198
functioning church, NM 674

house, NM 674
public art museum, CT 124
public building, NM 674
residential street, PA 198
seashore resort, NJ 191
state fair, MI 410
synagogue, RI 122
trading post, AZ 655
university, MA 102
zoo, PA 200
Olmsted, Frederick Law 97
Olympia, WA 701
Olympic Center, NY 186
Olympic Games, GA 305
Olympic Hall of Fame, AB 927
Olympic National Park, WA 706
Omaha, NE 488–491
on 641
Onation's Niagara Escarpment, ON 894
Ondaatje, Michael 852
only
accredited Buddhist university in the U.S., CO 596
backwards-flowing river in the world, IL 439
collection of prison tattoo art in U.S., ID 554
existing cast of Michelangelo's Moses, SD 472
granite dome in the U.S., WI 449
inter-tribal university in the U.S., KS 497
royal residence in America, HI 846
Shinto garden outside of Japan, BC 907
State Capitol heated with geothermal water, ID 554
state never to fly a foreign flag, ID 552
turreted castle in North America, ON 891
water-eroded bridge on continent, MA 116
Ontario 884–903
Algonquin Provincial Park 901
Ottawa 895–903
Stratford 895
Toronto 884–894
Orange County, CA 757–759
Orcas Island, WA 704

Oregon 716-??
 Ashland 730
 Astoria 724
 Bend 731
 Cannon Beach 724
 Columbia River Gorge
  723
 Crater Lake 729
 Eugene 726-729
 Hells Canyon 732
 Klamath Falls 729
 Mt. Hood 722
 Newport 725
 Portland 716-722
 Reedsport 726
 Wallowa Mountains 732
Oregon Dunes National
 Recreation Area, OR 726
Oregon Shakespeare
 Festival 730
Oregon Trail, NE 494
Organ Pipe Cactus
 National Monument, AZ
 666
Orlando, FL 362-370
Oswald, Lee Harvey 522
Ottawa, ON 895-903
outdoors. See camping and
 the outdoors
Outer Banks, NC 295
Ovens Natural Park, NS 856
Oxford, MS 332

P

Pacific Crest Trail, WA 712
Pacific Northwest 689-??
Pacific Rim National Park,
 BC 911
Padre Island, TX 542
Page, AZ 657
Pagosa Springs, CO 615
Painted Desert, AZ 659
Paiute peoples, UT 644
Palm Springs, CA 768
Palo Alto, CA 803
Palo Duro Canyon State
 Park, TX 545
Panama City, FL 391
Park City, UT 631
Parker, Charlie 511
Parliament Buildings, ON
 899
Parthenon, TN 272
Pasadena, CA 752
passports 5
Paul Revere House, MA 95
Payette National Forest, ID
 555
Pearl Harbor, HI 61, 844,
 846
Pecos Bill 543
Pecos National Historic

 Park, NM 676
Peggy's Cove, NS 854
Pei, I.M. 96, 98, 178, 398,
 483, 523
Pele 849
Penn, William 193
Pennsylvania 192-211
 Gettysburg 205
 Lancaster County 202
 Ohiopyle 210
 Philadelphia 193-202
 Pittsburgh 206-209
Pennsylvania Dutch 202
Perkins Cove, ME 72
Petoskey, MI 418
Petrified Forest National
 Park, AZ 659
Petroglyph National
 Monument, NM 681
Petty, Tom 391
Pez Memorabilia, CA 804
Philadelphia, PA 193-202
Phish 84
Phoenicia, NY 173
Phoenix, AZ 661-665
pi
 official value, IN 423
Pictured Rocks National
 Lakeshore, MI 421
Pike National Forest, CO
 608
pilgrims 105
Pine Hill, NY 173
Pinkham Notch, NH 80
Pinnacles National
 Monument, CA 777
Pioneer Square, WA 696
Pittsburgh, PA 206-209
planning your trip 1-21
Plessy v. Ferguson 59
Plymouth, MA 105
Poe, Edgar Allen 217, 247
Point Reyes National
 Seashore, CA 807
Polebridge, MT 566
Pony Express 586
Port Townsend, WA 705
Portland, ME 69-71
Portland, OR 716-722
postal system 53
Powers, Austin 894
Pow-Wow, OK 516
Presley, Elvis 281
Prince Edward Island 864-
 866
 Charlottetown 866
Prince Edward National
 Park, PEI 866
Prince Rupert, BC 913
Prince, artist formerly
 known as 460, 461

Pro Football Hall of Fame,
 OH 399
Prototype of the city of the
 future, PQ 873
Providence, RI 119-120
Provincetown, MA 109-111
Puff the Magic Dragon 850
Pullman, IL 439
Pyramid Lake, NV 625

Q

Quadratic Formula 492
Québec 866-883
 Montréal 867-878
 Québec City 878-883
Québec City, PQ 878-883
Queens, NY 158

R

Rachel Carson National
 Wildlife Refuge, ME 71
Radio City Music Hall, NY
 153
rafting
 Big Bend, TX 550
 Bryson City, NC 277
 Cody, WY 582
 Colorado Springs, CO 607
 Durango, CO 615
 Glenwood Springs, CO
  604
 Jackson Hole, WY 581
 Missoula, MT 564
 New River Gorge, WV
  254
 Ohiopyle, PA 210
 Sawtooth, ID 559
 Winter Park, CO 595
ragtime 499
Rainbow Bridge, AZ 657
Raleigh, NC 285
Rapid City, SD 478
Rattlesnake Wilderness
 National Recreation Area,
 MT 564
Reagan, Ronald 62, 747
recreational vehicles (RVs)
 47
Red Scare 61
Redwood National Park,
 CA 813
Reedsport, OR 726
Rehoboth Beach, DE 212
Reno, NV 623
Reorganized Church of
 Jesus Christ of Latter Day
 Saints 512
Research Triangle, NC 285-
 288
Revere, Paul 95, 104
Reversing Falls, NB 861
Revolutionary War 103

Rhode Island 118–123
  Block Island 122
  Newport 121–122
  Providence 119–120
Richmond, VA 236–240
rock 'n' roll 64
Rock and Roll Hall of Fame, OH 398
rock that blows, NC 292
Rockefeller, John D. 60
Rockland, ME 73
Rockwell, Norman 117
Rocky and Bullwinkle 466
Rocky Mountain National Park 599–602
rocky mountain oysters, MT 563
Rocky Mountains 551–616
Rodeo Capital of the World, WY 582
rodeos
  Mesquite, TX 524
Rogers, Will 614
Roosevelt National Forest, CO 597
Roosevelt, Franklin D. 61, 305
Roosevelt, Theodore 61
Root Beer Lady of Knife Lake, MN 464
Rose, Pete 404
Ross Lake, WA 714
Roswell, NM 687
roughing it safely 49
Rowan Oak, MS 332
Royal Ontario Museum, ON 891
rubber duckie race, AK 838
Ruth, Babe 100, 176, 217

S

Sacajawea 689
Sacramento, CA 815
safety and security 12
Saguaro National Park, AZ 668
Saint John, NB 860
Salem Witch Museum, MA 104
Salem, MA 104
sales tax 12
Salinas, CA 777
Salmon River, ID 557
Salt Lake City, UT 626–630
San Antonio Missions National Historical Park, TX 538
San Antonio, TX 535–541
San Diego Zoo, CA 764
San Diego, CA 760–767
San Francisco, CA 780–798
San Jose, CA 801

San Juan Islands, WA 703
San Juan National Forest, CO 615
San Juan National Historic Park, WA 704
San Luis Obispo, CA 774
San Mateo County, CA 804
Sandusky, OH 399
Sandwich, MA 107
Santa Barbara, CA 772–774
Santa Cruz, CA 777–779
Santa Fe National Forest, NM 672, 676
Santa Fe, NM 672–676
Santa Monica, CA 748
Saratoga, WY 589
Sargent, John Singer 70
Saturday Night Live 153
Sault Ste. Marie, MI 420
Savannah, GA 314–317
Sawtooth National Forest, ID 556, 557–559
Sawyer, Tom 499
Schaffer, Paul 891
Scotts Bluff National Monument, NE 494
seafaring lingo 127
Sears Tower, IL 436
Seattle, WA 690–700
Second City, IL 440
Sedona, AZ 659
Sedro Woolley, WA 713
Sendak, Maurice 199
Seneca Falls, NY 179
Seney National Wildlife Refuge, MI 421
Sesame Street 175
Seward, AK 833
Shaker Village, KY 267
Shakespeare in the Park, NY 155
shaking someone's left hand 448
Shatner, William 853
Shenandoah National Park, VA 248
Sheridan, WY 583
Sherman, William T. 288
shoofly pie 203
Short, Martin 894
shot heard 'round the world, MA 104
Siegel, Bugsy 744
Sierra Club 51
Sierra Design 45
Silver City, NM 685
Silverthorne, CO 596
Silverton, CO 615
Simpson, O.J. 747
Simpsons, The 118
Sioux Falls, SD 472

Sitting Bull 561
Siuslaw National Forest, OR 726
skateboard grandma, CA 748
Ski Hall of Fame, CO 602
skiing
  Adirondacks, NY 184
  Aspen, CO 603
  Badlands, SD 472
  Banff, AB 923
  Boone, NC 292
  Bozeman, MT 563
  Breckenridge, CO 596
  Catskills, NY 173
  Cooper Mountain, CO 596
  Crested Butte, CO 611
  Fairbanks, AK 837
  Flagstaff, AZ 653
  Franconia Notch, NH 79
  Glenwood Springs, CO 604
  Grand Teton, WY 579
  Jackson Hole, WY 581
  Jasper, AB 925
  Juneau, AK 841
  Keystone, CO 596
  Lake Placid, NY 185
  Lake Tahoe, CA 820
  Lead, SD 480
  McCall, ID 555
  Missoula, MT 564
  Monongahela, WV 256
  Mt. Hood, OR 722
  North Conway, NH 79
  Park City, UT 631
  Québec City, PQ 883
  Salt Lake City, UT 630
  Seattle, WA 698
  Stowe, VT 86
  Taos, NM 678
  Vail, CO 602
  White Mountains, NH 79
  Whitefish, MT 568
  Winter Park, CO 595
  Wolf Creek, CO 615
  Yosemite, CA 825
skinniest
  building in the world, BC 907
Sky Dome, ON 893
slavery 60
Sleeping Bear Dunes, MI 416
Sloss Furnaces National Historic Landmark, AL 323
Smithsonian, D.C. 229
Smokejumpers
  McCall, ID 555
  Missoula, MT 565

Smokey Range, ID 557
Snowy Mountain Range, WY 589
Sonny and Cher 747
Sonoma Valley, CA 810
Sonora, CA 815
Soudan, MN 464
Sound of Music 87
South 257-356
South Bay, CA 757
South Carolina 298-??
  Charleston 298-301
  Columbia 301-302
  Grand Strand 302-??
  Myrtle Beach 302-??
South Dakota 472-481
  Badlands 473
  Black Hills 475-481
  Crazy Horse Memorial 476
  Custer State Park 477
  Deadwood 480
  Hot Springs 478
  Jewel Cave 477
  Lead 480
  Mt. Rushmore 476
  Rapid City 478
  Sioux Falls 472
  Spearfish 480
  Wind Cave 477
  Wounded Knee 474
southernmost point in the U.S., FL 384
Southwest 617-688
Southwest Harbor, ME 74
Space Center Houston, TX 532
Spam Jam, TX 529
Spearfish, SD 480
specific concerns 16-21
  bisexual, gay, and lesbian travelers 17
  disabled travelers 18
  kosher 21
  minority travelers 19
  older travelers 17
  travelers with children 19
  vegetarians 19
  women travelers 16
Spirit Lake, IA 485
Spokane, WA 715
Springfield, IL 442
Springfield, MA 118
Springsteen, Bruce 64
St. Augustine, FL 357-360
St. Charles, MO 506
St. Ignatius, MT 565
St. Louis, MO 499-505
St. Paul, MN 455-461
St. Petersburg, FL 387-390
stand-by flights 25
  Airhitch 27

  Air-Tech 27
Stanislaus National Forest, CA 826
Stanley, ID 557
Stanton, Elizabeth Cady 179
Starr, Kenneth 63
Staten Island, NY 160
Statue of Liberty, NY 148
STDs 14
steak, 72 oz. 544
Steinbeck, John 776
Stipe, Michael 313
Stonehenge replicas
  Carhenge, NE 494
  Woodhenge, MO 506
Stonewall Inn, NY 149
Stonington, CT 127
Stowe, Harriet Beecher 123
Stowe, VT 86-87
Stratford Shakespeare Festival, ON 895
Stratford, ON 895
streetcar named "Desire," LA 339
Streisand, Barbra 746
student fares 31
student identitification cards 8
student visas 16
studying in the U.S. and Canada 15
Summit County, CO 596
Sun Valley, ID 555
Sundance Film Festival, UT 631
Sundance Kid 633
Sunset Crater Volcano National Monument, AZ 653
Superior National Forest, MN 465
sweet, sweet 604

T

Tabasco Factory, LA 349
tackiest monument in the world, WA 695
Tahlequah, OK 516
tallest in the world
  church, IL 436
  cross, MI 418
  free-standing structure, ON 892
  geyser, MT 574
  inclined tower, PQ 872
  mountain, HI 849
  tree, CA 814
tallest monument in the U.S., MO 502
tally me banana 387
Tampa, FL 385-387
Tanglewood, MA 117

Taos, NM 676-678
taxes 12
  goods and services tax (GST) 12
  sales tax 12
Taylor, Elizabeth 747
Tea, SD 472
teacher identification cards 8
telephones 53
  calling cards 55
  collect calls 55
  third-party billing 55
Telluride, CO 612
Tennessee 269-285
  Chattanooga 277
  Cherokee Reservation 276
  Great Smoky Mountains 275
  Knoxville 273-275
  Memphis 278-285
  Nashville 269-273
Tennis Hall of Fame, RI 122
Tensleep, WY 584
Testicle Festival, MT 563
Texas 519-550
  Amarillo 543
  Austin 525-529
  Big Bend 549
  Corpus Christi 541
  Dallas 520-524
  El Paso 546
  Fort Worth 524-525
  Fredericksburg 541
  Galveston Island 534-535
  Guadalupe Mountains 545-546
  Houston 529-534
  Padre Island 542
  Palo Duro Canyon 545
  San Antonio 535-541
  Western Texas 543-550
Thelma and Louise 645
Theodore Roosevelt National Park, ND 470
Thermopolis, WY 585
Thoreau, Henry David 64, 104
Thousand Island Seaway, NY 186
Three Capes Loop, OR 725
Times Square, NY 152
Timpanogos Cave National Monument, UT 630
tipping 12
Tombstone, AZ 670
Tongass National Forest, AK 839
Toronto, ON 884-894
Tour de l'île, PQ 876
Trail of Tears National

Historic Trail 516
trails
  Appalachian Trail 77, 277
  Bruce Trail, ON 895
  Oregon Trail, WY 586
trains 31
travel agencies 21
traveler's checks 10
travelers with children 19
Traverse City, MI 417
Tricky Dick 231
Trinity Site, NM 686
Trudeau, Pierre 852
Truman, Harry 512
Trump, Donald 190
Truro, MA 109
Truth or Consequences,
  NM 684
Tubman, Harriet 60
Tucson, AZ 666–670
Tulsa, OK 513–516
Turner, Frederick Jackson
  428
Turner, Ted 305, 312
Tuskegee, AL 321
Tuzigoot National
  Monument, AZ 660
Twain, Mark 124, 506, 815
Twisp, WA 714

U

U.S. Constitution 231
U.S. Mint, PA 197
U.S. Olympic Complex,
  CO 609
U.S.S. Alabama 325
U.S.S. Arizona National
  Memorial, AK 846
U.S.S. Drum 326
U.S.S. Lexington 542
Uinta National Forest, UT
  630
Unabomber 63
Underground Railroad 60
United Nations Building,
  NY 153
United States 58–850
United States Air Force
  Academy, CO 609
United States Olympic
  Team 607
Universal Studios, CA 752
Universal Studios, FL 370
Universities
  Amherst 118
  Arizona 668
  Brown 119
  California-Berkeley 799
  College of William &
    Mary 242
  Columbia 156
  Cornell 178

Duke 288
Florida 391
Harvard 102
Haskell Indian Nations,
  KS 497
Indiana 426
Iowa 485
Kansas 497
Massachusetts Institute of
  Technology 102
Massachusetts-Amherst
  118
McGill, PQ 872
Michigan 411
Middlebury 85
New York 149
North Carolina at Chapel
  Hill 285
Ohio State 400
Oregon 728
Pennsylvania 200
Stanford, CA 803
Texas at Austin 528
Toronto 891
Tuskegee 321
UCLA 746
Vermont 83
Virginia 247
Washington 697
Williams 116
Wisconsin 450
Yale 125
Upper Peninsula, MI 419–
  422
Utah 625–645
  Arches 636
  Bryce Canyon 640
  Canyonlands 637
  Capitol Reef 639
  Cedar City 643
  Dinosaur and Vernal 631
  Flaming Gorge 633
  Hovenweep 644
  Moab 634
  Natural Bridges 644
  Park City 631
  Salt Lake City 626–630
  Timpanogos Cave 630
  Zion 641

V

Vail, CO 602
Valley Forge, PA 202
Valley Girl 752
Valley of the Gods, UT 645
Vancouver Island, BC 909–
  911
Vancouver, BC 903–909
Vanderbilt, George 60
Vashon Island, WA 700
vegetarians 19
Venice, CA 748

Vermont 81–89
  Brattleboro 88
  Burlington 82–84
  Champlain Valley 84
  Middlebury 85
  Stowe 86–87
  White River Junction 88
Vernal, UT 631, 632
VIA Rail (800-561-3949) 32
Viagra 63
Vicksburg, MS 329
Victoria, BC 909
Virginia 236–251
  Charlottesville 245–248
  Jamestown 242
  Richmond 236–240
  Shenandoah 248
  Virginia Beach 243
  Williamsburg 240–243
  Yorktown 242
Virginia Beach, VA 243
Visa 11
visas
  student 16
  travel/business 6
  work in Canada 15
  work in U.S. 15
Voodoo Museum, LA 340
Voyageurs National Park,
  MN 466

W

Wadsworth Athenaeum,
  CT 124
Wadsworth-Longfellow,
  Henry 70
Waffle House, GA 310
Waimea, HI 850
Walden Pond, MA 104
Walker, MN 464
Wall Drug, SD 474
Wall Street, NY 147
Wall, SD 474
Wallowa Mountains, OR
  732
Walnut Canyon National
  Monument, AZ 653
Warren, Chief Justice Earl
  59
Washington 690–716
  Bellingham 702
  Cascade Range 709–715
  Marblemount 713
  Mt. Rainier National Park
    711
  Mt. St. Helens 709
  Olympia 701
  Olympic National Park
    706
  Olympic Peninsula 705–
    709
  Orcas Island 704

Port Townsend 705
Ross Lake 714
San Juan Islands 703
Seattle 690–700
Sedro Woolley 713
Spokane 715
Twisp 714
Vashon Island 700
Winthrop 714
Washington, Booker T. 321
Washington, D.C. 222–236
Watergate, D.C. 231
Waterton Lakes National
Park, AB 568
Waterton-Glacier Peace
Park, MT and AB 565–569
Wayne, John 484
Webster, Noah 123
Welles, Orson 741
Wellfleet, MA 109
werewolves, IN 425
West Virginia 251–256
Harpers Ferry 252
Monongahela 255
New River Gorge 254
West Yellowstone, MT 570,
573
Western Museum of
Mining and Industry, CO
609
Western Union 11
Weston, Edward 674
wettest spot on earth, HI
849
Wharton, Edith 117
White Cloud Mountains, ID
557
White Mountains National
Forest, NH 77
White Mountains, NH 77–
81
White River Junction, VT
88
White River National
Forest, CO 604
White Sands National
Monument, NM 686
Whitefish, MT 568
Whitehorse, YT 915
whitewater rafting
Charlemont, MA 116
Eugene, OR 728
Grand Canyon, AZ 649
Jasper, AB 925
Montréal, PQ 876
Seattle, WA 698
Tahoe Lake, CA 820
Taos, NM 678
whoopie pie 203
Wichita, KS 495

Willamette National Forest,
OR 727
Williams, Hank, Jr. 525
Williams, Roger 120
Williams, Tennessee 111
Williamsburg, VA 240–243
Wilmette, IL 439
Wind Cave National Park,
SD 477
windiest place in the U.S.,
NH 80
Window Rock, AZ 655
Wine Country, CA 807–811
wine tasting (how to) 809
Winter Olympic Museum,
NY 186
Winter Park, CO 595
Winthrop, WA 714
wiring money 11
Wisconsin 444–454
Apostle Islands 453
Door County 450–453
Madison 448
Milwaukee 444–448
WKRP in Cincinnati 404
Wolf Haven International,
WA 701
women travelers 16
Women's Hall of Fame, NY
179
Women's Rights National
Historic Park 179
women's suffrage 61
Woodstock, NY 172
working
in Canada 15
in the U.S. 15
World Center for Birds of
Prey, ID 554
World Championship
Barbecue Cooking
Contest, TN 279
World Wide Web 3
Wounded Knee, SD 474
Wrangell-St. Elias National
Park, AK 834
Wright Brothers 409
Wright, Frank Lloyd 210,
438, 443
Wrigley Field, IL 441
Wupatki National
Monument, AZ 654
Wyoming 570–590
Bighorn Mountains 584
Buffalo 583
Casper 586
Cheyenne 587
Cody 582
Devils Tower 585
Grand Teton 576–579

Jackson 579–582
Laramie 588
Saratoga 589
Sheridan 583
Thermopolis 585
Yellowstone 570–576

X
X
Not many words begin
with "x"
X-Files, The 687

Y
Yarmouth, NS 856
Yellowstone National Park,
WY 570–576
Yoho National Park, BC 912
Yorktown, VA 242
Yosemite National Park,
CA 821–826
Young Men's Christian
Association (YMCA) 41
Young Women's Christian
Association (YWCA) 41
Young, Neil 852
Yukon Territory 915–921
Dawson City 918
Kluane National Park 917
Whitehorse 915

Z
Zion National Park, UT 641
zoos
Albuquerque, NM 681
Anchorage, AK 832
Atlanta, GA 310
Baltimore, MD 217
Bronx, NY 159
Calgary, AB 928
Chicago, IL 438
Cincinnati, OH 404
Columbia, SC 302
Denver, CO 594
Disney, FL 368
Houston, TX 532
Indianapolis, IN 425
Kansas City, MO 511
Little Rock, AR 352
Los Angeles, CA 751
New Orleans, LA 341
Omaha, NE 490
Philadelphia, PA 200
Portland, OR 721
San Antonio, TX 539
San Diego, CA 764
Seattle, WA 698
St. Louis, MO 503
Tampa, FL 387
Washington, D.C. 233
Zozobra, NM 676

INDEX

Researcher-Writers

Frank Beidler   *Wisconsin, Upper Michigan, Minnesota*
Frank came out of retirement for another dance with Ma Let's Go, only to have his brand-new, well-loved pick-up truck chased by a twister right out of Hollywood. Taking on questionable medical devices and the Mall of America with his characteristic wit, Frank showed why he's a *Let's Go: USA* mainstay.

Rebe Glass   *The Carolinas, Georgia, Alabama, Florida*
Though post offices and restaurant owners often proved uncooperative, Rebe kept up a candor and enthusiasm on the job that most editors can only dream about. After learning the hard way about the hills of Columbia, SC, she went on to write copy as dazzling as the sands of the Florida Keys. Whether assessing fashion in Alabama eateries or raving over Disney's spanking-new Animal Kingdom, Rebe handed us a meticulous account of the South and Florida that spared no detail.

Ruth Halikman   *Utah, Colorado, Arizona, New Mexico, Western Texas*
Ruth, another veteran of the *Let's Go* trenches, ventured to the Southwest in search of ghost towns, hold-over hippies, and good regional literature. Despite a car that really wanted to quit, this Maryland native whipped her section of the book into shape; her perfect prose beautifully captured a landscape she was seeing for the first time. Kept busy by the longest USA 1999 itinerary and a steady parade of visitors, Ruth handled it all with admirable patience. We wish her much success as she sallies forth into New York City and beyond.

Joe McCannon   *Montana, the Dakotas, Wyoming, Iowa, Nebraska*
Joe can only be described as a ballsy researcher-writer, and a man who was never afraid to have a good conversation (with himself). Trading in a semester's worth of English airs for a pen and a gluestick, this self-described "winter activities fiend" found more Great Plains skiing hotspots than we ever dreamed existed. A real cowboy, Joe galloped across the plains of America's mid-section and through the Old West, then conquered the northern Rockies. En route, he churned out expertly written copy akin to a verbal field of dreams, keeping us laughing from start to finish.

Matt Ozug   *Idaho, Wyoming, Colorado, Utah*
The most open-faced researcher ever, Matt did his writing, and everything else, in his own unique style. After surviving two exploding tires in the first days of his itinerary, this rugged mountaineer traipsed across the Rockies with impressive passion, pressing on through June snowstorms to send back mountains of original copy. Captivated by quieter havens such as Stanley, ID, Matt refused to be sucked in by the hype surrounding more touristed spots, and uncovered hidden gems every step of the way.

Ann Schiff   *Pennsylvania, the Virginias, Maryland, New Jersey, Delaware*
Armed with an acrobatic vocabulary and the unique perspective of a caving and astronomy enthusiast, Ann tackled her home turf, sending back a steady stream of suggestions and formidably thorough write-ups. Neither rain nor sleet nor snow nor computer failure could keep her from her appointed rounds.

Jon Stein   *Texas, Louisiana, Oklahoma, Arkansas*
Beginning with his home state of Texas, Jon braved scorching temperatures to bring us the lowdown on his region. Whether drinking in some back-alley New Orleans dive, masquerading as Mr. Bubble, or giving the folks at the Oklahoma City Stockyards something to think about, never has a man so loved his job. His editors thank him for the flavor of the South, which he sent us in forms both edible and readable, and always good to the last spicy drop.

Emily VonKohorn *Ohio, Kentucky, Indiana, Missouri, Kansas, Tennessee, North Carolina*
Most Connecticut natives don't like country music; now this one does. Emily fell in love with many things Southern: barbecue, B&B's, and the Biltmore Estate not least among them. In search of a mythical three-legged calf, Emily stumbled upon Kansas

establishments still more bizarre, but these encounters couldn't dampen her unstoppable energy. Facing extra cities, piles of maps, and long-lost relatives with nary a complaint, Emily brightened our days with sparkling correspondence before racing off to explore the West. Rest assured, this is one Let's Go RW who *will* be going back.

Christian Lorentzen   *New York, Toronto*
Christian went over Niagara in a barrel and landed in Toronto, which he followed with a visit to the land of the Bard in Stratford, ON.

Leeore Schnairson   *Pittsburgh, Ohiopyle, Manhattan*
Chased by robotic dinosaurs from Pittsburgh to Cambridge, Leeore still managed to whip up some fabulous copy and finish *Let's Go: California,* an achievement in itself.

Eliot Schrefer   *Eastern Canada, Northern New England*
Determined to overcome the rigors of RW-ing, Eliot tamed the wilds of his personal Oz with astonishing speed. His spotless copy left us speechless with amazement, even inspiring our own trip to New Hampshire, for which we thank him.

Alex Speier   *New York, Cleveland, Allegheny*
"Publicity Hound" may be what the business card says, but it's quite clear that Alex is a sweet, sweet researcher-writer at heart.

Samantha VanGerbig   *Massachusetts, Connecticut*
Struck by illness two weeks into her journey across the mid-Atlantic, Sam only had enough time to take a whirlwind tour of southern New England and send us a hilarious illustrated account of her travels. Her contribution was sorely missed.

Vivek Waglé   *Chicago, Michigan*
Fresh from a *Let's Go* stint in India, Vivek came back to the New World and tackled an even greater challenge: Detroit. Trekking up and down the Lower Peninsula, he put a fresh face on the state that others might not have noticed. Bravó!

Drake Park Bennett	*Atlantic City, Brooklyn, the Bronx, Manhattan*
Ian Z. Pervil	*Long Island, Queens, Manhattan*
Clint Thacker	*Manhattan*
Eli Ceryak	*Manhattan*
Jace Clayton	*Manhattan*
John L. Lester	*Manhattan*
Katherine Model	*Staten Island*
John Orsini	*Washington, D.C.*
Julianna Tymoczko	*Washington, D.C.*
Joseph Cleemann	*California Desert, Las Vegas, San Diego*
James Eagan	*Los Angeles, South Bay, Orange County, Santa Barbara*
Elizabeth Feakins	*Central Coast, North Coast, Wine Country*
Robert MacDougall	*Bay Area, San Francisco*
Nancy Meakem	*Northern Interior, Reno, Sierra Nevada*
Kristy Garcia	*Washington, Eastern Oregon*
Anne Johnson	*Northern British Columbia, Coastal Alaska*
Jennifer Laine	*Alaska*
Thomas Lue	*Oregon, Central Washington*
Rebecca Reider	*Southern British Columbia, Alberta*
Paul Todgham	*British Columbia, the Yukon, Interior Alaska*
Paul Torres	*Tijuana*
Jim Stewart	*El Paso, Ciudad Juárez*
Rachel Farbiarz	*Editor, New York City*
Josh Gewolb	*Editor, Washington, D.C.*
Leeore Schnairson	*Editor, California*
Benjamin Lima	*Associate Editor, California*
Doug Rand	*Editor, Alaska & the Pacific Northwest*
Ben Florman	*Associate Editor, Alaska & the Pacific Northwest*

Acknowledgments

Congratulations, first and foremost, to our devoted RWs. Pioneers of cyber-RW-ing, they went way beyond the call of duty in defiance of sickness and crazy weather to bring this mammoth project to completion. Thanks to Monica for her support, watchful eye, and easygoing attitude. To the entire D-room for antics and fabulous crunch; to Derek for his map expertise; to Emily C. and Anne J., *pour le travail de vérifier les détails au téléphone;* and to the LG '99 RW's, who whipped up Boston copy so stellar it burned. *Merci beaucoup;* thank you and goodnight.**—Team USA**

Heaps o' thanks to TJ and Kaya for hilarity, brilliant editing, and impeccable judgment; you two are amazing. To ME, BW, MF, AA, & TE for perspective. Cheers to 20D and the K-house kids for keeping me going, and to Frank and Ruth for their counsel. Hugs for those of the 1999 office staff who stepped in during the eleventh hour; we couldn't have done it without you! I dedicate my work to Mom, Dad, Eunice, Lewis, and my family in Cali, who remind me every day what it means to be loved. **—IJH**

Irene and Kaya, I can't imagine a day not working with the both of you. John L. and my drinking buddies. Ben F. and the long walk home. Leeore, Farbs, Lucky Sharms, Leems, Monica, Josh, Doug, Angus, Comrade Gallagher, the *Politburo,* Bob Dylan, and Wyclef Jean. The Domestic Room lives, whether they like it or not—I loved it. Alex S., Derek G., and the Cougrz. 264 Willow #1 and the LDS. Mateo, Pierce, and Eli, I'm without words. Mom, Dad, Steve, Joan, and Ted. How about a beer?**—TJK**

To the hardest working duo in town-y'all made it a hell of a summer in the city: Crazy respect: to the never-weary Irene—your undying work ethic and passion for the book; T.J., your humor and obscure trivia kept it real day after day. Extra special thanks to mom and pops—a guy couldn't ask for 2 more caring folks—Becky, Carol, Julianna, the Bronx Bomber, the 3-ring circus they call the DR, and of course, the CRLS (the *true* Cambridge school) crew (Hilary, Matt, Eric, Steve and Meg).**—KS**

Editor	Irene J. Hahn
Associate Editor	T.J. Kelleher
Associate Editor	Kaya Stone
Managing Editor	Monica Eileen Eav
Publishing Director	Caroline R. Sherman
Publishing Director	Anna C. Portnoy
Production Manager	Dan Visel
Associate Production Manager	Maryanthe Elizabeth Malliaris
Cartography Manager	Derek McKee
Design Manager	Bentsion Harder
Editorial Manager	M. Allison Arwady
Editorial Manager	Lisa M. Nosal
Financial Manager	Monica Eileen Eav
Personnel Manager	Nicolas R. Rapold
Publicity Manager	Alexander Z. Speier
New Media Manager	Måns O. Larsson
Map Editors	Matthew R. Daniels, Dan Luskin
Production Associate	Heath Ritchie
Office Coordinator	Tom Moore, Jodie Kirschner, Eliza Harrington
Director of Advertising Sales	Gene Plotkin
Associate Sales Executives	Colleen Gaard, Mateo Jaramillo, Alexandra Price
President	Catherine J. Turco
General Manager	Richard Olken
Assistant General Manager	Anne E. Chisholm

Thanks to Our Readers...

Mano Aaron, CA; Jean-Marc Abela, CAN; George Adams, NH; Bob & Susan Adams, GA; Deborah Adeyanju, NY; Rita Alexander, MI; Shani Amory-Claxton, NY; Kate Anderson, AUS; Lindsey Anderson, ENG; Viki Anderson, NY; Ray Andrews, JPN; Robin J. Andrus, NJ; L. Asurmendi, CA; Anthony Atkinson, ENG; Deborah Bacek, GA; Jeffrey Bagdade, MI; Mark Baker, UK; Mary Baker, TN; Jeff Barkoff, PA; Regina Barsanti, NY; Ethan Beeler, MA; Damao Bell, CA; Rya Ben-Shir, IL; Susan Bennerstrom, WA; Marla Benton, CAN; Matthew Berenson, OR; Walter Bergstrom, OR; Caryl Bird, ENG; Charlotte Blanc, NY; Jeremy Boley, EL SAL; Oliver Bradley, GER; A.Braurstein, CO; Philip R. Brazil, WA; Henrik Brockdorff, DMK; Tony Bronco, NJ; Eileen Brouillard, SC; Mary Brown, ENG; Tom Brown, CA; Elizabeth Buckius, CO; Sue Buckley, UK; Christine Burer, SWITZ; Norman Butler, MO; Brett Carroll, WA; Susan Caswell, ISR; Carlos Cersosimo, ITA; Barbara Crary Chase, WA; Stella Cherry Carbost, SCOT; Oi Ling Cheung, HK; Simon Chinn, ENG; Charles Cho, AUS; Carolyn R. Christie, AUS; Emma Church, ENG; Kelley Coblentz, IN; Cathy Cohan, PA; Phyllis Cole, TX; Karina Collins, SWITZ; Michael Cox, CA; Mike Craig, MD; Rene Crusto, LA; Claudine D'Anjou, CAN; Lizz Daniels, CAN; Simon Davies, SCOT; Samantha Davis, AUS; Leah Davis, TX; Stephanie Dickman, MN; Philipp Dittrich,GER; Tim Donovan, IL; Reed Drew, OR; Wendy Duncan, SCOT; Melissa Dunlap, VA; P.A. Emery, UK; GCL Emery, SAF; Louise Evans, AUS; Christine Farr, AUS; David Fattel, NJ; Vivian Feen, MD; David Ferraro, SPN; Sue Ferrick, CO; Philip Fielden, UK; Nancy Fintel, IL; Jody Finver, FL; D. Ross Fisher, CAN; Abigail Flack, IL; Elizabeth Foster, NY; Bonnie Fritz, CAN; J. Fuson, OR; Michael K. Gasuad, NV; Raad German, TX; Mark Gilbert, NY; Betsy Gilliland, CA; Ana Goshko, NY; Patrick Goyenneche, CAN; David Greene, NY; Jennifer Griffin, ENG; Janet & Jeremy Griffith, ENG; Nanci Guartofierro, NY; Denise Guillemette, MA; Ilona Haayer, HON; Joseph Habboushe, PA; John Haddon, CA; Ladislav Hanka, MI; Michael Hanke, CA; Avital Harari, TX; Channing Hardy, KY; Patrick Harris, CA; Denise Hasher, PA; Jackie Hattori, UK; Guthrie Hebenstreit, ROM; Therase Hill, AUS; Denise Hines, NJ; Cheryl Horne, ENG; Julie Howell, IL; Naomi Hsu, NJ; Mark Hudgkinson, ENG; Brenda Humphrey, NC; Kelly Hunt, NY; Daman Irby, AUT; Bill Irwin, NY; Andrea B. Jackson, PA; John Jacobsen, FL; Pat Johanson, MD; Russell Jones, FL; J. Jones, AUS; Sharon Jones, MI; Craig Jones, CA; Wayne Jones, ENG; Jamie Kagan, NJ; Mirko Kaiser, GER; Scott Kauffman, NY; John Keanie, NIRE; Barbara Keary, FL; Jamie Kehoe, AUS; Alistair Kernick, SAF; Daihi Kielle, SWITZ; John Knutsen, CA; Rebecca Koepke, NY; Jeannine Kolb, ME; Elze Kollen, NETH; Lorne Korman, CAN; Robin Kortright, CAN; Isel Krinsky, CAN; George Landers, ENG; Jodie Lanthois, AUS; Roger Latzgo, PA; A. Lavery, AZ; Joan Lea, ENG; Lorraine Lee, NY; Phoebe Leed, MA; Tammy Leeper, CA; Paul Lejeune, ENG; Yee-Leng Leong, CA; Sam Levene, CA; Robin Levin, PA; Christianna Lewis, PA; Ernesto Licata, ITA; Wolfgang Lischtansky, AUT; Michelle Little, CAN; Dee Littrell, CA; Maria Lobosco, UK; Netii Ross, ITA; Didier Look, CAN; Alice Lorenzotti, MA; David Love, PA; Briege Mac Donagh, IRE; Brooke Madigan, NY; Helen Maltby, FL; Shyama Marchesi, ITA; Domenico Maria, ITA; Natasha Markovic, AUS; Edward Marshall, ECU; Rachel Marshall, TX; Kate Maynard, UK; Agnes McCann, IRE; Susan McGowan, NY; Brandi McGunigal, CAN; Neville McLean, NZ; Marty McLendon, MS; Matthew Melko, OH; Barry Mendelson, CA; Eric Middendorf, OH; Nancy Mike, AZ; Coren Milbury, NH; Margaret Mill, NY; David H. Miller, TX; Ralph Miller, NV; Susan Miller, CO; Larry Moeller, MI; Richard Moore, ENG; Anne & Andrea Mosher, MA; J. L. Mourne, TX; Athanassios Moustakas, GER; Laurel Naversen, ENG; Suzanne Neil, IA; Deborah Nickles, PA; Pieter & Agnes Noels, BEL; Werner Norr, GER; Ruth J. Nye, ENG; Heidi O'Brien, WA; Sherry O'Cain, SC; Aibhan O'Connor, IRE; Kevin O'Connor, CA; Margaret O'Rielly, IRE; Daniel O'Rourke, CA; Krissy Oechslin, OH; Johan Oelofse, SAF; Quinn Okamoto, CA; Juan Ramon Olaizola, SPN; Laura Onorato, NM; Bill Orkin, IL; K. Owusu-Agyenang, UK; Anne Paananen, SWD; Jenine Padget, AUS; Frank Pado, TX; G. Pajkich, Washington, DC; J. Parker, CA; Marian Parnat, AUS; Sandra Swift Parrino, NY; Iris Patten, NY; M. Pavini, CT; David Pawielski, MN; Jenny Pawson, ENG; Colin Peak, AUS; Marius Penderis, ENG; Jo-an Peters, AZ; Barbara Phillips, NY; Romain Picard, Washington, DC; Pati Pike, ENG; Mark Pollock, SWITZ; Minnie Adele Potter, FL; Martin Potter, ENG; Claudia Praetel, ENG; Bill Press, Washington, DC; David Prince, NC; Andrea Pronko, OH; C. Robert Pryor, OH; Phu Quy, VTNM; Adrian Rainbow, ENG; John Raven, AUS; Lynn Reddringer, VA; John Rennie, NZ; Ruth B.Robinson, FL; John & Adelaida Romagnoli, CA; Eva Romano, FRA; Mark A. Roscoe, NETH; Yolanda & Jason Ross, CAN; Sharee Rowe, ENG; W. Suzanne Rowell, NY; Vic Roych, AZ; John Russell, ENG; Jennifer Ruth, OH; William Sabino, NJ; Hideki Saito, JPN; Frank Schaer, HUN; Jeff Schultz, WI; Floretta Seeland-Connally, IL; Colette Shoulders, FRA; Shireen Sills, ITA; Virginia Simon, AUS; Beth Simon, NY; Gary Simpson, AUS; Barbara & Allen Sisarsky, GA; Alon Siton, ISR; Kathy Skeie, CA; Robyn Skillecorn, AUS; Erik & Kathy Skon, MN; Stine Skorpen, NOR; Philip Smart, CAN; Colin Smit, ENG; Kenneth Smith, DE; Caleb Smith, CA; Geoffrey Smith, TX; John Snyder, NC; Kathrin Speidel, GER; Lani Steele, PHIL; Julie Stelbracht, PA; Margaret Stires, TN; Donald Stumpf, NY; Samuel Suffern, TN; Michael Swerdlow, ENG; Brian Talley, TX; Serene-Marie Terrell, NY; B. Larry Thilson, CAN; J. Pelham Thomas, NC; Wright Thompson, ITA; Christine Timm, NY; Melinda Tong, HK; M. Tritica, AUS; Melanie Tritz, CAN; Mark Trop, FL; Chris Troxel, AZ; Rozana Tsiknaki, GRC; Lois Turner, NZ; Nicole Virgil, IL; Blondie Vucich, CO; Wendy Wan, SAF; Carrie & Simon Wedgwood, ENG; Frederick Weibgen, NJ; Richard Weil, MN; Alan Weissberg, OH; Ryan Wells, OH; Jill Wester, GER; Clinton White, AL; Gael White, CAN; Melanie Whitfield, SCOT; Bryn Williams, CAN; Amanda Williams, CAN; Wendy Willis, CAN; Sasha Wilson, NY; Kendra Wilson, CA; Olivia Wiseman, ENG; Gerry Wood, CA; Kelly Wooten, CA; Robert Worsley, ENG; C.A.Wright, ENG; Caroline Wright, ENG; Mary H. Yuhasz, CO; Margaret Zimmerman, WA.

★Let's Go 1999 Reader Questionnaire★

Please fill this out and return it to **Let's Go, St. Martin's Press,** 175 Fifth Ave., New York, NY 10010-7848. All respondents will receive a free subscription to **The Yellowjacket,** the Let's Go Newsletter. You can find a more extensive version of this survey on the web at http://www.letsgo.com.

Name: _____

Address: _____

City: _____ **State:** _____ **Zip/Postal Code:** _____

Email: _____ **Which book(s) did you use?**_____

How old are you? under 19   19-24   25-34   35-44   45-54   55 or over

Are you (circle one)   in high school   in college   in graduate school
  employed   retired   between jobs

Have you used Let's Go before? yes no **Would you use it again?** yes no

How did you first hear about Let's Go? friend   store clerk   television
  bookstore display   advertisement/promotion   review   other

Why did you choose Let's Go (circle up to two)? reputation budget focus
  price   writing style   annual updating   other: _____

Which other guides have you used, if any? Fodor's   Footprint Handbooks
  Frommer's $-a-day   Lonely Planet   Moon Guides   Rick Steve's
  Rough Guides   UpClose   other: _____

Which guide do you prefer? _____

**Please rank each of the following parts of Let's Go 1 to 5 (1=needs
  improvement, 5=perfect).** packaging/cover   practical information
  accommodations   food   cultural introduction   sights
  practical introduction ("Essentials")   directions   entertainment
  gay/lesbian information   maps   other: _____

**How would you like to see the books improved? (continue on separate page,
  if necessary)**_____

_____

How long was your trip?   one week   two weeks   three weeks
  one month   two months or more

Which countries did you visit? _____

What was your average daily budget, not including flights? _____

Have you traveled extensively before? yes no

Do you buy a separate map when you visit a foreign city? yes no

Have you used a Let's Go Map Guide? yes no

If you have, would you recommend them to others? yes no

Have you visited Let's Go's website? yes no

What would you like to see included on Let's Go's website? _____

_____

What percentage of your trip planning did you do on the Web? _____

Would you use a Let's Go: recreational (e.g. skiing) guide gay/lesbian guide
  adventure/trekking guide   phrasebook   general travel information guide

**Which of the following destinations do you hope to visit in the next three to
  five years (circle one)?** Canada Argentina Perú Kenya Middle East
  Caribbean Scandinavia other: _____

Where did you buy your guidebook?   Internet   independent bookstore
  chain bookstore   college bookstore   travel store   other: _____

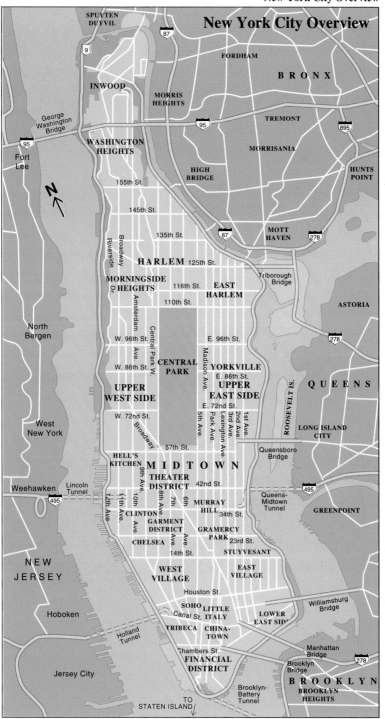

New York City Overview

SPUYTEN DUYVIL

FORDHAM

B R O N X

INWOOD

MORRIS HEIGHTS

TREMONT

George Washington Bridge

WASHINGTON HEIGHTS

MORRISANIA

Fort Lee

HIGH BRIDGE

HUNTS POINT

N

155th St.

145th St.

135th St.

MOTT HAVEN

Broadway
Riverside Dr.

HARLEM 125th St.

MORNINGSIDE HEIGHTS

116th St.

EAST HARLEM

Triborough Bridge

110th St.

ASTORIA

North Bergen

Amsterdam Ave.

Central Park W.

W. 96th St.

E. 96th St.

Madison Ave.

W. 86th St.

CENTRAL PARK

YORKVILLE E. 86th St.

UPPER EAST SIDE

Q U E E N S

UPPER WEST SIDE

ROOSEVELT IS.

E. 72nd St.

2nd Ave.

West New York

W. 72nd St.

Broadway

5th Ave.
Park Ave.
Lexington Ave.
3rd Ave.
1st Ave.

LONG ISLAND CITY

57th St.

HELL'S KITCHEN

Queensboro Bridge

M I D T O W N

THEATER DISTRICT 42nd St.

Weehawken

Lincoln Tunnel

9th Ave.
8th Ave.
7th
6th

Queens-Midtown Tunnel

12th Ave.
11th Ave.
10th

MURRAY HILL 34th St.

GREENPOINT

CLINTON Ave.

GARMENT DISTRICT

GRAMERCY PARK 23rd St.

CHELSEA

Ave.

14th St.

STUYVESANT

N E W
J E R S E Y

WEST VILLAGE

EAST VILLAGE

Houston St.

Hoboken

SOHO LITTLE
Canal St. ITALY

Williamsburg Bridge

Holland Tunnel

TRIBECA CHINA-TOWN

LOWER EAST SIDE

Chambers St.

Manhattan Bridge

FINANCIAL DISTRICT

Brooklyn Bridge

Jersey City

Brooklyn-Battery Tunnel

B R O O K L Y N

TO STATEN ISLAND

BROOKLYN HEIGHTS

New York City Subways

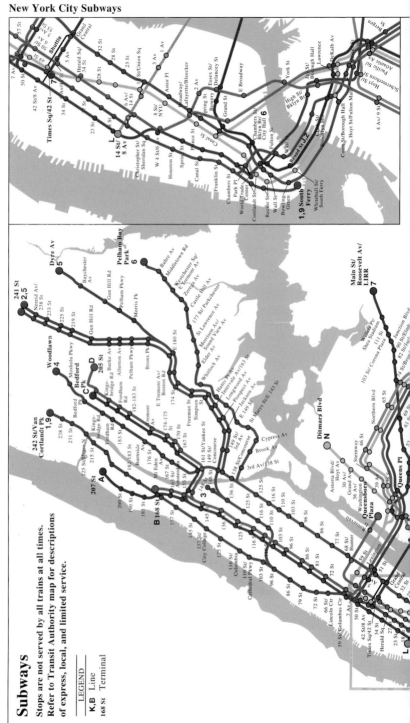

Subways

Stops are not served by all trains at all times.
Refer to Transit Authority map for descriptions
of express, local, and limited service.

LEGEND

K,B   Line

168 St   Terminal

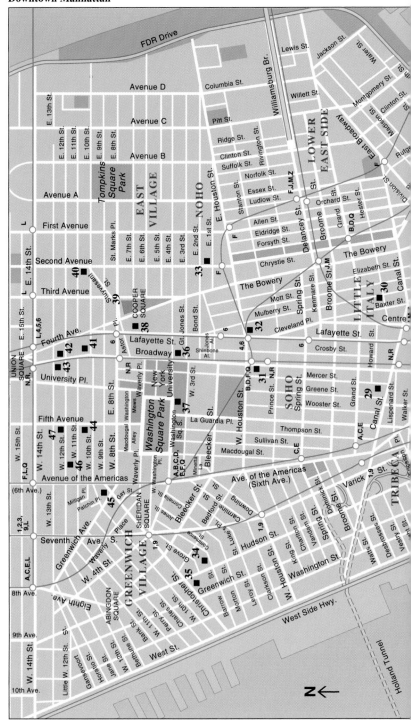

Midtown Manhattan

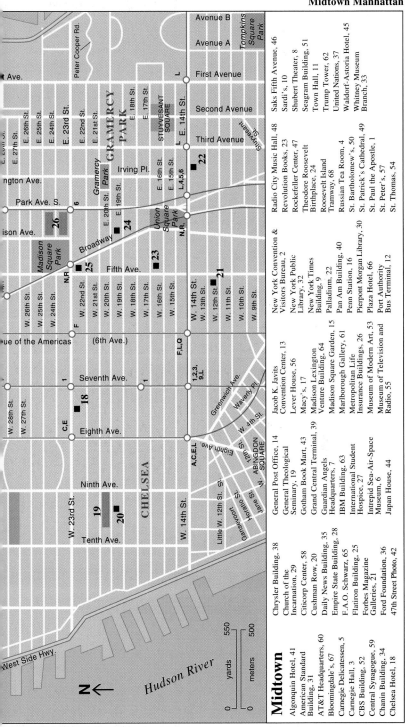

Midtown

Algonquin Hotel, 41
American Standard Building, 31
AT&T Headquarters, 60
Bloomingdale's, 67
Carnegie Delicatessen, 5
Carnegie Hall, 3
CBS Building, 52
Central Synagogue, 59
Chanin Building, 34
Chelsea Hotel, 18
Chrysler Building, 38
Church of the Incarnation, 29
Citicorp Center, 58
Cushman Row, 20
Daily News Building, 35
Empire State Building, 28
F.A.O. Schwarz, 65
Flatiron Building, 25
Forbes Magazine Galleries, 21
Ford Foundation, 36
47th Street Photo, 42
General Post Office, 14
General Theological Seminary, 19
Gotham Book Mart, 43
Grand Central Terminal, 39
Guardian Angels Headquarters, 7
IBM Building, 63
International Student Hospice, 27
Intrepid Sea-Air-Space Museum, 6
Japan House, 44
Jacob K. Javits Convention Center, 13
Lever House, 56
Macy's, 17
Madison Lexington Venture Building, 64
Madison Square Garden, 15
Marlborough Gallery, 61
Metropolitan Life Insurance Buildings, 26
Museum of Modern Art, 53
Museum of Television and Radio, 55
New York Convention & Visitors Bureau, 2
New York Public Library, 32
New York Times Building, 9
Palladium, 22
Pan Am Building, 40
Penn Station, 16
Pierpont Morgan Library, 30
Plaza Hotel, 66
Port Authority Bus Terminal, 12
Radio City Music Hall, 48
Revolution Books, 23
Rockefeller Center, 47
Theodore Roosevelt Birthplace, 24
Roosevelt Island Tramway, 68
Russian Tea Room, 4
St. Bartholomew's, 50
St. Patrick's Cathedral, 49
St. Paul the Apostle, 1
St. Peter's, 57
St. Thomas, 54
Saks Fifth Avenue, 46
Sardi's, 10
Shubert Theater, 8
Seagram Building, 51
Town Hall, 11
Trump Tower, 62
United Nations, 37
Waldorf-Astoria Hotel, 45
Whitney Museum Branch, 33

Uptown

American Museum of Natural History, 53
The Ansonia, 55
The Arsenal, 25
Asia Society, 14
Belvedere Castle, 36
Bethesda Fountain, 33
Blockhouse No. 1, 42
Bloomingdale's, 22
Bridle Path, 30
Cathedral of St. John the Divine, 47
Central Park Zoo, 24
Chess and Checkers House, 28
Children's Museum of Manhattan, 51
Children's Zoo, 26
China House, 19

Cleopatra's Needle, 38
Columbia University, 46
Conservatory Garden, 2
Cooper-Hewitt Museum, 7
The Dairy, 27
Dakota Apartments, 56
Delacorte Theater, 37
El Museo del Barrio, 1
Fordham University, 60
Frick Museum, 13
Gracie Mansion, 10
Grant's Tomb, 45
Great Lawn, 39
Guggenheim Museum, 9
Hayden Planetarium (at the American Museum of Natural History), 53
Hector Memorial, 50
Hotel des Artistes, 57

Hunter College, 16
International Center of Photography, 5
Jewish Museum, 6
The Juilliard School (at Lincoln Center), 59
Lincoln Center, 59
Loeb Boathouse, 34
Masjid Malcolm Shabazz , 43
Metropolitan Museum of Art, 11
Mt. Sinai Hospital, 4
Museum of American Folk Art, 58
Museum of American Illustration, 21
Museum of the City of New York, 3
National Academy of Design, 8
New York Convention & Visitors Bureau, 61

New York Historical Society, 54
New York Hospital, 15
Plaza Hotel, 23
Police Station (Central Park), 40
Rockefeller University, 20
7th Regiment Armory, 17
Shakespeare Garden, 35
Soldiers and Sailors Monument, 49
Strawberry Fields, 32
Studio Museum in Harlem, 44
Symphony Space, 48
Tavern on the Green, 31
Temple Emanu-El, 18
Tennis Courts, 41
Whitney Museum of American Art, 12
Wollman Rink, 29
Zabar's, 52

Central Washington, D.C.

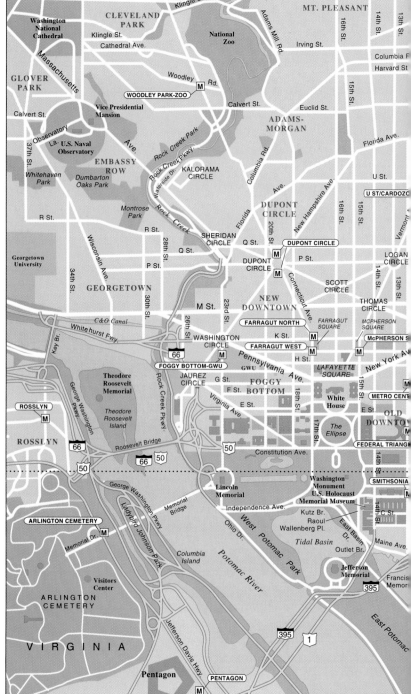

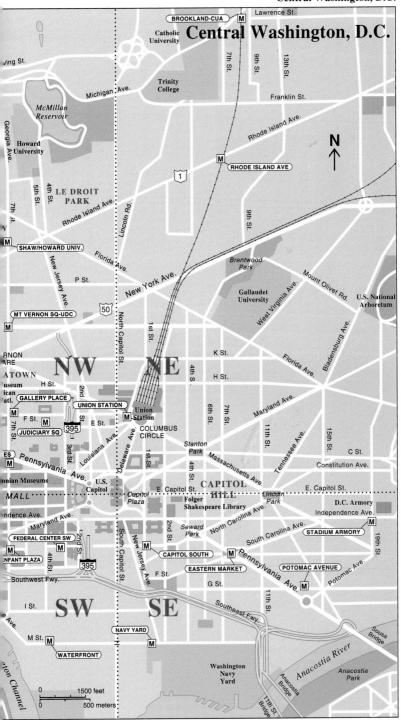

Central Washington, D.C.

The Mall Area, Washington, D.C.

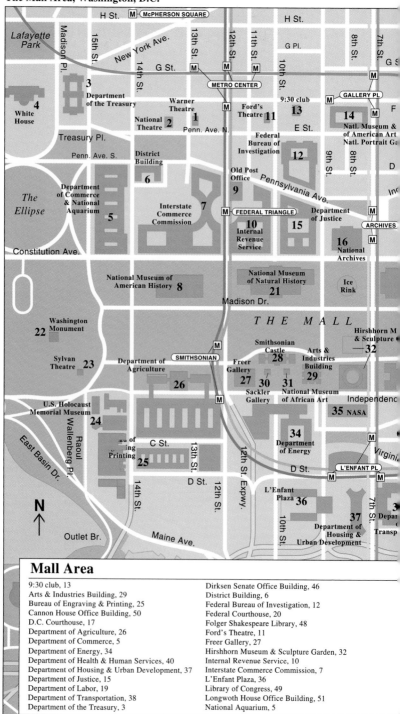

Mall Area

9:30 club, 13
Arts & Industries Building, 29
Bureau of Engraving & Printing, 25
Cannon House Office Building, 50
D.C. Courthouse, 17
Department of Agriculture, 26
Department of Commerce, 5
Department of Energy, 34
Department of Health & Human Services, 40
Department of Housing & Urban Development, 37
Department of Justice, 15
Department of Labor, 19
Department of Transportation, 38
Department of the Treasury, 3

Dirksen Senate Office Building, 46
District Building, 6
Federal Bureau of Investigation, 12
Federal Courthouse, 20
Folger Shakespeare Library, 48
Ford's Theatre, 11
Freer Gallery, 27
Hirshhorn Museum & Sculpture Garden, 32
Internal Revenue Service, 10
Interstate Commerce Commission, 7
L'Enfant Plaza, 36
Library of Congress, 49
Longworth House Office Building, 51
National Aquarium, 5

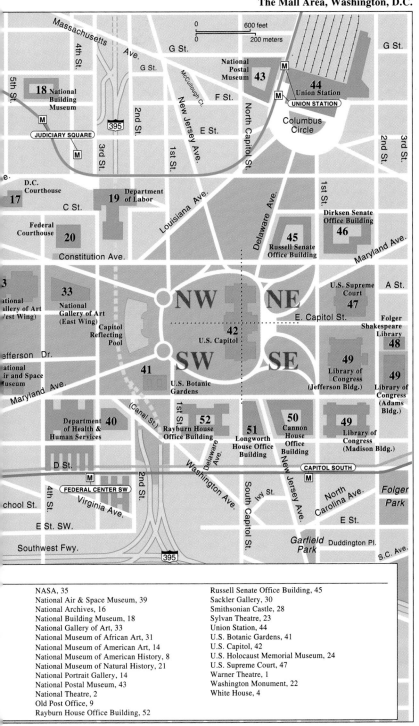

NASA, 35
National Air & Space Museum, 39
National Archives, 16
National Building Museum, 18
National Gallery of Art, 33
National Museum of African Art, 31
National Museum of American Art, 14
National Museum of American History, 8
National Museum of Natural History, 21
National Portrait Gallery, 14
National Postal Museum, 43
National Theatre, 2
Old Post Office, 9
Rayburn House Office Building, 52

Russell Senate Office Building, 45
Sackler Gallery, 30
Smithsonian Castle, 28
Sylvan Theatre, 23
Union Station, 44
U.S. Botanic Gardens, 41
U.S. Capitol, 42
U.S. Holocaust Memorial Museum, 24
U.S. Supreme Court, 47
Warner Theatre, 1
Washington Monument, 22
White House, 4

White House Area, Foggy Bottom, and Nearby Arlington

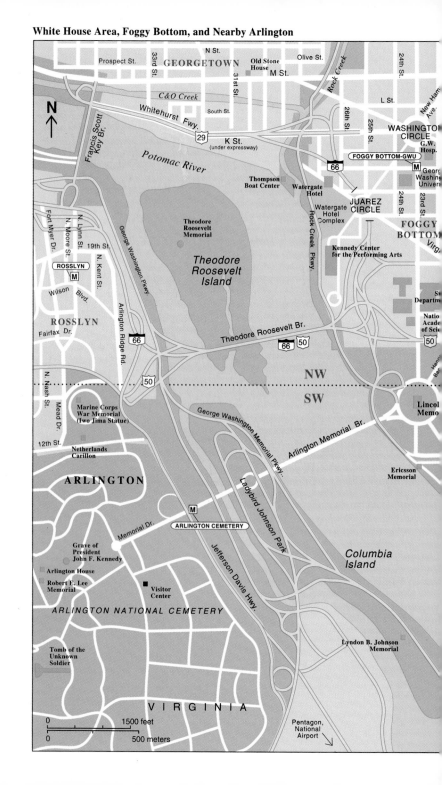

Jefferson Pl.

Connecticut Ave.

M St.

THOMAS CIRCLE

M St.

11th St.

8th St.

20th St.

19th St.

18th St.

DeSales St.

17th St.

National Geographic Society

15th St.

Vermont Ave.

Massachusetts Ave.

L St.

9th St.

The Washington Post

16th St.

13th St.

12th St.

K St.

MT. VERNON SQUARE

FARRAGUT NORTH M

K St.

FARRAGUT SQUARE

McPHERSON SQUARE

Franklin Park

New York Ave.

I St.

sylvania Ave.

FARRAGUT WEST M

U.S. Chamber of Commerce

St. John's Church

McPHERSON SQ M

National Museum of Women in the Arts

H St.

Convention Center

H St.

Decatur House

LAFAYETTE SQUARE

15th St.

14th St.

New York Ave. Presbyterian Church

Martin Luther King Jr. Library

G Pl.

G St.

World Bank

Renwick Gallery

Blair House

Jackson Pl.

Madison Pl.

U.S. Treasury

G St.

10th St.

G St.

F St.

Old Executive Office Building

Visitor Information Center

METRO CENTER M M

F St.

9:30 club

General Services Administration

Octagon

State Pl.

White House

Natl. Theatre

Warner Theatre

M

E St.

11th St.

Ford's Theatre

E St.

Corcoran Gallery

Treasury Pl.

Executive Ave.

E St.

Pennsylvania Ave.

Federal Bureau of Investigation

9th St.

District Building

Market Pl.

Interior Department

D St.

17th St.

Ellipse Rd.

FEDERAL TRIANGLE

Old Post Office

M

C St.

D.A.R. Constitution Hall

THE ELLIPSE

Department of Commerce

Internal Revenue Service

Department of Justice

National Archives

Organization of American States

onstitution Ave.

S. Executive Pl.

Constitution Ave.

Constitution Gardens

Natl. Museum of American History

Natl. Museum of Natural History

Madison Dr.

tnam erans morial

Memorial to the Signers of the Declaration of Independence

THE MALL

Arts & Industries Building

Reflecting Pool

Washington Monument

14th St.

Freer Gallery of Art

Smithsonian Castle

est Potomac Park

Sylvan Theatre

M

SMITHSONIAN

D.C. War Memorial

U.S. Holocaust Memorial Museum

Independence Ave.

Natl. Museum of African Art

pendence Ave.

Kutz Br.

East Basin Dr.

15th St.

Department of Agriculture

C St.

13th St.

12th St.

Department of Energy

L'Enfant Promenade

9th St.

D St.

Japanese Lantern

Bureau of Engraving & Printing

12th St. Expwy.

L'Enfant Plaza

West Potomac Dr.

W. Basin Dr.

Paddleboats

Tidal Basin

Outlet Br.

Maine Ave.

Cherry Trees

Ohio Dr.

Jefferson Memorial

Francis Case Memorial Br.

H St.

Maine Ave.

Water St.

Potomac River

395

George Mason Bridge

Williams Memorial Bridge

1

Washington Channel

Natl. Park Service Visitors Welcome Center & Park Police Headquarters

East Potomac Park

White House Area, Foggy Bottom, and Nearby Arlington

Metrorail System, Washington, D.C.

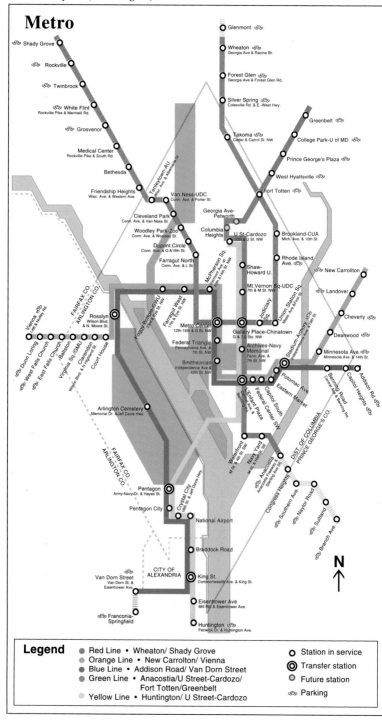

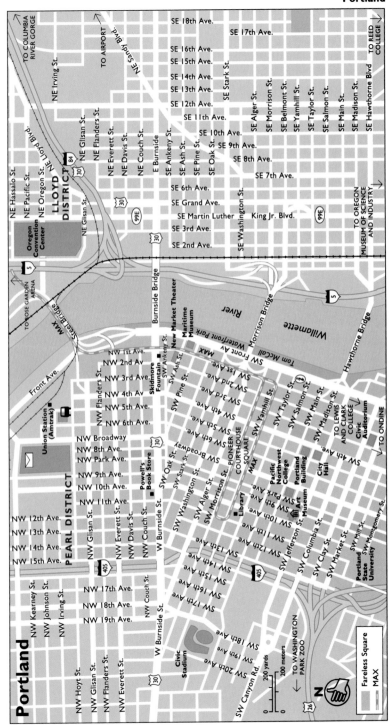

Portland

Seattle

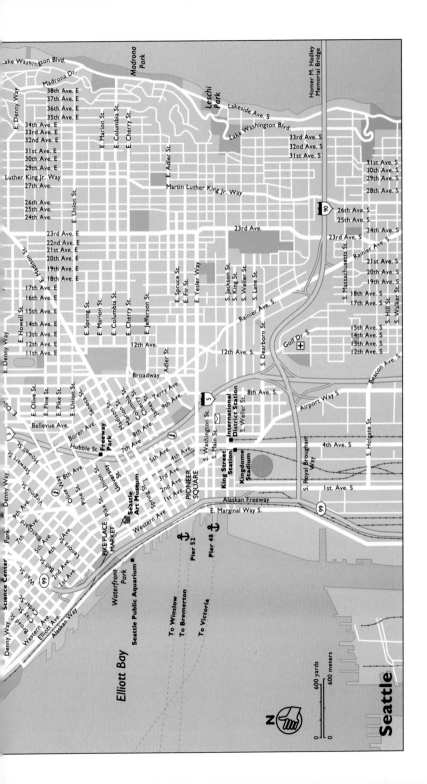

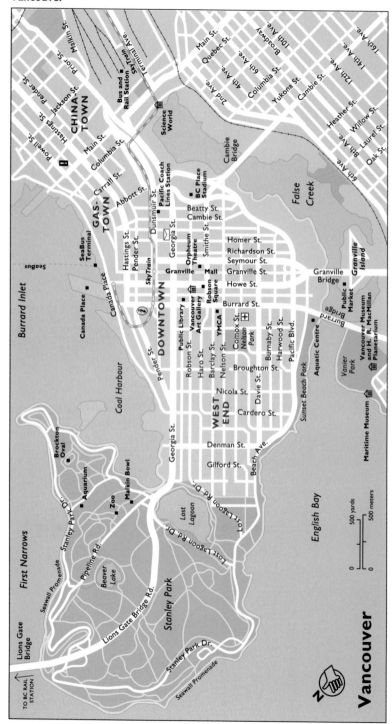

First Narrows

Burrard Inlet

Seabus

Coal Harbour

Lions Gate
Bridge

TO BC RAIL
STATION

Seawall Promenade

Stanley Park Dr.

Pipeline Rd.

Beaver
Lake

Brockton
Oval

Aquarium

Zoo

Malkin Bowl

Lost
Lagoon

Lost Lagoon Rd. Dr.

Stanley Park

Stanley Park Dr.

Seawall Promenade

English Bay

CHINA-
TOWN

Prior St.

Malkin St.

Pender St.

Jackson St.

Powell St.

Hastings St.

Main St.

Columbia St.

Bus and
Rail Station

SkyTrain

Terminal Ave.

Quebec St.

Main St.

2nd Ave

4th Ave

6th Ave

Broadway

10th Ave

12th Ave

14th Ave

16th Ave

Columbia St.

Yukona St.

Cambie St.

Heather St.

Willow St.

Laurel St.

Oak St.

8th Ave

6th Ave

Science
World

Cambie
Bridge

False
Creek

GAS-
TOWN

Carrall St.

Abbott St.

Dunsmuir St.

Pacific Coach
Lines Station

BC Place
Stadium

Beatty St.

Cambie St.

Georgia St.

Orpheum
Theatre

Smithe St.

Homer St.

Richardson St.

Seymour St.

Granville St.

Howe St.

Granville
Bridge

Granville
Island

SeaBus
Terminal

Canada Place

Hastings St.

Pender St.

SkyTrain

Granville

Mall

Public Library

Vancouver
Art Gallery

Robson
Square

Burrard St.

Granville
Bridge

Public
Market

Burrard
Bridge

DOWNTOWN

Pender St.

Robson St.

Haro St.

Barclay St.

Nelson St.

YMCA

Comox St.

Nelson
Park

Burnaby St.

Harwood St.

Pacific Blvd.

Broughton St.

Aquatic Centre

Vancouver Museum
and H. R. MacMillan
Planetarium

Vanier
Park

WEST
END

Nicola St.

Cardero St.

Denman St.

Gilford St.

Georgia St.

Beach Ave.

Sunset Beach Park

Maritime Museum

Davie St.

0   500 yards

0   500 meters

N

Vancouver

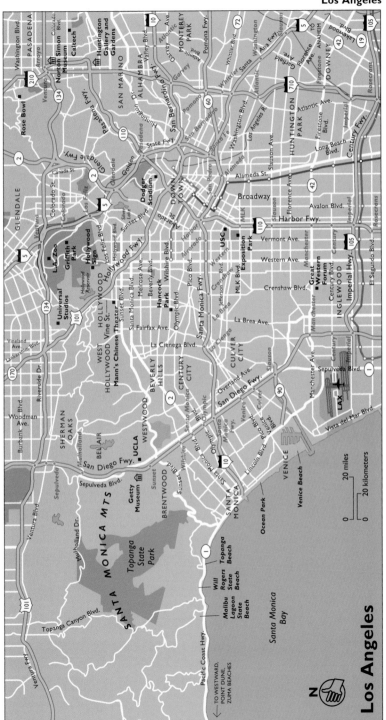

Los Angeles

Los Angeles

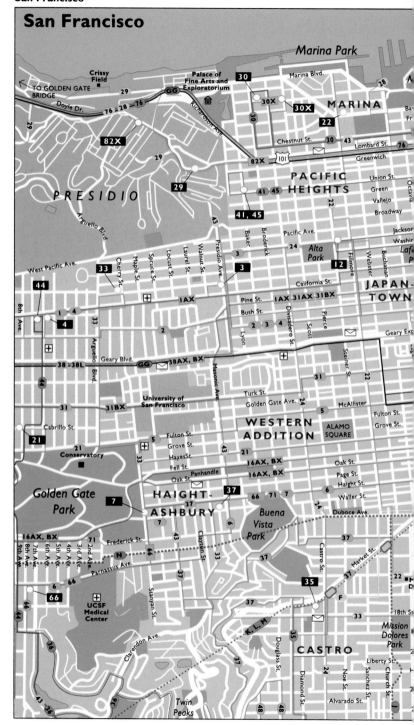

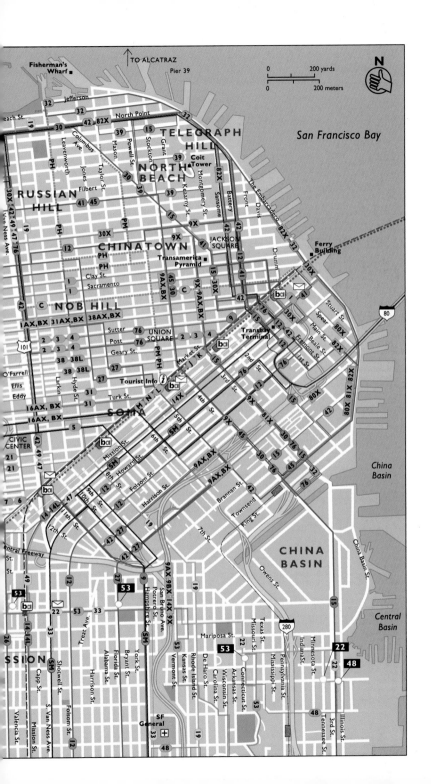

L.A. Westside

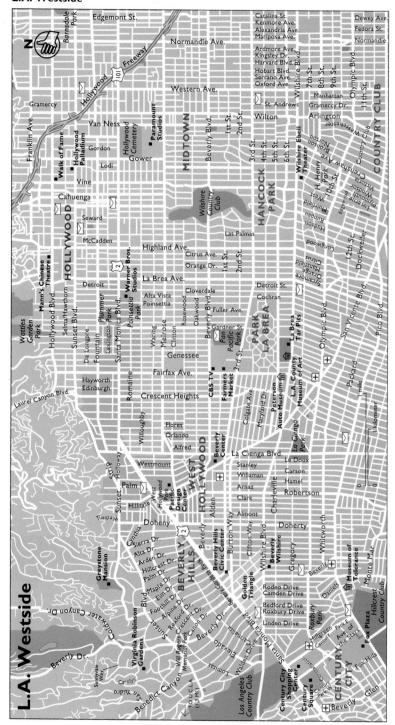